A COMEDY OF JUSTICE

JOB IS PARTLY OUTRAGEOUS,
INCREDIBLY THOUGHT-PROVOKING
AND ENDLESSLY FASCINATING!

"FOLLOWING WORLD WAR II ROBERT
A. HEINLEIN EMERGED AS NOT ONLY
AMERICA'S PREMIER WRITER OF SPEC-
ULATIVE FICTION, BUT AS THE
GREATEST WRITER OF SUCH FICTION
IN THE WORLD. HE REMAINS TODAY AS
A SORT OF TRADEMARK FOR ALL THAT
IS FINEST IN AMERICAN IMAGINATIVE
FICTION." —Stephen King

"JOB is an exhilarating romp through the
author's mental universe."
                                    —*New York Times Book Review*

Also by Robert A. Heinlein
Published by Ballantine Books:

ROBERT A. HEINLEIN
JOB:
A COMEDY OF JUSTICE

A Del Rey Book

BALLANTINE BOOKS • NEW YORK

A Del Rey Book
Published by Ballantine Books
Copyright © 1984 by Robert A. Heinlein

All rights reserved under International and Pan-American
Copyright Conventions. Published in the United States by
Ballantine Books, a division of Random House, Inc., New York,
and simultaneously in Canada by Random House of Canada
Limited, Toronto.

Library of Congress Catalog Card Number: 84-3091

ISBN 0-345-31650-9

Manufactured in the United States of America

First Hardcover Edition: September 1984
First Paperback Edition: November 1985

Cover art by Michael Whelan

To Clifford D. Simak

Behold, happy is the man whom God correcteth:
therefore despise not thou the chastening of
the Almighty.
Job 5:17

I

When thou walkest through the fire,
thou shalt not be burned.

Isaiah 43:2

The fire pit was about twenty-five feet long by ten feet wide, and perhaps two feet deep. The fire had been burning for hours. The bed of coals gave off a blast of heat almost unbearable even back where I was seated, fifteen feet from the side of the pit, in the second row of tourists.

I had given up my front-row seat to one of the ladies from the ship, delighted to accept the shielding offered by her well-fed carcass. I was tempted to move still farther back . . . but I *did* want to see the fire walkers close up. How often does one get to view a miracle?

"It's a hoax," the Well-Traveled Man said. "You'll see."

"Not really a hoax, Gerald," the Authority-on-Everything denied. "Just somewhat less than we were led to expect. It won't be the whole village—probably none of the hula dancers and certainly not those children. One or two of the young men, with calluses on their feet as thick as cowhide, and hopped up on opium

1

or some native drug, will go down the pit at a dead run. The villagers will cheer and our kanaka friend there who is translating for us will strongly suggest that we should tip each of the fire walkers, over and above what we've paid for the luau and the dancing and this show.

"Not a complete hoax," he went on. "The shore excursion brochure listed a 'demonstration of fire walking.' That's what we'll get. Never mind the talk about a whole village of fire walkers. Not in the contract." The Authority looked smug.

"Mass hypnosis," the Professional Bore announced.

I was tempted to ask for an explanation of "mass hypnosis"—but nobody wanted to hear from me; I was junior—not necessarily in years but in the cruise ship *Konge Knut.* That's how it is in cruise ships: Anyone who has been in the vessel since port of departure is senior to anyone who joins the ship later. The Medes and the Persians laid down this law and nothing can change it. I had flown down in the *Count von Zeppelin,* at Papeete I would fly home in the *Admiral Moffett,* so I was forever junior and should keep quiet while my betters pontificated.

Cruise ships have the best food and, all too often, the worst conversation in the world. Despite this I was enjoying the islands; even the Mystic and the Amateur Astrologer and the Parlor Freudian and the Numerologist did not trouble me, as I did not listen.

"They do it through the fourth dimension," the Mystic announced. "Isn't that true, Gwendolyn?"

"Quite true, dear," the Numerologist agreed. "Oh, here they come now! It will be an odd number, you'll see."

"You're so learned, dear."

"Humph," said the Skeptic.

The native who was assisting our ship's excursion host raised his arms and spread his palms for silence. "Please, will you all listen! *Mauruuru roa*. Thank you very much. The high priest and priestess will now pray the Gods to make the fire safe for the villagers. I ask you to remember that this is a religious ceremony, very ancient; please behave as you would in your own church. Because—"

An extremely old kanaka interrupted; he and the translator exchanged words in a language not known to me—Polynesian, I assumed; it had the right liquid flow to it. The younger kanaka turned back to us.

"The high priest tells me that some of the children are making their first walk through fire today, including that baby over there in her mother's arms. He asks all of you to keep perfectly silent during the prayers, to insure the safety of the children. Let me add that I am a Catholic. At this point I always ask our Holy Mother Mary to watch over our children—and I ask all of you to pray for them in your own way. Or at least keep silent and think good thoughts for them. If the high priest is not satisfied that there is a reverent attitude, he won't let the children enter the fire—I've even known him to cancel the entire ceremony."

"There you have it, Gerald," said the Authority-on-Everything in a third-balcony whisper. "The build-up. Now the switch, and they'll blame it on us." He snorted.

The Authority—his name was Cheevers—had been annoying me ever since I had joined the ship. I leaned forward and said quietly into his ear, "If those children walk through the fire, do you have the guts to do like-wise?"

Let this be a lesson to you. Learn by my bad example. Never let an oaf cause you to lose your judgment. Some seconds later I found that my challenge had been turned against me and—somehow!—all three, the Authority, the Skeptic, and the Well-Traveled Man, had each bet me a hundred that *I* would not dare walk the fire pit, stipulating that the children walked first.

Then the translator was shushing us again and the priest and priestess stepped down into the fire pit and everybody kept very quiet and I suppose some of us prayed. I know I did. I found myself reciting what popped into my mind:

"Now I lay me down to sleep.

"I pray the Lord my soul to keep—"

Somehow it seemed appropriate.

The priest and the priestess did not walk through the fire; they did something quietly more spectacular and (it seemed to me) far more dangerous. They simply stood in the fire pit, barefooted, and prayed for several minutes. I could see their lips move. Every so often the old priest sprinkled something into the pit. Whatever it was, as it struck the coals it burst into sparkles.

I tried to see what they were standing on, coals or rocks, but I could not tell . . . and could not guess which would be worse. Yet this old woman, skinny as gnawed bones, stood there quietly, face placid, and with no precautions other than having tucked up her lava-lava so that it was almost a diaper. Apparently she fretted about burning her clothes but not about burning her legs.

Three men with poles had been straightening out the burning logs, making sure that the bed of the pit was a firm and fairly even footing for the fire walkers. I took a deep interest in this, as I expected to be walking in that pit in a few minutes—if I didn't cave in and forfeit the bet. It seemed to me that they were making it possible to walk the length of the fire pit on rocks rather than burning coals. I hoped so!

Then I wondered what difference it would make— recalling sun-scorched sidewalks that had blistered my bare feet when I was a boy in Kansas. That fire had to be at least seven hundred degrees; those rocks had been soaking in that fire for several hours. At such temperatures was there any real choice between frying pan and fire?

Meanwhile the voice of reason was whispering in my ear that forfeiting three hundred was not much of a price to pay to get out of this bind . . . or would I rather walk the rest of my life on two barbecued stumps?

Would it help if I took an aspirin?

The three men finished fiddling with the burning logs and went to the end of the pit at our left; the rest of the villagers gathered behind them—including those darned kids! What were their parents thinking about, letting them risk something like this? Why weren't they in school where they belonged?

The three fire tenders led off, walking single file down the center of the fire, not hurrying, not dallying. The rest of the men of the village followed them, a slow, steady procession. Then came the women, including the young mother with a baby on her hip.

When the blast of heat struck the infant, it started to cry. Without varying her steady pace, its mother swung it up and gave it suck; the baby shut up.

The children followed, from pubescent girls and adolescent boys down to the kindergarten level. Last was a little girl (nine? eight?) who was leading her round-eyed little brother by the hand. He seemed to be about four and was dressed only in his skin.

I looked at this kid and knew with mournful certainty that I was about to be served up rare; I could no longer back out. Once the baby boy stumbled; his sister kept him from falling. He went on then, short sturdy steps. At the far end someone reached down and lifted him out.

And it was *my* turn.

The translator said to me, "You understand that the Polynesia Tourist Bureau takes no responsibility for your safety? That fire can burn you, it can kill you. These people can walk it safely because they have faith."

I assured him that I had faith, while wondering how I could be such a barefaced liar. I signed a release he presented.

All too soon I was standing at one end of the pit, with my trousers rolled up to my knees. My shoes and socks and hat and wallet were at the far end, waiting on a stool. That was my goal, my prize—if I didn't make it, would they cast lots for them? Or would they ship them to my next of kin?

He was saying: "Go right down the middle. Don't hurry but don't stand still." The high priest spoke up; my mentor listened, then said, "He says not to run, even if your feet burn. Because you might stumble and fall down. Then you might never get up. He means you might die. I must add that you probably would not die—unless you breathed flame. But you would certainly be terribly burned. So don't hurry and don't fall down. Now see that flat rock under you? That's your first step. *Que le bon Dieu vous garde.* Good luck."

"Thanks." I glanced over at the Authority-on-Everything, who was smiling ghoulishly, if ghouls smile. I gave him a mendaciously jaunty wave and stepped down.

I had taken three steps before I realized that I didn't feel anything at all. Then I did feel something: scared. Scared silly and wishing I were in Peoria. Or even Philadelphia. Instead of alone in this vast smoldering waste. The far end of the pit was a city block away. Maybe farther. But I kept plodding toward it while hoping that this numb paralysis would not cause me to collapse before reaching it.

I felt smothered and discovered that I had been holding my breath. So I gasped—and regretted it. Over a fire pit that vast there is blistering gas and smoke and carbon dioxide and carbon monoxide and something that may be Satan's halitosis, but not enough oxygen to matter. I chopped off that gasp with my eyes watering and my throat raw and tried to estimate whether or not I could reach the end without breathing.

Heaven help me, I could not *see* the far end! The smoke had billowed up and my eyes would barely open and would not focus. So I pushed on, while trying to remember the formula by which one made a deathbed confession and then slid into Heaven on a technicality.

Maybe there wasn't any such formula. My feet felt odd and my knees were coming unglued . . .

"Feeling better, Mr. Graham?"

I was lying on grass and looking up into a friendly,

brown face. "I guess so," I answered. "What happened? Did I walk it?"

"Certainly you walked it. Beautifully. But you fainted right at the end. We were standing by and grabbed you, hauled you out. But you tell me what happened. Did you get your lungs full of smoke?"

"Maybe. Am I burned?"

"No. Oh, you may form one blister on your right foot. But you held the thought perfectly. All but that faint, which must have been caused by smoke."

"I guess so." I sat up with his help. "Can you hand me my shoes and socks? Where is everybody?"

"The bus left. The high priest took your pulse and checked your breathing but he wouldn't let anyone disturb you. If you force a man to wake up when his spirit is still walking about, the spirit may not come back in. So he believes and no one dares argue with him."

"I won't argue with him; I feel fine. Rested. But how do I get back to the ship?" Five miles of tropical paradise would get tedious after the first mile. On foot. Especially as my feet seemed to have swelled a bit. For which they had ample excuse.

"The bus will come back to take the villagers to the boat that takes them back to the island they live on. It then could take you to your ship. But we can do better. My cousin has an automobile. He will take you."

"Good. How much will he charge me?" Taxis in Polynesia are always outrageous, especially when the drivers have you at their mercy, of which they have none. But it occurred to me that I could afford to be robbed as I was bound to show a profit on this jape. Three hundred minus one taxi fare. I picked up my hat. "Where's my wallet?"

"Your wallet?"

"My billfold. I left it in my hat. Where is it? This isn't funny; my money was in it. And my cards."

"Your money? *Oh! Votre portefeuille.* I am sorry; my English is not perfect. The officer from your ship, your excursion guide, took care of it."

"That was kind of him. But how am I to pay your cousin? I don't have a franc on me."

We got that straightened out. The ship's excursion escort, realizing that he would be leaving me strapped in rescuing my billfold, had prepaid my ride back to the ship. My kanaka friend took me to his cousin's car and introduced me to his cousin—not too effectively, as the cousin's English was limited to "Okay, Chief!" and I never did get his name straight.

His automobile was a triumph of baling wire and faith. We went roaring back to the dock at full throttle, frightening chickens and easily outrunning baby goats. I did not pay much attention as I was bemused by something that had happened just before we left. The villagers were waiting for their bus to return; we walked right through them. Or started to. I got kissed. I got kissed by all of them. I had already seen the Polynesian habit of kissing where we would just shake hands, but this was the first time it had happened to me.

My friend explained it to me: "You walked through their fire, so you are an honorary member of their village. They want to kill a pig for you. Hold a feast in your honor."

I tried to answer in kind while explaining that I had to return home across the great water but I would return someday, God willing. Eventually we got away.

But that was not what had me most bemused. Any

unbiased judge would have to admit that I am reasonably sophisticated. I am aware that some places do not have America's high moral standards and are careless about indecent exposure. I know that Polynesian women used to run around naked from the waist up until civilization came along—shucks, I read the *National Geographic*.

But I never expected to *see* it.

Before I made my fire walk the villagers were dressed just as you would expect: grass skirts but with the women's bosoms covered.

But when they kissed me hello-goodbye they were not. Not covered, I mean. Just like the *National Geographic*.

Now I appreciate feminine beauty. Those delightful differences, seen under proper circumstances with the shades decently drawn, can be dazzling. But forty-odd (no, even) of them are intimidating. I saw more human, feminine busts than I had ever seen before, total and cumulative, in my entire life. The Methodist Episcopal Society for Temperance and Morals would have been shocked right out of their wits.

With adequate warning I am sure that I could have enjoyed the experience. As it was, it was too new, too much, too fast. I could appreciate it only in retrospect.

Our tropical Rolls-Royce crunched to a stop with the aid of hand brake, foot brake, and first-gear compression; I looked up from bemused euphoria. My driver announced, "Okay, Chief!"

I said, "That's not my ship."

"Okay, Chief?"

"You've taken me to the wrong dock. Uh, it looks like the right dock but it's the wrong ship." Of that I was certain. M.V. *Konge Knut* has white sides and superstructure and a rakish false funnel. This ship was mostly red with four tall black stacks. Steam, it had to be—not a motor vessel. As well as years out of date. "No. No!"

"Okay, Chief. *Votre vapeur! Voilà!*"

"*Non!*"

"Okay, Chief." He got out, came around and opened the door on the passenger side, grabbed my arm, and pulled.

I'm in fairly good shape, but his arm had been toughened by swimming, climbing for coconuts, hauling in fishnets, and pulling tourists who don't want to go out of cars. I got out.

He jumped back in, called out, "Okay, Chief! *Merci bien! Au 'voir!*" and was gone.

I went, Hobson's choice, up the gangway of the strange vessel to learn, if possible, what had become of the *Konge Knut*. As I stepped aboard, the petty officer on gangway watch saluted and said, "Afternoon, sir. Mr. Graham, Mr. Nielsen left a package for you. One moment—" He lifted the lid of his watch desk, took out a large manila envelope. "Here you are, sir."

The package had written on it: *A. L. Graham, cabin C109*. I opened it, found a well-worn wallet.

"Is everything in order, Mr. Graham?"

"Yes, thank you. Will you tell Mr. Nielsen that I received it? And give him my thanks."

"Certainly, sir."

I noted that this was D deck, went up one flight to find cabin C109.

All was not quite in order. My name is not "Graham."

II

The thing that hath been, it is that which
shall be, and that which is done is that
which shall be done, and there is
no new thing under the sun.

Ecclesiastes 1:9

Thank heaven ships use a consistent numbering system. Stateroom C109 was where it should be: on C deck, starboard side forward, between C107 and C111; I reached it without having to speak to anyone. I tried the door; it was locked—Mr. Graham apparently believed the warnings pursers give about locking doors, especially in port.

The key, I thought glumly, is in Mr. Graham's pants pocket. But where is Mr. Graham? About to catch me snooping at his door? Or is he trying my door while I am trying his door?

There is a small but not zero chance that a given key will fit a strange lock. I had in my own pocket my room key from the *Konge Knut.* I tried it.

Well, it was worth trying. I stood there, wondering whether to sneeze or drop dead, when I heard a sweet voice behind me:

"Oh, Mr. Graham!"

A young and pretty woman in a maid's costume—

12

Correction: stewardess' uniform. She came bustling toward me, took a pass key that was chained to her belt, opened C109, while saying, "Margrethe asked me to watch for you. She told me that you had left your cabin key on your desk. She let it stay but told me to watch for you and let you in."

"That's most kind of you, Miss, uh—"

"I'm Astrid. I have the matching rooms on the port side, so Marga and I cover for each other. She's gone ashore this afternoon." She held the door for me. "Will that be all, sir?"

I thanked her, she left. I latched and bolted the door, collapsed in a chair and gave way to the shakes.

Ten minutes later I stood up, went into the bathroom, put cold water on my face and eyes. I had not solved anything and had not wholly calmed down, but my nerves were no longer snapping like a flag in a high wind. I had been holding myself in ever since I had begun to suspect that something was seriously wrong, which was—when? When nothing seemed quite right at the fire pit? Later? Well, with utter certainty when I saw one 20,000-ton ship substituted for another.

My father used to tell me, "Alex, there is nothing wrong with being scared . . . as long as you don't let it affect you until the danger is over. Being hysterical is okay, too . . . afterwards and in private. Tears are not unmanly . . . in the bathroom with the door locked. The difference between a coward and a brave man is mostly a matter of timing."

I'm not the man my father was but I try to follow his advice. If you can learn not to jump when the firecracker goes off—or whatever the surprise is—you stand a good chance of being able to hang tight until the emergency is over.

This emergency was not over but I had benefited by the catharsis of a good case of shakes. Now I could take stock.

Hypotheses:

a) Something preposterous has happened to the world around me, or

b) Something preposterous has happened to Alex Hergensheimer's mind; he should be locked up and sedated.

I could not think of a third hypothesis; those two seemed to cover all bases. The second hypothesis I need not waste time on. If I were raising snakes in my hat, eventually other people would notice and come around with a straitjacket and put me in a nice padded room.

So let's assume that I am sane (or nearly so; being a little bit crazy is helpful). If I am okay, then the world is out of joint. Let's take stock.

That wallet. Not mine. Most wallets are generally similar each to other and this one was much like mine. But carry a wallet for a few years and it fits you; it is distinctly yours. I had known at once that this one was not mine. But I did not want to say so to a ship's petty officer who insisted on "recognizing" me as "Mr. Graham."

I took out Graham's wallet and opened it.

Several hundred francs—count it later.

Eighty-five dollars in paper—legal tender of "The United States of North America."

A driver's license issued to A. L. Graham.

There were more items but I came across a window occupied by a typed notice, one that stopped me cold:

*   *   *

Anyone finding this wallet may keep any money in it as a reward if he will be so kind as to return the wallet to A. L. Graham, cabin C109, S.S. KONGE KNUT, Danish American Line, or to any purser or agent of the line. Thank you. A.L.G.

So now I knew what had happened to the *Konge Knut*; she had undergone a sea change.

Or had *I?* Was there truly a changed world and therefore a changed ship? Or were there two worlds and had I somehow walked through fire into the second one? Were there indeed two men and had they swapped destinies? Or had Alex Hergensheimer metamorphized into Alec Graham while M.V. *Konge Knut* changed into S.S. *Konge Knut?* (While the North American Union melted into the United States of North America?)

Good questions. I'm glad you brought them up. Now, class, are there any more questions—

When I was in middle school there was a spate of magazines publishing fantastic stories, not alone ghost stories but weird yarns of every sort. Magic ships plying the ether to other stars. Strange inventions. Trips to the center of the earth. Other "dimensions." Flying machines. Power from burning atoms. Monsters created in secret laboratories.

I used to buy them and hide them inside copies of *Youth's Companion* and of *Young Crusaders,* knowing instinctively that my parents would disapprove and confiscate. I loved them and so did my outlaw chum Bert.

It couldn't last. First there was an editorial in *Youth's Companion:* "Poison to the Soul—Stamp it Out!" Then our pastor, Brother Draper, preached a sermon against such mind-corrupting trash, with comparisons to the evil effects of cigarettes and booze. Then our state out-lawed such publications under the "standards of the community" doctrine even before passage of the national law and the parallel executive order.

And a cache I had hidden "perfectly" in our attic disappeared. Worse, the works of Mr. H. G. Wells and M. Jules Verne and some others were taken out of our public library.

You have to admire the motives of our spiritual leaders and elected officials in seeking to protect the minds of the young. As Brother Draper pointed out, there are enough exciting and adventurous stories in the Good Book to satisfy the needs of every boy and girl in the world; there was simply no need for profane literature. He was not urging censorship of books for adults, just for the impressionable young. If persons of mature years wanted to read such fantastic trash, suffer them to do so—although he, for one, could not see why any grown man would *want* to.

I guess I was one of the "impressionable young"—I still miss them.

I remember particularly one by Mr. Wells: *Men Like Gods*. These people were driving along in an automobile when an explosion happens and they find themselves in another world, much like their own but better. They meet the people who live there and there is explanation about parallel universes and the fourth dimension and such.

That was the first installment. The Protect-Our-Youth state law was passed right after that, so I never saw the later installments.

One of my English professors who was bluntly opposed to censorship once said that Mr. Wells had invented every one of the basic fantastic themes, and he cited this story as the origin of the multiple-universes concept. I was intending to ask this prof if he knew where I could find a copy, but I put it off to the end of the term when I would be legally "of mature years"— and waited too long; the academic senate committee on faith and morals voted against tenure for that professor, and he left abruptly without finishing the term.

Did something happen to me like that which Mr. Wells described in *Men Like Gods*? Did Mr. Wells have the holy gift of prophecy? For example, would men someday actually fly to the moon? Preposterous!

But was it more preposterous than what had happened to me?

As may be, here I was in *Konge Knut* (even though she was not *my Konge Knut*) and the sailing board at the gangway showed her getting underway at 6 p.m. It was already late afternoon and high time for me to decide.

What to do? I seemed to have mislaid my own ship, the Motor Vessel *Konge Knut*. But the crew (some of the crew) of the Steamship *Konge Knut* seemed ready to accept me as "Mr. Graham," passenger.

Stay aboard and try to brazen it out? What if Graham comes aboard (any minute now!) and demands to know what I am doing in his room?

Or go ashore (as I should) and go to the authorities with my problem?

Alex, the French colonial authorities will love you. No baggage, only the clothes on your back, no money, not a sou—no passport! Oh, they will love you so much they'll give you room and board for the rest of your life . . . in an oubliette with a grill over the top.

There's money in that wallet.

So? Ever heard of the Eighth Commandment? That's *his* money.

But it stands to reason that *he* walked through the fire at the same time you did but on this side, this world or whatever—or his wallet would not have been waiting for you. Now *he* has *your* wallet. That's logical.

Listen, my retarded friend, do you think logic has anything to do with the predicament we are in?

Well—

Speak up!

No, not really. Then how about this? Sit tight in this room. If Graham shows up before the ship sails, you get kicked off the ship, that's sure. But you would be no worse off than you will be if you leave now. If he does *not* show up, then you take his place at least as far as Papeete. That's a big city; your chances of coping with the situation are far better there. Consuls and such.

You talked me into it.

Passenger ships usually publish a daily newspaper for the passengers—just a single or double sheet filled with thrilling items such as "There will be a boat drill at ten o'clock this morning. All passengers are requested—" and "Yesterday's mileage pool was won by Mrs. Ephraim Glutz of Bethany, Iowa" and, usually, a few news items picked up by the wireless operator. I looked around for the ship's paper and for the "Welcome Aboard!" This latter is a booklet (perhaps with another name) intended to make the passenger newly aboard sophisticated in the little world of the ship: names of the officers, times of meals, location of barber shop, laundry, dining room, gift shop (notions, magazines, toothpaste), and how to place a morning call, plan of the ship by decks, location of life preservers, how to find your lifeboat station, where to get your table assignment—

"Table assignment"! Ouch! A passenger who has been aboard even one day does not have to ask how to find his table in the dining room. It's the little things that trip you. Well, I'd have to bull it through.

The welcome-aboard booklet was tucked into Graham's desk. I thumbed through it, with a mental note to memorize all key facts before I left this room— if I was still aboard when the ship sailed—then put it aside, as I had found the ship's newspaper:

The King's Skald it was headed and Graham, bless him, had saved all of them from the day he had boarded the ship . . . at Portland, Oregon, as I deduced from the place and date line of the earliest issue. That suggested that Graham was ticketed for the entire cruise, which could be important to me. I had expected to go back as I had arrived, by airship—but, even if the dirigible liner *Admiral Moffett* existed in this world or dimension or whatever, I no longer had a ticket for it and no money with which to buy one. What do these French colonials do to a tourist who has no money? Burn him at the stake? Or merely draw and quarter him? I did not want to find out. Graham's roundtrip ticket (if he had one) might keep me from having to find out.

(If he didn't show up in the next hour and have me kicked off the ship.)

I did not consider remaining in Polynesia. Being a penniless beachcomber on Bora-Bora or Moorea may have been practical a hundred years ago but today the only thing free in these islands is contagious disease.

It seemed likely that I would be just as broke and just as much a stranger in America but nevertheless I felt that I would be better off in my native land. Well, Graham's native land.

I read some of the wireless news items but could not make sense of them, so I put them aside for later study. What little I had learned from them was not comforting. I had cherished deep down an illogical hope that this would turn out to be just a silly mixup that would soon be straightened out (don't ask me how). But those news items ended all hoping.

I mean to say, what sort of world is it in which the "President" of Germany visits London? In my world Kaiser Wilhelm IV rules the German Empire. A "president" for Germany sounds as silly as a "king" for America.

This might be a pleasant world . . . but it was *not* the world I was born into. Not by those weird news items.

As I put away Graham's file of *The King's Skald* I noted on the top sheet today's prescribed dress for dinner: "Formal."

I was not surprised; the *Konge Knut* in her other incarnation as a motor vessel was quite formal. If the ship was underway, black tie was expected. If you didn't wear it, you were made to feel that you really ought to eat in your stateroom.

I don't own a tuxedo; our church does not encourage vanities. I had compromised by wearing a blue serge suit at dinners underway, with a white shirt and a snap-on black bow tie. Nobody said anything. It did not matter, as I was below the salt anyhow, having come aboard at Papeete.

I decided to see if Mr. Graham owned a dark suit. And a black tie.

Mr. Graham owned lots of clothes, far more than I did. I tried on a sports jacket; it fit me well enough. Trousers? Length seemed okay; I was not sure about the waistband—and too shy to try on a pair and thereby risk being caught by Graham with one leg in his trousers. What does one say? Hi, there! I was just waiting for you and thought I would pass the time by trying on your pants. Not convincing.

He had not one but two tuxedos, one in conventional black and the other in dark red—I had never heard of such frippery.

But I did not find a snap-on bow tie.

He had black bow ties, several. But I have never learned how to tie a bow tie.

I took a deep breath and thought about it.

There came a knock at the door. I didn't jump out of my skin, just almost. "Who's there!" (Honest, Mr. Graham, I was just waiting for you!)

"Stewardess, sir."

"Oh. Come in, come in!"

I heard her try her key, then I jumped to turn back the bolt. "Sorry, I had forgotten that I had used the dead bolt. Do come in."

Margréthe turned out to be about the age of Astrid, youngish, and even prettier, with flaxen hair and freckles across her nose. She spoke textbook-correct English with a charming lilt to it. She was carrying a short white jacket on a coat hanger. "Your mess jacket, sir. Karl says the other one will be ready tomorrow."

"Why, thank you, Margrethe! I had forgotten all about it."

"I thought you might. So I came back aboard a little early—the laundry was just closing. I'm glad I did; it's much too hot for you to wear black."

"You shouldn't have come back early; you're spoiling me."

"I like to take good care of my guests. As you know." She hung the jacket in the wardrobe, turned to leave. "I'll be back to tie your tie. Six-thirty as usual, sir?"

"Six-thirty is fine. What time is it now?" (Tarnation, my watch was gone wherever Motor Vessel *Konge Knut* had vanished; I had not worn it ashore.)

"Almost six o'clock." She hesitated. "I'll lay out your clothes before I go; you don't have much time."

"My dear girl! That's no part of your duties."

"No, it's my pleasure." She opened a drawer, took out a dress shirt, placed it on my/Graham's bunk. "And you know why." With the quick efficiency of a person who knows exactly where everything is, she opened a small desk drawer that I had not touched, took out a leather case, from it laid out by the shirt a watch, a ring, and shirt studs, then inserted studs into the shirt, placed fresh underwear and black silk socks on the pillow, placed evening pumps by the chair with shoe horn tucked inside, took from the wardrobe that mess jacket, hung it and black dress trousers (braces attached) and dark red cummerbund on the front of the wardrobe. She glanced over the layout, added a wing collar, a black tie, and a fresh handkerchief to the stack on the pillow—cast her eye over it again, placed the room key and the wallet by the ring and the watch—glanced again, nodded. "I must run or I'll miss dinner. I'll be back for the tie." And she was gone, not running but moving very fast.

Margrethe was so right. If she had not laid out everything, I would still be struggling to put myself together. That shirt alone would have stopped me; it was one of the dive-in-and-button-up-the-back sort. I had never worn one.

Thank heaven Graham used an ordinary brand of safety razor. By six-fifteen I had touched up my morning shave, showered (necessary!), and washed the smoke out of my hair.

His shoes fit me as if I had broken them in myself. His trousers were a bit tight in the waist—a Danish ship is no place to lose weight and I had been in the Motor Vessel *Konge Knut* for a fortnight. I was still struggling with that consarned backwards shirt when Margrethe let herself in with her pass key.

She came straight to me, said, "Hold still," and quickly buttoned the buttons I could not reach. Then she fitted that fiendish collar over its collar buttons, laid the tie around my neck. "Turn around, please."

Tying a bow tie properly involves magic. She knew the spell.

She helped me with the cummerbund, held my jacket for me, looked me over and announced, "You'll do. And I'm proud of you; at dinner the girls were talking about you. I wish I had seen it. You are very brave."

"Not brave. Foolish. I talked when I should have kept still."

"Brave. I must go—I left Kristina guarding a cherry tart for me. But if I stay away too long someone will steal it."

"You run along. And thank you loads! Hurry and save that tart."

"Aren't you going to pay me?"

"Oh. What payment would you like?"

"Don't tease me!" She moved a few inches closer, turned her face up. I don't know much about girls (who does?) but some signals are large print. I took her by her shoulders, kissed both her cheeks, hesitated just long enough to be certain that she was neither displeased nor surprised, then placed one right in the middle. Her lips were full and warm.

"Was that the payment you had in mind?"

"Yes, of course. But you can kiss better than that. You know you can." She pouted her lower lip, then dropped her eyes.

"Brace yourself."

Yes, I can kiss lots better than that. Or could by the time we had used up that kiss. By letting Margrethe lead it and heartily cooperating in whatever way she seemed to think a better kiss should go I learned more about kissing in the next two minutes than I had learned in my entire life up to then.

My ears roared.

For a moment after we broke she held still in my arms and looked up at me most soberly. "Alec," she said softly, "that's the best you've ever kissed me. Goodness. Now I'm going to run before I make you late for dinner." She slipped out of my arms and left as she did everything, quickly.

I inspected myself in the mirror. No marks. A kiss that emphatic ought to leave marks.

What sort of person was this Graham? I could wear his clothes . . . but could I cope with his woman? Or was she his? Who knows?—I did not. Was he a lecher, a womanizer? Or was I butting in on a perfectly nice if somewhat indiscreet romance?

How do you walk back through a fire pit?

And did I want to?

Go aft to the main companionway, then down two decks and go aft again—that's what the ship's plans in the booklet showed.

No problem. A man at the door of the dining saloon, dressed much as I was but with a menu under his arm, had to be the head waiter, the chief dining-room steward. He confirmed it with a big professional smile. "Good evening, Mr. Graham."

I paused. "Good evening. What's this about a change in seating arrangements? Where am I to sit tonight?" (If you grab the bull by the horns, you at least confuse him.)

"It's not a permanent change, sir. Tomorrow you will be back at table fourteen. But tonight the Captain has asked that you sit at his table. If you will follow me, sir."

He led me to an oversize table amidships, started to seat me on the Captain's right—and the Captain stood up and started to clap, the others at his table followed suit, and shortly everyone in the dining room (it seemed) was standing and clapping and some were cheering.

I learned two things at that dinner. First, it was clear that Graham had pulled the same silly stunt I had (but it still was not clear whether there was one of us or two of us—I tabled that question).

Second, but of major importance: Do not drink ice-cold Aalborg akvavit on an empty stomach, especially if you were brought up White Ribbon as I was.

III

Wine is a mocker, strong drink is raging—
Proverbs 20:1

I am not blaming Captain Hansen. I have heard that Scandinavians put ethanol into their blood as antifreeze, against their long hard winters, and consequently cannot understand people who cannot take strong drink. Besides that, nobody held my arms, nobody held my nose, nobody forced spirits down my throat. I did it myself.

Our church doesn't hold with the doctrine that the flesh is weak and therefore sin is humanly understandable and readily forgiven. Sin can be forgiven but just barely and you are surely going to catch it first. Sin should suffer.

I found out about some of that suffering. I'm told it is called a hangover.

That is what my drinking uncle called it. Uncle Ed maintained that no man can cope with temperance who has not had a full course of intemperance . . . otherwise when temptation came his way, he would not know how to handle it.

27

Maybe I proved Uncle Ed's point. He was considered a bad influence around our house and, if he had not been Mother's brother, Dad would not have allowed him in the house. As it was, he was never pressed to stay longer and was not urged to hurry back.

Before I even sat down at the table, the Captain offered me a glass of akvavit. The glasses used for this are not large; they are quite small—and that is the deceptive part of the danger.

The Captain had a glass like it in his hand. He looked me in the eye and said, "To our hero! *Skaal!*"— threw his head back and tossed it down.

There were echoes of *"Skaal!"* all around the table and everyone seemed to gulp it down just like the Captain.

So I did. I could say that being guest of honor laid certain obligations on me—"When in Rome" and all that. But the truth is I did not have the requisite strength of character to refuse. I told myself, "One tiny glass can't hurt," and gulped it down.

No trouble. It went down smoothly. One pleasant ice-cold swallow, then a spicy aftertaste with a hint of licorice. I did not know what I was drinking but I was not sure that it was alcoholic. It seemed not to be.

We sat down and somebody put food in front of me and the Captain's steward poured another glass of schnapps for me. I was about to start nibbling the food, Danish hors d'oeuvres and delicious—smorgasbord tidbits—when someone put a hand on my shoulder.

I looked up. The Well-Traveled Man—

With him were the Authority and the Skeptic.

Not the same names. Whoever (Whatever?) was playing games with my life had not gone that far.

"Gerald Fortescue" was now "Jeremy Forsyth," for example. But despite slight differences I had no trouble recognizing each of them and their new names were close enough to show that someone, or something, was continuing the joke.

(Then why wasn't my new name something like "Hergensheimer"? "Hergensheimer" has dignity about it, a rolling grandeur. Graham is a so-so name.)

"Alec," Mr. Forsyth said, "we misjudged you. Duncan and I and Pete are happy to admit it. Here's the three thousand we owe you, and—" He hauled his right hand out from behind his back, held up a large bottle. "—the best champagne in the ship as a mark of our esteem."

"Steward!" said the Captain.

Shortly the wine steward was going around, filling glasses at our table. But before that, I found myself again standing up, making *Skaal!* in akvavit three times, once to each of the losers, while clutching three thousand dollars (United States of North America dollars). I did not have time then to wonder why three hundred had changed to three thousand—besides, it was not as odd as what had happened to the *Konge Knut*. Both of her. And my wonder circuits were overloaded anyhow.

Captain Hansen told his waitress to place chairs at the table for Forsyth and company, but all three insisted that their wives and table mates expected them to return. Nor was there room. Not that it would have mattered to Captain Hansen. He is a Viking, half again as big as a house; hand him a hammer and he would be mistaken for Thor—he has muscles where other men don't even have places. It is very hard to argue with him.

But he jovially agreed to compromise. They could go back to their tables and finish their dinners but first they must join him and me in pledging Shadrach, Meshach, and Abed-nego, guardian angels of our shipmate Alec. In fact the whole table must join in. "Steward!"

So we said *"Skaal!"* three more times, while bouncing Danish antifreeze off our tonsils.

Have you kept count? That's seven, I think. You can stop counting, as that is where I lost track. I was beginning to feel a return of the numbness I had felt halfway through the fire pit.

The wine steward had completed pouring champagne, having renewed his supply at a gesture from the Captain. Then it was time to toast me again, and I returned the compliment to the three losers, then we all toasted Captain Hansen, and then we toasted the good ship *Konge Knut*.

The Captain toasted the United States and the whole room stood and drank with him, so I felt it incumbent to answer by toasting the Danish Queen, and that got me toasted again and the Captain demanded a speech from me. "Tell us how it feels to be in the fiery furnace!"

I tried to refuse and there were shouts of "Speech! Speech!" from all around me.

I stood up with some difficulty, tried to remember the speech I had made at the last foreign missions fundraising dinner. It evaded me. Finally I said, "Aw, shucks, it wasn't anything. Just put your ear to the ground and your shoulder to the wheel and your eyes on the stars and you can do it too. Thank you, thank you all and next time you must come to my house."

They cheered and we skaaled again, I forget why, and the lady on the Captain's left got up and came around and kissed me, whereupon all the ladies at the Captain's table clustered around and kissed me. That seemed to inspire the other ladies in the room, for there was a steady procession coming up to claim a buss from me, and usually kissing the Captain while they were about it, or perhaps the other way around.

During this parade someone removed a steak from in front of me, one I had had plans for. I didn't miss it too much, because that endless orgy of osculation had me bewildered, plus bemusement much like that caused by the female villagers of the fire walk.

Much of this bemusement started when I first walked into the dining room. Let me put it this way: My fellow passengers, female, really should have been in the *National Geographic*.

Yes. Like that. Well, maybe not quite, but what they did wear made them look nakeder than those friendly villagers. I'm not going to describe those "formal evening dresses" because I'm not sure I could—and I *am* sure I shouldn't. But none of them covered more than twenty percent of what ladies usually keep covered at fancy evening affairs in the world I grew up in. Above the waist I mean. Their skirts, long, some clear to the floor, were nevertheless cut or slit in most startling ways.

Some of the ladies had tops to their dresses that covered everything . . . but the material was transparent as glass. Or almost.

And some of the youngest ladies, girls really, actually did belong in the *National Geographic,* just like my villagers. Somehow, these younger ladies did not seem quite as immodest as their elders.

I had noticed this display almost the instant I walked in. But I tried not to stare and the Captain and others kept me so busy at first that I really did not have time to sneak glances at the incredible exposure. But, look—when a lady comes up and puts her arms around you and insists on kissing you, it is difficult *not* to notice that she isn't wearing enough to ward off pneumonia. Or other chest complaints.

But I kept a tight rein on myself despite increasing dizziness and numbness.

Even bare skin did not startle me as much as bare words—language I had never heard in public in my life and extremely seldom even in private among men only. "Men," I said, as gentlemen don't talk that way even with no ladies present—in the world I knew.

The most shocking thing that ever happened to me in my boyhood was one day crossing the town square, noticing a crowd on the penance side of the courthouse, joining it to see who was catching it and why . . . and finding my Scoutmaster in the stocks. I almost fainted.

His offense was profane language, so the sign on his chest told us. The accuser was his own wife; he did not dispute it and had thrown himself on the mercy of the court—the judge was Deacon Brumby, who didn't know the word.

Mr. Kirk, my Scoutmaster, left town two weeks later and nobody ever saw him again—being exposed in the stocks was likely to have that effect on a man. I don't know what the bad language was that Mr. Kirk had used, but it couldn't have been too bad, as all Deacon Brumby could give him was one dawn-to-dusk.

That night at the Captain's table in the *Konge Knut* I heard a sweet lady of the favorite-grandmother sort address her husband in a pattern of forbidden words involving blasphemy and certain criminal sensual acts. Had she spoken that way in public in my home town she would have received maximum exposure in stocks followed by being ridden out of town. (Our town did not use tar and feathers; that was regarded as brutal.)

Yet this dear lady in the ship was not even chided. Her husband simply smiled and told her that she worried too much.

Between shocking speech, incredible immodest exposure, and effects of two sorts of strange and deceptive potions lavishly administered, I was utterly confused. A stranger in a strange land, I was overcome by customs new and shocking. But through it all I clung to the conviction that I must appear to be sophisticated, at home, unsurprised. I must not let anyone suspect that I was not Alec Graham, shipmate, but instead Alexander Hergensheimer, total stranger . . . or something terrible might happen.

Of course I was wrong; something terrible had already happened. I was indeed a total stranger in an utterly strange and confusing land . . . but I do not think, in retrospect, that I would have made my condition worse had I simply blurted out my predicament.

I would not have been believed.

How else? I had trouble believing it myself.

Captain Hansen, a hearty no-nonsense man, would have bellowed with laughter at my "joke" and insisted on another toast. Had I persisted in my "delusion" he would have had the ship's doctor talk to me.

Still, I got through that amazing evening easier by holding tight to the notion that I must concentrate on acting the part of Alec Graham while never letting anyone suspect that I was a changeling, a cuckoo's egg.

There had just been placed in front of me a slice of princess cake, a beautiful multilayered confection I recalled from the other *Konge Knut,* and a small cup of coffee, when the Captain stood up. "Come, Alec! We go to the lounge now; the show is ready to start—but they can't start till I get there. So come on! You don't want all that sweet stuff; it's not good for you. You can have coffee in the lounge. But before that we have some man's drinks, henh? Not these joke drinks. You like Russian vodka?"

He linked his arm in mine. I discovered that I was going to the lounge. Volition did not enter into it.

That lounge show was much the mixture I had found earlier in M.V. *Konge Knut*—a magician who did improbable things but not as improbable as what I had done (or been done to?), a standup comedian who should have sat down, a pretty girl who sang, and dancers. The major differences were two I had already been exposed to: bare skin and bare words, and by then I was so numb from earlier shock and akvavit that these additional proofs of a different world had minimal effect.

The girl who sang just barely had clothes on and the lyrics of her songs would have caused her trouble even in the underworld of Newark, New Jersey. Or so I think; I have no direct experience with that notorious sink of iniquity. I paid more attention to her appearance, since here I need not avert my eyes; one is *expected* to stare at performers.

If one admits for the sake of argument that customs in dress can be wildly different without destroying the fabric of society (a possibility I do not concede but will stipulate), then it helps, I think, if the person exhibiting this difference is young and healthy and comely.

The singer was young and healthy and comely. I felt a twinge of regret when she left the spotlight.

The major event was a troupe of Tahitian dancers, and I was truly not surprised that they were costumed bare to the waist save for flowers or shell beads—by then I would have been surprised had they been otherwise. What was still surprising (although I suppose it should not have been) was the subsequent behavior of my fellow passengers.

First the troupe, eight girls, two men, danced for us, much the same dancing that had preceded the fire walk today, much the same as I had seen when a troupe had come aboard M.V. *Konge Knut* in Papeete. Perhaps you know that the hula of Tahiti differs from the slow and graceful hula of the Kingdom of Hawaii by being at a *much* faster beat and is much more energetic. I'm no expert on the arts of the dance but at least I have seen both styles of hula in the lands where each was native.

I prefer the Hawaiian hula, which I had seen when the *Count von Zeppelin* had stopped at Hilo for a day on her way to Papeete. The Tahitian hula strikes me as an athletic accomplishment rather than an art form. But its very energy and speed make it still more startling in the dress or undress these native girls wore.

There was more to come. After a long dance sequence

which included paired dancing between girls and each of the two young men—in which they did things that would have been astonishing even among barnyard fowl (I kept expecting Captain Hansen to put a stop to it), the ship's master of ceremonies or cruise director stepped forward.

"Ladeez and gentlemen," he announced, "and the rest of you intoxicated persons of irregular birth—" (I am forced to amend his language.) "Most of you setters and even a few pointers have made good use of the four days our dancers have been with us to add the Tahitian hula to your repertoire. Shortly you'll be given a chance to demonstrate what you've learned and to receive diplomas as authentic Papeete papayas. But what you don't know is that others in the good ole knutty *Knut* have been practicing, too. Maestro, strike up the band!"

Out from behind the lounge stage danced a dozen more hula dancers. But these girls were not Polynesian; these girls were Caucasian. They were dressed authentically, grass skirts and necklaces, a flower in the hair, nothing else. But instead of warm brown, their skins were white; most of them were blondes, two were redheads.

It makes a difference. By then I was ready to concede that Polynesian women were correctly and even modestly dressed in their native costume—other places, other customs. Was not Mother Eve modest in her simplicity before the Fall?

But white women are grossly out of place in South Seas garb.

However, this did not keep me from watching the dancing. I was amazed to see that these girls danced that fast and complex dance as well (to my untutored eye) as did the island girls. I remarked on it to the Captain. "They learned to dance that precisely in only four days?"

He snorted. "They practice every cruise, those who ship with us before. All have practiced at least since San Diego."

At that point I recognized one of the dancers—Astrid, the sweet young woman who had let me into "my" stateroom—and I then understood why they had had time and incentive to practice together: These girls were ship's crew. I looked at her—stared, in fact—with more interest. She caught my eye and smiled. Like a dolt, a bumpkin, instead of smiling back I looked away and blushed, and tried to cover my embarrassment by taking a big sip of the drink I found in my hand.

One of the kanaka dancers whirled out in front of the white girls and called one of them out for a pair dance. Heaven save me, it was Margrethe!

I choked up and could not breathe. She was the most blindingly beautiful sight I had ever seen in all my life.

"Behold, thou art fair, my love; behold, thou art fair; thou hast doves' eyes within thy locks: thy hair is as a flock of goats, that appear from Mount Gilead.

"Thy navel is like a round goblet, which wanteth not liquor: thy belly is like a heap of wheat set about with lilies.

"Thy two breasts are like two young roes that are twins.

"Thou art all fair, my love; there is no spot in thee."

IV

I slowly became aware of myself and wished I had not; a most terrible nightmare was chasing me. I jammed my eyes shut against the light and tried to go back to sleep.

Native drums were beating in my head; I tried to shut them out by covering my ears.

They got louder.

I gave up, opened my eyes and lifted my head. A mistake—my stomach flipflopped and my ears shook. My eyes would not track and those infernal drums were tearing my skull apart.

I finally got my eyes to track, although the focus was fuzzy. I looked around, found that I was in a strange room, lying on top of a bed and only half dressed.

That began to bring it back to me. A party aboard ship. Spirits. Lots of spirits. Noise. Nakedness. The Captain in a grass skirt, dancing heartily, and the orchestra keeping step with him. Some of the lady passengers wearing grass skirts and some wearing even less. Rattle of bamboo, boom of drums.

Drums—

Those weren't drums in my head; that was the booming of the worst headache of my life. Why in Ned did I let them—

Never mind "them." You did it yourself, chum.

Yes, but—

"Yes, but." Always "Yes, but." All your life it's been "Yes, but." When are you going to straighten up and take full responsibility for your life and all that happens to you?

Yes, but *this* isn't my fault. I'm not A. L. Graham. That isn't my name. This isn't my ship.

It isn't? You're not?

Of course not—

I sat up to shake off this bad dream. Sitting up was a mistake; my head did not fall off but a stabbing pain at the base of my neck added itself to the throbbing inside my skull. I was wearing black dress trousers and apparently nothing else and I was in a strange room that was rolling slowly.

Graham's trousers. Graham's room. And that long, slow roll was that of a ship with no stabilizers.

Not a dream. Or if it is, I can't shake myself out of it. My teeth itched, my feet didn't fit. Dried sweat all over me except where I was clammy. My armpits— Don't even think about armpits!

My mouth needed to have lye dumped into it.

I remembered everything now. Or almost. The fire pit. Villagers. Chickens scurrying out of the way. The ship that wasn't my ship—but was. Margrethe—

Margrethe!

"Thy two breasts are like two roes—thou art all fair, my love!"

Margrethe among the dancers, her bosom as bare as

her feet. Margrethe dancing with that villainous kanaka, and shaking her—

No wonder I got drunk!

Stow it, chum! You were drunk before that. All
you've got against that native lad is that it was he instead of *you*. You wanted to dance with her yourself.
Only *you* can't dance.

Dancing is a snare of Satan.

And don't you wish you knew how!

"*—like two roes*"! Yes. I do!

I heard a light tap at the door, then a rattle of keys.
Margrethe stuck her head in. "Awake? Good." She
came in, carrying a tray, closed the door, came to me.
"Drink this."

"What is it?"

"Tomato juice, mostly. Don't argue—drink it!"

"I don't think I can."

"Yes, you can. You must. Do it."

I sniffed it, then I took a small sip. To my amazement it did not nauseate me. So I drank some more.
After one minor quiver it went down smoothly and lay
quietly inside me. Margrethe produced two pills. "Take
these. Wash them down with the rest of the tomato
juice."

"I never take medicine."

She sighed, and said something I did not understand. Not English. Not quite. "What did you say?"

"Just something my grandmother used to say when
grandfather argued with her. Mr. Graham, take those
pills. They are just aspirin and you need them. If you
won't cooperate, I'll stop trying to help you. I'll— I'll
swap you to Astrid, that's what I'll do."

"Don't do that."

"I will if you keep objecting. Astrid would swap, I know she would. She likes you—she told me you were watching her dance last night."

I accepted the pills, washed them down with the rest of the tomato juice—ice-cold and very comforting. "I did until I spotted you. Then I watched you."

She smiled for the first time. "Yes? Did you like it?"

"You were beautiful." (And your dance was obscene. Your immodest dress and your behavior shocked me out of a year's growth. I hated it—and I wish I could see it all over again this very instant!) "You are very graceful."

The smile grew dimples. "I had hoped that you would like it, sir."

"I did. Now stop threatening me with Astrid."

"All right. As long as you behave. Now get up and into the shower. First very hot, then very cold. Like a sauna." She waited. "'Up,' I said. I'm not leaving until that shower is running and steam is pouring out."

"I'll shower. After you leave."

"And you'll run it lukewarm, I know. Get up, get those trousers off, get into that shower. While you're showering, I'll fetch your breakfast tray. There is just enough time before they shut down the galley to set up for lunch . . . so quit wasting time. Please!"

"Oh, I can't eat breakfast! Not today. No." Food— what a disgusting thought.

"You *must* eat. You drank too much last night, you know you did. If you don't eat, you will feel bad all day. Mr. Graham, I've finished making up for all my other guests, so I'm off watch now. I'm fetching your tray, then I'm going to stay and see that you eat it."

She looked at me. "I should have taken your trousers off when I put you to bed. But you were too heavy."

"You put me to bed?"

"Ori helped me. The boy I danced with." My face must have given me away, for she added hastily, "Oh, I didn't let him come into your room, sir. I undressed you myself. But I did have to have help to get you up the stairs."

"I wasn't criticizing." (Did you go back to the party then? Was he there? Did you dance with him again? *"—jealousy is cruel as the grave; the coals thereof are coals of fire—"* I have no right.) "I thank you both. I must have been a beastly nuisance."

"Well . . . brave men often drink too much, after danger is over. But it's not good for you."

"No, it's not." I got up off the bed, went into the bathroom, said, "I'll turn it up hot. Promise." I closed the door and bolted it, finished undressing. (So I got so stinking, rubber-limp drunk that a native boy had to help get me to bed. Alex, you're a disgusting mess! And you haven't any right to be jealous over a nice girl. You don't own her, her behavior is not wrong by the standards of this place—wherever this place is—and all she's done is mother you and take care of you. That does not give you a claim on her.)

I did turn it up hot, though it durn near kilt poor old Alex. But I left it hot until the nerve ends seemed cauterized—then suddenly switched it to cold, and screamed.

I let it stay cold until it no longer felt cold, then shut it off and dried down, having opened the door to let out the moisture-charged air. I stepped out into the room . . . and suddenly realized that I felt wonderful.

No headache. No feeling that the world is ending at noon. No stomach queasies. Just hunger. Alex, you must never get drunk again . . . but if you do, you must do exactly what Margrethe tells you to. You've got a smart head on her shoulders, boy—appreciate it.

I started to whistle and opened Graham's wardrobe.

I heard a key in the door, hastily grabbed his bathrobe, managed to cover up before she got the door open. She was slow about it, being hampered by a heavy tray. When I realized this I held the door for her. She put down the tray, then arranged dishes and food on my desk.

"You were right about the sauna-type shower," I told her. "It was just what the doctor ordered. Or the nurse, I should say."

"I know, it's what my grandmother used to do for my grandfather."

"A smart woman. My, this smells good!" (Scrambled eggs, bacon, lavish amounts of Danish pastry, milk, coffee—a side dish of cheeses, *fladbrød,* and thin curls of ham, some tropic fruit I can't name.) "What was that your grandmother used to say when your grandfather argued?"

"Oh, she was sometimes impatient."

"And you never are. Tell me."

"Well— She used to say that God created men to test the souls of women."

"She may have a point. Do you agree with her?"

Her smile produced dimples. "I think they have other uses as well."

Margrethe tidied my room and cleaned my bath (okay, okay, *Graham's* room, *Graham's* bath—satisfied?)

while I ate. She laid out a pair of slacks, a sport shirt in an island print, and sandals for me, then removed the tray and dishes while leaving coffee and the remaining fruit. I thanked her as she left, wondered if I should offer "payment" and wondered, too, if she performed such valet services for other passengers. It seemed unlikely. I found I could not ask.

I bolted the door after her and proceeded to search Graham's room.

I was wearing his clothes, sleeping in his bed, answering to his name—and now I must decide whether or not I would go whole hawg and *be* "A. L. Graham" . . . or should I go to some authority (American consul? If not, whom?), admit the impersonation, and ask for help?

Events were crowding me. Today's *King Skald* showed that S.S. *Konge Knut* was scheduled to dock at Papeete at 3 p.m. and sail for Mazatlán, Mexico, at 6 p.m. The purser notified all passengers wishing to change francs into dollars that a representative of the Bank of Papeete would be in the ship's square facing the purser's office from docking until fifteen minutes before sailing. The purser again wished to notify passengers that shipboard indebtedness such as bar and shop bills could be settled only in dollars, Danish crowns, or by means of validated letters of credit.

All very reasonable. And troubling. I had expected the ship to stop at Papeete for twenty-four hours at the very least. Docking for only three hours seemed preposterous—why, they would hardly finish tying up before it would be time to start singling up for sailing! Didn't they have to pay rent for twenty-four hours if they docked at all?

Then I reminded myself that managing the ship was not my business. Perhaps the Captain was taking advantage of a few hours between departure of one ship and arrival of another. Or there might be six other reasons. The only thing I should worry about was what I could accomplish between three and six, and what I *must* accomplish between now and three.

Forty minutes of intense searching turned up the following:

Clothes, all sorts—no problem other than about five pounds at my waistline.

Money—the francs in his billfold (must change them) and the eighty-five dollars there; three thousand dollars loose in the desk drawer that held the little case for Graham's watch, ring, shirt studs, etc. Since the watch and jewelry had been returned to this case, I assumed conclusively that Margrethe had conserved for me the proceeds of that bet that I (or Graham) had won from Forsyth and Jeeves and Henshaw. It is said that the Lord looks out for fools and drunkards; if so, in my case He operated through Margrethe.

Various impedimenta of no significance to my immediate problem—books, souvenirs, toothpaste, etc.

No passport.

When a first search failed to turn up Graham's passport, I went back and searched again, this time checking the pockets of all clothes hanging in his wardrobe as well as rechecking with care all the usual places and some unusual places that might hide a booklet the size of a passport.

No passport.

Some tourists are meticulous about keeping their passports on their persons whenever leaving a ship. I prefer not to carry my passport when I can avoid it because losing a passport is a sticky mess. I had not carried mine the day before . . . so now mine was gone where the woodbine twineth, gone to Fiddler's Green, gone where Motor Vessel *Konge Knut* had gone. And where was that? I had not had time to think about that yet; I was too busy coping with a strange new world.

If Graham had carried his passport yesterday, then it too was gone to Fiddler's Green through a crack in the fourth dimension. It was beginning to look that way.

While I fumed, someone slipped an envelope under the stateroom door.

I picked it up and opened it. Inside was the purser's billing for "my" (Graham's) bills aboard ship. Was Graham scheduled to leave the ship at Papeete? Oh, no! If he was, I might be marooned in the islands indefinitely.

No, maybe not. This appeared to be a routine end-of-a-month billing.

The size of Graham's bar bill shocked me . . . until I noticed some individual items. Then I was still more shocked but for another reason. When a Coca-Cola costs two dollars it does not mean that a Coke is bigger; it means that the dollar is smaller.

I now knew why a three-hundred-dollar bet on, uh, the *other* side turned out to be three thousand dollars on this side.

If I was going to have to live in this world, I was going to have to readjust my thinking about all prices. Treat dollars as I would a foreign currency and convert all prices in my head until I got used to them. For example, if these shipboard prices were representative, then a first-class dinner, steak or prime rib, in a first-class restaurant, let's say the main dining room of a hotel such as the Brown Palace or the Mark Hopkins—such a dinner could easily cost ten dollars. Whew!

With cocktails before dinner and wine with it, the tab might reach fifteen dollars! A week's wages. Thank heaven I don't drink!

You don't what?

Look—last night was a very special occasion.

So? So it was, because you lose your virginity only once. Once gone, it's gone forever. What was that you were drinking just before the lights went out? A Danish zombie? Wouldn't you like one of those about now? Just to readjust your stability?

I'll never touch one again!

See you later, chum.

Just one more chance but a good one—I hoped. The small case that Graham used for jewelry and such had in it a key, plain save for the number eighty-two stamped on its side. If fate was smiling, that was a key to a lockbox in the purser's office.

(And if fate was sneering at me today, it was a key to a lockbox in a bank somewhere in the forty-six states, a bank I would never see. But let's not borrow trouble; I have all I need.)

I went down one deck and aft. "Good morning, Purser."

"Ah, Mr. Graham! A fine party, was it not?"

"It certainly was. One more like that and I'm a corpse."

"Oh, come now. That from a man who walks through fire. You seemed to enjoy it—and I know I did. What can we do for you, sir?"

I brought out the key I had found. "Do I have the right key? Or does this one belong to my bank? I can never remember."

The purser took it. "That's one of ours. Poul! Take this and get Mr. Graham's box. Mr. Graham, do you want to come around behind and sit at a table?"

"Yes, thank you. Uh, do you have a sack or something that would hold the contents of a box that size? I would take it back to my desk for paper work."

"'A sack'— Mmm . . . I could get one from the gift shop. But— How long do you think this desk work will take you? Can you finish it by noon?"

"Oh, certainly."

"Then take the box itself back to your stateroom. There is a rule against it but I made the rule so we can risk breaking it. But try to be back by noon. We close from noon to thirteen—union rules—and if I have to sit here by myself with all my clerks gone to lunch, you'll have to buy me a drink."

"I'll buy you one anyhow."

"We'll roll for it. Here you are. Don't take it through any fires."

Right on top was Graham's passport. A tight lump in my chest eased. I know of no more lost feeling than being outside the Union without a passport . . . even though it's not truly the Union. I opened it, looked at the picture embossed inside. Do I look like that? I went into the bathroom, compared the face in the mirror with the face in the passport.

Near enough, I guess. No one expects much of a passport picture. I tried holding the photograph up to the mirror. Suddenly it was a good resemblance.

Chum, your face is lopsided . . . and so is yours, Mr. Graham.

Brother, if I'm going to have to assume your identity permanently—and it looks more and more as if I had no choice—it's a relief to know that we look so much alike. Fingerprints? We'll cope with that when we have to. Seems the U.S. of N.A. doesn't use fingerprints on passports; that's some help. Occupation: Executive. Executive of *what*? A funeral parlor? Or a worldwide chain of hotels? Maybe this is not going to be difficult but merely impossible.

Address: Care of O'Hara, Rigsbee, Crumpacker, and Rigsbee, Attys at Law, Suite 7000, Smith Building, Dallas. Oh, just dandy. Merely a mail drop. No business address, no home address, no business. Why, you phony, I'd love to poke you in the snoot!

(He can't be too repulsive; Margrethe thinks well of him. Well, yes—but he should keep his hands off Margrethe; he's taking advantage of her. Unfair. *Who* is taking advantage of her? Watch it, boy, you'll get a split personality.)

An envelope under the passport contained the passenger's file copy of his ticket—and it was indeed round trip, Portland to Portland. Twin, unless you show up before 6 p.m., I've got a trip home. Maybe you can use my ticket in the *Admiral Moffett*. I wish you luck.

There were some minor items but the bulk of the metal box was occupied by ten sealed fat envelopes, business size. I opened one.

It contained thousand-dollar bills, one hundred of them.

I made a fast check with the other nine. All alike. One million dollars in cash.

V

The wicked flee when no man pursueth:
but the righteous are bold as a lion.
Proverbs 28:1

Barely breathing, I used gummed tape I found in Graham's desk to seal the envelopes. I put everything back but the passport, placed it with that three thousand that I thought of as "mine" in the little drawer of the desk, then took the box back to the purser's office, carrying it carefully.

Someone else was at the front desk but the purser was in sight in his inner office; I caught his eye.

"Hi," he called out. "Back so soon?" He came out.

"Yes," I agreed. "For once, everything tallied." I passed the box to him.

"I'd like to hire you for this office. Here, nothing ever tallies. At least not earlier than midnight. Let's go find that drink. I need one."

"So do I! Let's."

The purser led me aft to an outdoor bar I had not noticed on the ship's plan. The deck above us ended and the deck we were on, D deck, continued on out as a weather deck, bright teak planks pleasant to walk on.

The break on C deck formed an overhang; under it was this outdoor spread canvas. At right angles to the bar were long tables offering a lavish buffet lunch; passengers were queued up for it. Farther aft was the ship's swimming pool; I could hear splashing, squeals, and yells.

He led me on aft to a small table occupied by two junior officers. We stopped there. "You two. Jump overboard."

"Right away, Purser." They stood up, picked up their beer glasses, and moved farther aft. One of them grinned at me and nodded, as if we knew each other, so I nodded and said, "Hi."

This table was partly shaded by awning. The purser said to me, "Do you want to sit in the sun and watch the girls, or sit in the shade and relax?"

"Either way. Sit where you wish; I'll take the other chair."

"Um. Let's move this table a little and both sit in the shade. There, that does it." He sat down facing forward; perforce I sat facing the swimming pool—and confirmed something I thought I had seen at first glance: This swimming pool did not require anything as redundant as swim suits.

I should have inferred it by logic had I thought about it—but I had not. The last time I had seen it—swimming without suits—I had been about twelve and it had been strictly a male privilege for boys that age or younger.

"I said, 'What will you drink, Mr. Graham?'"

"Oh! Sorry, I wasn't listening."

"I know. You were looking. What will it be?"

"Uh . . . a Danish zombie."

He blinked at me. "You don't want that at this time of day; that's a skull splitter. Mmm—" He waggled his fingers at someone behind me. "Sweetheart, come here."

I looked up as the summoned waitress approached. I looked and then looked twice. I had seen her last through an alcoholic haze the night before, one of two redheads in the hula chorus line.

"Tell Hans I want two silver fizzes. What's your name, dear?"

"Mr. Henderson, you pretend just one more time that you don't know my name and I'll pour your drink right on your bald spot."

"Yes, dear. Now hurry up. Get those fat legs moving."

She snorted and glided away on limbs that were slender and graceful. The purser added, "A fine girl, that. Her parents live just across from me in Odense; I've known her since she was a baby. A smart girl, too. Bodel is studying to be a veterinary surgeon, one more year to go."

"Really? How does she do this and go to school, too?"

"Most of our girls are at university. Some take a summer off, some take a term off—go to sea, have some fun, save up money for next term. In hiring I give preference to girls who are working their way through university; they are more dependable—and they know more languages. Take your room stewardess. Astrid?"

"No. Margrethe."

"Oh, yes, you are in one-oh-nine; Astrid has portside forward on your deck, Margrethe is on your side. Margrethe Svensdatter Gunderson. Schoolteacher. English language and history. But knows four more languages—not counting Scandinavian languages—and has certificates for two of them. On one-year leave from H. C. Andersen Middle School. I'm betting she won't go back."

"Eh? Why?"

"She'll marry a rich American. Are you rich?"

"*Me?* Do I look rich?" (Could he possibly know what is in that lockbox? Dear God, what does one do with a million dollars that isn't yours? I can't just throw it overboard. Why would Graham be traveling with that much in cash? I could think of several reasons, all bad. Any one of them could get me in more trouble than I had ever seen.)

"Rich Americans never look it; they practice not looking rich. North Americans, I mean; South Americans are another fish entirely. Gertrude, thank you. You are a good girl."

"You want this drink on your bald spot?"

"You want me to throw you into the pool with your clothes on? Behave yourself, dear, or I'll tell your mother. Put them down and give me the chit."

"No chit; Hans wanted to buy a drink for Mr. Graham. So he decided to include you, this once."

"You tell him that's the way the bar loses money. Tell him I take it out of his wages."

That's how I happened to drink two silver fizzes instead of one . . . and was well on my way toward a disaster such as the night before, when Mr. Henderson decided that we must eat. I wanted a third fizz. The first two had enabled me to quit worrying over that crazy box full of money while enhancing my appreciation of the poolside floor show. I was discovering that a lifetime of conditioning could wash away in only twenty-four hours. There was nothing sinful about looking at feminine loveliness unadorned. It was as sweetly innocent as looking at flowers or kittens—but far more fun.

In the meantime I wanted another drink.

Mr. Henderson vetoed it, called Bodel over, spoke to her rapidly in Danish. She left, returned a few minutes later carrying a loaded tray—smorgasbord, hot meat balls, sweet pastry shells stuffed with ice cream, strong coffee, all in large quantities.

Twenty-five minutes later I still appreciated the teen-agers at the pool, but I was no longer on my way to another alcoholic catastrophe. I had sobered up so much that I now realized that I not only could not solve my problems through spirits but must shun alcohol until I did solve them—as I did not know how to handle strong drink. Uncle Ed was right; vice required training and long practice—otherwise for pragmatic reasons virtue should rule even when moral instruction has ceased to bind.

My morals certainly had ceased to bind—or I could not have sat there with a glass of Devil's brew in my hand while I stared at naked female flesh.

I found that I had not even a twinge of conscience over anything. My only regret involved the sad knowledge that I could not handle the amount of alcohol I would have enjoyed. *"Easy is the descent into Hell."*

Mr. Henderson stood up. "We tie up in less than two hours and I have some figures to fudge before the agent comes aboard. Thanks for a nice time."

"Thank *you*, sir! *Tusind tak!* Is that how you say it?"

He smiled and left. I sat there for a bit and thought. Two hours till we docked, three hours in port—what could I do with the opportunities?

Go to the American consul? Tell him *what?* Dear Mr. Consul, I am not he whom I am presumed to be and I just happened to find this million dollars—

Ridiculous!

Say nothing to anyone, grab that million, go ashore and catch the next airship for Patagonia?

Impossible. My morals had slipped—apparently they were never very strong. But I still had this prejudice against stealing. It's not only wrong; it's undignified.

Bad enough that I'm wearing his clothes.

Take the three thousand that is "rightfully" yours, go ashore, wait for the ship to sail, then get back to America as best you can?

Stupid idea! You would wind up in a tropical jail and your silly gesture would not do Graham any good. It's Hobson's choice again, you knothead; you must stay aboard and wait for Graham to show up. He won't, but there might be a wireless message or something. Bite your nails until the ship sails. When it does, thank God for a trip home to God's country. While Graham does the same for his ticket home in the *Admiral Moffett*. I wonder how he likes being named Hergensheimer? Better than I like "Graham" I'll bet. A proud name, Hergensheimer.

I got up, ducked around to the far side, and went up two decks to the library, found it unoccupied save for a woman working on a crossword puzzle. Neither of us wanted to be disturbed, which made us good company.

Most of the bookcases were locked, the librarian not being present, but there was a battered encyclopedia— just what I needed as a start.

Two hours later I was startled by a blast indicating that we had a line to the dock; we had arrived. I was loaded with strange history and stranger ideas and none of it digested. To start with, in this world William Jennings Bryan was never president; in 1896 McKinley had been elected in his place, had served two terms and had been followed by someone named Roosevelt.

I recognized none of the twentieth-century presidents.

Instead of more than a century of peace under our traditional neutrality, the United States had repeatedly been involved in foreign wars: 1899, 1912–17, 1932 (with *Japan!*), 1950–52, 1980–84, and so on right up to the current year—or current when this encyclopedia was published; *King's Skald* did not report a war now going on.

Behind the glass of one of the locked cases I spotted several history books. If I was still in the ship three hours from now, I must plan on reading every history book in the ship's library during the long passage to America.

But names of presidents and dates of wars were not my most urgent need; these are not daily concerns. What I urgently needed to know, lest ignorance cause me anything from needless embarrassment to catastrophe, was the differences between my world and this world in how people lived, talked, behaved, ate, drank, played, prayed, and loved. While I was learning, I must be careful to talk as little as possible and to listen as much as possible.

I once had a neighbor whose knowledge of history seemed limited to two dates, 1492 and 1776, and even with those two he was mixed up as to what events each marked. His ignorance in other fields was just as profound; nevertheless he earned an excellent living as a paving contractor.

It does not require a broad education to function as a social and economic animal . . . as long as you know when to rub blue mud into your bellybutton. But a mistake in local customs can get you lynched.

I wondered how Graham was doing? It occurred to me that his situation was far more dangerous than mine . . . if I assumed (as apparently I must) that he and I had simply swapped places. It seemed that my background could make me appear eccentric here—but *his* background could get Graham into serious trouble in my world. A casual remark, an innocent act, could land him in the stocks. Or worse.

But he might find his worst trouble through attempting to fit himself fully into my role—if indeed he tried. Let me put it this way: On her birthday after we had been married a year I gave Abigail a fancy edition of *The Taming of the Shrew*. She never suspected that I had been making a statement; her conviction of her own righteousness did not embrace the possibility that in my heart I equated her to Kate. If Graham assumed my role as her husband, the relationship was bound to be interesting for each of them.

I would not knowingly wish Abigail on anyone. Since I had not been consulted, I did not cry crocodile tears.

(What would it be to bed with a woman who did not always refer to marital relations as "family duties"?)

*   *   *

Here I have in front of me a twenty-volume encyclopedia, millions of words packed with all the major facts of this world—facts I urgently need. What can I squeeze out of it quickly? Where to start? I don't want Greek art, or Egyptian history, or geology—but what *do* I want?

Well, what did you first notice about this world? This ship itself. Its old-fashioned appearance compared with the sleek lines of the M.V. *Konge Knut*. Then, once you were aboard, the lack of a telephone in your-Graham's stateroom. The lack of passenger elevators. Little things that gave it an air of the luxury of grandfather's day.

So let's see the article on "Ships"—volume eighteen.

Yes, sir! Three pages of pictures . . . and they all have that Mauve-Decade look. S.S. *Britannia*, biggest and fastest North Atlantic liner, 2000 passengers, only sixteen knots! And looks it.

Let's try the general article on "Transportation"—

Well, well! We aren't too surprised, are we? No mention of airships. But let's check the index volume— Airship, nothing; dirigible, zero; aeronautics—see "Balloon."

Ah, yes, a good article on free ballooning, with the Montgolfiers and the other daring pioneers—even Salomon Andrée's brave and tragic attack on the North Pole. But either Count von Zeppelin never lived, or he never turned his attention to aeronautics.

Possibly, after his service in the Civil War, he returned to Germany and there never found the atmosphere receptive to the idea of air travel that he enjoyed in Ohio in my world. As may be, this world does not have air travel. Alex, if you have to live here, how would you like to "invent" the airship? Be a pioneer and tycoon, and get rich and famous?

What makes you think you could?

Why, I made my first airship flight when I was only twelve years old! I know all about them; I could draw plans for one right now——

You could? Draw me production drawings for a lightweight diesel, not over one pound per horsepower. Specify the alloys used, give the heat treatments, show work diagrams for the actual operating cycles, specify fuels, state procurement sources, specify lubricants——

All those things can be worked out!

Yes, but can *you* do it? Even knowing that it can be done? Remember why you dropped out of engineering school and decided you had a call for the ministry? Comparative religion, homiletics, higher criticism, apologetics, Hebrew, Latin, Greek, all require scholarship . . . but the slipstick subjects require brains.

So I'm stupid, am I?

Would you have walked through that fire pit if you had brains enough to come in out of the rain?

Why didn't you stop me?

Stop you? When did you ever listen to *me*? Quit evading——what was your final mark in thermodynamics?

All right! Assume that I can't do it myself——

Big of you.

Lay off, will you? Knowing that something *can* be done is two thirds of the battle. I could be director of research and guide the efforts of some really sharp young engineers. They supply the brains; I supply the unique memory of what a dirigible balloon looks like and how it works. Okay?

That's the proper division of labor: You supply memory, they supply brains. Yes, that could work. But not quickly, not cheaply. How are you going to finance it?

Uh, sell shares?

Remember the summer you sold vacuum cleaners? Well . . . there's that million dollars.

Naughty, naughty!

"Mr. Graham?"

I looked up from my great plans to find a yeoman from the purser's office looking at me. "Yes?"

She handed me an envelope. "From Mr. Henderson, sir. He said you would probably have an answer."

"Thank you." The note read: "Dear Mr. Graham: There are three men down here in the square who claim to have an appointment with you. I don't like their looks or the way they talk—and this port has some very strange customers. If you are not expecting them or don't wish to see them, tell my messenger that she could not find you. Then I'll tell them that you've gone ashore. A.P.H."

I remained balanced between curiosity and caution for some long, uncomfortable moments. They did not want to see me; they wanted to see Graham . . . and whatever it was they wanted of Graham, I could not satisfy their want.

You *know* what they want!

So I suspect. But, even if they have a chit signed by Saint Peter, I can't turn over to them—or to anyone— that silly million dollars. You know that.

Certainly I know that. I wanted to be sure that you

knew it. All right, since there are no circumstances under which you will turn over to a trio of strangers the contents of Graham's lockbox, then why see them?

Because I've got to *know!* Now shut up. I said to the yeoman, "Please tell Mr. Henderson that I will be right down. And thank you for your trouble."

"My pleasure, sir. Uh, Mr. Graham . . . I saw you walk the fire. You were wonderful!"

"I was out of my silly mind. Thanks anyhow."

I stopped at the top of the companionway and sized up the three men waiting for me. They looked as if they had been type-cast for menace: one oversize job about six feet eight with the hands, feet, jaw, and ears of glandular giantism; one sissy type about one quarter the size of the big man; one nothing type with dead eyes. Muscles, brain, and gun—or was it my jumpy imagination?

A smart person would go quietly back up and hide. I'm not smart.

VI

Let us eat and drink, for tomorrow we shall die.
Isaiah 22:13

I walked down the stairs, not looking at the three, and went directly to the desk of the purser's office. Mr. Henderson was there, spoke quietly as I reached the counter. "Those three over there. Do you know them?"

"No, I don't know them. I'll see what they want. But keep an eye on us, will you, please?"

"Right!"

I turned and started to walk past that lovable trio. The smart boy said sharply, "Graham! Stop there! Where you going?"

I kept moving and snapped, "Shut up, you idiot! Are you trying to blow it?" Muscles stepped into my path and hung over me like a tall building. The gun stepped in behind me. In a fake prison-yard style, from the side of my mouth, I said, "Quit making a scene and get these apes off the ship! You and I must talk."

"Certainly we talk. *Ici!* Now. Here."

"You utter fool," I answered softly and glanced nervously up, to left and right. "Not here. Cows. Bugs.

62

Come with me. But have Mutt and Jeff wait on the dock."

"Non!"

"God save us! Listen carefully." I whispered, "You are going to tell these animals to leave the ship and wait at the foot of the gangway. Then you and I are going to walk out on the weather deck where we can talk without being overheard. Otherwise we do *nothing!*—and I report to Number-One that you blew the deal. Understand? Right *now!* Or go back and tell them the deal is off."

He hesitated, then spoke rapidly in French that I could not follow, my French being mostly of the *La plume de ma tante* sort. The gorilla seemed to hesitate but the gun type shrugged and started toward the gangway door. I said to the little wart, "Come on! Don't waste time; the ship is about to sail!" I headed aft without looking to see whether or not he was following. I set a brisk pace that forced him to follow or lose me. I was as much taller than he as that ape was taller than I; he had to trot to stay at my heels.

I kept right on going aft and outside, onto the weather deck, past the open bar and the tables, clear to the swimming pool.

It was, as I expected, unoccupied, the ship being in port. There was the usual sign up, CLOSED WHILE SHIP IS IN PORT, and a nominal barrier around it of a single strand of rope, but the pool was still filled. I stepped over the rope and stood with my back to the pool. He followed me; I held up a hand. "Stop right there." He stopped.

"Now we can talk," I said. "Explain yourself, and you'd better make it good! What do you mean, calling

attention to yourself by bringing that muscle aboard?
And a Danish ship at that! Mr. B. is going to be very,
very angry with you. What's your name?"

"Never mind my name. Where's the package?"

"What package?"

He started to sputter; I interrupted. "Cut the nonsense; I'm not impressed. This ship is getting ready to
sail; you have only minutes to tell me exactly what you
want and to convince me that you should get it. Keep
throwing your weight around and you'll find yourself
going back to your boss and telling him you failed. So
speak up! What do you want?"

"The package!"

I sighed. "My old and stupid, you are stuck in a rut.
We've been over that. What sort of a package? What's
in it?"

He hesitated. "Money."

"Interesting. How much money?"

This time he hesitated twice as long, so again I interrupted. "If you don't know how much money, I'll give
you a couple of francs for beer and send you on your
way. Is that what you want? Two francs?"

A man that skinny shouldn't have such high blood
pressure. He managed to say, "American dollars. One
million."

I laughed in his face. "What makes you think I've
got that much? And if I had, why should I give it to
you? How do I know you are supposed to get it?"

"You crazy, man? You know who am I."

"Prove it. Your eyes are funny and your voice sounds
different. I think you're a ringer."

" 'Ringer'?"

"A fake, a phony! An impostor."

He answered angrily—French, I suppose. I am sure it was not complimentary. I dug into my memory, repeated carefully and with feeling the remark that a lady had made last night which had caused her husband to say that she worried too much. It was not appropriate but I intended simply to anger him.

Apparently I succeeded. He raised a hand, I grabbed his wrist, tripped myself, fell backwards into the pool, pulling him with me. As we fell I shouted, "Help!"

We splashed. I got a firm grip on him, pulled myself up as I shoved him under again. "Help! He's drowning me!"

Down we went again, struggling with each other. I yelled for help each time my head was above water. Just as help came I went limp and let go.

I stayed limp until they started to give me mouth-to-mouth resuscitation. At that point I snorted and opened my eyes. "Where am I?"

Someone said, "He's coming around. He's okay."

I looked around. I was flat on my back alongside the pool. Someone had done a professional job of pulling me out with a dip-and-jerk; my left arm felt almost dislocated. Aside from that I was okay. "Where is he? The man who pushed me in."

"He got away."

I recognized the voice, turned my head. My friend Mr. Henderson, the purser.

"He did?"

That ended it. My rat-faced caller had scrambled out as I was being fished out and had streaked off the ship. By the time they had finished reviving me, Nasty and his bodyguards were long gone.

Mr. Henderson had me lie still until the ship's doctor arrived. He put a stethoscope on me and announced that I was okay. I told a couple of small fibs, some near truths, and an evasion. By then the gangway had been removed and shortly a loud blast announced that we had left the dock.

I did not find it necessary to tell anyone that I had played water polo in school.

The next many days were very sweet, in the fashion that grapes grow sweetest on the slopes of a live volcano.

I managed to get acquainted (reacquainted?) with my table mates without, apparently, anyone noticing that I was a stranger. I picked up names just by waiting until someone else spoke to someone by name—remembered the name and used it later. Everyone was pleasant to me—I not only was not "below the salt," since the record showed that I had been aboard the full trip, but also I was at least a celebrity if not a hero for having walked through the fire.

I did not use the swimming pool. I was not sure what swimming Graham had done, if any, and, having been "rescued," I did not want to exhibit a degree of skill inconsistent with that "rescue." Besides, while I grew accustomed to (and even appreciative of) a degree of nudity shocking in my former life, I did not feel that I could manage with aplomb being naked in company.

Since there was nothing I could do about it, I put the mystery of Nastyface and his bodyguard out of my mind.

The same was true of the all-embracing mystery of who I am and how I got here—nothing I could do about it, so don't worry about it. On reflection I realized that I was in exactly the same predicament as every other human being alive: We don't know who we are, or where we came from, or why we are here. My dilemma was merely fresher, not different.

One thing (possibly the only thing) I learned in seminary was to face calmly the ancient mystery of life, untroubled by my inability to solve it. Honest priests and preachers are denied the comforts of religion; instead they must live with the austere rewards of philosophy. I never became much of a metaphysician but I did learn not to worry about that which I could not solve.

I spent much time in the library or reading in deck chairs, and each day I learned more about and felt more at home in this world. Happy, golden days slipped past like a dream of childhood.

And every day there was Margrethe.

I felt like a boy undergoing his first attack of puppy love.

It was a strange romance. We could not speak of love. Or I could not, and she did not. Every day she was my servant (shared with her other passenger guests) . . . and my "mother" (shared with others? I did not think so . . . but I did not know). The relationship was close but not intimate. Then each day, for a few moments while I "paid" her for tying my bow tie, she was my wonderfully sweet and utterly passionate darling.

But only then.

At other times I was "Mr. Graham" to her and she called me "sir"—warmly friendly but not intimate. She was willing to chat, standing up and with the door open; she often had ship's gossip to share with me. But her manner was always that of the perfect servant. Correction: the perfect crew member assigned to personal service. Each day I learned a little more about her. I found no fault in her.

For me the day started with my first sight of her—usually on my way to breakfast when I would meet her in the passageway or spot her through an open door of a room she was making up . . . just "Good morning, Margrethe" and "Good morning, Mr. Graham," but the sun did not rise until that moment.

I would see her from time to time during the day, peaking each day with that golden ritual after she tied my tie.

Then I would see her briefly after dinner. Immediately after dinner each evening I would return to my room for a few minutes to refresh myself before the evening's activities—lounge show, concert, games, or perhaps just a return to the library. At that hour Margrethe would be somewhere in the starboard forward passageway of C deck, opening beds, tidying baths, and so forth—making her guests' staterooms inviting for the night. Again I would say hello, then wait in my room (whether she had yet reached it or not) because she would come in shortly, either to open my bed or simply to inquire, "Will you need anything more this evening, sir?"

And I would always smile and answer, "I don't need a thing, Margrethe. Thank you." Whereupon she would bid me good night and wish me sound sleep. That ended my day no matter what else I did before retiring.

Of course I was tempted—daily!—to answer, "You know what I need!" I could not. *Imprimis*: I was a married man. True, my wife was lost somewhere in another world (or I was). But from holy matrimony there is no release this side of the grave. Item: Her love affair (if such it was) was with Graham, whom I was impersonating. I could not refuse that evening kiss (I'm not that angelically perfect!) but in fairness to my beloved I could not go beyond it. Item: An honorable man must not offer less than matrimony to the object of his love . . . and that I was both legally and morally unable to offer.

So those golden days were bittersweet. Each day brought one day nearer the inescapable time when I must leave Margrethe, almost certainly never to see her again.

I was not free even to tell her what that loss would mean to me.

Nor was my love for her so selfless that I hoped the separation would not grieve her. Meanly, self-centered as an adolescent, I hoped that she would miss me as dreadfully as I was going to miss her. Childish puppy love—certainly! I offer in extenuation the fact that I had known only the "love" of a woman who loved Jesus so much that she had no real affection for any flesh-and-blood creature.

Never marry a woman who prays too much.

We were ten days out from Papeete with Mexico almost over the skyline when this precarious idyll ended. For several days Margrethe had seemed more withdrawn each day. I could not tax her with it as there was nothing I could put my finger on and certainly nothing of which I could complain. But it reached crisis that evening when she tied my tie.

As usual I smiled and thanked her and kissed her.

Then I stopped with her still in my arms and said, "What's wrong? I know you can kiss better than that. Is my breath bad?"

She answered levelly, "Mr. Graham, I think we had better stop this."

"So it's 'Mr. Graham,' is it? Margrethe, what have I done?"

"You've done nothing!"

"Then— My dear, you're crying!"

"I'm sorry. I didn't intend to."

I took my handkerchief, blotted her tears, and said gently, "I have never intended to hurt you. You must tell me what's wrong so that I can change it."

"If you don't know, sir, I don't see how I can explain it."

"Won't you try? Please!" (Could it be one of those cyclic emotional disturbances women are heir to?)

"Uh . . . Mr. Graham, I knew it could not last beyond the end of the voyage—and, believe me, I did not count on any more. I suppose it means more to me than it did to you. But I never thought that you would simply end it, with no explanation, sooner than we must."

"Margrethe . . . I do not understand."

"But you *do* know!"

"But I don't know."

"You *must* know. It's been eleven days. Each night I've asked you and each night you've turned me down. Mr. Graham, aren't you ever again going to ask me to come back later?"

"Oh. So *that's* what you meant! Margrethe—"

"Yes, sir?"

"I'm not 'Mr. Graham.'"

"Sir?"

"My name is 'Hergensheimer.' It has been exactly eleven days since I saw you for the first time in my life. I'm sorry. I'm terribly sorry. But that is the truth."

VII

Now therefore be content, look upon me;
for it is evident unto you if I lie.
Job 6:28

Margrethe is both a warm comfort and a civilized adult. Never once did she gasp, or expostulate, or say, "Oh, no!" or "I can't believe it!" At my first statement she held very still, waited, then said quietly, "I do not understand."

"I don't understand it either," I told her. "Something happened when I walked through that fire pit. The world changed. This ship——" I pounded the bulkhead beside us. "——is not the ship I was in before. And people call me 'Graham' . . . when I *know* that my name is Alexander Hergensheimer. But it's not just me and this ship; it's the whole world. Different history. Different countries. No airships here."

"Alec, what is an airship?"

"Uh, up in the air, like a balloon. It *is* a balloon, in a way. But it goes very fast, over a hundred knots."

She considered it soberly. "I think that I would find that frightening."

"Not at all; it's the best way to travel. I flew down

72

here in one, the *Count von Zeppelin* of North American Airlines. But this world doesn't have airships. That was the point that finally convinced me that this really is a different world—and not just some complicated hoax that someone had played on me. Air travel is so major a part of the economy of the world I knew that it changes everything else not to have it. Take— Look, do you believe me?"

She answered slowly and carefully, "I believe that you are telling the truth as you see it. But the truth I see is very different."

"I know and that's what makes it so hard. I— See here, if you don't hurry, you're going to miss dinner, right?"

"It does not matter."

"Yes, it does; you must not miss meals just because I made a stupid mistake and hurt your feelings. And if I don't show up, Inga will send somebody up to find out whether I'm ill or asleep or whatever; I've seen her do it with others at my table. Margrethe—my very dear!— I've wanted to tell you. I've waited to tell you. I've needed to tell you. And now I can and I must. But I can't do it in five minutes standing up. After you turn down beds tonight can you take time to listen to me?"

"Alec, I will always take all the time for you that you need."

"All right. You go down and eat, and I'll go down and touch base at least—get Inga off my neck—and I'll meet you here after you turn down beds. All right?"

She looked thoughtful. "All right. Alec— Will you kiss me again?"

That's how I knew she believed me. Or wanted to

believe me. I quit worrying. I even ate a good dinner, although I hurried.

She was waiting for me when I returned, and stood up as I came in. I took her in my arms, pecked her on the nose, picked her up by her elbows and sat her on my bunk; then I sat down in the only chair. "Dear one, do you think I'm crazy?"

"Alec, I don't know what to tink." (Yes, she said "tink." Once in a long while, under stress of emotion, Margrethe would lose the use of the theta sound. Otherwise her English accent was far better than my tall-corn accent, harsh as a rusty saw.)

"I know," I agreed. "I had the same problem. Only two ways to look at it. Either something incredible did happen when I walked through the fire, something that changed my whole world. Or I'm as crazy as a pet 'coon. I've spent days checking the facts . . . and the world *has* changed. Not just airships. Kaiser Wilhelm the Fourth is missing and some silly president named 'Schmidt' is in his place. Things like that."

"I would not call Herr Schmidt 'silly.' He is quite a good president as German presidents go."

"That's my point, dear. To me, any German president looks silly, as Germany is—in *my* world—one of the last western monarchies effectively unlimited. Even the Tsar is not as powerful."

"And that has to be my point, too, Alec. There is no Kaiser and there is no Tsar. The Grand Duke of Muscovy is a constitutional monarch and no longer claims to be suzerain over other Slavic states."

"Margrethe, we're both saying the same thing. The world I grew up in is gone. I'm having to learn about a different world. Not a totally different world. Geography does not seem to have changed, and not all of history. The two worlds seem to be the same almost up to the beginning of the twentieth century. Call it eighteen-ninety. About a hundred years back something strange happened and the two worlds split apart . . . and about twelve days ago something equally strange happened to me and I got bounced into this world." I smiled at her. "But I'm not sorry. Do you know why? Because *you* are in this world."

"Thank you. It is important to me that you are in it, too."

"Then you do believe me. Just as I have been forced to believe it. So much so that I've quit worrying about it. Just one thing really bothers me— What became of Alec Graham? Is he filling my place in my world? Or what?"

She did not answer at once, and when she did, her answer did not seem responsive. "Alec, will you please take down your trousers?"

"What did you say, Margrethe?"

"Please. I am not making a joke and I am not trying to entice you. I must see something. Please lower your trousers."

"I don't see— All right." I shut up and did as she asked—not easy in evening dress. I had to take off my mess jacket, then my cummerbund, before I was peeled enough to let me slide the braces off my shoulders.

Then, reluctantly, I started unbuttoning my fly. (Another shortcoming of this retarded world—no zippers. I did not appreciate zippers until I no longer had them.)

I took a deep breath, then lowered my trousers a few inches. "Is that enough?"

"A little more, please—and will you please turn your back to me?"

I did as she asked. Then I felt her hands, gentle and not invasive, at my right rear. She lifted a shirttail and pulled down the top of my underwear pants on the right.

A moment later she restored both garments. "That's enough. Thank you."

I tucked in my shirttails and buttoned up my fly, reshouldered the braces and reached for the cummerbund. She said, "Just a moment, Alec."

"Eh? I thought you were through."

"I am. But there is no need to get back into those formal clothes; let me get out casual trousers for you. And shirt. Unless you are going back to the lounge?"

"No. Not if you will stay."

"I will stay; we must talk." Quickly she took out casual trousers and a sports shirt for me, laid them on the bed. "Excuse me, please." She went into the bath.

I don't know whether she needed to use it or not, but she knew that I could change more comfortably in the stateroom than in that cramped shipboard bathroom.

I changed and felt better. A cummerbund and a boiled shirt are better than a straitjacket but not much. She came out, at once hung up the clothes I had taken off, all but the shirt and collar. She removed studs and collar buttons from these, put them away, and put shirt and collar into my laundry bag. I wondered what Abigail would think if she could see these wifely attentions. Abigail did not believe in spoiling me—and did not.

"What was that all about, Margrethe?"

"I had to see something. Alec, you were wondering what had become of Alec Graham. I now know the answer."

"Yes?"

"He's right here. You are he."

At last I said, "That, just from looking at a few square inches on my behind? What did you find, Margrethe? The strawberry mark that identifies the missing heir?"

"No, Alec. Your 'Southern Cross.'"

"My what?"

"Please, Alec. I had hoped that it would restore your memory. I saw it the first night we—" She hesitated, then looked me square in the eye. "—made love. You turned on the light, then turned over on your belly to see what time it was. That was when I noticed the moles on your right buttock cheek. I commented on the pattern they made, and we joked about it. You said that it was your Southern Cross and it let you know which end was up."

Margrethe turned slightly pink but continued to look me firmly in the eye. "And I showed you some moles on my body. Alec, I am sorry that you do not remember it but please believe me: By then we were well enough acquainted that we could be playful about such things without my being forward or rude."

"Margrethe, I don't think you could ever be forward or rude. But you're putting too much importance on a chance arrangement of moles. I've got moles all over me; it doesn't surprise me that some of them, back where I can't see easily, are arranged in a cross shape.

Or that Graham had some that were somewhat similar."

"Not 'similar.' Exactly the same."

"Well— There is a much better way to check. In the desk there in my wallet. Graham's wallet, actually. Driver's license. His. His thumbprint on it. I haven't checked it because I have never had the slightest doubt that he was Graham and that I am Hergensheimer and that we are not the same man. But we *can* check. Get it out, dear. Check it yourself. I'll put a thumbprint on the mirror in the bath. Compare them. Then you will know."

"Alec, I do know. You are the one who doesn't believe it; you check it."

"Well—" Margrethe's counterproposal was reasonable; I agreed to it.

I got out Graham's driver's license, then placed a print on the bath mirror by first rubbing my thumb over my nose for the nose's natural oil, so much greater than that of the pad of the thumb. I found that I could not see the pattern on the glass too well, so I shook a little talcum onto my palm, blew it toward the mirror.

Worse. The powder that detectives use must be much finer than shaving talcum. Or perhaps I don't know how to use it. I placed another print without powder, looked at both prints, at my right thumb, at the print on the driver's license, then checked to see that the license did indeed designate print of right thumb. It did. "Margrethe! Will you come look, please?"

She joined me in the bath. "Look at this," I said. "Look at all four—my thumb and three prints. The pattern in all four is basically an arch—but that simply trims it down to half the thumbprints in the world. I'll bet you even money that your own thumbprints have an arch pattern. Honest, can you tell whether or not the thumbprint on that card was made by *this* thumb? Or by my left thumb; they might have made a mistake."

"I cannot tell, Alec. I have no skill in this."

"Well— I don't think even an expert could tell in this light. We'll have to put it off till morning; we need bright sunlight out on deck. We also need glossy white paper, stamp-pad ink, and a magnifying glass . . . and I'll bet Mr. Henderson will have all three. Will tomorrow do?"

"Certainly. This test is not for me, Alec; I already know in my heart. And by seeing your 'Southern Cross.' Something has happened to your memory but you are still you . . . and someday we will find your memory again."

"It's not that easy, dear. I *know* that I am not Graham. Margrethe, do you have any idea what business he was in? Or why he was on this trip?"

"Must I say 'him'? I did not ask your business, Alec. And you never offered to tell me."

"Yes, I think you must say 'him,' at least until we check that thumbprint. Was he married?"

"Again, he did not say and I did not ask."

"But you implied— No, you flatly stated that you had 'made love' with this man whom you believe to be me, and that you have been in bed with him."

"Alec, are you reproaching me?"

"Oh, no, no, no!" (But I was, and she knew it.) "Whom you go to bed with is your business. But I must tell you that *I* am married."

She shut her face against me. "Alec, I did not try to seduce you into marriage."

"Graham, you mean. I was not there."

"Very well. Graham. I did not entrap Alec Graham. For our mutual happiness we made love. Matrimony was not mentioned by either of us."

"Look, I'm sorry I mentioned the matter! It seemed to have some bearing on the mystery; that's all. Margrethe, will you believe that I would rather strike off my arm—or pluck out my eye and cast it from me—than hurt you, ever, in any way?"

"Thank you, Alec. I believe you."

"All that Jesus ever said was: 'Go, and sin no more.' Surely you do not think I would ever set myself up as more severely judgmental than was Jesus? But I was not judging you; I was seeking information about Graham. His business, in particular. Uh, did you ever suspect that he might be engaged in something illegal?"

She gave a ghost of a smile. "Had I ever suspected anything of the sort, my loyalty to him is such that I would never express such suspicion. Since you insist that you are not he, then there it must stand."

"*Touché!*" I grinned sheepishly. Could I tell her about the lockbox? Yes, I must. I had to be frank with her and had to persuade her that she was not being disloyal to Graham/me were she to be equally frank. "Margrethe, I was not asking idly and I was not prying where I had no business to pry. I have still more trouble and I need your advice."

Her turn to be startled. "Alec . . . I do not often give advice. I do not like to."

"May I tell you my trouble? You need not advise me . . . but perhaps you may be able to analyze it for me."

I told her quickly about that truly damning million dollars. "Margrethe, can you think of any legitimate reason why an honest man would be carrying a million dollars in cash? Travelers checks, letters of credit, drafts for transferring monies, even bearer bonds— But *cash?* In that amount? I say that it is psychologically as unbelievable as what happened to me in the fire pit is physically unbelievable. Can you see any other way to look at it? For what *honest* reason would a man carry that much cash on a trip like this?"

"I will not pass judgment."

"I do not ask you to judge; I ask you to stretch your imagination and tell me why a man would carry with him a million dollars in cash. Can you think of a reason? One as farfetched as you like . . . but a reason."

"There could be many reasons."

"Can you think of one?"

I waited; she remained silent. I sighed and said, "I can't think of one, either. Plenty of criminal reasons, of course, as so-called 'hot money' almost always moves as cash. This is so common that most governments—all governments, I believe—assume that any large amount of cash being moved other than by a bank or by a government is indeed crime money until proved otherwise. Or counterfeit money, a still more depressing idea. The advice I need is this: Margrethe, what should I do with it? It's not mine; I can't take it off the ship. For the same reason I can't abandon it. I can't even throw it overboard. What *can* I do with it?"

My question was not rhetorical; I had to find an answer that would not cause me to wind up in jail for something Graham had done. So far, the only answer I could think of was to go to the only authority in the ship, the Captain, tell him all my troubles and ask him to take custody of that awkward million dollars.

Ridiculous. That would just give me a fresh set of bad answers, depending on whether or not the Captain believed me and on whether or not the Captain himself was honest—and possibly on other variables. But I could not see any outcome from telling the Captain that would not end in my being locked up, either in jail or in a mental hospital.

The simplest way to resolve the situation would be to throw the pesky stuff overboard!

I had moral objections to that. I've broken some of the Commandments and bent some others, but being financially honest has never been a problem to me. Granted, lately my moral fiber did not seem to be as strong as I had thought, but nevertheless I was not tempted to steal that million even to jettison it.

But there was a stronger objection: Do you know anyone who, having a million dollars in his hands, could bring himself to destroy it?

Maybe you do. I don't. In a pinch I might turn it over to the Captain but I would not destroy it.

Smuggle it ashore? Alex, if you ever take it out of that lockbox, you have stolen it. Will you destroy your self-respect for a million dollars? For ten million? For five dollars?

"Well, Margrethe?"

"Alec, it seems to me that the solution is evident."

"Eh?"

"But you have been trying to solve your problems in the wrong order. First you must regain your memory. Then you will know why you are carrying that money.

It will turn out to be for some innocent and logical purpose." She smiled. "I know you better than you know yourself. You are a good man, Alec; you are not a criminal."

I felt a mixture of exasperation at her and of pride in what she thought of me—but more exasperation than pride. "Confound it, dear, I have *not* lost my memory. I am not Alec Graham; I am Alexander Hergensheimer, and that's been my name all my life and my memory is sharp. Want to know the name of my second-grade teacher? Miss Andrews. Or how I happened to have my first airship ride when I was twelve? For I do indeed come from a world in which airships ply every ocean and even over the North Pole, and Germany is a monarchy and the North American Union has enjoyed a century of peace and prosperity and this ship we are in tonight would be considered so out of date and so miserably equipped and slow that no one would sail in it. I asked for help; I did not ask for a psychiatric opinion. If you think I'm crazy, say so . . . and we'll drop the subject."

"I did not mean to anger you."

"My dear! You did not anger me; I simply unloaded on you some of my worry and frustration—and I should not have done so. I'm sorry. But I do have real problems and they are not solved by telling me that my memory is at fault. If it were my memory, saying so would solve nothing; my problems would still be there. But I should not have snapped at you. Margrethe, you are all I have . . . in a strange and sometimes frightening world. I'm sorry."

She slid down off my bunk. "Nothing to be sorry about, dear Alec. But there is no point in further discussion tonight. Tomorrow— Tomorrow we will test that thumbprint carefully, in bright sunlight. Then you will see, and it could have an immediate effect on your memory."

"Or it could have an immediate effect on your stubbornness, best of girls."

She smiled. "We will see. Tomorrow. Now I think I must go to bed. We have reached the point where we are each repeating the same arguments . . . and upsetting each other. I don't want that, Alec. That is not good."

She turned and headed for the door, not even offering herself for a goodnight kiss.

"Margrethe!"

"Yes, Alec?"

"Come back and kiss me."

"Should I, Alec? You, a married man."

"Uh— Well, for heaven's sake, a kiss isn't the same as adultery."

She shook her head sadly. "There are kisses and kisses, Alec. I would not kiss the way we have kissed unless I was happily willing to go on from there and make love. To me that would be a happy and innocent thing . . . but to you it would be adultery. You pointed out what the Christ said to the woman taken in adultery. I have not sinned . . . and I will not cause you to sin." Again she turned to leave.

"Margrethe!"

"Yes, Alec?"

"You asked me if I intended ever again to ask you to come back later. I ask you now. Tonight. Will you come back later?"

"Sin, Alec. For you it would be sin . . . and that

would make it sin for me, knowing how you feel about it."

"'Sin.' I'm not sure what sin is. I do know I need you . . . and I think you need me."

"Goodnight, Alec." She left quickly.

After a long while I brushed my teeth and washed my face, then decided that another shower might help. I took it lukewarm and it seemed to calm me a little. But when I went to bed, I lay awake, doing something I call thinking but probably is not.

I reviewed in my mind all the many major mistakes I have made in my life, one after another, dusting them off and bringing them up sharp in my head, right to the silly, awkward, inept, self-righteous, asinine fool I had made of myself tonight, and, in so doing, how I had wounded and humiliated the best and sweetest woman I have ever known.

I can keep myself uselessly occupied with self-flagellation for an entire night when my latest attack of foot-in-mouth disease is severe. This current one bid fair to keep me staring at the ceiling for days.

Some long time later, after midnight and more, I was awakened by the sound of a key in the door. I fumbled for the bunk light switch, found it just as she dropped her robe and got into bed with me. I switched off the light.

She was warm and smooth and trembling and crying. I held her gently and tried to soothe her. She did not speak and neither did I. There had been too many words earlier and most of them had been mine. Now was a time simply to cuddle and hold and speak without words.

At last her trembling slowed, then stopped. Her breathing became even. Then she sighed and said very softly, "I could not stay away."

"Margrethe. I love you."

"Oh! I love you so much it hurts in my heart."

I think we were both asleep when the collision happened. I had not intended to sleep but for the first time since the fire walk I was relaxed and untroubled; I dropped off.

First came this incredible jar that almost knocked us out of my bunk, then a grinding, crunching noise at earsplitting level. I got the bunk light on—and the skin of the ship at the foot of the bunk was bending inward.

The general alarm sounded, adding to the already deafening noise. The steel side of the ship buckled, then ruptured as something dirty white and cold pushed into the hole. As the light went out.

I got out of that bunk any which way, dragging Margrethe with me. The ship rolled heavily to port, causing us to slide down into the angle of the deck and the inboard bulkhead. I slammed against the door handle, grabbed at it, and hung on with my right hand while I held Margrethe to me with my left arm. The ship rolled back to starboard, and wind and water poured in through the hole—we heard it and felt it, could not see it. The ship recovered, then rolled again to starboard—and I lost my grip on the door handle.

I have to reconstruct what happened next—pitch dark, mind you, and a bedlam of sound. We were falling—I never let go of her—and then we were in water.

Apparently when the ship rolled back to starboard,

we were tossed out through the hole. But that is just reconstruction; all I actually know is that we fell, together, into water, went down rather deep.

We came up and I had Margrethe under my left arm, almost in a proper lifesaver carry. I grabbed a look as I gulped air, then we went under again. The ship was right alongside us and moving. There was cold wind and rumbling noise; something high and dark was on the side away from the ship. But it was the ship that scared me—or rather its propeller, its screw. Stateroom C109 was far forward—but if I didn't get us well away from the ship almost at once, Margrethe and I were going to be chewed into hamburger by the screw. I hung onto her and stroked hard away from the ship, kicking strongly—and exulted as I felt us getting away from the hazard of the ship . . . and banged my head something brutal against blackness.

VIII

*So they took up Jonah, and cast him
forth into the sea: and the sea ceased
from her raging.*
Jonah 1:15

I was comfortable and did not want to wake up. But a slight throb in my head was annoying me and, willy-nilly, I did wake. I shook my head to get rid of that throb and got a snootful of water. I snorted it out.

"Alec?" Her voice was nearby.

I was on my back in blood-warm water, salt water by the taste, with blackness all around me—about as near to a return to the womb as can be accomplished this side of death. Or was this death? "Margrethe?"

"Oh! Oh, Alec, I am so relieved! You have been asleep a long time. How do you feel?"

I checked around, counted this and that, twitched that and this, found that I was floating on my back between Margrethe's limbs, she being also on her back with my head in her hands, in one of the standard Red-Cross lifesaving positions. She was using slow frog kicks, not so much moving us as keeping us afloat. "I'm all right. I think. How about you?"

"I'm just fine, dearest!—now that you're awake."

"What happened?"

"You bumped your head against the berg."

"Berg?"

"The ice mountain. Iceberg."

(Iceberg? I tried to remember what had happened.) "What iceberg?"

"The one that wrecked the ship."

Some of it came tumbling back, but it still did not make an understandable picture. A giant crash as if the ship had hit a reef, then we were dumped into water. A struggle to get clear—I did bump my head. "Margrethe, we're in the tropics, as far south as Hawaii. How can there be icebergs?"

"I don't know, Alec."

"But—" I started to say "impossible," then decided that, from me, that word was silly. "This water is too warm for icebergs. Look, you can quit working so hard; in salt water I float as easily as Ivory soap."

"All right. But do let me hold you. I almost lost you once in this darkness; I'm frightened that it might happen again. When we fell in, the water was cold. Now it's warm; so we must not be near the berg."

"Hang onto me, sure; I don't want to lose you, either." Yes, the water had been cold when we fell into it; I remembered. Or cold compared with a nice warm cuddle in bed. And a cold wind. "What happened to the iceberg?"

"Alec, I don't know. We fell into the water together. You grabbed me and got us away from the ship; I'm sure that saved us. But it was dark as December night and blowing hard and in the blackness you ran your head into the ice.

"That is when I almost lost you. It knocked you out,

dear, and you let go of me. I went under and gulped water and came up and spat it out and couldn't find you.

"Alec, I have never been so frightened in all my life. You weren't anywhere. I couldn't see you; I reached out, all sides, and could not touch you; I called out, you did not answer."

"I'm sorry."

"I should not have panicked. But I thought you had drowned. Or were drowning and I was not stopping it. But in paddling around my hand struck you, and then I grabbed you and everything was all right—until you didn't answer. But I checked and found that your heart was steady and strong, so everything was all right after all, and I took you in the back carry so that I could hold your face out of water. After a long time you woke up—and now everything is truly all right."

"You didn't panic; I'd be dead if you had. Not many people could do what you did."

"Oh, it's not so uncommon; I was a guard at a beach north of København two summers—on Fridays I gave lessons. Lots of boys and girls learned."

"Keeping your head in a crunch and doing it in pitch darkness isn't learned from lessons; don't be so modest. What about the ship? And the iceberg?"

"Alec, again I don't know. By the time I found you and made sure that you were all right and then got you into towing position—by the time I had time to look around, it was like this. Nothing. Just blackness."

"I wonder if she sank? That was one big wallop she took! No explosion? You didn't hear anything?"

"I didn't hear an explosion. Just wind and the collision sounds you must have heard, then some shouts after we were in the water. If she sank, I did not see it, but— Alec, for the past half hour, about, I've been swimming with my head pushed against a pillow or a pad or a mattress. Does that mean the ship sank? Flotsam in the water?"

"Not necessarily but it's not encouraging. Why have you been keeping your head against it?"

"Because we may need it. If it is one of the deck cushions or sunbathing mats from the pool, then it's stuffed with kapok and is an emergency lifesaver."

"That's what I meant. If it's a flotation cushion, why are you just keeping your head against it? Why aren't you on it, up out of the water?"

"Because I could not do that without letting go of you."

"Oh. Margrethe, when we get out of this, will you kindly give me a swift kick? Well, I'm awake now; let's find out what you've found. By Braille."

"All right. But I don't want to let go of you when I can't see you."

"Honey, I'm at least as anxious not to lose track of you. Okay, like this: You hang onto me with one hand; reach behind you with the other. Get a good grip on this cushion or whatever it is. I turn over and hang onto you and track you up to the hand you are using to grip the pillow thing. Then we'll see—we'll both feel what we have and decide how we can use it."

It was not just a pillow, or even a bench cushion; it was (by the feel of it) a large sunbathing pad, at least six feet wide and somewhat longer than that—big enough for two people, or three if they were well acquainted. Almost as good as finding a lifeboat! Better—this flotation pad included Margrethe. I was minded of a profane poem passed around privately at seminary: "A jug of wine, a loaf of bread, and thou—"

Getting up onto a mat that is limp as an angleworm on a night as black as the inside of a pile of coal is not merely difficult; it is impossible. We accomplished the impossible by my hanging on to it with both hands while Margrethe slowly slithered up over me. Then she gave me a hand while I inched up and onto it.

Then I leaned on one elbow and fell off and got lost. I followed Margrethe's voice and bumped into the pad, and again got slowly and cautiously aboard.

We found that the most practical way to make best use of the space and buoyancy offered by the mat was to lie on our backs, side by side, starfished like that Leonardo da Vinci drawing, in order to spread ourselves as widely as possible over the support.

I said, "You all right, hon?"

"Just fine!"

"Need anything?"

"Not anything we have here. I'm comfortable, and relaxed—and you are here."

"Me, too. But what would you have if you could have anything you want?"

"Well . . . a hot fudge sundae."

I considered it. "No. A chocolate sundae with marshmallow syrup, and a cherry on top. And a cup of coffee."

"A cup of chocolate. But make mine hot fudge. It's a taste I acquired in America. We Danes do lots of good things with ice cream, but putting a hot sauce on an ice-cold dish never occurred to us. A hot fudge sundae. Better make that a double."

"All right. I'll pay for a double if that's what you want. I'm a dead game sport, I am—and you saved my life."

Her inboard hand patted mine. "Alec, you're fun— and I'm happy. Do you think we're going to get out of this alive?"

"I don't know, hon. The supreme irony of life is that hardly anyone gets out of it alive. But I promise you this: I'm going to do my best to get you that hot fudge sundae."

We both woke up when it got light. Yes, I slept and I know Margrethe did, too, as I woke a little before she did, listened to her soft snores, and kept quiet until I saw her eyes open. I had not expected to be able to sleep but I am not surprised (now) that we did—perfect bed, perfect silence, perfect temperature, both of us very tired . . . and absolutely nothing to worry about that was worth worrying about because there was nothing, nothing whatever, to do about our problems earlier than daylight. I think I fell asleep thinking: Yes, Margrethe was right; a hot fudge sundae was a better choice than a chocolate marshmallow sundae. I know I dreamt about such a sundae—a quasi-nightmare in which I would dip into it, a big bite . . . lift the spoon to my mouth, and find it empty. I think that woke me.

She turned her head toward me, smiled and looked about sixteen and utterly heavenly. ("—like two young roes that are twins. Thou art all fair, my love; there is no spot in thee.") "Good morning, beautiful."

She giggled. "Good morning, Prince Charming. Did you sleep well?"

"Matter of fact, Margrethe, I haven't slept so well in a month. Odd. All I want now is breakfast in bed."

"Right away, sir. I'll hurry!"

"Go along with you. I should not have mentioned food. I'll settle for a kiss. Think we can manage a kiss without falling into the water?"

"Yes. But let's be careful. Just turn your face this way; don't roll over."

It was a kiss mostly symbolic rather than one of Margrethe's all-out specials. We were both quite careful not to disturb the precarious stability of our make-do life raft. We were worried about something more important than being dumped into the ocean—at least I was.

I decided to broach it, take it out where we could worry about it together. "Margrethe, by the map just outside the dining room we should have the coast of Mexico near Mazatlán just east of us. What time did the ship sink? If it sank. I mean, what time was the collision?"

"I don't know."

"Nor do I. After midnight, I'm sure of that. The *Konge Knut* was scheduled to arrive at eight a.m. So that coast line could be over a hundred miles east of us. Or it could be almost on top of us. Mountains over there, we may be able to see them when this overcast clears away. As it did yesterday, so it probably will today. Sweetheart, how are you on long-distance swimming? If we can see mountains, do you want to try for it?"

She was slow in answering. "Alec, if you wish, we will try it."

"That wasn't quite what I asked."

"That is true. In warm sea water I think I can swim as long as necessary. I did once swim the Great Belt, in water colder than this. But, Alec, in the Belt are no sharks. Here there are sharks. I have seen."

I let out a sigh. "I'm glad you said it; I didn't want to have to say it. Hon, I think we must stay right here and hold still. Not call attention to ourselves. I can skip breakfast—especially a shark's breakfast."

"One does not starve quickly."

"We won't starve. If you had your druthers, which would you pick? Starvation? Or death by sunburn? Sharks? Or dying of thirst? In all the lifeboat and Robinson Crusoe stories I've ever read our hero had something to work with. I don't have even a toothpick. Correction: I have you; that changes the odds. Margrethe, what do you think we ought to do?"

"I think we will be picked up."

I thought so, too, but for a reason I did not want to discuss with Margrethe. "I'm glad to hear you say that. But why do you think so?"

"Alec, have you been to Mazatlán before?"

"No."

"It is an important fishing port, both commercial fishing and sport fishing. Since dawn hundreds of boats have put out to sea. The largest and fastest go many kilometers out. If we wait, they will find us."

"May find us, you mean. There is a lot of ocean out here. But you're right; swimming for it is suicide; our best bet is to stay here and hold tight."

"They will be looking for us, Alec."

"They will? Why?"

"If *Konge Knut* did not sink, then the Captain knows when and where we were lost overboard; when he reaches port—about now—he will ask for a daylight search. But if she did sink, then they will be scouring the whole area for survivors."

"Sounds logical." (I had another idea, not at all logical.)

"Our problem is to stay alive till they find us, avoiding sharks and thirst and sunburn as best we can—and all of that means holding still. Quite still and all the time. Except that I think we should turn over now and then, after the sun is out, to spread the burn."

"And pray for cloudy weather. Yes, all of that. And maybe we should not talk. Not get quite so thirsty—eh?"

She kept silent so long that I thought she had started the discipline I had suggested. Then she said, "Beloved, we may not live."

"I know."

"If we are to die, I would choose to hear your voice, and I would not wish to be deprived of telling you that I love you—now that I may!—in a futile attempt to live a few minutes longer."

"Yes, my sweetheart. Yes."

Despite that decision we talked very little. For me it was enough to touch her hand; it appeared to be enough for her, too.

A long time later—three hours at a guess—I heard Margrethe gasp.

"Trouble?"

"Alec! Look there!" She pointed. I looked.

It should have been my turn to gasp, but I was somewhat braced for it: high up, a cruciform shape, somewhat like a bird gliding, but much larger and clearly artificial. A flying machine—

I knew that flying machines were impossible; in engineering school I had studied Professor Simon Newcomb's well-known mathematical proof that the efforts of Professor Langley and others to build an aerodyne capable of carrying a man were doomed, useless, because scale theory proved that no such contraption large enough to carry a man could carry a heat-energy plant large enough to lift it off the ground—much less a passenger.

That was science's final word on a folly and it put a stop to wasting public monies on a will-o'-the-wisp. Research and development money went into airships, where it belonged, with enormous success.

However, in the past few days I had gained a new angle on the idea of "impossible." When a veritable flying machine showed up in our sky, I was not greatly surprised.

I think Margrethe held her breath until it passed over us and was far toward the horizon. I started to, then forced myself to breathe calmly—it was such a beautiful thing, silvery and sleek and fast. I could not judge its size, but, if those dark spots in its side were windows, then it was enormous.

I could not see what pushed it along.

"Alec . . . is that an airship?"

"No. At least it is not what I meant when I told you about airships. This I would call a 'flying machine.' That's all I can say; I've never seen one before. But I can tell you one thing, now—something very important."

"Yes?"

"We are not going to die . . . and I now know why the ship was sunk."

"Why, Alec?"

"To keep me from checking a thumbprint."

IX

"Or, to put it more nearly exactly, the iceberg was there and the collision took place to keep me from checking my thumbprint against the thumbprint on Graham's driver's license. The ship may not have sunk; that may not have been necessary to the scheme."

Margrethe did not say anything.

So I added gently, "Go ahead, dear; say it. Get it off your chest; I won't mind. I'm crazy. Paranoid."

"Alec, I did not say that. I did not think it. I would not."

"No, you did not say it. But this time my aberration cannot be explained away as 'loss of memory.' That is, if we saw the same thing. What did you see?"

"I saw something strange in the sky. I heard it, too. You told me that it was a flying machine."

"Well, I think that is what it should be called—but you can call it a, uh, a 'gumpersaggle' for all of me. Something new and strange. What is this gumpersaggle? Describe it."

"It was something moving in the sky. It came from back that way, then passed almost over us, and disappeared there." (She pointed, a direction I had decided was north.) "It was shaped something like a cross, a crucifix. The crosspiece had bumps on it, four I think. The front end had eyes like a whale and the back end had flukes like a whale. A whale with wings—that's what it looked like, Alec; a whale flying through the sky!"

"You thought it was alive?"

"Uh, I don't know. I don't think so. I don't know what to think."

"I don't think it was alive; I think it was a machine. A flying machine. A boat with wings on it. But, either way—a machine or a flying whale—have you ever in your life seen anything like it?"

"Alec, it was so strange that I have trouble believing that I saw it."

"I know. But you saw it first and pointed it out to me—so I didn't trick you into thinking that you saw it."

"You wouldn't do that."

"No, I would not. But I'm glad you saw it first, dearest girl; that means it's real—not something dreamed up in my fevered brain. That thing did not come from the world you are used to . . . and I can promise you that it is not one of the airships I talked about; it is not from the world I grew up in. So we're now in still a third world." I sighed. "The first time it took a twenty-thousand-ton ocean liner to prove to me that I had changed worlds. This time just one sight of something that simply could not exist in my world is all I need to know that they are at it again. They shifted worlds when I was knocked out—I think that's when they did it. As may be, I think they did it to keep me from checking that thumbprint. Paranoia. The delusion that the whole world is a conspiracy. Only it's not a delusion."

I watched her eyes. "Well?"

"Alec . . . could it possibly be that both of us imagined it? Delirious, perhaps? We've both had a rough experience—you hit your head; I may have hit mine when the iceberg struck."

"Margrethe, we would not each have the same delirium dream. If you wake up and find that I'm gone, that could be your answer. But I'm not gone; I'm right here. Besides, you would still have to account for an iceberg as far south as we are. Paranoia is a simpler explanation. But the conspiracy is aimed at me; you just had the misfortune to be caught in it. I'm sorry." (I wasn't really sorry. A raft in the middle of the ocean is no place to be alone. But with Margrethe it was "paradise enow.")

"I still think that sharing the same dream is—*Alec, there it comes again!*" She pointed.

I didn't see anything at first, then I did: A dot that grew into a cruciform shape, a shape that I now identified as "flying machine." I watched it grow.

"Margrethe, it must have turned around. Maybe it saw us. Or they saw us. Or he saw us. Whatever."

"Perhaps."

As it came closer I saw that it was going to pass to our right rather than overhead. Margrethe said suddenly, "It's not the same one."

"And it's not a flying whale—unless flying whales hereabouts have wide red stripes down their sides."

"It's not a whale. I mean 'it's not alive.' You are right, Alec; it is a machine. Dear, do you really think it has people inside it? That scares me."

"I think I would be more scared if it did not have people inside it." (I remembered a fantastic story translated from the German about a world peopled by nothing but automatic machines—not a pleasant story.) "Actually, it's good news. We both know now that our seeing the first one was not a dream, not an illusion. That nails down the fact that we are in another world. Therefore we are going to be rescued."

She said hesitantly, "I don't quite follow that."

"That's because you are still trying to avoid calling me paranoid—and thank you, dear, but my being paranoid is the simplest hypothesis. If the joker pulling the strings had intended to kill me, the easy time to do it would have been with the iceberg. Or earlier, with the fire pit. But he's not out to kill me, at least not now. He's playing with me, cat and mouse. So I'll be rescued. So will you, because we're together. You were with me when the iceberg hit—your bad luck. You're still with me now, so you'll be rescued—your good luck. Don't fight it, dear. I've had some days to get used to it, and I find that it is all right once you relax. Paranoia is the only rational approach to a conspiracy world."

"But, Alec, the world ought not to be that way."

"There is no 'ought' to it, my love. The essence of philosophy is to accept the universe as it is, rather than try to force it into some preconceived shape." I added, "Wups! Don't roll off. You don't want to be a snack for a shark just after we've had proof that we are going to be picked up!"

*   *   *

For the next hour or so nothing happened—unless you count sighting two regal sailfish. The overcast burned away and I began to be anxious for an early rescue; I figured they owed me that much! Not let me get a third-degree sunburn. Margrethe might be able to take a bit more sun than I; she was blonde but she was tanned a warm toast color all over—lovely! But I was raw frog-belly white except for my face and hands—a full day of tropic sun could put me into hospital. Or worse.

The eastern horizon now seemed to show a gray unevenness that could be mountains—or so I kept telling myself, although there isn't much you can see when your viewpoint is about seven inches above water line. If those were indeed mountains or hills, then land was not many miles away. Boats from Mazatlán should be in sight any time now . . . if Mazatlán was still there in this world. If—

Then another flying machine showed up.

It was only vaguely like the other two. They had been flying parallel to the coast, the first from the south, the second from the north. This machine came out from the direction of the coast, flying mostly west, although it zigzagged.

It passed north of us, then turned back and circled around us. It came low enough that I could see that it did indeed have men in it, two I thought.

Its shape is hard to explain. Imagine first a giant box kite, about forty feet long, four feet wide, and about three feet between two kite surfaces.

Imagine this box kite placed at right angles to a boat

shape, somewhat like an Esquimau's kayak but larger, much larger—about as large as the box kite.

Underneath all this are two more kayak shapes, smaller, parallel to the main shape.

At one end of this shape is an engine (as I saw later) and at the front end of that is an air propeller, like a ship's water propeller—and this I saw later, also. When I first saw this unbelievable structure, the air screw was turning so extremely fast that one simply could not see it. But one could hear it! The noise made by this contraption was deafening and never stopped.

The machine turned toward us and tilted down so that it headed straight toward us—like nothing so much as a pelican gliding down to scoop up fish.

With us the fish. It was frightening. To me, at least; Margrethe never let out a peep. But she did squeeze my fingers very hard. The mere fact that we were not fish and that a machine could not eat us and would not want to did not make this dive at us less terrifying.

Despite my fright (or because of it) I now saw that this construction was at least twice as big as I had estimated when I saw it high in the sky. It had two teamsters operating it, seated side by side behind a window in the front end. The driving engine turned out to be two, mounted between the box-kite wings, one on the right of the teamsters' position, one on the left.

At the very last instant the machine lifted like a horse taking a hurdle, and barely missed us. The blast of wind it created almost knocked us off our raft and the blast of sound caused my ears to ring.

It went a little higher, curved back toward us, glided again but not quite toward us. The lower twin kayak shapes touched the water, creating a brave comet's tail of spume——and the thing slowed and stopped and stayed there, on the water, and did not sink!

Now the air screws moved very slowly and I saw them for the first time . . . and admired the engineering ingenuity that had gone into them. Not as efficient, I suspected, as the ducted air screws used in our dirigible airships, but an elegant solution to a problem in a place where ducting would be difficult or perhaps impossible.

But those infernally noisy driving engines! How any engineer could accept that, I could not see. As one of my professors said (back before thermodynamics convinced me that I had a call for the ministry), noise is always a byproduct of inefficiency. A correctly designed engine is as silent as the grave.

The machine turned and came at us again, moving very slowly. Its teamsters handled it so that it missed us by a few feet and almost stopped. One of the two inside it crawled out of the carriage space behind the window and was clinging by his left hand to one of the stanchions that held the two box-kite wings apart. His other hand held a coiled line.

As the flying machine passed us, he cast the line toward us. I snatched at it, got a hand on it, and did not myself go into the water because Margrethe snatched at me.

I handed the line to Margrethe. "Let him pull you in. I'll slide into the water and be right behind you."

"No!"

"What do you mean, 'No'? This is no time to argue. Do it!"

"Alec, be quiet! He's trying to tell us something."

I shut up, more than a little offended. Margrethe listened. (No point in my listening; my Spanish is limited to *"Gracias"* and *"Por favor."* Instead I read the lettering on the side of the machine: *EL GUARD-ACOSTAS REAL DE MÉXICO.*

"Alec, he is warning us to be very careful. Sharks."

"Ouch."

"Yes. We are to stay where we are. He will pull gently on this rope. I think he means to get us into his machine without us going into the water."

"A man after my own heart!"

We tried it; it did not work. A breeze had sprung up; it had much more effect on the flying machine than it had on us—that water-soaked sunbathing pad was practically nailed down, no sail area at all. Instead of being able to pull us to the flying machine, the man on the other end of the line was forced to let out more line to keep from pulling us off into the water.

He called out something; Margrethe answered. They shouted back and forth. She turned to me. "He says to let loose the rope. They will go out and come back, this time directly at us, but slowly. As they come closest, we are to try to scramble up into the *aeroplano.* The machine."

"All right."

The machine left us, went out on the water and curved back. While waiting, we were not bored; we had the dorsal fin of a huge shark to entertain us. It did not attack; apparently it had not made up its mind (what mind?) that we were good to eat. I suppose it saw only the underside of the kapok pad.

The flying machine headed directly toward us on the water, looking like some monstrous dragonfly skimming the surface. I said, "Darling, as it gets closest, you dive for the stanchion closest to you and I'll push you up. Then I'll come up behind you."

"No, Alec."

"What do you mean, 'No'?" I was vexed. Margrethe was such a good comrade—then suddenly so stubborn. At the wrong time.

"You can't push me; you have no foundation to push from. And you can't stand up; you can't even sit up. Uh, you scramble to the right; I'll scramble to the left. If either of us misses, then back onto the pad—fast! The *aeroplano* will come around again."

"But—"

"That's how he said to do it."

There was no time left; the machine was almost on top of us. The "legs" or stanchions joining the lower twin shapes to the body of the machine bridged the pad, one just missing me and the other just missing Margrethe. "Now!" she cried. I lunged toward my side, got a hand on a stanchion.

And almost jerked my right arm out by the roots but I kept on moving, monkey fashion—got both hands on that undercarriage, got a foot up on a horizontal kayak shape, turned my head.

Saw a hand reaching down to Margrethe—she climbed and was lifted onto the kite wing above, and disappeared. I turned to climb up my side—and suddenly levitated up and onto the wing. I do not ordinarily levitate but this time I had incentive: a dirty white fin too big for any decent fish, cutting the water right toward my foot.

I found myself alongside the little carriage house from which the teamsters directed their strange craft.

The second man (not the one who had climbed out to help) stuck his head out a window, grinned at me, reached back and opened a little door. I crawled inside, head first. Margrethe was already there.

The space had four seats, two in front where the teamsters sat, and two behind where we were.

The teamster on my side looked around and said something, and continued—I noticed!—to look at Margrethe. Certainly she was naked, but that was not her fault, and a gentleman would not stare.

"He says," Margrethe explained, "that we must fasten our belts. I think he means this." She held up a buckle on the end of a belt, the other end being secured to the frame of the carriage.

I discovered that I was sitting on a similar buckle, which was digging a hole into my sunburned backside. I hadn't noticed it up to then, too many other things demanding attention. (Why didn't he keep his eyes to himself! I felt myself ready to shout at him. That he had, at great peril to himself, just saved her life and mine did not that moment occur to me; I was simply growing furious that he would take such advantage of a helpless lady.)

I turned my attention to that pesky belt and tried to ignore it. He spoke to the other man beside him, who responded enthusiastically. Margrethe interrupted the discussion. "What are they saying?" I demanded.

"The poor man is about to give me the shirt off his back. I am protesting . . . but I'm not protesting so hard as to put a stop to it. It's very gallant of them, dear, and, while I'm not foolish about it, I do feel more at ease among strangers with some sort of clothing."

She listened, and added, "They're arguing as to which one has the privilege."

I shut up. In my mind I apologized to them. I'll bet even the Pope in Rome has sneaked a quick look a time or two in his life.

The one on the right apparently won the argument. He squirmed around in his seat—he could not stand up—and got his shirt off, turned and passed it back to Margrethe. *"Señorita. Por favor."* He added other remarks but they were beyond my knowledge.

Margrethe replied with dignity and grace, and chatted with them as she wiggled into his shirt. It covered her mostly. She turned to me. "Dear, the commander is *Teniente* Anibal Sanz Garcia and his assistant is *Sargento* Roberto Dominguez Jones, both of the Royal Mexican Coast Guard. Both the Lieutenant and the Sergeant wanted to give me a shirt, but the Sergeant won a finger-guessing game, so I have his shirt."

"It's mighty generous of him. Ask them if there is anything at all in the machine that I can wear."

"I'll try." She spoke several phrases; I heard my name. Then she shifted back to English. "Gentlemen, I have the honor to present my husband, *Señor* Alexandro Graham Hergensheimer." She shifted back to Spanish.

Shortly she was answered. "The Lieutenant is devastated to admit that they have nothing to offer you. But he promises on his mother's honor that something will be found for you just as quickly as we reach Mazatlán and the Coast Guard headquarters there. Now he urges both of us to fasten our belts tightly as we are about to fly. Alec, I'm scared!"

"Don't be. I'll hold your hand."

Sergeant Dominguez turned around again, held up a canteen. *"Agua?"*

"Goodness, yes!" agreed Margrethe. *"Sí sí sí!"*

Water has never tasted so good.

The Lieutenant looked around when we returned the canteen, gave a big smile and a thumbs-up sign old as the Colosseum, and did something that speeded up his driving engines. They had been turning over very slowly; now they speeded up to a horrible racket. The machine turned as he headed it straight into the wind. The wind had been freshening all morning; now it showed little curls of white on the tops of the wavelets. He speeded his engines still more, to an unbelievable violence, and we went bouncing over the water, shaking everything.

Then we started hitting about every tenth wave with incredible force. I don't know why we weren't wrecked.

Suddenly we were twenty feet off the water; the bumping stopped. The vibration and the noise continued. We climbed at a sharp angle—and turned and started down again, and I almost-not-quite threw up that welcome drink of water.

The ocean was right in front of us, a solid wall. The Lieutenant turned his head and shouted something.

I wanted to tell him to keep his eyes on the road!— but I did not. "What does he say?"

"He says to look where he points. He'll point us right at it. *El tiburón blanco grande*—the great white shark that almost got us."

(I could have done without it.) Sure enough, right in the middle of this wall of water was a gray ghost with a fin cutting the water. Just when I knew that we were going to splash right down on top of it, the wall tilted away from us, my buttocks were forced down hard against the seat, my ears roared, and I again missed throwing up on our host only by iron will.

The machine leveled off and suddenly the ride was almost comfortable, aside from the racket and the vibration.

Airships are ever so much nicer.

The rugged hills behind the shoreline, so hard to see from our raft, were clearly in sight once we were in the air, and so was the shore—a series of beautiful beaches and a town where we were headed. The Sergeant looked around, pointed down at the town, and spoke. "What did he say?"

"Sergeant Roberto says that we are home just in time for lunch. *Almuerzo*, he said, but notes that it's breakfast—*desayuno*—for us."

My stomach suddenly decided to stay awhile. "I don't care what he calls it. Tell him not to bother to cook the horse; I'll eat it raw."

Margrethe translated; both our hosts laughed, then the Lieutenant proceeded to swoop down and place his machine on the water while looking back over his shoulder to talk to Margrethe—who continued to smile while she drove her nails through the palm of my right hand.

We got down. No one was killed. But airships are much better.

Lunch! Everything was coming up roses.

X

In the sweat of thy face shalt thou eat bread,
till thou return unto the ground—
Genesis 3:19

A half hour after the flying machine splashed down in the harbor of Mazatlán Margrethe and I were seated with Sergeant Dominguez in the enlisted men's mess of the Coast Guard. We were late for the midday meal but we were served. And I was clothed. Some at least—a pair of dungaree trousers. But the difference between bare naked and a pair of pants is far greater than the difference between cheap work trousers and the finest ermine. Try it and you'll see.

A small boat had come out to the flying machine's mooring; then I had to walk across the dock where we had landed and into the headquarters building, there to wait until these pants could be found for me—with strangers staring at me the whole time, some of them women. I know now how it feels to be exposed in stocks. Dreadful! I haven't been so embarrassed since an unfortunate accident in Sunday school when I was five.

But now it was done with and there was food and drink in front of us and, for the time being, I was abundantly happy. The food was not what I was used to. Who said that hunger was the best sauce? Whoever he was, he was right; our lunch was delicious. Thin cornmeal pancakes soaked with gravy, fried beans, a scorching hot stew, a bowl of little yellow tomatoes, and coffee strong, black, and bitter—what more could a man want? No gourmet ever savored a meal as much as I enjoyed that one.

(At first I had been a bit miffed that we ate in the enlisted men's mess rather than going with Lieutenant Sanz to wherever the officers ate. Much later I had it pointed out to me that I suffered from a very common civilian syndrome, i.e., a civilian with no military experience unconsciously equates his social position to that of officers, never to that of enlisted men. On examination this notion is obviously ridiculous—but it is almost universal. Oh, perhaps not universal but it obtains throughout America . . . where every man is "as good as anyone else and better than most.")

Sergeant Dominguez now had his shirt back. While pants were being found for me, a woman—a charwoman, I believe; the Mexican Coast Guard did not seem to have female ratings—a woman at headquarters had been sent to fetch something for Margrethe, and that something turned out to be a blouse and a full skirt, each of cotton and in bright colors. A simple and obviously cheap costume but Margrethe looked beautiful in it.

As yet, neither of us had shoes. No matter—the weather was warm and dry; shoes could wait. We were fed, we were dressed, we were safe—and all with a warm hospitality that caused me to feel that Mexicans were the finest people on earth.

After my second cup of coffee I said, "Sweetheart, how do we excuse ourselves and leave without being rude? I think we should find the American consul as early as possible."

"We have to go back to the headquarters building."

"More red tape?"

"I suppose you could call it that. I think they want to question us in more detail as to how we came to be where we were found. One must admit that our story is odd."

"I suppose so." Our initial interview with the Commandant had been less than satisfactory. Had I been alone I think he simply would have called me a liar . . . but it is difficult for a male man bursting with masculine ego to talk that way to Margrethe.

The trouble was the good ship *Konge Knut*.

She had not sunk, she had not come into port—she had never existed.

I was only moderately surprised. Had she turned into a full-rigged ship or a quinquereme, I would not have been surprised. But I had expected some sort of vessel of that same name—I thought the rules required it. But now it was becoming clear that I did not understand the rules. If there were any.

Margrethe had pointed out to me a confirming factor: This Mazatlán was not the town she had visited before. This one was much smaller and was not a tourist town—indeed the long dock where the *Konge Knut* should have tied up did not exist in this world. I think that this convinced her quite as much as the flying machines in proving to her that my "paranoia" was in fact the least hypothesis. She had been here before; that dock was big and solid; it was gone. It shook her.

The Commandant had not been impressed. He spent more time questioning Lieutenant Sanz than he spent questioning us. He did not seem pleased with Sanz.

There was another factor that I did not understand at the time and have never fully understood. Sanz's boss was "Captain" (or *"Capitán"*); the Commandant also was "Captain." But they were not the same rank.

The Coast Guard used navy ranks. However, that small part of it that operated flying machines used army ranks. I think this trivial difference had an historical origin. As may be, there was friction at the interface; the four-stripes or seagoing Captain was not disposed to accept as gospel anything reported by a flying-machine officer.

Lieutenant Sanz had fetched in two naked survivors with a preposterous story; the four-striper seemed inclined to blame Sanz himself for the unbelievable aspects of our story.

Sanz was not intimidated. I think he had no real respect for an officer who had never been higher off the water than a crow's nest. (Having ridden in his death trap, I understood why he was not inclined to genuflect to a sea-level type. Even among dirigible balloon pilots I have encountered this tendency to divide the world into those who fly and those who do not.)

After a bit, finding himself unable to shake Sanz, unable to shake Margrethe, and unable to communicate with me except through Margrethe, the Commandant shrugged and gave instructions that resulted in us all going to lunch. I thought that ended it. But now we were going back for more, whatever it was.

Our second session with the Commandant was short. He told us that we would see the immigration judge at four that afternoon—the court with that jurisdiction; there was no separate immigration court. In the meantime here was a list of what we owed—arrange payment with the judge.

Margrethe looked startled as she accepted a piece of paper from him; I demanded to know what he had said.

She translated; I looked at that billing.

More than eight thousand pesos!

It did not take a deep knowledge of Spanish to read that bill; almost all the words were cognates. *"Tres horas"* is three hours, and we were charged for three hours' use of *"aeroplano"*—a word I had heard earlier from Margrethe; it meant their flying machine. We were charged also for the time of Lieutenant Sanz and Sergeant Dominguez. Plus a multiplying factor that I decided must mean applied overhead, or near enough.

And there was fuel for the *aeroplano,* and service for it.

"Trousers" are *"pantalones"*—and here was a bill for the pair I was wearing.

A *"falda"* was a skirt and a *"camisa"* was a blouse—and Margrethe's outfit was decidedly not cheap.

One item surprised me not by its price but by being included; I had thought we were guests: two lunches, each at twelve pesos.

There was even a separate charge for the Commandant's time.

I started to ask how much eight thousand pesos came to in dollars—then shut up, realizing that I had not the slightest idea of the buying power of a dollar in this new world we had been dumped into.

Margrethe discussed the billing with Lieutenant Sanz, who looked embarrassed. There was much expostulation and waving of hands. She listened, then told me, "Alec, it isn't Anibal's idea and it is not even the fault of the Commandant. The tariffs on these services—rescue at sea, use of the *aeroplano*, and so forth— are set from *el Distrito Real*, the Royal District—that's the same as Mexico City, I believe. Lieutenant Sanz tells me that there is an economy drive on at the top level, with great pressure on everyone to make all public services self-supporting. He says that, if the Commandant did not charge us for our rescue and the Inspector Royal ever found out about it, it would be deducted from the Commandant's pay. Plus whatever punitive measures a royal commission found appropriate. And Anibal wants you to know that he is devastated at this embarrassing situation. If he owned the *aeroplano* himself, we would simply be his guests. He will always look on you as his brother and me as his sister."

"Tell him I feel the same way about him and please make it at least as flowery as he made it."

"I will. And Roberto wants to be included."

"And the same goes for the Sergeant. But find out where and how to get to the American consul. We've got troubles."

Lieutenant Anibal Sanz was told to see to it that we appeared in court at four o'clock; with that we were dismissed. Sanz delegated Sergeant Roberto to escort us to the consul and back, expressed regret that his duty status kept him from escorting us personally—clicked his heels, bowed over Margrethe's hand, and kissed it. He got a lot of mileage out of that simple gesture; I could see that Margrethe was pleased. But they don't teach that grace in Kansas. My loss.

*   *   *

Mazatlán is on a peninsula; the Coast Guard station is on the south shore not far from the lighthouse (tallest in the world—impressive!); the American consulate is about a mile away across town at the north shore, straight down *Avenida* Miguel Alemán its entire length—a pleasant walk, graced about halfway by a lovely fountain.

But Margrethe and I were barefooted.

Sergeant Dominguez did not suggest a taxi—and I could not.

At first being barefooted did not seem important. There were other bare feet on that boulevard and by no means all of them on children. (Nor did I have the only bare chest.) As a youngster I had regarded bare feet as a luxury, a privilege. I went barefooted all summer and put on shoes most reluctantly when school opened.

After the first block I was wondering why, as a kid, I had always looked forward to going barefooted. Shortly thereafter I asked Margrethe to ask Sergeant Roberto, please, to slow down and let me pick my way for maximum shade; this pesky sidewalk is frying my feet!

(Margrethe had not complained and did not—and I was a bit vexed with her that she had not. I benefited constantly from Margrethe's angelic fortitude—and found it hard to live up to.)

From there on I gave my full attention to pampering my poor, abused, tender pink feet. I felt sorry for myself and wondered why I had ever left God's country.

"I wept that I had no shoes, until I met a man who had no feet." I don't know who said that first, but it is part of our cultural heritage and should be.

It happened to me.

Not quite halfway, where Miguel Alemán crosses *Calle* Aquiles Serdan at the fountain, we encountered a street beggar. He looked up at us and grinned, held up a handful of pencils—"looked up" because he was riding a little wheeled dolly; he had no feet.

Sergeant Roberto called him by name and flipped him a coin; the beggar caught it in his teeth, flipped it into his pocket, called out, *"Gracias!"*—and turned his attention to me.

I said quickly, "Margrethe, will you please explain to him that I have no money whatever."

"Yes, Alec." She squatted down, spoke with him eye to eye. Then she straightened up. "Pepe says to tell you, that's all right; he'll catch you someday when you are rich."

"Please tell him that I will be back. I promise."

She did so. Pepe grinned at me, threw Margrethe a kiss, and saluted the Sergeant and me. We went on.

And I stopped being so finicky careful to coddle my feet. Pepe had forced me to reassess my situation. Ever since I had learned that the Mexican government did not regard rescuing me as a privilege but expected me to pay for it, I had been feeling sorry for myself, abused, put upon. I had been muttering to myself that my compatriots who complained that all Mexicans were bloodsuckers, living on gringo tourists, were dead right! Not Roberto and the Lieutenant, of course—but the others. Lazy parasites, all of them!—with their hands out for the Yankee dollar.

Like Pepe.

I reviewed in my mind all the Mexicans I had met that day, each one I could remember, and asked forgiveness for my snide thoughts. Mexicans were simply fellow travelers on that long journey from dark to eternal darkness. Some carried their burdens well, some did not. And some carried very heavy burdens with gallantry and grace. Like Pepe.

Yesterday I had been living in luxury; today I was broke and in debt. But I have my health, I have my brain, I have my two hands—and I have Margrethe. My burdens were light; I should carry them joyfully. Thank you, Pepe!

The door of the consulate had a small American flag over it and the Great Seal in bronze on it. I pulled the bell wire beside it.

After a considerable wait the door opened a crack and a female voice told us to go away (I needed no translation; her meaning was clear). The door started to close. Sergeant Roberto whistled loudly and called out. The crack widened; a dialogue ensued. Margrethe said, "He's telling her to tell *Don* Ambrosio that two American citizens are here who must see him at once because they must appear in court at four this afternoon."

Again we waited. After about twenty minutes the maid let us in and ushered us into a dark office. The consul came in, fixed my eye with his, and demanded to know how I dared to interrupt his siesta?

Then he caught sight of Margrethe and slowed down. To her it was: "How can I serve you? In the meantime will you honor my poor house by accepting a glass of wine? Or a cup of coffee?"

Barefooted and in a garish dress, Margrethe was a lady—I was riffraff. Don't ask me why this was so; it just was. The effect was most marked with men. But it worked with women, too. Try to rationalize it and you find yourself using words like "royal," "noble," "gentry," and "to the manner born"—all involving concepts anathema to the American democratic ideal. Whether this proves something about Margrethe or something about the democratic ideal I will leave as an exercise for the student.

Don Ambrosio was a pompous zero but nevertheless he was a relief because he spoke American—real American, not English; he had been born in Brownsville, Texas. I feel certain that the backs of his parents were wet. He had parlayed a talent for politics among his fellow Chicanos into a cushy sinecure, telling gringo travelers in the land of Montezuma why they could not have what they desperately needed.

Which he eventually told us.

I let Margrethe do most of the talking because she was obviously so much more successful at it than I was. She called us "Mr. and Mrs. Graham"—we had agreed on that name during the walk here. When we were rescued, she had used "Graham Hergensheimer" and had explained to me later that this let me choose: I could select "Hergensheimer" simply by asserting that the listener's memory had had a minor bobble; the name had been offered as "Hergensheimer Graham." No? Well, then *I* must have miscalled it—sorry.

I let it stay "Graham Hergensheimer" and thereby used the name "Graham" in order to keep things simple; to her I had always been "Graham" and I had been using the name myself for almost two weeks. Before I got out of the consulate I had told a dozen more lies, trying to keep our story believable. I did not want unnecessary complication; "Mr. and Mrs. Alec Graham" was easiest.

(Minor theological note: Many people seem to believe

that the Ten Commandments forbid lying. Not at all!
The prohibition is against bearing false witness against
your neighbor—a specific, limited, and despicable sort
of lie. But there is no Biblical rule forbidding simple
untruth. Many theologians believe that no human social
organization could stand up under the strain of absolute
honesty. If you think their misgivings are unfounded,
try telling your friends the ungarnished truth about
what you think of their offspring—if you dare risk it.)

After endless repetitions (in which the *Konge Knut*
shrank and became our private cruiser) *Don* Ambrosio
said to me, "It's no use, Mr. Graham. I cannot issue
you even a temporary document to substitute for your
lost passport because you have offered me not one shred
of proof that you are an American citizen."

I answered, "*Don* Ambrosio, I am astonished. I know
that Mrs. Graham has a slight accent; we told you that
she was born in Denmark. But do you honestly think
that anyone not born amidst the tall corn could possibly
have my accent?"

He gave a most Latin shrug. "I'm not an expert in
midwest accents. To my ear you could have been born
to one of the harsher British accents, then have gone on
the stage—and everybody knows that a competent ac-
tor can acquire the accent for any role. The People's
Republic of England goes to any length these days to
plant their sleepers in the States; you might be from
Lincoln, England, rather than from somewhere near
Lincoln, Nebraska."

"Do you really believe that?"

"What I believe is not the question. The fact is that I
will not sign a piece of paper saying that you are an

American citizen when I don't know that you are. I'm sorry. Is there anything more that I can do for you?"

(How can you do "more" for me when you haven't done anything yet?) "Possibly you can advise us."

"Possibly. I am not a lawyer."

I offered him our copy of the billing against us, explained it. "Is this in order and are these charges appropriate?"

He looked it over. "These charges are certainly legal both by their laws and ours. Appropriate? Didn't you tell me that they saved your lives?"

"No question about it. Oh, there's an outside chance that a fishing boat might have picked us up if the Coast Guard had not found us. But the Coast Guard did find us and did save us."

"Is your life—your two lives—worth less than eight thousand pesos? Mine is worth considerably more, I assure you."

"It isn't that, sir. We have no money, not a cent. It all went down with the boat."

"So send for money. You can have it sent care of the consulate. I'll go that far."

"Thank you. It will take time. In the meantime how can I get them off my neck? I was told that this judge will want cash and immediately."

"Oh, it's not that bad. It's true that they don't permit bankruptcy the way we do, and they do have a rather old-fashioned debtors-prison law. But they don't use it—just the threat of it. Instead the court will see that you get a job that will let you settle your indebtedness. *Don* Clemente is a humane judge; he will take care of you."

Aside from flowery nonsense directed at Margrethe,

that ended it. We picked up Sergeant Roberto, who had been enjoying backstairs hospitality from the maid and the cook, and headed for the courthouse.

Don Clemente (Judge Ibañez) was as pleasant as *Don* Ambrosio had said he would be. Since we informed the clerk at once that we stipulated the debt but did not have the cash to pay it, there was no trial. We were simply seated in the uncrowded courtroom and told to wait while the judge disposed of cases on his docket. He handled several quickly. Some were minor offenses drawing fines; some were debt cases; some were hearings for later trial. I could not tell much about what was going on and whispering was frowned on, so Margrethe could not tell me much. But he was certainly no hanging judge.

The cases at hand were finished; at a word from the clerk we went out back with the "miscreants"—peasants, mostly—who owed fines or debts. We found ourselves lined up on a low platform, facing a group of men. Margrethe asked what this was—and was answered, *"La subasta."*

"What's that?" I asked her.

"Alec, I'm not sure. It's not a word I know."

Settlements were made quickly on the others; I gathered that most of them had been there before. Then there was just one man left of the group off the platform, just us on the platform. The man remaining looked sleekly prosperous. He smiled and spoke to me. Margrethe answered.

"What is he saying?" I asked.

"He asked you if you can wash dishes. I told him that you do not speak Spanish."

"Tell him that of course I can wash dishes. But that's hardly a job I want."

Five minutes later our debt had been paid, in cash, to the clerk of the court, and we had acquired a *patrón*, *Señor* Jaime Valera Guzman. He paid sixty pesos a day for Margrethe, thirty for me, plus our found. Court costs were twenty-five hundred pesos, plus fees for two nonresident work permits, plus war-tax stamps. The clerk figured our total indebtedness, then divided it out for us: In only a hundred and twenty-one days—four months—our obligation to our *patrón* would be discharged. Unless, of course, we spent some money during that time.

He also directed us to our *patrón*'s place of business, *Restaurante* Pancho Villa. Our *patrón* had already left in his private car. *Patrones* ride; *peones* walk.

XI

And Jacob served seven years for Rachel;
and they seemed unto him but a few days,
for the love he had to her.
Genesis 29:20

Sometimes, while washing dishes, I would amuse myself by calculating how high a stack of dishes I had washed since going to work for our *patrón, Don* Jaime. The ordinary plate used in Pancho Villa café stacked twenty plates to a foot. I arbitrarily decided that a cup and saucer, or two glasses, would count as one plate, since these items did not stack well. And so forth.

The great Mazatlán lighthouse is five hundred and fifteen feet tall, only forty feet shorter than the Washington Monument. I remember the day I completed my first "lighthouse stack." I had told Margrethe earlier that week that I was approaching my goal and expected to reach it by Thursday or early Friday.

And did so, Thursday evening—and left the scullery, stood in the door between the kitchen and the dining room, caught Margrethe's eye, raised my hands high and shook hands with myself like a pugilist.

Margrethe stopped what she was doing—taking orders from a family party—and applauded. This caused her to have to explain to her guests what was going on, and that resulted in her stopping by the scullery a few minutes later to pass to me a ten-peso note, a congratulatory gift from the father of that family. I asked her to thank him for me, and please tell him that I had just started my second lighthouse stack, which I was dedicating to him and his family.

Which in turn resulted in *Señora* Valera sending her husband, *Don* Jaime, to find out why Margrethe was wasting time and making a scene instead of paying attention to her work . . . which resulted in *Don* Jaime inquiring how much the diners had tipped me and then matching it.

The *Señora* had no reason to complain; Margrethe was not only her best waitress; she was her only bilingual waitress. The day we started to work for Sr. y Sra. Valera a sign painter was called in to paint a conspicuous sign: ENGLIS SPOKE HERE. Thereafter, in addition to being available for any English-speaking guests, Margrethe prepared menus in English (and the prices on the menus in English were about forty percent higher than the prices on the all-Spanish menus).

Don Jaime was not a bad boss. He was cheerful and, on the whole, kindly to his employees. When we had been there about a month, he told me that he would not have bid in my debt had it not been that the judge would not permit my contract to be separated from Margrethe's contract, we being a married couple (else I could have found myself a field hand able to see my wife only on rare occasions—as *Don* Ambrosio had told me, *Don* Clemente was a humane judge).

I told him that I was happy that the package included me but it simply showed his good judgment to want to hire Margrethe.

He agreed that that was true. He had attended the Wednesday labor auctions several weeks on end in search of a bilingual woman or girl who could be trained as a waitress, then had bid me in as well to obtain Margrethe—but he wished to tell me that he had not regretted it as he had never seen the scullery so clean, the dishes so immaculate, the silverware so shiny.

I assured him that it was my happy privilege to help uphold the honor and prestige of *Restaurante* Pancho Villa and its distinguished *patrón, el Don* Jaime.

In fact it would have been difficult for me *not* to improve that scullery. When I took over, I thought at first that the floor was dirt. And so it was—you could have planted potatoes!—but under the filth, about a half inch down, was sound concrete. I cleaned and then kept it clean—my feet were still bare. Then I demanded roach powder.

Each morning I killed roaches and cleaned the floor. Each evening, just before quitting for the day, I sprinkled roach powder. It is impossible (I think) to conquer roaches, but it is possible to fight them to a draw, force them back and maintain a holding action.

As to the quality of my dishwashing, it could not be otherwise; my mother had a severe dirt phobia and, because of my placement in a large family, I washed or wiped dishes under her eye from age seven through thirteen (at which time I graduated through taking on a newspaper route that left me no time for dishwashing).

But just because I did it well, do not think I was

enamored of dishwashing. It had bored me as a child; it bored me as a man.

Then why did I do it? Why didn't I run away?

Isn't that evident? Dishwashing kept me with Margrethe. Running away might be feasible for some debtors—I don't think much effort went into trying to track down and bring back debtors who disappeared some dark night—but running away was not feasible for a married couple, one of whom was a conspicuous blonde in a country in which any blonde is always conspicuous and the other was a man who could not speak Spanish.

While we both worked hard—eleven to eleven each day except Tuesday, with a nominal two hours off for siesta and a half hour each for lunch and dinner—we had the other twelve hours each day to ourselves, plus all day Tuesday.

Niagara Falls never supplied a finer honeymoon. We had a tiny attic room at the back of the restaurant building. It was hot but we weren't there much in the heat of the day—by eleven at night it was comfortable no matter how hot the day had been. In Mazatlán most residents of our social class (zero!) did not have inside plumbing. But we worked and lived in a restaurant building; there was a flush toilet we shared with other employees during working hours and shared with no one the other twelve hours of each day. (There was also a Maw Jones out back, which I sometimes used during working hours—I don't think Margrethe ever used it.)

We had the use of a shower on the ground floor, back to back with the employees' toilet, and the needs of the scullery were such that the building had a large water heater. *Señora* Valera scolded us regularly for using too much hot water ("Gas costs money!"); we listened in silence and went right on using whatever amount of hot water we needed.

Our *patrón*'s contract with the state required him to supply us with food and shelter (and clothing, under the law, but I did not learn this until too late to matter), which is why we slept there, and of course we ate there—not the chef's specialties, but quite good food.

"Better is a dinner of herbs where love is, than a stalled ox and hatred therewith." We had only ourselves; it was enough.

Margrethe, because she sometimes received tips, especially from gringos, was slowly accumulating cash money. We spent as little of this as possible—she bought shoes for each of us—and she saved against the day when we would be free of our peonage and able to go north. I had no illusions that the nation north of us was the land of my birth . . . but it was this world's analog of it; English was spoken there and I was sure that its culture would have to be closer to what we had been used to.

Tips to Margrethe brought us into friction with *Señora* Valera the very first week. While *Don* Jaime was legally our *patrón*, she owned the restaurant—or so we were told by Amanda the cook. Jaime Valera had once been headwaiter there and had married the owner's daughter. This made him permanent *maître d'hôtel*. When his father-in-law died, he became the owner in the eyes of the public. But his wife retained the purse strings and presided over the cash register.

(Perhaps I should add that he was "*Don* Jaime" to us because he was our *patrón;* he was not a *Don* to the public. The honorific "*Don*" will not translate into English, but owning a restaurant does not make a man a *Don*—but, for example, being a judge does.)

The first time Margrethe was seen to receive a tip, the *Señora* told her to turn it over—at the end of each week she would receive her percentage.

Margrethe came straight to me in the scullery. "Alec, what shall I do? Tips were my main income in the *Konge Knut* and no one ever asked me to share them. Can she do this to me?"

I told her not to turn her tips over to the *Señora* but to tell her that we would discuss it with her at the end of the day.

There is one advantage to being a *peón*: You don't get fired over a disagreement with your boss. Certainly we could be fired . . . but that would simply lose the Valeras some ten thousand pesos they had invested in us.

By the end of the day I knew exactly what to say and how to say it—how Margrethe must say it, as it was another month before I soaked up enough Spanish to maintain a minimum conversation:

"Sir and Madam, we do not understand this ruling about gifts to me. We want to see the judge and ask him what our contract requires."

As I had suspected, they were not willing to see the judge about it. They were legally entitled to Margrethe's service but they had no claim on money given to her by a third party.

This did not end it. *Señora* Valera was so angry at being balked by a mere waitress that she had a sign posted: NO PROPINAS—NO TIPS, and the same notice was placed in the menus.

Peones can't strike. But there were five other waitresses, two of them Amanda's daughters. The day

Señora Valera ordered no tipping she found that she had just one waitress (Margrethe) and no one in the kitchen. She gave up. But I am sure she never forgave us.

Don Jaime treated us as employees; his wife treated us as slaves. Despite that old cliché about "wage slaves," there is a world of difference. Since we both tried hard to be faithful employees while paying off our debt but flatly refused to be slaves, we were bound to tangle with *Señora* Valera.

Shortly after the disagreement over tips Margrethe became convinced that the *Señora* was snooping in our bedroom. If true, there was no way to stop her; there was no lock for the door and she could enter our room without fear of being caught any day while we were working.

I gave some thought to boobytraps until Margrethe vetoed the idea. She simply thereafter kept her money on her person. But it was a measure of what we thought of our "patroness" that Margrethe considered it necessary to take precautions against her stealing from us.

We did not let *Señora* Valera spoil our happiness. And we did not let our dubious status as a "married" couple spoil our somewhat irregular honeymoon. Oh, I would have spoiled it because I always have had this unholy itch to analyze matters I really do not know how to analyze. But Margrethe is much more practical than I am and simply did not permit it. I tried to rationalize our relationship to her by pointing out that polygamy was not forbidden by Hóly Writ but solely by modern law and custom—and she chopped me off briskly by saying that she had no interest in how many wives or concubines King Solomon had and did not regard him or any Old Testament character as a model for her own behavior. If I did not want to live with her, speak up! Say so!

I shut up. Some problems are best let be, not chewed over with words. This modern compulsion to "talk it out" is a mistake at least as often as it is a solution.

But her disdain for Biblical authority concerning the legality of one man having two wives was so sharp that I asked her about it later—not about polygamy; I stayed away from that touchy subject; I asked her how she felt about the authority of Holy Writ in general. I explained that the church I was brought up in believed in strict interpretation—"A whole Bible, not a Bible full of holes"—Scripture was the literal word of God . . . but that I knew that other churches felt that the spirit rather than the letter ruled . . . some being so liberal that they hardly bothered with the Bible. Yet all of them called themselves Christian.

"Margrethe my love, as deputy executive secretary of Churches United for Decency I was in daily contact with members of every Protestant sect in the country and in liaison association with many Roman Catholic clerics on matters where we could join in a united front. I learned that my own church did not have a monopoly on virtue. A man could be awfully mixed up in religious fundamentals and still be a fine citizen and a devout Christian."

I chuckled as I recalled something and went on, "Or to put it in reverse, one of my Catholic friends, Father Mahaffey, told me that even I could squeeze into Heaven, because the Good Lord in His infinite wisdom made allowances for the ignorance and wrongheadedness of Protestants."

This conversation took place on a Tuesday, our day

off, the one day a week the restaurant did not open, and in consequence we were on top of *el Cerro de la Nevería*—Icebox Hill, but it sounds better in Spanish—and just finishing a picnic lunch. This hill was downtown, close to Pancho Villa café, but was a bucolic oasis; the citizens had followed the Spanish habit of turning hills into parks rather than building on them. A happy place—

"My dear, I would never try to proselytize you into my church. But I do want to know as much about you as possible. I find that I don't know much about churches in Denmark. Mostly Lutheran, I think—but does Denmark have its own established state church like some other European nations? Either way, which church is yours, and is it strict interpretationist or liberal—and again, either way, how do *you* feel about it? And remember what Father Mahaffey said—I agree with him. I don't think that my church has the only door into Heaven."

I was lying stretched out; Margrethe was seated with her knees drawn up and holding them and was faced west, staring out to sea. This placed her with her face turned away from me. She did not answer my query. Presently I said gently, "My dear, did you hear me?"

"I heard you."

Again I waited, then added, "If I have been prying where I should not pry, I'm sorry and I withdraw the question."

"No. I knew that I would have to answer it some day. Alec, I am not a Christian." She let go her knees, swung around, and looked me in the eye. "You can have a divorce as simply as we married, just by telling me so. I won't fight it; I will go quietly away. But,

Alec, when you told me that you loved me, then later when you told me that we were married in the eyes of God, you did not ask me my religion."

"Margrethe."

"Yes, Alec?"

"First, wash out your mouth. Then ask my pardon."

"There may be enough wine left in the bottle to rinse out my mouth. But I cannot ask pardon for not telling you this. I would have answered truthfully at any time. You did not ask."

"Wash out your mouth for talking about divorce. Ask my pardon for daring to think that I would ever divorce you under any circumstances whatever. If you are ever naughty enough, I may beat you. But I would never put you away. For richer, for poorer, in sickness and health, now and forever. Woman, I love you! Get that through your head."

Suddenly she was in my arms, weeping for only the second time, and I was doing the only thing possible, namely, kissing her.

I heard a cheer behind me and turned my head. We had had the top of the hill to ourselves, it being a work day for most people. But I found that we had an audience of two streetwise urchins, so young that sex was unclear. Catching my eye, one of them cheered again, then made loud kissing noises.

"Beat it!" I called out. "Scram! *Vaya con Dios!* Is that what I wanted to say, Marga?"

She spoke to them and they did go away, after more high giggles. I needed the interruption. I had said to Margrethe what had to be said because she needed immediate reassurance after her silly, gallant speech. But nevertheless I was shaken to my depths.

I started to speak, then decided that I had said enough for one day. But Margrethe said nothing, too; the silence grew painful. I felt that matters could not be left so, balanced uncertainly on edge. "What is your faith, dear one? Judaism? I do remember now that there are Jews in Denmark. Not all Danes are Lutheran."

"Some Jews, yes. But barely one in a thousand. No, Alec. Uh— There are older Gods."

"Older than Jehovah? Impossible."

Margrethe said nothing—characteristically. If she disagreed, she usually said nothing. She seemed to have no interest in winning arguments, in which she must differ from 99 percent of the human race . . . many of whom appear willing to suffer any disaster rather than lose an argument.

So I found myself having to conduct both sides to keep the argument from dying through lack of nourishment. "I retract that. I should not have said, 'Impossible.' I was speaking from the accepted chronology as given by Bishop Ussher. If one accepts his dating, then the world was created five thousand nine hundred and ninety-eight years ago this coming October. Of course that dating is not itself a matter of Holy Writ; Hales arrived at a different figure, uh, seven thousand four hundred and five, I think—I do better when I write figures down. And other scholars get slightly different answers.

"But they all agree that some four or five thousand years before Christ occurred the unique event, Creation. At that point Jehovah created the world and, in so doing, created time. Time cannot exist alone. As a corollary, nothing and no one and no god can be older than Jehovah, since Jehovah created time. You see?"

"I wish I'd kept quiet."

"My dear! I am simply trying to have an intellectual discussion; I did not and do not and never do and never will intend to hurt you. I said that was the case by the orthodox way of dating. Clearly you are using another way. Will you explain it to me?—and not jump all over poor old Alex every time he opens his mouth? I was schooled as a minister in a church that emphasizes preaching; discussion comes as naturally to me as swimming does to fish. But now you preach and I'll listen. Tell me about these older gods."

"You know of them. The oldest and greatest we celebrate tomorrow; the middle day of each week is his."

"Today is Tuesday, tomorrow— Wednesday! *Wotan!* He is your God?"

"Odin. 'Wotan' is a German distortion of Old Norse. Father Odin and his two brothers created the world. In the beginning there was void, nothing—then the rest of it reads much like Genesis, even to Adam and Eve— but called Askr and Embla rather than Adam and Eve."

"Perhaps it *is* Genesis, Margrethe."

"What do you mean, Alec?"

"The Bible is the Word of God, in particular the English translation known as the King James version because every word of that translation was sustained by prayer and the best efforts of the world's greatest scholars—any difference in opinion was taken directly to the Lord in prayer. So the King James Bible *is* the Word of God.

"But nowhere is it written that this can be the only Word of God. A sacred writing of another race at another time in another language can also be inspired history . . . *if* it is compatible with the Bible. And that is what you have just described, is it not?"

"Ah, just on Creation and on Adam and Eve, Alec. The chronology does not match at all. You said that the world was created about six thousand years ago?"

"About. Hales makes it longer. The Bible does not give dates; dating is a modern invention."

"Even that longer time—Hales?—is much too short. A hundred thousand years would be more like it."

I started to expostulate—after all, some things are just too much to be swallowed—then remembered that I had warned myself not to say anything that could cause Margrethe to shut up. "Go on, dear. Do your religious writings tell what happened during all those millennia?"

"Almost all of it happened before writing was invented. Some was preserved in epic poems sung by skalds. But even that did not start until men learned to live in tribes and Odin taught them to sing. The longest period was ruled by the frost giants before mankind was more than wild animals, hunted for sport. But the real difference in the chronology is this, Alec. The Bible runs from Creation to Judgment Day, then Millennium—the Kingdom on Earth—then the War in Heaven and the end of the world. After that is the Heavenly City and Eternity—time has stopped. Is that correct?"

"Well, yes. A professional eschatologist would find that overly simplified but you have correctly described the main outlines. The details are given in Revelations—the Revelation of Saint John the Divine, I should say. Many prophets have witnessed the final things but Saint John is the only one with the complete story . . . because Christ Himself delivered the Revelation to John to stop the elect from being deceived by false prophets. Creation, the Fall from Grace, the long centuries of struggle and trial, then the final battle, followed by Judgment and the Kingdom. What does your faith say, my love?"

"The final battle we call Ragnarok rather than Armageddon—"

"I can't see that terminology matters."

"Please, dear. The name does not matter but what happens does. In your Judgment Day the goats are separated from the sheep. The saved go to eternal bliss; the damned go to eternal punishment. Correct?"

"Correct—while noting for purposes of scientific accuracy that some authorities assert that, while bliss is eternal, God so loves the world that even the damned may eventually be saved; no soul is utterly beyond redemption. Other theologians regard this as heresy— but it appeals to me; I have never liked the idea of eternal damnation. I'm a sentimentalist, my dear."

"I know you are, Alec, and I love you for it. You should find the old religion appealing . . . as it does not have eternal damnation."

"It does not?"

"No. At Ragnarok the world as we know it will be destroyed. But that is not the end. After a long time, a time of healing, a new universe will be created, one better and cleaner and free from the evils of this world. It too will last for countless millennia . . . until again the forces of evil and cold contend against the forces of goodness and light . . . and again there is a time of rest, followed by a new creation and another chance for men. Nothing is ever finished, nothing is ever perfect, but over and over again the race of men gets another chance to do better than last time, ever and again without end."

"And this you believe, Margrethe?"

"I find it easier to believe than the smugness of the saved and the desperate plight of the damned in the Christian faith. Jehovah is said to be all powerful. If this is true, then the poor damned souls in Hell are there because Jehovah planned it that way in every minute detail. Is this not so?"

I hesitated. The logical reconciliation of Omnipotence, Omniscience, and Omnibenevolence is the thorniest problem in theology, one causing even Jesuits to break their teeth. "Margrethe, some of the mysteries of the Almighty are not easily explained. We mortals must accept Our Father's benevolent intention toward us, whether or not we always understand His works."

"Must a baby understand God's benevolent intention when his brains are dashed out against a rock? Does he then go straight to Hell, praising the Lord for His infinite Wisdom and Goodness?"

"Margrethe! What in the world are you talking about?"

"I am talking about places in the Old Testament in which Jehovah gives direct orders to kill babies, sometimes ordering that they be killed by dashing them against rocks. See that Psalm that starts 'By the rivers of Babylon—' And see the word of the Lord Jehovah in Hosea: 'their infants shall be dashed in pieces, and their women with child shall be ripped up.' And there is the case of Elisha and the bears. Alec, do you believe in your heart that your God caused bears to tear up little children merely because they made fun of an old man's bald head?" She waited.

And I waited. Presently she said, "Is that story of the she bears and the forty-two children the literal Word of God?"

"Certainly it's the Word of God! But I don't pretend to understand it fully. Margrethe, if you want detailed explanations of everything the Lord has done, pray to Him for enlightenment. But don't crowd me about it."

"I did not intend to crowd you, Alec. I'm sorry."

"No need to be. I've never understood about those bears but I don't let it shake my faith. Perhaps it's a parable. But look, dear, doesn't your Father Odin have a pretty bloody history Himself?"

"Not on the same scale. Jehovah destroyed city after city, every man, woman, and child, down to the youngest baby. Odin killed only in combat against opponents his own size. But, most important difference of all, Father Odin is *not* all powerful and does *not* claim to be all wise."

(A theology that avoids the thorniest problem— But how can you call Him "God" if He is not omnipotent?)

She went on, "Alec my only love, I don't want to attack your faith. I don't enjoy it and never intended to—and hope that nothing like it will ever happen again. But you did ask me point blank whether or not I accepted the authority of 'Holy Writ'—by which you mean your Bible. I must answer just as point blank. I do not. The Jehovah or Yahweh of the Old Testament seems to me to be a sadistic, bloodthirsty, genocidal villain. I cannot understand how He can be identified with the gentle Christ of the New Testament. Even through a mystic Trinity."

I started to answer but she hurried on. "Dear heart, before we leave this subject I must tell you something I have been thinking about. Does your religion offer an explanation of the weird thing that has happened to us? Once to me, twice to you—this changed world?"

(It had been endlessly on my mind, too!) "No. I must confess it. I wish I had a Bible to search for an explanation. But I have been searching in my mind. I haven't been able to find anything that should have prepared me for this." I sighed. "It's a bleak feeling. But—" I smiled at her. "—Divine Providence placed you with me. No land is strange to me that has Margrethe in it."

"Dear Alec. I asked because the old religion does offer an explanation."

"What?"

"Not a cheerful one. At the beginning of this cycle Loki was overcome—do you know Loki?"

"Some. The mischief maker."

"'Mischief' is too mild a word; he works evil. For thousands of years he has been a prisoner, chained to a great rock. Alec, the end of every cycle in the story of man begins the same way. Loki manages to escape his bonds . . . and chaos results."

She looked at me with great sadness. "Alec, I am sorry . . . but I do believe that Loki is loose. The signs show it. Now *anything* can happen. We enter the Twilight of the Gods. Ragnarok comes. Our world ends."

XII

---

*And in the same hour was there a great earthquake,
and the tenth part of the city fell, and in the
earthquake were slain of men seven thousand:
and the remnant were affrighted, and gave glory
to the God of Heaven.*

Revelation 11:13

I washed another lighthouse stack of dishes while I pondered the things Margrethe had said to me that beautiful afternoon on Icebox Hill—but I never again mentioned the subject to Margrethe. And she did not speak of it to me; as Margrethe never argued about anything if she could reasonably keep silent.

Did I believe her theory about Loki and Ragnarok? Of course not! Oh, I had no objection to calling Armageddon by the name "Ragnarok." Jesus or Joshua or Jesu; Mary or Miriam or Maryam or Maria, Jehovah or Yahweh—any verbal symbol will do as long as speaker and listener agree on meaning. But Loki? Ask me to believe that a mythical demigod of an ignorant, barbarian race has wrought changes in the whole universe? Now, really!

I am a modern man, with an open mind—but not so empty that the wind blows through it. Somewhere in Holy Writ lay a rational explanation for the upsets that had happened to us. I need not look to ghost stories of long-dead pagans for explanation.

I missed not having a Bible at hand. Oh, no doubt there were Catholic Bibles at the basilica three blocks away . . . in Latin or in Spanish. I wanted the King James version. Again no doubt there were copies of it somewhere in this city—but I did not know where. For the first time in my life I envied the perfect memory of Preachin' Paul (Rev. Paul Balonius) who tramped up and down the central states the middle of last century, preaching the Word without carrying the Book with him. Brother Paul was reputed to be able to quote from memory any verse cited by book, chapter, and number of verse, or, conversely, correctly place by book, chapter, and number any verse read to him.

I was born too late to meet Preachin' Paul, so I never saw him do this—but perfect memory is a special gift God bestows not too infrequently; I have no reason to doubt that Brother Paul had it. Paul died suddenly, somewhat mysteriously, and possibly sinfully—in the words of my mission studies professor, one should exercise great prudence in praying alone with a married woman.

I don't have Paul's gift. I can quote the first few chapters of Genesis and several of the Psalms and the Christmas story according to Luke, and some other passages. But for today's problem I needed to study in exact detail *all* the prophets, especially the prophecy known as the Revelation of Saint John the Divine.

Was Armageddon approaching? Was the Second Coming at hand? Would I myself still be alive in the flesh when the great Trump sounds?

A thrilling thought, and not one to be discarded too quickly. Many millions will be alive on that great day; that mighty host could include Alexander Hergensheimer. Would I hear His Shout and see the dead rise up and then myself "be caught up together with them in the clouds, to meet the Lord in the air" and then ever be with the Lord, as promised? The most thrilling passage in the Great Book!

Not that I had any assurance that I myself would be among those saved on that great day, even if I lived in the flesh to that day. Being an ordained minister of the Gospel does not necessarily improve one's chances. Clergymen are aware of this cold truth (if they are honest with themselves) but laymen sometimes think that men of the cloth have an inside track.

Not true! For a clergyman, there are no excuses. He can never claim that "he didn't know it was loaded," or cite youth and inexperience as a reason to ask for mercy, or claim ignorance of the law, or any of the other many excuses by which a layman might show a touch less than moral perfection but still be saved.

Knowing this, I was forced to admit that my own record lately did not suggest that I was among the saved. Certainly, I was born again. Some people seem to think that this is a permanent condition, like a college degree. Brother, don't count on it! I was only too aware that I had racked up quite a number of sins lately: Sinful pride. Intemperance. Greed. Lechery. Adultery. Doubt. And others.

Worse yet, I felt no contrition for the very worst of these.

If the record did not show that Margrethe was saved and listed for Heaven, then I had no interest in going there myself. God help me, that was the truth.

I worried about Margrethe's immortal soul.

She could not claim the second chance of all pre-

Christian Era souls. She had been born into the Lutheran Church, not my church but ancestor to my church, ancestor to all Protestant churches, the first fruit of the Diet of Worms. (When I was a lad in Sunday school, "Diet of Worms" inspired mind pictures quite foreign to theology!)

The only way Margrethe could be saved would be by renouncing her heresy and seeking to be born again. But she must do this herself; I could not do it for her.

The most I could possibly do would be to urge her to seek salvation. But I would have to do it most carefully. One does not persuade a butterfly to light on one's hand by brandishing a sword. Margrethe was not a heathen ignorant of Christ and needing only to be instructed. No, she had been born into Christianity and had rejected it, eyes open. She could cite Scripture as readily as I could—at some time she had studied the Book most diligently, far more than most laymen. When and why I never asked, but I think it must have been at the time when she began to contemplate leaving the Christian faith. Margrethe was so serious and so *good* that I felt certain that she would never take such a drastic step without long, hard study.

How urgent was the problem of Margrethe? Did I have thirty years or so to learn her mind and feel out the best approach? Or was Armageddon so close upon us that even a day's delay could doom her for eternity?

The pagan Ragnarok and the Christian Armageddon have this in common: The final battle will be preceded by great signs and portents. Were we experiencing such omens? Margrethe thought so. Myself, I found the idea that this world changing presaged Armageddon more attractive than the alternative, i.e., paranoia on my part. Could a ship be wrecked and a world changed just to keep me from checking a thumbprint? I had thought so at the time but—oh, come now, Alex, you are not that important.

(Or was I?)

I have never been a Millenarianist. I am aware how often the number one thousand appears in the Bible, especially in prophecy—but I have never believed that the Almighty was constrained to work in even millennia—or any other numbering patterns—just to please numerologists.

On the other hand I know that many thousands of sensible and devout people place enormous importance on the forthcoming end of the Second Millennium, with Judgment Day and Armageddon and all that must follow—expected at that time. They find their proofs in the Bible and claim confirmation in the lines in the Great Pyramid and in a variety of Apocrypha.

But they differ among themselves as to the end of the millennium. 2000 A.D.? Or 2001 A.D.? Or is the correct dating 3 p.m. Jerusalem local time April 7, 2030 A.D.? If indeed scholars have the time and date of the Crucifixion—and the earthquake at the moment of His death—correctly figured against mundane time reckoning. Or should it be Good Friday 2030 A.D. as calculated by the lunar calendar? This is no trivial matter in view of what we are attempting to date.

But, if we take the birth of Christ rather than the date of the Crucifixion as the starting point from which to count the millennia, it is evident at once that neither the naive date of 2000 A.D. nor the slightly less naive date of 2001 can be the bimillenarian date *because Jesus was born in Bethlehem on Christmas Day year 5 B.C.*

Every educated person knows this and almost no one ever thinks about it.

How could the greatest event in all history, the birth of our Lord Incarnate, have been misdated by five years? Incredible!

Very easily. A sixth-century monk made a mistake in arithmetic. Our present dating ("Anno Domini") was not used until centuries after Christ was born. Anyone who has ever tried to decipher on a cornerstone a date written in Roman numerals can sympathize with the error of Brother Dionysius Exiguus. In the sixth century there were so few who could read at all that the error went undetected for many years—and by then it was too late to change all the records. So we have the ludicrous situation that Christ was born five years before Christ was born—an Irishism that can be resolved only by noting that one clause refers to fact and the other clause refers to a false-to-fact calendar.

For two thousand years the good monk's error was of little importance. But now it becomes of supreme importance. If the Millenarianists are correct, the end of the world can be expected *Christmas Day this year*.

Please note that I did not say "December 25th." The day and month of Christ's birth are unknown. Matthew notes that Herod was king; Luke states that Augustus was Caesar and that Cyrenius was governor of Syria, and we all know that Joseph and Mary had traveled from Nazareth to Bethlehem to be counted and taxed.

There are no other data, neither of Holy Writ nor of Roman civil records.

So there you have it. By Millenarianist theory the Final Judgment can be expected about thirty-five years from now . . . or later this afternoon!

Were it not for Margrethe this uncertainty would not

keep me awake nights. But how can I sleep if my beloved is in immediate danger of being cast down into the Bottomless Pit, there to suffer throughout eternity?

What would *you* do?

Envision me standing barefooted on a greasy floor, washing dishes to pay off my indenture, while thinking deep thoughts of last and first things. A laughable sight! But dishwashing does not occupy all the mind; I was better off with hard bread for the mind to chew on.

Sometimes I contrasted my sorry state with what I had so recently been, while wondering if I would ever find my way back through the maze into the place I had built for myself.

Would I want to go back? Abigail was there—and, while polygamy was acceptable in the Old Testament, it was not accepted in the forty-six states. That had been settled once and for all when the Union Army's artillery had destroyed the temple of the antichrist in Salt Lake City and the Army had supervised the breaking up and diaspora of those immoral "families."

Giving up Margrethe for Abigail would be far too high a price to pay to resume the position of power and importance I had until recently held. Yet I had enjoyed my work and the deep satisfaction over worthwhile accomplishment that went with it. We had achieved our best year since the foundation was formed—I refer to the nonprofit corporation Churches United for Decency. "Nonprofit" does not mean that such an organization cannot pay appropriate salaries and even bonuses, and I had been taking a well-earned vacation after the best fund-raising year of our history—primarily my accomplishment because, as deputy director, my first duty was to see that our coffers were kept filled.

But I took even greater satisfaction in our labors in the vineyards, as fund raising means nothing if our programs of spiritual welfare do not meet their goals.

The past year had seen the following positive accomplishments:

a) A federal law making abortion a capital offense;

b) A federal law making the manufacture, sale, possession, importation, transportation, and/or use of any contraceptive drug or device a felony carrying a mandatory prison sentence of not less than a year and a day but not more than twenty years for each offense—and eliminating the hypocritical subterfuge of "For Prevention of Disease Only";

c) A federal law that, while it did not abolish gambling, did make the control and licensing of it a federal jurisdiction. One step at a time—having built this foundation we could tackle those twin pits, Nevada and New Jersey, piece by piece. Divide and conquer!

d) A Supreme Court decision in which we had appeared as *amicus curiae* under which community standards of the typical or median-population community applied to all cities of each state (Tomkins v. Allied News Distributors);

e) Real progress in our drive to get tobacco defined as a prescription drug through the tactical device of separating snuff and chewing tobacco from the problem by inaugurating the definition "substances intended for burning and inhaling";

f) Progress at our annual national prayer meeting on several subjects in which I was interested. One was the matter of how to remove the tax-free status of any private school not affiliated with a Christian sect. Policy on this was not yet complete because of the thorny matter of Roman Catholic schools. Should our umbrella cover them? Or was it time to strike? Whether the Catholics were allies or enemies was always a deep problem to those of us out on the firing line.

At least as difficult was the Jewish problem—was a humane solution possible? If not, then what? Should we grasp the nettle? This was debated only *in camera*.

Another matter was a pet project of my own: the frustrating of astronomers. Few laymen realize what mischief astronomers are up to. I first noticed it when I was still in engineering school and took a course in descriptive astronomy under the requirements for breadth in each student's program. Give an astronomer a bigger telescope and turn him loose, leave him unsupervised, and the first thing he does is to come down with pestiferous, half-baked guesses denying the ancient truths of Genesis.

There is only one way to deal with this sort of nonsense: Hit them in the pocketbook! Redefine "educational" to exclude those colossal white elephants, astronomical observatories. Make the Naval Observatory the only one tax free, reduce its staff, and limit their activity to matters clearly related to navigation. (Some of the most blasphemous and subversive theories have come from tenured civil servants there who don't have enough legitimate work to keep them busy.)

Self-styled "scientists" are usually up to no good, but astronomers are the worst of the lot.

Another matter that comes up regularly at each annual prayer meeting I did not favor spending time or money on: "Votes for Women." These hysterical females styling themselves "suffragettes" are not a threat, can never win, and it just makes them feel self-important to pay attention to them. They should not be jailed and should not be displayed in stocks—never let them be martyrs! Ignore them.

There were other interesting and worthwhile goals that I kept off the agenda and did not suffer to be brought up from the floor in the sessions I moderated, but instead carried them on my "Maybe next year" list:

Separate schools for boys and girls.

Restoring the death penalty for witchcraft and satanism.

The Alaska option for the Negro problem.

Federal control of prostitution.

Homosexuals—what's the answer? Punishment? Surgery? Other?

There are endless good causes commending themselves to guardians of the public morals—the question is always how to pick and choose to the greater glory of God.

But all of these issues, fascinating as they are, I might never again pursue. A sculleryman who is just learning the local language (ungrammatically, I feel sure!) is not able to be a political force. So I did not worry about such matters and concentrated on my real problems: Margrethe's heresy and, more immediate but less important, getting legally free of peonage and going north.

We had served more than one hundred days when I asked *Don* Jaime to help me work out the exact date when we would have discharged the terms of our debt contract—a polite way of saying: Dear Boss, come the day, we are going to leave here like a scared rabbit. Plan on it.

I had figured on a total obligated time of one hundred and twenty-one days . . . and *Don* Jaime shocked me almost out of my Spanish by getting a result of one hundred and fifty-eight days.

More than six weeks to go when I figured that we would be free next week!

I protested, pointing out that our total obligation as listed by the court, divided by the auction value placed on our services (pesos sixty for Margrethe, half that for me, for each day), gave one hundred twenty-one days . . . of which we had served one hundred fifteen.

Not a hundred and fifteen—ninety-nine—he handed me a calendar and invited me to count. It was at that point that I discovered that our lovely Tuesdays did not reduce our committed time. Or so said our *patrón*.

"And besides that, Alexandro," he added, "you have failed to figure the interest on the unpaid balance; you haven't multiplied by the inflation factor; you haven't allowed for taxes, or even your contribution for Our Lady of Sorrows. If you fall ill, I should support you, eh?"

(Well, yes. While I had not thought about it, I did think a *patrón* had that duty toward his *peones*.) "*Don* Jaime, the day you bid in our debts, the clerk of the court figured the contract for me. He told me our obligation was one hundred and twenty-one days. He told me!"

"Then go talk to the clerk of the court about it." *Don* Jaime turned his back on me.

That chilled me. *Don* Jaime seemed as willing for me to take it up with the referee authority as he had been unwilling to discuss Margrethe's tips with the court. To me this meant that he had handled enough of these debt contracts to be certain how they worked and thus had no fear that the judge or his clerk might rule against him.

I was not able to speak with Margrethe about it in private until that night. "Marga, how could I be so mistaken about this? I thought the clerk worked it out for us before he had us countersign the assignment of debt. One hundred and twenty-one days. Right?"

She did not answer me at once. I persisted, "Isn't that what you told me?"

"Alec, despite the fact that I now usually think in English—or in Spanish, lately—when I must do arithmetic, I work it in Danish. The Danish word for sixty is *'tres'*—and that is also the Spanish word for three. Do you see how easily I could get mixed up? I don't know now whether I said to you, *'Ciento y veintiuno'* or *'Ciento y sesentiuno'*—because I remember numbers in Danish, not in English, not in Spanish. I thought you did the division yourself."

"Oh, I did. Certainly the clerk didn't say, 'A hundred and twenty-one.' He didn't use any English that I recall. And at that time I did not know any Spanish. *Señor* Muñoz explained it to you and you translated for me and later I did the arithmetic again and it seemed to confirm what he had said. Or you had said. Oh, shucks, I don't know!"

"Then why don't we forget it until we can ask *Señor* Muñoz?"

"Marga, doesn't it upset you to find that we are going to have to slave away in this dump an extra five weeks?"

"Yes, but not very much. Alec, I've always had to work. Working aboard ship was harder work than teaching school—but I got to travel and see strange places. Waiting tables here is a little harder than cleaning rooms in the *Konge Knut*—but I have you with me here and that more than makes up for it. I want to go with you to your homeland . . . but it's not my homeland, so I'm not as eager to leave here as you are. To me, today, where you are is my homeland."

"Darling, you are so logical and reasonable and civilized that you sometimes drive me right straight up the wall."

"Alec, I don't mean to do that. I just want us to stop worrying about it until we can see *Señor* Muñoz. But right this minute I want to rub your back until you relax."

"Madame, you've convinced me! But only if I have the privilege of rubbing your poor tired feet before you rub my back."

We did both. "Ah, wilderness were paradise enow!"

Beggars can't be choosy. I got up early the next morning, saw the clerk's runner, was told that I could not see the clerk until court adjourned for the day, so I made a semi-appointment for close-of-court on Tuesday—"semi" in that we were committed to show up; *Señor* Muñoz was not. (But would be there, *Deus volent.*)

So on Tuesday we went on our picnic outing as usual, as we could not see *Señor* Muñoz earlier than about 4 p.m. But we were Sunday-go-to-meeting rather than dressed for a picnic—meaning that we both wore our shoes, both had had baths that morning, and I had shaved, and I wore my best clothes, handed down from *Don* Jaime but clean and fresh, rather than the tired Coast Guard work pants I wore in the scullery. Margrethe wore the colorful outfit she had acquired our first day in Mazatlán.

Then we both endeavored not to get too sweaty or dusty. Why we thought it mattered I cannot say. But somehow each of us felt that propriety called for one's best appearance in visiting a court.

As usual we walked over to the fountain to see our friend Pepe before swinging back to climb our hill. He greeted us in the intimate mode of friends and we exchanged graceful amenities of the sort that fit so well in Spanish and are almost never encountered in English. Our weekly visit with Pepe had become an important part of our social life. We knew more about him now— from Amanda, not from him—and I respected him more than ever.

Pepe had not been born without legs (as I had once thought); he had formerly been a teamster, driving lorries over the mountains to Durango and beyond. Then there had been an accident and Pepe had been pinned under his rig for two days before he was rescued. He was brought in to Our Lady of Sorrows apparently D.O.A.

Pepe was tougher than that. Four months later he was released from hospital; someone passed the hat to buy him his little cart; he received his mendicant's license, and he took up his pitch by the fountain—friend to streetwalkers, friend to *Dons,* and a merry grin for the worst that fate could hand him.

When, after a decent interval for conversation and inquiries as to health and welfare and that of mutual acquaintances, we turned to leave, I offered our friend a one-peso note.

He handed it back. "Twenty-five centavos, my friend. Do you not have change? Or did you wish me to make change?"

"Pepe our friend, it was our intention and our wish that you keep this trivial gift."

"No no no. From tourists I take their teeth and ask for more. From you, my friend, twenty-five centavos."

I did not argue. In Mexico a man has his dignity, or he is dead.

El Cerro de la Nevería is one hundred meters high; we climbed it very slowly, with me hanging back because I wanted to be certain not to place any strain on Margrethe. From signs I was almost certain that she was in a family way. But she had not seen fit to discuss it with me and of course I could not raise the subject if she did not.

We found our favorite place, where we enjoyed shade from a small tree but nevertheless had a full view all around, three hundred and sixty degrees—northwest into the Gulf of California, west into the Pacific and what might or might not be clouds on the horizon capping a peak at the tip of Baja California two hundred miles away, southwest along our own peninsula to *Cerro Vigía* (Lookout Hill) with beautiful *Playa de las Olas Altas* between us and *Cerro Vigía,* then beyond it *Cerro Creston,* the site of the giant lighthouse, the *"Faro"* itself commanding the tip of the peninsula—south right across town to the Coast Guard landing. On the east and northeast were the mountains that concealed Durango a hundred and fifty miles away . . . but today the air was so clear that it felt as if we could reach out and touch those peaks.

Mazatlán was spread out below like a toy village. Even the basilica looked like an architect's scale model from up here, rather than a most imposing church—for the umpteenth time I wondered how the Catholics, with their (usually) poverty-stricken congregations, could build such fine churches while their Protestant opposite numbers had such a time raising the mortgages on more modest structures.

"Look, Alec!" said Margrethe. "Anibal and Roberto have their new *aeroplano*!" She pointed.

Sure enough, there were now *two aeroplanos* at the Coast Guard mooring. One was the grotesque giant dragonfly that had rescued us; the new one was quite different. At first I thought it had sunk at its moorings; the floats on which the older craft landed on the water were missing from this structure.

Then I realized that this new craft was literally a flying boat. The body of the *aeroplano* itself was a float, or a boat—a watertight structure. The propelling engines of this craft were mounted above the wings.

I was not sure that I trusted these radical changes. The homely certainties of the craft we had ridden in were more to my taste.

"Alec, let's go call on them next Tuesday."

"All right."

"Do you suppose that Anibal would possibly offer us a ride in his new *aeroplano*?"

"Not if the Commandant knows about it." I did not say that the newfangled rig did not look safe to me; Margrethe was always fearless. "But we'll call on them and ask to see it. Lieutenant Anibal will like that. Roberto, too. Let's eat."

"Piggy piggy," she answered, and spread out a *servilleta*, started covering it with food from a basket I had carried. Tuesdays gave Margrethe an opportunity to vary Amanda's excellent Mexican cooking with her own

Danish and international cooking. Today she had elected to make Danish open-face sandwiches so much enjoyed by all Danes—and by anyone else who has ever had a chance to enjoy them. Amanda allowed Margrethe to do what she liked in the kitchen, and *Señora Valera* did not interfere—she never came into the kitchen, under some armed truce arrived at before we joined the staff. Amanda was a woman of firm character.

Today's sandwiches featured heavily the tender, tasty shrimp for which Mazatlán is famous, but the shrimp were just a starter. I remember ham, turkey, crumbled crisp bacon, mayonnaise, three sorts of cheese, several sorts of pickle, little peppers, unidentified fish, thin slices of beef, fresh tomato, tomato paste, three sorts of lettuce, what I think was deep-fried eggplant. But thank goodness it is not necessary to understand food in order to enjoy it—Margrethe placed it in front of me; I happily chomped away, whether I knew what I was eating or not.

An hour later I was belching and pretending not to. "Margrethe, have I told you today that I love you?"

"Yes, but not lately."

"I do. You are not only beautiful, fair to see and of gainly proportions, you are also a fine cook."

"Thank you, sir."

"Do you wish to be admired for your intellectual excellence as well?"

"Not necessarily. No."

"As you wish. If you change your mind, let me know. Quit fiddling with the remnants; I'll tidy up later. Lie down here beside me and explain to me why you continue to live with me. It can't be for my cooking. Is it because I am the best dishwasher on the west coast of Mexico?"

"Yes." She went right on tidying things, did not stop until our picnic site was perfectly back in order, with all that was left back in the basket, ready to be returned to Amanda.

Then she lay down beside me, slid her arm under my neck—then raised her head. "What's that?"

"What's—" Then I heard it. A distant rumble increasing in volume, like a freight train coming 'round the bend. But the nearest railway, the line north to Chihuahua and south to Guadalajara, was distant, beyond the peninsula of Mazatlán.

The rumble grew louder; the ground started to sway. Margrethe sat up. "Alec, I'm frightened."

"Don't be afraid, dear; I'm here." I reached up and pulled her down to me, held her tight while the solid ground bounced up and down under us and the roaring rumble increased to unbelievable volume.

If you've ever been in an earthquake, even a small one, you know what we were feeling better than my words can say. If you have never been in one, you won't believe me—and the more accurately I describe it, the more certain you are not to believe me.

The worst part about a quake is that there is nothing solid to cling to anywhere . . . but the most startling thing is the noise, the infernal racket of every sort—the crash of rock grinding together under you, the ripping, rending sounds of buildings being torn apart, the screams of the frightened, the cries of the hurt and the lost, the howling and wailing of animals caught by disaster beyond their comprehension.

And none of it will stop.

This went on for an endless time—then the main earthquake hit us and the city fell down.

I could hear it. The noise that could not increase suddenly doubled. I managed to get up on one elbow and look. The dome of the basilica broke like a soap bubble. "Oh, Marga, look! No, don't—this is terrible."

She half sat up, said nothing and her face was blank. I kept my arm around her and looked down the peninsula past *Cerro Vigía* and at the lighthouse.

It was leaning.

While I watched it broke about halfway up, then slowly and with dignity collapsed to the ground.

Past the city I caught sight of the moored *aeroplanos* of the Coast Guard. They were dancing around in a frenzy; the new one dipped one wing; the water caught it—then I lost sight of it as a cloud rose up from the city, a cloud of dust from thousands and thousands of tons of shattered masonry.

I looked for the restaurant, and found it: EL RESTAURANTE PANCHO VILLA. Then while I watched, the wall on which the sign was painted crumpled and fell into the street. Dust rose up and concealed where it had been.

"Margrethe! It's gone. The restaurant. El Pancho Villa." I pointed.

"I don't see anything."

"It's gone, I tell you. Destroyed. Oh, thank the Lord that Amanda and the girls were not there today!"

"Yes. Alec, won't it ever stop?"

Suddenly it did stop—much more suddenly than it started. Miraculously the dust was gone; there was no racket, no screams of the hurt and dying, no howls of animals.

The lighthouse was back where it belonged.

I looked to the left of it, checking on the moored *aeroplanos*—nothing. Not even the driven piles to which they should be tied. I looked back at the city— all serene. The basilica was unhurt, beautiful. I looked for the Pancho Villa sign.

I could not find it. There was a building on what seemed the proper corner, but its shape was not quite right and it had different windows. "Marg— Where's the restaurant?"

"I don't know. Alec, what is happening?"

"They're at it again," I said bitterly. "The world changers. The earthquake is over but this is not the city we were in. It looks a lot like it but it's not the same."

I was only half right. Before we could make up our minds to start down the hill, the rumble started up again. Then the swaying . . . then the greatly increased noise and violent movement of the land, and *this* city was destroyed. Again I saw our towering lighthouse crack and fall. Again the church fell in on itself. Again the dust clouds rose and with it the screams and howls.

I raised my clenched fist and shook it at the sky. "God damn it! *Stop!* Twice is too much."

I was not blasted.

XIII

I have seen all the works that are done under the sun; and,
behold, all is vanity and vexation of the spirit.
Ecclesiastes 1:14

I am going to skip over the next three days, for there
was nothing good about them. "There was blood in the
streets and dust." Survivors, those of us who were not
hurt, not prostrate with grief, not dazed or hysterical
beyond action—few of us, in short—worked at the
rubble here and there trying to find living creatures under the bricks and stones and plaster. But how much
can you do with your naked fingers against endless tons
of rock?

And how much can you do when you do dig down
and discover that you were too late, that indeed it was
too late before you started? We heard this mewling,
something like a kitten, so we dug most carefully, trying not to put any pressure on whatever was underneath, trying not to let the stones we shifted dislodge
anything that would cause more grief underneath—and
found the source. An infant, freshly dead. Pelvis broken, one side of its head bashed. "Happy shall he be,
that taketh and dasheth thy little ones against the

stones." I turned my head away and threw up. Never will I read Psalm 137 again.

That night we spent on the lower slopes of Icebox Hill. When the sun went down, we perforce stopped trying. Not only did the darkness make it impossible to work but there was looting going on. I had a deep conviction that any looter was a potential rapist and murderer. I was prepared to die for Margrethe should it become necessary—but I had no wish to die gallantly but futilely, in a confrontation that could have been avoided.

Early the following afternoon the Mexican Army arrived. We had accomplished nothing useful in the meantime—more of the same picking away at rubble. Never mind what we found. The soldiers put a stop even to that; all civilians were herded back up the peninsula, away from the ruined city, to the railroad station across the river. There we waited—new widows, husbands freshly bereaved, lost children, injured on make-do stretchers, walking wounded, some with no marks on them but with empty eyes and no speech. Margrethe and I were of the lucky ones; we were merely hungry, thirsty, dirty, and covered with bruises from head to foot from lying on the ground during the earthquake. Correction: during two earthquakes.

Had anyone else experienced *two* earthquakes?

I hesitated to ask. I seemed to be the unique observer to this world-changing—save that, twice, Margrethe had come with me because I was holding her at the instant. Were there other victims around? Had there been others in *Konge Knut* who had kept their mouths shut about it as carefully as I had? How do you ask?

Excuse me, amigo, but is this the same city it was yesterday?

When we had waited at the railroad station about two hours an army water cart came through—a tin cup of water to each refugee and a soldier with a bayonet to enforce order in the queues.

Just before sundown the cart came back with more water and with loaves of bread; Margrethe and I were rationed a quarter of a loaf between us. A train backed into the station about then and the army people started loading it even as supplies were being unloaded. Marga and I were lucky; we were pushed into a passenger car—most rode in freight cars.

The train started north. We weren't asked whether or not we wanted to go north; we weren't asked for money for fares; all of Mazatlán was being evacuated. Until its water system could be restored, Mazatlán belonged to the rats and the dead.

No point in describing the journey. The train moved; we endured. The railway line leaves the coast at Guaymas and goes straight north across Sonora to Arizona—beautiful country but we were in no shape to appreciate it. We slept as much as we could and pretended to sleep the rest of the time. Every time the train stopped, some left it—unless the police herded them back on. By the time we reached Nogales, Sonora, the train was less than half full; the rest seemed headed for Nogales, Arizona, and of course we were.

We reached the international gate early afternoon three days after the quake.

We were herded into a detention building just over the line, and a man in a uniform made a speech in Spanish: "Welcome, amigos! The United States is

happy to help its neighbors in their time of trial and
the U.S. Immigration Service has streamlined its pro-
cedures so that we can take care of all of you quickly.
First we must ask you all to go through delousing.
Then you'll be issued green cards outside of quota so
that you can work at any job anywhere in the States.
But you will find labor agents to help you as you leave
the compound. And a soup kitchen! If you are hungry,
stop and have your first meal here as guests of Uncle
Sam. Welcome to *los Estados Unidos*!"

Several people had questions to ask but Margrethe
and I headed for the door that led to the delousing
setup. I resented the name assigned to this sanitary routine—a requirement that you take delousing is a way of
saying that you are lousy. Dirty and mussed we certainly were, and I had a three-day beard. But lousy?

Well, perhaps we were. After a day of picking
through the ruins and two days crowded in with other
unwashed in a railroad car that was not too clean when
we boarded it, could I honestly assert that I was com-
pletely free of vermin?

Delousing wasn't too bad. It was mostly a supervised
shower bath with exhortations in Spanish to scrub the
hairy places thoroughly with a medicated soft soap. In
the meantime my clothes went through some sort of
sterilization or fumigation—autoclave, I think—then I
had to wait, bare naked, for twenty minutes to reclaim
them, while I grew more and more angry with each
passing minute.

But once I was dressed again, I got over my anger,
realizing that no one was intentionally pushing me
around; it was simply that any improvised procedure for
handling crowds of people in an emergency is almost

certain to be destructive of human dignity. (The Mexican refugees seemed to find it offensive; I heard mutterings.)

Then again I had to wait, for Margrethe.

She came out the exit door from the distaff side, caught my eye, and smiled, and suddenly everything was all right. How could she come out of a delousing chamber and look as if she had just stepped out of a bandbox?

She came up to me and said, "Did I keep you waiting, dear? I'm sorry. There was an ironing board in there and I seized the chance to touch up my dress. It looked a sorry sight when it came out of the washer."

"I didn't mind waiting," I fibbed. "You're beautiful." (No fib!) "Shall we go to dinner? Soup kitchen dinner, I'm afraid."

"Isn't there some paper work we have to go through?"

"Oh. I think we can hit the soup kitchen first. We don't want green cards; they are for Mexican nationals. Instead I must explain about our lost passports." I had worked this out in my head and had explained it to Margrethe on the train. This is what I would say had happened to us: We were tourists, staying in *Hotel de las Olas Altas* on the beach. When the earthquake hit, we were on the beach. So we lost our clothes, our money, our passports, everything, as our hotel had been destroyed. We were lucky to be alive, and the clothes we were wearing had been given to us by Mexican Red Cross.

This story had two advantages: *Hotel de las Olas Altas* had indeed been destroyed, and the rest of the story had no easy way to be checked.

I found that we had to go through the green-card queue in order to reach the soup kitchen. Eventually we got as far as the table. A man there shoved a file card in front of me, saying in Spanish: "Print your name, last name first. List your address. If it was destroyed in the quake, say so, and give some other address—cousin, father, priest, somebody whose home was not destroyed."

I started my spiel. The functionary looked up and said, "Amigo, you're holding up the line."

"But," I said, "I don't need a green card. I don't want a green card. I'm an American citizen returning from abroad and I'm trying to explain why I don't have my passport. And the same for my wife."

He drummed on the table, "Look," he said, "your accent says that you're native American. But I can't do anything about your lost passport and I've got three hundred and fifty refugees still to process, and another trainload just pulling in. I won't get to bed before two. Why don't you do us both a favor and accept a green card? It won't poison you and it'll get you in. Tomorrow you can fight with the State Department about your passport—but not with me. Okay?"

I'm stupid but not stubborn. "Okay." For my Mexican accommodation address I listed *Don* Jaime; I figured he owed me that much. His address had the advantage of being in another universe.

The soup kitchen was what you would expect from a charity operation. But it was gringo cooking, the first I had had in months—and we were hungry. The Stark's Delicious apple I had for dessert was indeed delicious. It was still short of sundown when we were out on the streets of Nogales—free, bathed, fed, and inside the United States legally or almost. We were at least a thousand percent better off than those two naked survivors who had been picked up out of the ocean seventeen weeks ago.

But we were still orphans of fate, no money at all, no place to rest, no clothes but those we were wearing, and my three-day beard and the shape my clothes were in after going through an autoclave or whatever made me look like a skid row derelict.

The no-money situation was particularly annoying because we *did* have money, Margrethe's hoarded tips. But the paper money said *"Reino"* where it should have read *"República"* and the coins did not have the right faces. Some of the coins may have contained enough silver to have some minor intrinsic value. But, if so, there was no easy way to cash it in at once. And any attempt to spend any of this money would simply get us into major trouble.

How much had we lost? There are no interuniversal exchange rates. One might make a guess in terms of equivalent purchasing power—so many dozens of eggs, or so many kilos of sugar. But why bother? Whatever it was, we had lost it.

This paralleled a futility I had run into in Mazatlán. I had attempted, while lord of the scullery, to write to a) Alexander Hergensheimer's boss, the Reverend Dr. Dandy Danny Dover, D.D., director of Churches United for Decency, and b) Alec Graham's lawyers in Dallas.

Neither letter was answered; neither came back. Which was what I had expected, as neither Alec nor

Alexander came from a world having flying machines, *aeroplanos*.

I would try both again—but with small hope; I already knew that this world would feel strange both to Graham and to Hergensheimer. How? Nothing that I had noticed until we reached Nogales. But here, in that detention hall, was (hold tight to your chair) *television*. A handsome big box with a window in one side, and in that window living pictures of people . . . and sounds coming out of it of those selfsame people talking.

Either you have this invention and are used to it and take it for granted, or you live in a world that does not have it—and you don't believe me. Learn from me, as I have been forced to believe unbelievable things. There *is* such an invention; there is a world where it is as common as bicycles, and its name is television—or sometimes teevee or telly or video or even "idiot box"—and if you were to hear some of the purposes for which this great wonder is used, you would understand the last tag.

If you ever find yourself flat broke in a strange city and no one to turn to, and you do not want to turn yourself in at a police station and don't want to be mugged, there is just one best answer for emergency help. You will usually find it in the city's tenderloin, near skid row:

The Salvation Army.

Once I laid hands on a telephone book it took me no time at all to get the address of the Salvation Army mission (although it did take me a bit of time to recognize a telephone when I saw one—warning to interworld travelers: Minor changes can be even more confusing than major changes).

Twenty minutes and one wrong turn later Margrethe and I were at the mission. Outside on the sidewalk four of them—French horn, big drum, two tambourines— were gathering a crowd. They were working on "Rock of Ages" and doing well, but they needed a baritone and I was tempted to join them.

But a couple of store fronts before we reached the mission Margrethe stopped and plucked at my sleeve. "Alec . . . must we do this?"

"Eh? What's the trouble, dear? I thought we had agreed."

"No, sir. You simply told me."

"Mmm— Perhaps I did. You don't want to go to the Salvation Army?"

She took a deep breath and sighed it out. "Alec . . . I have not been inside a church since—since I left the Lutheran Church. To go to one now— I think it would be sinful."

(Dear Lord, what can I do with this child? She is apostate not because she is heathen . . . but because her rules are even more strict than Yours. Guidance, please—and do hurry it up!) "Sweetheart, if it feels sinful to you, we won't do it. But tell me what we are to do now; I've run out of ideas."

"Ah— Alec, are there not other institutions to which a person in distress may turn?"

"Oh, certainly. In a city this size the Roman Catholic Church is bound to have more than one refuge. And there will be other Protestant ones. Probably a Jewish one. And—"

"I meant, 'Not connected with a church.'"

"Ah, so. Margrethe, we both know that this is not really my home country; you probably know as much about how it works as I do. There may be refuges for the homeless here that are totally unconnected with a church. I'm not sure, as churches tend to monopolize the field—nobody else wants it. If it were early in the day instead of getting dark, I would try to find something called united charities or community chest or the equivalent, and look over the menu; there might be something. But now— Finding a policeman and asking for help is the only other thing I can think of this time of day . . . and I can tell you ahead of time what a cop in this part of town would do if you told him you had nowhere to sleep. He would point you toward the mission right there. Old Sal."

"In København—or Stockholm or Oslo—I would go straight to the main police station. You just ask for a place to sleep; they give it to you."

"I have to point out that this is not Denmark or Sweden or Norway. Here they might let us stay—by locking me in the drunk tank and locking you up in the holding pen for prostitutes. Then tomorrow morning we might or might not be charged with vagrancy. I don't know."

"Is America really so evil?"

"I don't know, dear—this isn't my America. But I don't want to find out the hard way. Sweetheart . . . if I *worked* for whatever they give us, could we spend a night with the Salvation Army without your feeling sinful about it?"

She considered it solemnly—Margrethe's greatest lack was a total absence of sense of humor. Good nature—loads. A child's delight in play, yes. Sense of humor? "Life is real and life is earnest—"

"Alec, if that can be arranged, I would not feel wrong in entering. I will work, too."

"Not necessary, dear; it will be my profession that is involved. When they finish feeding the derelicts tonight, there will be a high stack of dirty dishes—and you are looking at the heavyweight champion dishwasher in all of Mexico and *los Estados Unidos.*"

So I washed dishes. I also helped spread out hymnbooks and set up the evening services. And I borrowed a safety razor and a blade from Brother Eddie McCaw, the adjutant. I told him how we happened to be there—vacationing on the Mexican Riviera, sunbathing on the beach when the big one hit—all the string of lies I had prepared for the Immigration Service and hadn't been able to use. "Lost it all. Cash, travelers checks, passports, clothes, ticket home, the works. But just the same, we were lucky. We're alive."

"The Lord had His arms around you. You tell me that you are born again?"

"Years back."

"It will do our lost sheep good to rub shoulders with you. When it comes time for witnessing, will you tell them all about it? You're the first eyewitness. Oh, we felt it here but it just rattled the dishes."

"Glad to."

"Good. Let me get you that razor."

So I witnessed and gave them a truthful and horrendous description of the quake, but not as horrid as it really was—I never want to see another rat—or another dead baby—and I thanked the Lord publicly that Margrethe and I had not been hurt and found that it was the most sincere prayer I had said in years.

The Reverend Eddie asked that roomful of odorous outcasts to join him in a prayer of thanks that Brother and Sister Graham had been spared, and he made it a good rousing prayer that covered everything from Jonah to the hundredth sheep, and drew shouts of *"Amen!"* from around the room. One old wino came forward and said that he had at last seen God's grace and God's mercy and he was now ready to give his life to Christ.

Brother Eddie prayed over him, and invited others to come forward and two more did—a natural evangelist, he saw in our story a theme for his night's sermon and used it, hanging it on Luke fifteen, ten, and Matthew six, nineteen. I don't know that he had prepared from those two verses—probably not, as any preacher worth his salt can preach endlessly from either one of them. Either way, he could think on his feet and he made good use of our unplanned presence.

He was pleased with us, and I am sure that is why he told me, as we were cleaning up for the night, after the supper that followed the service, that while of course they didn't have separate rooms for married couples— they didn't often get married couples—still, it looked like Sister Graham would be the only one in the sisters' dormitory tonight, so why didn't I doss down in there instead of in the men's dormitory? No double bed, just stacked bunks—sorry! But at least we could be in the same room.

I thanked him and we happily went to bed. Two people can share a very narrow bed if they really want to sleep together.

*   *   *

The next morning Margrethe cooked breakfast for the derelicts. She went into the kitchen and volunteered and soon was doing it all as the regular cook did not cook breakfast; it was the job of whoever had the duty. Breakfast did not require a graduate chef—oatmeal porridge, bread, margarine, little valencia oranges (culls?), coffee. I left her there to wash dishes and to wait until I came back.

I went out and found a job.

I knew, from listening to wireless (called "radio" here) while washing dishes the night before, that there was unemployment in the United States, enough to be a political and social problem.

There is always work in the Southwest for agricultural labor but I had dodged that sort of work yesterday. I'm not too proud for that work; I had followed the harvest for several years from the time I was big enough to handle a pitchfork. But I could not take Margrethe into the fields.

I did not expect to find a job as a clergyman; I hadn't even told Brother Eddie that I was ordained. There is always an unemployment problem for preachers. Oh, there are always empty pulpits, true—but ones in which a church mouse would starve.

But I had a second profession.

Dishwasher.

No matter how many people are out of work, there are always dishwashing jobs going begging. Yesterday, in walking from the border gate to the Salvation Army mission, I had noticed three restaurants with "Dishwasher Wanted" signs in their windows—noticed them because I had had plenty of time on the long ride from

Mazatlán to admit to myself that I had no other salable skill.

No salable skill. I was not ordained in this world; I would not *be* ordained in this world as I could not show graduation from seminary or divinity school——or even the backing of a primitive sect that takes no mind of schools but depends on inspiration by the Holy Ghost.

I was certainly not an engineer.

I could not get a job teaching even those subjects I knew well because I no longer could show any formal preparation——I couldn't even show that I had graduated from middle school!

In general I was no salesman. True, I had shown an unexpected talent for the complex skills that make up a professional money-raiser . . . but here I had no record, no reputation. I might someday do this again——but we needed cash *today*.

What did that leave? I had looked at the help-wanted ads in a copy of the Nogales *Times* someone had left in the mission. I was not a tax accountant. I was not any sort of a mechanic. I did not know what a software designer was but I was not one, nor was I a "computer" anything. I was not a nurse or any sort of health care professional.

I could go on indefinitely listing the things I was not, and could not learn overnight. But that is point-less. What I could do, what would feed Margrethe and me while we sized up this new world and learned the angles, was what I had been forced to do as a *peón*.

A competent and reliable dishwasher never starves. (He's more likely to die of boredom.)

The first place did not smell good and its kitchen looked dirty; I did not linger. The second place was a major-chain hotel, with several people in the scullery. The boss looked me over and said, "This is a Chicano job; you wouldn't be happy here." I tried to argue; he shut me off.

But the third was okay, a restaurant only a little bigger than the Pancho Villa, with a clean kitchen and a manager no more than normally jaundiced.

He warned me, "This job pays minimum wage and there are no raises. One meal a day on the house. I catch you sneaking anything, even a toothpick, and out you go that instant—no second chance. You work the hours I set and I change 'em to suit me. Right now I need you for noon to four, six to ten, five days a week. Or you can work six days but no overtime scale for it. Overtime scale if I require you to work more than eight hours in one day, or more than forty-eight hours in one week."

"Okay."

"All right, let's see your Social Security card."

I handed him my green card.

He handed it back. "You expect me to pay you twelve dollars and a half an hour on the basis of a green card? You're no Chicano. You trying to get me in trouble with the government? Where did you get that card?"

So I gave him the song and dance I had prepared for the Immigration Service. "Lost everything. I can't even phone and tell somebody to send me money; I have to get home first before I can shake any assets loose."

"You could get public assistance."

"Mister, I'm too stinkin' proud." (I don't know how and I can't prove I'm me. Just don't quiz me and let me wash dishes.)

"Glad to hear it. 'Stinking proud,' I mean. This country could use more like you. Go over to the Social Security office and get them to issue you a new one. They will, even if you can't recall the number of your old one. Then come back here and go to work. Mmm— I'll start you on payroll right now. But you must come back and put in a full day to collect."

"More than fair. Where is the Social Security office?"

So I went to the Federal Building and told my lies over again, embroidering only as necessary. The serious young lady who issued the card insisted on giving me a lecture on Social Security and how it worked, a lecture she had apparently memorized. I'll bet you she never had a "client" (that's what she called me) who listened so carefully. It was all new to me.

I gave the name "Alec L. Graham." This was not a conscious decision. I had been using that name for weeks, answered with it by reflex—then was not in a good position to say, "Sorry, Miss, my name is actually Hergensheimer."

I started work. During my four-to-six break I went back to the mission—and learned that Margrethe had a job, too.

It was temporary, three weeks—but three weeks at just the right time. The mission cook had not had a vacation in over a year and wanted to go to Flagstaff to visit her daughter, who had just had a baby. So Margrethe had her job for the time being—and her bedroom, also for the time being.

So Brother and Sister Graham were in awfully good shape—for the time being.

XIV

*I returned, and saw under the sun, that the race
is not to the swift, nor the battle to the strong,
neither yet bread to the wise, nor yet riches to men of
understanding, nor yet favour to men of skill;
but time and chance happeneth to them all.*
Ecclesiastes 9:11

Pray tell me why there is not a dishwashing school of philosophy? The conditions would seem ideal for indulging in the dear delights of attempting to unscrew the inscrutable. The work keeps the body busy while demanding almost nothing of the brain. I had eight hours every day in which to try to find answers to questions.

What questions? *All* questions. Five months earlier I had been a prosperous and respected professional in the most respected of professions, in a world I understood thoroughly—or so I thought. Today I was sure of nothing and had nothing.

Correction—I had Margrethe. Wealth enough for any man, I would not trade her for all the riches of Cathay. But even Margrethe represented a solemn contract I could not yet fulfill. In the eyes of the Lord I had taken her to wife . . . but I was not supporting her.

Yes, I had a job—but in truth she was supporting herself. When Mr. Cowgirl hired me, I had not been daunted by "minimum wage and no raises." Twelve dollars and fifty cents per hour struck me as a dazzling sum—why, many a married man in Wichita (*my* Wichita, in another universe) supported a family on twelve and a half dollars per *week*.

What I did not realize was that here $12.50 would not buy a tuna sandwich in that same restaurant—not a fancy restaurant, either; cheap, in fact. I would have had less trouble adjusting to the economy in this strange-but-familiar world if its money had been described in unfamiliar terms—shillings, shekels, soles, anything but dollars. I had been brought up to think of a dollar as a substantial piece of wealth; the idea that a hundred dollars a day was a poverty-level minimum wage was not one I could grasp easily.

Twelve-fifty an hour, a hundred dollars a day, five hundred a week, twenty-six thousand dollars a year—*Poverty* level? Listen carefully. In the world in which I grew up, that was riches beyond dreams of avarice.

Getting used to price and wage levels in dollars that weren't really dollars was simply the most ubiquitous aspect of a strange economy; the main problem was how to cope, how to stay afloat, how to make a living for me and my wife (and our children, with one expected all too soon if I had guessed right) in a world in which I had no diplomas, no training, no friends, no references, no track record of any sort. Alex, what in God's truth *are* you good for? . . . other than dishwashing!

I could easily wash a lighthouse stack of dishes while worrying that problem alone. It *had* to be solved. To-day I washed dishes cheerfully . . . but soon I must do better for my beloved. Minimum wage was not enough.

Now at last we come to the prime question: Dear

Lord God Jehovah, what mean these signs and portents Thou hast placed on me Thy servant?

There comes a time when a faithful worshiper must get up off his knees and deal with his Lord God in blunt and practical terms. Lord, *tell* me what to believe! Are these the deceitful great signs and wonders of which You warned, sent by antichrist to seduce the very elect?

Or are these true signs of the final days? Will we hear Your Shout?

Or am I as mad as Nebuchadnezzar and all of these appearances merely vapors in my disordered mind?

If one of these be true, then the other two are false. How am I to choose? Lord God of Hosts, how have I offended Thee?

In walking back to the mission one night I saw a sign that could be construed as a direct answer to my prayers: MILLIONS NOW LIVING WILL NEVER DIE. The sign was carried by a man and with him was a small child handing out leaflets.

I contrived not to accept one. I had seen that sign many times throughout my life, but I had long tended to avoid Jehovah's Witnesses. They are so stiff-necked and stubborn that it is impossible to work with them, whereas Churches United for Decency is necessarily an ecumenical association. In fund raising and in political action one must (while of course shunning heresy) avoid arguments on fiddling points of doctrine. Word-splitting theologians are the death of efficient organization. How can you include a sect in practical labor in the vineyards of the Lord if that sect asserts that they alone know the Truth, the whole Truth, and nothing but the Truth and all who disagree are heretics, destined for the fires of Hell?

Impossible. So we left them out of C.U.D.

Still— Perhaps this time they were right.

Which brings me to the most urgent of all questions: How to lead Margrethe back to the Lord before the Trump and the Shout.

But "how" depends on "when." Premillenarian theologians differ greatly among themselves as to the date of the Last Trump.

I rely on the scientific method. On any disputed point there is always one sure answer: Look it up in the Book. And so I did, now that I was living at the Salvation Army mission and could borrow a copy of the Holy Bible. I looked it up again and again and again . . . and learned why premillenarians differed so on their dates.

The Bible is the literal Word of God; let there be no mistake about that. But nowhere did the Lord promise us that it would be easy to read.

Again and again Our Lord and His incarnation as the Son, Jesus of Nazareth, the Messiah, promises His disciples that their generation (i.e., first century A.D.) will see His return. Elsewhere, and again many times, He promises that He will return after a thousand years have passed . . . or is it two thousand years . . . or is it some other period, after the Gospel has been preached to all mankind in every country?

Which is true?

All are true, if you read them right. Jesus did indeed return in the generation of His twelve disciples; He did so at the first Easter, His resurrection. That was His first return, the utterly necessary one, the one that proved to all that He was indeed the Son of God and God Himself. He returned again after a thousand years and, in His infinite mercy, ruled that His children be given yet another grant of grace, a further period of trial, rather than let sinners be consigned forthwith to the fiery depths of Hell. His Mercy is infinite.

These dates are hard to read, and understandably so, as it was never His intention to encourage sinners to go on sinning because the day of reckoning had been postponed. What is precise, exact, and unmistakable, repeated again and again, is that He expects every one of His children to live every day, every hour, every heart beat, as if this one were the last. When is the end of this age? When is the Shout and the Trump? When is the Day of Judgment? *Now!* You will be given no warning whatever. No time for deathbed contrition. You must live in a state of grace . . . or, when the instant comes, you will be cast down into the Lake of Fire, there to burn in agony throughout all eternity.

So reads the Word of God.

And to me, so sounds the voice of doom. I had *no* period of grace in which to lead Margrethe back into the fold . . . as the Shout may come this very day.

What to do? What to do?

For mortal man, with any problem too great, there is only one thing to do: Take it to the Lord in prayer.

And so I did, again and again and again. Prayer is always answered. But it is necessary to recognize the answer . . . and it may not be the answer you want.

In the meantime one must render unto Caesar the things that are Caesar's. Of course I elected to work six days a week rather than five ($31,200 a year!)—as I needed every shekel I could garner. Margrethe needed everything!—and so did I. Especially we needed shoes. The shoes we had been wearing when disaster struck in Mazatlán had been quite good shoes—for peasants in Mazatlán. But they had been worn during two days of digging through rubble after the quake, then had been worn continuously since then; they were ready for the trash bin. So we needed shoes, at least two pairs each, one pair for work, one for Sunday-go-to-meeting.

And many other things. I don't know what all a woman needs, but it is more complex than what a man needs. I had to put money into Margrethe's hands and encourage her to buy what she needed. I could pig it with nothing much more than shoes and a pair of dungarees (to spare my one good outfit)—although I did buy a razor, and got a haircut at a barber's college near the mission, one where a haircut was only two dollars if one was willing to accept the greenest apprentice, and I was. Margrethe looked at it and said gently that she thought she could do as well herself, and save us that two dollars. Later she took scissors and straightened out what that untalented apprentice had done to me . . . and thereafter I never again spent money on barbers.

But saving two dollars did not offset a greater damage. I had honestly thought, when Mr. Cowgirl hired me, that I was going to be paid a hundred dollars every day I worked.

He didn't pay me that much and he didn't cheat me. Let me explain.

I finished that first day of work tired but happy. Happier than I had been since the earthquake struck, I mean—happiness is relative. I stopped at the cashier's stand where Mr. Cowgirl was working on his accounts;

Ron's Grill having closed for the day. He looked up. "How did it go, Alec?"

"Just fine, sir."

"Luke tells me that you are doing okay." Luke was a giant blackamoor, head cook and my nominal boss. In fact he had not supervised me other than to show me where things were and make sure that I knew what to do.

"That's pleasant to hear. Luke's a good cook." That one-meal-a-day bonus over minimum wage I had eaten at four o'clock as breakfast was ancient history by then. Luke had explained to me that the help could order anything on the menu but steaks or chops, and that today I could have all the seconds I wanted if I chose either the stew or the meat loaf.

I chose the meat loaf because his kitchen smelled and looked clean. You can tell far more about a cook by his meat loaf than you can from the way he grills a steak. I took seconds on the meat loaf—with no catsup.

Luke was generous in the slab of cherry pie he cut for me, then he added a scoop of vanilla ice cream . . . which I did not rate, as it was an either/or, not both.

"Luke seldom says a good word about white boys," my employer went on, "and never about a Chicano. So you must be doing okay."

"I hope so." I was growing a mite impatient. We are all the Lord's children but it was the first time in my life that a blackamoor's opinion of my work had mattered. I simply wanted to be paid so that I could hurry home to Margrethe—to the Salvation Army mission, that is.

Mr. Cowgirl folded his hands and twiddled his thumbs. "You want to be paid, don't you?"

I controlled my annoyance. "Yes, sir."

"Alec, with dishwashers I prefer to pay by the week."

I felt dismay and I am sure my face showed it.

"Don't misunderstand me," he added. "You're an hourly-rate employee, so you are paid at the end of each day if that's what you choose."

"Then I do choose. I need the money."

"Let me finish. The reason I prefer to pay dishwashers weekly instead of daily is that, all too often, if I hire one and pay him at the end of the day, he goes straight out and buys a jug of muscatel, then doesn't show up for a couple of days. When he does, he wants his job back. Angry at me. Ready to complain to the Labor Board. Funny part about it is that I may even be able to give him his job back—for another one-day shot at it—because the bum I've hired in his place has gone and done the same thing.

"This isn't likely to happen with Chicanos as they usually want to save money to send back to Mexico. But I've yet to see the Chicano who could handle the scullery to suit Luke . . . and I need Luke more than I need a particular dishwasher. Negras—Luke can usually tell me whether a spade is going to work out, and the good ones are better than a white boy any time. But the good ones are always trying to improve themselves . . . and if I don't promote them to pantry boy or assistant cook or whatever, soon they go across the street to somebody who will. So it's always a problem. If I can get a week's work out of a dishwasher, I figure I've won. If I get two weeks, I'm jubilant. Once I got a full month. But that's once in a lifetime."

"You're going to get three full weeks out of me," I said. "Now can I have my pay?"

"Don't rush me. If you elect to be paid once a week, I go for a dollar more on your hourly rate. That's forty dollars more at the end of the week. What do you say?"

(No, that's forty-eight more per week, I told myself. Almost $34,000 per year just for washing dishes. Whew!) "That's forty-eight dollars more each week," I answered. "Not forty. As I'm going for that six-days-a-week option. I do need the money."

"Okay. Then I pay you once a week."

"Just a moment. Can't we start it tomorrow? I need some cash today. My wife and I haven't anything, anything at all. I've got the clothes I'm standing in, nothing else. The same for my wife. I can sweat it out a few more days. But there are things a woman just has to have."

He shrugged. "Suit yourself. But you don't get the dollar-an-hour bonus for today's work. And if you are one minute late tomorrow, I'll assume you're sleeping it off and I put the sign back in the window."

"I'm no wino, Mr. Cowgirl."

"We'll see." He turned to his bookkeeping machine and did something to its keyboard. I don't know what because I never understood it. It was an arithmetic machine but nothing like a Babbage Numerator. It had keys on it somewhat like a typewriting machine. But there was a window above that where numbers and letters appeared by some sort of magic.

The machine whirred and tinkled and he reached into it and brought out a card, handed it to me. "There you are."

I took it and examined it, and again felt dismay.

It was a piece of pasteboard about three inches wide and seven long, with numerous little holes punched in it and with printing on it that stated that it was a draft on Nogales Commercial and Savings Bank by which Ron's Grill directed them to pay to Alec L. Graham— No, not one hundred dollars.

Fifty-one dollars and twenty-seven cents.

"Something wrong?" he asked.

"Uh, I had expected twelve-fifty an hour."

"That's what I paid you. Eight hours at minimum wage. You can check the deductions yourself. That's not my arithmetic; this is an IBM 1990 and it's instructed by IBM software, *Paymaster Plus* . . . and IBM has a standing offer of ten thousand dollars to any employee who can show that this model IBM and this mark of their software fouled up a pay check. Look at it. Gross pay, one hundred dollars. Deductions all listed. Add 'em up. Subtract them. Check your answer against IBM's answer. But don't blame me. I didn't write those laws—and I like them even less than you do. Do you realize that almost every dishwasher that comes in here, whether wetback or citizen, wants me to pay him in cash and forget the deductions? Do you know what the fine is if they catch me doing it just once? What happens if they catch me a second time? Don't look sour at me—go talk to the government."

"I just don't understand it. It's new to me, all of it. Can you tell me what these deductions mean? This one that says 'Admin,' for example."

"That stands for 'administration fee' but don't ask me why you have to pay it, as I am the one who has to do the bookkeeping and I certainly don't get paid to do it."

I tried to check the other deductions against the fine-print explanations. "SocSec" turned out to be "Social Security." The young lady had explained that to me this morning . . . but I had told her at the time that, while it was certainly an excellent idea, I felt that I would have to wait until later before subscribing to it; I could not afford it just yet. "MedIns" and "HospIns" and "DentIns" were simple enough but I could not afford them now, either. But what was "PL217?" The fine print simply referred to a date and page in "PubReg." What about "DepEduc" and "UNESCO?"

And what in the world was "Income Tax?"

"I still don't understand it. It's all new to me."

"Alec, you're not the only one who doesn't understand it. But why do you say it is new to you? It has been going on all your life . . . and your daddy's and your granddaddy's, at least."

"I'm sorry. What is 'Income Tax'?"

He blinked at me. "Are you sure you don't need to see a shrink?"

"What is a 'shrink'?"

He sighed. "Now I need to see one. Look, Alec. Just take it. Discuss the deductions with the government, not with me. You sound sincere, so maybe you were hit on the head when you got caught in the Mazatlán quake. I just want to go home and take a Miltown. So take it, please."

"All right. I guess. But I don't know anyone who would cash this for me."

"No problem. Endorse it back to me and I'll pay you cash. But keep the stub, as the IRS will insist on seeing all your deduction stubs before paying you back any overpayment."

I didn't understand that, either, but I kept the stub.

Despite the shock of learning that almost half my pay was gone before I touched it, we were better off each day, as, between us, Margrethe and I had over four hundred dollars a week that did not have to be spent just to stay alive but could be converted into clothing and other necessities. Theoretically she was being paid the same wages as had been the cook she replaced, or twenty-two dollars an hour for twenty-four hours a week, or $528/week.

In fact she had the same sort of deductions I had, which caused her net pay to come to just under $290/week. Again theoretically. But $54/week was checked off for lodging—fair enough, I decided, when I found out what rooming houses were charging. More than fair, in fact. Then we were assessed $105/week for meals. Brother McCaw at first had put us down for $140/week for meals and had offered to show by his books that Mrs. Owens, the regular cook, had always paid, by checkoff, $10 each day for her meals . . . so the two of us should be assessed $140/week.

I agreed that that was fair (having seen the prices on the menu at Ron's Grill)—fair in theory. But I was going to have my heaviest meal of the day where I worked. We compromised on ten a day for Marga, half that for me.

So Margrethe wound up with a hundred and thirty-one a week out of a gross of five hundred and twenty-eight.

If she could collect it. Like most churches, the Salvation Army lives from hand to mouth . . . and sometimes the hand doesn't quite reach the mouth.

Nevertheless we were well off and better off each week. At the end of the first week we bought new shoes for Margrethe, first quality and quite smart, for only $279.90, on sale at J. C. Penney's, marked down from $350.

Of course she fussed at getting new shoes for her before buying shoes for me. I pointed out that we still had over a hundred dollars toward shoes for me—next week—and would she please hold it for us so that I would not be tempted to spend it. Solemnly she agreed.

So the following Monday we got shoes for me even cheaper—Army surplus, good, stout comfortable shoes that would outlast anything bought from a regular shoe store. (I would worry about dress shoes for me after I had other matters under control. There is nothing like being barefoot broke to adjust one's mundane values.) Then we went to the Goodwill retail store and bought a dress and a summer suit for her, and dungaree pants for me.

Margrethe wanted to get more clothes for me—we still had almost sixty dollars. I objected.

"Why not, Alec? You need clothes every bit as badly as I do . . . yet we have spent almost all that you have saved on *me*. It's not fair."

I answered, "We've spent it where it was needed. Next week, if Mrs. Owens comes back on time, you'll be out of a job and we'll have to move. I think we should move on. So let's save what we can for bus fare."

"Move on where, dear?"

"To Kansas. This is a world strange to each of us. Yet it is familiar, too—same language, same geography, some of the same history. Here I'm just a dishwasher, not earning enough to support you. But I have a strong feeling that Kansas—Kansas in this world—will be so much like the Kansas I was born in that I'll be able to cope better."

"Whither thou goest, beloved."

The mission was almost a mile from Ron's Grill; instead of trying to go "home" at my four-to-six break, I usually spent my free time, after eating, at the downtown branch library, getting myself oriented. That, and newspapers that customers sometimes left in the restaurant, constituted my principal means of reeducation.

In this world Mr. William Jennings Bryan had indeed been President and his benign influence had kept us out of the Great European War. He then had offered his services for a negotiated peace. The Treaty of Philadelphia had more or less restored Europe to what it had been before 1913.

I didn't recognize any of the Presidents after Bryan, either from my own world or from Margrethe's world. Then I became utterly bemused when I first ran across the name of the current President: His Most Christian Majesty, John Edward the Second, Hereditary President of the United States and Canada, Duke of Hyannisport, Comte de Québec, Defender of the Faith, Protector of the Poor, Marshal in Chief of the Peace Force.

I looked at a picture of him, laying a cornerstone in Alberta. He was tall and broad-shouldered and blandly handsome and was wearing a fancy uniform with enough medals on his chest to ward off pneumonia. I studied his face and asked myself, "Would you buy a used car from this man?"

But the more I thought about it, the more logical it seemed. Americans, all during their two and a quarter centuries as a separate nation, had missed the royalty they had shucked off. They slobbered over European royalty whenever they got the chance. Their wealthiest citizens married their daughters to royalty whenever possible, even to Georgian princes—a "prince" in Georgia being a farmer with the biggest manure pile in the neighborhood.

I did not know where they had hired this royal dude. Perhaps they had sent to Estoril for him, or even had him shipped in from the Balkans. As one of my history profs had pointed out, there are always out-of-work royalty around, looking for jobs. When a man is out of work, he can't be fussy, as I knew too well. Laying cornerstones is probably no more boring than washing dishes. But the hours are longer. I think. I've never been a king. I'm not sure that I would take a job in the kinging business if it were offered to me; there are obvious drawbacks and not just the long hours.

On the other hand—

Refusing a crown that you know will never be offered to you is sour grapes, by definition. I searched my heart and concluded that I probably would be able to persuade myself that it was a sacrifice I should make for my fellow men. I would pray over it until I was convinced that the Lord *wanted* me to accept this burden.

Truly I am not being cynical. I know how frail men can be in persuading themselves that the Lord wants them to do something they wanted to do all along—and I am no better than my brethren in this.

But the thing that stonkered me was the idea of Canada united with us. Most Americans do not know why Canadians dislike us (I do not), but they do. The idea that Canadians would ever vote to unite with us boggles the mind.

I went to the library desk and asked for a recent general history of the United States. I had just started to study it when I noted by the wall clock that it was almost four o'clock . . . so I had to check it back in and hustle to get back to my scullery on time. I did not have library loan privileges as I could not as yet afford the deposit required of nonresidents.

More important than the political changes were technical and cultural changes. I realized almost at once that this world was more advanced in physical science and technology than my own. In fact I realized it almost as quickly as I saw a "television" display device.

I never did understand how televising takes place. I tried to learn about it in the public library and at once bumped into a subject called "electronics." (Not "electrics" but "electronics.") So I tried to study up about electronics and encountered the most amazing mathematical gibberish. Not since thermodynamics had caused me to decide that I had a call for the ministry have I seen such confusing and turgid equations. I don't think Rolla Tech could ever cope with such amphigory—at least not Rolla Tech when I was an undergraduate there.

But the superior technology of this world was evident in many more things than television. Consider "traffic lights." No doubt you have seen cities so choked with traffic that it is almost impossible to cross major streets other than through intervention by police officers. Also no doubt you have sometimes been annoyed when a policeman charged with controlling traffic has stopped the flow in your direction to accommodate some very important person from city hall or such.

Can you imagine a situation in which traffic could be controlled in great volume *with no police officers whatever* at hand—just an impersonal colored light?

Believe me, that is exactly what they had in Nogales.

Here is how it works:

At every busy intersection you place a minimum of twelve lights, four groups of three, a group facing each of the cardinal directions and so screened that each group can be seen only from its direction. Each group has one red light, one green light, one amber light. These lights are served by electrical power and each shines brightly enough to be seen at a distance of a mile, more or less, even in bright sunlight. These are not arc lights; these are very powerful Edison lamps—this is important because these lights must be turned on and off every few moments and must function without fail hours on end, even days on end, twenty-four hours a day.

These lights are placed up high, on telegraph poles, or suspended over intersections, so that they may be seen by teamsters or drivers or cyclists from a distance. When the green lights shine, let us say, north and south, the red lights shine east and west—traffic may flow north and south, while east and west traffic is required to stand and wait *exactly as if a police officer had blown his whistle and held up his hands, motioning traffic to move north and south while restraining traffic from moving east and west.*

Is that clear? The lights replace the policeman's hand signals.

The amber lights replace the policeman's whistle; they warn of an imminent change in the situation.

But what is the advantage?—since someone, presumably a policeman, must switch the lights on and off, as needed. Simply this: The switching is done *automatically* from a distance (even miles!) at a central switchboard.

There are many other marvels about this system, such as electrical counting devices to decide how long each light burns for best handling of the traffic, special lights for controlling left turns or to accommodate people on foot . . . but the truly great marvel is this: People *obey* these lights.

Think about it. With no policemen anywhere around people obey these blind and dumb bits of machinery *as if they were policemen.*

Are people here so sheeplike and peaceful that they can be controlled this easily? No. I wondered about it and found some statistics in the library. This world has a higher rate of violent crime than does the world in which I was born. Caused by these strange lights? I don't think so. I think that the people here, although disposed to violence against each other, accept obeying traffic lights as a logical thing to do. Perhaps.

As may be, it is passing strange.

Another conspicuous difference in technology lies in air traffic. Not the decent, cleanly, safe, and silent dirigible airships of my home world— No, no! These are more like the *aeroplanos* of the Mexicano world in which Margrethe and I sweated out our indentures before the great quake that destroyed Mazatlán. But they are so much bigger, faster, noisier, and fly so much higher than the *aeroplanos* we knew that they are almost another breed—or are indeed another breed, perhaps, as they are called "jet planes." Can you imagine a vehicle that flies eight miles above the ground? Can you imagine a giant car that moves faster than sound? Can you imagine a screaming whine so loud that it makes your teeth ache?

They call this "progress." I long for the comfort and graciousness of LTA *Count von Zeppelin*. Because you can't get away from these behemoths. Several times a day one of these things goes screaming over the mission, fairly low down, as it approaches a grounding at the flying field north of the city. The noise bothers me and makes Margrethe very nervous.

Still, most of the enhancements in technology really are progress—better plumbing, better lighting indoors and out, better roads, better buildings, many sorts of machinery that make human labor less onerous and more productive. I am never one of those back-to-nature freaks who sneer at engineering; I have more reason than most people to respect engineering. Most people who sneer at technology would starve to death if the engineering infrastructure were removed.

We had been in Nogales just short of three weeks when I was able to carry out a plan that I had dreamed of for nearly five months . . . and had actively plotted since our arrival in Nogales (but had to delay until I could afford it). I picked Monday to carry it out, that being my day off. I told Margrethe to dress up in her new clothes as I was taking my best girl out for a treat, and I dressed up, too—my one suit, my new shoes, and a clean shirt . . . and shaved and bathed and nails clean and trimmed.

It was a lovely day, sunny and not too hot. We both

felt cheerful because, first, Mrs. Owens had written to Brother McCaw saying that she was staying on another week if she could be spared, and second, we now had enough money for bus fares for both of us to Wichita, Kansas, although just barely—but the word from Mrs. Owens meant that we could squirrel away another four hundred dollars for eating money on the way and still arrive not quite broke.

I took Margrethe to a place I had spotted the day I looked for a job as a dishwasher—a nice little place outside the tenderloin, an old-fashioned ice cream parlor.

We stopped outside it. "Best girl, see this place? Do you remember a conversation we had when we were floating on the broad Pacific on a sunbathing mat and not really expecting to live much longer?—at least I was not."

"Beloved, how could I forget?"

"I asked you what you would have if you could have anything in the world that you wanted. Do you remember what you answered?"

"Of course I do! It was a hot fudge sundae."

"Right! Today is your unbirthday, dear. You are about to have that hot fudge sundae."

"Oh, Alec!"

"Don't blubber. Can't stand a woman who cries. Or you can have a chocolate malt. Or a sawdust sundae. Whatever your heart desires. But I did make sure that this place always has hot fudge sundaes before I brought you here."

"We can't afford it. We should save for the trip."

"We *can* afford it. A hot fudge sundae is five dollars. Two for ten dollars. And I'm going to be a dead game sport and tip the waitress a dollar. Man does not live by bread alone. Nor does woman, Woman. Come along!"

We were shown to a table by a pretty waitress (but not as pretty as my bride). I seated Margrethe with her back to the street, holding the chair for her, and then sat down opposite her. "I'm Tammy," the waitress said as she offered us a menu. "What would you folks like this lovely day?"

"We won't need the menu," I said. "Two hot fudge sundaes, please."

Tammy looked thoughtful. "All right, if you don't mind waiting a few minutes. We may have to make up the hot sauce."

"A few minutes, who cares? We've waited much longer than that."

She smiled and went away. I looked at Marga. "We've waited *much* longer. Haven't we?"

"Alec, you're a sentimentalist and that's part of why I love you."

"I'm a sentimental slob and right now I'm slavering at the thought of hot fudge sundae. But I wanted you to see this place for another reason, too. Marga, how would you like to run such a place as this? Us, that is. Together. You'd be boss, I'd be dishwasher, janitor, handyman, bouncer, and whatever was needed."

She looked very thoughtful. "You are serious?"

"Quite. Of course we couldn't go into business for ourselves right away; we will have to save some money first. But not much, the way I plan it. A dinky little place, but bright and cheerful—after I paint it. A soda fountain, plus a very limited menu. Hot dogs. Hamburgers. Danish open-face sandwiches. Nothing else.

Soup, maybe. But canned soups are no problem and not much inventory."

Margrethe looked shocked. "Not canned soups. I can serve a real soup . . . cheaper and better than anything out of a tin."

"I defer to your professional judgment, Ma'am. Kansas has half a dozen little college towns; any of them would welcome such a place. Maybe we pick a shop already existing, a mom-and-pop place—work for them a year, then buy them out. Change the name to The Hot Fudge Sundae. Or maybe Marga's Sandwiches."

"The Hot Fudge Sundae. Alec, do you really think we can do this?"

I leaned toward her and took her hand. "I'm sure we can, darling. And without working ourselves to death, too." I moved my head. "That traffic light is staring me right in the eye."

"I know. I can see it reflected in your eye every time it changes. Want to swap seats? It won't bother me."

"It doesn't bother me. It just has a somewhat hypnotic effect." I looked down at the table, looked back at the light. "Hey, it's gone out."

Margrethe twisted her neck to look. "I don't see it. Where?"

"Uh . . . pesky thing has disappeared. Looks like."

I heard a male voice at my elbow. "What'll it be for you two? Beer or wine; we're not licensed for the hard stuff."

I looked around, saw a waiter. "Where's Tammy?"

"Who's Tammy?"

I took a deep breath, tried to slow my heart, then said, "Sorry, brother; I shouldn't have come in here. I find I've left my wallet at home." I stood up. "Come, dear."

Wide-eyed and silent, Margrethe came with me. As we walked out, I looked around, noting changes. I suppose it was a decent enough place, as beer joints go. But it was not our cheerful ice cream parlor.

And not our world.

XV

Boast not thyself of tomorrow; for
thou knowest not what a day may bring forth.
Proverbs 27:1

Outside, without planning it, I headed us toward the
Salvation Army mission. Margrethe kept quiet and held
tight to my arm. I should have been frightened; instead
I was boiling angry. Presently I muttered, "Damn
them! Damn them!"

"Damn who, Alec?"

"I don't know. That's the worst of it. Whoever is
doing this to us. Your friend Loki, maybe."

"He is not my friend, any more than Satan is your
friend. I dread and fear what Loki is doing to our
world."

"I'm not afraid, I'm angry. Loki or Satan or whoever,
this last is too much. No sense to it. Why couldn't they
wait thirty minutes? That hot fudge sundae was practically under our nose—and they snatched it away!
Marga, that's not right, that's not fair! That's sheer,
unadulterated cruelty. Senseless. On a par with pulling
wings off flies. I despise them. Whoever."

Instead of continuing with useless talk about matters

we could not settle, Margrethe said, "Dear, where are we going?"

"Eh?" I stopped short. "Why, to the mission, I suppose."

"Is this the right way?"

"Why, yes, cert—" I paused to look around. "I don't know." I had been walking automatically, my attention fully on my anger. Now I found that I was unsure of any landmarks. "I guess I'm lost."

"I know I am."

It took us another half hour to get straightened out. The neighborhood was vaguely familiar but nothing was quite right. I found the block where Ron's Grill should be, could not find Ron's Grill. Eventually a policeman directed us to the mission . . . which was now in a different building. To my surprise, Brother McCaw was there. But he did not recognize us, and his name was now McNabb. We left, as gracefully as possible. Not very, that is.

I walked us back the way we had come—slowly, as I wasn't going anywhere. "Marga, we're right back where we were three weeks ago. Better shoes, that's all. A pocket full of money—but money we can't spend, as it is certain to be funny money here . . . good for a quiet rest behind bars if I tried to pass any of it."

"You're probably right, dear one."

"There is a bank on that corner just ahead. Instead of trying to spend any of it, I could walk in and simply ask whether or not it was worth anything."

"There couldn't be any harm in that. Could there?"

"There shouldn't be. But our friend Loki could have another practical joke up his sleeve. Uh, we've got to know. Here—you take everything but one bill. If they arrest me, you pretend not to know me."

"No!"

"What do you mean, 'No'? There is no point in both of us being in jail."

She looked stubborn and said nothing. How can you argue with a woman who won't talk? I sighed. "Look, dear, the only other thing I can think of is to look for another job washing dishes. Maybe Brother McNabb will let us sleep in the mission tonight."

"I'll look for a job, too. I can wash dishes. Or cook. Or something."

"We'll see. Come inside with me, Marga; we'll go to jail together. But I think I've figured out how to handle this without going to jail." I took out one treasury note, crumpled it, and tore one corner. Then we went into the bank together, me holding it in my hand as if I had just picked it up. I did not go to a teller's window; instead I went to that railing behind which bank officials sit at their desks.

I leaned on the railing and spoke to the man nearest to it; his desk sign marked him as assistant manager. "Excuse me, sir! Can you answer a question for me?"

He looked annoyed but his reply did not show it. "I'll try. What's on your mind?"

"Is this really money? Or is it stage money, or something?"

He looked at it, then looked more closely. "Interesting. Where did you get this?"

"My wife found it on a sidewalk. Is it money?"

"Of course it's not money. Whoever heard of a twenty-dollar note? Stage money, probably. Or an advertising promotion."

"Then it's not worth anything?"

"It's worth the paper it's printed on, that's all. I doubt that it could even be called counterfeit, since there has been no effort to make it look like the real thing. Still, the Treasury inspectors will want to see it."

"All right. Can you take care of it?"

"Yes. But they'll want to talk to you, I'm sure. Let's get your name and address. And your wife's, of course, since she found it."

"Okay. I want a receipt for it." I gave our names as "Mr. and Mrs. Alexander Hergensheimer" and gave the address—but not the name—of Ron's Grill. Then I solemnly accepted a receipt.

Once out on the sidewalk I said, "Well, we're no worse off than we thought we were. Time for me to look for some dirty dishes."

"Alec—"

"Yes, beloved?"

"We were going to Kansas."

"So we were. But our bus-fare money is not worth the paper it is printed on. I'll have to earn some more. I can. I did it once, I can do it again."

"Alec. Let us now go to Kansas."

A half hour later we were walking north on the highway to Tucson. Whenever anyone passed us, I signalled our hope of being picked up.

It took us three hitches simply to reach Tucson. At Tucson it would have made equal sense to head east toward El Paso, Texas, as to continue on Route 89, as 89 swings west before it goes north to Phoenix. It was settled for us by the chance that the first lift we were able to beg out of Tucson was with a teamster who was taking a load north.

This ride we were able to pick up at a truckers' stop at the intersection of 89 and 80, and I am forced to admit that the teamster listened to our plea because Margrethe is the beauty she is—had I been alone I might still be standing there. I might as well say right now that this whole trip depended throughout on Margrethe's beauty and womanly charm quite as much as it depended on my willingness to do any honest work whatever, no matter how menial, dirty, or difficult.

I found this fact unpleasant to face. I held dark thoughts of Potiphar's wife and of the story of Susanna and the Elders. I found myself being vexed with Margrethe when her only offense lay in being her usual gracious, warm, and friendly self. I came close to telling her not to smile at strangers and to keep her eyes to herself.

That temptation hit me sharpest that first day at sundown when this same trucker stopped at a roadside oasis centered around a restaurant and a fueling facility. "I'm going to have a couple of beers and a sirloin steak," he announced. "How about you, Maggie baby? Could you use a rare steak? This is the place where they just chase the cow through the kitchen."

She smiled at him. "Thank you, Steve. But I'm not hungry."

My darling was telling an untruth. She knew it, I knew it—and I felt sure that Steve knew it. Our last meal had been breakfast at the mission, eleven hours and a universe ago. I had tried to wash dishes for a meal at the truckers' stop outside Tucson, but had been dismissed rather abruptly. So we had had nothing all day but water from a public drinking faucet.

"Don't try to kid your grandmother, Maggie. We've been on the road four hours. You're hungry."

I spoke up quickly to keep Margrethe from persisting in an untruth—told, I felt certain, on my behalf. "What she means, Steve, is that she doesn't accept dinner invitations from other men. She expects me to provide her dinner." I added, "But I thank you on her behalf and we both thank you for the ride. It's been most pleasant."

We were still seated in the cab of his truck, Margrethe in the middle. He leaned forward and looked around her. "Alec, you think I'm trying to get into Maggie's pants, don't you?"

I answered stiffly that I did not think anything of the sort while thinking privately that that was exactly what I thought he had been trying to accomplish all along . . . and I resented not only his unchivalrous overtures but also the gross language he had just used. But I had learned the hard way that rules of polite speech in the world in which I had grown up were not necessarily rules in another universe.

"Oh, yes, you do think so. I wasn't born yesterday and a lot of my life has been spent on the road, getting my illusions knocked out. You think I'm trying to lay your woman because every stud who comes along tries to put the make on her. But let me clue you in, son. I don't knock when there's nobody at home. And I can always tell. Maggie ain't having any. I checked that out hours ago. And congratulations; a faithful woman is good to find. Isn't that true?"

"Yes, certainly," I agreed grudgingly.

"So get your feathers down. You're about to take your wife to dinner. You've already said thank you to me for the ride but why don't you really thank me by inviting me to dinner?—so I won't have to eat alone."

I hope that I did not look dismayed and that my instant of hesitation was not noticeable. "Certainly, Steve. We owe you that for your kindness. Uh, will you excuse me while I make some arrangements?" I started to get out of the cab.

"Alec, you don't lie any better than Maggie does."

"Excuse me?"

"You think I'm blind? You're broke. Or, if you aren't absolutely stony, you are so near flat you can't afford to buy me a sirloin steak. Or even the blueplate special."

"That is true," I answered with—I hope—dignity. "The arrangements I must make are with the restaurant manager. I hope to exchange dishwashing for the price of three dinners."

"I thought so. If you were just ordinary broke, you'd be riding Greyhound and you'd have some baggage. If you were broke but not yet hungry broke, you'd hitch-hike to save your money for eating but you would have some sort of baggage. A kiester each, or at least a bindle. But you've got no baggage . . . and you're both wearing suits—in the desert, for God's sake! The signs all spell disaster."

I remained mute.

"Now look," he went on. "Possibly the owner of this joint would let you wash dishes. More likely he's got three wetbacks pearl-diving this very minute and has turned down at least three more already today; this is on the main north-south route of *turistas* coming through holes in the Fence. In any case I can't wait while you wash dishes; I've got to herd this rig a lot of miles yet tonight. So I'll make you a deal. You take me to dinner but I lend you the money."

"I'm a poor risk."

"Nope, you're a good risk. What the bankers call a character loan, the very best risk there is. Sometime, this coming year, or maybe twenty years from now, you'll run across another young couple, broke and hungry. You'll buy them dinner on the same terms. That pays me back. Then when they do the same, down the line, that pays you back. Get it?"

"I'll pay you back sevenfold!"

"Once is enough. After that you do it for your own pleasure. Come on, let's eat."

Rimrock Restop restaurant was robust rather than fancy—about on a par with Ron's Grill in another world. It had both counter and tables. Steve led us to a table and shortly a fairly young and rather pretty waitress came over.

"Howdy, Steve! Long time."

"Hi, Babe! How'd the rabbit test come out?"

"The rabbit died. How about your blood test?" She smiled at me and at Margrethe. "Hi, folks! What'll you have?"

I had had time to glance at the menu, first down the right-hand side, of course—and was shocked at the prices. Shocked to find them back on the scale of the world I knew best, I mean. Hamburgers for a dime, coffee at five cents, *table d'hôte* dinners at seventy-five to ninety cents—these prices I understood.

I looked at it and said, "May I have a cheese super-burger, medium well?"

"Sure thing, Ace. How about you, dear?"

Margrethe took the same, but medium rare.

"Steve?" the waitress inquired.

"That'll be three beers—*Coors*—and three sirloin steaks, one rare, one medium rare, one medium. With the usual garbage. Baked potato, fried promises, whatever. The usual limp salad. Hot rolls. All the usual. Dessert later. Coffee."

"Gotcha."

"Wantcha to meet my friends. Maggie, this is Hazel. That's Alec, her husband."

"You lucky man! Hi, Maggie; glad to know you. Sorry to see you in such company, though. Has Steve tried to sell you anything?"

"No."

"Good. Don't buy anything, don't sign anything, don't bet with him. And be glad you're safely married; he's got wives in three states."

"Four," Steve corrected.

"Four now? Congratulations. Ladies' restroom is through the kitchen, Maggie; men go around behind." She left moving fast, with a swish of her skirt.

"That's a fine broad," Steve said. "You know what they say about waitresses, especially in truckers' joints. Well, Hazel is probably the only hash-slinger on this highway who *ain't* sellin' it. Come on, Alec." He got up and led me outdoors and around to the men's room. I followed him. By the time I understood what he had said, it was too late to resent his talking that way in a lady's presence. Then I was forced to admit that Margrethe had not resented it—had simply treated it as information. As praise of Hazel, in fact. I think my greatest trouble with all these worrisome world changes had to do, not with economics, not with social behavior, not with technology, but simply with language, and the *mores* and taboos thereto.

Beer was waiting for us when we returned, and so was Margrethe, looking cool and refreshed.

Steve toasted us. "Skoal!"

We echoed *"Skaal!"* and I took a sip and then a lot more—just what I needed after a long day on a desert highway. My moral downfall in S.S. *Konge Knut* had included getting reacquainted with beer, something I had not touched since my days as an engineering student, and very little then—no money for vices. This was excellent beer, it seemed to me, but not as good as the Danish Tuborg served in the ship. Did you know that there is not one word against beer in the Bible? In fact the word "beer" in the Bible means "fountain" or "well."

The steaks were delicious.

Under the mellowing influence of beer and good food I found myself trying to explain to Steve how we happened to be down on our luck and accepting the charity of strangers . . . without actually saying anything. Presently Margrethe said to me, "Alec. Tell him."

"You think I should?"

"I think Steve is entitled to know. And I trust him."

"Very well. Steve, we are strangers from another world."

He neither laughed nor smiled; he just looked interested. Presently he said, "Flying saucer?"

"No. I mean another universe, not just another

planet. Although it seems like the same planet. I mean, Margrethe and I were in a state called Arizona and a city called Nogales just earlier today. Then it changed. Nogales shrank down and nothing was quite the same. Arizona looks about the same, although I don't know this state very well."

"Territory."

"Excuse me?"

"Arizona is a territory, not a state. Statehood was voted down."

"Oh. That's the way it was in my world, too. Something about taxes. But we didn't come from my world. Nor from Marga's world. We came from—" I stopped. "I'm not telling this very well." I looked across at Margrethe. "Can you explain it?"

"I can't *explain* it," she answered, "because I don't understand it. But, Steve, it's true. I'm from one world, Alec is from another world, we've lived in still another world, and we were in yet again another world this morning. And now we are here. That is why we don't have any money. No, we do have money but it's not money of this world."

Steve said, "Could we take this one world at a time? I'm getting dizzy."

I said, "She left out two worlds."

"No, dear—three. You may have forgotten the iceberg world."

"No, I counted that. I— Excuse me, Steve. I'll try to take it one world at a time. But it isn't easy. This morning— We went into an ice cream parlor in Nogales because I wanted to buy Margrethe a hot fudge sundae. We sat down at a table, across from each other like right now, and that put me facing a set of traffic lights—"

"A set of what?"

"A set of traffic signal lights, red, green, and amber. That's how I spotted that we had changed worlds again. This world doesn't have signal lights, or at least I haven't seen any. Just traffic cops. But in the world we got up in this morning, instead of traffic cops, they do it with signal lights."

"Sounds like they do it with mirrors. What's this got to do with buying Maggie a hot fudge sundae?"

"That was because, when we were shipwrecked and floating around in the ocean, Margrethe wanted a hot fudge sundae. This morning was my first chance to buy one for her. When the traffic lights disappeared, I knew we had changed worlds again—and that meant that my money wasn't any good. So I could not buy her a hot fudge sundae. And could not buy her dinner tonight. No money. No spendable money, I mean. You see?"

"I think I fell off three turns back. What happened to your money?"

"Oh." I dug into my pocket, hauled out our carefully hoarded bus-fare money, picked out a twenty-dollar bill, handed it to Steve. "Nothing happened to it. Look at this."

He looked at it carefully. "'Lawful money for all debts public and private.' That sounds okay. But who's this joker with his picture on it? And when did they start printing twenty-dollar treasury notes?"

"Never, in your world. I guess. The picture is of William Jennings Bryan, President of the United States from 1913 to 1921."

"Not at Horace Mann School in Akron, he wasn't. Never heard of him."

"In my school he was elected in 1896, not sixteen years later. And in Margrethe's world Mr. Bryan was never president at all. Say! Margrethe! This just might be your world!"

"Why do you think so, dear?"

"Maybe, maybe not. As we came north out of Nogales I didn't notice a flying field or any signs concerning one. And I just remembered that I haven't heard or seen a jet plane all day long. Or any sort of a flying machine. Have you?"

"No. No, I haven't. But I haven't been thinking about them." She added, "I'm almost certain there haven't been any near us."

"There you have it! Or maybe this is my world. Steve, what's the situation on aeronautics here?"

"Arrow what?"

"Flying machines. Jet planes. Aeroplanes of any sort. And dirigibles—do you have dirigibles?"

"None of those things rings any bells with me. You're talking about flying, real flying, up in the air like a bird?"

"Yes, yes!"

"No, of course not. Or do you mean balloons? I've seen a balloon."

"Not balloons. Oh, a dirigible is a sort of a balloon. But it's long instead of round—sort of cigar-shaped. And it's propelled by engines something like your truck and goes a hundred miles an hour and more—and usually fairly high, one or two thousand feet. Higher over mountains."

For the first time Steve showed surprise rather than interest. "God A'mighty! You've actually *seen* something like that?"

"I've ridden in them. Many times. First when I was only twelve years old. You went to school in Akron? In my world Akron is world famous as the place where they build the biggest, fastest, and best dirigible airships in all the world."

Steve shook his head. "When the parade goes by, I'm out for a short beer. That's the story of my life. Maggie, you've seen airships? Ridden in them?"

"No. They are not in my world. But I've ridden in a flying machine. An *aeroplano*. Once. It was terribly exciting. Frightening, too. But I would like to do it again."

"I betcha would. Me, I reckon it would scare the tar out of me. But I would take a ride in one, even if it killed me. Folks, I'm beginning to believe you. You tell it so straight. That and this money. If it *is* money."

"It *is* money," I insisted, "from another world. Look at it closely, Steve. Obviously it's not money of your world. But it's not play money or stage money either. Would anybody bother to make steel engravings that perfect just for stage money? The engraver who made the plates expected that note to be accepted as money . . . yet it isn't even a correct denomination—that's the first thing you noticed. Wait a moment." I dug into another pocket. "Yup! Still here." I took out a ten-peso note—from the Kingdom of Mexico. I had burned most of the useless money we had accumulated before the quake—Margrethe's tips at El Pancho Villa—but I had saved a few souvenirs. "Look at this, too. Do you know Spanish?"

"Not really. TexMex. *Cantina* Spanish." He looked at the Mexican money. "This looks okay."

"Look more closely," Margrethe urged him. "Where it says '*Reino.*' Shouldn't that read '*República*'? Or is Mexico a kingdom in this world?"

"It's a republic . . . partly because I helped keep it that way. I was an election judge there when I was in the Marines. It's amazing what a few Marines armed to their eyebrows can do to keep an election honest. Okay, pals; you've sold me. Mexico is not a kingdom and hitchhikers who don't have the price of dinner on them ought not to be carrying around Mexicano money that says it *is* a kingdom. Maybe I'm crazy but I'm inclined to throw in with you. What's the explanation?"

"Steve," I said soberly, "I wish I knew. The simplest explanation is that I've gone crazy and that it's all imaginary—you, me, Marga, this restaurant, this world—all products of my brain fever."

"You can be imaginary if you want to, but leave Maggie and me out of it. Do you have any other explanations?"

"Uh . . . that depends. Do you read the Bible, Steve?"

"Well, yes and no. Being on the road, lots of times I find myself wide awake in bed with nothing around to read but a Gideon Bible. So sometimes I do."

"Do you recall Matthew twenty-four, twenty-four?"

"Huh? Should I?"

I quoted it for him. "That's one possibility, Steve. These world changes may be signs sent by the Devil himself, intended to deceive us. On the other hand they may be portents of the end of world and the coming of Christ into His kingdom. Hear the Word:

"'Immediately after the tribulation of those days shall the sun be darkened, and the moon shall not give her light, and the stars shall fall from heaven, and the powers of the heavens shall be shaken:

"'And then shall appear the sign of the Son of man in heaven: and then shall all the tribes of the earth mourn, and they shall see the Son of man coming in the clouds of heaven with power and great glory.

"'And he shall send his angels with a great sound of a trumpet, and they shall gather together his elect from the four winds, from one end of heaven to the other.'

"That's what it adds up to, Steve. Maybe these are the false signs of the tribulations before the end, or maybe these wonders foretell the Parousia, the coming of Christ. But, either way, we are coming to the end of the world. Are you born again?"

"Mmm, I can't rightly say that I am. I was baptized a long time ago, when I was too young to have much say in the matter. I'm not a churchgoer, except sometimes to see my friends married or buried. If I was washed clean once, I guess I'm a little dusty by now. I don't suppose I qualify."

"No, I'm certain that you do not. Steve, the end of the world is coming and Christ is returning soon. The most urgent business you have—that anyone has!—is to take your troubles to Jesus, be washed in His Blood, and be born again in Him. Because you will receive no warning. The Trump will sound and you will either be caught up into the arms of Jesus, safe and happy forevermore, or you will be cast down into the fire and brimstone, there to suffer agonies through all eternity. You must be ready."

"Cripes! Alec, have you ever thought about becoming a preacher?"

"I've thought about it."

"You should do more than think about it, you should be one. You said all that just like you believed every word of it."

"I do."

"Thought maybe. Well, I'll pay you the respect of giving it some hard thought. But in the meantime I hope they don't hold Kingdom Come tonight because I've still got this load to deliver. Hazel! Let me have the check, dear; I've got to get the show on the road."

Three steak dinners came to $3.90; six beers was another sixty cents, for a total of $4.50. Steve paid with a half eagle, a coin I had never seen outside a coin collection—I wanted to look at this one but had no excuse.

Hazel picked it up, looked at it. "Don't get much gold around here," she remarked. "Cartwheels are the usual thing. And some paper, although the boss doesn't like paper money. Sure you can spare this, Steve?"

"I found the Lost Dutchman."

"Go along with you; I'm not going to be your fifth wife."

"I had in mind just a temporary arrangement."

"Not that either—not for a five-dollar gold piece." She dug into an apron pocket, took out a silver half dollar. "Your change, dear."

He pushed it back toward her. "What'll you do for fifty cents?"

She picked it up, pocketed it. "Spit in your eye. Thanks. Night, folks. Glad you came in."

* * *

During the thirty-five miles or so on into Flagstaff Steve asked questions of us about the worlds we had seen but made no comments. He talked just enough to keep us talking. He was especially interested in my descriptions of airships, jet planes, and *aeroplanos,* but anything technical fascinated him. Television he found much harder to believe than flying machines—well, so did I. But Margrethe assured him that she had seen television herself, and Margrethe is hard to disbelieve. Me, I might be mistaken for a con man. But not Margrethe. Her voice and manner carry conviction.

In Flagstaff, just short of Route 66, Steve pulled over to the side and stopped, left his engine running. "All out," he said, "if you insist on heading east. If you want to go north, you're welcome."

I said, "We've got to get to Kansas, Steve."

"Yes, I know. While you can get there either way, Sixty-Six is your best bet . . . though why anyone should want to go to Kansas beats me. It's that intersection ahead, there. Keep right and keep going; you can't miss it. Watch out for the Santa Fe tracks. Where you planning to sleep tonight?"

"I don't have any plans. We'll walk until we get another ride. If we don't get an all-night ride and we get too sleepy, we can sleep by the side of the road—it's warm."

"Alec, you listen to your Uncle Dudley. You're not going to sleep on the desert tonight. It's warm now; it'll be freezing cold by morning. Maybe you haven't noticed but we've been climbing all the way from Phoenix. And if the Gila monsters don't get you, the sand fleas will. You've got to rent a cabin."

"Steve, I can't rent a cabin."

"The Lord will provide. You believe that, don't you?"

"Yes," I answered stiffly, "I believe that." (But He also helps those who help themselves.)

"So let the Lord provide. Maggie, about this end-of-the-world business, do you agree with Alec?"

"I certainly don't disagree!"

"Mmm. Alec, I'm going to give it a lot of thought . . . starting tonight, by reading a Gideon Bible. This time I don't want to miss the parade. You go on down Sixty-Six, look for a place saying 'cabins.' Not 'motel,' not 'roadside inn,' not a word about Simmons mattresses or private baths—just 'cabins.' If they ask more than two dollars, walk away. Keep dickering and you might get it for one."

I wasn't listening very hard as I was growing quite angry. Dicker with *what?* He knew that I was utterly without funds—didn't he believe me?

"So I'll say good-bye," Steve went on. "Alec, can you get that door? I don't want to get out."

"I can get it." I opened it, stepped down, then remembered my manners. "Steve, I want to thank you for everything. Dinner, and beer, and a long ride. May the Lord watch over you and keep you."

"Thank you and don't mention it. Here." He reached into a pocket, pulled out a card. "That's my business card. Actually it's my daughter's address. When you get to Kansas, drop me a card, let me know how you made out."

"I'll do that." I took the card, then started to hand Margrethe down.

Steve stopped her. "Maggie! Aren't you going to kiss ol' Steve good-bye?"

"Why, certainly, Steve!" She turned back and half faced him on the seat.

"That's better. Alec, you'd better turn your back."

I did not turn my back but I tried to ignore it, while watching out the corner of my eye.

If it had gone on one half-second longer, I would have dragged her out of that cab bodily. Yet I am forced to admit that Margrethe was not having attentions forced on her; she was cooperating fully, kissing him in a fashion no married woman should ever kiss another man.

I endured it.

At last it ended. I handed her down, and closed the door. Steve called out, "'Bye, kids!" and his truck moved forward. As it picked up speed he tooted his horn twice.

Margrethe said, "Alec, you are angry with me."

"No. Surprised, yes. Even shocked. Disappointed. Saddened."

"Don't sniff at me!"

"Eh?"

"Steve drove us two hundred and fifty miles and bought us a fine dinner and didn't laugh when we told him a preposterous story. And now you get hoity-toity and holier-than-thou because I kissed him hard enough to show that I appreciated what he had done for me *and* my husband. I won't stand for it, do you hear?"

"I just meant that—"

"Stop it! I won't listen to explanations. Because you're wrong! And now *I* am angry and I shall stay angry until you realize you are wrong. So think it over!" She turned and started walking rapidly toward the intersection of 66 with 89.

I hurried to catch up. "Margrethe!"

She did not answer and increased her pace.

"Margrethe!" Eyes straight ahead—

"Margrethe darling! I was wrong. I'm sorry, I apologize."

She stopped abruptly, turned and threw her arms around my neck, started to cry. "Oh, Alec, I love you so and you're such a fub!"

I did not answer at once as my mouth was busy. At last I said, "I love you, too, and what is a fub?"

"You are."

"Well— In that case I'm your fub and you're stuck with me. Don't walk away from me again."

"I won't. Not ever." We resumed what we had been doing.

After a while I pulled my face back just far enough to whisper: "We don't have a bed to our name and I've never wanted one more."

"Alec. Check your pockets."

"Huh?"

"While he was kissing me, Steve whispered to me to tell you to check your pockets and to say, 'The Lord will provide.'"

I found it in my left-hand coat pocket: a gold eagle. Never before had I held one in my hand. It felt warm and heavy.

XVI

At a drugstore in downtown Flagstaff I exchanged
that gold eagle for nine cartwheels, ninety-five cents in
change, and a bar of Ivory soap. Buying soap was Margrethe's idea. "Alec, a druggist is not a banker; changing money is something he may not want to do other
than as part of a sale. We need soap. I want to wash
your underwear and mine, and we both need baths . . .
and I suspect that, at the sort of cheap lodging Steve
urged us to take, soap may not be included in the
rent."

She was right on both points. The druggist raised his
eyebrows at the ten-dollar gold piece but said nothing.
He took the coin, let it ring on the glass top of a counter, then reached behind his cash register, fetched out a
small bottle, and subjected the coin to the acid test.

I made no comment. Silently he counted out nine
silver dollars, a half dollar, a quarter, and two dimes.
Instead of pocketing the coins at once, I stood fast, and
subjected each coin to the same ringing test he had

used, using his glass counter. Having done so, I pushed one cartwheel back at him.

Again he made no comment—he had heard the dull ring of that putatively silver coin as well as I. He rang up "No Sale," handed me another cartwheel (which rang clear as a bell), and put the bogus coin somewhere in the back of the cash drawer. Then he turned his back on me.

At the outskirts of town, halfway to Winona, we found a place shabby enough to meet our standards. Margrethe conducted the dicker, in Spanish. Our host asked five dollars. Marga called on the Virgin Mary and three other saints to witness what was being done to her. Then she offered him five pesos.

I did not understand this maneuver; I knew she had no pesos on her. Surely she would not be intending to offer those unspendable "royal" pesos I still carried?

I did not find out, as our host answered with a price of three dollars and that is final, *Señora,* as God is my witness.

They settled on a dollar and a half, then Marga rented clean sheets and a blanket for another fifty cents—paid for the lot with two silver dollars but demanded pillows and clean pillow-cases to seal the bargain. She got them but the *patrón* asked something for luck. Marga added a dime and he bowed deeply and assured us that his house was ours.

At seven the next morning we were on our way, rested, clean, happy, and hungry. A half hour later we were in Winona and much hungrier. We cured the latter at a little trailer-coach lunchroom: a stack of wheat cakes, ten cents; coffee, five cents—no charge for second cup, no limit on butter or syrup.

Margrethe could not finish her hot cakes—they were lavish—so we swapped plates and I salvaged what she had left.

A sign on the wall read: CASH WHEN SERVED — NO TIPPING — ARE YOU READY FOR JUDGMENT DAY? The cook-waiter (and owner, I think) had a copy of *The Watch Tower* propped up by his range. I asked, "Brother, do you have any late news on when to expect Judgment Day?"

"Don't joke about it. Eternity is a long time to spend in the Pit."

I answered, "I was not joking. By the signs and portents I think we are in the seven-year period prophesied in the eleventh chapter of Revelation, verses two and three. But I don't know how far we are into it."

"We're already well into the second half," he answered. "The two witnesses are now prophesying and the antichrist is abroad in the land. Are you in a state of grace? If not, you had better get cracking."

I answered, "'Therefore be ye also ready: for such an hour as ye think not the Son of man cometh.'"

"You'd better believe it!"

"I do believe it. Thanks for a good breakfast."

"Don't mention it. May the Lord watch over you."

"Thank you. May He bless you and keep you." Marga and I left.

We headed east again. "How is my sweetheart?"

"Full of food and happy."

"So am I. Something you did last night made me especially happy."

"Me, too. But you always do, darling man. Every time."

"Uh, yes, there's that. Me, too. Always. But I meant

something you said, earlier. When Steve asked if you agreed with me about Judgment Day and you told him you did agree. Marga, I can't tell you how much it has worried me that you have not chosen to be received back into the arms of Jesus. With Judgment Day rushing toward us and no way to know the hour—well, I've worried. I do worry. But apparently you are finding your way back to the light but had not yet discussed it with me."

We walked perhaps twenty paces while Margrethe did not say anything.

At last she said quietly, "Beloved, I would put your mind at rest. If I could. I cannot."

"So? I do not understand. Will you explain?"

"I did not tell Steve that I agreed with you. I said to him that I did not disagree."

"But that's the same thing!"

"No, darling. What I did not say to Steve but could have said in full honesty is that I will *never* publicly disagree with my husband about anything. Any disagreement with you I will discuss with you in private. Not in Steve's presence. Not anyone's."

I chewed that over, let several possible comments go unsaid—at last said, "Thank you, Margrethe."

"Beloved, I do it for my own dignity as well as for yours. All my life I have hated the sight of husband and wife disagreeing—disputing—quarreling in public. If you say that the sun is covered with bright green puppy dogs, I will not disagree in public."

"Ah, but it is!"

"Sir?" She stopped, and looked startled.

"My good Marga. Whatever the problem, you always find a gentle answer. If I ever do see bright green puppy dogs on the face of the sun, I will try to remember to discuss it with you in private, not face you with hard decisions in public. I love you. I read too much into what you said to Steve because I really do worry."

She took my hand and we walked a bit farther without talking.

"Alec?"

"Yes, my love?"

"I do not willingly worry you. If I am wrong and you are going to the Christian Heaven, I do want to go with you. If this means a return to faith in Jesus—and it seems that it does—then that is what I want. I will try. I cannot promise it, as faith is not a matter of simple volition. But I will try."

I stopped to kiss her, to the amusement of a carload of men passing by. "Darling, more I cannot ask. Shall we pray together?"

"Alec, I would rather not. Let me pray alone—and I will! When it comes time to pray together, I will tell you."

Not long after that we were picked up by a ranch couple who took us into Winslow. They dropped us there without asking any questions and without us offering any information, which must set some sort of record.

Winslow is much larger than Winona; it is a respectable town as desert communities go—seven thousand at a guess. We found there an opportunity to carry out something Steve had indirectly suggested and that we had discussed the night before.

Steve was correct; we were not dressed for the desert. True, we had had no choice, as we had been caught by a world change. But I did not see another man wearing a business suit in the desert. Nor did we see Anglo women dressed in women's suits. Indian women and Mexican women wore skirts, but Anglo women wore either shorts or trousers—slacks, jeans, cutoffs, riding pants, something. Rarely a skirt, never a suit.

Furthermore our suits were not right even as city wear. They looked as out of place as styles of the Mauve Decade would look. Don't ask me how as I am no expert on styles, especially for women. The suit that I wore had been both smart and expensive when worn by my *patrón, Don* Jaime, in Mazatlán in another world . . . but on me, in the Arizona desert in this world, it was something out of skid row.

In Winslow we found just the shop we needed: SECOND WIND — A Million Bargains — All Sales Cash, No Guarantees, No Returns — All Used Clothing Sterilized Before Being Offered For Sale. Above this were the same statements in Spanish.

An hour later, after much picking over of their stock and some heavy dickering by Margrethe, we were dressed for the desert. I was wearing khaki pants, a shirt to match, and a straw hat of vaguely western style. Margrethe was wearing considerably less: shorts that were both short and tight—indecently so—and an upper garment that was less than a bodice but slightly more than a brassière. It was termed a "halter."

When I saw Marga in this outfit, I whispered to her, "I positively will not permit you to appear in public in that shameless costume."

She answered, "Dear, don't be a fub so early in the day. It's too hot."

"I'm not joking. I forbid you to buy that."

"Alec, I don't recall asking your permission."

"Are you defying me?"

She sighed. "Perhaps I am. I don't want to. Did you get your razor?"

"You saw me!"

"I have your underpants and socks. Is there anything more you need now?"

"No. Margrethe! Quit evading me!"

"Darling, I told you that I will not quarrel with you in public. This outfit has a wrap-around skirt; I was about to put it on. Let me do so and settle the bill. Then we can go outside and talk in private."

Fuming, I went along with what she proposed. I might as well admit that, under her careful management, we came out of that bazaar with more money than we had had when we came in. How? That suit from my *patrón*, *Don* Jaime, that looked so ridiculous on me, looked just right on the owner of the shop—in fact he resembled *Don* Jaime. He had been willing to swap, even, for what I needed—khaki shirt and pants and straw hat.

But Margrethe insisted on something to boot. She demanded five dollars, got two.

I learned, as she settled our bill, that she had wrought similar magic in getting rid of that tailored suit she no longer needed. We entered the shop with $7.55; we left it with $8.80 . . . and desert outfits for each of us, a comb (for two), a toothbrush (also for two), a knapsack, a safety razor, plus a minimum of underwear and socks—all secondhand but alleged to be sterilized.

I am not good at tactics, not with women. We were outside and down the highway to an open place where we could talk privately before Margrethe would talk to me—and I did not realize that I had already lost.

Without stopping, she said, "Well, dear? You had something to discuss."

"Uh, with that skirt in place your clothing is acceptable. Barely. But you are not to appear in public in those shorts. Is that understood?"

"I intended to wear just the shorts. If the weather is warm. As it is."

"But, Margrethe, I told you not to—" She was unsnapping the skirt, taking it off. "You are defying me!"

She folded it up neatly. "May I place this in the knapsack? Please?"

"You are deliberately disobeying me!"

"But, Alec, I don't have to obey you and you don't have to obey me."

"But— Look, dear, be reasonable. You know I don't usually give orders. But a wife must obey her husband. Are you my wife?"

"You told me so. So I am until you tell me otherwise."

"Then it is your duty to obey me."

"No, Alec."

"But that is a wife's first duty!"

"I don't agree."

"But— This is madness! Are you leaving me?"

"No. Only if you divorce me."

"I don't believe in divorce. Divorce is wrong. Against Scripture."

She made no answer.

"Margrethe . . . *please* put your skirt on."

She said softly, "Almost you persuade me, dearest. Will you explain why you want me to do so?"

"What? Because those shorts, worn alone, are indecent!"

"I don't see how an article of clothing can be indecent, Alec. A person, yes. Are you saying that *I* am indecent?"

"Uh— You're twisting my words. When you wear those shorts—without a skirt—in public, you expose so much of yourself that the spectacle is indecent. Right now, walking this highway, your limbs are fully exposed . . . to the people in that car that just passed, for example. They saw you. I saw them staring!"

"Good. I hope they enjoyed it."

"*What?*"

"You tell me that I am beautiful. But you could be prejudiced. I hope that my appearance is pleasing to other people as well."

"Be serious, Margrethe; we're speaking of your naked limbs. Naked."

"You're saying my legs are bare. So they are. I prefer them bare when the weather is warm. What are you frowning at, dear? Are my legs ugly?"

(*"Thou art all fair, my love; there is no spot in thee!"*) "Your limbs are beautiful, my love; I have told you so many times. But I have no wish to share your beauty."

"Beauty is not diminished by being shared. Let's get back to the subject, Alec; you were explaining how my legs are indecent. If you can explain it. I don't think you can."

"But, Margrethe, nakedness is indecent by its very nature. It inspires lewd thoughts."

"Really? Does seeing my legs cause you to get an erection?"

"*Margrethe!*"

"Alec, stop being a fub! I asked a simple question."

"An improper question."

She sighed. "I don't see how that question can possibly be improper between husband and wife. And I will never concede that my legs are indecent. Or that nakedness is indecent. I have been naked in front of hundreds of people—"

"*Margrethe!*"

She looked surprised. "Surely you know that?"

"I did not know it and I am shocked to hear it."

"Truly, dear? But you know how well I swim."

"What's that got to do with it? I swim well, too. But I don't swim naked; I wear a bathing suit." (But I was remembering most sharply the pool in *Konge Knut*—of course my darling was used to nude swimming. I found myself out on a limb.)

"Oh. Yes, I've seen such suits, in Mazatlán. And in Spain. But, darling, we're going astray again. The problem is wider than whether or not bare legs are indecent or whether I should have kissed Steve good-bye or even whether I must obey you. You are expecting me to be what I am not. I want to be your wife for many years, for all my life—and I hope to share Heaven with you if Heaven is your destination. But, darling, I am not a child, I am not a slave. Because I love you I wish to please you. But I will not obey an order simply because I am a wife."

I could say that I overwhelmed her with the brilliance of my rebuttal. Yes, I could say that, but it would not be true. I was still trying to think of an answer when a car slowed down as it overtook us. I heard a whistle of the sort called "wolf." The car stopped beyond us and backed up. "Need a ride?" a voice called out.

"Yes!" Margrethe answered, and hurried. Perforce, I did, too.

It was a station wagon with a woman behind the wheel, a man riding with her. Both were my age or older. He reached back, opened the rear door. "Climb in!"

I handed Margrethe in, followed her and closed the door. "Got room enough?" he asked. "If not, throw that junk on the floor. We never sit in the back seat, so stuff sort o' gravitates to it. We're Clyde and Bessie Bulkey."

"He's Bulkey; I'm just well fed," the driver added.

"You're supposed to laugh at that; I've heard it before." He was indeed bulky, the sort of big-boned beefy man who is an athlete in school, then puts on weight later. His wife had correctly described both of them; she was not fat but carried some extra padding.

"How do you do, Mrs. Bulkey, Mr. Bulkey. We're Alec and Margrethe Graham. Thank you for picking us up."

"Don't be so formal, Alec," she answered. "How far you going?"

"Bessie, *please* keep one eye on the road."

"Clyde, if you don't like the way I'm herding this heap, I'll pull over and let you drive."

"Oh, no, no, you're doing fine!"

"Pipe down then, or I invoke rule K. Well, Alec?"

"We're going to Kansas."

"Coo! We're not going that far; we turn north at Chambers. That's just a short piece down the road, about ninety miles. But you're welcome to that much. What are you going to do in Kansas?"

(What was I going to do in Kansas? Open an ice cream parlor . . . bring my dear wife back to the fold . . . prepare for Judgment Day—) "I'm going to wash dishes."

"My husband is too modest," Margrethe said quietly. "We're going to open a small restaurant and soda fountain in a college town. But on our way to that goal we are likely to wash dishes. Or almost any work."

So I explained what had happened to us, with variations and omissions to avoid what they wouldn't believe. "The restaurant was wiped out, our Mexican partners were dead, and we lost everything we had. I said 'dishwashing' because that is the one job I can almost always find. But I'll take a swing at 'most anything."

Clyde said, "Alec, with that attitude you'll be back on your feet before you know it."

"We lost some money, that's all. We're not too old to start over again." (Dear Lord, will You hold off Judgment Day long enough for me to do it? Thy will be done. Amen.)

Margrethe reached over and squeezed my hand. Clyde noticed it. He had turned around in his seat so that he faced us as well as his wife. "You'll make it," he said. "With your wife backing you, you're bound to make it."

"I think so. Thank you." I knew why he was turned to face us: to stare at Margrethe. I wanted to tell him to keep his eyes to himself but, under the circumstances, I could not. Besides that, it was clear that Mr. and Mrs. Bulkey saw nothing wrong with the way my beloved was dressed; Mrs. Bulkey was dressed the same way, only more so. Or less so. Less costume, more bare skin. I must admit, too, that, while she was not the immortal beauty Margrethe is, she was quite comely.

At Painted Desert we stopped, got out, and stared at the truly unbelievable natural beauty. I had seen it once before; Margrethe had never seen it and was breathless. Clyde told me that they always stopped, even though they had seen it hundreds of times.

Correction: I had seen it once before . . . in another world. Painted Desert tended to prove what I had strongly suspected: It was not Mother Earth that changed in these wild changes; it was man and his works—and even those only in part. But the only obvious explanation seemed to lead straight to paranoia. If so, I must not surrender to it; I must take care of Margrethe.

Clyde bought us hot dogs and cold drinks and brushed aside my offer to pay. When we got back into their car, Clyde took the wheel and invited Margrethe to ride up front with him. I was not pleased but could not show it, as Bessie promptly said, "Poor Alec! Has to put up with the old bag. Don't sulk, dear; it's only twenty-three miles to the turn-off for Chambers . . . or less than twenty-three minutes the way Clyde drives."

This time Clyde took thirty minutes. But he waited and made sure that we had a ride to Gallup.

We reached Gallup long before dark. Despite $8.80 in our pockets, it seemed time to look for dirty dishes. Gallup has almost as many motels and cabin courts as it has Indians and almost half of these hostelries have restaurants. I checked a baker's dozen before I found one that needed a dishwasher.

Fourteen days later we were in Oklahoma City. If you think that is slow time, you are correct; it is less than fifty miles a day. But plenty had happened and I was feeling decidedly paranoid—world change after world change and always timed to cause me maximum trouble.

Ever seen a cat play with a mouse? The mouse never has a chance. If he has even the brains the good Lord gives a mouse, he knows that. Nevertheless the mouse keeps on trying . . . and is hauled back every time.

I was the mouse.

Or we were the mice, for Margrethe was with me . . . and she was all that kept me going. She didn't complain and she didn't quit. So I couldn't quit.

Example: I had figured out that, while paper money was never any good after a world change, hard money, gold and silver, would somehow be negotiable, as bullion if not as coin. So, when I got a chance to lay hands on hard money, I was stingy with it and refused to take paper money in change for hard money.

Smart boy. Alec, you're a real brain.

So on our third day in Gallup Marga and I took a nap in a room paid for by dishwashing (me) and by cleaning rooms (Margrethe). We didn't intend to go to sleep; we simply wanted to rest a bit before eating; it had been a long, hard day. We lay down on top of the bedspread.

I was just getting relaxed when I realized that something hard was pressing against my spine. I roused enough to figure out that our hoarded silver dollars had slipped out of my side pocket when I had turned over. So I eased my arm out from under Marga's head, retrieved the dollars, counted them, added the loose change, and placed it all on the bedside table a foot from my head, then got horizontal again, slid my arm under Marga's head and fell right to sleep.

When I woke up it was pitch dark.

I came wide awake. Margrethe was still snoring softly on my arm. I shook her a little "Honey. Wake up."

"Mrrrf?"

"It's late. We may have missed dinner."

She came quickly awake. "Can you switch on the bed lamp?"

I fumbled at the bedside table, nearly fell out of bed. "Can't find the pesky thing. It's dark as the inside of a pile of coal. Wait a sec, I'll get the overhead light."

I got cautiously off the bed, headed for the door, stumbled over a chair, could not find the door—groped for it, did find it, groped some more and found a light switch by it. The overhead light came on.

For a long, dismal moment neither of us said anything. Then I said, inanely and unnecessarily, "They did it again."

The room had the characterless anonymity of any cheap motel room anywhere. Nevertheless it was different in details from the room in which we had gone to sleep.

And our hoarded silver dollars were gone.

Everything but the clothes we were wearing was gone—knapsack, clean socks, spare underwear, comb, safety razor, everything. I inspected, made certain.

"Well, Marga, what now?"

"Whatever you say, sir."

"Mmm. I don't think they'll know me in the kitchen. But they still might let me wash dishes."

"Or they may need a waitress."

The door had a spring lock and I had no key, so I left it an inch ajar. The door led directly outdoors and looked across a parking court at the office—a corner room with a lighted sign reading OFFICE—all commonplace except that it did not match the appearance of the motel in which we had been working. In that establishment the manager's office had been in the front end of a central building, the rest of that central building being the coffee shop.

Yes, we had missed dinner.

And breakfast. This motel did not have a coffee shop.

"Well, Marga?"

"Which way is Kansas?"

"That way . . . I think. But we have two choices. We can go back into the room, go to bed properly, and sleep until daylight. Or we can get out there on the highway and try to thumb a ride. In the dark."

"Alec, I see only *one* choice. If we go back inside and go to bed, we'll get up at daylight, some hours hungrier and no better off. Maybe worse off, if they catch us sleeping in a room we didn't pay for—"

"I washed an awful lot of dishes!"

"Not here, you didn't. Here they might send for the police."

We started walking.

That was typical of the persecution we suffered in trying to get to Kansas. Yes, I said "persecution." If paranoia consists in believing that the world around you is a conspiracy against you, I had become paranoid. But it was either a "sane" paranoia (if you will pardon the Irishism), or I was suffering from delusions so monumental that I should be locked up and treated.

Maybe so. If so, Margrethe was part of my delusions—an answer I could not accept. It could not be *folie à deux;* Margrethe was sane in any world.

It was the middle of the day before we got anything to eat, and by then I was beginning to see ghosts where a healthy man would see only dust devils. My hat had gone where the woodbine twineth and the New Mexico sun on my head was not helping my state.

A carload of men from a construction site picked us up and took us into Grants, and bought us lunch before they left us there. I may be certifiably insane but I am not stupid; we owe that ride and that meal to the fact that Margrethe in shorts indecently tight is a sight that attracts the attention of men. That gave me plenty to think about while I enjoyed (and I did enjoy it!) that lunch they bought us. But I kept my ruminations to myself.

After they left us I said, "East?"

"Yes, sir. But first I would like to check the public library. If there is one."

"Oh, yes! Surely." Earlier, in the world of our friend Steve, the lack of any sort of air travel had caused me to suspect that Steve's world might be the world where Margrethe was born (and therefore the home of "Alec Graham" as well). In Gallup we had checked on this at the public library—I had looked up American history in an encyclopedia while Marga checked on Danish history. It took us each about five minutes to determine that Steve's world was not the world Marga was born in. I found that Bryan had been elected in 1896 but had died in office, succeeded by his vice president, Arthur Sewall—and that was all I needed to know; I then simply raced through presidents and wars I had never heard of.

Margrethe had finished her line of investigation with her nose twitching with indignation. Once outside where we didn't have to whisper I asked her what was troubling her. "This isn't your world, dear; I made sure of that."

"It certainly isn't!"

"But we didn't have anything but a negative to go on. There may be many worlds that have no aeronautics of any sort."

"I'm glad this isn't my world! Alec, in this world *Denmark is part of Sweden*. Isn't that terrible?"

Truthfully I did not understand her upset. Both countries are Scandinavian, pretty much alike—or so it seemed to me. "I'm sorry, dear. I don't know much about such things." (I had been to Stockholm once, liked the place. It didn't seem a good time to tell her so.)

"And that silly book says that Stockholm is the capital and that Carl Sixteenth is king. Alec, he isn't even royal! And now they tell me he's *my* king!"

"But, sweetheart, he's not your king. This isn't even your world."

"I know. Alec? If we have to settle here—if the world doesn't change again—couldn't I be naturalized?"

"Why, yes. I suppose so."

She sighed. "I don't want to be a Swede."

I kept quiet. There were some things I couldn't help her with.

So in Grants we again went to a public library to see what the latest changes had done to the world. Since we had seen no *aeroplanos* and no dirigibles, again it was possible that we were in Margrethe's world. This time I looked first under "Aeronautics"—did not find dirigibles but did find flying machines . . . invented by Dr. Alberto Santos-Dumont of Brazil early in this century—and I was bemused by the inventor's name, as, in my world, he had been a pioneer in dirigibles second only to Count von Zeppelin. Apparently the doctor's aerodynes were primitive compared with jet planes, or even *aeroplanos;* they seemed to be curiosities rather than commercial vehicles. I dropped it and turned to American history, checking first on William Jennings Bryan.

I couldn't find him at all. Well, I had known that this was not my world.

But Marga was all smiles, could hardly wait to get outside the no-talking area to tell me about it. "In this world Scandinavia is all one big country . . . and København is its capital!"

"Well, good!"

"Queen Margrethe's son Prince Frederik was crowned King Eric Gustav—no doubt to please the outlanders. But he is true Danish royalty and a Dane right down to his skull bone. This is as it should be!"

I tried to show her that I was happy, too. Without a cent between us, with no idea where we would sleep that night, she was delighted as a child at Christmas . . . over an event that I could not see mattered at all.

Two short rides got us into Albuquerque and I decided that it was prudent to stay there a bit—it's a big place—even if we had to throw ourselves on Salvation Army charity. But I quickly found a job as a dishwasher in the coffee shop of the local Holiday Inn and Margrethe went to work as a waitress in the same shop.

We had been working there less than two hours when she came back to the scullery and slid something into my hip pocket while I was bent over a sink. "A present for you, dear!"

I turned around. "Hi, Gorgeous." I checked my pocket—a safety razor of the travel sort—handle unscrews, and razor and handle and blades all fit into a waterproof case smaller than a pocket Testament, and intended to be carried in a pocket. "Steal it?"

"Not quite. Tips. Got it at the lobby notions stand. Dear, at your first break I want you to shave."

"Let me clue you, doll. You get hired for your looks. I get hired for my strong back, weak mind, and docile disposition. They don't care how I look."

"But I do."

"Your slightest wish is my command. Now get out of here; you're slowing up production."

That night Margrethe explained why she had bought me a razor ahead of anything else. "Dear, it's not just because I like your face smooth and your hair short—although I do! These Loki tricks have kept on and each time we have to find work at once just to eat. You say that nobody cares how a dishwasher looks . . . but I say looking clean and neat helps in getting hired for *any* job, and can't possibly hurt.

"But there is another reason. As a result of these changes, you've had to let your whiskers grow once, twice—I can count five times, once for over three days.

Dearest, when you are freshly shaved, you stand tall and look happy. And that makes me happy."

Margrethe made for me a sort of money belt—actually a cloth pocket and a piece of cloth tape—which she wanted me to wear in bed. "Dear, we've lost anything we didn't have on us whenever a shift took place. I want you to put your razor and our hard money into this when you undress for bed."

"I don't think we can outwit Satan that easily."

"Maybe not. We can try. We come through each change with the clothes we are wearing at the time and with whatever we have in our pockets. This seems to fit the rules."

"Chaos does not have rules."

"Perhaps this is not chaos. Alec, if you won't wear this to bed, do you mind if I do?"

"Oh, I'll wear it. It won't stop Satan if he really wants to take it away from us. Nor does it really worry me. Once he dumped us mother naked into the Pacific and we pulled out of it—remember? What *does* worry me is— Marga, have you noticed that every time we have gone through a change we've been holding each other? At least holding hands?"

"I've noticed."

"Change happens in the blink of an eye. What happens if we're not together, holding each other? At least touching? Tell me."

She kept quiet so long that I knew she did not intend to answer.

"Uh huh," I said. "Me, too. But we *can't* be Siamese twins, touching all the time. We have to work. My darling, my life, Satan or Loki or whatever bad spirit is doing this to us, can separate us forever simply by picking any instant when we are not touching."

"Alec."

"Yes, my love?"

"Loki has been able to do this to us at any moment for a long time. It has not happened."

"So it may happen the next second."

"Yes. But it may not happen at all."

We moved on, and suffered more changes. Margrethe's precautions did seem to work—although in one change they seemed to work almost too well; I barely missed a jail sentence for unlawful possession of silver coins. But a quick change (the quickest we had seen) got rid of the charge, the evidence, and the complaining witness. We found ourselves in a strange courtroom and were quickly evicted for lacking tickets entitling us to remain there.

But the razor stayed with me; no cop or sheriff or marshal seemed to want to confiscate that.

We were moving on by our usual method (my thumb and Margrethe's lovely legs; I had long since admitted to myself that I might as well enjoy the inevitable) and had been dropped in a pretty part of—Texas, it must have been—by a trucker who had turned north off 66 on a side road.

We had come out of the desert into low green hills. It was a beautiful day but we were tired, hungry, sweaty, and dirty, for our persecutors—Satan or whoever—had outdone themselves: three changes in thirty-six hours.

In one day I had had two dishwashing jobs in the

same town at the same address . . . and had collected nothing. It is difficult to collect from The Lonesome Cowboy Steak House when it turns into Vivian's Grill in front of your eyes. The same was true three hours later when Vivian's Grill melted into a used-car lot. The only thing good about these shocks was that by great good fortune (or conspiracy?) Margrethe was with me each time—in one case she had come to get me and was waiting with me while my boss was figuring my time, in the other she had been working with me.

The third change did us out of a night's lodging that had already been paid for in kind by Margrethe's labor.

So when that trucker dropped us, we were tired and hungry and dirty and my paranoia had reached a new high.

We had been walking a few hundred yards when we came to a sweet little stream, a sight in Texas precious beyond all else.

We stopped on the culvert bridging it. "Margrethe, how would you like to wade in that?"

"Darling, I'm going to do more than wade in it, I'm going to bathe in it."

"Hmm— Yes, go under the fence, along the stream about fifty, seventy-five yards, and I don't think anyone could see us from the road."

"Sweetheart, they can line up and cheer if they want to; I'm going to have a bath. And— That water looks clean. Would it be safe to drink?"

"The upstream side? Certainly. We've taken worse chances every day since the iceberg. Now if we had something to eat— Say, your hot fudge sundae. Or would you prefer scrambled eggs?" I held up the lower wire of the fence to let her crawl under.

"Will you settle for an Oh Henry bar?"

"Make that a Milky Way," I answered, "if I have my druthers."

"I'm afraid you don't, dear. An Oh Henry bar is all there is." She held the wire for me.

"Maybe we'd better stop talking about food we don't have," I said, and crawled under—straightened up and added, "I'm ready to eat raw skunk."

"Food we do have, dear man. I have an Oh Henry in my tote."

I stopped abruptly. "Woman, if you're joking, I'm going to beat you."

"I'm not joking."

"In Texas it is legal to correct a wife with a stick not thicker than one's thumb." I held up my thumb. "Do you see one about this size?"

"I'll find one."

"Where did you get a candy bar?"

"That roadside stop where Mr. Facelli treated us to coffee and doughnuts."

Mr. Facelli had been our middle-of-the-night ride just before the truck that had just dropped us. Two small cake doughnuts each and the sugar and cream for coffee had been our only calories for twenty-four hours.

"The beating can wait. Woman, if you stole it, tell me about it later. You really do have a real live Oh Henry? Or am I getting feverish?"

"Alec, do you think I would steal a candy bar? I bought it from a coin machine while you and Mr. Facelli were in the men's room after we ate."

"How? We don't have any money. Not from this world."

"Yes, Alec. But there was a dime in my tote, from

two changes back. Of course it was not a good dime, strictly speaking. But I couldn't see any real harm if the machine would take it. And it did. But I put it out of sight before you two got back . . . because I didn't have three dimes and could not offer a candy bar to Mr. Facelli." She added anxiously, "Do you think I cheated? Using that dime?"

"It's a technicality I won't go into . . . as long as I get to share in the proceeds of the crime. And that makes me equally guilty. Uh . . . eat first, or bathe first?"

We ate first, a picnic banquet washed down by delicious creek water. Then we bathed, with much splashing and laughing—I remember it as one of the happiest times of my life. Margrethe had soap in her tote bag, too, and I supplied the towel, my shirt. First I wiped Margrethe with it, then I wiped me with it. The dry, warm air finished the job.

What happened immediately after was inevitable. I had never in my life made love outdoors, much less in bright daylight. If anyone had asked me, I would have said that for me it would be a psychological impossibility; I would be too inhibited, too aware of the indecency involved.

I am amazed and happy to say that, while keenly aware of the circumstances, I was untroubled at the time and quite able . . . perhaps because of Margrethe's bubbling, infectious enthusiasm.

I have never slept naked on grass before, either. I think we slept about an hour.

When we woke up, Margrethe insisted on shaving me. I could not shave myself very well as I had no mirror, but she could and did, with her usual efficiency. We stood knee-deep in the water; I worked up soapsuds with my hands and slathered my face. She shaved and I renewed the lather as needed.

"There," she said at last, and gave me a sign-off kiss, "you'll do. Rinse off now and don't forget your ears. I'll find the towel. Your shirt." She climbed onto the bank while I leaned far over and splashed water on my face.

"Alec—"

"I can't hear you; the water's running."

"Please, dear!"

I straightened up, wiped the water out of my eyes, looked around.

Everything we owned was gone, everything but my razor.

XVII

*Behold, I go forward, but he is not there;
and backward, but I cannot perceive him: On the
left hand, where he doth work, but I cannot
behold him: he hideth himself on the right hand,
that I cannot see him.*

Job 23:8–10

Margrethe said, "What did you do with the soap?"

I took a deep breath, sighed it out. "Did I hear you correctly? You're asking what I did with the soap?"

"What would you rather I said?"

"Uh— I don't know. But not that. A miracle takes place . . . and you ask me about a bar of soap."

"Alec, a miracle that takes place again and again and again is no longer a miracle; it's just a nuisance. Too many, too much. I want to scream or break into tears. So I asked about the soap."

I had been halfway to hysteria myself when Margrethe's statement hit me like a dash of cold water. Margrethe? She who took icebergs and earthquakes in her stride, she who never whimpered in adversity . . . *she* wanted to scream?

"I'm sorry, dear. I had the soap in my hands when you were shaving me. I did not have it in my hands when I rinsed my face. I suppose I laid it on the bank. But I don't recall. Does it matter?"

"Not really, I suppose. Although that cake of Camay, used just once, would be half our worldly goods if I could find it, this razor being the other half. You may have placed it on the bank, but I don't see it."

"Then it's gone. Marga, we've got urgent things to worry about before we'll be dirty enough to need soap again. Food, clothing, shelter." I scrambled up onto the bank. "Shoes. We don't even have *shoes*. What do we do now? I'm stumped. If I had a wailing wall, I'd wail."

"Steady, dear, steady."

"Is it all right if I just whimper a little?"

She came close, put her arms around me, and kissed me. "Whimper all you want to, dear, whimper for both of us. Then let's decide what to do."

I can't stay depressed with Margrethe's arms around me. "Do you have any ideas? I can't think of anything but picking our way back to the highway and trying to thumb a ride . . . which doesn't appeal to me in the state I'm in. Not even a fig leaf. Do you see a fig tree?"

"Does Texas have fig trees?"

"Texas has everything. What do we do now?"

"We go back to the highway and start walking."

"Barefooted? Why not stand still and wave our thumbs? We can't go far enough barefooted to matter. My feet are tender."

"They'll toughen up. Alec, we *must* keep moving. For our morale, love. If we give up, we'll die. I know it."

Ten minutes later we were moving slowly east on the highway. But it was not the highway we had left. This one was four lanes instead of two, with wide paved shoulders. The fence marking the right of way, instead of three strands of barbed wire, was chain-link steel as high as my head. We would have had a terrible time reaching the highway had it not been for the stream. By going back into the water and holding our breaths, we managed to slither under the fence. This left us sopping wet again (and no towel-shirt) but the warm air corrected that in a few minutes.

There was much more traffic on this highway than there had been on the one we had left, both freight and what seemed to be passenger cars. And it was *fast*. How fast I could not guess, but it seemed at least twice as fast as any ground transportation I had ever seen. Perhaps as fast as transoceanic dirigibles.

There were big vehicles that had to be freight movers but looked more like railroad boxcars than they looked like lorries. And even longer than boxcars. But as I stared I figured out that each one was at least three cars, articulated. I figured this out by attempting to count wheels. Sixteen per car? Six more on some sort of locomotive up front, for a total of fifty-four wheels. Was this possible?

These behemoths moved with no sound but the noise of air rushing past them, plus a whoosh of tires against pavement. My dynamics professor would have approved.

In the lane nearest us were smaller vehicles that I assumed to be passenger cars, although I could not see anyone inside. Where one would expect windows appeared to be mirrors or burnished steel. They were long and low and as sleekly shaped as an airship.

And now I saw that this was not *one* highway, but *two*. All the traffic on the pavement nearest us was going east; at least a hundred yards away another stream of traffic was going west. Still farther away, seen only in glimpses, was a limit fence for the northern side of the widest right of way I have ever seen.

We trudged along on the edge of the shoulder. I began to feel gloomy about the chances of being picked up. Even if they could see us (which seemed uncertain), how could they stop quickly enough to pick up someone on the highway? Nevertheless I waved the hitchhikers' sign at each car.

I kept my misgivings to myself. After we had been walking a dismal time, a car that had just passed us dropped out of the traffic lane onto the shoulder, stopped at least a quarter mile ahead of us, then backed toward us at a speed I would regard as too fast if I were going forward. We got hastily off the shoulder.

It stopped alongside us. A mirrored section a yard wide and at least that high lifted up like a storm-cellar door, and I found myself looking into the passenger compartment. The operator looked out at us and grinned. "I don't believe it!"

I tried to grin back. "I don't believe it myself. But here we are. Will you give us a ride?"

"Could be." He looked Margrethe up and down. "My, aren't you the purty thing! What happened?"

Margrethe answered, "Sir, we are lost."

"Looks like. But how did you manage to lose your clothes, too? Kidnapped? Or what? Never mind, that can wait. I'm Jerry Farnsworth."

I answered, "We're Alec and Margrethe Graham."

"Good to meet you. Well, you don't look armed— except for that thing in your hand, Miz Graham. What is it?"

She held it out to him. "A razor."

He accepted it, looked at it, handed it back.

"Durned if it isn't. Haven't seen one like that since I was too young to shave. Well, I don't see how you can highjack me with that. Climb in. Alec, you can have the back seat; your sister can sit up here with me." Another section of the shell swung upward.

"Thank you," I answered, thinking sourly about beggars and choosers. "Marga is not my sister, she's my wife."

"Lucky man! Do you object to your wife riding with me?"

"Oh, of course not!"

"I think that answer would cause a tension meter to jingle. Dear, you'd better get back there with your husband."

"Sir, you invited me to sit with you and my husband voiced his approval." Margrethe slipped into the forward passenger seat. I opened my mouth and closed it, having found I had nothing to say. I climbed into the back seat, discovered that the car was bigger inside than out; the seat was roomy and comfortable. The doors closed down; the "mirrors" now were windows.

"I'm about to put her back into the flow," our host said, "so don't fight the safeties. Sometimes this buggy bucks like a Brahma bull, six gees or better. No, wait a sec. Where are you two going?" He looked at Margrethe.

"We're going to Kansas, Mr. Farnsworth."

"Call me Jerry, dear. In your skin?"

"We have no clothing, sir. We lost it."

I added, "Mr. Farnsworth—Jerry—we're in a distressed state. We lost everything. Yes, we are going to Kansas, but first we must find clothes somewhere—Red Cross, maybe, I don't know. And I've got to find a job and make us some money. Then we'll go to Kansas."

"I see. I think I do. Some of it. How are you going to get to Kansas?"

"I had in mind continuing straight on to Oklahoma City, then north. Stick to the main highways. Since we're hitchhiking."

"Alec, you really are lost. See that fence? Do you know the penalty for a pedestrian caught inside that fence?"

"No, I don't."

"Ignorance is bliss. You'll be much better off on the small side roads where hitching is still legal, or at least tolerated. If you're for Oke City, I can help you along. Hang on." He did something at controls in front of him. He didn't touch the wheel because there wasn't any wheel to touch. Instead there were two hand grips.

The car vibrated faintly, then jumped sideways. I felt as if I had fallen into soft mush and my skin tingled as with static electricity. The car bucked like a small boat in a heavy sea, but that "soft mush" kept me from being battered about. Suddenly it quieted down and only that faint vibration continued. The landscape was streaking past.

"Now," said Mr. Farnsworth, "tell me about it."

"Margrethe?"

"Of course, dearest. You must."

"Jerry . . . we're from another world."

"Oh, no!" He groaned. "Not another flying saucer! That makes four this week. That's your story?"

"No, no. I've never seen a flying saucer. We're from earth, but . . . different. We were hitchhiking on Highway Sixty-Six, trying to reach Kansas—"

"Wait a minute. You said, 'Sixty-Six.'"

"Yes, of course."

"That's what they used to call this road before they

rebuilt it. But it hasn't been called anything but Interstate Forty for, oh, over forty years, maybe fifty. Hey. *Time* travelers! Are you?"

"What year is this?" I asked.

"Nineteen-ninety-four."

"That's our year, too. Wednesday the eighteenth of May. Or was this morning. Before the change."

"It still is. But— Look, let's quit jumping around. Start at the beginning, whenever that was, and tell me how you wound up inside the fence, bare naked."

So I told him.

Presently he said, "That fire pit. Didn't burn you?"

"One small blister."

"Just a blister. I reckon you would be safe in Hell."

"Look, Jerry, they really do walk on live coals."

"I know, I've seen it. In New Guinea. Never hankered to try it. That iceberg— Something bothers me. How does an iceberg crash into the *side* of a vessel? An iceberg is dead in the water, always. Certainly a ship can bump into one but damage should be to the *bow*. Right?"

"Margrethe?"

"I don't know, Alec. What Jerry says sounds right. But it *did* happen."

"Jerry, I don't know either. We were in a forward stateroom; maybe the whole front end was crushed in. But, if Marga doesn't know, I surely do not, as I got banged on the head and went out like a light. Marga kept me afloat—I told you."

Farnsworth looked thoughtfully at me. He had swiveled his seat around to face both of us while I talked, and he had showed Margrethe how to unlock her chair so that it would turn, also, which brought us three into an intimate circle of conversation, knees almost touching—and left him with his back to the traffic. "Alec, what became of this Hergensheimer?"

"Maybe I didn't make that clear—it's not too clear to me, either. It's *Graham* who is missing. *I* am Hergensheimer. When I walked through the fire and found myself in a different world, I found myself in Graham's place, as I said. Everybody called me Graham and seemed to think that I *was* Graham—and Graham was missing. I guess you could say I took the easy way out . . . but there I was, thousands of miles from home, no money, no ticket, and nobody had ever heard of Alexander Hergensheimer." I shrugged and spread my hands helplessly. "I sinned. I wore his clothes, I ate at his table, I answered to his name."

"I still don't get the skinny of this. Maybe you look enough like Graham to fool almost anyone . . . but your wife would know the difference. Margie?"

Margrethe looked into my eyes with sadness and love, and answered steadily, "Jerry, my husband is confused. A strange amnesia. He is Alec Graham. There is no Alexander Hergensheimer. There never was."

I was left speechless. True, Margrethe and I had not discussed this matter for many weeks; true, she had never flatly admitted that I was not Alec Graham. I was learning again (again and again!) that one never won an argument with Margrethe. Any time I thought I had won, it always turned out that she had simply shut up.

Farnsworth said to me, "Maybe that knock in the head, Alec?"

"Look, that knock in the head was nothing—a few minutes unconsciousness, nothing more. And no gaps in my memory. Anyhow it happened two weeks *after* the fire walk. Jerry, my wife is a wonderful woman . . . but I *must* disagree with her on this. She wants to believe that I am Alec Graham because she fell in love with Graham before she ever met me. She believes it because she needs to believe it. But of course I know who I am: Hergensheimer. I admit that amnesia can have some funny effects . . . but there was one clue that I could not have faked, one that said emphatically that I, Alexander Hergensheimer, was not Alec Graham."

I slapped my stomach, where a bay window had been. "Here is the proof: I wore Graham's clothes, I told you. But his clothes did not fit me perfectly. At the time of the fire walk I was rather plump, too heavy, carrying a lot of flab right here." I slapped my stomach again. "Graham's clothes were too tight around the middle for me. I had to suck in hard and hold my breath to fasten the waistband on any pair of his trousers. That could not happen in the blink of an eye, while walking through a fire pit. Nor did it. Two weeks of rich food in a cruise ship gave me that bay window . . . and it proves that I am not Alec Graham."

Margrethe not only kept quiet, her expression said nothing. But Farnsworth insisted. "Margie?"

"Alec, you were having exactly that trouble with your clothes *before* the fire walk. For the same reason. Too much rich food." She smiled. "I'm sorry to contradict you, my beloved . . . but I'm awfully glad you're you."

Jerry said, "Alec, many is the man who would walk through fire to get a woman to look at him that way just once. When you get to Kansas, you had better go see the Menningers; you've got to get that amnesia untangled. Nobody can fool a woman about her husband. When she's lived with him, slept with him, given him enemas and listened to his jokes, a substitution is impossible no matter how much the ringer may look like him. Even an identical twin could not do it. There are all those little things a wife knows and the public never sees."

I said, "Marga, it's up to you."

She answered, "Jerry, my husband is saying that I must refute that—in part—myself. At that time I did not know Alec as well as a wife knows her husband. I was not his wife then; I was his lover—and I had been such only a few days." She smiled. "But you're right in essence; I recognized him."

Farnsworth frowned. "I'm getting mixed up again. We're talking about either one man or two. This Alexander Hergensheimer— Alec, tell me about him."

"I'm a Protestant preacher, Jerry, ordained in the Brothers of the Apocalypse Christian Church of the One Truth—the Apocalypse Brethren as you hear us referred to. I was born on my grandfather's farm outside Wichita on May twenty-second—"

"Hey, you've got a birthday this week!" Jerry remarked. Marga looked alert.

"So I have. I've been too busy to think about it. —in nineteen-sixty. My parents and grandparents are dead; my oldest brother is still working the family farm—"

"That's why you're going to Kansas? To find your brother?"

"No. That farm is in another world, the one I grew up in."

"Then why are you going to Kansas?"

I was slow in answering. "I don't have a logical answer. Perhaps it's the homing instinct. Or it may be something like horses running back into a burning barn. I don't know, Jerry. But I have to go back and try to find my roots."

"That's a reason I can understand. Go on."

I told him about my schooling, not hiding the fact that I had failed to make it in engineering—my switch to the seminary and my ordination on graduation, then my association with C.U.D. I did not mention Abigail, I did not mention that I hadn't been too successful as a parson largely (in my private opinion) because Abigail did not like people and my parishioners did not like Abigail. Impossible to put all details into a short biography—but the fact is that I could not mention Abigail at all without throwing doubt on the legitimacy of Margrethe's status . . . and this I could not do.

"That's about it. If we were in my native world, you could phone C.U.D. national headquarters in Kansas City, Kansas, and check on me. We had had a successful year and I was on vacation. I took a dirigible, the *Count von Zeppelin* of North American Airlines, from Kansas City airport to San Francisco, to Hilo, to Tahiti, and there I joined the Motor Vessel *Konge Knut* and that about brings us up to date, as I've told you the rest."

"You sound kosher, you talk a good game—are you born again?"

"Certainly! I'm afraid I'm not in a state of grace now . . . but I'm working on it. We're in the Last Days, brother; it's urgent. Are *you* born again?"

"Discuss it later. What's the second law of thermodynamics?"

I made a wry face. "Entropy always increases. That's the one that tripped me."

"Now tell me about Alec Graham."

"Not much I can tell. His passport showed that he

was born in Texas, and he gave a law firm in Dallas as an address. For the rest you had better ask Margrethe; she knew him, I didn't." (I did not mention an embarrassing million dollars. I could not explain it, so I left it out . . . and Marga had only my word for it; she had never seen it.)

"Margie? Can you fill us in on Alec Graham?"

She was slow in answering. "I'm afraid I can't add anything to what my husband has told you."

"Hey! You're letting me down. Your husband gave a detailed description of Dr. Jekyll; can't you describe Mr. Hyde? So far, he's a zero. A mail drop in Dallas, nothing more."

"Mr. Farnsworth, I'm sure you've never been a shipboard stewardess—"

"Nope, I haven't. But I was a room steward in a cargo liner—two trips when I was a kid."

"Then you'll understand. A stewardess knows many things about her passengers. She knows how often they bathe. She knows how often they change their clothes. She knows how they smell—and everyone does smell, some good, some bad. She knows what sort of books they read—or don't read. Most of all she knows whether or not they are truly gentlefolk, honest, generous, considerate, warmhearted. She knows everything one could need to know to judge a person. Yet she may not know a passenger's occupation, home town, schooling, or any of those details that a friend would know.

"Before the day of the fire walk I had been Alec Graham's stewardess for four weeks. For the last two of those weeks I was his mistress and was ecstatically in love with him. After the fire walk it was many days before his amnesia let us resume our happy relationship—and then it did, and I was happy again. And now I have been his wife for four months—months of some adversity but the happiest time of my whole life. And it still is and I think it always will be. And that is all I know about my husband Alec Graham." She smiled at me and her eyes were brimming with tears, and I found that mine were, too.

Jerry sighed and shook his head. "This calls for a Solomon. Which I am not. I believe both your stories—and one of them can't be correct. Never mind. My wife and I practice Muslim hospitality, something I learned in the late war. Will you accept our hospitality for a night or two? You had better say yes."

Marga glanced at me; I said, "Yes!"

"Good. Now to see if the boss is at home." He swiveled around to face forward, touched something. A few moments later a light came on and something went *beep!* once. His face lighted up and he spoke: "Duchess, this is your favorite husband."

"Oh, Ronny, it's been so *long.*"

"No, no. Try again."

"Albert? Tony? George, Andy, Jim—"

"Once more and get it right; I have company with me."

"Yes, Jerry?"

"Company for dinner and overnight and possibly more."

"Yes, my love. How many and what sexes and when will you be home?"

"Let me ask Hubert." Again he touched something. "Hubert says twenty-seven minutes. Two guests. The one seated by me is about twenty-three, give or take a bit, blonde, long, wavy hair, dark blue eyes, height about five seven, mass about one twenty, other basics I have not checked but about those of our daughter. Female. I am certain she is female as she is not wearing so much as a G-string."

"Yes, dear. I'll scratch her eyes out. After I've fed her, of course."

"Good. But she's no menace as her husband is with her and is watching her closely. Did I say that he is naked, too?"

"You did not. Interesting."

"Do you want his basic statistic? If so, do you want it relaxed or at attention?"

"My love, you are a dirty old man, I am happy to say. Quit trying to embarrass your guests."

"There is madness in my method, Duchess. They are naked because they have no clothes at all. Yet I suspect that they do embarrass easily. So please meet us at the gate with clothing. You have her statistics, except—Margie, hand me a foot." Marga promptly put a foot up high, without comment. He felt it. "A pair of your sandals will fit, I think. Zapatos for him. Of mine."

"His other sizes? Never mind the jokes."

"He's about my height and shoulders, but I am twenty pounds heavier, at least. So something from my skinny rack. If Sybil has a houseful of her junior barbarians, please use extreme prejudice to keep them away from the gate. These are gentle people; we'll introduce them after they have a chance to dress."

"Roger Wilco, Sergeant Bilko. But it is time that you introduced them to *me*."

"*Mea culpa*. My love, this is Margrethe Graham, Mrs. Alec Graham."

"Hello, Margrethe, welcome to our home."

"Thank you, Mrs. Farnsworth—"

"Katherine, dear. Or Kate."

"'Katherine.' I can't tell you how much you are doing for us . . . when we were so miserable!" My darling started to cry.

She stopped it abruptly. "And this is my husband, Alec Graham."

"Howdy, Mrs. Farnsworth. And thank you."

"Alec, you bring that girl straight here. I want to welcome her. Both of you."

Jerry cut in. "Hubert says twenty-two minutes, Duchess."

"*Hasta la vista.* Sign off and let me get busy."

"End." Jerry turned his seat around. "Kate will find you a pretty to wear, Margie . . . although in your case there ought to be a law. Say, are you cold? I've been yacking so much I didn't think of it. I keep this buggy cool enough for me, in clothes. But Hubert can change it to suit."

"I am a Viking, Jerry; I never get cold. Most rooms are too warm to suit me."

"How about you, Alec?"

"I'm warm enough," I answered, fibbing only a little.

"I believe—" Jerry started to say—

—as the heavens opened with the most brilliant light imaginable, outshining day, and I was gripped by sudden grief, knowing that I failed to lead my beloved back to grace.

XVIII

Then Satan answered the Lord, and said,
Doth Job fear God for nought?
Job 1:7

Canst thou by searching find out God? canst thou
find out the Almighty unto perfection?
Job 11:7

I waited for the Shout.

My feelings were mixed. Did I want the Rapture? Was I ready to be snatched up into the loving arms of Jesus? Yes, dear Lord. Yes! Without Margrethe? No, no! Then you choose to be cast down into the Pit? Yes—no, but— Make up your mind!

Mr. Farnsworth looked up. "See that baby go!"

I looked up through the roof of the car. There was a second sun directly overhead. It seemed to shrink and lose brilliance as I watched it.

Our host went on, "Right on time! Yesterday we had a hold, missed the window, and had to reslot. When you're sitting on the pad, and single-H is boiling away, even a hold for one orbit can kill your profit margin. And yesterday wasn't even a glitch; it was a totally worthless recheck ordered by a Nasa fatbottom. Figures."

He seemed to be talking English.

Margrethe said breathlessly, "Mr. Farnsworth—Jerry—what was it?"

"Eh? Never seen a lift-off before?"

"I don't know what a lift-off is."

"Mm . . . yes. Margie, the fact that you and Alec are from another world—or worlds—hasn't really soaked through my skull yet. Your world doesn't have space travel?"

"I'm not sure what you mean but I don't think we do."

I was fairly sure what he meant so I interrupted. "Jerry, you're talking about flying to the moon, aren't you? Like Jules Verne."

"Yes. Close enough."

"That was an ethership? Going to the moon? Golly Moses!" The profanity just slipped out.

"Slow down. That was not an ethership, it was an unmanned freight rocket. It is not going to Luna; it is going only as far as Leo—low Earth orbit. Then it comes back, ditches off Galveston, is ferried back to North Texas Port, where it will lift again sometime next week. But some of its cargo will go on to Luna City or Tycho Under—and some may go as far as the Asteroids. Clear?"

"Uh . . . not quite."

"Well, in Kennedy's second term—"

"Who?"

"John F. Kennedy. President. Sixty-one to sixty-nine."

"I'm sorry. I'm going to have to relearn history again. Jerry, the most confusing thing about being bounced around among worlds is not new technology, such as television or jet planes—or even space-travel ships. It is different history."

"Well— When we get home, I'll find you an American history, and a history of space travel. A lot of them around the house; I'm in space up to my armpits— started with model rockets as a kid. Now, besides Diana Freight Lines, I've got a piece of Jacob's Ladder and the Beanstalk, both—just a tax loss at present but—"

I think he caught sight of my face. "Sorry. You skim through the books I'll dig out for you, then we'll talk."

Farnsworth looked back at his controls, punched something, blinked at it, punched again, and said, "Hubert says that we'll have the sound in three minutes twenty-one seconds."

When the sound did arrive, I was disappointed. I had expected a thunderclap to match that incredible light. Instead it was a rumble that went on and on, then faded away without a distinct end.

A few minutes later the car left the highway, swung right in a large circle and went under the highway through a tunnel and came out on a smaller highway. We stayed on this highway (83, I noted) about five minutes, then there was a repeated beeping sound and a flash of lights. "I hear you," Mr. Farnsworth said. "Just hold your horses." He swung his chair around and faced forward, grasped the two hand grips.

The next several minutes were interesting. I was reminded of something the Sage of Hannibal said: "If it warn't for the honor, I'd druther uv walked." Mr. Farnsworth seemed to regard any collision avoided by a measurable distance as less than sporting. Again and again that "soft mush" saved us from bruises if not broken bones. Once that signal from the machinery went *Bee-bee-bee-beep!* at him; he growled in answer: "Pipe down! You mind your business; I'll mind mine," and subjected us to another near miss.

We turned off onto a narrow road, private I concluded, as there was an arch over the entrance reading FARNSWORTH'S FOLLY. We went up a grade. At the top, lost among trees, was a high gate that snapped out of the way as we approached it.

There we met Katie Farnsworth.

If you have read this far in this memoir, you know that I am in love with my wife. That is a basic, like the speed of light, like the love of God the Father. Know ye now that I learned that I could love another person, a woman, without detracting from my love for Margrethe, without wishing to take her from her lawful mate, without lusting to possess her. Or at least not much.

In meeting her I learned that five feet two inches is the perfect height for a woman, that forty is the perfect age, and that a hundred and ten pounds is the correct weight, just as for a woman's voice contralto is the right register. That my own beloved darling is none of these is irrelevant; Katie Farnsworth makes them perfect for *her* by being herself content with what *she* is.

But she startled me first by the most graceful gesture of warm hospitality I have ever encountered.

She knew from her husband that we were utterly without clothes; she knew also from him that he felt that we were embarrassed by our state. So she had fetched clothing for each of us.

And she herself was naked.

No, that's not right; I was naked, she was unclothed. That's not quite right, either. Nude? Bare? Stripped? Undressed? No, she was dressed in her own beauty, like Mother Eve before the Fall. She made it seem so utterly appropriate that I wondered how I had ever acquired the delusion that freedom from clothing equals obscenity.

Those clamshell doors lifted; I got out and handed Margrethe out. Mrs. Farnsworth dropped what she was carrying, put her arms around Margrethe and kissed her. "Margrethe! Welcome, dear."

My darling hugged her back and sniffled again.

Then she offered me her hand. "Welcome to you, too, Mr. Graham. Alec." I took her hand, did not shake it. Instead I handled it like rare china and bowed over it. I felt that I should kiss it but I had never learned how.

For Margrethe she had a summer dress the shade of Marga's eyes. Its styling suggested the Arcadia of myth; one could imagine a wood nymph wearing it. It hung on the left shoulder, was open all the way down on the right but wrapped around with generous overlap. Both sides of this simple garment ended in a long sash ribbon; the end that went under passed through a slot, which permitted both ends to go all the way around Marga's waist, then to tie at her right side.

It occurred to me that this was a fit-anyone dress. It would be tight or loose on any figure depending on how it was tied.

Katie had sandals for Marga in blue to match her dress. For me she had Mexican sandals, zapatos, of the cut-leather openwork sort that are almost as fit-anyone as that dress, simply by how they are tied. She offered me trousers and shirt that were superficially equivalent to those I had bought in Winslow at the SECOND WIND—but these were tailormade of summer-weight wool rather than mass-produced from cheap cotton. She also had for me socks that fitted themselves to my feet and knit shorts that seemed to be my size.

When she had dressed us, there was still clothing on the grass—hers. I then realized that she had walked to the gate dressed, stripped down there, and waited for us—"dressed" as we were.

That's politeness.

Dressed, we all got into the car. Mr. Farnsworth waited a moment before starting up his driveway. "Katie, our guests are Christians."

Mrs. Farnsworth seemed delighted. "Oh, how very interesting!"

"So I thought. Alec? *Verb. sap.* Not many Christians in these parts. Feel free to speak your mind in front of Katie and me . . . but when anyone else is around, you may be more comfortable not discussing your beliefs. Understand me?"

"Uh . . . I'm afraid I don't." My head was in a whirl and I felt a ringing in my ears.

"Well . . . being a Christian isn't against the law here; Texas has freedom of religion. Nevertheless Christians aren't at all popular and Christian worship is mostly underground. Uh, if you want to get in touch with your own people, I suppose we could manage to locate a catacomb. Kate?"

"Oh, I'm sure we could find someone who knows. I can put out some feelers."

"If Alec says to, dear. Alec, you're in no danger of being stoned; this country isn't some ignorant redneck backwoods. Or not much danger. But I don't want you to be discriminated against or insulted."

Katie Farnsworth said, "Sybil."

"Oh, oh! Yes. Alec, our daughter is a good girl and as civilized as one can expect in a teenager. But she is an apprentice witch, a recent convert to the Old Religion—and, being both a convert and a teenager, dead serious about it. Sybil would not be rude to a guest—Katie brought her up properly. Besides, she knows I would skin her alive. But it would be a favor to me if you will avoid placing too much strain on her. As I'm sure you know, every teenager is a time bomb waiting to go off."

Margrethe answered for me: "We will be most careful. This 'Old Religion'—is this the worship of Odin?"

I felt a chill . . . when I was already discombobulated beyond my capacity. But our host answered, "No. Or at least I don't think so. You could ask Sybil. If you are willing to risk having your ear talked off; she'll try to convert you. Very intense."

Katie Farnsworth added, "I have never heard Sybil mention Odin. Mostly she speaks just of 'the Goddess.' Don't Druids worship Odin? Truly I don't know. I'm afraid Sybil considers us so hopelessly old-fashioned that she doesn't bother to discuss theology with us."

"And let's not discuss it now," Jerry added, and started us up the drive.

The Farnsworth mansion was long, low, and rambling, with a flavor of lazy opulence. Jerry swung us under a *porte-cochère;* we all got out. He slapped the top of his car as one might slap the neck of a horse. It moved away and turned the corner of the house as we went inside.

I'm not going to say much about their house as, while it was beautiful and Texas lavish, it would not necessarily appear any one way long enough to justify describing it; most of what we saw Jerry called "hollow grams." How can I describe them? Frozen dreams? Three-dimensional pictures? Let me put it this way: Chairs were solid. So were table tops. Anything else in that house, better touch it cautiously and find out, as it might be as beautifully *there* as a rainbow . . . and just as insubstantial.

I don't know how these ghosts were produced. I think it is possible that the laws of physics in that world were somewhat different from those of the Kansas of my youth.

Katie led us into what Jerry called their "family room" and Jerry stopped abruptly. "Bloody Hindu whorehouse!"

It was a very large room with ceilings that seemed impossibly high for a one-storey ranch house. Every wall, arch, alcove, soffit, and beam was covered with sculptured figures. But such figures! I found myself blushing. These figures had apparently been copied from that notorious temple cavern in southern India, the one that depicts every possible vice of venery in obscene and blatant detail.

Katie said, "Sorry, dear! The youngsters were dancing in here." She hurried to the left, melted into one sculpture group and disappeared. "What will you have, Gerald?"

"Uh, Remington number two."

"Right away."

Suddenly the obscene figures disappeared, the ceiling lowered abruptly and changed to a beam-and-plaster

construction, one wall became a picture window looking out at mountains that belonged in Utah (not
Texas), the wall opposite it now carried a massive stone
fireplace with a goodly fire crackling in it, the furniture
changed to the style sometimes called "mission" and
the floor changed to flagstones covered with Amerin-
dian rugs.

"That's better. Thank you, Katherine. Sit down,
friends—pick a spot and squat."

I sat down, avoiding what was obviously the "papa"
chair—massive and leather upholstered. Katie and
Marga took a couch together. Jerry sat in that papa
chair. "My love, what will you drink?"

"Campari and soda, please."

"Sissy. And you, Margie?"

"Campari and soda would suit me, too."

"Two sissies. Alec?"

"I'll go along with the ladies."

"Son, I'll tolerate that in the weaker sex. But not
from a grown man. Try again."

"Uh, Scotch and soda."

"I'd horsewhip you, if I had a horse. Podnuh, you
have just one more chance."

"Uh . . . bourbon and branch?"

"Saved yourself. Jack Daniel's with water on the
side. Other day, man in Dallas tried to order *Irish*
whisky. Rode him out o' town on a rail. Then they
apologized to him. Turned out he was a Yankee and
didn't know any better." All this time our host was
drumming with his fingertips on a small table at his
elbow. He stopped this fretful drumming and, suddenly, at the table by my chair appeared a Texas jigger
of brown liquid and a tumbler of water. I found that

the others had been served, too. Jerry raised his glass. "Save your Confederate money! *Salud!*"

We drank and he went on, "Katherine, do you know where our rapscallion is hiding?"

"I think they are all in the pool, dear."

"So." Jerry resumed that nervous drumming. Suddenly there appeared in the air in front of our host, seated on a diving board that jutted out of nowhere, a young female. She was in bright sunlight although the room we were in was in cool shadow. Drops of water sprinkled on her. She faced Jerry, which placed her back toward me. "Hi, Pipsqueak."

"Hi, Daddy. Kiss kiss."

"In a pig's eye. When was the last time I spanked you?"

"My ninth birthday. When I set fire to Aunt Minnie. What did I do now?"

"By the great golden gawdy greasy gonads of God, what do you *mean* by leaving that vulgar, bawdy, pornic program running in the family room?"

"Don't give me that static, Daddy doll; I've seen your books."

"Never mind what I have in my private library; answer my question."

"I forgot to turn it off, Daddy. I'm sorry."

"That's what the cow said to Mrs. Murphy. But the fire burned on. Look, my dear, you know you are free to use the controls to suit yourself. But when you are through, you must put the display back the way you found it. Or, if you don't know how, you must put it back to zero for the default display."

"Yes, Daddy. I just *forgot.*"

"Don't go squirming around like that; I'm not

through chewing you out. By the big brass balls of Koshchei, *where* did you get *thát* program?"

"At campus. It was an instruction tape in my tantric yoga class."

"'Tantric yoga'? Swivel hips, you don't need such a course. Does your mother know about this?"

Katherine moved in smoothly: "I urged her to take it, dear one. Sybil is talented, as we know. But raw talent is not enough; she needed tutoring."

"So? I'll never argue with your mother on this subject, so I withdraw to a previously prepared position. That tape. How did you come by it? You are familiar with the applicable laws concerning copyrighted material; we both remember the hooraw over that *Jefferson Starship* tape—"

"Daddy, you're worse than an elephant! Don't you *ever* forget anything?"

"Never, and much worse. You are warned that anything you say may be taken down in writing and held against you at another time and place. How say you?"

"I demand to see an attorney!"

"Oh, so you *did* pirate it!"

"Don't you wish I had! So you could gloat. I'm sorry, Daddy, but I paid the catalog fee, in full, in cash, and the campus library service copied it for me. So there. Smarty."

"Smarty yourself. You wasted your money."

"I don't think so. I like it."

'So do I. But you wasted your money. You should have asked *me* for it."

"*Huh!*"

"Gotcha! I thought at first you had been picking

locks in my study or working a spell on 'em. Pleased to hear that you were merely extravagant. How much?"

"Uh . . . forty-nine fifty. That's at student's discount."

"Sounds fair; I paid sixty-five. All right. But if it shows up on your semester billing, I'll deduct it from your allowance. Just one thing, sugar plum— I brought two nice people home, a lady and a gentleman. We walk into the parlor. What had been the parlor. And these two gentlefolk are faced with the entire Kama Sutra, in panting, quivering color. What do you think of that?"

"I didn't *mean* to."

"So we'll forget it. But it is never polite to shock people, especially guests, so let's be more careful next time. Will you be at dinner?"

"Yes. If I can be excused early and run, run, run. Date, Daddy."

"What time will you be home?"

"Won't. All-night gathering. Rehearsal for Midsummer Night. Thirteen covens."

He sighed. "I suppose that I should thank the Three Crones that you are on the pill."

"Pill shmill. Don't be a cube, Daddy; nobody ever gets pregnant at a Sabbat; everybody knows that."

"Everybody but me. Well, let us offer thanks that you are willing to have dinner with us." Suddenly she shrieked as she fell forward off the board. The picture followed her down.

She splashed, then came up spouting water. "Daddy! You pushed me!"

"How could you say such a thing?" he answered in

self-righteous tones. The living picture suddenly vanished.

Katie Farnsworth said conversationally, "Gerald keeps trying to dominate his daughter. Hopelessly, of course. He should take her to bed and discharge his incestuous yearnings. But they are both too prissy for that."

"Woman, remind me to beat you."

"Yes, dearest. You wouldn't have to force her. Make your intentions plain and she will burst into tears and surrender. Then both of you will have the best time of your lives. Wouldn't you say so, Margrethe?"

"I would say so."

By then I was too numb to be shocked by Margrethe's words.

Dinner was a gourmet's delight and a social confusion. It was served in the formal dining hall, i.e., that same family room with a different program controlling the hollow grams. The ceiling was higher, the windows were tall, evenly spaced, framed by floor-length drapes, and they looked out on formal gardens.

One piece of furniture wheeled itself in, and was not a hollow gram—or not much so. It was a banquet table that (so far as I know) was, in itself, pantry, stove, icebox—all of a well-equipped kitchen. That's a conclusion, subject to refutation. All I can say is that I never saw a servant and never saw our hostess do any work. Nevertheless her husband congratulated her on her cooking—as well he might, and so did we.

Jerry did a little work; he carved a roast (prime rib, enough for a troop of hungry Boy Scouts) and he served the plates, serving them at his place. Once a plate was loaded, it went smoothly around to the person for whom it was intended, like a toy train on a track—but there was no train and no track. Machinery concealed by hollow grams? I suppose so. But that simply covers one mystery with another.

(I learned later that a swank Texas household in that world would have had human servants conspicuously in sight. But Jerry and Katie had simple tastes.)

There were six of us at the table, Jerry at one end, Katie at the other; Margrethe sat on Jerry's right, his daughter Sybil on his left; I was at the right of my hostess, and at her left was Sybil's young man, her date. This put him opposite me, and I had Sybil on my right.

The young man's name was Roderick Lyman Culverson III; he did not manage to catch my name. I have long suspected that the male of our species, in most cases, should be raised in a barrel and fed through the bunghole. Then, at age eighteen, a solemn decision can be made: whether to take him out of the barrel, or to drive in the bung.

Young Culverson gave me no reason to change my opinion—and I would have voted to drive in the bung.

Early on, Sybil made clear that they were at the same campus. But he seemed to be as much a stranger to the Farnsworths as he was to us. Katie asked, "Roderick, are you an apprentice witch, too?"

He looked as if he had sniffed something nasty, but Sybil saved him from having to answer such a crude question. "Mothuh! Rod received his athame *ages* ago."

"Sorry I goofed," Katie said tranquilly. "Is that a diploma you get when you finish your apprenticeship?"

"It's a sacred knife, Mama, used in ritual. It can be used to—"

"*Sybil!* There are gentiles present." Culverson frowned at Sybil, then glared at me. I thought how well he would look with a black eye but I endeavored to keep my thoughts out of my face.

Jerry said, "Then you're a graduate warlock, Rod?"

Sybil broke in again. "Daddy! The correct word is—"

"Pipe down, sugar plum! Let him answer for himself. Rod?"

"That word is used only by the ignorant—"

"Hold it! I am uninformed on some subjects, and then I seek information, as I am now doing. But you don't sit at my table and call me ignorant. Now, can you answer me without casting asparagus?"

Culverson's nostrils spread but he took a grip on himself. "'Witch' is the usual term for both male and female adepts in the Craft. 'Wizard' is an acceptable term but is not technically exact; it means 'sorcerer' or 'magician' . . . but not all magicians are witches and not all witches practice magic. But 'warlock' is considered to be offensive as well as incorrect because it is associated with Devil worship—and the Craft is *not* Devil worship—and the word itself by its derivation means 'oath breaker'—and witches do not break oaths. Correction: The Craft forbids the breaking of oaths. A witch who breaks an oath, even to a gentile, is subject to discipline, even expulsion if the oath is that major. So I am not a 'graduate warlock.' The correct designation for my present status is 'Accepted Craftsman,' that is to say: 'witch.'"

"Well stated! Thank you. I ask forgiveness for using

the term 'warlock' to you and about you—'' Jerry waited.

A long moment later Culverson said hastily, "Oh, certainly! No offense meant and none taken."

"Thank you. To add to your comments about derivations, 'witch' derives from 'wicca' meaning 'wise,' and from 'wicce' meaning 'woman' . . . which may account for most witches being female and suggests that our ancestors may have known something that we don't. In any case 'the Craft' is the short way of saying 'the Craft of Wisdom.' Correct?"

"Eh? Oh, certainly! Wisdom. That's what the Old Religion is all about."

"Good. Son, listen to me carefully. Wisdom includes not getting angry unnecessarily. The Law ignores trifles and the wise man does, too. Such trifles as a young girl defining an athame among gentiles—knowledge that isn't all that esoteric anyhow—and an old fool using a word inappropriately. Understand me?"

Again Jerry waited. Then he said very softly, "I said, 'Do you understand me?'"

Culverson took a deep breath. "I understood you. A wise man ignores trifles."

"Good. May I offer you another slice of the roast?"

Culverson kept quiet for some time then. As did I. As did Sybil. Katie and Jerry and Margrethe kept up a flow of polite chitchat that ignored the fact that a guest had just been thoroughly and publicly spanked. Presently Sybil said, "Daddy, are you and Mama expecting me to attend fire worship Friday?"

"'Expect' is hardly the word," Jerry answered, "when

you have picked another church of your own. 'Hope' would be closer."

Katie added, "Sybil, tonight you feel that your coven is all the church you will ever need. But that could change . . . and I understand that the Old Religion does not forbid its members to attend other religious services."

Culverson put in, "That reflects centuries, millennia, of persecution, Mrs. Farnsworth. It is still in our laws that each member of a coven must also belong publicly to some socially approved church. But we no longer try too hard to enforce it."

"I see," agreed Katie. "Thank you, Roderick. Sybil, since your new church encourages membership in another church, it might be prudent to attend fairly regularly just to protect your Brownie points. You may need them."

"Exactly," agreed her father. "'Brownie points.' Ever occur to you, hon, that your pop being a stalwart pillar of the congregation, with a fast checkbook, might have something to do with the fact that he also sells more Cadillacs than any other dealer in Texas?"

"Daddy, that sounds utterly shameless."

"It sure is. It also sells Cadillacs. And don't call it fire worship; you know it is not. It is not the flame we worship, but what it stands for."

Sybil twisted her serviette and, for the moment, looked a troubled thirteen instead of the mature woman her body showed her to be. "Papa, that's just it. All my life that flame has meant to me healing, cleansing, life everlasting—until I studied the Craft. Its history. Daddy, to a witch . . . *fire means the way they kill us!*"

I was shocked almost out of breathing. I think it had not really sunk into me emotionally that these two, obnoxious but commonplace young punk, and pretty and quite delightful young girl . . . daughter of Katie, daughter of Jerry, our two Good Samaritans without equal—that these two were *witches*.

Yes, yes, I know: Exodus twenty-two verse eighteen, "Thou shalt not suffer a witch to live." As solemn an injunction as the Ten Commandments, given to Moses directly by God, in the presence of all the children of Israel—

What was I doing breaking bread with witches?

Mark me for a coward. I did not stand up and denounce them. I sat tight.

Katie said, "Darling, darling! That was clear back in the middle ages! Not today, not now, not here."

Culverson said, "Mrs. Farnsworth, every witch knows that the terror can start up again any time. Even a season of bad crops could touch it off. And Salem wasn't very long ago. Nor very far away." He added, "There are still Christians around. They would set the fires if they could. Just like Salem."

This was a great chance to keep my mouth shut. I blurted out, "No witch was burned at Salem."

He looked at me. "What do you know about it?"

"The burnings were in Europe, not here. In Salem witches were hanged, except one who was pressed to death." (Fire should never have been used. The Lord God ordered us not to suffer them to live; He did *not* tell us to put them to death by torture.)

He eyed me again. "So? You seem to approve of the hangings."

"I never said anything of the sort!" (Dear God, for-give me!)

Jerry cut in. "I rule this subject out of order! There will be no further discussion of it at the table. Sybil, we don't want you to attend if it upsets you or reminds you of tragic occasions. Speaking of hanging, what shall we do about the backfield of the Dallas Cowboys?"

Two hours later Jerry Farnsworth and I were again seated in that room, this time it being Remington number three: a snow storm against the windows, an occasional cold draft across the floor, and once the howl of a wolf—a roaring fire felt good. He poured coffee for us, and brandy in huge snifters, big enough for gold-fish. "You hear of noble brandy," he said. "Napoleon, or Carlos Primero. But this is royal brandy—so royal it has hemophilia."

I gulped; I did not like the joke. I was still queasy from thinking about witches, dying witches. With a jerk of the heels, or dancing on flames. And all of them with Sybil's sweet face.

Does the Bible define "witch" somewhere? Could it be that these modern members of the Craft were not at all what Jehovah meant by "witch"?

Quit dodging, Alex! Assume that "witch" in Exodus means exactly what "witch" means here in Texas today. You're the judge and she has confessed. *Can you sentence Katie's teenager to hang? Will you spring the trap?* Don't dodge it, boy; you've been dodging all your life.

Pontius Pilate washed his hands.

I will not sentence a witch to die! So help me, Lord, I can do no other.

Jerry said, "Here's to the success of your venture,

yours and Margie's. Sip it slowly and it will not intoxicate; it will simply quiet your nerves while it sharpens your wits. Alec, tell me now why you expect the end of the world."

For the next hour I went over the evidence, pointing out that it was not just one prophecy that agreed on the signs, but many: Revelations, Daniel, Ezekiel, Isaiah, Paul in writing to the Thessalonians, and again to the Corinthians, Jesus himself in all four of the Gospels, again and again in each.

To my surprise Jerry had a copy of the Book. I picked out passages easy for laymen to understand, wrote down chapter and verse so that he could study them later. One Thessalonians 4:15—17 of course, and the 24th chapter of the Gospel according to Saint Matthew, all fifty-one verses of it, and the same prophecies in Saint Luke, chapter twenty-one—and Luke 21:32 with its clue to the confusion of many as to "this generation." What Christ actually said was that the generation which sees these signs and portents will live to see His return, hear the Shout, experience Judgment Day. The message is plain if you read *all* of it; the errors have arisen from picking out bits and pieces and ignoring the rest. The parable of the fig tree explains this.

I also picked out for him, in Isaiah and Daniel and elsewhere, the Old Testament prophecies that parallel the New Testament prophecies.

I handed him this list of prophecies and urged him to study them carefully, and, if he encountered difficulties, simply read more widely. And take it to God. "'Ask, and it shall be given you; seek, and ye shall find.'"

He said, "Alec, I can agree with one thing. The news

for the past several months has looked to me like Armageddon. Say tomorrow afternoon. Might as well be the end of the world and Judgment Day, as there won't be enough left to salvage after this one." He looked sad. "I used to worry about what kind of a world Sybil would grow up in. Now I wonder if she'll grow up."

"Jerry. Work on it. Find your way to grace. Then lead your wife and daughter. You don't need me, you don't need anyone but Jesus. He said, 'Behold, I stand at the door and knock; if anyone hears My voice, I will come in to him.' Revelations three, twenty."

"You believe."

"I do."

"Alec, I wish I could go along with you. It would be comforting, the world being what it is today. But I can't see proof in the dreams of long-dead prophets; you can read anything into them. Theology is never any help; it is searching in a dark cellar at midnight for a black cat that isn't there. Theologians can persuade themselves of anything. Oh, my church, too—but at least mine is honestly pantheistic. Anyone who can worship a trinity and insist that his religion is a monotheism can believe anything—just give him time to rationalize it. Forgive me for being blunt."

"Jerry, in religion bluntness is necessary. 'I know that my Redeemer liveth, and that He shall stand at the latter day upon the earth.' That's Job again, chapter nineteen. He's your Redeemer, too, Jerry—I pray that you find Him."

"Not much chance, I'm afraid." Jerry stood up.

"You haven't found Him *yet*. Don't quit. I'll pray for you."

"Thank you, and thanks for trying. How do the shoes feel?"

"Comfortable, quite."

"If you insist on hitting the road tomorrow, you must have shoes that won't give you bunions between here and Kansas. You're sure?"

"I'm sure. And sure that we must leave. If we stayed another day, you'd have us so spoiled we would never hit the road again." (The truth that I could not tell him was that I was so upset by witchcraft and fire worship that I had to leave. But I could not load my weakness onto him.)

"Let me show you to your bedroom. Quietly, as Margie may be asleep. Unless our ladies have stayed up even later than we have."

At the bedroom door he put out his hand. "If you're right and I'm wrong, you tell me that it's possible that even you can slip."

"True. I'm not in a state of grace, not now. I've got to work on it."

"Well, good luck. But if you do slip, look me up in Hell, will you?"

So far as I could tell, Jerry was utterly serious. "I don't know that it is permitted."

"Work on it. And so will I. I promise you"—he grinned—"some hellacious hospitality. Really warm!"

I grinned back. "It's a date."

Again my darling had fallen asleep without undressing. I smiled at her without making a sound, then got beside her and pillowed her head on my shoulder. I would let her wake up slowly, then undress the poor baby and put her to bed. Meanwhile I had a thousand—well, dozens—of thoughts to get untangled.

Presently I noticed that it was getting light. Then I noticed how scratchy and lumpy the bed was. The light increased and I saw that we were sprawled over bales of hay, in a barn.

XIX

And Ahab said to Elijah, Hast thou found me,
O mine enemy? And he answered, I have found thee:
because thou hast sold thyself to work evil
in the sight of the Lord.
1 Kings 21:20

We did the last ninety miles down 66 from Clinton to Oklahoma City pushing hard, ignoring the fact that we were flat broke again, nothing to eat, nowhere to sleep.

We had seen a dirigible.

Of course this changed everything. For months I had been nobody from nowhere, penniless, dishwashing my only trade, and a tramp in fact. But back in my own world— A well-paying job, a respected position in the community, a fat bank account. And an end to this truly infernal bouncing around between worlds.

We were riding into Clinton middle of the morning, guests of a farmer taking a load of produce into town. I heard Margrethe gasp. I looked where she was staring—and there she was!—silvery and sleek and beautiful. I could not make out her name, but her logo told me that she was Eastern Airlines.

"Dallas—Denver Express," our host remarked, and

hauled a watch out of his overalls. "Six minutes late. Unusual."

I tried to cover my excitement. "Does Clinton have an airport?"

"Oh, no. Oklahoma City, nearest. Goin' to give up hitchhiking and take to the air?"

"Would be nice."

"Wouldn't it, though. Beats farmin'."

I kept the conversation on inanities until he dropped us outside the city market a few minutes later. But, once Margrethe and I were alone, I could hardly contain myself. I started to kiss her, then suddenly stopped myself. Oklahoma is every bit as moral as Kansas; most communities have stiff laws about public lallygagging.

I wondered how hard I was going to find it to readjust, after many weeks in many worlds not one of which had the high moral standards of my home world. It could be difficult to stay out of trouble when (admit it!) I had grown used to kissing my wife in public and to other displays, innocent in themselves, but never seen in public in moral communities. Worse, could I keep my darling out of trouble? I had been born here and could slip back into its ways . . . but Marga was as affectionate as a collie pup and had no sense of shame whatever about showing it.

I said, "Sorry, dear, I was about to kiss you. But I must not."

"Why not?"

"Uh, I can't kiss you in public. Not here. Only in private. It's— It's a case of 'When in Rome, one must do as the Romans do.' But never mind that now. Darling, we're home! My home, and now it's your home. You saw the dirigible."

"That was an airship truly?"

"Really and truly . . . and the happiest sight I've seen in months. Except— Don't get your hopes up too high, too fast. We know how some of these shifting worlds strongly resemble each other in many ways. I suppose there is an outside possibility that this is a world with dirigibles . . . but not *my* world. Oh, I don't believe that—but let's not get too excited."

(I did not notice that Margrethe was not at all excited.)

"How will you tell that this is your world?"

"We could check just as we have before, at public libraries. But in this case there is something faster and better. I want to find the Bell Telephone office—I'll ask at that grocery store."

I wanted the telephone office rather than a public telephone because I wanted to consult telephone books before making telephone calls—was it my world?

Yes, it was! The office had telephone books for all of Oklahoma and also books from major cities in other states—including a most familiar telephone book for Kansas City, Kansas. "See, Margrethe?" I pointed to the listing for Churches United for Decency, National Office.

"I see."

"Isn't it exciting? Doesn't it make you want to dance and sing?"

"I am very happy for you, Alec."

(She made it sound like: "Doesn't he look natural? And so many lovely flowers.")

We had the alcove where the telephone books were to

ourselves. So I whispered urgently, "What's the trouble, dear? This is a happy occasion. Don't you understand? Once I get on that phone we'll have money. No more menial jobs, no more wondering how we will eat or where we will sleep. We'll go straight home by Pullman—no, by dirigible! You'll like that, I know you will! The ultimate in luxury. Our honeymoon, darling—the honeymoon we could never afford."

"You will not take me to Kansas City."

"What do you mean?"

"Alec . . . your wife is there."

Believe me when I say that I had not thought once about Abigail in many, many weeks. I had become convinced that I would never see her again (regaining my home world was totally unexpected) and I now had a wife, all the wife any man could ever want: Margrethe.

I wonder if that first shovelful of dirt hits a corpse with the same shock.

I pulled out of it. Some. "Marga, here's what we'll do. Yes, I have a problem, but we can solve it. Of course you go to Kansas City with me! You must. But there, because of Abigail, I must find a quiet place for you to stay while I get things straightened out." (Straightened out? Abigail was going to scream bloody murder.) "First I must get at my money. Then I must see a lawyer." (Divorce? In a state where there was only one legal ground and that one granted divorce only to the injured party? Margrethe the other woman? Impossible. Let Margrethe be exposed in stocks? Be ridden out of town on a rail if Abigail demanded it? Never mind what would be done to me, never mind that Abigail would strip me of every cent—Margrethe must not be subjected to the Scarlet Letter laws of my home world. No!)

"Then we will go to Denmark." (No, it can't be divorce.)

"We will?"

"We will. Darling, you are my wife, now and forever. I can't leave you here while I get things worked out in Kay See; the world might shift and I would lose you. But we can't go to Denmark until I lay hands on my money. All clear?" (What if Abigail has cleaned out my bank account?)

"Yes, Alec. We will go to Kansas City."

(That settled part of it. But it did not settle Abigail. Never mind, I would burn that bridge when I came to it.)

Thirty seconds later I had more problems. Certainly the girl in charge would place a call for me long distance collect. Kansas City? For Kansas City, either Kansas or Missouri, the fee to open the trunk line for query was twenty-five cents. Deposit it in the coin box, please, when I tell you. Booth two.

I went to the booth and dug into my pocket for coins, laid them out:

A twenty-cent piece;

Two threepenny coppers;

A Canadian quarter, with the face of the Queen (queen?);

A half dollar;

Three five-cent pieces that were *not* nickels, but smaller.

And not one of these coins carried the familiar "God Is Our Fortress" motto of the North American Union.

I stared at that ragbag collection and tried to figure

out when this last change had taken place. Since I last was paid evidently, which placed it later than yesterday afternoon but earlier than the hitch we had gotten just after breakfast. While we slept last night? But we had not lost our clothes, had not lost our money. I even had my razor, a lump in my breast pocket.

Never mind—any attempt to understand all the details of these changes led only to madness. The shift had indeed taken place; I was here in my native world . . . and it had left me with no money. With no legal money.

By Hobson's choice, that Canadian quarter looked awfully good. I did not try to tell myself that the Eighth Commandment did not apply to big corporations. Instead I did promise myself that I would pay it back. I picked it up and took the receiver off the hook.

"Number, please."

"Please place a collect call to Churches United for Decency in Kansas City, Kansas. The number is State Line 1224J. I'll speak to anyone who answers."

"Deposit twenty-five cents, please." I deposited that Canadian quarter and held my breath—heard it go *ting-thunk-thunk*. Then Central said, "Thank you. Do not hang up. Please wait."

I waited. And waited. And waited.

"On your call to Kansas City— Churches United for Decency reports that they do not accept collect calls."

"Hold it! Please tell them that the Reverend Alexander Hergensheimer is calling."

"Thank you. Please deposit twenty-five cents."

"Hey! I didn't get any use out of that first quarter. You hung up too soon."

"We did not disconnect; the party in Kansas City hung up."

"Well, call them back, please, and this time tell them not to hang up."

"Yes, sir. Please deposit twenty-five cents."

"Central, would I be calling collect if I had plenty of change on me? Get them on the line and tell them who I am. Reverend Alexander Hergensheimer, Deputy Executive Director."

"Please wait on the line."

So I waited again. And waited.

"Reverend? The party in Kansas City says to tell you that they do not accept collect calls from—I am quoting exactly—Jesus Christ Himself."

"That's no way to talk on the telephone. Or anywhere."

"I quite agree. There was more. This person said to tell you that he had never heard of you."

"Why, that—" I shut up, as I had no way to express myself within the dignity of the cloth.

"Yes, indeed. I tried to get his name. He hung up on me."

"Young man? Old man? Bass, tenor, baritone?"

"Boy soprano. I gathered an impression that it was the office boy, answering the phone during the lunch hour."

"I see. Well, thank you for your efforts. Above and beyond the call of duty, in my opinion."

"A pleasure, Reverend."

I left there, kicking myself. I did not explain to Margrethe until we were clear of the building. "Hoist by my own petard, dear one. I wrote that 'No Collect

Calls' order myself. An analysis of the telephone log proved to me beyond any possible doubt that collect calls to our office were never for the benefit of the association. Nine out of ten are begging calls . . . and Churches United for Decency is not a charity. It collects money; it does not give it away. The tenth call is either from a troublemaker or a crank. So I set this firm rule and enforced it . . . and it paid off at once. Saved hundreds of dollars a year just in telephone tolls." I managed to smile. "Never dreamed that I would be caught in my own net."

"What are your plans now, Alec?"

"Now? Get out on Highway Sixty-Six and start waving my thumb. I want us to reach Oklahoma City before five o'clock. It should be easy; it's not very far."

"Yes, sir. Why five o'clock, may I ask?"

"You can always ask anything and you know it. Knock off the Patient Griselda act, sweetheart; you've been moping ever since we saw that dirigible. Because there is a district office of C.U.D. in Oklahoma City and I want to be there before they close. Wait'll you see them roll out the red carpet, hon! Get to Oke City and our troubles are over."

That afternoon reminded me of wading through sorghum. January sorghum. We had no trouble getting rides—but the rides were mostly short distances. We averaged about twenty miles an hour on a highway that permitted sixty miles per hour. We lost fifty-five minutes for a good reason: a free meal. For the umpteenth time a trucker bought us something to eat when he ate . . . for the reason that there is almost no man alive who can stop to eat, and fail to invite Margrethe to eat if she is there. (Then I get fed, too, simply because I'm her property. I'm not complaining.)

We ate in twenty minutes, then he spent thirty minutes and endless quarters playing pinball machines . . . and I stood there and seethed and Margrethe stood beside him and clapped her hands and squealed when he made a good score. But her social instincts are sound; he then drove us all the rest of the way to Oklahoma City. There he went through town when he could have taken a bypass, and at four-twenty he dropped us at 36th and Lincoln, only two blocks from the C.U.D. district office.

I walked that two blocks whistling. Once I said, "Smile, hon! A month from now—or sooner—we'll eat in the Tivoli."

"Truly?"

"Truly. You've told me so much about it that I can't wait. There's the building!"

Our suite is on the second floor. It warmed the cockles to see the door with lettering on the glass: CHURCHES UNITED FOR DECENCY — Enter.

"After you, my love!" I grabbed the knob, to open for her.

The door was locked.

I banged on it, then spotted a doorbell and rang it. Then I alternated knocking and ringing. And again.

A blackamoor carrying a mop and a pail came down the corridor, started to pass us. I called, "Hey, Uncle! Do you have a key to this suite?"

"Sure don't, Captain. Ain't nobody in there now. They most generally locked up and gone by four o'clock."

"I see. Thanks."

"A pleasure, Captain."

Out on the street again, I grinned sheepishly at Margrethe. "Red carpet treatment. Closing at four. When the cat is away, the mice will play. Some heads will roll, I promise you. I can't think of another cliché to fit the situation. Oh, yes, I can. Beggars can't be choosers. Madam, would you like to sleep in the park tonight? Warm night, no rain expected. Chiggers and mosquitoes, no extra charge."

We slept in Lincoln Park, on the golf course, on a green that was living velvet—alive with chiggers.

It was a good night's sleep despite chiggers. We got up when the first early golfers showed up, and we got off the golf course with nothing worse than dirty looks. We made use of public washrooms in the park, and rejoined much neater, feeling fresher, me with a fresh shave, and both of us filled with free water for breakfast. On the whole I felt cheerful. It was too early to expect those self-appointed playboys at C.U.D. to show up, so, when we ran across a policeman, I asked the location of the public library, then I added, "By the way, where is the airport?"

"The what?"

"The dirigible flying field."

The cop turned to Margrethe. "Lady, is he sick?"

I did feel sick a half hour later when I checked the directory in the building we had visited the afternoon before . . . I felt sick but unsurprised to find no Churches United for Decency among its tenants. But to make certain I walked up to the second floor. That suite was now occupied by an insurance firm.

"Well, dear, let's go to the public library. Find out what kind of world we are in."

"Yes, Alec." She was looking cheerful. "Dearest, I'm sorry you are disappointed . . . but I am so relieved. I— I was frightened out of my wits at the thought of meeting your wife."

"You won't. Not ever. Promise. Uh, I'm sort of relieved, too. And hungry."

We walked a few more steps. "Alec. Don't be angry."

"I'll do no more than give you a fat lip. What is it?"

"I have five quarters. Good ones."

"At this point I am supposed to say, 'Daughter, were you a good girl in Philadelphy?' Out with it. Whom did you kill? Much blood?"

"Yesterday. Those pinball games. Every time Harry won free games he gave me a quarter. 'For luck,' he said."

I decided not to beat her. Of course they were not "good quarters" but they turned out to be good enough. Good enough, that is, to fit coin machines. We had passed a penny arcade; such places usually have coin-operated food dispensers and this one did. The prices were dreadfully high—fifty cents for a skimpy stale sandwich; twenty-five cents for a bare mouthful of chocolate. But it was better than some breakfasts we had had on the road. And we certainly did not steal, as the quarters from my world were real silver.

Then we went to the public library to find out what sort of world we must cope with now.

We found out quickly:

Marga's world.

XX

Margrethe was as elated as I had been the day before.
She bubbled, she smiled, she looked sixteen. I looked
around for a private place—back of book stacks or
somewhere—where I could kiss her without worrying
about a proctor. Then I remembered that this was Margrethe's world where nobody cared . . . and grabbed
her where she stood and bussed her properly.

And got scolded by a librarian.

No, not for what I had done, but because we had
been somewhat noisy about it. Public kissing did not in
itself disturb that library's decorum. Hardly. I noticed,
while I was promising to keep quiet and apologizing for
the breach, a display rack by that librarian's desk:

New Titles INSTRUCTIONAL PORNOGRAPHY —
Ages 6 to 12

Fifteen minutes later I was waving my thumb again
on Highway 77 to Dallas.

Why Dallas? A law firm: O'Hara, Rigsbee, Crumpacker, and Rigsbee.

As soon as we were outside the library, Marga had started talking excitedly about how she could now end our troubles: her bank account in Copenhagen.

I said, "Wait a minute, darling. Where's your checkbook? Where's your identification?"

What it came to was that Margrethe could possibly draw on her assets in Denmark after several days at a highly optimistic best or after several weeks at a more probable estimate . . . and that even the longer period involved quite a bit of money up front for cablegrams. Telephone across the Atlantic? Marga did not think such a thing existed. (And even if it did, I thought it likely that cablegrams were cheaper and more certain.)

Even after all arrangements had been made, it was possible that actual payment might involve postal delivery from Europe—in a world that had no airmail.

So we headed for Dallas, I having assured Marga that, at the very worst, Alec Graham's lawyers would advance Alec Graham enough money to get him (us) off the street, and, with luck, we would come at once into major assets.

(Or they might fail to recognize me as Alec Graham and prove that I was not he—by fingerprints, by signature, by something—and thereby lay the ghost of "Alec Graham" in Margrethe's sweet but addled mind. But I did not mention this to Margrethe.)

It is two hundred miles from Oklahoma City to Dallas; we arrived there at 2 p.m., having picked up a ride at the intersection of 66 and 77, and kept it clear into the Texas metropolis. We were dropped where 77 crosses 80 at the Trinity River, and we walked to the Smith Building; it took us half an hour.

The receptionist in suite 7000 looked like something out of the sort of stage show that C.U.D. has spent much time and money to suppress. She was dressed but not very much, and her makeup was what Marga calls "high style." She was nubile and pretty and, with my newly learned toleration, I simply enjoyed the sinful sight. She smiled and said, "May I help you?"

"This is a fine day for golf. Which of the partners is still in the office?"

"Only Mr. Crumpacker, I'm afraid."

"He's the one I want to see."

"And whom shall I say is calling?"

(First hurdle— I missed it. Or did she?) "Don't you recognize me?"

"I'm sorry. Should I?"

"How long have you been working here?"

"Just over three months."

"That accounts for it. Tell Crumpacker that Alec Graham is here."

I could not hear what Crumpacker said to her but I was watching her eyes; I think they widened—I feel sure of it. But all she said was, "Mr. Crumpacker will see you." Then she turned to Margrethe. "May I offer you a magazine while you wait? And would you like a reefer?"

I said, "She's coming with me."

"But—"

"Come along, Marga." I headed quickly for the inner offices.

Crumpacker's door was easy to find; it was the one

with the squawking issuing from it. This shut off as I opened the door and held it for Margrethe. As I followed her in, he was saying, "Miss, you'll have to wait outside!"

"No," I denied, as I closed the door behind me. "Mrs. Graham stays."

He looked startled. "Mrs. Graham?"

"Surprised you, didn't I? Got married since I saw you last. Darling, this is Sam Crumpacker, one of my attorneys." (I had picked his first name off his door.)

"How do you do, Mr. Crumpacker?"

"Uh, glad to meet you, Mrs. Graham. Congratulations. Congratulations to you, Alec—you always could pick 'em."

I said, "Thanks. Sit down, Marga."

"Just a moment, folks! Mrs. Graham can't stay— really she can't! You know that."

"I know no such thing. This time I'm going to have a witness." No, I did not know that he was crooked. But I had learned long ago, in dealing with legislators, that anyone who tries to keep you from having a witness is bad news. So C.U.D. always had witnesses and always stayed within the law; it was cheaper that way.

Marga was seated; I sat down beside her. Crumpacker had jumped up when we came in; he remained standing. His mouth worked nervously. "I ought to call the Federal prosecutor."

"Do that," I agreed. "Pick up the phone there and call him. Let's *both* of us go see him. Let's tell him *everything*. With witnesses. Let's call in the press. All of the press, not just the tame cats."

(What did I know? Nothing. But when it's necessary

to bluff, always bluff big. I was scared. This rat could turn and fight like a cornered mouse—a rabid one.)

"I should."

"Do it, do it! Let's name names, and tell who did what and who got paid. I want to get *everything* out into the open . . . before somebody slips cyanide into my soup."

"Don't talk that way."

"Who has a better right? Who pushed me overboard? *Who?*"

"Don't look at me!"

"No, Sammie, I don't think you did it; you weren't there. But it could be your godson. Eh?" Then I smiled my biggest right-hand-of-fellowship smile. "Just joking, Sam. My old friend would not want me dead. But you can tell me some things and help me out. Sam, it's not convenient to be dumped way off on the other side of the world—so you owe me." (No, I still knew nothing . . . nothing save the evident fact that here was a man with a guilty conscience—so crowd him.)

"Alec, let's not do anything hasty."

"I'm in no hurry. But I've got to have explanations. And money."

"Alec, I tell you on my word of honor all I know about what happened to you is that this squarehead ship came into Portland and you ain't aboard. And I have to go all the way to Oregon f' God's sake to witness them breaking into your strong-box. And there's only a hundred thousand in it; the rest is missing. Who got it, Alec? Who got to you?"

He had his eyes on me; I hope my face didn't show anything. But he had hulled me. Was this true? This shyster would lie as easily as he talked. Had my friend the purser, or the purser and the captain in cahoots, looted that lockbox?

As a working hypothesis, always prefer the simpler explanation. This man was more likely to lie than the purser was to steal. And it was likely—no, certain—that the captain would have to be present before the purser would force his way into the lockbox of a missing passenger. If these two responsible officers, with careers and reputations to lose, nevertheless combined to steal, why would they leave a hundred thousand behind? Why not take it all and be blandly ignorant about the contents of my lockbox?—as indeed they should be. Something fishy here.

"What are you implying was missing?"

"Huh?" He glanced at Margrethe. "Uh— Well, damn it, there should have been nine hundred grand more. The money you didn't pass over in Tahiti."

"Who says I didn't?"

"What? Alec, don't make things worse. Mr. Z. says so. You tried to drown his bagman."

I looked at him and laughed. "You mean those tropical gangsters? They tried to get the boodle without identifying themselves and without giving receipts. I told them an emphatic no—so the clever boy had his muscle throw me into the pool. Hmm— Sam, I see it now. Find out who came aboard the *Konge Knut* in Papeete."

"Why?"

"That's your man. He not only got the boodle; he pushed me overboard. When you know, don't bother to try to get him extradited, just tell me his name. I'll arrange the rest myself. Personally."

"Damn it, we want that million dollars."

"Do you think you can get it? It wound up in Mr. Z.'s hands . . . but you got no receipt. And I got a lot of grief from asking for a receipt. Don't be silly, Sam; the nine hundred thousand is gone. But not my fee. So pass over that hundred grand. Now."

"*What?* The Federal prosecutor in Portland kept that, impounded it as evidence."

"Sam, Sam boy, don't try to teach your grandmother how to steal sheep. As evidence for *what?* Who is charged? Who is indicted? What crime is alleged? Am I charged with stealing something out of my own lockbox? What crime?"

"'What crime?' Somebody stole that nine hundred grand, that's what!"

"Really? Who's the complainant? Who asserts that there ever was nine hundred thousand in that lockbox? I certainly never told anyone that—so *who says?* Pick up that phone, Sam; call the Federal prosecutor in Portland. Ask him why he held that money—on whose complaint? Let's get to the bottom of this. Pick it up, Sam. If that Federal clown has my money, I want to shake it loose from him."

"You're almighty anxious to talk to prosecutors! Strange talk from *you.*"

"Maybe I've had an acute attack of honesty. Sam, your unwillingness to call Portland tells me all I need to know. You were called out there to act on my behalf, as my attorney. American passenger lost overboard, ship of foreign registry, you betcha they get hold of the passenger's attorney to inventory his assets. Then they pass it all over to his attorney and he gives a receipt for it. Sam, what did you do with my clothes?"

"Eh? Gave 'em to the Red Cross. Of course."

"You did, eh?"

"After the prosecutor released 'em, I mean."

"Interesting. The Federal attorney keeps the money, although no one has complained that any money is missing . . . but lets the clothes out of his hands *when the only probable crime is murder.*"

"*Huh?*"

"Me, I mean. Who pushed me and who hired him to? Sam, we both know where the money is." I stood up, pointed. "In that safe. That's where it logically has to be. You wouldn't bank it; there would be a record. You wouldn't hide it at home; your wife might find it. And you certainly didn't split with your partners. Sam, open it. I want to see whether there is a hundred thousand in there . . . or a million."

"You're out of your mind!"

"Call the Federal prosecutor. Let him be our witness."

I had him so angry he couldn't talk. His hands trembled. It isn't safe to get a little man too angry—and I topped him by six inches, weight and other measurements to match. He wouldn't attack me himself—he was a lawyer—but I would need to be careful going through doorways, and such.

Time to try to cool him— "Sam, Sam, don't take it so seriously. You were leaning on me pretty heavily . . . so I leaned back. The good Lord alone knows why prosecutors do anything—the gonif most likely has stolen it by now . . . in the belief that I am dead and will never complain. So I'll go to Portland and lean on him, hard."

"There's paper out on you there."

"Really? What charges?"

"Seduction under promise of marriage. A female crewman of that ship." He had the grace to look apologetically at Margrethe. "Sorry, Mrs. Graham. But your husband asked me."

"Quite all right," she answered crisply.

"I do get around, don't I? What does she look like? Is she pretty? What's her name?"

"I never saw her; she wasn't there. Her name? Some Swede name. Let me think. Gunderson, that was it. Margaret S. Gunderson."

Margrethe, bless her heart, never let out a peep—not even at being called a Swede. I said in wonderment, "I'm accused of seducing this woman . . . aboard a foreign-flag vessel, somewhere in the South Seas. So there's a warrant out for me in Portland, Oregon. Sam, what kind of a lawyer are you? To let a client have paper slapped on him on that sort of charge."

"I'm a smart lawyer, that's the kind I am. Just as you said, no telling what a Federal attorney will do; they take their brains out when they appoint 'em. It simply wasn't important enough to talk about, you being dead, or so we all thought. I'm just looking out for your interests, letting you know about it before you step in it. Gimme some time, I'll get it quashed—*then* you go to Portland."

"Sounds reasonable. There aren't any charges outstanding on me here, are there?"

"No. Well, yes and no. You know the deal; we assured them that you would not be coming back, so they turned the blind eye when you left. But here you are, back. Alec, you can't afford to be seen here. Or elsewhere in Texas. Or anywhere in the States, actually.

Word gets around, and they'll dig up those old charges."

"I was innocent!"

He shrugged. "Alec, all my clients are innocent. I'm talking like a father, in your own interest. Get out of Dallas. If you go as far as Paraguay, so much the better."

"How? I'm broke. Sam, I've *got* to have some dough."

"Have I ever let you down?" He got out his wallet, counted out five one-hundred-dollar bills, laid them in front of me.

I looked at them. "What's that? A tip?" I picked them up, pocketed them. "That much won't get us to Brownsville. Now let's see some money."

"See me tomorrow."

"Don't play games, Sam. Open that safe and get me some real money. Or I don't come here tomorrow; I go see the Federal man and sing like the birdies. After I get square with him—and I will; the Feds love a state's witness, it's the only way they ever win a case—then I go to Oregon and pick up that hundred grand."

"Alec, are you threatening me?"

"You play games, I play games. Sam, I need a car and I don't mean a beat-up Ford. A Cadillac. Doesn't have to be new, but a cream puff, clean, and a good engine. A Cadillac and a few grand and we'll be in Laredo by midnight, and in Monterrey by morning. I'll call you from Mexico City and give you an address. If you really want me to go to Paraguay and stay there, you send the money to D.F. for me to do it."

It did not work out quite that way, but I settled for a used Pontiac and left with six thousand dollars in cash, and instructions to go to a particular used-car lot and accept the deal offered me—Sam would call and set it up. He agreed also to call the Hyatt and get us the bridal suite, and would see that they held it. Then I was to come back at ten the next morning.

I refused to get up that early. "Make that eleven. We're still on our honeymoon."

Sam chuckled, slapped me on the back, and agreed.

Out in the corridor we headed toward the elevators but went ten feet farther and I opened the door to the fire-escape trunk. Margrethe followed me without comment but once inside the staircase trunk and out of earshot of others she said, "Alec, that man is not your friend."

"No, he's not."

"I am afraid for you."

"I'm afraid for me, too."

"Terribly afraid. I fear for your life."

"My love, I fear for my life, too. And for yours. You are in danger as long as you are with me."

"I will *not* leave you!"

"I know. Whatever this is, we are in it together."

"Yes. What are our plans now?"

"Now we go to Kansas."

"Oh, good! Then we are not driving to Mexico?"

"Hon, I don't even know how to drive a car."

We came out in a basement garage and walked up a ramp to a side street. There we walked several blocks away from the Smith Building, picked up a cruising taxi, rode it to the Texas & Pacific Station, there picked up a taxi at the taxi rank, and rode it to Fort Worth, twenty-five miles west. Margrethe was very quiet on the trip. I did not ask her what she was thinking about because I knew: It can't be happy-making to discover that a person you fell in love with was mixed up in some shenanigan that smelled of gangsters and rackets. I made myself a solemn promise never to mention the matter to her.

In Fort Worth I had the hackie drop us on its most stylish shopping street, letting him pick it. Then I said to Marga, "Darling, I'm about to buy you a heavy gold chain."

"Goodness, darling! I don't need a gold chain."

"We need it. Marga, the first time I was in this world—with you, in *Konge Knut*—I learned that here the dollar was soft, not backed by gold, and every price I have seen today confirms that. So, if change comes again—and we never know—even the hard money of this world, quarters and half dollars and dimes, won't be worth anything because they're not really silver. As for the paper money I got from Crumpacker—waste paper!

"Unless I change it into something else. We'll start with that gold chain and from here on you wear it to bed, you even wear it to bathe—unless you hang it around my neck."

"I see. Yes."

"We'll buy some heavy gold jewelry for each of us, then I'm going to try to find a coin dealer—buy some silver cartwheels, maybe some gold coins. But my purpose is to get rid of most of this paper money in the next hour—all but the price of two bus tickets to Wichita, Kansas, three hundred and fifty miles north of here. Could you stand to ride a bus all night tonight? I want to get us out of Texas."

"Certainly! Oh, dear, I do want to get out of Texas! Truly, I'm still frightened."

"Truly, you are not alone."

"But—"

"'But' what, dear? And quit looking sad."

"Alec, I haven't had a bath for *four days*."

We found the jewelry shop, we found the coin shop; I spent about half that fiat money and saved the rest for bus fare and other purposes in this world—such as dinner, which we ate as soon as the shops started to close. A hamburger we had eaten in Gainesville seemed an awfully long way off in time and space. Then I determined that there was a bus going north—Oklahoma City, Wichita, Salina—at ten o'clock that evening. I bought tickets and paid an extra dollar on each ticket to reserve seats. Then I threw money away like a drunken sailor—took a room in a hotel across from the bus station, knowing that we would be checking out in less than two hours.

It was worth it. Hot baths for each of us, taking turns, each of us remaining fully dressed and carrying the other's clothing, jewelry, and all the money while the other was naked and wet. And carrying my razor, which had become a talisman of how to outwit Loki's playful tricks.

And new, clean underwear for each of us, purchased in passing while we were converting paper money into valuta.

I had hoped for time enough for love—but no; by

the time I was clean and dry we had to dress and check out to catch that bus. Never mind, there would be other times. We climbed into the bus, put the back-rests back, put Marga's head on my shoulder. As the bus headed north we fell asleep.

I woke up sometime later because the road was so rough. We were seated right behind the driver, so I leaned forward and asked, "Is this a detour?" I could not recall a rough stretch when we had ridden south on this same road about twelve hours earlier.

"No," he said. "We've crossed into Oklahoma, that's all. Not much pavement in Oklahoma. Some near Oke City and a little between there and Guthrie."

The talk had wakened Margrethe; she straightened up. "What is it, dear?"

"Nothing. Just Loki having fun with us. Go back to sleep."

XXI

I was driving a horse and buggy and not enjoying it.
The day was hot, the dust kicked up by horse's hooves
stuck to sweaty skin, flies were bad, there was no
breeze. We were somewhere near the corner of Missouri, Kansas, and Oklahoma, but I was not sure
where. I had not seen a map for days and the roads were
no longer marked with highway signs for the guidance
of automobilists—there were no automobiles.

The last two weeks (more or less—I had lost track of
the days) had been endless torments of Sisyphus, one
ridiculous frustration after another. Sell silver dollars to
a local dealer in exchange for that world's paper?—no
trouble; I did it several times. But it didn't always
help. Once I had sold silver for local paper money and
we had ordered dinner—when, boom, another world
change and we went hungry. Another time I was
cheated outrageously and when I complained, I was
told: "Neighbor, possession of that coin is illegal and
you know it. I've offered you a price anyhow because I

like you. Will you take it? Or shall I do my plain duty as a citizen?"

I took it. The paper money he gave us for five ounces of silver would not buy dinner for Marga and me at a backwoods gourmet spot called "Mom's Diner."

That was in a charming community called (by a sign at its outskirts):

THE TEN COMMANDMENTS
A Clean Community
Blackamoors, Kikes, Papists
Keep Moving!

We kept moving. That whole two weeks had been spent trying to travel the two hundred miles from Oklahoma City to Joplin, Missouri. I had been forced to give up the notion of avoiding Kansas City. I still had no intention of staying in or near Kansas City, not when a sudden change of worlds could land us in Abigail's lap. But I had learned in Oklahoma City that the fastest and indeed the only practical route to Wichita was a long detour through Kansas City. We had retrogressed to the horse-and-buggy era.

When you consider the total age of the earth, from Creation in 4004 B.C. to the year of Our Lord 1994, or 5998 years—call it 6000—in a period of 6000 years, 80 or 90 years is nothing much. And that is how short a time it has been since the horse-and-buggy day in my world. My father was born in that day (1909) and my paternal grandfather not only never owned an automobile but refused to ride in one. He claimed that they were spawn of the Devil, and used to quote passages from Ezekiel to prove it. Perhaps he was right.

But the horse-and-buggy era does have shortcomings. There are obvious ones such as no inside plumbing, no air conditioning, no modern medicine. But for us there was an unobvious but major one; where there are no trucks and no cars there is effectively no hitchhiking. Oh, it is sometimes possible to hitch rides on farm wagons—but the difference in speed between a human's walk and a horse's walk is not great. We rode when we could but, either way, fifteen miles was a good day's progress—too good; it left no time to work for meals and a place to sleep.

There is an old paradox, Achilles and the Tortoise, in which the remaining distance to your goal is halved at each step. The question is: How long does it take to reach your goal? The answer is: You can't get there from here.

That is the way we "progressed" from Oklahoma City to Joplin.

Something else compounded my frustration: I became increasingly persuaded that we were indeed in the latter days, and we could expect the return of Jesus and the Final Judgment at any moment—and my darling, my necessary one, was not yet back in the arms of Jesus. I refrained from nagging her about it, although it took all my will power to respect her wish to handle it alone. I began to sleep badly through worrying about her.

I became a bit crazy, too (in addition to my paranoid belief that these world changes were aimed at me personally)—crazy in that I acquired an unfounded but compelling belief that finishing this journey was essential to the safety of my darling's immortal soul. Just let us get as far as Kansas, dear Lord, and I will pray without ceasing until I have converted her and brought her to grace. O Lord God of Israel, grant me this boon!

I continued to look for dishwashing jobs (or anything) even while we still had silver and gold to trade for local money. But motels disappeared entirely; hotels became scarce and restaurants decreased in numbers and size to fit an economy in which travel was rare and almost all meals were eaten at home.

It became easier to find jobs cleaning stalls in livery stables. I preferred dishwashing to shoveling horse manure—especially as I had only one pair of shoes. But I stuck to the rule of take any honest work but *keep moving!*

You may wonder why we did not shift to hitching rides on freight trains. In the first place I did not know how, never having done it. Still more important, I could not guarantee Marga's safety. There were the hazards of mounting a moving freight car. But worse were dangers from people: railroad bulls and road kids—hobos, tramps, bindlestiffs, bums. No need to discuss those grisly dangers, as I kept her away from rail lines and hobo jungles.

And I worried. While abiding strictly by her request not to be pressured, I did take to praying aloud every night and in her presence, on my knees. And at last, to my great joy, my darling joined me, on her knees. She did not pray aloud and I stopped vocalizing myself, save for a final: "In Jesus' name, Amen." We still did not talk about it.

I wound up driving this horse and buggy (goodness, what a hot day!—"Cyclone weather," my grandmother Hergensheimer would have called it) as a result of a job cleaning stalls in a livery stable. As usual I had quit after one day, telling my temporary employer that my wife and I had to move on to Joplin; her mother was ill.

He told me that he had a rig that needed to be returned to the next town up the road. What he meant was that he had too many rigs and nags on hand, his own and others, or he would have waited until he could send it back by renting it to a passing drummer.

I offered to return it for one day's wages at the same extremely low rate that he had paid me to shovel manure and curry nags.

He pointed out that he was doing me a favor, since my wife and I had to get to Joplin.

He had both logic and strength of position on his side; I agreed. But his wife did put up a lunch for us, as well as giving us breakfast after we slept in their shed.

So I was not too unhappy driving that rig, despite the weather, despite the frustrations. We were getting a few miles closer to Joplin every day—and now my darling was praying. It was beginning to look like "Home Free!" after all.

We had just reached the outskirts of this town (Lowell? Racine? I wish I could remember) when we encountered something right straight out of my childhood: a camp meeting, an old-time revival. On the left side of the road was a cemetery, well kept but the grass was drying; facing it on the right was the revival tent, pitched in a pasture. I wondered whether the juxtaposition of graveyard and Bible meeting was accidental, or planned?—if the Reverend Danny had been involved, I would know it was planned; most people cannot see gravestones without thinking about the long hereafter.

Crowded ranks of buggies and farm wagons stood near the tent, and a temporary corral lay beyond them.

Picnic tables of the plank-and-sawhorse type were by the tent on the other side; I could see remains of lunch. This was a serious Bible meeting, one that started in the morning, broke for lunch, carried on in the afternoon—would no doubt break for supper, then adjourn only when the revivalist judged that there were no more souls to be saved that day.

(I despise these modern city preachers with their five-minute "inspirational messages." They say Billy Sunday could preach for seven hours on only a glass of water—then do it again in the evening *and* the next day. No wonder heathen cults have spread like a green bay tree!)

There was a two-horse caravan near the tent. Painted on its side was: Brother "Bible" Barnaby. Out front was a canvas sign on guys and stays:

> That Old-Time Religion!
> Brother "Bible" Barnaby
> Healing Every Session
> 10a.m. — 2p.m. — 7p.m.
> Every Day from Sunday June 5th till
> !!!JUDGMENT DAY!!!

I spoke to the nag and pulled on the reins to let her know that I wanted to stop. "Darling, look at that!"

Margrethe read the sign, made no comment.

"I admire his courage," I said. "Brother Barnaby is betting his reputation that Judgment Day will arrive before it's time to harvest wheat . . . which could be early this year, hot as it is."

"But you think Judgment Day is soon."

"Yes, but I'm not betting a professional reputation on it . . . just my immortal soul and hope of Heaven.

Marga, every Bible student reads the prophecies slightly differently. Or very differently. Most of the current crop of premillenarians don't expect the Day earlier than the year two thousand. I want to hear how Brother Barnaby reasons. He might have something. Do you mind if we stay here an hour?"

"We will stay however long you wish. But— Alec, you wish me to go in? Must I?"

"Uh—" (Yes, darling, I certainly do want you to go inside.) "You would rather wait in the buggy?"

Her silence was answer enough. "I see. Marga, I'm not trying to twist your arm. Just one thing— We have not been separated except when utterly necessary for several weeks. And you know why. With the changes coming almost every day, I would hate to have one hit while you were sitting out here and I was inside, quite a way off. Uh, we could stand outside the tent. I see they have the sides rolled up."

She squared her shoulders. "I was being silly. No, we will go inside. Alec, I do need to hold your hand; you are right: Change comes fast. But I will not ask you to stay away from a meeting of your coreligionists."

"Thank you, Marga."

"And, Alec— I will *try!*"

"Thank you. Thank you loads! Amen!"

"No need to tank me. If you go to your Heaven, I want to go, too!"

"Let's go inside, dear."

I put the buggy at the far end of a rank, then led the mare to the corral, Marga with me. As we came back to the tent I could hear:

*　　*　　*

"—the corner where you are!

"Brighten the corner where you are!

"Someone far from harbor you may guide across the bar!

"So—"

I chimed in: "—brighten the corner where you are!" It felt good.

Their instrumental music consisted of a foot-pumped organ and a slide trombone. The latter surprised me but pleased me; there is no other instrument that can get right down and rassle with *The Holy City* the way a trombone can, and it is almost indispensable for *The Son of God Goes Forth to War.*

The congregation was supported by a choir in white angel robes—a scratch choir, I surmised, as the white robes were homemade, from sheets. But what that choir may have lacked in professionalism it made up for in zeal. Church music does not have to be good as long as it is sincere—and loud.

The sawdust trail, six feet wide, led straight down the middle, benches on each side. It dead-ended against a chancel rail of two-by-fours. An usher led us down the trail in answer to my hope for seats down front. The place was crowded but he got people to squeeze over and we wound up on the aisle in the second row, me outside. Yes, there were still seats in the back, but every preacher despises people—their name is legion!— who sit clear at the back when there are seats open down front.

As the music stopped, Brother Barnaby stood up and came to the pulpit, placed his hand on the Bible. "It's all in the Book," he said quietly, almost in a whisper. The congregation became dead still.

He stepped forward, looked around. "Who loves you?"

"Jesus loves me!"

"Let Him hear you."

"JESUS LOVES ME!"

"How do you know that?"

"IT'S IN THE BOOK!"

I became aware of an odor I had not smelled in a long time. My professor of homiletics pointed out to us once in a workshop session that a congregation imbued with religious fervor has a strong and distinctive odor ("stink" is the word he used) compounded of sweat and both male and female hormones. "My sons," he told us, "if your assembled congregation smells too sweet, you aren't getting to them. If you can't make 'em sweat, if they don't break out in their own musk like a cat in rut, you might as well quit and go across the street to the papists. Religious ecstasy is the strongest human emotion; when it's there, you can smell it!"

Brother Barnaby got to them.

(And, I must confess, I never did. That's why I wound up as an organizer and money-raiser.)

"Yes, it's in the Book. The Bible is the Word of God, not just here and there, but every word. Not as allegory, but as literal truth. You shall know the truth and the truth will make you free. I read to you now from the Book: 'For the Lord Himself will descend from Heaven with a shout, with the voice of the archangel, and with the Trump of God: and the dead in Christ shall rise first.'

"That last line is great news, my brothers and sisters: —the dead in Christ shall rise first.' What does that say? It does not say that the dead shall rise first; it says that the *dead in Christ* shall rise first. Those who were washed in the blood of the Lamb, born again in Jesus, and then have died in a state of grace *before* His second coming, they will not be forgotten, they will be *first*. Their graves will open, they will be miraculously restored to life and health and physical perfection and will lead the parade to Heaven, there to dwell in happiness by the great white throne forevermore!"

Someone shouted, "Hallelujah!"

"Bless you, sister. Ah, the good news! All the dead in Christ, every one! Sister Ellen, taken from her family by the cruel hand of cancer, but who died with the name of Jesus on her lips, *she* will help lead the procession. Asa's beloved wife, who died giving birth but in a state of grace, she will be there! All your dear ones who died in Christ will be gathered up and you will see them in Heaven. Brother Ben, who lived a sinful life, but found God in a foxhole before an enemy bullet cut him down, *he* will be there . . . and his case is specially good news, witnessing that God can be found anywhere. Jesus is present not only in churches—in fact there are fancy-Dan churches where His Name is rarely heard—"

"You can say that again!"

"And I will. God is everywhere; He can hear you when you speak. He can hear you more easily when you are ploughing a field, or down on your knees by your bed, than He can in some ornate cathedral surrounded by the painted and perfumed. He is here *now,* and He promises you, 'I will never desert you, nor will I ever forsake you. I stand at the door and knock, if anyone hears My voice and opens the door, I will come in to Him, and will dine with Him, and he with Me.' That's

His promise, dearly beloved, in plain words. No obscurities, no highfalutin 'interpretation,' no so-called 'allegorical meanings.' Christ Himself is waiting for you, if only you will ask.

"And if you do ask, if you are born again in Jesus, if He washes away your sins and you reach that state of grace . . . what then? I read you the first half of God's promise to the faithful. You will hear the Shout, you will hear the great Trumpet sounding His advent, as He promised, and the dead in Christ shall rise again. Those dry bones will rise again and be covered with living, healthy flesh.

"*Then* what?

"Hear the words of the Lord: 'Then we which are alive'— That's you and me, brothers and sisters; God is talking about *us*. 'Then we which are alive and remain shall be caught up together with them in the clouds, to meet the Lord in the air and so shall we ever be with the Lord'!

"So shall we ever be! So shall we *ever* be! With the Lord in Heaven!"

"Hallelujah!"

"Bless His Name!"

"Amen! Amen!"

(I found that I was one of those saying "Amen!")

"But there's a price. There are no free tickets to Heaven. What happens if you *don't* ask Jesus to help you? What if you ignore His offer to be washed free of sin and reborn in the blood of the Lamb? What then? Well? Answer me!"

The congregation was still save for heavy breathing, then a voice from the back said, not loudly, "Hellfire."

"Hellfire and damnation! Not for just a little while

but through all eternity! Not some mystical, allegorical fire that singes only your peace of mind and burns no more than a Fourth of July sparkler. This is the real thing, a raging fire, as real as this." Brother Barnaby slapped the pulpit with a crack that could be heard throughout the tent. "The sort of fire that makes a baseburner glow cherry red, then white. And you are *in* that fire, Sinner, and the ghastly pain goes on and on, and it never stops. Never! There's no hope for you. No use asking for a second chance. You've *had* your second chance . . . and your millionth chance. And more. For two thousand years sweet Jesus has been begging you, *pleading* with you, to accept from Him that for which He died in agony on the Cross to give you. So, once you are burning in that fiery Pit and trying to cough up the brimstone—that's sulfur, plain ordinary sulfur, burning and stinking, and it will burn your lungs and blister your sinful hide!—when you're roasting deep in the Pit for your sins, don't go whining about how dreadful it hurts and how you didn't know it would be like that. Jesus knows all about pain; He died on the Cross. He died for *you*. But you wouldn't listen and now you're down in the Pit and whining.

"And there you'll *stay*, suffering burning agony throughout eternity! Your whines can't be heard from down in the Pit; they are drowned out by the screams of billions of other sinners!"

Brother Barnaby lowered his voice to conversational level. "Do you want to burn in the Pit?"

"No!" — "Never!" — "Jesus save us!"

"Jesus will save you, if you ask Him to. Those who died in Christ are saved, we read about them. Those alive when He returns will be saved if they are born again and remain in that state of grace. He promised us that He would return, and that Satan would be chained for a thousand years while He rules in peace and justice here on earth. That's the Millennium, folks, that's the great day at hand. After that thousand years Satan will be loosed for a little while and the final battle will be fought. There'll be war in Heaven. The Archangel Michael will be the general for our side, leading God's angels against the Dragon—that's Satan again—and his host of fallen angels. And Satan lost—will lose, that is, a thousand years from now. And nevermore will he be seen in Heaven.

"But that's a thousand years from now, dear friends. You will live to see it . . . *if* you accept Jesus and are born again before that Trumpet blast that signals His return. When will that be? Soon, soon! What does the Book say? In the Bible God tells you not once but many times, in Isaiah, in Daniel, in Ezekiel, and in all four of the Gospels, that you will *not* be told the exact hour of His return. Why? So you can't sweep the dirt under the rug, that's why! If He told you that He would arrive New Year's Day the year two thousand, there are those who would spend the next five and a half years consorting with lewd women, worshiping strange gods, breaking every one of the Ten Commandments . . . then, sometime Christmas Week nineteen ninety-nine you would find them in church, crying repentance, trying to make a deal.

"No siree Bob! No cheap deals. It's the same price to everyone. The Shout and the Trump may be months away . . . or you may hear it before I can finish this sentence. It's up to you to be ready when it comes.

"But we know that it is coming soon. How? Again

it's in the Book. Signs and portents. The first, without which the rest cannot happen, is the return of the Children of Israel to the Promised Land—see Ezekiel, see Matthew, see today's newspapers. They rebuild the Temple . . . and sure enough they have; it's in the *Kansas City Star.* There be other signs and portents, wonders of all sorts—but the greatest are tribulations, trials to test the souls of men the way Job was tested. Can there be a better word to describe the twentieth century than 'tribulations'?

"Wars and terrorists and assassinations and fires and plagues. And more wars. Never in history has mankind been tried so bitterly. But endure as Job endured and the end is happiness and eternal peace—the peace of God, which passeth all understanding. He offers you His hand, He loves you, He will save you."

Brother Barnaby stopped and wiped his forehead with a large handkerchief that was already soggy from such use. The choir (perhaps at a signal from him) started singing softly, "We shall gather at the river, the beautiful, beautiful river, that flows by the throne of God—" and presently segued into:

"Just as I am, without one plea—"

Brother Barnaby got down on one knee and held out his arms to us. "Please! Won't you answer Him? Come, accept Jesus, let Him gather you in His arms—"

The choir continued softly with:

"But that Thy blood was shed for me,
"And Thou bidd'st me come to Thee,
"O Lamb of God, I come, I come!"

And the Holy Ghost descended.

I felt Him overpower me and the joy of Jesus filled my heart. I stood up and stepped out into the aisle Only then did I remember that I had Margrethe with me. I turned and saw her staring back at me, her face filled with a sweet and deeply serious look. "Come, darling," I whispered, and led her into the aisle. Together we went down the sawdust trail to God.

There were others ahead of us at the chancel rail. I found us a place, pushed some crutches and a truss aside, and knelt down. I placed my right hand on the rail, rested my forehead on it, while I continued to hold Marga's hand with my left. I prayed Jesus to wash away our sins and receive us into His arms.

One of Brother Barnaby's helpers was whispering into my ear. "How is it with you, brother?"

"I'm fine," I said happily, "and so is my wife. Help someone who needs it."

"Bless you, brother." He moved on. A sister farther down was writhing and speaking in tongues; he stopped to comfort her.

I bowed my head again, then became aware of neighing and loud squeals of frightened horses and a great flapping and shaking of the canvas roof above us. I looked up and saw a split start and widen, then the canvas blew away. The ground trembled, the sky was dark.

The Trump shook my bones, the Shout was the loudest ever heard, joyous and triumphant. I helped Margrethe to her feet and smiled at her. "It's *now*, darling!"

We were swept up.

We were tumbled head over heels and tossed about by a funnel cloud, a Kansas twister. I was wrenched away from Marga and tried to twist back, but could not. You can't swim in a twister; you go where it takes you. But I knew she was safe.

The storm turned me upside down and held me there for a long moment, about two hundred feet up. The horses had broken out of the corral, and some of the people, not caught up, were milling about. The force of the twister turned me again and I stared down at the cemetery.

The graves were opening.

XXII

When the morning stars sang together,
and all the sons of God shouted for joy.
Job 38:7

The wind whipped me around, and I saw no more of the graves. By the time I was faced down again the ground was no longer in sight—just a boiling cloud glowing inside with a great light, amber and saffron and powder blue and green gold. I continued to search for Margrethe, but few people drifted near me and none was she. Never mind, the Lord would protect her. Her temporary absence could not dismay me; we had taken the only important hurdle together.

I thought about that hurdle. What a near thing! Suppose that old mare had thrown a shoe and the delay had caused us to reach that point on the road an hour later than we did? Answer: We would never have reached it. The Last Trump would have sounded while we were still on the road, with neither of us in a state of grace. Instead of being caught up into the Rapture, we would have gone to Judgment unredeemed, then straight to Hell.

Do I believe in predestination?

That is a good question. Let's move on to questions I can answer. I floated above those clouds for a time unmeasured by me. I sometimes saw other people but no one came close enough for talk. I began to wonder when I would see our Lord Jesus—He had promised specifically that He would meet us "in the air."

I had to remind myself that I was behaving like a little child who demands that Mama do it *now* and is answered, "Be patient, dear. Not yet." God's time and mine were not the same; the Bible said so. Judgment Day had to be a busy time and I had no concept of what duties Jesus had to carry out. Oh, yes, I did know of one; those graves opening up reminded me. Those who had died in Christ (millions? billions? more?) were to go *first* to meet our Father Who art in Heaven, and of course the Lord Jesus would be with them on that glorious occasion; He had promised them that.

Having figured out the reason for the delay, I relaxed. I was willing to wait my turn to see Jesus . . . and when I did see Him, I would ask Him to bring Margrethe and me together.

No longer worried, no longer hurried, utterly comfortable, neither hot nor cold, not hungry, not thirsty, floating as effortlessly as a cloud, I began to feel the bliss that had been promised. I slept.

I don't know how long I slept. A long time—I had been utterly exhausted; the last three weeks had been grinding. Running a hand across my face told me that I had slept a couple of days or more; my whiskers had reached the untidy state that meant at least two days of neglect. I touched my breast pocket—yes, my trusty Gillette, gift of Marga, was still buttoned safely inside. But I had no soap, no water, no mirror.

This irritated me as I had been awakened by a bugle call (not the Great Trumpet—probably just one wielded by an angel on duty), a call that I knew without being told meant, "Wake up there! It is now your turn."

It was indeed—so when the "roll was called up yonder" I showed up with a two-day beard. Embarrassing!

Angels handled us like traffic cops, herding us into the formations they wanted. I knew they were angels; they wore wings and white robes and were heroic in size—one that flew near me was nine or ten feet tall. They did not flap their wings (I learned later that wings were worn only for ceremony, or as badges of authority). I discovered that I could move as these traffic cops directed. I had not been able to control my motions earlier; now I could move in any direction by volition alone.

They brought us first into columns, single file, stretched out for miles (hundreds of miles? thousands?). Then they brought the columns into ranks, twelve abreast—these were stacked in layers, twelve deep. I was, unless I miscounted, number four in my rank, which was stacked three layers down. I was about two hundred places back in my column—estimated while forming up—but I could not guess how long the column was.

And we flew past the Throne of God.

But first an angel positioned himself in the air about fifty yards off our left flank. His voice carried well. "Now hear this! You will pass in review in this formation. Hold your position at all times. Guide on the creature on your left, the creature under you, and the one ahead of you. Leave ten cubits between ranks and between layers, five cubits elbow to elbow in ranks. No crowding, no breaking out of ranks, no slowing down as we pass the Throne. Anybody breaking flight discipline will be sent to the tail end of the flight . . . and I'm warning you now, the Son might be gone by then, with nobody but Peter or Paul or some other saint to receive the parade. Any questions?"

"How much is a cubit?"

"Two cubits is one yard. Any creature in this cohort who does not know how long a yard is?"

No one spoke up. The angel added, "Any more questions?"

A woman to my left and above me called out, "Yes! My daughter didn't have her cough medicine with her. So I fetched it. Can you take it to her?"

"Creature, please accept my assurance that any cough your daughter manages to take with her to Heaven will be purely psychosomatic."

"But her doctor said—"

"And in the meantime shut up and let's get on with this parade. Special requests can be filed after arriving in Heaven."

There were more questions, mostly silly, confirming an opinion I had kept to myself for years: Piety does not imply horse sense.

Again the trumpet sounded; our cohort's flightmaster called out, *"Forward!"* Seconds later there was a single blast; he shouted, *"Fly!"* We moved forward.

(Note: I call this angel "he" because he seemed male. Ones that seemed to be female I refer to as "she." I never have been sure about sex in an angel. If any. I think they are androgynous but I never had a chance to find out. Or the courage to ask.)

(Here's another one that bothers me. Jesus had brothers and sisters; is the Virgin Mary still a virgin? I have never had the courage to ask that question, either.)

We could see His throne for many miles ahead. This was not the great white Throne of God the Father in Heaven; this was just a field job for Jesus to use on this occasion. Nevertheless it was magnificent, carved out of a single diamond with its myriad facets picking up Jesus' inner light and refracting it in a shower of fire and ice in all directions. And that is what I saw best, as the face of Jesus shines with such blazing light that, without sunglasses, you can't really see His features.

Never mind; you knew Who He was. One could not help knowing. A feeling of overpowering awe grabbed me when we were still at least twenty-five miles away. Despite my professors of theology, for the first time in my life I understood (felt) that single emotion that is described in the Bible by two words used together: love and fear. I loved/feared the Entity on that throne, and now I knew why Peter and James had abandoned their nets and followed Him.

And of course I did not make my request to Him as we passed closest (about a hundred yards). In my life on earth I had addressed (prayed to) Jesus by name thousands of times; when I saw Him in the Flesh I simply reminded myself that the angel herding us had promised us a chance to file personal requests when we reached Heaven. Soon enough. In the meantime it pleased me to think about Margrethe, somewhere in this parade, seeing the Lord Jesus on His throne . . . and if I had not intervened, she might never have seen Him. It made me feel warm and good, on top of the ecstatic awe I felt in staring at His blinding light.

*   *   *

Some miles past the throne the column swung up and to the right, and we left the neighborhood first of earth and then of the solar system. We headed straight for Heaven and picked up speed.

Did you know that earth looks like a crescent moon when you look back at it? I wondered whether or not any flat-earthers had managed to attain the Rapture. It did not seem likely, but such ignorant superstition is not totally incompatible with believing in Christ. Some superstitions are absolutely forbidden—astrology, for example, and Darwinism. But the flat-earth nonsense is nowhere forbidden that I know of. If there were any flat-earthers with us, how did they feel to look back and *see* that the earth was round as a tennis ball?

(Or would the Lord in His mercy let them perceive it as flat? Can mortal man ever understand the viewpoint of God?)

It seemed to take about two hours to reach the neighborhood of Heaven. I say "seemed to" because it might have been any length of time; there was no human scale by which to judge. In the same vein, the total period of the Rapture seemed to me to be about two days . . . but I had reason later to believe that it may have been seven years—at least by some reckoning. Measures of time and space become very slippery when one lacks mundane clocks and yardsticks.

As we approached the Holy City our guides had us slow down and then make a sightseeing sweep around it before going in through one of the gates.

This was no minor jaunt. New Jerusalem (Heaven, the Holy City, Jehovah's capital) is laid out foursquare like the District of Columbia, but it is enormously bigger, one thousand three hundred and twenty miles on a side, five thousand two hundred and eighty miles around it, and that gives an area of one million seven hundred and forty-two thousand four hundred square miles.

This makes cities like Los Angeles or New York look tiny.

In solemn truth the Holy City covers an area more than six times as big as all of Texas! At that, it's crowded. But they are expecting only a few more after us.

It's a walled city, of course, and the walls are two hundred and sixteen feet high, and the same wide. The tops of the wall are laid out in twelve traffic lanes—and no guard rails. Scary. There are twelve gates, three in each wall, the famous pearly gates (and they are); these normally stand open—will not be closed, we were told, until the Final Battle.

The wall itself is of iridescent jasper but it has a dozen footings in horizontal layers that are more dazzling than the wall itself: sapphire, chalcedony, emerald, sardonyx, chrysolite, beryl, topaz, amethyst—I may have missed some. New Jerusalem is so dazzling everywhere that it is hard for a human to grasp it—impossible to grasp it all at once.

When we finished the sweep around the Holy City, our cohort's flightmaster herded us into a holding pattern like dirigibles at O'Hare and kept us there until he received a signal that one of the gates was free—and I was hoping to get at least a glimpse of Saint Peter, but no—his office is at the main gate, the Gate of Judah, whereas we went in by the opposite gate, named for

Asher, where we were registered by angels deputized to act for Peter.

Even with all twelve gates in use and dozens of Peter-deputized clerks at each gate and examination waived (since we all were caught up at the Rapture—guaranteed saved) we had to queue up quite a long time just to get registered in, receive temporary identifications, temporary bunking assignments, temporary eating assignments—

("Eating"?)

Yes, I thought so, too, and I asked the angel who booked me about it. He/she looked down at me. "Refection is optional. It will do you no harm never to eat and not to drink. But many creatures and some angels enjoy eating, especially in company. Suit yourself."

"Thank you. Now about this berthing assignment. It's a single. I want a double, for me and my wife. I want—"

"Your former wife, you mean. In Heaven there is no marriage or giving in marriage."

"Huh? Does that mean we can't live together?"

"Not at all. But both of you must apply, together, at Berthing General. See the office of Exchange and Readjustments. Be sure, each of you, to fetch your berthing chit."

"But that's the problem! I got separated from my wife. How do I find her?"

"Not part of my M.O.S. Ask at the information booth. In the meantime use your singles apartment in Gideon Barracks."

"But—"

He (she?) sighed. "Do you realize how many thousands of hours I have been sitting here? Can you guess how complex it is to provide for millions of creatures at once, some alive and never dead, others newly incarnate? This is the first time we have had to install plumbing for the use of fleshly creatures—do you even suspect how inconvenient *that* is? I say that, when you install plumbing, you are bound to get creatures who *need* plumbing—and there goes the neighborhood! But did they listen to me? Hunh! Pick up your papers, go through that door, draw a robe and a halo—harps are optional. Follow the green line to Gideon Barracks."

"*No!*"

I saw his (her) lips move; she (he) may have been praying. "Do you think it is proper to run around Heaven looking the way you do? You are quite untidy. We aren't used to living-flesh creatures. Uh . . . Elijah is the last I recall, and I must say that you look almost as disreputable as he did. In addition to discarding those rags and putting on a decent white robe, if I were you I would do something about that dandruff."

"Look," I said tensely. "Nobody knows the trouble I've seen, nobody knows but Jesus. While you've been sitting around in a clean white robe and a halo in an immaculate city with streets of gold, I've been struggling with Satan himself. I know I don't look very neat but I didn't choose to come here looking this way. Uh— Where can I pick up some razor blades?"

"Some what?"

"Razor blades. Gillette double-edged blades, or that type. For this." I took out my razor, showed it to her/him. "Preferably stainless steel."

"Here everything is stainless. But what in Heaven is *that?*"

"A safety razor. To take this untidy beard off my face."

"Really? If the Lord in His wisdom had intended His male creations not to have hair on their faces, He would have created them with smooth features. Here, let me dispose of that." He-she reached for my razor.

I snatched it back. "Oh, no, you don't! Where's that information booth?"

"To your left. Six hundred and sixty miles." She-he sniffed.

I turned away, fuming. Bureaucrats. Even in Heaven. I didn't ask any more questions there because I spotted a veiled meaning. Six hundred and sixty miles is a figure I recalled from our sightseeing tour: the exact distance from a center gate (such as Asher Gate, where I was) to the center of Heaven, i.e., the Great White Throne of the Lord God Jehovah, God the Father. He (she) was telling me, none too gently, that if I did not like the way I was being treated, I could take my complaints to the Boss—i.e., "Get lost!"

I picked up my papers and backed away, looked around for someone else in authority.

The one who organized this gymkhana, Gabriel or Michael or whoever, had anticipated that there would be lots of creatures milling around, each with problems that didn't quite fit the system. So scattered through the crowd were cherubs. Don't think of Michelangelo or Luca della Robbia; these were not bambinos with dimpled knees; these were people a foot and a half taller than we newcomers were—like angels but with little cherub wings and each with a badge reading "STAFF."

Or maybe they were indeed angels; I never have been sure about the distinction between angels and cherubim and seraphim and such; the Book seems to take it for granted that you know such things without being told. The papists list *nine* different classes of angels! By whose authority? It's not in the Book!

I found only two distinct classes in Heaven: angels and humans. Angels consider themselves superior and do not hesitate to let you know it. And they are indeed superior in position and power and privilege. Saved souls are second-class citizens. The notion, one that runs all through Protestant Christianity and maybe among papists as well, that a saved soul will practically sit in the lap of God—well, it ain't so! So you're saved and you go to Heaven—you find at once that you are the new boy on the block, junior to everybody there.

A saved soul in Heaven occupies much the position of a blackamoor in Arkansas. And it's the angels who really rub your nose in it.

I never met an angel I liked.

And this derives from how they feel about us. Let's look at it from the angelic viewpoint. According to Daniel there are a hundred million angels in Heaven. Before the Resurrection and the Rapture, Heaven must have been uncrowded, a nice place to live and offering a good career—some messenger work, some choral work, an occasional ritual. I'm sure the angels liked it.

Along comes a great swarm of immigrants, many millions (billions?), and some of them aren't even housebroken. All of them require nursemaiding. After untold eons of beatific living, suddenly the angels find themselves working overtime, running what amounts to an enormous orphan asylum. It's not surprising that they don't like us.

Still . . . I don't like them, either. Snobs!

*   *   *

I found a cherub (angel?) with a STAFF badge and asked the location of the nearest information booth. He hooked a thumb over his shoulder. "Straight down the boulevard six thousand furlongs. It's by the River that flows from the Throne."

I stared down the boulevard. At that distance God the Father on His Throne looked like a rising sun. I said, "Six thousand furlongs is over six hundred miles. Isn't there one in this neighborhood?"

"Creature, it was done that way on purpose. If we had placed a booth on each corner, every one of them would have crowds around it; asking silly questions. This way, a creature won't make the effort unless it has a truly important question to ask."

Logical. And infuriating. I found that I was again possessed by unheavenly thoughts. I had always pictured Heaven as a place of guaranteed beatitude—not filled with the same silly frustration so common on earth. I counted to ten in English, then in Latin. "Uh, what's the flight time? Is there a speed limit?"

"Surely you don't think that you would be allowed to *fly* there, do you?"

"Why not? Just earlier today I flew here and then all the way around the City."

"You just thought you did. Actually, your cohort leader did it all. Creature, let me give you a tip that may keep you out of trouble. When you get your wings—*if* you ever do get wings—don't try to fly over the Holy City. You'll be grounded so fast your teeth will ache. And your wings stripped away."

"Why?"

"Because you don't rate it, that's why. You Johnny-

Come-Latelies show up here and think you own the place. You'd carve your initials in the Throne if you could get that close to it. So let me put you wise. Heaven operates by just one rule: R.H.I.P. Do you know what that means?"

"No," I answered, not entirely truthfully.

"Listen and learn. You can forget the Ten Commandments. Here only two or three of them still apply and you'll find you can't break those even if you were to try. The golden rule everywhere in Heaven is: Rank Hath Its Privileges. At this eon you are a raw recruit in the Armies of the Lord, with the lowest rank possible. And the least privilege. In fact the only privilege I can think of that you rate is being here, just being here. The Lord in His infinite wisdom has decreed that you qualify to enter here. But that's all. Behave yourself and you will be allowed to stay. Now as to the traffic rule you asked about. Angels and nobody else fly over the Holy City. When on duty or during ceremonies. That does not mean you. Not even if you get wings. If you do. I emphasize this because a surprising number of you creatures have arrived here with the delusion that going to Heaven automatically changes a creature into an angel. It doesn't. It can't. Creatures *never* become angels. A saint sometimes. Though seldom. An angel, never."

I counted ten backwards, in Hebrew. "If you don't mind, I'm still trying to reach that information booth. Since I am not allowed to fly, how *do* I get there?"

"Why didn't you say that in the first place? Take the bus."

Sometime later I was seated in a chariot bus of the Holy City Transit Lines and we were rumbling toward the distant Throne. The chariot was open, boat-shaped, with an entrance in the rear, and had no discernible motive power and no teamster or conductor. It stopped at marked chariot stops and that is how I got aboard. I had not yet found out how to get it to stop.

Apparently everyone in the City rode these buses (except V.I.P.s who rated private chariots). Even angels. Most passengers were humans dressed in conventional white and wearing ordinary halos. But a few were humans in costumes of various eras and topped off by larger and fancier halos. I noticed that angels were fairly polite to these creatures in the fancier halos. But they did not sit with them. Angels sat in the front of the car, these privileged humans in the middle part, and the common herd (including yours truly) in the rear.

I asked one of my own sort how long it took to reach the Throne.

"I don't know," I was answered. "I don't go nearly that far."

This soul seemed to be female, middle-aged, and friendly, so I used a commonplace opener. "That's a Kansas accent, is it not?"

She smiled. "I don't think so. I was born in Flanders."

"Really? You speak very fluent English."

She shook her head gently. "I never learned English."

"But—"

"I know. You are a recent arrival. Heaven is not affected by the Curse of Babel. Here the Confusion of Tongues never took place . . . and a good thing for me as I have no skill in languages—a handicap before I died. Not so here." She looked at me with interest. "May I ask where you died? And when?"

"I did not die," I told her. "I was snatched up alive in the Rapture."

Her eyes widened. "Oh, how thrilling! You must be very holy."

"I don't think so. Why do you say that?"

"The Rapture will come—came?—without warning. Or so I was taught."

"That's right."

"Then with no warning, and no time for confession, and no priest to help you . . . you were ready! As free from sin as Mother Mary. You came straight to Heaven. You *must* be holy." She added, "That's what I thought when I saw your costume, since saints—martyrs especially—often dress as they did on earth. I saw too that you are not wearing your saint's halo. But that's your privilege." She looked suddenly shy. "Will you bless me? Or do I presume?"

"Sister, I am not a saint."

"You will not grant me your blessing?"

(Dear Jesus, how did this happen to me?) "Having heard me say that, to the best of my knowledge and belief, I am not a saint, do you still want me to bless you?"

"If you will . . . holy father."

"Very well. Turn and lower your head a little—" Instead she turned fully and dropped to her knees. I put a hand on her head. "By authority vested in me as an ordained minister of the one true catholic church of Jesus Christ the Son of God the Father and by the power of the Holy Ghost, I bless this our sister in Christ. So mote it be!"

I heard echoes of "Amen!" around us; we had had quite an audience. I felt embarrassed. I was not certain, and still am not certain, that I had any authority to bestow blessings in Heaven itself. But the dear woman had asked for it and I could not refuse.

She looked up at me with tears in her eyes. "I knew it, I knew it!"

"Knew what?"

"That you are a saint. Now you are wearing it!"

I started to say, "Wearing what?" when a minor miracle occurred. Suddenly I was looking at myself from outside: wrinkled and dirty khaki pants, Army-surplus shirt with dark sweat stains in the armpits and a bulge of razor in the left breast pocket, three-day growth of beard and in need of a haircut . . . and, floating over my head, a halo the size of a washtub, shining and sparkling!

"Up off your knees," I said instead, "and let's stop being conspicuous."

"Yes, father." She added, "You should not be seated back here."

"I'll be the judge of that, daughter. Now tell me about yourself." I looked around as she resumed her seat, and happened to catch the eye of an angel seated all alone, up forward. (S)he gestured to me to come forward.

I had had my fill of the arrogance of angels; at first I ignored the signal. But everyone was noticing and pretending not to, and my awe-struck companion was whispering urgently, "Most holy person, the angelic one wants to see you."

I gave in—partly because it was easier, partly because I wanted to ask the angel a question. I got up and went to the front of the bus.

"You wanted me?"

"Yes. You know the rules. Angels in front, creatures

in back, saints in the middle. If you sit in back with creatures, you are teaching them bad habits. How can you expect to maintain your saintly privileges if you ignore protocol? Don't let it happen again."

I thought of several retorts, all unheavenly. Instead I said, "May I ask a question?"

"Ask."

"How much longer until this bus reaches the River from the Throne?"

"Why do you ask? You have all eternity before you."

"Does that mean that you don't know? Or that you won't tell?"

"Go sit down in your proper section. At once!"

I went back and tried to find a seat in the after space. But my fellow creatures had closed in and left me no room. No one said anything and they would not meet my eye, but it was evident that no one would aid me in defying the authority of an angel. I sighed and sat down in the mid-section, in lonely splendor, as I was the only saint aboard. If I was a saint.

I don't know how long it took to reach the Throne. In Heaven the light doesn't vary and the weather does not change and I had no watch. It was simply a boringly long time. Boring? Yes. A gorgeous palace constructed of precious stones is a wonderful sight to see. A dozen palaces constructed of jewels can be a dozen wonderful sights, each different from the other. But a hundred miles of such palaces will put you to sleep, and six hundred miles of the same is deadly dull. I began to long for a used-car lot, or a dump, or (best yet) a stretch of green and open countryside.

New Jerusalem is a city of perfect beauty; I am witness to that. But that long ride taught me the uses of ugliness.

I never have found out who designed the Holy City. That God authorized the design and construction is axiomatic. But the Bible does not name the architect(s), or the builder(s). Freemasons speak of "the Great Architect," meaning Jehovah—but you won't find that in the Bible. Just once I asked an angel, "Who designed this city?" He didn't sneer at my ignorance, he didn't scold me—he appeared to be unable to conceive it as a question. But it remains a question to me: Did God create (design and build) the Holy City Himself, right down to the smallest jewel? Or did He farm it out to subordinates?

Whoever designed it, the Holy City has a major shortcoming, in my opinion—and never mind telling me that my presumption in passing judgment on God's design is blasphemous. It *is* a lack, a serious one.

It lacks a public library.

One reference librarian who had devoted her life to answering any and all questions, trivial and weighty, would be more use in Heaven than another cohort of arrogant angels. There must be plenty of such ladies in Heaven, as it takes a saintly disposition and the patience of Job to be a reference librarian and to stick with it for forty years. But to carry on their vocation they would need books and files and so forth, the tools of their profession. Given a chance, I'm sure they would set up the files and catalog the books—but where would they get the books? Heaven does not seem to have a book-publishing industry.

Heaven doesn't have industry. Heaven doesn't have an economy. When Jehovah decreed, after the expulsion from Eden, that we descendants of Adam must gain our bread by the sweat of our faces, He created economics and it has been operating ever since for ca. 6000 years.

But not in Heaven.

In Heaven He giveth us our daily bread *without* the sweat of our faces. In truth you don't need daily bread; you can't starve, you won't even get hungry enough to matter—just hungry enough to enjoy eating if you want to amuse yourself by stopping in any of the many restaurants, refectories, and lunchrooms. The best hamburger I ever ate in my life was in a small lunchroom off the Square of the Throne on the banks of the River. But again, I'm ahead of my story.

Another lack, not as serious for my taste but serious, is gardens. No gardens, I mean, except the grove of the Tree of Life by the River near the Throne, and a few, a very few, private gardens here and there. I think I know why this is so and, if I am right, it may be self-correcting. Until we reached Heaven (the people of the Rapture and the resurrected dead-in-Christ) almost all citizens of the Holy City were angels. The million or so exceptions were martyrs for the faith, children of Israel so holy that they made it without ever having personally experienced Christ (i.e., mostly before 30 A.D.), and another group from unenlightened lands—souls virtuous without ever knowing of Christ. So 99 percent of the citizens of the Holy City were angels.

Angels don't seem to be interested in horticulture. I suppose that figures—I can't imagine an angel down on his/her knees, mulching the soil around a plant. They just aren't the dirty-fingernails sort needed to grow prize roses.

Now that angels are outnumbered by humans by at least ten to one I expect that we will see gardens— gardens, garden clubs, lectures on how to prepare the soil, and so forth. All the endless ritual of the devoted gardener. Now they will have time for it.

Most humans in Heaven do what they want to do without the pressure of need. That nice lady (Suzanne) who wanted my blessing was a lacemaker in Flanders; now she teaches it in a school open to anyone who is interested. I have gathered a strong impression that, for most humans, the real problem of an eternity of bliss is how to pass the time. (Query: Could there be something to this reincarnation idea so prevalent in other religions but so firmly rejected by Christianity? Could a saved soul be rewarded, eventually, by being shoved back into the conflict? If not on earth, then elsewhere? I've got to lay hands on a Bible and do some searching. To my utter amazement, here in Heaven Bibles seem to be awfully hard to come by.)

The information booth was right where it was supposed to be, close to the bank of the River of the Water of Life that flows from the Throne of God and winds through the grove of the Tree of Life. The Throne soars up from the middle of the grove but you can't see it very well that close to its base. It's like looking up at the tallest of New York skyscrapers while standing on the sidewalk by it. Only more so. And of course you can't see the Face of God; you are looking straight up one thousand four hundred and forty cubits. What you see is the Radiance . . . and you can feel the Presence.

The information booth was as crowded as that cherub had led me to expect. The inquirers weren't queued up;

they were massed a hundred deep around it. I looked at that swarm and wondered how long it would take me to work my way up to the counter. Was it possible to work my way there other than by the nastiest of bargain-day tactics, stepping on corns, jabbing with elbows, all the things that make department stores so uninviting to males?

I stood back and looked at that mob and tried to figure out how to cope. Or was there some other way to locate Margrethe without stepping on corns?

I was still standing there when a STAFF cherub came up to me. "Holy one, are you trying to reach the information booth?"

"I surely am!"

"Come with me. Stay close behind me." He was carrying a long staff of the sort used by riot police. "Gangway! Make way for a saint! Step lively there!" In nothing flat I reached the counter of the booth. I don't think anyone was injured but there must have been some hurt feelings. I don't approve of that sort of action; I think that treatment should be even-handed for everyone. But, where R.H.I.P. is the rule, being even a corporal is vastly better than being a private.

I turned to thank the cherub; he was gone. A voice said, "Holy one, what do you want?" An angel back of the counter was looking down at me.

I explained that I wanted to locate my wife. He drummed on the counter. "That's not ordinarily a service we supply. There is a co-op run by creatures called 'Find Your Friends and Loved Ones' for that sort of thing."

"Where is it?"

"Near Asher Gate."

"*What?* I just came from there. That's where I registered in."

"You should have asked the angel who checked you in. You registered recently?"

"Quite recently; I was caught up in the Rapture. I did ask the angel who registered me . . . and got a fast brushoff. He, she, uh, that angel told me to come here."

"Mrf. Lemme see your papers."

I passed them over. The angel studied them, slowly and carefully, then called to another angel, who had stopped servicing the mob to watch. "Tirl! Look at this."

So the second angel looked over my papers, nodded sagely, handed them back—glanced at me, shook his head sadly. "Is something wrong?" I asked.

"No. Holy one, you had the misfortune to be serviced, if that is the word, by an angel who wouldn't help his closest friend, if he had one, which he doesn't. But I'm a bit surprised that she was so abrupt with a saint."

"I wasn't wearing this halo at the time."

"That accounts for it. You drew it later?"

"I did not draw it. I acquired it miraculously, on the way from Asher Gate to here."

"I see. Holy one, it's your privilege to put Khromitycinel on the report. On the other hand I could use the farspeaker to place your inquiry for you."

"I think that would be better."

"So do I. In the long run. For you. If I make my meaning clear."

"You do."

"But before I call that co-op let's check with Saint

Peter's office and make sure your wife has arrived. When did she die?"

"She didn't die. She was caught up in the Rapture, too."

"So? That means a quick and easy check, no searching of old rolls. Full name, age, sex if any, place and date of—no, we don't need that. Full name first."

"Margrethe Svensdatter Gunderson."

"Better spell that."

I did so.

"That's enough for now. If Peter's clerks can spell. You can't wait here; we don't have a waiting room. There is a little restaurant right opposite us—see the sign?"

I turned and looked. "'The Holy Cow'?"

"That's it. Good cooking, if you eat. Wait there; I'll send word to you."

"Thank you!"

"You are welcome—" She glanced again at my papers, then handed them back. "—Saint Alexander Hergensheimer."

The Holy Cow was the most homey sight I had seen since the Rapture: a small, neat lunchroom that would have looked at home in Saint Louis or Denver. I went inside. A tall blackamoor whose chef's hat stuck up through his halo was at the grill with his back to me. I sat down at the counter, cleared my throat.

"Just hold your horses." He finished what he was doing, turned around. "What can I— Well, well! Holy man, what can I fix for you? Name it, just name it!"

"Luke! It's good to see you!"

He stared at me. "We have met?"

"Don't you remember me? I used to work for you. Ron's Grill, Nogales. Alec. Your dishwasher."

He stared again, gave a deep sigh. "You sure fooled me . . . Saint Alec."

"Just 'Alec' to my friends. It's some sort of administrative mistake, Luke. When they catch it, I'll trade this Sunday job for an ordinary halo."

"Beg to doubt—Saint Alec. They don't make mistakes in Heaven. Hey! Albert! Take the counter. My friend Saint Alec and I are going to sit in the dining room. Albert's my sous-chef."

I shook hands with a fat little man who was almost a parody of what a French chef should look like. He was wearing a *Cordon Bleu* hat as well as his halo. Luke and I went through a side door into a small dining room, sat down at a table. We were joined by a waitress and I got another shock.

Luke said, "Hazel, I want you to meet an old friend of mine, Saint Alec—he and I used to be business associates. Hazel is hostess of The Holy Cow."

"I was Luke's dishwasher," I told her. "Hazel, it's wonderful to see you!" I stood up, started to shake hands, then changed my mind for the better, put my arms around her.

She smiled up at me, did not seem surprised. "Welcome, Alec! 'Saint Alec' now, I see. I'm not surprised."

"I am. It's a mistake."

"Mistakes don't happen in Heaven. Where is Margie? Still alive on earth?"

"No." I explained how we had been separated. "So I'm waiting here for word."

"You'll find her." She kissed me, quickly and warmly—which reminded me of my four-day beard. I seated her, sat down with my friends. "You are sure to find her quickly, because that is a promise we were made and is precisely carried out. Reunion in Heaven with friends and loved ones. 'We shall gather by the River—' and sure enough, there it is, right outside the door. Steve— Saint Alec, you do remember Steve? He was with you and Margie when we met."

"How could I forget him? He bought us dinner and gave us a gold eagle when we were stony. Do I remember Steve!"

"I'm happy to hear you say that . . . because Steve credits you with converting him—born-again conversion—and getting him into Heaven. You see, Steve was killed on the Plain of Meggido, and I was killed in the War, too, uh, that was about five years after we met you—"

"Five years?"

"Yes. I was killed fairly early in the War; Steve lasted clear to Armageddon—"

"Hazel . . . it hasn't been much over a month since Steve bought us that dinner at Rimrock."

"That's logical. You were caught up in the Rapture and that touched off the War. So you spent the War years up in the air, and that makes it work out that Steve and I are here first even though you left first. You can discuss it with Steve; he'll be in soon. By the way, I'm his concubine now—his wife, except that here there is no marrying or giving in marriage. Anyhow Steve went back into the Corps when war broke out and got up to captain before they killed him. His outfit landed at Haifa and Steve died battling for the Lord at the height of Armageddon. I'm real proud of him."

"You should be. Luke, did the War get you, too?"

Luke gave a big grin. "No, sir, Saint Alec. They hanged me."

"You're joking!"

"No joke. They hanged me fair and square. You remember when you quit me?"

"I didn't quit you. A miracle intervened. That's how I met Hazel. And Steve."

"Well . . . you know more about miracles than I do. Anyway, we had to get another dishwasher right fast, and we had to take a Chicano. Man, he was a real bad ass, that one. Pulled a knife on me. That was his mistake. Pull a knife on a cook in his own kitchen? He cut me up some, I cut him up proper. Jury mostly his cousins, I think. Anyhow the D.A. said it was time for an example. But it was all right. I had been baptized long before that; the prison chaplain helped me be born again. I spoke a sermon standing on that trap with the noose around my neck. Then I said, 'You can do it now! Send me to Jesus! Hallelujah!' And they did. Happiest day of my life!"

Albert stuck his head in. "Saint Alec, there's an angel here looking for you."

"Coming!"

The angel was waiting just outside for the reason that he was taller than the doorway and not inclined to stoop. "You are Saint Alexander Hergensheimer?"

"That's me."

"Your inquiry concerning a creature designated Margrethe Svensdatter Gunderson: The report reads: Subject was not caught up in the Rapture, and has not shown up in any subsequent draft. This creature, Margrethe Svensdatter Gunderson, is not in Heaven and is not expected. That is all."

XXIII

I cry unto Thee, and Thou dost not hear me:
I stand up, and Thou regardest me not.
Job 30:20

So of course I eventually wound up in Saint Peter's
ffice at the Gate of Judah—having chased all over
eaven first. On Hazel's advice I went back to the Gate
' Asher and looked up that co-op "Find Your Friends
d Loved Ones."

"Saint Alec, angels don't pass out misinformation
d the records they consult are accurate. But they may
ot have consulted the right records, and, in my opin-
n, they would not have searched as deeply as you
ould search if you were doing it yourself—angels
ing angels. Margie might be listed under her maiden
me."

"That was what I gave them!"

"Oh. I thought you asked them to search for 'Margie
raham'?"

"No. Should I go back and ask them to?"

"No. Not yet. And when you do—if you must—
n't ask again at this information booth. Go directly

to St. Peter's office. There you'll get personal attention from other humans, not from angels."

"That's for me!"

"Yes. But try first at 'Find Your Friends and Loved Ones.' That's not a bureaucracy; it's a co-op made up of volunteers, all of them people who really care. That's how Steve found me after he was killed. He didn't know my family name and I hadn't used it for years, anyhow. He didn't know my date and place of death. But a little old lady at 'Find Your Friends' kept right on searching females named Hazel until Steve said 'Bingo!' If he had just checked at the main personnel office—Saint Peter's—they would have reported 'insufficient data, no identification.'"

She smiled and went on, "But the co-op uses imagination. They brought Luke and me together, even though we hadn't even met before we died. After I got tired of loafing I decided that I wanted to manage a little restaurant—it's a wonderful way to meet people and make friends. So I asked the co-op and they set their computers on 'cook,' and after a lot of false starts and wrong numbers it got Luke and me together and we formed a partnership and set up the Holy Cow. A similar search got us Albert."

Hazel, like Katie Farnsworth, is the sort of woman who heals just by her presence. But she's practical about it, too, like my own treasure. She volunteered to launder my dirty clothes and lent me a robe of Steve's to wear while my clothes dried. She found me a mirror and a cake of soap; at long last I tackled a five-day (seven-year?) beard. My one razor blade was closer to being a saw than a knife by then, but a half hour's patient honing using the inside of a glass tumbler (a trick I had learned in seminary) restored it to temporary usefulness.

But now I needed a proper shave even though I had shaved—tried to shave—a couple of hours ago. I did not know how long I had been on this hunt but I did know that I had shaved four times . . . with cold water, twice without soap, and once by Braille—no mirror. Plumbing had indeed been installed for us fleshly types . . . but not up to *American Standard* quality. Hardly surprising, since angels don't use plumbing and don't need it, and since the overwhelming majority of the fleshly ones have little or no experience with inside plumbing.

The people who man the co-op were as helpful as Hazel said they would be (and I don't think my fancy halo had anything to do with it) but nothing they turned up gave me any clue to Margrethe, even though they patiently ran computer searches on every combination I could think of.

I thanked them and blessed them and headed for Judah Gate, all the way across Heaven, thirteen hundred and twenty miles away. I stopped only once, at the Square of the Throne, for one of Luke's heavenburgers and a cup of the best coffee in New Jerusalem, and some encouraging words from Hazel. I continued my weary search feeling much bucked up.

The Heavenly Bureau of Personnel occupies two colossal palaces on the right as you come through the gate. The first and smaller is for B.C. admissions; the second is for admissions since then, and includes Peter's office suite, on the second floor. I went straight there.

A big double door read SAINT PETER — Walk In,

so I did. But not into his office; here was a waiting room big enough for Grand Central Station. I pushed through a turnstile that operated by pulling a ticket out of a slot, and a mechanical voice said, "Thank you. Please sit down and wait to be called."

My ticket read "2013" and the place was crowded; I decided, as I looked around for an empty seat, that I was going to need another shave before my number would come up.

I was still looking when a nun bustled up to me, and ducked a knee in a quick curtsy. "Holy one, may I serve you?" I did not know enough about the costumes worn by Roman Catholic orders to know what sisterhood she belonged to, but she was dressed in what I would call "typical"—long black dress down to her ankles and to her wrists, white starched deal over her chest and around her neck and covering her ears, a black headdress covering everything else and giving her the silhouette of a sphinx, a *big* rosary hanging around her neck . . . and an ageless, serene face topped off by a lopsided pince-nez. And, of course, her halo.

The thing that impressed me most was that she was here. She was the first proof I had seen that papists can be saved. In seminary we used to argue about that in late-night bull sessions . . . although the official position of my church was that certainly they could be saved, as long as they believed as we did and were born again in Jesus. I made a mental note to ask her when and how she had been born again—it would be, I was sure, an inspiring story.

I said, "Why, thank you, Sister! That's most kind of you. Yes, you can help me—that is, I hope you can. I'm Alexander Hergensheimer and I'm trying to find my wife. This is the place to inquire, is it not? I'm new here."

"Yes, Saint Alexander, this is the place. But you did want to see Saint Peter, did you not?"

"I'd like to pay my respects. If he's not too busy."

"I'm sure he will want to see you, Holy Father. Let me tell my Sister Superior." She picked up the cross on her rosary, appeared to whisper into it, then looked up. "Is that spelled H,E,R,G,E,N,S,H,E,I,M,E,R, Saint Alexander?"

"Correct, Sister."

She spoke again to the rosary. Then she added, to me, "Sister Marie Charles is secretary to Saint Peter. I'm her assistant and general gopher." She smiled. "Sister Mary Rose."

"It is good to meet you, Sister Mary Rose. Tell me about yourself. What order are you?"

"I'm a Dominican, Holy Father. In life I was a hospital administrator in Frankfurt, Germany. Here, where there is no longer a need for nursing, I do this work because I like to mingle with people. Will you come with me, sir?"

The crowd parted like the waters of the Red Sea, whether in deference to the nun or to my gaudy halo, I cannot say. Maybe both. She took me to an unmarked side door and straight in, and I found myself in the office of her boss, Sister Marie Charles. She was a tall nun, as tall as I am, and handsome—or "beautiful" may be more accurate. She seemed younger than her assistant . . . but how is one to tell with nuns? She was seated at a big flattop desk piled high and with an old-style Underwood typewriter swung out from its side.

She got up quickly, faced me, and dropped that odd curtsy.

"Welcome, Saint Alexander! We are honored by your call. Saint Peter will be with you soon. Will you be seated? May we offer you refreshment? A glass of wine? A Coca-Cola?"

"Say, I would really enjoy a Coca-Cola! I haven't had one since I was on earth."

"A Coca-Cola, right away." She smiled. "I'll tell you a secret. Coca-Cola is Saint Peter's one vice. So we always have them on ice here."

A voice came out of the air above her desk—a strong, resonant baritone of the sort I think of as a good preaching voice—a voice like that of "Bible" Barnaby, may his name be blessed. "I heard that, Charlie. Let him have his Coke in here; I'm free now."

"Were you eavesdropping again, Boss?"

"None of your lip, girl. And fetch one for me, too."

Saint Peter was up and striding toward the door with his hand out as I was ushered in. I was taught in church history that he was believed to have been about ninety when he died. Or when he was executed (crucified?) by the Romans, if he was. (Preaching has always been a chancy vocation, but in the days of Peter's ministry it was as chancy as that of a Marine platoon sergeant.)

This man looked to be a strong and hearty sixty, or possibly seventy—an outdoor man, with a permanent suntan and the scars that come from sun damage. His hair and beard were full and seemed never to have been cut, streaked with gray but not white, and (to my surprise) he appeared to have been at one time a redhead. He was well muscled and broad shouldered, and his hands were calloused, as I learned when he gripped my hand. He was dressed in sandals, a brown robe of coarse wool, a halo like mine, and a dinky little skullcap resting in the middle of that fine head of hair.

I liked him on sight.

He led me around to a comfortable chair near his desk chair, seated me before he sat back down. Sister Marie Charles was right behind us with two Cokes on a tray, in the familiar pinchwaist bottles and with not-so-familiar (I had not seen them for years) Coke glasses with the tulip tops and the registered trademark. I wondered who had the franchise in Heaven and how such business matters were handled.

He said, "Thanks, Charlie. Hold all calls."

"Even?"

"Don't be silly. Beat it." He turned to me. "Alexander, I try to greet each newly arrived saint personally. But somehow I missed you."

"I arrived in the middle of a mob, Saint Peter. Those from the Rapture. And not at this gate. Asher Gate."

"That accounts for it. A busy day, that one, and we still aren't straightened out. But a saint should be escorted to the main gate . . . by twenty-four angels and two trumpets. I'll have to look into this."

"To be frank, Saint Peter," I blurted out, "I don't think I *am* a saint. But I can't get this fancy halo off."

He shook his head. "You are one, all right. And don't let your misgivings gnaw at you; no saint *ever* knows that he is one, he has to be told. It is a holy paradox that anyone who thinks he is a saint never is. Why, when I arrived here and they handed me the keys and told me I was in charge, I didn't believe it. I thought the Master was playing a joke on me in return for a couple of japes I pulled on Him back in the days when we were barnstorming around the Sea of Galilee. Oh, no! He meant it. Rabbi Simon bar Jona the old fisherman was gone and I've been Saint Peter ever since. As you are Saint Alexander, like it or not. And you will like it, in time."

He tapped on a fat file folder lying on his desk. "I've been reading your record. There is no doubt about your sanctity. Once I reviewed your record I recalled your trial. Devil's Advocate against you was Thomas Aquinas; he came up to me afterwards and told me that his attack was *pro forma,* as there had never been any doubt in his mind but what you qualified. Tell me, that first miracle, ordeal by fire—did your faith ever waver?"

"I guess it did. I got a blister out of it."

Saint Peter snorted. "One lonely blister! And you don't think you qualify. Son, if Saint Joan had had faith as firm as yours, she would have quenched the fire that martyred her. I know of—"

Sister Marie Charles' voice announced, "Saint Alexander's wife is here."

"Show her in!" To me he added, "Tell you later."

I hardly heard him; my heart was bursting.

The door opened; in walked Abigail.

I don't know how to describe the next few minutes. Heartbreaking disappointment coupled with embarrassment summarizes it.

Abigail looked at me and said severely, "Alexander, what in the world are you doing wearing that preposterous halo? Take it off instantly!"

Saint Peter rumbled, "Daughter, you are not 'in the world'; you are in my private office. You will not speak to Saint Alexander that way."

Abigail turned her gaze to him, and sniffed. "You call *him* a saint? And didn't your mother teach you to stand up for ladies? Or are saints exempt from such niceties?"

"I do stand up, for *ladies*. Daughter, you will address me with respect. And you will speak to your husband with the respect a wife owes her husband."

"He's not my husband!"

"Eh?" Saint Peter looked from her to me, then back. "Explain yourself."

"Jesus said, 'For in the resurrection they neither marry, nor are given in marriage, but are as the angels.' So there! And He said it again in Mark twelve, twenty-three."

"Yes," agreed Saint Peter, "I heard Him say it. To the Sadducees. By that rule you are no longer a wife."

"Yes! Hallelujah! Years I have waited to be rid of that clod—be rid of him without sinning."

"I'm unsure about the latter. But not being a wife does not relieve you of the duty to speak politely to this saint who was once your husband." Peter turned again to me. "Do you wish her to stay?"

"Me? No, no! There's been a mistake."

"So it appears. Daughter, you may go."

"Now you just wait! Having come all this way, I have things I've been planning to tell you. Perfectly scandalous goings-on I have seen around here. Why, without the slightest sense of decency—"

"Daughter, I dismissed you. Will you walk out on your own feet? Or shall I send for two stalwart angels and have you thrown out?"

"Why, the very idea! I was just going to say—"

"You are *not* going to say!"

"Well, I certainly have as much right to speak my mind as anyone!"

"Not in this office. Sister Marie Charles!"

"Yes, sir!"

"Do you still remember the judo they taught you when you were working with the Detroit police?"

"I do!"

"Get this yenta out of here."

The tall nun grinned and dusted her hands together. What happened next happened so fast that I can't describe it. But Abigail left very suddenly.

Saint Peter sat back down, sighed, and picked up his Coke. "That woman would try the patience of Job. How long were you married to her?"

"Uh, slightly over a thousand years."

"I understand you. Why did you send for her?"

"I didn't. Well, I didn't intend to." I started to try to explain.

He stopped me. "Of course! Why didn't you say that you were searching for your concubine? You misled Mary Rose. Yes, I know whom you mean: the zaftig shiksa who runs all through the latter part of your dossier. Very nice girl, she seemed to me. You are looking for her?"

"Yes, surely. The day of the Trump and the Shout we were snatched up together. But that whirlwind, a real Kansas twister, was so violent that we were separated."

"You inquired about her before. An inquiry relayed from the information booth by the River."

"That's right."

"Alexander, that inquiry is the last entry in your file. I can order the search repeated . . . but I can tell you ahead of time that it will be useful only to assure you. The answer will be the same: She is not here."

He stood up and came around to put a hand on my shoulder. "This is a tragedy that I have seen repeated endlessly. A loving couple, confident of eternity together: One comes here, the other does not. What can I do? I wish I could do something. I can't."

"Saint Peter, there has been a mistake!"

He did not answer.

"Listen to me! I know! She and I were side by side, kneeling at the chancel rail, praying . . . and just before the Trump and the Shout the Holy Ghost descended on us and we were in a perfect state of grace and were snatched up together. Ask Him! Ask Him! He will listen to you."

Peter sighed again. "He will listen to anyone, in any of His Aspects. But I will inquire." He picked up a telephone instrument so old-fashioned that Alexander Graham Bell could have assembled it. "Charlie, give me the Spook. Okay, I'll wait. Hi! This is Pete, down at the main gate. Heard any new ones? No? Neither have I. Listen, I got a problem. Please run Yourself back to the day of the Shout and the Trump, when You, in Your aspect as Junior, caught up alive all those incarnate souls who were at that moment in a state of grace. Place Yourself outside a wide place in the road called Lowell, Kansas—that's in North America—and at a tent meeting, a revival under canvas. Are You there? Now, at least a few femtoseconds before the Trump, it is alleged by one Alexander Hergensheimer, now canonized, that You descended on him and his beloved concubine Margrethe. She is described as about three and a half cubits tall, blonde, freckled, eighty mina— Oh, You do? Oh. Too late, huh? I was afraid of that. I'll tell him."

I interrupted, whispering urgently, "Ask Him where she is!"

"Boss, Saint Alexander is in agony. He wants to know where she is. Yes, I'll tell him." Saint Peter hung up. "Not in Heaven, not on earth. You can figure out the answer for yourself. And I'm sorry."

I must state that Saint Peter was endlessly patient with me. He assured me that I could talk with any One of the Trinity . . . but reminded me that, in consulting the Holy Ghost we had consulted all of Them. Peter had fresh searches made of the Rapture list, the graves-opened list, and of the running list of all arrivals since then—while telling me that no computer search could conceivably deny the infallible answers of God Himself speaking as the Holy Ghost . . . which I understood and agreed with, while welcoming new searches.

I said, "But how about on earth? Could she be alive somewhere there? Maybe in Copenhagen?"

Peter answered, "Alexander, He is as omniscient on earth as He is in Heaven. Can't you see that?"

I gave a deep sigh. "I see that. I've been dodging the obvious. All right, how do I get from here to Hell?"

"Alec! Don't talk that way!"

"The hell I won't talk that way! Peter, an eternity here without her is not an eternity of bliss; it is an eternity of boredom and loneliness and grief. You think this damned gaudy halo means anything to me when I *know*—yes, you've convinced me!—that my beloved is burning in the Pit? I didn't ask much. Just to be allowed to live with her. I was willing to wash dishes forever if only I could see her smile, hear her voice, touch her hand! She's been shipped on a technicality and you know it! Snobbish, bad-tempered angels get to live here without ever doing one lick to deserve it. But my Marga, who is a real angel if one ever lived, gets turned down and sent to Hell to everlasting torture on a childish twist in the rules. You can tell the Father and His sweet-talking Son and that sneaky Ghost that they can take their gaudy Holy City and shove it! If Margrethe has to be in Hell, that's where *I* want to be!"

Peter was saying, "Forgive him, Father; he's feverish with grief—he doesn't know what he is saying."

I quieted down a little. "Saint Peter, I know exactly what I am saying. I don't want to stay here. My beloved is in Hell, so that is where I want to be. Where I *must* be."

"Alec, you'll get over this."

"What you don't see is that I don't *want* to get over this. I want to be with my love and share her fate. You tell me she's in Hell—"

"No, I told you that it is certain that she is not in Heaven and not on earth."

"Is there a fourth place? Limbo, or some such?"

"Limbo is a myth. I know of no fourth place."

"Then I want to leave here at once and look all over Hell for her. How?"

Peter shrugged.

"Damn it, don't give me a run-around! That's all I've been handed since the day I walked through the fire— one run-around after another. Am I a prisoner?"

"No."

"Then tell me how to go to Hell."

"Very well. You can't wear that halo to Hell. They wouldn't let you in."

"I never wanted it. Let's go!"

Not long after that I stood on the threshold of Judah Gate, escorted there by two angels. Peter did not say good-bye to me; I guess he was disgusted. I was sorry about that; I liked him very much. But I could not make him understand that Heaven was not Heaven to me without Margrethe.

I paused at the brink. "I want you to take one message back to Saint Peter—"

They ignored me, grabbed me from both sides, and tossed me over.

I fell.

And fell.

XXIV

And still I fell.

For modern man one of the most troubling aspects of eternity lies in getting used to the slippery quality of time. With no clocks and no calendars and lacking even the alternation of day and night, or the phases of the moon, or the pageant of seasons, duration becomes subjective and "What time is it?" is a matter of opinion, not of fact.

I think I fell longer than twenty minutes; I do not think that I fell as long as twenty years.

But don't risk any money on it either way.

There was nothing to see but the insides of my eyeballs. There was not even the Holy City receding in the distance.

Early on, I tried to entertain myself by reliving in memory the happiest times in my life—and found that happy memories made me sad. So I thought about sad occasions and that was worse. Presently I slept. Or I think I did. How can you tell when you are totally cut off from sensation? I remember reading about one of those busybody "scientists" building something he called a "sensory deprivation chamber." What he achieved was a thrill-packed three-ring circus compared with the meager delights of falling from Heaven to Hell.

My first intimation that I was getting close to Hell was the stink. Rotten eggs. H_2S. Hydrogen sulfide. The stench of burning brimstone.

You don't die from it, but small comfort that may be, since those who encounter this stench are dead when they whiff it. Or usually so; I am not dead. They tell of other live ones in history and literature—Dante, Aeneas, Ulysses, Orpheus. But weren't all of those cases fiction? Am I the first living man to go to Hell, despite all those yarns?

If so, how long will I stay alive and healthy? Just long enough to hit the flaming surface of the Lake?— there to go *psst!* and become a rapidly disappearing grease spot? Had my Quixotic gesture been just a wee bit hasty? A rapidly disappearing grease spot could not be much help to Margrethe; perhaps I should have stayed in Heaven and bargained. A saint in full-dress halo picketing the Lord in front of His Throne might have caused Him to reverse His decision . . . since *His* decision it had to be, L. G. Jehovah being omnipotent.

A bit late to think of it, boy! You can see the red glow on the clouds now. That must be boiling lava down there. How far down? Not far enough! How fast am I falling? Too fast!

I can see what the famous Pit is now: the caldera of an incredibly enormous volcano. Its walls are all around me, miles high, yet the flames and the molten lava are still a long, long way below me. But coming up fast! How are your miracle-working powers today, Saint Alec? You coped with that other fire pit with only a blister; think you can handle this one? The difference is only a matter of degree.

"With patience and plenty of saliva the elephant deflowered the mosquito." That job was just a matter of degree, too; can you do as well as that elephant? Saint Alec, that was not a saintly thought; what has happened to your piety? Maybe it's the influence of this wicked neighborhood. Oh, well, you no longer need worry about sinful thoughts; it is too late to worry about any sin. You no longer risk going to Hell for your sins; you are now entering Hell—you are now *in* Hell. In roughly three seconds you are going to be a grease spot. 'Bye, Marga my own! I'm sorry I never managed to get you that hot fudge sundae. Satan, receive my soul; Jesus is a fink—

They netted me like a butterfly. But a butterfly would have needed asbestos wings to have been saved the way I was saved; my pants were smoldering. They threw a bucket of water over me when they had me on the bank.

"Just sign this chit."

"What chit?" I sat up and looked out at the flames.

"This chit." Somebody was holding a piece of paper under my nose and offering me a pen.

"Why do you want me to sign it?"

"You have to sign it. It acknowledges that we saved you from the burning Pit."

"I want to see a lawyer. Meanwhile I won't sign anything." The last time I was in this fix it got me tied down, washing dishes, for four months. This time I couldn't spare four months; I had to get busy at once, searching for Margrethe.

"Don't be stupid. Do you want to be tossed back into *that* stuff?"

A second voice said, "Knock it off, Bert. Try telling him the truth."

("Bert?" I thought that first voice was familiar!) "Bert! What are *you* doing here?" My boyhood chum, the one who shared my taste in literature. Verne and Wells and Tom Swift—"garbage," Brother Draper had called it.

The owner of the first voice looked at me more closely. "Well, I'll be a buggered baboon. Stinky Hergensheimer!"

"In the flesh."

"I'll be eternally damned. You haven't changed much. Rod, get the net spread again; this is the wrong fish. Stinky, you've cost us a nice fee; we were fishing for Saint Alexander."

"Saint who?"

"Alexander. A Mick holy man who decided to go slumming. Why he didn't come in by a Seven-Forty-Seven God only knows; we don't usually get carriage trade here at the Pit. As may be, you've probably cost us a major client by getting in the way just when this saint was expected . . . and you ought to pay us for that."

"How about that fin you owe me?"

"Boy, do you have a memory! That's outlawed by the statute of limitations."

"Show it to me in Hell's law books. Anyhow, limitations can't apply; you never answered me when I tried to collect. So it's five bucks, compounded quarterly at six percent, for . . . how many years?"

"Discuss it later, Stinky. I've got to keep an eye out for this saint."

"Bert."

"Later, Stinky."

"Do you recall my right name? The one my folks gave me?"

"Why, I suppose— *Alexander!* Oh, no, Stinky, it can't be! Why, you almost flunked out of that back-woods Bible college, after you did flunk out of Rolla." His face expressed pain and disbelief. "Life can't be that unfair."

"'The Lord moves in mysterious ways, His wonders to perform.' Meet Saint Alexander, Bert. Would you like me to bless you? In lieu of a fee, I mean."

"We insist on cash. Anyhow, I don't believe it."

"I believe it," the second man, the one Bert had called "Rod," put in. "And I'd like your blessing, fa-ther; I've never been blessed by a saint before. Bert, there's nothing showing on the distant-warning screen and, as you know, only one ballistic arrival was pro-jected for this watch—so this *has* to be Saint Alex-ander."

"Can't be. Rod, I know this character. If he's a saint, I'm a pink monkey—" There was a bolt of lightning out of a cloudless sky. When Bert picked himself up, his clothes hung on him loosely. But he did not need them, as he was now covered with pink fur.

The monkey looked up at me indignantly. "Is that any way to treat an old pal?"

"Bert, I didn't do it. Or at least I did not intend to

do it. Around me, miracles just happen; I don't do them on purpose."

"Excuses. If I had rabies, I'd bite you."

Twenty minutes later we were in a booth at a lakefront bar, drinking beer and waiting for a thaumaturgist reputed to be expert in shapes and appearances. I had been telling them why I was in Hell. "So I've got to find her. First I've got to check the Pit; if she's in there it's *really* urgent."

"She's not in there," said Rod.

"Huh? I hope you can prove that. How do you know?"

"There's never anyone in the Pit. That's a lot of malarkey thought up to keep the peasants in line. Sure, a lot of the hoi polloi arrive ballistically, and a percentage of them used to fall into the Pit until the manager set up this safety watch Bert and I are on. But falling into the Pit doesn't do a soul any harm . . . aside from scaring him silly. It burns, of course, so he comes shooting out even faster than he went in. But he's not damaged. A fire bath just cleans up his allergies, if any."

(Nobody in the Pit! No "burning in Hell's fires throughout eternity"—what a shock that was going to be to Brother "Bible" Barnaby . . . and a lot of others whose stock in trade depended on Hell's fires. But I was not here to discuss eschatology with two lost souls; I was here to find Marga.) "This 'manager' you speak of. Is that a euphemism for the Old One?"

The monkey—Bert, I mean—squeaked, "If you mean Satan, say so!"

"That's who I mean."

"Naw. Mr. Ashmedai is city manager; Satan never does any work. Why should he? He owns this planet."

"This is a planet?"

"You think maybe it's a comet? Look out that window. Prettiest planet in this galaxy. And the best kept. No snakes. No cockroaches. No chiggers. No poison ivy. No tax collectors. No rats. No cancer. No preachers. Only two lawyers."

"You make it sound like Heaven."

"Never been there. You say you just came from there; you tell us."

"Well . . . Heaven's okay, if you're an angel. It's not a planet; it's an artificial place, like Manhattan. I'm not here to plug Heaven; I'm here to find Marga. Should I try to see this Mr. Ashmedai? Or would I be better off going directly to Satan?"

The monkey tried to whistle, produced a mouselike squeak. Rod shook his head. "Saint Alec, you keep surprising me. I've been here since 1588, whenever that was, and I've never laid eyes on the Owner. I've never thought of trying to see him. I wouldn't know how to start. Bert, what do you think?"

"I think I need another beer."

"Where do you put it? Since that lightning hit you, you aren't big enough to put away one can of beer, let alone three."

"Don't be nosy and call the waiter."

The quality of discourse did not improve, as every question I asked turned up more questions and no answers. The thaumaturgist arrived and bore off Bert on her shoulder, Bert chattering angrily over her fee—she wanted half of all his assets and demanded a contract signed in blood before she would get to work. He wanted her to accept ten percent and wanted me to pay half of that.

When they left, Rod said it was time we found a pad for me; he would take me to a good hotel nearby.

I pointed out that I was without funds. "No problem, Saint Alec. All our immigrants arrive broke, but American Express and Diners Club and Chase Manhattan vie for the chance to extend first credit, knowing that whoever signs an immigrant first has a strong chance of keeping his business forever and six weeks past."

"Don't they lose a lot, extending unsecured credit that way?"

"No. Here in Hell, everybody pays up, eventually. Bear in mind that here a deadbeat can't even die to avoid his debts. So just sign in, and charge everything to room service until you set it up with one of the big three."

The Sans Souci Sheraton is on the Plaza, straight across from the Palace. Rod took me to the desk; I signed a registration card and asked for a single with bath. The desk clerk, a small female devil with cute little horns, looked at the card I had signed and her eyes widened. "Uh, *Saint* Alexander?"

"I'm Alexander Hergensheimer, just as I registered. I am sometimes called 'Saint Alexander,' but I don't think the title applies here."

She was busy not listening while she thumbed through her reservations. "Here it is, Your Holiness—the reservation for your suite."

"Huh? I don't need a suite. And I probably couldn't pay for it."

"Compliments of the management, sir."

XXV

*And he had seven hundred wives, princesses, and
three hundred concubines: and his wives turned
away his heart.*
1 Kings 11:3

*Shall mortal man be more just than God? shall a
man be more pure than his maker?*
Job 4:17

"Compliments of the management!!" *How?* Nobody
knew I was coming here until just before I was chucked
out Judah Gate. Did Saint Peter have a hotline to Hell?
Was there some sort of under-the-table cooperation
with the Adversary? Brother, how that thought would
scandalize the Board of Bishops back home!

Even more so, *why?* But I had no time to ponder it;
the little devil—imp?—on duty slapped the desk bell
and shouted, "Front!"

The bellhop who responded was human, and a very
attractive youngster. I wondered how he had died so
young and why he had missed going to Heaven. But it
was none of my business so I did not ask. I did notice
one thing: While he reminded me in his appearance of a
Philip Morris ad, when he walked in front of me, leading me to my suite, I was reminded of another cigarette
ad—"So round, so firm, so fully packed." That lad had
the sort of bottom that Hindu lechers write poetry

about—could it have been that sort of sin that caused him to wind up here?

I forgot the matter when I entered that suite.

The living room was too small for football but large enough for tennis. The furnishings would be described as "adequate" by any well-heeled oriental potentate. The alcove called "the buttery" had a cold-table collation laid out ample for forty guests, with a few hot dishes on the end—roast pig with apple in mouth, baked peacock with feathers restored, a few such tidbits. Facing this display was a bar that was well stocked—the chief purser of *Konge Knut* would have been impressed by it.

My bellhop ("Call me 'Pat.'") was moving around, opening drapes, adjusting windows, changing thermostats, checking towels—all of those things bellhops do to encourage a liberal tip—while I was trying to figure out how to tip. Was there a way to charge a tip for a bellhop to room service? Well, I would have to ask Pat. I went through the bedroom (a Sabbath Day's journey!) and tracked Pat down in the bath.

Undressing. Trousers at half-mast and about to be kicked off. Bare bottom facing me. I called out, "Here, lad! *No!* Thanks for the thought . . . but boys are not my weakness."

"They're my weakness," Pat answered, "but I'm not a boy"—and turned around, facing me.

Pat was right; she was emphatically not a boy.

I stood there with my chin hanging down, while she took off the rest of her clothes, dumped them into a hamper. "There!" she said, smiling. "Am I glad to get out of that monkey suit! I've been wearing it since you were reported as spotted on radar. What happened, Saint Alec? Did you stop for a beer?"

"Well . . . yes. Two or three beers."

"I thought so. Bert Kinsey had the watch, did he not? If the Lake ever overflows and covers this part of town with lava, Bert will stop for a beer before he runs for it. Say, what are you looking troubled about? Did I say something wrong?"

"Uh, Miss. You are very pretty—but I didn't ask for a girl, either."

She stepped closer to me, looked up and patted my cheek. I could feel her breath on my chin, smell its sweetness. "Saint Alec," she said softly, "I'm not trying to seduce you. Oh, I'm available, surely; a party girl, or two or three, comes with the territory for all our luxury suites. But I can do a lot more than make love to you." She reached out, grabbed a bath towel, draped it round her hips. "*Ichiban* bath girl, too. Prease, you like me wark arong spine?" She dimpled and tossed the towel aside. "I'm a number-one bartender, too. May I serve you a Danish zombie?"

"Who told you I liked Danish zombies?"

She had turned away to open a wardrobe. "Every saint I've ever met liked them. Do you like this?" She held up a robe that appeared to be woven from a light blue fog.

"It's lovely. How many saints have you met?"

"One. You. No, two, but the other one didn't drink zombies. I was just being flip. I'm sorry."

"I'm not; it may be a clue. Did the information come from a Danish girl? A blonde, about your size, about your weight, too. Margrethe, or Marga. Sometimes 'Margie.'"

"No. The scoop on you was in a printout I was given when I was assigned to you. This Margie—friend of yours?"

"Rather more than a friend. She's the reason I'm in Hell. On Hell. In?"

"Either way. I'm fairly certain I've never met your Margie."

"How does one go about finding another person here? Directories? Voting lists? What?"

"I've never seen either. Hell isn't very organized. It's an anarchy except for a touch of absolute monarchy on some points."

"Do you suppose I could ask Satan?"

She looked dubious. "There's no rule I know of that says you can't write a letter to His Infernal Majesty. But there is no rule that says He has to read it, either. I think it would be opened and read by some secretary; they wouldn't just dump it into the Lake. I don't think they would." She added, "Shall we go into the den? Or are you ready for bed?"

"Uh, I think I need a bath. I know I do."

"Good! I've never bathed a saint before. Fun!"

"Oh, I don't need help. I can bathe myself."

She bathed me.

Shé gave me a manicure. She gave me a pedicure and *tsk-tsked* over my toenails—"disgraceful" was the mildest term she used. She trimmed my hair. When I asked about razor blades, she showed me a cupboard in the bath stocking eight or nine different ways of coping with beards. "I recommend that electric razor with the

hree rotary heads but, if you will trust me, you will
earn that I am quite competent with an old-fashioned
straight razor."

"I'm just looking for some Gillette blades."

"I don't know that brand but there are brand-new
azors here to match all these sorts of blades."

"No, I want my own sort. Double-edged. Stainless."

"Wilkinson Sword, double-edged lifetime?"

"Maybe. Oh, here we are!—'Gillette Stainless —
Buy Two Packs, Get One Free.'"

"Good. I'll shave you."

"No, I can do it."

A half hour later I settled back against pillows in a
bed fit for a king's honeymoon. I had a fine Dagwood in
my belly, a Danish zombie nightcap in my hand, and I
was wearing brand-new silk pajamas in maroon and old
gold. Pat took off that translucent peignoir in blue
smoke that she had worn except while bathing me and
got in beside me, placed a drink for herself, Glenlivet
on rocks, where she could reach it.

(I said to myself, "Look, Marga, I didn't choose this.
There is only this one bed. But it's a big bed and she's
not trying to snuggle up. You wouldn't want me to
kick her out, would you? She's a nice kid; I don't want
to hurt her feelings. I'm tired; I'm going to drink this
and go right to sleep.")

I didn't go right to sleep. Pat was not the least bit
aggressive. But she was *very* cooperative. I found one
part of my mind devoting itself intensely to what Pat
had to offer (plenty!) while another part of my mind
was explaining to Marga that this wasn't anything se-

rious; I don't love her; I love you and only you and always will . . . but I haven't been able to sleep and—

Then we slept for a while. Then we watched a living hollow gram that Pat said was "X rated" and I learned about things I had never heard of, but it turned out that Pat had and could do them and could teach me and this time I paused just long enough to tell Marga was learning them for both of us, then I turned my whole attention to learning.

Then we napped again.

It was some time later that Pat reached out and touched my shoulder. "Turn over this way, dear; let me see your face. I thought so. Alec, I know you're carrying the torch for your sweetheart; that's why I'm here to make it easier. But I can't if you won't try. What did she do for you that I haven't done and can't do? Does she have that famous left-hand thread? Or what? Name it, describe it. I'll either do it, or fake it, or send out for it. Please, dear. You're beginning to hurt my professional pride."

"You're doing just fine." I patted her hand.

"I wonder. More girls like me, maybe, in various flavors? Drown you in tits?—chocolate, vanilla, strawberry, tutti-frutti. 'Tutti-frutti'—hmm . . . Maybe you'd like a San Francisco sandwich? Or some other Sodom-and-Gomorrah fancy? I have a male friend from Berkeley who isn't all that male; he has a delicious playful imagination; I've teamed with him many times. And he has on call others like him; he's a member of both Aleister Crowley Associates and Nero's Heroes and Zeroes. If you fancy a mob scene, Donny and I can cast it any way you like, and the Sans Souci will orchestrate it to suit your taste. Persian Garden, sorority house,

Turkish harem, jungle drums with obscene rites, nunnery— 'Nunnery'—did I tell you what I did before I died?"

"I wasn't certain you had died."

"Oh, certainly. I'm not an imp faking human; I'm human. You don't think anyone could get a job like this without human experience, do you? You have to be human right down to your toes to please a fellow human most; that stuff about the superior erotic ability of succubi is just their advertising. I was a nun, Alec, from adolescence to death, most of it spent teaching grammar and arithmetic to children who didn't want to learn.

"I soon learned that my vocation had not been a true one. What I did not know was how to get out of it. So I stayed. At about thirty I discovered just how miserably awful my mistake had been; my sexuality reached maturity. Mean to say I got horny, Saint Alec, and stayed horny and got more so every year.

"The worst thing about my predicament was not that I was subjected to temptation but that I was *not* subjected to temptation—as I would have grabbed any opportunity. Fat chance! My confessor might have looked upon me with lust had I been a choir boy—as it was, he sometimes snored while I was confessing. Not surprising; my sins were dull, even to me."

"What were your sins, Pat?"

"Carnal thoughts, most of which I did not confess. Not being forgiven, they went straight into Saint Peter's computers. Blasphemous adulterous fornication."

"Huh? Pat, you have quite an imagination."

"Not especially, just horny. You probably don't know just how hemmed in a nun is. She is a bride of

Christ; that's the contract. So even to *think* about the joys of sex makes of her an adulterous wife in the worst possible way."

"Be darned. Pat, I recently met two nuns, in Heaven. Both seemed like hearty wenches, one especially. Yet there they were."

"No inconsistency. Most nuns confess their sins regularly, are forgiven. Then they usually die in the bosom of their Family, with its chaplain or confessor at hand. So she gets the last rites with her sins all forgiven and she's shipped straight to Heaven, pure as Ivory soap.

"But not me!" She grinned. "I'm being punished for my sins and enjoying every wicked minute of it. I died a virgin in 1918, during the big flu epidemic, and so many died so fast that no priest got to me in time to grease me into Heaven. So I wound up here. At the end of my thousand-year apprenticeship—"

"Hold it! You died in 1918?"

"Yes. The great Spanish Influenza epidemic. Born in 1878, died in 1918, on my fortieth birthday. Would you prefer for me to look forty? I can, you know."

"No, you look just fine. Beautiful."

"I wasn't sure. Some men— Lots of eager motherhumpers around here and most of them never got a chance to do it while they were alive. It's one of my easier entertainments. I simply lead you into hypnotizing yourself, you supply the data. Then I look and sound exactly like your mother. Smell like her, too. Everything. Except that I am available to you in ways that your mother probably was not. I—"

"Patty, I don't even *like* my mother!"

"Oh. Didn't that cause you trouble at Judgment Day?"

"No. That's not in the rules. It says in the Book that you must honor thy father and thy mother. Not one word about loving them. I honored her, all the full protocol. Kept her picture on my desk. A letter every week. Telephoned her on her birthday. Called on her in person as my duties permitted. Listened to her eternal bitching and to her poisonous gossip about her women friends. Never contradicted her. Paid her hospital bills. Followed her to her grave. But weep I did not. She didn't like me and I didn't like her. Forget my mother! Pat, I asked you a question and you changed the subject."

"Sorry, dear. Hey, look what I've found!"

"Don't change the subject again; just keep it warm in your hand while you answer my question. You said something about your 'thousand-year apprenticeship.'"

"Yes?"

"But you said also that you died in 1918. The Final Trump sounded in 1994—I know; I was there. That's only seventy-six years later than your death. To me that Final Trump seems like only a few days ago, about a month, no more. I ran across something that seemed to make it seven years ago. But that still isn't over nine hundred, the best part of a thousand years. I'm not a spirit, I'm a living body. And I'm not Methuselah." (Damn it, is Margrethe separated from me by a thousand years? This isn't fair!)

"Oh. Alec, in eternity a thousand years isn't any particular time; it is simply a long time. Long enough in this case to test whether or not I had both the talent and the disposition for the profession. That took quite a while because, while I was horny enough—and stayed that way; almost any guest can send me right through the ceiling—as you noticed—I had arrived here knowing nothing about sex. Nothing! But I did learn and eventually Mary Magdalene gave me high marks and recommended me for permanent appointment."

"Is *she* down *here?*"

"Oh. She's a visiting professor here; she's on the permanent faculty in Heaven."

"What does she teach in Heaven?"

"I have no idea but it can't be what she teaches here. Or I don't *think* so. Hmm. Alec, she's one of the eternal greats; she makes her own rules. But this time you changed the subject. I was trying to tell you that I don't know how long my apprenticeship lasted because time is whatever you want it to be. How long have you and I been in bed together?"

"Uh, quite a while. But not long enough. I think it must be near midnight."

"It's midnight if you want it to be midnight. Want me to get on top?"

The next morning, whenever that was, Pat and I had breakfast on the balcony looking out over the Lake. She was dressed in Marga's favorite costume, shorts tight and short, and a halter with her breasts tending to overflow their bounds. I don't know when she got her clothes, but my pants and shirt had been cleaned and repaired in the night and my underwear and socks washed—in Hell there seem to be busy little imps everywhere. Besides, they could have driven a flock of geese through our bedroom the latter part of the night without disturbing me.

I looked at Pat across the table, appreciating her wholesome, girl-scout beauty, with her sprinkle of

reckles across her nose, and thought how strange it was
hat I had ever confused sex with sin. Sex can involve
in, surely—any human act can involve cruelty and in-
ustice. But sex alone held no taint of sin. I had arrived
ere tired, confused, and unhappy—Pat had first made
ne happy, then caused me to rest, then left me happy
his lovely morning.

Not any less anxious to find you, Marga my own—
ut in much better shape to push the search.

Would Margrethe see it that way?

Well, she had never seemed jealous of me.

How would I feel if she took a vacation, a sexual
acation, such as I had just enjoyed? That's a good
uestion. Better think about it, boy—because sauce for
he goose is not a horse of another color.

I looked out over the Lake, watched the smoke rise
nd the flames throwing red lights on the smoke . . .
while right and left were green and sunny early summer
ights, with snow-tipped mountains in the far distance.
Pat—"

"Yes, dear?"

"The Lake bank can't be more than a furlong from
ere. But I can't smell any brimstone."

"Notice how the breeze is blowing those banners?
'rom anywhere around the Pit the wind blows toward
he Pit. There it rises—incidentally slowing any soul
rriving ballistically—and then on the far side of the
lobe there is a corresponding down draft into a cold
it where the hydrogen sulfide reacts with oxygen to
orm water and sulfur. The sulfur is deposited; the
vater comes out as water vapor, and returns. The two
its and this circulation control the weather here some-

what the way the moon acts as a control on earth weather. But gentler."

"I was never too hot at physical sciences . . . but that doesn't sound like the natural laws I learned in school."

"Of course not. Different Boss here. He runs this planet to suit himself."

Whatever I meant to answer got lost in a mellow gong played inside the suite. "Shall I answer, sir?"

"Sure, but how dare you call me 'sir'? Probably just room service. Huh?"

"No, dear Alec, room service will just come in when they see that we are through." She got up, came back quickly with an envelope. "Letter by Imperial courier. For you, dear."

Me? I accepted it gingerly, and opened it. An embossed seal at the top: the conventional Devil in red, horns, hooves, tail, pitchfork, and standing in flames. Below it:

Saint Alexander Hergensheimer
Sans Souci Sheraton
The Capital

Greetings:

In response to your petition for an audience with His Infernal Majesty, Satan Mekratrig, Sovereign of Hell and His Colonies beyond, First of the Fallen Thrones, Prince of Lies, I have the honour to advise you that His Majesty requires you to substantiate your request by supplying to this office a full and frank memoir of your life. When this has been done, a decision on your request will be made.

May I add to His Majesty's message this advice:
Any attempt to omit, slur over, or color in the belief
that you will thereby please His Majesty will *not*
please Him.

> I have the honour to remain,
> Sincerely His,
> (s) Beelzebub
> Secretary to His Majesty

I read it aloud to Pat. She blinked her eyes and whis-
led. "Dear, you had better get busy!"

"I—" The paper burst into flames; I dropped it into
he dirty dishes. "Does that always happen?"

"I don't know; it's the first time I've ever seen a mes-
age from Number One. And the first time I've heard of
anyone being even conditionally granted an audience."

"Pat. I didn't ask for an audience. I planned to find
out how to do so today. But I have not put in the
request this answers."

"Then you must put in the request *at once*. It
wouldn't do to let it stay unbalanced. I'll help dear—
I'll type it for you."

The imps had been around again. In one corner of
hat vast living room I found that they had installed
two desks, one a writing desk, with stacks of paper and
a tumbler of pens, the other a more complex setup. Pat
went straight to that one. "Dear, it looks like I'm still
assigned to you. I'm your secretary now. The latest and
best Hewlett-Packard equipment—this is going to be
fun! Or do you know how to type?"

"I'm afraid not."

"Okay, you write it longhand; I'll put it into shape
. . and correct your spelling and your grammar—you

just whip it out. Now I know why I was picked for this job. Not my girlish smile, dear—my typing. Most of my guild can't type. Many of them took up whoring because shorthand and typing were too much for them. Not me. Well, let's get to work; this job will run days, weeks, I don't know. Do you want me to continue to sleep here?"

"Do you want to leave?"

"Dear, that's the guest's decision. Has to be."

"I don't want you to leave." (Marga! Do please understand!)

"Good thing you said that, or I would have burst into tears. Besides, a good secretary should stick around in case something comes up in the night."

"Pat, that was an old joke when I was in seminary."

"It was an old joke before you were born, dear. Let's get to work."

Visualize a calendar (that I don't have), its pages ripping off in the wind. This manuscript gets longer and longer but Pat insists that Prince Beelzebub's advice must be taken literally. Pat makes two copies of all that I write; one copy stacks up on my desk, the other copy disappears each night. Imps again. Pat tells me that I can assume that the vanishing copy is going to the Palace, at least as far as the Prince's desk . . . so what I am doing so far must be satisfactory.

In less than two hours each day Pat types out and prints out what takes me all day to write. But I stopped driving so hard when a handwritten note came in:

*　　*　　*

You are working too hard. Enjoy yourself. Take her to the theater. Go on a picnic. Don't be so wound up.

(s) B.

The note self-destroyed, so I knew it was authentic. So I obeyed. With pleasure! But I am not going to describe the fleshpots of Satan's capital city.

This morning I finally reached that odd point where I was (am) writing now about what is going on now—and I hand my last page to Pat.

Less than an hour after I completed that line above the gong sounded; Pat went out into the foyer, hurried back. She put her arms around me. "This is good-bye, dear. I won't be seeing you again."

"*What!*"

"Just that, dear. I was told this morning that my assignment was ending. And I have something I must tell you. You will find, you are bound to learn, that I have been reporting on you daily. Please don't be angry about it. I am a professional, part of the Imperial security staff."

"Be damned! So every kiss, every sigh, was a fake."

"Not one was fake! Not one! And, when you find your Marga, please tell her that I said she is lucky."

"Sister Mary Patricia, is this another lie?"

"Saint Alexander, I have never lied to you. I've had to hold back some things until I was free to speak, that's all." She took her arms from around me.

"Hey! Aren't you going to kiss me good-bye?"

"Alec, if you really want to kiss me, you won't ask."

I didn't ask; I did it. If Pat was faking, she's a better actress than I think she is.

Two giant fallen angels were waiting to take me to the Palace. They were heavily armed and fully armored. Pat had packaged my manuscript and told me that I was expected to bring it with me. I started to leave—then stopped most suddenly. "My razor!"

"Check your pocket, dear."

"Huh? How'd it get there?"

"I knew you weren't coming back, dear."

Again I learned that, in the company of angels, I could fly. Out my own balcony, around the Sans Souci Sheraton, across the Plaza, and we landed on a third-floor balcony of Satan's Palace. Then through several corridors, up a flight of stairs with lifts too high to be comfortable for humans. When I stumbled, one of my escorts caught me, then steadied me until we reached the top, but said nothing—neither ever said anything.

Great brass doors, as complex as the Ghiberti Doors, opened. I was shoved inside.

And saw Him.

A dark and smoky hall, armed guards down both sides, a high throne, a Being on it, at least twice as high as a man . . . a Being that was the conventional Devil such as you see on a Pluto bottle or a deviled-ham tin—tail and horns and fierce eyes, a pitchfork in lieu of scepter, a gleam from braziers glinting off Its dark red skin, sleek muscles. I had to remind myself that the Prince of Lies could look any way He wished; this was probably to daunt me.

His voice rumbled out like a foghorn: "Saint Alexander, you may approach Me."

XXVI

I am a brother to dragons, and a companion to owls.
Job 30:29

I started up the steps leading to the throne. Again, the lifts were too high, the treads too wide, and now I had no one to steady me. I was reduced to crawling up those confounded steps while Satan looked down at me with a sardonic smile. From all around came music from an unseen source, death music, vaguely Wagnerian but nothing I could identify. I think it was laced with that below-sonic frequency that makes dogs howl, horses run away, and causes men to think of flight or suicide.

That staircase kept stretching.

I didn't count the number of steps when I started up, but the flight looked to be about thirty steps, no more. When I had been crawling up it for several minutes, I realized that it looked as high as ever. The Prince of Lies!

So I stopped and waited.

Presently that rumbling voice said, "Something wrong, Saint Alexander?"

"Nothing wrong," I answered, "because You planned it this way. If You really want me to approach You, You will turn off the joke circuit. In the meantime there is no point in my trying to climb a treadmill."

"You think I am doing that to you?"

"I *know* that You are. A game. Cat and mouse."

"You are trying to make a fool of Me, in front of My gentlemen."

"No, Your Majesty, I cannot make a fool of You. Only You can do that."

"Ah so. Do you realize that I can blast you where you stand?"

"Your Majesty, I have been totally in Your power since I entered Your realm. What do You wish of me? Shall I continue trying to climb Your treadmill?"

"Yes."

So I did, and the staircase stopped stretching and the treads reduced to a comfortable seven inches. In seconds I reached the same level as Satan—the level of His cloven feet, that is. Which put me much too close to Him. Not only was His Presence terrifying—I had to keep a close grip on myself—but also He *stank*! Of filthy garbage cans, of rotting meat, of civet and skunk, of brimstone, of closed rooms and gas from diseased gut—all that and worse. I said to myself, Alex Hergensheimer, if you let Him prod you into throwing up and thereby kill any chance of getting you and Marga back together—just don't do it! Control yourself!

"The stool is for you," said Satan. "Be seated."

Near the throne was a backless stool, low enough to destroy the dignity of anyone who sat on it. I sat.

Satan picked up a manuscript with a hand so big that

the business-size sheets were like a deck of cards in His hand. "I've read it. Not bad. A bit wordy but My editors will cut it—better that way than too brief. We will need an ending for it . . . from you or by a ghost. Probably the latter; it needs more impact than you give it. Tell me, have you ever thought of writing for a living? Rather than preaching?"

"I don't think I have the talent."

"Talent shmalent. You should *see* the stuff that gets published. But you must hike up those sex scenes; today's cash customers demand such scenes *wet*. Never mind that now; I didn't call you here to discuss your literary style and its shortcomings. I called you in to make you an offer."

I waited. So did He. After a bit He said, "Aren't curious about the offer?"

"Your Majesty, certainly I am. But, if my race has earned one lesson concerning You, it is that a human should be extremely cautious in bargaining with You."

He chuckled and the foundations shook. "Poor little human, did you really think that I wanted to dicker for your scrawny soul?"

"I don't know what You want. But I'm not as smart as Dr. Faust, and not nearly as smart as Daniel Webster. It behooves me to be cautious."

"Oh, come! I don't want your soul. There's no market for souls today; there are far too many of them and quality is way down. I can pick them up at a nickel a bunch, like radishes. But I don't; I'm overstocked. No, Saint Alexander, I wish to retain your services. Your professional services."

(I was suddenly alarmed. What's the catch? Alex,

this is loaded! Look behind you! What's He after?)
"You need a dishwasher?"

He chuckled again, about 4.2 on the Richter scale.
"No, no, Saint Alexander! Your vocation—not the ex-
igency to which you were temporarily reduced. I want
to hire you as a gospel-shouter, a Bible-thumper. I
want you to work the Jesus business, just as you were
trained to. You won't have to raise money or pass the
collection plate; the salary will be ample and the duties
light. What do you say?"

"I say You are trying to trick me."

"Now that's not very kind. No tricks, Saint Alexander. You will be free to preach exactly as you please,
no restrictions. Your title will be personal chaplain to
Me, and Primate of Hell. You can devote the rest of
your time—as little or as much as you wish—to saving
lost souls . . . and there are plenty of those here. Salary
to be negotiated . . . but not less than the incumbent,
Pope Alexander the Sixth, a notoriously greedy soul.
You won't be pinched, I promise you. Well? How say
you?"

(Who's crazy? The Devil, or me? Or am I having
another of those nightmares that have been dogging me
lately?) "Your Majesty, You have not mentioned anything I want."

"Ah so? Everybody needs money. You're broke; you
can't stay in that fancy suite another day without finding a job." He tapped the manuscript. "This may bring
in something, some day. Not soon. I'm not going to
advance you anything on it; it might not sell. There are
too many I-Was-a-Prisoner-of-the-Evil-King extrava-
ganzas on the market already these days."

"Your Majesty, You have read my memoir; You *know* what I want."

"Eh? Name it."

"You know. My beloved. Margrethe Svensdatter Gunderson."

He looked surprised. "Didn't I send you a memo about that? She's not in Hell."

I felt like a patient who has kept his chin up right up to the minute the biopsy comes back . . . and then can't accept the bad news. "Are You *sure?*"

"Of course I am. Who do you think is in charge round here?"

(Prince of Liars, Prince of Lies!) "How can You be sure? The way I hear it, nobody keeps track. A person could be in Hell for years and You would never know, one way or the other."

"If that's the way you heard it, you heard wrong. Look, if you accept My offer, you'll be able to afford the best agents in history, from Sherlock Holmes to J. Edgar Hoover, to search all over Hell for you. But you'd be wasting your money; she is *not* in My jurisdiction. I'm telling you officially."

I hesitated. Hell is a big place; I could search it by myself throughout eternity and I might not find Marga. But plenty of money (how well I knew it!) made hard things easy and impossible things merely difficult.

However— Some of the things I had done as executive deputy of C.U.D. may have been a touch shoddy (meeting a budget isn't easy), but as an ordained minister I had never hired out to the Foe. Our Ancient Adversary. How can a minister of Christ be chaplain to Satan? Marga darling, I *can't*.

"No."

"I can't hear you. Let Me sweeten the deal. Accept
and I will assign My prize female agent Sister Mary
Patricia to you permanently. She'll be your slave—with
the minor reservation that you must not sell her. However, you can rent her out, if you wish. How say you
now?"

"No."

"Oh, come, come! You ask for one female; I offer you
a better one. You can't pretend not to be satisfied with
Pat; you've been shacked up with her for weeks. Shall I
play back some of the sighs and moans?"

"You unspeakable cad!"

"Tut, tut, don't be rude to Me in My own house.
You know and I know and we all know that there isn't
any great difference between one female and another—
save possibly in their cooking. I'm offering you one
slightly better in place of the one you mislaid. A year
from now you'll thank Me. Two years from now you'll
wonder why you ever fussed. Better accept, Saint Alexander; it is the best offer you can hope for, because, I
tell you solemnly, that Danish zombie you ask for is not
in Hell. Well?"

"*No!*"

Satan drummed on the arm of his throne and looked
vexed. "That's your last word?"

"Yes."

"Suppose I offered you the chaplain job *with* your id
maiden thrown in?"

"You said she wasn't in Hell!"

"I did not say that I did not know where she is."

"You can get her?"

"Answer My question. Will you accept service as My chaplain if the contract includes returning her to you?"

(Marga, Marga!) "No."

Satan said briskly, "Sergeant General, dismiss the guard. You come with me."

"Leftanright! . . . *Hace!* For'd! . . . *Harp!*"

Satan got down from His throne, went around behind it without further word to me. I had to hurry to catch up with His giant strides. Back of the throne was a long dark tunnel; I broke into a run when it seemed that He was getting away from me. His silhouette shrank rapidly against a dim light at the far end of the tunnel.

Then I almost stepped on His heels. He had not been receding as fast as I had thought; He had been changing in size. Or I had been. He and I were now much the same height. I skidded to a halt close behind Him as He reached a doorway at the end of the tunnel. It was barely lighted by a red glow.

Satan touched something at the door; a white fan light came on above the door. He opened it and turned toward me. "Come in, Alec."

My heart skipped and I gasped for breath. *"Jerry!* Jerry Farnsworth!"

XXVII

*For in much wisdom is much grief; and he that
increaseth knowledge increaseth sorrow.*
Ecclesiastes 1:18

*And Job spake, and said, Let the day
perish wherein I was born, and the night
in which it was said, There is a man
child conceived.*
Job 3:2–3

My eyes dimmed, my head started to spin, my knees
went rubbery. Jerry said sharply, "Hey, none of
that!"—grabbed me around the waist, dragged me inside, slammed the door.

He kept me from falling, then shook me and slapped
my face. I shook my head and caught my breath. I
heard Katie's voice: "Let's get him in where he can lie
down."

My eyes focused. "I'm okay. I was just taken all over
queer for a second." I looked around. We were in the
foyer of the Farnsworth house.

"You went into syncope, that's what you did. Not
surprising, you had a shock. Come into the family
room."

"All right. Hi, Katie. Gosh, it's good to see you."

"You, too, dear." She came closer, put her arms
around me, and kissed me. I learned again that, while
Marga was my be-all, Katie was my kind of woman,

too. And Pat. Marga, I wish you could have met Pat. (Marga!)

The family room seemed bare—unfinished furniture, no windows, no fireplace. Jerry said, "Katie, give us Remington number two, will you, please? I'm going to punch drinks."

"Yes, dear."

While they were busy, Sybil came tearing in, threw her arms around me (almost knocking me off my feet; the child is solid) and kissed me, a quick buss unlike Katie's benison. "Mr. Graham! You were terrific! I watched all of it. With Sister Pat. She thinks you're terrific, too."

The left wall changed into a picture window looking out at mountains; the opposite wall now had a field-stone fireplace with a brisk fire that looked the same as the last time I saw it. The ceiling now was low; furniture and floor and fixtures were all as I recalled "Remington number two." Katie turned away from the controls. "Sybil, let him be, dear. Alec, off your feet. Rest."

"All right." I sat down. "Uh . . . is this Texas? Or is it Hell?"

"Matter of opinion," Jerry said.

"Is there a difference?" asked Sybil.

"Hard to tell," said Katie. "Don't worry about it now, Alec. I watched you, too, and I agree with the girls. I was proud of you."

"He's a tough case," Jerry put in. "I didn't get a mite of change off him. Alec, you stubborn squarehead, I lost three bets on you." Drinks appeared at our places. Jerry raised his glass. "So here's to you."

"To Alec!"

"Right!"

"Here's to me," I agreed and took a big slug of Jack Daniel's. "Jerry? You're not *really*—"

He grinned at me. The tailored ranch clothes faded; the western boots gave way to cloven hooves, horns stuck up through His hair, His skin glowed ruddy red and oily over heavy muscles; in His lap a preposterously huge phallus thrust rampantly skyward.

Katie said gently, "I think You've convinced him, dear, and it's not one of Your prettier guises."

Quickly the conventional Devil faded and the equally conventional Texas millionaire returned. "That's better," said Sybil. "Daddy, why do You use that corny one?"

"It's an emphatic symbol. But what I'm wearing now is appropriate here. And you should be in Texas clothes, too."

"Must I? I think Patty has Mr. Graham used to skin by now."

"Her skin, not your skin. Do it before I fry you for lunch."

"Daddy, You're a fraud." Sybil grew blue jeans and a halter without moving out of her chair. "And I'm tired of being a teenager and see no reason to continue the charade. Saint Alec knows he was hoaxed."

"Sybil, you talk too much."

"Dear One, she may be right," Katie put in quietly.

Jerry shook His head. I sighed and said what I had to say. "Yes, Jerry, I know I've been hoaxed. By those who I thought were my friends. And Marga's friends, too. *You* have been behind it all? Then who am I? Job?"

"Yes and no."

"What does that mean . . . Your Majesty?"

"Alec, you need not call Me that. We met as friends.
hope we will stay friends."

"How can we be friends? If I am Job. Your Majesty
. . *where is my wife!*"

"Alec, I wish I knew. Your memoir gave Me some
lues and I have been following them. But I don't know
s yet. You must be patient."

"Uh . . . damn it, patient I'm not! *What* clues? Set
me on the trail! *Can't You see that I'm going out of my
mind?*"

"No, I can't, because you're not. I've just been grill-
ng you. I pushed you to what should have been your
breaking point. You can't be broken. However, you
an't help Me search for her, not at this point. Alec,
ou've got to remember that you are human . . . and I
m *not.* I have powers that you can't imagine. I have
imitations that you cannot imagine, too. So hold your
eace and listen.

"I am your friend. If you don't believe that I am, you
re free to leave My house and fend for yourself. There
re jobs to be had down at the Lake front—if you can
tand the reek of brimstone. You can search for Marga
our own way. I don't owe you two anything as *I am not
ehind your troubles.* Believe Me."

"Uh . . . I *want* to believe You."

"Perhaps you'll believe Katie."

Katie said, "Alec, the Old One speaks sooth to you.
He did not compass your troubles. Dear, did you ever
bandage a wounded dog . . . and have the poor beastie,
n its ignorance, gnaw away the dressing and damage
tself still more?"

"Uh, yes." (My dog Brownie. I was twelve. Browni died.)

"Don't be like that poor dog. Trust Jerry. If He is t help you, He must do things beyond your ken. Woul you try to direct a brain surgeon? Or attempt to hurr one?"

I smiled ruefully and reached out to pat her hand "I'll be good, Katie. I'll try."

"Yes, do try, for Marga's sake."

"I will. Uh, Jerry—stipulating that I'm merely hu man and can't understand everything, can You tell m *anything*?"

"What I can, I will. Where shall I start?"

"Well, when I asked if I was Job, You said, 'Yes an no.' What did You mean?"

"You are indeed another Job. With the original Job was, I confess, one of the villains. This time I'm no

"I'm not proud of the fashion in which I bedevile Job. I'm not proud of the fashion in which I have s often let My Brother Yahweh maneuver Me into doin His dirty work—starting clear back with Mothe Eve—and before that, in ways I cannot explain. An I've always been a sucker for a bet, any sort of a be . . . and I'm not proud of that weakness, either."

Jerry looked at the fire and brooded. "Eve was pretty one. As soon as I laid eyes on her I knew tha Yahweh had finally cooked up a creation worthy of a Artist. Then I found out He had copied most of th design."

"Huh? But—"

"Man, do not interrupt. Most of your errors—th My Brother actively encourages—arise from believin that your God is solitary and all powerful. In fact M

Brother—and I, too, of course—is no more than a corporal in the T.O. of the Commander in Chief. And, I must add, the Great One I think of as the C-in-C, the Chairman, the Final Power, may be a mere private to some higher Power I cannot comprehend.

"Behind every mystery lies another mystery. Infinite recession. But you don't need to know final answers—if there be such—and neither do I. You want to know what happened to you . . . and to Margrethe. Yahweh came to Me and offered the same wager We had made over Job, asserting that He had a follower who was even more stubborn than Job. I turned Him down. That bet over Job had not been much fun; long before it was concluded I grew tired of clobbering the poor schmo. So this time I told My Brother to take His shell games elsewhere.

"It was not until I saw you and Marga trudging along Interstate Forty, naked as kittens and just as helpless, that I realized that Yahweh had found someone else with whom to play His nasty games. So I fetched you here and kept you for a week or so—"

"What? Just one night!"

"Don't quibble. Kept you long enough to wring you dry, then sent you on your way . . . armed with some tips on how to cope, yes, but in fact you were doing all right on your own. You're a tough son of a bitch, Alec, so much so that I looked up the bitch you are the son of. A bitch she is and tough she was and the combo of that vixen and your sweet and gentle sire produced a creature able to survive. So I let you alone.

"I was notified that you were coming here; My spies are everywhere. Half of My Brother's personal staff are double agents."

"Saint Peter?"

"Eh? No, not Pete. Pete is a good old Joe, the mos
perfect Christian in Heaven or on earth. Denied hi
Boss thrice, been making up for it ever since. Utterl
delighted to be on nickname terms with his Master i
all three of His conventional Aspects. I like Pete. If h
ever has a falling out with My Brother, he's got a jo
here.

"Then you showed up in Hell. Do you recall an invi
tation I extended to you concerning Hell?"

("—look me up. I promise you some hellacious hos
pitality.") "Yes!"

"Did I deliver? Careful how you answer; Sister Pat i
listening."

"She's not listening," Katie denied. "Pat is a lady
Not much like some people. Darling, I can shorter
this. What Alec wants to know is why he was per
secuted, how he was persecuted, and what he can d
about it now. Meaning Marga. Alec, the why is simple
you were picked for the same reason that a pit bull i
picked to go into the pit and be torn to ribbons: be
cause Yahweh thought you could win. The how i
equally simple. You guessed right when you though
you were paranoid. Paranoid but not crazy; they wer
indeed conspiring against you. Every time you got clos
to the answer the razzle-dazzle started over again. Tha
million dollars. Minor razzle-dazzle, that money existe
only long enough to confuse you. I think that cover
everything but what you can do. What you can do an
all that you can do is to trust Jerry. He may fail—it
very dangerous—but He will try."

I looked at Katie with increased respect, and som
trepidation. She had referred to matters I had neve

mentioned to Jerry. "Katie? Are you human? Or are you, uh, a fallen throne or something like that?"

She giggled. "First time anyone has suspected that. I'm human, all too human, Alec love. Furthermore I'm no stranger to you; you know lots about me."

"I do?"

"Think back. April of the year one thousand four hundred and forty-six years before the birth of Yeshua of Nazareth."

"I should be able to identify it that way? I'm sorry; I can't."

"Then try it this way: exactly forty years after the exodus from Egypt of the Children of Israel."

"The conquest of Canaan."

"Oh, pshaw! Try the Book of Joshua, chapter two. What's my name, what's my trade; was I mother, wife, or maid?"

(One of the best-known stories in the Bible. *Her?* I'm *talking* to her?) "Uh . . . *Rahab?*"

"The harlot of Jericho. That's me. I hid General Joshua's spies in my house . . . and thereby saved my parents and my brothers and sisters from the massacre. Now tell me I'm 'well preserved.'"

Sybil snickered. "Go ahead. I dare you."

"Gosh, Katie, you're well preserved! That's been over three thousand years, about thirty-four hundred. Hardly a wrinkle. Well, not many."

"'Not many'! No breakfast for you, young man!"

"Katie, you're beautiful and you know it. You and Margrethe tie for first place."

"Have you looked at *me?*" demanded Sybil. "I have my fans. Anyhow, Mom is over four thousand years old. A hag."

"No, Sybil, the parting of the Red Sea was in fourteen-ninety-one B.C. Add that to the date of the Rapture, nineteen-ninety-four A.D. Then add seven years—"

"Alec."

"Yes, Jerry?"

"Sybil is right. You just haven't noticed it. The thousand years of peace between Armageddon and the War in Heaven is half over. My Brother, wearing his Jesus hat, is now ruling on earth, and I am chained and cast down into the Pit for this entire thousand years."

"You don't look chained from here. Could I have some more Jack Daniel's?—I'm confused."

"I'm chained enough for this purpose; I've ceased 'going to and fro in the earth and walking up and down in it.' Yahweh has it all to Himself for the short time remaining before He destroys it. I won't bother His games." Jerry shrugged. "I declined to take part in Armageddon—I pointed out to Him that He had plenty of homegrown villains for it. Alec, with My Brother writing the scripts, I was always supposed to fight fiercely, like Harvard, then lose. It got monotonous. He's got me scheduled to take another dive at the end of this Millennium, to fulfill His prophecies. That 'War in Heaven' He predicted in the so-called Book of Revelation. I'm not going to go. I've told My angels that they can form a foreign legion if they want to, but I'm sitting this one out. What's the point in a battle if the outcome is predetermined thousands of years before the whistle?"

He was watching me while He talked. He stopped abruptly. "What's eating on you now?"

"Jerry . . . if it has been five hundred years since I lost Margrethe, it's hopeless. Isn't it?"

"Hey! Damnation, boy, haven't I told you not to try to understand things you can't understand? Would I be working on it if it were hopeless?"

Katie said, "Jerry, I had Alec all quieted down . . . and You got him upset again."

"I'm sorry."

"You didn't mean to. Alec, Jerry is blunt, but He's right. For you, acting alone, the search was always hopeless. But with Jerry's help, you may find her. Not certain, but a hope worth pursuing. But time isn't relevant, five hundred years or five seconds. You don't have to understand it, but do please believe it."

"All right. I will. Because otherwise there would be no hope, none."

"But there *is* hope; all you have to do now is be patient."

"I'll try. But I guess Marga and I will never have our soda fountain and lunch counter in Kansas."

"Why not?" asked Jerry.

"Five centuries? They won't even speak the same language. There will be no one who knows a hot fudge sundae from curried goat. Customs change."

"So you reinvent the hot fudge sundae and make a killing. Don't be a pessimist, son."

"Would you like one right now?" asked Sybil.

"I don't think he had better mix it with Jack Daniel's," Jerry advised.

"Thanks, Sybil . . . but I'd probably cry in it. I associate it with Marga."

"So don't. Son, crying in your drink is bad enough; crying into a hot fudge sundae is disgusting."

"Do I get to finish the story of my scandalous youth, or won't anybody listen?"

I said, "Katie, I'm listening. You made a deal with Joshua."

"With his spies. Alec love, to anyone whose love and respect I want—you, I mean—I need to explain something. Some people who know who I am—and even more who don't—class Rahab the harlot as a traitor. Treason in time of war, betrayal of fellow citizens, all that. I—"

"I never thought so, Katie. Jehovah had decreed that Jericho would fall. Since it was ordained, you couldn't change it. What you did was to save your father and mother and the other kids."

"Yes, but there is more to it, Alec. Patriotism is a fairly late concept. Back then, in the land of Canaan, any loyalty other than to one's family was personal loyalty to a chief of some sort—usually a successful warrior who dubbed himself 'king.' Alec, a whore doesn't—didn't—have that sort of loyalty."

"So? Katie, in spite of studying at seminary I don't really have any sharp concept of what life was like back then. I keep trying to see it in terms of Kansas."

"Not too different. A whore at that time and place was either a temple prostitute, or a slave, or a self-owned private contractor. I was a free woman. Oh yeah? Whores don't fight city hall, they can't. An officer of the king comes in, he expects free tail and free drinks, same for the civic patrol—the cops. Same for any sort of politician. Alec, I tell you the truth; I gave away more tail than I sold—and often got a black eye a bonus. No, I did not feel loyalty to Jericho; the Jews weren't any more cruel and they were *much* cleaner!"

"Katie, I don't know of any Protestant Christian who thinks anything bad of Rahab. But I have long wondered about one detail in her—your—story. Your house was on the city wall?"

"Yes. It was inconvenient for housekeeping—carrying water up all those steps—but convenient for business, and the rent was low. It was the fact that I lived on the wall that let me save General Joshua's agents. Used a clothesline; they went out the window. Didn't get my clothesline back, either."

"How high was that wall?"

"Hunh? Goodness, I don't know. It was *high*."

"Twenty cubits."

"Was it, Jerry?"

"I was there. Professional interest. First use of nerve warfare in combination with sonic weapons."

"The reason I ask about the height, Katie, is because it states in the Book that you gathered all your family into your house and stayed there, all during the siege."

"We surely did, seven horrid days. My contract with the Israelite spies required it. My place was only two little rooms, not big enough for three adults and seven kids. We ran out of food, we ran out of water, the kids cried, and my father complained. He happily took the money I brought in; with seven kids he needed it. But he resented having to stay under the same roof where I entertained johns, and he was especially bitter about having to use my bed. My workbench. But use it he did, and I slept on the floor."

"Then your family were all in your house when the walls came tumbling down."

"Yes, surely. We didn't dare leave it until they came for us, the two spies. My house was marked at the window with red string."

"Katie, your house was on the wall, thirty feet up. The Bible says the wall fell down flat. Wasn't anyone hurt?"

She looked startled. "Why, no."

"Didn't the house collapse?"

"No. Alec, it's been a long time. But I remember the trumpets and the shout, and then the earthquake rumble as the city wall fell. But my house wasn't hurt."

"Saint Alec!"

"Yes, Jerry?"

"You should know; you're a saint. A miracle. If Yahweh hadn't been throwing miracles right and left, the Israelites would never have conquered the Canaanites. Here this ragged band of Okies comes into a rich country of walled cities—and they never lose a battle. Miracles. Ask the Canaanites. If you can find one. My Brother pretty regularly had them all put to the sword except some few cases where the young and pretty ones were saved as slaves."

"But it was the Promised Land, Jerry, and they were His Chosen People."

"They are indeed the Chosen People. Of course being chosen by Yahweh is no great shakes. Do you know your Book well enough to know how many times He crossed 'em up? My Brother is a bit of a jerk."

I had had too much Jack Daniel's and too many shocks. But Jerry's casual blasphemy triggered me. "The Lord God Jehovah is a just God!"

"You never played marbles with Him. Alec, 'justice' [i]s not a divine concept; it is a human illusion. The very [b]asis of the Judeo-Christian code is injustice, the [s]capegoat system. The scapegoat sacrifice runs all [th]rough the Old Testament, then it reaches its height [i]n the New Testament with the notion of the Martyred [R]edeemer. How can justice possibly be served by load-[in]g your sins on another? Whether it be a lamb having [it]s throat cut ritually, or a Messiah nailed to a cross and ['d]ying for your sins.' Somebody should tell all of Yah-[w]eh's followers, Jews and Christians, that there is no [su]ch thing as a free lunch.

"Or maybe there is. Being in that catatonic condi-[ti]on called 'grace' at the exact moment of death—or at [th]e Final Trump—will get you into Heaven. Right? [Y]ou got to Heaven that way, did you not?"

"That's correct. I hit it lucky. For I had racked up [q]uite a list of sins before then."

"A long and wicked life followed by five minutes of [p]erfect grace gets you into Heaven. An equally long life [o]f decent living and good works followed by one out-[b]urst of taking the name of the Lord in vain—then [h]ave a heart attack at that moment and be damned for [e]ternity. Is that the system?"

I answered stiffly, "If you read the words of the Bible [li]terally, that is the system. But the Lord moves in [m]ysterious—"

"Not mysterious to Me, bud: I've known Him too [l]ong. It's His world, His rules, His doing. His rules are [e]xact and anyone can follow them and reap the reward. [B]ut 'just' they are not. What do you think of what He [h]as done to you and your Marga? Is that justice?"

I took a deep breath. "I've been trying to figure that

out ever since Judgment Day . . . and Jack Daniel
isn't helping. No, I don't think it's what I signed u
for."

"Ah, but you did!"

"How?"

"My Brother Yahweh, wearing His Jesus face, said
'After this manner therefore pray ye:' Go ahead, say it.

"'Our Father, which art in heaven, Hallowed be th
name. Thy kingdom come. Thy will be done—'"

"Stop! Stop right there. 'Thy will be done—' N
Muslim claiming to be a 'slave of God' ever gave a mo
sweeping consent than that. In that prayer you invi
Him to do His worst. The perfect masochist. That's th
test of Job, boy. Job was treated unjustly in every wa
day after day for years—I know, I know, I was there;
did it—and My dear Brother stood by and let Me do i
Let Me? He urged Me, He connived in it, accessor
ahead of the fact.

"Now it's your turn. Your God did it to you. Wil
you curse Him? Or will you come wiggling back c
your belly like a whipped dog?"

XXVIII

Ask, and it shall be given you; seek, and ye shall find;
knock, and it shall be opened unto you.
Matthew 7:7

I was saved from answering that impossible question by an interruption—and was I glad! I suppose every man has doubts at times about God's justice. I admit that I had been much troubled lately and had been forced to remind myself again and again that God's ways are not man's ways, and that I could not expect always to understand the purposes of the Lord.

But I could not speak my misgivings aloud, and least of all to the Lord's Ancient Adversary. It was especially upsetting that Satan chose at this moment to have the shape and the voice of my only friend.

Debating with the Devil is a mug's game at best.

The interruption was mundane: a telephone ringing. Accidental interruption? I don't think Satan tolerates "accidents." As may be, I did not have to answer the question that I could not answer.

Katie said, "Shall I get it, dear?"

"Please."

A telephone handset appeared in Katie's hand. "Lu-

cifer's office, Rahab speaking. Repeat, please. I will in
quire." She looked at Jerry.

"I'll take it." Jerry operated without a visible tele
phone instrument. "Speaking. No. I said, no. No
damn it! Refer that to Mr. Ashmedai. Let Me have the
other call." He muttered something about the impos
sibility of getting competent help, then said, "Speak
ing. Yes, Sir!" Then He said nothing for quite a long
time. At last He said, "At once, Sir. Thank you."

Jerry stood up. "Please excuse Me, Alec; I have work
to do. I can't say when I will be back. Try to treat this
waiting as a vacation . . . and My house is yours. Ka
tie, take care of him. Sybil, keep him amused." Jerry
vanished.

"Will I keep him amused!" Sybil got up and stood in
front of me, rubbed her hands together. Her western
clothes faded out, leaving Sybil. She grinned.

Katie said mildly, "Sybil, stop that. Grow more
clothes at once or I'll send you home."

"Spoilsport." Sybil developed a skimpy bikini. "I
plan to make Saint Alec forget that Danish baggage."

"What'll you bet, dear? I've been talking to Pat."

"So? What did Pat say?"

"Margrethe can cook."

Sybil looked disgusted. "A girl spends fifty years o
her back, studying hard. Along comes some slottie wh
can make chicken and dumplings. It's not fair."

I decided to change the subject. "Sybil, those trick
you do with clothes are fascinating. Are you a gradua
witch now?"

Instead of answering me at once, Sybil glanced a
Katie, who said to her: "All over with, dear. Spea
freely."

"Okay. Saint Alec, I'm no witch. Witchcraft is poppycock. You know that verse in the Bible about not suffering witches to live?"

"Exodus twenty-two, eighteen."

"That's the one. The Old Hebrew word translated here as 'witch' actually means 'poisoner.' Not letting a poisoner continue to breathe strikes me as a good idea. But I wonder how many friendless old women have been hanged or burned as a result of a sloppy translation?"

(Could this really be true? What about the "literal word of God" concept on which I had been reared? Of course the word "witch" is English, not the original Hebrew . . . but the translators of the King James version were sustained by God—that's why that version of the Bible [and only that one] can be taken literally. But— No! Sybil must be mistaken. The Good Lord would not let hundreds, thousands, of innocent people be tortured to death over a mistranslation He could so easily have corrected.)

"So you did not attend a Sabbat that night. What did you do?"

"Not what you think; Israfel and I aren't quite that chummy. Chums, yes; buddies, no."

"'Israfel'? I thought he was in Heaven."

"That's his godfather. The trumpeter. This Israfel can't play a note. But he did ask me to tell you, if I ever got a chance, that he really isn't the pimple he pretended to be as 'Roderick Lyman Culverson, Third.'"

"I'm glad to hear that. As he certainly did a good job of portraying an unbearable young snot. I didn't see how a daughter of Katie and Jerry—or is it just of

Katie?—could have such poor taste as to pick that boo
as a pal. Not Israfel, of course, but the part he wa
playing."

"Oh. Better fix that, too. Katie, what relation ar
we?"

"I don't think even Dr. Darwin could find any ge
netic relationship, dear. But I am every bit as proud o
you as I would be were you my own daughter."

"Thank you, Mom!"

"But we all are related," I objected, "throug
Mother Eve. Since Katie, wrinkles and all, was bor
while the Children of Israel were wandering in the wil
derness, there are only about eighty begats from Eve t
Katie. With your birthdate and simple arithmetic w
could make a shrewd guess at how close your bloo
relationship is."

"Oh, oh! Here we go again. Saint Alec, Mama Kat
is descended from Eve; I am not. Different species. I'r
an imp. An afrit, if you want to get technical."

She again vanished her clothes and did a body trans
formation. "See?"

I said, "Say! Weren't you managing the desk at th
Sans Souci Sheraton the evening I arrived in Hell?"

"I certainly was. And I'm flattered that you re
member me, in my own shape." She resumed her hu
man appearance, plus the tiny bikini. "I was ther
because I knew you by sight. Pop didn't want anythin
to go wrong."

Katie stood up. "Let's continue this outside; I'd lik
a dip before dinner."

"I'm busy seducing Saint Alec."

"Dreamer. Continue it outdoors."

Outside it was a lovely Texas late afternoon, wit

engthening shadows. "Katie, a straight answer, please.
s this Hell? Or is this Texas?"

"Both."

"I withdraw the question."

I must have let my annoyance show in my voice, for
he turned and put a hand on my chest. "Alec, I was
ot jesting. For many centuries Lucifer has maintained
ieds-à-terre here and there on earth. In each He had an
stablished personality, a front. After Armageddon,
vhen His Brother set Himself up as king of earth for
he Millennium, He quit visiting earth. But some of
hese places were home to Him, so He pinched them off
nd took them with Him. You see?"

"I suppose I do. About as well as a cow understands
alculus."

"I don't understand the mechanism; it's on the God
vel. But those numerous changes you and Marga un-
erwent during your persecution: How deep did each
hange go? Do you think the entire planet was involved
ch time?"

Reality tumbled in my mind in a fashion it had not
nce the last of those "changes." "Katie, I don't know! I
was always too busy surviving. Wait a moment. Each
hange did cover the whole planet earth and about a
entury of its history. Because I always checked the his-
ory and memorized as much as I could. Cultural
nanges, too. The whole complex."

"Each change stopped not far beyond the end of your
ose, Alec, and no one but you—you two—was aware
 any change. You didn't check history; you checked
story books. At least this is the way Lucifer would have
andled it, had He been arranging the deception."

"Uh— Katie, do you realize how long it would take

to revise, rewrite, and print an entire encyclopedia
That's what I usually consulted."

"But, Alec, you have already been told that *time*
never a problem on the God level. Or space. Whateve
was needed to deceive you was provided. But no mor
than that. That is the conservative principle in art a
the God level. While I can't do it, not being at th
level, I have seen a lot of it done. A skillful Artist i
shapes and appearances does no more than necessary t
create His effect."

Rahab sat down on the edge of the pool, paddled h
feet in the water. "Come sit beside me. Consider th
edge of the 'big bang.' What is there out beyond th
limit where the red shift has the magnitude that mea
that the expansion of the universe equals the speed
light—what is beyond?"

I answered rather stiffly, "Katie, your hypothetic
question lacks meaning. I've kept up, more or les
with such silly notions as the 'big bang' and the 'e
panding universe' because a preacher of the Gosp
must keep track of such theories in order to be able
refute them. The two you mention imply an impossib
length of time—impossible because the world was cr
ated about six thousand years ago. 'About' because th
exact date of Creation is hard to calculate, and also b
cause I am uncertain as to the present date. But arou
six thousand years—not the billion years or so the bi
bangers need."

"Alec . . . your universe is about twenty-three b
lion years old."

I started to retort, closed my mouth. I will not flat
contradict my hostess.

She added, "And your universe was created in four
thousand and four B.C."

I stared at the water long enough for Sybil to surface
and splash us.

"Well, Alec?"

"You've left me with nothing to say."

"But notice carefully what I did say. I did *not* say
that the world was created twenty-three billion years
ago; I said that was its age. It was created old. Created
with fossils in the ground and craters on the moon, all
speaking of great age. Created that way by Yahweh,
because it amused Him to do so. One of those scientists
said, 'God does not roll dice with the universe.' Unfortunately not true. Yahweh rolls loaded dice with His
universe . . . to deceive His creatures."

"Why would He do that?"

"Lucifer says that it is because He is a poor Artist,
the sort who is always changing His mind and scraping
the canvas. And a practical joker. But I'm really not
entitled to an opinion; I'm not at that level. And Lucifer is prejudiced where His Brother is concerned; I
think that is obvious. You haven't remarked on the
greatest wonder."

"Maybe I missed it."

"No, I think you were being polite. How an old
whore happened to have opinions about cosmogony and
teleology and eschatology and other long words of
Greek derivation; that's the greatest wonder. Not?"

"Why, Rahab honey, I was just so busy counting
your wrinkles that I wasn't lis—"

This got me shoved into the water. I came up sput-
tering and spouting and found both women laughing at

me. So I placed both hands on the edge of the pool wi
Katie captured inside the circle. She did not seem
mind being captive; she leaned against me like a ca
"You were about to say?" I asked.

"Alec, to be able to read and write is as wonderful
sex. Or almost. You may not fully appreciate what
blessing it is because you probably learned how as
baby and have been doing it casually ever since. B
when I was a whore in Canaan almost four millenn
ago, I did not know how to read and write. I learned
listening . . . to johns, to neighbors, to gossip in t
market. But that's not a way to learn much, and ev
scribes and judges were ignorant then.

"I had been dead nearly three centuries before
learned to read and write, and when I did learn, I w
taught by the ghost of a harlot from what later becar
the great Cretan civilization. Saint Alec, this may sta
tle you but, in general throughout history, whor
learned to read and write long before respectab
women took up the dangerous practice. When I d
learn, brother! For a while it crowded sex out of n
life."

She grinned up at me. "Almost, anyhow. Presently
went back to a more healthy balance, reading and se
in equal amounts."

"I don't have the strength for that ratio."

"Women are different. My best education start
with the burning of the Library at Alexandria. Yahw
didn't want it, so Lucifer grabbed the ghosts of all tho
thousands of codices, took them to Hell, regenerat
them carefully—and Rahab had a picnic! And let
add: Lucifer has His eye on the Vatican Library, since
will be up for salvage soon. Instead of having to reger

ate ghosts, in the case of the Vatican Library, Lucifer
plans to pinch it off intact just before Time Stop, and
ake it unhurt to Hell. Won't that be grand?"

"Sounds as if it would be. The only thing about
which I've ever envied the papists is their library. But
. . 'regenerated ghosts'?"

"Slap my back."

"Huh?"

"Slap it. No, harder than that; I'm not a fragile little
butterfly. Harder. That's more like it. What you just
lapped is a regenerated ghost."

"Felt solid."

"Should be, I paid list price for the job. It was before
Lucifer noticed me and made me a bird in a gilded
cage, a pitiful sight to see. I understand that, if you are
saved and go to Heaven, regeneration goes with salvation . . . but here you buy it on credit, then work your
arse off to pay for it. That being exactly how I paid for
it. Saint Alec, you didn't die, I know. A regenerated
body is just like the one a person has before death, but
better. No contagious diseases, no allergies, no old-age
wrinkles—and 'wrinkles' my foot! I wasn't wrinkled
the day I died . . . or at least not much. How did you
get me talking about wrinkles? We were discussing rel-
ativity and the expanding universe, a really high-type
intellectual conversation."

That night Sybil made a strong effort to get into my
bed, an effort that Katie firmly thwarted—then went
to bed with me herself. "Pat said that you were not to
be allowed to sleep alone."

"Pat thinks I'm sick. I'm not."

"I won't argue it. And don't quiver your chin, dear
Mother Rahab will let you sleep."

Sometime in the night I woke up sobbing, and Kati
was there. She comforted me. I'm sure Pat told he
about my nightmares. With Katie there to quiet m
down I got back to sleep rather quickly.

It was a sweet Arcadian interlude . . . save for th
absence of Margrethe. But Katie had me convinced tha
I owed it to Jerry (and to her) to be patient and no
brood over my loss. So I did not, or not much, in th
daytime, and, while night could be bad, even lonel
nights are not too lonely with Mother Rahab to sooth
one after waking up emotionally defenseless. She wa
always there . . . except one night she had to be away
Sybil took that watch, carefully instructed by Katie
and carried it out the same way.

I discovered one amusing thing about Sybil. In slee
she slips back into her natural shape, imp or afrit, with
out knowing it. This makes her about six inches shorte
and she has those cute little horns that were the firs
thing I had noticed about her, at the Sans Souci.

Daytimes we swam and sunbathed and rode horse
back and picnicked out in the hills. In making th
enclave Jerry had apparently pinched off many squar
miles; we appeared to be able to go as far as we liked i
any direction.

Or perhaps I don't understand at all how such thing
are done.

Strike out "perhaps"—I know as much about oper
tions on the God level as a frog knows about Friday

Jerry had been gone about a week when Raha
showed up at the breakfast table with my memo

manuscript. "Saint Alec, Lucifer sent instructions that you are to bring this up to date and keep it up to date."

"All right. Will longhand do? Or, if there is a typewriter around, I guess I could hunt and peck."

"You do it longhand; I'll do a smooth draft. I've done lots of secretarial work for Prince Lucifer."

"Katie, sometimes you call Him Jerry, sometimes Lucifer, never Satan."

"Alec, He prefers 'Lucifer' but He answers to anything. 'Jerry' and 'Katie' were names invented for you and Marga—"

"And 'Sybil,'" Sybil amended.

"And 'Sybil.' Yes, Egret. Do you want your own name back now?"

"No, I think it's nice that Alec—and Marga—have names for us that no one else knows."

"Just a minute," I put in. "The day I met you, all three of you responded to those names as if you had worn them all your lives."

"Mom and I are pretty fast at extemporaneous drama," Sybil-Egret said. "They didn't know they were fire-worshipers until I slipped it into the conversation. And I didn't know I was a witch until Mom tipped me off. Israfel is pretty sharp, too. But he did have more time to think about his role."

"So we were snookered in all directions. A couple of country cousins."

"Alec," Katie said to me earnestly, "Lucifer always has reasons for what He does. He rarely explains. His intentions are malevolent only toward malicious people . . which you are not."

* * *

We three were sunbathing by the pool when Jerr
returned suddenly. He said abruptly to me, not ever
stopping first to speak to Katie: "Get your clothes on
We're leaving at once."

Katie bounced up, rushed in and got my clothes
The women had me dressed as fast as a fireman answer
ing an alarm. Katie shoved my razor into my pocket
buttoned it. I announced, "I'm ready!"

"Where's his manuscript?"

Again Katie rushed in, out again fast. "Here!"

In that brief time Jerry had grown twelve feet tall—
and changed. He was still Jerry, but I now knew wh
Lucifer was known as the most beautiful of all the an
gels. "So long!" he said. "Rahab, I'll call you if I can.
He started to pick me up.

"Wait! Egret and I must kiss him good-bye!"

"Oh. Make it snappy!"

They did, ritual pecks only, given simultaneously
Jerry grabbed me, held me like a child, and we wen
straight up. I had a quick glimpse of Sans Souci, th
Palace, and the Plaza, then smoke and flame from th
Pit covered them. We went on out of this world.

How we traveled, how long we traveled, where w
traveled I do not know. It was like that endless fall t
Hell, but made much more agreeable by Jerry's arms
It reminded me of times when I was very young, two o
three years old, when my father would sometimes pic
me up after supper and hold me until I fell asleep.

I suppose I did sleep. After a long time I becam
alert by feeling Jerry sweeping in for a landing. He pu
me down, set me on my feet.

There was gravity here; I felt weight and "down

gain had meaning. But I do not think we were on a
planet. We seemed to be on a platform or a porch of
ome immensely large building. I could not see it be-
ause we were right up against it. Elsewhere there was
nothing to see, just an amorphous twilight.

Jerry said, "Are you all right?"

"Yes. Yes, I think so."

"Good. Listen carefully. I am about to take you in to
ee—no, for you to be seen by—an Entity who is to
me, and to my brother your god Yahweh, as Yahweh is
o you. Understand me?"

"Uh . . . maybe. I'm not sure."

"A is to B as B is to C. To this Entity your lord god
Jehovah is equivalent to a child building sand castles at
beach, then destroying them in childish tantrums. To
Him I am a child, too. I look up to Him as you look up
o your triple deity—father, son, and holy ghost. I
don't worship this Entity as God; He does not demand,
does not expect, and does not want, that sort of boot-
icking. Yahweh may be the only god who ever thought
up that curious vice—at least I do not know of another
planet or place in any universe where god-worship is
practiced. But I am young and not much traveled."

Jerry was watching me closely. He appeared to be
roubled. "Alec, maybe this analogy will explain it.
When you were growing up, did you ever have to take
pet to a veterinarian?"

"Yes. I didn't like it because they always hated it
o."

"I don't like it, either. Very well, you know what it
s to take a sick or damaged animal to the vet. Then
ou had to wait while the doctor decided whether or
ot your pet could be made well. Or whether the kind

and gentle thing to do was to put the little creature ou
of its misery. Is this not true?"

"Yes. Jerry, you're telling me that things are dicey
Uncertain."

"Utterly uncertain. No precedent. A human bein
has never been taken to this level before. I don't know
what He will do."

"Okay. You told me before that there would be
risk."

"Yes. You are in great danger. And so am I, al
though I think your danger is much greater than mine
But, Alec, I can assure you of this: If It decides t
extinguish you, you will never know it. It is not a sa
distic God."

"'It'—is it 'It' or 'He'?"

"Uh . . . use 'he.' If It embodies, It will probabl
use a human appearance. If so, you can address Him a
'Mr. Chairman' or 'Mr. Koshchei.' Treat Him as yo
would a man much older than you are and one whom
you respect highly. *Don't* bow down or offer worship
Just stand your ground and tell the truth. If you die
die with dignity."

The guard who stopped us at the door was not hu
man—until I looked again and then he was human
And that characterizes the uncertainty of everything
saw at the place Jerry referred to as "The Branch Of
fice."

The guard said to me, "Strip down, please. Leav
your clothes with me; you can pick them up later
What is that metal object?"

I explained that it was just a safety razor.

"And what is it for?"

"It's a . . . a knife for cutting hair off the face."

"You grow hair on your face?"

I tried to explain shaving.

"If you don't want hair there, why do you grow it here? Is it a material of economic congress?"

"Jerry, I think I'm out of my depth."

"I'll handle it." I suppose He then talked to the guard but I didn't hear anything. Jerry said to me, "Leave your razor with your clothes. He thinks you are crazy but he thinks I am crazy, too. It doesn't matter."

Mr. Koshchei may be an "It" but to me He looked like a twin brother of Dr. Simmons, the vet back home in Kansas to whom I used to take cats and dogs, and once a turtle—the procession of small animals who shared my childhood. And the Chairman's office looked exactly like Dr. Simmons' office, even to the rolltop desk the doctor must have inherited from his grandfather. There was a well-remembered Seth Thomas eight-day clock on a little shelf over the doctor's desk.

I realized (being cold sober and rested) that this was not Dr. Simmons and that the semblance was intentional but not intended to deceive. The Chairman, whatever He or It or She may be, had reached into my mind with some sort of hypnosis to create an ambience in which I could relax. Dr. Simmons used to pet an animal and talk to it, before he got down to the uncomfortable, unfamiliar, and often painful things that he had to do to that animal.

It had worked. It worked with me, too. I knew that Mr. Koshchei was not the old veterinary surgeon of my childhood . . . but this simulacrum brought out in me the same feeling of trust.

Mr. Koshchei looked up as we came in. He nodded to Jerry, glanced at me. "Sit down."

We sat down. Mr. Koshchei turned back to His desk. My manuscript was on it. He picked it up, jogged the sheets straight, put them down. "How are things in your own bailiwick, Lucifer? Any problems?"

"No, Sir. Oh, the usual gripes about the air conditioning. Nothing I can't handle."

"Do you want to rule earth this millennium?"

"Hasn't my brother claimed it?"

"Yahweh has claimed it, yes—he has pronounced Time Stop and torn it down. But I am not bound to let him rebuild. Do you want it? Answer Me."

"Sir, I would much rather start with all-new materials."

"All your guild prefer to start fresh. With no thought of the expense, of course. I could assign you to the Glaroon for a few cycles. How say you?"

Jerry was slow in answering. "I must leave it to the Chairman's judgment."

"You are quite right; you must. So we will discuss it later. Why have you interested yourself in this creature of your brother's?"

I must have dropped off to sleep, for I saw puppies and kittens playing in a courtyard—and there was nothing of that sort there. I heard Jerry saying, "Mr. Chairman, almost everything about a human creature is ridiculous, except its ability to suffer bravely and die gallantly for whatever it loves and believes in. The validity of that belief, the appropriateness of that love, is irrelevant; it is the bravery and the gallantry that count. These are uniquely human qualities, independent of mankind's creator, who has none of them himself—as I know, since he is my brother . . . and I lack them, too.

"You ask, why *this* animal, and why me? This one I picked up beside a road, a stray—and, putting aside its own troubles—much too big for it!—it devoted itself to a valiant (and fruitless) attempt to save my 'soul' by the rules it had been taught. That its attempt was misguided and useless does not matter; it tried hard on my behalf when it believed me to be in extreme danger. Now that it is in trouble I owe it an equal effort."

Mr. Koshchei pushed his spectacles down His nose and looked over them. "You offer no reason why I should interfere with local authority."

"Sir, is there not a guild rule requiring artists to be kind in their treatment of their volitionals?"

"No."

Jerry looked daunted. "Sir, I must have misunderstood my training."

"Yes, I think you have. There is an artistic principle—not a rule—that volitionals should be treated consistently. But to insist on kindness would be to eliminate that degree of freedom for which volition in creatures was invented. Without the possibility of tragedy the volitionals might as well be golems."

"Sir, I think I understand that. But would the Chairman please amplify the artistic principle of consistent treatment?"

"Nothing complex about it, Lucifer. For a creature to act out its own minor art, the rules under which it acts must be either known to it or be such that the rules can become known through trial and error—with error not always fatal. In short the creature must be able to learn and to benefit by its experience."

"Sir, that is exactly my complaint about my brother
See that record before You. Yahweh baited a trap and
thereby lured this creature into a contest that it could
not win—then declared the game over and took the
prize from it. And, although this is an extreme case, a
destruction test, this nevertheless is typical of his treat
ment of all his volitionals. Games so rigged that his
creatures cannot win. For six millennia I got his losers
. . . and many of them arrived in Hell catatonic with
fear—fear of me, fear of an eternity of torture. They
can't believe they've been lied to. My therapists have to
work hard to reorient the poor slobs. It's not funny."

Mr. Koshchei did not appear to listen. He leaned
back in His old wooden swivel chair, making it creak—
and, yes, I do know that the creak came out of my
memories—and looked again at my memoir. He
scratched the gray fringe around His bald pate and
made an irritating noise, half whistle, half hum—also
out of my buried memories of Doc Simmons, but ut
terly real.

"This female creature, the bait. A volitional?"

"In my opinion, yes, Mr. Chairman."

(Good heavens, Jerry! Don't you *know*?)

"Then I think we may assume that this one would
not be satisfied with a simulacrum." He hummed and
whistled through His teeth. "So let us look deeper."

Mr. Koshchei's office seemed small when we were ad
mitted; now there were several others present: another
angel who looked a lot like Jerry but older and with a
pinched expression unlike Jerry's expansive joviality
another older character who wore a long coat, a big
broad-brimmed hat, a patch over one eye, and had

crow sitting on his shoulder, and—why, confound his
arrogance!—Sam Crumpacker, that Dallas shyster.

Back of Crumpacker three men were lined up, well-
fed types, and all vaguely familiar. I knew I had seen
them before.

Then I got it. I had won a hundred (or was it a
thousand?) from each of them on a most foolhardy bet.

I looked back at Crumpacker, and was angrier than
ever—the scoundrel was now wearing my face!

I turned to Jerry and started to whisper urgently.
"See that man over there? The one—"

"Shut up."

"But—"

"Be quiet and listen."

Jerry's brother was speaking. "So who's complaining?
You want I should put on my Jesus hat and prove it?
The fact that some of them make it proves it ain't too
hard—seven point one percent in this last batch, not
counting golems. Not good enough? Who says?"

The old boy in the black hat said, "I count anything
less than fifty percent a failure."

"So who's talking? Who lost ground to me every year
for a millennium? How you handle your creatures;
that's your business. What I do with mine; that's my
business."

"That's why I'm here," the big hat replied. "You
grossly interfered with one of mine."

"Not me!" Yahweh hooked a thumb at the man who
managed to look like both me and Sam Crumpacker.
"That one! My Shabbes goy. A little rough? So whose
boy is he? Answer that!"

Mr. Koshchei tapped my memoir, spoke to the man

with my face. "Loki, how many places do you figure i
this story?"

"Depends on how You figure it, Chief. Eight or nin
places, if You count the walk-ons. All through it, whe
You consider that I spent four solid weeks softening up
this foxy schoolteacher so that she would roll over and
pant when Joe Nebbish came along."

Jerry had a big fist around my upper left arm. "Keep
quiet!"

Loki went on: "And Yahweh didn't pay up."

"So why should I? Who won?"

"You cheated. I had your champion, your prize
bigot, ready to crack when you pulled Judgment Day
early. There he sits. Ask him. Ask him if he still swear
by you. Or at you? Ask him. Then pay up. I have mu
nition bills to meet."

Mr. Koshchei stated, "I declare this discussion out o
order. This office is not a collection agency. Yahweh
the principal complaint against you seems to be tha
you are not consistent in your rules for your creatures."

"Should I kiss them? For omelets you break eggs."

"Speak to the case in point. You ran a destruction
test. Whether it was artistically necessary is moot. But
at the end of the test, you took one to Heaven, left the
other behind—and thereby punished both of them
Why?"

"One rule for all. She didn't make it."

"Aren't you the god that announced the rule con
cerning binding the mouths of the kine that tread the
grain?"

The next thing I knew I was standing on Mr
Koshchei's desk, staring right into His enormous face.

suppose Jerry put me there. He was saying, "This is yours?"

I looked in the direction He indicated—and had to keep from fainting. Marga!

Margrethe cold and dead and encased in a coffin-shaped cake of ice. It occupied much of the desk top and was beginning to melt onto it.

I tried to throw myself onto it, found I could not move.

"I think that answers Me," Mr. Koshchei went on. "Odin, what is its destiny?"

"She died fighting, at Ragnarok. She has earned a cycle in Valhalla."

"Listen to him!" Loki sneered. "Ragnarok is not over. And this time I'm winning. This *pige* is mine! All Danish broads are willing . . . but this one is explosive!" He smirked and winked at me. "Isn't she?"

The Chairman said quietly, "Loki, you weary Me"—and suddenly Loki was missing. Even his chair was gone. "Odin, will you spare her for part of that cycle?"

"For how long? She has earned the right to Valhalla."

"An indeterminate time. This creature had stated its willingness to wash dishes 'forever' in order to take care of her. One may doubt that it realizes just how long a period 'forever' is . . . yet its story does show earnestness of purpose."

"Mr. Chairman, my warriors, male and female, dead in honorable combat, are my equals, not my slaves—I am proud to be first among such equals. I raise no objections . . . if *she* consents."

My heart soared. Then Jerry, from clear across the room, whispered into my ear, "Don't get your hopes

up. To her it may be as long as a thousand years
Women do forget."

The Chairman was saying, "The web patterns ar
still intact, are they not?"

Yahweh answered, "So who destroys file copies?"

"Regenerate as necessary."

"And who is paying for this?"

"You are. A fine to teach you to pay attention t
consistency."

"Oy! Every prophecy I fulfilled! And now He tel.
me consistent I am not! This is justice?"

"No. It is Art. Alexander. Look at Me."

I looked at that great face; Its eyes held me. They g
bigger, and bigger, and bigger. I slumped forward an
fell into them.

XXIX

*There is no remembrance of former things; neither shall
there be any remembrance of things that are to come
with those that shall come after.*

Ecclesiastes 1:11

This week Margrethe and I, with help from our daughter Gerda, are giving our house and our shop a real Scandahoovian cleaning, because the Farnsworths, our friends from Texas—our best friends anywhere—are coming to see us. To Marga and me, a visit from Jerry and Katie is Christmas and the Fourth of July rolled into one. And for our kids, too; Sybil Farnsworth is Inga's age; the girls are chums.

This time will be extra special; they are bringing Patricia Marymount with them. Pat is almost as old a friend as the Farnsworths and the sweetest person in the world—an old-maid schoolmarm but not a bit prissy.

The Farnsworths changed our luck. Marga and I were down in Mexico on our honeymoon when the earthquake that destroyed Mazatlán hit. We weren't hurt but we had a bad time getting out—passports, money, and travelers checks gone. Halfway home we met the Farnsworths and that changed everything—no more trouble. Oh, I got back to Kansas with no baggage but a razor (sentimental value, Marga gave it to me on ou honeymoon; I've used it ever since).

When we reached my home state, we found just th mom-and-pop shop we wanted—a lunchroom in th little college town, Eden, Kansas, southeast of Wichit. The shop was owned by Mr. and Mrs. A. S. Modeu they wanted to retire. We started as their employees; i less than a month we were their tenants. Then I wer into hock to the bank up to my armpits and that made u owners-of-record of MARGA'S HOT FUDGE SUN DAE—soda fountain, hot dogs, hamburgers, an Marga's heavenly Danish open-face sandwiches.

Margrethe wanted to name it Marga-and-Alex's H Fudge Sundae—I vetoed that; it doesn't scan. Beside. she is the one who meets the public; she's our best ac vertising. I work back where I'm not seen—dish washer, janitor, porter, you name it. Margrethe handl the front, with help from Astrid. And from me; all us can cook or concoct anything on our menu, even th open-face sandwiches. However, with the latter we fo low Marga's color photographs and lists of ingredient in fairness to our customers only Margrethe is allowe to be creative.

Our namesake item, the hot fudge sundae, is ready all times and I have kept the price at ten cents, a though that allows only a one-and-a-half-cent gro profit. Any customer having a birthday gets one free along with our singing *Happy Birthday!* with lou banging on a drum, and a kiss. College boys appreciat kissing Margrethe more than they do the free sundae Understandable. But Pop Graham doesn't do too badl with the co-eds, either. (I don't force kisses on a "birth day girl.")

Our shop was a success from day one. The location is good—facing Elm Street gate and Old Main. Plentiful trade was guaranteed by low prices and Margrethe's magic touch with food . . . *and* her beauty and her sweet personality; we aren't selling calories, we're selling happiness. She piles a lavish serving of happiness on each plate; she has it to spare.

With me to watch the pennies, our team could not lose. And I do watch pennies; if the cost of ingredients ever kills that narrow margin on a hot fudge sundae, the price goes up. Mr. Belial, president of our bank, says that the country is in a long, steady period of gentle prosperity. I hope he is right; meanwhile I watch the gross profit.

The town is enjoying a real estate boom, caused by the Farnsworths plus the change in climate. It used to be that the typical wealthy Texan had a summer home in Colorado Springs, but now that we no longer fry eggs on our sidewalks, Texans are beginning to see the charms of Kansas. They say it's a change in the Jet Stream. (Or is it the Gulf Stream? I never was strong in science.) Whatever, our summers now are balmy and our winters are mild; many of Jerry's friends or associates are buying land in Eden and building summer homes. Mr. Ashmedai, manager of some of Jerry's interests, now lives here year round—and Dr. Adramelech, chancellor of Eden College, caused him to be elected to the board of trustees, along with an honorary doctorate—as a former money-raiser I can see why.

We welcome them all and not just for their money . . but I would not want Eden to grow as crowded as Dallas.

Not that it could. This is a bucolic place; the college

is our only "industry." One community church serve
all sects, The Church of the Divine Orgasm—Sabbath
school at 9:30 a.m., church services at 11, picnic an
orgy immediately following.

We don't believe in shoving religion down a kid'
throat but the truth is that young people like our com
munity church—thanks to our pastor, the Reverend
Dr. M. O. Loch. Malcolm is a Presbyterian, I think; h
still has a Scottish burr in his speech. But there is noth
ing of the dour Scot about him and kids love him. H
leads the revels and directs the rituals—our daughter
Elise is a Novice Ecdysiast under him and she talks c
having a vocation. (Piffle. She'll marry right out of hig
school; I could name the young man—though I can
see what she sees in him.)

Margrethe serves in the Altar Guild; I pass the plat
on the Sabbath and serve on the finance board. I'v
never given up my membership in the Apocalyps
Brethren but I must admit that we Brethren read
wrong; the end of the millennium came and went an
the Shout was never heard.

A man who is happy at home doesn't lie awak
nights worrying about the hereafter.

What is success? My classmates at Rolla Tech, bac
when, may think that I've settled for too little, owne
with-the-bank of a tiny restaurant in a nowhere towr
But I have what I want. I would not want to be a sair
in Heaven if Margrethe was not with me; I wouldn
fear going to Hell if she was there—not that I believ
in Hell or ever stood a chance of being a saint i
Heaven.

Samuel Clemens put it: "Where she was, there was
den." Omar phrased it: "—thou beside me in the wil-
erness, ah wilderness were paradise enow." Browning
ermed it: "Summum Bonum." All were asserting the
ame great truth, which is for me:

Heaven is where Margrethe is.

A Note From the Publisher

Blue Willow, Inc. has made a serious effort to ensure that information provided in this book is as accurate as possible. Over 10,000 person-hours have gone into the research, collection, verification, and editing necessary to complete *Measure for Measure*, however, the publisher and authors do not guarantee that all of the information included in this book is error free or exact. It simply is not possible to create a work of this size without having errors, typos, inaccuracies or omissions. If you discover any errors, we would greatly appreciate it if you would report them to us. We also welcome any suggestions that you might have concerning future editions of any of our products.

Blue Willow, Inc.
P.O. Box 621227, Dept. 101
Littleton, Colorado 80162
(303) 932-1600
World Wide Web Home Page:
http://www. bluewillow. com

Preface

No book of this magnitude is put together by one or two people, and *Measure For Measure* is no exception. Many people have been involved in the conception and creation of this volume.

Many thanks to my friend and co-author, Thomas, for the idea for *Measure For Measure* and for the opportunity to compile and compute the data presented in it. Without his vision, support, and expertise in desktop publishing and database manipulation there would be no *Measure For Measure*. My deepest thanks to you, my friend.

Many talented people helped gather and compile the information on which *Measure For Measure* is based. My sincere thanks to Trisha Glover, Donna Baumgarten, Amy Full, Liz Young, Stephanie Young, Carrie Glover, and Chris Young for their support and hours of dedicated help.

A very special thanks to my beautiful wife, Millie, for the use of her artistic talents in designing the cover for *Measure For Measure* and for her love and support during our twenty-nine years of mutual respect and love. I love you my lady!

Richard

Producing a book like *Measure for Measure* has got to be asking for trouble!! The shear magnitude of this project would have been enough to scare most people out of their wits and if you couple that with the frustration of resolving why 25 different sources can't agree on a simple little conversion like Cambodian chongs to Lebanese chinbuls . . . well, you'll begin to understand what is special about my co-author and friend Richard Young. Many thanks to Millie Young for the beautiful cover art work - how does it feel to have become a graphics guru?

Special thanks are due to my family and friends for their understanding and acceptance of the sacrifices that we all must make in order to publish a book. Mom and Dad, Pat, Mary, Trish, and Carrie, without your love and support over the years, none of this would have been possible. To my new and very special children, Eric, Dena and David, welcome to my world. You have all helped to make my life complete and I love you all very much.

Thomas

Table of Contents

Blue Willow Products

Measure for Measure

Richard A. Young and Thomas J. Glover, 1996
ISBN 1-889796-00-X, 864 pages, soft cover, 4"x 6"

1 The International System of Units

Introduction

In the United States, the International System of Units is known simply as the "Metric System" or, more appropriately, the Modernized Metric System. The name is translated from the French *Le Système International d'Unités* and is abbreviated **SI** in all languages. **SI** was formally adopted in 1960. **SI** is a coherent system of units which, in thirty-six years, has grown to become an almost universally accepted system of units in engineering, science, trade, and commerce.

Brief History of SI

The International System of Units has evolved out of a unit of length (the **meter**) and a unit of mass (the **kilogram**). These units were created by the Paris Academy of Sciences and adopted by the National Assembly of France in 1795. On May 20, 1875, an international treaty known as the Treaty of the Meter or the Meter Convention (*Convention du Mètre*) was signed by representatives from 17 countries, including the United States.

The Treaty of the Meter established three organizations to conduct activities relating to a uniform system of units. The General Conference on Weights and Measures (CGPM, *Conférence Générale des Poids et Mesures*), the International Committee of Weights and Measures (CIPM, *Comité International des Poids et Mesures*), and the International Bureau of Weights and Measures (BIPM, *Bureau International des Poids et Mesures*) are the organizations that have ultimate control over The International System of Units. The National Institute of Standards and Technology (NIST) of the U.S. Department of Commerce is the United States representative to all three of these international organizations.

In 1960, the Eleventh General Conference on Weight and Measures adopted The International System of Units. This system is based on the **meter, kilogram, second, ampere, kelvin,** and **candela**. In 1971, the Fourteenth General Conference on Weights and Measures added the **mole** as the **SI** unit for the amount of substance.

Brief History of SI in the United States

The Congress of the United States legalized the use of a metric system throughout the United States in 1866. On April 5, 1893, the Mendenhall Order, named for T.C. Mendenhall, U.S. Superintendent of Standard Weights, established metric units as the ultimate base of all U.S. Customary Units. Thus, the pound was defined in terms of the kilogram and the yard was defined in terms of the meter. The Metric Conversion Act of 1975 designated the "metric system of measurement as the preferred system of weights and measures for United States trade and commerce," and furthermore, the "metric system of measurement" was defined as The International System of Units.

Since 1975, additional federal laws, regulations, and executive orders have extolled the <u>voluntary</u> use of **SI** in the United States. Unfortunately (or fortunately, depending on your point of view), **SI** has never been <u>mandated</u> by law as the official system of units in the United States. Although many professional societies and associations in the United States have officially adopted **SI** for use in their journals, conference proceedings, magazines, and books, the English or Imperial units remain firmly entrenched in every day American life.

SI Basics

SI has seven *base* units (**meter, kilogram, second, ampere, kelvin, mole,** and **candela**) and two *supplementary* units (**radian** and **steradian**). The seven base units are fundamental, independent quantities (length, mass, time, electric current, thermodynamic temperature, amount of substance, and luminous intensity) which have been defined and measured with a high degree of certainty. A definition and brief history of each base unit is included later in this chapter in the section entitled **SI Base Units** (page 22.).

SI is a coherent system of units, which means that all necessary units can be formed as products and quotients of the base and supplementary units. All units formed in this manner are called derived units. Nineteen of these derived units have been given special names (becquerel, coulomb, degree Celsius, farad, gray, henry, hertz, joule, lumen, lux, newton, ohm, pascal, siemens, sievert, tesla, volt, watt, and weber).

Table 1, on page 10, presents the names of quantities approved for use in **SI**, the name of the **SI** unit for each quantity, the unit symbol, and the expression for each unit in terms of either base or derived units. Figure 1 on page 21 illustrates the relationships between the base and supplementary units and the nineteen derived units with special names.

SI is a decimal system meaning that subdivisions of units are based on multiples of 10. Multiples or subdivisions are noted in **SI** by prefix names which express the power of 10 (exponent) to be applied to a given multiple or subdivision. Table 2, on page 20, presents the multiplication factors, exponents, prefix names, prefix symbols, and pronunciation for all prefixes in **SI**.

Table 1 - Units

Unit	Type of Unit

SI Base Units

ampere	electric current
candela	luminous intensity
kelvin	thermodynamic temperature
kilogram	mass
meter	length
mole	amount of substance
second	time

SI Supplementary Units

radian	plane angle
steradian	solid angle

SI Derived Units With Special Names

becquerel	activity (of a radionuclide)
coulomb	electric charge, quantity of electricity
farad	capacitance
gray	absorbed dose, kerma, absorbed dose index
henry	electric inductance
joule	energy, work, quantity of heat
lumen	luminous flux
lux	illuminance, luminous flux density
newton	force
ohm	electric resistance
pascal	pressure, stress
siemens	electric conductance
sievert	dose equivalent, dose equivalent index
tesla	magnetic flux density
volt	electric potential, potential difference, electromotive force
watt	power, radiant flux
weber	magnetic flux

Table 1 - Units

Unit	SI Unit Symbol	Expression in Other Units	Expression in SI Base Units
SI Base Units			
ampere	A		
candela	cd		
kelvin	K		
kilogram	kg		
meter	m		
mole	mol		
second	s		
SI Supplementary Units			
radian	rad		
steradian	sr		
SI Derived Units With Special Names			
becquerel	Bq		$1 / s$
coulomb	C		$A \bullet s$
farad	F	C / V	$s^4 \bullet A^2 / m^2 \bullet kg$
gray	Gy	J / kg	m^2 / s^2
henry	H	Wb / A	$m^2 \bullet kg / s^2 \bullet A^2$
joule	J	$N \bullet m$	$m^2 \bullet kg / s^2$
lumen	lm		$cd \bullet sr$
lux	lx	lm / m^2	$cd \bullet sr / m^2$
newton	N		$m \bullet kg / s^2$
ohm	Ω	V / A	$m^2 \bullet kg / s^3 \bullet A^2$
pascal	Pa	N / m^2	$kg / m \bullet s^2$
siemens	S	A / V	$s^3 \bullet A^2 / m^2 \bullet kg$
sievert	Sv	J / kg	m^2 / s^2
tesla	T	Wb / m^2	$kg / s^2 \bullet A$
volt	V	W / A	$m^2 \bullet kg / s^3 \bullet A$
watt	W	J / s	$m^2 \bullet kg / s^3$
weber	Wb	$V \bullet s$	$m^2 \bullet kg / s^2 \bullet A$

Table 1 - Units

Unit	Type of Unit	➡

SI Derived Units

1/cubic meter second	neutron source density
1/henry	electric reluctance
1/joule cubic meter	density of states
1/meter	reciprocal length, phase coefficient, attenuation coefficient
1/pascal	compressibility
1/second	frequency, circular frequency, angular velocity
ampere square meter	electromagnetic moment
ampere/meter	magnetic field strength, linear electric current density
ampere/square meter	electric current density
becquerel/cubic meter	volume activity (of a radionuclide)
becquerel/kilogram	specific activity (of a radionuclide)
bel	sound pressure level
candela/square meter	luminance
coulomb meter	electric dipole moment
coulomb square meter/volt	electric polarizability
coulomb/cubic meter	electric charge density
coulomb/kilogram	exposure (x and gamma rays)
coulomb/kilogram second	exposure rate (x and gamma rays)
coulomb/square meter	electric flux density, electric surface charge density
cubic meter	volume
cubic meter/kilogram	specific volume
cubic meter/mole	molar volume
cubic meter/second	flow rate (volume basis)
farad/meter	electric permittivity
gray/second	absorbed dose rate
henry/meter	electric permeability
joule second	moment of momentum
joule square meter/kilogram	total mass stopping power
joule/cubic meter	energy density

Table 1 - Units

Unit	Expression in Other Units	Expression in SI Base Units
SI Derived Units		
1/cubic meter second		$1 / m^3 \bullet s$
1/henry	A / Wb	$A^2 \bullet s^2 / m^2 \bullet kg$
1/joule cubic meter		$s^2 / kg \bullet m^5$
1/meter		$1 / m$
1/pascal	m^2 / N	$m \bullet s^2 / kg$
1/second		$1 / s$
ampere square meter	J / T	$A \bullet m^2$
ampere/meter	N / Wb	A / m
ampere/square meter		A / m^2
becquerel/cubic meter		$1 / m^3 \bullet s$
becquerel/kilogram		$1 / kg \bullet s$
bel	dimensionless	
candela/square meter		cd / m^2
coulomb meter		$A \bullet s \bullet m$
coulomb square meter/volt	$F \bullet m^2$	$A^2 \bullet s^4 / kg$
coulomb/cubic meter		$A \bullet s / m^3$
coulomb/kilogram	$A \bullet m^2 / J \bullet s$	$A \bullet s / kg$
coulomb/kilogram second		A / kg
coulomb/square meter		$A \bullet s / m^2$
cubic meter		m^3
cubic meter/kilogram		m^3 / kg
cubic meter/mole		m^3 / mol
cubic meter/second		m^3 / s
farad/meter	$C / V \bullet m$	$A^2 \bullet s^4 / m^3 \bullet kg$
gray/second	W / kg	m^2 / s^3
henry/meter	N / A^2	$m \bullet kg / s^2 \bullet A^2$
joule second	$N \bullet m \bullet s$	$m^2 \bullet kg / s$
joule square meter/kilogram		m^4 / s^2
joule/cubic meter	N / m^2	$kg / m \bullet s^2$

Table 1 - Units

Unit	Type of Unit	

SI Derived Units (continued)

Unit	Type of Unit
joule/kelvin	specific heat, heat capacity, entropy
joule/kilogram	specific thermodynamic energy
joule/kilogram kelvin	specific heat capacity, specific entropy
joule/meter	linear energy transfer
joule/mole	molar energy
joule/mole kelvin	molar entropy, molar heat capacity
joule/square meter	energy fluence, radiant exposure
kelvin/watt	thermal resistance
kilogram meter/second	momentum, impluse
kilogram square meter	moment of inertia of a mass
kilogram/cubic meter	density, mass density
kilogram/meter	linear density
kilogram/mole	molar mass
kilogram/second	flow rate (mass basis)
kilogram/square meter	surface density
lumen second	quantity of light, luminous energy
lumen/watt	luminous efficacy
lux second	light exposure
meter/second	velocity, speed
meter/square second	acceleration
meter^4	second moment of area, moment of inertia of area
mole/cubic meter	concentration of amount of substance (mole basis)
mole/kilogram	molality
newton meter	torque, moment of force, bending moment
newton second/meter	mechanical impedance
newton/meter	surface tension
ohm meter	electric resistivity
pascal second	dynamic viscosity
pascal second/cubic meter	acoustic impedance
pascal/kelvin	pressure coefficient

Table 1 · Units

Unit	Expression in Other Units	Expression in SI Base Units

SI Derived Units (continued)

Unit	Expression in Other Units	Expression in SI Base Units
joule/kelvin		$m^2 \bullet kg / s^2 \bullet K$
joule/kilogram	$W \bullet s / kg$	m^2 / s^2
joule/kilogram kelvin		$m^2 / s^2 \bullet K$
joule/meter	N	$m \bullet kg / s^2$
joule/mole		$m^2 \bullet kg / s^2 \bullet mol$
joule/mole kelvin		$m^2 \bullet kg / s^2 \bullet mol \bullet K$
joule/square meter	N / m	kg / s^2
kelvin/watt		$s^3 \bullet K / m^2 \bullet kg$
kilogram meter/second	N / s	$kg \bullet m / s$
kilogram square meter		$kg \bullet m^2$
kilogram/cubic meter		kg / m^3
kilogram/meter		kg / m
kilogram/mole		kg / mol
kilogram/second		kg / s
kilogram/square meter		kg / m^2
lumen second		$s \bullet cd \bullet sr$
lumen/watt		$s^3 \bullet cd \bullet sr / m^2 \bullet kg$
lux second		$s \bullet cd \bullet sr / m^2$
meter/second		m / s
meter/square second		m / s^2
meter^4		m^4
mole/cubic meter		mol / m^3
mole/kilogram		mol / kg
newton meter	J	$m^2 \bullet kg / s^2$
newton second/meter		kg / s
newton/meter	J / m^2	kg / s^2
ohm meter		$m^3 \bullet kg / s^3 \bullet A^2$
pascal second	$N \bullet s / m^2$	$kg / m \bullet s$
pascal second/cubic meter	$N \bullet s / m^5$	$kg / m^4 \bullet s$
pascal/kelvin		$kg / m \bullet s^2 \bullet K$

Table 1 - Units

SI Derived Units (continued)

phon ....loudness level
radian/square second...............angular acceleration
siemens/meter ....electric conductivity
square meter..............................area
square meter kelvin/watt..........coefficient of thermal insulation
square meter/joule.....................spectral cross-section
square meter/second.................kinematic viscosity
square meter/volt second ....mobility (drift)
volt/kelvin.................................seebeck coefficient
volt/meter..................................electric field strength
watt/kelvin.................................thermal conductance
watt/meter kelvin ....thermal conductivity
watt/square meter.....................heat flux density, irradiance power
density, heat flow rate
watt/square meter kelvin...........coefficient of heat transfer
watt/square meter steradian .....radiance
watt/steradian...........................radiant intensity
weber meter...............................magnetic dipole moment
weber/meter ....magnetic vector potential

Derived Units - Not Approved For Use With SI

1/farad ....electric elastance
coulomb/meter ....electric dipole moment per unit area
cubic meter/cubic meter...........concentration (volume basis)
cubic meter/joule......................specific fuel consumption (volume basis)
cubic meter/meter ....fuel consumption (SI)
gal/centimeter...........................acceleration gradient
kelvin/meter ....geothermal gradient
kilogram meter/pascal square second
permeability (water)
kilogram/joule ....specific fuel consumption (mass basis)
kilogram/kilogram.....................concentration (mass basis), ore grading
kilogram/square meter second ......flow rate per unit area (mass basis)
liter ....champagne bottle size

Table 1 - Units

Unit	Expression in Other Units	Expression in SI Base Units

SI Derived Units (continued)

Unit	Expression in Other Units	Expression in SI Base Units
phon		dimensionless
radian/square second		rad / s^2
siemens/meter		$s^3 \bullet A^2 / m^3 \bullet kg$
square meter		m^2
square meter kelvin/watt		$s^3 \bullet K / kg$
square meter/joule		s^2 / kg
square meter/second		m^2 / s
square meter/volt second	m^2 / Wb	$s^2 \bullet A / kg$
volt/kelvin		V / K
volt/meter		$m \bullet kg / s^3 \bullet A$
watt/kelvin		$m^2 \bullet kg / s^3 \bullet K$
watt/meter kelvin	$J / m \bullet s \bullet K$	$m \bullet kg / s^3 \bullet K$
watt/square meter	$J / m^2 \bullet s$	kg / s^3
watt/square meter kelvin	$J / m^2 \bullet s \bullet K$	$kg / s^3 \bullet K$
watt/square meter steradian		$kg / s^3 \bullet sr$
watt/steradian		$m^2 \bullet kg / s^3 \bullet sr$
weber meter	$V \bullet s \bullet m$	$m^3 \bullet kg / s^2 \bullet A$
weber/meter	$V \bullet s / m$	$m \bullet kg / s^2 \bullet A$

Derived Units - Not Approved For Use With SI

Unit	Expression in Other Units	Expression in SI Base Units
1/farad	V / C	$m^2 \bullet kg / s^4 \bullet A^2$
coulomb/meter		$A \bullet s / m$
cubic meter/cubic meter		1
cubic meter/joule		m^2 / N
cubic meter/meter		m^2
gal/centimeter		$1 / s^2$
kelvin/meter		K / m
kilogram meter/pascal square second		m^2
kilogram/joule	$kg / N \bullet m$	s^2 / m^2
kilogram/kilogram		1
kilogram/square meter second		$kg / m^2 \bullet s$
liter		m^3

Table 1 - Units

Derived Units - Not Approved For Use With SI (cont.)

Unit	Type of Unit
meter kelvin/watt	thermal resistivity
meter/cubic meter	fuel consumption (US)
meter/kelvin	geothermal step
mole/second	flow rate (mole basis)
mole/square meter	surface concentration
newton meter/meter	torque per unit length
pascal second/meter	specific acoustic impedance
pascal/meter	pressure gradient
second	sedimentation coefficient
square meter	sound absorption
square meter/cubic meter	area per unit volume
square meter/kilogram	specific area
square meter/pascal second	mobility
unit	units, count, pure numbers
watt/cubic meter	heat release rate
watt/cubic meter kelvin	heat transfer coefficient
watt/square meter hertz	energy flux density

For units not included in *Measure for Measure*, see Appendix page 864.

Table 1 - Units

Unit	Expression in Other Units	Expression in SI Base Units

Derived Units - Not Approved For Use With SI (cont.)

Unit	Expression in Other Units	Expression in SI Base Units
meter kelvin/watt	$m \bullet s \bullet K / J$	$s^3 \bullet K / m \bullet kg$
meter/cubic meter		$1 / m^2$
meter/kelvin		m / K
mole/second		mol / s
mole/square meter		mol / m^2
newton meter/meter	N	$m \bullet kg / s^2$
pascal second/meter	$N \bullet s / m^3$	$kg / m^2 \bullet s$
pascal/meter		$kg / m^2 \bullet s^2$
second		s
square meter		m^2
square meter/cubic meter		$1 / m$
square meter/kilogram		m^2 / kg
square meter/pascal second		$m^3 \bullet s / kg$
unit		1
watt/cubic meter		$kg / m \bullet s^3$
watt/cubic meter kelvin		$kg / m \bullet s^3 \bullet K$
watt/square meter hertz		kg / s^2

For units not included in *Measure for Measure,* **see Appendix page 864.**

Table 2 - Decimal System Prefixes

Multiplication Factor	Exponent	Prefix
1 000 000 000 000 000 000 000 000	10^{24}	yotta
1 000 000 000 000 000 000 000	10^{21}	zetta
1 000 000 000 000 000 000	10^{18}	exa
1 000 000 000 000 000	10^{15}	peta
1 000 000 000 000	10^{12}	tera
1 000 000 000	10^{9}	giga
1 000 000	10^{6}	mega
1 000	10^{3}	kilo
100	10^{2}	hecto
10	10^{1}	deka
0.1	10^{-1}	deci
0.01	10^{-2}	centi
0.001	10^{-3}	milli
0.000 001	10^{-6}	micro
0.000 000 001	10^{-9}	nano
0.000 000 000 001	10^{-12}	pico
0.000 000 000 000 001	10^{-15}	femto
0.000 000 000 000 000 001	10^{-18}	atto
0.000 000 000 000 000 000 001	10^{-21}	zepto
0.000 000 000 000 000 000 000 001	10^{-24}	yocto

Prefix	Symbol	Pronunciation
yotta	Y	YOTT-a (a as in about)
zetta	Z	ZETT-a (a as in about)
exa	E	EX-a (a as in about)
peta	P	PET-a (as in petal)
tera	T	TERR-a (as in terrace)
giga	G	GIG-a (gig as in giggle, a as in about)
mega	M	MEG-a (as in megaphone)
kilo	k	KILL-oh
hecto	h	HECK-toe
deka	da	DECK-a (as in decahedron)
deci	d	DESS-ih (as in decimal)
centi	c	SENT-ih (as in centipede)
milli	m	MILL-ih (as in military)
micro	μ	MIKE-roe (as in microbe)
nano	n	NAN-oh (a as in ant)
pico	p	PEEK-oh
femto	f	FEM-toe
atto	a	AT-toe (a as in hat)
zepto	z	ZEP-toe (e as in step)
yocto	y	YOCK-toe

Figure 1 - Relationships of SI Units

From: *Interpretation of the SI for the United States and Metric Conversion Policy for Federal Agencies,* NIST Special Publication 814, Barry N. Taylor, Editor, October 1991.

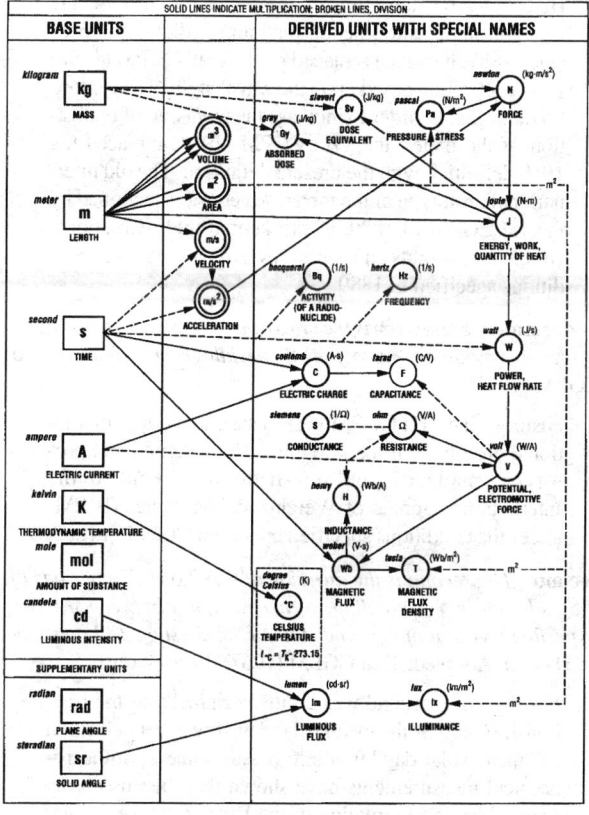

SI Base Units

meter - *The meter is the length of the path traveled by light in a vacuum during the time interval of 1/299,792,458 of a second.* Adopted : 17th CGPM (1983), Resolution 1.

History - The definition of the meter based upon the international prototype of platinum-iridium, in force since 1889, had been replaced by the 11th CGPM (1960) with a definition based upon the wavelength of a krypton-86 radiation. In order to increase the precision of realization of the meter, the 17th CGPM (1983) replaced the 1960 definition with the present definition. The old international prototype of the meter, which was sanctioned by the 1st CGPM in 1889, is still kept at the International Bureau of Weights and Measures (BIPM) under the conditions specified in 1889.

kilogram - *The kilogram is the unit of mass; it is equal to the mass of the international prototype of the kilogram.* Adopted: 3rd CGPM (1901).

History - The 1st CGPM (1889) sanctioned the international prototype of the kilogram. This international prototype, made of platinum-iridium, is kept at the International Bureau of Weights and Measures (BIPM) under the conditions specified by the 1st CGPM in 1889.

second - *The second is the duration of 9,192,631,770 periods of the radiation corresponding to the transition between the two hyperfine levels of the ground state of the caesium-133 (cesium-133) atom.* Adopted: 13th CGPM (1967), Resolution 1.

History - The second was defined originally as the fraction 1/86,400 of the mean solar day. The exact definition of "mean solar day" was left to astronomers. But astronomical measurements have shown that, because of irregularities in the rotation of the Earth, the "mean solar day" does not guarantee the desired accuracy for the second. In order to define the unit of time more precisely, the 11th CGPM (1960) adopted a definition given by the International Astronomical Union (IAU) which was based on the "tropical year". Experimental work had, however, already shown that an atomic standard of time-interval, based on a transition between two energy levels of an atom or molecule, could be realized and reproduced much more accurately. Considering that a very precise definition of the second is indispensable for the needs of advanced metrology, the 13th CGPM (1967) decided to replace the definition on the second with the present definition.

ampere - *The ampere is that constant current which, if maintained in two straight parallel conductors of infinite length, of negligible circular cross section, and placed 1 meter apart in vacuum, would produce between these conductors a force equal to 2 x 10^{-7} newton per meter of length.* Adopted: 9th CGPM (1948).

History - Electric units, called "international," for current and resistance had been introduced by the International Electrical Congress held in Chicago in 1893, and the definitions of the "international" ampere and the "international" ohm were confirmed by the International Conference of London in 1908. Although it was already obvious on the occasion of the 8th CGPM (1933) that there was a unanimous desire to replace those "international" units by the so-called "absolute" units, the official decision to abolish the "international" units was only taken by the 9th CGPM (1948) which adopted the present definition.

kelvin - *The kelvin, unit of thermodynamic temperature, is the fraction 1/273.16 of the thermodynamic temperature of the triple point of water.* Adopted: 13th CGPM (1967), Resolution 4.

History - The definition of the unit of thermodynamic temperature was given in substance by the 10th CGPM (1954) which selected the triple point of water as the fundamental fixed point and assigned to it the temperature 273.16 K. The 13th CGPM (1967) adopted the name *kelvin* (symbol K) instead of "degree Kelvin" (symbol °K) and adopted the present definition of the unit of thermodynamic temperature.

mole - *The mole is the amount of substance of a system which contains as many elementary entities as there are atoms in 0.012 kilogram of carbon-12. When the mole is used, the elementary entities may be atoms, molecules, ions, electrons, other particles, or specified groups of such particles.* Adopted: 14th CGPM (1971), Resolution 3.

History - Since the discovery of the fundamental laws of chemistry, units of amount of substance, called for instance, "gram-atom" and "gram-molecule," have been used to specify amounts of chemical elements or compounds. These units had a direct connection with "atomic weights" and "molecular weights." "Atomic weights" were originally referenced to the atomic weight of oxygen (by general agreement taken as 16). But physicists separated isotopes in mass spectrograph and attributed the value 16 to one of the isotopes of oxygen, while chemists attributed that same value to the (slightly variable) mixture of isotopes 16, 17 and 18, which was for them the naturally occurring element oxygen. Finally, in 1960, an agreement between the International Union of Pure and Applied Physics (IUPAP) and the International Union of Pure and Applied Chemistry (IUPAC) brought this dispute to an end. Physicists and chemists have ever since agreed to assign the value 12 to the isotope 12 of carbon. The unified scale thus obtained gives values of "relative atomic mass." It remained to define the unit of amount of substance by fixing the corresponding mass of carbon-12.

By international agreement, this mass has been fixed at 0.012 kg, and the unit of the quantity "amount of substance" has been given the name *mole* (symbol mol). Following proposals of IUPAP, IUPAC, and ISO (International Organization for Standardization), the CIPM gave in 1967, and confirmed in 1969, the present definition of the mole, which was finally adopted by the 14th CGPM (1971).

candela - *The candela is the luminous intensity, in a given direction, of a source that emits monochromatic radiation of frequency 540×10^{12} hertz and that has a radiant intensity in that direction of 1/683 watt per steradian.* Adopted: 16th CGPM (1979), Resolution 3.

History - The units of luminous intensity based on flame or incandescent standards in use in various countries before 1948 were replaced initially by the "new candle" based on the luminance of a Planckian radiator (a blackbody) at the temperature of freezing platinum. This decision had been prepared by the International Commission on Illumination (CIE) and by CIPM before 1937, and was promulgated by the CIPM in 1946, and then ratified in 1948 by the 9th CGPM which adopted a new international name for this unit, the *candela* (symbol cd); in 1967 the 13th CGPM gave an amended version of the 1946 definition.

Because of experimental difficulties in realizing a Planckian radiator at high temperatures and the new possibilities offered by radiometry, i.e., the measurement of optical radiation power, the 16th CGPM (1979) adopted the present definition.

2 About Measure For Measure

Measure For Measure has been compiled over a three year period. Approximately 5,100 units were selected from over 140 sources. These units and their definitions were used to calculate over 178,000 conversion factors. The authors then selected more than 39,000 of the most useful conversion factors for inclusion in *Measure For Measure*.

Conventions Used in *Measure For Measure*

Conventions used by the authors in *Measure For Measure* are in accordance with ASTM E 380-92, Standard Practice for Use of the International System of Units (SI) and ANSI/IEEE 268-1992, American National Standard for Metric Practice. A few of these conventions differ from official **SI** convention as stated in International Standards ISO 31:1992 and ISO 1000:1992. The main differences are the spelling of the units *meter* (ISO: metre) and *liter* (ISO: litre) and the spelling of the prefix deka (ISO: deca).

In ASTM E-380-92 and ANSI/IEEE 268-1992 the units *electronvolt, watthour,* and *wattsecond* are written as single words. Other references and dictionaries write these units either as two words or as a hyphenated word. *Measure For Measure* uses the spelling given in ASTM E-380-92 and ANSI/IEEE 268-1992 for these units and their derivatives.

Units containing exponent names, such as units for area or volume, will have the exponent name in front of the unit name. So the **SI** unit of area is the **square meter** not **meter squared** and the **SI** unit of volume is the **cubic meter** not the **meter cubed**.

How To Use *Measure For Measure*

Measure For Measure is easy to use. Units are listed alphabetically. Units listed in the *Convert From* column are shown in **bold face type** while units in the *Convert To* column are shown in normal type face. Conversion factors are given in both scientific notation (to seven decimal places) - in the column labeled *Scientific* - and in decimal notation - in the column labeled *Standard*. Modifiers are enclosed in brackets [ ] and give clarifying information about the units listed in either the *Convert From* or *Convert To* columns. The **<Type of Unit>** field is a guide to the type of quantity the Convert From unit represents. Additional information on all of the different **<Type of Unit>** choices is included in Table 1 on page 10.

For most units in the *Convert From* column there will be at least one **SI** unit in the *Convert To* column. There are a few units in *Measure For Measure* for which there are no approved **SI** units, these have been included for completeness.

Displaying conversion factors in both scientific and standard notation presents problems with rounding. The authors held the scientific notation constant at 8 significant digits, one digit left of the decimal and 7 right of the decimal. With standard notation, however, the digits were set to a <u>maximum</u> of 7 right of the decimal and a <u>maximum</u> of 8 left of the decimal. A number which in scientific notation has 8 significant digits may appear quite differently when displayed in standard or decimal notation, depending on the location of the decimal. In all cases, the number with the greatest number of significant digits is the more accurate number. For example:

ampere second/square meter
    franklin/square centimeter ------- 299,792.4<u>58</u>-------2.997 924 <u>6</u>E+05
                                                          Std. Notation----Scientific Notation

Note that the last digit in scientific notation has been rounded off to 6 from the more accurate standard notation value.

Examples of Converting

Example 1: Simple Conversion

> To convert 3 feet to inches: Locate **foot** in the *Convert From* column. Scroll down the *Convert To* column until **inch** is located. In the *Standard* column opposite **inch** locate the desired conversion factor, 12, in other words, 1 **foot** = 12 **inches**. To convert, simply multiply the number of **feet** (3 in this case) by 12 to obtain 36 **inches**.

Example 2: Complex conversion

> Calculate the factor to convert from **foot** to **inch** using conversion factors for the **meter** which is an SI unit common to both the **foot** and the **inch**. Locate 1 **foot** = 0.3048 **meter** and 1 **inch** = 2.54 E-02 **meter**. Combine these conversion factors as follows:

$$1\, foot = \frac{0.3048\ meter}{\dfrac{2.54\ E-02\ meter}{1\ inch}}$$

$$1\, foot = \frac{0.3048}{2.54\ E-02}\ inch$$

$$1\, foot = 12\ inch$$

The technique demonstrated in Example 2 may be used to find conversion factors not listed in *Measure For Measure*. As long as the two units of interest have a third unit common to both, the conversion factor from one unit to the other may be calculated.

Units From Other Countries and Ancient Units

The authors have used many references to collect both modern and ancient conversion factors for units from countries around the world. Most units presented in *Measure For Measure* are modern units which predate the use of **SI** as the official system of units for each country. They are presented in *Measure For Measure* for completeness and some of these units may still be in use in local trade and commerce. Most units labeled as "ancient" are from the Roman or Greek empires, Chinese or Japanese dynasties, or from ancient countries of the Middle East referenced in the Bible. Because of variations between references in the spelling of unit names and in the accuracy of conversion factors, the reader should regard all conversion factors for units from other countries and ancient units as estimates. These units are marked with one of the following **<Type of Unit>** labels:

> **<mass, special - see page 29>**
> **<volume, special - see page 29>**
> **<area, special - see page 29>**
> **<length, special - see page 29>**

Please note again, the above labels indicate that the conversion factors are the authors <u>best estimate</u> for these units.

Units and Modifiers

The authors have been as specific as possible when identifying units. Modifiers have been used extensively to help differentiate between similar units. For example, the **British thermal unit -** the **Btu -** is listed nine times in the *Convert From* column because, over the years, the **Btu** has had nine separate definitions and the **Btu [international table]** is different from the **Btu [mean]** or the **Btu [thermochemical].** Similarly the **calorie** is listed seven times, the **carat** is listed six times, etc..

Some derived units may have more than one modifier such as **ounce [troy]/ton [long]**. In *Measure For Measure* this unit is given in either *Convert* column as **ounce/ton** with **[troy/long]** as the modifier. For the unit **ounce/ton [long]** where no modifier is given for the unit **ounce**, the modifier will be **[- /long]**.

When one or more units are combined into a derived unit, the order of the units in either the numerator or denominator is not significant. A derived unit such as **Btu/hour cubic foot** may also be written as **Btu/cubic foot hour** or the unit **foot pound-force** may be written as **pound-force foot**. When searching for derived units in *Measure For Measure* be sure to check all possible combinations of unit order.

Mixed Units

Mixed units are formed when two or more units from different unit systems are combined into one unit. An example of a mixed unit would be **ounce/cubic meter** which mixes an Imperial mass unit (the **ounce**) with the **SI** unit of volume (the **cubic meter**). Mixed units are strongly discouraged in **SI** and should be avoided whenever possible. Mixed units have been minimized in *Measure For Measure*.

Units of Mass and Force

In the English or Imperial system of units, force and mass are often incorrectly used as being interchangeable. For example, when the unit **pound** is used it is often unclear if the user means mass or force. **SI** avoids this confusion by using the **kilogram** as the unit of mass and the **newton** as the unit of force. To avoid confusion in *Measure For Measure* the authors have chosen to mark English units of force by attaching "-force" to the end of the unit name. Thus, **pound** is a mass unit which would convert to the **kilogram** and **pound-force** is a force unit which would convert to the **newton**.

Equivalent Units

Equivalent units are, as the name implies, units that are equal. Conversion factors for equivalent units are always equal to 1. Examples of equivalent units would be: *Convert From:* **joule**; *Convert To:* **newton meter**; *Scientific: 1.000 000 0E+00* or *Convert From:* **volt**; *Convert To:* **watt/ampere**; *Scientific: 1.000 000 0E+00.* Equivalent units usually involve the definition of one unit in terms of two or more units in the same system of units. In the above examples the **SI** unit **joule** is defined as a **newton meter** and the **SI** unit **volt** is defined as a **watt per ampere**.

Units Not Currently in *Measure for Measure*

During the compiling process, the authors discovered a number of units for which there was either no exact definition or for which there was disagreement between authoritative sources on an exact definition. The authors have listed these units in the Appendix (page 864) in hopes that users of *Measure for Measure* might drop Blue Willow a note if they become aware of additional sources that might help resolve these problems.

At this time, it has been decided to not include units that are "approximate" in the main Conversion Factor section. As additional research is completed, the authors may elect to include these units in future editions of *Measure for Measure*. (An exception to this rule has been made for the "pinch" and the "dash", which are commonly used quantities in cooking. The approximate conversions for each have been included in the main section.)

Abbreviations Used in *Measure For Measure*

The use of abbreviations has been minimized in *Measure For Measure*, however, the use of some abbreviations was unavoidable. The following list is provided for easy interpretation of all abbreviations used in *Measure For Measure*:

ANSI	American National Standards Institute
ASTM	American Society for Testing and Standards
BIPM	International Bureau of Weights and Measures
Btu	British thermal unit
C-12	stable isotope of carbon with a mass number of 12
CGPM	General Conference on Weights and Measures
cgs system	centimeter-gram-second system of units
CIE	International Commission on Illumination
CIPM	International Committee of Weights and Measures
°C	degree Celsius
°F	degree Fahrenheit
EEC	European Economic Community
eq. energy	equivalent energy
IEEE	Institute of Electrical and Electronics Engineers
I.T.	International Table
ISO	International Organization for Standardization
IST-90	International Temperature Scale-1990
IUPAC	International Union of Pure and Applied Chemistry
IUPAP	International Union of Pure and Applied Physics
kPa	kilopascal
NATO	North Atlantic Treaty Organization
NBS	National Bureau of Standards (now NIST, National Institute of Standards and Technology)
NIST	National Institute of Standards and Technology (formerly NBS, National Bureau of Standards)
SI	International System of Units (*Le Système International d'Unités*)
thermoc.	thermochemical
THz	terahertz
UK	United Kingdom
UN	United Nations
US	United States
USSR	Union of Soviet Socialist Republics
UTC	Coordinated Universal Time
WWII	Second World War
>>>	number larger than 10,000,000
<<<	number smaller than 0.000 000 1

References

Over 140 major sources were used to compile and verify the information presented in *Measure For Measure*. The following is a list of some of the more important sources :

A Guide To Metrics, Terry Richardson, Prakken Publications, Inc., 275 Metty Drive, Ann Arbor, MI 48103, USA, 1978.

American National Standard For Metric Practice, ANSI/IEEE Standard 268-1992, The Institute of Electrical and Electronics Engineers, Inc., 345 East 47th Street, New York, NY 10017, USA, 1992.

ASME Steam Tables, Fifth Edition, The American Society Of Mechanical Engineers, United Engineering Center, 345 East 47th Street, New York, NY 10017, USA, 1983.

Dictionary Of Scientific Units, Sixth Edition, H.G. Jerrard and D.B. McNeill, Chapman and Hall, 29 West 35th Street, New York, NY 10001, USA, 1992.

Elsevier's Lexicon Of International And National Units, W.E. Clason, Elsevier Publishing Company, 52 Vanderbilt Avenue, New York, New York, USA, 1964.

Energy Interrelationships, Report Number FEA/B-77/166, Federal Energy Administration, Office of Energy Information and Analysis, Office of Energy Systems Data, Washington, DC 20465, USA, 1977.

Energy Reference Handbook, First Edition, N.C. McNerney and Thomas F.P. Sullivan, Government Institutes, Inc., 4733 Bethesda Ave., Washington, DC 20014, USA, 1974.

Flow Measurement Engineering Handbook, R.W. Miller, Second Edition, McGraw-Hill Publishing Company, 11 West 19th Street, New York, NY 10011, 1989.

Geigy Scientific Tables, Eight Edition, C. Lentner, Medical Education Division, Ciba-Giegy Corporation, West Caldwell, NJ 07006, USA, 1981.

Guide For The Use Of The International System of Units, The Modernized Metric System, NIST Special Publication 811, Arthur

O. McCoubrey, US Department of Commerce, National Institute of Standards and Technology, Gaithersburg, MD 20899, USA, September, 1991.

Handbook Of Hydrology, David R. Maidment, McGraw-Hill Companies, Inc., 11 West 19th Street, New York, NY 10011, 1993.

Handbook Of Physical Calculations, Second Edition, Jan J. Tuma, McGraw-Hill Book Company, New York, New York, USA, 1983.

IES Lighting Handbook, Reference Volume, Illuminating Engineering Society of North America, Waverly Press, Inc., Baltimore, Maryland, USA, 1984.

International And Metric Units Of Measurement, Marvin H. Green, Chemical Publishing Company, Inc., New York, New York, 1973.

Interpretation Of The SI For The United States And Metric Conversion Policy For Federal Agencies, NIST Special Publication 814, Barry N. Taylor, Editor, US Department of Commerce, National Institute of Standards and Technology, Gaithersburg, MD 20899, USA, October 1991.

Land Survey Systems, John G. McEntyre, John Wiley and Sons, New York, New York, USA, 1978.

Lighting For Energy-Efficient Luminous Environments, Ronald N. Helms and M. Clay Belcher, Prentice Hall, Englewood Cliffs, NJ 07632, USA, 1991.

Lighting Handbook, Reference And Application, Mark S. Rea, Illuminating Engineering Society of North America, Publications Department, IESNA, 120 Wall Street, 17th Floor, New York, NY 10005, USA, 1993.

Marks' Standard Handbook For Mechanical Engineers, Ninth Edition, Eugene A. Avallone and Theodore Baumeister III, McGraw-Hill Book Company, 11 West 19th Street, New York, NY 10011, USA, 1986.

McGraw-Hill Dictionary Of Scientific And Technical Terms, Fourth Edition, Sybil P. Parker, McGraw-Hill Book Company, New York, New York, USA, 1989.

Metric In Minutes, Dennis R, Brownridge, Professional Publications, Inc., 1250 Fifth Avenue, Belmont, CA 94002, USA, 1994.

Quantification In Science, The VNR Dictionary of Engineering Units and Measures, Michele Melaragno, Van Nostrand Reinhold, 115 Fifth Avenue, New York, NY 10003, USA, 1991.

Quantities And Units Of Measurement, A Dictionary and Handbook, J.V. Drazil, Mansell Publishing Limited, 6 All Saints Street, London N1 9RL, 1983.

Quantities And Units, ISO Standards Handbook, Third Edition, International Organization for Standardization, Case postale 56, CH-1211 Geneve 20, Switzerland, 1993 (available from American National Standards Institute, 11 West 42nd Street, New York, NY 10036, USA).

Scales And Weights, A Historical Outline, Bruno Kisch, Yale University Press, USA, 1965.

Sizes: The Illustrated Encyclopedia, John Lord, HarperCollins Publishers, Inc, 10 East 53rd Street, New York, NY 10022, USA, 1995.

Specifications, Tolerances, and Other Technical Requirements For Weighing And Measuring Devices, NIST Handbook 44, 1993 Edition, Henry V. Oppermann, Editor, US Department of Commerce, National Institute of Standards and Technology, Gaithersburg, MD 20899, USA, 1993.

Standard Practice For Use Of The International System Of Units (SI) (The Modernized Metric System), ASTM Designation: E 380-92, American Society for Testing and Materials, 1916 Race Street, Philadelphia, PA 19103, USA, June 1993.

Surveying For Civil Engineers, Philip Kissam, McGraw-Hill Book Company, 11 West 19th Street, New York, NY 10011, 1981.

Tables of Physical And Chemical Constants, 16th Edition, G.W.C. Kaye and T.H. Laby, Longman Group Limited, Longman House, Burnt Mill, Harlow, Essex CM20 2JE, England, 1995.

The 1986 CODATA Recommended Values Of The Fundamental Physical Constants, E. Richard Cohen and Barry N. Taylor, Journal of Research of the National Bureau of Standards, Volume

92, Number 85, US Department of Commerce, National Bureau of Standards, Gaithersburg, MD 20899, USA, 1987.

The Astronomical Almanac For The Year 1995, Richard E. Blumberg and Alexander Boksenberg, US Government Printing Office, Washington, DC 20402, USA, 1994.

The Eerdmans Bible Dictionary, Allen C. Myers, William B. Eerdmans Publishing Company, Grand Rapids, Michigan, USA, 1987.

The International System Of Units (SI), NIST Special Publication 330, 1991 Edition, Barry N. Taylor, US Department of Commerce, National Institute of Standards and Technology, Gaithersburg, MD 20899, USA, August 1991.

The International System Of Units, Physical Constants And Conversion Factors, Second Edition, E.A. Mechtly, Scientific and Technical Information Office, National Aeronautics and Space Administration, Washington, DC 20546, USA, 1973.

The Macmillan Dictionary Of Measurement, Mike Darton and John Clark, Macmillian Publishing Company, 866 Third Avenue, New York, NY 10022, USA, 1994.

The New York Public Library Desk Reference, John Masten, Prentice Hall General Reference, 15 Columbus Circle, New York, NY 10023, 1993.

The Oxford Campanion To The Bible, Bruce M. Metzger and Michael D. Coogan, Oxford University Press, 200 Madison Avenue, New York, NY 10016, USA, 1993.

The Water Encyclopedia, Second Edition, Frits van der Leeden, Fred L. Troise, and David Keith Todd, Lewis Publishers, Inc., 121 South Main St., Chelsea, MI 48118, USA, 1990.

The World Measurement Guide, Fourth Edition, The Economist Newspaper Limited, 25 St. James's Street, London, England SW1A 1HG, 1980.

Units Of Measurement, Stephen Dresner, Hasting House, Publishers, 10 East 40th Street, New York, NY 10016, USA, 1971.

3 Physical Constants

Committe on Data for Science and Technology,
International Council of Scientific Unions
1986 recommended values of the fundamental physical constants.

Quantity	Symbol	Value	Units
GENERAL CONSTANTS			
Speed of light in a vacuum	c	299 792 458	m / s
Permeability of vacuum	μ_0	$4\pi \times 10^{-7}$	N / A^2
		= 12.566 370 614 ...	10^{-7} N / A^2
Permittivity of vacuum, $1 / \mu_0 c^2$	ε_0	8.854 187 817 ...	10^{-12} F / m
Newtonian constant of gravitation	G	6.672 59 (±85)	10^{-11} $m^3 / kg\, s^2$
Planck constant	h	6.626 075 5 (±40)	10^{-34} J s
in electron volts, $h / \{e\}$		4.135 669 2 (±12)	10^{-15} eV s
$h / 2\pi$	$\hbar$	1.054 572 66 (±63)	10^{-34} J s
in electron volts, $\hbar / \{e\}$		6.582 122 0 (±20)	10^{-16} eV s
Planck mass, $(\hbar c / G)^{1/2}$	m_P	2.176 71 (±14)	10^{-8} kg
Planck length, $\hbar / m_P c = (\hbar G / c^3)^{1/2}$	l_P	1.616 05 (±10)	10^{-34} m
Planck time, $l_P / c = (\hbar G / c^5)^{1/2}$	t_P	5.390 56 (±34)	10^{-44} s
Electromagnetic constants			
Elementary charge	e	1.602 177 33 (±49)	10^{-19} C
	e / h	2.417 988 36 (±72)	10^{14} A / J
Magnetic flux quantum, $h / 2e$	Φ_0	2.067 834 61 (±61)	10^{-15} Wb
Josephson frequency-voltage quotient	$2e / h$	4.835 976 7 (±14)	10^{14} Hz / V
Quantized Hall conductance	e^2 / h	3.874 046 14 (±17)	10^{-5} S
Quantized Hall resistance, $h/e^2 = \mu_0 c / 2\alpha$	R_H	25 812.805 6 (±12)	Ω
Bohr magneton, $e\hbar / 2\, m_e$	μ_B	9.274 015 4 (±31)	10^{-24} J / T
in electron volts, $\mu_B / \{e\}$		5.788 382 63 (±52)	10^{-5} eV / T
in hertz, μ_B / h		1.399 624 18 (±42)	10^{10} Hz / T
in wavenumbers, μ_B / hc		46.686 437 (±14)	1 / m T
in kelvins, μ_B / k		0.671 709 9 (±57)	K / T
Nuclear magneton, $e\hbar / 2\, m_p$	μ_N	5.050 786 6 (±17)	10^{-27} J / T
in electron volts, $\mu_N / \{e\}$		3.152 451 66 (±28)	10^{-8} eV / T
in hertz, μ_N / h		7.622 591 4 (±23)	Mhz / T
in wavenumbers, μ_N / hc		2.542 622 81 (±77)	10^{-2} / m T
in kelvins, μ_N / k		3.658 246 (±31)	10^{-4} K / T
ATOMIC CONSTANTS			
Fine-structure constant, $\mu_0 c e^2 / 2h$	α	7.297 353 08 (±33)	10^{-3}
Inverse fine-structure constant	$1 / \alpha$	137.035 989 5 (±61)	
Rydberg constant, $m_e c \alpha^2 / 2h$	$R\infty$	10 973 731.534 (±13)	1 / m
in hertz, $R_\infty c$		3.289 841 949 9 (±39)	10^{15} Hz
in joules, $R_\infty hc$		2.179 874 1 (±13)	10^{-18} J
in electron volts, $R_\infty hc / \{e\}$		13.605 698 1 (±40)	eV
Bohr radius, $\alpha / 4\pi\, R_\infty$	a_0	0.529 177 249 (±24)	10^{-10} m
Hartree energy, $e^2 / 4\pi\, \varepsilon_0\, a_0 = 2\, R_\infty\, hc$	E_h	4.359 748 2 (±26)	10^{-18} J
in electron volts, $E_h / \{e\}$		27.211 396 1 (±81)	eV
Quantum of circulation	$h / 2\, m_e$	3.636 948 07 (±33)	10^{-4} m^2 / s
	h / m_e	7.273 896 14 (±65)	10^{-4} m^2 / s
Electron			
Electron mass	m_e	9.109 389 7 (±54)	10^{-31} kg
		5.485 799 03 (±13)	10^{-4} u
in electron volts, $m_e c^2 / \{e\}$		0.510 999 06 (±15)	MeV

Electron-muon mass ratio	m_e / m_μ	4.836 332 18 ($\pm$71)	. . . . 10^{-3}
Electron-proton mass ratio	m_e / m_p	5.446 170 13 ($\pm$11)	. . . . 10^{-4}
Electron-deuteron mass ratio	m_e / m_d	2.724 437 07 ($\pm$06)	. . . . 10^{-4}
Electron-α-particle mass ratio	m_e / m_α	1.370 933 54 ($\pm$03)	. . . . 10^{-4}
Electron specific charge	$-e / m_e$	-1.758 819 62 ($\pm$53)	10^{11} C / kg
Electron molar mass	$M(e)$, M_e	5.485 799 03 ($\pm$13)	10^{-7} kg / mol
Compton wavelength, $h / m_e c$	λ_C	2.426 310 58 ($\pm$22)	. . . . 10^{-12} m
$\lambda_C / 2\pi = \alpha\, a_0 = \alpha^2 / 4\pi\; R_\infty$	$\lambda_C / 2\pi$	3.861 593 23 ($\pm$35)	. . . . 10^{-13} m
Classical electron radius, $\alpha^2 a_0$	r_e	2.817 940 92 ($\pm$38)	. . . . 10^{-15} m
Thomson cross section, $(8\pi / 3)\, r_e^{\;2}$	σ_e	0.665 246 16 ($\pm$18)	. . . . 10^{-28} m^2
Electron magnetic moment	μ_e	928.477 01 ($\pm$31)	. . . 10^{-26} J / T
in Bohr magnetons	μ_e / μ_B	1.001 159 652 193 ($\pm$10)	
in nuclear magnetons	μ_e / μ_N	1 838.282 000 ($\pm$37)	
Electron magnetic moment anomaly, μ_e / μ_B-1	a_e	1.159 652 193 ($\pm$10)	. . . . 10^{-3}
Electron g factor, $2 (1 + a_e)$	g_e	2.002 319 304 386 ($\pm$20)	
Electron-muon magnetic moment ratio	μ_e / μ_μ	206.766 967 ($\pm$30)	
Electron-proton magnetic moment ratio	μ_e / μ_p	658.210 688 1 ($\pm$66)	

Muon --

Muon mass	m_μ	1.883 532 7 ($\pm$11)	. . . 10^{-28} kg
		0.113 428 913 ($\pm$17)	. . . . u
in electron volts, $m_\mu c^2 / \{e\}$		105.658 389 ($\pm$34)	. . . MeV
Muon-electron mass ratio	m_μ / m_e	206.768 262 ($\pm$30)	
Muon molar mass	$M(\mu)$, M_μ	1.134 289 13 ($\pm$17)	10^{-4} kg / mol
Muon magnetic moment	μ_μ	4.490 451 4 ($\pm$15)	. . 10^{-26} J / T
in Bohr magnetons	μ_μ / μ_B	4.841 970 97 ($\pm$71)	. . . . 10^{-3}
in nuclear magnetons	μ_μ / μ_N	8.890 598 1 ($\pm$13)	
Muon magnetic moment anomaly, $[\mu_\mu / (e\hbar / 2m_\mu)]$-1	a_μ	1.165 923 0 ($\pm$84)	. . . . 10^{-3}
Muon g factor, $2 (1 + a_\mu)$	g_μ	2.002 331 846 ($\pm$17)	
Muon-proton magnetic moment ratio	μ_μ / μ_p	3.183 345 47 ($\pm$47)	

Proton --

Proton mass	m_p	1.672 623 1 ($\pm$10)	. . . 10^{-27} kg
		1.007 276 470 ($\pm$12)	. . . . u
in electron volts, $m_p c^2 / \{e\}$		938.272 31 ($\pm$28)	. . . . MeV
Proton-electron mass ratio	m_p / m_e	1 836.152 701 ($\pm$37)	
Proton-muon mass ratio	m_p / m_μ	8.880 244 4 ($\pm$13)	
Proton specific charge	e / m_p	9.578 830 9 ($\pm$29)	10^7 C / kg
Proton molar mass	$M(p)$, M_p	1.007 276 470 ($\pm$12)	10^{-3} kg/mol
Proton Compton wavelength, $h / m_p c$	$\lambda_{C,p}$	1.321 410 02 ($\pm$12)	. . . 10^{-15} m
	$\lambda_{C,p} / 2\pi$	2.103 089 37 ($\pm$19)	. . . 10^{-16} m
Proton magnetic moment	μ_p	1.410 607 61 ($\pm$47)	10^{-26} J / T
in Bohr magnetons	μ_p / μ_B	1.521 032 202 ($\pm$15)	. . . 10^{-3}
in nuclear magnetons	μ_p / μ_N	2.792 847 386 ($\pm$63)	
Diamagnetic shielding correction for protons (pure water, spherical sample, 25°C) $1 - \mu'_p / \mu_p$	σ_{H2O}	25.689 ($\pm$15)	. . . . 10^{-6}
Shielded proton moment (pure water, spherical sample, 25°C)	μ'_p	1.410 571 38 ($\pm$47)	10^{-26} J / T
in Bohr magneton	μ'_p / μ_B	1.520 993 129 ($\pm$17)	. . . 10^{-3}
in nuclear megneton	μ'_p / μ_N	2.792 775 642 ($\pm$64)	
Proton gyromagnetic ratio	γ_p	26 752.212 8 ($\pm$81)	. 10^4 / s T
	$\gamma_p / 2\pi$	42.577 469 ($\pm$13)	. . Mhz / T
uncorrected (pure water, spherical sample, 25°C)	γ'_p	26 751.525 5 ($\pm$81)	. 10^4 / s T
	$\gamma'_p / 2\pi$	42.576 375 ($\pm$13)	. . . Mhz / T

Neutron

Neutron mass	m_n	1.674 928 6 (± 10)	10^{-27} kg
		1.008 664 904 (± 14)	u
in electron volts, $m_n c^2 / \{e\}$		939.565 63 (± 28)	MeV
Neutron-electron mass ratio	m_n / m_e	1 838.683 662 (± 40)	
Neutron-proton mass ratio	m_n / m_p	1.001 378 404 (± 09)	
Neutron molar mass	$M(n), M_n$	1.008 664 904 (± 14)	10^{-3} kg/mol
Neutron Compton wavelength, $h / m_n c$	$\lambda_{C,n}$	1.319 591 10 (± 12)	10^{-15} m
$\lambda_{C,n} / 2\pi$	$\lambda_{C,n}$	2.100 194 45 (± 19)	10^{-16} m
Neutron magnetic moment	μ_n	0.966 237 07 (± 40)	10^{-26} J / T
in Bohr magnetons	μ_n / μ_B	1.041 875 63 (± 25)	10^{-3}
in nuclear magnetons	μ_n / μ_N	1.913 042 75 (± 45)	
Neutron-electron magnetic moment ratio	μ_n / μ_e	1.040 668 82 (± 25)	10^{-3}
Neutron-proton magnetic moment ratio	μ_n / μ_p	0.684 979 34 (± 16)	

Deuteron

Deuteron mass	m_d	3.343 586 0 (± 20)	10^{-27} kg
		2.013 553 214 (± 24)	u
in electron volts, $m_d c^2 / \{e\}$		1 875.613 39 (± 57)	MeV
Deuteron-electron mass ratio	m_d / m_e	3 670.483 014 (± 75)	
Deuteron-proton mass ratio	m_d / m_p	1.999 007 496 (± 06)	
Deuteron molar mass	$M(d), M_d$	2.013 553 214 (± 24)	10^{-3} kg/mol
Deuteron magnetic moment	μ_d	0.433 073 75 (± 15)	10^{-26} J / T
in Bohr magnetons	μ_d / μ_B	0.466 975 447 9 (± 91)	10^{-3}
in nuclear magnetons	μ_d / μ_N	0.857 438 230 (± 24)	
Deuteron-electron magnetic moment ratio	μ_d / μ_e	0.466 434 546 0 (± 91)	10^{-3}
Deuteron-proton magnetic moment ratio	μ_d / μ_p	0.307 012 203 5 (± 51)	

PHYSICO-CHEMICAL CONSTANTS

Avogadro constant	N_A, L	6.022 136 7 (± 36)	10^{23} /mol
Atomic mass constant, $m_u = 1/12\, m\, (^{12}C)$	m_u	1.660 540 2 (± 10)	10^{-27} kg
in electron volts, $m_u c^2 / \{e\}$		931.494 32 (± 28)	MeV
Faraday constant, $N_A e$	F	96 485.309 (± 29)	C / mol
Molar Planck constant	$N_A h$	3.990 313 23 (± 36)	10^{-10} J s/mol
	$N_A h c$	0.119 626 58 (± 11)	J m / mol
Molar gas constant	R	8.314 510 (± 70)	J / mol K
Boltzmann constant, R / N_A	k	1.380 658 (± 12)	10^{-23} J / K
in electron volts, $k / \{e\}$		8.617 385 (± 73)	10^{-5} eV / K
in hertz, k / h		2.083 674 (± 18)	10^{10} Hz / K
in wavenumbers, k / hc		69.503 87 (± 59)	1 /m K
Molar volume (ideal gas), $R T / p$, $T = 273.15$ K,			
$p = 101\,325$ Pa	V_m	0.022 414 10 (± 19)	m^3/ mol
Loschmidt constant, N_A / V_m	n_0	2.686 763 (± 23)	10^{25} / mol^3
$T = 273.15$ K, $p = 100$ kPa	V_m	0.022 711 08 (± 19)	m^3 / mol
Sackur-Tetrode constant (absolute entropy constant), $5/2 + \ln[(2\pi\, m_u k\, T_1 / h^2)^{3/2} k\, T_1 / p_0]$			
$T_1 = 1$ K, $p_0 = 100$ kPa	S_0 / R	-1.151 693 (± 21)	
$T_1 = 1$ K, $p_0 = 101\,235$ Pa		-1.164 856 (± 21)	
Stefan-Boltzmann constant, $(\pi^2 / 60) k^4 / \hbar^3 c^2$	σ	5.670 51 (± 19)	10^{-8} W / m^2 K^4
First radition constant, $2\pi\, h c^2$	c_1	3.741 774 9 (± 22)	10^{-16} W m^2
Second radition constant, $h c / k$	c_2	0.014 387 69 (± 12)	m K
Wien displacement law constant, $b = \lambda_{max}\, T = c_2 / 4.965\,114\,23...$	b	2.897 756 (± 24)	10^{-3} m K

MAINTAINED UNITS AND STANDARD VALUES

Standard values

Electron volt, (e / C) J = $\{e\}$ J		eV	1.602 177 33 (± 49)	10^{-19} J

(Unified) atomic mass unit, $1u = m_u = 1/12\ m(^{12}C)$	u	1.660 540 2 (±10)	10^{-27} kg
Standard atmosphere	atm	101 325	Pa
Standard acceleration of gravity	g_n	9.806 65	m / s^2

"As-maintained" electrical units

BIPM maintained ohm, Ω_{69-BI},
$\Omega_{BI85} \equiv \Omega_{69-BI}$ (January 1, 1985) $\quad \Omega_{BI85}\quad$ 1 - 1.563 (±50) x 10^{-6}
$$= 0.999\ 998\ 437\ (\pm50)\ \dots\ \Omega$$

BIPM maintained volt,
$V_{76-BI} \equiv 483\ 594.0\ Ghz\ (h\,/2e)\quad V_{76-BI}\quad$ 1 - 7.59 (±30) x 10^{-6}
$$= 0.999\ 992\ 41(\pm30)\ \dots\ V$$

BIPM maintained ampere,
$A_{BIPM} = V_{76-BI}\,/\,\Omega_{69-BI}\quad\quad A_{BI85}\quad$ 1 - 6.03 (±30) x 10^{-6}
$$= 0.999\ 993\ 97\ (\pm30)\ \dots\ A$$

X-ray standards

Cu x unit: $\lambda(CuK\alpha_1) \equiv 1\ 537.400$ xu	xu($CuK\alpha_1$)	1.002 077 89 (±70)	10^{-13} m
Mo x unit: $\lambda(MoK\alpha_1) \equiv 707.831$ xu	xu($MoK\alpha_1$)	1.002 099 38 (±45)	10^{-13} m
Å*: $\lambda(WK\alpha_1) \equiv 0.209\ 100$ Å*	Å*	1.000 014 81 (±92)	10^{-10} m
Lattice spacing of Si (in vacuum, 22.5 °C)	a	0.543 101 96 (±11)	nm
$d_{220} = a\,/\sqrt{8}$	d_{220}	0.192 015 540 (±40)	nm
Molar volume of Si, $M(Si)\,/\,\rho\,(Si) = N_A\,a^3/8$	V_m(Si)	12.058 817 9 (±89)	cm^3/ mol

IAU** (1976) System Of Astronomical Constants

Quantity	Symbol	Value	Unit
DEFINING CONSTANTS			
Gaussian gravitational constant	k	0.017 202 098 95	
Speed of light	c	299 792 458	m / s
PRIMARY CONSTANTS			
Light-time for unit distance	τ_A	499.004 783 7	s
Equatorial radius for Earth	a_e	6 378.140	m
IUGG*** value	a_e	6 378.137	m
Dynamical form-factor for Earth	J_2	0.001 082 63	
Geocentric gravitational constant	GE	3.986 004 48	10^{14} m^3 / s^2
Constant of gravitation	G	6.672	10^{-11} m^3 / kg s^2
Ratio of mass of Moon to mass of Earth	μ	0.012 300 034	
General precession in longitude, per Julian century, at standard epoch 2000	ρ	5 029".096 6	
Obliquity of the ecliptic, at std. epoch 2000	ε	23° 26' 21".411 9	
DERIVED CONSTANTS			
Constant of nutation, at std. epoch 2000	N	9".202 5	
Unit distance, $c\,\tau_A =$	A	1.495 978 706 6	10^{11} m
Solar parallax, arcsin (a_e/A)	$\pi_\odot$	8".794 148	
Constant of aberration, for std. epoch 2000	κ	20".495 52	
Flattening factor for the Earth	f	0.003 352 81	
		= 1 / 298.257	
Heliocentric gravitational constant, $A^3 k^2/\,D^2 =$	GS	1.327 124 38	10^{20} m^3 / s^2
Ratio of Sun mass to Earth mass, $(GS)/(GE) = S\,/\,E$		332 946.038	
Ratio of Sun mass to (Earth + Moon) mass $(S/E)/(1+\mu)$		328 900.55	
Mass of the Sun, $(GS)\,/\,G =$	S	1.989 1	10^{30} kg

** IAU, International Astronomical Union
*** IUGG, International Union of Geodesy and Geophysics

4 Conversion Factors

Convert From		<Type of Unit>
Convert To	Standard	Scientific

1/ siemens — <electric resistance>
ohm	1	1.000 000 0E+00
statohm	<<<	1.112 650 1E-12

1/abhenry — <electric reluctance>
1/henry	>>>	1.000 000 0E+09
1/stathenry	>>>	8.987 551 8E+20

1/Btu cubic foot [-/ I.T.] — <density of states>
1/joule cubic meter	0.033 471 8	3.347 184 6E-02

1/calorie cubic centimeter [-/ I.T.] — <density of states>
1/joule cubic meter	238,845.9	2.388 459 0E+05

1/centimeter — <reciprocal length, phase coefficient>
1/foot	30.48	3.048 000 0E+01
1/meter	100	1.000 000 0E+02
radian/meter	100	1.000 000 0E+02

1/centimeter [atomic physics, eq. energy] — <energy>
atomic mass unit [unified, C-12, 1986, eq. energy]	<<<	1.331 025 2E-13
deuteron rest mass [atomic physics, eq. energy]	<<<	6.610 330 5E-14
electron rest mass [atomic physics, eq. energy]	<<<	2.426 310 6E-10
electronvolt	0.000 124	1.239 842 4E-04
hartree [atomic physics, eq. energy]	0.000 004 6	4.556 335 3E-06
hertz [atomic physics, eq. energy]	>>>	2.997 924 6E+10
joule	<<<	1.986 447 5E-23
kayser [atomic physics, eq. energy]	1	1.000 000 0E+00
kelvin [atomic physics, eq. energy]	1.438 768 7	1.438 768 7E+00
muon rest mass [atomic physics, eq. energy]	<<<	1.173 444 6E-12
neutron rest mass [atomic physics, eq. energy]	<<<	1.319 591 1E-13
proton rest mass [atomic physics, eq. energy]	<<<	1.321 410 0E-13
rydberg [atomic physics, eq. energy]	0.000 009 1	9.112 562 3E-06
yoctojoule	19.864 475	1.986 447 5E+01

1/cubic centimeter day — <neutron source density>
1/cubic foot minute	19.664 477	1.966 447 7E+01
1/cubic meter second	11.574 074	1.157 407 4E+01
1/cubic yard second	8.849 014 6	8.849 014 6E+00

1/cubic foot minute — <neutron source density>
1/cubic centimeter day	0.050 853 1	5.085 312 0E-02
1/cubic meter second	0.588 577 8	5.885 777 8E-01
1/cubic yard second	0.45	4.500 000 0E-01

1/cubic meter second — <neutron source density>
1/cubic centimeter day	0.086 4	8.640 000 0E-02
1/cubic foot minute	1.699 010 8	1.699 010 8E+00
1/cubic yard second	0.764 554 9	7.645 548 6E-01

1/cubic yard second — <neutron source density>
1/cubic centimeter day	0.113 006 9	1.130 069 3E-01
1/cubic foot minute	2.222 222 2	2.222 222 2E+00
1/cubic meter second	1.307 950 6	1.307 950 6E+00

1/electronvolt cubic meter — <density of states>
1/joule cubic meter	>>>	6.241 506 4E+18

1/erg cubic centimeter — <density of states>
1/joule cubic meter	>>>	1.000 000 0E+13

Convert From / Convert To	Standard	Type of Unit / Scientific
1/farad		**<electric elastance>**
daraf	1	1.000 000 0E+00
1/foot		**<reciprocal length, phase coefficient>**
1/centimeter	0.032 808 4	3.280 839 9E−02
1/inch	0.083 333 3	8.333 333 3E−02
1/meter	3.280 839 9	3.280 839 9E+00
diopter	3.280 839 9	3.280 839 9E+01
radian/meter	3.280 839 9	3.280 839 9E+00
1/henry		**<electric reluctance>**
1/abhenry	<<<	1.000 000 0E−09
1/ohm second	1	1.000 000 0E+00
1/stathenry	>>>	8.987 551 8E+11
ampere/volt second	1	1.000 000 0E+00
ampere/weber	1	1.000 000 0E+00
square ampere/joule	1	1.000 000 0E+00
1/inch		**<reciprocal length, phase coefficient>**
1/foot	12	1.200 000 0E+01
radian/meter	39.370 079	3.937 007 9E+01
1/joule cubic meter		**<density of states>**
1/Btu cubic foot [-/ I.T.]	29.875 855	2.987 585 5E+01
1/electronvolt cubic meter	<<<	1.602 177 3E−19
1/watthour cubic meter	3,600	3.600 000 0E+03
1/meter		**<reciprocal length, phase coefficient>**
1/centimeter	0.01	1.000 000 0E−02
1/foot	0.304 8	3.048 000 0E−01
diopter	1	1.000 000 0E+00
radian/meter	1	1.000 000 0E+00
1/meter [atomic physics, eq. energy]		**<energy>**
atomic mass unit [unified, C-12, 1986, eq. energy]	<<<	1.331 025 2E−15
deuteron rest mass [atomic physics, eq. energy]	<<<	6.610 330 5E−16
electron rest mass [atomic physics, eq. energy]	<<<	2.426 310 6E−12
electronvolt	0.000 001 2	1.239 842 4E−06
hartree [atomic physics, eq. energy]	<<<	4.556 335 3E−08
hertz [atomic physics, eq. energy]	>>>	2.997 924 6E+08
joule	<<<	1.986 447 5E−25
kayser [atomic physics, eq. energy]	0.01	1.000 000 0E−02
kelvin [atomic physics, eq. energy]	0.014 387 7	1.438 768 7E−02
muon rest mass [atomic physics, eq. energy]	<<<	1.173 444 4E−14
neutron rest mass [atomic physics, eq. energy]	<<<	1.319 591 1E−15
proton rest mass [atomic physics, eq. energy]	<<<	1.321 410 0E−15
rydberg [atomic physics, eq. energy]	<<<	9.112 562 3E−08
yoctojoule	0.198 644 8	1.986 447 5E−01
1/mho		**<electric resistance>**
1/siemens	1	1.000 000 0E+00
abohm	>>>	1.000 000 0E+09
ohm	1	1.000 000 0E+00
statohm	<<<	1.112 650 1E−12
1/ohm		**<electric conductance>**
absiemens	<<<	1.000 000 0E−09
ampere/volt	1	1.000 000 0E+00
second/henry	1	1.000 000 0E+00
siemens	1	1.000 000 0E+00
statsiemens	>>>	8.987 551 8E+11
1/ohm meter		**<electric conductivity>**
mho/meter	1	1.000 000 0E+00
rom	1	1.000 000 0E+00
siemens/meter	1	1.000 000 0E+00
1/ohm second		**<electric reluctance>**
1/abhenry	<<<	1.000 000 0E−09
1/henry	1	1.000 000 0E+00

1/stathenry	>>>	8.987 551 8E+11
1/pascal		**<compressibility>**
brewster	>>>	1.000 000 0E+12
square centimeter/dyne	0.1	1.000 000 0E−01
square foot/pound-force	47.880 259	4.788 025 9E+01
square foot/poundal	1.488 163 9	1.488 163 9E+00
square meter/kilogram-force	9.806 65	9.806 650 0E+00
square meter/kilopond	9.806 65	9.806 650 0E+00
square meter/newton	1	1.000 000 0E+00
1/second		**<radionuclide activity>**
becquerel	1	1.000 000 0E+00
millicurie	<<<	2.702 702 7E−08
rutherford	0.000 001	1.000 000 0E−06
1/second		**<frequency>**
cycle/second	1	1.000 000 0E+00
degree/hour	1,296,000	1.296 000 0E+06
degree/minute	21,600	2.160 000 0E+04
degree/second	360	3.600 000 0E+02
hertz	1	1.000 000 0E+00
radian/hour	22,619.467	2.261 946 7E+04
radian/minute	376.991 12	3.769 911 2E+02
radian/second	6.283 185 3	6.283 185 3E+00
revolution/hour	3,600	3.600 000 0E+03
revolution/minute	60	6.000 000 0E+01
revolution/second	1	1.000 000 0E+00
1/siemens		**<electric resistance>**
1/mho	1	1.000 000 0E+00
abohm	>>>	1.000 000 0E+09
1/stathenry		**<electric reluctance>**
1/abhenry	<<<	1.112 650 1E−21
1/henry	<<<	1.112 650 1E−12
1/watthour cubic meter		**<density of states>**
1/joule cubic meter	0.000 277 8	2.777 777 8E−04
aam [Germany]		**<volume, special - see page 29>**
liter	155	1.550 000 0E+02
aam [Netherlands]		**<volume, special - see page 29>**
liter	155.2	1.552 000 0E+02
abada [Ethiopia]		**<mass, special - see page 29>**
kilogram	15.6	1.560 000 0E+01
abampere		**<electric current>**
ampere	10	1.000 000 0E+01
biot	1	1.000 000 0E+00
coulomb/second	10	1.000 000 0E+01
gilbert	12.566 370 6	1.256 637 1E+01
statampere	>>>	2.997 924 6E+10
abampere square centimeter		**<electromagnetic moment>**
ampere square inch	1,550,003.1	1.550 003 1E+06
ampere square meter	1,000	1.000 000 0E+03
statampere square centimeter	>>>	2.997 924 6E+16
abampere/centimeter		**<magnetic field strength>**
ampere/inch	25.4	2.540 000 0E+01
ampere/meter	1,000	1.000 000 0E+03
oersted	12.566 370 6	1.256 637 1E+01
statampere/centimeter	>>>	2.997 924 6E+10
abampere/square centimeter		**<electric current density>**
ampere/square inch	64.516	6.451 600 0E+01
ampere/square meter	100,000	1.000 000 0E+05
ampere/square millimeter	0.1	1.000 000 0E−01

abas [Iran] — <mass, special - see page 29>
milligram ---- 187.5 --- 1.875 000 0E+02

abbas [Iran] — <mass, special - see page 29>
gram ---- 0.185 58 --- 1.855 800 0E−01

abbassi [Iran] — <mass, special - see page 29>
gram ---- 375 --- 3.750 000 0E+02

abcoulomb — <electric charge>
ampere second ---- 10 --- 1.000 000 0E+01
coulomb ---- 10 --- 1.000 000 0E+01
dekacoulomb ---- 1 --- 1.000 000 0E+00
electromagnetic unit of charge [cgs system] ---- 1 --- 1.000 000 0E+00
farad volt ---- 10 --- 1.000 000 0E+01
statcoulomb ---- >>> --- 2.997 924 6E+10

abcoulomb centimeter — <electric dipole moment>
ampere second meter ---- 0.1 --- 1.000 000 0E−01
coulomb meter ---- 0.1 --- 1.000 000 0E−01
farad volt meter ---- 0.1 --- 1.000 000 0E−01

abcoulomb/centimeter — <electric dipole moment/unit area>
coulomb/meter ---- 1,000 --- 1.000 000 0E+03
coulomb/millimeter ---- 1 --- 1.000 000 0E+00
kilocoulomb/meter ---- 1 --- 1.000 000 0E+00

abcoulomb/cubic centimeter — <electric charge density>
coulomb/cubic centimeter ---- 10 --- 1.000 000 0E+01
coulomb/cubic meter ---- >>> --- 1.000 000 0E+07
megacoulomb/cubic meter ---- 10 --- 1.000 000 0E+01

abcoulomb/square centimeter — <electric flux density>
ampere hour/square meter ---- 27.777 777 8 --- 2.777 777 8E+01
coulomb/square inch ---- 64.516 --- 6.451 600 0E+01
coulomb/square meter ---- 100,000 --- 1.000 000 0E+05
franklin/square centimeter ---- >>> --- 2.997 924 6E+10
statcoulomb/square centimeter ---- >>> --- 2.997 924 6E+10

abdah [Egypt, ancient] — <length, special - see page 29>
centimeter ---- 7.49 --- 7.490 000 0E+00

abe [Persia, ancient] — <volume, special - see page 29>
liter ---- 56 --- 5.600 000 0E+01

abfarad — <capacitance>
coulomb/volt ---- >>> --- 1.000 000 0E+09
electromagnetic unit of capacitance [cgs system] ---- 1 --- 1.000 000 0E+00
farad ---- >>> --- 1.000 000 0E+09
gigafarad ---- 1 --- 1.000 000 0E+00
statfarad ---- >>> --- 8.987 551 8E+20

abfarad/centimeter — <electric permittivity>
coulomb/volt meter ---- >>> --- 1.000 000 0E+07
farad/meter ---- >>> --- 1.000 000 0E+07
statfarad/centimeter ---- >>> --- 8.987 551 8E+20

abhenry — <electric inductance>
electromagnetic unit of inductance [cgs system] ---- 1 --- 1.000 000 0E+00
henry ---- <<< --- 1.000 000 0E−09
joule/square ampere ---- <<< --- 1.000 000 0E−09
ohm second ---- <<< --- 1.000 000 0E−09
stathenry ---- <<< --- 1.112 650 1E−21
weber/ampere ---- <<< --- 1.000 000 0E−09

abmho — <electric conductance>
ampere/volt ---- >>> --- 1.000 000 0E+09
electromagnetic unit of conductance [cgs system] ---- 1 --- 1.000 000 0E+00
mho ---- >>> --- 1.000 000 0E+09
siemens ---- >>> --- 1.000 000 0E+09
statmho ---- >>> --- 8.987 551 8E+20

Convert From	<Type of Unit>	
Convert To	Standard	Scientific

abmho/centimeter — <electric conductivity>
absiemens/centimeter	1	1.000 000 0E+00
mho/meter	>>>	1.000 000 0E+11
siemens/meter	>>>	1.000 000 0E+11
statmho/centimeter	>>>	8.987 551 8E+20

abohm — <electric resistance>
1/ siemens	<<<	1.000 000 0E−09
nanoohm	1	1.000 000 0E+00
ohm	<<<	1.000 000 0E−09
statohm	<<<	1.112 650 1E−21

abohm centimeter — <electric resistivity>
microohm inch	0.000 393 7	3.937 007 9E−04
ohm circular mil/foot	0.006 015 3	6.015 304 9E−03
ohm meter	<<<	1.000 000 0E−11
ohm square millimeter/meter	0.000 01	1.000 000 0E−05
statohm centimeter	<<<	1.112 650 1E−21

abraa [Morocco] — <area, special - see page 29>
| hectare | 0.18 | 1.800 000 0E−01 |

absiemens — <electric conductance>
1/ohm	>>>	1.000 000 0E+09
electromagnetic unit of conductance [cgs system]	1	1.000 000 0E+00
gigasiemens	1	1.000 000 0E+00
siemens	>>>	1.000 000 0E+09
statsiemens	>>>	8.987 551 8E+20

absiemens/centimeter — <electric conductivity>
abmho/centimeter	1	1.000 000 0E+00
mho/meter	>>>	1.000 000 0E+11
siemens/meter	>>>	1.000 000 0E+11
statsiemens/centimeter	>>>	8.987 551 8E+20

abtesla — <magnetic flux density>
electromagnetic unit of magnetic flux density [cgs system]	1	1.000 000 0E+00
gauss	1	1.000 000 0E+00
tesla	0.000 1	1.000 000 0E−04

abucco [Burma] — <mass, special - see page 29>
| kilogram | 20 | 2.000 000 0E+01 |

abvolt — <electric potential>
coulomb/farad	<<<	1.000 000 0E−08
electromagnetic unit of electric potential [cgs system]	1	1.000 000 0E+00
nanovolt	10	1.000 000 0E+01
statvolt	<<<	3.335 641 0E−11
volt	<<<	1.000 000 0E−08

abvolt/centimeter — <electric field strength>
microvolt/meter	1	1.000 000 0E+00
statvolt/centimeter	<<<	3.335 641 0E−11
volt/inch	<<<	2.540 000 0E−08
volt/meter	0.000 001	1.000 000 0E−06

abweber — <magnetic flux>
| maxwell | 1 | 1.000 000 0E+00 |
| weber | <<< | 1.000 000 0E−08 |

abweber centimeter — <magnetic dipole moment>
| statweber centimeter | <<< | 3.335 641 0E−11 |
| weber meter | <<< | 1.256 637 1E−09 |

abweber/centimeter — <magnetic vector potential>
| statweber/centimeter | <<< | 3.335 641 0E−11 |
| weber/meter | 0.000 001 | 1.000 000 0E−06 |

acetabulum [Rome, ancient] — <volume, special - see page 29>
| milliliter | 67 | 6.700 000 0E+01 |

acheintaya [Burma] — <mass, special - see page 29>
| kilogram | 163.29 | 1.632 900 0E+02 |

Convert From	<Type of Unit>	
Convert To	Standard	Scientific

achtel [Austria] <volume, special - see page 29>
liter --- 7.69 --- 7.690 000 0E+00

achtel [Denmark] <volume, special - see page 29>
liter --- 2.17 --- 2.170 000 0E+00

acino [Italy] <mass, special - see page 29>
gram -- 0.038 --- 3.800 000 0E−02

acoustic ohm <acoustic impedance>
dyne second/centimeter[5] ---------------------------- 1 --- 1.000 000 0E+00
pascal second/cubic meter ------------------------ 100,000 --- 1.000 000 0E+05

acre [Bangladesh] <area, special - see page 29>
hectare --- 0.404 7 --- 4.047 000 0E−01

acre [commerical] <area>
acre [international] ------------------------------ 0.826 446 3 --- 8.264 462 8E−01
acre [US, survey] ---------------------------------- 0.826 443 --- 8.264 428 8E−01
are -- 33.445 094 --- 3.344 509 4E+01
hectare -- 0.334 450 9 --- 3.344 509 4E−01
rood --- 3.305 771 9 --- 3.305 771 9E+00
square -- 360 --- 3.600 000 0E+02
square arpent [US, survey] ----------------------- 0.978 235 8 --- 9.782 357 6E−01
square cable length [US, survey] ----------------- 0.069 444 2 --- 6.944 416 7E−02
square chain [Gunter or US, survey] -------------- 8.264 429 8 --- 8.264 429 8E+00
square chain [Ramden or Engineer] ---------------- 3.599 985 6 --- 3.599 985 6E+00
square foot [international] ---------------------------- 36,000 --- 3.600 000 0E+04
square hectometer -------------------------------- 0.334 450 9 --- 3.344 509 4E−01
square meter ------------------------------------- 3,344.509 4 --- 3.344 509 4E+03
square mile [international] ----------------------- 0.001 291 3 --- 1.291 322 3E−03
square pole [US, survey] -------------------------- 132.230 88 --- 1.322 308 8E+02
square rope -- 90 --- 9.000 000 0E+01

acre [France] <area, special - see page 29>
are --- 52 --- 5.200 000 0E+01

acre [international] <area>
acre [commerical] -------------------------------------- 1.21 --- 1.210 000 0E+00
acre [US, survey] -------------------------------- 0.999 996 --- 9.999 960 0E−01
are -- 40.468 564 --- 4.046 856 4E+01
hectare -- 0.404 685 6 --- 4.046 856 4E−01
rood --- 3.999 984 --- 3.999 984 0E+00
square -- 435.6 --- 4.356 000 0E+02
square arpent [US, survey] ----------------------- 1.183 665 3 --- 1.183 665 3E+00
square chain [Gunter or US, survey] -------------- 9.999 96 --- 9.999 960 0E+00
square chain [Ramden or Engineer] ---------------- 4.355 982 6 --- 4.355 982 6E+00
square foot [international] ---------------------------- 43,560 --- 4.356 000 0E+04
square meter ------------------------------------- 4,046.856 4 --- 4.046 856 4E+03
square mile [international] ----------------------- 0.001 562 5 --- 1.562 500 0E−03
square perch [US, survey] ------------------------ 159.999 36 --- 1.599 993 6E+02
square rope -- 108.9 --- 1.089 000 0E+02

acre [Ireland] <area, special - see page 29>
hectare --- 0.655 5 --- 6.555 000 0E−01

acre [Netherlands] <area, special - see page 29>
hectare --- 0.426 4 --- 4.264 000 0E−01

acre [Pakistan] <area, special - see page 29>
hectare --- 0.405 --- 4.050 000 0E−01

acre [Rome, ancient] <area, special - see page 29>
hectare -- 0.252 --- 2.520 000 0E−01

acre [US, survey] <area>
acre [commerical] -------------------------------- 1.210 004 8 --- 1.210 004 8E+00
acre [international] ------------------------------ 1.000 004 --- 1.000 004 0E+00
are -- 40.468 726 --- 4.046 872 6E+01
hectare -- 0.404 687 3 --- 4.046 872 6E−01
rood -- 4 --- 4.000 000 0E+00
square -- 435.601 74 --- 4.356 017 4E+02

Convert From	<Type of Unit>	
Convert To	Standard	Scientific

square arpent [US, survey]---	1.183 67----	1.183 670 0E+00
square chain [Gunter or US, survey]--	10----	1.000 000 0E+01
square chain [Ramden or Engineer]--	4.356----	4.356 000 0E+00
square foot [international]---	43,560.174----	4.356 017 4E+04
square foot [US, survey]--	43,560----	4.356 000 0E+04
square furlong [US, survey]--	0.1----	1.000 000 0E−01
square meter--	4,046.872 6----	4.046 872 6E+03
square perch [US, survey]--	160----	1.600 000 0E+02
square rope---	108.900 44----	1.089 004 4E+02

acre foot   **\<volume>**

acre foot [US, survey]---	0.999 994 2----	9.999 941 9E−01
acre inch--	12----	1.200 000 0E+01
barrel [US, liquid]--	10,344.49----	1.034 449 0E+04
barrel [US, petroleum]---	7,758.367 3----	7.758 367 3E+03
cubic decimeter--	1,233,481.8----	1.233 481 8E+06
cubic foot--	43,560----	4.356 000 0E+04
cubic inch--	>>>----	7.527 168 0E+07
cubic meter--	1,233.481 8----	1.233 481 8E+03
cubic mile--	0.000 000 3----	2.959 280 3E−07
cubic yard--	1,613.333 3----	1.613 333 3E+03
drum [US, liquid]---	5,924.571 4----	5.924 571 4E+03
gallon [Canada, liquid]---	271,328.07----	2.713 280 7E+05
gallon [UK, dry or liquid]---	271,328.07----	2.713 280 7E+05
gallon [US, liquid]--	325,851.43----	3.258 514 3E+05
hectare meter--	0.123 348 2----	1.233 481 8E−01
liter---	1,233,481.8----	1.233 481 8E+06
megaliter---	1.233 481 8----	1.233 481 8E+00
million acre foot--	0.000 001----	1.000 000 0E−06
ounce [US, liquid]--	>>>----	4.170 898 3E+07
pint [US, liquid]--	2,606,811.4----	2.606 811 4E+06
quart [US, liquid]---	1,303,405.7----	1.303 405 7E+06
stere--	1,233.481 8----	1.233 481 8E+03
thousand cubic foot---	43.56----	4.356 000 0E+01

acre foot [US, survey]   **\<volume>**

acre foot--	1.000 005 8----	1.000 005 8E+00
acre inch--	12.000 07----	1.200 007 0E+01
barrel [US, liquid]--	10,344.55----	1.034 455 0E+04
barrel [US, petroleum]---	7,758.412 4----	7.758 412 4E+03
billion cubic foot--	0.000 043 6----	4.356 025 3E−05
cubic decimeter--	1,233,489----	1.233 489 0E+06
cubic foot--	43,560.253----	4.356 025 3E+04
cubic inch--	>>>----	7.527 211 7E+07
cubic meter--	1,233.489----	1.233 489 0E+03
cubic mile--	0.000 000 3----	2.959 297 5E−07
cubic yard--	1,613.342 7----	1.613 342 7E+03
drum [US, liquid]---	5,924.605 8----	5.924 605 8E+03
gallon [Canada, liquid]---	271,329.65----	2.713 296 5E+05
gallon [UK, dry or liquid]---	271,329.65----	2.713 296 5E+05
gallon [US, liquid]--	325,853.32----	3.258 533 2E+05
hectare meter--	0.123 348 9----	1.233 489 0E−01
liter---	1,233,489----	1.233 489 0E+06
megaliter---	1.233 489----	1.233 489 0E+00
million acre foot--	0.000 001----	1.000 005 8E−06
pint [UK]--	2,170,637.2----	2.170 637 2E+06
pint [US, liquid]--	2,606,826.6----	2.606 826 6E+06
quart [UK]--	1,085,318.6----	1.085 318 6E+06
quart [US, liquid]---	1,303,413.3----	1.303 413 3E+06
stere--	1,233.489----	1.233 489 0E+03
thousand cubic foot---	43.560 253----	4.356 025 3E+01

acre foot/day   **\<flow rate, volume basis>**

acre foot/day [US, survey]---	0.999 994----	9.999 940 0E−01
acre inch/day---	12----	1.200 000 0E+01
acre inch/hour--	0.5----	5.000 000 0E−01

	Standard	Scientific
barrel/minute [UK]	5.233 952	5.233 952 0E+00
barrel/minute [US, federal]	7.299 539 2	7.299 539 2E+00
barrel/minute [US, liquid]	7.183 673 5	7.183 673 5E+00
barrel/minute [US, petroleum]	5.387 755 1	5.387 755 1E+00
barrel/second [US, federal]	0.121 659	1.216 590 9E−01
barrel/second [US, liquid]	0.119 727 9	1.197 278 9E−01
cubic decimeter/second	14.276 410 2	1.427 641 0E+01
cubic dekameter/day	1.233 481 8	1.233 481 8E+00
cubic foot/minute	30.25	3.025 000 0E+01
cubic foot/second	0.504 166 7	5.041 666 7E−01
cubic meter/hour	51.395 076 6	5.139 507 7E+01
cubic meter/minute	0.856 584 6	8.565 846 1E−01
cubic meter/second	0.014 276 4	1.427 641 0E−02
cubic yard/hour	67.222 222 2	6.722 222 2E+01
cubic yard/minute	1.120 370 4	1.120 370 4E+00
cusec	0.504 166 7	5.041 666 7E−01
dekaliter/minute	85.658 460 9	8.565 846 1E+01
dekaliter/second	1.427 641	1.427 641 0E+00
gallon/second [UK]	3.140 371 2	3.140 371 2E+00
gallon/second [US, liquid]	3.771 428 6	3.771 428 6E+00
hectare meter/day	0.123 348 2	1.233 481 8E−01
hectoliter/minute	8.565 846 1	8.565 846 1E+00
hectoliter/second	0.142 764 1	1.427 641 0E+00
kiloliter/hour	51.395 076 6	5.139 507 7E+01
kiloliter/minute	0.856 584 6	8.565 846 1E−01
liter/second	14.276 410 2	1.427 641 0E+01
liter/second [pre-1964]	14.276 010 4	1.427 601 0E+01
stere/hour	51.395 077	5.139 507 7E+01
stere/minute	0.856 584 6	8.565 846 1E−01
thousand cubic foot/day	43.56	4.356 000 0E+01
thousand cubic foot/hour	1.815	1.815 000 0E+00

acre foot/day [US, survey] — \<flow rate, volume basis\>

	Standard	Scientific
acre foot/day	1.000 006	1.000 006 0E+00
acre inch/day	12.000 072	1.200 007 2E+01
acre inch/hour	0.500 003	5.000 030 0E−01
barrel/minute [UK]	5.233 983 4	5.233 983 4E+00
barrel/minute [US, federal]	7.299 583	7.299 583 0E+00
barrel/minute [US, liquid]	7.183 716 6	7.183 716 6E+00
barrel/minute [US, petroleum]	5.387 787 4	5.387 787 4E+00
barrel/second [US, federal]	0.121 659 7	1.216 597 2E−01
barrel/second [US, liquid]	0.119 728 6	1.197 286 7E−01
cubic decimeter/second	14.276 495 8	1.427 649 6E+01
cubic dekameter/day	1.233 489 2	1.233 489 2E+00
cubic foot/minute	30.250 181 5	3.025 018 2E+01
cubic foot/second	0.504 169 7	5.041 696 9E−01
cubic meter/hour	51.395 384 9	5.139 538 5E+01
cubic meter/minute	0.856 589 7	8.565 897 5E−01
cubic meter/second	0.014 276 5	1.427 649 6E−02
cubic yard/hour	67.222 625 6	6.722 262 6E+01
cubic yard/minute	1.120 377 1	1.120 377 1E+00
dekaliter/minute	85.658 974 9	8.565 897 5E+01
dekaliter/second	1.427 649 6	1.427 649 6E+00
gallon/second [UK]	3.140 390 1	3.140 390 1E+00
gallon/second [US, liquid]	3.771 451 2	3.771 451 2E+00
hectare meter/day	0.123 348 9	1.233 489 2E−01
hectoliter/minute	8.565 897 5	8.565 897 5E+00
hectoliter/second	0.142 765	1.427 649 6E−01
kiloliter/hour	51.395 384 9	5.139 538 5E+01
kiloliter/minute	0.856 589 7	8.565 897 5E−01
liter/second	14.276 495 8	1.427 649 6E+01
liter/second [pre-1964]	14.276 096 1	1.427 609 6E+01
stere/hour	51.395 385	5.139 538 5E+01
stere/minute	0.856 589 8	8.565 897 5E−01

Convert To	Standard	Scientific
thousand cubic foot/day	43.560 261	4.356 026 1E+01
thousand cubic foot/hour	1.815 010 9	1.815 010 9E+00
acre foot/hour	**\<flow rate, volume basis\>**	
acre foot/day	24	2.400 000 0E+01
acre foot/day [US, survey]	23.999 856	2.399 985 6E+01
acre foot/hour [US, survey]	0.999 994	9.999 940 0E-01
acre inch/hour	12	1.200 000 0E+01
acre inch/minute	0.2	2.000 000 0E-01
barrel/second [UK]	2.093 580 8	2.093 580 8E+00
barrel/second [US, federal]	2.919 815 7	2.919 815 7E+00
barrel/second [US, liquid]	2.873 469 4	2.873 469 4E+00
barrel/second [US, petroleum]	2.155 102	2.155 102 0E+00
cubic dekameter/day	29.603 564 1	2.960 356 4E+01
cubic dekameter/hour	1.233 481 8	1.233 481 8E+00
cubic foot/second	12.1	1.210 000 0E+01
cubic meter/minute	20.558 030 6	2.055 803 1E+01
cubic meter/second	0.342 633 8	3.426 338 4E-01
cubic yard/minute	26.888 888 9	2.688 889 9E+01
cubic yard/second	0.448 148 1	4.481 481 5E-01
dekaliter/second	34.263 384	3.426 338 4E+01
gallon/second [UK]	75.368 909 1	7.536 890 9E+00
gallon/second [US, liquid]	90.514 285 7	9.051 428 6E+00
hectare meter/day	2.960 356 4	2.960 356 4E+00
hectare meter/hour	0.123 348 2	1.233 481 8E-01
hectoliter/second	3.426 338 4	3.426 338 4E+00
kiloliter/minute	20.558 030 6	2.055 803 1E+01
kiloliter/second	0.342 633 8	3.426 338 4E-01
stere/minute	20.558 031	2.055 803 1E+01
stere/second	0.342 633 8	3.426 338 4E-01
thousand cubic foot/hour	43.56	4.356 000 0E+01
thousand cubic foot/minute	0.726	7.260 000 0E-01
acre foot/hour [US, survey]	**\<flow rate, volume basis\>**	
acre foot/day	24.000 144	2.400 014 4E+01
acre foot/day [US, survey]	24	2.400 000 0E+01
acre foot/hour	1.000 006	1.000 006 0E+00
acre inch/hour	12.000 072	1.200 007 2E+01
acre inch/minute	0.200 001 2	2.000 012 0E-01
barrel/second [UK]	2.093 593 4	2.093 593 4E+00
barrel/second [US, federal]	2.919 833 2	2.919 833 2E+00
barrel/second [US, liquid]	2.873 486 6	2.873 486 6E+00
barrel/second [US, petroleum]	2.155 115	2.155 115 0E+00
cubic dekameter/day	29.603 741 7	2.960 374 2E+01
cubic dekameter/hour	1.233 489 2	1.233 489 2E+00
cubic foot/second	12.100 072 6	1.210 007 3E+01
cubic meter/minute	20.558 154	2.055 815 4E+01
cubic meter/second	0.342 635 9	3.426 359 0E-01
cubic yard/minute	26.889 050 2	2.688 905 0E+01
cubic yard/second	0.448 150 8	4.481 508 4E-01
dekaliter/second	34.263 59	3.426 359 0E+01
gallon/second [UK]	75.369 361	7.536 936 1E+00
gallon/second [US, liquid]	90.514 828 8	9.051 482 9E+00
hectare meter/day	2.960 374 2	2.960 374 2E+00
hectare meter/hour	0.123 348 9	1.233 489 2E-01
hectoliter/second	3.426 359	3.426 359 0E+00
kiloliter/minute	20.558 154	2.055 815 4E+01
kiloliter/second	0.342 635 9	3.426 359 0E-01
petrograd standard/minute	4.400 026 4	4.400 026 4E+00
stere/minute	20.558 154	2.055 815 4E+01
stere/second	0.342 635 9	3.426 359 0E-01
thousand cubic foot/hour	43.560 261	4.356 026 1E+01
thousand cubic foot/minute	0.726 004 4	7.260 043 6E-01
acre foot/minute	**\<flow rate, volume basis\>**	
acre foot/day	1,440	1.440 000 0E+03

Convert From Convert To	Standard	\<Type of Unit\> Scientific
acre foot/hour	60	6.000 000 0E+01
acre foot/hour [US, survey]	59.999 64	5.999 964 0E+01
acre foot/minute [US, survey]	0.999 994	9.999 940 0E-01
acre foot/second	0.016 666 7	1.666 666 7E-02
acre foot/second [US, survey]	0.016 666 6	1.666 656 7E-02
acre inch/hour	720	7.200 000 0E+02
acre inch/minute	12	1.200 000 0E+01
acre inch/second	0.2	2.000 000 0E-01
barrel/second [UK]	125.614 848	1.256 148 5E+02
barrel/second [US, federal]	175.188 94	1.751 889 4E+02
barrel/second [US, liquid]	172.408 163	1.724 081 6E+02
barrel/second [US, petroleum]	129.306 122	1.293 061 2E+02
billion cubic foot/day	0.062 726 4	6.272 640 0E-02
cubic dekameter/hour	74.008 910 3	7.400 891 0E+01
cubic dekameter/minute	1.233 481 8	1.233 481 8E+00
cubic dekameter/second	0.020 558	2.055 803 1E-02
cubic foot/minute	43,560	4.356 000 0E+04
cubic foot/second	726	7.260 000 0E+02
cubic meter/second	20.558 030 6	2.055 803 1E+01
cubic yard/hour	96,800	9.680 000 0E+04
cubic yard/second	26.888 888 9	2.688 888 9E+01
hectare meter/day	177.621 385	1.776 213 9E+02
hectare meter/hour	7.400 891	7.400 891 0E+00
hectare meter/minute	0.123 348 2	1.233 481 8E-01
hectoliter/second	205.580 306	2.055 803 1E+02
kiloliter/second	20.558 030 6	2.055 803 1E+01
million acre foot/hour	0.000 06	6.000 000 0E-05
petrograd standard/minute	264	2.640 000 0E+02
petrograd standard/second	4.4	4.400 000 0E+00
stere/second	20.558 031	2.055 803 1E+01
thousand cubic foot/minute	43.56	4.356 000 0E+01
thousand cubic foot/second	0.726	7.260 000 0E-01
acre foot/minute [US, survey]	**\<flow rate, volume basis\>**	
acre foot/day [US, survey]	1,440	1.440 000 0E+03
acre foot/hour	60.000 36	6.000 036 0E+01
acre foot/hour [US, survey]	60	6.000 000 0E+01
acre foot/minute	1.000 006	1.000 006 0E+00
acre foot/second	0.016 666 8	1.666 676 7E-02
acre foot/second [US, survey]	0.016 666 7	1.666 666 7E-02
acre inch/hour	720.004 32	7.200 043 2E+02
acre inch/minute	12.000 072	1.200 007 2E+01
acre inch/second	0.200 001 2	2.000 012 0E-01
barrel/second [UK]	125.615 602	1.256 156 0E+02
barrel/second [US, federal]	175.189 991	1.751 899 9E+02
barrel/second [US, liquid]	172.409 198	1.724 092 0E+02
barrel/second [US, petroleum]	129.306 898	1.293 069 0E+02
billion cubic foot/day	0.062 726 8	6.272 677 6E-02
cubic dekameter/hour	74.009 354 3	7.400 935 4E+01
cubic dekameter/minute	1.233 489 2	1.233 489 2E+00
cubic dekameter/second	0.020 558 2	2.055 815 4E-02
cubic foot/second	726.004 356	7.260 043 6E+02
cubic meter/second	20.558 154	2.055 815 4E+01
cubic yard/second	26.889 050 2	2.688 905 0E+01
hectare meter/day	177.622 45	1.776 224 5E+02
hectare meter/hour	7.400 935 4	7.400 935 4E+00
hectare meter/minute	0.123 348 9	1.233 489 2E-01
hectoliter/second	205.581 54	2.055 815 4E+02
kiloliter/second	20.558 154	2.055 815 4E+01
liter/second	20.558.154	2.055 815 4E+04
petrograd standard/minute	264.001 58	2.640 015 8E+02
petrograd standard/second	4.400 026 4	4.400 026 4E+00
stere/second	20.558 154	2.055 815 4E+01
thousand cubic foot/minute	43.560 261	4.356 026 1E+01

	Standard	Scientific
thousand cubic foot/second	0.726 004 4	7.260 043 6E−01

acre foot/second — \<flow rate, volume basis\>

	Standard	Scientific
acre foot/hour	3,600	3.600 000 0E+03
acre foot/hour [US, survey]	3,599.978 4	3.599 978 4E+03
acre foot/minute	60.000 00	6.000 000 0E+01
acre foot/minute [US, survey]	59.999 64	5.999 964 0E+01
acre foot/second [US, survey]	0.999 994	9.999 940 0E−01
acre inch/minute	720	7.200 000 0E+02
acre inch/second	12	1.200 000 0E+01
barrel/second [UK]	7,536.890 91	7.536 890 9E+03
billion cubic foot/day	3.763 584	3.763 584 0E+00
billion cubic foot/minute	0.002 613 6	2.613 600 0E−03
cubem/day	0.025 568 2	2.556 818 2E−02
cubem/hour	0.001 065 3	1.065 340 9E−03
cubic dekameter/hour	4,440.534 62	4.440 534 6E+03
cubic dekameter/minute	74.008 910 3	7.400 891 0E+01
cubic dekameter/second	1.233 481 8	1.233 481 8E+00
cubic kilometer/day	0.106 572 8	1.065 728 3E−01
cubic kilometer/hour	0.004 440 5	4.440 534 6E−03
cubic meter/second	1,233.481 84	1.233 481 8E+03
cubic mile/day	0.025 568 2	2.556 818 2E−02
cubic mile/hour	0.001 065 3	1.065 340 9E−03
cubic yard/second	1,613.333 33	1.613 333 3E+03
hectare meter/hour	444.053 462	4.440 534 6E+02
hectare meter/minute	7.400 891 0	7.400 891 0E+00
hectare meter/second	0.123 348 2	1.233 481 8E−01
kiloliter/second	1,233.481 84	1.233 481 8E+03
million acre foot/day	0.086 4	8.640 000 0E−02
million acre foot/hour	0.003 6	3.600 000 0E−03
petrograd standard/second	264	2.640 000 0E+02
stere/second	1,233.481 8	1.233 481 8E+03
thousand cubic foot/minute	2,613.6	2.613 600 0E+03
thousand cubic foot/second	43.56	4.356 000 0E+01
trillion cubic foot/day	0.003 763 6	3.763 584 0E−03

acre foot/second [US, survey] — \<flow rate, volume basis\>

	Standard	Scientific
acre foot/hour	3,600.021 6	3.600 021 6E+03
acre foot/hour [US, survey]	3,600	3.600 000 0E+03
acre foot/minute	60.000 36	6.000 036 0E+01
acre foot/minute [US, survey]	60	6.000 000 0E+01
acre foot/second	1.000 006	1.000 006 0E+00
acre inch/minute	720.004 32	7.200 043 2E+02
acre inch/second	12.000 072	1.200 007 2E+01
barrel/second [UK]	7,536.936 13	7.536 936 1E+03
barrel/second [US, petroleum]	7,758.413 9	7.758 413 9E+03
billion cubic foot/day	3.763 606 6	3.763 606 6E+00
billion cubic foot/hour	0.156 816 9	1.568 169 4E−01
billion cubic foot/minute	0.002 613 6	2.613 615 7E−03
cubem/day	0.025 568 3	2.556 833 5E−02
cubem/hour	0.001 065 3	1.065 347 3E−03
cubic dekameter/hour	4,440.561 26	4.440 561 3E+03
cubic dekameter/minute	74.009 354 3	7.400 935 4E+01
cubic dekameter/second	1.233 489 2	1.233 489 2E+00
cubic kilometer/day	0.106 573 5	1.065 734 7E−01
cubic kilometer/hour	0.004 440 6	4.440 561 3E−03
cubic meter/second	1,233.489 24	1.233 489 2E+03
cubic mile/day	0.025 568 3	2.556 833 5E−02
cubic mile/hour	0.001 065 3	1.065 347 3E−03
cubic yard/second	1,613.343 01	1.613 343 0E+03
hectare meter/hour	444.056 126	4.440 561 3E+02
hectare meter/minute	7.400 935 4	7.400 935 4E+00
hectare meter/second	0.123 348 9	1.233 489 2E−01
kiloliter/second	1,233.489 24	1.233 489 2E+03
million acre foot/day	0.086 400 5	8.640 051 8E−02

Convert From	<Type of Unit>	
Convert To	Standard	Scientific

million acre foot/hour	0.003 6	3.600 021 6E-03
petrograd standard/second	264.001 58	2.640 015 8E+02
stere/second	1,233.489 2	1.233 489 2E+03
thousand cubic foot/minute	2,613.615 7	2.613 615 7E+03
thousand cubic foot/second	43.560 261	4.356 026 1E+01
trillion cubic foot/day	0.003 763 6	3.763 606 6E-03

acre inch <volume>

acre foot	0.083 333 3	8.333 333 3E-02
acre foot [US, survey]	0.083 332 8	8.333 284 9E-02
barrel [UK]	628.074 24	6.280 742 4E+02
barrel [US, liquid]	862.040 82	8.620 408 2E+02
barrel [US, petroleum]	646.530 61	6.465 306 1E+02
billion cubic foot	0.000 003 6	3.630 000 0E-06
cubic decimeter	102,790.15	1.027 901 5E+05
cubic foot	3,630	3.630 000 0E+03
cubic inch	6,272,640	6.272 640 0E+06
cubic meter	102.790 15	1.027 901 5E+02
cubic mile	<<<	2.466 066 9E-08
cubic yard	134.444 44	1.344 444 4E+02
drum [US, liquid]	493.714 29	4.937 142 9E+02
gallon [Canada, liquid]	22,610.673	2.261 067 3E+04
gallon [UK, dry or liquid]	22,610.673	2.261 067 3E+04
gallon [US, liquid]	27,154.286	2.715 428 6E+04
hectare meter	0.010 279	1.027 901 5E-02
liter	102,790.15	1.027 901 5E+05
million acre foot	<<<	8.333 333 3E-08
petrograd standard	22	2.200 000 0E+01
quart [US, liquid]	108,617.14	1.086 171 4E+05
stere	102.790 15	1.027 901 5E+02
thousand cubic foot	3.63	3.630 000 0E+00

acre inch/day <flow rate, volume basis>

barrel/hour [UK]	26.169 760 1	2.616 976 0E+01
barrel/hour [US, liquid]	35.918 367 3	3.591 836 7E+01
barrel/hour [US, petroleum]	26.938 775 5	2.693 877 6E+01
barrel/minute [UK]	0.436 162 7	4.361 626 7E-01
barrel/minute [US, liquid]	0.598 639 5	5.986 394 6E-01
barrel/minute [US, petroleum]	0.448 979 6	4.489 795 9E-01
cubic decimeter/second	1.189 700 9	1.189 700 9E+00
cubic dekameter/day	0.102 790 2	1.027 901 5E-01
cubic foot/minute	2.520 833 3	2.520 833 3E+00
cubic inch/second	72.6	7.260 000 0E+01
cubic meter/hour	4.282 923 1	4.282 923 1E+00
cubic meter/second	0.001 189 7	1.189 700 9E-03
cubic yard/hour	5.601 851 9	5.601 851 9E+00
deciliter/second	11.897 008 5	1.189 700 9E+01
dekaliter/minute	7.138 205 1	7.138 205 1E+00
dekaliter/second	0.118 970 1	1.189 700 9E-01
gallon/minute [UK]	15.701 856 1	1.570 185 6E+01
gallon/minute [US, liquid]	18.857 142 9	1.885 714 3E+01
gallon/second [UK]	0.261 697 6	2.616 976 0E-01
gallon/second [US, liquid]	0.314 285 7	3.142 857 1E-01
hectoliter/hour	42.829 230 5	4.282 923 1E+01
hectoliter/minute	0.713 820 5	7.138 205 1E-01
kiloliter/hour	4.282 923 1	4.282 923 1E+00
liter/minute	71.382 050 8	7.138 205 1E+01
liter/minute [pre-1964]	71.380 052 1	7.138 005 2E+01
liter/second	1.189 700 9	1.189 700 9E+00
liter/second [pre-1964]	1.189 667 5	1.189 667 5E+00
ounce/second [UK, liquid]	41.871 616	4.187 161 6E+01
ounce/second [US, liquid]	40.228 571	4.022 857 1E+01
petrograd standard/day	22	2.200 000 0E+01
stere/hour	4.282 923	4.282 923 0E+00
thousand cubic foot/day	3.63	3.630 000 0E+00

Convert To	Standard	Scientific
acre inch/hour		**<flow rate, volume basis>**
acre foot/day	2	2.000 000 0E+00
acre foot/day [US, survey]	1.999 988	1.999 988 0E+00
acre inch/day	24	2.400 000 0E+01
barrel/minute [UK]	10.467 904	1.046 790 4E+01
barrel/minute [US, federal]	14.599 078 3	1.459 907 8E+01
barrel/minute [US, liquid]	14.367 346 9	1.436 734 7E+01
barrel/minute [US, petroleum]	10.775 510 2	1.077 551 0E+01
barrel/second [UK]	0.174 465 1	1.744 650 7E−01
barrel/second [US, federal]	0.243 318	2.433 179 7E−01
barrel/second [US, liquid]	0.239 455 8	2.394 557 8E−01
barrel/second [US, petroleum]	0.179 591 8	1.795 918 4E−01
cubic decimeter/second	28.552 820 3	2.855 282 0E+00
cubic dekameter/day	2.466 963 7	2.466 963 7E+00
cubic dekameter/hour	0.102 790 2	1.027 901 5E−01
cubic foot/minute	60.5	6.050 000 0E+01
cubic foot/second	1.008 333 3	1.008 333 3E+00
cubic meter/minute	1.713 169 2	1.713 169 2E+00
cubic meter/second	0.028 552 8	2.855 282 0E−02
cubic yard/minute	2.240 740 7	2.240 740 7E+00
dekaliter/second	2.855 282	2.855 282 0E+00
gallon/second [UK]	6.280 742 4	6.280 742 4E+00
gallon/second [US, liquid]	7.542 857 1	7.542 857 1E+00
hectare meter/day	0.246 696 4	2.466 963 7E−01
hectoliter/minute	17.131 692	1.713 169 2E+00
hectoliter/second	0.285 528 2	2.855 282 0E−01
kiloliter/minute	1.713 169 2	1.713 169 2E+00
liter/second	28.552 820 3	2.855 282 0E+00
liter/second [pre-1964]	28.552 020 9	2.855 202 1E+00
petrograd standard/hour	22	2.200 000 0E+01
petrograd standard/minute	0.366 666 7	3.666 666 7E−01
stere/minute	1.713 169 2	1.713 169 2E+00
thousand cubic foot/hour	3.63	3.630 000 0E+00
acre inch/minute		**<flow rate, volume basis>**
acre foot/hour	5	5.000 000 0E+00
acre foot/hour [US, survey]	4.999 97	4.999 970 0E+00
acre foot/minute	0.083 333 3	8.333 333 3E−02
acre foot/minute [US, survey]	0.083 333	8.333 283 3E−02
acre inch/hour	60	6.000 000 0E+01
barrel/minute [UK]	628.074 242	6.280 742 4E+02
barrel/minute [US, liquid]	862.040 816	8.620 408 2E+02
barrel/minute [US, petroleum]	646.530 612	6.465 306 1E+02
barrel/second [UK]	10.467 904	1.046 790 4E+01
barrel/second [US, liquid]	14.367 346 9	1.436 734 7E+01
barrel/second [US, petroleum]	10.775 510 2	1.077 551 0E+01
cubic dekameter/day	148.017 821	1.480 178 2E+02
cubic dekameter/hour	6.167 409 2	6.167 409 2E+00
cubic dekameter/minute	0.102 790 2	1.027 901 5E−01
cubic foot/second	60.5	6.050 000 0E+01
cubic meter/minute	102.790 153	1.027 901 5E+02
cubic meter/second	1.713 169 2	1.713 169 2E+00
cubic yard/minute	134.444 444	1.344 444 4E+02
cubic yard/second	2.240 740 7	2.240 740 7E+00
dekaliter/second	171.316 922	1.713 169 2E+02
gallon/second [UK]	376.844 545	3.768 445 5E+02
gallon/second [US, liquid]	452.571 429	4.525 714 3E+02
hectare meter/day	14.801 782 1	1.480 178 2E+01
hectare meter/hour	0.616 740 9	6.167 409 2E−01
hectare meter/minute	0.010 279	1.027 901 5E−02
hectoliter/second	17.131 692	1.713 169 2E+01
kiloliter/minute	102.790 153	1.027 901 5E+02
kiloliter/second	1.713 169 2	1.713 169 2E+00
petrograd standard/minute	22	2.200 000 0E+01

Convert From Convert To	Standard	<Type of Unit> Scientific
stere/second	1.713 169 2	1.713 169 2E+00
thousand cubic foot/hour	217.8	2.178 000 0E+02
thousand cubic foot/minute	3.63	3.630 000 0E+00
thousand cubic foot/second	0.060 5	6.050 000 0E-02
acre inch/second		**<flow rate, volume basis>**
acre foot/day	7,200	7.200 000 0E+03
acre foot/hour	300	3.000 000 0E+02
acre foot/hour [US, survey]	299.998 2	2.999 982 0E+02
acre foot/minute	5	5.000 000 0E+00
acre foot/minute [US, survey]	4.999 97	4.999 970 0E+00
acre foot/second	0.083 333 3	8.333 333 3E-02
acre foot/second [US, survey]	0.083 332 8	8.333 283 3E-02
acre inch/day	86,400	8.640 000 0E+04
acre inch/hour	3,600	3.600 000 0E+03
acre inch/minute	60	6.000 000 0E+01
barrel/second [UK]	628.074 242	6.280 742 4E+02
barrel/second [US, federal]	875.944 7	8.759 447 0E+02
barrel/second [US, liquid]	862.040 816	8.620 408 2E+02
barrel/second [US, petroleum]	646.530 612	6.465 306 1E+02
billion cubic foot/day	0.313 632	3.136 320 0E-01
billion cubic foot/hour	0.013 068	1.306 800 0E-02
cubic dekameter/hour	370.044 551	3.700 445 5E+02
cubic dekameter/minute	6.167 409 2	6.167 409 2E+00
cubic dekameter/second	0.102 790 2	1.027 901 5E-01
cubic meter/second	102.790 153	1.027 901 5E+02
cubic yard/second	134.444 444	1.344 444 4E+02
hectare meter/day	888.106 923	8.881 069 2E+02
hectare meter/hour	37.004 455 1	3.700 445 5E+01
hectare meter/minute	0.616 740 9	6.167 409 2E-01
hectare meter/second	0.010 279	1.027 901 5E-02
kiloliter/second	102.790 153	1.027 901 5E+02
petrograd standard/second	22	2.200 000 0E+01
stere/second	102.790 15	1.027 901 5E+02
thousand cubic foot/minute	217.8	2.178 000 0E+02
thousand cubic foot/second	3.63	3.630 000 0E+00
acre/pound		**<specific area>**
square foot/pound	43,560	4.356 000 0E+04
square meter/kilogram	8,921.791 2	8.921 791 2E+03
actus [Rome, ancient]		**<length, special - see page 29>**
meter	35.5	3.550 000 0E+01
actus quadratus [Rome, ancient]		**<area, special - see page 29>**
hectare	0.126	1.260 000 0E-01
actus simplex [Rome, ancient]		**<area, special - see page 29>**
square meter	42.1	4.210 000 0E+01
adarme [Argentina]		**<mass, special - see page 29>**
gram	1.79	1.790 000 0E+00
adarme [Chile]		**<mass, special - see page 29>**
gram	1.79	1.790 000 0E+00
adarme [Honduras]		**<mass, special - see page 29>**
gram	1.79	1.790 000 0E+00
adarme [Mexico]		**<mass, special - see page 29>**
gram	1.79	1.790 000 0E+00
adarme [Peru]		**<mass, special - see page 29>**
gram	1.79	1.790 000 0E+00
adarme [Spain]		**<mass, special - see page 29>**
gram	1.79	1.790 000 0E+00
adoulie [India]		**<volume, special - see page 29>**
liter	6.881	6.881 000 0E+00
adowlie [India, heavy]		**<mass, special - see page 29>**
kilogram	2.031	2.031 000 0E+00

	Standard	Scientific
adowly [India]		\<mass, special - see page 29\>
kilogram	1.866	1.866 000 0E+00
ady [India]		\<length, special - see page 29\>
centimeter	26.6	2.660 000 0E+01
aftari [Morocco]		\<area, special - see page 29\>
square meter	900	9.000 000 0E+02
agate [print]		\<length\>
barleycorn	0.228 311	2.283 105 0E-01
caliber	7.610 35	7.610 350 0E+00
centimeter	0.193 302 9	1.933 028 9E-01
didot point [print]	5.134 428 7	5.134 428 7E+00
douzieme [print]	10.958 904	1.095 890 4E+01
em [pica, print]	0.458 333 3	4.583 333 3E-01
inch [international]	0.076 103 5	7.610 350 0E-02
iron [print]	0.018 333 3	1.833 333 3E-02
ligne [print]	0.913 242	9.132 420 0E-01
line [print]	0.913 242	9.132 420 0E-01
meter	0.001 933	1.933 028 9E-03
mil	76.103 5	7.610 350 0E+01
millimeter	1.933 028 9	1.933 028 9E+00
nonpareil [print]	0.916 666 7	9.166 666 7E-01
pearl [print]	1.1	1.100 000 0E+00
pica [print]	0.458 333 3	4.583 333 3E-01
point [print]	5.5	5.500 000 0E+00
agito [Burma]		\<mass, special - see page 29\>
gram	392.9	3.929 000 0E+02
ahm [South Africa]		\<volume, special - see page 29\>
liter	143.841 6	1.438 416 0E+02
ahm [Sweden]		\<volume, special - see page 29\>
hectoliter	1.57	1.570 000 0E+00
aime [Germany]		\<volume, special - see page 29\>
liter	68.7	6.870 000 0E+01
aimer [Germany]		\<volume, special - see page 29\>
liter	68.7	6.870 000 0E+01
akey [Sudan]		\<mass, special - see page 29\>
gram	1.3	1.300 000 0E+00
ako [Hungary]		\<volume, special - see page 29\>
liter	54.3	5.430 000 0E+01
akov [Yugoslavia]		\<volume, special - see page 29\>
liter	56.6	5.660 000 0E+01
albrun [Denmark]		\<area, special - see page 29\>
are	2.955 1	2.955 100 0E+00
album [Denmark]		\<area, special - see page 29\>
square meter	57.461	5.746 100 0E+01
aldan [Mongolia]		\<length, special - see page 29\>
meter	1.6	1.600 000 0E+00
alen [Denmark]		\<length, special - see page 29\>
meter	0.627 7	6.277 000 0E-01
alen [Sweden]		\<length, special - see page 29\>
meter	0.593 8	5.938 000 0E-01
alin [Iceland]		\<length, special - see page 29\>
meter	0.627 7	6.277 000 0E-01
alma [Turkey]		\<volume, special - see page 29\>
liter	5.24	5.240 000 0E+00
almane [India]		\<mass, special - see page 29\>
gram	1,126.67	1.126 670 0E+03
almenn turma [Iceland]		\<volume, special - see page 29\>
liter	115.9	1.159 000 0E+02

Convert From	<Type of Unit>	
Convert To	Standard	Scientific

almud [Belize] — <volume, special - see page 29>
liter ---------- 5.683 --- 5.683 000 0E+00

almud [Brazil] — <volume, special - see page 29>
liter ---------- 31.95 --- 3.195 000 0E+01

almud [British Honduras] — <volume, special - see page 29>
liter ---------- 5.682 --- 5.682 000 0E+00

almud [Chile] — <volume, special - see page 29>
liter ---------- 8.08 --- 8.080 000 0E+00

almud [Ecuador] — <mass, special - see page 29>
kilogram ---------- 12.88 --- 1.288 000 0E+01

almud [Mexico] — <volume, special - see page 29>
liter ---------- 7.567 2 --- 7.567 200 0E+00

almud [Paraguay] — <volume, special - see page 29>
liter ---------- 24 --- 2.400 000 0E+01

almud [Portugal] — <volume, special - see page 29>
liter ---------- 16.5 --- 1.650 000 0E+01

almude [Brazil] — <volume, special - see page 29>
liter ---------- 31.944 --- 3.194 400 0E+01

almude [Ecuador] — <mass, special - see page 29>
kilogram ---------- 12.88 --- 1.288 000 0E+01

almude [Mexico] — <volume, special - see page 29>
liter ---------- 7.568 --- 7.568 000 0E+00

almude [Paraguay] — <volume, special - see page 29>
liter ---------- 24 --- 2.400 000 0E+01

almude [Portugal] — <volume, special - see page 29>
liter ---------- 16.75 --- 1.675 000 0E+01

almude [Spain] — <volume, special - see page 29>
liter ---------- 4.625 --- 4.625 000 0E+00

almude [Spanish North Africa] — <volume, special - see page 29>
liter ---------- 14 --- 1.400 000 0E+01

almude [Turkey] — <volume, special - see page 29>
liter ---------- 5.24 --- 5.240 000 0E+00

aln [Sweden] — <length, special - see page 29>
meter ---------- 0.593 802 --- 5.938 020 0E−01

alqueire [Portugal] — <volume, special - see page 29>
liter ---------- 13.96 --- 1.396 000 0E+01

alqueire carree [Portugal] — <area, special - see page 29>
are ---------- 241.68 --- 2.416 800 0E+02

alquier [Portugal] — <volume, special - see page 29>
liter ---------- 13.8 --- 1.380 000 0E+01

am [Sweden] — <volume, special - see page 29>
liter ---------- 157.03 --- 1.570 300 0E+02

Amagat density unit — <concentration, mole basis>
mole/cubic meter ---------- 44.615 769 --- 4.461 576 9E+01

Amagat volume unit — <volume>
cubic foot ---------- 0.791 528 8 --- 7.915 288 1E−01
cubic meter ---------- 0.022 413 6 --- 2.241 360 0E−02
gallon [US, liquid] ---------- 5.921 046 7 --- 5.921 046 7E+00

amat [Batavia] — <mass, special - see page 29>
kilogram ---------- 123.5 --- 1.235 000 0E+02

ambar [Turkey] — <volume, special - see page 29>
cubic meter ---------- 0.435 --- 4.350 000 0E−01

amma [Greece, ancient] — <length, special - see page 29>
meter ---------- 18.5 --- 1.850 000 0E+01

amma [Hebrew, ancient] — <length, special - see page 29>
meter ---------- 0.443 --- 4.430 000 0E−01

Convert From Convert To	\<Type of Unit\> Standard	Scientific

ammah [Hebrew, ancient, large] \<length, special - see page 29\>
centimeter-- 52.5----5.250 000 0E+01

ammah [Hebrew, ancient] \<length, special - see page 29\>
centimeter-- 54----5.400 000 0E+01

ammonam [Sri Lanka] \<volume, special - see page 29\>
hectoliter-- 2.04----2.040 000 0E+00

amomam [Sri Lanka] \<volume, special - see page 29\>
hectoliter-- 2.04----2.040 000 0E+00

ampere \<electric current\>
abampere-- 0.1----1.000 000 0E-01
ampere [international]--------------------------------------- 1.000 15----1.000 150 0E+00
biot-- 0.1----1.000 000 0E-01
coulomb/second-- 1----1.000 000 0E+00
electromagnetic unit of current [cgs system]----------------------- 1----1.000 000 0E+00
electrostatic unit of current [cgs system]----------------------- 0.1----1.000 000 0E-01
franklin/second--- >>>----2.997 924 6E+09
gaussian electric current------------------------------------- >>>----2.997 924 6E+09
gilbert-- 1.256 637 1----1.256 637 1E+00
siemens volt--- 1----1.000 000 0E+00
statampere-- >>>----2.997 924 6E+09
volt/ohm--- 1----1.000 000 0E+00
watt/volt-- 1----1.000 000 0E+00
weber/henry-- 1----1.000 000 0E+00

ampere [international] \<electric current\>
abampere--- 0.099 985----9.998 500 7E-02
ampere-- 0.999 850 1----9.998 500 7E-01
biot--- 0.099 985----9.998 500 7E-02
gilbert-- 1.256 448 7----1.256 448 7E+00
statampere-- >>>----2.997 475 1E+09

ampere circular mil \<electromagnetic moment\>
ampere square meter--- <<<----5.067 074 8E-10

ampere henry \<magnetic flux\>
gauss square centimeter-------------------------------------- >>>----1.000 000 0E+08
joule/ampere--- 1----1.000 000 0E+00
maxwell--- >>>----1.000 000 0E+08
statweber-- 0.003 335 6----3.335 641 0E-03
tesla square meter-- 1----1.000 000 0E+00
unit pole--- 7,957,747.54----7.957 747 5E+06
volt second-- 1----1.000 000 0E+00
weber-- 1----1.000 000 0E+00

ampere henry/square meter \<magnetic flux density\>
electromagnetic unit of magnetic flux density [cgs system] -- 10,000----1.000 000 0E+04
gauss--- 10,000----1.000 000 0E+04
line/square centimeter [of magnetic force]------------------ 10,000----1.000 000 0E+04
maxwell/square meter--- 1----1.000 000 0E+00
tesla-- 1----1.000 000 0E+00

ampere hour \<electric charge\>
abcoulomb--- 360----3.600 000 0E+02
coulomb--- 3,600----3.600 000 0E+03
farad volt--- 3,600----3.600 000 0E+03
kilocoulomb-- 3.6----3.600 000 0E+00
statcoulomb-- >>>----1.079 252 9E+13

ampere hour meter \<electric dipole moment\>
ampere second meter-- 3,600----3.600 000 0E+03
coulomb meter-- 3,600----3.600 000 0E+03
kilocoulomb meter-- 3.6----3.600 000 0E+00

ampere hour/cubic meter \<electric charge density\>
ampere second/cubic meter------------------------------------ 3,600----3.600 000 0E+03
coulomb/cubic meter-- 3,600----3.600 000 0E+03
kilocoulomb/cubic meter--------------------------------------- 3.6----3.600 000 0E+00

Convert From / Convert To	Standard	Scientific
ampere hour/meter	<electric dipole moment/unit area>	
coulomb/meter	3,600	3.600 000 0E+03
ampere hour/square meter	<electric flux density>	
abcoulomb/square centimeter	0.036	3.600 000 0E-02
coulomb/square inch	2.322 576	2.322 576 0E+00
coulomb/square meter	3,600	3.600 000 0E+03
franklin/square centimeter	>>>	1.079 252 9E+09
statcoulomb/square centimeter	>>>	1.079 252 9E+09
ampere minute	<electric charge>	
coulomb	60	6.000 000 0E+01
ampere ohm	<electric potential>	
abvolt	>>>	1.000 000 0E+08
statvolt	0.003 335 6	3.335 641 0E-03
volt	1	1.000 000 0E+00
watt/ampere	1	1.000 000 0E+00
ampere ohm/meter	<electric field strength>	
coulomb/farad meter	1	1.000 000 0E+00
joule/coulomb meter	1	1.000 000 0E+00
newton/coulomb	1	1.000 000 0E+00
volt/inch	0.025 4	2.540 000 0E-02
volt/meter	1	1.000 000 0E+00
ampere second	<electric charge>	
abcoulomb	0.1	1.000 000 0E-01
coulomb	1	1.000 000 0E+00
electromagnetic unit of charge [cgs system]	0.1	1.000 000 0E-01
farad volt	1	1.000 000 0E+00
statcoulomb	>>>	2.997 924 6E+09
ampere second meter	<electric dipole moment>	
abcoulomb centimeter	10	1.000 000 0E+01
coulomb meter	1	1.000 000 0E+00
farad volt meter	1	1.000 000 0E+00
ampere second/cubic meter	<electric charge density>	
abcoulomb/cubic centimeter	0.000 000 1	1.000 000 0E-07
coulomb/cubic meter	1	1.000 000 0E+00
franklin/cubic centimeter	2,997.924 58	2.997 924 6E+03
statcoulomb/cubic centimeter	2,997.924 58	2.997 924 6E+03
ampere second/kilogram	<exposure, gamma and X rays>	
coulomb/kilogram	1	1.000 000 0E+00
roentgen	3,875.969	3.875 969 0E+03
röntgen	3,875.969	3.875 969 0E+03
ampere second/meter	<electric dipole moment/unit area>	
coulomb/meter	1	1.000 000 0E+00
farad volt/meter	1	1.000 000 0E+00
ampere second/square meter	<electric flux density>	
abcoulomb/square centimeter	0.000 01	1.000 000 0E-05
ampere hour/square meter	0.000 277 8	2.777 777 8E-04
coulomb/square inch	0.000 645 2	6.451 600 0E-04
coulomb/square meter	1	1.000 000 0E+00
franklin/square centimeter	299,792.458	2.997 924 6E+05
statcoulomb/square centimeter	299,792.458	2.997 924 6E+05
ampere second/volt	<capacitance>	
abfarad	<<<	1.000 000 0E-09
coulomb/volt	1	1.000 000 0E+00
farad	1	1.000 000 0E+00
second/ohm	1	1.000 000 0E+00
statfarad	>>>	8.987 551 8E+11
ampere second/volt meter	<electric permittivity>	
abfarad/centimeter	0.000 000 1	1.000 000 0E-07
farad/meter	1	1.000 000 0E+00
statfarad/centimeter	>>>	8.987 551 8E+13

ampere square centimeter   <electromagnetic moment>

Convert To	Standard	Scientific
ampere square inch	0.155 000 3	1.550 003 1E-01
ampere square meter	0.000 1	1.000 000 0E-04
statampere square centimeter	>>>	2.997 924 6E+09

ampere square inch   <electromagnetic moment>

Convert To	Standard	Scientific
ampere square centimeter	6.451 6	6.451 600 0E+00
ampere square meter	0.000 645 2	6.451 600 0E-04
statampere square centimeter	>>>	1.934 141 0E+10

ampere square meter   <electromagnetic moment>

Convert To	Standard	Scientific
abampere square centimeter	0.001	1.000 000 0E-03
ampere circular mil	>>>	1.973 525 2E+09
ampere square inch	1,550.003 1	1.550 003 1E+03
ampere square millimeter	1,000,000	1.000 000 0E+06
statampere square centimeter	>>>	2.997 924 6E+13

ampere square meter/joule second   <exposure, gamma and X rays>

Convert To	Standard	Scientific
coulomb/kilogram	1	1.000 000 0E+00
roentgen	3,875.969	3.875 969 0E+03
röntgen	3,875.969	3.875 969 0E+03

ampere square millimeter   <electromagnetic moment>

Convert To	Standard	Scientific
ampere square inch	0.001 55	1.550 003 1E-03
ampere square meter	0.000 001	1.000 000 0E-06
statampere square centimeter	>>>	2.997 924 6E+07

ampere/centimeter   <magnetic field strength>

Convert To	Standard	Scientific
ampere/inch	2.54	2.540 000 0E+00
ampere/meter	100	1.000 000 0E+02
oersted	1.256 637 1	1.256 637 1E+00
statampere/centimeter	>>>	2.997 924 6E+09

ampere/inch   <magnetic field strength>

Convert To	Standard	Scientific
abampere/centimeter	0.039 370 1	3.937 007 9E-02
ampere/meter	39.370 078 7	3.937 007 9E+01
newton/weber	39.370 079	3.937 007 9E+01
oersted	0.494 739	4.947 390 0E-01
statampere/centimeter	>>>	1.180 285 3E+09

ampere/kilogram   <exposure rate, gamma and X rays>

Convert To	Standard	Scientific
coulomb/kilogram second	1	1.000 000 0E+00
roentgen/second	3,875.969	3.875 969 0E+03
röntgen/second	3,875.969	3.875 969 0E+03

ampere/meter   <magnetic field strength>

Convert To	Standard	Scientific
abampere/centimeter	0.001	1.000 000 0E-03
ampere/inch	0.025 4	2.540 000 0E-02
gilbert/centimeter	0.012 566 4	1.256 637 1E-02
newton/weber	1	1.000 000 0E+00
oersted	0.012 566 4	1.256 637 1E-02
statampere/centimeter	>>>	2.997 924 6E+07

ampere/millimeter   <magnetic field strength>

Convert To	Standard	Scientific
abampere/centimeter	1	1.000 000 0E+00
ampere/inch	25.4	2.540 000 0E+01
ampere/meter	1,000	1.000 000 0E+03
oersted	12.566 370 6	1.256 637 1E+01
statampere/centimeter	>>>	2.997 924 6E+10

ampere/square centimeter   <electric current density>

Convert To	Standard	Scientific
abampere/square centimeter	0.1	1.000 000 0E-01
ampere/square inch	6.451 6	6.451 600 0E+00
ampere/square meter	10,000	1.000 000 0E+04

ampere/square inch   <electric current density>

Convert To	Standard	Scientific
ampere/square centimeter	0.155 000 3	1.550 003 1E-01
ampere/square meter	1,550.003 1	1.550 003 1E+03
kiloampere/square meter	1.550 003 1	1.550 003 1E+00

ampere/square meter   <electric current density>

Convert To	Standard	Scientific
ampere/square centimeter	0.000 1	1.000 000 0E-04

Convert From / Convert To	Standard	Scientific
ampere/square inch	0.000 645 2	6.451 600 0E−04
kiloampere/square meter	0.001	1.000 000 0E−03
statampere/square centimeter	299,792.458	2.997 924 6E+05
ampere/square millimeter		**<electric current density>**
abampere/square centimeter	10	1.000 000 0E+01
ampere/square inch	645.16	6.451 600 0E+02
ampere/square meter	1,000,000	1.000 000 0E+06
megaampere/square meter	1	1.000 000 0E+00
ampere/volt		**<electric conductance>**
1/ohm	1	1.000 000 0E+00
mho	1	1.000 000 0E+00
second/henry	1	1.000 000 0E+00
siemens	1	1.000 000 0E+00
statsiemens	>>>	8.987 551 8E+11
ampere/volt second		**<electric reluctance>**
1/abhenry	<<<	1.000 000 0E−09
1/henry	1	1.000 000 0E+00
1/ohm second	1	1.000 000 0E+00
1/stathenry	>>>	8.987 551 8E+11
ampere/weber	1	1.000 000 0E+00
square ampere/joule	1	1.000 000 0E+00
ampere/weber		**<electric reluctance>**
1/abhenry	<<<	1.000 000 0E−09
1/henry	1	1.000 000 0E+00
1/ohm second	1	1.000 000 0E+00
1/stathenry	>>>	8.987 551 8E+11
ampere/volt second	1	1.000 000 0E+00
square ampere/joule	1	1.000 000 0E+00
amphora [Greece, ancient]		**<volume, special - see page 29>**
liter	38.8	3.880 000 0E+01
amphora [Rome, ancient]		**<volume, special - see page 29>**
liter	26	2.600 000 0E+01
amunam [Ceylon]		**<volume, special - see page 29>**
liter	203.4	2.034 000 0E+02
ancre [Germany]		**<volume, special - see page 29>**
liter	34.35	3.435 000 0E+01
ancre [Netherlands]		**<volume, special - see page 29>**
liter	38.8	3.880 000 0E+01
angstrom		**<length>**
bicron	100	1.000 000 0E+02
fermi	100,000	1.000 000 0E+05
inch [international]	<<<	3.937 007 9E−09
meter	<<<	1.000 000 0E−10
microinch	0.003 937	3.937 007 9E−03
micrometer	0.000 1	1.000 000 0E−04
micromicron	100	1.000 000 0E+02
micron	0.000 1	1.000 000 0E−04
mil	0.000 003 9	3.937 007 9E−06
millimicron	0.1	1.000 000 0E−01
siegbahn	997.932 09	9.979 320 9E+02
stigma	100	1.000 000 0E+02
tenthmeter	1	1.000 000 0E+00
wavelength of orange-red spectral line of krypton-86	0.000 165 1	1.650 763 7E−04
x-unit	997.932 09	9.979 320 9E+02
angula [India]		**<length, special - see page 29>**
centimeter	1.905	1.905 000 0E+00
anguli [India]		**<length, special - see page 29>**
centimeter	1.905	1.905 000 0E+00
ankare [Sweden]		**<volume, special - see page 29>**
liter	39.256 7	3.925 670 0E+01

Convert From Convert To			
		<Type of Unit>	
		Standard	Scientific

anker
cubic foot		1.336 805 6	1.336 805 6E+00
cubic meter		0.037 854 1	3.785 411 8E−02
gallon [US, liquid]		10	1.000 000 0E+01

<volume>

anker [Germany] — **<volume, special - see page 29>**
liter		38.8	3.880 000 0E+01

anker [Iceland] — **<volume, special - see page 29>**
liter		37.676	3.767 600 0E+01

anker [Netherlands] — **<volume, special - see page 29>**
liter		38.8	3.880 000 0E+01

anker [South Africa] — **<volume, special - see page 29>**
liter		35.960 41	3.596 041 0E+01

anker [UK] — **<volume, special - see page 29>**
liter		45	4.500 000 0E+01

ankre [Denmark] — **<volume, special - see page 29>**
liter		38.645	3.864 500 0E+01

anna [Bangladesh] — **<mass, special - see page 29>**
milligram		729	7.290 000 0E+02

anna [Pakistan] — **<area, special - see page 29>**
square meter		16.862	1.686 200 0E+01

annual — **<time>**
quarter		4	4.000 000 0E+00
year [normal calendar]		1	1.000 000 0E+00

annuk [Cambodia] — **<length, special - see page 29>**
millimeter		0.001 51	1.510 000 0E−03

anoman [Sri Lanka] — **<volume, special - see page 29>**
hectoliter		2.04	2.040 000 0E+00

ansyr [Russia] — **<mass, special - see page 29>**
gram		546	5.460 000 0E+02

antal [Hungary] — **<volume, special - see page 29>**
liter		51	5.100 000 0E+01

antel [Hebrew, ancient] — **<volume, special - see page 29>**
cubic centimeter		137.347 83	1.373 478 3E+02

anukabiet [Thailand] — **<length, special - see page 29>**
centimeter		0.260 416 7	2.604 166 7E−01

apatan [Philippines] — **<volume, special - see page 29>**
liter		0.094	9.400 000 0E−02

apostilb [German Hefner] — **<luminance>**
apostilb [international]		0.9	9.000 000 0E−01
blondel		0.9	9.000 000 0E−01
candela/square foot		0.026 614 8	2.661 476 0E−02
candela/square meter		0.286 478 9	2.864 789 0E−01
footlambert		0.083 612 7	8.361 273 6E−02
lambert		0.000 09	9.000 000 0E−05
nit		0.286 478 9	2.864 789 0E−01
stilb		0.000 028 6	2.864 789 0E−05

apostilb [international] — **<luminance>**
apostilb [German Hefner]		1.111 111 1	1.111 111 1E+00
blondel		1	1.000 000 0E+00
candela/square foot		0.029 572	2.957 195 6E−02
candela/square meter		0.318 309 9	3.183 098 9E−01
footlambert		0.092 903	9.290 304 0E−02
lambert		0.000 1	1.000 000 0E−04
nit		0.318 309 9	3.183 098 9E−01
skot		1,000	1.000 000 0E+03
stilb		0.000 031 8	3.183 098 9E−05

aranjada [Spain] — **<area, special - see page 29>**
are		44.719 2	4.471 920 0E+01

| Convert From | <Type of Unit> | |
Convert To	Standard	Scientific
aratel [Brazil]	<mass, special - see page 29>	
gram	454.25	4.542 500 0E+02
archin [Bahrain]	<length, special - see page 29>	
centimeter	48.26	4.826 000 0E+01
archin [Cyprus]	<length, special - see page 29>	
centimeter	60.96	6.096 000 0E+01
archin [Greece]	<length, special - see page 29>	
centimeter	75	7.500 000 0E+01
archin [Iraq]	<length, special - see page 29>	
centimeter	74.5	7.450 000 0E+01
archin [Jordan, land]	<length, special - see page 29>	
centimeter	75.8	7.580 000 0E+01
archin [Jordan, textiles]	<length, special - see page 29>	
centimeter	68	6.800 000 0E+01
archin [Lebanon, land]	<length, special - see page 29>	
centimeter	75.8	7.580 000 0E+01
archin [Lebanon, textiles]	<length, special - see page 29>	
centimeter	68	6.800 000 0E+01
archin [Morocco]	<length, special - see page 29>	
centimeter	55.88	5.588 000 0E+01
archin [Russia]	<length, special - see page 29>	
centimeter	71.12	7.112 000 0E+01
archin [Saudi Arabia]	<length, special - see page 29>	
centimeter	45.7	4.570 000 0E+01
archin [Syria]	<length, special - see page 29>	
centimeter	70	7.000 000 0E+01
archin [Turkey]	<length, special - see page 29>	
meter	1	1.000 000 0E+00
ardab [Egypt]	<volume, special - see page 29>	
hectoliter	1.98	1.980 000 0E+00
ardab [Saudi Arabia]	<volume, special - see page 29>	
hectoliter	1.98	1.980 000 0E+00
ardab [Sudan]	<volume, special - see page 29>	
hectoliter	1.98	1.980 000 0E+00
ardeb [Egypt]	<area, special - see page 29>	
hectare	0.275	2.750 000 0E-01
ardeb [Ethiopia]	<volume, special - see page 29>	
cubic meter	0.011	1.100 000 0E-02
ardeb [Saudi Arabia]	<volume, special - see page 29>	
hectoliter	1.98	1.980 000 0E+00
ardeb [Sudan]	<volume, special - see page 29>	
liter	198	1.980 000 0E+02
are		<area>
acre [commerical]	0.029 899 8	2.989 975 1E-02
acre [France]	0.019 230 8	1.923 076 9E-02
acre [international]	0.024 710 5	2.471 053 8E-02
acre [US, survey]	0.024 710 4	2.471 043 9E-02
albrun [Denmark]	0.338 398	3.383 980 2E-01
alqueire carree [Portugal]	0.004 137 7	4.137 702 7E-03
aranjada [Spain]	0.022 361 8	2.236 176 0E-02
arpent [Belgium]	0.005 924 2	5.924 170 6E-03
arpent [France]	0.029 239 8	2.923 976 6E-02
arpent [Mauritius]	0.023 692 2	2.369 219 1E-02
arpent [Seychelles]	0.023 692 2	2.369 219 1E-02
arpent codatral [Hungary]	0.703 234 9	7.032 348 8E-01
balita [Philippines]	0.035 778 2	3.577 817 5E-02
braza [Panama]	35.842 294	3.584 229 4E+01

are (continued)   **<area>**

Convert To	Standard	Scientific
braza [Philippines]	35.842 294	3.584 229 4E+01
braza carree [Philippines]	3.577 817 5	3.577 817 5E+00
cape morgen [South Africa]	0.011 675	1.167 500 1E-02
carreau de terre [Haiti]	0.007 751 9	7.751 938 0E-03
celemin [Spain]	0.186 219 7	1.862 197 4E-01
chungbo [South Korea]	0.010 083 3	1.008 331 8E-02
cuadra cuadrada [Ecuador]	0.014 312 3	1.431 229 4E-02
cuadra cuadrada [Paraguay]	0.013 315 6	1.331 557 9E-02
dan chung [Hong Kong]	0.148 258	1.482 579 7E-01
dan oranja [Yugoslavia]	0.027 800 9	2.780 094 5E-02
darat [Somalia]	0.012 5	1.250 000 0E-02
dareb [Somalia]	0.04	4.000 000 0E-02
denum [Libya]	0.108 813 9	1.088 139 3E-01
djarib [Iran]	0.092 592 6	9.259 259 3E-02
fanega [Spain]	0.015 529	1.552 901 1E-02
fanga [Spain]	0.015 529	1.552 901 1E-02
fanga carree [Portugal]	0.020 688 5	2.068 851 4E-02
feddan masri [Egypt]	0.023 803 9	2.380 385 6E-02
ferrado [Portugal]	0.137 931	1.379 310 3E-01
geira [Portugal]	0.017 232 5	1.723 246 6E-02
ghamaon [India]	0.018 456 6	1.845 663 8E-02
giornata [Italy]	0.026 315 8	2.631 578 9E-02
gong mu [China]	1	1.000 000 0E+00
hectare	0.01	1.000 000 0E-02
hold [Hungary]	0.023 170 1	2.317 013 8E-02
jareeb [Pakistan]	0.247 105 4	2.471 054 1E-01
jerib [Iran]	0.092 592 6	9.259 259 3E-02
jitro [Czechoslovakia]	0.017 376 2	1.737 619 5E-02
joch [Austria]	0.017 376 2	1.737 619 5E-02
joch [Hungary]	0.023 169 6	2.316 960 1E-02
juchart [Switzerland]	0.027 777 8	2.777 777 8E-02
juchert [Germany]	0.029 348 8	2.934 875 1E-02
kadastral hold [Hungary]	0.703 234 9	7.032 348 8E-01
kanal [India]	0.037 374 7	3.737 468 3E-02
kerad kamel [Egypt]	0.571 428 6	5.714 285 7E-01
kish [China]	0.649 350 7	6.493 506 5E-01
korec [Czechoslovakia]	0.034 758 4	3.475 842 9E-02
kung mou [Taiwan]	1	1.000 000 0E+00
kung mu [China]	1	1.000 000 0E+00
lanaz [Yugoslavia]	0.017 391 3	1.739 130 4E-02
line [Paraguay]	0.013 333 3	1.333 333 3E-02
loan [Philippines]	0.357 781 8	3.577 817 5E-01
maal [Norway]	0.1	1.000 000 0E-01
mal [Norway]	0.1	1.000 000 0E-01
manzana [British Honduras]	0.011 976	1.197 604 8E-02
manzana [Colombia]	0.014 308 2	1.430 819 9E-02
manzana [Costa Rica]	0.014 306 2	1.430 615 2E-02
manzana [El Salvador]	0.014 306 2	1.430 615 2E-02
manzana [Guatemala]	0.014 306 2	1.430 615 2E-02
manzana [Honduras]	0.014 343 1	1.434 308 7E-02
manzana [Nicaragua]	0.014 196 5	1.419 647 9E-02
manzana [Spain]	0.014 311 5	1.431 153 6E-02
marco real [Spain]	0.015 529	1.552 901 1E-02
mau [Vietnam]	0.027 777 8	2.777 777 8E-02
mecate [Belize]	0.191 570 9	1.915 708 8E-01
metze [Austria]	0.052 132 2	5.213 220 7E-02
mil covas [Brazil]	0.033 057 9	3.305 785 1E-02
mira [Czechoslovakia]	0.052 137 6	5.213 764 3E-02
morg [Poland]	0.017 860 3	1.786 033 2E-02
morga [Poland]	0.017 860 3	1.786 033 2E-02
morgen [Germany, Baden]	0.027 777 8	2.777 777 8E-02
morgen [Germany, Bavaria]	0.036 683 8	3.668 378 6E-02

are (continued)   **\<area\>**

Convert To	Standard	Scientific
morgen [Germany, Hanover]	0.038 153 4	3.815 337 7E-02
morgen [Germany, Prussia]	0.039 165 3	3.916 530 9E-02
morgen [Germany, Wurttemberg]	0.031 725 9	3.172 588 8E-02
morgen [Swaziland]	0.011 675	1.167 500 1E-02
mou [China]	0.162 760 4	1.627 604 2E-01
mukhamma [Sudan]	0.030 970 3	3.097 029 9E-02
petit arpent codastral [Hungary]	0.023 170 1	2.317 013 8E-02
pondermaat [Netherlands]	0.027 210 9	2.721 088 4E-02
qada [Sudan]	0.004 534 3	4.534 324 8E-03
quadra [Brazil]	0.574 052 8	5.740 528 1E-01
quadrato [Italy]	0.019 802 0	1.980 198 0E-02
ralica [Yugoslavia]	0.04	4.000 000 0E-02
ralo [Yugoslavia]	0.04	4.000 000 0E-02
roede [Belgium]	1	1.000 000 0E+00
rolo [Yugoslavia]	0.04	4.000 000 0E-02
rood	0.098 841 8	9.884 175 7E-02
saa [Libya]	0.010 416 7	1.041 666 7E-02
shih mow [China]	0.15	1.500 000 0E-01
solares [Ecuador]	0.057 247 5	5.724 753 8E-02
square	10.763 91	1.076 391 0E+01
square arpent [US, survey]	0.029 249	2.924 900 6E-02
square cape rood [South Africa]	7.005 253 9	7.005 253 9E+00
square chain [Gunter or US, survey]	0.247 104 4	2.471 043 9E-01
square chain [Ramden or Engineer]	0.107 638 7	1.076 386 7E-01
square dekameter	1	1.000 000 0E+00
square kafiz [Iran]	1	1.000 000 0E+00
square meter	100	1.000 000 0E+02
square mile [international]	0.000 038 6	3.861 021 6E-05
square pace	172.222 57	1.722 225 7E+02
square perch [US, survey]	3.953 670 3	3.953 670 3E+00
square pole [US, survey]	3.953 670 3	3.953 670 3E+00
square rod [US, survey]	3.953 670 3	3.953 670 3E+00
square rope	2.690 977 6	2.690 977 6E+00
square vara [US, survey, California]	142.332 13	1.423 321 3E+02
square vara [US, survey, Texas]	139.499 72	1.394 997 2E+02
square yard [based on US, survey foot]	119.598 53	1.195 985 3E+02
square yard [international]	119.599	1.195 990 0E+02
stemma [Greece, ancient]	0.078 727 8	7.872 775 9E-02
stremma [Greece, ancient]	0.078 727 8	7.872 775 9E-02
stremma [Switzerland]	0.1	1.000 000 0E-01
strych [Czechoslovakia]	0.034 746 4	3.474 635 2E-02
tagwerk [Germany, Bavaria]	0.029 348 8	2.934 875 1E-02
tagwerk [Germany, Wurttemberg]	0.856 017 8	8.560 178 1E-01
tan [Japan]	0.100 806 5	1.008 064 5E-01
task [Belize]	0.191 570 9	1.915 708 8E-01
tonde hartkorn [Denmark]	0.003 525	3.524 974 4E-03
topo [Peru]	0.036 954 9	3.695 491 5E-02
tundagslatta [Iceland]	0.031 333 2	3.133 322 9E-02
tunland [Finland]	0.020 259 3	2.025 931 9E-02
tunland [Sweden]	0.020 259 3	2.025 931 9E-02
tunnland [Finland]	0.020 259 3	2.025 931 9E-02
tunnland [Sweden]	0.020 259 3	2.025 931 9E-02
vara cuadrada [Guatemala]	143.122 94	1.431 229 4E+02
yoke [Austria]	0.017 376 2	1.737 619 5E-02
yoke [Hungary]	0.023 169 6	2.316 960 1E-02

argienco [Spain]   **\<mass, special - see page 29\>**

Convert To	Standard	Scientific
gram	1.75	1.750 000 0E+00

argienso [Spain]   **\<mass, special - see page 29\>**

Convert To	Standard	Scientific
gram	1.75	1.750 000 0E+00

arine [Belgium]   **\<length, special - see page 29\>**

Convert To	Standard	Scientific
meter	1.2	1.200 000 0E+00

Convert From	<Type of Unit>	
Convert To	Standard	Scientific

arish [Iran]   \<length, special - see page 29\>
  meter-- 1.04----1.040 000 0E+00

arkana [Greece, ancient]   \<length, special - see page 29\>
  meter-- 3.08----3.080 000 0E+00

aroura [Egypt, ancient]   \<area, special - see page 29\>
  square meter---2,034.91----2.034 910 0E+03

arpent [Belgium]   \<area, special - see page 29\>
  are --- 168.8----1.688 000 0E+02

arpent [Canada]   \<length, special - see page 29\>
  meter--58.47----5.847 000 0E+01

arpent [Canada]   \<area, special - see page 29\>
  hectare---0.342----3.420 000 0E-01

arpent [France]   \<area, special - see page 29\>
  are -- 34.2----3.420 000 0E+01

arpent [France]   \<length\>
  chain [Gunter or US, survey]------------------------------- 2.906 585 1----2.906 585 1E+00
  chain [Ramden or Engineer]------------------------------------1.918 35----1.918 350 0E+00
  foot [France]-- 180----1.800 000 0E+02
  foot [international]--- 191.835----1.918 350 0E+02
  foot [US, survey]-- 191.834 62----1.918 346 2E+02
  inch [based on US, survey foot]----------------------- 2,302.015 4----2.302 015 4E+03
  inch [international]--2,302.02----2.302 020 0E+03
  link [Gunter or US, survey] ------------------------------- 290.658 51----2.906 585 1E+02
  link [Ramden or Engineer]-------------------------------------191.835----1.918 350 0E+02
  meter-- 58.471 308----5.847 130 8E+01
  pace [geometrical]--- 3.836 7----3.836 700 0E+00
  pace [US, survey]--------------------------------------- 76.733 847----7.673 384 7E+01
  perch [US, survey]-- 11.626 34----1.162 634 0E+01
  perche [France]-- 10----1.000 000 0E+01
  pied [France]-- 180----1.800 000 0E+02
  rope--9.591 75----9.591 750 0E+00
  yard [based on US, survey foot]----------------------- 63.944 872----6.394 487 2E+01
  yard [international]--63.945----6.394 500 0E+01
  yard [UK]-- 63.945 111----6.394 511 1E+01

arpent [Mauritius]   \<area, special - see page 29\>
  are --- 42.208----4.220 800 0E+01

arpent [Seychelles]   \<area, special - see page 29\>
  are --- 42.208----4.220 800 0E+01

arpent codatral [Hungary]   \<area, special - see page 29\>
  are -- 1.422----1.422 000 0E+00

arratel [Argentina]   \<mass, special - see page 29\>
  gram--- 459.4----4.594 000 0E+02

arratel [Bolivia]   \<mass, special - see page 29\>
  gram--- 460----4.600 000 0E+02

arratel [Brazil]   \<mass, special - see page 29\>
  gram--- 459.05----4.590 500 0E+02

arratel [Chile]   \<mass, special - see page 29\>
  gram--- 460----4.600 000 0E+02

arratel [Colombia]   \<mass, special - see page 29\>
  gram--- 500----5.000 000 0E+02

arratel [Costa Rica]   \<mass, special - see page 29\>
  gram--- 460----4.600 000 0E+02

arratel [Cuba]   \<mass, special - see page 29\>
  gram--- 460.09----4.600 900 0E+02

arratel [Ecuador]   \<mass, special - see page 29\>
  gram--- 460----4.600 000 0E+02

arratel [El Salvador]   \<mass, special - see page 29\>
  gram--- 460----4.600 000 0E+02

| Convert From | | \<Type of Unit\> |
Convert To	Standard	Scientific
arratel [Guatemala]	\<mass, special - see page 29\>	
gram	460 ---	4.600 000 0E+02
arratel [Honduras]	\<mass, special - see page 29\>	
gram	460 ---	4.600 000 0E+02
arratel [Mexico]	\<mass, special - see page 29\>	
gram	460.2 ---	4.602 000 0E+02
arratel [Paraguay]	\<mass, special - see page 29\>	
gram	459 ---	4.590 000 0E+02
arratel [Peru]	\<mass, special - see page 29\>	
gram	460 ---	4.600 000 0E+02
arratel [Philippines]	\<mass, special - see page 29\>	
gram	460 ---	4.600 000 0E+02
arratel [Portugal]	\<mass, special - see page 29\>	
gram	459.05 ---	4.590 500 0E+02
arratel [Spain]	\<mass, special - see page 29\>	
gram	460.09 ---	4.600 900 0E+02
arratel [Venezuela]	\<mass, special - see page 29\>	
gram	460.9 ---	4.609 000 0E+02
arroa [Spain]	\<mass, special - see page 29\>	
kilogram	11.502 ---	1.150 200 0E+01
arroba [Argentina]	\<mass, special - see page 29\>	
kilogram	11.48 ---	1.148 000 0E+01
arroba [Belize]	\<mass, special - see page 29\>	
kilogram	11.34 ---	1.134 000 0E+01
arroba [Bolivia]	\<volume, special - see page 29\>	
liter	30.46 ---	3.046 000 0E+01
arroba [Bolivia]	\<mass, special - see page 29\>	
kilogram	11.5 ---	1.150 000 0E+01
arroba [Brazil]	\<mass, special - see page 29\>	
kilogram	15 ---	1.500 000 0E+01
arroba [British Honduras]	\<mass, special - see page 29\>	
kilogram	11.339 81 ---	1.133 981 0E+01
arroba [Chile]	\<volume, special - see page 29\>	
liter	40 ---	4.000 000 0E+01
arroba [Chile]	\<mass, special - see page 29\>	
kilogram	11.5 ---	1.150 000 0E+01
arroba [Colombia]	\<volume, special - see page 29\>	
liter	16.14 ---	1.614 000 0E+01
arroba [Colombia]	\<mass, special - see page 29\>	
kilogram	12.5 ---	1.250 000 0E+01
arroba [Costa Rica]	\<volume, special - see page 29\>	
liter	17 ---	1.700 000 0E+01
arroba [Costa Rica]	\<mass, special - see page 29\>	
kilogram	11.5 ---	1.150 000 0E+01
arroba [Cuba]	\<volume, special - see page 29\>	
liter	16.14 ---	1.614 000 0E+01
arroba [Cuba]	\<mass, special - see page 29\>	
kilogram	11.502 ---	1.150 200 0E+01
arroba [Dominican Republic]	\<mass, special - see page 29\>	
kilogram	11.34 ---	1.134 000 0E+01
arroba [Ecuador]	\<volume, special - see page 29\>	
liter	16.14 ---	1.614 000 0E+01
arroba [Ecuador]	\<mass, special - see page 29\>	
kilogram	11.5 ---	1.150 000 0E+01

| Convert From | | <Type of Unit> |
Convert To	Standard	Scientific
arroba [El Salvador]	<mass, special - see page 29>	
kilogram	11.5	1.150 000 0E+01
arroba [Guatemala]	<volume, special - see page 29>	
liter	16.14	1.614 000 0E+01
arroba [Guatemala]	<mass, special - see page 29>	
kilogram	11.502	1.150 200 0E+01
arroba [Honduras]	<volume, special - see page 29>	
liter	16.6	1.660 000 0E+01
arroba [Honduras]	<mass, special - see page 29>	
kilogram	11.502	1.150 200 0E+01
arroba [Mexico]	<mass, special - see page 29>	
kilogram	11.506	1.150 600 0E+01
arroba [Nicaragua]	<mass, special - see page 29>	
kilogram	11.5	1.150 000 0E+01
arroba [Paraguay]	<mass, special - see page 29>	
kilogram	11.48	1.148 000 0E+01
arroba [Peru]	<volume, special - see page 29>	
liter	12.563	1.256 300 0E+01
arroba [Peru]	<mass, special - see page 29>	
kilogram	11.502	1.150 200 0E+01
arroba [Philippines]	<mass, special - see page 29>	
kilogram	11.5	1.150 000 0E+01
arroba [Portugal]	<mass, special - see page 29>	
kilogram	14.69	1.469 000 0E+01
arroba [Spain, oil]	<volume, special - see page 29>	
liter	12.563	1.256 300 0E+01
arroba [Spain]	<volume, special - see page 29>	
liter	16.14	1.614 000 0E+01
arroba [Spain]	<mass, special - see page 29>	
kilogram	11.502	1.150 200 0E+01
arroba [Uruguay]	<mass, special - see page 29>	
kilogram	10	1.000 000 0E+01
arroba [Venezuela]	<volume, special - see page 29>	
liter	16.136	1.613 600 0E+01
arroba [Venezuela]	<mass, special - see page 29>	
kilogram	11.5	1.150 000 0E+01
arsheen [Russia]	<length, special - see page 29>	
centimeter	71.12	7.112 000 0E+01
arshin [Bahrain]	<length, special - see page 29>	
centimeter	48.26	4.826 000 0E+01
arshin [Cyprus]	<length, special - see page 29>	
centimeter	60.96	6.096 000 0E+01
arshin [Iran]	<length, special - see page 29>	
meter	1.04	1.040 000 0E+00
arshin [Iraq]	<length, special - see page 29>	
centimeter	74.5	7.450 000 0E+01
arshin [Jordan, land]	<length, special - see page 29>	
centimeter	75.8	7.580 000 0E+01
arshin [Jordan, textiles]	<length, special - see page 29>	
centimeter	68	6.800 000 0E+01
arshin [Lebanon, land]	<length, special - see page 29>	
centimeter	75.8	7.580 000 0E+01
arshin [Morocco]	<length, special - see page 29>	
centimeter	55.88	5.588 000 0E+01

Convert From		\<Type of Unit\>
Convert To	Standard	Scientific

arshin [Russia] — \<length, special - see page 29\>
centimeter — 71.12 — 7.112 000 0E+01

arshin [Saudi Arabia] — \<length, special - see page 29\>
centimeter — 45.7 — 4.570 000 0E+01

arshin [Syria] — \<length, special - see page 29\>
centimeter — 70 — 7.000 000 0E+01

arshin [Turkey] — \<length, special - see page 29\>
meter — 1 — 1.000 000 0E+00

arshyn [Turkey] — \<length, special - see page 29\>
centimeter — 71.1 — 7.110 000 0E+01

artaba [Egypt, ancient] — \<volume, special - see page 29\>
liter — 46.7 — 4.670 000 0E+01

artaba [Iran] — \<volume, special - see page 29\>
liter — 66 — 6.600 000 0E+01

artabe [Rome, ancient] — \<volume, special - see page 29\>
liter — 36.45 — 3.645 000 0E+01

artal [Ethiopia] — \<mass, special - see page 29\>
gram — 311 — 3.110 000 0E+02

artal [Israel] — \<mass, special - see page 29\>
kilogram — 2.88 — 2.880 000 0E+00

artal [Turkey] — \<mass, special - see page 29\>
gram — 641.472 5 — 6.414 725 0E+02

as [Rome, ancient] — \<mass, special - see page 29\>
gram — 327 — 3.270 000 0E+02

as [Sweden] — \<mass, special - see page 29\>
gram — 0.048 042 — 4.804 200 0E-02

asba [Egypt, ancient] — \<length, special - see page 29\>
centimeter — 3.125 — 3.125 000 0E+00

ass [Germany] — \<mass, special - see page 29\>
gram — 0.048 — 4.800 000 0E-02

ass [Italy] — \<mass, special - see page 29\>
gram — 0.038 — 3.800 000 0E-02

astronomical unit — \<length\>
bevameter — 149.597 87 — 1.495 978 7E+02
foot [international] — >>> — 4.908 066 6E+11
foot [US, survey] — >>> — 4.908 056 8E+11
kiloparsec — <<< — 4.848 136 8E-09
light year [based on mean Julian year] — 0.000 015 8 — 1.581 250 7E-05
megaparsec — <<< — 4.848 136 8E-12
meter — >>> — 1.495 978 7E+11
mile [international] — >>> — 9.295 580 7E+07
mile [US, statute] — >>> — 9.295 562 1E+07
mile [US, survey] — >>> — 9.295 562 1E+07
myriameter — >>> — 1.495 978 7E+07
parsec — 0.000 004 8 — 4.848 136 8E-06
siriometer — 0.000 001 — 1.000 000 0E-06

atado [Costa Rica] — \<mass, special - see page 29\>
kilogram — 1.035 — 1.035 000 0E+00

atmosphere [metric] — \<pressure\>
atmosphere [standard] — 0.967 841 1 — 9.678 411 1E-01
atmosphere [technical] — 1 — 1.000 000 0E+00
bar — 0.980 665 — 9.806 650 0E-01
centimeter of mercury [0 °C, by convention] — 73.555 914 — 7.355 591 4E+01
foot of mercury [0 °C, by convention] — 2.413 251 8 — 2.413 251 8E+00
gram-force/square centimeter — 1,000 — 1.000 000 0E+03
inch of mercury [0 °C, by convention] — 28.959 021 — 2.895 902 1E+01
inch of water [4 °C, by convention] — 393.700 79 — 3.937 007 9E+02
kilogram-force/square centimeter — 1 — 1.000 000 0E+00

Convert To	Standard	Scientific
kilopond/square centimeter	1	1.000 000 0E+00
kip/square foot	2.048 161 4	2.048 161 4E+00
millimeter of mercury [0 °C, by convention]	735.559 14	7.355 591 4E+02
millimeter of water [4 °C, by convention]	10,000	1.000 000 0E+04
ounce-force/square inch	227.573 49	2.275 734 9E+00
pascal	98,066.5	9.806 650 0E+04
pieze [France]	98.066 5	9.806 650 0E+01
pound-force/square inch	14.223 343	1.422 334 3E+01
sthene/square meter [France]	98.066 5	9.806 650 0E+01
ton-force/square foot [short]	1.024 080 7	1.024 080 7E+00
ton-force/square meter [metric]	10	1.000 000 0E+01
torr	735.559 24	7.355 592 4E+02

atmosphere [physical]   \<pressure\>

Convert To	Standard	Scientific
atmosphere [standard]	1	1.000 000 0E+00
atmosphere [technical]	1.033 227 5	1.033 227 5E+00
bar	1.013 25	1.013 250 0E+00
centimeter of mercury [0 °C, by convention]	75.999 989	7.599 998 9E+01
foot of mercury [0 °C, by convention]	2.493 438	2.493 438 0E+00
foot of water [4 °C, by convention]	33.898 538	3.389 853 8E+01
inch of mercury [0 °C, by convention]	29.921 256	2.992 125 6E+01
inch of water [4 °C, by convention]	406.782 46	4.067 824 6E+02
kilogram-force/square centimeter	1.033 227 5	1.033 227 5E+00
kilopond/square centimeter	1.033 227 5	1.033 227 5E+00
kip/square foot	2.116 216	2.116 216 6E+00
millimeter of mercury [0 °C, by convention]	759.999 89	7.599 998 9E+02
millimeter of water [4 °C, by convention]	10,332.275	1.033 227 5E+04
newton/square millimeter	0.101 325	1.013 250 0E-01
ounce-force/square inch	235.135 18	2.351 351 8E+02
pascal	101,325	1.013 250 0E+05
pound-force/square inch	14.695 949	1.469 594 9E+01
ton-force/square foot [short]	1.058 108 3	1.058 108 3E+00
ton-force/square meter [metric]	10.332 275	1.033 227 5E+01
torr	760	7.600 000 0E+02

atmosphere [standard, pre-1954]   \<pressure\>

Convert To	Standard	Scientific
atmosphere [standard]	1.000 000 1	1.000 000 1E+00
atmosphere [technical]	1.033 227 6	1.033 227 6E+00
bar	1.013 250 1	1.013 250 1E+00
centimeter of mercury [0 °C, by convention]	76	7.600 000 0E+01
centimeter of water [4 °C, by convention]	1,033.227 6	1.033 227 6E+03
foot of mercury [0 °C, by convention]	2.493 438 3	2.493 438 3E+00
foot of water [4 °C, by convention]	33.898 543	3.389 854 3E+01
gram-force/square centimeter	1.033 227 6	1.033 227 6E+00
inch of mercury [0 °C, by convention]	29.921 26	2.992 126 0E+01
inch of water [4 °C, by convention]	406.782 52	4.067 825 2E+02
kilogram-force/square centimeter	1.033 227 6	1.033 227 6E+00
kilopond/square centimeter	1.033 227 6	1.033 227 6E+00
kip/square foot	2.116 216 9	2.116 216 9E+00
millimeter of mercury [0 °C, by convention]	760	7.600 000 0E+02
newton/square millimeter	0.101 325	1.013 250 0E-01
ounce-force/square inch	235.135 21	2.351 352 1E+02
pascal	101,325.01	1.013 250 1E+05
pound-force/square inch	14.695 951	1.469 595 1E+01
ton-force/square foot [short]	1.058 108 5	1.058 108 5E+00
ton-force/square meter [metric]	10.332 276	1.033 227 6E+01
torr	760.000 11	7.600 001 1E+02

atmosphere [standard]   \<pressure\>

Convert To	Standard	Scientific
atmosphere [physical]	1	1.000 000 0E+00
atmosphere [technical]	1.033 227 5	1.033 227 5E+00
bar	1.013 25	1.013 250 0E+00
centimeter of mercury [0 °C, by convention]	75.999 989	7.599 998 9E+01
centimeter of water [4 °C, by convention]	1,033.227 5	1.033 227 5E+03
foot of mercury [0 °C, by convention]	2.493 438	2.493 438 0E+00
foot of water [4 °C, by convention]	33.898 538	3.389 853 8E+01

	Standard	Scientific
inch of mercury [0 °C, by convention]	29.921 256	2.992 125 6E+01
inch of water [4 °C, by convention]	406.782 46	4.067 824 6E+02
kilogram-force/square centimeter	1.033 227 5	1.033 227 5E+00
kilopond/square centimeter	1.033 227 5	1.033 227 5E+00
kip/square foot	2.116 216 6	2.116 216 6E+00
millimeter of mercury [0 °C, by convention]	759.999 89	7.599 998 9E+02
millimeter of water [4 °C, by convention]	10,332.275	1.033 227 5E+04
newton/square millimeter	0.101 325	1.013 250 0E-01
pascal	101,325	1.013 250 0E+05
pieze [France]	101.325	1.013 250 0E+02
pound-force/square inch	14.695 949	1.469 594 9E+01
sthene/square meter [France]	101.325	1.013 250 0E+02
ton-force/square foot [short]	1.058 108 3	1.058 108 3E+00
ton-force/square meter [metric]	10.332 275	1.033 227 5E+01
torr	760	7.600 000 0E+02
atmosphere [technical]		**\<pressure\>**
atmosphere [metric]	1	1.000 000 0E+00
atmosphere [standard]	0.967 841 1	9.678 411 1E-01
bar	0.980 665	9.806 650 0E-01
centimeter of mercury [0 °C, by convention]	73.555 914	7.355 591 4E+01
centimeter of water [4 °C, by convention]	1,000	1.000 000 0E+03
decibar	9.806 65	9.806 650 0E+00
foot of mercury [0 °C, by convention]	2.413 251 8	2.413 251 8E+00
foot of water [4 °C, by convention]	32.808 399	3.280 839 9E+01
gram-force/square centimeter	1,000	1.000 000 0E+03
inch of mercury [0 °C, by convention]	28.959 021	2.895 902 1E+01
inch of water [4 °C, by convention]	393.700 79	3.937 007 9E+02
kilogram-force/square centimeter	1	1.000 000 0E+00
kilopond/square centimeter	1	1.000 000 0E+00
kip/square foot	2.048 161 4	2.048 161 4E+00
millimeter of mercury [0 °C, by convention]	735.559 14	7.355 591 4E+02
millimeter of water [4 °C, by convention]	10,000	1.000 000 0E+04
pascal	98,065.5	9.806 650 0E+04
pieze [France]	98.066 5	9.806 650 0E+01
pound-force/square inch	14.223 343	1.422 334 3E+01
sthene/square meter [France]	98.066 5	9.806 650 0E+01
ton-force/square foot [short]	1.024 080 7	1.024 080 7E+00
ton-force/square meter [metric]	10	1.000 000 0E+01
torr	735.559 24	7.355 592 4E+02
atomic mass unit [chemical, 1960, eq. energy]		**\<energy\>**
atomic mass unit [physical, 1960, eq. energy]	1.000 272 8	1.000 272 8E+00
atomic mass unit [unified, C-12, 1973, eq. energy]	0.999 887 3	9.998 872 8E-01
atomic mass unit [unified, C-12, 1986, eq. energy]	0.999 893 4	9.998 933 8E-01
deuteron rest mass [atomic physics, eq. energy]	0.496 581 6	4.965 815 5E-01
electron rest mass [atomic physics, eq. energy]	1,822.694 2	1.822 694 2E+03
electronvolt	>>>	9.313 950 0E+08
gigaelectronvolt	0.931 395	9.313 950 0E-01
hartree [atomic physics, eq. energy]	>>>	3.422 812 2E+07
joule	<<<	1.492 260 0E-10
kayser [atomic physics, eq. energy]	>>>	7.512 204 5E+12
kelvin [atomic physics, eq. energy]	>>>	1.080 832 4E+13
kiloelectronvolt	931,395	9.313 950 0E+05
megaelectronvolt	931.395	9.313 950 0E+02
muon rest mass [atomic physics, eq. energy]	8.815 154 3	8.815 154 3E+00
neutron rest mass [atomic physics, eq. energy]	0.991 303 8	9.913 038 2E-01
proton rest mass [atomic physics, eq. energy]	0.992 670 2	9.926 702 4E-01
rydberg [atomic physics, eq. energy]	>>>	6.845 543 2E+07
teraelectronvolt	0.000 931 4	9.313 950 0E-04
atomic mass unit [chemical, 1960]		**\<mass\>**
atomic mass unit [physical, 1960]	1.000 275	1.000 275 0E+00
atomic mass unit [unified, C-12,1986]	0.999 821 1	9.998 210 9E-01
avogram	0.999 821 1	9.998 210 9E-01
dalton	0.999 821 1	9.998 210 9E-01

grain		<<<----2.562 146 7E-23
kilogram		<<<----1.660 243 1E-27
yoctogram	1.660 243 1	1.660 243 1E+00

atomic mass unit [chemical, 1973] <mass>

atomic mass unit [physical, 1973]	1.000 275 0	1.000 275 0E+00
atomic mass unit [unified, C-12,1973]	0.999 957	9.999 570 0E-01
atomic mass unit [unified, C-12,1986]	0.999 972 2	9.999 722 4E-01
avogram	0.999 972 3	9.999 722 5E-01
dalton	0.999 972 2	9.999 722 4E-01
grain		<<<----2.562 534 0E-23
kilogram		<<<----1.660 494 1E-27
yoctogram	1.660 494 1	1.660 494 1E+00

atomic mass unit [chemical, 1986] <mass>

atomic mass unit [physical, 1986]	1.000 275 0	1.000 275 0E+00
atomic mass unit [unified, C-12,1986]	0.999 957	9.999 570 0E-01
avogram	0.999 957	9.999 570 1E-01
dalton	0.999 957	9.999 570 0E-01
grain		<<<----2.562 495 0E-23
kilogram		<<<----1.660 468 8E-27
yoctogram	1.660 468 8	1.660 468 8E+00

atomic mass unit [physical, 1960, eq. energy] <energy>

atomic mass unit [chemical, 1960, eq. energy]	0.999 727 3	9.997 272 9E-01
atomic mass unit [unified, C-12, 1973, eq. energy]	0.999 614 6	9.996 146 0E-01
atomic mass unit [unified, C-12, 1986, eq. energy]	0.999 620 7	9.996 207 0E-01
deuteron rest mass [atomic physics, eq. energy]	0.496 446 1	4.964 461 3E-01
electron rest mass [atomic physics, eq. energy]	1,822.197 1	1.822 197 1E+03
electronvolt		>>>----9.311 410 0E+08
gram [atomic physics, eq. energy]		<<<----1.659 910 3E-24
hartree [atomic physics, eq. energy]		>>>----3.421 878 8E+07
joule		<<<----1.491 853 0E-10
kiloelectronvolt	931,141	9.311 410 0E+05
megaelectronvolt	931,141	9.311 410 0E+02
muon rest mass [atomic physics, eq. energy]	8.812 750 3	8.812 750 3E+00
neutron rest mass [atomic physics, eq. energy]	0.991 033 5	9.910 334 8E-01
proton rest mass [atomic physics, eq. energy]	0.992 399 5	9.923 995 3E-01
rydberg [atomic physics, eq. energy]		>>>----6.843 676 3E+07

atomic mass unit [physical, 1960] <mass>

atomic mass unit [chemical, 1960]	0.999 725 1	9.997 250 9E-01
atomic mass unit [unified, C-12,1986]	0.999 546 2	9.995 462 2E-01
avogram	0.999 546 2	9.995 462 3E-01
dalton	0.999 546 2	9.995 462 2E-01
grain		<<<----2.561 442 3E-23
kilogram		<<<----1.659 786 7E-27
yoctogram	1.659 786 7	1.659 786 7E+00

atomic mass unit [physical, 1973] <mass>

atomic mass unit [chemical, 1973]	0.999 725 1	9.997 250 9E-01
atomic mass unit [unified, C-12,1973]	0.999 682 1	9.996 821 0E-01
atomic mass unit [unified, C-12,1986]	0.999 697 3	9.996 973 4E-01
avogram	0.999 697 3	9.996 973 4E-01
dalton	0.999 697 3	9.996 973 4E-01
grain		<<<----2.561 829 5E-23
kilogram		<<<----1.660 037 6E-27
yoctogram	1.660 037 6	1.660 037 6E+00

atomic mass unit [physical, 1986] <mass>

atomic mass unit [chemical, 1986]	0.999 725 1	9.997 250 9E-01
atomic mass unit [unified, C-12,1986]	0.999 682 1	9.996 821 0E-01
avogram	0.999 682 1	9.996 821 1E-01
dalton	0.999 682 1	9.996 821 0E-01
grain		<<<----2.561 790 5E-23
kilogram		<<<----1.660 012 3E-27
yoctogram	1.660 012 3	1.660 012 3E+00

Convert From / Convert To	Standard	\<Type of Unit\> Scientific

atomic mass unit [unified, C-12, 1973, eq. energy] \<energy\>

Convert To	Standard	Scientific
atomic mass unit [chemical, 1960, eq. energy]	1.000 112 7	1.000 112 7E+00
atomic mass unit [physical, 1960, eq. energy]	1.000 385 5	1.000 385 5E+00
atomic mass unit [unified, C-12, 1986, eq. energy]	1.000 006 1	1.000 006 1E+00
deuteron rest mass [atomic physics, eq. energy]	0.496 637 5	4.966 375 3E-01
electron rest mass [atomic physics, eq. energy]	1,822.899 6	1.822 899 6E+03
electronvolt	>>>	9.315 000 0E+08
hartree [atomic physics, eq. energy]	>>>	3.423 198 1E+07
joule	<<<	1.492 428 2E-10
kiloelectronvolt	931,500	9.315 000 0E+05
megaelectronvolt	931.5	9.315 000 0E+02
muon rest mass [atomic physics, eq. energy]	8.816 148	8.816 148 0E+00
neutron rest mass [atomic physics, eq. energy]	0.991 415 6	9.914 155 8E-01
proton rest mass [atomic physics, eq. energy]	0.992 782 2	9.927 821 5E-01
rydberg [atomic physics, eq. energy]	>>>	6.846 314 9E+07
teraelectronvolt	0.000 931 5	9.315 000 0E-04

atomic mass unit [unified, C-12, 1986, eq. energy] \<energy\>

Convert To	Standard	Scientific
atomic mass unit [chemical, 1960, eq. energy]	1.000 106 6	1.000 106 6E+00
atomic mass unit [physical, 1960, eq. energy]	1.000 379 4	1.000 379 4E+00
atomic mass unit [unified, C-12, 1973, eq. energy]	0.999 993 9	9.999 939 0E-01
deuteron rest mass [atomic physics, eq. energy]	0.496 634 5	4.966 345 0E-01
electron rest mass [atomic physics, eq. energy]	1,822.888 5	1.822 888 5E+03
electronvolt	>>>	9.314 943 0E+08
hartree [atomic physics, eq. energy]	>>>	3.423 177 2E+07
hertz [atomic physics, eq. energy]	>>>	2.252 342 4E+23
joule	<<<	1.492 419 1E-10
kiloelectronvolt	931,494.32	9.314 943 0E+05
megaelectronvolt	931.494 32	9.314 943 2E+02
muon rest mass [atomic physics, eq. energy]	8.816 094 3	8.816 094 0E+00
neutron rest mass [atomic physics, eq. energy]	0.991 409 5	9.914 095 3E-01
proton rest mass [atomic physics, eq. energy]	0.992 776 1	9.927 761 0E-01
rydberg [atomic physics, eq. energy]	>>>	6.846 273 1E+07
teraelectronvolt	0.000 931 5	9.314 943 2E-04

atomic mass unit [unified, C-12,1960] \<mass\>

Convert To	Standard	Scientific
atomic mass unit [chemical, 1960]	1.000 043	1.000 043 0E+00
atomic mass unit [physical, 1960]	1.000 318	1.000 318 0E+00
atomic mass unit [unified, C-12,1986]	0.999 864 1	9.998 640 8E-01
avogram	0.999 864 1	9.998 640 8E-01
dalton	0.999 864 1	9.998 640 8E-01
grain	<<<	2.562 256 8E-23
kilogram	<<<	1.660 314 5E-27
yoctogram	1.660 314 5	1.660 314 5E+00

atomic mass unit [unified, C-12,1973] \<mass\>

Convert To	Standard	Scientific
atomic mass unit [chemical, 1973]	1.000 043	1.000 043 0E+00
atomic mass unit [physical, 1973]	1.000 318	1.000 318 0E+00
atomic mass unit [unified, C-12,1986]	1.000 015 2	1.000 015 2E+00
avogram	1.000 015 2	1.000 015 2E+00
dalton	1.000 015 2	1.000 015 2E+00
grain	<<<	2.562 644 2E-23
kilogram	<<<	1.660 565 5E-27
yoctogram	1.660 565 5	1.660 565 5E+00

atomic mass unit [unified, C-12,1986] \<mass\>

Convert To	Standard	Scientific
atomic mass unit [chemical, 1986]	1.000 043	1.000 043 0E+00
atomic mass unit [physical, 1986]	1.000 318	1.000 318 0E+00
avogram	1	1.000 000 0E+00
dalton	1	1.000 000 0E+00
grain	<<<	2.562 605 1E-23
kilogram	<<<	1.660 540 2E-27
milli-mass-unit	1,000	1.000 000 0E+03
yoctogram	1.660 540 2	1.660 540 2E+00

atting [Sweden] \<volume, special - see page 29\>

Convert To	Standard	Scientific
liter	15.702 7	1.570 270 0E+01

attobar \<pressure\>

atmosphere [standard]	<<<	9.869 232 7E-19
atmosphere [technical]	<<<	1.019 716 2E-18
bar	<<<	1.000 000 0E-18
barye [France]	<<<	1.000 000 0E-12
centimeter of water [4 °C, by convention]	<<<	1.019 716 2E-15
dyne/square centimeter	<<<	1.000 000 0E-12
micrometer of water [4 °C, by convention]	<<<	1.019 716 2E-11
millimeter of water [4 °C, by convention]	<<<	1.019 716 2E-14
pascal	<<<	1.000 000 0E-13
picopascal	0.1	1.000 000 0E-01
poundal/square foot	<<<	6.719 689 8E-14
torr	<<<	7.500 616 8E-16

attocandela \<luminous intensity\>

candela	<<<	1.000 000 0E-18

attogram \<mass\>

atomic mass unit [chemical, 1986]	602,239.56	6.022 395 6E+05
atomic mass unit [physical, 1986]	602,405.17	6.024 051 7E+05
atomic mass unit [unified, C-12,1986]	602,213.67	6.022 136 7E+05
avogram	602,213.67	6.022 136 7E+05
dalton	602,213.67	6.022 136 7E+05
gamma	<<<	1.000 000 0E-12
grain	<<<	1.543 235 8E-17
kilogram	<<<	1.000 000 0E-21
zeptogram	1,000	1.000 000 0E+03

attojoule \<energy\>

1/centimeter [atomic physics, eq. energy]	50,341.125	5.034 112 5E+04
atomic mass unit [chemical, 1960, eq. energy]	<<<	6.701 245 5E-09
atomic mass unit [physical, 1960, eq. energy]	<<<	6.703 073 3E-09
atomic mass unit [unified, C-12, 1973, eq. energy]	<<<	6.700 489 9E-09
atomic mass unit [unified, C-12, 1986, eq. energy]	<<<	6.700 530 8E-09
deuteron rest mass [atomic physics, eq. energy]	<<<	3.327 714 8E-09
electron rest mass [atomic physics, eq. energy]	0.000 012 2	1.221 432 1E-05
electronvolt	6.241 506 4	6.241 506 4E+00
femtojoule	0.001	1.000 000 0E-03
hartree [atomic physics, eq. energy]	0.229 371	2.293 710 4E-01
joule	<<<	1.000 000 0E-18
kayser [atomic physics, eq. energy]	50,341.125	5.034 112 5E+04
kelvin [atomic physics, eq. energy]	72,429.233	7.242 923 3E+04
muon rest mass [atomic physics, eq. energy]	<<<	5.907 251 1E-08
neutron rest mass [atomic physics, eq. energy]	<<<	6.642 970 1E-09
proton rest mass [atomic physics, eq. energy]	<<<	6.652 126 8E-09
rydberg [atomic physics, eq. energy]	0.458 736 6	4.587 366 4E-01

attoliter \<volume\>

cubic inch	<<<	6.102 374 4E-17
cubic meter	<<<	1.000 000 0E-21
cubic micrometer	0.001	1.000 000 0E-03
dram [US, liquid]	<<<	2.705 121 8E-16
drop [US, liquid]	<<<	1.217 304 8E-14
femtoliter	0.001	1.000 000 0E-03
lambda	<<<	1.000 000 0E-12
liter	<<<	1.000 000 0E-18
scruple [UK, liquid]	<<<	8.446 819 1E-16

attometer \<length\>

bicron	0.000 001	1.000 000 0E-06
fermi	0.001	1.000 000 0E-03
meter	<<<	1.000 000 0E-18
microinch	<<<	3.937 007 9E-11
micromicron	0.000 001	1.000 000 0E-06
micron	<<<	1.000 000 0E-12
mil	<<<	3.937 007 9E-14
millimicron	<<<	1.000 000 0E-09

stigma	0.000 001	1.000 000 0E-06
tenthmeter	\<\<\<	1.000 000 0E-08
thou	\<\<\<	3.937 007 9E-14
x-unit	0.000 01	9.979 320 9E-06

attomole   \<amount of substance\>

mole	\<\<\<	1.000 000 0E-18

attonewton   \<force\>

crinal	\<\<\<	1.000 000 0E-17
dyne	\<\<\<	1.000 000 0E-13
grain-force	\<\<\<	1.573 662 6E-15
gram-force	\<\<\<	1.019 716 2E-16
newton	\<\<\<	1.000 000 0E-18
ounce-force	\<\<\<	3.596 943 1E-18
pound-force	\<\<\<	2.248 089 4E-19
poundal	\<\<\<	7.233 013 8E-18

attopascal   \<pressure\>

atmosphere [standard]	\<\<\<	9.869 232 7E-24
atmosphere [technical]	\<\<\<	1.019 716 2E-23
micrometer of mercury [0 °C, by convention]	\<\<\<	7.500 615 8E-18
micrometer of water [4 °C, by convention]	\<\<\<	1.019 716 2E-16
pascal	\<\<\<	1.000 000 0E-18
yoctobar	10	1.000 000 0E+01

attowatt   \<power\>

calorie/hour [I.T.]	\<\<\<	8.598 452 3E-16
cubic meter atmosphere/hour	\<\<\<	3.552 923 8E-14
dyne centimeter/hour	\<\<\<	3.600 000 0E-08
erg/hour	\<\<\<	3.600 000 0E-08
foot pound-force/hour	\<\<\<	2.655 223 7E-15
foot poundal/hour	\<\<\<	8.542 929 7E-14
gram-force centimeter/hour	\<\<\<	3.670 978 4E-11
joule/hour	\<\<\<	3.600 000 0E-15
kilogram-force meter/hour	\<\<\<	3.670 978 4E-16
kilopond meter/hour	\<\<\<	3.670 978 4E-16
lumen [green light at 100% efficiency]	\<\<\<	6.850 000 0E-16
newton meter/hour	\<\<\<	3.600 000 0E-15
volt ampere	\<\<\<	1.000 000 0E-18
watt	\<\<\<	1.000 000 0E-18

aum [South Africa]   \<volume, special - see page 29\>

liter	143.841 6	1.438 416 0E+02

aune [Belgium]   \<length, special - see page 29\>

meter	1.2	1.200 000 0E+00

aune [Dominican Republic]   \<length, special - see page 29\>

meter	1.188	1.188 000 0E+00

aune [France]   \<length, special - see page 29\>

meter	1.188	1.188 000 0E+00

aune [Germany]   \<length, special - see page 29\>

centimeter	66.69	6.669 000 0E+01

aune [Haiti]   \<length, special - see page 29\>

meter	1.191	1.191 000 0E+00

aune [Switzerland]   \<length, special - see page 29\>

meter	1.2	1.200 000 0E+00

aureus [Rome, ancient]   \<mass, special - see page 29\>

gram	7.8	7.800 000 0E+00

avogram   \<mass\>

atomic mass unit [chemical, 1986]	1.000 043	1.000 043 0E+00
atomic mass unit [physical, 1986]	1.000 318	1.000 318 0E+00
atomic mass unit [unified, C-12,1986]	1	1.000 000 0E+00
dalton	1	1.000 000 0E+00
grain	\<\<\<	2.562 605 1E-23
gram	\<\<\<	1.660 540 2E-24

| Convert From | <Type of Unit> | |
Convert To	Standard	Scientific
kilogram	<<<1.660 540 2E–27	
milli-mass-unit	1,000	1.000 000 0E+03
yoctogram	1.660 540 2	1.660 540 2E+00
azba [Hebrew, ancient]	<length, special - see page 29>	
millimeter	18.72	1.872 000 0E+01
azumbre [Colombia]	<volume, special - see page 29>	
liter	2.02	2.020 000 0E+00
azumbre [Panama]	<volume, special - see page 29>	
liter	2.02	2.020 000 0E+00
azumbre [Spain]	<volume, special - see page 29>	
liter	2.02	2.020 000 0E+00
baa [Egypt]	<length, special - see page 29>	
meter	3	3.000 000 0E+00
baa [Oman]	<length, special - see page 29>	
meter	1.44	1.440 000 0E+00
baa [Saudi Arabia]	<length, special - see page 29>	
centimeter	13.97	1.397 000 0E+01
baar [Batavia, large]	<mass, special - see page 29>	
kilogram	277.834	2.778 340 0E+02
baar [Batavia, small]	<mass, special - see page 29>	
kilogram	185.223	1.852 230 0E+02
baar [Sumatra]	<mass, special - see page 29>	
kilogram	192.026	1.920 260 0E+02
baer [Batavia, large]	<mass, special - see page 29>	
kilogram	277.834	2.778 340 0E+02
baer [Batavia, small]	<mass, special - see page 29>	
kilogram	185.223	1.852 230 0E+02
baer [Sumatra]	<mass, special - see page 29>	
kilogram	192.026	1.920 260 0E+02
bag [Burma]	<volume, special - see page 29>	
hectoliter	1.227	1.227 000 0E+00
bag [Sierra Leone]	<volume, special - see page 29>	
liter	80	8.000 000 0E+01
bag [UK]	<volume, special - see page 29>	
liter	109.103	1.091 030 0E+02
bag of cement [US, dry]	<mass>	
kilogram	42.637 683	4.263 768 3E+01
pound	94	9.400 000 0E+01
bahar [Batavia, large]	<mass, special - see page 29>	
kilogram	277.834	2.778 340 0E+02
bahar [Batavia, small]	<mass, special - see page 29>	
kilogram	185.223	1.852 230 0E+02
bahar [India]	<mass, special - see page 29>	
kilogram	261.27	2.612 700 0E+02
bahar [Iran]	<length, special - see page 29>	
centimeter	3.25	3.250 000 0E+00
bahar [Oman]	<mass, special - see page 29>	
kilogram	807.96	8.079 600 0E+02
bahar [Saudi Arabia]	<mass, special - see page 29>	
kilogram	204.1	2.041 000 0E+02
bahar [Sumatra]	<mass, special - see page 29>	
kilogram	192.026	1.920 260 0E+02
baht [Burma]	<mass, special - see page 29>	
gram	16.33	1.633 000 0E+01
baht [Laos]	<mass, special - see page 29>	
gram	15	1.500 000 0E+01

Convert From		<Type of Unit>
Convert To	Standard	Scientific

baht [Thailand] <mass, special - see page 29>
gram ----15--- 1.500 000 0E+01

bahu [Indonesia] <area, special - see page 29>
hectare ----0.709 65--- 7.096 500 0E-01

bai [Laos] <mass, special - see page 29>
gram ----37.5--- 3.750 000 0E+01

bak [Laos] <mass, special - see page 29>
gram ----3.75--- 3.750 000 0E+00

bak [Thailand] <mass, special - see page 29>
gram ----3.75--- 3.750 000 0E+00

baker's dozen <units>
unit ----13--- 1.300 000 0E+01

balde [Ecuador] <volume, special - see page 29>
liter ----10--- 1.000 000 0E+01

bale [Belgium] <mass, special - see page 29>
kilogram ----93.732--- 9.373 200 0E+01

bale [Indonesia] <mass, special - see page 29>
kilogram ----180--- 1.800 000 0E+02

bale [Netherlands] <mass, special - see page 29>
kilogram ----93.732--- 9.373 200 0E+01

bale [New Zealand] <mass, special - see page 29>
kilogram ----152--- 1.520 000 0E+02

bale [Philippines] <mass, special - see page 29>
kilogram ----126.5--- 1.265 000 0E+02

bale [UK] <mass, special - see page 29>
kilogram ----108.872--- 1.088 720 0E+02

balita [Philippines] <area, special - see page 29>
are ----27.95--- 2.795 000 0E+01

ballen [Belgium] <mass, special - see page 29>
kilogram ----93.732--- 9.373 200 0E+01

ballen [Netherlands] <mass, special - see page 29>
kilogram ----93.732--- 9.373 200 0E+01

balli [South Africa] <volume, special - see page 29>
liter ----46--- 4.600 000 0E+01

balthazar [champagne bottle] <champagne bottle size>
bottle [wine, standard] ----16--- 1.600 000 0E+01
liter ----12--- 1.200 000 0E+01

bamboo [Burma] <length, special - see page 29>
meter ----3.2--- 3.200 000 0E+00

ban [Thailand] <volume, special - see page 29>
liter ----1,000--- 1.000 000 0E+03

bandle [Ireland] <length, special - see page 29>
meter ----0.61--- 6.100 000 0E-01

bandu [Malaysia] <volume, special - see page 29>
liter ----45.46--- 4.546 000 0E+01

bandu [Singapore] <volume, special - see page 29>
liter ----45.46--- 4.546 000 0E+01

baquila [Egypt] <mass, special - see page 29>
gram ----2.34--- 2.340 000 0E+00

bar <pressure>
atmosphere [standard] ----0.986 923 3--- 9.869 232 7E-01
atmosphere [technical] ----1.019 716 2--- 1.019 716 2E+00
centimeter of mercury [0 °C, by convention] ----75.006 158--- 7.500 615 8E+01
centimeter of water [4 °C, by convention] ----1,019.716 2--- 1.019 716 2E+03
foot of mercury [0 °C, by convention] ----2.460 831 9--- 2.460 831 9E+00
foot of water [4 °C, by convention] ----33.455 256--- 3.345 525 6E+01

Convert From	<Type of Unit>	
Convert To	Standard	Scientific

	Standard	Scientific
gram-force/square centimeter	1,019.716 2	1.019 716 2E+03
inch of mercury [0 °C, by convention]	29.529 983	2.952 998 3E+01
inch of water [4 °C, by convention]	401.463 08	4.014 630 8E+02
kilogram-force/square centimeter	1.019 716 2	1.019 716 2E+00
kilopond/square centimeter	1.019 716 2	1.019 716 2E+00
kip/square foot	2.088 543 4	2.088 543 4E+00
millimeter of mercury [0 °C, by convention]	750.061 58	7.500 615 8E+02
millimeter of water [4 °C, by convention]	10,197.162	1.019 716 2E+04
newton/square millimeter	0.1	1.000 000 0E−01
ounce-force/square inch	232.060 38	2.320 603 8E+02
pascal	100,000	1.000 000 0E+05
pieze [France]	100	1.000 000 0E+02
pound-force/square inch	14.503 774	1.450 377 4E+01
sthene/square meter [France]	100	1.000 000 0E+02
ton-force/square foot [short]	1.044 271 7	1.044 271 7E+00
ton-force/square meter [metric]	10.197 162	1.019 716 2E+01
torr	750.061 68	7.500 616 8E+02
bar [Batavia, large]	**<mass, special - see page 29>**	
kilogram	277.834	2.778 340 2E+02
bar [Batavia, small]	**<mass, special - see page 29>**	
kilogram	185.223	1.852 230 0E+02
bar [Sumatra]	**<mass, special - see page 29>**	
kilogram	192.026	1.920 260 0E+02
bara [Singapore]	**<mass, special - see page 29>**	
kilogram	181.4	1.814 000 0E+02
barad	**<pressure>**	
dyne/square centimeter	1	1.000 000 0E+00
pascal	0.1	1.000 000 0E−01
pound-force/square foot	0.000 014 5	1.450 377 4E−05
baril [Argentina]	**<volume, special - see page 29>**	
liter	76	7.600 000 0E+01
baril [France]	**<volume, special - see page 29>**	
liter	158.982 8	1.589 828 0E+02
baril [Greece]	**<volume, special - see page 29>**	
liter	40	4.000 000 0E+01
baril [Libya]	**<volume, special - see page 29>**	
liter	64.44	6.444 000 0E+01
baril [Mexico]	**<volume, special - see page 29>**	
liter	74.2	7.420 000 0E+01
barile [Greece]	**<volume, special - see page 29>**	
liter	74.2	7.420 000 0E+01
barile [Italy, oil]	**<volume, special - see page 29>**	
liter	33.4	3.340 000 0E+01
barile [Italy, wine]	**<volume, special - see page 29>**	
liter	45.6	4.560 000 0E+01
barile [Italy]	**<volume, special - see page 29>**	
liter	58.34	5.834 000 0E+01
barile [Libya]	**<volume, special - see page 29>**	
liter	64.4	6.440 000 0E+01
barleycorn	**<length>**	
agate [print]	4.38	4.380 000 0E+00
caliber	33.333 333	3.333 333 3E+01
didot point [print]	22.488 798	2.248 879 8E+01
douzieme [print]	48	4.800 000 0E+01
em [pica, print]	2.007 5	2.007 500 0E+00
inch [based on US, survey foot]	0.333 332 7	3.333 326 7E−01
inch [international]	0.333 333	3.333 333 3E−01
iron [print]	0.080 3	8.030 000 1E−02
iron [shoe leather]	16	1.600 000 0E+01

Convert From / Convert To	Standard	Scientific
ligne [print]	4	4.000 000 0E+00
line [print]	4	4.000 000 0E+00
meter	0.008 466 7	8.466 666 7E−03
microinch	333,333.33	3.333 333 3E+05
micron	8,466.666 7	8.466 666 7E+03
mil	333.333 33	3.333 333 3E+02
millimeter	8.466 666 7	8.466 666 7E+00
nonpareil [print]	4.015	4.015 000 0E+00
pearl [print]	4.818	4.818 000 0E+00
pica [print]	2.007 5	2.007 500 0E+00
point [print]	24.09	2.409 000 0E+01
thou	333.333 33	3.333 333 3E+02

barmil [Malta] — <volume, special - see page 29>
| liter | 43.188 | 4.318 800 0E+01 |

barmil [Mexico] — <volume, special - see page 29>
| liter | 76 | 7.600 000 0E+01 |

barmil [Paraguay] — <volume, special - see page 29>
| liter | 96.93 | 9.693 000 0E+01 |

barn — <area>
circular microinch	<<<	1.973 525 2E−13
square angstrom	<<<	1.000 000 0E−08
square bicron	0.000 1	1.000 000 0E−04
square femtometer	100	1.000 000 0E+02
square fermi	100	1.000 000 0E+02
square inch [international]	<<<	1.550 003 1E−25
square meter	<<<	1.000 000 0E−28
square microinch	<<<	1.550 003 1E−13
square micromicron	0.000 1	1.000 000 0E−04
square micron	<<<	1.000 000 0E−16
square millimicron	0.000 1	1.000 000 0E−10
square stigma	0.000 1	1.000 000 0E−04
square tenthmeter	<<<	1.000 000 0E−08
square x-unit	0.009 958 7	9.958 684 5E−03

barn/electronvolt — <spectral cross-section>
| square meter/joule | <<< | 6.241 506 4E−10 |

barn/erg — <spectral cross-section>
foot/pound-force	<<<	1.459 390 3E−20
square meter/joule	<<<	1.000 000 0E−21
square second/kilogram	<<<	1.000 000 0E−21

barrel [UK, wine] — <volume>
barrel [UK]	0.875	8.750 000 0E−01
barrel [US, federal]	1.220 320 1	1.220 320 1E+00
barrel [US, federal proof spirits]	0.945 748 1	9.457 480 7E−01
barrel [US, liquid]	1.200 949 9	1.200 949 9E+00
bushel [UK]	3.937 5	3.937 500 0E+00
cubic foot	5.057 125 1	5.057 125 1E+00
cubic inch	8,738.712 1	8.738 712 1E+03
cubic meter	0.143 201 8	1.432 018 4E−01
cubic yard	0.187 300 9	1.873 009 3E−01
cup [Canada, measuring]	630	6.300 000 0E+02
cup [US, measuring]	605.278 76	6.052 787 6E+02
drum [US, liquid]	0.687 816 8	6.878 167 8E−01
firkin [UK]	3.5	3.500 000 0E+00
firkin [US]	4.203 324 7	4.203 324 7E+00
gallon [UK, dry or liquid]	31.5	3.150 000 0E+01
gallon [US, liquid]	37.829 923	3.782 992 3E+01
hogshead [UK]	0.5	5.000 000 0E−01
hogshead [US]	0.600 475	6.004 749 6E−01
liter	143.201 84	1.432 018 4E+02
ounce [UK, liquid]	5,040	5.040 000 0E+03
ounce [US, liquid]	4,842.230 1	4.842 230 1E+03

	Standard	Scientific
peck [UK]	15.75	1.575 000 0E+01
peck [US]	16.254 894	1.625 489 4E+01
pint [UK]	252	2.520 000 0E+02
pint [US, liquid]	302.639 38	3.026 393 8E+02
quart [UK]	126	1.260 000 0E+02
quart [US, liquid]	151.319 69	1.513 196 9E+02

barrel [UK]   <volume>

	Standard	Scientific
barrel [US, dry]	1.415 405 3	1.415 405 3E+00
barrel [US, liquid]	1.372 514 2	1.372 514 2E+00
barrel [US, petroleum]	1.029 385 7	1.029 385 7E+00
bushel [UK]	4.5	4.500 000 0E+00
chaldron [UK, dry]	0.125	1.250 000 0E-01
chaldron [UK, liquid]	0.125	1.250 000 0E-01
chaldron [US, dry]	0.129 007 1	1.290 070 9E-01
cubic foot	5.779 571 5	5.779 571 5E+00
cubic inch	9.987 099 6	9.987 099 6E+03
cubic meter	0.163 659 2	1.636 592 4E-01
cubic yard	0.214 058 2	2.140 582 0E-01
firkin [UK]	4	4.000 000 0E+00
firkin [US]	4.803 799 7	4.803 799 7E+00
gallon [Canada, liquid]	36	3.600 000 0E+01
gallon [UK, dry or liquid]	36	3.600 000 0E+01
gallon [US, dry]	37.154 043	3.715 404 3E+01
gallon [US, liquid]	43.234 197	4.323 419 7E+01
kilderkin [UK, liquid]	2	2.000 000 0E+00
liter	163.659 24	1.636 592 4E+02
peck [UK]	18	1.800 000 0E+01
peck [US]	18.577 021	1.857 702 1E+01
pint [UK]	288	2.880 000 0E+02
pint [US, dry]	297.232 34	2.972 323 4E+02
pint [US, liquid]	345.873 58	3.458 735 8E+02
quart [UK]	144	1.440 000 0E+02
quart [US, dry]	148.616 17	1.486 161 7E+02
quart [US, liquid]	172.936 79	1.729 367 9E+02

barrel [US, dry commodities except cranberry]   <volume>

	Standard	Scientific
barrel [US, dry]	1.000 009 3	1.000 009 3E+00
barrel [US, standard, cranberry]	1.211 029	1.211 029 0E+00
bushel [UK]	3.179 331	3.179 331 0E+00
bushel [US, dry]	3.281 25	3.281 250 0E+00
bushel [US, heaped]	2.567 975 8	2.567 975 8E+00
bushel [US, struck measure]	3.281 25	3.281 250 0E+00
chaldron [UK, dry]	0.088 314 8	8.831 475 0E-02
chaldron [US, dry]	0.091 145 8	9.114 583 3E-02
cubic foot	4.083 371 3	4.083 371 3E+00
cubic inch	7,056.065 6	7.056 065 6E+03
cubic meter	0.115 628 2	1.156 282 0E-01
cubic yard	0.151 236	1.512 359 7E-01
gallon [UK, dry or liquid]	25.434 648	2.543 464 8E+01
gallon [US, dry]	26.25	2.625 000 0E+01
pint [UK]	203.477 18	2.034 771 8E+02
pint [US, dry]	210	2.100 000 0E+02
quart [UK]	101.738 59	1.017 385 9E+02
quart [US, dry]	105	1.050 000 0E+02

barrel [US, dry]   <volume>

	Standard	Scientific
barrel [US, dry commodities except cranberry]	0.999 990 7	9.999 907 0E-01
barrel [US, standard, cranberry]	1.211 017 8	1.211 017 8E+00
bushel [US, dry]	3.281 219 5	3.281 219 5E+00
bushel [US, heaped]	2.567 951 9	2.567 951 9E+00
bushel [US, struck measure]	3.281 219 5	3.281 219 5E+00
chaldron [US, dry]	0.091 145	9.114 498 6E-02
cubic foot	4.083 333 3	4.083 333 3E+00
cubic inch	7,056	7.056 000 0E+03
cubic meter	0.115 627 1	1.156 271 2E-01

| Convert From | <Type of Unit> | |
Convert To	Standard	Scientific
cubic yard	0.151 234 6	1.512 345 7E-01
gallon [UK, dry or liquid]	25.434 411	2.543 441 1E+01
gallon [US, dry]	26.249 756	2.624 975 6E+01
peck [UK]	12.717 206	1.271 720 6E+01
peck [US]	13.124 878	1.312 487 8E+01
pint [US, dry]	209.998 05	2.099 980 5E+02
quart [US, dry]	104.999 02	1.049 990 2E+02
stere	0.115 627 1	1.156 271 2E-01
barrel [US, federal proof spirits]		**<volume>**
barrel [UK]	0.925 193 5	9.251 935 4E-01
barrel [UK, wine]	1.057 364	1.057 364 0E+00
barrel [US, federal]	1.290 322 6	1.290 322 6E+00
barrel [US, liquid]	1.269 841 3	1.269 841 3E+00
cubic foot	5.347 222 2	5.347 222 2E+00
cubic inch	9,240	9.240 000 0E+03
cubic meter	0.151 416 5	1.514 164 7E-01
cubic yard	0.198 045 3	1.980 452 7E-01
cup [US, measuring]	640	6.400 000 0E+02
dram [US, liquid]	40,960	4.096 000 0E+04
firkin [US]	4.444 444 4	4.444 444 4E+00
gallon [US, liquid]	40	4.000 000 0E+01
kilderkin [US, liquid]	2.222 222 2	2.222 222 2E+00
liter	151.416 47	1.514 164 7E+02
ounce [US, liquid]	5,120	5.120 000 0E+03
pint [US, liquid]	320	3.200 000 0E+02
quart [US, liquid]	160	1.600 000 0E+02
tablespoon [US, measuring]	10,240	1.024 000 0E+04
teaspoon [US, measuring]	30,720	3.072 000 0E+04
Winchester wine gallon [UK]	40	4.000 000 0E+01
barrel [US, federal]		**<volume>**
barrel [US, federal proof spirits]	0.775	7.750 000 0E-01
barrel [US, liquid]	0.984 127	9.841 269 8E-01
cubic foot	4.144 097 2	4.144 097 2E+00
cubic inch	7,161	7.161 000 0E+03
cubic meter	0.117 347 8	1.173 477 7E-01
cubic yard	0.153 485 1	1.534 850 8E-01
cup [US, measuring]	496	4.960 000 0E+02
firkin [UK]	2.868 1	2.868 100 0E+00
firkin [US]	3.444 444 4	3.444 444 4E+00
gallon [UK, dry or liquid]	25.812 9	2.581 290 0E+01
gallon [US, liquid]	31	3.100 000 0E+01
gill [UK]	826.012 79	8.260 127 9E+02
gill [US]	992	9.920 000 0E+02
liter	117.347 77	1.173 477 7E+02
ounce [US, liquid]	3,968	3.968 000 0E+03
pint [US, liquid]	248	2.480 000 0E+02
quart [US, liquid]	124	1.240 000 0E+02
tablespoon [US, measuring]	7,936	7.936 000 0E+03
teaspoon [US, measuring]	23,808	2.380 800 0E+04
Winchester wine gallon [UK]	31	3.100 000 0E+01
barrel [US, liquid]		**<volume>**
barrel [US, federal]	1.016 129	1.016 129 0E+00
barrel [US, federal proof spirits]	0.787 5	7.875 000 0E-01
barrel [US, petroleum]	0.75	7.500 000 0E-01
cubic foot	4.210 937 5	4.210 937 5E+00
cubic inch	7,276.5	7.276 500 0E+03
cubic meter	0.119 240 5	1.192 404 7E-01
cubic yard	0.155 960 7	1.559 606 5E-01
cup [US, measuring]	504	5.040 000 0E+02
firkin [UK]	2.914 359 6	2.914 359 6E+00
firkin [US]	3.5	3.500 000 0E+00
gallon [UK, dry or liquid]	26.229 237	2.622 923 7E+01
gallon [US, liquid]	31.5	3.150 000 0E+01

Convert From Convert To	<Type of Unit>	
	Standard	Scientific
gill [UK]	839.335 58	8.393 355 8E+02
gill [US]	1,008	1.008 000 0E+03
hogshead [UK]	0.416 337 1	4.163 370 9E-01
hogshead [US]	0.5	5.000 000 0E-01
liter	119.240 47	1.192 404 7E+02
ounce [US, liquid]	4,032	4.032 000 0E+03
pint [US, liquid]	252	2.520 000 0E+02
pipe [US, liquid]	0.25	2.500 000 0E-01
quart [US, liquid]	126	1.260 000 0E+02
stere	0.119 240 5	1.192 404 7E-01
Winchester wine gallon [UK]	31.5	3.150 000 0E+01
barrel [US, petroleum]		**<volume>**
barrel [UK]	0.971 453 2	9.714 532 2E-01
barrel [US, federal proof spirits]	1.05	1.050 000 0E+00
barrel [US, liquid]	1.333 333 3	1.333 333 3E+00
cubic foot	5.614 583 3	5.614 583 3E+00
cubic inch	9,702	9.702 000 0E+03
cubic meter	0.158 987 3	1.589 872 9E-01
cubic yard	0.207 947 5	2.079 475 3E-01
drum [US, liquid]	0.763 636 4	7.636 363 6E-01
gallon [UK, dry or liquid]	34.972 316	3.497 231 6E+01
gallon [US, liquid]	42	4.200 000 0E+01
hectoliter	1.589 872 9	1.589 872 9E+00
liter	158.987 29	1.589 872 9E+02
ounce [US, liquid]	5,376	5.376 000 0E+03
pint [US, liquid]	336	3.360 000 0E+02
quart [US, liquid]	168	1.680 000 0E+02
stere	0.158 987 3	1.589 872 9E-01
barrel [US, standard, cranberry]		**<volume>**
barrel [US, dry]	0.825 751 7	8.257 517 3E-01
barrel [US, dry commodities except cranberry]	0.825 744 1	8.257 440 5E-01
bushel [UK]	2.625 313 6	2.625 313 6E+00
bushel [US, dry]	2.709 472 7	2.709 472 7E+00
cubic foot	3.371 819 6	3.371 819 6E+00
cubic inch	5,826.504 2	5.826 504 2E+03
cubic meter	0.095 479 3	9.547 929 7E-02
cubic yard	0.124 882 2	1.248 822 1E-01
gallon [UK, dry or liquid]	21.002 509	2.100 250 9E+01
gallon [US, dry]	21.675 781	2.167 578 1E+01
pint [US, dry]	173.406 25	1.734 062 5E+02
quart [US, dry]	86.703 125	8.670 312 5E+01
stere	0.095 479 3	9.547 929 7E-02
barrel/day [UK]		**<flow rate, volume basis>**
barrel/day [US, federal]	1.394 651 5	1.394 651 5E+00
barrel/day [US, liquid]	1.372 514 2	1.372 514 2E+00
barrel/day [US, petroleum]	1.029 385 7	1.029 385 7E+00
centiliter/minute	11.365 225	1.136 522 5E+01
centiliter/second	0.189 420 4	1.894 204 2E-01
cubic centimeter/second	1.894 204 2	1.894 204 2E+00
cubic decimeter/hour	6.819 135 0	6.819 135 0E+00
cubic decimeter/minute	0.113 652 3	1.136 522 5E-01
cubic foot/day	5.779 571 5	5.779 571 5E+00
cubic foot/hour	0.240 815 5	2.408 154 8E-01
cubic inch/minute	6.935 485 8	6.935 485 8E+00
cubic inch/second	0.115 591 4	1.155 914 3E-01
cubic meter/day	0.163 659 2	1.636 592 4E-01
cubic meter/second	0.000 001 9	1.894 204 2E-06
cubic yard/day	0.214 058 2	2.140 582 0E-01
cubic yard/hour	0.008 919 1	8.919 091 9E-03
deciliter/hour	68.191 35	6.819 135 0E+01
deciliter/minute	1.136 522 5	1.136 522 5E+00
dekaliter/day	16.365 924	1.636 592 4E+01
dekaliter/hour	0.681 913 5	6.819 135 0E-01

Convert From	<Type of Unit>	
Convert To	Standard	Scientific
gallon/day [UK]	36	3.600 000 0E+01
gallon/day [US, liquid]	43.234 197 3	4.323 419 7E+01
gallon/hour [UK]	1.5	1.500 000 0E+00
gallon/hour [US, liquid]	1.801 424 9	1.801 424 9E+00
hectoliter/day	1.636 592 4	1.636 592 4E+00
kiloliter/day	0.163 659 2	1.636 592 4E−01
liter/hour	6.819 135	6.819 135 0E+00
liter/hour [pre-1964]	6.818 944 1	6.818 944 1E+00
liter/minute	0.113 652 3	1.136 522 5E−01
liter/minute [pre-1964]	0.113 649 1	1.136 490 7E−01
milliliter/second	1.894 204 2	1.894 204 2E+00
ounce/minute [UK, liquid]	4	4.000 000 0E+00
ounce/minute [US, liquid]	3.843 039 8	3.843 039 8E+00
stere/day	0.163 659 2	1.636 592 4E−01
barrel/day [US, federal]	**<flow rate, volume basis>**	
barrel/day [UK]	0.717 025	7.170 249 9E−01
barrel/day [US, liquid]	0.984 127	9.841 269 8E−01
barrel/day [US, petroleum]	0.738 095 2	7.380 952 4E−01
centiliter/minute	8.149 150 4	8.149 150 4E+00
centiliter/second	0.135 819 2	1.358 191 7E−01
cubic centimeter/minute	81.491 503 7	8.149 150 4E+01
cubic centimeter/second	1.358 191 7	1.358 191 7E+00
cubic decimeter/hour	4.889 490 2	4.889 490 2E+00
cubic foot/day	4.144 097 2	4.144 097 2E+00
cubic foot/hour	0.172 670 7	1.726 707 2E−01
cubic inch/minute	4.972 916 7	4.972 916 7E+00
cubic meter/day	0.117 347 8	1.173 477 7E−01
cubic meter/second	0.000 001 4	1.358 191 7E−06
cubic yard/day	0.153 485 1	1.534 850 8E−01
deciliter/hour	48.894 902 2	4.889 490 2E+01
deciliter/minute	0.814 915	8.149 150 4E−01
dekaliter/day	11.734 776 5	1.173 477 7E+00
dekaliter/hour	0.488 949	4.889 490 2E−01
gallon/day [UK]	25.812 899 7	2.581 290 0E+01
gallon/day [US, liquid]	31	3.100 000 0E+01
gallon/hour [UK]	1.075 537 5	1.075 537 5E+00
gallon/hour [US, liquid]	1.291 666 7	1.291 666 7E+00
hectoliter/day	1.173 477 7	1.173 477 7E+00
kiloliter/day	0.117 347 8	1.173 477 7E−01
liter/hour	4.889 490 2	4.889 490 2E+00
liter/hour [pre-1964]	4.889 353 3	4.889 353 3E+00
milliliter/minute	81.491 503 7	8.149 150 4E+01
milliliter/second	1.358 191 7	1.358 191 7E+00
ounce/minute [UK, liquid]	2.868 1	2.868 100 0E+00
ounce/minute [US, liquid]	2.755 555 6	2.755 555 6E+00
stere/day	0.117 347 8	1.173 477 7E−01
barrel/day [US, liquid]	**<flow rate, volume basis>**	
barrel/day [UK]	0.728 589 9	7.285 899 1E−01
barrel/day [US, federal]	1.016 129	1.016 129 0E+00
barrel/day [US, petroleum]	0.75	7.500 000 0E−01
centiliter/minute	8.280 588 3	8.280 588 3E+00
centiliter/second	0.138 009 8	1.380 098 1E−01
cubic centimeter/minute	82.805 882 8	8.280 588 3E+01
cubic centimeter/second	1.380 098 1	1.380 098 1E+00
cubic decimeter/hour	4.968 353	4.968 353 0E+00
cubic foot/day	4.210 937 5	4.210 937 5E+00
cubic foot/hour	0.175 455 7	1.754 557 3E−01
cubic inch/minute	5.053 125	5.053 125 0E+00
cubic yard/day	0.155 960 6	1.559 606 5E−01
deciliter/hour	49.683 529 7	4.968 353 0E+01
deciliter/minute	0.828 058 8	8.280 588 3E−01
dekaliter/day	11.924 047 1	1.192 404 7E+00
dekaliter/hour	0.496 835 3	4.968 353 0E−01

	Standard	Scientific
gallon/day [US, liquid]	31.5	3.150 000 0E+01
gallon/hour [US, liquid]	1.312 5	1.312 500 0E+00
gallon/minute [US, liquid]	0.021 875	2.187 500 0E−02
gallon/second [US, liquid]	0.000 364 6	3.645 833 3E−04
hectoliter/day	1.192 404 7	1.192 404 7E+00
kiloliter/day	0.119 240 5	1.192 404 7E−01
liter/hour	4.968 353	4.968 353 0E+00
liter/hour [pre-1964]	4.968 213 9	4.968 213 9E+00
milliliter/minute	82.805 882 8	8.280 588 3E+01
milliliter/second	1.380 098 1	1.380 098 1E+00
ounce/minute [UK, liquid]	2.914 359 6	2.914 359 6E+00
ounce/minute [US, liquid]	2.8	2.800 000 0E+00
stere/day	0.119 240 5	1.192 404 7E−01

barrel/day [US, petroleum] <flow rate, volume basis>

	Standard	Scientific
barrel/day [UK]	0.971 453 2	9.714 532 2E−01
barrel/day [US, federal]	1.354 838 7	1.354 838 7E+00
barrel/day [US, liquid]	1.333 333 3	1.333 333 3E+00
centiliter/minute	11.040 784 4	1.104 078 4E+01
centiliter/second	0.184 013 1	1.840 130 7E−01
cubic centimeter/second	1.840 130 7	1.840 130 7E+00
cubic decimeter/hour	6.624 470 6	6.624 470 6E+00
cubic decimeter/minute	0.110 407 8	1.104 078 4E−01
cubic foot/day	5.614 583	5.614 583 3E+00
cubic foot/hour	0.233 941	2.339 409 7E−01
cubic inch/minute	6.737 5	6.737 500 0E+00
cubic inch/second	0.112 291 7	1.122 916 7E−01
cubic meter/day	0.158 987 3	1.589 873 0E−01
cubic meter/second	0.000 001 8	1.840 130 7E−06
cubic yard/day	0.207 947 5	2.079 475 3E−01
deciliter/hour	66.244 706 2	6.624 470 6E+00
deciliter/minute	1.104 078 4	1.104 078 4E+00
dekaliter/day	15.898 729 5	1.589 873 0E+00
dekaliter/hour	0.662 447 1	6.624 470 6E−01
gallon/day [US, liquid]	42	4.200 000 0E+01
gallon/hour [US, liquid]	1.75	1.750 000 0E+00
gallon/minute [US, liquid]	0.029 166 7	2.916 666 7E−02
gallon/second [US, liquid]	0.000 486 1	4.861 111 1E−04
hectoliter/day	1.589 873	1.589 873 0E+00
kiloliter/day	0.158 987 3	1.589 873 0E−01
liter/hour	6.624 470 6	6.624 470 6E+00
liter/hour [pre-1964]	6.624 285 1	6.624 285 1E+00
liter/minute	0.110 407 8	1.104 078 4E−01
liter/minute [pre-1964]	0.110 404 8	1.104 047 5E−01
milliliter/second	1.840 130 7	1.840 130 7E+00
ounce/minute [UK, liquid]	3.885 812 9	3.885 812 9E+00
ounce/minute [US, liquid]	3.733 333 3	3.733 333 3E+00
stere/day	0.158 987 3	1.589 872 9E−01

barrel/hour [UK] <flow rate, volume basis>

	Standard	Scientific
barrel/hour [UK]	24	2.400 000 0E+01
barrel/hour [US, federal]	1.394 651 5	1.394 651 5E+00
barrel/hour [US, liquid]	1.372 514 2	1.372 514 2E+00
barrel/hour [US, petroleum]	1.029 385 7	1.029 385 7E+00
cubic foot/hour	5.779 571 5	5.779 571 5E+00
cubic inch/second	2.774 194 3	2.774 194 3E+00
cubic meter/day	3.927 821 8	3.927 821 8E+00
cubic meter/second	0.000 045 5	4.546 090 0E−05
cubic yard/day	5.137 396 9	5.137 396 9E+00
deciliter/minute	27.276 54	2.727 654 0E+01
dekaliter/hour	16.365 924	1.636 592 4E+01
gallon/day [UK]	36	3.600 000 0E+01
gallon/hour [US, liquid]	43.234 197 3	4.323 419 7E+01
gallon/minute [UK]	0.6	6.000 000 0E−01
gallon/minute [US, liquid]	0.720 57	7.205 699 6E−01

Convert From / Convert To	Standard	\<Type of Unit\> Scientific

Convert From Convert To	Standard	\<Type of Unit\> Scientific
gallon/second [UK]	0.01	1.000 000 0E−02
hectoliter/day	39.278 217 6	3.927 821 8E+01
hectoliter/hour	1.636 592 4	1.636 592 4E+00
kiloliter/day	3.927 821 8	3.927 821 8E+00
liter/minute	2.727 654	2.727 654 E+00
liter/minute [pre-1964]	2.727 577 6	2.727 577 6E+00
milliliter/second	45.460 9	4.546 090 0E+01
ounce/minute [UK, liquid]	96	9.600 000 0E+01
ounce/minute [US, liquid]	92.232 954	9.223 295 4E+01
ounce/second [UK, liquid]	1.6	1.600 000 0E+00
ounce/second [US, liquid]	1.537 215 9	1.537 215 9E+00
petrograd standard/day	0.840 665	8.406 649 5E−01
stere/day	3.927 821 8	3.927 821 8E+00
thousand cubic foot/day	0.138 709 7	1.387 097 2E−01
barrel/hour [US, federal]		**\<flow rate, volume basis\>**
barrel/day [US, federal]	24	2.400 000 0E+01
centiliter/second	3.259 660 2	3.259 660 2E+00
cubic decimeter/minute	1.955 796 1	1.955 796 1E+00
cubic foot/hour	4.144 097 2	4.144 097 2E+00
cubic inch/second	1.989 166 7	1.989 166 7E+00
cubic meter/day	2.816 346 4	2.816 346 4E+00
cubic meter/second	0.000 032 6	3.259 660 2E−05
cubic yard/day	3.683 642	3.683 642 0E+00
deciliter/minute	19.557 960 9	1.955 796 1E+01
dekaliter/hour	11.734 776 5	1.173 477 7E+01
gallon/hour [US, liquid]	31	3.100 000 0E+01
gallon/minute [UK]	0.430 215	4.302 150 0E−01
gallon/minute [US, liquid]	0.516 666 7	5.166 666 7E−01
hectoliter/day	28.163 463 7	2.816 346 4E+01
hectoliter/hour	1.173 477 7	1.173 477 7E+00
kiloliter/day	2.816 346 4	2.816 346 4E+00
kiloliter/hour	0.117 348	1.173 477 7E−01
liter/minute	1.955 796 1	1.955 796 1E+00
liter/minute [pre-1964]	1.955 741 3	1.955 741 3E+00
milliliter/second	32.596 601 5	3.259 660 2E+01
ounce/minute [UK, liquid]	68.834 399	6.883 439 9E+01
ounce/minute [US, liquid]	66.133 333	6.613 333 3E+01
ounce/second [UK, liquid]	1.147 24	1.147 240 0E+00
ounce/second [US, liquid]	1.102 222 2	1.102 222 2E+00
petrograd standard/day	0.602 777 8	6.027 777 8E−01
stere/day	2.816 346 4	2.816 346 4E+00
stere/hour	0.117 347 8	1.173 477 7E−01
barrel/hour [US, liquid]		**\<flow rate, volume basis\>**
barrel/day [US, liquid]	24	2.400 000 0E+01
barrel/day [US, petroleum]	18	1.800 000 0E+01
barrel/hour [US, federal]	1.016 129	1.016 129 0E+00
barrel/hour [US, petroleum]	0.75	7.500 000 0E−01
centiliter/second	3.312 235 3	3.312 235 3E+00
cubic centimeter/second	33.122 353 1	3.312 235 3E+01
cubic decimeter/minute	1.987 341 2	1.987 341 2E+00
cubic foot/hour	4.210 937 5	4.210 937 5E+00
cubic inch/second	2.021 25	2.021 250 0E+00
cubic meter/day	2.861 771 3	2.861 771 3E+00
cubic meter/second	0.000 033 1	3.312 235 3E−05
cubic yard/day	3.743 055 6	3.743 055 6E+00
deciliter/minute	19.873 411 9	1.987 341 2E+01
dekaliter/hour	11.924 047 1	1.192 404 7E+01
gallon/hour [US, liquid]	31.5	3.150 000 0E+01
gallon/minute [US, liquid]	0.525	5.250 000 0E−01
hectoliter/hour	1.192 404 7	1.192 404 7E+00
kiloliter/day	2.861 771 3	2.861 771 3E+00
liter/minute	1.987 341 2	1.987 341 2E+00
liter/minute [pre-1964]	1.987 285 5	1.987 285 5E+00

Convert From Convert To	\<Type of Unit\> Standard	Scientific

	Standard	Scientific
ounce/minute [US, liquid]	67.2	6.720 000 0E+01
ounce/second [UK, liquid]	1.165 743 9	1.165 743 9E+00
ounce/second [US, liquid]	1.12	1.120 000 0E+00
petrograd standard/day	0.612 5	6.125 000 0E−01
stere/day	2.861 771 3	2.861 771 3E+00
stere/hour	0.119 240 5	1.192 404 7E−01
thousand cubic foot/day	0.101 062 5	1.010 625 0E−01

barrel/hour [US, petroleum] \<flow rate, volume basis\>

	Standard	Scientific
barrel/day [US, liquid]	32	3.200 000 0E+01
barrel/day [US, petroleum]	24	2.400 000 0E+01
barrel/day [US, federal]	1.354 838 7	1.354 838 7E+00
barrel/hour [US, liquid]	1.333 333 3	1.333 333 3E+00
centiliter/second	4.416 313 8	4.416 313 8E+00
cubic centimeter/second	44.163 137 5	4.416 313 8E+01
cubic decimeter/minute	2.649 788 3	2.649 788 3E+00
cubic foot/hour	5.614 583 3	5.614 583 3E+00
cubic inch/second	2.695	2.695 000 0E+00
cubic meter/day	3.815 695 1	3.815 695 1E+00
cubic meter/second	0.000 044 2	4.416 313 8E−05
cubic yard/day	4.990 740 7	4.990 740 7E+00
deciliter/minute	26.497 882 5	2.649 788 3E+01
gallon/hour [US, liquid]	42	4.200 000 0E+01
gallon/minute [US, liquid]	0.7	7.000 000 0E−01
hectoliter/hour	1.589 873	1.589 873 0E+00
kiloliter/day	3.815 695 1	3.815 695 1E+00
liter/minute	2.649 788 3	2.649 788 3E+00
liter/minute [pre-1964]	2.649 714 1	2.649 714 1E+00
ounce/minute [US, liquid]	89.6	8.960 000 0E+01
ounce/second [US, liquid]	1.493 333 3	1.493 333 3E+00
petrograd standard/day	0.816 666 7	8.166 666 7E−01
stere/day	3.815 695 1	3.815 695 1E+00

barrel/minute [UK] \<flow rate, volume basis\>

	Standard	Scientific
acre inch/day	2.292 722 6	2.292 722 6E+00
barrel/day [UK]	1,440	1.440 000 0E+03
barrel/hour [UK]	60	6.000 000 0E+01
barrel/hour [US, liquid]	82.350 852	8.235 085 2E+01
barrel/minute [US, federal]	1.394 651 5	1.394 651 5E+00
barrel/minute [US, liquid]	1.372 514 2	1.372 514 2E+00
barrel/minute [US, petroleum]	1.029 385 7	1.029 385 7E+00
cubic decimeter/second	2.727 654	2.727 654 0E+00
cubic foot/minute	5.779 571 5	5.779 571 5E+00
cubic meter/hour	9.819 554 4	9.819 554 4E+00
cubic meter/second	0.002 727 7	2.727 654 0E−03
cubic yard/hour	12.843 492 3	1.284 349 2E+01
gallon/minute [UK]	36	3.600 000 0E+01
gallon/second [UK]	0.6	6.000 000 0E−01
hectoliter/minute	1.636 592 4	1.636 592 4E+00
kiloliter/hour	9.819 554 4	9.819 554 4E+00
liter/second	2.727 654	2.727 654 0E+00
liter/second [pre-1964]	2.727 577 6	2.727 577 6E+00
ounce/day [UK, liquid]	8,294,400	8.294 400 0E+06
ounce/hour [UK, liquid]	345,600	3.456 000 0E+05
ounce/minute [UK, liquid]	5,760	5.760 000 0E+03
ounce/second [UK, liquid]	96	9.600 000 0E+01
petrograd standard/hour	2.101 662 4	2.101 662 4E+00
stere/hour	9.819 554 4	9.819 554 4E+00
thousand cubic foot/day	8.322 583	8.322 583 0E+00

barrel/minute [US, federal] \<flow rate, volume basis\>

	Standard	Scientific
acre inch/day	1.643 939 4	1.643 939 4E+00
barrel/day [US, federal]	1,440	1.440 000 0E+03
barrel/hour [US, federal]	60	6.000 000 0E+01
barrel/minute [US, liquid]	0.984 127	9.841 269 8E−01
barrel/minute [US, petroleum]	0.738 095 2	7.380 952 4E−01

Convert From Convert To	Standard	<Type of Unit> Scientific
cubic decimeter/second	1.955 796 1	1.955 796 1E+00
cubic foot/minute	4.144 097 2	4.144 097 2E+00
cubic inch/minute	7,161	7.161 000 0E+03
cubic meter/hour	7.040 865 9	7.040 865 9E+00
cubic meter/second	0.001 955 8	1.955 796 1E-03
cubic yard/hour	9.209 104 9	9.209 104 9E+00
gallon/minute [US, liquid]	31	3.100 000 0E+01
hectoliter/minute	1.173 477 7	1.173 477 7E+00
kiloliter/hour	7.040 865 9	7.040 865 9E+00
liter/second	1.955 796 1	1.955 796 1E+00
liter/second [pre-1964]	1.955 741 3	1.955 741 3E+00
petrograd standard/hour	1.506 944 4	1.506 944 4E+00
stere/hour	7.040 865 9	7.040 865 9E+00
thousand cubic foot/day	5.967 5	5.967 500 0E+00
barrel/minute [US, liquid]		**<flow rate, volume basis>**
acre inch/day	1.670 454 6	1.670 454 6E+00
barrel/day [US, liquid]	1,440	1.440 000 0E+03
barrel/day [US, petroleum]	1,080	1.080 000 0E+03
barrel/hour [US, liquid]	60	6.000 000 0E+01
barrel/hour [US, petroleum]	45	4.500 000 0E+01
barrel/minute [US, federal]	1.016 129	1.016 129 0E+00
barrel/minute [US, petroleum]	0.75	7.500 000 0E-01
cubic decimeter/second	1.987 341 2	1.987 341 2E+00
cubic foot/minute	4.210 937 5	4.210 937 5E+00
cubic meter/hour	7.154 428 3	7.154 428 3E+00
cubic meter/second	0.001 987 3	1.987 341 2E-03
cubic yard/hour	9.357 638 9	9.357 638 9E+00
gallon/hour [US, liquid]	1,890	1.890 000 0E+03
gallon/minute [US, liquid]	31.5	3.150 000 0E+01
gallon/second [US, liquid]	0.525	5.250 000 0E-01
hectoliter/minute	1.192 404 7	1.192 404 7E+00
kiloliter/hour	7.154 428 3	7.154 428 3E+00
liter/second	1.987 341 2	1.987 341 2E+00
liter/second [pre-1964]	1.987 285 5	1.987 285 5E+00
ounce/second [US, liquid]	67.2	6.720 000 0E+01
petrograd standard/day	36.75	3.675 000 0E+01
petrograd standard/hour	1.531 25	1.531 250 0E+00
stere/hour	7.154 428 3	7.154 428 3E+00
thousand cubic foot/day	6.063 75	6.063 750 0E+00
barrel/minute [US, petroleum]		**<flow rate, volume basis>**
acre inch/day	2.227 272 7	2.227 272 7E+00
barrel/day [US, liquid]	1,920	1.920 000 0E+03
barrel/day [US, petroleum]	1,440	1.440 000 0E+03
barrel/hour [US, liquid]	80	8.000 000 0E+01
barrel/hour [US, petroleum]	60	6.000 000 0E+01
barrel/minute [US, federal]	1.354 838 7	1.354 838 7E+00
barrel/minute [US, liquid]	1.333 333 3	1.333 333 3E+00
cubic decimeter/second	2.649 788 3	2.649 788 3E+00
cubic foot/day	8,085	8.085 000 0E+03
cubic foot/minute	5.614 583 3	5.614 583 3E+00
cubic inch/minute	9,702	9.702 000 0E+03
cubic meter/hour	9.539 237 7	9.539 237 7E+00
cubic meter/second	0.002 649 8	2.649 788 3E-03
gallon/hour [US, liquid]	2,520	2.520 000 0E+03
gallon/minute [US, liquid]	42	4.200 000 0E+01
gallon/second [US, liquid]	0.7	7.000 000 0E-01
hectoliter/minute	1.589 873	1.589 873 0E+00
kiloliter/hour	9.539 237 7	9.539 237 7E+00
liter/second	2.649 788 3	2.649 788 3E+00
liter/second [pre-1964]	2.649 714 1	2.649 714 1E+00
ounce/minute [US, liquid]	5,376	5.376 000 0E+03
petrograd standard/day	49	4.900 000 0E+01
petrograd standard/hour	2.041 666 7	2.041 666 7E+00

	Standard	Scientific
stere/hour	9.539 237 7	9.539 237 7E+00
thousand cubic foot/day	8.085	8.085 000 0E+00
barrel/second [UK]	**\<flow rate, volume basis\>**	
acre inch/hour	5.731 806 5	5.731 806 5E+00
barrel/day [UK]	86,400	8.640 000 0E+04
barrel/hour [UK]	3,600	3.600 000 0E+03
barrel/minute [UK]	60	6.000 000 0E+01
barrel/second [US, federal]	1.394 651 5	1.394 651 5E+00
barrel/second [US, liquid]	1.372 514 2	1.372 514 2E+00
barrel/second [US, petroleum]	1.029 385 7	1.029 385 7E+00
cubic foot/second	5.779 571 5	5.779 571 5E+00
cubic meter/minute	9.819 554 4	9.819 554 4E+00
cubic meter/second	0.163 659 2	1.636 592 4E-01
gallon/minute [UK]	2,160	2.160 000 0E+03
gallon/second [UK]	36	3.600 000 0E+01
hectare meter/day	1.414 015 8	1.414 015 8E+00
hectoliter/second	1.636 592 4	1.636 592 4E+00
kiloliter/minute	9.819 554 4	9.819 554 4E+00
liter/second	163.659 24	1.636 592 4E+02
ounce/second [UK, liquid]	5,760	5.760 000 0E+03
petrograd standard/minute	2.101 662 4	2.101 662 4E+00
stere/minute	9.819 554 4	9.819 554 4E+00
barrel/second [US, federal]	**\<flow rate, volume basis\>**	
acre foot/day	8.219 697	8.219 697 0E+00
acre foot/day [US, survey]	8.219 647 7	8.219 647 7E+00
acre inch/hour	4.109 848 5	4.109 848 5E+00
barrel/hour [US, federal]	3,600	3.600 000 0E+03
barrel/minute [US, federal]	60	6.000 000 0E+01
cubic foot/second	4.144 097 2	4.144 097 2E+00
cubic meter/minute	7.040 865 9	7.040 865 9E+00
cubic meter/second	0.117 347 8	1.173 477 7E-01
cubic yard/minute	9.209 104 9	9.209 104 9E+00
gallon/minute [US, liquid]	1,860	1.860 000 0E+03
gallon/second [US, liquid]	31	3.100 000 0E+01
hectare meter/day	1.013 884 7	1.013 884 7E+00
hectoliter/second	1.173 477 7	1.173 477 7E+00
kiloliter/minute	7.040 865 9	7.040 865 9E+00
ounce/second [US, liquid]	3,968	3.968 000 0E+03
petrograd standard/day	2,170	2.170 000 0E+03
petrograd standard/minute	1.506 944 4	1.506 944 4E+00
stere/minute	7.040 865 9	7.040 865 9E+00
barrel/second [US, liquid]	**\<flow rate, volume basis\>**	
acre foot/day	8.352 272 7	8.352 272 7E+00
acre foot/day [US, survey]	8.352 222 6	8.352 222 6E+00
acre inch/hour	4.176 136 4	4.176 136 4E+00
barrel/hour [US, liquid]	3,600	3.600 000 0E+03
barrel/hour [US, petroleum]	2,700	2.700 000 0E+03
barrel/minute [US, liquid]	60	6.000 000 0E+01
barrel/minute [US, petroleum]	45	4.500 000 0E+01
barrel/second [US, federal]	1.016 129	1.016 129 0E+00
barrel/second [US, petroleum]	0.75	7.500 000 0E-01
cubic foot/second	4.210 937 5	4.210 937 5E+00
cubic meter/minute	7.154 428 3	7.154 428 3E+00
cubic meter/second	0.119 240 5	1.192 404 7E-01
cubic yard/minute	9.357 638 9	9.357 638 9E+00
gallon/minute [US, liquid]	1,890	1.890 000 0E+03
gallon/second [US, liquid]	31.5	3.150 000 0E+01
hectare meter/day	1.030 237 7	1.030 237 7E+00
hectoliter/second	1.192 404 7	1.192 404 7E+00
kiloliter/minute	7.154 428 3	7.154 428 3E+00
ounce/second [US, liquid]	4,032	4.032 000 0E+03
petrograd standard/day	2,205	2.205 000 0E+03
petrograd standard/minute	1.531 25	1.531 250 0E+00

Convert From / Convert To	Standard	Scientific
stere/minute	7.154 428 3	7.154 428 3E+00
barrel/second [US, petroleum]	\<flow rate, volume basis\>	
acre inch/hour	5.568 181 8	5.568 181 8E+00
barrel/hour [US, liquid]	4,800	4.800 000 0E+03
barrel/hour [US, petroleum]	3,600	3.600 000 0E+03
barrel/minute [US, liquid]	80	8.000 000 0E+01
barrel/minute [US, petroleum]	60	6.000 000 0E+01
barrel/second [US, federal]	1.354 838 7	1.354 838 7E+00
barrel/second [US, liquid]	1.333 333 3	1.333 333 3E+00
cubic foot/second	5.614 583 3	5.614 583 3E+00
cubic inch/second	9,702	9.702 000 0E+03
cubic meter/minute	9.539 237 7	9.539 237 7E+00
cubic meter/second	0.158 987 3	1.589 873 0E−01
gallon/second [US, liquid]	42	4.200 000 0E+01
hectare meter/day	1.373 650 2	1.373 650 2E+00
hectoliter/second	1.589 873	1.589 873 0E+00
kiloliter/minute	9.539 237 7	9.539 237 7E+00
petrograd standard/day	2,940	2.940 000 0E+03
stere/minute	9.539 237 7	9.539 237 7E+00
barril [Argentina]	\<volume, special - see page 29\>	
liter	76	7.600 000 0E+01
barril [Malta]	\<volume, special - see page 29\>	
liter	43.188	4.318 800 0E+01
barril [Mexico]	\<volume, special - see page 29\>	
liter	76	7.600 000 0E+01
barril [Paraguay]	\<volume, special - see page 29\>	
liter	96.93	9.693 000 0E+01
barril [Venezuela]	\<volume, special - see page 29\>	
liter	85	8.500 000 0E+01
barrique [France, wine]	\<volume, special - see page 29\>	
hectoliter	2.262	2.262 000 0E+00
barrique [France]	\<volume, special - see page 29\>	
liter	225	2.250 000 0E+02
barrique [Germany]	\<volume, special - see page 29\>	
hectoliter	2.061	2.061 000 0E+00
barrique [Haiti]	\<volume, special - see page 29\>	
liter	227.12	2.271 200 0E+02
barrique [Malta]	\<volume, special - see page 29\>	
liter	43.188	4.318 800 0E+01
barrique [Mexico]	\<volume, special - see page 29\>	
liter	76	7.600 000 0E+01
barrique [Paraguay]	\<volume, special - see page 29\>	
liter	96.93	9.693 000 0E+01
barrique [Portugal]	\<volume, special - see page 29\>	
liter	215	2.150 000 0E+02
barye [France]	\<pressure\>	
atmosphere [standard]	0.000 001	9.869 232 7E−07
atmosphere [technical]	0.000 001	1.019 716 2E−06
bar	0.000 001	1.000 000 0E−06
decipascal	1	1.000 000 0E+00
dyne/square centimeter	1	1.000 000 0E+00
gram-force/square centimeter	0.001 019 7	1.019 716 2E−03
kilogram-force/square meter	0.010 197 2	1.019 716 2E−02
kilopond/square meter	0.010 197 2	1.019 716 2E−02
microbar	1	1.000 000 0E+00
micrometer of mercury [0 °C, by convention]	0.750 061 6	7.500 615 8E−01
micrometer of water [4 °C, by convention]	10.197 162	1.019 716 2E+01
millimeter of mercury [0 °C, by convention]	0.000 750 1	7.500 615 8E−04
millimeter of water [4 °C, by convention]	0.010 197 2	1.019 716 2E−02

	Standard	Scientific
newton/square meter	0.1	1.000 000 0E-01
ounce-force/square inch	0.000 232 1	2.320 603 8E-04
pascal	0.1	1.000 000 0E-01
pound-force/square foot	0.002 088 5	2.088 543 4E-03
poundal/square foot	0.067 196 9	6.719 689 8E-02
sthene/square meter [France]	0.000 1	1.000 000 0E-04
ton-force/square foot [short]	0.000 001	1.044 271 7E-06
ton-force/square meter [metric]	0.000 010 2	1.019 716 2E-05
torr	0.000 750 1	7.500 616 8E-04

barzina [Hebrew, ancient]   <volume, see page 29>
cubic centimeter — 17.168 479 — 1.716 847 9E+01

base box [for tin-plated steel sheet]   <area>
square foot [international] — 217.777 777 8 — 2.177 777 8E+02
square inch [international] — 31,360 — 3.136 000 0E+04
square meter — 20.232 218 — 2.023 221 8E+01

basket [Burma]   <volume, special - see page 29>
liter — 40.915 — 4.091 500 0E+01

bat [Burma]   <mass, special - see page 29>
gram — 16.33 — 1.633 000 0E+01

bat [Hebrew, ancient]   <volume, special - see page 29>
liter — 22 — 2.200 000 0E+01

bat [Laos]   <mass, special - see page 29>
gram — 15 — 1.500 000 0E+01

bat [Thailand]   <mass, special - see page 29>
gram — 15 — 1.500 000 0E+01

bat [Vietnam]   <volume, special - see page 29>
centiliter — 50 — 5.000 000 0E+01

bath [Burma]   <mass, special - see page 29>
gram — 16.33 — 1.633 000 0E+01

bath [Hebrew, ancient]   <volume, special - see page 29>
liter — 22 — 2.200 000 0E+01

bath [Israel]   <volume, special - see page 29>
liter — 40 — 4.000 000 0E+01

bath [Laos]   <mass, special - see page 29>
gram — 15 — 1.500 000 0E+01

bath [Rome, ancient]   <volume, special - see page 29>
liter — 39 — 3.900 000 0E+01

bath [Thailand]   <mass, special - see page 29>
gram — 15 — 1.500 000 0E+01

batman [Iran, large]   <mass, special - see page 29>
kilogram — 10.205 — 1.020 500 0E+01

batman [Iran, small]   <mass, special - see page 29>
kilogram — 2.551 — 2.551 000 0E+00

batman [Iran]   <mass, special - see page 29>
kilogram — 3 — 3.000 000 0E+00

batman [Turkey, large]   <mass, special - see page 29>
kilogram — 10.205 — 1.020 500 0E+01

batman [Turkey, small]   <mass, special - see page 29>
kilogram — 2.551 — 2.551 000 0E+00

batman [Turkey]   <mass, special - see page 29>
kilogram — 7.698 — 7.698 000 0E+00

batmar [Iran, large]   <mass, special - see page 29>
kilogram — 10.205 — 1.020 500 0E+01

batmar [Iran, small]   <mass, special - see page 29>
kilogram — 2.551 — 2.551 000 0E+00

batmar [Iran]   <mass, special - see page 29>
gram — 5,942 — 5.942 000 0E+03

Convert From	<Type of Unit>	
Convert To	Standard	Scientific

batmar [Turkey, large] <mass, special - see page 29>
  kilogram -- 10.205 --- 1.020 500 0E+01

batmar [Turkey, small] <mass, special - see page 29>
  kilogram -- 2.551 --- 2.551 000 0E+00

batmar [Turkey] <mass, special - see page 29>
  kilogram -- 3.827 --- 3.827 000 0E+00

batos [Greece, ancient] <volume, special - see page 29>
  liter --- 39.5 --- 3.950 000 0E+01

batt [Iceland] <mass, special - see page 29>
  kilogram -- 160 --- 1.600 000 0E+02

battim [Hebrew, ancient] <volume, special - see page 29>
  liter --- 38 --- 3.800 000 0E+01

bau [Indonesia] <area, special - see page 29>
  hectare -- 0.709 65 --- 7.096 500 0E-01

bazer [Indonesia] <mass, special - see page 29>
  kilogram -- 185.223 --- 1.852 230 0E+02

becher [Austria] <volume, special - see page 29>
  liter --- 0.48 --- 4.800 000 0E-01

becker [Austria] <volume, special - see page 29>
  liter --- 0.48 --- 4.800 000 0E-01

becquerel <radionuclide activity>
  1/second --- 1 --- 1.000 000 0E+00
  curie --- <<< 2.702 702 7E-11
  disintegration/second -------------------------------- 1 --- 1.000 000 0E+00
  kilobecquerel -- 0.001 --- 1.000 000 0E-03
  millicurie -- <<< 2.702 702 7E-08
  rutherford --- 0.000 001 --- 1.000 000 0E-06

becquerel/cubic meter <radionuclide volume activity>
  curie/cubic meter ------------------------------------ <<< 2.702 702 7E-11
  rutherford/cubic meter ------------------------------- 0.000 001 --- 1.000 000 0E-06

becquerel/kilogram <radionuclide specific activity>
  curie/kilogram --------------------------------------- <<< 2.702 702 7E-11
  rutherford/kilogram ---------------------------------- 0.000 001 --- 1.000 000 0E-06

beczka [Poland] <volume, special - see page 29>
  liter --- 100 --- 1.000 000 0E+02

behar [Indonesia] <mass, special - see page 29>
  gram --- 270.658 --- 2.706 580 0E+02

behar [Iran] <length, special - see page 29>
  centimeter --- 3.25 --- 3.250 000 0E+00

behar [Saudi Arabia] <mass, special - see page 29>
  kilogram -- 204.1 --- 2.041 000 0E+02

bei ke [China] <mass, special - see page 29>
  gram --- 100 --- 1.000 000 0E+02

bei mi [China] <length, special - see page 29>
  meter -- 100 --- 1.000 000 0E+02

bei sheng [China] <volume, special - see page 29>
  hectoliter -- 1 --- 1.000 000 0E+00

beit sea [Hebrew, ancient] <area, special - see page 29>
  square meter --- 740 --- 7.400 000 0E+02

beit zemed [Hebrew, ancient] <area, special - see page 29>
  hectare -- 0.22 --- 2.200 000 0E-01

beka [Hebrew, ancient] <mass, special - see page 29>
  gram --- 5.75 --- 5.750 000 0E+00

bekah [Hebrew, ancient] <mass, special - see page 29>
  gram --- 6 --- 6.000 000 0E+00

Convert From / Convert To	Standard	Scientific
bekaim [Hebrew, ancient]		**<mass, special - see page 29>**
gram	6.3	6.300 000 0E+00
bel		**<sound pressure level>**
brig	1	1.000 000 0E+00
decibel	10	1.000 000 0E+01
decineper	11.512 925 5	1.151 292 6E+01
dex	1	1.000 000 0E+00
neper	1.151 292 6	1.151 292 6E+00
bema [Greece, ancient]		**<length, special - see page 29>**
centimeter	74	7.400 000 0E+01
benda [Central Africa]		**<mass, special - see page 29>**
gram	64	6.400 000 0E+01
benequen [Belize]		**<volume, special - see page 29>**
liter	17.048	1.704 800 0E+01
benz		**<velocity>**
foot/minute	196.850 39	1.968 503 9E+02
meter/second	1	1.000 000 0E+00
mile/hour	2.236 936 3	2.236 936 3E+00
beqa [Egypt, ancient]		**<mass, special - see page 29>**
gram	15.6	1.560 000 0E+01
beqa [Hebrew, ancient]		**<mass, special - see page 29>**
gram	5.712	5.712 000 0E+00
bercherect [Russia]		**<mass, special - see page 29>**
kilogram	163.597	1.635 970 0E+02
berkovec [Russia]		**<mass, special - see page 29>**
kilogram	163.8	1.638 000 0E+02
berkovet [Russia]		**<mass, special - see page 29>**
kilogram	163.8	1.638 000 0E+02
berkovetz [Russia]		**<mass, special - see page 29>**
kilogram	163.805	1.638 050 0E+02
berkowetz [Russia]		**<mass, special - see page 29>**
kilogram	163.597	1.635 970 0E+02
berkowitz [Russia]		**<mass, special - see page 29>**
kilogram	163.597	1.635 970 0E+02
beru [Babylon, ancient]		**<length, special - see page 29>**
kilometer	10.8	1.080 000 0E+01
bes [Rome, ancient]		**<mass, special - see page 29>**
gram	218.3	2.183 000 0E+02
besana [Cuba]		**<area, special - see page 29>**
square meter	2,588.77	2.588 770 0E+03
beswa [Afghanistan]		**<area, special - see page 29>**
square meter	97.6	9.760 000 0E+01
bevameter		**<length>**
astronomical unit	0.006 684 6	6.684 587 2E−03
chain [Gunter or US, survey]	>>>	4.970 959 6E+07
chain [Ramden or Engineer]	>>>	3.280 839 9E+07
foot [international]	>>>	3.280 839 9E+09
foot [US, survey]	>>>	3.280 839 9E+09
furlong [US, survey]	4,970,959.6	4.970 959 6E+06
gigameter	1	1.000 000 0E+00
league [international, nautical]	179,985.6	1.799 856 0E+05
league [UK, nautical]	179,870.61	1.798 706 1E+05
league [US, statute]	207,123.32	2.071 233 2E+05
meter	>>>	1.000 000 0E+09
mile [international]	621,371.19	6.213 711 9E+05
mile [US, statute]	621,369.95	6.213 699 5E+05
mile [US, survey]	621,369.95	6.213 699 5E+05
myriameter	100,000	1.000 000 0E+05

	Standard	Scientific
range [US, survey]	103,561.66	1.035 616 6E+05
spat	0.001	1.000 000 0E−03
township [US, survey]	103,561.66	1.035 616 6E+05
bezah [Hebrew, ancient]	<volume, special - see page 29>	
cubic centimeter	91.565 223	9.156 522 3E+01
bhar [Batavia, large]	<mass, special - see page 29>	
kilogram	277.834	2.778 340 0E+02
bhar [Batavia, small]	<mass, special - see page 29>	
kilogram	185.223	1.852 230 0E+02
bhar [Sumatra]	<mass, special - see page 29>	
kilogram	192.026	1.920 260 0E+02
bhara [Brunei]	<mass, special - see page 29>	
kilogram	181.437	1.814 370 0E+02
bhara [Malaysia]	<mass, special - see page 29>	
kilogram	181.4	1.814 000 0E+02
bhari [Bangladesh]	<mass, special - see page 29>	
gram	11.664	1.166 400 0E+01
bhari [India]	<mass, special - see page 29>	
gram	11.663 8	1.166 380 0E+01
bia [Laos]	<mass, special - see page 29>	
gram	37.5	3.750 000 0E+01
bicentennial	<time>	
year [normal calendar]	200	2.000 000 0E+02
bicron	<length>	
angstrom	0.01	1.000 000 0E−02
caliber	<<<	3.937 007 9E−09
fermi	1,000	1.000 000 0E+03
inch [international]	<<<	3.937 007 9E−11
meter	<<<	1.000 000 0E−12
microinch	0.000 039 4	3.937 007 9E−05
micromicron	1	1.000 000 0E+00
mil	<<<	3.937 007 9E−08
picometer	1	1.000 000 0E+00
stigma	1	1.000 000 0E+00
tenthmeter	0.01	1.000 000 0E−02
thou	<<<	3.937 007 9E−08
wavelength of orange-red spectral line of krypton-86	0.000 001 7	1.650 763 7E−06
x-unit	9.979 320 9	9.979 320 9E+00
biennial	<time>	
biennium	1	1.000 000 0E+00
quarter	8	8.000 000 0E+00
year [normal calendar]	2	2.000 000 0E+00
biennium	<time>	
biennial	1	1.000 000 0E+00
quarter	8	8.000 000 0E+00
year [normal calendar]	2	2.000 000 0E+00
bigha [Bangladesh]	<area, special - see page 29>	
hectare	0.135	1.350 000 0E−01
bigha [India]	<area, special - see page 29>	
hectare	0.134	1.340 000 0E−01
bigha [Nepal]	<area, special - see page 29>	
hectare	0.677 141	6.771 410 0E−01
bigha [Pakistan]	<area, special - see page 29>	
hectare	0.202 34	2.023 400 0E−01
billion [UK]	<units>	
unit	>>>	1.000 000 0E+12
billion [US]	<units>	
milliard [UK]	1	1.000 000 0E+00

	Standard	Scientific
unit	>>>	1.000 000 0E+09
billion cubic foot		**<volume>**
acre foot	22,956.841	2.295 684 1E+04
barrel [US, liquid]	>>>	2.374 768 1E+08
barrel [US, petroleum]	>>>	1.781 076 1E+08
cubem	0.006 793 6	6.793 572 8E−03
cubic foot	>>>	1.000 000 0E+09
cubic meter	>>>	2.831 684 7E+07
cubic mile	0.006 793 6	6.793 572 8E−03
cubic yard	>>>	3.703 703 7E+07
gallon [US, liquid]	>>>	7.480 519 5E+09
hectare meter	2,831.684 7	2.831 684 7E+03
liter	>>>	2.831 684 7E+10
million acre foot	0.022 956 8	2.295 684 1E−02
million board foot	12,000	1.200 000 0E+04
thousand cubic foot	1,000,000	1.000 000 0E+06
trillion cubic foot	0.001	1.000 000 0E−03
billion cubic foot/day		**<flow rate, volume basis>**
acre foot/hour	956.535 047	9.565 350 5E+02
acre foot/hour [US, survey]	956.529 308	9.565 293 1E+02
acre foot/minute	15.942 250 8	1.594 225 1E+01
acre foot/minute [US, survey]	15.942 155 1	1.594 215 5E+01
acre foot/second	0.265 704 2	2.657 041 8E−01
acre foot/second [US, survey]	0.265 702 6	2.657 025 9E−01
acre inch/minute	191.307 009	1.913 070 1E+02
acre inch/second	3.188 450 2	3.188 450 2E+00
billion cubic foot/second	0.041 666 7	4.166 666 7E−02
cubic dekameter/minute	19.664 476 8	1.966 447 7E+01
cubic dekameter/second	0.327 741 3	3.277 412 8E−01
cubic foot/day	>>>	1.000 000 0E+09
cubic inch/minute	>>>	1.200 000 0E+09
cubic inch/second	>>>	2.000 000 0E+07
cubic kilometer/day	0.028 316 8	2.831 684 7E−02
cubic meter/second	327.741 28	3.277 412 8E+02
cubic yard/second	428.669 41	4.286 694 1E+02
hectare meter/hour	117.986 861	1.179 868 6E+02
hectare meter/minute	1.966 447 7	1.966 447 7E+00
hectare meter/second	0.032 774 1	3.277 412 8E−02
kiloliter/second	327.741 28	3.277 412 8E+02
million acre foot/day	0.022 956 8	2.295 684 1E−02
petrograd standard/second	70.145 903	7.014 590 3E+01
stere/second	327.741 28	3.277 412 8E+02
thousand cubic foot/minute	694.444 44	6.944 444 4E+02
thousand cubic foot/second	11.574 074	1.157 407 4E+01
trillion cubic foot/day	0.001	1.000 000 0E−03
billion cubic foot/hour		**<flow rate, volume basis>**
acre foot/second	6.376 900 3	6.376 900 3E+00
acre foot/second [US, survey]	6.376 862 1	6.376 862 1E+00
billion cubic foot/day	24	2.400 000 0E+01
cubic dekameter/second	7.865 790 7	7.865 790 7E+00
cubic foot/hour	>>>	1.000 000 0E+09
cubic inch/second	>>>	4.800 000 0E+08
cubic kilometer/day	0.679 604 3	6.796 043 2E−01
cubic meter/second	7,865.790 72	7.865 790 7E+03
cubic mile/day	0.163 045 7	1.630 457 5E−01
gallon/second [US, liquid]	2,077,922.08	2.077 922 1E+06
hectare meter/minute	47.194 744 3	4.719 474 4E+01
hectare meter/second	0.786 579 1	7.865 790 7E−01
liter/second	7,865,790.72	7.865 790 7E+06
million acre foot/hour	0.022 956 8	2.295 684 1E−02
thousand cubic foot/day	>>>	2.400 000 0E+07
thousand cubic foot/hour	1,000,000	1.000 000 0E+06
trillion cubic foot/day	0.024	2.400 000 0E−02

trillion cubic foot/hour	0.001	1.000 000 0E−03
billion cubic foot/minute		**<flow rate, volume basis>**
acre foot/second	382.614 019	3.826 140 2E+02
acre foot/second [US, survey]	382.611 723	3.826 117 2E+02
acre inch/second	4,591.368 23	4.591 368 2E+03
billion cubic foot/day	1,440	1.440 000 0E+03
billion cubic foot/hour	60	6.000 000 0E+01
billion cubic foot/second	0.016 666 7	1.666 666 7E−02
cubem/day	9.782 744 8	9.782 744 8E+00
cubem/hour	0.407 614 4	4.076 143 7E−01
cubem/minute	0.006 793 6	6.793 572 8E−03
cubic dekameter/second	471.947 443	4.719 474 4E+02
cubic foot/hour	>>>	6.000 000 0E+10
cubic inch/second	>>>	2.880 000 0E+10
cubic kilometer/day	40.776 259 1	4.077 625 9E+01
cubic kilometer/hour	1.699 010 8	1.699 010 8E+00
cubic kilometer/minute	0.028 316 8	2.831 684 7E−02
cubic meter/second	471,947.443	4.719 474 4E+05
cubic mile/day	9.782 744 8	9.782 744 8E+00
cubic mile/hour	0.407 614 4	4.076 143 7E−01
cubic mile/minute	0.006 793 6	6.793 572 8E−03
gallon/second [US, liquid]	>>>	1.246 753 3E+08
hectare meter/minute	2,831.684 66	2.831 684 7E+03
liter/second	>>>	4.719 474 4E+08
million acre foot/day	33.057 851 2	3.305 785 1E+01
million acre foot/hour	1.377 410 5	1.377 410 5E+00
million acre foot/minute	0.022 956 8	2.295 684 1E−02
thousand cubic foot/hour	>>>	6.000 000 0E+07
thousand cubic foot/minute	1,000,000	1.000 000 0E+06
trillion cubic foot/day	1.44	1.440 000 0E+00
trillion cubic foot/hour	0.06	6.000 000 0E−02
trillion cubic foot/minute	0.001	1.000 000 0E−03
billion cubic foot/second		**<flow rate, volume basis>**
billion cubic foot/day	86,400	8.640 000 0E+04
billion cubic foot/hour	3,600	3.600 000 0E+03
billion cubic foot/minute	60	6.000 000 0E+01
cubem/day	586.964 688	5.869 646 9E+02
cubem/hour	24.456 862	2.445 686 2E+01
cubem/minute	0.407 614 4	4.076 143 7E−01
cubem/second	0.006 793 6	6.793 572 8E−03
cubic dekameter/second	28,316.846 6	2.831 684 7E+04
cubic foot/second	>>>	1.000 000 0E+09
cubic kilometer/day	2,446.575 55	2.446 575 6E+03
cubic kilometer/hour	101.940 648	1.019 406 5E+02
cubic kilometer/minute	1.699 010 8	1.699 010 8E+00
cubic kilometer/second	0.028 316 8	2.831 684 7E−02
cubic meter/second	>>>	2.831 684 7E+07
cubic mile/day	586.964 688	5.869 646 9E+02
cubic mile/hour	24.456 862	2.445 686 2E+01
cubic mile/minute	0.407 614 4	4.076 143 7E−01
cubic mile/second	0.006 793 6	6.793 572 8E−03
million acre foot/day	1,983.471 07	1.983 471 1E+03
million acre foot/hour	82.644 628 1	8.264 462 8E+01
million acre foot/minute	1.377 410 5	1.377 410 5E+00
million acre foot/second	0.022 956 8	2.295 684 1E−02
trillion cubic foot/day	86.4	8.640 000 0E+01
trillion cubic foot/hour	3.6	3.600 000 0E+00
trillion cubic foot/minute	0.06	6.000 000 0E−02
trillion cubic foot/second	0.001	1.000 000 0E−03
biltu [Babylon, ancient]		**<mass, special - see page 29>**
kilogram	30	3.000 000 0E+01

bin [Taiwan]		<area, special - see page 29>
square meter	3.306	3.306 000 0E+00
binae sextulae [Rome, ancient]		<mass, special - see page 29>
gram	9.096	9.096 000 0E+00
bing fang kung chih [Taiwan]		<area, special - see page 29>
square meter	1	1.000 000 0E+00
biot		<electric current>
abampere	1	1.000 000 0E+00
ampere	10	1.000 000 0E+01
electromagnetic unit of current [cgs system]	1	1.000 000 0E+00
gilbert	12.566 370 6	1.256 637 1E+01
statampere	>>>	2.997 924 6E+10
bis [Burma]		<mass, special - see page 29>
gram	1,536.9	1.536 900 0E+03
bismar pound [Denmark]		<mass, special - see page 29>
gram	5,993	5.993 000 0E+03
bismerpund [Denmark]		<mass, special - see page 29>
kilogram	6	6.000 000 0E+00
bismerpund [Norway]		<mass, special - see page 29>
kilogram	6	6.000 000 0E+00
bissmar pound [Denmark]		<mass, special - see page 29>
gram	5,993	5.993 000 0E+03
bitta [Nepal]		<length, special - see page 29>
centimeter	22.86	2.286 000 0E+01
blink		<time>
day	0.000 01	1.000 000 0E-05
second	0.864	8.640 000 0E-01
blondel		<luminance>
apostilb [German Hefner]	1.111 111 1	1.111 111 1E+00
apostilb [international]	1	1.000 000 0E+00
bril	10	1.000 000 0E+01
candela/square foot	0.029 572	2.957 195 6E-02
candela/square meter	0.318 309 9	3.183 098 9E-01
footlambert	0.092 903	9.290 304 0E-02
millilambert	0.1	1.000 000 0E-01
nit	0.318 309 9	3.183 098 9E-01
skot	1,000	1.000 000 0E+03
stilb	0.000 031 8	3.183 098 9E-05
board foot		<volume>
bushel [US, dry]	0.066 963 7	6.696 366 3E-02
cord [firewood]	0.000 651	6.510 416 7E-04
cord foot [timber]	0.005 208 3	5.208 333 3E-03
cubic decimeter	2.359 737 2	2.359 737 2E+00
cubic foot	0.083 333 3	8.333 333 3E-02
cubic inch	144	1.440 000 0E+02
cubic meter	0.002 359 7	2.359 737 2E-03
cubic yard	0.003 086 4	3.086 419 8E-03
million board foot	0.000 001	1.000 000 0E-06
stere	0.002 359 7	2.359 737 2E-03
thousand board foot	0.001	1.000 000 0E-03
Board of Trade Unit		<energy>
cheval vapeur heure [France]	1.359 621 6	1.359 621 6E+00
horsepower hour	1.341 022 1	1.341 022 1E+00
joule	3,600,000	3.600 000 0E+06
kilowatthour	1	1.000 000 0E+00
boccale [Italy]		<volume, special - see page 29>
liter	1.823	1.823 000 0E+00
bochka [Russia]		<volume, special - see page 29>
liter	491.96	4.919 600 0E+02

Convert From	<Type of Unit>	
Convert To	Standard	Scientific

bocka [Russia] — <volume, special - see page 29>
hectoliter -- 4.92 --- 4.920 000 0E+00

bocoy [Cuba] — <volume, special - see page 29>
hectoliter -- 6.624 --- 6.624 000 0E+00

bohar [Indochina] — <mass, special - see page 29>
gram --- 45.38 --- 4.538 000 0E+01

bohar [Sumatra] — <mass, special - see page 29>
gram --48 --- 4.800 000 0E+01

bois equarris [Norway] — <volume, special - see page 29>
cubic meter --2.654 704 --- 2.654 704 0E+00

bois ronds [Norway] — <volume, special - see page 29>
cubic meter --2.123 763 --- 2.123 763 0E+00

bois scies [Norway] — <volume, special - see page 29>
cubic meter --2.920 175 --- 2.920 175 0E+00

boisseau [Belgium] — <volume, special - see page 29>
liter ---15 --- 1.500 000 0E+01

boisseau [France] — <volume, special - see page 29>
liter ---12.5 --- 1.250 000 0E+01

boisseau [Switzerland] — <volume, special - see page 29>
liter ---15 --- 1.500 000 0E+01

bojote [Venezuela] — <mass, special - see page 29>
gram ---250 --- 2.500 000 0E+02

bok [Laos] — <volume, special - see page 29>
liter ---20 --- 2.000 000 0E+01

bok louang [Laos] — <volume, special - see page 29>
liter -- 4 --- 4.000 000 0E+00

bole — <momentum>
dyne second -- 1 --- 1.000 000 0E+00
gram centimeter/second --- 1 --- 1.000 000 0E+00
newton second -- 0.000 01 --- 1.000 000 0E-05
pound foot/second -------------------------------------- 0.000 072 3 --- 7.233 013 9E-05
pound-force second ------------------------------------- 0.000 072 2 --- 2.248 089 4E-06

boll [UK, avoirdupois] — <mass, special - see page 29>
kilogram ---63.503 --- 6.350 300 0E+01

bolt [cloth] — <length>
barleycorn --4,320 --- 4.320 000 0E+03
cubit --80 --- 8.000 000 0E+01
dekameter ---3.657 6 --- 3.657 600 0E+00
digit ---1,920 --- 1.920 000 0E+03
ell [cloth] ---32 --- 3.200 000 0E+01
foot [international] ---120 --- 1.200 000 0E+02
inch [international] ---1,440 --- 1.440 000 0E+03
meter --36.576 --- 3.657 600 0E+01
myriameter --- 0.003 657 6 --- 3.657 600 0E-03
nail [cloth] ---640 --- 6.400 000 0E+02
pace [geometrical] --2.4 --- 2.400 000 0E+00
palm --480 --- 4.800 000 0E+02
quarter [cloth] ---160 --- 1.600 000 0E+02
rope -- 6 --- 6.000 000 0E+00
skein [cloth] --0.333 333 3 --- 3.333 333 3E-01
span --160 --- 1.600 000 0E+02
yard [international] --40 --- 4.000 000 0E+01

bongkal [Malaysia] — <mass, special - see page 29>
gram ---53.913 --- 5.391 300 0E+01

boo [Japan] — <length, special - see page 29>
millimeter ---3.03 --- 3.030 000 0E+00

boot [Netherlands] — <volume, special - see page 29>
hectoliter ---5.3 --- 5.300 000 0E+00

Convert From Convert To		Standard	\<Type of Unit\> Scientific

bota [Portugal]	\<volume, special - see page 29\>		
liter		435	4.350 000 0E+02
bota [Spain, wine]	\<volume, special - see page 29\>		
hectoliter		4.838	4.838 000 0E+00
botchka [Russia]	\<volume, special - see page 29\>		
liter		491.96	4.919 600 0E+02
botella [Costa Rica]	\<volume, special - see page 29\>		
liter		0.67	6.700 000 0E−01
botella [Cuba]	\<volume, special - see page 29\>		
liter		0.725	7.250 000 0E−01
botella [El Salvador]	\<volume, special - see page 29\>		
liter		0.75	7.500 000 0E−01
botella [Guatemala]	\<volume, special - see page 29\>		
liter		0.65	6.500 000 0E−01
botella [Honduras]	\<volume, special - see page 29\>		
centiliter		69.12	6.912 000 0E+01
botella [Nicaragua]	\<volume, special - see page 29\>		
liter		0.67	6.700 000 0E−01
botella [Panama]	\<volume, special - see page 29\>		
liter		0.757	7.570 000 0E−01
botellon [Venezuela]	\<volume, special - see page 29\>		
liter		0.666	6.660 000 0E−01
botija [Ecuador]	\<mass, special - see page 29\>		
kilogram		5.75	5.750 000 0E+00
botijuela [Venezuela]	\<mass, special - see page 29\>		
kilogram		5	5.000 000 0E+00
botsa [Greece]	\<mass, special - see page 29\>		
kilogram		2.56	2.560 000 0E+00
botte [Italy]	\<volume, special - see page 29\>		
hectoliter		9.33	9.330 000 0E+00
bottle [Sri Lanka]	\<volume, special - see page 29\>		
centiliter		75.7	7.570 000 0E+01
bottle [UK, small]	\<volume, special - see page 29\>		
milliliter		275	2.750 000 0E+02
bottle [wine, standard]	\<champagne bottle size\>		
balthazar [champagne bottle]		0.062 5	6.250 000 0E−02
jeroboam [champagne bottle]		0.25	2.500 000 0E−01
liter		0.75	7.500 000 0E−01
magnum [champagne bottle]		0.5	5.000 000 0E−01
methuselah [champagne bottle]		0.125	1.250 000 0E−01
nebuchadnezzar [champagne bottle]		0.05	5.000 000 0E−02
rehoboam [champagne bottle]		0.166 666 7	1.666 666 7E−01
salmanazar [champagne bottle]		0.083 333 3	8.333 333 3E−02
bougie decimale [France]	\<luminous intensity\>		
bougie nouvelle [France]		0.977 928 7	9.779 286 9E−01
candela		0.977 928 7	9.779 286 9E−01
candle [international standard]		0.96	9.600 000 0E−01
Hefner candle [Germany]		1.065 482 8	1.065 482 8E+00
watt/steradian [at 540 THz]		0.001 431 8	1.431 813 6E−03
bougie nouvelle [France]	\<luminous intensity\>		
bougie decimale [France]		1.022 569 4	1.022 569 4E+00
candela		1	1.000 000 0E+00
candle [new]		1	1.000 000 0E+00
Hefner candle [Germany]		1.089 530 2	1.089 530 2E+00
lumen/steradian		1	1.000 000 0E+00
watt/steradian [at 540 THz]		0.001 464 1	1.464 128 8E−03
boutylka [Russia, vodka]	\<volume, special - see page 29\>		
centiliter		61.5	6.150 000 0E+01

Convert From	<Type of Unit>	
Convert To	Standard	Scientific

boutylka [Russia]   <volume, special - see page 29>
liter ---------- 0.769 --- 7.690 000 0E−01

bouw [Indonesia]   <area, special - see page 29>
hectare ---------- 0.709 65 --- 7.096 500 0E−01

bow [India]   <length, special - see page 29>
meter ---------- 1.828 8 --- 1.828 800 0E+00

bow [Pakistan]   <length, special - see page 29>
meter ---------- 1.828 8 --- 1.828 800 0E+00

bozze [Libya]   <volume, special - see page 29>
liter ---------- 2.685 --- 2.685 000 0E+00

braca [Argentina]   <length, special - see page 29>
meter ---------- 1.733 --- 1.733 000 0E+00

braca [Brazil]   <length, special - see page 29>
meter ---------- 2.222 --- 2.222 000 0E+00

braca [Chile]   <length, special - see page 29>
meter ---------- 1.672 --- 1.672 000 0E+00

braca [Colombia]   <length, special - see page 29>
meter ---------- 1.6 --- 1.600 000 0E+00

braca [El Salvador]   <length, special - see page 29>
meter ---------- 1.672 --- 1.672 000 0E+00

braca [Portugal]   <length, special - see page 29>
meter ---------- 2.2 --- 2.200 000 0E+00

braca quadrada [Brazil]   <area, special - see page 29>
square meter ---------- 4.84 --- 4.840 000 0E+00

braccio d'ara [Italy]   <length, special - see page 29>
centimeter ---------- 70 --- 7.000 000 0E+01

brace   <units>
couple ---------- 1 --- 1.000 000 0E+00
one ---------- 2 --- 2.000 000 0E+00
pair ---------- 1 --- 1.000 000 0E+00
single ---------- 2 --- 2.000 000 0E+00
unit ---------- 2 --- 2.000 000 0E+00

brache [Switzerland]   <length, special - see page 29>
centimeter ---------- 60 --- 6.000 000 0E+01

brasse [Argentina]   <length, special - see page 29>
meter ---------- 1.733 --- 1.733 000 0E+00

brasse [Belgium]   <length, special - see page 29>
meter ---------- 1.4 --- 1.400 000 0E+00

brasse [Chile]   <length, special - see page 29>
meter ---------- 1.672 --- 1.672 000 0E+00

brasse [Colombia]   <length, special - see page 29>
meter ---------- 1.6 --- 1.600 000 0E+00

brasse [El Salvador]   <length, special - see page 29>
meter ---------- 1.672 --- 1.672 000 0E+00

brasse [France]   <length, special - see page 29>
meter ---------- 1.62 --- 1.620 000 0E+00

braza [Argentina]   <length, special - see page 29>
meter ---------- 1.733 --- 1.733 000 0E+00

braza [Chile]   <length, special - see page 29>
meter ---------- 1.672 --- 1.672 000 0E+00

braza [Colombia]   <length, special - see page 29>
meter ---------- 1.6 --- 1.600 000 0E+00

braza [Costa Rica]   <length, special - see page 29>
meter ---------- 1.672 --- 1.672 000 0E+00

braza [El Salvador]   <length, special - see page 29>
meter ---------- 1.672 --- 1.672 000 0E+00

Convert From Convert To	<Type of Unit> Standard	Scientific

braza [Guatemala]
<length, special - see page 29>
meter -------------------------------------- 1.672 ---- 1.672 000 0E+00

braza [Panama]
<area, special - see page 29>
are -------------------------------------- 0.027 9 ---- 2.790 000 0E−02

braza [Peru]
<length, special - see page 29>
meter -------------------------------------- 1.672 ---- 1.672 000 0E+00

braza [Philippines]
<area, special - see page 29>
are -------------------------------------- 0.027 9 ---- 2.790 000 0E−02

braza [Spain]
<length, special - see page 29>
meter -------------------------------------- 1.67 ---- 1.670 000 0E+00

braza carree [Philippines]
<area, special - see page 29>
are -------------------------------------- 0.279 5 ---- 2.795 000 0E−01

brazada [Argentina]
<length, special - see page 29>
meter -------------------------------------- 1.733 ---- 1.733 000 0E+00

brazada [Chile]
<length, special - see page 29>
meter -------------------------------------- 1.672 ---- 1.672 000 0E+00

brazada [Colombia]
<length, special - see page 29>
meter -------------------------------------- 1.6 ---- 1.600 000 0E+00

brazada [El Salvador]
<length, special - see page 29>
meter -------------------------------------- 1.672 ---- 1.672 000 0E+00

brente [Switzerland]
<volume, special - see page 29>
liter -------------------------------------- 37.5 ---- 3.750 000 0E+01

brewster
<compressibility>
1/pascal -------------------------------------- <<< 1.000 000 0E−12

brig
<sound pressure level>
bel -------------------------------------- 1 ---- 1.000 000 0E+00
neper -------------------------------------- 1.151 292 6 ---- 1.151 292 6E+00

bril
<luminance>
blondel -------------------------------------- 0.1 ---- 1.000 000 0E−01
candela/square meter -------------------------------------- 0.031 831 ---- 3.183 098 9E−02
millilambert -------------------------------------- 0.01 ---- 1.000 000 0E−02
skot -------------------------------------- 100 ---- 1.000 000 0E+02

briquette [Indonesia]
<mass, special - see page 29>
kilogram -------------------------------------- 0.5 ---- 5.000 000 0E−01

Btu [15 °C]
<energy>
Btu [15.6 °C] -------------------------------------- 1.000 117 6 ---- 1.000 117 6E+00
Btu [15.8 °C, Canada] -------------------------------------- 1.000 179 2 ---- 1.000 179 2E+00
Btu [15.8 °C, ISO] -------------------------------------- 1.000 288 3 ---- 1.000 288 3E+00
Btu [3.9 °C] -------------------------------------- 0.995 408 ---- 9.954 080 0E−01
Btu [I.T.] -------------------------------------- 0.999 761 3 ---- 9.997 612 9E−01
Btu [I.T., pre-1956] -------------------------------------- 0.999 776 3 ---- 9.997 763 1E−01
Btu [mean] -------------------------------------- 0.998 990 4 ---- 9.989 904 1E−01
Btu [thermoc.] -------------------------------------- 1.000 430 3 ---- 1.000 430 3E+00
calorie [15 °C, CIPM, 1950] -------------------------------------- 252.013 86 ---- 2.520 138 6E+02
calorie [15 °C, NBS, 1939] -------------------------------------- 251.995 8 ---- 2.519 958 0E+02
calorie [I.T.] -------------------------------------- 251.935 61 ---- 2.519 356 1E+02
calorie [kilogram, I.T.] -------------------------------------- 0.251 935 6 ---- 2.519 356 1E−01
centigrade heat unit [15 °C] -------------------------------------- 0.555 555 6 ---- 5.555 555 6E−01
cubic foot atmosphere -------------------------------------- 0.367 629 4 ---- 3.676 294 3E−01
frigorie [France] -------------------------------------- 0.251 995 8 ---- 2.519 958 0E−01
joule -------------------------------------- 1,054.804 ---- 1.054 804 0E+03
kilocalorie [I.T.] -------------------------------------- 0.251 935 6 ---- 2.519 356 1E−01
liter atmosphere -------------------------------------- 10.410 106 ---- 1.041 010 6E+01
watthour -------------------------------------- 0.293 001 1 ---- 2.930 011 1E−01

Btu [15.6 °C]
<energy>
Btu [15 °C] -------------------------------------- 0.999 882 4 ---- 9.998 824 4E−01
Btu [15.8 °C, Canada] -------------------------------------- 1.000 061 6 ---- 1.000 061 6E+00
Btu [15.8 °C, ISO] -------------------------------------- 1.000 170 7 ---- 1.000 170 7E+00
Btu [3.9 °C] -------------------------------------- 0.995 291 ---- 9.952 909 9E−01

Convert From Convert To	Standard	\<Type of Unit\> Scientific
Btu [I.T.]	0.999 643 8	9.996 437 6E−01
Btu [I.T. , pre-1956]	0.999 658 8	9.996 587 8E−01
Btu [mean]	0.998 873	9.988 729 7E−01
Btu [thermoc.]	1.000 312 7	1.000 312 7E+00
calorie [I.T.]	251.905 99	2.519 059 9E+02
calorie [kilogram, I.T.]	0.251 906	2.519 059 9E−01
centigrade heat unit [15.6 °C]	0.555 555 6	5.555 555 6E−01
cubic foot atmosphere	0.367 586 2	3.675 862 1E−01
frigorie [France]	0.251 966 2	2.519 661 7E−01
joule	1,054.68	1.054 680 0E+03
kilocalorie [I.T.]	0.251 906	2.519 059 9E−01
kilogram calorie [15 °C, NBS, 1939]	0.251 966 2	2.519 661 7E−01
liter atmosphere	10.408 882	1.040 888 2E+01
watthour	0.292 966 7	2.929 666 7E−01
Btu [15.8 °C, Canada]		\<energy\>
Btu [15 °C]	0.999 820 8	9.998 208 2E−01
Btu [15.6 °C]	0.999 938 4	9.999 383 7E−01
Btu [15.8 °C, ISO]	1.000 109 1	1.000 109 1E+00
Btu [3.9 °C]	0.995 229 7	9.952 296 5E−01
Btu [I.T.]	0.999 582 1	9.995 821 5E−01
Btu [I.T. , pre-1956]	0.999 597 2	9.995 971 7E−01
Btu [mean]	0.998 811 4	9.988 114 1E−01
Btu [thermoc.]	1.000 251 1	1.000 251 1E+00
calorie [I.T.]	251.890 47	2.518 904 7E+02
calorie [kilogram, I.T.]	0.251 890 5	2.518 904 7E−01
centigrade heat unit [15.8 °C, Canada]	0.555 555 6	5.555 555 6E−01
cubic foot atmosphere	0.367 563 6	3.675 635 6E−01
frigorie [France]	0.251 950 6	2.519 506 4E−01
joule	1,054.615	1.054 615 0E+03
kilocalorie [I.T.]	0.251 890 5	2.518 904 7E−01
kilogram calorie [15 °C, NBS, 1939]	0.251 950 6	2.519 506 4E−01
liter atmosphere	10.408 241	1.040 824 1E+01
watthour	0.292 948 6	2.929 486 0E−01
Btu [15.8 °C, ISO]		\<energy\>
Btu [15 °C]	0.999 711 8	9.997 117 9E−01
Btu [15.6 °C]	0.999 829 3	9.998 293 9E−01
Btu [15.8 °C, Canada]	0.999 891	9.998 909 6E−01
Btu [3.9 °C]	0.995 121 1	9.951 211 2E−01
Btu [I.T.]	0.999 473 2	9.994 731 5E−01
Btu [I.T. , pre-1956]	0.999 488 2	9.994 881 7E−01
Btu [mean]	0.998 702 5	9.987 024 9E−01
Btu [thermoc.]	1.000 142	1.000 142 0E+00
calorie [I.T.]	251.863	2.518 630 0E+02
calorie [kilogram, I.T.]	0.251 863	2.518 630 0E−01
centigrade heat unit [15.8 °C, ISO]	0.555 555 6	5.555 555 6E−01
cubic foot atmosphere	0.367 523 5	3.675 234 7E−01
frigorie [France]	0.251 923 2	2.519 231 7E−01
joule	1,054.5	1.054 500 0E+03
kilocalorie [I.T.]	0.251 863	2.518 630 0E−01
kilogram calorie [15 °C, NBS, 1939]	0.251 923 2	2.519 231 7E−01
kilojoule	1.054 5	1.054 500 0E+00
liter atmosphere	10.407 106	1.040 710 6E+01
watthour	0.292 916 7	2.929 166 7E−01
Btu [3.9 °C]		\<energy\>
Btu [15 °C]	1.004 613 2	1.004 613 2E+00
Btu [15.6 °C]	1.004 731 3	1.004 731 3E+00
Btu [15.8 °C, Canada]	1.004 793 2	1.004 793 2E+00
Btu [15.8 °C, ISO]	1.004 902 8	1.004 902 8E+00
Btu [I.T.]	1.004 373 4	1.004 373 4E+00
Btu [I.T. , pre-1956]	1.004 388 5	1.004 388 5E+00
Btu [mean]	1.003 598 9	1.003 598 9E+00
Btu [thermoc.]	1.005 045 5	1.005 045 5E+00
calorie [I.T.]	253.097 83	2.530 978 3E+02

	Standard	Scientific
calorie [kilogram, I.T.]	0.253 097 8	2.530 978 3E-01
centigrade heat unit [3.9 °C]	0.555 555 6	5.555 555 6E-01
cubic foot atmosphere	0.369 325 4	3.693 253 7E-01
frigorie [France]	0.253 158 3	2.531 583 0E-01
joule	1,059.67	1.059 670 0E+03
kilocalorie [I.T.]	0.253 097 8	2.530 978 3E-01
kilogram calorie [15 °C, NBS, 1939]	0.253 158 3	2.531 583 0E-01
liter atmosphere	10.458 13	1.045 813 0E+01
watthour	0.294 352 8	2.943 527 8E-01

Btu [I.T., pre-1956] \<energy\>

	Standard	Scientific
Btu [15 °C]	1.000 223 7	1.000 223 7E+00
Btu [15.6 °C]	1.000 341 3	1.000 341 3E+00
Btu [15.8 °C, Canada]	1.000 403	1.000 403 0E+00
Btu [15.8 °C, ISO]	1.000 512 1	1.000 512 1E+00
Btu [3.9 °C]	0.995 630 7	9.956 307 2E-01
Btu [I.T.]	0.999 985	9.999 849 7E-01
Btu [mean]	0.999 213 9	9.992 139 2E-01
Btu [thermoc.]	1.000 654 2	1.000 654 2E+00
calorie [I.T.]	251.991 97	2.519 919 7E+02
calorie [kilogram, I.T.]	0.251 992	2.519 919 7E-01
centigrade heat unit [I.T., pre-1956]	0.555 555 6	5.555 555 6E-01
frigorie [France]	0.252 052 2	2.520 521 8E-01
joule	1,055.04	1.055 040 0E+03
kilocalorie [I.T.]	0.251 992	2.519 919 7E-01
kilogram calorie [15 °C, NBS, 1939]	0.252 052	2.520 521 8E-01
liter atmosphere	10.412 435	1.041 243 5E+01
watthour	0.293 066 7	2.930 666 7E-01

Btu [I.T.] \<energy\>

	Standard	Scientific
Btu [15 °C]	1.000 238 8	1.000 238 8E+00
Btu [15.6 °C]	1.000 356 4	1.000 356 4E+00
Btu [15.8 °C, Canada]	1.000 418	1.000 418 0E+00
Btu [15.8 °C, ISO]	1.000 527 1	1.000 527 1E+00
Btu [3.9 °C]	0.995 645 7	9.956 456 8E-01
Btu [I.T., pre-1956]	1.000 015	1.000 015 0E+00
Btu [mean]	0.999 228 9	9.992 289 3E-01
Btu [thermoc.]	1.000 669 2	1.000 669 2E+00
calorie [I.T.]	251.995 76	2.519 957 6E+02
calorie [kilogram, I.T.]	0.251 995	2.519 957 6E-01
centigrade heat unit [I.T.]	0.555 555 6	5.555 555 6E-01
cubic foot atmosphere	0.367 717 2	3.677 172 1E-01
cubic foot of liquified petroleum gas [standard]	0.000 396 5	3.965 107 1E-04
frigorie [France]	0.252 056	2.520 559 6E-01
joule	1,055.055 9	1.055 055 9E+03
kilocalorie [I.T.]	0.251 995 8	2.519 957 6E-01
kilogram calorie [15 °C, NBS, 1939]	0.252 056	2.520 559 6E-01
kilogram of water [evaporated from and at 100 °C]	0.000 467 5	4.674 593 9E-04
kilogram of water [heated from 16.7 °C to 100 °C]	0.003 026 1	3.026 098 8E-03
liter atmosphere	10.412 592	1.041 259 2E+01
pound of water [evaporated from and at 100 °C]	0.001 030 6	1.030 571 6E-03
pound of water [heated form 16.7 °C to 100 °C]	0.006 671	6.671 405 9E-03
q-unit	<<<	1.000 000 0E-18
watthour	0.293 071 1	2.930 710 7E-01

Btu [mean] \<energy\>

	Standard	Scientific
Btu [15 °C]	1.001 010 6	1.001 010 6E+00
Btu [15.6 °C]	1.001 128 3	1.001 128 3E+00
Btu [15.8 °C, Canada]	1.001 19	1.001 190 0E+00
Btu [15.8 °C, ISO]	1.001 299 2	1.001 299 2E+00
Btu [3.9 °C]	0.996 414	9.964 139 8E-01
Btu [I.T.]	1.000 771 7	1.000 771 7E+00
Btu [I.T., pre-1956]	1.000 786 7	1.000 786 7E+00
Btu [thermoc.]	1.001 441 4	1.001 441 4E+00
calorie [I.T.]	252.190 22	2.521 902 2E+02
calorie [kilogram, I.T.]	0.252 190 2	2.521 902 2E-01

Convert From Convert To	Standard	\<Type of Unit\> Scientific
centigrade heat unit [mean]	0.555 555 6	5.555 555 6E-01
cubic foot atmosphere	0.368 001	3.680 009 6E-01
frigorie [France]	0.252 250 5	2.522 504 7E-01
gram calorie	252.250 47	2.522 504 7E+02
joule	1,055.87	1.055 870 0E+03
kilocalorie [mean]	0.251 996 4	2.519 964 1E-01
kilogram calorie [15 °C, NBS, 1939]	0.252 250 5	2.522 504 7E-01
kilojoule	1.055 87	1.055 870 0E+00
liter atmosphere	10.420 627	1.042 062 7E+01
watthour	0.293 297 2	2.932 972 2E-01

Btu [thermoc.] \<energy\>

Convert To	Standard	Scientific
Btu [15 °C]	0.999 569 8	9.995 698 4E-01
Btu [15.6 °C]	0.999 687 4	9.996 873 6E-01
Btu [15.8 °C, Canada]	0.999 749	9.997 489 7E-01
Btu [15.8 °C, ISO]	0.999 858	9.998 580 0E-01
Btu [3.9 °C]	0.994 979 8	9.949 798 2E-01
Btu [I.T.]	0.999 331 2	9.993 312 3E-01
Btu [I.T. , pre-1956]	0.999 346 3	9.993 462 5E-01
Btu [mean]	0.998 560 7	9.985 606 8E-01
calorie [I.T.]	251.827 23	2.518 272 3E+02
calorie [kilogram, I.T.]	0.251 827 2	2.518 272 3E-01
centigrade heat unit [thermoc.]	0.555 555 6	5.555 555 6E-01
cubic foot atmosphere	0.367 471 3	3.674 712 9E-01
frigorie [France]	0.251 887 4	2.518 874 0E-01
joule	1,054.350 3	1.054 350 3E+03
kilocalorie [I.T.]	0.251 827 2	2.518 272 3E-01
kilocalorie [thermoc.]	0.251 995 8	2.519 957 6E-01
kilogram calorie [15 °C, NBS, 1939]	0.251 887 4	2.518 874 0E-01
liter atmosphere	10.405 628	1.040 562 8E+01
watthour	0.292 875 1	2.928 750 7E-01

Btu foot/hour square foot °F [I.T.] \<thermal conductivity\>

Convert To	Standard	Scientific
Btu foot/hour square foot °F [thermoc.]	1.000 669 5	1.000 669 5E+00
Btu inch/hour square foot °F [I.T.]	12	1.200 000 0E+01
Btu/hour foot °F [I.T.]	1	1.000 000 0E+00
Btu/hour foot °F [thermoc.]	1.000 669 5	1.000 669 5E+00
calorie centimeter/hour square centimeter °C [I.T.]	14.881 639	1.488 163 9E+01
joule/second meter kelvin	1.730 734 7	1.730 734 7E+00
kilocalorie/hour meter °C [I.T.]	1.488 163 9	1.488 163 9E+00
watt/foot °C	0.527 527 9	5.275 279 3E-01
watt/meter kelvin	1.730 734 7	1.730 734 7E+00

Btu foot/hour square foot °F [thermoc.] \<thermal conductivity\>

Convert To	Standard	Scientific
Btu foot/hour square foot °F [I.T.]	0.999 331	9.993 309 8E-01
Btu inch/hour square foot °F [I.T.]	11.991 972	1.199 197 2E+01
Btu inch/hour square foot °F [thermoc.]	12	1.200 000 0E+01
Btu/hour foot °F [I.T.]	0.999 331	9.993 309 8E-01
Btu/hour foot °F [thermoc.]	1	1.000 000 0E+00
joule/second meter kelvin	1.729 576 8	1.729 576 8E+00
watt/foot °C	0.527 175	5.271 750 7E-01
watt/meter kelvin	1.729 576 8	1.729 576 8E+00

Btu foot/hour square foot degree Rankine [I.T.] \<thermal conductivity\>

Convert To	Standard	Scientific
Btu foot/hour square foot °F [I.T.]	1	1.000 000 0E+00
Btu foot/hour square foot °F [thermoc.]	1.000 669 5	1.000 669 5E+00
Btu inch/hour square foot °F [I.T.]	12	1.200 000 0E+01
Btu inch/hour square foot degree Rankine [I.T.]	12	1.200 000 0E+01
Btu/hour foot °F [I.T.]	1	1.000 000 0E+00
Btu/hour foot degree Rankine [I.T.]	1	1.000 000 0E+00
joule/second meter kelvin	1.730 734 7	1.730 734 7E+00
kilocalorie/hour meter °C [I.T.]	1.488 163 9	1.488 163 9E+00
watt/foot °C	0.527 527 9	5.275 279 3E-01
watt/meter kelvin	1.730 734 7	1.730 734 7E+00

Btu foot/second square foot °F [I.T.] \<thermal conductivity\>

Convert To	Standard	Scientific
Btu foot/hour square foot °F [I.T.]	3,600	3.600 000 0E+03

Convert From Convert To	<Type of Unit> Standard	Scientific
Btu foot/second square foot degree Rankine [I.T.]		
Btu inch/second square foot °F [I.T.]	12	1.200 000 0E+01
Btu/second foot °F [I.T.]	1	1.000 000 0E+00
calorie/second centimeter °C [I.T.]	14.881 639	1.488 163 9E+01
joule/second meter kelvin	6,230.644 8	6.230 644 8E+03
kilowatt/meter kelvin	6.230 644 8	6.230 644 8E+00
watt/foot °C	1,899.100 5	1.899 100 5E+03
watt/meter kelvin	6,230.644 8	6.230 644 8E+03
Btu foot/second square foot degree Rankine [I.T.]		<thermal conductivity>
Btu foot/hour square foot °F [I.T.]	3,600	3.600 000 0E+03
Btu inch/second square foot °F [I.T.]	1	1.000 000 0E+00
Btu inch/second square foot °F [I.T.]	12	1.200 000 0E+01
Btu/hour foot °F [I.T.]	3,600	3.600 000 0E+03
Btu/second foot °F [I.T.]	1	1.000 000 0E+00
calorie/second centimeter °C [I.T.]	14.881 639	1.488 163 9E+01
kilowatt/meter kelvin	6.230 644 8	6.230 644 8E+00
watt/foot °C	1,899.100 5	1.899 100 5E+03
watt/meter kelvin	6,230.644 8	6.230 644 8E+03
Btu inch/day square foot °F [I.T.]		<thermal conductivity>
Btu inch/hour square foot °F [I.T.]	0.003 472 2	3.472 222 2E–03
Btu inch/day square foot degree Rankine [I.T.]	1	1.000 000 0E+00
Btu inch/hour square foot °F [thermoc.]	0.041 666 7	4.166 666 7E–02
Btu/hour foot °F [thermoc.]	0.003 474 5	3.474 546 8E–03
calorie centimeter/hour square centimeter °C [I.T.]	0.051 672 3	5.167 235 9E–02
kilocalorie/hour meter °C [I.T.]	0.005 167 2	5.167 235 9E–03
watt/foot °C	0.001 831 7	1.831 694 2E–03
watt/meter kelvin	0.006 009 5	6.009 495 4E–03
Btu inch/day square foot degree Rankine [I.T.]		<thermal conductivity>
Btu inch/hour square foot °F [I.T.]	0.003 472 2	3.472 222 2E–03
Btu inch/day square foot °F [I.T.]	1	1.000 000 0E+00
Btu inch/hour square foot °F [thermoc.]	0.041 666 7	4.166 666 7E–02
Btu/hour foot °F [I.T.]	0.003 472 2	3.472 222 2E–03
calorie centimeter/hour square centimeter °C [I.T.]	0.051 672 3	5.167 235 9E–02
kilocalorie/hour meter °C [I.T.]	0.005 167 2	5.167 235 9E–03
watt/foot °C	0.001 831 7	1.831 694 2E–03
watt/meter kelvin	0.006 009 5	6.009 495 4E–03
Btu inch/hour square foot °F [I.T.]		<thermal conductivity>
Btu inch/day square foot °F [I.T.]	24	2.400 000 0E+01
Btu/hour foot °F [I.T.]	0.083 333 3	8.333 333 3E–02
calorie centimeter/hour square centimeter °C [I.T.]	1.240 136 6	1.240 136 6E+00
kilocalorie/hour meter °C [I.T.]	0.124 013 7	1.240 136 6E–01
watt/foot °C	0.043 960 7	4.396 066 1E–02
watt/meter kelvin	0.144 227 9	1.442 278 9E–01
Btu inch/hour square foot °F [thermoc.]		<thermal conductivity>
Btu foot/hour square foot °F [thermoc.]	0.083 333 3	8.333 333 3E–02
Btu inch/day square foot °F [I.T.]	23.983 944	2.398 394 4E+01
Btu inch/hour square foot °F [I.T.]	0.999 331	9.993 309 8E–01
Btu/hour foot °F [I.T.]	0.083 277 6	8.327 758 2E–02
Btu/hour foot °F [thermoc.]	0.083 333 3	8.333 333 3E–02
calorie centimeter/hour square centimeter °C [I.T.]	1.239 306 9	1.239 306 9E+00
kilocalorie/hour meter °C [I.T.]	0.123 930 7	1.239 306 9E–01
watt/foot °C	0.043 931 3	4.393 125 0E–02
watt/meter kelvin	0.144 131 4	1.441 314 0E–01
Btu inch/hour square foot degree Rankine [I.T.]		<thermal conductivity>
Btu inch/day square foot °F [I.T.]	24	2.400 000 0E+01
Btu inch/hour square foot °F [I.T.]	1	1.000 000 0E+00
Btu inch/hour square foot °F [thermoc.]	1.000 669 5	1.000 669 5E+00
Btu/hour foot °F [I.T.]	0.083 333 3	8.333 333 3E–02
calorie centimeter/hour square centimeter °C [I.T.]	1.240 136 6	1.240 136 6E+00
kilocalorie/hour meter °C [I.T.]	0.124 013 7	1.240 136 6E–01

Convert From Convert To	Standard	<Type of Unit> Scientific
watt/foot °C	0.043 960 7	4.396 066 1E-02
watt/meter kelvin	0.144 227 9	1.442 278 9E-01

Btu inch/second square foot °F [I.T.]   <thermal conductivity>

Btu foot/hour square foot °F [I.T.]	300	3.000 000 0E+02
Btu foot/second square foot °F [I.T.]	0.083 333 3	8.333 333 3E-02
Btu inch/hour square foot °F [I.T.]	3,600	3.600 000 0E+03
Btu inch/hour square foot degree Rankine [I.T.]	3,600	3.600 000 0E+03
Btu/hour foot °F [I.T.]	300	3.000 000 0E+02
Btu/second foot °F [I.T.]	0.083 333 3	8.333 333 3E-02
calorie centimeter/second square centimeter °C [I.T.]	1.240 136 6	1.240 136 6E+00
calorie/second centimeter °C [I.T.]	1.240 136 6	1.240 136 6E+00
calorie/second centimeter °C [thermoc.]	1.240 966 5	1.240 966 5E+00
watt centimeter/square centimeter °C	5.192 204	5.192 204 0E+00
watt/centimeter kelvin	5.192 204	5.192 204 0E+00
watt/foot °C	158.258 38	1.582 583 8E+02
watt/meter kelvin	519.220 4	5.192 204 0E+02

Btu inch/second square foot °F [thermoc.]   <thermal conductivity>

Btu foot/hour square foot °F [I.T.]	299.799 29	2.997 992 9E+02
Btu foot/second square foot °F [thermoc.]	300	3.000 000 0E+02
Btu inch/hour square foot °F [I.T.]	3,597.591 5	3.597 591 5E+03
Btu inch/hour square foot °F [thermoc.]	3,600	3.600 000 0E+03
Btu/hour foot °F [I.T.]	299.799 29	2.997 992 9E+02
Btu/hour foot °F [thermoc.]	300	3.000 000 0E+02
calorie centimeter/second square centimeter °C [I.T.]	1.239 306 9	1.239 306 9E+00
calorie/second centimeter °C [I.T.]	1.239 306 9	1.239 306 9E+00
calorie/second centimeter °C [thermoc.]	1.240 136 3	1.240 136 3E+00
watt/centimeter kelvin	5.188 730 3	5.188 730 3E+00
watt/foot °C	158.152 5	1.581 525 0E+02
watt/meter kelvin	518.873 03	5.188 730 3E+02

Btu inch/second square foot degree Rankine [I.T.]   <thermal conductivity>

Btu foot/hour square foot °F [I.T.]	300	3.000 000 0E+02
Btu foot/hour square foot °F [thermoc.]	300.200 84	3.002 008 4E+02
Btu inch/second square foot °F [I.T.]	1	1.000 000 0E+00
Btu inch/second square foot °F [thermoc.]	1.000 669 5	1.000 669 5E+00
Btu/hour foot °F [I.T.]	300	3.000 000 0E+02
Btu/hour foot °F [thermoc.]	300.200 84	3.002 008 4E+02
calorie centimeter/second square centimeter °C [I.T.]	1.240 136 6	1.240 136 6E+00
calorie/second centimeter °C [I.T.]	1.240 136 6	1.240 136 6E+00
calorie/second centimeter °C [thermoc.]	1.240 966 5	1.240 966 5E+00
watt/centimeter kelvin	5.192 204	5.192 204 0E+00
watt/foot °C	158.258 38	1.582 583 8E+02
watt/meter kelvin	519.220 4	5.192 204 0E+02

Btu square foot/pound [I.T.]   <total mass stopping power>

calorie square centimeter/gram [I.T.]	516.128	5.161 280 0E+02
joule square meter/kilogram	216.092 47	2.160 924 7E+02

Btu/cubic foot [I.T.]   <energy density>

joule/cubic meter	37,258.946	3.725 894 6E+04

Btu/cubic foot hour [I.T.]   <heat release rate>

joule/cubic meter second	10.349 707	1.034 970 7E+01
kilocalorie/cubic meter hour [I.T.]	8.899 146 3	8.899 146 3E+00
watt/cubic meter	10.349 707	1.034 970 7E+01

Btu/day square foot [I.T.]   <heat flux density>

Btu/day square foot [thermoc.]	1.000 669 2	1.000 669 2E+00
calorie/day square centimeter [I.T.]	0.271 246	2.712 459 8E-01
calorie/day square centimeter [thermoc.]	0.271 427 5	2.714 275 0E-01
kilocalorie/hour square meter [I.T.]	0.113 019 2	1.130 191 6E-01
kilocalorie/hour square meter [thermoc.]	0.113 094 8	1.130 947 9E-01
watt/square foot	0.012 211 3	1.221 129 5E-02
watt/square meter	0.131 441 3	1.314 412 8E-01

Convert From	<Type of Unit>	
Convert To	Standard	Scientific
Btu/day square foot [thermoc.]	<heat flux density>	
Btu/day square foot [I.T.]	0.999 331 2	9.993 312 3E-01
calorie/day square centimeter [I.T.]	0.271 064 6	2.710 645 8E-01
calorie/day square centimeter [thermoc.]	0.271 246	2.712 459 8E-01
kilocalorie/hour square meter [I.T.]	0.112 943 6	1.129 435 7E-01
kilocalorie/hour square meter [thermoc.]	0.113 019 2	1.130 191 6E-01
watt/square meter	0.131 353 4	1.313 533 8E-01
Btu/day square foot °F [I.T.]	<heat transfer coefficient>	
Btu/hour square foot °F [thermoc.]	0.041 694 6	4.169 456 1E-02
calorie/hour square centimeter °C [I.T.]	0.020 343 4	2.034 344 8E-02
watt/square foot °C	0.021 980 3	2.198 033 0E-02
watt/square meter kelvin	0.236 594 3	2.365 943 1E-01
Btu/°F [I.T.]	<specific heat>	
Btu/°F [thermoc.]	1.000 669 5	1.000 669 5E+00
clausius	0.453 592 4	4.535 923 7E-01
joule/kelvin	1,899.100 5	1.899 100 5E+03
kilocalorie/°C [I.T.]	0.453 592 4	4.535 923 7E-01
Btu/°F [thermoc.]	<specific heat>	
Btu/°F [I.T.]	0.999 331	9.993 309 8E-01
joule/kelvin	1,897.83	1.897 830 0E+03
kilocalorie/°C [I.T.]	0.453 592 3	4.535 922 6E-01
Btu/foot [I.T.]	<linear energy transfer>	
electronvolt/meter	>>>	2.160 478 3E+22
joule/meter	3,461.469 3	3.461 469 3E+03
kilocalorie/meter [I.T.]	0.826 757 8	8.267 577 5E-01
Btu/hour [15 °C]	<power>	
Btu/hour [15.6 °C]	1.000 117 6	1.000 117 6E+00
Btu/hour [I.T.]	0.999 761 2	9.997 612 9E-01
Btu/hour [thermoc.]	1.000 430 3	1.000 430 3E+00
calorie/minute [15 °C, CIPM, 1950]	4.200 231	4.200 231 0E+00
calorie/minute [I.T.]	4.198 926 8	4.198 926 8E+00
calorie/minute [thermoc.]	4.201 736 8	4.201 736 8E+00
centigrade heat unit/hour [mean]	0.554 994 7	5.549 946 7E-01
cubic meter atmosphere/second	2.891 696 1	2.891 696 1E+00
dyne centimeter/second	2,930,011.1	2.930 011 1E+06
erg/second	2,930,011.1	2.930 011 1E+06
foot pound-force/minute	12.966 392	1.296 639 2E+01
foot poundal/second	6.953 022	6.953 022 0E+00
gram-force centimeter/second	2,987.779 8	2.987 779 8E+03
horsepower	0.000 392 9	3.929 209 6E-04
horsepower [metric]	0.000 398 4	3.983 706 4E-04
joule/minute	17.580 067	1.758 006 7E+01
kilocalorie/hour [I.T.]	0.251 935 6	2.519 356 1E-01
kilogram square meter/cubic second	0.293 001 1	2.930 011 1E-01
kilogram-force meter/minute	1.792 667 9	1.792 667 9E+00
kilopond meter/minute	1.792 667 9	1.792 667 9E+00
million Btu/hour [I.T.]	0.000 001	9.997 612 9E-07
newton meter/minute	17.580 067	1.758 006 7E+01
pound square foot/cubic second	6.953 022	6.953 022 0E+00
volt ampere	0.293 001 1	2.930 011 1E-01
watt	0.293 001 1	2.930 011 1E-01
Btu/hour [15.6 °C]	<power>	
Btu/hour [15.8 °C, ISO]	1.000 170 7	1.000 170 7E+00
Btu/hour [I.T.]	0.999 643 8	9.996 437 6E-01
Btu/hour [thermoc.]	1.000 312 7	1.000 312 7E+00
calorie/minute [I.T.]	4.198 433 2	4.198 433 2E+00
calorie/minute [thermoc.]	4.201 242 8	4.201 242 8E+00
centigrade heat unit/hour [mean]	0.554 929 4	5.549 294 3E-01
cubic meter atmosphere/second	2.891 356 2	2.891 356 2E+00
dyne centimeter/second	2,929,666.7	2.929 666 7E+06
erg/second	2,929,666.7	2.929 666 7E+06
foot pound-force/minute	12.964 867	1.296 486 7E+01

	Standard	Scientific
foot poundal/second	6.952 204 6	6.952 204 6E+00
gram-force centimeter/second	2,987.428 6	2.987 428 6E+03
horsepower	0.000 392 9	3.928 747 7E−04
horsepower [metric]	0.000 398 3	3.983 238 1E−04
joule/minute	17.578	1.757 800 0E+01
kilocalorie/hour [I.T.]	0.251 906	2.519 059 9E−01
kilogram square meter/cubic second	0.292 966 7	2.929 666 7E−01
kilogram-force meter/minute	1.792 457 2	1.792 457 2E+00
kilopond meter/minute	1.792 457 2	1.792 457 2E+00
lumen [green light at 100% efficiency]	200.682 17	2.006 821 7E+02
million Btu/hour [I.T.]	0.000 001	9.996 437 6E−07
newton meter/minute	17.578	1.757 800 0E+01
pound square foot/cubic second	6.952 204 6	6.952 204 6E+00
volt ampere	0.292 966 7	2.929 666 7E−01
watt	0.292 966 7	2.929 666 7E−01

Btu/hour [15.8 °C, Canada] <power>

	Standard	Scientific
Btu/hour [15.8 °C, ISO]	1.000 109 1	1.000 109 1E+00
Btu/hour [thermoc.]	1.000 251 1	1.000 251 1E+00
calorie/minute [I.T.]	4.198 174 4	4.198 174 4E+00
centigrade heat unit/hour [mean]	0.554 895 2	5.548 952 3E−01
cubic meter atmosphere/second	2.891 178	2.891 178 0E+00
dyne centimeter/second	2,929,486.1	2.929 486 1E+06
erg/second	2,929,486.1	2.929 486 1E+06
foot pound-force/minute	12.964 068	1.296 406 8E+01
foot poundal/second	6.951 776 1	6.951 776 1E+00
gram-force centimeter/second	2,987.244 5	2.987 244 5E+03
horsepower	0.000 392 9	3.928 505 6E−04
horsepower [metric]	0.000 398 3	3.982 992 6E−04
joule/minute	17.576 917	1.757 691 7E+01
kilocalorie/hour [I.T.]	0.251 890 5	2.518 904 7E−01
kilogram square meter/cubic second	0.292 948 6	2.929 486 1E−01
kilogram-force meter/minute	1.792 346 7	1.792 346 7E+00
kilopond meter/minute	1.792 346 7	1.792 346 7E+00
million Btu/hour [I.T.]	0.000 001	9.995 821 5E−07
newton meter/minute	17.576 917	1.757 691 7E+01
pound square foot/cubic second	6.951 776 1	6.951 776 1E+00
volt ampere	0.292 948 6	2.929 486 1E−01
watt	0.292 948 6	2.929 486 1E−01

Btu/hour [15.8 °C, ISO] <power>

	Standard	Scientific
Btu/hour [I.T.]	0.999 473 2	9.994 731 5E−01
Btu/hour [thermoc.]	1.000 142	1.000 142 0E+00
calorie/minute [I.T.]	4.197 716 6	4.197 716 6E+00
centigrade heat unit/hour [mean]	0.554 834 7	5.548 347 2E−01
cubic meter atmosphere/second	2.890 862 7	2.890 862 7E+00
dyne centimeter/second	2,929,166.7	2.929 166 7E+06
erg/second	2,929,166.7	2.929 166 7E+06
foot pound-force/minute	12.962 655	1.296 265 5E+01
foot poundal/second	6.951 018 1	6.951 018 1E+00
gram-force centimeter/second	2,986.918 7	2.986 918 7E+03
horsepower	0.000 392 8	3.928 077 2E−04
horsepower [metric]	0.000 398 3	3.982 558 3E−04
joule/minute	17.575	1.757 500 0E+01
kilocalorie/hour [I.T.]	0.251 863	2.518 630 0E−01
kilogram square meter/cubic second	0.292 916 7	2.929 166 7E−01
kilogram-force meter/minute	1.792 151 2	1.792 151 2E+00
kilopond meter/minute	1.792 151 2	1.792 151 2E+00
newton meter/minute	17.575	1.757 500 0E+01
pound square foot/cubic second	6.951 018 1	6.951 018 1E+00
volt ampere	0.292 916 7	2.929 166 7E−01
watt	0.292 916 7	2.929 166 7E−01

Btu/hour [3.9 °C] <power>

	Standard	Scientific
Btu/hour [I.T.]	1.004 373 4	1.004 373 4E+00
Btu/hour [thermoc.]	1.005 045 5	1.005 045 5E+00

| Convert From | | <Type of Unit> |
Convert To	Standard	Scientific
calorie/minute [I.T.]	4.218 297 2	4.218 297 2E+00
calorie/minute [thermoc.]	4.221 120 1	4.221 120 1E+00
centigrade heat unit/hour [mean]	0.557 555	5.575 549 6E-01
cubic meter atmosphere/second	2.905 036 1	2.905 036 1E+00
dyne centimeter/second	2,943,527.8	2.943 527 8E+06
erg/second	2,943,527.8	2.943 527 8E+06
foot pound-force/second	0.217 103 5	2.171 034 7E-01
foot poundal/second	6.985 097 5	6.985 097 5E+00
gram-force centimeter/second	3,001.563	3.001 563 0E+03
horsepower	0.000 394 7	3.947 335 8E-04
horsepower [metric]	0.000 400 2	4.002 084 0E-04
joule/minute	17.661 167	1.766 116 7E+01
kilocalorie/hour [I.T.]	0.253 097 8	2.530 978 3E-01
kilogram-force meter/minute	1.800 937 8	1.800 937 8E+00
kilopond meter/minute	1.800 937 8	1.800 937 8E+00
million Btu/hour [I.T.]	0.000 001	1.004 373 4E-06
newton meter/minute	17.661 167	1.766 116 7E+01
pound square foot/cubic second	6.985 097 5	6.985 097 5E+00
volt ampere	0.294 352 8	2.943 527 8E-01
watt	0.294 352 8	2.943 527 8E-01

Btu/hour [I.T., pre-1956]		<power>
Btu/hour [I.T.]	0.999 985	9.999 849 7E-01
calorie/minute [I.T.]	4.199 866 2	4.199 866 2E+00
centigrade heat unit/hour [mean]	0.555 118 4	5.551 188 4E-01
cubic meter atmosphere/second	2.892 343 1	2.892 343 1E+00
dyne centimeter/second	2,930,666.7	2.930 666 7E+06
erg/second	2,930,666.7	2.930 666 7E+06
foot pound-force/minute	12.969 293	1.296 929 3E+01
foot poundal/second	6.954 577 6	6.954 577 6E+00
gram-force centimeter/second	2,988.448 3	2.988 448 3E+03
horsepower	0.000 393	3.930 088 7E-04
horsepower [metric]	0.000 398 5	3.984 597 6E-04
joule/minute	17.584	1.758 400 0E+01
kilocalorie/hour [I.T.]	0.251 992	2.519 919 7E-01
kilogram-force meter/minute	1.793 069	1.793 069 0E+00
kilopond meter/minute	1.793 069	1.793 069 0E+00
newton meter/minute	17.584	1.758 400 0E+01
pound square foot/cubic second	6.954 577 6	6.954 577 6E+00
volt ampere	0.293 066 7	2.930 666 7E-01
watt	0.293 066 7	2.930 666 7E-01

Btu/hour [I.T.]		<power>
Btu/hour [thermoc.]	1.000 669 2	1.000 669 2E+00
calorie/minute [I.T.]	4.199 929 4	4.199 929 4E+00
calorie/minute [thermoc.]	4.202 74	4.202 740 0E+00
centigrade heat unit/hour [mean]	0.555 127 1	5.551 271 4E-01
cubic meter atmosphere/second	2.892 386 6	2.892 386 6E+00
dyne centimeter/second	2,930,710.7	2.930 710 7E+06
erg/second	2,930,710.7	2.930 710 7E+06
foot pound-force/minute	12.969 488	1.296 948 8E+01
foot poundal/second	6.954 682 1	6.954 682 1E+00
gram-force centimeter/second	2,988.493 2	2.988 493 2E+03
horsepower	0.000 393	3.930 147 8E-04
horsepower [metric]	0.000 398 5	3.984 657 6E-04
joule/minute	17.584 264	1.758 426 4E+01
kilocalorie/hour [I.T.]	0.251 992 6	2.519 957 6E-01
kilogram-force meter/minute	1.793 095 9	1.793 095 9E+00
kilopond meter/minute	1.793 095 9	1.793 095 9E+00
million Btu/hour [I.T.]	0.000 001	1.000 000 0E-06
newton meter/minute	17.584 264	1.758 426 4E+01
pound square foot/cubic second	6.954 682 1	6.954 682 1E+00
var	0.293 071 1	2.930 710 7E-01
volt ampere	0.293 071 1	2.930 710 7E-01
watt	0.293 071 1	2.930 710 7E-01

Convert From   **\<Type of Unit\>**

Convert To	Standard	Scientific
Btu/hour [mean]		**\<power\>**
Btu/hour [I.T.]	1.000 771 7	1.000 771 7E+00
Btu/hour [thermoc.]	1.001 441 4	1.001 441 4E+00
calorie/minute [I.T.]	4.203 170 3	4.203 170 3E+00
centigrade heat unit/hour [mean]	0.555 555 6	5.555 555 6E−01
cubic meter atmosphere/second	2.894 618 5	2.894 618 5E+00
dyne centimeter/second	2,932,972.2	2.932 972 2E+06
erg/second	2,932,972.2	2.932 972 2E+06
foot pound-force/minute	12.979 496	1.297 949 6E+01
foot poundal/second	6.960 048 8	6.960 048 8E+00
gram-force centimeter/second	2,990.799 3	2.990 799 3E+03
horsepower	0.000 393 3	3.933 180 5E−04
horsepower [metric]	0.000 398 8	3.987 732 4E−04
joule/minute	17.597 833	1.759 783 3E+01
kilocalorie/hour [I.T.]	0.252 190 2	2.521 902 2E−01
kilogram square meter/cubic second	0.293 297 2	2.932 972 2E−01
kilogram-force meter/minute	1.794 479 6	1.794 479 6E+00
kilopond meter/minute	1.794 479 6	1.794 479 6E+00
million Btu/hour [I.T.]	0.000 001	1.000 771 7E−06
newton meter/minute	17.597 833	1.759 783 3E+01
pound square foot/cubic second	6.960 048 8	6.960 048 8E+00
volt ampere	0.293 297 2	2.932 972 2E−01
watt	0.293 297 2	2.932 972 2E−01
Btu/hour [thermoc.]		**\<power\>**
Btu/hour [I.T.]	0.999 331 2	9.993 312 3E−01
calorie/minute [I.T.]	4.197 120 6	4.197 120 6E+00
calorie/minute [thermoc.]	4.199 929 4	4.199 929 4E+00
centigrade heat unit/hour [mean]	0.554 755 9	5.547 559 5E−01
cubic meter atmosphere/second	2.890 452 2	2.890 452 2E+00
dyne centimeter/second	2,928,750.7	2.928 750 7E+06
erg/second	2,928,750.7	2.928 750 7E+06
foot pound-force/minute	12.960 814	1.296 081 4E+01
foot poundal/second	6.950 031	6.950 031 0E+00
gram-force centimeter/second	2,986.494 6	2.986 494 6E+03
horsepower	0.000 392 8	3.927 519 4E−04
horsepower [metric]	0.000 398 2	3.981 992 8E−04
joule/minute	17.572 504	1.757 250 4E+01
kilocalorie/hour [I.T.]	0.251 827 2	2.518 272 3E−01
kilogram square meter/cubic second	0.292 875 1	2.928 750 7E−01
kilogram-force meter/minute	1.791 896 8	1.791 896 8E+00
kilopond meter/minute	1.791 896 8	1.791 896 8E+00
newton meter/minute	17.572 504	1.757 250 4E+01
pound square foot/cubic second	6.950 031	6.950 031 0E+00
volt ampere	0.292 875 1	2.928 750 7E−01
watt	0.292 875 1	2.928 750 7E−01
Btu/hour cubic foot °F [I.T.]		**\<heat transfer coefficient\>**
calorie/second cubic centimeter °C [I.T.]	0.000 004 4	4.449 573 2E−06
kilocalorie/hour cubic meter °C [I.T.]	16.018 463	1.601 846 3E+01
watt/cubic meter kelvin	18.629 473	1.862 947 3E+01
Btu/hour foot °F [I.T.]		**\<thermal conductivity\>**
Btu foot/hour square foot °F [I.T.]	1	1.000 000 0E+00
Btu foot/hour square foot °F [thermoc.]	1.000 669 5	1.000 669 5E+00
Btu inch/hour square foot °F [I.T.]	12	1.200 000 0E+01
Btu inch/hour square foot °F [thermoc.]	12.008 034	1.200 803 4E+01
Btu/hour foot °F [thermoc.]	1.000 669 5	1.000 669 5E+00
Btu/hour foot degree Rankine [I.T.]	1	1.000 000 0E+00
calorie centimeter/hour square centimeter °C [I.T.]	14.881 639	1.488 163 9E+01
joule/second meter kelvin	1.730 734 7	1.730 734 7E+00
kilocalorie/hour meter °C [I.T.]	1.488 163 9	1.488 163 9E+00
watt/foot °C	0.527 527 9	5.275 279 3E−01
watt/meter kelvin	1.730 734 7	1.730 734 7E+00

Btu/hour foot °F [thermoc.] \<thermal conductivity\>

	Standard	Scientific
Btu foot/hour square foot °F [I.T.]	0.999 331	9.993 309 8E−01
Btu foot/hour square foot °F [thermoc.]	1	1.000 000 0E+00
Btu inch/hour square foot °F [I.T.]	11.991 972	1.199 197 2E+01
Btu inch/hour square foot °F [thermoc.]	12	1.200 000 0E+01
Btu/hour foot °F [I.T.]	0.999 331	9.993 309 8E−01
calorie centimeter/hour square foot °C [I.T.]	14.871 683	1.487 168 3E+01
joule/second meter kelvin	1.729 576 8	1.729 576 8E+00
kilocalorie/hour meter °C [I.T.]	1.487 168 3	1.487 168 3E+00
watt/foot °C	0.527 175	5.271 750 0E−01
watt/meter kelvin	1.729 576 8	1.729 576 8E+00

Btu/hour foot degree Rankine [I.T.] \<thermal conductivity\>

	Standard	Scientific
Btu foot/hour square foot °F [I.T.]	1	1.000 000 0E+00
Btu foot/hour square foot °F [thermoc.]	1.000 669 5	1.000 669 5E+00
Btu inch/hour square foot °F [I.T.]	12	1.200 000 0E+01
Btu inch/hour square foot °F [thermoc.]	12.008 034	1.200 803 4E+01
Btu/hour foot °F [I.T.]	1	1.000 000 0E+00
Btu/hour foot °F [thermoc.]	1.000 669 5	1.000 669 5E+00
calorie centimeter/hour square foot °C [I.T.]	14.881 639	1.488 163 9E+01
joule/second meter kelvin	1.730 734 7	1.730 734 7E+00
kilocalorie/hour meter °C [I.T.]	1.488 163 9	1.488 163 9E+00
watt/foot °C	0.527 527 9	5.275 279 3E−01
watt/meter kelvin	1.730 734 7	1.730 734 7E+00

Btu/hour square foot [I.T.] \<heat flux density\>

	Standard	Scientific
Btu/hour square foot [thermoc.]	1.000 669 2	1.000 669 2E+00
calorie/day square centimeter [I.T.]	6.509 903 5	6.509 903 5E+00
calorie/day square centimeter [thermoc.]	6.514 26	6.514 260 0E+00
kilocalorie/hour square meter [I.T.]	2.712 459 8	2.712 459 8E+00
kilocalorie/hour square meter [thermoc.]	2.714 275	2.714 275 0E+00
watt/square meter	3.154 590 7	3.154 590 7E+00

Btu/hour square foot [thermoc.] \<heat flux density\>

	Standard	Scientific
Btu/hour square foot [I.T.]	0.999 331 2	9.993 312 3E−01
calorie/day square centimeter [I.T.]	6.505 549 9	6.505 549 9E+00
calorie/day square centimeter [thermoc.]	6.509 903 5	6.509 903 5E+00
kilocalorie/hour square meter [I.T.]	2.710 645 8	2.710 645 8E+00
kilocalorie/hour square meter [thermoc.]	2.712 459 8	2.712 459 8E+00
watt/square meter	3.152 481 1	3.152 481 1E+00

Btu/hour square foot °F [I.T.] \<heat transfer coefficient\>

	Standard	Scientific
Btu/hour square foot °F [thermoc.]	1.000 669 5	1.000 669 5E+00
calorie/hour square centimeter °C [I.T.]	0.488 242 8	4.882 427 6E−01
watt/square foot °C	0.527 527 9	5.275 279 3E−01
watt/square foot °F	0.293 071 1	2.930 710 7E−01
watt/square meter °C	5.678 263 3	5.678 263 3E+00

Btu/hour square foot °F [thermoc.] \<heat transfer coefficient\>

	Standard	Scientific
Btu/day square foot °F [I.T.]	23.983 944	2.398 394 4E+01
kilocalorie/hour square meter °C [I.T.]	4.879 161 2	4.879 161 2E+00
watt/square foot °C	0.527 175	5.271 750 0E−01
watt/square meter °C	5.674 464 5	5.674 464 5E+00

Btu/minute [15 °C] \<power\>

	Standard	Scientific
Btu/hour [I.T.]	59.985 677	5.998 567 7E+01
Btu/minute [thermoc.]	1.000 430 3	1.000 430 3E+00
calorie/second [I.T.]	4.198 926 8	4.198 926 8E+00
centigrade heat unit/hour [mean]	33.299 68	3.329 968 0E+01
cubic meter atmosphere/second	173.501 77	1.735 017 7E+02
dyne centimeter/second	>>>	1.758 006 7E+08
erg/second	>>>	1.758 006 7E+08
foot pound-force/second	12.966 392	1.296 639 2E+01
foot poundal/second	417.181 32	4.171 813 2E+02
gram-force centimeter/second	179,266.79	1.792 667 9E+05
horsepower	0.023 575 3	2.357 525 8E−02
horsepower [metric]	0.023 902 2	2.390 223 8E−02
joule/second	17.580 067	1.758 006 7E+01

Convert From / Convert To	Standard	<Type of Unit> Scientific

Convert From
Convert To | Standard | <Type of Unit> Scientific

	Standard	Scientific
kilocalorie/hour [I.T.]	15.116 136	1.511 613 6E+01
kilogram square meter/cubic second	17.580 067	1.758 006 7E+01
kilogram-force meter/second	1.792 667 9	1.792 667 9E+00
kilopond meter/second	1.792 667 9	1.792 667 9E+00
newton meter/second	17.580 067	1.758 006 7E+01
pound square foot/cubic second	417.181 32	4.171 813 2E+02
volt ampere	17.580 067	1.758 006 7E+01
watt	17.580 067	1.758 006 7E+01

Btu/minute [15.6 °C] <power>

	Standard	Scientific
Btu/minute [15.8 °C, Canada]	1.000 061 6	1.000 061 6E+00
Btu/minute [I.T.]	0.999 643 8	9.996 437 6E-01
Btu/minute [thermoc.]	1.000 312 7	1.000 312 7E+00
calorie/second [I.T.]	4.198 433 2	4.198 433 2E+00
calorie/second [thermoc.]	4.201 242 8	4.201 242 8E+00
centigrade heat unit/hour [mean]	33.295 766	3.329 576 6E+01
cubic meter atmosphere/second	173.481 37	1.734 813 7E+02
dyne centimeter/second	>>>	1.757 800 0E+08
erg/second	>>>	1.757 800 0E+08
foot pound-force/second	12.964 867	1.296 486 7E+01
foot poundal/second	417.132 28	4.171 322 8E+02
gram-force centimeter/second	179,245.72	1.792 457 2E+05
horsepower	0.023 572 5	2.357 248 6E-02
horsepower [metric]	0.023 899 4	2.389 942 9E-02
joule/second	17.578	1.757 800 0E+01
kilocalorie/hour [I.T.]	15.114 359	1.511 435 9E+01
kilogram square meter/cubic second	17.578	1.757 800 0E+01
kilogram-force meter/second	1.792 457 2	1.792 457 2E+00
kilopond meter/second	1.792 457 2	1.792 457 2E+00
newton meter/second	17.578	1.757 800 0E+01
pound square foot/cubic second	417.132 28	4.171 322 8E+02
volt ampere	17.578	1.757 800 0E+01
watt	17.578	1.757 800 0E+01

Btu/minute [15.8 °C, Canada] <power>

	Standard	Scientific
Btu/minute [15.8 °C, ISO]	1.000 109 1	1.000 109 1E+00
Btu/minute [I.T.]	0.999 582 1	9.995 821 5E-01
Btu/minute [thermoc.]	1.000 251 1	1.000 251 1E+00
calorie/second [I.T.]	4.198 174 4	4.198 174 4E+00
centigrade heat unit/hour [mean]	33.293 714	3.329 371 4E+01
cubic meter atmosphere/second	173.470 68	1.734 706 8E+02
dyne centimeter/second	>>>	1.757 691 7E+08
erg/second	>>>	1.757 691 7E+08
foot pound-force/second	12.964 068	1.296 406 8E+01
foot poundal/second	417.106 57	4.171 065 7E+02
gram-force centimeter/second	179,234.67	1.792 346 7E+05
horsepower	0.023 571	2.357 103 4E-02
horsepower [metric]	0.023 898	2.389 795 6E-02
joule/second	17.576 917	1.757 691 7E+01
kilocalorie/hour [I.T.]	15.113 428	1.511 342 8E+01
kilogram-force meter/second	1.792 346 7	1.792 346 7E+00
kilopond meter/second	1.792 346 7	1.792 346 7E+00
newton meter/second	17.576 917	1.757 691 7E+01
volt ampere	17.576 917	1.757 691 7E+01
watt	17.576 917	1.757 691 7E+01

Btu/minute [15.8 °C, ISO] <power>

	Standard	Scientific
Btu/hour [I.T.]	59.968 389	5.996 838 9E+01
Btu/minute [thermoc.]	1.000 142	1.000 142 0E+00
calorie/second [I.T.]	4.197 716 6	4.197 716 6E+00
calorie/second [thermoc.]	4.200 525 8	4.200 525 8E+00
centigrade heat unit/hour [mean]	33.290 083	3.329 008 3E+01
cubic meter atmosphere/second	173.451 76	1.734 517 6E+02
dyne centimeter/second	>>>	1.757 500 0E+08
erg/second	>>>	1.757 500 0E+08
foot pound-force/second	12.962 655	1.296 265 5E+01

Convert From	<Type of Unit>	
Convert To	Standard	Scientific

foot poundal/second	417.061 08	4.170 610 8E+02
gram-force centimeter/second	179,215.12	1.792 151 2E+05
horsepower	0.023 568 5	2.356 846 3E-02
horsepower [metric]	0.023 895 4	2.389 535 0E-02
joule/second	17.575	1.757 500 0E+01
kilocalorie/hour [I.T.]	15.111 78	1.511 178 0E+01
kilogram square meter/cubic second	17.575	1.757 500 0E+01
kilogram-force meter/second	1.792 151 2	1.792 151 2E+00
kilopond meter/second	1.792 151 2	1.792 151 2E+00
newton meter/second	17.575	1.757 500 0E+01
pound square foot/cubic second	417.061 08	4.170 610 8E+02
volt ampere	17.575	1.757 500 0E+01
watt	17.575	1.757 500 0E+01

Btu/minute [3.9 °C] <power>

Btu/minute [I.T.]	1.004 373 4	1.004 373 4E+00
Btu/minute [thermoc.]	1.005 045 5	1.005 045 5E+00
calorie/second [I.T.]	4.218 297 2	4.218 297 2E+00
calorie/second [thermoc.]	4.221 120 1	4.221 120 1E+00
centigrade heat unit/hour [mean]	33.453 298	3.345 329 8E+01
cubic meter atmosphere/second	174.302 16	1.743 021 6E+02
dyne centimeter/second	>>>	1.766 116 7E+08
erg/second	>>>	1.766 116 7E+08
foot pound-force/second	13.026 208	1.302 620 8E+01
foot poundal/second	419.105 85	4.191 058 5E+02
gigawatt	<<<	1.766 116 7E-08
gram-force centimeter/second	180,093.78	1.800 937 8E+05
horsepower	0.023 684	2.368 401 5E-02
horsepower [metric]	0.024 012 5	2.401 250 4E-02
joule/second	17.661 167	1.766 116 7E+01
kilocalorie/hour [I.T.]	15.185 87	1.518 587 0E+01
kilogram square meter/cubic second	17.661 167	1.766 116 7E+01
kilogram-force meter/second	1.800 937 8	1.800 937 8E+00
kilopond meter/second	1.800 937 8	1.800 937 8E+00
newton meter/second	17.661 167	1.766 116 7E+01
pound square foot/cubic second	419.105 85	4.191 058 5E+02
volt ampere	17.661 167	1.766 116 7E+01
watt	17.661 167	1.766 116 7E+01

Btu/minute [I.T. , pre-1956] <power>

Btu/minute [I.T.]	0.999 985	9.999 849 7E-01
Btu/minute [thermoc.]	1.000 654 2	1.000 654 2E+00
calorie/second [I.T.]	4.199 866 2	4.199 866 2E+00
calorie/second [thermoc.]	4.202 676 9	4.202 676 9E+00
centigrade heat unit/hour [mean]	33.307 131	3.330 713 1E+01
cubic meter atmosphere/second	173.540 59	1.735 405 9E+02
dyne centimeter/second	>>>	1.758 400 0E+08
erg/second	>>>	1.758 400 0E+08
foot pound-force/second	12.969 293	1.296 929 3E+01
foot poundal/second	417.274 66	4.172 746 6E+02
gram-force centimeter/second	179,306.9	1.793 069 0E+05
horsepower	0.023 580 5	2.358 053 2E-02
horsepower [metric]	0.023 907 6	2.390 758 7E-02
joule/second	17.584	1.758 400 0E+01
kilocalorie/hour [I.T.]	15.119 518	1.511 951 8E+01
kilogram square meter/cubic second	17.584	1.758 400 0E+01
kilogram-force meter/second	1.793 069	1.793 069 0E+00
kilopond meter/second	1.793 069	1.793 069 0E+00
newton meter/second	17.584	1.758 400 0E+01
pound square foot/cubic second	417.274 66	4.172 746 6E+02
volt ampere	17.584	1.758 400 0E+01
watt	17.584	1.758 400 0E+01

Btu/minute [I.T.] <power>

Btu/hour [I.T.]	60	6.000 000 0E+01
Btu/minute [I.T. , pre-1956]	1.000 015	1.000 015 0E+00

Convert From	<Type of Unit>	
Convert To	Standard	Scientific

	Standard	Scientific
Btu/minute [thermoc.]	1.000 669 2	1.000 669 2E+00
calorie/second [I.T.]	4.199 929 4	4.199 929 4E+00
calorie/second [thermoc.]	4.202 74	4.202 740 0E+00
centigrade heat unit/hour [mean]	33.307 631	3.330 763 1E+01
cubic meter atmosphere/second	173.543 19	1.735 431 9E+02
dyne centimeter/second	>>>	1.758 426 4E+08
erg/second	>>>	1.758 426 4E+08
foot pound-force/second	12.969 488	1.296 948 8E+01
foot poundal/second	417.280 93	4.172 809 3E+02
gram-force centimeter/second	179,309.59	1.793 095 9E+05
horsepower	0.023 580 9	2.358 088 7E−02
horsepower [metric]	0.023 907 9	2.390 794 6E−02
joule/second	17.584 264	1.758 426 4E+01
kilocalorie/hour [I.T.]	15.119 746	1.511 974 6E+01
kilogram square meter/cubic second	17.584 264	1.758 426 4E+01
kilogram-force meter/second	1.793 095 9	1.793 095 9E+00
kilopond meter/second	1.793 095 9	1.793 095 9E+00
million Btu/hour [I.T.]	0.000 06	6.000 000 0E−05
newton meter/second	17.584 264	1.758 426 4E+01
pound square foot/cubic second	417.280 93	4.172 809 3E+02
ton of refrigeration	0.005	5.000 000 0E−03
volt ampere	17.584 264	1.758 426 4E+01
watt	17.584 264	1.758 426 4E+01

Btu/minute [mean] <power>

	Standard	Scientific
Btu/minute [I.T.]	1.000 771 7	1.000 771 7E+00
Btu/minute [thermoc.]	1.001 441 4	1.001 441 4E+00
calorie/second [I.T.]	4.203 170 3	4.203 170 3E+00
calorie/second [thermoc.]	4.205 983 1	4.205 983 1E+00
centigrade heat unit/hour [mean]	33.333 333	3.333 333 3E+01
cubic meter atmosphere/second	173.677 11	1.736 771 1E+02
dyne centimeter/second	>>>	1.759 783 3E+08
erg/second	>>>	1.759 783 3E+08
foot pound-force/second	12.979 496	1.297 949 6E+01
foot poundal/second	417.602 93	4.176 029 3E+02
gram-force centimeter/second	179,447.96	1.794 479 6E+05
horsepower	0.023 599 1	2.359 908 3E−02
horsepower [UK]	0.023 599 1	2.359 908 3E−02
joule/second	17.597 833	1.759 783 3E+01
kilocalorie/hour [I.T.]	15.131 413	1.513 141 3E+01
kilogram square meter/cubic second	17.597 833	1.759 783 3E+01
kilogram-force meter/second	1.794 479 6	1.794 479 6E+00
kilopond meter/second	1.794 479 6	1.794 479 6E+00
newton meter/second	17.597 833	1.759 783 3E+01
pound square foot/cubic second	417.602 93	4.176 029 3E+02
volt ampere	17.597 833	1.759 783 3E+01
watt	17.597 833	1.759 783 3E+01

Btu/minute [thermoc.] <power>

	Standard	Scientific
Btu/hour [I.T. , pre-1956]	59.960 775	5.996 077 5E+01
Btu/hour [thermoc.]	60	6.000 000 0E+01
calorie/second [I.T.]	4.197 120 6	4.197 120 6E+00
calorie/second [thermoc.]	4.199 929 4	4.199 929 4E+00
centigrade heat unit/hour [mean]	33.285 356	3.328 535 6E+01
cubic meter atmosphere/second	173.427 13	1.734 271 3E+02
dyne centimeter/second	>>>	1.757 250 4E+08
erg/second	>>>	1.757 250 4E+08
foot pound-force/second	12.960 814	1.296 081 4E+01
foot poundal/second	417.001 86	4.170 018 6E+02
gram-force centimeter/second	179,189.68	1.791 896 8E+05
horsepower	0.023 565 1	2.356 511 7E−02
horsepower [metric]	0.023 892	2.389 195 7E−02
joule/second	17.572 504	1.757 250 4E+01
kilocalorie/hour [I.T.]	15.109 634	1.510 963 4E+01
kilogram square meter/cubic second	17.572 504	1.757 250 4E+01

Convert From Convert To	<Type of Unit> Standard	Scientific
kilogram-force meter/second	1.791 896 8	1.791 896 8E+00
kilopond meter/second	1.791 896 8	1.791 896 8E+00
newton meter/second	17.572 504	1.757 250 4E+01
pound square foot/cubic second	417.001 86	4.170 018 6E+02
volt ampere	17.572 504	1.757 250 4E+01
watt	17.572 504	1.757 250 4E+01

Btu/minute square foot [I.T.]   <heat flux density>

Convert To	Standard	Scientific
Btu/hour square foot [I.T.]	60	6.000 000 0E+01
Btu/hour square foot [thermoc.]	60.040 153	6.004 015 3E+01
Btu/minute square foot [thermoc.]	1.000 669 2	1.000 669 2E+00
pyron	0.271 246	2.712 459 8E−01
watt/square foot	17.584 264	1.758 426 4E+01
watt/square meter	189.275 44	1.892 754 4E+02

Btu/minute square foot [thermoc.]   <heat flux density>

Convert To	Standard	Scientific
Btu/hour square foot [I.T.]	59.959 874	5.995 987 4E+01
Btu/hour square foot [thermoc.]	60	6.000 000 0E+01
Btu/minute square foot [I.T.]	0.999 331 2	9.993 312 3E−01
pyron	0.271 064 6	2.710 645 8E−01
watt/square foot	17.572 504	1.757 250 4E+01
watt/square meter	189.148 86	1.891 488 6E+02

Btu/pound [I.T.]   <specific thermodynamic energy>

Convert To	Standard	Scientific
Btu/pound [thermoc.]	1.000 669 2	1.000 669 2E+00
calorie/gram [I.T.]	0.555 555 6	5.555 555 6E−01
calorie/gram [thermoc.]	0.555 927 3	5.559 273 4E−01
joule/kilogram	2,326	2.326 000 0E+03

Btu/pound [thermoc.]   <specific thermodynamic energy>

Convert To	Standard	Scientific
Btu/pound [I.T.]	0.999 331 2	9.993 312 3E−01
calorie/gram [I.T.]	0.555 184	5.551 840 2E−01
calorie/gram [thermoc.]	0.555 555 6	5.555 555 6E−01
joule/kilogram	2,324.444 4	2.324 444 4E+03

Btu/pound °F [I.T.]   <specific heat capacity>

Convert To	Standard	Scientific
Btu/pound °F [thermoc.]	1.000 669 2	1.000 669 2E+00
calorie/gram °C [I.T.]	1	1.000 000 0E+00
calorie/gram °C [thermoc.]	1.000 669 2	1.000 669 2E+00
joule/kilogram kelvin	4,186.8	4.186 800 0E+03
mayer	4.186 8	4.186 800 0E+00

Btu/pound °F [thermoc.]   <specific heat capacity>

Convert To	Standard	Scientific
Btu/pound °F [I.T.]	0.999 331 2	9.993 312 3E−01
calorie/gram °C [I.T.]	0.999 331 2	9.993 312 3E−01
calorie/gram °C [thermoc.]	1	1.000 000 0E+00
joule/kilogram kelvin	4,184	4.184 000 0E+03

Btu/second [15 °C]   <power>

Convert To	Standard	Scientific
Btu/second [I.T.]	0.999 761 3	9.997 612 9E−01
Btu/second [thermoc.]	1.000 430 3	1.000 430 3E+00
calorie/second [I.T.]	251.935 61	2.519 356 1E+02
calorie/second [thermoc.]	252.104 21	2.521 042 1E+02
centigrade heat unit/minute [mean]	33.299 68	3.329 968 0E+01
cheval vapeur [France]	1.434 134 3	1.434 134 3E+00
cubic meter atmosphere/second	10,410.106	1.041 010 6E+04
dyne centimeter/second	>>>	1.054 804 0E+10
erg/second	>>>	1.054 804 0E+10
foot pound-force/second	777.983 51	7.779 835 1E+02
foot poundal/second	25,030.879	2.503 087 9E+04
gram-force centimeter/second	>>>	1.075 600 7E+07
horsepower	1.414 515 5	1.414 515 5E+00
horsepower [metric]	1.434 134 3	1.434 134 3E+00
joule/second	1,054.804	1.054 804 0E+03
kilocalorie/minute [I.T.]	15.116 136	1.511 613 6E+01
kilogram square meter/cubic second	1,054.804	1.054 804 0E+03
kilogram-force meter/second	107.560 07	1.075 600 7E+02
kilopond meter/second	107.560 07	1.075 600 7E+02

| Convert From | | <Type of Unit> |
Convert To	Standard	Scientific
kilowatt	1.054 804	1.054 804 0E+00
newton meter/second	1,054.804	1.054 804 0E+03
pferdestarke [Germany]	1.434 134 3	1.434 134 3E+00
poncelet [France]	1.075 600 7	1.075 600 7E+00
pound square foot/cubic second	25,030.879	2.503 087 9E+04
ton of refrigeration	0.299 928 4	2.999 283 9E−01
volt ampere	1,054.804	1.054 804 0E+03
watt	1,054.804	1.054 804 0E+03

Btu/second [15.6 °C]   \<power\>

Convert To	Standard	Scientific
Btu/second [I.T.]	0.999 643 8	9.996 437 6E−01
Btu/second [thermoc.]	1.000 312 7	1.000 312 7E+00
calorie/second [I.T.]	251.905 99	2.519 059 9E+02
calorie/second [thermoc.]	252.074 57	2.520 745 7E+02
centigrade heat unit/minute [mean]	33.295 766	3.329 576 6E+01
cubic meter atmosphere/second	10,408.882	1.040 888 2E+04
dyne centimeter/second	>>>	1.054 680 0E+10
erg/second	>>>	1.054 680 0E+10
foot pound-force/second	777.892 05	7.778 920 5E+02
foot poundal/second	25,027.937	2.502 793 7E+04
gram-force centimeter/second	>>>	1.075 474 3E+07
horsepower	1.414 349 2	1.414 349 2E+00
horsepower [metric]	1.433 965 7	1.433 965 7E+00
joule/second	1,054.68	1.054 680 0E+03
kilocalorie/minute [I.T.]	15.114 359	1.511 435 9E+01
kilogram-force meter/second	107.547 43	1.075 474 3E+02
kilopond meter/second	107.547 43	1.075 474 3E+02
kilowatt	1.054 68	1.054 680 0E+00
newton meter/second	1,054.68	1.054 680 0E+03
pferdestarke [Germany]	1.433 965 7	1.433 965 7E+00
poncelet [France]	1.075 474 3	1.075 474 3E+00
pound square foot/cubic second	25,027.937	2.502 793 7E+04
ton of refrigeration	0.299 893 1	2.998 931 3E−01
volt ampere	1,054.68	1.054 680 0E+03
watt	1,054.68	1.054 680 0E+03

Btu/second [15.8 °C, Canada]   \<power\>

Convert To	Standard	Scientific
Btu/second [I.T.]	0.999 582 1	9.995 821 5E−01
Btu/second [thermoc.]	1.000 251 1	1.000 251 1E+00
calorie/second [I.T.]	251.890 47	2.518 904 7E+02
calorie/second [thermoc.]	252.059 03	2.520 590 3E+02
centigrade heat unit/minute [mean]	33.293 714	3.329 371 4E+01
cheval vapeur [France]	1.433 877 4	1.433 877 4E+00
cubic meter atmosphere/second	10,408.241	1.040 824 1E+04
dyne centimeter/second	>>>	1.054 615 0E+10
erg/second	>>>	1.054 615 0E+10
foot pound-force/second	777.844 11	7.778 441 1E+02
foot poundal/second	25,026.394	2.502 639 4E+04
gram-force centimeter/second	>>>	1.075 408 0E+07
horsepower	1.414 262	1.414 262 0E+00
horsepower [metric]	1.433 877 4	1.433 877 4E+00
joule/second	1,054.615	1.054 615 0E+03
kilocalorie/minute [I.T.]	15.113 428	1.511 342 8E+01
kilogram square meter/cubic second	1,054.615	1.054 615 0E+03
kilogram-force meter/second	107.540 8	1.075 408 0E+02
kilopond meter/second	107.540 8	1.075 408 0E+02
kilowatt	1.054 615	1.054 615 0E+00
newton meter/second	1,054.615	1.054 615 0E+03
pferdestarke [Germany]	1.433 877 4	1.433 877 4E+00
poncelet [France]	1.075 408	1.075 408 0E+00
pound square foot/cubic second	25,026.394	2.502 639 4E+04
ton of refrigeration	0.299 874 7	2.998 746 5E−01
volt ampere	1,054.615	1.054 615 0E+03
watt	1,054.615	1.054 615 0E+03

Btu/second [15.8 °C, ISO] <power>

Btu/second [I.T.]	0.999 473 2	9.994 731 5E−01
Btu/second [thermoc.]	1.000 142	1.000 142 0E+00
calorie/second [I.T.]	251.863	2.518 630 0E+02
calorie/second [thermoc.]	252.031 55	2.520 315 5E+02
centigrade heat unit/minute [mean]	33.290 083	3.329 008 3E+01
cheval vapeur [France]	1.433 721	1.433 721 0E+00
cubic meter atmosphere/second	10,407.106	1.040 710 6E+04
dyne centimeter/second	>>>	1.054 500 0E+10
erg/second	>>>	1.054 500 0E+10
foot pound-force/second	777.759 29	7.777 592 9E+02
foot poundal/second	25,023.665	2.502 366 5E+04
gram-force centimeter/second	>>>	1.075 290 7E+07
horsepower	1.414 107 8	1.414 107 8E+00
horsepower [metric]	1.433 721	1.433 721 0E+00
joule/second	1,054.5	1.054 500 0E+03
kilocalorie/minute [I.T.]	15.111 78	1.511 178 0E+01
kilogram square meter/cubic second	1,054.5	1.054 500 0E+03
kilogram-force meter/second	107.529 07	1.075 290 7E+02
kilopond meter/second	107.529 07	1.075 290 7E+02
kilowatt	1.054 5	1.054 500 0E+00
newton meter/second	1,054.5	1.054 500 0E+03
pferdestarke [Germany]	1.433 721	1.433 721 0E+00
poncelet [France]	1.075 290 7	1.075 290 7E+00
ton of refrigeration	0.299 842	2.998 419 5E−01
volt ampere	1,054.5	1.054 500 0E+03
watt	1,054.5	1.054 500 0E+03

Btu/second [3.9 °C] <power>

Btu/second [I.T.]	1.004 373 4	1.004 373 4E+00
Btu/second [thermoc.]	1.005 045 5	1.005 045 5E+00
calorie/second [I.T.]	253.097 83	2.530 978 3E+02
calorie/second [thermoc.]	253.267 21	2.532 672 1E+02
centigrade heat unit/minute [mean]	33.453 298	3.345 329 8E+01
cheval vapeur [France]	1.440 750 2	1.440 750 2E+00
cubic meter atmosphere/second	10,458.13	1.045 813 0E+04
dyne centimeter/second	>>>	1.059 670 0E+10
erg/second	>>>	1.059 670 0E+10
foot pound-force/second	781.572 48	7.815 724 8E+02
foot poundal/second	25,146.351	2.514 635 1E+04
gram-force centimeter/second	>>>	1.080 562 7E+07
horsepower	1.421 040 9	1.421 040 9E+00
horsepower [metric]	1.440 750 2	1.440 750 2E+00
joule/second	1,059.67	1.059 670 0E+03
kilocalorie/minute [I.T.]	15.185 87	1.518 587 0E+01
kilogram square meter/cubic second	1,059.67	1.059 670 0E+03
kilogram-force meter/second	108.056 27	1.080 562 7E+02
kilopond meter/second	108.056 27	1.080 562 7E+02
kilowatt	1.059 67	1.059 670 0E+00
newton meter/second	1,059.67	1.059 670 0E+03
pferdestarke [Germany]	1.440 750 2	1.440 750 2E+00
poncelet [France]	1.080 562 7	1.080 562 7E+00
pound square foot/cubic second	25,146.351	2.514 635 1E+04
ton of refrigeration	0.301 312	3.013 120 1E−01
volt ampere	1,059.67	1.059 670 0E+03
watt	1,059.67	1.059 670 0E+03

Btu/second [I.T. , pre-1956] <power>

Btu/second [I.T.]	0.999 985	9.999 849 7E−01
Btu/second [thermoc.]	1.000 654 2	1.000 654 2E+00
calorie/second [I.T.]	251.991 97	2.519 919 7E+02
calorie/second [thermoc.]	252.160 61	2.521 606 1E+02
centigrade heat unit/minute [mean]	33.307 131	3.330 713 1E+01
cheval vapeur [France]	1.434 455 2	1.434 455 2E+00
cubic meter atmosphere/second	10,412.435	1.041 243 5E+04

Convert From Convert To	<Type of Unit>	
	Standard	Scientific
dyne centimeter/second ----------->>>	---	1.055 040 0E+10
erg/second ----------->>>	---	1.055 040 0E+10
foot pound-force/second-----------	778.157 57	--- 7.781 575 7E+02
foot poundal/second-----------	25,036.479	--- 2.503 647 9E+04
gram-force centimeter/second ----------->>>	---	1.075 841 4E+07
horsepower-----------	1.414 831 9	--- 1.414 831 9E+00
horsepower [metric]-----------	1.434 455 2	--- 1.434 455 2E+00
joule/second-----------	1,055.04	--- 1.055 040 0E+03
kilocalorie/minute [I.T.]-----------	15.119 518	--- 1.511 951 8E+01
kilogram square meter/cubic second-----------	1,055.04	--- 1.055 040 0E+03
kilogram-force meter/second-----------	107.584 14	--- 1.075 841 4E+02
kilopond meter/second-----------	107.584 14	--- 1.075 841 4E+02
kilowatt-----------	1.055 04	--- 1.055 040 0E+00
newton meter/second-----------	1,055.04	--- 1.055 040 0E+03
pferdestarke [Germany]-----------	1.434 455 2	--- 1.434 455 2E+00
poncelet [France]-----------	1.075 841 4	--- 1.075 841 4E+00
ton of refrigeration-----------	0.299 995 5	--- 2.999 954 9E-01
volt ampere-----------	1,055.04	--- 1.055 040 0E+03
watt-----------	1,055.04	--- 1.055 040 0E+03
Btu/second [I.T.]		**<power>**
Btu/second [I.T., pre-1956]-----------	1.000 015	--- 1.000 015 0E+00
Btu/second [thermoc.]-----------	1.000 669 2	--- 1.000 669 2E+00
calorie/second [I.T.]-----------	251.995 76	--- 2.519 957 6E+02
calorie/second [thermoc.]-----------	252.164 4	--- 2.521 644 0E+02
centigrade heat unit/minute [mean]-----------	33.307 631	--- 3.330 763 1E+01
cheval vapeur [France]-----------	1.434 476 7	--- 1.434 476 7E+00
cubic meter atmosphere/second-----------	10,412.592	--- 1.041 259 2E+04
dyne centimeter/second ----------->>>	---	1.055 055 9E+10
erg/second ----------->>>	---	1.055 055 9E+10
foot pound-force/second-----------	778.169 26	--- 7.781 692 6E+02
foot poundal/second-----------	25,036.856	--- 2.503 685 6E+04
gram-force centimeter/second ----------->>>	---	1.075 857 6E+07
horsepower-----------	1.414 853 2	--- 1.414 853 2E+00
horsepower [metric]-----------	1.434 476 7	--- 1.434 476 7E+00
joule/second-----------	1,055.055 9	--- 1.055 055 9E+03
kilocalorie/minute [I.T.]-----------	15.119 746	--- 1.511 974 6E+01
kilogram square meter/cubic second-----------	1,055.055 9	--- 1.055 055 9E+03
kilogram-force meter/second-----------	107.585 76	--- 1.075 857 6E+02
kilopond meter/second-----------	107.585 76	--- 1.075 857 6E+02
kilowatt-----------	1.055 055 9	--- 1.055 055 9E+00
million Btu/hour [I.T.]-----------	0.003 6	--- 3.600 000 0E-03
newton meter/second-----------	1,055.055 9	--- 1.055 055 9E+03
pferdestarke [Germany]-----------	1.434 476 7	--- 1.434 476 7E+00
poncelet [France]-----------	1.075 857 6	--- 1.075 857 6E+00
pound square foot/cubic second-----------	25,036.856	--- 2.503 685 6E+04
ton of refrigeration-----------	0.3	--- 3.000 000 0E-01
volt ampere-----------	1,055.055 9	--- 1.055 055 9E+03
watt-----------	1,055.055 9	--- 1.055 055 9E+03
Btu/second [mean]		**<power>**
Btu/second [I.T.]-----------	1.000 771 7	--- 1.000 771 7E+00
Btu/second [thermoc.]-----------	1.001 441 4	--- 1.001 441 4E+00
calorie/second [I.T.]-----------	252.190 22	--- 2.521 902 2E+02
calorie/second [thermoc.]-----------	252.358 99	--- 2.523 589 9E+02
centigrade heat unit/hour [mean]-----------	2,000	--- 2.000 000 0E+03
cheval vapeur [France]-----------	1.435 583 7	--- 1.435 583 7E+00
cubic meter atmosphere/second-----------	10,420.627	--- 1.042 062 7E+04
dyne centimeter/second ----------->>>	---	1.055 870 0E+10
erg/second ----------->>>	---	1.055 870 0E+10
foot pound-force/second-----------	778.769 75	--- 7.787 697 5E+02
foot poundal/second-----------	25,056.176	--- 2.505 617 6E+04
gram-force centimeter/second ----------->>>	---	1.076 687 8E+07
horsepower-----------	1.415 945	--- 1.415 945 0E+00
horsepower [metric]-----------	1.435 583 7	--- 1.435 583 7E+00

Convert From		<Type of Unit>
Convert To	Standard	Scientific

joule/second		
kilocalorie/minute [I.T.]	1,055.87	1.055 870 0E+03
kilogram square meter/cubic second	15.131 413	1.513 141 3E+01
kilogram-force meter/second	1,055.87	1.055 870 0E+03
kilopond meter/second	107.668 78	1.076 687 8E+02
kilowatt	107.668 78	1.076 687 8E+02
newton meter/second	1,055.87	1.055 870 0E+00
pferdestarke [Germany]	1,055.87	1.055 870 0E+03
poncelet [France]	1.435 583 7	1.435 583 7E+00
pound square foot/cubic second	1.076 687 8	1.076 687 8E+00
ton of refrigeration	25,056.176	2.505 617 6E+04
volt ampere	0.300 231 5	3.002 315 0E−01
watt	1,055.87	1.055 870 0E+03

Btu/second [thermoc.]		<power>
Btu/minute [I.T.]	59.959 874	5.995 987 4E+01
Btu/minute [thermoc.]	60	6.000 000 0E+01
calorie/second [I.T.]	251.827 23	2.518 272 3E+02
calorie/second [thermoc.]	251.995 76	2.519 957 6E+02
centigrade heat unit/minute [mean]	33.285 356	3.328 535 6E+01
cheval vapeur [France]	1.433 517 4	1.433 517 4E+00
cubic meter atmosphere/second	10,405.628	1.040 562 8E+04
dyne centimeter/second	>>>	1.054 350 3E+10
erg/second	>>>	1.054 350 3E+10
foot pound-force/second	777.648 85	7.776 488 5E+02
foot poundal/second	25,020.112	2.502 011 2E+04
gram-force centimeter/second	>>>	1.075 138 1E+07
horsepower	1.413 907	1.413 907 0E+00
horsepower [metric]	1.433 517 4	1.433 517 4E+00
joule/second	1,054.350 3	1.054 350 3E+03
kilocalorie/minute [I.T.]	15.109 634	1.510 963 4E+01
kilogram square meter/cubic second	1,054.350 3	1.054 350 3E+03
kilogram-force meter/second	107.513 81	1.075 138 1E+02
kilopond meter/second	107.513 81	1.075 138 1E+02
kilowatt	1.054 350 3	1.054 350 3E+00
newton meter/second	1,054.350 3	1.054 350 3E+03
pferdestarke [Germany]	1.433 517 4	1.433 517 4E+00
poncelet [France]	1.075 138 1	1.075 138 1E+00
ton of refrigeration	0.299 799 4	2.997 993 7E−01
volt ampere	1,054.350 3	1.054 350 3E+03
watt	1,054.350 3	1.054 350 3E+03

Btu/second °F [I.T.]		<thermal conductance>
kilocalorie/second °C [I.T.]	0.453 592 4	4.535 923 7E−01
watt/kelvin	1,899.100 5	1.899 100 5E+03

Btu/second foot °F [I.T.]		<thermal conductivity>
Btu foot/second square foot °F [I.T.]	1	1.000 000 0E+00
Btu inch/second square foot °F [I.T.]	12	1.200 000 0E+01
Btu inch/second square foot °F [thermoc.]	12.008 034	1.200 803 4E+01
Btu/second foot degree Rankine [I.T.]	1	1.000 000 0E+00
calorie centimeter/second square centimeter °C [I.T.]	14.881 639	1.488 163 9E+01
calorie/second centimeter °C [I.T.]	14.881 639	1.488 163 9E+01
calorie/second centimeter °C [thermoc.]	14.891 598	1.489 159 8E+01
kilowatt/meter °C	6.230 644 8	6.230 644 8E+00
kilowatt/meter kelvin	6.230 644 8	6.230 644 8E+00
watt/foot °C	1,899.100 5	1.899 100 5E+03
watt/meter kelvin	6,230.644 8	6.230 644 8E+00

Btu/second foot degree Rankine [I.T.]		<thermal conductivity>
Btu foot/second square foot °F [I.T.]	1	1.000 000 0E+00
Btu inch/second square foot °F [I.T.]	12	1.200 000 0E+01
Btu inch/second square foot °F [thermoc.]	12.008 034	1.200 803 4E+01
Btu/second foot °F [I.T.]	1	1.000 000 0E+00
calorie centimeter/second square centimeter °C [I.T.]	14.881 639	1.488 163 9E+01
calorie/second centimeter °C [I.T.]	14.881 639	1.488 163 9E+01

Convert From Convert To	Standard	Scientific
calorie/second centimeter °C [thermoc.]	14.891 598	1.489 159 8E+01
kilowatt/meter °C	6.230 644 8	6.230 644 8E+00
kilowatt/meter kelvin	6.230 644 8	6.230 644 8E+00
watt/foot °C	1,899.100 5	1.899 100 5E+03
watt/meter kelvin	6,230.644 8	6.230 644 8E+03

Btu/second square foot [I.T.]   \<heat flux density\>

	Standard	Scientific
Btu/minute square foot [I.T.]	60	6.000 000 0E+01
Btu/minute square foot [thermoc.]	60.040 153	6.004 015 3E+01
Btu/second square foot [thermoc.]	1.000 669 2	1.000 669 2E+00
calorie/second square centimeter [I.T.]	0.271 246	2.712 459 8E-01
calorie/second square centimeter [thermoc.]	0.271 427 5	2.714 275 0E-01
finsen unit	0.113 565 3	1.135 652 7E-01
watt/square inch	7.326 776 8	7.326 776 8E+00
watt/square meter	11,356.527	1.135 652 7E+04

Btu/second square foot [thermoc.]   \<heat flux density\>

	Standard	Scientific
Btu/minute square foot [I.T.]	59.959 847	5.995 987 4E+01
Btu/minute square foot [thermoc.]	60	6.000 000 0E+01
Btu/second square foot [I.T.]	0.999 331 2	9.993 312 3E-01
pyron	16.263 875	1.626 387 5E+01
watt/square inch	7.321 876 8	7.321 876 8E+00
watt/square meter	11,348.932	1.134 893 2E+04

Btu/second square foot °F [I.T.]   \<heat transfer coefficient\>

	Standard	Scientific
Btu/second square foot °F [thermoc.]	1.000 669 2	1.000 669 2E+00
calorie/second square centimeter °C [I.T.]	0.488 242 8	4.882 427 6E-01
watt/square foot °C	1,899.100 5	1.899 100 5E+03
watt/square meter kelvin	20,441.748	2.044 174 8E+04

Btu/second square foot °F [thermoc.]   \<heat transfer coefficient\>

	Standard	Scientific
Btu/second square foot °F [I.T.]	0.999 331	9.993 309 8E-01
calorie/hour square centimeter °C [I.T.]	1,756.498	1.756 498 0E+03
watt/square foot °C	1,897.83	1.897 830 0E+03
watt/square meter kelvin	20,428.072	2.042 807 2E+04

Btu/second square inch [I.T.]   \<heat flux density\>

	Standard	Scientific
Btu/second square inch [thermoc.]	1.000 669 2	1.000 669 2E+00
calorie/second square centimeter [I.T.]	39.059 421	3.905 942 1E+01
calorie/second square centimeter [thermoc.]	39.085 56	3.908 556 0E+01
watt/square inch	1,055.055 9	1.055 055 9E+03
watt/square meter	1,635,339.8	1.635 339 8E+06
watt/square millimeter	1.635 339 8	1.635 339 8E+00

Btu/second square inch [thermoc.]   \<heat flux density\>

	Standard	Scientific
Btu/second square inch [I.T.]	0.999 331 2	9.993 312 3E-01
calorie/second square centimeter [I.T.]	39.033 299	3.903 329 9E+01
calorie/second square centimeter [thermoc.]	39.059 421	3.905 942 1E+01
pyron	2,341.998	2.341 998 0E+03
watt/square inch	1,054.350 3	1.054 350 3E+03
watt/square meter	1,634,246.2	1.634 246 2E+06

Btu/square foot [I.T.]   \<energy fluence\>

	Standard	Scientific
electronvolt/square meter	>>>	7.088 183 4E+22
joule/square meter	11,356.527	1.135 652 7E+04
kilocalorie/square meter [I.T.]	2.712 459 8	2.712 459 8E+00

Btu/square foot [thermoc.]   \<energy fluence\>

	Standard	Scientific
joule/square meter	11,348.932	1.134 893 2E+04

bu [Japan]   \<area, special - see page 29\>

	Standard	Scientific
square meter	3.306	3.306 000 0E+00

bucket [UK]   \<volume, special - see page 29\>

	Standard	Scientific
liter	18.183 84	1.818 384 0E+01

bugday [Turkey]   \<mass, special - see page 29\>

	Standard	Scientific
milligram	50.1	5.010 000 0E+01

bulto [Philippines]   \<volume, special - see page 29\>

	Standard	Scientific
liter	75	7.500 000 0E+01

bulto [Philippines]   \<mass, special - see page 29\>
  kilogram -- 61.35----6.135 000 0E+01

bulto [Venezuela]   \<mass, special - see page 29\>
  kilogram -- 49----4.900 000 0E+01

buncal [Indochina]   \<mass, special - see page 29\>
  gram --- 45.38----4.538 000 0E+01

buncal [Sumatra]   \<mass, special - see page 29\>
  gram -- 48----4.800 000 0E+01

bunder [Netherlands]   \<area, special - see page 29\>
  hectare-- 1----1.000 000 0E+00

bundle [South Africa]   \<mass, special - see page 29\>
  kilogram ------------------------------------ 3.175 147----3.175 147 0E+00

bunkal [Indochina]   \<mass, special - see page 29\>
  gram --- 45.38----4.538 000 0E+01

bunkal [Sumatra]   \<mass, special - see page 29\>
  gram -- 48----4.800 000 0E+01

busa [Saudi Arabia, ancient]   \<length, special - see page 29\>
  centimeter-- 2.54----2.540 000 0E+00

busa [Sudan]   \<length, special - see page 29\>
  centimeter-- 2.54----2.540 000 0E+00

bushel [UK, struck measure]   \<volume\>
  barrel [UK] ------------------------------------ 0.222 222 7----2.222 226 8E-01
  bushel [US, dry] ------------------------------ 1.032 058 9----1.032 058 9E+00
  bushel [US, struck measure] ------------- 1.032 058 9----1.032 058 9E+00
  cubic foot ------------------------------------- 1.284 351 9----1.284 351 9E+00
  cubic inch --2,219.36----2.219 360 0E+03
  cubic meter ---------------------------------- 0.036 368 8----3.636 879 4E-02
  cubic yard ----------------------------------- 0.047 568 6----4.756 858 7E-02
  gallon [UK, dry or liquid] ------------------ 8.000 016 4----8.000 016 4E+00
  gallon [US, dry] ---------------------------- 8.256 470 8----8.256 470 8E+00
  peck [UK] ------------------------------------ 4.000 008 2----4.000 008 2E+00
  peck [US] ----------------------------------- 4.128 235 4----4.128 235 4E+00
  pint [UK] -------------------------------------- 64.000 131----6.400 013 1E+01
  pint [US, dry] ------------------------------- 66.051 767----6.605 176 7E+01
  quart [UK] ----------------------------------- 32.000 065----3.200 006 5E+01
  quart [US, dry] ----------------------------- 33.025 883----3.302 588 3E+01
  stere -- 0.036 368 8----3.636 879 4E-02

bushel [UK]   \<volume\>
  board foot --------------------------------- 15.412 191----1.541 219 1E+01
  bushel [US, dry] ------------------------------ 1.032 056 7----1.032 056 7E+00
  chaldron [UK, dry]---------------------------- 0.027 777 8----2.777 777 8E-02
  chaldron [US, dry]---------------------------- 0.028 668 2----2.866 824 3E-02
  cubic foot ------------------------------------- 1.284 349 2----1.284 349 2E+00
  cubic inch ---------------------------------- 2,219.355 5----2.219 355 5E+03
  cubic meter ---------------------------------- 0.036 368 7----3.636 872 0E-02
  cubic yard ----------------------------------- 0.047 568 5----4.756 849 0E-02
  gallon [UK, dry or liquid] ----------------------------8----8.000 000 0E+00
  gallon [US, dry] ---------------------------- 8.256 453 9----8.256 453 9E+00
  peck [UK] --4----4.000 000 0E+00
  peck [US] ----------------------------------- 4.128 227 0----4.128 227 0E+00
  pint [UK] ---64----6.400 000 0E+01
  pint [US, dry] ------------------------------- 66.051 632----6.605 163 2E+01
  quart [UK] --32----3.200 000 0E+01
  quart [US, dry] ----------------------------- 33.025 816----3.302 581 6E+01
  quarter [UK] --- 0.125----1.250 000 0E-01
  stere -- 0.036 368 7----3.636 872 0E-02

bushel [US, dry]   \<volume\>
  barrel [US, dry] ---------------------------- 0.304 764 7----3.047 647 4E-01
  barrel [US, dry commodities except cranberry]---------- 0.304 761 9----3.047 619 0E-01
  bushel [UK] -------------------------------------- 0.968 939----9.689 389 7E-01

| Convert From | | <Type of Unit> |
Convert To	Standard	Scientific
cubic foot	1.244 456	1.244 456 0E+00
cubic inch	2,150.42	2.150 420 0E+03
cubic meter	0.035 239 1	3.523 907 0E-02
cubic yard	0.046 091	4.609 096 4E-02
gallon [UK, dry or liquid]	7.751 511 8	7.751 511 8E+00
gallon [US, dry]	8	8.000 000 0E+00
peck [UK]	3.875 755 9	3.875 755 9E+00
peck [US]	4	4.000 000 0E+00
pint [UK]	62.012 094	6.201 209 4E+01
pint [US, dry]	64	6.400 000 0E+01
quart [UK]	31.006 047	3.100 604 7E+01
quart [US, dry]	32	3.200 000 0E+01
stere	0.035 239 1	3.523 907 0E-02
bushel [US, heaped]		<volume>
barrel [US, dry]	0.389 415 4	3.894 153 9E-01
barrel [US, dry commodities except cranberry]	0.389 411 8	3.894 117 7E-01
bushel [UK]	1.238 068 9	1.238 068 9E+00
bushel [US, dry]	1.277 757 4	1.277 757 4E+00
cubic foot	1.590 112 8	1.590 112 8E+00
cubic inch	2,747.715	2.747 715 0E+03
cubic meter	0.045 027	4.502 698 2E-02
cubic yard	0.058 893 1	5.889 306 8E-02
gallon [UK, dry or liquid]	9.904 551 3	9.904 551 3E+00
gallon [US, dry]	10.222 059	1.022 205 9E+01
peck [UK]	4.952 275 6	4.952 275 6E+00
peck [US]	5.111 029 5	5.111 029 5E+00
pint [US, dry]	81.776 472	8.177 647 2E+01
quart [US, dry]	40.888 236	4.088 823 6E+01
stere	0.045 027	4.502 698 2E-02
bushel [US, struck measure]		<volume>
barrel [US, dry]	0.304 764 7	3.047 647 4E-01
barrel [US, dry commodities except cranberry]	0.304 761 9	3.047 619 0E-01
bushel [US, heaped]	0.782 621 2	7.826 212 0E-01
cubic foot	1.244 456	1.244 456 0E+00
cubic inch	2,150.42	2.150 420 0E+03
cubic meter	0.035 239 1	3.523 907 0E-02
cubic yard	0.046 091	4.609 096 4E-02
gallon [UK, dry or liquid]	7.751 511 8	7.751 511 8E+00
gallon [US, dry]	8	8.000 000 0E+00
peck [UK]	3.875 755 9	3.875 755 9E+00
peck [US]	4	4.000 000 0E+00
pint [US, dry]	64	6.400 000 0E+01
quart [US, dry]	32	3.200 000 0E+01
stere	0.035 239 1	3.523 907 0E-02
buttima [Persia]		<mass, special - see page 29>
kilogram	11.482	1.148 200 0E+01
byce [Malaya and Singapore]		<volume, special - see page 29>
liter	0.505	5.050 000 0E-01
byee [Burma]		<volume, special - see page 29>
liter	0.505	5.050 000 0E-01
cab [Hebrew, ancient]		<volume, special - see page 29>
liter	1	1.000 000 0E+00
caba [Eritrea]		<volume, special - see page 29>
liter	2	2.000 000 0E+00
caba [Somalia]		<volume, special - see page 29>
liter	0.453	4.530 000 0E-01
cabaho [Eritrea]		<volume, special - see page 29>
liter	6	6.000 000 0E+00
caballeria [Canada]		<area, special - see page 29>
hectare	43.7	4.370 000 0E+01

caballeria [Costa Rica]
hectare — <area, special - see page 29>
— 45.25 — 4.525 000 0E+01

caballeria [Cuba]
hectare — <area, special - see page 29>
— 13.42 — 1.342 000 0E+01

caballeria [Dominican Republic]
hectare — <area, special - see page 29>
— 75.46 — 7.546 000 0E+01

caballeria [Ecuador]
hectare — <area, special - see page 29>
— 11.29 — 1.129 000 0E+01

caballeria [El Salvador]
hectare — <area, special - see page 29>
— 44.965 — 4.496 500 0E+01

caballeria [Guatemala]
hectare — <area, special - see page 29>
— 44.72 — 4.472 000 0E+01

caballeria [Honduras]
hectare — <area, special - see page 29>
— 44.97 — 4.497 000 0E+01

caballeria [Mexico]
hectare — <area, special - see page 29>
— 42.8 — 4.280 000 0E+01

caballeria [Nicaragua]
hectare — <area, special - see page 29>
— 45.158 — 4.515 800 0E+01

caballeria [Spain]
hectare — <area, special - see page 29>
— 38.64 — 3.864 000 0E+01

caban [Philippines]
liter — <volume, special - see page 29>
— 75 — 7.500 000 0E+01

cabda [Arabia, ancient]
centimeter — <length, special - see page 29>
— 7.9 — 7.900 000 0E+00

cabelleria [Nicaragua]
hectare — <area, special - see page 29>
— 45.08 — 4.508 000 0E+01

cable length [US, survey]

Convert To	Standard	Scientific
chain [Gunter or US, survey]	10.909 091	1.090 909 1E+01
chain [Ramden or Engineer]	7.200 014 4	7.200 014 4E+00
fathom [US, survey]	120	1.200 000 0E+02
foot [international]	720.001 44	7.200 014 4E+02
foot [US, survey]	720	7.200 000 0E+02
furlong [US, survey]	1.090 909 1	1.090 909 1E+00
inch [based on US, survey foot]	8,640	8.640 000 0E+03
meter	219.456 44	2.194 564 4E+02
out [US, survey]	2.181 818 2	2.181 818 2E+00
pace [geometrical]	14.400 029	1.440 002 9E+01
pace [US, survey]	288	2.880 000 0E+02
perch [US, survey]	43.636 364	4.363 636 4E+01
pole [US, survey]	43.636 364	4.363 636 4E+01
rod [US, survey]	43.636 364	4.363 636 4E+01
yard [based on US, survey foot]	240	2.400 000 0E+02
yard [international]	240.000 48	2.400 004 8E+02
yard [UK]	240.000 9	2.400 009 0E+02

cabulla [Venezuela]
kilogram — <mass, special - see page 29>
— 20 — 2.000 000 0E+01

cabulla [Venezuela]
meter — <length, special - see page 29>
— 80 — 8.000 000 0E+01

cadaa [Egypt, ancient]
liter — <volume, special - see page 29>
— 2.06 — 2.060 000 0E+00

cadastral denum [Lebanon]
square meter — <area, special - see page 29>
— 1,000 — 1.000 000 0E+03

cadastral yoke [Hungary]
hectare — <area, special - see page 29>
— 0.575 464 — 5.754 640 0E-01

cadne [Lebanon]
hectare — <area, special - see page 29>
— 0.29 — 2.900 000 0E-01

cafa [Guatemala]
kilogram — <mass, special - see page 29>
— 16 — 1.600 000 0E+01

Convert From / Convert To	Standard	Scientific
caffiso [Algeria]	<volume, special - see page 29>	
liter	317.47	3.174 700 0E+02
caffiso [Italy]	<volume, special - see page 29>	
liter	21.2	2.120 000 0E+01
caffiso [Malta]	<volume, special - see page 29>	
liter	20.4	2.040 000 0E+01
caffiz [Tunisia]	<volume, special - see page 29>	
liter	640	6.400 000 0E+02
cafiso [Italy]	<volume, special - see page 29>	
liter	21.2	2.120 000 0E+01
cafiso [Tunisia]	<volume, special - see page 29>	
hectoliter	5.819	5.819 000 0E+00
cafisso [Tunisia]	<volume, special - see page 29>	
liter	640	6.400 000 0E+02
cafiz [Spain]	<volume, special - see page 29>	
liter	250	2.500 000 0E+02
cafla [Arabia, ancient]	<mass, special - see page 29>	
gram	3.167	3.167 000 0E+00
cahaho [Eritrea]	<volume, special - see page 29>	
liter	6	6.000 000 0E+00
cahia [Nicaragua]	<volume, special - see page 29>	
liter	607.6	6.076 000 0E+02
cahiz [Spain]	<volume, special - see page 29>	
liter	666	6.660 000 0E+02
caja [Costa Rica]	<mass, special - see page 29>	
kilogram	16	1.600 000 0E+01
caja [El Salvador]	<mass, special - see page 29>	
kilogram	16	1.600 000 0E+01
caja [Honduras]	<mass, special - see page 29>	
kilogram	16	1.600 000 0E+01
caja [Nicaragua]	<mass, special - see page 29>	
kilogram	16	1.600 000 0E+01
caja [Venezuela]	<mass, special - see page 29>	
kilogram	41	4.100 000 0E+01
cajon [Venezuela, dry]	<volume, special - see page 29>	
liter	40	4.000 000 0E+01
cajuela [Costa Rica]	<volume, special - see page 29>	
liter	17	1.700 000 0E+01
cajuela [El Salvador]	<volume, special - see page 29>	
liter	16.6	1.660 000 0E+01
cajuela [Guatemala]	<volume, special - see page 29>	
liter	16.6	1.660 000 0E+01
cajuela [Honduras]	<volume, special - see page 29>	
liter	16.6	1.660 000 0E+01
cajuela [Nicaragua]	<volume, special - see page 29>	
liter	16.6	1.660 000 0E+01
cal [Poland]	<length, special - see page 29>	
millimeter	24	2.400 000 0E+01
calc [Greece, ancient]	<mass, special - see page 29>	
milligram	101	1.010 000 0E+02
caliber		<length>
barleycorn	0.03	3.000 000 0E-02
foot [international]	0.000 833 3	8.333 333 3E-04
inch [based on US, survey foot]	0.01	9.999 980 0E-03
inch [international]	0.01	1.000 000 0E-02
link [Gunter or US, survey]	0.001 262 6	1.262 623 7E-03

Convert To	Standard	Scientific

link [Ramden or Engineer]

Convert To	Standard	Scientific
meter	0.000 833 3	8.333 333 3E-04
microinch	0.000 254	2.540 000 0E-04
micron	10,000	1.000 000 0E+04
mil	254	2.540 000 0E+02
millimicron	10	1.000 000 0E+01
thou	254,000	2.540 000 0E+05
wavelength of orange-red spectral line of krypton-86	419.293 99	4.192 939 9E+02

calorie [15 °C, CIPM, 1950] <energy>

Convert To	Standard	Scientific
Btu [I.T.]	0.003 967 1	3.967 088 6E-03
calorie [15 °C, NBS, 1939]	0.999 928 3	9.999 283 3E-01
calorie [20 °C]	1.000 860 9	1.000 860 9E+00
calorie [I.T.]	0.999 689 5	9.996 895 0E-01
calorie [mean]	0.998 921 3	9.989 212 5E-01
calorie [thermoc.]	1.000 358 5	1.000 358 5E+00
cubic centimeter atmosphere	41.307 673	4.130 767 3E+01
foot pound-force	3.087 066 4	3.087 066 4E+00
gigaelectronvolt	99.323 423	9.932 342 3E+01
gram calorie	>>>	2.612 382 5E+10
inch pound-force	0.999 928 3	9.999 283 3E-01
joule	37.044 797	3.704 479 7E+01
kilogram square meter/square second	4.185 5	4.185 500 0E+00
kilopond meter	0.426 802 2	4.268 022 2E-01
megaerg	41.855	4.185 500 0E+01
megalerg	41.855	4.185 500 0E+01
meter kilogram-force	0.426 802 2	4.268 022 2E-01
newton meter	4.185 5	4.185 500 0E+00
wattsecond	4.185 5	4.185 500 0E+00

calorie [15 °C, NBS, 1939] <energy>

Convert To	Standard	Scientific
Btu [I.T.]	0.003 967 4	3.967 372 9E-03
calorie [15 °C, CIPM, 1950]	1.000 071 7	1.000 071 7E+00
calorie [20 °C]	1.000 932 6	1.000 932 6E+00
calorie [I.T.]	0.999 761 0	9.997 611 5E-01
calorie [mean]	0.998 992 8	9.989 928 4E-01
calorie [thermoc.]	1.000 430 2	1.000 430 2E+00
cubic centimeter atmosphere	41.310 634	4.131 063 4E+01
foot pound-force	3.087 287 6	3.087 287 6E+00
foot poundal	99.330 543	9.933 054 3E+01
gigaelectronvolt	>>>	2.612 569 7E+10
gram calorie	1	1.000 000 0E+00
inch pound-force	37.047 452	3.704 745 2E+01
joule	4.185 8	4.185 800 0E+00
kilogram square meter/square second	4.185 8	4.185 800 0E+00
kilopond meter	0.426 832 8	4.268 328 1E-01
megaerg	41.858	4.185 800 0E+01
megalerg	41.858	4.185 800 0E+01
meter kilogram-force	0.426 832 8	4.268 328 1E-01
newton meter	4.185 8	4.185 800 0E+00
wattsecond	4.185 8	4.185 800 0E+00

calorie [20 °C] <energy>

Convert To	Standard	Scientific
Btu [I.T.]	0.003 963 7	3.963 676 4E-03
calorie [15 °C, CIPM, 1950]	0.999 139 9	9.991 398 9E-01
calorie [15 °C, NBS, 1939]	0.999 068 3	9.990 682 8E-01
calorie [I.T.]	0.998 829 7	9.988 296 6E-01
calorie [mean]	0.998 062 1	9.980 620 6E-01
calorie [thermoc.]	0.999 498 1	9.994 980 9E-01
cubic centimeter atmosphere	41.272 144	4.127 214 4E+01
foot pound-force	3.084 411 2	3.084 411 2E+00
foot poundal	99.237 994	9.923 799 4E+01
gigaelectronvolt	>>>	2.610 135 5E+10
gram calorie	0.999 068 3	9.990 682 8E-01
inch pound-force	37.012 934	3.701 293 4E+01

Convert From / Convert To	Standard	Scientific

Convert From Convert To	Standard	Scientific (Type of Unit)
joule	4.181 9	4.181 900 0E+00
kilogram square meter/square second	4.181 9	4.181 900 0E+00
kilopond meter	0.426 435 1	4.264 351 2E-01
megaerg	41.819	4.181 900 0E+01
megalerg	41.819	4.181 900 0E+01
meter kilogram-force	0.426 435 1	4.264 351 2E-01
newton meter	4.181 9	4.181 900 0E+00
wattsecond	4.181 9	4.181 900 0E+00
calorie [I.T.]		**\<energy\>**
Btu [I.T.]	0.003 968 3	3.968 320 7E-03
calorie [15 °C, CIPM, 1950]	1.000 310 6	1.000 310 6E+00
calorie [15 °C, NBS, 1939]	1.000 238 9	1.000 238 9E+00
calorie [20 °C]	1.001 171 7	1.001 171 7E+00
calorie [kilogram, I.T.]	0.001	1.000 000 0E-03
calorie [mean]	0.999 231 5	9.992 315 1E-01
calorie [thermoc.]	1.000 669 2	1.000 669 2E+00
cubic centimeter atmosphere	41.320 503	4.132 050 3E+01
foot pound-force	3.088 025 2	3.088 025 2E+00
foot poundal	99.354 273	9.935 427 3E+01
gram calorie	1.000 238 9	1.000 238 9E+00
inch pound-force	37.056 302	3.705 630 2E+01
joule	4.186 8	4.186 800 0E+00
kilogram square meter/square second	4.186 8	4.186 800 0E+00
kilopond meter	0.426 934 8	4.269 347 8E-01
megaerg	41.868	4.186 800 0E+01
megalerg	41.868	4.186 800 0E+01
meter kilogram-force	0.426 934 8	4.269 347 8E-01
newton meter	4.186 8	4.186 800 0E+00
wattsecond	4.186 8	4.186 800 0E+00
calorie [kilogram, I.T.]		**\<energy\>**
Btu [I.T.]	3.968 320 7	3.968 320 7E+00
calorie [I.T.]	1,000	1.000 000 0E+03
calorie [kilogram, mean]	0.999 231 5	9.992 315 1E-01
calorie [kilogram, thermoc.]	1.000 669 2	1.000 669 2E+00
calorie [nutritional]	1.000 669 2	1.000 669 2E+00
centigrade heat unit [I.T.]	2.204 622 6	2.204 622 6E+00
cubic foot atmosphere	1.459 219 8	1.459 219 8E+00
dekawatthour	0.116 3	1.163 000 0E-01
frigorie [France]	1.000 238 9	1.000 238 9E+00
joule	4,186.8	4.186 800 0E+03
kilocalorie [I.T.]	1	1.000 000 0E+00
kilogram calorie [15 °C, NBS, 1939]	1.000 238 9	1.000 238 9E+00
liter atmosphere	41.320 503	4.132 050 3E+01
watthour	1.163	1.163 000 0E+00
calorie [kilogram, mean]		**\<energy\>**
Btu [I.T.]	3.971 372 7	3.971 372 7E+00
Btu [mean]	3.968 310 5	3.968 310 5E+00
calorie [I.T.]	1,000.769 1	1.000 769 1E+03
calorie [kilogram, I.T.]	1.000 769 1	1.000 769 1E+00
calorie [kilogram, thermoc.]	1.001 438 8	1.001 438 8E+00
calorie [nutritional]	1.001 438 8	1.001 438 8E+00
centigrade heat unit [mean]	2.204 616 9	2.204 616 9E+00
cubic foot atmosphere	1.460 342 1	1.460 342 1E+00
dekawatthour	0.116 389 4	1.163 894 4E-01
frigorie [France]	1.001 008 2	1.001 008 2E+00
joule	4,190.02	4.190 020 0E+03
kilocalorie [mean]	1	1.000 000 0E+00
kilogram calorie [15 °C, NBS, 1939]	1.001 008 2	1.001 008 2E+00
liter atmosphere	41.352 282	4.135 228 2E+01
watthour	1.163 894 4	1.163 894 4E+00
calorie [kilogram, thermoc.]		**\<energy\>**
Btu [I.T.]	3.965 666 8	3.965 666 8E+00

Convert To	Standard	Scientific
Btu [thermoc.]	3.968 320 7	3.968 320 7E+00
calorie [I.T.]	999.331 23	9.993 312 3E+02
calorie [kilogram, I.T.]	0.999 331 2	9.993 312 3E-01
calorie [kilogram, mean]	0.998 563 3	9.985 632 5E-01
calorie [nutritional]	1	1.000 000 0E+00
centigrade heat unit [thermoc.]	2.204 622 6	2.204 622 6E+00
cubic foot atmosphere	1.458 243 9	1.458 243 9E+00
dekawatthour	0.116 222 2	1.162 222 2E-01
frigorie [France]	0.999 57	9.995 699 7E-01
joule	4,184	4.184 000 0E+03
kilocalorie [I.T.]	0.999 331 2	9.993 312 3E-01
kilocalorie [mean]	0.998 563 3	9.985 632 5E-01
kilocalorie [thermoc.]	1	1.000 000 0E+00
kilogram calorie [15 °C, NBS, 1939]	0.999 57	9.995 699 7E-01
liter atmosphere	41.292 869	4.129 286 9E+01
watthour	1.162 222 2	1.162 222 2E+00

calorie [mean] \<energy\>

Convert To	Standard	Scientific
Btu [I.T.]	0.003 971 4	3.971 372 7E-03
Btu [mean]	0.003 968 3	3.968 310 5E-03
calorie [15 °C, CIPM, 1950]	1.001 079 9	1.001 079 9E+00
calorie [15 °C, NBS, 1939]	1.001 008 2	1.001 008 2E+00
calorie [20 °C]	1.001 941 7	1.001 941 7E+00
calorie [I.T.]	1.000 769 1	1.000 769 1E+00
calorie [thermoc.]	1.001 438 8	1.001 438 8E+00
cubic centimeter atmosphere	41.352 282	4.135 228 2E+01
foot pound-force	3.090 400 2	3.090 400 2E+00
foot poundal	99.430 685	9.943 068 5E+01
gram calorie	1.001 008 2	1.001 008 2E+00
inch pound-force	37.084 802	3.708 480 2E+01
joule	4.190 02	4.190 020 0E+00
kilogram square meter/square second	4.190 02	4.190 020 0E+00
kilopond meter	0.427 263 1	4.272 631 3E-01
megaerg	41.900 2	4.190 020 0E+01
megalerg	41.900 2	4.190 020 0E+01
meter kilogram-force	0.427 263 1	4.272 631 3E-01
newton meter	4.190 02	4.190 020 0E+00
wattsecond	4.190 02	4.190 020 0E+00

calorie [nutritional] \<energy\>

Convert To	Standard	Scientific
Btu [I.T.]	3.965 666 8	3.965 666 8E+00
calorie [I.T.]	999.331 23	9.993 312 3E+02
calorie [kilogram, I.T.]	0.999 331 2	9.993 312 3E-01
calorie [kilogram, mean]	0.998 563 3	9.985 632 5E-01
calorie [kilogram, thermoc.]	1	1.000 000 0E+00
calorie [thermoc.]	1,000	1.000 000 0E+03
centigrade heat unit [thermoc.]	2.204 622 6	2.204 622 6E+00
cubic foot atmosphere	1.458 243 9	1.458 243 9E+00
dekawatthour	0.116 222 2	1.162 222 2E-01
frigorie [France]	0.999 57	9.995 699 7E-01
joule	4,184	4.184 000 0E+03
kilocalorie [thermoc.]	1	1.000 000 0E+00
kilogram calorie [15 °C, NBS, 1939]	0.999 57	9.995 699 7E-01
liter atmosphere	41.292 869	4.129 286 9E+01
watthour	1.162 222 2	1.162 222 2E+00

calorie [thermoc.] \<energy\>

Convert To	Standard	Scientific
Btu [I.T.]	0.003 965 7	3.965 666 8E-03
Btu [thermoc.]	0.003 968 3	3.968 320 7E-03
calorie [15 °C, CIPM, 1950]	0.999 641 6	9.996 416 0E-01
calorie [15 °C, NBS, 1939]	0.999 57	9.995 699 7E-01
calorie [20 °C]	1.000 502 2	1.000 502 2E+00
calorie [I.T.]	0.999 331 2	9.993 312 3E-01
calorie [kilogram, thermoc.]	0.001	1.000 000 0E-03
calorie [mean]	0.998 563 3	9.985 632 5E-01
calorie [nutritional]	0.001	1.000 000 0E-03

Convert From	<Type of Unit>	
Convert To	Standard	Scientific

cubic centimeter atmosphere	41.292 869	4.129 286 9E+01
foot pound-force	3.085 96	3.085 960 0E+00
foot poundal	99.287 828	9.928 782 8E+01
gram calorie	0.999 57	9.995 699 7E−01
inch pound-force	37.031 52	3.703 152 0E+01
joule	4.184	4.184 000 0E+00
kilogram square meter/square second	4.184	4.184 000 0E+00
kilopond meter	0.426 649 3	4.266 492 6E−01
kiloton [metric, explosive energy]	<<<	1.000 000 0E−12
megaerg	41.84	4.184 000 0E+01
megalerg	41.84	4.184 000 0E+01
meter kilogram-force	0.426 649 3	4.266 492 6E−01
newton meter	4.184	4.184 000 0E+00
wattsecond	4.184	4.184 000 0E+00

calorie centimeter/hour square centimeter °C [I.T.]   <thermal conductivity>

Btu foot/hour square foot °F [I.T.]	0.067 196 9	6.719 689 8E−02
Btu foot/hour square foot °F [thermoc.]	0.067 241 9	6.724 188 4E−02
Btu inch/day square foot °F [I.T.]	19.352 706	1.935 270 6E+01
Btu inch/hour square foot °F [I.T.]	0.806 362 8	8.063 627 7E−01
Btu inch/hour square foot °F [thermoc.]	0.806 902 6	8.069 026 0E−01
kilocalorie/hour meter °C [I.T.]	0.1	1.000 000 0E−01
watt/foot °C	0.035 448 2	3.544 824 0E−02
watt/meter kelvin	0.116 3	1.163 000 0E−01

calorie centimeter/second square centimeter °C [I.T.]   <thermal conductivity>

Btu foot/hour square foot °F [I.T.]	241.908 83	2.419 088 3E+02
Btu foot/hour square foot °F [thermoc.]	242.070 78	2.420 707 8E+02
Btu inch/second square foot °F [I.T.]	0.806 362 8	8.063 627 7E−01
Btu inch/second square foot °F [thermoc.]	0.806 902 6	8.069 026 0E−01
Btu/hour foot °F [I.T.]	241.908 83	2.419 088 3E+02
Btu/hour foot °F [thermoc.]	242.070 78	2.420 707 8E+02
calorie/second centimeter °C [I.T.]	1	1.000 000 0E+00
calorie/second centimeter °C [thermoc.]	1.000 669 2	1.000 669 2E+00
watt centimeter/square centimeter °C	4.186 8	4.186 800 0E+00
watt/centimeter kelvin	4.186 8	4.186 800 0E+00
watt/foot °C	127.613 66	1.276 136 6E+02
watt/meter kelvin	418.68	4.186 800 0E+02

calorie square centimeter/gram [I.T.]   <total mass stopping power>

Btu square foot/pound [I.T.]	0.001 937 5	1.937 503 9E−03
joule square meter/kilogram	0.418 68	4.186 800 0E−01

calorie/cubic centimeter [I.T.]   <energy density>

joule/cubic meter	4,186,800	4.186 800 0E+06

calorie/cubic centimeter second [I.T.]   <heat release rate>

Btu/cubic foot hour [I.T.]	404,533.18	4.045 331 8E+05
joule/cubic meter second	4,186,800	4.186 800 0E+06
watt/cubic meter	4,186,800	4.186 800 0E+06

calorie/day square centimeter [I.T.]   <heat flux density>

Btu/day square foot [I.T.]	3.686 690 6	3.686 690 6E+00
Btu/day square foot [thermoc.]	3.689 157 8	3.689 157 8E+00
calorie/day square centimeter [thermoc.]	1.000 669 2	1.000 669 2E+00
kilocalorie/hour square meter [I.T.]	0.416 666 7	4.166 666 7E−01
kilocalorie/hour square meter [thermoc.]	0.416 945 5	4.169 455 1E−01
watt/square meter	0.484 583 3	4.845 833 3E−01

calorie/day square centimeter [thermoc.]   <heat flux density>

Btu/day square foot [I.T.]	3.684 225	3.684 225 0E+00
Btu/day square foot [thermoc.]	3.686 690 6	3.686 690 6E+00
calorie/day square centimeter [I.T.]	0.999 331 2	9.993 312 3E−01
kilocalorie/hour square meter [I.T.]	0.416 388	4.163 880 1E−01
kilocalorie/hour square meter [thermoc.]	0.416 666 7	4.166 666 7E−01
watt/square meter	0.484 259 3	4.842 592 6E−01

calorie/°C [I.T.]   <specific heat>

Btu/°F [I.T.]	0.002 204 6	2.204 622 6E−03

Convert From
Convert To   **<Type of Unit>**
Standard   Scientific

	Standard	Scientific
calorie/°C [thermoc.]		
calorie/°C [thermoc.]	1.000 669 2	1.000 669 2E+00
clausius	0.001	1.000 000 0E−03
joule/kelvin	4.186 8	4.186 800 0E+00
calorie/°C [thermoc.]		**<specific heat>**
Btu/°F [thermoc.]	0.002 204 6	2.204 623 2E−03
calorie/°C [I.T.]	0.999 331 2	9.993 312 3E−01
joule/kelvin	4.184	4.184 000 0E+00
calorie/gram [I.T.]		**<specific thermodynamic energy>**
Btu/pound [I.T.]	1.8	1.800 000 0E+00
Btu/pound [thermoc.]	1.801 204 6	1.801 204 6E+00
calorie/gram [thermoc.]	1.000 669 2	1.000 669 2E+00
joule/kilogram	4,186.8	4.186 800 0E+03
calorie/gram [thermoc.]		**<specific thermodynamic energy>**
Btu/pound [I.T.]	1.798 796 2	1.798 796 2E+00
Btu/pound [thermoc.]	1.8	1.800 000 0E+00
calorie/gram [I.T.]	0.999 331 2	9.993 312 3E−01
joule/kilogram	4,184	4.184 000 0E+03
calorie/gram °C [I.T.]		**<specific heat capacity>**
Btu/pound °F [I.T.]	1	1.000 000 0E+00
Btu/pound °F [thermoc.]	1.000 669 2	1.000 669 2E+00
calorie/gram °C [thermoc.]	1.000 669 2	1.000 669 2E+00
joule/kilogram kelvin	4,186.8	4.186 800 0E+03
calorie/gram °C [thermoc.]		**<specific heat capacity>**
Btu/pound °F [I.T.]	0.999 331 2	9.993 312 3E−01
Btu/pound °F [thermoc.]	1	1.000 000 0E+00
calorie/gram °C [I.T.]	0.999 331 2	9.993 312 3E−01
joule/kilogram kelvin	4,184	4.184 000 0E+03
calorie/hour [15 °C, CIPM, 1950]		**<power>**
Btu/hour [I.T.]	0.003 967 1	3.967 088 6E−03
Btu/hour [thermoc.]	0.003 969 7	3.969 743 4E−03
calorie/hour [I.T.]	0.999 689 5	9.996 895 0E−01
calorie/hour [thermoc.]	1.000 358 5	1.000 358 5E+00
centigrade heat unit/hour [mean]	0.002 202 4	2.202 238 7E−03
cubic meter atmosphere/hour	41.307 673	4.130 767 3E+01
dyne centimeter/second	11,626.389	1.162 638 9E+04
erg/second	11,626.389	1.162 638 9E+04
foot pound-force/hour	3.087 066 4	3.087 066 4E+00
foot poundal/minute	1.655 390 4	1.655 390 4E+00
gram-force centimeter/second	11.855 617	1.185 561 7E+01
horsepower	0.000 001 6	1.559 124 4E−06
horsepower [metric]	0.000 001 6	1.580 749 0E−06
joule/hour	4.185 5	4.185 500 0E+00
kilocalorie/hour [thermoc.]	0.001 000 4	1.000 358 5E−03
kilogram square meter/cubic second	0.001 162 6	1.162 638 9E−03
kilogram-force meter/hour	0.426 802 2	4.268 022 2E−01
kilopond meter/hour	0.426 802 2	4.268 022 2E−01
milliwatt	1.162 638 9	1.162 638 9E+00
newton meter/hour	4.185 5	4.185 500 0E+00
pound square foot/cubic second	0.027 589 8	2.758 984 2E−02
volt ampere	0.001 162 6	1.162 638 9E−03
watt	0.001 162 6	1.162 638 9E−03
calorie/hour [15 °C, NBS, 1939]		**<power>**
calorie/hour [I.T.]	0.999 761 2	9.997 611 5E−01
calorie/hour [thermoc.]	1.000 430 2	1.000 430 2E+00
centigrade heat unit/hour [mean]	0.002 202 4	2.202 396 5E−03
cubic meter atmosphere/hour	41.310 634	4.131 063 4E+01
dyne centimeter/second	11,627.222	1.162 722 2E+04
erg/second	11,627.222	1.162 722 2E+04
foot pound-force/hour	3.087 287 6	3.087 287 6E+00
foot poundal/minute	1.655 509	1.655 509 0E+00
gram-force centimeter/second	11.856 467	1.185 646 7E+01

	Standard	Scientific
horsepower	0.000 001 6	1.559 236 2E−06
horsepower [metric]	0.000 001 6	1.580 862 3E−06
joule/hour	4.185 8	4.185 800 0E+00
kilocalorie/hour [thermoc.]	0.001 000 4	1.000 430 3E−03
kilogram square meter/cubic second	0.001 162 7	1.162 722 2E−03
kilogram-force meter/hour	0.426 832 8	4.268 328 1E−01
kilopond meter/hour	0.426 832 8	4.268 328 1E−01
milliwatt	1.162 722 2	1.162 722 2E+00
newton meter/hour	4.185 8	4.185 800 0E+00
pound square foot/cubic second	0.027 591 8	2.759 181 7E−02
volt ampere	0.001 162 7	1.162 722 2E−03
watt	0.001 162 7	1.162 722 2E−03
calorie/hour [20 °C]		**\<power\>**
Btu/hour [I.T.]	0.003 963 7	3.963 676 4E−03
Btu/hour [thermoc.]	0.003 966 3	3.966 329 0E−03
calorie/hour [I.T.]	0.998 829 7	9.988 296 6E−01
calorie/hour [thermoc.]	0.999 498 1	9.994 980 9E−01
centigrade heat unit/hour [mean]	0.002 200 3	2.200 344 5E−03
cubic meter atmosphere/hour	41.272 144	4.127 214 4E+01
dyne centimeter/second	11,616.389	1.161 638 9E+04
erg/second	11,616.389	1.161 638 9E+04
foot pound-force/hour	3.084 411 2	3.084 411 2E+00
foot poundal/minute	1.653 966 6	1.653 966 6E+00
gram-force centimeter/second	11.845 42	1.184 542 0E+01
hectowatt	0.000 011 6	1.161 638 9E−05
horsepower	0.000 001 6	1.557 783 4E−06
horsepower [metric]	0.000 001 6	1.579 389 3E−06
joule/hour	4.181 9	4.181 900 0E+00
kilocalorie/hour [I.T.]	0.000 998 8	9.988 296 6E−04
kilogram-force meter/hour	0.426 435 1	4.264 351 2E−01
kilopond meter/hour	0.426 435 1	4.264 351 2E−01
newton meter/hour	4.181 9	4.181 900 0E+00
pound square foot/cubic second	0.027 566 1	2.756 610 9E−02
volt ampere	0.001 161 6	1.161 638 9E−03
watt	0.001 161 6	1.161 638 9E−03
calorie/hour [I.T.]		**\<power\>**
Btu/hour [I.T.]	0.003 968 3	3.968 320 7E−03
Btu/hour [thermoc.]	0.003 971	3.970 976 4E−03
calorie/hour [thermoc.]	1.000 669 2	1.000 669 2E+00
centigrade heat unit/hour [mean]	0.002 202 9	2.202 922 7E−03
cubic meter atmosphere/hour	41.320 503	4.132 050 3E+01
dyne centimeter/second	11,630	1.163 000 0E+04
erg/second	11,630	1.163 000 0E+04
foot pound-force/hour	3.088 025 2	3.088 025 2E+00
foot poundal/minute	1.655 904 5	1.655 904 5E+00
gram-force centimeter/second	11.859 3	1.185 930 0E+01
horsepower	0.000 001 6	1.559 608 7E−06
horsepower [metric]	0.000 001 6	1.581 239 9E−06
joule/hour	4.186 8	4.186 800 0E+00
kilocalorie/hour [I.T.]	0.001	1.000 000 0E−03
kilogram square meter/cubic second	0.001 163	1.163 000 0E−04
kilogram-force meter/hour	0.426 934 8	4.269 347 8E−01
kilopond meter/hour	0.426 934 8	4.269 347 8E−01
lumen [green light at 100% efficiency]	0.796 655	7.966 550 0E−01
lumen [green light at 5,550 angstrom]	0.790 84	7.908 400 2E−01
lumen [monochromatic radiation of 540 THz]	0.794 329	7.943 290 0E−01
milliwatt	1.163	1.163 000 0E+00
newton meter/hour	4.186 8	4.186 800 0E+00
pound square foot/cubic second	0.027 598 4	2.759 840 9E−02
volt ampere	0.001 163	1.163 000 0E−03
watt	0.001 163	1.163 000 0E−03
calorie/hour [mean]		**\<power\>**
Btu/hour [I.T.]	0.003 971 4	3.971 372 7E−03

	Standard	Scientific
Btu/hour [thermoc.]	0.003 974	3.974 030 4E-03
calorie/hour [I.T.]	1.000 769 1	1.000 769 1E+00
calorie/hour [thermoc.]	1.001 438 8	1.001 438 8E+00
centigrade heat unit/hour [mean]	0.002 204 6	2.204 616 9E-03
cubic meter atmosphere/hour	41.352 282	4.135 228 2E+01
dyne centimeter/second	11,638.944	1.163 894 4E+04
erg/second	11,638.944	1.163 894 4E+04
foot pound-force/hour	3.090 400 2	3.090 400 2E+00
foot poundal/minute	1.657 178 1	1.657 178 1E+00
gram-force centimeter/second	11.868 42	1.186 842 0E+01
horsepower	0.000 001 6	1.560 808 2E-06
horsepower [metric]	0.000 001 6	1.582 456 0E-06
joule/hour	4.190 02	4.190 020 0E+00
kilocalorie/hour [I.T.]	0.001 000 8	1.000 769 1E-03
kilogram square meter/cubic second	0.001 163 9	1.163 894 4E-03
kilogram-force meter/hour	0.427 263 1	4.272 631 3E-01
kilopond meter/hour	0.427 263 1	4.272 631 3E-01
milliwatt	1.163 894 4	1.163 894 4E+00
newton meter/hour	4.190 02	4.190 020 0E+00
pound square foot/cubic second	0.027 619 6	2.761 963 5E-02
volt ampere	0.001 163 9	1.163 894 4E-03
watt	0.001 163 9	1.163 894 4E-03

calorie/hour [thermoc.]   \<power\>

	Standard	Scientific
Btu/hour [I.T.]	0.003 965 7	3.965 666 8E-03
Btu/hour [thermoc.]	0.003 968 3	3.968 320 7E-03
calorie/hour [20 °C]	1.000 502 2	1.000 502 2E+00
calorie/hour [I.T.]	0.999 331 2	9.993 312 3E-01
centigrade heat unit/hour [mean]	0.002 201 4	2.201 449 5E-03
cubic meter atmosphere/hour	41.292 869	4.129 286 9E+01
dyne centimeter/second	11,622.222	1.162 222 2E+04
erg/second	11,622.222	1.162 222 2E+04
foot pound-force/hour	3.085 96	3.085 960 0E+00
foot poundal/minute	1.654 797 1	1.654 797 1E+00
gram-force centimeter/second	11.851 368	1.185 136 8E+01
horsepower	0.000 001 6	1.558 565 7E-06
horsepower [metric]	0.000 001 6	1.580 182 5E-06
joule/hour	4.184	4.184 000 0E+00
kilocalorie/hour [I.T.]	0.000 999 3	9.993 312 3E-04
kilocalorie/hour [thermoc.]	0.001	1.000 000 0E-03
kilogram square meter/cubic second	0.001 162 2	1.162 222 2E-03
kilogram-force meter/hour	0.426 649 3	4.266 492 6E-01
kilopond meter/hour	0.426 649 3	4.266 492 6E-01
milliwatt	1.162 222 2	1.162 222 2E+00
newton meter/hour	4.184	4.184 000 0E+00
pound square foot/cubic second	0.027 58	2.757 995 2E-02
volt ampere	0.001 162 2	1.162 222 2E-03
watt	0.001 162 2	1.162 222 2E-03

calorie/hour square centimeter °C [I.T.]   \<heat transfer coefficient\>

	Standard	Scientific
Btu/hour square foot °F [I.T.]	2.048 161 4	2.048 161 4E+00
Btu/hour square foot °F [thermoc.]	2.049 532 6	2.049 532 6E+00
kilocalorie/hour square meter °C [I.T.]	10	1.000 000 0E+01
watt/square foot °C	1.080 462 4	1.080 462 4E+00
watt/square meter kelvin	11.63	1.163 000 0E+01

calorie/minute [15 °C, CIPM, 1950]   \<power\>

	Standard	Scientific
Btu/hour [I.T.]	0.238 025 3	2.380 253 1E-01
Btu/hour [thermoc.]	0.238 184 6	2.381 846 0E-01
calorie/minute [I.T.]	0.999 689 5	9.996 895 0E-01
calorie/minute [thermoc.]	1.000 358 5	1.000 358 5E+00
centiwatt	6.975 833 3	6.975 833 3E+00
cubic meter atmosphere/minute	41.307 673	4.130 767 3E+01
dyne centimeter/second	697,583.33	6.975 833 3E+05
erg/second	697,583.33	6.975 833 3E+05
foot pound-force/minute	3.087 066 4	3.087 066 4E+00

Convert From Convert To	\<Type of Unit\>	
	Standard	Scientific
foot poundal/second	1.655 390 4	1.655 390 4E+00
gram-force centimeter/second	711.337 03	7.113 370 3E+02
hectowatt	0.000 697 6	6.975 833 3E-04
horsepower	0.000 093 5	9.354 746 6E-05
horsepower [metric]	0.000 094 8	9.484 493 8E-05
joule/minute	4.185 5	4.185 500 0E+00
kilocalorie/hour [I.T.]	0.059 981 4	5.998 137 0E-02
kilogram square meter/cubic second	0.069 758 3	6.975 833 3E-02
kilogram-force meter/hour	25.608 133	2.560 813 3E+01
kilopond meter/hour	25.608 133	2.560 813 3E+01
lumen [green light at 100% efficiency]	47.784 458	4.778 445 8E+01
lumen [green light at 5,550 angstrom]	47.435 668	4.743 566 8E+01
newton meter/minute	4.185 5	4.185 500 0E+00
pound square foot/cubic second	1.655 390 4	1.655 390 4E+00
volt ampere	0.069 758 3	6.975 833 3E-02
watt	0.069 758 3	6.975 833 3E-02

calorie/minute [15 °C, NBS, 1939] \<power\>

Convert To	Standard	Scientific
Btu/hour [I.T.]	0.238 042 4	2.380 423 7E-01
Btu/hour [thermoc.]	0.238 201 7	2.382 016 8E-01
calorie/minute [I.T.]	0.999 761 2	9.997 611 5E-01
calorie/minute [thermoc.]	1.000 430 2	1.000 430 2E+00
centigrade heat unit/hour [mean]	0.132 143 8	1.321 437 9E-01
centiwatt	6.976 333 3	6.976 333 3E+00
cubic meter atmosphere/minute	41.310 634	4.131 063 4E+01
dyne centimeter/second	697,633.33	6.976 333 3E+05
erg/second	697,633.33	6.976 333 3E+05
foot pound-force/minute	3.087 287 6	3.087 287 6E+00
foot poundal/second	1.655 509	1.655 509 0E+00
gram-force centimeter/second	711.388 02	7.113 880 2E+02
horsepower	0.000 093 6	9.355 417 1E-05
horsepower [metric]	0.000 094 9	9.485 173 6E-05
joule/minute	4.185 8	4.185 800 0E+00
kilocalorie/hour [I.T.]	0.059 985 7	5.998 566 9E-02
kilogram square meter/cubic second	0.069 763 3	6.976 333 3E-02
kilogram-force meter/hour	25.609 969	2.560 996 9E+01
kilopond meter/hour	25.609 969	2.560 996 9E+01
lumen [green light at 100% efficiency]	47.787 883	4.778 788 3E+01
lumen [green light at 5,550 angstrom]	47.439 068	4.743 906 8E+01
newton meter/minute	4.185 8	4.185 800 0E+00
pound square foot/cubic second	1.655 509	1.655 509 0E+00
volt ampere	0.069 763 3	6.976 333 3E-02
watt	0.069 763 3	6.976 333 3E-02

calorie/minute [20 °C] \<power\>

Convert To	Standard	Scientific
Btu/hour [I.T.]	0.237 820 6	2.378 205 8E-01
Btu/hour [thermoc.]	0.237 979 7	2.379 797 4E-01
calorie/hour [I.T.]	59.929 779	5.992 977 9E+01
calorie/hour [thermoc.]	59.969 885	5.996 988 5E+01
centigrade heat unit/hour [mean]	0.132 020 7	1.320 206 7E-01
centiwatt	6.969 833 3	6.969 833 3E+00
cubic meter atmosphere/minute	41.272 144	4.127 214 4E+01
dyne centimeter/second	696,983.33	6.969 833 3E+05
erg/second	696,983.33	6.969 833 3E+05
foot pound-force/minute	3.084 411 2	3.084 411 2E+00
foot poundal/second	1.653 966 6	1.653 966 6E+00
gram-force centimeter/second	710.725 21	7.107 252 1E+02
horsepower	0.000 093 5	9.346 700 5E-05
horsepower [metric]	0.000 094 8	9.476 336 1E-05
joule/minute	4.181 9	4.181 900 0E+00
kilocalorie/hour [I.T.]	0.059 929 8	5.992 977 9E-02
kilogram square meter/cubic second	0.069 698 3	6.969 833 3E-02
kilogram-force meter/hour	25.586 107	2.558 610 7E+01
kilopond meter/hour	25.586 107	2.558 610 7E+01
lumen [green light at 100% efficiency]	47.743 358	4.774 335 8E+01

Convert From Convert To	Standard	<Type of Unit> Scientific
lumen [green light at 5,550 angstrom]	47.394 868	4.739 486 8E+01
newton meter/minute	4.181 9	4.181 900 0E+00
pound square foot/cubic second	1.653 966 6	1.653 966 6E+00
volt ampere	0.069 698 3	6.969 833 3E−02
watt	0.069 698 3	6.969 833 3E−02

calorie/minute [I.T.] <power>

Convert To	Standard	Scientific
Btu/hour [I.T.]	0.238 099 2	2.380 992 4E−01
Btu/hour [thermoc.]	0.238 258 6	2.382 585 8E−01
calorie/minute [20 °C]	1.001 171 7	1.001 171 7E+00
calorie/minute [thermoc.]	1.000 669 2	1.000 669 2E+00
centigrade heat unit/hour [mean]	0.132 175 4	1.321 753 6E−01
centiwatt	6.978	6.978 000 0E+00
cubic meter atmosphere/minute	41.320 503	4.132 050 3E+01
dyne centimeter/second	697,800	6.978 000 0E+05
erg/second	697,800	6.978 000 0E+05
foot pound-force/minute	3.088 025 2	3.088 025 2E+00
foot poundal/second	1.655 904 5	1.655 904 5E+00
gram-force centimeter/second	711.557 97	7.115 579 7E+02
horsepower	0.000 093 6	9.357 652 1E−05
horsepower [metric]	0.000 094 9	9.487 439 6E−05
joule/minute	4.186 8	4.186 800 0E+00
kilocalorie/hour [I.T.]	0.06	6.000 000 0E−02
kilogram square meter/cubic second	0.069 78	6.978 000 0E−02
kilogram-force meter/hour	25.616 087	2.561 608 7E+01
kilopond meter/hour	25.616 087	2.561 608 7E+01
lumen [green light at 100% efficiency]	47.799 3	4.779 930 0E+01
lumen [green light at 5,550 angstrom]	47.450 401	4.745 040 1E+01
newton meter/minute	4.186 8	4.186 800 0E+00
pound square foot/cubic second	1.655 904 5	1.655 904 5E+00
volt ampere	0.069 78	6.978 000 0E−02
watt	0.069 78	6.978 000 0E−02

calorie/minute [mean] <power>

Convert To	Standard	Scientific
Btu/hour [I.T.]	0.238 282 4	2.382 823 6E−01
Btu/hour [thermoc.]	0.238 441 8	2.384 418 2E−01
calorie/minute [20 °C]	1.001 941 7	1.001 941 7E+00
calorie/minute [thermoc.]	1.001 438 8	1.001 438 8E+00
centigrade heat unit/hour [mean]	0.132 277 0	1.322 770 2E−01
centiwatt	6.983 366 7	6.983 366 7E+00
cubic meter atmosphere/minute	41.352 282	4.135 228 2E+01
dyne centimeter/second	698,336.67	6.983 366 7E+05
erg/second	698,336.67	6.983 366 7E+05
foot pound-force/minute	3.090 400 2	3.090 400 2E+00
foot poundal/second	1.657 178 1	1.657 178 1E+00
gram-force centimeter/second	712.105 22	7.121 052 2E+02
horsepower	0.000 093 6	9.364 849 0E−05
horsepower [metric]	0.000 094 9	9.494 736 3E−05
joule/minute	4.190 02	4.190 020 0E+00
kilocalorie/hour [I.T.]	0.060 046 1	6.004 614 5E−02
kilogram square meter/cubic second	0.069 833 7	6.983 366 7E−02
kilogram-force meter/hour	25.635 788	2.563 578 8E+01
kilopond meter/hour	25.635 788	2.563 578 8E+01
lumen [green light at 100% efficiency]	47.836 062	4.783 606 2E+01
lumen [green light at 5,550 angstrom]	47.486 894	4.748 689 4E+01
newton meter/minute	4.190 02	4.190 020 0E+00
pound square foot/cubic second	1.657 178 1	1.657 178 1E+00
volt ampere	0.069 833 7	6.983 366 7E−02
watt	0.069 833 7	6.983 366 7E−02

calorie/minute [thermoc.] <power>

Convert To	Standard	Scientific
Btu/hour [I.T.]	0.237 94	2.379 400 1E−01
Btu/hour [thermoc.]	0.238 099 2	2.380 992 4E−01
calorie/minute [20 °C]	1.000 502 2	1.000 502 2E+00
calorie/minute [I.T.]	0.999 331 2	9.993 312 3E−01
centigrade heat unit/hour [mean]	0.132 087	1.320 869 7E−01

Convert From Convert To	<Type of Unit> Standard	Scientific

centiwatt	6.973 333 3	6.973 333 3E+00
cubic meter atmosphere/minute	41.292 869	4.129 286 9E+01
dyne centimeter/second	697,333.33	6.973 333 3E+05
erg/second	697,333.33	6.973 333 3E+05
foot pound-force/minute	3.085 96	3.085 960 0E+00
foot poundal/second	1.654 797 1	1.654 797 1E+00
gram-force centimeter/second	711.082 11	7.110 821 1E+02
horsepower	0.000 093 5	9.351 394 0E-05
horsepower [metric]	0.000 094 8	9.481 094 7E-05
joule/minute	4.184	4.184 000 0E+00
kilocalorie/hour [thermoc.]	0.06	6.000 000 0E-02
kilogram square meter/cubic second	0.069 733 3	6.973 333 3E-02
kilogram-force meter/hour	25.598 956	2.559 895 6E+01
kilopond meter/hour	25.598 956	2.559 895 6E+01
lumen [green light at 100% efficiency]	47.767 333	4.776 733 3E+01
lumen [green light at 5,550 angstrom]	47.418 668	4.741 866 8E+01
newton meter/minute	4.184	4.184 000 0E+00
pound square foot/cubic second	1.654 797 1	1.654 797 1E+00
volt ampere	0.069 733 3	6.973 333 3E-02
watt	0.069 733 3	6.973 333 3E-02

calorie/minute square centimeter [I.T.] \<heat flux density>
| watt/square meter | 697.8 | 6.978 000 0E+02 |

calorie/minute square centimeter [thermoc.] \<heat flux density>
| watt/square meter | 697.333 333 3 | 6.973 333 3E+02 |

calorie/second [15 °C, CIPM, 1950] \<power>
Btu/hour [I.T.]	14.281 519	1.428 151 9E+01
Btu/hour [thermoc.]	14.291 076	1.429 107 6E+01
calorie/second [20 °C]	1.000 860 9	1.000 860 9E+00
calorie/second [thermoc.]	1.000 358 5	1.000 358 5E+00
centigrade heat unit/hour [mean]	7.928 059 3	7.928 059 3E+00
cubic meter atmosphere/second	41.307 673	4.130 767 3E+01
dyne centimeter/second	>>>	4.185 500 0E+07
erg/second	>>>	4.185 500 0E+07
foot pound-force/second	3.087 066 4	3.087 066 4E+00
foot poundal/second	99.323 423	9.932 342 3E+01
gram-force centimeter/second	42,680.222	4.268 022 2E+04
horsepower	0.005 612 8	5.612 848 0E-03
horsepower [metric]	0.005 690 7	5.690 696 3E-03
joule/second	4.185 5	4.185 500 0E+00
kilocalorie/hour [I.T.]	3.598 882 2	3.598 882 2E+00
kilocalorie/minute [I.T.]	0.059 981 4	5.998 137 0E-02
kilocalorie/second [thermoc.]	0.001 000 4	1.000 358 5E-03
kilogram square meter/cubic second	4.185 5	4.185 500 0E+00
kilogram-force meter/minute	25.608 133	2.560 813 3E+01
kilopond meter/minute	25.608 133	2.560 813 3E+01
newton meter/second	4.185 5	4.185 500 0E+00
pound square foot/cubic second	99.323 423	9.932 342 3E+01
volt ampere	4.185 5	4.185 500 0E+00
watt	4.185 5	4.185 500 0E+00

calorie/second [15 °C, NBS, 1939] \<power>
Btu/hour [I.T.]	14.282 542	1.428 254 2E+01
Btu/hour [thermoc.]	14.292 101	1.429 210 1E+01
calorie/second [15 °C, CIPM, 1950]	1.000 071 7	1.000 071 7E+00
calorie/second [20 °C]	0.999 761 2	9.997 611 5E-01
calorie/second [I.T.]	1.000 430 2	1.000 430 2E+00
calorie/second [thermoc.]	1.000 430 2	1.000 430 2E+00
centigrade heat unit/hour [mean]	7.928 627 6	7.928 627 6E+00
cubic meter atmosphere/second	41.310 634	4.131 063 4E+01
dyne centimeter/second	>>>	4.185 800 0E+07
erg/second	>>>	4.185 800 0E+07
foot pound-force/second	3.087 287 6	3.087 287 6E+00
foot poundal/second	99.330 543	9.933 054 3E+01
gram-force centimeter/second	42,683.281	4.268 328 1E+04

	Standard	Scientific
horsepower	0.005 613 3	5.613 250 3E-03
horsepower [metric]	0.005 691 1	5.691 104 2E-03
joule/second	4.185 8	4.185 800 0E+00
kilocalorie/hour [I.T.]	3.599 140 2	3.599 140 2E+00
kilogram square meter/cubic second	4.185 8	4.185 800 0E+00
kilogram-force meter/minute	25.609 969	2.560 996 9E+01
kilopond meter/minute	25.609 969	2.560 996 9E+01
newton meter/second	4.185 8	4.185 800 0E+00
pound square foot/cubic second	99.330 543	9.933 054 3E+01
volt ampere	4.185 8	4.185 800 0E+00
watt	4.185 8	4.185 800 0E+00

calorie/second [20 °C] <power>

	Standard	Scientific
Btu/hour [I.T.]	14.269 235	1.426 923 5E+01
Btu/hour [thermoc.]	14.278 784	1.427 878 4E+01
calorie/second [I.T.]	0.998 829 7	9.988 296 6E-01
calorie/second [thermoc.]	0.999 498 1	9.994 980 9E-01
centigrade heat unit/hour [mean]	7.921 240 3	7.921 240 3E+00
cubic meter atmosphere/second	41.272 144	4.127 214 4E+01
dyne centimeter/second	>>>	4.181 900 0E+07
erg/second	>>>	4.181 900 0E+07
foot pound-force/second	3.084 411 2	3.084 411 2E+00
foot poundal/second	99.237 994	9.923 799 4E+01
gram-force centimeter/second	42,643.512	4.264 351 2E+04
horsepower	0.005 608	5.608 020 3E-03
horsepower [metric]	0.005 685 8	5.685 801 6E-03
joule/second	4.181 9	4.181 900 0E+00
kilocalorie/hour [I.T.]	3.595 786 8	3.595 786 8E+00
kilogram square meter/cubic second	4.181 9	4.181 900 0E+00
kilogram-force meter/minute	25.586 107	2.558 610 7E+01
kilopond meter/minute	25.586 107	2.558 610 7E+01
newton meter/second	4.181 9	4.181 900 0E+00
pound square foot/cubic second	99.237 994	9.923 799 4E+01
volt ampere	4.181 9	4.181 900 0E+00
watt	4.181 9	4.181 900 0E+00

calorie/second [I.T.] <power>

	Standard	Scientific
Btu/hour [I.T.]	14.285 955	1.428 595 5E+01
Btu/hour [thermoc.]	14.295 515	1.429 551 5E+01
calorie/second [20 °C]	1.001 171 7	1.001 171 7E+00
calorie/second [thermoc.]	1.000 669 2	1.000 669 2E+00
centigrade heat unit/hour [mean]	7.930 521 7	7.930 521 7E+00
cubic meter atmosphere/second	41.320 503	4.132 050 3E+01
dyne centimeter/second	>>>	4.186 800 0E+07
erg/second	>>>	4.186 800 0E+07
foot pound-force/second	3.088 025 2	3.088 025 2E+00
foot poundal/second	99.354 273	9.935 427 3E+01
gram-force centimeter/second	42,693.478	4.269 347 8E+04
horsepower	0.005 614 6	5.614 591 3E-03
horsepower [metric]	0.005 692 5	5.692 463 8E-03
joule/second	4.186 8	4.186 800 0E+00
kilocalorie/hour [I.T.]	3.6	3.600 000 0E+00
kilogram square meter/cubic second	4.186 8	4.186 800 0E+00
kilogram-force meter/minute	25.616 087	2.561 608 7E+01
kilopond meter/minute	25.616 087	2.561 608 7E+01
newton meter/second	4.186 8	4.186 800 0E+00
pound square foot/cubic second	99.354 273	9.935 427 3E+01
volt ampere	4.186 8	4.186 800 0E+00
watt	4.186 8	4.186 800 0E+00

calorie/second [mean] <power>

	Standard	Scientific
Btu/hour [I.T.]	14.296 942	1.429 694 2E+01
Btu/hour [thermoc.]	14.306 509	1.430 650 9E+01
calorie/second [I.T.]	1.000 769 1	1.000 769 1E+00
calorie/second [thermoc.]	1.001 438 8	1.001 438 8E+00
centigrade heat unit/hour [mean]	7.936 621	7.936 621 0E+00

Convert From Convert To	\<Type of Unit\> Standard	Scientific
cubic meter atmosphere/second	41.352 282	4.135 228 2E+01
dyne centimeter/second	>>>	4.190 020 0E+07
erg/second	>>>	4.190 020 0E+07
foot pound-force/second	3.090 400 2	3.090 400 2E+00
foot poundal/second	99.430 685	9.943 068 5E+01
gram-force centimeter/second	42,726.313	4.272 631 3E+04
horsepower	0.005 618 9	5.618 909 4E-03
horsepower [metric]	0.005 696 8	5.696 841 8E-03
joule/second	4.190 02	4.190 020 0E+00
kilocalorie/hour [mean]	3.6	3.600 000 0E+00
kilogram square meter/cubic second	4.190 02	4.190 020 0E+00
kilogram-force meter/minute	25.635 788	2.563 578 8E+01
kilopond meter/minute	25.635 788	2.563 578 8E+01
newton meter/second	4.190 02	4.190 020 0E+00
pound square foot/cubic second	99.430 685	9.943 068 5E+01
volt ampere	4.190 02	4.190 020 0E+00
watt	4.190 02	4.190 020 0E+00
calorie/second [thermoc.]	**\<power\>**	
Btu/hour [I.T.]	14.276 401	1.427 640 1E+01
Btu/hour [thermoc.]	14.285 955	1.428 595 5E+01
calorie/second [20 °C]	1.000 502 2	1.000 502 2E+00
calorie/second [I.T.]	0.999 331 2	9.993 312 3E-01
centigrade heat unit/hour [mean]	7.925 218 1	7.925 218 1E+00
cubic meter atmosphere/second	41.292 869	4.129 286 9E+01
dyne centimeter/second	>>>	4.184 000 0E+07
erg/second	>>>	4.184 000 0E+07
foot pound-force/second	3.085 96	3.085 960 0E+00
foot poundal/second	99.287 828	9.928 782 8E+01
gram-force centimeter/second	42,664.926	4.266 492 6E+04
horsepower	0.005 610 8	5.610 836 4E-03
horsepower [metric]	0.005 688 7	5.688 656 8E-03
joule/second	4.184	4.184 000 0E+00
kilocalorie/hour [I.T.]	3.597 592 4	3.597 592 4E+00
kilocalorie/hour [thermoc.]	3.6	3.600 000 0E+00
kilogram square meter/cubic second	4.184	4.184 000 0E+00
kilogram-force meter/minute	25.598 956	2.559 895 6E+01
kilopond meter/minute	25.598 956	2.559 895 6E+01
newton meter/second	4.184	4.184 000 0E+00
pound square foot/cubic second	99.287 828	9.928 782 8E+01
volt ampere	4.184	4.184 000 0E+00
watt	4.184	4.184 000 0E+00
calorie/second centimeter °C [I.T.]	**\<thermal conductivity\>**	
Btu foot/hour square foot °F [I.T.]	241.908 83	2.419 088 3E+02
Btu foot/hour square foot °F [thermoc.]	242.070 78	2.420 707 8E+02
Btu inch/second square foot °F [I.T.]	0.806 362 8	8.063 627 7E-01
Btu inch/second square foot °F [thermoc.]	0.806 902 6	8.069 026 0E-01
Btu/hour foot °F [I.T.]	241.908 83	2.419 088 3E+02
Btu/hour foot °F [thermoc.]	242.070 78	2.420 707 8E+02
calorie centimeter/hour square centimeter °C [I.T.]	3,600	3.600 000 0E+03
calorie centimeter/second square centimeter °C [I.T.]	1	1.000 000 0E+00
calorie/second centimeter °C [thermoc.]	1.000 669 2	1.000 669 2E+00
kilowatt/meter kelvin	0.418 68	4.186 800 0E-01
watt/centimeter kelvin	4.186 8	4.186 800 0E+00
watt/foot °C	127.613 66	1.276 136 6E+02
watt/meter kelvin	418.68	4.186 800 0E+02
calorie/second centimeter °C [thermoc.]	**\<thermal conductivity\>**	
Btu foot/hour square foot °F [I.T.]	241.747 05	2.417 470 5E+02
Btu foot/hour square foot °F [thermoc.]	241.908 89	2.419 088 9E+02
Btu inch/second square foot °F [I.T.]	0.805 823 5	8.058 235 0E-01
Btu inch/second square foot °F [thermoc.]	0.806 363	8.063 629 7E-01
Btu/hour foot °F [I.T.]	241.747 05	2.417 470 5E+02
Btu/hour foot °F [thermoc.]	241.908 89	2.419 088 9E+02
calorie centimeter/second square centimeter °C [I.T.]	0.999 331 2	9.993 312 3E-01

Convert From	<Type of Unit>	
Convert To	Standard	Scientific

calorie/second centimeter °C [I.T.]		
watt centimeter/square centimeter °C	4.184	4.184 000 0E+00
watt/centimeter kelvin	4.184	4.184 000 0E+00
watt/foot °C	127.528 32	1.275 283 2E+02
watt/meter kelvin	418.4	4.184 000 0E+02
calorie/second cubic centimeter °C [I.T.]	**<heat transfer coefficient>**	
Btu/hour cubic foot °F [I.T.]	224,740.66	2.247 406 6E+05
kilocalorie/hour cubic meter °C [I.T.]	3,600,000	3.600 000 0E+06
watt/cubic meter kelvin	4,186,800	4.186 800 0E+06
calorie/second °C [I.T.]	**<thermal conductance>**	
Btu/second °F [I.T.]	0.002 204 6	2.204 622 6E-03
kilocalorie/second °C [I.T.]	0.001	1.000 000 0E-03
watt/kelvin	4.186 8	4.186 800 0E+00
calorie/second square centimeter [I.T.]	**<heat flux density>**	
Btu/second square foot [I.T.]	3.686 690 6	3.686 690 6E+00
Btu/second square foot [thermoc.]	3.689 157 8	3.689 157 8E+00
calorie/second square centimeter [thermoc.]	1.000 669 2	1.000 669 2E+00
finsen unit	0.418 68	4.186 800 0E-01
pyron	60	6.000 000 0E+01
watt/square inch	27.011 559	2.701 155 9E+01
watt/square meter	41,868	4.186 800 0E+04
calorie/second square centimeter [thermoc.]	**<heat flux density>**	
Btu/second square foot [I.T.]	3.684 225	3.684 225 0E+00
Btu/second square foot [thermoc.]	3.686 690 6	3.686 690 6E+00
calorie/second square centimeter [I.T.]	0.999 331 2	9.993 312 3E-01
pyron	59.959 874	5.995 987 4E+01
watt/square inch	26.993 494	2.699 349 4E+01
watt/square meter	41,840	4.184 000 0E+04
calorie/second square centimeter °C [I.T.]	**<heat transfer coefficient>**	
Btu/second square foot °F [I.T.]	2.048 161 4	2.048 161 4E+00
Btu/second square foot °F [thermoc.]	2.049 532 6	2.049 532 6E+00
calorie/second square centimeter °C [thermoc.]	1.000 669 2	1.000 669 2E+00
watt/square foot °C	3,889.664 5	3.889 664 5E+03
watt/square meter kelvin	41,868	4.186 800 0E+04
calorie/second square centimeter °C [thermoc.]	**<heat transfer coefficient>**	
Btu/second square foot °F [I.T.]	2.046 791 7	2.046 791 7E+00
Btu/second square foot °F [thermoc.]	2.048 162	2.048 162 0E+00
calorie/second square centimeter °C [I.T.]	0.999 331 2	9.993 312 3E-01
watt/square foot °C	3,887.063 2	3.887 063 2E+03
watt/square meter kelvin	41,840	4.184 000 0E+04
calorie/square centimeter [15 °C, CIPM, 1950]	**<energy fluence>**	
joule/square meter	41,855	4.185 500 0E+04
langley [15 °C, CIPM, 1950]	1	1.000 000 0E+00
calorie/square centimeter [I.T.]	**<energy fluence>**	
joule/square meter	41,868	4.186 800 0E+04
langley [I.T.]	1	1.000 000 0E+00
calorie/square centimeter [thermoc.]	**<energy fluence>**	
joule/square meter	41,840	4.184 000 0E+04
langley [thermoc.]	1	1.000 000 0E+00
calow [Poland]	**<length, special - see page 29>**	
centimeter	2.4	2.400 000 0E+00
camionada [El Salvador]	**<volume, special - see page 29>**	
cubic meter	3	3.000 000 0E+00
can [Philippines]	**<volume, special - see page 29>**	
liter	18.926 53	1.892 653 0E+01
can [Vietnam]	**<mass, special - see page 29>**	
kilogram	0.6	6.000 000 0E-01
cana [Netherlands Antilles]	**<mass, special - see page 29>**	
kilogram	0.75	7.500 000 0E-01

| Convert From | <Type of Unit> | |
Convert To	Standard	Scientific

canada [Brazil] — <volume, special - see page 29>
liter — 2.662 — 2.662 000 0E+00

canada [Portugal] — <volume, special - see page 29>
liter — 1.38 — 1.380 000 0E+00

candareen [Cambodia] — <mass, special - see page 29>
gram — 0.375 — 3.750 000 0E-01

candareen [China] — <mass, special - see page 29>
gram — 0.5 — 5.000 000 0E-01

candareen [Hong Kong] — <mass, special - see page 29>
gram — 0.378 — 3.780 000 0E-01

candareen [Japan] — <mass, special - see page 29>
gram — 0.375 — 3.750 000 0E-01

candareen [Laos] — <mass, special - see page 29>
gram — 0.375 — 3.750 000 0E-01

candarin [China] — <mass, special - see page 29>
gram — 0.377 993 7 — 3.779 937 0E-01

candel [Portuguese India] — <volume, special - see page 29>
liter — 159.7 — 1.597 000 0E+02

candela — <luminous intensity>

	Standard	Scientific
bougie decimale [France]	1.022 569 4	1.022 569 4E+00
bougie nouvelle [France]	1	1.000 000 0E+00
candle [international standard]	0.981 666 7	9.816 666 7E-01
candle [new]	1	1.000 000 0E+00
carcel	0.102 150 5	1.021 505 4E-01
Hefner candle [Germany]	1.089 530 2	1.089 530 2E+00
hefnerkerze [Germany]	1.089 530 2	1.089 530 2E+00
lumen/steradian	1	1.000 000 0E+00
lux square meter/steradian	1	1.000 000 0E+00
violle	0.049 578 6	4.957 858 2E-02
watt/steradian [at 540 THz]	0.001 464 1	1.464 128 8E-03
watt/steradian [at 5550 angstrom]	0.001 470 6	1.470 588 2E-03
watt/steradian [green light at 100% efficiency]	0.001 459 9	1.459 854 0E-03

candela second steradian — <quantity of light>

	Standard	Scientific
joule	0.001 464 1	1.464 128 8E-03
lumen second	1	1.000 000 0E+00
lux second square meter	1	1.000 000 0E+00
talbot	1	1.000 000 0E+00
wattsecond [light at 540 THz]	0.001 464 1	1.464 128 8E-03

candela steradian — <luminous flux>

	Standard	Scientific
lumen	1	1.000 000 0E+00
lux square meter	1	1.000 000 0E+00
watt [at 5550 angstrom]	0.001 470 6	1.470 588 2E-03

candela steradian/square meter — <illuminance>

	Standard	Scientific
footcandle	0.092 903	9.290 304 0E-02
lumen/square foot	0.092 903	9.290 304 0E-02
lumen/square meter	1	1.000 000 0E+00
lux	1	1.000 000 0E+00
nox	1,000	1.000 000 0E+03
phot	0.000 1	1.000 000 0E-04

candela steradian/watt — <luminous efficacy>

	Standard	Scientific
lumen/watt	1	1.000 000 0E+00
lux square meter/watt	1	1.000 000 0E+00

candela/square centimeter — <luminance>

	Standard	Scientific
blondel	31,415.927	3.141 592 7E+04
candela/square inch	6.451 6	6.451 600 0E+00
candela/square meter	10,000	1.000 000 0E+04
footlambert	2,918.635 1	2.918 635 1E+03
lambert	3.141 592 7	3.141 592 7E+00
nit	10,000	1.000 000 0E+04

Convert From	<Type of Unit>	
Convert To	Standard	Scientific
stilb --	1 ----	1.000 000 0E+00
candela/square foot	**<luminance>**	
apostilb [international] --	33.815 822 ----	3.381 582 2E+01
blondel ---	33.815 822 ----	3.381 582 2E+01
candela/square inch ---	0.006 944 4 ----	6.944 444 4E-03
candela/square meter ---	10.763 91 ----	1.076 391 0E+01
footlambert --	3.141 592 7 ----	3.141 592 7E+00
millilambert ---	3.381 582 2 ----	3.381 582 2E+00
nit ---	10.763 91 ----	1.076 391 0E+01
stilb ---	0.001 076 4 ----	1.076 391 0E-03
candela/square inch	**<luminance>**	
apostilb [international] --	4,869.478 4 ----	4.869 478 4E+03
blondel ---	4,869.478 4 ----	4.869 478 4E+03
candela/square foot --	144 ----	1.440 000 0E+02
candela/square meter ---	1,550.003 1 ----	1.550 003 1E+03
footlambert --	452.389 34 ----	4.523 893 4E+02
lambert ---	0.486 947 8 ----	4.869 478 4E-01
nit ---	1,550.003 1 ----	1.550 003 1E+03
stilb ---	0.155 000 3 ----	1.550 003 1E-01
candela/square meter	**<luminance>**	
apostilb [international] --	3.141 592 7 ----	3.141 592 7E+00
blondel ---	3.141 592 7 ----	3.141 592 7E+00
bril --	31.415 927 ----	3.141 592 7E+01
candela/square foot --	0.092 903 ----	9.290 304 0E-02
footlambert --	0.291 863 5 ----	2.918 635 1E-01
lumen/steradian square meter ---------------------------------	1 ----	1.000 000 0E+00
lux steradian --	1 ----	1.000 000 0E+00
millilambert ---	0.314 159 3 ----	3.141 592 7E-01
nit ---	1 ----	1.000 000 0E+00
skot ---	3,141.592 7 ----	3.141 592 7E+03
stilb ---	0.000 1 ----	1.000 000 0E-04
candil [East India]	**<mass, special - see page 29>**	
kilogram ---	254.029 ----	2.540 290 0E+02
candil [Portuguese India]	**<volume, special - see page 29>**	
liter ---	159.7 ----	1.597 000 0E+02
candle [international standard]	**<luminous intensity>**	
bougie decimale [France] --------------------------------------	1.041 666 7 ----	1.041 666 7E+00
bougie nouvelle [France] --------------------------------------	1.018 675 7 ----	1.018 675 7E+00
candela --	1.018 675 7 ----	1.018 675 7E+00
carcel --	0.104 058 3 ----	1.040 582 7E-01
Hefner candle [Germany] --------------------------------------	1.109 877 9 ----	1.109 877 9E+00
watt/steradian [at 540 THz] -----------------------------------	0.001 491 5 ----	1.491 472 5E-03
candle [new]	**<luminous intensity>**	
bougie nouvelle [France] --------------------------------------	1 ----	1.000 000 0E+00
candela --	1 ----	1.000 000 0E+00
candle [international standard] -------------------------------	0.981 666 7 ----	9.816 666 7E-01
lumen/steradian ---	1 ----	1.000 000 0E+00
lux square meter/steradian -----------------------------------	1 ----	1.000 000 0E+00
watt/steradian [at 540 THz] -----------------------------------	0.001 464 1 ----	1.464 128 8E-03
candy [Burma]	**<mass, special - see page 29>**	
kilogram ---	8,164.663 ----	8.164 663 0E+03
candy [India]	**<mass, special - see page 29>**	
kilogram ---	254 ----	2.540 000 0E+02
candy [Sri Lanka]	**<mass, special - see page 29>**	
kilogram ---	226.8 ----	2.268 000 0E+02
candy [Yemen]	**<mass, special - see page 29>**	
kilogram ---	304.8 ----	3.048 000 0E+02
caneca [Cuba]	**<volume, special - see page 29>**	
liter ---	21.75 ----	2.175 000 0E+01

canna [Italy]   <length, special - see page 29>
    meter -- 2 --- 2.000 000 0E+00

canna [Malta]   <length, special - see page 29>
    meter -- 2.095 --- 2.095 000 0E+00

canna [Spanish North Africa]   <length, special - see page 29>
    centimeter -------------------------------------- 53.3 --- 5.330 000 0E+01

cantar [Cyprus, Aleppo]   <mass, special - see page 29>
    kilogram -------------------------------- 228.611 --- 2.286 110 0E+02

cantar [Cyprus]   <mass, special - see page 29>
    kilogram ----------------------------------- 55.883 --- 5.588 300 0E+01

cantar [Egypt]   <mass, special - see page 29>
    kilogram ----------------------------------- 44.928 --- 4.492 800 0E+01

cantar [Greece]   <mass, special - see page 29>
    kilogram ------------------------------------ 56.32 --- 5.632 000 0E+01

cantar [Iraq]   <mass, special - see page 29>
    kilogram ----------------------------------- 44.928 --- 4.492 800 0E+01

cantar [Lebanon]   <mass, special - see page 29>
    kilogram ----------------------------------- 256.4 --- 2.564 000 0E+02

cantar [Malta]   <mass, special - see page 29>
    kilogram ----------------------------------- 79.379 --- 7.937 900 0E+01

cantar [Morocco]   <mass, special - see page 29>
    kilogram ------------------------------------ 51.26 --- 5.126 000 0E+01

cantar [Romania]   <mass, special - see page 29>
    kilogram ---------------------------------------56 --- 5.600 000 0E+01

cantar [Sudan, large]   <mass, special - see page 29>
    kilogram ------------------------------------ 141.5 --- 1.415 000 0E+02

cantar [Sudan, small]   <mass, special - see page 29>
    kilogram ----------------------------------- 44.928 --- 4.492 800 0E+01

cantar [Syria]   <mass, special - see page 29>
    kilogram ----------------------------------- 256.5 --- 2.565 000 0E+02

cantar [Tunisia]   <mass, special - see page 29>
    kilogram ------------------------------------ 50.38 --- 5.038 000 0E+01

cantar [Turkey]   <mass, special - see page 29>
    kilogram ------------------------------------ 56.45 --- 5.645 000 0E+01

cantara [Bolivia]   <mass, special - see page 29>
    kilogram ------------------------------------ 11.5 --- 1.150 000 0E+01

cantara [Brazil]   <mass, special - see page 29>
    kilogram ------------------------------------ 14.7 --- 1.470 000 0E+01

cantara [Chile]   <mass, special - see page 29>
    kilogram ------------------------------------ 11.5 --- 1.150 000 0E+01

cantara [Colombia]   <mass, special - see page 29>
    kilogram ------------------------------------ 12.5 --- 1.250 000 0E+01

cantara [Cuba]   <mass, special - see page 29>
    kilogram --------------------------------- 11.502 --- 1.150 200 0E+01

cantara [Dominican Republic]   <mass, special - see page 29>
    kilogram ------------------------------------ 11.34 --- 1.134 000 0E+01

cantara [Ecuador]   <mass, special - see page 29>
    kilogram ------------------------------------ 11.5 --- 1.150 000 0E+01

cantara [Mexico]   <mass, special - see page 29>
    kilogram ------------------------------------ 11.51 --- 1.151 000 0E+01

cantara [Paraguay]   <mass, special - see page 29>
    kilogram ---------------------------------- 11.475 --- 1.147 500 0E+01

cantara [Peru]   <volume, special - see page 29>
    liter --- 16.1 --- 1.610 000 0E+01

| Convert From | | <Type of Unit> |
Convert To	Standard	Scientific
cantara [Peru]	<mass, special - see page 29>	
kilogram	11.5	1.150 000 0E+01
cantara [Philippines]	<mass, special - see page 29>	
kilogram	11.5	1.150 000 0E+01
cantara [Portugal]	<mass, special - see page 29>	
kilogram	15	1.500 000 0E+01
cantara [Spain]	<volume, special - see page 29>	
liter	16.128	1.612 800 0E+01
cantara [Spain]	<mass, special - see page 29>	
kilogram	11.502	1.150 200 0E+01
cantara [Uruguay]	<mass, special - see page 29>	
kilogram	11.485	1.148 500 0E+01
cantara [Venezuela]	<mass, special - see page 29>	
kilogram	11.52	1.152 000 0E+01
cantarelli [Italy, Genoa]	<mass, special - see page 29>	
kilogram	52.325	5.232 500 0E+01
cantarelli [Romania]	<mass, special - see page 29>	
kilogram	56.726	5.672 600 0E+01
cantarelli [Syria]	<mass, special - see page 29>	
kilogram	189.988	1.899 880 0E+02
cantaro [Egypt]	<mass, special - see page 29>	
kilogram	44.928	4.492 800 0E+01
cantaro [Iraq]	<mass, special - see page 29>	
kilogram	44.928	4.492 800 0E+01
cantaro [Italy]	<mass, special - see page 29>	
kilogram	47.517	4.751 700 0E+01
cantaro [Mexico]	<mass, special - see page 29>	
kilogram	11.506	1.150 600 0E+01
cantaro [Portugal]	<volume, special - see page 29>	
liter	8.27	8.270 000 0E+00
cantaro [Romania]	<mass, special - see page 29>	
kilogram	56.726	5.672 600 0E+01
cantaro [Sardinia]	<mass, special - see page 29>	
kilogram	40.118	4.011 800 0E+01
cantaro [Spain]	<volume, special - see page 29>	
liter	16.133	1.613 300 0E+01
cantaro [Syria, Damascus]	<mass, special - see page 29>	
kilogram	256.5	2.565 000 0E+02
cantaro [Syria]	<mass, special - see page 29>	
kilogram	189.988	1.899 880 0E+02
cantaro barbaresco [Spain]	<mass, special - see page 29>	
kilogram	42.03	4.203 000 0E+01
cantaro grosso [Italy, Rome]	<mass, special - see page 29>	
kilogram	339.295	3.392 950 0E+02
cantaro grosso [Italy]	<mass, special - see page 29>	
kilogram	89	8.900 000 0E+01
cantaro grosso [Sicily]	<mass, special - see page 29>	
kilogram	87.351	8.735 100 0E+01
cantaro sottile [Sicily]	<mass, special - see page 29>	
kilogram	79.413	7.941 300 0E+01
cantero [Ecuador]	<area, special - see page 29>	
square meter	441	4.410 000 0E+02
cao [Vietnam]	<area, special - see page 29>	
square meter	360	3.600 000 0E+02

Convert From		<Type of Unit>
Convert To	Standard	Scientific

cap [Vietnam]   <volume, special - see page 29>
centiliter --- 20 --- 2.000 000 0E+01

cape foot [South Africa]   <length, special - see page 29>
meter --- 0.314 86 --- 3.148 600 0E-01

cape inch [South Africa]   <length, special - see page 29>
centimeter --------------------------------------- 2.624 --- 2.624 000 0E+00

cape morgen [South Africa]   <area, special - see page 29>
are --- 85.653 1 --- 8.565 310 0E+01

cape rood [South Africa]   <length, special - see page 29>
meter --- 3.778 3 --- 3.778 300 0E+00

capicha [Iran]   <volume, special - see page 29>
liter --- 2.63 --- 2.630 000 0E+00

caractero [Spain]   <mass, special - see page 29>
gram --- 0.2 --- 2.000 000 0E-01

carak [Persia]   <mass, special - see page 29>
gram --- 750 --- 7.500 000 0E+02

carat [gemstones]   <mass>

	Standard	Scientific
carat [international]	1	1.000 000 0E+00
carat [metric]	1	1.000 000 0E+00
carat [UK]	0.771 617 9	7.716 179 2E-01
carat [US, after 1913]	1	1.000 000 0E+00
carat [US, before 1913]	0.974 184 1	9.741 841 2E-01
decigram	2	2.000 000 0E+00
drachm [UK, apothecary]	0.051 441 2	5.144 119 5E-02
dram [avoirdupois]	0.112 876 7	1.128 766 8E-01
dram [US, apothecary]	0.051 441 2	5.144 119 5E-02
grain	3.086 471 7	3.086 471 7E+00
grain [apothecary]	3.086 471 7	3.086 471 7E+00
grain [avoirdupois]	3.086 471 7	3.086 471 7E+00
grain [troy]	3.086 471 7	3.086 471 7E+00
kilogram	0.000 2	2.000 000 0E-04
ounce [apothecary]	0.006 430 1	6.430 149 3E-03
ounce [troy]	0.006 430 1	6.430 149 3E-03
pennyweight	0.128 603	1.286 029 9E-01
point [jewelers']	100	1.000 000 0E+02
scruple [UK]	0.154 323 6	1.543 235 8E-01
scruple [US, apothecary]	0.154 323 6	1.543 235 8E-01

carat [international]   <mass>

	Standard	Scientific
carat [gemstones]	1	1.000 000 0E+00
carat [metric]	1	1.000 000 0E+00
carat [UK]	0.771 617 9	7.716 179 2E-01
carat [US, after 1913]	1	1.000 000 0E+00
carat [US, before 1913]	0.974 184 1	9.741 841 2E-01
decigram	2	2.000 000 0E+00
drachm [UK, apothecary]	0.051 441 2	5.144 119 5E-02
dram [avoirdupois]	0.112 876 7	1.128 766 8E-01
dram [US, apothecary]	0.051 441 2	5.144 119 5E-02
grain	3.086 471 7	3.086 471 7E+00
grain [apothecary]	3.086 471 7	3.086 471 7E+00
grain [avoirdupois]	3.086 471 7	3.086 471 7E+00
grain [troy]	3.086 471 7	3.086 471 7E+00
kilogram	0.000 2	2.000 000 0E-04
milligram	200	2.000 000 0E+02
ounce [apothecary]	0.006 430 1	6.430 149 3E-03
ounce [troy]	0.006 430 1	6.430 149 3E-03
pennyweight	0.128 603	1.286 029 9E-01
point [jewelers']	100	1.000 000 0E+02
scruple [UK]	0.154 323 6	1.543 235 8E-01
scruple [US, apothecary]	0.154 323 6	1.543 235 8E-01

Convert From Convert To	<Type of Unit> Standard	Scientific
carat [Iran]	**<mass, special - see page 29>**	
milligram	195	1.950 000 0E+02
carat [Italy, Bologna, gold, silver and jewels]	**<mass, special - see page 29>**	
gram	0.108	1.080 000 0E-01
carat [Italy, Florence, gold, silver and jewels]	**<mass, special - see page 29>**	
gram	14.15	1.415 000 0E+01
carat [Italy, Genoa, gold, silver and jewels]	**<mass, special - see page 29>**	
gram	13.22	1.322 000 0E+01
carat [Italy, Milan, gold, silver and jewels]	**<mass, special - see page 29>**	
gram	9.8	9.800 000 0E+00
carat [Italy, Turin, gold, silver and jewels]	**<mass, special - see page 29>**	
gram	10.25	1.025 000 0E+01
carat [Italy, Venice, gold, silver and jewels]	**<mass, special - see page 29>**	
gram	0.2	2.000 000 0E-01
carat [metric]	**<mass>**	
carat [gemstones]	1	1.000 000 0E+00
carat [international]	1	1.000 000 0E+00
carat [UK]	0.771 617 9	7.716 179 2E-01
carat [US, after 1913]	1	1.000 000 0E+00
carat [US, before 1913]	0.974 184 1	9.741 841 2E-01
decigram	2	2.000 000 0E+00
drachm [UK, apothecary]	0.051 441 2	5.144 119 5E-02
dram [avoirdupois]	0.112 876 7	1.128 766 8E-01
dram [US, apothecary]	0.051 441 2	5.144 119 5E-02
grain	3.086 471 7	3.086 471 7E+00
grain [apothecary]	3.086 471 7	3.086 471 7E+00
grain [avoirdupois]	3.086 471 7	3.086 471 7E+00
grain [troy]	3.086 471 7	3.086 471 7E+00
kilogram	0.000 2	2.000 000 0E-04
milligram	200	2.000 000 0E+02
ounce [apothecary]	0.006 430 1	6.430 149 3E-03
ounce [troy]	0.006 430 1	6.430 149 3E-03
pennyweight [troy]	0.128 603	1.286 029 9E-01
point [jewelers']	100	1.000 000 0E+02
scruple [UK]	0.154 323 6	1.543 235 8E-01
scruple [US, apothecary]	0.154 323 6	1.543 235 8E-01
carat [Thailand]	**<mass, special - see page 29>**	
gram	0.2	2.000 000 0E-01
carat [UK]	**<mass>**	
carat [gemstones]	1.295 978 2	1.295 978 2E+00
carat [international]	1.295 978 2	1.295 978 2E+00
carat [metric]	1.295 978 2	1.295 978 2E+00
carat [US, after 1913]	1.295 978 2	1.295 978 2E+00
carat [US, before 1913]	1.262 521 4	1.262 521 4E+00
decigram	2.591 956 4	2.591 956 4E+00
drachm [UK, apothecary]	0.066 666 7	6.666 666 7E-02
dram [avoirdupois]	0.146 285 7	1.462 857 1E-01
dram [US, apothecary]	0.066 666 7	6.666 666 7E-02
grain	4	4.000 000 0E+00
grain [apothecary]	4	4.000 000 0E+00
grain [avoirdupois]	4	4.000 000 0E+00
grain [troy]	4	4.000 000 0E+00
kilogram	0.000 259 2	2.591 956 4E-04
ounce [apothecary]	0.008 333 3	8.333 333 3E-03
ounce [troy]	0.008 333 3	8.333 333 3E-03
pennyweight [troy]	0.166 666 7	1.666 666 7E-01
point [jewelers']	129.597 82	1.295 978 2E+02
scruple [UK]	0.2	2.000 000 0E-01
scruple [US, apothecary]	0.2	2.000 000 0E-01

carat [US, after 1913] \<mass\>

Convert To	Standard	Scientific
carat [gemstones]	1	1.000 000 0E+00
carat [international]	1	1.000 000 0E+00
carat [metric]	1	1.000 000 0E+00
carat [UK]	0.771 617 9	7.716 179 2E−01
carat [US, before 1913]	0.974 184 1	9.741 841 2E−01
decigram	2	2.000 000 0E+00
drachm [UK, apothecary]	0.051 441 2	5.144 119 5E−02
dram [avoirdupois]	0.112 876 7	1.128 766 8E−01
dram [US, apothecary]	0.051 441 2	5.144 119 5E−02
grain	3.086 471 7	3.086 471 7E+00
grain [apothecary]	3.086 471 7	3.086 471 7E+00
grain [avoirdupois]	3.086 471 7	3.086 471 7E+00
grain [troy]	3.086 471 7	3.086 471 7E+00
kilogram	0.000 2	2.000 000 0E−04
milligram	200	2.000 000 0E+02
ounce [apothecary]	0.006 430 1	6.430 149 3E−03
ounce [troy]	0.006 430 1	6.430 149 3E−03
pennyweight [troy]	0.128 603	1.286 029 9E−01
point [jewelers']	100	1.000 000 0E+02
scruple [UK]	0.154 323 6	1.543 235 8E−01
scruple [US, apothecary]	0.154 323 6	1.543 235 8E−01

carat [US, before 1913] \<mass\>

Convert To	Standard	Scientific
carat [gemstones]	1.026 5	1.026 500 0E+00
carat [international]	1.026 5	1.026 500 0E+00
carat [metric]	1.026 5	1.026 500 0E+00
carat [UK]	0.792 065 8	7.920 657 9E−01
carat [US, after 1913]	1.026 5	1.026 500 0E+00
decigram	2.053	2.053 000 0E+00
drachm [UK, apothecary]	0.052 804 4	5.280 438 6E−02
dram [avoirdupois]	0.115 867 9	1.158 679 1E−01
dram [US, apothecary]	0.052 804 4	5.280 438 6E−02
grain	3.168 263 2	3.168 263 2E+00
grain [apothecary]	3.168 263 2	3.168 263 2E+00
grain [avoirdupois]	3.168 263 2	3.168 263 2E+00
grain [troy]	3.168 263 2	3.168 263 2E+00
kilogram	0.000 205 3	2.053 000 0E−04
milligram	205.3	2.053 000 0E+02
ounce [apothecary]	0.006 600 5	6.600 548 3E−03
ounce [troy]	0.006 600 5	6.600 548 3E−03
pennyweight [troy]	0.132 011	1.320 109 7E−01
point [jewelers']	102.65	1.026 500 0E+02
scruple [UK]	0.158 413 2	1.584 131 6E−01
scruple [US, apothecary]	0.158 413 2	1.584 131 6E−01

carate [Germany, gold and silver] \<mass, special - see page 29\>

Convert To	Standard	Scientific
gram	10.62	1.062 000 0E+01

carate [Germany, jewels and pearls] \<mass, special - see page 29\>

Convert To	Standard	Scientific
gram	0.198	1.980 000 0E−01

carate [Switzerland, gold and silver] \<mass, special - see page 29\>

Convert To	Standard	Scientific
gram	10.2	1.020 000 0E+01

carcel \<luminous intensity\>

Convert To	Standard	Scientific
bougie nouvelle [France]	9.789 473 7	9.789 473 7E+00
candela	9.789 473 7	9.789 473 7E+00
candle [international standard]	9.61	9.610 000 0E+00
Hefner candle [Germany]	10.665 927	1.066 592 7E+01
watt/steradian [at 540 THz]	0.014 333 1	1.433 305 1E−02

carga [Colombia] \<mass, special - see page 29\>

Convert To	Standard	Scientific
kilogram	125	1.250 000 0E+02

carga [Costa Rica] \<mass, special - see page 29\>

Convert To	Standard	Scientific
kilogram	161	1.610 000 0E+02

| Convert From | | <Type of Unit> |
Convert To	Standard	Scientific
carga [El Salvador] kilogram	<mass, special - see page 29> 92	9.200 000 0E+01
carga [Mexico] liter	<volume, special - see page 29> 181.61	1.816 100 0E+02
carga [Mexico] kilogram	<mass, special - see page 29> 140	1.400 000 0E+02
carga [Nicaragua] kilogram	<mass, special - see page 29> 161	1.610 000 0E+02
carga [Spain] liter	<volume, special - see page 29> 222	2.220 000 0E+02
carga [Venezuela] kilogram	<mass, special - see page 29> 184	1.840 000 0E+02
carga [Venezuela] hectare	<area, special - see page 29> 1	1.000 000 0E+00
carga de papa [Costa Rica] kilogram	<mass, special - see page 29> 828	8.280 000 0E+02
cargo [Belize] liter	<volume, special - see page 29> 68.19	6.819 000 0E+01
cargo [Belize] kilogram	<mass, special - see page 29> 90.72	9.072 000 0E+01
cargo [British Honduras] liter	<volume, special - see page 29> 68.189 4	6.818 940 0E+01
cargo [British Honduras] kilogram	<mass, special - see page 29> 90.718 5	9.071 850 0E+01
caro [Dominican Republic] hectare	<area, special - see page 29> 1.293	1.293 000 0E+00
carreau [Dominican Republic] hectare	<area, special - see page 29> 1.293	1.293 000 0E+00
carreau de terre [Haiti] are	<area, special - see page 29> 129	1.290 000 0E+02
carree [France] square meter	<area, special - see page 29> 51.072	5.107 200 0E+01
carretada [El Salvador] cubic meter	<volume, special - see page 29> 1	1.000 000 0E+00
carsi [Turkey, textiles] centimeter	<length, special - see page 29> 68	6.800 000 0E+01
case [Fiji, bananas] kilogram	<mass, special - see page 29> 32.7	3.270 000 0E+01
cash [China] milligram	<mass, special - see page 29> 50	5.000 000 0E+01
cash [India] milligram	<mass, special - see page 29> 1.215	1.215 000 0E+01
cass [Cyprus] liter	<volume, special - see page 29> 4.73	4.730 000 0E+00
cassaba [Egypt, ancient] meter	<length, special - see page 29> 3.55	3.550 000 0E+00
cassaba [Iraq] meter	<length, special - see page 29> 3.8	3.800 000 0E+00
cast [Russia] milliliter	<volume, special - see page 29> 109.3	1.093 000 0E+02
castellano [Spain] gram	<mass, special - see page 29> 4.793	4.793 000 0E+00
cate [China] kilogram	<mass, special - see page 29> 0.5	5.000 000 0E-01

Convert From	<Type of Unit>	
Convert To	Standard	Scientific

cate [Indonesia] <mass, special - see page 29>
kilogram ----------------------------------- 0.618 --- 6.180 000 0E−01

cate [Japan] <mass, special - see page 29>
kilogram ----------------------------------- 0.6 --- 6.000 000 0E−01

cate [South Korea] <mass, special - see page 29>
kilogram ----------------------------------- 0.6 --- 6.000 000 0E−01

cate [Thailand] <mass, special - see page 29>
kilogram ----------------------------------- 0.6 --- 6.000 000 0E−01

catta [India] <area, special - see page 29>
square meter ------------------------ 66.890 189 --- 6.689 018 9E+01

catti [Batavia] <mass, special - see page 29>
gram ----------------------------------- 617.5 --- 6.175 000 0E+02

catti [China] <mass, special - see page 29>
gram ----------------------------------- 604.875 --- 6.048 750 0E+02

catti [Japan] <mass, special - see page 29>
gram ----------------------------------- 594 --- 5.940 000 0E+02

catti [Sumatra] <mass, special - see page 29>
gram ----------------------------------- 604.875 --- 6.048 750 0E+02

cattie [Burma] <mass, special - see page 29>
gram ----------------------------------- 544.310 8 --- 5.443 108 0E+02

catty [Batavia] <mass, special - see page 29>
gram ----------------------------------- 617.5 --- 6.175 000 0E+02

catty [Brunei] <mass, special - see page 29>
kilogram ----------------------------------- 0.605 --- 6.050 000 0E−01

catty [China] <mass, special - see page 29>
kilogram ----------------------------------- 0.5 --- 5.000 000 0E−01

catty [Indonesia] <mass, special - see page 29>
kilogram ----------------------------------- 0.618 --- 6.180 000 0E−01

catty [Japan] <mass, special - see page 29>
kilogram ----------------------------------- 0.6 --- 6.000 000 0E−01

catty [Java] <mass, special - see page 29>
gram ----------------------------------- 615 --- 6.150 000 0E+02

catty [Malaysia] <mass, special - see page 29>
gram ----------------------------------- 922.7 --- 9.227 000 0E+02

catty [Philippines] <mass, special - see page 29>
gram ----------------------------------- 594.375 --- 5.943 750 0E+02

catty [South Korea] <mass, special - see page 29>
kilogram ----------------------------------- 0.6 --- 6.000 000 0E−01

catty [Sumatra] <mass, special - see page 29>
gram ----------------------------------- 960.25 --- 9.602 500 0E+02

catty [Taiwan] <mass, special - see page 29>
kilogram ----------------------------------- 0.6 --- 6.000 000 0E−01

catty [Thailand] <mass, special - see page 29>
kilogram ----------------------------------- 0.6 --- 6.000 000 0E−01

cavan [Philippines] <volume, special - see page 29>
liter ----------------------------------- 75 --- 7.500 000 0E+01

cavan [Philippines] <mass, special - see page 29>
kilogram ----------------------------------- 61.35 --- 6.135 000 0E+01

cawney [India] <area, special - see page 29>
hectare ----------------------------------- 0.535 --- 5.350 000 0E−01

cawnie [India] <area, special - see page 29>
hectare ----------------------------------- 0.535 --- 5.350 000 0E−01

cay [Vietnam] <length, special - see page 29>
meter ----------------------------------- 18.75 --- 1.875 000 0E+01

| Convert From | <Type of Unit> | |
Convert To	Standard	Scientific
cazuela [El Salvador]	<volume, special - see page 29>	
liter	16.6	1.660 000 0E+01
ceira [Portuguese India]	<mass, special - see page 29>	
gram	933.1	9.331 000 0E+02
ceki [Turkey]	<mass, special - see page 29>	
kilogram	225.798 3	2.257 983 0E+02
cekirdek [Turkey]	<mass, special - see page 29>	
milligram	401	4.010 000 0E+02
celemin [Spain]	<area, special - see page 29>	
are	5.37	5.370 000 0E+00
celo	<acceleration>	
foot/square second	1	1.000 000 0E+00
galileo	30.48	3.048 000 0E+01
g_n [due to gravity]	0.031 081	3.108 095 0E−02
leo	0.030 48	3.048 000 0E−02
meter/square second	0.304 8	3.048 000 0E−01
cental [US]	<mass>	
centner [UK]	0.892 857 1	8.928 571 4E−01
doppelzentner [Germany]	0.453 592 4	4.535 923 7E−01
hundredweight [long]	0.892 857 1	8.928 571 4E−01
hundredweight [short]	1	1.000 000 0E+00
hyl	4.625 354	4.625 354 9E+00
kilogram	45.359 237	4.535 923 7E+01
myriagram	4.535 923 7	4.535 923 7E+00
pound	100	1.000 000 0E+02
pound [troy]	121.527 78	1.215 277 8E+02
pound [UK]	100.000 01	1.000 000 1E+02
pound [unified]	100	1.000 000 0E+02
pound [US, avoirdupois]	99.999 987	9.999 998 7E+01
pound [US, troy]	121.527 76	1.215 277 6E+02
quarter [long]	0.178 571 4	1.785 714 3E−01
quarter [short]	0.2	2.000 000 0E−01
quarter [US]	4	4.000 000 0E+00
quintal [US]	1	1.000 000 0E+00
slug	3.108 095	3.108 095 0E+00
stone [UK]	7.142 857 1	7.142 857 1E+00
ton [long]	0.044 642 9	4.464 285 7E−02
ton [short]	0.05	5.000 000 0E−02
ton [UK]	0.044 642 9	4.464 285 7E−02
tonne	0.045 359 2	4.535 923 7E−02
centenaar [Netherlands]	<mass, special - see page 29>	
kilogram	100	1.000 000 0E+02
centenary	<time>	
centennial	1	1.000 000 0E+00
century	1	1.000 000 0E+00
year [normal calendar]	100	1.000 000 0E+02
centennial	<time>	
centenary	1	1.000 000 0E+00
century	1	1.000 000 0E+00
year [normal calendar]	100	1.000 000 0E+02
centiampere	<electric current>	
abampere	0.001	1.000 000 0E−03
ampere	0.01	1.000 000 0E−02
statampere	>>>	2.997 924 6E+07
centiare	<area>	
acre [international]	0.000 247 1	2.471 053 8E−04
hectare	0.000 1	1.000 000 0E−04
square	0.107 639 1	1.076 391 0E−01
square cubit	4.783 960 2	4.783 960 2E+00
square digit	2,755.561 1	2.755 561 1E+03

Convert From	\<Type of Unit\>	
Convert To	Standard	Scientific

square foot [international]	10.763 91	1.076 391 0E+01
square foot [US, survey]	10.763 867	1.076 386 7E+01
square link [Gunter or US, survey]	24.710 439	2.471 043 9E+01
square link [Ramden or Engineer]	10.763 867	1.076 386 7E+01
square meter	1	1.000 000 0E+00
square pace	1.722 225 7	1.722 225 7E+00
square perch [US, survey]	0.039 536 7	3.953 670 3E−02
square span	19.135 841	1.913 584 1E+01
square vara [US, survey, California]	1.423 321 3	1.423 321 3E+00
square vara [US, survey, Texas]	1.394 997 2	1.394 997 2E+00
square yard [based on US, survey foot]	1.195 985 3	1.195 985 3E+00
square yard [international]	1.195 99	1.195 990 0E+00

centibar		**\<pressure\>**
atmosphere [standard]	0.009 869 2	9.869 232 7E−03
atmosphere [technical]	0.010 197 2	1.019 716 2E−02
bar	0.01	1.000 000 0E−02
barye [France]	10,000	1.000 000 0E+04
centimeter of mercury [0 °C, by convention]	0.750 061 6	7.500 615 8E−01
centimeter of water [4 °C, by convention]	10.197 162	1.019 716 2E+01
dyne/square centimeter	10,000	1.000 000 0E+04
foot of mercury [0 °C, by convention]	0.024 608 3	2.460 831 9E−02
foot of water [4 °C, by convention]	0.334 552 6	3.345 525 6E−01
gram-force/square centimeter	10.197 162	1.019 716 2E+01
inch of mercury [0 °C, by convention]	0.295 299 8	2.952 998 3E−01
inch of water [4 °C, by convention]	4.014 630 8	4.014 630 8E+00
kilogram-force/square meter	101.971 62	1.019 716 2E+02
kilopascal	1	1.000 000 0E+00
kilopond/square meter	101.971 62	1.019 716 2E+02
kip/square foot	0.020 885 4	2.088 543 4E−02
millimeter of mercury [0 °C, by convention]	7.500 615 8	7.500 615 8E+00
millimeter of water [4 °C, by convention]	101.971 62	1.019 716 2E+02
newton/square meter	1,000	1.000 000 0E+03
ounce-force/square inch	2.320 603 8	2.320 603 8E+00
pascal	1,000	1.000 000 0E+03
pieze [France]	1	1.000 000 0E+00
pound-force/square foot	20.885 434	2.088 543 4E+01
sthene/square meter [France]	1	1.000 000 0E+00
ton-force/square foot [short]	0.010 442 7	1.044 271 7E−02
ton-force/square meter [metric]	0.101 971 6	1.019 716 2E−01
torr	7.500 616 8	7.500 616 8E+00

centicandela		**\<luminous intensity\>**
candela	0.01	1.000 000 0E−02

centicoulomb		**\<electric charge\>**
abcoulomb	0.001	1.000 000 0E−03
coulomb	0.01	1.000 000 0E−02
electromagnetic unit of charge [cgs system]	0.001	1.000 000 0E−03
farad volt	0.01	1.000 000 0E−02
statcoulomb	>>>	2.997 924 6E+07

centifarad		**\<capacitance\>**
abfarad	<<<	1.000 000 0E−11
coulomb/volt	0.01	1.000 000 0E−02
farad	0.01	1.000 000 0E−02
statfarad	>>>	8.987 551 8E+09

centigal		**\<acceleration\>**
foot/square second	0.000 328 1	3.280 839 9E−04
galileo	0.01	1.000 000 0E−02
g_n [due to gravity]	0.000 010 2	1.019 716 2E−05
meter/square second	0.000 1	1.000 000 0E−04
millimeter/square second	0.1	1.000 000 0E−01

centigrade heat unit [15 °C]		**\<energy\>**
Btu [15 °C]	1.8	1.800 000 0E+00
Btu [I.T.]	1.799 570 3	1.799 570 3E+00

calorie [kilogram, I.T.]	0.453 484 1	4.534 840 9E-01
centigrade heat unit [I.T.]	0.999 761 3	9.997 612 9E-01
cubic foot atmosphere	0.661 733	6.617 329 7E-01
frigorie [France]	0.453 592 4	4.535 924 3E-01
joule	1,898.647 2	1.898 647 2E+03
kilocalorie [I.T.]	0.453 484 1	4.534 840 9E-01
kilogram calorie [15 °C, NBS, 1939]	0.453 592 4	4.535 924 3E-01
liter atmosphere	18.738 191	1.873 819 1E+01
watthour	0.527 402	5.274 020 0E-01

centigrade heat unit [15.6 °C] <energy>

Btu [15.6 °C]	1.8	1.800 000 0E+00
Btu [I.T.]	1.799 358 8	1.799 358 8E+00
calorie [kilogram, I.T.]	0.453 430 8	4.534 307 8E-01
centigrade heat unit [I.T.]	0.999 643 8	9.996 437 6E-01
cubic foot atmosphere	0.661 655 2	6.616 551 8E-01
frigorie [France]	0.453 539 1	4.535 391 1E-01
joule	1,898.424	1.898 424 0E+03
kilocalorie [I.T.]	0.453 430 8	4.534 307 8E-01
kilocalorie [mean]	0.453 082 3	4.530 823 2E-01
kilocalorie [thermoc.]	0.453 734 2	4.537 342 3E-01
kilogram calorie [15 °C, NBS, 1939]	0.453 539 1	4.535 391 1E-01
liter atmosphere	18.735 988	1.873 598 8E+01
watthour	0.527 34	5.273 400 0E-01

centigrade heat unit [15.8 °C, Canada] <energy>

Btu [15.8 °C, Canada]	1.8	1.800 000 0E+00
Btu [I.T.]	1.799 247 9	1.799 247 9E+00
calorie [kilogram, I.T.]	0.453 402 8	4.534 028 4E-01
centigrade heat unit [I.T.]	0.999 582 1	9.995 821 5E-01
cubic foot atmosphere	0.661 614 4	6.616 144 0E-01
frigorie [France]	0.453 511 2	4.535 111 6E-01
joule	1,898.307	1.898 307 0E+03
kilocalorie [I.T.]	0.453 402 8	4.534 028 4E-01
kilogram calorie [15 °C, NBS, 1939]	0.453 511 2	4.535 111 6E-01
liter atmosphere	18.734 833	1.873 483 3E+01
watthour	0.527 307 5	5.273 075 0E-01

centigrade heat unit [15.8 °C, ISO] <energy>

Btu [15.8 °C, ISO]	1.8	1.800 000 0E+00
Btu [I.T.]	1.799 051 7	1.799 051 7E+00
calorie [kilogram, I.T.]	0.453 353 0	4.533 534 0E-01
centigrade heat unit [I.T.]	0.999 473 2	9.994 731 5E-01
cubic foot atmosphere	0.661 542 3	6.615 422 5E-01
frigorie [France]	0.453 461 7	4.534 617 0E-01
joule	1,898.1	1.898 100 0E+03
kilocalorie [I.T.]	0.453 353 0	4.533 534 0E-01
kilogram calorie [15 °C, NBS, 1939]	0.453 461 7	4.534 617 0E-01
liter atmosphere	18.732 791	1.873 279 1E+01
watthour	0.527 25	5.272 500 0E-01

centigrade heat unit [3.9 °C] <energy>

Btu [3.9 °C]	1.8	1.800 000 0E+00
Btu [I.T.]	1.807 872 1	1.807 872 1E+00
calorie [kilogram, I.T.]	0.455 576 1	4.555 761 0E-01
centigrade heat unit [I.T.]	1.004 373 4	1.004 373 4E+00
cubic foot atmosphere	0.664 785 7	6.647 856 6E-01
frigorie [France]	0.455 684 9	4.556 849 3E-01
joule	1,907.406	1.907 406 0E+03
kilocalorie [I.T.]	0.455 576 1	4.555 761 0E-01
kilogram calorie [15 °C, NBS, 1939]	0.455 684 9	4.556 849 3E-01
liter atmosphere	18.824 634	1.882 463 4E+01
watthour	0.529 835	5.298 350 0E-01

centigrade heat unit [I.T. , pre-1956] <energy>

Btu [I.T.]	1.799 973	1.799 973 0E+00
Btu [I.T. , pre-1956]	1.8	1.800 000 0E+00

Convert From Convert To	Standard	\<Type of Unit\> Scientific

	Standard	Scientific
calorie [kilogram, I.T.]	0.453 585 6	4.535 855 5E-01
centigrade heat unit [I.T.]	0.999 985	9.999 849 7E-01
cubic foot atmosphere	0.661 881	6.618 810 2E-01
frigorie [France]	0.453 693 9	4.536 939 2E-01
kilocalorie [I.T.]	0.453 585 6	4.535 855 5E-01
kilogram calorie [15 °C, NBS, 1939]	0.453 693 9	4.536 939 2E-01
liter atmosphere	18.742 383	1.874 238 3E+01
watthour	0.527 52	5.275 200 0E-01

centigrade heat unit [I.T.] \<energy\>

	Standard	Scientific
Btu [I.T.]	1.8	1.800 000 0E+00
calorie [kilogram, I.T.]	0.453 592 4	4.535 923 7E-01
centigrade heat unit [I.T., pre-1956]	1.000 015	1.000 015 0E+00
cubic foot atmosphere	0.661 891	6.618 909 7E-01
frigorie [France]	0.453 700 7	4.537 007 3E-01
joule	1,899.100 5	1.899 100 5E+03
kilocalorie [I.T.]	0.453 592 4	4.535 923 7E-01
kilogram calorie [15 °C, NBS, 1939]	0.453 700 7	4.537 007 3E-01
liter atmosphere	18.742 665	1.874 266 5E+01
watthour	0.527 527 9	5.275 279 3E-01

centigrade heat unit [mean] \<energy\>

	Standard	Scientific
Btu [I.T.]	1.801 389	1.801 389 0E+00
Btu [mean]	1.8	1.800 000 0E+00
calorie [kilogram, I.T.]	0.453 942 4	4.539 423 9E-01
calorie [kilogram, mean]	0.453 593 5	4.535 935 4E-01
centigrade heat unit [I.T.]	1.000 771 7	1.000 771 7E+00
cubic foot atmosphere	0.662 401 7	6.624 017 3E-01
frigorie [France]	0.454 050 8	4.540 508 4E-01
joule	1,900.566	1.900 566 0E+03
kilocalorie [mean]	0.453 593 5	4.535 935 4E-01
kilogram calorie [15 °C, NBS, 1939]	0.454 050 8	4.540 508 4E-01
liter atmosphere	18.757 128	1.875 712 8E+01
watthour	0.527 935	5.279 350 0E-01

centigrade heat unit [thermoc.] \<energy\>

	Standard	Scientific
Btu [I.T.]	1.798 796 2	1.798 796 2E+00
Btu [thermoc.]	1.8	1.800 000 0E+00
calorie [kilogram, I.T.]	0.453 289	4.532 890 2E-01
calorie [kilogram, thermoc.]	0.453 592 4	4.535 923 7E-01
centigrade heat unit [I.T.]	0.999 331 2	9.993 312 3E-01
cubic foot atmosphere	0.661 448 3	6.614 483 2E-01
frigorie [France]	0.453 397 3	4.533 973 1E-01
joule	1,897.830 5	1.897 830 5E+03
kilocalorie [thermoc.]	0.453 592 4	4.535 923 7E-01
kilogram calorie [15 °C, NBS, 1939]	0.453 397 3	4.533 973 1E-01
kilojoule	1.897 830 5	1.897 830 5E+00
liter atmosphere	18.730 131	1.873 013 1E+01
watthour	0.527 175 1	5.271 751 0E-01

centigrade heat unit/hour [mean] \<power\>

	Standard	Scientific
Btu/hour [I.T.]	1.801 389	1.801 389 0E+00
Btu/hour [mean]	1.8	1.800 000 0E+00
calorie/minute [I.T.]	7.565 706 5	7.565 706 5E+00
calorie/minute [mean]	7.559 892 3	7.559 892 3E+00
cubic meter atmosphere/second	5.210 313 3	5.210 313 3E+00
deciwatt	5.279 35	5.279 350 0E+00
dyne centimeter/second	5,279,350	5.279 350 0E+06
erg/second	5,279,350	5.279 350 0E+06
foot pound-force/minute	23.363 092	2.336 309 2E+01
foot poundal/second	12.528 088	1.252 808 8E+01
gram-force centimeter/second	5,383.438 8	5.383 438 8E+03
horsepower	0.000 708	7.079 725 0E-04
horsepower [metric]	0.000 717 8	7.177 918 4E-04
joule/minute	31.676 1	3.167 610 0E+01
kilocalorie/hour [I.T.]	0.453 942 4	4.539 423 9E-01

	Standard	Scientific
kilogram-force meter/minute	3.230 063 3	3.230 063 3E+00
kilopond meter/minute	3.230 063 3	3.230 063 3E+00
newton meter/minute	31.676 1	3.167 610 0E+01
pound square foot/cubic second	12.528 088	1.252 808 8E+01
volt ampere	0.527 935	5.279 350 0E-01
watt	0.527 935	5.279 350 0E-01

centigrade heat unit/minute [mean] \<power\>

	Standard	Scientific
Btu/minute [I.T.]	1.801 389	1.801 389 0E+00
Btu/minute [mean]	1.8	1.800 000 0E+00
calorie/second [I.T.]	7.565 706 5	7.565 706 5E+00
calorie/second [thermoc.]	7.570 769 6	7.570 769 6E+00
centigrade heat unit/hour [mean]	60	6.000 000 0E+01
cubic meter atmosphere/second	312.618 8	3.126 188 0E+02
dekawatt	3.167 61	3.167 610 0E+00
dyne centimeter/second	>>>	3.167 610 0E+08
erg/second	>>>	3.167 610 0E+08
foot pound-force/second	23.363 092	2.336 309 2E+01
foot poundal/second	751.685 27	7.516 852 7E+02
gram-force centimeter/second	323,006.33	3.230 063 3E+05
horsepower	0.042 478 4	4.247 835 0E-02
horsepower [metric]	0.043 067 5	4.306 751 0E-02
joule/second	31.676 1	3.167 610 0E+01
kilocalorie/hour [I.T.]	27.236 543	2.723 654 3E+01
kilogram square meter/cubic second	31.676 1	3.167 610 0E+01
kilogram-force meter/second	3.230 063 3	3.230 063 3E+00
kilopond meter/second	3.230 063 3	3.230 063 3E+00
newton meter/second	31.676 1	3.167 610 0E+01
pound square foot/cubic second	751.685 27	7.516 852 7E+02
volt ampere	31.676 1	3.167 610 0E+01
watt	31.676 1	3.167 610 0E+01

centigrade heat unit/second [mean] \<power\>

	Standard	Scientific
Btu/second [I.T.]	1.801 389	1.801 389 0E+00
Btu/second [mean]	1.8	1.800 000 0E+00
Btu/second [thermoc.]	1.802 594 5	1.802 594 5E+00
calorie/second [I.T.]	453.942 39	4.539 423 9E+02
calorie/second [thermoc.]	454.246 18	4.542 461 8E+02
centigrade heat unit/minute [mean]	60	6.000 000 0E+01
cheval vapeur [France]	2.584 050 6	2.584 050 6E+00
cubic meter atmosphere/second	18,757.128	1.875 712 8E+04
dyne centimeter/second	>>>	1.900 566 0E+10
erg/second	>>>	1.900 566 0E+10
foot pound-force/second	1,401.785 5	1.401 785 5E+03
foot poundal/second	45,101.116	4.510 111 6E+04
gram-force centimeter/second	>>>	1.938 038 0E+07
horsepower	2.548 701	2.548 701 0E+00
horsepower [metric]	2.584 050 6	2.584 050 6E+00
joule/second	1,900.566	1.900 566 0E+03
kilocalorie/minute [I.T.]	27.236 543	2.723 654 3E+01
kilogram-force meter/second	193.803 8	1.938 038 0E+02
kilopond meter/second	193.803 8	1.938 038 0E+02
kilowatt	1.900 566	1.900 566 0E+00
newton meter/second	1,900.566	1.900 566 0E+03
pferdestarke [Germany]	2.584 050 6	2.584 050 6E+00
poncelet [France]	1.938 038	1.938 038 0E+00
ton of refrigeration	0.540 416 7	5.404 167 0E-01
volt ampere	1,900.566	1.900 566 0E+03
watt	1,900.566	1.900 566 0E+03

centigram \<mass\>

	Standard	Scientific
carat [gemstones]	0.05	5.000 000 0E-02
carat [international]	0.05	5.000 000 0E-02
carat [metric]	0.05	5.000 000 0E-02
carat [UK]	0.038 580 9	3.858 089 6E-02
carat [US, after 1913]	0.05	5.000 000 0E-02

Convert From Convert To	Standard	Scientific
carat [US, before 1913]	0.048 709 2	4.870 920 6E-02
drachm [UK, apothecary]	0.002 572 1	2.572 059 7E-03
dram [avoirdupois]	0.005 643 8	5.643 833 9E-03
dram [US, apothecary]	0.002 572 1	2.572 059 7E-03
grain	0.154 323 6	1.543 235 8E-01
grain [apothecary]	0.154 323 6	1.543 235 8E-01
grain [avoirdupois]	0.154 323 6	1.543 235 8E-01
grain [troy]	0.154 323 6	1.543 235 8E-01
kilogram	0.000 01	1.000 000 0E-05
ounce	0.000 352 7	3.527 396 2E-04
ounce [apothecary]	0.000 321 5	3.215 074 7E-04
ounce [avoirdupois]	0.000 352 7	3.527 396 2E-04
ounce [troy]	0.000 321 5	3.215 074 7E-04
pennyweight [troy]	0.006 430 1	6.430 149 3E-03
point [jewelers']	5	5.000 000 0E+00
scruple [UK]	0.007 716 2	7.716 179 2E-03
scruple [US, apothecary]	0.007 716 2	7.716 179 2E-03

centihenry — <electric inductance>

Convert To	Standard	Scientific
abhenry	>>>	1.000 000 0E+11
henry	100	1.000 000 0E+02
joule/square ampere	100	1.000 000 0E+02
ohm second	100	1.000 000 0E+02
stathenry	<<<	1.112 650 1E-10

centibar — <pressure>

Convert To	Standard	Scientific
atmosphere [standard]	0.013 157 9	1.315 789 7E-02
atmosphere [technical]	0.013 595 1	1.359 510 0E-02
bar	0.013 332 2	1.333 223 9E-02
centibar	1.333 223 9	1.333 223 9E+00
centimeter of mercury [0 °C, by convention]	1	1.000 000 0E+00
centimeter of water [4 °C, by convention]	13.595 1	1.359 510 0E+01
foot of mercury [0 °C, by convention]	0.032 808 4	3.280 839 5E-02
foot of water [4 °C, by convention]	0.446 033 5	4.460 334 6E-01
gram-force/square centimeter	13.595 1	1.359 510 0E+01
inch of mercury [0 °C, by convention]	0.393 700 8	3.937 007 9E-01
inch of water [4 °C, by convention]	5.352 401 6	5.352 401 6E+00
kilogram-force/square meter	135.951	1.359 510 0E+02
kilopascal	1.333 223 9	1.333 223 9E+00
kilopond/square meter	135.951	1.359 510 0E+02
kip/square foot	0.027 845	2.784 496 0E-02
millimeter of mercury [0 °C, by convention]	10	1.000 000 0E+01
millimeter of water [4 °C, by convention]	135.951	1.359 510 0E+02
newton/square meter	1,333.223 9	1.333 223 9E+03
ounce-force/square inch	3.093 884 4	3.093 884 4E+00
pascal	1,333.223 9	1.333 223 9E+03
pieze [France]	1.333 223 9	1.333 223 9E+00
pound-force/square foot	27.844 96	2.784 496 0E+01
poundal/square foot	895.885 08	8.958 850 8E+02
sthene/square meter [France]	1.333 223 9	1.333 223 9E+00
ton-force/square foot [short]	0.013 922 5	1.392 248 0E-02
ton-force/square meter [metric]	0.135 951	1.359 510 0E-01
torr	10.000 001	1.000 000 1E+01

centijoule — <energy>

Convert To	Standard	Scientific
calorie [I.T.]	0.002 388 5	2.388 459 0E-03
calorie [mean]	0.002 386 6	2.386 623 5E-03
calorie [thermoc.]	0.002 390 1	2.390 057 4E-03
centimeter gram-force	101.971 62	1.019 716 2E+02
cubic centimeter atmosphere	0.098 692 3	9.869 232 7E-02
foot pound-force	0.007 375 6	7.375 621 5E-03
foot poundal	0.237 303 6	2.373 036 0E-01
gram calorie	0.002 389	2.389 029 6E-03
inch ounce-force	1.416 119 3	1.416 119 3E+00
inch pound-force	0.088 507 5	8.850 745 8E-02
joule	0.01	1.000 000 0E-02

Convert To	Standard	Scientific
kilogram square meter/square second	0.01	1.000 000 0E-02
kilopond meter	0.001 019 7	1.019 716 2E-03
megaerg	0.1	1.000 000 0E-01
megalerg	0.1	1.000 000 0E-01
meter kilogram-force	0.001 019 7	1.019 716 2E-03
newton meter	0.01	1.000 000 0E-02
wattsecond	0.01	1.000 000 0E-02

centiliter		**\<volume\>**
barrel [US, liquid]	0.000 083 9	8.386 414 4E-05
bat [Vietnam]	0.02	2.000 000 0E-02
botella [Honduras]	0.014 467 6	1.446 759 3E-02
bottle [Sri Lanka]	0.013 21	1.321 004 0E-02
boutylka [Russia, vodka]	0.016 260 2	1.626 016 3E-02
cap [Vietnam]	0.05	5.000 000 0E-02
cubic foot	0.000 353 1	3.531 466 7E-04
cubic inch	0.610 237 4	6.102 374 4E-01
cubic meter	0.000 01	1.000 000 0E-05
cubic yard	0.000 013 1	1.307 950 6E-05
cup [Sierra Leone]	0.030 03	3.003 003 0E-02
drachm [UK, liquid]	2.815 606 4	2.815 606 4E+00
dram [Canada, liquid]	2.815 606 4	2.815 606 4E+00
dram [US, liquid]	2.705 121 8	2.705 121 8E+00
drop [US, liquid]	121.730 48	1.217 304 8E+02
fan sheng [China]	0.1	1.000 000 0E-01
fillette angevine [France, wine]	0.028 571 4	2.857 142 9E-02
gallon [UK, dry or liquid]	0.002 199 7	2.199 692 5E-03
gallon [US, liquid]	0.002 641 7	2.641 720 5E-03
he [China]	0.1	1.000 000 0E-01
hop [Hong Kong]	0.1	1.000 000 0E-01
kung ho [Taiwan]	0.1	1.000 000 0E-01
kung so [Taiwan]	1	1.000 000 0E+00
lang [Malaysia, dry]	0.017 597 6	1.759 757 9E-02
li sheng [China]	1	1.000 000 0E+00
liter	0.01	1.000 000 0E-02
lugim [Hebrew, ancient]	0.018 867 9	1.886 792 5E-02
mana [Nepal, cereals]	0.017 596 3	1.759 604 0E-02
minim [UK]	168.936 38	1.689 363 8E+02
minim [US]	162.307 31	1.623 073 1E+02
moselle [Germany]	0.014 285 7	1.428 571 4E-02
nofs [Malta, oil and milk]	0.015 649 5	1.564 945 2E-02
onza [Honduras]	0.347 222 2	3.472 222 2E-01
ounce [US, liquid]	0.338 140 2	3.381 402 3E-01
pint [US, liquid]	0.021 133 8	2.113 376 4E-02
pot beaujolais [France]	0.022 222 2	2.222 222 2E-02
quart [US, liquid]	0.010 566 9	1.056 688 2E-02
quart de bouteille [Mauritius]	0.013 197 8	1.319 783 6E-02
rhine [Germany]	0.014 285 7	1.428 571 4E-02
scruple [UK, liquid]	8.446 819 1	8.446 819 1E+00
shao [China]	1	1.000 000 0E+00
shih sho [China]	1	1.000 000 0E+00
shin [Mongolia]	0.015 384 6	1.538 461 5E-02
stein [Germany]	0.013 333 3	1.333 333 3E-02
stere	0.000 01	1.000 000 0E-05
tablespoon [US, measuring]	0.676 280 5	6.762 804 5E-01
teacup [UK]	0.04	4.000 000 0E-02
teaspoon [US, measuring]	2.028 841 4	2.028 841 4E+00
thuoc [Vietnam, cereal]	0.5	5.000 000 0E-01
vingerhoed [Netherlands]	1	1.000 000 0E+00

centiliter/day		**\<flow rate, volume basis\>**
centiliter/hour	0.041 666 7	4.166 666 7E-02
cubic centimeter/day	10	1.000 000 0E+01
cubic centimeter/hour	0.416 666 7	4.166 666 7E-01
cubic decimeter/day	0.01	1.000 000 0E-02

Convert From Convert To	<Type of Unit> Standard	Scientific
cubic inch/day	0.610 237 4	6.102 374 4E-01
cubic inch/hour	0.025 426 6	2.542 656 0E-02
cubic meter/day	0.000 01	1.000 000 0E-05
cubic meter/second	<<<	1.157 407 4E-10
cubic millimeter/day	10,000	1.000 000 0E+04
cubic millimeter/hour	416.666 667	4.166 666 7E+02
cubic millimeter/minute	6.944 444 4	6.944 444 4E+00
cubic millimeter/second	0.115 740 7	1.157 407 4E-01
deciliter/day	0.1	1.000 000 0E-01
deciliter/hour	0.004 166 7	4.166 666 7E-03
dekaliter/day	0.001	1.000 000 0E-03
gallon/day [UK]	0.002 199 7	2.199 692 5E-03
gallon/day [US, liquid]	0.002 641 7	2.641 720 5E-03
lambda/day	10,000	1.000 000 0E+04
lambda/hour	416.666 667	4.166 666 7E+02
lambda/minute	6.944 444 4	6.944 444 4E+00
lambda/second	0.115 740 7	1.157 407 4E-01
liter/day	0.01	1.000 000 0E-02
liter/day [pre-1964]	0.009 999 7	9.999 720 0E-03
milliliter/day	10	1.000 000 0E+01
milliliter/hour	0.416 666 7	4.166 666 7E-01
ounce/day [UK, liquid]	0.351 950 8	3.519 508 0E-01
ounce/day [US, liquid]	0.338 140 2	3.381 402 3E-01
ounce/hour [UK, liquid]	0.014 664 6	1.466 461 7E-02
ounce/hour [US, liquid]	0.014 089 2	1.408 917 6E-02
stere/day	0.000 01	1.000 000 0E-05
centiliter/hour	**<flow rate, volume basis>**	
barrel/day [US, liquid]	0.002 012 7	2.012 739 5E-03
barrel/day [US, petroleum]	0.001 509 6	1.509 554 6E-03
centiliter/day	24	2.400 000 0E+01
cubic centimeter/hour	10	1.000 000 0E+01
cubic decimeter/hour	0.01	1.000 000 0E-02
cubic foot/day	0.008 475 5	8.475 520 0E-03
cubic inch/day	14.645 698 6	1.464 569 9E+01
cubic meter/second	<<<	2.777 777 8E-09
cubic millimeter/second	2.777 777 8	2.777 777 8E+00
deciliter/day	2.4	2.400 000 0E+00
deciliter/hour	0.1	1.000 000 0E-01
dekaliter/day	0.024	2.400 000 0E-02
gallon/day [US, liquid]	0.063 401 3	6.340 129 3E-02
hectoliter/day	0.002 4	2.400 000 0E-03
lambda/second	2.777 777 8	2.777 777 8E+00
liter/day	0.24	2.400 000 0E-01
liter/day [pre-1964]	0.239 993 3	2.399 932 8E-01
milliliter/hour	10	1.000 000 0E+01
ounce/day [US, liquid]	8.115 365 4	8.115 365 4E+00
ounce/hour [US, liquid]	0.338 140 2	3.381 402 3E-01
ounce/minute [US, liquid]	0.005 635 7	5.635 670 5E-03
centiliter/minute	**<flow rate, volume basis>**	
barrel/day [US, federal]	0.122 712 2	1.227 121 8E-01
barrel/day [US, liquid]	0.120 764 4	1.207 643 7E-01
centiliter/hour	60	6.000 000 0E+01
cubic centimeter/minute	10	1.000 000 0E+01
cubic centimeter/second	0.166 666 7	1.666 666 7E-01
cubic decimeter/day	14.4	1.440 000 0E+01
cubic decimeter/hour	0.6	6.000 000 0E-01
cubic foot/day	0.508 531 2	5.085 312 0E-01
cubic inch/hour	36.614 246 5	3.661 424 7E+01
cubic inch/minute	0.610 237 4	6.102 374 4E-01
cubic meter/day	0.014 4	1.440 000 0E-02
cubic meter/second	0.000 000 2	1.666 666 7E-07
deciliter/hour	6	6.000 000 0E+00
deciliter/minute	0.1	1.000 000 0E-01

Convert From	<Type of Unit>	
Convert To	Standard	Scientific

dekaliter/day	1.44	1.440 000 0E+00
gallon/day [UK]	3.167 557 2	3.167 557 2E+00
gallon/day [US, liquid]	3.804 077 6	3.804 077 6E+00
gallon/hour [UK]	0.131 981 5	1.319 815 5E−01
gallon/hour [US, liquid]	0.158 503 2	1.585 032 3E−01
hectoliter/day	0.144	1.440 000 0E−01
liter/day	14.4	1.440 000 0E+00
liter/day [pre-1964]	14.399 596 8	1.439 959 7E+00
liter/hour	0.6	6.000 000 0E−01
liter/hour [pre-1964]	0.599 983 2	5.999 832 0E−01
milliliter/minute	1	1.000 000 0E+00
milliliter/second	0.166 666 7	1.666 666 7E−01
ounce/hour [UK, liquid]	21.117 048	2.111 704 8E+01
ounce/hour [US, liquid]	20.288 414	2.028 841 4E+01
ounce/minute [UK, liquid]	0.351 950 8	3.519 508 0E−01
ounce/minute [US, liquid]	0.338 140 2	3.381 402 3E−01

centiliter/second **<flow rate, volume basis>**

barrel/day [US, liquid]	7.245 862	7.245 862 0E+00
barrel/day [US, petroleum]	5.434 396 5	5.434 396 5E+00
barrel/hour [US, liquid]	0.301 910 9	3.019 109 2E−01
barrel/hour [US, petroleum]	0.226 433 2	2.264 331 9E−01
cubic centimeter/second	10	1.000 000 0E+01
cubic foot/hour	1.271 328	1.271 328 0E+00
cubic inch/minute	36.614 246 5	3.661 424 7E+01
cubic meter/day	0.864	8.640 000 0E−01
cubic meter/second	0.000 01	1.000 000 0E−05
cubic yard/day	1.130 069 3	1.130 069 3E+00
deciliter/minute	6	6.000 000 0E+00
dekaliter/hour	3.6	3.600 000 0E+00
gallon/hour [US, liquid]	9.510 193 9	9.510 193 9E+00
gallon/minute [US, liquid]	0.158 503 2	1.585 032 3E−01
hectoliter/day	8.64	8.640 000 0E+00
kiloliter/day	0.864	8.640 000 0E−01
liter/hour	36	3.600 000 0E+01
liter/hour [pre-1964]	35.998 992	3.599 899 2E+01
milliliter/second	10	1.000 000 0E+01
ounce/minute [US, liquid]	20.288 414	2.028 841 4E+01
petrograd standard/day	0.184 920 4	1.849 204 4E−01
stere/day	0.864	8.640 000 0E−01

centillion [UK] **<units>**

unit	>>> 1.000 000 0E+600	

centimeter **<length>**

abdah [Egypt, ancient]	0.133 511 4	1.335 113 5E−01
ady [India]	0.037 594	3.759 398 5E−02
ammah [Hebrew, ancient]	0.018 518 5	1.851 851 9E−02
ammah [Hebrew, ancient, large]	0.019 047 6	1.904 761 9E−02
angstrom	>>> 1.000 000 0E+08	
angula [India]	0.524 934 4	5.249 343 8E−01
anguli [India]	0.524 934 4	5.249 343 8E−01
anukabiet [Thailand]	3.84	3.840 000 0E+00
archin [Bahrain]	0.020 721 1	2.072 109 4E−02
archin [Cyprus]	0.016 404 2	1.640 419 9E−02
archin [Greece]	0.013 333 3	1.333 333 3E−02
archin [Iraq]	0.013 422 8	1.342 281 9E−02
archin [Jordan, land]	0.013 192 6	1.319 261 2E−02
archin [Jordan, textiles]	0.014 705 9	1.470 588 2E−02
archin [Lebanon, land]	0.013 192 6	1.319 261 2E−02
archin [Lebanon, textiles]	0.014 705 9	1.470 588 2E−02
archin [Morocco]	0.017 895 5	1.789 549 0E−02
archin [Russia]	0.014 060 7	1.406 074 2E−02
archin [Saudi Arabia]	0.021 881 8	2.188 183 9E−02
archin [Syria]	0.014 285 7	1.428 571 4E−02
arsheen [Russia]	0.014 060 7	1.406 074 2E−02

Convert From		<Type of Unit>
Convert To	Standard	Scientific

centimeter (continued)   <length>

arshin [Bahrain]	0.020 721 1	2.072 109 4E-02
arshin [Cyprus]	0.016 404 2	1.640 419 9E-02
arshin [Iraq]	0.013 422 8	1.342 281 9E-02
arshin [Jordan, land]	0.013 192 6	1.319 261 2E-02
arshin [Jordan, textiles]	0.014 705 9	1.470 588 2E-02
arshin [Lebanon, land]	0.013 192 6	1.319 261 2E-02
arshin [Morocco]	0.017 895 5	1.789 549 0E-02
arshin [Russia]	0.014 060 7	1.406 074 2E-02
arshin [Saudi Arabia]	0.021 881 8	2.188 183 8E-02
arshin [Syria]	0.014 285 7	1.428 571 4E-02
arshyn [Turkey]	0.014 064 7	1.406 469 8E-02
asba [Egypt, ancient]	0.32	3.200 000 0E-01
aune [Germany]	0.014 994 8	1.499 475 2E-02
baa [Saudi Arabia]	0.071 582	7.158 196 1E-02
bahar [Iran]	0.307 692 3	3.076 923 1E-01
barleycorn	1.181 102 4	1.181 102 4E+00
behar [Iran]	0.307 692 3	3.076 923 1E-01
bema [Greece, ancient]	0.013 513 5	1.351 351 4E-02
bitta [Nepal]	0.043 744 5	4.374 453 2E-02
braccio d'ara [Italy]	0.014 285 7	1.428 571 4E-02
brache [Switzerland]	0.016 666 7	1.666 666 7E-02
busa [Saudi Arabia, ancient]	0.393 700 8	3.937 007 9E-01
busa [Sudan]	0.393 700 8	3.937 007 9E-01
cabda [Arabia, ancient]	0.126 582 3	1.265 822 8E-01
caliber	39.370 079	3.937 007 9E+01
calow [Poland]	0.416 666 7	4.166 666 7E-01
canna [Spanish North Africa]	0.018 761 7	1.876 172 6E-02
cape inch [South Africa]	0.381 097 6	3.810 975 6E-01
carsi [Turkey, textiles]	0.014 705 9	1.470 588 2E-02
cham am [Cambodia]	0.04	4.000 000 0E-02
check [Malaysia]	0.026 691 6	2.669 157 9E-02
chi [Mongolia]	0.031 25	3.125 000 0E-02
chi [South Korea]	0.330 000 3	3.300 003 3E-01
chih [China]	0.027 922	2.792 204 2E-02
chinese foot [China]	0.031 25	3.125 000 0E-02
choryos [Egypt, ancient]	0.133 511 4	1.335 113 5E-01
chuhm [Malaysia]	0.266 915 8	2.669 157 9E-01
chuhm [Singapore]	0.266 915 8	2.669 157 9E-01
chum [Malaysia]	0.266 915 8	2.669 157 9E-01
chum [Singapore]	0.266 915 8	2.669 157 9E-01
covada [Portugal]	0.015 151 5	1.515 151 5E-02
covado [Portugal]	0.015 151 5	1.515 151 5E-02
covido [India]	0.021 872 3	2.187 226 6E-02
covido [Saudi Arabia, ancient]	0.021 881 8	2.188 183 8E-02
cuarta [Colombia]	0.05	5.000 000 0E-02
cuarto [Colombia]	0.05	5.000 000 0E-02
cubi [Eritrea]	0.031 25	3.125 000 0E-02
cubit [Babylon, ancient]	0.019 047 6	1.904 761 9E-02
cubit [Egypt, ancient, long]	0.019 098 5	1.909 854 9E-02
cubit [Egypt, ancient, short]	0.022 271 7	2.227 171 5E-02
cubit [Greece, ancient]	0.021 505 4	2.150 537 6E-02
cubit [India]	0.021 872 3	2.187 226 6E-02
cubit [Mesopotamia, ancient]	0.020 202	2.020 202 0E-02
cubit [Rome, ancient]	0.022 522 5	2.252 252 3E-02
cubit [Spanish North Africa]	0.018 761 7	1.876 172 6E-02
cubit [Syria, textiles]	0.015 873	1.587 301 6E-02
cubito [Somaliland]	0.017 889 1	1.788 908 8E-02
cun [Hong Kong]	0.269 197 1	2.691 971 2E-01
daktylos [Greece, ancient]	0.393 700 8	3.937 007 9E-01
dedo [Spain]	0.574 712 6	5.747 126 4E-01
deido [Spain]	0.574 227 5	5.742 275 2E-01
deraga [Iraq, ancient]	0.018 761 7	1.876 172 6E-02

centimeter (continued) <length>

	Standard	Scientific
deraga akhdam [Iraq, ancient]	0.015 873	1.587 301 6E−02
deraga cabda [Iraq, ancient]	0.021 097	2.109 704 6E−02
derah [Eritrea]	0.021 739 1	2.173 913 0E−02
dhara [Bahrain]	0.020 721 1	2.072 109 4E−02
dhara [Cyprus]	0.016 404 2	1.640 419 9E−02
dhara [Iraq]	0.013 422 8	1.342 281 9E−02
dhara [Jordan, land]	0.013 192 6	1.319 261 2E−02
dhara [Jordan, textiles]	0.014 705 9	1.470 588 2E−02
dhara [Lebanon, land]	0.013 192 6	1.319 261 2E−02
dhara [Lebanon, textiles]	0.014 705 9	1.470 588 2E−02
dhara [Morocco]	0.017 895 5	1.789 549 0E−02
dhara [Oman]	0.021 881 8	2.188 183 8E−02
dhara [Russia]	0.014 060 7	1.406 074 2E−02
dhara [Saudi Arabia]	0.021 881 8	2.188 183 8E−02
dhara [Syria, textiles]	0.014 285 7	1.428 571 4E−02
dhira [Bahrain]	0.020 721 1	2.072 109 4E−02
dhira [Cyprus]	0.016 404 2	1.640 419 9E−02
dhira [Iraq]	0.013 422 8	1.342 281 9E−02
dhira [Jordan, land]	0.013 192 6	1.319 261 2E−02
dhira [Jordan, textiles]	0.014 705 9	1.470 588 2E−02
dhira [Lebanon, land]	0.013 192 6	1.319 261 2E−02
dhira [Lebanon, textiles]	0.014 705 9	1.470 588 2E−02
dhira [Morocco]	0.017 895 5	1.789 549 0E−02
dhira [Russia]	0.014 060 7	1.406 074 2E−02
dhira [Saudi Arabia]	0.021 881 8	2.188 183 8E−02
dhira [Syria]	0.013 333 3	1.333 333 3E−02
dhira [Syria, textiles]	0.014 285 7	1.428 571 4E−02
dhiraa [Bahrain]	0.020 721 1	2.072 109 4E−02
dhiraa [Cyprus]	0.016 404 2	1.640 419 9E−02
dhiraa [Iraq]	0.013 422 8	1.342 281 9E−02
dhiraa [Jordan, land]	0.013 192 6	1.319 261 2E−02
dhiraa [Jordan, textiles]	0.014 705 9	1.470 588 2E−02
dhiraa [Lebanon, land]	0.013 192 6	1.319 261 2E−02
dhiraa [Lebanon, textiles]	0.014 705 9	1.470 588 2E−02
dhiraa [Morocco]	0.017 895 5	1.789 549 0E−02
dhiraa [Russia]	0.014 060 7	1.406 074 2E−02
dhiraa [Saudi Arabia]	0.021 881 8	2.188 183 8E−02
dhiraa [Syria, textiles]	0.014 285 7	1.428 571 4E−02
dhra [Bahrain]	0.020 721 1	2.072 109 4E−02
dhra [Cyprus]	0.016 404 2	1.640 419 9E−02
dhra [Iraq]	0.013 422 8	1.342 281 9E−02
dhra [Jordan, land]	0.013 192 6	1.319 261 2E−02
dhra [Jordan, textiles]	0.014 705 9	1.470 588 2E−02
dhra [Lebanon, land]	0.013 192 6	1.319 261 2E−02
dhra [Lebanon, textiles]	0.014 705 9	1.470 588 2E−02
dhra [Morocco]	0.017 895 5	1.789 549 0E−02
dhra [Russia]	0.014 060 7	1.406 074 2E−02
dhra [Saudi Arabia]	0.021 881 8	2.188 183 8E−02
dhra [Syria, textiles]	0.014 285 7	1.428 571 4E−02
dhra d'alep [Iraq]	0.014 598 5	1.459 854 0E−02
digit	0.524 934 4	5.249 343 4E−01
digit [Iraq, ancient]	0.303 030 3	3.030 303 0E−01
digit [Mesopotamia, ancient]	0.606 060 6	6.060 606 1E−01
digitus [Rome, ancient]	0.540 540 5	5.405 405 4E−01
dira [Bahrain]	0.020 721 1	2.072 109 4E−02
dira [Cyprus]	0.016 404 2	1.640 419 9E−02
dira [Greece]	0.013 333 3	1.333 333 3E−02
dira [Iraq]	0.013 422 8	1.342 281 9E−02
dira [Jordan, land]	0.013 192 6	1.319 261 2E−02
dira [Jordan, textiles]	0.014 705 9	1.470 588 2E−02
dira [Lebanon, land]	0.013 192 6	1.319 261 2E−02
dira [Lebanon, textiles]	0.014 705 9	1.470 588 2E−02

centimeter (continued)   **\<length>**

Convert To	Standard	Scientific
dira [Morocco]	0.017 895 5	1.789 549 0E−02
dira [Russia]	0.014 060 7	1.406 074 2E−02
dira [Saudi Arabia]	0.022 757 3	2.275 727 1E−02
dira [Saudi Arabia, ancient]	0.021 881 8	2.188 183 8E−02
dira [Sudan]	0.017 244 4	1.724 435 2E−02
dira [Syria, textiles]	0.014 285 7	1.428 571 4E−02
dira [Yemen]	0.021 881 8	2.188 183 8E−02
dira baladi [Egypt]	0.017 241 4	1.724 137 9E−02
dira minari [Greece]	0.015 432 1	1.543 209 9E−02
diraa [Bahrain]	0.020 721 1	2.072 109 4E−02
diraa [Cyprus]	0.016 404 2	1.640 419 9E−02
diraa [Egypt, ancient, textiles]	0.017 241 4	1.724 137 9E−02
diraa [Iraq]	0.013 422 8	1.342 281 9E−02
diraa [Jordan, land]	0.013 192 6	1.319 261 2E−02
diraa [Jordan, textiles]	0.014 705 9	1.470 588 2E−02
diraa [Lebanon, land]	0.013 192 6	1.319 261 2E−02
diraa [Lebanon, textiles]	0.014 705 9	1.470 588 2E−02
diraa [Morocco]	0.017 895 5	1.789 549 0E−02
diraa [Russia]	0.014 060 7	1.406 074 2E−02
diraa [Saudi Arabia]	0.021 881 8	2.188 183 8E−02
diraa [Sudan]	0.017 244 4	1.724 435 2E−02
diraa [Syria, textiles]	0.014 285 7	1.428 571 4E−02
diraa memari [Egypt, ancient, building]	0.013 333 3	1.333 333 3E−02
dong [Vietnam]	0.428 571 4	4.285 714 3E−01
doron [Greece, ancient]	0.520 833 3	5.208 333 3E−01
dra [Bahrain]	0.020 721 1	2.072 109 4E−02
dra [Cyprus]	0.016 404 2	1.640 419 9E−02
dra [Iraq]	0.013 422 8	1.342 281 9E−02
dra [Jordan, land]	0.013 192 6	1.319 261 2E−02
dra [Jordan, textiles]	0.014 705 9	1.470 588 2E−02
dra [Lebanon, land]	0.013 192 6	1.319 261 2E−02
dra [Lebanon, textiles]	0.014 705 9	1.470 588 2E−02
dra [Morocco]	0.017 895 5	1.789 549 0E−02
dra [Russia]	0.014 060 7	1.406 074 2E−02
dra [Saudi Arabia]	0.021 881 8	2.188 183 8E−02
dra [Syria, textiles]	0.014 285 7	1.428 571 4E−02
dra arbi [Libya, textiles]	0.020 408 2	2.040 816 3E−02
dra maghmari [Syria, land]	0.013 192 6	1.319 261 2E−02
draa arbi [Libya, textiles]	0.020 408 2	2.040 816 3E−02
draa milki [Libya, land]	0.02	2.000 000 0E−02
drah [Bahrain]	0.020 721 1	2.072 109 4E−02
drah [Cyprus]	0.016 404 2	1.640 419 9E−02
drah [Iraq]	0.013 422 8	1.342 281 9E−02
drah [Jordan, land]	0.013 192 6	1.319 261 2E−02
drah [Jordan, textiles]	0.014 705 9	1.470 588 2E−02
drah [Lebanon, land]	0.013 192 6	1.319 261 2E−02
drah [Lebanon, textiles]	0.014 727 5	1.472 754 1E−02
drah [Russia]	0.014 060 7	1.406 074 2E−02
drah [Saudi Arabia]	0.021 881 8	2.188 183 8E−02
drah [Syria, textiles]	0.014 285 7	1.428 571 4E−02
drahi [Bahrain]	0.020 721 1	2.072 109 4E−02
drahi [Cyprus]	0.016 404 2	1.640 419 9E−02
drahi [Iraq]	0.013 422 8	1.342 281 9E−02
drahi [Jordan, land]	0.013 192 6	1.319 261 2E−02
drahi [Jordan, textiles]	0.014 705 9	1.470 588 2E−02
drahi [Lebanon, land]	0.013 192 6	1.319 261 2E−02
drahi [Lebanon, textiles]	0.014 705 9	1.470 588 2E−02
drahi [Morocco]	0.017 895 5	1.789 549 0E−02
drahi [Russia]	0.014 060 7	1.406 074 2E−02
drahi [Saudi Arabia]	0.021 881 8	2.188 183 8E−02
drahi [Syria, textiles]	0.014 285 7	1.428 571 4E−02
duim [Netherlands]	1	1.000 000 0E+00

centimeter (continued)

	Standard	Scientific
duim [Russia]	0.393 700 8	3.937 007 9E-01
duime [Russia]	0.393 700 8	3.937 007 9E-01
ell [Belgium]	0.014 581 5	1.458 151 1E-02
elle [Latvia]	0.018 622	1.862 197 4E-02
em [pica, print]	2.371 063	2.371 063 0E+00
emmet [Eritrea]	0.021 739 1	2.173 913 0E-02
endaze [Turkey]	0.015 384 6	1.538 461 5E-02
endazeh [Turkey]	0.015 384 6	1.538 461 5E-02
etzba [Hebrew, ancient]	0.526 315 8	5.263 157 9E-01
etzbah [Hebrew, ancient]	0.526 315 8	5.263 157 9E-01
ezba [Hebrew, ancient]	0.515 463 9	5.154 639 2E-01
fatar [Oman]	0.055 555 6	5.555 555 6E-02
fen mi [China]	0.1	1.000 000 0E-01
finger [Egypt, ancient]	0.549 450 5	5.494 505 5E-01
finger [Hebrew, ancient]	0.540 540 5	5.405 405 4E-01
finger [Sumeria, ancient]	0.598 802 4	5.988 024 0E-01
fitr [Saudi Arabia, ancient]	0.065 616 8	6.561 679 8E-02
fod [Denmark]	0.031 862 4	3.186 235 5E-02
foot [Babylon, ancient]	0.028 256 6	2.825 657 0E-02
foot [Egypt, ancient]	0.027 777 8	2.777 777 8E-02
foot [Greece, ancient]	0.032 372 9	3.237 293 6E-02
foot [Greece, ancient, olympic]	0.031 201 2	3.120 124 8E-02
foot [international]	0.032 808 4	3.280 839 9E-02
foot [Iraq, ancient]	0.031 645 6	3.164 557 0E-02
foot [Netherlands]	0.035 319 5	3.531 946 5E-02
foot [Rome, ancient]	0.033 783 8	3.378 378 4E-02
foot [Russia]	0.032 808 4	3.280 839 9E-02
foot [US, survey]	0.032 808 3	3.280 833 3E-02
fot [Finland]	0.037 467 2	3.746 721 6E-02
fot [Norway]	0.031 872 5	3.187 251 0E-02
fot [Sweden]	0.033 681 4	3.368 137 4E-02
fuss [Russia]	0.028 089 9	2.808 988 8E-02
fuss [Switzerland]	0.033 333 3	3.333 333 3E-02
fusz [Austria]	0.031 637 6	3.163 756 0E-02
fut [Russia]	0.032 808 4	3.280 839 9E-02
gareh [Iran]	0.153 846 2	1.538 461 5E-01
gat [Ethiopia]	0.133 333 3	3.333 333 3E-01
gaz [India]	0.010 936 1	1.093 613 9E-02
gaz gareeb [Afghanistan]	0.013 587	1.358 695 7E-02
gazi jerib [Afghanistan]	0.013 575 9	1.357 588 9E-02
gazi memar [Afghanistan]	0.012 303 2	1.230 315 0E-02
geerah [India]	0.174 978 1	1.749 781 3E-01
gereh gaz sha [Afghanistan]	0.151 515 2	1.515 151 5E-01
gereh gazi sha [Afghanistan]	0.149 981 3	1.499 812 5E-01
girah [Iran]	0.153 846 2	1.538 461 5E-01
girah [Pakistan]	0.174 978 1	1.749 781 3E-01
gireh [India]	0.174 978 1	1.749 781 3E-01
gireh [Iran]	0.153 846 2	1.538 461 5E-01
gran [Sweden]	33.681 261	3.368 126 1E+01
great ovido [Saudi Arabia, ancient]	0.014 577 3	1.457 725 9E-02
greater pic [Turkey]	0.014 705 9	1.470 588 2E-02
greater pic [Turkey, land]	0.013 192 6	1.319 261 2E-02
gudge [Saudi Arabia, ancient]	0.015 748	1.574 803 1E-02
guereh [Iran]	0.153 846 2	1.538 461 5E-01
guz [India, Bombay]	0.014 492 8	1.449 275 4E-02
haat [Nepal, textiles]	0.021 872 3	2.187 226 6E-02
handaza [Libya, textiles]	0.014 705 9	1.470 588 2E-02
handbreadth [Hebrew, ancient]	0.125	1.250 000 0E-01
handbreadth [Iraq, ancient]	0.101 010 1	1.010 101 0E-01
hasit [Hebrew, ancient]	0.053 553 6	5.355 358 6E-02
hasta [India]	0.021 872 3	2.187 226 6E-02
hat [Cambodia]	0.02	2.000 000 0E-02

centimeter (continued)   \<length\>

	Standard	Scientific
hath [India]	0.021 872 3	2.187 226 6E-02
haut [India]	0.021 872 3	2.187 226 6E-02
hemipodion [Greece, ancient]	0.064 935 1	6.493 506 5E-02
hindaza [Saudi Arabia, ancient]	0.014 577 3	1.457 725 9E-02
hollegada [Brazil]	0.363 636 4	3.636 363 6E-01
huvelik [Hungary]	0.380 228 1	3.802 281 4E-01
imagu [Mongolia]	0.312 5	3.125 000 0E-01
inch [based on US, survey foot]	0.393 7	3.937 000 0E-01
inch [international]	0.393 700 8	3.937 007 9E-01
jacob [India]	1.587 301 6	1.587 301 6E+00
jalka [Finland]	0.037 467 2	3.746 721 6E-02
jaob [India]	1.574 803 1	1.574 803 1E+00
jenghal [Singapore]	0.043 744 5	4.374 453 2E-02
jengkal [Malaysia]	0.043 744 5	4.374 453 2E-02
jengkal [Singapore]	0.043 744 5	4.374 453 2E-02
jow [India]	1.587 301 6	1.587 301 6E+00
kabda [Egypt]	0.062 111 8	6.211 180 1E-02
kabiet [Thailand]	1.92	1.920 000 0E+00
kala [Morocco, Tangier]	0.017 889 1	1.788 908 8E-02
kam [Laos]	0.1	1.000 000 0E-01
kam louang [Laos]	0.08	8.000 000 0E-02
kama [Morocco, Tangier]	0.007 874	7.874 015 7E-03
kerat [Turkey]	0.349 956 3	3.499 562 6E-01
keup [Thailand]	0.04	4.000 000 0E-02
khat [Turkey]	1	1.000 000 0E+00
khub [Laos]	0.05	5.000 000 0E-02
khub louang [Laos]	0.04	4.000 000 0E-02
khup [Laos]	0.05	5.000 000 0E-02
khup [Thailand]	0.04	4.000 000 0E-02
kind [Eritrea]	0.02	2.000 000 0E-02
kirat [Lebanon, land]	0.316 455 7	3.164 557 0E-01
kirat [Lebanon, textiles]	0.353 356 9	3.533 568 9E-01
kirat [Sudan]	0.413 907 3	4.139 072 8E-01
kondylos [Greece, ancient]	0.259 740 3	2.597 402 6E-01
kovid [India]	0.021 872 3	2.187 226 6E-02
kung fen [China]	1	1.000 000 0E+00
kung fun [Taiwan]	1	1.000 000 0E+00
kung tsun [Taiwan]	0.1	1.000 000 0E-01
kup [Thailand]	0.04	4.000 000 0E-02
kus [Iraq, ancient, large]	0.010 101	1.010 101 0E-02
kus [Iraq, ancient, small]	0.020 242 9	2.024 291 5E-02
kvarter [Sweden]	0.067 362 3	6.736 229 5E-02
lesser pic [Turkey]	0.015 384 6	1.538 461 5E-02
li mi [China]	1	1.000 000 0E+00
lichar [Greece, ancient]	0.052 083 3	5.208 333 3E-02
liin [Russia]	0.393 7	3.937 000 0E-01
likot [Ukraine]	0.012 853 5	1.285 347 0E-02
line [print]	4.724 409 4	4.724 409 4E+00
line [UK]	4.724 408 7	4.724 408 7E+00
linia [Chile]	5.167 958 7	5.167 958 7E+00
linie [Denmark]	4.588 082	4.588 082 0E+00
link [Gunter or US, survey]	0.049 709 6	4.970 959 6E-02
link [Ramden or Engineer]	0.032 808 4	3.280 839 9E-02
loket [Czechoslovakia]	0.016 863 4	1.686 340 6E-02
mekyas cubit [Egypt, ancient]	0.018 518 5	1.851 851 9E-02
meter	0.01	1.000 000 0E-02
mil	393.700 79	3.937 007 9E+02
mimar [Turkey, land]	0.013 192 6	1.319 261 2E-02
mimari [Greece]	0.013 333 3	1.333 333 3E-02
min [Thailand]	0.480 000 1	4.800 000 8E-01
mira [Ukraine]	0.013 157 9	1.315 789 5E-02
mkono [Tanganyika]	0.021 739 1	2.173 913 0E-02

centimeter (continued) <length>

	Standard	Scientific
mkono [Tanzania]	0.021 872 3	2.187 226 6E-02
moot [India]	0.131 233 6	1.312 336 0E-01
niew [Thailand]	0.480 000 1	4.800 000 8E-01
niou [Laos]	0.599 88	5.998 800 2E-01
niou [Thailand]	0.480 076 8	4.800 768 1E-01
niou louang [Laos]	0.480 000 1	4.800 000 8E-01
niu [Laos]	0.599 88	5.998 800 2E-01
niu [Thailand]	0.480 076 8	4.800 768 1E-01
node [Antigua]	0.087 719 3	8.771 929 8E-02
nus [Algeria]	0.040 322 6	4.032 258 1E-02
ourob [Iran]	0.076 923 1	7.692 307 7E-02
ouroub [Iran]	0.076 923 1	7.692 307 7E-02
ovido [Saudi Arabia, ancient]	0.021 881 8	2.188 183 8E-02
pace [Hebrew, ancient]	0.017 851 2	1.785 119 5E-02
palag [Yugoslavia]	0.275 178 9	2.751 788 7E-01
palaiste [Greece, ancient]	0.129 870 1	1.298 701 3E-01
paleste [Greece, ancient]	0.520 833 3	5.208 333 3E-01
paletz [Russia]	0.787 401 6	7.874 015 7E-01
palgat [Burma]	0.393 700 8	3.937 007 9E-01
palm [Egypt, ancient]	0.133 333 3	1.333 333 3E-01
palm [Greece, ancient]	0.520 833 3	5.208 333 3E-01
palm [Iraq, ancient]	0.101 010 1	1.010 101 0E-01
palma [Rome, ancient]	0.135 318	1.353 180 0E-01
palmi [Libya]	0.04	4.000 000 0E-02
palmi [Malta]	0.038 182 5	3.818 251 2E-02
palmi [Spain]	0.047 846 9	4.784 689 0E-02
palmipes [Rome, ancient]	0.027 027	2.702 702 7E-02
palmo [Brazil]	0.045 454 5	4.545 454 5E-02
palmo [Ecuador]	0.047 619	4.761 904 8E-02
palmo [Italy]	0.1	1.000 000 0E-01
palmo [Libya]	0.04	4.000 000 0E-02
palmo [Malta]	0.038 182 5	3.818 251 2E-02
palmo [Portugal]	0.045 454 5	4.545 454 5E-02
palmo [Spain]	0.047 846 9	4.784 689 0E-02
palmus [Rome, ancient]	0.135 135 1	1.351 351 4E-01
palmus maior [Rome, ancient]	0.045 045	4.504 504 5E-02
parasang [Hebrew, ancient]	0.000 002 2	2.231 399 4E-06
Paris inch [France]	0.369 412 6	3.694 126 3E-01
parmack [Turkey]	0.239 808 2	2.398 081 5E-01
parmah [Turkey]	0.239 808 2	2.398 081 5E-01
parmak [Turkey, land]	0.316 756 4	3.167 564 1E-01
pe [Brazil]	0.030 303	3.030 303 0E-02
pe [Macao]	0.030 303	3.030 303 0E-02
pe [Portugal]	0.030 303	3.030 303 0E-02
pes [Rome, ancient]	0.033 818 1	3.381 805 9E-02
pes drusianus [Rome, ancient]	0.029 940 1	2.994 012 0E-02
pesiah [Hebrew, ancient]	0.017 851 2	1.785 119 5E-02
pic [Bahrain]	0.020 721 1	2.072 109 4E-02
pic [Cyprus]	0.016 404 2	1.640 419 9E-02
pic [Greece]	0.013 333 3	1.333 333 3E-02
pic [Iraq, Baghdad]	0.013 422 8	1.342 281 9E-02
pic [Iraq, Mosul]	0.014 285 7	1.428 571 4E-02
pic [Jordan, land]	0.013 192 6	1.319 261 2E-02
pic [Jordan, textiles]	0.014 705 9	1.470 588 2E-02
pic [Lebanon, land]	0.013 192 6	1.319 261 2E-02
pic [Lebanon, textiles]	0.014 727 5	1.472 754 1E-02
pic [Morocco]	0.017 895 5	1.789 549 0E-02
pic [Saudi Arabia]	0.021 881 8	2.188 183 8E-02
pic [Spanish North Africa]	0.016 393 4	1.639 344 3E-02
pic [Syria, textiles]	0.014 285 7	1.428 571 4E-02
pic [Turkey, land]	0.013 197 8	1.319 783 6E-02

centimeter (continued) \<length\>

	Standard	Scientific
pic [Turkey, textiles]	0.014 705 9	1.470 588 2E-02
pic arabe [Tunisia]	0.020 284	2.028 397 6E-02
pic turc [Tunisia]	0.015 528	1.552 795 0E-02
picki [Greece]	0.013 333 3	1.333 333 3E-02
pie [Argentina]	0.034 614 1	3.461 405 3E-02
pie [Chile]	0.032 808 4	3.280 839 9E-02
pie [El Salvador]	0.035 893 8	3.589 375 4E-02
pie [Honduras]	0.035 928 6	3.592 857 4E-02
pied [Belgium]	0.030 778 7	3.077 870 1E-02
pied [Switzerland]	0.033 333 3	3.333 333 3E-02
pied anglais [Haiti]	0.032 808 4	3.280 839 9E-02
pied de roi [France]	0.030 781 5	3.078 154 3E-02
piede [Paraguay]	0.034 614 1	3.461 405 3E-02
pik [Bahrain]	0.020 721 1	2.072 109 4E-02
pik [Cyprus]	0.016 404 2	1.640 419 9E-02
pik [Egypt]	0.017 241 4	1.724 137 9E-02
pik [Greece]	0.013 333 3	1.333 333 3E-02
pik [Iraq]	0.013 422 8	1.342 281 9E-02
pik [Jordan, land]	0.013 192 6	1.319 261 2E-02
pik [Jordan, textiles]	0.014 705 9	1.470 588 2E-02
pik [Lebanon, land]	0.013 192 6	1.319 261 2E-02
pik [Lebanon, textiles]	0.014 705 9	1.470 588 2E-02
pik [Libya]	0.017 895 5	1.789 549 0E-02
pik [Morocco]	0.014 060 7	1.406 074 2E-02
pik [Russia]	0.021 881 8	2.188 183 8E-02
pik [Saudi Arabia]	0.014 285 7	1.428 571 4E-02
pik [Syria, textiles]	0.013 192 6	1.319 261 2E-02
pik [Turkey, land]	0.015 408 3	1.540 832 0E-02
pik andoulsi [Tunisia, wool]	0.020 284	2.028 397 6E-02
pik arbi [Tunisia, linen]	0.017 244 4	1.724 435 2E-02
pik baladi [Sudan]	0.015 503 9	1.550 387 6E-02
pik turki [Tunisia, silk]	0.013 333 3	1.333 333 3E-02
pike [Greece]	0.013 192 6	1.319 261 2E-02
piq [Lebanon, land]	0.014 705 9	1.470 588 2E-02
piq [Lebanon, textiles]	28.452 756	2.845 275 6E+01
point [print]	0.363 636 4	3.636 363 6E-01
polegada [Brazil]	0.363 636 4	3.636 363 6E-01
polegada [Portugal]	0.365 230 1	3.652 300 9E-01
polegada [Portugal]	0.265 957 5	2.659 574 5E-01
ponto [Macao]	0.333 333 3	3.333 333 3E-01
pouce [Belgium]	0.369 412 6	3.694 126 3E-01
pouce [France]	0.415 454 9	4.154 549 2E-01
pouce [Paraguay]	0.333 333 3	3.333 333 3E-01
pouce [Switzerland]	0.032 020 5	3.202 049 3E-02
pous [Greece, ancient]	0.415 454 9	4.154 549 2E-01
pulgada [Argentina]	0.415 627 6	4.156 276 0E-01
pulgada [Bolivia]	0.4	4.000 000 0E-01
pulgada [Colombia]	0.430 663 2	4.306 632 2E-01
pulgada [El Salvador]	0.430 663 2	4.306 632 2E-01
pulgada [Guatemala]	0.431 034 5	4.310 344 8E-01
pulgada [Panama]	0.430 663 2	4.306 632 2E-01
pulgada [Philippines]	0.431 034 5	4.310 344 8E-01
pulgada [Spain]	0.393 700 8	3.937 007 9E-01
pulgada inglesa [Chile]	5.464 480 9	5.464 480 9E+00
punkt [Austria]	0.028 901 7	2.890 173 4E-02
pygme [Greece, ancient]	0.025 974	2.597 402 6E-02
pygon [Greece, ancient]	0.08	8.000 000 0E-02
qabdah [Egypt]	11.494 253	1.149 425 3E+01
qirat barsoun [Egypt]	0.021 276 6	2.127 659 6E-02
quan diem xich [Vietnam]	0.333 333 3	3.333 333 3E-01
rajabah [Oman]	0.080 645 2	8.064 516 1E-02
rebia [Algeria]		

centimeter (continued)

centimeter (continued)   <length>

Convert To	Standard	Scientific
remen [Egypt, ancient]	0.022 271 7	2.227 171 5E−02
roupi [Cyprus]	0.131 233 6	1.312 336 0E−01
roupi [Greece]	0.123 456 8	1.234 567 9E−01
sandong [Burma]	0.017 895 5	1.789 549 0E−02
sauk [Laos]	0.025	2.500 000 0E−02
sauk [Thailand]	0.02	2.000 000 0E−02
sawk [Laos]	0.025	2.500 000 0E−02
sawk [Thailand]	0.02	2.000 000 0E−02
scale cubit [Islam]	0.006 868 1	6.868 131 9E−03
schibr [Egypt, ancient]	0.044 444 4	4.444 444 4E−02
schuh [Switzerland]	0.033 333 3	3.333 333 3E−02
sedri [Eritrea]	0.043 478 3	4.347 826 1E−02
senzer [Eritrea]	0.043 478 3	4.347 826 1E−02
sett [Antigua]	0.043 668 1	4.366 812 2E−02
shibiri [Tanganyika]	0.043 478 3	4.347 826 1E−02
shibr [Oman]	0.041 666 7	4.166 666 7E−02
shibr [Saudi Arabia]	0.056 243	5.624 297 0E−02
shih chih [China]	0.03	3.000 000 0E−02
shih tsun [China]	0.3	3.000 000 0E−01
shusi [Iraq, ancient]	0.606 060 6	6.060 606 1E−01
sinjer [Abyssinia, ancient]	0.043 478 3	4.347 826 1E−02
sinzer [Abyssinia, ancient]	0.043 478 3	4.347 826 1E−02
sinzer [Ethiopia]	0.043 744 5	4.374 453 2E−02
skrupel [Sweden]	336.812 61	3.368 126 1E+02
sok [Laos]	0.025	2.500 000 0E−02
sok [Thailand]	0.02	2.000 000 0E−02
sok louang [Laos]	0.02	2.000 000 0E−02
sotka [Russia]	0.468 603 6	4.686 035 6E−01
span [Greece, ancient]	0.043 29	4.329 004 3E−02
span [Hebrew, ancient]	0.044 444 4	4.444 444 4E−02
spithame [Greece, ancient]	0.043 29	4.329 004 3E−02
stadium [Hebrew, ancient]	0.000 066 9	6.694 198 2E−05
stopa [Poland]	0.034 722 2	3.472 222 2E−02
stopa [Russia]	0.032 808 4	3.280 839 9E−02
stopa [Yugoslavia]	0.031 645 6	3.164 557 0E−02
stopy [Ukraine]	0.031 645 6	3.164 557 0E−02
su bad [Sumeria, ancient]	0.04	4.000 000 0E−02
sun [Japan]	0.330 033	3.300 330 0E−01
sun [Japan, textiles]	0.263 991 6	2.639 915 5E−01
susi [Sumeria, ancient]	0.598 802 4	5.988 024 0E−01
tac [Vietnam]	0.25	2.500 000 0E−01
taim [India]	0.021 872 3	2.187 226 6E−02
tat [Abyssinia, ancient]	0.4	4.000 000 0E−01
tat [Ethiopia]	0.5	5.000 000 0E−01
tcharak [Iran]	0.038 461 5	3.846 153 8E−02
tcheirek [Iran]	0.038 461 5	3.846 153 8E−02
tefah [Hebrew, ancient]	0.128 205 1	1.282 051 3E−01
tephah [Hebrew, ancient]	0.107 526 9	1.075 268 8E−01
tercia [Colombia]	0.035 880 9	3.588 087 5E−02
terto [Egypt, ancient]	0.044 444 4	4.444 444 4E−02
theb [Egypt, ancient]	0.534 759 4	5.347 593 6E−01
thneap [Cambodia]	0.480 076 8	4.800 768 1E−01
thou	393.700 79	3.937 007 9E+02
thumlumgur [Iceland]	0.384 615 4	3.846 153 8E−01
thuoc may [Vietnam]	0.016	1.600 000 0E−02
thuoc moc [Vietnam]	0.025	2.500 000 0E−02
tokhoi [Mongolia]	0.031 25	3.125 000 0E−02
tomini [Morocco]	0.140 056	1.400 560 2E−01
tomma [Iceland]	0.393 700 8	3.937 007 9E−01
tomme [Denmark]	0.382 339	3.823 390 0E−01
tonni [Spanish North Africa]	0.131 147 5	1.311 475 4E−01
tophah [Hebrew, ancient]	0.128 205 1	1.282 051 3E−01

centimeter (continued)

Convert To	Standard	Scientific
tschak [Iran]	0.038 461 5	3.846 153 8E-02
tser [Egypt, ancient]	0.027 777 8	2.777 777 8E-02
tsun [China]	0.279 220 4	2.792 204 2E-01
tsun [Hong Kong]	0.269 197 1	2.691 971 2E-01
tum [Finland]	0.404 858 3	4.048 583 0E-01
tum [Sweden]	0.336 700 3	3.367 003 0E-01
tumma [Finland]	0.404 858 3	4.048 583 0E-01
ubanu [Akkadian, ancient]	0.598 802 4	5.988 024 0E-01
ulna [Rome, ancient]	0.022 553	2.255 300 0E-02
uncia [Rome, ancient]	0.405 844 2	4.058 441 6E-01
unglee [India]	0.529 100 5	5.291 005 3E-01
unglie [Pakistan]	0.524 934 4	5.249 343 8E-01
ungul [India]	0.524 934 4	5.249 343 8E-01
ungul [Pakistan]	0.524 934 4	5.249 343 8E-01
unguli [India]	0.524 934 4	5.249 343 8E-01
usbaa [Egypt]	0.303 030 3	3.030 303 0E-01
vara [Argentina]	0.011 547 3	1.154 734 4E-02
vara [Chile]	0.011 963 2	1.196 315 3E-02
vara [Colombia]	0.012 5	1.250 000 0E-02
vara [Costa Rica]	0.011 961 7	1.196 172 2E-02
vara [Cuba]	0.011 792 5	1.179 245 3E-02
vara [Dominican Republic]	0.011 961 7	1.196 172 2E-02
vara [Ecuador]	0.011 904 8	1.190 476 2E-02
vara [El Salvador]	0.011 961 7	1.196 172 2E-02
vara [Guatemala]	0.011 976	1.197 604 8E-02
vara [Honduras]	0.011 933 2	1.193 317 4E-02
vara [Mexico]	0.011 904 8	1.190 476 2E-02
vara [Nicaragua]	0.012 5	1.250 000 0E-02
vara [Panama]	0.011 534	1.153 402 5E-02
vara [Paraguay]	0.011 933 2	1.193 317 4E-02
vara [Peru]	0.011 963 2	1.196 315 3E-02
vara [Spain]	0.011 641 4	1.164 144 4E-02
vara [Uruguay]	0.012 5	1.250 000 0E-02
vara granadina [Colombia]	0.224 971 9	2.249 718 8E-01
verchok [Russia]	4.850 107 4	4.850 107 4E+00
verklinje [Sweden]	0.404 176	4.041 759 5E-01
verkturn [Sweden]	0.224 971 9	2.249 718 8E-01
versock [Russia]	0.031 172 1	3.117 207 0E-02
vilasti [India]	0.035 335 7	3.533 568 9E-02
voet [Netherlands]	0.010 989	1.098 901 1E-02
wari [Tanganyika]	16,507.637	1.650 763 7E+04
wavelength of orange-red spectral line of krypton-86	0.224 971 9	2.249 718 8E-01
werchok [Russia]	0.04	4.000 000 0E-01
xiber [Libya]	0.045 454 5	4.545 454 5E-02
xiber [Macao]	0.038 182 5	3.818 251 2E-02
xiber [Malta]	0.047 846 9	4.784 689 0E-02
xiber [Spain]	0.043 478 3	4.347 826 1E-02
zereth [Hebrew, ancient]	0.013 428 8	1.342 281 9E-02
ziraa [Iraq]	0.013 192 6	1.319 261 2E-02
zirah [Lebanon, land]	0.014 727 5	1.472 754 1E-02
zirah [Lebanon, textiles]	0.379 650 7	3.796 507 2E-01
zoll [Austria]	0.381 679 4	3.816 793 9E-01
zoll [Germany]	0.411 150 4	4.111 504 0E-01
zoll [Germany, Bavaria]	0.382 339	3.823 390 0E-01
zoll [Germany, Prussia]	0.349 052 3	3.490 523 2E-01
zoll [Germany, Wurttemberg]	0.336 813 7	3.368 137 4E-01
zoll [Sweden]	0.333 333 3	3.333 333 3E-01
zoll [Switzerland]	0.379 650 7	3.796 507 2E-01
zollpfund [Austria]		\<energy\>

centimeter gram-force

Convert To	Standard	Scientific
Btu [I.T.]	\<\<\< 9.294 910 8E-08	

Convert To	Standard	Scientific
calorie [I.T.]	0.000 023 4	2.342 278 1E-05
centigrade heat unit [I.T.]	<<<	5.163 839 3E-08
cubic centimeter atmosphere	0.000 967 8	9.678 411 1E-04
dyne centimeter	980.665	9.806 650 0E+02
erg	980.665	9.806 650 0E+02
foot pound-force	0.000 072 3	7.233 013 9E-05
foot poundal	0.002 327 2	2.327 153 4E-03
inch ounce-force	0.013 887 4	1.388 738 7E-02
inch pound-force	0.000 868	8.679 616 6E-04
joule	0.000 098 1	9.806 650 0E-05
megaerg	0.000 980 7	9.806 650 0E-04
megalerg	0.000 980 7	9.806 650 0E-04
wattsecond	0.000 098 1	9.806 650 0E-05
centimeter gram-force		**<torque>**
foot ounce-force	0.001 157 3	1.157 282 2E-03
meter kilogram-force	0.000 01	1.000 000 0E-05
newton meter	0.000 098 1	9.806 650 0E-05
centimeter kelvin/watt		**<thermal resistivity>**
meter kelvin/watt	0.01	1.000 000 0E-02
centimeter of mercury [0 °C, by convention]		**<pressure>**
atmosphere [standard]	0.013 157 9	1.315 789 7E-02
atmosphere [technical]	0.013 595 1	1.359 510 0E-02
bar	0.013 332 2	1.333 223 9E-02
centibar	1.333 223 9	1.333 223 9E+00
centihg	1	1.000 000 0E+00
centimeter of water [4 °C, by convention]	13.595 1	1.359 510 0E+01
foot of mercury [0 °C, by convention]	0.032 808 4	3.280 839 9E-02
foot of water [4 °C, by convention]	0.446 033 5	4.460 334 6E-01
gram-force/square centimeter	13.595 1	1.359 510 0E+01
inch of mercury [0 °C, by convention]	0.393 700 8	3.937 007 9E-01
inch of water [4 °C, by convention]	5.352 401 6	5.352 401 6E+00
kilogram-force/square meter	135.951	1.359 510 0E+02
kilopascal	1.333 223 9	1.333 223 9E+00
kilopond/square meter	135.951	1.359 510 0E+02
kip/square foot	0.027 845	2.784 496 0E-02
millimeter of mercury [0 °C, by convention]	10	1.000 000 0E+01
millimeter of water [4 °C, by convention]	135.951	1.359 510 0E+02
ounce-force/square inch	3.093 884 4	3.093 884 4E+00
pascal	1,333.223 9	1.333 223 9E+03
pieze [France]	1.333 223 9	1.333 223 9E+00
pound-force/square foot	27.844 96	2.784 496 0E+01
sthene/square meter [France]	1.333 223 9	1.333 223 9E+00
ton-force/square foot [short]	0.013 922 5	1.392 248 0E-02
ton-force/square meter [metric]	0.135 951	1.359 510 0E-01
torr	10.000 001	1.000 000 1E+01
centimeter of water [4 °C, by convention]		**<pressure>**
atmosphere [standard]	0.000 967 8	9.678 411 1E-04
atmosphere [technical]	0.001	1.000 000 0E-03
bar	0.000 980 7	9.806 650 0E-04
barye [France]	980.665	9.806 650 0E+02
centimeter of mercury [0 °C, by convention]	0.073 555 9	7.355 591 4E-02
decitorr	7.355 592 4	7.355 592 4E+00
dekapascal	9.806 65	9.806 650 0E+00
dyne/square centimeter	980.665	9.806 650 0E+02
foot of mercury [0 °C, by convention]	0.002 413 3	2.413 251 8E-03
foot of water [4 °C, by convention]	0.032 808 4	3.280 839 9E-02
gram-force/square centimeter	1	1.000 000 0E+00
inch of mercury [0 °C, by convention]	0.028 959	2.895 902 1E-02
inch of water [4 °C, by convention]	0.393 700 8	3.937 007 9E-01
kilogram-force/square meter	10	1.000 000 0E+01
kilopond/square meter	10	1.000 000 0E+01
millimeter of mercury [0 °C, by convention]	0.735 559 1	7.355 591 4E-01

Convert From Convert To	<Type of Unit> Standard	Scientific
		10 — 1.000 000 0E+01
millimeter of water [4 °C, by convention]	98.066 5	9.806 650 0E+01
newton/square meter	0.227 573 5	2.275 734 9E-01
ounce-force/square inch	98.066 5	9.806 650 0E+01
pascal	0.098 066 5	9.806 650 0E-02
pieze [France]	2.048 161 4	2.048 161 4E+00
pound-force/square foot	65.897 646	6.589 764 6E+01
poundal/square foot	0.098 066 5	9.806 650 0E-02
sthene/square meter [France]	0.01	1.000 000 0E-02
ton-force/square meter [metric]	0.735 559 2	7.355 592 4E-01
torr	0.735 559 2	7.355 592 4E-01
centimeter second °C/erg		<thermal resistivity>
meter kelvin/watt	100,000	1.000 000 0E+05
centimeter/day		<velocity>
foot/day	0.032 808 4	3.280 839 9E-02
inch/day	0.393 700 8	3.937 007 9E-01
meter/second	0.000 000 1	1.157 407 4E-07
mile/day	0.000 006 2	6.213 711 9E-06
yard/day	0.010 936 1	1.093 613 3E-02
centimeter/dyne		<spectral cross-section>
foot/pound-force	14,593.903	1.459 390 3E+04
square centimeter/erg	1	1.000 000 0E+00
square meter/joule	1,000	1.000 000 0E+03
square second/kilogram	1,000	1.000 000 0E+03
centimeter/hour		<velocity>
foot/day	0.787 401 6	7.874 015 8E-01
inch/day	9.448 818 9	9.448 818 9E+00
meter/second	0.000 002 8	2.777 777 8E-06
mile/day	0.000 149 1	1.491 290 9E-04
yard/day	0.262 467 2	2.624 671 9E-01
centimeter/minute		<velocity>
foot/hour	1.968 503 9	1.968 503 9E+00
inch/hour	23.622 047	2.362 204 7E+01
meter/second	0.000 166 7	1.666 666 7E-04
mile/day	0.008 947 7	8.947 745 2E-03
yard/day	15.748 031 5	1.574 803 2E+01
centimeter/second		<velocity>
foot/minute	1.968 503 9	1.968 503 9E+00
inch/minute	23.622 047	2.362 204 7E+01
meter/second	0.01	1.000 000 0E-02
mile/day	0.536 864 7	5.368 647 1E-01
yard/hour	39.370 078 7	3.937 007 9E+01
centimeter/square second		<acceleration>
foot/square second	0.032 808 4	3.280 839 9E-02
galileo	1	1.000 000 0E+00
g_n [due to gravity]	0.001 019 7	1.019 716 2E-03
leo	0.001	1.000 000 0E-03
meter/square second	0.01	1.000 000 0E-02
centimeter⁴		<second moment of area>
foot⁴	0.000 001 2	1.158 617 7E-06
inch⁴	0.024 025 1	2.402 509 6E-02
meter⁴	<<<	1.000 000 0E-08
centimole		<amount of substance>
mole	0.01	1.000 000 0E-02
centinewton		<force>
crinal	0.1	1.000 000 0E-01
dyne	1,000	1.000 000 0E+03
grain-force	15.736 626	1.573 662 6E+01
gram-force	1.019 716 2	1.019 716 2E+00
newton	0.01	1.000 000 0E-02
ounce-force	0.035 969 4	3.596 943 1E-02
pond	1.019 716 2	1.019 716 2E+00

	Standard	Scientific
pound-force	0.002 248 1	2.248 089 4E-03
poundal	0.072 330 1	7.233 013 9E-02
centiohm		**<electric resistance>**
1/ siemens	0.01	1.000 000 0E-02
abohm	>>>	1.000 000 0E+07
ohm	0.01	1.000 000 0E-02
statohm	<<<	1.112 650 1E-14
centipascal		**<pressure>**
atmosphere [standard]	<<<	9.869 232 7E-08
atmosphere [technical]	0.000 000 1	1.019 716 2E-08
bar	0.000 000 1	1.000 000 0E-07
barye [France]	0.1	1.000 000 0E-01
dyne/square centimeter	0.1	1.000 000 0E-01
gram-force/square centimeter	0.000 102	1.019 716 2E-04
kilogram-force/square meter	0.001 019 7	1.019 716 2E-03
kilopond/square meter	0.001 019 7	1.019 716 2E-03
microbar	0.1	1.000 000 0E-01
micrometer of mercury [0 °C, by convention]	0.075 006 2	7.500 615 8E-02
micrometer of water [4 °C, by convention]	1.019 716 2	1.019 716 2E+00
newton/square meter	0.01	1.000 000 0E-02
pascal	0.01	1.000 000 0E-02
pound-force/square foot	0.000 208 9	2.088 543 4E-04
poundal/square foot	0.006 719 7	6.719 689 8E-03
torr	0.000 075	7.500 616 8E-05
centipoise		**<dynamic viscosity>**
dyne second/square centimeter	0.01	1.000 000 0E-02
gram/centimeter second	0.01	1.000 000 0E-02
kilogram/meter hour	3.6	3.600 000 0E+00
pascal second	0.001	1.000 000 0E-03
poise	0.01	1.000 000 0E-02
pound/foot hour	2.419 088 3	2.419 088 3E+00
poundal hour/square foot	2.419 088 3	2.419 088 3E+00
centisecond		**<time>**
second	0.01	1.000 000 0E-02
centisiemens		**<electric conductance>**
absiemens	<<<	1.000 000 0E-11
siemens	0.01	1.000 000 0E-02
statsiemens	>>>	8.987 551 8E+09
centistokes		**<kinematic viscosity>**
square centimeter/hour	36	3.600 000 0E+01
square foot/day	0.930 001 9	9.300 018 6E-01
square inch/hour	5.580 011 2	5.580 011 2E+00
square meter/second	0.000 001	1.000 000 0E-06
square millimeter/second	1	1.000 000 0E+00
stokes	0.01	1.000 000 0E-02
centitesla		**<magnetic flux density>**
electromagnetic unit of magnetic flux density [cgs system]	100	1.000 000 0E+02
gauss	100	1.000 000 0E+02
line/square centimeter [of magnetic force]	100	1.000 000 0E+02
maxwell/square meter	0.01	1.000 000 0E-02
tesla	0.01	1.000 000 0E-02
centitorr		**<pressure>**
atmosphere [standard]	0.000 013 2	1.315 789 5E-05
atmosphere [technical]	0.000 013 6	1.359 509 8E-05
bar	0.000 013 3	1.333 223 7E-05
barye [France]	13.332 237	1.333 223 7E+01
gram-force/square centimeter	0.013 595 1	1.359 509 8E-02
kilogram-force/square meter	0.135 951	1.359 509 8E-01
kilopond/square meter	0.135 951	1.359 509 8E-01
microbar	13.332 237	1.333 223 7E+01
micrometer of mercury [0 °C, by convention]	9.999 998 6	9.999 998 6E+00

	Standard	Scientific
micrometer of water [4 °C, by convention]	135.950 98	1.359 509 8E+02
newton/square meter	1.333 223 7	1.333 223 7E+00
pascal	1.333 223 7	1.333 223 7E+00
pieze [France]	0.001 333 2	1.333 223 7E-03
pound-force/square foot	0.027 845	2.784 495 6E-02
poundal/square foot	0.895 885	8.958 849 5E-01
sthene/square meter [France]	0.001 333 2	1.333 223 7E-03
torr	0.01	1.000 000 0E-02

centivolt \<electric potential\>

	Standard	Scientific
ampere ohm	0.01	1.000 000 0E-02
joule/coulomb	0.01	1.000 000 0E-02
statvolt	0.000 033 4	3.335 641 0E-05
volt	0.01	1.000 000 0E-02
watt/ampere	0.01	1.000 000 0E-02

centiwatt \<power\>

	Standard	Scientific
Btu/hour [I.T.]	0.034 121 4	3.412 141 6E-02
Btu/hour [thermoc.]	0.034 144 3	3.414 425 1E-02
calorie/hour [I.T.]	8.598 452 3	8.598 452 3E+00
calorie/hour [thermoc.]	8.604 205 5	8.604 206 5E+00
centigrade heat unit/hour [mean]	0.018 941 7	1.894 172 6E-02
cubic meter atmosphere/minute	5.921 539 6	5.921 539 6E+00
dyne centimeter/second	100,000	1.000 000 0E+05
erg/second	100,000	1.000 000 0E+05
foot pound-force/hour	26.552 237	2.655 223 7E+01
foot poundal/minute	14.238 216	1.423 821 6E+01
gram-force centimeter/second	101.971 62	1.019 716 2E+02
horsepower	0.000 013 4	1.341 022 1E-05
horsepower [metric]	0.000 013 6	1.359 621 6E-05
joule/hour	36	3.600 000 0E+01
kilocalorie/hour [I.T.]	0.008 598 5	8.598 452 3E-03
kilogram square meter/cubic second	0.01	1.000 000 0E-02
kilogram-force meter/hour	3.670 978 4	3.670 978 4E+00
kilopond meter/hour	3.670 978 4	3.670 978 4E+00
lumen [green light at 100% efficiency]	6.85	6.850 000 0E+00
lumen [green light at 5,550 angstrom]	6.800 000 2	6.800 000 2E+00
newton meter/hour	36	3.600 000 0E+01
pound square foot/cubic second	0.237 303 6	2.373 036 0E-01
volt ampere	0.01	1.000 000 0E-02
watt	0.01	1.000 000 0E-02

centiweber \<magnetic flux\>

	Standard	Scientific
electrostatic unit of magnetic flux [cgs system]	0.000 033 4	3.335 641 0E-05
gauss square centimeter	1,000,000	1.000 000 0E+06
maxwell	1,000,000	1.000 000 0E+06
statweber	0.000 033 4	3.335 641 0E-05
unit pole	79,577.475 4	7.957 747 5E+04
weber	0.01	1.000 000 0E-02

centnar [Poland] \<mass, special - see page 29\>

		Scientific
kilogram	40.550 4	4.055 040 0E+01

centner [Denmark] \<mass, special - see page 29\>

		Scientific
kilogram	50	5.000 000 0E+01

centner [Germany] \<mass, special - see page 29\>

		Scientific
kilogram	50	5.000 000 0E+01

centner [Norway] \<mass, special - see page 29\>

		Scientific
kilogram	49.81	4.981 000 0E+01

centner [Sweden] \<mass, special - see page 29\>

		Scientific
kilogram	42.515	4.251 500 0E+01

centner [Switzerland] \<mass, special - see page 29\>

		Scientific
kilogram	50	5.000 000 0E+01

centner [UK] \<mass\>

	Standard	Scientific
cental [US]	1.12	1.120 000 0E+00
doppelzentner [Germany]	0.508 023 5	5.080 234 5E-01

	Standard	Scientific
hundredweight [long]	1	1.000 000 0E+00
hundredweight [short]	1.12	1.120 000 0E+00
hundredweight [UK]	1	1.000 000 0E+00
kilogram	50.802 345	5.080 234 5E+01
pound	112	1.120 000 0E+02
pound [avoirdupois]	112	1.120 000 0E+02
pound [troy]	136.111 11	1.361 111 1E+02
pound [UK]	112.000 01	1.120 000 1E+02
pound [US, avoirdupois]	111.999 99	1.119 999 9E+02
quarter [long]	0.2	2.000 000 0E−01
quarter [short]	0.224	2.240 000 0E−01
quarter [UK]	4	4.000 000 0E+00
quarter [US]	4.48	4.480 000 0E+00
quintal [UK]	1	1.000 000 0E+00
quintal [US]	1.12	1.120 000 0E+00
stone [UK]	8	8.000 000 0E+00
ton [long]	0.05	5.000 000 0E−02
ton [short]	0.056	5.600 000 0E−02
ton [UK]	0.05	5.000 000 0E−02
tonne	0.050 802 3	5.080 234 5E−02
centrad		**<plane angle>**
degree [angular]	0.572 957 8	5.729 578 0E−01
radian	0.01	1.000 000 0E−02
central [South Africa]		**<mass, special - see page 29>**
kilogram	45.359 237	4.535 923 7E+01
centuria [Rome, ancient]		**<area, special - see page 29>**
hectare	50.4	5.040 000 0E+01
century		**<time>**
centenary	1	1.000 000 0E+00
centennial	1	1.000 000 0E+00
year [normal calendar]	100	1.000 000 0E+02
ceston [Venezuela]		**<volume, special - see page 29>**
liter	70	7.000 000 0E+01
cha [South Korea]		**<length, special - see page 29>**
meter	0.303 03	3.030 300 0E−01
chabba [Iraq, ancient]		**<mass, special - see page 29>**
milligram	65	6.500 000 0E+01
chabba [Iraq, ancient]		**<length, special - see page 29>**
millimeter	3.3	3.300 000 0E+00
chai meu [Thailand]		**<volume, special - see page 29>**
liter	0.125	1.250 000 0E−01
chain [Gunter or US, survey]		**<length>**
chain [Ramden or Engineer]	0.660 001 3	6.600 013 2E−01
foot [international]	66.000 132	6.600 013 2E+01
foot [US, survey]	66	6.600 000 0E+01
inch [based on US, survey foot]	792	7.920 000 0E+02
inch [international]	792.001 58	7.920 015 8E+02
link [Gunter or US, survey]	100	1.000 000 0E+02
link [Ramden or Engineer]	66.000 132	6.600 013 2E+01
meter	20.116 84	2.011 684 0E+01
mile [international]	0.012 5	1.250 002 5E−02
mile [US, statute]	0.012 5	1.250 000 0E−02
mile [US, survey]	0.012 5	1.250 000 0E−02
out [US, survey]	0.2	2.000 000 0E−01
pace [geometrical]	1.320 002 6	1.320 002 6E+00
pace [US, survey]	26.4	2.640 000 0E+01
perch [US, survey]	4	4.000 000 0E+00
perche [France]	3.440 463 5	3.440 463 5E+00
pole [US, survey]	4	4.000 000 0E+00
rod [US, survey]	4	4.000 000 0E+00
yard [based on US, survey foot]	22	2.200 000 0E+01

yard [international]	22.000 044	2.200 004 4E+01
chain [Ramden or Engineer]		**<length>**
chain [Gunter or US, survey]	1.515 148 5	1.515 148 5E+00
foot [international]	100	1.000 000 0E+02
foot [US, survey]	99.999 8	9.999 980 0E+01
furlong [US, survey]	0.151 514 9	1.515 148 5E−01
inch [based on US, survey foot]	1,199.997 6	1.199 997 6E+03
inch [international]	1,200	1.200 000 0E+03
link [Gunter or US, survey]	151.514 85	1.515 148 5E+02
link [Ramden or Engineer]	100	1.000 000 0E+02
meter	30.48	3.048 000 0E+01
mile [international]	0.018 939 4	1.893 939 4E−02
mile [US, statute]	0.018 939 4	1.893 935 6E−02
mile [US, survey]	0.018 939 4	1.893 935 6E−02
out [US, survey]	0.303 029 7	3.030 297 0E−01
pace [geometrical]	2	2.000 000 0E+00
pace [US, survey]	39.999 92	3.999 992 0E+01
perch [US, survey]	6.060 593 9	6.060 593 9E+00
pole [US, survey]	6.060 593 9	6.060 593 9E+00
rod [US, survey]	6.060 593 9	6.060 593 9E+00
rope	5	5.000 000 0E+00
yard [based on US, survey foot]	33.333 267	3.333 326 7E+01
yard [international]	33.333 333	3.333 333 3E+01
chaldron [UK, dry]		**<volume>**
barrel [UK]	8	8.000 000 0E+00
barrel [US, dry]	11.323 242	1.132 324 2E+01
bushel [UK]	36	3.600 000 0E+01
bushel [US, dry]	37.154 043	3.715 404 3E+01
chaldron [UK, liquid]	1	1.000 000 0E+00
chaldron [US, dry]	1.032 056 7	1.032 056 7E+00
cubic foot	46.236 572	4.623 657 2E+01
cubic inch	79,896.797	7.989 679 7E+04
cubic meter	1.309 273 9	1.309 273 9E+00
cubic yard	1.712 465 6	1.712 465 6E+00
gallon [UK, dry or liquid]	288	2.880 000 0E+02
gallon [US, dry]	297.232 34	2.972 323 4E+02
peck [UK]	144	1.440 000 0E+02
peck [US]	148.616 17	1.486 161 7E+02
pint [UK]	2,304	2.304 000 0E+03
pint [US, dry]	2,377.858 7	2.377 858 7E+03
quart [UK]	1,152	1.152 000 0E+03
quart [US, dry]	1,188.929 4	1.188 929 4E+03
quarter [UK]	4.5	4.500 000 0E+00
stere	1.309 273 9	1.309 273 9E+00
chaldron [UK, liquid]		**<volume>**
barrel [UK]	8	8.000 000 0E+00
barrel [UK, wine]	9.142 857 1	9.142 857 1E+00
barrel [US, federal proof spirits]	8.646 839 5	8.646 839 5E+00
bushel [UK]	36	3.600 000 0E+01
chaldron [UK, dry]	1	1.000 000 0E+00
cubic foot	46.236 572	4.623 657 2E+01
cubic inch	79,896.797	7.989 679 7E+04
cubic meter	1.309 273 9	1.309 273 9E+00
cubic yard	1.712 465 6	1.712 465 6E+00
cup [Canada, measuring]	5,760	5.760 000 0E+03
firkin [UK]	32	3.200 000 0E+01
firkin [US]	38.430 398	3.843 039 8E+01
gallon [Canada, liquid]	288	2.880 000 0E+02
gallon [UK, dry or liquid]	288	2.880 000 0E+02
gallon [US, liquid]	345.873 58	3.458 735 8E+02
gill [UK]	9,216	9.216 000 0E+03
hogshead [UK]	4.571 428 6	4.571 428 6E+00
hogshead [US]	5.490 056 8	5.490 056 8E+00

	Standard	Scientific
kiloliter	1.309 273 9	1.309 273 9E+00
liter	1,309.273 9	1.309 273 9E+03
ounce [UK, liquid]	46,080	4.608 000 0E+04
peck [UK]	144	1.440 000 0E+02
pint [UK]	2,304	2.304 000 0E+03
quart [UK]	1,152	1.152 000 0E+03
quarter [UK]	4.5	4.500 000 0E+00
stere	1.309 273 9	1.309 273 9E+00

chaldron [US, dry] — `<volume>`

	Standard	Scientific
barrel [US, dry]	10.971 531	1.097 153 1E+01
barrel [US, dry commodities except cranberry]	10.971 429	1.097 142 9E+01
bushel [US, dry]	36	3.600 000 0E+01
bushel [US, struck measure]	36	3.600 000 0E+01
cubic foot	44.800 417	4.480 041 7E+01
cubic inch	77,415.12	7.741 512 0E+04
cubic meter	1.268 606 5	1.268 606 5E+00
cubic yard	1.659 274 7	1.659 274 7E+00
gallon [UK, dry or liquid]	279.054 42	2.790 544 2E+02
gallon [US, dry]	288	2.880 000 0E+02
peck [US]	144	1.440 000 0E+02
pint [US, dry]	2,304	2.304 000 0E+03
quart [US, dry]	1,152	1.152 000 0E+03
stere	1.268 606 5	1.268 606 5E+00

chalkos [Greece, ancient] — `<mass, special - see page 29>`

	Standard	Scientific
gram	8.6	8.600 000 0E+00

chalque [Greece, ancient] — `<mass, special - see page 29>`

	Standard	Scientific
milligram	101	1.010 000 0E+02

cham am [Cambodia] — `<length, special - see page 29>`

	Standard	Scientific
centimeter	25	2.500 000 0E+01

chang [China] — `<length, special - see page 29>`

	Standard	Scientific
meter	3.581	3.581 000 0E+00

chang [Mongolia] — `<length, special - see page 29>`

	Standard	Scientific
meter	3.2	3.200 000 0E+00

chang [Thailand] — `<mass, special - see page 29>`

	Standard	Scientific
kilogram	1.2	1.200 000 0E+00

chang awn [Thailand] — `<volume, special - see page 29>`

	Standard	Scientific
liter	0.5	5.000 000 0E−01

chapah [Malaysia] — `<mass, special - see page 29>`

	Standard	Scientific
kilogram	0.816	8.160 000 0E−01

charac [Iran] — `<length, special - see page 29>`

	Standard	Scientific
meter	0.26	2.600 000 0E−01

charak [Afghanistan] — `<mass, special - see page 29>`

	Standard	Scientific
kilogram	1.776 5	1.776 500 0E+00

charge [Belgium] — `<mass, special - see page 29>`

	Standard	Scientific
kilogram	187.464	1.874 640 0E+02

charge [France] — `<mass, special - see page 29>`

	Standard	Scientific
kilogram	146.852	1.468 520 0E+02

charge [Holland] — `<mass, special - see page 29>`

	Standard	Scientific
kilogram	187.464	1.874 640 0E+02

chariot [Netherlands, wool] — `<mass, special - see page 29>`

	Standard	Scientific
kilogram	77.353	7.735 300 0E+01

charka [Russia] — `<volume, special - see page 29>`

	Standard	Scientific
liter	0.123	1.230 000 0E−01

charruba [Libya] — `<mass, special - see page 29>`

	Standard	Scientific
gram	0.191 718	1.917 180 0E−01

chast [Russia] — `<area, special - see page 29>`

	Standard	Scientific
square meter	38	3.800 000 0E+01

Convert From	<Type of Unit>	
Convert To	Standard	Scientific

chattack [Bangladesh] `<mass, special - see page 29>`
gram-- 58.32 --- 5.832 000 0E+01

chattack [India] `<mass, special - see page 29>`
gram-- 58.32 --- 5.832 000 0E+01

chattack [Pakistan] `<mass, special - see page 29>`
gram-- 58.32 --- 5.832 000 0E+01

chattak [Ceylon] `<mass, special - see page 29>`
gram--58.319 02 --- 5.831 902 0E+01

chattak [India] `<area, special - see page 29>`
square meter--------------------------------4.180 636 8 --- 4.180 636 8E+00

chattak [Pakistan] `<mass, special - see page 29>`
gram--58.319 --- 5.831 900 0E+01

chattauck [India] `<mass, special - see page 29>`
gram--58.319 --- 5.831 900 0E+01

chauseemeile [Germany] `<length, special - see page 29>`
kilometer--7.414 5 --- 7.414 500 0E+00

chawal [Pakistan] `<mass, special - see page 29>`
gram-- 0.015 187 2 --- 1.518 724 0E-02

che [China] `<length, special - see page 29>`
meter-- 0.333 333 3 --- 3.333 333 3E-01

che [Hong Kong] `<length, special - see page 29>`
meter--0.371 475 --- 3.714 750 0E-01

che [Singapore] `<length, special - see page 29>`
meter--0.374 6 --- 3.746 000 0E-01

check [China, new] `<length, special - see page 29>`
meter-- 0.333 333 3 --- 3.333 333 3E-01

check [China, old] `<length, special - see page 29>`
meter-- 0.358 14 --- 3.581 400 0E-01

check [Hong Kong] `<length, special - see page 29>`
meter--0.374 6 --- 3.746 000 0E-01

check [Malaysia] `<length, special - see page 29>`
centimeter--37.465 --- 3.746 500 0E+01

check [Singapore] `<length, special - see page 29>`
meter--0.374 6 --- 3.746 000 0E-01

chee [Malaysia] `<mass, special - see page 29>`
gram-- 3.78 --- 3.780 000 0E+00

cheh [China] `<length, special - see page 29>`
meter-- 0.333 333 3 --- 3.333 333 3E-01

cheh [Hong Kong] `<length, special - see page 29>`
meter--0.371 475 --- 3.714 750 0E-01

cheh [Singapore] `<length, special - see page 29>`
meter--0.374 6 --- 3.746 000 0E-01

chek [China, new] `<length, special - see page 29>`
meter-- 0.333 333 3 --- 3.333 333 3E-01

chek [China, old] `<length, special - see page 29>`
meter-- 0.358 14 --- 3.581 400 0E-01

chek [Hong Kong] `<length, special - see page 29>`
meter--0.371 475 --- 3.714 750 0E-01

chek [Singapore] `<length, special - see page 29>`
meter--0.374 6 --- 3.746 000 0E-01

cheky [Turkey] `<mass, special - see page 29>`
gram--318.667 --- 3.186 670 0E+02

chela [Somalia] `<volume, special - see page 29>`
liter-- 1.359 --- 1.359 000 0E+00

cheli [Turkey]   \<mass, special - see page 29\>
  kilogram --------------------------------------- 230.930 1 ----2.309 301 0E+02

chemica [Iran]   \<volume, special - see page 29\>
  liter--- 1.316 ----1.316 000 0E+00

chequi [Turkey]   \<mass, special - see page 29\>
  gram-- 318.667 ----3.186 670 0E+02

chetverik [Russia]   \<volume, special - see page 29\>
  liter-- 26.2 ----2.620 000 0E+01

chetvert [Russia]   \<volume, special - see page 29\>
  hectoliter -- 2.1 ----2.100 000 0E+00

chetvertinka [Russia]   \<volume, special - see page 29\>
  liter-- 0.25 ----2.500 000 0E-01

cheung [Hong Kong]   \<length, special - see page 29\>
  meter---3.714 75 ----3.714 750 0E+00

cheung [Malaysia]   \<length, special - see page 29\>
  meter--- 3.746 ----3.746 000 0E+00

cheung [Singapore]   \<length, special - see page 29\>
  meter-- 3.746 5 ----3.746 500 0E+00

cheval vapeur [France]   \<power\>

	Standard	Scientific
Btu/minute [I.T.]	41.827 098	4.182 709 8E+01
Btu/minute [thermoc.]	41.855 09	4.185 509 0E+01
calorie/second [I.T.]	175.670 86	1.756 708 6E+02
calorie/second [thermoc.]	175.788 42	1.757 884 2E+02
centigrade heat unit/minute [mean]	23.219 359	2.321 935 9E+01
cubic meter atmosphere/second	7,258.808 3	7.258 808 3E+03
dyne centimeter/second	>>>	7.354 987 5E+09
erg/second	>>>	7.354 987 5E+09
foot pound-force/second	542.476 04	5.424 760 4E+02
foot poundal/second	17,453.65	1.745 365 0E+04
gram-force centimeter/second	7,500,000	7.500 000 0E+06
hectowatt	7.354 987 5	7.354 987 5E+00
horsepower	0.986 320 1	9.863 200 7E-01
horsepower [metric]	1	1.000 000 0E+00
joule/second	735.498 75	7.354 987 5E+02
kilocalorie/minute [I.T.]	10.540 252	1.054 025 2E+01
kilogram square meter/cubic second	735.498 75	7.354 987 5E+02
kilogram-force meter/second	75	7.500 000 0E+01
kilopond meter/second	75	7.500 000 0E+01
newton meter/second	735.498 75	7.354 987 5E+02
pferdestarke [Germany]	1	1.000 000 0E+00
poncelet [France]	0.75	7.500 000 0E-01
ton of refrigeration	0.209 135 5	2.091 354 9E-01
volt ampere	735.498 75	7.354 987 5E+02
watt	735.498 75	7.354 987 5E+02

cheval vapeur heure [France]   \<energy\>

	Standard	Scientific
Board of Trade Unit	0.735 498 8	7.354 987 5E-01
Btu [I.T.]	2,509.625 9	2.509 625 9E+03
calorie [I.T.]	632,415.09	6.324 150 9E+05
calorie [kilogram, I.T.]	632.415 09	6.324 150 9E+02
calorie [kilogram, mean]	631.929 08	6.319 290 8E+02
calorie [kilogram, thermoc.]	632.838 31	6.328 383 1E+02
centigrade heat unit [I.T.]	1,394.236 6	1.394 236 6E+03
coal equivalent kilogram [UN, standard]	0.090 345	9.034 501 3E-02
cubic foot atmosphere	922.832 62	9.228 326 2E+02
dekawatthour	73.549 875	7.354 987 5E+01
foot pound-force	1,952,913.7	1.952 913 7E+06
foot poundal	>>>	6.283 314 1E+07
frigorie [France]	632.566 18	6.325 661 8E+02
hectowatthour	7.354 987 5	7.354 987 5E+00
horsepower hour	0.986 320 1	9.863 200 7E-01

Convert From Convert To	<Type of Unit> Standard	Scientific
horsepower hour [metric]	1	1.000 000 0E+00
joule	2,647,795.5	2.647 795 5E+06
kilocalorie [I.T.]	632.415 09	6.324 150 9E+02
kilogram calorie [15 °C, NBS, 1939]	632.566 18	6.325 661 8E+02
kilowatthour	0.735 498 8	7.354 987 5E−01
megajoule	2.647 795 5	2.647 795 5E+00
myriawatthour	0.073 549 9	7.354 987 5E−02
newton meter	2,647,795.5	2.647 795 5E+06
pferdestarkenstunde [Germany]	1	1.000 000 0E+00
quad	<<<	2.509 625 9E−12
therm [EEC]	0.025 096 3	2.509 625 9E−02
therm [US]	0.025 102 3	2.510 225 1E−02
thermie [France]	0.632 566 2	6.325 661 8E−01
watthour	735.498 75	7.354 987 5E+02
chevron [Cambodia] cubic meter	<volume, special - see page 29> 0.1	1.000 000 0E−01
chhatak [Bangladesh] gram	<mass, special - see page 29> 58.319	5.831 900 0E+01
chhatak [India] gram	<mass, special - see page 29> 58.319	5.831 900 0E+01
chhatak [Pakistan] gram	<mass, special - see page 29> 58.319	5.831 900 0E+01
chhek [China, new] meter	<length, special - see page 29> 0.333 333 3	3.333 333 3E−01
chhek [China, old] meter	<length, special - see page 29> 0.358 14	3.581 400 0E−01
chhek [Hong Kong] meter	<length, special - see page 29> 0.374 6	3.746 000 0E−01
chhek [Singapore] meter	<length, special - see page 29> 0.374 6	3.746 000 0E−01
chi [Cambodia] gram	<mass, special - see page 29> 3.75	3.750 000 0E+00
chi [China] meter	<length, special - see page 29> 0.333 333 3	3.333 333 3E−01
chi [Hong Kong] gram	<mass, special - see page 29> 3.78	3.780 000 0E+00
chi [Mongolia] gram	<mass, special - see page 29> 3.75	3.750 000 0E+00
chi [Mongolia] centimeter	<length, special - see page 29> 32	3.200 000 0E+01
chi [South Korea] centimeter	<length, special - see page 29> 3.030 3	3.030 300 0E+00
chi [Vietnam] kilogram	<mass, special - see page 29> 3.75	3.750 000 0E+00
chia [Taiwan] hectare	<area, special - see page 29> 0.969 9	9.699 000 0E−01
chien [China] gram	<mass, special - see page 29> 3.779 9	3.779 900 0E+00
chien [Singapore] gram	<mass, special - see page 29> 3.444 74	3.444 740 0E+00
chih [China] centimeter	<length, special - see page 29> 35.814	3.581 400 0E+01
chih [Hong Kong] meter	<length, special - see page 29> 0.371 475	3.714 750 0E−01
chih [Singapore] meter	<length, special - see page 29> 0.374 6	3.746 000 0E−01

| Convert From | | **\<Type of Unit\>** |
Convert To	Standard	Scientific
chiliad		**\<time\>**
millenarian	1	1.000 000 0E+00
millenary	1	1.000 000 0E+00
millennium	1	1.000 000 0E+00
year [normal calendar]	1,000	1.000 000 0E+03
chin [Cambodia]	**\<mass, special - see page 29\>**	
gram	3.75	3.750 000 0E+00
chin [China, new]	**\<mass, special - see page 29\>**	
kilogram	0.5	5.000 000 0E-01
chin [China, old]	**\<mass, special - see page 29\>**	
gram	604.789 8	6.047 898 0E+02
chin [Hong Kong]	**\<mass, special - see page 29\>**	
gram	3.779 9	3.779 900 0E+00
chin [Indonesia]	**\<mass, special - see page 29\>**	
kilogram	0.618	6.180 000 0E-01
chin [Japan]	**\<mass, special - see page 29\>**	
kilogram	0.6	6.000 000 0E-01
chin [Mongolia]	**\<mass, special - see page 29\>**	
gram	3.75	3.750 000 0E+00
chin [South Korea]	**\<mass, special - see page 29\>**	
kilogram	0.6	6.000 000 0E-01
chin [Thailand]	**\<mass, special - see page 29\>**	
kilogram	0.6	6.000 000 0E-01
chinanda [Philippines]	**\<mass, special - see page 29\>**	
kilogram	6.325	6.325 000 0E+00
chinbul [Lebanon]	**\<mass, special - see page 29\>**	
kilogram	150	1.500 000 0E+02
chinese foot [China]	**\<length, special - see page 29\>**	
centimeter	32	3.200 000 0E+01
chinese foot [Hong Kong]	**\<length, special - see page 29\>**	
meter	0.371 475	3.714 750 0E-01
chinese inch [Hong Kong]	**\<length, special - see page 29\>**	
millimeter	37.147 5	3.714 750 0E+01
chinese mile [Hong Kong]	**\<length, special - see page 29\>**	
kilometer	0.557 21	5.572 100 0E-01
chinese yard [Hong Kong, textiles]	**\<length, special - see page 29\>**	
meter	0.891 54	8.915 400 0E-01
ching [China]	**\<area, special - see page 29\>**	
square meter	11.241	1.124 100 0E+01
chittack [India]	**\<mass, special - see page 29\>**	
gram	58.319	5.831 900 0E+01
chittak [India]	**\<mass, special - see page 29\>**	
gram	58.319 02	5.831 902 0E+01
chkalik [Russia]	**\<volume, special - see page 29\>**	
liter	0.061	6.100 000 0E-02
cho [Japan]	**\<length, special - see page 29\>**	
meter	109.09	1.090 900 0E+02
choinix [Greece, ancient]	**\<volume, special - see page 29\>**	
liter	1.2	1.200 000 0E+00
chok [South Korea]	**\<length, special - see page 29\>**	
meter	0.303 03	3.030 300 0E-01
chombol [Lebanon, wheat]	**\<mass, special - see page 29\>**	
kilogram	150	1.500 000 0E+02
chomor [Hebrew, ancient]	**\<volume, special - see page 29\>**	
hectoliter	3.8	3.800 000 0E+00

Convert From / Convert To	Standard	Scientific
chong [Cambodia]	\<mass, special - see page 29\>	
kilogram	30	3.000 000 0E+01
chopin [France]	\<volume, special - see page 29\>	
liter	0.465 5	4.655 000 0E−01
chopin [Scotland]	\<volume, special - see page 29\>	
liter	1.136 5	1.136 500 0E+00
chopine [France]	\<volume, special - see page 29\>	
liter	0.5	5.000 000 0E−01
choryos [Egypt, ancient]	\<length, special - see page 29\>	
centimeter	7.49	7.490 000 0E+00
chou [Greece, ancient]	\<volume, special - see page 29\>	
liter	21	2.100 000 0E+01
chous [Greece, ancient]	\<volume, special - see page 29\>	
liter	3.236 3	3.236 300 0E+00
chu [Greece, ancient]	\<volume, special - see page 29\>	
liter	21	2.100 000 0E+01
chuchok [Brunei, gold]	\<mass, special - see page 29\>	
milligram	378	3.780 000 0E+02
chuhm [Malaysia]	\<length, special - see page 29\>	
centimeter	3.746 5	3.746 500 0E+00
chuhm [Singapore]	\<length, special - see page 29\>	
centimeter	3.746 5	3.746 500 0E+00
chum [Malaysia]	\<length, special - see page 29\>	
centimeter	3.746 5	3.746 500 0E+00
chum [Singapore]	\<length, special - see page 29\>	
centimeter	3.746 5	3.746 500 0E+00
chung [South Korea]	\<length, special - see page 29\>	
meter	109.09	1.090 900 0E+02
chungbo [Japan]	\<length, special - see page 29\>	
meter	109.09	1.090 900 0E+02
chungbo [South Korea]	\<area, special - see page 29\>	
are	99.173 7	9.917 370 0E+01
chuo [China]	\<area, special - see page 29\>	
square meter	168.62	1.686 200 0E+02
chupa [Philippines]	\<volume, special - see page 29\>	
liter	0.375	3.750 000 0E−01
circle [angular]	\<plane angle\>	
grade [angular]	400	4.000 000 0E+02
mil [military artillery, angle, NATO]	6,400	6.400 000 0E+03
radian	6.283 185 3	6.283 185 3E+00
revolution [angular]	1	1.000 000 0E+00
circular centimeter	\<area\>	
circular foot [international]	0.001 076 4	1.076 391 0E−03
circular foot [US, survey]	0.001 076 4	1.076 386 7E−03
circular inch [based on US, survey foot]	0.154 999 7	1.549 996 9E−01
circular inch [international]	0.155 000 3	1.550 003 1E−01
square barleycorn	1.095 632 6	1.095 632 6E+00
square caliber	1,217.369 6	1.217 369 6E+03
square centimeter	0.785 398 2	7.853 981 6E−01
square digit	0.216 421 3	2.164 212 6E−01
square inch [based on US, survey foot]	0.121 736 5	1.217 364 7E−01
square inch [international]	0.121 737	1.217 369 6E−01
square meter	0.000 078 5	7.853 981 6E−05
square millimeter	78.539 816	7.853 981 6E+01
square palm	0.013 526 3	1.352 632 9E−02
square span	0.001 502 9	1.502 925 4E−03
circular foot [international]	\<area\>	
are	0.000 729 7	7.296 587 7E−04

circular centimeter

circular foot [US, survey]	929.030 4	9.290 304 0E+02
circular inch [based on US, survey foot]	0.999 996	9.999 960 0E-01
circular inch [international]	143.999 42	1.439 994 2E+02
square cubit	144	1.440 000 0E+02
square foot [international]	0.349 065 9	3.490 658 5E-01
square foot [US, survey]	0.785 398 2	7.853 981 6E-01
square link [Gunter or US, survey]	0.785 395	7.853 950 2E-01
square link [Ramden or Engineer]	1.803 018 9	1.803 018 9E+00
square meter	0.785 395	7.853 950 2E-01
square pace	0.072 965 9	7.296 587 7E-02
square palm	0.125 663 7	1.256 637 1E-01
square span	12.566 371	1.256 637 1E+01
square vara [US, survey, California]	1.396 263 4	1.396 263 4E+00
square vara [US, survey, Texas]	0.103 853 9	1.038 538 9E-01
	0.101 787 2	1.017 871 9E-01

circular foot [US, survey] \<area\>

circular centimeter	929.034 12	9.290 341 2E+02
circular foot [international]	1.000 004	1.000 004 0E+00
circular inch [based on US, survey foot]	144	1.440 000 0E+02
circular inch [international]	144.000 58	1.440 005 8E+02
square digit	201.062 73	2.010 627 3E+02
square foot [international]	0.785 401 3	7.854 013 0E-01
square foot [US, survey]	0.785 398 2	7.853 981 6E-01
square inch [based on US, survey foot]	113.097 34	1.130 973 4E+02
square inch [international]	113.097 79	1.130 977 9E+02
square link [Gunter or US, survey]	1.803 026 1	1.803 026 1E+00
square link [Ramden or Engineer]	0.785 398 2	7.853 981 6E-01
square meter	0.072 966 2	7.296 616 9E-02
square yard [based on US, survey foot]	0.087 266 5	8.726 646 3E-02
square yard [international]	0.087 266 8	8.726 681 2E-02

circular inch [based on US, survey foot] \<area\>

circular centimeter	6.451 625 8	6.451 625 8E+00
circular inch [international]	1.000 004	1.000 004 0E+00
square barleycorn	7.068 611 7	7.068 611 7E+00
square centimeter	5.067 095 1	5.067 095 1E+00
square foot [international]	0.005 454 2	5.454 175 7E-03
square foot [US, survey]	0.005 454 2	5.454 153 9E-03
square inch [based on US, survey foot]	0.785 398 2	7.853 981 6E-01
square inch [international]	0.785 401 3	7.854 013 0E-01
square meter	0.000 506 7	5.067 095 1E-04

circular inch [international] \<area\>

circular centimeter	6.451 6	6.451 600 0E+00
circular foot [international]	0.006 944 4	6.944 444 4E-03
circular foot [US, survey]	0.006 944 4	6.944 416 7E-03
circular inch [based on US, survey foot]	0.999 996	9.999 960 0E-01
square barleycorn	7.068 583 5	7.068 583 5E+00
square caliber	7.853 981 6	7.853 981 6E+03
square centimeter	5.067 074 8	5.067 074 8E+00
square foot [international]	0.005 454 2	5.454 153 9E-03
square foot [US, survey]	0.005 454 1	5.454 132 1E-03
square inch [based on US, survey foot]	0.785 395	7.853 950 2E-01
square inch [international]	0.785 398 2	7.853 981 6E-01
square meter	0.000 506 7	5.067 074 8E-04

circular microinch \<area\>

circular micrometer	0.000 645 2	6.451 600 0E-04
circular mil	0.000 001	1.000 000 0E-06
square angstrom	50,670.748	5.067 074 8E+04
square bicron	>>>	5.067 074 8E+08
square caliber	<<<	7.853 981 6E-09
square inch [based on US, survey foot]	<<<	7.853 950 2E-13
square inch [international]	<<<	7.853 981 6E-13
square meter	<<<	5.067 074 8E-16

square microinch	0.785 398 2	7.853 981 6E-01
square micromicron	>>>	5.067 074 8E+08
square micron	0.000 506 7	5.067 074 8E-04
square mil	0.000 000 8	7.853 981 6E-07
square millimicron	506.707 48	5.067 074 8E+02
square stigma	>>>	5.067 074 8E+08
square tenthmeter	50,670.748	5.067 074 8E+04
square thou	0.000 000 8	7.853 981 6E-07

circular micrometer <area>

circular inch [based on US, survey foot]	<<<	1.549 996 9E-09
circular inch [international]	<<<	1.550 003 1E-09
circular microinch	1,550.003 1	1.550 003 1E+03
circular mil	0.001 55	1.550 003 1E-03
square caliber	0.000 012 2	1.217 369 6E-05
square inch [based on US, survey foot]	<<<	1.217 364 7E-09
square inch [international]	<<<	1.217 369 6E-09
square meter	<<<	7.853 981 6E-13
square microinch	1,217.369 6	1.217 369 6E+03
square micrometer	0.785 398 2	7.853 981 6E-01
square micron	0.785 398 2	7.853 981 6E-01
square mil	0.001 217 4	1.217 369 6E-03
square millimicron	785,398.16	7.853 981 6E+05
square tenthmeter	>>>	7.853 981 6E+07
square thou	0.001 217 4	1.217 369 6E-03

circular mil <area>

circular inch [based on US, survey foot]	0.000 001	9.999 960 0E-07
circular inch [international]	0.000 001	1.000 000 0E-06
circular microinch	1,000,000	1.000 000 0E+06
circular micrometer	645.16	6.451 600 0E+02
circular millimeter	0.000 645 2	6.451 600 0E-04
square caliber	0.007 854	7.853 981 6E-03
square inch [based on US, survey foot]	0.000 000 8	7.853 950 2E-07
square inch [international]	0.000 000 8	7.853 981 6E-07
square meter	<<<	5.067 074 8E-10
square microinch	785,398.16	7.853 981 6E+05
square micrometer	506.707 48	5.067 074 8E+02
square micron	506.707 48	5.067 074 8E+02
square mil	0.785 398 2	7.853 981 6E-01
square thou	0.785 398 2	7.853 981 6E-01

circular millimeter <area>

circular inch [based on US, survey foot]	0.001 55	1.549 996 9E-03
circular inch [international]	0.001 55	1.550 003 1E-03
circular mil	1,550.003 1	1.550 003 1E+03
square caliber	12.173 696	1.217 369 6E+01
square centimeter	0.007 854	7.853 981 6E-03
square inch [based on US, survey foot]	0.001 217 4	1.217 364 7E-03
square inch [international]	0.001 217 4	1.217 369 6E-03
square microinch	>>>	1.217 369 6E+09
square micron	785,398.16	7.853 981 6E+05
square mil	0.785 398 2	7.853 981 6E-01
square millimeter	0.785 398 2	7.853 981 6E-01
square thou	1,217.369 6	1.217 369 6E+03

clausius <specific heat>

Btu/°F [I.T.]	2.204 622 6	2.204 622 6E+00
calorie/°C [I.T.]	1,000	1.000 000 0E+03
joule/kelvin	4,186.8	4.186 800 0E+03
kilocalorie/°C [I.T.]	1	1.000 000 0E+00

clima [Rome, ancient] <area, special - see page 29>

square meter	315	3.150 000 0E+02

clo [for clothing] <thermal insulation coefficient>

square meter °C/watt	0.155	1.550 000 0E-01
square meter kelvin/watt	0.155	1.550 000 0E-01

	Standard	Scientific
tog [for clothing]	1.55	1.550 000 0E+00
clove [UK]	\<mass, special - see page 29\>	
gram	3,628.739	3.628 739 0E+03
clusec		\<power\>
watt	0.000 001 3	1.333 223 7E-06
coal equivalent kilogram [UN, standard]		\<energy\>
Btu [I.T.]	27,778.245	2.777 824 5E+04
calorie [kilogram, I.T.]	7,000	7.000 000 0E+03
cheval vapeur heure [France]	11.068 68	1.106 868 0E+01
coal equivalent metric ton [UN, standard]	0.001	1.000 000 0E-03
dekawatthour	814.1	8.141 000 0E+02
foot pound-force	>>>	2.161 617 6E+07
foot poundal	>>>	6.954 799 1E+08
frigorie [France]	7,001.672 3	7.001 672 3E+03
hectowatthour	81.41	8.141 000 0E+01
horsepower hour	10.917 261	1.091 726 1E+01
horsepower hour [metric]	11.068 68	1.106 868 0E+01
joule	>>>	2.930 760 0E+07
kilocalorie [I.T.]	7,000	7.000 000 0E+03
kilogram calorie [15 °C, NBS, 1939]	7,001.672 3	7.001 672 3E+03
kilowatthour	8.141	8.141 000 0E+00
megawatthour	0.008 141	8.141 000 0E-03
myriawatthour	0.814 1	8.141 000 0E-01
pferdestarkenstunde [Germany]	11.068 68	1.106 868 0E+01
therm [EEC]	0.277 782 5	2.777 824 5E-01
therm [US]	0.277 848 8	2.778 487 8E-01
thermie [France]	7.001 672 3	7.001 672 3E+00
ton [metric, explosive energy]	0.007 004 7	7.004 684 5E-03
watthour	8,141	8.141 000 0E+03
coal equivalent metric ton [UN, standard]		\<energy\>
Btu [I.T.]	>>>	2.777 824 5E+07
calorie [I.T.]	>>>	7.000 000 0E+09
calorie [kilogram, I.T.]	7,000,000	7.000 000 0E+06
cheval vapeur heure [France]	11,068.68	1.106 868 0E+04
coal equivalent kilogram [UN, standard]	1,000	1.000 000 0E+03
dekawatthour	814,100	8.141 000 0E+05
gigawatthour	0.008 141	8.141 000 0E-03
gram [atomic physics, eq. energy]	0.000 326 1	3.260 910 3E-04
hectowatthour	81,410	8.141 000 0E+04
horsepower hour	10,917.261	1.091 726 1E+04
horsepower hour [metric]	11,068.68	1.106 868 0E+04
joule	>>>	2.930 760 0E+10
kiloton [metric, explosive energy]	0.007 004 7	7.004 684 5E-03
kilowatthour	8,141	8.141 000 0E+03
megajoule	29,307.6	2.930 760 0E+04
megawatthour	8.141	8.141 000 0E+00
myriawatthour	814.1	8.141 000 0E+02
pferdestarkenstunde [Germany]	11,068.68	1.106 868 0E+04
therm [EEC]	277.782 45	2.777 824 5E+02
therm [US]	277.848 78	2.778 487 8E+02
thermie [France]	7,001.672 3	7.001 672 3E+03
ton [metric, explosive energy]	7.004 684 5	7.004 684 5E+00
watthour	8,141,000	8.141 000 0E+06
cob [Israel]	\<volume, special - see page 29\>	
liter	2.22	2.220 000 0E+00
coccio [Italy]	\<mass, special - see page 29\>	
gram	0.55	5.500 000 0E-01
cochliarion [Greece, ancient]	\<volume, special - see page 29\>	
milliliter	4.9	4.900 000 0E+00
codo [Spain, wine]	\<volume, special - see page 29\>	
liter	0.126 04	1.260 400 0E-01

Convert From Convert To	Standard	<Type of Unit> Scientific
codo [Spain]		<length, special - see page 29>
meter	0.418	4.180 000 0E−01
cojang [Sumatra]		<mass, special - see page 29>
kilogram	2,952.6	2.952 600 0E+03
cola [Syria]		<mass, special - see page 29>
kilogram	66.496	6.649 600 0E+01
collothum [Iran]		<volume, special - see page 29>
liter	8.23	8.230 000 0E+00
commerzlast [Germany]		<mass, special - see page 29>
kilogram	2,422.296	2.422 296 0E+03
cong [Vietnam]		<area, special - see page 29>
square meter	1,000	1.000 000 0E+03
conge [Greece, ancient]		<volume, special - see page 29>
liter	3.51	3.510 000 0E+00
congius [Rome, ancient]		<volume, special - see page 29>
liter	3.24	3.240 000 0E+00
coomb [UK, dry]		<volume, special - see page 29>
hectoliter	1.454 707	1.454 707 0E+00
copa [Spain]		<volume, special - see page 29>
liter	0.126	1.260 000 0E−01
cor [Hebrew, ancient]		<volume, special - see page 29>
liter	220	2.200 000 0E+02
cord [firewood]		<volume>
barrel [US, dry]	31.346 939	3.134 693 9E+01
board foot	1,536	1.536 000 0E+03
bushel [US, dry]	102.856 19	1.028 561 9E+02
cord foot [timber]	8	8.000 000 0E+00
cubic foot	128	1.280 000 0E+02
cubic inch	221,184	2.211 840 0E+05
cubic meter	3.624 556 4	3.624 556 4E+00
cubic yard	4.740 740 7	4.740 740 7E+00
English water ton [UK]	3.559 334 5	3.559 334 5E+00
freight ton	3.2	3.200 000 0E+00
measurement ton	3.2	3.200 000 0E+00
ocean ton	3.2	3.200 000 0E+00
register ton	1.28	1.280 000 0E+00
shipping ton	3.2	3.200 000 0E+00
stere	3.624 556 4	3.624 556 4E+00
thousand board foot	1.536	1.536 000 0E+00
cord foot [timber]		<volume>
board foot	192	1.920 000 0E+02
cord [firewood]	0.125	1.250 000 0E−01
cubic foot	16	1.600 000 0E+01
cubic inch	27,648	2.764 800 0E+04
cubic meter	0.453 069 6	4.530 695 5E−01
cubic yard	0.592 592 6	5.925 925 9E−01
freight ton	0.4	4.000 000 0E−01
measurement ton	0.4	4.000 000 0E−01
ocean ton	0.4	4.000 000 0E−01
register ton	0.16	1.600 000 0E−01
shipping ton	0.4	4.000 000 0E−01
stere	0.453 069 6	4.530 695 5E−01
thousand board foot	0.192	1.920 000 0E−01
thousand cubic foot	0.016	1.600 000 0E−02
cordel [Cuba]		<length, special - see page 29>
meter	20.352	2.035 200 0E+01
cordel [Paraguay]		<length, special - see page 29>
meter	69.88	6.988 000 0E+01

| Convert From | | <Type of Unit> |
Convert To	Standard	Scientific

cordel cuadrado [Cuba] — <area, special – see page 29>
square meter -------- 414.2 ---- 4.142 000 0E+02

coss [India] — <length, special – see page 29>
meter -------- 3,657.6 ---- 3.657 600 0E+03

cotyla [Greece, ancient] — <volume, special – see page 29>
liter -------- 0.273 ---- 2.730 000 0E-01

coudee [Israel] — <length, special – see page 29>
meter -------- 0.446 5 ---- 4.465 000 0E-01

coulomb — <electric charge>
abcoulomb -------- 0.1 ---- 1.000 000 0E-01
ampere hour -------- 0.000 277 8 ---- 2.777 777 8E-04
ampere minute -------- 0.016 666 7 ---- 1.666 666 7E-02
ampere second -------- 1 ---- 1.000 000 0E+00
coulomb [international] -------- 1.000 15 ---- 1.000 150 0E+00
electromagnetic unit of charge [cgs system] -------- 0.1 ---- 1.000 000 0E-01
electron charge -------- >>> 6.241 506 4E+18
electrostatic unit of charge [cgs system] -------- >>> 2.997 924 6E+09
elementary charge -------- >>> 6.241 506 4E+18
farad volt -------- 1 ---- 1.000 000 0E+00
faraday [based on carbon-12] -------- 0.000 010 4 ---- 1.036 427 2E-05
faraday [chemical] -------- 0.000 010 4 ---- 1.036 315 6E-05
faraday [physical] -------- 0.000 010 4 ---- 1.036 034 3E-05
franklin -------- >>> 2.997 924 6E+09
gaussian electric charge -------- >>> 2.997 924 6E+09
statcoulomb -------- >>> 2.997 924 6E+09

coulomb [international] — <electric charge>
abcoulomb -------- 0.099 985 ---- 9.998 500 0E-02
ampere second -------- 0.999 85 ---- 9.998 500 0E-01
coulomb -------- 0.999 85 ---- 9.998 500 0E-01
electromagnetic unit of charge [cgs system] -------- 0.099 985 ---- 9.998 500 0E-02
farad volt -------- 0.999 85 ---- 9.998 500 0E-01

coulomb centimeter — <electric dipole moment>
abcoulomb centimeter -------- 0.1 ---- 1.000 000 0E-01
coulomb meter -------- 0.01 ---- 1.000 000 0E-02
millicoulomb meter -------- 10 ---- 1.000 000 0E+01

coulomb meter — <electric dipole moment>
abcoulomb centimeter -------- 10 ---- 1.000 000 0E+01
ampere second meter -------- 1 ---- 1.000 000 0E+00
debye unit -------- >>> 2.997 924 6E+29
farad volt meter -------- 1 ---- 1.000 000 0E+00
franklin centimeter -------- >>> 2.997 924 6E+11
statcoulomb centimeter -------- >>> 2.997 924 6E+11

coulomb millimeter — <electric dipole moment>
abcoulomb centimeter -------- 0.01 ---- 1.000 000 0E-02
coulomb meter -------- 0.001 ---- 1.000 000 0E-03
statcoulomb centimeter -------- >>> 2.997 924 6E+08

coulomb square centimeter/volt — <electric polarizability>
coulomb square meter/volt -------- 0.000 1 ---- 1.000 000 0E-04

coulomb square meter/volt — <electric polarizability>
farad square meter -------- 1 ---- 1.000 000 0E+00

coulomb/centimeter — <electric dipole moment/unit area>
coulomb/meter -------- 100 ---- 1.000 000 0E+02

coulomb/cubic centimeter — <electric charge density>
abcoulomb/cubic centimeter -------- 0.1 ---- 1.000 000 0E-01
coulomb/cubic meter -------- 1,000,000 ---- 1.000 000 0E+06
franklin/cubic centimeter -------- >>> 2.997 924 6E+09
statcoulomb/cubic centimeter -------- >>> 2.997 924 6E+09

coulomb/cubic meter — <electric charge density>
ampere second/cubic meter -------- 1 ---- 1.000 000 0E+00
franklin/cubic centimeter -------- 2,997.924 58 ---- 2.997 924 6E+03

Convert From		<Type of Unit>
Convert To	Standard	Scientific

| statcoulomb/cubic centimeter | 2,997.924 58 | 2.997 924 6E+03 |

coulomb/cubic millimeter   **<electric charge density>**

coulomb/cubic meter	>>>	1.000 000 0E+09
gigacoulomb/cubic meter	1	1.000 000 0E+00
statcoulomb/cubic centimeter	>>>	2.997 924 6E+12

coulomb/farad   **<electric potential>**

ampere ohm	1	1.000 000 0E+00
joule/coulomb	1	1.000 000 0E+00
statvolt	0.003 335 6	3.335 641 0E-03
volt	1	1.000 000 0E+00
watt/ampere	1	1.000 000 0E+00

coulomb/farad meter   **<electric field strength>**

joule/coulomb meter	1	1.000 000 0E+00
newton/coulomb	1	1.000 000 0E+00
volt/inch	0.025 4	2.540 000 0E-02
volt/meter	1	1.000 000 0E+00

coulomb/kilogram   **<exposure, gamma and X rays>**

ampere second/kilogram	1	1.000 000 0E+00
ampere square meter/joule second	1	1.000 000 0E+00
roentgen	3,875.969	3.875 969 0E+03
röntgen	3,875.969	3.875 969 0E+03

coulomb/kilogram second   **<exposure rate, gamma and X rays>**

ampere/kilogram	1	1.000 000 0E+00
roentgen/second	3,875.969	3.875 969 0E+03
röntgen/second	3,875.969	3.875 969 0E+03

coulomb/meter   **<electric dipole moment/unit area>**

abcoulomb/centimeter	0.001	1.000 000 0E-03
ampere hour/meter	0.000 277 8	2.777 777 8E-04
ampere second/meter	1	1.000 000 0E+00
coulomb/centimeter	0.01	1.000 000 0E-02
coulomb/millimeter	0.001	1.000 000 0E-03
debye unit/square angstrom	>>>	2.997 924 6E+09
farad volt/meter	1	1.000 000 0E+00
franklin/centimeter	>>>	2.997 924 6E+07
helmholtz	>>>	2.997 924 6E+09
kilocoulomb/meter	0.001	1.000 000 0E-03
millicoulomb/meter	1,000	1.000 000 0E+03
statcoulomb/centimeter	>>>	2.997 924 6E+07

coulomb/millimeter   **<electric dipole moment/unit area>**

| abcoulomb/centimeter | 1 | 1.000 000 0E+00 |
| coulomb/meter | 1,000 | 1.000 000 0E+03 |

coulomb/second   **<electric current>**

ampere	1	1.000 000 0E+00
biot	0.1	1.000 000 0E-01
franklin/second	>>>	2.997 924 6E+09
gilbert	1.256 637 1	1.256 637 1E+00
volt/ohm	1	1.000 000 0E+00
watt/volt	1	1.000 000 0E+00

coulomb/square centimeter   **<electric flux density>**

abcoulomb/square centimeter	0.1	1.000 000 0E-01
ampere hour/square meter	2.777 777 8	2.777 777 8E+00
coulomb/square inch	6.451 6	6.451 600 0E+00
coulomb/square meter	10,000	1.000 000 0E+04
franklin/square centimeter	>>>	2.997 924 6E+09
statcoulomb/square centimeter	>>>	2.997 924 6E+09

coulomb/square inch   **<electric flux density>**

abcoulomb/square centimeter	0.015 5	1.550 003 1E-02
ampere hour/square meter	0.430 556 4	4.305 564 2E-01
coulomb/square meter	1,550.003 1	1.550 003 1E+03
franklin/square centimeter	>>>	4.646 792 4E+08
statcoulomb/square centimeter	>>>	4.646 792 4E+08

Convert From		<Type of Unit>
Convert To	Standard	Scientific

coulomb/square meter   \<electric flux density\>

	Standard	Scientific
abcoulomb/square centimeter	0.000 01	1.000 000 0E−05
ampere hour/square meter	0.000 277 8	2.777 777 8E−04
ampere second/square meter	1	1.000 000 0E+00
coulomb/square inch	0.000 645 2	6.451 600 0E−04
franklin/square centimeter	299,792.458	2.997 924 6E+05
statcoulomb/square centimeter	299,792.458	2.997 924 6E+05

coulomb/square millimeter   \<electric flux density\>

	Standard	Scientific
abcoulomb/square centimeter	10	1.000 000 0E+01
ampere hour/square meter	277.777 778	2.777 777 8E+02
coulomb/square inch	645.16	6.451 600 0E+02
coulomb/square meter	1,000,000	1.000 000 0E+06
franklin/square centimeter	>>>	2.997 924 6E+11
statcoulomb/square centimeter	>>>	2.997 924 6E+11

coulomb/volt   \<capacitance\>

	Standard	Scientific
abfarad	<<<	1.000 000 0E−09
ampere second/volt	1	1.000 000 0E+00
farad	1	1.000 000 0E+00
second/ohm	1	1.000 000 0E+00
statfarad	>>>	8.987 551 8E+11

coulomb/volt meter   \<electric permittivity\>

	Standard	Scientific
abfarad/centimeter	0.000 000 1	1.000 000 0E−07
farad/meter	1	1.000 000 0E+00
statfarad/centimeter	>>>	8.987 551 8E+13

couple   \<units\>

	Standard	Scientific
brace	1	1.000 000 0E+00
one	2	2.000 000 0E+00
pair	1	1.000 000 0E+00
single	2	2.000 000 0E+00
unit	2	2.000 000 0E+00

courd [Morocco]   \<area, special - see page 29\>

	Standard	Scientific
square meter	450	4.500 000 0E+02

covada [Portugal]   \<length, special - see page 29\>

	Standard	Scientific
centimeter	66	6.600 000 0E+01

covado [Brazil]   \<length, special - see page 29\>

	Standard	Scientific
meter	68.49	6.849 000 0E+01

covado [Portugal]   \<length, special - see page 29\>

	Standard	Scientific
centimeter	66	6.600 000 0E+01

covido [India]   \<length, special - see page 29\>

	Standard	Scientific
centimeter	45.72	4.572 000 0E+01

covido [Saudi Arabia, ancient]   \<length, special - see page 29\>

	Standard	Scientific
centimeter	45.7	4.570 000 0E+01

coyan [Thailand]   \<mass, special - see page 29\>

	Standard	Scientific
kilogram	1,200	1.200 000 0E+03

crinal   \<force\>

	Standard	Scientific
decinewton	1	1.000 000 0E+00
dekagram-force	1.019 716 2	1.019 716 2E+00
dyne	10,000	1.000 000 0E+04
grain-force	157.366 26	1.573 662 6E+02
gram-force	10.197 162 1	1.019 716 2E+01
newton	0.1	1.000 000 0E−01
ounce-force	0.359 694 3	3.596 943 1E−01
pond	10.197 162 1	1.019 716 2E+01
pound-force	0.022 480 9	2.248 089 4E−02
poundal	0.723 301 4	7.233 013 9E−01

crith   \<mass\>

	Standard	Scientific
kilogram	0.000 089 9	8.988 500 0E−05

crocodile   \<electric potential\>

	Standard	Scientific
megavolt	1	1.000 000 0E+00

Convert From		<Type of Unit>
Convert To	Standard	Scientific

volt --- 1,000,000 --- 1.000 000 0E+06

crosh [Bangladesh]   **<length, special - see page 29>**
  kilometer --- 3.218 --- 3.218 000 0E+00

crown [Switzerland] **<mass, special - see page 29>**
  gram --- 3.37 --- 3.370 000 0E+00

cuada [Argentina] **<length, special - see page 29>**
  meter --- 129.9 --- 1.299 000 0E+02

cuadra [Argentina] **<length, special - see page 29>**
  meter --- 130 --- 1.300 000 0E+02

cuadra [Chile] **<length, special - see page 29>**
  meter -- 125.39 --- 1.253 900 0E+02

cuadra [Colombia] **<length, special - see page 29>**
  meter ---80 --- 8.000 000 0E+01

cuadra [Ecuador] **<length, special - see page 29>**
  meter ---84 --- 8.400 000 0E+01

cuadra [El Salvador] **<area, special - see page 29>**
  square meter -- 70.258 --- 7.025 800 0E+01

cuadra [Paraguay] **<length, special - see page 29>**
  meter --- 86.66 --- 8.666 000 0E+01

cuadra [Peru] **<area, special - see page 29>**
  hectare -- 1 --- 1.000 000 0E+00

cuadra [Spain] **<length, special - see page 29>**
  meter --- 125.4 --- 1.254 000 0E+02

cuadra [Uruguay] **<length, special - see page 29>**
  meter --- 85.9 --- 8.590 000 0E+01

cuadra cuadrada [Chile] **<area, special - see page 29>**
  hectare -- 1.572 5 --- 1.572 500 0E+00

cuadra cuadrada [Ecuador] **<area, special - see page 29>**
  are --- 69.87 --- 6.987 000 0E+01

cuadra cuadrada [Paraguay] **<area, special - see page 29>**
  are --- 75.1 --- 7.510 000 0E+01

cuadra cuadrada [Uruguay] **<area, special - see page 29>**
  square meter -- 7,380 --- 7.380 000 0E+03

cuadro [Venezuela] **<area, special - see page 29>**
  hectare --- 0.64 --- 6.400 000 0E-01

cuarta [Argentina] **<volume, special - see page 29>**
  liter -- 0.594 --- 5.940 000 0E-01

cuarta [Brazil] **<area, special - see page 29>**
  hectare --- 0.371 --- 3.710 000 0E-01

cuarta [Colombia] **<length, special - see page 29>**
  centimeter ---20 --- 2.000 000 0E+01

cuarta [Nicaragua] **<volume, special - see page 29>**
  milliliter -- 167 --- 1.670 000 0E+02

cuarta [Paraguay] **<volume, special - see page 29>**
  liter -- 0.757 --- 7.570 000 0E-01

cuarter [Argentina] **<volume, special - see page 29>**
  liter -- 114 --- 1.140 000 0E+02

cuarteron [Mexico] **<volume, special - see page 29>**
  liter ---25 --- 2.500 000 0E+01

cuarteron [Spain, oil] **<volume, special - see page 29>**
  liter -- 0.126 --- 1.260 000 0E-01

cuartilla [Argentina] **<volume, special - see page 29>**
  liter --- 34.3 --- 3.430 000 0E+01

cuartilla [Ecuador] **<mass, special - see page 29>**
  kilogram ---23 --- 2.300 000 0E+01

cuartilla [Spain, dry]		<volume, special - see page 29>
liter	13.875	1.387 500 0E+01
cuartilla [Spain, liquid]		<volume, special - see page 29>
liter	4.03	4.030 000 0E+00
cuartilla [Spain, oil]		<volume, special - see page 29>
liter	3.140 8	3.140 800 0E+00
cuartilla [Spain, wine]		<volume, special - see page 29>
liter	4.033 3	4.033 300 0E+00
cuartilla [Venezuela]		<mass, special - see page 29>
kilogram	2	2.000 000 0E+00
cuartilla [Venezuela]		<area, special - see page 29>
square meter	100	1.000 000 0E+02
cuartillo [Costa Rica]		<volume, special - see page 29>
liter	4.25	4.250 000 0E+00
cuartillo [Cuba]		<volume, special - see page 29>
liter	0.86	8.600 000 0E-01
cuartillo [Mexico, dry]		<volume, special - see page 29>
liter	1.891 8	1.891 800 0E+00
cuartillo [Mexico, liquid]		<volume, special - see page 29>
liter	0.456 264	4.562 640 0E-01
cuartillo [Mexico, oil]		<volume, special - see page 29>
liter	0.506 162	5.061 620 0E-01
cuartillo [Spain, dry]		<volume, special - see page 29>
liter	1.156 3	1.156 300 0E+00
cuartillo [Spain, liquid]		<volume, special - see page 29>
liter	0.504	5.040 000 0E-01
cuartillo habanero [Cuba]		<volume, special - see page 29>
liter	0.86	8.600 000 0E-01
cuarto [Colombia]		<length, special - see page 29>
centimeter	20	2.000 000 0E+01
cubem		<volume>
acre foot	3,379,200	3.379 200 0E+06
billion cubic foot	147.197 95	1.471 979 5E+02
cubic foot	>>>	1.471 979 5E+11
cubic kilometer	4.168 181 8	4.168 181 8E+00
cubic meter	>>>	4.168 181 8E+09
cubic mile	1	1.000 000 0E+00
cubic yard	>>>	5.451 776 0E+09
gallon [UK, dry or liquid]	>>>	9.168 718 2E+11
gallon [US, liquid]	>>>	1.101 117 1E+12
hectare meter	416,818.18	4.168 181 8E+05
liter	>>>	4.168 181 8E+12
million acre foot	3.379 2	3.379 200 0E+00
stere	>>>	4.168 181 8E+09
teraliter	4.168 181 8	4.168 181 8E+00
trillion cubic foot	0.147 198	1.471 979 5E-01
cubem/day		<flow rate, volume basis>
acre foot/minute	2,346.666 67	2.346 666 7E+03
acre foot/minute [US, survey]	2,346.652 59	2.346 652 6E+03
acre foot/second	39.111 111 1	3.911 111 1E+01
acre foot/second [US, survey]	39.110 876 4	3.911 087 6E+01
acre inch/second	469.333 333	4.693 333 3E+02
billion cubic foot/day	147.197 952	1.471 979 5E+02
billion cubic foot/hour	6.133 248	6.133 248 0E+00
billion cubic foot/minute	0.102 220 8	1.022 208 0E-01
billion cubic foot/second	0.001 703 7	1.703 680 0E-03
cubem/hour	0.041 666 7	4.166 666 7E-02
cubic dekameter/minute	2,894.570 71	2.894 570 7E+03
cubic dekameter/second	48.242 845 2	4.824 284 5E+01

	Standard	Scientific
cubic kilometer/day	4.168 181 8	4.168 181 8E+00
cubic kilometer/hour	0.173 674 2	1.736 742 4E−01
cubic kilometer/minute	0.002 894 6	2.894 570 7E−03
cubic meter/second	48,242.845 2	4.824 284 5E+04
cubic mile/day	1	1.000 000 0E+00
cubic mile/hour	0.041 666 7	4.166 666 7E−02
hectare meter/minute	289.457 071	2.894 570 7E+02
hectare meter/second	4.824 284 5	4.824 284 5E+00
million acre foot/day	3.379 2	3.379 200 0E+00
million acre foot/hour	0.140 8	1.408 000 0E−01
million acre foot/minute	0.002 346 7	2.346 666 7E−03
thousand cubic foot/second	1,703.68	1.703 680 0E+03
trillion cubic foot/day	0.147 198	1.471 979 5E−01
trillion cubic foot/hour	0.006 133 2	6.133 248 0E−03
cubem/hour		**\<flow rate, volume basis\>**
acre foot/minute	56,320	5.632 000 0E+04
acre foot/minute [US, survey]	56,319.662 1	5.631 966 2E+04
acre foot/second	938.666 667	9.386 666 7E+02
acre foot/second [US, survey]	938.661 035	9.386 610 4E+02
acre inch/second	11,264	1.126 400 0E+04
billion cubic foot/day	147.197 952	1.471 979 5E+02
billion cubic foot/minute	2.453 299 2	2.453 299 2E+00
billion cubic foot/second	0.040 888 3	4.088 832 0E−02
cubem/day	24	2.400 000 0E+01
cubem/minute	0.016 666 7	1.666 666 7E−02
cubem/second	0.000 277 8	2.777 777 8E−04
cubic dekameter/second	69,469.697 1	6.946 969 7E+04
cubic kilometer/day	100.036 364	1.000 363 6E+02
cubic kilometer/hour	4.168 181 8	4.168 181 8E+00
cubic kilometer/minute	0.069 469 7	6.946 969 7E−02
cubic kilometer/second	0.001 157 8	1.157 828 3E−03
cubic meter/second	1,157,828.28	1.157 828 3E+06
cubic mile/day	24	2.400 000 0E+01
cubic mile/hour	1	1.000 000 0E+00
cubic mile/minute	0.016 666 7	1.666 666 7E−02
cubic mile/second	0.000 277 8	2.777 777 8E−04
hectare meter/minute	6,946.969 71	6.946 969 7E+03
hectare meter/second	115.782 828	1.157 828 3E+02
million acre foot/day	81.100 8	8.110 080 0E+01
million acre foot/hour	3.379 2	3.379 200 0E+00
million acre foot/minute	0.056 32	5.632 000 0E−02
million acre foot/second	0.000 938 7	9.386 666 7E−04
thousand cubic foot/second	40,888.32	4.088 832 0E+04
trillion cubic foot/day	3.532 750 8	3.532 750 8E+00
trillion cubic foot/hour	0.147 198	1.471 979 5E−01
trillion cubic foot/minute	0.002 453 3	2.453 299 2E−03
cubem/minute		**\<flow rate, volume basis\>**
acre foot/second	56,320	5.632 000 0E+04
acre foot/second [US, survey]	56,319.662 1	5.631 966 2E+04
billion cubic foot/minute	8,831.877 12	8.831 877 1E+03
billion cubic foot/second	147.197 952	1.471 979 5E+02
cubem/day	2.453 299 2	2.453 299 2E+00
cubem/hour	1,440	1.440 000 0E+03
cubem/second	60	6.000 000 0E+01
cubic dekameter/second	0.016 666 7	1.666 666 7E−02
cubic kilometer/day	69,469.697 1	6.946 969 7E+04
cubic kilometer/hour	6,002.181 83	6.002 181 8E+03
cubic kilometer/minute	250.090 91	2.500 909 1E+02
cubic kilometer/second	4.168 181 8	4.168 181 8E+00
cubic meter/second	0.069 469 7	6.946 969 7E−02
cubic mile/day	>>>	6.946 969 7E+07
cubic mile/hour	1,440	1.440 000 0E+03
	60	6.000 000 0E+01

Convert From		<Type of Unit>
Convert To	Standard	Scientific

	Standard	Scientific
cubic mile/minute	1	1.000 000 0E+00
cubic mile/second	0.016 666 7	1.666 666 7E−02
hectare meter/second	6,946.969 71	6.946 969 7E+03
million acre foot/day	4,866.048	4.866 048 0E+03
million acre foot/hour	202.752	2.027 520 0E+02
million acre foot/minute	3.379 2	3.379 200 0E+00
million acre foot/second	0.056 32	5.632 000 0E−02
trillion cubic foot/day	211.965 05	2.119 650 5E+02
trillion cubic foot/hour	8.831 877 1	8.831 877 1E+00
trillion cubic foot/minute	0.147 198	1.471 979 5E−01
trillion cubic foot/second	0.002 453 3	2.453 299 2E−03

cubem/second	<flow rate, volume basis>	
acre foot/second	3,379,200	3.379 200 0E+06
acre foot/second [US, survey]	3,379,179.72	3.379 179 7E+06
billion cubic foot/hour	529,912.627	5.299 126 3E+05
billion cubic foot/minute	8,831.877 12	8.831 877 1E+03
billion cubic foot/second	147.197 952	1.471 979 5E+02
cubem/day	86,400	8.640 000 0E+04
cubem/hour	3,600	3.600 000 0E+03
cubem/minute	60	6.000 000 0E+01
cubic dekameter/second	4,168,181.83	4.168 181 8E+06
cubic kilometer/day	360,130.91	3.601 309 1E+05
cubic kilometer/hour	15,005.454 6	1.500 545 5E+04
cubic kilometer/minute	250.090 91	2.500 909 1E+02
cubic kilometer/second	4.168 181 8	4.168 181 8E+00
cubic meter/second	>>>	4.168 181 8E+09
cubic mile/day	86,400	8.640 000 0E+04
cubic mile/hour	3,600	3.600 000 0E+03
cubic mile/minute	60	6.000 000 0E+01
cubic mile/second	1	1.000 000 0E+00
hectare meter/second	416,818.183	4.168 181 8E+05
million acre foot/day	291,962.88	2.919 628 8E+05
million acre foot/hour	12,165.12	1.216 512 0E+04
million acre foot/minute	202.752	2.027 520 0E+02
million acre foot/second	3.379 2	3.379 200 0E+00
trillion cubic foot/day	12,717.903	1.271 790 3E+04
trillion cubic foot/hour	529.912 63	5.299 126 3E+02
trillion cubic foot/minute	8.831 877 1	8.831 877 1E+00
trillion cubic foot/second	0.147 198	1.471 979 5E−01

cubi [Eritrea]	<length, special - see page 29>	
centimeter	32	3.200 000 0E+01

cubic archine [Russia]	<volume, special - see page 29>	
cubic meter	0.359 728 8	3.597 288 0E−01

cubic attometer		<volume>
barrel [US, liquid]	<<<	8.386 414 4E−54
cubic foot	<<<	3.531 466 7E−53
cubic meter	<<<	1.000 000 0E−54
liter	<<<	1.000 000 0E−51
stere	<<<	1.000 000 0E−54

cubic centimeter		<volume>
antel [Hebrew, ancient]	0.007 280 8	7.280 784 0E−03
barrel [US, liquid]	0.000 008 4	8.386 414 4E−06
barzina [Hebrew, ancient]	0.058 246 3	5.824 627 8E−02
bezah [Hebrew, ancient]	0.010 921 2	1.092 117 7E−02
bushel [US, dry]	0.000 028 4	2.837 759 3E−05
cubic duim [Russia]	0.061 023 7	6.102 374 4E−02
cubic foot	0.000 035 3	3.531 466 7E−05
cubic inch	0.061 023 7	6.102 374 4E−02
cubic meter	0.000 001	1.000 000 0E−06
cubic verchok [Russia]	0.011 386 4	1.138 635 7E−02
cubic yard	0.000 001 3	1.307 950 6E−06
cubic zoll [Germany]	0.069 507 2	6.950 719 4E−02

Convert From	<Type of Unit>	
Convert To	Standard	Scientific
egg [Hebrew, ancient]	0.010 921 2	1.092 117 7E-02
gallon [US, liquid]	0.000 264 2	2.641 720 5E-04
geriwa [Hebrew, ancient, dry]	0.000 075 8	7.584 698 3E-05
kapiza [Hebrew, ancient]	0.000 910 1	9.100 980 8E-04
khoinix [Greece, ancient]	0.000 927	9.269 730 6E-04
kortab [Hebrew, ancient]	0.116 492 6	1.164 925 6E-01
kubieke duim [Netherlands]	1	1.000 000 0E+00
kubieke palm [Netherlands]	0.001	1.000 000 0E-03
kuza [Hebrew, ancient, liquid]	0.000 303 4	3.033 879 3E-04
kyathys [Greece, ancient]	0.022 247 4	2.224 743 6E-02
lambda	1,000	1.000 000 0E+03
liter	0.001	1.000 000 0E-03
metarta [Hebrew, ancient]	0.000 025 3	2.528 232 8E-05
milliliter	1	1.000 000 0E+00
minim [US]	16.230 731	1.623 073 1E+01
ounce [US, liquid]	0.033 814	3.381 402 3E-02
pesikta [Hebrew, ancient, dry]	0.000 005 1	5.056 465 6E-06
pie cubica [Mexico]	0.000 045 9	4.587 997 8E-05
pint [US, dry]	0.001 816 2	1.816 166 0E-03
pint [US, liquid]	0.002 113 4	2.113 376 4E-03
pulgada cubica [Mexico]	0.079 283 3	7.928 327 9E-02
stere	0.000 001	1.000 000 0E-06
tablespoon [US, measuring]	0.067 628	6.762 804 5E-02
teaspoon [US, measuring]	0.202 884 1	2.028 841 4E-01
tuman [Hebrew, ancient]	0.003 640 4	3.640 392 3E-03
ukla [Hebrew, ancient]	0.009 101 3	9.101 309 6E-03
xeste [Hebrew, ancient]	0.001 820 2	1.820 196 2E-03
cubic centimeter atmosphere		**<energy>**
Btu [I.T.]	0.000 096	9.603 757 0E-05
calorie [I.T.]	0.024 201 1	2.420 106 0E-02
calorie [kilogram, I.T.]	0.000 024 2	2.420 106 0E-05
centigrade heat unit [I.T.]	0.000 053 4	5.335 420 5E-05
cubic foot atmosphere	0.000 035 3	3.531 466 7E-05
cubic meter atmosphere	0.000 001	1.000 000 0E-06
foot pound-force	0.074 733 5	7.473 348 5E-02
foot poundal	2.404 478 8	2.404 478 8E+00
gram calorie	0.024 206 8	2.420 684 2E-02
inch ounce-force	14.348 829	1.434 882 9E+01
inch pound-force	0.896 801 8	8.968 018 2E-01
joule	0.101 325	1.013 250 0E-01
kilogram square meter/square second	0.101 325	1.013 250 0E-01
kilopond meter	0.010 332 3	1.033 227 5E-02
liter atmosphere	0.001	1.000 000 0E-03
megaerg	1.013 25	1.013 250 0E+00
megalerg	1.013 25	1.013 250 0E+00
meter kilogram-force	0.010 332 3	1.033 227 5E-02
newton meter	0.101 325	1.013 250 0E-01
wattsecond	0.101 325	1.013 250 0E-01
cubic centimeter second/gram		**<mobility>**
cubic foot second/pound	0.016 018 5	1.601 846 3E-02
cubic inch second/pound	27.679 905	2.767 990 5E+01
square meter/pascal second	0.001	1.000 000 0E-03
cubic centimeter/calorie [-/ I.T.]	**<specific fuel consumption, volume basis>**	
cubic foot/Btu [-/ I.T.]	0.008 899 1	8.899 146 3E-03
cubic meter/joule	0.000 000 2	2.388 459 0E-07
gallon/horsepower hour [US, liquid]	169.383 55	1.693 835 5E+02
cubic centimeter/day		**<flow rate, volume basis>**
centiliter/day	0.1	1.000 000 0E-01
centiliter/hour	0.004 166 7	4.166 666 7E-03
cubic centimeter/hour	0.041 666 7	4.166 666 7E-02
cubic centimeter/minute	0.000 694 4	6.944 444 4E-04
cubic decimeter/day	0.001	1.000 000 0E-03

Convert From Convert To	Standard	\<Type of Unit\> Scientific

cubic inch/day

Convert To	Standard	Scientific
cubic inch/day	0.061 023 7	6.102 374 4E-02
cubic inch/hour	0.002 542 7	2.542 656 0E-03
cubic meter/second	<<<	1.157 407 4E-11
cubic millimeter/day	1,000	1.000 000 0E+03
cubic millimeter/hour	41.666 666 7	4.166 666 7E+01
cubic millimeter/minute	0.694 444 4	6.944 444 4E-01
cubic millimeter/second	0.011 574 1	1.157 407 4E-02
deciliter/day	0.01	1.000 000 0E-02
lambda/day	1,000	1.000 000 0E+03
lambda/hour	41.666 666 7	4.166 666 7E+01
lambda/minute	0.694 444 4	6.944 444 4E-01
lambda/second	0.011 574 1	1.157 407 4E-02
liter/day	0.001	1.000 000 0E-03
liter/day [pre-1964]	0.001	9.999 720 0E-04
milliliter/day	1	1.000 000 0E+00
milliliter/hour	0.041 666 7	4.166 666 7E-02
ounce/day [UK, liquid]	0.035 195 1	3.519 508 0E-02
ounce/day [US, liquid]	0.033 814	3.381 402 3E-02
ounce/hour [UK, liquid]	0.001 466 5	1.466 461 7E-03
ounce/hour [US, liquid]	0.001 408 9	1.408 917 6E-03
stere/day	0.000 000 1	1.000 000 0E-06

cubic centimeter/gram   \<specific volume\>

Convert To	Standard	Scientific
cubic foot/pound	0.016 018 5	1.601 846 3E-02
cubic inch/pound	27.679 905	2.767 990 5E+01
cubic meter/kilogram	0.001	1.000 000 0E-03

cubic centimeter/hour   \<flow rate, volume basis\>

Convert To	Standard	Scientific
centiliter/day	2.4	2.400 000 0E+00
centiliter/hour	0.1	1.000 000 0E-01
centiliter/minute	0.001 666 7	1.666 666 7E-03
cubic centimeter/day	24	2.400 000 0E+01
cubic centimeter/minute	0.016 666 7	1.666 666 7E-02
cubic decimeter/day	0.024	2.400 000 0E-02
cubic decimeter/hour	0.001	1.000 000 0E-03
cubic inch/day	1.464 569 9	1.464 569 9E+00
cubic inch/hour	0.061 023 7	6.102 374 4E-02
cubic inch/minute	0.001 017 1	1.017 062 4E-03
cubic meter/second	<<<	2.777 777 8E-10
cubic millimeter/hour	1,000	1.000 000 0E+03
cubic millimeter/minute	16.666 666 7	1.666 666 7E+01
cubic millimeter/second	0.277 777 8	2.777 777 8E-01
deciliter/day	0.24	2.400 000 0E-01
deciliter/hour	0.01	1.000 000 0E-02
dekaliter/day	0.002 4	2.400 000 0E-03
gallon/day [UK]	0.005 279 3	5.279 262 0E-03
gallon/day [US, liquid]	0.006 340 1	6.340 129 3E-03
lambda/hour	1,000	1.000 000 0E+03
lambda/minute	16.666 666 7	1.666 666 7E+01
lambda/second	0.277 777 8	2.777 777 8E-01
liter/day	0.024	2.400 000 0E-02
liter/day [pre-1964]	0.023 999 3	2.399 932 8E-02
liter/hour	0.001	1.000 000 0E-03
liter/hour [pre-1964]	0.001	9.999 720 0E-04
milliliter/day	24	2.400 000 0E+01
milliliter/hour	1	1.000 000 0E+00
milliliter/minute	0.016 666 7	1.666 666 7E-02
ounce/day [UK, liquid]	0.844 681 9	8.446 819 1E-01
ounce/day [US, liquid]	0.811 536 5	8.115 365 4E-01
ounce/hour [UK, liquid]	0.035 195 1	3.519 508 0E-02
ounce/hour [US, liquid]	0.033 814	3.381 402 3E-02

cubic centimeter/minute   \<flow rate, volume basis\>

Convert To	Standard	Scientific
barrel/day [US, liquid]	0.012 076 4	1.207 643 7E-02
centiliter/hour	6	6.000 000 0E+00
cubic centimeter/hour	60	6.000 000 0E+01

Convert From	<Type of Unit>	
Convert To	Standard	Scientific

cubic decimeter/day	1.44	1.440 000 0E+00
cubic foot/day	0.050 853 1	5.085 312 0E-02
cubic inch/day	87.874 191 5	8.787 419 1E+01
cubic inch/hour	3.661 424 7	3.661 424 7E+00
cubic meter/second	<<<	1.666 666 7E-08
cubic millimeter/second	16.666 666 7	1.666 666 7E+01
deciliter/day	14.4	1.440 000 0E+01
dekaliter/day	0.144	1.440 000 0E-01
gallon/day [UK]	0.316 755 7	3.167 557 2E-01
gallon/day [US, liquid]	0.380 407 8	3.804 077 6E-01
hectoliter/day	0.014 4	1.440 000 0E-02
lambda/second	16.666 666 7	1.666 666 7E+01
liter/day	1.44	1.440 000 0E+00
liter/day [pre-1964]	1.439 959 7	1.439 959 7E+00
milliliter/hour	60	6.000 000 0E+01
milliliter/minute	1	1.000 000 0E+00
ounce/hour [UK, liquid]	2.111 704 8	2.111 704 8E+00
ounce/hour [US, liquid]	2.028 841 4	2.028 841 4E+00

cubic centimeter/mole	<molar volume>	
cubic meter/mole	0.000 001	1.000 000 0E-06
liter/mole	0.001	1.000 000 0E-03

cubic centimeter/second	<flow rate, volume basis>	
barrel/day [UK]	0.527 926 2	5.279 262 0E-01
barrel/day [US, federal]	0.736 273 1	7.362 730 8E-01
barrel/day [US, liquid]	0.724 586 2	7.245 862 0E-01
barrel/day [US, petroleum]	0.543 439 7	5.434 396 5E-01
centiliter/minute	6	6.000 000 0E+00
centiliter/second	0.1	1.000 000 0E-01
cubic centimeter/minute	60	6.000 000 0E+01
cubic decimeter/day	86.4	8.640 000 0E+01
cubic decimeter/hour	3.6	3.600 000 0E+00
cubic foot/day	3.051 187 2	3.051 187 2E+00
cubic foot/hour	0.127 132 8	1.271 328 0E-01
cubic inch/minute	3.661 424 7	3.661 424 7E+00
cubic meter/second	0.000 001	1.000 000 0E-06
cubic yard/day	0.113 006 9	1.130 069 3E-01
deciliter/hour	36	3.600 000 0E+01
deciliter/minute	0.6	6.000 000 0E-01
dekaliter/day	8.64	8.640 000 0E+00
dekaliter/hour	0.36	3.600 000 0E-01
gallon/day [UK]	19.005 343 1	1.900 534 3E+01
gallon/day [US, liquid]	22.824 465 3	2.282 446 5E+01
gallon/hour [UK]	0.791 889 3	7.918 892 9E-01
gallon/hour [US, liquid]	0.951 019 4	9.510 193 9E-01
hectoliter/day	0.864	8.640 000 0E-01
liter/day	86.4	8.640 000 0E+01
liter/day [pre-1964]	86.397 580 9	8.639 758 1E+01
liter/hour	3.6	3.600 000 0E+00
liter/hour [pre-1964]	3.599 899 2	3.599 899 2E+00
milliliter/minute	60	6.000 000 0E+01
milliliter/second	1	1.000 000 0E+00
ounce/minute [UK, liquid]	2.111 704 8	2.111 704 8E+00
ounce/minute [US, liquid]	2.028 841 4	2.028 841 4E+00

cubic cubit [Egypt, ancient]	<volume, special - see page 29>	
cubic meter	0.144	1.440 000 0E-01

cubic decimeter	<volume>	
barrel [US, dry]	0.008 648 5	8.648 489 0E-03
barrel [US, liquid]	0.008 386 4	8.386 414 4E-03
bushel [US, dry]	0.028 377 6	2.837 759 3E-02
cubic fod [Denmark]	0.032 345 7	3.234 571 1E-02
cubic foot	0.035 314 7	3.531 466 7E-02
cubic gareh [Iran]	1	1.000 000 0E+00

	Standard	Scientific
cubic inch	61.023 744	6.102 374 4E+01
cubic meter	0.001	1.000 000 0E−03
cubic yard	0.001 308	1.307 950 6E−03
cup [Canada, measuring]	4.399 385	4.399 385 0E+00
cup [US, measuring]	4.226 752 8	4.226 752 8E+00
gallon [UK, dry or liquid]	0.219 969 3	2.199 692 5E−01
gallon [US, dry]	0.227 020 8	2.270 207 5E−01
gallon [US, liquid]	0.264 172 1	2.641 720 5E−01
gill [UK]	7.039 015 9	7.039 015 9E+00
gill [US]	8.453 505 7	8.453 505 7E+00
jae [South Korea]	0.299 490 9	2.994 908 7E−01
liter	1	1.000 000 0E+00
ounce [UK, liquid]	35.195 08	3.519 508 0E+01
ounce [US, liquid]	33.814 023	3.381 402 3E+01
pint [UK]	1.759 754	1.759 754 0E+00
pint [US, dry]	1.816 166	1.816 166 0E+00
pint [US, liquid]	2.113 376 4	2.113 376 4E+00
pulgada maderera [Chile]	0.042 378 3	4.237 826 8E−02
quart [UK]	0.879 877	8.798 769 9E−01
quart [US, dry]	0.908 083	9.080 829 8E−01
quart [US, liquid]	1.056 688 2	1.056 688 2E+00
sai [Japan]	0.035 937 6	3.593 761 2E−02
stere	0.001	1.000 000 0E−03
cubic decimeter/day		**\<flow rate, volume basis\>**
centiliter/day	100	1.000 000 0E+02
centiliter/hour	4.166 666 7	4.166 666 7E+00
cubic centimeter/hour	41.666 666 7	4.166 666 7E+01
cubic decimeter/hour	0.041 666 7	4.166 666 7E−02
cubic foot/day	0.035 314 7	3.531 466 7E−02
cubic inch/day	61.023 744 1	6.102 374 4E+01
cubic inch/hour	2.542 656	2.542 656 0E+00
cubic meter/second	\<\<\<	1.157 407 4E−08
cubic millimeter/second	11.574 074 1	1.157 407 4E+01
deciliter/day	10	1.000 000 0E+01
dekaliter/day	0.1	1.000 000 0E−01
gallon/day [US, liquid]	0.264 172 1	2.641 720 5E−01
hectoliter/day	0.01	1.000 000 0E−02
lambda/second	11.574 074 1	1.157 407 4E+01
liter/day	1	1.000 000 0E+00
liter/day [pre-1964]	0.999 972	9.999 720 0E−01
milliliter/hour	41.666 666 7	4.166 666 7E+01
milliliter/minute	0.694 444 4	6.944 444 4E−01
ounce/day [UK, liquid]	35.195 08	3.519 508 0E+01
ounce/day [US, liquid]	33.814 023	3.381 402 3E+01
ounce/hour [UK, liquid]	1.466 461 7	1.466 461 7E+00
ounce/hour [US, liquid]	1.408 917 6	1.408 917 6E+00
stere/day	0.001	1.000 000 0E−03
cubic decimeter/hour		**\<flow rate, volume basis\>**
barrel/day [UK]	0.146 646 2	1.466 461 7E−01
barrel/day [US, federal]	0.204 520 3	2.045 203 0E−01
barrel/day [US, liquid]	0.201 273 9	2.012 739 5E−01
barrel/day [US, petroleum]	0.150 955 5	1.509 554 6E−01
centiliter/minute	1.666 666 7	1.666 666 7E+00
cubic centimeter/minute	16.666 666 7	1.666 666 7E+01
cubic centimeter/second	0.277 777 8	2.777 777 8E−01
cubic decimeter/day	24	2.400 000 0E+01
cubic foot/day	0.847 552	8.475 520 0E−01
cubic inch/hour	61.023 744 1	6.102 374 4E+01
cubic inch/minute	1.017 062 4	1.017 062 4E+00
cubic meter/second	0.000 000 3	2.777 777 8E−07
deciliter/hour	10	1.000 000 0E+01
deciliter/minute	0.166 666 7	1.666 666 7E−01
dekaliter/day	2.4	2.400 000 0E+00

Convert From Convert To	Standard	<Type of Unit> Scientific
dekaliter/hour	0.1	1.000 000 0E-01
gallon/day [UK]	5.279 262	5.279 262 0E+00
gallon/day [US, liquid]	6.340 129 3	6.340 129 3E+00
gallon/hour [UK]	0.219 969 2	2.199 692 5E-01
gallon/hour [US, liquid]	0.264 172 1	2.641 720 5E-01
hectoliter/day	0.24	2.400 000 0E-01
liter/day	24	2.400 000 0E+01
liter/day [pre-1964]	23.999 328	2.399 932 8E+01
liter/hour	1	1.000 000 0E+00
liter/hour [pre-1964]	0.999 972	9.999 720 0E-01
milliliter/minute	16.666 666 7	1.666 666 7E+01
milliliter/second	0.277 777 8	2.777 777 8E-01
ounce/hour [UK, liquid]	35.195 08	3.519 508 0E+01
ounce/hour [US, liquid]	33.814 023	3.381 402 3E+01
ounce/minute [UK, liquid]	0.586 584 7	5.865 846 6E-01
ounce/minute [US, liquid]	0.563 567 1	5.635 670 5E-01
cubic decimeter/minute		**<flow rate, volume basis>**
barrel/day [UK]	8.798 769 9	8.798 769 9E+00
barrel/day [US, federal]	12.271 217 9	1.227 121 8E+00
barrel/day [US, liquid]	12.076 436 7	1.207 643 7E+00
barrel/day [US, petroleum]	9.057 327 5	9.057 327 5E+00
centiliter/second	1.666 666 7	1.666 666 7E+00
cubic decimeter/hour	60	6.000 000 0E+01
cubic foot/hour	2.118 88	2.118 880 0E+00
cubic inch/second	1.017 062 4	1.017 062 4E+00
cubic meter/day	1.44	1.440 000 0E+00
cubic meter/second	0.000 016 7	1.666 666 7E-05
cubic yard/day	1.883 448 9	1.883 448 9E+00
deciliter/minute	10	1.000 000 0E+01
dekaliter/hour	6	6.000 000 0E+00
gallon/hour [UK]	13.198 154 9	1.319 815 5E+01
gallon/hour [US, liquid]	15.850 323 1	1.585 032 3E+01
hectoliter/day	14.4	1.440 000 0E+00
hectoliter/hour	0.6	6.000 000 0E-01
kiloliter/day	1.44	1.440 000 0E+00
liter/minute	1	1.000 000 0E+00
liter/minute [pre-1964]	0.999 972	9.999 720 0E-01
milliliter/second	16.666 666 7	1.666 666 7E+01
ounce/minute [UK, liquid]	35.195 08	3.519 508 0E+01
ounce/minute [US, liquid]	33.814 023	3.381 402 3E+01
petrograd standard/day	0.308 200 7	3.082 007 3E-01
stere/day	1.44	1.440 000 0E+00
cubic decimeter/mole		**<molar volume>**
cubic meter/mole	0.001	1.000 000 0E-03
liter/mole	1	1.000 000 0E+00
cubic decimeter/second		**<flow rate, volume basis>**
acre inch/day	0.840 547 4	8.405 474 4E-01
barrel/hour [UK]	21.996 924 8	2.199 692 5E+01
barrel/hour [US, federal]	30.678 044 8	3.067 804 5E+01
barrel/hour [US, liquid]	30.191 091 7	3.019 109 2E+01
barrel/hour [US, petroleum]	22.643 318 8	2.264 331 9E+01
cubic decimeter/minute	60	6.000 000 0E+01
cubic foot/minute	2.118 88	2.118 880 0E+00
cubic inch/second	61.023 744 1	6.102 374 4E+01
cubic meter/hour	3.6	3.600 000 0E+00
cubic meter/second	0.001	1.000 000 0E-03
cubic yard/hour	4.708 622 2	4.708 622 2E+00
deciliter/second	10	1.000 000 0E+01
dekaliter/minute	6	6.000 000 0E+00
gallon/minute [UK]	13.198 154 9	1.319 815 5E+01
gallon/minute [US, liquid]	15.850 323 1	1.585 032 3E+01
gallon/second [UK]	0.219 969 2	2.199 692 5E-01
gallon/second [US, liquid]	0.264 172 1	2.641 720 5E-01

Convert From	<Type of Unit>	
Convert To	Standard	Scientific

hectoliter/hour	36	3.600 000 0E+01
kiloliter/hour	3.6	3.600 000 0E+00
liter/second	1	1.000 000 0E+00
liter/second [pre-1964]	0.999 972	9.999 720 0E−01
petrograd standard/day	18.492 044	1.849 204 4E+01
stere/hour	3.6	3.600 000 0E+00
thousand cubic foot/day	3.051 187 2	3.051 187 2E+00

cubic dekameter   **\<volume>**

acre inch	9.728 558 3	9.728 558 3E+00
barrel [US, dry]	8,648.489 8	8.648 489 8E+03
barrel [US, liquid]	8,386.414 4	8.386 414 4E+03
bushel [US, dry]	28,377.593	2.837 759 3E+04
cubic foot	35,314.667	3.531 466 7E+04
cubic inch	>>>	6.102 374 4E+07
cubic meter	1,000	1.000 000 0E+03
cubic yard	1,307.950 6	1.307 950 6E+03
gallon [US, dry]	227,020.75	2.270 207 5E+05
gallon [US, liquid]	264,172.05	2.641 720 5E+05
hectare meter	0.1	1.000 000 0E−01
liter	1,000,000	1.000 000 0E+06
megaliter	1	1.000 000 0E+00
stere	1,000	1.000 000 0E+03
thousand cubic foot	35.314 667	3.531 466 7E+01

cubic dekameter/day   **\<flow rate, volume basis>**

acre foot/day	0.810 713 2	8.107 131 9E−01
acre foot/day [US, survey]	0.810 708 3	8.107 083 3E−01
acre inch/day	9.728 558 3	9.728 558 3E+00
barrel/minute [UK]	4.243 234	4.243 234 0E+00
barrel/minute [US, federal]	5.917 832 7	5.917 832 7E+00
barrel/minute [US, liquid]	5.823 898 9	5.823 898 9E+00
barrel/minute [US, petroleum]	4.367 924 2	4.367 924 2E+00
cubic decimeter/second	11.574 074 1	1.157 407 4E+01
cubic foot/minute	24.524 074 1	2.452 407 4E+01
cubic meter/hour	41.666 666 7	4.166 666 7E+01
cubic meter/second	0.011 574 1	1.157 407 4E−02
cubic yard/hour	54.497 942	5.449 794 2E+01
dekaliter/second	1.157 407 4	1.157 407 4E+00
gallon/second [UK]	2.545 940 4	2.545 940 4E+00
gallon/second [US, liquid]	3.057 546 9	3.057 546 9E+00
hectare meter/day	0.1	1.000 000 0E−01
hectoliter/minute	6.944 444 4	6.944 444 4E+00
kiloliter/hour	41.666 666 7	4.166 666 7E+01
liter/second	11.574 074 1	1.157 407 4E+01
liter/second [pre-1964]	11.573 75	1.157 375 0E+01
petrograd standard/hour	8.917 845 1	8.917 845 1E+00
stere/hour	41.666 667	4.166 666 7E+01
thousand cubic foot/day	35.314 667	3.531 466 7E+01
thousand cubic foot/hour	1.471 444 4	1.471 444 4E+00

cubic dekameter/hour   **\<flow rate, volume basis>**

acre foot/day	19.457 116 7	1.945 711 7E+01
acre foot/day [US, survey]	19.456 999 9	1.945 700 0E+01
acre inch/hour	9.728 558 3	9.728 558 3E+00
barrel/second [UK]	1.697 293 6	1.697 293 6E+00
barrel/second [US, federal]	2.367 133 1	2.367 133 1E+00
barrel/second [US, liquid]	2.329 559 5	2.329 559 5E+00
barrel/second [US, petroleum]	1.747 169 7	1.747 169 7E+00
cubic dekameter/day	24	2.400 000 0E+01
cubic foot/second	9.809 629 6	9.809 629 6E+00
cubic meter/minute	16.666 666 7	1.666 666 7E+01
cubic meter/second	0.277 777 8	2.777 777 8E−01
cubic yard/minute	21.799 177	2.179 917 7E+01
dekaliter/second	27.777 777 8	2.777 777 8E+01
gallon/second [UK]	61.102 569	6.110 256 9E+01

Convert From	<Type of Unit>	
Convert To	Standard	Scientific

gallon/second [US, liquid]	73.381 125 7	7.338 112 6E+01
hectare meter/day	2.4	2.400 000 0E+00
hectoliter/second	2.777 777 8	2.777 777 8E+00
kiloliter/minute	16.666 666 7	1.666 666 7E+01
liter/second	277.777 778	2.777 777 8E+02
liter/second [pre-1964]	277.77	2.777 700 0E+02
petrograd standard/second	3.567 138 1	3.567 138 1E+00
stere/minute	16.666 667	1.666 666 7E+01
thousand cubic foot/hour	35.314 667	3.531 466 7E+01

cubic dekameter/minute   \<flow rate, volume basis\>

acre foot/hour	48.642 791 6	4.864 279 2E+01
acre foot/hour [US, survey]	48.642 499 8	4.864 250 0E+01
acre foot/minute	0.810 713 2	8.107 131 9E-01
acre foot/minute [US, survey]	0.810 708 3	8.107 083 3E-01
acre foot/second	0.013 511 9	1.351 188 7E-02
acre foot/second [US, survey]	0.013 511 8	1.351 180 6E-02
acre inch/hour	583.713 5	5.837 135 0E+02
acre inch/minute	9.728 558 3	9.728 558 3E+00
acre inch/second	0.162 142 6	1.621 426 4E-01
barrel/second [UK]	101.837 615	1.018 376 2E+02
barrel/second [US, federal]	142.027 985	1.420 279 9E+02
barrel/second [US, liquid]	139.773 573	1.397 735 7E+02
barrel/second [US, petroleum]	104.830 18	1.048 301 8E+02
billion cubic foot/day	0.050 853 1	5.085 312 0E-02
cubic dekameter/hour	60	6.000 000 0E+01
cubic dekameter/second	0.016 666 7	1.666 666 7E-02
cubic meter/second	16.666 666 7	1.666 666 7E+01
cubic yard/second	21.799 177	2.179 917 7E+01
hectare meter/day	144	1.440 000 0E+02
hectare meter/hour	6	6.000 000 0E+00
hectare meter/minute	0.1	1.000 000 0E-01
hectoliter/second	166.666 667	1.666 666 7E+02
kiloliter/second	16.666 667	1.666 666 7E+01
petrograd standard/minute	214.028 28	2.140 282 8E+02
petrograd standard/second	3.567 138 1	3.567 138 1E+00
stere/second	16.666 667	1.666 666 7E+01
thousand cubic foot/minute	35.314 667	3.531 466 7E+01
thousand cubic foot/second	0.588 577 8	5.885 777 8E-01

cubic dekameter/second   \<flow rate, volume basis\>

acre foot/minute	48.642 791 6	4.864 279 2E+01
acre foot/minute [US, survey]	48.642 499 8	4.864 250 0E+01
acre foot/second	0.810 713 2	8.107 131 9E-01
acre foot/second [US, survey]	0.810 708 3	8.107 083 3E-01
acre inch/minute	583.713 5	5.837 135 0E+02
acre inch/second	9.728 558 3	9.728 558 3E+00
barrel/second [UK]	6,110.256 9	6.110 256 9E+03
barrel/second [US, federal]	8,521.679 11	8.521 679 1E+03
barrel/second [US, liquid]	8,386.414 36	8.386 414 4E+03
barrel/second [US, petroleum]	6,289.810 77	6.289 810 8E+03
billion cubic foot/day	3.051 187 2	3.051 187 2E+00
billion cubic foot/hour	0.127 132 8	1.271 328 0E-01
cubem/day	0.020 728 5	2.072 846 2E-02
cubic dekameter/minute	60	6.000 000 0E+01
cubic kilometer/day	0.086 4	8.640 000 0E-02
cubic meter/second	1,000	1.000 000 0E+03
cubic mile/day	0.020 728 5	2.072 846 2E-02
cubic yard/second	1,307.950 6	1.307 950 6E+03
hectare meter/hour	360	3.600 000 0E+02
hectare meter/minute	6	6.000 000 0E+00
hectare meter/second	0.1	1.000 000 0E-01
kiloliter/second	1,000	1.000 000 0E+03
million acre foot/day	0.070 045 6	7.004 562 0E-02
petrograd standard/second	214.028 28	2.140 282 8E+02

stere/second	1,000	1.000 000 0E+03
thousand cubic foot/second	35.314 667	3.531 466 7E+01
trillion cubic foot/day	0.003 051 2	3.051 187 2E-03

cubic duim [Russia]   <volume, special - see page 29>
cubic centimeter	16.387 064	1.638 706 4E+01

cubic exameter   <volume>
acre foot	>>>	8.107 131 9E+50
cubem	>>>	2.399 127 6E+44
cubic foot	>>>	3.531 466 7E+55
cubic meter	>>>	1.000 000 0E+54
cubic mile	>>>	2.399 127 6E+44
exaliter	>>>	1.000 000 0E+39
gallon [US, dry]	>>>	2.270 207 5E+56
gallon [US, liquid]	>>>	2.641 720 5E+56
hectare meter	>>>	1.000 000 0E+50
liter	>>>	1.000 000 0E+57
million acre foot	>>>	8.107 131 9E+44
trillion cubic foot	>>>	3.531 466 7E+43
yottaliter	>>>	1.000 000 0E+33

cubic femtometer   <volume>
cubic inch	<<<	6.102 374 4E-41
cubic meter	<<<	1.000 000 0E-45
drop [US, liquid]	<<<	1.217 304 8E-38
liter	<<<	1.000 000 0E-42
yoctoliter	<<<	1.000 000 0E-18

cubic fod [Denmark]   <volume, special - see page 29>
cubic decimeter	30.916	3.091 600 0E+01

cubic foot   <volume>
Amagat volume unit	1.263 377 9	1.263 377 9E+00
anker	0.748 052	7.480 519 5E-01
barrel [US, dry]	0.244 898	2.448 979 6E-01
barrel [US, liquid]	0.237 476 8	2.374 768 1E-01
board foot	12	1.200 000 0E+01
bushel [US, dry]	0.803 564	8.035 639 5E-01
chaldron [UK, dry]	0.021 627 9	2.162 790 1E-02
chaldron [US, dry]	0.022 321 2	2.232 122 1E-02
cord [firewood]	0.007 812 5	7.812 500 0E-03
cord foot [timber]	0.062 5	6.250 000 0E-02
cubic inch	1,728	1.728 000 0E+03
cubic meter	0.028 316 8	2.831 684 7E-02
cubic yard	0.037 037	3.703 703 7E-02
dekaliter	2.831 684 7	2.831 684 7E+00
freight ton	0.025	2.500 000 0E-02
gallon [US, dry]	6.428 511 6	6.428 511 6E+00
gallon [US, liquid]	7.480 519 5	7.480 519 5E+00
liter	28.316 847	2.831 684 7E+01
measurement ton	0.025	2.500 000 0E-02
ocean ton	0.025	2.500 000 0E-02
peck [UK]	3.114 417 7	3.114 417 7E+00
peck [US]	3.214 255 8	3.214 255 8E+00
pint [US, dry]	51.428 093	5.142 809 3E+01
pint [US, liquid]	59.844 156	5.984 415 6E+01
pound of water [at 4 °C, 101.325 kPa, using IST-90 density equation]	62.426 212	6.242 621 2E+01
pound of water [at 60 °F, 14.696 pound-force/square inch, using IST-90 density equation]	62.366 374	6.236 637 4E+01
register ton	0.01	1.000 000 0E-02
shipping ton	0.025	2.500 000 0E-02
stere	0.028 316 8	2.831 684 7E-02
Winchester wine gallon [UK]	7.480 519 5	7.480 519 5E+00

cubic foot atmosphere   <energy>
Btu [I.T.]	2.719 481 1	2.719 481 1E+00

calorie [I.T.]	685.297 72	6.852 977 2E+02
calorie [kilogram, I.T.]	0.685 297 7	6.852 977 2E−01
centigrade heat unit [I.T.]	1.510 822 8	1.510 822 8E+00
cubic centimeter atmosphere	28,316.847	2.831 684 7E+04
frigorie [France]	0.685 461 4	6.854 614 4E−01
joule	2,869.204 5	2.869 204 5E+03
kilocalorie [I.T.]	0.685 297 7	6.852 977 2E−01
kilogram calorie [15 °C, NBS, 1939]	0.685 461 4	6.854 614 4E−01
liter atmosphere	28.316 847	2.831 684 7E+01
watthour	0.797 001 2	7.970 012 4E−01

cubic foot of cement [US, dry, in bag] <mass>

kilogram	42.637 683	4.263 768 3E+01
pound	94	9.400 000 0E+01

cubic foot of liquified petroleum gas [standard] <energy>

Btu [I.T.]	2,522	2.522 000 0E+03
joule	2,660,850.9	2.660 850 9E+06

cubic foot of natural gas [standard] <energy>

joule	1,087,200	1.087 200 0E+06
kilowatthour	0.302	3.020 000 0E−01

cubic foot second/pound <mobility>

cubic centimeter second/gram	62.427 961	6.242 796 1E+01
cubic inch second/pound	1,728	1.728 000 0E+03
square meter/pascal second	0.062 428	6.242 796 1E−02

cubic foot/Btu [−/ I.T.] <specific fuel consumption, volume basis>

cubic meter/joule	0.000 026 8	2.683 919 2E−05
cubic meter/kilocalorie [−/ I.T.]	0.112 370 3	1.123 703 3E−01
gallon/horsepower hour [US, liquid]	19,033.685	1.903 368 5E+04

cubic foot/cubic foot <concentration, volume basis>

cubic foot/gallon [−/US, liquid]	0.133 680 6	1.336 805 6E−01
cubic meter/cubic meter	1	1.000 000 0E+00
gallon/cubic foot [US, liquid]	7.480 519 5	7.480 519 5E+00

cubic foot/day <flow rate, volume basis>

barrel/day [UK]	0.173 023 2	1.730 232 1E−01
barrel/day [US, federal]	0.241 307 1	2.413 070 8E−01
barrel/day [US, liquid]	0.237 476 8	2.374 768 1E−01
barrel/day [US, petroleum]	0.178 107 6	1.781 076 1E−01
centiliter/minute	1.966 447 7	1.966 447 7E+00
cubic centimeter/minute	19.664 476 8	1.966 447 7E+01
cubic centimeter/second	0.327 741 3	3.277 412 8E−01
cubic decimeter/day	28.316 846 6	2.831 684 7E+01
cubic decimeter/hour	1.179 868 6	1.179 868 6E+00
cubic inch/hour	72	7.200 000 0E+01
cubic inch/minute	1.2	1.200 000 0E+00
cubic meter/second	0.000 000 3	3.277 412 8E−07
deciliter/hour	11.798 686 1	1.179 868 6E+01
deciliter/minute	0.196 644 8	1.966 447 7E−01
dekaliter/day	2.831 684 7	2.831 684 7E+00
dekaliter/hour	0.117 986 9	1.179 868 6E−01
gallon/day [UK]	6.228 835 5	6.228 835 5E+00
gallon/day [US, liquid]	7.480 519 5	7.480 519 5E+00
gallon/hour [UK]	0.259 534 8	2.595 348 1E−01
gallon/hour [US, liquid]	0.311 688 3	3.116 883 1E−01
hectoliter/day	0.283 168 5	2.831 684 7E−01
liter/day	28.316 846 6	2.831 684 7E+01
liter/day [pre-1964]	28.316 053 7	2.831 605 4E+01
liter/hour	1.179 868 6	1.179 868 6E+00
liter/hour [pre-1964]	1.179 835 6	1.179 835 6E+00
milliliter/minute	19.664 476 8	1.966 447 7E+01
milliliter/second	0.327 741 3	3.277 412 8E−01
ounce/hour [UK, liquid]	41.525 57	4.152 557 0E+01
ounce/hour [US, liquid]	39.896 104	3.989 610 4E+01

| Convert From | <Type of Unit> | |
Convert To	Standard	Scientific
ounce/minute [UK, liquid]	0.692 092 8	6.920 928 3E-01
ounce/minute [US, liquid]	0.664 935 1	6.649 350 6E-01
cubic foot/gallon [-/US, liquid]	<concentration, volume basis>	
cubic foot/cubic foot	7.480 519 5	7.480 519 5E+00
cubic meter/cubic meter	7.480 519 5	7.480 519 5E+00
gallon/cubic foot [US, liquid]	55.958 172	5.595 817 2E+01
cubic foot/hour	<flow rate, volume basis>	
barrel/day [US, liquid]	5.699 443 4	5.699 443 4E+00
barrel/day [US, petroleum]	4.274 582 6	4.274 582 6E+00
barrel/hour [US, liquid]	0.237 476 8	2.374 768 1E-01
barrel/hour [US, petroleum]	0.178 107 6	1.781 076 1E-01
centiliter/minute	47.194 744 3	4.719 474 4E+01
cubic centimeter/second	7.865 790 7	7.865 790 7E+00
cubic decimeter/hour	28.316 846 6	2.831 684 7E+01
cubic foot/day	24	2.400 000 0E+01
cubic inch/minute	28.8	2.880 000 0E+01
cubic meter/second	0.000 007 9	7.865 790 7E-06
deciliter/minute	4.719 474 4	4.719 474 4E+00
dekaliter/day	67.960 431 9	6.796 043 2E+01
dekaliter/minute	2.831 684 7	2.831 684 7E+00
gallon/hour [US, liquid]	7.480 519 5	7.480 519 5E+00
gallon/minute [US, liquid]	0.124 675 3	1.246 753 3E-01
hectoliter/day	6.796 043 2	6.796 043 2E+00
kiloliter/day	0.679 604 3	6.796 043 2E-01
liter/hour	28.316 846 6	2.831 684 7E+01
liter/hour [pre-1964]	28.316 053 7	2.831 605 4E+01
milliliter/second	7.865 790 7	7.865 790 7E+00
ounce/minute [US, liquid]	15.958 442	1.595 844 2E+01
ounce/second [US, liquid]	0.265 974	2.659 740 3E-01
petrograd standard/day	0.145 454 5	1.454 545 5E-01
stere/day	0.679 604 3	6.796 043 2E-01
cubic foot/minute	<flow rate, volume basis>	
acre inch/day	0.396 694 2	3.966 942 2E-01
barrel/hour [US, liquid]	14.248 608 5	1.424 860 9E+01
barrel/hour [US, petroleum]	10.686 456 4	1.068 645 6E+01
barrel/minute [US, liquid]	0.237 476 8	2.374 768 1E-01
barrel/minute [US, petroleum]	0.178 107 6	1.781 076 1E-01
centiliter/second	47.194 744 3	4.719 474 4E+01
cubic decimeter/minute	28.316 846 6	2.831 684 7E+01
cubic foot/hour	60	6.000 000 0E+01
cubic inch/second	28.8	2.880 000 0E+01
cubic meter/day	40.776 259 1	4.077 625 9E+01
cubic meter/hour	1.699 010 8	1.699 010 8E+00
cubic meter/second	0.000 471 9	4.719 474 4E-04
cubic yard/day	53.333 333 3	5.333 333 3E+01
cubic yard/hour	2.222 222 2	2.222 222 2E+00
deciliter/second	4.719 474 4	4.719 474 4E+00
dekaliter/minute	2.831 684 7	2.831 684 7E+00
gallon/minute [UK]	6.228 835 5	6.228 835 5E+00
gallon/minute [US, liquid]	7.480 519 5	7.480 519 5E+00
hectoliter/hour	16.990 108	1.699 010 8E+00
kiloliter/day	40.776 259 1	4.077 625 9E+01
kiloliter/hour	1.699 010 8	1.699 010 8E+00
liter/minute	28.316 846 6	2.831 684 7E+01
liter/minute [pre-1964]	28.316 053 7	2.831 605 4E+01
ounce/second [UK, liquid]	16.610 228	1.661 022 8E+01
ounce/second [US, liquid]	15.958 442	1.595 844 2E+01
petrograd standard/day	8.727 272 7	8.727 272 7E+00
stere/day	40.776 259	4.077 625 9E+01
stere/hour	1.699 010 8	1.699 010 8E+00
thousand cubic foot/day	1.44	1.440 000 0E+00

Convert From	\<Type of Unit>	
Convert To	Standard	Scientific

cubic foot/pound — \<specific volume>
cubic inch/pound	1,728	1.728 000 0E+03
cubic meter/kilogram	0.062 428	6.242 796 1E−02

cubic foot/second — \<flow rate, volume basis>
acre foot/day	1.983 471 1	1.983 471 1E+00
acre foot/day [US, survey]	1.983 459 2	1.983 459 2E+00
acre inch/day	23.801 652 9	2.380 165 3E+01
acre inch/hour	0.991 735 5	9.917 355 4E−01
barrel/minute [UK]	10.381 392 4	1.038 139 2E+01
barrel/minute [US, federal]	14.478 424 8	1.447 842 5E+01
barrel/minute [US, liquid]	14.248 608 5	1.424 860 9E+01
barrel/minute [US, petroleum]	10.686 456 4	1.068 645 6E+01
cubic decimeter/second	28.316 846 6	2.831 684 7E+01
cubic dekameter/day	2.446 575 6	2.446 575 6E+00
cubic dekameter/hour	0.101 940 6	1.019 406 5E−01
cubic foot/minute	60	6.000 000 0E+01
cubic meter/minute	1.699 010 8	1.699 010 8E+00
cubic meter/second	0.028 316 8	2.831 684 7E−02
cubic yard/minute	2.222 222 2	2.222 222 2E+00
cusec	1	1.000 000 0E+00
dekaliter/second	2.831 684 7	2.831 684 7E+00
gallon/second [UK]	6.228 835 5	6.228 835 5E+00
gallon/second [US, liquid]	7.480 519 5	7.480 519 5E+00
hectare meter/day	0.244 657 6	2.446 575 6E−01
hectoliter/minute	16.990 108	1.699 010 8E+01
hectoliter/second	0.283 168 5	2.831 684 7E−01
kiloliter/minute	1.699 010 8	1.699 010 8E+00
liter/second	28.316 846 6	2.831 684 7E+01
liter/second [pre-1964]	28.316 053 7	2.831 605 4E+01
miner's inch [AZ, CA, MT, OR]	40	4.000 000 0E+01
miner's inch [British Columbia, Canada]	35.714 286	3.571 428 6E+01
miner's inch [Colorado]	38.4	3.840 000 0E+01
miner's inch [ID, KS, NE, NM, NV, ND, SD, UT]	50	5.000 000 0E+01
petrograd standard/hour	21.818 182	2.181 818 2E+01
stere/minute	1.699 010 8	1.699 010 8E+00
thousand cubic foot/day	86.4	8.640 000 0E+01
thousand cubic foot/hour	3.6	3.600 000 0E+00

cubic fot [Sweden] — \<volume, special - see page 29>
liter	26.172	2.617 200 0E+01

cubic fut [Russia] — \<volume, special - see page 29>
cubic meter	0.028 316 9	2.831 685 0E−02

cubic gareh [Iran] — \<volume, special - see page 29>
cubic decimeter	1	1.000 000 0E+00

cubic gigameter — \<volume>
acre foot	>>>	8.107 131 9E+23
barrel [US, dry]	>>>	8.648 489 8E+27
barrel [US, liquid]	>>>	8.386 414 4E+27
cubem	>>>	2.399 127 6E+17
cubic foot	>>>	3.531 466 7E+28
cubic meter	>>>	1.000 000 0E+27
cubic yard	>>>	1.307 950 6E+27
gallon [US, dry]	>>>	2.270 207 5E+29
gallon [US, liquid]	>>>	2.641 720 5E+29
liter	>>>	1.000 000 0E+30
million acre foot	>>>	8.107 131 9E+17
stere	>>>	1.000 000 0E+27
trillion cubic foot	>>>	3.531 466 7E+16
yottaliter	1,000,000	1.000 000 0E+06

cubic hectometer — \<volume>
acre foot	810.713 19	8.107 131 9E+02
barrel [US, dry]	8,648,489.8	8.648 489 8E+06
barrel [US, liquid]	8,386,414.4	8.386 414 4E+06

Convert From Convert To	Standard	\<Type of Unit\> Scientific
billion cubic foot		
cubem	0.035 314 7	3.531 466 7E-02
cubic foot	0.000 239 9	2.399 127 6E-04
cubic inch	>>>	3.531 466 7E+07
cubic meter	1,000,000	6.102 374 4E+10
cubic mile	0.000 239 9	1.000 000 0E+06
cubic yard	1,307,950.6	2.399 127 6E-04
gallon [US, dry]	>>>	1.307 950 6E+06
gallon [US, liquid]	>>>	2.270 207 5E+08
gigaliter	1	2.641 720 5E+08
hectare meter	100	1.000 000 0E+00
liter	>>>	1.000 000 0E+02
million acre foot	0.000 810 7	1.000 000 0E+09
million board foot	423.776	8.107 131 9E-04
stere	1,000,000	4.237 760 0E+02
		1.000 000 0E+06
cubic inch		\<volume\>
barrel [US, dry]	0.000 141 7	1.417 233 6E-04
barrel [US, liquid]	0.000 137 4	1.374 287 1E-04
bushel [US, dry]	0.000 465	4.650 254 4E-04
centiliter	1.638 706 4	1.638 706 4E+00
cubic centimeter	16.387 064	1.638 706 4E+01
cubic foot	0.000 578 7	5.787 037 0E-04
cubic meter	0.000 016 4	1.638 706 4E-05
cubic yard	0.000 021 4	2.143 347 1E-05
cup [Canada, measuring]	0.072 093	7.209 300 3E-02
cup [metric]	0.081 935 3	8.193 532 0E-02
cup [US, measuring]	0.069 264 1	6.926 406 9E-02
drachm [UK, liquid]	4.613 952 2	4.613 952 2E+00
dram [Canada, liquid]	4.613 952 2	4.613 952 2E+00
dram [US, liquid]	4.432 900 4	4.432 900 4E+00
fifth [US, liquid]	0.021 645	2.164 502 2E-02
gallon [US, dry]	0.003 720 2	3.720 203 5E-03
gallon [US, liquid]	0.004 329	4.329 004 3E-03
jigger [US, liquid]	0.369 408 4	3.694 083 7E-01
kilderkin [US, liquid]	0.000 240 5	2.405 002 4E-04
liter	0.016 387 1	1.638 706 4E-02
ounce [US, liquid]	0.554 112 6	5.541 125 5E-01
pint [US, dry]	0.029 761 6	2.976 162 8E-02
pint [US, liquid]	0.034 632	3.463 203 5E-02
pony [US, liquid]	0.554 112 6	5.541 125 5E-01
pound of water [at 4 °C, 101.325 kPa, using IST-90 density equation]	0.036 126 3	3.612 628 0E-02
pound of water [at 60 °F, 14.696 pound-force/square inch, using IST-90 density equation]	0.036 091 7	3.609 165 1E-02
quart [US, dry]	0.014 880 8	1.488 081 4E-02
quart [US, liquid]	0.017 316	1.731 601 7E-02
shot [US, liquid]	0.554 112 6	5.541 125 5E-01
stere	0.000 016 4	1.638 706 4E-05
tablespoon [US, measuring]	1.108 225 1	1.108 225 1E+00
teaspoon [US, measuring]	3.324 675 3	3.324 675 3E+00
cubic inch second/pound		\<mobility\>
cubic centimeter second/gram	0.036 127 3	3.612 729 2E-02
cubic foot second/pound	0.000 578 7	5.787 037 0E-04
square meter/pascal second	0.000 036 1	3.612 729 2E-05
cubic inch/day		\<flow rate, volume basis\>
centiliter/day	1.638 706 4	1.638 706 4E+00
centiliter/hour	0.068 279 4	6.827 943 3E-02
centiliter/minute	0.001 138	1.137 990 6E-03
cubic centimeter/day	16.387 064	1.638 706 4E+01
cubic centimeter/hour	0.682 794 3	6.827 943 3E-01
cubic centimeter/minute	0.011 379 9	1.137 990 6E-02
cubic decimeter/day	0.016 387 1	1.638 706 4E-02
cubic inch/hour	0.041 666 7	4.166 666 7E-02

Convert From	<Type of Unit>	
Convert To	Standard	Scientific

	Standard	Scientific
cubic meter/second	<<<	1.896 650 9E–10
cubic millimeter/hour	682.794 333	6.827 943 3E+02
cubic millimeter/minute	11.379 905 6	1.137 990 6E+01
cubic millimeter/second	0.189 665 1	1.896 650 9E–01
deciliter/day	0.163 870 6	1.638 706 4E–01
deciliter/hour	0.006 827 9	6.827 943 3E–03
dekaliter/day	0.001 638 7	1.638 706 4E–03
gallon/day [UK]	0.003 604 7	3.604 650 2E–03
gallon/day [US, liquid]	0.004 329	4.329 004 3E–03
lambda/hour	682.794 333	6.827 943 3E+02
lambda/minute	11.379 905 6	1.137 990 6E+01
lambda/second	0.189 665 1	1.896 650 9E–01
liter/day	0.016 387 1	1.638 706 4E–02
liter/day [pre-1964]	0.016 386 6	1.638 660 5E–02
milliliter/day	16.387 064	1.638 706 4E+01
milliliter/hour	0.682 794 3	6.827 943 3E–01
milliliter/minute	0.011 379 9	1.137 990 6E–02
ounce/day [UK, liquid]	0.576 744	5.767 440 2E–01
ounce/day [US, liquid]	0.554 112 6	5.541 125 5E–01
ounce/hour [UK, liquid]	0.024 031	2.403 100 1E–02
ounce/hour [US, liquid]	0.023 088	2.308 802 3E–02
cubic inch/hour	**<flow rate, volume basis>**	
centiliter/day	39.328 953 6	3.932 895 4E+01
centiliter/hour	1.638 706 4	1.638 706 4E+00
centiliter/minute	0.027 311 8	2.731 177 3E–02
cubic centimeter/day	393.289 536	3.932 895 4E+02
cubic centimeter/hour	16.387 064	1.638 706 4E+01
cubic centimeter/minute	0.273 117 7	2.731 177 3E–01
cubic decimeter/day	0.393 289 5	3.932 895 4E–01
cubic decimeter/hour	0.016 387 1	1.638 706 4E–02
cubic foot/day	0.013 888 9	1.388 888 9E–02
cubic inch/day	24	2.400 000 0E+01
cubic inch/minute	0.016 666 7	1.666 666 7E–02
cubic millimeter/minute	273.117 733	2.731 177 3E+02
cubic millimeter/second	4.551 962 2	4.551 962 2E+00
deciliter/day	3.932 895 4	3.932 895 4E+00
deciliter/hour	0.163 870 6	1.638 706 4E–01
dekaliter/day	0.039 329	3.932 895 4E–02
gallon/day [UK]	0.086 511 6	8.651 160 4E–02
gallon/day [US, liquid]	0.103 896 1	1.038 961 0E–01
lambda/minute	273.117 733	2.731 177 3E+02
lambda/second	4.551 962 2	4.551 962 2E+00
liter/day	0.393 289 5	3.932 895 4E–01
liter/day [pre-1964]	0.393 278 5	3.932 785 2E–01
liter/hour	0.016 387 1	1.638 706 4E–02
liter/hour [pre-1964]	0.016 386 6	1.638 660 5E–02
milliliter/day	393.289 536	3.932 895 4E+02
milliliter/hour	16.387 064	1.638 706 4E+01
milliliter/minute	0.273 117 7	2.731 177 3E–01
ounce/day [UK, liquid]	13.841 857	1.384 185 7E+01
ounce/day [US, liquid]	13.298 701	1.329 870 1E+01
ounce/hour [UK, liquid]	0.576 744	5.767 440 2E–01
ounce/hour [US, liquid]	0.554 112 6	5.541 125 5E–01
cubic inch/minute	**<flow rate, volume basis>**	
barrel/day [UK]	0.144 186	1.441 860 1E–01
barrel/day [US, federal]	0.201 089 2	2.010 892 3E–01
barrel/day [US, liquid]	0.197 897 3	1.978 973 4E–01
barrel/day [US, petroleum]	0.148 423	1.484 230 1E–01
centiliter/hour	98.322 384	9.832 238 4E+01
centiliter/minute	1.638 706 4	1.638 706 4E+00
cubic centimeter/minute	16.387 064	1.638 706 4E+01
cubic centimeter/second	0.273 117 7	2.731 177 3E–01
cubic decimeter/day	23.597 372 2	2.359 737 2E+01

Convert From		<Type of Unit>
Convert To	Standard	Scientific

cubic decimeter/hour	0.983 223 8	9.832 238 4E-01
cubic foot/day	0.833 333 3	8.333 333 3E-01
cubic inch/hour	60	6.000 000 0E+01
deciliter/hour	9.832 238 4	9.832 238 4E+00
deciliter/minute	0.163 870 6	1.638 706 4E+00
dekaliter/day	2.359 737 2	2.359 737 2E+00
gallon/day [UK]	5.190 696 2	5.190 696 2E+00
gallon/day [US, liquid]	6.233 766 2	6.233 766 2E+00
gallon/hour [UK]	0.216 279	2.162 790 1E-01
gallon/hour [US, liquid]	0.259 740 3	2.597 402 6E-01
hectoliter/day	0.235 973 7	2.359 737 2E-01
liter/day	23.597 372	2.359 737 2E+01
liter/day [pre-1964]	23.596 711 5	2.359 671 2E+01
liter/hour	0.983 223 8	9.832 238 4E-01
liter/hour [pre-1964]	0.983 196 3	9.831 963 1E-01
milliliter/minute	16.387 064	1.638 706 4E+01
milliliter/second	0.273 117 7	2.731 177 3E-01
ounce/hour [UK, liquid]	34.604 641	3.460 464 1E+01
ounce/hour [US, liquid]	33.246 753	3.324 675 3E+01
ounce/minute [UK, liquid]	0.576 744	5.767 440 2E-01
ounce/minute [US, liquid]	0.554 112 5	5.541 125 5E-01
cubic inch/pound		**<specific volume>**
cubic foot/pound	0.000 578 7	5.787 037 0E-04
cubic meter/kilogram	0.000 036 1	3.612 729 2E-05
cubic inch/second		**<flow rate, volume basis>**
barrel/day [US, liquid]	11.873 840 4	1.187 384 0E+01
barrel/day [US, petroleum]	8.905 380 3	8.905 380 3E+00
barrel/hour [US, liquid]	0.494 743 4	4.947 433 5E-01
barrel/hour [US, petroleum]	0.371 057 5	3.710 575 1E-01
centiliter/second	1.638 706 4	1.638 706 4E+00
cubic centimeter/second	16.387 064	1.638 706 4E+01
cubic decimeter/hour	58.993 430 4	5.899 343 0E+01
cubic foot/day	50	5.000 000 0E+01
cubic foot/hour	2.083 333 3	2.083 333 3E+00
cubic inch/minute	60	6.000 000 0E+01
cubic meter/day	1.415 842 3	1.415 842 3E+00
cubic meter/second	0.000 016 4	1.638 706 4E-05
cubic yard/day	1.851 851 9	1.851 851 9E+00
deciliter/minute	9.832 238 4	9.832 238 4E+00
dekaliter/hour	5.899 343	5.899 343 0E+00
gallon/hour [UK]	12.976 740 5	1.297 674 1E+01
gallon/hour [US, liquid]	15.584 415 6	1.558 441 6E+01
hectoliter/day	14.158 423	1.415 842 3E+01
kiloliter/day	1.415 842 3	1.415 842 3E+00
liter/hour	58.993 430 4	5.899 343 0E+01
liter/hour [pre-1964]	58.991 778 6	5.899 177 9E+01
milliliter/second	16.387 064	1.638 706 4E+01
ounce/minute [UK, liquid]	34.604 641	3.460 464 1E+01
ounce/minute [US, liquid]	33.246 753	3.324 675 3E+01
petrograd standard/day	0.303 030 3	3.030 303 0E-01
stere/day	1.415 842 3	1.415 842 3E+00
cubic kilometer		**<volume>**
acre foot	810,713.19	8.107 131 9E+05
barrel [US, dry]	>>>	8.648 489 8E+09
barrel [US, liquid]	>>>	8.386 414 4E+09
billion cubic foot	35.314 667	3.531 466 7E+01
cubem	0.239 912 8	2.399 127 6E-01
cubic foot	>>>	3.531 466 7E+10
cubic meter	>>>	1.000 000 0E+09
cubic mile	0.239 912 8	2.399 127 6E-01
cubic yard	>>>	1.307 950 6E+09
hectare meter	100,000	1.000 000 0E+05
liter	>>>	1.000 000 0E+12

	Standard	Scientific
million board foot	423,776	4.237 760 0E+05
stere	>>>	1.000 000 0E+09
teraliter	1	1.000 000 0E+00
trillion cubic foot	0.035 314 7	3.531 466 7E-02
cubic kilometer/day		**<flow rate, volume basis>**
acre foot/minute	562.995 273	5.629 952 7E+02
acre foot/minute [US, survey]	562.991 896	5.629 919 0E+02
acre foot/second	9.383 254 6	9.383 254 6E+00
acre foot/second [US, survey]	9.383 198 3	9.383 198 3E+00
acre inch/minute	6,755.943 28	6.755 943 3E+03
acre inch/second	112.599 055	1.125 990 6E+02
billion cubic foot/day	35.314 666 7	3.531 466 7E+01
billion cubic foot/hour	1.471 444 5	1.471 444 5E+00
billion cubic foot/minute	0.024 524 1	2.452 407 4E-02
cubem/day	0.239 912 8	2.399 127 6E-01
cubem/hour	0.009 996 4	9.996 364 9E-03
cubic dekameter/minute	694.444 444	6.944 444 4E+02
cubic dekameter/second	11.574 074 1	1.157 407 4E+01
cubic kilometer/hour	0.041 666 7	4.166 666 7E-02
cubic meter/second	11.574.074 1	1.157 407 4E+04
cubic mile/day	0.239 912 8	2.399 127 6E-01
cubic mile/hour	0.009 996 4	9.996 364 9E-03
hectare meter/hour	4,166.666 67	4.166 666 7E+03
hectare meter/minute	69.444 444 4	6.944 444 4E+01
hectare meter/second	1.157 407 4	1.157 407 4E+00
million acre foot/day	0.810 713 2	8.107 131 9E-01
million acre foot/hour	0.033 779 7	3.377 971 6E-02
petrograd standard/second	2,477.179 2	2.477 179 2E+03
thousand cubic foot/second	408.734 57	4.087 345 7E+02
trillion cubic foot/day	0.035 314 7	3.531 466 7E-02
trillion cubic foot/hour	0.001 471 4	1.471 444 4E-03
cubic kilometer/hour		**<flow rate, volume basis>**
acre foot/second	225.198 109	2.251 981 1E+02
acre foot/second [US, survey]	225.196 758	2.251 967 6E+02
acre inch/second	2,702.377 31	2.702 377 3E+03
billion cubic foot/day	847.552 001	8.475 520 0E+02
billion cubic foot/hour	35.314 666 7	3.531 466 7E+01
billion cubic foot/minute	0.588 577 8	5.885 777 8E-01
billion cubic foot/second	0.009 809 6	9.809 629 6E-03
cubem/day	5.757 906 2	5.757 906 2E+00
cubem/hour	0.239 912 8	2.399 127 6E-01
cubem/minute	0.003 998 5	3.998 546 0E-03
cubic dekameter/second	277.777 778	2.777 777 8E+02
cubic kilometer/day	24	2.400 000 0E+01
cubic kilometer/minute	0.016 666 7	1.666 666 7E-02
cubic meter/second	277,777.778	2.777 777 8E+05
cubic mile/day	5.757 906 2	5.757 906 2E+00
cubic mile/hour	0.239 912 8	2.399 127 6E-01
cubic mile/minute	0.003 998 5	3.998 546 0E-03
hectare meter/minute	1,666.666 67	1.666 666 7E+03
hectare meter/second	27.777 777 8	2.777 777 8E+01
million acre foot/day	19.457 116 7	1.945 711 7E+01
million acre foot/hour	0.810 713 2	8.107 131 9E-01
million acre foot/minute	0.013 511 9	1.351 188 7E-02
thousand cubic foot/second	9,809.629 6	9.809 629 6E+03
trillion cubic foot/day	0.847 552	8.475 520 0E-01
trillion cubic foot/hour	0.035 314 7	3.531 466 7E-02
cubic kilometer/minute		**<flow rate, volume basis>**
billion cubic foot/hour	2,118.88	2.118 880 0E+03
billion cubic foot/minute	35.314 666 7	3.531 466 7E+01
billion cubic foot/second	0.588 577 8	5.885 777 8E-01
cubem/day	345.474 372	3.454 743 7E+02
cubem/hour	14.394 765 5	1.439 476 6E+01

	Standard	Scientific
cubem/minute	0.239 912 8	2.399 127 6E−01
cubem/second	0.003 998 5	3.998 546 0E−03
cubic kilometer/day	1,440	1.440 000 0E+03
cubic kilometer/hour	60	6.000 000 0E+01
cubic kilometer/second	0.016 666 7	1.666 666 7E−02
cubic meter/second	>>>	1.666 666 7E+07
cubic mile/day	345.474 372	3.454 743 7E+02
cubic mile/hour	14.394 765 5	1.439 476 6E+01
cubic mile/minute	0.239 912 8	2.399 127 6E−01
cubic mile/second	0.003 998 5	3.998 546 0E−03
hectare meter/second	1,666.666 67	1.666 666 7E+03
million acre foot/day	1,167.427	1.167 427 0E+03
million acre foot/hour	48.642 791 6	4.864 279 2E+01
million acre foot/minute	0.810 713 2	8.107 131 9E−01
million acre foot/second	0.013 511 9	1.351 188 7E−02
trillion cubic foot/day	50.853 12	5.085 312 0E+01
trillion cubic foot/hour	2.118 88	2.118 880 0E+00
trillion cubic foot/minute	0.035 314 7	3.531 466 7E−02
cubic kilometer/second		**<flow rate, volume basis>**
billion cubic foot/minute	2,118.88	2.118 880 0E+03
billion cubic foot/second	35.314 666 7	3.531 466 7E+01
cubem/day	20,728.462 3	2.072 846 2E+04
cubem/hour	863.685 931	8.636 859 3E+02
cubem/minute	14.394 765 5	1.439 476 6E+01
cubem/second	0.239 912 8	2.399 127 6E−01
cubic kilometer/day	86,400	8.640 000 0E+04
cubic kilometer/hour	3,600	3.600 000 0E+03
cubic kilometer/minute	60	6.000 000 0E+01
cubic meter/second	>>>	1.000 000 0E+09
cubic mile/day	20,728.462 3	2.072 846 2E+04
cubic mile/hour	863.685 931	8.636 859 3E+02
cubic mile/minute	14.394 765 5	1.439 476 6E+01
cubic mile/second	0.239 912 8	2.399 127 6E−01
million acre foot/day	70,045.619 9	7.004 562 0E+04
million acre foot/hour	2,918.567 5	2.918 567 5E+03
million acre foot/minute	48.642 791 6	4.864 279 2E+01
million acre foot/second	0.810 713 2	8.107 131 9E−01
trillion cubic foot/day	3,051.187 2	3.051 187 2E+03
trillion cubic foot/hour	127.132 8	1.271 328 0E+02
trillion cubic foot/minute	2.118 88	2.118 880 0E+00
trillion cubic foot/second	0.035 314 7	3.531 466 7E−02
cubic klafter [Austria]		**<volume, special - see page 29>**
cubic meter	6.821	6.821 000 0E+00
cubic megameter		**<volume>**
acre foot	>>>	8.107 131 9E+14
cubem	>>>	2.399 127 6E+08
cubic foot	>>>	3.531 466 7E+19
cubic meter	>>>	1.000 000 0E+18
cubic mile	>>>	2.399 127 6E+08
cubic yard	>>>	1.307 950 6E+18
gallon [US, dry]	>>>	2.270 227 0E+20
gallon [US, liquid]	>>>	2.641 720 5E+20
hectare meter	>>>	1.000 000 0E+14
liter	>>>	1.000 000 0E+21
million acre foot	>>>	8.107 131 9E+08
million board foot	>>>	4.237 760 0E+14
stere	>>>	1.000 000 0E+18
trillion cubic foot	>>>	3.531 466 7E+07
zettaliter	1	1.000 000 0E+00
cubic meter		**<volume>**
acre foot	0.000 810 7	8.107 131 9E−04
Amagat volume unit	44.615 769	4.461 576 9E+01

cubic meter (continued) <volume>

	Standard	Scientific
ambar [Turkey]	2.298 850 6	2.298 850 6E+00
anker	26.417 205	2.641 720 5E+01
ardeb [Ethiopia]	90.909 091	9.090 909 1E+01
barrel [UK]	6.110 256 9	6.110 256 9E+00
barrel [US, dry]	8.648 489 8	8.648 489 8E+00
barrel [US, liquid]	8.386 414 4	8.386 414 4E+00
barrel [US, petroleum]	6.289 810 8	6.289 810 8E+00
bois equarris [Norway]	0.376 689 8	3.766 898 3E-01
bois ronds [Norway]	0.470 862 3	4.708 623 3E-01
bois scies [Norway]	0.342 445 2	3.424 452 3E-01
bushel [UK]	27.496 156	2.749 615 6E+01
bushel [US, dry]	28.377 593	2.837 759 3E+01
camionada [El Salvador]	0.333 333 3	3.333 333 3E-01
carretada [El Salvador]	1	1.000 000 0E+00
chevron [Cambodia]	10	1.000 000 0E+01
cord foot [timber]	2.207 166 7	2.207 166 7E+00
cubic archine [Russia]	2.779 871 9	2.779 871 9E+00
cubic cubit [Egypt, ancient]	6.944 444 4	6.944 444 4E+00
cubic foot	35.314 667	3.531 466 7E+01
cubic fut [Russia]	35.314 662	3.531 466 2E+01
cubic inch	61,023.744	6.102 374 4E+04
cubic klafter [Austria]	0.146 606 1	1.466 060 7E-01
cubic sagene [Russia]	0.102 958 2	1.029 582 2E-01
cubic yard	1.307 950 6	1.307 950 6E+00
cup [metric]	5,000	5.000 000 0E+03
drum [US, liquid]	4.803 128 2	4.803 128 2E+00
ertragsfestmeter [Austria, solid wood]	1	1.000 000 0E+00
famn [Finland]	0.25	2.500 000 0E-01
favn [Norway, firewood]	0.416 666 7	4.166 666 7E-01
favn braende [Denmark]	0.449 248 4	4.492 484 1E-01
favne [Denmark]	0.449 236 3	4.492 363 0E-01
fifth [US, liquid]	1,320.860 3	1.320 860 3E+03
gallon [UK, dry or liquid]	219.969 25	2.199 692 5E+02
gallon [US, dry]	227.020 75	2.270 207 5E+02
gallon [US, liquid]	264.172 05	2.641 720 5E+02
hogshead [UK]	3.491 575 4	3.491 575 4E+00
hogshead [US]	4.193 207 2	4.193 207 2E+00
holzklafter [Switzerland]	0.342 935 5	3.429 355 3E-01
ippyong [South Korea]	0.166 389 4	1.663 893 5E-01
jigger [US, liquid]	22,542.682	2.254 268 2E+04
kavan [Cambodia]	6.578 947 4	6.578 947 4E+00
kilderkin [UK, liquid]	12.220 514	1.222 051 4E+01
kilderkin [US, liquid]	14.676 225	1.467 622 5E+01
kiloliter	1	1.000 000 0E+00
kubieke el [Netherlands]	1	1.000 000 0E+00
kubikfot [Sweden]	38.208 919	3.820 891 9E+01
lai [Vietnam]	15.625	1.562 500 0E+01
liter	1,000	1.000 000 0E+03
mau [Vietnam, soil measure]	0.000 694 4	6.944 444 4E-04
mieng [Vietnam, soil measure]	0.069 444 4	6.944 444 4E-02
moule [Switzerland]	0.25	2.500 000 0E-01
o [Vietnam]	15.625	1.562 500 0E+01
palmo cubica [Macao]	93.896 714	9.389 671 4E+01
panchang [Malaysia]	0.326 797 4	3.267 973 9E-01
pe cubica [Macao]	27.824 151	2.782 415 1E+01
petrograd standard	0.214 028 3	2.140 282 8E-01
phlan [Cambodia]	10	1.000 000 0E+01
pinometer [Czechoslovakia]	1	1.000 000 0E+00
pipe [UK]	2.036 752 3	2.036 752 3E+00
pipe [US, liquid]	2.096 603 6	2.096 603 6E+00
pony [US, liquid]	33,814.023	3.381 402 3E+04

pound of water
[at 4 °C, 101.325 kPa, using IST-90 density equation] 2,204.560 9 ---- 2.204 560 9E+03

pound of water [at 60 °F, 14.696 pound-force/square
inch, using IST-90 density equation] ---------------- 2,202.447 7 ---- 2.202 447 7E+03

	Standard	Scientific
puncheon [UK]	3.144 900 3	3.144 900 3E+00
pyong [South Korea, timber]	0.499 126 5	4.991 265 3E-01
qasba xubu [Malta and Gozo]	0.108 676 9	1.086 768 7E-01
quarter [UK]	3.437 019 5	3.437 019 5E+00
raummeter [Austria, piled wood]	1	1.000 000 0E+00
ryutsubo [Japan]	0.166 389 4	1.663 893 5E-01
sao [Vietnam, soil measure]	0.006 944 4	6.944 444 4E-03
shot [US, liquid]	33,814.023	3.381 402 3E+04
stere	1	1.000 000 0E+00
stero [Italy]	1	1.000 000 0E+00
syli [Finland]	0.25	2.500 000 0E-01
tat [Ethiopia]	40	4.000 000 0E+01
teningsfet [Iceland]	32.362 46	3.236 246 0E+01
than [Vietnam, soil measure]	0.625	6.250 000 0E-01
tonel [Argentina]	0.971 817 3	9.718 173 0E-01
tonneau [Argentina]	0.971 817 3	9.718 173 0E-01
tonneau de jauge international [France]	0.353 146 7	3.531 466 6E-01
tonneau de mer [France]	0.694 444 4	6.944 444 4E-01
tonnelada [Argentina]	0.971 817 3	9.718 173 0E-01
tun [UK, liquid]	1.018 376 1	1.018 376 1E+00
tun [US, liquid]	1.048 301 8	1.048 301 8E+00
vara cubica [Macao]	0.751 314 8	7.513 148 0E-01
vara cubica [Mexico]	1.699 293 1	1.699 293 1E+00
vara cubica [Spain]	1.712 100 1	1.712 100 1E+00
wisse [Netherlands]	1	1.000 000 0E+00
xiber xubu [Malta and Gozo]	55.642 42	5.564 242 0E+01

cubic meter atmosphere <energy>

	Standard	Scientific
cubic centimeter atmosphere	1,000,000	1.000 000 0E+06
joule	101,325	1.013 250 0E+05

cubic meter atmosphere/hour <power>

	Standard	Scientific
Btu/hour [I.T.]	0.000 096	9.603 757 0E-05
Btu/hour [thermoc.]	0.000 096 1	9.610 184 0E-05
calorie/hour [I.T.]	0.024 201	2.420 106 0E-02
calorie/hour [thermoc.]	0.024 217 3	2.421 725 6E-02
centigrade heat unit/hour [mean]	0.000 053 3	5.331 306 6E-05
dyne centimeter/second	281.458 33	2.814 583 3E+02
erg/second	281.458 33	2.814 583 3E+02
foot pound-force/hour	0.074 733 5	7.473 348 5E-02
foot poundal/hour	2.404 478 8	2.404 478 8E+00
gram-force centimeter/minute	17.220 458	1.722 045 8E+01
horsepower	<<<	3.774 418 4E-08
horsepower [metric]	<<<	3.826 768 3E-08
joule/hour	0.101 325	1.013 250 0E-01
kilocalorie/hour [I.T.]	0.000 024 2	2.420 106 0E-05
kilogram force meter/hour	0.010 332 3	1.033 227 5E-02
kilopond meter/hour	0.010 332 3	1.033 227 5E-02
lumen [green light at 100% efficiency]	0.019 279 9	1.927 989 6E-02
lumen [green light at 5,550 angstrom]	0.019 139 2	1.913 916 7E-02
newton meter/hour	0.101 325	1.013 250 0E-01
volt ampere	0.000 028 1	2.814 583 3E-05
watt	0.000 028 1	2.814 583 3E-05

cubic meter atmosphere/minute <power>

	Standard	Scientific
Btu/hour [I.T.]	0.005 762 3	5.762 254 2E-03
Btu/hour [thermoc.]	0.005 766 1	5.766 110 4E-03
calorie/hour [I.T.]	1.452 063 6	1.452 063 6E+00
calorie/hour [thermoc.]	1.453 035 4	1.453 035 4E+00
centigrade heat unit/hour [mean]	0.003 198 8	3.198 783 9E-03
cubic meter atmosphere/hour	60	6.000 000 0E+01
dyne centimeter/second	16,887.5	1.688 750 0E+04

Convert From / Convert To	Standard	Scientific
erg/second	16,887.5	1.688 750 0E+04
foot pound-force/hour	4.484 009 1	4.484 009 1E+00
foot poundal/minute	2.404 478 8	2.404 478 8E+00
gram-force centimeter/second	17.220 458	1.722 045 8E+01
horsepower	0.000 002 3	2.264 651 1E-06
horsepower [metric]	0.000 002 3	2.296 061 0E-06
joule/hour	6.079 5	6.079 500 0E+00
kilocalorie/hour [I.T.]	0.001 452 1	1.452 063 6E-03
kilogram-force meter/hour	0.619 936 5	6.199 364 7E-01
kilopond meter/hour	0.619 936 5	6.199 364 7E-01
lumen [green light at 100% efficiency]	1.156 793 8	1.156 793 8E+00
lumen [green light at 5,550 angstrom]	1.148 35	1.148 350 0E+00
milliwatt	1.688 75	1.688 750 0E+00
newton meter/hour	6.079 5	6.079 500 0E+00
pound square foot/cubic second	0.040 074 6	4.007 464 6E-02
volt ampere	0.001 688 8	1.688 750 0E-03
watt	0.001 688 8	1.688 750 0E-03
cubic meter atmosphere/second		**<power>**
Btu/hour [I.T.]	0.345 735 3	3.457 352 5E-01
Btu/hour [thermoc.]	0.345 966 6	3.459 666 2E-01
calorie/minute [I.T.]	1.452 063 6	1.452 063 6E+00
calorie/minute [thermoc.]	1.453 035 4	1.453 035 4E+00
centigrade heat unit/hour [mean]	0.191 927	1.919 270 4E-01
cubic meter atmosphere/minute	60	6.000 000 0E+01
deciwatt	1.013 25	1.013 250 0E+00
dyne centimeter/second	1,013,250	1.013 250 0E+06
erg/second	1,013,250	1.013 250 0E+06
foot pound-force/minute	4.484 009 1	4.484 009 1E+00
foot poundal/second	2.404 478 8	2.404 478 8E+00
gram-force centimeter/second	1,033.227 5	1.033 227 5E+03
horsepower	0.000 135 9	1.358 790 6E-04
horsepower [metric]	0.000 137 8	1.377 636 6E-04
joule/minute	6.079 5	6.079 500 0E+00
kilocalorie/hour [I.T.]	0.087 123 8	8.712 381 8E-02
kilogram square meter/cubic second	0.101 325	1.013 250 0E-01
kilogram-force meter/hour	37.196 188	3.719 618 8E+01
kilopond meter/hour	37.196 188	3.719 618 8E+01
lumen [green light at 100% efficiency]	69.407 625	6.940 762 5E+01
lumen [green light at 5,550 angstrom]	68.901 002	6.890 100 2E+01
newton meter/minute	6.079 5	6.079 500 0E+00
pound square foot/cubic second	2.404 478 8	2.404 478 8E+00
volt ampere	0.101 325	1.013 250 0E-01
watt	0.101 325	1.013 250 0E-01
cubic meter second/kilogram		**<mobility>**
cubic foot second/pound	16.018 463	1.601 846 3E+01
cubic inch second/pound	27,679.905	2.767 990 5E+04
square meter/pascal second	1	1.000 000 0E+00
cubic meter/cubic meter		**<concentration, volume basis>**
cubic foot/cubic foot	1	1.000 000 0E+00
cubic foot/gallon [-/US, liquid]	0.133 680 6	1.336 805 6E-01
gallon/cubic foot [US, liquid]	7.480 519 5	7.480 519 5E+00
cubic meter/day		**<flow rate, volume basis>**
barrel/day [UK]	6.110 256 9	6.110 256 9E+00
barrel/day [US, federal]	8.521 679 1	8.521 679 1E+00
barrel/day [US, liquid]	8.386 414 4	8.386 414 4E+00
barrel/day [US, petroleum]	6.289 810 8	6.289 810 8E+00
centiliter/minute	69.444 444 4	6.944 444 4E+01
centiliter/second	1.157 407 4	1.157 407 4E+00
cubic centimeter/second	11.574 074 1	1.157 407 4E+01
cubic decimeter/hour	41.666 666 7	4.166 666 7E+01
cubic foot/day	35.314 666 7	3.531 466 7E+01
cubic foot/hour	1.471 444 5	1.471 444 5E+00

| Convert From | <Type of Unit> | |
Convert To	Standard	Scientific
cubic inch/minute	42.377 600 1	4.237 760 0E+01
cubic yard/day	1.307 950 6	1.307 950 6E+00
deciliter/minute	6.944 444 4	6.944 444 4E+00
dekaliter/hour	4.166 666 7	4.166 666 7E+00
gallon/hour [UK]	9.165 385 3	9.165 385 3E+00
gallon/hour [US, liquid]	11.007 168 8	1.100 716 9E+01
hectoliter/day	10	1.000 000 0E+01
kiloliter/day	1	1.000 000 0E+00
liter/hour	41.666 666 7	4.166 666 7E+01
liter/hour [pre-1964]	41.665 5	4.166 550 0E+01
milliliter/second	11.574 074 1	1.157 407 4E+01
ounce/minute [UK, liquid]	24.441 028	2.444 102 8E+01
ounce/minute [US, liquid]	23.481 96	2.348 196 0E+01
petrograd standard/day	0.214 028 3	2.140 282 8E−01
stere/day	1	1.000 000 0E+00
cubic meter/hour	**<flow rate, volume basis>**	
acre inch/day	0.233 485 4	2.334 854 0E−01
barrel/hour [UK]	6.110 256 9	6.110 256 9E+00
barrel/hour [US, federal]	8.521 679 1	8.521 679 1E+00
barrel/hour [US, liquid]	8.386 414 4	8.386 414 4E+00
barrel/hour [US, petroleum]	6.289 810 8	6.289 810 8E+00
centiliter/second	27.777 777 8	2.777 777 8E+01
cubic decimeter/minute	16.666 666 7	1.666 666 7E+01
cubic foot/hour	35.314 666 7	3.531 466 7E+01
cubic inch/second	16.951 04	1.695 104 0E+01
cubic meter/day	24	2.400 000 0E+01
cubic meter/second	0.000 277 8	2.777 777 8E−04
cubic yard/day	31.390 814 9	3.139 081 5E+01
cubic yard/hour	1.307 950 6	1.307 950 6E+00
deciliter/second	2.777 777 8	2.777 777 8E+00
dekaliter/minute	1.666 666 7	1.666 666 7E+00
gallon/minute [UK]	3.666 154 7	3.666 154 1E+00
gallon/minute [US, liquid]	4.402 867 5	4.402 867 5E+00
hectoliter/hour	10	1.000 000 0E+01
kiloliter/day	24	2.400 000 0E+01
kiloliter/hour	1	1.000 000 0E+00
liter/minute	16.666 666 7	1.666 666 7E+01
liter/minute [pre-1964]	16.666 2	1.666 620 0E+01
ounce/second [UK, liquid]	9.776 411	9.776 411 0E+00
ounce/second [US, liquid]	9.392 784 1	9.392 784 1E+00
petrograd standard/day	5.136 678 8	5.136 678 8E+00
stere/day	24	2.400 000 0E+01
stere/hour	1	1.000 000 0E+00
thousand cubic foot/day	0.847 552	8.475 520 0E−01
cubic meter/joule	**<specific fuel consumption, volume basis>**	
cubic foot/Btu [-/ I.T.]	37,258.946	3.725 894 6E+04
cubic meter/kilocalorie [-/ I.T.]	4,186.8	4.186 800 0E+03
gallon/horsepower hour [US, liquid]	>>>	7.091 750 4E+08
liter/joule	1,000	1.000 000 0E+03
liter/kilowatthour	>>>	3.600 000 0E+09
cubic meter/kilocalorie [-/ I.T.]	**<specific fuel consumption, volume basis>**	
cubic foot/Btu [-/ I.T.]	8.899 146 3	8.899 146 3E+00
cubic meter/joule	0.000 238 8	2.388 459 0E−04
gallon/horsepower hour [US, liquid]	169,383.55	1.693 835 5E+05
cubic meter/kilogram	**<specific volume>**	
cubic centimeter/gram	1,000	1.000 000 0E+03
cubic foot/pound	16.018 463	1.601 846 3E+01
cubic inch/pound	27,679.905	2.767 990 5E+04
cubic meter/liter	**<concentration, volume basis>**	
cubic foot/cubic foot	1,000	1.000 000 0E+03
cubic foot/gallon [-/US, liquid]	133.680 56	1.336 805 6E+02
cubic meter/cubic meter	1,000	1.000 000 0E+03

Convert From	<Type of Unit>	
Convert To	Standard	Scientific

gallon/cubic foot [US, liquid]	7,480.519 5	7.480 519 5E+03

cubic meter/meter <fuel consumption, SI>

gallon/mile	425,143.71	4.251 437 1E+05
liter/100 kilometer	10,000	1.000 000 0E+04
liter/kilometer	1,000,000	1.000 000 0E+06
liter/meter	1,000	1.000 000 0E+03

cubic meter/minute <flow rate, volume basis>

acre foot/day	1.167 427	1.167 427 0E+00
acre foot/day [US, survey]	1.167 42	1.167 420 0E+00
acre inch/day	14.009 124	1.400 912 4E+01
barrel/minute [UK]	6.110 256 9	6.110 256 9E+00
barrel/minute [US, federal]	8.521 679 1	8.521 679 1E+00
barrel/minute [US, liquid]	8.386 414 4	8.386 414 4E+00
barrel/minute [US, petroleum]	6.289 810 8	6.289 810 8E+00
cubic decimeter/second	16.666 666 7	1.666 666 7E+01
cubic dekameter/day	1.44	1.440 000 0E+00
cubic foot/minute	35.314 666 7	3.531 466 7E+01
cubic foot/second	0.588 577 8	5.885 777 8E-01
cubic meter/hour	60	6.000 000 0E+01
cubic meter/second	0.016 666 7	1.666 666 7E-02
cubic yard/hour	78.477 037	7.847 703 7E+01
cubic yard/minute	1.307 950 6	1.307 950 6E+00
dekaliter/second	1.666 666 7	1.666 666 7E+00
gallon/second [UK]	3.666 154 1	3.666 154 1E+00
gallon/second [US, liquid]	4.402 867 5	4.402 867 5E+00
hectare meter/day	0.144	1.440 000 0E-01
hectoliter/minute	10	1.000 000 0E+01
hectoliter/second	0.166 666 7	1.666 666 7E-01
kiloliter/hour	60	6.000 000 0E+01
kiloliter/minute	1	1.000 000 0E+00
liter/second	16.666 666 7	1.666 666 7E+01
liter/second [pre-1964]	16.666 2	1.666 620 0E+01
petrograd standard/hour	12.841 697	1.284 169 7E+01
petrograd standard/minute	0.214 028 3	2.140 282 8E-01
stere/hour	60	6.000 000 0E+01
stere/minute	1	1.000 000 0E+00
thousand cubic foot/day	50.853 12	5.085 312 0E+01
thousand cubic foot/hour	2.118 88	2.118 880 0E+00

cubic meter/mole <molar volume>

liter/mole	1,000	1.000 000 0E+03

cubic meter/second <flow rate, volume basis>

acre foot/day	70.045 619 9	7.004 562 0E+01
acre foot/day [US, survey]	70.045 199 7	7.004 520 0E+01
acre foot/hour	2.918 567 5	2.918 567 5E+00
acre foot/hour [US, survey]	2.918 55	2.918 550 0E+00
acre inch/hour	35.022 81	3.502 281 0E+01
acre inch/minute	0.583 713 5	5.837 135 0E-01
barrel/second [UK]	6.110 256 9	6.110 256 9E+00
barrel/second [US, federal]	8.521 679 1	8.521 679 1E+00
barrel/second [US, liquid]	8.386 414 4	8.386 414 4E+00
barrel/second [US, petroleum]	6.289 810 8	6.289 810 8E+00
billion cubic foot/day	0.003 051 2	3.051 187 2E-03
centiliter/second	100,000	1.000 000 0E+05
cubem/day	0.000 020 7	2.072 846 2E-05
cubic centimeter/second	1,000,000	1.000 000 0E+06
cubic decimeter/second	1,000	1.000 000 0E+03
cubic dekameter/hour	3.6	3.600 000 0E+00
cubic foot/second	35.314 666 7	3.531 466 7E+01
cubic inch/second	61,023.744 1	6.102 374 4E+04
cubic kilometer/day	0.000 086 4	8.640 000 0E-05
cubic meter/minute	60	6.000 000 0E+01
cubic mile/day	0.000 020 7	2.072 846 2E-05

	Standard	Scientific
cubic millimeter/second	>>>	1.000 000 0E+09
cubic yard/second	1.307 950 6	1.307 950 6E+00
cusec	35.314 666 7	3.531 466 7E+01
deciliter/second	10,000	1.000 000 0E+04
dekaliter/second	100	1.000 000 0E+02
gallon/second [UK]	219.969 248	2.199 692 5E+02
gallon/second [US, liquid]	264.172 052	2.641 720 5E+02
hectare meter/day	8.64	8.640 000 0E+00
hectoliter/second	10	1.000 000 0E+01
kiloliter/second	1	1.000 000 0E+00
lambda/second	>>>	1.000 000 0E+09
liter/second	1,000	1.000 000 0E+03
liter/second [pre-1964]	999.972 001	9.999 720 0E+02
milliliter/second	1,000,000	1.000 000 0E+06
million acre foot/day	0.000 07	7.004 562 0E−05
miner's inch [AZ, CA, MT, OR]	1,412.586 7	1.412 586 7E+03
miner's inch [British Columbia, Canada]	1,261.238 1	1.261 238 1E+03
miner's inch [Colorado]	1,356.083 2	1.356 083 2E+03
miner's inch [ID, KS, NE, NM, NV, ND, SD, UT]	1,765.733 333	1.765 733 3E+03
ounce/second [UK, liquid]	35,195.08	3.519 508 0E+04
ounce/second [US, liquid]	33,814.023	3.381 402 3E+04
petrograd standard/minute	12.841 697	1.284 169 7E+01
stere/second	1	1.000 000 0E+00
thousand cubic foot/minute	2.118 88	2.118 880 0E+00
trillion cubic foot/day	0.000 003 1	3.051 187 2E−06
cubic micrometer		**<volume>**
cubic inch	<<<	6.102 374 4E−14
cubic meter	<<<	1.000 000 0E−18
dram [US, liquid]	<<<	2.705 121 8E−13
drop [US, liquid]	<<<	1.217 304 8E−11
femtoliter	1	1.000 000 0E+00
lambda	<<<	1.000 000 0E−09
liter	<<<	1.000 000 0E−15
ounce [UK, liquid]	<<<	3.519 508 0E−14
ounce [US, liquid]	<<<	3.381 402 3E−14
cubic mile		**<volume>**
acre foot	3,379,200	3.379 200 0E+06
barrel [US, dry]	>>>	3.604 847 8E+10
barrel [US, liquid]	>>>	3.495 610 0E+10
barrel [US, petroleum]	>>>	2.621 707 5E+10
billion cubic foot	147.197 95	1.471 979 5E+02
cubem	1	1.000 000 0E+00
cubic foot	>>>	1.471 979 5E+11
cubic kilometer	4.168 181 8	4.168 181 8E+00
cubic meter	>>>	4.168 181 8E+09
cubic yard	>>>	5.451 776 0E+09
gallon [US, dry]	>>>	9.462 637 5E+11
gallon [US, liquid]	>>>	1.101 117 1E+12
hectare meter	416,818.18	4.168 181 8E+05
liter	>>>	4.168 181 8E+12
million acre foot	3.379 2	3.379 200 0E+00
teraliter	4.168 181 8	4.168 181 8E+00
trillion cubic foot	0.147 198	1.471 979 5E−01
cubic mile/day		**<flow rate, volume basis>**
acre foot/minute	2,346.666 67	2.346 666 7E+03
acre foot/minute [US, survey]	2,346.652 59	2.346 652 6E+03
acre foot/second	39.111 111 1	3.911 111 1E+01
acre foot/second [US, survey]	39.110 876 4	3.911 087 6E+01
acre inch/second	469.333 333	4.693 333 3E+02
billion cubic foot/day	147.197 952	1.471 979 5E+02
billion cubic foot/hour	6.133 248	6.133 248 0E+00
billion cubic foot/minute	0.102 220 8	1.022 208 0E−01
cubem/day	1	1.000 000 0E+00

Convert To	Standard	Scientific
cubem/hour	0.041 666 7	4.166 666 7E−02
cubic dekameter/second	48.242 845 2	4.824 284 5E+01
cubic kilometer/day	4.168 181 8	4.168 181 8E+00
cubic kilometer/hour	0.173 674 2	1.736 742 4E−01
cubic meter/second	48,242.845 2	4.824 284 5E+04
cubic mile/hour	0.041 666 7	4.166 666 7E−02
hectare meter/minute	289.457 071	2.894 570 7E+02
hectare meter/second	4.824 284 5	4.824 284 5E+00
million acre foot/day	3.379 2	3.379 200 0E+00
million acre foot/hour	0.140 8	1.408 000 0E−01
thousand cubic foot/second	1,703.68	1.703 680 0E+03
trillion cubic foot/day	0.147 198	1.471 979 5E−01
cubic mile/hour		**<flow rate, volume basis>**
acre foot/second	938.666 667	9.386 666 7E+02
acre foot/second [US, survey]	938.661 035	9.386 610 4E+02
billion cubic foot/hour	147.197 952	1.471 979 5E+02
billion cubic foot/minute	2.453 299 2	2.453 299 2E+00
cubem/day	24	2.400 000 0E+01
cubem/hour	1	1.000 000 0E+00
cubem/minute	0.016 666 7	1.666 666 7E−02
cubic dekameter/second	1,157.828 28	1.157 828 3E+03
cubic kilometer/day	100.036 364	1.000 363 6E+02
cubic kilometer/hour	4.168 181 8	4.168 181 8E+00
cubic kilometer/minute	0.069 469 7	6.946 969 7E−02
cubic meter/second	1,157,828.28	1.157 828 3E+06
cubic mile/day	24	2.400 000 0E+01
hectare meter/second	115.782 828	1.157 828 3E+02
million acre foot/day	81.100 8	8.110 080 0E+01
million acre foot/hour	3.379 2	3.379 200 0E+00
trillion cubic foot/day	3.532 750 8	3.532 750 8E+00
trillion cubic foot/hour	0.147 198	1.471 979 5E−01
cubic mile/minute		**<flow rate, volume basis>**
acre foot/second	56,320	5.632 000 0E+04
acre foot/second [US, survey]	56,319.662 1	5.631 966 2E+04
billion cubic foot/hour	8,831.877 12	8.831 877 1E+03
billion cubic foot/minute	147.197 952	1.471 979 5E+02
billion cubic foot/second	2.453 299 2	2.453 299 2E+00
cubem/day	1,440	1.440 000 0E+03
cubem/hour	60	6.000 000 0E+01
cubem/minute	1	1.000 000 0E+00
cubic dekameter/second	69,469.697 1	6.946 969 7E+04
cubic kilometer/day	6,002.181 83	6.002 181 8E+03
cubic kilometer/hour	250.090 91	2.500 909 1E+02
cubic kilometer/minute	4.168 181 8	4.168 181 8E+00
cubic meter/second	>>>	6.946 969 7E+07
cubic mile/day	1,440	1.440 000 0E+03
cubic mile/hour	60	6.000 000 0E+01
hectare meter/second	6,946.969 71	6.946 969 7E+03
million acre foot/day	4,866.048	4.866 048 0E+03
million acre foot/hour	202.752	2.027 520 0E+02
million acre foot/minute	3.379 2	3.379 200 0E+00
trillion cubic foot/day	211.965 05	2.119 650 5E+02
trillion cubic foot/hour	8.831 877 1	8.831 877 1E+00
trillion cubic foot/minute	0.147 198	1.471 979 5E−01
cubic mile/second		**<flow rate, volume basis>**
acre foot/second	3,379,200	3.379 200 0E+06
acre foot/second [US, survey]	3,379,179.72	3.379 179 7E+06
barrel/second [US, liquid]	>>>	3.495 610 0E+10
billion cubic foot/second	147.197 952	1.471 979 5E+02
cubem/minute	60	6.000 000 0E+01
cubem/second	1	1.000 000 0E+00
cubic dekameter/second	4,168,181.83	4.168 181 8E+06
cubic kilometer/minute	250.090 91	2.500 909 1E+02

cubic kilometer/second	4.168 181 8	4.168 181 8E+00
cubic meter/second	>>>	4.168 181 8E+09
cubic mile/hour	3,600	3.600 000 0E+03
cubic mile/minute	60	6.000 000 0E+01
hectare meter/second	416,818.183	4.168 181 8E+05
million acre foot/hour	12,165.12	1.216 512 0E+04
million acre foot/minute	202.752	2.027 520 0E+02
million acre foot/second	3.379 2	3.379 200 0E+00
trillion cubic foot/day	12,717.903	1.271 790 3E+04
trillion cubic foot/hour	529.912 63	5.299 126 3E+02
trillion cubic foot/minute	8.831 877 1	8.831 877 1E+00
trillion cubic foot/second	0.147 198	1.471 979 5E-01
cubic millimeter		**<volume>**
cubic foot	<<<	3.531 466 7E-08
cubic inch	0.000 061	6.102 374 4E-05
cubic meter	<<<	1.000 000 0E-09
drop [US, liquid]	0.012 173	1.217 304 8E-02
gallon [US, dry]	0.000 000 2	2.270 207 5E-07
gallon [US, liquid]	0.000 000 3	2.641 720 5E-07
lambda	1	1.000 000 0E+00
linea cubica [Mexico]	0.136 999 4	1.369 994 4E-01
liter	0.000 001	1.000 000 0E-06
microliter	1	1.000 000 0E+00
ounce [US, liquid]	0.000 033 8	3.381 402 3E-05
stere	<<<	1.000 000 0E-09
cubic millimeter/day		**<flow rate, volume basis>**
barrel/day [US, liquid]	<<<	8.386 414 4E-09
barrel/day [US, petroleum]	<<<	6.289 810 8E-09
centiliter/day	0.000 1	1.000 000 0E-04
cubic centimeter/day	0.001	1.000 000 0E-03
cubic inch/day	0.000 061	6.102 374 4E-05
cubic meter/second	<<<	1.157 407 4E-14
cubic millimeter/hour	0.041 666 7	4.166 666 7E-02
lambda/day	1	1.000 000 0E+00
liter/day	0.000 001	1.000 000 0E-06
liter/day [pre-1964]	0.000 001	9.999 720 0E-07
milliliter/day	0.001	1.000 000 0E-03
ounce/day [UK, liquid]	0.000 035 2	3.519 508 0E-05
ounce/day [US, liquid]	0.000 033 8	3.381 402 3E-05
cubic millimeter/hour		**<flow rate, volume basis>**
barrel/day [UK]	0.000 000 1	1.466 461 7E-07
barrel/day [US, federal]	0.000 000 2	2.045 203 0E-07
centiliter/day	0.002 4	2.400 000 0E-03
cubic centimeter/day	0.024	2.400 000 0E-02
cubic inch/day	0.001 464 6	1.464 569 9E-03
cubic meter/second	<<<	2.777 777 8E-13
cubic millimeter/day	24	2.400 000 0E+01
lambda/day	24	2.400 000 0E+01
lambda/hour	1	1.000 000 0E+00
liter/day	0.000 024	2.400 000 0E-05
liter/day [pre-1964]	0.000 024	2.399 932 8E-05
milliliter/day	0.024	2.400 000 0E-02
ounce/day [UK, liquid]	0.000 844 7	8.446 819 1E-04
ounce/day [US, liquid]	0.000 811 5	8.115 365 4E-04
cubic millimeter/minute		**<flow rate, volume basis>**
barrel/day [US, liquid]	0.000 012 1	1.207 643 7E-05
centiliter/day	0.144	1.440 000 0E-01
cubic centimeter/day	1.44	1.440 000 0E+00
cubic decimeter/day	0.001 44	1.440 000 0E-03
cubic foot/day	0.000 050 9	5.085 312 0E-05
cubic inch/day	0.087 874 2	8.787 419 2E-02
cubic meter/second	<<<	1.666 666 7E-11

Convert From		<Type of Unit>
Convert To	Standard	Scientific

cubic millimeter/hour	60	6.000 000 0E+01
deciliter/day	0.014 4	1.440 000 0E-02
gallon/day [UK]	0.000 316 8	3.167 557 2E-04
gallon/day [US, liquid]	0.000 380 4	3.804 077 6E-04
lambda/minute	1	1.000 000 0E+00
liter/day	0.001 44	1.440 000 0E-03
liter/day [pre-1964]	0.001 44	1.439 959 7E-03
milliliter/day	1.44	1.440 000 0E+00
ounce/day [UK, liquid]	0.050 680 9	5.068 091 5E-02
ounce/day [US, liquid]	0.048 692 2	4.869 219 3E-02

cubic millimeter/second		<flow rate, volume basis>
barrel/day [UK]	0.000 527 9	5.279 262 0E-04
barrel/day [US, federal]	0.000 736 3	7.362 730 8E-04
barrel/day [US, liquid]	0.000 724 6	7.245 862 0E-04
barrel/day [US, petroleum]	0.000 543 4	5.434 396 5E-04
centiliter/day	8.64	8.640 000 0E+00
cubic centimeter/hour	3.6	3.600 000 0E+00
cubic decimeter/day	0.086 4	8.640 000 0E-02
cubic foot/day	0.003 051 2	3.051 187 2E-03
cubic inch/day	5.272 451 5	5.272 451 5E+00
cubic meter/second	<<<	1.000 000 0E-09
cubic millimeter/minute	60	6.000 000 0E+01
cubic yard/day	0.000 113	1.130 069 3E-04
deciliter/day	0.864	8.640 000 0E-01
gallon/day [UK]	0.019 005 3	1.900 534 3E-02
gallon/day [US, liquid]	0.022 824 5	2.282 446 5E-02
lambda/second	1	1.000 000 0E+00
liter/day	0.086 4	8.640 000 0E-02
liter/day [pre-1964]	0.086 397 6	8.639 758 1E-02
milliliter/hour	3.6	3.600 000 0E+00
ounce/day [UK, liquid]	3.040 854 9	3.040 854 9E+00
ounce/day [US, liquid]	2.921 531 6	2.921 531 6E+00

cubic nanometer		<volume>
cubic inch	<<<	6.102 374 4E-23
cubic meter	<<<	1.000 000 0E-27
drop [US, liquid]	<<<	1.217 304 8E-20
liter	<<<	1.000 000 0E-24
yoctoliter	1	1.000 000 0E+00

cubic petameter		<volume>
acre foot	>>>	8.107 131 9E+41
barrel [US, dry]	>>>	8.648 489 8E+45
barrel [US, liquid]	>>>	8.386 414 4E+45
bushel [US, dry]	>>>	2.837 759 3E+46
cubic foot	>>>	3.531 466 7E+46
cubic meter	>>>	1.000 000 0E+45
cubic yard	>>>	1.307 950 6E+45
hectare meter	>>>	1.000 000 0E+41
liter	>>>	1.000 000 0E+48
million acre foot	>>>	8.107 131 9E+35
million board foot	>>>	4.237 760 0E+41
stere	>>>	1.000 000 0E+45
trillion cubic foot	>>>	3.531 466 7E+34
yottaliter	>>>	1.000 000 0E+24

cubic picometer		<volume>
cubic inch	<<<	6.102 374 4E-32
cubic meter	<<<	1.000 000 0E-36
drop [US, liquid]	<<<	1.217 304 8E-29
liter	<<<	1.000 000 0E-33
ounce [US, liquid]	<<<	3.381 402 3E-32
teaspoon [US, measuring]	<<<	2.028 841 4E-31
yoctoliter	<<<	1.000 000 0E-09

	Standard	Scientific
cubic sagene [Russia]		<volume, special - see page 29>
cubic meter	9.712 678	9.712 678 0E+00
cubic terameter		<volume>
acre foot	>>>	8.107 131 9E+32
cubem	>>>	2.399 127 6E+26
cubic meter	>>>	1.000 000 0E+36
cubic mile	>>>	2.399 127 6E+26
cubic yard	>>>	1.307 950 6E+36
gallon [US, dry]	>>>	2.270 207 5E+38
gallon [US, liquid]	>>>	2.641 720 5E+38
hectare meter	>>>	1.000 000 0E+32
liter	>>>	1.000 000 0E+39
trillion cubic foot	>>>	3.531 466 7E+25
yottaliter	>>>	1.000 000 0E+15
cubic verchok [Russia]		<volume, special - see page 29>
cubic centimeter	87.824 4	8.782 440 0E+01
cubic yard		<volume>
acre foot	0.000 619 8	6.198 347 1E−04
barrel [US, dry]	6.612 244 9	6.612 244 9E+00
barrel [US, liquid]	6.411 873 8	6.411 873 8E+00
board foot	324	3.240 000 0E+02
bushel [UK]	21.022 32	2.102 232 0E+01
bushel [US, dry]	21.696 227	2.169 622 7E+01
cord foot [timber]	1.687 5	1.687 500 0E+00
cubic foot	27	2.700 000 0E+01
cubic inch	46,656	4.665 600 0E+04
cubic meter	0.764 554 9	7.645 548 6E−01
cubic mile	<<<	1.834 264 7E−10
drum [US, liquid]	3.672 255	3.672 255 0E+00
gallon [US, dry]	173.569 81	1.735 698 1E+02
gallon [US, liquid]	201.974 03	2.019 740 3E+02
hectare meter	0.000 076 5	7.645 548 6E−05
hectoliter	7.645 548 6	7.645 548 6E+00
liter	764.554 86	7.645 548 6E+02
quarter [UK]	2.627 79	2.627 790 0E+00
stere	0.764 554 9	7.645 548 6E−01
thousand board foot	0.324	3.240 000 0E−01
thousand cubic foot	0.027	2.700 000 0E−02
trillion cubic foot	<<<	2.700 000 0E−11
Winchester wine gallon [UK]	201.974 03	2.019 740 3E+02
cubic yard/day		<flow rate, volume basis>
acre inch/day	0.007 438	7.438 016 5E−03
barrel/day [UK]	4.671 626 6	4.671 626 6E+00
barrel/day [US, federal]	6.515 291 2	6.515 291 2E+00
barrel/day [US, liquid]	6.411 873 8	6.411 873 8E+00
barrel/day [US, petroleum]	4.808 905 4	4.808 905 4E+00
centiliter/minute	53.094 087	5.309 408 7E+01
cubic centimeter/second	8.849 014 6	8.849 014 6E+00
cubic decimeter/hour	31.856 452 4	3.185 645 2E+01
cubic foot/hour	1.125	1.125 000 0E+00
cubic inch/minute	32.4	3.240 000 0E+01
cubic meter/second	0.000 008 8	8.849 014 6E−06
cubic yard/hour	0.041 666 7	4.166 666 7E−02
deciliter/minute	5.309 408 7	5.309 408 7E+00
dekaliter/hour	3.185 645 2	3.185 645 2E+00
gallon/hour [UK]	7.007 439 9	7.007 439 9E+00
gallon/hour [US, liquid]	8.415 584 4	8.415 584 4E+00
hectoliter/hour	7.645 548 6	7.645 548 6E+00
lambda/second	8,849.014 56	8.849 014 6E+03
liter/hour	31.856 452 4	3.185 645 2E+01
liter/hour [pre-1964]	31.855 560 5	3.185 556 1E+01
milliliter/second	8.849 014 6	8.849 014 6E+00

Convert To	Standard	Scientific
miner's inch [AZ, CA, MT, OR]	0.012 5	1.250 000 0E-02
miner's inch [British Columbia, Canada]	0.011 160 7	1.116 071 4E-02
miner's inch [Colorado]	0.012	1.200 000 0E-02
miner's inch [ID, KS, NE, NM, NV, ND, SD, UT]	0.015 625	1.562 500 0E-02
ounce/minute [UK, liquid]	18.686 506	1.868 650 6E+01
ounce/minute [US, liquid]	17.953 247	1.795 324 7E+01
petrograd standard/day	0.163 636 4	1.636 363 6E-01
stere/day	0.764 554 9	7.645 548 6E-01
thousand cubic foot/day	0.027	2.700 000 0E-02
cubic yard/hour		**<flow rate, volume basis>**
acre foot/day	0.014 876	1.487 603 3E-02
acre foot/day [US, survey]	0.014 875 9	1.487 594 4E-02
acre inch/day	0.178 512 4	1.785 124 0E-01
barrel/hour [UK]	4.671 626 6	4.671 626 6E+00
barrel/hour [US, federal]	6.515 291 2	6.515 291 2E+00
barrel/hour [US, liquid]	6.411 873 8	6.411 873 8E+00
barrel/hour [US, petroleum]	4.808 905 4	4.808 905 4E+00
centiliter/second	21.237 634 9	2.123 763 5E+01
cubic centimeter/second	212.376 349	2.123 763 5E+02
cubic decimeter/minute	12.742 581	1.274 258 1E+01
cubic foot/hour	27	2.700 000 0E+01
cubic inch/second	12.96	1.296 000 0E+01
cubic meter/second	0.000 212 4	2.123 763 5E-04
cubic yard/day	24	2.400 000 0E+01
deciliter/second	2.123 763 5	2.123 763 5E+00
dekaliter/minute	1.274 258 1	1.274 258 1E+00
gallon/minute [UK]	2.802 976	2.802 976 0E+00
gallon/minute [US, liquid]	3.366 233 8	3.366 233 8E+00
hectoliter/hour	7.645 548 6	7.645 548 6E+00
kiloliter/day	18.349 316 6	1.834 931 7E+01
liter/minute	12.742 581	1.274 258 1E+01
liter/minute [pre-1964]	12.742 224 2	1.274 222 4E+01
ounce/second [UK, liquid]	7.474 602 6	7.474 602 6E+00
ounce/second [US, liquid]	7.181 298 7	7.181 298 7E+00
petrograd standard/day	3.927 272 7	3.927 272 7E+00
stere/day	18.349 317	1.834 931 7E+01
thousand cubic foot/day	0.648	6.480 000 0E-01
cubic yard/minute		**<flow rate, volume basis>**
acre foot/day	0.892 562	8.925 619 8E-01
acre foot/day [US, survey]	0.892 556 6	8.925 566 3E-01
acre inch/day	10.710 743 8	1.071 074 4E+01
barrel/minute [UK]	4.671 626 6	4.671 626 6E+00
barrel/minute [US, federal]	6.515 291 2	6.515 291 2E+00
barrel/minute [US, liquid]	6.411 873 8	6.411 873 8E+00
barrel/minute [US, petroleum]	4.808 905 4	4.808 905 4E+00
cubic decimeter/second	12.742 581	1.274 258 1E+01
cubic dekameter/day	1.100 959	1.100 959 0E+00
cubic foot/minute	27	2.700 000 0E+01
cubic inch/second	777.6	7.776 000 0E+02
cubic meter/second	0.012 742 6	1.274 258 1E-02
cubic yard/hour	60	6.000 000 0E+01
deciliter/second	127.425 81	1.274 258 1E+02
dekaliter/second	1.274 258 1	1.274 258 1E+00
gallon/second [UK]	2.802 976	2.802 976 0E+00
gallon/second [US, liquid]	3.366 233 8	3.366 233 8E+00
hectare meter/day	0.110 095 9	1.100 959 0E-01
hectoliter/minute	7.645 548 6	7.645 548 6E+00
kiloliter/hour	45.873 291 5	4.587 329 2E+01
liter/second	12.742 581	1.274 258 1E+01
liter/second [pre-1964]	12.742 224 2	1.274 222 4E+01
ounce/second [UK, liquid]	448.476 15	4.484 761 5E+02
ounce/second [US, liquid]	430.877 92	4.308 779 2E+02
petrograd standard/hour	9.818 181 8	9.818 181 8E+00

Convert From Convert To	Standard	<Type of Unit> Scientific

Convert From Convert To	Standard	Scientific
stere/hour	45.873 291	4.587 329 1E+01
thousand cubic foot/hour	1.62	1.620 000 0E+00

cubic yard/second   **<flow rate, volume basis>**

Convert To	Standard	Scientific
acre foot/hour	2.231 405	2.231 405 0E+00
acre foot/hour [US, survey]	2.231 391 6	2.231 391 6E+00
acre inch/hour	26.776 859 5	2.677 686 0E+01
barrel/second [UK]	4.671 626 6	4.671 626 6E+00
barrel/second [US, federal]	6.515 291 2	6.515 291 2E+00
barrel/second [US, liquid]	6.411 873 8	6.411 873 8E+00
barrel/second [US, petroleum]	4.808 905 4	4.808 905 4E+00
billion cubic foot/day	0.002 332 8	2.332 800 0E−03
cubic dekameter/hour	2.752 397 5	2.752 397 5E+00
cubic foot/second	27	2.700 000 0E+01
cubic inch/second	46,656	4.665 600 0E+04
cubic meter/second	0.764 554 9	7.645 548 6E−01
cubic yard/minute	60	6.000 000 0E+01
deciliter/second	7,645.548 58	7.645 548 6E+03
dekaliter/second	76.455 485 8	7.645 548 6E+01
gallon/second [UK]	168.178 557	1.681 785 6E+02
gallon/second [US, liquid]	201.974 026	2.019 740 3E+02
hectare meter/day	6.605 754	6.605 754 0E+00
hectoliter/second	7.645 548 6	7.645 548 6E+00
kiloliter/minute	45.873 291 5	4.587 329 2E+01
liter/second	764.554 858	7.645 548 6E+02
liter/second [pre-1964]	764.533 451	7.645 334 5E+02
ounce/second [UK, liquid]	26,908.569	2.690 856 9E+04
ounce/second [US, liquid]	25,852.675	2.585 267 5E+04
petrograd standard/minute	9.818 181 8	9.818 181 8E+00
stere/minute	45.873 291	4.587 329 1E+01
thousand cubic foot/minute	1.62	1.620 000 0E+00

cubic yoctometer   **<volume>**

Convert To	Standard	Scientific
cubic inch	<<<	6.102 374 4E−68
cubic meter	<<<	1.000 000 0E−72
drop [US, liquid]	<<<	1.217 304 8E−65
liter	<<<	1.000 000 0E−69
yoctoliter	<<<	1.000 000 0E−45

cubic yottameter   **<volume>**

Convert To	Standard	Scientific
acre foot	>>>	8.107 131 9E+68
billion cubic foot	>>>	3.531 466 7E+64
cubem	>>>	2.399 127 6E+62
cubic foot	>>>	3.531 466 7E+73
cubic meter	>>>	1.000 000 0E+72
cubic mile	>>>	2.399 127 6E+62
gallon [US, dry]	>>>	2.270 207 5E+74
gallon [US, liquid]	>>>	2.641 720 5E+74
hectare meter	>>>	1.000 000 0E+68
liter	>>>	1.000 000 0E+75
million acre foot	>>>	8.107 131 9E+62
trillion cubic foot	>>>	3.531 466 7E+61
yottaliter	>>>	1.000 000 0E+51

cubic zeptometer   **<volume>**

Convert To	Standard	Scientific
cubic inch	<<<	6.102 374 4E−59
cubic meter	<<<	1.000 000 0E−63
drop [US, liquid]	<<<	1.217 304 8E−56
liter	<<<	1.000 000 0E−60
yoctoliter	<<<	1.000 000 0E−36

cubic zettameter   **<volume>**

Convert To	Standard	Scientific
acre foot	>>>	8.107 131 9E+59
cubem	>>>	2.399 127 6E+53
cubic meter	>>>	1.000 000 0E+63
cubic mile	>>>	2.399 127 6E+53
hectare meter	>>>	1.000 000 0E+59

Convert From		<Type of Unit>
Convert To	Standard	Scientific

	Standard	Scientific
liter ----------	--->>>	1.000 000 0E+66
million board foot ----------	--->>>	4.237 760 0E+59
trillion cubic foot ----------	--->>>	3.531 466 7E+52
yottaliter----------	--->>>	1.000 000 0E+42

cubic zoll [Germany] <volume, special - see page 29>
cubic centimeter---------- 14.387 1 --- 1.438 700 0E+01

cubit <length>
caliber----------	1,800	1.800 000 0E+03
digit----------	24	2.400 000 0E+01
foot [international]----------	1.5	1.500 000 0E+00
foot [US, survey]----------	1.499 997	1.499 997 0E+00
hand [horses]----------	4.5	4.500 000 0E+00
inch [based on US, survey foot]----------	17.999 964	1.799 996 4E+01
inch [international]----------	18	1.800 000 0E+01
meter----------	0.457 2	4.572 000 0E-01
mil----------	18,000	1.800 000 0E+04
nail [cloth]----------	8	8.000 000 0E+00
pace [geometrical]----------	0.03	3.000 000 0E-02
palm----------	6	6.000 000 0E+00
pied [France]----------	1.407 459 5	1.407 459 5E+00
quarter [cloth]----------	2	2.000 000 0E+00
span----------	2	2.000 000 0E+00
yard [based on US, survey foot]----------	0.499 999	4.999 990 0E-01
yard [international]----------	0.5	5.000 000 0E-01
yard [UK]----------	0.500 000 9	5.000 008 7E-01

cubit [Babylon, ancient] <length, special - see page 29>
centimeter---------- 52.5 --- 5.250 000 0E+01

cubit [Burma] <length, special - see page 29>
meter ---------- 0.457 2 --- 4.572 000 0E-01

cubit [Cambodia] <length, special - see page 29>
meter ---------- 0.5 --- 5.000 000 0E-01

cubit [Egypt, ancient, long] <length, special - see page 29>
centimeter---------- 52.36 --- 5.236 000 0E+01

cubit [Egypt, ancient, short] <length, special - see page 29>
centimeter---------- 44.9 --- 4.490 000 0E+01

cubit [Greece, ancient] <length, special - see page 29>
centimeter---------- 46.5 --- 4.650 000 0E+01

cubit [Hebrew, ancient, long] <length, special - see page 29>
meter ---------- 0.5 --- 5.000 000 0E-01

cubit [Hebrew, ancient, short] <length, special - see page 29>
meter ---------- 0.45 --- 4.500 000 0E-01

cubit [India] <length, special - see page 29>
centimeter---------- 45.72 --- 4.572 000 0E+01

cubit [Malaysia] <length, special - see page 29>
meter ---------- 0.457 2 --- 4.572 000 0E-01

cubit [Mesopotamia, ancient] <length, special - see page 29>
centimeter---------- 49.5 --- 4.950 000 0E+01

cubit [Pakistan] <length, special - see page 29>
meter ---------- 0.457 2 --- 4.572 000 0E-01

cubit [Rome, ancient] <length, special - see page 29>
centimeter---------- 44.4 --- 4.440 000 0E+01

cubit [Singapore] <length, special - see page 29>
meter ---------- 0.457 --- 4.570 000 0E-01

cubit [Somalia] <length, special - see page 29>
meter ---------- 0.558 8 --- 5.588 000 0E-01

cubit [Spanish North Africa] <length, special - see page 29>
centimeter---------- 53.3 --- 5.330 000 0E+01

Convert From Convert To	Standard	<Type of Unit> Scientific
cubit [Syria, textiles]		<length, special - see page 29>
centimeter	63	6.300 000 0E+01
cubito [Cambodia]		<length, special - see page 29>
meter	0.5	5.000 000 0E−01
cubito [Somalia]		<length, special - see page 29>
meter	0.558 8	5.588 000 0E−01
cubito [Somaliland]		<length, special - see page 29>
centimeter	55.9	5.590 000 0E+01
cubitus [Rome, ancient]		<length, special - see page 29>
meter	0.444	4.440 000 0E−01
cuddy [Arabia]		<volume, special - see page 29>
liter	3.78	3.780 000 0E+00
cuerda [Cuba]		<length, special - see page 29>
meter	20.352	2.035 200 0E+01
cuerda [Paraguay]		<length, special - see page 29>
meter	69.88	6.988 000 0E+01
cuerda [Philippines]		<area, special - see page 29>
hectare	0.393	3.930 000 0E−01
cuerda [Puerto Rico]		<area, special - see page 29>
hectare	0.393	3.930 000 0E−01
culleus [Rome, ancient]		<volume, special - see page 29>
liter	524	5.240 000 0E+02
cun [Hong Kong]		<length, special - see page 29>
centimeter	3.714 75	3.714 750 0E+00
cunningham acre [Ireland]		<area, special - see page 29>
hectare	0.522 6	5.226 000 0E−01
cup [Canada, measuring]		<volume>
bushel [UK]	0.006 25	6.250 000 0E−03
cubic foot	0.008 027 2	8.027 182 7E−03
cubic inch	13.870 972	1.387 097 2E+01
cubic meter	0.000 227 3	2.273 045 0E−04
cup [US, measuring]	0.960 759 9	9.607 599 4E−01
deciliter	2.273 045	2.273 045 0E+00
drachm [UK, liquid]	64	6.400 000 0E+01
dram [Canada, liquid]	64	6.400 000 0E+01
gallon [Canada, liquid]	0.05	5.000 000 0E−02
gallon [UK, dry or liquid]	0.05	5.000 000 0E−02
gallon [US, dry]	0.051 602 8	5.160 283 7E−02
gallon [US, liquid]	0.060 047 5	6.004 749 6E−02
gill [UK]	1.6	1.600 000 0E+00
gill [US]	1.921 519 9	1.921 519 9E+00
liter	0.227 304 5	2.273 045 0E−01
milliliter	227.304 5	2.273 045 0E+02
ounce [UK, liquid]	8	8.000 000 0E+00
ounce [US, liquid]	7.686 079 5	7.686 079 5E+00
pint [UK]	0.4	4.000 000 0E−01
pint [US, dry]	0.412 822 7	4.128 227 0E−01
pint [US, liquid]	0.480 38	4.803 799 7E−01
quart [UK]	0.2	2.000 000 0E−01
quart [US, dry]	0.206 411 4	2.064 113 5E−01
quart [US, liquid]	0.240 19	2.401 899 9E−01
scruple [UK, liquid]	192	1.920 000 0E+02
tablespoon [Canada, measuring]	16.000 027	1.600 002 7E+01
tablespoon [US, measuring]	15.372 159	1.537 215 9E+01
teaspoon [Canada, measuring]	48.000 081	4.800 008 1E+01
teaspoon [US, measuring]	46.116 477	4.611 647 7E+01
cup [metric]		<volume>
cubic inch	12.204 749	1.220 474 9E+01
cubic meter	0.000 2	2.000 000 0E−04

Convert From Convert To	Standard	<Type of Unit> Scientific
cup [US, measuring]-------------------	0.845 350 6	8.453 505 7E-01
deciliter -----------------------------	2	2.000 000 0E+00
liter ---------------------------------	0.2	2.000 000 0E-01
milliliter----------------------------	200	2.000 000 0E+02
ounce [US, liquid]--------------------	6.762 804 5	6.762 804 5E+01
cup [Sierra Leone]		<volume, special - see page 29>
centiliter----------------------------	33.3	3.330 000 0E+01
cup [US, measuring]		<volume>
cubic foot --------------------------	0.008 355	8.355 034 7E-03
cubic inch --------------------------	14.437 5	1.443 750 0E+01
cubic meter -------------------------	0.000 236 6	2.365 882 4E-04
cup [Canada, measuring]-------------	1.040 842 7	1.040 842 7E+00
cup [metric]-------------------------	1.182 941 2	1.182 941 2E+00
deciliter ----------------------------	2.365 882 4	2.365 882 4E+00
dram [US, liquid]--------------------	64	6.400 000 0E+01
drop [US, liquid]--------------------	2,880	2.880 000 0E+03
gallon [US, liquid]------------------	0.062 5	6.250 000 0E-02
gill [UK]----------------------------	1.665 348 4	1.665 348 4E+00
gill [US]----------------------------	2	2.000 000 0E+00
liter --------------------------------	0.236 588 2	2.365 882 4E-01
ounce [UK, liquid] ------------------	8.326 741 8	8.326 741 8E+00
ounce [US, liquid] ------------------	8	8.000 000 0E+00
pint [UK] ---------------------------	0.416 337 1	4.163 370 9E-01
pint [US, dry]-----------------------	0.429 683 5	4.296 835 0E-01
pint [US, liquid]--------------------	0.5	5.000 000 0E-01
quart [UK] --------------------------	0.208 168 6	2.081 685 5E-01
quart [US, dry]----------------------	0.214 841 8	2.148 417 5E-01
quart [US, liquid]-------------------	0.25	2.500 000 0E-01
tablespoon [Canada, measuring]------	16.653 512	1.665 351 2E+01
tablespoon [US, measuring]----------	16	1.600 000 0E+01
teaspoon [Canada, measuring]--------	49.960 536	4.996 053 6E+01
teaspoon [US, measuring]------------	48	4.800 000 0E+01
Winchester wine gallon [UK] --------	0.062 5	6.250 000 0E-02
curie		<radionuclide activity>
becquerel---------------------------	>>>	3.700 000 0E+10
rutherford---------------------------	37,000	3.700 000 0E+04
curie/cubic meter		<radionuclide volume activity>
becquerel/cubic meter ---------------	>>>	3.700 000 0E+10
rutherford/cubic meter --------------	37,000	3.700 000 0E+04
curie/kilogram		<radionuclide specific activity>
becquerel/kilogram ------------------	>>>	3.700 000 0E+10
millicurie/kilogram ------------------	1,000	1.000 000 0E+03
rutherford/kilogram------------------	37,000	3.700 000 0E+04
curo [Portuguese India]		<volume, special - see page 29>
liter --------------------------------	7.986	7.986 000 0E+00
cusec		<flow rate, volume basis>
acre foot/day------------------------	1.983 471 1	1.983 471 1E+00
cubic foot/second -------------------	1	1.000 000 0E+00
cubic meter/second ------------------	0.028 316 8	2.831 684 7E-02
custom centner [Germany]		<mass, special - see page 29>
kilogram----------------------------	50	5.000 000 0E+01
custom quintal [Czechoslovakia, hops]		<mass, special - see page 29>
kilogram----------------------------	50	5.000 000 0E+01
cwierc [Poland]		<volume, special - see page 29>
liter --------------------------------	32	3.200 000 0E+01
cyathus [Rome, ancient]		<volume, special - see page 29>
liter --------------------------------	0.045 5	4.550 000 0E-02
cyathys [Greece, ancient]		<volume, special - see page 29>
liter --------------------------------	0.044 949	4.494 900 0E-02

Convert From Convert To	<Type of Unit>	
	Standard	Scientific

cycle/second   **\<frequency>**

	Standard	Scientific
1/second	1	1.000 000 0E+00
degree/second	360	3.600 000 0E+02
hertz	1	1.000 000 0E+00
kilohertz	0.001	1.000 000 0E−03
radian/second	6.283 185 3	6.283 185 3E+00
revolution/second	1	1.000 000 0E+00

dai [South Korea]   **\<volume, special - see page 29>**

liter	1.803 9	1.803 900 0E+00

dain [Burma]   **\<length, special - see page 29>**

kilometer	3.912	3.912 000 0E+00

daktylos [Greece, ancient]   **\<length, special - see page 29>**

centimeter	2.54	2.540 000 0E+00

dalton   **\<mass>**

atomic mass unit [unified, C-12,1986]	1	1.000 000 0E+00
avogram	1	1.000 000 0E+00
grain	<<<	2.562 605 1E−23
kilogram	<<<	1.660 540 2E−27
milli-mass-unit	1,000	1.000 000 0E+03
yoctogram	1.660 540 2	1.660 540 2E+00

dam [East India]   **\<mass, special - see page 29>**

gram	20.96	2.096 000 0E+01

damleng [Brunei]   **\<mass, special - see page 29>**

gram	37.8	3.780 000 0E+01

damleng [Cambodia]   **\<mass, special - see page 29>**

gram	37.5	3.750 000 0E+01

damleng [China]   **\<mass, special - see page 29>**

gram	37.8	3.780 000 0E+01

damleng [Hong Kong]   **\<mass, special - see page 29>**

gram	37.8	3.780 000 0E+01

dan [Cambodia]   **\<mass, special - see page 29>**

kilogram	60	6.000 000 0E+01

dan [China]   **\<mass, special - see page 29>**

kilogram	100	1.000 000 0E+02

dan [Indonesia]   **\<mass, special - see page 29>**

kilogram	61.761	6.176 100 0E+01

dan [Japan]   **\<mass, special - see page 29>**

kilogram	60	6.000 000 0E+01

dan [Laos]   **\<mass, special - see page 29>**

kilogram	60	6.000 000 0E+01

dan [Mongolia]   **\<volume, special - see page 29>**

liter	65	6.500 000 0E+01

dan [Philippines]   **\<mass, special - see page 29>**

kilogram	63.249	6.324 900 0E+01

dan [Thailand]   **\<mass, special - see page 29>**

kilogram	60	6.000 000 0E+01

dan [Vietnam]   **\<mass, special - see page 29>**

kilogram	60.453	6.045 300 0E+01

dan chung [Hong Kong]   **\<area, special - see page 29>**

are	6.745	6.745 000 0E+00

dan oranja [Yugoslavia]   **\<area, special - see page 29>**

are	35.97	3.597 000 0E+01

danar [Iran]   **\<mass, special - see page 29>**

gram	187.5	1.875 000 0E+02

daneq [Egypt]   **\<area, special - see page 29>**

square meter	29.172	2.917 200 0E+01

Convert From		<Type of Unit>
Convert To	Standard	Scientific

danich [Arabia] <mass, special - see page 29>
gram --- 0.4 --- 4.000 000 0E-01

daraf <electric elastance>
1/farad --- 1 --- 1.000 000 0E+00

darat [Somalia] <area, special - see page 29>
are --- 80 --- 8.000 000 0E+01

darchini [Arabia] <mass, special - see page 29>
gram --- 0.4 --- 4.000 000 0E-01

darcy [20 °C] <permeability, water>
millidarcy [20 °C] --- 1,000 --- 1.000 000 0E+03
perm [20 °C] --- 0.000 439 5 --- 4.394 644 0E-04
square centimeter --- <<< --- 9.869 232 7E-09
square foot --- <<< --- 1.062 315 4E-11
square meter --- <<< --- 9.869 232 7E-13

dareb [Somalia] <area, special - see page 29>
are --- 25 --- 2.500 000 0E+01

dareikos [Persia, ancient, gold] <mass, special - see page 29>
gram --- 8.41 --- 8.410 000 0E+00

dariba [Egypt] <volume, special - see page 29>
hectoliter --- 15.84 --- 1.584 000 0E+01

daribah [Egypt] <volume, special - see page 29>
hectoliter --- 15.84 --- 1.584 000 0E+01

daric [Hebrew, ancient, gold] <mass, special - see page 29>
gram --- 8 --- 8.000 000 0E+00

daric [Persia, ancient, gold] <mass, special - see page 29>
gram --- 8.41 --- 8.410 000 0E+00

darm [Cambodia] <mass, special - see page 29>
kilogram --- 60 --- 6.000 000 0E+01

darm [China] <mass, special - see page 29>
kilogram --- 50 --- 5.000 000 0E+01

darm [Indonesia] <mass, special - see page 29>
kilogram --- 61.761 --- 6.176 100 0E+01

darm [Japan] <mass, special - see page 29>
kilogram --- 60 --- 6.000 000 0E+01

darm [Laos] <mass, special - see page 29>
kilogram --- 60 --- 6.000 000 0E+01

darm [Philippines] <mass, special - see page 29>
kilogram --- 63.249 --- 6.324 900 0E+01

darm [Thailand] <mass, special - see page 29>
kilogram --- 60 --- 6.000 000 0E+01

darm [Vietnam] <mass, special - see page 29>
kilogram --- 60.453 --- 6.045 300 0E+01

dartung [Iran] <mass, special - see page 29>
gram --- 1.020 7 --- 1.020 700 0E+00

dash [US, an approximate measurement] <volume>
teaspoon --- less than 1/8 teaspoon

dau [Hong Kong] <volume, special - see page 29>
liter --- 10 --- 1.000 000 0E+01

dau [Vietnam] <volume, special - see page 29>
liter --- 1 --- 1.000 000 0E+00

dau chung [Hong Kong] <area, special - see page 29>
square meter --- 674.5 --- 6.745 000 0E+02

daula [Ethiopia] <volume, special - see page 29>
hectoliter --- 0.88 --- 8.800 000 0E-01

dawala [Ethiopia] <mass, special - see page 29>
kilogram --- 80 --- 8.000 000 0E+01

	Standard	Scientific
		<Type of Unit>

dawulla [Ethiopia]   **<mass, special - see page 29>**

Convert To	Standard	Scientific
kilogram	100	1.000 000 0E+02

day   **<time>**

Convert To	Standard	Scientific
blink	100,000	1.000 000 0E+05
day [Coordinated Universal Time (UTC)]	1	1.000 000 0E+00
day [mean solar]	1	1.000 000 0E+00
hour	24	2.400 000 0E+01
minute	1,440	1.440 000 0E+03
second	86,400	8.640 000 0E+04
year [normal calendar]	0.002 739 7	2.739 726 0E-03

day [Coordinated Universal Time (UTC)]   **<time>**

Convert To	Standard	Scientific
day	1	1.000 000 0E+00
hour	24	2.400 000 0E+01
minute	1,440	1.440 000 0E+03
month [mean sidereal]	0.036 601	3.660 099 5E-02
second	86,400	8.640 000 0E+04
year [normal calendar]	0.002 739 7	2.739 726 0E-03

day [mean sidereal]   **<time>**

Convert To	Standard	Scientific
day	0.997 269 6	9.972 695 7E-01
hour	23.934 469 6	2.393 447 0E+01
hour [mean sidereal]	24	2.400 000 0E+01
minute	1,436.068 18	1.436 068 2E+03
minute [mean sidereal]	1,440	1.440 000 0E+03
second	86,164.090 5	8.616 409 1E+04
second [mean sidereal]	86,400	8.640 000 0E+04
year [mean sidereal]	0.002 730 3	2.730 327 7E-03
year [normal calendar]	0.002 732 2	2.732 245 4E-03

day [mean solar]   **<time>**

Convert To	Standard	Scientific
day	1	1.000 000 0E+00
day [Coordinated Universal Time (UTC)]	1	1.000 000 0E+00
hour	24	2.400 000 0E+01
hour [mean solar]	24	2.400 000 0E+01
minute	1,440	1.440 000 0E+03
minute [mean solar]	1,440	1.440 000 0E+03
month [mean sidereal]	0.036 601	3.660 099 5E-02
second	86,400	8.640 000 0E+04
second [mean solar]	86,400	8.640 000 0E+04
year [normal calendar]	0.002 739 7	2.739 726 0E-03

day square foot °F/Btu inch [-/ I.T.]   **<thermal resistivity>**

Convert To	Standard	Scientific
meter kelvin/watt	166.403 32	1.664 033 2E+02

day square foot degree Rankine/Btu inch [-/ I.T.]   **<thermal resistivity>**

Convert To	Standard	Scientific
meter kelvin/watt	166.403 32	1.664 033 2E+02

dbn [Egypt, ancient]   **<mass, special - see page 29>**

Convert To	Standard	Scientific
gram	91	9.100 000 0E+01

debbie [Zambia]   **<volume, special - see page 29>**

Convert To	Standard	Scientific
liter	18.184	1.818 400 0E+01

deben [Egypt, ancient]   **<mass, special - see page 29>**

Convert To	Standard	Scientific
gram	91	9.100 000 0E+01

debye unit   **<electric dipole moment>**

Convert To	Standard	Scientific
coulomb meter	<<<	3.335 641 0E-30
franklin centimeter	<<<	1.000 000 0E-18

debye unit/square angstrom   **<electric dipole moment/unit area>**

Convert To	Standard	Scientific
coulomb/meter	<<<	3.335 641 0E-10
helmholtz	1	1.000 000 0E+00

decade   **<units>**

Convert To	Standard	Scientific
ten	1	1.000 000 0E+00
unit	10	1.000 000 0E+01

decade   **<time>**

Convert To	Standard	Scientific
decennary	1	1.000 000 0E+00
decennial	1	1.000 000 0E+00

Convert From Convert To	Standard	<Type of Unit> Scientific

Convert From Convert To	Standard	Scientific
decennium		
decade	1	1.000 000 0E+00
year [normal calendar]	10	1.000 000 0E+01
decempeda [Rome, ancient]		<length, special - see page 29>
meter	2.96	2.960 000 0E+00
decempeda quadrata [Rome, ancient]		<area, special - see page 29>
square meter	8.76	8.760 000 0E+00
decennary		<time>
decade	1	1.000 000 0E+00
decennial	1	1.000 000 0E+00
decennium	1	1.000 000 0E+00
year [normal calendar]	10	1.000 000 0E+01
decennial		<time>
decade	1	1.000 000 0E+00
decennary	1	1.000 000 0E+00
decennium	1	1.000 000 0E+00
year [normal calendar]	10	1.000 000 0E+01
decennium		<time>
decade	1	1.000 000 0E+00
decennary	1	1.000 000 0E+00
decennial	1	1.000 000 0E+00
year [normal calendar]	10	1.000 000 0E+01
deciampere		<electric current>
abampere	0.01	1.000 000 0E-02
ampere	0.1	1.000 000 0E-01
biot	0.01	1.000 000 0E-02
franklin/second	>>>	2.997 924 6E+08
gilbert	0.125 663 7	1.256 637 1E-01
statampere	>>>	2.997 924 6E+08
deciatine [Russia]		<area, special - see page 29>
hectare	1.092 54	1.092 540 0E+00
decibar		<pressure>
atmosphere [standard]	0.098 692 3	9.869 232 7E-02
atmosphere [technical]	0.101 971 6	1.019 716 2E-01
bar	0.1	1.000 000 0E-01
centimeter of mercury [0 °C, by convention]	7.500 615 8	7.500 615 8E+00
centimeter of water [4 °C, by convention]	101.971 62	1.019 716 2E+02
foot of mercury [0 °C, by convention]	0.246 083 2	2.460 831 9E-01
foot of water [4 °C, by convention]	3.345 525 6	3.345 525 6E+00
gram-force/square centimeter	101.971 62	1.019 716 2E+02
inch of mercury [0 °C, by convention]	2.952 998 3	2.952 998 3E+00
inch of water [4 °C, by convention]	40.146 308	4.014 630 8E+01
kilogram-force/square centimeter	0.101 971 6	1.019 716 2E-01
kilopascal	10	1.000 000 0E+01
kilopond/square centimeter	0.101 971 6	1.019 716 2E-01
kip/square foot	0.208 854 3	2.088 543 4E-01
millimeter of mercury [0 °C, by convention]	75.006 158	7.500 615 8E+01
millimeter of water [4 °C, by convention]	1,019.716 2	1.019 716 2E+03
newton/square millimeter	0.01	1.000 000 0E-02
ounce-force/square inch	23.206 038	2.320 603 8E+01
pascal	10,000	1.000 000 0E+04
pieze [France]	10	1.000 000 0E+01
pound-force/square inch	1.450 377 4	1.450 377 4E+00
sthene/square meter [France]	10	1.000 000 0E+01
ton-force/square foot [short]	0.104 427 2	1.044 271 7E-01
ton-force/square meter [metric]	1.019 716 2	1.019 716 2E+00
torr	75.006 168	7.500 616 8E+01
decibel		<sound pressure level>
bel	0.1	1.000 000 0E-01
neper	0.115 129 3	1.151 292 6E-01
decicandela		<luminous intensity>
candela	0.1	1.000 000 0E-01

decicoulomb <electric charge>

	Standard	Scientific
abcoulomb	0.01	1.000 000 0E-02
coulomb	0.1	1.000 000 0E-01
electromagnetic unit of charge [cgs system]	0.01	1.000 000 0E-02
statcoulomb	>>>	2.997 924 6E+08

decifarad <capacitance>

	Standard	Scientific
abfarad	<<<	1.000 000 0E-10
coulomb/volt	0.1	1.000 000 0E-01
farad	0.1	1.000 000 0E-01
statfarad	>>>	8.987 551 8E+10

decigal <acceleration>

	Standard	Scientific
foot/square second	0.003 280 8	3.280 839 9E-03
galileo	0.1	1.000 000 0E-01
gn [due to gravity]	0.000 102	1.019 716 2E-04
meter/square second	0.001	1.000 000 0E-03
millimeter/square second	1	1.000 000 0E+00

decigram <mass>

	Standard	Scientific
carat [gemstones]	0.5	5.000 000 0E-01
carat [international]	0.5	5.000 000 0E-01
carat [metric]	0.5	5.000 000 0E-01
carat [UK]	0.385 809	3.858 089 6E-01
carat [US, after 1913]	0.5	5.000 000 0E-01
carat [US, before 1913]	0.487 092 1	4.870 920 6E-01
drachm [UK, apothecary]	0.025 720 6	2.572 059 7E-02
dram [avoirdupois]	0.056 438 3	5.643 833 9E-02
dram [US, apothecary]	0.025 720 6	2.572 059 7E-02
grain	1.543 235 8	1.543 235 8E+00
grain [apothecary]	1.543 235 8	1.543 235 8E+00
grain [avoirdupois]	1.543 235 8	1.543 235 8E+00
grain [troy]	1.543 235 8	1.543 235 8E+00
kilogram	0.000 1	1.000 000 0E-04
ounce	0.003 527 4	3.527 396 2E-03
ounce [apothecary]	0.003 215 1	3.215 074 7E-03
ounce [avoirdupois]	0.003 527 4	3.527 396 2E-03
ounce [troy]	0.003 215 1	3.215 074 7E-03
pennyweight [troy]	0.064 301 5	6.430 149 3E-02
point [jewelers']	50	5.000 000 0E+01
scruple [UK]	0.077 161 8	7.716 179 2E-02
scruple [US, apothecary]	0.077 161 8	7.716 179 2E-02

decigram-force <force>

	Standard	Scientific
crinal	0.009 806 7	9.806 650 0E-03
dyne	98.066 5	9.806 650 0E+01
grain-force	1.543 235 8	1.543 235 8E+00
gram-force	0.1	1.000 000 0E-01
newton	0.000 980 7	9.806 650 0E-04
pond	0.1	1.000 000 0E-01
pound-force	0.000 220 5	2.204 622 6E-04
poundal	0.007 093 2	7.093 163 5E-03

decihenry <electric inductance>

	Standard	Scientific
abhenry	>>>	1.000 000 0E+08
henry	0.1	1.000 000 0E-01
joule/square ampere	0.1	1.000 000 0E-01
ohm second	0.1	1.000 000 0E-01
stathenry	<<<	1.112 650 1E-13

decijoule <energy>

	Standard	Scientific
Btu [I.T.]	0.000 094 8	9.478 171 2E-05
calorie [I.T.]	0.023 884 6	2.388 459 0E-02
calorie [mean]	0.023 866 2	2.386 623 5E-02
calorie [thermoc.]	0.023 900 6	2.390 057 4E-02
centigrade heat unit [I.T.]	0.000 052 7	5.265 650 7E-05
centimeter gram-force	1,019.716 2	1.019 716 2E+03
cubic centimeter atmosphere	0.986 923 3	9.869 232 7E-01

Convert From Convert To	\<Type of Unit\> Standard	\<Type of Unit\> Scientific
dyne centimeter	1,000,000	1.000 000 0E+06
erg	1,000,000	1.000 000 0E+06
foot pound-force	0.073 756 2	7.375 621 5E-02
foot poundal	2.373 036	2.373 036 0E+00
gram calorie	0.023 890 3	2.389 029 6E-02
inch ounce-force	14.161 193	1.416 119 3E+01
inch pound-force	0.885 074 6	8.850 745 8E-01
joule	0.1	1.000 000 0E-01
kilogram square meter/square second	0.1	1.000 000 0E-01
kilopond meter	0.010 197 2	1.019 716 2E-02
megaerg	1	1.000 000 0E+00
megalerg	1	1.000 000 0E+00
meter kilogram-force	0.010 197 2	1.019 716 2E-02
newton meter	0.1	1.000 000 0E-01
wattsecond	0.1	1.000 000 0E-01
deciliter		**\<volume\>**
barrel [US, dry]	0.000 864 8	8.648 489 8E-04
barrel [US, liquid]	0.000 838 6	8.386 414 5E-04
barrel [US, petroleum]	0.000 629	6.289 810 8E-04
board foot	0.042 377 6	4.237 760 0E-02
bushel [US, dry]	0.002 837 8	2.837 759 3E-03
cubic foot	0.003 531 5	3.531 466 7E-03
cubic inch	6.102 374 4	6.102 374 4E+00
cubic meter	0.000 1	1.000 000 0E-04
cup [Canada, measuring]	0.439 938 5	4.399 385 0E-01
cup [metric]	0.5	5.000 000 0E-01
cup [US, measuring]	0.422 675 3	4.226 752 8E-01
drachm [UK, liquid]	28.156 064	2.815 606 4E+01
dram [Canada, liquid]	28.156 064	2.815 606 4E+01
dram [US, liquid]	27.051 218	2.705 121 8E+01
gallon [US, dry]	0.022 702 1	2.270 207 5E-02
gallon [US, liquid]	0.026 417 2	2.641 720 5E-02
gill [UK]	0.703 901 6	7.039 015 9E-01
gill [US]	0.845 350 6	8.453 505 7E-01
liter	0.1	1.000 000 0E-01
ounce [UK, liquid]	3.519 508	3.519 508 0E+00
ounce [US, liquid]	3.381 402 3	3.381 402 3E+00
pint [UK]	0.175 975 4	1.759 754 0E-01
pint [US, dry]	0.181 616 6	1.816 166 0E-01
pint [US, liquid]	0.211 337 6	2.113 376 4E-01
quart [UK]	0.087 987 7	8.798 769 9E-02
quart [US, dry]	0.090 808 3	9.080 829 8E-02
quart [US, liquid]	0.105 668 8	1.056 688 2E-01
scruple [US, liquid]	84.468 191	8.446 819 1E+01
shih ho [China]	1	1.000 000 0E+00
stere	0.000 1	1.000 000 0E-04
tablespoon [Canada, measuring]	7.039 027 9	7.039 027 9E+00
tablespoon [US, measuring]	6.762 804 5	6.762 804 5E+00
teaspoon [Canada, measuring]	21.117 084	2.111 708 4E+01
teaspoon [US, measuring]	20.288 414	2.028 841 4E+01
deciliter/day		**\<flow rate, volume basis\>**
barrel/day [UK]	0.000 611	6.110 256 9E-04
barrel/day [US, federal]	0.000 852 2	8.521 679 1E-04
barrel/day [US, liquid]	0.000 838 6	8.386 414 4E-04
barrel/day [US, petroleum]	0.000 629	6.289 810 8E-04
centiliter/day	10	1.000 000 0E+01
cubic centimeter/hour	4.166 666 7	4.166 666 7E+00
cubic decimeter/day	0.1	1.000 000 0E-01
cubic foot/day	0.003 531 5	3.531 466 7E-03
cubic inch/day	6.102 374 4	6.102 374 4E+00
cubic meter/second	\<\<\<	1.157 407 4E-09
cubic millimeter/second	1.157 407 4	1.157 407 4E+00
dekaliter/day	0.01	1.000 000 0E-02

| Convert From | | <Type of Unit> | |
Convert To	Standard	Scientific

	Standard	Scientific
gallon/day [UK]	0.021 996 9	2.199 692 5E-02
gallon/day [US, liquid]	0.026 417 2	2.641 720 5E-02
hectoliter/day	0.001	1.000 000 0E-03
lambda/second	1.157 407 4	1.157 407 4E+00
liter/day	0.1	1.000 000 0E-01
liter/day [pre-1964]	0.099 997 2	9.999 720 0E-02
milliliter/hour	4.166 666 7	4.166 666 7E+00
ounce/day [UK, liquid]	3.519 508	3.519 508 0E+00
ounce/day [US, liquid]	3.381 402 3	3.381 402 3E+00
stere/day	0.000 1	1.000 000 0E-04

deciliter/hour — <flow rate, volume basis>

Convert To	Standard	Scientific
acre inch/day	0.000 023 3	2.334 854 0E-05
barrel/day [UK]	0.014 664 6	1.466 461 7E-02
barrel/day [US, federal]	0.020 452	2.045 203 0E-02
barrel/day [US, liquid]	0.020 127 4	2.012 739 5E-02
barrel/day [US, petroleum]	0.015 095 5	1.509 554 6E-02
centiliter/hour	10	1.000 000 0E+01
cubic centimeter/minute	1.666 666 7	1.666 666 7E+00
cubic decimeter/day	2.4	2.400 000 0E+00
cubic foot/day	0.084 755 2	8.475 520 0E-02
cubic inch/hour	6.102 374 4	6.102 374 4E+00
cubic meter/second	<<<	2.777 777 8E-08
cubic millimeter/second	27.777 777 8	2.777 777 8E+01
cubic yard/day	0.003 139 1	3.139 081 5E-03
deciliter/day	24	2.400 000 0E+01
dekaliter/day	0.24	2.400 000 0E-01
gallon/day [UK]	0.527 926 2	5.279 262 0E-01
gallon/day [US, liquid]	0.634 012 9	6.340 129 3E-01
hectoliter/day	0.024	2.400 000 0E-02
lambda/second	27.777 777 8	2.777 777 8E+01
liter/day	2.4	2.400 000 0E+00
liter/day [pre-1964]	2.399 932 8	2.399 932 8E+00
milliliter/minute	1.666 666 7	1.666 666 7E+00
ounce/hour [UK, liquid]	3.519 508	3.519 508 0E+00
ounce/hour [US, liquid]	3.381 402 3	3.381 402 3E+00
stere/day	0.002 4	2.400 000 0E-03

deciliter/minute — <flow rate, volume basis>

Convert To	Standard	Scientific
acre inch/day	0.001 400 9	1.400 912 4E-03
barrel/day [UK]	0.879 877	8.798 769 9E-01
barrel/day [US, federal]	1.227 121 8	1.227 121 8E+00
barrel/day [US, liquid]	1.207 643 7	1.207 643 7E+00
barrel/day [US, petroleum]	0.905 732 8	9.057 327 5E-01
centiliter/minute	10	1.000 000 0E+01
cubic centimeter/second	1.666 666 7	1.666 666 7E+00
cubic decimeter/hour	6	6.000 000 0E+00
cubic foot/day	5.085 312	5.085 312 0E+00
cubic inch/minute	6.102 374 4	6.102 374 4E+00
cubic meter/second	0.000 001 7	1.666 666 7E-06
cubic millimeter/second	1,666.666 67	1.666 666 7E+03
cubic yard/day	0.188 344 9	1.883 448 9E-01
deciliter/hour	60	6.000 000 0E+01
dekaliter/day	14.4	1.440 000 0E+01
gallon/hour [UK]	1.319 815 5	1.319 815 5E+00
gallon/day [US, liquid]	1.585 032 3	1.585 032 3E+00
hectoliter/day	1.44	1.440 000 0E+00
kiloliter/day	0.144	1.440 000 0E-01
lambda/second	1,666.666 67	1.666 666 7E+03
liter/hour	6	6.000 000 0E+00
liter/hour [pre-1964]	5.999 832	5.999 832 0E+00
milliliter/second	1.666 666 7	1.666 666 7E+00
ounce/minute [UK, liquid]	3.519 508	3.519 508 0E+00
ounce/minute [US, liquid]	3.381 402 3	3.381 402 3E+00
stere/day	0.144	1.440 000 0E-01

Convert From	\<Type of Unit>	
Convert To	Standard	Scientific

thousand cubic foot/day	0.005 085 3	5.085 312 0E−03

deciliter/second \<flow rate, volume basis>

Convert To	Standard	Scientific
acre foot/day	0.007 004 6	7.004 562 0E−03
acre foot/day [US, survey]	0.007 004 5	7.004 520 0E−03
acre inch/day	0.084 054 7	8.405 474 4E−02
barrel/hour [UK]	2.199 692 5	2.199 692 5E+00
barrel/hour [US, federal]	3.067 804 5	3.067 804 5E+00
barrel/hour [US, liquid]	3.019 109 2	3.019 109 2E+00
barrel/hour [US, petroleum]	2.264 331 9	2.264 331 9E+00
centiliter/second	10	1.000 000 0E+01
cubic centimeter/second	100	1.000 000 0E+02
cubic decimeter/minute	6	6.000 000 0E+00
cubic foot/hour	12.713 28	1.271 328 0E+01
cubic inch/second	6.102 374 4	6.102 374 4E+00
cubic meter/day	8.64	8.640 000 0E+00
cubic meter/second	0.000 1	1.000 000 0E−04
cubic yard/day	11.300 693 4	1.130 069 3E+01
deciliter/minute	60	6.000 000 0E+01
dekaliter/hour	36	3.600 000 0E+01
gallon/minute [UK]	1.319 815 5	1.319 815 5E+00
gallon/minute [US, liquid]	1.585 032 3	1.585 032 3E+00
hectoliter/hour	3.6	3.600 000 0E+00
kiloliter/day	8.64	8.640 000 0E+00
liter/minute	6	6.000 000 0E+00
liter/minute [pre-1964]	5.999 832	5.999 832 0E+00
ounce/second [UK, liquid]	3.519 508	3.519 508 0E+00
ounce/second [US, liquid]	3.381 402 3	3.381 402 3E+00
petrograd standard/day	1.849 204 4	1.849 204 4E+00
stere/day	8.64	8.640 000 0E+00
thousand cubic foot/day	0.305 118 7	3.051 187 2E−01

decillion [UK] \<units>

Convert To	Standard	Scientific
novemdecillion [US]	1	1.000 000 0E+00
unit	>>>	1.000 000 0E+60

decillion [US] \<units>

Convert To	Standard	Scientific
unit	>>>	1.000 000 0E+33

decimeter \<length>

Convert To	Standard	Scientific
agate [print]	51.732 284	5.173 228 4E+01
barleycorn	11.811 024	1.181 102 4E+01
douzieme [print]	566.929 13	5.669 291 3E+02
foot [France]	0.307 843 3	3.078 432 9E−01
foot [international]	0.328 084	3.280 839 9E−01
foot [US, survey]	0.328 083 3	3.280 833 3E−01
inch [based on US, survey foot]	3.937	3.937 000 0E+00
inch [international]	3.937 007 9	3.937 007 9E+00
ligne [print]	47.244 094	4.724 409 4E+01
line [print]	47.244 094	4.724 409 4E+01
meter	0.1	1.000 000 0E−01
mil	3,937.007 9	3.937 007 9E+03
nail [cloth]	1.749 781 3	1.749 781 3E+00
nonpareil [print]	47.421 26	4.742 126 0E+01
palm	1.312 336	1.312 336 0E+00
pearl [print]	56.905 512	5.690 551 2E+01
pica [print]	23.710 63	2.371 063 0E+01
point [print]	284.527 56	2.845 275 6E+02
thou	3,937.007 9	3.937 007 9E+03
yard [based on US, survey foot]	0.109 361 1	1.093 611 1E−01
yard [international]	0.109 361 3	1.093 613 3E−01
yard [UK]	0.109 361 5	1.093 615 2E−01

decimeter/square second \<acceleration>

Convert To	Standard	Scientific
foot/square second	0.328 084	3.280 839 9E−01
galileo	10	1.000 000 0E+01
g$_n$ [due to gravity]	0.010 197 2	1.019 716 2E−02

| Convert From | <Type of Unit> | |
Convert To	Standard	Scientific
meter/square second	0.1	1.000 000 0E-01
mile/hour minute	13.421 617 8	1.342 161 8E+01
decimole	**<amount of substance>**	
mole	0.1	1.000 000 0E-01
decina [Italy]	**<mass, special - see page 29>**	
kilogram	3.393	3.393 000 0E+00
decineper	**<sound pressure level>**	
bel	0.086 858 9	8.685 889 6E-02
neper	0.1	1.000 000 0E-01
decinewton		**<force>**
crinal	1	1.000 000 0E+00
dyne	10,000	1.000 000 0E+04
grain-force	157.366 26	1.573 662 6E+02
gram-force	10.197 162 1	1.019 716 2E+01
newton	0.1	1.000 000 0E-01
ounce-force	0.359 694 3	3.596 943 1E-01
pond	10.197 162 1	1.019 716 2E+01
pound-force	0.022 480 9	2.248 089 4E-02
poundal	0.723 301 4	7.233 013 9E-01
deciohm		**<electric resistance>**
1/ siemens	0.1	1.000 000 0E-01
abohm	>>>	1.000 000 0E+08
ohm	0.1	1.000 000 0E-01
statohm	<<<	1.112 650 1E-13
decipascal		**<pressure>**
atmosphere [standard]	0.000 001	9.869 232 7E-07
atmosphere [technical]	0.000 001	1.019 716 2E-06
bar	0.000 001	1.000 000 0E-06
barye [France]	1	1.000 000 0E+00
dyne/square centimeter	1	1.000 000 0E+00
gram-force/square centimeter	0.001 019 7	1.019 716 2E-03
kilogram-force/square meter	0.010 197 2	1.019 716 2E-02
kilopond/square meter	0.010 197 2	1.019 716 2E-02
microbar	1	1.000 000 0E+00
micrometer of mercury [0 °C, by convention]	0.750 061 6	7.500 615 8E-01
micrometer of water [4 °C, by convention]	10.197 162	1.019 716 2E+01
newton/square meter	0.1	1.000 000 0E-01
pascal	0.1	1.000 000 0E-01
pound-force/square foot	0.002 088 5	2.088 543 4E-03
poundal/square foot	0.067 196 9	6.719 689 8E-02
torr	0.000 750 1	7.500 616 8E-04
decipoise		**<dynamic viscosity>**
dyne second/square centimeter	0.1	1.000 000 0E-01
gram/centimeter second	0.1	1.000 000 0E-01
kilogram/meter hour	36	3.600 000 0E+01
pascal second	0.01	1.000 000 0E-02
poise	0.1	1.000 000 0E-01
pound/foot hour	24.190 883 1	2.419 088 3E+01
poundal hour/square foot	24.190 883 1	2.419 088 3E+01
decisiemens		**<electric conductance>**
absiemens	<<<	1.000 000 0E-10
siemens	0.1	1.000 000 0E-01
statsiemens	>>>	8.987 551 8E+10
decitesla		**<magnetic flux density>**
electromagnetic unit of magnetic flux density [cgs system]	1,000	1.000 000 0E+03
gauss	1,000	1.000 000 0E+03
line/square centimeter [of magnetic force]	1,000	1.000 000 0E+03
maxwell/square meter	0.1	1.000 000 0E-01
tesla	0.1	1.000 000 0E-01
decitonne		**<mass>**
cental [US]	2.204 622 6	2.204 622 6E+00

Convert From	\<Type of Unit\>	
Convert To	Standard	Scientific
centner [UK]	1.968 413 1	1.968 413 1E+00
doppelzentner [Germany]	1	1.000 000 0E+00
hundredweight [long]	1.968 413 1	1.968 413 1E+00
hundredweight [short]	2.204 622 6	2.204 622 6E+00
hundredweight [UK]	1.968 413 1	1.968 413 1E+00
kilogram	100	1.000 000 0E+02
millier	0.1	1.000 000 0E−01
quarter [long]	0.393 682 6	3.936 826 1E−01
quarter [short]	0.440 924 5	4.409 245 2E−01
quarter [UK]	7.873 652 2	7.873 652 2E+00
quarter [US]	8.818 490 5	8.818 490 5E+00
quintal [metric]	1	1.000 000 0E+00
quintal [UK]	1.968 413 1	1.968 413 1E+00
quintal [US]	2.204 622 6	2.204 622 6E+00
slug	6.852 176 6	6.852 176 6E+00
stone [UK]	15.747 304	1.574 730 4E+01
ton [long]	0.098 420 7	9.842 065 3E−02
ton [metric]	0.1	1.000 000 0E−01
ton [short]	0.110 231 1	1.102 311 3E−01
tonne	0.1	1.000 000 0E−01
decitorr		**\<pressure\>**
atmosphere [standard]	0.000 131 6	1.315 789 5E−04
atmosphere [technical]	0.000 136	1.359 509 8E−04
bar	0.000 133 3	1.333 223 7E−04
barye [France]	133.322 37	1.333 223 7E+02
centimeter of mercury [0 °C, by convention]	0.01	9.999 998 6E−03
centimeter of water [4 °C, by convention]	0.135 951	1.359 509 8E−01
dekapascal	1.333 223 7	1.333 223 7E+00
dyne/square centimeter	133.322 37	1.333 223 7E+02
gram-force/square centimeter	0.135 951	1.359 509 8E−01
kilogram-force/square meter	1.359 509 8	1.359 509 8E+00
kilopond/square meter	1.359 509 8	1.359 509 8E+00
micrometer of mercury [0 °C, by convention]	99.999 986	9.999 998 6E+01
micrometer of water [4 °C, by convention]	1,359.509 8	1.359 509 8E+03
millimeter of mercury [0 °C, by convention]	0.1	9.999 998 6E−02
millimeter of water [4 °C, by convention]	1.359 509 8	1.359 509 8E+00
newton/square meter	13.332 237	1.333 223 7E+01
pascal	13.332 237	1.333 223 7E+01
pieze [France]	0.013 332 2	1.333 223 7E−02
pound-force/square foot	0.278 449 6	2.784 495 6E−01
poundal/square foot	8.958 849 5	8.958 849 5E+00
sthene/square meter [France]	0.013 332 2	1.333 223 7E−02
ton-force/square meter [metric]	0.001 359 5	1.359 509 8E−03
torr	0.1	1.000 000 0E−01
decivolt		**\<electric potential\>**
ampere ohm	0.1	1.000 000 0E−01
joule/coulomb	0.1	1.000 000 0E−01
statvolt	0.000 333 6	3.335 641 0E−04
volt	0.1	1.000 000 0E−01
watt/ampere	0.1	1.000 000 0E−01
deciwatt		**\<power\>**
Btu/hour [I.T.]	0.341 214 2	3.412 141 6E−01
Btu/hour [thermoc.]	0.341 442 5	3.414 425 1E−01
calorie/minute [I.T.]	1.433 075 4	1.433 075 4E+00
calorie/minute [thermoc.]	1.434 034 4	1.434 034 4E+00
centigrade heat unit/hour [mean]	0.189 417 3	1.894 172 6E−01
cubic meter atmosphere/minute	59.215 396	5.921 539 6E+01
dyne centimeter/second	1,000,000	1.000 000 0E+06
erg/second	1,000,000	1.000 000 0E+06
foot pound-force/minute	4.425 372 9	4.425 372 9E+00
foot poundal/second	2.373 036	2.373 036 0E+00
gram-force centimeter/second	1,019.716 2	1.019 716 2E+03
horsepower	0.000 134 1	1.341 022 1E−04

Convert From Convert To	Standard	\<Type of Unit\> Scientific
horsepower [metric]	0.000 136	1.359 621 6E−04
joule/minute	6	6.000 000 0E+00
kilocalorie/hour [I.T.]	0.085 984 5	8.598 452 3E−02
kilogram square meter/cubic second	0.1	1.000 000 0E−01
kilogram-force meter/hour	36.709 784	3.670 978 4E+01
kilopond meter/hour	36.709 784	3.670 978 4E+01
lumen [green light at 100% efficiency]	68.5	6.850 000 0E+01
lumen [green light at 5,550 angstrom]	68.000 000	6.800 000 2E+01
newton meter/minute	6	6.000 000 0E+00
pound square foot/cubic second	2.373 036	2.373 036 0E+00
volt ampere	0.1	1.000 000 0E−01
watt	0.1	1.000 000 0E−01

deciweber   **\<magnetic flux\>**

	Standard	Scientific
electrostatic unit of magnetic flux [cgs system]	0.000 333 6	3.335 641 0E−04
gauss square centimeter	>>>	1.000 000 0E+07
line [of magnetic force]	>>>	1.000 000 0E+07
maxwell	>>>	1.000 000 0E+07
statweber	0.000 333 6	3.335 641 0E−04
unit pole	795,774.754	7.957 747 5E+05
weber	0.1	1.000 000 0E−01

decunx [Rome, ancient]   **\<mass, special - see page 29\>**

	Standard	Scientific
gram	272.88	2.728 800 0E+02

dedo [Spain]   **\<length, special - see page 29\>**

	Standard	Scientific
centimeter	1.74	1.740 000 0E+00

degree [angular]   **\<plane angle\>**

	Standard	Scientific
centrad	1.745 329 3	1.745 329 3E+00
grade [angular]	1.111 111 1	1.111 111 1E+00
mil [military artillery, angle, USSR]	17.5	1.750 000 0E+01
minute [angular]	60	6.000 000 0E+01
radian	0.017 453 3	1.745 329 3E−02
second [angular]	3,600	3.600 000 0E+03
sign	0.033 333 3	3.333 333 3E−02

degree Celsius   **\<thermodynamic temperature\>**

°F	(1.8 x degree Celsius) + 32
degree Rankine	(1.8 x degree Celsius) + 491.67
degree Reaumur [France]	degree Celsius / 1.25
kelvin	degree Celsius + 273.15

degreeCelsius/kilowatt   **\<thermal resistance\>**

	Standard	Scientific
hour °F/Btu [-/ I.T.]	0.000 527 5	5.275 279 3E−04
kelvin/watt	0.001	1.000 000 0E−03
second °C/calorie [-/ I.T.]	0.004 186 8	4.186 800 0E−03

degree Celsius/meter   **\<geothermal gradient\>**

	Standard	Scientific
kelvin/meter	1	1.000 000 0E+00

degree Celsius/watt   **\<thermal resistance\>**

	Standard	Scientific
hour °F/Btu [-/ I.T.]	0.527 527 9	5.275 279 3E−01
kelvin/watt	1	1.000 000 0E+00
second °C/calorie [-/ I.T.]	4.186 8	4.186 800 0E+00
second kelvin/joule	1	1.000 000 0E+00

degree Fahrenheit   **\<thermodynamic temperature\>**

°C	(degree Fahrenheit − 32) / 1.8
degree Rankine	degree Fahrenheit + 459.67
degree Reaumur [France]	(degree Fahrenheit − 32) / 2.25
kelvin	[(degree Fahrenheit − 32) / 1.8] + 273.15

degree Fahrenheit/foot   **\<geothermal gradient\>**

	Standard	Scientific
kelvin/meter	1.822 688 8	1.822 688 8E+00

degree Rankine   **\<thermodynamic temperature\>**

°C	(degree Rankine − 491.67) / 1.8
°F	degree Rankine − 459.67
degree Reaumur [France]	(degree Rankine − 491.67) / 2.25
kelvin	degree Rankine / 1.8

degree Reaumur [France] \<thermodynamic temperature\>
°C ---------- 1.25 x degree Reaumur
°F ---------- (2.25 x degree Reaumur) + 32
degree Rankine ---------- (2.25 x degree Reaumur) + 491.67
kelvin ---------- (1.25 x degree Reaumur) + 273.15

degree/foot \<reciprocal length, phase coefficient\>
1/foot ---------- 0.017 453 3 --- 1.745 329 3E-02
degree/inch ---------- 0.083 333 3 --- 8.333 333 3E-02
radian/meter ---------- 0.057 261 5 --- 5.726 145 8E-02

degree/hour \<frequency\>
1/second ---------- 0.000 000 8 --- 7.716 049 4E-07
degree/minute ---------- 0.016 666 7 --- 1.666 666 7E-02
hertz ---------- 0.000 000 8 --- 7.716 049 4E-07
radian/hour ---------- 0.017 453 3 --- 1.745 329 3E-02
revolution/hour ---------- 0.002 777 8 --- 2.777 777 8E-03

degree/inch \<reciprocal length, phase coefficient\>
degree/foot ---------- 12 --- 1.200 000 0E+01
radian/meter ---------- 0.687 137 5 --- 6.871 375 0E-01

degree/minute \<frequency\>
1/second ---------- 0.000 046 3 --- 4.629 629 6E-05
degree/hour ---------- 60 --- 6.000 000 0E+01
millihertz ---------- 0.046 296 3 --- 4.629 629 6E-02
radian/hour ---------- 1.047 197 6 --- 1.047 197 6E+00
revolution/hour ---------- 0.166 666 7 --- 1.666 666 7E-01

degree/second \<frequency\>
1/second ---------- 0.002 777 8 --- 2.777 777 8E-03
degree/minute ---------- 60 --- 6.000 000 0E+01
millihertz ---------- 2.777 777 8 --- 2.777 777 8E+00
radian/minute ---------- 1.047 197 6 --- 1.047 197 6E+00
revolution/hour ---------- 10 --- 1.000 000 0E+01

degree/square second \<angular acceleration\>
radian/square second ---------- 0.017 453 3 --- 1.745 329 3E-02

deido [Spain] \<length, special - see page 29\>
centimeter ---------- 1.741 47 --- 1.741 470 0E+00

dekaampere \<electric current\>
abampere ---------- 1 --- 1.000 000 0E+00
ampere ---------- 10 --- 1.000 000 0E+01
electromagnetic unit of current [cgs system] ---------- 1 --- 1.000 000 0E+00
franklin/second ---------- >>> --- 2.997 924 6E+10
statampere ---------- >>> --- 2.997 924 6E+10

dekabar \<pressure\>
atmosphere [standard] ---------- 9.869 232 7 --- 9.869 232 7E+00
atmosphere [technical] ---------- 10.197 162 --- 1.019 716 2E+01
bar ---------- 10 --- 1.000 000 0E+01
foot of mercury [0 °C, by convention] ---------- 24.608 319 --- 2.460 831 9E+01
foot of water [4 °C, by convention] ---------- 334.552 56 --- 3.345 525 6E+02
kilogram-force/square centimeter ---------- 10.197 162 --- 1.019 716 2E+01
kilopond/square centimeter ---------- 10.197 162 --- 1.019 716 2E+01
kip/square foot ---------- 20.885 434 --- 2.088 543 4E+01
megapascal ---------- 1 --- 1.000 000 0E+00
newton/square millimeter ---------- 1 --- 1.000 000 0E+00
pascal ---------- 1,000,000 --- 1.000 000 0E+06
pound-force/square inch ---------- 145.037 74 --- 1.450 377 4E+02
sthene/square meter [France] ---------- 1,000 --- 1.000 000 0E+03
ton-force/square foot [long] ---------- 9.323 854 6 --- 9.323 854 6E+00
ton-force/square meter [metric] ---------- 101.971 62 --- 1.019 716 2E+02
torr ---------- 7,500.616 8 --- 7.500 616 8E+03

dekacandela \<luminous intensity\>
candela ---------- 10 --- 1.000 000 0E+01

| Convert From | <Type of Unit> | |
Convert To	Standard	Scientific
dekacoulomb		**<electric charge>**
abcoulomb	1	1.000 000 0E+00
ampere second	10	1.000 000 0E+01
coulomb	10	1.000 000 0E+01
electromagnetic unit of charge [cgs system]	1	1.000 000 0E+00
farad volt	10	1.000 000 0E+01
dekafarad		**<capacitance>**
abfarad	<<<	1.000 000 0E-08
coulomb/volt	10	1.000 000 0E+01
farad	10	1.000 000 0E+01
statfarad	>>>	8.987 551 8E+12
dekagram		**<mass>**
carat [international]	50	5.000 000 0E+01
carat [UK]	38.580 896	3.858 089 6E+01
carat [US, before 1913]	48.709 206	4.870 920 6E+01
drachm [UK, apothecary]	2.572 059 7	2.572 059 7E+00
dram [avoirdupois]	5.643 833 9	5.643 833 9E+00
dram [US, apothecary]	2.572 059 7	2.572 059 7E+00
kilogram	0.01	1.000 000 0E-02
ounce	0.352 739 6	3.527 396 2E-01
ounce [apothecary]	0.321 507 5	3.215 074 7E-01
ounce [avoirdupois]	0.352 739 6	3.527 396 2E-01
ounce [troy]	0.321 507 5	3.215 074 7E-01
pennyweight [troy]	6.430 149 3	6.430 149 3E+00
scruple [UK]	7.716 179 2	7.716 179 2E+00
scruple [US, apothecary]	7.716 179 2	7.716 179 2E+00
ton [UK, assay or assay, long]	0.306 122 5	3.061 224 5E-01
ton [US, assay or assay, short]	0.342 857 1	3.428 571 4E-01
dekagram-force		**<force>**
crinal	0.980 665	9.806 650 0E-01
dyne	9,806.65	9.806 650 0E+03
gram-force	10	1.000 000 0E+01
newton	0.098 066 5	9.806 650 0E-02
ounce-force	0.352 739 6	3.527 396 2E-01
pond	10	1.000 000 0E+01
pound-force	0.022 046 2	2.204 622 6E-02
poundal	0.709 316 4	7.093 163 5E-01
dekahenry		**<electric inductance>**
abhenry	>>>	1.000 000 0E+10
henry	10	1.000 000 0E+01
joule/square ampere	10	1.000 000 0E+01
ohm second	10	1.000 000 0E+01
stathenry	<<<	1.112 650 1E-11
dekajoule		**<energy>**
Btu [I.T.]	0.009 478 2	9.478 171 2E-03
calorie [I.T.]	2.388 459	2.388 459 0E+00
calorie [mean]	2.386 623 5	2.386 623 5E+00
calorie [thermoc.]	2.390 057 4	2.390 057 4E+00
cubic centimeter atmosphere	98.692 327	9.869 232 7E+01
dyne centimeter	>>>	1.000 000 0E+08
erg	>>>	1.000 000 0E+08
foot pound-force	7.375 621 5	7.375 621 5E+00
foot poundal	237.303 6	2.373 036 0E+02
gram calorie	2.389 029 6	2.389 029 6E+00
inch ounce-force	1,416.119 3	1.416 119 3E+03
inch pound-force	88.507 458	8.850 745 8E+01
joule	10	1.000 000 0E+01
kilogram square meter/square second	10	1.000 000 0E+01
kilopond meter	1.019 716 2	1.019 716 2E+00
liter atmosphere	0.098 692 3	9.869 232 7E-02
megaerg	100	1.000 000 0E+02
megalerg	100	1.000 000 0E+02

Convert From Convert To	Standard	\<Type of Unit> Scientific
meter kilogram-force	1.019 716 2	1.019 716 2E+00
newton meter	10	1.000 000 0E+01
wattsecond	10	1.000 000 0E+01
dekaliter		**\<volume>**
barrel [US, dry]	0.086 484 9	8.648 489 8E−02
barrel [US, liquid]	0.083 864 1	8.386 414 4E−02
barrel [US, petroleum]	0.062 898 1	6.289 810 8E−02
board foot	4.237 76	4.237 760 0E+00
bushel [UK]	0.274 961 6	2.749 615 6E−01
bushel [US, dry]	0.283 775 9	2.837 759 3E−01
cubic foot	0.353 146 7	3.531 466 7E−01
cubic inch	610.237 44	6.102 374 4E+02
cubic meter	0.01	1.000 000 0E−02
cubic yard	0.013 079 5	1.307 950 6E−02
cup [Canada, measuring]	43.993 85	4.399 385 0E+01
cup [US, measuring]	42.267 528	4.226 752 8E+01
gallon [Canada, liquid]	2.199 692 5	2.199 692 5E+00
gallon [UK, dry or liquid]	2.199 692 5	2.199 692 5E+00
gallon [US, dry]	2.270 207 5	2.270 207 5E+00
gallon [US, liquid]	2.641 720 5	2.641 720 5E+00
gill [UK]	70.390 159	7.039 015 9E+01
gill [US]	84.535 057	8.453 505 7E+01
liter	10	1.000 000 0E+01
peck [UK]	1.099 846 2	1.099 846 2E+00
peck [US]	1.135 103 7	1.135 103 7E+00
pint [UK]	17.597 54	1.759 754 0E+01
pint [US, dry]	18.161 66	1.816 166 0E+01
pint [US, liquid]	21.133 764	2.113 376 4E+01
quart [UK]	8.798 769 9	8.798 769 9E+00
quart [US, dry]	9.080 829 8	9.080 829 8E+00
quart [US, liquid]	10.566 882	1.056 688 2E+01
shih dao [China]	1	1.000 000 0E+00
stere	0.01	1.000 000 0E−02
Winchester wine gallon [UK]	2.641 720 5	2.641 720 5E+00
dekaliter/day		**\<flow rate, volume basis>**
barrel/day [UK]	0.061 102 6	6.110 256 9E−02
barrel/day [US, federal]	0.085 216 8	8.521 679 1E−02
barrel/day [US, liquid]	0.083 864 1	8.386 414 4E−02
barrel/day [US, petroleum]	0.062 898 1	6.289 810 8E−02
centiliter/day	1,000	1.000 000 0E+03
centiliter/hour	41.666 666 7	4.166 666 7E+01
cubic centimeter/day	10,000	1.000 000 0E+04
cubic centimeter/minute	6.944 444 4	6.944 444 4E+00
cubic decimeter/day	10	1.000 000 0E+01
cubic foot/day	0.353 146 7	3.531 466 7E−01
cubic inch/hour	25.426 56	2.542 656 0E+01
cubic meter/day	0.01	1.000 000 0E−02
cubic meter/second	0.000 000 1	1.157 407 4E−07
cubic millimeter/second	115.740 741	1.157 407 4E+02
cubic yard/day	0.013 079 5	1.307 950 6E−02
deciliter/day	100	1.000 000 0E+02
deciliter/hour	4.166 666 7	4.166 666 7E+00
gallon/day [UK]	2.199 692 5	2.199 692 5E+00
gallon/day [US, liquid]	2.641 720 5	2.641 720 5E+00
hectoliter/day	0.1	1.000 000 0E−01
kiloliter/day	0.01	1.000 000 0E−02
lambda/second	115.740 741	1.157 407 4E+02
liter/day	10	1.000 000 0E+01
liter/day [pre-1964]	9.999 72	9.999 720 0E+00
milliliter/minute	6.944 444 4	6.944 444 4E+00
ounce/hour [UK, liquid]	14.664 617	1.466 461 7E+01
ounce/hour [US, liquid]	14.089 176	1.408 917 6E+01
stere/day	0.01	1.000 000 0E−02

dekaliter/hour — \<flow rate, volume basis\>

Convert To	Standard	Scientific
acre inch/day	0.002 334 9	2.334 854 0E-03
barrel/day [UK]	1.466 461 7	1.466 461 7E+00
barrel/day [US, federal]	2.045 203	2.045 203 0E+00
barrel/day [US, liquid]	2.012 739 5	2.012 739 5E+00
barrel/day [US, petroleum]	1.509 554 6	1.509 554 6E+00
centiliter/minute	16.666 666 7	1.666 666 7E+01
cubic centimeter/second	2.777 777 8	2.777 777 8E+00
cubic decimeter/hour	10	1.000 000 0E+01
cubic foot/day	8.475 52	8.475 520 0E+00
cubic inch/minute	10.170 624	1.017 062 4E+01
cubic meter/day	0.24	2.400 000 0E-01
cubic meter/second	0.000 002 8	2.777 777 8E-06
cubic millimeter/second	2,777.777 78	2.777 777 8E+03
cubic yard/day	0.313 908 1	3.139 081 5E-01
deciliter/minute	1.666 666 7	1.666 666 7E+00
dekaliter/day	24	2.400 000 0E+01
gallon/hour [UK]	2.199 692 5	2.199 692 5E+00
gallon/hour [US, liquid]	2.641 720 5	2.641 720 5E+00
hectoliter/day	2.4	2.400 000 0E+00
kiloliter/day	0.24	2.400 000 0E-01
lambda/second	2,777.777 78	2.777 777 8E+03
liter/hour	10	1.000 000 0E+01
liter/hour [pre-1964]	9.999 72	9.999 720 0E+00
milliliter/second	2.777 777 8	2.777 777 8E+00
ounce/minute [UK, liquid]	5.865 846 6	5.865 846 6E+00
ounce/minute [US, liquid]	5.635 670 5	5.635 670 5E+00
stere/day	0.24	2.400 000 0E-01
thousand cubic foot/day	0.008 475 5	8.475 520 0E-03

dekaliter/minute — \<flow rate, volume basis\>

Convert To	Standard	Scientific
acre foot/day	0.011 674 3	1.167 427 0E-02
acre foot/day [US, survey]	0.011 674 2	1.167 420 0E-02
acre inch/day	0.140 091 2	1.400 912 4E-01
barrel/hour [UK]	3.666 154 1	3.666 154 1E+00
barrel/hour [US, federal]	5.113 007 5	5.113 007 5E+00
barrel/hour [US, liquid]	5.031 848 6	5.031 848 6E+00
barrel/hour [US, petroleum]	3.773 886 5	3.773 886 5E+00
centiliter/second	16.666 666 7	1.666 666 7E+01
cubic centimeter/second	166.666 667	1.666 666 7E+02
cubic decimeter/minute	10	1.000 000 0E+01
cubic foot/hour	21.188 80	2.118 880 0E+01
cubic inch/second	10.170 624	1.017 062 4E+01
cubic meter/day	14.4	1.440 000 0E+01
cubic meter/second	0.000 166 7	1.666 666 7E-04
cubic yard/day	18.834 488 9	1.883 448 9E+01
deciliter/second	1.666 666 7	1.666 666 7E+00
gallon/minute [UK]	2.199 692 5	2.199 692 5E+00
gallon/minute [US, liquid]	2.641 720 5	2.641 720 5E+00
hectoliter/hour	6	6.000 000 0E+00
kiloliter/day	14.4	1.440 000 0E+01
liter/minute	10	1.000 000 0E+01
liter/minute [pre-1964]	9.999 72	9.999 720 0E+00
milliliter/day	>>>	1.440 000 0E+07
milliliter/hour	600,000	6.000 000 0E+05
milliliter/minute	10,000	1.000 000 0E+04
milliliter/second	166.666 667	1.666 666 7E+02
ounce/second [UK, liquid]	5.865 846 6	5.865 846 6E+00
ounce/second [US, liquid]	5.635 670 5	5.635 670 5E+00
petrograd standard/day	3.082 007 3	3.082 007 3E+00
stere/day	14.4	1.440 000 0E+01
thousand cubic foot/day	0.508 531 2	5.085 312 0E-01

dekaliter/second — \<flow rate, volume basis\>

Convert To	Standard	Scientific
acre foot/day	0.700 456 2	7.004 562 0E-01

Convert From	\<Type of Unit\>
Convert To	Standard	Scientific

acre foot/day [US, survey]	0.700 452	7.004 520 0E−01
acre inch/day	8.405 474 4	8.405 474 4E+00
barrel/minute [UK]	3.666 154 1	3.666 154 1E+00
barrel/minute [US, federal]	5.113 007 5	5.113 007 5E+00
barrel/minute [US, liquid]	5.031 848 6	5.031 848 6E+00
barrel/minute [US, petroleum]	3.773 886 5	3.773 886 5E+00
centiliter/second	1,000	1.000 000 0E+03
cubic decimeter/second	10	1.000 000 0E+01
cubic dekameter/day	0.864	8.640 000 0E−01
cubic foot/minute	21.188 8	2.118 880 0E+01
cubic inch/second	610.237 441	6.102 374 4E+02
cubic meter/hour	36	3.600 000 0E+01
cubic meter/second	0.01	1.000 000 0E−02
cubic yard/hour	47.086 222	4.708 622 2E+01
deciliter/second	100	1.000 000 0E+02
dekaliter/minute	60	6.000 000 0E+01
gallon/second [UK]	2.199 692 5	2.199 692 5E+00
gallon/second [US, liquid]	2.641 720 5	2.641 720 5E+00
hectare meter/day	0.086 4	8.640 000 0E−02
hectoliter/minute	6	6.000 000 0E+00
kiloliter/hour	36	3.600 000 0E+01
liter/second	10	1.000 000 0E+01
liter/second [pre-1964]	9.999 72	9.999 720 0E+00
ounce/second [UK, liquid]	351.950 8	3.519 508 0E+02
ounce/second [US, liquid]	338.140 23	3.381 402 3E+02
petrograd standard/hour	7.705 018 2	7.705 018 2E+00
stere/hour	36	3.600 000 0E+01
thousand cubic foot/hour	1.271 328	1.271 328 0E+00

dekameter		\<length\>
cubit	21.872 266	2.187 226 6E+01
digit	524.934 38	5.249 343 8E+02
fathom [US, survey]	5.468 055 6	5.468 055 6E+00
foot [France]	30.784 329	3.078 432 9E+01
foot [international]	32.808 399	3.280 839 9E+01
foot [US, survey]	32.808 333	3.280 833 3E+01
inch [based on US, survey foot]	393.7	3.937 000 0E+02
inch [international]	393.700 79	3.937 007 9E+02
link [Gunter or US, survey]	49.709 596	4.970 959 6E+01
link [Ramden or Engineer]	32.808 399	3.280 839 9E+01
meter	10	1.000 000 0E+01
myriameter	0.001	1.000 000 0E−03
palm	131.233 6	1.312 336 0E+02
perch [US, survey]	1.988 383 8	1.988 383 8E+00
perche [France]	1.710 240 5	1.710 240 5E+00
pied [France]	30.784 329	3.078 432 9E+01
pole [US, survey]	1.988 383 8	1.988 383 8E+00
rod [US, survey]	1.988 383 8	1.988 383 8E+00
rope	1.640 419 9	1.640 419 9E+00
span	43.744 532	4.374 453 2E+01
yard [based on US, survey foot]	10.936 111	1.093 611 1E+01
yard [international]	10.936 133	1.093 613 3E+01
yard [UK]	10.936 152	1.093 615 2E+01

dekameter/day		\<velocity\>
foot/hour	1.367 016 6	1.367 016 6E+00
inch/hour	16.404 199 5	1.640 420 0E+01
knot [international]	0.000 225	2.249 820 0E−04
meter/second	0.000 115 7	1.157 407 4E−04
mile/day	0.006 213 7	6.213 711 9E−03
nautical mile/day [international]	0.005 399 6	5.399 568 0E−03
yard/day	10.936 133	1.093 613 3E+01

dekameter/hour		\<velocity\>
foot/hour	32.808 399	3.280 839 9E+01
inch/minute	6.561 679 8	6.561 679 8E+00

	Standard	Scientific
knot [international]	0.005 399 6	5.399 568 0E-03
meter/second	0.002 777 8	2.777 777 8E-03
mile/day	0.149 129 1	1.491 290 9E-01
nautical mile/day [international]	0.129 589 6	1.295 896 3E-01
yard/hour	10.936 133	1.093 613 3E+01

dekameter/minute   \<velocity\>

	Standard	Scientific
foot/minute	32.808 399	3.280 839 9E+01
inch/second	6.561 679 8	6.561 679 8E+00
knot [international]	0.323 974 1	3.239 740 8E-01
meter/second	0.166 666 7	1.666 666 7E-01
mile/day	8.947 745 2	8.947 745 2E+00
nautical mile/day [international]	7.775 378	7.775 378 0E+00
yard/minute	10.936 133	1.093 613 3E+01

dekameter/second   \<velocity\>

	Standard	Scientific
foot/second	32.808 399	3.280 839 9E+01
inch/second	393.700 787	3.937 007 9E+02
knot [international]	19.438 444 9	1.943 844 5E+01
meter/second	10	1.000 000 0E+01
mile/hour	22.369 362 9	2.236 936 3E+01
nautical mile/hour [international]	19.438 444 9	1.943 844 5E+01
yard/second	10.936 133	1.093 613 3E+01

dekameter/square second   \<acceleration\>

	Standard	Scientific
foot/square second	32.808 399	3.280 839 9E+01
galileo	1,000	1.000 000 0E+03
gn [due to gravity]	1.019 716 2	1.019 716 2E+00
meter/square second	10	1.000 000 0E+01

dekamole   \<amount of substance\>

	Standard	Scientific
mole	10	1.000 000 0E+01

dekanewton   \<force\>

	Standard	Scientific
crinal	100	1.000 000 0E+02
dyne	1,000,000	1.000 000 0E+06
joule/meter	10	1.000 000 0E+01
newton	10	1.000 000 0E+01
ounce-force	35.969 430 9	3.596 943 1E+01
pond	1,019.716 21	1.019 716 2E+03
pound-force	2.248 089 4	2.248 089 4E+00
poundal	72.330 138	7.233 013 9E+01

dekaohm   \<electric resistance\>

	Standard	Scientific
1/ siemens	10	1.000 000 0E+01
abohm	>>>	1.000 000 0E+10
ohm	10	1.000 000 0E+01
statohm	<<<	1.112 650 1E-11

dekapascal   \<pressure\>

	Standard	Scientific
atmosphere [standard]	0.000 098 7	9.869 232 7E-05
atmosphere [technical]	0.000 102	1.019 716 2E-04
bar	0.000 1	1.000 000 0E-04
barye [France]	100	1.000 000 0E+02
centimeter of mercury [0 °C, by convention]	0.007 500 6	7.500 615 8E-03
centimeter of water [4 °C, by convention]	0.101 971 6	1.019 716 2E-01
centitorr	7.500 616 8	7.500 616 8E+00
dyne/square centimeter	100	1.000 000 0E+02
gram-force/square centimeter	0.101 971 6	1.019 716 2E-01
inch of mercury [0 °C, by convention]	0.002 953	2.952 998 3E-03
inch of water [4 °C, by convention]	0.040 146 3	4.014 630 8E-02
kilogram-force/square meter	1.019 716 2	1.019 716 2E+00
kilopond/square meter	1.019 716 2	1.019 716 2E+00
micrometer of mercury [0 °C, by convention]	75.006 158	7.500 615 8E+01
micrometer of water [4 °C, by convention]	1,019.716 2	1.019 716 8E+03
millimeter of mercury [0 °C, by convention]	0.075 006 2	7.500 615 8E-02
millimeter of water [4 °C, by convention]	1.019 716 2	1.019 716 2E+00
newton/square meter	10	1.000 000 0E+01

Convert From	<Type of Unit>	
Convert To	Standard	Scientific

ounce-force/square inch	0.023 206	2.320 603 8E-02
pascal	10	1.000 000 0E+01
pieze [France]	0.01	1.000 000 0E-02
pound-force/square foot	0.208 854 3	2.088 543 4E-01
poundal/square foot	6.719 689 8	6.719 689 8E+00
sthene/square meter [France]	0.01	1.000 000 0E-02
ton-force/square meter [metric]	0.001 019 7	1.019 716 2E-03
torr	0.075 006 2	7.500 616 8E-02

dekasiemens <electric conductance>

absiemens	<<<	1.000 000 0E-08
siemens	10	1.000 000 0E+01
statsiemens	>>>	8.987 551 8E+12

dekatesla <magnetic flux density>

electromagnetic unit of magnetic flux density [cgs system]	100,000	1.000 000 0E+05
gauss	100,000	1.000 000 0E+05
line/square centimeter [of magnetic force]	100,000	1.000 000 0E+05
maxwell/square meter	10	1.000 000 0E+01
tesla	10	1.000 000 0E+01

dekavolt <electric potential>

ampere ohm	10	1.000 000 0E+01
joule/coulomb	10	1.000 000 0E+01
statvolt	0.033 356 4	3.335 641 0E-02
volt	10	1.000 000 0E+01
watt/ampere	10	1.000 000 0E+01

dekawatt <power>

Btu/hour [I.T.]	34.121 416	3.412 141 6E+01
Btu/hour [thermoc.]	34.144 251	3.414 425 1E+01
calorie/second [I.T.]	2.388 459	2.388 459 0E+00
calorie/second [thermoc.]	2.390 057 4	2.390 057 4E+00
centigrade heat unit/hour [mean]	18.941 726	1.894 172 6E+01
cheval vapeur [France]	0.013 596 2	1.359 621 6E-02
cubic meter atmosphere/second	98.692 327	9.869 232 7E+01
dyne centimeter/second	>>>	1.000 000 0E+08
erg/second	>>>	1.000 000 0E+08
foot pound-force/second	7.375 621 5	7.375 621 5E+00
foot poundal/second	237.303 6	2.373 036 0E+02
gram-force centimeter/second	101,971.62	1.019 716 2E+05
horsepower	0.013 410 2	1.341 022 1E-02
horsepower [metric]	0.013 596 2	1.359 621 6E-02
joule/second	10	1.000 000 0E+01
kilocalorie/hour [I.T.]	8.598 452 3	8.598 452 3E+00
kilogram square meter/cubic second	10	1.000 000 0E+01
kilogram-force meter/second	1.019 716 2	1.019 716 2E+00
kilopond meter/second	1.019 716 2	1.019 716 2E+00
newton meter/second	10	1.000 000 0E+01
pferdestarke [Germany]	0.013 596 2	1.359 621 6E-02
poncelet [France]	0.010 197 2	1.019 716 2E-02
pound square foot/cubic second	237.303 6	2.373 036 0E+02
volt ampere	10	1.000 000 0E+01
watt	10	1.000 000 0E+01

dekawatthour <energy>

Btu [I.T.]	34.121 416	3.412 141 6E+01
calorie [kilogram, I.T.]	8.598 452 3	8.598 452 3E+00
calorie [kilogram, mean]	8.591 844 4	8.591 844 4E+00
calorie [kilogram, thermoc.]	8.604 206 5	8.604 206 5E+00
calorie [nutritional]	8.604 206 5	8.604 206 5E+00
centigrade heat unit [I.T.]	18.956 342	1.895 634 2E+01
centimeter gram-force	>>>	3.670 978 4E+08
cubic foot atmosphere	12.547 032	1.254 703 2E+01
foot pound-force	26,552.237	2.655 223 7E+04
foot poundal	854,292.97	8.542 929 7E+05
frigorie [France]	8.600 506 5	8.600 506 5E+00

Convert From Convert To	<Type of Unit>	
	Standard	Scientific
horsepower hour	0.013 410 2	1.341 022 1E-02
horsepower hour [metric]	0.013 596 2	1.359 621 6E-02
inch ounce-force	5,098,029.6	5.098 029 6E+06
inch pound-force	318,626.85	3.186 268 5E+05
joule	36,000	3.600 000 0E+04
kilocalorie [I.T.]	8.598 452 3	8.598 452 3E+00
kilogram calorie [15 °C, NBS, 1939]	8.600 506 5	8.600 506 5E+00
liter atmosphere	355.292 38	3.552 923 8E+02
newton meter	36,000	3.600 000 0E+04
pferdestarkenstunde [Germany]	0.013 596 2	1.359 621 6E-02
thermie [France]	0.008 600 5	8.600 506 5E-03
watthour	10	1.000 000 0E+01
wattsecond	36,000	3.600 000 0E+04
dekaweber	**<magnetic flux>**	
electrostatic unit of magnetic flux [cgs system]	0.033 356 4	3.335 641 0E-02
gauss square centimeter	>>>	1.000 000 0E+09
maxwell	>>>	1.000 000 0E+09
statweber	0.033 356 4	3.335 641 0E-02
unit pole	>>>	7.957 747 5E+07
weber	10	1.000 000 0E+01
demikilo [France]	**<mass, special - see page 29>**	
gram	500	5.000 000 0E+02
denaro [France]	**<mass, special - see page 29>**	
gram	1.27	1.270 000 0E+00
denaro [Italy, Milan]	**<mass, special - see page 29>**	
gram	1	1.000 000 0E+00
denaro [Italy, Rome]	**<mass, special - see page 29>**	
gram	1.17	1.170 000 0E+00
denaro [Italy, Venice]	**<mass, special - see page 29>**	
gram	1	1.000 000 0E+00
denaro [Italy]	**<mass, special - see page 29>**	
gram	1.75	1.750 000 0E+00
denaro [Libya]	**<mass, special - see page 29>**	
gram	1.18	1.180 000 0E+00
denaro [Switzerland]	**<mass, special - see page 29>**	
gram	1	1.000 000 0E+00
denat [Austria]	**<mass, special - see page 29>**	
gram	1.093 8	1.093 800 0E+00
denheiro [Portugal]	**<mass, special - see page 29>**	
gram	19.13	1.913 000 0E+01
denier	**<linear density>**	
drex	1.111 111 1	1.111 111 1E+00
kilogram/meter	0.000 000 1	1.111 111 1E-07
kilotex	0.000 111 1	1.111 111 1E-04
ounce/foot	0.000 001 2	1.194 611 5E-06
pound/yard	0.000 000 2	2.239 896 6E-07
tex	0.111 111 1	1.111 111 1E-01
denier [France]	**<mass, special - see page 29>**	
gram	1.275	1.275 000 0E+00
denier [Italy, Milan]	**<mass, special - see page 29>**	
gram	1	1.000 000 0E+00
denier [Italy, Rome]	**<mass, special - see page 29>**	
gram	1.17	1.170 000 0E+00
denier [Italy, Venice]	**<mass, special - see page 29>**	
gram	1	1.000 000 0E+00
denier [Italy]	**<mass, special - see page 29>**	
gram	1.75	1.750 000 0E+00

Convert From Convert To	Standard	<Type of Unit> Scientific
denier [Switzerland]	<mass, special - see page 29>	
gram	1	1.000 000 0E+00
denk [Turkey]	<mass, special - see page 29>	
gram	0.802	8.020 000 0E-01
denum [Cyprus]	<area, special - see page 29>	
square meter	1,337.8	1.337 800 0E+03
denum [Libya]	<area, special - see page 29>	
are	9.19	9.190 000 0E+00
denum [Syria]	<area, special - see page 29>	
square meter	800	8.000 000 0E+02
depa [Singapore]	<length, special - see page 29>	
meter	1.828 8	1.828 800 0E+00
deraga [Iraq, ancient]	<length, special - see page 29>	
centimeter	53.3	5.330 000 0E+01
deraga akhdam [Iraq, ancient]	<length, special - see page 29>	
centimeter	63	6.300 000 0E+01
deraga cabda [Iraq, ancient]	<length, special - see page 29>	
centimeter	47.4	4.740 000 0E+01
derah [Eritrea]	<length, special - see page 29>	
centimeter	46	4.600 000 0E+01
derham [Lebanon]	<mass, special - see page 29>	
gram	3.205	3.205 000 0E+00
derham [Persia, gold and silver]	<mass, special - see page 29>	
gram	9.36	9.360 000 0E+00
derhem [Egypt]	<mass, special - see page 29>	
gram	3.12	3.120 000 0E+00
derhem [Iran]	<mass, special - see page 29>	
gram	9.375	9.375 000 0E+00
derhem [Iraq]	<mass, special - see page 29>	
gram	3.12	3.120 000 0E+00
derhem [Persia, gold and silver]	<mass, special - see page 29>	
gram	9.36	9.360 000 0E+00
derhem [Sudan]	<mass, special - see page 29>	
gram	3.12	3.120 000 0E+00
derime [Ethiopia]	<mass, special - see page 29>	
gram	2.59	2.590 000 0E+00
desatine [Russia]	<area, special - see page 29>	
hectare	1.093	1.093 000 0E+00
desiatyny [Russia]	<area, special - see page 29>	
hectare	1.09	1.090 000 0E+00
dessetine [Russia]	<area, special - see page 29>	
hectare	1.093	1.093 000 0E+00
dessiatina [Russia]	<area, special - see page 29>	
hectare	1.092 54	1.092 540 0E+00
deunam [Near East]	<area, special - see page 29>	
square meter	2,500	2.500 000 0E+03
deunum [Cyprus]	<area, special - see page 29>	
square meter	1,337.8	1.337 800 0E+03
deunum [Middle East]	<area, special - see page 29>	
square meter	919	9.190 000 0E+02
deunum [Turkey]	<area, special - see page 29>	
hectare	25	2.500 000 0E+01
deunx [Rome, ancient]	<mass, special - see page 29>	
gram	300.16	3.001 600 0E+02

Convert From Convert To	Standard	\<Type of Unit> Scientific
deusquin [Netherlands]		\<mass, special - see page 29>
gram	0.097	9.700 000 0E−02
deuteron rest mass [atomic physics, eq. energy]		\<energy>
atomic mass unit [unified, C-12, 1986, eq. energy]	2.013 553 2	2.013 553 2E+00
dyne centimeter	0.003 005 1	3.005 065 3E−03
electron rest mass [atomic physics, eq. energy]	3,670.483 1	3.670 483 1E+03
erg	0.003 005 1	3.005 065 3E−03
gigaelectronvolt	1.875 613 4	1.875 613 4E+00
hartree [atomic physics, eq. energy]	>>>	6.892 749 5E+07
joule	<<<	3.005 065 3E−10
kiloelectronvolt	1,875,613.4	1.875 613 4E+06
megaelectronvolt	1,875.613 4	1.875 613 4E+03
muon rest mass [atomic physics, eq. energy]	17.751 675	1.775 167 5E+01
neutron rest mass [atomic physics, eq. energy]	1.996 255 9	1.996 255 9E+00
proton rest mass [atomic physics, eq. energy]	1.999 007 5	1.999 007 5E+00
teraelectronvolt	0.001 875 6	1.875 613 4E−03
dex		\<sound pressure level>
bel	1	1.000 000 0E+00
neper	1.151 292 6	1.151 292 6E+00
dextan [Rome, ancient]		\<mass, special - see page 29>
gram	272.88	2.728 800 0E+02
dha [Burma]		\<length, special - see page 29>
meter	3.2	3.200 000 0E+00
dhan [Bangladesh, precious metals]		\<mass, special - see page 29>
milligram	30.4	3.040 000 0E+01
dhan [India]		\<mass, special - see page 29>
milligram	36.4	3.640 000 0E+01
dhanu [India]		\<length, special - see page 29>
meter	1.828 8	1.828 800 0E+00
dhara [Bahrain]		\<length, special - see page 29>
centimeter	48.26	4.826 000 0E+01
dhara [Cyprus]		\<length, special - see page 29>
centimeter	60.96	6.096 000 0E+01
dhara [Iraq]		\<length, special - see page 29>
centimeter	74.5	7.450 000 0E+01
dhara [Jordan, land]		\<length, special - see page 29>
centimeter	75.8	7.580 000 0E+01
dhara [Jordan, textiles]		\<length, special - see page 29>
centimeter	68	6.800 000 0E+01
dhara [Lebanon, land]		\<length, special - see page 29>
centimeter	75.8	7.580 000 0E+01
dhara [Lebanon, textiles]		\<length, special - see page 29>
centimeter	68	6.800 000 0E+01
dhara [Morocco]		\<length, special - see page 29>
centimeter	55.88	5.588 000 0E+01
dhara [Oman]		\<length, special - see page 29>
centimeter	45.7	4.570 000 0E+01
dhara [Russia]		\<length, special - see page 29>
centimeter	71.12	7.112 000 0E+01
dhara [Saudi Arabia]		\<length, special - see page 29>
centimeter	45.7	4.570 000 0E+01
dhara [Syria, textiles]		\<length, special - see page 29>
centimeter	70	7.000 000 0E+01
dharana [India, ancient, gold]		\<mass, special - see page 29>
gram	396.8	3.968 000 0E+02
dharana [India, ancient, silver]		\<mass, special - see page 29>
gram	3.968	3.968 000 0E+00

| Convert From | | <Type of Unit> |
Convert To	Standard	Scientific
dharana [India, ancient]	<mass, special - see page 29>	
gram	9.696	9.696 000 0E+00
dharni [Nepal]	<mass, special - see page 29>	
kilogram	2.332 8	2.332 800 0E+00
dhira [Bahrain]	<length, special - see page 29>	
centimeter	48.26	4.826 000 0E+01
dhira [Cyprus]	<length, special - see page 29>	
centimeter	60.96	6.096 000 0E+01
dhira [Iraq]	<length, special - see page 29>	
centimeter	74.5	7.450 000 0E+01
dhira [Jordan, land]	<length, special - see page 29>	
centimeter	75.8	7.580 000 0E+01
dhira [Jordan, textiles]	<length, special - see page 29>	
centimeter	68	6.800 000 0E+01
dhira [Lebanon, land]	<length, special - see page 29>	
centimeter	75.8	7.580 000 0E+01
dhira [Lebanon, textiles]	<length, special - see page 29>	
centimeter	68	6.800 000 0E+01
dhira [Morocco]	<length, special - see page 29>	
centimeter	55.88	5.588 000 0E+01
dhira [Russia]	<length, special - see page 29>	
centimeter	71.12	7.112 000 0E+01
dhira [Saudi Arabia]	<length, special - see page 29>	
centimeter	45.7	4.570 000 0E+01
dhira [Syria, textiles]	<length, special - see page 29>	
centimeter	70	7.000 000 0E+01
dhira [Syria]	<length, special - see page 29>	
centimeter	75	7.500 000 0E+01
dhiraa [Bahrain]	<length, special - see page 29>	
centimeter	48.26	4.826 000 0E+01
dhiraa [Cyprus]	<length, special - see page 29>	
centimeter	60.96	6.096 000 0E+01
dhiraa [Iraq]	<length, special - see page 29>	
centimeter	74.5	7.450 000 0E+01
dhiraa [Jordan, land]	<length, special - see page 29>	
centimeter	75.8	7.580 000 0E+01
dhiraa [Jordan, textiles]	<length, special - see page 29>	
centimeter	68	6.800 000 0E+01
dhiraa [Lebanon, land]	<length, special - see page 29>	
centimeter	75.8	7.580 000 0E+01
dhiraa [Lebanon, textiles]	<length, special - see page 29>	
centimeter	68	6.800 000 0E+01
dhiraa [Morocco]	<length, special - see page 29>	
centimeter	55.88	5.588 000 0E+01
dhiraa [Russia]	<length, special - see page 29>	
centimeter	71.12	7.112 000 0E+01
dhiraa [Saudi Arabia]	<length, special - see page 29>	
centimeter	45.7	4.570 000 0E+01
dhiraa [Syria, textiles]	<length, special - see page 29>	
centimeter	70	7.000 000 0E+01
dhra [Bahrain]	<length, special - see page 29>	
centimeter	48.26	4.826 000 0E+01
dhra [Cyprus]	<length, special - see page 29>	
centimeter	60.96	6.096 000 0E+01

Convert From		\<Type of Unit\>
Convert To	Standard	Scientific

dhra [Iraq] <length, special - see page 29>
centimeter--- 74.5----7.450 000 0E+01

dhra [Jordan, land] <length, special - see page 29>
centimeter--- 75.8----7.580 000 0E+01

dhra [Jordan, textiles] <length, special - see page 29>
centimeter--- 68----6.800 000 0E+01

dhra [Lebanon, land] <length, special - see page 29>
centimeter--- 75.8----7.580 000 0E+01

dhra [Lebanon, textiles] <length, special - see page 29>
centimeter--- 68----6.800 000 0E+01

dhra [Morocco] <length, special - see page 29>
centimeter--- 55.88----5.588 000 0E+01

dhra [Russia] <length, special - see page 29>
centimeter-- 71.12----7.112 000 0E+01

dhra [Saudi Arabia] <length, special - see page 29>
centimeter--- 45.7----4.570 000 0E+01

dhra [Syria, textiles] <length, special - see page 29>
centimeter--- 70----7.000 000 0E+01

dhra d'alep [Iraq] <length, special - see page 29>
centimeter--- 68.5----6.850 000 0E+01

dhumd [Egypt] <area, special - see page 29>
hectare--- 0.42----4.200 000 0E-01

dhumd [Iraq] <area, special - see page 29>
hectare--- 5----5.000 000 0E+00

dhumd [Saudi Arabia] <area, special - see page 29>
hectare--- 0.42----4.200 000 0E-01

dhumd [Sudan] <area, special - see page 29>
hectare--- 0.42----4.200 000 0E-01

dhumd [Yemen] <area, special - see page 29>
hectare--- 0.405----4.050 000 0E-01

dhur [Nepal] <area, special - see page 29>
square meter------------------------------------- 16.929----1.692 900 0E+01

dhura [India] <mass, special - see page 29>
kilogram --------------------------------------- 4.665 522----4.665 522 0E+00

dhurree [India] <mass, special - see page 29>
kilogram --- 4.665----4.665 000 0E+00

diciatine [Russia] <area, special - see page 29>
hectare--- 1.092 54----1.092 540 0E+00

didot point [print] <length>
agate [print]--- 0.194 763 6----1.947 636 4E-01
caliber-- 1.482 219 4----1.482 194 4E+00
douzieme [print] ----------------------------------- 2.134 396----2.134 396 0E+00
em [pica, print]------------------------------------ 0.089 266 7----8.926 666 7E-02
inch [based on US, survey foot]------------------- 0.014 822 2----1.482 216 5E-02
inch [international]-------------------------------- 0.014 822 2----1.482 219 4E-02
iron [print] --- 0.003 570 7----3.570 666 7E-03
ligne [print]-- 0.177 866 3----1.778 663 3E-01
line [print]--- 0.177 866 3----1.778 663 3E-01
meter-- 0.000 376 5----3.764 837 4E-04
microinch-- 14,822.194----1.482 219 4E+04
micron-- 376.483 74----3.764 837 4E+02
mil-- 14.822 194----1.482 219 4E+01
nonpareil [print]------------------------------------ 0.178 533 3----1.785 333 3E-01
pearl [print]--- 0.214 24----2.142 400 0E-01
pica [print]--- 0.089 266 7----8.926 666 7E-02
point [print]-- 1.071 2----1.071 200 0E+00
thou--- 14.822 194----1.482 219 4E+01

Convert From	<Type of Unit>	
Convert To	Standard	Scientific

didrachm [Egypt, ancient] — <mass, special - see page 29>
  gram —————————————————————— 7.78 --- 7.780 000 0E+00

didrachm [Greece, ancient] — <mass, special - see page 29>
  gram —————————————————————— 9.72 --- 9.720 000 0E+00

didrachma [Greece, ancient] — <mass, special - see page 29>
  gram —————————————————————— 8.6 --- 8.600 000 0E+00

digit — <length>
  agate [print] ——————————————— 9.855 000 1 --- 9.855 000 1E+00
  barleycorn —————————————————— 2.25 --- 2.250 000 0E+00
  caliber ———————————————————————— 75 --- 7.500 000 0E+01
  centimeter ——————————————————— 1.905 --- 1.905 000 0E+00
  cubit ———————————————————— 0.041 666 7 --- 4.166 666 7E-02
  didot point [print] ——————————— 50.599 795 --- 5.059 979 5E+01
  douzieme [print] —————————————————— 108 --- 1.080 000 0E+02
  em [pica, print] —————————————— 4.516 875 --- 4.516 875 0E+00
  inch [based on US, survey foot] ———— 0.749 998 5 --- 7.499 985 0E-01
  inch [international] ————————————————— 0.75 --- 7.500 000 0E-01
  ligne [print] ———————————————————————— 9 --- 9.000 000 0E+00
  line [print] ————————————————————————— 9 --- 9.000 000 0E+00
  meter ————————————————————— 0.019 05 --- 1.905 000 0E-02
  mil ————————————————————————— 750 --- 7.500 000 0E+02
  nonpareil [print] ————————————— 9.033 750 1 --- 9.033 750 1E+00
  pica [print] —————————————————— 4.516 875 --- 4.516 875 0E+00
  point [print] ————————————————— 54.202 501 --- 5.420 250 1E+01
  thou ————————————————————————— 750 --- 7.500 000 0E+02

digit [Egypt, ancient] — <length, special - see page 29>
  millimeter ————————————————————— 18.72 --- 1.872 000 0E+00

digit [Greece, ancient] — <length, special - see page 29>
  millimeter ————————————————————— 19.25 --- 1.925 000 0E+00

digit [Hebrew, ancient] — <length, special - see page 29>
  millimeter ———————————————————————— 19 --- 1.900 000 0E+01

digit [Iraq, ancient] — <length, special - see page 29>
  centimeter ——————————————————————— 3.3 --- 3.300 000 0E+00

digit [Mesopotamia, ancient] — <length, special - see page 29>
  centimeter —————————————————————— 1.65 --- 1.650 000 0E+00

digitus [Rome, ancient] — <length, special - see page 29>
  centimeter —————————————————————— 1.85 --- 1.850 000 0E+00

dilepton [Hebrew, ancient] — <mass, special - see page 29>
  gram ——————————————————————————— 1.5 --- 1.500 000 0E+00

dimerlie [Romania] — <volume, special - see page 29>
  liter ———————————————————————— 24.6 --- 2.460 000 0E+01

dimidia sextula [Rome, ancient] — <mass, special - see page 29>
  gram ————————————————————— 2.274 --- 2.274 000 0E+00

dinar [Arabia] — <mass, special - see page 29>
  gram ——————————————————————————— 4.2 --- 4.200 000 0E+00

diopter — <reciprocal length, phase coefficient>
  1/foot ——————————————————————— 0.304 8 --- 3.048 000 0E-01
  1/meter ———————————————————————————— 1 --- 1.000 000 0E+00
  radian/meter ——————————————————————— 1 --- 1.000 000 0E+00

dipondium [Rome, ancient] — <mass, special - see page 29>
  gram ————————————————————————— 12.4 --- 1.240 000 0E+01

dira [Bahrain] — <length, special - see page 29>
  centimeter ————————————————————— 48.26 --- 4.826 000 0E+01

dira [Cyprus] — <length, special - see page 29>
  centimeter ————————————————————— 60.96 --- 6.096 000 0E+01

dira [Greece] — <length, special - see page 29>
  centimeter ———————————————————————— 75 --- 7.500 000 0E+01

Convert From	<Type of Unit>	
Convert To	Standard	Scientific

dira [Iraq] <length, special - see page 29>
centimeter--- 74.5----7.450 000 0E+01

dira [Jordan, land] <length, special - see page 29>
centimeter--- 75.8----7.580 000 0E+01

dira [Jordan, textiles] <length, special - see page 29>
centimeter--- 68----6.800 000 0E+01

dira [Lebanon, land] <length, special - see page 29>
centimeter--- 75.8----7.580 000 0E+01

dira [Lebanon, textiles] <length, special - see page 29>
centimeter--- 68----6.800 000 0E+01

dira [Morocco] <length, special - see page 29>
centimeter--- 55.88----5.588 000 0E+01

dira [Russia] <length, special - see page 29>
centimeter--- 71.12----7.112 000 0E+01

dira [Saudi Arabia, ancient] <length, special - see page 29>
centimeter--- 45.7----4.570 000 0E+01

dira [Saudi Arabia] <length, special - see page 29>
centimeter--- 43.942----4.394 200 0E+01

dira [Sudan] <length, special - see page 29>
centimeter--- 57.99----5.799 000 0E+01

dira [Syria, textiles] <length, special - see page 29>
centimeter--- 70----7.000 000 0E+01

dira [Yemen] <length, special - see page 29>
centimeter--- 45.7----4.570 000 0E+01

dira baladi [Egypt] <length, special - see page 29>
centimeter--- 58----5.800 000 0E+01

dira minari [Greece] <length, special - see page 29>
centimeter--- 64.8----6.480 000 0E+01

diraa [Bahrain] <length, special - see page 29>
centimeter--- 48.26----4.826 000 0E+01

diraa [Cyprus] <length, special - see page 29>
centimeter--- 60.96----6.096 000 0E+01

diraa [Egypt, ancient, textiles] <length, special - see page 29>
centimeter--- 58----5.800 000 0E+01

diraa [Iraq] <length, special - see page 29>
centimeter--- 74.5----7.450 000 0E+01

diraa [Jordan, land] <length, special - see page 29>
centimeter--- 75.8----7.580 000 0E+01

diraa [Jordan, textiles] <length, special - see page 29>
centimeter--- 68----6.800 000 0E+01

diraa [Lebanon, land] <length, special - see page 29>
centimeter--- 75.8----7.580 000 0E+01

diraa [Lebanon, textiles] <length, special - see page 29>
centimeter--- 68----6.800 000 0E+01

diraa [Morocco] <length, special - see page 29>
centimeter--- 55.88----5.588 000 0E+01

diraa [Russia] <length, special - see page 29>
centimeter--- 71.12----7.112 000 0E+01

diraa [Saudi Arabia] <length, special - see page 29>
centimeter--- 45.7----4.570 000 0E+01

diraa [Sudan] <length, special - see page 29>
centimeter--- 57.99----5.799 000 0E+01

diraa [Syria, textiles] <length, special - see page 29>
centimeter--- 70----7.000 000 0E+01

Convert From		<Type of Unit>
Convert To	Standard	Scientific

diraa baladi [Egypt] <length, special - see page 29>
  meter --- 0.58 --- 5.800 000 0E−01

diraa memari [Egypt, ancient, building] <length, special - see page 29>
  centimeter --------------------------------------- 75 --- 7.500 000 0E+01

dirham [Iran] <mass, special - see page 29>
  gram ------------------------------------ 9.375 --- 9.375 000 0E+00

dirhem [Iran] <mass, special - see page 29>
  gram ------------------------------------ 9.375 --- 9.375 000 0E+00

dirhem [Persia, gold and silver] <mass, special - see page 29>
  gram -------------------------------------- 9.36 --- 9.360 000 0E+00

dirhem [Turkey] <mass, special - see page 29>
  gram --------------------------------------- 10 --- 1.000 000 0E+01

disintegration/second <radionuclide activity>
  1/second ------------------------------------- 1 --- 1.000 000 0E+00
  becquerel ----------------------------------- 1 --- 1.000 000 0E+00
  curie --------------------------------- <<< --- 2.702 702 7E−11
  rutherford -------------------------- 0.000 001 --- 1.000 000 0E−06

djarib [Iran] <area, special - see page 29>
  are -------------------------------------- 10.8 --- 1.080 000 0E+01

djerib [Turkey] <area, special - see page 29>
  hectare -- 1 --- 1.000 000 0E+00

djevil [Turkey] <area, special - see page 29>
  hectare -- 1 --- 1.000 000 0E+00

djung [Indonesia] <area, special - see page 29>
  hectare ---------------------------------- 1.419 3 --- 1.419 300 0E+00

dodran [Rome, ancient] <mass, special - see page 29>
  gram ------------------------------------ 245.59 --- 2.455 900 0E+02

doi [South Korea] <volume, special - see page 29>
  liter ---------------------------------- 1.803 91 --- 1.803 910 0E+00

doli [Russia] <mass, special - see page 29>
  milligram ------------------------------- 44.435 --- 4.443 500 0E+01

dolia [Russia] <mass, special - see page 29>
  milligram ------------------------------- 44.435 --- 4.443 500 0E+01

dolja [Russia] <mass, special - see page 29>
  milligram ------------------------------- 44.435 --- 4.443 500 0E+01

doly [Russia] <mass, special - see page 29>
  milligram --------------------------------- 44.4 --- 4.440 000 0E+01

don [South Korea] <mass, special - see page 29>
  gram -------------------------------------- 3.75 --- 3.750 000 0E+00

donchung [South Korea] <mass, special - see page 29>
  gram -------------------------------------- 3.75 --- 3.750 000 0E+00

dong [Iran] <mass, special - see page 29>
  milligram ----------------------------------- 781 --- 7.810 000 0E+02

dong [Vietnam] <mass, special - see page 29>
  gram ------------------------------------- 3.778 --- 3.778 000 0E+00

dong [Vietnam] <length, special - see page 29>
  centimeter --------------------------- 2.333 333 3 --- 2.333 333 3E+00

donum [Cyprus] <area, special - see page 29>
  square meter ---------------------------- 1,337.8 --- 1.337 800 0E+03

donum [Israel] <area, special - see page 29>
  square meter ------------------------------ 1,000 --- 1.000 000 0E+03

donum [Jordan] <area, special - see page 29>
  square meter ------------------------------ 1,000 --- 1.000 000 0E+03

donum [Lebanon] <area, special - see page 29>
  square meter -------------------------------- 919 --- 9.190 000 0E+02

Convert From	<Type of Unit>	
Convert To	Standard	Scientific

donum [Libya]	<area, special - see page 29>	
square meter	919	9.190 000 0E+02
donum [Syria]	<area, special - see page 29>	
square meter	919	9.190 000 0E+02
donum [Turkey]	<area, special - see page 29>	
square meter	919	9.190 000 0E+02
donum [Yugoslavia]	<area, special - see page 29>	
square meter	700	7.000 000 0E+02
doon [Thailand]	<mass, special - see page 29>	
kilogram	24	2.400 000 0E+01
doppelzentner [Germany]	<mass>	
cental [US]	2.204 622 6	2.204 622 6E+00
centner [UK]	1.968 413 1	1.968 413 1E+00
decitonne	1	1.000 000 0E+00
hundredweight [long]	1.968 413 1	1.968 413 1E+00
hundredweight [short]	2.204 622 6	2.204 622 6E+00
hundredweight [UK]	1.968 413 1	1.968 413 1E+00
hyl	10.197 162	1.019 716 2E+01
quarter [long]	0.393 682 6	3.936 826 1E-01
quarter [short]	0.440 924 5	4.409 245 2E-01
quarter [UK]	7.873 652 2	7.873 652 2E+00
quarter [US]	8.818 490 5	8.818 490 5E+00
quintal [metric]	1	1.000 000 0E+00
quintal [UK]	1.968 413 1	1.968 413 1E+00
quintal [US]	2.204 622 6	2.204 622 6E+00
slug	6.852 176 6	6.852 176 6E+00
slug [metric]	10.197 162	1.019 716 2E+01
stone [UK]	15.747 304	1.574 730 4E+01
ton [long]	0.098 420 7	9.842 065 3E-02
ton [metric]	0.1	1.000 000 0E-01
ton [short]	0.110 231 1	1.102 311 3E-01
tonne	0.1	1.000 000 0E-01
doron [Greece, ancient]	<length, special - see page 29>	
centimeter	1.92	1.920 000 0E+00
dou [China]	<volume, special - see page 29>	
liter	10	1.000 000 0E+01
double fanega [Uruguay]	<volume, special - see page 29>	
hectoliter	2.745	2.745 000 0E+00
double stadion [Mesopotamia, ancient]	<length, special - see page 29>	
meter	360.7	3.607 000 0E+02
douzieme [print]	<length>	
agate [print]	0.091 25	9.125 000 1E-02
barleycorn	0.020 833 3	2.083 333 3E-02
didot point [print]	0.468 516 6	4.685 166 2E-01
digit	0.009 259 3	9.259 259 3E-03
em [pica, print]	0.041 822 9	4.182 291 7E-02
inch [based on US, survey foot]	0.006 944 4	6.944 430 6E-03
inch [international]	0.006 944 4	6.944 444 4E-03
iron [print]	0.001 672 9	1.672 916 7E-03
ligne [print]	0.083 333 3	8.333 333 3E-02
line [print]	0.083 333 3	8.333 333 3E-02
meter	0.000 176 4	1.763 888 9E-04
microinch	6,944.444 4	6.944 444 4E+03
micron	176.388 89	1.763 888 9E+02
mil	6.944 444 4	6.944 444 4E+00
nonpareil [print]	0.083 645 8	8.364 583 3E-02
pearl [print]	0.100 375	1.003 750 0E-01
pica [print]	0.041 822 9	4.182 291 7E-02
point [print]	0.501 875	5.018 750 1E-01
thou	6.944 444 4	6.944 444 4E+00

Convert From		<Type of Unit>
Convert To	Standard	Scientific

dozen   **<units>**

Convert To	Standard	Scientific
brace	6	6.000 000 0E+00
duodecal	1	1.000 000 0E+00
hexad	2	2.000 000 0E+00
pair	6	6.000 000 0E+00
unit	12	1.200 000 0E+01

dra [Bahrain]   **<length, special - see page 29>**
centimeter	48.26	4.826 000 0E+01

dra [Cyprus]   **<length, special - see page 29>**
centimeter	60.96	6.096 000 0E+01

dra [Iraq] **<length, special - see page 29>**
centimeter	74.5	7.450 000 0E+01

dra [Jordan, land] **<length, special - see page 29>**
centimeter	75.8	7.580 000 0E+01

dra [Jordan, textiles] **<length, special - see page 29>**
centimeter	68	6.800 000 0E+01

dra [Lebanon, land] **<length, special - see page 29>**
centimeter	75.8	7.580 000 0E+01

dra [Lebanon, textiles] **<length, special - see page 29>**
centimeter	68	6.800 000 0E+01

dra [Morocco] **<length, special - see page 29>**
centimeter	55.88	5.588 000 0E+01

dra [Russia] **<length, special - see page 29>**
centimeter	71.12	7.112 000 0E+01

dra [Saudi Arabia] **<length, special - see page 29>**
centimeter	45.7	4.570 000 0E+01

dra [Syria, textiles] **<length, special - see page 29>**
centimeter	70	7.000 000 0E+01

dra [Yemen] **<length, special - see page 29>**
meter	0.67	6.700 000 0E-01

dra arbi [Libya, textiles] **<length, special - see page 29>**
centimeter	49	4.900 000 0E+01

dra maghmari [Syria, land] **<length, special - see page 29>**
centimeter	75.8	7.580 000 0E+01

draa arbi [Libya, textiles] **<length, special - see page 29>**
centimeter	49	4.900 000 0E+01

draa milki [Libya, land] **<length, special - see page 29>**
centimeter	50	5.000 000 0E+01

drachm [Egypt, ancient] **<mass, special - see page 29>**
gram	3.89	3.890 000 0E+00

drachm [Ethiopia] **<mass, special - see page 29>**
gram	2.59	2.590 000 0E+00

drachm [Netherlands] **<mass, special - see page 29>**
gram	3.906	3.906 000 0E+00

drachm [Poland] **<mass, special - see page 29>**
gram	3.15	3.150 000 0E+00

drachm [UK, apothecary] **<mass>**
Convert To	Standard	Scientific
carat [gemstones]	19.439 673	1.943 967 3E+01
carat [international]	19.439 673	1.943 967 3E+01
carat [metric]	19.439 673	1.943 967 3E+01
carat [UK]	15	1.500 000 0E+01
carat [US, after 1913]	19.439 673	1.943 967 3E+01
carat [US, before 1913]	18.937 821	1.893 782 1E+01
dram [avoirdupois]	2.194 285 7	2.194 285 7E+00
dram [US, apothecary]	1	1.000 000 0E+00
grain	60	6.000 000 0E+01
grain [apothecary]	60	6.000 000 0E+01

grain [avoirdupois]	60	6.000 000 0E+01
grain [troy]	60	6.000 000 0E+01
gram	3.887 934 6	3.887 934 6E+00
kilogram	0.003 887 9	3.887 934 6E-03
ounce	0.137 142 9	1.371 428 6E-01
ounce [apothecary]	0.125	1.250 000 0E-01
ounce [avoirdupois]	0.137 142 9	1.371 428 6E-01
ounce [troy]	0.125	1.250 000 0E-01
pennyweight [troy]	2.5	2.500 000 0E+00
scruple [UK]	3	3.000 000 0E+00
scruple [US, apothecary]	3	3.000 000 0E+00
ton [UK, assay or assay, long]	0.119 018 4	1.190 184 1E-01
ton [US, assay or assay, short]	0.133 300 6	1.333 006 1E-01

drachm [UK, liquid]   **<volume>**

cubic centimeter	3.551 632 8	3.551 632 8E+00
cubic foot	0.000 125 4	1.254 247 3E-04
cubic inch	0.216 733 9	2.167 339 3E-01
cubic meter	0.000 003 6	3.551 632 8E-06
cup [Canada, measuring]	0.015 625	1.562 500 0E-02
cup [US, measuring]	0.015 011 9	1.501 187 4E-02
dram [Canada, liquid]	1	1.000 000 0E+00
dram [US, liquid]	0.960 759 9	9.607 599 4E-01
drop [US, liquid]	43.234 197	4.323 419 7E+01
gill [UK]	0.025	2.500 000 0E-02
gill [US]	0.030 023 7	3.002 374 8E-02
liter	0.003 551 6	3.551 632 8E-03
milliliter	3.551 632 8	3.551 632 8E+00
minim [UK]	60	6.000 000 0E+01
minim [US]	57.645 596	5.764 559 6E+01
ounce [UK, liquid]	0.125	1.250 000 0E-01
ounce [US, liquid]	0.120 095	1.200 949 9E-01
scruple [UK, liquid]	3	3.000 000 0E+00
tablespoon [Canada, measuring]	0.250 000 4	2.500 004 2E-01
tablespoon [US, measuring]	0.240 19	2.401 899 9E-01
teaspoon [Canada, measuring]	0.750 001 3	7.500 012 7E-01
teaspoon [US, measuring]	0.720 57	7.205 699 6E-01

drachma [Austria]   **<mass, special - see page 29>**

gram	4.68	4.680 000 0E+00

drachma [Cyprus]   **<mass, special - see page 29>**

gram	3.175	3.175 000 0E+00

drachma [Egypt]   **<mass, special - see page 29>**

gram	3.12	3.120 000 0E+00

drachma [Germany]   **<mass, special - see page 29>**

gram	3.76	3.760 000 0E+00

drachma [Greece]   **<mass, special - see page 29>**

gram	4.36	4.360 000 0E+00

drachma [Iran]   **<mass, special - see page 29>**

gram	9.375	9.375 000 0E+00

drachma [Iraq]   **<mass, special - see page 29>**

gram	3.207 5	3.207 500 0E+00

drachma [Italy]   **<mass, special - see page 29>**

gram	3.57	3.570 000 0E+00

drachma [Jordan]   **<mass, special - see page 29>**

gram	3.205	3.205 000 0E+00

drachma [Lebanon]   **<mass, special - see page 29>**

gram	3.205	3.205 000 0E+00

drachma [Libya]   **<mass, special - see page 29>**

gram	3.205	3.205 000 0E+00

drachma [Netherlands]   **<mass, special - see page 29>**

gram	3.86	3.860 000 0E+00

drachma [Rome, ancient]
gram ──────────────────────────── <mass, special - see page 29>
3.4 --- 3.400 000 0E+00

drachma [Russia, apothecary]
gram ──────────────────────────── <mass, special - see page 29>
3.732 --- 3.732 000 0E+00

drachma [Sudan]
gram ──────────────────────────── <mass, special - see page 29>
3.12 --- 3.120 000 0E+00

drachma [Switzerland]
gram ──────────────────────────── <mass, special - see page 29>
3.1 --- 3.100 000 0E+00

drachma [Syria]
gram ──────────────────────────── <mass, special - see page 29>
3.205 --- 3.205 000 0E+00

drachma [Turkey]
gram ──────────────────────────── <mass, special - see page 29>
3.207 5 --- 3.207 500 0E+00

drachme [Austria, apothecary]
gram ──────────────────────────── <mass, special - see page 29>
4.375 1 --- 4.375 100 0E+00

drachme [Cyprus]
gram ──────────────────────────── <mass, special - see page 29>
3.175 147 --- 3.175 147 0E+00

drachme [France]
gram ──────────────────────────── <mass, special - see page 29>
3.824 --- 3.824 000 0E+00

drachme [Greece, ancient]
gram ──────────────────────────── <mass, special - see page 29>
14.175 --- 1.417 500 0E+01

drachme [Iraq, ancient]
gram ──────────────────────────── <mass, special - see page 29>
3.12 --- 3.120 000 0E+00

drachme [Poland]
gram ──────────────────────────── <mass, special - see page 29>
3.15 --- 3.150 000 0E+00

drachme [Switzerland]
gram ──────────────────────────── <mass, special - see page 29>
3.906 --- 3.906 000 0E+00

drachme [Turkey, gold and silver]
gram ──────────────────────────── <mass, special - see page 29>
3.1 --- 3.100 000 0E+00

drachme [Turkey]
gram ──────────────────────────── <mass, special - see page 29>
3.2 --- 3.200 000 0E+00

drah [Bahrain]
centimeter ──────────────────────── <length, special - see page 29>
48.26 --- 4.826 000 0E+01

drah [Cyprus]
centimeter ──────────────────────── <length, special - see page 29>
60.96 --- 6.096 000 0E+01

drah [Iraq]
centimeter ──────────────────────── <length, special - see page 29>
74.5 --- 7.450 000 0E+01

drah [Jordan, land]
centimeter ──────────────────────── <length, special - see page 29>
75.8 --- 7.580 000 0E+01

drah [Jordan, textiles]
centimeter ──────────────────────── <length, special - see page 29>
68 --- 6.800 000 0E+01

drah [Lebanon, land]
centimeter ──────────────────────── <length, special - see page 29>
75.8 --- 7.580 000 0E+01

drah [Lebanon, textiles]
centimeter ──────────────────────── <length, special - see page 29>
67.9 --- 6.790 000 0E+01

drah [Morocco]
meter ──────────────────────────── <length, special - see page 29>
0.5 --- 5.000 000 0E-01

drah [Russia]
centimeter ──────────────────────── <length, special - see page 29>
71.12 --- 7.112 000 0E+01

drah [Saudi Arabia]
centimeter ──────────────────────── <length, special - see page 29>
45.7 --- 4.570 000 0E+01

drah [Syria, textiles]
centimeter ──────────────────────── <length, special - see page 29>
70 --- 7.000 000 0E+01

drahi [Bahrain]
centimeter ──────────────────────── <length, special - see page 29>
48.26 --- 4.826 000 0E+01

drahi [Cyprus] <length, special - see page 29>
centimeter-- 60.96----6.096 000 0E+01

drahi [Iraq] <length, special - see page 29>
centimeter-- 74.5----7.450 000 0E+01

drahi [Jordan, land] <length, special - see page 29>
centimeter-- 75.8----7.580 000 0E+01

drahi [Jordan, textiles] <length, special - see page 29>
centimeter-- 68----6.800 000 0E+01

drahi [Lebanon, land] <length, special - see page 29>
centimeter-- 75.8----7.580 000 0E+01

drahi [Lebanon, textiles] <length, special - see page 29>
centimeter-- 68----6.800 000 0E+01

drahi [Morocco] <length, special - see page 29>
centimeter-- 55.88----5.588 000 0E+01

drahi [Russia] <length, special - see page 29>
centimeter-- 71.12----7.112 000 0E+01

drahi [Saudi Arabia] <length, special - see page 29>
centimeter-- 45.7----4.570 000 0E+01

drahi [Syria, textiles] <length, special - see page 29>
centimeter-- 70----7.000 000 0E+01

dram [avoirdupois] <mass>

Convert To	Standard	Scientific
carat [international]	8.859 226	8.859 226 0E+00
carat [UK]	6.835 937 5	6.835 937 5E+00
carat [US, before 1913]	8.630 517 3	8.630 517 3E+00
drachm [UK, apothecary]	0.455 729 2	4.557 291 7E−01
dram [US, apothecary]	0.455 729 2	4.557 291 7E−01
grain	27.343 75	2.734 375 0E+01
grain [apothecary]	27.343 75	2.734 375 0E+01
grain [avoirdupois]	27.343 75	2.734 375 0E+01
grain [troy]	27.343 75	2.734 375 0E+01
gram	1.771 845 2	1.771 845 2E+00
kilogram	0.001 771 8	1.771 845 2E−03
ounce	0.062 5	6.250 000 0E−02
ounce [apothecary]	0.056 966 1	5.696 614 6E−02
ounce [avoirdupois]	0.062 5	6.250 000 0E−02
pennyweight [troy]	1.139 322 9	1.139 322 9E+00
point [jewelers']	885.922 6	8.859 226 0E+02
scruple [UK]	1.367 187 5	1.367 187 5E+00
scruple [US, apothecary]	1.367 187 5	1.367 187 5E+00
ton [UK, assay or assay, long]	0.054 240 2	5.424 015 9E−02
ton [US, assay or assay, short]	0.060 749	6.074 897 8E−02

dram [Canada, liquid] <volume>

Convert To	Standard	Scientific
cubic centimeter	3.551 632 8	3.551 632 8E+00
cubic foot	0.000 125 4	1.254 247 3E−04
cubic inch	0.216 733 9	2.167 339 3E−01
cubic meter	0.000 003 6	3.551 632 8E−06
cup [Canada, measuring]	0.015 625	1.562 500 0E−02
cup [US, measuring]	0.015 011 9	1.501 187 4E−02
drachm [UK, liquid]	1	1.000 000 0E+00
dram [US, liquid]	0.960 759 9	9.607 599 4E−01
drop [US, liquid]	43.234 197	4.323 419 7E+01
liter	0.003 551 6	3.551 632 8E−03
milliliter	3.551 632 8	3.551 632 8E+00
minim [UK]	60	6.000 000 0E+01
minim [US]	57.645 596	5.764 559 6E+01
ounce [UK, liquid]	0.125	1.250 000 0E−01
ounce [US, liquid]	0.120 095	1.200 949 9E−01
pint [UK]	0.006 25	6.250 000 0E−03
pint [US, dry]	0.006 450 4	6.450 354 0E−03
pint [US, liquid]	0.007 505 9	7.505 937 0E−03

	Standard	Scientific
quart [UK]	0.003 125	3.125 000 0E−03
quart [US, dry]	0.003 225 2	3.225 177 3E−03
quart [US, liquid]	0.003 753	3.752 968 5E−03
scruple [UK, liquid]	3	3.000 000 0E+00
tablespoon [Canada, measuring]	0.250 000 4	2.500 004 2E−01
tablespoon [US, measuring]	0.240 19	2.401 899 9E−01
teaspoon [Canada, measuring]	0.750 001 3	7.500 012 7E−01
teaspoon [US, measuring]	0.720 57	7.205 699 6E−01

dram [Cyprus] — <mass, special - see page 29>
| gram | 3.175 | 3.175 000 0E+00 |

dram [Egypt] — <mass, special - see page 29>
| gram | 3.12 | 3.120 000 0E+00 |

dram [Greece] — <mass, special - see page 29>
| gram | 3.2 | 3.200 000 0E+00 |

dram [Iran] — <mass, special - see page 29>
| gram | 9.375 | 9.375 000 0E+00 |

dram [Iraq, Baghdad] — <mass, special - see page 29>
| gram | 3.25 | 3.250 000 0E+00 |

dram [Iraq] — <mass, special - see page 29>
| gram | 3.207 5 | 3.207 500 0E+00 |

dram [Jordan] — <mass, special - see page 29>
| gram | 3.205 | 3.205 000 0E+00 |

dram [Lebanon] — <mass, special - see page 29>
| gram | 3.205 | 3.205 000 0E+00 |

dram [Libya] — <mass, special - see page 29>
| gram | 3.205 | 3.205 000 0E+00 |

dram [Romania] — <mass, special - see page 29>
| gram | 3.22 | 3.220 000 0E+00 |

dram [Sudan] — <mass, special - see page 29>
| gram | 3.12 | 3.120 000 0E+00 |

dram [Turkey] — <mass, special - see page 29>
| gram | 3.207 5 | 3.207 500 0E+00 |

dram [US, apothecary] — <mass>
	Standard	Scientific
carat [international]	19.439 673	1.943 967 3E+01
carat [UK]	15	1.500 000 0E+01
carat [US, before 1913]	18.937 821	1.893 782 1E+01
drachm [UK, apothecary]	1	1.000 000 0E+00
dram [avoirdupois]	2.194 285 7	2.194 285 7E+00
grain	60	6.000 000 0E+01
grain [apothecary]	60	6.000 000 0E+01
grain [avoirdupois]	60	6.000 000 0E+01
grain [troy]	60	6.000 000 0E+01
gram	3.887 934 6	3.887 934 6E+00
kilogram	0.003 887 9	3.887 934 6E−03
ounce	0.137 142 9	1.371 428 6E−01
ounce [apothecary]	0.125	1.250 000 0E−01
ounce [avoirdupois]	0.137 142 9	1.371 428 6E−01
ounce [troy]	0.125	1.250 000 0E−01
pennyweight [troy]	2.5	2.500 000 0E+00
scruple [UK]	3	3.000 000 0E+00
scruple [US, apothecary]	3	3.000 000 0E+00
ton [UK, assay or assay, long]	0.119 018 4	1.190 184 1E−01
ton [US, assay or assay, short]	0.133 300 6	1.333 006 1E−01

dram [US, liquid] — <volume>
	Standard	Scientific
cubic centimeter	3.696 691 2	3.696 691 2E+00
cubic foot	0.000 130 5	1.305 474 2E−04
cubic inch	0.225 585 9	2.255 859 4E−01
cubic meter	0.000 003 7	3.696 691 2E−06
cup [Canada, measuring]	0.016 263 2	1.626 316 8E−02

Convert From Convert To	<Type of Unit>	
	Standard	Scientific
cup [US, measuring]	0.015 625	1.562 500 0E-02
drachm [UK, liquid]	1.040 842 7	1.040 842 7E+00
dram [Canada, liquid]	1.040 842 7	1.040 842 7E+00
drop [US, liquid]	45	4.500 000 0E+01
liter	0.003 696 7	3.696 691 2E-03
milliliter	3.696 691 2	3.696 691 2E+00
minim [UK]	62.450 564	6.245 056 4E+01
minim [US]	60	6.000 000 0E+01
ounce [UK, liquid]	0.130 105 3	1.301 053 4E-01
ounce [US, liquid]	0.125	1.250 000 0E-01
pint [UK]	0.006 505 3	6.505 267 1E-03
pint [US, dry]	0.006 713 8	6.713 804 7E-03
pint [US, liquid]	0.007 812 5	7.812 500 0E-03
quart [UK]	0.003 252 6	3.252 633 5E-03
quart [US, dry]	0.003 356 9	3.356 902 4E-03
quart [US, liquid]	0.003 906 3	3.906 250 0E-03
scruple [UK, liquid]	3.122 528 2	3.122 528 2E+00
tablespoon [Canada, measuring]	0.260 211 1	2.602 111 2E-01
tablespoon [US, measuring]	0.25	2.500 000 0E-01
teaspoon [Canada, measuring]	0.780 633 4	7.806 333 7E-01
teaspoon [US, measuring]	0.75	7.500 000 0E-01

drame [Iraq]   <mass, special - see page 29>
| gram | 3.25 | 3.250 000 0E+00 |

drame [Romania]   <mass, special - see page 29>
| gram | 3.22 | 3.220 000 0E+00 |

dramm [Yugoslavia]   <mass, special - see page 29>
| gram | 3.2 | 3.200 000 0E+00 |

dramma [Cyprus]   <mass, special - see page 29>
| gram | 3.175 | 3.175 000 0E+00 |

dramma [Egypt]   <mass, special - see page 29>
| gram | 3.12 | 3.120 000 0E+00 |

dramma [Iran]   <mass, special - see page 29>
| gram | 9.375 | 9.375 000 0E+00 |

dramma [Libya, gold, silver and silk]   <mass, special - see page 29>
| gram | 3.067 48 | 3.067 480 0E+00 |

dramma [Sudan]   <mass, special - see page 29>
| gram | 3.12 | 3.120 000 0E+00 |

dramme [Greece]   <mass, special - see page 29>
| gram | 3.23 | 3.230 000 0E+00 |

dreiling [Austria]   <volume, special - see page 29>
| hectoliter | 16.98 | 1.698 000 0E+01 |

dreissiger [Germany]   <volume, special - see page 29>
| liter | 1.158 1 | 1.158 100 0E+00 |

drex   <linear density>
denier	0.9	9.000 000 0E-01
kilogram/meter	0.000 000 1	1.000 000 0E-07
ounce/foot	0.000 000 1	1.075 150 4E-06
pound/yard	0.000 000 2	2.015 906 9E-07
tex	0.1	1.000 000 0E-01

drop [US, liquid]   <volume>
cubic foot	0.000 002 9	2.901 053 7E-06
cubic inch	0.005 013	5.013 020 8E-03
cubic meter	<<<	8.214 869 3E-08
drachm [UK, liquid]	0.023 129 8	2.312 983 8E-02
dram [Canada, liquid]	0.023 129 8	2.312 983 8E-02
dram [US, liquid]	0.022 222 2	2.222 222 2E-02
fifth [US, liquid]	0.000 108 5	1.085 069 4E-04
jigger [US, liquid]	0.001 851 9	1.851 851 9E-03
lambda	82.148 693	8.214 869 3E+01
liter	0.000 082 1	8.214 869 3E-05

Convert From	Standard	<Type of Unit>
Convert To		Scientific

microliter	82.148 693	8.214 869 3E+01
minim [UK]	1.387 790 3	1.387 790 3E+00
minim [US]	1.333 333 3	1.333 333 3E+00
ounce [UK, liquid]	0.002 891 2	2.891 229 8E-03
ounce [US, liquid]	0.002 777 8	2.777 777 8E-03
pony [US, liquid]	0.002 777 8	2.777 777 8E-03
scruple [UK, liquid]	0.069 389 5	6.938 951 5E-02
shot [US, liquid]	0.002 777 8	2.777 777 8E-03
tablespoon [Canada, measuring]	0.005 782 5	5.782 469 4E-03
tablespoon [US, measuring]	0.005 555 6	5.555 555 6E-03
teaspoon [Canada, measuring]	0.017 347 4	1.734 740 8E-02
teaspoon [US, measuring]	0.016 666 7	1.666 666 7E-02

drum [US, liquid] <volume>

barrel [US, federal proof spirits]	1.375	1.375 000 0E+00
barrel [US, liquid]	1.746 031 7	1.746 031 7E+00
barrel [US, petroleum]	1.309 523 8	1.309 523 8E+00
chaldron [UK, liquid]	0.159 017 6	1.590 176 4E-01
cubic foot	7.352 430 6	7.352 430 6E+00
cubic inch	12,705	1.270 500 0E+04
cubic meter	0.208 197 7	2.081 976 5E-01
cup [Canada, measuring]	915.941 6	9.159 416 0E+02
cup [US, measuring]	880	8.800 000 0E+02
dram [US, liquid]	56,320	5.632 000 0E+04
firkin [UK]	5.088 564 5	5.088 564 5E+00
firkin [US]	6.111 111 1	6.111 111 1E+00
gallon [Canada, liquid]	45.797 08	4.579 708 0E+01
gallon [UK, dry or liquid]	45.797 08	4.579 708 0E+01
gallon [US, liquid]	55	5.500 000 0E+01
gill [UK]	1,465.506 6	1.465 506 6E+03
gill [US]	1,760	1.760 000 0E+03
hectoliter	2.081 976 5	2.081 976 5E+00
liter	208.197 65	2.081 976 5E+02
ounce [UK, liquid]	7,327.532 8	7.327 532 8E+03
ounce [US, liquid]	7,040	7.040 000 0E+03
pint [UK]	366.376 64	3.663 766 4E+02
pint [US, liquid]	440	4.400 000 0E+02
quart [UK]	183.188 32	1.831 883 2E+02
quart [US, liquid]	220	2.200 000 0E+02
stere	0.208 197 7	2.081 976 5E-01
tablespoon [Canada, measuring]	14,655.09	1.465 509 0E+04
tablespoon [US, measuring]	14,080	1.408 000 0E+04
teaspoon [Canada, measuring]	43,965.271	4.396 527 1E+04
teaspoon [US, measuring]	42,240	4.224 000 0E+04
tun [UK, liquid]	0.212 023 5	2.120 235 2E-01
tun [US, liquid]	0.218 254	2.182 539 7E-01
Winchester wine gallon [UK]	55	5.500 000 0E+01

du [Mongolia] <volume, special - see page 29>

liter	6.5	6.500 000 0E+00

ducat [Austria] <mass, special - see page 29>

gram	3.52	3.520 000 0E+00

ducat ass [Germany] <mass, special - see page 29>

gram	0.056	5.600 000 0E-02

duella [France, apothecary] <mass, special - see page 29>

gram	10.2	1.020 000 0E+01

duella [Rome, ancient] <mass, special - see page 29>

gram	9.096	9.096 000 0E+00

duelle [France, apothecary] <mass, special - see page 29>

gram	10.2	1.020 000 0E+01

duim [Netherlands] <length, special - see page 29>

centimeter	1	1.000 000 0E+00

duim [Russia]
centimeter-- <length, special - see page 29>
2.54----2.540 000 0E+00

duime [Russia]
centimeter-- <length, special - see page 29>
2.54----2.540 000 0E+00

dulum [Cyprus]
square meter-- <area, special - see page 29>
1,337.8----1.337 800 0E+03

dulum [Israel]
square meter-- <area, special - see page 29>
1,000----1.000 000 0E+03

dulum [Jordan]
square meter-- <area, special - see page 29>
1,000----1.000 000 0E+03

dulum [Lebanon]
square meter-- <area, special - see page 29>
919----9.190 000 0E+02

dulum [Libya]
square meter-- <area, special - see page 29>
919----9.190 000 0E+02

dulum [Syria]
square meter-- <area, special - see page 29>
919----9.190 000 0E+02

dulum [Turkey]
square meter-- <area, special - see page 29>
919----9.190 000 0E+02

dulum [Yugoslavia]
square meter-- <area, special - see page 29>
1,000----1.000 000 0E+03

dun [Cambodia]
kilogram --- <mass, special - see page 29>
60----6.000 000 0E+01

dun [China]
kilogram --- <mass, special - see page 29>
50----5.000 000 0E+01

dun [Indonesia]
kilogram --- <mass, special - see page 29>
61.761----6.176 100 0E+01

dun [Japan]
kilogram --- <mass, special - see page 29>
60----6.000 000 0E+01

dun [Laos]
kilogram --- <mass, special - see page 29>
60----6.000 000 0E+01

dun [Philippines]
kilogram --- <mass, special - see page 29>
63.249----6.324 900 0E+01

dun [Thailand]
kilogram --- <mass, special - see page 29>
60----6.000 000 0E+01

dun [Vietnam]
kilogram --- <mass, special - see page 29>
60.453----6.045 300 0E+01

dunam [Cyprus]
square meter-- <area, special - see page 29>
1,337.8----1.337 800 0E+03

dunam [Israel]
square meter-- <area, special - see page 29>
1,000----1.000 000 0E+03

dunam [Jordan]
square meter-- <area, special - see page 29>
1,000----1.000 000 0E+03

dunam [Lebanon]
square meter-- <area, special - see page 29>
919----9.190 000 0E+02

dunam [Libya]
square meter-- <area, special - see page 29>
919----9.190 000 0E+02

dunam [Syria]
square meter-- <area, special - see page 29>
919----9.190 000 0E+02

dunam [Turkey]
square meter-- <area, special - see page 29>
919----9.190 000 0E+02

dung [Iran]
milligram--- <mass, special - see page 29>
781----7.810 000 0E+02

dung [Persia, gold and silver]
gram--- <mass, special - see page 29>
0.778----7.780 000 0E-01

Convert From Convert To	Standard	<Type of Unit> Scientific
dunum [Cyprus]		<area, special - see page 29>
square meter	1,337.8	1.337 800 0E+03
dunum [Israel]		<area, special - see page 29>
square meter	1,000	1.000 000 0E+03
dunum [Jordan]		<area, special - see page 29>
square meter	1,000	1.000 000 0E+03
dunum [Lebanon]		<area, special - see page 29>
square meter	919	9.190 000 0E+02
dunum [Libya]		<area, special - see page 29>
square meter	919	9.190 000 0E+02
dunum [Syria]		<area, special - see page 29>
square meter	919	9.190 000 0E+02
dunum [Turkey]		<area, special - see page 29>
square meter	919	9.190 000 0E+02
dunum [Yugoslavia]		<area, special - see page 29>
square meter	1,000	1.000 000 0E+03
duodecal		<units>
dozen	1	1.000 000 0E+00
hexad	2	2.000 000 0E+00
unit	12	1.200 000 0E+01
duodecillion [UK]		<units>
unit	>>>	1.000 000 0E+72
duodecillion [US]		<units>
unit	>>>	1.000 000 0E+39
dyne		<force>
crinal	0.000 1	1.000 000 0E-04
erg/centimeter	1	1.000 000 0E+00
grain-force	0.015 736 6	1.573 662 6E-02
gram-force	0.001 019 7	1.019 716 2E-03
newton	0.000 01	1.000 000 0E-05
ounce-force	0.000 036	3.596 943 1E-05
pond	0.001 019 7	1.019 716 2E-03
pound-force	0.000 002 2	2.248 089 4E-06
poundal	0.000 072 3	7.233 013 9E-05
dyne		<linear energy transfer>
Btu/foot [I.T.]	<<<	2.888 946 6E-09
electronvolt/meter	>>>	6.241 506 4E+13
joule/meter	0.000 01	1.000 000 0E-05
kilocalorie/meter [I.T.]	<<<	2.388 459 0E-09
dyne centimeter		<energy>
atomic mass unit [unified, C-12, 1986, eq. energy]	670.053 08	6.700 530 8E+02
Btu [I.T.]	<<<	9.478 171 2E-11
calorie [I.T.]	<<<	2.388 459 0E-08
calorie [kilogram, I.T.]	<<<	2.388 459 0E-11
centimeter gram-force	0.001 019 7	1.019 716 2E-03
erg	1	1.000 000 0E+00
foot pound-force	<<<	7.375 621 5E-08
foot poundal	0.000 002 4	2.373 036 0E-06
gigaelectronvolt	624.150 64	6.241 506 4E+02
inch ounce-force	0.000 014 2	1.416 119 3E-05
inch pound-force	0.000 000 9	8.850 745 8E-07
joule	0.000 000 1	1.000 000 0E-07
megaelectronvolt	624,150.64	6.241 506 4E+05
megaerg	0.000 001	1.000 000 0E-06
megalerg	0.000 001	1.000 000 0E-06
muon rest mass [atomic physics, eq. energy]	5,907.251 1	5.907 251 1E+03
neutron rest mass [atomic physics, eq. energy]	664.297 01	6.642 970 1E+02
proton rest mass [atomic physics, eq. energy]	665.212 68	6.652 126 8E+02
teraelectronvolt	0.624 150 6	6.241 506 4E-01

| Convert From | | <Type of Unit> |
| Convert To | Standard | Scientific |

dyne centimeter — `<torque>`

	Standard	Scientific
centimeter gram-force	0.001 019 7	1.019 716 2E-03
foot ounce-force	0.000 001 2	1.180 099 4E-06
newton meter	0.000 000 1	1.000 000 0E-07

dyne centimeter second — `<moment of momentum>`

	Standard	Scientific
erg second	1	1.000 000 0E+00
gram square centimeter/second	1	1.000 000 0E+00
kilogram square meter/second	0.000 000 1	1.000 000 0E-07
pound square foot/second	0.000 002 4	2.373 036 0E-06

dyne centimeter/hour — `<power>`

	Standard	Scientific
Btu/hour [I.T.]	<<<	9.478 171 2E-11
calorie/hour [I.T.]	<<<	2.388 459 0E-08
centigrade heat unit/hour [mean]	<<<	5.261 590 5E-11
cubic meter atmosphere/hour	0.000 001	9.869 232 7E-07
dyne centimeter/minute	0.016 666 7	1.666 666 7E-02
erg/hour	1	1.000 000 0E+00
foot pound-force/hour	<<<	7.375 621 5E-08
foot poundal/hour	0.000 002 4	2.373 036 0E-06
gram-force centimeter/hour	0.001 019 7	1.019 716 2E-03
horsepower	<<<	3.725 061 4E-14
horsepower [metric]	<<<	3.776 726 7E-14
joule/hour	0.000 000 1	1.000 000 0E-07
kilocalorie/hour [I.T.]	<<<	2.388 459 0E-11
kilogram-force meter/hour	<<<	1.019 716 2E-08
kilopond meter/hour	<<<	1.019 716 2E-08
newton meter/hour	0.000 000 1	1.000 000 0E-07
volt ampere	<<<	2.777 777 8E-11
watt	<<<	2.777 777 8E-11

dyne centimeter/minute — `<power>`

	Standard	Scientific
Btu/hour [I.T.]	<<<	5.686 902 7E-09
Btu/hour [thermoc.]	<<<	5.690 708 5E-09
calorie/hour [I.T.]	0.000 001 4	1.433 075 4E-06
calorie/hour [thermoc.]	0.000 001 4	1.434 034 4E-06
centigrade heat unit/hour [mean]	<<<	3.156 954 3E-09
cubic meter atmosphere/hour	0.000 059 2	5.921 539 6E-05
dyne centimeter/hour	60	6.000 000 0E+01
erg/minute	1	1.000 000 0E+00
foot pound-force/hour	0.000 004 4	4.425 372 9E-06
foot poundal/hour	0.000 142 4	1.423 821 6E-04
gram-force centimeter/hour	0.061 183	6.118 297 3E-02
horsepower	<<<	2.235 036 8E-12
horsepower [metric]	<<<	2.266 036 0E-12
joule/hour	0.000 006	6.000 000 0E-06
kilocalorie/hour [I.T.]	<<<	1.433 075 4E-09
kilogram-force meter/hour	0.000 000 6	6.118 297 3E-07
kilopond meter/hour	0.000 000 6	6.118 297 3E-07
nanowatt	1.666 666 7	1.666 666 7E+00
newton meter/hour	0.000 006	6.000 000 0E-06
volt ampere	<<<	1.666 666 7E-09
watt	<<<	1.666 666 7E-09

dyne centimeter/second — `<power>`

	Standard	Scientific
Btu/hour [I.T.]	0.000 000 3	3.412 141 6E-07
Btu/hour [thermoc.]	0.000 000 3	3.414 425 1E-07
calorie/hour [I.T.]	0.000 086	8.598 452 3E-05
calorie/hour [thermoc.]	0.000 086	8.604 206 5E-05
centigrade heat unit/hour [mean]	0.000 000 2	1.894 172 6E-07
cubic meter atmosphere/hour	0.003 552 9	3.552 923 8E-03
dyne centimeter/minute	60	6.000 000 0E+01
erg/second	1	1.000 000 0E+00
foot pound-force/hour	0.000 265 5	2.655 223 7E-04
foot poundal/hour	0.008 542 9	8.542 929 7E-03
gram-force centimeter/hour	3.670 978 4	3.670 978 4E+00

| Convert From | | <Type of Unit> |
Convert To	Standard	Scientific

horsepower	<<<	1.341 022 1E-10
horsepower [metric]	<<<	1.359 621 6E-10
joule/hour	0.000 36	3.600 000 0E-04
kilocalorie/hour [I.T.]	<<<	8.598 452 3E-08
kilogram-force meter/hour	0.000 036 7	3.670 978 4E-05
kilopond meter/hour	0.000 036 7	3.670 978 4E-05
newton meter/hour	0.000 36	3.600 000 0E-04
volt ampere	0.000 000 1	1.000 000 0E-07
watt	0.000 000 1	1.000 000 0E-07

dyne second <momentum>

bole	1	1.000 000 0E+00
gram centimeter/second	1	1.000 000 0E+00
newton second	0.000 01	1.000 000 0E-05
pound foot/second	0.000 072 3	7.233 013 9E-05
pound-force second	0.000 002 2	2.248 089 4E-06

dyne second/centimeter <mechanical impedance>

kilogram-force second/meter	0.000 102	1.019 716 2E-04
pound-force second/foot	0.000 068 5	6.852 176 6E-05
poundal second/foot	0.002 204 6	2.204 622 6E-03

dyne second/centimeter <mechanical impedance>

newton second/meter	0.001	1.000 000 0E-03

dyne second/centimeter^5 <acoustic impedance>

acoustic ohm	1	1.000 000 0E+00
newton second/meter^5	100,000	1.000 000 0E+05
pascal second/cubic meter	100,000	1.000 000 0E+05

dyne second/cubic centimeter <specific acoustic impedance>

kilogram-force second/cubic meter	1.019 716 2	1.019 716 2E+00
pascal second/meter	10	1.000 000 0E+01
pound-force second/cubic foot	0.063 658 8	6.365 880 4E-02
poundal second/cubic foot	2.048 161 4	2.048 161 4E+00
rayl	1	1.000 000 0E+00

dyne second/square centimeter <dynamic viscosity>

gram/centimeter second	1	1.000 000 0E+00
kilogram/meter second	0.1	1.000 000 0E-01
newton second/square meter	0.1	1.000 000 0E-01
pascal second	0.1	1.000 000 0E-01
poise	1	1.000 000 0E+00
poiseuille [France]	0.1	1.000 000 0E-01

dyne square second/centimeter <mass>

carat [gemstones]	5	5.000 000 0E+00
carat [international]	5	5.000 000 0E+00
carat [metric]	5	5.000 000 0E+00
carat [US, after 1913]	5	5.000 000 0E+00
gram	1	1.000 000 0E+00
hyl	0.000 102	1.019 716 2E-04
kilogram	0.001	1.000 000 0E-03
kilogram-force square second/meter	0.000 102	1.019 716 2E-04
newton square second/meter	0.001	1.000 000 0E-03
pound-force square second/foot	0.000 068 5	6.852 176 6E-05
poundal square second/foot	0.002 204 6	2.204 622 6E-03
quintal [metric]	0.000 01	1.000 000 0E-05
slug [metric]	0.000 102	1.019 716 2E-04

dyne/centimeter <energy fluence>

Btu/square foot [I.T.]	<<<	8.805 509 2E-08
joule/square meter	0.001	1.000 000 0E-03
kilocalorie/square meter [I.T.]	0.000 000 2	2.388 459 0E-07

dyne/centimeter <surface tension>

gram-force/meter	0.101 971 6	1.019 716 2E-01
millinewton/meter	1	1.000 000 0E+00
newton/meter	0.001	1.000 000 0E-03
ounce-force/foot	0.001 096 3	1.096 348 3E-03

	Standard	Scientific
pound-force/foot	0.000 068 5	6.852 176 6E−05
dyne/meter		**\<surface tension\>**
gram-force/meter	0.001 019 7	1.019 716 2E−03
newton/meter	0.000 01	1.000 000 0E−05
ounce-force/foot	0.000 011	1.096 348 3E−05
dyne/square centimeter		**\<pressure\>**
atmosphere [standard]	0.000 001	9.869 232 7E−07
atmosphere [technical]	0.000 001	1.019 716 2E−06
bar	0.000 001	1.000 000 0E−06
barad	1	1.000 000 0E+00
barye [France]	1	1.000 000 0E+00
decipascal	1	1.000 000 0E+00
gram-force/square centimeter	0.001 019 7	1.019 716 2E−03
kilogram-force/square meter	0.010 197 2	1.019 716 2E−02
kilopond/square meter	0.010 197 2	1.019 716 2E−02
microbar	1	1.000 000 0E+00
micrometer of mercury [0 °C, by convention]	0.750 061 6	7.500 615 8E−01
micrometer of water [4 °C, by convention]	10.197 162	1.019 716 2E+01
newton/square meter	0.1	1.000 000 0E−01
pascal	0.1	1.000 000 0E−01
pound-force/square foot	0.002 088 5	2.088 543 4E−03
poundal/square foot	0.067 196 9	6.719 689 8E−02
torr	0.000 750 1	7.500 616 8E−04
dyne/square centimeter		**\<energy density\>**
erg/cubic centimeter	1	1.000 000 0E+00
joule/cubic meter	0.1	1.000 000 0E−01
dynia [Greece, ancient]		**\<length, special - see page 29\>**
meter	1.848	1.848 000 0E+00
dzhin [Mongolia]		**\<mass, special - see page 29\>**
gram	600	6.000 000 0E+02
efa [Hebrew, ancient]		**\<volume, special - see page 29\>**
liter	38	3.800 000 0E+01
efot [Hebrew, ancient]		**\<volume, special - see page 29\>**
liter	38	3.800 000 0E+01
egg [Hebrew, ancient]		**\<volume, special - see page 29\>**
cubic centimeter	91.565 223	9.156 522 3E+01
eimer [Austria]		**\<volume, special - see page 29\>**
liter	56.604	5.660 400 0E+01
eimer [Germany]		**\<volume, special - see page 29\>**
liter	64.137	6.413 700 0E+01
el [Indonesia]		**\<length, special - see page 29\>**
meter	0.687 8	6.878 000 0E−01
el [Malaysia]		**\<length, special - see page 29\>**
meter	0.914 4	9.144 000 0E−01
el [Netherlands]		**\<length, special - see page 29\>**
meter	1	1.000 000 0E+00
el [Surinam]		**\<length, special - see page 29\>**
meter	0.687 8	6.878 000 0E−01
el cotejo [Venezuela]		**\<mass, special - see page 29\>**
kilogram	5	5.000 000 0E+00
electromagnetic unit of capacitance [cgs system]		**\<capacitance\>**
abfarad	1	1.000 000 0E+00
coulomb/volt	>>>	1.000 000 0E+09
electrostatic unit of capacitance [cgs system]	>>>	8.987 551 8E+20
farad	>>>	1.000 000 0E+09
statfarad	>>>	8.987 551 8E+20
electromagnetic unit of charge [cgs system]		**\<electric charge\>**
abcoulomb	1	1.000 000 0E+00
ampere second	10	1.000 000 0E+01

Convert From / Convert To	Standard	Scientific
coulomb	10	1.000 000 0E+01
dekacoulomb	1	1.000 000 0E+00
farad volt	10	1.000 000 0E+01

electromagnetic unit of conductance [cgs system] <electric conductance>

Convert To	Standard	Scientific
absiemens	1	1.000 000 0E+00
gigasiemens	1	1.000 000 0E+00
siemens	>>>	1.000 000 0E+09
statsiemens	>>>	8.987 551 8E+20

electromagnetic unit of current [cgs system] <electric current>

Convert To	Standard	Scientific
abampere	1	1.000 000 0E+00
ampere	10	1.000 000 0E+01
biot	1	1.000 000 0E+00
dekaampere	1	1.000 000 0E+00
gilbert	12.566 370 6	1.256 637 1E+01
statampere	>>>	2.997 924 6E+10

electromagnetic unit of electric potential [cgs system] <electric potential>

Convert To	Standard	Scientific
abvolt	1	1.000 000 0E+00
nanovolt	10	1.000 000 0E+01
statvolt	<<<	3.335 641 0E−11
volt	<<<	1.000 000 0E−08

electromagnetic unit of inductance [cgs system] <electric inductance>

Convert To	Standard	Scientific
abhenry	1	1.000 000 0E+00
electrostatic unit of inductance [cgs system]	<<<	1.112 650 1E−21
henry	<<<	1.000 000 0E−09
ohm second	<<<	1.000 000 0E−09
stathenry	<<<	1.112 650 1E−21

electromagnetic unit of magnetic flux [cgs system] <magnetic flux>

Convert To	Standard	Scientific
electrostatic unit of magnetic flux [cgs system]	<<<	3.335 641 0E−11
gauss square centimeter	1	1.000 000 0E+00
line [of magnetic force]	1	1.000 000 0E+00
maxwell	1	1.000 000 0E+00
statweber	<<<	3.335 641 0E−11
unit pole	0.079 577 5	7.957 747 5E−02
weber	<<<	1.000 000 0E−08

electromagnetic unit of magnetic flux density [cgs system] <magnetic flux density>

Convert To	Standard	Scientific
abtesla	1	1.000 000 0E+00
electrostatic unit of magnetic flux density [cgs system]	<<<	3.335 641 0E−11
gauss	1	1.000 000 0E+00
line/square centimeter [of magnetic force]	1	1.000 000 0E+00
maxwell/square meter	0.000 1	1.000 000 0E−04
tesla	0.000 1	1.000 000 0E−04

electromagnetic unit of resistance [cgs system] <electric resistance>

Convert To	Standard	Scientific
1/ siemens	<<<	1.000 000 0E−09
abohm	1	1.000 000 0E+00
ohm	<<<	1.000 000 0E−09
statohm	<<<	1.112 650 1E−21

electron charge <electric charge>

Convert To	Standard	Scientific
abcoulomb	<<<	1.602 177 3E−20
coulomb	<<<	1.602 177 3E−19
elementary charge	1	1.000 000 0E+00
statcoulomb	<<<	4.803 206 8E−10

electron rest mass [atomic physics, eq. energy] <energy>

Convert To	Standard	Scientific
atomic mass unit [unified, C-12, 1986, eq. energy]	0.000 548 6	5.485 799 0E−04
deuteron rest mass [atomic physics, eq. energy]	0.000 272 4	2.724 437 0E−04
electronvolt	510,999.06	5.109 990 6E+05
gigaelectronvolt	0.000 511	5.109 990 6E−04
hartree [atomic physics, eq. energy]	18,778.862	1.877 886 2E+04
joule	<<<	8.187 111 1E−14
kiloelectronvolt	510.999 06	5.109 990 6E+02
megaelectronvolt	0.510 999 1	5.109 990 6E−01
muon rest mass [atomic physics, eq. energy]	0.004 836 3	4.836 332 1E−03

Convert From Convert To	Standard	<Type of Unit> Scientific
neutron rest mass [atomic physics, eq. energy]	0.000 543 9	5.438 673 4E-04
proton rest mass [atomic physics, eq. energy]	0.000 544 6	5.446 170 1E-04
rydberg [atomic physics, eq. energy]	37,557.278	3.755 727 8E+04
electronvolt		**<energy>**
1/centimeter [atomic physics, eq. energy]	8,065.540 9	8.065 540 9E+03
1/meter [atomic physics, eq. energy]	806,554.09	8.065 540 9E+05
atomic mass unit [unified, C-12, 1986, eq. energy]	<<<	1.073 543 9E-09
deuteron rest mass [atomic physics, eq. energy]	<<<	5.331 589 2E-10
electron rest mass [atomic physics, eq. energy]	0.000 002	1.956 950 8E-06
femtojoule	0.000 160 2	1.602 177 3E-04
hartree [atomic physics, eq. energy]	0.036 749 3	3.674 930 9E-02
joule	<<<	1.602 177 3E-19
kayser [atomic physics, eq. energy]	8,065.540 9	8.065 540 9E+03
kelvin [atomic physics, eq. energy]	11,604.448	1.160 444 8E+04
kiloelectronvolt	0.001	1.000 000 0E-03
megaelectronvolt	0.000 001	1.000 000 0E-06
muon rest mass [atomic physics, eq. energy]	<<<	9.464 463 8E-09
neutron rest mass [atomic physics, eq. energy]	<<<	1.064 321 6E-09
proton rest mass [atomic physics, eq. energy]	<<<	1.065 788 7E-09
rydberg [atomic physics, eq. energy]	0.073 497 7	7.349 774 4E-02
electronvolt/gram		**<specific thermodynamic energy>**
joule/kilogram	<<<	1.602 177 3E-16
electronvolt/meter		**<linear energy transfer>**
Btu/foot [I.T.]	<<<	4.628 604 7E-23
dyne	<<<	1.602 177 3E-14
joule/meter	<<<	1.602 177 3E-19
kilocalorie/meter [I.T.]	<<<	3.826 734 8E-23
electronvolt/square meter		**<energy fluence>**
Btu/square foot [I.T.]	<<<	1.410 798 7E-23
joule/square meter	<<<	1.602 177 3E-19
kilocalorie/square meter [I.T.]	<<<	3.826 734 8E-23
electrostatic unit of capacitance [cgs system]		**<capacitance>**
abfarad	<<<	1.112 650 1E-21
coulomb/volt	<<<	1.112 650 1E-12
electromagnetic unit of capacitance [cgs system]	<<<	1.112 650 1E-21
farad	<<<	1.112 650 1E-12
gaussian electric capacitance	1	1.000 000 0E+00
statfarad	1	1.000 000 0E+00
electrostatic unit of charge [cgs system]		**<electric charge>**
coulomb	<<<	3.335 641 0E-10
franklin	1	1.000 000 0E+00
gaussian electric charge	1	1.000 000 0E+00
statcoulomb	1	1.000 000 0E+00
electrostatic unit of conductance [cgs system]		**<electric conductance>**
absiemens	<<<	1.112 650 1E-21
gaussian electric conductance	1	1.000 000 0E+00
siemens	<<<	1.112 650 1E-12
statsiemens	1	1.000 000 0E+00
electrostatic unit of current [cgs system]		**<electric current>**
abampere	<<<	3.335 641 0E-11
ampere	<<<	3.335 641 0E-10
franklin/second	1	1.000 000 0E+00
gaussian electric current	1	1.000 000 0E+00
statampere	1	1.000 000 0E+00
electrostatic unit of electric potential [cgs system]		**<electric potential>**
erg/franklin	1	1.000 000 0E+00
gaussian electric potential	1	1.000 000 0E+00
statvolt	1	1.000 000 0E+00
volt	299.792 458	2.997 924 6E+02
electrostatic unit of inductance [cgs system]		**<electric inductance>**
abhenry	>>>	8.987 551 8E+20

| Convert From | | **\<Type of Unit\>** |
Convert To	Standard	Scientific
gaussian electric inductance	1	1.000 000 0E+00
henry	>>>	8.987 551 8E+11
ohm second	>>>	8.987 551 8E+11
stathenry	1	1.000 000 0E+00

electrostatic unit of magnetic flux [cgs system] | | **\<magnetic flux\>**

electromagnetic unit of magnetic flux [cgs system]	>>>	2.997 924 6E+10
gauss square centimeter	>>>	2.997 924 6E+10
gaussian magnetic flux	1	1.000 000 0E+00
maxwell	>>>	2.997 924 6E+10
statweber	1	1.000 000 0E+00
unit pole	299.792 458	2.385 672 7E+09
weber	>>>	2.997 924 6E+02

electrostatic unit of magnetic flux density [cgs system] | | **\<magnetic flux density\>**

gaussian magnetic flux density	1	1.000 000 0E+00
line/square centimeter [of magnetic force]	>>>	2.997 924 6E+10
maxwell/square meter	2,997,924.58	2.997 924 6E+06
megatesla	2.997 924 6	2.997 924 6E+00
stattesla	1	1.000 000 0E+00
tesla	2,997,924.58	2.997 924 6E+06

electrostatic unit of resistance [cgs system] | | **\<electric resistance\>**

1/ siemens	>>>	8.987 551 8E+11
abohm	>>>	8.987 551 8E+20
gaussian electric resistance	1	1.000 000 0E+00
ohm	>>>	8.987 551 8E+11
statohm	1	1.000 000 0E+00

elementary charge | | **\<electric charge\>**

ampere second	<<<	1.602 177 3E-19
coulomb	<<<	1.602 177 3E-19
electron charge	1	1.000 000 0E+00
farad volt	<<<	1.602 177 3E-19
statcoulomb	<<<	4.803 206 8E-10

ell [Austria] | | **\<length, special - see page 29\>**
| meter | 0.779 2 | 7.792 000 0E-01 |

ell [Babylon, ancient] | | **\<length, special - see page 29\>**
| millimeter | 495 | 4.950 000 0E+02 |

ell [Belgium] | | **\<length, special - see page 29\>**
| centimeter | 68.58 | 6.858 000 0E+01 |

ell [cloth] | | **\<length\>**

bolt [cloth]	0.031 25	3.125 000 0E-02
cubit	2.5	2.500 000 0E+00
digit	60	6.000 000 0E+01
foot [France]	3.518 648 8	3.518 648 8E+00
foot [international]	3.75	3.750 000 0E+00
foot [US, survey]	3.749 992 5	3.749 992 5E+00
inch [based on US, survey foot]	44.999 91	4.499 991 0E+01
inch [international]	45	4.500 000 0E+01
iron [shoe leather]	2,160	2.160 000 0E+03
meter	1.143	1.143 000 0E+00
mil	45,000	4.500 000 0E+04
nail [cloth]	20	2.000 000 0E+01
palm	15	1.500 000 0E+01
quarter [cloth]	5	5.000 000 0E+00
skein [cloth]	0.010 416 7	1.041 666 7E-02
span	5	5.000 000 0E+00
thou	45,000	4.500 000 0E+04
yard [based on US, survey foot]	1.249 997 5	1.249 997 5E+00
yard [international]	1.25	1.250 000 0E+00
yard [UK]	1.250 002 2	1.250 002 2E+00

ell [Hebrew, ancient] | | **\<length, special - see page 29\>**
| millimeter | 495 | 4.950 000 0E+02 |

Convert From	<Type of Unit>	
Convert To	Standard	Scientific

ell [Indonesia] — <length, special - see page 29>
  meter --- 0.687 8 ---- 6.878 000 0E-01

ell [Malaysia] — <length, special - see page 29>
  meter --- 0.914 4 ---- 9.144 000 0E-01

ell [Netherlands] — <length, special - see page 29>
  meter --- 0.687 8 ---- 6.878 000 0E-01

elle [Germany] — <length, special - see page 29>
  meter --- 0.833 01 ---- 8.330 100 0E-01

elle [Latvia] — <length, special - see page 29>
  centimeter -- 53.7 ---- 5.370 000 0E+01

elle [South Africa] — <length, special - see page 29>
  meter -- 0.685 ---- 6.850 000 0E-01

elle [Switzerland] — <length, special - see page 29>
  meter -- 0.6 ---- 6.000 000 0E-01

em [pica, print] — <length>
  agate [print] ---------------------------------- 2.181 818 2 ---- 2.181 818 2E+00
  barleycorn ----------------------------------- 0.498 132 ---- 4.981 320 0E-01
  caliber -------------------------------------- 16.604 4 ---- 1.660 440 0E+01
  didot point [print] ----------------------------- 11.202 39 ---- 1.120 239 0E+01
  douzieme [print] ----------------------------- 23.910 336 ---- 2.391 033 6E+01
  foot [international] ----------------------------- 0.013 837 ---- 1.383 700 0E-02
  foot [US, survey] ----------------------------- 0.013 837 ---- 1.383 697 2E-02
  inch [based on US, survey foot] ------------- 0.166 043 7 ---- 1.660 436 7E-01
  inch [international] ---------------------------- 0.166 044 ---- 1.660 440 0E-01
  iron [print] --------------------------------------- 0.04 ---- 4.000 000 0E-02
  ligne [print] ---------------------------------- 1.992 528 ---- 1.992 528 0E+00
  line [print] ----------------------------------- 1.992 528 ---- 1.992 528 0E+00
  meter -- 0.004 217 5 ---- 4.217 517 6E-03
  mil --- 166.044 ---- 1.660 440 0E+02
  nonpareil [print] -------------------------------------- 2 ---- 2.000 000 0E+00
  pearl [print] -------------------------------------- 2.4 ---- 2.400 000 0E+00
  pica [print] -- 1 ---- 1.000 000 0E+00
  point [print] ------------------------------------- 12 ---- 1.200 000 0E+01
  thou --- 166.044 ---- 1.660 440 0E+02

emine [Switzerland] — <volume, special - see page 29>
  liter -- 1.5 ---- 1.500 000 0E+00

emmet [Eritrea] — <length, special - see page 29>
  centimeter --- 46 ---- 4.600 000 0E+01

encaa [Eritrea] — <volume, special - see page 29>
  liter -- 1.5 ---- 1.500 000 0E+00

encablure [France] — <length, special - see page 29>
  meter --- 200 ---- 2.000 000 0E+02

endaze [Turkey] — <length, special - see page 29>
  centimeter --- 65 ---- 6.500 000 0E+01

endazeh [Turkey] — <length, special - see page 29>
  centimeter --- 65 ---- 6.500 000 0E+01

endere [Romania] — <length, special - see page 29>
  meter -- 0.662 ---- 6.620 000 0E-01

engel [Holland, troy] — <mass, special - see page 29>
  gram --- 1.56 ---- 1.560 000 0E+00

engelot [Holland, troy] — <mass, special - see page 29>
  gram --- 1.56 ---- 1.560 000 0E+00

engelsen [Holland, troy] — <mass, special - see page 29>
  gram --- 1.56 ---- 1.560 000 0E+00

engjateigur [Iceland] — <area, special - see page 29>
  hectare -- 0.319 ---- 3.190 000 0E-01

English water ton [UK] — <volume>
  barrel [UK] ---------------------------------- 6.222 222 2 ---- 6.222 222 2E+00

Convert From — Convert To — Standard — `<Type of Unit>` Scientific

Convert To	Standard	Scientific
barrel [US, dry]	8.806 966 1	8.806 966 1E+00
barrel [US, liquid]	8.540 088 4	8.540 088 4E+00
barrel [US, petroleum]	6.405 066 3	6.405 066 3E+00
bushel [UK]	28	2.800 000 0E+01
bushel [US, dry]	28.897 589	2.889 758 9E+01
cord foot [timber]	2.247 611 1	2.247 611 1E+00
cubic foot	35.961 447	3.596 177 8E+01
cubic inch	62,141.953	6.214 195 3E+04
cubic meter	1.018 324 2	1.018 324 2E+00
cubic yard	1.331 917 7	1.331 917 7E+00
drum [US, liquid]	4.891 141 5	4.891 141 5E+00
freight ton	0.899 044 5	8.990 444 6E-01
gallon [UK, dry or liquid]	224	2.240 000 0E+02
gallon [US, dry]	231.180 71	2.311 807 1E+02
gallon [US, liquid]	269.012 78	2.690 127 8E+02
hogshead [UK]	3.555 555 6	3.555 555 6E+00
hogshead [US]	4.270 044 2	4.270 044 2E+00
kiloliter	1.018 324 2	1.018 324 2E+00
liter	1,018.324 2	1.018 324 2E+03
ocean ton	0.899 044 5	8.990 444 6E-01
petrograd standard	0.217 950 2	2.179 501 7E-01
pipe [UK]	2.074 074 1	2.074 074 1E+00
pipe [US, liquid]	2.135 022 1	2.135 022 1E+00
quarter [UK]	3.5	3.500 000 0E+00
register ton	0.359 617 8	3.596 177 8E-01
shipping ton	0.899 044 5	8.990 444 6E-01
stere	1.018 324 2	1.018 324 2E+00
tun [UK, liquid]	1.037 037	1.037 037 0E+00
tun [US, liquid]	1.067 511	1.067 511 0E+00
Winchester wine gallon [UK]	269.012 78	2.690 127 8E+02

entelam [Eritrea] `<volume, special - see page 29>`

Convert To	Standard	Scientific
liter	192	1.920 000 0E+02

Eötvös unit `<acceleration gradient>`

Convert To	Standard	Scientific
gal/centimeter	<<<	1.000 000 0E-09

epha [Hebrew, ancient] `<volume, special - see page 29>`

Convert To	Standard	Scientific
liter	22.9	2.290 000 0E+01

ephah [Babylon, ancient] `<volume, special - see page 29>`

Convert To	Standard	Scientific
liter	39.3	3.930 000 0E+01

ephah [Hebrew, ancient] `<volume, special - see page 29>`

Convert To	Standard	Scientific
liter	22	2.200 000 0E+01

erg `<energy>`

Convert To	Standard	Scientific
atomic mass unit [unified, C-12, 1986, eq. energy]	670.053 08	6.700 530 8E+02
Btu [I.T.]	<<<	9.478 171 2E-11
calorie [I.T.]	<<<	2.388 459 0E-08
calorie [kilogram, I.T.]	<<<	2.388 459 0E-11
centigrade heat unit [I.T.]	<<<	5.265 650 7E-11
centimeter gram-force	0.001 019 7	1.019 716 2E-03
cubic centimeter atmosphere	0.000 001	9.869 232 7E-07
cubic foot atmosphere	<<<	3.485 286 6E-11
deuteron rest mass [atomic physics, eq. energy]	332.771 48	3.327 714 8E+02
dyne centimeter	1	1.000 000 0E+00
electron rest mass [atomic physics, eq. energy]	1,221,432.1	1.221 432 1E+06
foot pound-force	<<<	7.375 621 5E-08
foot poundal	0.000 002 4	2.373 036 0E-06
gigaelectronvolt	624.150 64	6.241 506 4E+02
horsepower hour	<<<	3.725 061 4E-14
horsepower hour [metric]	<<<	3.776 726 7E-14
inch ounce-force	0.000 014 2	1.416 119 3E-05
inch pound-force	0.000 000 9	8.850 745 8E-07
joule	0.000 000 1	1.000 000 0E-07
kilowatthour	<<<	2.777 777 8E-14
liter atmosphere	<<<	9.869 232 7E-10

Convert From		<Type of Unit>
Convert To	Standard	Scientific

megaelectronvolt	624,150.64	6.241 506 4E+05
megaerg	0.000 001	1.000 000 0E-06
megalerg	0.000 001	1.000 000 0E-06
muon rest mass [atomic physics, eq. energy]	5,907.251 1	5.907 251 1E+03
neutron rest mass [atomic physics, eq. energy]	664.297 01	6.642 970 1E+02
proton rest mass [atomic physics, eq. energy]	665.212 68	6.652 126 8E+02
teraelectronvolt	0.624 150 6	6.241 506 4E-01
wattsecond	0.000 001	1.000 000 0E-07

erg second <moment of momentum>

dyne centimeter second	1	1.000 000 0E+00
gram square centimeter/second	1	1.000 000 0E+00
kilogram square meter/second	0.000 01	1.000 000 0E-07
pound square foot/second	0.000 002 4	2.373 036 0E-06

erg square centimeter/gram <total mass stopping power>

Btu square foot/pound [I.T.]	<<<	4.627 648 5E-11
calorie square centimeter/gram [I.T.]	<<<	2.388 459 0E-08
joule square meter/kilogram	<<<	1.000 000 0E-08

erg/centimeter <force>

crinal	0.000 1	1.000 000 0E-04
dyne	1	1.000 000 0E+00
gram-force	0.001 019 7	1.019 716 2E-03
newton	0.000 01	1.000 000 0E-05
ounce-force	0.000 036	3.596 943 1E-05
pond	0.001 019 7	1.019 716 2E-03
pound-force	0.000 002 2	2.248 089 4E-06
poundal	0.000 072 3	7.233 013 9E-05

erg/centimeter <linear energy transfer>

Btu/foot [I.T.]	<<<	2.888 946 6E-09
electronvolt/meter	>>>	6.241 506 4E+13
joule/meter	0.000 01	1.000 000 0E-05
kilocalorie/meter [I.T.]	<<<	2.388 459 0E-09

erg/centimeter second °C <thermal conductivity>

watt/meter kelvin	0.000 01	1.000 000 0E-05

erg/cubic centimeter <energy density>

dyne/square centimeter	1	1.000 000 0E+00
joule/cubic meter	0.1	1.000 000 0E-01

erg/cubic centimeter second <heat release rate>

Btu/cubic foot hour [I.T.]	0.009 662 1	9.662 109 1E-03
joule/cubic meter second	0.1	1.000 000 0E-01
watt/cubic meter	0.1	1.000 000 0E-01

erg/franklin <electric potential>

abvolt	>>>	2.997 924 6E+10
electrostatic unit of electric potential [cgs system]	1	1.000 000 0E+00
gaussian electric potential	1	1.000 000 0E+00
statvolt	1	1.000 000 0E+00
volt	299.792 458	2.997 924 6E+02

erg/gram <absorbed dose>

gray	0.000 1	1.000 000 0E-04
rad	0.01	1.000 000 0E-02
rep	0.011 933 2	1.193 317 4E-02

erg/gram <specific thermodynamic energy>

joule/kilogram	0.000 1	1.000 000 0E-04

erg/gram °C <specific heat capacity>

joule/kilogram kelvin	0.000 1	1.000 000 0E-04

erg/gram second <absorbed dose rate>

gray/second	0.000 1	1.000 000 0E-04
rad/second	0.01	1.000 000 0E-02

erg/hour <power>

Btu/hour [I.T.]	<<<	9.478 171 2E-11
Btu/hour [thermoc.]	<<<	9.484 514 1E-11

Convert From Convert To	Standard	<Type of Unit> Scientific
calorie/hour [I.T.]	<<<	2.388 459 0E-08
calorie/hour [thermoc.]	<<<	2.390 057 4E-08
centigrade heat unit/hour [mean]	<<<	5.261 590 5E-11
cubic meter atmosphere/hour	0.000 001	9.869 232 7E-07
dyne centimeter/hour	1	1.000 000 0E+00
foot pound-force/hour	<<<	7.375 621 5E-08
foot poundal/hour	0.000 002 4	2.373 036 0E-06
gram-force centimeter/hour	0.001 019 7	1.019 716 2E-03
horsepower	<<<	3.725 061 4E-14
horsepower [metric]	<<<	3.776 726 7E-14
joule/hour	0.000 000 1	1.000 000 0E-07
kilocalorie/hour [I.T.]	<<<	2.388 459 0E-11
kilogram-force meter/hour	<<<	1.019 716 2E-08
kilopond meter/hour	<<<	1.019 716 2E-08
newton meter/hour	0.000 000 1	1.000 000 0E-07
picowatt	27.777 778	2.777 777 8E+01
volt ampere	<<<	2.777 777 8E-11
watt	<<<	2.777 777 8E-11

erg/kelvin   <specific heat>
joule/kelvin	0.000 000 1	1.000 000 0E-07

erg/minute   <power>
Btu/hour [I.T.]	<<<	5.686 902 7E-09
Btu/hour [thermoc.]	<<<	5.690 708 5E-09
calorie/hour [I.T.]	0.000 001 4	1.433 075 4E-06
calorie/hour [thermoc.]	0.000 001 4	1.434 034 4E-06
centigrade heat unit/hour [mean]	<<<	3.156 954 3E-09
cubic meter atmosphere/hour	0.000 059 2	5.921 539 6E-05
dyne centimeter/minute	1	1.000 000 0E+00
erg/hour	60	6.000 000 0E+01
foot pound-force/hour	0.000 004 4	4.425 372 9E-06
foot poundal/hour	0.000 142 4	1.423 821 6E-04
gram-force centimeter/hour	0.061 183	6.118 297 3E-02
horsepower	<<<	2.235 036 8E-12
horsepower [metric]	<<<	2.266 036 0E-12
joule/hour	0.000 006	6.000 000 0E-06
kilocalorie/hour [I.T.]	<<<	1.433 075 4E-09
kilogram-force meter/hour	0.000 000 6	6.118 297 3E-07
kilopond meter/hour	0.000 000 6	6.118 297 3E-07
nanowatt	1.666 666 7	1.666 666 7E+00
newton meter/hour	0.000 006	6.000 000 0E-06
volt ampere	<<<	1.666 666 7E-09
watt	<<<	1.666 666 7E-09

erg/second   <power>
Btu/hour [I.T.]	0.000 000 3	3.412 141 6E-07
Btu/hour [thermoc.]	0.000 000 3	3.414 425 1E-07
calorie/hour [I.T.]	0.000 086	8.598 452 3E-05
calorie/hour [thermoc.]	0.000 086	8.604 206 5E-05
centigrade heat unit/hour [mean]	0.000 000 2	1.894 172 6E-07
cubic meter atmosphere/hour	0.003 552 9	3.552 923 8E-03
dyne centimeter/second	1	1.000 000 0E+00
erg/minute	60	6.000 000 0E+01
foot pound-force/hour	0.000 265 5	2.655 223 7E-04
foot poundal/hour	0.008 542 9	8.542 929 7E-03
gram-force centimeter/hour	3.670 978 4	3.670 978 4E+00
horsepower	<<<	1.341 022 1E-10
horsepower [metric]	<<<	1.359 621 6E-10
joule/hour	0.000 36	3.600 000 0E-04
kilocalorie/hour [I.T.]	<<<	8.598 452 3E-08
kilogram-force meter/hour	0.000 036 7	3.670 978 4E-05
kilopond meter/hour	0.000 036 7	3.670 978 4E-05
microwatt	0.1	1.000 000 0E-01
newton meter/hour	0.000 36	3.600 000 0E-04
volt ampere	0.000 000 1	1.000 000 0E-07

Convert From Convert To	<Type of Unit> Standard	Scientific
watt	0.000 000 1	1.000 000 0E−07
erg/second square centimeter	**<heat flux density>**	
Btu/day square foot [I.T.]	0.007 608	7.607 959 9E−03
Btu/day square foot [thermoc.]	0.007 613 1	7.613 051 3E−03
calorie/day square centimeter [I.T.]	0.002 063 6	2.063 628 5E−03
calorie/day square centimeter [thermoc.]	0.002 065	2.065 009 6E−03
joule/second square meter	0.001	1.000 000 0E−03
watt/square meter	0.001	1.000 000 0E−03
erg/second steradian	**<radiant intensity>**	
joule/second steradian	0.000 000 1	1.000 000 0E−07
watt/steradian	0.000 000 1	1.000 000 0E−07
erg/second steradian square centimeter	**<radiance>**	
joule/second steradian square meter	0.001	1.000 000 0E−03
watt/steradian square meter	0.001	1.000 000 0E−03
erg/square centimeter	**<energy fluence>**	
Btu/square foot [I.T.]	<<<	8.805 509 2E−08
joule/square meter	0.001	1.000 000 0E−03
kilocalorie/square meter [I.T.]	0.000 000 2	2.388 459 0E−07
erg/square centimeter second °C	**<heat transfer coefficient>**	
watt/square meter kelvin	0.001	1.000 000 0E−03
erklein [Germany]	**<volume, special - see page 29>**	
liter	1,710.3	1.710 300 0E+03
erlek [Cyprus]	**<area, special - see page 29>**	
square meter	334.450 9	3.344 509 0E+02
ertragsfestmeter [Austria, solid wood]	**<volume, special - see page 29>**	
cubic meter	1	1.000 000 0E+00
esba [Hebrew, ancient]	**<length, special - see page 29>**	
meter	0.019	1.900 000 0E−02
escropulo [Brazil]	**<mass, special - see page 29>**	
gram	1.195 44	1.195 440 0E+00
escrupulo [Brazil]	**<mass, special - see page 29>**	
gram	1.2	1.200 000 0E+00
escrupulo [Portugal]	**<mass, special - see page 29>**	
gram	1.195 4	1.195 400 0E+00
esschen [Germany]	**<mass, special - see page 29>**	
gram	0.048	4.800 000 0E−02
estadal [Nicaragua]	**<area, special - see page 29>**	
square meter	11.28	1.128 000 0E+01
estadal [Spain]	**<area, special - see page 29>**	
square meter	11.18	1.118 000 0E+01
estadel [Venezuela]	**<length, special - see page 29>**	
meter	4.18	4.180 000 0E+00
estadio [Portugal]	**<length, special - see page 29>**	
meter	258	2.580 000 0E+02
estadio [Spain]	**<length, special - see page 29>**	
meter	174.148	1.741 480 0E+02
estado [Spain]	**<length, special - see page 29>**	
meter	1.67	1.670 000 0E+00
estelin [France, troy]	**<mass, special - see page 29>**	
gram	2	2.000 000 0E+00
estodal [Spain]	**<area, special - see page 29>**	
square meter	11.179 8	1.117 980 0E+01
etzba [Hebrew, ancient]	**<length, special - see page 29>**	
centimeter	1.9	1.900 000 0E+00
etzbah [Hebrew, ancient]	**<length, special - see page 29>**	
centimeter	1.9	1.900 000 0E+00

Convert From		<Type of Unit>
Convert To	Standard	Scientific

evieh [Turkey] — <area, special - see page 29>
square meter --- 1,000 --- 1.000 000 0E+03

evlek [Cyprus] — <area, special - see page 29>
square meter --- 334.5 --- 3.345 000 0E+02

evlek [Turkey] — <area, special - see page 29>
square meter --- 0.144 --- 1.440 000 0E-01

exabar — <pressure>
atmosphere [standard]	>>>	9.869 232 7E+17
atmosphere [technical]	>>>	1.019 716 2E+18
bar	>>>	1.000 000 0E+18
exapascal	100,000	1.000 000 0E+05
foot of mercury [0 °C, by convention]	>>>	2.460 831 9E+18
foot of water [4 °C, by convention]	>>>	3.345 525 6E+19
kilogram-force/square millimeter	>>>	1.019 716 2E+16
kilopond/square millimeter	>>>	1.019 716 2E+16
kip/square inch	>>>	1.450 377 4E+16
newton/square millimeter	>>>	1.000 000 0E+18
pascal	>>>	1.000 000 0E+23
pound-force/square inch	>>>	1.450 377 4E+19
ton-force/square inch [short]	>>>	7.251 886 9E+15
torr	>>>	7.500 616 8E+20
zettapascal	100	1.000 000 0E+02

exacandela — <luminous intensity>
| candela | >>> | 1.000 000 0E+18 |

exagram — <mass>
kilogram	>>>	1.000 000 0E+15
megaton [metric]	1,000,000	1.000 000 0E+06
megatonne	1,000,000	1.000 000 0E+06
ton [long]	>>>	9.842 065 3E+11
ton [metric]	>>>	1.000 000 0E+12
ton [short]	>>>	1.102 311 3E+12
ton [UK]	>>>	9.842 065 3E+11
ton [US, displacement]	>>>	9.842 065 3E+11
ton [US, gross]	>>>	9.842 065 3E+11
ton [US, net]	>>>	1.102 311 3E+12
ton [US, shipping]	>>>	9.842 065 3E+11
zettagram	0.001	1.000 000 0E-03

exajoule — <energy>
cheval vapeur heure [France]	>>>	3.776 726 7E+11
coal equivalent kilogram [UN, standard]	>>>	3.412 084 2E+10
coal equivalent metric ton [UN, standard]	>>>	3.412 084 2E+07
exawatthour	0.000 277 8	2.777 777 8E-04
gigawatthour	277,777.78	2.777 777 8E+05
gram [atomic physics, eq. energy]	11,126.501	1.112 650 1E+04
horsepower hour	>>>	3.725 061 4E+11
horsepower hour [metric]	>>>	3.776 726 7E+11
joule	>>>	1.000 000 0E+18
kilogram [atomic physics, eq. energy]	11.126 501	1.112 650 1E+01
kiloton [metric, explosive energy]	239,005.74	2.390 057 4E+05
kilowatthour	>>>	2.777 777 8E+11
megaton [metric, explosive energy]	239.005 74	2.390 057 4E+02
megawatthour	>>>	2.777 777 8E+08
myriawatthour	>>>	2.777 777 8E+10
petawatthour	0.277 777 8	2.777 777 8E-01
pferdestarkenstunde [Germany]	>>>	3.776 726 7E+11
quad	0.947 817 1	9.478 171 2E-01
terawatthour	277.777 78	2.777 777 8E+02
therm [EEC]	>>>	9.478 171 2E+09
therm [US]	>>>	9.480 434 3E+09
thermie [France]	>>>	2.389 029 6E+11
ton [metric, explosive energy]	>>>	2.390 057 4E+08
yottawatthour	<<<	2.777 777 8E-10

Convert From	<Type of Unit>	
Convert To	Standard	Scientific
zettawatthour	0.000 000 3	2.777 777 8E-07

exaliter   **<volume>**

barrel [US, dry]	>>>	8.648 489 8E+15
barrel [US, liquid]	>>>	8.386 414 4E+15
barrel [US, petroleum]	>>>	6.289 810 8E+15
billion cubic foot	>>>	3.531 466 7E+07
cubem	239,912.76	2.399 127 6E+05
cubic foot	>>>	3.531 466 7E+16
cubic meter	>>>	1.000 000 0E+15
cubic mile	239,912.76	2.399 127 6E+05
cubic yard	>>>	1.307 950 6E+15
hectare meter	>>>	1.000 000 0E+11
liter	>>>	1.000 000 0E+18
million acre foot	810,713.19	8.107 131 9E+05
trillion cubic foot	35,314.667	3.531 466 7E+04
zettaliter	0.001	1.000 000 0E-03

exameter   **<length>**

astronomical unit	6,684,587.2	6.684 587 2E+06
bevameter	>>>	1.000 000 0E+09
kiloparsec	0.032 407 8	3.240 779 8E-02
light year [based on mean Julian year]	105.700 08	1.057 000 8E+02
megaparsec	0.000 032 4	3.240 779 8E-05
meter	>>>	1.000 000 0E+18
mile [international]	>>>	6.213 711 9E+14
mile [US, statute]	>>>	6.213 699 5E+14
mile [US, survey]	>>>	6.213 699 5E+14
myriameter	>>>	1.000 000 0E+14
parsec	32.407 793	3.240 779 3E+01
yard [based on US, survey foot]	>>>	1.093 611 1E+18
yard [international]	>>>	1.093 613 3E+18
yard [UK]	>>>	1.093 615 2E+18

examole   **<amount of substance>**

mole	>>>	1.000 000 0E+18

exanewton   **<force>**

crinal	>>>	1.000 000 0E+19
dyne	>>>	1.000 000 0E+23
gram-force	>>>	1.019 716 2E+20
newton	>>>	1.000 000 0E+18
ounce-force	>>>	3.596 943 1E+18
pond	>>>	1.019 716 2E+20
pound-force	>>>	2.248 089 4E+17
poundal	>>>	7.233 013 9E+18

exapascal   **<pressure>**

atmosphere [standard]	>>>	9.869 232 7E+12
atmosphere [technical]	>>>	1.019 716 2E+13
bar	>>>	1.000 000 0E+13
foot of mercury [0 °C, by convention]	>>>	2.460 831 9E+13
foot of water [4 °C, by convention]	>>>	3.345 525 6E+14
kilogram-force/square millimeter	>>>	1.019 716 2E+11
kilopond/square millimeter	>>>	1.019 716 2E+11
kip/square inch	>>>	1.450 377 4E+11
newton/square millimeter	>>>	1.000 000 0E+12
pascal	>>>	1.000 000 0E+18
pound-force/square inch	>>>	1.450 377 4E+14
terabar	10	1.000 000 0E+01
ton-force/square inch [short]	>>>	7.251 886 9E+10
torr	>>>	7.500 616 8E+15

exawatt   **<power>**

Btu/second [I.T.]	>>>	9.478 171 2E+14
Btu/second [thermoc.]	>>>	9.484 514 1E+14
calorie/second [I.T.]	>>>	2.388 459 0E+17
calorie/second [thermoc.]	>>>	2.390 057 4E+17

Convert From Convert To	Standard	<Type of Unit> Scientific
centigrade heat unit/second [mean]	>>>	5.261 590 5E+14
cubic meter atmosphere/second	>>>	9.869 232 7E+18
dyne centimeter/second	>>>	1.000 000 0E+25
erg/second	>>>	1.000 000 0E+25
foot pound-force/second	>>>	7.375 621 5E+17
foot poundal/second	>>>	2.373 036 0E+19
gram-force centimeter/second	>>>	1.019 716 2E+22
horsepower	>>>	1.341 022 1E+15
horsepower [metric]	>>>	1.359 621 6E+15
joule/second	>>>	1.000 000 0E+18
kilocalorie/second [I.T.]	>>>	2.388 459 0E+14
kilogram-force meter/second	>>>	1.019 716 2E+17
kilopond meter/second	>>>	1.019 716 2E+17
newton meter/second	>>>	1.000 000 0E+18
volt ampere	>>>	1.000 000 0E+18
watt	>>>	1.000 000 0E+18

exawatthour   <energy>

coal equivalent kilogram [UN, standard]	>>>	1.228 350 3E+14
coal equivalent metric ton [UN, standard]	>>>	1.228 350 3E+11
exajoule	3,600	3.600 000 0E+03
foot pound-force	>>>	2.655 223 7E+21
foot poundal	>>>	8.542 929 7E+22
gigajoule	>>>	3.600 000 0E+12
gram [atomic physics, eq. energy]	>>>	4.005 540 2E+07
horsepower hour	>>>	1.341 022 1E+15
horsepower hour [metric]	>>>	1.359 621 6E+15
joule	>>>	3.600 000 0E+21
kilogram [atomic physics, eq. energy]	40,055.402	4.005 540 2E+04
kilopond meter	>>>	3.670 978 4E+20
kiloton [metric, explosive energy]	>>>	8.604 206 5E+08
megaton [metric, explosive energy]	860,420.65	8.604 206 5E+05
petajoule	3,600,000	3.600 000 0E+06
quad	3,412.141 6	3.412 141 6E+03
terajoule	>>>	3.600 000 0E+09
ton [metric, explosive energy]	>>>	8.604 206 5E+11
yottajoule	0.003 6	3.600 000 0E−03
zettajoule	3.6	3.600 000 0E+00

ezba [Hebrew, ancient]   <length, special - see page 29>

centimeter	1.94 --- 1.940 000 0E+00

fad ol [Denmark]   <volume, special - see page 29>

hectoliter	9.275 --- 9.275 000 0E+00

faddan [Iraq]   <area, special - see page 29>

hectare	5 --- 5.000 000 0E+00

faddan [Yemen]   <area, special - see page 29>

hectare	0.405 --- 4.050 000 0E−01

famn [Denmark]   <length, special - see page 29>

meter	1.883 --- 1.883 000 0E+00

famn [Finland]   <volume, special - see page 29>

cubic meter	4 --- 4.000 000 0E+00

famn [Sweden]   <length, special - see page 29>

meter	1.78 --- 1.780 000 0E+00

fan [Cambodia]   <mass, special - see page 29>

gram	0.375 --- 3.750 000 0E−01

fan [Hong Kong]   <mass, special - see page 29>

gram	0.377 993 6 --- 3.779 936 0E−01

fan [Hong Kong]   <length, special - see page 29>

millimeter	3.714 75 --- 3.714 750 0E+00

fan [Japan]   <mass, special - see page 29>

gram	0.375 --- 3.750 000 0E−01

| Convert From | | <Type of Unit> |
Convert To	Standard	Scientific

fan [Laos] <mass, special - see page 29>
gram ---- 0.375 ---- 3.750 000 0E-01

fan gong li [China] <area, special - see page 29>
square kilometer ---- 1 ---- 1.000 000 0E+00

fan mi [China] <area, special - see page 29>
square meter ---- 1 ---- 1.000 000 0E+00

fan sheng [China] <volume, special - see page 29>
centiliter ---- 10 ---- 1.000 000 0E+01

fanega [Argentina] <volume, special - see page 29>
liter ---- 137 ---- 1.370 000 0E+02

fanega [Chile] <volume, special - see page 29>
liter ---- 97 ---- 9.700 000 0E+01

fanega [Costa Rica, coffee] <mass, special - see page 29>
kilogram ---- 348.36 ---- 3.483 600 0E+02

fanega [Costa Rica] <volume, special - see page 29>
liter ---- 408 ---- 4.080 000 0E+02

fanega [Cuba] <volume, special - see page 29>
liter ---- 105.75 ---- 1.057 500 0E+02

fanega [Ecuador, grain] <mass, special - see page 29>
kilogram ---- 113 ---- 1.130 000 0E+02

fanega [El Salvador] <volume, special - see page 29>
liter ---- 259.61 ---- 2.596 100 0E+02

fanega [Honduras] <volume, special - see page 29>
liter ---- 110.28 ---- 1.102 800 0E+02

fanega [Mexico] <volume, special - see page 29>
liter ---- 90.81 ---- 9.081 000 0E+01

fanega [Mexico] <area, special - see page 29>
hectare ---- 3.566 28 ---- 3.566 280 0E+00

fanega [Morocco, grain] <mass, special - see page 29>
kilogram ---- 44 ---- 4.400 000 0E+01

fanega [Nicaragua] <mass, special - see page 29>
kilogram ---- 161 ---- 1.610 000 0E+02

fanega [Paraguay] <volume, special - see page 29>
liter ---- 288 ---- 2.880 000 0E+02

fanega [Peru] <area, special - see page 29>
square meter ---- 6,536 ---- 6.536 000 0E+03

fanega [Spain] <area, special - see page 29>
are ---- 64.395 6 ---- 6.439 560 0E+01

fanega [Trinidad and Tobago] <mass, special - see page 29>
kilogram ---- 49.9 ---- 4.990 000 0E+01

fanega [Uruguay] <mass, special - see page 29>
kilogram ---- 100 ---- 1.000 000 0E+02

fanega [Venezuela] <volume, special - see page 29>
liter ---- 117.5 ---- 1.175 000 0E+02

fanegada [Spain] <area, special - see page 29>
square meter ---- 6,400 ---- 6.400 000 0E+03

fanegada [Venezuela] <area, special - see page 29>
hectare ---- 0.699 ---- 6.990 000 0E-01

fanga [Brazil] <volume, special - see page 29>
liter ---- 145 ---- 1.450 000 0E+02

fanga [Spain] <area, special - see page 29>
are ---- 64.395 6 ---- 6.439 560 0E+01

fanga carree [Portugal] <area, special - see page 29>
are ---- 48.336 ---- 4.833 600 0E+01

fanoe [East India, troy]   **<mass, special - see page 29>**
- gram -- 0.378 --- 3.780 000 0E−01

faon [Denmark]   **<length, special - see page 29>**
- meter -- 1.883 14 --- 1.883 140 0E+00

farad   **<capacitance>**
- abfarad -- <<< 1.000 000 0E−09
- ampere second/volt --- 1 --- 1.000 000 0E+00
- coulomb/volt --- 1 --- 1.000 000 0E+00
- electromagnetic unit of capacitance [cgs system] ------------ <<< 1.000 000 0E−09
- electrostatic unit of capacitance [cgs system] -------------- >>> 8.987 551 8E+11
- farad [international] ---------------------------- 1.000 490 2 --- 1.000 490 2E+00
- gaussian electric capacitance ------------------------------- >>> 8.987 551 8E+11
- jar -- >>> 8.987 551 8E+08
- puff --- >>> 1.000 000 0E+12
- second/ohm --- 1 --- 1.000 000 0E+00
- statfarad -- >>> 8.987 551 8E+11

farad [international]   **<capacitance>**
- abfarad -- <<< 9.995 100 0E−10
- coulomb/volt --------------------------------------- 0.999 51 --- 9.995 100 0E−01
- farad -- 0.999 51 --- 9.995 100 0E−01
- second/ohm --- 0.999 51 --- 9.995 100 0E−01
- statfarad -- >>> 8.983 147 9E+11

farad square meter   **<electric polarizability>**
- coulomb square meter/volt ----------------------------------- 1 --- 1.000 000 0E+00

farad volt   **<electric charge>**
- abcoulomb -- 0.1 --- 1.000 000 0E−01
- ampere second --- 1 --- 1.000 000 0E+00
- coulomb --- 1 --- 1.000 000 0E+00
- electromagnetic unit of charge [cgs system] --------- 0.1 --- 1.000 000 0E−01

farad volt meter   **<electric dipole moment>**
- abcoulomb centimeter --------------------------------- 10 --- 1.000 000 0E+01
- ampere second meter ----------------------------------- 1 --- 1.000 000 0E+00
- coulomb meter --- 1 --- 1.000 000 0E+00
- statcoulomb centimeter ------------------------------------- 2.997 924 6E+11

farad volt/meter   **<electric dipole moment/unit area>**
- ampere second/meter ----------------------------------- 1 --- 1.000 000 0E+00
- coulomb/meter --- 1 --- 1.000 000 0E+00

farad/meter   **<electric permittivity>**
- abfarad/centimeter ----------------------------- 0.000 000 1 --- 1.000 000 0E−07
- ampere second/volt meter ------------------------------ 1 --- 1.000 000 0E+00
- coulomb/volt meter ------------------------------------ 1 --- 1.000 000 0E+00
- second/ohm meter -------------------------------------- 1 --- 1.000 000 0E+00
- statfarad/centimeter --------------------------------------- >>> 8.987 551 8E+13

faraday [based on carbon-12]   **<electric charge>**
- abcoulomb --------------------------------------- 9,648.530 9 --- 9.648 530 9E+03
- coulomb -- 96,485.309 --- 9.648 530 9E+04
- faraday [chemical] --------------------------- 0.999 892 3 --- 9.998 923 2E−01
- faraday [physical] --------------------------- 0.999 620 9 --- 9.996 209 1E−01
- statcoulomb --- >>> 2.892 556 8E+14

faraday [chemical]   **<electric charge>**
- abcoulomb --- 9,649.57 --- 9.649 570 0E+03
- coulomb -- 96,495.7 --- 9.649 570 0E+04
- faraday [based on carbon-12] ----------------- 1.000 107 7 --- 1.000 107 7E+00
- faraday [physical] --------------------------- 0.999 728 6 --- 9.997 285 6E−01
- statcoulomb --- >>> 2.892 868 3E+14

faraday [physical]   **<electric charge>**
- ampere hour --------------------------------- 26.811 638 9 --- 2.681 163 9E+01
- coulomb -- 96,521.9 --- 9.652 190 0E+04
- electromagnetic unit of charge [cgs system] ------- 9,652.19 --- 9.652 190 0E+03
- faraday [based on carbon-12] ----------------- 1.000 379 2 --- 1.000 379 2E+00

Convert From		<Type of Unit>
Convert To	Standard	Scientific

faraday [chemical] -------------------------	1.000 271 5	1.000 271 5E+00
statcoulomb ------------------------------	>>>	2.893 653 8E+14
farasala [Muscat and Oman]	<mass, special - see page 29>	
kilogram --------------------------	40.398	4.039 800 0E+01
farasalah [Oman]	<mass, special - see page 29>	
kilogram ---------------------------	40.4	4.040 000 0E+01
fardo [Honduras, tobacco]	<mass, special - see page 29>	
kilogram ----------------------------	46	4.600 000 0E+01
fardo [Philippines]	<mass, special - see page 29>	
kilogram ---------------------------	15.2	1.520 000 0E+01
fardo de tabaco [Costa Rica]	<mass, special - see page 29>	
kilogram ---------------------------	57.6	5.760 000 0E+01
farsakh [Abyssinia, ancient]	<length, special - see page 29>	
kilometer ---------------------------	5.07	5.070 000 0E+00
farsakh [Arabia]	<length, special - see page 29>	
kilometer ---------------------------	4.83	4.830 000 0E+00
farsakh [Ethiopia]	<length, special - see page 29>	
meter---------------------------	5,070	5.070 000 0E+03
farsakh [Iran]	<length, special - see page 29>	
kilometer ---------------------------	6.24	6.240 000 0E+00
farsakh [Oman]	<length, special - see page 29>	
kilometer ---------------------------	4.8	4.800 000 0E+00
farsakh song [Iran]	<length, special - see page 29>	
kilometer ---------------------------	6.24	6.240 000 0E+00
farsalah [Somalia]	<mass, special - see page 29>	
kilogram ---------------------------	16.128	1.612 800 0E+01
farsalah [Tanzania]	<mass, special - see page 29>	
kilogram ---------------------------	16.33	1.633 000 0E+01
farsang [Abyssinia, ancient]	<length, special - see page 29>	
kilometer ---------------------------	5.07	5.070 000 0E+00
farsang [Iran]	<length, special - see page 29>	
kilometer ---------------------------	6.24	6.240 000 0E+00
fass [Austria]	<volume, special - see page 29>	
liter--------------------------------	566.6	5.666 000 0E+02
fat [Sweden]	<volume, special - see page 29>	
liter------------------------	157.027	1.570 270 0E+02
fatar [Oman]	<length, special - see page 29>	
centimeter----------------------------	18	1.800 000 0E+01
fathmur [Iceland]	<length, special - see page 29>	
meter--------------------------	1.883 1	1.883 100 0E+00
fathom [Greece, ancient]	<length, special - see page 29>	
meter--------------------------	1.848	1.848 000 0E+00
fathom [Hebrew, ancient]	<length, special - see page 29>	
meter--------------------------	1.85	1.850 000 0E+00
fathom [Hungary]	<length, special - see page 29>	
meter--------------------------	1.896	1.896 000 0E+00
fathom [US, survey]		<length>
cable length [US, survey] -----------------------	0.008 333 3	8.333 333 3E-03
caliber-------------------------------------	7,200.014 4	7.200 014 4E+03
chain [Gunter or US, survey] ------------------	0.090 909 1	9.090 909 1E-02
chain [Ramden or Engineer] -------------------	0.060 000 1	6.000 012 0E-02
foot [international]-------------------------	6.000 012	6.000 012 0E+00
foot [US, survey] -------------------------------	6	6.000 000 0E+00
furlong [US, survey] ---------------------------	0.009 090 9	9.090 909 1E-03
inch [based on US, survey foot] ---------------	72	7.200 000 0E+01
inch [international] ------------------------------	72.000 144	7.200 014 4E+01
link [Gunter or US, survey] -------------------	9.090 909 1	9.090 909 1E+00

Convert From Convert To	Standard	<Type of Unit> Scientific
link [Ramden or Engineer]	6.000 012	6.000 012 0E+00
meter	1.828 803 7	1.828 803 7E+00
out [US, survey]	0.018 181 8	1.818 181 8E−02
pace [US, survey]	2.4	2.400 000 0E+00
perch [US, survey]	0.363 636 4	3.636 363 6E−01
pole [US, survey]	0.363 636 4	3.636 363 6E−01
range [US, survey]	0.000 189 4	1.893 939 4E−04
rod [US, survey]	0.363 636 4	3.636 363 6E−01
yard [based on US, survey foot]	2	2.000 000 0E+00
yard [international]	2.000 004	2.000 004 0E+00
yard [UK]	2.000 007 5	2.000 007 5E+00
fatil [Islam]		**<mass, special - see page 29>**
gram	0.045	4.500 000 0E−02
faunt [Saudi Arabia]		**<mass, special - see page 29>**
kilogram	1.769	1.769 000 0E+00
faust [Hungary]		**<length, special - see page 29>**
meter	0.105 36	1.053 600 0E−01
favn [Norway, firewood]		**<volume, special - see page 29>**
cubic meter	2.4	2.400 000 0E+00
favn [Sweden]		**<length, special - see page 29>**
meter	1.781 5	1.781 500 0E+00
favn braende [Denmark]		**<volume, special - see page 29>**
cubic meter	2.225 94	2.225 940 0E+00
favne [Denmark]		**<volume, special - see page 29>**
cubic meter	2.226	2.226 000 0E+00
feddan [Iraq]		**<area, special - see page 29>**
hectare	5	5.000 000 0E+00
feddan [Yemen]		**<area, special - see page 29>**
hectare	0.405	4.050 000 0E−01
feddan masri [Egypt]		**<area, special - see page 29>**
are	42.01	4.201 000 0E+01
felin [France, troy]		**<mass, special - see page 29>**
gram	0.38	3.800 000 0E−01
femtobar		**<pressure>**
atmosphere [standard]	<<<	9.869 232 7E−16
atmosphere [technical]	<<<	1.019 716 2E−15
bar	<<<	1.000 000 0E−15
dyne/square centimeter	<<<	1.000 000 0E−09
gram-force/square centimeter	<<<	1.019 716 2E−12
kilogram-force/square meter	<<<	1.019 716 2E−11
kilopond/square meter	<<<	1.019 716 2E−11
micrometer of mercury [0 °C, by convention]	<<<	7.500 615 8E−10
micrometer of water [4 °C, by convention]	<<<	1.019 716 2E−08
newton/square meter	<<<	1.000 000 0E−10
pascal	<<<	1.000 000 0E−10
picopascal	100	1.000 000 0E+02
poundal/square foot	<<<	6.719 689 8E−11
torr	<<<	7.500 616 8E−13
femtocandela		**<luminous intensity>**
candela	<<<	1.000 000 0E−15
femtogram		**<mass>**
atomic mass unit [unified, C-12,1986]	>>>	6.022 136 7E+08
avogram	>>>	6.022 136 7E+08
dalton	>>>	6.022 136 7E+08
gamma	<<<	1.000 000 0E−09
grain	<<<	1.543 235 8E−14
kilogram	<<<	1.000 000 0E−18
femtojoule		**<energy>**
1/centimeter [atomic physics, eq. energy]	>>>	5.034 112 5E+07

Convert From Convert To	Standard	<Type of Unit> Scientific
atomic mass unit [unified, C-12, 1986, eq. energy]	0.000 006 7	6.700 530 5E–06
deuteron rest mass [atomic physics, eq. energy]	0.000 003 3	3.327 714 8E–06
dyne centimeter	<<<	1.000 000 0E–08
electron rest mass [atomic physics, eq. energy]	0.012 214 3	1.221 432 1E–02
electronvolt	6,241.506 4	6.241 506 4E+03
erg	<<<	1.000 000 0E–08
gigaelectronvolt	0.000 006 2	6.241 506 4E–06
hartree [atomic physics, eq. energy]	229.371 04	2.293 710 4E+02
joule	<<<	1.000 000 0E–15
kayser [atomic physics, eq. energy]	>>>	5.034 112 5E+07
kelvin [atomic physics, eq. energy]	>>>	7.242 923 3E+07
kiloelectronvolt	6.241 506 4	6.241 506 4E+00
megaelectronvolt	0.006 241 5	6.241 506 4E–03
muon rest mass [atomic physics, eq. energy]	0.000 059 1	5.907 251 1E–05
neutron rest mass [atomic physics, eq. energy]	0.000 006 6	6.642 970 1E–06
proton rest mass [atomic physics, eq. energy]	0.000 006 7	6.652 126 8E–06
rydberg [atomic physics, eq. energy]	458.736 64	4.587 366 4E+02

femtoliter		<volume>
cubic inch	<<<	6.102 374 4E–14
cubic meter	<<<	1.000 000 0E–18
cubic micrometer	1	1.000 000 0E+00
drachm [UK, liquid]	<<<	2.815 606 4E–13
dram [Canada, liquid]	<<<	2.815 606 4E–13
dram [US, liquid]	<<<	2.705 121 8E–13
drop [US, liquid]	<<<	1.217 304 8E–11
lambda	<<<	1.000 000 0E–09
liter	<<<	1.000 000 0E–15
ounce [UK, liquid]	<<<	3.519 508 0E–14
ounce [US, liquid]	<<<	3.381 402 3E–14
scruple [UK, liquid]	<<<	8.446 819 1E–13

femtometer		<length>
angstrom	0.000 01	1.000 000 0E–05
bicron	0.001	1.000 000 0E–03
caliber	<<<	3.937 007 9E–12
fermi	1	1.000 000 0E+00
inch [based on US, survey foot]	<<<	3.937 007 9E–14
inch [international]	<<<	3.937 007 9E–14
meter	<<<	1.000 000 0E–15
microinch	<<<	3.937 007 9E–08
micromicron	0.001	1.000 000 0E–03
mil	<<<	3.937 007 9E–11
millimicron	0.000 001	1.000 000 0E–06
stigma	0.001	1.000 000 0E–03
tenthmeter	0.000 01	1.000 000 0E–05
thou	<<<	3.937 007 9E–11
x-unit	0.009 979 3	9.979 320 9E–03

femtomole		<amount of substance>
mole	<<<	1.000 000 0E–15

femtonewton		<force>
crinal	<<<	1.000 000 0E–14
dyne	<<<	1.000 000 0E–10
gram-force	<<<	1.019 716 2E–13
newton	<<<	1.000 000 0E–15
ounce-force	<<<	3.596 943 1E–15
pond	<<<	1.019 716 2E–13
pound-force	<<<	2.248 089 4E–16
poundal	<<<	7.233 013 9E–15

femtopascal		<pressure>
atmosphere [standard]	<<<	9.869 232 7E–21
atmosphere [technical]	<<<	1.019 716 2E–20
bar	<<<	1.000 000 0E–20
micrometer of mercury [0 °C, by convention]	<<<	7.500 615 8E–15

Convert From / Convert To	Standard	Scientific
micrometer of water [4 °C, by convention]	<<<	1.019 716 2E–13
newton/square meter	<<<	1.000 000 0E–15
pascal	<<<	1.000 000 0E–15
poundal/square foot	<<<	6.719 689 8E–16
zeptobar	–10	1.000 000 0E+01

femtowatt   **<power>**

Convert To	Standard	Scientific
Btu/hour [I.T.]	<<<	3.412 141 6E–15
Btu/hour [thermoc.]	<<<	3.414 425 1E–15
calorie/hour [I.T.]	<<<	8.598 452 3E–13
calorie/hour [thermoc.]	<<<	8.604 206 5E–13
centigrade heat unit/hour [mean]	<<<	1.894 172 6E–15
cubic meter atmosphere/hour	<<<	3.552 923 8E–11
dyne centimeter/hour	0.000 036	3.600 000 0E–05
erg/hour	0.000 036	3.600 000 0E–05
foot pound-force/hour	<<<	2.655 223 7E–12
foot poundal/hour	<<<	8.542 929 7E–11
gram-force centimeter/hour	<<<	3.670 978 4E–08
horsepower	<<<	1.341 022 1E–18
horsepower [metric]	<<<	1.359 621 6E–18
joule/hour	<<<	3.600 000 0E–12
kilocalorie/hour [I.T.]	<<<	8.598 452 3E–16
kilogram-force meter/hour	<<<	3.670 978 4E–13
kilopond meter/hour	<<<	3.670 978 4E–13
newton meter/hour	<<<	3.600 000 0E–12
volt ampere	<<<	1.000 000 0E–15
watt	<<<	1.000 000 0E–15

fen [China, silver]   **<mass, special - see page 29>**

Convert To	Standard	Scientific
gram	0.378	3.780 000 0E–01

fen [China]   **<length, special - see page 29>**

Convert To	Standard	Scientific
millimeter	3.581 4	3.581 400 0E+00

fen ke [China]   **<mass, special - see page 29>**

Convert To	Standard	Scientific
milligram	100	1.000 000 0E+02

fen mi [China]   **<length, special - see page 29>**

Convert To	Standard	Scientific
centimeter	10	1.000 000 0E+01

feralin [Iceland]   **<area, special - see page 29>**

Convert To	Standard	Scientific
square meter	0.394 01	3.940 100 0E–01

ferasla [Ethiopia]   **<mass, special - see page 29>**

Convert To	Standard	Scientific
kilogram	17	1.700 000 0E+01

ferfathmur [Iceland]   **<area, special - see page 29>**

Convert To	Standard	Scientific
square meter	3.546	3.546 000 0E+00

ferfet [Iceland]   **<area, special - see page 29>**

Convert To	Standard	Scientific
square meter	0.098 5	9.850 000 0E–02

ferlino [Italy]   **<mass, special - see page 29>**

Convert To	Standard	Scientific
gram	1.73	1.730 000 0E+00

fermi   **<length>**

Convert To	Standard	Scientific
angstrom	0.000 01	1.000 000 0E–05
bicron	0.001	1.000 000 0E–03
femtometer	1	1.000 000 0E+00
inch [based on US, survey foot]	<<<	3.937 000 0E–14
inch [international]	<<<	3.937 007 9E–14
meter	<<<	1.000 000 0E–15
microinch	<<<	3.937 007 9E–08
micromicron	0.001	1.000 000 0E–03
mil	<<<	3.937 007 9E–11
millimicron	0.000 001	1.000 000 0E–06
stigma	0.001	1.000 000 0E–03
tenthmeter	0.000 01	1.000 000 0E–05
x-unit	0.009 979 3	9.979 320 9E–03

fermila [Iceland]   **<area, special - see page 29>**

Convert To	Standard	Scientific
square kilometer	56.738	5.673 800 0E+01

Convert From	<Type of Unit>	
Convert To	Standard	Scientific

fern [Singapore, troy]   `<mass, special - see page 29>`
gram --- 0.344 47 ---- 3.444 700 0E-01

ferrado [Portugal]   `<area, special - see page 29>`
are --- 7.25 ---- 7.250 000 0E+00

ferrah [Oman]   `<mass, special - see page 29>`
kilogram --- 11.3 ---- 1.130 000 0E+01

fershi kadim [Turkey]   `<length, special - see page 29>`
kilometer -- 5.685 ---- 5.685 000 0E+00

ferthumiungur [Iceland]   `<area, special - see page 29>`
square centimeter -- 6.84 ---- 6.840 000 0E+00

fet [Iceland]   `<length, special - see page 29>`
meter -- 0.313 85 ---- 3.138 500 0E-01

feuillette [France, wine]   `<volume, special - see page 29>`
liter --- 114 ---- 1.140 000 0E+02

feun [China]   `<area, special - see page 29>`
square meter --- 40 ---- 4.000 000 0E+01

fierding [Iceland]   `<mass, special - see page 29>`
kilogram -- 20 ---- 2.000 000 0E+01

fifth [US, liquid]   `<volume>`
cubic inch --- 46.2 ---- 4.620 000 0E+01
cubic meter --- 0.000 757 1 ---- 7.570 823 6E-04
drop [US, liquid] -- 9,216 ---- 9.216 000 0E+03
gallon [US, liquid] --- 0.2 ---- 2.000 000 0E-01
liter --- 0.757 082 4 ---- 7.570 823 6E-01
ounce [US, liquid] --- 25.6 ---- 2.560 000 0E+01

fillette angevine [France, wine]   `<volume, special - see page 29>`
centiliter -- 35 ---- 3.500 000 0E+01

finger [Egypt, ancient]   `<length, special - see page 29>`
centimeter --- 1.82 ---- 1.820 000 0E+00

finger [Greece, ancient]   `<length, special - see page 29>`
millimeter -- 19.25 ---- 1.925 000 0E+01

finger [Hebrew, ancient]   `<length, special - see page 29>`
centimeter --- 1.85 ---- 1.850 000 0E+00

finger [Sumeria, ancient]   `<length, special - see page 29>`
centimeter --- 1.67 ---- 1.670 000 0E+00

fingerbreadth [Egypt, ancient]   `<length, special - see page 29>`
meter -- 0.019 ---- 1.900 000 0E-02

fingerbreadth [Hebrew, ancient]   `<length, special - see page 29>`
meter -- 0.022 ---- 2.200 000 0E-02

finsen unit   `<heat flux density>`
Btu/second square foot [I.T.] ------------------------- 8.805 509 2 ---- 8.805 509 2E+00
calorie/second square centimeter [I.T.] -------------- 2.388 459 ---- 2.388 459 0E+00
watt/square centimeter --- 10 ---- 1.000 000 0E+01
watt/square meter -- 100,000 ---- 1.000 000 0E+05

firkin [Rome, ancient]   `<volume, special - see page 29>`
liter -- 39 ---- 3.900 000 0E+01

firkin [UK]   `<volume>`
barrel [UK] --- 0.25 ---- 2.500 000 0E-01
barrel [US, dry] --- 0.353 851 3 ---- 3.538 513 2E-01
barrel [US, liquid] -- 0.343 128 6 ---- 3.431 285 5E-01
barrel [US, petroleum] ----------------------------------- 0.257 346 4 ---- 2.573 464 1E-01
bushel [UK] -- 1.125 ---- 1.125 000 0E+00
chaldron [UK, liquid] ------------------------------------- 0.031 25 ---- 3.125 000 0E-02
cubic foot --- 1.444 892 9 ---- 1.444 892 9E+00
cubic inch --- 2,496.774 9 ---- 2.496 774 9E+03
cubic meter -- 0.040 914 8 ---- 4.091 481 0E-02
cubic yard --- 0.053 514 6 ---- 5.351 455 1E-02
cup [Canada, measuring] --------------------------------------- 180 ---- 1.800 000 0E+02

Convert From / Convert To	Standard	\<Type of Unit\> Scientific
cup [US, measuring]	172.936 79	1.729 367 9E+02
dekaliter	4.091 481	4.091 481 0E+00
firkin [US]	1.200 949 9	1.200 949 9E+00
gallon [Canada, liquid]	9	9.000 000 0E+00
gallon [UK, dry or liquid]	9	9.000 000 0E+00
gallon [US, dry]	9.288 510 7	9.288 510 7E+00
gallon [US, liquid]	10.808 549	1.080 854 9E+01
gill [UK]	288	2.880 000 0E+02
gill [US]	345.873 58	3.458 735 8E+02
kilderkin [UK, liquid]	0.5	5.000 000 0E-01
liter	40.914 81	4.091 481 0E+01
peck [UK]	4.5	4.500 000 0E+00
peck [US]	4.644 255 3	4.644 255 3E+00
pint [UK]	72	7.200 000 0E+01
pint [US, dry]	74.308 086	7.430 808 6E+01
pint [US, liquid]	86.468 395	8.646 839 5E+01
quart [UK]	36	3.600 000 0E+01
quart [US, dry]	37.154 043	3.715 404 3E+01
quart [US, liquid]	43.234 197	4.323 419 7E+01
stere	0.040 914 8	4.091 481 0E-02
Winchester wine gallon [UK]	10.808 549	1.080 854 9E+01

firkin [US] \<volume\>

Convert To	Standard	Scientific
barrel [US]	0.208 168 6	2.081 685 5E-01
barrel [US, federal proof spirits]	0.225	2.250 000 0E-01
barrel [US, liquid]	0.285 714 3	2.857 142 9E-01
cubic foot	1.203 125	1.203 125 0E+00
cubic inch	2,079	2.079 000 0E+03
cubic meter	0.034 068 7	3.406 870 6E-02
cubic yard	0.044 560 2	4.456 018 5E-02
cup [Canada, measuring]	149.881 35	1.498 813 5E+02
cup [US, measuring]	144	1.440 000 0E+02
dekaliter	3.406 870 6	3.406 870 6E+00
drachm [UK, liquid]	9,592.406 6	9.592 406 6E+03
dram [US, liquid]	9,216	9.216 000 0E+03
firkin [UK]	0.832 674 2	8.326 741 8E-01
gallon [UK, dry or liquid]	7.494 067 7	7.494 067 7E+00
gallon [US, liquid]	9	9.000 000 0E+00
gill [UK]	239.810 17	2.398 101 7E+02
gill [US]	288	2.880 000 0E+02
kilderkin [US, liquid]	0.5	5.000 000 0E-01
liter	34.068 706	3.406 870 6E+01
ounce [UK, liquid]	1,199.050 8	1.199 050 8E+03
ounce [US, liquid]	1,152	1.152 000 0E+03
pint [UK]	59.952 541	5.995 254 1E+01
pint [US, liquid]	72	7.200 000 0E+01
quart [UK]	29.976 271	2.997 627 1E+01
quart [US, liquid]	36	3.600 000 0E+01
stere	0.034 068 7	3.406 870 6E-02
tablespoon [Canada, measuring]	2,398.105 7	2.398 105 7E+03
tablespoon [US, measuring]	2,304	2.304 000 0E+03
teaspoon [Canada, measuring]	7,194.317 1	7.194 317 1E+03
teaspoon [US, measuring]	6,912	6.912 000 0E+03
Winchester wine gallon [UK]	9	9.000 000 0E+00

firlot [UK, barley] \<mass, special - see page 29\>

Convert To	Standard	Scientific
kilogram	33.112	3.311 200 0E+01

firlot [UK, oats] \<mass, special - see page 29\>

Convert To	Standard	Scientific
kilogram	25.855	2.585 500 0E+01

firlot [UK, wheat] \<mass, special - see page 29\>

Convert To	Standard	Scientific
kilogram	27.216	2.721 600 0E+01

fisk [Iceland] \<mass, special - see page 29\>

Convert To	Standard	Scientific
kilogram	4	4.000 000 0E+00

| Convert From | <Type of Unit> | |
Convert To	Standard	Scientific

fitil [Turkey] <mass, special - see page 29>
milligram-- 12.5----1.250 000 0E+01

fitr [Saudi Arabia, ancient] <length, special - see page 29>
centimeter--- 15.24----1.524 000 0E+01

fjarding [Sweden, dry] <volume, special - see page 29>
liter---18.319 8----1.831 980 0E+01

fjarding [Sweden, liquid] <volume, special - see page 29>
liter---31.405 4----3.140 540 0E+01

fjerding [Denmark] <volume, special - see page 29>
liter-- 34.78----3.478 000 0E+01

fjerdingkar [Denmark] <volume, special - see page 29>
liter--4.347 54----4.347 540 0E+00

fjerdingkar [Denmark] <area, special - see page 29>
square meter------------------------------------ 172.382----1.723 820 0E+02

flagon [UK] <volume, special - see page 29>
milliliter-- 1,130----1.130 000 0E+03

flask of mercury <mass>
| cental [US]--- 0.76----7.600 000 0E-01 |
| centner [UK]----------------------------------- 0.678 571 4----6.785 714 3E-01 |
| geepound------------------------------------- 2.362 152 2----2.362 152 2E+00 |
| hyl-- 3.515 269 8----3.515 269 8E+00 |
| kilogram------------------------------------- 34.473 02----3.447 302 0E+01 |
| myriagram------------------------------------ 3.447 302----3.447 302 0E+00 |
| pound-- 76----7.600 000 0E+01 |
| pound [avoirdupois]------------------------------ 76----7.600 000 0E+01 |
| pound [troy]---------------------------------- 92.361 111----9.236 111 1E+01 |
| poundal square second/foot----------------------- 76----7.600 000 0E+01 |
| quarter [long]------------------------------- 0.135 714 3----1.357 142 9E-01 |
| quarter [short]----------------------------------- 0.152----1.520 000 0E-01 |
| quarter [UK]---------------------------------- 2.714 285 7----2.714 285 7E+00 |
| quarter [US]--------------------------------------- 3.04----3.040 000 0E+00 |
| slug--- 2.362 152 2----2.362 152 2E+00 |
| slug [metric]-------------------------------- 3.515 269 8----3.515 269 8E+00 |
| stone [UK]---------------------------------- 5.428 571 4----5.428 571 4E+00 |

flux unit <energy flux density>
watt/square meter hertz -------------------------- <<<----1.000 000 0E-26

fod [Denmark] <length, special - see page 29>
centimeter------------------------------------ 31.385----3.138 500 0E+01

foder [Sweden] <volume, special - see page 29>
hectoliter--------------------------------------- 9.42----9.420 000 0E+00

foglietta [Italy, liquid] <volume, special - see page 29>
milliliter-- 456----4.560 000 0E+02

folha [Cape Verde, liquid] <volume, special - see page 29>
liter--- 1.05----1.050 000 0E+00

foot [Babylon, ancient] <length, special - see page 29>
centimeter-------------------------------------35.39----3.539 000 0E+01

foot [Canada, Quebec] <length, special - see page 29>
meter---0.325----3.250 000 0E-01

foot [Egypt, ancient] <length, special - see page 29>
centimeter-- 36----3.600 000 0E+01

foot [France] <length>
| arpent [France]------------------------------ 0.005 555 6----5.555 555 6E-03 |
| chain [Gunter or US, survey]---------------- 0.016 147 7----1.614 769 5E-02 |
| chain [Ramden or Engineer]----------------- 0.010 657 5----1.065 750 0E-02 |
| foot [international]--------------------------- 1.065 75----1.065 750 0E+00 |
| foot [US, survey]-------------------------- 1.065 747 9----1.065 747 9E+00 |
| inch [based on US, survey foot]---------- 12.788 974----1.278 897 4E+01 |
| inch [international]------------------------ 12.789----1.278 900 0E+01 |

| Convert From | | <Type of Unit> |
Convert To	Standard	Scientific
link [Gunter or US, survey]	1.614 769 5	1.614 769 5E+00
link [Ramden or Engineer]	1.065 75	1.065 750 0E+00
meter	0.324 840 6	3.248 406 0E-01
mile [international]	0.000 201 8	2.018 465 9E-04
mile [US, statute]	0.000 201 8	2.018 461 9E-04
mile [US, survey]	0.000 201 8	2.018 461 9E-04
out [US, survey]	0.003 229 5	3.229 539 0E-03
pace [US, survey]	0.426 299 2	4.262 991 5E-01
pied [France]	1	1.000 000 0E+00
span	1.421	1.421 000 0E+00
yard [based on US, survey foot]	0.355 249 3	3.552 492 9E-01
yard [international]	0.355 25	3.552 500 0E-01
yard [UK]	0.355 250 6	3.552 506 2E-01

foot [Greece, ancient, olympic]   <length, special - see page 29>

centimeter	32.05	3.205 000 0E+01

foot [Greece, ancient]   <length, special - see page 29>

centimeter	30.89	3.089 000 0E+01

foot [international]   <length>

Convert To	Standard	Scientific
astronomical unit	<<<	2.037 462 2E-12
barleycorn	36	3.600 000 0E+01
bolt [cloth]	0.008 333 3	8.333 333 3E-03
cable length [US, survey]	0.001 388 9	1.388 886 1E-03
caliber	1,200	1.200 000 0E+03
chain [Gunter or US, survey]	0.015 151 5	1.515 148 5E-02
chain [Ramden or Engineer]	0.01	1.000 000 0E-02
digit	16	1.600 000 0E+01
fathom [US, survey]	0.166 666 3	1.666 663 3E-01
foot [US, survey]	0.999 998	9.999 980 0E-01
furlong [US, survey]	0.001 515 1	1.515 148 5E-03
hand [horses]	3	3.000 000 0E+00
inch [based on US, survey foot]	11.999 976	1.199 997 6E+01
inch [international]	12	1.200 000 0E+01
kilometer	0.000 304 8	3.048 000 0E-04
lea [US, cotton yarn]	0.002 777 8	2.777 777 8E-03
lea [US, linen yarn]	0.001 111 1	1.111 111 1E-03
lea [US, silk yarn]	0.002 777 8	2.777 777 8E-03
lea [US, wool yarn]	0.004 166 7	4.166 666 7E-03
link [Gunter or US, survey]	1.515 148 5	1.515 148 5E+00
link [Ramden or Engineer]	1	1.000 000 0E+00
meter	0.304 8	3.048 000 0E-01
mile [international]	0.000 189 4	1.893 939 4E-04
mile [US, statute]	0.000 189 4	1.893 935 6E-04
mile [US, survey]	0.000 189 4	1.893 935 6E-04
pace [geometrical]	0.02	2.000 000 0E-02
pace [US, survey]	0.399 999 2	3.999 992 0E-01
pole [US, survey]	0.060 605 9	6.060 593 9E-02
span	1.333 333 3	1.333 333 3E+00
vara [US, survey, California]	0.363 635 6	3.636 356 4E-01
vara [US, survey, Texas]	0.359 999 3	3.599 992 8E-01
yard [based on US, survey foot]	0.333 332 7	3.333 326 7E-01
yard [international]	0.333 333 3	3.333 333 3E-01
yard [UK]	0.333 333 9	3.333 339 1E-01

foot [Iraq, ancient]   <length, special - see page 29>

centimeter	31.6	3.160 000 0E+01

foot [Netherlands]   <length, special - see page 29>

centimeter	28.313	2.831 300 0E+01

foot [Phoenicia, ancient]   <length, special - see page 29>

millimeter	495	4.950 000 0E+02

foot [Rome, ancient]   <length, special - see page 29>

centimeter	29.6	2.960 000 0E+01

Convert From		<Type of Unit>
Convert To	Standard	Scientific

foot [Russia]   \<length, special - see page 29\>

	Standard	Scientific
centimeter	30.48	3.048 000 0E+01

foot [South Africa]   \<length, special - see page 29\>

	Standard	Scientific
meter	0.304 797 3	3.047 972 7E-01

foot [US, survey]   \<length\>

	Standard	Scientific
arpent [France]	0.005 212 8	5.212 823 5E-03
cable length [US, survey]	0.001 388 9	1.388 888 9E-03
chain [Gunter or US, survey]	0.015 151 5	1.515 151 5E-02
chain [Ramden or Engineer]	0.01	1.000 002 0E-02
fathom [US, survey]	0.166 666 7	1.666 666 7E-01
foot [international]	1.000 002	1.000 002 0E+00
furlong [US, survey]	0.001 515 2	1.515 151 5E-03
inch [based on US, survey foot]	12	1.200 002 0E+01
inch [international]	12.000 024	1.200 002 4E+01
link [Gunter or US, survey]	1.515 151 5	1.515 151 5E+00
link [Ramden or Engineer]	1.000 002	1.000 002 0E+00
meter	0.304 800 6	3.048 006 1E-01
mile [international]	0.000 189 4	1.893 943 2E-04
mile [US, statute]	0.000 189 4	1.893 939 4E-04
mile [US, survey]	0.000 189 4	1.893 939 4E-04
out [US, survey]	0.003 030 3	3.030 303 0E-03
pace [geometrical]	0.02	2.000 004 0E-02
pace [US, survey]	0.4	4.000 000 0E-01
perch [US, survey]	0.060 606 1	6.060 606 1E-02
pole [US, survey]	0.060 606 1	6.060 606 1E-02
range [US, survey]	0.000 031 6	3.156 565 7E-05
rod [US, survey]	0.060 606 1	6.060 606 1E-02
township [US, survey]	0.000 031 6	3.156 565 7E-05
vara [US, survey, California]	0.363 636 4	3.636 363 6E-01
vara [US, survey, Texas]	0.36	3.600 000 0E-01
yard [based on US, survey foot]	0.333 333 3	3.333 333 3E-01
yard [international]	0.333 334	3.333 340 0E-01
yard [UK]	0.333 334 6	3.333 345 8E-01

foot °C/watt   \<thermal resistivity\>

	Standard	Scientific
meter kelvin/watt	0.304 8	3.048 000 0E-01

foot of air [dry, CO_2 free, at 101325 Pa and 0 °C]   \<pressure\>

	Standard	Scientific
pascal	3.864 088 8	3.864 088 8E+00

foot of air [dry, CO_2 free, at 101325 Pa and 15 °C]   \<pressure\>

	Standard	Scientific
pascal	3.662 293 1	3.662 293 1E+00

foot of mercury [0 °C, by convention]   \<pressure\>

	Standard	Scientific
atmosphere [standard]	0.401 052 7	4.010 526 9E-01
atmosphere [technical]	0.414 378 7	4.143 786 5E-01
bar	0.406 366 6	4.063 666 4E-01
centimeter of mercury [0 °C, by convention]	30.48	3.048 000 0E+01
centimeter of water [4 °C, by convention]	414.378 65	4.143 786 5E+02
decibar	4.063 666 4	4.063 666 4E+00
foot of water [4 °C, by convention]	13.595 1	1.359 510 0E+01
gram-force/square centimeter	414.378 65	4.143 786 5E+02
inch of mercury [0 °C, by convention]	12	1.200 000 0E+01
inch of water [4 °C, by convention]	163.141 2	1.631 412 0E+02
kilogram-force/square centimeter	0.414 378 7	4.143 786 5E-01
kilopond/square centimeter	0.414 378 7	4.143 786 5E-01
kip/square foot	0.848 714 4	8.487 143 7E-01
millimeter of mercury [0 °C, by convention]	304.8	3.048 000 0E+02
millimeter of water [4 °C, by convention]	4,143.786 5	4.143 786 5E+03
newton/square millimeter	0.040 636 7	4.063 666 4E-02
ounce-force/square inch	94.301 596	9.430 159 6E+01
pascal	40,636.664	4.063 666 4E+04
pound-force/square inch	5.893 849 8	5.893 849 8E+00
sthene/square meter [France]	40.636 664	4.063 666 4E+01
ton-force/square foot [short]	0.424 357 2	4.243 571 8E-01
ton-force/square meter [metric]	4.143 786 5	4.143 786 5E+00

torr	304.800 04	3.048 000 4E+02

foot of water [4 °C, by convention]   **<pressure>**

atmosphere [standard]	0.029 499 8	2.949 979 7E-02
atmosphere [technical]	0.030 48	3.048 000 0E-02
bar	0.029 890 7	2.989 066 9E-02
centibar	2.989 066 9	2.989 066 9E+00
centihg	2.241 984 2	2.241 984 2E+00
centimeter of mercury [0 °C, by convention]	2.241 984 2	2.241 984 2E+00
centimeter of water [4 °C, by convention]	30.48	3.048 000 0E+01
foot of mercury [0 °C, by convention]	0.073 555 9	7.355 591 4E-02
gram-force/square centimeter	30.48	3.048 000 0E+01
inch of mercury [0 °C, by convention]	0.882 671	8.826 709 6E-01
inch of water [4 °C, by convention]	12	1.200 000 0E+01
kilogram-force/square meter	304.8	3.048 000 0E+02
kilopascal	2.989 066 9	2.989 066 9E+00
kilopond/square meter	304.8	3.048 000 0E+02
kip/square foot	0.062 428	6.242 796 1E-02
millimeter of mercury [0 °C, by convention]	22.419 842	2.241 984 2E+01
millimeter of water [4 °C, by convention]	304.8	3.048 000 0E+02
ounce-force/square inch	6.936 440 1	6.936 440 1E+00
pascal	2.989.066 9	2.989 066 9E+03
pieze [France]	2.989 066 9	2.989 066 9E+00
pound-force/square foot	62.427 961	6.242 796 1E+01
sthene/square meter [France]	2.989 066 9	2.989 066 9E+00
ton-force/square foot [short]	0.031 214	3.121 398 0E-02
ton-force/square meter [metric]	0.304 8	3.048 000 0E-01
torr	22.419 846	2.241 984 6E+01

foot ounce-force   **<torque>**

centimeter gram-force	864.093 46	8.640 934 6E+02
foot pound-force	0.062 5	6.250 000 0E-02
foot poundal	2.010 878	2.010 878 0E+00
inch ounce-force	12	1.200 000 0E+01
meter kilogram-force	0.008 640 9	8.640 934 6E-03
newton meter	0.084 738 6	8.473 862 2E-02

foot pound-force   **<energy>**

Btu [I.T.]	0.001 285 1	1.285 067 5E-03
calorie [I.T.]	0.323 831 6	3.238 315 5E-01
calorie [mean]	0.323 582 7	3.235 826 9E-01
calorie [thermoc.]	0.324 048 3	3.240 482 7E-01
centigrade heat unit [I.T.]	0.000 713 9	7.139 263 7E-04
cubic centimeter atmosphere	13.380 883	1.338 088 3E+01
dyne centimeter	>>>	1.355 817 9E+07
erg	>>>	1.355 817 9E+07
foot poundal	32.174 049	3.217 404 9E+01
frigorie [France]	0.000 323 9	3.239 089 2E-04
gram calorie	0.323 908 9	3.239 089 2E-01
horsepower hour	0.000 000 5	5.050 505 1E-07
horsepower hour [metric]	0.000 000 5	5.120 553 9E-07
inch ounce-force	192	1.920 000 0E+02
inch pound-force	12	1.200 000 0E+01
joule	1.355 817 9	1.355 817 9E+00
kilogram square meter/square second	1.355 817 9	1.355 817 9E+00
kilopond meter	0.138 255	1.382 549 5E-01
liter atmosphere	0.013 380 9	1.338 088 3E-02
megaerg	13.558 179	1.355 817 9E+01
megalerg	13.558 179	1.355 817 9E+01
meter kilogram-force	0.138 255	1.382 549 5E-01
newton meter	1.355 817 9	1.355 817 9E+00
watthour	0.000 376 6	3.766 161 0E-04
wattsecond	1.355 817 9	1.355 817 9E+00

foot pound-force   **<torque>**

foot ounce-force	16	1.600 000 0E+01

Convert From	<Type of Unit>	
Convert To	Standard	Scientific

foot pound-force/hour **\<power\>**
Btu/hour [I.T.]	0.001 285 1	1.285 067 5E–03
Btu/hour [thermoc.]	0.001 285 9	1.285 927 5E–03
calorie/hour [I.T.]	0.323 831 6	3.238 315 5E–01
calorie/hour [thermoc.]	0.324 048 3	3.240 482 7E–01
centigrade heat unit/hour [mean]	0.000 713 4	7.133 758 8E–04
cubic meter atmosphere/hour	13.380 883	1.338 088 3E+01
dyne centimeter/second	3,766.161	3.766 161 0E+03
erg/second	3,766.161	3.766 161 0E+03
foot poundal/hour	32.174 049	3.217 404 9E+01
gram-force centimeter/second	3.840 415 4	3.840 415 4E+00
horsepower	0.000 000 5	5.050 505 1E–07
horsepower [metric]	0.000 000 5	5.120 553 9E–07
inch ounce-force revolution/minute	0.509 295 8	5.092 958 2E–01
joule/hour	1.355 817 9	1.355 817 9E+00
kilocalorie/hour [I.T.]	0.000 323 8	3.238 315 5E–04
kilogram-force meter/hour	0.138 255	1.382 549 5E–01
kilopond meter/hour	0.138 255	1.382 549 5E–01
lumen [green light at 100% efficiency]	0.257 982	2.579 820 3E–01
lumen [green light at 5,550 angstrom]	0.256 099	2.560 989 5E–01
lumen [monochromatic radiation of 540 THz]	0.257 228 8	2.572 287 9E–01
milliwatt	0.376 616 1	3.766 161 0E–01
newton meter/hour	1.355 817 9	1.355 817 9E+00
volt ampere	0.000 376 6	3.766 161 0E–04
watt	0.000 376 6	3.766 161 0E–04

foot pound-force/inch **\<torque/unit length\>**
newton meter/meter	53.378 659	5.337 865 9E+01

foot pound-force/minute **\<power\>**
Btu/hour [I.T., pre-1956]	0.077 105 2	7.710 520 6E–02
Btu/hour [thermoc.]	0.077 155 6	7.715 564 7E–02
calorie/hour [I.T.]	19.429 893	1.942 989 3E+01
calorie/hour [thermoc.]	19.442 896	1.944 289 6E+01
centigrade heat unit/hour [mean]	0.042 802 6	4.280 255 3E–02
centiwatt	2.259 696 6	2.259 696 6E+00
cubic meter atmosphere/minute	13.380 883	1.338 088 3E+01
dyne centimeter/second	225,969.66	2.259 696 6E+05
erg/second	225,969.66	2.259 696 6E+05
foot pound-force/hour	60	6.000 000 0E+01
foot poundal/minute	32.174 049	3.217 404 9E+01
gram-force centimeter/second	230.424 92	2.304 249 2E+02
horsepower	0.000 030 3	3.030 303 0E–05
horsepower [metric]	0.000 030 7	3.072 332 3E–05
joule/minute	1.355 817 9	1.355 817 9E+00
kilocalorie/hour [I.T.]	0.019 429 9	1.942 989 3E–02
kilogram square meter/cubic second	0.022 597	2.259 696 6E–02
kilogram-force meter/hour	8.295 297 3	8.295 297 3E+00
kilopond meter/hour	8.295 297 3	8.295 297 3E+00
lumen [green light at 100% efficiency]	15.478 922	1.547 892 2E+01
lumen [green light at 5,550 angstrom]	15.365 937	1.536 593 7E+01
newton meter/minute	1.355 817 9	1.355 817 9E+00
pound square foot/cubic second	0.536 234 1	5.362 341 4E–01
volt ampere	0.022 597	2.259 696 6E–02
watt	0.022 597	2.259 696 6E–02

foot pound-force/pound **\<specific thermodynamic energy\>**
joule/kilogram	2.989 066 9	2.989 066 9E+00

foot pound-force/pound °F **\<specific heat capacity\>**
joule/kilogram kelvin	5.380 320 5	5.380 320 5E+00

foot pound-force/second **\<power\>**
Btu/hour [I.T.]	4.626 242 9	4.626 242 9E+00
Btu/hour [thermoc.]	4.629 338 8	4.629 338 8E+00
calorie/minute [I.T.]	19.429 893	1.942 989 3E+01
calorie/minute [thermoc.]	19.442 896	1.944 289 6E+01

	Standard	Scientific
centigrade heat unit/hour [mean]	2.568 153 2	2.568 153 2E+00
cubic meter atmosphere/second	13.380 883	1.338 088 3E+01
dyne centimeter/second	>>>	1.355 817 9E+07
erg/second	>>>	1.355 817 9E+07
foot pound-force/minute	60	6.000 000 0E+01
foot poundal/second	32.174 049	3.217 404 9E+01
gram-force centimeter/second	13,825.495	1.382 549 5E+04
horsepower	0.001 818 2	1.818 181 8E-03
horsepower [metric]	0.001 843 4	1.843 399 4E-03
joule/second	1.355 817 9	1.355 817 9E+00
kilocalorie/hour [I.T.]	1.165 793 6	1.165 793 6E+00
kilogram square meter/cubic second	1.355 817 9	1.355 817 9E+00
kilogram-force meter/minute	8.295 297 3	8.295 297 3E+00
kilopond meter/minute	8.295 297 3	8.295 297 3E+00
lumen [green light at 100% efficiency]	928.735 29	9.287 352 9E+02
lumen [green light at 5,550 angstrom]	921.956 23	9.219 562 3E+02
newton meter/second	1.355 817 9	1.355 817 9E+00
pound square foot/cubic second	32.174 049	3.217 404 9E+01
volt ampere	1.355 817 9	1.355 817 9E+00
watt	1.355 817 9	1.355 817 9E+00
foot poundal		**\<energy\>**
Btu [I.T.]	0.000 039 9	3.994 111 8E-05
calorie [I.T.]	0.010 065	1.006 499 2E-02
calorie [mean]	0.010 057 3	1.005 725 8E-02
calorie [thermoc.]	0.010 071 7	1.007 172 8E-02
centimeter gram-force	429.709 53	4.297 095 3E+02
cubic centimeter atmosphere	0.415 890 6	4.158 905 5E-01
cubic foot atmosphere	0.000 014 7	1.468 703 6E-05
dyne centimeter	421,401.1	4.214 011 0E+05
erg	421,401.1	4.214 011 0E+05
foot pound-force	0.031 081	3.108 095 0E-02
gram calorie	0.010 067 4	1.006 739 7E-02
horsepower hour	<<<	1.569 745 0E-08
horsepower hour [metric]	<<<	1.591 516 8E-08
inch ounce-force	5.967 542 4	5.967 542 4E+00
inch pound-force	0.372 971 4	3.729 714 0E-01
joule	0.042 140 1	4.214 011 0E-02
kilogram square meter/square second	0.042 140 1	4.214 011 0E-02
kilopond meter	0.004 297 1	4.297 095 3E-03
kilowatthour	<<<	1.170 558 6E-08
megaerg	0.421 401 1	4.214 011 0E-01
megalerg	0.421 401 1	4.214 011 0E-01
meter kilogram-force	0.004 297 1	4.297 095 3E-03
newton meter	0.042 140 1	4.214 011 0E-02
watthour	0.000 011 7	1.170 558 6E-05
wattsecond	0.042 140 1	4.214 011 0E-02
foot poundal		**\<torque\>**
foot ounce-force	0.497 295 2	4.972 952 0E-01
foot poundal/hour		**\<power\>**
Btu/hour [I.T.]	0.000 039 9	3.994 111 8E-05
Btu/hour [thermoc.]	0.000 04	3.996 784 9E-05
calorie/hour [I.T.]	0.010 065	1.006 499 2E-02
calorie/hour [thermoc.]	0.010 071 7	1.007 172 8E-02
centigrade heat unit/hour [mean]	0.000 022 2	2.217 240 0E-05
cubic meter atmosphere/hour	0.415 890 6	4.158 905 5E-01
dyne centimeter/second	117.055 86	1.170 558 6E+02
erg/second	117.055 86	1.170 558 6E+02
foot pound-force/hour	0.031 081	3.108 095 0E-02
foot poundal/minute	0.016 666 7	1.666 666 7E-02
gram-force centimeter/minute	7.161 825 6	7.161 825 6E+00
horsepower	<<<	1.569 745 0E-08
horsepower [UK]	<<<	1.569 745 0E-08
joule/hour	0.042 140 1	4.214 011 0E-02

Convert From Convert To	Standard	<Type of Unit> Scientific
kilocalorie/hour [I.T.]	0.000 010 1	1.006 499 2E-05
kilogram-force meter/hour	0.004 297 1	4.297 095 3E-03
kilopond meter/hour	0.004 297 1	4.297 095 3E-03
newton meter/hour	0.042 140 1	4.214 011 0E-02
volt ampere	0.000 011 7	1.170 558 6E-05
watt	0.000 011 7	1.170 558 6E-05
foot poundal/minute		**<power>**
Btu/hour [I.T.]	0.002 396 5	2.396 467 1E-03
Btu/hour [thermoc.]	0.002 398 1	2.398 070 8E-03
calorie/hour [I.T.]	0.603 899 5	6.038 995 4E-01
calorie/hour [thermoc.]	0.604 303 7	6.043 036 8E-01
centigrade heat unit/hour [mean]	0.001 330 3	1.330 344 0E-03
cubic meter atmosphere/hour	24.953 433	2.495 343 3E+01
dyne centimeter/second	7,023.351 7	7.023 351 7E+03
erg/second	7,023.351 7	7.023 351 7E+03
foot pound-force/hour	1.864 857	1.864 857 0E+00
foot poundal/hour	60	6.000 000 0E+01
gram-force centimeter/second	7.161 825 6	7.161 825 6E+00
horsepower	0.000 000 9	9.418 469 7E-07
horsepower [metric]	0.000 001	9.549 100 8E-07
joule/hour	2.528 406 6	2.528 406 6E+00
kilocalorie/hour [I.T.]	0.000 603 9	6.038 995 4E-04
kilogram-force meter/hour	0.257 825 7	2.578 257 2E-01
kilopond meter/hour	0.257 825 7	2.578 257 2E-01
lumen [green light at 100% efficiency]	0.481 099 6	4.810 995 9E-01
lumen [green light at 5,550 angstrom]	0.477 587 9	4.775 879 3E-01
milliwatt	0.702 335 2	7.023 351 7E-01
newton meter/hour	2.528 406 6	2.528 406 6E+00
pound square foot/cubic second	0.016 666 7	1.666 666 7E-02
volt ampere	0.000 702 3	7.023 351 7E-04
watt	0.000 702 3	7.023 351 7E-04
foot poundal/second		**<power>**
Btu/hour [I.T.]	0.143 788	1.437 880 2E-01
Btu/hour [thermoc.]	0.143 884 3	1.438 842 5E-01
calorie/hour [I.T.]	36.233 973	3.623 397 3E+01
calorie/hour [thermoc.]	36.258 221	3.625 822 1E+01
centigrade heat unit/hour [mean]	0.079 820 6	7.982 064 1E-02
centiwatt	4.214 011	4.214 011 0E+00
cubic meter atmosphere/minute	24.953 433	2.495 343 3E+01
dyne centimeter/second	421,401.1	4.214 011 0E+05
erg/second	421,401.1	4.214 011 0E+05
foot pound-force/minute	1.864 857	1.864 857 0E+00
foot poundal/minute	60	6.000 000 0E+01
gram-force centimeter/second	429.709 53	4.297 095 3E+02
horsepower	0.000 056 5	5.651 081 8E-05
horsepower [metric]	0.000 057 3	5.729 460 5E-05
joule/minute	2.528 406 6	2.528 406 6E+00
kilocalorie/hour [I.T.]	0.036 234	3.623 397 3E-02
kilogram square meter/cubic second	0.042 140 1	4.214 011 0E-02
kilogram-force meter/hour	15.469 543	1.546 954 3E+01
kilopond meter/hour	15.469 543	1.546 954 3E+01
lumen [green light at 100% efficiency]	28.865 975	2.886 597 5E+01
lumen [green light at 5,550 angstrom]	28.655 276	2.865 527 6E+01
newton meter/minute	2.528 406 6	2.528 406 6E+00
pound square foot/cubic second	1	1.000 000 0E+00
volt ampere	0.042 140 1	4.214 011 0E-02
watt	0.042 140 1	4.214 011 0E-02
foot/day		**<velocity>**
centimeter/hour	1.27	1.270 000 0E+00
hectometer/day	0.003 048	3.048 000 0E-03
inch/day	12	1.200 000 0E+01
knot [international]	0.000 006 9	6.857 451 4E-06
meter/day	0.304 8	3.048 000 0E-01

| Convert From | | <Type of Unit> |
Convert To	Standard	Scientific
meter/second--	0.000 003 5	3.527 777 8E-06
mile/day---	0.000 189 4	1.893 939 4E-04
millimeter/hour---	12.7	1.270 000 0E+01
nautical mile/day [international]-------------------------	0.000 164 6	1.645 788 3E-04
yard/day--	0.333 333 3	3.333 333 3E-01

foot/°F   **\<geothermal step\>**

	Standard	Scientific
meter/kelvin--	0.548 64	5.486 400 0E-01

foot/hour   **\<velocity\>**

	Standard	Scientific
centimeter/hour--	30.48	3.048 000 0E+01
dekameter/day---	0.731 52	7.315 200 0E-01
foot/day--	24	2.400 000 0E+01
hectometer/day--	0.073 152	7.315 200 0E-02
inch/hour---	12	1.200 000 0E+01
knot [international] --------------------------------------	0.000 164 6	1.645 788 3E-04
meter/day--	7.315 2	7.315 200 0E+00
meter/second--	0.000 084 7	8.466 666 7E-05
mile/day--	0.004 545 5	4.545 466 6E-03
millimeter/minute--	5.08	5.080 000 0E+00
yard/day--	8	8.000 000 0E+00

foot/minute   **\<velocity\>**

	Standard	Scientific
benz--	0.005 08	5.080 000 0E-03
centimeter/minute---------------------------------------	30.48	3.048 000 0E+01
dekameter/hour---	1.828 8	1.828 800 0E+00
foot/hour---	60	6.000 000 0E+01
hectometer/day--	4.389 12	4.389 120 0E+00
inch/minute---	12	1.200 000 0E+01
kilometer/day--	0.438 912	4.389 120 0E-01
knot [international] --------------------------------------	0.009 874 7	9.874 730 0E-03
meter/hour---	18.288	1.828 800 0E+01
meter/second--	0.005 08	5.080 000 0E-03
mile/day--	0.272 727 3	2.727 272 7E-01
millimeter/second---------------------------------------	5.08	5.080 000 0E+00
nautical mile/day [international]-------------------------	0.236 993 5	2.369 935 2E-01
yard/hour---	20	2.000 000 0E+01

foot/pound-force   **\<spectral cross-section\>**

	Standard	Scientific
meter/newton--	0.068 521 8	6.852 176 6E-02
square meter/joule--------------------------------------	0.068 521 8	6.852 176 6E-02
square second/kilogram--------------------------------	0.068 521 8	6.852 176 6E-02

foot/second   **\<velocity\>**

	Standard	Scientific
centimeter/second--------------------------------------	30.48	3.048 000 0E+01
dekameter/minute---------------------------------------	1.828 8	1.828 800 0E+00
foot/minute---	60	6.000 000 0E+01
hectometer/hour---	10.972 8	1.097 280 0E+01
inch/second--	12	1.200 000 0E+01
kilometer/hour---	1.097 28	1.097 280 0E+00
knot [international] --------------------------------------	0.592 483 8	5.924 838 0E-01
meter/minute--	18.288	1.828 800 0E+01
meter/second--	0.304 8	3.048 000 0E-01
mile/day--	16.363 636 4	1.636 363 6E+01
millimeter/second---------------------------------------	304.8	3.048 000 0E+02
nautical mile/day [international]-------------------------	14.219 611 2	1.421 961 1E+01
yard/minute--	20	2.000 000 0E+01

foot/square second   **\<acceleration\>**

	Standard	Scientific
celo---	1	1.000 000 0E+00
galileo--	30.48	3.048 000 0E+01
g$_n$ [due to gravity] ------------------------------------	0.031 081	3.108 095 0E-02
leo--	0.030 48	3.048 000 0E-02
meter/square second-----------------------------------	0.304 8	3.048 000 0E-01

foot^4   **\<second moment of area\>**

	Standard	Scientific
inch^4---	20,736	2.073 600 0E+04
meter^4---	0.008 631	8.630 974 8E-03

Convert From Convert To	Standard	<Type of Unit> Scientific
footcandle		<illuminance>
lumen/square foot	1	1.000 000 0E+00
lumen/square meter	10.763 91	1.076 391 0E+01
lux	10.763 91	1.076 391 0E+01
nox	10,763.91	1.076 391 0E+04
phot	0.001 076 4	1.076 391 0E−03
footcandle second		<light exposure>
lumen second/square foot	1	1.000 000 0E+00
lumen second/square inch	0.006 944 4	6.944 444 4E−03
lux second	10.763 91	1.076 391 0E+01
milliphot second	1.076 391	1.076 391 0E+00
footlambert		<luminance>
apostilb [international]	10.763 91	1.076 391 0E+01
blondel	10.763 91	1.076 391 0E+01
candela/square foot	0.318 309 9	3.183 098 9E−01
candela/square meter	3.426 259 1	3.426 259 1E+00
millilambert	1.076 391	1.076 391 0E+00
nit	3.426 259 1	3.426 259 1E+00
stilb	0.000 342 6	3.426 259 1E−04
foring [Iceland]		<mass, special - see page 29>
gram	4,994	4.994 000 0E+03
forten [Turkey]		<volume, special - see page 29>
liter	400	4.000 000 0E+02
fortin [Turkey]		<volume, special - see page 29>
hectoliter	1.41	1.410 000 0E+00
fortnight		<time>
day	14	1.400 000 0E+01
week	2	2.000 000 0E+00
fot [Finland]		<length, special - see page 29>
centimeter	26.69	2.669 000 0E+01
fot [Norway]		<length, special - see page 29>
centimeter	31.375	3.137 500 0E+01
fot [Sweden]		<length, special - see page 29>
centimeter	29.69	2.969 000 0E+01
fount [Russia, apothecary]		<mass, special - see page 29>
gram	358.323 4	3.583 234 0E+02
founte [Russia]		<mass, special - see page 29>
gram	409.5	4.095 000 0E+02
fout [Russia]		<mass, special - see page 29>
gram	409.512 4	4.095 124 0E+02
frail [Spain]		<mass, special - see page 29>
kilogram	22.7	2.270 000 0E+01
franklin		<electric charge>
ampere second	<<<	3.335 641 0E−10
coulomb	<<<	3.335 641 0E−10
electrostatic unit of charge [cgs system]	1	1.000 000 0E+00
gaussian electric charge	1	1.000 000 0E+00
statcoulomb	1	1.000 000 0E+00
franklin centimeter		<electric dipole moment>
coulomb meter	<<<	3.335 641 0E−12
debye unit	>>>	1.000 000 0E+18
statcoulomb centimeter	1	1.000 000 0E+00
franklin/centimeter		<electric dipole moment/unit area>
coulomb/meter	<<<	3.335 641 0E−08
statcoulomb/centimeter	1	1.000 000 0E+00
franklin/cubic centimeter		<electric charge density>
coulomb/cubic meter	0.000 333 6	3.335 641 0E−04
millicoulomb/cubic meter	0.333 564 1	3.335 641 0E−01

statcoulomb/cubic centimeter ----- 1 --- 1.000 000 0E+00

franklin/second \<electric current\>
abampere ----- \<<--- 3.335 641 0E−11
ampere ----- \<<< --- 3.335 641 0E−10
electrostatic unit of current [cgs system] ----- 1 --- 1.000 000 0E+00
gaussian electric current ----- 1 --- 1.000 000 0E+00
statampere ----- 1 --- 1.000 000 0E+00

franklin/square centimeter \<electric flux density\>
abcoulomb/square centimeter ----- \<<--- 3.335 641 0E−11
ampere hour/square meter ----- \<<--- 9.265 669 3E−10
coulomb/square inch ----- \<<--- 2.152 022 1E−09
coulomb/square meter ----- 0.000 003 3 --- 3.335 641 0E−06
microcoulomb/square meter ----- 3.335 641 --- 3.335 641 0E+00
statcoulomb/square centimeter ----- 1 --- 1.000 000 0E+00

frasala [Ethiopia] \<mass, special - see page 29\>
kilogram ----- 17 --- 1.700 000 0E+01

frasala [Somalia] \<mass, special - see page 29\>
kilogram ----- 16.128 --- 1.612 800 0E+01

frasala [Tanzania] \<mass, special - see page 29\>
kilogram ----- 16.33 --- 1.633 000 0E+01

frasala [Yemen] \<mass, special - see page 29\>
kilogram ----- 12.7 --- 1.270 000 0E+01

frasco [Argentina] \<volume, special - see page 29\>
liter ----- 2.375 --- 2.375 000 0E+00

frasco [Cuba] \<volume, special - see page 29\>
liter ----- 2.175 --- 2.175 000 0E+00

frasco [Mexico] \<volume, special - see page 29\>
liter ----- 2.366 --- 2.366 000 0E+00

frasco [Paraguay] \<volume, special - see page 29\>
liter ----- 3.029 --- 3.029 000 0E+00

frasila [Ethiopia] \<mass, special - see page 29\>
kilogram ----- 17 --- 1.700 000 0E+01

frasila [Somalia] \<mass, special - see page 29\>
kilogram ----- 16.128 --- 1.612 800 0E+01

frasila [Tanganyika] \<volume, special - see page 29\>
liter ----- 24 --- 2.400 000 0E+01

frasila [Tanzania] \<mass, special - see page 29\>
kilogram ----- 15.88 --- 1.588 000 0E+01

frasila [Yemen] \<mass, special - see page 29\>
kilogram ----- 12.7 --- 1.270 000 0E+01

frasilla [Ethiopia] \<mass, special - see page 29\>
kilogram ----- 17 --- 1.700 000 0E+01

frasla [Somalia] \<mass, special - see page 29\>
kilogram ----- 16.308 --- 1.630 800 0E+01

frasla [Tanzania] \<mass, special - see page 29\>
kilogram ----- 16.33 --- 1.633 000 0E+01

frasla [Yemen] \<mass, special - see page 29\>
kilogram ----- 11.22 --- 1.122 000 0E+01

frasoulla [Ethiopia] \<mass, special - see page 29\>
kilogram ----- 17 --- 1.700 000 0E+01

frasoulla [Somalia] \<mass, special - see page 29\>
kilogram ----- 16.128 --- 1.612 800 0E+01

frasoulla [Tanzania] \<mass, special - see page 29\>
kilogram ----- 16.33 --- 1.633 000 0E+01

frazila [Tanzania] \<mass, special - see page 29\>
kilogram ----- 16.33 --- 1.633 000 0E+01

Convert From Convert To	<Type of Unit>	
	Standard	Scientific

frazula [Ethiopia, coffee] <mass, special - see page 29>
kilogram -- 16.75 ---- 1.675 000 0E+01

freight ton <volume>
board foot -- 480 ---- 4.800 000 0E+02
bushel [US, dry] -- 32.142 558 ---- 3.214 255 8E+01
cord foot [timber] -------------------------------------- 2.5 ---- 2.500 000 0E+00
cubic foot -- 40 ---- 4.000 000 0E+01
cubic inch -- 69,120 ---- 6.912 000 0E+04
cubic meter -- 1.132 673 9 ---- 1.132 673 9E+00
cubic yard --- 1.481 481 5 ---- 1.481 481 5E+00
English water ton [UK] -------------------------------- 1.112 292 ---- 1.112 292 0E+00
kiloliter --- 1.132 673 9 ---- 1.132 673 9E+00
liter --- 1,132.673 9 ---- 1.132 673 9E+03
measurement ton -------------------------------------- 1 ---- 1.000 000 0E+00
ocean ton -- 1 ---- 1.000 000 0E+00
petrograd standard ------------------------------------ 0.242 424 2 ---- 2.424 242 4E−01
register ton -- 0.4 ---- 4.000 000 0E−01
shipping ton --- 1 ---- 1.000 000 0E+00
stere -- 1.132 673 9 ---- 1.132 673 9E+00
thousand board foot ----------------------------------- 0.48 ---- 4.800 000 0E−01
thousand cubic foot ----------------------------------- 0.04 ---- 4.000 000 0E−02

fresnel <frequency>
hertz --- >>> 1.000 000 0E+12
terahertz --- 1 ---- 1.000 000 0E+00

frigorie [France] <energy>
Btu [I.T.] --- 3.967 372 9 ---- 3.967 372 9E+00
Btu [mean] --- 3.964 313 8 ---- 3.964 313 8E+00
Btu [thermoc.] --- 3.970 027 9 ---- 3.970 027 9E+00
calorie [kilogram, I.T.] -------------------------------- 0.999 761 2 ---- 9.997 611 5E−01
calorie [kilogram, mean] ------------------------------ 0.998 992 8 ---- 9.989 928 4E−01
calorie [kilogram, thermoc.] -------------------------- 1.000 430 2 ---- 1.000 430 2E+00
calorie [nutritional] ----------------------------------- 1.000 430 2 ---- 1.000 430 2E+00
centigrade heat unit [I.T.] ---------------------------- 2.204 096 1 ---- 2.204 096 1E+00
cheval vapeur heure [France] ------------------------- 0.001 580 9 ---- 1.580 862 3E−03
cubic foot atmosphere -------------------------------- 1.458 871 2 ---- 1.458 871 2E+00
foot pound-force -------------------------------------- 3,087.287 6 ---- 3.087 287 6E+03
foot poundal --- 99,330.543 ---- 9.933 054 3E+04
gram calorie --- 1,000 ---- 1.000 000 0E+03
horsepower hour -------------------------------------- 0.001 559 2 ---- 1.559 236 2E−03
horsepower hour [metric] ----------------------------- 0.001 580 9 ---- 1.580 862 3E−03
inch ounce-force -------------------------------------- 592,759.23 ---- 5.927 592 3E+05
inch pound-force -------------------------------------- 37,047.452 ---- 3.704 745 2E+04
joule -- 4,185.8 ---- 4.185 800 0E+03
kilocalorie [I.T.] -------------------------------------- 0.999 761 2 ---- 9.997 611 5E−01
kilocalorie [mean] ------------------------------------ 0.998 992 8 ---- 9.989 928 4E−01
kilocalorie [thermoc.] -------------------------------- 1.000 430 2 ---- 1.000 430 2E+00
kilogram calorie [15 °C, NBS, 1939] ----------------- 1 ---- 1.000 000 0E+00
liter atmosphere --------------------------------------- 41.310 634 ---- 4.131 063 4E+01
watthour -- 1.162 722 2 ---- 1.162 722 2E+00

fudder [Luxembourg] <volume, special - see page 29>
hectoliter --- 10 ---- 1.000 000 0E+01

fuder [Germany] <volume, special - see page 29>
hectoliter --- 8.244 ---- 8.244 000 0E+00

fuder [Netherlands, wine] <volume, special - see page 29>
hectoliter --- 10 ---- 1.000 000 0E+01

fuen [China, troy] <mass, special - see page 29>
gram -- 0.378 ---- 3.780 000 0E−01

fun [Hong Kong] <length, special - see page 29>
millimeter -- 3.714 75 ---- 3.714 750 0E+00

funal <force>
kilonewton --- 1 ---- 1.000 000 0E+00

newton	1,000	1.000 000 0E+03
sthene	1	1.000 000 0E+00
ton meter/square second [metric]	1	1.000 000 0E+00

funda [Russia, troy] — <mass, special - see page 29>
| gram | 409.16 | 4.091 600 0E+02 |

funt [Poland] — <mass, special - see page 29>
| gram | 500 | 5.000 000 0E+02 |

funt [Russia] — <mass, special - see page 29>
| gram | 409.5 | 4.095 000 0E+02 |

funta [Russia, troy] — <mass, special - see page 29>
| gram | 409.16 | 4.091 600 0E+02 |

furlong [Palestine, ancient] — <length, special - see page 29>
| meter | 185 | 1.850 000 0E+02 |

furlong [US, survey] — <length>
cable length [US, survey]	0.916 666 7	9.166 666 7E-01
chain [Gunter or US, survey]	10	1.000 000 0E+01
chain [Ramden or Engineer]	6.600 013 2	6.600 013 2E+00
fathom [US, survey]	110	1.100 000 0E+02
foot [international]	660.001 32	6.600 013 2E+02
foot [US, survey]	660	6.600 000 0E+02
inch [based on US, survey foot]	7,920	7.920 000 0E+03
inch [international]	7,920.015 8	7.920 015 8E+03
league [US, statute]	0.041 666 7	4.166 666 7E-02
link [Gunter or US, survey]	1,000	1.000 000 0E+03
link [Ramden or Engineer]	660.001 32	6.600 013 2E+02
meter	201.168 4	2.011 684 0E+02
mile [international]	0.125 000 3	1.250 002 5E-01
mile [US, statute]	0.125	1.250 000 0E-01
mile [US, survey]	0.125	1.250 000 0E-01
out [US, survey]	2	2.000 000 0E+00
pace [geometrical]	13.200 026	1.320 002 6E+01
pace [US, survey]	264	2.640 000 0E+02
perch [US, survey]	40	4.000 000 0E+01
pole [US, survey]	40	4.000 000 0E+01
range [US, survey]	0.020 833 3	2.083 333 3E-02
rod [US, survey]	40	4.000 000 0E+01
township [US, survey]	0.020 833 3	2.083 333 3E-02
vara [US, survey, California]	240	2.400 000 0E+02
vara [US, survey, Texas]	237.6	2.376 000 0E+02
yard [based on US, survey foot]	220	2.200 000 0E+02
yard [international]	220.000 44	2.200 004 4E+02
yard [UK]	220.000 82	2.200 008 2E+02

furlong/fortnight — <velocity>
| mile/hour [Campbell factor] | 0.000 372 | 3.720 245 6E-04 |

fuss [Austria] — <length, special - see page 29>
| meter | 0.316 08 | 3.160 800 0E-01 |

fuss [Germany] — <length, special - see page 29>
| meter | 0.291 86 | 2.918 600 0E-01 |

fuss [Russia] — <length, special - see page 29>
| centimeter | 35.6 | 3.560 000 0E+01 |

fuss [Switzerland] — <length, special - see page 29>
| centimeter | 30 | 3.000 000 0E+01 |

fusz [Austria] — <length, special - see page 29>
| centimeter | 31.608 | 3.160 800 0E+01 |

fut [Russia] — <length, special - see page 29>
| centimeter | 30.48 | 3.048 000 0E+01 |

futtermassel [Austria] — <volume, special - see page 29>
| liter | 0.96 | 9.600 000 0E-01 |

g-unit \<acceleration\>
foot/square second	32.174 048 6	3.217 404 9E+01
galileo	980.665	9.806 650 0E+02
gₙ [due to gravity]	1	1.000 000 0E+00
grav	1	1.000 000 0E+00
meter/square second	9.806 65	9.806 650 0E+00

gab [Hebrew, ancient] \<volume, special - see page 29\>
liter	1.3	1.300 000 0E+00

gadula [Libya] \<area, special - see page 29\>
square meter	12.25	1.225 000 0E+01

gal \<acceleration\>
centimeter/square second	1	1.000 000 0E+00
foot/square second	0.032 808 4	3.280 839 9E−02
galileo	1	1.000 000 0E+00
gₙ [due to gravity]	0.001 019 7	1.019 716 2E−03
leo	0.001	1.000 000 0E−03
meter/square second	0.01	1.000 000 0E−02

gal/centimeter \<acceleration gradient\>
Eötvös unit	>>>	1.000 000 0E+09
gal/foot	30.48	3.048 000 0E+01
gal/inch	2.54	2.540 000 0E+00
gal/meter	100	1.000 000 0E+02

gal/foot \<acceleration gradient\>
gal/centimeter	0.032 808 4	3.280 839 9E−02
gal/inch	0.083 333 3	8.333 333 3E−02

gal/inch \<acceleration gradient\>
gal/centimeter	0.393 700 8	3.937 007 9E−01
gal/foot	12	1.200 000 0E+01

gal/meter \<acceleration gradient\>
gal/centimeter	0.01	1.000 000 0E−02

galao [Cape Verde] \<volume, special - see page 29\>
liter	3.7	3.700 000 0E+00

galileo \<acceleration\>
centimeter/square second	1	1.000 000 0E+00
foot/square second	0.032 808 4	3.280 839 9E−02
gal	1	1.000 000 0E+00
gₙ [due to gravity]	0.001 019 7	1.019 716 2E−03
meter/square second	0.01	1.000 000 0E−02

gallon [British Honduras] \<volume, special - see page 29\>
liter	3.785 306	3.785 306 0E+00

gallon [Canada, liquid] \<volume\>
barrel [UK]	0.027 777 8	2.777 777 8E−02
barrel [US, liquid]	0.038 125 4	3.812 539 4E−02
barrel [US, petroleum]	0.028 594	2.859 404 6E−02
cubic decimeter	4.546 09	4.546 090 0E+00
cubic foot	0.160 543 7	1.605 436 5E−01
cubic inch	277.419 43	2.774 194 3E+02
cubic meter	0.004 546 1	4.546 090 0E−03
cup [Canada, measuring]	20	2.000 000 0E+01
cup [US, measuring]	19.215 199	1.921 519 9E+01
drachm [UK, liquid]	1,280	1.280 000 0E+03
dram [Canada, liquid]	1,280	1.280 000 0E+03
dram [US, liquid]	1,229.772 7	1.229 772 7E+03
gallon [UK, dry or liquid]	1	1.000 000 0E+00
gallon [US, liquid]	1.200 949 9	1.200 949 9E+00
gill [UK]	32	3.200 000 0E+01
gill [US]	38.430 398	3.843 039 8E+01
liter	4.546 09	4.546 090 0E+00
minim [UK]	76,800	7.680 000 0E+04
minim [US]	73,786.363	7.378 636 3E+04

	Standard	Scientific
ounce [UK, liquid]	160	1.600 000 0E+02
ounce [US, liquid]	153.721 59	1.537 215 9E+02
peck [UK]	0.5	5.000 000 0E-01
peck [US]	0.516 028 4	5.160 283 7E-01
pint [UK]	8	8.000 000 0E+00
pint [US, liquid]	9.607 599 4	9.607 599 4E+00
quart [UK]	4	4.000 000 0E+00
quart [US, liquid]	4.803 799 7	4.803 799 7E+00
scruple [UK, liquid]	3,840	3.840 000 0E+03
stere	0.004 546 1	4.546 090 0E-03
Winchester wine gallon [UK]	1.200 949 9	1.200 949 9E+00
gallon [Haiti]	**<volume, special - see page 29>**	
liter	3.785 31	3.785 310 0E+00
gallon [Hebrew, ancient]	**<volume, special - see page 29>**	
liter	39.4	3.940 000 0E+01
gallon [Peru]	**<volume, special - see page 29>**	
liter	4.545 96	4.545 960 0E+00
gallon [South Africa]	**<volume, special - see page 29>**	
liter	3.785 306	3.785 306 0E+00
gallon [UK, dry or liquid]		**<volume>**
barrel [UK]	0.027 777 8	2.777 777 8E-02
barrel [US, dry]	0.039 316 8	3.931 681 3E-02
barrel [US, liquid]	0.038 125 4	3.812 539 4E-02
barrel [US, petroleum]	0.028 594	2.859 404 6E-02
board foot	1.926 523 8	1.926 523 8E+00
bushel [UK]	0.125	1.250 000 0E-01
bushel [US, dry]	0.129 007 1	1.290 070 1E-01
cubic decimeter	4.546 09	4.546 090 0E+00
cubic foot	0.160 543 7	1.605 436 5E-01
cubic inch	277.419 43	2.774 194 3E+02
cubic meter	0.004 546 1	4.546 090 0E-03
cubic yard	0.005 946 1	5.946 061 2E-03
cup [Canada, measuring]	20	2.000 000 0E+01
cup [US, measuring]	19.215 199	1.921 519 9E+01
drachm [UK, liquid]	1,280	1.280 000 0E+03
dram [Canada, liquid]	1,280	1.280 000 0E+03
gallon [Canada, liquid]	1	1.000 000 0E+00
gallon [US, dry]	1.032 056 7	1.032 056 7E+00
gallon [US, liquid]	1.200 949 9	1.200 949 9E+00
gill [UK]	32	3.200 000 0E+01
gill [US]	38.430 398	3.843 039 8E+01
kilderkin [UK, liquid]	0.055 555 6	5.555 555 5E-02
liter	4.546 09	4.546 090 0E+00
ounce [UK, liquid]	160	1.600 000 0E+02
ounce [US, liquid]	153.721 59	1.537 215 9E+02
peck [UK]	0.5	5.000 000 0E-01
peck [US]	0.516 028 4	5.160 283 7E-01
pint [UK]	8	8.000 000 0E+00
pint [US, dry]	8.256 453 9	8.256 453 9E+00
pint [US, liquid]	9.607 599 4	9.607 599 4E+00
quart [UK]	4	4.000 000 0E+00
quart [US, dry]	4.128 227	4.128 227 0E+00
quart [US, liquid]	4.803 799 7	4.803 799 7E+00
scruple [UK, liquid]	3,840	3.840 000 0E+03
stere	0.004 546 1	4.546 090 0E-03
tablespoon [Canada, measuring]	320.000 54	3.200 005 4E+02
tablespoon [US, measuring]	307.443 18	3.074 431 8E+02
teaspoon [Canada, measuring]	960.001 62	9.600 016 2E+02
teaspoon [US, measuring]	922.329 54	9.223 295 4E+02
Winchester wine gallon [UK]	1.200 949 9	1.200 949 9E+00
gallon [US, dry]		**<volume>**
barrel [UK]	0.026 915	2.691 497 1E-02

barrel [US, dry]	0.038 095 6	3.809 559 2E-02
board foot	1.866 684	1.866 684 0E+00
bushel [US, dry]	0.125	1.250 000 0E-01
bushel [US, struck measure]	0.125	1.250 000 0E-01
cubic decimeter	4.404 883 8	4.404 883 8E+00
cubic foot	0.155 557	1.555 570 0E-01
cubic inch	268.802 5	2.688 025 0E+02
cubic meter	0.004 404 9	4.404 883 8E-03
cubic yard	0.005 761 4	5.761 370 5E-03
gallon [UK, dry or liquid]	0.968 939	9.689 389 7E-01
liter	4.404 883 8	4.404 883 8E+00
peck [UK]	0.484 469 5	4.844 694 9E-01
peck [US]	0.5	5.000 000 0E-01
pint [UK]	7.751 511 8	7.751 511 8E+00
pint [US, dry]	8	8.000 000 0E+00
quart [UK]	3.875 755 9	3.875 755 9E+00
quart [US, dry]	4	4.000 000 0E+00
stere	0.004 404 9	4.404 883 8E-03

gallon [US, liquid] <volume>

Amagat volume unit	0.168 889 1	1.688 890 6E-01
anker	0.1	1.000 000 0E-01
barrel [UK]	0.023 129 8	2.312 983 8E-02
barrel [US, federal proof spirits]	0.025	2.500 000 0E-02
barrel [US, liquid]	0.031 746	3.174 603 2E-02
barrel [US, petroleum]	0.023 809 5	2.380 952 4E-02
cubic decimeter	3.785 411 8	3.785 411 8E+00
cubic foot	0.133 680 6	1.336 805 6E-01
cubic inch	231	2.310 000 0E+02
cubic meter	0.003 785 4	3.785 411 8E-03
cubic yard	0.004 951 1	4.951 131 7E-03
cup [Canada, measuring]	16.653 484	1.665 348 4E+01
cup [US, measuring]	16	1.600 000 0E+01
drachm [UK, liquid]	1,065.823	1.065 823 0E+03
dram [Canada, liquid]	1,065.823	1.065 823 0E+03
dram [US, liquid]	1,024	1.024 000 0E+03
drop [US, liquid]	46,080	4.608 000 0E+04
drum [US, liquid]	0.018 181 8	1.818 181 8E-02
fifth [US, liquid]	5	5.000 000 0E+00
gallon [Canada, liquid]	0.832 674 2	8.326 741 8E-01
gallon [UK, dry or liquid]	0.832 674 2	8.326 741 8E-01
gill [UK]	26.645 574	2.664 557 4E+01
gill [US]	32	3.200 000 0E+01
kilderkin [US, liquid]	0.055 555 6	5.555 555 6E-02
liter	3.785 411 8	3.785 411 8E+00
ounce [UK, liquid]	133.227 87	1.332 278 7E+02
ounce [US, liquid]	128	1.280 000 0E+02
pint [UK]	6.661 393 5	6.661 393 5E+00
pint [US, liquid]	8	8.000 000 0E+00
pound of water [at 4 °C, 101.325 kPa, using IST-90 density equation]	8.345 170 7	8.345 170 7E+00
pound of water [at 60 °F, 14.696 pound-force/square inch, using IST-90 density equation]	8.337 171 5	8.337 171 5E+00
quart [UK]	3.330 696 7	3.330 696 7E+00
quart [US, liquid]	4	4.000 000 0E+00
tablespoon [Canada, measuring]	266.456 19	2.664 561 9E+02
tablespoon [US, measuring]	256	2.560 000 0E+02
teaspoon [Canada, measuring]	799.368 57	7.993 685 7E+02
teaspoon [US, measuring]	768	7.680 000 0E+02
Winchester wine gallon [UK]	1	1.000 000 0E+00

gallon of automotive gasoline [US, liquid] <energy>

joule	>>>	1.317 600 0E+08
kilowatthour	36.6	3.660 000 0E+01

gallon of aviation gasoline [US, liquid] \<energy\>
joule	>>>	1.317 600 0E+08
kilowatthour	36.6	3.660 000 0E+01

gallon of diesel oil [US, liquid] \<energy\>
joule	>>>	1.465 200 0E+08
kilowatthour	40.7	4.070 000 0E+01

gallon of distillate #2 fuel oil [US, liquid] \<energy\>
joule	>>>	1.465 200 0E+08
kilowatthour	40.7	4.070 000 0E+01

gallon of jet fuel, kerosene type [US, liquid] \<energy\>
joule	>>>	1.422 000 0E+08
kilowatthour	39.5	3.950 000 0E+01

gallon of jet fuel, naphtha type [US, liquid] \<energy\>
joule	>>>	1.339 200 0E+08
kilowatthour	37.2	3.720 000 0E+01

gallon of kerosene [US, liquid] \<energy\>
joule	>>>	1.422 000 0E+08
kilowatthour	39.5	3.950 000 0E+01

gallon of residual fuel oil [US, liquid] \<energy\>
joule	>>>	1.580 400 0E+08
kilowatthour	43.9	4.390 000 0E+01

gallon/cubic foot [US, liquid] \<concentration, volume basis\>
cubic foot/cubic foot	0.133 680 6	1.336 805 6E-01
cubic foot/gallon [-/US, liquid]	0.017 870 5	1.787 049 1E-02
cubic meter/cubic meter	0.133 680 6	1.336 805 6E-01

gallon/day [UK] \<flow rate, volume basis\>
acre inch/day	0.000 044 2	4.422 690 2E-05
barrel/day [UK]	0.027 777 8	2.777 777 8E-02
barrel/day [US, federal]	0.038 740 3	3.874 032 0E-02
barrel/day [US, liquid]	0.038 125 4	3.812 539 5E-02
barrel/day [US, petroleum]	0.028 594	2.859 404 6E-02
centiliter/day	18.942 041 7	1.894 204 2E+01
cubic centimeter/minute	3.157 006 9	3.157 006 9E+00
cubic decimeter/day	4.546 09	4.546 090 0E+00
cubic foot/day	0.160 543 7	1.605 436 5E-01
cubic inch/hour	11.559 143	1.155 914 3E+01
cubic meter/second	<<<	5.261 678 2E-08
cubic millimeter/second	52.616 782 4	5.261 678 2E+01
cubic yard/day	0.005 946 1	5.946 061 2E-03
deciliter/hour	1.894 204 2	1.894 204 2E+00
dekaliter/day	0.454 609	4.546 090 0E-01
gallon/day [US, liquid]	1.200 949 9	1.200 949 9E+00
hectoliter/day	0.045 460 9	4.546 090 0E-02
lambda/second	52.616 782 4	5.261 678 2E+01
liter/day	4.546 09	4.546 090 0E+00
liter/day [pre-1964]	4.545 962 7	4.545 962 7E+00
ounce/hour [UK, liquid]	6.666 666 7	6.666 666 7E+00
ounce/hour [US, liquid]	6.405 066 3	6.405 066 3E+00
stere/day	0.004 546 1	4.546 090 0E-03
thousand cubic foot/day	0.000 160 5	1.605 436 5E-04

gallon/day [US, liquid] \<flow rate, volume basis\>
acre foot/day	0.000 003 1	3.068 883 3E-06
acre foot/day [US, survey]	0.000 003 1	3.068 864 3E-06
acre inch/day	0.000 036 8	3.682 659 9E-05
barrel/day [UK]	0.023 129 8	2.312 983 9E-02
barrel/day [US, federal]	0.032 258 1	3.225 806 5E-02
barrel/day [US, liquid]	0.031 746	3.174 603 2E-02
barrel/day [US, petroleum]	0.023 809 5	2.380 952 4E-02
centiliter/hour	15.772 549 1	1.577 254 9E+01
cubic centimeter/minute	2.628 758 2	2.628 758 2E+00
cubic decimeter/day	3.785 411 8	3.785 411 8E+00

	Standard	Scientific
cubic foot/day	0.133 680 6	1.336 805 6E-01
cubic inch/hour	9.625	9.625 000 0E+00
cubic meter/second	<<<	4.381 263 6E-08
cubic millimeter/second	43.812 636 4	4.381 263 6E+01
cubic yard/day	0.004 951 1	4.951 131 7E-03
deciliter/hour	1.577 254 9	1.577 254 9E+00
dekaliter/day	0.378 541 2	3.785 411 8E-01
gallon/day [UK]	0.832 674 2	8.326 741 9E-01
hectoliter/day	0.037 854 1	3.785 411 8E-02
kiloliter/day	0.003 785 4	3.785 411 8E-03
lambda/second	43.812 636 4	4.381 263 6E+01
liter/day	3.785 411 8	3.785 411 8E+00
liter/day [pre-1964]	3.785 305 8	3.785 305 8E+00
milliliter/minute	2.628 758 2	2.628 758 2E+00
ounce/hour [UK, liquid]	5.551 161 2	5.551 161 2E+00
ounce/hour [US, liquid]	5.333 333 3	5.333 333 3E+00
stere/day	0.003 785 4	3.785 411 8E-03

gallon/horsepower hour [US, liquid]   <specific fuel consumption, volume basis>

	Standard	Scientific
cubic centimeter/calorie [-/ I.T.]	0.005 903 8	5.903 761 1E-03
cubic foot/Btu [-/ I.T.]	0.000 052 5	5.253 843 4E-05
cubic meter/joule	<<<	1.410 089 1E-09
cubic meter/kilocalorie [-/ I.T.]	0.000 005 9	5.903 761 1E-06

gallon/hour [UK]   <flow rate, volume basis>

	Standard	Scientific
acre inch/day	0.001 061 4	1.061 445 6E-03
barrel/day [UK]	0.666 666 7	6.666 666 7E-01
barrel/day [US, federal]	0.929 767 7	9.297 676 8E-01
barrel/day [US, liquid]	0.915 009 5	9.150 094 7E-01
barrel/day [US, petroleum]	0.686 257 1	6.862 571 0E-01
centiliter/minute	7.576 816 7	7.576 816 7E+00
cubic centimeter/second	1.262 802 8	1.262 802 8E+00
cubic decimeter/hour	4.546 09	4.546 090 0E+00
cubic foot/day	3.853 047 7	3.853 047 7E+00
cubic inch/minute	4.623 657 2	4.623 657 2E+00
cubic meter/day	0.109 106 2	1.091 061 6E-01
cubic meter/second	0.000 001 3	1.262 802 8E-06
cubic yard/day	0.142 750 5	1.427 054 7E-01
deciliter/hour	45.460 9	4.546 090 0E+01
dekaliter/day	10.910 616	1.091 061 6E+01
gallon/day [UK]	24	2.400 000 0E+01
gallon/day [US, liquid]	28.822 798 2	2.882 279 8E+01
gallon/hour [US, liquid]	1.200 949 9	1.200 949 9E+00
hectoliter/day	1.091 061 6	1.091 061 6E+00
lambda/second	1,262.802 78	1.262 802 8E+03
liter/hour	4.546 09	4.546 090 0E+00
liter/hour [pre-1964]	4.545 962 7	4.545 962 7E+00
milliliter/second	1.262 802 8	1.262 802 8E+00
ounce/minute [UK, liquid]	2.666 666 7	2.666 666 7E+00
ounce/minute [US, liquid]	2.562 026 5	2.562 026 5E+00
stere/day	0.109 106 2	1.091 061 6E-01
thousand cubic foot/day	0.003 853	3.853 047 7E-03

gallon/hour [US, liquid]   <flow rate, volume basis>

	Standard	Scientific
acre inch/day	0.000 883 8	8.838 383 8E-04
barrel/day [UK]	0.555 116 1	5.551 161 2E-01
barrel/day [US, federal]	0.774 193 5	7.741 935 5E-01
barrel/day [US, liquid]	0.761 904 8	7.619 047 6E-01
barrel/day [US, petroleum]	0.571 428 6	5.714 285 7E-01
centiliter/minute	6.309 019 6	6.309 019 6E+00
cubic centimeter/second	1.051 503 3	1.051 503 3E+00
cubic decimeter/hour	3.785 411 8	3.785 411 8E+00
cubic foot/day	3.208 333 3	3.208 333 3E+00
cubic inch/minute	3.85	3.850 000 0E+00
cubic meter/day	0.090 849 9	9.084 988 3E-02
cubic meter/second	0.000 001 1	1.051 503 3E-06

	Standard	Scientific
cubic yard/day	0.118 827 2	1.188 271 6E-01
deciliter/hour	37.854 117 8	3.785 411 8E+01
dekaliter/hour	9.084 988 3	9.084 988 3E+00
gallon/day [UK]	19.984 180 4	1.998 418 0E+01
gallon/day [US, liquid]	24	2.400 000 0E+01
gallon/hour [UK]	0.832 674 2	8.326 741 9E-01
hectoliter/day	0.908 498 8	9.084 988 3E-01
kiloliter/day	0.090 849 9	9.084 988 3E-02
lambda/second	1,051.503 27	1.051 503 3E+03
liter/hour	3.785 411 8	3.785 411 8E+00
liter/hour [pre-1964]	3.785 305 8	3.785 305 8E+00
milliliter/second	1.051 503 3	1.051 503 3E+00
ounce/minute [UK, liquid]	2.220 464 5	2.220 464 5E+00
ounce/minute [US, liquid]	2.133 333 3	2.133 333 3E+00
petrograd standard/day	0.019 444 4	1.944 444 4E-02
stere/day	0.090 849 9	9.084 988 3E-02
thousand cubic foot/day	0.003 208 3	3.208 333 3E-03

gallon/mile [US, liquid/international]   <fuel consumption, SI>

	Standard	Scientific
cubic meter/meter	0.000 002 4	2.352 145 8E-06
liter/100 kilometer	0.023 521 5	2.352 145 8E-02
liter/kilometer	2.352 145 8	2.352 145 8E+00
liter/meter	0.002 352 1	2.352 145 8E-03

gallon/minute [UK]   <flow rate, volume basis>

	Standard	Scientific
acre inch/day	0.063 686 7	6.368 673 9E-02
barrel/hour [UK]	1.666 666 7	1.666 666 7E+00
barrel/hour [US, federal]	2.324 419 2	2.324 419 2E+00
barrel/hour [US, liquid]	2.287 523 7	2.287 523 7E+00
barrel/hour [US, petroleum]	1.715 642 8	1.715 642 8E+00
centiliter/second	7.576 816 7	7.576 816 7E+00
cubic centimeter/second	75.768 166 7	7.576 816 7E+01
cubic decimeter/minute	4.546 09	4.546 090 0E+00
cubic foot/hour	9.632 619 2	9.632 619 2E+00
cubic inch/second	4.623 657 2	4.623 657 2E+00
cubic meter/day	6.546 369 6	6.546 369 6E+00
cubic meter/second	0.000 075 8	7.576 816 7E-05
cubic yard/day	8.562 328 2	8.562 328 2E+00
deciliter/minute	45.460 9	4.546 090 0E+01
dekaliter/hour	27.276 54	2.727 654 0E+01
gallon/hour [UK]	60	6.000 000 0E+01
gallon/hour [US, liquid]	72.056 995 5	7.205 699 6E+01
gallon/minute [US, liquid]	1.200 949 9	1.200 949 9E+00
hectoliter/day	2.727 654	2.727 654 0E+00
kiloliter/day	6.546 369 6	6.546 369 6E+00
liter/minute	4.546 09	4.546 090 0E+00
liter/minute [pre-1964]	4.545 962 7	4.545 962 7E+00
milliliter/second	75.768 166 7	7.576 816 7E+01
ounce/second [UK, liquid]	2.666 666 7	2.666 666 7E+00
ounce/second [US, liquid]	2.562 026 5	2.562 026 5E+00
petrograd standard/day	1.401 108 2	1.401 108 2E+00
stere/day	6.546 369 6	6.546 369 6E+00
thousand cubic foot/day	0.231 182 9	2.311 828 6E-01

gallon/minute [US, liquid]   <flow rate, volume basis>

	Standard	Scientific
acre inch/day	0.053 030 3	5.303 030 3E-02
barrel/hour [UK]	1.387 790 3	1.387 790 3E+00
barrel/hour [US, federal]	1.935 483 9	1.935 483 9E+00
barrel/hour [US, liquid]	1.904 761 9	1.904 761 9E+00
barrel/hour [US, petroleum]	1.428 571 4	1.428 571 4E+00
centiliter/second	6.309 019 6	6.309 019 6E+00
cubic centimeter/second	63.090 196 4	6.309 019 6E+01
cubic decimeter/minute	3.785 411 8	3.785 411 8E+00
cubic foot/hour	8.020 833 3	8.020 833 3E+00
cubic inch/second	3.85	3.850 000 0E+00
cubic meter/day	5.450 993	5.450 993 0E+00

	Standard	Scientific
cubic meter/second	0.000 063 1	6.309 019 6E−05
cubic yard/day	7.129 629 6	7.129 629 6E+00
deciliter/minute	37.854 117 8	3.785 411 8E+01
dekaliter/hour	22.712 470 7	2.271 247 1E+01
gallon/hour [UK]	49.960 451 1	4.996 045 1E+01
gallon/hour [US, liquid]	60	6.000 000 0E+01
gallon/minute [UK]	0.832 674 2	8.326 741 9E−01
hectoliter/hour	2.271 247 1	2.271 247 1E+00
kiloliter/day	5.450 993	5.450 993 0E+00
liter/minute	3.785 411 8	3.785 411 8E+00
liter/minute [pre-1964]	3.785 305 8	3.785 305 8E+00
milliliter/second	63.090 196 4	6.309 019 6E+01
ounce/second [UK, liquid]	2.220 464 5	2.220 464 5E+00
ounce/second [US, liquid]	2.133 333 3	2.133 333 3E+00
petrograd standard/day	1.166 666 7	1.166 666 7E+00
stere/day	5.450 993	5.450 993 0E+00
thousand cubic foot/day	0.192 5	1.925 000 0E−01
gallon/second [UK]		**<flow rate, volume basis>**
acre foot/day	0.318 433 7	3.184 336 9E−01
acre foot/day [US, survey]	0.318 431 8	3.184 317 8E−01
acre inch/day	3.821 204 3	3.821 204 3E+00
barrel/hour [UK]	100	1.000 000 0E+02
barrel/minute [UK]	1.666 666 7	1.666 666 7E+00
barrel/minute [US, federal]	2.324 419 2	2.324 419 2E+00
barrel/minute [US, liquid]	2.287 523 7	2.287 523 7E+00
barrel/minute [US, petroleum]	1.715 642 8	1.715 642 8E+00
centiliter/second	454.609	4.546 090 0E+02
cubic centimeter/second	4,546.09	4.546 090 0E+03
cubic decimeter/second	4.546 09	4.546 090 0E+00
cubic foot/minute	9.632 619 2	9.632 619 2E+00
cubic inch/second	277.419 433	2.774 194 3E+02
cubic meter/second	0.004 546 1	4.546 090 0E−03
cubic yard/hour	21.405 82	2.140 582 0E+01
deciliter/second	45.460 9	4.546 090 0E+01
dekaliter/minute	27.276 54	2.727 654 0E+01
gallon/minute [UK]	60	6.000 000 0E+01
gallon/minute [US, liquid]	72.056 995 5	7.205 699 6E+01
gallon/second [US, liquid]	1.200 949 9	1.200 949 9E+00
hectare meter/day	0.039 278 2	3.927 821 8E−02
hectoliter/minute	2.727 654	2.727 654 0E+00
kiloliter/hour	16.365 924	1.636 592 4E+01
liter/second	4.546 09	4.546 090 0E+00
liter/second [pre-1964]	4.545 962 7	4.545 962 7E+00
ounce/second [UK, liquid]	160	1.600 000 0E+02
ounce/second [US, liquid]	153.721 59	1.537 215 9E+02
petrograd standard/hour	3.502 770 6	3.502 770 6E+00
stere/hour	16.365 924	1.636 592 4E+01
thousand cubic foot/day	13.870 972	1.387 097 2E+01
gallon/second [US, liquid]		**<flow rate, volume basis>**
acre foot/day	0.265 151 5	2.651 515 2E−01
acre foot/day [US, survey]	0.265 149 9	2.651 499 2E−01
acre inch/day	3.181 818	3.181 818 0E+00
barrel/minute [UK]	1.387 790 3	1.387 790 3E+00
barrel/minute [US, federal]	1.935 483 9	1.935 483 9E+00
barrel/minute [US, liquid]	1.904 761 9	1.904 761 9E+00
barrel/minute [US, petroleum]	1.428 571 4	1.428 571 4E+00
centiliter/second	378.541 178	3.785 411 8E+02
cubic centimeter/second	3,785.411 78	3.785 411 8E+03
cubic decimeter/second	3.785 411 8	3.785 411 8E+00
cubic dekameter/day	0.327 059 6	3.270 595 8E−01
cubic foot/minute	8.020 833 3	8.020 833 3E+00
cubic inch/second	231	2.310 000 0E+02
cubic meter/hour	13.627 482 4	1.362 748 2E+01

Convert From Convert To	Standard	<Type of Unit> Scientific
cubic meter/second	0.003 785 4	3.785 411 8E-03
cubic yard/hour	17.824 074	1.782 407 4E+01
deciliter/second	37.854 117 8	3.785 411 8E+01
dekaliter/minute	22.712 470 7	2.271 247 1E+01
gallon/minute [UK]	49.960 451 1	4.996 045 1E+01
gallon/minute [US, liquid]	60	6.000 000 0E+01
gallon/second [US, liquid]	0.832 674 2	8.326 741 9E-01
hectare meter/day	0.032 706	3.270 595 8E-02
hectoliter/minute	2.271 247 1	2.271 247 1E+00
kiloliter/hour	13.627 482 4	1.362 748 2E+01
liter/second	3.785 411 8	3.785 411 8E+00
liter/second [pre-1964]	3.785 305 8	3.785 305 8E+00
ounce/second [UK, liquid]	133.227 87	1.332 278 7E+02
ounce/second [US, liquid]	128	1.280 000 0E+02
petrograd standard/day	70	7.000 000 0E+01
petrograd standard/hour	2.916 666 7	2.916 666 7E+00
stere/hour	13.627 482	1.362 748 2E+01
thousand cubic foot/day	11.55	1.155 000 0E+01

galon [Argentina]
<volume, special - see page 29>

liter	3.8	3.800 000 0E+00

galon [Bolivia]
<volume, special - see page 29>

liter	3.36	3.360 000 0E+00

galon [Chile]
<volume, special - see page 29>

liter	4.54	4.540 000 0E+00

galon [Dominican Republic]
<volume, special - see page 29>

liter	3.240 1	3.240 100 0E+00

galon [El Salvador]
<volume, special - see page 29>

liter	3.75	3.750 000 0E+00

galon [Honduras]
<volume, special - see page 29>

liter	3.456	3.456 000 0E+00

galon [Peru]
<volume, special - see page 29>

liter	3.36	3.360 000 0E+00

galon [Venezuela]
<volume, special - see page 29>

liter	3.5	3.500 000 0E+00

gamma
<magnetic flux density>

electromagnetic unit of magnetic flux density [cgs system]	0.000 01	1.000 000 0E-05
gauss	0.000 01	1.000 000 0E-05
line/square centimeter [of magnetic force]	0.000 01	1.000 000 0E-05
maxwell/square meter	<<<	1.000 000 0E-09
nanotesla	1	1.000 000 0E+00
tesla	<<<	1.000 000 0E-09
volt second/square meter	<<<	1.000 000 0E-09
weber/square meter	<<<	1.000 000 0E-09

gamma
<mass>

carat [international]	0.000 005	5.000 000 0E-06
carat [metric]	0.000 005	5.000 000 0E-06
carat [US, after 1913]	0.000 005	5.000 000 0E-06
drachm [UK, apothecary]	0.000 000 3	2.572 059 7E-07
dram [avoirdupois]	0.000 000 6	5.643 833 9E-07
dram [US, apothecary]	0.000 000 3	2.572 059 7E-07
grain	0.000 015 4	1.543 235 8E-05
grain [apothecary]	0.000 015 4	1.543 235 8E-05
grain [avoirdupois]	0.000 015 4	1.543 235 8E-05
grain [troy]	0.000 015 4	1.543 235 8E-05
gram	0.000 001	1.000 000 0E-06
kilogram	<<<	1.000 000 0E-09
microgram	1	1.000 000 0E+00

gammil
<density>

gram/cubic meter	1	1.000 000 0E+00
kilogram/cubic meter	0.001	1.000 000 0E-03

| Convert From | | <Type of Unit> |
Convert To	Standard	Scientific
milligram/cubic decimeter	1	1.000 000 0E+00
milligram/liter	1	1.000 000 0E+00
pound/cubic yard	0.001 685 6	1.685 554 9E−03

gan [Iraq, ancient]   <area, special - see page 29>

hectare	2.7	2.700 000 0E+00

gana [Libya, textiles]   <length, special - see page 29>

meter	1.6	1.600 000 0E+00

gandom [Iran]   <mass, special - see page 29>

milligram	48.83	4.883 000 0E+01

gandum [Iran]   <mass, special - see page 29>

milligram	48.83	4.883 000 0E+01

gang [Vietnam]   <area, special - see page 29>

square meter	0.04	4.000 000 0E−02

ganta [Indonesia]   <volume, special - see page 29>

liter	8.577	8.577 000 0E+00

ganta [Malaysia]   <volume, special - see page 29>

liter	4.546	4.546 000 0E+00

ganta [Philippines]   <volume, special - see page 29>

liter	3	3.000 000 0E+00

gantang [Indonesia]   <volume, special - see page 29>

liter	8.576 6	8.576 600 0E+00

gantang [Philippines]   <volume, special - see page 29>

liter	3	3.000 000 0E+00

gantang [South Africa]   <volume, special - see page 29>

liter	9.2	9.200 000 0E+00

ganu [Akkadian, ancient]   <length, special - see page 29>

meter	3	3.000 000 0E+00

gar [Iraq, ancient]   <length, special - see page 29>

meter	11.9	1.190 000 0E+01

garava [Syria]   <volume, special - see page 29>

liter	14.5	1.450 000 0E+01

garce [India]   <volume, special - see page 29>

hectoliter	49.06	4.906 000 0E+01

gareh [Iran]   <length, special - see page 29>

centimeter	6.5	6.500 000 0E+00

garmida [Hebrew, ancient]   <area, special - see page 29>

square meter	0.3	3.000 000 0E−01

garnetz [Russia, dry]   <volume, special - see page 29>

liter	3.28	3.280 000 0E+00

garniec [Poland]   <volume, special - see page 29>

liter	4	4.000 000 0E+00

garra [Malta]   <volume, special - see page 29>

liter	10.797	1.079 700 0E+01

garrafa [Brazil]   <volume, special - see page 29>

liter	0.666	6.660 000 0E−01

garrafon [Cuba]   <volume, special - see page 29>

liter	18.125	1.812 500 0E+01

garsa [India, rice, milled]   <mass, special - see page 29>

kilogram	3,522.54	3.522 540 0E+03

garwoke [Burma]   <length, special - see page 29>

kilometer	20.483	2.048 300 0E+01

gasab [Egypt, ancient]   <length, special - see page 29>

meter	3.55	3.550 000 0E+00

gasha [Eritrea]   <area, special - see page 29>

hectare	40	4.000 000 0E+01

Convert From		<Type of Unit>
Convert To	Standard	Scientific

gasha [Ethiopia] — — — — — — — — — — — <area, special - see page 29>
hectare---40 --- 4.000 000 0E+01

gat [Ethiopia] — — — — — — — — — — — — <length, special - see page 29>
centimeter--7.5 --- 7.500 000 0E+00

gatsar [Mongolia] — — — — — — — — — — <length, special - see page 29>
meter---576 --- 5.760 000 0E+02

gaulette [Mauritius] — — — — — — — — — <length, special - see page 29>
meter---3.248 4 --- 3.248 400 0E+00

gauss — — — — — — — — — — — — — — — — — — <magnetic flux density>
abtesla --1 --- 1.000 000 0E+00
electromagnetic unit of magnetic flux density [cgs system] ---------- 1 --- 1.000 000 0E+00
gamma---100,000 --- 1.000 000 0E+05
line/square centimeter [of magnetic force] ---------------------- 1 --- 1.000 000 0E+00
maxwell/square meter --------------------------------------0.000 1 --- 1.000 000 0E-04
tesla --0.000 1 --- 1.000 000 0E-04

gauss square centimeter — — — — — — — — — — — — <magnetic flux>
electromagnetic unit of magnetic flux [cgs system]---------------- 1 --- 1.000 000 0E+00
electrostatic unit of magnetic flux [cgs system]----------<<< 3.335 641 0E-11
line [of magnetic force] --- 1 --- 1.000 000 0E+00
maxwell--- 1 --- 1.000 000 0E+00
statweber---<<< 3.335 641 0E-11
unit pole---0.079 577 5 --- 7.957 747 5E-02
weber--<<< 1.000 000 0E-08

gaussian electric capacitance — — — — — — — — — — <capacitance>
abfarad---<<< 1.112 650 1E-21
electrostatic unit of capacitance [cgs system]------------------- 1 --- 1.000 000 0E+00
farad---<<< 1.112 650 1E-12
statfarad--- 1 --- 1.000 000 0E+00

gaussian electric charge — — — — — — — — — — — — <electric charge>
ampere second ---<<< 3.335 641 0E-10
coulomb --<<< 3.335 641 0E-10
electrostatic unit of charge [cgs system] ----------------------- 1 --- 1.000 000 0E+00
franklin -- 1 --- 1.000 000 0E+00
statcoulomb--- 1 --- 1.000 000 0E+00

gaussian electric conductance — — — — — — — — <electric conductance>
absiemens---<<< 1.112 650 1E-21
electrostatic unit of conductance [cgs system]------------------- 1 --- 1.000 000 0E+00
picosiemens---1.112 650 1 --- 1.112 650 1E+00
siemens---<<< 1.112 650 1E-12
statsiemens--- 1 --- 1.000 000 0E+00

gaussian electric current — — — — — — — — — — — — <electric current>
abampere--<<< 3.335 641 0E-11
ampere--<<< 3.335 641 0E-10
electrostatic unit of current [cgs system] ---------------------- 1 --- 1.000 000 0E+00
franklin/second--- 1 --- 1.000 000 0E+00
statampere-- 1 --- 1.000 000 0E+00

gaussian electric inductance — — — — — — — — — — <electric inductance>
abhenry--->>> 8.987 551 8E+20
electrostatic unit of inductance [cgs system] ------------------- 1 --- 1.000 000 0E+00
henry--->>> 8.987 551 8E+11
ohm second -->>> 8.987 551 8E+11
stathenry--- 1 --- 1.000 000 0E+00

gaussian electric potential — — — — — — — — — — — <electric potential>
abvolt--->>> --- 2.997 924 6E+10
electrostatic unit of electric potential [cgs system]--------------- 1 --- 1.000 000 0E+00
erg/franklin-- 1 --- 1.000 000 0E+00
statvolt-- 1 --- 1.000 000 0E+00
volt--- 299.792 458 --- 2.997 924 6E+02

gaussian electric resistance — — — — — — — — — — <electric resistance>
1/ siemens-->>> --- 8.987 551 8E+11

Convert From		<Type of Unit>
Convert To	Standard	Scientific

abohm -------	>>>----	8.987 551 8E+20
electrostatic unit of resistance [cgs system]----	1----	1.000 000 0E+00
ohm----	>>>----	8.987 551 8E+11
statohm----	1----	1.000 000 0E+00

gaussian magnetic flux <magnetic flux>
electrostatic unit of magnetic flux [cgs system]----	1----	1.000 000 0E+00
gauss square centimeter----	>>>----	2.997 924 6E+10
line [of magnetic force] ----	>>>----	2.997 924 6E+10
maxwell----	>>>----	2.997 924 6E+10
statweber----	1----	1.000 000 0E+00
unit pole ----	>>>----	2.385 672 7E+09
weber ----	299.792 458----	2.997 924 6E+02

gaussian magnetic flux density <magnetic flux density>
electrostatic unit of magnetic flux density [cgs system] ----	1----	1.000 000 0E+00
line/square centimeter [of magnetic force]----	>>>----	2.997 924 6E+10
maxwell/square meter ----	2,997,924.58----	2.997 924 6E+06
stattesla ----	1----	1.000 000 0E+00
tesla ----	2,997,924.58----	2.997 924 6E+06

gauza [Islam] <mass, special - see page 29>
gram----	29.75----	2.975 000 0E+01

gaz [India] <length, special - see page 29>
centimeter----	91.44----	9.144 000 0E+01

gaz [Iran] <length, special - see page 29>
meter----	1.04----	1.040 000 0E+00

gaz gareeb [Afghanistan] <length, special - see page 29>
centimeter----	73.6----	7.360 000 0E+01

gaz memar [Afghanistan] <length, special - see page 29>
meter----	0.838----	8.380 000 0E-01

gaz sha [Afghanistan] <length, special - see page 29>
meter----	1.066----	1.066 000 0E+00

gazi jerib [Afghanistan] <length, special - see page 29>
centimeter----	73.66----	7.366 000 0E+01

gazi memar [Afghanistan] <length, special - see page 29>
centimeter----	81.28----	8.128 000 0E+01

gazi sha [Afghanistan] <length, special - see page 29>
meter----	1.066 8----	1.066 800 0E+00

gedang [Spice Islands, pepper] <mass, special - see page 29>
gram----	1,976----	1.976 000 0E+03

geepound <mass>
cental [US]----	0.321 740 5----	3.217 404 9E-01
centner [UK]----	0.287 268 3----	2.872 682 9E-01
decitonne----	0.145 939----	1.459 390 3E-01
doppelzentner [Germany]----	0.145 939----	1.459 390 3E-01
flask of mercury ----	0.423 342 7----	4.233 427 4E-01
hundredweight [long]----	0.287 268 3----	2.872 682 9E-01
hundredweight [short]----	0.321 740 5----	3.217 404 9E-01
hundredweight [UK] ----	0.287 268 3----	2.872 682 9E-01
hyl ----	1.488 163 9----	1.488 163 9E+00
kilogram ----	14.593 903----	1.459 390 3E+01
pound ----	32.174 049----	3.217 404 9E+01
pound [avoirdupois] ----	32.174 049----	3.217 404 9E+01
pound [troy] ----	39.100 406----	3.910 040 6E+01
pound [unified] ----	32.174 049----	3.217 404 9E+01
pound-force square second/foot ----	1----	1.000 000 0E+00
poundal square second/foot----	32.174 049----	3.217 404 9E+01
slug----	1----	1.000 000 0E+00
slug [metric] ----	1.488 163 9----	1.488 163 9E+00
stone [UK]----	2.298 146 3----	2.298 146 3E+00

Convert From		<Type of Unit>
Convert To	Standard	Scientific

geerah [India] <length, special - see page 29>
  centimeter--- 5.715 --- 5.715 000 0E+00

geira [Brazil] <area, special - see page 29>
  hectare---19 --- 1.900 000 0E+01

geira [Portugal] <area, special - see page 29>
  are --- 58.03 --- 5.803 000 0E+01

gemmho <electric conductance>
  micromho--- 1 --- 1.000 000 0E+00
  microsiemens -- 1 --- 1.000 000 0E+00
  siemens--------------------------------------0.000 001 --- 1.000 000 0E−06

gera [Hebrew, ancient] <mass, special - see page 29>
  gram -- 0.818 --- 8.180 000 0E−01

gerah [Hebrew, ancient] <mass, special - see page 29>
  gram--- 0.5 --- 5.000 000 0E−01

gerbe [Spanish North Africa] <mass, special - see page 29>
  kilogram --- 3 --- 3.000 000 0E+00

gereeb [Afghanistan] <area, special - see page 29>
  square meter ----------------------------------- 1,952 --- 1.952 000 0E+03

gereh gaz sha [Afghanistan] <length, special - see page 29>
  centimeter---6.6 --- 6.600 000 0E+00

gereh gazi sha [Afghanistan] <length, special - see page 29>
  centimeter--6.667 5 --- 6.667 500 0E+00

geriwa [Hebrew, ancient, dry] <volume, special - see page 29>
  cubic centimeter-----------------------------13,184.44 --- 1.318 444 0E+04

gerot [Hebrew, ancient] <mass, special - see page 29>
  milligram --633 --- 6.330 000 0E+02

ghamaon [India] <area, special - see page 29>
  are --54.181 05 --- 5.418 105 0E+01

ghe [Vietnam] <area, special - see page 29>
  square meter ------------------------------------- 0.16 --- 1.600 000 0E−01

ghebeta [Eritrea] <volume, special - see page 29>
  liter --24 --- 2.400 000 0E+01

ghirara [Syria] <mass, special - see page 29>
  kilogram --208.74 --- 2.087 400 0E+02

ghumaon [Pakistan] <area, special - see page 29>
  hectare--- 0.405 --- 4.050 000 0E−01

gi [Sumeria, ancient] <length, special - see page 29>
  meter --- 3 --- 3.000 000 0E+00

gia [Vietnam, rice paddy] <volume, special - see page 29>
  liter ---40 --- 4.000 000 0E+01

gia chiec [Vietnam] <volume, special - see page 29>
  liter ---20 --- 2.000 000 0E+01

gia nan [Vietnam] <volume, special - see page 29>
  liter ---45 --- 4.500 000 0E+01

gian [China] <mass, special - see page 29>
  gram --- 5 --- 5.000 000 0E+00

gian sheng [China] <volume, special - see page 29>
  kiloliter --- 1 --- 1.000 000 0E+00

giarra [Libya, liquid] <volume, special - see page 29>
  liter ---14,128 --- 1.412 800 0E+04

giarra [Libya] <mass, special - see page 29>
  kilogram ---75 --- 7.500 000 0E+01

gibbs <surface concentration>
  mole/square meter-----------------------------0.000 001 --- 1.000 000 0E−06

gigabar <pressure>
  atmosphere [standard]--------------------------------->>> --- 9.869 232 7E+08

	Standard	Scientific
atmosphere [technical]	>>>	1.019 716 2E+09
bar	>>>	1.000 000 0E+09
dyne/square centimeter	>>>	1.000 000 0E+15
foot of mercury [0 °C, by convention]	>>>	2.460 831 9E+09
foot of water [4 °C, by convention]	>>>	3.345 525 6E+10
kilogram-force/square millimeter	>>>	1.019 716 2E+07
kilopond/square millimeter	>>>	1.019 716 2E+07
kip/square inch	>>>	1.450 377 4E+07
newton/square millimeter	>>>	1.000 000 0E+08
pascal	>>>	1.000 000 0E+14
petapascal	0.1	1.000 000 0E−01
pound-force/square inch	>>>	1.450 377 4E+10
ton-force/square inch [short]	7,251,886.9	7.251 886 9E+06
torr	>>>	7.500 616 8E+11

gigabecquerel		**\<radionuclide activity\>**
1/second	>>>	1.000 000 0E+09
becquerel	>>>	1.000 000 0E+09
curie	0.027 027	2.702 702 7E−02
rutherford	1,000	1.000 000 0E+03

gigacandela		**\<luminous intensity\>**
candela	>>>	1.000 000 0E+09

gigacoulomb		**\<electric charge\>**
ampere second	>>>	1.000 000 0E+09
coulomb	>>>	1.000 000 0E+09
electromagnetic unit of charge [cgs system]	>>>	1.000 000 0E+08
farad volt	>>>	1.000 000 0E+09
franklin	>>>	2.997 924 6E+18

gigacoulomb/cubic meter		**\<electric charge density\>**
coulomb/cubic meter	>>>	1.000 000 0E+09
coulomb/cubic millimeter	1	1.000 000 0E+00
statcoulomb/cubic centimeter	>>>	2.997 924 6E+12

gigaelectronvolt		**\<energy\>**
atomic mass unit [unified, C-12, 1986, eq. energy]	1.073 543 9	1.073 543 9E+00
deuteron rest mass [atomic physics, eq. energy]	0.533 158 9	5.331 589 2E−01
dyne centimeter	0.001 602 2	1.602 177 3E−03
electron rest mass [atomic physics, eq. energy]	1,956.950 8	1.956 950 8E+03
erg	0.001 602 2	1.602 177 3E−03
joule	<<<	1.602 177 3E−10
muon rest mass [atomic physics, eq. energy]	9.464 463 8	9.464 463 8E+00
neutron rest mass [atomic physics, eq. energy]	1.064 321 6	1.064 321 6E+00
proton rest mass [atomic physics, eq. energy]	1.065 788 7	1.065 788 7E+00
rydberg [atomic physics, eq. energy]	>>>	7.349 774 4E+07

gigafarad		**\<capacitance\>**
abfarad	1	1.000 000 0E+00
coulomb/volt	>>>	1.000 000 0E+09
electromagnetic unit of capacitance [cgs system]	1	1.000 000 0E+00
farad	>>>	1.000 000 0E+09
statfarad	>>>	8.987 551 8E+20

gigagram		**\<mass\>**
kilogram	1,000,000	1.000 000 0E+06
kiloton [metric]	1	1.000 000 0E+00
kilotonne	1	1.000 000 0E+00
megaton [metric]	0.001	1.000 000 0E−03
megatonne	0.001	1.000 000 0E−03
millier	1,000	1.000 000 0E+03
ton [long]	984.206 53	9.842 065 3E+02
ton [metric]	1	1.000 000 0E+00
ton [short]	1,102.311 3	1.102 311 3E+03
ton [UK]	984.206 53	9.842 065 3E+02
tonne	1,000	1.000 000 0E+03

| Convert From | | <Type of Unit> |
| Convert To | Standard | Scientific |

gigahenry <electric inductance>
abhenry	>>>	1.000 000 0E+18
electrostatic unit of inductance [cgs system]	0.001 112 7	1.112 650 1E−03
henry	>>>	1.000 000 0E+09
ohm second	>>>	1.000 000 0E+09
stathenry	0.001 112 7	1.112 650 1E−03

gigahertz <frequency>
1/second	>>>	1.000 000 0E+09
degree/second	>>>	3.600 000 0E+11
megahertz	1,000	1.000 000 0E+03
radian/second	>>>	6.283 185 3E+09
revolution/second	>>>	1.000 000 0E+09

gigajoule <energy>
Btu [I.T.]	947,817.12	9.478 171 2E+05
calorie [I.T.]	>>>	2.388 459 0E+08
calorie [kilogram, I.T.]	238,845.9	2.388 459 0E+05
centigrade heat unit [I.T.]	526,565.07	5.265 650 7E+05
cheval vapeur heure [France]	377.672 67	3.776 726 7E+02
coal equivalent kilogram [UN, standard]	34.120 842	3.412 084 2E+01
coal equivalent metric ton [UN, standard]	0.034 120 8	3.412 084 2E−02
dekawatthour	27,777.778	2.777 777 8E+04
foot pound-force	>>>	7.375 621 5E+08
foot poundal	>>>	2.373 036 0E+10
horsepower hour	372.506 14	3.725 061 4E+02
horsepower hour [metric]	377.672 67	3.776 726 7E+02
joule	>>>	1.000 000 0E+09
kiloton [metric, explosive energy]	0.000 239	2.390 057 4E−04
kilowatthour	277.777 78	2.777 777 8E+02
myriawatthour	27.777 778	2.777 777 8E+01
pferdestarkenstunde [Germany]	377.672 67	3.776 726 7E+02
therm [EEC]	9.478 171 2	9.478 171 2E+00
therm [US]	9.480 434 3	9.480 434 3E+00
thermie [France]	238.902 96	2.389 029 6E+02
ton [metric, explosive energy]	0.239 005 7	2.390 057 4E−01
watthour	277,777.78	2.777 777 8E+05
wattsecond	>>>	1.000 000 0E+09

gigaliter <volume>
acre foot	810.713 19	8.107 131 9E+02
acre inch	9,728.558 3	9.728 558 3E+03
barrel [UK]	6,110,256.9	6.110 256 9E+06
barrel [US, dry]	8,648,489.8	8.648 489 8E+06
barrel [US, liquid]	8,386,414.4	8.386 414 4E+06
barrel [US, petroleum]	6,289,810.8	6.289 810 8E+06
cubic foot	>>>	3.531 466 7E+07
cubic hectometer	1	1.000 000 0E+00
cubic inch	>>>	6.102 374 4E+10
cubic meter	1,000,000	1.000 000 0E+06
cubic yard	1,307,950.6	1.307 950 6E+06
drum [US, liquid]	4,803,128.2	4.803 128 2E+06
hectare meter	100	1.000 000 0E+02
liter	>>>	1.000 000 0E+09
million acre foot	0.000 810 7	8.107 131 9E−04
stere	1,000,000	1.000 000 0E+06
Winchester wine gallon [UK]	>>>	2.641 720 5E+08

gigameter <length>
astronomical unit	0.006 684 6	6.684 587 2E−03
bevameter	1	1.000 000 0E+00
fathom [US, survey]	>>>	5.468 055 6E+08
foot [international]	>>>	3.280 839 9E+09
foot [US, survey]	>>>	3.280 833 3E+09
furlong [US, survey]	4,970,959.6	4.970 959 6E+06
league [US, statute]	207,123.32	2.071 233 2E+05

Convert From
Convert To   **<Type of Unit>**
Standard   Scientific

Convert To	Standard	Scientific
light year [based on mean Julian year]	0.000 000 1	1.057 000 8E-07
meter	>>>	1.000 000 0E+00
mile [international]	621,371.19	6.213 711 9E+05
mile [US, statute]	621,369.95	6.213 699 5E+05
mile [US, survey]	621,369.95	6.213 699 5E+05
myriameter	100,000	1.000 000 0E+05
spat	0.001	1.000 000 0E-03
terameter	0.001	1.000 000 0E-03
township [US, survey]	103,561.66	1.035 616 6E+05
yard [based on US, survey foot]	>>>	1.093 611 1E+09
yard [international]	>>>	1.093 613 3E+09
yard [UK]	>>>	1.093 615 2E+09

gigamole   <amount of substance>

Convert To	Standard	Scientific
mole	>>>	1.000 000 0E+09

giganewton   <force>

Convert To	Standard	Scientific
crinal	>>>	1.000 000 0E+10
dyne	>>>	1.000 000 0E+14
gram-force	>>>	1.019 716 2E+11
newton	>>>	1.000 000 0E+09
ounce-force	>>>	3.596 943 1E+09
pond	>>>	1.019 716 2E+11
pound-force	>>>	2.248 089 4E+08
poundal	>>>	7.233 013 9E+09

gigaohm   <electric resistance>

Convert To	Standard	Scientific
1/ siemens	>>>	1.000 000 0E+09
abohm	>>>	1.000 000 0E+18
ohm	>>>	1.000 000 0E+09
statohm	0.001 112 7	1.112 650 1E-03

gigaohm meter   <electric resistivity>

Convert To	Standard	Scientific
abohm centimeter	>>>	1.000 000 0E+20
microohm inch	>>>	3.937 007 9E+16
ohm circular mil/foot	>>>	6.015 304 9E+17
ohm meter	>>>	1.000 000 0E+09
ohm square millimeter/meter	>>>	1.000 000 0E+15
statohm centimeter	0.111 265	1.112 650 1E-01

gigapascal   <pressure>

Convert To	Standard	Scientific
atmosphere [standard]	9,869.232 7	9.869 232 7E+03
atmosphere [technical]	10,197.162	1.019 716 2E+04
bar	10,000	1.000 000 0E+04
foot of mercury [0 °C, by convention]	24,608.319	2.460 831 9E+04
foot of water [4 °C, by convention]	334,552.56	3.345 525 6E+05
kilobar	10	1.000 000 0E+01
kilogram-force/square millimeter	101.971 62	1.019 716 2E+02
kilopond/square millimeter	101.971 62	1.019 716 2E+02
kip/square inch	145.037 74	1.450 377 4E+02
newton/square millimeter	1,000	1.000 000 0E+03
pascal	>>>	1.000 000 0E+09
pound-force/square inch	145,037.74	1.450 377 4E+05
ton-force/square inch [short]	72.518 869	7.251 886 9E+01
ton-force/square meter [metric]	101,971.62	1.019 716 2E+05
torr	7,500,616.8	7.500 616 8E+06

gigasiemens   <electric conductance>

Convert To	Standard	Scientific
absiemens	1	1.000 000 0E+00
electromagnetic unit of conductance [cgs system]	1	1.000 000 0E+00
siemens	>>>	1.000 000 0E+09
statsiemens	>>>	8.987 551 8E+20

gigatesla   <magnetic flux density>

Convert To	Standard	Scientific
electrostatic unit of magnetic flux density [cgs system]	333.564 095	3.335 641 0E+02
gaussian magnetic flux density	333.564 095	3.335 641 0E+02
maxwell/square meter	>>>	1.000 000 0E+09
tesla	>>>	1.000 000 0E+09

Convert From Convert To	Standard	<Type of Unit> Scientific

gigavolt   **<electric potential>**

abvolt	>>>	$1.000\ 000\ 0E{+}17$
electrostatic unit of electric potential [cgs system]	3,335,640.95	$3.335\ 641\ 0E{+}06$
statvolt	3,335,640.95	$3.335\ 641\ 0E{+}06$
volt	>>>	$1.000\ 000\ 0E{+}09$

gigawatt   **<power>**

Btu/second [I.T., pre-1956]	947,831.36	$9.478\ 313\ 6E{+}05$
Btu/second [thermoc.]	948,451.41	$9.484\ 514\ 1E{+}05$
calorie/second [I.T.]	>>>	$2.388\ 459\ 0E{+}08$
calorie/second [thermoc.]	>>>	$2.390\ 057\ 4E{+}08$
centigrade heat unit/second [mean]	526,159.05	$5.261\ 590\ 5E{+}05$
cubic meter atmosphere/second	>>>	$9.869\ 232\ 7E{+}09$
dyne centimeter/second	>>>	$1.000\ 000\ 0E{+}16$
erg/second	>>>	$1.000\ 000\ 0E{+}16$
foot pound-force/second	>>>	$7.375\ 621\ 5E{+}08$
foot poundal/second	>>>	$2.373\ 036\ 0E{+}10$
gram-force centimeter/second	>>>	$1.019\ 716\ 2E{+}13$
horsepower	1,341,022.1	$1.341\ 022\ 1E{+}06$
horsepower [metric]	1,359,621.6	$1.359\ 621\ 6E{+}06$
joule/second	>>>	$1.000\ 000\ 0E{+}09$
kilocalorie/second [I.T.]	238,845.9	$2.388\ 459\ 0E{+}05$
kilogram-force meter/second	>>>	$1.019\ 716\ 2E{+}08$
kilopond meter/second	>>>	$1.019\ 716\ 2E{+}08$
million Btu/hour [I.T.]	3,412.141 6	$3.412\ 141\ 6E{+}03$
newton meter/second	>>>	$1.000\ 000\ 0E{+}09$
ton of refrigeration	284,345.14	$2.843\ 451\ 4E{+}05$
volt ampere	>>>	$1.000\ 000\ 0E{+}09$
watt	>>>	$1.000\ 000\ 0E{+}09$

gigawatthour   **<energy>**

Btu [I.T.]	>>>	$3.412\ 141\ 6E{+}09$
calorie [I.T.]	>>>	$8.598\ 452\ 3E{+}11$
calorie [kilogram, I.T.]	>>>	$8.598\ 452\ 3E{+}08$
centigrade heat unit [I.T.]	>>>	$1.895\ 634\ 2E{+}09$
cheval vapeur heure [France]	1,359,621.6	$1.359\ 621\ 6E{+}06$
coal equivalent kilogram [UN, standard]	122,835.03	$1.228\ 350\ 3E{+}05$
coal equivalent metric ton [UN, standard]	122.835 03	$1.228\ 350\ 3E{+}02$
foot pound-force	>>>	$2.655\ 223\ 7E{+}12$
foot poundal	>>>	$8.542\ 929\ 7E{+}13$
gram [atomic physics, eq. energy]	0.040 055 4	$4.005\ 540\ 2E{-}02$
horsepower hour	1,341,022.1	$1.341\ 022\ 1E{+}06$
horsepower hour [metric]	1,359,621.6	$1.359\ 621\ 6E{+}06$
joule	>>>	$3.600\ 000\ 0E{+}12$
kilogram [atomic physics, eq. energy]	0.000 040 1	$4.005\ 540\ 2E{-}05$
kiloton [metric, explosive energy]	0.000 860 4	$8.604\ 206\ 5E{-}01$
megaton [metric, explosive energy]	0.000 000 8	$8.604\ 206\ 5E{-}04$
myriawatthour	100,000	$1.000\ 000\ 0E{+}05$
pferdestarkenstunde [Germany]	1,359,621.6	$1.359\ 621\ 6E{+}06$
quad	0.000 003 4	$3.412\ 141\ 6E{-}06$
therm [EEC]	34,121.416	$3.412\ 141\ 6E{+}04$
therm [US]	34,129.563	$3.412\ 956\ 3E{+}04$
thermie [France]	860,050.65	$8.600\ 506\ 5E{+}05$
ton [metric, explosive energy]	860.420 65	$8.604\ 206\ 5E{+}02$
watthour	>>>	$1.000\ 000\ 0E{+}09$

gigaweber   **<magnetic flux>**

electrostatic unit of magnetic flux [cgs system]	3,335,640.95	$3.335\ 641\ 0E{+}06$
gauss square centimeter	>>>	$1.000\ 000\ 0E{+}17$
maxwell	>>>	$1.000\ 000\ 0E{+}17$
statweber	3,335,640.95	$3.335\ 641\ 0E{+}06$
unit pole	>>>	$7.957\ 747\ 5E{+}15$
weber	>>>	$1.000\ 000\ 0E{+}09$

gilbert   **<electric current>**

abampere	0.079 577 5	$7.957\ 747\ 2E{-}02$

| Convert From | | <Type of Unit> |
Convert To	Standard	Scientific
ampere	0.795 774 7	7.957 747 2E-01
deciampere	7.957 747 2	7.957 747 2E+00
statampere	>>>	2.385 672 6E+09

gilbert/centimeter <magnetic field strength>

	Standard	Scientific
ampere/inch	2.021 267 8	2.021 267 8E+00
ampere/meter	79.577 471 5	7.957 747 1E+01
oersted	1	1.000 000 0E+00
statampere/centimeter	>>>	2.385 672 6E+09

gill [UK] <volume>

	Standard	Scientific
bushel [UK]	0.003 906 3	3.906 250 0E-03
cubic foot	0.005 017	5.016 989 2E-03
cubic inch	8.669 357 3	8.669 357 3E+00
cubic meter	0.000 142 1	1.420 653 1E-04
cubic yard	0.000 185 8	1.858 144 1E-04
cup [Canada, measuring]	0.625	6.250 000 0E-01
cup [US, measuring]	0.600 475	6.004 749 6E-01
deciliter	1.420 653 1	1.420 653 1E+00
drachm [UK, liquid]	40	4.000 000 0E+01
dram [Canada, liquid]	40	4.000 000 0E+01
dram [US, liquid]	38.430 398	3.843 039 8E+01
gallon [Canada, liquid]	0.031 25	3.125 000 0E-02
gallon [UK, dry or liquid]	0.031 25	3.125 000 0E-02
gallon [US, liquid]	0.037 529 7	3.752 968 5E-02
gill [US]	1.200 949 9	1.200 949 9E+00
liter	0.142 065 3	1.420 653 1E-01
minim [UK]	2,400	2.400 000 0E+03
minim [US]	2,305.823 9	2.305 823 9E+03
ounce [UK, liquid]	5	5.000 000 0E+00
ounce [US, liquid]	4.803 799 7	4.803 799 7E+00
pint [UK]	0.25	2.500 000 0E-01
quart [UK]	0.125	1.250 000 0E-01
scruple [UK, liquid]	120	1.200 000 0E+02
tablespoon [Canada, measuring]	10.000 017	1.000 001 7E+01
tablespoon [US, measuring]	9.607 599 4	9.607 599 4E+00
teaspoon [Canada, measuring]	30.000 051	3.000 005 1E+01
teaspoon [US, measuring]	28.822 798	2.882 279 8E+01

gill [US] <volume>

	Standard	Scientific
barrel [UK]	0.000 722 8	7.228 074 5E-04
barrel [US, liquid]	0.000 992 1	9.920 634 9E-04
barrel [US, petroleum]	0.000 744	7.440 476 2E-04
cubic decimeter	0.118 294 1	1.182 941 2E-01
cubic foot	0.004 177 5	4.177 517 4E-03
cubic inch	7.218 75	7.218 750 0E+00
cubic meter	0.000 118 3	1.182 941 2E-04
cup [Canada, measuring]	0.520 421 4	5.204 213 7E-01
cup [US, measuring]	0.5	5.000 000 0E-01
drachm [UK, liquid]	33.306 967	3.330 696 7E+01
dram [Canada, liquid]	33.306 967	3.330 696 7E+01
dram [US, liquid]	32	3.200 000 0E+01
drop [US, liquid]	1,440	1.440 000 0E+03
gallon [Canada, liquid]	0.026 021 1	2.602 106 8E-02
gallon [UK, dry or liquid]	0.026 021 1	2.602 106 8E-02
gallon [US, liquid]	0.031 25	3.125 000 0E-02
gill [UK]	0.832 674 2	8.326 741 8E-01
liter	0.118 294 1	1.182 941 2E-01
minim [UK]	1,998.418	1.998 418 0E+03
minim [US]	1,920	1.920 000 0E+03
ounce [UK, liquid]	4.163 370 9	4.163 370 9E+00
ounce [US, liquid]	4	4.000 000 0E+00
pint [UK]	0.208 168 6	2.081 685 5E-01
pint [US, liquid]	0.25	2.500 000 0E-01
quart [UK]	0.104 084 3	1.040 842 7E-01
quart [US, liquid]	0.125	1.250 000 0E-01

scruple [UK, liquid]	99.920 902	9.992 090 2E+01
tablespoon [Canada, measuring]	8.326 755 9	8.326 755 9E+00
tablespoon [US, measuring]	8	8.000 000 0E+00
teaspoon [Canada, measuring]	24.980 268	2.498 026 8E+01
teaspoon [US, measuring]	24	2.400 000 0E+01
Winchester wine gallon [UK]	0.031 25	3.125 000 0E-02

gin [Batavia] <mass, special - see page 29>
gram — 617.5 — 6.175 000 0E+02

gin [Iraq, ancient] <volume, special - see page 29>
liter — 4.82 — 4.820 000 0E+00

gin [Iraq, ancient] <area, special - see page 29>
square meter — 0.25 — 2.500 000 0E-01

gin [Japan] <mass, special - see page 29>
gram — 594 — 5.940 000 0E+02

gin [Java] <mass, special - see page 29>
gram — 615 — 6.150 000 0E+02

gin [Malaysia] <mass, special - see page 29>
kilogram — 0.604 775 — 6.047 750 0E-01

gin [Philippines] <mass, special - see page 29>
gram — 594.375 — 5.943 750 0E+02

gin [Sumatra] <mass, special - see page 29>
gram — 960.25 — 9.602 500 0E+02

giornata [Italy] <area, special - see page 29>
are — 38 — 3.800 000 0E+01

girah [Iran] <length, special - see page 29>
centimeter — 6.5 — 6.500 000 0E+00

girah [Pakistan] <length, special - see page 29>
centimeter — 5.715 — 5.715 000 0E+00

gireh [India] <length, special - see page 29>
centimeter — 5.715 — 5.715 000 0E+00

gireh [Iran] <length, special - see page 29>
centimeter — 6.5 — 6.500 000 0E+00

girib [Turkey] <area, special - see page 29>
hectare — 0.207 — 2.070 000 0E-01

girla [Tanzania] <mass, special - see page 29>
kilogram — 163.3 — 1.633 000 0E+02

giro [Burma, troy] <mass, special - see page 29>
gram — 392.9 — 3.929 000 0E+02

gis [Sumeria, ancient] <length, special - see page 29>
meter — 360.7 — 3.607 000 0E+02

gisla [Eritrea] <mass, special - see page 29>
kilogram — 163.08 — 1.630 800 0E+02

gisla [Somalia, dry] <volume, special - see page 29>
liter — 163.08 — 1.630 800 0E+02

gisla [Tanzania] <mass, special - see page 29>
kilogram — 163.3 — 1.633 000 0E+02

gisla [Yugoslavia] <mass, special - see page 29>
kilogram — 163 — 1.630 000 0E+02

gizla [Somalia, dry] <volume, special - see page 29>
hectoliter — 1.631 — 1.631 000 0E+00

gizla [Somalia] <mass, special - see page 29>
kilogram — 163.08 — 1.630 800 0E+02

glied [Germany, wool] <mass, special - see page 29>
kilogram — 10.719 — 1.071 900 0E+01

glug <mass>
hyl — 0.1 — 1.000 000 0E-01

Convert From	<Type of Unit>	
Convert To	Standard	Scientific

kilogram	0.980 665	9.806 650 0E-01
kilogram-force square second/meter	0.1	1.000 000 0E-01

g_n [due to gravity] `<acceleration>`
foot/square second	32.174 048 6	3.217 404 9E+01
g-unit	1	1.000 000 0E+00
galileo	980.665	9.806 650 0E+02
grav	1	1.000 000 0E+00
meter/square second	9.806 65	9.806 650 0E+00

go [Japan] `<volume, special - see page 29>`
liter	0.18	1.800 000 0E-01

go [Japan] `<area, special - see page 29>`
square meter	0.330 58	3.305 800 0E-01

goduk [Turkey] `<volume, special - see page 29>`
liter	25.2	2.520 000 0E+01

gomari [Cyprus] `<volume, special - see page 29>`
liter	163.659	1.636 590 0E+02

gomor [Hebrew, ancient] `<volume, special - see page 29>`
liter	3.8	3.800 000 0E+00

gomor [Rome, ancient, large] `<volume, special - see page 29>`
liter	120	1.200 000 0E+02

gomor [Rome, ancient, small] `<volume, special - see page 29>`
liter	96	9.600 000 0E+01

gon [angular] `<plane angle>`
degree [angular]	0.9	9.000 000 0E-01
grade [angular]	1	1.000 000 0E+00
mil [military artillery, angle, US, WWII]	10	1.000 000 0E+01
radian	0.015 708	1.570 796 3E-02
right angle	0.01	1.000 000 0E-02

gon [Persia] `<mass, special - see page 29>`
gram	0.045	4.500 000 0E-02

gon [Vietnam] `<length, special - see page 29>`
meter	187.5	1.875 000 0E+02

gong li [China] `<length, special - see page 29>`
kilometer	1	1.000 000 0E+00

gong mu [China] `<area, special - see page 29>`
are	1	1.000 000 0E+00

gong qing [China] `<area, special - see page 29>`
hectare	1	1.000 000 0E+00

googol `<units>`
unit	>>>	1.000 000 0E+100

googolplex [defined as 10 to the power of googol] `<units>`

unit $10^{10^{100}}$ (ten to the tenth power to the hundredth power)

gorraf [Libya] `<mass, special - see page 29>`
kilogram	12.5	1.250 000 0E+01

gouffa [Morocco] `<area, special - see page 29>`
hectare	0.5	5.000 000 0E-01

goundo [Ethiopia] `<volume, special - see page 29>`
liter	3	3.000 000 0E+00

grade [angular] `<plane angle>`
gon [angular]	1	1.000 000 0E+00
mil [military artillery, angle, NATO]	16	1.600 000 0E+01
mil [military artillery, angle, US, WWII]	10	1.000 000 0E+01
minute [angular]	54	5.400 000 0E+01
radian	0.015 708	1.570 796 3E-02
right angle	0.01	1.000 000 0E-02

	Standard	Scientific
second [angular]	3,240	3.240 000 0E+03
gradula [Libya]	<area, special - see page 29>	
square meter	12.25	1.225 000 0E+01
gradus [Rome, ancient]	<length, special - see page 29>	
meter	0.74	7.400 000 0E-01
grain		<mass>
carat [international]	0.323 994 6	3.239 945 5E-01
carat [UK]	0.25	2.500 000 0E-01
carat [US, after 1913]	0.323 994 6	3.239 945 5E-01
centigram	6.479 891	6.479 891 0E+00
drachm [UK, apothecary]	0.016 666 7	1.666 666 7E-02
dram [avoirdupois]	0.036 571 4	3.657 142 9E-02
dram [US, apothecary]	0.016 666 7	1.666 666 7E-02
grain	1	1.000 000 0E+00
grain [apothecary]	1	1.000 000 0E+00
grain [avoirdupois]	1	1.000 000 0E+00
grain [troy]	1	1.000 000 0E+00
kilogram	0.000 064 8	6.479 891 0E-05
ounce	0.002 285 7	2.285 714 3E-03
ounce [apothecary]	0.002 083 3	2.083 333 3E-03
ounce [avoirdupois]	0.002 285 7	2.285 714 3E-03
ounce [troy]	0.002 083 3	2.083 333 3E-03
pennyweight [troy]	0.041 666 7	4.166 666 7E-02
point [jewelers']	32.399 455	3.239 945 5E+01
grain [apothecary]		<mass>
carat [international]	0.323 994 6	3.239 945 5E-01
carat [UK]	0.25	2.500 000 0E-01
carat [US, after 1913]	0.323 994 6	3.239 945 5E-01
centigram	6.479 891	6.479 891 0E+00
drachm [UK, apothecary]	0.016 666 7	1.666 666 7E-02
dram [avoirdupois]	0.036 571 4	3.657 142 9E-02
dram [US, apothecary]	0.016 666 7	1.666 666 7E-02
grain	1	1.000 000 0E+00
grain [avoirdupois]	1	1.000 000 0E+00
grain [troy]	1	1.000 000 0E+00
kilogram	0.000 064 8	6.479 891 0E-05
ounce	0.002 285 7	2.285 714 3E-03
ounce [apothecary]	0.002 083 3	2.083 333 3E-03
ounce [avoirdupois]	0.002 285 7	2.285 714 3E-03
ounce [troy]	0.002 083 3	2.083 333 3E-03
pennyweight [troy]	0.041 666 7	4.166 666 7E-02
point [jewelers']	32.399 455	3.239 945 5E+01
scruple [UK]	0.05	5.000 000 0E-02
scruple [US, apothecary]	0.05	5.000 000 0E-02
grain [avoirdupois]		<mass>
carat [international]	0.323 994 6	3.239 945 5E-01
carat [UK]	0.25	2.500 000 0E-01
carat [US, after 1913]	0.323 994 6	3.239 945 5E-01
centigram	6.479 891	6.479 891 0E+00
drachm [UK, apothecary]	0.016 666 7	1.666 666 7E-02
dram [avoirdupois]	0.036 571 4	3.657 142 9E-02
dram [US, apothecary]	0.016 666 7	1.666 666 7E-02
grain	1	1.000 000 0E+00
grain [apothecary]	1	1.000 000 0E+00
grain [troy]	1	1.000 000 0E+00
kilogram	0.000 064 8	6.479 891 0E-05
ounce	0.002 285 7	2.285 714 3E-03
ounce [apothecary]	0.002 083 3	2.083 333 3E-03
ounce [avoirdupois]	0.002 285 7	2.285 714 3E-03
ounce [troy]	0.002 083 3	2.083 333 3E-03
pennyweight [troy]	0.041 666 7	4.166 666 7E-02
point [jewelers']	32.399 455	3.239 945 5E+01

Convert From		<Type of Unit>
Convert To	Standard	Scientific

scruple [UK]	0.05	5.000 000 0E−02
scruple [US, apothecary]	0.05	5.000 000 0E−02

grain [Bahrain] <mass, special - see page 29>
milligram	64.8	6.480 000 0E+01

grain [France, 1800 definition] <mass, special - see page 29>
gram	0.1	1.000 000 0E−01

grain [France] <mass, special - see page 29>
gram	0.053 1	5.310 000 0E−02

grain [India] <mass, special - see page 29>
gram	0.064 798 9	6.479 891 0E−02

grain [metric] <mass>
kilogram	0.000 05	5.000 000 0E−05

grain [Pakistan] <mass, special - see page 29>
gram	0.064 798 9	6.479 891 0E−02

grain [Russia] <mass, special - see page 29>
milligram	62.2	6.220 000 0E+01

grain [Switzerland, apothecary] <mass, special - see page 29>
gram	0.065 104 2	6.510 417 0E−02

grain [Switzerland] <mass, special - see page 29>
milligram	65.104	6.510 400 0E+01

grain [troy] <mass>
carat [international]	0.323 994 6	3.239 945 5E−01
carat [UK]	0.25	2.500 000 0E−01
carat [US, after 1913]	0.323 994 6	3.239 945 5E−01
centigram	6.479 891	6.479 891 0E+00
drachm [UK, apothecary]	0.016 666 7	1.666 666 7E−02
dram [avoirdupois]	0.036 571 4	3.657 142 9E−02
dram [US, apothecary]	0.016 666 7	1.666 666 7E−02
grain	1	1.000 000 0E+00
grain [apothecary]	1	1.000 000 0E+00
grain [avoirdupois]	1	1.000 000 0E+00
kilogram	0.000 064 8	6.479 891 0E−05
ounce	0.002 285 7	2.285 714 3E−03
ounce [apothecary]	0.002 083 3	2.083 333 3E−03
ounce [avoirdupois]	0.002 285 7	2.285 714 3E−03
ounce [troy]	0.002 083 3	2.083 333 3E−03
pennyweight [troy]	0.041 666 7	4.166 666 7E−02
point [jewelers']	32.399 455	3.239 945 5E+01
scruple [UK]	0.05	5.000 000 0E−02
scruple [US, apothecary]	0.05	5.000 000 0E−02

grain [Turkey] <mass, special - see page 29>
milligram	50.1	5.010 000 0E+01

grain-force <force>
crinal	0.006 354 6	6.354 602 3E−03
dyne	63.546 023 1	6.354 602 3E+01
gram-force	0.064 798 9	6.479 891 0E−02
newton	0.000 635 5	6.354 602 3E−04
ounce-force	0.002 285 7	2.285 714 3E−03
pond	0.064 798 9	6.479 891 0E−02
pound-force	0.000 142 9	1.428 571 4E−04
poundal	0.004 596 3	4.596 292 7E−03

grain/cubic foot <density>
grain/cubic yard	27	2.700 000 0E+01
grain/gallon [-/US, liquid]	0.133 680 6	1.336 805 6E−01
gram/cubic meter	2.288 351 9	2.288 351 9E+00
gram/liter	0.002 288 4	2.288 351 9E−03
kilogram/cubic meter	0.002 288 4	2.288 351 9E−03
kilogram/liter	0.000 002 3	2.288 351 9E−06
milligram/liter	2.288 351 9	2.288 351 9E+00
ounce/cubic yard	0.061 714 3	6.171 428 6E−02

pound/cubic inch	<<<	8.267 195 8E–08
pound/gallon [-/US, liquid]	0.000 019 1	1.909 722 2E–05
slug/cubic inch	<<<	2.569 523 0E–09
ton/cubic yard [short]	0.000 001 9	1.928 571 4E–06

grain/cubic inch <density>

grain/cubic foot	1,728	1.728 000 0E+03
grain/cubic yard	46,656	4.665 600 0E+04
grain/gallon [-/US, liquid]	231	2.310 000 0E+02
gram/liter	3.954 272 1	3.954 272 1E+00
kilogram/cubic meter	3.954 272 1	3.954 272 1E+00
milligram/milliliter	3.954 272 1	3.954 272 1E+00
ounce/cubic foot	3.949 714 3	3.949 714 3E+00
ounce/cubic foot [troy]	3.6	3.600 000 0E+00
ounce/gallon [-/US, liquid]	0.528	5.280 000 0E–01
pound/cubic yard	6.665 142 9	6.665 142 9E+00
pound/gallon [-/US, liquid]	0.033	3.300 000 0E–02
slug/cubic yard	0.207 159	2.071 589 7E–01
tonne/cubic meter	0.003 954 3	3.954 272 1E–03

grain/cubic yard <density>

grain/cubic foot	0.037 037	3.703 703 7E–02
grain/gallon [-/US, liquid]	0.004 951 1	4.951 131 7E–03
gram/cubic meter	0.084 753 8	8.475 377 4E–02
kilogram/cubic meter	0.000 084 8	8.475 377 4E–05
milligram/cubic meter	84.753 774	8.475 377 4E+01
ounce/cubic yard	0.002 285 7	2.285 714 3E–03
ounce/cubic yard [troy]	0.002 083 3	2.083 333 3E–03
pound/cubic yard	0.000 142 9	1.428 571 4E–04
slug/cubic yard	0.000 004 4	4.440 135 7E–06

grain/gallon [-/UK, liquid] <density>

grain/cubic foot	6.228 835 5	6.228 835 5E+00
grain/gallon [-/US, liquid]	0.832 674 2	8.326 741 8E–01
gram/liter	0.014 253 8	1.425 376 8E–02
kilogram/cubic meter	0.014 253 8	1.425 376 8E–02
milligram/cubic decimeter	14.253 768	1.425 376 8E+01
ounce/cubic yard	0.384 408 1	3.844 081 3E–01
ounce/cubic yard [troy]	0.350 372	3.503 719 9E–01
pound/cubic yard	0.024 025 5	2.402 550 8E–02
slug/cubic yard	0.000 746 7	7.467 356 2E–04

grain/gallon [-/US, liquid] <density>

grain/cubic foot	7.480 519 5	7.480 519 5E+00
grain/gallon [-/UK, liquid]	1.200 949 9	1.200 949 9E+00
gram/cubic meter	17.118 061	1.711 806 1E+01
kilogram/cubic meter	0.017 118 1	1.711 806 1E–02
milligram/liter	17.118 061	1.711 806 1E+01
ounce/cubic yard	0.461 654 9	4.616 549 2E–01
pound/cubic yard	0.028 853 4	2.885 343 2E–02
slug/cubic yard	0.000 896 8	8.967 920 9E–04

grain/square foot <surface density>

grain/square yard	9	9.000 000 0E+00
kilogram/are	0.069 749	6.974 896 6E–02
kilogram/hectare	6.974 896 6	6.974 896 6E+00
kilogram/square meter	0.000 697 5	6.974 896 6E–04
ounce/square yard	0.020 571 4	2.057 142 9E–02
pound/acre	6.222 857 1	6.222 857 1E+00
pound/square yard	0.001 285 7	1.285 714 3E–03
slug/square yard	0.000 04	3.996 122 2E–05

grain/square inch <surface density>

grain/square foot	144	1.440 000 0E+02
gram/square meter	100.438 51	1.004 385 1E+02
kilogram/are	10.043 851	1.004 385 1E+01
kilogram/square meter	0.100 438 5	1.004 385 1E–01
milligram/square centimeter	10.043 851	1.004 385 1E+01

ounce/square yard	2.962 285 7	2.962 285 7E+00
pound/acre	896.091 43	8.960 914 3E+02
pound/square yard	0.185 142 9	1.851 428 6E−01
slug/square yard	0.005 754 4	5.754 415 9E−03
tonne/square meter	0.000 100 4	1.004 385 1E−04
grain/square yard		**\<surface density>**
grain/square foot	0.111 111 1	1.111 111 1E−01
kilogram/hectare	0.774 988 5	7.749 885 1E−01
kilogram/square meter	0.000 077 5	7.749 885 1E−05
milligram/square meter	77.498 851	7.749 885 1E+01
ounce/square yard	0.002 285 7	2.285 714 3E−03
pound/acre	0.691 428 6	6.914 285 7E−01
pound/square yard	0.000 142 9	1.428 571 4E−04
gram		**\<mass>**
abbas [Iran]	5.388 511 7	5.388 511 7E+00
abbassi [Iran]	0.002 666 7	2.666 666 7E−03
acino [Italy]	26.315 789	2.631 578 9E+01
adarme [Argentina]	0.558 659 2	5.586 592 2E−01
adarme [Chile]	0.558 659 2	5.586 592 2E−01
adarme [Honduras]	0.558 659 2	5.586 592 2E−01
adarme [Mexico]	0.558 659 2	5.586 592 2E−01
adarme [Peru]	0.558 659 2	5.586 592 2E−01
adarme [Spain]	0.558 659 2	5.586 592 2E−01
agito [Burma]	0.002 545 2	2.545 176 9E−03
akey [Sudan]	0.769 230 8	7.692 307 7E−01
almane [India]	0.000 887 6	8.875 713 4E−04
ansyr [Russia]	0.001 831 5	1.831 501 8E−03
aratel [Brazil]	0.002 201 4	2.201 430 9E−03
argienco [Spain]	0.571 428 6	5.714 285 7E−01
argienso [Spain]	0.571 428 6	5.714 285 7E−01
arratel [Argentina]	0.002 176 8	2.176 752 2E−03
arratel [Bolivia]	0.002 173 9	2.173 913 0E−03
arratel [Brazil]	0.002 178 4	2.178 411 9E−03
arratel [Chile]	0.002 173 9	2.173 913 0E−03
arratel [Colombia]	0.002	2.000 000 0E−03
arratel [Costa Rica]	0.002 173 9	2.173 913 0E−03
arratel [Cuba]	0.002 173 5	2.173 487 8E−03
arratel [Ecuador]	0.002 173 9	2.173 913 0E−03
arratel [El Salvador]	0.002 173 9	2.173 913 0E−03
arratel [Guatemala]	0.002 173 9	2.173 913 0E−03
arratel [Honduras]	0.002 173 9	2.173 913 0E−03
arratel [Mexico]	0.002 173	2.172 968 3E−03
arratel [Paraguay]	0.002 178 6	2.178 649 2E−03
arratel [Peru]	0.002 173 9	2.173 913 0E−03
arratel [Philippines]	0.002 173 9	2.173 913 0E−03
arratel [Portugal]	0.002 178 4	2.178 411 9E−03
arratel [Spain]	0.002 173 5	2.173 487 8E−03
arratel [Venezuela]	0.002 169 7	2.169 668 0E−03
artal [Ethiopia]	0.003 215 4	3.215 434 1E−03
artal [Turkey]	0.001 558 9	1.558 913 3E−03
as [Rome, ancient]	0.003 058 1	3.058 104 0E−03
as [Sweden]	20.815 12	2.081 512 0E+01
ass [Germany]	20.833 333	2.083 333 3E+01
ass [Italy]	26.315 789	2.631 578 9E+01
aureus [Rome, ancient]	0.128 205 1	1.282 051 3E−01
baht [Burma]	0.061 237	6.123 698 7E−02
baht [Laos]	0.066 666 7	6.666 666 7E−02
baht [Thailand]	0.066 666 7	6.666 666 7E−02
bai [Laos]	0.026 666 7	2.666 666 7E−02
bak [Laos]	0.266 666 7	2.666 666 7E−01
bak [Thailand]	0.266 666 7	2.666 666 7E−01
baquila [Egypt]	0.427 350 4	4.273 504 3E−01
bat [Burma]	0.061 237	6.123 698 7E−02

gram (continued) \<mass\>

	Standard	Scientific
bat [Laos]	0.066 666 7	6.666 666 7E–02
bat [Thailand]	0.066 666 7	6.666 666 7E–02
bath [Burma]	0.061 237	6.123 698 7E–02
bath [Laos]	0.066 666 7	6.666 666 7E–02
bath [Thailand]	0.066 666 7	6.666 666 7E–02
batman [Iran]	0.000 168 3	1.682 935 0E–04
behar [Indonesia]	0.003 694 7	3.694 699 6E–03
bei ke [China]	0.01	1.000 000 0E–02
beka [Hebrew, ancient]	0.173 913	1.739 130 4E–01
bekah [Hebrew, ancient]	0.166 666 7	1.666 666 7E–01
bekaim [Hebrew, ancient]	0.158 730 2	1.587 301 6E–01
benda [Central Africa]	0.015 625	1.562 500 0E–02
beqa [Egypt, ancient]	0.064 102 6	6.410 256 4E–02
beqa [Hebrew, ancient]	0.175 07	1.750 700 3E–01
bes [Rome, ancient]	0.004 580 9	4.580 852 0E–03
bhan [Bangladesh]	0.085 733 9	8.573 388 2E–02
bhari [India]	0.085 735 4	8.573 535 2E–02
bia [Laos]	0.026 666 7	2.666 666 7E–02
binae sextulae [Rome, ancient]	0.109 938 4	1.099 384 3E–01
bis [Burma]	0.000 650 7	6.506 604 2E–04
bismar pound [Denmark]	0.000 166 9	1.668 613 4E–04
bissmar pound [Denmark]	0.000 166 9	1.668 613 4E–04
bohar [Indochina]	0.022 036 1	2.203 613 9E–02
bohar [Sumatra]	0.020 833 3	2.083 333 3E–02
bojote [Venezuela]	0.004	4.000 000 0E–03
bongkal [Malaysia]	0.018 548 4	1.854 840 2E–02
buncal [Indochina]	0.022 036 1	2.203 613 9E–02
buncal [Sumatra]	0.020 833 3	2.083 333 3E–02
bunkal [Indochina]	0.022 036 1	2.203 613 9E–02
bunkal [Sumatra]	0.020 833 3	2.083 333 3E–02
cafla [Arabia, ancient]	0.315 756 2	3.157 562 4E–01
candareen [Cambodia]	2.666 666 7	2.666 666 7E+00
candareen [China]	2	2.000 000 0E+00
candareen [Hong Kong]	2.645 502 6	2.645 502 6E+00
candareen [Japan]	2.666 666 7	2.666 666 7E+00
candareen [Laos]	2.666 666 7	2.666 666 7E+00
candarin [China]	2.645 546 7	2.645 546 7E+00
caractero [Spain]	5	5.000 000 0E+00
carak [Persia]	0.001 333 3	1.333 333 3E–03
carat [international]	5	5.000 000 0E+00
carat [Italy, Bologna, gold, silver and jewels]	9.259 259 3	9.259 259 3E+00
carat [Italy, Florence, gold, silver and jewels]	0.070 671 4	7.067 137 8E–02
carat [Italy, Genoa, gold, silver and jewels]	0.075 643	7.564 296 5E–02
carat [Italy, Milan, gold, silver and jewels]	0.102 040 8	1.020 408 2E–01
carat [Italy, Turin, gold, silver and jewels]	0.097 561	9.756 097 6E–02
carat [Italy, Venice, gold, silver and jewels]	5	5.000 000 0E+00
carat [Thailand]	5	5.000 000 0E+00
carat [UK]	3.858 089 6	3.858 089 6E+00
carat [US, after 1913]	5	5.000 000 0E+00
carate [Germany, gold and silver]	0.094 162	9.416 195 9E–02
carate [Germany, jewels and pearls]	5.050 505 1	5.050 505 1E+00
carate [Switzerland, gold and silver]	0.098 039 2	9.803 921 6E–02
castellano [Spain]	0.208 637 6	2.086 376 0E–01
catti [Batavia]	0.001 619 4	1.619 433 2E–03
catti [China]	0.001 653 2	1.653 234 1E–03
catti [Japan]	0.001 683 5	1.683 501 7E–03
catti [Sumatra]	0.001 653 2	1.653 234 1E–03
cattie [Burma]	0.001 837 2	1.837 168 7E–03
catty [Batavia]	0.001 619 4	1.619 433 2E–03
catty [Java]	0.001 626	1.626 016 3E–03
catty [Malaysia]	0.001 083 8	1.083 775 9E–03
catty [Philippines]	0.001 682 4	1.682 439 5E–03

gram (continued)   \<mass\>

	Standard	Scientific
catty [Sumatra]	0.001 041 4	1.041 395 5E–03
ceira [Portuguese India]	0.001 071 7	1.071 696 5E–03
chalkos [Greece, ancient]	0.116 279 1	1.162 790 7E–01
charruba [Libya]	5.215 994 3	5.215 994 3E+00
chattack [Bangladesh]	0.017 146 8	1.714 677 6E–02
chattack [India]	0.017 146 8	1.714 677 6E–02
chattack [Pakistan]	0.017 146 8	1.714 677 6E–02
chattak [Ceylon]	0.017 147 1	1.714 706 5E–02
chattak [Pakistan]	0.017 147 1	1.714 707 0E–02
chattauck [India]	0.017 147 1	1.714 707 0E–02
chawal [Pakistan]	65.844 749	6.584 474 9E+01
chee [Malaysia]	0.264 550 3	2.645 502 6E–01
cheky [Turkey]	0.003 138 1	3.138 072 0E–03
chequi [Turkey]	0.003 138 1	3.138 072 0E–03
chhatak [Bangladesh]	0.017 147 1	1.714 707 0E–02
chhatak [India]	0.017 147 1	1.714 707 0E–02
chhatak [Pakistan]	0.017 147 1	1.714 707 0E–02
chi [Cambodia]	0.266 666 7	2.666 666 7E–01
chi [Hong Kong]	0.264 550 3	2.645 502 6E–01
chi [Mongolia]	0.266 666 7	2.666 666 7E–01
chien [China]	0.264 557 3	2.645 572 6E–01
chien [Singapore]	0.290 297 7	2.902 976 7E–01
chin [Cambodia]	0.266 666 7	2.666 666 7E–01
chin [China, old]	0.001 653 5	1.653 467 0E–03
chin [Hong Kong]	0.264 557 3	2.645 572 6E–01
chin [Mongolia]	0.266 666 7	2.666 666 7E–01
chittack [India]	0.017 147 1	1.714 707 0E–02
chittak [India]	0.017 147 1	1.714 706 5E–02
clove [UK]	0.000 275 6	2.755 778 3E–04
coccio [Italy]	1.818 181 8	1.818 181 8E+00
crown [Switzerland]	0.296 735 9	2.967 359 1E–01
dam [East India]	0.047 709 9	4.770 992 4E–02
damleng [Brunei]	0.026 455	2.645 502 6E–02
damleng [Cambodia]	0.026 666 7	2.666 666 7E–02
damleng [China]	0.026 455	2.645 502 6E–02
damleng [Hong Kong]	0.026 455	2.645 502 6E–02
danar [Iran]	0.005 333 3	5.333 333 3E–03
danich [Arabia]	2.5	2.500 000 0E+00
darchini [Arabia]	2.5	2.500 000 0E+00
dareikos [Persia, ancient, gold]	0.118 906 1	1.189 060 6E–01
daric [Hebrew, ancient, gold]	0.125	1.250 000 0E–01
daric [Persia, ancient, gold]	0.118 906 1	1.189 060 6E–01
dartung [Iran]	0.979 719 8	9.797 198 0E–01
dbn [Egypt, ancient]	0.010 989	1.098 901 1E–02
deben [Egypt, ancient]	0.010 989	1.098 901 1E–02
decunx [Rome, ancient]	0.003 664 6	3.664 614 5E–03
demikilo [France]	0.002	2.000 000 0E–03
denaro [France]	0.787 401 6	7.874 015 7E–01
denaro [Italy]	0.571 428 6	5.714 285 7E–01
denaro [Italy, Milan]	1	1.000 000 0E+00
denaro [Italy, Rome]	0.854 700 9	8.547 008 5E–01
denaro [Italy, Venice]	1	1.000 000 0E+00
denaro [Libya]	0.847 457 6	8.474 576 3E–01
denaro [Switzerland]	1	1.000 000 0E+00
denat [Austria]	0.914 243 9	9.142 439 2E–01
denheiro [Portugal]	0.052 273 9	5.227 391 5E–02
denier [France]	0.784 313 7	7.843 137 3E–01
denier [Italy]	0.571 428 6	5.714 285 7E–01
denier [Italy, Milan]	1	1.000 000 0E+00
denier [Italy, Rome]	0.854 700 9	8.547 008 5E–01
denier [Italy, Venice]	1	1.000 000 0E+00
denier [Switzerland]	1	1.000 000 0E+00

gram (continued)   **<mass>**

Convert To	Standard	Scientific
denk [Turkey]	1.246 882 8	1.246 882 8E+00
derham [Lebanon]	0.312 012 5	3.120 124 8E−01
derham [Persia, gold and silver]	0.106 837 6	1.068 376 1E−01
derhem [Egypt]	0.320 512 8	3.205 128 2E−01
derhem [Iran]	0.106 666 7	1.066 666 7E−01
derhem [Iraq]	0.320 512 8	3.205 128 2E−01
derhem [Persia, gold and silver]	0.106 837 6	1.068 376 1E−01
derhem [Sudan]	0.320 512 8	3.205 128 2E−01
derime [Ethiopia]	0.386 100 4	3.861 003 9E−01
deunx [Rome, ancient]	0.003 331 6	3.331 556 5E−03
deusquin [Netherlands]	10.309 278	1.030 927 8E+01
dextan [Rome, ancient]	0.003 664 6	3.664 614 5E−03
dharana [India, ancient]	0.103 135 3	1.031 353 1E−01
dharana [India, ancient, gold]	0.002 520 2	2.520 161 3E−03
dharana [India, ancient, silver]	0.252 016 1	2.520 161 3E−01
didrachm [Egypt, ancient]	0.128 534 7	1.285 347 0E−01
didrachm [Greece, ancient]	0.102 880 7	1.028 806 6E−01
didrachma [Greece, ancient]	0.116 279 1	1.162 790 7E−01
dilepton [Hebrew, ancient]	0.666 666 7	6.666 666 7E−01
dimidia sextula [Rome, ancient]	0.439 753 7	4.397 537 4E−01
dinar [Arabia]	0.238 095 2	2.380 952 4E−01
dipondium [Rome, ancient]	0.080 645 2	8.064 516 1E−02
dirham [Iran]	0.106 666 7	1.066 666 7E−01
dirhem [Iran]	0.106 666 7	1.066 666 7E−01
dirhem [Persia, gold and silver]	0.106 837 6	1.068 376 1E−01
dirhem [Turkey]	0.1	1.000 000 0E−01
dodran [Rome, ancient]	0.004 071 8	4.071 827 0E−03
don [South Korea]	0.266 666 7	2.666 666 7E−01
donchung [South Korea]	0.266 666 7	2.666 666 7E−01
dong [Vietnam]	0.264 690 3	2.646 903 1E−01
drachm [Egypt, ancient]	0.257 069 4	2.570 694 1E−01
drachm [Ethiopia]	0.386 100 4	3.861 003 9E−01
drachm [Netherlands]	0.256 016 4	2.560 163 9E−01
drachm [Poland]	0.317 460 3	3.174 603 2E−01
drachm [UK, apothecary]	0.257 206	2.572 059 7E−01
drachma [Austria]	0.213 675 2	2.136 752 1E−01
drachma [Cyprus]	0.314 960 6	3.149 606 3E−01
drachma [Egypt]	0.320 512 8	3.205 128 2E−01
drachma [Germany]	0.265 957 5	2.659 574 5E−01
drachma [Greece]	0.229 357 8	2.293 578 0E−01
drachma [Iran]	0.106 666 7	1.066 666 7E−01
drachma [Iraq]	0.311 769 3	3.117 692 9E−01
drachma [Italy]	0.280 112	2.801 120 4E−01
drachma [Jordan]	0.312 012 5	3.120 124 8E−01
drachma [Lebanon]	0.312 012 5	3.120 124 8E−01
drachma [Libya]	0.312 012 5	3.120 124 8E−01
drachma [Netherlands]	0.259 067 4	2.590 673 6E−01
drachma [Rome, ancient]	0.294 117 7	2.941 176 5E−01
drachma [Russia, apothecary]	0.267 952 8	2.679 528 4E−01
drachma [Sudan]	0.320 512 8	3.205 128 2E−01
drachma [Switzerland]	0.322 580 7	3.225 806 5E−01
drachma [Syria]	0.312 012 5	3.120 124 8E−01
drachma [Turkey]	0.311 769 3	3.117 692 9E−01
drachme [Austria, apothecary]	0.228 566 2	2.285 662 0E−01
drachme [Cyprus]	0.314 946 1	3.149 460 5E−01
drachme [France]	0.261 506 3	2.615 062 8E−01
drachme [Greece, ancient]	0.070 546 7	7.054 673 7E−02
drachme [Iraq, ancient]	0.320 512 8	3.205 128 2E−01
drachme [Poland]	0.317 460 3	3.174 603 2E−01
drachme [Switzerland]	0.256 016 4	2.560 163 9E−01
drachme [Turkey]	0.312 5	3.125 000 0E−01
drachme [Turkey, gold and silver]	0.322 580 7	3.225 806 5E−01

gram (continued)

<mass>

	Standard	Scientific
dram [avoirdupois]	0.564 383 4	5.643 833 9E-01
dram [Cyprus]	0.314 960 6	3.149 606 3E-01
dram [Egypt]	0.320 512 8	3.205 128 2E-01
dram [Greece]	0.312 5	3.125 000 2E-01
dram [Iran]	0.106 666 7	1.066 666 7E-01
dram [Iraq]	0.311 769 3	3.117 692 9E-01
dram [Iraq, Baghdad]	0.307 692 3	3.076 923 1E-01
dram [Jordan]	0.312 012 5	3.120 124 8E-01
dram [Lebanon]	0.312 012 5	3.120 124 8E-01
dram [Libya]	0.312 012 5	3.120 124 8E-01
dram [Romania]	0.310 559	3.105 590 1E-01
dram [Sudan]	0.320 512 8	3.205 128 2E-01
dram [Turkey]	0.311 769 3	3.117 692 9E-01
dram [US, apothecary]	0.257 206	2.572 059 7E-01
drame [Iraq]	0.307 692 3	3.076 923 1E-01
drame [Romania]	0.310 559	3.105 590 1E-01
dramm [Yugoslavia]	0.312 5	3.125 000 0E-01
dramma [Cyprus]	0.314 960 6	3.149 606 3E-01
dramma [Egypt]	0.320 512 8	3.205 128 2E-01
dramma [Iran]	0.106 666 7	1.066 666 7E-01
dramma [Libya, gold, silver and silk]	0.326 005	3.260 005 0E-01
dramma [Sudan]	0.320 512 8	3.205 128 2E-01
dramme [Greece]	0.309 597 5	3.095 975 2E-01
ducat [Austria]	0.284 090 9	2.840 909 1E+01
ducat ass [Germany]	17.857 143	1.785 714 3E+01
duella [France, apothecary]	0.098 039 2	9.803 921 6E-02
duella [Rome, ancient]	0.109 938 4	1.099 384 3E-01
duelle [France, apothecary]	0.098 039 2	9.803 921 6E-02
dung [Persia, gold and silver]	1.285 347	1.285 347 0E+00
dyne square second/centimeter	1	1.000 000 0E+00
dzhin [Mongolia]	0.001 666 7	1.666 666 7E-03
engel [Holland, troy]	0.641 025 6	6.410 256 4E-01
engelot [Holland, troy]	0.641 025 6	6.410 256 4E-01
engelsen [Holland, troy]	0.641 025 6	6.410 256 4E-01
escropulo [Brazil]	0.836 512 1	8.365 120 8E-01
escrupulo [Brazil]	0.833 333 3	8.333 333 3E-01
escrupulo [Portugal]	0.836 540 1	8.365 400 7E-01
esschen [Germany]	20.833 333	2.083 333 3E+01
estelin [France, troy]	0.5	5.000 000 0E-01
fan [Cambodia]	2.666 666 7	2.666 666 7E+00
fan [Hong Kong]	2.645 547 4	2.645 547 4E+00
fan [Japan]	2.666 666 7	2.666 666 7E+00
fan [Laos]	2.666 666 7	2.666 666 7E+00
fanoe [East India, troy]	2.645 502 6	2.645 502 6E+00
fatil [Islam]	22.222 222	2.222 222 2E+01
felin [France, troy]	2.631 578 9	2.631 578 9E+00
fen [China, silver]	2.645 502 6	2.645 502 6E+00
ferlino [Italy]	0.578 034 7	5.780 346 8E-01
fern [Singapore, troy]	2.903 010 4	2.903 010 4E+00
foring [Iceland]	0.000 200 2	2.002 402 6E-04
fount [Russia, apothecary]	0.002 790 8	2.790 775 0E-03
founte [Russia]	0.002 442	2.442 002 4E-03
fout [Russia]	0.002 441 9	2.441 928 5E-03
fuen [China, troy]	2.645 502 6	2.645 502 6E+00
funda [Russia, troy]	0.002 444	2.444 031 7E-03
funt [Poland]	0.002	2.000 000 0E-03
funt [Russia]	0.002 442	2.442 002 4E-03
funta [Russia, troy]	0.002 444	2.444 031 7E-03
gauza [Islam]	0.033 613 4	3.361 344 5E-02
gedang [Spice Islands, pepper]	0.000 506 1	5.060 728 7E-04
gera [Hebrew, ancient]	1.222 493 9	1.222 493 9E+00
gerah [Hebrew, ancient]	2	2.000 000 0E+00

gram (continued) <mass>

gian [China]	0.2	2.000 000 0E-01
gin [Batavia]	0.001 619 4	1.619 433 2E-03
gin [Japan]	0.001 683 5	1.683 501 7E-03
gin [Java]	0.001 626	1.626 016 3E-03
gin [Philippines]	0.001 682 4	1.682 439 5E-03
gin [Sumatra]	0.001 041 4	1.041 395 5E-03
giro [Burma, troy]	0.002 545 2	2.545 176 9E-03
gon [Persia]	22.222 222	2.222 222 2E+01
grain	15.432 358	1.543 235 8E+01
grain [apothecary]	15.432 358	1.543 235 8E+01
grain [avoirdupois]	15.432 358	1.543 235 8E+01
grain [France]	18.832 392	1.883 239 2E+01
grain [France, 1800 definition]	10	1.000 000 0E+01
grain [India]	15.432 358	1.543 235 8E+01
grain [Pakistan]	15.432 358	1.543 235 8E+01
grain [Switzerland, apothecary]	15.359 999	1.535 999 9E+01
grain [troy]	15.432 358	1.543 235 8E+01
gramma [Greece, ancient]	0.617 284	6.172 839 5E-01
gran [Austria]	1.694 915 3	1.694 915 3E+00
gran [Austria, apothecary]	13.404 826	1.340 482 6E+01
gran [Belgium, gold]	3.125	3.125 000 0E+00
gran [Belgium, silver]	1.173 708 9	1.173 708 9E+00
gran [Denmark]	1.173 708 9	1.173 708 9E+00
gran [Germany]	1.219 512 2	1.219 512 2E+00
gran [India, troy]	0.085 910 7	8.591 065 3E-02
gran [Switzerland, apothecary]	20	2.000 000 0E+01
gran [UK]	15.384 615	1.538 461 5E+01
grani [Thailand]	1.066 666 7	1.066 666 7E+00
grano [Argentina]	20	2.000 000 0E+01
grano [Chile]	20.030 727	2.003 072 7E+01
grano [Germany]	20	2.000 000 0E+01
grano [Netherlands]	14.925 373	1.492 537 3E+01
grano [Sweden, apothecary]	15.873 016	1.587 301 6E+01
grano [Switzerland, apothecary]	20	2.000 000 0E+01
granottino [Italy, troy]	500	5.000 000 0E+02
granow [Poland]	23.255 814	2.325 581 4E+01
granow [Russia, hay]	0.000 122 2	1.222 045 7E-04
grao [Brazil]	20.076 25	2.007 625 0E+01
grao [Portugal]	20.076 29	2.007 629 0E+01
grein [Netherlands]	15.625	1.562 500 0E+01
grivna [Russia]	0.002 441 8	2.441 787 8E-03
gros [France]	0.261 485 8	2.614 857 6E-01
gros [France, 1800 definition]	0.1	1.000 000 0E-01
gros poid [Switzerland]	0.001 815 9	1.815 903 7E-03
gyrath [Algeria, troy]	4.830 917 9	4.830 917 9E+00
half mina [Greece, ancient]	0.003 199 8	3.199 795 2E-03
hang [Cambodia]	0.026 666 7	2.666 666 7E-02
hang [China]	0.02	2.000 000 0E-02
hardal [Islam, mustard grain]	1,408.450 7	1.408 450 7E+03
harruba [Islam]	5.128 205 1	5.128 205 1E+00
harsela [Egypt]	0.000 783 5	7.834 564 6E-04
heller [Germany, troy]	2.222 222 2	2.222 222 2E+00
heller [UK, apothecary]	66.666 667	6.666 666 7E+01
hiyaka me [Japan]	0.002 666 7	2.666 666 7E-03
hong [Laos]	0.026 666 7	2.666 666 7E-02
hoon [Cambodia]	2.666 666 7	2.666 666 7E+00
hoon [Japan]	2.666 666 7	2.666 666 7E+00
hoon [Laos]	2.666 666 7	2.666 666 7E+00
houn [Hong Kong]	2.645 502 6	2.645 502 6E+00
huitieme [Seychelles]	0.016 343 1	1.634 307 4E-02
hukka [Iraq, Istanbul]	0.779 423 2	7.794 232 3E-01
hyaku me [Japan]	0.002 666 7	2.666 666 7E-03

gram (continued)   \<mass\>

Convert To	Standard	Scientific
kamha [Egypt]	20.512 821	2.051 282 1E+01
kancha [India]	0.068 588 2	6.858 823 5E−02
kanchha [Bangladesh]	0.068 587 1	6.858 710 6E−02
kara [Austria, jewels and pearls]	4.807 692 3	4.807 692 3E+00
kara [Batavia, jewels and pearls]	5.050 505 1	5.050 505 1E+00
kara [East India, jewels and pearls]	5.050 505 1	5.050 505 1E+00
kara [Germany, gold and silver]	0.094 162	9.416 195 9E−02
kara [Germany, jewels and pearls]	4.854 368 9	4.854 368 9E+00
kara [Netherlands, Amsterdam, jewels and pearls]	4.830 917 9	4.830 917 9E+00
kara [Switzerland, Bern, gold and silver]	0.098 039 2	9.803 921 6E−02
kara [UK, London, jewels and pearls]	4.784 689	4.784 689 0E+00
karaat [Netherlands]	3.885 914 2	3.885 914 2E+00
karat [Austria, jewels and pearls]	4.807 692 3	4.807 692 3E+00
karat [Batavia, jewels and pearls]	5.050 505 1	5.050 505 1E+00
karat [East India, jewels and pearls]	5.050 505 1	5.050 505 1E+00
karat [Germany, gold and silver]	0.094 162	9.416 195 9E−02
karat [Germany, jewels and pearls]	4.854 368 9	4.854 368 9E+00
karat [Netherlands, Amsterdam, jewels and pearls]	4.830 917 9	4.830 917 9E+00
karat [Portugal, Lisbon, jewels]	4.859 086 5	4.859 086 5E+00
karat [UK, London, jewels and pearls]	4.784 689	4.784 689 0E+00
karsha [India, ancient]	0.100 806 5	1.008 064 5E−01
karshapana [Hindu, ancient, copper]	0.100 806 5	1.008 064 5E−01
kat [Egypt]	0.107 169 2	1.071 691 6E−01
kati [Burma]	0.001 838 2	1.838 235 3E−03
kati [North Borneo]	0.001 653 5	1.653 466 8E−03
kati [Sarawak]	0.001 653 5	1.653 467 0E−03
kdt [Egypt, ancient]	0.109 890 1	1.098 901 1E−01
ke [China]	1	1.000 000 0E+00
kedet [Egypt, ancient]	0.106 383	1.063 829 8E−01
khaskha [Pakistan]	5.267 577 1	5.267 577 1E+00
khord [Afghanistan]	0.009 057 5	9.057 478 8E−03
kilogram	0.001	1.000 000 0E−03
kirat [Egypt]	5.128 205 1	5.128 205 1E+00
kite [Egypt]	0.109 890 1	1.098 901 1E−01
kiya [Oman]	0.005 941 8	5.941 770 6E−03
klam [Thailand]	4.266 666 7	4.266 666 7E+00
klom [Thailand]	8.533 333 3	8.533 333 3E+00
kon [South Korea]	0.001 666 7	1.666 666 7E−03
kona [India, ancient]	0.142 892 2	1.428 922 1E−01
korn [Sweden]	23.525 205	2.352 520 5E+01
korrel [Netherlands]	10	1.000 000 0E+01
kramergewicht [Germany]	0.002 126 4	2.126 392 8E−03
krinne [Switzerland, large]	0.001 441 3	1.441 337 6E−03
kung chien [Taiwan]	0.1	1.000 000 0E−01
kung fen [China]	1	1.000 000 0E+00
kung ko [Taiwan]	1	1.000 000 0E+00
kung liang [China]	0.01	1.000 000 0E−02
kung liang [Taiwan]	0.01	1.000 000 0E−02
kunke [India]	0.003 547 1	3.547 105 6E−03
kvint [Denmark]	0.2	2.000 000 0E−01
kvintin [Sweden]	0.301 122 3	3.011 222 8E−01
kyaku me [Japan]	0.002 666 7	2.666 666 7E−03
kyat [Burma]	0.061 237	6.123 698 7E−02
kyat [Laos]	0.066 666 7	6.666 666 7E−02
kyat [Romania]	0.061 237	6.123 698 7E−02
kyat [Thailand]	0.066 666 7	6.666 666 7E−02
lan [Mongolia]	0.026 666 7	2.666 666 7E−02
lana [Russia]	0.029 411 8	2.941 176 5E−02
lang [Vietnam]	0.026 455	2.645 502 6E−02
lata [Costa Rica]	0.002 207	2.207 018 3E−03
leang [China]	0.026 456 4	2.645 642 6E−02
leung [Brunei]	0.026 455	2.645 502 6E−02

gram (continued)

		<mass>
leung [Cambodia]	0.026 666 7	2.666 666 7E-02
leung [China]	0.02	2.000 000 0E-02
leung [Hong Kong]	0.026 455	2.645 502 6E-02
li [Cambodia]	26.666 667	2.666 666 7E+01
liang [Brunei]	0.026 455	2.645 502 6E-02
liang [Cambodia]	0.026 666 7	2.666 666 7E-02
liang [China]	0.026 456 4	2.645 642 6E-02
liang [Hong Kong]	0.026 455	2.645 502 6E-02
libbra [Brazil]	0.002 179 6	2.179 599 0E-03
libbra [Italy]	0.002 949 9	2.949 852 5E-03
libbra [Italy, Bologna]	0.002 763 6	2.763 576 1E-03
libbra [Italy, Florence]	0.002 945 5	2.945 508 1E-03
libbra [Italy, Naples]	0.003 117 6	3.117 605 4E-03
libbra [Italy, Palermo, gold and silver]	0.003 149 1	3.149 110 4E-03
libbra [Italy, Parma]	0.003 048 8	3.048 780 5E-03
libbra [Italy, Rome]	0.002 947 2	2.947 244 3E-03
libbra [Italy, Turin]	0.002 711 2	2.711 165 9E-03
libbra [Portugal]	0.002 178 6	2.178 649 2E-03
libbra [Rome, ancient]	0.003 096	3.095 975 2E-03
libbra [Vatican City]	0.002 948 5	2.948 495 7E-03
libbra metrica [Italy, Milan]	0.001	1.000 000 0E-03
libra [Argentina]	0.002 176 8	2.176 752 3E-03
libra [Bolivia]	0.002 173 9	2.173 913 0E-03
libra [Brazil]	0.002 178 4	2.178 411 9E-03
libra [Cape Verde]	0.002 178 6	2.178 649 2E-03
libra [Chile]	0.002 173 5	2.173 473 6E-03
libra [Colombia]	0.002	2.000 000 0E-03
libra [Costa Rica]	0.002 173 9	2.173 913 0E-03
libra [Cuba]	0.002 173 5	2.173 487 8E-03
libra [Dominican Republic]	0.002 204 6	2.204 585 5E-03
libra [Ecuador]	0.002 173 9	2.173 913 0E-03
libra [El Salvador]	0.002 173 9	2.173 913 0E-03
libra [Guatemala]	0.002 173 9	2.173 913 0E-03
libra [Honduras]	0.002 173 9	2.173 913 0E-03
libra [Malta]	0.002 204 6	2.204 585 5E-03
libra [Mexico]	0.002 172 7	2.172 732 2E-03
libra [Nicaragua]	0.002 173 9	2.173 913 0E-03
libra [Paraguay]	0.002 178 6	2.178 649 2E-03
libra [Peru]	0.002 173 9	2.173 913 0E-03
libra [Philippines]	0.002 173 9	2.173 913 0E-03
libra [Portugal]	0.002 178 4	2.178 411 9E-03
libra [Puerto Rico]	0.002 169 2	2.169 197 4E-03
libra [Rome, ancient]	0.003 067 5	3.067 484 7E-03
libra [Spain]	0.002 173 5	2.173 487 8E-03
libra [Uruguay]	0.002 176 8	2.176 752 3E-03
libra [Venezuela]	0.002 169 7	2.169 668 0E-03
libra de farmacia [Argentina]	0.002 901 9	2.901 915 3E-03
libre subtile [France]	0.003 142 3	3.142 282 6E-03
lira [Brazil]	0.002 179 6	2.179 599 0E-03
lira [Italy, Bologna, gold, silver and jewels]	0.002 753 8	2.753 834 7E-03
lira [Italy, Naples]	0.003 115 3	3.115 264 8E-03
lira [Italy, Rome]	0.002 947 2	2.947 244 3E-03
lira [Portugal]	0.002 178 6	2.178 649 2E-03
litra [Greece, ancient]	0.003 063 7	3.063 725 5E-03
litra [Rome, ancient]	0.003 053 9	3.053 901 4E-03
litre [Ethiopia]	0.003 215 4	3.215 434 1E-03
litre [Greece]	0.002 202 6	2.202 643 2E-03
litre [Romania]	0.003 102 7	3.102 699 3E-03
littre [Romania]	0.003 102 7	3.102 699 3E-03
livre [Cambodia]	0.001 666 7	1.666 666 7E-03
livre [France]	0.002 042 9	2.042 875 9E-03
livre [Russia, apothecary]	0.002 790 8	2.790 775 0E-03

gram (continued) <mass>

	Standard	Scientific
livre [Spain]	0.002 173 5	2.173 473 6E-03
livre commune [France]	0.002 042 9	2.042 900 9E-03
livre de Charlemagne [France]	0.002 724 1	2.724 053 4E-03
livre de pharmacie [Switzerland]	0.002 666 7	2.666 666 7E-03
livre esterlin [France]	0.002 724 1	2.724 053 4E-03
livre francaise [Haiti]	0.005 276 9	5.276 882 0E-03
livre poids de table [France]	0.002 451 4	2.451 401 0E-03
livre usuelle [France]	0.002	2.000 000 0E-03
lod [Denmark]	0.064	6.400 000 0E-02
lod [Norway]	0.064 226 1	6.422 607 6E-02
lod [Sweden]	0.075 280 8	7.528 079 7E-02
logarike litra [Greece, ancient]	0.003 125	3.125 000 0E-03
lofti [Russia]	0.078 125	7.812 500 0E-02
lood [Indonesia]	0.064 766 8	6.476 683 9E-02
loode [Netherlands]	0.1	1.000 000 0E-01
loot [Netherlands]	0.064 935 1	6.493 506 5E-02
lot [Germany]	0.1	1.000 000 0E-01
lot [Russia]	0.078 141 7	7.814 172 7E-02
lot [Switzerland]	0.064	6.400 000 0E-02
loth [Austria]	0.057 142 9	5.714 285 7E-02
loth [Germany]	0.1	1.000 000 0E-01
loth [Netherlands]	0.1	1.000 000 0E-01
loth [Norway]	0.064 102 6	6.410 256 4E-02
loth [Poland]	0.078 926 6	7.892 659 8E-02
loth [Russia]	0.078 125	7.812 500 0E-02
loth [Switzerland]	0.064	6.400 000 0E-02
lut [Poland]	0.078 914 1	7.891 414 1E-02
lutow [Poland]	0.078 926 6	7.892 659 8E-02
lyang [China]	0.026 469	2.646 903 1E-02
mace [China]	0.264 690 3	2.646 903 1E-01
mace [Hong Kong]	0.264 690 7	2.646 907 3E-01
mace [India, jewels and pearls]	22.222 222	2.222 222 2E+01
mace [Malaysia]	0.165 343 9	1.653 439 2E-01
mace [Sumatra]	0.094 339 6	9.433 962 3E-02
mahs [India, gold and silver]	0.869 565 2	8.695 652 2E-01
mahs [Sumatra]	0.094 339 6	9.433 962 3E-02
maille [France, gold and silver]	1.282 051 3	1.282 051 3E+00
mandel gewichtsgran [Austria]	1.694 915 3	1.694 915 3E+00
mane [Hebrew, ancient, gold]	0.001 579 8	1.579 778 8E-03
maneh [Hebrew, ancient]	0.001 750 7	1.750 700 3E-03
maneh [Italy]	0.002 931 9	2.931 889 3E-03
mangal [India, jewels and pearls]	4	4.000 000 0E+00
mangalis [India, jewels and pearls]	4	4.000 000 0E+00
mangelin [India, jewels and pearls]	4	4.000 000 0E+00
mangelin [India, Madras]	2.572 059 5	2.572 059 5E+00
manhe [Hebrew, ancient, gold]	0.001 579 8	1.579 778 8E-03
manim [Hebrew, ancient, gold]	0.001 579 8	1.579 778 8E-03
manne [Japan]	0.266 666 7	2.666 666 7E-01
manojo [Venezuela]	0.004	4.000 000 0E+00
manu [Babylon, ancient]	0.001 022 5	1.022 494 9E-03
maqar [Egypt]	0.284 900 3	2.849 002 8E-01
marc [Austria]	0.003 563 8	3.563 791 8E-03
marc [Denmark]	0.004 005 3	4.005 287 0E-03
marc [France]	0.004 085 8	4.085 751 8E-03
marc [Germany]	0.004 278 1	4.278 074 9E-03
marc [Switzerland, heavy]	0.004 085 8	4.085 751 8E-03
marca [Italy]	0.004 255 3	4.255 319 1E-03
marca [Spain]	0.004 347 8	4.347 826 1E-03
marck [Denmark]	0.004 005 3	4.005 287 0E-03
marck [Germany]	0.004 278 1	4.278 074 9E-03
marco [Bolivia]	0.004 347 8	4.347 826 1E-03
marco [Brazil]	0.003 338 9	3.338 898 2E-03

gram (continued) <mass>

Convert To	Standard	Scientific
marco [Honduras]	0.004 346 9	4.346 881 1E-03
marco [Italy, gold and silver]	0.004 066 8	4.066 759 9E-03
marco [Mexico]	0.004 345 4	4.345 370 0E-03
marco [Portugal]	0.004 356 7	4.356 729 0E-03
marco [Spain]	0.004 346 9	4.346 937 8E-03
mario [Spain]	0.004 346 9	4.346 937 8E-03
mark [Austria, Vienna, gold and silver]	0.003 563 2	3.563 233 1E-03
mark [France]	0.004	4.000 000 0E-03
mark [Germany, Augsburg]	0.004 239 1	4.239 084 4E-03
mark [Germany, Cologne]	0.004 278 1	4.278 074 9E-03
mark [Germany, Nuremberg]	0.004 191 7	4.191 659 4E-03
mark [Netherlands]	0.004 048 6	4.048 583 0E-03
mark [Spain]	0.004 346 5	4.346 503 2E-03
mark [Sweden]	0.004 749	4.748 992 0E-03
markgewicht [Belgium]	0.002 031 9	2.031 900 8E-03
mas [Brunei, gold]	0.264 550 3	2.645 502 6E-01
mas [India]	0.857 632 9	8.576 329 3E-01
mas [India, gold and silver]	0.869 565 2	8.695 652 2E-01
mas [India, jewels and pearls]	22.222 222	2.222 222 2E+01
mas [Sumatra]	0.094 339 6	9.433 962 3E-02
masha [Ceylon]	1.028 823 8	1.028 823 8E+00
masha [India]	1.028 823 6	1.028 823 6E+00
masha [India, gold and silver]	0.869 565 2	8.695 652 2E-01
masha [Sumatra]	0.094 339 6	9.433 962 3E-02
massa [India, gold and silver]	0.869 565 2	8.695 652 2E-01
massa [India, jewels and pearls]	22.222 222	2.222 222 2E+01
massa [Sumatra]	0.094 339 6	9.433 962 3E-02
mat [Burma]	0.244 958 1	2.449 580 9E-01
mayam [Malaysia, precious metals]	0.296 735 9	2.967 359 1E-01
mayam [Singapore, precious metals]	0.296 735 9	2.967 359 1E-01
me [Japan]	0.266 666 7	2.666 666 7E-01
me [Sumatra]	1.666 666 7	1.666 666 7E+00
media [Argentina]	0.021 767 5	2.176 752 3E-02
media [Belize]	0.022 045 9	2.204 585 5E-02
mesghal [Iran]	0.215 535 8	2.155 358 2E-01
meteka [Algiers]	0.214 132 8	2.141 327 6E-01
meteka [Egypt]	0.213 675 2	2.136 752 1E-01
meteka [Libya, Tripoli]	0.208 333 3	2.083 333 3E-01
meteka [Syria]	0.208 333 3	2.083 333 3E-01
methgal [Afghanistan]	0.217 391 3	2.173 913 0E-01
methkal [Algiers]	0.214 132 8	2.141 327 6E-01
methkal [Egypt]	0.213 675 2	2.136 752 1E-01
methkal [Libya, Tripoli]	0.208 333 3	2.083 333 3E-01
methkal [Syria]	0.208 333 3	2.083 333 3E-01
metical [Algeria]	0.138 888 9	1.388 888 9E-01
metical [Tunisia]	0.254 065	2.540 650 4E-01
metir [Eritrea]	0.002 202 6	2.202 643 2E-03
metkal [Afghanistan]	0.217 391 3	2.173 913 0E-01
metkal [Iran]	0.213 333 3	2.133 333 3E-01
metkal [Libya, gold]	0.217 344 1	2.173 440 6E-01
metska [Algiers]	0.214 132 8	2.141 327 6E-01
metska [Egypt]	0.213 675 2	2.136 752 1E-01
metska [Libya, Tripoli]	0.208 333 3	2.083 333 3E-01
metska [Syria]	0.208 333 3	2.083 333 3E-01
metskal [Algeria, gold]	0.214 132 8	2.141 327 6E-01
mian [Malacca, gold and silver]	0.374 531 8	3.745 318 4E-01
mian [Singapore, gold and silver]	0.374 531 8	3.745 318 4E-01
migr [Egypt]	0.284 900 3	2.849 002 8E-01
migrab [Anatolia, medieval]	0.001 333 3	1.333 333 3E-03
mina [Babylon, ancient]	0.001 022 2	1.022 181 9E-03
mina [Babylon, ancient, heavy]	0.001 017 9	1.017 915 3E-03
mina [Babylon, ancient, royal]	0.000 990 1	9.900 990 1E-04

gram (continued) <mass>

	Standard	Scientific
mina [Egypt]	0.001 323 3	1.323 329 0E-03
mina [Hebrew, ancient]	0.001 666 7	1.666 666 7E-03
mina [Hebrew, ancient, light]	0.001 980 2	1.980 198 0E-03
mina [Italy]	0.002 789 4	2.789 400 3E-03
mina [Mesopotamia, ancient]	0.002 083 3	2.083 333 3E-03
mina [Phoenicia, ancient, silver]	0.002 747 3	2.747 252 7E-03
mina [Rome, ancient]	0.002 941 2	2.941 176 5E-03
mina [Syria]	0.001 696 8	1.696 842 2E-03
minah [Egypt, ancient]	0.001 285 3	1.285 347 0E-03
minah [Hebrew, ancient, gold]	0.001 579 8	1.579 778 8E-03
miscal [Afghanistan]	0.217 391 3	2.173 913 0E-01
miscal [Iran]	0.215 535 8	2.155 358 2E-01
miscal [Libya, gold]	0.217 344 1	2.173 440 6E-01
miskal [Afghanistan]	0.217 391 3	2.173 913 0E-01
miskal [Algeria]	0.234 192	2.341 920 4E-01
miskal [Egypt]	0.213 675 2	2.136 752 1E-01
miskal [Iran]	0.215 517 2	2.155 172 4E-01
miskal [Libya]	0.217 344 1	2.173 440 6E-01
miskal [Sudan]	0.213 675 2	2.136 752 1E-01
miskal [Turkey]	0.207 857	2.078 569 9E-01
mismal [Persia]	0.217 864 9	2.178 649 2E-01
misqal [Afghanistan]	0.217 391 3	2.173 913 0E-01
misqal [Iran]	0.213 333	2.133 333 3E-01
misqal [Libya, gold]	0.217 344 1	2.173 440 6E-01
misri [Islam]	0.002 247 7	2.247 696 1E-03
mithkal [Muslim India]	0.181 818	1.818 181 8E-01
mithkal [Sudan]	0.213 675 2	2.136 752 1E-01
mitiga [Algiers]	0.214 132 8	2.141 327 6E-01
mitiga [Egypt]	0.213 675 2	2.136 752 1E-01
mitiga [Libya, Tripoli]	0.208 333 3	2.083 333 3E-01
mitiga [Syria]	0.208 333 3	2.083 333 3E-01
mitkal [Iraq, ancient]	0.213 675 2	2.136 752 1E-01
mitkal [Turkey]	0.207 857	2.078 569 9E-01
mitqal [Islam]	0.224 014 3	2.240 143 4E-01
mitqual [Islam]	0.224 014 3	2.240 143 4E-01
mitsal [Egypt]	0.213 675 2	2.136 752 1E-01
mna [Egypt]	0.001 677 3	1.677 289 5E-03
mna [Greece, ancient]	0.002 325 6	2.325 581 4E-03
mna [Syria]	0.001 696 8	1.696 842 2E-03
mocha [Ethiopia]	0.032 154 3	3.215 434 1E-02
mokka pound [Yemen]	0.002 471 1	2.471 149 3E-03
momme [Japan]	0.266 666 7	2.666 666 7E-01
momme [South Korea]	0.266 666 7	2.666 666 7E-01
monme [Japan]	0.266 666 7	2.666 666 7E-01
monme [Sumatra]	1.666 666 7	1.666 666 7E+00
moo [Burma]	0.489 955 9	4.899 559 0E-01
mozetta [Greece, Ionian Islands, salt]	0.001 004 9	1.004 924 1E-03
mudd [Lebanon]	0.312 012 5	3.120 124 8E-01
naqir [Islam]	22.222 222	2.222 222 2E+01
nass [Arabia]	0.016	1.600 000 0E-02
nawa [Arabia]	0.064 102 6	6.410 256 4E-02
neal [Cambodia]	0.001 666 7	1.666 666 7E-03
neset [Hebrew, ancient]	0.101 626	1.016 260 2E-01
neseph [Hebrew, ancient]	0.095 102 3	9.510 223 5E-02
neter [Ethiopia]	0.002 222 2	2.222 222 2E-03
netir [Eritrea]	0.002 202 6	2.202 643 2E-03
netseph [Hebrew, ancient]	0.101 626	1.016 260 2E-01
ngamu [Burma]	0.122 474	1.224 739 7E-01
nijo [Japan]	0.066 666 7	6.666 666 7E-02
nishka [Hindu, ancient, gold]	0.025 201 6	2.520 161 3E-02
nohod [Persia]	5.555 555 6	5.555 555 6E+00
nouaia [Tunisia]	5.080 139 2	5.080 139 2E+00

gram (continued) \<mass\>

	Standard	Scientific
nsp [Hebrew, ancient]	0.1	1.000 000 0E−01
nuge [Anatolia, medieval]	0.003 998 4	3.998 400 6E−03
obol [Greece, ancient]	1.408 450 7	1.408 450 7E+00
obolos [Greece, ancient]	1.369 863	1.369 863 0E+00
obolus [Rome, ancient]	1.760 563 4	1.760 563 4E+00
ochava [Macao]	0.278 551 5	2.785 515 3E−01
ochava [Mexico]	0.278 11	2.781 099 6E−01
ochava [Spain]	0.278 204 4	2.782 043 6E−01
octava [Brazil, gold and silver]	0.277 777 8	2.777 777 8E−01
octava [Italy, gold, silver and jewels]	0.588 235 3	5.882 352 9E−01
octava [Portugal, gold and silver]	0.277 777 8	2.777 777 8E−01
oitava [Brazil]	0.278 836 6	2.788 365 8E−01
oitava [Macao]	0.278 551 5	2.785 515 3E−01
oitava [Mexico]	0.277 777 8	2.777 777 8E−01
oket [Ethiopia]	0.035 629	3.562 903 1E−02
okia [Egypt]	0.026 709 4	2.670 940 2E−02
okia [Eritrea]	0.035 587 2	3.558 718 9E−02
okia [Ethiopia]	0.035 629	3.562 903 1E−02
okia [Iraq, Mosul]	0.007 794 2	7.794 232 3E−03
okia [Jordan, Nabulsi]	0.004 159 7	4.159 733 8E−03
okia [Jordan, Shami]	0.004 679 5	4.679 457 2E−03
okia [Lebanon]	0.004 679 5	4.679 457 2E−03
okia [Libya]	0.031 201 2	3.120 124 8E−02
okia [Somalia]	0.035 714 3	3.571 428 6E−02
okia [Somaliland]	0.035 319 5	3.531 946 5E−02
okia [Sudan]	0.026 709 4	2.670 940 2E−02
okia [Syria]	0.004 679 5	4.679 457 2E−03
okiya [Ethiopia]	0.038 61	3.861 003 9E−02
okiya [Iraq, Istanbul]	0.003 117 7	3.117 692 9E−03
okiya [Jordan, Nabulsi]	0.004 159 7	4.159 733 8E−03
okiya [Jordan, Shami]	0.004 679 5	4.679 457 2E−03
okiya [Lebanon]	0.004 679 5	4.679 457 2E−03
okiya [Libya]	0.031 201 2	3.120 124 8E−02
okiya [Somalia]	0.035 714 3	3.571 428 6E−02
okiya [Sudan]	0.026 709 4	2.670 940 2E−02
okiya [Syria]	0.004 679 5	4.679 457 2E−03
onca [Brazil]	0.034 854 6	3.485 462 1E−02
onca [Portugal]	0.034 854 1	3.485 413 5E−02
onca [Portuguese India]	0.034 855 4	3.485 535 0E−02
once [Ethiopia]	0.038 61	3.861 003 9E−02
once [Holland, medical]	0.032	3.200 000 0E−02
once [Holland, troy]	0.01	1.000 000 0E−02
once [Jordan, Nabulsi]	0.004 159 7	4.159 733 8E−03
once [Jordan, Shami]	0.004 679 5	4.679 457 2E−03
once [Lebanon]	0.004 679 5	4.679 457 2E−03
once [Libya]	0.031 201 2	3.120 124 8E−02
once [Somalia]	0.035 714 3	3.571 428 6E−02
once [Sudan]	0.026 709 4	2.670 940 2E−02
once [Switzerland]	0.032	3.200 000 0E−02
once [Syria]	0.004 677 3	4.677 268 5E−03
once [Tunisia]	0.031 750 8	3.175 076 9E−02
once arabi [Zanzibar and Pemba]	0.035 714 3	3.571 428 6E−02
oncia [Italy, heavy]	0.027 777 8	2.777 777 8E−02
oncia [Italy, light]	0.039 682 5	3.968 254 0E−02
oncia [Italy, Milan]	0.01	1.000 000 0E−02
onckie [Iraq, ancient]	0.026 738	2.673 796 8E−02
ons [Indonesia]	0.032 383 4	3.238 342 0E−02
ons [Netherlands]	0.032 362 5	3.236 246 0E−02
ons [Surinam]	0.01	1.000 000 0E−02
onza [Argentina]	0.034 831 1	3.483 106 9E−02
onza [Chile]	0.034 782 6	3.478 260 9E−02
onza [Colombia]	0.032	3.200 000 0E−02

gram (continued)

<mass>

	Standard	Scientific
onza [Cuba]	0.034 775 4	3.477 535 1E-02
onza [Dominican Republic]	0.035 273 4	3.527 336 9E-02
onza [El Salvador]	0.034 782 6	3.478 260 9E-02
onza [Guatemala]	0.034 782 6	3.478 260 9E-02
onza [Honduras]	0.034 775 4	3.477 535 1E-02
onza [Mexico]	0.034 764 5	3.476 447 1E-02
onza [Nicaragua]	0.034 782 6	3.478 260 9E-02
onza [Paraguay]	0.034 855 4	3.485 535 0E-02
onza [Peru]	0.034 782 6	3.478 260 9E-02
onza [Philippines]	0.034 782 6	3.478 260 9E-02
onza [Spain]	0.034 775 4	3.477 535 1E-02
onza [Venezuela]	0.034 782 6	3.478 260 9E-02
opuia [Jordan, Nabulsi]	0.004 160 3	4.160 252 9E-03
opuia [Jordan, Shami]	0.004 680 3	4.680 333 2E-03
oqiya [Ethiopia]	0.038 61	3.861 003 9E-02
oqiya [Iraq, Istanbul]	0.003 117 7	3.117 692 9E-03
oqiya [Iraq, Mosul]	0.007 794 2	7.794 232 3E-03
oqiya [Jordan, Nabulsi]	0.004 159 7	4.159 733 8E-03
oqiya [Jordan, Shami]	0.004 679 5	4.679 457 2E-03
oqiya [Lebanon]	0.004 679 5	4.679 457 2E-03
oqiya [Libya]	0.031 201 2	3.120 124 8E-02
oqiya [Somalia]	0.035 714 3	3.571 428 6E-02
oqiya [Sudan]	0.026 709 4	2.670 940 2E-02
oqiya [Syria]	0.004 679 5	4.679 457 2E-03
oquia [Ethiopia]	0.038 61	3.861 003 9E-02
oquia [Iraq, Mosul]	0.007 794 2	7.794 232 3E-03
oquia [Jordan, Nabulsi]	0.004 159 7	4.159 733 8E-03
oquia [Jordan, Shami]	0.004 679 5	4.679 457 2E-03
oquia [Lebanon]	0.004 679 5	4.679 457 2E-03
oquia [Libya]	0.031 201 2	3.120 124 8E-02
oquia [Somalia]	0.035 714 3	3.571 428 6E-02
oquia [Sudan]	0.026 709 4	2.670 940 2E-02
oquia [Syria]	0.004 679 5	4.679 457 2E-03
ore [Iceland]	0.037 306 5	3.730 647 3E-02
ore [Norway]	0.037 306 5	3.730 647 3E-02
ore [Sweden]	0.037 306 5	3.730 647 3E-02
ort [Denmark]	2	2.000 000 0E+00
ort [Sweden]	0.235 211 1	2.352 111 0E-01
osira [Portuguese India]	0.001 071 7	1.071 696 5E-03
ottava [Brazil, gold and silver]	0.277 777 8	2.777 777 8E-01
ottava [Italy, gold, silver and jewels]	0.588 235 3	5.882 352 9E-01
ottava [Portugal, gold and silver]	0.277 777 8	2.777 777 8E-01
oukeia [Morocco]	0.008	8.000 000 0E-03
ounce	0.035 274	3.527 396 2E-02
ounce [avoirdupois]	0.035 274	3.527 396 2E-02
ounce [Ethiopia]	0.038 61	3.861 003 9E-02
ounce [France, 1800 definition]	0.032	3.200 000 0E-02
ounce [France, 1800 definition]	0.01	1.000 000 0E-02
ounce [Holland, troy]	0.032 520 3	3.252 032 5E-02
ounce [Iraq, ancient]	0.026 738	2.673 796 8E-02
ounce [Italy, Rome]	0.037 306 5	3.730 647 3E-02
ounce [Norway]	0.032 154 3	3.215 434 1E-02
ounce [Pakistan]	0.035 274	3.527 396 6E-02
ounce [Russia, apothecary]	0.033 489 6	3.348 961 8E-02
ounce [Syria, gold and silver]	0.033 613 4	3.361 344 5E-02
ounce [troy]	0.032 150 7	3.215 074 7E-02
outava [Brazil, gold and silver]	0.277 777 8	2.777 777 8E-01
outava [Italy, gold, silver and jewels]	0.588 235 3	5.882 352 9E-01
outava [Portugal, gold and silver]	0.277 777 8	2.777 777 8E-01
pa [India]	0.004 286 7	4.286 694 1E-03
pagoda [India]	0.285 787 8	2.857 877 7E-01
pai [Burma]	0.979 431 9	9.794 319 3E-01

gram (continued) \<mass\>

	Standard	Scientific
pai [Thailand]	2.133 333 3	2.133 333 3E+00
pala [Hindu, ancient, gold]	0.025 201 6	2.520 161 3E-02
pala [India, ancient]	0.025 201 6	2.520 161 3E-02
pali [Oman, cereals]	0.003 571 4	3.571 428 6E-03
pallie [India, Calcutta, grain]	0.000 242 8	2.427 773 7E-04
pao [Bangladesh]	0.004 286 8	4.286 767 6E-03
pao [India, Calcutta]	0.004 286 8	4.286 765 8E-03
pao [India, Madras]	0.014 289 2	1.428 918 5E-02
pao [Nepal]	0.005 144	5.144 032 9E-03
pao [Pakistan]	0.004 286 8	4.286 765 8E-03
parto [Italy, gold]	90.909 091	9.090 909 1E+01
payim [Hebrew, ancient]	0.131 164 7	1.311 647 4E-01
pennyweight [troy]	0.643 014 9	6.430 149 3E-01
peso grosso [Italy, Venice]	0.002 096 4	2.096 436 1E-03
peso sottile [Italy, Genoa]	0.003 154 9	3.154 872 7E-03
peso sottile [Italy, Venice]	0.003 319 5	3.319 502 1E-03
pfennig [Austria]	0.914 243 9	9.142 439 2E-01
pfund [Brazil, gold and silver]	0.002 201 4	2.201 430 9E-03
pfund [Poland]	0.002 471 6	2.471 576 9E-03
pim [Hebrew, ancient]	0.131 406	1.314 060 4E-01
pinar [Iran]	0.010 666 7	1.066 666 7E-02
poids de marc [France]	0.002 042 9	2.042 900 9E-03
poids de soie [France]	0.002 179 1	2.179 067 0E-03
poids de ville [France]	0.002 388	2.388 002 7E-03
point [jewelers']	500	5.000 000 0E+02
pollam [India]	0.042 868 8	4.286 877 9E-02
pond [Indonesia]	0.002 023 9	2.023 881 8E-03
pond [Netherlands]	0.002 023 9	2.023 881 8E-03
pond [Surinam]	0.002	2.000 000 0E-03
pondo [Rome, ancient]	0.003 053 9	3.053 901 4E-03
pong [Laos, opium]	0.002 666 7	2.666 666 7E-03
pound [Austria, Vienna, commercial]	0.001 785 7	1.785 676 0E-03
pound [Austria, Vienna, medicinal]	0.002 380 9	2.380 901 4E-03
pound [Belgium, Antwerp]	0.002 133 1	2.133 105 8E-03
pound [Belgium, Brussels]	0.002 138 3	2.138 259 9E-03
pound [Czechoslovakia]	0.001 944 2	1.944 201 4E-03
pound [Germany]	0.001 785 5	1.785 523 0E-03
pound [Hebrew, ancient]	0.003 154 6	3.154 574 1E-03
pound [Italy, heavy]	0.002 867 9	2.867 901 6E-03
pound [Italy, light]	0.003 154 9	3.154 872 7E-03
pound [Latvia]	0.002 387 6	2.387 603 6E-03
pound [Lebanon]	0.001 966 1	1.966 065 7E-03
pound [Malta, gold and silver]	0.003 158 5	3.158 459 9E-03
pound [Netherlands, medicinal]	0.002 666 7	2.666 666 7E-03
pound [Netherlands, troy]	0.002 031 8	2.031 826 5E-03
pound [Pakistan]	0.002 204 6	2.204 622 6E-03
pound [Portugal]	0.002 178 6	2.178 649 2E-03
pound [Russia, apothecary]	0.002 790 8	2.790 778 2E-03
pound [Spain, Valencia, small]	0.002 808 9	2.808 909 9E-03
pound [Sweden]	0.002 351 1	2.351 060 3E-03
pound [Switzerland, apothecary]	0.002	2.000 000 0E-03
pow [Afghanistan]	0.002 264 4	2.264 364 6E-03
powa [Bangladesh]	0.004 286 8	4.286 767 6E-03
powa [India]	0.004 286 8	4.286 765 8E-03
powa [Pakistan]	0.004 286 8	4.286 767 6E-03
powa chhatak [Bangladesh]	0.068 587 1	6.858 710 6E-02
pund [Norway]	0.002 007 6	2.007 629 0E-03
pund [Sweden]	0.002	2.000 000 0E-03
punto [Philippines]	0.004 743 8	4.743 833 0E-03
purana [Hindu, ancient, silver]	0.252 016 1	2.520 161 3E-01
qamhah [Egypt]	20.512 821	2.051 282 1E+01
qdt [Egypt, ancient]	0.109 890 1	1.098 901 1E-01

| Convert From | <Type of Unit> | |
| Convert To | Standard | Scientific |

gram (continued) `<mass>`

qesita [Arabia, ancient]	0.000 699 8	6.997 900 6E-04
qirat [Egypt]	5.128 205 1	5.128 205 1E+00
qirath [Islam]	5.128 205 1	5.128 205 1E+00
quadran [Rome, ancient]	0.322 580 7	3.225 806 5E-01
quamha [Islam]	20	2.000 000 0E+01
quentchen [Austria]	0.228 566 2	2.285 662 0E-01
quenten [Norway]	0.257 069 4	2.570 694 1E-01
quilat [Austria, jewels and pearls]	4.807 692 3	4.807 692 3E+00
quilat [Batavia, jewels and pearls]	5.050 505 1	5.050 505 1E+00
quilat [Germany, gold and silver]	0.094 162	9.416 195 9E-02
quilat [Germany, jewels and pearls]	4.854 368 9	4.854 368 9E+00
quilat [India, jewels and pearls]	5.050 505 1	5.050 505 1E+00
quilat [Netherlands, jewels and pearls]	4.830 917 9	4.830 917 9E+00
quilat [Portugal, jewels]	4.859 086 5	4.859 086 5E+00
quilat [Switzerland, gold and silver]	0.098 039 2	9.803 921 6E-02
quilat [UK, jewels and pearls]	4.784 689	4.784 689 0E+00
quilate [Philippines]	4.878 048 8	4.878 048 8E+00
quilate [Spain]	5.007 686 8	5.007 686 8E+00
quincunx [Rome, ancient]	0.007 329 2	7.329 229 0E-03
quintal [Argentina]	0.021 767 5	2.176 752 3E-02
quintal [Belize]	0.022 045 9	2.204 585 5E-02
rabaa [Morocco]	0.004	4.000 000 0E-03
ratal [Morocco]	0.002	2.000 000 0E-03
ratel [Morocco]	0.002	2.000 000 0E-03
ratili [Morocco]	0.002	2.000 000 0E-03
ratili [Tanganyika]	0.002 204 6	2.204 622 6E-03
ratl [Iraq]	0.002 489 6	2.489 581 1E-03
ratl [Morocco]	0.002	2.000 000 0E-03
ratl [North Africa]	0.002 037 9	2.037 905 0E-03
ratl [Spain]	0.001 985 4	1.985 387 5E-03
ratl [Yemen]	0.002 204 6	2.204 585 5E-03
ratl djarwi [Islam]	0.001 037 3	1.037 344 4E-03
ratl laythi [Islam]	0.001 618 2	1.618 227 7E-03
ratl rumi [Muslim, ancient]	0.002 697	2.697 046 2E-03
rattel [Morocco]	0.002	2.000 000 0E-03
real [Indonesia, precious metals]	0.036 975 4	3.697 541 1E-02
rebah [Hebrew, ancient]	0.312 5	3.125 000 0E-01
retal [Algeria]	0.002	2.000 000 0E-03
revaim [Hebrew, ancient]	0.312 5	3.125 000 0E-01
rotal [Morocco]	0.001 949 3	1.949 317 7E-03
rotal [Spanish North Africa]	0.001 970 4	1.970 443 3E-03
rotel fedhy [Algeria, silver]	0.002 010 3	2.010 312 9E-03
rotl [Eritrea]	0.002 227 2	2.227 171 5E-03
rotl [Ethiopia]	0.003 215 4	3.215 434 1E-03
rotl [Morocco]	0.002	2.000 000 0E-03
rotl [Saudi Arabia]	0.002 204 6	2.204 585 5E-03
rotle [Yemen]	0.001 488 1	1.488 095 2E-03
rotol [Morocco]	0.002	2.000 000 0E-03
rotoli [Egypt]	0.002 225 7	2.225 684 4E-03
rotoli [Turkey]	0.001 558 9	1.558 913 3E-03
rotolo [Morocco]	0.002	2.000 000 0E-03
rottel [Tunisia]	0.001 984 9	1.984 914 6E-03
rottle [Morocco]	0.002	2.000 000 0E-03
rottle [Saudi Arabia]	0.002 204 6	2.204 585 5E-03
rottle [Saudi Arabia, ancient]	0.002 162 2	2.162 162 2E-03
rottol [Morocco]	0.002	2.000 000 0E-03
rottolo [Abyssinia, ancient]	0.003 215 4	3.215 434 1E-03
rottolo [Cyprus]	0.001 789 5	1.789 466 4E-03
rottolo [Ethiopia]	0.003 215 4	3.215 434 1E-03
rottolo [Morocco]	0.001 900 1	1.900 057 0E-03
rottolo [Somaliland]	0.002 207 5	2.207 505 5E-03
rottolo [Tunisia]	0.001 985 7	1.985 702 9E-03

gram (continued)

<mass>

	Standard	Scientific
rottolo a kebyr [Algeria]	0.001 220 9	1.220 852 2E-03
rottolo a khadhary [Algeria]	0.001 627 9	1.627 869 1E-03
rottolo a thary [Algeria]	0.001 831 2	1.831 166 5E-03
rottolo attari [Tunisia]	0.001 984 4	1.984 426 2E-03
rova [Hebrew, ancient]	0.312 5	3.125 000 0E-01
rtel [Morocco]	0.002	2.000 000 0E-03
salung [Laos]	0.266 666 7	2.666 666 7E-01
salung [Thailand]	0.266 666 7	2.666 666 7E-01
scripula [Iceland]	1.048 218	1.048 218 0E+00
scripula [Norway]	1.048 218	1.048 218 0E+00
scripula [Sweden]	1.048 218	1.048 218 0E+00
scripulum [Rome, ancient]	0.879 507 5	8.795 074 8E-01
scrupel [Austria, apothecary]	0.685 682 9	6.856 829 4E-01
scrupel [Netherlands]	0.777 182 5	7.771 825 4E-01
scruple [France]	0.784 313 7	7.843 137 3E-01
scruple [Switzerland]	0.768 049 2	7.680 491 6E-01
scruple [UK]	0.771 617 9	7.716 179 2E-01
scruple [US, apothecary]	0.771 617 9	7.716 179 2E-01
scrupulum [Rome, ancient]	0.877 193	8.771 929 8E-01
scrupulum [Russia, apothecary]	0.803 858 5	8.038 585 2E-01
seer [Iran]	0.013 333 3	1.333 333 3E-02
semis [Rome, ancient]	0.006 107 6	6.107 616 2E-03
semisextula [Rome, ancient]	0.438 596 5	4.385 964 9E-01
semiuncia [Rome, ancient]	0.072 992 7	7.299 270 1E-02
semuncia [Rome, ancient]	0.073 292 3	7.329 229 0E-02
septunx [Rome, ancient]	0.005 235 1	5.235 053 9E-03
seqel [Hebrew, ancient]	0.087 565 7	8.756 567 4E-02
sescuncia [Rome, ancient]	0.024 432	2.443 195 7E-02
sesterce [Rome, ancient]	0.039 370 1	3.937 007 9E-02
seu [Babylon, ancient]	21.739 13	2.173 913 0E+01
sextan [Rome, ancient]	0.018 321 7	1.832 173 0E-02
sextula [Rome, ancient]	0.219 780 2	2.197 802 2E-01
shatamana [Hindu, ancient, silver]	0.025 201 6	2.520 161 3E-02
shekalim [Hebrew, ancient]	0.078 740 2	7.874 015 7E-02
shekel [Babylon, ancient]	0.121 654 5	1.216 545 0E-01
shekel [Egypt, ancient]	0.064 102 6	6.410 256 4E-02
shekel [Greece, ancient]	0.102 880 7	1.028 806 6E-01
shekel [Hebrew, ancient]	0.087 565 7	8.756 567 4E-02
shekel [Iraq, ancient, silver]	0.124 688 3	1.246 882 8E-01
shekel [Mesopotamia, ancient]	0.125	1.250 000 0E-01
shekel [Palestine, ancient]	0.061 237	6.123 698 7E-02
shekel [Rome, ancient]	0.070 077 1	7.007 708 5E-02
shekel hamelech [Hebrew, ancient]	0.068 728 5	6.872 852 2E-02
sheqel [Hebrew, ancient]	0.005 672 5	5.672 471 5E-03
shi ke [China]	0.1	1.000 000 0E-01
shiglu [Babylon, ancient]	0.120 481 9	1.204 819 3E-01
shih chien [China]	0.32	3.200 000 0E-01
shih chin [China]	0.002	2.000 000 0E-03
shih liang [China]	0.032	3.200 000 0E-02
sicca [India, gold and silver]	0.066 666 7	6.666 666 7E-02
sicilicus [Rome, ancient]	0.146 412 9	1.464 128 8E-01
siglos [Greece, ancient]	0.178 571 4	1.785 714 3E-01
siglos [Hebrew, ancient]	0.011 560 7	1.156 069 4E-02
sihr [Iran]	0.013 333 3	1.333 333 3E-02
siki [Bangladesh]	0.342 465 8	3.424 657 5E-01
siki [India]	0.342 941 2	3.429 411 7E-01
siliqua [Rome, ancient]	5.291 005	5.291 005 3E+00
sir [Iran]	0.013 471	1.347 098 9E-02
skaalpund [Sweden]	0.002 352 1	2.352 111 0E-03
skalpund [Sweden]	0.002 352 1	2.352 111 0E-03
solidus [Rome, ancient]	0.219 876 9	2.198 768 7E-01
solotnik [Russia]	0.235 294 1	2.352 941 0E-01

gram (continued)

\<mass\>

Convert To	Standard	Scientific
solung [Thailand]	0.266 666 7	2.666 666 7E-01
sompay [Thailand]	1.066 666 7	1.066 666 7E+00
star pagoda [India, gold and silver]	0.293 685 8	2.936 857 6E-01
stater [Greece, ancient]	0.102 880 7	1.028 806 6E-01
suku [Indonesia]	0.147 907 1	1.479 071 1E-01
suvarna [Hindu, ancient, gold]	0.100 806 5	1.008 064 5E-01
suvarna [India, ancient]	0.100 806 5	1.008 064 5E-01
swin [China, silver]	2.645 502 6	2.645 502 6E+00
tael [Brunei]	0.026 455	2.645 502 6E-02
tael [Cambodia]	0.026 666 7	2.666 666 7E-02
tael [China]	0.026 469	2.646 903 1E-02
tael [Hong Kong]	0.026 455	2.645 572 6E-02
tael [Japan]	0.026 666 7	2.666 666 7E-02
tael [Macao]	0.026 455 7	2.645 572 6E-02
tael [Philippines]	0.025 296 6	2.529 660 3E-02
tael [Singapore, precious metals and medicine]	0.029 029 8	2.902 976 7E-02
tael [Thailand]	0.016 666 7	1.666 666 7E-02
tael [Vietnam]	0.026 466 9	2.646 693 0E-02
tahil [Brunei]	0.026 455	2.645 502 6E-02
tahil [Cambodia]	0.026 666 7	2.666 666 7E-02
tahil [China]	0.02	2.000 000 0E-02
tahil [Hong Kong]	0.026 455	2.645 502 6E-02
tahil [Macao]	0.026 455	2.645 502 6E-02
tahil [Malaysia]	0.026 456 4	2.645 642 6E-02
tahil [North Borneo]	0.026 455 5	2.645 547 4E-02
tahil [Sarawak]	0.026 455 5	2.645 547 4E-02
tahil [Singapore]	0.026 455 7	2.645 572 6E-02
tai [Taiwan]	0.001 666 7	1.666 666 7E-03
tale [China]	0.026 469	2.646 903 1E-02
tale [Sumatra, gold and silver]	0.016 254 9	1.625 487 6E-02
talent [Babylon, ancient]	0.020 362 5	2.036 245 2E-02
taler [Germany, silver]	0.059 988	5.998 800 2E-02
tali [Indonesia]	0.295 770 5	2.957 704 8E-01
tamlung [Thailand]	0.016 666 7	1.666 666 7E-02
tang [India, pearls]	0.077 160 5	7.716 049 4E-02
tank [India, pearls]	0.077 160 5	7.716 049 4E-02
tartimar [Hebrew, ancient]	0.005 578 8	5.578 800 6E-03
tauk [India, pearls]	0.214 132 8	2.141 327 6E-01
tcharak [Iran]	1.333 333 3	1.333 333 3E+00
ten drachma [Greece, ancient]	0.015 862 9	1.586 294 4E-02
termini [Tunisia]	0.254 065	2.540 650 4E-01
teruncius [Rome, ancient]	0.012 216	1.221 597 8E-02
tetradrachm [Egypt, ancient]	0.064 102 6	6.410 256 4E-02
tetradrachm [Greece, ancient]	0.051 546 4	5.154 639 2E-02
tetradrachma [Greece, ancient]	0.057 471 3	5.747 126 4E-02
tetradrachma [Hebrew, ancient]	0.071 428 6	7.142 857 1E-02
thail [Indonesia, diamonds]	0.018 487 7	1.848 770 6E-02
thail [Indonesia, opium]	0.025 906 1	2.590 606 5E-02
thail [Indonesia, precious metals]	0.018 487 7	1.848 770 6E-02
thaler [Oman, Maria Theresa]	0.035 650 6	3.565 062 4E-02
then [Tunisia]	0.254 006 3	2.540 063 1E-01
tia [Yemen]	0.857 632 9	8.576 329 3E-01
tical [Burma]	0.061 237	6.123 698 7E-02
tical [Laos]	0.066 666 7	6.666 666 7E-02
tical [Thailand]	0.066 666 7	6.666 666 7E-02
tien [Vietnam]	0.264 690 3	2.646 903 1E-01
tikal [Burma]	0.061 237	6.123 698 7E-02
tji [Indonesia, opium]	0.259 067 4	2.590 673 6E-01
tola [Bahrain]	0.085 763 3	8.576 329 3E-02
tola [Bangladesh]	0.085 733 9	8.573 388 2E-02
tola [Ceylon]	0.085 735 4	8.573 535 2E-02
tola [India]	0.085 733 9	8.573 388 2E-02

gram (continued) \<mass\>

	Standard	Scientific
tola [Pakistan]	0.085 733 9	8.573 388 2E-02
tola [Yemen]	0.085 733 9	8.573 388 2E-02
tola [Zanzibar and Pemba]	0.087 734 7	8.773 469 0E-02
tolah [India, gold and silver]	0.068 728 5	6.872 852 2E-02
tomin [Spain]	1.669 228 9	1.669 228 9E+00
ton [UK, assay or assay, long]	0.030 612 2	3.061 224 5E-02
ton [US, assay or assay, short]	0.034 285 7	3.428 571 4E-02
triens [Rome, ancient]	0.009 161 7	9.161 704 1E-03
tscheki [Turkey]	0.003 138 1	3.138 072 0E-03
tsein [China]	0.264 557 3	2.645 572 6E-01
tsin [Cambodia]	0.266 666 7	2.666 666 7E-01
tsin [Hong Kong]	0.264 550 3	2.645 502 6E-01
tsin [Mongolia]	0.266 666 7	2.666 666 7E-01
tuht [Turkey]	0.006 234 4	6.234 414 0E-03
uckir [Tunisia]	0.031 750 8	3.175 076 9E-02
ughia [Somaliland]	0.035 319 5	3.531 946 5E-02
ugija [Malta and Gozo]	0.037 793 5	3.779 352 3E-02
ukia [Ethiopia]	0.038 61	3.861 003 9E-02
ukia [Jordan, Nabulsi]	0.004 159 7	4.159 733 8E-03
ukia [Lebanon]	0.004 679 5	4.679 457 2E-03
ukia [Libya]	0.031 201 2	3.120 124 8E-02
ukia [Somalia]	0.035 714 3	3.571 428 6E-02
ukia [Sudan]	0.026 709 4	2.670 940 2E-02
ukia [Syria, Damascus]	0.004 679 5	4.679 457 2E-03
ukie [Libya, ostrich feathers and spinning wools]	0.031 201 2	3.120 124 8E-02
ukkia [Algeria]	0.029 299 7	2.929 973 6E-02
uncia [Rome, ancient]	0.036 646 1	3.664 614 5E-02
uncya [Poland]	0.039 457 1	3.945 707 1E-02
uns [Sweden]	0.037 640 3	3.764 025 7E-02
unser [Denmark]	0.033 999 7	3.399 972 8E-02
unze [Algeria]	0.029 299 7	2.929 973 6E-02
unze [Austria]	0.028 570 6	2.857 061 2E-02
unze [France, 1800 definition]	0.01	1.000 000 0E-02
unze [Germany]	0.032	3.200 000 0E-02
unze [Switzerland]	0.032	3.200 000 0E-02
unzen [Germany]	0.034 211 4	3.421 142 7E-02
uqija [Malta]	0.037 735 8	3.773 584 9E-02
uqije [Islam]	0.025 641	2.564 102 6E-02
uye [Lebanon]	0.005	5.000 000 0E-03
uzan [Tunisia]	0.031 759 1	3.175 913 9E-02
vall [India, gold and silver]	0.265 392 8	2.653 927 8E-01
vierding [Austria]	0.007 142 9	7.142 857 1E-03
viertellot [Switzerland]	0.256 016 4	2.560 163 9E-01
wagia [Ethiopia]	0.038 61	3.861 003 9E-02
wagia [Iraq]	0.007 794 2	7.794 232 7E-03
wagia [Jordan]	0.004 159 7	4.159 733 8E-03
wagia [Lebanon]	0.004 679 5	4.679 457 2E-03
wagia [Libya]	0.031 201 2	3.120 124 8E-02
wagia [Somalia]	0.035 714 3	3.571 428 6E-02
wagia [Sudan]	0.026 709 4	2.670 940 2E-02
wagia [Syria]	0.004 679 5	4.679 457 2E-03
wagia dahabia [Sudan, gold]	0.031 25	3.125 000 0E-02
wakea [Ethiopia]	0.038 61	3.861 003 9E-02
wakea [Jordan]	0.004 159 7	4.159 733 8E-03
wakea [Lebanon]	0.004 679 5	4.679 457 2E-03
wakea [Libya]	0.031 201 2	3.120 124 8E-02
wakea [Somalia]	0.035 714 3	3.571 428 6E-02
wakea [Sudan]	0.026 709 4	2.670 940 2E-02
wakea [Syria]	0.004 679 5	4.679 457 2E-03
wakega [Yemen]	0.031 645 6	3.164 557 0E-02
wakia [Tanganyika]	0.035 274	3.527 396 6E-02
wakiah [Zanzibar and Pemba]	0.035 714 3	3.571 428 6E-02

gram (continued)   `<mass>`

	Standard	Scientific
wang [Indonesia]	0.887 311 5	8.873 114 5E−01
wichtje [Netherlands]	1	1.000 000 0E+00
woket [Eritrea]	0.035 587 2	3.558 718 9E−02
woket [Ethiopia]	0.038 61	3.861 003 9E−02
woket [Jordan]	0.004 159 7	4.159 733 8E−03
woket [Lebanon]	0.004 679 5	4.679 457 2E−03
woket [Libya]	0.031 201 2	3.120 124 8E−02
woket [Somalia]	0.035 714 3	3.571 428 6E−02
woket [Sudan]	0.026 709 4	2.670 940 2E−02
woket [Syria]	0.004 679 5	4.679 457 2E−03
wukiyeh [Iraq, ancient]	0.026 738	2.673 796 8E−02
yang [South Korea]	0.026 666 7	2.666 666 7E−02
yusdroman [Iraq, ancient]	0.002 673 8	2.673 796 8E−03
ywegi [Burma]	1.959 664 6	1.959 664 6E+00
ywegyi [Burma]	1.960 784 3	1.960 784 3E+00
zollpfund [Germany]	0.002	2.000 000 0E−03
zollverein pound [Germany]	0.002	2.000 000 0E−03
zolotnik [Russia]	0.234 411 6	2.344 116 3E−01
zuz [Hebrew, ancient]	0.278 94	2.789 400 3E−01

gram [atomic physics, eq. energy]   `<energy>`

	Standard	Scientific
Btu [I.T.]	>>>	8.518 555 5E+10
calorie [I.T.]	>>>	2.146 639 9E+13
calorie [kilogram, I.T.]	>>>	2.146 639 9E+10
centigrade heat unit [I.T.]	>>>	4.732 530 8E+10
cheval vapeur heure [France]	>>>	3.394 352 7E+07
coal equivalent kilogram [UN, standard]	3,066,628.4	3.066 628 4E+06
coal equivalent metric ton [UN, standard]	3,066,628.4	3.066 628 4E+03
horsepower hour	>>>	3.347 918 2E+07
horsepower hour [metric]	>>>	3.394 352 7E+07
joule	>>>	8.987 551 8E+13
kilogram [atomic physics, eq. energy]	0.001	1.000 000 0E−03
kiloton [metric, explosive energy]	21.480 764	2.148 076 4E+01
megaton [metric, explosive energy]	0.021 480 8	2.148 076 4E−02
pferdestarkenstunde [Germany]	>>>	3.394 352 7E+07
quad	0.000 085 2	8.518 555 5E−05
therm [EEC]	851,855.55	8.518 555 5E+05
therm [US]	852,058.94	8.520 589 4E+05
thermie [France]	2,147 152	2.147 152 7E+07
ton [metric, explosive energy]	21,480.764	2.148 076 4E+04

gram calorie   `<energy>`

	Standard	Scientific
Btu [I.T.]	0.003 967 4	3.967 372 9E−03
calorie [15 °C, NBS, 1939]	1	1.000 000 0E+00
calorie [I.T.]	0.999 761	9.997 611 5E−01
calorie [kilogram, I.T.]	0.000 999 8	9.997 611 5E−04
centigrade heat unit [I.T.]	0.002 204 1	2.204 096 1E−03
centimeter gram-force	42,683.281	4.268 328 1E+04
cubic centimeter atmosphere	41.310 634	4.131 063 4E+01
cubic foot atmosphere	0.001 458 9	1.458 871 3E−03
dyne centimeter	>>>	4.185 800 0E+07
erg	>>>	4.185 800 0E+07
foot pound-force	3.087 287 6	3.087 287 6E+00
foot poundal	99.330 543	9.933 054 3E+01
frigorie [France]	0.001	1.000 000 0E−03
horsepower hour	0.000 001 6	1.559 236 2E−06
horsepower hour [metric]	0.000 001 6	1.580 862 3E−06
inch ounce-force	592.759 23	5.927 592 3E+02
inch pound-force	37.047 452	3.704 745 2E+01
joule	4.185 8	4.185 800 0E+00
kilogram square meter/square second	4.185 8	4.185 800 0E+00
kilopond meter	0.426 832 8	4.268 328 1E−01
liter atmosphere	0.041 310 6	4.131 063 4E−02

| Convert From | | **\<Type of Unit\>** |
Convert To	Standard	Scientific

megaerg	41.858	4.185 800 0E+01
megalerg	41.858	4.185 800 0E+01
meter kilogram-force	0.426 832 8	4.268 328 1E−01
newton meter	4.185 8	4.185 800 0E+00
watthour	0.001 162 7	1.162 722 2E−03
wattsecond	4.185 8	4.185 800 0E+00

gram centimeter/second <momentum>
bole	1	1.000 000 0E+00
dyne second	1	1.000 000 0E+00
newton second	0.000 01	1.000 000 0E−05
poundal second	0.000 072 3	7.233 013 9E−05
slug foot/second	0.000 002 2	2.248 089 4E−06

gram centimeter/square second <force>
crinal	0.000 1	1.000 000 0E−04
dyne	1	1.000 000 0E+00
gram-force	0.001 019 7	1.019 716 2E−03
newton	0.000 01	1.000 000 0E−05
ounce-force	0.000 036	3.596 943 1E−05
pond	0.001 019 7	1.019 716 2E−03
pound-force	0.000 002 2	2.248 089 4E−06
poundal	0.000 072 3	7.233 013 9E−05

gram square centimeter <moment of inertia of a mass>
gram-force centimeter square second	0.001 019 7	1.019 716 2E−03
kilogram square meter	0.000 000 1	1.000 000 0E−07
ounce square inch	0.005 467 5	5.467 475 0E−03
pond centimeter square second	0.001 019 7	1.019 716 2E−03
pound square inch	0.000 341 7	3.417 171 9E−04

gram square centimeter/second <moment of momentum>
dyne centimeter second	1	1.000 000 0E+00
erg second	1	1.000 000 0E+00
kilogram square meter/second	0.000 000 1	1.000 000 0E−07
pound square foot/second	0.000 002 4	2.373 036 0E−06

gram square meter <moment of inertia of a mass>
gram-force centimeter square second	10.197 162	1.019 716 2E+01
kilogram square meter	0.001	1.000 000 0E−03
ounce square inch	54.674 75	5.467 475 0E+01
pond centimeter square second	10.197 162	1.019 716 2E+01
pound square inch	3.417 171 9	3.417 171 9E+00

gram-force <force>
crinal	0.098 066 5	9.806 650 0E−02
dyne	980.665	9.806 650 0E+02
newton	0.009 806 7	9.806 650 0E−03
ounce-force	0.035 274	3.527 396 2E−02
pond	1	1.000 000 0E+00
pound-force	0.002 204 6	2.204 622 6E−03
poundal	0.070 931 6	7.093 163 5E−02

gram-force centimeter square second <moment of inertia of a mass>
kilogram square centimeter	0.980 665	9.806 650 0E−01
kilogram square meter	0.000 098 1	9.806 650 0E−05
ounce square inch	5.361 761 4	5.361 761 4E+00
pond centimeter square second	1	1.000 000 0E+00
pound square inch	0.335 110 1	3.351 100 9E−01

gram-force centimeter/hour <power>
Btu/hour [I.T.]	<<<	9.294 910 8E−08
Btu/hour [thermoc.]	<<<	9.301 131 1E−08
calorie/hour [I.T.]	0.000 023 4	2.342 278 1E−05
calorie/hour [thermoc.]	0.000 023 4	2.343 845 6E−05
centigrade heat unit/hour [mean]	<<<	5.159 857 6E−08
cubic meter atmosphere/hour	0.000 967 8	9.678 411 1E−04
dyne centimeter/minute	16.344 417	1.634 441 7E+01
erg/minute	16.344 417	1.634 441 7E+01

Convert From		<Type of Unit>
Convert To	Standard	Scientific

	Standard	Scientific
foot pound-force/hour	0.000 072 3	7.233 013 9E-05
foot poundal/hour	0.002 327 2	2.327 153 4E-03
gram-force centimeter/minute	0.016 666 7	1.666 666 7E-02
horsepower	<<<	3.653 037 3E-11
horsepower [metric]	<<<	3.703 703 7E-11
joule/hour	0.000 098 1	9.806 650 0E-05
kilocalorie/hour [I.T.]	<<<	2.342 278 1E-08
kilogram-force meter/hour	0.000 01	1.000 000 0E-05
kilopond meter/hour	0.000 01	1.000 000 0E-05
nanowatt	27.240 694	2.724 069 4E+01
newton meter/hour	0.000 098 1	9.806 650 0E-05
volt ampere	<<<	2.724 069 4E-08
watt	<<<	2.724 069 4E-08

gram-force centimeter/minute <power>

	Standard	Scientific
Btu/hour [I.T.]	0.000 005 6	5.576 946 5E-06
Btu/hour [thermoc.]	0.000 005 6	5.580 678 6E-06
calorie/hour [I.T.]	0.001 405 4	1.405 366 9E-03
calorie/hour [thermoc.]	0.001 406 3	1.406 307 4E-03
centigrade heat unit/hour [mean]	0.000 003 1	3.095 914 6E-06
cubic meter atmosphere/hour	0.058 070 5	5.807 046 6E-02
dyne centimeter/second	16.344 417	1.634 441 7E+01
erg/second	16.344 417	1.634 441 7E+01
foot pound-force/hour	0.004 339 8	4.339 808 3E-03
foot poundal/hour	0.139 629 2	1.396 292 0E-01
gram-force centimeter/hour	60	6.000 000 0E+01
horsepower	<<<	2.191 822 4E-09
horsepower [metric]	<<<	2.222 222 2E-09
joule/hour	0.005 884	5.883 990 0E-03
kilocalorie/hour [I.T.]	0.000 014	1.405 366 9E-06
kilogram-force meter/hour	0.000 6	6.000 000 0E-04
kilopond meter/hour	0.000 6	6.000 000 0E-04
microwatt	1.634 441 7	1.634 441 7E+00
newton meter/hour	0.005 884	5.883 990 0E-03
pound square foot/cubic second	0.000 038 8	3.878 589 0E-05
volt ampere	0.000 001 6	1.634 441 7E-06
watt	0.000 001 6	1.634 441 7E-06

gram-force centimeter/second <power>

	Standard	Scientific
Btu/hour [I.T.]	0.000 334 6	3.346 167 9E-04
Btu/hour [thermoc.]	0.000 334 8	3.348 407 2E-04
calorie/hour [I.T.]	0.084 322	8.432 201 2E-02
calorie/hour [thermoc.]	0.084 378 4	8.437 844 2E-02
centigrade heat unit/hour [mean]	0.000 185 8	1.857 548 8E-04
cubic meter atmosphere/hour	3.484 228	3.484 228 0E+00
dyne centimeter/second	980.665	9.806 650 0E+02
erg/second	980.665	9.806 650 0E+02
foot pound-force/hour	0.260 388 5	2.603 885 0E-01
foot poundal/hour	8.377 752 2	8.377 752 2E+00
gram-force centimeter/minute	60	6.000 000 0E+01
horsepower	0.000 000 1	1.315 093 4E-07
horsepower [metric]	0.000 000 1	1.333 333 3E-07
joule/hour	0.353 039 4	3.530 394 0E-01
kilocalorie/hour [I.T.]	0.000 084 3	8.432 201 2E-05
kilogram-force meter/hour	0.036	3.600 000 0E-02
kilopond meter/hour	0.036	3.600 000 0E-02
lumen [green light at 100% efficiency]	0.067 175 6	6.717 555 3E-02
lumen [green light at 5,550 angstrom]	0.066 685 2	6.668 522 2E-02
microwatt	98.066 5	9.806 650 0E+01
newton meter/hour	0.353 039 4	3.530 394 0E-01
poncelet [France]	0.000 000 1	1.000 000 0E-07
pound square foot/cubic second	0.002 327 2	2.327 153 4E-03
volt ampere	0.000 098 1	9.806 650 0E-05
watt	0.000 098 1	9.806 650 0E-05

gram-force meter square second   \<moment of inertia of a mass>

gram square meter	9.806 65	9.806 650 0E+00
kilogram square meter	0.009 806 7	9.806 650 0E−03
ounce square foot	3.723 445 4	3.723 445 4E+00
ounce-force inch square second	1.388 738 7	1.388 738 7E+00
pond meter square second	1	1.000 000 0E+00
slug square inch	1.041 554	1.041 554 0E+00

gram-force second/square centimeter   \<dynamic viscosity>

kilogram-force second/square meter	10	1.000 000 0E+01
pascal second	98.066 5	9.806 650 0E+01
pound-force second/square foot	2.048 161 4	2.048 161 4E+00
pound/foot second	65.897 645 5	6.589 764 6E+01
slug/foot second	2.048 161 4	2.048 161 4E+00

gram-force/centimeter   \<surface tension>

dyne/centimeter	980.665	9.806 650 0E+02
gram-force/meter	100	1.000 000 0E+02
kilopond/meter	0.1	1.000 000 0E−01
millinewton/centimeter	9.806 65	9.806 650 0E+00
newton/meter	0.980 665	9.806 650 0E−01
ounce-force/foot	1.075 150 4	1.075 150 4E+00
pound-force/foot	0.067 196 9	6.719 689 8E−02

gram-force/meter   \<surface tension>

dyne/centimeter	9.806 65	9.806 650 0E+00
kilogram-force/meter	0.001	1.000 000 0E−03
kilopond/meter	0.001	1.000 000 0E−03
millinewton/meter	9.806 65	9.806 650 0E+00
newton/meter	0.009 806 7	9.806 650 0E−03
ounce-force/foot	0.010 751 5	1.075 150 4E−02
pound-force/foot	0.000 672	6.719 689 8E−04

gram-force/square centimeter   \<pressure>

atmosphere [standard]	0.000 967 8	9.678 411 1E−04
atmosphere [technical]	0.001	1.000 000 0E−03
bar	0.000 980 7	9.806 650 0E−04
barye [France]	980.665	9.806 650 0E+02
centimeter of mercury [0 °C, by convention]	0.073 555 9	7.355 591 4E−02
centimeter of water [4 °C, by convention]	1	1.000 000 0E+00
decitorr	7.355 592 4	7.355 592 4E+00
dekapascal	9.806 65	9.806 650 0E+00
dyne/square centimeter	980.665	9.806 650 0E+02
inch of mercury [0 °C, by convention]	0.028 959	2.895 902 1E−02
inch of water [4 °C, by convention]	0.393 700 8	3.937 007 9E−01
kilogram-force/square meter	10	1.000 000 0E+01
kilopond/square meter	10	1.000 000 0E+01
kip/square foot	0.002 048 2	2.048 161 4E−03
micrometer of mercury [0 °C, by convention]	735.559 14	7.355 591 4E+02
micrometer of water [4 °C, by convention]	10,000	1.000 000 0E+04
millimeter of mercury [0 °C, by convention]	0.735 559 1	7.355 591 4E−01
millimeter of water [4 °C, by convention]	10	1.000 000 0E+01
newton/square meter	98.066 5	9.806 650 0E+01
ounce-force/square inch	0.227 573 5	2.275 734 9E−01
pascal	98.066 5	9.806 650 0E+01
pound-force/square foot	2.048 161 4	2.048 161 4E+00
poundal/square foot	65.897 646	6.589 764 6E+01
ton-force/square foot [short]	0.001 024 1	1.024 080 7E−03
ton-force/square meter [metric]	0.01	1.000 000 0E−02
torr	0.735 559 2	7.355 592 4E−01

gram/calorie [-/ I.T.]   \<specific fuel consumption, mass basis>

kilogram/joule	0.000 238 8	2.388 459 0E−04
pound/Btu [-/ I.T.]	0.555 555 6	5.555 555 6E−01
pound/horsepower hour	1,413.574 2	1.413 574 2E+03

gram/centimeter second   \<dynamic viscosity>

dyne second/square centimeter	1	1.000 000 0E+00

| Convert From | | <Type of Unit> |
Convert To	Standard	Scientific
kilogram/meter second	0.1	1.000 000 0E-01
pascal second	0.1	1.000 000 0E-01
poise	1	1.000 000 0E+00
poiseuille [France]	0.1	1.000 000 0E-01
gram/cubic centimeter		**<density>**
gram/milliliter	1	1.000 000 0E+00
kilogram/cubic decimeter	1	1.000 000 0E+00
kilogram/cubic meter	1,000	1.000 000 0E+03
kilogram/liter	1	1.000 000 0E+00
megagram/cubic meter	1	1.000 000 0E+00
ounce/cubic inch	0.578 036 7	5.780 366 7E-01
pound/cubic foot	62.427 961	6.242 796 1E+01
pound/gallon [-/US, liquid]	8.345 404 5	8.345 404 5E+00
slug/cubic foot	1.940 320 3	1.940 320 3E+00
ton/cubic yard [long]	0.752 479 9	7.524 798 8E-01
ton/cubic yard [short]	0.842 777 5	8.427 774 7E-01
tonne/cubic meter	1	1.000 000 0E+00
gram/cubic decimeter		**<density>**
grain/cubic inch	0.252 891	2.528 910 4E-01
grain/gallon [-/US, liquid]	58.417 831	5.841 783 1E+01
gram/liter	1	1.000 000 0E+00
kilogram/cubic meter	1	1.000 000 0E+00
milligram/cubic centimeter	1	1.000 000 0E+00
milligram/milliliter	1	1.000 000 0E+00
ounce/cubic inch	26.968 879	2.696 887 9E+01
ounce/gallon [-/US, liquid]	0.133 526 5	1.335 264 7E-01
pound/cubic yard	1.685 554 9	1.685 554 9E+00
slug/cubic yard	0.052 388 6	5.238 864 9E-02
ton/cubic yard [short]	0.000 842 8	8.427 774 7E-04
tonne/cubic meter	0.001	1.000 000 0E-03
gram/cubic meter		**<density>**
gammil	1	1.000 000 0E+00
grain/cubic yard	11.798 885	1.179 888 5E+01
gram/liter	0.001	1.000 000 0E-03
kilogram/cubic meter	0.001	1.000 000 0E-03
micril	1	1.000 000 0E+00
milligram/cubic decimeter	1	1.000 000 0E+00
milligram/liter	1	1.000 000 0E+00
ounce/cubic yard	0.026 968 9	2.696 887 9E-02
pound/cubic yard	0.001 685 6	1.685 554 9E-03
slug/cubic yard	0.000 052 4	5.238 864 9E-05
ton/cubic yard [short]	0.000 000 8	8.427 774 7E-07
tonne/cubic meter	0.000 001	1.000 000 0E-06
gram/hour		**<flow rate, mass basis>**
kilogram/second	0.000 000 3	2.777 777 8E-07
pound/hour	0.002 204 6	2.204 622 6E-03
gram/kilometer		**<linear density>**
denier	9	9.000 000 0E+00
drex	10	1.000 000 0E+01
kilogram/meter	0.000 001	1.000 000 0E-06
ounce/foot	0.000 010 8	1.075 150 4E-05
pound/yard	0.000 002	2.015 906 9E-06
tex	1	1.000 000 0E+00
gram/liter		**<density>**
grain/cubic inch	0.252 891	2.528 910 4E-01
grain/gallon [-/US, liquid]	58.417 831	5.841 783 1E+01
gram/cubic decimeter	1	1.000 000 0E+00
kilogram/cubic meter	1	1.000 000 0E+00
milligram/cubic centimeter	1	1.000 000 0E+00
milligram/milliliter	1	1.000 000 0E+00
ounce/cubic yard	26.968 879	2.696 887 9E+01
ounce/gallon [-/US, liquid]	0.133 526 5	1.335 264 7E-01

	Standard	Scientific
ounce/gallon [troy/US, liquid]	0.121 703 8	1.217 038 1E-01
pound/cubic foot	0.062 428	6.242 796 1E-02
pound/cubic yard	1.685 554 9	1.685 554 9E+00
ton/cubic yard [short]	0.000 842 8	8.427 774 7E-04
tonne/cubic meter	0.001	1.000 000 0E-03

gram/meter   \<linear density\>

	Standard	Scientific
denier	9,000	9.000 000 0E+03
drex	10,000	1.000 000 0E+04
kilogram/meter	0.001	1.000 000 0E-03
kilotex	1	1.000 000 0E+00
ounce/foot	0.010 751 5	1.075 150 4E-02
pound/yard	0.002 015 9	2.015 906 9E-03
tex	1,000	1.000 000 0E+03

gram/milliliter   \<density\>

	Standard	Scientific
grain/cubic inch	252.891 04	2.528 910 4E+02
gram/cubic centimeter	1	1.000 000 0E+00
kilogram/cubic decimeter	1	1.000 000 0E+00
kilogram/cubic meter	1,000	1.000 000 0E+03
kilogram/liter	1	1.000 000 0E+00
megagram/cubic meter	1	1.000 000 0E+00
ounce/cubic foot	998.847 37	9.988 473 7E+02
pound/cubic foot	62.427 961	6.242 796 1E+01
pound/gallon [-/US, liquid]	8.345 404 5	8.345 404 5E+00
slug/cubic foot	1.940 320 3	1.940 320 3E+00
tonne/cubic meter	1	1.000 000 0E+00

gram/minute   \<flow rate, mass basis\>

	Standard	Scientific
kilogram/second	0.000 016 7	1.666 666 7E-05
pound/hour	0.132 277 4	1.322 773 6E-01

gram/mole   \<molar mass\>

	Standard	Scientific
kilogram/kilomole	1	1.000 000 0E+00
kilogram/mole	0.001	1.000 000 0E-03

gram/second   \<flow rate, mass basis\>

	Standard	Scientific
kilogram/second	0.001	1.000 000 0E-03
pound/hour	7.936 641 4	7.936 641 4E+00

gram/square centimeter   \<surface density\>

	Standard	Scientific
grain/square inch	99.563 403	9.956 340 3E+01
kilogram/are	1,000	1.000 000 0E+03
kilogram/square meter	10	1.000 000 0E+01
ounce/square foot	32.770 583	3.277 058 3E+01
pound/acre	89,217.912	8.921 791 2E+04
pound/square foot	2.048 161 4	2.048 161 4E+00
slug/square yard	0.572 929 2	5.729 292 3E-01
ton/square foot [short]	0.001 024 1	1.024 080 7E-03
tonne/square meter	0.01	1.000 000 0E-02

gram/square meter   \<surface density\>

	Standard	Scientific
grain/square meter	1.433 713	1.433 713 0E+00
kilogram/hectare	10	1.000 000 0E+01
kilogram/square meter	0.001	1.000 000 0E-03
ounce/square yard	0.029 493 5	2.949 352 5E-02
pound/acre	8.921 791 2	8.921 791 2E+00
pound/square yard	0.001 843 3	1.843 345 3E-03
slug/square yard	0.000 057 3	5.729 292 3E-05

gram/square meter second   \<flow rate/unit area, mass basis\>

	Standard	Scientific
kilogram/square meter second	0.001	1.000 000 0E-03
ounce/square foot second	0.003 277 1	3.277 058 3E-03
pound/acre second	8.921 791 2	8.921 791 2E+00
pound/square foot second	0.000 204 8	2.048 161 4E-04

gram/ton [-/long]   \<concentration, mass basis\>

	Standard	Scientific
karat	0.000 023 6	2.362 095 7E-05
kilogram/kilogram	0.000 001	9.842 065 3E-07
milligram/ton [-/long]	1,000	1.000 000 0E+03

Convert From / Convert To	Standard	Scientific
ounce/ton [-/short]	0.031 494 6	3.149 460 9E-02
ounce/ton [troy/short]	0.028 706	2.870 602 4E-02
part/million	0.984 206 5	9.842 065 3E-01
pennyweight/ton [troy/short]	0.574 120 5	5.741 204 7E-01
percent	0.000 098 4	9.842 065 3E-05
pound/ton [-/short]	0.001 968 4	1.968 413 1E-03
gram/ton [-/metric]		**<concentration, mass basis>**
gram/ton [-/long]	1.016 046 9	1.016 046 9E+00
gram/tonne	1	1.000 000 0E+00
karat	0.000 024	2.400 000 0E-05
kilogram/kilogram	0.000 001	1.000 000 0E-06
milligram/kilogram	1	1.000 000 0E+00
milligram/ton [-/metric]	1,000	1.000 000 0E+03
ounce/ton [-/short]	0.032	3.200 000 0E-02
part/million	1	1.000 000 0E+00
percent	0.000 1	1.000 000 0E-04
pound/ton [-/long]	0.002 24	2.240 000 0E-03
pound/ton [-/short]	0.002	2.000 000 0E-03
gram/ton [-/short]		**<concentration, mass basis>**
gram/ton [-/long]	1.12	1.120 000 0E+00
karat	0.000 026 5	2.645 547 2E-05
kilogram/kilogram	0.000 001 1	1.102 311 3E-06
milligram/kilogram	1.102 311 3	1.102 311 3E+00
milligram/ton [-/long]	1,120	1.120 000 0E+03
milligram/ton [-/short]	1,000	1.000 000 0E+03
ounce/ton [-/metric]	0.038 882 9	3.888 288 7E-02
ounce/ton [troy/short]	0.032 150 7	3.215 074 7E-02
part/million	1.102 311 3	1.102 311 3E+00
pennyweight/ton [troy/short]	0.643 014 9	6.430 149 3E-01
percent	0.000 110 2	1.102 311 3E-04
pound/ton [-/short]	0.002 204 6	2.204 622 6E-03
gram/ton [-/UK, assay or assay, long]		**<concentration, mass basis>**
gram/ton [-/US, assay or assay, short]	0.892 857 1	8.928 571 4E-01
karat	0.734 693 9	7.346 938 8E-01
kilogram/kilogram	0.030 612 2	3.061 224 5E-02
milligram/ton [-/UK, assay or assay, long]	1,000	1.000 000 0E+03
ounce/ton [troy/long]	1,000	1.000 000 0E+03
part/million	30,612.244 9	3.061 224 5E+04
pennyweight/ton [troy/long]	20,000	2.000 000 0E+04
percent	3.061 224 5	3.061 224 5E+00
pound/ton [-/metric]	67.488 447 6	6.748 844 8E+01
gram/ton [-/US, assay or assay, short]		**<concentration, mass basis>**
gram/ton [-/UK, assay or assay, long]	1.12	1.120 000 0E+00
karat	0.822 857 1	8.228 571 4E-01
kilogram/kilogram	0.034 285 7	3.428 571 4E-02
milligram/ton [-/US, assay or assay, short]	1,000	1.000 000 0E+03
ounce/ton [-/US, assay or assay, short]	0.035 274	3.527 396 2E-02
part/million	34,285.714 3	3.428 571 4E+04
pennyweight/ton [troy/short]	20,000	2.000 000 0E+04
percent	3.428 571 4	3.428 571 4E+00
pound/ton [-/long]	76.8	7.680 000 0E+01
gram/tonne		**<concentration, mass basis>**
gram/ton [-/long]	1.016 046 9	1.016 046 9E+00
gram/ton [-/metric]	1	1.000 000 0E+00
karat	0.000 024	2.400 000 0E-05
kilogram/kilogram	0.000 001	1.000 000 0E-06
milligram/gram	0.001	1.000 000 0E-03
milligram/kilogram	1	1.000 000 0E+00
milligram/ton [-/metric]	1,000	1.000 000 0E+03
ounce/ton [-/short]	0.032	3.200 000 0E-02
part/million	1	1.000 000 0E+00
pennyweight/ton [troy/short]	0.583 333 3	5.833 333 3E-01

| Convert From | | <Type of Unit> |
Convert To	Standard	Scientific
percent	0.000 1	1.000 000 0E-04
pound/ton [-/short]	0.002	2.000 000 0E-03

gramma [Greece, ancient]   <mass, special - see page 29>
gram --- 1.62 --- 1.620 000 0E+00

gramme [Greece]   <length, special - see page 29>
millimeter --- 2.12 --- 2.120 000 0E+00

gran [Austria, apothecary]   <mass, special - see page 29>
gram --- 0.074 6 --- 7.460 000 0E-02

gran [Austria]   <mass, special - see page 29>
gram --- 0.59 --- 5.900 000 0E-01

gran [Belgium, gold]   <mass, special - see page 29>
gram --- 0.32 --- 3.200 000 0E-01

gran [Belgium, silver]   <mass, special - see page 29>
gram --- 0.852 --- 8.520 000 0E-01

gran [Denmark]   <mass, special - see page 29>
gram --- 0.852 --- 8.520 000 0E-01

gran [Germany]   <mass, special - see page 29>
gram --- 0.82 --- 8.200 000 0E-01

gran [India, troy]   <mass, special - see page 29>
gram --- 11.64 --- 1.164 000 0E+01

gran [Sweden]   <length, special - see page 29>
centimeter --- 0.029 690 1 --- 2.969 010 0E-02

gran [Switzerland, apothecary]   <mass, special - see page 29>
gram --- 0.05 --- 5.000 000 0E-02

gran [UK]   <mass, special - see page 29>
gram --- 0.065 --- 6.500 000 0E-02

grande litra [Greece]   <mass, special - see page 29>
kilogram --- 48 --- 4.800 000 0E+01

grani [Thailand]   <mass, special - see page 29>
gram --- 0.937 5 --- 9.375 000 0E-01

grano [Argentina]   <mass, special - see page 29>
gram --- 0.05 --- 5.000 000 0E-02

grano [Chile]   <mass, special - see page 29>
gram --- 0.049 923 3 --- 4.992 330 0E-02

grano [Germany]   <mass, special - see page 29>
gram --- 0.05 --- 5.000 000 0E-02

grano [Honduras]   <mass, special - see page 29>
milligram --- 49.92 --- 4.992 000 0E+01

grano [Italy]   <mass, special - see page 29>
milligram --- 49.05 --- 4.905 000 0E+01

grano [Netherlands]   <mass, special - see page 29>
gram --- 0.067 --- 6.700 000 0E-02

grano [Spain]   <mass, special - see page 29>
milligram --- 49.9 --- 4.990 000 0E+01

grano [Sweden, apothecary]   <mass, special - see page 29>
gram --- 0.063 --- 6.300 000 0E-02

grano [Switzerland, apothecary]   <mass, special - see page 29>
gram --- 0.05 --- 5.000 000 0E-02

granottino [Italy, troy]   <mass, special - see page 29>
gram --- 0.002 --- 2.000 000 0E-03

granow [Poland]   <mass, special - see page 29>
gram --- 0.043 --- 4.300 000 0E-02

granow [Russia, hay]   <mass, special - see page 29>
gram --- 8,183 --- 8.183 000 0E+03

granum [Russia, apothecary]   <mass, special - see page 29>
milligram --- 62.209 --- 6.220 900 0E+01

Convert From / Convert To	Standard	Scientific
grao [Brazil]	<mass, special - see page 29>	
gram	0.049 810 1	4.981 010 0E-02
grao [Portugal]	<mass, special - see page 29>	
gram	0.049 81	4.981 000 0E-02
grav	<acceleration>	
foot/square second	32.174 048 6	3.217 404 9E+01
g-unit	1	1.000 000 0E+00
galileo	980.665	9.806 650 0E+02
g_n [due to gravity]	1	1.000 000 0E+00
meter/square second	9.806 65	9.806 650 0E+00
gray	<absorbed dose>	
joule/kilogram	1	1.000 000 0E+00
rad	100	1.000 000 0E+02
rep	119.331 74	1.193 317 4E+02
gray/second	<absorbed dose rate>	
joule/kilogram second	1	1.000 000 0E+00
rad/second	100	1.000 000 0E+02
rep/second	119.331 74	1.193 317 4E+02
watt/kilogram	1	1.000 000 0E+00
great gross	<units>	
hexad	288	2.880 000 0E+02
unit	1,728	1.728 000 0E+03
great hin [Hebrew, ancient]	<volume, special - see page 29>	
liter	9.18	9.180 000 0E+00
great mina [Iraq, ancient]	<mass, special - see page 29>	
kilogram	0.962	9.620 000 0E-01
great ovido [Saudi Arabia, ancient]	<length, special - see page 29>	
centimeter	68.6	6.860 000 0E+01
greater pic [Turkey, land]	<length, special - see page 29>	
centimeter	75.8	7.580 000 0E+01
greater pic [Turkey]	<length, special - see page 29>	
centimeter	68	6.800 000 0E+01
grein [Netherlands]	<mass, special - see page 29>	
gram	0.064	6.400 000 0E-02
grivna [Russia]	<mass, special - see page 29>	
gram	409.536	4.095 360 0E+02
gros [France, 1800 definition]	<mass, special - see page 29>	
gram	10	1.000 000 0E+01
gros [France]	<mass, special - see page 29>	
gram	3.824 3	3.824 300 0E+00
gros poid [Switzerland]	<mass, special - see page 29>	
gram	550.69	5.506 900 0E+02
gross	<units>	
hexad	24	2.400 000 0E+01
unit	144	1.440 000 0E+02
gubiar [Mongolia]	<area, special - see page 29>	
hectare	9.216	9.216 000 0E+00
gudge [India]	<length, special - see page 29>	
meter	0.685 8	6.858 000 0E-01
gudge [Iran]	<length, special - see page 29>	
meter	1.04	1.040 000 0E+00
gudge [Pakistan]	<length, special - see page 29>	
meter	0.914 4	9.144 000 0E-01
gudge [Saudi Arabia, ancient]	<length, special - see page 29>	
centimeter	63.5	6.350 000 0E+01
guereh [Iran]	<length, special - see page 29>	
centimeter	6.5	6.500 000 0E+00

Convert From Convert To	Standard	<Type of Unit> Scientific
gulg slug [metric]	0.1	**<mass>** 1.000 000 0E−01
gun [China] kilogram	<mass, special - see page 29> 0.5	5.000 000 0E−01
gunja [India, seed] milligram	<mass, special - see page 29> 65	6.500 000 0E+01
guntha [Pakistan] square meter	<area, special - see page 29> 101.17	1.011 700 0E+02
gur [Iraq, ancient] hectoliter	<volume, special - see page 29> 2.89	2.890 000 0E+00
gur [Mesopotamia, ancient] liter	<volume, special - see page 29> 246	2.460 000 0E+02
gurraf [Libya] liter	<volume, special - see page 29> 2.306 6	2.306 600 0E+00
guz [Ceylon] meter	<length, special - see page 29> 0.914 4	9.144 000 0E−01
guz [India, Bombay] centimeter	<length, special - see page 29> 69	6.900 000 0E+01
guz [India] meter	<length, special - see page 29> 0.914 4	9.144 000 0E−01
guz [Iran] meter	<length, special - see page 29> 1.04	1.040 000 0E+00
guz [Nepal, textiles] meter	<length, special - see page 29> 0.914 4	9.144 000 0E−01
guz [Pakistan] meter	<length, special - see page 29> 0.914 4	9.144 000 0E−01
gyrath [Algeria, troy] gram	<mass, special - see page 29> 0.207	2.070 000 0E−01
haat [Nepal, textiles] centimeter	<length, special - see page 29> 45.72	4.572 000 0E+01
hab [Cambodia] kilogram	<mass, special - see page 29> 60	6.000 000 0E+01
hab [China] kilogram	<mass, special - see page 29> 50	5.000 000 0E+01
hab [Indonesia] kilogram	<mass, special - see page 29> 61.761	6.176 100 0E+01
hab [Japan] kilogram	<mass, special - see page 29> 60	6.000 000 0E+01
hab [Laos] kilogram	<mass, special - see page 29> 60	6.000 000 0E+01
hab [Philippines] kilogram	<mass, special - see page 29> 63.249	6.324 900 0E+01
hab [Thailand] kilogram	<mass, special - see page 29> 60	6.000 000 0E+01
hab [Vietnam] kilogram	<mass, special - see page 29> 60.453	6.045 300 0E+01
habba [Egypt] square meter	<area, special - see page 29> 58.344	5.834 400 0E+01
habba [Sudan] milligram	<mass, special - see page 29> 100	1.000 000 0E+02
habba shair [Egypt] millimeter	<length, special - see page 29> 5.22	5.220 000 0E+00
habbe [Turkey] milligram	<mass, special - see page 29> 0.783	7.830 000 0E−01

Convert From Convert To	Standard	<Type of Unit> Scientific
habl [Libya]	<length, special - see page 29>	
meter	35	3.500 000 0E+01
hak [Turkey]	<volume, special - see page 29>	
liter	33.7	3.370 000 0E+01
hal [Cambodia]	<mass, special - see page 29>	
kilogram	60	6.000 000 0E+01
hal [China]	<mass, special - see page 29>	
kilogram	50	5.000 000 0E+01
hal [Indonesia]	<mass, special - see page 29>	
kilogram	61.761	6.176 100 0E+01
hal [Japan]	<mass, special - see page 29>	
kilogram	60	6.000 000 0E+01
hal [Laos]	<mass, special - see page 29>	
kilogram	60	6.000 000 0E+01
hal [Philippines]	<mass, special - see page 29>	
kilogram	63.249	6.324 900 0E+01
hal [Thailand]	<mass, special - see page 29>	
kilogram	60	6.000 000 0E+01
hal [Vietnam]	<mass, special - see page 29>	
kilogram	60.453	6.045 300 0E+01
halbe [Austria]	<volume, special - see page 29>	
liter	0.707	7.070 000 0E-01
halbe [Hungary]	<volume, special - see page 29>	
liter	0.848	8.480 000 0E-01
halbstuck [Netherlands]	<volume, special - see page 29>	
liter	600	6.000 000 0E+02
half anker [UK]	<volume, special - see page 29>	
liter	22.7	2.270 000 0E+01
half barrel [UK]	<volume, special - see page 29>	
liter	82	8.200 000 0E+01
half chest [Ceylon, tea]	<mass, special - see page 29>	
kilogram	31.751 47	3.175 147 0E+01
half hogshead [UK]	<volume, special - see page 29>	
liter	123	1.230 000 0E+02
half homer [Hebrew, ancient]	<volume, special - see page 29>	
liter	110	1.100 000 0E+02
half mina [Greece, ancient]	<mass, special - see page 29>	
gram	312.52	3.125 200 0E+02
halibin [Romania]	<length, special - see page 29>	
meter	0.701	7.010 000 0E-01
halvstop [Sweden]	<volume, special - see page 29>	
liter	0.654 279	6.542 790 0E-01
hami [Sudan]	<mass, special - see page 29>	
kilogram	312	3.120 000 0E+02
hand [horses]		<length>
barleycorn	12	1.200 000 0E+01
caliber	400	4.000 000 0E+02
cubit	0.222 222 2	2.222 222 2E-01
decimeter	1.016	1.016 000 0E+00
digit	5.333 333 3	5.333 333 3E+00
foot [international]	0.333 333 3	3.333 333 3E-01
inch [international]	4	4.000 000 0E+00
link [Gunter or US, survey]	0.505 049 5	5.050 494 9E-01
link [Ramden or Engineer]	0.333 333 3	3.333 333 3E-01
meter	0.101 6	1.016 000 0E-01
mil	4,000	4.000 000 0E+03
nail [cloth]	1.777 777 8	1.777 777 8E+00

	Standard	Scientific
pace [geometrical]		
palm	0.006 666 7	6.666 666 7E–03
palm	1.333 333 3	1.333 333 3E+00
span	0.444 444 4	4.444 444 4E–01
thou	4,000	4.000 000 0E+03
handaza [Libya, textiles]	<length, special - see page 29>	
centimeter	68	6.800 000 0E+01
handbreadth [Hebrew, ancient]	<length, special - see page 29>	
centimeter	8	8.000 000 0E+00
handbreadth [Iraq, ancient]	<length, special - see page 29>	
centimeter	9.9	9.900 000 0E+00
hang [Cambodia]	<mass, special - see page 29>	
gram	37.5	3.750 000 0E+01
hang [China]	<mass, special - see page 29>	
gram	50	5.000 000 0E+01
hao [China]	<mass, special - see page 29>	
milligram	3.779 937	3.779 937 0E+00
hao ke [China]	<mass, special - see page 29>	
milligram	1	1.000 000 0E+00
hao mi [China]	<length, special - see page 29>	
millimeter	1	1.000 000 0E+00
hao sheng [China]	<volume, special - see page 29>	
milliliter	1	1.000 000 0E+00
hap [Cambodia]	<mass, special - see page 29>	
kilogram	60	6.000 000 0E+01
hap [China]	<mass, special - see page 29>	
kilogram	50	5.000 000 0E+01
hap [Indonesia]	<mass, special - see page 29>	
kilogram	61.761	6.176 100 0E+01
hap [Laos]	<mass, special - see page 29>	
kilogram	60	6.000 000 0E+01
hap [Philippines]	<mass, special - see page 29>	
kilogram	63.249	6.324 900 0E+01
hap [Thailand]	<mass, special - see page 29>	
kilogram	60	6.000 000 0E+01
hap [Vietnam]	<mass, special - see page 29>	
kilogram	60.453	6.045 300 0E+01
harbour ton [South Africa]	<mass, special - see page 29>	
kilogram	907.184 7	9.071 847 0E+02
hardal [Islam, mustard grain]	<mass, special - see page 29>	
gram	0.000 71	7.100 000 0E–04
harruba [Islam]	<mass, special - see page 29>	
gram	0.195	1.950 000 0E–01
harsela [Egypt]	<mass, special - see page 29>	
gram	1,276.4	1.276 400 0E+03
hartree [atomic physics, eq. energy]		<energy>
1/centimeter [atomic physics, eq. energy]	219,474.63	2.194 746 3E+05
1/meter [atomic physics, eq. energy]	>>>	2.194 746 3E+07
atomic mass unit [unified, C-12, 1986, eq. energy]	<<<	2.921 262 7E–08
deuteron rest mass [atomic physics, eq. energy]	<<<	1.450 799 9E–08
electron rest mass [atomic physics, eq. energy]	0.000 053 3	5.325 136 3E–05
electronvolt	27.211 396	2.721 139 6E+01
gigaelectronvolt	<<<	2.721 139 6E–08
joule	<<<	4.359 748 2E–18
kayser [atomic physics, eq. energy]	219,474.63	2.194 746 3E+05
kelvin [atomic physics, eq. energy]	315,773.22	3.157 732 2E+05
kiloelectronvolt	0.027 211 4	2.721 139 6E–02
megaelectronvolt	0.000 027 2	2.721 139 6E–05

Convert From Convert To	Standard	\<Type of Unit> Scientific

Convert From / Convert To	Standard	Scientific
muon rest mass [atomic physics, eq. energy]	0.000 000 3	2.575 412 8E−07
neutron rest mass [atomic physics, eq. energy]	<<<	2.896 167 7E−08
picojoule	0.000 004 4	4.359 748 2E−06
proton rest mass [atomic physics, eq. energy]	<<<	2.900 159 8E−08
rydberg [atomic physics, eq. energy]	1.999 976 3	1.999 976 3E+00
hasit [Hebrew, ancient]		\<length, special - see page 29>
centimeter	18.672 886	1.867 288 6E+01
hasta [India]		\<length, special - see page 29>
centimeter	45.72	4.572 000 0E+01
hasta [Malaysia]		\<length, special - see page 29>
meter	0.457 2	4.572 000 0E−01
hasta [Singapore]		\<length, special - see page 29>
meter	0.457 2	4.572 000 0E−01
hat [Cambodia]		\<length, special - see page 29>
centimeter	50	5.000 000 0E+01
hat [Somalia]		\<length, special - see page 29>
meter	0.558 8	5.588 000 0E−01
hath [Cambodia]		\<length, special - see page 29>
meter	0.5	5.000 000 0E−01
hath [India]		\<length, special - see page 29>
centimeter	45.72	4.572 000 0E+01
hath [Somalia]		\<length, special - see page 29>
meter	0.558 8	5.588 000 0E−01
hatt [Turkey]		\<length, special - see page 29>
millimeter	0.346	3.460 000 0E−01
haut [India]		\<length, special - see page 29>
centimeter	45.72	4.572 000 0E+01
he [China]		\<volume, special - see page 29>
centiliter	10	1.000 000 0E+01
hebbeh [Iraq, ancient]		\<mass, special - see page 29>
milligram	65	6.500 000 0E+01
hectare		\<area>
abraa [Morocco]	5.555 555 6	5.555 555 6E+00
acre [Bangladesh]	2.470 966 1	2.470 966 1E+00
acre [commerical]	2.989 975 1	2.989 975 1E+00
acre [international]	2.471 053 8	2.471 053 8E+00
acre [Ireland]	1.525 553	1.525 553 E+00
acre [Netherlands]	2.345 215 8	2.345 215 8E+00
acre [Pakistan]	2.469 135 8	2.469 135 8E+00
acre [Rome, ancient]	3.968 254	3.968 254 0E+00
acre [US, survey]	2.471 043 9	2.471 043 9E+00
actus quadratus [Rome, ancient]	7.936 507 9	7.936 507 9E+00
ardeb [Egypt]	3.636 363 6	3.636 363 6E+00
are	100	1.000 000 0E+02
arpent [Canada]	2.923 976 6	2.923 976 6E+00
bahu [Indonesia]	1.409 145 4	1.409 145 4E+00
bau [Indonesia]	1.409 145 4	1.409 145 4E+00
beit zemed [Hebrew, ancient]	4.545 454 5	4.545 454 5E+00
bigha [Bangladesh]	7.407 407 4	7.407 407 4E+00
bigha [India]	7.462 686 6	7.462 686 6E+00
bigha [Nepal]	1.476 797 3	1.476 797 3E+00
bigha [Pakistan]	4.942 176 5	4.942 176 5E+00
bouw [Indonesia]	1.409 145 4	1.409 145 4E+00
bunder [Netherlands]	1	1.000 000 0E+00
caballeria [Canada]	0.022 883 3	2.288 329 5E−02
caballeria [Costa Rica]	0.022 099 4	2.209 944 8E−02
caballeria [Cuba]	0.074 515 6	7.451 564 8E−02
caballeria [Dominican Republic]	0.013 252 1	1.325 205 4E−02
caballeria [Ecuador]	0.088 574	8.857 395 9E−02

Convert From
Convert To   Standard   \<Type of Unit\>
     Scientific

hectare (continued)   \<area\>

Convert To	Standard	Scientific
caballeria [El Salvador]	0.022 239 5	2.223 952 0E−02
caballeria [Guatemala]	0.022 361 4	2.236 136 0E−02
caballeria [Honduras]	0.022 237	2.223 704 7E−02
caballeria [Mexico]	0.023 364 5	2.336 448 6E−02
caballeria [Nicaragua]	0.022 144 5	2.214 447 1E−02
caballeria [Spain]	0.025 879 9	2.587 991 7E−02
cabelleria [Nicaragua]	0.022 182 8	2.218 278 6E−02
cadastral yoke [Hungary]	1.737 728 2	1.737 728 2E+00
cadne [Lebanon]	3.448 275 9	3.448 275 9E+00
carga [Venezuela]	1	1.000 000 0E+00
caro [Dominican Republic]	0.773 395 2	7.733 952 0E−01
carreau [Dominican Republic]	0.773 395 2	7.733 952 0E−01
cawney [India]	1.869 158 9	1.869 158 9E+00
cawnie [India]	1.869 158 9	1.869 158 9E+00
centuria [Rome, ancient]	0.019 841 3	1.984 127 0E−02
chia [Taiwan]	1.031 034 1	1.031 034 1E+00
cuadra [Peru]	1	1.000 000 0E+00
cuadra cuadrada [Chile]	0.635 930 1	6.359 300 5E−01
cuadro [Venezuela]	1.562 5	1.562 500 0E+00
cuarta [Brazil]	2.695 417 8	2.695 417 8E+00
cuerda [Philippines]	2.544 529 3	2.544 529 3E+00
cuerda [Puerto Rico]	2.544 529 3	2.544 529 3E+00
cunningham acre [Ireland]	1.913 509 4	1.913 509 4E+00
deciatine [Russia]	0.915 298 3	9.152 983 0E−01
desatine [Russia]	0.914 913 1	9.149 130 8E−01
desiatiny [Russia]	0.917 431 2	9.174 311 9E−01
dessetine [Russia]	0.914 913 1	9.149 130 8E−01
dessiatina [Russia]	0.915 298 3	9.152 983 0E−01
deunum [Turkey]	0.04	4.000 000 0E−02
dhumd [Egypt]	2.380 952 4	2.380 952 4E+00
dhumd [Iraq]	0.2	2.000 000 0E−01
dhumd [Saudi Arabia]	2.380 952 4	2.380 952 4E+00
dhumd [Sudan]	2.380 952 4	2.380 952 4E+00
dhumd [Yemen]	2.469 135 8	2.469 135 8E+00
diciatine [Russia]	0.915 298 3	9.152 983 0E−01
djerib [Turkey]	1	1.000 000 0E+00
djevil [Turkey]	1	1.000 000 0E+00
djung [Indonesia]	0.704 572 7	7.045 726 8E−01
engjateigur [Iceland]	3.134 796 2	3.134 796 2E+00
faddan [Iraq]	0.2	2.000 000 0E−01
faddan [Yemen]	2.469 135 8	2.469 135 8E+00
fanega [Mexico]	0.280 404 2	2.804 042 3E−01
fanegada [Venezuela]	1.430 615 2	1.430 615 2E+00
feddan [Iraq]	0.2	2.000 000 0E−01
feddan [Yemen]	2.469 135 8	2.469 135 8E+00
gan [Iraq, ancient]	0.370 370 4	3.703 703 7E−01
gasha [Eritrea]	0.025	2.500 000 0E−02
gasha [Ethiopia]	0.025	2.500 000 0E−02
geira [Brazil]	0.052 631 6	5.263 157 9E−02
ghumaon [Pakistan]	2.469 135 8	2.469 135 8E+00
girib [Turkey]	4.830 917 9	4.830 917 9E+00
gong qing [China]	1	1.000 000 0E+00
gouffa [Morocco]	2	2.000 000 0E+00
gubiar [Mongolia]	0.108 506 9	1.085 069 4E−01
heredium [Rome, ancient]	1.984 127	1.984 127 0E+00
izenbi [Morocco]	5.555 555 6	5.555 555 6E+00
jerib [Afghanistan]	5.118 755 1	5.118 755 1E+00
juger [Rome, ancient]	3.968 254	3.968 254 0E+00
jugerum [Rome, ancient]	3.944 773 2	3.944 773 2E+00
jungbo [Japan]	1.008 369 5	1.008 369 5E+00
jungbo [North Korea]	1.008 369 5	1.008 369 5E+00
jungbo [South Korea]	1.008 369 5	1.008 369 5E+00

hectare (continued) <area>

	Standard	Scientific
kalad [Ethiopia]	0.025	2.500 000 E−02
kanee [Pakistan]	6.176 652 3	6.176 652 3E+00
katastarsko jutro [Yugoslavia]	1.737 619 5	1.737 619 5E+00
katasztralis hold [Hungary]	1.737 728 2	1.737 728 2E+00
keila [Libya]	3.125	3.125 000 0E+00
khedem [Morocco]	10	1.000 000 0E+01
kila [Libya]	3.125	3.125 000 0E+00
kin [China]	0.162 760 4	1.627 604 2E−01
king [China]	1.483 679 5	1.483 679 5E+00
ko [Taiwan]	1.031 034 1	1.031 034 1E+00
kordofan [Sudan]	1.376 273 1	1.376 273 1E+00
kordofan mukhamas [Sudan, land]	1.376 235 2	1.376 235 2E+00
kulba [Afghanistan]	0.127 975 4	1.279 754 3E−01
kung ching [China]	1	1.000 000 0E+00
kung ching [Taiwan]	1	1.000 000 0E+00
lan [Czechoslovakia]	0.057 903 9	5.790 388 0E−02
lanac [Yugoslavia]	1.390 820 6	1.390 820 6E+00
makhammus [Sudan]	3.095 975 2	3.095 975 2E+00
man [China]	14.925 373	1.492 537 3E+01
manzana [Argentina]	1	1.000 000 0E+00
manzana [Belize]	1.197 604 8	1.197 604 8E+00
marabba [Pakistan]	0.098 842 2	9.884 216 3E−02
maw [China]	14.925 373	1.492 537 3E+01
medio [Venezuela]	2	2.000 000 0E+00
meshara [Iraq]	4	4.000 000 0E+00
mishara [Iraq]	4	4.000 000 0E+00
modd [Malta]	0.556 173 5	5.561 735 3E−01
moraba [Pakistan]	0.098 843 5	9.884 353 1E−02
morg [Lithuania]	1.403 902 8	1.403 902 8E+00
morg [Ukraine]	1.739 130 4	1.739 130 4E+00
morgan [South Africa]	1.162 790 7	1.162 790 7E+00
morgen [Botswana]	1.166 861 1	1.166 861 1E+00
morgen [Netherlands]	1.172 607 9	1.172 607 9E+00
morgen [South Africa]	1.167 501 4	1.167 501 4E+00
mow [China]	14.925 373	1.492 537 3E+01
mu [China]	15.015 015	1.501 501 5E+01
mud [Netherlands]	1	1.000 000 0E+00
mudde [Netherlands]	1	1.000 000 0E+00
muddle [Netherlands]	1	1.000 000 0E+00
orlong [Malaysia]	1.869 158 9	1.869 158 9E+00
orlong [Singapore]	1.869 158 9	1.869 158 9E+00
panchar [Indonesia]	0.352 236 7	3.522 367 0E−01
penjuru [Malaysia]	7.474 958 9	7.474 958 9E+00
penjuru [Singapore]	7.462 686 6	7.462 686 6E+00
qadaa [Sudan]	0.453 720 5	4.537 205 1E−01
qing [China]	0.15	1.500 000 0E−01
quadra de sesmaria [Brazil]	0.011 481 1	1.148 105 6E−02
quarta [Cape Verde]	2.152 203 9	2.152 203 9E+00
quinon [Philippines]	0.357 781 8	3.577 817 5E−01
rai [Laos]	6.25	6.250 000 0E+00
rai [Thailand]	6.25	6.250 000 0E+00
relong [Malaysia]	3.484 320 6	3.484 320 6E+00
relong [Singapore]	3.484 320 6	3.484 320 6E+00
rhineland acre [Surinam]	2.345 215 8	2.345 215 8E+00
rhynland acre [Guyana]	2.347 417 8	2.347 417 8E+00
rood	9.884 175 7	9.884 175 7E+00
rosa [Cuba]	1.340 482 6	1.340 482 6E+00
roza [Cuba]	1.340 482 6	1.340 482 6E+00
saltus [Rome, ancient]	0.004 950 5	4.950 495 0E−03
sdal [Morocco]	5.555 555 6	5.555 555 6E+00
set [Egypt, ancient]	3.636 363 6	3.636 363 6E+00
shih ching [China]	0.15	1.500 000 0E−01

hectare (continued) <area>

Convert To	Standard	Scientific
sitio [Mexico]	0.000 569 6	5.696 025 9E–04
spanland [Sweden]	4.048 583	4.048 583 0E+00
square arpent [US, survey]	2.924 900 6	2.924 900 6E+00
square chain [Gunter or US, survey]	24.710 439	2.471 043 9E+01
square chain [Ramden or Engineer]	10.763 867	1.076 386 7E+01
square cuadra [Chile]	0.636 132 3	6.361 323 2E–01
square cuadra [Ecuador]	1.417 233 6	1.417 233 6E+00
square furlong [US, survey]	0.247 104 4	2.471 043 9E–01
square hectometer	1	1.000 000 0E+00
square meter	10,000	1.000 000 0E+04
square mile [international]	0.003 861	3.861 021 6E–03
square mile [US, statute]	0.003 861	3.861 006 1E–03
square mile [US, survey]	0.003 861	3.861 006 1E–03
square perch [US, survey]	395.367 03	3.953 670 3E+02
square rope	269.097 76	2.690 977 6E+02
square sen [Thailand]	6.25	6.250 000 0E+00
suerte [Nicaragua]	0.709 219 9	7.092 198 6E–01
tarialte [Morocco]	2.777 777 8	2.777 777 8E+00
tchetvert [Russia]	1.830 596 9	1.830 596 9E+00
tomna [Malta]	8.928 571 4	8.928 571 4E+00
tonde [Denmark]	0.352 497 4	3.524 974 4E–01
tonde land [Denmark]	1.811 594 2	1.811 594 2E+00
tzemed [Mesopotamia, ancient]	5	5.000 000 0E+00
vierkante mijl [Netherlands]	0.01	1.000 000 0E–02
vloka [Poland]	0.059 538	5.953 798 5E–02
yugada [Peru]	0.030 959 8	3.095 975 2E–02
yugada [Spain]	0.031 057 8	3.105 783 0E–02

hectare meter <volume>

Convert To	Standard	Scientific
acre foot	8.107 131 9	8.107 131 9E+00
acre inch	97.285 583	9.728 558 3E+01
barrel [UK]	61,102.569	6.110 256 9E+04
barrel [US, liquid]	83,864.144	8.386 414 4E+04
barrel [US, petroleum]	62,898.108	6.289 810 8E+04
cubic foot	353,146.67	3.531 466 7E+05
cubic meter	10,000	1.000 000 0E+04
cubic yard	13,079.506	1.307 950 6E+04
gallon [Canada, liquid]	2,199,692.5	2.199 692 5E+06
gallon [UK, dry or liquid]	2,199,692.5	2.199 692 5E+06
gallon [US, liquid]	2,641,720.5	2.641 720 5E+06
liter	>>>	1.000 000 0E+07
petrograd standard	2,140.282 8	2.140 282 8E+03
stere	10,000	1.000 000 0E+04

hectare meter/day <flow rate, volume basis>

Convert To	Standard	Scientific
acre foot/day	8.107 131 9	8.107 131 9E+00
acre foot/day [US, survey]	8.107 083 3	8.107 083 3E+00
acre inch/hour	4.053 566	4.053 566 0E+00
barrel/minute [UK]	42.432 339 6	4.243 234 0E+01
barrel/minute [US, federal]	59.178 327 1	5.917 832 7E+01
barrel/minute [US, liquid]	58.238 988 6	5.823 898 9E+01
barrel/minute [US, petroleum]	43.679 241 5	4.367 924 2E+01
centiliter/day	>>>	1.000 000 0E+09
cubic centimeter/day	>>>	1.000 000 0E+10
cubic decimeter/day	>>>	1.000 000 0E+07
cubic dekameter/day	10	1.000 000 0E+01
cubic foot/second	4.087 345 7	4.087 345 7E+00
cubic inch/second	7,062.933 34	7.062 933 3E+03
cubic kilometer/day	0.000 01	1.000 000 0E–05
cubic meter/minute	6.944 444 4	6.944 444 4E+00
cubic meter/second	0.115 740 7	1.157 407 4E–01
cubic yard/minute	9.082 990 4	9.082 990 4E+00
dekaliter/second	11.574 074 1	1.157 407 4E+01

	Standard	Scientific
gallon/second [UK]	25.459 403 7	2.545 940 4E+01
gallon/second [US, liquid]	30.575 469	3.057 546 9E+01
hectare meter/hour	0.041 666 7	4.166 666 7E-02
hectoliter/day	100,000	1.000 000 0E+05
hectoliter/second	1.157 407 4	1.157 407 4E+00
kiloliter/day	10,000	1.000 000 0E+04
kiloliter/minute	6.944 444 4	6.944 444 4E+00
liter/second	115.740 741	1.157 407 4E+02
liter/second [pre-1964]	115.737 5	1.157 375 0E+02
ounce/second [UK, liquid]	4,073.504 66	4.073 504 6E+03
ounce/second [US, liquid]	3,913.66	3.913 660 0E+03
petrograd standard/minute	1.486 307 5	1.486 307 5E+00
stere/minute	6.944 444 4	6.944 444 4E+00
thousand cubic foot/hour	14.714 444	1.471 444 4E+01
hectare meter/hour		**<flow rate, volume basis>**
acre foot/hour	8.107 131 9	8.107 131 9E+00
acre foot/hour [US, survey]	8.107 083 3	8.107 083 3E+00
acre inch/minute	1.621 426 4	1.621 426 4E+00
barrel/second [UK]	16.972 935 8	1.697 293 6E+01
barrel/second [US, federal]	23.671 330 9	2.367 133 1E+01
barrel/second [US, liquid]	23.295 593 9	2.329 559 5E+01
barrel/second [US, petroleum]	17.471 696 6	1.747 169 7E+01
cubic dekameter/hour	10	1.000 000 0E+01
cubic foot/second	98.096 296 4	9.809 629 6E+01
cubic meter/second	2.777 777 8	2.777 777 8E+00
cubic yard/second	3.633 196 2	3.633 196 2E+00
gallon/second [UK]	611.025 69	6.110 256 9E+02
gallon/second [US, liquid]	733.811 257	7.338 112 6E+02
hectare meter/day	24	2.400 000 0E+01
hectoliter/second	27.777 777 8	2.777 777 8E+01
kiloliter/second	2.777 777 8	2.777 777 8E+00
liter/second	2,777.777 78	2.777 777 8E+03
liter/second [pre-1964]	2,777.7	2.777 700 0E+03
ounce/second [UK, liquid]	97,764.11	9.776 411 0E+04
ounce/second [US, liquid]	93,927.841	9.392 784 1E+04
petrograd standard/minute	35.671 381	3.567 138 1E+01
stere/second	2.777 777 8	2.777 777 8E+00
thousand cubic foot/minute	5.885 777 8	5.885 777 8E+00
hectare meter/minute		**<flow rate, volume basis>**
acre foot/minute	8.107 131 9	8.107 131 9E+00
acre foot/minute [US, survey]	8.107 083 3	8.107 083 3E+00
acre inch/second	1.621 426 4	1.621 426 4E+00
barrel/second [UK]	1,018.376 15	1.018 376 2E+03
barrel/second [US, federal]	1,420.279 84	1.420 279 9E+03
barrel/second [US, liquid]	1,397.735 73	1.397 735 7E+03
barrel/second [US, petroleum]	1,048.301 8	1.048 301 8E+03
billion cubic foot/day	0.508 531 2	5.085 312 0E-01
cubem/day	0.003 454 7	3.454 743 7E-03
cubic dekameter/minute	10	1.000 000 0E+01
cubic kilometer/day	0.014 4	1.440 000 0E-02
cubic meter/second	166.666 667	1.666 666 7E+02
cubic yard/second	217.991 77	2.179 917 7E+02
gallon/second [UK]	36,661.541 4	3.666 154 1E+04
gallon/second [US, liquid]	44,028.675 4	4.402 867 5E+04
hectare meter/hour	60	6.000 000 0E+01
kiloliter/second	166.666 667	1.666 666 7E+02
liter/second	166,666.667	1.666 666 7E+05
liter/second [pre-1964]	166,662	1.666 620 0E+05
million acre foot/day	0.011 674 3	1.167 427 0E-02
petrograd standard/second	35.671 381	3.567 138 1E+01
stere/second	166.666 67	1.666 666 7E+02
thousand cubic foot/second	5.885 777 8	5.885 777 8E+00

	<Type of Unit>
Standard	Scientific

hectare meter/second <flow rate, volume basis>
Convert To	Standard	Scientific
acre foot/second	8.107 131 9	8.107 131 9E+00
acre foot/second [US, survey]	8.107 083 3	8.107 083 3E+00
acre inch/second	97.285 583 3	9.728 558 3E+01
barrel/second [UK]	61,102.569	6.110 256 9E+04
barrel/second [US, federal]	85,216.791 1	8.521 679 1E+04
barrel/second [US, liquid]	83,864.143 6	8.386 414 4E+04
barrel/second [US, petroleum]	62,898.107 7	6.289 810 8E+04
billion cubic foot/hour	1.271 328	1.271 328 0E+00
cubem/day	0.207 284 6	2.072 846 2E−01
cubic dekameter/second	10	1.000 000 0E+01
cubic kilometer/day	0.864	8.640 000 0E−01
cubic meter/second	10,000	1.000 000 0E+04
cubic mile/day	0.207 284 6	2.072 846 2E−01
hectare meter/minute	60	6.000 000 0E+01
million acre foot/day	0.700 456 2	7.004 562 0E−01
petrograd standard/second	2,140.282 8	2.140 282 8E+03
thousand cubic foot/second	353.146 67	3.531 466 7E+02
trillion cubic foot/day	0.030 511 9	3.051 187 2E−02

hectare/kilogram <specific area>
Convert To	Standard	Scientific
square foot/pound	48,824.276	4.882 427 6E+04
square meter/kilogram	10,000	1.000 000 0E+04

hectoampere <electric current>
Convert To	Standard	Scientific
abampere	10	1.000 000 0E+01
ampere	100	1.000 000 0E+02
electromagnetic unit of current [cgs system]	10	1.000 000 0E+01
gilbert	125.663 706	1.256 637 1E+02
statampere	>>>	2.997 924 6E+11

hectobar <pressure>
Convert To	Standard	Scientific
atmosphere [standard]	98.692 327	9.869 232 7E+01
atmosphere [technical]	101.971 62	1.019 716 2E+02
bar	100	1.000 000 0E+02
foot of mercury [0 °C, by convention]	246.083 19	2.460 831 9E+02
foot of water [4 °C, by convention]	3,345.525 6	3.345 525 6E+03
kilogram-force/square millimeter	1.019 716 2	1.019 716 2E+00
kilopond/square millimeter	1.019 716 2	1.019 716 2E+00
kip/square inch	1.450 377 4	1.450 377 4E+00
megapascal	10	1.000 000 0E+01
newton/square millimeter	10	1.000 000 0E+01
ounce-force/square inch	23,206.038	2.320 603 8E+04
pascal	>>>	1.000 000 0E+07
pound-force/square inch	1,450.377 4	1.450 377 4E+03
ton-force/square inch [short]	0.725 188 7	7.251 886 9E−01
ton-force/square meter [metric]	1,019.716 2	1.019 716 2E+03
torr	75,006.168	7.500 616 8E+04

hectocandela <luminous intensity>
Convert To	Standard	Scientific
candela	100	1.000 000 0E+02

hectocoulomb <electric charge>
Convert To	Standard	Scientific
abcoulomb	10	1.000 000 0E+01
coulomb	100	1.000 000 0E+02
electromagnetic unit of charge [cgs system]	10	1.000 000 0E+01
farad volt	100	1.000 000 0E+02
statcoulomb	>>>	2.997 924 6E+11

hectofarad <capacitance>
Convert To	Standard	Scientific
abfarad	0.000 000 1	1.000 000 0E−07
coulomb/volt	100	1.000 000 0E+02
farad	100	1.000 000 0E+02
statfarad	>>>	8.987 551 8E+13

hectogram <mass>
Convert To	Standard	Scientific
carat [international]	500	5.000 000 0E+02
carat [UK]	385.808 96	3.858 089 6E+02

Convert From Convert To	Standard	<Type of Unit> Scientific

Convert From / Convert To — Standard — Scientific

	Standard	Scientific
carat [US, after 1913]	500	5.000 000 0E+02
drachm [UK, apothecary]	25.720 597	2.572 059 7E+01
dram [avoirdupois]	56.438 339	5.643 833 9E+01
dram [US, apothecary]	25.720 597	2.572 059 7E+01
hyl	0.010 197 2	1.019 716 2E−02
kilogram	0.1	1.000 000 0E−01
onca [France, 1800 definition]	1	1.000 000 0E+00
once [France, 1800 definition]	1	1.000 000 0E+00
oncia [France, 1800 definition]	1	1.000 000 0E+00
ounce	3.527 396 2	3.527 396 2E+00
ounce [apothecary]	3.215 074 7	3.215 074 7E+00
ounce [avoirdupois]	3.527 396 2	3.527 396 2E+00
ounce [troy]	3.215 074 7	3.215 074 7E+00
pennyweight [troy]	64.301 493	6.430 149 3E+01
pound	0.220 462 3	2.204 622 6E−01
pound [troy]	0.267 922 9	2.679 228 9E−01
pound [unified]	0.220 462 3	2.204 622 6E−01
pound [US, avoirdupois]	0.220 462 3	2.204 622 6E−01
pound [US, troy]	0.267 922 9	2.679 228 9E−01
scruple [UK]	77.161 792	7.716 179 2E+01
scruple [US, apothecary]	77.161 792	7.716 179 2E+01
ton [UK, assay or assay, long]	3.061 224 5	3.061 224 5E+00
ton [US, assay or assay, short]	3.428 571 4	3.428 571 4E+00

hectohenry — <electric inductance>

	Standard	Scientific
abhenry	>>>	1.000 000 0E+11
henry	100	1.000 000 0E+02
ohm second	100	1.000 000 0E+02
stathenry	<<<	1.112 650 1E−10

hectojoule — <energy>

	Standard	Scientific
Btu [I.T.]	0.094 781 7	9.478 171 2E−02
Btu [mean]	0.094 708 6	9.470 862 9E−02
Btu [thermoc.]	0.094 845 1	9.484 514 1E−02
calorie [I.T.]	23.884 59	2.388 459 0E+01
calorie [kilogram, I.T.]	0.023 884 6	2.388 459 0E−02
calorie [mean]	23.866 235	2.386 623 5E+01
calorie [thermoc.]	23.900 574	2.390 057 4E+01
cubic centimeter atmosphere	986.923 27	9.869 232 7E+02
cubic foot atmosphere	0.034 852 9	3.485 286 6E−02
foot pound-force	73.756 215	7.375 621 5E+01
foot poundal	2,373.036	2.373 036 0E+03
gram calorie	23.890 296	2.389 029 6E+01
inch pound-force	885.074 58	8.850 745 8E+02
joule	100	1.000 000 0E+02
kilocalorie [I.T.]	0.023 884 6	2.388 459 0E−02
kilojoule	0.1	1.000 000 0E−01
kilopond meter	10.197 162	1.019 716 2E+01
liter atmosphere	0.986 923 3	9.869 232 7E−01
meter kilogram-force	10.197 162	1.019 716 2E+01
newton meter	100	1.000 000 0E+02
watthour	0.027 777 8	2.777 777 8E−02
wattsecond	100	1.000 000 0E+02

hectoliter — <volume>

	Standard	Scientific
acre foot	0.000 081 1	8.107 131 9E−05
acre inch	0.000 972 9	9.728 558 3E−04
ahm [Sweden]	0.636 942 7	6.369 426 8E−01
ammonam [Sri Lanka]	0.490 196 1	4.901 960 8E−01
amomam [Sri Lanka]	0.490 196 1	4.901 960 8E−01
anoman [Sri Lanka]	0.490 196 1	4.901 960 8E−01
ardab [Egypt]	0.505 050 5	5.050 505 1E−01
ardab [Saudi Arabia]	0.505 050 5	5.050 505 1E−01
ardab [Sudan]	0.505 050 5	5.050 505 1E−01
ardeb [Saudi Arabia]	0.505 050 5	5.050 505 1E−01
bag [Burma]	0.814 995 9	8.149 959 3E−01

hectoliter (continued) \<volume\>

Convert To	Standard	Scientific
barrel [UK]	0.611 025 7	6.110 256 9E-01
barrel [US, dry]	0.864 849	8.648 489 8E-01
barrel [US, liquid]	0.838 641 4	8.386 414 4E-01
barrel [US, petroleum]	0.628 981 1	6.289 810 8E-01
barrique [France, wine]	0.442 086 7	4.420 866 5E-01
barrique [Germany]	0.485 201 4	4.852 013 6E-01
bei sheng [China]	1	1.000 000 0E+00
board foot	42.377 6	4.237 760 0E+01
bocka [Russia]	0.203 252	2.032 520 3E-01
bocoy [Cuba]	0.150 966 2	1.509 661 8E-01
boot [Netherlands]	0.188 679 3	1.886 792 5E-01
bota [Spain, wine]	0.206 697	2.066 969 8E-01
botte [Italy]	0.107 181 1	1.071 811 4E-01
bushel [UK]	2.749 615 6	2.749 615 6E+00
bushel [US, dry]	2.837 759 3	2.837 759 3E+00
cafiso [Tunisia]	0.171 850 8	1.718 508 3E-01
chetvert [Russia]	0.476 190 5	4.761 904 8E-01
chomor [Hebrew, ancient]	0.263 157 9	2.631 578 9E-01
coomb [UK, dry]	0.687 423 7	6.874 236 5E-01
cord foot [timber]	0.220 716 7	2.207 166 7E-01
cubic foot	3.531 466 7	3.531 466 7E+00
cubic inch	6,102.374 4	6.102 374 4E+03
cubic meter	0.1	1.000 000 0E-01
cubic yard	0.130 795 1	1.307 950 6E-01
cup [Canada, measuring]	439.938 5	4.399 385 2E+02
cup [US, measuring]	422.675 28	4.226 752 8E+02
dariba [Egypt]	0.063 131 3	6.313 131 3E-02
daribah [Egypt]	0.063 131 3	6.313 131 3E-02
daula [Ethiopia]	1.136 363 6	1.136 363 6E+00
double fanega [Uruguay]	0.364 298 7	3.642 987 2E-01
dreiling [Austria]	0.058 892 8	5.889 281 5E-02
fad ol [Denmark]	0.107 816 7	1.078 167 1E-01
firkin [UK]	2.444 102 8	2.444 102 8E+00
firkin [US]	2.935 245	2.935 245 0E+00
foder [Sweden]	0.106 157 1	1.061 571 1E-01
fortin [Turkey]	0.709 219 9	7.092 198 6E-01
fudder [Luxembourg]	0.1	1.000 000 0E-01
fuder [Germany]	0.121 300 3	1.213 003 4E-01
fuder [Netherlands, wine]	0.1	1.000 000 0E-01
gallon [Canada, liquid]	21.996 925	2.199 692 5E+01
gallon [UK, dry or liquid]	21.996 925	2.199 692 5E+01
gallon [US, dry]	22.702 075	2.270 207 5E+01
gallon [US, liquid]	26.417 205	2.641 720 5E+01
garce [India]	0.020 383 2	2.038 320 4E-02
gill [UK]	703.901 59	7.039 015 9E+02
gill [US]	845.350 57	8.453 505 7E+02
gizla [Somalia, dry]	0.613 120 8	6.131 207 8E-01
gur [Iraq, ancient]	0.346 020 8	3.460 207 6E-01
hogshead [Germany]	0.485 201 4	4.852 013 6E-01
kfiz [Tunisia, cereals]	0.171 850 8	1.718 508 3E-01
khakoon [India]	0.057 471 3	5.747 126 4E-02
kollast [Sweden]	0.050 530 6	5.053 057 1E-02
kor [Egypt, ancient]	1.041 666 7	1.041 666 7E+00
korn topmaal [Norway]	0.625	6.250 000 0E-01
koyan [Malaysia]	0.027 495 2	2.749 518 8E-02
koyan [Sarawak]	0.027 496 9	2.749 694 2E-02
koyan [Singapore]	0.027 495 2	2.749 518 8E-02
kul tonde [Denmark]	0.588 107 3	5.881 072 9E-01
kung shih [China]	1	1.000 000 0E+00
kung tan [Taiwan]	1	1.000 000 0E+00
kwien [Thailand]	0.05	5.000 000 0E-02
last [Germany, dry]	0.025 271 7	2.527 167 0E-02

hectoliter (continued)

<volume>

	Standard	Scientific
last [Sweden]	0.033 694 9	3.369 487 9E−02
letakhim [Hebrew, ancient, dry]	0.526 315 8	5.263 157 9E−01
liter	100	1.000 000 0E+02
makuk [Syria]	0.125	1.250 000 0E−01
malter [Germany, dry]	0.151 63	1.516 300 2E−01
malter [Switzerland, dry]	0.666 666 7	6.666 666 7E−01
marco real [Argentina]	0.728 863	7.288 629 7E−01
marco real [Honduras]	0.090 678 3	9.067 827 3E−02
marco real [Paraguay]	0.347 222 2	3.472 222 2E−01
minot [Canada]	0.025 700 3	2.570 033 4E−02
modd [Malta, cereals]	0.343 760 7	3.437 607 4E−01
moio [Brazil]	0.045 955 9	4.595 588 2E−02
moio [Cape Verde, dry]	0.040 070 8	4.007 084 5E−02
moio [Portugal]	0.120 481 9	1.204 819 3E−01
mud [Netherlands]	1	1.000 000 0E+00
mud [South Africa]	0.916 565 1	9.165 650 8E−01
mudde [Netherlands]	1	1.000 000 0E+00
muid [Brazil]	0.045 955 9	4.595 588 2E−02
muid [France, dry]	0.053 384 6	5.338 458 3E−02
muid [Netherlands]	1	1.000 000 0E+00
muid [South Africa]	0.916 565 1	9.165 650 8E−01
mula [Argentina]	0.728 863	7.288 629 7E−01
mula [Honduras]	0.090 678 3	9.067 827 3E−02
mula [Paraguay]	0.347 222 2	3.472 222 2E−01
muth [Austria]	0.054 209 4	5.420 935 7E−02
ohm [Germany, liquid]	0.727 802	7.278 020 4E−01
oltonde [Denmark]	0.761 035	7.610 350 1E−01
oltunna [Iceland]	0.761 035	7.610 350 1E−01
osmin [Russia]	0.952 381	9.523 809 5E−01
osmina [Russia]	0.952 381	9.523 809 5E−01
ounce [UK, liquid]	3,519.508	3.519 508 0E+03
ounce [US, liquid]	3,381.402 3	3.381 402 3E+03
petrograd standard	0.021 402 8	2.140 282 8E−02
pijp [Netherlands]	0.185 185 2	1.851 851 9E−01
pint [UK]	175.975 4	1.759 754 0E+02
pint [US, liquid]	211.337 64	2.113 376 4E+02
pipa [Argentina]	0.219 298 3	2.192 982 5E−01
pipa [Dominican Republic]	0.174 581	1.745 810 1E−01
pipa [Paraguay]	0.171 939 5	1.719 394 8E−01
pipa [Singapore]	0.174 581	1.745 810 1E−01
pipe [Argentina]	0.219 298 3	2.192 982 5E−01
pipe [Cuba]	0.209 687 6	2.096 875 7E−01
pipe [Dominican Republic]	0.174 581	1.745 810 1E−01
pipe [Netherlands, wine]	0.242 571 3	2.425 712 6E−01
pipe [Paraguay]	0.171 939 5	1.719 394 8E−01
pipe [Russia, liquid]	0.225 835 6	2.258 355 9E−01
pipe [Singapore]	0.174 581	1.745 810 1E−01
quart [UK]	87.987 699	8.798 769 9E+01
quart [US, liquid]	105.668 82	1.056 688 2E+02
quarteau [France, dry]	0.213 538 3	2.135 383 3E−01
quarto [Italy, dry]	1.358 695 7	1.358 695 7E+00
rubbiatella [Italy, dry]	0.679 347 8	6.793 478 3E−01
sac [Switzerland, dry]	0.666 666 7	6.666 666 7E−01
sack [Egypt, ancient]	1.041 666 7	1.041 666 7E+00
salma tumoli [Malta, cereals]	0.343 760 7	3.437 607 4E−01
seh [Hong Kong]	1	1.000 000 0E+00
setier [France, dry]	0.640 615	6.406 149 9E−01
shih dan [China]	1	1.000 000 0E+00
sildar mal [Iceland]	0.666 666 7	6.666 666 7E−01
square cuadra [Uruguay]	0.728 332 1	7.283 321 2E−01
stere	0.1	1.000 000 0E−01
tan [China]	0.965 717	9.657 170 4E−01

hectoliter (continued) <volume>

tiercon [Mauritius]	0.584 795 3	5.847 953 2E-01
tjaere tonde [Denmark]	0.862 559 7	8.625 597 3E-01
tonde korn [Denmark]	0.718 798 7	7.187 987 4E-01
tonde ol [Denmark]	0.761 081 3	7.610 813 4E-01
tonde sild [Denmark]	0.924 171 7	9.241 717 1E-01
tonel [Brazil]	0.104 349 3	1.043 492 8E-01
tonneau [France, wine]	0.110 521 7	1.105 216 6E-01
tumoli [Malta, cereals]	0.013 748 2	1.374 816 1E-02
tun [Malaysia]	0.087 290 5	8.729 050 3E-02
tun [Singapore]	0.087 290 5	8.729 050 3E-02
ueba [Libya]	0.344 234 1	3.442 340 8E-01
vat [Belgium]	1	1.000 000 0E+00
Winchester wine gallon [UK]	26.417 205	2.641 720 5E+01
winspel [Germany, dry]	0.075 815	7.581 501 1E-02

hectoliter/day <flow rate, volume basis>

barrel/day [UK]	0.611 025 7	6.110 256 9E-01
barrel/day [US, federal]	0.852 167 9	8.521 679 1E-01
barrel/day [US, liquid]	0.838 641 4	8.386 414 4E-01
barrel/day [US, petroleum]	0.628 981 1	6.289 810 8E-01
centiliter/minute	6.944 444 4	6.944 444 4E+00
cubic centimeter/second	1.157 407 4	1.157 407 4E+00
cubic decimeter/day	100	1.000 000 0E+02
cubic decimeter/hour	4.166 666 7	4.166 666 7E+00
cubic foot/day	3.531 466 7	3.531 466 7E+00
cubic inch/minute	4.237 76	4.237 760 0E+00
cubic meter/day	0.1	1.000 000 0E-01
cubic meter/second	0.000 001 2	1.157 407 4E-06
cubic millimeter/second	1,157.407 41	1.157 407 4E+03
cubic yard/day	0.130 795 1	1.307 950 6E-01
deciliter/day	1,000	1.000 000 0E+03
deciliter/hour	41.666 666 7	4.166 666 7E+01
dekaliter/day	10	1.000 000 0E+01
gallon/hour [UK]	0.916 538 5	9.165 385 4E-01
gallon/hour [US, liquid]	1.100 716 9	1.100 716 9E+00
hectoliter/hour	0.041 666 7	4.166 666 7E-02
kiloliter/day	0.1	1.000 000 0E-01
lambda/second	1,157.407 41	1.157 407 4E+03
liter/hour	4.166 666 7	4.166 666 7E+00
liter/hour [pre-1964]	4.166 55	4.166 550 0E+00
milliliter/second	1.157 407 4	1.157 407 4E+00
ounce/minute [UK, liquid]	2.444 102 8	2.444 102 8E+00
ounce/minute [US, liquid]	2.348 196	2.348 196 0E+00
petrograd standard/day	0.021 402 8	2.140 282 8E-02
stere/day	0.1	1.000 000 0E-01
thousand cubic foot/day	0.003 531 5	3.531 466 7E-03

hectoliter/hour <flow rate, volume basis>

acre inch/day	0.023 348 5	2.334 854 0E-02
barrel/day [UK]	14.664 616 6	1.466 461 7E+01
barrel/day [US, federal]	20.452 029 9	2.045 203 0E+01
barrel/day [US, liquid]	20.127 394 5	2.012 739 5E+01
barrel/day [US, petroleum]	15.095 545 8	1.509 554 6E+01
centiliter/second	2.777 777 8	2.777 777 8E+00
cubic centimeter/second	27.777 777 8	2.777 777 8E+01
cubic decimeter/hour	100	1.000 000 0E+02
cubic decimeter/minute	1.666 666 7	1.666 666 7E+00
cubic decimeter/second	0.027 777 8	2.777 777 8E-02
cubic dekameter/day	0.002 4	2.400 000 0E-03
cubic foot/hour	3.531 466 7	3.531 466 7E+00
cubic inch/second	1.695 104	1.695 104 0E+00
cubic meter/day	2.4	2.400 000 0E+00
cubic meter/second	0.000 027 8	2.777 777 8E-05

	Standard	Scientific
cubic yard/day	3.139 081 5	3.139 081 5E+00
deciliter/minute	16.666 666 7	1.666 666 7E+01
dekaliter/hour	10	1.000 000 0E+01
gallon/hour [UK]	21.996 924 8	2.199 692 5E+01
gallon/hour [US, liquid]	26.417 205 2	2.641 720 5E+01
hectoliter/day	24	2.400 000 0E+01
kiloliter/day	2.4	2.400 000 0E+00
liter/minute	1.666 666 7	1.666 666 7E+00
liter/minute [pre-1964]	1.666 62	1.666 620 0E+00
milliliter/second	27.777 777 8	2.777 777 8E+01
ounce/minute [UK, liquid]	58.658 466	5.865 846 6E+01
ounce/minute [US, liquid]	56.356 705	5.635 670 5E+01
petrograd standard/day	0.513 667 9	5.136 678 8E−01
stere/day	2.4	2.400 000 0E+00
hectoliter/minute		**\<flow rate, volume basis\>**
acre foot/day	0.116 742 7	1.167 427 4E−01
acre foot/day [US, survey]	0.116 742	1.167 420 0E−01
acre inch/day	1.400 912 4	1.400 912 4E+00
barrel/hour [UK]	36.661 541 4	3.666 154 1E+01
barrel/hour [US, federal]	51.130 074 6	5.113 007 5E+01
barrel/hour [US, liquid]	50.318 486 2	5.031 848 6E+01
barrel/hour [US, petroleum]	37.738 864 6	3.773 886 5E+01
centiliter/second	166.666 667	1.666 666 7E+02
cubic decimeter/minute	100	1.000 000 0E+02
cubic decimeter/second	1.666 666 7	1.666 666 7E+00
cubic dekameter/day	0.144	1.440 000 0E−01
cubic foot/minute	3.531 466 7	3.531 466 7E+00
cubic meter/hour	6	6.000 000 0E+00
cubic meter/second	0.001 666 7	1.666 666 7E−03
cubic yard/hour	7.847 703 7	7.847 703 7E+00
deciliter/second	16.666 666 7	1.666 666 7E+01
dekaliter/minute	10	1.000 000 0E+01
gallon/minute [UK]	21.996 924 8	2.199 692 5E+01
gallon/minute [US, liquid]	26.417 205 2	2.641 720 5E+01
hectare meter/day	0.014 4	1.440 000 0E−02
hectoliter/hour	60	6.000 000 0E+01
kiloliter/hour	6	6.000 000 0E+00
liter/second	1.666 666 7	1.666 666 7E+00
liter/second [pre-1964]	1.666 62	1.666 620 0E+00
ounce/second [UK, liquid]	58.658 466	5.865 846 6E+01
ounce/second [US, liquid]	56.356 705	5.635 670 5E+01
petrograd standard/hour	1.284 169 7	1.284 169 7E+00
stere/hour	6	6.000 000 0E+00
thousand cubic foot/day	5.085 312	5.085 312 0E+00
hectoliter/second		**\<flow rate, volume basis\>**
acre foot/day	7.004 562	7.004 562 0E+00
acre foot/day [US, survey]	7.004 52	7.004 520 0E+00
acre inch/hour	3.502 281	3.502 281 0E+00
barrel/minute [UK]	36.661 541 4	3.666 154 1E+01
barrel/minute [US, federal]	51.130 074 6	5.113 007 5E+01
barrel/minute [US, liquid]	50.318 486 2	5.031 848 6E+01
barrel/minute [US, petroleum]	37.738 864 6	3.773 886 5E+01
cubic decimeter/second	100	1.000 000 0E+02
cubic dekameter/day	8.64	8.640 000 0E+00
cubic foot/second	3.531 466 7	3.531 466 7E+00
cubic meter/minute	6	6.000 000 0E+00
cubic meter/second	0.1	1.000 000 0E−01
cubic yard/minute	7.847 703 7	7.847 703 7E+00
dekaliter/second	10	1.000 000 0E+01
gallon/second [UK]	21.996 924 8	2.199 692 5E+01
gallon/second [US, liquid]	26.417 205 2	2.641 720 5E+01
hectare meter/day	0.864	8.640 000 0E−01
hectoliter/minute	60	6.000 000 0E+01

Convert From Convert To	<Type of Unit> Standard	Scientific
kiloliter/minute	6	6.000 000 0E+00
liter/second	100	1.000 000 0E+02
liter/second [pre-1964]	99.997 200 1	9.999 720 0E+01
ounce/second [UK, liquid]	3,519.508	3.519 508 0E+03
ounce/second [US, liquid]	3,381.402 3	3.381 402 3E+03
petrograd standard/minute	1.284 169 7	1.284 169 7E+00
stere/minute	6	6.000 000 0E+00
thousand cubic foot/hour	12.713 28	1.271 328 0E+01

hectometer <length>

	Standard	Scientific
cable length [US, survey]	0.455 671 3	4.556 713 0E-01
chain [Gunter or US, survey]	4.970 959 6	4.970 959 6E+00
chain [Ramden or Engineer]	3.280 839 9	3.280 839 9E+00
fathom [US, survey]	54.680 556	5.468 055 6E+01
foot [international]	328.083 99	3.280 839 9E+02
foot [US, survey]	328.083 33	3.280 833 3E+02
furlong [US, survey]	0.497 096	4.970 959 6E-01
inch [based on US, survey foot]	3,937	3.937 000 0E+03
inch [international]	3,937.007 9	3.937 007 9E+03
link [Gunter or US, survey]	497.095 96	4.970 959 6E+02
link [Ramden or Engineer]	328.083 99	3.280 839 9E+02
meter	100	1.000 000 0E+02
mile [international]	0.062 137 1	6.213 711 9E-02
mile [US, statute]	0.062 137	6.213 699 5E-02
mile [US, survey]	0.062 137	6.213 699 5E-02
myriameter	0.01	1.000 000 0E-02
pace [geometrical]	6.561 679 8	6.561 679 8E+00
pace [US, survey]	131.233 33	1.312 333 3E+02
perch [US, survey]	19.883 838	1.988 383 8E+01
range [US, survey]	0.010 356 2	1.035 616 6E-02
township [US, survey]	0.010 356 2	1.035 616 6E-02
yard [based on US, survey foot]	109.361 11	1.093 611 1E+02
yard [international]	109.361 33	1.093 613 3E+02

hectometer/day <velocity>

	Standard	Scientific
foot/hour	13.670 166 2	1.367 016 6E+01
inch/minute	2.734 033 3	2.734 033 3E+00
knot [international]	0.002 249 8	2.249 820 0E-03
meter/hour	4.166 666 7	4.166 666 7E+00
meter/second	0.001 157 4	1.157 407 4E-03
mile/day	0.062 137 1	6.213 711 9E-02
millimeter/second	1.157 407 4	1.157 407 4E+00
nautical mile/day [international]	0.053 995 7	5.399 568 0E-02
yard/hour	4.556 722 1	4.556 722 1E+00

hectometer/hour <velocity>

	Standard	Scientific
foot/minute	5.468 066 5	5.468 066 5E+00
inch/second	1.093 613 3	1.093 613 3E+00
kilometer/day	2.4	2.400 000 0E+00
knot [international]	0.053 995 7	5.399 568 0E-02
meter/second	0.027 777 8	2.777 777 8E-02
mile/day	1.491 290 9	1.491 290 9E+00
nautical mile/day [international]	1.295 896 3	1.295 896 3E+00
yard/minute	1.822 688 8	1.822 688 8E+00

hectometer/minute <velocity>

	Standard	Scientific
foot/second	5.468 066 5	5.468 066 5E+00
inch/second	65.616 797 9	6.561 679 8E+01
knot [international]	3.239 740 8	3.239 740 8E+00
meter/second	1.666 666 7	1.666 666 7E+00
mile/hour	3.728 227 2	3.728 227 2E+00
nautical mile/hour [international]	3.239 740 8	3.239 740 8E+00
yard/second	1.822 688 8	1.822 688 8E+00

hectometer/second <velocity>

	Standard	Scientific
foot/second	328.083 99	3.280 839 9E+02
inch/second	3,937.007 87	3.937 007 9E+03

Convert From	**<Type of Unit>**	
Convert To	Standard	Scientific

knot [international]		
knot [international]	194.384 449	1.943 844 5E+02
meter/second	100	1.000 000 0E+02
mile/hour	223.693 629	2.236 936 3E+02
mile/minute	3.728 227 2	3.728 227 2E+00
nautical mile/minute [international]	3.239 740 8	3.239 740 8E+00
yard/second	109.361 33	1.093 613 3E+02

hectometer/square second   **<acceleration>**

foot/square second	328.083 99	3.280 839 9E+02
gn [due to gravity]	10.197 162 1	1.019 716 2E+01
meter/square second	100	1.000 000 0E+02

hectomole   **<amount of substance>**

mole	100	1.000 000 0E+02

hectonewton   **<force>**

crinal	1,000	1.000 000 0E+03
dyne	>>>	1.000 000 0E+07
gram-force	10,197.162 1	1.019 716 2E+04
newton	100	1.000 000 0E+02
ounce-force	359.694 309	3.596 943 1E+02
pond	10,197.162 1	1.019 716 2E+04
pound-force	22.480 894 3	2.248 089 4E+01
poundal	723.301 385	7.233 013 9E+02
sthene	0.1	1.000 000 0E-01

hectoohm   **<electric resistance>**

1/ siemens	100	1.000 000 0E+02
abohm	>>>	1.000 000 0E+11
ohm	100	1.000 000 0E+02
statohm	<<<	1.112 650 1E-10

hectopascal   **<pressure>**

atmosphere [standard]	0.000 986 9	9.869 232 7E-04
atmosphere [technical]	0.001 019 7	1.019 716 2E-03
bar	0.001	1.000 000 0E-03
barye [France]	1,000	1.000 000 0E+03
centimeter of mercury [0 °C, by convention]	0.075 006 2	7.500 615 8E-02
centimeter of water [4 °C, by convention]	1.019 716 2	1.019 716 2E+00
decitorr	7.500 616 8	7.500 616 8E+00
dyne/square centimeter	1,000	1.000 000 0E+03
gram-force/square centimeter	1.019 716 2	1.019 716 2E+00
inch of mercury [0 °C, by convention]	0.029 53	2.952 998 3E-02
inch of water [4 °C, by convention]	0.401 463	4.014 630 8E-01
kilogram-force/square meter	10.197 162	1.019 716 2E+01
kilopond/square meter	10.197 162	1.019 716 2E+01
kip/square foot	0.002 088 5	2.088 543 4E-03
millibar	1	1.000 000 0E+00
millimeter of mercury [0 °C, by convention]	0.750 061 6	7.500 615 8E-01
millimeter of water [4 °C, by convention]	10.197 162	1.019 716 2E+01
newton/square meter	100	1.000 000 0E+02
ounce-force/square inch	0.232 060 4	2.320 603 8E-01
pascal	100	1.000 000 0E+02
pieze [France]	0.1	1.000 000 0E-01
pound-force/square foot	2.088 543 4	2.088 543 4E+00
poundal/square foot	67.196 898	6.719 689 8E+01
sthene/square meter [France]	0.1	1.000 000 0E-01
ton-force/square foot [short]	0.001 044 3	1.044 271 7E-03
ton-force/square meter [metric]	0.010 197 2	1.019 716 2E-02
torr	0.750 061 7	7.500 616 8E-01

hectosecond   **<time>**

second	100	1.000 000 0E+02

hectosiemens   **<electric conductance>**

absiemens	0.000 000 1	1.000 000 0E-07
electromagnetic unit of conductance [cgs system]	0.000 000 1	1.000 000 0E-07
siemens	100	1.000 000 0E+02

Convert From		<Type of Unit>
Convert To	Standard	Scientific

| statsiemens | >>> | 8.987 551 8E+13 |

hectotesla — <magnetic flux density>

Convert To	Standard	Scientific
electromagnetic unit of magnetic flux density [cgs system]	1,000,000	1.000 000 0E+06
electrostatic unit of magnetic flux density [cgs system]	0.000 033 4	3.335 641 0E-05
gauss	1,000,000	1.000 000 0E+06
gigatesla	0.000 000 1	1.000 000 0E-07
line/square centimeter [of magnetic force]	1,000,000	1.000 000 0E+06
maxwell/square meter	100	1.000 000 0E+02
tesla	100	1.000 000 0E+02

hectovolt — <electric potential>

Convert To	Standard	Scientific
abvolt	>>>	1.000 000 0E+10
electrostatic unit of electric potential [cgs system]	0.333 564 1	3.335 641 0E-01
statvolt	0.333 564 1	3.335 641 0E-01
volt	100	1.000 000 0E+02

hectowatt — <power>

Convert To	Standard	Scientific
Btu/minute [I.T.]	5.686 902 7	5.686 902 7E+00
Btu/minute [thermoc.]	5.690 708 5	5.690 708 5E+00
calorie/second [I.T.]	23.884 59	2.388 459 0E+01
calorie/second [thermoc.]	23.900 574	2.390 057 4E+01
centigrade heat unit/minute [mean]	3.156 954 3	3.156 954 3E+00
cheval vapeur [France]	0.135 962 2	1.359 621 6E-01
cubic meter atmosphere/second	986.923 27	9.869 232 7E-02
dyne centimeter/second	>>>	1.000 000 0E+09
erg/second	>>>	1.000 000 0E+09
foot pound-force/second	73.756 215	7.375 621 5E+01
foot poundal/second	2,373.036	2.373 036 0E+03
gram-force centimeter/second	1,019,716.2	1.019 716 2E+06
horsepower	0.134 102 2	1.341 022 1E-01
horsepower [metric]	0.135 962 2	1.359 621 6E-01
joule/second	100	1.000 000 0E+02
kilocalorie/minute [I.T.]	1.433 075 4	1.433 075 4E+00
kilogram square meter/cubic second	100	1.000 000 0E+02
kilogram-force meter/second	10.197 162	1.019 716 2E+01
kilopond meter/second	10.197 162	1.019 716 2E+01
newton meter/second	100	1.000 000 0E+02
pferdestarke [Germany]	0.135 962 2	1.359 621 6E-01
poncelet [France]	0.101 971 6	1.019 716 2E-01
pound square foot/cubic second	2,373.036	2.373 036 0E+03
ton of refrigeration	0.028 434 5	2.843 451 4E-02
volt ampere	100	1.000 000 0E+02
watt	100	1.000 000 0E+02

hectowatthour — <energy>

Convert To	Standard	Scientific
Btu [I.T.]	341.214 16	3.412 141 6E+02
calorie [kilogram, I.T.]	85.984 523	8.598 452 3E+01
calorie [kilogram, mean]	85.918 444	8.591 844 4E+01
calorie [kilogram, thermoc.]	86.042 065	8.604 206 5E+01
calorie [nutritional]	86.042 065	8.604 206 5E+01
centigrade heat unit [I.T.]	189.563 42	1.895 634 2E+02
cheval vapeur heure [France]	0.135 962 2	1.359 621 6E-01
cubic centimeter atmosphere	3,552,923.8	3.552 923 8E+06
cubic foot atmosphere	125.470 32	1.254 703 2E+02
frigorie [France]	86.005 065	8.600 506 5E+01
horsepower hour	0.134 102 2	1.341 022 1E-01
horsepower hour [metric]	0.135 962 2	1.359 621 6E-01
joule	360,000	3.600 000 0E+05
kilocalorie [I.T.]	85.984 523	8.598 452 3E+01
kilogram calorie [15 °C, NBS, 1939]	86.005 065	8.600 506 5E+01
kilowatthour	0.1	1.000 000 0E-01
meter kilogram-force	36,709.784	3.670 978 4E+04
newton meter	360,000	3.600 000 0E+05
pferdestarkenstunde [Germany]	0.135 962 2	1.359 621 6E-01
watthour	100	1.000 000 0E+02

wattsecond	360,000	3.600 000 0E+05
hectoweber		**\<magnetic flux\>**
electrostatic unit of magnetic flux [cgs system]	0.333 564 1	3.335 641 0E−01
gauss square centimeter	>>>	1.000 000 0E+10
maxwell	>>>	1.000 000 0E+10
statweber	0.333 564 1	3.335 641 0E−01
unit pole	>>>	7.957 747 5E+08
weber	100	1.000 000 0E+02
Hefner candle [Germany]		**\<luminous intensity\>**
bougie decimale [France]	0.938 541 7	9.385 416 7E−01
candela	0.917 826 8	9.178 268 3E−01
candle [international standard]	0.901	9.010 000 0E−01
carcel	0.093 756 5	9.375 650 4E−02
hefnerkerze [Germany]	1	1.000 000 0E+00
watt/steradian [at 540 THz]	0.001 343 8	1.343 816 7E−03
hefnerkerze [Germany]		**\<luminous intensity\>**
candela	0.917 826 8	9.178 268 3E−01
Hefner candle [Germany]	1	1.000 000 0E+00
lumen/steradian	0.917 826 8	9.178 268 3E−01
hekat [Egypt, ancient]		**\<volume, special - see page 29\>**
liter	4.89	4.890 000 0E+00
hekat [Hebrew, ancient]		**\<volume, special - see page 29\>**
liter	4.77	4.770 000 0E+00
hekt [Egypt, ancient]		**\<volume, special - see page 29\>**
liter	4.8	4.800 000 0E+00
heller [Germany, troy]		**\<mass, special - see page 29\>**
gram	0.45	4.500 000 0E−01
heller [UK, apothecary]		**\<mass, special - see page 29\>**
gram	0.015	1.500 000 0E−02
helmholtz		**\<electric dipole moment/unit area\>**
coulomb/meter	<<<	3.335 641 0E−10
debye unit/square angstrom	1	1.000 000 0E+00
franklin/centimeter	0.01	1.000 000 0E−02
hema [Greece, ancient]		**\<length, special - see page 29\>**
meter	0.77	7.700 000 0E−01
hembl [Sudan]		**\<mass, special - see page 29\>**
kilogram	312	3.120 000 0E+02
hemikotylion [Greece, ancient]		**\<volume, special - see page 29\>**
milliliter	146	1.460 000 0E+02
hemina [Rome, ancient]		**\<volume, special - see page 29\>**
liter	0.273	2.730 000 0E−01
hemipodion [Greece, ancient]		**\<length, special - see page 29\>**
centimeter	15.4	1.540 000 0E+01
hemisphere		**\<solid angle\>**
spat	0.5	5.000 000 0E−01
spheradian	6.283 185 3	6.283 185 3E+00
sphere	0.5	5.000 000 0E−01
spherical degree	360	3.600 000 0E+02
spherical right angle	4	4.000 000 0E+00
spherical solid angle	0.5	5.000 000 0E−01
square degree	20,626.481	2.062 648 1E+04
square grade	25,464.791	2.546 479 1E+04
steradian	6.283 185 3	6.283 185 3E+00
steregon	0.5	5.000 000 0E−01
heml [Egypt, ancient]		**\<mass, special - see page 29\>**
kilogram	249.6	2.496 000 0E+02
hemla [Sudan]		**\<mass, special - see page 29\>**
kilogram	74.88	7.488 000 0E+01

Convert From		<Type of Unit>
Convert To	Standard	Scientific

hen [Egypt, ancient] — <volume, special - see page 29>
liter	0.455	4.550 000 0E−01

henry — <electric inductance>
abhenry	>>>	1.000 000 0E+09
electromagnetic unit of inductance [cgs system]	>>>	1.000 000 0E+09
electrostatic unit of inductance [cgs system]	<<<	1.112 650 1E−12
gaussian electric inductance	<<<	1.112 650 1E−12
henry [international]	0.999 510 2	9.995 102 4E−01
joule/square ampere	1	1.000 000 0E+00
ohm second	1	1.000 000 0E+00
stathenry	<<<	1.112 650 1E−12
volt second/ampere	1	1.000 000 0E+00
weber/ampere	1	1.000 000 0E+00

henry [international] — <electric inductance>
abhenry	>>>	1.000 490 0E+09
henry	1.000 49	1.000 490 0E+00
ohm second	1.000 49	1.000 490 0E+00
stathenry	<<<	1.113 195 3E−12

henry/centimeter — <electric permeability>
henry/meter	100	1.000 000 0E+02
magn	100	1.000 000 0E+02

henry/meter — <electric permeability>
henry/centimeter	0.01	1.000 000 0E−02
magn	1	1.000 000 0E+00

henry/millimeter — <electric permeability>
henry/meter	1,000	1.000 000 0E+03

henry/second — <electric resistance>
1/ siemens	1	1.000 000 0E+00
abohm	>>>	1.000 000 0E+09
ohm	1	1.000 000 0E+00
statohm	<<<	1.112 650 1E−12

henu [Egypt, ancient] — <volume, special - see page 29>
milliliter	300	3.000 000 0E+02

heptad — <units>
unit	7	7.000 000 0E+00

heredium [Rome, ancient] — <area, special - see page 29>
hectare	0.504	5.040 000 0E−01

hertz — <frequency>
1/second	1	1.000 000 0E+00
cycle/second	1	1.000 000 0E+00
degree/second	360	3.600 000 0E+02
fresnel	<<<	1.000 000 0E−12
millihertz	1,000	1.000 000 0E+03
radian/second	6.283 185 3	6.283 185 3E+00
revolution/second	1	1.000 000 0E+00

hertz [atomic physics, eq. energy] — <energy>
atomic mass unit [unified, C-12, 1986, eq. energy]	<<<	4.439 822 3E−24
deuteron rest mass [atomic physics, eq. energy]	<<<	2.204 968 9E−24
electronvolt	<<<	4.135 669 2E−15
hartree [atomic physics, eq. energy]	<<<	1.519 829 9E−16
joule	<<<	6.626 075 5E−34
kayser [atomic physics, eq. energy]	<<<	3.335 641 0E−11
kelvin [atomic physics, eq. energy]	<<<	4.799 215 7E−11
kiloelectronvolt	<<<	4.135 669 2E−18
megaelectronvolt	<<<	4.135 669 2E−21
muon rest mass [atomic physics, eq. energy]	<<<	3.914 189 2E−23
neutron rest mass [atomic physics, eq. energy]	<<<	4.401 682 1E−24
proton rest mass [atomic physics, eq. energy]	<<<	4.407 749 4E−24
rydberg [atomic physics, eq. energy]	<<<	3.039 623 6E−16

hesta [Cambodia]   <length, special - see page 29>
  meter ---- 0.5 ---- 5.000 000 0E-01

hesta [Somalia]   <length, special - see page 29>
  meter ---- 0.558 8 ---- 5.588 000 0E-01

hexad   <units>
  duodecal ---- 0.5 ---- 5.000 000 0E-01
  unit ---- 6 ---- 6.000 000 0E+00

hin [Egypt, ancient]   <volume, special - see page 29>
  liter ---- 0.48 ---- 4.800 000 0E-01

hin [Hebrew, ancient]   <volume, special - see page 29>
  liter ---- 4 ---- 4.000 000 0E+00

hindaza [Saudi Arabia, ancient]   <length, special - see page 29>
  centimeter ---- 68.6 ---- 6.860 000 0E+01

hinim [Hebrew, ancient]   <volume, special - see page 29>
  liter ---- 6.3 ---- 6.300 000 0E+00

hippicon [Greece, ancient]   <length, special - see page 29>
  meter ---- 739 ---- 7.390 000 0E+02

hiro [Japan]   <length, special - see page 29>
  meter ---- 1.515 ---- 1.515 000 0E+00

hiyaka me [Japan]   <mass, special - see page 29>
  gram ---- 375 ---- 3.750 000 0E+02

hkt [Egypt, ancient]   <volume, special - see page 29>
  liter ---- 5.03 ---- 5.030 000 0E+00

hoc [Vietnam]   <volume, special - see page 29>
  liter ---- 60 ---- 6.000 000 0E+01

hog [Israel]   <volume, special - see page 29>
  liter ---- 0.555 ---- 5.550 000 0E-01

hogga [Iraq]   <mass, special - see page 29>
  kilogram ---- 1.270 059 ---- 1.270 059 0E+00

hogshead [Australia]   <volume, special - see page 29>
  liter ---- 295 ---- 2.950 000 0E+02

hogshead [Germany]   <volume, special - see page 29>
  hectoliter ---- 2.061 ---- 2.061 000 0E+00

hogshead [Singapore]   <volume, special - see page 29>
  liter ---- 286.4 ---- 2.864 000 0E+02

hogshead [South Africa]   <volume, special - see page 29>
  liter ---- 295 ---- 2.950 000 0E+02

hogshead [UK]   <volume>
  barrel [UK] ---- 1.75 ---- 1.750 000 0E+00
  barrel [UK, wine] ---- 2 ---- 2.000 000 0E+00
  barrel [US, liquid] ---- 2.401 899 9 ---- 2.401 899 9E+00
  barrel [US, petroleum] ---- 1.801 424 9 ---- 1.801 424 9E+00
  chaldron [UK, dry] ---- 0.218 75 ---- 2.187 500 0E-01
  chaldron [UK, liquid] ---- 0.218 75 ---- 2.187 500 0E-01
  cubic foot ---- 10.114 25 ---- 1.011 425 0E+01
  cubic inch ---- 17,477.424 ---- 1.747 742 4E+04
  cubic meter ---- 0.286 403 7 ---- 2.864 036 7E-01
  cup [Canada, measuring] ---- 1,260 ---- 1.260 000 0E+03
  cup [US, measuring] ---- 1,210.557 5 ---- 1.210 557 5E+03
  drachm [UK, liquid] ---- 80,640 ---- 8.064 000 0E+04
  dram [Canada, liquid] ---- 80,640 ---- 8.064 000 0E+04
  dram [US, liquid] ---- 77,475.682 ---- 7.747 568 2E+04
  drum [US, liquid] ---- 1.375 633 6 ---- 1.375 633 6E+00
  firkin [UK] ---- 7 ---- 7.000 000 0E+00
  firkin [US] ---- 8.406 649 5 ---- 8.406 649 5E+00
  gallon [Canada, liquid] ---- 63 ---- 6.300 000 0E+01
  gallon [UK, dry or liquid] ---- 63 ---- 6.300 000 0E+01
  gallon [US, liquid] ---- 75.659 845 ---- 7.565 984 5E+01

gill [UK]	2,016	2.016 000 0E+03
gill [US]	2,421.115	2.421 115 0E+03
hectoliter	2.864 036 7	2.864 036 7E+00
hogshead [US]	1.200 949 9	1.200 949 9E+00
liter	286.403 67	2.864 036 7E+02
ounce [UK, liquid]	10,080	1.008 000 0E+04
ounce [US, liquid]	9,684.460 2	9.684 460 2E+03
pint [UK]	504	5.040 000 0E+02
pint [US, liquid]	605.278 76	6.052 787 6E+02
quart [UK]	252	2.520 000 0E+02
quart [US, liquid]	302.639 38	3.026 393 8E+02
stere	0.286 403 7	2.864 036 7E-01
Winchester wine gallon [UK]	75.659 845	7.565 984 5E+01

hogshead [US]   **<volume>**

barrel [UK]	1.457 179 8	1.457 179 8E+00
barrel [US, federal proof spirits]	1.575	1.575 000 0E+00
barrel [US, liquid]	2	2.000 000 0E+00
barrel [US, petroleum]	1.5	1.500 000 0E+00
cubic foot	8.421 875	8.421 875 0E+00
cubic inch	14,553	1.455 300 0E+04
cubic meter	0.238 480 9	2.384 809 4E-01
cubic yard	0.311 921 3	3.119 213 0E-01
cup [Canada, measuring]	1,049.169 5	1.049 169 5E+03
cup [US, measuring]	1,008	1.008 000 0E+03
drum [US, liquid]	1.145 454 5	1.145 454 5E+00
firkin [UK]	5.828 719 3	5.828 719 3E+00
firkin [US]	7	7.000 000 0E+00
gallon [Canada, liquid]	52.458 474	5.245 847 4E+01
gallon [UK, dry or liquid]	52.458 474	5.245 847 4E+01
gallon [US, liquid]	63	6.300 000 0E+01
gill [UK]	1,678.671 2	1.678 671 2E+03
gill [US]	2,016	2.016 000 0E+03
hectoliter	2.384 809 4	2.384 809 4E+00
hogshead [UK]	0.832 674 2	8.326 741 8E-01
liter	238.480 94	2.384 809 4E+02
ounce [UK, liquid]	8,393.355 8	8.393 355 8E+03
ounce [US, liquid]	8,064	8.064 000 0E+03
pint [UK]	419.667 79	4.196 677 9E+02
pint [US, liquid]	504	5.040 000 0E+02
quart [UK]	209.833 89	2.098 338 9E+02
quart [US, liquid]	252	2.520 000 0E+02
stere	0.238 480 9	2.384 809 4E-01
tun [UK, liquid]	0.242 863 3	2.428 633 0E-01
tun [US, liquid]	0.25	2.500 000 0E-01
Winchester wine gallon [UK]	63	6.300 000 0E+01

hoi [Laos]   **<mass, special - see page 29>**

kilogram	0.15	1.500 000 0E-01

hold [Hungary]   **<area, special - see page 29>**

are	43.159	4.315 900 0E+01

hollegada [Brazil]   **<length, special - see page 29>**

centimeter	2.75	2.750 000 0E+00

holzklafter [Switzerland]   **<volume, special - see page 29>**

cubic meter	2.916	2.916 000 0E+00

homer [Babylon, ancient]   **<volume, special - see page 29>**

liter	100	1.000 000 0E+02

homer [Hebrew, ancient]   **<volume, special - see page 29>**

liter	220	2.200 000 0E+02

hong [Laos]   **<mass, special - see page 29>**

gram	37.5	3.750 000 0E+01

hong euk louang [Laos]   **<length, special - see page 29>**

meter	1	1.000 000 0E+00

hoon [Cambodia] \<mass, special - see page 29\>
  gram--0.375----3.750 000 0E-01

hoon [Indonesia, opium] \<mass, special - see page 29\>
  milligram-- 386.01----3.860 100 0E+02

hoon [Japan] \<mass, special - see page 29\>
  gram--0.375----3.750 000 0E-01

hoon [Laos] \<mass, special - see page 29\>
  gram--0.375----3.750 000 0E-01

hop [Hong Kong] \<volume, special - see page 29\>
  centiliter --10----1.000 000 0E+01

hop [South Korea] \<volume, special - see page 29\>
  liter--0.180 391----1.803 910 0E-01

horsepower \<power\>
  Btu/minute [I.T.] -- 42.407 226----4.240 722 6E+01
  Btu/minute [thermoc.]-------------------------------- 42.435 606----4.243 560 6E+01
  calorie/second [I.T.] ------------------------------------ 178.107 35----1.781 073 5E+02
  calorie/second [thermoc.]-------------------------- 178.226 55----1.782 265 5E+02
  centigrade heat unit/minute [mean] --------------- 23.541 404----2.354 140 4E+01
  cheval vapeur [France]------------------------------- 1.013 869 7----1.013 869 7E+00
  cubic meter atmosphere/second----------------- 7,359.485 5----7.359 485 5E+03
  dyne centimeter/second----------------------------------- >>>----7.456 998 7E+09
  erg/second-- >>>----7.456 998 7E+09
  foot pound-force/second ----------------------------------- 550----5.500 000 0E+02
  foot poundal/second------------------------------- 17,695.727----1.769 572 7E+04
  gram-force centimeter/second------------------- 7,604,022.5----7.604 022 5E+06
  hectowatt--- 7.456 998 7----7.456 998 7E+00
  horsepower [550 foot pound-force/second] ---------------1----1.000 000 0E+00
  horsepower [mechanical]---------------------------------------1----1.000 000 0E+00
  horsepower [metric] ---------------------------------- 1.013 869 7----1.013 869 7E+00
  horsepower [UK] ---1----1.000 000 0E+00
  horsepower [US] ---1----1.000 000 0E+00
  joule/second--- 745.699 87----7.456 998 7E+02
  kilocalorie/minute [I.T.] --------------------------- 10.686 441----1.068 644 1E+01
  kilogram square meter/cubic second-------------- 745.699 87----7.456 998 7E+02
  kilogram-force meter/second--------------------- 76.040 225----7.604 022 5E+01
  kilopond meter/second---------------------------- 76.040 225----7.604 022 5E+01
  newton meter/second ----------------------------- 745.699 87----7.456 998 7E+02
  pferdestarke [Germany] --------------------------- 1.013 869 7----1.013 869 7E+00
  poncelet [France] -------------------------------------- 0.760 402 2----7.604 022 5E-01
  ton of refrigeration --------------------------------- 0.212 036 1----2.120 361 3E-01
  volt ampere -- 745.699 87----7.456 998 7E+02
  watt -- 745.699 87----7.456 998 7E+02

horsepower [550 foot pound-force/second] \<power\>
  Btu/minute [I.T.] -- 42.407 226----4.240 722 6E+01
  Btu/minute [thermoc.]-------------------------------- 42.435 606----4.243 560 6E+01
  calorie/second [I.T.] ------------------------------------ 178.107 35----1.781 073 5E+02
  calorie/second [thermoc.]-------------------------- 178.226 55----1.782 265 5E+02
  centigrade heat unit/minute [mean] --------------- 23.541 404----2.354 140 4E+01
  cheval vapeur [France]------------------------------- 1.013 869 7----1.013 869 7E+00
  cubic meter atmosphere/second----------------- 7,359.485 5----7.359 485 5E+03
  dyne centimeter/second----------------------------------- >>>----7.456 998 7E+09
  erg/second-- >>>----7.456 998 7E+09
  foot pound-force/second ----------------------------------- 550----5.500 000 0E+02
  foot poundal/second------------------------------- 17,695.727----1.769 572 7E+04
  gram-force centimeter/second------------------- 7,604,022.5----7.604 022 5E+06
  hectowatt--- 7.456 998 7----7.456 998 7E+00
  horsepower---1----1.000 000 0E+00
  horsepower [mechanical]---------------------------------------1----1.000 000 0E+00
  horsepower [metric] ---------------------------------- 1.013 869 7----1.013 869 7E+00
  horsepower [UK] ---1----1.000 000 0E+00
  horsepower [US] ---1----1.000 000 0E+00

Convert From	<Type of Unit>	
Convert To	Standard	Scientific

	Standard	Scientific
joule/second	745.699 87	7.456 998 7E+02
kilocalorie/minute [I.T.]	10.686 441	1.068 644 1E+01
kilogram square meter/cubic second	745.699 87	7.456 998 7E+02
kilogram-force meter/second	76.040 225	7.604 022 5E+01
kilopond meter/second	76.040 225	7.604 022 5E+01
million Btu/hour [I.T.]	0.002 544 4	2.544 433 6E−03
newton meter/second	745.699 87	7.456 998 7E+02
pferdestarke [Germany]	1.013 869 7	1.013 869 7E+00
poncelet [France]	0.760 402 2	7.604 022 5E−01
ton of refrigeration	0.212 036 1	2.120 361 3E−01
volt ampere	745.699 87	7.456 998 7E+02
watt	745.699 87	7.456 998 7E+02

horsepower [boiler]   `<power>`

	Standard	Scientific
Btu/second [I.T.]	9.297 612	9.297 612 0E+00
Btu/second [thermoc.]	9.303 834 2	9.303 834 2E+00
calorie/second [I.T.]	2,342.958 8	2.342 958 8E+03
calorie/second [thermoc.]	2,344.526 8	2.344 526 8E+03
centigrade heat unit/second [mean]	5.161 357 2	5.161 357 2E+00
cheval vapeur [France]	13.337 208	1.333 720 8E+01
cubic meter atmosphere/second	96,812.238	9.681 223 8E+04
dyne centimeter/second	>>>	9.809 500 0E+10
erg/second	>>>	9.809 500 0E+10
foot pound-force/second	7,235.115 9	7.235 115 9E+03
foot poundal/second	232,782.97	2.327 829 7E+05
gram-force centimeter/second	>>>	1.000 290 6E+08
horsepower	13.154 756	1.315 475 6E+01
horsepower [metric]	13.337 208	1.333 720 8E+01
joule/second	9,809.5	9.809 500 0E+03
kilocalorie/minute [I.T.]	2.342 958 8	2.342 958 8E+00
kilogram square meter/cubic second	9,809.5	9.809 500 0E+03
kilogram-force meter/second	1,000.290 6	1.000 290 6E+03
kilopond meter/second	1,000.290 6	1.000 290 6E+03
kilowatt	9.809 5	9.809 500 0E+00
million Btu/hour [I.T.]	0.033 471 4	3.347 140 3E−02
newton meter/second	9,809.5	9.809 500 0E+03
pferdestarke [Germany]	13.337 208	1.333 720 8E+01
poncelet [France]	10.002 906	1.000 290 6E+01
ton of refrigeration	2.789 283 6	2.789 283 6E+00
volt ampere	9,809.5	9.809 500 0E+03
watt	9,809.5	9.809 500 0E+03

horsepower [electric]   `<power>`

	Standard	Scientific
Btu/minute [I.T.]	42.424 294	4.242 429 4E+01
Btu/minute [thermoc.]	42.452 685	4.245 268 5E+01
calorie/second [I.T.]	178.179 04	1.781 790 4E+02
calorie/second [thermoc.]	178.298 28	1.782 982 8E+02
centigrade heat unit/minute [mean]	23.550 879	2.355 087 9E+01
cheval vapeur [France]	1.014 277 7	1.014 277 7E+00
cubic meter atmosphere/second	7,362.447 6	7.362 447 6E+03
dyne centimeter/second	>>>	7.460 000 0E+09
erg/second	>>>	7.460 000 0E+09
foot pound-force/second	550.221 36	5.502 213 6E+02
foot poundal/second	17,702.849	1.770 284 9E+04
gram-force centimeter/second	7,607,082.9	7.607 082 9E+06
hectowatt	7.46	7.460 000 0E+00
horsepower	1.000 402 5	1.000 402 5E+00
horsepower [metric]	1.014 277 7	1.014 277 7E+00
joule/second	746	7.460 000 0E+02
kilocalorie/minute [I.T.]	10.690 742	1.069 074 2E+01
kilogram square meter/cubic second	746	7.460 000 0E+02
kilogram-force meter/second	76.070 829	7.607 082 9E+01
kilopond meter/second	76.070 829	7.607 082 9E+01
million Btu/hour [I.T.]	0.002 545 5	2.545 457 7E−03
newton meter/second	746	7.460 000 0E+02

	Standard	Scientific
pferdestarke [Germany]	1.014 277 7	1.014 277 7E+00
poncelet [France]	0.760 708 3	7.607 082 9E−01
ton of refrigeration	0.212 121 5	2.121 214 7E−01
volt ampere	746	7.460 000 0E+02
watt	746	7.460 000 0E+02

horsepower [mechanical]   <power>

	Standard	Scientific
Btu/minute [I.T.]	42.407 226	4.240 722 6E+01
Btu/minute [thermoc.]	42.435 606	4.243 560 6E+01
calorie/second [I.T.]	178.107 35	1.781 073 5E+02
calorie/second [thermoc.]	178.226 55	1.782 265 5E+02
centigrade heat unit/minute [mean]	23.541 404	2.354 140 4E+01
cheval vapeur [France]	1.013 869 7	1.013 869 7E+00
cubic meter atmosphere/second	7,359.485 5	7.359 485 5E+03
dyne centimeter/second	>>>	7.456 998 7E+09
erg/second	>>>	7.456 998 7E+09
foot pound-force/second	550	5.500 000 0E+02
foot poundal/second	17,695.727	1.769 572 7E+04
gram-force centimeter/second	7,604,022.5	7.604 022 5E+06
hectowatt	7.456 998 7	7.456 998 7E+00
horsepower	1	1.000 000 0E+00
horsepower [550 foot pound-force/second]	1	1.000 000 0E+00
horsepower [UK]	1	1.000 000 0E+00
horsepower [US]	1	1.000 000 0E+00
joule/second	745.699 87	7.456 998 7E+02
kilocalorie/minute [I.T.]	10.686 441	1.068 644 1E+01
kilogram square meter/cubic second	745.699 87	7.456 998 7E+02
kilogram-force meter/second	76.040 225	7.604 022 5E+01
kilopond meter/second	76.040 225	7.604 022 5E+01
million Btu/hour [I.T.]	0.002 544 4	2.544 433 6E−03
newton meter/second	745.699 87	7.456 998 7E+02
pferdestarke [Germany]	1.013 869 7	1.013 869 7E+00
poncelet [France]	0.760 402 5	7.604 022 5E−01
pound square foot/cubic second	17,695.727	1.769 572 7E+04
ton of refrigeration	0.212 036 1	2.120 361 3E−01
volt ampere	745.699 87	7.456 998 7E+02
watt	745.699 87	7.456 998 7E+02

horsepower [metric]   <power>

	Standard	Scientific
Btu/minute [I.T.]	41.827 098	4.182 709 8E+01
Btu/minute [thermoc.]	41.855 09	4.185 509 0E+01
calorie/second [I.T.]	175.670 86	1.756 708 6E+02
calorie/second [thermoc.]	175.788 42	1.757 884 2E+02
centigrade heat unit/minute [mean]	23.219 359	2.321 935 9E+01
cheval vapeur [France]	1	1.000 000 0E+00
cubic meter atmosphere/second	7,258.808 3	7.258 808 3E+03
dyne centimeter/second	>>>	7.354 987 5E+09
erg/second	>>>	7.354 987 5E+09
foot pound-force/second	542.476 04	5.424 760 4E+02
foot poundal/second	17,453.65	1.745 365 0E+04
gram-force centimeter/second	7,500,000.0	7.500 000 0E+06
hectowatt	7.354 987 5	7.354 987 5E+00
horsepower	0.986 320 1	9.863 200 7E−01
joule/second	735.498 75	7.354 987 5E+02
kilocalorie/minute [I.T.]	10.540 252	1.054 025 2E+01
kilogram square meter/cubic second	735.498 75	7.354 987 5E+02
kilogram-force meter/second	75	7.500 000 0E+01
kilopond meter/second	75	7.500 000 0E+01
million Btu/hour [I.T.]	0.002 509 6	2.509 625 9E−03
newton meter/second	735.498 75	7.354 987 5E+02
pferdestarke [Germany]	1	1.000 000 0E+00
poncelet [France]	0.75	7.500 000 0E−01
pound square foot/cubic second	17,453.65	1.745 365 0E+04
ton of refrigeration	0.209 135 5	2.091 354 9E−01
volt ampere	735.498 75	7.354 987 5E+02

Convert From	<Type of Unit>	
Convert To	Standard	Scientific

| watt | 735.498 75 | 7.354 987 5E+02 |

horsepower [UK]   **<power>**

Convert To	Standard	Scientific
Btu/minute [I.T.]	42.407 226	4.240 722 6E+01
Btu/minute [thermoc.]	42.435 606	4.243 560 6E+01
calorie/second [I.T.]	178.107 35	1.781 073 5E+02
calorie/second [thermoc.]	178.226 55	1.782 265 5E+02
centigrade heat unit/minute [mean]	23.541 404	2.354 140 4E+01
cheval vapeur [France]	1.013 869 7	1.013 869 7E+00
cubic meter atmosphere/second	7,359.485 5	7.359 485 5E+03
dyne centimeter/second	>>>	7.456 998 7E+09
erg/second	>>>	7.456 998 7E+09
foot pound-force/second	550	5.500 000 0E+02
foot poundal/second	17,695.727	1.769 572 7E+04
gram-force centimeter/second	7,604,022.5	7.604 022 5E+06
hectowatt	7.456 998 7	7.456 998 7E+00
horsepower	1	1.000 000 0E+00
horsepower [550 foot pound-force/second]	1	1.000 000 0E+00
horsepower [mechanical]	1	1.000 000 0E+00
horsepower [metric]	1.013 869 7	1.013 869 7E+00
horsepower [US]	1	1.000 000 0E+00
joule/second	745.699 87	7.456 998 7E+02
kilocalorie/minute [I.T.]	10.686 441	1.068 644 1E+01
kilogram square meter/cubic second	745.699 87	7.456 998 7E+02
kilogram-force meter/second	76.040 225	7.604 022 5E+01
kilopond meter/second	76.040 225	7.604 022 5E+01
newton meter/second	745.699 87	7.456 998 7E+02
pferdestarke [Germany]	1.013 869 7	1.013 869 7E+00
poncelet [France]	0.760 402 2	7.604 022 5E-01
ton of refrigeration	0.212 036 1	2.120 361 3E-01
volt ampere	745.699 87	7.456 998 7E+02
watt	745.699 87	7.456 998 7E+02

horsepower [US]   **<power>**

Convert To	Standard	Scientific
Btu/minute [I.T.]	42.407 226	4.240 722 6E+01
Btu/minute [thermoc.]	42.435 606	4.243 560 6E+01
calorie/second [I.T.]	178.107 35	1.781 073 5E+02
calorie/second [thermoc.]	178.226 55	1.782 265 5E+02
centigrade heat unit/minute [mean]	23.541 404	2.354 140 4E+01
cheval vapeur [France]	1.013 869 7	1.013 869 7E+00
cubic meter atmosphere/second	7,359.485 5	7.359 485 5E+03
dyne centimeter/second	>>>	7.456 998 7E+09
erg/second	>>>	7.456 998 7E+09
foot pound-force/second	550	5.500 000 0E+02
foot poundal/second	17,695.727	1.769 572 7E+04
gram-force centimeter/second	7,604,022.5	7.604 022 5E+06
hectowatt	7.456 998 7	7.456 998 7E+00
horsepower	1	1.000 000 0E+00
horsepower [550 foot pound-force/second]	1	1.000 000 0E+00
horsepower [mechanical]	1	1.000 000 0E+00
horsepower [metric]	1.013 869 7	1.013 869 7E+00
horsepower [UK]	1	1.000 000 0E+00
joule/second	745.699 87	7.456 998 7E+02
kilocalorie/minute [I.T.]	10.686 441	1.068 644 1E+01
kilogram square meter/cubic second	745.699 87	7.456 998 7E+02
kilogram-force meter/second	76.040 225	7.604 022 5E+01
kilopond meter/second	76.040 225	7.604 022 5E+01
million Btu/hour [I.T.]	0.002 544 4	2.544 433 6E-03
newton meter/second	745.699 87	7.456 998 7E+02
pferdestarke [Germany]	1.013 869 7	1.013 869 7E+00
poncelet [France]	0.760 402 2	7.604 022 5E-01
ton of refrigeration	0.212 036 1	2.120 361 3E-01
volt ampere	745.699 87	7.456 998 7E+02
watt	745.699 87	7.456 998 7E+02

Convert From	<Type of Unit>	
Convert To	Standard	Scientific

horsepower [water]   <power>

Convert To	Standard	Scientific
Btu/minute [I.T.]	42.426 74	4.242 674 0E+01
Btu/minute [thermoc.]	42.455 132	4.245 513 2E+01
calorie/second [I.T.]	178.189 31	1.781 893 1E+02
calorie/second [thermoc.]	178.308 56	1.783 085 6E+02
centigrade heat unit/minute [mean]	23.552 237	2.355 223 7E+01
cheval vapeur [France]	1.014 336 2	1.014 336 2E+00
cubic meter atmosphere/second	7,362.871 9	7.362 871 9E+03
dyne centimeter/second	>>>	7.460 430 0E+09
erg/second	>>>	7.460 430 0E+09
foot pound-force/second	550.253 08	5.502 530 8E+02
foot poundal/second	17,703.869	1.770 386 9E+04
gram-force centimeter/second	7,607,521.4	7.607 521 4E+06
hectowatt	7.460 43	7.460 430 0E+00
horsepower	1.000 460 1	1.000 460 1E+00
horsepower [metric]	1.014 336 2	1.014 336 2E+00
joule/second	746.043	7.460 430 0E+02
kilocalorie/minute [I.T.]	10.691 359	1.069 135 9E+01
kilogram square meter/cubic second	746.043	7.460 430 0E+02
kilogram-force meter/second	76.075 214	7.607 521 4E+01
kilopond meter/second	76.075 214	7.607 521 4E+01
million Btu/hour [I.T.]	0.002 545 6	2.545 604 4E-03
newton meter/second	746.043	7.460 430 0E+02
pferdestarke [Germany]	1.014 336 2	1.014 336 2E+00
poncelet [France]	0.760 752 1	7.607 521 4E-01
ton of refrigeration	0.212 133 7	2.121 337 0E-01
volt ampere	746.043	7.460 430 0E+02
watt	746.043	7.460 430 0E+02

horsepower hour   <energy>

Convert To	Standard	Scientific
Board of Trade Unit	0.745 699 9	7.456 998 7E-01
Btu [I.T.]	2,544.433 6	2.544 433 6E+03
calorie [I.T.]	641,186.48	6.411 864 8E+05
calorie [kilogram, I.T.]	641.186 48	6.411 864 8E+02
calorie [kilogram, mean]	640.693 73	6.406 937 3E+02
calorie [kilogram, thermoc.]	641.615 57	6.416 155 7E+02
centimeter gram-force	>>>	2.737 448 1E+10
cheval vapeur heure [France]	1.013 869 7	1.013 869 7E+00
coal equivalent kilogram [UN, standard]	0.091 598 1	9.159 806 8E-02
cubic centimeter atmosphere	>>>	2.649 414 8E+07
cubic foot atmosphere	935.632	9.356 320 0E+02
dyne centimeter	>>>	2.684 519 5E+13
erg	>>>	2.684 519 5E+13
foot pound-force	1,980,000	1.980 000 0E+06
foot poundal	>>>	6.370 461 6E+07
frigorie [France]	641.339 66	6.413 396 6E+02
gram calorie	641,339.66	6.413 396 6E+05
hectowatthour	7.456 998 7	7.456 998 7E+00
horsepower hour [metric]	1.013 869 7	1.013 869 7E+00
inch ounce-force	>>>	3.801 600 0E+08
inch pound-force	>>>	2.376 000 0E+07
joule	2,684,519.5	2.684 519 5E+06
kilocalorie [I.T.]	641.186 48	6.411 864 8E+02
kilocalorie [mean]	640.693 73	6.406 937 3E+02
kilocalorie [thermoc.]	641.615 57	6.416 155 7E+02
kilogram calorie [15 °C, NBS, 1939]	641.339 66	6.413 396 6E+02
kilowatthour	0.745 699 9	7.456 998 7E-01
myriawatthour	0.074 57	7.456 998 7E-02
pferdestarkenstunde [Germany]	1.013 869 7	1.013 869 7E+00
therm [EEC]	0.025 444 3	2.544 433 6E-02
therm [US]	0.025 450 4	2.545 041 1E-02
thermie [France]	0.641 339 7	6.413 396 6E-01
watthour	745.699 87	7.456 998 7E+02
wattsecond	2,684,519.5	2.684 519 5E+06

Convert From		
Convert To	Standard	<Type of Unit> Scientific

horsepower hour [metric] <energy>
Btu [I.T.]	2,509.625 9	2.509 625 9E+03
calorie [I.T.]	632,415.09	6.324 150 9E+05
calorie [kilogram, I.T.]	632.415 09	6.324 150 9E+02
centimeter gram-force	>>>	2.700 000 0E+10
cheval vapeur heure [France]	1	1.000 000 0E+00
coal equivalent kilogram [UN, standard]	0.090 345	9.034 501 3E-02
cubic centimeter atmosphere	2,613.17	2.613 170 4E+07
cubic foot atmosphere	922.832 62	9.228 326 2E+02
dyne centimeter	>>>	2.647 795 5E+13
erg	>>>	2.647 795 5E+13
foot pound-force	1,952,913.7	1.952 913 7E+06
foot poundal	>>>	6.283 314 1E+07
frigorie [France]	632.566 18	6.325 661 8E+02
gram calorie	632,566.18	6.325 661 8E+05
horsepower hour	0.986 320 1	9.863 200 7E-01
joule	2,647,795.5	2.647 795 5E+06
kilocalorie [I.T.]	632.415 09	6.324 150 9E+02
kilocalorie [mean]	631.929 08	6.319 290 8E+02
kilocalorie [thermoc.]	632.838 31	6.328 383 1E+02
kilogram calorie [15 °C, NBS, 1939]	632.566 18	6.325 661 8E+02
kilopond meter	270,000	2.700 000 0E+05
kilowatthour	0.735 498 8	7.354 987 5E-01
meter kilogram-force	270,000	2.700 000 0E+05
myriawatthour	0.073 549 9	7.354 987 5E-02
pferdestarkenstunde [Germany]	1	1.000 000 0E+00
therm [EEC]	0.025 096 3	2.509 625 9E-02
therm [US]	0.025 102 3	2.510 225 1E-02
thermie [France]	0.632 566 2	6.325 661 8E-01
watthour	735.498 75	7.354 987 5E+02
wattsecond	2,647,795.5	2.647 795 5E+06

hot [Vietnam] <mass, special - see page 29>
milligram	0.037 78	3.778 000 0E-02

hot [Vietnam] <length, special - see page 29>
micrometer	0.4	4.000 000 0E-01

houn [Hong Kong] <mass, special - see page 29>
gram	0.378	3.780 000 0E-01

hour <time>
day	0.041 666 7	4.166 666 7E-02
hour [mean solar]	1	1.000 000 0E+00
minute	60	6.000 000 0E+01
month [mean sidereal]	0.001 525	1.525 041 4E-03
second	3,600	3.600 000 0E+03
year [normal calendar]	0.000 114 2	1.141 552 5E-04

hour [Coordinated Universal Time (UTC)] <time>
day	0.041 666 7	4.166 666 7E-02
hour	1	1.000 000 0E+00
minute	60	6.000 000 0E+01
month [mean sidereal]	0.001 525	1.525 041 4E-03
second	3,600	3.600 000 0E+03
year [normal calendar]	0.000 114 2	1.141 552 5E-04

hour [mean sidereal] <time>
day	0.041 552 9	4.155 289 9E-02
day [mean sidereal]	0.041 666 7	4.166 666 7E-02
hour	0.997 269 6	9.972 695 7E-01
minute	59.836 174	5.983 617 4E+01
minute [mean sidereal]	60	6.000 000 0E+01
month [mean sidereal]	0.001 520 9	1.520 877 4E-03
second	3,590.170 44	3.590 170 4E+03
second [mean sidereal]	3,600	3.600 000 0E+03
year [mean sidereal]	0.000 113 8	1.137 636 5E-04
year [normal calendar]	0.000 113 8	1.138 435 6E-04

Convert From Convert To	<Type of Unit> Standard	Scientific
hour [mean solar]		**<time>**
day	0.041 666 7	4.166 666 7E-02
day [mean solar]	0.041 666 7	4.166 666 7E-02
hour	1	1.000 000 0E+00
minute	60	6.000 000 0E+01
minute [mean solar]	60	6.000 000 0E+01
month [mean sidereal]	0.001 525	1.525 041 4E-03
second	3,600	3.600 000 0E+03
second [mean solar]	3,600	3.600 000 0E+03
year [mean sidereal]	0.000 114 1	1.140 751 3E-04
year [normal calendar]	0.000 114 2	1.141 552 5E-04
hour °C/kilocalorie [-/ I.T.]		**<thermal resistance>**
hour °F/Btu [-/ I.T.]	0.453 592 4	4.535 923 7E-01
kelvin/watt	0.859 845 2	8.598 452 3E-01
second °C/calorie [-/ I.T.]	3.6	3.600 000 0E+00
hour °F/Btu [-/ I.T.]		**<thermal resistance>**
°C/watt	1.895 634 2	1.895 634 2E+00
hour °C/kilocalorie [-/ I.T.]	2.204 622 6	2.204 622 6E+00
kelvin/watt	1.895 634 2	1.895 634 2E+00
hour foot °F/Btu [-/ I.T.]		**<thermal resistivity>**
meter kelvin/watt	0.577 789 3	5.777 893 2E-01
hour foot °F/Btu [-/ thermoc.]		**<thermal resistivity>**
meter kelvin/watt	0.578 176 1	5.781 761 3E-01
hour foot degree Rankine/Btu [-/ I.T.]		**<thermal resistivity>**
meter kelvin/watt	0.577 789 3	5.777 893 2E-01
hour meter °C/kilocalorie [-/ I.T.]		**<thermal resistivity>**
meter kelvin/watt	0.859 845 2	8.598 452 3E-01
hour square centimeter °C/calorie centimeter [-/ I.T.]		**<thermal resistivity>**
meter kelvin/watt	8.598 452 3	8.598 452 3E+00
hour square foot °F/Btu foot [-/ I.T.]		**<thermal resistivity>**
meter kelvin/watt	0.577 789 3	5.777 893 2E-01
hour square foot °F/Btu foot [-/ thermoc.]		**<thermal resistivity>**
meter kelvin/watt	0.578 176 1	5.781 761 3E-01
hour square foot °F/Btu inch [-/ I.T.]		**<thermal resistivity>**
meter kelvin/watt	6.933 471 8	6.933 471 8E+00
hour square foot °F/Btu inch [-/ thermoc.]		**<thermal resistivity>**
meter kelvin/watt	6.938 113 5	6.938 113 5E+00
hour square foot degree Rankine/Btu foot [-/ I.T.]		**<thermal resistivity>**
meter kelvin/watt	0.577 789 3	5.777 893 2E-01
hour square foot degree Rankine/Btu inch [-/ I.T.]		**<thermal resistivity>**
meter kelvin/watt	6.933 471 8	6.933 471 8E+00
hout [Netherlands]		**<area, special - see page 29>**
square meter	1,421.3	1.421 300 0E+03
hu [China]		**<volume, special - see page 29>**
liter	51.773	5.177 300 0E+01
hu mi [China]		**<length, special - see page 29>**
micrometer	10	1.000 000 0E+01
huacal [Venezuela]		**<volume, special - see page 29>**
liter	28	2.800 000 0E+01
huitieme [Seychelles]		**<mass, special - see page 29>**
gram	61.188	6.118 800 0E+01
hukka [Iraq, Baghdad]		**<mass, special - see page 29>**
kilogram	4.167	4.167 000 0E+00
hukka [Iraq, Istanbul]		**<mass, special - see page 29>**
gram	1.283	1.283 000 0E+00
hundred		**<units>**
unit	100	1.000 000 0E+02

Convert From		<Type of Unit>
Convert To	Standard	Scientific

hundredweight [long]   <mass>

cental [US]	1.12	1.120 000 0E+00
centner [UK]	1	1.000 000 0E+00
flask of mercury	1.473 684 2	1.473 684 2E+00
geepound	3.481 066 4	3.481 066 4E+00
hundredweight [short]	1.12	1.120 000 0E+00
hundredweight [UK]	1	1.000 000 0E+00
hundredweight [US, gross]	1	1.000 000 0E+00
hundredweight [US, net]	1.12	1.120 000 0E+00
hyl	5.180 397 5	5.180 397 5E+00
kilogram	50.802 345	5.080 234 5E+01
kilogram-force square second/meter	5.180 397 5	5.180 397 5E+00
myriagram	5.080 234 5	5.080 234 5E+00
pound-force square second/foot	3.481 066 4	3.481 066 4E+00
quarter [UK]	4	4.000 000 0E+00
quarter [US]	4.48	4.480 000 0E+00
quintal [UK]	1	1.000 000 0E+00
quintal [US]	1.12	1.120 000 0E+00
slug	3.481 066 4	3.481 066 4E+00
slug [metric]	5.180 397 5	5.180 397 5E+00
stone [UK]	8	8.000 000 0E+00

hundredweight [Pakistan]   <mass, special - see page 29>

kilogram	50.802 35	5.080 235 0E+01

hundredweight [short]   <mass>

cental [US]	1	1.000 000 0E+00
centner [UK]	0.892 857 1	8.928 571 4E-01
flask of mercury	1.315 789 5	1.315 789 5E+00
geepound	3.108 095	3.108 095 0E+00
hundredweight [long]	0.892 857 1	8.928 571 4E-01
hundredweight [UK]	0.892 857 1	8.928 571 4E-01
hundredweight [US, gross]	0.892 857 1	8.928 571 4E-01
hundredweight [US, net]	1	1.000 000 0E+00
hyl	4.625 354 9	4.625 354 9E+00
kilogram	45.359 237	4.535 923 7E+01
kilogram-force square second/meter	4.625 354 9	4.625 354 9E+00
myriagram	4.535 923 7	4.535 923 7E+00
pound-force square second/foot	3.108 095	3.108 095 0E+00
quarter [short]	0.2	2.000 000 0E-01
quarter [UK]	3.571 428 6	3.571 428 6E+00
quarter [US]	4	4.000 000 0E+00
quintal [metric]	0.453 592 4	4.535 923 7E-01
quintal [UK]	0.892 857 1	8.928 571 4E-01
quintal [US]	1	1.000 000 0E+00
slug	3.108 095	3.108 095 0E+00
slug [metric]	4.625 354 9	4.625 354 9E+00
stone [UK]	7.142 857 1	7.142 857 1E+00

hundredweight [UK]   <mass>

cental [US]	1.12	1.120 000 0E+00
centner [UK]	1	1.000 000 0E+00
flask of mercury	1.473 684 2	1.473 684 2E+00
geepound	3.481 066 4	3.481 066 4E+00
hundredweight [long]	1	1.000 000 0E+00
hundredweight [short]	1.12	1.120 000 0E+00
hundredweight [US, gross]	1	1.000 000 0E+00
hundredweight [US, net]	1.12	1.120 000 0E+00
hyl	5.180 397 5	5.180 397 5E+00
kilogram	50.802 345	5.080 234 5E+01
kilogram-force square second/meter	5.180 397 5	5.180 397 5E+00
myriagram	5.080 234 5	5.080 234 5E+00
pound-force square second/foot	3.481 066 4	3.481 066 4E+00
quarter [UK]	4	4.000 000 0E+00
quarter [US]	4.48	4.480 000 0E+00

Convert To	Standard	Scientific
quintal [UK]	1	1.000 000 0E+00
quintal [US]	1.12	1.120 000 0E+00
slug	3.481 066 4	3.481 066 4E+00
slug [metric]	5.180 397 5	5.180 397 5E+00
stone [UK]	8	8.000 000 0E+00

hundredweight [US, gross] <mass>

Convert To	Standard	Scientific
cental [US]	1.12	1.120 000 0E+00
centner [UK]	1	1.000 000 0E+00
flask of mercury	1.473 684 2	1.473 684 2E+00
geepound	3.481 066 4	3.481 066 4E+00
hundredweight [long]	1	1.000 000 0E+00
hundredweight [short]	1.12	1.120 000 0E+00
hundredweight [UK]	1	1.000 000 0E+00
hundredweight [US, net]	1.12	1.120 000 0E+00
hyl	5.180 397 5	5.180 397 5E+00
kilogram	50.802 345	5.080 234 5E+01
kilogram-force square second/meter	5.180 397 5	5.180 397 5E+00
myriagram	5.080 234 5	5.080 234 5E+00
pound-force square second/foot	3.481 066 4	3.481 066 4E+00
quarter [UK]	4	4.000 000 0E+00
quarter [US]	4.48	4.480 000 0E+00
quintal [UK]	1	1.000 000 0E+00
quintal [US]	1.12	1.120 000 0E+00
slug	3.481 066 4	3.481 066 4E+00
slug [metric]	5.180 397 5	5.180 397 5E+00
stone [UK]	8	8.000 000 0E+00

hundredweight [US, net] <mass>

Convert To	Standard	Scientific
cental [US]	1	1.000 000 0E+00
centner [UK]	0.892 857 1	8.928 571 4E-01
flask of mercury	1.315 789 5	1.315 789 5E+00
geepound	3.108 095	3.108 095 0E+00
hundredweight [long]	0.892 857 1	8.928 571 4E-01
hundredweight [short]	1	1.000 000 0E+00
hundredweight [UK]	0.892 857 1	8.928 571 4E-01
hundredweight [US, gross]	0.892 857 1	8.928 571 4E-01
hyl	4.625 354 9	4.625 354 9E+00
kilogram	45.359 237	4.535 923 7E+01
kilogram-force square second/meter	4.625 354 9	4.625 354 9E+00
pound-force square second/foot	3.108 095	3.108 095 0E+00
quarter [UK]	3.571 428 6	3.571 428 6E+00
quarter [US]	4	4.000 000 0E+00
quintal [metric]	0.453 592 4	4.535 923 7E-01
quintal [UK]	0.892 857 1	8.928 571 4E-01
quintal [US]	1	1.000 000 0E+00
slug	3.108 095	3.108 095 0E+00
slug [metric]	4.625 354 9	4.625 354 9E+00
stone [UK]	7.142 857 1	7.142 857 1E+00

huvelik [Hungary] <length, special - see page 29>

Convert To	Standard	Scientific
centimeter	2.63	2.630 000 0E+00

hvat [Yugoslavia] <length, special - see page 29>

Convert To	Standard	Scientific
meter	1.896	1.896 000 0E+00

hyaku me [Japan] <mass, special - see page 29>

Convert To	Standard	Scientific
gram	375	3.750 000 0E+02

hyl <mass>

Convert To	Standard	Scientific
glug	10	1.000 000 0E+01
kilogram	9.806 65	9.806 650 0E+00
kilogram-force square second/meter	1	1.000 000 0E+00
newton square second/meter	9.806 65	9.806 650 0E+00
pound	21.619 962	2.161 996 2E+01
pound [apothecary]	26.274 26	2.627 426 0E+01
pound [avoirdupois]	21.619 962	2.161 996 2E+01
pound [international]	21.619 962	2.161 996 2E+01

Convert To	Standard	Scientific
pound [troy]	26.274 26	2.627 426 0E+01
pound [US, avoirdupois]	21.619 96	2.161 996 2E+01
pound [US, troy]	26.274 257	2.627 425 7E+01
poundal square second/foot	21.619 962	2.161 996 2E+01
slug [metric]	1	1.000 000 0E+00
stone [UK]	1.544 283	1.544 283 0E+00

hyl meter/square second   **\<force\>**

Convert To	Standard	Scientific
crinal	98.066 5	9.806 650 0E+01
dyne	980,665	9.806 650 0E+05
gram-force	1,000	1.000 000 0E+03
newton	9.806 65	9.806 650 0E+00
ounce-force	35.273 961 9	3.527 396 2E+01
pond	1,000	1.000 000 0E+03
pound-force	2.204 622 6	2.204 622 6E+00
poundal	70.931 635 3	7.093 163 5E+01
ton-force [metric]	0.001	1.000 000 0E−03

hyl/meter second   **\<dynamic viscosity\>**

Convert To	Standard	Scientific
kilogram-force second/square meter	1	1.000 000 0E+00
kilogram/meter second	9.806 65	9.806 650 0E+00
pascal second	9.806 65	9.806 650 0E+00
pound/foot second	6.589 764 6	6.589 764 6E+00
poundal second/square foot	6.589 764 6	6.589 764 6E+00

imagu [Mongolia]   **\<length, special - see page 29\>**

Convert To	Standard	Scientific
centimeter	3.2	3.200 000 0E+00

imeru [Assyrian, ancient]   **\<mass, special - see page 29\>**

Convert To	Standard	Scientific
kilogram	90	9.000 000 0E+01

imi [Germany]   **\<volume, special - see page 29\>**

Convert To	Standard	Scientific
liter	18.37	1.837 000 0E+01

immi [Switzerland]   **\<volume, special - see page 29\>**

Convert To	Standard	Scientific
liter	1.5	1.500 000 0E+00

inch [based on US, survey foot]   **\<length\>**

Convert To	Standard	Scientific
cable length [US, survey]	0.000 115 7	1.157 407 4E−04
chain [Gunter or US, survey]	0.001 262 6	1.262 626 3E−03
chain [Ramden or Engineer]	0.000 833 3	8.333 350 0E−04
fathom [US, survey]	0.013 888 9	1.388 888 9E−02
foot [international]	0.083 333 5	8.333 350 0E−02
foot [US, survey]	0.083 333 3	8.333 333 3E−02
furlong [US, survey]	0.000 126 3	1.262 626 3E−04
inch [international]	1.000 002	1.000 002 0E+00
link [Gunter or US, survey]	0.126 262 6	1.262 626 3E−01
link [Ramden or Engineer]	0.083 333 5	8.333 350 0E−02
meter	0.025 400 1	2.540 005 1E−02
out [US, survey]	0.000 252 5	2.525 252 5E−04
pace [US, survey]	0.033 333 3	3.333 333 3E−02
perch [US, survey]	0.005 050 5	5.050 505 1E−03
vara [US, survey, California]	0.030 303	3.030 303 0E−02
vara [US, survey, Texas]	0.03	3.000 000 0E−02
yard [based on US, survey foot]	0.027 777 8	2.777 777 8E−02
yard [international]	0.027 777 8	2.777 783 3E−02

inch [international]   **\<length\>**

Convert To	Standard	Scientific
angstrom	>>>	2.540 000 0E+08
barleycorn	3	3.000 000 0E+00
caliber	100	1.000 000 0E+02
centimeter	2.54	2.540 000 0E+00
chain [Gunter or US, survey]	0.001 262 6	1.262 623 7E−03
chain [Ramden or Engineer]	0.000 833 3	8.333 333 3E−04
cubit	0.055 555 6	5.555 555 6E−02
digit	1.333 333	1.333 333 3E+00
foot [France]	0.078 192 2	7.819 219 6E−02
foot [international]	0.083 333 3	8.333 333 3E−02
foot [US, survey]	0.083 333 2	8.333 316 7E−02

Convert From Convert To	Standard	Type of Unit Scientific
hand [horses]	0.25	2.500 000 0E-01
inch [based on US, survey foot]	0.999 998	9.999 980 0E-01
ligne [print]	12	1.200 000 0E+01
line [print]	12	1.200 000 0E+01
link [Gunter or US, survey]	0.126 262 4	1.262 623 7E-01
link [Ramden or Engineer]	0.083 333 3	8.333 333 3E-02
meter	0.025 4	2.540 000 0E-02
micron	25,400	2.540 000 0E+04
mil	1,000	1.000 000 0E+03
thou	1,000	1.000 000 0E+03
vara [US, survey, California]	0.030 303	3.030 297 0E-02
vara [US, survey, Texas]	0.029 999 9	2.999 994 0E-02
wavelength of orange-red spectral line of krypton-86	41,929.399	4.192 939 9E+04
yard [based on US, survey foot]	0.027 777 7	2.777 772 2E-02
yard [international]	0.027 777 8	2.777 777 8E-02
yard [UK]	0.027 777 8	2.777 782 6E-02

inch of air [dry, CO_2 free, at 101325 Pa and 0 °C]		pressure
pascal	0.322 007 4	3.220 074 0E-01

inch of air [dry, CO_2 free, at 101325 Pa and 15 °C]		pressure
pascal	0.305 191 1	3.051 910 9E-01

inch of mercury [0 °C, by convention]		pressure
atmosphere [standard]	0.033 421 1	3.342 105 7E-02
atmosphere [technical]	0.034 531 6	3.453 155 4E-02
bar	0.033 863 9	3.386 388 6E-02
centibar	3.386 388 6	3.386 388 6E+00
centihg	2.54	2.540 000 0E+00
centimeter of mercury [0 °C, by convention]	2.54	2.540 000 0E+00
centimeter of water [4 °C, by convention]	34.531 554	3.453 155 4E+01
foot of mercury [0 °C, by convention]	0.083 333 3	8.333 333 3E-02
foot of water [4 °C, by convention]	1.132 925 1	1.132 925 0E+00
gram-force/square centimeter	34.531 554	3.453 155 4E+01
inch of water [4 °C, by convention]	13.595 1	1.359 510 0E+01
kilogram-force/square meter	345.315 54	3.453 155 4E+02
kilopascal	3.386 388 6	3.386 388 6E+00
kilopond/square meter	345.315 54	3.453 155 4E+02
kip/square foot	0.070 726 2	7.072 619 7E-02
millihg	25.4	2.540 000 0E+01
millimeter of mercury [0 °C, by convention]	25.4	2.540 000 0E+01
millimeter of water [4 °C, by convention]	345.315 54	3.453 155 4E+02
newton/square meter	3,386.388 6	3.386 388 6E+03
ounce-force/square inch	7.858 466 4	7.858 466 4E+00
pascal	3,386.388 6	3.386 388 6E+03
pieze [France]	3.386 388 6	3.386 388 6E+00
pound-force/square foot	70.726 197	7.072 619 7E+01
sthene/square meter [France]	3.386 388 6	3.386 388 6E+00
ton-force/square foot [short]	0.035 363 1	3.536 309 9E-02
ton-force/square meter [metric]	0.345 315 5	3.453 155 4E-01
torr	25.400 004	2.540 000 4E+01

inch of water [4 °C, by convention]		pressure
atmosphere [standard]	0.002 458 3	2.458 316 4E-03
atmosphere [technical]	0.002 54	2.540 000 0E-03
bar	0.002 490 9	2.490 889 1E-03
barye [France]	2,490.889 1	2.490 889 1E+03
centimeter of mercury [0 °C, by convention]	0.186 832	1.868 320 2E-01
centimeter of water [4 °C, by convention]	2.54	2.540 000 0E+00
dyne/square centimeter	2,490.889 1	2.490 889 1E+03
foot of mercury [0 °C, by convention]	0.006 129 7	6.129 659 5E-03
foot of water [4 °C, by convention]	0.083 333 3	8.333 333 3E-02
gram-force/square centimeter	2.54	2.540 000 0E+00
hectopascal	2.490 889 1	2.490 889 1E+00
inch of mercury [0 °C, by convention]	0.073 555 9	7.355 591 4E-02
kilogram-force/square meter	25.4	2.540 000 0E+01

Convert From Convert To	Standard	<Type of Unit> Scientific
kilopond/square meter	25.4	2.540 000 0E+01
millibar	2.490 889 1	2.490 889 1E+00
milling	1.868 320 2	1.868 320 2E+00
millimeter of mercury [0 °C, by convention]	1.868 320 2	1.868 320 2E+00
millimeter of water [4 °C, by convention]	25.4	2.540 000 0E+01
newton/square meter	249.088 91	2.490 889 1E+02
ounce-force/square inch	0.578 036 7	5.780 366 7E−01
pascal	249.088 91	2.490 889 1E+02
pieze [France]	0.249 088 9	2.490 889 1E−01
pound-force/square foot	5.202 33	5.202 330 0E+00
poundal/square foot	167.380 02	1.673 800 2E+02
sthene/square meter [France]	0.249 088 9	2.490 889 1E−01
ton-force/square foot [short]	0.002 601 2	2.601 165 0E−03
ton-force/square meter [metric]	0.025 4	2.540 000 0E−02
torr	1.868 320 5	1.868 320 5E+00

inch ounce-force   <energy>

Convert To	Standard	Scientific
Btu [I.T.]	0.000 006 7	6.693 059 7E−06
calorie [I.T.]	0.001 686 6	1.686 622 7E−03
calorie [mean]	0.001 685 3	1.685 326 5E−03
calorie [thermoc.]	0.001 687 8	1.687 751 4E−03
centimeter gram-force	72.007 789	7.200 778 9E+01
cubic centimeter atmosphere	0.069 692 1	6.969 209 8E−02
cubic foot atmosphere	0.000 002 5	2.461 153 2E−06
dyne centimeter	70,615.518	7.061 551 8E+04
erg	70,615.518	7.061 551 8E+04
foot pound-force	0.005 208 3	5.208 333 3E−03
foot poundal	0.167 573 2	1.675 731 7E−01
gram calorie	0.001 687	1.687 025 6E−03
inch pound-force	0.062 5	6.250 000 0E−02
joule	0.007 061 6	7.061 551 8E−03
kilogram square meter/square second	0.007 061 6	7.061 551 8E−03
kilopond meter	0.000 720 1	7.200 778 9E−04
megaerg	0.070 615 5	7.061 551 8E−02
megalerg	0.070 615 5	7.061 551 8E−02
meter kilogram-force	0.000 720 1	7.200 778 9E−04
newton meter	0.007 061 6	7.061 551 8E−03
teraelectronvolt	44,074.721	4.407 472 1E+04
watthour	0.000 002	1.961 542 2E−06
wattsecond	0.007 061 6	7.061 551 8E−03

inch ounce-force   <torque>

Convert To	Standard	Scientific
foot ounce-force	0.083 333 3	8.333 333 3E−02

inch ounce-force revolution/minute   <power>

Convert To	Standard	Scientific
foot pound-force/hour	1.963 495 4	1.963 495 4E+00
watt	0.000 739 5	7.394 839 8E−04

inch pound-force   <energy>

Convert To	Standard	Scientific
Btu [I.T.]	0.000 107 1	1.070 889 6E−04
calorie [I.T.]	0.026 986	2.698 596 3E−02
calorie [mean]	0.026 965 2	2.696 522 4E−02
calorie [thermoc.]	0.027 004	2.700 402 2E−02
centimeter gram-force	1,152.124 6	1.152 124 6E+03
cubic centimeter atmosphere	1.115 073 6	1.115 073 6E+00
foot pound-force	0.083 333 3	8.333 333 3E−02
foot poundal	2.681 170 7	2.681 170 7E+00
gram calorie	0.026 992 4	2.699 241 0E−02
inch ounce-force	16	1.600 000 0E+01
joule	0.112 984 8	1.129 848 3E−01
kilogram square meter/square second	0.112 984 8	1.129 848 3E−01
kilopond meter	0.011 521 2	1.152 124 6E−02
megaerg	1.129 848 3	1.129 848 3E+00
megalerg	1.129 848 3	1.129 848 3E+00
meter kilogram-force	0.011 521 2	1.152 124 6E−02
newton meter	0.112 984 8	1.129 848 3E−01

| Convert From | | <Type of Unit> |
Convert To	Standard	Scientific
watthour	0.000 031 4	3.138 467 5E−05
wattsecond	0.112 984 8	1.129 848 3E−01
inch pound-force		**<torque>**
foot ounce-force	1.333 333 3	1.333 333 3E+00
inch pound-force/inch		**<torque/unit length>**
newton meter/meter	4.448 221 6	4.448 221 6E+00
inch/day		**<velocity>**
centimeter/day	2.54	2.540 000 0E+00
dekameter/day	0.002 54	2.540 000 0E−03
foot/day	0.083 333 3	8.333 333 3E−02
knot [international]	0.000 000 6	5.714 542 8E−07
meter/day	0.025 4	2.540 000 0E−02
meter/second	0.000 000 3	2.939 814 8E−07
mile/day	0.000 015 8	1.578 282 8E−05
millimeter/hour	1.058 333 3	1.058 333 3E+00
nautical mile/day [international]	0.000 013 7	1.371 490 3E−05
yard/day	0.027 777 8	2.777 777 8E−02
inch/hour		**<velocity>**
centimeter/hour	2.54	2.540 000 0E+00
dekameter/day	0.060 96	6.096 000 0E−02
foot/day	2	2.000 000 0E+01
inch/day	24	2.400 000 0E+01
knot [international]	0.000 013 7	1.371 490 3E−05
meter/day	0.609 6	6.096 000 0E−01
meter/second	0.000 007 1	7.055 555 6E−06
millimeter/hour	25.4	2.540 000 0E+01
yard/day	0.666 666 7	6.666 666 7E−01
inch/minute		**<velocity>**
centimeter/minute	2.54	2.540 000 0E+00
dekameter/day	3.657 6	3.657 600 0E+00
foot/hour	5	5.000 000 0E+00
hectometer/day	0.365 76	3.657 600 0E−01
inch/hour	60	6.000 000 0E+01
knot [international]	0.000 822 9	8.228 941 7E−04
meter/hour	1.524	1.524 000 0E+00
meter/second	0.000 423 3	4.233 333 3E−04
mile/day	0.022 727 3	2.272 727 3E−02
millimeter/minute	25.4	2.540 000 0E+01
nautical mile/day [international]	0.019 749 5	1.974 946 0E−02
yard/day	40	4.000 000 0E+01
yard/hour	1.666 666 7	1.666 666 7E+00
inch/second		**<velocity>**
centimeter/second	2.54	2.540 000 0E+00
dekameter/hour	9.144	9.144 000 0E+00
foot/minute	5	5.000 000 0E+00
inch/minute	60	6.000 000 0E+01
kilometer/day	2.194 56	2.194 560 0E+00
knot [international]	0.049 373 7	4.937 365 0E−02
meter/minute	1.524	1.524 000 0E+00
mile/day	1.363 636 4	1.363 636 4E+00
millimeter/second	25.4	2.540 000 0E+01
nautical mile/day [international]	1.184 967 6	1.184 967 6E+00
yard/minute	1.666 666 7	1.666 666 7E+00
inch/square second		**<acceleration>**
foot/square second	0.083 333 3	8.333 333 3E−02
galileo	2.54	2.540 000 0E+00
leo	0.002 54	2.540 000 0E−03
meter/square second	0.025 4	2.540 000 0E−02
inch⁴		**<second moment of area>**
foot⁴	0.000 048 2	4.822 530 9E−05
meter⁴	0.000 000 4	4.162 314 3E−07

millimeter[4]	416,231.43	4.162 314 3E+05
ippyong [South Korea]		<volume, special - see page 29>
cubic meter	6.01	6.010 000 0E+00
iron [print]		<length>
agate [print]	54.545 455	5.454 545 5E+01
caliber	415.11	4.151 100 0E+02
didot point [print]	280.059 75	2.800 597 5E+02
digit	5.534 8	5.534 800 0E+00
douzieme [print]	597.758 4	5.977 584 0E+02
em [pica, print]	25	2.500 000 0E+01
inch [international]	4.151 1	4.151 100 0E+00
ligne [print]	49.813 2	4.981 320 0E+01
line [print]	49.813 2	4.981 320 0E+01
meter	0.105 437 9	1.054 379 4E-01
microinch	4,151,100	4.151 100 0E+06
mil	4,151.1	4.151 100 0E+03
nonpareil [print]	50	5.000 000 0E+01
pearl [print]	60	6.000 000 0E+01
pica [print]	25	2.500 000 0E+01
point [print]	300	3.000 000 0E+02
thou	4,151.1	4.151 100 0E+03
iron [shoe leather]		<length>
barleycorn	0.062 5	6.250 000 0E-02
caliber	2.083 333 3	2.083 333 3E+00
cubit	0.001 157 4	1.157 407 4E-03
foot [international]	0.001 736 1	1.736 111 1E-03
inch [international]	0.020 833 3	2.083 333 3E-02
meter	0.000 529 2	5.291 666 7E-04
microinch	20,833.333	2.083 333 3E+04
micron	529.166 67	5.291 666 7E+02
mil	20.833 333	2.083 333 3E+01
thou	20.833 333	2.083 333 3E+01
issaron [Hebrew, ancient]		<volume, special - see page 29>
liter	2.299	2.299 000 0E+00
itce [Hungary]		<volume, special - see page 29>
liter	0.848	8.480 000 0E-01
itcze [Hungary]		<volume, special - see page 29>
liter	0.848	8.480 000 0E-01
iugerum [Rome, ancient]		<area, special - see page 29>
square meter	2,523.3	2.523 300 0E+03
izenbi [Morocco]		<area, special - see page 29>
hectare	0.18	1.800 000 0E-01
jabia [Libya]		<area, special - see page 29>
square meter	1,225	1.225 000 0E+03
jacob [India]		<length, special - see page 29>
centimeter	0.63	6.300 000 0E-01
jae [South Korea]		<volume, special - see page 29>
cubic decimeter	3.339	3.339 000 0E+00
jak [South Korea]		<volume, special - see page 29>
milliliter	18.039	1.803 900 0E+01
jak [South Korea]		<area, special - see page 29>
square meter	0.033 058	3.305 800 0E-02
jalka [Finland]		<length, special - see page 29>
centimeter	26.69	2.669 000 0E+01
jaob [India]		<length, special - see page 29>
centimeter	0.635	6.350 000 0E-01
jar		<capacitance>
farad	<<<	1.112 650 1E-09
statfarad	1,000	1.000 000 0E+03

jarda [Cape Verde]
meter -- \<length, special - see page 29\>
0.88 ---- 8.800 000 0E−01

jareeb [Pakistan]
meter -- \<length, special - see page 29\>
20.116 8 ---- 2.011 680 0E+01

jareeb [Pakistan]
are -- \<area, special - see page 29\>
4.046 856 ---- 4.046 856 0E+00

jarib [India]
meter -- \<length, special - see page 29\>
54.864 ---- 5.486 400 0E+01

jarra [Libya]
liter --- \<volume, special - see page 29\>
14.13 ---- 1.413 000 0E+01

jarra [Mexico]
liter --- \<volume, special - see page 29\>
8.21 ---- 8.210 000 0E+00

java paal [Indonesia]
kilometer --- \<length, special - see page 29\>
1.507 ---- 1.507 000 0E+00

jemba [Malaysia]
square meter -- \<area, special - see page 29\>
13.378 ---- 1.337 800 0E+01

jemba [Singapore]
square meter -- \<area, special - see page 29\>
13.378 ---- 1.337 800 0E+01

jenghal [Singapore]
centimeter -- \<length, special - see page 29\>
22.86 ---- 2.286 000 0E+01

jengkal [Malaysia]
centimeter -- \<length, special - see page 29\>
22.86 ---- 2.286 000 0E+01

jengkal [Singapore]
centimeter -- \<length, special - see page 29\>
22.86 ---- 2.286 000 0E+01

jerib [Afghanistan]
hectare --- \<area, special - see page 29\>
0.195 36 ---- 1.953 600 0E−01

jerib [Iran]
are --- \<area, special - see page 29\>
10.8 ---- 1.080 000 0E+01

jeroboam [champagne bottle]
bottle [wine, standard] -- \<champagne bottle size\>
4 ---- 4.000 000 0E+00
liter --- 3 ---- 3.000 000 0E+00

jigger [US, liquid]
cubic inch -------------------------------- 2.707 031 3 ---- 2.707 031 3E+00 \<volume\>
cubic meter ------------------------------- 0.000 044 4 ---- 4.436 029 4E−05
drop [US, liquid] ------------------------- 540 ---- 5.400 000 0E+02
liter ------------------------------------- 0.044 360 3 ---- 4.436 029 4E−02
ounce [US, liquid] ------------------------ 1.5 ---- 1.500 000 0E+00

jin [Brunei]
kilogram -- \<mass, special - see page 29\>
0.605 ---- 6.050 000 0E−01

jin [China, new]
kilogram -- \<mass, special - see page 29\>
0.5 ---- 5.000 000 0E−01

jin [China, old]
kilogram -- \<mass, special - see page 29\>
0.605 ---- 6.050 000 0E−01

jin [Hong Kong]
kilogram -- \<mass, special - see page 29\>
0.605 ---- 6.050 000 0E−01

jin [Indonesia]
kilogram -- \<mass, special - see page 29\>
0.618 ---- 6.180 000 0E−01

jin [Japan]
kilogram -- \<mass, special - see page 29\>
0.6 ---- 6.000 000 0E−01

jin [Malaysia]
kilogram -- \<mass, special - see page 29\>
0.605 ---- 6.050 000 0E−01

jin [Singapore]
kilogram -- \<mass, special - see page 29\>
0.605 ---- 6.050 000 0E−01

jin [South Korea]
kilogram -- \<mass, special - see page 29\>
0.6 ---- 6.000 000 0E−01

Convert From Convert To	Standard	<Type of Unit> Scientific
jin [Thailand]	<mass, special - see page 29>	
kilogram ----------	---------- 0.6 ---	6.000 000 0E-01
jirib [Afghanistan]	<area, special - see page 29>	
square meter ----------	---------- 1.952 ---	1.952 000 0E+00
jitro [Czechoslovakia]	<area, special - see page 29>	
are ----------	---------- 57.55 ---	5.755 000 0E+01
jizla [Tanganyika]	<volume, special - see page 29>	
liter----------	---------- 240 ---	2.400 000 0E+02
jo [Japan]	<length, special - see page 29>	
meter ----------	---------- 3.03 ---	3.030 000 0E+00
joch [Austria]	<area, special - see page 29>	
are ----------	---------- 57.55 ---	5.755 000 0E+01
joch [Hungary]	<area, special - see page 29>	
are ----------	---------- 43.16 ---	4.316 000 0E+01
joule [energy]		<energy>
1/meter [atomic physics, eq. energy]----------	>>>	5.034 112 5E+24
atomic mass unit [unified, C-12, 1986, eq. energy]----------	>>>	6.700 530 8E+09
Board of Trade Unit----------	0.000 000 3 ---	2.777 777 8E-07
Btu [15 °C]----------	0.000 948 ---	9.480 434 3E-04
Btu [15.6 °C]----------	0.000 948 2 ---	9.481 548 9E-04
Btu [15.8 °C, Canada]----------	0.000 948 2 ---	9.482 133 3E-04
Btu [15.8 °C, ISO]----------	0.000 948 3 ---	9.483 167 4E-04
Btu [3.9 °C]----------	0.000 943 7 ---	9.436 900 2E-04
Btu [I.T.]----------	0.000 947 8 ---	9.478 171 2E-04
Btu [I.T., pre-1956]----------	0.000 947 8 ---	9.478 313 6E-04
Btu [mean]----------	0.000 947 1 ---	9.470 862 9E-04
Btu [thermoc.]----------	0.000 948 5 ---	9.484 514 1E-04
calorie [15 °C, CIPM, 1950]----------	0.238 920 1 ---	2.389 200 8E-01
calorie [15 °C, NBS, 1939]----------	0.238 903 ---	2.389 029 6E-01
calorie [20 °C]----------	0.239 125 8 ---	2.391 257 6E-01
calorie [I.T.]----------	0.238 845 9 ---	2.388 459 0E-01
calorie [kilogram, I.T.]----------	0.000 238 8 ---	2.388 459 0E-04
calorie [kilogram, mean]----------	0.000 238 7 ---	2.386 623 5E-04
calorie [kilogram, thermoc.]----------	0.000 239 ---	2.390 057 4E-04
calorie [mean]----------	0.238 662 4 ---	2.386 623 5E-01
calorie [nutritional]----------	0.000 239 ---	2.390 057 4E-04
calorie [thermoc.]----------	0.239 005 7 ---	2.390 057 4E-01
centigrade heat unit [I.T.]----------	0.000 526 6 ---	5.265 650 7E-04
centigrade heat unit [mean]----------	0.000 526 2 ---	5.261 590 5E-04
centigrade heat unit [thermoc.]----------	0.000 526 9 ---	5.269 174 5E-04
centimeter gram-force ----------	10,197.162 ---	1.019 716 2E+04
cheval vapeur heure [France]----------	0.000 000 4 ---	3.776 726 7E-07
coal equivalent kilogram [UN, standard]----------	<<<	3.412 084 2E-08
coal equivalent metric ton [UN, standard]----------	<<<	3.412 084 2E-11
cubic centimeter atmosphere ----------	9.869 232 7 ---	9.869 232 7E+00
cubic foot atmosphere ----------	0.000 348 5 ---	3.485 286 6E-04
cubic foot of liquified petroleum gas [standard] ----------	0.000 000 4 ---	3.758 196 4E-07
cubic foot of natural gas [standard]----------	0.000 000 9 ---	9.197 939 7E-07
cubic meter atmosphere ----------	0.000 009 9 ---	9.869 232 7E-06
deuteron rest mass [atomic physics, eq. energy]----------	>>>	3.327 714 8E+09
dyne centimeter ----------	>>>	1.000 000 0E+07
electron rest mass [atomic physics, eq. energy]----------	>>>	1.221 432 1E+13
electronvolt ----------	>>>	6.241 506 4E+18
erg ----------	>>>	1.000 000 0E+07
foot pound-force ----------	0.737 562 2 ---	7.375 621 5E-01
foot poundal----------	23.730 36 ---	2.373 036 0E+01
frigorie [France]----------	0.000 238 9 ---	2.389 029 6E-04
gallon of automotive gasoline [US, liquid]----------	<<<	7.589 556 8E-09
gallon of aviation gasoline [US, liquid]----------	<<<	7.589 556 8E-09
gallon of diesel oil [US, liquid]----------	<<<	6.825 006 8E-09
gallon of distillate #2 fuel oil [US, liquid]----------	<<<	6.825 006 8E-09

joule [energy] (continued)   <energy>

Convert To	Standard	Scientific
gallon of jet fuel, kerosene type [US, liquid]	<<<	7.032 348 8E-09
gallon of jet fuel, naphtha type [US, liquid]	<<<	7.467 144 6E-09
gallon of kerosene [US, liquid]	<<<	7.032 348 8E-09
gallon of residual fuel oil [US, liquid]	<<<	6.327 512 0E-09
gram [atomic physics, eq. energy]	<<<	1.112 650 1E-14
gram calorie	0.238 903	2.389 029 6E-01
hartree [atomic physics, eq. energy]	>>>	2.293 710 4E+17
hertz [atomic physics, eq. energy]	>>>	1.509 189 0E+33
horsepower hour	0.000 000 4	3.725 061 4E-07
horsepower hour [metric]	0.000 000 4	3.776 726 7E-07
inch ounce-force	141.611 93	1.416 119 3E+02
inch pound-force	8.850 745 8	8.850 745 8E+00
joule [US, international]	0.999 818	9.998 180 3E-01
joule [US, legal, 1948]	0.999 983 5	9.999 835 0E-01
kayser [atomic physics, eq. energy]	>>>	5.034 112 5E+22
kelvin [atomic physics, eq. energy]	>>>	7.242 923 3E+22
kilocalorie [I.T.]	0.000 238 8	2.388 459 0E-04
kilocalorie [mean]	0.000 238 7	2.386 623 5E-04
kilocalorie [thermoc.]	0.000 239	2.390 057 4E-04
kilogram [atomic physics, eq. energy]	<<<	1.112 650 1E-17
kilogram calorie [15 °C, NBS, 1939]	0.000 238 9	2.389 029 6E-04
kilogram of water [evaporated from and at 100 °C]	0.000 000 4	4.430 660 2E-07
kilogram of water [heated from 16.7 °C to 100 °C]	0.000 002 9	2.868 188 3E-06
kilogram square meter/square second	1	1.000 000 0E+00
kilopond meter	0.101 971 6	1.019 716 2E-01
kiloton [metric, explosive energy]	<<<	2.390 057 4E-13
kilowatthour	0.000 000 3	2.777 777 8E-07
liter atmosphere	0.009 869 2	9.869 232 7E-03
megaerg	10	1.000 000 0E+01
megalerg	10	1.000 000 0E+01
meter kilogram-force	0.101 971 6	1.019 716 2E-01
muon rest mass [atomic physics, eq. energy]	>>>	5.907 251 1E+10
neutron rest mass [atomic physics, eq. energy]	>>>	6.642 970 1E+09
newton meter	1	1.000 000 0E+00
pferdestarkenstunde [Germany]	0.000 000 4	3.776 726 7E-07
pound of water [evaporated from and at 100 °C]	0.000 000 1	9.767 933 6E-07
pound of water [heated from 16.7 °C to 100 °C]	0.000 006 3	6.323 272 6E-06
proton rest mass [atomic physics, eq. energy]	>>>	6.652 126 8E+09
q-unit	<<<	9.478 171 2E-22
quad	<<<	9.478 171 2E-19
radian/second [atomic physics, eq. energy]	<<<	1.054 572 7E-34
rydberg [atomic physics, eq. energy]	>>>	4.587 366 4E+17
therm [EEC]	<<<	9.478 171 2E-09
therm [US]	<<<	9.480 434 3E-09
thermie [France]	0.000 000 2	2.389 029 6E-07
ton of anthracite coal [short]	<<<	3.733 572 3E-11
ton of bituminous coal [short]	<<<	3.836 709 6E-11
watthour	0.000 277 8	2.777 777 8E-04
wattsecond	1	1.000 000 0E+00

joule [quantity of light]   <quantity of light>

Convert To	Standard	Scientific
candela second steradian	683	6.830 000 0E+02
lumen hour	0.189 722 2	1.897 222 2E-01
lumen second	683	6.830 000 0E+02
lux second square meter	683	6.830 000 0E+02
talbot	683	6.830 000 0E+02
wattsecond [green light at 100% efficiency]	0.997 080 3	9.970 802 9E-01
wattsecond [light at 540 THz]	1	1.000 000 0E+00
wattsecond [light at 5550 angstrom]	1.004 411 8	1.004 411 8E+00

joule [US, international]   <energy>

Convert To	Standard	Scientific
Btu [I.T.]	0.000 948	9.479 896 2E-04
calorie [I.T.]	0.238 889 4	2.388 893 7E-01

Convert From	Standard	<Type of Unit>
Convert To		Scientific

	Standard	Scientific
calorie [kilogram, I.T.]	0.000 238 9	2.388 893 7E-04
calorie [mean]	0.238 705 8	2.387 057 0E-01
calorie [thermoc.]	0.239 049 2	2.390 492 4E-01
cubic centimeter atmosphere	9.871 028 9	9.871 028 9E+00
cubic foot atmosphere	0.000 348 6	3.485 920 9E-04
foot pound-force	0.737 696 4	7.376 963 9E-01
foot poundal	23.734 679	2.373 467 9E+01
gram calorie	0.238 946 4	2.389 464 4E-01
inch ounce-force	141.637 71	1.416 377 1E+02
inch pound-force	8.852 356 6	8.852 356 6E+00
joule	1.000 182	1.000 182 0E+00
joule [US, legal, 1948]	1.000 165 5	1.000 165 5E+00
kilogram square meter/square second	1.000 182	1.000 182 0E+00
kilopond meter	0.101 990 2	1.019 901 8E-01
liter atmosphere	0.009 871	9.871 028 9E-03
megaerg	10.001 82	1.000 182 0E+01
megalerg	10.001 82	1.000 182 0E+01
meter kilogram-force	0.101 990 2	1.019 901 8E-01
millijoule	1,000.182	1.000 182 0E+03
newton meter	1.000 182	1.000 182 0E+00
watthour	0.000 277 8	2.778 283 3E-04
wattsecond	1.000 182	1.000 182 0E+00

joule [US, legal, 1948] <energy>

	Standard	Scientific
Btu [I.T.]	0.000 947 8	9.478 327 6E-04
calorie [I.T.]	0.238 849 8	2.388 498 4E-01
calorie [kilogram, I.T.]	0.000 238 8	2.388 498 4E-04
calorie [mean]	0.238 666 3	2.386 662 8E-01
calorie [thermoc.]	0.239 009 7	2.390 096 8E-01
cubic centimeter atmosphere	9.869 395 5	9.869 395 5E+00
cubic foot atmosphere	0.000 348 5	3.485 344 1E-04
dyne centimeter	>>>	1.000 016 5E+07
erg	>>>	1.000 016 5E+07
foot pound-force	0.737 574 3	7.375 743 2E-01
foot poundal	23.730 752	2.373 075 2E+01
gram calorie	0.238 906 9	2.389 069 0E-01
hectojoule	0.010 000 2	1.000 016 5E-02
inch ounce-force	141.614 27	1.416 142 7E+02
inch pound-force	8.850 891 8	8.850 891 8E+00
joule	1.000 016 5	1.000 016 5E+00
joule [US, international]	0.999 834 5	9.998 345 3E-01
kilogram square meter/square second	1.000 016 5	1.000 016 5E+00
kilopond meter	0.101 973 3	1.019 733 0E-01
liter atmosphere	0.009 869 4	9.869 395 5E-03
megaerg	10.000 165	1.000 016 5E+01
megalerg	10.000 165	1.000 016 5E+01
meter kilogram-force	0.101 973 3	1.019 733 0E-01
newton meter	1.000 016 5	1.000 016 5E+00
watthour	0.000 277 8	2.777 823 6E-04
wattsecond	1.000 016 5	1.000 016 5E+00

joule second <moment of momentum>

	Standard	Scientific
kilogram square meter/second	1	1.000 000 0E+00
newton meter second	1	1.000 000 0E+00
planck	1	1.000 000 0E+00
pound foot square/second	23.730 36	2.373 036 0E+01

joule second/square meter <mechanical impedance>

	Standard	Scientific
dyne second/centimeter	1,000	1.000 000 0E+03
kilogram-force second/meter	0.101 971 6	1.019 716 2E-01
newton second/meter	1	1.000 000 0E+00
pound-force second/foot	0.068 521 8	6.852 176 6E-02
poundal second/foot	2.204 622 6	2.204 622 6E+00

joule square meter/kilogram <total mass stopping power>

	Standard	Scientific
Btu square foot/pound [I.T.]	0.004 627 6	4.627 648 5E-03

Convert From Convert To	Standard	\<Type of Unit> Scientific
calorie square centimeter/gram [I.T.]	2.388 459	2.388 459 0E+00
joule/ampere		**\<magnetic flux>**
ampere henry	1	1.000 000 0E+00
gauss square centimeter	>>>	1.000 000 0E+08
maxwell	>>>	1.000 000 0E+08
statweber	0.003 335 6	3.335 641 0E-03
tesla square meter	1	1.000 000 0E+00
unit pole	7,957,747.54	7.957 747 5E+06
volt second	1	1.000 000 0E+00
weber	1	1.000 000 0E+00
joule/ampere square meter		**\<magnetic flux density>**
ampere henry/square meter	1	1.000 000 0E+00
electromagnetic unit of magnetic flux density [cgs system]	10,000	1.000 000 0E+04
gauss	10,000	1.000 000 0E+04
line/square centimeter [of magnetic force]	10,000	1.000 000 0E+04
maxwell/square meter	1	1.000 000 0E+00
newton/ampere meter	1	1.000 000 0E+00
tesla	1	1.000 000 0E+00
joule/coulomb		**\<electric potential>**
ampere ohm	1	1.000 000 0E+00
coulomb/farad	1	1.000 000 0E+00
statvolt	0.003 335 6	3.335 641 0E-03
volt	1	1.000 000 0E+00
watt/ampere	1	1.000 000 0E+00
joule/coulomb meter		**\<electric field strength>**
abvolt/centimeter	1,000,000	1.000 000 0E+06
volt/inch	0.025 4	2.540 000 0E-02
volt/meter	1	1.000 000 0E+00
watt/ampere meter	1	1.000 000 0E+00
joule/cubic meter		**\<energy density>**
Btu/cubic foot [I.T.]	0.000 026 8	2.683 919 2E-05
calorie/cubic centimeter [I.T.]	0.000 000 2	2.388 459 0E-07
dyne/square centimeter	10	1.000 000 0E+01
newton/square meter	1	1.000 000 0E+00
joule/cubic meter second		**\<heat release rate>**
Btu/cubic foot hour [I.T.]	0.096 621 1	9.662 109 1E-02
calorie/cubic centimeter second [I.T.]	0.000 000 2	2.388 459 0E-07
erg/cubic centimeter second	10	1.000 000 0E+01
kilocalorie/cubic meter hour [I.T.]	0.859 845 2	8.598 452 3E-01
watt/cubic meter	1	1.000 000 0E+00
joule/hour		**\<power>**
Btu/hour [I.T.]	0.000 947 8	9.478 171 2E-04
Btu/hour [thermoc.]	0.000 948 5	9.484 514 1E-04
calorie/hour [I.T.]	0.238 845 9	2.388 459 0E-01
calorie/hour [thermoc.]	0.239 005 7	2.390 057 4E-01
centigrade heat unit/hour [mean]	0.000 526 2	5.261 590 5E-04
cubic meter atmosphere/hour	9.869 232 7	9.869 232 7E+00
dyne centimeter/second	2,777.777 8	2.777 777 8E+03
erg/second	2,777.777 8	2.777 777 8E+03
foot pound-force/hour	0.737 562 2	7.375 621 5E-01
foot poundal/hour	23.730 36	2.373 036 0E+01
gram-force centimeter/second	2.832 545	2.832 545 0E+00
horsepower	0.000 000 4	3.725 061 4E-07
horsepower [metric]	0.000 000 4	3.776 726 7E-07
joule/minute	0.016 666 7	1.666 666 7E-02
kilocalorie/hour [I.T.]	0.000 238 8	2.388 459 0E-04
kilogram-force meter/hour	0.101 971 6	1.019 716 2E-01
kilopond meter/hour	0.101 971 6	1.019 716 2E-01
lumen [green light at 100% efficiency]	0.190 277 8	1.902 777 8E-01
lumen [green light at 5,550 angstrom]	0.188 888 9	1.888 888 9E-01
newton meter/hour	1	1.000 000 0E+00

Convert From / Convert To	Standard	Scientific	<Type of Unit>

	Standard	Scientific
pound square foot/cubic second	0.006 591 8	6.591 766 8E–03
volt ampere	0.000 277 8	2.777 777 8E–04
watt	0.000 277 8	2.777 777 8E–04

joule/kelvin — <specific heat>

	Standard	Scientific
Btu/°F [I.T.]	0.000 526 6	5.265 650 7E–04
Btu/°F [thermoc.]	0.000 526 9	5.269 175 8E–04
calorie/°C [I.T.]	0.238 845 9	2.388 459 0E–01
calorie/°C [thermoc.]	0.239 005 7	2.390 057 4E–01
clausius	0.000 238 8	2.388 459 0E–04
erg/kelvin	>>>	1.000 000 0E+07
kilocalorie/°C [I.T.]	0.000 238 8	2.388 459 0E–04
kilocalorie/°C [thermoc.]	0.000 239	2.390 057 4E–04

joule/kilogram — <absorbed dose>

	Standard	Scientific
gray	1	1.000 000 0E+00
rad	100	1.000 000 0E+02
rep	119.331 74	1.193 317 4E+02

joule/kilogram — <dose equivalent>

	Standard	Scientific
newton meter/kilogram	1	1.000 000 0E+00
sievert	1	1.000 000 0E+00
square meter/square second	1	1.000 000 0E+00

joule/kilogram — <specific thermodynamic energy>

	Standard	Scientific
Btu/pound [I.T.]	0.000 429 9	4.299 226 1E–04
Btu/pound [thermoc.]	0.000 430 2	4.302 103 3E–04
calorie/gram [I.T.]	0.000 238 8	2.388 459 0E–04
calorie/gram [thermoc.]	0.000 239	2.390 057 4E–04
electronvolt/gram	>>>	6.241 506 4E+15
erg/gram	10,000	1.000 000 0E+04
foot pound-force/pound	0.334 552 6	3.345 525 6E–01
kilogram-force meter/kilogram	0.101 971 6	1.019 716 2E–01
watt second/kilogram	1	1.000 000 0E+00

joule/kilogram kelvin — <specific heat capacity>

	Standard	Scientific
Btu/pound °F [I.T.]	0.000 238 8	2.388 459 0E–04
Btu/pound °F [thermoc.]	0.000 239	2.390 057 4E–04
calorie/gram °C [I.T.]	0.000 238 8	2.388 459 0E–04
calorie/gram °C [thermoc.]	0.000 239	2.390 057 4E–04
erg/gram °C	10,000	1.000 000 0E+04
foot pound-force/pound °F	0.185 862 5	1.858 625 4E–01
kilocalorie/kilogram °C [I.T.]	0.000 238 8	2.388 459 0E–04
kilocalorie/kilogram °C [thermoc.]	0.000 239	2.390 057 4E–04
kilogram-force meter/kilogram °C	0.101 971 6	1.019 716 2E–01
kilopond meter/kilogram °C	0.101 971 6	1.019 716 2E–01
mayer	0.001	1.000 000 0E–03

joule/kilogram second — <absorbed dose rate>

	Standard	Scientific
gray/second	1	1.000 000 0E+00
rad/second	100	1.000 000 0E+02
rep/second	119.331 74	1.193 317 4E+02

joule/meter — <force>

	Standard	Scientific
crinal	10	1.000 000 0E+01
dyne	100,000	1.000 000 0E+05
gram-force	101.971 621	1.019 716 2E+02
kilogram meter/square second	1	1.000 000 0E+00
newton	1	1.000 000 0E+00
ounce-force	3.596 943 1	3.596 943 1E+00
pascal square meter	1	1.000 000 0E+00
pond	101.971 621	1.019 716 2E+02
pound-force	0.224 808 9	2.248 089 4E–01
poundal	7.233 013 9	7.233 013 9E+00

joule/meter — <linear energy transfer>

	Standard	Scientific
Btu/foot [I.T.]	0.000 288 9	2.888 946 6E–04
electronvolt/meter	>>>	6.241 506 4E+18
kilocalorie/meter [I.T.]	0.000 238 8	2.388 459 0E–04

Convert From / Convert To	Standard	<Type of Unit> Scientific
joule/minute		<power>
Btu/hour [I.T.]	0.056 869	5.686 902 7E-02
Btu/hour [thermoc.]	0.056 907 1	5.690 708 5E-02
calorie/hour [I.T.]	14.330 754	1.433 075 4E+01
calorie/hour [thermoc.]	14.340 344	1.434 034 4E+01
centigrade heat unit/hour [mean]	0.031 569 5	3.156 954 3E-02
centiwatt	1.666 666 7	1.666 666 7E+00
cubic meter atmosphere/minute	9.869 232 7	9.869 232 7E+00
dyne centimeter/second	166,666.67	1.666 666 7E+05
erg/second	166,666.67	1.666 666 7E+05
foot pound-force/hour	44.253 729	4.425 372 9E+01
foot poundal/minute	23.730 36	2.373 036 0E+01
gram-force centimeter/second	169.952 7	1.699 527 0E+02
horsepower	0.000 022 4	2.235 036 8E-05
horsepower [metric]	0.000 022 7	2.266 036 0E-05
joule/hour	60	6.000 000 0E+01
kilocalorie/hour [I.T.]	0.014 330 8	1.433 075 4E-02
kilogram square meter/cubic second	0.016 666 7	1.666 666 7E-02
kilogram-force meter/hour	6.118 297 3	6.118 297 3E+00
kilopond meter/hour	6.118 297 3	6.118 297 3E+00
lumen [green light at 100% efficiency]	11.416 667	1.141 666 7E+01
lumen [green light at 5,550 angstrom]	11.333 334	1.133 333 4E+01
newton meter/minute	1	1.000 000 0E+00
pound square foot/cubic second	0.395 506	3.955 060 1E-01
volt ampere	0.016 666 7	1.666 666 7E-02
watt	0.016 666 7	1.666 666 7E-02
joule/mole		<molar energy>
kilojoule/mole	0.001	1.000 000 0E-03
millijoule/mole	1,000	1.000 000 0E+03
joule/mole kelvin		<molar entropy>
kilojoule/mole kelvin	0.001	1.000 000 0E-03
millijoule/mole kelvin	1,000	1.000 000 0E+03
joule/second		<power>
Btu/hour [I.T.]	3.412 141 6	3.412 141 6E+00
Btu/hour [thermoc.]	3.414 425 1	3.414 425 1E+00
calorie/minute [I.T.]	14.330 754	1.433 075 4E+01
calorie/minute [thermoc.]	14.340 344	1.434 034 4E+01
centigrade heat unit/hour [mean]	1.894 172 6	1.894 172 6E+00
cubic meter atmosphere/second	9.869 232 7	9.869 232 7E+00
dyne centimeter/second	>>>	1.000 000 0E+07
erg/second	>>>	1.000 000 0E+07
foot pound-force/minute	44.253 729	4.425 372 9E+01
foot poundal/second	23.730 36	2.373 036 0E+01
gram-force centimeter/second	10,197.162	1.019 716 2E+04
horsepower	0.001 341	1.341 022 1E-03
horsepower [metric]	0.001 359 6	1.359 621 6E-03
joule/minute	60	6.000 000 0E+01
kilocalorie/hour [I.T.]	0.859 845 2	8.598 452 3E-01
kilogram square meter/cubic second	1	1.000 000 0E+00
kilogram-force meter/minute	6.118 297 3	6.118 297 3E+00
kilopond meter/minute	6.118 297 3	6.118 297 3E+00
lumen [green light at 100% efficiency]	685	6.850 000 0E+02
lumen [green light at 5,550 angstrom]	680.000 02	6.800 000 2E+02
newton meter/second	1	1.000 000 0E+00
pferdestarke [Germany]	0.001 359 6	1.359 621 6E-03
poncelet [France]	0.001 019 7	1.019 716 2E-03
pound square foot/cubic second	23.730 36	2.373 036 0E+01
ton of refrigeration	0.000 284 3	2.843 451 4E-04
volt ampere	1	1.000 000 0E+00
watt	1	1.000 000 0E+00
joule/second cubic meter kelvin		<heat transfer coefficient>
Btu/hour cubic foot °F [I.T.]	0.053 678 4	5.367 838 4E-02

kilocalorie/hour cubic meter °C [I.T.]	0.859 845 2	8.598 452 3E-01
watt/cubic meter kelvin	1	1.000 000 0E+00
joule/second kelvin		**<thermal conductance>**
Btu/second °F [I.T.]	0.000 526 6	5.265 650 7E-04
calorie/second °C [I.T.]	0.238 845 9	2.388 459 0E-01
watt/kelvin	1	1.000 000 0E+00
joule/second meter kelvin		**<thermal conductivity>**
Btu foot/hour square foot °F [I.T.]	0.577 789 3	5.777 893 2E-01
Btu foot/hour square foot °F [thermoc.]	0.578 176 1	5.781 761 3E-01
Btu inch/hour square foot °F [I.T.]	6.933 471 8	6.933 471 8E+00
Btu inch/hour square foot °F [thermoc.]	6.938 113 5	6.938 113 5E+00
Btu/hour foot °F [I.T.]	0.577 789 3	5.777 893 2E-01
Btu/hour foot °F [thermoc.]	0.578 176 1	5.781 761 3E-01
calorie centimeter/hour square centimeter °C [I.T.]	8.598 452 3	8.598 452 3E+00
kilocalorie/hour meter °C [I.T.]	0.859 845 2	8.598 452 3E-01
watt/foot °C	0.304 8	3.048 000 0E-01
watt/meter kelvin	1	1.000 000 0E+00
joule/second square meter		**<heat flux density>**
Btu/day square foot [I.T.]	7.607 959 9	7.607 959 9E+00
Btu/day square foot [thermoc.]	7.613 051 3	7.613 051 3E+00
calorie/day square centimeter [I.T.]	2.063 628 5	2.063 628 5E+00
calorie/day square centimeter [thermoc.]	2.065 009 6	2.065 009 6E+00
erg/second square centimeter	1,000	1.000 000 0E+03
watt/square foot	0.092 903	9.290 304 0E-02
watt/square meter	1	1.000 000 0E+00
joule/second square meter kelvin		**<heat transfer coefficient>**
Btu/day square foot °F [I.T.]	4.226 644 4	4.226 644 4E+00
calorie/hour square centimeter °C [I.T.]	0.085 984 5	8.598 452 3E-02
watt/square meter °C	0.092 903	9.290 304 0E-02
watt/square meter kelvin	1	1.000 000 0E+00
joule/second steradian		**<radiant intensity>**
erg/second steradian	>>> 1.000 000 0E+07
watt/steradian	1	1.000 000 0E+00
joule/second steradian square meter		**<radiance>**
erg/second steradian square centimeter	1,000	1.000 000 0E+03
watt/steradian square meter	1	1.000 000 0E+00
joule/square ampere		**<electric inductance>**
abhenry	>>> 1.000 000 0E+09
henry	1	1.000 000 0E+00
ohm second	1	1.000 000 0E+00
stathenry	<<< 1.112 650 1E-12
volt second/ampere	1	1.000 000 0E+00
weber/ampere	1	1.000 000 0E+00
joule/square meter		**<energy fluence>**
Btu/square foot [I.T.]	0.000 088 1	8.805 509 2E-05
Btu/square foot [thermoc.]	0.000 088 1	8.811 402 0E-05
calorie/square centimeter [15 °C, CIPM, 1950]	0.000 023 9	2.389 200 8E-05
calorie/square centimeter [I.T.]	0.000 023 9	2.388 459 0E-05
calorie/square centimeter [thermoc.]	0.000 023 9	2.390 057 4E-05
dyne/centimeter	1,000	1.000 000 0E+03
erg/square centimeter	1,000	1.000 000 0E+03
kilocalorie/square meter [I.T.]	0.000 238 8	2.388 459 0E-04
kilocalorie/square meter [thermoc.]	0.000 239	2.390 057 4E-04
langley [15 °C, CIPM, 1950]	0.000 023 9	2.389 200 8E-05
langley [I.T.]	0.000 023 9	2.388 459 0E-05
langley [thermoc.]	0.000 023 9	2.390 057 4E-05
newton/meter	1	1.000 000 0E+00
jow [India]		**<length, special - see page 29>**
centimeter	0.63	6.300 000 0E-01
juchart [Switzerland]		**<area, special - see page 29>**
are	36	3.600 000 0E+01

| Convert From | | <Type of Unit> |
| Convert To | Standard | Scientific |

juchert [Germany]
are --- 34.073 ---- 3.407 300 0E+01 `<area, special - see page 29>`

juger [Rome, ancient]
hectare -- 0.252 ---- 2.520 000 0E-01 `<area, special - see page 29>`

jugerum [Rome, ancient]
hectare --- 0.253 5 ---- 2.535 000 0E-01 `<area, special - see page 29>`

jumba [Malacca]
meter --- 3.658 ---- 3.658 000 0E+00 `<length, special - see page 29>`

jumfru [Sweden]
liter -- 0.082 ---- 8.200 000 0E-02 `<volume, special - see page 29>`

jungbo [Japan]
meter -- 109.09 ---- 1.090 900 0E+02 `<length, special - see page 29>`

jungbo [Japan]
hectare --- 0.991 7 ---- 9.917 000 0E-01 `<area, special - see page 29>`

jungbo [North Korea]
hectare --- 0.991 7 ---- 9.917 000 0E-01 `<area, special - see page 29>`

jungbo [South Korea]
hectare --- 0.991 7 ---- 9.917 000 0E-01 `<area, special - see page 29>`

jungfru [Sweden]
liter ------------------------------------- 0.081 784 8 ---- 8.178 480 0E-02 `<volume, special - see page 29>`

ka [Laos]
milligram ------------------------------------- 937.5 ---- 9.375 000 0E+02 `<mass, special - see page 29>`

kab [Babylon, ancient]
liter -- 2 ---- 2.000 000 0E+00 `<volume, special - see page 29>`

kab [Hebrew, ancient]
liter -- 1.3 ---- 1.300 000 0E+00 `<volume, special - see page 29>`

kabda [Egypt]
centimeter -------------------------------------- 16.1 ---- 1.610 000 0E+01 `<length, special - see page 29>`

kabellangd [Sweden]
meter --- 178.141 ---- 1.781 410 0E+02 `<length, special - see page 29>`

kabellengte [Netherlands, nautical]
meter --- 225 ---- 2.250 000 0E+02 `<length, special - see page 29>`

kabiet [Laos]
millimeter --------------------------------------- 4.167 ---- 4.167 000 0E+00 `<length, special - see page 29>`

kabiet [Thailand]
centimeter --------------------------------- 0.520 833 3 ---- 5.208 333 3E-01 `<length, special - see page 29>`

kabiet louang [Laos]
millimeter ---------------------------------- 5.208 333 ---- 5.208 333 0E+00 `<length, special - see page 29>`

kada [Yemen]
liter --- 40 ---- 4.000 000 0E+01 `<volume, special - see page 29>`

kadah [Egypt]
liter -- 2.062 5 ---- 2.062 500 0E+00 `<volume, special - see page 29>`

kadah [Sudan]
liter -- 2.06 ---- 2.060 000 0E+00 `<volume, special - see page 29>`

kadastral hold [Hungary]
are --- 1.422 ---- 1.422 000 0E+00 `<area, special - see page 29>`

kahun [India, grain]
kilogram --------------------------------------- 1,318.17 ---- 1.318 170 0E+03 `<mass, special - see page 29>`

kaila [Tanzania]
kilogram -- 2.722 ---- 2.722 000 0E+00 `<mass, special - see page 29>`

kairi [Japan]
kilometer -- 1.852 ---- 1.852 000 0E+00 `<length, special - see page 29>`

kala [Morocco, Tangier]
centimeter --------------------------------------- 55.9 ---- 5.590 000 0E+01 `<length, special - see page 29>`

| Convert From | | **\<Type of Unit\>** |
Convert To	Standard	Scientific

kala [Morocco]
meter -- 0.558 8 --- 5.588 000 0E−01 \<length, special - see page 29\>

kalad [Ethiopia] \<area, special - see page 29\>
hectare --40 --- 4.000 000 0E+01

kaledje [Egypt, ancient] \<volume, special - see page 29\>
liter -- 2.06 --- 2.060 000 0E+00

kalong [Laos] \<volume, special - see page 29\>
liter --20 --- 2.000 000 0E+01

kalvar [Persia] \<mass, special - see page 29\>
kilogram --- 594.2 --- 5.942 000 0E+02

kam [Laos] \<length, special - see page 29\>
centimeter--10 --- 1.000 000 0E+01

kam louang [Laos] \<length, special - see page 29\>
centimeter--12.5 --- 1.250 000 0E+01

kam meu [Thailand] \<volume, special - see page 29\>
liter -- 0.125 --- 1.250 000 0E−01

kama [Morocco, Tangier] \<length, special - see page 29\>
centimeter--127 --- 1.270 000 0E+02

kambeh [Iraq, ancient] \<mass, special - see page 29\>
milligram -- 48.75 --- 4.875 000 0E+01

kamha [Egypt] \<mass, special - see page 29\>
gram -- 0.048 75 --- 4.875 000 0E−02

kamha [Iraq, ancient] \<mass, special - see page 29\>
milligram -- 48.75 --- 4.875 000 0E+01

kamha [Turkey] \<mass, special - see page 29\>
milligram -- 50.1 --- 5.010 000 0E+01

kamian [Poland] \<mass, special - see page 29\>
kilogram --- 10.137 6 --- 1.013 760 0E+01

kamian [Russia] \<mass, special - see page 29\>
kilogram --- 10.237 81 --- 1.023 781 0E+01

kamlah [Egypt] \<mass, special - see page 29\>
kilogram --- 74.88 --- 7.488 000 0E+01

kamme [Japan] \<mass, special - see page 29\>
kilogram --- 3.75 --- 3.750 000 0E+00

kan [Brunei] \<mass, special - see page 29\>
kilogram --- 0.605 --- 6.050 000 0E−01

kan [China] \<mass, special - see page 29\>
kilogram --- 0.5 --- 5.000 000 0E−01

kan [Finland] \<volume, special - see page 29\>
liter -- 1.994 2 --- 1.994 200 0E+00

kan [Hong Kong] \<mass, special - see page 29\>
kilogram --- 0.605 --- 6.050 000 0E−01

kan [Indonesia] \<mass, special - see page 29\>
kilogram --- 0.618 --- 6.180 000 0E−01

kan [Japan] \<mass, special - see page 29\>
kilogram --- 3.75 --- 3.750 000 0E+00

kan [Malaysia] \<mass, special - see page 29\>
kilogram --- 0.605 --- 6.050 000 0E−01

kan [Netherlands] \<volume, special - see page 29\>
liter -- 1 --- 1.000 000 0E+00

kan [Singapore] \<mass, special - see page 29\>
kilogram --- 0.605 --- 6.050 000 0E−01

kan [South Korea] \<mass, special - see page 29\>
kilogram --- 0.6 --- 6.000 000 0E−01

kan [Thailand]
kilogram ———————————————————— <mass, special - see page 29>
———————————— 0.6 ——— 6.000 000 0E−01

kanahn [Thailand]
liter ——————————————————————— <volume, special - see page 29>
————————————— 1 ——— 1.000 000 0E+00

kanal [India]
are ————————————————————————— <area, special - see page 29>
———————————— 26.756 08 ——— 2.675 608 0E+01

kanal [Pakistan]
square meter ——————————————————— <area, special - see page 29>
————————————— 505.86 ——— 5.058 600 0E+02

kancha [India]
gram ———————————————————————— <mass, special - see page 29>
———————————— 14.579 76 ——— 1.457 976 0E+01

kanchha [Bangladesh]
gram ———————————————————————— <mass, special - see page 29>
————————————— 14.58 ——— 1.458 000 0E+01

kande [Denmark]
liter ——————————————————————— <volume, special - see page 29>
————————————— 1.932 2 ——— 1.932 200 0E+00

kandi [Yemen]
kilogram ————————————————————— <mass, special - see page 29>
————————————— 304.8 ——— 3.048 000 0E+02

kandy [Burma]
tonne ——————————————————————— <mass, special - see page 29>
————————————— 8.165 ——— 8.165 000 0E+00

kandy [India]
kilogram ————————————————————— <mass, special - see page 29>
————————————— 254 ——— 2.540 000 0E+02

kanee [Pakistan]
hectare —————————————————————— <area, special - see page 29>
————————————— 0.161 9 ——— 1.619 000 0E−01

kaneh [Israel]
meter ——————————————————————— <length, special - see page 29>
————————————— 2.679 ——— 2.679 000 0E+00

kanna [South Africa]
liter ——————————————————————— <volume, special - see page 29>
————————————— 1.488 ——— 1.488 000 0E+00

kanna [Sweden]
liter ——————————————————————— <volume, special - see page 29>
————————————— 2.617 12 ——— 2.617 120 0E+00

kanne [Germany]
liter ——————————————————————— <volume, special - see page 29>
————————————— 1 ——— 1.000 000 0E+00

kanne [South Africa]
liter ——————————————————————— <volume, special - see page 29>
————————————— 1.488 ——— 1.488 000 0E+00

kannland [Sweden]
square meter ——————————————————— <area, special - see page 29>
————————————— 44.08 ——— 4.408 000 0E+01

kannu [Finland]
liter ——————————————————————— <volume, special - see page 29>
————————————— 2.62 ——— 2.620 000 0E+00

kantaing [Cambodia]
liter ——————————————————————— <volume, special - see page 29>
————————————— 7.5 ——— 7.500 000 0E+00

kantar [Arab]
kilogram ————————————————————— <mass, special - see page 29>
————————————— 50.802 08 ——— 5.080 208 0E+01

kantar [Cyprus]
kilogram ————————————————————— <mass, special - see page 29>
————————————— 55.883 ——— 5.588 300 0E+01

kantar [Egypt, ancient]
kilogram ————————————————————— <mass, special - see page 29>
————————————— 44.93 ——— 4.493 000 0E+01

kantar [Ethiopia]
kilogram ————————————————————— <mass, special - see page 29>
————————————— 45.5 ——— 4.550 000 0E+01

kantar [Greece]
kilogram ————————————————————— <mass, special - see page 29>
————————————— 56.32 ——— 5.632 000 0E+01

kantar [Iraq, ancient]
kilogram ————————————————————— <mass, special - see page 29>
————————————— 44.928 ——— 4.492 800 0E+01

kantar [Jordan]
kilogram ————————————————————— <mass, special - see page 29>
————————————— 288.44 ——— 2.884 400 0E+02

kantar [Lebanon]
kilogram ————————————————————— <mass, special - see page 29>
————————————— 256.4 ——— 2.564 000 0E+02

Convert From Convert To	<Type of Unit> Standard	Scientific
kantar [Libya]	<mass, special - see page 29>	
kilogram	64.1	6.410 000 0E+01
kantar [Malta]	<mass, special - see page 29>	
kilogram	79.38	7.938 000 0E+01
kantar [Morocco]	<mass, special - see page 29>	
kilogram	100	1.000 000 0E+02
kantar [Saudi Arabia, ancient]	<mass, special - see page 29>	
kilogram	51.35	5.135 000 0E+01
kantar [Spanish North Africa]	<mass, special - see page 29>	
kilogram	50.75	5.075 000 0E+01
kantar [Sudan, large]	<mass, special - see page 29>	
kilogram	141.523	1.415 230 0E+02
kantar [Sudan]	<mass, special - see page 29>	
kilogram	44.928	4.492 800 0E+01
kantar [Syria]	<mass, special - see page 29>	
kilogram	256.5	2.565 000 0E+02
kantar [Turkey]	<mass, special - see page 29>	
kilogram	56.449 58	5.644 958 0E+01
kantar attari [Tunisia]	<mass, special - see page 29>	
kilogram	503.924	5.039 240 0E+02
kantar d'leppo [Cyprus]	<mass, special - see page 29>	
kilogram	228.610 6	2.286 106 0E+02
kantje [Germany]	<mass, special - see page 29>	
kilogram	74	7.400 000 0E+01
kapiza [Hebrew, ancient]	<volume, special - see page 29>	
cubic centimeter	1,098.782 7	1.098 782 7E+03
kappa [Finland]	<volume, special - see page 29>	
liter	5	5.000 000 0E+00
kappe [Sweden]	<volume, special - see page 29>	
liter	4.579 95	4.579 950 0E+00
kappland [Sweden]	<area, special - see page 29>	
square meter	154.263	1.542 630 0E+02
kara [Austria, jewels and pearls]	<mass, special - see page 29>	
gram	0.208	2.080 000 0E-01
kara [Batavia, jewels and pearls]	<mass, special - see page 29>	
gram	0.198	1.980 000 0E-01
kara [East India, jewels and pearls]	<mass, special - see page 29>	
gram	0.198	1.980 000 0E-01
kara [Germany, gold and silver]	<mass, special - see page 29>	
gram	10.62	1.062 000 0E+01
kara [Germany, jewels and pearls]	<mass, special - see page 29>	
gram	0.206	2.060 000 0E-01
kara [Netherlands, Amsterdan, jewels and pearls]	<mass, special - see page 29>	
gram	0.207	2.070 000 0E-01
kara [Switzerland, Bern, gold and silver]	<mass, special - see page 29>	
gram	10.2	1.020 000 0E+01
kara [UK, London, jewels and pearls]	<mass, special - see page 29>	
gram	0.209	2.090 000 0E-01
karaat [Netherlands]	<mass, special - see page 29>	
gram	0.257 339 7	2.573 397 0E-01
karam [Pakistan]	<length, special - see page 29>	
meter	1.676	1.676 000 0E+00
karat	<concentration, mass basis>	
gram/ton [-/UK, assay or assay, long]	1.361 111 1	1.361 111 1E+00
gram/ton [-/US, assay or assay, short]	1.215 277 8	1.215 277 8E+00
kilogram/kilogram	0.041 666 7	4.166 666 7E-02

	Standard	Scientific
ounce/ton [-/short]	1,333.333 33	1.333 333 3E+03
part/million	41,666.666 7	4.166 666 7E+04
pennyweight/ton [troy/long]	27,222.222 2	2.722 222 2E+04
percent	4.166 666 7	4.166 666 7E+00
pound/ton [-/long]	93.333 333 3	9.333 333 3E+01

karat [Austria, jewels and pearls] <mass, special - see page 29>
  gram — 0.208 — 2.080 000 0E-01

karat [Batavia, jewels and pearls] <mass, special - see page 29>
  gram — 0.198 — 1.980 000 0E-01

karat [East India, jewels and pearls] <mass, special - see page 29>
  gram — 0.198 — 1.980 000 0E-01

karat [Germany, gold and silver] <mass, special - see page 29>
  gram — 10.62 — 1.062 000 0E+01

karat [Germany, jewels and pearls] <mass, special - see page 29>
  gram — 0.206 — 2.060 000 0E-01

karat [Netherlands, Amsterdam, jewels and pearls] <mass, special - see page 29>
  gram — 0.207 — 2.070 000 0E-01

karat [Portugal, Lisbon, jewels] <mass, special - see page 29>
  gram — 0.205 8 — 2.058 000 0E-01

karat [UK, London, jewels and pearls] <mass, special - see page 29>
  gram — 0.209 — 2.090 000 0E-01

karch [Austria] <mass, special - see page 29>
  kilogram — 224 — 2.240 000 0E+02

kard [Morocco] <volume, special - see page 29>
  liter — 10 — 1.000 000 0E+01

karsha [India, ancient] <mass, special - see page 29>
  gram — 9.92 — 9.920 000 0E+00

karshapana [Hindu, ancient, copper] <mass, special - see page 29>
  gram — 9.92 — 9.920 000 0E+00

kartocc [Malta, beer, wine and spirits] <volume, special - see page 29>
  liter — 1.136 — 1.136 000 0E+00

kartos [Cyprus] <volume, special - see page 29>
  liter — 5.11 — 5.110 000 0E+00

karvar [Iran] <mass, special - see page 29>
  kilogram — 296.934 — 2.969 340 0E+02

kasaba [Egypt] <length, special - see page 29>
  meter — 3.55 — 3.550 000 0E+00

kasaba hakimiyya [Egypt] <length, special - see page 29>
  meter — 3.85 — 3.850 000 0E+00

kasbu [Iraq, ancient] <length, special - see page 29>
  kilometer — 21.3 — 2.130 000 0E+01

kasm [Ethiopia] <mass, special - see page 29>
  kilogram — 3.9 — 3.900 000 0E+00

kassaba [Egypt] <length, special - see page 29>
  meter — 3.55 — 3.550 000 0E+00

kassabah [Egypt] <length, special - see page 29>
  meter — 3.55 — 3.550 000 0E+00

kassabe [Syria] <area, special - see page 29>
  square meter — 23.814 — 2.381 400 0E+01

kat [Egypt] <mass, special - see page 29>
  gram — 9.331 043 — 9.331 043 0E+00

katang [Cambodia, dry] <volume, special - see page 29>
  liter — 7.5 — 7.500 000 0E+00

katastarsko jutro [Yugoslavia] <area, special - see page 29>
  hectare — 0.575 5 — 5.755 000 0E-01

katasztralis hold [Hungary]
hectare — <area, special - see page 29>
0.575 464 --- 5.754 640 0E−01

katha [Bangladesh]
square meter — <area, special - see page 29>
67.4 --- 6.740 000 0E+01

kathouah [Iraq, ancient]
meter — <length, special - see page 29>
1.9 --- 1.900 000 0E+00

kati [Brunei]
kilogram — <mass, special - see page 29>
0.605 --- 6.050 000 0E−01

kati [Burma]
gram — <mass, special - see page 29>
544 --- 5.440 000 0E+02

kati [China]
kilogram — <mass, special - see page 29>
0.5 --- 5.000 000 0E−01

kati [Hong Kong]
kilogram — <mass, special - see page 29>
0.605 --- 6.050 000 0E−01

kati [Indonesia]
kilogram — <mass, special - see page 29>
0.618 --- 6.180 000 0E−01

kati [Japan]
kilogram — <mass, special - see page 29>
0.6 --- 6.000 000 0E−01

kati [Malaysia]
kilogram — <mass, special - see page 29>
0.605 --- 6.050 000 0E−01

kati [North Borneo]
gram — <mass, special - see page 29>
604.789 9 --- 6.047 899 0E+02

kati [Sarawak]
gram — <mass, special - see page 29>
604.789 8 --- 6.047 898 0E+02

kati [Singapore]
kilogram — <mass, special - see page 29>
0.605 --- 6.050 000 0E−01

kati [South Korea]
kilogram — <mass, special - see page 29>
0.6 --- 6.000 000 0E−01

kati [Thailand]
kilogram — <mass, special - see page 29>
0.6 --- 6.000 000 0E−01

kattha [Nepal]
square meter — <area, special - see page 29>
338.57 --- 3.385 700 0E+02

katti [Brunei]
kilogram — <mass, special - see page 29>
0.605 --- 6.050 000 0E−01

katti [China]
kilogram — <mass, special - see page 29>
0.5 --- 5.000 000 0E−01

katti [Hong Kong]
kilogram — <mass, special - see page 29>
0.605 --- 6.050 000 0E−01

katti [Indonesia]
kilogram — <mass, special - see page 29>
0.618 --- 6.180 000 0E−01

katti [Japan]
kilogram — <mass, special - see page 29>
0.6 --- 6.000 000 0E−01

katti [Malaysia]
kilogram — <mass, special - see page 29>
0.605 --- 6.050 000 0E−01

katti [Singapore]
kilogram — <mass, special - see page 29>
0.605 --- 6.050 000 0E−01

katti [South Korea]
kilogram — <mass, special - see page 29>
0.6 --- 6.000 000 0E−01

katti [Thailand]
kilogram — <mass, special - see page 29>
0.6 --- 6.000 000 0E−01

kav [Hebrew, ancient]
liter — <volume, special - see page 29>
1.2 --- 1.200 000 0E+00

kavan [Cambodia]
cubic meter — <volume, special - see page 29>
0.152 --- 1.520 000 0E−01

kawtha [Burma] \<length, special - see page 29\>
kilometer --- 5.121 ---- 5.121 000 0E+00

kayser [atomic physics, eq. energy] \<energy\>
1/centimeter [atomic physics, eq. energy] -------------------- 1 ---- 1.000 000 0E+00
1/meter [atomic physics, eq. energy] ------------------------ 100 ---- 1.000 000 0E+02
atomic mass unit [unified, C-12, 1986, eq. energy] ---------- \<\<\< ---- 1.331 025 2E-13
electron rest mass [atomic physics, eq. energy] ------------- \<\<\< ---- 2.426 310 6E-10
electronvolt --- 0.000 124 ---- 1.239 842 4E-04
hartree [atomic physics, eq. energy] ------------------------ 0.000 004 6 ---- 4.556 335 3E-06
hertz [atomic physics, eq. energy] -------------------------- \>\>\> ---- 2.997 924 6E+10
joule --- \<\<\< ---- 1.986 447 5E-23
kelvin [atomic physics, eq. energy] -------------------------- 1.438 768 7 ---- 1.438 768 7E+00
kiloelectronvolt --- 0.000 000 1 ---- 1.239 842 4E-07
megaelectronvolt -- \<\<\< ---- 1.239 842 4E-10
muon rest mass [atomic physics, eq. energy] --------------- \<\<\< ---- 1.173 444 4E-12
neutron rest mass [atomic physics, eq. energy] ------------ \<\<\< ---- 1.319 591 1E-13
proton rest mass [atomic physics, eq. energy] ------------- \<\<\< ---- 1.321 410 0E-13
rydberg [atomic physics, eq. energy] ------------------------ 0.000 009 1 ---- 9.112 562 3E-06
watthour -- \<\<\< ---- 5.517 909 6E-27

kdt [Egypt, ancient] \<mass, special - see page 29\>
gram --- 9.1 ---- 9.100 000 0E+00

ke [China] \<mass, special - see page 29\>
gram --- 1 ---- 1.000 000 0E+00

keddah [Egypt] \<volume, special - see page 29\>
liter -- 2.06 ---- 2.060 000 0E-04

kedet [Egypt, ancient] \<mass, special - see page 29\>
gram --- 9.4 ---- 9.400 000 0E+00

keila [Egypt] \<volume, special - see page 29\>
liter -- 16.5 ---- 1.650 000 0E+01

keila [Libya] \<area, special - see page 29\>
hectare -- 0.32 ---- 3.200 000 0E-01

keila [Sudan] \<volume, special - see page 29\>
liter -- 16.5 ---- 1.650 000 0E+01

keila [Yemen] \<volume, special - see page 29\>
liter -- 36 ---- 3.600 000 0E+01

kejla [Malta] \<area, special - see page 29\>
square meter -- 18.735 ---- 1.873 500 0E+01

kela [Saudi Arabia] \<mass, special - see page 29\>
kilogram --- 3.175 3 ---- 3.175 300 0E+00

keleh [Egypt] \<volume, special - see page 29\>
liter -- 16.5 ---- 1.650 000 0E+01

kelvin \<thermodynamic temperature\>
°C --- kelvin − 273.15
°F --- [1.8 x (kelvin − 273.15)] + 32
degree Rankine --- 1.8 x kelvin
degree Reaumur [France] ----------------------------------- (kelvin − 273.15) / 1.25

kelvin [atomic physics, eq. energy] \<energy\>
1/centimeter [atomic physics, eq. energy] -------------------- 0.695 038 8 ---- 6.950 387 7E-01
1/meter [atomic physics, eq. energy] ------------------------ 69.503 877 ---- 6.950 387 7E+01
atomic mass unit [unified, C-12, 1986, eq. energy] ---------- \<\<\< ---- 9.251 141 4E-14
deuteron rest mass [atomic physics, eq. energy] ------------ \<\<\< ---- 4.594 436 0E-14
electron rest mass [atomic physics, eq. energy] ------------- \<\<\< ---- 1.686 379 9E-10
electronvolt --- 0.000 086 2 ---- 8.617 385 7E-05
gigaelectronvolt -- \<\<\< ---- 8.617 385 7E-14
hartree [atomic physics, eq. energy] ------------------------ 0.000 003 2 ---- 3.166 829 7E-06
hertz [atomic physics, eq. energy] -------------------------- \>\>\> ---- 2.083 673 8E+10
joule --- \<\<\< ---- 1.380 658 0E-23
kayser [atomic physics, eq. energy] -------------------------- 0.695 038 8 ---- 6.950 387 7E-01
kiloelectronvolt --- \<\<\< ---- 8.617 385 7E-08

Convert From Convert To	Standard	<Type of Unit> Scientific

Convert From / Convert To	Standard	Scientific
megaelectronvolt --<<< ---		8.617 385 7E-11
muon rest mass [atomic physics, eq. energy] ----------------------<<< ---		8.155 893 5E-13
neutron rest mass [atomic physics, eq. energy] -------------------<<< ---		9.171 669 8E-14
proton rest mass [atomic physics, eq. energy] --------------------<<< ---		9.184 312 1E-14
rydberg [atomic physics, eq. energy] ------------------------ 0.000 006 3		6.333 584 1E-06
watthour --<<< ---		3.835 161 1E-27

kelvin/kilowatt   \<thermal resistance\>

	Standard	Scientific
hour °C/kilocalorie [-/ I.T.] ----------------------------------- 0.001 163		1.163 000 0E-03
hour °F/Btu [-/ I.T.] -- 0.000 527 5		5.275 279 3E-04
kelvin/watt --- 0.001		1.000 000 0E-03
second °C/calorie [-/ I.T.] --------------------------------- 0.004 186 8		4.186 800 0E-03

kelvin/meter   \<geothermal gradient\>

	Standard	Scientific
°C/meter -- 1		1.000 000 0E+00
°F/foot --- 0.548 64		5.486 400 0E-01

kelvin/watt   \<thermal resistance\>

	Standard	Scientific
°C/kilowatt -- 1,000		1.000 000 0E+03
°C/watt -- 1		1.000 000 0E+00
hour °C/kilocalorie [-/ I.T.] ---------------------------------- 1.163		1.163 000 0E+00
hour °F/Btu [-/ I.T.] -- 0.527 527 9		5.275 279 3E-01
kelvin/kilowatt --- 1,000		1.000 000 0E+03
second °C/calorie [-/ I.T.] ------------------------------------ 4.186 8		4.186 800 0E+00
second kelvin/joule -- 1		1.000 000 0E+00

keml [Egypt]   \<mass, special - see page 29\>
kilogram --- 249.6 --- 2.496 000 0E+02

kemple [UK, straw]   \<mass, special - see page 29\>
kilogram --- 199.581 --- 1.995 810 0E+02

ken [Japan]   \<length, special - see page 29\>
meter --- 1.818 --- 1.818 000 0E+00

ken [South Korea]   \<length, special - see page 29\>
meter --- 1.818 --- 1.818 000 0E+00

ken [Thailand]   \<length, special - see page 29\>
meter --- 1.016 --- 1.016 000 0E+00

kend [Ethiopia]   \<length, special - see page 29\>
meter --- 0.5 --- 5.000 000 0E-01

kental [Turkey]   \<mass, special - see page 29\>
kilogram -- 17.96 --- 1.796 000 0E+01

kerad kamel [Egypt]   \<area, special - see page 29\>
are --- 1.75 --- 1.750 000 0E+00

kerat [Turkey]   \<length, special - see page 29\>
centimeter -------------------------------------- 2.857 5 --- 2.857 500 0E+00

kette [Germany]   \<length, special - see page 29\>
meter --- 10 --- 1.000 000 0E+01

kettle [Sierra Leone]   \<volume, special - see page 29\>
liter -- 9.99 --- 9.990 000 0E+00

keun [Brunei]   \<mass, special - see page 29\>
kilogram -- 0.605 --- 6.050 000 0E-01

keun [China]   \<mass, special - see page 29\>
kilogram -- 0.5 --- 5.000 000 0E-01

keun [Hong Kong]   \<mass, special - see page 29\>
kilogram -- 0.605 --- 6.050 000 0E-01

keun [Indonesia]   \<mass, special - see page 29\>
kilogram -- 0.618 --- 6.180 000 0E-01

keun [Japan]   \<mass, special - see page 29\>
kilogram -- 0.6 --- 6.000 000 0E-01

keun [Malaysia]   \<mass, special - see page 29\>
kilogram -- 0.605 --- 6.050 000 0E-01

keun [Singapore]   <mass, special - see page 29>
  kilogram --0.605----6.050 000 0E-01

keun [South Korea]   <mass, special - see page 29>
  kilogram ---0.6----6.000 000 0E-01

keun [Thailand]   <mass, special - see page 29>
  kilogram ---0.6----6.000 000 0E-01

keup [Thailand]   <length, special - see page 29>
  centimeter--25----2.500 000 0E+01

kfiz [Tunisia, cereals]   <volume, special - see page 29>
  hectoliter ---5.819----5.819 000 0E+00

khakoon [India]   <volume, special - see page 29>
  hectoliter --17.4----1.740 000 0E+01

khalad [Ethiopia]   <length, special - see page 29>
  meter---65----6.500 000 0E+01

khanan [Laos]   <volume, special - see page 29>
  liter--5----5.000 000 0E+00

khanan louang [Laos]   <volume, special - see page 29>
  liter--1----1.000 000 0E+00

khandi [Oman, cereals]   <mass, special - see page 29>
  kilogram --227----2.270 000 0E+02

khar [Egypt]   <volume, special - see page 29>
  liter---97.8----9.780 000 0E+01

kharouba [Egypt]   <volume, special - see page 29>
  liter---0.129----1.290 000 0E-01

kharrouba [Morocco]   <volume, special - see page 29>
  liter---40----4.000 000 0E+01

kharruba [Egypt]   <volume, special - see page 29>
  liter--0.128 91----1.289 100 0E-01

kharvar [Afghanistan]   <mass, special - see page 29>
  kilogram --565.28----5.652 800 0E+02

kharvar [Iran]   <mass, special - see page 29>
  kilogram --296.934----2.969 340 0E+02

kharwar [Afghanistan]   <mass, special - see page 29>
  kilogram --565.28----5.652 800 0E+02

kharwar [Iran]   <mass, special - see page 29>
  kilogram --300----3.000 000 0E+02

kharwar [Persia]   <mass, special - see page 29>
  kilogram --297----2.970 000 0E+02

khashkha [Pakistan]   <mass, special - see page 29>
  milligram---1.898----1.898 000 0E+00

khaskha [Pakistan]   <mass, special - see page 29>
  gram---0.189 840 6----1.898 406 0E-01

khat [Turkey]   <length, special - see page 29>
  centimeter---1----1.000 000 0E+00

khau [Vietnam]   <area, special - see page 29>
  square meter---0.16----1.600 000 0E-01

khedem [Morocco]   <area, special - see page 29>
  hectare--0.1----1.000 000 0E-01

khet [Egypt, ancient]   <length, special - see page 29>
  meter--52.4----5.240 000 0E+01

khluon chay [Cambodia]   <length, special - see page 29>
  millimeter---0.217----2.170 000 0E-01

khoinix [Greece, ancient]   <volume, special - see page 29>
  cubic centimeter---------------------------------1,078.78----1.078 780 0E+03

| Convert From | <Type of Unit> | |
Convert To	Standard	Scientific
khord [Afghanistan]	<mass, special - see page 29>	
gram	110.406	1.104 060 0E+02
khos aldan [Mongolia]	<length, special - see page 29>	
meter	3.2	3.200 000 0E+00
khou [Mongolia]	<mass, special - see page 29>	
milligram	3.75	3.750 000 0E+00
khoubhie [Syria]	<volume, special - see page 29>	
liter	6.5	6.500 000 0E+00
khous [Greece, ancient]	<volume, special - see page 29>	
liter	3.236 3	3.236 300 0E+00
khub [Laos]	<length, special - see page 29>	
centimeter	20	2.000 000 0E+01
khub louang [Laos]	<length, special - see page 29>	
centimeter	25	2.500 000 0E+01
khubi [Mongolia]	<length, special - see page 29>	
meter	57.6	5.760 000 0E+01
khup [Laos]	<length, special - see page 29>	
centimeter	20	2.000 000 0E+01
khup [Thailand]	<length, special - see page 29>	
centimeter	25	2.500 000 0E+01
khvat [Yugoslavia]	<length, special - see page 29>	
meter	1.896	1.896 000 0E+00
khwe [Burma]	<volume, special - see page 29>	
liter	20.457	2.045 700 0E+01
khwet [Burma]	<volume, special - see page 29>	
liter	1.279	1.279 000 0E+00
kibaba [Tanganyika]	<volume, special - see page 29>	
liter	1	1.000 000 0E+00
kibaba [Tanzania]	<volume, special - see page 29>	
liter	1	1.000 000 0E+00
kiccar [Hebrew, ancient]	<mass, special - see page 29>	
kilogram	38	3.800 000 0E+01
kikar [Hebrew, ancient]	<mass, special - see page 29>	
kilogram	49.11	4.911 000 0E+01
kikkar [Hebrew, ancient]	<mass, special - see page 29>	
kilogram	34.3	3.430 000 0E+01
kikkar [Iraq, ancient]	<mass, special - see page 29>	
kilogram	56.16	5.616 000 0E+01
kikkor [Hebrew, ancient]	<mass, special - see page 29>	
kilogram	38	3.800 000 0E+01
kila [Egypt, wheat]	<mass, special - see page 29>	
kilogram	12.5	1.250 000 0E+01
kila [Egypt]	<volume, special - see page 29>	
liter	16.5	1.650 000 0E+01
kila [Libya]	<area, special - see page 29>	
hectare	0.32	3.200 000 0E-01
kila [Sudan]	<volume, special - see page 29>	
liter	16.5	1.650 000 0E+01
kilah [Egypt]	<volume, special - see page 29>	
liter	16.5	1.650 000 0E+01
kilderkin [UK, liquid]	<volume>	
barrel [UK]	0.5	5.000 000 0E-01
cubic meter	0.081 829 6	8.182 962 0E-02
firkin [UK]	2	2.000 000 0E+00
gallon [UK, dry or liquid]	18	1.800 000 0E+01

Convert From	<Type of Unit>	
Convert To	Standard	Scientific

kilderkin [US, liquid]   **<volume>**

	Standard	Scientific
barrel [US, federal proof sprits]	0.45	4.500 000 0E-01
cubic inch	4,158	4.158 000 0E+03
cubic meter	0.068 137 4	6.813 741 2E-02
firkin [US]	2	2.000 000 0E+00
gallon [US, liquid]	18	1.800 000 0E+01

kile [Cyprus, rye]   **<mass, special - see page 29>**

	Standard	Scientific
kilogram	27.216	2.721 600 0E+01

kile [Cyprus, wheat]   **<mass, special - see page 29>**

	Standard	Scientific
kilogram	26.671	2.667 100 0E+01

kile [Cyprus]   **<volume, special - see page 29>**

	Standard	Scientific
liter	36.37	3.637 000 0E+01

kile [Greece]   **<volume, special - see page 29>**

	Standard	Scientific
liter	37.7	3.770 000 0E+01

kile [Libya]   **<volume, special - see page 29>**

	Standard	Scientific
liter	36	3.600 000 0E+01

kile [Turkey, barley]   **<mass, special - see page 29>**

	Standard	Scientific
kilogram	26	2.600 000 0E+01

kile [Turkey, oats]   **<mass, special - see page 29>**

	Standard	Scientific
kilogram	24	2.400 000 0E+01

kile [Turkey, rye]   **<mass, special - see page 29>**

	Standard	Scientific
kilogram	28	2.800 000 0E+01

kile [Turkey, wheat]   **<mass, special - see page 29>**

	Standard	Scientific
kilogram	30	3.000 000 0E+01

kileh [Cyprus]   **<volume, special - see page 29>**

	Standard	Scientific
liter	36.37	3.637 000 0E+01

kileh [Libya]   **<volume, special - see page 29>**

	Standard	Scientific
liter	36	3.600 000 0E+01

kileh [Turkey]   **<volume, special - see page 29>**

	Standard	Scientific
liter	37	3.700 000 0E+01

kilesi [Cyprus]   **<volume, special - see page 29>**

	Standard	Scientific
liter	36.37	3.637 000 0E+01

kilesi [Libya]   **<volume, special - see page 29>**

	Standard	Scientific
liter	36	3.600 000 0E+01

kilesi [Turkey]   **<volume, special - see page 29>**

	Standard	Scientific
liter	37	3.700 000 0E+01

kilo [Greece]   **<volume, special - see page 29>**

	Standard	Scientific
liter	100	1.000 000 0E+02

kilo [Romania]   **<volume, special - see page 29>**

	Standard	Scientific
liter	393.6	3.936 000 0E+02

kiloampere   **<electric current>**

	Standard	Scientific
abampere	100	1.000 000 0E+02
ampere	1,000	1.000 000 0E+03
electromagnetic unit of current [cgs system]	100	1.000 000 0E+02
statampere	>>>	2.997 924 6E+12

kiloampere square meter   **<electromagnetic moment>**

	Standard	Scientific
abampere square centimeter	1	1.000 000 0E+00
ampere square inch	1,550,003.1	1.550 003 1E+06
ampere square meter	1,000	1.000 000 0E+03
statampere square centimeter	>>>	2.997 924 6E+16

kiloampere/meter   **<magnetic field strength>**

	Standard	Scientific
abampere/centimeter	1	1.000 000 0E+00
ampere/inch	25.4	2.540 000 0E+01
ampere/meter	1,000	1.000 000 0E+03
oersted	12.566 370 6	1.256 637 1E+01
statampere/centimeter	>>>	2.997 924 6E+10

Convert From Convert To	Standard	<Type of Unit> Scientific
kiloampere/square meter		**<electric current density>**
ampere/square centimeter	0.1	1.000 000 0E-01
ampere/square inch	0.645 16	6.451 600 0E-01
ampere/square meter	1,000	1.000 000 0E+03
kilobar		**<pressure>**
atmosphere [standard]	986.923 27	9.869 232 7E+02
atmosphere [technical]	1,019.716 2	1.019 716 2E+03
bar	1,000	1.000 000 0E+03
foot of mercury [0 °C, by convention]	2,460.831 9	2.460 831 9E+03
foot of water [4 °C, by convention]	33,455.256	3.345 525 6E+04
kilogram-force/square millimeter	10.197 162	1.019 716 2E+01
kilopond/square millimeter	10.197 162	1.019 716 2E+01
kip/square inch	14.503 774	1.450 377 4E+01
newton/square millimeter	100	1.000 000 0E+02
pascal	>>>	1.000 000 0E+08
pound-force/square inch	14,503.774	1.450 377 4E+04
ton-force/square foot [long]	932.385 46	9.323 854 6E+02
ton-force/square inch [short]	7.251 886 9	7.251 886 9E+00
torr	750,061.68	7.500 616 8E+05
kilobecquerel		**<radionuclide activity>**
1/second	1,000	1.000 000 0E+03
becquerel	1,000	1.000 000 0E+03
curie	<<<	2.702 702 7E-08
rutherford	0.001	1.000 000 0E-03
kilobecquerel/cubic meter		**<radionuclide volume activity>**
becquerel/cubic meter	1,000	1.000 000 0E+03
curie/cubic meter	<<<	2.702 702 7E-08
rutherford/cubic meter	0.001	1.000 000 0E-03
kilobecquerel/kilogram		**<radionuclide specific activity>**
becquerel/kilogram	1,000	1.000 000 0E+03
curie/kilogram	<<<	2.702 702 7E-08
rutherford/kilogram	0.001	1.000 000 0E-03
kilocalorie [I.T.]		**<energy>**
Btu [I.T.]	3.968 320 7	3.968 320 7E+00
Btu [mean]	3.965 260 9	3.965 260 9E+00
Btu [thermoc.]	3.970 976 4	3.970 976 4E+00
calorie [I.T.]	1,000	1.000 000 0E+03
calorie [kilogram, I.T.]	1	1.000 000 0E+00
calorie [kilogram, mean]	0.999 231 5	9.992 315 1E-01
calorie [kilogram, thermoc.]	1.000 669 2	1.000 669 2E+00
calorie [nutritional]	1.000 669 2	1.000 669 2E+00
calorie [thermoc.]	1.000 669 2	1.000 669 2E+00
centigrade heat unit [I.T.]	2.204 622 6	2.204 622 6E+00
cheval vapeur heure [France]	0.001 581 2	1.581 239 9E-03
cubic centimeter atmosphere	41,320.503	4.132 050 3E+04
cubic foot atmosphere	1.459 219 8	1.459 219 8E+00
foot pound-force	3,088.025 2	3.088 025 2E+03
foot poundal	99,354.273	9.935 427 3E+04
frigorie [France]	1.000 238 9	1.000 238 9E+00
inch ounce-force	592,900.84	5.929 008 4E+05
inch pound-force	37,056.302	3.705 630 2E+04
joule	4,186.8	4.186 800 0E+03
kilocalorie [mean]	0.999 231 5	9.992 315 1E-01
kilocalorie [thermoc.]	1.000 669 2	1.000 669 2E+00
kilogram calorie [15 °C, NBS, 1939]	1.000 238 9	1.000 238 9E+00
liter atmosphere	41.320 503	4.132 050 3E+01
meter kilogram-force	426.934 78	4.269 347 8E+02
newton meter	4,186.8	4.186 800 0E+03
watthour	1.163	1.163 000 0E+00
wattsecond	4,186.8	4.186 800 0E+03
kilocalorie [mean]		**<energy>**
Btu [I.T.]	3.971 372 7	3.971 372 7E+00

Convert From	<Type of Unit>	
Convert To	Standard	Scientific
Btu [mean]	3.968 310 5	3.968 310 5E+00
Btu [thermoc.]	3.974 030 4	3.974 030 4E+00
calorie [I.T.]	1,000.769 1	1.000 769 1E+03
calorie [kilogram, I.T.]	1.000 769 1	1.000 769 1E+00
calorie [kilogram, mean]	1	1.000 000 0E+00
calorie [kilogram, thermoc.]	1.001 438 8	1.001 438 8E+00
calorie [mean]	1,000.	1.000 000 0E+03
calorie [nutritional]	1.001 438 8	1.001 438 8E+00
calorie [thermoc.]	1.001 438 8	1.001 438 8E+03
centigrade heat unit [15.6 °C]	2.207 104 4	2.207 104 4E+00
centigrade heat unit [mean]	2.204 616 9	2.204 616 9E+00
centimeter gram-force	>>>	4.272 631 3E+07
cubic centimeter atmosphere	41,352.282	4.135 228 2E+04
cubic foot atmosphere	1.460 342 1	1.460 342 1E+00
foot pound-force	3,090.400 2	3.090 400 2E+03
foot poundal	99,430.685	9.943 068 5E+04
frigorie [France]	1.001 008 2	1.001 008 2E+00
joule	4,190.02	4.190 020 0E+03
kilocalorie [I.T.]	1.000 769 1	1.000 769 1E+00
kilocalorie [thermoc.]	1.001 438 8	1.001 438 8E+00
kilogram calorie [15 °C, NBS, 1939]	1.001 008 2	1.001 008 2E+00
liter atmosphere	41.352 282	4.135 228 2E+01
meter kilogram-force	427.263 13	4.272 631 3E+02
newton meter	4,190.02	4.190 020 0E+03
pferdestarkenstunde [Germany]	0.001 582 5	1.582 456 0E-03
watthour	1.163 894 4	1.163 894 4E+00

kilocalorie [thermoc.] <energy>

Btu [I.T.]	3.965 666 8	3.965 666 8E+00
Btu [mean]	3.962 609	3.962 609 0E+00
Btu [thermoc.]	3.968 320 7	3.968 320 7E+00
calorie [I.T.]	999.331 23	9.993 312 3E+02
calorie [kilogram, I.T.]	0.999 331 2	9.993 312 3E-01
calorie [kilogram, mean]	0.998 563 3	9.985 632 5E-01
calorie [kilogram, thermoc.]	1	1.000 000 0E+00
calorie [mean]	998.563 25	9.985 632 5E+02
calorie [nutritional]	1	1.000 000 0E+00
calorie [thermoc.]	1,000.	1.000 000 0E+03
centigrade heat unit [mean]	2.201 449 5	2.201 449 5E+00
cubic centimeter atmosphere	41,292.869	4.129 286 9E+04
cubic foot atmosphere	1.458 243 9	1.458 243 9E+00
erg	>>>	4.184 000 0E+10
foot pound-force	3,085.96	3.085 960 0E+03
foot poundal	99,287.828	9.928 782 8E+04
frigorie [France]	0.999 57	9.995 699 7E-01
inch ounce-force	592,504.33	5.925 043 3E+05
inch pound-force	37,031.52	3.703 152 0E+04
joule	4,184.	4.184 000 0E+03
kilocalorie [I.T.]	0.999 331 2	9.993 312 3E-01
kilocalorie [mean]	0.998 563 3	9.985 632 5E-01
kilogram calorie [15 °C, NBS, 1939]	0.999 57	9.995 699 7E-01
kilojoule	4.184	4.184 000 0E+00
liter atmosphere	41.292 869	4.129 286 9E+01
watthour	1.162 222	1.162 222 2E+00

kilocalorie meter/square meter hour °C [I.T.] <thermal conductivity>

watt/meter kelvin	1.163	1.163 000 0E+00

kilocalorie square meter/kilogram [I.T.] <total mass stopping power>

Btu square foot/pound [I.T.]	19.375 039	1.937 503 9E+01
joule square meter/kilogram	4,186.8	4.186 800 0E+03

kilocalorie/cubic meter [I.T.] <energy density>

Btu/cubic foot [I.T.]	0.112 370 3	1.123 703 3E-01
joule/cubic meter	4,186.8	4.186 800 0E+03

kilocalorie/cubic meter hour [I.T.] <heat release rate>

	Standard	Scientific
Btu/cubic foot hour [I.T.]	0.112 370 3	1.123 703 3E−01
joule/cubic meter second	1.163	1.163 000 0E+00
watt/cubic meter	1.163	1.163 000 0E+00

kilocalorie/°C [I.T.] <specific heat>

	Standard	Scientific
Btu/°F [I.T.]	2.204 622 6	2.204 622 6E+00
calorie/°C [I.T.]	1,000	1.000 000 0E+03
clausius	1	1.000 000 0E+00
joule/kelvin	4,186.8	4.186 800 0E+03

kilocalorie/°C [thermoc.] <specific heat>

	Standard	Scientific
Btu/°F [thermoc.]	2.204 623 2	2.204 623 2E+00
calorie/°C [thermoc.]	1,000	1.000 000 0E+03
joule/kelvin	4,184	4.184 000 0E+03

kilocalorie/hour [I.T.] <power>

	Standard	Scientific
Btu/hour [I.T.]	3.968 320 7	3.968 320 7E+00
Btu/hour [thermoc.]	3.970 976 4	3.970 976 4E+00
calorie/minute [I.T.]	16.666 667	1.666 666 7E+01
calorie/minute [thermoc.]	16.677 82	1.667 782 0E+01
centigrade heat unit/hour [mean]	2.202 922 7	2.202 922 7E+00
cubic meter atmosphere/second	11.477 918	1.147 791 8E+01
dyne centimeter/second	>>>	1.163 000 0E+07
erg/second	>>>	1.163 000 0E+07
foot pound-force/minute	51.467 087	5.146 708 7E+01
foot poundal/second	27.598 409	2.759 840 9E+01
gram-force centimeter/second	11,859.3	1.185 930 1E+04
horsepower	0.001 559 6	1.559 608 7E−03
horsepower [metric]	0.001 581 2	1.581 239 9E−03
joule/second	1.163	1.163 000 0E+00
kilocalorie/hour [thermoc.]	1.000 669 2	1.000 669 2E+00
kilogram square meter/cubic second	1.163	1.163 000 0E+00
kilogram-force meter/minute	7.115 579 7	7.115 579 7E+00
kilopond meter/minute	7.115 579 7	7.115 579 7E+00
lumen [green light at 100% efficiency]	796.655	7.966 550 0E+02
lumen [green light at 5,550 angstrom]	790.840 02	7.908 400 2E+02
newton meter/second	1.163	1.163 000 0E+00
pferdestarke [Germany]	0.001 581 2	1.581 239 9E−03
poncelet [France]	0.001 185 9	1.185 930 0E−03
pound square foot/cubic second	27.598 409	2.759 840 9E+01
ton of refrigeration	0.000 330 7	3.306 933 9E−04
volt ampere	1.163	1.163 000 0E+00
watt	1.163	1.163 000 0E+00

kilocalorie/hour [mean] <power>

	Standard	Scientific
Btu/hour [I.T.]	3.971 372 7	3.971 372 7E+00
Btu/hour [thermoc.]	3.974 030 4	3.974 030 4E+00
calorie/minute [I.T.]	16.679 485	1.667 948 5E+01
calorie/minute [thermoc.]	16.690 647	1.669 064 7E+01
centigrade heat unit/hour [mean]	2.204 616 9	2.204 616 9E+00
cubic meter atmosphere/second	11.486 745	1.148 674 5E+01
dyne centimeter/second	>>>	1.163 894 4E+07
erg/second	>>>	1.163 894 4E+07
foot pound-force/minute	51.506 669	5.150 666 9E+01
foot poundal/second	27.619 635	2.761 963 5E+01
gram-force centimeter/second	11,868.42	1.186 842 0E+04
horsepower	0.001 560 8	1.560 808 2E−03
horsepower [metric]	0.001 582 5	1.582 456 0E−03
joule/second	1.163 894 4	1.163 894 4E+00
kilocalorie/hour [I.T.]	1.000 769 1	1.000 769 1E+00
kilogram square meter/cubic second	1.163 894 4	1.163 894 4E+00
kilogram-force meter/minute	7.121 052 2	7.121 052 2E+00
kilopond meter/minute	7.121 052 2	7.121 052 2E+00
lumen [green light at 100% efficiency]	797.267 69	7.972 676 9E+02
lumen [green light at 5,550 angstrom]	791.448 24	7.914 482 4E+02

Convert From		\<Type of Unit\>
Convert To	Standard	Scientific

newton meter/second	1.163 894 4	1.163 894 4E+00
pferdestarke [Germany]	0.001 582 5	1.582 456 0E-03
poncelet [France]	0.001 186 8	1.186 842 0E-03
pound square foot/cubic second	27.619 635	2.761 963 5E+01
volt ampere	1.163 894 4	1.163 894 4E+00
watt	1.163 894 4	1.163 894 4E+00

kilocalorie/hour [thermoc.] \<power\>

Btu/hour [I.T.]	3.965 666 8	3.965 666 8E+00
Btu/hour [thermoc.]	3.968 320 7	3.968 320 7E+00
calorie/minute [I.T.]	16.655 521	1.665 552 1E+01
calorie/minute [thermoc.]	16.666 667	1.666 666 7E+01
centigrade heat unit/hour [mean]	2.201 449 5	2.201 449 5E+00
cubic meter atmosphere/second	11.470 242	1.147 024 2E+01
dyne centimeter/second	>>>	1.162 222 2E+07
erg/second	>>>	1.162 222 2E+07
foot pound-force/minute	51.432 667	5.143 266 7E+01
foot poundal/second	27.579 952	2.757 995 2E+01
gram-force centimeter/second	11,851.368	1.185 136 8E+04
horsepower	0.001 558 6	1.558 565 7E-03
horsepower [metric]	0.001 580 2	1.580 182 5E-03
joule/second	1.162 222 2	1.162 222 2E+00
kilocalorie/hour [mean]	0.998 563 2	9.985 632 5E-01
kilogram square meter/cubic second	1.162 222 2	1.162 222 2E+00
kilogram-force meter/minute	7.110 821 1	7.110 821 1E+00
kilopond meter/minute	7.110 821 1	7.110 821 1E+00
lumen [green light at 100% efficiency]	796.122 22	7.961 222 2E+02
lumen [green light at 5,550 angstrom]	790.311 13	7.903 111 3E+02
newton meter/second	1.162 222 2	1.162 222 2E+00
pferdestarke [Germany]	0.001 580 2	1.580 182 5E-03
poncelet [France]	0.001 185 1	1.185 136 8E-03
pound square foot/cubic second	27.579 952	2.757 995 2E+01
volt ampere	1.162 222 2	1.162 222 2E+00
watt	1.162 222 2	1.162 222 2E+00

kilocalorie/hour cubic meter °C [I.T.] \<heat transfer coefficient\>

Btu/hour cubic foot °F [I.T.]	0.062 428	6.242 796 1E-02
calorie/second cubic centimeter °C [I.T.]	0.000 000 3	2.777 777 8E-07
watt/cubic meter kelvin	1.163	1.163 000 0E+00

kilocalorie/hour meter °C [I.T.] \<thermal conductivity\>

Btu foot/hour square foot °F [I.T.]	0.671 969	6.719 689 8E-01
Btu foot/hour square foot °F [thermoc.]	0.672 418 8	6.724 188 4E-01
Btu inch/hour square foot °F [I.T.]	8.063 627	8.063 627 7E+00
Btu inch/hour square foot °F [thermoc.]	8.069 026	8.069 026 0E+00
Btu/hour foot °F [I.T.]	0.671 969	6.719 689 8E-01
Btu/hour foot °F [thermoc.]	0.672 418 8	6.724 188 4E-01
calorie centimeter/hour square centimeter °C [I.T.]	10	1.000 000 0E+01
joule/second meter kelvin	1.163	1.163 000 0E+00
watt/foot °C	0.354 482 4	3.544 824 0E-01
watt/meter kelvin	1.163	1.163 000 0E+00

kilocalorie/hour square meter [I.T.] \<heat flux density\>

Btu/day square foot [I.T.]	8.848 057 4	8.848 057 4E+00
Btu/day square foot [thermoc.]	8.853 978 7	8.853 978 7E+00
calorie/day square centimeter [I.T.]	2.4	2.400 000 0E+00
calorie/day square centimeter [thermoc.]	2.401 606 1	2.401 606 1E+00
kilocalorie/hour square meter [thermoc.]	1.000 669 2	1.000 669 2E+00
watt/square meter	1.163	1.163 000 0E+00

kilocalorie/hour square meter [thermoc.] \<heat flux density\>

Btu/day square foot [I.T.]	8.842 140 1	8.842 140 1E+00
Btu/day square foot [thermoc.]	8.848 057 4	8.848 057 4E+00
calorie/day square centimeter [I.T.]	2.398 395	2.398 395 0E+00
calorie/day square centimeter [thermoc.]	2.4	2.400 000 0E+00
kilocalorie/hour square meter [I.T.]	0.999 331 2	9.993 312 3E-01
watt/square foot	0.107 974	1.079 739 8E-01

	Standard	Scientific
watt/square meter	1.162 222 2	1.162 222 2E+00
kilocalorie/hour square meter °C [I.T.]	<heat transfer coefficient>	
Btu/day square foot °F [I.T.]	4.915 587 4	4.915 587 4E+00
calorie/hour square centimeter °C [I.T.]	0.1	1.000 000 0E−01
watt/square foot °C	0.108 046 2	1.080 462 4E−01
watt/square meter kelvin	1.163	1.163 000 0E+00
kilocalorie/kilogram [I.T.]	<specific thermodynamic energy>	
Btu/pound [I.T.]	1.8	1.800 000 0E+00
Btu/pound [thermoc.]	1.801 204 6	1.801 204 6E+00
calorie/gram [I.T.]	1	1.000 000 0E+00
calorie/gram [thermoc.]	1.000 669 2	1.000 669 2E+00
joule/kilogram	4,186.8	4.186 800 0E+03
kilocalorie/kilogram [thermoc.]	<specific thermodynamic energy>	
Btu/pound [I.T.]	1.798 796 2	1.798 796 2E+00
Btu/pound [thermoc.]	1.8	1.800 000 0E+00
calorie/gram [I.T.]	0.999 331 2	9.993 312 3E−01
calorie/gram [thermoc.]	1	1.000 000 0E+00
joule/kilogram	4,184	4.184 000 0E+03
kilocalorie/kilogram °C [I.T.]	<specific heat capacity>	
Btu/pound °F [I.T.]	1	1.000 000 0E+00
Btu/pound °F [thermoc.]	1.000 669 2	1.000 669 2E+00
calorie/gram °C [I.T.]	1	1.000 000 0E+00
calorie/gram °C [thermoc.]	1.000 669 2	1.000 669 2E+00
joule/kilogram kelvin	4,186.8	4.186 800 0E+03
mayer	4.186 8	4.186 800 0E+00
kilocalorie/kilogram °C [thermoc.]	<specific heat capacity>	
Btu/pound °F [I.T.]	0.999 331 2	9.993 312 3E−01
Btu/pound °F [thermoc.]	1	1.000 000 0E+00
calorie/gram °C [I.T.]	0.999 331 2	9.993 312 3E−01
calorie/gram °C [thermoc.]	1	1.000 000 0E+00
joule/kilogram kelvin	4,184	4.184 000 0E+03
kilocalorie/meter [I.T.]	<linear energy transfer>	
Btu/foot [I.T.]	1.209 544 2	1.209 544 2E+00
electronvolt/meter	>>>	2.613 193 9E+22
erg/centimeter	>>>	4.186 800 0E+08
joule/meter	4,186.8	4.186 800 0E+03
kilocalorie/minute [I.T.]		<power>
Btu/minute [I.T.]	3.968 320 7	3.968 320 7E+00
Btu/minute [thermoc.]	3.970 976 4	3.970 976 4E+00
calorie/second [I.T.]	16.666 667	1.666 666 7E+01
calorie/second [thermoc.]	16.677 82	1.667 782 0E+01
centigrade heat unit/minute [mean]	2.202 922 7	2.202 922 7E+00
cheval vapeur [France]	0.094 874 4	9.487 439 6E−02
cubic meter atmosphere/second	688.675 06	6.886 750 6E+02
dekawatt	6.978	6.978 000 0E+00
dyne centimeter/second	>>>	6.978 000 0E+08
erg/second	>>>	6.978 000 0E+08
foot pound-force/second	51.467 087	5.146 708 7E+01
foot poundal/second	1,655.904 5	1.655 904 5E+03
gram-force centimeter/second	711,557.97	7.115 579 7E+05
horsepower	0.093 576 5	9.357 652 1E−02
horsepower [metric]	0.094 874 4	9.487 439 6E−02
joule/second	69.78	6.978 000 0E+01
kilocalorie/minute [thermoc.]	1.000 669 2	1.000 669 2E+00
kilogram square meter/cubic second	69.78	6.978 000 0E+01
kilogram-force meter/second	7.115 579 7	7.115 579 7E+00
kilopond meter/second	7.115 579 7	7.115 579 7E+00
newton meter/second	69.78	6.978 000 0E+01
pferdestarke [Germany]	0.094 874 4	9.487 439 6E−02
poncelet [France]	0.071 155 8	7.115 579 7E−02
pound square foot/cubic second	1,655.904 5	1.655 904 5E+03

ton of refrigeration	0.019 841 6	1.984 160 4E–02
volt ampere	69.78	6.978 000 0E+01
watt	69.78	6.978 000 0E+01

kilocalorie/minute [mean] <power>

Btu/minute [I.T.]	3.971 372 7	3.971 372 7E+00
Btu/minute [thermoc.]	3.974 030 4	3.974 030 4E+00
calorie/second [I.T.]	16.679 485	1.667 948 5E+01
calorie/second [thermoc.]	16.690 647	1.669 064 7E+01
centigrade heat unit/minute [mean]	2.204 616 9	2.204 616 9E+00
cheval vapeur [France]	0.094 947 4	9.494 736 3E–02
cubic meter atmosphere/second	689.204 7	6.892 047 0E+02
dekawatt	6.983 366 7	6.983 366 7E+00
dyne centimeter/second	>>>	6.983 366 7E+08
erg/second	>>>	6.983 366 7E+08
foot pound-force/second	51.506 669	5.150 666 9E+01
foot poundal/second	1,657.178 1	1.657 178 1E+03
gram-force centimeter/second	712,105.22	7.121 052 2E+05
horsepower	0.093 648 5	9.364 849 0E–02
horsepower [metric]	0.094 947 4	9.494 736 3E–02
joule/second	69.833 667	6.983 366 7E+01
kilocalorie/minute [I.T.]	1.000 769 1	1.000 769 1E+00
kilogram square meter/cubic second	69.833 667	6.983 366 7E+01
kilogram-force meter/second	7.121 052 2	7.121 052 2E+00
kilopond meter/second	7.121 052 2	7.121 052 2E+00
newton meter/second	69.833 667	6.983 366 7E+01
pferdestarke [Germany]	0.094 947 4	9.494 736 3E–02
poncelet [France]	0.071 210 5	7.121 052 2E–02
pound square foot/cubic second	1,657.178 1	1.657 178 1E+03
ton of refrigeration	0.019 856 9	1.985 686 3E–02
volt ampere	69.833 667	6.983 366 7E+01
watt	69.833 667	6.983 366 7E+01

kilocalorie/minute [thermoc.] <power>

Btu/minute [I.T.]	3.965 666 8	3.965 666 8E+00
Btu/minute [thermoc.]	3.968 320 7	3.968 320 7E+00
calorie/second [I.T.]	16.655 521	1.665 552 1E+01
calorie/second [thermoc.]	16.666 667	1.666 666 7E+01
centigrade heat unit/minute [mean]	2.201 449 5	2.201 449 5E+00
cheval vapeur [France]	0.094 810 9	9.481 094 7E–02
cubic meter atmosphere/second	688.214 49	6.882 144 9E+02
dekawatt	6.973 333 3	6.973 333 3E+00
dyne centimeter/second	>>>	6.973 333 3E+08
erg/second	>>>	6.973 333 3E+08
foot pound-force/second	51.432 667	5.143 266 7E+01
foot poundal/second	1,654.797 1	1.654 797 1E+03
gram-force centimeter/second	711,082.11	7.110 821 1E+05
horsepower	0.093 513 9	9.351 394 0E–02
horsepower [metric]	0.094 810 9	9.481 094 7E–02
joule/second	69.733 333	6.973 333 3E+01
kilocalorie/hour [thermoc.]	60	6.000 000 0E+01
kilogram square meter/cubic second	69.733 333	6.973 333 3E+01
kilogram-force meter/second	7.110 821 1	7.110 821 1E+00
kilopond meter/second	7.110 821 1	7.110 821 1E+00
newton meter/second	69.733 333	6.973 333 3E+01
pferdestarke [Germany]	0.094 810 9	9.481 094 7E–02
poncelet [France]	0.071 108 2	7.110 821 1E–02
pound square foot/cubic second	1,654.797 1	1.654 797 1E+03
ton of refrigeration	0.019 828 3	1.982 833 4E–02
volt ampere	69.733 333	6.973 333 3E+01
watt	69.733 333	6.973 333 3E+01

kilocalorie/second [I.T.] <power>

Btu/second [I.T.]	3.968 320 7	3.968 320 7E+00
Btu/second [thermoc.]	3.970 976 4	3.970 976 4E+00
calorie/second [I.T.]	1,000	1.000 000 0E+03

	Standard	Scientific
calorie/second [thermoc.]	1,000.669 2	1.000 669 2E+03
centigrade heat unit/second [mean]	2.202 922 7	2.202 922 7E+00
cheval vapeur [France]	5.692 463 8	5.692 463 8E+00
cubic meter atmosphere/second	41,320.503	4.132 050 3E+04
dyne centimeter/second	>>>	4.186 800 0E+10
erg/second	>>>	4.186 800 0E+10
foot pound-force/second	3,088.025 2	3.088 025 2E+03
foot poundal/second	99,354.273	9.935 427 3E+04
gram-force centimeter/second	>>>	4.269 347 8E+07
horsepower	5.614 591 3	5.614 591 3E+00
horsepower [metric]	5.692 463 8	5.692 463 8E+00
joule/second	4,186.8	4.186 800 0E+03
kilocalorie/second [thermoc.]	1.000 669 2	1.000 669 2E+00
kilogram square meter/cubic second	4,186.8	4.186 800 0E+03
kilogram-force meter/second	426.934 78	4.269 347 8E+02
kilopond meter/second	426.934 78	4.269 347 8E+02
kilowatt	4.186 8	4.186 800 0E+00
million Btu/hour [I.T.]	0.014 286	1.428 595 5E−02
newton meter/second	4,186.8	4.186 800 0E+03
pferdestarke [Germany]	5.692 463 8	5.692 463 8E+00
poncelet [France]	4.269 347 8	4.269 347 8E+00
ton of refrigeration	1.190 496 2	1.190 496 2E+00
volt ampere	4,186.8	4.186 800 0E+03
watt	4,186.8	4.186 800 0E+03

kilocalorie/second [mean] \<power\>

	Standard	Scientific
Btu/second [I.T.]	3.971 372 7	3.971 372 7E+00
Btu/second [thermoc.]	3.974 030 4	3.974 030 4E+00
calorie/second [I.T.]	1,000.769 1	1.000 769 1E+03
calorie/second [thermoc.]	1,001.438 8	1.001 438 8E+03
centigrade heat unit/second [mean]	2.204 616 9	2.204 616 9E+00
cheval vapeur [France]	5.696 841 8	5.696 841 8E+00
cubic meter atmosphere/second	41,352.282	4.135 228 2E+04
dyne centimeter/second	>>>	4.190 020 0E+10
erg/second	>>>	4.190 020 0E+10
foot pound-force/second	3,090.400 2	3.090 400 2E+03
foot poundal/second	99,430.685	9.943 068 5E+04
gram-force centimeter/second	>>>	4.272 631 3E+07
horsepower	5.618 909 4	5.618 909 4E+00
joule/second	4,190.02	4.190 020 0E+03
kilocalorie/second [I.T.]	1.000 769 1	1.000 769 1E+00
kilogram square meter/cubic second	4,190.02	4.190 020 0E+03
kilogram-force meter/second	427.263 13	4.272 631 3E+02
kilopond meter/second	427.263 13	4.272 631 3E+02
kilowatt	4.190 02	4.190 020 0E+00
million Btu/hour [I.T.]	0.014 296 9	1.429 694 2E−02
nanowatt	>>>	4.190 020 0E+12
newton meter/second	4,190.02	4.190 020 0E+03
pferdestarke [Germany]	5.696 841 8	5.696 841 8E+00
poncelet [France]	4.272 631 3	4.272 631 3E+00
ton of refrigeration	1.191 411 8	1.191 411 8E+00
volt ampere	4,190.02	4.190 020 0E+03
watt	4,190.02	4.190 020 0E+03

kilocalorie/second [thermoc.] \<power\>

	Standard	Scientific
Btu/second [I.T.]	3.965 666 8	3.965 666 8E+00
Btu/second [thermoc.]	3.968 320 7	3.968 320 7E+00
calorie/second [I.T.]	999.331 23	9.993 312 3E+02
calorie/second [thermoc.]	1,000	1.000 000 0E+03
centigrade heat unit/second [mean]	2.201 449 5	2.201 449 5E+00
cheval vapeur [France]	5.688 656 8	5.688 656 8E+00
cubic meter atmosphere/second	41,292.869	4.129 286 9E+04
dyne centimeter/second	>>>	4.184 000 0E+10
erg/second	>>>	4.184 000 0E+10
foot pound-force/second	3,085.96	3.085 960 0E+03

	Standard	Scientific
foot poundal/second	99,287.828	9.928 782 8E+04
gram-force centimeter/second	>>>	4.266 492 6E+07
horsepower	5.610 836 4	5.610 836 4E+00
horsepower [metric]	5.688 656 8	5.688 656 8E+00
joule/second	4,184	4.184 000 0E+03
kilocalorie/minute [I.T.]	59.959 874	5.995 987 4E+01
kilocalorie/minute [thermoc.]	60	6.000 000 0E+01
kilogram square meter/cubic second	4,184	4.184 000 0E+03
kilogram-force meter/second	426.649 26	4.266 492 6E+02
kilopond meter/second	426.649 26	4.266 492 6E+02
kilowatt	4.184	4.184 000 0E+00
million Btu/hour [I.T.]	0.014 276 4	1.427 640 1E−02
newton meter/second	4,184	4.184 000 0E+03
pferdestarke [Germany]	5.688 656 8	5.688 656 8E+00
poncelet [France]	4.266 492 6	4.266 492 6E+00
ton of refrigeration	1.189 7	1.189 700 0E+00
volt ampere	4,184	4.184 000 0E+03
watt	4,184	4.184 000 0E+03
kilocalorie/second °C [I.T.]		**\<thermal conductance\>**
Btu/second °F [I.T.]	2.204 622 6	2.204 622 6E+00
calorie/second °C [I.T.]	1,000	1.000 000 0E+03
watt/kelvin	4,186.8	4.186 800 0E+03
kilocalorie/square meter [I.T.]		**\<energy fluence\>**
Btu/square foot [I.T.]	0.368 669 1	3.686 690 6E−01
joule/square meter	4,186.8	4.186 800 0E+03
kilocalorie/square meter [thermoc.]		**\<energy fluence\>**
joule/square meter	4,184	4.184 000 0E+03
kilocandela		**\<luminous intensity\>**
candela	1,000	1.000 000 0E+03
kilocandela/square meter		**\<luminance\>**
apostilb [international]	3,141.592 7	3.141 592 7E+03
blondel	3,141.592 7	3.141 592 7E+03
candela/square foot	92.903 04	9.290 304 0E+01
candela/square meter	1,000	1.000 000 0E+03
footlambert	291.863 51	2.918 635 1E+02
lambert	0.314 159 3	3.141 592 7E−01
nit	1,000	1.000 000 0E+03
stilb	0.1	1.000 000 0E−01
kilocoulomb		**\<electric charge\>**
abcoulomb	100	1.000 000 0E+02
ampere second	1,000	1.000 000 0E+03
coulomb	1,000	1.000 000 0E+03
electromagnetic unit of charge [cgs system]	100	1.000 000 0E+02
faraday [based on carbon-12]	0.010 364 3	1.036 427 2E−02
kilocoulomb meter		**\<electric dipole moment\>**
ampere hour meter	0.277 777 8	2.777 777 8E−01
ampere second meter	1,000	1.000 000 0E+03
coulomb meter	1,000	1.000 000 0E+03
statcoulomb centimeter	>>>	2.997 924 6E+14
kilocoulomb/cubic meter		**\<electric charge density\>**
abcoulomb/cubic centimeter	0.000 1	1.000 000 0E−04
coulomb/cubic meter	1,000	1.000 000 0E+03
statcoulomb/cubic centimeter	2,997,924.58	2.997 924 6E+06
kilocoulomb/meter		**\<electric dipole moment/unit area\>**
abcoulomb/centimeter	1	1.000 000 0E+00
coulomb/meter	1,000	1.000 000 0E+03
kilocoulomb/square meter		**\<electric flux density\>**
abcoulomb/square centimeter	0.01	1.000 000 0E−02
ampere hour/square meter	0.277 777 8	2.777 777 8E−01
coulomb/square inch	0.645 16	6.451 600 0E−01
coulomb/square meter	1,000	1.000 000 0E+03

| franklin/square centimeter | >>> | 2.997 924 6E+08 |
| statcoulomb/square centimeter | >>> | 2.997 924 6E+08 |

kiloelectronvolt   **<energy>**

1/centimeter [atomic physics, eq. energy]	8,065,540.9	8.065 540 9E+06
1/meter [atomic physics, eq. energy]	>>>	8.065 540 9E+08
atomic mass unit [unified, C-12, 1986, eq. energy]	0.000 001 1	1.073 543 9E-06
deuteron rest mass [atomic physics, eq. energy]	0.000 000 5	5.331 589 2E-07
electron rest mass [atomic physics, eq. energy]	0.001 957	1.956 950 8E-03
electronvolt	1,000	1.000 000 0E+03
hartree [atomic physics, eq. energy]	36.749 309	3.674 930 9E+01
joule	<<<	1.602 177 3E-16
kayser [atomic physics, eq. energy]	8,065,540.9	8.065 540 9E+06
kelvin [atomic physics, eq. energy]	>>>	1.160 444 8E+07
megaelectronvolt	0.001	1.000 000 0E-03
muon rest mass [atomic physics, eq. energy]	0.000 009 5	9.464 463 8E-06
neutron rest mass [atomic physics, eq. energy]	0.000 001 1	1.064 321 6E-06
proton rest mass [atomic physics, eq. energy]	0.000 001 1	1.065 788 7E-06
rydberg [atomic physics, eq. energy]	73.497 744	7.349 774 4E+01
teraelectronvolt	<<<	1.000 000 0E-09

kilofarad   **<capacitance>**

abfarad	0.000 001	1.000 000 0E-06
coulomb/volt	1,000	1.000 000 0E+03
farad	1,000	1.000 000 0E+03
statfarad	>>>	8.987 551 8E+14

kilofarad/meter   **<electric permittivity>**

abfarad/centimeter	0.000 1	1.000 000 0E-04
farad/meter	1,000	1.000 000 0E+03
statfarad/centimeter	>>>	8.987 551 8E+16

kilogram   **<mass>**

abada [Ethiopia]	0.064 102 6	6.410 256 4E-02
abucco [Burma]	0.05	5.000 000 0E-02
acheintaya [Burma]	0.006 124 1	6.124 073 7E-03
adowlie [India, heavy]	0.492 368 3	4.923 682 9E-01
adowly [India]	0.535 905 7	5.359 056 8E-01
almud [Ecuador]	0.077 639 8	7.763 975 2E-02
almude [Ecuador]	0.077 639 8	7.763 975 2E-02
amat [Batavia]	0.008 097 2	8.097 166 0E-03
arroa [Spain]	0.086 941 4	8.694 140 1E-02
arroba [Argentina]	0.087 108	8.710 801 4E-02
arroba [Belize]	0.088 183 4	8.818 342 2E-02
arroba [Bolivia]	0.086 956 5	8.695 652 2E-02
arroba [Brazil]	0.066 666 7	6.666 666 7E-02
arroba [British Honduras]	0.088 184 9	8.818 489 9E-02
arroba [Chile]	0.086 956 5	8.695 652 2E-02
arroba [Colombia]	0.08	8.000 000 0E-02
arroba [Costa Rica]	0.086 956 5	8.695 652 2E-02
arroba [Cuba]	0.086 941 4	8.694 140 1E-02
arroba [Dominican Republic]	0.088 183 4	8.818 342 2E-02
arroba [Ecuador]	0.086 956 5	8.695 652 2E-02
arroba [El Salvador]	0.086 956 5	8.695 652 2E-02
arroba [Guatemala]	0.086 941 4	8.694 140 1E-02
arroba [Honduras]	0.086 941 4	8.694 140 1E-02
arroba [Mexico]	0.086 911 2	8.691 117 7E-02
arroba [Nicaragua]	0.086 956 5	8.695 652 2E-02
arroba [Paraguay]	0.087 108	8.710 801 4E-02
arroba [Peru]	0.086 941 4	8.694 140 1E-02
arroba [Philippines]	0.086 956 5	8.695 652 2E-02
arroba [Portugal]	0.068 073 5	6.807 351 9E-02
arroba [Spain]	0.086 941 4	8.694 140 1E-02
arroba [Uruguay]	0.1	1.000 000 0E-01
arroba [Venezuela]	0.086 956 5	8.695 652 2E-02
artal [Israel]	0.347 222 2	3.472 222 2E-01

kilogram (continued)   <mass>

Convert To	Standard	Scientific
atado [Costa Rica]	0.966 183 6	9.661 835 7E−01
atomic mass unit [chemical, 1986]	>>>	6.022 395 6E+26
atomic mass unit [physical, 1986]	>>>	6.024 051 7E+26
atomic mass unit [unified, C-12,1986]	>>>	6.022 136 7E+26
avogram	>>>	6.022 136 7E+26
baar [Batavia, large]	0.003 599 3	3.599 271 5E−03
baar [Batavia, small]	0.005 398 9	5.398 897 5E−03
baar [Sumatra]	0.005 207 6	5.207 628 1E−03
baer [Batavia, large]	0.003 599 3	3.599 271 5E−03
baer [Batavia, small]	0.005 398 9	5.398 897 5E−03
baer [Sumatra]	0.005 207 6	5.207 628 1E−03
bag of cement [US, dry]	0.023 453 4	2.345 343 2E−02
bahar [Batavia, large]	0.003 599 3	3.599 271 5E−03
bahar [Batavia, small]	0.005 398 9	5.398 897 5E−03
bahar [India]	0.003 827 5	3.827 458 2E−03
bahar [Oman]	0.001 237 7	1.237 685 0E−03
bahar [Saudi Arabia]	0.004 899 6	4.899 559 0E−03
bahar [Sumatra]	0.005 207 6	5.207 628 1E−03
bale [Belgium]	0.010 668 7	1.066 871 5E−02
bale [Indonesia]	0.005 555 6	5.555 555 6E−03
bale [Netherlands]	0.010 668 7	1.066 871 5E−02
bale [New Zealand]	0.006 578 9	6.578 947 4E−03
bale [Philippines]	0.007 905 1	7.905 138 3E−03
bale [UK]	0.009 185 1	9.185 098 1E−03
ballen [Belgium]	0.010 668 7	1.066 871 5E−02
ballen [Netherlands]	0.010 668 7	1.066 871 5E−02
bar [Batavia, large]	0.003 599 3	3.599 271 5E−03
bar [Batavia, small]	0.005 398 9	5.398 897 5E−03
bar [Sumatra]	0.005 207 6	5.207 628 1E−03
bara [Singapore]	0.005 512 7	5.512 679 2E−03
batman [Iran]	0.333 333 3	3.333 333 3E−01
batman [Iran, large]	0.097 991 2	9.799 118 1E−02
batman [Iran, small]	0.392 003 1	3.920 031 4E−01
batman [Turkey]	0.129 903 9	1.299 038 7E−01
batman [Turkey, large]	0.097 991 2	9.799 118 1E−02
batman [Turkey, small]	0.392 003 1	3.920 031 4E−01
batmar [Iran, large]	0.097 991 2	9.799 118 1E−02
batmar [Iran, small]	0.392 003 1	3.920 031 4E−01
batmar [Turkey]	0.261 301 3	2.613 012 8E−01
batmar [Turkey, large]	0.097 991 2	9.799 118 1E−02
batmar [Turkey, small]	0.392 003 1	3.920 031 4E−01
batt [Iceland]	0.006 25	6.250 000 0E−03
bazer [Indonesia]	0.005 398 9	5.398 897 5E−03
behar [Saudi Arabia]	0.004 899 6	4.899 559 0E−03
bercherect [Russia]	0.006 112 6	6.112 581 5E−03
berkovec [Russia]	0.006 105	6.105 006 1E−03
berkovet [Russia]	0.006 105	6.105 006 1E−03
berkovetz [Russia]	0.006 104 8	6.104 819 8E−03
berkowetz [Russia]	0.006 112 6	6.112 581 5E−03
berkowitz [Russia]	0.006 112 6	6.112 581 5E−03
bhar [Batavia, large]	0.003 599 3	3.599 271 5E−03
bhar [Batavia, small]	0.005 398 9	5.398 897 5E−03
bhar [Sumatra]	0.005 207 6	5.207 628 1E−03
bhara [Brunei]	0.005 511 6	5.511 555 0E−03
bhara [Malaysia]	0.005 512 7	5.512 679 2E−03
biltu [Babylon, ancient]	0.033 333 3	3.333 333 3E−02
bismerpund [Denmark]	0.166 666 7	1.666 666 7E−01
bismerpund [Norway]	0.166 666 7	1.666 666 7E−01
boll [UK, avoirdupois]	0.015 747 3	1.574 728 8E−02
botija [Ecuador]	0.173 913	1.739 130 4E−01
botijuela [Venezuela]	0.2	2.000 000 0E−01
botsa [Greece]	0.390 625	3.906 250 0E−01

kilogram (continued)   \<mass\>

briquette [Indonesia]	2	2.000 000 0E+00
bulto [Philippines]	0.016 299 9	1.629 991 9E-02
bulto [Venezuela]	0.020 408 2	2.040 816 3E-02
bundle [South Africa]	0.314 946 1	3.149 460 5E-01
buttima [Persia]	0.087 092 8	8.709 284 1E-02
cabulla [Venezuela]	0.05	5.000 000 0E-02
cafa [Guatemala]	0.062 5	6.250 000 0E-02
caja [Costa Rica]	0.062 5	6.250 000 0E-02
caja [El Salvador]	0.062 5	6.250 000 0E-02
caja [Honduras]	0.062 5	6.250 000 0E-02
caja [Nicaragua]	0.062 5	6.250 000 0E-02
caja [Venezuela]	0.024 390 2	2.439 024 4E-02
can [Vietnam]	1.666 666 7	1.666 666 7E+00
cana [Netherlands Antilles]	1.333 333 3	1.333 333 3E+00
candil [East India]	0.003 936 6	3.936 558 4E-03
candy [Burma]	0.000 122 5	1.224 790 3E-04
candy [India]	0.003 937	3.937 007 9E-03
candy [Sri Lanka]	0.004 409 2	4.409 171 1E-03
candy [Yemen]	0.003 280 8	3.280 839 9E-03
cantar [Cyprus]	0.017 894 5	1.789 453 0E-02
cantar [Cyprus, Aleppo]	0.004 374 2	4.374 242 7E-03
cantar [Egypt]	0.022 257 8	2.225 783 5E-02
cantar [Greece]	0.017 755 7	1.775 568 2E-02
cantar [Iraq]	0.022 257 8	2.225 783 5E-02
cantar [Lebanon]	0.003 900 2	3.900 156 0E-03
cantar [Malta]	0.012 597 8	1.259 779 0E-02
cantar [Morocco]	0.019 508 4	1.950 838 9E-02
cantar [Romania]	0.017 857 1	1.785 714 3E-02
cantar [Sudan, large]	0.007 067 1	7.067 137 8E-03
cantar [Sudan, small]	0.022 257 8	2.225 783 5E-02
cantar [Syria]	0.003 898 6	3.898 635 5E-03
cantar [Tunisia]	0.019 849 1	1.984 914 6E-02
cantar [Turkey]	0.017 714 8	1.771 479 2E-02
cantara [Bolivia]	0.086 956 5	8.695 652 2E-02
cantara [Brazil]	0.068 027 2	6.802 721 1E-02
cantara [Chile]	0.086 956 5	8.695 652 2E-02
cantara [Colombia]	0.08	8.000 000 0E-02
cantara [Cuba]	0.086 941 4	8.694 140 1E-02
cantara [Dominican Republic]	0.088 183 4	8.818 342 2E-02
cantara [Ecuador]	0.086 956 5	8.695 652 2E-02
cantara [Mexico]	0.086 881	8.688 097 3E-02
cantara [Paraguay]	0.087 146	8.714 596 9E-02
cantara [Peru]	0.086 956 5	8.695 652 2E-02
cantara [Philippines]	0.086 956 5	8.695 652 2E-02
cantara [Portugal]	0.066 666 7	6.666 666 7E-02
cantara [Spain]	0.086 941 4	8.694 140 1E-02
cantara [Uruguay]	0.087 070 1	8.707 009 1E-02
cantara [Venezuela]	0.086 805 6	8.680 555 6E-02
cantarelli [Italy, Genoa]	0.019 111 3	1.911 132 3E-02
cantarelli [Romania]	0.017 628 6	1.762 860 1E-02
cantarelli [Syria]	0.005 263 5	5.263 490 3E-03
cantaro [Egypt]	0.022 257 8	2.225 783 5E-02
cantaro [Iraq]	0.022 257 8	2.225 783 5E-02
cantaro [Italy]	0.021 045 1	2.104 510 0E-02
cantaro [Mexico]	0.086 911 2	8.691 117 7E-02
cantaro [Romania]	0.017 628 6	1.762 860 1E-02
cantaro [Sardinia]	0.024 926 5	2.492 646 7E-02
cantaro [Syria]	0.005 263 5	5.263 490 3E-03
cantaro [Syria, Damascus]	0.003 898 6	3.898 635 5E-03
cantaro barbaresco [Spain]	0.023 792 5	2.379 252 9E-02
cantaro grosso [Italy]	0.011 236	1.123 595 5E-02
cantaro grosso [Italy, Rome]	0.002 947 3	2.947 287 8E-03

	<Type of Unit>
Standard	Scientific

kilogram (continued)   **<mass>**

Convert To	Standard	Scientific
cantaro grosso [Sicily]	0.011 448 1	1.144 806 6E−02
cantaro sottile [Sicily]	0.012 592 4	1.259 239 7E−02
carat [gemstones]	5,000	5.000 000 0E+03
carat [international]	5,000	5.000 000 0E+03
carat [metric]	5,000	5.000 000 0E+03
carat [UK]	3,858.089 6	3.858 089 6E+03
carat [US, after 1913]	5,000	5.000 000 0E+03
carat [US, before 1913]	4,870.920 6	4.870 920 6E+03
carga [Colombia]	0.008	8.000 000 0E−03
carga [Costa Rica]	0.006 211 2	6.211 180 1E−03
carga [El Salvador]	0.010 869 6	1.086 956 5E−02
carga [Mexico]	0.007 142 9	7.142 857 1E−03
carga [Nicaragua]	0.006 211 2	6.211 180 1E−03
carga [Venezuela]	0.005 434 8	5.434 782 6E−03
carga de papa [Costa Rica]	0.001 207 7	1.207 729 5E−03
cargo [Belize]	0.011 022 9	1.102 292 8E−02
cargo [British Honduras]	0.011 023 1	1.102 311 0E−02
case [Fiji, bananas]	0.030 581	3.058 104 0E−02
cate [China]	2	2.000 000 0E+00
cate [Indonesia]	1.618 123	1.618 123 0E+00
cate [Japan]	1.666 666 7	1.666 666 7E+00
cate [South Korea]	1.666 666 7	1.666 666 7E+00
cate [Thailand]	1.666 666 7	1.666 666 7E+00
catty [Brunei]	1.652 892 6	1.652 892 6E+00
catty [China]	2	2.000 000 0E+00
catty [Indonesia]	1.618 123	1.618 123 0E+00
catty [Japan]	1.666 666 7	1.666 666 7E+00
catty [South Korea]	1.666 666 7	1.666 666 7E+00
catty [Taiwan]	1.666 666 7	1.666 666 7E+00
catty [Thailand]	1.666 666 7	1.666 666 7E+00
cavan [Philippines]	0.016 299 9	1.629 991 9E−02
ceki [Turkey]	0.004 428 1	4.428 731 3E−03
cental [US]	0.022 046 2	2.204 622 6E−02
centenaar [Netherlands]	0.01	1.000 000 0E−02
centnar [Poland]	0.024 660 7	2.466 066 9E−02
centner [Denmark]	0.02	2.000 000 0E−02
centner [Germany]	0.02	2.000 000 0E−02
centner [Norway]	0.020 076 3	2.007 629 0E−02
centner [Sweden]	0.023 521 1	2.352 111 0E−02
centner [Switzerland]	0.02	2.000 000 0E−02
centner [UK]	0.019 684 1	1.968 413 1E−02
central [South Africa]	0.022 046 2	2.204 622 6E−02
chang [Thailand]	0.833 333 3	8.333 333 3E−01
chapah [Malaysia]	1.225 490 2	1.225 490 2E+00
charak [Afghanistan]	0.562 904 6	5.629 045 9E−01
charge [Belgium]	0.005 334 4	5.334 357 5E−03
charge [France]	0.006 809 6	6.809 577 0E−03
charge [Holland]	0.005 334 4	5.334 357 5E−03
chariot [Netherlands, wool]	0.012 927 7	1.292 774 7E−02
cheli [Turkey]	0.004 330 3	4.330 314 7E−03
chi [Vietnam]	0.266 666 7	2.666 666 7E−01
chin [China, new]	2	2.000 000 0E+00
chin [Indonesia]	1.618 123	1.618 123 0E+00
chin [Japan]	1.666 666 7	1.666 666 7E+00
chin [South Korea]	1.666 666 7	1.666 666 7E+00
chin [Thailand]	1.666 666 7	1.666 666 7E+00
chinanda [Philippines]	0.158 102 8	1.581 027 7E−01
chinbul [Lebanon]	0.006 666 7	6.666 666 7E−03
chombol [Lebanon, wheat]	0.006 666 7	6.666 666 7E−03
chong [Cambodia]	0.033 333 3	3.333 333 3E−02
cojang [Sumatra]	0.000 338 7	3.386 845 5E−04
cola [Syria]	0.015 038 5	1.503 849 9E−02

kilogram (continued)

<mass>

Convert To	Standard	Scientific
commerzlast [Germany]	0.000 412 8	4.128 314 6E−04
coyan [Thailand]	0.000 833 3	8.333 333 3E−04
crith	11,125.327	1.112 532 7E+04
cuartilla [Ecuador]	0.043 478 3	4.347 826 1E−02
cuartilla [Venezuela]	0.5	5.000 000 0E−01
cubic foot of cement [US, dry, in bag]	0.023 453 4	2.345 343 2E−02
custom centner [Germany]	0.02	2.000 000 0E−02
custom quintal [Czechoslovakia, hops]	0.02	2.000 000 0E−02
dalton	>>>	6.022 136 7E+26
dan [Cambodia]	0.016 666 7	1.666 666 7E−02
dan [China]	0.01	1.000 000 0E−02
dan [Indonesia]	0.016 191 4	1.619 144 8E−02
dan [Japan]	0.016 666 7	1.666 666 7E−02
dan [Laos]	0.016 666 7	1.666 666 7E−02
dan [Philippines]	0.015 810 5	1.581 052 7E−02
dan [Thailand]	0.016 666 7	1.666 666 7E−02
dan [Vietnam]	0.016 541 8	1.654 177 6E−02
darm [Cambodia]	0.016 666 7	1.666 666 7E−02
darm [China]	0.02	2.000 000 0E−02
darm [Indonesia]	0.016 191 4	1.619 144 8E−02
darm [Japan]	0.016 666 7	1.666 666 7E−02
darm [Laos]	0.016 666 7	1.666 666 7E−02
darm [Philippines]	0.015 810 5	1.581 052 7E−02
darm [Thailand]	0.016 666 7	1.666 666 7E−02
darm [Vietnam]	0.016 541 8	1.654 177 6E−02
dawala [Ethiopia]	0.012 5	1.250 000 0E−02
dawulla [Ethiopia]	0.01	1.000 000 0E−02
decina [Italy]	0.294 724 4	2.947 244 3E−01
decitonne	0.01	1.000 000 0E−02
dharni [Nepal]	0.428 669 4	4.286 694 1E−01
dhura [India]	0.214 338 3	2.143 382 9E−01
dhurree [India]	0.214 362 3	2.143 622 7E−01
doon [Thailand]	0.041 666 7	4.166 666 7E−02
doppelzentner [Germany]	0.01	1.000 000 0E−02
drachm [UK, apothecary]	257.205 97	2.572 059 7E+02
dram [avoirdupois]	564.383 39	5.643 833 9E+02
dram [US, apothecary]	257.205 97	2.572 059 7E+02
dun [Cambodia]	0.016 666 7	1.666 666 7E−02
dun [China]	0.02	2.000 000 0E−02
dun [Indonesia]	0.016 191 4	1.619 144 8E−02
dun [Japan]	0.016 666 7	1.666 666 7E−02
dun [Laos]	0.016 666 7	1.666 666 7E−02
dun [Philippines]	0.015 810 5	1.581 052 7E−02
dun [Thailand]	0.016 666 7	1.666 666 7E−02
dun [Vietnam]	0.016 541 8	1.654 177 6E−02
dyne square second/centimeter	1,000.	1.000 000 0E+03
el cotejo [Venezuela]	0.2	2.000 000 0E−01
fanega [Costa Rica, coffee]	0.002 870 6	2.870 593 6E−03
fanega [Ecuador, grain]	0.008 849 6	8.849 557 5E−03
fanega [Morocco, grain]	0.022 727 3	2.272 727 3E−02
fanega [Nicaragua]	0.006 211 2	6.211 180 1E−03
fanega [Trinidad and Tobago]	0.020 040 1	2.004 008 0E−02
fanega [Uruguay]	0.01	1.000 000 0E−02
farasala [Muscat and Oman]	0.024 753 7	2.475 370 1E−02
farasalah [Oman]	0.024 752 5	2.475 247 5E−02
fardo [Honduras, tobacco]	0.021 739 1	2.173 913 0E−02
fardo [Philippines]	0.065 789 5	6.578 947 4E−02
fardo de tabaco [Costa Rica]	0.017 361 1	1.736 111 1E−02
farsalah [Somalia]	0.062 004	6.200 396 8E−02
farsalah [Tanzania]	0.061 237	6.123 698 7E−02
faunt [Saudi Arabia]	0.565 291 1	5.652 911 2E−01
ferasla [Ethiopia]	0.058 823 5	5.882 352 9E−02

kilogram (continued)   **<mass>**

Convert To	Standard	Scientific
ferrah [Oman]	0.088 495 6	8.849 557 5E-02
fierding [Iceland]	0.05	5.000 000 0E-02
firlot [UK, barley]	0.030 200 5	3.020 053 2E-02
firlot [UK, oats]	0.038 677 2	3.867 723 8E-02
firlot [UK, wheat]	0.036 743 1	3.674 309 2E-02
fisk [Iceland]	0.25	2.500 000 0E-01
flask of mercury	0.029 008 2	2.900 819 2E-02
frail [Spain]	0.044 052 9	4.405 286 3E-02
frasala [Ethiopia]	0.058 823 5	5.882 352 9E-02
frasala [Somalia]	0.062 004	6.200 396 8E-02
frasala [Tanzania]	0.061 237	6.123 698 7E-02
frasala [Yemen]	0.078 740 2	7.874 015 7E-02
frasila [Ethiopia]	0.058 823 5	5.882 352 9E-02
frasila [Somalia]	0.062 004	6.200 396 8E-02
frasila [Tanzania]	0.062 972 3	6.297 229 2E-02
frasila [Yemen]	0.078 740 2	7.874 015 7E-02
frasilla [Ethiopia]	0.058 823 5	5.882 352 9E-02
frasla [Somalia]	0.061 319 6	6.131 959 8E-02
frasla [Tanzania]	0.061 237	6.123 698 7E-02
frasla [Yemen]	0.089 126 6	8.912 656 0E-02
frasoulla [Ethiopia]	0.058 823 5	5.882 352 9E-02
frasoulla [Somalia]	0.062 004	6.200 396 8E-02
frasoulla [Tanzania]	0.061 237	6.123 698 7E-02
frazila [Tanzania]	0.061 237	6.123 698 7E-02
frazila [Ethiopia, coffee]	0.059 701 5	5.970 149 3E-02
gamma	>>>	1.000 000 0E+09
garsa [India, rice, milled]	0.000 283 9	2.838 860 6E-04
geepound	0.068 521 8	6.852 176 6E-02
gerbe [Spanish North Africa]	0.333 333 3	3.333 333 3E-01
ghirara [Syria]	0.004 790 6	4.790 648 7E-03
giarra [Libya]	0.013 333 3	1.333 333 3E-02
gin [Malaysia]	1.653 507 5	1.653 507 5E+00
girla [Tanzania]	0.006 123 7	6.123 698 7E-03
gisla [Eritrea]	0.006 132	6.131 959 8E-03
gisla [Tanzania]	0.006 123 7	6.123 698 7E-03
gisla [Yugoslavia]	0.006 135	6.134 969 3E-03
gizla [Somalia]	0.006 132	6.131 959 8E-03
glied [Germany, wool]	0.093 292 3	9.329 228 5E-02
glug	1.019 716 2	1.019 716 2E+00
gorraf [Libya]	0.08	8.000 000 0E-02
grain	15,432.358	1.543 235 8E+04
grain [apothecary]	15,432.358	1.543 235 8E+04
grain [avoirdupois]	15,432.358	1.543 235 8E+04
grain [metric]	20,000	2.000 000 0E+04
grain [troy]	15,432.358	1.543 235 8E+04
gram	1,000	1.000 000 0E+03
grande litra [Greece]	0.020 833 3	2.083 333 3E-02
great mina [Iraq, ancient]	1.039 501	1.039 501 0E+00
gun [China]	2	2.000 000 0E+00
hab [Cambodia]	0.016 666 7	1.666 666 7E-02
hab [China]	0.02	2.000 000 0E-02
hab [Indonesia]	0.016 191 4	1.619 144 8E-02
hab [Japan]	0.016 666 7	1.666 666 7E-02
hab [Laos]	0.016 666 7	1.666 666 7E-02
hab [Philippines]	0.015 810 5	1.581 052 7E-02
hab [Thailand]	0.016 666 7	1.666 666 7E-02
hab [Vietnam]	0.016 541 8	1.654 177 6E-02
hal [Cambodia]	0.016 666 7	1.666 666 7E-02
hal [China]	0.02	2.000 000 0E-02
hal [Indonesia]	0.016 191 4	1.619 144 8E-02
hal [Japan]	0.016 666 7	1.666 666 7E-02
hal [Laos]	0.016 666 7	1.666 666 7E-02

kilogram (continued)   <mass>

	Standard	Scientific
hal [Philippines]	0.015 810 5	1.581 052 7E-02
hal [Thailand]	0.016 666 7	1.666 666 7E-02
hal [Vietnam]	0.016 541 8	1.654 177 6E-02
half chest [Ceylon, tea]	0.031 494 6	3.149 460 5E-02
haml [Sudan]	0.003 205 1	3.205 128 2E-03
hap [Cambodia]	0.016 666 7	1.666 666 7E-02
hap [China]	0.02	2.000 000 0E-02
hap [Indonesia]	0.016 191 4	1.619 144 8E-02
hap [Laos]	0.016 666 7	1.666 666 7E-02
hap [Philippines]	0.015 810 5	1.581 052 7E-02
hap [Thailand]	0.016 666 7	1.666 666 7E-02
hap [Vietnam]	0.016 541 8	1.654 177 6E-02
harbour ton [South Africa]	0.001 102 3	1.102 311 4E-03
hembl [Sudan]	0.003 205 1	3.205 128 2E-03
heml [Egypt, ancient]	0.004 006 4	4.006 410 3E-03
hemla [Sudan]	0.013 354 7	1.335 470 1E-02
hogga [Iraq]	0.787 365	7.873 650 0E-01
hoi [Laos]	6.666 666 7	6.666 666 7E+00
hukka [Iraq, Baghdad]	0.239 980 8	2.399 808 0E-01
hundredweight [long]	0.019 684 1	1.968 413 1E-02
hundredweight [Pakistan]	0.019 684 1	1.968 412 9E-02
hundredweight [short]	0.022 046 2	2.204 622 6E-02
hundredweight [UK]	0.019 684 1	1.968 413 1E-02
hundredweight [US, gross]	0.019 684 1	1.968 413 1E-02
hundredweight [US, net]	0.022 046 2	2.204 622 6E-02
hyl	0.101 971 6	1.019 716 2E-01
imeru [Assyrian, ancient]	0.011 111 1	1.111 111 1E-02
jin [Brunei]	1.652 892 6	1.652 892 6E+00
jin [China, new]	2	2.000 000 0E+00
jin [China, old]	1.652 892 6	1.652 892 6E+00
jin [Hong Kong]	1.652 892 6	1.652 892 6E+00
jin [Indonesia]	1.618 123	1.618 123 0E+00
jin [Japan]	1.666 666 7	1.666 666 7E+00
jin [Malaysia]	1.652 892 6	1.652 892 6E+00
jin [Singapore]	1.652 892 6	1.652 892 6E+00
jin [South Korea]	1.666 666 7	1.666 666 7E+00
jin [Thailand]	1.666 666 7	1.666 666 7E+00
kahun [India, grain]	0.000 758 6	7.586 274 9E-04
kaila [Tanzania]	0.367 376 9	3.673 769 3E-01
kalvar [Persia]	0.001 682 9	1.682 935 0E-03
kamian [Poland]	0.098 642 7	9.864 267 0E-02
kamian [Russia]	0.097 677 1	9.767 714 0E-02
kamlah [Egypt]	0.013 354 7	1.335 470 1E-02
kamme [Japan]	0.266 666 7	2.666 666 7E-01
kan [Brunei]	1.652 892 6	1.652 892 6E+00
kan [China]	2	2.000 000 0E+00
kan [Hong Kong]	1.652 892 6	1.652 892 6E+00
kan [Japan]	0.266 666 7	2.666 666 7E-01
kan [Indonesia]	1.618 123	1.618 123 0E+00
kan [Malaysia]	1.652 892 6	1.652 892 6E+00
kan [Singapore]	1.652 892 6	1.652 892 6E+00
kan [South Korea]	1.666 666 7	1.666 666 7E+00
kan [Thailand]	1.666 666 7	1.666 666 7E+00
kandi [Yemen]	0.003 280 8	3.280 839 9E-03
kandy [India]	0.003 937	3.937 007 9E-03
kantar [Arab]	0.019 684 2	1.968 423 3E-02
kantar [Cyprus]	0.017 894 5	1.789 453 0E-02
kantar [Egypt, ancient]	0.022 256 8	2.225 684 4E-02
kantar [Ethiopia]	0.021 978	2.197 802 0E-02
kantar [Greece]	0.017 755 7	1.775 568 2E-02
kantar [Iraq, ancient]	0.022 257 8	2.225 783 5E-02
kantar [Jordan]	0.003 466 9	3.466 925 5E-03

kilogram (continued)   <mass>

	Standard	Scientific
kantar [Lebanon]	0.003 900 2	3.900 156 0E–03
kantar [Libya]	0.015 600 6	1.560 062 4E–02
kantar [Malta]	0.012 597 6	1.259 763 2E–02
kantar [Morocco]	0.01	1.000 000 0E–02
kantar [Saudi Arabia, ancient]	0.019 474 2	1.947 419 7E–02
kantar [Spanish North Africa]	0.019 704 4	1.970 443 3E–02
kantar [Sudan]	0.022 257 8	2.225 783 5E–02
kantar [Sudan, large]	0.007 066	7.065 989 5E–03
kantar [Syria]	0.003 898 6	3.898 635 5E–03
kantar [Turkey]	0.017 714 9	1.771 492 4E–02
kantar attari [Tunisia]	0.001 984 4	1.984 426 2E–03
kantar d'leppo [Cyprus]	0.004 374 3	4.374 250 4E–03
kantje [Germany]	0.013 513 5	1.351 351 4E–02
karch [Austria]	0.004 464 3	4.464 285 7E–03
karvar [Iran]	0.003 367 8	3.367 751 8E–03
kasm [Ethiopia]	0.256 410 3	2.564 102 6E–01
kati [Brunei]	1.652 892 6	1.652 892 6E+00
kati [China]	2	2.000 000 0E+00
kati [Hong Kong]	1.652 892 6	1.652 892 6E+00
kati [Indonesia]	1.618 123	1.618 123 0E+00
kati [Japan]	1.666 666 7	1.666 666 7E+00
kati [Malaysia]	1.652 892 6	1.652 892 6E+00
kati [Singapore]	1.652 892 6	1.652 892 6E+00
kati [South Korea]	1.666 666 7	1.666 666 7E+00
kati [Thailand]	1.666 666 7	1.666 666 7E+00
katti [Brunei]	1.652 892 6	1.652 892 6E+00
katti [China]	2	2.000 000 0E+00
katti [Hong Kong]	1.652 892 6	1.652 892 6E+00
katti [Indonesia]	1.618 123	1.618 123 0E+00
katti [Japan]	1.666 666 7	1.666 666 7E+00
katti [Malaysia]	1.652 892 6	1.652 892 6E+00
katti [Singapore]	1.652 892 6	1.652 892 6E+00
katti [South Korea]	1.666 666 7	1.666 666 7E+00
katti [Thailand]	1.666 666 7	1.666 666 7E+00
kela [Saudi Arabia]	0.314 930 9	3.149 308 7E–01
keml [Egypt]	0.004 006 4	4.006 410 3E–03
kemple [UK, straw]	0.005 010 5	5.010 497 0E–03
kental [Turkey]	0.055 679 3	5.567 928 7E–02
keun [Brunei]	1.652 892 6	1.652 892 6E+00
keun [China]	2	2.000 000 0E+00
keun [Hong Kong]	1.652 892 6	1.652 892 6E+00
keun [Indonesia]	1.618 123	1.618 123 0E+00
keun [Japan]	1.666 666 7	1.666 666 7E+00
keun [Malaysia]	1.652 892 6	1.652 892 6E+00
keun [Singapore]	1.652 892 6	1.652 892 6E+00
keun [South Korea]	1.666 666 7	1.666 666 7E+00
keun [Thailand]	1.666 666 7	1.666 666 7E+00
khandi [Oman, cereals]	0.004 405 3	4.405 286 3E–03
kharvar [Afghanistan]	0.001 769	1.769 034 8E–03
kharvar [Iran]	0.003 367 8	3.367 751 8E–03
kharwar [Afghanistan]	0.001 769	1.769 034 8E–03
kharwar [Iran]	0.003 333 3	3.333 333 3E–03
kharwar [Persia]	0.003 367	3.367 003 4E–03
kiccar [Hebrew, ancient]	0.026 315 8	2.631 578 9E–02
kikar [Hebrew, ancient]	0.020 362 5	2.036 245 2E–02
kikkar [Hebrew, ancient]	0.029 154 5	2.915 451 9E–02
kikkar [Iraq, ancient]	0.017 806 3	1.780 626 8E–02
kikkor [Hebrew, ancient]	0.026 315 8	2.631 578 9E–02
kila [Egypt, wheat]	0.08	8.000 000 0E–02
kile [Cyprus, rye]	0.036 743 1	3.674 309 2E–02
kile [Cyprus, wheat]	0.037 493 9	3.749 390 7E–02
kile [Turkey, barley]	0.038 461 5	3.846 153 8E–02

Convert From	<Type of Unit>	
Convert To	Standard	Scientific

kilogram (continued)   \<mass>

Convert To	Standard	Scientific
kile [Turkey, oats]	0.041 666 7	4.166 666 7E-02
kile [Turkey, rye]	0.035 714 3	3.571 428 6E-02
kile [Turkey, wheat]	0.033 333 3	3.333 333 3E-02
kilogram-force square second/meter	0.101 971 6	1.019 716 2E-01
kilolitra [Greece]	0.002 083 3	2.083 333 3E-03
kiloton [metric]	0.000 001	1.000 000 0E-06
kilotonne	0.000 001	1.000 000 0E-06
kin [Japan]	1.666 666 7	1.666 666 7E+00
kinn [Brunei]	1.652 892 6	1.652 892 6E+00
kinn [China]	1.652 892 6	1.652 892 6E+00
kinn [Hong Kong]	1.652 892 6	1.652 892 6E+00
kinn [Indonesia]	1.618 123	1.618 123 0E+00
kinn [Japan]	1.666 666 7	1.666 666 7E+00
kinn [Malaysia]	1.652 892 6	1.652 892 6E+00
kinn [Singapore]	1.652 892 6	1.652 892 6E+00
kinn [South Korea]	1.666 666 7	1.666 666 7E+00
kinn [Thailand]	1.666 666 7	1.666 666 7E+00
kintar [Cyprus]	0.017 894 5	1.789 453 0E-02
kintar [Egypt]	0.022 257 8	2.225 783 5E-02
kintar [Greece]	0.017 755 7	1.775 568 2E-02
kintar [Iraq]	0.003 645 6	3.645 643 2E-03
kintar [Lebanon]	0.003 900 2	3.900 156 0E-03
kintar [Malta]	0.012 597 6	1.259 763 2E-02
kintar [Morocco]	0.01	1.000 000 0E-02
kintar [Sudan, large]	0.007 067 1	7.067 137 8E-03
kintar [Sudan, small]	0.022 257 8	2.225 783 5E-02
kintar [Syria]	0.003 898 6	3.898 635 5E-03
kintar [Turkey]	0.017 714 8	1.771 479 2E-02
kiyak kin [Japan]	0.016 638 7	1.663 874 1E-02
kiyaka me [Japan]	0.002 662	2.661 992 9E-03
klender [Germany, wool]	0.095 093 2	9.509 319 1E-02
kleud [Germany, wool]	0.095 093 2	9.509 319 1E-02
kolle [Lebanon, olive oil]	0.029 989 5	2.998 950 4E-02
koret [Poland]	0.02	2.000 000 0E-02
korn tonde [Denmark, oats]	0.014 285 7	1.428 571 4E-02
korn tonde [Denmark, wheat]	0.009 302 3	9.302 325 6E-03
kouna [Ethiopia]	0.25	2.500 000 0E-01
koyan [Brunei]	0.000 413 4	4.133 939 6E-04
koyan [Malaysia]	0.000 413 4	4.133 939 6E-04
koyan [Singapore]	0.000 413 4	4.133 939 6E-04
koyang [Batavia]	0.000 599 9	5.998 800 2E-04
kula [Spanish North Africa]	0.089 565 6	8.956 560 7E-02
kulack [Batavia, grain and rice]	0.232 342	2.323 420 1E-01
kung chin [China]	1	1.000 000 0E+00
kung chin [Taiwan]	1	1.000 000 0E+00
kung heng [Taiwan]	0.1	1.000 000 0E-01
kung shi [China]	0.01	1.000 000 0E-02
kung tan [Taiwan]	0.01	1.000 000 0E-02
kung ton [China]	0.001	1.000 000 0E-03
kunna [Ethiopia]	0.2	2.000 000 0E-01
kurr [Islam, wheat]	0.000 353 5	3.534 818 0E-04
kurr [Mesopotamia, ancient, wheat]	0.001 296 7	1.296 680 5E-03
kurr [Persia, ancient, wheat]	0.000 996	9.960 916 4E-04
kwamme [Japan]	0.266 666 7	2.666 666 7E-01
kwan [Japan]	0.266 666 7	2.666 666 7E-01
kwan [South Korea]	0.266 666 7	2.666 666 7E-01
lachsa [Philippines]	0.032 938 1	3.293 807 6E-02
ladan [Ethiopia]	0.025	2.500 000 0E-02
lagel [Austria, steel]	0.014 282 7	1.428 265 4E-02
lane [Laos]	0.000 833 3	8.333 333 3E-04
last [Denmark]	0.000 5	5.000 000 0E-04
li [South Korea]	0.254 629 2	2.546 291 6E-01

Convert From Convert To	Standard	Scientific

kilogram (continued)   **<mass>**

Convert To	Standard	Scientific
libra [Italy]	1	1.000 000 0E+00
libra [Libya]	2.941 176 5	2.941 176 5E+00
liespfund [Germany]	0.147 470 9	1.474 708 7E−01
liespund [Iceland]	0.031 25	3.125 000 0E−02
lispond [Norway]	0.125 486 3	1.254 862 6E−01
lispound [Denmark]	0.125 000 4	1.250 004 1E−01
lispound [Sweden]	0.117 619 1	1.176 190 8E−01
lispund [Denmark]	0.125	1.250 000 0E−01
lispund [Sweden]	0.117 626	1.176 260 2E−01
litre [Cyprus]	0.437 445 3	4.374 453 2E−01
litre [Indonesia, rice, milled]	1.25	1.250 000 0E+00
litro [Venezuela]	0.4	4.000 000 0E−01
livre [Belgium]	2	2.000 000 0E+00
livre [Switzerland]	2	2.000 000 0E+00
livre poids de marc [France]	0.002 042 9	2.042 859 2E−03
load [Gambia, cocoa]	0.036 764 7	3.676 470 6E−02
load [Ghana, cocoa]	0.036 764 7	3.676 470 6E−02
load [Nigeria, cocoa]	0.036 764 7	3.676 470 6E−02
load [Sierra Leone, cocoa]	0.036 764 7	3.676 470 6E−02
lood [Netherlands]	0.1	1.000 000 0E−01
ludra [Turkey]	1.773 049 6	1.773 049 6E+00
luong [Vietnam]	0.026 666 7	2.666 666 7E−02
mahn [Afghanistan]	0.223 214 3	2.232 142 9E−01
mahnd [Arab]	1.080 697 4	1.080 697 4E+00
mahud [Saudi Arabia, ancient]	1.081 081 1	1.081 081 1E+00
makkuk [Islam, ancient, wheat]	0.067 069 1	6.706 908 1E−02
man [Iran]	0.333 333 3	3.333 333 3E−01
man [Iraq]	0.039 368 3	3.936 826 5E−02
man [Muslim India]	0.026 795 3	2.679 528 4E−02
man chah [Iran]	0.168 387 3	1.683 873 0E−01
man i bandar abbassi [Iran]	0.256 590 5	2.565 905 3E−01
man i hashemi [Iran]	0.018 709 7	1.870 970 4E−02
man i kahneh [Iran]	0.215 535 8	2.155 358 2E−01
man i noh abbassi [Iran]	0.299 355 5	2.993 554 9E−01
man i rey [Iran]	0.084 193 5	8.419 351 0E−02
man i shah [Iran]	0.168 387 3	1.683 873 0E−01
man i tabriz [Iran]	0.333 333 3	3.333 333 3E−01
man tabriz [Iran]	0.336 775 2	3.367 751 8E−01
mancuema [Honduras]	0.695 652 2	6.956 521 7E−01
maneh [Babylon, ancient]	1.980 198	1.980 198 0E+00
mann [Iraq, Baghdad]	0.04	4.000 000 0E−02
mann [Iraq, Basra, coffee]	0.015 588 5	1.558 846 5E−02
mann [Persia, ancient]	0.333 333 3	3.333 333 3E−01
mann [Turkey, silk]	0.261 301 3	2.613 012 8E−01
mano [Honduras, maize or corn]	0.881 834 2	8.818 342 2E−01
mao [Portuguese India]	0.026 795 3	2.679 528 4E−02
maon [India, Bombay]	0.078 740 2	7.874 015 7E−02
maon [India, Calcutta]	0.091 549 9	9.154 994 0E−02
maon [India, Madras]	0.088 183 4	8.818 342 2E−02
marco real [Bolivia]	0.010 869 6	1.086 956 5E−02
marco real [Ecuador]	0.010 869 6	1.086 956 5E−02
marco real [Nicaragua]	0.006 211 2	6.211 180 1E−03
marco real [Trinidad and Tobago]	0.020 040 1	2.004 008 0E−02
marco real [Uruguay]	0.01	1.000 000 0E−02
marfold [Venezuela]	0.002 5	2.500 000 0E−03
mark [Austria]	0.003 571 3	3.571 301 0E−03
mark [Denmark]	4.277 16	4.277 160 0E+00
mark [Iceland]	1	1.000 000 0E+00
mark [Norway]	4.746 084 5	4.746 084 5E+00
matar [Islam, ancient, oil]	0.058 823 5	5.882 352 9E−02
maund [Afghanistan]	0.028 304 6	2.830 455 7E−02
maund [Bahrain]	0.039 370 1	3.937 007 9E−02

kilogram (continued) <mass>

	Standard	Scientific
maund [Bangladesh]	0.026 795 3	2.679 528 4E-02
maund [Ceylon]	0.026 792 3	2.679 229 0E-02
maund [India]	0.026 792 4	2.679 241 2E-02
maund [India, bazaar]	0.026 845 6	2.684 563 8E-02
maund [India, Bombay]	0.076 558	7.655 795 4E-02
maund [India, Surat]	0.059 056 3	5.905 628 1E-02
maund [Kuwait]	0.039 370 1	3.937 007 9E-02
maund [Muscat and Oman]	0.247 524 8	2.475 247 5E-01
maund [Nepal]	0.026 792 3	2.679 226 9E-02
maund [Pakistan]	0.026 795 3	2.679 528 4E-02
maund [Saudi Arabia]	0.026 820 4	2.682 043 7E-02
maund [Singapore, rice, milled]	0.026 881 7	2.688 172 0E-02
maund [Sumatra, rice, milled]	0.029 403 1	2.940 311 7E-02
maund [Tanzania]	0.747 384 2	7.473 841 6E-01
maund [Yemen]	0.026 795 3	2.679 528 4E-02
maund [Zanzibar and Pemba]	0.752 445 5	7.524 454 5E-01
mazsa [Hungary]	0.01	1.000 000 0E+00
media [Bolivia]	0.021 739 1	2.173 913 0E-02
media [Chile]	0.021 739 1	2.173 913 0E-02
media [Colombia]	0.02	2.000 000 0E-02
media [Costa Rica]	0.021 739 1	2.173 913 0E-02
media [Cuba]	0.02	2.000 000 0E-02
media [Czechoslovakia]	0.021 734 9	2.173 487 8E-02
media [Dominican Republic]	0.022 045 9	2.204 585 5E-02
media [Ecuador]	0.021 739 1	2.173 913 0E-02
media [Guatemala]	0.021 739 1	2.173 913 0E-02
media [Honduras]	0.021 739 1	2.173 913 0E-02
media [Macao]	0.017 020 7	1.702 069 7E-02
media [Mexico]	0.021 729 7	2.172 968 3E-02
media [Paraguay]	0.021 786 5	2.178 649 2E-02
media [Peru]	0.021 739 1	2.173 913 0E-02
media [Philippines]	0.021 739 1	2.173 913 0E-02
media [Portugal]	0.016 666 7	1.666 666 7E-02
media [Spain]	0.021 734 9	2.173 487 8E-02
media [Venezuela]	0.021 696 7	2.169 668 0E-02
megaton [metric]	<<<	1.000 000 0E-09
megatonne	<<<	1.000 000 0E-09
meile [Venezuela]	0.002 5	2.500 000 0E-03
meterzentner [Austria]	0.01	1.000 000 0E+00
metric-technical unit of mass	0.101 971 6	1.019 716 2E-01
metrischer [Germany]	0.01	1.000 000 0E+00
mil [Venezuela]	0.002 5	2.500 000 0E-03
milli-mass-unit	>>>	6.022 136 7E+29
millier	0.001	1.000 000 0E-03
mina [Greece, ancient]	0.666 666 7	6.666 666 7E-01
minah [Iraq, ancient]	1.112 347 1	1.112 347 1E+00
modd [Malta, wheat]	0.004 499 2	4.499 235 1E-03
moio [Portugal]	0.028 323 8	2.832 379 8E-02
mon [Bahrain]	0.039 370 1	3.937 007 9E-02
mon [Bangladesh]	0.026 795 3	2.679 528 4E-02
mon [India]	0.026 795 3	2.679 528 4E-02
mon [Muscat and Oman]	0.247 524 8	2.475 247 5E-01
mon [Pakistan]	0.026 795 3	2.679 528 4E-02
mon [Yemen]	0.026 795 3	2.679 528 4E-02
moosa [Cyprus]	0.019 684 1	1.968 412 9E-02
mounce	40	4.000 000 0E+01
mound [India]	0.026 809 7	2.680 965 1E-02
mudu [Nigeria]	0.884 955 8	8.849 557 5E-01
mula [Bolivia]	0.010 869 6	1.086 956 5E-02
mula [Ecuador]	0.010 869 6	1.086 956 5E-02
mula [Nicaragua]	0.006 211 2	6.211 180 1E-03
mula [Trinidad and Tobago]	0.020 040 1	2.004 008 0E-02

kilogram (continued)   \<mass>

Unit	Standard	Scientific
mula [Uruguay]	0.01	1.000 000 0E-02
mule load [Belize]	0.011 022 9	1.102 292 8E-02
mun [Laos]	0.083 333 3	8.333 333 3E-02
mune [Laos]	0.083 333 3	8.333 333 3E-02
mutagalla [Ethiopia]	0.128 205 1	1.282 051 3E-01
myriagram	0.1	1.000 000 0E-01
nagel [Belgium]	0.355 618 8	3.556 187 8E-01
nagel [Holland]	0.355 618 8	3.556 187 8E-01
nagel [UK, wool]	0.319 795 3	3.197 953 3E-01
nail [Belgium]	0.355 618 8	3.556 187 8E-01
nail [Holland]	0.355 618 8	3.556 187 8E-01
nail [UK, wool]	0.319 795 3	3.197 953 3E-01
natr [Ethiopia]	1.187 634 4	1.187 634 4E+00
nelli [Sumatra, rice, milled]	0.068 516 6	6.851 661 5E-02
newton square second/meter	1	1.000 000 0E+00
nim man [Iran]	0.666 666 7	6.666 666 7E-01
occa [Egypt, ancient]	0.801 282 1	8.012 820 5E-01
occa [Iraq, ancient]	0.801 282 1	8.012 820 5E-01
occa [Romania]	0.775 795 2	7.757 951 9E-01
ock [Cyprus]	0.787 401 6	7.874 015 7E-01
ock [Greece]	0.781 25	7.812 500 0E-01
ock [Jordan]	0.780 031 2	7.800 312 0E-01
ock [Lebanon]	0.780 031 2	7.800 312 0E-01
ock [Libya]	0.780 031 2	7.800 312 0E-01
ock [Saudi Arabia]	0.801 282 1	8.012 820 5E-01
ock [Syria]	0.780 031 2	7.800 312 0E-01
ock [Turkey]	0.779 423 2	7.794 232 3E-01
ocque [Lebanon]	0.780 037 3	7.800 372 9E-01
ogga [Turkey, ancient]	0.779 423 2	7.794 232 3E-01
oka [Egypt, ancient]	0.801 282 1	8.012 820 5E-01
oka [Greece]	0.781 25	7.812 500 0E-01
oka [Iraq, ancient]	0.801 282 1	8.012 820 5E-01
oka [Jordan]	0.780 031 2	7.800 312 0E-01
oka [Lebanon]	0.780 031 2	7.800 312 0E-01
oka [Libya]	0.801 282 1	8.012 820 5E-01
oka [Saudi Arabia]	0.801 282 1	8.012 820 5E-01
oka [Syria]	0.780 031 2	7.800 312 0E-01
oka [Turkey]	0.779 423 2	7.794 232 3E-01
oka [Yugoslavia]	0.781 25	7.812 500 0E-01
oke [Afghanistan]	0.892 857 1	8.928 571 4E-01
oke [Bulgaria]	0.776 397 5	7.763 975 2E-01
oke [Cyprus]	0.787 401 6	7.874 015 7E-01
oke [Egypt]	0.801 282 1	8.012 820 5E-01
oke [Greece]	0.781 25	7.812 500 0E-01
oke [Iraq]	0.801 282 1	8.012 820 5E-01
oke [Jordan]	0.780 031 2	7.800 312 0E-01
oke [Lebanon]	0.780 031 2	7.800 312 0E-01
oke [Libya]	0.780 031 2	7.800 312 0E-01
oke [Romania]	0.787 401 6	7.874 015 7E-01
oke [Saudi Arabia]	0.787 339 6	7.873 395 8E-01
oke [Sudan]	0.801 282 1	8.012 820 5E-01
oke [Syria]	0.780 031 2	7.800 312 0E-01
oke [Turkey]	0.779 423 2	7.794 232 3E-01
oke [Yugoslavia]	0.781 25	7.812 500 0E-01
okia [Iraq, Baghdad]	0.959 692 9	9.596 929 0E-01
okiya [Iraq, Baghdad]	0.959 692 9	9.596 929 0E-01
okka [Cyprus]	0.787 401 6	7.874 015 7E-01
okka [Greece]	0.781 25	7.812 500 0E-01
okka [Jordan]	0.780 031 2	7.800 312 0E-01
okka [Lebanon]	0.780 031 2	7.800 312 0E-01
okka [Libya]	0.780 031 2	7.800 312 0E-01
okka [Saudi Arabia]	0.801 282 1	8.012 820 5E-01

kilogram (continued)   \<mass\>

	Standard	Scientific
okka [Syria]	0.780 031 2	7.800 312 0E–01
okka [Turkey]	0.779 456 6	7.794 566 4E–01
okka [Turkey, ancient]	0.779 423 2	7.794 232 3E–01
okka [Yemen]	1.176 470 6	1.176 470 6E+00
once [Iraq]	0.959 692 9	9.596 929 0E–01
oqa [Islam]	0.797 448 2	7.974 481 7E–01
oqiya [Iraq, Baghdad]	0.959 692 9	9.596 929 0E–01
oquia [Iraq, Baghdad]	0.959 692 9	9.596 929 0E–01
ounce	35.273 962	3.527 396 2E+01
ounce [apothecary]	32.150 747	3.215 074 7E+01
ounce [avoirdupois]	35.273 962	3.527 396 2E+01
ounce [metric]	40	4.000 000 0E+01
ounce [troy]	32.150 747	3.215 074 7E+01
paca [Venezuela]	0.02	2.000 000 0E–02
pachen [Russia]	0.002 034 9	2.034 940 0E–03
pack [UK]	0.009 185 9	9.185 941 8E–03
package [Bangladesh, tea]	0.021 198 1	2.119 811 8E–02
packen [Russia]	0.002 037 5	2.037 531 3E–03
palie [India]	0.587 889 5	5.878 894 8E–01
pallie [India]	0.587 889 5	5.878 894 8E–01
pally [India]	0.214 338 3	2.143 382 9E–01
paloin [India]	0.587 889 5	5.878 894 8E–01
parah [Sumatra, rice, milled]	0.021 081 5	2.108 148 0E–02
passeree [India]	0.214 362 3	2.143 622 7E–01
pauseri [India]	0.214 338 3	2.143 382 9E–01
pecul [Batavia]	0.020 386 5	2.038 652 9E–02
pecul [Brunei]	0.016 534 7	1.653 466 5E–02
pecul [Cambodia]	0.016 666 7	1.666 666 7E–02
pecul [China]	0.02	2.000 000 0E–02
pecul [China, Canton]	0.016 534 9	1.653 493 8E–02
pecul [Hong Kong]	0.016 534 7	1.653 466 5E–02
pecul [India]	0.016 934 2	1.693 422 7E–02
pecul [India, Madras]	0.016 701 5	1.670 146 1E–02
pecul [Indonesia]	0.016 191 4	1.619 144 8E–02
pecul [Japan]	0.016 666 7	1.666 666 7E–02
pecul [Laos]	0.016 666 7	1.666 666 7E–02
pecul [Macao]	0.016 534 7	1.653 466 5E–02
pecul [Malaysia]	0.016 534 7	1.653 466 5E–02
pecul [Philippines]	0.015 810 5	1.581 052 7E–02
pecul [Thailand]	0.016 666 7	1.666 666 7E–02
pecul [Vietnam]	0.016 541 8	1.654 177 6E–02
pedra [Cape Verde]	0.726 216 4	7.262 164 1E–01
peiktha [Burma]	0.612 369 9	6.123 698 7E–01
pekul [India]	0.016 934 2	1.693 422 7E–02
pennyweight [troy]	643.014 93	6.430 149 3E+02
perma [Russia, hay]	0.000 254 7	2.546 862 3E–04
peso [Italy]	0.110 460 6	1.104 606 2E–01
peso grosso [Italy, Genoa]	0.038 223 4	3.822 337 7E–02
pfund [Austria]	2	2.000 000 0E+00
pfund [Denmark]	2	2.000 000 0E+00
pfund [Germany]	2	2.000 000 0E+00
pfund [Switzerland]	2	2.000 000 0E+00
phan [Laos]	0.833 333 3	8.333 333 3E–01
pic [India]	0.016 934 2	1.693 422 7E–02
pico [Brunei]	0.016 534 7	1.653 466 5E–02
pico [Cambodia]	0.016 666 7	1.666 666 7E–02
pico [China]	0.02	2.000 000 0E–02
pico [Hong Kong]	0.016 534 7	1.653 466 5E–02
pico [Indonesia]	0.016 191 4	1.619 144 8E–02
pico [Japan]	0.016 666 7	1.666 666 7E–02
pico [Laos]	0.016 666 7	1.666 666 7E–02
pico [Macao]	0.016 534 7	1.653 466 5E–02

kilogram (continued)   \<mass\>

Convert To	Standard	Scientific
pico [Malaysia]	0.016 534 7	1.653 466 5E-02
pico [Philippines]	0.015 810 5	1.581 052 7E-02
pico [Singapore]	0.016 534 7	1.653 466 5E-02
pico [Thailand]	0.016 666 7	1.666 666 7E-02
pico [Vietnam]	0.016 541 8	1.654 177 6E-02
picol [Brunei]	0.016 534 7	1.653 466 5E-02
picol [Cambodia]	0.016 666 7	1.666 666 7E-02
picol [China]	0.016 534 9	1.653 493 8E-02
picol [Hong Kong]	0.016 534 7	1.653 466 5E-02
picol [India]	0.016 934 2	1.693 422 7E-02
picol [Indonesia]	0.016 191 4	1.619 144 8E-02
picol [Japan]	0.016 666 7	1.666 666 7E-02
picol [Laos]	0.016 666 7	1.666 666 7E-02
picol [Macao]	0.016 534 7	1.653 466 5E-02
picol [Malaysia]	0.016 534 7	1.653 466 5E-02
picol [Philippines]	0.015 810 5	1.581 052 7E-02
picol [Singapore]	0.016 534 7	1.653 466 5E-02
picol [Thailand]	0.016 666 7	1.666 666 7E-02
picol [Vietnam]	0.016 541 8	1.654 177 6E-02
picul [Brunei]	0.016 534 7	1.653 466 5E-02
picul [Cambodia]	0.016 666 7	1.666 666 7E-02
picul [China]	0.016 534 7	1.653 467 0E-02
picul [Hong Kong]	0.016 534 7	1.653 466 5E-02
picul [India]	0.016 934 2	1.693 422 7E-02
picul [Indonesia]	0.016 191 4	1.619 144 8E-02
picul [Japan]	0.016 666 7	1.666 666 7E-02
picul [Laos]	0.016 666 7	1.666 666 7E-02
picul [Macao]	0.016 534 7	1.653 466 5E-02
picul [Malaysia]	0.016 534 7	1.653 466 5E-02
picul [North Borneo]	0.016 534 7	1.653 467 0E-02
picul [Philippines]	0.015 810 5	1.581 052 7E-02
picul [Singapore]	0.016 534 7	1.653 466 5E-02
picul [South Korea]	0.016 535 1	1.653 507 5E-02
picul [Thailand]	0.016 666 7	1.666 666 7E-02
picul [Vietnam]	0.016 541 8	1.654 177 6E-02
pikul [Brunei]	0.016 534 7	1.653 466 5E-02
pikul [Cambodia]	0.016 666 7	1.666 666 7E-02
pikul [China]	0.016 534 7	1.653 466 5E-02
pikul [Hong Kong]	0.016 534 7	1.653 466 5E-02
pikul [Indonesia]	0.016 191 4	1.619 144 8E-02
pikul [Japan]	0.016 666 7	1.666 666 7E-02
pikul [Laos]	0.016 666 7	1.666 666 7E-02
pikul [Macao]	0.016 534 7	1.653 466 5E-02
pikul [Malaysia]	0.016 534 7	1.653 466 5E-02
pikul [North Borneo]	0.016 534 7	1.653 467 0E-02
pikul [Philippines]	0.015 810 5	1.581 052 7E-02
pikul [Singapore]	0.016 534 7	1.653 466 5E-02
pikul [Thailand]	0.016 666 7	1.666 666 7E-02
pikul [Vietnam]	0.016 541 8	1.654 177 6E-02
pintji [Netherlands Antilles]	2.666 666 7	2.666 666 7E+00
pocket [Swaziland, rice, milled]	0.022 046 3	2.204 634 1E-02
pocket [Zambia, rice, milled]	0.022 222 2	2.222 222 2E-02
poids de Paris [France]	0.002 042 9	2.042 859 2E-03
point [jewelers]	500,000	5.000 000 0E+05
pood [Russia]	0.061 050 1	6.105 006 1E-02
poud [Russia]	0.061 050 1	6.105 006 1E-02
pound	2.204 622 6	2.204 622 6E+00
pound [apothecary]	2.679 228 9	2.679 228 9E+00
pound [Argentina]	2.179 836 5	2.179 836 5E+00
pound [avoirdupois]	2.204 622 6	2.204 622 6E+00
pound [Denmark]	2	2.000 000 0E+00
pound [France]	2	2.000 000 0E+00

kilogram (continued) \<mass\>

	Standard	Scientific
pound [international]	2.204 622 6	2.204 622 6E+00
pound [Netherlands, Amsterdam]	2.024 291 5	2.024 291 5E+00
pound [Rome, ancient]	3.067 484 7	3.067 484 7E+00
pound [Russia, avoirdupois]	2.441 928 4	2.441 928 4E+00
pound [Spain]	2.173 913	2.173 913 0E+00
pound [troy]	2.679 228 9	2.679 228 9E+00
pound [UK]	2.204 622 6	2.204 622 6E+00
pound [unified]	2.204 622 6	2.204 622 6E+00
pound [US, avoirdupois]	2.204 622 3	2.204 622 3E+00
pound [US, troy]	2.679 228 5	2.679 228 5E+00
pound-force square second/foot	0.068 521 8	6.852 176 6E-02
poundal square second/foot	2.204 622 6	2.204 622 6E+00
pud [Russia]	0.061 349 7	6.134 969 3E-02
pund [Denmark]	2	2.000 000 0E+00
pund [Germany]	2	2.000 000 0E+00
pund [Iceland]	2	2.000 000 0E+00
punto [Venezuela]	0.001 666 7	1.666 666 7E-03
pushuri [Bangladesh]	0.214 316 3	2.143 163 3E-01
pyi [Burma, rice, milled]	0.470 366 9	4.703 668 9E-01
qadah [Yemen]	0.011 022 9	1.102 292 8E-02
qantar [Cyprus]	0.017 894 5	1.789 453 0E-02
qantar [Egypt]	0.022 257 8	2.225 783 5E-02
qantar [Greece]	0.017 755 7	1.775 568 2E-02
qantar [Iraq, ancient]	0.022 257 8	2.225 783 5E-02
qantar [Islam]	0.022 377 4	2.237 737 2E-02
qantar [Lebanon]	0.003 900 2	3.900 156 0E-03
qantar [Libya]	0.019 500 8	1.950 078 0E-02
qantar [Malta]	0.012 597 8	1.259 779 0E-02
qantar [Morocco]	0.01	1.000 000 0E-02
qantar [Sudan, large]	0.007 067 1	7.067 137 8E-03
qantar [Sudan, small]	0.022 257 8	2.225 783 5E-02
qantar [Syria]	0.003 898 6	3.898 635 5E-03
qantar [Turkey]	0.017 714 8	1.771 479 2E-02
qasa [Yemen]	0.881 834 2	8.818 342 2E-01
qili [Lebanon, olive oil]	0.029 989 5	2.998 950 4E-02
qintar [Egypt, ancient]	0.022 257 8	2.225 783 5E-02
qintar [Iraq, ancient]	0.022 257 8	2.225 783 5E-02
quantar [Cyprus]	0.017 894 5	1.789 453 0E-02
quantar [Egypt]	0.022 257 8	2.225 783 5E-02
quantar [Greece]	0.017 755 7	1.775 568 2E-02
quantar [Lebanon]	0.003 900 2	3.900 156 0E-03
quantar [Libya]	0.019 500 8	1.950 078 0E-02
quantar [Malta]	0.012 597 6	1.259 763 2E-02
quantar [Morocco]	0.01	1.000 000 0E-02
quantar [Sudan, large]	0.007 067 1	7.067 137 8E-03
quantar [Sudan, small]	0.022 257 8	2.225 783 5E-02
quantar [Syria]	0.003 898 6	3.898 635 5E-03
quantar [Turkey]	0.017 714 8	1.771 479 2E-02
quarter [long]	0.003 936 8	3.936 826 1E-03
quarter [short]	0.004 409 2	4.409 245 2E-03
quarter [UK]	0.078 736 5	7.873 652 2E-02
quarter [US]	0.088 184 9	8.818 490 5E-02
quintal [Algiers, copper and wax]	0.018 501 4	1.850 138 8E-02
quintal [Algiers, cotton and almonds]	0.016 819 4	1.681 944 3E-02
quintal [Algiers, flax]	0.009 250 7	9.250 693 8E-03
quintal [Algiers, iron, lead, and wool]	0.012 334 3	1.233 425 8E-02
quintal [Algiers, oil, soap, butter, honey, and dates]	0.011 145 4	1.114 541 4E-02
quintal [Bolivia]	0.021 739 1	2.173 913 0E-02
quintal [Brazil]	0.017 018 8	1.701 884 5E-02
quintal [British Honduras]	0.022 046 2	2.204 622 6E-02
quintal [Chile]	0.021 734 7	2.173 473 6E-02
quintal [Colombia]	0.02	2.000 000 0E-02

	Standard	Scientific

kilogram (continued)   **<mass>**

Convert To	Standard	Scientific
quintal [Costa Rica]	0.021 739 1	2.173 913 0E–02
quintal [Cuba]	0.021 734 9	2.173 487 8E–02
quintal [Czechoslovakia]	0.02	2.000 000 0E–02
quintal [Dominican Republic]	0.022 045 9	2.204 585 5E–02
quintal [Ecuador]	0.021 739 1	2.173 913 0E–02
quintal [Egypt, ancient]	0.022 257 8	2.225 783 5E–02
quintal [El Salvador]	0.022 037 1	2.203 711 0E–02
quintal [France]	0.020 428 6	2.042 859 2E–02
quintal [France, Paris]	0.01	1.000 000 0E–02
quintal [Greece]	0.017 755 7	1.775 568 2E–02
quintal [Guatemala]	0.021 739 1	2.173 913 0E–02
quintal [Honduras]	0.021 739 1	2.173 913 0E–02
quintal [Iraq, ancient]	0.022 257 8	2.225 783 5E–02
quintal [Macao]	0.017 020 7	1.702 069 7E–02
quintal [metric]	0.01	1.000 000 0E–02
quintal [Mexico]	0.021 729 7	2.172 968 3E–02
quintal [Morocco]	0.019 508 4	1.950 838 9E–02
quintal [Nicaragua]	0.021 739 1	2.173 913 0E–02
quintal [Paraguay]	0.021 786 5	2.178 649 2E–02
quintal [Peru]	0.021 739 1	2.173 913 0E–02
quintal [Philippines]	0.021 739 1	2.173 913 0E–02
quintal [Portugal]	0.016 666 7	1.666 666 7E–02
quintal [Romania]	0.017 628 6	1.762 860 1E–02
quintal [Spain]	0.021 734 9	2.173 487 8E–02
quintal [Switzerland]	0.01	1.000 000 0E–02
quintal [Turkey]	0.01	1.000 000 0E–02
quintal [UK]	0.019 684 1	1.968 413 1E–02
quintal [Uruguay]	0.021 767 5	2.176 752 3E–02
quintal [US]	0.022 046 2	2.204 622 6E–02
quintal [Venezuela]	0.021 696 7	2.169 668 0E–02
quintar [Saudi Arabia]	0.019 683 5	1.968 348 9E–02
quintaux [France]	0.020 429	2.042 900 9E–02
rafa [Bahrain]	0.003 937	3.937 007 9E–03
raik [India]	0.857 353 5	8.573 535 2E–01
ratal [Egypt]	2.227 171 5	2.227 171 5E+00
ratal [Iran]	2.132 196 2	2.132 196 2E+00
ratal [Jordan]	0.390 015 6	3.900 156 0E–01
ratal [Lebanon]	0.390 015 6	3.900 156 0E–01
ratal [Libya]	1.949 317 7	1.949 317 7E+00
ratal [Malta]	1.259 445 8	1.259 445 8E+00
ratal [Saudi Arabia]	2.164 502 2	2.164 502 2E+00
ratal [Somalia]	2.232 142 9	2.232 142 9E+00
ratal [Sudan]	2.227 171 5	2.227 171 5E+00
ratal [Syria]	0.389 863 6	3.898 635 5E–01
ratal [Tanzania]	2.202 643 2	2.202 643 2E+00
ratel [Egypt]	2.227 171 5	2.227 171 5E+00
ratel [Iran]	2.132 196 2	2.132 196 2E+00
ratel [Jordan]	0.390 015 6	3.900 156 0E–01
ratel [Lebanon]	0.390 015 6	3.900 156 0E–01
ratel [Libya]	1.949 317 7	1.949 317 7E+00
ratel [Malta]	1.259 445 8	1.259 445 8E+00
ratel [Saudi Arabia]	2.164 502 2	2.164 502 2E+00
ratel [Somalia]	2.232 142 9	2.232 142 9E+00
ratel [Sudan]	2.227 171 5	2.227 171 5E+00
ratel [Syria]	0.389 863 6	3.898 635 5E–01
ratel [Tanzania]	2.202 643 2	2.202 643 2E+00
ratili [Egypt]	2.227 171 5	2.227 171 5E+00
ratili [Iran]	2.132 196 2	2.132 196 2E+00
ratili [Jordan]	0.390 015 6	3.900 156 0E–01
ratili [Lebanon]	0.390 015 6	3.900 156 0E–01
ratili [Libya]	1.949 317 7	1.949 317 7E+00
ratili [Malta]	1.259 445 8	1.259 445 8E+00

kilogram (continued)   <mass>

	Standard	Scientific
ratili [Saudi Arabia]	2.164 502 2	2.164 502 2E+00
ratili [Somalia]	2.232 142 9	2.232 142 9E+00
ratili [Sudan]	2.227 171 5	2.227 171 5E+00
ratili [Syria]	2.227 171 5	2.227 171 5E+00
ratili [Tanzania]	0.389 863 6	3.898 635 5E-01
ratl [Bahrain]	2.202 643 2	2.202 643 2E+00
ratl [Egypt]	2.227 171 5	2.227 171 5E+00
ratl [Iran]	2.132 196 2	2.132 196 2E+00
ratl [Jordan]	0.390 015 6	3.900 156 0E-01
ratl [Lebanon]	0.390 015 6	3.900 156 0E-01
ratl [Libya]	1.949 317 7	1.949 317 7E+00
ratl [Malta]	1.259 445 8	1.259 445 8E+00
ratl [Saudi Arabia]	2.164 502 2	2.164 502 2E+00
ratl [Somalia]	2.232 142 9	2.232 142 9E+00
ratl [Sudan]	2.227 171 5	2.227 171 5E+00
ratl [Syria]	0.389 863 6	3.898 635 5E-01
ratl [Syria, heavy]	0.539 665 4	5.396 654 1E-01
ratl [Tanzania]	2.202 643 2	2.202 643 2E+00
rattel [Egypt]	2.227 171 5	2.227 171 5E+00
rattel [Iran]	2.132 196 2	2.132 196 2E+00
rattel [Jordan]	0.390 015 6	3.900 156 0E-01
rattel [Lebanon]	0.390 015 6	3.900 156 0E-01
rattel [Libya]	1.949 317 7	1.949 317 7E+00
rattel [Malta]	1.259 445 8	1.259 445 8E+00
rattel [Saudi Arabia]	2.164 502 2	2.164 502 2E+00
rattel [Somalia]	2.232 142 9	2.232 142 9E+00
rattel [Sudan]	2.227 171 5	2.227 171 5E+00
rattel [Syria]	0.389 863 6	3.898 635 5E-01
rattel [Tanzania]	2.202 643 2	2.202 643 2E+00
red [Honduras, maize or corn]	0.022 046 3	2.204 634 1E-02
rey [Iran]	0.083 333 3	8.333 333 3E-02
roba [Bahrain]	0.551 267 9	5.512 679 2E-01
rotal [Egypt]	2.227 171 5	2.227 171 5E+00
rotal [Saudi Arabia]	2.164 502 2	2.164 502 2E+00
rotal [Somalia]	2.232 142 9	2.232 142 9E+00
rotal [Sudan]	2.227 171 5	2.227 171 5E+00
rotal [Syria]	0.389 863 6	3.898 635 5E-01
rotal [Tanzania]	2.202 643 2	2.202 643 2E+00
rotl [Egypt, ancient]	2.227 171 5	2.227 171 5E+00
rotl [Iran]	2.132 196 2	2.132 196 2E+00
rotl [Israel, North]	0.416 666 7	4.166 666 7E-01
rotl [Israel, South]	0.347 222 2	3.472 222 2E-01
rotl [Jordan]	0.390 015 6	3.900 156 0E-01
rotl [Lebanon]	0.390 015 6	3.900 156 0E-01
rotl [Libya]	1.949 317 7	1.949 317 7E+00
rotl [Somalia]	2.232 142 9	2.232 142 9E+00
rotl [Sudan]	2.227 171 5	2.227 171 5E+00
rotl [Syria]	0.389 863 6	3.898 635 5E-01
rotl [Tanzania]	2.202 643 2	2.202 643 2E+00
rotol [Egypt]	2.227 171 5	2.227 171 5E+00
rotol [Libya]	1.949 317 7	1.949 317 7E+00
rotol [Malta]	1.259 445 8	1.259 445 8E+00
rotol [Saudi Arabia]	2.164 502 2	2.164 502 2E+00
rotol [Somalia]	2.232 142 9	2.232 142 9E+00
rotol [Sudan]	2.227 171 5	2.227 171 5E+00
rotol [Syria]	0.389 863 6	3.898 635 5E-01
rotol [Tanzania]	2.202 643 2	2.202 643 2E+00
rotolo [Egypt]	2.227 171 5	2.227 171 5E+00
rotolo [Iran]	2.132 196 2	2.132 196 2E+00
rotolo [Jordan]	0.390 015 6	3.900 156 0E-01
rotolo [Lebanon]	0.390 015 6	3.900 156 0E-01
rotolo [Libya]	1.949 317 7	1.949 317 7E+00

		<Type of Unit>
	Standard	Scientific

kilogram (continued)		<mass>
rotolo [Malta]	1.259 445 8	1.259 445 8E+00
rotolo [Saudi Arabia]	2.164 502 2	2.164 502 2E+00
rotolo [Somalia]	2.232 142 9	2.232 142 9E+00
rotolo [Sudan]	2.227 171 5	2.227 171 5E+00
rotolo [Syria]	0.389 863 6	3.898 635 5E-01
rotolo [Tanzania]	2.202 643 2	2.202 643 2E+00
rottel [Egypt]	2.227 171 5	2.227 171 5E+00
rottel [Iran]	2.132 196 2	2.132 196 2E+00
rottel [Jordan]	0.390 015 6	3.900 156 0E-01
rottel [Lebanon]	0.390 015 6	3.900 156 0E-01
rottel [Libya]	1.949 317 7	1.949 317 7E+00
rottel [Malta]	1.259 445 8	1.259 445 8E+00
rottel [Saudi Arabia]	2.164 502 2	2.164 502 2E+00
rottel [Somalia]	2.232 142 9	2.232 142 9E+00
rottel [Sudan]	2.227 171 5	2.227 171 5E+00
rottel [Syria]	0.389 863 6	3.898 635 5E-01
rottel [Tanzania]	2.202 643 2	2.202 643 2E+00
rottle [Egypt]	2.227 171 5	2.227 171 5E+00
rottle [Iran]	2.132 196 2	2.132 196 2E+00
rottle [Jordan]	0.390 015 6	3.900 156 0E-01
rottle [Lebanon]	0.390 015 6	3.900 156 0E-01
rottle [Libya]	1.949 317 7	1.949 317 7E+00
rottle [Malta]	1.259 445 8	1.259 445 8E+00
rottle [Somalia]	2.232 142 9	2.232 142 9E+00
rottle [Sudan]	2.227 171 5	2.227 171 5E+00
rottle [Syria]	0.389 863 6	3.898 635 5E-01
rottle [Tanzania]	2.202 643 2	2.202 643 2E+00
rotto [Syria]	0.451 06	4.510 599 9E-01
rottol [Egypt]	2.227 171 5	2.227 171 5E+00
rottol [Iran]	2.132 196 2	2.132 196 2E+00
rottol [Jordan]	0.390 015 6	3.900 156 0E-01
rottol [Lebanon]	0.389 863 6	3.898 635 5E-01
rottol [Libya]	1.949 317 7	1.949 317 7E+00
rottol [Malta]	1.259 445 8	1.259 445 8E+00
rottol [Saudi Arabia]	2.164 502 2	2.164 502 2E+00
rottol [Somalia]	2.232 142 9	2.232 142 9E+00
rottol [Sudan]	2.227 171 5	2.227 171 5E+00
rottol [Syria]	0.389 863 6	3.898 635 5E-01
rottol [Tanzania]	2.202 643 2	2.202 643 2E+00
rottol [Turkey]	0.389 711 6	3.897 116 1E-01
rottolo [Egypt]	2.227 171 5	2.227 171 5E+00
rottolo [Iran]	2.132 196 2	2.132 196 2E+00
rottolo [Jordan]	0.390 015 6	3.900 156 0E-01
rottolo [Lebanon]	0.390 015 6	3.900 156 0E-01
rottolo [Libya]	1.949 317 7	1.949 317 7E+00
rottolo [Malta]	1.259 445 8	1.259 445 8E+00
rottolo [Somalia]	2.232 142 9	2.232 142 9E+00
rottolo [Sudan]	2.227 171 5	2.227 171 5E+00
rottolo [Syria]	0.389 863 6	3.898 635 5E-01
rottolo [Tanzania]	2.202 643 2	2.202 643 2E+00
ruba [Bahrain]	0.551 267 9	5.512 679 2E-01
ruba [Saudi Arabia]	0.107 281 2	1.072 811 7E-01
rubbio [Italy]	0.126 270 6	1.262 706 0E-01
sac [Colombia]	0.016	1.600 000 0E-02
sac [Haiti, coffee]	0.016 666 7	1.666 666 7E-02
sac [Zaire, coffee]	0.016 666 7	1.666 666 7E-02
sacco [Brazil, coffee]	0.016 666 7	1.666 666 7E-02
sacco [Colombia, coffee]	0.014 492 8	1.449 275 4E-02
sacco [Costa Rica, coffee]	0.014 492 8	1.449 275 4E-02
sacco [Cuba, coffee]	0.011 111 1	1.111 111 1E-02
sacco [Guatemala, coffee]	0.014 492 8	1.449 275 4E-02
sack [Brazil, rice paddy]	0.02	2.000 000 0E-02

Convert From

Convert To
                                          `<Type of Unit>`

kilogram (continued)

	Standard	Scientific
sack [Egypt, rice, milled]	0.01	$1.000\ 000\ 0E{-}02$
sack [Ghana, rice paddy]	0.013 122 7	$1.312\ 267\ 1E{-}02$
sack [Ghana, rice, milled]	0.009 185 9	$9.185\ 941\ 8E{-}03$
sack [Malawi, rice paddy]	0.013 778 8	$1.377\ 884\ 9E{-}02$
sack [Malawi, rice, milled]	0.011 023 2	$1.102\ 317\ 1E{-}02$
sack [South Africa, rice paddy]	0.014 697 5	$1.469\ 745\ 3E{-}02$
sack [South Africa, rice, milled]	0.013 778 8	$1.377\ 884\ 9E{-}02$
sack [Surinam, rice paddy]	0.014 285 7	$1.428\ 571\ 4E{-}02$
sack [Surinam, rice, milled]	0.01	$1.000\ 000\ 0E{-}02$
sack [Taiwan, rice paddy]	0.008 474 6	$8.474\ 576\ 3E{-}03$
sack [Taiwan, rice, milled]	0.01	$1.000\ 000\ 0E{-}02$
sack [UK]	0.007 873 6	$7.873\ 643\ 8E{-}03$
sack [Zambia, rice paddy]	0.014 705 9	$1.470\ 588\ 2E{-}02$
saco [Colombia]	0.016	$1.600\ 000\ 0E{-}02$
saco [Colombia, coffee]	0.014 285 7	$1.428\ 571\ 4E{-}02$
saco [Cuba]	0.016	$1.600\ 000\ 0E{-}02$
saco [Cuba, coffee]	0.014 285 7	$1.428\ 571\ 4E{-}02$
saco [Dominican Republic, coffee]	0.013 333 3	$1.333\ 333\ 3E{-}02$
saco [Haiti]	0.016 666 7	$1.666\ 666\ 7E{-}02$
saco [Honduras, coffee]	0.014 492 8	$1.449\ 275\ 4E{-}02$
saco [Nicaragua, coffee]	0.014 492 8	$1.449\ 275\ 4E{-}02$
saco [Peru, coffee]	0.014 492 8	$1.449\ 275\ 4E{-}02$
saco de cafe [Colombia, coffee]	0.016	$1.600\ 000\ 0E{-}02$
saco de cafe [Costa Rica, coffee]	0.014 492 8	$1.449\ 275\ 4E{-}02$
saddirham [Iran]	0.666 666 7	$6.666\ 666\ 7E{-}01$
salm [Malta]	0.004 498 4	$4.498\ 425\ 6E{-}03$
salme [Malta and Gozo]	0.004 499 4	$4.499\ 437\ 6E{-}03$
sang [Iran]	1	$1.000\ 000\ 0E{+}00$
sang [Laos]	0.833 333 3	$8.333\ 333\ 3E{-}01$
satlijh [Yugoslavia]	3.125	$3.125\ 000\ 0E{+}00$
saum [Austria]	0.006 493 5	$6.493\ 506\ 5E{-}03$
scruple [UK]	771.617 92	$7.716\ 179\ 2E{+}02$
scruple [US, apothecary]	771.617 92	$7.716\ 179\ 2E{+}02$
seer [Afghanistan]	0.141 522 8	$1.415\ 227\ 9E{-}01$
seer [Bangladesh]	1.071 811 4	$1.071\ 811\ 4E{+}00$
seer [Ceylon]	1.071 691 6	$1.071\ 691\ 6E{+}00$
seer [India]	1.071 696 5	$1.071\ 696\ 5E{+}00$
seer [Nepal]	1.071 696 5	$1.071\ 696\ 5E{+}00$
seer [Pakistan]	1.071 811 4	$1.071\ 811\ 4E{+}00$
seer [Yemen]	1.071 811 4	$1.071\ 811\ 4E{+}00$
sene [Laos]	0.008 333 3	$8.333\ 333\ 3E{-}03$
sentner [Scandinavia]	0.019 684 2	$1.968\ 423\ 3E{-}02$
sep [Egypt, ancient]	1.063 829 8	$1.063\ 829\ 8E{+}00$
ser [Bangladesh]	1.071 696 5	$1.071\ 696\ 5E{+}00$
ser [Muslim India]	1.071 811 4	$1.071\ 811\ 4E{+}00$
shih tan [China]	0.02	$2.000\ 000\ 0E{-}02$
ship last [France]	0.000 5	$5.000\ 000\ 0E{-}04$
ship pound [Russia]	0.006 112 6	$6.112\ 581\ 5E{-}03$
ship pund [Sweden]	0.005 882 4	$5.882\ 352\ 9E{-}03$
shippond [Norway]	0.006 273 5	$6.273\ 525\ 7E{-}03$
sihr [Afghanistan]	0.141 522 8	$1.415\ 227\ 9E{-}01$
sihr [Bangladesh]	1.071 811 4	$1.071\ 811\ 4E{+}00$
sihr [India]	1.071 811 4	$1.071\ 811\ 4E{+}00$
sihr [Pakistan]	1.071 811 4	$1.071\ 811\ 4E{+}00$
sihr [Yemen]	1.071 811 4	$1.071\ 811\ 4E{+}00$
skaalpund [Netherlands]	2.369 668 2	$2.369\ 668\ 2E{+}00$
skaalpund [Norway]	2.007 629	$2.007\ 629\ 0E{+}00$
skalpunt [Finland]	2.352 520 5	$2.352\ 520\ 5E{+}00$
skeppslast [Sweden]	0.000 235 3	$2.352\ 520\ 5E{-}04$
skeppund [Sweden]	0.005 881 3	$5.881\ 315\ 1E{-}03$
skiblast [Denmark]	0.000 384 6	$3.846\ 153\ 8E{-}04$
skibpund [Denmark]	0.006 25	$6.250\ 000\ 0E{-}03$

kilogram (continued)   **\<mass>**

	Standard	Scientific
skippund [Iceland]	0.006 25	6.250 000 0E-03
skippunt [Finland]	0.005 881 3	5.881 315 1E-03
slug	0.068 521 8	6.852 176 6E-02
slug [metric]	0.101 971 6	1.019 716 2E-01
stater [Greece]	0.017 755 7	1.775 568 2E-02
stein [Austria]	0.089 285 7	8.928 571 4E-02
stone [Cyprus]	0.157 473 1	1.574 730 5E-01
stone [Scotland]	0.091 861 1	9.186 110 6E-02
stone [UK]	0.157 473	1.574 730 4E-01
suk [South Korea, barley]	0.010 101	1.010 101 0E-02
suk [South Korea, rice paddy]	0.01	1.000 000 0E-02
suk [South Korea, rice, milled]	0.006 944 4	6.944 444 4E-03
suk [South Korea, wheat]	0.007 246 4	7.246 376 8E-03
sus [Somalia]	0.677 966 1	6.779 661 0E-01
ta [Brunei]	0.016 534 7	1.653 466 5E-02
ta [Cambodia]	0.016 666 7	1.666 666 7E-02
ta [China]	0.016 534 7	1.653 466 5E-02
ta [Hong Kong]	0.016 534 7	1.653 466 5E-02
ta [Indonesia]	0.016 191 4	1.619 144 8E-02
ta [Japan]	0.016 666 7	1.666 666 7E-02
ta [Laos]	0.016 666 7	1.666 666 7E-02
ta [Macao]	0.016 534 7	1.653 466 5E-02
ta [Malaysia]	0.016 534 7	1.653 466 5E-02
ta [Philippines]	0.015 810 5	1.581 052 7E-02
ta [Singapore]	0.016 534 7	1.653 466 5E-02
ta [Thailand]	0.016 666 7	1.666 666 7E-02
ta [Vietnam]	0.016 542 6	1.654 259 7E-02
ta [Vietnam, rice paddy]	0.014 705 9	1.470 588 2E-02
ta [Vietnam, rice, milled]	0.01	1.000 000 0E-02
taam [Brunei]	0.016 534 7	1.653 466 5E-02
taam [Cambodia]	0.016 666 7	1.666 666 7E-02
taam [China]	0.016 534 7	1.653 466 5E-02
taam [Hong Kong]	0.016 534 7	1.653 466 5E-02
taam [Indonesia]	0.016 191 4	1.619 144 8E-02
taam [Japan]	0.016 666 7	1.666 666 7E-02
taam [Laos]	0.016 666 7	1.666 666 7E-02
taam [Macao]	0.016 534 7	1.653 466 5E-02
taam [Malaysia]	0.016 534 7	1.653 466 5E-02
taam [Philippines]	0.015 810 5	1.581 052 7E-02
taam [Singapore]	0.016 534 7	1.653 466 5E-02
taam [Thailand]	0.016 666 7	1.666 666 7E-02
taam [Vietnam]	0.016 541 8	1.654 177 6E-02
table [Lebanon, cereals]	0.066 666 7	6.666 666 7E-02
talanton [Greece, ancient]	0.034 246 6	3.424 657 5E-02
talent [Egypt, ancient]	0.021 413 3	2.141 327 6E-02
talent [Greece, ancient]	0.038 173 8	3.817 376 7E-02
talent [Hebrew, ancient]	0.029 154 5	2.915 451 9E-02
talent [Mesopotamia, ancient]	0.034 722 2	3.472 222 2E-02
talenton [Greece, ancient]	0.006 666 7	6.666 666 7E-03
talentum [Rome, ancient]	0.038 759 7	3.875 969 0E-02
tam [Brunei]	0.016 534 7	1.653 466 5E-02
tam [Cambodia]	0.016 666 7	1.666 666 7E-02
tam [China]	0.016 534 7	1.653 466 5E-02
tam [Hong Kong]	0.016 534 7	1.653 466 5E-02
tam [Indonesia]	0.016 191 4	1.619 144 8E-02
tam [Japan]	0.016 666 7	1.666 666 7E-02
tam [Laos]	0.016 666 7	1.666 666 7E-02
tam [Macao]	0.016 534 7	1.653 466 5E-02
tam [Malaysia]	0.016 534 7	1.653 466 5E-02
tam [Philippines]	0.015 810 5	1.581 052 7E-02
tam [Singapore]	0.016 534 7	1.653 466 5E-02
tam [Thailand]	0.016 666 7	1.666 666 7E-02

	Standard	<Type of Unit> Scientific

kilogram (continued)

<mass>

Convert To	Standard	Scientific
tam [Vietnam]	0.016 541 8	1.654 177 6E–02
tamuga [Costa Rica, solidified sugar cane juice]	0.483 091 8	4.830 917 9E–01
tan [Brunei]	0.016 534 7	1.653 466 5E–02
tan [Cambodia]	0.016 666 7	1.666 666 7E–02
tan [China]	0.02	2.000 000 0E–02
tan [Hong Kong]	0.016 534 7	1.653 466 5E–02
tan [Japan]	0.016 666 7	1.666 666 7E–02
tan [Laos]	0.016 666 7	1.666 666 7E–02
tan [Macao]	0.016 534 7	1.653 466 5E–02
tan [Malaysia]	0.016 534 7	1.653 466 5E–02
tan [Philippines]	0.015 810 5	1.581 052 7E–02
tan [Singapore]	0.016 534 7	1.653 466 5E–02
tan [Thailand]	0.016 666 7	1.666 666 7E–02
tan [Vietnam]	0.016 541 8	1.654 177 6E–02
tao [Cambodia, rice paddy]	0.083 333 3	8.333 333 3E–02
tao [Cambodia, rice, milled]	0.066 666 7	6.666 666 7E–02
tcheirek [Iran]	1.347 098 9	1.347 098 9E+00
tcheki [Turkey]	0.004 428 7	4.428 698 0E–03
tercio [Cuba, tobacco]	0.019 782 4	1.978 239 4E–02
tercio [Ecuador]	0.027 173 9	2.717 391 3E–02
tercio [Mexico]	0.013 579 6	1.357 957 6E–02
tercio [Venezuela]	0.025	2.500 000 0E–02
thamin [Yemen]	0.419 991 6	4.199 916 0E–01
thang [Cambodia, rice paddy]	0.041 666 7	4.166 666 7E–02
thang [Cambodia, rice, milled]	0.033 333 3	3.333 333 3E–02
thumn [Muslim Spain, olive oil]	0.892 857 1	8.928 571 4E–01
tillis [Islam, flour]	0.014 984 6	1.498 464 1E–02
tiya [Nigeria]	0.440 528 6	4.405 286 3E–01
tod [UK, avoirdupois]	0.078 734	7.873 395 8E–02
tomande [Saudi Arabia, ancient]	0.011 778 6	1.177 856 3E–02
ton [dead weight]	0.000 984 2	9.842 065 3E–04
ton [long]	0.000 984 2	9.842 065 3E–04
ton [metric]	0.001	1.000 000 0E–03
ton [Pakistan]	0.000 984 2	9.842 064 4E–04
ton [short]	0.001 102 3	1.102 311 3E–03
ton [UK]	0.000 984 2	9.842 065 3E–04
ton [UK, assay or assay, long]	30.612 245	3.061 224 5E+01
ton [US, assay or assay, short]	34.285 714	3.428 571 4E+01
ton [US, displacement]	0.000 984 2	9.842 065 3E–04
ton [US, gross]	0.000 984 2	9.842 065 3E–04
ton [US, net]	0.001 102 3	1.102 311 3E–03
ton [US, shipping]	0.000 984 2	9.842 065 3E–04
tonelada [Brazil]	0.001 260 7	1.260 655 7E–03
tonelada [Honduras]	0.001 102 3	1.102 311 3E–03
tonelada [Spain]	0.001 086 7	1.086 728 8E–03
tonelada [Spanish]	0.001 087 1	1.087 091 2E–03
tonne	0.001	1.000 000 0E–03
tonneau [Greece]	0.015 318 6	1.531 862 7E–02
tovar [Bulgaria]	0.007 764	7.763 975 2E–03
tovar [Yugoslavia]	0.007 812 5	7.812 500 0E–03
tschak [Iran]	1.347 098 9	1.347 098 9E+00
tughar [Iraq]	0.000 492 1	4.921 032 2E–04
tumna [Sudan]	0.178 062 7	1.780 626 8E–01
tunna smjors [Iceland]	0.008 928 6	8.928 571 4E–03
ugga [Sudan]	0.801 282 1	8.012 820 5E–01
ukia [Iraq]	0.959 692 9	9.596 929 0E–01
vamfort [Hungary]	2	2.000 000 0E+00
vammazsa [Hungary]	0.02	2.000 000 0E–02
vis [Burma]	0.612 369 9	6.123 698 7E–01
vis [India]	0.214 362 3	2.143 622 7E–01
vis [Romania]	0.612 369 9	6.123 698 7E–01
visham [India]	0.214 362 3	2.143 622 7E–01

Convert From	<Type of Unit>	
Convert To	Standard	Scientific

kilogram (continued) <mass>

viss [Burma]	0.612 369 9	6.123 698 7E−01
viss [India]	0.214 362 3	2.143 622 7E−01
wag [Netherlands, wool]	0.012 927 7	1.292 774 7E−02
wagla [Iraq]	0.959 692 9	9.596 929 0E−01
wakea [Iraq]	0.959 692 9	9.596 929 0E−01
wazma [Iraq]	0.009 842 1	9.842 064 4E−03
wazna [Saudi Arabia]	0.629 881 6	6.298 815 8E−01
windle [UK, wheat]	0.010 021	1.002 104 4E−02
wizna [Malta]	0.251 952 6	2.519 526 3E−01
wog [Netherlands, wool]	0.012 927 7	1.292 774 7E−02
woket [Iraq]	0.959 692 9	9.596 929 0E−01
woog [Denmark]	0.055 555 6	5.555 555 6E−02
xang [Laos]	0.833 333 3	8.333 333 3E−01
yan [China]	0.008 267 3	8.267 332 5E−03
yen [Vietnam]	0.166 666 7	1.666 666 7E−01
zentner [Austria]	0.017 856 8	1.785 682 4E−02
zentner [Denmark]	0.02	2.000 000 0E−02
zentner [Germany]	0.02	2.000 000 0E−02
zentner [Switzerland]	0.02	2.000 000 0E−02
zentner [UK]	0.022 045 9	2.204 585 5E−02
zhang [Thailand]	0.833 333 3	8.333 333 3E−01
zollcentner [Germany]	0.02	2.000 000 0E−02
zugtierlast [Switzerland]	0.001 333 3	1.333 333 3E−03

kilogram [atomic physics, eq. energy] <energy>

coal equivalent kilogram [UN, standard]	>>>	3.066 628 4E+09
coal equivalent metric ton [UN, standard]	3,066,628.4	3.066 628 4E+06
exawatthour	0.000 025	2.496 542 2E−05
gigawatthour	24,965.422	2.496 542 2E+04
gram [atomic physics, eq. energy]	1,000	1.000 000 0E+03
joule	>>>	8.987 551 8E+16
kiloton [metric, explosive energy]	21,480.764	2.148 076 4E+04
megaton [metric, explosive energy]	21.480 764	2.148 076 4E+01
megawatthour	>>>	2.496 542 2E+07
myriawatthour	>>>	2.496 542 2E+09
petawatthour	0.024 965 4	2.496 542 2E−02
quad	0.085 185 6	8.518 555 5E−02
terawatthour	24.965 422	2.496 542 2E+01
therm [EEC]	>>>	8.518 555 5E+08
therm [US]	>>>	8.520 589 4E+08
ton [metric, explosive energy]	>>>	2.148 076 4E+07

kilogram calorie [15 °C, NBS, 1939] <energy>

Btu [I.T.]	3.967 372 9	3.967 372 9E+00
Btu [mean]	3.964 313 8	3.964 313 8E+00
Btu [thermoc.]	3.970 027 9	3.970 027 9E+00
calorie [15 °C, NBS, 1939]	1,000	1.000 000 0E+03
calorie [kilogram, I.T.]	0.999 761 2	9.997 611 5E−01
calorie [nutritional]	1.000 430 2	1.000 430 2E+00
centigrade heat unit [15 °C]	2.204 622 3	2.204 622 3E+00
centigrade heat unit [I.T.]	2.204 096 1	2.204 096 1E+00
cubic centimeter atmosphere	41,310.634	4.131 063 4E+04
cubic foot atmosphere	1.458 871 3	1.458 871 3E+00
frigorie [France]	1	1.000 000 0E+00
gram calorie	1,000	1.000 000 0E+03
horsepower hour	0.001 559 2	1.559 236 2E−03
horsepower hour [metric]	0.001 580 9	1.580 862 3E−03
joule	4,185.8	4.185 800 0E+03
kilocalorie [thermoc.]	1.000 430 2	1.000 430 2E+00
kilogram square meter/square second	4,185.8	4.185 800 0E+03
kilopond meter	426.832 81	4.268 328 1E+02
liter atmosphere	41.310 634	4.131 063 4E+01
meter kilogram-force	426.832 81	4.268 328 1E+02

Convert From		\<Type of Unit\>
Convert To	**Standard**	**Scientific**
pferdestarkenstunde [Germany]	0.001 580 9	1.580 862 3E−03
thermie [France]	0.001	1.000 000 0E−03
watthour	1.162 722 2	1.162 722 2E+00
wattsecond	4,185.8	4.185 800 0E+03

kilogram meter/pascal square second \<permeability, water\>
| square meter | 1 | 1.000 000 0E+00 |

kilogram meter/second \<momentum\>
dyne second	100,000	1.000 000 0E+05
newton second	1	1.000 000 0E+00
pound foot/second	7.233 013 9	7.233 013 9E+00
pound-force second	0.224 808 9	2.248 089 4E−01

kilogram meter/square second \<force\>
crinal	10	1.000 000 0E+01
dyne	100,000	1.000 000 0E+05
gram-force	101.971 621	1.019 716 2E+02
joule/meter	1	1.000 000 0E+00
newton	1	1.000 000 0E+00
ounce-force	3.596 943 1	3.596 943 1E+00
pascal square meter	1	1.000 000 0E+00
pond	101.971 621	1.019 716 2E+02
pound-force	0.224 808 9	2.248 089 4E−01
poundal	7.233 013 9	7.233 013 9E+00

kilogram of water [evaporated from and at 100 °C] \<energy\>
| Btu [I.T.] | 2,139.223 2 | 2.139 223 2E+03 |
| joule | 2,257,000 | 2.257 000 0E+06 |

kilogram of water [heated from 16.7 °C to 100 °C] \<energy\>
| Btu [I.T.] | 330.458 48 | 3.304 584 8E+02 |
| joule | 348,652.15 | 3.486 521 5E+05 |

kilogram square centimeter \<moment of inertia of a mass\>
gram-force centimeter square second	1.019 716 2	1.019 716 2E+00
kilogram square meter	0.000 1	1.000 000 0E−04
ounce square inch	5.467 475	5.467 475 0E+00
pond centimeter square second	1.019 716 2	1.019 716 2E+00
pound square inch	0.341 717 2	3.417 171 9E−01

kilogram square meter \<moment of inertia of a mass\>
kilogram square centimeter	10,000	1.000 000 0E+04
kilopond centimeter square second	10.197 162	1.019 716 2E+01
ounce-force foot square second	11.800 994	1.180 099 4E+01
pound square foot	23.730 36	2.373 036 0E+01
pound-force inch square second	8.850 745 8	8.850 745 8E+00

kilogram square meter/cubic second \<power\>
Btu/hour [I.T.]	3.412 141 6	3.412 141 6E+00
Btu/hour [thermoc.]	3.414 425 1	3.414 425 1E+00
calorie/minute [I.T.]	14.330 754	1.433 075 4E+01
calorie/minute [thermoc.]	14.340 344	1.434 034 4E+01
centigrade heat unit/hour [mean]	1.894 172 6	1.894 172 6E+00
cheval vapeur [France]	0.001 359 6	1.359 621 6E−03
cubic meter atmosphere/second	9.869 232 7	9.869 232 7E+00
dyne centimeter/second	>>>	1.000 000 0E+07
erg/second	>>>	1.000 000 0E+07
foot pound-force/minute	44.253 729	4.425 372 9E+01
foot poundal/second	23.730 36	2.373 036 0E+01
gram-force centimeter/second	10,197.162	1.019 716 2E+04
horsepower	0.001 341	1.341 022 1E−03
horsepower [metric]	0.001 359 6	1.359 621 6E−03
joule/second	1	1.000 000 0E+00
kilocalorie/hour [I.T.]	0.859 845 2	8.598 452 3E−01
kilogram force meter/minute	6.118 297 3	6.118 297 3E+00
kilopond meter/minute	6.118 297 3	6.118 297 3E+00
lumen [green light at 100% efficiency]	685	6.850 000 0E+02
lumen [green light at 5,550 angstrom]	680.000 02	6.800 000 2E+02

Convert From / Convert To	Standard	\<Type of Unit\> Scientific

<table>

Convert From / Convert To — **Standard** — **\<Type of Unit\> Scientific**

	Standard	Scientific
newton meter/second	1	1.000 000 0E+00
pferdestarke [Germany]	0.001 359 6	1.359 621 6E−03
poncelet [France]	0.001 019 7	1.019 716 2E−03
pound square foot/cubic second	23.730 36	2.373 036 0E+01
volt ampere	1	1.000 000 0E+00
watt	1	1.000 000 0E+00

kilogram square meter/second   \<moment of momentum\>

	Standard	Scientific
joule second	1	1.000 000 0E+00
newton meter second	1	1.000 000 0E+00
planck	1	1.000 000 0E+00
pound square foot/second	23.730 36	2.373 036 0E+01

kilogram square meter/square second   \<energy\>

	Standard	Scientific
Btu [I.T.]	0.000 947 8	9.478 171 2E−04
Btu [mean]	0.000 947 1	9.470 862 9E−04
Btu [thermoc.]	0.000 948 5	9.484 514 1E−04
calorie [I.T.]	0.238 845 9	2.388 459 0E−01
calorie [mean]	0.238 662 4	2.386 623 5E−01
calorie [thermoc.]	0.239 005 7	2.390 057 4E−01
centigrade heat unit [I.T.]	0.000 526 6	5.265 650 7E−04
cubic centimeter atmosphere	9.869 232 7	9.869 232 7E+00
cubic foot atmosphere	0.000 348 5	3.485 286 6E−04
dyne centimeter	>>>	1.000 000 0E+07
erg	>>>	1.000 000 0E+07
foot pound-force	0.737 562 2	7.375 621 5E−01
foot poundal	23.730 36	2.373 036 0E+01
gram calorie	0.238 903	2.389 029 6E−01
inch ounce-force	141.611 93	1.416 119 3E+02
inch pound-force	8.850 745 8	8.850 745 8E+00
joule	1	1.000 000 0E+00
kilocalorie [I.T.]	0.000 238 8	2.388 459 0E−04
kilopond meter	0.101 971 6	1.019 716 2E−01
megaerg	10	1.000 000 0E+01
megalerg	10	1.000 000 0E+01
meter kilogram-force	0.101 971 6	1.019 716 2E−01
newton meter	1	1.000 000 0E+00
watthour	0.000 277 8	2.777 777 8E−04
wattsecond	1	1.000 000 0E+00

kilogram-force   \<force\>

	Standard	Scientific
crinal	98.066 5	9.806 650 0E+01
dyne	980,665	9.806 650 0E+05
gram-force	1,000	1.000 000 0E+03
hyl meter/square second	9.806 65	9.806 650 0E+00
joule/meter	9.806 65	9.806 650 0E+00
kilopond	1	1.000 000 0E+00
newton	9.806 65	9.806 650 0E+00
pond	1,000	1.000 000 0E+03
pound-force	2.204 622 6	2.204 622 6E+00
poundal	70.931 635 3	7.093 163 5E+01

kilogram-force centimeter square second   \<moment of inertia of a mass\>

	Standard	Scientific
gram-force meter square second	10	1.000 000 0E+01
kilogram square meter	0.098 066 5	9.806 650 0E−02
kilopond centimeter square second	1	1.000 000 0E+00
ounce-force foot square second	1.157 282 2	1.157 282 2E+00
pond meter square second	10	1.000 000 0E+01
pound square foot	2.327 153 4	2.327 153 4E+00
slug square inch	10.415 54	1.041 554 0E+01

kilogram-force meter square second   \<moment of inertia of a mass\>

	Standard	Scientific
kilogram square meter	9.806 65	9.806 650 0E+00
kilogram-force centimeter square second	100	1.000 000 0E+02
kilopond centimeter square second	100	1.000 000 0E+02
kilopond meter square second	1	1.000 000 0E+00
pound-force foot square second	7.233 013 9	7.233 013 9E+00

</table>

Convert From Convert To	Standard	Scientific
slug square foot	7.233 013 9	7.233 013 9E+00

kilogram-force meter/hour   \<power>

	Standard	Scientific
Btu/hour [I.T.]	0.009 294 9	9.294 910 8E-03
Btu/hour [thermoc.]	0.009 301 1	9.301 131 1E-03
calorie/hour [I.T.]	2.342 278 1	2.342 278 1E+00
calorie/hour [thermoc.]	2.343 845 6	2.343 845 6E+00
centigrade heat unit/hour [mean]	0.005 159 9	5.159 857 6E-03
cubic meter atmosphere/minute	1.613 068 5	1.613 068 5E+00
dyne centimeter/second	27,240.694	2.724 069 4E+04
erg/second	27,240.694	2.724 069 4E+04
foot pound-force/hour	7.233 013 9	7.233 013 9E+00
foot poundal/minute	3.878 589	3.878 589 0E+00
gram-force centimeter/second	27.777 778	2.777 777 8E+01
horsepower	0.000 003 7	3.653 037 3E-06
joule/hour	9.806 65	9.806 650 0E+00
kilocalorie/hour [I.T.]	0.002 342 3	2.342 278 1E-03
kilogram-force meter/minute	0.016 666 7	1.666 666 7E-02
kilopond meter/hour	1	1.000 000 0E+00
lumen [green light at 100% efficiency]	1.865 987 6	1.865 987 6E+00
lumen [green light at 5,550 angstrom]	1.852 367 3	1.852 367 3E+00
milliwatt	2.724 069 4	2.724 069 4E+00
newton meter/hour	9.806 65	9.806 650 0E+00
pound square foot/cubic second	0.064 643 2	6.464 315 0E-02
volt ampere	0.002 724 1	2.724 069 4E-03
watt	0.002 724 1	2.724 069 4E-03

kilogram-force meter/kilogram   \<specific thermodynamic energy>

	Standard	Scientific
joule/kilogram	9.806 65	9.806 650 0E+00

kilogram-force meter/kilogram °C   \<specific heat capacity>

	Standard	Scientific
joule/kilogram kelvin	9.806 65	9.806 650 0E+00

kilogram-force meter/minute   \<power>

	Standard	Scientific
Btu/hour [I.T.]	0.557 694 7	5.576 946 5E-01
Btu/hour [thermoc.]	0.558 067 9	5.580 678 6E-01
calorie/minute [I.T.]	2.342 278 1	2.342 278 1E+00
calorie/minute [thermoc.]	2.343 845 6	2.343 845 6E+00
centigrade heat unit/hour [mean]	0.309 591 5	3.095 914 6E-01
cubic meter atmosphere/second	1.613 068 5	1.613 068 5E+00
deciwatt	1.634 441 7	1.634 441 7E+00
dyne centimeter/second	1,634,441.7	1.634 441 7E+06
erg/second	1,634,441.7	1.634 441 7E+06
foot pound-force/minute	7.233 013 9	7.233 013 9E+00
foot poundal/second	3.878 589	3.878 589 0E+00
gram-force centimeter/second	1,666.666 7	1.666 666 7E+03
horsepower	0.000 219 2	2.191 822 4E-04
horsepower [metric]	0.000 222 2	2.222 222 2E-04
joule/minute	9.806 65	9.806 650 0E+00
kilocalorie/hour [I.T.]	0.140 536 7	1.405 366 9E-01
kilogram-force meter/hour	60	6.000 000 0E+01
kilopond meter/minute	1	1.000 000 0E+00
lumen [green light at 100% efficiency]	111.959 25	1.119 592 5E+02
lumen [green light at 5,550 angstrom]	111.142 04	1.111 420 4E+02
newton meter/minute	9.806 65	9.806 650 0E+00
pound square foot/cubic second	3.878 589	3.878 589 0E+00
volt ampere	0.163 444 2	1.634 441 7E-01
watt	0.163 444 2	1.634 441 7E-01

kilogram-force meter/second   \<power>

	Standard	Scientific
Btu/hour [I.T.]	33.461 679	3.346 167 9E+01
Btu/hour [thermoc.]	33.484 072	3.348 407 2E+01
calorie/second [I.T.]	2.342 278 1	2.342 278 1E+00
calorie/second [thermoc.]	2.343 845 6	2.343 845 6E+00
centigrade heat unit/hour [mean]	18.575 488	1.857 548 8E+01
cheval vapeur [France]	0.013 333 3	1.333 333 3E-02
cubic meter atmosphere/second	96.784 111	9.678 411 1E+01

Convert From / Convert To	Standard	Scientific
dyne centimeter/second	>>>	9.806 650 0E+07
erg/second	>>>	9.806 650 0E+07
foot pound-force/second	7.233 013 9	7.233 013 9E+00
foot poundal/second	232.715 34	2.327 153 4E+02
gram-force centimeter/second	100,000	1.000 000 0E+05
horsepower	0.013 150 9	1.315 093 4E-02
horsepower [metric]	0.013 333 3	1.333 333 3E-02
joule/second	9.806 65	9.806 650 0E+00
kilocalorie/hour [I.T.]	8.432 201 2	8.432 201 2E+00
kilogram square meter/cubic second	9.806 65	9.806 650 0E+00
kilogram-force meter/minute	60	6.000 000 0E+01
kilopond meter/second	1	1.000 000 0E+00
newton meter/second	9.806 65	9.806 650 0E+00
pferdestarke [Germany]	0.013 333 3	1.333 333 3E-02
poncelet [France]	0.01	1.000 000 0E-02
pound square foot/cubic second	232.715 34	2.327 153 4E+02
ton of refrigeration	0.002 788 5	2.788 473 2E-03
volt ampere	9.806 65	9.806 650 0E+00
watt	9.806 65	9.806 650 0E+00

kilogram-force second/cubic meter   \<specific acoustic impedance\>

	Standard	Scientific
pascal second/meter	9.806 65	9.806 650 0E+00
pound-force second/cubic foot	0.062 428	6.242 796 1E-02
poundal second/cubic foot	2.008 560 2	2.008 560 2E+00

kilogram-force second/meter   \<mechanical impedance\>

	Standard	Scientific
joule second/square meter	9.806 65	9.806 650 0E+00
newton second/meter	9.806 65	9.806 650 0E+00
pound-force second/foot	0.671 969	6.719 689 8E-01
poundal second/foot	21.619 962	2.161 996 2E+01

kilogram-force second/square meter   \<dynamic viscosity\>

	Standard	Scientific
hyl/meter second	1	1.000 000 0E+00
kilogram/meter second	9.806 65	9.806 650 0E+00
newton second/square meter	9.806 65	9.806 650 0E+00
pascal second	9.806 65	9.806 650 0E+00
pound/foot second	6.589 764 6	6.589 764 6E+00
poundal second/square foot	6.589 764 6	6.589 764 6E+00

kilogram-force square second/meter   \<mass\>

	Standard	Scientific
glug	10	1.000 000 0E+01
hyl	1	1.000 000 0E+00
kilogram	9.806 65	9.806 650 0E+00
newton square second/meter	9.806 65	9.806 650 0E+00
pound	21.619 962	2.161 996 2E+01
pound [apothecary]	26.274 26	2.627 426 0E+01
pound [avoirdupois]	21.619 962	2.161 996 2E+01
pound [troy]	26.274 26	2.627 426 0E+01
pound [UK]	21.619 964	2.161 996 4E+01
pound [US, avoirdupois]	21.619 96	2.161 996 0E+01
pound [US, troy]	26.274 257	2.627 425 7E+01
poundal square second/foot	21.619 962	2.161 996 2E+01
slug [metric]	1	1.000 000 0E+00
stone [UK]	1.544 283	1.544 283 0E+00

kilogram-force/centimeter   \<surface tension\>

	Standard	Scientific
gram-force/centimeter	1,000	1.000 000 0E+03
kilopond/centimeter	1	1.000 000 0E+00
newton/centimeter	9.806 65	9.806 650 0E+00
newton/meter	980.665	9.806 650 0E+02
ounce-force/inch	89.595 863	8.959 586 3E+01
pound-force/inch	5.599 741 5	5.599 741 5E+00

kilogram-force/meter   \<surface tension\>

	Standard	Scientific
gram-force/centimeter	10	1.000 000 0E+01
kilogram-force/centimeter	0.01	1.000 000 0E-02
newton/meter	9.806 65	9.806 650 0E+00
ounce-force/foot	10.751 504	1.075 150 4E+01

Convert From Convert To	Standard	Scientific
pound-force/foot	0.671 969	6.719 689 8E−01
kilogram-force/meter second °C		**‹heat transfer coefficient›**
watt/square meter kelvin	9.806 65	9.806 650 0E+00
kilogram-force/second °C		**‹thermal conductivity›**
watt/meter kelvin	9.806 65	9.806 650 0E+00
kilogram-force/square centimeter		**‹pressure›**
atmosphere [metric]	1	1.000 000 0E+00
atmosphere [standard]	0.967 841 1	9.678 411 1E−01
atmosphere [technical]	1	1.000 000 0E+00
bar	0.980 665	9.806 650 0E−01
centimeter of mercury [0 °C, by convention]	73.555 914	7.355 591 4E+01
centimeter of water [4 °C, by convention]	1,000	1.000 000 0E+03
decibar	9.806 65	9.806 650 0E+00
foot of mercury [0 °C, by convention]	2.413 251 8	2.413 251 8E+00
foot of water [4 °C, by convention]	32.808 399	3.280 839 9E+01
gram-force/square centimeter	1,000	1.000 000 0E+03
inch of mercury [0 °C, by convention]	28.959 021	2.895 902 1E+01
inch of water [4 °C, by convention]	393.700 79	3.937 007 9E+02
kilogram-force/square millimeter	0.01	1.000 000 0E−02
kilopascal	98.066 5	9.806 650 0E+01
kilopond/square centimeter	1	1.000 000 0E+00
kip/square foot	2.048 161 4	2.048 161 4E+00
newton/square millimeter	0.098 066 5	9.806 650 0E−02
ounce-force/square inch	227.573 49	2.275 734 9E+02
pascal	98,066.5	9.806 650 0E+04
pieze [France]	98.066 5	9.806 650 0E+01
pound-force/square inch	14.223 343	1.422 334 3E+01
sthene/square meter [France]	98.066 5	9.806 650 0E+01
ton-force/square foot [short]	1.024 080 7	1.024 080 7E+00
ton-force/square meter [metric]	10	1.000 000 0E+01
torr	735.559 24	7.355 592 4E+02
kilogram-force/square meter		**‹pressure›**
atmosphere [standard]	0.000 096 8	9.678 411 1E−05
atmosphere [technical]	0.000 1	1.000 000 0E−04
bar	0.000 098 1	9.806 650 0E−05
barye [France]	98.066 5	9.806 650 0E+01
centimeter of mercury [0 °C, by convention]	0.007 355 6	7.355 591 4E−03
centimeter of water [4 °C, by convention]	0.1	1.000 000 0E−01
centitorr	7.355 592 4	7.355 592 4E+00
dyne/square centimeter	98.066 5	9.806 650 0E+01
gram-force/square centimeter	0.1	1.000 000 0E−01
kilopond/square meter	1	1.000 000 0E+00
micrometer of mercury [0 °C, by convention]	73.555 914	7.355 591 4E+01
micrometer of water [4 °C, by convention]	1,000	1.000 000 0E+03
millimeter of mercury [0 °C, by convention]	0.073 555 9	7.355 591 4E−02
millimeter of water [4 °C, by convention]	1	1.000 000 0E+00
newton/square meter	9.806 65	9.806 650 0E+00
ounce-force/square inch	0.022 757 3	2.275 734 9E−02
pascal	9.806 65	9.806 650 0E+00
pound-force/square foot	0.204 816 1	2.048 161 4E−01
poundal/square foot	6.589 764 6	6.589 764 6E+00
ton-force/square foot [short]	0.000 102 4	1.024 080 7E−04
ton-force/square meter [metric]	0.001	1.000 000 0E−03
torr	0.073 555 9	7.355 592 4E−02
kilogram-force/square millimeter		**‹pressure›**
atmosphere [metric]	100	1.000 000 0E+02
atmosphere [standard]	96.784 111	9.678 411 1E+01
atmosphere [technical]	100	1.000 000 0E+02
bar	98.066 5	9.806 650 0E+01
centimeter of mercury [0 °C, by convention]	7,355.591 4	7.355 591 4E+03
centimeter of water [4 °C, by convention]	100,000	1.000 000 0E+05
dekabar	9.806 65	9.806 650 0E+00

	Standard	Scientific
foot of mercury [0 °C, by convention]	241.325 18	2.413 251 8E+02
foot of water [4 °C, by convention]	3,280.839 9	3.280 839 9E+03
gram-force/square centimeter	100,000	1.000 000 0E+05
inch of mercury [0 °C, by convention]	2,895.902 1	2.895 902 1E+03
inch of water [4 °C, by convention]	39,370.079	3.937 007 9E+04
kilogram-force/square centimeter	100	1.000 000 0E+02
kilopond/square millimeter	1	1.000 000 0E+00
kip/square inch	1.422 334 3	1.422 334 3E+00
megapascal	9.806 65	9.806 650 0E+00
newton/square millimeter	9.806 65	9.806 650 0E+00
pascal	9,806,650	9.806 650 0E+06
pound-force/square inch	1,422.334 3	1.422 334 3E+03
ton-force/square foot [long]	91.435 778	9.143 577 8E+01
ton-force/square inch [short]	0.711 167 2	7.111 671 7E−01
ton-force/square meter [metric]	1,000	1.000 000 0E+03
torr	73,555.924	7.355 592 4E+04

kilogram/are \<surface density\>

	Standard	Scientific
grain/square foot	14.337 13	1.433 713 0E+01
kilogram/hectare	100	1.000 000 0E+02
kilogram/square meter	0.01	1.000 000 0E−02
milligram/square centimeter	1	1.000 000 0E+00
ounce/square yard	0.294 935 3	2.949 352 5E−01
pound/acre	89.217 912	8.921 791 2E+01
pound/square yard	0.018 433 5	1.843 345 0E−02
slug/square yard	0.000 572 9	5.729 292 3E−04
tonne/square meter	0.000 01	1.000 000 0E−05

kilogram/are second \<flow rate/unit area, mass basis\>

	Standard	Scientific
gram/square meter second	10	1.000 000 0E+01
kilogram/hectare second	100	1.000 000 0E+02
kilogram/square meter second	0.01	1.000 000 0E−02
ounce/square foot second	0.032 770 6	3.277 058 3E−02
pound/acre second	89.217 912	8.921 791 2E+01

kilogram/cubic centimeter \<density\>

	Standard	Scientific
grain/gallon [-/US, liquid]	\>\>\>	5.841 783 1E+07
kilogram/cubic meter	1,000,000	1.000 000 0E+06
kilogram/milliliter	1	1.000 000 0E+00
megagram/cubic decimeter	1	1.000 000 0E+00
ounce/cubic inch	578.036 67	5.780 366 7E+02
pound/cubic inch	36.127 292	3.612 729 2E+01
slug/cubic inch	1.122 870 6	1.122 870 6E+00
ton/cubic foot [short]	31.213 98	3.121 398 0E+01
ton/gallon [short/US, liquid]	4.172 702 2	4.172 702 2E+00
tonne/liter	1	1.000 000 0E+00

kilogram/cubic decimeter \<density\>

	Standard	Scientific
grain/cubic inch	252.891 04	2.528 910 4E+02
gram/cubic centimeter	1	1.000 000 0E+00
gram/milliliter	1	1.000 000 0E+00
kilogram/cubic meter	1,000	1.000 000 0E+03
kilogram/liter	1	1.000 000 0E+00
megagram/cubic meter	1	1.000 000 0E+00
ounce/cubic foot	998.847 37	9.988 473 7E+02
pound/cubic foot	62.427 961	6.242 796 1E+01
pound/gallon [-/US, liquid]	8.345 404 5	8.345 404 5E+00
slug/cubic foot	1.940 320 3	1.940 320 3E+00
slug/gallon [-/US, liquid]	0.259 383 1	2.593 831 0E−01
tonne/cubic meter	1	1.000 000 0E+00

kilogram/cubic meter \<density\>

	Standard	Scientific
gammil	1,000	1.000 000 0E+03
grain/cubic inch	0.252 891	2.528 910 4E−01
gram/cubic decimeter	1	1.000 000 0E+00
gram/liter	1	1.000 000 0E+00
kilogram/liter	0.001	1.000 000 0E−03

Convert From Convert To	Standard	<Type of Unit> Scientific
micril	1,000	1.000 000 0E+03
milligram/cubic centimeter	1	1.000 000 0E+00
milligram/milliliter	1	1.000 000 0E+00
ounce/cubic foot	0.998 847 4	9.988 473 7E-01
ounce/cubic yard	26.968 879	2.696 887 9E+01
pound/circular mil foot	<<<	3.404 917 1E-10
pound/acre yard	1.685 554 9	1.685 554 9E+00
slug/cubic yard	0.052 388 6	5.238 864 9E-02
tonne/cubic meter	0.001	1.000 000 0E-03
kilogram/cubic second kelvin		**<heat transfer coefficient>**
watt/square meter kelvin	1	1.000 000 0E+00
kilogram/hectare		**<surface density>**
grain/square yard	1.290 341 7	1.290 341 7E+00
kilogram/are	0.01	1.000 000 0E-02
kilogram/square meter	0.000 1	1.000 000 0E-04
ounce/square yard	0.002 949 4	2.949 352 5E-03
pound/acre	0.892 179 1	8.921 791 2E-01
pound/square yard	0.000 184 3	1.843 345 3E-04
slug/square yard	0.000 005 7	5.729 292 3E-06
kilogram/hectare second		**<flow rate/unit area, mass basis>**
gram/square meter second	0.1	1.000 000 0E-01
kilogram/are second	0.01	1.000 000 0E-02
kilogram/square meter second	0.000 1	1.000 000 0E-04
pound/acre second	0.892 179 1	8.921 791 2E-01
kilogram/hour		**<flow rate, mass basis>**
kilogram/second	0.000 277 8	2.777 777 8E-04
pound/hour	2.204 622 6	2.204 622 6E+00
kilogram/joule		**<specific fuel consumption, mass basis>**
gram/calorie [-/ I.T.]	4,186.8	4.186 800 0E+03
pound/Btu [-/ I.T.]	2,326	2.326 000 0E+03
pound/horsepower hour	5,918,352.5	5.918 352 5E+06
kilogram/kilocalorie [-/ I.T.]		**<specific fuel consumption, mass basis>**
kilogram/joule	0.000 238 8	2.388 459 0E-04
pound/Btu [-/ I.T.]	0.555 555 6	5.555 555 6E-01
pound/horsepower hour	1,413.574 2	1.413 574 2E+03
kilogram/kilogram		**<concentration, mass basis>**
gram/ton [-/metric]	1,000,000	1.000 000 0E+06
gram/tonne	1,000,000	1.000 000 0E+06
karat	24	2.400 000 0E+01
milligram/gram	1,000	1.000 000 0E+03
milligram/kilogram	1,000,000	1.000 000 0E+06
ounce/ton [-/short]	32,000	3.200 000 0E+04
ounce/ton [-/US, assay or assay, short]	1.028 823 9	1.028 823 9E+00
ounce/ton [troy/UK, assay or assay, long]	1.050 257 7	1.050 257 7E+00
part/million	1,000,000	1.000 000 0E+06
percent	100	1.000 000 0E+02
pound/ton [-/long]	2,240	2.240 000 0E+03
pound/ton [-/short]	2,000	2.000 000 0E+03
kilogram/kilometer		**<linear density>**
denier	9,000	9.000 000 0E+03
drex	10,000	1.000 000 0E+04
kilogram/meter	0.001	1.000 000 0E-03
kilotex	1	1.000 000 0E+00
ounce/foot	0.010 751 5	1.075 150 4E-02
pound/yard	0.002 015 9	2.015 906 9E-03
tex	1,000	1.000 000 0E+03
kilogram/kilomole		**<molar mass>**
gram/mole	1	1.000 000 0E+00
kilogram/mole	0.001	1.000 000 0E-03
kilogram/liter		**<density>**
grain/cubic inch	252.891 04	2.528 910 4E+02

	Standard	Scientific
gram/cubic centimeter	1.000 000	1.000 000 0E+00
gram/milliliter	1.000 000	1.000 000 0E+00
kilogram/cubic decimeter	1.000 000	1.000 000 0E+00
kilogram/cubic meter	1,000.000	1.000 000 0E+03
megagram/cubic meter	1.000 000	1.000 000 0E+00
ounce/cubic foot	998.847 37	9.988 473 7E+02
ounce/gallon [-/US, liquid]	133.526 47	1.335 264 7E+02
pound/cubic foot	62.427 961	6.242 796 1E+01
pound/gallon [-/US, liquid]	8.345 404 5	8.345 404 5E+00
slug/cubic foot	1.940 320 3	1.940 320 3E+00
ton/cubic yard [short]	0.842 777 5	8.427 774 7E-01
tonne/cubic meter	1.000 000	1.000 000 0E+00
kilogram/meter		**<linear density>**
denier	9,000,000	9.000 000 0E+06
drex	>>>	1.000 000 0E+07
kilotex	1,000.000	1.000 000 0E+03
ounce/foot	10.751 504	1.075 150 4E+01
pli	0.055 997 4	5.599 741 5E-02
poumar	2,015,906.9	2.015 906 9E+06
pound/yard	2.015 906 9	2.015 906 9E+00
tex	1,000,000	1.000 000 0E+00
tonne/kilometer	1.000 000	1.000 000 0E+00
kilogram/meter hour		**<dynamic viscosity>**
kilogram-force second/square meter	0.000 028 3	2.832 545 0E-05
pascal second	0.000 277 7	2.777 777 8E-04
pound/foot hour	0.671 969	6.719 689 8E-01
poundal hour/square foot	0.671 969	6.719 689 8E-01
kilogram/meter second		**<dynamic viscosity>**
dyne second/square centimeter	10.000	1.000 000 0E+01
gram/centimeter second	10.000	1.000 000 0E+01
hyl/meter second	0.101 971 6	1.019 716 2E-01
kilogram-force second/square meter	0.101 971 6	1.019 716 2E-01
newton second/square meter	1.000 000	1.000 000 0E+00
pascal second	1.000 000	1.000 000 0E+00
poise	10.000	1.000 000 0E+01
pound/foot second	0.671 969	6.719 689 8E-01
poundal second/square foot	0.671 969	6.719 689 8E-01
kilogram/meter square second		**<pressure>**
pascal	1.000 000	1.000 000 0E+00
kilogram/milliliter		**<density>**
grain/cubic inch	252,891.04	2.528 910 4E+05
gram/cubic centimeter	1,000.000	1.000 000 0E+03
kilogram/cubic centimeter	1.000 000	1.000 000 0E+00
kilogram/cubic meter	1,000,000	1.000 000 0E+06
megagram/cubic decimeter	1.000 000	1.000 000 0E+00
megagram/liter	1.000 000	1.000 000 0E+00
ounce/cubic inch	578.036 67	5.780 366 7E+02
pound/cubic inch	36.127 292	3.612 729 2E+01
slug/cubic inch	1.122 870 6	1.122 870 6E+00
ton/cubic foot [short]	31.213 98	3.121 398 0E+01
ton/gallon [short/US, liquid]	4.172 702 2	4.172 702 2E+00
tonne/liter	1.000 000	1.000 000 0E+00
kilogram/minute		**<flow rate, mass basis>**
kilogram/second	0.016 666 7	1.666 666 7E-02
pound/minute	2.204 622 6	2.204 622 6E+00
kilogram/mole		**<molar mass>**
gram/mole	1,000.000	1.000 000 0E+03
kilogram/kilomole	1,000.000	1.000 000 0E+03
kilogram/second		**<flow rate, mass basis>**
gram/hour	3,600,000	3.600 000 0E+06
gram/minute	60,000	6.000 000 0E+04

	Standard	Scientific
gram/second	1,000	1.000 000 0E+03
kilogram/hour	3,600	3.600 000 0E+03
kilogram/minute	60	6.000 000 0E+01
pound/hour	7,936.641 4	7.936 641 4E+03
pound/minute	132.277 36	1.322 773 6E+02
pound/second	2.204 622 6	2.204 622 6E+00
ton/hour [long]	3.543 143 5	3.543 143 5E+00
ton/hour [metric]	3.6	3.600 000 0E+00
ton/hour [short]	3.968 320 7	3.968 320 7E+00
ton/minute [long]	0.059 052 4	5.905 239 2E−02
ton/minute [metric]	0.06	6.000 000 0E−02
ton/minute [short]	0.066 138 7	6.613 867 9E−02
ton/second [long]	0.000 984 2	9.842 065 3E−04
ton/second [metric]	0.001	1.000 000 0E−03
ton/second [short]	0.001 102 3	1.102 311 3E−03

kilogram/square centimeter <surface density>

	Standard	Scientific
grain/square inch	99,563.403	9.956 340 3E+04
kilogram/are	1,000,000	1.000 000 0E+06
kilogram/square meter	10,000	1.000 000 0E+04
ounce/square inch	227.573 49	2.275 734 9E+02
pound/square inch	14.223 343	1.422 334 3E+01
slug/square foot	63.658 804	6.365 880 4E+01
ton/square foot [short]	1.024 080 7	1.024 080 7E+00
ton/square yard [short]	9.216 726 5	9.216 726 5E+00
tonne/square meter	10	1.000 000 0E+01

kilogram/square meter <surface density>

	Standard	Scientific
grain/square foot	1,433.713	1.433 713 0E+03
grain/square inch	9.956 340 3	9.956 340 3E+00
grain/square yard	12,903.417	1.290 341 7E+04
kilogram/are	100	1.000 000 0E+02
milligram/square centimeter	100	1.000 000 0E+02
ounce/square foot	3.277 058 3	3.277 058 3E+00
pound/acre	8,921.791 2	8.921 791 2E+03
pound/square foot	0.204 816 1	2.048 161 4E−01
pound/square inch	0.001 422 3	1.422 334 3E−03
pound/square yard	1.843 345 3	1.843 345 3E+00
slug/square yard	0.057 292 9	5.729 292 9E−02
ton/square foot [short]	0.000 102 4	1.024 080 7E−04
ton/square yard [short]	0.000 921 7	9.216 726 5E−04
tonne/square meter	0.001	1.000 000 0E−03

kilogram/square meter second <flow rate/unit area, mass basis>

	Standard	Scientific
kilogram/are second	100	1.000 000 0E+02
ounce/square foot second	3.277 058 3	3.277 058 3E+00
pound/acre second	8,921.791 2	8.921 791 2E+03
pound/square foot second	0.204 816 1	2.048 161 4E−01
slug/square foot second	0.006 365 9	6.365 880 4E−03
tonne/square meter second	0.001	1.000 000 0E−03

kilogram/square meter square second <pressure gradient>

	Standard	Scientific
pascal/meter	1	1.000 000 0E+00
pound-force/square foot foot	0.006 365 9	6.365 880 4E−03
pound/square foot square second	0.204 816 1	2.048 161 4E−01

kilohenry <electric inductance>

	Standard	Scientific
abhenry	>>>	1.000 000 0E+12
henry	1,000	1.000 000 0E+03
joule/square ampere	1,000	1.000 000 0E+03
ohm second	1,000	1.000 000 0E+03
stathenry	<<<	1.112 650 1E−09

kilohertz <frequency>

	Standard	Scientific
1/second	1,000	1.000 000 0E+03
degree/second	360,000	3.600 000 0E+05
hertz	1,000	1.000 000 0E+03
radian/second	6,283.185 3	6.283 185 3E+03

revolution/second --	1,000 ----	1.000 000 0E+03
kilohm		**\<electric resistance\>**
1/ siemens --	1,000 ----	1.000 000 0E+03
abohm ---	>>> ----	1.000 000 0E+12
ohm --	1,000 ----	1.000 000 0E+03
statohm ---	<<< ----	1.112 650 1E-09
kilohm meter		**\<electric resistivity\>**
abohm centimeter ---	>>> ----	1.000 000 0E+14
microhm inch --	>>> ----	3.937 007 9E+10
ohm circular mil/foot ---	>>> ----	6.015 304 9E+11
ohm meter ---	1,000 ----	1.000 000 0E+03
ohm square millimeter/meter ----------------------------------	>>> ----	1.000 000 0E+09
statohm centimeter --	0.000 000 1 ----	1.112 650 1E-07
kilojoule		**\<energy\>**
Btu [I.T.] --	0.947 817 1 ----	9.478 171 2E-01
Btu [mean] --	0.947 086 3 ----	9.470 862 9E-01
Btu [thermoc.] --	0.948 451 4 ----	9.484 514 1E-01
calorie [I.T.] --	238.845 9 ----	2.388 459 0E+02
calorie [kilogram, I.T.] ---------------------------------------	0.238 845 9 ----	2.388 459 0E-01
calorie [kilogram, mean] -------------------------------------	0.238 662 4 ----	2.386 623 5E-01
calorie [kilogram, thermoc.] ---------------------------------	0.239 005 7 ----	2.390 057 4E-01
calorie [mean] --	238.662 35 ----	2.386 623 5E+02
calorie [nutritional] --	0.239 005 7 ----	2.390 057 4E-01
calorie [thermoc.] --	239.005 74 ----	2.390 057 4E+02
centigrade heat unit [I.T.] -----------------------------------	0.526 565 7 ----	5.265 650 7E-01
cubic centimeter atmosphere ---------------------------------	9,869.232 7 ----	9.869 232 7E+03
cubic foot atmosphere --	0.348 528 7 ----	3.485 286 6E-01
foot pound-force --	737.562 15 ----	7.375 621 5E+02
foot poundal --	23,730.36 ----	2.373 036 0E+04
frigorie [France] ---	0.238 903 ----	2.389 029 6E-01
horsepower hour --	0.000 372 5 ----	3.725 061 4E-04
horsepower hour [metric] -------------------------------------	0.000 377 7 ----	3.776 726 7E-04
joule ---	1,000 ----	1.000 000 0E+03
kilocalorie [I.T.] --	0.238 845 9 ----	2.388 459 0E-01
kilocalorie [mean] --	0.238 662 4 ----	2.386 623 5E-01
kilocalorie [thermoc.] --	0.239 005 7 ----	2.390 057 4E-01
kilogram calorie [15 °C, NBS, 1939] ------------------------	0.238 903 ----	2.389 029 6E-01
liter atmosphere --	9.869 232 7 ----	9.869 232 7E+00
megaerg ---	10,000 ----	1.000 000 0E+04
megalerg --	10,000 ----	1.000 000 0E+04
meter kilogram-force ---	101.971 62 ----	1.019 716 2E+02
newton meter --	1,000 ----	1.000 000 0E+03
pferdestarkenstunde [Germany] ------------------------------	0.000 377 7 ----	3.776 726 7E-04
watthour ---	0.277 777 8 ----	2.777 777 8E-01
wattsecond --	1,000 ----	1.000 000 0E+03
kilojoule/kilogram		**\<specific thermodynamic energy\>**
Btu/pound [I.T.] --	0.429 922 6 ----	4.299 226 1E-01
Btu/pound [thermoc.] ---	0.430 210 3 ----	4.302 103 0E-01
calorie/gram [I.T.] --	0.238 845 9 ----	2.388 459 0E-01
calorie/gram [thermoc.] --------------------------------------	0.239 005 7 ----	2.390 057 4E-01
joule/kilogram --	1,000 ----	1.000 000 0E+03
kilojoule/mole		**\<molar energy\>**
joule/mole ---	1,000 ----	1.000 000 0E+03
millijoule/mole --	1,000,000 ----	1.000 000 0E+06
kilojoule/mole kelvin		**\<molar entropy\>**
joule/mole kelvin ---	1,000 ----	1.000 000 0E+03
millijoule/mole kelvin --	1,000,000 ----	1.000 000 0E+06
kiloliter		**\<volume\>**
acre foot --	0.000 810 7 ----	8.107 131 9E-04
acre inch --	0.009 728 6 ----	9.728 558 3E-03
barrel [UK] --	6.110 256 9 ----	6.110 256 9E+00

	Standard	Scientific
barrel [US, dry]	8.648 489 8	8.648 489 8E+00
barrel [US, liquid]	8.386 414 4	8.386 414 4E+00
barrel [US, petroleum]	6.289 810 8	6.289 810 8E+00
cubic foot	35.314 667	3.531 466 7E+01
cubic inch	61,023.744	6.102 374 4E+04
cubic meter	1	1.000 000 0E+00
cubic yard	1.307 950 6	1.307 950 6E+00
drum [US, liquid]	4.803 128 2	4.803 128 2E+00
firkin [UK]	24.441 028	2.444 102 8E+01
firkin [US]	29.352 45	2.935 245 0E+01
gallon [Canada, liquid]	219.969 25	2.199 692 5E+02
gallon [UK, dry or liquid]	219.969 25	2.199 692 5E+02
gallon [US, liquid]	264.172 05	2.641 720 5E+02
gian sheng [China]	1	1.000 000 0E+00
hogshead [UK]	3.491 575 4	3.491 575 4E+00
hogshead [US]	4.193 207 2	4.193 207 2E+00
kung ping [Taiwan]	1	1.000 000 0E+00
liter	1,000	1.000 000 0E+03
ounce [UK, liquid]	35,195.08	3.519 508 0E+04
ounce [US, liquid]	33,814.023	3.381 402 3E+04
pint [UK]	1,759.754	1.759 754 0E+03
pint [US, liquid]	2,113.376 4	2.113 376 4E+03
quart [UK]	879.876 99	8.798 769 9E+02
quart [US, liquid]	1,056.688 2	1.056 688 2E+03
stere	1	1.000 000 0E+00
tun [UK, liquid]	1.018 376 1	1.018 376 1E+00
tun [US, liquid]	1.048 301 8	1.048 301 8E+00
Winchester wine gallon [UK]	264.172 05	2.641 720 5E+02
kiloliter/day		**\<flow rate, volume basis\>**
acre inch/day	0.009 728 6	9.728 558 3E-03
barrel/day [UK]	6.110 256 9	6.110 256 9E+00
barrel/day [US, federal]	8.521 679 1	8.521 679 1E+00
barrel/day [US, liquid]	8.386 414 4	8.386 414 4E+00
barrel/day [US, petroleum]	6.289 810 8	6.289 810 8E+00
centiliter/second	1.157 407 4	1.157 407 4E+00
cubic centimeter/second	11.574 074 1	1.157 407 4E+01
cubic decimeter/hour	41.666 666 7	4.166 666 7E+01
cubic foot/hour	1.471 444 5	1.471 444 5E+00
cubic inch/minute	42.377 600 1	4.237 760 0E+01
cubic meter/day	1	1.000 000 0E+00
cubic meter/second	0.000 011 6	1.157 407 4E-05
cubic yard/day	1.307 950 6	1.307 950 6E+00
deciliter/minute	6.944 444 4	6.944 444 4E+00
dekaliter/hour	4.166 666 7	4.166 666 7E+00
gallon/hour [UK]	9.165 385 3	9.165 385 3E+00
gallon/hour [US, liquid]	11.007 168 8	1.100 716 9E+01
hectoliter/day	10	1.000 000 0E+01
liter/hour	41.666 666 7	4.166 666 7E+01
liter/hour [pre-1964]	41.665 5	4.166 550 0E+01
milliliter/second	11.574 074 1	1.157 407 4E+01
ounce/minute [UK, liquid]	24.441 028	2.444 102 8E+01
ounce/minute [US, liquid]	23.481 96	2.348 196 0E+01
petrograd standard/day	0.214 028 3	2.140 282 8E-01
stere/day	1	1.000 000 0E+00
thousand cubic foot/day	0.035 314 7	3.531 466 7E-02
kiloliter/hour		**\<flow rate, volume basis\>**
acre foot/day	0.019 457 1	1.945 711 7E-02
acre foot/day [US, survey]	0.019 457	1.945 700 0E-02
acre inch/day	0.233 485 4	2.334 854 0E-01
barrel/hour [UK]	6.110 256 9	6.110 256 9E+00
barrel/hour [US, federal]	8.521 679 1	8.521 679 1E+00
barrel/hour [US, liquid]	8.386 414 4	8.386 414 4E+00
barrel/hour [US, petroleum]	6.289 810 8	6.289 810 8E+00

	Standard	Scientific
centiliter/second	27.777 777 8	2.777 777 8E+01
cubic centimeter/second	277.777 778	2.777 777 8E+02
cubic decimeter/minute	16.666 666 7	1.666 666 7E+01
cubic dekameter/day	0.024	2.400 000 0E-02
cubic foot/hour	35.314 666 7	3.531 466 7E+01
cubic inch/second	16.951 04	1.695 104 0E+01
cubic meter/hour	1	1.000 000 0E+00
cubic meter/second	0.000 277 8	2.777 777 8E-04
cubic yard/hour	1.307 950 6	1.307 950 6E+00
deciliter/second	2.777 777 8	2.777 777 8E+00
dekaliter/minute	1.666 666 7	1.666 666 7E+00
gallon/minute [UK]	3.666 154 1	3.666 154 1E+00
gallon/minute [US, liquid]	4.402 867 5	4.402 867 5E+00
hectoliter/hour	10	1.000 000 0E+01
kiloliter/day	24	2.400 000 0E+01
liter/minute	16.666 666 7	1.666 666 7E+01
liter/minute [pre-1964]	16.666 2	1.666 620 0E+01
milliliter/second	277.777 778	2.777 777 8E+02
ounce/second [UK, liquid]	9.776 411	9.776 411 0E+00
ounce/second [US, liquid]	9.392 784	9.392 784 1E+00
petrograd standard/day	5.136 678 8	5.136 678 8E+00
stere/hour	1	1.000 000 0E+00
thousand cubic foot/day	0.847 552	8.475 520 0E-01

kiloliter/minute   <flow rate, volume basis>

	Standard	Scientific
acre foot/day	1.167 427	1.167 427 0E+00
acre foot/day [US, survey]	1.167 42	1.167 420 0E+00
acre inch/day	14.009 124	1.400 912 4E+01
barrel/minute [UK]	6.110 256 9	6.110 256 9E+00
barrel/minute [US, federal]	8.521 679 1	8.521 679 1E+00
barrel/minute [US, liquid]	8.386 414 4	8.386 414 4E+00
barrel/minute [US, petroleum]	6.289 810 8	6.289 810 8E+00
cubic decimeter/second	16.666 666 7	1.666 666 7E+01
cubic dekameter/day	1.44	1.440 000 0E+00
cubic foot/minute	35.314 666 7	3.531 466 7E+01
cubic inch/second	1,017.062 4	1.017 062 4E+03
cubic meter/minute	1	1.000 000 0E+00
cubic meter/second	0.016 666 7	1.666 666 7E-02
cubic yard/minute	1.307 950 6	1.307 950 6E+00
dekaliter/second	1.666 666 7	1.666 666 7E+00
gallon/second [UK]	3.666 154 1	3.666 154 1E+00
gallon/second [US, liquid]	4.402 867 5	4.402 867 5E+00
hectare meter/day	0.144	1.440 000 0E-01
hectoliter/minute	10	1.000 000 0E+01
kiloliter/hour	60	6.000 000 0E+01
liter/second	16.666 666 7	1.666 666 7E+01
liter/second [pre-1964]	16.666 2	1.666 620 0E+01
ounce/second [UK, liquid]	586.584 66	5.865 846 6E+02
ounce/second [US, liquid]	563.567 05	5.635 670 5E+02
petrograd standard/hour	12.841 697	1.284 169 7E+01
stere/minute	1	1.000 000 0E+00
thousand cubic foot/hour	2.118 88	2.118 880 0E+00

kiloliter/second   <flow rate, volume basis>

	Standard	Scientific
acre foot/hour	2.918 567 5	2.918 567 5E+00
acre foot/hour [US, survey]	2.918 55	2.918 550 0E+00
acre inch/hour	35.022 81	3.502 281 0E+01
barrel/second [UK]	6.110 256 9	6.110 256 9E+00
barrel/second [US, federal]	8.521 679 1	8.521 679 1E+00
barrel/second [US, liquid]	8.386 414 4	8.386 414 4E+00
barrel/second [US, petroleum]	6.289 810 8	6.289 810 8E+00
cubic dekameter/hour	3.6	3.600 000 0E+00
cubic foot/second	35.314 666 7	3.531 466 7E+01
cubic meter/second	1	1.000 000 0E+00
cubic yard/second	1.307 950 6	1.307 950 6E+00

	Standard	Scientific
dekaliter/second	100	1.000 000 0E+02
gallon/second [UK]	219.969 248	2.199 692 5E+02
gallon/second [US, liquid]	264.172 052	2.641 720 5E+02
hectare meter/day	8.64	8.640 000 0E+00
hectoliter/second	10	1.000 000 0E+01
kiloliter/minute	60	6.000 000 0E+01
liter/second	1,000	1.000 000 0E+03
liter/second [pre-1964]	999.972 001	9.999 720 0E+02
ounce/second [UK, liquid]	35,195.08	3.519 508 0E+04
ounce/second [US, liquid]	33,814.023	3.381 402 3E+04
petrograd standard/minute	12.841 697	1.284 169 7E+01
stere/second	1	1.000 000 0E+00
thousand cubic foot/minute	2.118 88	2.118 880 0E+00

kilolitra [Greece]	<mass, special - see page 29>	
kilogram	480	4.800 000 0E+02

kilolux	<illuminance>	
footcandle	92.903 04	9.290 304 0E+01
lumen/square inch	0.645 16	6.451 600 0E-01
lumen/square meter	1,000	1.000 000 0E+03
lux	1,000	1.000 000 0E+03
nox	1,000,000	1.000 000 0E+06
phot	0.1	1.000 000 0E-01

kilolux second	<light exposure>	
footcandle second	92.903 04	9.290 304 0E+01
lumen second/square foot	92.903 04	9.290 304 0E+01
lumen second/square inch	0.645 16	6.451 600 0E-01
lux second	1,000	1.000 000 0E+03

kilometer	<length>	
beru [Babylon, ancient]	0.092 592 6	9.259 259 3E-02
cable length [US, survey]	4.556 713	4.556 713 0E+00
chain [Gunter or US, survey]	49.709 596	4.970 959 6E+01
chain [Ramden or Engineer]	32.808 399	3.280 839 9E+01
chauseemeile [Germany]	0.134 870 9	1.348 708 6E-01
chinese mile [Hong Kong]	1.794 655 5	1.794 655 5E+00
crosh [Bangladesh]	0.310 752	3.107 520 2E-01
dain [Burma]	0.255 623 7	2.556 237 2E-01
farsakh [Abyssinia, ancient]	0.197 238 7	1.972 386 6E-01
farsakh [Arabia]	0.207 039 3	2.070 393 4E-01
farsakh [Iran]	0.160 256 4	1.602 564 1E-01
farsakh [Oman]	0.208 333 3	2.083 333 3E-01
farsakh song [Iran]	0.160 256 4	1.602 564 1E-01
farsang [Abyssinia, ancient]	0.197 238 7	1.972 386 6E-01
farsang [Iran]	0.160 256 4	1.602 564 1E-01
fathom [US, survey]	546.805 56	5.468 055 6E+02
fershi kadim [Turkey]	0.175 901 5	1.759 015 0E-01
foot [international]	3,280.839 9	3.280 839 9E+03
foot [US, survey]	3,280.833 3	3.280 833 3E+03
furlong [US, survey]	4.970 959 6	4.970 959 6E+00
garwoke [Burma]	0.048 821	4.882 097 3E-02
gong li [China]	1	1.000 000 0E+00
inch [based on US, survey foot]	39,370	3.937 000 0E+04
inch [international]	39,370.079	3.937 007 9E+04
java paal [Indonesia]	0.663 57	6.635 700 1E-01
kairi [Japan]	0.539 956 8	5.399 568 0E-01
kasbu [Iraq, ancient]	0.046 948 4	4.694 835 7E-02
kawtha [Burma]	0.195 274 4	1.952 743 6E-01
konak [Turkey]	0.033 333 3	3.333 333 3E-02
kor [India]	0.546 806 6	5.468 066 5E-01
kor [Pakistan]	0.546 806 6	5.468 066 5E-01
kosh [Nepal]	0.310 655 5	3.106 554 8E-01
koss [India]	0.546 806 6	5.468 066 5E-01
koss [Pakistan]	0.546 806 6	5.468 066 5E-01

kilometer (continued)   <length>

Convert To	Standard	Scientific
kung li [China]	1	1.000 000 0E+00
kung li [Taiwan]	1	1.000 000 0E+00
lackilo [Laos]	1	1.000 000 0E+00
lan [Chile]	0.221 533	2.215 330 1E−01
lan [Cuba]	0.235 849 1	2.358 490 6E−01
lan [Ecuador]	0.2	2.000 000 0E+00
lan [El Salvador]	0.25	2.500 000 0E−01
lan [Guatemala]	0.179 436 5	1.794 365 7E−01
lan [Mexico]	0.238 663 5	2.386 634 8E−01
lan [Paraguay]	0.230 946 9	2.309 468 8E−01
lan [Peru]	0.179 856 1	1.798 561 2E−01
lan [Portugal]	0.181 818 2	1.818 181 8E−01
lan [Spain]	0.179 436 6	1.794 365 7E−01
lan [Uruguay]	0.194 174 8	1.941 747 6E−01
landmil [Denmark]	0.132 756 8	1.327 568 1E−01
league [Chile]	0.221 533	2.215 330 1E−01
league [Cuba]	0.235 849 1	2.358 490 6E−01
league [Ecuador]	0.2	2.000 000 0E+00
league [El Salvador]	0.25	2.500 000 0E−01
league [France]	0.25	2.500 000 0E−01
league [Guatemala]	0.179 436 6	1.794 365 7E−01
league [Mexico]	0.238 663 5	2.386 634 8E−01
league [Paraguay]	0.230 946 9	2.309 468 8E−01
league [Peru]	0.179 856 1	1.798 561 2E−01
league [Portugal]	0.181 818 2	1.818 181 8E−01
league [Spain]	0.179 436 6	1.794 365 7E−01
league [Uruguay]	0.194 174 8	1.941 747 6E−01
league [US, statute]	0.207 123 3	2.071 233 2E−01
legoa [Brazil]	0.151 515 2	1.515 151 5E−01
legoa [Mexico]	0.238 663 5	2.386 634 8E−01
legoa [Portugal]	0.161 550 9	1.615 508 9E−01
legoa [Venezuela]	0.199 044 6	1.990 445 9E−01
legua [Argentina]	0.192 307 7	1.923 076 9E−01
legua [Brazil]	0.151 515 2	1.515 151 5E−01
legua [Chile]	0.221 729 5	2.217 294 9E−01
legua [Colombia]	0.2	2.000 000 0E+00
legua [Cuba]	0.235 849 1	2.358 490 6E−01
legua [Ecuador]	0.2	2.000 000 0E+00
legua [El Salvador]	0.25	2.500 000 0E−01
legua [Guatemala]	0.179 436 6	1.794 365 7E−01
legua [Honduras]	0.239 521	2.395 209 6E−01
legua [Mexico]	0.238 663 5	2.386 634 8E−01
legua [Paraguay]	0.230 946 9	2.309 468 8E−01
legua [Peru]	0.179 856 1	1.798 561 2E−01
legua [Portugal]	0.181 818 2	1.818 181 8E−01
legua [Spain]	0.179 436 6	1.794 365 7E−01
legua [Uruguay]	0.194 174 8	1.941 747 6E−01
lei [Hong Kong]	1.794 655 5	1.794 655 5E+00
lei [South Korea]	0.254 647 3	2.546 473 1E−01
li [South Korea]	0.254 629 8	2.546 298 1E−01
lieue [Chile]	0.221 533	2.215 330 1E−01
lieue [Cuba]	0.235 849 1	2.358 490 6E−01
lieue [Ecuador]	0.2	2.000 000 0E+00
lieue [El Salvador]	0.25	2.500 000 0E−01
lieue [France]	0.225 002 3	2.250 022 5E−01
lieue [Guatemala]	0.179 436 6	1.794 365 7E−01
lieue [Mexico]	0.238 663 5	2.386 634 8E−01
lieue [Paraguay]	0.230 787	2.307 869 8E−01
lieue [Peru]	0.179 856 1	1.798 561 2E−01
lieue [Portugal]	0.181 818 2	1.818 181 8E−01
lieue [Spain]	0.179 436 6	1.794 365 7E−01
lieue [Switzerland]	0.208 333 3	2.083 333 3E−01

kilometer (continued) <length>

	Standard	Scientific
lieue [Uruguay]	0.194 174 8	1.941 747 6E-01
lieue de poste [France]	0.256 541 8	2.565 418 2E-01
link [Gunter or US, survey]	4,970.959 6	4.970 959 6E+03
link [Ramden or Engineer]	3,280.839 9	3.280 839 9E+03
marfold [Denmark]	0.132 758 1	1.327 580 5E-01
marfold [Hungary]	0.119 760 5	1.197 604 8E-01
marfold [Sweden]	0.1	1.000 000 0E-01
marhala [Arabia]	0.025 906 7	2.590 673 6E-02
marhala [Iraq, ancient]	0.021 978	2.197 802 2E-02
meile [Austria]	0.131 823 5	1.318 235 1E-01
meile [Denmark]	0.132 758 1	1.327 580 5E-01
meile [Hungary]	0.119 708 9	1.197 088 7E-01
meile [Sweden]	0.1	1.000 000 0E-01
merfold [Hungary]	0.119 703 1	1.197 031 4E-01
mertfold [Hungary]	0.119 708 9	1.197 088 7E-01
meter	1,000	1.000 000 0E+03
miglio [Italy]	1	1.000 000 0E+00
miglio [Rome, ancient]	0.676 59	6.765 899 9E-01
mijl [Netherlands]	0.179 985 6	1.799 856 0E-01
mil [Denmark]	0.132 802 1	1.328 021 2E-01
mil [Hungary]	0.119 760 5	1.197 604 8E-01
mil [Norway]	0.088 534 8	8.853 475 0E-02
mil [Sweden]	0.1	1.000 000 0E-01
mil [Turkey]	1	1.000 000 0E+00
mila [Iceland]	0.132 759 8	1.327 598 1E-01
mila [Poland]	0.117 233 3	1.172 332 9E-01
mila a landi [Iceland]	0.132 802 1	1.328 021 2E-01
mile [Austria]	0.131 821 8	1.318 217 8E-01
mile [Bangladesh]	0.621 504	6.215 040 4E-01
mile [Czechoslovakia, Bohemia]	0.142 795 9	1.427 959 4E-01
mile [Czechoslovakia, Silesia]	0.154 249 6	1.542 495 8E-01
mile [Denmark]	0.133 333 3	1.333 333 3E-01
mile [Hebrew, ancient]	0.674 763 8	6.747 638 3E-01
mile [international]	0.621 371 2	6.213 711 9E-01
mile [Ireland]	0.488 209 7	4.882 097 3E-01
mile [Portugal]	0.479 087 8	4.790 878 2E-01
mile [Rome, ancient]	0.675 675 7	6.756 756 8E-01
mile [Russia]	0.133 911 8	1.339 118 3E-01
mile [Scotland]	0.552 333 6	5.523 336 1E-01
mile [Sweden]	0.1	1.000 000 0E-01
mile [US, statute]	0.621 369 9	6.213 699 5E-01
mile [US, survey]	0.621 369 9	6.213 699 5E-01
mile passum [Rome, ancient]	0.676 59	6.765 899 9E-01
milha [Brazil]	0.454 545 5	4.545 454 5E-01
milha [Portugal]	0.484 496 1	4.844 961 2E-01
miliarum [Rome, ancient]	0.676 59	6.765 899 9E-01
milion [Greece, ancient]	0.674 763 8	6.747 638 3E-01
mill [Turkey]	1	1.000 000 0E+00
milla [Ecuador]	0.714 285 7	7.142 857 1E-01
milla [Honduras]	0.540 540 5	5.405 405 4E-01
milla [Nicaragua]	0.535 905 7	5.359 056 8E-01
milla [Spain]	0.717 782 3	7.177 823 4E-01
milla [Venezuela]	0.538 213 1	5.382 131 3E-01
mille [Belgium, ancient]	0.496 277 9	4.962 779 2E-01
milliare [Rome, ancient]	0.676 59	6.765 899 9E-01
myriameter	0.1	1.000 000 0E-01
nymil [Sweden]	0.1	1.000 000 0E-01
out [US, survey]	9.941 919 2	9.941 919 2E+00
paal [Java]	0.663 57	6.635 700 1E-01
paal [Sumatra]	0.539 956 8	5.399 568 0E-01
pace [US, survey]	1,312.333 3	1.312 333 3E+03
pal [Indonesia]	0.663 57	6.635 700 1E-01

Convert From
Convert To

	Standard	Scientific

kilometer (continued)   \<length\>

Convert To	Standard	Scientific
parasang [Greece, ancient]	0.180 375 2	1.803 751 8E-01
parasang [Iran]	0.160 256 4	1.602 564 1E-01
parasang [Iraq, ancient]	0.175 746 9	1.757 469 2E-01
parasange [Iran]	0.160 256 4	1.602 564 1E-01
peninkulma [Finland]	0.1	1.000 000 0E-01
perch [US, survey]	198.838 38	1.988 383 8E+02
persakh [Iran]	0.160 256 4	1.602 564 1E-01
pharoagh [Turkey]	0.1	1.000 000 0E-01
range [US, survey]	0.103 561 7	1.035 616 6E-01
ri [Japan]	0.254 452 9	2.544 529 3E-01
river [Egypt, ancient]	0.5	5.000 000 0E-01
roeneng [Thailand]	0.25	2.500 000 0E-01
schoenus [Rome, ancient]	0.169 147 5	1.691 475 0E-01
schoinos [Greece, ancient]	0.178 571 4	1.785 714 3E-01
siriometer	<<<	6.684 587 2E-15
stunde [Switzerland]	0.208 333 3	2.083 333 3E-01
taing [Burma]	0.255 754 5	2.557 544 8E-01
township [US, survey]	0.103 561 7	1.035 616 6E-01
tu [China]	0.006 205	6.205 013 7E-03
vara [US, survey, California]	1,193.030 3	1.193 030 3E+03
vara [US, survey, Texas]	1,181.1	1.181 100 0E+03
verst [Russia]	0.937 207 1	9.372 071 2E-01
versta [Russia]	0.937 207 1	9.372 071 2E-01
verste [Russia]	0.937 382 8	9.373 828 3E-01
walk of a Babylonian hour [Mesopotamia, ancient]	0.084 602 4	8.460 236 9E-02
werst [Russia]	0.937 207 1	9.372 071 2E-01
yard [based on US, survey foot]	1,093.611 1	1.093 611 1E+03
yard [international]	1,093.613 3	1.093 613 3E+03
yard [UK]	1,093.615 2	1.093 615 2E+03
yoch [Cambodia]	0.062 5	6.250 000 0E-02
yoch [Thailand]	0.062 5	6.250 000 0E-02
yot [Thailand]	0.25	2.500 000 0E-01
yote [Cambodia]	0.062 5	6.250 000 0E-02
yote [Thailand]	0.062 5	6.250 000 0E-02
yoyana [India]	0.126 262 6	1.262 626 3E-01
yuzanar [Burma]	0.013 186 7	1.318 669 7E-02

kilometer/cubic meter   \<fuel consumption, US\>

Convert To	Standard	Scientific
mile/gallon [international/US, liquid]	0.002 352 1	2.352 145 8E-03

kilometer/day   \<velocity\>

Convert To	Standard	Scientific
foot/minute	2.278 361	2.278 361 0E+00
inch/minute	27.340 332 5	2.734 033 3E+01
knot [international]	0.022 498 2	2.249 820 0E-02
mile/day	0.621 371 2	6.213 711 9E-01
nautical mile/day [international]	0.539 956 8	5.399 568 0E-01
yard/hour	45.567 220 8	4.556 722 1E+01

kilometer/hour   \<velocity\>

Convert To	Standard	Scientific
foot/minute	54.680 664 9	5.468 066 5E+01
inch/second	10.936 133	1.093 613 3E+01
knot [international]	0.539 956 8	5.399 568 0E-01
meter/second	0.277 777 8	2.777 777 8E-01
mile/day	14.912 908 6	1.491 290 9E+01
nautical mile/day [international]	12.958 963 3	1.295 896 3E+01
yard/minute	18.226 888 3	1.822 688 8E+01

kilometer/hour second   \<acceleration\>

Convert To	Standard	Scientific
foot/square second	0.911 344 4	9.113 444 2E-01
galileo	27.777 777 8	2.777 777 8E+01
gn [due to gravity]	0.028 325 5	2.832 545 0E-02
meter/square second	0.277 777 8	2.777 777 8E-01

kilometer/liter   \<fuel consumption, US\>

Convert To	Standard	Scientific
mile/gallon [international/US, liquid]	2.352 145 8	2.352 145 8E+00

kilometer/minute <velocity>

foot/second	54.680 664 9	5.468 066 5E+01
inch/second	656.167 979	6.561 679 8E+02
knot [international]	32.397 408 2	3.239 740 8E+01
meter/second	16.666 666 7	1.666 666 7E+01
mile/hour	37.282 271 5	3.728 227 2E+01
nautical mile/hour [international]	32.397 408 2	3.239 740 8E+01
yard/second	18.226 888 3	1.822 688 8E+01

kilometer/second <velocity>

foot/second	3,280.839 9	3.280 839 9E+03
inch/second	39,370.078 7	3.937 007 9E+04
knot [international]	1,943.844 49	1.943 844 5E+03
meter/second	1,000	1.000 000 0E+03
mile/minute	37.282 271 5	3.728 227 2E+01
nautical mile/minute [international]	32.397 408 2	3.239 740 8E+01
yard/second	1,093.613 3	1.093 613 3E+03

kilometer/square second <acceleration>

foot/square second	3,280.839 9	3.280 839 9E+03
galileo	100,000	1.000 000 0E+05
gₙ [due to gravity]	101.971 621	1.019 716 2E+02
meter/square second	1,000	1.000 000 0E+03

(gₙ shown as g_n [due to gravity])

kilomole <amount of substance>

mole	1,000	1.000 000 0E+03
number of atoms in 0.012 kg of carbon-12	1,000	1.000 000 0E+03
one atom of carbon-12	>>>	6.022 136 7E+26

kilomole/cubic meter <concentration, mole basis>

mole/cubic meter	1,000	1.000 000 0E+03
mole/liter	1	1.000 000 0E+00

kilomole/kilogram <molality>

mole/gram	1	1.000 000 0E+00
mole/kilogram	1,000	1.000 000 0E+03

kilonewton <force>

crinal	10,000	1.000 000 0E+04
dyne	>>>	1.000 000 0E+08
funal	1	1.000 000 0E+00
gram-force	101,971.621	1.019 716 2E+05
newton	1,000	1.000 000 0E+03
ounce-force	3,596.943 09	3.596 943 1E+03
pond	101,971.621	1.019 716 2E+05
pound-force	224.808 943	2.248 089 4E+02
poundal	7,233.013 85	7.233 013 9E+03
ton meter/square second [metric]	1	1.000 000 0E+00

kilonewton meter <torque>

foot pound-force	737.562 15	7.375 621 5E+02
inch pound-force	8,850.745 8	8.850 745 8E+03
kilopond meter	101.971 62	1.019 716 2E+02
meter kilogram-force	101.971 62	1.019 716 2E+02
newton meter	1,000	1.000 000 0E+03

kiloparsec <length>

astronomical unit	>>>	2.062 648 1E+08
bevameter	>>>	3.085 677 6E+10
light year [based on mean Julian year]	3,261.563 8	3.261 563 8E+03
megaparsec	0.001	1.000 000 0E-03
meter	>>>	3.085 677 6E+19
mile [international]	>>>	1.917 351 1E+16
mile [US, statute]	>>>	1.917 347 3E+16
mile [US, survey]	>>>	1.917 347 3E+16
myriameter	>>>	3.085 677 6E+15
parsec	1,000	1.000 000 0E+03
siriometer	206.264 81	2.062 648 1E+02

| Convert From | | <Type of Unit> |
Convert To	Standard	Scientific
kilopascal		**<pressure>**
atmosphere [standard]	0.009 869 2	9.869 232 7E-03
atmosphere [technical]	0.010 197 2	1.019 716 2E-02
bar	0.01	1.000 000 0E-02
centibar	1	1.000 000 0E+00
centimeter of mercury [0 °C, by convention]	0.750 061 6	7.500 615 8E-01
centimeter of water [4 °C, by convention]	10.197 162	1.019 716 2E+01
dyne/square centimeter	10,000	1.000 000 0E+04
gram-force/square centimeter	10.197 162	1.019 716 2E+01
inch of mercury [0 °C, by convention]	0.295 299 8	2.952 998 3E-01
inch of water [4 °C, by convention]	4.014 630 8	4.014 630 8E+00
kilogram-force/square meter	101.971 62	1.019 716 2E+02
kilopond/square meter	101.971 62	1.019 716 2E+02
kip/square foot	0.020 885 4	2.088 543 4E-02
millimeter of mercury [0 °C, by convention]	7.500 615 8	7.500 615 8E+00
millimeter of water [4 °C, by convention]	101.971 62	1.019 716 2E+02
newton/square meter	1,000	1.000 000 0E+03
ounce-force/square inch	2.320 603 8	2.320 603 8E+00
pascal	1,000	1.000 000 0E+03
pieze [France]	1	1.000 000 0E+00
pound-force/square foot	20.885 434	2.088 543 4E+01
poundal/square foot	671.968 98	6.719 689 8E+02
sthene/square meter [France]	1	1.000 000 0E+00
ton-force/square foot [short]	0.010 442 7	1.044 271 7E-02
ton-force/square meter [metric]	0.101 971 62	1.019 716 2E-01
torr	7.500 616 8	7.500 616 8E+00
kilopond		**<force>**
crinal	98.066 5	9.806 650 0E+01
dyne	980,665	9.806 650 0E+05
gram-force	1,000	1.000 000 0E+03
hyl meter/square second	1	1.000 000 0E+00
kilogram-force	1	1.000 000 0E+00
newton	9.806 65	9.806 650 0E+00
pond	1,000	1.000 000 0E+03
pound-force	2.204 622 6	2.204 622 6E+00
poundal	70.931 635 3	7.093 163 5E+01
kilopond centimeter square second		**<moment of inertia of a mass>**
gram-force meter square second	10	1.000 000 0E+01
kilogram square meter	0.098 066 5	9.806 650 0E-02
kilogram-force centimeter square second	1	1.000 000 0E+00
ounce-force foot square second	1.157 282 2	1.157 282 2E+00
pound square foot	2.327 153 4	2.327 153 4E+00
slug square inch	10.415 54	1.041 554 0E+01
kilopond meter		**<energy>**
Btu [I.T.]	0.009 294 9	9.294 910 8E-03
calorie [I.T.]	2.342 278 1	2.342 278 1E+00
calorie [kilogram, I.T.]	0.002 342 3	2.342 278 1E-03
calorie [kilogram, mean]	0.002 340 5	2.340 478 1E-03
calorie [kilogram, thermoc.]	0.002 343 8	2.343 845 6E-03
calorie [mean]	2.340 478 1	2.340 478 1E+00
calorie [nutritional]	0.002 343 8	2.343 845 6E-03
calorie [thermoc.]	2.343 845 6	2.343 845 6E+00
centigrade heat unit [I.T.]	0.005 163 8	5.163 839 3E-03
centimeter gram-force	100,000	1.000 000 0E+05
cubic centimeter atmosphere	96.784 111	9.678 411 1E+01
cubic foot atmosphere	0.003 417 9	3.417 898 6E-03
foot pound-force	7.233 013 9	7.233 013 9E+00
foot poundal	232.715 34	2.327 153 4E+02
gram calorie	2.342 837 7	2.342 837 7E+00
inch ounce-force	1,388.738 7	1.388 738 7E+03
inch pound-force	86.796 166	8.679 616 6E+01
joule	9.806 65	9.806 650 0E+00

Convert From Convert To	Standard	\<Type of Unit\> Scientific
kilogram square meter/square second	9.806 65	9.806 650 0E+00
liter atmosphere	0.096 784 1	9.678 411 1E−02
megaerg	98.066 5	9.806 650 0E+01
megalerg	98.066 5	9.806 650 0E+01
meter kilogram-force	1	1.000 000 0E+00
newton meter	9.806 65	9.806 650 0E+00
watthour	0.002 724 1	2.724 069 4E−03
wattsecond	9.806 65	9.806 650 0E+00

kilopond meter		**\<torque\>**
foot ounce-force	115.728 22	1.157 282 2E+02

kilopond meter square second		**\<moment of inertia of a mass\>**
kilogram square meter	9.806 65	9.806 650 0E+00
kilogram-force centimeter square second	100	1.000 000 0E+02
kilogram-force meter square second	1	1.000 000 0E+00
pound-force foot square second	7.233 013 9	7.233 013 9E+00
slug square foot	7.233 013 9	7.233 013 9E+00

kilopond meter/hour		**\<power\>**
Btu/hour [I.T.]	0.009 294 9	9.294 910 8E−03
Btu/hour [thermoc.]	0.009 301 1	9.301 131 1E−03
calorie/hour [I.T.]	2.342 278 1	2.342 278 1E+00
calorie/hour [thermoc.]	2.343 845 6	2.343 845 6E+00
centigrade heat unit/hour [mean]	0.005 159 9	5.159 857 6E−03
cubic meter atmosphere/minute	1.613 068 5	1.613 068 5E+00
dyne centimeter/second	27,240.694	2.724 069 4E+04
erg/second	27,240.694	2.724 069 4E+04
foot pound-force/hour	7.233 013 9	7.233 013 9E+00
foot poundal/minute	3.878 589	3.878 589 0E+00
gram-force centimeter/second	27.777 778	2.777 777 8E+01
horsepower	0.000 003 7	3.653 037 3E−06
horsepower [metric]	0.000 003 7	3.703 703 7E−06
joule/hour	9.806 65	9.806 650 0E+00
kilocalorie/hour [I.T.]	0.002 342 3	2.342 278 1E−03
kilogram square meter/cubic second	0.002 724 1	2.724 069 4E−03
kilogram-force meter/hour	1	1.000 000 0E+00
kilopond meter/minute	0.016 666 7	1.666 666 7E−02
lumen [green light at 100% efficiency]	1.865 987 6	1.865 987 6E+00
lumen [green light at 5,550 angstrom]	1.852 367 3	1.852 367 3E+00
milliwatt	2.724 069 4	2.724 069 4E+00
newton meter/hour	9.806 65	9.806 650 0E+00
pound square foot/cubic second	0.064 643 2	6.464 315 0E−02
volt ampere	0.002 724 1	2.724 069 4E−03
watt	0.002 724 1	2.724 069 4E−03

kilopond meter/kilogram °C		**\<specific heat capacity\>**
joule/kilogram kelvin	9.806 65	9.806 650 0E+00

kilopond meter/minute		**\<power\>**
Btu/hour [I.T.]	0.557 694 7	5.576 946 5E−01
Btu/hour [thermoc.]	0.558 067 9	5.580 678 6E−01
calorie/minute [I.T.]	2.342 278 1	2.342 278 1E+00
calorie/minute [thermoc.]	2.343 845 6	2.343 845 6E+00
centigrade heat unit/hour [mean]	0.309 591 5	3.095 914 6E−01
cubic meter atmosphere/second	1.613 068 5	1.613 068 5E+00
deciwatt	1.634 441 7	1.634 441 7E+00
dyne centimeter/second	1,634,441.7	1.634 441 7E+06
erg/second	1,634,441.7	1.634 441 7E+06
foot pound-force/minute	7.233 013 9	7.233 013 9E+00
foot poundal/second	3.878 589	3.878 589 0E+00
gram-force centimeter/second	1,666.666 7	1.666 666 7E+03
horsepower	0.000 219 2	2.191 822 4E−04
horsepower [metric]	0.000 222 2	2.222 222 2E−04
joule/minute	9.806 65	9.806 650 0E+00
kilocalorie/hour [I.T.]	0.140 536 7	1.405 366 9E−01
kilogram square meter/cubic second	0.163 444 2	1.634 441 7E−01

	Standard	Scientific
kilogram-force meter/minute	1	1.000 000 0E+00
kilopond meter/hour	60	6.000 000 0E+01
newton meter/minute	9.806 65	9.806 650 0E+00
pound square foot/cubic second	3.878 589	3.878 589 0E+00
volt ampere	0.163 444 2	1.634 441 7E−01
watt	0.163 444 2	1.634 441 7E−01

kilopond meter/second   <power>

	Standard	Scientific
Btu/hour [I.T.]	33.461 679	3.346 167 9E+01
Btu/hour [thermoc.]	33.484 072	3.348 407 2E+01
calorie/second [I.T.]	2.342 278 1	2.342 278 1E+00
calorie/second [thermoc.]	2.343 845 6	2.343 845 6E+00
centigrade heat unit/hour [mean]	18.575 488	1.857 548 8E+01
cheval vapeur [France]	0.013 333 3	1.333 333 3E−02
cubic meter atmosphere/second	96.784 111	9.678 411 1E+01
dyne centimeter/second	>>>	9.806 650 0E+07
erg/second	>>>	9.806 650 0E+07
foot pound-force/second	7.233 013 9	7.233 013 9E+00
foot poundal/second	232.715 34	2.327 153 4E+02
gram-force centimeter/second	100,000	1.000 000 0E+05
horsepower	0.013 150 9	1.315 093 4E−02
horsepower [metric]	0.013 333 3	1.333 333 3E−02
joule/second	9.806 65	9.806 650 0E+00
kilocalorie/hour [I.T.]	8.432 201 2	8.432 201 2E+00
kilogram square meter/cubic second	9.806 65	9.806 650 0E+00
kilogram-force meter/second	1	1.000 000 0E+00
kilopond meter/minute	60	6.000 000 0E+01
newton meter/second	9.806 65	9.806 650 0E+00
pferdestarke [Germany]	0.013 333 3	1.333 333 3E−02
poncelet [France]	0.01	1.000 000 0E−02
pound square foot/cubic second	232.715 34	2.327 153 4E+02
ton of refrigeration	0.002 788 5	2.788 473 2E−03
volt ampere	9.806 65	9.806 650 0E+00
watt	9.806 65	9.806 650 0E+00

kilopond/centimeter   <surface tension>

	Standard	Scientific
dyne/centimeter	980,665	9.806 650 0E+05
gram-force/centimeter	1,000	1.000 000 0E+03
kilogram-force/centimeter	1	1.000 000 0E+00
newton/centimeter	9.806 65	9.806 650 0E+00
newton/meter	980.665	9.806 650 0E+02
ounce-force/inch	89.595 863	8.959 586 3E+01
pound-force/inch	5.599 741 5	5.599 741 5E+00

kilopond/meter   <surface tension>

	Standard	Scientific
dyne/centimeter	9,806.65	9.806 650 0E+03
gram-force/centimeter	10	1.000 000 0E+01
kilogram-force/meter	1	1.000 000 0E+00
newton/meter	9.806 65	9.806 650 0E+00
ounce-force/foot	10.751 504	1.075 150 4E+01
pound-force/foot	0.671 969	6.719 689 8E−01

kilopond/square centimeter   <pressure>

	Standard	Scientific
atmosphere [metric]	1	1.000 000 0E+00
atmosphere [standard]	0.967 841 1	9.678 411 1E−01
atmosphere [technical]	1	1.000 000 0E+00
bar	0.980 665	9.806 650 0E−01
centimeter of mercury [0 °C, by convention]	73.555 914	7.355 591 4E+01
centimeter of water [4 °C, by convention]	1,000	1.000 000 0E+03
decibar	9.806 65	9.806 650 0E+00
dyne/square centimeter	980,665	9.806 650 0E+05
foot of mercury [0 °C, by convention]	2.413 251 8	2.413 251 8E+00
foot of water [4 °C, by convention]	32.808 399	3.280 839 9E+01
gram-force/square centimeter	1,000	1.000 000 0E+03
inch of mercury [0 °C, by convention]	28.959 021	2.895 902 1E+01
inch of water [4 °C, by convention]	393.700 79	3.937 007 9E+02

	Standard	Scientific
kilogram-force/square centimeter	1	1.000 000 0E+00
kilopond/square millimeter	0.01	1.000 000 0E-02
kip/square foot	2.048 161 4	2.048 161 4E+00
newton/square millimeter	0.098 066 5	9.806 650 0E-02
ounce-force/square inch	227.573 49	2.275 734 9E+02
pascal	98,066.5	9.806 650 0E+04
pound-force/square inch	14.223 343	1.422 334 3E+01
ton-force/square foot [short]	1.024 080 7	1.024 080 7E+00
ton-force/square meter [metric]	10	1.000 000 0E+01
torr	735.559 24	7.355 592 4E+02

kilopond/square meter \<pressure\>

	Standard	Scientific
atmosphere [standard]	0.000 096 8	9.678 411 1E-05
atmosphere [technical]	0.000 1	1.000 000 0E-04
bar	0.000 098 1	9.806 650 0E-05
barye [France]	98.066 5	9.806 650 0E+01
centimeter of mercury [0 °C, by convention]	0.007 355 6	7.355 591 4E-03
centimeter of water [4 °C, by convention]	0.1	1.000 000 0E-01
centitorr	7.355 592 4	7.355 592 4E+00
dyne/square centimeter	98.066 5	9.806 650 0E+01
gram-force/square centimeter	0.1	1.000 000 0E-01
inch of mercury [0 °C, by convention]	0.002 895 9	2.895 902 1E-03
inch of water [4 °C, by convention]	0.039 370 1	3.937 007 9E-02
kilogram-force/square meter	1	1.000 000 0E+00
kip/square foot	0.000 204 8	2.048 161 4E-04
micrometer of mercury [0 °C, by convention]	73.555 914	7.355 591 4E+01
micrometer of water [4 °C, by convention]	1,000	1.000 000 0E+03
millimeter of mercury [0 °C, by convention]	0.073 555 9	7.355 591 4E-02
millimeter of water [4 °C, by convention]	1	1.000 000 0E+00
newton/square meter	9.806 65	9.806 650 0E+00
ounce-force/square inch	0.022 757 3	2.275 734 9E-02
pascal	9.806 65	9.806 650 0E+00
pound-force/square foot	0.204 816 1	2.048 161 4E-01
poundal/square foot	6.589 764 6	6.589 764 6E+00
ton-force/square foot [short]	0.000 102 4	1.024 080 7E-04
ton-force/square meter [metric]	0.001	1.000 000 0E-03
torr	0.073 555 9	7.355 592 4E-02

kilopond/square millimeter \<pressure\>

	Standard	Scientific
atmosphere [standard]	96.784 111	9.678 411 1E+01
atmosphere [technical]	100	1.000 000 0E+02
bar	98.066 5	9.806 650 0E+01
dekabar	9.806 65	9.806 650 0E+00
foot of mercury [0 °C, by convention]	241.325 18	2.413 251 8E+02
foot of water [4 °C, by convention]	3,280.839 9	3.280 839 9E+03
gram-force/square centimeter	100,000	1.000 000 0E+05
kilogram-force/square millimeter	1	1.000 000 0E+00
kip/square inch	1.422 334 3	1.422 334 3E+00
megapascal	9.806 65	9.806 650 0E+00
newton/square millimeter	9.806 65	9.806 650 0E+00
pascal	9,806,650	9.806 650 0E+06
pound-force/square inch	1,422.334 3	1.422 334 3E+03
ton-force/square foot [long]	91.435 778	9.143 577 8E+01
ton-force/square foot [short]	102.408 07	1.024 080 7E+02
ton-force/square meter [metric]	1,000	1.000 000 0E+03
torr	73,555.924	7.355 592 4E+04

kilosecond \<time\>

	Standard	Scientific
second	1,000	1.000 000 0E+03

kilosiemens \<electric conductance\>

	Standard	Scientific
absiemens	0.000 001	1.000 000 0E-06
siemens	1,000	1.000 000 0E+03

kilosiemens/meter \<electric conductivity\>

	Standard	Scientific
absiemens/centimeter	\<\<\<	1.000 000 0E-08
mho/meter	1,000	1.000 000 0E+03

	Standard	Scientific
siemens/meter	1,000	1.000 000 0E+03
statsiemens/centimeter		8.987 551 8E+12
kilotesla		**\<magnetic flux density\>**
tesla	1,000	1.000 000 0E+03
kilotex		**\<linear density\>**
denier	9,000	9.000 000 0E+03
gram/meter	1	1.000 000 0E+00
kilogram/kilometer	1	1.000 000 0E+00
kilogram/meter	0.001	1.000 000 0E-03
ounce/foot	0.010 751 5	1.075 150 4E-02
kiloton [metric, explosive energy]		**\<energy\>**
calorie [kilogram, I.T.]	>>>	9.993 312 3E+08
calorie [kilogram, mean]	>>>	9.985 632 5E+08
calorie [kilogram, thermoc.]	>>>	1.000 000 0E+09
cheval vapeur heure [France]	1,580,182.5	1.580 182 5E+06
coal equivalent kilogram [UN, standard]	142,761.6	1.427 616 0E+05
coal equivalent metric ton [UN, standard]	142.761 6	1.427 616 0E+02
dekawatthour	>>>	1.162 222 2E+08
frigorie [France]	>>>	9.995 699 7E+08
gigawatthour	1.162 222 2	1.162 222 2E+00
gram [atomic physics, eq. energy]	0.046 553 3	4.655 327 8E-02
hectowatthour	>>>	1.162 222 2E+07
horsepower hour	1,558,565.7	1.558 565 7E+06
horsepower hour [metric]	1,580,182.5	1.580 182 5E+06
joule	>>>	4.184 000 0E+12
kilocalorie [I.T.]	>>>	9.993 312 3E+08
kilocalorie [mean]	>>>	9.985 632 5E+08
kilocalorie [thermoc.]	>>>	1.000 000 0E+09
kilogram [atomic physics, eq. energy]	0.000 046 6	4.655 327 8E-05
kilogram calorie [15 °C, NBS, 1939]	>>>	9.995 699 7E+08
kilowatthour	1,162,222.2	1.162 222 2E+06
megaton [metric, explosive energy]	0.001	1.000 000 0E-03
megawatthour	1,162.222 2	1.162 222 2E+03
myriawatthour	116,222.22	1.162 222 2E+05
petawatthour	0.000 001 2	1.162 222 2E-06
pferdestarkenstunde [Germany]	1,580,182.5	1.580 182 5E+06
quad	0.000 004	3.965 666 8E-06
terawatthour	0.001 162 2	1.162 222 2E-03
therm [EEC]	39,656.668	3.965 666 8E+04
therm [US]	39,666.137	3.966 613 7E+04
thermie [France]	999,569.97	9.995 699 7E+05
ton [metric, explosive energy]	1,000	1.000 000 0E+03
kiloton [metric]		**\<mass\>**
decitonne	10,000	1.000 000 0E+04
doppelzentner [Germany]	10,000	1.000 000 0E+04
gigagram	1	1.000 000 0E+00
hundredweight [long]	19,684.131	1.968 413 1E+04
hundredweight [short]	22,046.226	2.204 622 6E+04
hundredweight [UK]	19,684.131	1.968 413 1E+04
kilogram	1,000,000	1.000 000 0E+06
kilotonne	1	1.000 000 0E+00
megaton [metric]	0.001	1.000 000 0E-03
megatonne	0.001	1.000 000 0E-03
millier	1,000	1.000 000 0E+03
quarter [long]	3,936.826 1	3.936 826 1E+03
quarter [short]	4,409.245 2	4.409 245 2E+03
quintal [metric]	10,000	1.000 000 0E+04
ton [long]	984.206 53	9.842 065 3E+02
ton [metric]	1,000	1.000 000 0E+03
ton [short]	1,102.311 3	1.102 311 3E+03
ton [UK]	984.206 53	9.842 065 3E+02
tonne	1,000	1.000 000 0E+03

Convert From		<Type of Unit>
Convert To	Standard	Scientific

kilotonne <mass>

gigagram	1	1.000 000 0E+00
kilogram	1,000,000	1.000 000 0E+06
kiloton [metric]	1	1.000 000 0E+00
megaton [metric]	0.001	1.000 000 0E−03
megatonne	0.001	1.000 000 0E−03
millier	1,000	1.000 000 0E+03
quarter [long]	3,936.826 1	3.936 826 1E+03
quarter [short]	4,409.245 2	4.409 245 2E+03
ton [long]	984.206 53	9.842 065 3E+02
ton [metric]	1,000	1.000 000 0E+03
ton [short]	1,102.311 3	1.102 311 3E+03
ton [UK]	984.206 53	9.842 065 3E+02
tonne	1,000	1.000 000 0E+03

kilovolt <electric potential>

abvolt	>>>	1.000 000 0E+11
erg/franklin	3.335 641	3.335 641 0E+00
joule/coulomb	1,000	1.000 000 0E+03
statvolt	3.335 641	3.335 641 0E+00
volt	1,000	1.000 000 0E+03

kilovolt/meter <electric field strength>

statvolt/centimeter	0.033 356 4	3.335 641 0E−02
volt/inch	25.4	2.540 000 0E+01
volt/meter	1,000	1.000 000 0E+03
volt/millimeter	1	1.000 000 0E+00

kilowatt <power>

Btu/minute [I.T.]	56.869 027	5.686 902 7E+01
Btu/minute [thermoc.]	56.907 085	5.690 708 5E+01
calorie/second [I.T.]	238.845 9	2.388 459 0E+02
calorie/second [thermoc.]	239.005 74	2.390 057 4E+02
centigrade heat unit/minute [mean]	31.569 543	3.156 954 3E+01
cheval vapeur [France]	1.359 621 6	1.359 621 6E+00
cubic meter atmosphere/second	9,869.232 7	9.869 232 7E+03
dyne centimeter/second	>>>	1.000 000 0E+10
erg/second	>>>	1.000 000 0E+10
foot pound-force/second	737.562 15	7.375 621 5E+02
foot poundal/second	23,730.36	2.373 036 0E+04
gram-force centimeter/second	>>>	1.019 716 2E+07
horsepower	1.341 022 1	1.341 022 1E+00
horsepower [metric]	1.359 621 6	1.359 621 6E+00
joule/second	1,000	1.000 000 0E+03
kilocalorie/minute [I.T.]	14.330 754	1.433 075 4E+01
kilogram square meter/cubic second	1,000	1.000 000 0E+03
kilogram-force meter/second	101.971 62	1.019 716 2E+02
kilopond meter/second	101.971 62	1.019 716 2E+02
newton meter/second	1,000	1.000 000 0E+03
pferdestarke [Germany]	1.359 621 6	1.359 621 6E+00
poncelet [France]	1.019 716 2	1.019 716 2E+00
ton of refrigeration	0.284 345 1	2.843 451 4E−01
volt ampere	1,000	1.000 000 0E+03
watt	1,000	1.000 000 0E+03

kilowatt/cubic meter kelvin <heat transfer coefficient>

Btu/hour cubic foot °F [I.T.]	53.678 384	5.367 838 4E+01
kilocalorie/hour cubic meter °C [I.T.]	859.845 23	8.598 452 3E+02
watt/cubic meter kelvin	1,000	1.000 000 0E+03

kilowatt/meter °C <thermal conductivity>

Btu foot/second square foot °F [I.T.]	0.160 497	1.604 970 3E−01
Btu inch/second square foot °F [I.T.]	1.925 964 4	1.925 964 4E+00
Btu inch/second square foot °F [thermoc.]	1.927 253 8	1.927 253 8E+00
Btu/second foot °F [I.T.]	0.160 497	1.604 970 3E−01
calorie centimeter/second square centimeter °C [I.T.]	2.388 459	2.388 459 0E+00
calorie/second centimeter °C [I.T.]	2.388 459	2.388 459 0E+00

| Convert From | | <Type of Unit> |
Convert To	Standard	Scientific
calorie/second centimeter °C [thermoc.]	2.390 057 4	2.390 057 4E+00
kilowatt/meter kelvin	1	1.000 000 0E+00
watt/foot °C	304.8	3.048 000 0E+02
watt/meter kelvin	1,000	1.000 000 0E+03

kilowatt/meter kelvin <thermal conductivity>
Convert To	Standard	Scientific
Btu foot/second square foot °F [I.T.]	0.160 497	1.604 970 3E−01
Btu inch/second square foot °F [I.T.]	1.925 964 4	1.925 964 4E+00
Btu inch/second square foot °F [thermoc.]	1.927 253 8	1.927 253 8E+00
Btu/second square foot °F [I.T.]	0.160 497	1.604 970 3E−01
calorie centimeter/second square centimeter °C [I.T.]	2.388 459	2.388 459 0E+00
calorie/second centimeter °C [I.T.]	2.388 459	2.388 459 0E+00
calorie/second centimeter °C [thermoc.]	2.390 057 4	2.390 057 4E+00
kilowatt/meter °C	1	1.000 000 0E+00
watt centimeter/square centimeter °C	10	1.000 000 0E+01
watt/centimeter kelvin	10	1.000 000 0E+01
watt/foot °C	304.8	3.048 000 0E+02
watt/meter kelvin	1,000	1.000 000 0E+03

kilowatt/square meter <heat flux density>
Convert To	Standard	Scientific
Btu/minute square foot [I.T.]	5.283 305 5	5.283 305 5E+00
Btu/minute square foot [thermoc.]	5.286 841 2	5.286 841 2E+00
joule/second square meter	1,000	1.000 000 0E+03
pyron	1.433 075 4	1.433 075 4E+00
watt/square foot	92.903 04	9.290 304 0E+01
watt/square meter	1,000	1.000 000 0E+03

kilowatt/square meter °C <heat transfer coefficient>
Convert To	Standard	Scientific
Btu/hour square foot °F [I.T.]	176.110 18	1.761 101 8E+02
Btu/hour square foot °F [thermoc.]	176.228 08	1.762 280 8E+02
calorie/hour square centimeter °C [I.T.]	85.984 523	8.598 452 3E+01
kilowatt/square meter kelvin	1	1.000 000 0E+00
watt/square foot °C	92.903 04	9.290 304 0E+01
watt/square meter kelvin	1,000	1.000 000 0E+03

kilowatt/square meter kelvin <heat transfer coefficient>
Convert To	Standard	Scientific
Btu/hour square foot °F [I.T.]	176.110 18	1.761 101 8E+02
calorie/hour square centimeter °C [I.T.]	85.984 523	8.598 452 3E+01
kilowatt/square meter °C	1	1.000 000 0E+00
watt/square foot °C	92.903 04	9.290 304 0E+01
watt/square meter kelvin	1,000	1.000 000 0E+03

kilowatthour <energy>
Convert To	Standard	Scientific
Board of Trade Unit	1	1.000 000 0E+00
Btu [I.T.]	3,412.141 6	3.412 141 6E+03
calorie [I.T.]	859,845.23	8.598 452 3E+05
calorie [kilogram, I.T.]	859,845.23	8.598 452 3E+02
centigrade heat unit [I.T.]	1,895.634 2	1.895 634 2E+03
centimeter gram-force	>>>	3.670 978 4E+10
cheval vapeur heure [France]	1.359 621 6	1.359 621 6E+00
coal equivalent kilogram [UN, standard]	0.122 835	1.228 350 3E−01
cubic centimeter atmosphere	>>>	3.552 923 8E+07
cubic foot atmosphere	1,254.703 2	1.254 703 2E+03
cubic foot of natural gas [standard]	3.311 258 3	3.311 258 3E+00
dyne centimeter	>>>	3.600 000 0E+13
erg	>>>	3.600 000 0E+13
foot pound-force	2,655,223.7	2.655 223 7E+06
foot poundal	>>>	8.542 929 7E+07
frigorie [France]	860.050 65	8.600 506 5E+02
gallon of automotive gasoline [US, liquid]	0.027 322 4	2.732 240 4E−02
gallon of aviation gasoline [US, liquid]	0.027 322 4	2.732 240 4E−02
gallon of diesel oil [US, liquid]	0.024 57	2.457 002 0E−02
gallon of distillate #2 fuel oil [US, liquid]	0.024 57	2.457 002 0E−02
gallon of jet fuel, kerosene type [US, liquid]	0.025 316 5	2.531 645 6E−02
gallon of jet fuel, naphtha type [US, liquid]	0.026 881 7	2.688 172 0E−02
gallon of kerosene [US, liquid]	0.025 316 5	2.531 645 6E−02
gallon of residual fuel oil [US, liquid]	0.022 779	2.277 904 3E−02

Convert From		
	\<Type of Unit\>	
Convert To	Standard	Scientific

	Standard	Scientific
horsepower hour	1.341 022 1	1.341 022 1E+00
horsepower hour [metric]	1.359 621 6	1.359 621 6E+00
joule	3,600,000	3.600 000 0E+06
kilocalorie [I.T.]	859.845 23	8.598 452 3E+02
kilogram calorie [15 °C, NBS, 1939]	860.050 65	8.600 506 5E+02
kilojoule	3,600	3.600 000 0E+03
kilowatthour [international, 1948]	0.999 836 1	9.998 361 4E−01
meter kilogram-force	367,097.84	3.670 978 4E+05
newton meter	3,600,000	3.600 000 0E+06
pferdestarkenstunde [Germany]	1.359 621 6	1.359 621 6E+00
therm [EEC]	0.034 121 4	3.412 141 6E−02
therm [US]	0.034 129 6	3.412 956 3E−02
thermie [France]	0.860 050 7	8.600 506 5E−01
ton of anthracite coal [short]	0.000 134 4	1.344 086 0E−04
ton of bituminous coal [short]	0.000 138 1	1.381 215 5E−04
watthour	1,000	1.000 000 0E+03

kilowatthour [international, 1948] \<energy\>

	Standard	Scientific
Btu [I.T.]	3,412.700 8	3.412 700 8E+03
calorie [I.T.]	859,986.15	8.599 861 5E+05
calorie [kilogram, I.T.]	859.986 15	8.599 861 5E+02
cheval vapeur heure [France]	1.359 844 4	1.359 844 4E+00
coal equivalent kilogram [UN, standard]	0.122 855 2	1.228 551 6E−01
cubic centimeter atmosphere	>>>	3.553 506 0E+07
cubic foot atmosphere	1,254.908 8	1.254 908 8E+03
dyne centimeter	>>>	3.600 590 0E+13
erg	>>>	3.600 590 0E+13
foot pound-force	2,655,658.9	2.655 658 9E+06
foot poundal	>>>	8.544 329 8E+07
frigorie [France]	860.191 6	8.601 916 0E+02
hectowatthour	10.001 639	1.000 163 9E+01
horsepower hour	1.341 241 9	1.341 241 9E+00
horsepower hour [metric]	1.359 844 4	1.359 844 4E+00
joule	3,600,590	3.600 590 0E+06
kilocalorie [I.T.]	859.986 15	8.599 861 5E+02
kilogram calorie [15 °C, NBS, 1939]	860.191 6	8.601 916 0E+02
kilowatthour	1.000 163 9	1.000 163 9E+00
meter kilogram-force	367,158	3.671 580 0E+05
newton meter	3,600,590	3.600 590 0E+06
pferdestarkenstunde [Germany]	1.359 844 4	1.359 844 4E+00
therm [EEC]	0.034 127	3.412 700 8E−02
therm [US]	0.034 135 2	3.413 515 7E−02
thermie [France]	0.860 191 6	8.601 916 0E−01
watthour	1,000.163 9	1.000 163 9E+03

kiloweber \<magnetic flux\>

	Standard	Scientific
gauss square centimeter	>>>	1.000 000 0E+11
maxwell	>>>	1.000 000 0E+11
statweber	3.335 641	3.335 641 0E+00
unit pole	>>>	7.957 747 5E+09
weber	1,000	1.000 000 0E+03

kiloweber meter \<magnetic dipole moment\>

	Standard	Scientific
abweber centimeter	>>>	7.957 747 2E+11
statweber centimeter	26.544 187 3	2.654 418 7E+01
weber meter	1,000	1.000 000 0E+03

kiloweber/meter \<magnetic vector potential\>

	Standard	Scientific
abweber/centimeter	>>>	1.000 000 0E+09
statweber/centimeter	0.033 356 4	3.335 641 0E−02
weber/meter	1,000	1.000 000 0E+03

kin [China] \<area, special - see page 29\>

	Standard	Scientific
hectare	6.144	6.144 000 0E+00

kin [Japan] \<mass, special - see page 29\>

	Standard	Scientific
kilogram	0.6	6.000 000 0E−01

Convert From / Convert To	Standard	Scientific
kind [Eritrea]	<length, special - see page 29>	
centimeter	50	5.000 000 0E+01
king [China]	<area, special - see page 29>	
hectare	0.674	6.740 000 0E-01
kinn [Brunei]	<mass, special - see page 29>	
kilogram	0.605	6.050 000 0E-01
kinn [China]	<mass, special - see page 29>	
kilogram	0.605	6.050 000 0E-01
kinn [Hong Kong]	<mass, special - see page 29>	
kilogram	0.605	6.050 000 0E-01
kinn [Indonesia]	<mass, special - see page 29>	
kilogram	0.618	6.180 000 0E-01
kinn [Japan]	<mass, special - see page 29>	
kilogram	0.6	6.000 000 0E-01
kinn [Malaysia]	<mass, special - see page 29>	
kilogram	0.605	6.050 000 0E-01
kinn [Singapore]	<mass, special - see page 29>	
kilogram	0.605	6.050 000 0E-01
kinn [South Korea]	<mass, special - see page 29>	
kilogram	0.6	6.000 000 0E-01
kinn [Thailand]	<mass, special - see page 29>	
kilogram	0.6	6.000 000 0E-01
kintar [Cyprus]	<mass, special - see page 29>	
kilogram	55.883	5.588 300 0E+01
kintar [Egypt]	<mass, special - see page 29>	
kilogram	44.928	4.492 800 0E+01
kintar [Greece]	<mass, special - see page 29>	
kilogram	56.32	5.632 000 0E+01
kintar [Iraq]	<mass, special - see page 29>	
kilogram	274.3	2.743 000 0E+02
kintar [Lebanon]	<mass, special - see page 29>	
kilogram	256.4	2.564 000 0E+02
kintar [Malta]	<mass, special - see page 29>	
kilogram	79.38	7.938 000 0E+01
kintar [Morocco]	<mass, special - see page 29>	
kilogram	100	1.000 000 0E+02
kintar [Sudan, large]	<mass, special - see page 29>	
kilogram	141.5	1.415 000 0E+02
kintar [Sudan, small]	<mass, special - see page 29>	
kilogram	44.928	4.492 800 0E+01
kintar [Syria]	<mass, special - see page 29>	
kilogram	256.5	2.565 000 0E+02
kintar [Turkey]	<mass, special - see page 29>	
kilogram	56.45	5.645 000 0E+01
kip		<force>
crinal	44,482.216 2	4.448 221 6E+04
grain-force	7,000,000	7.000 000 0E+06
gram-force	453,592.37	4.535 923 7E+05
newton	4,448.221 62	4.448 221 6E+03
ounce-force	16,000	1.600 000 0E+04
pond	453,592.37	4.535 923 7E+05
pound-force	1,000	1.000 000 0E+03
poundal	32,174.048 6	3.217 404 9E+04
slug foot/square second	1,000	1.000 000 0E+03
ton-force [short]	0.5	5.000 000 0E-01
kip/square foot		<pressure>
atmosphere [standard]	0.472 541 4	4.725 414 2E-01

Convert From	<Type of Unit>	
Convert To	Standard	Scientific

	Standard	Scientific
atmosphere [technical]	0.488 242 8	4.882 427 6E−01
bar	0.478 802 6	4.788 025 9E−01
centimeter of mercury [0 °C, by convention]	35.913 143	3.591 314 3E+01
centimeter of water [4 °C, by convention]	488.242 76	4.882 427 6E+02
decibar	4.788 025 9	4.788 025 9E+00
foot of mercury [0 °C, by convention]	1.178 252 7	1.178 252 7E+00
foot of water [4 °C, by convention]	16.018 463	1.601 846 3E+01
gram-force/square centimeter	488.242 76	4.882 427 6E+02
inch of mercury [0 °C, by convention]	14.139 032	1.413 903 2E+01
inch of water [4 °C, by convention]	192.221 56	1.922 215 6E+02
kilogram-force/square centimeter	0.488 242 8	4.882 427 6E−01
kilopond/square centimeter	0.488 242 8	4.882 427 6E−01
newton/square millimeter	0.047 880 3	4.788 025 9E−02
ounce-force/square inch	111.111 11	1.111 111 1E+02
pieze [France]	47.880 259	4.788 025 9E+01
pound-force/square foot	1,000	1.000 000 0E+03
pound-force/square inch	6.944 444 4	6.944 444 4E+00
sthene/square meter [France]	47.880 259	4.788 025 9E+01
ton-force/square foot [short]	0.5	5.000 000 0E−01
ton-force/square meter [metric]	4.882 427 6	4.882 427 6E+00
torr	359.131 48	3.591 314 8E+02

kip/square inch <pressure>
	Standard	Scientific
atmosphere [standard]	68.045 964	6.804 596 4E+01
atmosphere [technical]	70.306 958	7.030 695 8E+01
bar	68.947 573	6.894 757 3E+01
centimeter of mercury [0 °C, by convention]	5,171.492 5	5.171 492 5E+03
centimeter of water [4 °C, by convention]	70,306.958	7.030 695 8E+04
dekabar	6.894 757 3	6.894 757 3E+00
foot of mercury [0 °C, by convention]	169.668 39	1.696 683 9E+02
foot of water [4 °C, by convention]	2,306.658 7	2.306 658 7E+03
gram-force/square centimeter	70,306.958	7.030 695 8E+04
inch of mercury [0 °C, by convention]	2,036.020 7	2.036 020 7E+03
inch of water [4 °C, by convention]	27,679.905	2.767 990 5E+04
kilogram-force/square centimeter	70.306 958	7.030 695 8E+01
kilopond/square centimeter	70.306 958	7.030 695 8E+01
kip/square foot	144	1.440 000 0E+02
megapascal	6.894 757 3	6.894 757 3E+00
newton/square millimeter	6.894 757 3	6.894 757 3E+00
pound-force/square inch	1,000	1.000 000 0E+03
ton-force/square foot [short]	72	7.200 000 0E+01
ton-force/square meter [metric]	703.069 58	7.030 695 8E+02
torr	51,714.933	5.171 493 3E+04

kirat [Egypt, ancient] <length, special - see page 29>
	Standard	Scientific
millimeter	0.87	8.700 000 0E−01

kirat [Egypt, ancient] <area, special - see page 29>
	Standard	Scientific
square meter	175.035	1.750 350 0E+02

kirat [Egypt] <volume, special - see page 29>
	Standard	Scientific
liter	0.064 453	6.445 300 0E−02

kirat [Egypt] <mass, special - see page 29>
	Standard	Scientific
gram	0.195	1.950 000 0E−01

kirat [Egypt] <area, special - see page 29>
	Standard	Scientific
square meter	175.03	1.750 300 0E+02

kirat [Iraq, ancient] <mass, special - see page 29>
	Standard	Scientific
milligram	195	1.950 000 0E+02

kirat [Lebanon, land] <length, special - see page 29>
	Standard	Scientific
centimeter	3.16	3.160 000 0E+00

kirat [Lebanon, textiles] <length, special - see page 29>
	Standard	Scientific
centimeter	2.83	2.830 000 0E+00

kirat [Sudan] <mass, special - see page 29>
	Standard	Scientific
milligram	195	1.950 000 0E+02

kirat [Sudan] <length, special - see page 29>
centimeter---2.416----2.416 000 0E+00

kish [China] <area, special - see page 29>
are --- 1.54----1.540 000 0E+00

kist [Islam, oil] <volume, special - see page 29>
liter --2.106----2.106 000 0E+00

kite [Egypt] <mass, special - see page 29>
gram--9.1----9.100 000 0E+00

kitmir [Turkey] <mass, special - see page 29>
milligram --- 3.13----3.130 000 0E+00

kiya [Oman] <mass, special - see page 29>
gram-- 168.3----1.683 000 0E+02

kiyak kin [Japan] <mass, special - see page 29>
kilogram ---60.100 7----6.010 070 0E+01

kiyaka me [Japan] <mass, special - see page 29>
kilogram --------------------------------------- 375.658 4----3.756 584 0E+02

klafter [Austria] <length, special - see page 29>
meter--- 1.896 5----1.896 500 0E+00

klafter [Germany] <length, special - see page 29>
meter--- 1.74----1.740 000 0E+00

klafter [Switzerland] <length, special - see page 29>
meter--- 1.8----1.800 000 0E+00

klam [Thailand] <mass, special - see page 29>
gram--0.234 375----2.343 750 0E-01

klender [Germany, wool] <mass, special - see page 29>
kilogram -- 10.516----1.051 600 0E+01

kleud [Germany, wool] <mass, special - see page 29>
kilogram -- 10.516----1.051 600 0E+01

klom [Thailand] <mass, special - see page 29>
gram-- 0.117 187 5----1.171 875 0E-01

knot [international] <velocity>
centimeter/second ---------------------------------51.444 444 4----5.144 444 4E+01
dekameter/minute---------------------------------- 3.086 666 7----3.086 666 7E+00
foot/second --- 1.687 809 9----1.687 809 9E+00
hectometer/hour--- 18.52----1.852 000 0E+01
inch/second ---20.253 718 3----2.025 371 8E+01
kilometer/hour --1.852----1.852 000 0E+00
meter/minute --30.866 666 7----3.086 666 7E+01
mile/hour -- 1.150 779 5----1.150 779 5E+00
millimeter/second -----------------------------------514.444 444----5.144 444 4E+02
nautical mile/hour [international] ------------------------1----1.000 000 0E+00
yard/minute ------------------------------------ 33.756 197 1----3.375 619 7E+01

ko [China] <volume, special - see page 29>
liter-- 0.103 544----1.035 440 0E-01

ko [Taiwan] <area, special - see page 29>
hectare --- 0.969 9----9.699 000 0E-01

kob [Laos] <volume, special - see page 29>
liter---2.5----2.500 000 0E+00

kob louang [Laos] <volume, special - see page 29>
liter--- 0.5----5.000 000 0E-01

koddi [Arab] <volume, special - see page 29>
liter---7.58----7.580 000 0E+00

koibon [Greece] <volume, special - see page 29>
liter-- 33.166----3.316 600 0E+01

koilon [Greece] <volume, special - see page 29>
liter-- 33.2----3.320 000 0E+01

koku [Japan]
liter ———————————————————— \<volume, special - see page 29\>
———————————————— 180.390 7 --- 1.803 907 0E+02

kolla [Tunisia]
liter ———————————————————— \<volume, special - see page 29\>
———————————————————— 10.102 --- 1.010 200 0E+01

kollast [Sweden]
hectoliter ———————————————— \<volume, special - see page 29\>
———————————————————— 19.79 --- 1.979 000 0E+01

kolle [Lebanon, olive oil]
kilogram ———————————————— \<mass, special - see page 29\>
———————————————————— 33.345 --- 3.334 500 0E+01

koltuk [Turkey]
square meter ——————————————— \<area, special - see page 29\>
———————————————————————— 1.48 --- 1.480 000 0E+00

koltunna [Sweden]
liter ———————————————————— \<volume, special - see page 29\>
———————————————————— 164.9 --- 1.649 000 0E+02

kon [South Korea]
gram ————————————————————— \<mass, special - see page 29\>
———————————————————————— 600 --- 6.000 000 0E+02

kona [India, ancient]
gram ————————————————————— \<mass, special - see page 29\>
———————————————— 6.998 282 3 --- 6.998 282 3E+00

konak [Turkey]
kilometer ——————————————— \<length, special - see page 29\>
———————————————————————— 30 --- 3.000 000 0E+01

kondylos [Greece, ancient]
centimeter ——————————————— \<length, special - see page 29\>
———————————————————— 3.85 --- 3.850 000 0E+00

konge [Greece, ancient]
liter ———————————————————— \<volume, special - see page 29\>
———————————————————— 3.51 --- 3.510 000 0E+00

kop [Netherlands]
liter ———————————————————— \<volume, special - see page 29\>
———————————————— 0.851 9 --- 8.519 000 0E-01

kor [Babylon, ancient]
liter ———————————————————— \<volume, special - see page 29\>
———————————————————————— 360 --- 3.600 000 0E+02

kor [Egypt, ancient]
hectoliter ———————————————— \<volume, special - see page 29\>
———————————————————— 0.96 --- 9.600 000 0E-01

kor [Hebrew, ancient]
liter ———————————————————— \<volume, special - see page 29\>
———————————————————————— 230 --- 2.300 000 0E+02

kor [India]
kilometer ——————————————— \<length, special - see page 29\>
———————————————————— 1.828 8 --- 1.828 800 0E+00

kor [Pakistan]
kilometer ——————————————— \<length, special - see page 29\>
———————————————————— 1.828 8 --- 1.828 800 0E+00

korce [Russia]
liter ———————————————————— \<volume, special - see page 29\>
———————————————— 122.994 1 --- 1.229 941 0E+02

kordofan [Sudan]
hectare ————————————————— \<area, special - see page 29\>
———————————————————— 0.726 6 --- 7.266 000 0E-01

kordofan mukhamas [Sudan, land]
hectare ————————————————— \<area, special - see page 29\>
———————————————————— 0.726 62 --- 7.266 200 0E-01

korec [Czechoslovakia]
liter ———————————————————— \<volume, special - see page 29\>
———————————————————— 93.592 --- 9.359 200 0E+01

korec [Czechoslovakia]
are ————————————————————— \<area, special - see page 29\>
———————————————————— 28.77 --- 2.877 000 0E+01

korec [Russia]
liter ———————————————————— \<volume, special - see page 29\>
———————————————————— 123.33 --- 1.233 300 0E+02

koret [Poland]
kilogram ———————————————— \<mass, special - see page 29\>
———————————————————————— 50 --- 5.000 000 0E+01

korn [Sweden]
gram ————————————————————— \<mass, special - see page 29\>
———————————————— 0.042 507 6 --- 4.250 760 0E-02

korn skeppa [Iceland]
liter ———————————————————— \<volume, special - see page 29\>
———————————————————— 17.39 --- 1.739 000 0E+01

korn tonde [Denmark, oats]
kilogram ———————————————— \<mass, special - see page 29\>
———————————————————————— 70 --- 7.000 000 0E+01

Convert From / Convert To	Standard	Scientific
korn tonde [Denmark, wheat] kilogram	<mass, special - see page 29> 107.5	1.075 000 0E+02
korn tonde [Denmark] liter	<volume, special - see page 29> 139.12	1.391 200 0E+02
korn tonde [Norway] liter	<volume, special - see page 29> 138.97	1.389 700 0E+02
korn topmaal [Norway] hectoliter	<volume, special - see page 29> 1.6	1.600 000 0E+00
korn tunna [Iceland] liter	<volume, special - see page 29> 139.11	1.391 100 0E+02
koros [Greece, ancient] liter	<volume, special - see page 29> 525	5.250 000 0E+02
korrel [Netherlands] gram	<mass, special - see page 29> 0.1	1.000 000 0E-01
kortab [Hebrew, ancient] cubic centimeter	<volume, special - see page 29> 8.584 239	8.584 239 0E+00
koryec [Poland] liter	<volume, special - see page 29> 128	1.280 000 0E+02
korzec [Poland] liter	<volume, special - see page 29> 128	1.280 000 0E+02
kosh [Nepal] kilometer	<length, special - see page 29> 3.219	3.219 000 0E+00
koss [India] kilometer	<length, special - see page 29> 1.828 8	1.828 800 0E+00
koss [Pakistan] kilometer	<length, special - see page 29> 1.828 8	1.828 800 0E+00
kotyle [Greece, ancient] milliliter	<volume, special - see page 29> 292	2.920 000 0E+02
kouna [Ethiopia] kilogram	<mass, special - see page 29> 4	4.000 000 0E+00
kouza [Cyprus] liter	<volume, special - see page 29> 10.2	1.020 000 0E+01
kovid [India] centimeter	<length, special - see page 29> 45.72	4.572 000 0E+01
koyan [Brunei] kilogram	<mass, special - see page 29> 2,419	2.419 000 0E+03
koyan [Malaysia] hectoliter	<volume, special - see page 29> 36.37	3.637 000 0E+01
koyan [Malaysia] kilogram	<mass, special - see page 29> 2,419	2.419 000 0E+03
koyan [Sarawak] hectoliter	<volume, special - see page 29> 36.367 68	3.636 768 0E+01
koyan [Singapore] hectoliter	<volume, special - see page 29> 36.37	3.637 000 0E+01
koyan [Singapore] kilogram	<mass, special - see page 29> 2,419	2.419 000 0E+03
koyan [Thailand] liter	<volume, special - see page 29> 2,000	2.000 000 0E+03
koyang [Batavia] kilogram	<mass, special - see page 29> 1,667	1.667 000 0E+03
kramergewicht [Germany] gram	<mass, special - see page 29> 470.28	4.702 800 0E+02
krap sran [Cambodia] millimeter	<length, special - see page 29> 2.604	2.604 000 0E+00

Convert From	<Type of Unit>	
Convert To	Standard	Scientific

krat [Turkey] — <mass, special - see page 29>
milligram ------- 200 --- 2.000 000 0E+02

krina [Bulgaria] — <volume, special - see page 29>
liter ------- 20 --- 2.000 000 0E+01

krinne [Switzerland, large] — <mass, special - see page 29>
gram ------- 693.8 --- 6.938 000 0E+02

krishnala [Hindu, ancient, gold] — <mass, special - see page 29>
milligram ------- 124 --- 1.240 000 0E+02

krouchka [Russia] — <volume, special - see page 29>
liter ------- 1.23 --- 1.230 000 0E+00

kruska [Russia, liquid] — <volume, special - see page 29>
liter ------- 1.23 --- 1.230 000 0E+00

kuba [Abyssinia, ancient] — <volume, special - see page 29>
liter ------- 1.02 --- 1.020 000 0E+00

kuba [Ethiopia] — <volume, special - see page 29>
liter ------- 1 --- 1.000 000 0E+00

kuba [Liberia] — <volume, special - see page 29>
liter ------- 1.02 --- 1.020 000 0E+00

kubieke duim [Netherlands] — <volume, special - see page 29>
cubic centimeter ------- 1 --- 1.000 000 0E+00

kubieke el [Netherlands] — <volume, special - see page 29>
cubic meter ------- 1 --- 1.000 000 0E+00

kubieke palm [Netherlands] — <volume, special - see page 29>
cubic centimeter ------- 1,000 --- 1.000 000 0E+03

kubikfot [Sweden] — <volume, special - see page 29>
cubic meter ------- 0.026 171 9 --- 2.617 190 0E-02

kujira shaku [Japan] — <length, special - see page 29>
meter ------- 0.379 --- 3.790 000 0E-01

kul tonde [Denmark] — <volume, special - see page 29>
hectoliter ------- 1.700 37 --- 1.700 370 0E+00

kula [Morocco, oil] — <volume, special - see page 29>
liter ------- 24.047 --- 2.404 700 0E+01

kula [Spanish North Africa] — <mass, special - see page 29>
kilogram ------- 11.165 --- 1.116 500 0E+01

kulack [Batavia, grain and rice] — <mass, special - see page 29>
kilogram ------- 4.304 --- 4.304 000 0E+00

kulba [Afghanistan] — <area, special - see page 29>
hectare ------- 7.814 --- 7.814 000 0E+00

kulimet [Estonia] — <volume, special - see page 29>
liter ------- 11.48 --- 1.148 000 0E+01

kulla [North Africa, ancient] — <volume, special - see page 29>
liter ------- 10.08 --- 1.008 000 0E+01

kulmet [Latvia] — <volume, special - see page 29>
liter ------- 10.93 --- 1.093 000 0E+01

kuna [Eritrea] — <volume, special - see page 29>
liter ------- 5 --- 5.000 000 0E+00

kuna [Ethiopia] — <volume, special - see page 29>
liter ------- 5 --- 5.000 000 0E+00

kuncha [Malaysia] — <volume, special - see page 29>
liter ------- 727.353 6 --- 7.273 536 0E+02

kuncha [Singapore] — <volume, special - see page 29>
liter ------- 727.353 6 --- 7.273 536 0E+02

kung [China] — <length, special - see page 29>
meter ------- 2.006 --- 2.006 000 0E+00

Convert From / Convert To	Standard <Type of Unit>	Scientific
kung chang [Taiwan] meter	<length, special - see page 29> 10	1.000 000 0E+01
kung chien [Taiwan] gram	<mass, special - see page 29> 10	1.000 000 0E+01
kung chih [China] meter	<length, special - see page 29> 1	1.000 000 0E+00
kung chih [Taiwan] meter	<length, special - see page 29> 1	1.000 000 0E+00
kung chin [China] kilogram	<mass, special - see page 29> 1	1.000 000 0E+00
kung chin [Taiwan] kilogram	<mass, special - see page 29> 1	1.000 000 0E+00
kung ching [China] hectare	<area, special - see page 29> 1	1.000 000 0E+00
kung ching [Taiwan] hectare	<area, special - see page 29> 1	1.000 000 0E+00
kung chu [Taiwan] milligram	<mass, special - see page 29> 100	1.000 000 0E+02
kung fen [China] gram	<mass, special - see page 29> 1	1.000 000 0E+00
kung fen [China] centimeter	<length, special - see page 29> 1	1.000 000 0E+00
kung fun [Taiwan] centimeter	<length, special - see page 29> 1	1.000 000 0E+00
kung hao [Taiwan] milligram	<mass, special - see page 29> 10	1.000 000 0E+01
kung heng [Taiwan] kilogram	<mass, special - see page 29> 10	1.000 000 0E+01
kung ho [China] liter	<volume, special - see page 29> 0.1	1.000 000 0E−01
kung ho [Taiwan] centiliter	<volume, special - see page 29> 10	1.000 000 0E+01
kung ko [Taiwan] gram	<mass, special - see page 29> 1	1.000 000 0E+00
kung li [China] kilometer	<length, special - see page 29> 1	1.000 000 0E+00
kung li [Taiwan] kilometer	<length, special - see page 29> 1	1.000 000 0E+00
kung liang [China] gram	<mass, special - see page 29> 100	1.000 000 0E+02
kung liang [Taiwan] gram	<mass, special - see page 29> 100	1.000 000 0E+02
kung mou [Taiwan] are	<area, special - see page 29> 1	1.000 000 0E+00
kung mu [China] are	<area, special - see page 29> 1	1.000 000 0E+00
kung ping [Taiwan] kiloliter	<volume, special - see page 29> 1	1.000 000 0E+00
kung sheng [China] liter	<volume, special - see page 29> 1	1.000 000 0E+00
kung sheng [Taiwan] liter	<volume, special - see page 29> 1	1.000 000 0E+00
kung shi [China] kilogram	<mass, special - see page 29> 100	1.000 000 0E+02

Convert From	<Type of Unit>	
Convert To	Standard	Scientific

kung shih [China]
hectoliter --- <volume, special - see page 29>
------------------- 1 --- 1.000 000 0E+00

kung so [Taiwan]
centiliter --- <volume, special - see page 29>
------------------- 1 --- 1.000 000 0E+00

kung sun [China]
milligram --- <mass, special - see page 29>
------------------- 1 --- 1.000 000 0E+00

kung szu [Taiwan]
milligram --- <mass, special - see page 29>
------------------- 1 --- 1.000 000 0E+00

kung tan [Taiwan]
hectoliter --- <volume, special - see page 29>
------------------- 1 --- 1.000 000 0E+00

kung tan [Taiwan]
kilogram --- <mass, special - see page 29>
------------------- 100 --- 1.000 000 0E+02

kung ton [China]
kilogram --- <mass, special - see page 29>
------------------- 1,000 --- 1.000 000 0E+03

kung tou [China]
liter --- <volume, special - see page 29>
------------------- 10 --- 1.000 000 0E+01

kung tou [Taiwan]
liter --- <volume, special - see page 29>
------------------- 10 --- 1.000 000 0E+01

kung tso [Taiwan]
milliliter --- <volume, special - see page 29>
------------------- 1 --- 1.000 000 0E+00

kung tsun [Taiwan]
centimeter --- <length, special - see page 29>
------------------- 10 --- 1.000 000 0E+01

kung tun [Taiwan]
tonne --- <mass, special - see page 29>
------------------- 1 --- 1.000 000 0E+00

kung yin [Taiwan]
meter --- <length, special - see page 29>
------------------- 100 --- 1.000 000 0E+02

kunke [India]
gram --- <mass, special - see page 29>
------------------- 281.92 --- 2.819 200 0E+02

kunna [Ethiopia]
liter --- <volume, special - see page 29>
------------------- 4.4 --- 4.400 000 0E+00

kunna [Ethiopia]
kilogram --- <mass, special - see page 29>
------------------- 5 --- 5.000 000 0E+00

kup [Thailand]
centimeter --- <length, special - see page 29>
------------------- 25 --- 2.500 000 0E+01

kupang [Brunei, gold]
milligram --- <mass, special - see page 29>
------------------- 37.8 --- 3.780 000 0E+01

kurr [Islam, wheat]
kilogram --- <mass, special - see page 29>
------------------- 2,829 --- 2.829 000 0E+03

kurr [Mesopotamia, ancient, wheat]
kilogram --- <mass, special - see page 29>
------------------- 771.2 --- 7.712 000 0E+02

kurr [Persia, ancient, wheat]
kilogram --- <mass, special - see page 29>
------------------- 1,004 --- 1.004 000 0E+03

kurru [Babylon, ancient]
liter --- <volume, special - see page 29>
------------------- 180 --- 1.800 000 0E+02

kus [Iraq, ancient, large]
centimeter --- <length, special - see page 29>
------------------- 99 --- 9.900 000 0E+01

kus [Iraq, ancient, small]
centimeter --- <length, special - see page 29>
------------------- 49.4 --- 4.940 000 0E+01

kutu [Turkey]
liter --- <volume, special - see page 29>
------------------- 4.6 --- 4.600 000 0E+00

kuza [Hebrew, ancient, liquid]
cubic centimeter --- <volume, special - see page 29>
------------------- 3,296.11 --- 3.296 110 0E+03

kvadratfot [Sweden]
square meter --- <area, special - see page 29>
------------------- 0.088 150 2 --- 8.815 020 0E−02

| Convert From | <Type of Unit> | |
Convert To	Standard	Scientific

kvadratni khvat [Yugoslavia] — <area, special - see page 29>
square meter ---- 3.596 6 ----3.596 600 0E+00

kvarter [Sweden, liquid] — <volume, special - see page 29>
liter ---- 0.327 139 ----3.271 390 0E-01

kvarter [Sweden] — <length, special - see page 29>
centimeter ----14.845 1 ----1.484 510 0E+01

kvint [Denmark] — <mass, special - see page 29>
gram ----5 ----5.000 000 0E+00

kvintin [Sweden] — <mass, special - see page 29>
gram ----3.320 91 ----3.320 910 0E+00

kwai [Burma] — <volume, special - see page 29>
liter ---- 4.04 ----4.040 000 0E+00

kwak [India] — <volume, special - see page 29>
liter ---- 0.34 ----3.400 000 0E-01

kwamme [Japan] — <mass, special - see page 29>
kilogram ---- 3.75 ----3.750 000 0E+00

kwan [Japan] — <mass, special - see page 29>
kilogram ---- 3.75 ----3.750 000 0E+00

kwan [South Korea] — <mass, special - see page 29>
kilogram ---- 3.75 ----3.750 000 0E+00

kwarta [Malta, beer, wine and spirits] — <volume, special - see page 29>
liter ----5.398 ----5.398 000 0E+00

kwarta [Malta, oil and milk] — <volume, special - see page 29>
liter ----5.114 ----5.114 000 0E+00

kwarta [Poland] — <volume, special - see page 29>
liter ----1 ----1.000 000 0E+00

kwarteka [Poland] — <volume, special - see page 29>
liter ---- 0.25 ----2.500 000 0E-01

kwarterka [Poland] — <volume, special - see page 29>
liter ---- 0.25 ----2.500 000 0E-01

kwarti [Poland, dry] — <volume, special - see page 29>
liter ---- 0.919 ----9.190 000 0E-01

kwarti [Poland, liquid] — <volume, special - see page 29>
liter ---- 0.948 ----9.480 000 0E-01

kwe [Burma] — <volume, special - see page 29>
liter ----20.46 ----2.046 000 0E+01

kwien [Thailand] — <volume, special - see page 29>
hectoliter ----20 ----2.000 000 0E+01

kyaku me [Japan] — <mass, special - see page 29>
gram ---- 375 ----3.750 000 0E+02

kyat [Burma] — <mass, special - see page 29>
gram ----16.33 ----1.633 000 0E+01

kyat [Laos] — <mass, special - see page 29>
gram ----15 ----1.500 000 0E+01

kyat [Romania] — <mass, special - see page 29>
gram ----16.33 ----1.633 000 0E+01

kyat [Thailand] — <mass, special - see page 29>
gram ---- 15 ----1.500 000 0E+01

kyathos [Greece, ancient] — <volume, special - see page 29>
milliliter ----49 ----4.900 000 0E+01

kyathys [Greece, ancient] — <volume, special - see page 29>
cubic centimeter ----44.949 ----4.494 900 0E+01

laang [Thailand] — <volume, special - see page 29>
liter ----0.5 ----5.000 000 0E-01

| Convert From | \<Type of Unit\> | |
Convert To	Standard	Scientific

labor [Canada] — \<area, special - see page 29\>
square meter — 716.8 — 7.168 000 0E+02

labor [US, survey] — \<area\>
acre [commerical]	214.340 26	2.143 402 6E+02
acre [international]	177.140 71	1.771 407 1E+02
acre [US, survey]	177.14	1.771 400 0E+02
are	7,168.630 1	7.168 630 1E+03
hectare	71.686 301	7.168 630 1E+01
rood	708.56	7.085 600 0E+02
section [US, survey]	0.276 781 3	2.767 812 5E-01
square arpent [US, survey]	209.675 3	2.096 753 0E+02
square foot [international]	7,716,249.3	7.716 249 3E+06
square foot [US, survey]	7,716,218.4	7.716 218 4E+06
square furlong [US, survey]	17.714	1.771 400 0E+01
square league [US, statute]	0.030 753 5	3.075 347 2E-02
square meter	716,863.01	7.168 630 1E+05
square mile [international]	0.276 782 4	2.767 823 6E-01
square mile [US, statute]	0.276 781 3	2.767 812 5E-01
square mile [US, survey]	0.276 781 3	2.767 812 5E-01
township [US, survey]	0.007 688 4	7.688 368 1E-03

lachsa [Philippines] — \<mass, special - see page 29\>
kilogram — 30.36 — 3.036 000 0E+01

lackilo [Laos] — \<length, special - see page 29\>
kilometer — 1 — 1.000 000 0E+00

ladan [Ethiopia] — \<mass, special - see page 29\>
kilogram — 40 — 4.000 000 0E+01

lagel [Austria, steel] — \<mass, special - see page 29\>
kilogram — 70.015 — 7.001 500 0E+01

lai [Vietnam] — \<volume, special - see page 29\>
cubic meter — 0.064 — 6.400 000 0E-02

lamang [Malaya and Singapore] — \<volume, special - see page 29\>
liter — 0.063 1 — 6.310 000 0E-02

lamany [Burma] — \<volume, special - see page 29\>
liter — 0.063 64 — 6.364 000 0E-02

lambda — \<volume\>
cubic foot	<<<	3.531 466 7E-08
cubic inch	0.000 061	6.102 374 4E-05
cubic meter	<<<	1.000 000 0E-09
cubic millimeter	1	1.000 000 0E+00
drachm [UK, liquid]	0.000 281 6	2.815 606 4E-04
dram [Canada, liquid]	0.000 281 6	2.815 606 4E-04
dram [US, liquid]	0.000 270 5	2.705 121 8E-04
drop [US, liquid]	0.012 173	1.217 304 8E-02
gallon [Canada, liquid]	0.000 000 2	2.199 692 5E-07
gallon [UK, dry or liquid]	0.000 000 2	2.199 692 5E-07
gallon [US, liquid]	0.000 000 3	2.641 720 5E-07
liter	0.000 001	1.000 000 0E-06
microliter	1	1.000 000 0E+00
ounce [UK, liquid]	0.000 035 2	3.519 508 0E-05
ounce [US, liquid]	0.000 033 8	3.381 402 3E-05
scruple [UK, liquid]	0.000 844 7	8.446 819 1E-04
tablespoon [Canada, measuring]	0.000 070 4	7.039 027 9E-05
tablespoon [US, measuring]	0.000 067 6	6.762 804 5E-05
teaspoon [Canada, measuring]	0.000 211 2	2.111 708 4E-04
teaspoon [US, measuring]	0.000 202 9	2.028 841 4E-04

lambda/day — \<flow rate, volume basis\>
centiliter/day	0.000 1	1.000 000 0E-04
cubic centimeter/day	0.001	1.000 000 0E-03
cubic millimeter/day	1	1.000 000 0E+00
deciliter/day	0.000 01	1.000 000 0E-05

	Standard	Scientific
		<Type of Unit>

Convert To	Standard	Scientific
lambda/hour	0.041 666 7	4.166 666 7E-02
milliliter/day	0.001	1.000 000 0E-03
lambda/hour		**<flow rate, volume basis>**
centiliter/day	0.002 4	2.400 000 0E-03
cubic centimeter/day	0.024	2.400 000 0E-02
cubic inch/hour	0.000 061	6.102 374 4E-05
cubic meter/day	<<<	2.400 000 0E-08
cubic mile/day	<<<	5.757 906 2E-18
cubic millimeter/hour	1	1.000 000 0E+00
deciliter/day	0.000 24	2.400 000 0E-04
lambda/day	24	2.400 000 0E+01
milliliter/day	0.024	2.400 000 0E-02
ounce/day [UK, liquid]	0.000 844 7	8.446 819 1E-04
ounce/day [US, liquid]	0.000 811 5	8.115 365 4E-04
lambda/minute		**<flow rate, volume basis>**
centiliter/day	0.144	1.440 000 0E-01
cubic centimeter/day	1.44	1.440 000 0E+00
cubic decimeter/day	0.001 44	1.440 000 0E-03
cubic inch/day	0.087 874 2	8.787 419 2E-02
cubic millimeter/minute	1	1.000 000 0E+00
deciliter/day	0.014 4	1.440 000 0E-02
gallon/day [UK]	0.000 316 8	3.167 557 2E-04
gallon/day [US, liquid]	0.000 380 4	3.804 077 6E-04
lambda/hour	60	6.000 000 0E+01
liter/day	0.001 44	1.440 000 0E-03
liter/day [pre-1964]	0.001 44	1.439 959 7E-03
milliliter/day	1.44	1.440 000 0E+00
ounce/day [UK, liquid]	0.050 680 9	5.068 091 5E-02
ounce/day [US, liquid]	0.048 692 2	4.869 219 3E-02
lambda/second		**<flow rate, volume basis>**
barrel/day [UK]	0.000 527 9	5.279 262 0E-04
barrel/day [US, federal]	0.000 736 3	7.362 730 8E-04
barrel/day [US, liquid]	0.000 724 6	7.245 862 0E-04
barrel/day [US, petroleum]	0.000 543 4	5.434 396 5E-04
centiliter/day	8.64	8.640 000 0E+00
cubic centimeter/hour	3.6	3.600 000 0E+00
cubic foot/day	0.003 051 2	3.051 187 2E-03
cubic inch/day	5.272 451 5	5.272 451 5E+00
cubic meter/second	<<<	1.000 000 0E-09
cubic millimeter/second	1	1.000 000 0E+00
deciliter/day	0.864	8.640 000 0E-01
dekaliter/day	0.008 64	8.640 000 0E-03
gallon/day [UK]	0.019 005 3	1.900 534 3E-02
gallon/day [US, liquid]	0.022 824 5	2.282 446 5E-02
lambda/minute	60	6.000 000 0E+01
liter/day	0.086 4	8.640 000 0E-02
liter/day [pre-1964]	0.086 397 6	8.639 758 1E-02
milliliter/hour	3.6	3.600 000 0E+00
ounce/day [UK, liquid]	3.040 854 9	3.040 854 9E+00
ounce/day [US, liquid]	2.921 531 6	2.921 531 6E+00
lambert		**<luminance>**
apostilb [international]	10,000	1.000 000 0E+04
blondel	10,000	1.000 000 0E+04
candela/square inch	2.053 608 1	2.053 608 1E+00
candela/square meter	3,183.098 9	3.183 098 9E+03
footlambert	929.030 4	9.290 304 0E+02
nit	3,183.098 9	3.183 098 9E+03
skot	>>>	1.000 000 0E+07
stilb	0.318 309 9	3.183 098 9E-01
lame [Burma]		**<volume, special - see page 29>**
liter	0.319 637 8	3.196 378 0E-01

Convert From	<Type of Unit>	
Convert To	Standard	Scientific

Ian [Burma]   \<length, special - see page 29\>
meter--- 1.829 --- 1.829 000 0E+00

Ian [Chile]   \<length, special - see page 29\>
kilometer--- 4.514 --- 4.514 000 0E+00

Ian [Cuba]   \<length, special - see page 29\>
kilometer--- 4.24 --- 4.240 000 0E+00

Ian [Czechoslovakia]   \<area, special - see page 29\>
hectare-- 17.27 --- 1.727 000 0E+01

Ian [Ecuador]   \<length, special - see page 29\>
kilometer--- 5 --- 5.000 000 0E+00

Ian [El Salvador]   \<length, special - see page 29\>
kilometer--- 4 --- 4.000 000 0E+00

Ian [Guatemala]   \<length, special - see page 29\>
kilometer--- 5.573 --- 5.573 000 0E+00

Ian [Mexico]   \<length, special - see page 29\>
kilometer--- 4.19 --- 4.190 000 0E+00

Ian [Mongolia]   \<mass, special - see page 29\>
gram --- 37.5 --- 3.750 000 0E+01

Ian [Paraguay]   \<length, special - see page 29\>
kilometer--- 4.33 --- 4.330 000 0E+00

Ian [Peru]   \<length, special - see page 29\>
kilometer--- 5.56 --- 5.560 000 0E+00

Ian [Portugal]   \<length, special - see page 29\>
kilometer--- 5.5 --- 5.500 000 0E+00

Ian [Spain]   \<length, special - see page 29\>
kilometer--- 5.573 --- 5.573 000 0E+00

Ian [Uruguay]   \<length, special - see page 29\>
kilometer--- 5.15 --- 5.150 000 0E+00

Iana [Russia]   \<mass, special - see page 29\>
gram --- 34 --- 3.400 000 0E+01

Ianac [Yugoslavia]   \<area, special - see page 29\>
hectare-- 0.719 --- 7.190 000 0E-01

Ianaz [Yugoslavia]   \<area, special - see page 29\>
are -- 57.5 --- 5.750 000 0E+01

Ianca [Cape Verde]   \<length, special - see page 29\>
meter-- 4.4 --- 4.400 000 0E+00

Iandmil [Denmark]   \<length, special - see page 29\>
kilometer-- 7.532 57 --- 7.532 570 0E+00

Iane [Laos]   \<mass, special - see page 29\>
kilogram -- 1,200 --- 1.200 000 0E+03

Iang [Malaysia, dry]   \<volume, special - see page 29\>
centiliter-- 56.826 --- 5.682 600 0E+01

Iang [Sarawak]   \<volume, special - see page 29\>
liter --- 0.568 245 --- 5.682 450 0E-01

Iang [Vietnam]   \<mass, special - see page 29\>
gram -- 37.8 --- 3.780 000 0E+01

langley [15 °C, CIPM, 1950]   \<energy fluence\>
calorie/square centimeter [15 °C, CIPM, 1950]------------------------- 1 --- 1.000 000 0E+00
joule/square meter -- 41,855 --- 4.185 500 0E+04

langley [I.T.]   \<energy fluence\>
calorie/square centimeter [I.T.] ------------------------------------ 1 --- 1.000 000 0E+00
joule/square meter -- 41,868 --- 4.186 800 0E+04

langley [thermoc.]   \<energy fluence\>
calorie/square centimeter [thermoc.] -------------------------------- 1 --- 1.000 000 0E+00
joule/square meter -- 41,840 --- 4.184 000 0E+04

| Convert From | <Type of Unit> | |
Convert To	Standard	Scientific
last [Denmark]	<mass, special - see page 29>	
kilogram	2,000	2.000 000 0E+03
last [Germany, dry]	<volume, special - see page 29>	
hectoliter	39.57	3.957 000 0E+01
last [Netherlands]	<volume, special - see page 29>	
liter	3,000	3.000 000 0E+03
last [Sweden]	<volume, special - see page 29>	
hectoliter	29.678 1	2.967 810 0E+01
last [UK]	<volume, special - see page 29>	
liter	2,909.414	2.909 414 0E+03
last [US]	<mass, special - see page 29>	
tonne	1.814 4	1.814 400 0E+00
lasta [Ceylon]	<length, special - see page 29>	
meter	0.656	6.560 000 0E−01
lastre [Argentina]	<volume, special - see page 29>	
liter	2,057.966	2.057 966 0E+03
lata [Costa Rica]	<mass, special - see page 29>	
gram	453.1	4.531 000 0E+02
lath [India]	<length, special - see page 29>	
meter	2.743 2	2.743 200 0E+00
latro [Czechoslovakia]	<length, special - see page 29>	
meter	1.917	1.917 000 0E+00
le [China]	<mass, special - see page 29>	
milligram	37.799	3.779 900 0E+01
le [Vietnam]	<volume, special - see page 29>	
liter	0.1	1.000 000 0E−01
lea [Singapore, precious metals and medicine]	<mass, special - see page 29>	
milligram	34.447	3.444 700 0E+01
lea [US, cotton yarn]		<length>
foot [international]	360	3.600 000 0E+02
meter	109.728	1.097 280 0E+02
yard [international]	120	1.200 000 0E+02
lea [US, linen yarn]		<length>
foot [international]	900	9.000 000 0E+02
meter	274.32	2.743 200 0E+02
yard [international]	300	3.000 000 0E+02
lea [US, silk yarn]		<length>
foot [international]	360	3.600 000 0E+02
meter	109.728	1.097 280 0E+02
yard [international]	120	1.200 000 0E+02
lea [US, wool yarn]		<length>
foot [international]	240	2.400 000 0E+02
meter	73.152	7.315 200 0E+01
yard [international]	80	8.000 000 0E+01
league [Chile]	<length, special - see page 29>	
kilometer	4.514	4.514 000 0E+00
league [Cuba]	<length, special - see page 29>	
kilometer	4.24	4.240 000 0E+00
league [Ecuador]	<length, special - see page 29>	
kilometer	5	5.000 000 0E+00
league [El Salvador]	<length, special - see page 29>	
kilometer	4	4.000 000 0E+00
league [France]	<length, special - see page 29>	
kilometer	4	4.000 000 0E+00
league [Guatemala]	<length, special - see page 29>	
kilometer	5.573	5.573 000 0E+00

| Convert From | <Type of Unit> | |
Convert To	Standard	Scientific
league [international, nautical]		<length>
cable length [US, survey]	25.317 097	2.531 709 7E+01
fathom [US, survey]	3,038.051 7	3.038 051 7E+03
foot [international]	18,228.346	1.822 834 6E+04
foot [US, survey]	18,228.31	1.822 831 0E+04
furlong [US, survey]	27.618 652	2.761 865 2E+01
league [UK, nautical]	0.999 361 1	9.993 611 0E-01
league [US, statute]	1.150 777 1	1.150 777 1E+00
meter	5,556	5.556 000 0E+03
mile [international]	3.452 338 3	3.452 338 3E+00
mile [international, nautical]	3	3.000 000 0E+00
mile [UK, nautical]	2.998 083 3	2.998 083 3E+00
mile [US, nautical]	3	3.000 000 0E+00
mile [US, statute]	3.452 331 4	3.452 331 4E+00
mile [US, survey]	3.452 331 4	3.452 331 4E+00
out [US, survey]	55.237 303	5.523 730 3E+01
perch [US, survey]	1,104.746 1	1.104 746 1E+03
yard [based on US, survey foot]	6,076.103 3	6.076 103 3E+03
yard [international]	6,076.115 5	6.076 115 5E+03
yard [UK]	6,076.126 1	6.076 126 1E+03
league [Mexico]		<length, special - see page 29>
kilometer	4.19	4.190 000 0E+00
league [Paraguay]		<length, special - see page 29>
kilometer	4.33	4.330 000 0E+00
league [Peru]		<length, special - see page 29>
kilometer	5.56	5.560 000 0E+00
league [Portugal]		<length, special - see page 29>
kilometer	5.5	5.500 000 0E+00
league [Spain]		<length, special - see page 29>
kilometer	5.573	5.573 000 0E+00
league [UK, nautical]		<length>
cable length [US, survey]	25.333 283	2.533 328 3E+01
chain [Gunter or US, survey]	276.363 08	2.763 630 8E+02
chain [Ramden or Engineer]	182.4	1.824 000 0E+02
fathom [US, survey]	3,039.993 9	3.039 993 9E+03
foot [international]	18,240	1.824 000 0E+04
foot [US, survey]	18,239.964	1.823 996 4E+04
furlong [US, survey]	27.636 308	2.763 630 8E+01
inch [based on US, survey foot]	218,879.56	2.188 795 6E+05
inch [international]	218,880	2.188 800 0E+05
league [international, nautical]	1.000 639 3	1.000 639 3E+00
league [US, statute]	1.151 512 8	1.151 512 8E+00
link [Gunter or US, survey]	27,636.308	2.763 630 8E+04
link [Ramden or Engineer]	18,240	1.824 000 0E+04
meter	5,559.552	5.559 552 0E+03
mile [international]	3.454 545 5	3.454 545 5E+00
mile [international, nautical]	3.001 917 9	3.001 917 9E+00
mile [UK, nautical]	3	3.000 000 0E+00
mile [US, nautical]	3.001 917 9	3.001 917 9E+00
mile [US, statute]	3.454 538 5	3.454 538 5E+00
mile [US, survey]	3.454 538 5	3.454 538 5E+00
out [US, survey]	55.272 617	5.527 261 7E+01
perch [US, survey]	1,105.452 3	1.105 452 3E+03
rope	912	9.120 000 0E+02
span	24,320	2.432 000 0E+04
yard [based on US, survey foot]	6,079.987 8	6.079 987 8E+03
yard [international]	6,080	6.080 000 0E+03
yard [UK]	6,080.010 6	6.080 010 6E+03
league [Uruguay]		<length, special - see page 29>
kilometer	5.15	5.150 000 0E+00

league [US, statute]   **\<length>**

Convert To	Standard	Scientific
cable length [US, survey]	22	2.200 000 0E+01
chain [Gunter or US, survey]	240	2.400 000 0E+02
chain [Ramden or Engineer]	158.400 32	1.584 003 2E+02
fathom [US, survey]	2,640	2.640 000 0E+03
foot [international]	15,840.032	1.584 003 2E+04
foot [US, survey]	15,840	1.584 000 0E+04
furlong [US, survey]	24	2.400 000 0E+01
inch [based on US, survey foot]	190,080	1.900 800 0E+05
inch [international]	190,080.38	1.900 803 8E+05
league [international, nautical]	0.868 978	8.689 779 8E−01
league [UK, nautical]	0.868 422 8	8.684 227 9E−01
link [Gunter or US, survey]	24,000	2.400 000 0E+04
link [Ramden or Engineer]	15,840.032	1.584 003 2E+04
meter	4,828.041 7	4.828 041 7E+03
mile [international]	3.000 006	3.000 006 0E+00
mile [international, nautical]	2.606 933 9	2.606 933 9E+00
mile [UK, nautical]	2.605 268 4	2.605 268 4E+00
mile [US, nautical]	2.606 933 9	2.606 933 9E+00
mile [US, statute]	3	3.000 000 0E+00
mile [US, survey]	3	3.000 000 0E+00
out [US, survey]	48	4.800 000 0E+01
perch [US, survey]	960	9.600 000 0E+02
pole [US, survey]	960	9.600 000 0E+02
range [US, survey]	0.5	5.000 000 0E−01
rod [US, survey]	960	9.600 000 0E+02
township [US, survey]	0.5	5.000 000 0E−01
yard [based on US, survey foot]	5,280	5.280 000 0E+03
yard [international]	5,280.010 6	5.280 010 6E+03
yard [UK]	5,280.019 7	5.280 019 7E+03

leaguer [South Africa]   **\<volume, special - see page 29>**

liter	575.366 5	5.753 665 0E+02

leaguer [Swaziland]   **\<volume, special - see page 29>**

liter	575.064	5.750 640 0E+02

leang [China]   **\<mass, special - see page 29>**

gram	37.798	3.779 800 0E+01

legana [Iran]   **\<volume, special - see page 29>**

liter	39.48	3.948 000 0E+01

legger [Netherlands]   **\<volume, special - see page 29>**

liter	582	5.820 000 0E+02

legger [South Africa]   **\<volume, special - see page 29>**

liter	575.366 5	5.753 665 0E+02

legoa [Brazil]   **\<length, special - see page 29>**

kilometer	6.6	6.600 000 0E+00

legoa [Mexico]   **\<length, special - see page 29>**

kilometer	4.19	4.190 000 0E+00

legoa [Portugal]   **\<length, special - see page 29>**

kilometer	6.19	6.190 000 0E+00

legoa [Venezuela]   **\<length, special - see page 29>**

kilometer	5.024	5.024 000 0E+00

legua [Argentina]   **\<length, special - see page 29>**

kilometer	5.2	5.200 000 0E+00

legua [Brazil]   **\<length, special - see page 29>**

kilometer	6.6	6.600 000 0E+00

legua [Chile]   **\<length, special - see page 29>**

kilometer	4.51	4.510 000 0E+00

legua [Colombia]   **\<length, special - see page 29>**

kilometer	5	5.000 000 0E+00

Convert From　　　　　　　　　　　　　　　　　　**<Type of Unit>**
　Convert To　　　　　　　　　　　　　　　Standard　　　Scientific

legua [Cuba]　　　　　　　　　　　　<length, special - see page 29>
　kilometer--4.24 --- 4.240 000 0E+00

legua [Ecuador]　　　　　　　　　　　<length, special - see page 29>
　kilometer---5 --- 5.000 000 0E+00

legua [El Salvador]　　　　　　　　　<length, special - see page 29>
　kilometer---4 --- 4.000 000 0E+00

legua [Guatemala]　　　　　　　　　　<length, special - see page 29>
　kilometer--5.573 --- 5.573 000 0E+00

legua [Honduras]　　　　　　　　　　<length, special - see page 29>
　kilometer--4.175 --- 4.175 000 0E+00

legua [Mexico]　　　　　　　　　　　<length, special - see page 29>
　kilometer---4.19 --- 4.190 000 0E+00

legua [Paraguay]　　　　　　　　　　<length, special - see page 29>
　kilometer---4.33 --- 4.330 000 0E+00

legua [Peru]　　　　　　　　　　　　<length, special - see page 29>
　kilometer---5.56 --- 5.560 000 0E+00

legua [Portugal]　　　　　　　　　　<length, special - see page 29>
　kilometer--5.5 --- 5.500 000 0E+00

legua [Spain]　　　　　　　　　　　　<length, special - see page 29>
　kilometer--5.573 --- 5.573 000 0E+00

legua [Uruguay]　　　　　　　　　　　<length, special - see page 29>
　kilometer---5.15 --- 5.150 000 0E+00

legua cuadrada [Paraguay]　　　　　　<area, special - see page 29>
　square kilometer------------------------------------18.77 --- 1.877 000 0E+01

legua cuadrada [Uruguay]　　　　　　<area, special - see page 29>
　square kilometer-------------------------------------26.6 --- 2.660 000 0E+01

legua quadrada [Brazil]　　　　　　　<area, special - see page 29>
　square kilometer-------------------------------------43.6 --- 4.360 000 0E+01

lei [China]　　　　　　　　　　　　　<length, special - see page 29>
　meter --500 --- 5.000 000 0E+02

lei [Hong Kong]　　　　　　　　　　　<length, special - see page 29>
　kilometer--0.557 21 --- 5.572 100 0E-01

lei [South Korea]　　　　　　　　　　<length, special - see page 29>
　kilometer--3.927 --- 3.927 000 0E+00

lekha [Bulgaria]　　　　　　　　　　　<area, special - see page 29>
　square meter ---------------------------------------229.8 --- 2.298 000 0E+02

lelong [Malaysia]　　　　　　　　　　<area, special - see page 29>
　square meter --------------------------------------222.97 --- 2.229 700 0E+02

lelong [Singapore]　　　　　　　　　　<area, special - see page 29>
　square meter --------------------------------------222.97 --- 2.229 700 0E+02

lentor　　　　　　　　　　　　　　　<kinematic viscosity>
　poise cubic centimeter/gram -----------------------------1 --- 1.000 000 0E+00
　square centimeter/second --------------------------------1 --- 1.000 000 0E+00
　square foot/hour -----------------------------3.875 007 8 --- 3.875 007 8E+00
　square meter/second----------------------------------0.000 1 --- 1.000 000 0E-04
　stokes --1 --- 1.000 000 0E+00

leo　　　　　　　　　　　　　　　　<acceleration>
　celo --32.808 399 --- 3.280 839 9E+01
　centimeter/square second ---------------------------1,000 --- 1.000 000 0E+03
　foot/square second------------------------------32.808 399 --- 3.280 839 9E+01
　gal--1,000 --- 1.000 000 0E+03
　inch/square second------------------------------393.700 79 --- 3.937 007 9E+02
　meter/square second-------------------------------------10 --- 1.000 000 0E+01

lesser pic [Turkey]　　　　　　　　　<length, special - see page 29>
　centimeter---65 --- 6.500 000 0E+01

letakhim [Hebrew, ancient, dry]　　　<volume, special - see page 29>
　hectoliter---1.9 --- 1.900 000 0E+00

Convert From / Convert To	Standard	Scientific
letek [Hebrew, ancient]	<volume, special - see page 29>	
liter	114.8	1.148 000 0E+02
letekh [Hebrew, ancient]	<volume, special - see page 29>	
liter	110	1.100 000 0E+02
lethech [Hebrew, ancient]	<volume, special - see page 29>	
liter	114.8	1.148 000 0E+02
lethek [Hebrew, ancient]	<volume, special - see page 29>	
liter	110	1.100 000 0E+02
lethekh [Hebrew, ancient]	<volume, special - see page 29>	
liter	114.956	1.149 560 0E+02
leung [Brunei]	<mass, special - see page 29>	
gram	37.8	3.780 000 0E+01
leung [Cambodia]	<mass, special - see page 29>	
gram	37.5	3.750 000 0E+01
leung [China]	<mass, special - see page 29>	
gram	50	5.000 000 0E+01
leung [Hong Kong]	<mass, special - see page 29>	
gram	37.8	3.780 000 0E+01
li [Cambodia]	<mass, special - see page 29>	
gram	0.037 5	3.750 000 0E-02
li [China]	<mass, special - see page 29>	
milligram	37.799 37	3.779 937 0E+01
li [China]	<length, special - see page 29>	
meter	644.65	6.446 500 0E+02
li [Hong Kong]	<length, special - see page 29>	
meter	557.213	5.572 130 0E+02
li [Laos]	<mass, special - see page 29>	
milligram	37.5	3.750 000 0E+01
li [Mongolia]	<mass, special - see page 29>	
milligram	37.5	3.750 000 0E+01
li [Mongolia]	<length, special - see page 29>	
millimeter	0.32	3.200 000 0E-01
li [South Korea]	<mass, special - see page 29>	
kilogram	3.927 28	3.927 280 0E+00
li [South Korea]	<length, special - see page 29>	
kilometer	3.927 27	3.927 270 0E+00
li ke [China]	<mass, special - see page 29>	
milligram	10	1.000 000 0E+01
li mi [China]	<length, special - see page 29>	
centimeter	1	1.000 000 0E+00
li sheng [China]	<volume, special - see page 29>	
centiliter	1	1.000 000 0E+00
liang [Brunei]	<mass, special - see page 29>	
gram	37.8	3.780 000 0E+01
liang [Cambodia]	<mass, special - see page 29>	
gram	37.5	3.750 000 0E+01
liang [China]	<mass, special - see page 29>	
gram	37.798	3.779 800 0E+01
liang [Hong Kong]	<mass, special - see page 29>	
gram	37.8	3.780 000 0E+01
libbra [Brazil]	<mass, special - see page 29>	
gram	458.8	4.588 000 0E+02
libbra [Italy, Bologna]	<mass, special - see page 29>	
gram	361.85	3.618 500 0E+02

| Convert From | <Type of Unit> | |
Convert To	Standard	Scientific
libbra [Italy, Florence]	<mass, special - see page 29>	
gram	339.5	3.395 000 0E+02
libbra [Italy, Naples]	<mass, special - see page 29>	
gram	320.759	3.207 590 0E+02
libbra [Italy, Palermo, gold and silver]	<mass, special - see page 29>	
gram	317.55	3.175 500 0E+02
libbra [Italy, Parma]	<mass, special - see page 29>	
gram	328	3.280 000 0E+02
libbra [Italy, Rome]	<mass, special - see page 29>	
gram	339.3	3.393 000 0E+02
libbra [Italy, Turin]	<mass, special - see page 29>	
gram	368.845	3.688 450 0E+02
libbra [Italy]	<mass, special - see page 29>	
gram	339	3.390 000 0E+02
libbra [Portugal]	<mass, special - see page 29>	
gram	459	4.590 000 0E+02
libbra [Rome, ancient]	<mass, special - see page 29>	
gram	323	3.230 000 0E+02
libbra [Vatican City]	<mass, special - see page 29>	
gram	339.156	3.391 560 0E+02
libbra metrica [Italy, Milan]	<mass, special - see page 29>	
gram	1,000	1.000 000 0E+03
libra [Argentina]	<mass, special - see page 29>	
gram	459.4	4.594 000 0E+02
libra [Bolivia]	<mass, special - see page 29>	
gram	460	4.600 000 0E+02
libra [Brazil]	<mass, special - see page 29>	
gram	459.05	4.590 500 0E+02
libra [Cape Verde]	<mass, special - see page 29>	
gram	459	4.590 000 0E+02
libra [Chile]	<mass, special - see page 29>	
gram	460.093	4.600 930 0E+02
libra [Colombia]	<mass, special - see page 29>	
gram	500	5.000 000 0E+02
libra [Costa Rica]	<mass, special - see page 29>	
gram	460	4.600 000 0E+02
libra [Cuba]	<mass, special - see page 29>	
gram	460.09	4.600 900 0E+02
libra [Dominican Republic]	<mass, special - see page 29>	
gram	453.6	4.536 000 0E+02
libra [Ecuador]	<mass, special - see page 29>	
gram	460	4.600 000 0E+02
libra [El Salvador]	<mass, special - see page 29>	
gram	460	4.600 000 0E+02
libra [Guatemala]	<mass, special - see page 29>	
gram	460	4.600 000 0E+02
libra [Honduras]	<mass, special - see page 29>	
gram	460	4.600 000 0E+02
libra [Italy]	<mass, special - see page 29>	
kilogram	1	1.000 000 0E+00
libra [Libya]	<mass, special - see page 29>	
kilogram	0.34	3.400 000 0E-01
libra [Malta]	<mass, special - see page 29>	
gram	453.6	4.536 000 0E+02

| Convert From | | | <Type of Unit> |
Convert To		Standard	Scientific

Convert From / To	Type of Unit	Standard	Scientific
libra [Mexico]	<mass, special - see page 29>		
gram		460.25	4.602 500 E+02
libra [Nicaragua]	<mass, special - see page 29>		
gram		460	4.600 000 E+02
libra [Paraguay]	<mass, special - see page 29>		
gram		459	4.590 000 E+02
libra [Peru]	<mass, special - see page 29>		
gram		460	4.600 000 E+02
libra [Philippines]	<mass, special - see page 29>		
gram		460	4.600 000 E+02
libra [Portugal]	<mass, special - see page 29>		
gram		459.05	4.590 500 E+02
libra [Puerto Rico]	<mass, special - see page 29>		
gram		461	4.610 000 E+02
libra [Rome, ancient]	<mass, special - see page 29>		
gram		326	3.260 000 E+02
libra [Spain]	<mass, special - see page 29>		
gram		460.09	4.600 900 E+02
libra [Uruguay]	<mass, special - see page 29>		
gram		459.4	4.594 000 E+02
libra [Venezuela]	<mass, special - see page 29>		
gram		460.9	4.609 000 E+02
libra de farmacia [Argentina]	<mass, special - see page 29>		
gram		344.6	3.446 000 E+02
libre subtile [France]	<mass, special - see page 29>		
gram		318.24	3.182 400 E+02
lichar [Greece, ancient]	<length, special - see page 29>		
centimeter		19.2	1.920 000 E+01
liespfund [Germany]	<mass, special - see page 29>		
kilogram		6.781	6.781 000 E+00
liespund [Iceland]	<mass, special - see page 29>		
kilogram		32	3.200 000 E+01
lieue [Chile]	<length, special - see page 29>		
kilometer		4.514	4.514 000 E+00
lieue [Cuba]	<length, special - see page 29>		
kilometer		4.24	4.240 000 E+00
lieue [Ecuador]	<length, special - see page 29>		
kilometer		5	5.000 000 E+00
lieue [El Salvador]	<length, special - see page 29>		
kilometer		4	4.000 000 E+00
lieue [France]	<length, special - see page 29>		
kilometer		4.444 4	4.444 400 E+00
lieue [Guatemala]	<length, special - see page 29>		
kilometer		5.573	5.573 000 E+00
lieue [Mexico]	<length, special - see page 29>		
kilometer		4.19	4.190 000 E+00
lieue [Paraguay]	<length, special - see page 29>		
kilometer		4.333	4.333 000 E+00
lieue [Peru]	<length, special - see page 29>		
kilometer		5.56	5.560 000 E+00
lieue [Portugal]	<length, special - see page 29>		
kilometer		5.5	5.500 000 E+00
lieue [Spain]	<length, special - see page 29>		
kilometer		5.573	5.573 000 E+00

| Convert From | | <Type of Unit> |
Convert To	Standard	Scientific

lieue [Switzerland] <length, special - see page 29>
kilometer -- 4.8 --- 4.800 000 0E+00

lieue [Uruguay] <length, special - see page 29>
kilometer -- 5.15 --- 5.150 000 0E+00

lieue de poste [France] <length, special - see page 29>
kilometer -- 3.898 --- 3.898 000 0E+00

light year [based on anomalistic year] <length>
meter -->>> 9.460 980 0E+15

light year [based on mean Julian year] <length>
astronomical unit --- 63,241.077 --- 6.324 107 7E+04
bevameter --- 9,460,730.5 --- 9.460 730 5E+06
exameter --- 0.009 460 7 --- 9.460 730 5E-03
kilometer -->>> 9.460 730 5E+12
kiloparsec -- 0.000 306 6 --- 3.066 014 0E-04
megaparsec -- 0.000 000 3 --- 3.066 014 0E-07
meter --->>> 9.460 730 5E+15
mile [international] -->>> 5.878 625 4E+12
mile [US, statute] -->>> 5.878 613 6E+12
mile [US, survey] -->>> 5.878 613 6E+12
myriameter --->>> 9.460 730 5E+11
parsec --- 0.306 601 4 --- 3.066 014 0E-01
petameter --- 9.460 730 5 --- 9.460 730 5E+00
spat --- 9,460.730 5 --- 9.460 730 5E+03

light year [based on sidereal year] <length>
meter -->>> 9.460 895 3E+15

light year [based on tropical year] <length>
meter -->>> 9.460 528 2E+15

ligne [France] <length, special - see page 29>
millimeter --- 2.256 --- 2.256 000 0E+00

ligne [Haiti] <length, special - see page 29>
millimeter --- 2.256 --- 2.256 000 0E+00

ligne [Paraguay] <length, special - see page 29>
millimeter --- 2.006 --- 2.006 000 0E+00

ligne [print] <length>
agate [print] -- 1.095 --- 1.095 000 0E+00
barleycorn -- 0.25 --- 2.500 000 0E-01
caliber --- 8.333 333 3 --- 8.333 333 3E+00
didot point [print] --- 5.622 199 5 --- 5.622 199 5E+00
douzieme [print] -- 12 --- 1.200 000 0E+01
em [pica, print] -- 0.501 875 --- 5.018 750 1E-01
foot [international] --------------------------------------- 0.006 944 4 --- 6.944 444 4E-03
inch [international] -- 0.083 333 3 --- 8.333 333 3E-02
iron [print] -- 0.020 075 --- 2.007 500 0E-02
line [print] --- 1 --- 1.000 000 0E+00
meter --- 0.002 116 7 --- 2.116 666 7E-03
mil -- 83.333 333 --- 8.333 333 3E+01
millimeter --- 2.116 666 7 --- 2.116 666 7E+00
nonpareil [print] --- 1.003 75 --- 1.003 750 0E+00
pearl [print] --- 1.204 5 --- 1.204 500 0E+00
pica [print] --- 0.501 875 --- 5.018 750 1E-01
point [print] --- 6.022 500 1 --- 6.022 500 1E+00

ligne [Switzerland] <length, special - see page 29>
millimeter --- 2.083 3 --- 2.083 300 0E+00

ligula [Rome, ancient] <volume, special - see page 29>
liter -- 0.011 067 7 --- 1.106 770 0E-02

liin [Russia] <length, special - see page 29>
centimeter -- 2.540 005 --- 2.540 005 0E+00

likot [Ukraine] <length, special - see page 29>
centimeter --- 77.8 --- 7.780 000 0E+01

	Standard	Scientific
lin [Cambodia]	\<mass, special - see page 29\>	
milligram	37.5	3.750 000 0E+01
lin [China]	\<mass, special - see page 29\>	
milligram	50	5.000 000 0E+01
lin [Laos]	\<mass, special - see page 29\>	
milligram	37.5	3.750 000 0E+01
lina [Iceland]	\<length, special - see page 29\>	
millimeter	2.18	2.180 000 0E+00
line [France]	\<length, special - see page 29\>	
millimeter	2.256	2.256 000 0E+00
line [Greece]	\<length, special - see page 29\>	
millimeter	2.12	2.120 000 0E+00
line [of magnetic force]		\<magnetic flux\>
electromagnetic unit of magnetic flux [cgs system]	1	1.000 000 0E+00
gauss square centimeter	1	1.000 000 0E+00
maxwell	1	1.000 000 0E+00
statweber	\<\<\<	3.335 641 0E-11
unit pole	0.079 577 5	7.957 747 5E-02
weber	\<\<\<	1.000 000 0E-08
line [Paraguay]		\<area, special - see page 29\>
are	75	7.500 000 0E+01
line [print]		\<length\>
agate [print]	1.095	1.095 000 0E+00
barleycorn	0.25	2.500 000 0E-01
caliber	8.333 333 3	8.333 333 3E+00
didot point [print]	5.622 199 5	5.622 199 5E+00
douzieme [print]	12	1.200 000 0E+01
em [pica, print]	0.501 875	5.018 750 1E-01
foot [international]	0.006 944 4	6.944 444 4E-03
inch [international]	0.083 333 3	8.333 333 3E-02
iron [print]	0.020 075	2.007 500 0E-02
ligne [print]	1	1.000 000 0E+00
meter	0.002 116 7	2.116 666 7E-03
mil	83.333 333	8.333 333 3E+01
millimeter	2.116 666 7	2.116 666 7E+00
nonpareil [print]	1.003 75	1.003 750 0E+00
pearl [print]	1.204 5	1.204 500 0E+00
pica [print]	0.501 875	5.018 750 1E-01
point [print]	6.022 500 1	6.022 500 1E+00
thou	83.333 333	8.333 333 3E+01
line [Russia]	\<length, special - see page 29\>	
millimeter	2.54	2.540 000 0E+00
line [UK]	\<length, special - see page 29\>	
centimeter	0.211 666 7	2.116 667 0E-01
line/square centimeter [of magnetic force]		\<magnetic flux density\>
electromagnetic unit of magnetic flux density [cgs system]	1	1.000 000 0E+00
gamma	100,000	1.000 000 0E+05
gauss	1	1.000 000 0E+00
maxwell/square meter	0.000 1	1.000 000 0E-04
tesla	0.000 1	1.000 000 0E-04
linea [Argentina]	\<length, special - see page 29\>	
millimeter	2	2.000 000 0E+00
linea [Chile]	\<length, special - see page 29\>	
millimeter	1.93	1.930 000 0E+00
linea [Honduras]	\<length, special - see page 29\>	
millimeter	1.93	1.930 000 0E+00
linea [Mexico]	\<length, special - see page 29\>	
millimeter	1.94	1.940 000 0E+00

Convert From	<Type of Unit>	
Convert To	Standard	Scientific

linea [Paraguay] <length, special - see page 29>
millimeter ----- 2.006 --- 2.006 000 0E+00

linea [Spain] <length, special - see page 29>
millimeter ----- 1.934 97 --- 1.934 970 0E+00

linea cuadrada [Mexico] <area, special - see page 29>
square millimeter ----- 3.762 9 --- 3.762 900 0E+00

linea cubica [Mexico] <volume, special - see page 29>
cubic millimeter ----- 7.299 3 --- 7.299 300 0E+00

linha [Brazil] <length, special - see page 29>
millimeter ----- 2.3 --- 2.300 000 0E+00

linha [Portugal] <length, special - see page 29>
millimeter ----- 2.29 --- 2.290 000 0E+00

linhada [Cape Verde] <length, special - see page 29>
meter ----- 22 --- 2.200 000 0E+01

linia [Chile] <length, special - see page 29>
centimeter ----- 0.193 5 --- 1.935 000 0E-01

linia [Sudan] <length, special - see page 29>
millimeter ----- 3.175 --- 3.175 000 0E+00

linie [Austria] <length, special - see page 29>
millimeter ----- 2.195 --- 2.195 000 0E+00

linie [Denmark] <length, special - see page 29>
centimeter ----- 0.217 956 --- 2.179 560 0E-01

linie [Germany, Bavaria] <length, special - see page 29>
millimeter ----- 2.026 81 --- 2.026 810 0E+00

linie [Germany, Prussia] <length, special - see page 29>
millimeter ----- 2.179 57 --- 2.179 570 0E+00

linie [Switzerland] <length, special - see page 29>
millimeter ----- 2.083 3 --- 2.083 300 0E+00

liniya [Russia] <length, special - see page 29>
millimeter ----- 2.54 --- 2.540 000 0E+00

linja [Poland] <length, special - see page 29>
millimeter ----- 2 --- 2.000 000 0E+00

linje [Sweden] <length, special - see page 29>
millimeter ----- 2.97 --- 2.970 000 0E+00

link [Gunter or US, survey] <length>
cable length [US, survey] ----- 0.000 916 7 --- 9.166 666 7E-04
chain [Gunter or US, survey] ----- 0.01 --- 1.000 000 0E-02
chain [Ramden or Engineer] ----- 0.006 6 --- 6.600 013 2E-03
fathom [US, survey] ----- 0.11 --- 1.100 000 0E-01
foot [international] ----- 0.660 001 3 --- 6.600 013 2E-01
foot [US, survey] ----- 0.66 --- 6.600 000 0E-01
furlong [US, survey] ----- 0.001 --- 1.000 000 0E-03
inch [based on US, survey foot] ----- 7.92 --- 7.920 000 0E+00
inch [international] ----- 7.920 015 8 --- 7.920 015 8E+00
league [US, statute] ----- 0.000 041 7 --- 4.166 666 7E-05
link [Ramden or Engineer] ----- 0.660 001 3 --- 6.600 013 2E-01
meter ----- 0.201 168 4 --- 2.011 684 0E-01
mile [international] ----- 0.000 125 --- 1.250 002 5E-04
mile [US, statute] ----- 0.000 125 --- 1.250 000 0E-04
mile [US, survey] ----- 0.000 125 --- 1.250 000 0E-04
out [US, survey] ----- 0.002 --- 2.000 000 0E-03
pace [US, survey] ----- 0.264 --- 2.640 000 0E-01
perch [US, survey] ----- 0.04 --- 4.000 000 0E-02
pole [US, survey] ----- 0.04 --- 4.000 000 0E-02
range [US, survey] ----- 0.000 020 8 --- 2.083 333 3E-05
rod [US, survey] ----- 0.04 --- 4.000 000 0E-02
township [US, survey] ----- 0.000 020 8 --- 2.083 333 3E-05
vara [US, survey, California] ----- 0.24 --- 2.400 000 0E-01

Convert From / Convert To	Standard	Scientific \<Type of Unit\>
vara [US, survey, Texas]	0.237 6	2.376 000 0E−01
yard [based on US, survey foot]	0.22	2.200 000 0E−01
yard [international]	0.220 000 4	2.200 004 4E−01
link [Ramden or Engineer]		**\<length\>**
cable length [US, survey]	0.001 388 9	1.388 886 1E−03
caliber	1,200	1.200 000 0E+03
chain [Gunter or US, survey]	0.015 151 5	1.515 148 5E−02
chain [Ramden or Engineer]	0.01	1.000 000 0E−02
fathom [US, survey]	0.166 666 3	1.666 663 3E−01
foot [international]	1	1.000 000 0E+00
foot [US, survey]	0.999 998	9.999 980 0E−01
furlong [US, survey]	0.001 515 1	1.515 148 5E−03
inch [based on US, survey foot]	11.999 976	1.199 997 6E+01
inch [international]	12	1.200 000 0E+01
league [US, survey, nautical]	0.000 054 9	5.485 961 1E−05
league [US, statute]	0.000 063 1	6.313 118 7E−05
link [Gunter or US, survey]	1.515 148 5	1.515 148 5E+00
meter	0.304 8	3.048 000 0E−01
mile [international]	0.000 189 4	1.893 939 4E−04
mile [US, statute]	0.000 189 4	1.893 935 6E−04
mile [US, survey]	0.000 189 4	1.893 935 6E−04
out [US, survey]	0.003 030 3	3.030 297 0E−03
pace [geometrical]	0.02	2.000 000 0E−02
pace [US, survey]	0.399 999 2	3.999 992 0E−01
perch [US, survey]	0.060 605 9	6.060 593 9E−02
rope	0.05	5.000 000 0E−02
township [US, survey]	0.000 031 6	3.156 559 5E−05
yard [based on US, survey foot]	0.333 332 7	3.333 326 7E−01
yard [international]	0.333 333 3	3.333 333 3E−01
lino [Paraguay]		**\<area, special - see page 29\>**
square meter	75.1	7.510 000 0E+01
lira [Brazil]		**\<mass, special - see page 29\>**
gram	458.8	4.588 000 0E+02
lira [Italy, Bologna, gold, silver and jewels]		**\<mass, special - see page 29\>**
gram	363.13	3.631 300 0E+02
lira [Italy, Naples]		**\<mass, special - see page 29\>**
gram	321	3.210 000 0E+02
lira [Italy, Rome]		**\<mass, special - see page 29\>**
gram	339.3	3.393 000 0E+02
lira [Portugal]		**\<mass, special - see page 29\>**
gram	459	4.590 000 0E+02
lispond [Norway]		**\<mass, special - see page 29\>**
kilogram	7.969	7.969 000 0E+00
lispound [Denmark]		**\<mass, special - see page 29\>**
kilogram	7.999 973 7	7.999 973 7E+00
lispound [Sweden]		**\<mass, special - see page 29\>**
kilogram	8.502 022	8.502 022 0E+00
lispund [Denmark]		**\<mass, special - see page 29\>**
kilogram	8	8.000 000 0E+00
lispund [Sweden]		**\<mass, special - see page 29\>**
kilogram	8.501 52	8.501 520 0E+00
liter		**\<champagne bottle size\>**
balthazar [champagne bottle]	0.083 333 3	8.333 333 3E−02
bottle [wine, standard]	1.333 333 3	1.333 333 3E+00
jeroboam [champagne bottle]	0.333 333 3	3.333 333 3E−01
magnum [champagne bottle]	0.666 666 7	6.666 666 7E−01
methuselah [champagne bottle]	0.166 666 7	1.666 666 7E−01
nebuchadnezzar [champagne bottle]	0.066 666 7	6.666 666 7E−02
rehoboam [champagne bottle]	0.222 222 2	2.222 222 2E−01
salmanazar [champagne bottle]	0.111 111 1	1.111 111 1E−01

Convert From		\<Type of Unit\>
Convert To	Standard	Scientific

liter   \<volume\>

Convert To	Standard	Scientific
aam [Germany]	0.006 451 6	6.451 612 9E-03
aam [Netherlands]	0.006 443 3	6.443 299 0E-03
abe [Persia, ancient]	0.017 857 1	1.785 714 3E-02
achtel [Austria]	0.130 039	1.300 390 1E-01
achtel [Denmark]	0.460 829 5	4.608 294 9E-01
acre inch	0.000 009 7	9.728 558 3E-06
adoulie [India]	0.145 327 7	1.453 277 1E-01
ahm [South Africa]	0.006 952 1	6.952 091 7E-03
aime [Germany]	0.014 556	1.455 604 1E-02
aimer [Germany]	0.014 556	1.455 604 1E-02
ako [Hungary]	0.018 416 2	1.841 620 6E-02
akov [Yugoslavia]	0.017 667 8	1.766 784 5E-02
alma [Turkey]	0.190 839 7	1.908 396 9E-01
almenn turma [Iceland]	0.008 628 1	8.628 127 7E-03
almud [Belize]	0.175 963 4	1.759 634 0E-01
almud [Brazil]	0.031 298 9	3.129 890 5E-02
almud [British Honduras]	0.175 994 3	1.759 943 7E-01
almud [Chile]	0.123 762 4	1.237 623 8E-01
almud [Mexico]	0.132 149 3	1.321 492 8E-01
almud [Paraguay]	0.041 666 7	4.166 666 7E-02
almud [Portugal]	0.060 606 1	6.060 606 1E-02
almude [Brazil]	0.031 304 8	3.130 478 3E-02
almude [Mexico]	0.132 135 3	1.321 353 1E-01
almude [Paraguay]	0.041 666 7	4.166 666 7E-02
almude [Portugal]	0.059 701 5	5.970 149 3E-02
almude [Spain]	0.216 216 2	2.162 162 1E-01
almude [Spanish North Africa]	0.071 428 6	7.142 857 1E-02
almude [Turkey]	0.190 839 7	1.908 396 9E-01
alqueire [Portugal]	0.071 633 2	7.163 323 8E-02
alquier [Portugal]	0.072 463 8	7.246 376 8E-02
am [Sweden]	0.006 368 2	6.368 209 9E-03
amphora [Greece, ancient]	0.025 773 2	2.577 319 6E-02
amphora [Rome, ancient]	0.038 461 5	3.846 153 8E-02
amunam [Ceylon]	0.004 916 4	4.916 420 8E-03
ancre [Germany]	0.029 112 1	2.911 208 2E-02
ancre [Netherlands]	0.025 773 2	2.577 319 6E-02
ankare [Sweden]	0.025 473 4	2.547 335 9E-02
anker [Germany]	0.025 773 2	2.577 319 6E-02
anker [Iceland]	0.026 542 1	2.654 209 2E-02
anker [Netherlands]	0.025 773 2	2.577 319 6E-02
anker [South Africa]	0.027 808 4	2.780 835 9E-02
anker [UK]	0.022 222 2	2.222 222 2E-02
ankre [Denmark]	0.025 876 6	2.587 656 9E-02
antal [Hungary]	0.019 607 8	1.960 784 3E-02
apatan [Philippines]	10.638 298	1.063 829 8E+01
ardeb [Sudan]	0.005 050 5	5.050 505 1E-03
arroba [Bolivia]	0.032 829 9	3.282 994 1E-02
arroba [Chile]	0.025	2.500 000 0E-02
arroba [Colombia]	0.061 957 9	6.195 786 9E-02
arroba [Costa Rica]	0.058 823 5	5.882 352 9E-02
arroba [Cuba]	0.061 957 9	6.195 786 9E-02
arroba [Ecuador]	0.061 957 9	6.195 786 9E-02
arroba [Guatemala]	0.061 957 9	6.195 786 9E-02
arroba [Honduras]	0.060 241	6.024 096 4E-02
arroba [Peru]	0.079 598 8	7.959 882 2E-02
arroba [Spain]	0.061 957 9	6.195 786 9E-02
arroba [Spain, oil]	0.079 598 8	7.959 882 2E-02
arroba [Venezuela]	0.061 973 2	6.197 322 8E-02
artaba [Egypt, ancient]	0.021 413 3	2.141 327 6E-02
artaba [Iran]	0.015 151 5	1.515 151 5E-02
artabe [Rome, ancient]	0.027 434 8	2.743 484 2E-02
atting [Sweden]	0.063 683 3	6.368 331 6E-02

liter (continued) \<volume\>

aum [South Africa]	0.006 952 1	6.952 091 7E–03
azumbre [Colombia]	0.495 049 5	4.950 495 0E–01
azumbre [Panama]	0.495 049 5	4.950 495 0E–01
azumbre [Spain]	0.495 049 5	4.950 495 0E–01
bag [Sierra Leone]	0.012 5	1.250 000 0E–02
bag [UK]	0.009 165 7	9.165 650 8E–03
balde [Ecuador]	0.1	1.000 000 0E–01
balli [South Africa]	0.021 739 1	2.173 913 0E–02
ban [Thailand]	0.001	1.000 000 0E–03
bandu [Malaysia]	0.021 997 4	2.199 736 0E–02
bandu [Singapore]	0.021 997 4	2.199 736 0E–02
baril [Argentina]	0.013 157 9	1.315 789 5E–02
baril [France]	0.006 29	6.289 988 6E–03
baril [Greece]	0.025	2.500 000 0E–02
baril [Libya]	0.015 518 3	1.551 831 2E–02
baril [Mexico]	0.013 477 1	1.347 708 9E–02
barile [Greece]	0.013 477 1	1.347 708 9E–02
barile [Italy]	0.017 140 9	1.714 089 8E–02
barile [Italy, oil]	0.029 940 1	2.994 012 0E–02
barile [Italy, wine]	0.021 929 8	2.192 982 5E–02
barile [Libya]	0.015 528	1.552 795 0E–02
barmil [Malta]	0.023 154 6	2.315 458 0E–02
barmil [Mexico]	0.013 157 9	1.315 789 5E–02
barmil [Paraguay]	0.010 316 7	1.031 672 3E–02
barrel [UK]	0.006 110 3	6.110 256 9E–03
barrel [US, federal]	0.008 521 7	8.521 679 1E–03
barrel [US, federal proof spirits]	0.006 604 3	6.604 301 3E–03
barrel [US, liquid]	0.008 386 4	8.386 414 4E–03
barrel [US, petroleum]	0.006 289 8	6.289 810 8E–03
barril [Argentina]	0.013 157 9	1.315 789 5E–02
barril [Mexico]	0.013 157 9	1.315 789 5E–02
barril [Paraguay]	0.010 316 7	1.031 672 3E–02
barril [Venezuela]	0.011 764 7	1.176 470 6E–02
barrique [France]	0.004 444 4	4.444 444 4E–03
barrique [Haiti]	0.004 403	4.402 958 8E–03
barrique [Malta]	0.023 154 6	2.315 458 0E–02
barrique [Mexico]	0.013 157 9	1.315 789 5E–02
barrique [Paraguay]	0.010 316 7	1.031 672 3E–02
barrique [Portugal]	0.004 651 2	4.651 162 8E–03
basket [Burma]	0.024 440 9	2.444 091 4E–02
bat [Hebrew, ancient]	0.045 454	4.545 454 5E–02
bath [Hebrew, ancient]	0.045 454	4.545 454 5E–02
bath [Israel]	0.025	2.500 000 0E–02
bath [Rome, ancient]	0.025 641	2.564 102 6E–02
batos [Greece, ancient]	0.025 316 5	2.531 645 6E–02
battim [Hebrew, ancient]	0.026 315 8	2.631 578 9E–02
becher [Austria]	2.083 333 3	2.083 333 3E+00
becker [Austria]	2.083 333 3	2.083 333 3E+00
beczka [Poland]	0.01	1.000 000 0E–02
benequen [Belize]	0.058 657 9	5.865 790 7E–02
boccale [Italy]	0.548 546 4	5.485 463 5E–01
bochka [Russia]	0.002 032 7	2.032 685 6E–03
boisseau [Belgium]	0.066 666 7	6.666 666 7E–02
boisseau [France]	0.08	8.000 000 0E–02
boisseau [Switzerland]	0.066 666 7	6.666 666 7E–02
bok [Laos]	0.05	5.000 000 0E–02
bok louang [Laos]	0.25	2.500 000 0E–01
bota [Portugal]	0.002 298 9	2.298 850 6E–03
botchka [Russia]	0.002 032 7	2.032 685 6E–03
botella [Costa Rica]	1.492 537 3	1.492 537 3E+00
botella [Cuba]	1.379 310 3	1.379 310 3E+00

Convert From		<Type of Unit>
Convert To	Standard	Scientific

liter (continued) <volume>

botella [El Salvador]	1.333 333 3	1.333 333 3E+00
botella [Guatemala]	1.538 461 5	1.538 461 5E+00
botella [Nicaragua]	1.492 537 3	1.492 537 3E+00
botella [Panama]	1.321 004	1.321 004 0E+00
botellon [Venezuela]	1.501 501 5	1.501 501 5E+00
boutylka [Russia]	1.300 390 1	1.300 390 1E+00
bozze [Libya]	0.372 439 5	3.724 394 8E-01
brente [Switzerland]	0.026 666 7	2.666 666 7E-02
bucket [UK]	0.054 993 9	5.499 388 5E-02
bulto [Philippines]	0.013 333 3	1.333 333 3E-02
byce [Malaya and Singapore]	1.980 198	1.980 198 0E+00
byee [Burma]	1.980 198	1.980 198 0E+00
cab [Hebrew, ancient]	1	1.000 000 0E+00
caba [Eritrea]	0.5	5.000 000 0E-01
caba [Somalia]	2.207 505 5	2.207 505 5E+00
cabaho [Eritrea]	0.166 666 7	1.666 666 7E-01
caban [Philippines]	0.013 333 3	1.333 333 3E-02
cadaa [Egypt, ancient]	0.485 436 9	4.854 368 9E-01
caffiso [Algeria]	0.003 149 9	3.149 903 9E-03
caffiso [Italy]	0.047 169 8	4.716 981 1E-02
caffiso [Malta]	0.049 019 6	4.901 960 8E-02
caffiz [Tunisia]	0.001 562 5	1.562 500 0E-03
cafiso [Italy]	0.047 169 8	4.716 981 1E-02
cafisso [Tunisia]	0.001 562 5	1.562 500 0E-03
cafiz [Spain]	0.004	4.000 000 0E-03
cahaho [Eritrea]	0.166 666 7	1.666 666 7E-01
cahia [Nicaragua]	0.001 645 8	1.645 819 6E-03
cahiz [Spain]	0.001 501 5	1.501 501 5E-03
cajon [Venezuela, dry]	0.025	2.500 000 0E-02
cajuela [Costa Rica]	0.058 823 5	5.882 352 9E-02
cajuela [El Salvador]	0.060 241	6.024 096 4E-02
cajuela [Guatemala]	0.060 241	6.024 096 4E-02
cajuela [Honduras]	0.060 241	6.024 096 4E-02
cajuela [Nicaragua]	0.060 241	6.024 096 4E-02
can [Philippines]	0.052 835 9	5.283 588 7E-02
canada [Brazil]	0.375 657 4	3.756 574 0E-01
canada [Portugal]	0.724 637 7	7.246 376 8E-01
candel [Portuguese India]	0.006 261 7	6.261 740 8E-03
candil [Portuguese India]	0.006 261 7	6.261 740 8E-03
caneca [Cuba]	0.045 977	4.597 701 1E-02
cantara [Peru]	0.062 111 8	6.211 180 1E-02
cantara [Spain]	0.062 004	6.200 396 8E-02
cantaro [Portugal]	0.120 919	1.209 189 8E-01
cantaro [Spain]	0.061 984 8	6.198 475 2E-02
capicha [Iran]	0.380 228 1	3.802 281 4E-01
carga [Mexico]	0.005 506 3	5.506 304 7E-03
carga [Spain]	0.004 504 5	4.504 504 5E-03
cargo [Belize]	0.014 664 9	1.466 490 7E-02
cargo [British Honduras]	0.014 665	1.466 503 6E-02
cass [Cyprus]	0.211 416 5	2.114 164 9E-01
cavan [Philippines]	0.013 333 3	1.333 333 3E-02
cazuela [El Salvador]	0.060 241	6.024 096 4E-02
ceston [Venezuela]	0.014 285 7	1.428 571 4E-02
chai meu [Thailand]	8	8.000 000 0E+00
chaldron [UK, liquid]	0.000 763 8	7.637 821 1E-04
chang awn [Thailand]	2	2.000 000 0E+00
charka [Russia]	8.130 081 3	8.130 081 3E+00
chela [Somalia]	0.735 835 2	7.358 351 7E-01
chemica [Iran]	0.759 878 4	7.598 784 2E-01
chetverik [Russia]	0.038 167 9	3.816 793 9E-02
chetvertinka [Russia]	4	4.000 000 0E+00
chkalik [Russia]	16.393 443	1.639 344 3E+01

Convert From   **<Type of Unit>**

Convert To	Standard	Scientific

liter (continued)   **<volume>**

Convert To	Standard	Scientific
choinix [Greece, ancient]	0.833 333 3	8.333 333 3E−01
chopin [France]	2.148 227 7	2.148 227 7E+00
chopin [Scotland]	0.879 894 4	8.798 944 1E−01
chopine [France]	2	2.000 000 0E+00
chou [Greece, ancient]	0.047 619	4.761 904 8E−02
chous [Greece, ancient]	0.308 994 8	3.089 948 4E−01
chu [Greece, ancient]	0.047 619	4.761 904 8E−02
chupa [Philippines]	2.666 666 7	2.666 666 7E+00
cob [Israel]	0.450 450 5	4.504 504 5E−01
codo [Spain, wine]	7.933 989 2	7.933 989 2E+00
collothum [Iran]	0.121 506 7	1.215 066 7E−01
conge [Greece, ancient]	0.284 900 3	2.849 002 8E−01
congius [Rome, ancient]	0.308 642	3.086 419 8E−01
copa [Spain]	7.936 507 9	7.936 507 9E+00
cor [Hebrew, ancient]	0.004 545 5	4.545 454 5E−03
cotyla [Greece, ancient]	3.663 003 7	3.663 003 7E+00
cuarta [Argentina]	1.683 501 7	1.683 501 7E+00
cuarta [Paraguay]	1.321 004	1.321 004 0E+00
cuarter [Argentina]	0.008 771 9	8.771 929 8E−03
cuarteron [Mexico]	0.04	4.000 000 0E−02
cuarteron [Spain, oil]	7.936 507 9	7.936 507 9E+00
cuartilla [Argentina]	0.029 154 5	2.915 451 9E−02
cuartilla [Spain, dry]	0.072 072 1	7.207 207 2E−02
cuartilla [Spain, liquid]	0.248 139	2.481 389 6E−01
cuartilla [Spain, oil]	0.318 390 2	3.183 902 2E−01
cuartilla [Spain, wine]	0.247 935 9	2.479 359 3E−01
cuartillo [Costa Rica]	0.235 294 1	2.352 941 2E−01
cuartillo [Cuba]	1.162 790 7	1.162 790 7E+00
cuartillo [Mexico, dry]	0.528 597 1	5.285 971 0E−01
cuartillo [Mexico, liquid]	2.191 713 6	2.191 713 6E+00
cuartillo [Mexico, oil]	1.975 652 1	1.975 652 1E+00
cuartillo [Spain, dry]	0.864 827 5	8.648 274 7E−01
cuartillo [Spain, liquid]	1.984 127	1.984 127 0E+00
cuartillo habanero [Cuba]	1.162 790 7	1.162 790 7E+00
cubic decimeter	1	1.000 000 0E+00
cubic foot	0.035 314 7	3.531 466 7E−02
cubic fot [Sweden]	0.038 208 8	3.820 877 3E−02
cubic inch	61.023 744	6.102 374 4E+01
cubic meter	0.001	1.000 000 0E−03
cubic yard	0.001 308	1.307 950 6E−03
cuddy [Arabia]	0.264 550 3	2.645 502 6E−01
culleus [Rome, ancient]	0.001 908 4	1.908 396 9E−03
cup [Canada, measuring]	4.399 385	4.399 385 0E+00
cup [metric]	5	5.000 000 0E+00
cup [US, measuring]	4.226 752 8	4.226 752 8E+00
curo [Portuguese India]	0.125 219 1	1.252 191 3E−01
cwierc [Poland]	0.031 25	3.125 000 0E−02
cyathus [Rome, ancient]	21.978 022	2.197 802 2E+01
cyathys [Greece, ancient]	22.247 436	2.224 743 6E+01
dai [South Korea]	0.554 354 5	5.543 544 5E−01
dan [Mongolia]	0.015 384 6	1.538 461 5E−02
dau [Hong Kong]	0.1	1.000 000 0E−01
dau [Vietnam]	1	1.000 000 0E+00
debbie [Zambia]	0.054 993 4	5.499 340 1E−02
dimerlie [Romania]	0.040 650 4	4.065 040 7E−02
doi [South Korea]	0.554 351 4	5.543 513 8E−01
dou [China]	0.1	1.000 000 0E−01
drachm [UK, liquid]	281.560 64	2.815 606 4E+02
dram [Canada, liquid]	281.560 64	2.815 606 4E+02
dram [US, liquid]	270.512 18	2.705 121 8E+02
dreissiger [Germany]	0.863 483 3	8.634 832 9E−01
drop [US, liquid]	12,173.048	1.217 304 8E+04

	Standard	Scientific
Convert From Convert To	Standard	<Type of Unit> Scientific

liter (continued)   <volume>

Convert To	Standard	Scientific
du [Mongolia]	0.153 846 2	$1.538\ 461\ 5E{-}01$
efa [Hebrew, ancient]	0.026 315 8	$2.631\ 578\ 9E{-}02$
efot [Hebrew, ancient]	0.026 315 8	$2.631\ 578\ 9E{-}02$
eimer [Austria]	0.017 666 6	$1.766\ 659\ 6E{-}02$
eimer [Germany]	0.015 591 6	$1.559\ 162\ 4E{-}02$
emine [Switzerland]	0.666 666 7	$6.666\ 666\ 7E{-}01$
encaa [Eritrea]	0.666 666 7	$6.666\ 666\ 7E{-}01$
entelam [Eritrea]	0.005 208 3	$5.208\ 333\ 3E{-}03$
epha [Hebrew, ancient]	0.043 668 1	$4.366\ 812\ 3E{-}02$
ephah [Babylon, ancient]	0.025 445 3	$2.544\ 529\ 3E{-}02$
ephah [Hebrew, ancient]	0.045 454 5	$4.545\ 454\ 5E{-}02$
erklein [Germany]	0.000 584 7	$5.846\ 927\ 4E{-}04$
fanega [Argentina]	0.007 299 3	$7.299\ 270\ 1E{-}03$
fanega [Chile]	0.010 309 3	$1.030\ 927\ 8E{-}02$
fanega [Costa Rica]	0.002 451	$2.450\ 980\ 4E{-}03$
fanega [Cuba]	0.009 456 3	$9.456\ 264\ 8E{-}03$
fanega [El Salvador]	0.003 851 9	$3.851\ 931\ 7E{-}03$
fanega [Honduras]	0.009 067 8	$9.067\ 827\ 3E{-}03$
fanega [Mexico]	0.011 012	$1.101\ 200\ 3E{-}02$
fanega [Paraguay]	0.003 472 2	$3.472\ 222\ 2E{-}03$
fanega [Venezuela]	0.008 510 6	$8.510\ 638\ 3E{-}03$
fanga [Brazil]	0.006 896 6	$6.896\ 551\ 7E{-}03$
fass [Austria]	0.001 764 9	$1.764\ 913\ 5E{-}03$
fat [Sweden]	0.006 368 3	$6.368\ 331\ 6E{-}03$
feuillette [France, wine]	0.008 771 9	$8.771\ 929\ 8E{-}03$
fifth [US, liquid]	1.320 860 3	$1.320\ 860\ 3E{+}00$
firkin [Rome, ancient]	0.025 641	$2.564\ 102\ 6E{-}02$
firkin [UK]	0.024 441	$2.444\ 102\ 8E{-}02$
firkin [US]	0.029 352 5	$2.935\ 245\ 0E{-}02$
fjarding [Sweden, dry]	0.054 585 7	$5.458\ 574\ 9E{-}02$
fjarding [Sweden, liquid]	0.031 841 7	$3.184\ 165\ 8E{-}02$
fjerding [Denmark]	0.028 752 2	$2.875\ 215\ 6E{-}02$
fjerdingkar [Denmark]	0.230 015 1	$2.300\ 151\ 3E{-}01$
folha [Cape Verde, liquid]	0.952 381	$9.523\ 809\ 5E{-}01$
forten [Turkey]	0.002 5	$2.500\ 000\ 0E{-}03$
frasco [Argentina]	0.421 052 6	$4.210\ 526\ 3E{-}01$
frasco [Cuba]	0.459 770 1	$4.597\ 701\ 1E{-}01$
frasco [Mexico]	0.422 654 3	$4.226\ 542\ 7E{-}01$
frasco [Paraguay]	0.330 142	$3.301\ 419\ 6E{-}01$
frasila [Tanganyika]	0.041 666 7	$4.166\ 666\ 7E{-}02$
futtermassel [Austria]	1.041 666 7	$1.041\ 666\ 7E{+}00$
gab [Hebrew, ancient]	0.769 230 8	$7.692\ 307\ 7E{-}01$
galao [Cape Verde]	0.270 270 3	$2.702\ 702\ 7E{-}01$
gallon [British Honduras]	0.264 179 4	$2.641\ 794\ 3E{-}01$
gallon [Canada, liquid]	0.219 969 3	$2.199\ 692\ 5E{-}01$
gallon [Haiti]	0.264 179 2	$2.641\ 791\ 6E{-}01$
gallon [Hebrew, ancient]	0.025 380 7	$2.538\ 071\ 1E{-}02$
gallon [Peru]	0.219 975 5	$2.199\ 755\ 4E{-}01$
gallon [South Africa]	0.264 179 4	$2.641\ 794\ 3E{-}01$
gallon [UK, dry or liquid]	0.219 969 3	$2.199\ 692\ 5E{-}01$
gallon [US, liquid]	0.264 172 1	$2.641\ 720\ 5E{-}01$
galon [Argentina]	0.263 157 9	$2.631\ 578\ 9E{-}01$
galon [Bolivia]	0.297 619 1	$2.976\ 190\ 5E{-}01$
galon [Chile]	0.220 264 3	$2.202\ 643\ 2E{-}01$
galon [Dominican Republic]	0.308 632 5	$3.086\ 324\ 5E{-}01$
galon [El Salvador]	0.266 666 7	$2.666\ 666\ 7E{-}01$
galon [Honduras]	0.289 351 9	$2.893\ 518\ 5E{-}01$
galon [Peru]	0.297 619 1	$2.976\ 190\ 5E{-}01$
galon [Venezuela]	0.285 714 3	$2.857\ 142\ 9E{-}01$
ganta [Indonesia]	0.116 590 9	$1.165\ 908\ 8E{-}01$
ganta [Malaysia]	0.219 973 6	$2.199\ 736\ 0E{-}01$
ganta [Philippines]	0.333 333 3	$3.333\ 333\ 3E{-}01$

liter (continued) | | <volume>

Convert To	Standard	Scientific
gantang [Indonesia]	0.116 596 3	1.165 963 2E-01
gantang [Philippines]	0.333 333 3	3.333 333 3E-01
gantang [South Africa]	0.108 695 7	1.086 956 5E-01
garava [Syria]	0.068 965 5	6.896 551 7E-02
garnetz [Russia, dry]	0.304 878 1	3.048 780 5E-01
garniec [Poland]	0.25	2.500 000 0E-01
garra [Malta]	0.092 618 3	9.261 832 0E-02
garrafa [Brazil]	1.501 501 5	1.501 501 5E+00
garrafon [Cuba]	0.055 172 4	5.517 241 4E-02
ghebeta [Eritrea]	0.041 666 7	4.166 666 7E-02
gia [Vietnam, rice paddy]	0.025	2.500 000 0E-02
gia chiec [Vietnam]	0.05	5.000 000 0E-02
gia nan [Vietnam]	0.022 222 2	2.222 222 2E-02
giarra [Libya, liquid]	0.000 070 8	7.078 142 7E-05
gill [UK]	7.039 015 9	7.039 015 9E+00
gill [US]	8.453 505 7	8.453 505 7E+00
gin [Iraq, ancient]	0.207 468 9	2.074 688 8E-01
gisla [Somalia, dry]	0.006 132	6.131 959 8E-03
go [Japan]	5.555 555 6	5.555 555 6E+00
goduk [Turkey]	0.039 682 5	3.968 254 0E-02
gomari [Cyprus]	0.006 110 3	6.110 265 9E-03
gomor [Hebrew, ancient]	0.263 157 9	2.631 578 9E-01
gomor [Rome, ancient, large]	0.008 333 3	8.333 333 3E-03
gomor [Rome, ancient, small]	0.010 416 7	1.041 666 7E-02
goundo [Ethiopia]	0.333 333 3	3.333 333 3E-01
great hin [Hebrew, ancient]	0.108 932 5	1.089 324 6E-01
gur [Mesopotamia, ancient]	0.004 065	4.065 040 7E-03
gurraf [Libya]	0.433 538 5	4.335 385 4E-01
hak [Turkey]	0.029 673 6	2.967 359 1E-02
halbe [Austria]	1.414 427 2	1.414 427 2E+00
halbe [Hungary]	1.179 245 3	1.179 245 3E+00
halbstuck [Netherlands]	0.001 666 7	1.666 666 7E-03
half anker [UK]	0.044 052 9	4.405 286 3E-02
half barrel [UK]	0.012 195 1	1.219 512 2E-02
half hogshead [UK]	0.008 130 1	8.130 081 3E-03
half homer [Hebrew, ancient]	0.009 090 9	9.090 909 1E-03
halvstop [Sweden]	1.528 4	1.528 400 0E+00
hekat [Egypt, ancient]	0.204 499	2.044 989 8E-01
hekat [Hebrew, ancient]	0.209 643 6	2.096 436 1E-01
hekt [Egypt, ancient]	0.208 333 3	2.083 333 3E-01
hemina [Rome, ancient]	3.663 003 7	3.663 003 7E+00
hen [Egypt, ancient]	2.197 802 2	2.197 802 2E+00
hin [Egypt, ancient]	2.083 333 3	2.083 333 3E+00
hin [Hebrew, ancient]	0.25	2.500 000 0E-01
hinim [Hebrew, ancient]	0.158 730 2	1.587 301 6E-01
hkt [Egypt, ancient]	0.198 807 2	1.988 071 6E-01
hoc [Vietnam]	0.016 666 7	1.666 666 7E-02
hog [Israel]	1.801 801 8	1.801 801 8E+00
hogshead [Australia]	0.003 389 8	3.389 830 5E-03
hogshead [Singapore]	0.003 491 6	3.491 620 1E-03
hogshead [South Africa]	0.003 389 8	3.389 830 5E-03
hogshead [UK]	0.003 491 6	3.491 575 4E-03
hogshead [US]	0.004 193 2	4.193 207 2E-03
homer [Babylon, ancient]	0.01	1.000 000 0E-02
homer [Hebrew, ancient]	0.004 545 5	4.545 454 5E-03
hop [South Korea]	5.543 513 8	5.543 513 8E+00
hu [China]	0.019 315 1	1.931 508 7E-02
huacal [Venezuela]	0.035 714 3	3.571 428 6E-02
imi [Germany]	0.054 436 6	5.443 658 1E-02
immi [Switzerland]	0.666 666 7	6.666 666 7E-01
issaron [Hebrew, ancient]	0.434 971 7	4.349 717 3E-01
itce [Hungary]	1.179 245 3	1.179 245 3E+00

liter (continued)   **<volume>**

Convert To	Standard	Scientific
itcze [Hungary]	1.179 245 3	1.179 245 3E+00
jarra [Libya]	0.070 771 4	7.077 140 0E-02
jarra [Mexico]	0.121 802 7	1.218 026 8E-01
jigger [US, liquid]	22.542 682	2.254 268 2E+01
jizia [Tanganyika]	0.004 166 7	4.166 666 7E-03
jumfru [Sweden]	12.195 122	1.219 512 2E+01
jungfru [Sweden]	12.227 211	1.222 721 1E+01
kab [Babylon, ancient]	0.5	5.000 000 0E-01
kab [Hebrew, ancient]	0.769 230 8	7.692 307 0E-01
kada [Yemen]	0.025	2.500 000 0E-02
kadah [Egypt]	0.484 848 5	4.848 484 8E-01
kadah [Sudan]	0.485 436 9	4.854 368 9E-01
kaledje [Egypt, ancient]	0.485 436 9	4.854 368 9E-01
kalong [Laos]	0.05	5.000 000 0E-02
kam meu [Thailand]	8	8.000 000 0E+00
kan [Finland]	0.501 454 2	5.014 542 2E-01
kan [Netherlands]	1	1.000 000 0E+00
kanahn [Thailand]	1	1.000 000 0E+00
kande [Denmark]	0.517 544 8	5.175 447 7E-01
kanna [South Africa]	0.672 043	6.720 430 1E-01
kanna [Sweden]	0.382 099 4	3.820 994 1E-01
kanne [Germany]	1	1.000 000 0E+00
kanne [South Africa]	0.672 043	6.720 430 1E-01
kannu [Finland]	0.381 679 4	3.816 793 9E-01
kantaing [Cambodia]	0.133 333 3	1.333 333 3E-01
kappa [Finland]	0.2	2.000 000 0E-01
kappe [Sweden]	0.218 343	2.183 430 0E-01
kard [Morocco]	0.1	1.000 000 0E-01
kartocc [Malta, beer, wine and spirits]	0.880 281 7	8.802 816 9E-01
kartos [Cyprus]	0.195 694 7	1.956 947 2E-01
katang [Cambodia, dry]	0.133 333 3	1.333 333 3E-01
kav [Hebrew, ancient]	0.833 333 3	8.333 333 3E-01
keddah [Egypt]	0.485 436 9	4.854 368 9E-01
keila [Egypt]	0.060 606 1	6.060 606 1E-02
keila [Sudan]	0.060 606 1	6.060 606 1E-02
keila [Yemen]	0.027 777 8	2.777 777 8E-02
keleh [Egypt]	0.060 606 1	6.060 606 1E-02
kettle [Sierra Leone]	0.100 100 1	1.001 001 0E-01
khanan [Laos]	0.2	2.000 000 0E-01
khanan louang [Laos]	1	1.000 000 0E+00
khar [Egypt]	0.010 224 9	1.022 494 9E-02
kharouba [Egypt]	7.751 938	7.751 938 0E+00
kharrouba [Morocco]	0.025	2.500 000 0E-02
kharruba [Egypt]	7.757 350 1	7.757 350 1E+00
khoubhie [Syria]	0.153 846 2	1.538 461 5E-01
khous [Greece, ancient]	0.308 994 8	3.089 948 4E-01
khwe [Burma]	0.048 883	4.888 302 3E-02
khwet [Burma]	0.781 860 8	7.818 608 3E-01
kibaba [Tanganyika]	1	1.000 000 0E+00
kibaba [Tanzania]	1	1.000 000 0E+00
kila [Egypt]	0.060 606 1	6.060 606 1E-02
kila [Sudan]	0.060 606 1	6.060 606 1E-02
kilah [Egypt]	0.060 606 1	6.060 606 1E-02
kile [Cyprus]	0.027 495 2	2.749 518 8E-02
kile [Greece]	0.026 525 2	2.652 519 9E-02
kile [Libya]	0.027 777 8	2.777 777 8E-02
kileh [Cyprus]	0.027 495 2	2.749 518 8E-02
kileh [Libya]	0.027 777 8	2.777 777 8E-02
kileh [Turkey]	0.027 027	2.702 702 7E-02
kilesi [Cyprus]	0.027 495 2	2.749 518 8E-02
kilesi [Libya]	0.027 777 8	2.777 777 8E-02
kilesi [Turkey]	0.027 027	2.702 702 7E-02

Convert From		<Type of Unit>
Convert To	Standard	Scientific

liter (continued)   \<volume\>

	Standard	Scientific
kilo [Greece]	0.01	1.000 000 0E−02
kilo [Romania]	0.002 540 7	2.540 650 4E−03
kirat [Egypt]	15.515 182	1.551 518 2E+01
kist [Islam, oil]	0.474 833 8	4.748 338 1E−01
ko [China]	9.657 73	9.657 730 0E+00
kob [Laos]	0.4	4.000 000 0E−01
kob louang [Laos]	2	2.000 000 0E+00
koddi [Arab]	0.131 926 1	1.319 261 2E−01
koibon [Greece]	0.030 151 4	3.015 136 0E−02
koilon [Greece]	0.030 120 5	3.012 048 2E−02
koku [Japan]	0.005 543 5	5.543 523 0E−03
kolla [Tunisia]	0.098 990 3	9.899 029 9E−02
koltunna [Sweden]	0.006 064 3	6.064 281 4E−03
konge [Greece, ancient]	0.284 900 3	2.849 002 8E−01
kop [Netherlands]	1.173 846 7	1.173 846 7E+00
kor [Babylon, ancient]	0.002 777 8	2.777 777 8E−03
kor [Hebrew, ancient]	0.004 347 8	4.347 826 1E−03
korce [Russia]	0.008 130 5	8.130 471 3E−03
korec [Czechoslovakia]	0.010 684 7	1.068 467 4E−02
korec [Russia]	0.008 108 3	8.108 327 3E−03
korn skeppa [Iceland]	0.057 504 3	5.750 431 3E−02
korn tonde [Denmark]	0.007 188	7.188 039 1E−03
korn tonde [Norway]	0.007 195 8	7.195 797 7E−03
korn tunna [Iceland]	0.007 188 6	7.188 555 8E−03
koros [Greece, ancient]	0.001 904 8	1.904 761 9E−03
koryec [Poland]	0.007 812 5	7.812 500 0E−03
korzec [Poland]	0.007 812 5	7.812 500 0E−03
kouza [Cyprus]	0.098 039 2	9.803 921 6E−02
koyan [Thailand]	0.000 5	5.000 000 0E−04
krina [Bulgaria]	0.05	5.000 000 0E−02
krouchka [Russia]	0.813 008 1	8.130 081 3E−01
kruska [Russia, liquid]	0.813 008 1	8.130 081 3E−01
kuba [Abyssinia, ancient]	0.980 392 2	9.803 921 6E−01
kuba [Ethiopia]	1	1.000 000 0E+00
kuba [Liberia]	0.980 392 2	9.803 921 6E−01
kuba [Morocco, oil]	0.041 585 2	4.158 522 9E−02
kula [Morocco, oil]	0.041 585 2	4.158 522 9E−02
kulimet [Estonia]	0.087 108	8.710 801 4E−02
kulla [North Africa, ancient]	0.099 206 3	9.920 634 9E−02
kulmet [Latvia]	0.091 491 3	9.149 130 8E−02
kuna [Eritrea]	0.2	2.000 000 0E−01
kuna [Ethiopia]	0.2	2.000 000 0E−01
kuncha [Malaysia]	0.001 374 8	1.374 847 1E−03
kuncha [Singapore]	0.001 374 8	1.374 847 1E−03
kung ho [China]	10	1.000 000 0E+01
kung sheng [China]	1	1.000 000 0E+00
kung sheng [Taiwan]	1	1.000 000 0E+00
kung tou [China]	0.1	1.000 000 0E+00
kung tou [Taiwan]	0.1	1.000 000 0E+00
kunna [Ethiopia]	0.227 272 7	2.272 727 3E−01
kurru [Babylon, ancient]	0.005 555 6	5.555 555 6E−03
kutu [Turkey]	0.217 391 3	2.173 913 0E−01
kvarter [Sweden, liquid]	3.056 804 6	3.056 804 6E+00
kwai [Burma]	0.247 524 8	2.475 247 5E−01
kwak [India]	2.941 176 5	2.941 176 5E+00
kwarta [Malta, beer, wine and spirits]	0.185 253 8	1.852 538 0E−01
kwarta [Malta, oil and milk]	0.195 541 7	1.955 416 5E−01
kwarta [Poland]	1	1.000 000 0E+00
kwarteka [Poland]	4	4.000 000 0E+00
kwarterka [Poland]	4	4.000 000 0E+00
kwarti [Poland, dry]	1.088 139 3	1.088 139 3E+00
kwarti [Poland, liquid]	1.054 852 3	1.054 852 3E+00
kwe [Burma]	0.048 875 9	4.887 585 5E−02

liter (continued) <volume>

	Standard	Scientific
laang [Thailand]	2	2.000 000 0E+00
lamang [Malaya and Singapore]	15.847 861	1.584 786 1E+01
lamany [Burma]	15.713 388	1.571 338 8E+01
lambda	1,000,000	1.000 000 0E+06
lame [Burma]	3.128 541 1	3.128 541 1E+00
lang [Sarawak]	1.759 804 3	1.759 804 3E+00
last [Netherlands]	0.000 333 3	3.333 333 3E−04
last [UK]	0.000 343 7	3.437 118 3E−04
lastre [Argentina]	0.000 485 9	4.859 166 8E−04
le [Vietnam]	10	1.000 000 0E+01
leaguer [South Africa]	0.001 738	1.738 022 6E−03
leaguer [Swaziland]	0.001 738 9	1.738 936 9E−03
legana [Iran]	0.025 329 3	2.532 928 1E−02
legger [Netherlands]	0.001 718 2	1.718 213 1E−03
legger [South Africa]	0.001 738	1.738 022 6E−03
letek [Hebrew, ancient]	0.008 710 8	8.710 801 4E−03
letekh [Hebrew, ancient]	0.009 090 9	9.090 909 1E−03
lethech [Hebrew, ancient]	0.008 710 8	8.710 801 4E−03
lethek [Hebrew, ancient]	0.009 090 9	9.090 909 1E−03
lethekh [Hebrew, ancient]	0.008 699	8.698 980 5E−03
ligula [Rome, ancient]	90.353 009	9.035 300 9E+01
liter [pre-1964]	0.999 972	9.999 720 0E−01
litre [Cyprus]	0.314 267 8	3.142 677 6E−01
litron [France, dry]	1.230 012 3	1.230 012 3E+00
load [Cyprus]	0.006 110 4	6.110 430 1E−03
lof [Russia]	0.015 450 6	1.545 064 4E−02
log [Hebrew, ancient]	2.857 142 9	2.857 142 9E+00
logh [Hebrew, ancient]	3.134 796 2	3.134 796 2E+00
logh [Rome, ancient]	1.886 792 5	1.886 792 5E+00
maass [Germany]	0.544 365 8	5.443 658 1E−01
maass [Switzerland]	0.666 666 7	6.666 666 7E−01
maatje [Netherlands]	10	1.000 000 0E+01
maess [Germany]	1.164 144 4	1.164 144 4E+00
mal [South Korea, large]	0.055 435 4	5.543 544 5E−02
mal [South Korea, small]	0.110 870 9	1.108 708 9E−01
malouah [Egypt]	0.242 718 5	2.427 184 5E−01
maltaro [Libya]	0.042 881 6	4.288 164 7E−02
malwa [Egypt]	0.242 424 2	2.424 242 4E−01
malwa [Sudan]	0.242 424 2	2.424 242 4E−01
mandu [North Borneo]	0.021 997 6	2.199 755 4E−02
marcal [India, grain]	0.081 367	8.136 696 5E−02
marco real [Chile]	0.010 310 3	1.031 034 1E−02
marco real [Colombia]	0.018 018	1.801 801 8E−02
marco real [Dominican Republic]	0.018 018	1.801 801 8E−02
marco real [Mexico]	0.011 011 4	1.101 139 7E−02
marco real [Spain]	0.018 018	1.801 801 8E−02
maris [Babylon, ancient]	0.033 003 3	3.300 330 0E−02
marta [Libya]	0.048 192 8	4.819 277 1E−02
mass [Austria]	0.704 225 4	7.042 253 5E−01
mass [Germany]	1.164 144 4	1.164 144 4E+00
masse [Austria]	0.706 663 8	7.066 638 4E−01
massel [Germany]	0.215 866 2	2.158 661 6E−01
masskanne [Germany]	0.935 453 7	9.354 537 0E−01
mattaro [Libya]	0.042 881 6	4.288 164 7E−02
measure [Hebrew, ancient]	0.129 870 1	1.298 701 3E−01
measure [Sri Lanka, dry]	0.943 396 2	9.433 962 3E−01
medida [Honduras]	0.348 189 4	3.481 894 2E−01
medimno [Cyprus]	0.013 324 6	1.332 462 8E−02
medimnos [Greece, ancient]	0.025 641	2.564 102 6E−02
medimnus [Greece, ancient]	0.019 290 1	1.929 012 3E−02
medio [Honduras]	0.021 762 8	2.176 278 6E−02
medio [Spain]	0.432 900 4	4.329 004 3E−01

	Standard	<Type of Unit> Scientific

liter (continued)   **<volume>**

Convert To	Standard	Scientific
medio almud [El Salvador]	0.092 447 1	9.244 707 4E–02
megarikon [Greece, ancient]	0.009 756 1	9.756 097 6E–03
meias canada [Portugal, liquid]	1.451 378 8	1.451 378 8E+00
meio [Portugal]	1.432 87	1.432 870 0E+00
mengel [Netherlands]	0.825 082 5	8.250 825 1E–01
menor [Iran]	0.079 700 3	7.970 032 7E–02
mercal [India]	0.081 566 1	8.156 606 9E–02
merica [Czechoslovakia]	0.014 164 3	1.416 430 6E–02
merice [Czechoslovakia]	0.014 184 4	1.418 439 7E–02
messe [Eritrea]	0.666 666 7	6.666 666 7E–01
messe [Ethiopia]	0.666 666 7	6.666 666 7E–01
meter [Turkey]	0.190 839 7	1.908 396 9E–01
metreta [Greece, ancient]	0.034 246 6	3.424 657 5E–02
metretes [Greece, ancient]	0.034 246 6	3.424 657 5E–02
metretes [Hebrew, ancient]	0.025 445 3	2.544 529 3E–02
metro [Turkey]	0.088 261 3	8.826 125 3E–02
mettar [Tunisia]	0.049 485 4	4.948 535 2E–02
metter [Tunisia, oil]	0.050 761 4	5.076 142 1E–02
metter [Tunisia]	0.050 761 4	5.076 142 1E–02
metze [Austria]	0.016 260 2	1.626 016 3E–02
metze [Denmark]	0.032 341 5	3.234 152 7E–02
metze [Germany, Bavaria]	0.026 983 3	2.698 327 0E–02
metze [Germany, Prussia]	0.291 120 8	2.911 208 2E–01
metze [Hungary]	0.018 761 7	1.876 172 6E–02
mid [Jordan, oil]	0.055 555 6	5.555 555 6E–02
midd [Sudan]	0.242 424 2	2.424 242 4E–01
millerole [Tunisia]	0.015 625	1.562 500 0E–02
minae [Babylon, ancient]	1.980 198	1.980 198 0E+00
mine [France, dry]	0.012 812 3	1.281 230 0E–02
mingel [Netherlands]	0.824 402 3	8.244 023 1E–01
minim [UK]	16,893.638	1.689 363 8E+04
minim [US]	16,230.731	1.623 073 1E+04
minot [France, dry]	0.025 624 6	2.562 460 0E–02
mirze [Romania]	0.005 081 3	5.081 300 8E–03
misura [Libya]	0.050 505 1	5.050 505 1E–02
modion [Rome, ancient, dry]	0.114 468 9	1.144 688 6E–01
modios [Greece, ancient]	0.118 231 3	1.182 312 6E–01
modius [Rome, ancient]	0.117 647 2	1.176 472 0E–01
moio [Spain]	0.003 874	3.874 017 0E–03
moyo [Spain]	0.003 874	3.874 017 0E–03
mudd [Morocco]	0.021 413 3	2.141 327 6E–02
mudd [North Africa]	0.004 975 1	4.975 124 4E–03
mudd [Spanish North Africa]	0.071 428 6	7.142 857 1E–02
mudd [Syria]	0.038 461 5	3.846 153 8E–02
muid [Switzerland]	0.006 666 7	6.666 666 7E–03
mula [Chile]	0.010 310 3	1.031 034 1E–02
mula [Colombia]	0.018 018	1.801 801 8E–02
mula [Mexico]	0.011 011 4	1.101 139 7E–02
mula [Spain]	0.018 018	1.801 801 8E–02
musa kibaba [Tanganyika]	2	2.000 000 0E+00
musu kibaba [Tanzania]	2	2.000 000 0E+00
muthmassel [Austria]	0.260 206 6	2.602 066 0E–01
mutsje [Netherlands]	6.666 666 7	6.666 666 7E+00
mystram [Greece]	100	1.000 000 0E+02
nafer [Yemen]	1.6	1.600 000 0E+00
nalih [Singapore]	0.013 748 5	1.374 847 1E–02
nigida [Mesopotamia, ancient]	0.020 325 2	2.032 520 3E–02
niou [Thailand]	100	1.000 000 0E+02
nisf kadah [Egypt]	0.969 65	9.696 499 6E–01
nisf keddah [Egypt]	0.969 932 1	9.699 321 0E–01
noggin [UK]	7.039 214 8	7.039 214 8E+00
nozibu [Burma]	3.128 541 1	3.128 541 1E+00

liter (continued) \<volume\>

	Standard	Scientific
nusfiah [Arabia]	1.052 631 6	1.052 631 6E+00
ock [Cyprus]	0.785 546	7.855 459 5E-01
octava [Argentina]	6.738 544 5	6.738 544 5E+00
octavillo [Spain, liquid]	3.968 254	3.968 254 0E+00
oitava [Portugal]	0.706 713 8	7.067 137 8E-01
oka [Bulgaria]	0.781 25	7.812 500 0E-01
oka [Cyprus]	0.781 25	7.812 500 0E-01
oka [Turkey]	0.781 25	7.812 500 0E-01
oka [Yugoslavia]	0.706 713 8	7.067 137 8E-01
oke [Bulgaria]	0.781 25	7.812 500 0E-01
oke [Cyprus]	0.781 25	7.812 500 0E-01
oke [Romania, dry]	0.650 195 1	6.501 950 6E-01
oke [Romania, liquid]	0.706 713 8	7.067 137 8E-01
oke [Turkey]	0.781 25	7.812 500 0E-01
okka [Cyprus]	0.785 546	7.855 459 5E-01
okka [Turkey]	0.882 612 5	8.826 125 3E-01
okshoofd [Netherlands]	0.004 295 5	4.295 532 6E-03
olcek [Turkey]	0.054 054 1	5.405 405 4E-02
ollock [India]	5.219 206 7	5.219 206 7E+00
omarium [Hebrew, ancient, dry]	0.263 157 9	2.631 578 9E-01
omer [Babylon, ancient]	0.454 545 5	4.545 454 5E-01
omer [Hebrew, ancient]	0.252 270 4	2.522 704 3E-01
oms [Russia]	0.013 550 8	1.355 078 5E-02
oner [Hebrew, ancient, dry]	0.263 157 9	2.631 578 9E-01
orna [Italy, wine]	0.017 543 9	1.754 386 0E-02
ottinger [Finland]	0.063 653 7	6.365 372 4E-02
ottingkar [Denmark]	0.057 504 3	5.750 431 3E-02
ottinkar [Denmark]	0.057 504 3	5.750 431 3E-02
ouiba [Tunisia]	0.025	2.500 000 0E-02
ounce [UK, liquid]	35.195 08	3.519 508 0E+01
ounce [US, liquid]	33.814 023	3.381 402 3E+01
oxhoft [Germany]	0.004 851 9	4.851 872 3E-03
oxhoft [Russia]	0.004 516 9	4.516 928 1E-03
oxhuvud [Sweden]	0.004 245 6	4.245 563 4E-03
paegel [Denmark]	4.132 231 4	4.132 231 4E+00
paegl [Denmark]	4.132 231 4	4.132 231 4E+00
paimoneh [Iran]	1	1.000 000 0E+00
pajak [Russia]	0.019 054 9	1.905 487 8E-02
pajmaneh [Iran]	1	1.000 000 0E+00
pajok [Russia]	0.019 054 9	1.905 487 8E-02
pally [India]	0.183 823 5	1.838 235 3E-01
panu [Babylon, ancient]	0.027 777 8	2.777 777 8E-02
para [Ceylon]	0.039 370 1	3.937 007 9E-02
para [Malaysia]	0.021 997 4	2.199 736 0E-02
para [Singapore]	0.021 997 4	2.199 736 0E-02
para [Straits Settlements]	0.021 997 4	2.199 736 0E-02
paraffin [Zambia]	0.054 993 4	5.499 340 1E-02
parah [Ceylon]	0.039 370 1	3.937 007 9E-02
parah [Sri Lanka, dry]	0.039 215 7	3.921 568 6E-02
parah [Straits Settlements]	0.021 997 4	2.199 736 0E-02
parak [Malaysia]	0.021 997 6	2.199 755 4E-02
parak [Singapore]	0.021 997 6	2.199 755 4E-02
parrah [Ceylon]	0.039 370 1	3.937 007 9E-02
parrah [Straits Settlements]	0.021 997 4	2.199 736 0E-02
parrak [India]	0.009 082 7	9.082 652 1E-03
pathi [Nepal]	0.219 973 6	2.199 736 0E-01
pau [North Borneo]	3.519 608 6	3.519 608 6E+00
pau [Straits Settlements]	3.521 126 8	3.521 126 8E+00
pfiff [Austria]	5.555 555 6	5.555 555 6E+00
phai mu [Laos]	0.8	8.000 000 0E-01
phai mu louang [Laos]	4	4.000 000 0E+00
phlang [Cambodia]	0.01	1.000 000 0E-02

Convert From
Convert To | | Standard | Scientific
Standard | <Type of Unit>
Scientific

liter (continued) | | | <volume>

Convert To	Standard	Scientific
phuong [Vietnam]	0.033 333 3	3.333 333 3E-02
pie de madera [Cuba]	0.423 728 8	4.237 288 1E-01
pin [UK]	0.048 780 5	4.878 048 8E-02
pint [Netherlands]	1.649 348 5	1.649 348 5E+00
pint [UK]	1.759 754	1.759 754 0E+00
pint [US, liquid]	2.113 376 4	2.113 376 4E+00
pinta [Chile]	1.785 714 3	1.785 714 3E+00
pinte [France]	1.074 113 9	1.074 113 9E+00
pipa [Brazil]	0.002 087	2.086 985 6E-03
pipa [Cuba]	0.002 096 7	2.096 743 8E-03
pipa [Portugal]	0.002 297 3	2.297 266 3E-03
pipa [Sweden]	0.002 122 8	2.122 777 2E-03
pipe [Portugal, Lisbon]	0.001 886 8	1.886 792 5E-03
pipe [Portugal, wine]	0.001 869 2	1.869 158 9E-03
pipe [South Africa]	0.002 401 6	2.401 631 6E-03
pipe [Spain, wine]	0.229 621 1	2.296 211 3E-01
pipe [UK]	0.002 036 8	2.036 752 3E-03
pipe [US, liquid]	0.002 096 6	2.096 603 6E-03
pishi [Tanganyika]	0.25	2.500 000 0E-01
pishi [Tanzania]	0.25	2.500 000 0E-01
pjak [Russia]	0.019 055 8	1.905 579 7E-02
pliashka [Russia, liquid]	1.639 344 3	1.639 344 3E+00
podd [Portuguese India]	1.001 702 9	1.001 702 9E+00
poisson [France]	8.620 689 7	8.620 689 7E+00
polugarnetz [Russia]	0.609 756 1	6.097 561 0E-01
polygarnetz [Russia]	0.609 756 1	6.097 561 0E-01
pony [US, liquid]	0.029 573 5	2.957 353 0E-02
pot [Belgium, dry]	0.666 666 7	6.666 666 7E-01
pot [Belgium, liquid]	2	2.000 000 0E+00
pot [Denmark]	1.030 927 8	1.030 927 8E+00
pot [France]	0.537 634 4	5.376 344 1E-01
pot [Hebrew, ancient]	1.886 792 5	1.886 792 5E+00
pot [Norway]	1	1.000 000 0E+00
pot [Portugal, liquid]	0.120 919	1.209 189 8E-01
pot [Switzerland]	0.666 666 7	6.666 666 7E-01
pottar [Iceland]	1.035 132 4	1.035 132 4E+00
pottle [UK]	0.439 951 1	4.399 510 8E-01
pottur [Iceland]	1.030 927 8	1.030 927 8E+00
pound of water [at 4 °C, 101.325 kPa, using IST-90 density equation]	2.204 560 9	2.204 560 9E+00
pound of water [at 60 °F, 14.696 pound-force/square inch, using IST-90 density equation]	2.202 447 7	2.202 447 7E+00
probmetze [Austria]	16.653 344	1.665 334 4E+01
puddee [India]	0.652 315 7	6.523 157 0E-01
puili [Portuguese India]	0.250 438 3	2.504 382 7E-01
pyi [Burma, dry]	0.391 083 3	3.910 833 0E-01
qab [Hebrew, ancient]	0.783 699 1	7.836 990 6E-01
qabh [Hebrew, ancient]	0.783 085 4	7.830 853 6E-01
qabim [Hebrew, ancient]	0.476 190 5	4.761 904 8E-01
qabin [Hebrew, ancient, dry]	0.476 190 5	4.761 904 8E-01
qadah [Egypt]	0.485 436 9	4.854 368 9E-01
qadah [Sudan]	0.484 848 5	4.848 484 8E-01
qav [Hebrew, ancient]	0.476 190 5	4.761 904 8E-01
qirat [Egypt]	15.515 182	1.551 518 2E+01
qu [Babylon, ancient]	1	1.000 000 0E+00
quadrantal [Rome, ancient, liquid]	0.038 759 7	3.875 969 0E-02
quart [Germany]	0.873 331 9	8.733 319 4E-01
quart [Hebrew, ancient]	0.925 925 5	9.259 259 3E-01
quart [UK]	0.879 877	8.798 769 9E-01
quart [US, liquid]	1.056 688 2	1.056 688 2E+00
quarta [Cape Verde, dry]	0.096 172 3	9.617 234 1E-02
quartarella [Italy, dry]	0.027 173 9	2.717 391 3E-02

liter (continued) <volume>

	Standard	Scientific
quartarius [Rome, ancient]	7.352 941 2	7.352 941 2E+00
quartarius [Rome, ancient, dry]	7.352 941 2	7.352 941 2E+00
quartarius [Rome, ancient, liquid]	7.299 270 1	7.299 270 1E+00
quartaut [France]	0.014 912	1.491 201 9E-02
quartaut [Portugal, wine]	0.007 462 7	7.462 686 6E-03
quarte [France]	0.307 692 3	3.076 923 1E-01
quarter [UK]	0.003 437	3.437 019 5E-03
quartern [UK, dry]	0.439 951 1	4.399 510 8E-01
quartern [UK, liquid]	7.039 214 8	7.039 214 8E+00
quarteron [Switzerland]	0.066 666 7	6.666 666 7E-02
quartia [Belize]	0.351 988 7	3.519 887 4E-01
quartier [Germany]	1.164 144 4	1.164 144 4E+00
quartilho [Brazil]	1.502 629 6	1.502 629 6E+00
quartilho [Portugal, liquid]	2.898 550 7	2.898 550 7E+00
quartillo [Portugal]	2.865 329 5	2.865 329 5E+00
quarto [Brazil]	0.110 253 6	1.102 535 8E-01
quarto [Portugal]	0.289 017 3	2.890 173 4E-01
quiba [Tunisia, cereals]	0.027 495 9	2.749 594 4E-02
quilo [Greece]	0.026 525 2	2.652 519 9E-02
racin [Spain]	3.459 369 7	3.459 369 7E+00
racione [Spain, dry]	3.448 275 9	3.448 275 9E+00
raik [India]	0.726 744 2	7.267 441 9E-01
rebee [Syria]	0.210 526 3	2.105 263 2E-01
rob [Egypt, ancient]	0.121 212 1	1.212 121 2E-01
robbah [Egypt]	1.937 984 5	1.937 984 5E+00
robo kibaba [Tanganyika]	4	4.000 000 0E+00
robo kibaba [Tanzania]	4	4.000 000 0E+00
roquille [France]	34.364 261	3.436 426 1E+01
rotl [Sudan, liquid]	1.759 804 3	1.759 804 3E+00
rottol [Turkey]	0.625	6.250 000 0E-01
roub [Egypt]	0.121 212 1	1.212 121 2E-01
roubouh [Egypt]	0.121 212 1	1.212 121 2E-01
rub [Egypt]	0.121 212 1	1.212 121 2E-01
rub [Eritrea]	0.555 555 6	5.555 555 6E-01
ruba [Sudan]	0.121 212 1	1.212 121 2E-01
rubia [Eritrea]	0.555 555 6	5.555 555 6E-01
rundlet [UK]	0.012 195 1	1.219 512 2E-02
ruplagi [Turkey]	0.039 682 5	3.968 254 0E-02
sa [Tunisia, cereals]	0.329 924 1	3.299 241 2E-01
saa [Jordan, oil]	0.166 666 7	1.666 666 7E-01
saa [Libya, dry]	0.008 417 5	8.417 508 4E-03
saa [Tunisia, dry]	0.300 300 3	3.003 003 0E-01
saa [Tunisia, liquid]	0.881 834 2	8.818 342 2E-01
saagh [Syria]	0.102 774 9	1.027 749 2E-01
saah [Algeria]	0.017 241 4	1.724 137 9E-02
sabbitha [Iran]	0.138 178 8	1.381 788 0E-01
sacco [Eritrea]	0.009 259 3	9.259 259 3E-03
sack [Philippines]	0.013 333 3	1.333 333 3E-02
saha [Syria]	0.076 923 1	7.692 307 7E-02
saha [Tunisia, cereals]	0.329 924 1	3.299 241 2E-01
sahh [Morocco]	0.017 857 1	1.785 714 3E-02
sahh [Spanish North Africa]	0.017 857 1	1.785 714 3E-02
sale [Burma]	1.564 270 6	1.564 270 6E+00
sat [Egypt, ancient]	0.085 470 1	8.547 008 5E-02
sat [Hebrew, ancient, dry]	0.078 740 2	7.874 015 7E-02
sat [Laos]	0.005	5.000 000 0E-03
sat [Thailand]	0.05	5.000 000 0E-02
saton [Hebrew, ancient, dry]	0.078 740 2	7.874 015 7E-02
saum [Switzerland]	0.006 666 7	6.666 666 7E-03
saw [Tunisia, cereals]	0.329 924 1	3.299 241 2E-01
sayut [Burma]	0.195 541 7	1.955 416 5E-01
scheffel [Germany, Bavaria]	0.004 497 2	4.497 211 7E-03

liter (continued) \<volume\>

Convert To	Standard	Scientific
scheffel [Germany, Prussia]	0.018 194 5	1.819 445 5E−02
scheffel [Germany, Wurttemberg]	0.005 642 7	5.642 704 0E−03
schepel [Netherlands]	0.1	1.000 000 0E−01
scheppel [South Africa]	0.036 662 6	3.666 259 0E−02
schoppe [Germany]	2.177 463 3	2.177 463 3E+00
schoppen [Germany]	2	2.000 000 0E+00
schtaff [Russia]	0.813 047 1	8.130 471 3E−01
scruple [UK, liquid]	844.681 91	8.446 819 1E+02
sea [Hebrew, ancient]	0.129 870 1	1.298 701 3E−01
seah [Babylon, ancient]	0.151 515 2	1.515 151 5E−01
seah [Hebrew, ancient]	0.066 666 7	6.666 666 7E−02
seak [Macao]	0.009 699 3	9.699 321 0E−03
seam [UK]	0.003 437 1	3.437 118 3E−03
seer [Sri Lanka, liquid]	0.943 396 2	9.433 962 3E−01
seidel [Austria, beer]	2.828 054 3	2.828 054 3E+00
seik [Burma, dry]	0.097 761 3	9.776 126 7E−02
seik [Burma, liquid]	0.495 049 5	4.950 495 0E−02
seim [Hebrew, ancient, dry]	0.078 740 2	7.874 015 7E−02
seit [Burma, dry]	0.097 196 7	9.719 674 9E−02
seit [Burma, liquid]	0.495 049 5	4.950 495 0E−02
selemin [Portugal]	2.292 526 4	2.292 526 4E+00
semimodius [Rome, ancient, dry]	0.229 357 8	2.293 578 0E−01
semodius [Rome, ancient, dry]	0.232 558 1	2.325 581 4E−01
seste [Thailand]	0.001 25	1.250 000 0E−03
setier [France, liquid]	2.147 305 1	2.147 305 1E+00
setier [Switzerland]	0.026 666 7	2.666 666 7E−02
sextarius [Babylon, ancient]	2	2.000 000 0E+00
sextarius [Rome, ancient]	1.831 501 8	1.831 501 8E+00
sexto [Venezuela]	6.024 096 4	6.024 096 4E+00
shen [China]	0.965 773	9.657 730 0E−01
sheng [China]	0.966 183 6	9.661 835 7E−01
shi sheng [China]	0.1	1.000 000 0E−01
shih sen [China]	1	1.000 000 0E+00
shinik [Turkey]	0.1	1.000 000 0E−01
sho [China]	96.577 3	9.657 730 0E+01
sho [Japan]	0.554 352 3	5.543 523 0E−01
shot [US, liquid]	33.814 023	3.381 402 3E+01
shushack [Belize]	0.043 994 7	4.399 472 1E−02
sila [Iraq, ancient]	1.038 421 6	1.038 421 6E+00
sila [Mesopotamia, ancient]	1.219 512 2	1.219 512 2E+00
sila [Sumeria, ancient]	1	1.000 000 0E+00
simri [Germany]	0.045 140 6	4.514 061 3E−02
sing [Hong Kong]	1	1.000 000 0E+00
sinik [Turkey]	0.108 695 7	1.086 956 5E−01
six [UK]	0.036 63	3.663 003 7E−02
skaepper [Denmark]	0.057 504 3	5.750 431 5E−02
skeppe [Denmark]	0.057 504 3	5.750 431 5E−02
skieppe [Denmark]	0.057 504 3	5.750 431 5E−02
skjeppe [Norway]	0.057 570 5	5.757 052 4E−02
spann [Sweden]	0.013 646 3	1.364 628 8E−02
spint [Netherlands]	0.2	2.000 000 0E−01
stajo [Italy, dry]	0.040 766 4	4.076 640 8E−02
stangiew [Poland]	0.003 661 9	3.661 930 6E−03
starello [Italy, dry]	0.054 347 8	5.434 782 6E−02
steekkan [Netherlands]	0.051 546 4	5.154 639 2E−02
stere	0.001	1.000 000 0E−03
stof [Russia]	6.504 378 1	6.504 378 1E+00
stoop [Netherlands]	0.412 371 1	4.123 711 3E−01
stop [Sweden]	0.764 198 8	7.641 988 1E−01
strike [UK]	0.013 748 5	1.374 847 1E−02
strych [Czechoslovakia]	0.010 684 7	1.068 467 4E−02
stubchen [Denmark]	0.258 799 2	2.587 991 7E−01

Convert From		
Convert To	Standard	Scientific
liter (continued)		**<volume>**
suk [South Korea]	0.005 543 1	5.543 513 8E-03
sulga [Mongolia]	0.153 846 2	1.538 461 5E-01
sultchek [Turkey]	1	1.000 000 0E+00
sutu [Assyrian, ancient]	0.074 626 9	7.462 686 6E-02
sutu [Babylon, ancient]	0.166 666 7	1.666 666 7E-01
tabla [Somalia]	0.049 055 7	4.905 567 8E-02
tabla [Somaliland]	0.049 019 6	4.901 960 8E-02
tablespoon [Canada, measuring]	70.390 279	7.039 027 9E+01
tablespoon [US, measuring]	67.628 045	6.762 804 5E+01
tamlaum [Thailand]	0.002 5	2.500 000 0E-03
tanan [Thailand]	1	1.000 000 0E+00
tanica [Eritrea]	0.055 555 6	5.555 555 6E-02
tanica [Iraq]	0.054 993 4	5.499 340 1E-02
tanica [Somalia]	0.055 555 6	5.555 555 6E-02
tanica [Somaliland]	0.055 555 6	5.555 555 6E-02
tao [Cambodia]	0.066 666 7	6.666 666 7E-02
tarri [Algeria]	0.050 398 1	5.039 814 5E-02
tau [China]	0.096 574 5	9.657 450 2E-02
tcharka [Russia]	8.130 471 3	8.130 471 3E+00
tchast [Russia]	9.146 779 3	9.146 779 3E+00
tchetverik [Russia]	0.038 111 6	3.811 158 6E-02
tchetvert [Russia, dry]	0.004 763 9	4.763 948 7E-03
teaspoon [Canada, measuring]	211.170 84	2.111 708 4E+02
teaspoon [US, measuring]	202.884 14	2.028 841 4E+02
teman [Arabia]	0.011 764 7	1.176 470 6E-02
teman [Libya]	0.037 285 6	3.728 560 8E-02
teminye [Syria]	0.414 937 8	4.149 377 6E-01
teneka [Iraq]	0.054 993 4	5.499 340 1E-02
teneka [Somalia]	0.055 555 6	5.555 555 6E-02
teng [Burma, dry]	0.024 440 9	2.444 091 4E-02
thamardi tin [Burma, dry]	0.024 440 9	2.444 091 4E-02
thamardi tinn [Burma]	0.008 147 2	8.147 243 5E-03
thanan [Thailand]	1	1.000 000 0E+00
thang [Cambodia]	0.033 333 3	3.333 333 3E-02
thang [Laos]	0.005	5.000 000 0E-03
thang [Thailand]	0.05	5.000 000 0E-02
thang [Vietnam]	0.5	5.000 000 0E-01
thang louang [Laos]	0.025	2.500 000 0E-02
thoum [Yemen]	0.02	2.000 000 0E-02
thung [Vietnam]	0.05	5.000 000 0E-02
tierce [UK]	0.005 235 6	5.235 602 1E-03
tin [Burma]	0.024 441 7	2.444 172 7E-02
tin han [Burma]	0.024 441 7	2.444 172 7E-02
tinaja [Philippines]	0.020 833 3	2.083 333 3E-02
tinja [Philippines]	0.020 833 3	2.083 333 3E-02
tipree [Ceylon]	1.161 440 2	1.161 440 2E+00
tipree [India]	1.162 520 3	1.162 520 3E+00
to [Japan]	0.055 435 4	5.543 544 5E-02
tomini [Morocco]	0.171 526 6	1.715 265 9E-01
tomna [Malta]	0.054 993 4	5.499 340 1E-02
tonde [Denmark, dry]	0.007 189 1	7.189 072 6E-03
tonde [Denmark, liquid]	0.007 610 4	7.610 350 1E-03
tonel [Portugal]	0.001 162 8	1.162 790 7E-03
tonelada [Argentina]	0.000 971 8	9.718 361 9E-04
tonelada [Portugal]	0.001 148 8	1.148 765 1E-03
tonneau [Belgium, wine]	0.01	1.000 000 0E-02
tonneau [Portugal]	0.001 162 8	1.162 790 7E-03
tonnelada [Portugal]	0.001 148 1	1.148 105 6E-03
toque [Seychelles]	0.045 454 5	4.545 454 5E-02
tou [China]	0.1	1.000 000 0E-01
toumnah [Egypt]	3.878 976	3.878 976 0E+00
touque [Cambodia]	0.055 555 6	5.555 555 6E-02

Convert From
Convert To

Convert From / Convert To	Standard	Scientific
		<Type of Unit>
	Standard	Scientific

liter (continued) <volume>

	Standard	Scientific
touque [Seychelles]	0.043 975 8	4.397 576 1E−02
trug [US, mortar]	0.042 568	4.256 804 5E−02
tun [Straits Settlements]	0.000 872 9	8.729 050 3E−04
tun [UK, liquid]	0.001 018 4	1.018 376 1E−03
tun [US, liquid]	0.001 048 3	1.048 301 8E−03
tunna [Finland]	0.007 959 9	7.959 882 2E−03
tunna [Sweden]	0.006 821 3	6.821 282 4E−03
tunnia [Finland, grain]	0.006 065	6.065 017 0E−03
tunnia [Finland, liquid]	0.007 959 9	7.959 882 2E−03
urna [Rome, ancient, liquid]	0.076 923 1	7.692 307 7E−02
uyen [Vietnam, rice, milled]	1	1.000 000 0E+00
vadra [Romania]	0.065 789 5	6.578 947 4E−02
vat [Netherlands]	0.001 073 9	1.073 883 2E−03
vedro [Bulgaria]	0.1	1.000 000 0E−01
vedro [Russia]	0.081 300 8	8.130 081 3E−02
velte [France, liquid]	0.134 210 2	1.342 101 7E−01
velte [Mauritius]	0.134 219 2	1.342 191 8E−01
viacka [Romania]	0.070 671 4	7.067 137 8E−02
vidro [Russia]	0.081 300 8	8.130 081 3E−02
vierd [Netherlands]	0.146 735 1	1.467 351 4E−01
vierling [Germany]	0.180 564 1	1.805 640 8E−01
viertel [Austria]	0.064 935 1	6.493 506 5E−02
viertel [Denmark]	0.129 366 1	1.293 661 1E−01
viertel [Germany, dry]	0.072 780 2	7.278 020 4E−02
viertel [Switzerland]	0.066 666 7	6.666 666 7E−02
viertelein [Germany]	5.778 008 9	5.778 008 9E+00
viertelsaum [Switzerland, liquid]	0.026 666 7	2.666 666 7E−02
wanche [Ethiopia]	3.333 333 3	3.333 333 3E+00
weba [Tunisia, cereals]	0.027 495 9	2.749 594 4E−02
wedro [Russia]	0.081 300 8	8.130 081 3E−02
weiba [Egypt]	0.030 303	3.030 303 0E−02
wey [UK]	0.000 687 4	6.874 236 5E−04
whiba [Tunisia]	0.025	2.500 000 0E−02
wiba [Tunisia, cereals]	0.027 495 9	2.749 594 4E−02
Winchester wine gallon [UK]	0.264 172 1	2.641 720 5E−01
wise [Netherlands]	0.001	1.000 000 0E−03
xeste [Greece, ancient]	1.886 792 5	1.886 792 5E+00
zah [Tunisia, cereals]	0.329 924 1	3.299 241 2E−01
zak [Netherlands]	0.012 227 9	1.222 792 9E−02
zalay [Burma]	7.917 656 4	7.917 656 4E+00
zarf [Turkey]	0.434 782 6	4.347 826 1E−01
zayoot [Burma]	0.990 099	9.900 990 1E−01
zudda [Arabia]	0.158 227 9	1.582 278 5E−01

liter [pre-1964] <volume>

	Standard	Scientific
barrel [UK]	0.006 110 4	6.110 428 0E−03
barrel [US, liquid]	0.008 386 6	8.386 649 2E−03
barrel [US, petroleum]	0.006 29	6.289 986 9E−03
cubic decimeter	1.000 028	1.000 028 0E+00
cubic foot	0.035 315 7	3.531 565 6E−02
cubic inch	61.025 453	6.102 545 3E+01
cubic meter	0.001	1.000 028 0E−03
cup [Canada, measuring]	4.399 508 1	4.399 508 1E+00
cup [US, measuring]	4.226 871 2	4.226 871 2E+00
drachm [UK, liquid]	281.568 52	2.815 685 2E+02
dram [Canada, liquid]	281.568 52	2.815 685 2E+02
dram [US, liquid]	270.519 76	2.705 197 6E+02
drop [US, liquid]	12,173.389	1.217 338 9E+04
drum [US, liquid]	0.004 803 3	4.803 262 7E−03
gallon [Canada, liquid]	0.219 975 4	2.199 754 1E−01
gallon [UK, dry or liquid]	0.219 975 4	2.199 754 1E−01
gallon [US, liquid]	0.264 179 5	2.641 794 5E−01

Convert To	Standard	Scientific
gill [UK]	7.039 213	7.039 213 0E+00
gill [US]	8.453 742 4	8.453 742 4E+00
liter	1.000 028	1.000 028 0E+00
ounce [UK, liquid]	35.196 065	3.519 606 5E+01
ounce [US, liquid]	33.814 969	3.381 496 9E+01
pint [UK]	1.759 803 3	1.759 803 3E+00
pint [US, liquid]	2.113 435 6	2.113 435 6E+00
quart [UK]	0.879 901 6	8.799 016 3E−01
quart [US, liquid]	1.056 717 8	1.056 717 8E+00
scruple [UK, liquid]	844.705 56	8.447 055 6E+02
tablespoon [Canada, measuring]	70.392 25	7.039 225 0E+01
tablespoon [US, measuring]	67.629 939	6.762 993 9E+01
teaspoon [Canada, measuring]	211.176 75	2.111 767 5E+02
teaspoon [US, measuring]	202.889 82	2.028 898 2E+02
Winchester wine gallon [UK]	0.264 179 5	2.641 794 5E−01

liter atmosphere   <energy>

Convert To	Standard	Scientific
Btu [I.T.]	0.096 037 6	9.603 757 6E−02
calorie [I.T.]	24.201 06	2.420 106 0E+01
calorie [kilogram, I.T.]	0.024 201 1	2.420 106 0E−02
centigrade heat unit [I.T.]	0.053 354 2	5.335 420 5E−02
centimeter gram-force	1,033,227.5	1.033 227 5E+06
cubic centimeter atmosphere	1,000	1.000 000 0E+03
cubic foot atmosphere	0.035 314 7	3.531 466 7E−02
foot pound-force	74.733 485	7.473 348 5E+01
foot poundal	2,404.478 8	2.404 478 8E+03
gram calorie	24.206 842	2.420 684 2E+01
horsepower hour	0.000 037 7	3.774 418 4E−05
horsepower hour [metric]	0.000 038 3	3.826 768 3E−05
inch ounce-force	14,348.829	1.434 882 9E+04
inch pound-force	896.801 82	8.968 018 2E+02
joule	101.325	1.013 250 0E+02
kilocalorie [I.T.]	0.024 201 1	2.420 106 0E−02
kilogram calorie [15 °C, NBS, 1939]	0.024 206 8	2.420 684 2E−02
kilogram square meter/square second	101.325	1.013 250 0E+02
kilopond meter	10.332 275	1.033 227 5E+01
liter atmosphere [pre-1964]	0.999 972	9.999 720 0E−01
megaerg	1,013.25	1.013 250 0E+03
megalerg	1,013.25	1.013 250 0E+03
meter kilogram-force	10.332 275	1.033 227 5E+01
newton meter	101.325	1.013 250 0E+02
pferdestarkenstunde [Germany]	0.000 038 3	3.826 768 3E−05
watthour	0.028 145 8	2.814 583 3E−02
wattsecond	101.325	1.013 250 0E+02

liter atmosphere [pre-1964]   <energy>

Convert To	Standard	Scientific
Btu [I.T.]	0.096 040 3	9.604 025 9E−02
calorie [I.T.]	24.201 738	2.420 173 8E+01
calorie [kilogram, I.T.]	0.024 201 7	2.420 173 8E−02
centigrade heat unit [I.T.]	0.053 355 7	5.335 569 9E−02
cubic centimeter atmosphere	1,000.028	1.000 028 0E+03
cubic foot atmosphere	0.035 315 7	3.531 565 6E−02
foot pound-force	74.735 577	7.473 557 7E+01
foot poundal	2,404.546 1	2.404 546 1E+03
frigorie [France]	0.024 207 5	2.420 752 0E+01
gram calorie	24.207 52	2.420 752 0E+01
horsepower hour	0.000 037 7	3.774 524 1E−05
horsepower hour [metric]	0.000 038 3	3.826 875 0E−05
inch ounce-force	14,349.231	1.434 923 1E+04
inch pound-force	896.826 93	8.968 269 3E+02
joule	101.327 84	1.013 278 4E+02
kilocalorie [I.T.]	0.024 201 7	2.420 173 8E−02
kilogram calorie [15 °C, NBS, 1939]	0.024 207 5	2.420 752 0E−02
kilopond meter	10.332 564	1.033 256 4E+01
liter atmosphere	1.000 028	1.000 028 0E+00

Convert To	Standard	Scientific
meter kilogram-force	10.332 564	1.033 256 4E+01
newton meter	101.327 84	1.013 278 4E+02
watthour	0.028 146 6	2.814 662 1E-02
wattsecond	101.327 84	1.013 278 4E+02
liter/100 kilometer		**<fuel consumption, SI>**
cubic meter/meter	0.000 1	1.000 000 0E-04
gallon/mile [US, liquid/international]	42.514 371	4.251 437 1E+01
mile/gallon [international/US, liquid]	2.352 145 8E+02 / (liter/100 kilometer)	
liter/centimeter day		**<kinematic viscosity>**
centistokes	1.157 407 4	1.157 407 4E+00
square centimeter/hour	41.666 666 7	4.166 666 7E+01
square foot/day	1.076 391	1.076 391E+00
square inch/hour	6.458 346 3	6.458 346 3E+00
square meter/second	0.000 001 2	1.157 407 4E-06
square millimeter/second	1.157 407 4	1.157 407 4E+00
liter/centimeter hour		**<kinematic viscosity>**
centistokes	27.777 777 8	2.777 777 8E+01
liter/centimeter day	24	2.400 000 0E+01
square centimeter/minute	16.666 666 7	1.666 666 7E+01
square foot/hour	1.076 391	1.076 391E+00
square inch/minute	2.583 338 5	2.583 338 5E+00
square meter/day	2.4	2.400 000 0E+00
square meter/second	0.000 027 8	2.777 777 8E-05
square millimeter/second	27.777 777 8	2.777 777 8E+01
liter/centimeter minute		**<kinematic viscosity>**
liter/centimeter hour	60	6.000 000 0E+01
poise cubic centimeter/gram	16.666 666 7	1.666 666 7E+01
square centimeter/second	16.666 666 7	1.666 666 7E+01
square foot/minute	1.076 391	1.076 391E+00
square inch/second	2.583 338 5	2.583 338 5E+00
square meter/hour	6	6.000 000 0E+00
square meter/second	0.001 666 7	1.666 666 7E-03
square millimeter/second	1,666.666 67	1.666 666 7E+03
stokes	16.666 666 7	1.666 666 7E+01
liter/centimeter second		**<kinematic viscosity>**
liter/centimeter minute	60	6.000 000 0E+01
square centimeter/second	1,000	1.000 000 0E+03
square foot/second	1.076 391	1.076 391E+00
square inch/second	155.000 31	1.550 003 1E+02
square meter/minute	6	6.000 000 0E+00
square meter/second	0.1	1.000 000 0E-01
stokes	1,000	1.000 000 0E+03
liter/cubic meter		**<concentration, volume basis>**
cubic foot/cubic foot	0.001	1.000 000 0E-03
cubic meter/cubic meter	0.001	1.000 000 0E-03
gallon/cubic foot [US, liquid]	0.007 480 5	7.480 519 5E-03
liter/day		**<flow rate, volume basis>**
barrel/day [UK]	0.006 110 3	6.110 256 9E-03
barrel/day [US, federal]	0.008 521 7	8.521 679 1E-03
barrel/day [US, liquid]	0.008 386 4	8.386 414 4E-03
barrel/day [US, petroleum]	0.006 289 8	6.289 810 8E-03
centiliter/day	100	1.000 000 0E+02
centiliter/hour	4.166 666 7	4.166 666 7E+00
cubic centimeter/day	1,000	1.000 000 0E+03
cubic centimeter/hour	41.666 666 7	4.166 666 7E+01
cubic decimeter/day	1	1.000 000 0E+00
cubic foot/day	0.035 314 7	3.531 466 7E-02
cubic inch/hour	2.542 656	2.542 656 0E+00
cubic meter/day	0.001	1.000 000 0E-03
cubic meter/second	<<<	1.157 407 4E-08
cubic millimeter/second	11.574 074 1	1.157 407 4E+01

| Convert From | | <Type of Unit> |
Convert To	Standard	Scientific
deciliter/day	10	1.000 000 0E+01
dekaliter/day	0.1	1.000 000 0E−01
gallon/day [UK]	0.219 969 2	2.199 692 5E−01
gallon/day [US, liquid]	0.264 172 1	2.641 720 5E−01
hectoliter/day	0.01	1.000 000 0E−02
kiloliter/day	0.001	1.000 000 0E−03
lambda/second	11.574 074 1	1.157 407 4E+01
liter/day [pre-1964]	0.999 972	9.999 720 0E−01
milliliter/day	1,000	1.000 000 0E+03
milliliter/hour	41.666 666 7	4.166 666 7E+01
ounce/hour [UK, liquid]	1.466 461 7	1.466 461 7E+00
ounce/hour [US, liquid]	1.408 917 6	1.408 917 6E+00
stere/day	0.001	1.000 000 0E−03
liter/day [pre-1964]		**<flow rate, volume basis>**
barrel/day [UK]	0.006 110 4	6.110 428 0E−03
barrel/day [US, federal]	0.008 521 9	8.521 917 7E−03
barrel/day [US, liquid]	0.008 386 6	8.386 649 2E−03
barrel/day [US, petroleum]	0.006 29	6.289 986 9E−03
centiliter/day	100.002 8	1.000 028 0E+02
centiliter/hour	4.166 783 3	4.166 783 3E+00
cubic centimeter/day	1,000.028	1.000 028 0E+03
cubic centimeter/hour	41.667 833 3	4.166 783 3E+01
cubic decimeter/day	1.000 028	1.000 028 0E+00
cubic foot/day	0.035 315 7	3.531 565 6E−02
cubic inch/hour	2.542 727 2	2.542 727 2E+00
cubic meter/day	0.001	1.000 028 0E−03
cubic meter/second	<<<	1.157 439 8E−08
cubic millimeter/second	11.574 398 1	1.157 439 8E+01
cubic yard/day	0.001 308	1.307 987 2E−03
deciliter/day	10.000 28	1.000 028 0E+01
dekaliter/day	0.100 002 8	1.000 028 0E+01
gallon/day [UK]	0.219 975 4	2.199 754 1E−01
gallon/day [US, liquid]	0.264 179 4	2.641 794 5E−01
hectoliter/day	0.010 000 3	1.000 028 0E−02
kiloliter/day	0.001	1.000 028 0E−03
liter/day	1.000 028	1.000 028 0E+00
milliliter/day	1,000.028	1.000 028 0E+00
milliliter/hour	41.667 833 3	4.166 783 3E+01
ounce/hour [UK, liquid]	1.466 502 7	1.466 502 7E+00
ounce/hour [US, liquid]	1.408 957 1	1.408 957 1E+00
stere/day	0.001	1.000 028 0E−03
liter/hour		**<flow rate, volume basis>**
barrel/day [UK]	0.146 646 2	1.466 461 7E−01
barrel/day [US, federal]	0.204 520 3	2.045 203 0E−01
barrel/day [US, liquid]	0.201 273 9	2.012 739 5E−01
barrel/day [US, petroleum]	0.150 955 5	1.509 554 6E−01
centiliter/hour	100	1.000 000 0E+02
centiliter/minute	1.666 666 7	1.666 666 7E+00
cubic centimeter/hour	1,000	1.000 000 0E+03
cubic centimeter/minute	16.666 666 7	1.666 666 7E+01
cubic decimeter/hour	1	1.000 000 0E+00
cubic foot/hour	0.847 552	8.475 520 0E−01
cubic inch/minute	1.017 062 4	1.017 062 4E+00
cubic meter/hour	0.001	1.000 000 0E−03
cubic meter/second	0.000 000 3	2.777 777 8E−07
cubic millimeter/second	277.777 778	2.777 777 8E+02
deciliter/hour	10	1.000 000 0E+01
dekaliter/day	2.4	2.400 000 0E+00
gallon/day [UK]	5.279 262	5.279 262 0E+00
gallon/day [US, liquid]	6.340 129 3	6.340 129 3E+00
hectoliter/day	0.24	2.400 000 0E+00
lambda/second	277.777 778	2.777 777 8E+02
liter/hour [pre-1964]	0.999 972	9.999 720 0E−01

	Standard	Scientific
milliliter/minute	16.666 666 7	1.666 666 7E+01
ounce/hour [UK, liquid]	35.195 08	3.519 508 0E+01
ounce/hour [US, liquid]	33.814 023	3.381 402 3E+01
stere/day	0.024	2.400 000 0E-02
stere/hour	0.001	1.000 000 0E-03

liter/hour [pre-1964] <flow rate, volume basis>

	Standard	Scientific
barrel/day [UK]	0.146 650 3	1.466 502 7E-01
barrel/day [US, federal]	0.204 526	2.045 260 3E-01
barrel/day [US, liquid]	0.201 279 6	2.012 795 8E-01
barrel/day [US, petroleum]	0.150 959 9	1.509 596 9E-01
centiliter/minute	1.666 713 3	1.666 713 3E+00
cubic centimeter/minute	16.667 133 3	1.666 713 3E+01
cubic decimeter/hour	1.000 028	1.000 028 0E+00
cubic foot/day	0.847 575 7	8.475 757 3E-01
cubic inch/minute	1.017 090 9	1.017 090 9E+00
cubic meter/day	0.024 000 7	2.400 067 2E-02
cubic millimeter/second	277.785 556	2.777 855 6E+02
cubic yard/day	0.031 391 7	3.139 169 4E-02
deciliter/hour	10.000 28	1.000 028 0E+01
dekaliter/day	2.400 067 2	2.400 067 2E+00
gallon/day [UK]	5.279 409 8	5.279 409 8E+00
gallon/day [US, liquid]	6.340 306 8	6.340 306 8E+00
hectoliter/day	0.240 006 7	2.400 067 2E-01
kiloliter/day	0.024 000 7	2.400 067 2E-02
lambda/second	277.785 556	2.777 855 6E+02
liter/day	24.000 672	2.400 067 2E+01
liter/day [pre-1964]	24	2.400 000 0E+01
liter/hour	1.000 028	1.000 028 0E+00
milliliter/minute	16.667 133 3	1.666 713 3E+01
ounce/hour [UK, liquid]	35.196 065	3.519 606 5E+01
ounce/hour [US, liquid]	33.814 969	3.381 496 9E+01
stere/day	0.024 000 7	2.400 067 2E-02

liter/joule <specific fuel consumption, volume basis>

	Standard	Scientific
cubic meter/joule	0.001	1.000 000 0E-03

liter/kilometer <fuel consumption, SI>

	Standard	Scientific
cubic meter/meter	0.000 001	1.000 000 0E-06
gallon/mile [US, liquid/international]	0.425 143 7	4.251 437 1E-01

liter/kilowatthour <specific fuel consumption, volume basis>

	Standard	Scientific
cubic meter/joule	<<<	2.777 777 8E-10

liter/meter <fuel consumption, SI>

	Standard	Scientific
cubic meter/meter	0.001	1.000 000 0E-03
gallon/mile [US, liquid/international]	425.143 71	4.251 437 1E+02

liter/minute <flow rate, volume basis>

	Standard	Scientific
acre foot/day	0.001 167 4	1.167 427 0E-03
acre foot/day [US, survey]	0.001 167 4	1.167 420 0E-03
acre inch/day	0.014 009 1	1.400 912 4E-02
barrel/day [UK]	8.798 769 9	8.798 769 9E+00
barrel/day [US, federal]	12.271 217 9	1.227 121 8E+01
barrel/day [US, liquid]	12.076 436 7	1.207 643 7E+01
barrel/day [US, petroleum]	9.057 327 5	9.057 327 5E+00
centiliter/minute	100	1.000 000 0E+02
centiliter/second	1.666 666 7	1.666 666 7E+00
cubic centimeter/second	16.666 666 7	1.666 666 7E+01
cubic decimeter/minute	1	1.000 000 0E+00
cubic dekameter/day	0.001 44	1.440 000 0E-03
cubic foot/hour	2.118 88	2.118 880 0E+00
cubic inch/second	1.017 062 4	1.017 062 4E+00
cubic meter/day	1.44	1.440 000 0E+00
cubic meter/second	0.000 016 7	1.666 666 7E-05
cubic yard/day	1.883 448 9	1.883 448 9E+00
deciliter/minute	10	1.000 000 0E+01
dekaliter/hour	6	6.000 000 0E+00

Convert From / Convert To	Standard	Scientific
gallon/hour [UK]	13.198 154 9	1.319 815 5E+01
gallon/hour [US, liquid]	15.850 323 1	1.585 032 3E+01
hectoliter/day	14.4	1.440 000 0E+01
kiloliter/day	1.44	1.440 000 0E+00
liter/hour	60	6.000 000 0E+01
liter/hour [pre-1964]	59.998 32	5.999 832 0E+01
liter/minute [pre-1964]	0.999 972	9.999 720 0E-01
milliliter/minute	1,000	1.000 000 0E+03
milliliter/second	16.666 666 7	1.666 666 7E+01
ounce/minute [UK, liquid]	35.195 08	3.519 508 0E+01
ounce/minute [US, liquid]	33.814 023	3.381 402 3E+01
petrograd standard/day	0.308 200 7	3.082 007 3E-01
stere/day	1.44	1.440 000 0E+00
thousand cubic foot/day	0.050 853 1	5.085 312 0E-02
liter/minute [pre-1964]	**<flow rate, volume basis>**	
acre foot/day	0.001 167 5	1.167 459 7E-03
acre foot/day [US, survey]	0.001 167 5	1.167 452 7E-03
acre inch/day	0.014 009 5	1.400 951 6E-02
barrel/day [UK]	8.799 016 3	8.799 016 3E+00
barrel/day [US, federal]	12.271 561 5	1.227 156 2E+01
barrel/day [US, liquid]	12.076 774 8	1.207 677 5E+01
barrel/day [US, petroleum]	9.057 581 1	9.057 581 1E+00
centiliter/minute	100.002 8	1.000 028 0E+02
centiliter/second	1.666 713 3	1.666 713 3E+00
cubic centimeter/minute	1,000.028	1.000 028 0E+03
cubic centimeter/second	16.667 133 3	1.666 713 3E+01
cubic decimeter/minute	1.000 028	1.000 028 0E+00
cubic foot/hour	2.118 939 3	2.118 939 3E+00
cubic inch/second	1.017 090 9	1.017 090 9E+00
cubic meter/day	1.440 040 3	1.440 040 3E+00
cubic meter/second	0.000 016 7	1.666 713 3E-05
cubic yard/day	1.883 501 6	1.883 501 6E+00
dekaliter/hour	6.000 168	6.000 168 0E+00
dekaliter/minute	0.100 002 8	1.000 028 0E-01
gallon/hour [UK]	13.198 524 4	1.319 852 4E+01
gallon/hour [US, liquid]	15.850 767	1.585 076 7E+01
hectoliter/day	14.400 403 2	1.440 040 3E+01
kiloliter/day	1.440 040 3	1.440 040 3E+00
liter/minute	1.000 028	1.000 028 0E+00
milliliter/second	16.667 133 3	1.666 713 3E+01
ounce/minute [UK, liquid]	35.196 065	3.519 606 5E+01
ounce/minute [US, liquid]	33.814 969	3.381 496 9E+01
petrograd standard/day	0.308 209 4	3.082 093 6E-01
stere/day	1.440 040 3	1.440 040 3E+00
thousand cubic foot/day	0.050 854 5	5.085 454 4E-02
liter/mole	**<molar volume>**	
cubic decimeter/mole	1	1.000 000 0E+00
cubic meter/mole	0.001	1.000 000 0E-03
liter/second	**<flow rate, volume basis>**	
acre foot/day	0.070 045 6	7.004 562 0E-02
acre foot/day [US, survey]	0.070 045 2	7.004 520 0E-02
acre inch/day	0.840 547 4	8.405 474 4E-01
barrel/hour [UK]	21.996 924 8	2.199 692 5E+01
barrel/hour [US, federal]	30.678 044 8	3.067 804 5E+01
barrel/hour [US, liquid]	30.191 091 7	3.019 109 2E+01
barrel/hour [US, petroleum]	22.643 318 8	2.264 331 9E+01
centiliter/second	100	1.000 000 0E+02
cubic centimeter/second	1,000	1.000 000 0E+03
cubic decimeter/second	1	1.000 000 0E+00
cubic foot/minute	2.118 88	2.118 880 0E+00
cubic inch/second	61.023 744 1	6.102 374 4E+01
cubic meter/hour	3.6	3.600 000 0E+00
cubic yard/hour	4.708 622 2	4.708 622 2E+00

	Standard	Scientific
deciliter/second	10	1.000 000 0E+01
dekaliter/minute	6	6.000 000 0E+00
gallon/minute [UK]	13.198 154 9	1.319 815 5E+01
gallon/minute [US, liquid]	15.850 323 1	1.585 032 3E+01
hectoliter/hour	36	3.600 000 0E+01
kiloliter/hour	3.6	3.600 000 0E+00
liter/minute	60	6.000 000 0E+01
liter/minute [pre-1964]	59.998 32	5.999 832 0E+01
liter/second [pre-1964]	0.999 972	9.999 720 0E-01
ounce/second [UK, liquid]	35.195 08	3.519 508 0E+01
ounce/second [US, liquid]	33.814 023	3.381 402 3E+01
petrograd standard/day	18.492 044	1.849 204 4E+01
stere/hour	3.6	3.600 000 0E+00
thousand cubic foot/day	3.051 187 2	3.051 187 2E+00

liter/second [pre-1964] \<flow rate, volume basis\>

	Standard	Scientific
acre foot/day	0.070 047 6	7.004 758 1E-02
acre foot/day [US, survey]	0.070 047 2	7.004 716 1E-02
acre inch/day	0.840 571	8.405 709 8E-01
barrel/hour [UK]	21.997 540 7	2.199 754 1E+01
barrel/hour [US, federal]	30.678 903 8	3.067 890 4E+01
barrel/hour [US, liquid]	30.191 937	3.019 193 7E+01
barrel/hour [US, petroleum]	22.643 952 8	2.264 395 3E+01
centiliter/second	100.002 8	1.000 028 0E+02
cubic centimeter/second	1,000.028	1.000 028 0E+03
cubic decimeter/second	1.000 028	1.000 028 0E+00
cubic dekameter/day	0.086 402 4	8.640 241 9E-02
cubic foot/minute	2.118 939 3	2.118 939 3E+00
cubic inch/second	61.025 452 8	6.102 545 3E+01
cubic meter/hour	3.600 100 8	3.600 100 8E+00
cubic meter/second	0.001	1.000 028 0E-03
cubic yard/hour	4.708 754 1	4.708 754 1E+00
deciliter/second	10.000 28	1.000 028 0E+01
dekaliter/minute	6.000 168	6.000 168 0E+01
gallon/minute [UK]	13.198 524 4	1.319 852 4E+01
gallon/minute [US, liquid]	15.850 767	1.585 076 7E+01
hectoliter/hour	36.001 008	3.600 100 8E+01
kiloliter/hour	3.600 100 8	3.600 100 8E+00
liter/second	1.000 028	1.000 028 0E+00
ounce/second [UK, liquid]	35.196 065	3.519 606 5E+01
ounce/second [US, liquid]	33.814 969	3.381 496 9E+01
petrograd standard/day	18.492 561	1.849 256 1E+01
stere/hour	3.600 100 8	3.600 100 8E+00
thousand cubic foot/day	3.051 272 6	3.051 272 6E+00

litra [Greece, ancient] \<mass, special - see page 29\>

	Standard	Scientific
gram	326.4	3.264 000 0E+02

litra [Rome, ancient] \<mass, special - see page 29\>

	Standard	Scientific
gram	327.45	3.274 500 0E+02

litre [Cyprus] \<volume, special - see page 29\>

	Standard	Scientific
liter	3.182	3.182 000 0E+00

litre [Cyprus] \<mass, special - see page 29\>

	Standard	Scientific
kilogram	2.286	2.286 000 0E+00

litre [Ethiopia] \<mass, special - see page 29\>

	Standard	Scientific
gram	311	3.110 000 0E+02

litre [Greece] \<mass, special - see page 29\>

	Standard	Scientific
gram	454	4.540 000 0E+02

litre [Indonesia, rice, milled] \<mass, special - see page 29\>

	Standard	Scientific
kilogram	0.8	8.000 000 0E-01

litre [Romania] \<mass, special - see page 29\>

	Standard	Scientific
gram	322.3	3.223 000 0E+02

litro [Venezuela] \<mass, special - see page 29\>

	Standard	Scientific
kilogram	2.5	2.500 000 0E+00

| Convert From | | \<Type of Unit\> |
Convert To	Standard	Scientific
litro [Venezuela]		\<area, special - see page 29\>
square meter	625	6.250 000 0E+02
litron [France, dry]		\<volume, special - see page 29\>
liter	0.813	8.130 000 0E-01
littre [Romania]		\<mass, special - see page 29\>
gram	322.3	3.223 000 0E+02
livre [Belgium]		\<mass, special - see page 29\>
kilogram	0.5	5.000 000 0E-01
livre [Cambodia]		\<mass, special - see page 29\>
gram	600	6.000 000 0E+02
livre [France]		\<mass, special - see page 29\>
gram	489.506	4.895 060 0E+02
livre [Russia, apothecary]		\<mass, special - see page 29\>
gram	358.323 4	3.583 234 0E+02
livre [Spain]		\<mass, special - see page 29\>
gram	460.093	4.600 930 0E+02
livre [Switzerland]		\<mass, special - see page 29\>
kilogram	0.5	5.000 000 0E-01
livre commune [France]		\<mass, special - see page 29\>
gram	489.5	4.895 000 0E+02
livre de Charlemagne [France]		\<mass, special - see page 29\>
gram	367.1	3.671 000 0E+02
livre de pharmacie [Switzerland]		\<mass, special - see page 29\>
gram	375	3.750 000 0E+02
livre esterlin [France]		\<mass, special - see page 29\>
gram	367.1	3.671 000 0E+02
livre francaise [Haiti]		\<mass, special - see page 29\>
gram	189.505 85	1.895 058 5E+02
livre poids de marc [France]		\<mass, special - see page 29\>
kilogram	489.51	4.895 100 0E+02
livre poids de table [France]		\<mass, special - see page 29\>
gram	407.93	4.079 300 0E+02
livre usuelle [France]		\<mass, special - see page 29\>
gram	500	5.000 000 0E+02
load [Cyprus]		\<volume, special - see page 29\>
liter	163.654 6	1.636 546 0E+02
load [Gambia, cocoa]		\<mass, special - see page 29\>
kilogram	27.2	2.720 000 0E+01
load [Ghana, cocoa]		\<mass, special - see page 29\>
kilogram	27.2	2.720 000 0E+01
load [Nigeria, cocoa]		\<mass, special - see page 29\>
kilogram	27.2	2.720 000 0E+01
load [Sierra Leone, cocoa]		\<mass, special - see page 29\>
kilogram	27.2	2.720 000 0E+01
loan [Philippines]		\<area, special - see page 29\>
are	2.795	2.795 000 0E+00
lod [Denmark]		\<mass, special - see page 29\>
gram	15.625	1.562 500 0E+01
lod [Norway]		\<mass, special - see page 29\>
gram	15.57	1.557 000 0E+01
lod [Sweden]		\<mass, special - see page 29\>
gram	13.283 6	1.328 360 0E+01
lof [Russia]		\<volume, special - see page 29\>
liter	64.722 22	6.472 222 0E+01

Convert From	<Type of Unit>	
Convert To	Standard	Scientific

log [Hebrew, ancient] — <volume, special - see page 29>
  liter --- 0.35 ---- 3.500 000 0E-01

logarike litra [Greece, ancient] — <mass, special - see page 29>
  gram -- 320 ---- 3.200 000 0E+02

logh [Hebrew, ancient] — <volume, special - see page 29>
  liter -- 0.319 ---- 3.190 000 0E-01

logh [Rome, ancient] — <volume, special - see page 29>
  liter -- 0.53 ---- 5.300 000 0E-01

loket [Czechoslovakia] — <length, special - see page 29>
  centimeter --- 59.3 ---- 5.930 000 0E+01

lokiec [Poland] — <length, special - see page 29>
  meter --- 0.576 ---- 5.760 000 0E-01

lolti [Russia] — <mass, special - see page 29>
  gram -- 12.8 ---- 1.280 000 0E+01

lood [Indonesia] — <mass, special - see page 29>
  gram -- 15.44 ---- 1.544 000 0E+01

lood [Netherlands] — <mass, special - see page 29>
  kilogram --- 10 ---- 1.000 000 0E+01

loode [Netherlands] — <mass, special - see page 29>
  gram -- 10 ---- 1.000 000 0E+01

loot [Netherlands] — <mass, special - see page 29>
  gram -- 15.4 ---- 1.540 000 0E+01

lot [Germany] — <mass, special - see page 29>
  gram -- 10 ---- 1.000 000 0E+01

lot [Russia] — <mass, special - see page 29>
  gram -- 12.797 26 ---- 1.279 726 0E+01

lot [Switzerland] — <mass, special - see page 29>
  gram -- 15.625 ---- 1.562 500 0E+01

loth [Austria] — <mass, special - see page 29>
  gram -- 17.5 ---- 1.750 000 0E+01

loth [Germany] — <mass, special - see page 29>
  gram -- 10 ---- 1.000 000 0E+01

loth [Netherlands] — <mass, special - see page 29>
  gram -- 10 ---- 1.000 000 0E+01

loth [Norway] — <mass, special - see page 29>
  gram -- 15.6 ---- 1.560 000 0E+01

loth [Poland] — <mass, special - see page 29>
  gram -- 12.67 ---- 1.267 000 0E+01

loth [Russia] — <mass, special - see page 29>
  gram -- 12.8 ---- 1.280 000 0E+01

loth [Switzerland] — <mass, special - see page 29>
  gram -- 15.625 ---- 1.562 500 0E+01

loudness unit — <loudness level>
  noy --- 0.001 ---- 1.000 000 0E-03
  phon -- 0.04 ---- 4.000 000 0E-02
  sone -- 0.001 ---- 1.000 000 0E-03

ludra [Turkey] — <mass, special - see page 29>
  kilogram --- 0.564 ---- 5.640 000 0E-01

lugim [Hebrew, ancient] — <volume, special - see page 29>
  centiliter -- 53 ---- 5.300 000 0E+01

lumen — <luminous flux>
  candela steradian ---------------------------------- 1 ---- 1.000 000 0E+00
  lux square meter ----------------------------------- 1 ---- 1.000 000 0E+00
  watt [at 540 THz] ------------------------------- 0.001 464 1 ---- 1.464 128 8E-03
  watt [at 5550 angstrom] ------------------- 0.001 470 6 ---- 1.470 588 2E-03
  watt [green light at 100% efficiency] ---------- 0.001 459 9 ---- 1.459 854 0E-03

Convert From	<Type of Unit>	
Convert To	Standard	Scientific

lumen [green light at 100% efficiency] `<power>`

Btu/hour [I.T.]	0.004 981 2	4.981 228 7E–03
Btu/hour [thermoc.]	0.004 984 6	4.984 562 5E–03
calorie/hour [I.T.]	1.255 248 5	1.255 248 5E+00
calorie/hour [thermoc.]	1.256 088 5	1.256 088 5E+00
centigrade heat unit/hour [mean]	0.002 765 2	2.765 215 4E–03
cubic meter atmosphere/hour	51.867 5	5.186 750 0E+01
dyne centimeter/second	14,598.54	1.459 854 0E+04
erg/second	14,598.54	1.459 854 0E+04
foot pound-force/hour	3.876 239	3.876 239 0E+00
foot poundal/minute	2.078 571 7	2.078 571 7E+00
gram-force centimeter/second	14.886 368	1.488 636 8E+01
horsepower	0.000 002	1.957 696 5E–06
horsepower [metric]	0.000 002	1.984 849 1E–06
joule/hour	5.255 474 5	5.255 474 5E+00
kilocalorie/hour [I.T.]	0.001 255 2	1.255 248 5E–03
kilogram square meter/cubic second	0.001 459 9	1.459 854 0E–03
kilogram-force meter/hour	0.535 909 3	5.359 092 5E–01
kilopond meter/hour	0.535 909 3	5.359 092 5E–01
lumen [green light at 5,550 angstrom]	0.992 700 8	9.927 007 5E–01
milliwatt	1.459 854	1.459 854 0E+00
newton meter/hour	5.255 474 5	5.255 474 5E+00
pound square foot/cubic second	0.034 642 9	3.464 286 2E–02
volt ampere	0.001 459 9	1.459 854 0E–03
watt	0.001 459 9	1.459 854 0E–03

lumen [green light at 5,550 angstrom] `<power>`

Btu/hour [I.T.]	0.005 017 9	5.017 855 2E–03
Btu/hour [thermoc.]	0.005 021 2	5.021 213 3E–03
calorie/hour [I.T.]	1.264 478 2	1.264 478 2E+00
calorie/hour [thermoc.]	1.265 324 5	1.265 324 5E+00
centigrade heat unit/hour [mean]	0.002 785 5	2.785 547 8E–03
cubic meter atmosphere/hour	52.248 878	5.224 887 8E+01
dyne centimeter/second	14,705.882	1.470 588 2E+04
erg/second	14,705.882	1.470 588 2E+04
foot pound-force/hour	3.904 740 7	3.904 740 7E+00
foot poundal/minute	2.093 855 3	2.093 855 3E+00
gram-force centimeter/second	14.995 826	1.499 582 6E+01
horsepower	0.000 002	1.972 091 5E–06
horsepower [metric]	0.000 002	1.999 443 5E–06
joule/hour	5.294 117 5	5.294 117 5E+00
kilocalorie/hour [I.T.]	0.001 264 5	1.264 478 2E–03
kilogram square meter/cubic second	0.001 470 6	1.470 588 2E–03
kilogram-force meter/hour	0.539 849 8	5.398 497 5E–01
kilopond meter/hour	0.539 849 8	5.398 497 5E–01
lumen [green light at 100% efficiency]	1.007 352 9	1.007 352 9E+00
milliwatt	1.470 588 2	1.470 588 2E+00
newton meter/hour	5.294 117 5	5.294 117 5E+00
pound square foot/cubic second	0.034 897 6	3.489 758 8E–02
volt ampere	0.001 470 6	1.470 588 2E–03
watt	0.001 470 6	1.470 588 2E–03

lumen [monochromatic radiation of 540 THz] `<power>`

calorie/hour [I.T.]	1.258 924 2	1.258 924 2E+00
foot pound-force/hour	3.887 589 7	3.887 589 7E+00
watt	0.001 464 1	1.464 128 8E–03

lumen hour `<quantity of light>`

joule	5.270 863 8	5.270 863 8E+00
lumen second	3,600	3.600 000 0E+03
lux second square meter	3,600	3.600 000 0E+03
wattsecond [light at 540 THz]	5.270 863 8	5.270 863 8E+00

lumen second `<quantity of light>`

candela second steradian	1	1.000 000 0E+00
joule	0.001 464 1	1.464 128 8E–03

Convert From Convert To	Standard	<Type of Unit> Scientific
lux second square meter	1	1.000 000 0E+00
talbot	1	1.000 000 0E+00
wattsecond [light at 540 THz]	0.001 464 1	1.464 128 8E-03
lumen second/square centimeter		**<light exposure>**
footcandle second	929.030 4	9.290 304 0E+02
lumen second/square foot	929.030 4	9.290 304 0E+02
lumen second/square inch	6.451 6	6.451 600 0E+00
lux second	10,000	1.000 000 0E+04
phot second	1	1.000 000 0E+00
lumen second/square foot		**<light exposure>**
footcandle second	1	1.000 000 0E+00
lumen second/square inch	0.006 944 4	6.944 444 4E-03
lux second	10.763 91	1.076 391 0E+01
milliphot second	1.076 391	1.076 391 0E+00
lumen second/square inch		**<light exposure>**
footcandle second	144	1.440 000 0E+02
kilolux second	1.550 003 1	1.550 003 1E+00
lux second	1,550.003 1	1.550 003 1E+03
phot second	0.155 000 3	1.550 003 1E-01
lumen second/square meter		**<light exposure>**
footcandle second	0.092 903	9.290 304 0E-02
lumen second/square inch	0.000 645 2	6.451 600 0E-04
lux second	1	1.000 000 0E+00
metercandle second	1	1.000 000 0E+00
lumen/square centimeter		**<illuminance>**
footcandle	929.030 4	9.290 304 0E+02
lumen/square inch	6.451 6	6.451 600 0E+00
lumen/square meter	10,000	1.000 000 0E+04
lux	10,000	1.000 000 0E+04
nox	>>>	1.000 000 0E+07
phot	1	1.000 000 0E+00
lumen/square foot		**<illuminance>**
footcandle	1	1.000 000 0E+00
lumen/square inch	0.006 944 4	6.944 444 4E-03
lumen/square meter	10.763 91	1.076 391 0E+01
lux	10.763 91	1.076 391 0E+01
nox	10,763.91	1.076 391 0E+04
phot	0.001 076 4	1.076 391 0E-03
lumen/square inch		**<illuminance>**
footcandle	144	1.440 000 0E+02
lumen/square foot	144	1.440 000 0E+02
lumen/square meter	1,550.003 1	1.550 003 1E+03
lux	1,550.003 1	1.550 003 1E+03
nox	1,550,003.1	1.550 003 1E+06
phot	0.155 000 3	1.550 003 1E-01
lumen/square meter		**<illuminance>**
candela steradian/square meter	1	1.000 000 0E+00
footcandle	0.092 903	9.290 304 0E-02
lumen/square inch	0.000 645 2	6.451 600 0E-04
lux	1	1.000 000 0E+00
metercandle	1	1.000 000 0E+00
nox	1,000	1.000 000 0E+03
phot	0.000 1	1.000 000 0E-04
lumen/steradian		**<luminous intensity>**
bougie nouvelle [France]	1	1.000 000 0E+00
candela	1	1.000 000 0E+00
candle [new]	1	1.000 000 0E+00
hefnerkerze [Germany]	1.089 530 2	1.089 530 2E+00
lux square meter/steradian	1	1.000 000 0E+00
violle	0.049 578 6	4.957 858 2E-02
watt/steradian [at 540 THz]	0.001 464 1	1.464 128 8E-03

lumen/steradian square meter <luminance>

	Standard	Scientific
apostilb [German Hefner]	3.490 658 5	3.490 658 5E+00
apostilb [international]	3.141 592 7	3.141 592 7E+00
blondel	3.141 592 7	3.141 592 7E+00
candela/square foot	0.092 903	9.290 304 0E-02
candela/square meter	1	1.000 000 0E+00
footlambert	0.291 863 5	2.918 635 1E-01
lux steradian	1	1.000 000 0E+00
millilambert	0.314 159 3	3.141 592 7E-01
nit	1	1.000 000 0E+00
stilb	0.000 1	1.000 000 0E-04

lumen/watt <luminous efficacy>

	Standard	Scientific
candela steradian/watt	1	1.000 000 0E+00
lux square meter/watt	1	1.000 000 0E+00

luong [Vietnam] <mass, special - see page 29>

	Standard	Scientific
kilogram	37.5	3.750 000 0E+01

lut [Poland] <mass, special - see page 29>

	Standard	Scientific
gram	12.672	1.267 200 0E+01

lutow [Poland] <mass, special - see page 29>

	Standard	Scientific
gram	12.67	1.267 000 0E+01

lux <illuminance>

	Standard	Scientific
candela steradian/square meter	1	1.000 000 0E+00
footcandle	0.092 903	9.290 304 0E-02
lumen/square centimeter	0.000 1	1.000 000 0E-04
lumen/square foot	0.092 903	9.290 304 0E-02
lumen/square inch	0.000 645 2	6.451 600 0E-04
lumen/square meter	1	1.000 000 0E+00
metercandle	1	1.000 000 0E+00
nox	1,000	1.000 000 0E+03
phot	0.000 1	1.000 000 0E-04

lux hour <light exposure>

	Standard	Scientific
kilolux second	3.6	3.600 000 0E+00
lumen second/square foot	334.450 94	3.344 509 4E+02
lumen second/square inch	2.322 576	2.322 576 0E+00
lux second	3,600	3.600 000 0E+03

lux second <light exposure>

	Standard	Scientific
footcandle second	0.092 903	9.290 304 0E-02
lumen second/square centimeter	0.000 1	1.000 000 0E-04
lumen second/square inch	0.000 645 2	6.451 600 0E-04
lumen second/square meter	1	1.000 000 0E+00
metercandle second	1	1.000 000 0E+00
milliphot second	0.1	1.000 000 0E-01
nox second	1,000	1.000 000 0E+03

lux second square meter <quantity of light>

	Standard	Scientific
candela second steradian	1	1.000 000 0E+00
joule	0.001 464 1	1.464 128 8E-03
lumen second	1	1.000 000 0E+00
talbot	1	1.000 000 0E+00
wattsecond [light at 540 THz]	0.001 464 1	1.464 128 8E-03

lux square meter <luminous flux>

	Standard	Scientific
candela steradian	1	1.000 000 0E+00
lumen	1	1.000 000 0E+00
watt [at 5550 angstrom]	0.001 470 6	1.470 588 2E-03

lux square meter/steradian <luminous intensity>

	Standard	Scientific
bougie nouvelle [France]	1	1.000 000 0E+00
candela	1	1.000 000 0E+00
candle [new]	1	1.000 000 0E+00
lumen/steradian	1	1.000 000 0E+00
watt/steradian [at 540 THz]	0.001 464 1	1.464 128 8E-03

lux square meter/watt — <luminous efficacy>
candela steradian/watt ---- 1 ---- 1.000 000 0E+00
lumen/watt ---- 1 ---- 1.000 000 0E+00

lux steradian — <luminance>
apostilb [international] ---- 3.141 592 7 ---- 3.141 592 7E+00
blondel ---- 3.141 592 7 ---- 3.141 592 7E+00
candela/square foot ---- 0.092 903 ---- 9.290 304 0E-02
candela/square meter ---- 1 ---- 1.000 000 0E+00
footlambert ---- 0.291 863 5 ---- 2.918 635 1E-01
lumen/steradian square meter ---- 1 ---- 1.000 000 0E+00
millilambert ---- 0.314 159 3 ---- 3.141 592 7E-01
nit ---- 1 ---- 1.000 000 0E+00
stilb ---- 0.000 1 ---- 1.000 000 0E-04

ly [Vietnam] — <mass, special - see page 29>
milligram ---- 37.78 ---- 3.778 000 0E+01

ly [Vietnam] — <length, special - see page 29>
millimeter ---- 0.4 ---- 4.000 000 0E-01

ly [Vietnam] — <area, special - see page 29>
square centimeter ---- 333.35 ---- 3.333 500 0E+02

lyang [China] — <mass, special - see page 29>
gram ---- 37.78 ---- 3.778 000 0E+01

ma [Hong Kong, textiles] — <length, special - see page 29>
meter ---- 0.891 54 ---- 8.915 400 0E-01

maal [Norway] — <area, special - see page 29>
are ---- 10 ---- 1.000 000 0E+01

maass [Germany] — <volume, special - see page 29>
liter ---- 1.837 ---- 1.837 000 0E+00

maass [Switzerland] — <volume, special - see page 29>
liter ---- 1.5 ---- 1.500 000 0E+00

maatje [Netherlands] — <volume, special - see page 29>
liter ---- 0.1 ---- 1.000 000 0E-01

mace [China] — <mass, special - see page 29>
gram ---- 3.778 ---- 3.778 000 0E+00

mace [Hong Kong] — <mass, special - see page 29>
gram ---- 3.777 994 ---- 3.777 994 0E+00

mace [India, jewels and pearls] — <mass, special - see page 29>
gram ---- 0.045 ---- 4.500 000 0E-02

mace [Malaysia] — <mass, special - see page 29>
gram ---- 6.048 ---- 6.048 000 0E+00

mace [Sumatra] — <mass, special - see page 29>
gram ---- 10.6 ---- 1.060 000 0E+01

maess [Germany] — <volume, special - see page 29>
liter ---- 0.859 ---- 8.590 000 0E-01

magn — <electric permeability>
henry/centimeter ---- 0.01 ---- 1.000 000 0E-02
henry/meter ---- 1 ---- 1.000 000 0E+00

magnum [champagne bottle] — <champagne bottle size>
bottle [wine, standard] ---- 2 ---- 2.000 000 0E+00
liter ---- 1.5 ---- 1.500 000 0E+00

mahn [Afghanistan] — <mass, special - see page 29>
kilogram ---- 4.48 ---- 4.480 000 0E+00

mahnd [Arab] — <mass, special - see page 29>
kilogram ---- 0.925 328 4 ---- 9.253 284 0E-01

mahs [India, gold and silver] — <mass, special - see page 29>
gram ---- 1.15 ---- 1.150 000 0E+00

mahs [Sumatra] — <mass, special - see page 29>
gram ---- 10.6 ---- 1.060 000 0E+01

Convert From Convert To	**\<Type of Unit\>** Standard	Scientific

mahud [Saudi Arabia, ancient] — \<mass, special - see page 29\>
kilogram -- 0.925 --- 9.250 000 0E−01

maille [France, gold and silver] — \<mass, special - see page 29\>
gram -- 0.78 --- 7.800 000 0E−01

makhammus [Sudan] — \<area, special - see page 29\>
hectare --- 0.323 --- 3.230 000 0E−01

makkuk [Islam, ancient, wheat] — \<mass, special - see page 29\>
kilogram -- 14.91 --- 1.491 000 0E+01

makuk [Syria] — \<volume, special - see page 29\>
hectoliter --- 8 --- 8.000 000 0E+00

mal [Norway] — \<area, special - see page 29\>
are --- 10 --- 1.000 000 0E+01

mal [South Korea, large] — \<volume, special - see page 29\>
liter -- 18.039 --- 1.803 900 0E+01

mal [South Korea, small] — \<volume, special - see page 29\>
liter -- 9.019 5 --- 9.019 500 0E+00

malouah [Egypt] — \<volume, special - see page 29\>
liter -- 4.12 --- 4.120 000 0E+00

maltaro [Libya] — \<volume, special - see page 29\>
liter -- 23.32 --- 2.332 000 0E+01

malter [Germany, dry] — \<volume, special - see page 29\>
hectoliter -- 6.595 --- 6.595 000 0E+00

malter [Switzerland, dry] — \<volume, special - see page 29\>
hectoliter -- 1.5 --- 1.500 000 0E+00

malwa [Egypt] — \<volume, special - see page 29\>
liter -- 4.125 --- 4.125 000 0E+00

malwa [Sudan] — \<volume, special - see page 29\>
liter -- 4.125 --- 4.125 000 0E+00

man [China] — \<area, special - see page 29\>
hectare --- 0.067 --- 6.700 000 0E−02

man [Iran] — \<mass, special - see page 29\>
kilogram --- 3 --- 3.000 000 0E+00

man [Iraq] — \<mass, special - see page 29\>
kilogram -- 25.401 17 --- 2.540 117 0E+01

man [Muslim India] — \<mass, special - see page 29\>
kilogram -- 37.32 --- 3.732 000 0E+01

man chah [Iran] — \<mass, special - see page 29\>
kilogram -- 5.938 69 --- 5.938 690 0E+00

man i bandar abbassi [Iran] — \<mass, special - see page 29\>
kilogram -- 3.897 26 --- 3.897 260 0E+00

man i hashemi [Iran] — \<mass, special - see page 29\>
kilogram --- 53.448 2 --- 5.344 820 0E+01

man i kahneh [Iran] — \<mass, special - see page 29\>
kilogram --- 4.639 6 --- 4.639 600 0E+00

man i noh abbassi [Iran] — \<mass, special - see page 29\>
kilogram -- 3.340 51 --- 3.340 510 0E+00

man i rey [Iran] — \<mass, special - see page 29\>
kilogram --- 11.877 4 --- 1.187 740 0E+01

man i shah [Iran] — \<mass, special - see page 29\>
kilogram -- 5.938 69 --- 5.938 690 0E+00

man i tabriz [Iran] — \<mass, special - see page 29\>
kilogram --- 3 --- 3.000 000 0E+00

man tabriz [Iran] — \<mass, special - see page 29\>
kilogram -- 2.969 34 --- 2.969 340 0E+00

Convert From Convert To	Standard	<Type of Unit> Scientific
mana [Nepal, cereals] centiliter ------------------------------------	<volume, special - see page 29> 56.83	5.683 000 0E+01
mancuema [Honduras] kilogram ------------------------------------	<mass, special - see page 29> 1.437 5	1.437 500 0E+00
mandel gewichtsgran [Austria] gram ------------------------------------	<mass, special - see page 29> 0.59	5.900 000 0E−01
mandu [North Borneo] liter------------------------------------	<volume, special - see page 29> 45.459 6	4.545 960 0E+01
mane [Hebrew, ancient, gold] gram ------------------------------------	<mass, special - see page 29> 633	6.330 000 0E+02
maneh [Babylon, ancient] kilogram ------------------------------------	<mass, special - see page 29> 0.505	5.050 000 0E−01
maneh [Hebrew, ancient] gram ------------------------------------	<mass, special - see page 29> 571.2	5.712 000 0E+02
maneh [Italy] gram ------------------------------------	<mass, special - see page 29> 341.077	3.410 770 0E+02
mangal [India, jewels and pearls] gram------------------------------------	<mass, special - see page 29> 0.25	2.500 000 0E−01
mangalis [India, jewels and pearls] gram ------------------------------------	<mass, special - see page 29> 0.25	2.500 000 0E−01
mangelin [India, jewels and pearls] gram ------------------------------------	<mass, special - see page 29> 0.25	2.500 000 0E−01
mangelin [India, Madras] gram ------------------------------------	<mass, special - see page 29> 0.388 793 5	3.887 935 0E−01
manhe [Hebrew, ancient, gold] gram ------------------------------------	<mass, special - see page 29> 633	6.330 000 0E+02
manim [Hebrew, ancient, gold] gram ------------------------------------	<mass, special - see page 29> 633	6.330 000 0E+02
mann [Iraq, Baghdad] kilogram ------------------------------------	<mass, special - see page 29> 25	2.500 000 0E+01
mann [Iraq, Basra, coffee] kilogram ------------------------------------	<mass, special - see page 29> 64.15	6.415 000 0E+01
mann [Persia, ancient] kilogram ------------------------------------	<mass, special - see page 29> 3	3.000 000 0E+00
mann [Turkey, silk] kilogram ------------------------------------	<mass, special - see page 29> 3.827	3.827 000 0E+00
manne [Japan] gram------------------------------------	<mass, special - see page 29> 3.75	3.750 000 0E+00
mano [Honduras, maize or corn] kilogram ------------------------------------	<mass, special - see page 29> 1.134	1.134 000 0E+00
manojo [Venezuela] gram------------------------------------	<mass, special - see page 29> 250	2.500 000 0E+02
manu [Babylon, ancient] gram ------------------------------------	<mass, special - see page 29> 978	9.780 000 0E+02
manzana [Argentina] hectare------------------------------------	<area, special - see page 29> 1	1.000 000 0E+00
manzana [Belize] hectare------------------------------------	<area, special - see page 29> 0.835	8.350 000 0E−01
manzana [British Honduras] are ------------------------------------	<area, special - see page 29> 83.5	8.350 000 0E+01
manzana [Colombia] are ------------------------------------	<area, special - see page 29> 69.89	6.989 000 0E+01
manzana [Costa Rica] are ------------------------------------	<area, special - see page 29> 69.9	6.990 000 0E+01

manzana [El Salvador]

Convert To		Standard	Scientific
are		69.9	6.990 000 0E+01

<Type of Unit>

Convert From / To	Standard	Scientific
manzana [El Salvador] — <area, special - see page 29>		
are	69.9	6.990 000 0E+01
manzana [Guatemala] — <area, special - see page 29>		
are	69.9	6.990 000 0E+01
manzana [Honduras] — <area, special - see page 29>		
are	69.72	6.972 000 0E+01
manzana [Nicaragua] — <area, special - see page 29>		
are	70.44	7.044 000 0E+01
manzana [Spain] — <area, special - see page 29>		
are	69.873 7	6.987 370 0E+01
mao [Portuguese India] — <mass, special - see page 29>		
kilogram	37.32	3.732 000 0E+01
maon [India, Bombay] — <mass, special - see page 29>		
kilogram	12.7	1.270 000 0E+01
maon [India, Calcutta] — <mass, special - see page 29>		
kilogram	10.923	1.092 300 0E+01
maon [India, Madras] — <mass, special - see page 29>		
kilogram	11.34	1.134 000 0E+01
maqar [Egypt] — <mass, special - see page 29>		
gram	3.51	3.510 000 0E+00
marabba [Pakistan] — <area, special - see page 29>		
hectare	10.117 14	1.011 714 0E+01
marasseh [Lebanon] — <area, special - see page 29>		
square meter	50	5.000 000 0E+01
marc [Austria] — <mass, special - see page 29>		
gram	280.6	2.806 000 0E+02
marc [Denmark] — <mass, special - see page 29>		
gram	249.67	2.496 700 0E+02
marc [France] — <mass, special - see page 29>		
gram	244.753	2.447 530 0E+02
marc [Germany] — <mass, special - see page 29>		
gram	233.75	2.337 500 0E+02
marc [Switzerland, heavy] — <mass, special - see page 29>		
gram	244.753	2.447 530 0E+02
marca [Italy] — <mass, special - see page 29>		
gram	235	2.350 000 0E+02
marca [Spain] — <mass, special - see page 29>		
gram	230	2.300 000 0E+02
marcal [India, grain] — <volume, special - see page 29>		
liter	12.29	1.229 000 0E+01
marck [Denmark] — <mass, special - see page 29>		
gram	249.67	2.496 700 0E+02
marck [Germany] — <mass, special - see page 29>		
gram	233.75	2.337 500 0E+02
marco [Bolivia] — <mass, special - see page 29>		
gram	230	2.300 000 0E+02
marco [Brazil] — <mass, special - see page 29>		
gram	299.5	2.995 000 0E+02
marco [Honduras] — <mass, special - see page 29>		
gram	230.05	2.300 500 0E+02
marco [Italy, gold and silver] — <mass, special - see page 29>		
gram	245.896	2.458 960 0E+02
marco [Mexico] — <mass, special - see page 29>		
gram	230.13	2.301 300 0E+02

| Convert From | | <Type of Unit> |
Convert To	Standard	Scientific
marco [Portugal]	<mass, special - see page 29>	
gram	229.53	2.295 300 0E+02
marco [Spain]	<mass, special - see page 29>	
gram	230.047	2.300 470 0E+02
marco real [Argentina]	<volume, special - see page 29>	
hectoliter	1.372	1.372 000 0E+00
marco real [Bolivia]	<mass, special - see page 29>	
kilogram	92	9.200 000 0E+01
marco real [Chile]	<volume, special - see page 29>	
liter	96.99	9.699 000 0E+01
marco real [Colombia]	<volume, special - see page 29>	
liter	55.5	5.550 000 0E+01
marco real [Dominican Republic]	<volume, special - see page 29>	
liter	55.5	5.550 000 0E+01
marco real [Ecuador]	<mass, special - see page 29>	
kilogram	92	9.200 000 0E+01
marco real [Honduras]	<volume, special - see page 29>	
hectoliter	11.028	1.102 800 0E+01
marco real [Mexico]	<volume, special - see page 29>	
liter	90.815	9.081 500 0E+01
marco real [Nicaragua]	<mass, special - see page 29>	
kilogram	161	1.610 000 0E+02
marco real [Paraguay]	<volume, special - see page 29>	
hectoliter	2.88	2.880 000 0E+00
marco real [Spain]	<volume, special - see page 29>	
liter	55.5	5.550 000 0E+01
marco real [Spain]	<area, special - see page 29>	
are	64.395 6	6.439 560 0E+01
marco real [Trinidad and Tobago]	<mass, special - see page 29>	
kilogram	49.9	4.990 000 0E+01
marco real [Uruguay]	<mass, special - see page 29>	
kilogram	100	1.000 000 0E+02
marfold [Denmark]	<length, special - see page 29>	
kilometer	7.532 5	7.532 500 0E+00
marfold [Hungary]	<length, special - see page 29>	
kilometer	8.35	8.350 000 0E+00
marfold [Sweden]	<length, special - see page 29>	
kilometer	10	1.000 000 0E+01
marfold [Venezuela]	<mass, special - see page 29>	
kilogram	400	4.000 000 0E+02
marhala [Arabia]	<length, special - see page 29>	
kilometer	38.6	3.860 000 0E+01
marhala [Iraq, ancient]	<length, special - see page 29>	
kilometer	45.5	4.550 000 0E+01
mario [Spain]	<mass, special - see page 29>	
gram	230.047	2.300 470 0E+02
maris [Babylon, ancient]	<volume, special - see page 29>	
liter	30.3	3.030 000 0E+01
mark [Austria, Vienna, gold and silver]	<mass, special - see page 29>	
gram	280.644	2.806 440 0E+02
mark [Austria]	<mass, special - see page 29>	
kilogram	280.01	2.800 100 0E+02
mark [Denmark]	<mass, special - see page 29>	
kilogram	0.233 8	2.338 000 0E-01

mark [France]
gram --- <mass, special - see page 29>
250 --- 2.500 000 0E+02

mark [Germany, Augsburg]
gram --- <mass, special - see page 29>
235.9 --- 2.359 000 0E+02

mark [Germany, Cologne]
gram --- <mass, special - see page 29>
233.75 --- 2.337 500 0E+02

mark [Germany, Nuremberg]
gram --- <mass, special - see page 29>
238.569 --- 2.385 690 0E+02

mark [Iceland]
kilogram --- <mass, special - see page 29>
1 --- 1.000 000 0E+00

mark [Netherlands]
gram --- <mass, special - see page 29>
247 --- 2.470 000 0E+02

mark [Norway]
kilogram --- <mass, special - see page 29>
0.210 7 --- 2.107 000 0E-01

mark [Spain]
gram --- <mass, special - see page 29>
230.07 --- 2.300 700 0E+02

mark [Sweden]
gram --- <mass, special - see page 29>
210.571 --- 2.105 710 0E+02

markgewicht [Belgium]
gram --- <mass, special - see page 29>
492.15 --- 4.921 500 0E+02

marla [India]
square meter --- <area, special - see page 29>
164.2 --- 1.642 000 0E+02

marla [Pakistan]
square meter --- <area, special - see page 29>
25.293 --- 2.529 300 0E+01

marok [Hungary]
meter --- <length, special - see page 29>
0.105 36 --- 1.053 600 0E-01

marta [Libya]
liter --- <volume, special - see page 29>
20.75 --- 2.075 000 0E+01

mas [Brunei, gold]
gram --- <mass, special - see page 29>
3.78 --- 3.780 000 0E+00

mas [India, gold and silver]
gram --- <mass, special - see page 29>
1.15 --- 1.150 000 0E+00

mas [India, jewels and pearls]
gram --- <mass, special - see page 29>
0.045 --- 4.500 000 0E-02

mas [India]
gram --- <mass, special - see page 29>
1.166 --- 1.166 000 0E+00

mas [Sumatra]
gram --- <mass, special - see page 29>
10.6 --- 1.060 000 0E+01

masha [Bangladesh, precious metals]
milligram --- <mass, special - see page 29>
972 --- 9.720 000 0E+02

masha [Ceylon]
gram --- <mass, special - see page 29>
0.971 983 7 --- 9.719 837 0E-01

masha [Hindu, ancient, gold]
milligram --- <mass, special - see page 29>
620 --- 6.200 000 0E+02

masha [Hindu, ancient, silver]
milligram --- <mass, special - see page 29>
248 --- 2.480 000 0E+02

masha [India, ancient, silver]
milligram --- <mass, special - see page 29>
606 --- 6.060 000 0E+02

masha [India, gold and silver]
gram --- <mass, special - see page 29>
1.15 --- 1.150 000 0E+00

masha [India]
gram --- <mass, special - see page 29>
0.971 983 9 --- 9.719 839 0E-01

masha [Pakistan]
milligram --- <mass, special - see page 29>
972 --- 9.720 000 0E+02

masha [Sumatra]
gram --- <mass, special - see page 29>
--- 10.6 ---- 1.060 000 0E+01

mass [Austria]
liter --- <volume, special - see page 29>
--- 1.42 ---- 1.420 000 0E+00

mass [Germany]
liter --- <volume, special - see page 29>
--- 0.859 ---- 8.590 000 0E−01

massa [India, gold and silver]
gram --- <mass, special - see page 29>
--- 1.15 ---- 1.150 000 0E+00

massa [India, jewels and pearls]
gram --- <mass, special - see page 29>
--- 0.045 ---- 4.500 000 0E−02

massa [Sumatra]
gram --- <mass, special - see page 29>
--- 10.6 ---- 1.060 000 0E+01

masse [Austria]
liter --- <volume, special - see page 29>
--- 1.415 1 ---- 1.415 100 0E+00

massel [Germany]
liter --- <volume, special - see page 29>
--- 4.632 5 ---- 4.632 500 0E+00

masskanne [Germany]
liter --- <volume, special - see page 29>
--- 1.069 ---- 1.069 000 0E+00

mat [Burma]
gram --- <mass, special - see page 29>
--- 4.082 331 ---- 4.082 331 0E+00

mata [Indonesia, opium]
milligram --- <mass, special - see page 29>
--- 386.01 ---- 3.860 100 0E+02

matar [Islam, ancient, oil]
kilogram --- <mass, special - see page 29>
--- 17 ---- 1.700 000 0E+01

matomana [Nepal]
square meter --- <area, special - see page 29>
--- 0.795 ---- 7.950 000 0E−01

matomuri [Nepal]
square meter --- <area, special - see page 29>
--- 127.18 ---- 1.271 800 0E+02

matopathi [Nepal]
square meter --- <area, special - see page 29>
--- 6.359 ---- 6.359 000 0E+00

mattaro [Libya]
liter --- <volume, special - see page 29>
--- 23.32 ---- 2.332 000 0E+01

mau [Vietnam, soil measure]
cubic meter --- <volume, special - see page 29>
--- 1,440 ---- 1.440 000 0E+03

mau [Vietnam]
are --- <area, special - see page 29>
--- 36 ---- 3.600 000 0E+01

maund [Afghanistan]
kilogram --- <mass, special - see page 29>
--- 35.33 ---- 3.533 000 0E+01

maund [Bahrain]
kilogram --- <mass, special - see page 29>
--- 25.4 ---- 2.540 000 0E+01

maund [Bangladesh]
kilogram --- <mass, special - see page 29>
--- 37.32 ---- 3.732 000 0E+01

maund [Ceylon]
kilogram --- <mass, special - see page 29>
--- 37.324 17 ---- 3.732 417 0E+01

maund [India, bazaar]
kilogram --- <mass, special - see page 29>
--- 37.25 ---- 3.725 000 0E+01

maund [India, Bombay]
kilogram --- <mass, special - see page 29>
--- 13.062 ---- 1.306 200 0E+01

maund [India, Surat]
kilogram --- <mass, special - see page 29>
--- 16.933 ---- 1.693 300 0E+01

maund [India]
kilogram --- <mass, special - see page 29>
--- 37.324 ---- 3.732 400 0E+01

maund [Kuwait]
kilogram --- <mass, special - see page 29>
--- 25.4 ---- 2.540 000 0E+01

Convert From		\<Type of Unit\>
Convert To	Standard	Scientific

maund [Muscat and Oman] · \<mass, special - see page 29\>
kilogram -- 4.04 --- 4.040 000 0E+00

maund [Nepal] · \<mass, special - see page 29\>
kilogram -- 37.324 2 --- 3.732 420 0E+01

maund [Pakistan] · \<mass, special - see page 29\>
kilogram --- 37.32 --- 3.732 000 0E+01

maund [Saudi Arabia] · \<mass, special - see page 29\>
kilogram --- 37.285 --- 3.728 500 0E+01

maund [Singapore, rice, milled] · \<mass, special - see page 29\>
kilogram -- 37.2 --- 3.720 000 0E+01

maund [Sumatra, rice, milled] · \<mass, special - see page 29\>
kilogram --- 34.01 --- 3.401 000 0E+01

maund [Tanzania] · \<mass, special - see page 29\>
kilogram --- 1.338 --- 1.338 000 0E+00

maund [Yemen] · \<mass, special - see page 29\>
kilogram --- 37.32 --- 3.732 000 0E+01

maund [Zanzibar and Pemba] · \<mass, special - see page 29\>
kilogram --- 1.329 --- 1.329 000 0E+00

maw [China] · \<area, special - see page 29\>
hectare -- 0.067 --- 6.700 000 0E-02

maxwell · \<magnetic flux\>
abweber --- 1 --- 1.000 000 0E+00
electromagnetic unit of magnetic flux [cgs system] ------------ 1 --- 1.000 000 0E+00
gauss square centimeter ------------------------------------- 1 --- 1.000 000 0E+00
line [of magnetic force] -------------------------------------- 1 --- 1.000 000 0E+00
statweber --- \<\<\< 3.335 641 0E-11
unit pole -- 0.079 577 5 --- 7.957 747 5E-02
weber --- \<\<\< 1.000 000 0E-08

maxwell/square meter · \<magnetic flux density\>
ampere henry/square meter ------------------------------------ 1 --- 1.000 000 0E+00
gauss -- 10,000 --- 1.000 000 0E+04
joule/ampere square meter ------------------------------------ 1 --- 1.000 000 0E+00
line/square centimeter [of magnetic force] ------------- 10,000 --- 1.000 000 0E+04
newton/ampere meter --- 1 --- 1.000 000 0E+00
tesla -- 1 --- 1.000 000 0E+00
volt second/square meter ------------------------------------- 1 --- 1.000 000 0E+00
weber/square meter --- 1 --- 1.000 000 0E+00

mayam [Malaysia, precious metals] · \<mass, special - see page 29\>
gram --- 3.37 --- 3.370 000 0E+00

mayam [Singapore, precious metals] · \<mass, special - see page 29\>
gram --- 3.37 --- 3.370 000 0E+00

mayer · \<specific heat capacity\>
Btu/pound °F [I.T.] --------------------------------- 0.238 845 9 --- 2.388 459 0E-01
joule/kilogram kelvin -- 1,000 --- 1.000 000 0E+03
kilocalorie/kilogram °C [I.T.] ----------------------- 0.238 845 9 --- 2.388 459 0E-01

maz [Macao] · \<area, special - see page 29\>
square meter -- 761.4 --- 7.614 000 0E+02

mazsa [Hungary] · \<mass, special - see page 29\>
kilogram --- 100 --- 1.000 000 0E+02

me [Japan] · \<mass, special - see page 29\>
gram --- 3.75 --- 3.750 000 0E+00

me [Sumatra] · \<mass, special - see page 29\>
gram -- 0.6 --- 6.000 000 0E-01

measure [Hebrew, ancient] · \<volume, special - see page 29\>
liter --- 7.7 --- 7.700 000 0E+00

measure [Sri Lanka, dry] · \<volume, special - see page 29\>
liter --- 1.06 --- 1.060 000 0E+00

measurement ton		**<volume>**
board foot	480	4.800 000 0E+02
bushel [UK]	31.144 177	3.114 417 7E+01
bushel [US, dry]	32.142 558	3.214 255 8E+01
cord [firewood]	0.312 5	3.125 000 0E−01
cord foot [timber]	2.5	2.500 000 0E+00
cubic foot	40	4.000 000 0E+01
cubic inch	69,120	6.912 000 0E+04
cubic meter	1.132 673 9	1.132 673 9E+00
cubic yard	1.481 481 5	1.481 481 5E+00
drum [US, liquid]	5.440 377 8	5.440 377 8E+00
English water ton [UK]	1.112 292	1.112 292 0E+00
freight ton	1	1.000 000 0E+00
gallon [UK, dry or liquid]	249.153 42	2.491 534 2E+02
gallon [US, liquid]	299.220 78	2.992 207 8E+02
kiloliter	1.132 673 9	1.132 673 9E+00
liter	1,132.673 9	1.132 673 9E+03
million board foot	0.000 48	4.800 000 0E−04
ocean ton	1	1.000 000 0E+00
peck [UK]	124.576 71	1.245 767 1E+02
peck [US]	128.570 23	1.285 702 3E+02
petrograd standard	0.242 424 2	2.424 242 4E−01
quarter [UK]	3.893 022 2	3.893 022 2E+00
register ton	0.4	4.000 000 0E−01
shipping ton	1	1.000 000 0E+00
stere	1.132 673 9	1.132 673 9E+00
thousand board foot	0.48	4.800 000 0E−01
thousand cubic foot	0.04	4.000 000 0E−02
tun [UK, liquid]	1.153 488	1.153 488 0E+00
tun [US, liquid]	1.187 384	1.187 384 0E+00
Winchester wine gallon [UK]	299.220 78	2.992 207 8E+02
measurette [France, dry]		**<volume, special - see page 29>**
milliliter	50.814	5.081 400 0E+01
mecate [Belize]		**<area, special - see page 29>**
are	5.22	5.220 000 0E+00
mecate [British Honduras]		**<area, special - see page 29>**
square meter	522	5.220 000 0E+02
mecate [Costa Rica]		**<length, special - see page 29>**
meter	20.06	2.006 000 0E+01
mecate [Guatemala]		**<length, special - see page 29>**
meter	20.062	2.006 200 0E+01
mecate [Honduras]		**<length, special - see page 29>**
meter	20.04	2.004 000 0E+01
mecate [Nicaragua]		**<length, special - see page 29>**
meter	20.14	2.014 000 0E+01
media [Argentina]		**<mass, special - see page 29>**
gram	45.94	4.594 000 0E+01
media [Belize]		**<mass, special - see page 29>**
gram	45.36	4.536 000 0E+01
media [Bolivia]		**<mass, special - see page 29>**
kilogram	46	4.600 000 0E+01
media [Chile]		**<mass, special - see page 29>**
kilogram	46	4.600 000 0E+01
media [Colombia]		**<mass, special - see page 29>**
kilogram	50	5.000 000 0E+01
media [Costa Rica]		**<mass, special - see page 29>**
kilogram	46	4.600 000 0E+01
media [Cuba]		**<mass, special - see page 29>**
kilogram	46.009	4.600 900 0E+01

| Convert From | | **\<Type of Unit\>** |
Convert To	Standard	Scientific

media [Czechoslovakia] <mass, special - see page 29>
kilogram ---50 --- 5.000 000 0E+01

media [Dominican Republic] <mass, special - see page 29>
kilogram --- 45.36 --- 4.536 000 0E+01

media [Ecuador] <mass, special - see page 29>
kilogram --46 --- 4.600 000 0E+01

media [Guatemala] <mass, special - see page 29>
kilogram --46 --- 4.600 000 0E+01

media [Honduras] <mass, special - see page 29>
kilogram --46 --- 4.600 000 0E+01

media [Macao] <mass, special - see page 29>
kilogram --- 58.752 --- 5.875 200 0E+01

media [Mexico] <mass, special - see page 29>
kilogram -- 46.02 --- 4.602 000 0E+01

media [Paraguay] <mass, special - see page 29>
kilogram --- 45.9 --- 4.590 000 0E+01

media [Peru] <mass, special - see page 29>
kilogram --46 --- 4.600 000 0E+01

media [Philippines] <mass, special - see page 29>
kilogram --46 --- 4.600 000 0E+01

media [Portugal] <mass, special - see page 29>
kilogram --60 --- 6.000 000 0E+01

media [Spain] <mass, special - see page 29>
kilogram --- 46.009 --- 4.600 900 0E+01

media [Venezuela] <mass, special - see page 29>
kilogram -- 46.09 --- 4.609 000 0E+01

medida [Honduras] <volume, special - see page 29>
liter --- 2.872 --- 2.872 000 0E+00

medida [Venezuela] <area, special - see page 29>
square meter -- 625 --- 6.250 000 0E+02

medimno [Cyprus] <volume, special - see page 29>
liter -- 75.049 --- 7.504 900 0E+01

medimnos [Greece, ancient] <volume, special - see page 29>
liter --39 --- 3.900 000 0E+01

medimnus [Greece, ancient] <volume, special - see page 29>
liter -- 51.84 --- 5.184 000 0E+01

medio [Honduras] <volume, special - see page 29>
liter --- 45.95 --- 4.595 000 0E+01

medio [Spain] <volume, special - see page 29>
liter -- 2.31 --- 2.310 000 0E+00

medio [Venezuela] <area, special - see page 29>
hectare -- 0.5 --- 5.000 000 0E-01

medio almud [El Salvador] <volume, special - see page 29>
liter --- 10.817 --- 1.081 700 0E+01

megaampere <electric current>
abampere -- 100,000 --- 1.000 000 0E+05
ampere---1,000,000 --- 1.000 000 0E+06
gilbert--1,256,637.06 --- 1.256 637 1E+06
stamampere--->>> --- 2.997 924 6E+15

megaampere/square meter <electric current density>
ampere/square inch --------------------------------------645.16 --- 6.451 600 0E+02
ampere/square meter ---------------------------------------1,000,000 --- 1.000 000 0E+06
ampere/square millimeter ------------------------------ 1 --- 1.000 000 0E+00

megabar <pressure>
atmosphere [standard]------------------------------------986,923.27 --- 9.869 232 7E+05
atmosphere [technical]-----------------------------------1,019,716.2 --- 1.019 716 2E+06

Convert From / Convert To	Standard	Scientific
bar	1,000,000	1.000 000 0E+06
dyne/square centimeter	>>>	1.000 000 0E+12
foot of mercury [0 °C, by convention]	2,460,831.9	2.460 831 9E+06
foot of water [4 °C, by convention]	>>>	3.345 525 6E+07
kilogram-force/square millimeter	10,197.162	1.019 716 2E+04
kilopond/square millimeter	10,197.162	1.019 716 2E+04
kip/square inch	14,503.774	1.450 377 4E+04
newton/square millimeter	100,000	1.000 000 0E+05
pascal	>>>	1.000 000 0E+11
pound-force/square inch	>>>	1.450 377 4E+07
ton-force/square inch [long]	6,474.899	6.474 899 0E+03
ton-force/square inch [short]	7,251.886 9	7.251 886 9E+03
torr	>>>	7.500 616 8E+08
megabecquerel		**\<radionuclide activity\>**
1/second	1,000,000	1.000 000 0E+06
becquerel	1,000,000	1.000 000 0E+06
curie	0.000 027	2.702 702 7E−05
rutherford	1	1.000 000 0E+00
megabecquerel/cubic meter		**\<radionuclide volume activity\>**
becquerel/cubic meter	1,000,000	1.000 000 0E+06
curie/cubic meter	0.000 027	2.702 702 7E−05
rutherford/cubic meter	1	1.000 000 0E+00
megabecquerel/kilogram		**\<radionuclide specific activity\>**
becquerel/kilogram	1,000,000	1.000 000 0E+06
curie/kilogram	0.000 027	2.702 702 7E−05
rutherford/kilogram	1	1.000 000 0E+00
megacandela		**\<luminous intensity\>**
candela	1,000,000	1.000 000 0E+06
megacoulomb		**\<electric charge\>**
ampere hour	277.777 778	2.777 777 8E+02
coulomb	1,000,000	1.000 000 0E+06
faraday [based on carbon-12]	10.364 272 1	1.036 427 2E+01
statcoulomb	>>>	2.997 924 6E+15
megacoulomb/cubic meter		**\<electric charge density\>**
coulomb/cubic centimeter	1	1.000 000 0E+00
coulomb/cubic meter	1,000,000	1.000 000 0E+06
statcoulomb/cubic centimeter	>>>	2.997 924 6E+09
megacoulomb/square meter		**\<electric flux density\>**
abcoulomb/square centimeter	10	1.000 000 0E+01
ampere hour/square meter	277.777 778	2.777 777 8E+02
coulomb/square inch	645.16	6.451 600 0E+02
coulomb/square meter	1,000,000	1.000 000 0E+06
coulomb/square millimeter	1	1.000 000 0E+00
franklin/square centimeter	>>>	2.997 924 6E+11
statcoulomb/square centimeter	>>>	2.997 924 6E+11
megaelectronvolt		**\<energy\>**
atomic mass unit [unified, C-12, 1986, eq. energy]	0.001 073 5	1.073 543 9E−03
deuteron rest mass [atomic physics, eq. energy]	0.000 533 2	5.331 589 2E−04
dyne centimeter	0.000 001 6	1.602 177 3E−06
electron rest mass [atomic physics, eq. energy]	1.956 950 8	1.956 950 8E+00
electronvolt	1,000,000	1.000 000 0E+06
erg	0.000 001 6	1.602 177 3E−06
gigaelectronvolt	0.001	1.000 000 0E−03
hartree [atomic physics, eq. energy]	36,749.309	3.674 930 9E+04
joule	<<<	1.602 177 3E−13
kiloelectronvolt	1,000	1.000 000 0E+03
muon rest mass [atomic physics, eq. energy]	0.009 464 5	9.464 463 8E−03
neutron rest mass [atomic physics, eq. energy]	0.001 064 3	1.064 321 6E−03
proton rest mass [atomic physics, eq. energy]	0.001 065 8	1.065 788 7E−03
rydberg [atomic physics, eq. energy]	73,497.744	7.349 774 4E+04
teraelectronvolt	0.000 001	1.000 000 0E−06

Convert From		<Type of Unit>
Convert To	Standard	Scientific

megaerg <energy>
Btu [I.T.]	0.000 094 8	9.478 171 2E−05
calorie [I.T.]	0.023 884 6	2.388 459 0E−02
calorie [kilogram, I.T.]	0.000 023 9	2.388 459 0E−05
centigrade heat unit [I.T.]	0.000 052 7	5.265 650 7E−05
centimeter gram-force	1,019.716 2	1.019 716 2E+03
cubic centimeter atmosphere	0.986 923 3	9.869 232 7E−01
cubic foot atmosphere	0.000 034 9	3.485 286 6E−05
dyne centimeter	1,000,000	1.000 000 0E+06
erg	1,000,000	1.000 000 0E+06
foot pound-force	0.073 756 2	7.375 621 5E−02
foot poundal	2.373 036	2.373 036 0E+00
frigorie [France]	0.000 023 9	2.389 029 6E−05
gram calorie	0.023 890 3	2.389 029 6E−02
horsepower hour	<<<	3.725 061 4E−08
horsepower hour [metric]	<<<	3.776 726 7E−08
inch ounce-force	14.161 193	1.416 119 3E+01
inch pound-force	0.885 074 6	8.850 745 8E−01
joule	0.1	1.000 000 0E−01
kilogram square meter/square second	0.1	1.000 000 0E−01
kilopond meter	0.010 197 2	1.019 716 2E−02
liter atmosphere	0.000 986 9	9.869 232 7E−04
megalerg	1	1.000 000 0E+00
meter kilogram-force	0.010 197 2	1.019 716 2E−02
newton meter	0.1	1.000 000 0E−01
watthour	0.000 027 8	2.777 777 8E−05
wattsecond	0.1	1.000 000 0E−01

megafarad <capacitance>
abfarad	0.001	1.000 000 0E−03
coulomb/volt	1,000,000	1.000 000 0E+06
farad	1,000,000	1.000 000 0E+06
statfarad	>>>	8.987 551 8E+17

megagram <mass>
decitonne	10	1.000 000 0E+01
doppelzentner [Germany]	10	1.000 000 0E+01
hundredweight [long]	19.684 131	1.968 413 1E+01
hundredweight [short]	22.046 226	2.204 622 6E+01
hundredweight [UK]	19.684 131	1.968 413 1E+01
kilogram	1,000	1.000 000 0E+03
millier	1	1.000 000 0E+00
pound-force square second/foot	68.521 766	6.852 176 6E+01
quarter [long]	3.936 826 1	3.936 826 1E+00
quarter [short]	4.409 245 2	4.409 245 2E+00
quarter [UK]	78.736 522	7.873 652 2E+01
quarter [US]	88.184 905	8.818 490 5E+01
quintal [metric]	10	1.000 000 0E+01
quintal [UK]	19.684 131	1.968 413 1E+01
quintal [US]	22.046 226	2.204 622 6E+01
slug	68.521 766	6.852 176 6E+01
ton [long]	0.984 206 5	9.842 065 3E−01
ton [metric]	1	1.000 000 0E+00
ton [short]	1.102 311 3	1.102 311 3E+00
ton [UK]	0.984 206 5	9.842 065 3E−01
tonne	1	1.000 000 0E+00

megagram/cubic centimeter <density>
gram/cubic centimeter	1,000,000	1.000 000 0E+06
kilogram/cubic centimeter	1,000	1.000 000 0E+03
kilogram/cubic meter	>>>	1.000 000 0E+09
megagram/milliliter	1	1.000 000 0E+00
ounce/cubic inch	578,036.67	5.780 366 7E+05
pound/cubic inch	36,127.292	3.612 729 2E+04
slug/cubic inch	1,122.870 6	1.122 870 6E+03

	Standard	Scientific
ton/cubic inch [short]	18.063 646	1.806 364 6E+01
ton/gallon [short/US, liquid]	4,172.702 2	4.172 702 2E+03
tonne/cubic centimeter	1	1.000 000 0E+00
tonne/milliliter	1	1.000 000 0E+00

megagram/cubic decimeter <density>

	Standard	Scientific
gram/cubic centimeter	1,000	1.000 000 0E+03
kilogram/cubic meter	1,000,000	1.000 000 0E+06
kilogram/milliliter	1	1.000 000 0E+00
megagram/liter	1	1.000 000 0E+00
ounce/cubic inch	578.036 67	5.780 366 7E+02
pound/cubic inch	36.127 292	3.612 729 2E+01
slug/cubic inch	1.122 870 6	1.122 870 6E+00
ton/cubic foot [short]	31.213 98	3.121 398 0E+01
ton/gallon [short/US, liquid]	4.172 702 2	4.172 702 2E+00
tonne/cubic decimeter	1	1.000 000 0E+00
tonne/liter	1	1.000 000 0E+00

megagram/cubic meter <density>

	Standard	Scientific
grain/cubic inch	252.891 04	2.528 910 4E+02
gram/cubic centimeter	1	1.000 000 0E+00
gram/milliliter	1	1.000 000 0E+00
kilogram/cubic meter	1,000	1.000 000 0E+03
kilogram/liter	1	1.000 000 0E+00
ounce/cubic inch	0.578 036 7	5.780 366 7E−01
pound/cubic foot	62.427 961	6.242 796 1E+01
pound/gallon [-/US, liquid]	8.345 404 5	8.345 404 5E+00
slug/cubic foot	1.940 320 3	1.940 320 3E+00
ton/cubic yard [short]	0.842 777 5	8.427 774 7E−01
tonne/cubic meter	1	1.000 000 0E+00

megagram/liter <density>

	Standard	Scientific
grain/cubic inch	252,891.04	2.528 910 4E+05
gram/cubic centimeter	1,000	1.000 000 0E+03
kilogram/cubic meter	1,000,000	1.000 000 0E+06
kilogram/liter	1,000	1.000 000 0E+03
megagram/cubic decimeter	1	1.000 000 0E+00
ounce/cubic inch	578.036 67	5.780 366 7E+02
pound/cubic inch	36.127 292	3.612 729 2E+01
pound/gallon [-/US, liquid]	8,345.404 5	8.345 404 5E+03
slug/cubic inch	1.122 870 6	1.122 870 6E+00
ton/cubic foot [short]	31.213 98	3.121 398 0E+01
ton/gallon [short/US, liquid]	4.172 702 2	4.172 702 2E+00
tonne/liter	1	1.000 000 0E+00

megagram/milliliter <density>

	Standard	Scientific
grain/cubic inch	>>>	2.528 910 4E+08
gram/cubic centimeter	1,000,000	1.000 000 0E+06
kilogram/cubic meter	>>>	1.000 000 0E+09
megagram/cubic centimeter	1	1.000 000 0E+00
ounce/cubic inch	578,036.67	5.780 366 7E+05
pound/cubic inch	36,127.292	3.612 729 2E+04
slug/cubic inch	1,122.870 6	1.122 870 6E+03
ton/cubic inch [short]	18.063 646	1.806 364 6E+01
ton/gallon [short/US, liquid]	4,172.702 2	4.172 702 2E+03
tonne/milliliter	1	1.000 000 0E+00

megahenry <electric inductance>

	Standard	Scientific
abhenry	>>>	1.000 000 0E+15
henry	1,000,000	1.000 000 0E+06
joule/square ampere	1,000,000	1.000 000 0E+06
ohm second	1,000,000	1.000 000 0E+06
stathenry	0.000 001 1	1.112 650 1E−06

megahertz <frequency>

	Standard	Scientific
1/second	1,000,000	1.000 000 0E+06
degree/second	>>>	3.600 000 0E+08
kilohertz	1,000	1.000 000 0E+03

Convert From	**<Type of Unit>**	
Convert To	Standard	Scientific

radian/second	6,283,185.3	6.283 185 3E+06
revolution/second	1,000,000	1.000 000 0E+06

megajoule   **<energy>**

Btu [I.T.]	947.817 12	9.478 171 2E+02
calorie [I.T.]	238,845.9	2.388 459 0E+05
calorie [kilogram, I.T.]	238.845 9	2.388 459 0E+02
centigrade heat unit [I.T.]	526.565 07	5.265 650 7E+02
cheval vapeur heure [France]	0.377 672 7	3.776 726 7E-01
coal equivalent kilogram [UN, standard]	0.034 120 8	3.412 084 2E-02
cubic centimeter atmosphere	9,869,232.7	9.869 232 7E+06
cubic foot atmosphere	348.528 66	3.485 286 6E+02
frigorie [France]	238.902 96	2.389 029 6E+02
gram calorie	238,902.96	2.389 029 6E+05
horsepower hour	0.372 506 1	3.725 061 4E-01
horsepower hour [metric]	0.377 672 7	3.776 726 7E-01
joule	1,000,000	1.000 000 0E+06
kilocalorie [I.T.]	238.845 9	2.388 459 0E+02
kilogram calorie [15 °C, NBS, 1939]	238.902 96	2.389 029 6E+02
kilowatthour	0.277 777 8	2.777 777 8E-01
pferdestarkenstunde [Germany]	0.377 672 7	3.776 726 7E-01
thermie [France]	0.238 903	2.389 029 6E-01
watthour	277.777 78	2.777 777 8E+02
wattsecond	1,000,000	1.000 000 0E+06

megajoule/kilogram   **<specific thermodynamic energy>**

Btu/pound [I.T.]	429.922 61	4.299 226 1E+02
Btu/pound [thermoc.]	430.210 33	4.302 103 3E+02
calorie/gram [I.T.]	238.845 9	2.388 459 0E+02
calorie/gram [thermoc.]	239.005 74	2.390 057 4E+02
joule/kilogram	1,000,000	1.000 000 0E+06

megalerg   **<energy>**

Btu [I.T.]	0.000 094 8	9.478 171 2E-05
calorie [I.T.]	0.023 884 6	2.388 459 0E-02
calorie [kilogram, I.T.]	0.000 023 9	2.388 459 0E-05
cubic centimeter atmosphere	0.986 923 3	9.869 232 7E-01
cubic foot atmosphere	0.000 034 9	3.485 286 6E-05
dyne centimeter	1,000,000	1.000 000 0E+06
erg	1,000,000	1.000 000 0E+06
foot pound-force	0.073 756 2	7.375 621 5E-02
foot poundal	2.373 036	2.373 036 0E+00
inch ounce-force	14.161 193	1.416 119 3E+01
inch pound-force	0.885 074 6	8.850 745 8E-01
joule	0.1	1.000 000 0E-01
kilogram square meter/square second	0.1	1.000 000 0E-01
kilopond meter	0.010 197 2	1.019 716 2E-02
liter atmosphere	0.000 986 9	9.869 232 7E-04
megaerg	1	1.000 000 0E+00
meter kilogram-force	0.010 197 2	1.019 716 2E-02
newton meter	0.1	1.000 000 0E-01
watthour	0.000 027 8	2.777 777 8E-05
wattsecond	0.1	1.000 000 0E-01

megaliter   **<volume>**

acre foot	0.810 713 2	8.107 131 9E-01
acre inch	9.728 558 3	9.728 558 3E+00
barrel [UK]	6,110.256 9	6.110 256 9E+03
barrel [US, liquid]	8,386.414 4	8.386 414 4E+03
barrel [US, petroleum]	6,289.810 8	6.289 810 8E+03
chaldron [UK, liquid]	763.782 11	7.637 821 1E+02
cubic dekameter	1	1.000 000 0E+00
cubic foot	35,314.667	3.531 466 7E+04
cubic inch	>>>	6.102 374 4E+07
cubic meter	1,000	1.000 000 0E+03
cubic yard	1,307.950 6	1.307 950 6E+03

| Convert From | | \<Type of Unit\> |
Convert To	Standard	Scientific
gallon [UK, dry or liquid]	219,969.25	2.199 692 5E+05
gallon [US, liquid]	264,172.05	2.641 720 5E+05
hectare meter	0.1	1.000 000 0E-01
liter	1,000,000	1.000 000 0E+06
shipping ton	882.866 67	8.828 666 7E+02
stere	1,000	1.000 000 0E+03

megameter   \<length\>

Convert To	Standard	Scientific
astronomical unit	0.000 006 7	6.684 587 2E-06
bevameter	0.001	1.000 000 0E-03
chain [Gunter or US, survey]	49,709.596	4.970 959 6E+04
chain [Ramden or Engineer]	32,808.399	3.280 839 9E+04
foot [international]	3,280,839.9	3.280 839 9E+06
foot [US, survey]	3,280,833.3	3.280 833 3E+06
furlong [US, survey]	4,970.959 6	4.970 959 6E+03
league [international, nautical]	179.985 6	1.799 856 0E+02
league [US, statute]	207.123 32	2.071 233 2E+02
link [Gunter or US, survey]	4,970,959.6	4.970 959 6E+06
link [Ramden or Engineer]	3,280,839.9	3.280 839 9E+06
meter	1,000,000	1.000 000 0E+06
mile [international]	621.371 19	6.213 711 9E+02
mile [US, statute]	621.369 95	6.213 699 5E+02
mile [US, survey]	621.369 95	6.213 699 5E+02
myriameter	100	1.000 000 0E+02
out [US, survey]	9,941.919 2	9.941 919 2E+03
pace [geometrical]	65,616.798	6.561 679 8E+04
pace [US, survey]	1,312,333.3	1.312 333 3E+06
perch [US, survey]	198,838.38	1.988 383 8E+05
perche [France]	171,024.05	1.710 240 5E+05
range [US, survey]	103.561 66	1.035 616 6E+02
township [US, survey]	103.561 66	1.035 616 6E+02
yard [based on US, survey foot]	1,093,611.1	1.093 611 1E+06
yard [international]	1,093,613.3	1.093 613 3E+06
yard [UK]	1,093,615.2	1.093 615 2E+06

megameter/day   \<velocity\>

Convert To	Standard	Scientific
foot/second	37.972 684	3.797 268 4E+01
inch/second	455.672 208	4.556 722 1E+02
knot [international]	22.498 200 1	2.249 820 0E+01
meter/second	11.574 074 1	1.157 407 4E+01
mile/hour	25.890 466 3	2.589 046 6E+01
nautical mile/hour [international]	22.498 200 1	2.249 820 0E+01
yard/second	12.657 561 3	1.265 756 1E+01

megameter/hour   \<velocity\>

Convert To	Standard	Scientific
foot/second	911.344 415	9.113 444 2E+02
inch/second	10,936.133	1.093 613 3E+04
knot [international]	539.956 803	5.399 568 0E+02
meter/second	277.777 778	2.777 777 8E+02
mile/minute	10.356 186 5	1.035 618 6E+01
nautical mile/minute [international]	8.999 280 1	8.999 280 1E+00
yard/second	303.781 472	3.037 814 7E+02

megameter/minute   \<velocity\>

Convert To	Standard	Scientific
foot/second	54,680.664 9	5.468 066 5E+04
inch/second	656,167.979	6.561 679 8E+05
knot [international]	32,397.408 2	3.239 740 8E+04
meter/second	16,666.666 7	1.666 666 7E+04
mile/second	10.356 186 5	1.035 618 7E+01
nautical mile/second [international]	8.999 280 1	8.999 280 1E+00
yard/second	18,226.888 3	1.822 688 8E+04

megameter/second   \<velocity\>

Convert To	Standard	Scientific
foot/second	3,280,839.9	3.280 839 9E+06
inch/second	>>>	3.937 007 9E+07
knot [international]	1,943,844.49	1.943 844 5E+06
meter/second	1,000,000	1.000 000 0E+06

Convert From Convert To	Standard	<Type of Unit> Scientific
mile/second	621.371 192	6.213 711 9E+02
nautical mile/second [international]	539.956 803	5.399 568 0E+02
speed of light	0.003 335 6	3.335 641 0E-03

megamho | | <electric conductance>
absiemens	0.001	1.000 000 0E-03
electromagnetic unit of conductance [cgs system]	0.001	1.000 000 0E-03
megasiemens	1	1.000 000 0E+00
siemens	1,000,000	1.000 000 0E+06
statsiemens	>>>	8.987 551 8E+17

megamole | | <amount of substance>
| mole | 1,000,000 | 1.000 000 0E+06 |

meganewton | | <force>
crinal	>>>	1.000 000 0E+07
dyne	>>>	1.000 000 0E+11
gram-force	>>>	1.019 716 2E+08
newton	1,000,000	1.000 000 0E+06
ounce-force	3,596,943.09	3.596 943 1E+06
pond	>>>	1.019 716 2E+08
pound-force	224,808.943	2.248 089 4E+05
poundal	7,233,013.85	7.233 013 9E+06

meganewton meter | | <torque>
foot pound-force	737,562.15	7.375 621 5E+05
kilonewton meter	1,000	1.000 000 0E+03
kilopond meter	101,971.62	1.019 716 2E+05
meter kilogram-force	101,971.62	1.019 716 2E+05
newton meter	1,000,000	1.000 000 0E+06

megaparsec | | <length>
astronomical unit	>>>	2.062 648 1E+11
bevameter	>>>	3.085 677 6E+13
exameter	30,856.776	3.085 677 6E+04
kiloparsec	1,000	1.000 000 0E+03
light year [based on mean Julian year]	3,261,563.8	3.261 563 8E+06
meter	>>>	3.085 677 6E+22
mile [international]	>>>	1.917 351 1E+19
mile [US, statute]	>>>	1.917 347 3E+19
mile [US, survey]	>>>	1.917 347 3E+19
myriameter	>>>	3.085 677 6E+18
parsec	1,000,000	1.000 000 0E+06
siriometer	206,264.81	2.062 648 1E+05
zettameter	30.856 776	3.085 677 6E+01

megapascal | | <pressure>
atmosphere [standard]	9.869 232 7	9.869 232 7E+00
atmosphere [technical]	10.197 162	1.019 716 2E+01
bar	10	1.000 000 0E+01
centimeter of mercury [0 °C, by convention]	750.061 58	7.500 615 8E+02
centimeter of water [4 °C, by convention]	10,197.162	1.019 716 2E+04
dekabar	1	1.000 000 0E+00
dyne/square centimeter	>>>	1.000 000 0E+07
foot of mercury [0 °C, by convention]	24.608 319	2.460 831 9E+01
foot of water [4 °C, by convention]	334.552 56	3.345 525 6E+02
gram-force/square centimeter	10,197.162	1.019 716 2E+04
kilogram-force/square centimeter	10.197 162	1.019 716 2E+01
kilopond/square centimeter	10.197 162	1.019 716 2E+01
kip/square foot	20.885 434	2.088 543 4E+01
newton/square millimeter	1	1.000 000 0E+00
ounce-force/square inch	2,320.603 8	2.320 603 8E+03
pascal	1,000,000	1.000 000 0E+06
pound-force/square inch	145.037 74	1.450 377 4E+02
ton-force/square foot [long]	9.323 854 6	9.323 854 6E+00
ton-force/square foot [short]	10.442 717	1.044 271 7E+01
ton-force/square meter [metric]	101.971 62	1.019 716 2E+02
torr	7,500.616 8	7.500 616 8E+03

Convert From / Convert To	Standard	Scientific

megarikon [Greece, ancient] — <volume, special - see page 29>

	Standard	Scientific
liter	102.5	1.025 000 0E+02

megasecond — <time>

	Standard	Scientific
second	1,000,000	1.000 000 0E+06

megasiemens — <electric conductance>

	Standard	Scientific
absiemens	0.001	1.000 000 0E−03
electromagnetic unit of conductance [cgs system]	0.001	1.000 000 0E−03
megamho	1	1.000 000 0E+00
siemens	1,000,000	1.000 000 0E+06
statsiemens	>>>	8.987 551 8E+17

megasiemens/meter — <electric conductivity>

	Standard	Scientific
absiemens/centimeter	0.000 01	1.000 000 0E−05
mho/meter	1,000,000	1.000 000 0E+06
siemens/meter	1,000,000	1.000 000 0E+06
statsiemens/centimeter	>>>	8.987 551 8E+15

megatesla — <magnetic flux density>

	Standard	Scientific
electrostatic unit of magnetic flux density [cgs system]	0.333 564 1	3.335 641 0E−01
gaussian magnetic flux density	0.333 564 1	3.335 641 0E−01
line/square centimeter [of magnetic force]	>>>	1.000 000 0E+10
maxwell/square meter	1,000,000	1.000 000 0E+06
tesla	1,000,000	1.000 000 0E+06

megaton [metric, explosive energy] — <energy>

	Standard	Scientific
coal equivalent kilogram [UN, standard]	>>>	1.427 616 0E+08
coal equivalent metric ton [UN, standard]	142,761.6	1.427 616 0E+05
exawatthour	0.000 001 2	1.162 222 2E−06
gigawatthour	1,162.222 2	1.162 222 2E+03
gram [atomic physics, eq. energy]	46.553 278	4.655 327 8E+01
hectowatthour	>>>	1.162 222 2E+10
joule	>>>	4.184 000 0E+15
kilogram [atomic physics, eq. energy]	0.046 553 3	4.655 327 8E−02
kiloton [metric, explosive energy]	1,000	1.000 000 0E+03
petawatthour	0.001 162 2	1.162 222 2E−03
quad	0.003 965 7	3.965 666 8E−03
terawatthour	1.162 222 2	1.162 222 2E+00
therm [EEC]	>>>	3.965 666 8E+07
therm [US]	>>>	3.966 613 7E+07
thermie [France]	>>>	9.995 699 7E+08
ton [metric, explosive energy]	1,000,000	1.000 000 0E+06

megaton [metric] — <mass>

	Standard	Scientific
kilogram	>>>	1.000 000 0E+09
kiloton [metric]	1,000	1.000 000 0E+03
kilotonne	1,000	1.000 000 0E+03
megatonne	1	1.000 000 0E+00
miller	1,000,000	1.000 000 0E+06
quarter [long]	3,936,826.1	3.936 826 1E+06
quarter [short]	4,409,245.2	4.409 245 2E+06
teragram	1	1.000 000 0E+00
ton [long]	984,206.53	9.842 065 3E+05
ton [metric]	1,000,000	1.000 000 0E+06
ton [short]	1,102,311.3	1.102 311 3E+06
ton [UK]	984,206.53	9.842 065 3E+05
tonne	1,000,000	1.000 000 0E+06

megatonne — <mass>

	Standard	Scientific
kilogram	>>>	1.000 000 0E+09
kiloton [metric]	1,000	1.000 000 0E+03
kilotonne	1,000	1.000 000 0E+03
megaton [metric]	1	1.000 000 0E+00
miller	1,000,000	1.000 000 0E+06
quarter [long]	3,936,826.1	3.936 826 1E+06
quarter [short]	4,409,245.2	4.409 245 2E+06
teragram	1	1.000 000 0E+00

ton [long]	984,206.53	9.842 065 3E+05
ton [metric]	1,000,000	1.000 000 0E+06
ton [short]	1,102,311.3	1.102 311 3E+06
ton [UK]	984,206.53	9.842 065 3E+05
tonne	1,000,000	1.000 000 0E+06

megavolt   \<electric potential\>

abvolt	>>>	1.000 000 0E+14
crocodile	1	1.000 000 0E+00
erg/franklin	3,335.640 95	3.335 641 0E+03
statvolt	3,335.640 95	3.335 641 0E+03
volt	1,000,000	1.000 000 0E+06

megavolt/meter   \<electric field strength\>

abvolt/centimeter	>>>	1.000 000 0E+12
statvolt/centimeter	33.356 409 5	3.335 641 0E+01
volt/inch	25,400	2.540 000 0E+04
volt/meter	1,000,000	1.000 000 0E+06

megawatt   \<power\>

Btu/second [I.T.]	947.817 12	9.478 171 2E+02
Btu/second [thermoc.]	948.451 41	9.484 514 1E+02
calorie/second [I.T.]	238,845.9	2.388 459 0E+05
calorie/second [thermoc.]	239,005.74	2.390 057 4E+05
centigrade heat unit/second [mean]	526.159 05	5.261 590 5E+02
cheval vapeur [France]	1,359.621 6	1.359 621 6E+03
cubic meter atmosphere/second	9,869,232.7	9.869 232 7E+06
dyne centimeter/second	>>>	1.000 000 0E+13
erg/second	>>>	1.000 000 0E+13
foot pound-force/second	737,562.15	7.375 621 5E+05
foot poundal/second	>>>	2.373 036 0E+07
gram-force centimeter/second	>>>	1.019 716 2E+10
horsepower	1,341.022 1	1.341 022 1E+03
horsepower [metric]	1,359.621 6	1.359 621 6E+03
joule/second	1,000,000	1.000 000 0E+06
kilocalorie/second [I.T.]	238.845 9	2.388 459 0E+02
kilogram-force meter/second	101,971.62	1.019 716 2E+05
kilopond meter/second	101,971.62	1.019 716 2E+05
million Btu/hour [I.T.]	3.412 141 6	3.412 141 6E+00
newton meter/second	1,000,000	1.000 000 0E+06
pferdestarke [Germany]	1,359.621 6	1.359 621 6E+03
poncelet [France]	1,019.716 2	1.019 716 2E+03
ton of refrigeration	284.345 14	2.843 451 4E+02
volt ampere	1,000,000	1.000 000 0E+06
watt	1,000,000	1.000 000 0E+06

megawatt/square meter   \<heat flux density\>

Btu/second square foot [I.T.]	88.055 092	8.805 509 2E+01
Btu/second square foot [thermoc.]	88.114 02	8.811 402 0E+01
calorie/second square centimeter [I.T.]	23.884 59	2.388 459 0E+01
calorie/second square centimeter [thermoc.]	23.900 574	2.390 057 4E+01
watt/square inch	645.16	6.451 600 0E+02
watt/square meter	1,000,000	1.000 000 0E+06

megawatthour   \<energy\>

cheval vapeur heure [France]	1,359.621 6	1.359 621 6E+03
coal equivalent kilogram [UN, standard]	122.835 03	1.228 350 3E+02
coal equivalent metric ton [UN, standard]	0.122 835	1.228 350 3E−01
horsepower hour	1,341.022 1	1.341 022 1E+03
horsepower hour [metric]	1,359.621 6	1.359 621 6E+03
joule	>>>	3.600 000 0E+09
kilocalorie [I.T.]	859,845.23	8.598 452 3E+05
kilogram calorie [15 °C, NBS, 1939]	860,050.65	8.600 506 5E+05
kiloton [metric, explosive energy]	0.000 860 4	8.604 206 5E−04
megaton [metric, explosive energy]	0.000 000 9	8.604 206 5E−07
myriawatthour	100	1.000 000 0E+02
pferdestarkenstunde [Germany]	1,359.621 6	1.359 621 6E+03

	Standard	Scientific
therm [EEC]	34.121 416	3.412 141 6E+01
therm [US]	34.129 563	3.412 956 3E+01
thermie [France]	860.050 65	8.600 506 5E+02
ton [metric, explosive energy]	0.860 420 7	8.604 206 5E-01
megaweber		**<magnetic flux>**
gauss square centimeter	>>>	1.000 000 0E+14
maxwell	>>>	1.000 000 0E+14
statweber	3,335.640 95	3.335 641 0E+03
unit pole	>>>	7.957 747 5E+12
weber	1,000,000	1.000 000 0E+06
megohm		**<electric resistance>**
1/ siemens	1,000,000	1.000 000 0E+06
abohm	>>>	1.000 000 0E+15
ohm	1,000,000	1.000 000 0E+06
statohm	0.000 001 1	1.112 650 1E-06
megohm meter		**<electric resistivity>**
abohm centimeter	>>>	1.000 000 0E+17
microohm inch	>>>	3.937 007 9E+13
ohm circular mil/foot	>>>	6.015 304 9E+14
ohm meter	1,000,000	1.000 000 0E+06
ohm square millimeter/meter	>>>	1.000 000 0E+12
statohm centimeter	0.000 111 3	1.112 650 1E-04
meias canada [Portugal, liquid]		**<volume, special - see page 29>**
liter	0.689	6.890 000 0E-01
meile [Austria]		**<length, special - see page 29>**
kilometer	7.585 9	7.585 900 0E+00
meile [Denmark]		**<length, special - see page 29>**
kilometer	7.532 5	7.532 500 0E+00
meile [Germany]		**<length, special - see page 29>**
meter	7,422	7.422 000 0E+03
meile [Hungary]		**<length, special - see page 29>**
kilometer	8.353 6	8.353 600 0E+00
meile [Sweden]		**<length, special - see page 29>**
kilometer	10	1.000 000 0E+01
meile [Venezuela]		**<mass, special - see page 29>**
kilogram	400	4.000 000 0E+02
meio [Portugal]		**<volume, special - see page 29>**
liter	0.697 9	6.979 000 0E-01
mekyas cubit [Egypt, ancient]		**<length, special - see page 29>**
centimeter	54	5.400 000 0E+01
mengel [Netherlands]		**<volume, special - see page 29>**
liter	1.212	1.212 000 0E+00
menor [Iran]		**<volume, special - see page 29>**
liter	12.547	1.254 700 0E+01
mercal [India]		**<volume, special - see page 29>**
liter	12.26	1.226 000 0E+01
merfold [Hungary]		**<length, special - see page 29>**
kilometer	8.354	8.354 000 0E+00
merica [Czechoslovakia]		**<volume, special - see page 29>**
liter	70.6	7.060 000 0E+01
merice [Czechoslovakia]		**<volume, special - see page 29>**
liter	70.5	7.050 000 0E+01
merice [Czechoslovakia]		**<area, special - see page 29>**
square meter	1.918	1.918 000 0E+00
merrassi [Syria]		**<area, special - see page 29>**
square meter	50	5.000 000 0E+01

Convert From / Convert To	Standard	Scientific
mertfold [Hungary]	<length, special - see page 29>	
kilometer	8.353 6	8.353 600 0E+00
mesana [Cuba]	<area, special - see page 29>	
square meter	2,588.77	2.588 770 0E+03
mesghal [Iran]	<mass, special - see page 29>	
gram	4.639 6	4.639 600 0E+00
meshara [Iraq]	<area, special - see page 29>	
hectare	0.25	2.500 000 0E-01
messe [Eritrea]	<volume, special - see page 29>	
liter	1.5	1.500 000 0E+00
messe [Ethiopia]	<volume, special - see page 29>	
liter	1.5	1.500 000 0E+00
metarta [Hebrew, ancient]	<volume, special - see page 29>	
cubic centimeter	39,553.32	3.955 332 0E+04
meteka [Algiers]	<mass, special - see page 29>	
gram	4.67	4.670 000 0E+00
meteka [Egypt]	<mass, special - see page 29>	
gram	4.68	4.680 000 0E+00
meteka [Libya, Tripoli]	<mass, special - see page 29>	
gram	4.8	4.800 000 0E+00
meteka [Syria]	<mass, special - see page 29>	
gram	4.8	4.800 000 0E+00
meter	<length>	
actus [Rome, ancient]	0.028 169	2.816 901 4E-02
agate [print]	517.322 84	5.173 228 4E+02
aldan [Mongolia]	0.625	6.250 000 0E-01
alen [Denmark]	1.593 117 7	1.593 117 7E+00
alen [Sweden]	1.684 068 7	1.684 068 7E+00
alin [Iceland]	1.593 117 7	1.593 117 7E+00
aln [Sweden]	1.684 063	1.684 063 0E+00
amma [Greece, ancient]	0.054 054 1	5.405 405 4E-02
amma [Hebrew, ancient]	2.257 336 3	2.257 336 3E+00
angstrom	>>>	1.000 000 0E+10
archin [Turkey]	1	1.000 000 0E+00
arine [Belgium]	0.833 333 3	8.333 333 3E-01
arish [Iran]	0.961 538 5	9.615 384 6E-01
arkana [Greece, ancient]	0.324 675 3	3.246 753 2E-01
arpent [Canada]	0.017 102 8	1.710 278 8E-02
arpent [France]	0.017 102 4	1.710 240 1E-02
arshin [Iran]	0.961 538 5	9.615 384 6E-01
arshin [Turkey]	1	1.000 000 0E+00
astronomical unit	<<<	6.684 587 2E-12
aune [Belgium]	0.833 333 3	8.333 333 3E-01
aune [Dominican Republic]	0.841 750 8	8.417 508 4E-01
aune [France]	0.841 750 8	8.417 508 4E-01
aune [Haiti]	0.839 630 6	8.396 305 6E-01
aune [Switzerland]	0.833 333 3	8.333 333 3E-01
baa [Egypt]	0.333 333 3	3.333 333 3E-01
baa [Oman]	0.694 444 4	6.944 444 4E-01
bamboo [Burma]	0.312 5	3.125 000 0E-01
bandle [Ireland]	1.639 344 3	1.639 344 3E+00
barleycorn	118.110 24	1.181 102 4E+02
bei mi [China]	0.01	1.000 000 0E-02
bevameter	<<<	1.000 000 0E-09
bicron	>>>	1.000 000 0E+12
bolt [cloth]	0.027 340 3	2.734 033 2E-02
bow [India]	0.546 806 6	5.468 066 5E-01
bow [Pakistan]	0.546 806 6	5.468 066 5E-01
braca [Argentina]	0.577 034 1	5.770 340 5E-01
braca [Brazil]	0.450 045	4.500 450 0E-01

		<Type of Unit>
	Standard	Scientific

meter (continued)   \<length\>

Convert From / To	Standard	Scientific
braca [Chile]	0.598 086 1	5.980 861 2E-01
braca [Colombia]	0.625	6.250 000 0E-01
braca [El Salvador]	0.598 086 1	5.980 861 2E-01
braca [Portugal]	0.454 545 5	4.545 454 5E-01
brasse [Argentina]	0.577 034 1	5.770 340 5E-01
brasse [Belgium]	0.714 285 7	7.142 857 1E-01
brasse [Chile]	0.598 086 1	5.980 861 2E-01
brasse [Colombia]	0.625	6.250 000 0E-01
brasse [El Salvador]	0.598 086 1	5.980 861 2E-01
brasse [France]	0.617 284	6.172 839 5E-01
braza [Argentina]	0.577 034 1	5.770 340 5E-01
braza [Chile]	0.598 086 1	5.980 861 2E-01
braza [Colombia]	0.625	6.250 000 0E-01
braza [Costa Rica]	0.598 086 1	5.980 861 2E-01
braza [El Salvador]	0.598 086 1	5.980 861 2E-01
braza [Guatemala]	0.598 086 1	5.980 861 2E-01
braza [Peru]	0.598 086 1	5.980 861 2E-01
braza [Spain]	0.598 802 4	5.988 024 0E-01
brazada [Argentina]	0.577 034 1	5.770 340 5E-01
brazada [Chile]	0.598 086 1	5.980 861 2E-01
brazada [Colombia]	0.625	6.250 000 0E-01
brazada [El Salvador]	0.598 086 1	5.980 861 2E-01
cable length [US, survey]	0.004 556 7	4.556 713 0E-03
cabulla [Venezuela]	0.012 5	1.250 000 0E-02
caliber	3,937.007 9	3.937 007 9E+03
canna [Italy]	0.5	5.000 000 0E-01
canna [Malta]	0.477 327	4.773 269 7E-01
cape foot [South Africa]	3.176 014 7	3.176 014 7E+00
cape rood [South Africa]	0.264 669 3	2.646 693 0E-01
cassaba [Egypt, ancient]	0.281 690 1	2.816 901 4E-01
cassaba [Iraq]	0.263 157 9	2.631 578 9E-01
cay [Vietnam]	0.053 333 3	5.333 333 3E-02
centimeter	100	1.000 000 0E+02
cha [South Korea]	3.300 003 3	3.300 003 3E+00
chain [Gunter or US, survey]	0.049 709 6	4.970 959 6E-02
chain [Ramden or Engineer]	0.032 808 4	3.280 839 9E-02
chang [China]	0.279 251 6	2.792 516 1E-01
chang [Mongolia]	0.312 5	3.125 000 0E-01
charac [Iran]	3.846 153 8	3.846 153 8E+00
che [China]	3	3.000 000 0E+00
che [Hong Kong]	2.691 971 2	2.691 971 2E+00
che [Singapore]	2.669 514 1	2.669 514 1E+00
check [China, new]	3	3.000 000 0E+00
check [China, old]	2.792 204 2	2.792 204 2E+00
check [Hong Kong]	2.669 514 1	2.669 514 1E+00
check [Singapore]	2.669 514 1	2.669 514 1E+00
cheh [China]	3	3.000 000 0E+00
cheh [Hong Kong]	2.691 971 2	2.691 971 2E+00
cheh [Singapore]	2.669 514 1	2.669 514 1E+00
chek [China, new]	3	3.000 000 0E+00
chek [China, old]	2.792 204 2	2.792 204 2E+00
chek [Hong Kong]	2.691 971 2	2.691 971 2E+00
chek [Singapore]	2.669 514 1	2.669 514 1E+00
cheung [Hong Kong]	0.269 197 1	2.691 971 2E-01
cheung [Malaysia]	0.266 951 4	2.669 514 1E-01
cheung [Singapore]	0.266 915 8	2.669 157 9E-01
chhek [China, new]	3	3.000 000 0E+00
chhek [China, old]	2.792 204 2	2.792 204 2E+00
chhek [Hong Kong]	2.669 514 1	2.669 514 1E+00
chhek [Singapore]	2.669 514 1	2.669 514 1E+00
chi [China]	3	3.000 000 0E+00
chih [Hong Kong]	2.691 971 2	2.691 971 2E+00

meter (continued)   <length>

Convert To	Standard	Scientific
chih [Singapore]	2.669 514 1	2.669 514 1E+00
chinese foot [Hong Kong]	2.691 971 2	2.691 971 2E+00
chinese yard [Hong Kong, textiles]	1.121 654 7	1.121 654 7E+00
cho [Japan]	0.009 166 7	9.166 743 1E-03
chok [South Korea]	3.300 003 3	3.300 003 3E+00
chung [South Korea]	0.009 166 7	9.166 743 1E-03
chungbo [Japan]	0.009 166 7	9.166 743 1E-03
codo [Spain]	2.392 344 5	2.392 344 5E+00
cordel [Cuba]	0.049 135 2	4.913 522 0E-02
cordel [Paraguay]	0.014 310 2	1.431 024 6E-02
coss [India]	0.000 273 4	2.734 033 0E-04
coudee [Israel]	2.239 641 7	2.239 641 7E+00
covado [Brazil]	0.014 600 7	1.460 067 2E-02
cuada [Argentina]	0.007 698 2	7.698 229 4E-03
cuadra [Argentina]	0.007 692 3	7.692 307 7E-03
cuadra [Chile]	0.007 975 1	7.975 117 6E-03
cuadra [Colombia]	0.012 5	1.250 000 0E-02
cuadra [Ecuador]	0.011 904 8	1.190 476 2E-02
cuadra [Paraguay]	0.011 539 3	1.153 934 9E-02
cuadra [Spain]	0.007 974 5	7.974 481 7E-03
cuadra [Uruguay]	0.011 641 4	1.164 144 4E-02
cubit	2.187 226 6	2.187 226 6E+00
cubit [Burma]	2.187 226 6	2.187 226 6E+00
cubit [Cambodia]	2	2.000 000 0E+00
cubit [Hebrew, ancient, long]	2	2.000 000 0E+00
cubit [Hebrew, ancient, short]	2.222 222 2	2.222 222 2E+00
cubit [Malaysia]	2.187 226 6	2.187 226 6E+00
cubit [Pakistan]	2.187 226 6	2.187 226 6E+00
cubit [Singapore]	2.188 183 8	2.188 183 8E+00
cubit [Somalia]	1.789 549	1.789 549 0E+00
cubito [Cambodia]	2	2.000 000 0E+00
cubito [Somalia]	1.789 549	1.789 549 0E+00
cubitus [Rome, ancient]	2.252 252 3	2.252 252 3E+00
cuerda [Cuba]	0.049 135 2	4.913 522 0E-02
cuerda [Paraguay]	0.014 310 2	1.431 024 6E-02
decempeda [Rome, ancient]	0.337 837 8	3.378 378 4E-01
decimeter	10	1.000 000 0E+01
dekameter	0.1	1.000 000 0E-01
depa [Singapore]	0.546 806 6	5.468 066 5E-01
dha [Burma]	0.312 5	3.125 000 0E-01
dhanu [India]	0.546 806 6	5.468 066 5E-01
didot point [print]	2,656.157 2	2.656 157 2E+03
digit	52.493 438	5.249 343 8E+01
diraa baladi [Egypt]	1.724 137 9	1.724 137 9E+00
double stadion [Mesopotamia, ancient]	0.002 772 4	2.772 387 0E-03
douzieme [print]	5,669.291 3	5.669 291 3E+03
dra [Yemen]	1.492 537 3	1.492 537 3E+00
drah [Morocco]	2	2.000 000 0E+00
dynia [Greece, ancient]	0.541 125 5	5.411 255 4E-01
el [Indonesia]	1.453 911	1.453 911 0E+00
el [Malaysia]	1.093 613 3	1.093 613 3E+00
el [Netherlands]	1	1.000 000 0E+00
el [Surinam]	1.453 911	1.453 911 0E+00
ell [Austria]	1.283 367 6	1.283 367 6E+00
ell [cloth]	0.874 890 6	8.748 906 4E-01
ell [Indonesia]	1.453 911	1.453 911 0E+00
ell [Malaysia]	1.093 613 3	1.093 613 3E+00
ell [Netherlands]	1.453 911	1.453 911 0E+00
elle [Germany]	1.200 465 8	1.200 465 8E+00
elle [South Africa]	1.459 854	1.459 854 0E+00
elle [Switzerland]	1.666 666 7	1.666 666 7E+00
em [pica, print]	237.106 3	2.371 063 0E+02

meter (continued) — \<length\>

	Standard	Scientific
encablure [France]	0.005	5.000 000 0E–03
endere [Romania]	1.510 574	1.510 574 0E+00
esba [Hebrew, ancient]	52.631 579	5.263 157 9E+01
estadel [Venezuela]	0.239 234 5	2.392 344 5E–01
estadio [Portugal]	0.003 876	3.875 969 0E–03
estadio [Spain]	0.005 742 2	5.742 242 2E–03
estado [Spain]	0.598 802 4	5.988 024 0E–01
famn [Denmark]	0.531 067 5	5.310 674 5E–01
famn [Sweden]	0.561 797 8	5.617 977 5E–01
faon [Denmark]	0.531 028	5.310 279 6E–01
farsakh [Ethiopia]	0.000 197 2	1.972 386 6E–04
fathmur [Iceland]	0.531 039 2	5.310 392 4E–01
fathom [Greece, ancient]	0.541 125 5	5.411 255 4E–01
fathom [Hebrew, ancient]	0.540 540 5	5.405 405 4E–01
fathom [Hungary]	0.527 426 2	5.274 261 6E–01
fathom [US, survey]	0.546 805 6	5.468 055 6E–01
faust [Hungary]	9.491 268	9.491 268 0E+00
favn [Sweden]	0.561 324 7	5.613 247 3E–01
fermi	>>> 1.000 000 0E+15	
fet [Iceland]	3.186 235 5	3.186 235 5E+00
fingerbreadth [Egypt, ancient]	52.631 579	5.263 157 9E+01
fingerbreadth [Hebrew, ancient]	45.454 545	4.545 454 5E+01
foot [Canada, Quebec]	3.076 923 1	3.076 923 1E+00
foot [France]	3.078 432 9	3.078 432 9E+00
foot [international]	3.280 839 9	3.280 839 9E+00
foot [South Africa]	3.280 869 3	3.280 869 3E+00
foot [US, survey]	3.280 833 3	3.280 833 3E+00
furlong [Palestine, ancient]	0.005 405 4	5.405 405 4E–03
furlong [US, survey]	0.004 971	4.970 959 6E–03
fuss [Austria]	3.163 756	3.163 756 0E+00
fuss [Germany]	3.426 300 3	3.426 300 3E+00
gana [Libya, textiles]	0.625	6.250 000 0E–01
ganu [Akkadian, ancient]	0.333 333 3	3.333 333 3E–01
gar [Iraq, ancient]	0.084 033 6	8.403 361 3E–02
gasab [Egypt, ancient]	0.281 690 1	2.816 901 4E–01
gatsar [Mongolia]	0.001 736 1	1.736 111 1E–03
gaulette [Mauritius]	0.307 843 9	3.078 438 6E–01
gaz [Iran]	0.961 538 5	9.615 384 6E–01
gaz memar [Afghanistan]	1.193 317 4	1.193 317 4E+00
gaz sha [Afghanistan]	0.938 086 3	9.380 863 0E–01
gazi sha [Afghanistan]	0.937 382 8	9.373 828 3E–01
gi [Sumeria, ancient]	0.333 333 3	3.333 333 3E–01
gigameter	<<< 1.000 000 0E–09	
gis [Sumeria, ancient]	0.002 772 4	2.772 387 0E–03
gon [Vietnam]	0.005 333 3	5.333 333 3E–03
gradus [Rome, ancient]	1.351 351 4	1.351 351 4E+00
gudge [India]	1.458 151 1	1.458 151 1E+00
gudge [Iran]	0.961 538 5	9.615 384 6E–01
gudge [Pakistan]	1.093 613 3	1.093 613 3E+00
guz [Ceylon]	1.093 613 3	1.093 613 3E+00
guz [India]	1.093 613 3	1.093 613 3E+00
guz [Iran]	0.961 538 5	9.615 384 6E–01
guz [Nepal, textiles]	1.093 613 3	1.093 613 3E+00
guz [Pakistan]	1.093 613 3	1.093 613 3E+00
habl [Libya]	0.028 571 4	2.857 142 9E–02
halibin [Romania]	1.426 533 5	1.426 533 5E+00
hand [horses]	9.842 519 7	9.842 519 7E+00
hasta [Malaysia]	2.187 226 6	2.187 226 6E+00
hasta [Singapore]	2.187 226 6	2.187 226 6E+00
hat [Somalia]	1.789 549	1.789 549 0E+00
hath [Cambodia]	2	2.000 000 0E+00
hath [Somalia]	1.789 549	1.789 549 0E+00

	\<Type of Unit>	
	Standard	Scientific

meter (continued) \<length>

Convert To	Standard	Scientific
hectometer	0.01	1.000 000 0E–02
hema [Greece, ancient]	1.298 701 3	1.298 701 3E+00
hesta [Cambodia]	2	2.000 000 0E+00
hesta [Somalia]	1.789 549	1.789 549 0E+00
hippicon [Greece, ancient]	0.001 353 2	1.353 180 0E–03
hiro [Japan]	0.660 066	6.600 660 1E–01
hong euk louang [Laos]	1	1.000 000 0E+00
hvat [Yugoslavia]	0.527 426 2	5.274 261 6E–01
inch [based on US, survey foot]	39.37	3.937 000 0E+01
inch [international]	39.370 079	3.937 007 9E+01
iron [print]	9.484 252 1	9.484 252 1E+00
iron [shoe leather]	1 889.763 8	1.889 763 8E+03
jarda [Cape Verde]	1.136 363 6	1.136 363 6E+00
jareeb [Pakistan]	0.049 709 7	4.970 969 5E–02
jarib [India]	0.018 226 9	1.822 688 8E–02
jo [Japan]	0.330 033	3.300 330 0E–01
jumba [Malacca]	0.273 373 4	2.733 734 3E–01
jungbo [Japan]	0.009 166 7	9.166 743 1E–03
kabellangd [Sweden]	0.005 613 5	5.613 530 9E–03
kabellengte [Netherlands, nautical]	0.004 444 4	4.444 444 4E–03
kala [Morocco]	1.789 549	1.789 549 0E+00
kaneh [Israel]	0.373 273 6	3.732 736 1E–01
karam [Pakistan]	0.596 658 7	5.966 587 1E–01
kasaba [Egypt]	0.281 690 1	2.816 901 4E–01
kasaba hakimiyya [Egypt]	0.259 740 3	2.597 402 6E–01
kassaba [Egypt]	0.281 690 1	2.816 901 4E–01
kassabah [Egypt]	0.281 690 1	2.816 901 4E–01
kathouah [Iraq, ancient]	0.526 315 8	5.263 157 9E–01
ken [Japan]	0.550 055	5.500 550 1E–01
ken [South Korea]	0.550 055	5.500 550 1E–01
ken [Thailand]	0.984 252	9.842 519 7E–01
kend [Ethiopia]	2	2.000 000 0E+00
kette [Germany]	0.1	1.000 000 0E–01
khalad [Ethiopia]	0.015 384 6	1.538 461 5E–02
khet [Egypt, ancient]	0.019 084	1.908 396 9E–02
khos aldan [Mongolia]	0.312 5	3.125 000 0E–01
khubi [Mongolia]	0.017 361 1	1.736 111 1E–02
khvat [Yugoslavia]	0.527 426 2	5.274 261 6E–01
kilometer	0.001	1.000 000 0E–03
kiloparsec	<<<	3.240 779 3E–20
klafter [Austria]	0.527 287 1	5.272 871 1E–01
klafter [Germany]	0.574 712 6	5.747 126 4E–01
klafter [Switzerland]	0.555 555 6	5.555 555 6E–01
kujira shaku [Japan]	2.638 522 4	2.638 522 4E+00
kung [China]	0.498 504 5	4.985 044 9E–01
kung chang [Taiwan]	0.1	1.000 000 0E–01
kung chih [China]	1	1.000 000 0E+00
kung chih [Taiwan]	1	1.000 000 0E+00
kung yin [Taiwan]	0.01	1.000 000 0E–02
lan [Burma]	0.546 746 9	5.467 468 6E–01
lanca [Cape Verde]	0.227 272 7	2.272 727 3E–01
lasta [Ceylon]	1.524 390 2	1.524 390 2E+00
lath [India]	0.364 537 8	3.645 377 7E–01
latro [Czechoslovakia]	0.521 648 4	5.216 484 1E–01
lea [US, cotton yarn]	0.009 113 4	9.113 444 2E–03
lea [US, linen yarn]	0.003 645 4	3.645 377 7E–03
lea [US, silk yarn]	0.009 113 4	9.113 444 2E–03
lea [US, wool yarn]	0.013 670 2	1.367 016 6E–02
league [international, nautical]	0.000 18	1.799 856 0E–04
league [UK, nautical]	0.000 179 9	1.798 706 1E–04
league [US, statute]	0.000 207 1	2.071 233 2E–04
lei [China]	0.002	2.000 000 0E–03

meter (continued) <length>

Convert To	Standard	Scientific
li [China]	0.001 551 2	1.551 229 3E−03
li [Hong Kong]	0.001 794 6	1.794 645 9E−03
light year [based on anomalistic year]	<<<	1.056 973 0E−16
light year [based on mean Julian year]	<<<	1.057 000 8E−16
light year [based on sidereal year]	<<<	1.056 982 4E−16
light year [based on tropical year]	<<<	1.057 023 4E−16
ligne [print]	472.440 94	4.724 409 4E+02
line [print]	472.440 94	4.724 409 4E+02
linhada [Cape Verde]	0.045 454 5	4.545 454 5E−02
link [Gunter or US, survey]	4.970 959 6	4.970 959 6E+00
link [Ramden or Engineer]	3.280 839 9	3.280 839 9E+00
lokiec [Poland]	1.736 111 1	1.736 111 1E+00
ma [Hong Kong, textiles]	1.121 654 7	1.121 654 7E+00
marok [Hungary]	9.491 268	9.491 268 0E+00
mecate [Costa Rica]	0.049 850 4	4.985 044 9E−02
mecate [Guatemala]	0.049 845 5	4.984 547 9E−02
mecate [Honduras]	0.049 900 2	4.990 020 0E−02
mecate [Nicaragua]	0.049 652 4	4.965 243 3E−02
megaparsec	<<<	3.240 779 3E−23
meile [Germany]	0.000 134 7	1.347 345 7E−04
mi [China]	1	1.000 000 0E+00
microinch	>>>	3.937 007 9E+07
micrometer	1,000,000	1.000 000 0E+06
micromicron	>>>	1.000 000 0E+12
micron	1,000,000	1.000 000 0E+06
mil	39,370.079	3.937 007 9E+04
mile [Germany]	0.000 133 3	1.333 333 3E−04
mile [international]	0.000 621 4	6.213 711 9E−04
mile [international, nautical]	0.000 54	5.399 568 0E−04
mile [UK, nautical]	0.000 539 6	5.396 118 2E−04
mile [US, nautical]	0.000 54	5.399 568 0E−04
mile [US, statute]	0.000 621 4	6.213 699 5E−04
mile [US, survey]	0.000 621 4	6.213 699 5E−04
milion [Rome, ancient]	0.000 676 1	6.761 325 2E−04
mille [France, nautical]	0.000 54	5.400 034 0E−04
mille passus [Rome, ancient]	0.000 676 1	6.761 325 2E−04
mille passuum [Rome, ancient]	0.000 675 7	6.756 756 8E−04
millimeter	1,000	1.000 000 0E+03
millimicron	>>>	1.000 000 0E+09
million [Hebrew, ancient]	0.000 676 4	6.763 611 8E−04
mkono [Kenya]	2.187 226 6	2.187 226 6E+00
mkono [Uganda]	2.187 226 6	2.187 226 6E+00
moolum [Ceylon]	2.187 226 6	2.187 226 6E+00
moolum [India]	2.187 226 6	2.187 226 6E+00
moreas plethron [Greece, ancient]	0.028 058 4	2.805 836 1E−02
mylia [Ukraine]	0.000 107 8	1.077 818 5E−04
myriameter	0.000 1	1.000 000 0E−04
nail [cloth]	17.497 813	1.749 781 3E+01
ngu [Thailand]	0.410 424 8	4.104 247 9E−01
ngu [Vietnam]	0.5	5.000 000 0E−01
ninda [Sumeria, ancient]	0.166 666 7	1.666 666 7E−01
niranja [India]	0.109 361 3	1.093 613 3E−01
noeud de loch [France]	0.064 800 4	6.480 041 5E−02
nonpareil [print]	474.212 6	4.742 126 0E+02
oke thapa [Burma]	0.015 623	1.562 304 7E−02
oke thapal [Burma]	0.012 782 5	1.278 249 3E−02
ona [Dominican Republic]	0.841 750 8	8.417 508 4E−01
orguia [Greece, ancient]	0.543 773 8	5.437 737 9E−01
orgyia [Greece, ancient]	0.540 540 5	5.405 405 4E−01
out [US, survey]	0.009 941 9	9.941 919 2E−03
pace [geometrical]	0.065 616 8	6.561 679 8E−02
pace [Greece, ancient]	1.298 701 3	1.298 701 3E+00

meter (continued) <length>

Convert To	Standard	Scientific
pace [US, survey]	1.312 333 3	1.312 333 3E+00
palame [Greece]	1	1.000 000 0E+00
palm	13.123 36	1.312 336 0E+01
palm [Hebrew, ancient]	12.5	1.250 000 0E+01
palm [Netherlands]	10	1.000 000 0E+01
palma [Spain]	4.785 238 5	4.785 238 5E+00
Paris foot [Canada, Quebec]	3.078 438 6	3.078 438 6E+00
Paris foot [France]	3.078 438 6	3.078 438 6E+00
parsec	<<<	3.240 779 3E-17
pas [Belgium]	1.111 111 1	1.111 111 1E+00
paso [Spain]	0.719 424 5	7.194 244 6E-01
passo [Brazil]	0.606 060 6	6.060 606 1E-01
passo [Libya]	1	1.000 000 0E+00
passus [Rome, ancient]	0.676 59	6.765 918 9E-01
pe [Cape Verde]	3.280 839 9	3.280 839 9E+00
pearl [print]	569.055 12	5.690 551 2E+02
pechus [Greece, ancient]	2.192 982 5	2.192 982 5E+00
perch [Ireland]	0.156 230 5	1.562 304 7E-01
perch [US, survey]	0.198 838 4	1.988 383 8E-01
perche [Belgium]	0.153 917 2	1.539 171 9E-01
perche [Canada, Quebec]	0.171 027 9	1.710 278 8E-01
perche [France]	0.171 024 1	1.710 240 5E-01
perche [France]	0.139 938 4	1.399 384 1E-01
perche [Switzerland]	0.333 333 3	3.333 333 3E-01
perestril [Ukraine]	0.015 384 6	1.538 461 5E-02
pertica [Rome, ancient]	0.337 837 8	3.378 378 4E-01
pes sestertius [Rome, ancient]	1.351 351 4	1.351 351 4E+00
phyeam [Cambodia]	0.5	5.000 000 0E-01
pic [Cyprus, textiles]	1.640 419 9	1.640 419 9E+00
pica [print]	237.106 3	2.371 063 0E+02
picheus [Greece]	0.666 666 7	6.666 666 7E-01
pie [Bolivia]	3.460 207 6	3.460 207 6E+00
pie [Costa Rica]	3.584 229 4	3.584 229 4E+00
pie [Cuba]	3.537 318 7	3.537 318 7E+00
pie [Ecuador]	3.280 839 9	3.280 839 9E+00
pie [Guatemala]	3.584 229 4	3.584 229 4E+00
pie [Haiti]	3.078 817 7	3.078 817 7E+00
pie [Italy]	3.571 428 6	3.571 428 6E+00
pie [Mexico]	3.584 229 4	3.584 229 4E+00
pie [Nicaragua]	3.571 428 6	3.571 428 6E+00
pie [Paraguay]	3.460 207 6	3.460 207 6E+00
pie [Spain]	3.584 229 4	3.584 229 4E+00
pied [Canada, Quebec]	3.078 438 6	3.078 438 6E+00
pied [Costa Rica]	3.584 229 4	3.584 229 4E+00
pied [Cuba]	3.537 318 7	3.537 318 7E+00
pied [France]	3.078 432 9	3.078 432 9E+00
pied [France]	3.078 438 6	3.078 438 6E+00
pied [Guatemala]	3.584 229 4	3.584 229 4E+00
pied [Haiti]	3.078 817 7	3.078 817 7E+00
pied [Mexico]	3.584 229 4	3.584 229 4E+00
pied [Nicaragua]	3.571 428 6	3.571 428 6E+00
pied [Paraguay]	3.460 207 6	3.460 207 6E+00
pied [Spain]	3.584 229 4	3.584 229 4E+00
pik [Algeria]	2.020 202	2.020 202 0E+00
plethron [Greece, ancient]	0.032 467 5	3.246 753 2E-02
point [print]	2,845.275 6	2.845 275 6E+03
pole [Ireland]	0.156 230 5	1.562 304 7E-01
pole [US, survey]	0.198 838 4	1.988 383 8E-01
postav [Ukraine]	0.035 714 3	3.571 428 6E-02
pret [Poland]	0.231 481 5	2.314 814 8E-01
pu [China]	0.555 555 6	5.555 555 6E-01
qadam [Sudan]	3.280 839 9	3.280 839 9E+00

meter (continued) — \<length\>

Convert To	Standard	Scientific
qama [Yemen]	0.606 060 6	6.060 606 1E-01
qasab [Egypt, ancient]	0.281 690 1	2.816 901 4E-01
qasaba [Egypt]	0.281 690 1	2.816 901 4E-01
qasba [Malta]	0.477 327	4.773 269 7E-01
quarter [cloth]	4.374 453 2	4.374 453 2E+00
rageil [Sudan]	0.596 658 7	5.966 587 1E-01
ragil [Sudan]	0.596 658 7	5.966 587 1E-01
ragil bergedawi [Sudan]	0.410 172 3	4.101 722 7E-01
range [US, survey]	0.000 103 6	1.035 616 6E-04
reed [Egypt, ancient]	0.317 460 3	3.174 603 2E-01
reed [Hebrew, ancient]	0.322 580 7	3.225 806 5E-01
reed [Israel]	0.373 273 6	3.732 736 1E-01
ref [Sweden]	0.033 681 4	3.368 137 4E-02
ri [North Korea]	0.002 546 3	2.546 298 1E-03
rif [Yugoslavia]	1.287 001 3	1.287 001 3E+00
rod [Egypt, ancient]	0.019 120 5	1.912 045 9E-02
rod [Mesopotamia, ancient]	0.333 333 3	3.333 333 3E-01
rod [US, survey]	0.198 838 4	1.988 383 8E-01
rode [Denmark]	0.318 674 3	3.186 743 1E-01
roe [Netherlands]	0.265 252	2.652 519 9E-01
roede [Indonesia]	0.265 435 1	2.654 350 5E-01
roede [Netherlands]	0.271 756 1	2.717 561 2E-01
rood [Swaziland]	0.264 669 3	2.646 693 0E-01
rope	0.164 042	1.640 419 9E-01
rope [Mesopotamia, ancient, rope]	0.016 666 7	1.666 666 7E-02
rope [UK]	0.164 042	1.640 419 9E-01
rute [Germany]	0.265 533 7	2.655 337 2E-01
rute [Switzerland]	0.333 333 3	3.333 333 3E-01
ruthe [Denmark]	0.318 616 4	3.186 164 4E-01
ruthe [Germany]	0.342 63	3.426 300 3E-01
ruthe [Switzerland]	0.555 555 6	5.555 555 6E-01
sabbath day's journey [Hebrew, ancient]	0.001 030 9	1.030 927 8E-03
sadzhen [Russia]	0.468 691 4	4.686 914 1E-01
sagen [Russia]	0.468 603 6	4.686 035 6E-01
sagene [Russia]	0.468 691 4	4.686 914 1E-01
sah [Czechoslovakia]	0.527 426 2	5.274 261 6E-01
sajon [Russia]	0.468 603 6	4.686 035 6E-01
sao [Thailand]	0.136 808 3	1.368 082 6E-01
saschen [Russia]	0.468 603 6	4.686 035 6E-01
sazem [Poland]	0.578 034 7	5.780 346 8E-01
sazhen [Ukraine]	0.526 315 8	5.263 157 9E-01
sazhene [Russia]	0.468 603 6	4.686 035 6E-01
sen [Cambodia]	0.025	2.500 000 0E-02
sen [Laos]	0.025	2.500 000 0E-02
sen [Thailand]	0.025	2.500 000 0E-02
senh [Cambodia]	0.025	2.500 000 0E-02
senh [Laos]	0.025	2.500 000 0E-02
senh [Thailand]	0.025	2.500 000 0E-02
senzer [Ethiopia]	4.347 826 1	4.347 826 1E+00
sesma [Spain]	7.177 823 4	7.177 823 4E+00
seu [Thailand]	0.004 8	4.800 000 0E-03
shaku [Japan]	3.300 33	3.300 330 0E+00
shi mi [China]	0.1	1.000 000 0E-01
shih chang [China]	0.3	3.000 000 0E-01
shih yin [China]	0.03	3.000 000 0E-02
side of a besana [Cuba]	0.019 654 1	1.965 408 8E-02
side of a beswa [Afghanistan]	0.101 224 8	1.012 248 2E-01
side of a beswax [Afghanistan]	0.045 269 4	4.526 935 3E-02
side of a gereeb [Afghanistan]	0.022 634 7	2.263 467 6E-02
side of a jerib [Afghanistan]	0.022 634 7	2.263 467 6E-02
siegbahn	>>>	9.979 320 9E+12
sinjer [Ethiopia]	4.347 826 1	4.347 826 1E+00

meter (continued)   **<length>**

Convert To	Standard	Scientific
siriometer	<<<	6.684 587 2E-18
sjomil [Finland]	0.000 54	5.399 568 0E-04
sjomila [Iceland]	0.000 539 1	5.390 835 6E-04
sjomill [Finland]	0.000 54	5.399 568 0E-04
skein [cloth]	0.009 113 4	9.113 444 2E-03
span	4.374 453 2	4.374 453 2E+00
span [Egypt, ancient]	4.444 444 4	4.444 444 4E+00
spat	<<<	1.000 000 0E-12
square braca [Cape Verde]	0.454 545 5	4.545 454 5E-01
staab [Switzerland]	0.833 333 3	8.333 333 3E-01
stab [Germany]	1	1.000 000 0E+00
stade [Greece, ancient]	0.005 405 4	5.405 405 4E-03
stadia [Greece, ancient]	0.005 414 2	5.414 185 2E-03
stadion [Greece, ancient, olympic]	0.005 208 3	5.208 333 3E-03
stadion [Hebrew, ancient]	0.006 178 3	6.178 331 4E-03
stadion [Iraq, ancient]	0.001 406 5	1.406 469 8E-03
stadion [Mesopotamia, ancient]	0.005 555 6	5.555 555 6E-03
stadion [Rome, ancient]	0.005 410 4	5.410 377 1E-03
stadium [Rome, ancient]	0.005 393 2	5.393 161 5E-03
stang [Sweden]	0.336 700 3	3.367 003 4E-01
stanjen [Romania]	0.448 430 5	4.484 304 9E-01
step [Greece, ancient]	1.298 701 3	1.298 701 3E+00
stigma	>>>	1.000 000 0E+12
stina [Ukraine]	0.142 857 1	1.428 571 4E-01
stinka [Ukraine]	0.142 857 1	1.428 571 4E-01
stong [Sweden]	0.336 791	3.367 910 5E-01
stopa [Czechoslovakia, Bohemia]	3.374 957 8	3.374 957 8E+00
stopa [Czechoslovakia, Moravia]	3.521 126 8	3.521 126 8E+00
stoppa [Poland]	3.472 222 2	3.472 222 2E+00
stringene [Romania]	0.510 204 1	5.102 040 8E-01
taim [Burma]	2.187 226 6	2.187 226 6E+00
taim [Cambodia]	2	2.000 000 0E+00
taim [Malaysia]	2.187 226 6	2.187 226 6E+00
taim [Pakistan]	2.187 226 6	2.187 226 6E+00
taim [Singapore]	2.188 183 8	2.188 183 8E+00
taim [Somalia]	1.789 549	1.789 549 0E+00
tar [Burma]	0.312 5	3.125 000 0E-01
task [Costa Rica]	0.049 840 5	4.984 051 0E-02
task [Guatemala]	0.049 840 5	4.984 051 0E-02
task [Nicaragua]	0.049 603 2	4.960 317 5E-02
taung [Burma]	2.187 226 6	2.187 226 6E+00
taung [Cambodia]	2	2.000 000 0E+00
taung [India]	2.187 226 6	2.187 226 6E+00
taung [Malaysia]	2.187 226 6	2.187 226 6E+00
taung [Pakistan]	2.187 226 6	2.187 226 6E+00
taung [Singapore]	2.188 183 8	2.188 183 8E+00
taung [Somalia]	1.789 549	1.789 549 0E+00
tenthmeter	>>>	1.000 000 0E+10
tepah [Hebrew, ancient]	13.513 514	1.351 351 4E+01
tercia [Costa Rica]	3.584 229 4	3.584 229 4E+00
tercia [Cuba]	3.537 318 7	3.537 318 7E+00
tercia [Guatemala]	3.584 229 4	3.584 229 4E+00
tercia [Haiti]	3.078 817 7	3.078 817 7E+00
tercia [Mexico]	3.584 229 4	3.584 229 4E+00
tercia [Nicaragua]	3.571 428 6	3.571 428 6E+00
tercia [Paraguay]	3.460 207 6	3.460 207 6E+00
tercia [Spain]	3.584 229 4	3.584 229 4E+00
tereia [Spain]	3.588 924 6	3.588 924 6E+00
thou	39,370.079	3.937 007 9E+04
thuoc [Thailand]	2.052 123 9	2.052 123 9E+00
tjengkal [Indonesia]	0.265 435 1	2.654 350 5E-01
toesa [Macao]	0.505 050 5	5.050 505 1E-01

Convert From		<Type of Unit>
Convert To	Standard	Scientific

meter (continued)   **\<length\>**

Convert To	Standard	Scientific
toise [Belgium]	0.496 277 9	4.962 779 2E-01
toise [France]	0.513 083 6	5.130 836 3E-01
toise [Mauritius]	0.513 083 6	5.130 836 3E-01
toise [Switzerland]	0.555 555 6	5.555 555 6E-01
top [Somalia]	0.255 754 4	2.557 544 8E-01
top [Somaliland]	0.255 754 4	2.557 544 8E-01
township [US, survey]	0.000 103 6	1.035 616 6E-04
truong [Vietnam]	0.25	2.500 000 0E-01
ud [Sudan]	0.431 034 5	4.310 344 8E-01
ush [Iraq, ancient]	0.001 406 5	1.406 469 8E-03
va [Laos]	0.5	5.000 000 0E-01
va [Thailand]	0.5	5.000 000 0E-01
va louang [Laos]	0.5	5.000 000 0E-01
va yiet [Laos]	0.5	5.000 000 0E-01
vadem [Netherlands]	0.546 448 1	5.464 480 9E-01
vara [Bolivia]	1.154 734 4	1.154 734 4E+00
vara [Brazil]	0.909 090 9	9.090 909 1E-01
vara [Canada]	1.180 637 5	1.180 637 5E+00
vara [Macao]	0.909 090 9	9.090 909 1E-01
vara [Philippines]	1.196 286 7	1.196 286 7E+00
vara [Portugal]	0.909 090 9	9.090 909 1E-01
vara [US, survey, California]	1.193 030 3	1.193 030 3E+00
vara [US, survey, Texas]	1.181 1	1.181 100 0E+00
vara [Venezuela]	1.25	1.250 000 0E+00
ver [India]	1.458 151 1	1.458 151 1E+00
ver [Iran]	0.961 538 5	9.615 384 6E-01
ver [Pakistan]	1.093 613 3	1.093 613 3E+00
verge [France]	0.139 938 4	1.399 384 3E-01
verste [Finland]	0.000 935 5	9.354 537 0E-04
vilasti [Ceylon]	3.048 780 5	3.048 780 5E+00
wa [Laos]	0.5	5.000 000 0E-01
wa [Thailand]	0.5	5.000 000 0E-01
wah [Laos]	0.5	5.000 000 0E-01
wah [Thailand]	0.5	5.000 000 0E-01
war [Yemen]	1.093 613 3	1.093 613 3E+00
wari [Tanzania]	1.093 613 3	1.093 613 3E+00
wavelength of orange-red spectral line of krypton-86	1,650,763.7	1.650 763 7E+06
x-unit	>>>	9.979 320 9E+12
xich [Vietnam]	2.5	2.500 000 0E+00
yard [based on US, survey foot]	1.093 611 1	1.093 611 1E+00
yard [international]	1.093 613 3	1.093 613 3E+00
yard [Pakistan]	1.093 613 3	1.093 613 3E+00
yard [UK]	1.093 615 2	1.093 615 2E+00
yarda [Colombia]	1.111 111 1	1.111 111 1E+00
yarda [Yemen]	1.093 613 3	1.093 613 3E+00
yin [China]	0.027 922	2.792 204 2E-02
ying [China]	0.027 922	2.792 204 2E-02
zar [India]	1.458 151 1	1.458 151 1E+00
zar [Iran]	0.961 538 5	9.615 384 6E-01
zar [Pakistan]	1.093 613 3	1.093 613 3E+00
zaz [Iran]	0.961 538 5	9.615 384 6E-01
zer [Iran]	0.961 538 5	9.615 384 6E-01
zer [Sumeria, ancient]	0.016 666 7	1.666 666 7E-02
zeret [Hebrew, ancient]	4.524 886 9	4.524 886 9E+00
zhang [China]	0.279 251 6	2.792 516 1E-01
zira [Turkey]	1	1.000 000 0E+00
zirai [Turkey]	1	1.000 000 0E+00
zogol [Hungary]	0.527 426 2	5.274 261 6E-01

meter [Turkey]   **\<volume, special - see page 29\>**

Convert To	Standard	Scientific
liter	5.24	5.240 000 0E+00

Convert From	<Type of Unit>	
Convert To	Standard	Scientific

meter °C/kilowatt   <thermal resistivity>
| meter kelvin/watt | 0.001 | 1.000 000 0E−03 |

meter °C/watt   <thermal resistivity>
| meter kelvin/watt | 1 | 1.000 000 0E+00 |

meter kelvin/kilowatt   <thermal resistivity>
| meter kelvin/watt | 0.001 | 1.000 000 0E−03 |

meter kelvin/watt   <thermal resistivity>
centimeter kelvin/watt	100	1.000 000 0E+02
centimeter second °C/erg	0.000 01	1.000 000 0E−05
day square foot °F/Btu inch [-/ I.T.]	0.006 009 5	6.009 495 4E−03
day square foot degree Rankine/Btu inch [-/ I.T.]	0.006 009 5	6.009 495 4E−03
foot °C/watt	3.280 839 9	3.280 839 9E+00
hour foot °F/Btu [-/ I.T.]	1.730 734 7	1.730 734 7E+00
hour foot °F/Btu [-/ thermoc.]	1.729 576 8	1.729 576 8E+00
hour foot degree Rankine/Btu [-/ I.T.]	1.730 734 7	1.730 734 7E+00
hour meter °C/kilocalorie [-/ I.T.]	1.163	1.163 000 0E+00
hour square centimeter °C/calorie centimeter [-/ I.T.]	0.116 3	1.163 000 0E−01
hour square foot °F/Btu foot [-/ I.T.]	1.730 734 7	1.730 734 7E+00
hour square foot °F/Btu foot [-/ thermoc.]	1.729 576 8	1.729 576 8E+00
hour square foot °F/Btu inch [-/ I.T.]	0.144 227 9	1.442 278 9E−01
hour square foot °F/Btu inch [-/ thermoc.]	0.144 131 4	1.441 314 0E−01
hour square foot degree Rankine/Btu foot [-/ I.T.]	1.730 734 7	1.730 734 7E+00
hour square foot degree Rankine/Btu inch [-/ I.T.]	0.144 227 9	1.442 278 9E−01
meter °C/kilowatt	1,000	1.000 000 0E+03
meter °C/watt	1	1.000 000 0E+00
meter kelvin/kilowatt	1,000	1.000 000 0E+03
second centimeter °C/calorie [-/ I.T.]	418.68	4.186 800 0E+02
second centimeter °C/calorie [-/ thermoc.]	418.4	4.184 000 0E+02
second °C/kilogram-force	9.806 65	9.806 650 0E+00
second foot °F/Btu [-/ I.T.]	6,230.644 8	6.230 644 8E+03
second foot degree Rankine/Btu [-/ I.T.]	6,230.644 8	6.230 644 8E+03
second kelvin/newton	1	1.000 000 0E+00
second meter kelvin/joule	1	1.000 000 0E+00
second square centimeter °C/calorie centimeter [-/ I.T.]	418.68	4.186 800 0E+02
second square foot °F/Btu foot [-/ I.T.]	6,230.644 8	6.230 644 8E+03
second square foot °F/Btu inch [-/ I.T.]	519.220 4	5.192 204 0E+02
second square foot °F/Btu inch [-/ thermoc.]	518.873 03	5.188 730 3E+02
second square foot degree Rankine/Btu foot [-/ I.T.]	6,230.644 8	6.230 644 8E+03
second square foot degree Rankine/Btu inch [-/ I.T.]	519.220 4	5.192 204 0E+02
square meter °C/watt centimeter	100	1.000 000 0E+02
square meter hour °C/ kilocalorie meter [-/ I.T.]	1.163	1.163 000 0E+00

meter kilogram-force   <energy>
Btu [I.T.]	0.009 294 9	9.294 910 6E−03
Btu [mean]	0.009 287 7	9.287 743 8E−03
Btu [thermoc.]	0.009 301 1	9.301 131 1E−03
calorie [I.T.]	2.342 278 1	2.342 278 1E+00
calorie [mean]	2.340 478 1	2.340 478 1E+00
calorie [thermoc.]	2.343 845 6	2.343 845 6E+00
centigrade heat unit [I.T.]	0.005 163 8	5.163 839 3E−03
cubic centimeter atmosphere	96.784 111	9.678 411 1E+01
cubic foot atmosphere	0.003 417 9	3.417 898 6E−03
foot pound-force	7.233 013 9	7.233 013 9E+00
foot poundal	232.715 34	2.327 153 4E+02
frigorie [France]	0.002 342 8	2.342 837 7E−03
gram calorie	2.342 837 7	2.342 837 7E+00
horsepower hour	0.000 003 7	3.653 037 3E−06
horsepower hour [metric]	0.000 003 7	3.703 703 7E−06
inch ounce-force	1,388.738 7	1.388 738 7E+03
inch pound-force	86.796 166	8.679 616 6E+01
joule	9.806 65	9.806 650 0E+00
kilogram square meter/square second	9.806 65	9.806 650 0E+00
kilopond meter	1	1.000 000 0E+00

liter atmosphere	0.096 784 1	9.678 411 1E-02
megaerg	98.066 5	9.806 650 0E+01
megaerg	98.066 5	9.806 650 0E+01
newton meter	9.806 65	9.806 650 0E+00
watthour	0.002 724 1	2.724 069 4E-03
wattsecond	9.806 65	9.806 650 0E+00

meter kilogram-force   **<torque>**

foot ounce-force	115.728 22	1.157 282 2E+02

meter of air [dry, CO_2 free, at 101325 Pa and 0 °C]   **<pressure>**

pascal	12.677 457	1.267 745 7E+01

meter of air [dry, CO_2 free, at 101325 Pa and 15 °C]   **<pressure>**

pascal	12.015 397	1.201 539 7E+01

meter/cubic meter   **<fuel consumption, US>**

mile/gallon [international/US, liquid]	0.000 002 4	2.352 145 8E-06

meter/day   **<velocity>**

foot/day	3.280 839 9	3.280 839 9E+00
inch/hour	1.640 42	1.640 420 0E+00
knot [international]	0.000 022 5	2.249 820 0E-05
mile/day	0.000 621 4	6.213 711 9E-04
nautical mile/day [international]	0.000 54	5.399 568 0E-04
yard/day	1.093 613 3	1.093 613 3E+00

meter/°C   **<geothermal step>**

meter/kelvin	1	1.000 000 0E+00

meter/hour   **<velocity>**

foot/hour	3.280 839 9	3.280 839 9E+00
inch/hour	39.370 078 7	3.937 007 9E+01
knot [international]	0.000 54	5.399 568 0E-04
mile/day	0.014 912 9	1.491 290 9E-02
nautical mile/day [international]	0.012 959	1.295 896 3E-02
yard/hour	1.093 613 3	1.093 613 3E+00

meter/kelvin   **<geothermal step>**

foot/°F	1.822 688 8	1.822 688 8E+00
meter/°C	1	1.000 000 0E+00

meter/liter   **<fuel consumption, US>**

mile/gallon [international/US, liquid]	0.002 352 1	2.352 145 8E-03

meter/minute   **<velocity>**

foot/minute	3.280 839 9	3.280 839 9E+00
inch/minute	39.370 078 7	3.937 007 9E+01
knot [international]	0.032 397 4	3.239 740 8E-02
meter/second	0.016 666 7	1.666 666 7E-02
mile/day	0.894 774 5	8.947 745 2E-01
nautical mile/day [international]	0.777 537 8	7.775 378 0E-01
yard/minute	1.093 613 3	1.093 613 3E+00

meter/newton   **<spectral cross-section>**

foot/pound-force	14.593 903	1.459 390 3E+01
square meter/joule	1	1.000 000 0E+00
square second/kilogram	1	1.000 000 0E+00

meter/second   **<velocity>**

benz	1	1.000 000 0E+00
dekameter/minute	6	6.000 000 0E+00
foot/second	3.280 839 9	3.280 839 9E+00
hectometer/hour	36	3.600 000 0E+01
inch/second	39.370 078 7	3.937 007 9E+01
kilometer/hour	3.6	3.600 000 0E+00
knot [international]	1.943 844 5	1.943 844 5E+00
mile/hour	2.236 936 3	2.236 936 3E+00
nautical mile/hour [international]	1.943 844 5	1.943 844 5E+00
yard/second	1.093 613 3	1.093 613 3E+00

meter/square second   **<acceleration>**

celo	3.280 839 9	3.280 839 9E+00

Convert From / Convert To	Standard	Scientific
foot/square second	3.280 839 9	3.280 839 9E+00
galileo	100	1.000 000 0E+02
gn [due to gravity]	0.101 971 6	1.019 716 2E−01
leo	0.1	1.000 000 0E−01
meter^4		**<second moment of area>**
foot^4	115.861 77	1.158 617 7E+02
inch^4	2,402,509.6	2.402 509 6E+06
metercandle		**<illuminance>**
candela steradian/square meter	1	1.000 000 0E+00
footcandle	0.092 903	9.290 304 0E−02
lumen/square meter	1	1.000 000 0E+00
lux	1	1.000 000 0E+00
milliphot	0.1	1.000 000 0E−01
nox	1,000	1.000 000 0E+03
metercandle second		**<light exposure>**
lumen second/square foot	0.092 903	9.290 304 0E−02
lumen second/square meter	1	1.000 000 0E+00
lux second	1	1.000 000 0E+00
milliphot second	0.1	1.000 000 0E−01
meterzentner [Austria]		**<mass, special - see page 29>**
kilogram	100	1.000 000 0E+02
methgal [Afghanistan]		**<mass, special - see page 29>**
gram	4.6	4.600 000 0E+00
methkal [Algiers]		**<mass, special - see page 29>**
gram	4.67	4.670 000 0E+00
methkal [Egypt]		**<mass, special - see page 29>**
gram	4.68	4.680 000 0E+00
methkal [Libya, Tripoli]		**<mass, special - see page 29>**
gram	4.8	4.800 000 0E+00
methkal [Syria]		**<mass, special - see page 29>**
gram	4.8	4.800 000 0E+00
methuselah [champagne bottle]		**<champagne bottle size>**
bottle [wine, standard]	8	8.000 000 0E+00
liter	6	6.000 000 0E+00
metical [Algeria]		**<mass, special - see page 29>**
gram	7.2	7.200 000 0E+00
metical [Tunisia]		**<mass, special - see page 29>**
gram	3.936	3.936 000 0E+00
metir [Eritrea]		**<mass, special - see page 29>**
gram	454	4.540 000 0E+02
metkal [Afghanistan]		**<mass, special - see page 29>**
gram	4.6	4.600 000 0E+00
metkal [Iran]		**<mass, special - see page 29>**
gram	4.687 5	4.687 500 0E+00
metkal [Libya, gold]		**<mass, special - see page 29>**
gram	4.601	4.601 000 0E+00
metreta [Greece, ancient]		**<volume, special - see page 29>**
liter	29.2	2.920 000 0E+01
metretes [Greece, ancient]		**<volume, special - see page 29>**
liter	29.2	2.920 000 0E+01
metretes [Hebrew, ancient]		**<volume, special - see page 29>**
liter	39.3	3.930 000 0E+01
metric-technical unit of mass		**<mass>**
kilogram	9.806 65	9.806 650 0E+00
metrischer [Germany]		**<mass, special - see page 29>**
kilogram	100	1.000 000 0E+02

Convert From Convert To	\<Type of Unit\> Standard	Scientific

metro [Turkey]
liter-- \<volume, special - see page 29\>
-- 11.33----1.133 000 0E+01

metska [Algiers]
gram--- \<mass, special - see page 29\>
--- 4.67----4.670 000 0E+00

metska [Egypt]
gram--- \<mass, special - see page 29\>
--- 4.68----4.680 000 0E+00

metska [Libya, Tripoli]
gram--- \<mass, special - see page 29\>
--- 4.8----4.800 000 0E+00

metska [Syria]
gram--- \<mass, special - see page 29\>
--- 4.8----4.800 000 0E+00

metskal [Algeria, gold]
gram--- \<mass, special - see page 29\>
--- 4.67----4.670 000 0E+00

mettar [Tunisia, oil]
liter-- \<volume, special - see page 29\>
-- 19.7----1.970 000 0E+01

mettar [Tunisia]
liter-- \<volume, special - see page 29\>
-- 20.208----2.020 800 0E+01

metter [Tunisia]
liter-- \<volume, special - see page 29\>
-- 19.7----1.970 000 0E+01

metze [Austria]
liter-- \<volume, special - see page 29\>
-- 61.5----6.150 000 0E+01

metze [Austria]
are--- \<area, special - see page 29\>
--- 19.182----1.918 200 0E+01

metze [Denmark]
liter-- \<volume, special - see page 29\>
-- 30.92----3.092 000 0E+01

metze [Germany, Bavaria]
liter-- \<volume, special - see page 29\>
-- 37.06----3.706 000 0E+01

metze [Germany, Prussia]
liter-- \<volume, special - see page 29\>
-- 3.435----3.435 000 0E+00

metze [Hungary]
liter-- \<volume, special - see page 29\>
-- 53.3----5.330 000 0E+01

mho
1/ohm -- \<electric conductance\>
1/ohm --1----1.000 000 0E+00
ampere/volt--1----1.000 000 0E+00
second/henry--1----1.000 000 0E+00
siemens ---1----1.000 000 0E+00
statsiemens -----------------------------------\>\>\>----8.987 551 8E+11

mho/meter
1/ohm meter-- \<electric conductivity\>
1/ohm meter--1----1.000 000 0E+00
abmho/centimeter-----------------------------\<\<\<----1.000 000 0E-11
rom --1----1.000 000 0E+00
siemens/meter--------------------------------------1----1.000 000 0E+00
statmho/centimeter --------------------------\>\>\>----8.987 551 8E+09

mi [China]
meter--- \<length, special - see page 29\>
---1----1.000 000 0E+00

mian [Malacca, gold and silver]
gram--- \<mass, special - see page 29\>
--- 2.67----2.670 000 0E+00

mian [Singapore, gold and silver]
gram--- \<mass, special - see page 29\>
--- 2.67----2.670 000 0E+00

micoohm centimeter
abohm centimeter-------------------------------- \<electric resistivity\>
abohm centimeter--------------------------------1,000----1.000 000 0E+03
microhm inch----------------------------------- 0.393 700 8----3.937 007 9E-01
ohm circular mil/foot----------------------- 6.015 304 9----6.015 304 9E+00
ohm meter--\<\<\<----1.000 000 0E-08
ohm square millimeter/meter---------------- 0.01----1.000 000 0E-02
statohm centimeter ---------------------------\<\<\<----1.112 650 1E-18

micril
gram/cubic meter------------------------------------ \<density\>
gram/cubic meter------------------------------------1----1.000 000 0E+00

	Standard	Scientific
kilogram/cubic meter	0.001	1.000 000 0E-03
milligram/cubic decimeter	1	1.000 000 0E+00
milligram/liter	1	1.000 000 0E+00
pound/cubic yard	0.001 685 6	1.685 554 9E-03

microampere <electric current>

	Standard	Scientific
abampere	0.000 000 1	1.000 000 0E-07
ampere	0.000 001	1.000 000 0E-06
electrostatic unit of current [cgs system]	2,997.924 58	2.997 924 6E+03
statampere	2,997.924 58	2.997 924 6E+03

microbar <pressure>

	Standard	Scientific
atmosphere [standard]	0.000 001	9.869 232 7E-07
atmosphere [technical]	0.000 001	1.019 716 2E-06
bar	0.000 001	1.000 000 0E-06
barye [France]	1	1.000 000 0E+00
decipascal	1	1.000 000 0E+00
dyne/square centimeter	1	1.000 000 0E+00
gram-force/square centimeter	0.001 019 7	1.019 716 2E-03
inch of mercury [0 °C, by convention]	0.000 029 5	2.952 998 3E-05
inch of water [4 °C, by convention]	0.000 401 5	4.014 630 8E-04
kilogram-force/square meter	0.010 197 2	1.019 716 2E-02
kilopond/square meter	0.010 197 2	1.019 716 2E-02
micrometer of mercury [0 °C, by convention]	0.750 061 6	7.500 615 8E-01
micrometer of water [4 °C, by convention]	10.197 162	1.019 716 2E+01
millitorr	0.750 061 7	7.500 616 8E-01
newton/square meter	0.1	1.000 000 0E-01
pascal	0.1	1.000 000 0E-01
pound-force/square foot	0.002 088 5	2.088 543 4E-03
poundal/square foot	0.067 196 9	6.719 689 8E-02
ton-force/square foot [short]	0.000 001	1.044 271 7E-06
torr	0.000 750 1	7.500 616 8E-04

microcandela <luminous intensity>

	Standard	Scientific
candela	0.000 001	1.000 000 0E-06

microcoulomb <electric charge>

	Standard	Scientific
abcoulomb	0.000 000 1	1.000 000 0E-07
coulomb	0.000 001	1.000 000 0E-06
electrostatic unit of charge [cgs system]	2,997.924 58	2.997 924 6E+03
franklin	2,997.924 58	2.997 924 6E+03
statcoulomb	2,997.924 58	2.997 924 6E+03

microcoulomb/cubic meter <electric charge density>

	Standard	Scientific
coulomb/cubic meter	0.000 001	1.000 000 0E-06
franklin/cubic centimeter	0.002 997 9	2.997 924 6E-03
statcoulomb/cubic centimeter	0.002 997 9	2.997 924 6E-03

microcoulomb/kilogram <exposure, gamma and X rays>

	Standard	Scientific
coulomb/kilogram	0.000 001	1.000 000 0E-06
roentgen	0.003 876	3.875 969 0E-03
röntgen	0.003 876	3.875 969 0E-03

microcoulomb/kilogram second <exposure rate, gamma and X rays>

	Standard	Scientific
coulomb/kilogram second	0.000 001	1.000 000 0E-06
roentgen/second	0.003 876	3.875 969 0E-03
röntgen/second	0.003 876	3.875 969 0E-03

microcoulomb/square meter <electric flux density>

	Standard	Scientific
abcoulomb/square centimeter	<<<	1.000 000 0E-11
ampere hour/square meter	<<<	2.777 777 8E-10
coulomb/square inch	<<<	6.451 600 0E-10
coulomb/square meter	0.000 001	1.000 000 0E-06
franklin/square centimeter	0.299 792 5	2.997 924 6E-01
statcoulomb/square centimeter	0.299 792 5	2.997 924 6E-01

microfarad <capacitance>

	Standard	Scientific
abfarad	<<<	1.000 000 0E-15
coulomb/volt	0.000 001	1.000 000 0E-06
farad	0.000 001	1.000 000 0E-06

Convert From Convert To	Standard	<Type of Unit> Scientific
statfarad	898,755.179	8.987 551 8E+05
microfarad/meter		**<electric permittivity>**
abfarad/centimeter	<<<	1.000 000 0E-13
farad/meter	0.000 001	1.000 000 0E-06
statfarad/centimeter	>>>	8.987 551 8E+07
microgram		**<mass>**
carat [international]	0.000 005	5.000 000 0E-06
carat [US, after 1913]	0.000 005	5.000 000 0E-06
carat [US, before 1913]	0.000 004 9	4.870 920 6E-06
drachm [UK, apothecary]	0.000 000 3	2.572 059 7E-07
dram [avoirdupois]	0.000 000 6	5.643 833 9E-07
dram [US, apothecary]	0.000 000 3	2.572 059 7E-07
gamma	1	1.000 000 0E+00
grain	0.000 015 4	1.543 235 8E-05
grain [apothecary]	0.000 015 4	1.543 235 8E-05
grain [avoirdupois]	0.000 015 4	1.543 235 8E-05
grain [troy]	0.000 015 4	1.543 235 8E-05
kilogram	<<<	1.000 000 0E-09
milligram	0.001	1.000 000 0E-03
pennyweight [troy]	0.000 000 6	6.430 149 3E-07
point [jewelers']	0.000 5	5.000 000 0E-04
scruple [UK]	0.000 000 8	7.716 179 2E-07
scruple [US, apothecary]	0.000 000 8	7.716 179 2E-07
microhenry		**<electric inductance>**
abhenry	1,000	1.000 000 0E+03
electromagnetic unit of inductance [cgs system]	1,000	1.000 000 0E+03
henry	0.000 001	1.000 000 0E-06
ohm second	0.000 001	1.000 000 0E-06
stathenry	<<<	1.112 650 1E-18
microhenry/meter		**<electric permeability>**
henry/meter	0.000 001	1.000 000 0E-06
microinch		**<length>**
angstrom	254	2.540 000 0E+02
barleycorn	0.000 003	3.000 000 0E-06
bicron	25,400	2.540 000 0E+04
caliber	0.000 1	1.000 000 0E-04
inch [based on US, survey foot]	0.000 001	9.999 980 0E-07
inch [international]	0.000 001	1.000 000 0E-06
meter	<<<	2.540 000 0E-08
micromicron	25,400	2.540 000 0E+04
micron	0.025 4	2.540 000 0E-02
mil	0.001	1.000 000 0E-03
millimicron	25.4	2.540 000 0E+01
stigma	25,400	2.540 000 0E+04
tenthmeter	254	2.540 000 0E+02
thou	0.001	1.000 000 0E-03
wavelength of orange-red spectral line of krypton-86	0.041 929 4	4.192 939 9E-02
x-unit	253,474.75	2.534 747 5E+05
microjoule		**<energy>**
atomic mass unit [unified, C-12, 1986, eq. energy]	6,700.530 8	6.700 530 8E+03
Btu [I.T.]	<<<	9.478 171 2E-10
calorie [I.T.]	0.000 000 2	2.388 459 0E-07
calorie [kilogram, I.T.]	<<<	2.388 459 0E-10
centimeter gram-force	0.010 197 2	1.019 716 2E-02
deuteron rest mass [atomic physics, eq. energy]	3,327.714 8	3.327 714 8E+03
dyne centimeter	10	1.000 000 0E+01
erg	10	1.000 000 0E+01
foot pound-force	0.000 000 7	7.375 621 5E-07
foot poundal	0.000 023 7	2.373 036 0E-05
inch ounce-force	0.000 141 6	1.416 119 3E-04
inch pound-force	0.000 008 9	8.850 745 8E-06
joule	0.000 001	1.000 000 0E-06

Convert From / Convert To	Standard	\<Type of Unit\> Scientific
kilogram square meter/square second	0.000 001	1.000 000 0E−06
kilopond meter	0.000 1	1.019 716 2E−07
liter atmosphere	\<\<\<	9.869 232 7E−09
muon rest mass [atomic physics, eq. energy]	59,072.511	5.907 251 1E+04
neutron rest mass [atomic physics, eq. energy]	6,642.970 1	6.642 970 1E+03
newton meter	0.000 001	1.000 000 0E−06
proton rest mass [atomic physics, eq. energy]	6,652.126 8	6.652 126 8E+03
teraelectronvolt	6.241 506 4	6.241 506 4E+00
microliter		**\<volume\>**
cubic foot	\<\<\<	3.531 466 7E−08
cubic inch	0.000 061	6.102 374 4E−05
cubic meter	\<\<\<	1.000 000 0E−09
cubic millimeter	1	1.000 000 0E+00
cubic yard	\<\<\<	1.307 950 6E−09
drachm [UK, liquid]	0.000 281 6	2.815 606 4E−04
dram [Canada, liquid]	0.000 281 6	2.815 606 4E−04
dram [US, liquid]	0.000 270 5	2.705 121 8E−04
drop [US, liquid]	0.012 173	1.217 304 8E−02
gallon [UK, dry or liquid]	0.000 000 2	2.199 692 5E−07
gallon [US, liquid]	0.000 000 3	2.641 720 5E−07
lambda	1	1.000 000 0E+00
liter	0.000 001	1.000 000 0E−06
ounce [UK, liquid]	0.000 035 2	3.519 508 0E−05
ounce [US, liquid]	0.000 033 8	3.381 402 3E−05
stere	\<\<\<	1.000 000 0E−09
micrometer		**\<length\>**
angstrom	10,000	1.000 000 0E+04
barleycorn	0.000 118 1	1.181 102 4E−04
bicron	1,000,000	1.000 000 0E+06
caliber	0.003 937	3.937 007 9E−03
cubit	0.000 002 2	2.187 226 6E−06
fermi	\>\>\>	1.000 000 0E+09
foot [France]	0.000 003 1	3.078 432 9E−06
foot [international]	0.000 003 3	3.280 839 9E−06
foot [US, survey]	0.000 003 3	3.280 833 3E−06
hot [Vietnam]	2.5	2.500 000 0E+00
hu mi [China]	0.1	1.000 000 0E−01
inch [based on US, survey foot]	0.000 039 4	3.937 007 9E−05
inch [international]	0.000 039 4	3.937 007 9E−05
meter	0.000 001	1.000 000 0E−06
microinch	39.370 079	3.937 007 9E+01
micromicron	1,000,000	1.000 000 0E+06
micron	1	1.000 000 0E+00
mil	0.039 370 1	3.937 007 9E−02
millimicron	1,000	1.000 000 0E+03
mo [South Korea]	0.033	3.300 003 3E−02
stigma	1,000,000	1.000 000 0E+06
tenthmeter	10,000	1.000 000 0E+04
thou	0.039 370 1	3.937 007 9E−02
ti [Vietnam]	0.25	2.500 000 0E−01
wavelength of orange-red spectral line of krypton-86	1.650 763 7	1.650 763 7E+00
wei mi [China]	1	1.000 000 0E+00
x-unit	9,979,320.9	9.979 320 9E+06
yard [based on US, survey foot]	0.000 001 1	1.093 611 1E−06
yard [international]	0.000 001 1	1.093 613 3E−06
micrometer of mercury [0 °C, by convention]		**\<pressure\>**
atmosphere [standard]	0.000 001 3	1.315 789 7E−06
atmosphere [technical]	0.000 001 4	1.359 510 0E−06
bar	0.000 001 3	1.333 223 9E−06
barye [France]	1.333 223 9	1.333 223 9E+00
decipascal	1.333 223 9	1.333 223 9E+00
dyne/square centimeter	1.333 223 9	1.333 223 9E+00
gram-force/square centimeter	0.001 359 5	1.359 510 0E−03

kilogram-force/square meter	0.013 595 1	1.359 510 0E−02
kilopond/square meter	0.013 595 1	1.359 510 0E−02
microbar	1.333 223 9	1.333 223 9E+00
micrometer of water [4 °C, by convention]	13.595 1	1.359 510 0E+01
micron of mercury [0 °C, by convention]	1	1.000 000 0E+00
millitorr	1.000 000 1	1.000 000 1E+00
newton/square meter	0.133 322 4	1.333 223 9E−01
pascal	0.133 322 4	1.333 223 9E−01
pound-force/square foot	0.002 784 5	2.784 496 0E−03
poundal/square foot	0.089 588 5	8.958 850 8E−02
torr	0.001	1.000 000 1E−03

micrometer of water [4 °C, by convention]   \<pressure\>

atmosphere [standard]	<<<	9.678 411 1E−08
atmosphere [technical]	0.000 000 1	1.000 000 0E−07
bar	<<<	9.806 650 0E−08
barye [France]	0.098 066 5	9.806 650 0E−02
dyne/square centimeter	0.098 066 5	9.806 650 0E−02
gram-force/square centimeter	0.000 1	1.000 000 0E−04
kilogram-force/square meter	0.001	1.000 000 0E−03
kilopond/square meter	0.001	1.000 000 0E−03
micrometer of mercury [0 °C, by convention]	0.073 555 9	7.355 591 4E−02
micron of mercury [0 °C, by convention]	0.073 555 9	7.355 591 4E−02
millimeter of mercury [0 °C, by convention]	0.000 073 6	7.355 591 4E−05
millimeter of water [4 °C, by convention]	0.001	1.000 000 0E−03
millipascal	9.806 65	9.806 650 0E+00
newton/square meter	0.009 806 7	9.806 650 0E−03
pascal	0.009 806 7	9.806 650 0E−03
pound-force/square foot	0.000 204 8	2.048 161 4E−04
poundal/square foot	0.006 589 8	6.589 764 6E−03
ton-force/square meter [metric]	0.000 001	1.000 000 0E−06
torr	0.000 073 6	7.355 592 4E−05

micromho   \<electric conductance\>

absiemens	<<<	1.000 000 0E−15
gemmho	1	1.000 000 0E+00
microsiemens	1	1.000 000 0E+00
siemens	0.000 001	1.000 000 0E−06
statsiemens	898,755.179	8.987 551 8E+05

micromicron   \<length\>

angstrom	0.01	1.000 000 0E−02
bicron	1	1.000 000 0E+00
caliber	<<<	3.937 007 9E−09
fermi	1,000	1.000 000 0E+03
inch [based on US, survey foot]	<<<	3.937 007 9E−11
inch [international]	<<<	3.937 007 9E−11
meter	<<<	1.000 000 0E−12
microinch	0.000 039 4	3.937 007 9E−05
micron	0.000 001	1.000 000 0E−06
mil	<<<	3.937 007 9E−08
millimicron	0.001	1.000 000 0E−03
picometer	1	1.000 000 0E+00
stigma	1	1.000 000 0E+00
tenthmeter	0.01	1.000 000 0E−02
thou	<<<	3.937 007 9E−08
wavelength of orange-red spectral line of krypton-86	0.000 001 7	1.650 763 7E−06
x-unit	9.979 320 9	9.979 320 9E+00

micromole   \<amount of substance\>

mole	0.000 001	1.000 000 0E−06
number of atoms in 0.012 kg of carbon-12	0.000 001	1.000 000 0E−06
one atom of carbon-12	>>>	6.022 136 7E+17

micromole/cubic centimeter   \<concentration, mole basis\>

millimole/liter	1	1.000 000 0E+00
mole/cubic meter	1	1.000 000 0E+00

| Convert From | <Type of Unit> | |
Convert To	Standard	Scientific
mole/liter	0.001	1.000 000 0E–03
micromole/gram		**<molality>**
millimole/kilogram	1	1.000 000 0E+00
mole/kilogram	0.001	1.000 000 0E–03
micromole/liter		**<concentration, mole basis>**
micromole/cubic centimeter	0.001	1.000 000 0E–03
millimole/cubic meter	1	1.000 000 0E+00
mole/cubic meter	0.001	1.000 000 0E–03
micron		**<length>**
angstrom	10,000	1.000 000 0E+04
bicron	1,000,000	1.000 000 0E+06
caliber	0.003 937	3.937 007 9E–03
fermi	>>>	1.000 000 0E+09
inch [based on US, survey foot]	0.000 039 4	3.937 007 9E–05
inch [international]	0.000 039 4	3.937 007 9E–05
meter	0.000 001	1.000 000 0E–06
microinch	39.370 079	3.937 007 9E+01
micrometer	1	1.000 000 0E+00
micromicron	1,000,000	1.000 000 0E+06
mil	0.039 370 1	3.937 007 9E–02
millimicron	1,000	1.000 000 0E+03
stigma	1,000,000	1.000 000 0E+06
tenthmeter	10,000	1.000 000 0E+04
thou	0.039 370 1	3.937 007 9E–02
wavelength of orange-red spectral line of krypton-86	1.650 763 7	1.650 763 7E+00
x-unit	9,979,320.9	9.979 320 9E+06
yard [based on US, survey foot]	0.000 001 1	1.093 611 1E–06
yard [international]	0.000 001 1	1.093 613 3E–06
yard [UK]	0.000 001 1	1.093 615 2E–06
micron of mercury [0 °C, by convention]		**<pressure>**
atmosphere [standard]	0.000 001 3	1.315 789 7E–06
atmosphere [technical]	0.000 001 4	1.359 510 0E–06
bar	0.000 001 3	1.333 223 9E–06
barye [France]	1.333 223 9	1.333 223 9E+00
centimeter of mercury [0 °C, by convention]	0.000 1	1.000 000 0E–04
centimeter of water [4 °C, by convention]	0.001 359 5	1.359 510 0E–03
decipascal	1.333 223 9	1.333 223 9E+00
dyne/square centimeter	1.333 223 9	1.333 223 9E+00
gram-force/square centimeter	0.001 359 5	1.359 510 0E–03
kilogram-force/square meter	0.013 595 1	1.359 510 0E–02
kilopond/square meter	0.013 595 1	1.359 510 0E–02
microbar	1.333 223 9	1.333 223 9E+00
micrometer of mercury [0 °C, by convention]	1	1.000 000 0E+00
micrometer of water [4 °C, by convention]	13.595 1	1.359 510 0E+01
millimeter of mercury [0 °C, by convention]	0.001	1.000 000 0E–03
millimeter of water [4 °C, by convention]	0.013 595 1	1.359 510 0E–02
millitorr	1.000 000 1	1.000 000 1E+00
newton/square meter	0.133 322 4	1.333 223 9E–01
pascal	0.133 322 4	1.333 223 9E–01
pound-force/square foot	0.002 784 5	2.784 496 0E–03
poundal/square foot	0.089 588 5	8.958 850 8E–02
torr	0.001	1.000 000 1E–03
micronewton		**<force>**
crinal	0.000 01	1.000 000 0E–05
dyne	0.1	1.000 000 0E–01
gram-force	0.000 102	1.019 716 2E–04
newton	0.000 001	1.000 000 0E–06
ounce-force	0.000 003 6	3.596 943 1E–06
pond	0.000 102	1.019 716 2E–04
pound-force	0.000 000 2	2.248 089 4E–07
poundal	0.000 007 2	7.233 013 9E–06

micronewton meter   **<torque>**

	Standard	Scientific
centimeter gram-force	0.010 197 2	1.019 716 2E−02
dyne centimeter	10	1.000 000 0E+01
inch ounce-force	0.000 141 6	1.416 119 3E−04
newton meter	0.000 001	1.000 000 0E−06

microohm   **<electric resistance>**

	Standard	Scientific
1/ siemens	0.000 001	1.000 000 0E−06
abohm	1,000	1.000 000 0E+03
ohm	0.000 001	1.000 000 0E−06
statohm	<<<	1.112 650 1E−18

microohm inch   **<electric resistivity>**

	Standard	Scientific
abohm centimeter	2,540	2.540 000 0E+03
micoohm centimeter	2.54	2.540 000 0E+00
ohm circular mil/foot	15.278 874 5	1.527 887 5E+01
ohm meter	<<<	2.540 000 0E−08
ohm square millimeter/meter	0.025 4	2.540 000 0E−02
statohm centimeter	<<<	2.826 131 1E−18

microohm meter   **<electric resistivity>**

	Standard	Scientific
abohm centimeter	100,000	1.000 000 0E+05
microhm inch	39.370 078 7	3.937 007 9E+01
ohm circular mil/foot	601.530 494	6.015 304 9E+02
ohm meter	0.000 001	1.000 000 0E−06
ohm square millimeter/meter	1	1.000 000 0E+00
statohm centimeter	<<<	1.112 650 1E−16

micropascal   **<pressure>**

	Standard	Scientific
atmosphere [standard]	<<<	9.869 232 7E−12
atmosphere [technical]	<<<	1.019 716 2E−11
bar	<<<	1.000 000 0E−11
barye [France]	0.000 01	1.000 000 0E−05
dyne/square centimeter	0.000 01	1.000 000 0E−05
gram-force/square centimeter	<<<	1.019 716 2E−08
kilogram-force/square meter	0.000 000 1	1.019 716 2E−07
kilopond/square meter	0.000 000 1	1.019 716 2E−07
micrometer of mercury [0 °C, by convention]	0.000 000 7	7.500 615 8E−06
micrometer of water [4 °C, by convention]	0.000 102	1.019 716 2E−04
newton/square meter	0.000 001	1.000 000 0E−06
pascal	0.000 001	1.000 000 0E−06
picobar	10	1.000 000 0E+01
pound-force/square foot	<<<	2.088 543 4E−08
poundal/square foot	0.000 007	6.719 689 8E−07
torr	<<<	7.500 616 8E−09

microradian   **<plane angle>**

	Standard	Scientific
degree [angular]	0.000 057 3	5.729 578 0E−05
mil [military infantry, angle, UK]	0.001	1.000 000 0E−03
milliradian	0.001	1.000 000 0E−03
radian	0.000 001	1.000 000 0E−06

microsecond   **<time>**

	Standard	Scientific
second	0.000 001	1.000 000 0E−06
shake	100	1.000 000 0E+02

microsiemens   **<electric conductance>**

	Standard	Scientific
absiemens	<<<	1.000 000 0E−15
gemmho	1	1.000 000 0E+00
micromho	1	1.000 000 0E+00
siemens	0.000 001	1.000 000 0E−06
statsiemens	898,755.179	8.987 551 8E+05

microsteradian   **<solid angle>**

	Standard	Scientific
hemisphere	0.000 000 2	1.591 549 4E−07
spat	<<<	7.957 747 2E−08
spheradian	0.000 001	1.000 000 0E−06
sphere	<<<	7.957 747 2E−08
spherical degree	0.000 057 3	5.729 578 0E−05

spherical right angle	0.000 000 6	6.366 197 7E-07
spherical solid angle	<<<	7.957 747 2E-08
square degree	0.003 282 8	3.282 806 4E-03
square grade	0.004 052 8	4.052 847 3E-03
sterad	0.000 001	1.000 000 0E-06
steradian	0.000 001	1.000 000 0E-06
steregon	<<<	7.957 747 2E-08

microtesla <magnetic flux density>

electromagnetic unit of magnetic flux density [cgs system]	0.01	1.000 000 0E-02
gamma	1,000	1.000 000 0E+03
gauss	0.01	1.000 000 0E-02
line/square centimeter [of magnetic force]	0.01	1.000 000 0E-02
maxwell/square meter	0.000 001	1.000 000 0E-06
tesla	0.000 001	1.000 000 0E-06

microvolt <electric potential>

abvolt	100	1.000 000 0E+02
electromagnetic unit of electric potential [cgs system]	100	1.000 000 0E+02
electrostatic unit of electric potential [cgs system]	<<<	3.335 641 0E-09
statvolt	<<<	3.335 641 0E-09
volt	0.000 001	1.000 000 0E-06

microvolt/meter <electric field strength>

abvolt/centimeter	1	1.000 000 0E+00
statvolt/centimeter	<<<	3.335 641 0E-11
volt/inch	<<<	2.540 000 0E-08
volt/meter	0.000 001	1.000 000 0E-06

microwatt <power>

Btu/hour [I.T.]	0.000 003 4	3.412 141 6E-06
Btu/hour [thermoc.]	0.000 003 4	3.414 425 1E-06
calorie/hour [I.T.]	0.000 859 8	8.598 452 3E-04
calorie/hour [thermoc.]	0.000 860 4	8.604 206 5E-04
centigrade heat unit/hour [mean]	0.000 001 9	1.894 172 6E-06
cubic meter atmosphere/hour	0.035 529 2	3.552 923 8E-02
dyne centimeter/second	10	1.000 000 0E+01
erg/second	10	1.000 000 0E+01
foot pound-force/hour	0.002 655 2	2.655 223 7E-03
foot poundal/hour	0.085 429 3	8.542 929 7E-02
gram-force centimeter/hour	36.709 784	3.670 978 4E+01
horsepower	<<<	1.341 022 1E-09
horsepower [metric]	<<<	1.359 621 6E-09
joule/hour	0.003 6	3.600 000 0E-03
kilocalorie/hour [I.T.]	0.000 000 9	8.598 452 3E-07
kilogram-force meter/hour	0.000 367 1	3.670 978 4E-04
kilopond meter/hour	0.000 367 1	3.670 978 4E-04
newton meter/hour	0.003 6	3.600 000 0E-03
pound square foot/cubic second	0.000 023 7	2.373 036 0E-05
volt ampere	0.000 001	1.000 000 0E-06
watt	0.000 001	1.000 000 0E-06

microwatt/square meter <heat flux density>

Btu/day square foot [I.T.]	0.000 007 6	7.607 959 9E-06
Btu/day square foot [thermoc.]	0.000 007 6	7.613 051 3E-06
calorie/day square centimeter [I.T.]	0.000 002 1	2.063 628 5E-06
calorie/day square centimeter [thermoc.]	0.000 002 1	2.065 009 6E-06
watt/square foot	<<<	9.290 304 0E-08
watt/square meter	0.000 001	1.000 000 0E-06

microweber <magnetic flux>

gauss square centimeter	100	1.000 000 0E+02
maxwell	100	1.000 000 0E+02
statweber	<<<	3.335 641 0E-09
unit pole	7.957 747 5	7.957 747 5E+00
weber	0.000 001	1.000 000 0E-06

mid [Jordan, oil]		\<volume, special - see page 29\>
liter	18	1.800 000 0E+01
midd [Sudan]		\<volume, special - see page 29\>
liter	4.125	4.125 000 0E+00
mieng [Vietnam, soil measure]		\<volume, special - see page 29\>
cubic meter	14.4	1.440 000 0E+01
mieng [Vietnam]		\<area, special - see page 29\>
square meter	36	3.600 000 0E+01
miglio [Italy]		\<length, special - see page 29\>
kilometer	1	1.000 000 0E+00
miglio [Rome, ancient]		\<length, special - see page 29\>
kilometer	1.478	1.478 000 0E+00
migr [Egypt]		\<mass, special - see page 29\>
gram	3.51	3.510 000 0E+00
migrab [Anatolia, medieval]		\<mass, special - see page 29\>
gram	750	7.500 000 0E+02
mijl [Netherlands]		\<length, special - see page 29\>
kilometer	5.556	5.556 000 0E+00
mil		\<length\>
angstrom	254,000	2.540 000 0E+05
barleycorn	0.003	3.000 000 0E-03
caliber	0.1	1.000 000 0E-01
inch [based on US, survey foot]	0.001	9.999 980 0E-04
inch [international]	0.001	1.000 000 0E-03
link [Gunter or US, survey]	0.000 126 3	1.262 623 7E-04
link [Ramden or Engineer]	0.000 083 3	8.333 333 3E-05
meter	0.000 025 4	2.540 000 0E-05
microinch	1,000	1.000 000 0E+03
micrometer	25.4	2.540 000 0E+01
micromicron	>>>	2.540 000 0E+07
micron	25.4	2.540 000 0E+01
millimeter	0.025 4	2.540 000 0E-02
millimicron	25,400	2.540 000 0E+04
stigma	>>>	2.540 000 0E+07
tenthmeter	254,000	2.540 000 0E+05
thou	1	1.000 000 0E+00
wavelength of orange-red spectral line of krypton-86	41.929 399	4.192 939 9E+01
yard [based on US, survey foot]	0.000 027 8	2.777 772 2E-05
yard [international]	0.000 027 8	2.777 777 8E-05
yard [UK]	0.000 027 8	2.777 782 6E-05
mil [Denmark]		\<length, special - see page 29\>
kilometer	7.53	7.530 000 0E+00
mil [Hungary]		\<length, special - see page 29\>
kilometer	8.35	8.350 000 0E+00
mil [military artillery, angle, NATO]		\<plane angle\>
grade [angular]	0.062 5	6.250 000 0E-02
mil [military artillery, angle, US, WWII]	0.625	6.250 000 0E-01
minute [angular]	3.375	3.375 000 0E+00
radian	0.000 981 7	9.817 477 0E-04
second [angular]	202.5	2.025 000 0E+02
mil [military artillery, angle, US, WWII]		\<plane angle\>
grade [angular]	0.1	1.000 000 0E-01
mil [military artillery, angle, NATO]	1.6	1.600 000 0E+00
minute [angular]	5.4	5.400 000 0E+00
radian	0.001 570 8	1.570 796 3E-03
second [angular]	324	3.240 000 0E+02
mil [military artillery, angle, USSR]		\<plane angle\>
degree [angular]	0.057 142 9	5.714 285 7E-02
grade [angular]	0.063 492 1	6.349 206 3E-02

mil [military artillery, angle, NATO]	1.015 873	1.015 873 0E+00
radian	0.000 997 3	9.973 310 0E−04
mil [military infantry, angle, UK]		<plane angle>
grade [angular]	0.063 662	6.366 197 7E−02
microradian	1,000	1.000 000 0E+03
milliradian	1	1.000 000 0E+00
radian	0.001	1.000 000 0E−03
mil [Norway]		<length, special - see page 29>
kilometer	11.295	1.129 500 0E+01
mil [Sweden]		<length, special - see page 29>
kilometer	10	1.000 000 0E+01
mil [Turkey]		<length, special - see page 29>
kilometer	1	1.000 000 0E+00
mil [Venezuela]		<mass, special - see page 29>
kilogram	400	4.000 000 0E+02
mil covas [Brazil]		<area, special - see page 29>
are	30.25	3.025 000 0E+01
mila [Iceland]		<length, special - see page 29>
kilometer	7.532 4	7.532 400 0E+00
mila [Poland]		<length, special - see page 29>
kilometer	8.53	8.530 000 0E+00
mila a landi [Iceland]		<length, special - see page 29>
kilometer	7.53	7.530 000 0E+00
mile [Austria]		<length, special - see page 29>
kilometer	7.586	7.586 000 0E+00
mile [Bangladesh]		<length, special - see page 29>
kilometer	1.609	1.609 000 0E+00
mile [Czechoslovakia, Bohemia]		<length, special - see page 29>
kilometer	7.003	7.003 000 0E+00
mile [Czechoslovakia, Silesia]		<length, special - see page 29>
kilometer	6.483	6.483 000 0E+00
mile [Denmark]		<length, special - see page 29>
kilometer	7.5	7.500 000 0E+00
mile [Germany]		<length, special - see page 29>
meter	7,500	7.500 000 0E+03
mile [Hebrew, ancient]		<length, special - see page 29>
kilometer	1.482	1.482 000 0E+00
mile [international, nautical]		<length>
cable length [US, survey]	8.439 032 4	8.439 032 4E+00
fathom [US, survey]	1,012.683 9	1.012 683 9E+03
foot [international]	6,076.115 5	6.076 115 5E+03
foot [US, survey]	6,076.103 3	6.076 103 3E+03
kilometer	1.852	1.852 000 0E+00
league [international, nautical]	0.333 333 3	3.333 333 3E−01
league [UK, nautical]	0.333 120 4	3.331 203 7E−01
league [US, statute]	0.383 592 4	3.835 923 8E−01
meter	1,852	1.852 000 0E+03
mile [international]	1.150 779 4	1.150 779 4E+00
mile [UK, nautical]	0.999 361 1	9.993 611 0E−01
mile [US, nautical]	1	1.000 000 0E+00
mile [US, statute]	1.150 777 1	1.150 777 1E+00
mile [US, survey]	1.150 777 1	1.150 777 1E+00
myriameter	0.185 2	1.852 000 0E−01
yard [based on US, survey foot]	2,025.367 8	2.025 367 8E+03
yard [international]	2,025.371 8	2.025 371 8E+03
yard [UK]	2,025.375 4	2.025 375 4E+03
mile [international]		<length>
astronomical unit	<<<	1.075 780 0E−08

Convert From / Convert To	Standard	Scientific
Convert From		**<Type of Unit>**
Convert To	Standard	Scientific
chain [Gunter or US, survey]	79.999 84	7.999 984 0E+01
chain [Ramden or Engineer]	52.8	5.280 000 0E+01
foot [international]	5,280	5.280 000 0E+03
foot [US, survey]	5,279.989 4	5.279 989 4E+03
inch [based on US, survey foot]	63,359.873	6.335 987 3E+04
inch [international]	63,360	6.336 000 0E+04
kilometer	1.609 344	1.609 344 0E+00
league [international, nautical]	0.289 658 8	2.896 587 5E−01
league [UK, nautical]	0.289 473 7	2.894 736 8E−01
league [US, statute]	0.333 332 7	3.333 326 7E−01
meter	1,609.344	1.609 344 0E+03
mile [international, nautical]	0.868 976 2	8.689 762 4E−01
mile [UK, nautical]	0.868 421 1	8.684 210 5E−01
mile [US, nautical]	0.868 976 2	8.689 762 4E−01
mile [US, statute]	0.999 998	9.999 980 0E−01
mile [US, survey]	0.999 998	9.999 980 0E−01
myriameter	0.160 934 4	1.609 344 0E−01
pace [geometrical]	105.6	1.056 000 0E+02
parsec	<<<	5.215 528 7E−14
perch [US, survey]	319.999 36	3.199 993 6E+02
perche [France]	275.236 53	2.752 365 3E+02
range [US, survey]	0.166 666 3	1.666 663 3E−01
siriometer	<<<	1.075 780 0E−14
spat	<<<	1.609 344 0E−09
yard [based on US, survey foot]	1,759.996 5	1.759 996 5E+03
yard [international]	1,760	1.760 000 0E+03
yard [UK]	1,760.003 1	1.760 003 1E+03
mile [Ireland]		**<length, special - see page 29>**
kilometer	2.048 3	2.048 300 0E+00
mile [Portugal]		**<length, special - see page 29>**
kilometer	2.087 3	2.087 300 0E+00
mile [Rome, ancient]		**<length, special - see page 29>**
kilometer	1.48	1.480 000 0E+00
mile [Russia]		**<length, special - see page 29>**
kilometer	7.467 6	7.467 600 0E+00
mile [Scotland]		**<length, special - see page 29>**
kilometer	1.810 5	1.810 500 0E+00
mile [Sweden]		**<length, special - see page 29>**
kilometer	10	1.000 000 0E+01
mile [UK, nautical]		**<length>**
cable length [US, survey]	8.444 427 6	8.444 427 6E+00
chain [Gunter or US, survey]	92.121 028	9.212 102 8E+01
chain [Ramden or Engineer]	60.8	6.080 000 0E+01
fathom [US, survey]	1,013.331 3	1.013 331 3E+03
foot [France]	5,704.902 7	5.704 902 7E+03
foot [international]	6,080	6.080 000 0E+03
foot [US, survey]	6,079.987 8	6.079 987 8E+03
furlong [US, survey]	9.212 102 8	9.212 102 8E+00
kilometer	1.853 184	1.853 184 0E+00
league [international, nautical]	0.333 546 4	3.335 464 4E−01
league [UK, nautical]	0.333 333 3	3.333 333 3E−01
league [US, statute]	0.383 837 6	3.838 376 2E−01
meter	1,853.184	1.853 184 0E+03
mile [international]	1.151 515 2	1.151 515 2E+00
mile [international, nautical]	1.000 639 3	1.000 639 3E+00
mile [US, nautical]	1.000 639 3	1.000 639 3E+00
mile [US, statute]	1.151 512 8	1.151 512 8E+00
mile [US, survey]	1.151 512 8	1.151 512 8E+00
rope	304	3.040 000 0E+02
yard [based on US, survey foot]	2,026.662 6	2.026 662 6E+03
yard [international]	2,026.666 7	2.026 666 7E+03

Convert From / Convert To	Standard	Scientific
yard [UK]	2,026.670 2	2.026 670 2E+03
mile [US, nautical]		**<length>**
cable length [US, survey]	8.439 032 4	8.439 032 4E+00
chain [Gunter or US, survey]	92.062 172	9.206 217 2E+01
chain [Ramden or Engineer]	60.761 155	6.076 115 5E+01
fathom [US, survey]	1,012.683 9	1.012 683 9E+03
foot [international]	6,076.115 5	6.076 115 5E+03
foot [US, survey]	6,076.103 3	6.076 103 3E+03
furlong [US, survey]	9.206 217 2	9.206 217 2E+00
inch [based on US, survey foot]	72,913.24	7.291 324 0E+04
inch [international]	72,913.386	7.291 338 6E+04
kilometer	1.852	1.852 000 0E+00
league [international, nautical]	0.333 333 3	3.333 333 3E−01
league [UK, nautical]	0.333 120 4	3.331 203 7E−01
league [US, statute]	0.383 592 4	3.835 923 8E−01
meter	1,852	1.852 000 0E+03
mile [international]	1.150 779 4	1.150 779 4E+00
mile [international, nautical]	1	1.000 000 0E+00
mile [UK, nautical]	0.999 361 1	9.993 611 0E−01
mile [US, statute]	1.150 777 1	1.150 777 1E+00
mile [US, survey]	1.150 777 1	1.150 777 1E+00
myriameter	0.185 2	1.852 000 0E−01
yard [based on US, survey foot]	2,025.367 8	2.025 367 8E+03
yard [international]	2,025.371 8	2.025 371 8E+03
yard [UK]	2,025.375 4	2.025 375 4E+03
mile [US, statute]		**<length>**
cable length [US, survey]	7.333 333 3	7.333 333 3E+00
chain [Gunter or US, survey]	80	8.000 000 0E+01
chain [Ramden or Engineer]	52.800 106	5.280 010 6E+01
fathom [US, survey]	880	8.800 000 0E+02
foot [France]	4,954.267 5	4.954 267 5E+03
foot [international]	5,280.010 6	5.280 010 6E+03
foot [US, survey]	5,280	5.280 000 0E+03
furlong [US, survey]	8	8.000 000 0E+00
inch [based on US, survey foot]	63,360	6.336 000 0E+04
inch [international]	63,360.127	6.336 012 7E+04
kilometer	1.609 347 2	1.609 347 2E+00
league [international, nautical]	0.289 659 3	2.896 593 0E−01
league [UK, nautical]	0.289 474 3	2.894 742 6E−01
league [US, statute]	0.333 333 3	3.333 333 3E−01
link [Gunter or US, survey]	8,000	8.000 000 0E+03
link [Ramden or Engineer]	5,280.010 6	5.280 010 6E+03
meter	1,609.347 2	1.609 347 2E+03
mile [international]	1.000 002	1.000 002 0E+00
mile [international, nautical]	0.868 978	8.689 779 8E−01
mile [UK, nautical]	0.868 422 8	8.684 227 9E−01
mile [US, nautical]	0.868 978	8.689 779 8E−01
mile [US, survey]	1	1.000 000 0E+00
out [US, survey]	16	1.600 000 0E+01
pace [geometrical]	105.600 21	1.056 002 1E+02
pace [US, survey]	2,112	2.112 000 0E+03
perch [US, survey]	320	3.200 000 0E+02
range [US, survey]	0.166 666 7	1.666 666 7E−01
yard [based on US, survey foot]	1,760	1.760 000 0E+03
yard [international]	1,760.003 5	1.760 003 5E+03
yard [UK]	1,760.006 6	1.760 006 6E+03
mile [US, survey]		**<length>**
arpent [France]	27.523 708	2.752 370 8E+01
bevameter	0.000 001 6	1.609 347 2E−06
cable length [US, survey]	7.333 333 3	7.333 333 3E+00
chain [Gunter or US, survey]	80	8.000 000 0E+01
chain [Ramden or Engineer]	52.800 106	5.280 010 6E+01
fathom [US, survey]	880	8.800 000 0E+02

Convert From / Convert To	Standard	<Type of Unit> Scientific
foot [international]	5,280.010 6	5.280 010 6E+03
foot [US, survey]	5,280	5.280 000 0E+03
furlong [US, survey]	8	8.000 000 0E+00
inch [based on US, survey foot]	63,360	6.336 000 0E+04
inch [international]	63,360.127	6.336 012 7E+04
kilometer	1.609 347 2	1.609 347 2E+00
league [international, nautical]	0.289 659 3	2.896 593 3E−01
league [UK, nautical]	0.289 474 3	2.894 742 6E−01
league [US, statute]	0.333 333 3	3.333 333 3E−01
link [Gunter or US, survey]	8,000	8.000 000 0E+03
link [Ramden or Engineer]	5,280.010 6	5.280 010 6E+03
meter	1,609.347 2	1.609 347 2E+03
mile [international]	1.000 002	1.000 002 0E+00
mile [international, nautical]	0.868 978	8.689 78E−01
mile [UK, nautical]	0.868 422 8	8.684 227 9E−01
mile [US, nautical]	0.868 978	8.689 779 8E−01
mile [US, statute]	1	1.000 000 0E+00
myriameter	0.160 934 7	1.609 347 2E−01
out [US, survey]	16	1.600 000 0E+01
pace [geometrical]	105.600 21	1.056 002 1E+02
pace [US, survey]	2,112	2.112 000 0E+03
perch [US, survey]	320	3.200 000 0E+02
perche [France]	275.237 08	2.752 370 8E+02
pied [France]	4,954.267 5	4.954 267 5E+03
pole [US, survey]	320	3.200 000 0E+02
range [US, survey]	0.166 666 7	1.666 666 7E−01
rod [US, survey]	320	3.200 000 0E+02
township [US, survey]	0.166 666 7	1.666 666 7E−01
vara [US, survey, California]	1,920	1.920 000 0E+03
vara [US, survey, Texas]	1,900.8	1.900 800 0E+03
yard [based on US, survey foot]	1,760	1.760 000 0E+03
yard [international]	1,760.003 5	1.760 003 5E+03
yard [UK]	1,760.006 6	1.760 006 6E+03
mile passum [Rome, ancient]	<length, special - see page 29>	
kilometer	1.478	1.478 000 0E+00
mile/day	<velocity>	
centimeter/second	1.862 666 7	1.862 666 7E+00
dekameter/hour	6.705 6	6.705 600 0E+00
foot/minute	3.666 666 7	3.666 666 7E+00
hectometer/day	16.093 44	1.609 344 0E+01
inch/minute	44	4.400 000 0E+01
kilometer/day	1.609 344	1.609 344 0E+00
knot [international]	0.036 207 3	3.620 734 3E−02
meter/minute	1.117 6	1.117 600 0E+00
mile/hour	0.041 666 7	4.166 666 7E−02
millimeter/second	18.626 666 7	1.862 666 7E+01
nautical mile/day [international]	0.868 976 2	8.689 762 4E−01
yard/minute	1.222 222 2	1.222 222 2E+00
mile/gallon [international/US, liquid]	<fuel consumption, US>	
kilometer/cubic meter	425.143 71	4.251 437 1E+02
kilometer/liter	0.425 143 7	4.251 437 1E−01
liter/100 kilometer	2.352 145 8E+02 / (mile / gallon)	
meter/cubic meter	425,143.71	4.251 437 1E+05
meter/liter	425.143 71	4.251 437 1E+02
mile/hour	<velocity>	
benz	0.447 04	4.470 400 0E−01
centimeter/second	44.704	4.470 400 0E+01
dekameter/minute	2.682 24	2.682 240 0E+00
foot/minute	88	8.800 000 0E+01
foot/second	1.466 666 7	1.466 666 7E+00
hectometer/hour	16.093 44	1.609 344 0E+01
inch/second	17.6	1.760 000 0E+01

Convert From		
Convert To	Standard	Scientific

	Standard	Scientific
kilometer/hour	1.609 344	1.609 344 0E+00
knot [international]	0.868 976 2	8.689 762 4E-01
meter/minute	26.822 4	2.682 240 0E+01
mile/day	24	2.400 000 0E+01
millimeter/second	447.04	4.470 400 0E+02
nautical mile/day [international]	20.855 429 8	2.085 543 0E+01
yard/minute	29.333 333 3	2.933 333 3E+01

mile/hour [Campbell factor]   **\<velocity>**

	Standard	Scientific
furlong/fortnight [US, survey]	2,687.994 6	2.687 994 6E+03

mile/hour minute   **\<acceleration>**

	Standard	Scientific
foot/square second	0.024 444 4	2.444 440 0E-02
galileo	0.745 066 7	7.450 666 7E-01
gn [due to gravity]	0.000 759 8	7.597 565 6E-04
meter/square second	0.007 450 7	7.450 666 7E-03

mile/hour second   **\<acceleration>**

	Standard	Scientific
foot/square second	1.466 666 7	1.466 666 7E+00
galileo	44.704	4.470 400 0E+01
gn [due to gravity]	0.045 585 4	4.558 539 4E-02
meter/square second	0.447 04	4.470 400 0E-01

mile/minute   **\<velocity>**

	Standard	Scientific
centimeter/second	2,682.24	2.682 240 0E+03
dekameter/second	2.682 24	2.682 240 0E+00
foot/second	88	8.800 000 0E+01
hectometer/minute	16.093 44	1.609 344 0E+01
inch/second	1,056	1.056 000 0E+03
kilometer/minute	1.609 344	1.609 344 0E+00
knot [international]	52.138 574 5	5.213 857 5E+01
megameter/day	2.317 455 4	2.317 455 4E+00
meter/second	26.822 4	2.682 240 0E+01
nautical mile/hour [international]	52.138 574 5	5.213 857 5E+01
yard/second	29.333 333 3	2.933 333 3E+01

mile/second   **\<velocity>**

	Standard	Scientific
dekameter/second	160.934 4	1.609 344 0E+02
foot/minute	316,800	3.168 000 0E+05
foot/second	5,280	5.280 000 0E+03
hectometer/second	16.093 44	1.609 344 0E+01
inch/second	63,360	6.336 000 0E+04
kilometer/second	1.609 344	1.609 344 0E+00
knot [international]	3,128.314 47	3.128 314 5E+03
megameter/hour	5.793 638 4	5.793 638 4E+00
meter/second	1,609.344	1.609 344 0E+03
mile/minute	60	6.000 000 0E+01
nautical mile/minute [international]	52.138 574 5	5.213 857 5E+01
yard/second	1,760	1.760 000 0E+03

mile/square second   **\<acceleration>**

	Standard	Scientific
foot/square second	5,280	5.280 000 0E+03
gn [due to gravity]	164.107 417	1.641 074 2E+02
grav	164.107 417	1.641 074 2E+02
meter/square second	1,609.344	1.609 344 0E+03

milha [Brazil]   **\<length, special - see page 29>**

	Standard	Scientific
kilometer	2.2	2.200 000 0E+00

milha [Portugal]   **\<length, special - see page 29>**

	Standard	Scientific
kilometer	2.064	2.064 000 0E+00

milha quadrada [Brazil]   **\<area, special - see page 29>**

	Standard	Scientific
square kilometer	4.84	4.840 000 0E+00

miliarum [Rome, ancient]   **\<length, special - see page 29>**

	Standard	Scientific
kilometer	1.478	1.478 000 0E+00

milion [Greece, ancient]   **\<length, special - see page 29>**

	Standard	Scientific
kilometer	1.482	1.482 000 0E+00

milion [Rome, ancient]   \<length, special - see page 29\>
  meter --1,479----1.479 000 0E+03

mill [Turkey]   \<length, special - see page 29\>
  kilometer --1----1.000 000 0E+00

milla [Ecuador]   \<length, special - see page 29\>
  kilometer ---1.4----1.400 000 0E+00

milla [Honduras]   \<length, special - see page 29\>
  kilometer --1.85----1.850 000 0E+00

milla [Nicaragua]   \<length, special - see page 29\>
  kilometer --1.866----1.866 000 0E+00

milla [Spain]   \<length, special - see page 29\>
  kilometer ---1.393 18----1.393 180 0E+00

milla [Venezuela]   \<length, special - see page 29\>
  kilometer --1.858----1.858 000 0E+00

mille [Belgium, ancient]   \<length, special - see page 29\>
  kilometer ---2.015----2.015 000 0E+00

mille [France, nautical]   \<length, special - see page 29\>
  meter ---1,851.84----1.851 840 0E+03

mille passus [Rome, ancient]   \<length, special - see page 29\>
  meter --1,479----1.479 000 0E+03

mille passuum [Rome, ancient]   \<length, special - see page 29\>
  meter --1,480----1.480 000 0E+03

millenarian   \<time\>
  chiliad --1----1.000 000 0E+00
  millenary---1----1.000 000 0E+00
  millennium---1----1.000 000 0E+00
  year [normal calendar]--1,000----1.000 000 0E+03

millenary   \<time\>
  chiliad --1----1.000 000 0E+00
  millenarian--1----1.000 000 0E+00
  millennium---1----1.000 000 0E+00
  year [normal calendar]--1,000----1.000 000 0E+03

millennium   \<time\>
  chiliad --1----1.000 000 0E+00
  millenarian--1----1.000 000 0E+00
  millenary--1----1.000 000 0E+00
  year [normal calendar]--1,000----1.000 000 0E+03

millerole [Tunisia]   \<volume, special - see page 29\>
  liter--64----6.400 000 0E+01

milli-mass-unit   \<mass\>
  atomic mass unit [unified, C-12, 1986] ------------------------0.001----1.000 000 0E-03
  avogram --0.001----1.000 000 0E-03
  dalton ---0.001----1.000 000 0E-03
  kilogram --- \<\<\<----1.660 540 2E-30

milliampere   \<electric current\>
  abampere---0.000 1----1.000 000 0E-04
  ampere --0.001----1.000 000 0E-03
  gilbert ---0.001 256 6----1.256 637 1E-03
  volt/ohm---0.001----1.000 000 0E-03

milliampere square meter   \<electromagnetic moment\>
  ampere square inch-----------------------------------1.550 003 1----1.550 003 1E+00
  ampere square meter--------------------------------------0.001----1.000 000 0E-03
  statampere square centimeter-------------------------- \>\>\>----2.997 924 6E+10

milliard [UK]   \<units\>
  billion [US]--1----1.000 000 0E+00
  unit-- \>\>\>----1.000 000 0E+09

milliare [Rome, ancient]   \<length, special - see page 29\>
  kilometer --1.478----1.478 000 0E+00

| Convert From | | <Type of Unit> |
Convert To	Standard	Scientific
millibar		**<pressure>**
atmosphere [standard]	0.000 986 9	9.869 232 7E−04
atmosphere [technical]	0.001 019 7	1.019 716 2E−03
bar	0.001	1.000 000 0E−03
barye [France]	1,000	1.000 000 0E+03
centimeter of mercury [0 °C, by convention]	0.075 006 2	7.500 615 8E−02
centimeter of water [4 °C, by convention]	1.019 716 2	1.019 716 2E+00
decitorr	7.500 616 8	7.500 616 8E+00
dyne/square centimeter	1,000	1.000 000 0E+03
gram-force/square centimeter	1.019 716 2	1.019 716 2E+00
hectopascal	1	1.000 000 0E+00
inch of mercury [0 °C, by convention]	0.029 53	2.952 998 3E−02
inch of water [4 °C, by convention]	0.401 463 1	4.014 630 8E−01
kilogram-force/square meter	10.197 162	1.019 716 2E+01
kilopond/square meter	10.197 162	1.019 716 2E+01
kip/square foot	0.002 088 5	2.088 543 4E−03
micrometer of mercury [0 °C, by convention]	750.061 58	7.500 615 8E+02
micrometer of water [4 °C, by convention]	10,197.162	1.019 716 2E+04
millimeter of mercury [0 °C, by convention]	0.750 061 6	7.500 615 8E−01
millimeter of water [4 °C, by convention]	10.197 162	1.019 716 2E+01
newton/square meter	100	1.000 000 0E+02
ounce-force/square inch	0.232 060 4	2.320 603 8E−01
pascal	100	1.000 000 0E+02
pieze [France]	0.1	1.000 000 0E−01
pound-force/square foot	2.088 543 4	2.088 543 4E+00
poundal/square foot	67.196 898	6.719 689 8E+01
sthene/square meter [France]	0.1	1.000 000 0E−01
ton-force/square foot [short]	0.001 044 3	1.044 271 7E−03
torr	0.750 061 7	7.500 616 8E−01
millicandela		**<luminous intensity>**
candela	0.001	1.000 000 0E−03
millicoulomb		**<electric charge>**
abcoulomb	0.000 1	1.000 000 0E−04
ampere second	0.001	1.000 000 0E−03
coulomb	0.001	1.000 000 0E−03
farad volt	0.001	1.000 000 0E−03
statcoulomb	2,997,924.58	2.997 924 6E+06
millicoulomb meter		**<electric dipole moment>**
abcoulomb centimeter	0.01	1.000 000 0E−02
coulomb meter	0.001	1.000 000 0E−03
statcoulomb centimeter	>>>	2.997 924 6E+08
millicoulomb/cubic meter		**<electric charge density>**
coulomb/cubic meter	0.001	1.000 000 0E−03
franklin/cubic centimeter	2.997 924 6	2.997 924 6E+00
statcoulomb/cubic centimeter	2.997 924 6	2.997 924 6E+00
millicoulomb/kilogram		**<exposure, gamma and X rays>**
coulomb/kilogram	0.001	1.000 000 0E−03
roentgen	3.875 969	3.875 969 0E+00
röntgen	3.875 969	3.875 969 0E+00
millicoulomb/kilogram second		**<exposure rate, gamma and X rays>**
coulomb/kilogram second	0.001	1.000 000 0E−03
roentgen/second	3.875 969	3.875 969 0E+00
röntgen/second	3.875 969	3.875 969 0E+00
millicoulomb/meter		**<electric dipole moment/unit area>**
coulomb/meter	0.001	1.000 000 0E−03
millicoulomb/square meter		**<electric flux density>**
abcoulomb/square centimeter	<<<	1.000 000 0E−08
ampere hour/square meter	0.000 000 3	2.777 777 8E−07
coulomb/square inch	0.000 000 6	6.451 600 0E−07
coulomb/square meter	0.001	1.000 000 0E−03
franklin/square centimeter	299.792 458	2.997 924 6E+02

	Standard	Scientific
statcoulomb/square centimeter	299.792 458	2.997 924 6E+02
millicurie		**\<radionuclide activity\>**
1/second	>>>	3.700 000 0E+07
becquerel	>>>	3.700 000 0E+07
curie	0.001	1.000 000 0E-03
rutherford	37	3.700 000 0E+01
millicurie/cubic meter		**\<radionuclide volume activity\>**
becquerel/cubic meter	>>>	3.700 000 0E+07
curie/cubic meter	0.001	1.000 000 0E-03
rutherford/cubic meter	37	3.700 000 0E+01
millicurie/kilogram		**\<radionuclide specific activity\>**
becquerel/kilogram	>>>	3.700 000 0E+07
curie/kilogram	0.001	1.000 000 0E-03
rutherford/kilogram	37	3.700 000 0E+01
millidarcy [20 °C]		**\<permeability, water\>**
darcy [20 °C]	0.001	1.000 000 0E-03
square foot	<<<	1.062 315 4E-14
square meter	<<<	9.869 232 7E-16
millier		**\<mass\>**
cental [US]	22.046 226	2.204 622 6E+01
centner [UK]	19.684 131	1.968 413 1E+01
doppelzentner [Germany]	10	1.000 000 0E+01
hundredweight [long]	19.684 131	1.968 413 1E+01
hundredweight [short]	22.046 226	2.204 622 6E+01
hundredweight [UK]	19.684 131	1.968 413 1E+01
kilogram	1,000	1.000 000 0E+03
megagram	1	1.000 000 0E+00
quarter [long]	3.936 826 1	3.936 826 1E+00
quarter [short]	4.409 245 2	4.409 245 2E+00
quarter [UK]	78.736 522	7.873 652 2E+01
quarter [US]	88.184 905	8.818 490 5E+01
quintal [metric]	10	1.000 000 0E+01
quintal [UK]	19.684 131	1.968 413 1E+01
quintal [US]	22.046 226	2.204 622 6E+01
slug	68.521 766	6.852 176 6E+01
ton [long]	0.984 206 5	9.842 065 3E-01
ton [metric]	1	1.000 000 0E+00
ton [short]	1.102 311 3	1.102 311 3E+00
ton [UK]	0.984 206 5	9.842 065 3E-01
tonne	1	1.000 000 0E+00
millifarad		**\<capacitance\>**
abfarad	<<<	1.000 000 0E-12
coulomb/volt	0.001	1.000 000 0E-03
farad	0.001	1.000 000 0E-03
statfarad	>>>	8.987 551 8E+08
millifarad/meter		**\<electric permittivity\>**
abfarad/centimeter	<<<	1.000 000 0E-10
farad/meter	0.001	1.000 000 0E-03
statfarad/centimeter	>>>	8.987 551 8E+10
milligal		**\<acceleration\>**
foot/square second	0.000 032 8	3.280 839 9E-05
galileo	0.001	1.000 000 0E-03
g_n [due to gravity]	0.000 001	1.019 716 2E-06
meter/square second	0.000 01	1.000 000 0E-05
milligram		**\<mass\>**
abas [Iran]	0.005 333 3	5.333 333 3E-03
anna [Bangladesh]	0.001 371 7	1.371 742 1E-03
bugday [Turkey]	0.019 960 1	1.996 008 0E-02
calc [Greece, ancient]	0.009 901	9.900 990 1E-03
carat [international]	0.005	5.000 000 0E-03
carat [Iran]	0.005 128 2	5.128 205 0E-03

milligram (continued)

<mass>

Convert To	Standard	Scientific
carat [US, after 1913]	0.005	5.000 000 0E-03
cash [China]	0.02	2.000 000 0E-02
cash [India]	0.823 045 3	8.230 452 7E-01
cekirdek [Turkey]	0.002 493 8	2.493 765 6E-03
chabba [Iraq, ancient]	0.015 384 6	1.538 461 5E-02
chalque [Greece, ancient]	0.009 901	9.900 990 1E-03
chuchok [Brunei, gold]	0.002 645 5	2.645 502 6E-03
dhan [Bangladesh, precious metals]	0.032 894 7	3.289 473 7E-02
dhan [India]	0.027 472 5	2.747 252 7E-02
doli [Russia]	0.022 504 8	2.250 478 2E-02
dolia [Russia]	0.022 504 8	2.250 478 2E-02
dolja [Russia]	0.022 504 8	2.250 478 2E-02
doly [Russia]	0.022 525 5	2.252 252 3E-02
dong [Iran]	0.001 280 4	1.280 409 7E-03
drachm [UK, apothecary]	0.000 257 2	2.572 059 7E-04
dram [avoirdupois]	0.000 564 4	5.643 833 9E-04
dram [US, apothecary]	0.000 257 2	2.572 059 7E-04
dung [Iran]	0.001 280 4	1.280 409 7E-03
dyne square second/centimeter	0.001	1.000 000 0E-03
fen ke [China]	0.01	1.000 000 0E-02
fitil [Turkey]	0.08	8.000 000 0E-02
gamma	1,000	1.000 000 0E+03
gandom [Iran]	0.020 479 2	2.047 921 4E-02
gandum [Iran]	0.020 479 2	2.047 921 4E-02
gerot [Hebrew, ancient]	0.001 579 8	1.579 778 8E-03
grain	0.015 432 4	1.543 235 8E-02
grain [apothecary]	0.015 432 4	1.543 235 8E-02
grain [avoirdupois]	0.015 432 4	1.543 235 8E-02
grain [Bahrain]	0.015 432 1	1.543 209 9E-02
grain [Russia]	0.016 077 2	1.607 717 0E-02
grain [Switzerland]	0.015 36	1.536 003 9E-02
grain [troy]	0.015 432 4	1.543 235 8E-02
grain [Turkey]	0.019 960 1	1.996 008 0E-02
grano [Honduras]	0.020 032 1	2.003 205 1E-02
grano [Italy]	0.020 387 4	2.038 736 0E-02
grano [Spain]	0.020 040 1	2.004 008 0E-02
granum [Russia, apothecary]	0.016 074 8	1.607 484 0E-02
gunja [India, seed]	0.015 384 6	1.538 461 5E-02
habba [Sudan]	0.01	1.000 000 0E-02
habbe [Turkey]	1.277 139 2	1.277 139 2E+00
hao [China]	0.264 554 7	2.645 546 7E-01
hao ke [China]	1	1.000 000 0E+00
hebbeh [Iraq, ancient]	0.015 384 6	1.538 461 5E-02
hoon [Indonesia, opium]	0.002 590 6	2.590 606 5E-03
hot [Vietnam]	26.469 031	2.646 903 1E+01
ka [Laos]	0.001 066 7	1.066 666 7E-03
kambeh [Iraq, ancient]	0.020 512 8	2.051 282 1E-02
kamha [Iraq, ancient]	0.020 512 8	2.051 282 1E-02
kamha [Turkey]	0.019 960 1	1.996 008 0E-02
khashkha [Pakistan]	0.526 870 4	5.268 703 9E-01
khou [Mongolia]	0.266 666 7	2.666 666 7E-01
kilogram	0.000 001	1.000 000 0E-06
kirat [Iraq, ancient]	0.005 128 2	5.128 205 1E-03
kirat [Sudan]	0.005 128 2	5.128 205 1E-03
kitmir [Turkey]	0.319 488 8	3.194 888 2E-01
krat [Turkey]	0.005	5.000 000 0E-03
krishnala [Hindu, ancient, gold]	0.008 064 5	8.064 516 1E-03
kung chu [Taiwan]	0.01	1.000 000 0E-02
kung hao [Taiwan]	0.1	1.000 000 0E-01
kung sun [China]	1	1.000 000 0E+00
kung szu [Taiwan]	1	1.000 000 0E+00
kupang [Brunei, gold]	0.026 455	2.645 502 6E-02

Convert From		\<Type of Unit\>
Convert To	Standard	Scientific

milligram (continued) \<mass\>

le [China]	0.026 455 7	2.645 572 6E–02
lea [Singapore, precious metals and medicine]	0.029 030 1	2.903 010 4E–02
li [China]	0.026 455 5	2.645 546 7E–02
li [Laos]	0.026 666 7	2.666 666 7E–02
li [Mongolia]	0.026 666 7	2.666 666 7E–02
li ke [China]	0.1	1.000 000 0E–01
lin [Cambodia]	0.026 666 7	2.666 666 7E–02
lin [China]	0.02	2.000 000 0E–02
lin [Laos]	0.026 666 7	2.666 666 7E–02
ly [Vietnam]	0.026 469	2.646 903 1E–02
masha [Bangladesh, precious metals]	0.001 028 8	1.028 806 6E–03
masha [Hindu, ancient, gold]	0.001 612 9	1.612 903 2E–03
masha [Hindu, ancient, silver]	0.004 032 3	4.032 258 1E–03
masha [India, ancient, silver]	0.001 650 2	1.650 165 0E–03
masha [Pakistan]	0.001 028 8	1.028 806 6E–03
mata [Indonesia, opium]	0.002 590 6	2.590 606 5E–03
mite [UK]	0.308 642	3.086 419 8E–01
mo [Japan]	0.266 666 7	2.666 666 7E–01
nakhod [Afghanistan]	0.005 213 8	5.213 764 3E–03
nakhod [Iran]	0.005 128 2	5.128 205 1E–03
nakir [Turkey]	0.159 744 4	1.597 444 1E–01
nokhod [Afghanistan]	0.005 213 8	5.213 764 3E–03
nokhod [Iran]	0.005 128 2	5.128 205 1E–03
obol [Greece]	0.001 397 9	1.397 858 5E–03
obol [Hebrew, ancient]	0.001 579 8	1.579 778 8E–03
pank [India]	0.131 689 5	1.316 894 5E–01
phan [Vietnam]	0.002 646 9	2.646 903 1E–03
point [jewelers']	0.5	5.000 000 0E–01
pun [Mongolia]	0.002 666 7	2.666 666 7E–03
punk [India]	0.109 769 5	1.097 694 8E–01
punkho [India]	0.109 769 5	1.097 694 8E–01
punko [India]	0.131 689 5	1.316 894 5E–01
quilate [Brazil]	0.005 019 1	5.019 072 5E–03
quilate [Colombia]	0.05	5.000 000 0E–02
rati [Bangladesh, precious metals]	0.008 230 5	8.230 452 7E–03
rati [India]	0.008 333 3	8.333 333 3E–03
retti [India]	0.006 849 3	6.849 315 1E–03
rin [Japan]	0.026 666 7	2.666 666 7E–02
ruay [Burma]	0.003 921 6	3.921 568 6E–03
ruttee [India]	0.006 849 3	6.849 315 1E–03
ruttee [Pakistan]	0.008 230 5	8.230 452 7E–03
saga [Malaysia, precious metals]	0.003 561 3	3.561 253 6E–03
saga [Singapore, precious metals]	0.003 561 3	3.561 253 6E–03
se [Iraq, ancient]	0.022 222 2	2.222 222 2E–02
shan [India]	0.032 922 4	3.292 236 8E–02
she [Iraq, ancient]	0.022 222 2	2.222 222 2E–02
shih fen [China]	0.003 2	3.200 000 0E–03
shih hao [China]	0.32	3.200 000 0E–01
shih li [China]	0.032	3.200 000 0E–02
shih sze [China]	3.2	3.200 000 0E+00
si [China]	2	2.000 000 0E+00
sitarion [Greece, ancient]	0.014 705 9	1.470 588 2E–02
ssu [China]	2.645 546 7	2.645 546 7E+00
suvarnamasha [India, ancient]	0.001 612 9	1.612 903 2E–03
ti [Vietnam]	2.646 903 1	2.646 903 1E+00
timbang [Indonesia, opium]	0.002 590 6	2.590 606 5E–03
una [Iran]	0.081 900 1	8.190 008 2E–02
vi [Vietnam]	264.690 31	2.646 903 1E+02
ywegale [Burma]	0.003 921 6	3.921 568 6E–03
zevre [Turkey]	0.478 468 9	4.784 689 0E–01

	Standard	Scientific
milligram/cubic centimeter		**<density>**
grain/gallon [-/US, liquid]	58.417 831	5.841 783 1E+01
gram/cubic decimeter	1	1.000 000 0E+00
gram/liter	1	1.000 000 0E+00
kilogram/cubic meter	1	1.000 000 0E+00
milligram/milliliter	1	1.000 000 0E+00
ounce/cubic yard	26.968 879	2.696 887 9E+01
ounce/gallon [-/US, liquid]	0.133 526 5	1.335 264 7E-01
pound/cubic yard	1.685 554 9	1.685 554 9E+00
slug/cubic yard	0.052 388 6	5.238 864 9E-02
ton/cubic yard [long]	0.000 752 5	7.524 798 8E-04
tonne/cubic meter	0.001	1.000 000 0E-03
milligram/cubic decimeter		**<density>**
gammil	1	1.000 000 0E+00
grain/cubic foot	0.436 995 7	4.369 957 2E-01
gram/cubic meter	1	1.000 000 0E+00
kilogram/cubic meter	0.001	1.000 000 0E-03
micril	1	1.000 000 0E+00
milligram/liter	1	1.000 000 0E+00
ounce/cubic yard	0.026 968 9	2.696 887 9E-02
pound/cubic yard	0.001 685 6	1.685 554 9E-03
slug/cubic yard	0.000 052 4	5.238 864 9E-05
ton/cubic yard [short]	0.000 000 8	8.427 774 7E-07
tonne/cubic meter	0.000 001	1.000 000 0E-06
milligram/cubic meter		**<density>**
grain/cubic yard	0.011 798 9	1.179 888 5E-02
gram/cubic meter	0.001	1.000 000 0E-03
kilogram/cubic meter	0.000 001	1.000 000 0E-06
milligram/liter	0.001	1.000 000 0E-03
ounce/cubic yard	0.000 027	2.696 887 9E-05
pound/cubic yard	0.000 001 7	1.685 554 9E-06
slug/cubic yard	<<<	5.238 864 9E-08
ton/cubic yard [short]	<<<	8.427 774 7E-10
tonne/cubic meter	<<<	1.000 000 0E-09
milligram/gram		**<concentration, mass basis>**
gram/ton [-/metric]	1,000	1.000 000 0E+03
gram/tonne	1,000	1.000 000 0E+03
kilogram/kilogram	0.001	1.000 000 0E-03
milligram/kilogram	1,000	1.000 000 0E+03
milligram/ton [-/metric]	1,000,000	1.000 000 0E+06
ounce/ton [-/short]	32	3.200 000 0E+01
ounce/ton [troy/long]	32.666 666 7	3.266 666 7E+01
part/million	1,000	1.000 000 0E+03
pennyweight/ton [troy/long]	653.333 333	6.533 333 3E+02
percent	0.1	1.000 000 0E-01
pound/ton [-/long]	2.24	2.240 000 0E+00
pound/ton [-/metric]	2.204 622 6	2.204 622 6E+00
pound/ton [-/short]	2	2.000 000 0E+00
milligram/hour		**<flow rate, mass basis>**
kilogram/second	<<<	2.777 777 8E-10
pound/hour	0.000 002 2	2.204 622 6E-06
milligram/kilogram		**<concentration, mass basis>**
gram/ton [-/long]	1.016 046 9	1.016 046 9E+00
gram/ton [-/metric]	1	1.000 000 0E+00
gram/tonne	1	1.000 000 0E+00
karat	0.000 024	2.400 000 0E-05
kilogram/kilogram	0.000 001	1.000 000 0E-06
milligram/gram	0.001	1.000 000 0E-03
milligram/ton [-/metric]	1,000	1.000 000 0E+03
ounce/ton [troy/long]	0.032 666 7	3.266 666 7E-02
part/million	1	1.000 000 0E+00
pennyweight/ton [troy/short]	0.583 333 3	5.833 333 3E-01

Convert From Convert To	Standard	<Type of Unit> Scientific
percent	0.000 1	1.000 000 0E−04
pound/ton [-/long]	0.002 24	2.240 000 0E−03
pound/ton [-/short]	0.002	2.000 000 0E−03
milligram/kilometer		**<linear density>**
denier	0.009	9.000 000 0E−03
drex	0.01	1.000 000 0E−02
kilogram/meter	<<<	1.000 000 0E−09
ounce/foot	<<<	1.075 150 4E−08
pound/yard	<<<	2.015 906 9E−09
tex	0.001	1.000 000 0E−03
milligram/liter		**<density>**
gammil	1	1.000 000 0E+00
grain/cubic yard	11.798 885	1.179 888 5E+01
gram/cubic meter	1	1.000 000 0E+00
kilogram/cubic meter	0.001	1.000 000 0E−03
micril	1	1.000 000 0E+00
milligram/cubic decimeter	1	1.000 000 0E+00
ounce/cubic yard	0.026 968 9	2.696 887 9E−02
pound/cubic yard	0.001 685 6	1.685 554 9E−03
slug/cubic yard	0.000 052 4	5.238 864 9E−05
ton/cubic yard [short]	0.000 000 8	8.427 774 7E−07
tonne/cubic meter	0.000 001	1.000 000 0E−06
milligram/meter		**<linear density>**
denier	9	9.000 000 0E+00
drex	10	1.000 000 0E+01
kilogram/meter	0.000 001	1.000 000 0E−06
ounce/foot	0.000 010 8	1.075 150 4E−05
pound/yard	0.000 002	2.015 906 9E−06
tex	1	1.000 000 0E+00
milligram/milliliter		**<density>**
grain/cubic inch	0.252 891	2.528 910 4E−01
gram/cubic decimeter	1	1.000 000 0E+00
gram/liter	1	1.000 000 0E+00
kilogram/cubic meter	1	1.000 000 0E+00
milligram/cubic centimeter	1	1.000 000 0E+00
ounce/cubic foot	0.998 847 4	9.988 473 7E−01
ounce/gallon [-/US, liquid]	0.133 526 5	1.335 264 7E−01
pound/cubic yard	1.685 554 9	1.685 554 9E+00
slug/cubic yard	0.052 388 6	5.238 864 9E−02
ton/cubic yard [short]	0.000 842 8	8.427 774 7E−04
tonne/cubic meter	0.001	1.000 000 0E−03
milligram/minute		**<flow rate, mass basis>**
kilogram/second	<<<	1.666 666 7E−08
pound/hour	0.000 132 3	1.322 773 6E−04
milligram/second		**<flow rate, mass basis>**
kilogram/second	0.000 001	1.000 000 0E−06
pound/hour	0.007 936 6	7.936 641 4E−03
milligram/square centimeter		**<surface density>**
grain/square foot	14.337 13	1.433 713 0E+01
kilogram/are	1	1.000 000 0E+00
kilogram/square meter	0.01	1.000 000 0E−02
ounce/square yard	0.294 935 3	2.949 352 5E−01
pound/acre	89.217 912	8.921 791 2E+01
pound/square yard	0.018 433 5	1.843 345 3E−02
slug/square yard	0.000 572 9	5.729 292 3E−04
milligram/square meter		**<surface density>**
grain/square yard	0.012 903 4	1.290 341 7E−02
kilogram/hectare	0.01	1.000 000 0E−02
kilogram/square meter	0.000 001	1.000 000 0E−06
ounce/square yard	0.000 029 5	2.949 352 5E−05
pound/acre	0.008 921 8	8.921 791 2E−03

| Convert From | | <Type of Unit> |
Convert To	Standard	Scientific
pound/square yard	0.000 001 8	1.843 345 3E-06
milligram/square meter second	**<flow rate/unit area, mass basis>**	
gram/square meter second	0.001	1.000 000 0E-03
kilogram/hectare second	0.01	1.000 000 0E-02
kilogram/square meter second	0.000 001	1.000 000 0E-06
pound/acre second	0.008 921 8	8.921 791 2E-03
milligram/ton [-/long]	**<concentration, mass basis>**	
gram/ton [-/long]	0.001	1.000 000 0E-03
karat	<<<	2.362 095 7E-08
kilogram/kilogram	<<<	9.842 065 3E-10
milligram/ton [-/metric]	0.984 206 5	9.842 065 3E-01
milligram/ton [-/short]	0.892 857 1	8.928 571 4E-01
part/million	0.000 984 2	9.842 065 3E-04
percent	<<<	9.842 065 3E-08
milligram/ton [-/metric]	**<concentration, mass basis>**	
gram/ton [-/metric]	0.001	1.000 000 0E-03
gram/tonne	0.001	1.000 000 0E-03
karat	<<<	2.400 000 0E-08
kilogram/kilogram	<<<	1.000 000 0E-09
milligram/kilogram	0.001	1.000 000 0E-03
milligram/ton [-/long]	1.016 046 9	1.016 046 9E+00
ounce/ton [-/short]	0.000 032	3.200 000 0E-05
part/million	0.001	1.000 000 0E-03
percent	0.000 000 1	1.000 000 0E-07
milligram/ton [-/short]	**<concentration, mass basis>**	
gram/ton [-/long]	0.001 12	1.120 000 0E-03
gram/ton [-/short]	0.001	1.000 000 0E-03
karat	<<<	2.645 547 2E-08
kilogram/kilogram	<<<	1.102 311 3E-09
milligram/ton [-/long]	1.12	1.120 000 0E+00
milligram/ton [-/metric]	1.102 311 3	1.102 311 3E+00
part/million	0.001 102 3	1.102 311 3E-03
percent	0.000 000 1	1.102 311 3E-07
milligram/ton [-/UK, assay or assay, long]	**<concentration, mass basis>**	
gram/ton [-/UK, assay or assay, long]	0.001	1.000 000 0E-03
karat	0.000 734 7	7.346 938 8E-04
kilogram/kilogram	0.000 030 6	3.061 224 5E-05
milligram/kilogram	30.612 244 9	3.061 224 5E+01
ounce/ton [-/long]	1.097 142 9	1.097 142 9E+00
ounce/ton [-/metric]	1.079 815 2	1.079 815 2E+00
ounce/ton [troy/long]	1	1.000 000 0E+00
part/million	30.612 244 9	3.061 224 5E+01
pennyweight/ton [troy/long]	20	2.000 000 0E+01
percent	0.003 061 2	3.061 224 5E-03
milligram/ton [-/US, assay or assay, short]	**<concentration, mass basis>**	
gram/ton [-/US, assay or assay, short]	0.001	1.000 000 0E-03
kilogram/kilogram	0.000 034 3	3.428 571 4E-05
milligram/ton [-/UK, assay or assay, long]	1.12	1.120 000 0E+00
ounce/ton [-/long]	1.228 8	1.228 800 0E+00
ounce/ton [troy/long]	1.12	1.120 000 0E+00
ounce/ton [troy/short]	1	1.000 000 0E+00
part/million	34.285 714 3	3.428 571 4E+01
pennyweight/ton [troy/short]	20	2.000 000 0E+01
percent	0.003 428 6	3.428 571 4E-03
milligray	**<absorbed dose>**	
gray	0.001	1.000 000 0E-03
rad	0.1	1.000 000 0E-01
rep	0.119 331 7	1.193 317 4E-01
milligray/second	**<absorbed dose rate>**	
gray/second	0.001	1.000 000 0E-03
rad/second	0.1	1.000 000 0E-01

| Convert From | <Type of Unit> | |
Convert To	Standard	Scientific
rep/second	0.119 331 7	1.193 317 4E−01
millihenry		**<electric inductance>**
abhenry	1,000,000	1.000 000 0E+06
henry	0.001	1.000 000 0E−03
ohm second	0.001	1.000 000 0E−03
stathenry	<<<	1.112 650 1E−15
millihertz		**<frequency>**
1/second	0.001	1.000 000 0E−03
degree/minute	21.6	2.160 000 0E+01
hertz	0.001	1.000 000 0E−03
radian/hour	22.619 467	2.261 946 7E+01
revolution/hour	3.6	3.600 000 0E+00
millihg		**<pressure>**
atmosphere [standard]	0.001 315 8	1.315 789 7E−03
atmosphere [technical]	0.001 359 5	1.359 510 0E−03
bar	0.001 333 2	1.333 223 9E−03
barye [France]	1,333.223 9	1.333 223 9E+03
centimeter of mercury [0 °C, by convention]	0.1	1.000 000 0E−01
centimeter of water [4 °C, by convention]	1.359 51	1.359 510 0E+00
dyne/square centimeter	1,333.223 9	1.333 223 9E+03
gram-force/square centimeter	1.359 51	1.359 510 0E+00
hectopascal	1.333 223 9	1.333 223 9E+00
inch of mercury [0 °C, by convention]	0.039 370 1	3.937 007 9E−02
inch of water [4 °C, by convention]	0.535 240 2	5.352 401 6E−01
kilogram-force/square meter	13.595 1	1.359 510 0E+01
kilopond/square meter	13.595 1	1.359 510 0E+01
kip/square foot	0.002 784 5	2.784 496 0E−03
millibar	1.333 223 9	1.333 223 9E+00
millimeter of mercury [0 °C, by convention]	1	1.000 000 0E+00
millimeter of water [4 °C, by convention]	13.595 1	1.359 510 0E+01
newton/square meter	133.322 39	1.333 223 9E+02
ounce-force/square inch	0.309 388 4	3.093 884 4E−01
pascal	133.322 39	1.333 223 9E+02
pound-force/square foot	2.784 496	2.784 496 0E+00
poundal/square foot	89.588 508	8.958 850 8E+01
ton-force/square foot [long]	0.001 243 1	1.243 078 0E−03
ton-force/square foot [short]	0.001 392 2	1.392 248 0E−03
ton-force/square meter [metric]	0.013 595 1	1.359 510 0E−02
torr	1.000 000 1	1.000 000 1E+00
millijoule		**<energy>**
Btu [I.T.]	0.000 000 9	9.478 171 2E−07
calorie [I.T.]	0.000 238 8	2.388 459 0E−04
calorie [kilogram, I.T.]	0.000 000 2	2.388 459 0E−07
centimeter gram-force	10.197 162	1.019 716 2E+01
cubic centimeter atmosphere	0.009 869 2	9.869 232 7E−03
cubic foot atmosphere	0.000 000 3	3.485 286 6E−07
dyne centimeter	10,000	1.000 000 0E+04
erg	10,000	1.000 000 0E+04
foot pound-force	0.000 737 6	7.375 621 5E−04
foot poundal	0.023 730 4	2.373 036 0E−02
gram calorie	0.000 238 9	2.389 029 6E−04
inch ounce-force	0.141 611 9	1.416 119 3E−01
inch pound-force	0.008 850 7	8.850 745 8E−03
joule	0.001	1.000 000 0E−03
kilogram square meter/square second	0.001	1.000 000 0E−03
kilopond meter	0.000 102	1.019 716 2E−04
liter atmosphere	0.000 009	9.869 232 7E−06
megaerg	0.01	1.000 000 0E−02
megalerg	0.01	1.000 000 0E−02
meter kilogram-force	0.000 102	1.019 716 2E−04
newton meter	0.001	1.000 000 0E−03
teraelectronvolt	6,241.506 4	6.241 506 4E+03

Convert From		<Type of Unit>
Convert To	Standard	Scientific

watthour	0.000 000 3	2.777 777 8E-07
wattsecond	0.001	1.000 000 0E-03

millijoule/kilogram   **<absorbed dose>**

gray	0.001	1.000 000 0E-03
rad	0.1	1.000 000 0E-01
rep	0.119 331 7	1.193 317 4E-01

millijoule/kilogram second   **<absorbed dose rate>**

gray/second	0.001	1.000 000 0E-03
rad/second	0.1	1.000 000 0E-01
rep/second	0.119 331 7	1.193 317 4E-01

millijoule/mole   **<molar energy>**

joule/mole	0.001	1.000 000 0E-03
kilojoule/mole	0.000 001	1.000 000 0E-06

millijoule/mole kelvin   **<molar entropy>**

joule/mole kelvin	0.001	1.000 000 0E-03
kilojoule/mole kelvin	0.000 001	1.000 000 0E-06

millilambert   **<luminance>**

apostilb [German Hefner]	11.111 111	1.111 111 1E+01
apostilb [international]	10	1.000 000 0E+01
blondel	10	1.000 000 0E+01
bril	100	1.000 000 0E+02
candela/square foot	0.295 719 6	2.957 195 6E-01
candela/square meter	3.183 098 9	3.183 098 9E+00
footlambert	0.929 030 4	9.290 304 0E-01
lambert	0.001	1.000 000 0E-03
nit	3.183 098 9	3.183 098 9E+00
stilb	0.000 318 3	3.183 098 9E-04

milliliter   **<volume>**

acetabulum [Rome, ancient]	0.014 925 4	1.492 537 3E-02
barrel [UK]	0.000 006 1	6.110 256 9E-06
barrel [US, liquid]	0.000 008 4	8.386 414 4E-06
barrel [US, petroleum]	0.000 006 3	6.289 810 8E-06
bottle [UK, small]	0.003 636 4	3.636 363 6E-03
cast [Russia]	0.009 149 1	9.149 130 8E-03
cochliarion [Greece, ancient]	0.204 081 6	2.040 816 3E-01
cuarta [Nicaragua]	0.005 988	5.988 024 0E-03
cubic centimeter	1	1.000 000 0E+00
cubic foot	0.000 035 3	3.531 466 7E-05
cubic inch	0.061 023 7	6.102 374 4E-02
cubic meter	0.000 001	1.000 000 0E-06
cup [metric]	0.005	5.000 000 0E-03
drachm [UK, liquid]	0.281 560 6	2.815 606 4E-01
dram [Canada, liquid]	0.281 560 6	2.815 606 4E-01
dram [US, liquid]	0.270 512 2	2.705 121 8E-01
drop [US, liquid]	12.173 048	1.217 304 8E+01
flagon [UK]	0.000 885	8.849 557 5E-04
foglietta [Italy, liquid]	0.002 193	2.192 982 5E-03
gallon [Canada, liquid]	0.000 22	2.199 692 5E-04
gallon [UK, dry or liquid]	0.000 22	2.199 692 5E-04
gallon [US, liquid]	0.000 264 2	2.641 720 5E-04
gill [UK]	0.007 039	7.039 015 7E-03
gill [US]	0.008 453 5	8.453 505 7E-03
hao sheng [China]	1	1.000 000 0E+00
hemikotylion [Greece, ancient]	0.006 849 3	6.849 315 1E-03
henu [Egypt, ancient]	0.003 333 3	3.333 333 3E-03
jak [South Korea]	0.055 435 4	5.543 544 5E-02
kotyle [Greece, ancient]	0.003 424 7	3.424 657 5E-03
kung tso [Taiwan]	1	1.000 000 0E+00
kyathos [Greece, ancient]	0.020 408 2	2.040 816 3E-02
lifer	0.001	1.000 000 0E-03
measurette [France, dry]	0.019 679 6	1.967 961 6E-02
minim [UK]	16.893 638	1.689 363 8E+01

	Standard	Scientific
minim [US]	16.230 731	1.623 073 1E+01
noessel [Germany, liquid]	0.002 331	2.331 002 3E−03
nofs [Malta, beer, wine and spirits]	0.001 760 6	1.760 563 4E−03
ort [Germany, liquid]	0.004 651 2	4.651 162 8E−03
ounce [UK, liquid]	0.035 195 1	3.519 508 0E−02
ounce [US, liquid]	0.033 814	3.381 402 3E−02
oxybaphon [Greece, ancient]	0.013 698 6	1.369 863 0E−02
paegle [Denmark]	0.004 140 3	4.140 272 4E−03
paele [Germany, liquid]	0.004 651 2	4.651 162 8E−03
pau [Brunei]	0.003 521 1	3.521 126 8E−03
pau [Malaysia]	0.003 521 1	3.521 126 8E−03
pau [Singapore]	0.003 521 1	3.521 126 8E−03
pegel [Germany, liquid]	0.004 651 2	4.651 162 8E−03
pinta [Malta, beer, wine and spirits]	0.007 042 3	7.042 253 5E−03
planken [Germany, liquid]	0.002 331	2.331 002 3E−03
posson [France, liquid]	0.008 591 1	8.591 065 3E−03
quartel [Germany, liquid]	0.002 331	2.331 002 3E−03
quartuccio [Italy, liquid]	0.008 771 9	8.771 929 8E−03
que [Vietnam, cereal]	50	5.000 000 0E+01
quei [China]	100	1.000 000 0E+02
sao [Vietnam, cereal]	5	5.000 000 0E+00
scruple [UK, liquid]	0.844 681 9	8.446 819 1E−01
seidel [Germany, liquid]	0.002 331	2.331 002 3E−03
sextario [Iran]	0.003 039 5	3.039 513 7E−03
shaku [Japan]	0.055 435 4	5.543 544 5E−02
shih se [China]	1	1.000 000 0E+00
sun [Japan]	55.435 23	5.543 523 0E+01
tablespoon [Canada, measuring]	0.070 390 3	7.039 027 9E−02
tablespoon [US, measuring]	0.067 628	6.762 804 5E−02
taza [Cuba]	0.004 237 3	4.237 288 1E−03
teacup [Scandinavia]	0.008	8.000 000 0E−03
teaspoon [Canada, measuring]	0.211 170 8	2.111 708 4E−01
teaspoon [US, measuring]	0.202 884 1	2.028 841 4E−01
terz [Malta, beer, wine and spirits]	0.003 519 9	3.519 887 4E−03
terz [Malta, oil and milk]	0.003 128 9	3.128 911 1E−03
toat [Vietnam]	5	5.000 000 0E+00
tot [UK]	0.042 235 1	4.223 508 0E−02
tuc [Vietnam, cereal]	303.030 3	3.030 303 0E+02
viertel [Germany, liquid]	0.002 331	2.331 002 3E−03
milliliter/day		**<flow rate, volume basis>**
centiliter/day	0.1	1.000 000 0E−01
cubic centimeter/day	1	1.000 000 0E+00
cubic decimeter/day	0.001	1.000 000 0E−03
cubic inch/day	0.061 023 7	6.102 374 4E−02
cubic meter/second	<<<	1.157 407 4E−11
cubic millimeter/day	1,000	1.000 000 0E+03
cubic millimeter/hour	41.666 666 7	4.166 666 7E+01
deciliter/day	0.01	1.000 000 0E−02
lambda/day	1,000	1.000 000 0E+03
lambda/hour	41.666 666 7	4.166 666 7E+01
liter/day	0.001	1.000 000 0E−03
liter/day [pre-1964]	0.001	9.999 720 0E−04
milliliter/hour	0.041 666 7	4.166 666 7E−02
ounce/day [UK, liquid]	0.035 195 1	3.519 508 0E−02
ounce/day [US, liquid]	0.033 814	3.381 402 3E−02
milliliter/hour		**<flow rate, volume basis>**
centiliter/day	2.4	2.400 000 0E+00
centiliter/hour	0.1	1.000 000 0E−01
cubic centimeter/hour	1	1.000 000 0E+00
cubic decimeter/day	0.024	2.400 000 0E−02
cubic inch/day	1.464 569	1.464 569 9E+00
cubic millimeter/minute	16.666 666 7	1.666 666 7E+01
deciliter/day	0.24	2.400 000 0E−01

	Standard	Scientific
dekaliter/day		
gallon/day [UK]	0.002 4	$2.400\ 000\text{E}{-}03$
gallon/day [US, liquid]	0.005 279 3	$5.279\ 262\text{E}{-}03$
hectoliter/day	0.006 340 1	$6.340\ 129\ 3\text{E}{-}03$
lambda/minute	0.000 24	$2.400\ 000\text{E}{-}04$
liter/day	0.024	$2.400\ 000\text{E}{-}02$
liter/day [pre-1964]	16.666 666 7	$1.666\ 666\ 7\text{E}{+}01$
milliliter/day	0.023 999 3	$2.399\ 932\ 8\text{E}{-}02$
ounce/day [UK, liquid]	24	$2.400\ 000\text{E}{+}01$
ounce/day [US, liquid]	0.844 681 9	$8.446\ 819\ 1\text{E}{-}01$
	0.811 536 5	$8.115\ 365\ 4\text{E}{-}01$
milliliter/minute		<flow rate, volume basis>
barrel/day [UK]	0.008 798 8	$8.798\ 769\ 9\text{E}{-}03$
barrel/day [US, federal]	0.012 271 2	$1.227\ 121\ 8\text{E}{-}02$
barrel/day [US, liquid]	0.012 076 4	$1.207\ 643\ 7\text{E}{-}02$
barrel/day [US, petroleum]	0.009 057 3	$9.057\ 327\ 5\text{E}{-}03$
centiliter/hour	6	$6.000\ 000\text{E}{+}00$
cubic centimeter/minute	1	$1.000\ 000\text{E}{+}00$
cubic decimeter/day	1.44	$1.440\ 000\text{E}{+}00$
cubic foot/day	0.050 853 1	$5.085\ 312\ 0\text{E}{-}02$
cubic inch/hour	3.661 424 7	$3.661\ 424\ 7\text{E}{+}00$
cubic meter/day	0.001 44	$1.440\ 000\text{E}{-}03$
cubic millimeter/second	16.666 666 7	$1.666\ 666\ 7\text{E}{+}01$
deciliter/day	14.4	$1.440\ 000\text{E}{+}01$
dekaliter/day	0.144	$1.440\ 000\text{E}{-}01$
gallon/day [UK]	0.316 755 7	$3.167\ 557\ 2\text{E}{-}01$
gallon/day [US, liquid]	0.380 407 8	$3.804\ 077\ 6\text{E}{-}01$
hectoliter/day	0.014 4	$1.440\ 000\text{E}{-}02$
kiloliter/day	0.001 44	$1.440\ 000\text{E}{-}03$
lambda/minute	1,000	$1.000\ 000\text{E}{+}03$
lambda/second	16.666 666 7	$1.666\ 666\ 7\text{E}{+}01$
liter/day	1.44	$1.440\ 000\text{E}{+}00$
liter/day [pre-1964]	1.439 959 7	$1.439\ 959\ 7\text{E}{+}00$
milliliter/hour	60	$6.000\ 000\text{E}{+}01$
ounce/hour [UK, liquid]	2.111 704 8	$2.111\ 704\ 8\text{E}{+}00$
ounce/hour [US, liquid]	2.028 841 4	$2.028\ 841\ 4\text{E}{+}00$
stere/day	0.001 44	$1.440\ 000\text{E}{-}03$
milliliter/second		<flow rate, volume basis>
acre inch/day	0.000 840 5	$8.405\ 474\ 4\text{E}{-}04$
barrel/day [UK]	0.527 926 2	$5.279\ 262\ 0\text{E}{-}01$
barrel/day [US, federal]	0.736 273 1	$7.362\ 730\ 8\text{E}{-}01$
barrel/day [US, liquid]	0.724 586 2	$7.245\ 862\ 0\text{E}{-}01$
barrel/day [US, petroleum]	0.543 439 7	$5.434\ 396\ 5\text{E}{-}01$
centiliter/minute	6	$6.000\ 000\text{E}{+}00$
centiliter/second	0.1	$1.000\ 000\text{E}{-}01$
cubic centimeter/second	1	$1.000\ 000\text{E}{+}00$
cubic decimeter/hour	3.6	$3.600\ 000\text{E}{+}00$
cubic foot/day	3.051 187 2	$3.051\ 187\ 2\text{E}{+}00$
cubic inch/minute	3.661 424 7	$3.661\ 424\ 7\text{E}{+}00$
cubic meter/day	0.086 4	$8.640\ 000\text{E}{-}02$
cubic meter/second	0.000 001	$1.000\ 000\text{E}{-}06$
cubic millimeter/second	1,000	$1.000\ 000\text{E}{+}03$
cubic yard/day	0.113 006 9	$1.130\ 069\ 3\text{E}{-}01$
deciliter/hour	36	$3.600\ 000\text{E}{+}01$
dekaliter/day	8.64	$8.640\ 000\text{E}{+}00$
gallon/day [UK]	19.005 343 1	$1.900\ 534\ 3\text{E}{+}01$
gallon/day [US, liquid]	22.824 465 3	$2.282\ 446\ 5\text{E}{+}01$
hectoliter/day	0.864	$8.640\ 000\text{E}{-}01$
kiloliter/day	0.086 4	$8.640\ 000\text{E}{-}02$
lambda/second	1,000	$1.000\ 000\text{E}{+}03$
liter/hour	3.6	$3.600\ 000\text{E}{+}00$
liter/hour [pre-1964]	3.599 899 2	$3.599\ 899\ 2\text{E}{+}00$
milliliter/minute	60	$6.000\ 000\text{E}{+}01$
ounce/minute [UK, liquid]	2.111 704 8	$2.111\ 704\ 8\text{E}{+}00$

	Standard	Scientific
ounce/minute [US, liquid]	2.028 841 4	2.028 841 4E+00
petrograd standard/day	0.018 492	1.849 204 4E-02
stere/day	0.086 4	8.640 000 0E-02
thousand cubic foot/day	0.003 051 2	3.051 187 2E-03

millimeter   **\<length\>**

	Standard	Scientific
angstrom	>>>	1.000 000 0E+07
annuk [Cambodia]	662.251 66	6.622 516 6E+02
azba [Hebrew, ancient]	0.053 418 8	5.341 880 3E-02
barleycorn	0.118 110 2	1.181 102 4E-01
boo [Japan]	0.330 033	3.300 330 3E-01
cal [Poland]	0.041 666 7	4.166 666 7E-02
caliber	3.937 007 9	3.937 007 9E+00
centimeter	0.1	1.000 000 0E-01
chabba [Iraq, ancient]	0.303 030 3	3.030 303 0E-01
chinese inch [Hong Kong]	0.026 919 7	2.691 971 2E-02
digit	0.052 493	5.249 343 8E-02
digit [Egypt, ancient]	0.053 418 8	5.341 880 3E-02
digit [Greece, ancient]	0.051 948 1	5.194 805 2E-02
digit [Hebrew, ancient]	0.052 631 6	5.263 157 9E-02
ell [Babylon, ancient]	0.002 020 2	2.020 202 0E-03
ell [Hebrew, ancient]	0.002 020 2	2.020 202 0E-03
em [pica, print]	0.237 106 3	2.371 063 0E-01
fan [Hong Kong]	0.269 197 1	2.691 971 2E-01
fen [China]	0.279 204 2	2.792 204 2E-01
finger [Greece, ancient]	0.051 948 1	5.194 805 2E-02
foot [France]	0.003 078 4	3.078 432 9E-03
foot [international]	0.003 280 8	3.280 839 9E-03
foot [Phoenicia, ancient]	0.002 020 2	2.020 202 0E-03
foot [US, survey]	0.003 280 8	3.280 833 3E-03
fun [Hong Kong]	0.269 197 1	2.691 971 2E-01
gramme [Greece]	0.471 698 1	4.716 981 1E-01
habba shair [Egypt]	0.191 570 8	1.915 708 8E-01
hao mi [China]	1	1.000 000 0E+00
hatt [Turkey]	2.890 173 4	2.890 173 4E+00
inch [based on US, survey foot]	0.039 37	3.937 000 0E-02
inch [international]	0.039 370 1	3.937 007 9E-02
kabiet [Laos]	0.239 980 8	2.399 808 0E-01
kabiet louang [Laos]	0.192	1.920 000 0E-01
khluon chay [Cambodia]	4.608 294 9	4.608 294 9E+00
kirat [Egypt, ancient]	1.149 425	1.149 425 3E+00
krap sran [Cambodia]	0.384 024 5	3.840 245 8E-01
li [Mongolia]	3.125	3.125 000 0E+00
ligne [France]	0.443 262 4	4.432 624 1E-01
ligne [Haiti]	0.443 262 4	4.432 624 1E-01
ligne [Paraguay]	0.498 504 5	4.985 044 9E-01
ligne [Switzerland]	0.480 007 7	4.800 076 8E-01
lina [Iceland]	0.458 715 6	4.587 156 0E-01
line [France]	0.443 262 4	4.432 624 1E-01
line [Greece]	0.471 698 1	4.716 981 1E-01
line [Russia]	0.393 700 8	3.937 007 9E-01
linea [Argentina]	0.5	5.000 000 0E-01
linea [Chile]	0.518 134 7	5.181 347 2E-01
linea [Honduras]	0.518 134 7	5.181 347 2E-01
linea [Mexico]	0.515 463 9	5.154 639 2E-01
linea [Paraguay]	0.498 504 5	4.985 044 9E-01
linea [Spain]	0.516 803 9	5.168 038 8E-01
linha [Brazil]	0.434 782 6	4.347 826 1E-01
linha [Portugal]	0.436 681 2	4.366 812 2E-01
linia [Sudan]	0.314 960 6	3.149 606 3E-01
linie [Austria]	0.455 580 9	4.555 808 7E-01
linie [Germany, Bavaria]	0.493 386 1	4.933 861 6E-01
linie [Germany, Prussia]	0.458 806 1	4.588 060 9E-01
linie [Switzerland]	0.480 007 7	4.800 076 8E-01

Convert From <Type of Unit>
Convert To Standard Scientific

millimeter (continued) <length>

	Standard	Scientific
liniya [Russia]	0.393 700 8	3.937 007 9E−01
linja [Poland]	0.5	5.000 000 0E−01
linje [Sweden]	0.336 700 3	3.367 003 4E−01
ly [Vietnam]	2.5	2.500 000 0E−01
meter	0.001	1.000 000 0E−03
microinch	39,370.079	3.937 007 9E+04
micromicron	>>>	1.000 000 0E+09
micron	1,000.	1.000 000 0E+03
mil	39.370 079	3.937 007 9E+01
millimicron	1,000,000.	1.000 000 0E+06
mo [Japan]	33.333 333	3.333 333 3E+01
mou [Iran]	1	1.000 000 0E+00
nocktat [Turkey]	3.448 275 9	3.448 275 9E+00
palaz [Yugoslavia]	0.027 517 9	2.751 788 7E−02
Paris line [France]	0.443 262 4	4.432 624 1E−01
phan [Vietnam]	0.25	2.500 000 0E−01
pied de perche [UK, land]	0.003 584 2	3.584 229 4E−03
point [Denmark]	5.505 698 4	5.505 698 4E+00
point [France]	5.319 148 9	5.319 148 9E+00
point [print]	2.845 275 6	2.845 275 6E+00
polegada [Macao]	0.036 363 6	3.636 363 6E−02
pong chay [Cambodia]	55.248 619	5.524 861 9E+01
ponto [Brazil]	5.235 602 1	5.235 602 1E+00
pouce [Haiti]	0.036 941 3	3.694 126 3E−02
pulgada [Cuba]	0.042 372 9	4.237 288 1E−02
pulgada [Honduras]	0.043 103 4	4.310 344 8E−02
pulgada [Mexico]	0.042 918 5	4.291 845 5E−02
pulgada [Nicaragua]	0.042 918 5	4.291 845 5E−02
pulgada [Paraguay]	0.041 493 8	4.149 377 6E−02
pulzier [Malta]	0.045 808 5	4.580 852 0E−02
pun [Mongolia]	0.312 5	3.125 000 0E−01
pun [South Korea]	0.330 033	3.300 330 0E−01
punto [Honduras]	6.211 180 1	6.211 180 1E+00
punto [Italy]	0.280 112	2.801 120 4E−01
qirat [Egypt, ancient]	1.149 425 3	1.149 425 3E+00
ri [South Korea]	3.300 33	3.300 330 0E+00
rin [Japan]	3.300 33	3.300 330 0E+00
shi [Japan]	330	3.300 330 0E+02
shih fen [China]	0.3	3.000 000 0E−01
shih hao [China]	30	3.000 000 0E+01
shih li [China]	3	3.000 000 0E+00
shih tze [China]	300	3.000 000 0E+02
si mi [China]	10	1.000 000 0E+01
sossus [Iraq, ancient]	0.606 060 6	6.060 606 1E−01
stich [Germany]	1	1.000 000 0E+00
streep [Netherlands]	1	1.000 000 0E+00
strich [Germany]	1	1.000 000 0E+00
strich [Switzerland]	0.480 000 1	4.800 000 8E−01
stritch [Switzerland]	3.333 333 3	3.333 333 3E+00
thou	39.370 079	3.937 007 9E+01
totchka [Russia]	3.937 007 9	3.937 007 9E+00
totschka [Russia]	3.937 007 9	3.937 007 9E+00
totska [Russia]	3.937 007 9	3.937 007 9E+00
trait [Switzerland]	3.333 333 3	3.333 333 3E+00
tsal [Ukraine]	0.040 322 6	4.032 258 1E−02
yard [based on US, survey foot]	0.001 093 6	1.093 611 1E−03
yard [international]	0.001 093 6	1.093 613 3E−03
yard [UK]	0.001 093 6	1.093 615 2E−03
zebo [Egypt, ancient]	0.053 418 8	5.341 880 3E−02

millimeter of mercury [0 °C, by convention] <pressure>

	Standard	Scientific
atmosphere [standard]	0.001 315 8	1.315 789 7E−03

Convert From Convert To	Standard	<Type of Unit> Scientific
atmosphere [technical]	0.001 359 5	1.359 510 0E-03
bar	0.001 333 2	1.333 223 9E-03
barye [France]	1,333.223 9	1.333 223 9E+03
centimeter of mercury [0 °C, by convention]	0.1	1.000 000 0E-01
centimeter of water [4 °C, by convention]	1.359 51	1.359 510 0E+00
dyne/square centimeter	1,333.223 9	1.333 223 9E+03
gram-force/square centimeter	1.359 51	1.359 510 0E+00
hectopascal	1.333 223 9	1.333 223 9E+00
inch of mercury [0 °C, by convention]	0.039 370 1	3.937 007 9E-02
inch of water [4 °C, by convention]	0.535 240 2	5.352 401 6E-01
kilogram-force/square meter	13.595 1	1.359 510 0E+01
kilopond/square meter	13.595 1	1.359 510 0E+01
kip/square foot	0.002 784 5	2.784 496 0E-03
micrometer of mercury [0 °C, by convention]	1,000	1.000 000 0E+03
micrometer of water [4 °C, by convention]	13,595.1	1.359 510 0E+04
millibar	1.333 223 9	1.333 223 9E+00
millihg	1	1.000 000 0E+00
millimeter of water [4 °C, by convention]	13.595 1	1.359 510 0E+01
newton/square meter	133.322 39	1.333 223 9E+02
ounce-force/square inch	0.309 388 4	3.093 884 4E-01
pascal	133.322 39	1.333 223 9E+02
pound-force/square foot	2.784 496	2.784 496 0E+00
poundal/square foot	89.588 508	8.958 850 8E+01
ton-force/square foot [long]	0.001 243 1	1.243 078 6E-03
ton-force/square foot [short]	0.001 392 2	1.392 248 0E-03
torr	1.000 000	1.000 000 1E+00
millimeter of water [4 °C, by convention]		**<pressure>**
atmosphere [standard]	0.000 096 8	9.678 411 1E-05
atmosphere [technical]	0.000 1	1.000 000 0E-04
bar	0.000 098 1	9.806 650 0E-05
barye [France]	98.066 5	9.806 650 0E+01
centimeter of mercury [0 °C, by convention]	0.007 355 6	7.355 591 4E-03
centimeter of water [4 °C, by convention]	0.1	1.000 000 0E-01
centitorr	7.355 592	7.355 592 4E+00
dyne/square centimeter	98.066 5	9.806 650 0E+01
gram-force/square centimeter	0.1	1.000 000 0E-01
inch of mercury [0 °C, by convention]	0.002 895 9	2.895 902 1E-03
inch of water [4 °C, by convention]	0.039 370 1	3.937 007 9E-02
kilogram-force/square meter	1	1.000 000 0E+00
kilopond/square meter	1	1.000 000 0E+00
kip/square foot	0.000 204 8	2.048 161 4E-04
micrometer of mercury [0 °C, by convention]	73.555 914	7.355 591 4E+01
micrometer of water [4 °C, by convention]	1,000	1.000 000 0E+03
millimeter of mercury [0 °C, by convention]	0.073 555 9	7.355 591 4E-02
newton/square meter	9.806 65	9.806 650 0E+00
ounce-force/square inch	0.022 757 3	2.275 734 9E-02
pascal	9.806 65	9.806 650 0E+00
pound-force/square foot	0.204 816 1	2.048 161 4E-01
poundal/square foot	6.589 764 6	6.589 764 6E+00
ton-force/square foot [short]	0.000 102 4	1.024 080 7E-04
ton-force/square meter [metric]	0.001	1.000 000 0E-03
torr	0.073 555 9	7.355 592 4E-02
millimeter/day		**<velocity>**
centimeter/day	0.1	1.000 000 0E-01
foot/day	0.003 280 8	3.280 839 9E-03
inch/day	0.039 370 1	3.937 007 9E-02
knot [international]	<<<	2.249 820 0E-08
meter [international]	0.001	1.000 000 0E-03
meter/second	<<<	1.157 407 4E-08
millimeter/hour	0.041 666 7	4.166 666 7E-02
yard/day	0.001 093 6	1.093 613 3E-03
millimeter/hour		**<velocity>**
centimeter/day	2.4	2.400 000 0E+00

Convert To	Standard	Scientific
foot/day	0.078 740 2	7.874 015 8E-02
inch/day	0.944 881 9	9.448 818 9E-01
knot [international]	0.000 000 5	5.399 568 0E-07
meter/second	0.000 000 3	2.777 777 8E-07
mile/day	0.000 014 9	1.491 290 9E-05
nautical mile/day [international]	0.000 013	1.295 896 3E-05
yard/day	0.026 246 7	2.624 671 9E-02
millimeter/minute		**<velocity>**
centimeter/hour	6	6.000 000 0E+00
foot/day	4.724 409 5	4.724 409 5E+00
inch/hour	2.362 204 7	2.362 204 7E+00
knot [international]	0.000 032 4	3.239 740 8E-05
meter/day	1.44	1.440 000 0E+00
meter/second	0.000 016 7	1.666 666 7E-05
mile/day	0.000 894 8	8.947 745 2E-04
millimeter/hour	60	6.000 000 0E+01
nautical mile/day [international]	0.000 777 5	7.775 378 0E-04
yard/day	1.574 803 2	1.574 803 2E+00
millimeter/second		**<velocity>**
centimeter/minute	6	6.000 000 0E+00
dekameter/day	8.64	8.640 000 0E+00
foot/hour	11.811 023 6	1.181 102 4E+01
inch/minute	2.362 204 7	2.362 204 7E+00
knot [international]	0.001 943 8	1.943 844 5E-03
meter/hour	3.6	3.600 000 0E+00
meter/second	0.001	1.000 000 0E-03
mile/day	0.053 686 5	5.368 647 1E-02
millimeter/minute	60	6.000 000 0E+01
nautical mile/day [international]	0.046 652 3	4.665 226 8E-02
yard/hour	3.937 007 9	3.937 007 9E+00
millimeter/square second		**<acceleration>**
decigal	1	1.000 000 0E+00
foot/square second	0.003 280 8	3.280 839 9E-03
galileo	0.1	1.000 000 0E-01
meter/square second	0.001	1.000 000 0E-03
millimeter^4		**<second moment of area>**
foot^4	<<<	1.158 617 7E-10
inch^4	0.000 002 4	2.402 509 6E-06
meter^4	<<<	1.000 000 0E-12
millimho		**<electric conductance>**
absiemens	<<<	1.000 000 0E-12
millisiemens	1	1.000 000 0E+00
siemens	0.001	1.000 000 0E-03
statsiemens	>>>	8.987 551 8E+08
millimicron		**<length>**
angstrom	10	1.000 000 0E+01
bicron	1,000	1.000 000 0E+03
caliber	0.000 003 9	3.937 007 9E-06
fermi	1,000,000	1.000 000 0E+06
inch [based on US, survey foot]	<<<	3.937 000 0E-08
inch [international]	<<<	3.937 007 9E-08
meter	<<<	1.000 000 0E-09
microinch	0.039 370 1	3.937 007 9E-02
micromicron	1,000	1.000 000 0E+03
micron	0.001	1.000 000 0E-03
mil	0.000 039 4	3.937 007 9E-05
nanometer	1	1.000 000 0E+00
stigma	1,000	1.000 000 0E+03
tenthmeter	10	1.000 000 0E+01
thou	0.000 039 4	3.937 007 9E-05
wavelength of orange-red spectral line of krypton-86	0.001 650 8	1.650 763 7E-03
x-unit	9,979.320 9	9.979 320 9E+03

millimole <amount of substance>

	Standard	Scientific
mole	0.001	1.000 000 0E−03
number of atoms in 0.012 kg of carbon-12	0.001	1.000 000 0E−03
one atom of carbon-12	>>>	6.022 136 7E+20

millimole/cubic centimeter <concentration, mole basis>

	Standard	Scientific
mole/cubic meter	1,000	1.000 000 0E+03
mole/liter	1	1.000 000 0E+00

millimole/cubic meter <concentration, mole basis>

	Standard	Scientific
micromole/liter	1	1.000 000 0E+00
mole/cubic meter	0.001	1.000 000 0E−03

millimole/gram <molality>

	Standard	Scientific
micromole/gram	1,000	1.000 000 0E+03
millimole/kilogram	1,000	1.000 000 0E+03
mole/kilogram	1	1.000 000 0E+00

millimole/hour <flow rate, mole basis>

	Standard	Scientific
mole/second	0.000 000 3	2.777 777 8E−07

millimole/kilogram <molality>

	Standard	Scientific
micromole/gram	1	1.000 000 0E+00
mole/kilogram	0.001	1.000 000 0E−03

millimole/liter <concentration, mole basis>

	Standard	Scientific
micromole/cubic centimeter	1	1.000 000 0E+00
mole/cubic meter	1	1.000 000 0E+00

millimole/milliliter <concentration, mole basis>

	Standard	Scientific
mole/cubic meter	1,000	1.000 000 0E+03
mole/liter	1	1.000 000 0E+00

millimole/minute <flow rate, mole basis>

	Standard	Scientific
mole/second	0.000 016 7	1.666 666 7E−05

millimole/second <flow rate, mole basis>

	Standard	Scientific
mole/second	0.001	1.000 000 0E−03

millinewton <force>

	Standard	Scientific
crinal	0.01	1.000 000 0E−02
dyne	100	1.000 000 0E+02
gram-force	0.001	1.000 000 0E−03
newton	0.101 971 6	1.019 716 2E−01
ounce-force	0.001	1.000 000 0E−03
pond	0.003 596 9	3.596 943 1E−03
pound-force	0.101 971 6	1.019 716 2E−01
poundal	0.000 224 8	2.248 089 4E−04
	0.007 233	7.233 013 9E−03

millinewton meter <torque>

	Standard	Scientific
centimeter gram-force	10.197 162	1.019 716 2E+01
foot ounce-force	0.011 801	1.180 099 4E−02
foot poundal	0.023 730 4	2.373 036 0E−02
inch ounce-force	0.141 611 9	1.416 119 3E−01
newton meter	0.001	1.000 000 0E−03

millinewton/centimeter <surface tension>

	Standard	Scientific
dyne/centimeter	100	1.000 000 0E+02
kilogram-force/meter	0.010 197 2	1.019 716 2E−02
kilopond/meter	0.010 197 2	1.019 716 2E−02
newton/meter	0.1	1.000 000 0E−01
ounce-force/foot	0.109 634 8	1.096 348 3E−01
pound-force/foot	0.006 852 2	6.852 176 6E−03

millinewton/meter <surface tension>

	Standard	Scientific
dyne/centimeter	1	1.000 000 0E+00
gram-force/meter	0.101 971 6	1.019 716 2E−01
millinewton/centimeter	0.01	1.000 000 0E−02
newton/meter	0.001	1.000 000 0E−03
ounce-force/foot	0.001 096 3	1.096 348 3E−03

milliohm <electric resistance>

	Standard	Scientific
1/ siemens	0.001	1.000 000 0E−03

| Convert From | | <Type of Unit> |
Convert To	Standard	Scientific
abohm		**<electric resistivity>**
ohm	1,000,000	1.000 000 0E+06
statohm	0.001	1.000 000 0E−03
	<<<	1.112 650 1E−15
milliohm meter		**<electric resistivity>**
abohm centimeter	>>>	1.000 000 0E+08
microohm inch	39,370.078 7	3.937 007 9E+04
ohm circular mil/foot	601,530.494	6.015 304 9E+05
ohm meter	0.001	1.000 000 0E−03
ohm square millimeter/meter	1,000	1.000 000 0E+03
statohm centimeter	<<<	1.112 650 1E−13
million		**<units>**
unit	1,000,000	1.000 000 0E+06
million [Hebrew, ancient]		**<length, special - see page 29>**
meter	1,478.5	1.478 500 0E+03
million acre foot		**<volume>**
acre foot	1,000,000	1.000 000 0E+06
acre inch	>>>	1.200 000 0E+07
barrel [UK]	>>>	7.536 890 9E+09
barrel [US, liquid]	>>>	1.034 449 0E+10
barrel [US, petroleum]	>>>	7.758 367 3E+09
billion cubic foot	43.56	4.356 000 0E+01
cubem	0.295 928	2.959 280 3E−01
cubic foot	>>>	4.356 000 0E+10
cubic kilometer	1.233 481 8	1.233 481 8E+00
cubic meter	>>>	1.233 481 8E+09
cubic mile	0.295 928	2.959 280 3E−01
cubic yard	>>>	1.613 333 3E+09
gallon [Canada, liquid]	>>>	2.713 280 7E+11
gallon [UK, dry or liquid]	>>>	2.713 280 7E+11
gallon [US, liquid]	>>>	3.258 514 3E+11
hectare meter	123,348.18	1.233 481 8E+05
liter	>>>	1.233 481 8E+12
stere	>>>	1.233 481 8E+09
teraliter	1.233 481 8	1.233 481 8E+00
trillion cubic foot	0.043 56	4.356 000 0E−02
million acre foot/day		**<flow rate, volume basis>**
acre foot/second	11.574 074 1	1.157 407 4E+01
acre foot/second [US, survey]	11.574 004 6	1.157 400 5E+01
acre inch/second	138.888 889	1.388 888 9E+02
billion cubic foot/hour	1.815	1.815 000 0E+00
cubem/day	0.295 928	2.959 280 3E−01
cubic dekameter/second	14.276 410 2	1.427 641 0E+01
cubic kilometer/day	1.233 481 8	1.233 481 8E+00
cubic meter/second	14,276.410 2	1.427 641 0E+04
cubic mile/day	0.295 928	2.959 280 3E−01
hectare meter/second	1.427 641	1.427 641 0E+00
petrograd standard/second	3,055.555 6	3.055 555 6E+03
thousand cubic foot/second	504.166 67	5.041 666 7E+02
trillion cubic foot/day	0.043 56	4.356 000 0E−02
million acre foot/hour		**<flow rate, volume basis>**
acre foot/second	277.777 778	2.777 777 8E+02
acre foot/second [US, survey]	277.776 111	2.777 761 1E+02
acre inch/second	3,333.333 33	3.333 333 3E+03
billion cubic foot/hour	43.56	4.356 000 0E+01
cubem/day	7.102 272 7	7.102 272 7E+00
cubic dekameter/second	342.633 844	3.426 338 4E+02
cubic kilometer/hour	1.233 481 8	1.233 481 8E+00
cubic meter/second	342,633.844	3.426 338 4E+05
cubic mile/day	7.102 272 7	7.102 272 7E+00
hectare meter/second	34.263 384 4	3.426 338 4E+01
million acre foot/day	24	2.400 000 0E+01
petrograd standard/second	73,333.333	7.333 333 3E+04

| Convert From | | <Type of Unit> |
Convert To	Standard	Scientific
thousand cubic foot/second	12,100	1.210 000 0E+04
trillion cubic foot/day	1.045 44	1.045 440 0E+00

million acre foot/minute   <flow rate, volume basis>

Convert To	Standard	Scientific
acre foot/second	16,666.666 7	1.666 666 7E+04
acre foot/second [US, survey]	16,666.566 7	1.666 656 7E+04
billion cubic foot/minute	43.56	4.356 000 0E+01
cubem/hour	17.755 681 8	1.775 568 2E+01
cubic dekameter/second	20,558.030 6	2.055 803 1E+04
cubic kilometer/minute	1.233 481 8	1.233 481 8E+00
cubic mile/hour	17.755 681 8	1.775 568 2E+01
hectare meter/second	2,055.803 06	2.055 803 1E+03
million acre foot/hour	60	6.000 000 0E+01
trillion cubic foot/minute	2.613 6	2.613 600 0E+00

million acre foot/second   <flow rate, volume basis>

Convert To	Standard	Scientific
billion cubic foot/second	43.56	4.356 000 0E+01
cubem/minute	17.755 681 8	1.775 568 2E+01
cubic kilometer/second	1.233 481 8	1.233 481 8E+00
cubic mile/minute	17.755 681 8	1.775 568 2E+01
million acre foot/minute	60	6.000 000 0E+01
trillion cubic foot/minute	2.613 6	2.613 600 0E+00

million board foot   <volume>

Convert To	Standard	Scientific
acre foot	1.913 070 1	1.913 070 1E+00
acre inch	22.956 841	2.295 684 1E+01
billion cubic foot	0.000 083 3	8.333 333 3E-05
board foot	1,000,000	1.000 000 0E+06
cord [firewood]	651.041 67	6.510 416 7E+02
cord foot [timber]	5,208.333 3	5.208 333 3E+03
cubic dekameter	2.359 737 2	2.359 737 2E+00
cubic foot	83,333.333	8.333 333 3E+04
cubic inch	>>>	1.440 000 0E+08
cubic meter	2,359.737 2	2.359 737 2E+03
cubic mile	0.000 000 6	5.661 310 7E-07
cubic yard	3,086.419 8	3.086 419 8E+03
freight ton	2,083.333 3	2.083 333 3E+03
gallon [UK, dry or liquid]	519,069.62	5.190 696 2E+05
gallon [US, dry]	535,709.3	5.357 093 0E+05
liter	2,359,737.2	2.359 737 2E+06
megaliter	2.359 737 2	2.359 737 2E+00
petrograd standard	505.050 51	5.050 505 1E+02
register ton	833.333 33	8.333 333 3E+02
shipping ton	2,083.333 3	2.083 333 3E+03
stere	2,359.737 2	2.359 737 2E+03
thousand board foot	1,000	1.000 000 0E+03
thousand cubic foot	83,333.333	8.333 333 3E+01
trillion cubic foot	<<<	8.333 333 3E-08

million Btu/hour [I.T.]   <power>

Convert To	Standard	Scientific
Btu/second [I.T.]	277.777 78	2.777 777 8E+02
Btu/second [thermoc.]	277.963 67	2.779 636 7E+02
calorie/second [I.T.]	69,998.823	6.999 882 3E+04
calorie/second [thermoc.]	70,045.667	7.004 566 7E+04
centigrade heat unit/second [mean]	154.202	1.542 020 0E+02
cheval vapeur [France]	398.465 76	3.984 657 6E+02
cubic meter atmosphere/second	2,892.386 6	2.892 386 6E+06
dyne centimeter/second	>>>	2.930 710 7E+12
erg/second	>>>	2.930 710 7E+12
foot pound-force/second	216,158.13	2.161 581 3E+05
foot poundal/second	6,954,682.1	6.954 682 1E+06
gram-force centimeter/second	>>>	2.988 493 2E+09
horsepower	393.014 78	3.930 147 8E+02
horsepower [metric]	398.465 76	3.984 657 6E+02
joule/second	293,071.07	2.930 710 7E+05
kilocalorie/second [I.T.]	69.998 823	6.999 882 3E+01

| Convert From | | <Type of Unit> |
Convert To	Standard	Scientific
kilogram-force meter/second	29,884.932	2.988 493 2E+04
kilopond meter/second	29,884.932	2.988 493 2E+04
newton meter/second	293,071.07	2.930 710 7E+05
pferdestarke [Germany]	398.465 76	3.984 657 6E+02
poncelet [France]	298.849 32	2.988 493 2E+02
ton of refrigeration	83.333 333	8.333 333 3E+01
volt ampere	293,071.07	2.930 710 7E+05
watt	293,071.07	2.930 710 7E+05

millipascal <pressure>
	Standard	Scientific
atmosphere [standard]	<<<	9.869 232 7E-09
atmosphere [technical]	<<<	1.019 716 2E-08
bar	<<<	1.000 000 0E-08
barye [France]	0.01	1.000 000 0E-02
dyne/square centimeter	0.01	1.000 000 0E-02
gram-force/square centimeter	0.000 010 2	1.019 716 2E-05
kilogram-force/square meter	0.000 102	1.019 716 2E-04
kilopond/square meter	0.000 102	1.019 716 2E-04
micrometer of mercury [0 °C, by convention]	0.007 500 6	7.500 615 8E-03
micrometer of water [4 °C, by convention]	0.101 971 6	1.019 716 2E-01
newton/square meter	0.001	1.000 000 0E-03
pascal	0.001	1.000 000 0E-03
pound-force/square foot	0.000 020 9	2.088 543 4E-05
poundal/square foot	0.000 672	6.719 689 8E-04
ton-force/square foot [short]	<<<	1.044 271 7E-08
ton-force/square meter [metric]	0.000 000 1	1.019 716 2E-07
torr	0.000 007 5	7.500 616 8E-06

millipascal second <dynamic viscosity>
	Standard	Scientific
kilogram/meter hour	3.6	3.600 000 0E+00
millipoise	10	1.000 000 0E+01
pascal second	0.001	1.000 000 0E-03
pound/foot hour	2.419 088 3	2.419 088 3E+00
poundal hour/square foot	2.419 088 3	2.419 088 3E+00

milliphot <illuminance>
	Standard	Scientific
footcandle	0.929 030 4	9.290 304 0E-01
lumen/square inch	0.006 451 6	6.451 600 0E-03
lumen/square meter	10	1.000 000 0E+01
lux	10	1.000 000 0E+01
nox	10,000	1.000 000 0E+04
phot	0.001	1.000 000 0E-03

milliphot second <light exposure>
	Standard	Scientific
footcandle second	0.929 030 4	9.290 304 0E-01
lumen second/square foot	0.929 030 4	9.290 304 0E-01
lumen second/square inch	0.006 451 6	6.451 600 0E-03
lux second	10	1.000 000 0E+01

millipoise <dynamic viscosity>
	Standard	Scientific
kilogram/meter hour	0.36	3.600 000 0E-01
newton second/square meter	0.000 1	1.000 000 0E-04
pascal second	0.000 1	1.000 000 0E-04
poise	0.001	1.000 000 0E-03
pound/foot hour	0.241 908 8	2.419 088 3E-01
poundal hour/square foot	0.241 908 8	2.419 088 3E-01

milliradian <plane angle>
	Standard	Scientific
degree [angular]	0.057 295 8	5.729 578 0E-02
grade [angular]	0.063 662	6.366 197 0E-02
microradian	1,000	1.000 000 0E+03
mil [military infantry, angle, UK]	1	1.000 000 0E+00
radian	0.001	1.000 000 0E-03

millisecond <time>
	Standard	Scientific
second	0.001	1.000 000 0E-03

millisiemens <electric conductance>
	Standard	Scientific
absiemens	<<<	1.000 000 0E-12

Convert From	<Type of Unit>	
Convert To	Standard	Scientific

millimho		
siemens	1	1.000 000 0E+00
statsiemens	0.001	1.000 000 0E−03
	>>>	8.987 551 8E+08

millisievert <dose equivalent>

rem	0.1	1.000 000 0E+00
sievert	0.001	1.000 000 0E−03

millitesla <magnetic flux density>

electromagnetic unit of magnetic flux density [cgs system]	10	1.000 000 0E+01
gauss	10	1.000 000 0E+01
line/square centimeter [of magnetic force]	10	1.000 000 0E+01
maxwell/square meter	0.001	1.000 000 0E−03
tesla	0.001	1.000 000 0E−03

millitorr <pressure>

atmosphere [standard]	0.000 001 3	1.315 789 5E−06
atmosphere [technical]	0.000 001 4	1.359 509 8E−06
bar	0.000 001 3	1.333 223 7E−06
barye [France]	1.333 223 7	1.333 223 7E+00
decipascal	1.333 223 7	1.333 223 7E+00
dyne/square centimeter	1.333 223 7	1.333 223 7E+00
gram-force/square centimeter	0.001 359 5	1.359 509 8E−03
kilogram-force/square meter	0.013 595 1	1.359 509 8E−02
kilopond/square meter	0.013 595 1	1.359 509 8E−02
microbar	1.333 223 7	1.333 223 7E+00
micrometer of mercury [0 °C, by convention]	0.999 999 9	9.999 998 6E−01
micrometer of water [4 °C, by convention]	13.595 098	1.359 509 8E+01
newton/square meter	0.133 322 4	1.333 223 7E−01
ounce-force/square inch	0.000 309 4	3.093 884 0E−04
pascal	0.133 322 4	1.333 223 7E−01
pound-force/square foot	0.002 784 5	2.784 495 6E−03
poundal/square foot	0.089 588 5	8.958 849 5E−02
torr	0.001	1.000 000 0E−03

millivolt <electric potential>

abvolt	100,000	1.000 000 0E+05
electrostatic unit of electric potential [cgs system]	0.000 003 3	3.335 641 0E−06
joule/coulomb	0.001	1.000 000 0E−03
statvolt	0.000 003 3	3.335 641 0E−06
volt	0.001	1.000 000 0E−03

millivolt/meter <electric field strength>

joule/coulomb meter	0.001	1.000 000 0E−03
statvolt/centimeter	<<<	3.335 641 0E−08
volt/inch	0.000 025 4	2.540 000 0E−05
volt/meter	0.001	1.000 000 0E−03

milliwatt <power>

Btu/hour [I.T.]	0.003 412 1	3.412 141 6E−03
Btu/hour [thermoc.]	0.003 414 4	3.414 425 1E−03
calorie/hour [I.T.]	0.859 845 2	8.598 452 3E−01
calorie/hour [thermoc.]	0.860 420 7	8.604 206 5E−01
centigrade heat unit/hour [mean]	0.001 894 2	1.894 172 6E−03
cubic meter atmosphere/hour	35.529 238	3.552 923 8E+01
dyne centimeter/second	10,000	1.000 000 0E+04
erg/second	10,000	1.000 000 0E+04
foot pound-force/hour	2.655 223 7	2.655 223 7E+00
foot poundal/minute	1.423 821 6	1.423 821 6E+00
gram-force centimeter/second	10.197 162	1.019 716 2E+01
horsepower	0.000 001 3	1.341 022 1E−06
horsepower [metric]	0.000 001 4	1.359 621 6E−06
joule/hour	3.6	3.600 000 0E+00
kilocalorie [I.T.]	0.000 859 8	8.598 452 3E−04
kilogram square meter/cubic second	0.001	1.000 000 0E−03
kilogram-force meter/hour	0.367 097 8	3.670 978 4E−01
kilopond meter/hour	0.367 097 8	3.670 978 4E−01
lumen [green light at 100% efficiency]	0.685	6.850 000 0E−01

| Convert From | <Type of Unit> | |
Convert To	Standard	Scientific
lumen [green light at 5,550 angstrom]	0.68	6.800 000 2E-01
newton meter/hour	3.6	3.600 000 0E+00
pound square foot/cubic second	0.023 730 4	2.373 036 0E-02
volt ampere	0.001	1.000 000 0E-03
watt	0.001	1.000 000 0E-03

milliwatt/square meter — **<heat flux density>**

Convert To	Standard	Scientific
Btu/day square foot [I.T.]	0.007 608	7.607 959 9E-03
Btu/day square foot [thermoc.]	0.007 613 1	7.613 051 3E-03
calorie/day square centimeter [I.T.]	0.002 063 6	2.063 628 5E-03
calorie/day square centimeter [thermoc.]	0.002 065	2.065 009 6E-03
erg/second square centimeter	1	1.000 000 0E+00
watt/square foot	0.000 092 9	9.290 304 0E-05
watt/square meter	0.001	1.000 000 0E-03

milliweber — **<magnetic flux>**

Convert To	Standard	Scientific
gauss square centimeter	100,000	1.000 000 0E+05
maxwell	100,000	1.000 000 0E+05
statweber	0.000 003 3	3.335 641 0E-06
unit pole	7,957.747 54	7.957 747 5E+03
weber	0.001	1.000 000 0E-03

milliweber meter — **<magnetic dipole moment>**

Convert To	Standard	Scientific
abweber centimeter	795,774.715	7.957 747 2E+05
statweber centimeter	0.000 026 5	2.654 418 7E-05
weber meter	0.001	1.000 000 0E-03

milliweber/meter — **<magnetic vector potential>**

Convert To	Standard	Scientific
abweber/centimeter	1,000	1.000 000 0E+03
statweber/centimeter	<<<	3.335 641 0E-08
weber/meter	0.001	1.000 000 0E-03

mimar [Turkey, land] — **<length, special - see page 29>**

Convert To	Standard	Scientific
centimeter	75.8	7.580 000 0E+01

mimari [Greece] — **<length, special - see page 29>**

Convert To	Standard	Scientific
centimeter	75	7.500 000 0E+01

min [Thailand] — **<length, special - see page 29>**

Convert To	Standard	Scientific
centimeter	2.083 333	2.083 333 0E+00

mina [Babylon, ancient, heavy] — **<mass, special - see page 29>**

Convert To	Standard	Scientific
gram	982.4	9.824 000 0E+02

mina [Babylon, ancient, royal] — **<mass, special - see page 29>**

Convert To	Standard	Scientific
gram	1,010	1.010 000 0E+03

mina [Babylon, ancient] — **<mass, special - see page 29>**

Convert To	Standard	Scientific
gram	978.3	9.783 000 0E+02

mina [Egypt] — **<mass, special - see page 29>**

Convert To	Standard	Scientific
gram	755.67	7.556 700 0E+02

mina [Greece, ancient] — **<mass, special - see page 29>**

Convert To	Standard	Scientific
kilogram	1.5	1.500 000 0E+00

mina [Hebrew, ancient, light] — **<mass, special - see page 29>**

Convert To	Standard	Scientific
gram	505	5.050 000 0E+02

mina [Hebrew, ancient] — **<mass, special - see page 29>**

Convert To	Standard	Scientific
gram	600	6.000 000 0E+02

mina [Italy] — **<mass, special - see page 29>**

Convert To	Standard	Scientific
gram	358.5	3.585 000 0E+02

mina [Mesopotamia, ancient] — **<mass, special - see page 29>**

Convert To	Standard	Scientific
gram	480	4.800 000 0E+02

mina [Phoenicia, ancient, silver] — **<mass, special - see page 29>**

Convert To	Standard	Scientific
gram	364	3.640 000 0E+02

mina [Rome, ancient] — **<mass, special - see page 29>**

Convert To	Standard	Scientific
gram	340	3.400 000 0E+02

mina [Syria] — **<mass, special - see page 29>**

Convert To	Standard	Scientific
gram	589.33	5.893 300 0E+02

Convert From Convert To	<Type of Unit> Standard	Scientific
minae [Babylon, ancient]	<volume, special - see page 29>	
liter	0.505	5.050 000 0E−01
minah [Egypt, ancient]	<mass, special - see page 29>	
gram	778	7.780 000 0E+02
minah [Hebrew, ancient, gold]	<mass, special - see page 29>	
gram	633	6.330 000 0E+02
minah [Iraq, ancient]	<mass, special - see page 29>	
kilogram	0.899	8.990 000 0E−01
mine [France, dry]	<volume, special - see page 29>	
liter	78.05	7.805 000 0E+01
miner's inch [AZ, CA, MT, OR]	<flow rate, volume basis>	
cubic foot/second	0.025	2.500 000 0E−02
cubic meter/second	0.000 707 9	7.079 211 6E−04
cubic yard/day	80	8.000 000 0E+01
miner's inch [British Columbia, Canada]	<flow rate, volume basis>	
cubic foot/second	0.028	2.800 000 0E−02
cubic meter/second	0.000 792 9	7.928 717 0E−04
cubic yard/day	89.6	8.960 000 0E+01
miner's inch [Colorado]	<flow rate, volume basis>	
cubic foot/second	0.026 041 7	2.604 166 7E−02
cubic meter/second	0.000 737 4	7.374 178 8E−04
cubic yard/day	83.333 333 3	8.333 333 3E+01
miner's inch [ID, KS, NE, NM, NV, ND, SD, UT]	<flow rate, volume basis>	
cubic foot/second	0.02	2.000 000 0E−02
cubic meter/second	0.000 566 3	5.663 369 3E−04
cubic yard/day	64	6.400 000 0E+01
mingel [Netherlands]	<volume, special - see page 29>	
liter	1.213	1.213 000 0E+00
minim [UK]	<volume>	
barrel [UK]	0.000 000 4	3.616 898 1E−07
barrel [US, liquid]	0.000 000 5	4.964 244 1E−07
barrel [US, petroleum]	0.000 000 4	3.723 183 1E−07
cubic foot	0.000 002 1	2.090 412 2E−06
cubic inch	0.003 612 2	3.612 232 2E−03
cubic meter	<<<	5.919 388 0E−08
gallon [Canada, liquid]	0.000 013	1.302 083 3E−05
gallon [UK, dry or liquid]	0.000 013	1.302 083 3E−05
gallon [US, liquid]	0.000 015 6	1.563 736 9E−05
lambda	59.193 88	5.919 388 0E+01
liter	0.000 059 2	5.919 388 0E−05
minim [US]	0.960 759 9	9.607 599 4E−01
ounce [UK, liquid]	0.002 083 3	2.083 333 3E−03
ounce [US, liquid]	0.002 001 6	2.001 583 2E−03
pint [UK]	0.000 104 2	1.041 666 7E−04
pint [US, liquid]	0.000 125 1	1.250 989 5E−04
quart [UK]	0.000 052 1	5.208 333 3E−05
quart [US, liquid]	0.000 062 5	6.254 947 5E−05
scruple [UK, liquid]	0.05	5.000 000 0E−02
minim [US]	<volume>	
barrel [UK]	0.000 000 4	3.764 622 1E−07
barrel [US, liquid]	0.000 000 5	5.166 997 4E−07
barrel [US, petroleum]	0.000 000 4	3.875 248 0E−07
cubic foot	0.000 002 2	2.175 790 3E−06
cubic inch	0.003 759 8	3.759 765 6E−03
cubic meter	<<<	6.161 152 0E−08
drachm [UK, liquid]	0.017 347 4	1.734 737 9E−02
dram [Canada, liquid]	0.017 347 4	1.734 737 9E−02
dram [US, liquid]	0.016 666 7	1.666 666 7E−02
drop [US, liquid]	0.75	7.500 000 0E−01
gallon [Canada, liquid]	0.000 013 6	1.355 264 0E−05

Convert From Convert To	Standard	Scientific <Type of Unit>
gallon [UK, dry or liquid]	0.000 013 6	1.355 264 0E–05
gallon [US, liquid]	0.000 016 3	1.627 604 2E–05
lambda	61.611 52	6.161 152 0E+01
liter	0.000 061 6	6.161 152 0E–05
minim [UK]	1.040 842 7	1.040 842 7E+00
ounce [UK, liquid]	0.002 168 4	2.168 422 4E–03
ounce [US, liquid]	0.002 083 3	2.083 333 3E–03
pint [UK]	0.000 108 4	1.084 211 2E–04
pint [US, liquid]	0.000 130 2	1.302 083 3E–04
scruple [UK, liquid]	0.052 042 1	5.204 213 7E–02
tablespoon [Canada, measuring]	0.004 336 9	4.336 852 1E–03
tablespoon [US, measuring]	0.004 166 7	4.166 666 7E–03
teaspoon [Canada, measuring]	0.013 010 6	1.301 055 6E–02
teaspoon [US, measuring]	0.012 5	1.250 000 0E–02

minot [Canada]   <volume, special - see page 29>
hectoliter	38.91	3.891 000 0E+01

minot [France, dry]   <volume, special - see page 29>
liter	39.025	3.902 500 0E+01

minute   <time>
day	0.000 694 4	6.944 444 4E–04
day [mean solar]	0.000 694 4	6.944 444 4E–04
hour	0.016 666 7	1.666 666 7E–02
hour [mean solar]	0.016 666 7	1.666 666 7E–02
minute [mean solar]	1	1.000 000 0E+00
month [mean sidereal]	0.000 025 4	2.541 735 7E–05
second	60	6.000 000 0E+01
second [Coordinated Universal Time (UTC)]	60	6.000 000 0E+01
second [mean solar]	60	6.000 000 0E+01
year [mean sidereal]	0.000 001 9	1.901 252 2E–06
year [normal calendar]	0.000 001 9	1.902 587 5E–06

minute [angular]   <plane angle>
degree [angular]	0.016 666 7	1.666 666 7E–02
grade [angular]	0.018 518 5	1.851 851 9E–02
radian	0.000 290 9	2.908 882 1E–04
second [angular]	60	6.000 000 0E+01
sign	0.000 555 6	5.555 555 6E–04

minute [Coordinated Universal Time (UTC)]   <time>
day	0.000 694 4	6.944 444 4E–04
day [mean solar]	0.000 694 4	6.944 444 4E–04
hour	0.016 666 7	1.666 666 7E–02
hour [mean solar]	0.016 666 7	1.666 666 7E–02
minute	1	1.000 000 0E+00
minute [mean sidereal]	1.002 737 9	1.002 737 9E+00
minute [mean solar]	1	1.000 000 0E+00
month [mean sidereal]	0.000 025 4	2.541 735 7E–05
second	60	6.000 000 0E+01
second [Coordinated Universal Time (UTC)]	60	6.000 000 0E+01
second [mean solar]	60	6.000 000 0E+01
year [mean sidereal]	0.000 001 9	1.901 252 2E–06
year [normal calendar]	0.000 001 9	1.902 587 5E–06

minute [mean sidereal]   <time>
day	0.000 692 5	6.925 483 1E–04
day [mean solar]	0.000 692 5	6.925 483 1E–04
hour	0.016 621 2	1.662 115 9E–02
hour [mean solar]	0.016 621 2	1.662 115 9E–02
minute	0.997 269 6	9.972 695 7E–01
minute [mean solar]	0.997 269 6	9.972 695 7E–01
month [mean sidereal]	0.000 025 3	2.534 795 7E–05
second	59.836 174	5.983 617 4E+01
second [mean sidereal]	60	6.000 000 0E+01
second [mean solar]	59.836 174	5.983 617 4E+01
year [mean sidereal]	0.000 001 9	1.896 060 9E–06

Convert From Convert To	Standard	<Type of Unit> Scientific
year [normal calendar]	0.000 001 9	1.897 392 6E-06
minute [mean solar]		**<time>**
day	0.000 694 4	6.944 444 4E-04
day [mean solar]	0.000 694 4	6.944 444 4E-04
hour	0.016 666 7	1.666 666 7E-02
hour [mean solar]	0.016 666 7	1.666 666 7E-02
minute	1	1.000 000 0E+00
minute [Coordinated Universal Time (UTC)]	1	1.000 000 0E+00
minute [mean sidereal]	1.002 737 9	1.002 737 9E+00
month [mean solar]	0.000 025 4	2.541 735 7E-05
second	60	6.000 000 0E+01
second [Coordinated Universal Time (UTC)]	60	6.000 000 0E+01
second [mean solar]	60	6.000 000 0E+01
year [mean sidereal]	0.000 001 9	1.901 252 2E-06
year [normal calendar]	0.000 001 9	1.902 587 5E-06
mira [Czechoslovakia]		**<area, special - see page 29>**
are	19.18	1.918 000 0E+01
mira [Ukraine]		**<length, special - see page 29>**
centimeter	76	7.600 000 0E+01
mirze [Romania]		**<volume, special - see page 29>**
liter	196.8	1.968 000 0E+02
miscal [Afghanistan]		**<mass, special - see page 29>**
gram	4.6	4.600 000 0E+00
miscal [Iran]		**<mass, special - see page 29>**
gram	4.639 6	4.639 600 0E+00
miscal [Libya, gold]		**<mass, special - see page 29>**
gram	4.601	4.601 000 0E+00
mishara [Iraq]		**<area, special - see page 29>**
hectare	0.25	2.500 000 0E-01
miskal [Afghanistan]		**<mass, special - see page 29>**
gram	4.6	4.600 000 0E+00
miskal [Algeria]		**<mass, special - see page 29>**
gram	4.27	4.270 000 0E+00
miskal [Egypt]		**<mass, special - see page 29>**
gram	4.68	4.680 000 0E+00
miskal [Iran]		**<mass, special - see page 29>**
gram	4.64	4.640 000 0E+00
miskal [Libya]		**<mass, special - see page 29>**
gram	4.601	4.601 000 0E+00
miskal [Sudan]		**<mass, special - see page 29>**
gram	4.68	4.680 000 0E+00
miskal [Turkey]		**<mass, special - see page 29>**
gram	4.811	4.811 000 0E+00
mismal [Persia]		**<mass, special - see page 29>**
gram	4.59	4.590 000 0E+00
misqal [Afghanistan]		**<mass, special - see page 29>**
gram	4.6	4.600 000 0E+00
misqal [Iran]		**<mass, special - see page 29>**
gram	4.687 5	4.687 500 0E+00
misqal [Libya, gold]		**<mass, special - see page 29>**
gram	4.601	4.601 000 0E+00
misri [Islam]		**<mass, special - see page 29>**
gram	444.9	4.449 000 0E+02
misura [Libya]		**<volume, special - see page 29>**
liter	19.8	1.980 000 0E+01
mite [UK]		**<mass, special - see page 29>**
milligram	3.24	3.240 000 0E+00

mithkal [Muslim India]
gram -- <mass, special - see page 29>
5.5 --- 5.500 000 0E+00

mithkal [Sudan]
gram -- <mass, special - see page 29>
4.68 --- 4.680 000 0E+00

mitiga [Algiers]
gram -- <mass, special - see page 29>
4.67 --- 4.670 000 0E+00

mitiga [Egypt]
gram -- <mass, special - see page 29>
4.68 --- 4.680 000 0E+00

mitiga [Libya, Tripoli]
gram -- <mass, special - see page 29>
4.8 --- 4.800 000 0E+00

mitiga [Syria]
gram -- <mass, special - see page 29>
4.8 --- 4.800 000 0E+00

mitkal [Iraq, ancient]
gram -- <mass, special - see page 29>
4.68 --- 4.680 000 0E+00

mitkal [Turkey]
gram -- <mass, special - see page 29>
4.811 --- 4.811 000 0E+00

mitqal [Islam]
gram -- <mass, special - see page 29>
4.464 --- 4.464 000 0E+00

mitqual [Islam]
gram -- <mass, special - see page 29>
4.464 --- 4.464 000 0E+00

mitsal [Egypt]
gram -- <mass, special - see page 29>
4.68 --- 4.680 000 0E+00

mkono [Kenya]
meter -- <length, special - see page 29>
0.457 2 --- 4.572 000 0E-01

mkono [Tanganyika]
centimeter -- <length, special - see page 29>
46 --- 4.600 000 0E+01

mkono [Tanzania]
centimeter -- <length, special - see page 29>
45.72 --- 4.572 000 0E+01

mkono [Uganda]
meter -- <length, special - see page 29>
0.457 2 --- 4.572 000 0E-01

mna [Egypt]
gram -- <mass, special - see page 29>
596.2 --- 5.962 000 0E+02

mna [Greece, ancient]
gram -- <mass, special - see page 29>
430 --- 4.300 000 0E+02

mna [Syria]
gram -- <mass, special - see page 29>
589.33 --- 5.893 300 0E+02

mo [Japan]
milligram -- <mass, special - see page 29>
3.75 --- 3.750 000 0E+00

mo [Japan]
millimeter -- <length, special - see page 29>
0.03 --- 3.000 000 0E-02

mo [South Korea]
micrometer -- <length, special - see page 29>
30.303 --- 3.030 300 0E+01

mocha [Ethiopia]
gram -- <mass, special - see page 29>
31.1 --- 3.110 000 0E+01

modd [Malta, cereals]
hectoliter -- <volume, special - see page 29>
2.909 --- 2.909 000 0E+00

modd [Malta, wheat]
kilogram -- <mass, special - see page 29>
222.26 --- 2.222 600 0E+02

modd [Malta]
hectare -- <area, special - see page 29>
1.798 --- 1.798 000 0E+00

modion [Rome, ancient, dry]
liter -- <volume, special - see page 29>
8.736 --- 8.736 000 0E+00

modios [Greece, ancient]
liter -- <volume, special - see page 29>
8.458 --- 8.458 000 0E+00

Convert From Convert To	Standard	<Type of Unit> Scientific
modius [Rome, ancient] liter	<volume, special - see page 29> 8.499 99	8.499 990 E+00
moio [Brazil] hectoliter	<volume, special - see page 29> 21.76	2.176 000 E+01
moio [Cape Verde, dry] hectoliter	<volume, special - see page 29> 24.955 8	2.495 580 0E+01
moio [Portugal] hectoliter	<volume, special - see page 29> 8.3	8.300 000 E+00
moio [Portugal] kilogram	<mass, special - see page 29> 35.306	3.530 600 E+01
moio [Spain] liter	<volume, special - see page 29> 258.13	2.581 300 E+02
mokka pound [Yemen] gram	<mass, special - see page 29> 404.67	4.046 700 0E+02
mole number of atoms in 0.012 kg of carbon-12 one atom of carbon-12	<amount of substance> 1 >>>6.022 136 7E+23	1.000 000 0E+00
mole/cubic decimeter mole/cubic meter mole/liter	<concentration, mole basis> 1,000 1	1.000 000 0E+03 1.000 000 0E+00
mole/cubic meter Amagat density unit micromole/cubic centimeter millimole/liter mole/liter	<concentration, mole basis> 0.022 413 6 1 1 0.001	2.241 360 0E−02 1.000 000 0E+00 1.000 000 0E+00 1.000 000 0E−03
mole/gram kilomole/kilogram mole/kilogram	<molality> 1 1,000	1.000 000 0E+00 1.000 000 0E+03
mole/hour mole/second	<flow rate, mole basis> 0.000 277 8	2.777 777 8E−04
mole/kilogram micromole/gram millimole/gram millimole/kilogram	<molality> 1,000 1 1,000	1.000 000 0E+03 1.000 000 0E+00 1.000 000 0E+03
mole/liter kilomole/cubic meter millimole/cubic centimeter millimole/milliliter mole/cubic meter	<concentration, mole basis> 1 1 1 1,000	1.000 000 0E+00 1.000 000 0E+00 1.000 000 0E+00 1.000 000 0E+03
mole/minute mole/second	<flow rate, mole basis> 0.016 666 7	1.666 666 7E−02
mole/second mole/minute	<flow rate, mole basis> 60	6.000 000 0E+01
mole/square meter gibbs	<surface concentration> 1,000,000	1.000 000 0E+06
momme [Japan] gram	<mass, special - see page 29> 3.75	3.750 000 0E+00
momme [South Korea] gram	<mass, special - see page 29> 3.75	3.750 000 0E+00
mon [Bahrain] kilogram	<mass, special - see page 29> 25.4	2.540 000 0E+01
mon [Bangladesh] kilogram	<mass, special - see page 29> 37.32	3.732 000 0E+01
mon [India] kilogram	<mass, special - see page 29> 37.32	3.732 000 0E+01
mon [Muscat and Oman] kilogram	<mass, special - see page 29> 4.04	4.040 000 0E+00

Convert From Convert To	<Type of Unit> Standard	Scientific

mon [Pakistan] <mass, special - see page 29>
kilogram -- 37.32 --- 3.732 000 0E+01

mon [Yemen] <mass, special - see page 29>
kilogram -- 37.32 --- 3.732 000 0E+01

monme [Japan] <mass, special - see page 29>
gram --- 3.75 --- 3.750 000 0E+00

monme [Sumatra] <mass, special - see page 29>
gram -- 0.6 --- 6.000 000 0E−01

month [anomalistic or perihelion] <time>
day --- 27.554 55 --- 2.755 455 0E+01
day [mean solar] -- 27.554 55 --- 2.755 455 0E+01
hour -- 661.309 2 --- 6.613 092 0E+02
hour [mean solar] -- 661.309 2 --- 6.613 092 0E+02
minute -- 39,678.552 --- 3.967 855 2E+04
month [mean sidereal] -- 1.008 523 9 --- 1.008 523 9E+00
second --- 2,380,713.12 --- 2.380 713 1E+06
year [anomalistic or perihelion] ------------------------------------ 0.075 438 3 --- 7.543 825 6E−02
year [normal calendar] --- 0.075 491 9 --- 7.549 191 8E−02

month [draconic] <time>
day --- 27.212 221 --- 2.721 222 1E+01
hour --- 653.093 304 --- 6.530 933 0E+02
minute -- 39,185.598 2 --- 3.918 559 8E+04
month [mean sidereal] -- 0.995 994 4 --- 9.959 943 5E−01
second -- 2,351,135.89 --- 2.351 135 9E+06
year [mean solar] --- 0.074 501 7 --- 7.450 170 3E−02
year [normal calendar] --- 0.074 554 --- 7.455 403 0E−02

month [lunar or phase or synodic] <time>
day --- 29.530 589 --- 2.953 058 9E+01
hour --- 708.734 136 --- 7.087 341 4E+02
minute -- 42,524.048 2 --- 4.252 404 8E+04
month [mean sidereal] -- 1.080 848 9 --- 1.080 848 9E+00
month [seasonal or tropical] --- 1.080 852 1 --- 1.080 852 1E+00
second -- 2,551,442.89 --- 2.551 442 9E+06
year [normal calendar] --- 0.080 905 7 --- 8.090 572 3E−02

month [mean sidereal] <time>
day --- 27.321 662 --- 2.732 166 2E+01
day [mean sidereal] --- 27.396 466 2 --- 2.739 646 6E+01
hour --- 655.719 888 --- 6.557 198 9E+02
hour [mean sidereal] --- 657.515 189 --- 6.575 151 9E+02
minute -- 39,343.193 3 --- 3.934 319 3E+04
minute [mean sidereal] --- 39,450.911 4 --- 3.945 091 1E+04
month [seasonal or tropical] --- 1.000 002 9 --- 1.000 002 9E+00
second -- 2,360,591.6 --- 2.360 591 6E+06
second [mean sidereal] --------------------------------------- 2,367,054.68 --- 2.367 054 7E+06
year [mean solar] --- 0.074 801 3 --- 7.480 133 1E−02
year [normal calendar] --- 0.074 853 9 --- 7.485 386 9E−02

month [seasonal or tropical] <time>
day --- 27.321 582 --- 2.732 158 2E+01
hour --- 655.717 968 --- 6.557 179 7E+02
minute -- 39,343.078 1 --- 3.934 307 8E+04
month [mean sidereal] -- 0.999 997 1 --- 9.999 970 7E−01
second -- 2,360,584.68 --- 2.360 584 7E+06
year [seasonal or tropical] -- 0.074 804 --- 7.480 401 4E−02

moo [Burma] <mass, special - see page 29>
gram --- 2.041 --- 2.041 000 0E+00

moolum [Ceylon] <length, special - see page 29>
meter -- 0.457 2 --- 4.572 000 0E−01

moolum [India] <length, special - see page 29>
meter -- 0.457 2 --- 4.572 000 0E−01

Convert From   **<Type of Unit>**
  Convert To   Standard   Scientific

moosa [Cyprus]   <mass, special - see page 29>
  kilogram ----------------------------------- 50.802 35 ---- 5.080 235 0E+01

moot [India]   <length, special - see page 29>
  centimeter --------------------------------- 7.62 ---- 7.620 000 0E+00

moraba [Pakistan]   <area, special - see page 29>
  hectare ------------------------------------ 10.117 ---- 1.011 700 0E+01

moreas plethron [Greece, ancient]   <length, special - see page 29>
  meter -------------------------------------- 35.64 ---- 3.564 000 0E+01

moreas stremma [Greece, ancient]   <area, special - see page 29>
  square meter ------------------------------- 1,270 ---- 1.270 000 0E+03

morg [Lithuania]   <area, special - see page 29>
  hectare ------------------------------------ 0.712 3 ---- 7.123 000 0E-01

morg [Poland]   <area, special - see page 29>
  are -- 55.99 ---- 5.599 000 0E+01

morg [Ukraine]   <area, special - see page 29>
  hectare ------------------------------------ 0.575 ---- 5.750 000 0E-01

morga [Poland]   <area, special - see page 29>
  are -- 55.99 ---- 5.599 000 0E+01

morgan [South Africa]   <area, special - see page 29>
  hectare ------------------------------------ 0.86 ---- 8.600 000 0E-01

morgen [Botswana]   <area, special - see page 29>
  hectare ------------------------------------ 0.857 ---- 8.570 000 0E-01

morgen [Germany, Baden]   <area, special - see page 29>
  are -- 36 ---- 3.600 000 0E+01

morgen [Germany, Bavaria]   <area, special - see page 29>
  are -- 27.26 ---- 2.726 000 0E+01

morgen [Germany, Hanover]   <area, special - see page 29>
  are -- 26.21 ---- 2.621 000 0E+01

morgen [Germany, Prussia]   <area, special - see page 29>
  are -- 25.532 8 ---- 2.553 280 0E+01

morgen [Germany, Wurttemberg] <area, special - see page 29>
  are -- 31.52 ---- 3.152 000 0E+01

morgen [Netherlands]   <area, special - see page 29>
  hectare ------------------------------------ 0.852 8 ---- 8.528 000 0E-01

morgen [South Africa]   <area, special - see page 29>
  hectare ------------------------------------ 0.856 53 ---- 8.565 300 0E-01

morgen [Swaziland]   <area, special - see page 29>
  hectare ------------------------------------ 85.653 1 ---- 8.565 310 0E-01

moselle [Germany]   <volume, special - see page 29>
  centiliter --------------------------------- 70 ---- 7.000 000 0E+01

motyka [Yugoslavia]   <area, special - see page 29>
  square meter ------------------------------- 800 ---- 8.000 000 0E+02

mou [China]   <area, special - see page 29>
  are -- 6.144 ---- 6.144 000 0E+00

mou [Iran]   <length, special - see page 29>
  millimeter --------------------------------- 1 ---- 1.000 000 0E+00

moud [Morocco]   <area, special - see page 29>
  square meter ------------------------------- 450 ---- 4.500 000 0E+02

moule [Switzerland]   <volume, special - see page 29>
  cubic meter -------------------------------- 4 ---- 4.000 000 0E+00

mounce   <mass>
  kilogram ----------------------------------- 0.025 ---- 2.500 000 0E-02

mound [India]   <mass, special - see page 29>
  kilogram ----------------------------------- 37.3 ---- 3.730 000 0E+01

| Convert From | | <Type of Unit> |
| Convert To | Standard | Scientific |

mow [China]
area, special - see page 29
hectare --- 0.067 --- 6.700 000 0E-02

mow [Hong Kong]
area, special - see page 29
square meter --- 842.8 --- 8.428 000 0E+02

moyo [Spain]
volume, special - see page 29
liter --- 258.13 --- 2.581 300 0E+02

mozetta [Greece, Ionian Islands, salt]
mass, special - see page 29
gram --- 995.1 --- 9.951 000 0E+02

mu [China]
area, special - see page 29
hectare -- 0.066 6 --- 6.660 000 0E-02

mud [Netherlands]
volume, special - see page 29
hectoliter --- 1 --- 1.000 000 0E+00

mud [Netherlands]
area, special - see page 29
hectare -- 1 --- 1.000 000 0E+00

mud [South Africa]
volume, special - see page 29
hectoliter --- 1.091 03 --- 1.091 030 0E+00

mudd [Lebanon]
mass, special - see page 29
gram --- 3.205 --- 3.205 000 0E+00

mudd [Morocco]
volume, special - see page 29
liter --- 46.7 --- 4.670 000 0E+01

mudd [North Africa]
volume, special - see page 29
liter --- 201 --- 2.010 000 0E+02

mudd [Spanish North Africa]
volume, special - see page 29
liter --- 14 --- 1.400 000 0E+01

mudd [Syria]
volume, special - see page 29
liter --- 26 --- 2.600 000 0E+01

mudde [Netherlands]
volume, special - see page 29
hectoliter --- 1 --- 1.000 000 0E+00

mudde [Netherlands]
area, special - see page 29
hectare -- 1 --- 1.000 000 0E+00

muddle [Netherlands]
area, special - see page 29
hectare -- 1 --- 1.000 000 0E+00

mudu [Nigeria]
mass, special - see page 29
kilogram -- 1.13 --- 1.130 000 0E+00

muid [Brazil]
volume, special - see page 29
hectoliter --- 21.76 --- 2.176 000 0E+01

muid [France, dry]
volume, special - see page 29
hectoliter --- 18.732 --- 1.873 200 0E+01

muid [Netherlands]
volume, special - see page 29
hectoliter --- 1 --- 1.000 000 0E+00

muid [South Africa]
volume, special - see page 29
hectoliter --- 1.091 03 --- 1.091 030 0E+00

muid [Switzerland]
volume, special - see page 29
liter --- 150 --- 1.500 000 0E+02

mukhamma [Sudan]
area, special - see page 29
are -- 32.289 --- 3.228 900 0E+01

mula [Argentina]
volume, special - see page 29
hectoliter --- 1.372 --- 1.372 000 0E+00

mula [Bolivia]
mass, special - see page 29
kilogram -- 92 --- 9.200 000 0E+01

mula [Chile]
volume, special - see page 29
liter --- 96.99 --- 9.699 000 0E+01

mula [Colombia]
volume, special - see page 29
liter --- 55.5 --- 5.550 000 0E+01

Convert From Convert To	Standard	<Type of Unit> Scientific
mula [Ecuador]		<mass, special - see page 29>
kilogram	92	9.200 000 0E+01
mula [Honduras]		<volume, special - see page 29>
hectoliter	11.028	1.102 800 0E+01
mula [Mexico]		<volume, special - see page 29>
liter	90.815	9.081 500 0E+01
mula [Nicaragua]		<mass, special - see page 29>
kilogram	161	1.610 000 0E+02
mula [Paraguay]		<volume, special - see page 29>
hectoliter	2.88	2.880 000 0E+00
mula [Spain]		<volume, special - see page 29>
liter	55.5	5.550 000 0E+01
mula [Trinidad and Tobago]		<mass, special - see page 29>
kilogram	49.9	4.990 000 0E+01
mula [Uruguay]		<mass, special - see page 29>
kilogram	100	1.000 000 0E+02
mule load [Belize]		<mass, special - see page 29>
kilogram	90.72	9.072 000 0E+01
mun [Laos]		<mass, special - see page 29>
kilogram	12	1.200 000 0E+01
mune [Laos]		<mass, special - see page 29>
kilogram	12	1.200 000 0E+01
muon rest mass [atomic physics, eq. energy]		<energy>
atomic mass unit [unified, C-12, 1986, eq. energy]	0.113 428 9	1.134 289 1E−01
deuteron rest mass [atomic physics, eq. energy]	0.056 332 7	5.633 271 2E−02
dyne centimeter	0.000 169 3	1.692 834 8E−04
electron rest mass [atomic physics, eq. energy]	206.768 26	2.067 682 6E+02
erg	0.000 169 3	1.692 834 8E−04
gigaelectronvolt	0.105 658 4	1.056 583 9E−01
hartree [atomic physics, eq. energy]	3,882,872.7	3.882 872 7E+06
joule	<<<	1.692 834 8E−11
kiloelectronvolt	105,658.39	1.056 583 9E+05
megaelectronvolt	105.658 39	1.056 583 9E+02
microjoule	0.000 016 9	1.692 834 8E−05
neutron rest mass [atomic physics, eq. energy]	0.112 454 5	1.124 545 1E−01
proton rest mass [atomic physics, eq. energy]	0.112 609 5	1.126 095 1E−01
rydberg [atomic physics, eq. energy , eq. energy]	7,765,653.3	7.765 653 3E+06
teraelectronvolt	0.000 105 7	1.056 583 9E−04
musa kibaba [Tanganyika]		<volume, special - see page 29>
liter	0.5	5.000 000 0E−01
musu kibaba [Tanzania]		<volume, special - see page 29>
liter	0.5	5.000 000 0E−01
mutagalla [Ethiopia]		<mass, special - see page 29>
kilogram	7.8	7.800 000 0E+00
muth [Austria]		<volume, special - see page 29>
hectoliter	18.447	1.844 700 0E+01
muthmassel [Austria]		<volume, special - see page 29>
liter	3.843 1	3.843 100 0E+00
mutsje [Netherlands]		<volume, special - see page 29>
liter	0.15	1.500 000 0E−01
mylia [Ukraine]		<length, special - see page 29>
meter	9,278	9.278 000 0E+03
myo [South Korea]		<area, special - see page 29>
square meter	99.173 7	9.917 370 0E+01
myriagram		<mass>
hyl	1.019 716 2	1.019 716 2E+00
kilogram	10	1.000 000 0E+01
kilogram-force square second/meter	1.019 716 2	1.019 716 2E+00

Convert From Convert To	Standard	<Type of Unit> Scientific
newton square second/meter	10	1.000 000 0E+01
pound	22.046 226	2.204 622 6E+01
pound [apothecary]	26.792 289	2.679 228 9E+01
pound [avoirdupois]	22.046 226	2.204 622 6E+01
pound [international]	22.046 226	2.204 622 6E+01
pound [troy]	26.792 289	2.679 228 9E+01
pound [US, avoirdupois]	22.046 223	2.204 622 3E+01
pound [US, troy]	26.792 285	2.679 228 5E+01
poundal square second/foot	22.046 226	2.204 622 6E+01
slug [metric]	1.019 716 2	1.019 716 2E+00
stone [UK]	1.574 730 4	1.574 730 4E+00
ton [UK, assay or assay, long]	306.122 45	3.061 224 5E+02
ton [US, assay or assay, short]	342.857 14	3.428 571 4E+02
myriameter		**<length>**
astronomical unit	<<<	6.684 587 2E−08
cable length [US, survey]	45.567 13	4.556 713 0E+01
chain [Gunter or US, survey]	497.095 96	4.970 959 6E+02
chain [Ramden or Engineer]	328.083 99	3.280 839 9E+02
foot [France]	30,784.329	3.078 432 9E+04
foot [international]	32,808.399	3.280 839 9E+04
foot [US, survey]	32,808.333	3.280 833 3E+04
furlong [US, survey]	49.709 596	4.970 959 6E+01
kilometer	10	1.000 000 0E+01
league [international, nautical]	1.799 856	1.799 856 0E+00
league [UK, nautical]	1.798 706 1	1.798 706 1E+00
league [US, statute]	2.071 233 2	2.071 233 2E+00
meter	10,000	1.000 000 0E+04
mile [international]	6.213 711 9	6.213 711 9E+00
mile [international, nautical]	5.399 568	5.399 568 0E+00
mile [US, statute]	6.213 699 5	6.213 699 5E+00
mile [US, survey]	6.213 699 5	6.213 699 5E+00
perch [US, survey]	1,988.383 8	1.988 383 8E+03
range [US, survey]	1.035 616 6	1.035 616 6E+00
yard [based on US, survey foot]	10,936.111	1.093 611 1E+04
yard [international]	10,936.133	1.093 613 3E+04
yard [UK]	10,936.152	1.093 615 2E+04
myriawatthour		**<energy>**
Btu [I.T.]	34,121.416	3.412 141 6E+04
calorie [I.T.]	8,598,452.3	8.598 452 3E+06
calorie [kilogram, I.T.]	8,598.452 3	8.598 452 3E+03
centigrade heat unit [I.T.]	18,956.342	1.895 634 2E+04
cheval vapeur heure [France]	13.596 216	1.359 621 6E+01
coal equivalent kilogram [UN, standard]	1.228 350 3	1.228 350 3E+00
coal equivalent metric ton [UN, standard]	0.001 228 4	1.228 350 3E−03
frigorie [France]	8,600.506 5	8.600 506 5E+03
horsepower hour	13.410 221	1.341 022 1E+01
horsepower hour [metric]	13.596 216	1.359 621 6E+01
joule	>>>	3.600 000 0E+07
kilocalorie [I.T.]	8,598.452 3	8.598 452 3E+03
kilogram calorie [15 °C, NBS, 1939]	8,600.506 5	8.600 506 5E+03
kilowatthour	10	1.000 000 0E+01
meter kilogram-force	3,670,978.4	3.670 978 4E+06
newton meter	>>>	3.600 000 0E+07
pferdestarkenstunde [Germany]	13.596 216	1.359 621 6E+01
therm [EEC]	0.341 214 2	3.412 141 6E−01
therm [US]	0.341 295 6	3.412 956 3E−01
thermie [France]	8.600 506 5	8.600 506 5E+00
ton [metric, explosive energy]	0.008 604 2	8.604 206 5E−03
mystram [Greece]		**<volume, special - see page 29>**
liter	0.01	1.000 000 0E−02
nafer [Yemen]		**<volume, special - see page 29>**
liter	0.625	6.250 000 0E−01

nagel [Belgium] <mass, special - see page 29>
kilogram --- 2.812 ---- 2.812 000 0E+00

nagel [Holland] <mass, special - see page 29>
kilogram --- 2.812 ---- 2.812 000 0E+00

nagel [UK, wool] <mass, special - see page 29>
kilogram --- 3.127 ---- 3.127 000 0E+00

nail [Belgium] <mass, special - see page 29>
kilogram --- 2.812 ---- 2.812 000 0E+00

nail [cloth] <length>
barleycorn --- 6.75 ---- 6.750 000 0E+00
bolt [cloth] -- 0.001 562 5 ---- 1.562 500 0E-03
centimeter -- 5.715 ---- 5.715 000 0E+00
cubit -- 0.125 ---- 1.250 000 0E-01
digit -- 3 ---- 3.000 000 0E+00
ell [cloth] --- 0.05 ---- 5.000 000 0E-02
foot [international] -------------------------------------- 0.187 5 ---- 1.875 000 0E-01
foot [US, survey] ---------------------------------- 0.187 499 6 ---- 1.874 996 3E-01
inch [based on US, survey foot] --------------- 2.249 995 5 ---- 2.249 995 5E+00
inch [international] --- 2.25 ---- 2.250 000 0E+00
iron [shoe leather] --- 108 ---- 1.080 000 0E+02
meter -- 0.057 15 ---- 5.715 000 0E-02
palm --- 0.75 ---- 7.500 000 0E-01
quarter [cloth] --- 0.25 ---- 2.500 000 0E-01
skein [cloth] ------------------------------------- 0.000 520 8 ---- 5.208 333 3E-04
span --- 0.25 ---- 2.500 000 0E-01
yard [based on US, survey foot] ------------- 0.062 499 9 ---- 6.249 987 5E-02
yard [international] -------------------------------- 0.062 5 ---- 6.250 000 0E-02

nail [Holland] <mass, special - see page 29>
kilogram --- 2.812 ---- 2.812 000 0E+00

nail [UK, wool] <mass, special - see page 29>
kilogram --- 3.127 ---- 3.127 000 0E+00

nakhod [Afghanistan] <mass, special - see page 29>
milligram --- 191.8 ---- 1.918 000 0E+02

nakhod [Iran] <mass, special - see page 29>
milligram --- 195 ---- 1.950 000 0E+02

nakir [Turkey] <mass, special - see page 29>
milligram --- 6.26 ---- 6.260 000 0E+00

nalih [Singapore] <volume, special - see page 29>
liter --- 72.735 36 ---- 7.273 536 0E+01

nanoampere <electric current>
abampere --- <<< ---- 1.000 000 0E-10
ampere -- <<< ---- 1.000 000 0E-09
electrostatic unit of current [cgs system] ------- 2.997 924 6 ---- 2.997 924 6E+00
statampere --------------------------------------- 2.997 924 6 ---- 2.997 924 6E+00

nanobar <pressure>
atmosphere [standard] ----------------------------------- <<< ---- 9.869 232 7E-10
atmosphere [technical] ------------------------------------ <<< ---- 1.019 716 2E-09
bar -- <<< ---- 1.000 000 0E-09
barye [France] --- 0.001 ---- 1.000 000 0E-03
dyne/square centimeter -------------------------------- 0.001 ---- 1.000 000 0E-03
gram-force/square centimeter ------------------- 0.000 001 ---- 1.019 716 2E-06
kilogram-force/square meter ------------------- 0.000 010 2 ---- 1.019 716 2E-05
kilopond/square meter ----------------------------- 0.000 010 2 ---- 1.019 716 2E-05
micrometer of mercury [0 °C, by convention] ----------- 0.000 750 1 ---- 7.500 615 8E-04
micrometer of water [4 °C, by convention] ------- 0.010 197 2 ---- 1.019 716 2E-02
newton/square meter ----------------------------- 0.000 1 ---- 1.000 000 0E-04
pascal -- 0.000 1 ---- 1.000 000 0E-04
pound-force/square foot ----------------------- 0.000 002 1 ---- 2.088 543 4E-06
poundal/square foot ------------------------------ 0.000 067 2 ---- 6.719 689 8E-05
torr --- 0.000 000 8 ---- 7.500 616 8E-07

Convert From		<Type of Unit>
Convert To	Standard	Scientific

nanocandela — <luminous intensity>
| candela | <<< --- | 1.000 000 0E−09 |

nanocoulomb — <electric charge>
abcoulomb	<<< ---	1.000 000 0E−10
coulomb	<<< ---	1.000 000 0E−09
franklin	2.997 924 6 ---	2.997 924 6E+00
statcoulomb	2.997 924 6 ---	2.997 924 6E+00

nanocoulomb/kilogram — <exposure, gamma and X rays>
coulomb/kilogram	<<< ---	1.000 000 0E−09
roentgen	0.000 003 9 ---	3.875 969 0E−06
röntgen	0.000 003 9 ---	3.875 969 0E−06

nanocoulomb/kilogram second — <exposure rate, gamma and X rays>
coulomb/kilogram second	<<< ---	1.000 000 0E−09
roentgen/second	0.000 003 9 ---	3.875 969 0E−06
röntgen/second	0.000 003 9 ---	3.875 969 0E−06

nanofarad — <capacitance>
abfarad	<<< ---	1.000 000 0E−18
coulomb/volt	<<< ---	1.000 000 0E−09
farad	<<< ---	1.000 000 0E−09
statfarad	898.755 179 ---	8.987 551 8E+02

nanofarad/meter — <electric permittivity>
abfarad/centimeter	<<< ---	1.000 000 0E−16
farad/meter	<<< ---	1.000 000 0E−09
statfarad/centimeter	89,875.517 9 ---	8.987 551 8E+04

nanogram — <mass>
gamma	0.001 ---	1.000 000 0E−03
grain	<<< ---	1.543 235 8E−08
grain [apothecary]	<<< ---	1.543 235 8E−08
grain [avoirdupois]	<<< ---	1.543 235 8E−08
grain [troy]	<<< ---	1.543 235 8E−08
kilogram	<<< ---	1.000 000 0E−12
picogram	1,000 ---	1.000 000 0E+03
point [jewelers']	0.000 000 5 ---	5.000 000 0E−07

nanohenry — <electric inductance>
abhenry	1 ---	1.000 000 0E+00
electromagnetic unit of inductance [cgs system]	1 ---	1.000 000 0E+00
henry	<<< ---	1.000 000 0E−09
ohm second	<<< ---	1.000 000 0E−09
stathenry	<<< ---	1.112 650 1E−21

nanohenry/meter — <electric permeability>
| henry/meter | <<< --- | 1.000 000 0E−09 |

nanojoule — <energy>
atomic mass unit [unified, C-12, 1986, eq. energy]	6.700 530 8 ---	6.700 530 8E+00
centimeter gram-force	0.000 010 2 ---	1.019 716 2E−05
deuteron rest mass [atomic physics, eq. energy]	3.327 714 8 ---	3.327 714 8E+00
dyne centimeter	0.01 ---	1.000 000 0E−02
electron rest mass [atomic physics, eq. energy]	12,214.321 ---	1.221 432 1E+04
erg	0.01 ---	1.000 000 0E−02
gigaelectronvolt	6.241 506 4 ---	6.241 506 4E+00
joule	<<< ---	1.000 000 0E−09
kiloelectronvolt	6,241,506.4 ---	6.241 506 4E+06
kilogram square meter/square second	<<< ---	1.000 000 0E−09
megaelectronvolt	6,241.506 4 ---	6.241 506 4E+03
meter kilogram-force	0.000 000 1 ---	1.019 716 2E−10
muon rest mass [atomic physics, eq. energy]	59.072 511 ---	5.907 251 1E+01
neutron rest mass [atomic physics, eq. energy]	6.642 970 1 ---	6.642 970 1E+00
newton meter	<<< ---	1.000 000 0E−09
proton rest mass [atomic physics, eq. energy]	6.652 126 8 ---	6.652 126 8E+00
teraelectronvolt	0.006 241 5 ---	6.241 506 4E−03
wattsecond	<<< ---	1.000 000 0E−09

Convert From	<Type of Unit>	
Convert To	Standard	Scientific

nanoliter   \<volume\>

	Standard	Scientific
cubic inch	<<<	6.102 374 4E-08
cubic meter	<<<	1.000 000 0E-12
drachm [UK, liquid]	0.000 000 3	2.815 606 4E-07
dram [Canada, liquid]	0.000 000 3	2.815 606 4E-07
dram [US, liquid]	0.000 000 3	2.705 121 8E-07
drop [US, liquid]	0.000 012 2	1.217 304 8E-05
gallon [Canada, liquid]	<<<	2.199 692 5E-10
gallon [UK, dry or liquid]	<<<	2.199 692 5E-10
gallon [US, liquid]	<<<	2.641 720 5E-10
lambda	0.001	1.000 000 0E-03
liter	<<<	1.000 000 0E-09
minim [UK]	0.000 016 9	1.689 363 8E-05
minim [US]	0.000 016 2	1.623 073 1E-05
ounce [UK, liquid]	<<<	3.519 508 0E-08
ounce [US, liquid]	<<<	3.381 402 3E-08
scruple [UK, liquid]	0.000 000 8	8.446 819 1E-07
tablespoon [Canada, measuring]	<<<	7.039 027 9E-08
tablespoon [US, measuring]	<<<	6.762 804 5E-08
teaspoon [Canada, measuring]	0.000 000 2	2.111 708 4E-07
teaspoon [US, measuring]	0.000 000 2	2.028 841 4E-07

nanometer   \<length\>

	Standard	Scientific
angstrom	10	1.000 000 0E+01
bicron	1,000	1.000 000 0E+03
caliber	0.000 003 9	3.937 007 9E-06
fermi	1,000,000	1.000 000 0E+06
inch [based on US, survey foot]	<<<	3.937 007 9E-08
inch [international]	<<<	3.937 007 9E-08
meter	<<<	1.000 000 0E-09
microinch	0.039 370 1	3.937 007 9E-02
micromicron	1,000	1.000 000 0E+03
micron	0.001	1.000 000 0E-03
mil	0.000 039 4	3.937 007 9E-05
millimicron	1	1.000 000 0E+00
stigma	1,000	1.000 000 0E+03
tenthmeter	10	1.000 000 0E+01
thou	0.000 039 4	3.937 007 9E-05
vi [Vietnam]	0.025	2.500 000 0E-02
wavelength of orange-red spectral line of krypton-86	0.001 650 8	1.650 763 7E-03
x-unit	9,979.320 9	9.979 320 9E+03

nanomole   \<amount of substance\>

	Standard	Scientific
mole	<<<	1.000 000 0E-09

nanonewton   \<force\>

	Standard	Scientific
crinal	<<<	1.000 000 0E-08
dyne	0.000 1	1.000 000 0E-04
gram-force	0.000 000 1	1.019 716 2E-07
newton	<<<	1.000 000 0E-09
ounce-force	<<<	3.596 943 1E-09
pond	0.000 000 1	1.019 716 2E-07
pound-force	<<<	2.248 089 4E-10
poundal	<<<	7.233 013 9E-09

nanoohm   \<electric resistance\>

	Standard	Scientific
1/ siemens	<<<	1.000 000 0E-09
abohm	1	1.000 000 0E+00
ohm	<<<	1.000 000 0E-09
statohm	<<<	1.112 650 1E-21

nanoohm meter   \<electric resistivity\>

	Standard	Scientific
abohm centimeter	100	1.000 000 0E+02
microohm inch	0.039 370 1	3.937 007 9E-02
ohm circular mil/foot	0.601 530 5	6.015 304 9E-01
ohm meter	<<<	1.000 000 0E-09
ohm square millimeter/meter	0.001	1.000 000 0E-03

statohm centimeter ----------- <<< --- 1.112 650 1E-19

nanopascal   \<pressure\>
atmosphere [standard] ----------- <<< --- 9.869 232 7E-15
atmosphere [technical] ----------- <<< --- 1.019 716 2E-14
bar ----------- <<< --- 1.000 000 0E-14
barye [France] ----------- <<< --- 1.000 000 0E-08
dyne/square centimeter ----------- <<< --- 1.000 000 0E-08
femtobar ----------- -10 --- 1.000 000 0E+01
kilogram-force/square meter ----------- <<< --- 1.019 716 2E-10
kilopond/square meter ----------- <<< --- 1.019 716 2E-10
micrometer of mercury [0 °C, by convention] ----------- <<< --- 7.500 615 8E-09
micrometer of water [4 °C, by convention] ----------- 0.000 000 1 --- 1.019 716 8E-07
pascal ----------- <<< --- 1.000 000 0E-09
pound-force/square foot ----------- <<< --- 2.088 543 4E-11
poundal/square foot ----------- <<< --- 6.719 689 8E-10
torr ----------- <<< --- 7.500 616 8E-12

nanosiemens   \<electric conductance\>
absiemens ----------- <<< --- 1.000 000 0E-18
electrostatic unit of conductance [cgs system] ----------- 898.755 179 --- 8.987 551 8E+02
gaussian electric conductance ----------- 898.755 179 --- 8.987 551 8E+02
siemens ----------- <<< --- 1.000 000 0E-09
statsiemens ----------- 898.755 179 --- 8.987 551 8E+02

nanotesla   \<magnetic flux density\>
electromagnetic unit of magnetic flux density [cgs system] 0.000 01 --- 1.000 000 0E-05
gamma ----------- 1 --- 1.000 000 0E+00
gauss ----------- 0.000 01 --- 1.000 000 0E-05
line/square centimeter [of magnetic force] ----------- 0.000 01 --- 1.000 000 0E-05
maxwell/square meter ----------- 0.000 01 --- 1.000 000 0E-05
tesla ----------- <<< --- 1.000 000 0E-09

nanovolt   \<electric potential\>
abvolt ----------- 0.1 --- 1.000 000 0E-01
electromagnetic unit of electric potential [cgs system] ----------- 0.1 --- 1.000 000 0E-01
statvolt ----------- <<< --- 3.335 641 0E-12
volt ----------- <<< --- 1.000 000 0E-09

nanowatt   \<power\>
Btu/hour [I.T.] ----------- <<< --- 3.412 141 6E-09
Btu/hour [thermoc.] ----------- <<< --- 3.414 425 1E-09
calorie/hour [I.T.] ----------- 0.000 000 9 --- 8.598 452 3E-07
calorie/hour [thermoc.] ----------- 0.000 000 9 --- 8.604 206 5E-07
centigrade heat unit/hour [mean] ----------- <<< --- 1.894 172 6E-09
cubic meter atmosphere/hour ----------- 0.000 035 5 --- 3.552 923 8E-05
dyne centimeter/hour ----------- -36 --- 3.600 000 0E+01
erg/hour ----------- -36 --- 3.600 000 0E+01
foot pound-force/hour ----------- 0.000 002 7 --- 2.655 223 7E-06
foot poundal/hour ----------- 0.000 085 4 --- 8.542 929 7E-05
gram-force centimeter/hour ----------- 0.036 709 8 --- 3.670 978 4E-02
horsepower ----------- <<< --- 1.341 022 1E-12
horsepower [metric] ----------- <<< --- 1.359 621 6E-12
joule/hour ----------- 0.000 003 6 --- 3.600 000 0E-06
kilocalorie/hour [I.T.] ----------- <<< --- 8.598 452 3E-10
kilogram-force meter/hour ----------- 0.000 000 4 --- 3.670 978 4E-07
kilopond meter/hour ----------- 0.000 000 4 --- 3.670 978 4E-07
newton meter/hour ----------- 0.000 003 6 --- 3.600 000 0E-06
volt ampere ----------- <<< --- 1.000 000 0E-09
watt ----------- <<< --- 1.000 000 0E-09

nanowatt/square meter   \<heat flux density\>
Btu/day square foot [I.T.] ----------- <<< --- 7.607 959 9E-09
Btu/day square foot [thermoc.] ----------- <<< --- 7.613 051 3E-09
calorie/day square centimeter [I.T.] ----------- <<< --- 2.063 628 5E-09
calorie/day square centimeter [thermoc.] ----------- <<< --- 2.065 009 6E-09
watt/square foot ----------- <<< --- 9.290 304 0E-11
watt/square meter ----------- <<< --- 1.000 000 0E-09

Convert From		<Type of Unit>
Convert To	Standard	Scientific

nanoweber <magnetic flux>
gauss square centimeter	0.1	1.000 000 0E-01
maxwell	0.1	1.000 000 0E-01
statweber	<<<	3.335 641 0E-12
unit pole	0.007 957 7	7.957 747 5E-03
weber	<<<	1.000 000 0E-09

naqir [Islam] <mass, special - see page 29>
gram	0.045	4.500 000 0E-02

nass [Arabia] <mass, special - see page 29>
gram	62.5	6.250 000 0E+01

natr [Ethiopia] <mass, special - see page 29>
kilogram	0.842 01	8.420 100 0E-01

nautical mile/day [international] <velocity>
centimeter/second	2.143 518 5	2.143 518 5E+00
dekameter/hour	7.716 666 7	7.716 666 7E+00
foot/minute	4.219 524 6	4.219 524 6E+00
hectometer/day	18.52	1.852 000 0E+01
inch/minute	50.634 295 7	5.063 429 6E+01
kilometer/day	1.852	1.852 000 0E+00
knot [international]	0.041 666 7	4.166 666 7E-02
meter/minute	1.286 111 1	1.286 111 1E+00
meter/second	0.021 435 2	2.143 518 5E-02
mile/day	1.150 779 5	1.150 779 5E+00
millimeter/second	21.435 185 2	2.143 518 5E+01
nautical mile/hour [international]	0.041 666 7	4.166 666 7E-02
yard/minute	1.406 508 2	1.406 508 2E+00

nautical mile/hour [international] <velocity>
centimeter/second	51.444 444 4	5.144 444 4E+01
dekameter/minute	3.086 666 7	3.086 666 7E+00
foot/second	1.687 809 9	1.687 809 9E+00
hectometer/hour	18.52	1.852 000 0E+01
inch/second	20.253 718 3	2.025 371 8E+01
kilometer/hour	1.852	1.852 000 0E+00
knot [international]	1	1.000 000 0E+00
meter/second	0.514 444 4	5.144 444 4E-01
mile/hour	1.150 779 5	1.150 779 5E+00
millimeter/second	514.444 444	5.144 444 4E+02
nautical mile/day [international]	24	2.400 000 0E+01
yard/minute	33.756 197 1	3.375 619 7E+01

nautical mile/minute [international] <velocity>
dekameter/second	3.086 666 7	3.086 666 7E+00
foot/second	101.268 591	1.012 685 9E+02
hectometer/minute	18.52	1.852 000 0E+01
inch/second	1,215.223 1	1.215 223 1E+03
kilometer/minute	1.852	1.852 000 0E+00
knot [international]	60	6.000 000 0E+01
megameter/day	2.666 88	2.666 880 0E+00
meter/second	30.866 666 7	3.086 666 7E+01
mile/minute	1.150 779 5	1.150 779 5E+00
nautical mile/hour [international]	60	6.000 000 0E+01
yard/second	33.756 197 1	3.375 619 7E+01

nautical mile/second [international] <velocity>
dekameter/second	185.2	1.852 000 0E+02
foot/second	6,076.115 49	6.076 115 5E+03
hectometer/second	18.52	1.852 000 0E+01
kilometer/second	1.852	1.852 000 0E+00
knot [international]	3,600	3.600 000 0E+03
megameter/hour	6.667 2	6.667 200 0E+00
meter/second	1,852	1.852 000 0E+03
mile/second	1.150 779 5	1.150 779 5E+00
nautical mile/minute [international]	60	6.000 000 0E+01

Convert From / Convert To	Standard	\<Type of Unit\> Scientific

	Standard	Scientific
yard/second ---	-2,025.371 83 ---	2.025 371 8E+03

nawa [Arabia] — \<mass, special - see page 29\>
| gram --- | ---- 15.6 --- | 1.560 000 0E+01 |

neal [Cambodia] — \<mass, special - see page 29\>
| gram --- | ---- 600 --- | 6.000 000 0E+02 |

nebuchadnezzar [champagne bottle] — \<champagne bottle size\>
| bottle [wine, standard] ---------------------------- | ----20 --- | 2.000 000 0E+01 |
| liter --- | ----15 --- | 1.500 000 0E+01 |

nelli [Sumatra, rice, milled] — \<mass, special - see page 29\>
| kilogram --- | ---- 14.595 --- | 1.459 500 0E+01 |

neper — \<sound pressure level\>
bel ---	-0.868 589 ---	8.685 889 6E-01
brig ---	-0.868 589 ---	8.685 889 6E-01
decibel --	8.685 889 6 ---	8.685 889 6E+00
dex ---	-0.868 589 ---	8.685 889 6E-01

nesef [Hebrew, ancient] — \<mass, special - see page 29\>
| gram --- | ---- 9.84 --- | 9.840 000 0E+00 |

neseph [Hebrew, ancient] — \<mass, special - see page 29\>
| gram --- | ---- 10.515 --- | 1.051 500 0E+01 |

neter [Ethiopia] — \<mass, special - see page 29\>
| gram --- | ----450 --- | 4.500 000 0E+02 |

netir [Eritrea] — \<mass, special - see page 29\>
| gram --- | ----454 --- | 4.540 000 0E+02 |

netseph [Hebrew, ancient] — \<mass, special - see page 29\>
| gram --- | ---- 9.84 --- | 9.840 000 0E+00 |

neutron rest mass [atomic physics, eq. energy] — \<energy\>
atomic mass unit [unified, C-12, 1986, eq. energy] -----	1.008 664 9 ---	1.008 664 9E+00
centimeter gram-force ------------------------------	0.000 001 5 ---	1.535 030 6E-06
deuteron rest mass [atomic physics, eq. energy] -------	0.500 937 8 ---	5.009 377 9E-01
dyne centimeter -----------------------------------	0.001 505 4 ---	1.505 350 8E-03
electron rest mass [atomic physics, eq. energy] -------	1,838.683 7 ---	1.838 683 7E+03
electronvolt ---------------------------------------	>>>	9.395 656 3E+08
erg --	0.001 505 4 ---	1.505 350 8E-03
gigaelectronvolt -----------------------------------	0.939 565 6 ---	9.395 656 3E-01
inch ounce-force ----------------------------------	<<<	2.131 756 3E-08
inch pound-force ----------------------------------	<<<	1.332 347 7E-09
joule --	<<<	1.505 350 8E-10
kiloelectronvolt ------------------------------------	939,565.63 ---	9.395 656 3E+05
megaelectronvolt ----------------------------------	939.565 63 ---	9.395 656 3E+02
muon rest mass [atomic physics, eq. energy] ---------	8.892 484 9 ---	8.892 484 9E+00
proton rest mass [atomic physics, eq. energy] --------	1.001 378 4 ---	1.001 378 4E+00
teraelectronvolt -----------------------------------	0.000 939 6 ---	9.395 656 3E-04
watthour --	<<<	4.181 529 9E-14

newton — \<force\>
crinal--	----10 ---	1.000 000 0E+01
decigram-force ------------------------------------	-1,019.716 21 ---	1.019 716 2E+03
dyne --	---- 100,000 ---	1.000 000 0E+05
erg/centimeter ------------------------------------	---- 100,000 ---	1.000 000 0E+05
funal --	---- 0.001 ---	1.000 000 0E-03
grain-force --	---- 1,573.662 6 ---	1.573 662 6E+03
gram centimeter/square second ---------------------	---- 100,000 ---	1.000 000 0E+05
gram-force --	101.971 621 ---	1.019 716 2E+02
hyl meter/square second ---------------------------	0.101 971 6 ---	1.019 716 2E-01
joule/meter ---------------------------------------	---- 1 ---	1.000 000 0E+00
kilogram meter/square second ----------------------	---- 1 ---	1.000 000 0E+00
kilogram-force ------------------------------------	0.101 971 6 ---	1.019 716 2E-01
kilopond --	0.101 971 6 ---	1.019 716 2E-01
kip --	0.000 224 8 ---	2.248 089 4E-04
ounce foot/square second --------------------------	115.728 22 ---	1.157 282 2E+02
ounce-force ---------------------------------------	3.596 943 1 ---	3.596 943 1E+00

Convert From Convert To	<Type of Unit> Standard	Scientific
ouncedal --	115.728 22 ----	1.157 282 2E+02
pascal square meter ------------------------------	1 ----	1.000 000 0E+00
pond---	101.971 621 ----	1.019 716 2E+02
pound foot/square second-----------------------	7.233 013 9 ----	7.233 013 9E+00
pound-force--	0.224 808 9 ----	2.248 089 4E-01
poundal---	7.233 013 9 ----	7.233 013 9E+00
slug foot/square second---------------------------	0.224 808 9 ----	2.248 089 4E-01
sthene --	0.001 ----	1.000 000 0E-03
ton foot/square second [long]-------------------	0.003 229 ----	3.229 024 0E-03
ton foot/square second [short]------------------	0.003 616 5 ----	3.616 506 9E-03
ton meter/square second [metric]--------------	0.001 ----	1.000 000 0E-03
ton-force [long]------------------------------------	0.000 100 4 ----	1.003 611 4E-04
ton-force [metric]---------------------------------	0.000 102 ----	1.019 716 2E-04
ton-force [short]----------------------------------	0.000 112 4 ----	1.124 044 7E-04
tondal --	0.003 229 ----	3.229 024 0E-03
volt ampere second/meter-----------------------	1 ----	1.000 000 0E+00
watt second/meter---------------------------------	1 ----	1.000 000 0E+00
newton	**<linear energy transfer>**	
Btu/foot [I.T.]-------------------------------------	0.000 288 9 ----	2.888 946 6E-04
electronvolt/meter---------------------------------	>>> ----	6.241 506 4E+18
kilocalorie/meter [I.T.]---------------------------	0.000 238 8 ----	2.388 459 0E-04
newton meter	**<energy>**	
Btu [I.T.] ---	0.000 947 8 ----	9.478 171 2E-04
calorie [I.T.] --------------------------------------	0.238 845 9 ----	2.388 459 0E-01
calorie [kilogram, I.T.] --------------------------	0.000 238 8 ----	2.388 459 0E-04
centigrade heat unit [I.T.]-----------------------	0.000 526 6 ----	5.265 650 7E-04
centimeter gram-force ----------------------------	10,197.162 ----	1.019 716 2E+04
cubic centimeter atmosphere -------------------	9.869 232 7 ----	9.869 232 7E+00
cubic foot atmosphere ---------------------------	0.000 348 5 ----	3.485 286 6E-04
dyne centimeter -----------------------------------	>>> ----	1.000 000 0E+07
erg ---	>>> ----	1.000 000 0E+07
foot pound-force----------------------------------	0.737 562 2 ----	7.375 621 5E-01
foot poundal --------------------------------------	23.730 36 ----	2.373 036 0E+01
frigorie [France]----------------------------------	0.000 238 9 ----	2.389 029 6E-04
gram calorie --------------------------------------	0.238 903 ----	2.389 029 6E-01
horsepower hour ---------------------------------	0.000 000 4 ----	3.725 061 4E-07
horsepower hour [metric] ------------------------	0.000 000 4 ----	3.776 726 7E-07
inch ounce-force ----------------------------------	141.611 93 ----	1.416 119 3E+02
inch pound-force ---------------------------------	8.850 745 8 ----	8.850 745 8E+00
joule --	1 ----	1.000 000 0E+00
kilocalorie [I.T.] ---------------------------------	0.000 238 8 ----	2.388 459 0E-04
kilogram calorie [15 °C, NBS, 1939] -----------	0.000 238 9 ----	2.389 029 6E-04
kilogram square meter/square second ---------	1 ----	1.000 000 0E+00
kilopond meter ------------------------------------	0.101 971 6 ----	1.019 716 2E-01
megaerg--	10 ----	1.000 000 0E+01
megalerg ---	10 ----	1.000 000 0E+01
meter kilogram-force -----------------------------	0.101 971 6 ----	1.019 716 2E-01
pferdestarkenstunde [Germany] ----------------	0.000 000 4 ----	3.776 726 7E-07
watthour ---	0.000 277 8 ----	2.777 777 8E-04
wattsecond ---------------------------------------	1 ----	1.000 000 0E+00
newton meter	**<torque>**	
foot ounce-force ---------------------------------	11.800 994 ----	1.180 099 4E+01
meter kilogram-force -----------------------------	0.101 971 6 ----	1.019 716 2E-01
newton meter second	**<moment of momentum>**	
joule second---------------------------------------	1 ----	1.000 000 0E+00
kilogram square meter/second -----------------	1 ----	1.000 000 0E+00
planck---	1 ----	1.000 000 0E+00
pound square foot/second-----------------------	23.730 36 ----	2.373 036 0E+01
newton meter/hour	**<power>**	
Btu/hour [I.T.] ------------------------------------	0.000 947 8 ----	9.478 171 2E-04
Btu/hour [thermoc.] -----------------------------	0.000 948 5 ----	9.484 514 1E-04
calorie/hour [I.T.] --------------------------------	0.238 845 9 ----	2.388 459 0E-01

Convert From Convert To	Standard	<Type of Unit> Scientific
calorie/hour [thermoc.]	0.239 005 7	2.390 057 4E-01
centigrade heat unit/hour [mean]	0.000 526 2	5.261 590 5E-04
cubic meter atmosphere/hour	9.869 232 7	9.869 232 7E+00
dyne centimeter/second	2,777.777 8	2.777 777 8E+03
erg/second	2,777.777 8	2.777 777 8E+03
foot pound-force/hour	0.737 562 2	7.375 621 5E-01
foot poundal/hour	23.730 36	2.373 036 0E+01
gram-force centimeter/second	2.832 545	2.832 545 0E+00
horsepower	0.000 000 4	3.725 061 4E-07
horsepower [metric]	0.000 000 4	3.776 726 7E-07
joule/hour	1	1.000 000 0E+00
kilocalorie/hour [I.T.]	0.000 238 8	2.388 459 0E-04
kilogram-force meter/hour	0.101 971 6	1.019 716 2E-01
kilopond meter/hour	0.101 971 6	1.019 716 2E-01
lumen [green light at 100% efficiency]	0.190 277 8	1.902 777 8E-01
lumen [green light at 5,550 angstrom]	0.188 888 9	1.888 888 9E-01
newton meter/minute	0.016 666 7	1.666 666 7E-02
pound square foot/cubic second	0.006 591 8	6.591 766 8E-03
volt ampere	0.000 277 8	2.777 777 8E-04
watt	0.000 277 8	2.777 777 8E-04
newton meter/kilogram		**<dose equivalent>**
joule/kilogram	1	1.000 000 0E+00
sievert	1	1.000 000 0E+00
square meter/square second	1	1.000 000 0E+00
newton meter/meter		**<torque/unit length>**
foot pound-force/inch	0.018 734 1	1.873 407 9E-02
inch pound-force/inch	0.224 808 9	2.248 089 4E-01
newton meter/minute		**<power>**
Btu/hour [I.T.]	0.056 869	5.686 902 7E-02
Btu/hour [thermoc.]	0.056 907 1	5.690 708 5E-02
calorie/hour [I.T.]	14.330 754	1.433 075 4E+01
calorie/hour [thermoc.]	14.340 344	1.434 034 4E+01
centigrade heat unit/hour [mean]	0.031 569 5	3.156 954 3E-02
centiwatt	1.666 666 7	1.666 666 7E+00
cubic meter atmosphere/minute	9.869 232 7	9.869 232 7E+00
dyne centimeter/second	166,666.67	1.666 666 7E+05
erg/second	166,666.67	1.666 666 7E+05
foot pound-force/hour	44.253 729	4.425 372 9E+01
foot poundal/minute	23.730 36	2.373 036 0E+01
gram-force centimeter/second	169.952 7	1.699 527 0E+02
horsepower	0.000 022 4	2.235 036 8E-05
horsepower [metric]	0.000 022 7	2.266 036 0E-05
joule/minute	1	1.000 000 0E+00
kilocalorie/hour [I.T.]	0.014 330 8	1.433 075 4E-02
kilogram square meter/cubic second	0.016 666 7	1.666 666 7E-02
kilogram-force meter/hour	6.118 297 3	6.118 297 3E+00
kilopond meter/hour	6.118 297 3	6.118 297 3E+00
lumen [green light at 100% efficiency]	11.416 667	1.141 666 7E+01
lumen [green light at 5,550 angstrom]	11.333 334	1.133 333 4E+01
newton meter/hour	60	6.000 000 0E+01
pound square foot/cubic second	0.395 506	3.955 060 1E-01
volt ampere	0.016 666 7	1.666 666 7E-02
watt	0.016 666 7	1.666 666 7E-02
newton meter/second		**<power>**
Btu/hour [I.T.]	3.412 141 6	3.412 141 6E+00
Btu/hour [thermoc.]	3.414 425 1	3.414 425 1E+00
calorie/minute [I.T.]	14.330 754	1.433 075 4E+01
calorie/minute [thermoc.]	14.340 344	1.434 034 4E+01
centigrade heat unit/hour [mean]	1.894 172 6	1.894 172 6E+00
cheval vapeur [France]	0.001 359 6	1.359 621 6E-03
cubic meter atmosphere/second	9.869 232 7	9.869 232 7E+00
dyne centimeter/second	>>>	1.000 000 0E+07

| Convert From | | **\<Type of Unit\>** |
Convert To	Standard	Scientific
erg/second	>>>	1.000 000 0E+07
foot pound-force/minute	44.253 729	4.425 372 9E+01
foot poundal/second	23.730 36	2.373 036 0E+01
gram-force centimeter/second	10,197.162	1.019 716 2E+04
horsepower	0.001 341	1.341 022 1E−03
horsepower [metric]	0.001 359 6	1.359 621 6E−03
joule/second	1	1.000 000 0E+00
kilocalorie/hour [I.T.]	0.859 845 2	8.598 452 3E−01
kilogram square meter/cubic second	1	1.000 000 0E+00
kilogram-force meter/minute	6.118 297 3	6.118 297 3E+00
kilopond meter/minute	6.118 297 3	6.118 297 3E+00
lumen [green light at 100% efficiency]	685	6.850 000 0E+02
lumen [green light at 5,550 angstrom]	680.000 02	6.800 000 2E+02
newton meter/minute	60	6.000 000 0E+01
pferdestarke [Germany]	0.001 359 6	1.359 621 6E−03
poncelet [France]	0.001 019 7	1.019 716 2E−03
pound square foot/cubic second	23.730 36	2.373 036 0E+01
ton of refrigeration	0.000 284 3	2.843 451 4E−04
volt ampere	1	1.000 000 0E+00
watt	1	1.000 000 0E+00
newton second		**\<momentum\>**
bole	100,000	1.000 000 0E+05
dyne second	100,000	1.000 000 0E+05
kilogram meter/second	1	1.000 000 0E+00
pound foot/second	7.233 013 9	7.233 013 9E+00
pound-force second	0.224 808 9	2.248 089 4E−01
newton second/cubic meter		**\<specific acoustic impedance\>**
kilogram-force second/cubic meter	0.101 971 6	1.019 716 2E−01
pascal second/meter	1	1.000 000 0E+00
pound-force second/cubic foot	0.006 365 9	6.365 880 4E−03
poundal second/cubic foot	0.204 816 1	2.048 161 0E−01
newton second/meter		**\<mechanical impedance\>**
joule second/square meter	1	1.000 000 0E+00
kilogram-force second/meter	0.101 971 6	1.019 716 2E−01
pound-force second/foot	0.068 521 8	6.852 176 6E−02
poundal second/foot	2.204 622 6	2.204 622 6E+00
newton second/meter^5		**\<acoustic impedance\>**
dyne second/centimeter^5	0.000 01	1.000 000 0E−05
pascal second/cubic meter	1	1.000 000 0E+00
newton second/square meter		**\<dynamic viscosity\>**
gram/centimeter second	10	1.000 000 0E+01
kilogram-force second/square meter	0.101 971 6	1.019 716 2E−01
kilogram/meter second	1	1.000 000 0E+00
pascal second	1	1.000 000 0E+00
poise	10	1.000 000 0E+01
poiseuille [France]	1	1.000 000 0E+00
pound/foot second	0.671 969	6.719 689 8E−01
poundal second/square foot	0.671 969	6.719 689 8E−01
newton square meter/ampere		**\<magnetic dipole moment\>**
abweber centimeter	>>>	7.957 747 2E+08
statweber centimeter	0.026 544 2	2.654 418 7E−02
volt second meter	1	1.000 000 0E+00
weber meter	1	1.000 000 0E+00
newton square second/meter		**\<mass\>**
hyl	0.101 971 6	1.019 716 2E−01
kilogram	1	1.000 000 0E+00
ounce	35.273 962	3.527 396 2E+01
ounce [apothecary]	32.150 747	3.215 074 7E+01
ounce [avoirdupois]	35.273 962	3.527 396 2E+01
ounce [troy]	32.150 747	3.215 074 7E+01
pound	2.204 622 6	2.204 622 6E+00

Measure for Measure 581

Convert From Convert To	Standard	<Type of Unit> Scientific
pound [apothecary]	2.679 228 9	2.679 228 9E+00
pound [avoirdupois]	2.204 622 6	2.204 622 6E+00
pound [international]	2.204 622 6	2.204 622 6E+00
pound [troy]	2.679 228 9	2.679 228 9E+00
pound [US, avoirdupois]	2.204 622 3	2.204 622 3E+00
pound [US, troy]	2.679 228 5	2.679 228 5E+00
poundal square second/foot	2.204 622 6	2.204 622 6E+00
quintal [metric]	0.01	1.000 000 0E-02
ton [UK, assay or assay, long]	30.612 245	3.061 224 5E+01
ton [US, assay or assay, short]	34.285 714	3.428 571 4E+01

newton/ampere <magnetic vector potential>

abweber/centimeter	1,000,000	1.000 000 0E+06
statweber/centimeter	0.000 033 4	3.335 641 0E-05
volt second/meter	1	1.000 000 0E+00
weber/meter	1	1.000 000 0E+00

newton/ampere meter <magnetic flux density>

ampere henry/square meter	1	1.000 000 0E+00
electromagnetic unit of magnetic flux density [cgs system]	10,000	1.000 000 0E+04
gauss	10,000	1.000 000 0E+04
joule/ampere square meter	1	1.000 000 0E+00
line/square centimeter [of magnetic force]	10,000	1.000 000 0E+04
maxwell/square meter	1	1.000 000 0E+00
tesla	1	1.000 000 0E+00
volt second/square meter	1	1.000 000 0E+00
weber/square meter	1	1.000 000 0E+00

newton/centimeter <surface tension>

gram-force/centimeter	101.971 62	1.019 716 2E+02
kilogram-force/meter	10.197 162	1.019 716 2E+01
kilopond/meter	10.197 162	1.019 716 2E+01
newton/meter	100	1.000 000 0E+02
ounce-force/foot	109.634 83	1.096 348 3E+02
pound-force/inch	0.571 014 7	5.710 147 2E-01

newton/coulomb <electric field strength>

joule/coulomb	1	1.000 000 0E+00
statvolt/centimeter	0.000 033 4	3.335 641 0E-05
volt/inch	0.025 4	2.540 000 0E-02
volt/meter	1	1.000 000 0E+00
watt/ampere meter	1	1.000 000 0E+00

newton/meter <energy fluence>

Btu/square foot [I.T.]	0.000 088 1	8.805 509 2E-05
dyne/centimeter	1,000	1.000 000 0E+03
erg/square centimeter	1,000	1.000 000 0E+03
joule/square meter	1	1.000 000 0E+00

newton/meter <surface tension>

gram-force/centimeter	1.019 716 2	1.019 716 2E+00
kilogram-force/meter	0.101 971 6	1.019 716 2E-01
kilopond/meter	0.101 971 6	1.019 716 2E-01
ounce-force/foot	1.096 348 3	1.096 348 3E+00
pound-force/foot	0.068 521 8	6.852 176 6E-02

newton/second kelvin <thermal conductivity>

watt/meter kelvin	1	1.000 000 0E+00

newton/square meter <pressure>

atmosphere [standard]	0.000 009 9	9.869 232 7E-06
atmosphere [technical]	0.000 010 2	1.019 716 2E-05
bar	0.000 01	1.000 000 0E-05
barye [France]	10	1.000 000 0E+01
dyne/square centimeter	10	1.000 000 0E+01
gram-force/square centimeter	0.010 197 2	1.019 716 2E-02
kilogram-force/square meter	0.101 971 6	1.019 716 2E-01
kilopond/square meter	0.101 971 6	1.019 716 2E-01
kip/square foot	0.000 020 9	2.088 543 4E-05

Convert From		<Type of Unit>
Convert To	Standard	Scientific

micrometer of mercury [0 °C, by convention]	7.500 615 8	7.500 615 8E+00
micrometer of water [4 °C, by convention]	101.971 62	1.019 716 2E+02
millitorr	7.500 616 8	7.500 616 8E+00
ounce-force/square inch	0.002 320 6	2.320 603 8E−03
pascal	1	1.000 000 0E+00
pieze [France]	0.001	1.000 000 0E−03
pound-force/square foot	0.020 885 4	2.088 543 4E−02
poundal/square foot	0.671 969	6.719 689 8E−01
sthene/square meter [France]	0.001	1.000 000 0E−03
ton-force/square foot [short]	0.000 010 4	1.044 271 7E−05
ton-force/square meter [metric]	0.000 102	1.019 716 2E−04
torr	0.007 500 6	7.500 616 8E−03
newton/square meter		**<energy density>**
Btu/cubic foot [I.T.]	0.000 026 8	2.683 919 2E−05
joule/cubic meter	1	1.000 000 0E+00
newton/square millimeter		**<pressure>**
atmosphere [standard]	9.869 232 7	9.869 232 7E+00
atmosphere [technical]	10.197 162	1.019 716 2E+01
bar	10	1.000 000 0E+01
centimeter of mercury [0 °C, by convention]	750.061 58	7.500 615 8E+02
centimeter of water [4 °C, by convention]	10,197.162	1.019 716 2E+04
dekabar	1	1.000 000 0E+00
foot of mercury [0 °C, by convention]	24.608 319	2.460 831 9E+01
foot of water [4 °C, by convention]	334.552 56	3.345 525 6E+02
inch of mercury [0 °C, by convention]	295.299 83	2.952 998 3E+02
inch of water [4 °C, by convention]	4,014.630 8	4.014 630 8E+03
kilogram-force/square centimeter	10.197 162	1.019 716 2E+01
kilopond/square centimeter	10.197 162	1.019 716 2E+01
kip/square foot	20.885 434	2.088 543 4E+01
megapascal	1	1.000 000 0E+00
ounce-force/square inch	2,320.603 8	2.320 603 8E+03
pascal	1,000,000	1.000 000 0E+06
pound-force/square inch	145.037 74	1.450 377 4E+02
ton-force/square foot [long]	9.323 854 6	9.323 854 6E+00
ton-force/square foot [short]	10.442 717	1.044 271 7E+01
ton-force/square meter [metric]	101.971 62	1.019 716 2E+02
torr	7,500.616 8	7.500 616 8E+03
newton/weber		**<magnetic field strength>**
ampere/inch	0.025 4	2.540 000 0E−02
ampere/meter	1	1.000 000 0E+00
ngamu [Burma]		**<mass, special - see page 29>**
gram	8.165	8.165 000 0E+00
ngan [Laos]		**<area, special - see page 29>**
square meter	400	4.000 000 0E+02
ngan [Thailand]		**<area, special - see page 29>**
square meter	400	4.000 000 0E+02
ngane [Laos]		**<area, special - see page 29>**
square meter	400	4.000 000 0E+02
ngane [Thailand]		**<area, special - see page 29>**
square meter	400	4.000 000 0E+02
ngu [Thailand]		**<length, special - see page 29>**
meter	2.436 5	2.436 500 0E+00
ngu [Vietnam]		**<length, special - see page 29>**
meter	2	2.000 000 0E+00
niew [Thailand]		**<length, special - see page 29>**
centimeter	2.083 333	2.083 333 0E+00
nigida [Mesopotamia, ancient]		**<volume, special - see page 29>**
liter	49.2	4.920 000 0E+01
nijo [Japan]		**<mass, special - see page 29>**
gram	15	1.500 000 0E+01

| Convert From | <Type of Unit> | |
Convert To	Standard	Scientific

nim man [Iran] <mass, special - see page 29>
kilogram -- 1.5 --- 1.500 000 0E+00

ninda [Sumeria, ancient] <length, special - see page 29>
meter --- 6 --- 6.000 000 0E+00

niou [Laos] <length, special - see page 29>
centimeter -- 1.667 --- 1.667 000 0E+00

niou [Thailand] <volume, special - see page 29>
liter --- 0.01 --- 1.000 000 0E-02

niou [Thailand] <length, special - see page 29>
centimeter --- 2.083 --- 2.083 000 0E+00

niou louang [Laos] <length, special - see page 29>
centimeter ----------------------------------- 2.083 333 --- 2.083 333 0E+00

niranja [India] <length, special - see page 29>
meter -- 9.144 --- 9.144 000 0E+00

nisf kadah [Egypt] <volume, special - see page 29>
liter --- 1.031 3 --- 1.031 300 0E+00

nisf keddah [Egypt] <volume, special - see page 29>
liter --- 1.031 --- 1.031 000 0E+00

nishka [Hindu, ancient, gold] <mass, special - see page 29>
gram --- 39.68 --- 3.968 000 0E+01

nit <luminance>
apostilb [international] -------------------------------- 3.141 592 7 --- 3.141 592 7E+00
blondel -- 3.141 592 7 --- 3.141 592 7E+00
candela/square foot ------------------------------- 0.092 903 --- 9.290 304 0E-02
candela/square meter --------------------------------------- 1 --- 1.000 000 0E+00
footlambert -- 0.291 863 5 --- 2.918 635 1E-01
lumen/steradian square meter --------------------------------- 1 --- 1.000 000 0E+00
lux steradian --- 1 --- 1.000 000 0E+00
millilambert -- 0.314 159 3 --- 3.141 592 7E-01
stilb -- 0.000 1 --- 1.000 000 0E-04

niu [Laos] <length, special - see page 29>
centimeter -- 1.667 --- 1.667 000 0E+00

niu [Thailand] <length, special - see page 29>
centimeter --- 2.083 --- 2.083 000 0E+00

nocktat [Turkey] <length, special - see page 29>
millimeter -- 0.29 --- 2.900 000 0E-01

node [Antigua] <length, special - see page 29>
centimeter -- 11.4 --- 1.140 000 0E+01

noessel [Germany, liquid] <volume, special - see page 29>
milliliter -- 429 --- 4.290 000 0E+02

noeud de loch [France] <length, special - see page 29>
meter -- 15.432 --- 1.543 200 0E+01

nofs [Malta, beer, wine and spirits] <volume, special - see page 29>
milliliter -- 568 --- 5.680 000 0E+02

nofs [Malta, oil and milk] <volume, special - see page 29>
centiliter -- 63.9 --- 6.390 000 0E+01

noggin [UK] <volume, special - see page 29>
liter --- 0.142 061 3 --- 1.420 613 0E-01

nohod [Persia] <mass, special - see page 29>
gram -- 0.18 --- 1.800 000 0E-01

nokhod [Afghanistan] <mass, special - see page 29>
milligram -- 191.8 --- 1.918 000 0E+02

nokhod [Iran] <mass, special - see page 29>
milligram --- 195 --- 1.950 000 0E+02

nonillion [UK] <units>
septendecillion [US] --- 1 --- 1.000 000 0E+00
unit --- >>> --- 1.000 000 0E+54

nonillion [US] \<units\>
quintillion [UK] -- 1 ---- 1.000 000 0E+00
unit --- >>> ---- 1.000 000 0E+30

nonpareil [print] \<length\>
agate [print] -------------------------------------- 1.090 909 1 ---- 1.090 909 1E+00
didot point [print] --------------------------------- 5.601 194 9 ---- 5.601 194 9E+00
douzieme [print] --------------------------------- 11.955 168 ---- 1.195 516 8E+01
em [pica, print] --- 0.5 ---- 5.000 000 0E-01
inch [based on US, survey foot] ------------ 0.083 021 8 ---- 8.302 183 4E-02
inch [international] ------------------------------ 0.083 022 ---- 8.302 200 0E-02
iron [print] -- 0.02 ---- 2.000 000 0E-02
ligne [print] ------------------------------------- 0.996 264 ---- 9.962 640 0E-01
line [print] -------------------------------------- 0.996 264 ---- 9.962 640 0E-01
meter -- 0.002 108 8 ---- 2.108 758 8E-03
microinch --- 83,022 ---- 8.302 200 0E+04
micron --- 2,108.758 8 ---- 2.108 758 8E+03
mil --- 83.022 ---- 8.302 200 0E+01
millimeter --------------------------------------- 2.108 758 8 ---- 2.108 758 8E+00
pearl [print] --- 1.2 ---- 1.200 000 0E+00
pica [print] -- 0.5 ---- 5.000 000 0E-01
point [print] -- 6 ---- 6.000 000 0E+00
thou --- 83.022 ---- 8.302 200 0E+01

nouaia [Tunisia] \<mass, special - see page 29\>
gram -- 0.196 845 ---- 1.968 450 0E-01

novemdecillion [UK] \<units\>
unit --- >>> ---- 1.000 000 0E+114

novemdecillion [US] \<units\>
decillion [UK] -- 1 ---- 1.000 000 0E+00
unit --- >>> ---- 1.000 000 0E+60

nox \<illuminance\>
footcandle --- 0.000 092 9 ---- 9.290 304 0E-05
lumen/square inch ------------------------------ 0.000 000 6 ---- 6.451 600 0E-07
lumen/square meter ------------------------------- 0.001 ---- 1.000 000 0E-03
lux --- 0.001 ---- 1.000 000 0E-03
milliphot --- 0.000 1 ---- 1.000 000 0E-04

nox second \<light exposure\>
footcandle second ------------------------------ 0.000 092 9 ---- 9.290 304 0E-05
lumen second/square inch ------------------- 0.000 000 6 ---- 6.451 600 0E-07
lux second --- 0.001 ---- 1.000 000 0E-03
phot second --- 0.000 1 ---- 1.000 000 0E-07

noy \<loudness level\>
loudness unit -- 1,000 ---- 1.000 000 0E+03
phon --- 40 ---- 4.000 000 0E+01
sone --- 1 ---- 1.000 000 0E+00

nozibu [Burma] \<volume, special - see page 29\>
liter --- 0.319 637 8 ---- 3.196 378 0E-01

nsp [Hebrew, ancient] \<mass, special - see page 29\>
gram --- 10 ---- 1.000 000 0E+01

nuge [Anatolia, medieval] \<mass, special - see page 29\>
gram --- 250.1 ---- 2.501 000 0E+02

number of atoms in 0.012 kg of carbon-12 \<amount of substance\>
mole --- 1 ---- 1.000 000 0E+00
one atom of carbon-12 ---------------------------- >>> ---- 6.022 136 7E+23

nus [Algeria] \<length, special - see page 29\>
centimeter --- 24.8 ---- 2.480 000 0E+01

nusfiah [Arabia] \<volume, special - see page 29\>
liter --- 0.95 ---- 9.500 000 0E-01

nymil [Sweden] \<length, special - see page 29\>
kilometer --- 10 ---- 1.000 000 0E+01

	Standard	Scientific
o [Vietnam]	<volume, special - see page 29>	
cubic meter	0.064	6.400 000 0E-02
o [Vietnam]	<area, special - see page 29>	
square meter	0.16	1.600 000 0E-01
obol [Greece, ancient]	<mass, special - see page 29>	
gram	0.71	7.100 000 0E-01
obol [Greece]	<mass, special - see page 29>	
milligram	715.38	7.153 800 0E+02
obol [Hebrew, ancient]	<mass, special - see page 29>	
milligram	633	6.330 000 0E+02
obolos [Greece, ancient]	<mass, special - see page 29>	
gram	0.73	7.300 000 0E-01
obolus [Rome, ancient]	<mass, special - see page 29>	
gram	0.568	5.680 000 0E-01
occa [Egypt, ancient]	<mass, special - see page 29>	
kilogram	1.248	1.248 000 0E+00
occa [Iraq, ancient]	<mass, special - see page 29>	
kilogram	1.248	1.248 000 0E+00
occa [Romania]	<mass, special - see page 29>	
kilogram	1.289	1.289 000 0E+00
ocean ton	<ocean ton>	
barrel [US, dry]	9.795 918 4	9.795 918 4E+00
board foot	480	4.800 000 0E+02
bushel [UK]	31.144 177	3.114 417 7E+01
bushel [US, dry]	32.142 558	3.214 255 8E+01
cord [firewood]	0.312 5	3.125 000 0E-01
cord foot [timber]	2.5	2.500 000 0E+00
cubic foot	40	4.000 000 0E+01
cubic inch	69,120	6.912 000 0E+04
cubic meter	1.132 673 9	1.132 673 9E+00
cubic yard	1.481 481 5	1.481 481 5E+00
English water ton [UK]	1.112 292	1.112 292 0E+00
freight ton	1	1.000 000 0E+00
hectare meter	0.000 113 3	1.132 673 9E-04
kiloliter	1.132 673 9	1.132 673 9E+00
liter	1,132.673 9	1.132 673 9E+03
measurement ton	1	1.000 000 0E+00
million board foot	0.000 48	4.800 000 0E-04
petrograd standard	0.242 424 2	2.424 242 4E-01
register ton	0.4	4.000 000 0E-01
shipping ton	1	1.000 000 0E+00
stere	1.132 673 9	1.132 673 9E+00
thousand board foot	0.48	4.800 000 0E-01
thousand cubic foot	0.04	4.000 000 0E-02
ochava [Macao]	<mass, special - see page 29>	
gram	3.59	3.590 000 0E+00
ochava [Mexico]	<mass, special - see page 29>	
gram	3.595 7	3.595 700 0E+00
ochava [Spain]	<mass, special - see page 29>	
gram	3.594 48	3.594 480 0E+00
ock [Cyprus]	<volume, special - see page 29>	
liter	1.273	1.273 000 0E+00
ock [Cyprus]	<mass, special - see page 29>	
kilogram	1.27	1.270 000 0E+00
ock [Greece]	<mass, special - see page 29>	
kilogram	1.28	1.280 000 0E+00
ock [Jordan]	<mass, special - see page 29>	
kilogram	1.282	1.282 000 0E+00

	Standard	Scientific
ock [Lebanon]	<mass, special - see page 29>	
kilogram	1.282	1.282 000 0E+00
ock [Libya]	<mass, special - see page 29>	
kilogram	1.282	1.282 000 0E+00
ock [Saudi Arabia]	<mass, special - see page 29>	
kilogram	1.248	1.248 000 0E+00
ock [Syria]	<mass, special - see page 29>	
kilogram	1.282	1.282 000 0E+00
ock [Turkey]	<mass, special - see page 29>	
kilogram	1.283	1.283 000 0E+00
ocque [Lebanon]	<mass, special - see page 29>	
kilogram	1.281 99	1.281 990 0E+00
octad	<units>	
unit	8	8.000 000 0E+00
octava [Argentina]	<volume, special - see page 29>	
liter	0.148 4	1.484 000 0E-01
octava [Brazil, gold and silver]	<mass, special - see page 29>	
gram	3.6	3.600 000 0E+00
octava [Italy, gold, silver and jewels]	<mass, special - see page 29>	
gram	1.7	1.700 000 0E+00
octava [Portugal, gold and silver]	<mass, special - see page 29>	
gram	3.6	3.600 000 0E+00
octavillo [Spain, liquid]	<volume, special - see page 29>	
liter	0.252	2.520 000 0E-01
octillion [UK]	<units>	
quindecillion [US]	1	1.000 000 0E+00
unit	>>>	1.000 000 0E+48
octillion [US]	<units>	
unit	>>>	1.000 000 0E+27
octodecillion [UK]	<units>	
unit	>>>	1.000 000 0E+108
octodecillion [US]	<units>	
unit	>>>	1.000 000 0E+57
oersted	<magnetic field strength>	
ampere/inch	2.021 267 8	2.021 267 8E+00
ampere/meter	79.577 471 5	7.957 747 2E+01
gilbert/centimeter	1	1.000 000 0E+00
statampere/centimeter	2.385 672 6E+09	
ogga [Turkey, ancient]	<mass, special - see page 29>	
kilogram	1.283	1.283 000 0E+00
ohm	<electric resistance>	
1/ siemens	1	1.000 000 0E+00
1/mho	1	1.000 000 0E+00
abohm	>>>	1.000 000 0E+09
electromagnetic unit of resistance [cgs system]	>>>	1.000 000 0E+09
electrostatic unit of resistance [cgs system]	<<<	1.112 650 1E-12
gaussian electric resistance	<<<	1.112 650 1E-12
henry/second	1	1.000 000 0E+00
ohm [international]	0.999 510 2	9.995 102 4E-01
statohm	<<<	1.112 650 1E-12
volt/ampere	1	1.000 000 0E+00
ohm [Germany, liquid]	<volume, special - see page 29>	
hectoliter	1.374	1.374 000 0E+00
ohm [international]	<electric resistance>	
1/ siemens	1.000 49	1.000 490 0E+00
abohm	>>>	1.000 490 0E+09
ohm	1.000 49	1.000 490 0E+00
statohm	<<<	1.113 195 3E-12

ohm centimeter <electric resistivity>
abohm centimeter -->>> --- 1.000 000 0E+09
microohm inch -- 393,700.787 --- 3.937 007 9E+05
ohm circular mil/foot --------------------------------- -6,015,304.94 --- 6.015 304 9E+06
ohm meter --- 0.01 --- 1.000 000 0E-02
ohm square millimeter/meter ---------------------------------- 10,000 --- 1.000 000 0E+04
statohm centimeter --<<< --- 1.112 650 1E-12

ohm circular mil/foot <electric resistivity>
abohm centimeter -- 166.242 611 --- 1.662 426 1E+02
microohm inch -- 0.065 449 8 --- 6.544 984 7E-02
ohm meter --<<< --- 1.662 426 1E-09
ohm square millimeter/meter ------------------------------ 0.001 662 4 --- 1.662 426 1E-03
preece ---<<< --- 1.662 426 1E-22
statohm centimeter --<<< --- 1.849 698 5E-19

ohm foot <electric resistivity>
ohm meter --- 0.304 8 --- 3.048 000 0E-01
preece ---<<< --- 3.048 000 0E-14

ohm inch <electric resistivity>
ohm meter --- 0.025 4 --- 2.540 000 0E-02

ohm meter <electric resistivity>
abohm centimeter -->>> --- 1.000 000 0E+11
microohm inch -->>> --- 3.937 007 9E+07
ohm centimeter --- 100 --- 1.000 000 0E+02
ohm circular mil/foot -->>> --- 6.015 304 9E+08
ohm foot --- 3.280 839 9 --- 3.280 839 9E+00
ohm inch --- 39.370 079 --- 3.937 007 9E+01
ohm square millimeter/meter ---------------------------- 1,000,000 --- 1.000 000 0E+06
preece ---<<< --- 1.000 000 0E-13
statohm centimeter --<<< --- 1.112 650 1E-10

ohm second <electric inductance>
abhenry -->>> --- 1.000 000 0E+09
henry -- 1 --- 1.000 000 0E+00
joule/square ampere --- 1 --- 1.000 000 0E+00
stathenry ---<<< --- 1.112 650 1E-12
volt second/ampere -- 1 --- 1.000 000 0E+00
weber/ampere --- 1 --- 1.000 000 0E+00

ohm square millimeter/meter <electric resistivity>
abohm centimeter -- 100,000 --- 1.000 000 0E+05
microohm inch --39.370 078 7 --- 3.937 007 9E+01
microohm meter --- 1 --- 1.000 000 0E+00
ohm circular mil/foot ----------------------------------- 601.530 494 --- 6.015 304 9E+02
ohm meter --- 0.000 001 --- 1.000 000 0E-06
statohm centimeter --<<< --- 1.112 650 1E-16

oitava [Brazil] <mass, special - see page 29>
gram -- 3.586 33 --- 3.586 330 0E+00

oitava [Macao] <mass, special - see page 29>
gram -- 3.59 --- 3.590 000 0E+00

oitava [Mexico] <mass, special - see page 29>
gram -- 3.6 --- 3.600 000 0E+00

oitava [Portugal] <volume, special - see page 29>
liter --- 1.415 --- 1.415 000 0E+00

oka [Bulgaria] <volume, special - see page 29>
liter -- 1.28 --- 1.280 000 0E+00

oka [Cyprus] <volume, special - see page 29>
liter -- 1.28 --- 1.280 000 0E+00

oka [Egypt, ancient] <mass, special - see page 29>
kilogram --- 1.248 --- 1.248 000 0E+00

oka [Greece] <mass, special - see page 29>
kilogram -- 1.28 --- 1.280 000 0E+00

oka [Iraq, ancient]		\<mass, special - see page 29\>
kilogram	1.248	1.248 000 0E+00
oka [Jordan]		\<mass, special - see page 29\>
kilogram	1.282	1.282 000 0E+00
oka [Lebanon]		\<mass, special - see page 29\>
kilogram	1.282	1.282 000 0E+00
oka [Libya]		\<mass, special - see page 29\>
kilogram	1.282	1.282 000 0E+00
oka [Saudi Arabia]		\<mass, special - see page 29\>
kilogram	1.248	1.248 000 0E+00
oka [Syria]		\<mass, special - see page 29\>
kilogram	1.282	1.282 000 0E+00
oka [Turkey]		\<volume, special - see page 29\>
liter	1.28	1.280 000 0E+00
oka [Turkey]		\<mass, special - see page 29\>
kilogram	1.283	1.283 000 0E+00
oka [Yugoslavia]		\<volume, special - see page 29\>
liter	1.415	1.415 000 0E+00
oka [Yugoslavia]		\<mass, special - see page 29\>
kilogram	1.28	1.280 000 0E+00
oke [Afghanistan]		\<mass, special - see page 29\>
kilogram	1.12	1.120 000 0E+00
oke [Bulgaria]		\<volume, special - see page 29\>
liter	1.28	1.280 000 0E+00
oke [Bulgaria]		\<mass, special - see page 29\>
kilogram	1.288	1.288 000 0E+00
oke [Cyprus]		\<volume, special - see page 29\>
liter	1.28	1.280 000 0E+00
oke [Cyprus]		\<mass, special - see page 29\>
kilogram	1.27	1.270 000 0E+00
oke [Egypt]		\<mass, special - see page 29\>
kilogram	1.248	1.248 000 0E+00
oke [Greece]		\<mass, special - see page 29\>
kilogram	1.28	1.280 000 0E+00
oke [Iraq]		\<mass, special - see page 29\>
kilogram	1.248	1.248 000 0E+00
oke [Jordan]		\<mass, special - see page 29\>
kilogram	1.282	1.282 000 0E+00
oke [Lebanon]		\<mass, special - see page 29\>
kilogram	1.282	1.282 000 0E+00
oke [Libya]		\<mass, special - see page 29\>
kilogram	1.282	1.282 000 0E+00
oke [Romania, dry]		\<volume, special - see page 29\>
liter	1.538	1.538 000 0E+00
oke [Romania, liquid]		\<volume, special - see page 29\>
liter	1.415	1.415 000 0E+00
oke [Romania]		\<mass, special - see page 29\>
kilogram	1.27	1.270 000 0E+00
oke [Saudi Arabia]		\<mass, special - see page 29\>
kilogram	1.270 1	1.270 100 0E+00
oke [Sudan]		\<mass, special - see page 29\>
kilogram	1.248	1.248 000 0E+00
oke [Syria]		\<mass, special - see page 29\>
kilogram	1.282	1.282 000 0E+00

Convert From	<Type of Unit>	
Convert To	Standard	Scientific

oke [Turkey]
liter --- <volume, special - see page 29>
-- 1.28 --- 1.280 000 0E+00

oke [Turkey]
kilogram --- <mass, special - see page 29>
-- 1.283 --- 1.283 000 0E+00

oke [Yugoslavia]
kilogram --- <mass, special - see page 29>
-- 1.28 --- 1.280 000 0E+00

oke thapa [Burma]
meter --- <length, special - see page 29>
--------------------------------------- 64.008 --- 6.400 800 0E+01

oke thapal [Burma]
meter --- <length, special - see page 29>
--------------------------------------- 78.232 --- 7.823 200 0E+01

oket [Ethiopia]
gram --- <mass, special - see page 29>
------------------------------------- 28.067 --- 2.806 700 0E+01

okia [Egypt]
gram --- <mass, special - see page 29>
------------------------------------- 37.44 --- 3.744 000 0E+01

okia [Eritrea]
gram --- <mass, special - see page 29>
-------------------------------------- 28.1 --- 2.810 000 0E+01

okia [Ethiopia]
gram --- <mass, special - see page 29>
------------------------------------- 28.067 --- 2.806 700 0E+01

okia [Iraq, Baghdad]
kilogram --- <mass, special - see page 29>
-- 1.042 --- 1.042 000 0E+00

okia [Iraq, Mosul]
gram --- <mass, special - see page 29>
-------------------------------------- 128.3 --- 1.283 000 0E+02

okia [Jordan, Nabulsi]
gram --- <mass, special - see page 29>
-------------------------------------- 240.4 --- 2.404 000 0E+02

okia [Jordan, Shami]
gram --- <mass, special - see page 29>
-------------------------------------- 213.7 --- 2.137 000 0E+02

okia [Lebanon]
gram --- <mass, special - see page 29>
-------------------------------------- 213.7 --- 2.137 000 0E+02

okia [Libya]
gram --- <mass, special - see page 29>
-------------------------------------- 32.05 --- 3.205 000 0E+01

okia [Somalia]
gram --- <mass, special - see page 29>
--28 --- 2.800 000 0E+01

okia [Somaliland]
gram --- <mass, special - see page 29>
-------------------------------------- 28.313 --- 2.831 300 0E+01

okia [Sudan]
gram --- <mass, special - see page 29>
-------------------------------------- 37.44 --- 3.744 000 0E+01

okia [Syria]
gram --- <mass, special - see page 29>
-------------------------------------- 213.7 --- 2.137 000 0E+02

okiya [Ethiopia]
gram --- <mass, special - see page 29>
-------------------------------------- 25.9 --- 2.590 000 0E+01

okiya [Iraq, Baghdad]
kilogram --- <mass, special - see page 29>
-- 1.042 --- 1.042 000 0E+00

okiya [Iraq, Istanbul]
gram --- <mass, special - see page 29>
-------------------------------------- 320.75 --- 3.207 500 0E+02

okiya [Jordan, Nabulsi]
gram --- <mass, special - see page 29>
-------------------------------------- 240.4 --- 2.404 000 0E+02

okiya [Jordan, Shami]
gram --- <mass, special - see page 29>
-------------------------------------- 213.7 --- 2.137 000 0E+02

okiya [Lebanon]
gram --- <mass, special - see page 29>
-------------------------------------- 213.7 --- 2.137 000 0E+02

okiya [Libya]
gram --- <mass, special - see page 29>
-------------------------------------- 32.05 --- 3.205 000 0E+01

okiya [Somalia]
gram --- <mass, special - see page 29>
--28 --- 2.800 000 0E+01

Convert From
Convert To
<Type of Unit>
Standard   Scientific

okiya [Sudan]   <mass, special - see page 29>
  gram -- 37.44 ---- 3.744 000 0E+01

okiya [Syria]   <mass, special - see page 29>
  gram -- 213.7 ---- 2.137 000 0E+02

okka [Cyprus]   <volume, special - see page 29>
  liter -- 1.273 ---- 1.273 000 0E+00

okka [Cyprus]   <mass, special - see page 29>
  kilogram --- 1.27 ---- 1.270 000 0E+00

okka [Greece]   <mass, special - see page 29>
  kilogram --- 1.28 ---- 1.280 000 0E+00

okka [Jordan]   <mass, special - see page 29>
  kilogram --- 1.282 ---- 1.282 000 0E+00

okka [Lebanon]   <mass, special - see page 29>
  kilogram --- 1.282 ---- 1.282 000 0E+00

okka [Libya]   <mass, special - see page 29>
  kilogram --- 1.282 ---- 1.282 000 0E+00

okka [Saudi Arabia]   <mass, special - see page 29>
  kilogram --- 1.248 ---- 1.248 000 0E+00

okka [Syria]   <mass, special - see page 29>
  kilogram --- 1.282 ---- 1.282 000 0E+00

okka [Turkey, ancient]   <mass, special - see page 29>
  kilogram --- 1.283 ---- 1.283 000 0E+00

okka [Turkey]   <volume, special - see page 29>
  liter -- 1.133 ---- 1.133 000 0E+00

okka [Turkey]   <mass, special - see page 29>
  kilogram -- 1.282 945 ---- 1.282 945 0E+00

okka [Yemen]   <mass, special - see page 29>
  kilogram --- 0.85 ---- 8.500 000 0E−01

okshoofd [Netherlands]   <volume, special - see page 29>
  liter -- 232.8 ---- 2.328 000 0E+02

olc [Iraq]   <area, special - see page 29>
  square meter --- 100 ---- 1.000 000 0E+02

olcek [Turkey]   <volume, special - see page 29>
  liter -- 18.5 ---- 1.850 000 0E+01

ollock [India]   <volume, special - see page 29>
  liter --- 0.191 6 ---- 1.916 000 0E−01

oltonde [Denmark]   <volume, special - see page 29>
  hectoliter -- 1.314 ---- 1.314 000 0E+00

oltunna [Iceland]   <volume, special - see page 29>
  hectoliter -- 1.314 ---- 1.314 000 0E+00

omarium [Hebrew, ancient, dry]   <volume, special - see page 29>
  liter -- 3.8 ---- 3.800 000 0E+00

omer [Babylon, ancient]   <volume, special - see page 29>
  liter -- 2.2 ---- 2.200 000 0E+00

omer [Hebrew, ancient]   <volume, special - see page 29>
  liter -- 3.964 ---- 3.964 000 0E+00

oms [Russia]   <volume, special - see page 29>
  liter --- 73.796 46 ---- 7.379 646 0E+01

ona [Dominican Republic]   <length, special - see page 29>
  meter --- 1.188 ---- 1.188 000 0E+00

onca [Brazil]   <mass, special - see page 29>
  gram -- 28.690 6 ---- 2.869 060 0E+01

onca [Cape Verde]   <area, special - see page 29>
  square meter --------------------------------------- 1,161.6 ---- 1.161 600 0E+03

Convert From	<Type of Unit>	
Convert To	Standard	Scientific

onca [France, 1800 definition]	<mass, special - see page 29>	
hectogram	1	1.000 000 0E+00
onca [Portugal]	<mass, special - see page 29>	
gram	28.691	2.869 100 0E+01
onca [Portuguese India]	<mass, special - see page 29>	
gram	28.69	2.869 000 0E+01
once [Ethiopia]	<mass, special - see page 29>	
gram	25.9	2.590 000 0E+01
once [France, 1800 definition]	<mass, special - see page 29>	
hectogram	1	1.000 000 0E+00
once [Holland, medical]	<mass, special - see page 29>	
gram	31.25	3.125 000 0E+01
once [Holland, troy]	<mass, special - see page 29>	
gram	100	1.000 000 0E+02
once [Iraq]	<mass, special - see page 29>	
kilogram	1.042	1.042 000 0E+00
once [Jordan, Nabulsi]	<mass, special - see page 29>	
gram	240.4	2.404 000 0E+02
once [Jordan, Shami]	<mass, special - see page 29>	
gram	213.7	2.137 000 0E+02
once [Lebanon]	<mass, special - see page 29>	
gram	213.7	2.137 000 0E+02
once [Libya]	<mass, special - see page 29>	
gram	32.05	3.205 000 0E+01
once [Somalia]	<mass, special - see page 29>	
gram	28	2.800 000 0E+01
once [Sudan]	<mass, special - see page 29>	
gram	37.44	3.744 000 0E+01
once [Switzerland]	<mass, special - see page 29>	
gram	31.25	3.125 000 0E+01
once [Syria]	<mass, special - see page 29>	
gram	213.8	2.138 000 0E+02
once [Tunisia]	<mass, special - see page 29>	
gram	31.495 3	3.149 530 0E+01
once arabi [Zanzibar and Pemba]	<mass, special - see page 29>	
gram	28	2.800 000 0E+01
oncia [France, 1800 definition]	<mass, special - see page 29>	
hectogram	1	1.000 000 0E+00
oncia [Italy, heavy]	<mass, special - see page 29>	
gram	36	3.600 000 0E+01
oncia [Italy, light]	<mass, special - see page 29>	
gram	25.2	2.520 000 0E+01
oncia [Italy, Milan]	<mass, special - see page 29>	
gram	100	1.000 000 0E+02
onckie [Iraq, ancient]	<mass, special - see page 29>	
gram	37.4	3.740 000 0E+01
one	<units>	
single	1	1.000 000 0E+00
unit	1	1.000 000 0E+00
one atom of carbon-12	<amount of substance>	
mole	<<< 1.660 540 2E−24	
number of atoms in 0.012 kg of carbon-12	<<< 1.660 540 2E−24	
oner [Hebrew, ancient, dry]	<volume, special - see page 29>	
liter	3.8	3.800 000 0E+00
ons [Indonesia]	<mass, special - see page 29>	
gram	30.88	3.088 000 0E+01

Convert From Convert To	<Type of Unit> Standard	Scientific
ons [Netherlands]	<mass, special - see page 29>	
gram	30.9	3.090 000 0E+01
ons [Surinam]	<mass, special - see page 29>	
gram	100	1.000 000 0E+02
onza [Argentina]	<mass, special - see page 29>	
gram	28.71	2.871 000 0E+01
onza [Chile]	<mass, special - see page 29>	
gram	28.75	2.875 000 0E+01
onza [Colombia]	<mass, special - see page 29>	
gram	31.25	3.125 000 0E+01
onza [Cuba]	<mass, special - see page 29>	
gram	28.756	2.875 600 0E+01
onza [Dominican Republic]	<mass, special - see page 29>	
gram	28.35	2.835 000 0E+01
onza [El Salvador]	<mass, special - see page 29>	
gram	28.75	2.875 000 0E+01
onza [Guatemala]	<mass, special - see page 29>	
gram	28.75	2.875 000 0E+01
onza [Honduras]	<volume, special - see page 29>	
centiliter	2.88	2.880 000 0E+00
onza [Honduras]	<mass, special - see page 29>	
gram	28.756	2.875 600 0E+01
onza [Mexico]	<mass, special - see page 29>	
gram	28.765	2.876 500 0E+01
onza [Nicaragua]	<mass, special - see page 29>	
gram	28.75	2.875 000 0E+01
onza [Paraguay]	<mass, special - see page 29>	
gram	28.69	2.869 000 0E+01
onza [Peru]	<mass, special - see page 29>	
gram	28.75	2.875 000 0E+01
onza [Philippines]	<mass, special - see page 29>	
gram	28.75	2.875 000 0E+01
onza [Spain]	<mass, special - see page 29>	
gram	28.756	2.875 600 0E+01
onza [Venezuela]	<mass, special - see page 29>	
gram	28.75	2.875 000 0E+01
open window unit	<sound absorption>	
square foot	1	1.000 000 0E+00
square meter	0.092 903	9.290 304 0E−02
opuia [Jordan, Nabulsi]	<mass, special - see page 29>	
gram	240.37	2.403 700 0E+02
opuia [Jordan, Shami]	<mass, special - see page 29>	
gram	213.66	2.136 600 0E+02
oqa [Islam]	<mass, special - see page 29>	
kilogram	1.254	1.254 000 0E+00
oqiya [Ethiopia]	<mass, special - see page 29>	
gram	25.9	2.590 000 0E+01
oqiya [Iraq, Baghdad]	<mass, special - see page 29>	
kilogram	1.042	1.042 000 0E+00
oqiya [Iraq, Istanbul]	<mass, special - see page 29>	
gram	320.75	3.207 500 0E+02
oqiya [Iraq, Mosul]	<mass, special - see page 29>	
gram	128.3	1.283 000 0E+02
oqiya [Jordan, Nabulsi]	<mass, special - see page 29>	
gram	240.4	2.404 000 0E+02

| Convert From | | <Type of Unit> |
Convert To	Standard	Scientific
oqiya [Jordan, Shami]	<mass, special - see page 29>	
gram	213.7	2.137 000 0E+02
oqiya [Lebanon]	<mass, special - see page 29>	
gram	213.7	2.137 000 0E+02
oqiya [Libya]	<mass, special - see page 29>	
gram	32.05	3.205 000 0E+01
oqiya [Somalia]	<mass, special - see page 29>	
gram	28	2.800 000 0E+01
oqiya [Sudan]	<mass, special - see page 29>	
gram	37.44	3.744 000 0E+01
oqiya [Syria]	<mass, special - see page 29>	
gram	213.7	2.137 000 0E+02
oquia [Ethiopia]	<mass, special - see page 29>	
gram	25.9	2.590 000 0E+01
oquia [Iraq, Baghdad]	<mass, special - see page 29>	
kilogram	1.042	1.042 000 0E+00
oquia [Iraq, Mosul]	<mass, special - see page 29>	
gram	128.3	1.283 000 0E+02
oquia [Jordan, Nabulsi]	<mass, special - see page 29>	
gram	240.4	2.404 000 0E+02
oquia [Jordan, Shami]	<mass, special - see page 29>	
gram	213.7	2.137 000 0E+02
oquia [Lebanon]	<mass, special - see page 29>	
gram	213.7	2.137 000 0E+02
oquia [Libya]	<mass, special - see page 29>	
gram	32.05	3.205 000 0E+01
oquia [Somalia]	<mass, special - see page 29>	
gram	28	2.800 000 0E+01
oquia [Sudan]	<mass, special - see page 29>	
gram	37.44	3.744 000 0E+01
oquia [Syria]	<mass, special - see page 29>	
gram	213.7	2.137 000 0E+02
ore [Iceland]	<mass, special - see page 29>	
gram	26.805	2.680 500 0E+01
ore [Norway]	<mass, special - see page 29>	
gram	26.805	2.680 500 0E+01
ore [Sweden]	<mass, special - see page 29>	
gram	26.805	2.680 500 0E+01
orguia [Greece, ancient]	<length, special - see page 29>	
meter	1.839	1.839 000 0E+00
orgyia [Greece, ancient]	<length, special - see page 29>	
meter	1.85	1.850 000 0E+00
orlong [Malaysia]	<area, special - see page 29>	
hectare	0.535	5.350 000 0E-01
orlong [Singapore]	<area, special - see page 29>	
hectare	0.535	5.350 000 0E-01
orna [Italy, wine]	<volume, special - see page 29>	
liter	57	5.700 000 0E+01
ort [Denmark]	<mass, special - see page 29>	
gram	0.5	5.000 000 0E-01
ort [Germany, liquid]	<volume, special - see page 29>	
milliliter	215	2.150 000 0E+02
ort [Sweden]	<mass, special - see page 29>	
gram	4.251 5	4.251 500 0E+00

osira [Portuguese India] — <mass, special - see page 29>
gram ---- 933.1 ---- 9.331 000 0E+02

osmin [Russia] — <volume, special - see page 29>
hectoliter ---- 1.05 ---- 1.050 000 0E+00

osmina [Russia] — <volume, special - see page 29>
hectoliter ---- 1.05 ---- 1.050 000 0E+00

ottava [Brazil, gold and silver] — <mass, special - see page 29>
gram ---- 3.6 ---- 3.600 000 0E+00

ottava [Italy, gold, silver and jewels] — <mass, special - see page 29>
gram ---- 1.7 ---- 1.700 000 0E+00

ottava [Portugal, gold and silver] — <mass, special - see page 29>
gram ---- 3.6 ---- 3.600 000 0E+00

ottinger [Finland] — <volume, special - see page 29>
liter ---- 15.71 ---- 1.571 000 0E+01

ottingkar [Denmark] — <volume, special - see page 29>
liter ---- 17.39 ---- 1.739 000 0E+01

ottinkar [Denmark] — <volume, special - see page 29>
liter ---- 17.39 ---- 1.739 000 0E+01

ouiba [Tunisia] — <volume, special - see page 29>
liter ---- 40 ---- 4.000 000 0E+01

oukeia [Morocco] — <mass, special - see page 29>
gram ---- 125 ---- 1.250 000 0E+02

ounce — <mass>

Convert To	Standard	Scientific
carat [international]	141.747 62	1.417 476 2E+02
carat [US, after 1913]	141.747 62	1.417 476 2E+02
dekagram	2.834 952 3	2.834 952 3E+00
drachm [UK, apothecary]	7.291 666 7	7.291 666 7E+00
dram [avoirdupois]	16	1.600 000 0E+01
dram [US, apothecary]	7.291 666 7	7.291 666 7E+00
grain	437.5	4.375 000 0E+02
kilogram	0.028 349 5	2.834 952 3E−02
ounce [avoirdupois]	1	1.000 000 0E+00
ounce [troy]	0.911 458 3	9.114 583 3E−01
pennyweight [troy]	18.229 167	1.822 916 7E+01
pound	0.062 5	6.250 000 0E−02
pound [apothecary]	0.075 954 9	7.595 486 1E−02
pound [avoirdupois]	0.062 5	6.250 000 0E−02
pound [international]	0.062 5	6.250 000 0E−02
pound [troy]	0.075 954 9	7.595 486 1E−02
pound [unified]	0.062 5	6.250 000 0E−02
scruple [UK]	21.875	2.187 500 0E+01
scruple [US, apothecary]	21.875	2.187 500 0E+01

ounce [apothecary] — <mass>

Convert To	Standard	Scientific
carat [international]	155.517 38	1.555 173 8E+02
carat [UK]	120	1.200 000 0E+02
carat [US, after 1913]	155.517 38	1.555 173 8E+02
dekagram	3.110 347 7	3.110 347 7E+00
drachm [UK, apothecary]	8	8.000 000 0E+00
dram [avoirdupois]	17.554 286	1.755 428 6E+01
dram [US, apothecary]	8	8.000 000 0E+00
grain	480	4.800 000 0E+02
grain [apothecary]	480	4.800 000 0E+02
kilogram	0.031 103 5	3.110 347 7E−02
ounce	1.097 142 9	1.097 142 9E+00
ounce [troy]	1	1.000 000 0E+00
pennyweight [troy]	20	2.000 000 0E+01
pound [apothecary]	0.083 333 3	8.333 333 3E−02
pound [avoirdupois]	0.068 571 4	6.857 142 9E−02
pound [troy]	0.083 333 3	8.333 333 3E−02
scruple [UK]	24	2.400 000 0E+01

	Standard	Scientific
scruple [US, apothecary]	24	2.400 000 0E+01
ton [UK, assay or assay, long]	0.952 147 3	9.521 472 5E−01
ton [US, assay or assay, short]	1.066 404 9	1.066 404 9E+00
ounce [avoirdupois]		**<mass>**
carat [international]	141.747 62	1.417 476 2E+02
carat [metric]	141.747 62	1.417 476 2E+02
carat [US, after 1913]	141.747 62	1.417 476 2E+02
dekagram	2.834 952 3	2.834 952 3E+00
drachm [UK, apothecary]	7.291 666 7	7.291 666 7E+00
dram [avoirdupois]	16	1.600 000 0E+01
dram [US, apothecary]	7.291 666 7	7.291 666 7E+00
grain	437.5	4.375 000 0E+02
grain [avoirdupois]	437.5	4.375 000 0E+02
grain [troy]	437.5	4.375 000 0E+02
kilogram	0.028 349 5	2.834 952 3E−02
ounce	1	1.000 000 0E+00
ounce [apothecary]	0.911 458 3	9.114 583 3E−01
ounce [troy]	0.911 458 3	9.114 583 3E−01
pennyweight [troy]	18.229 167	1.822 916 7E+01
pound [avoirdupois]	0.062 5	6.250 000 0E−02
pound [international]	0.062 5	6.250 000 0E−02
pound [troy]	0.075 954 9	7.595 486 1E−02
scruple [UK]	21.875	2.187 500 0E+01
scruple [US, apothecary]	21.875	2.187 500 0E+01
ounce [Ethiopia]		**<mass, special - see page 29>**
gram	25.9	2.590 000 0E+01
ounce [France, 1800 definition]		**<mass, special - see page 29>**
gram	100	1.000 000 0E+02
ounce [France]		**<mass, special - see page 29>**
gram	31.25	3.125 000 0E+01
ounce [Holland, troy]		**<mass, special - see page 29>**
gram	30.75	3.075 000 0E+01
ounce [Iraq, ancient]		**<mass, special - see page 29>**
gram	37.4	3.740 000 0E+01
ounce [Italy, Rome]		**<mass, special - see page 29>**
gram	26.805	2.680 500 0E+01
ounce [metric]		**<mass>**
kilogram	0.025	2.500 000 0E−02
ounce [Norway]		**<mass, special - see page 29>**
gram	31.1	3.110 000 0E+01
ounce [Pakistan]		**<mass, special - see page 29>**
gram	28.349 52	2.834 952 0E+01
ounce [Russia, apothecary]		**<mass, special - see page 29>**
gram	29.86	2.986 000 0E+01
ounce [Syria, gold and silver]		**<mass, special - see page 29>**
gram	29.75	2.975 000 0E+01
ounce [troy]		**<mass>**
carat [international]	155.517 38	1.555 173 8E+02
carat [US, after 1913]	155.517 38	1.555 173 8E+02
dekagram	3.110 347 7	3.110 347 7E+00
drachm [UK, apothecary]	8	8.000 000 0E+00
dram [avoirdupois]	17.554 286	1.755 428 6E+01
dram [US, apothecary]	8	8.000 000 0E+00
grain [avoirdupois]	480	4.800 000 0E+02
grain [troy]	480	4.800 000 0E+02
kilogram	0.031 103 5	3.110 347 7E−02
ounce	1.097 142 9	1.097 142 9E+00
ounce [apothecary]	1	1.000 000 0E+00
ounce [avoirdupois]	1.097 142 9	1.097 142 9E+00
pennyweight [troy]	20	2.000 000 0E+01

	Standard	Scientific
pound	0.068 571 4	6.857 142 9E–02
pound [apothecary]	0.083 333 3	8.333 333 3E–02
pound [troy]	0.083 333 3	8.333 333 3E–02
scruple [UK]	24	2.400 000 0E+01
scruple [US, apothecary]	24	2.400 000 0E+01
ton [UK, assay or assay, long]	0.952 147 3	9.521 472 5E–01
ton [US, assay or assay, short]	1.066 404 9	1.066 404 9E+00

ounce [UK, liquid]		**<volume>**
barrel [UK]	0.000 173 6	1.736 111 1E–04
barrel [US, liquid]	0.000 238 3	2.382 837 2E–04
barrel [US, petroleum]	0.000 178 7	1.787 127 9E–04
centiliter	2.841 306 3	2.841 306 3E+00
cubic foot	0.001 003 4	1.003 397 8E–03
cubic inch	1.733 871 5	1.733 871 5E+00
cubic meter	0.000 028 4	2.841 306 3E–05
cup [Canada, measuring]	0.125	1.250 000 0E–01
cup [US, measuring]	0.120 095	1.200 949 9E–01
drachm [UK, liquid]	8	8.000 000 0E+00
dram [Canada, liquid]	8	8.000 000 0E+00
dram [US, liquid]	7.686 079 5	7.686 079 5E+00
drop [US, liquid]	345.873 58	3.458 735 8E+02
gallon [Canada, liquid]	0.006 25	6.250 000 0E–03
gallon [UK, dry or liquid]	0.006 25	6.250 000 0E–03
gallon [US, liquid]	0.007 505 9	7.505 937 0E–03
gill [UK]	0.2	2.000 000 0E–01
gill [US]	0.240 19	2.401 899 9E–01
lambda	28,413.063	2.841 306 3E+04
liter	0.028 413 1	2.841 306 3E–02
minim [UK]	480	4.800 000 0E+02
minim [US]	461.164 77	4.611 647 7E+02
ounce [US, liquid]	0.960 759 9	9.607 599 4E–01
pint [UK]	0.05	5.000 000 0E–02
pint [US, liquid]	0.060 047 5	6.004 749 6E–02
quart [UK]	0.025	2.500 000 0E–02
quart [US, liquid]	0.030 023 7	3.002 374 8E–02
scruple [UK, liquid]	24	2.400 000 0E+01
tablespoon [Canada, measuring]	2.000 003 4	2.000 003 4E+00
tablespoon [US, measuring]	1.921 519 9	1.921 519 9E+00
teaspoon [Canada, measuring]	6.000 010 2	6.000 010 2E+00
teaspoon [US, measuring]	5.764 559 6	5.764 559 6E+00
Winchester wine gallon [UK]	0.007 505 9	7.505 937 0E–03

ounce [US, liquid]		**<volume>**
barrel [UK]	0.000 180 7	1.807 018 6E–04
barrel [US, liquid]	0.000 248	2.480 158 7E–04
barrel [US, petroleum]	0.000 186	1.860 119 0E–04
centiliter	2.957 353	2.957 353 0E+00
cubic foot	0.001 044 4	1.044 379 3E–03
cubic inch	1.804 687 5	1.804 687 5E+00
cubic meter	0.000 029 6	2.957 353 0E–05
cup [Canada, measuring]	0.130 105 3	1.301 053 4E–01
cup [metric]	0.147 867 7	1.478 676 5E–01
cup [US, measuring]	0.125	1.250 000 0E–01
drachm [UK, liquid]	8.326 741 8	8.326 741 8E+00
dram [Canada, liquid]	8.326 741 8	8.326 741 8E+00
dram [US, liquid]	8	8.000 000 0E+00
drop [US, liquid]	360	3.600 000 0E+02
fifth [US, liquid]	0.039 062 5	3.906 250 0E–02
gallon [Canada, liquid]	0.006 505 3	6.505 267 1E–03
gallon [UK, dry or liquid]	0.006 505 3	6.505 267 1E–03
gallon [US, liquid]	0.007 812 5	7.812 500 0E–03
gill [UK]	0.208 168 6	2.081 685 5E–01
gill [US]	0.25	2.500 000 0E–01
jigger [US, liquid]	0.666 666 7	6.666 666 7E–01

Convert From		<Type of Unit>
Convert To	Standard	Scientific

lambda	29,573.53	2.957 353 0E+04
liter	0.029 573 5	2.957 353 0E-02
minim [UK]	499.604 51	4.996 045 1E+02
minim [US]	480	4.800 000 0E+02
ounce [UK, liquid]	1.040 842 7	1.040 842 7E+00
pint [UK]	0.052 042 1	5.204 213 7E-02
pint [US, liquid]	0.062 5	6.250 000 0E-02
pony [US, liquid]	1	1.000 000 0E+00
quart [UK]	0.026 021 1	2.602 106 8E-02
quart [US, liquid]	0.031 25	3.125 000 0E-02
scruple [UK, liquid]	24.980 226	2.498 022 6E+01
shot [US, liquid]	1	1.000 000 0E+00
tablespoon [Canada, measuring]	2.081 689	2.081 689 0E+00
tablespoon [US, measuring]	2	2.000 000 0E+00
teaspoon [Canada, measuring]	6.245 067	6.245 067 0E+00
teaspoon [US, measuring]	6	6.000 000 0E+00

ounce foot/square second — <force>

newton	0.008 640 9	8.640 934 6E-03
ouncedal	1	1.000 000 0E+00
pound foot/square second	0.062 5	6.250 000 0E-02
poundal	0.062 5	6.250 000 0E-02

ounce square foot — <moment of inertia of a mass>

gram square meter	2.633 756 9	2.633 756 9E+00
kilogram square meter	0.002 633 8	2.633 756 9E-03
kilopond centimeter square second	0.026 856 8	2.685 684 6E-02
ounce square inch	144	1.440 000 0E+02
pound square inch	9	9.000 000 0E+00

ounce square inch — <moment of inertia of a mass>

gram square centimeter	182.899 78	1.828 997 8E+02
kilogram square meter	0.000 018 3	1.828 997 8E-05
pond centimeter square second	0.186 505 9	1.865 058 7E-01
pound square inch	0.062 5	6.250 000 0E-02
slug square inch	0.001 942 6	1.942 559 4E-03

ounce-force — <force>

crinal	2.780 138 5	2.780 138 5E+00
dyne	27,801.385 1	2.780 138 5E+04
grain-force	437.5	4.375 000 0E+02
gram-force	28.349 523 1	2.834 952 3E+01
newton	0.278 013 9	2.780 138 5E-01
pond	28.349 523 1	2.834 952 3E+01
pound-force	0.062 5	6.250 000 0E-02
poundal	2.010 878	2.010 878 0E+00

ounce-force foot square second — <moment of inertia of a mass>

gram-force meter square second	8.640 934 6	8.640 934 6E+00
kilogram square meter	0.084 738 6	8.473 862 2E-02
ounce-force inch square second	12	1.200 000 0E+01
pond meter square second	8.640 934 6	8.640 934 6E+00
pound square foot	2.010 878	2.010 878 0E+00
slug square inch	9	9.000 000 0E+00

ounce-force inch square second — <moment of inertia of a mass>

gram square meter	7.061 551 8	7.061 551 8E+00
kilogram square meter	0.007 061 6	7.061 551 8E-03
kilopond centimeter square second	0.072 007 8	7.200 778 9E-02
ounce square foot	2.681 170 7	2.681 170 7E+00
pound square inch	24.130 536	2.413 053 6E+01

ounce-force/foot — <surface tension>

dyne/centimeter	912.118 93	9.121 189 3E+02
gram-force/meter	93.010 246	9.301 024 6E+01
millinewton/centimeter	9.121 189 3	9.121 189 3E+00
newton/meter	0.912 118 9	9.121 189 3E-01
ounce-force/inch	0.083 333 3	8.333 333 3E-02

| Convert From | | <Type of Unit> |
| Convert To | Standard | Scientific |

pound-force/foot	0.062 5	6.250 000 0E-02
ounce-force/inch		**<surface tension>**
dyne/centimeter	10,945.427	1.094 542 7E+04
gram-force/centimeter	11.161 23	1.116 123 0E+01
kilogram-force/meter	1.116 123	1.116 123 0E+00
kilopond/meter	1.116 123	1.116 123 0E+00
newton/meter	10.945 427	1.094 542 7E+01
ounce-force/foot	12	1.200 000 0E+01
pound-force/foot	0.75	7.500 000 0E-01
ounce-force/square inch		**<pressure>**
atmosphere [standard]	0.004 252 9	4.252 872 7E-03
atmosphere [technical]	0.004 394 2	4.394 184 9E-03
bar	0.004 309 2	4.309 223 3E-03
barye [France]	4,309.223 3	4.309 223 3E+03
centimeter of mercury [0 °C, by convention]	0.323 218 3	3.232 182 8E-01
centimeter of water [4 °C, by convention]	4.394 184 9	4.394 184 9E+00
dyne/square centimeter	4,309.223 3	4.309 223 3E+03
gram-force/square centimeter	4.394 184 9	4.394 184 9E+00
hectopascal	4.309 223 3	4.309 223 3E+00
inch of mercury [0 °C, by convention]	0.127 251 3	1.272 512 9E-01
inch of water [4 °C, by convention]	1.729 994	1.729 994 0E+00
kilogram-force/square meter	43.941 849	4.394 184 9E+01
kilopond/square meter	43.941 849	4.394 184 9E+01
kip/square foot	0.009	9.000 000 0E-03
millibar	4.309 223 3	4.309 223 3E+00
millihg	3.232 182 8	3.232 182 8E+00
millimeter of mercury [0 °C, by convention]	3.232 182 8	3.232 182 8E+00
millimeter of water [4 °C, by convention]	43.941 849	4.394 184 9E+01
newton/square meter	430.922 33	4.309 223 3E+02
pascal	430.922 33	4.309 223 3E+02
pound-force/square foot	9	9.000 000 0E+00
poundal/square foot	289.566 44	2.895 664 4E+02
ton-force/square foot [long]	0.004 017 9	4.017 857 1E-03
ton-force/square foot [short]	0.004 5	4.500 000 0E-03
ton-force/square meter [metric]	0.043 941 8	4.394 184 9E-02
torr	3.232 183	3.232 183 0E+00
ounce/cubic foot		**<density>**
grain/cubic inch	0.253 182 9	2.531 828 7E-01
gram/cubic decimeter	1.001 154	1.001 154 0E+00
gram/liter	1.001 154	1.001 154 0E+00
kilogram/cubic meter	1.001 154	1.001 154 0E+00
milligram/cubic centimeter	1.001 154	1.001 154 0E+00
milligram/milliliter	1.001 154	1.001 154 0E+00
ounce/cubic foot [troy]	0.911 458 3	9.114 583 3E-01
ounce/cubic yard	27	2.700 000 0E+01
pound/cubic yard	1.687 5	1.687 500 0E+00
slug/cubic yard	0.052 449 1	5.244 910 3E-02
ton/cubic yard [short]	0.000 843 8	8.437 500 0E-04
tonne/cubic meter	0.001 001 2	1.001 154 0E-03
ounce/cubic foot [troy]		**<density>**
grain/cubic inch	0.277 777 8	2.777 777 8E-01
gram/liter	1.098 408 9	1.098 408 9E+00
kilogram/cubic meter	1.098 408 9	1.098 408 9E+00
milligram/milliliter	1.098 408 9	1.098 408 9E+00
ounce/cubic foot	1.097 142 9	1.097 142 9E+00
ounce/cubic yard	29.622 857	2.962 285 7E+01
ounce/cubic yard [troy]	27	2.700 000 0E+01
pound/cubic yard	1.851 428 6	1.851 428 6E+00
slug/cubic yard	0.057 544 2	5.754 415 9E-02
ton/cubic yard [short]	0.000 925 7	9.257 142 9E-04
tonne/cubic meter	0.001 098 4	1.098 408 9E-03

ounce/cubic inch   \<density\>

	Standard	Scientific
grain/cubic inch	437.5	4.375 000 0E+02
gram/cubic centimeter	1.729 994	1.729 994 0E+00
kilogram/cubic meter	1,729.994	1.729 994 0E+03
kilogram/liter	1.729 994	1.729 994 0E+00
megagram/cubic meter	1.729 994	1.729 994 0E+00
pound/cubic foot	108	1.080 000 0E+02
slug/cubic foot	3.356 742 6	3.356 742 6E+00
ton/cubic yard [short]	1.458	1.458 000 0E+00
tonne/cubic meter	1.729 994	1.729 994 0E+00

ounce/cubic inch [troy]   \<density\>

	Standard	Scientific
grain/cubic inch	480	4.800 000 0E+02
gram/milliliter	1.898 050 6	1.898 050 6E+00
kilogram/cubic meter	1,898.050 6	1.898 050 6E+03
kilogram/liter	1.898 050 6	1.898 050 6E+00
megagram/cubic meter	1.898 050 6	1.898 050 6E+00
ounce/cubic inch	1.097 142 9	1.097 142 9E+00
ounce/gallon [troy/US, liquid]	231	2.310 000 0E+02
pound/cubic foot	118.491 43	1.184 914 3E+02
slug/cubic foot	3.682 826 2	3.682 826 2E+00
ton/cubic foot [short]	0.059 245 7	5.924 571 4E−02
ton/cubic yard [short]	1.599 634 3	1.599 634 3E+00
tonne/cubic meter	1.898 050 6	1.898 050 6E+00

ounce/cubic yard   \<density\>

	Standard	Scientific
grain/cubic foot	16.203 704	1.620 370 4E+01
gram/cubic meter	37.079 776	3.707 977 6E+01
kilogram/cubic meter	0.037 079 8	3.707 977 6E−02
milligram/liter	37.079 776	3.707 977 6E+01
ounce/cubic foot	0.037 037	3.703 703 7E−02
ounce/cubic yard [troy]	0.911 458 3	9.114 583 3E−01
pound/cubic yard	0.062 5	6.250 000 0E−02
slug/cubic yard	0.001 942 6	1.942 559 4E−03
ton/cubic yard [short]	0.000 031 3	3.125 000 0E−05
tonne/cubic meter	0.000 037 1	3.707 977 6E−05

ounce/cubic yard [troy]   \<density\>

	Standard	Scientific
grain/cubic foot	17.777 778	1.777 777 8E+01
grain/gallon [-/US, liquid]	2.376 543 2	2.376 543 2E+00
gram/cubic meter	40.681 812	4.068 181 2E+01
kilogram/cubic meter	0.040 681 8	4.068 181 2E−02
milligram/liter	40.681 812	4.068 181 2E+01
ounce/cubic yard	1.097 142 9	1.097 142 9E+00
pound/cubic yard	0.068 571 4	6.857 142 9E−02
slug/cubic yard	0.002 131 3	2.131 265 2E−03
ton/cubic yard [short]	0.000 034 3	3.428 571 4E−05
tonne/cubic meter	0.000 040 7	4.068 181 2E−05

ounce/day [UK, liquid]   \<flow rate, volume basis\>

	Standard	Scientific
barrel/day [UK]	0.000 173 6	1.736 111 1E−04
barrel/day [US, federal]	0.000 242 1	2.421 270 0E−04
barrel/day [US, liquid]	0.000 238 3	2.382 837 2E−04
barrel/day [US, petroleum]	0.000 178 7	1.787 127 9E−04
centiliter/day	2.841 306 3	2.841 306 3E+00
cubic centimeter/hour	1.183 877 6	1.183 877 6E+00
cubic decimeter/day	0.028 413 1	2.841 306 3E−02
cubic foot/day	0.001 003 4	1.003 397 8E−03
cubic inch/day	1.733 871 5	1.733 871 5E+00
cubic millimeter/minute	19.731 293 4	1.973 129 3E+01
deciliter/day	0.284 130 6	2.841 306 3E−01
dekaliter/day	0.002 841 3	2.841 306 3E−03
gallon/day [UK]	0.006 25	6.250 000 0E−03
gallon/day [US, liquid]	0.007 505 9	7.505 937 0E−03
lambda/minute	19.731 293 4	1.973 129 3E+01
liter/day	0.028 413 1	2.841 306 3E−02

	Standard	Scientific
liter/day [pre-1964]	0.028 412 3	2.841 226 7E–02
milliliter/hour	1.183 877 6	1.183 877 6E+00
ounce/day [US, liquid]	0.960 759 9	9.607 599 4E–01
ounce/hour [UK, liquid]	0.041 666 7	4.166 666 7E–02
ounce/hour [US, liquid]	0.040 031 7	4.003 164 4E–02

ounce/day [US, liquid] \<flow rate, volume basis\>

	Standard	Scientific
barrel/day [UK]	0.000 180 7	1.807 018 6E–04
barrel/day [US, federal]	0.000 252	2.520 161 3E–04
barrel/day [US, liquid]	0.000 248	2.480 158 7E–04
barrel/day [US, petroleum]	0.000 186	1.860 119 1E–04
centiliter/day	2.957 353	2.957 353 0E+00
cubic centimeter/hour	1.232 230	1.232 230 4E+00
cubic foot/day	0.001 044 4	1.044 379 3E–03
cubic inch/day	1.804 687 5	1.804 687 5E+00
cubic meter/second	\<\<\<	3.422 862 2E–10
cubic millimeter/minute	20.537 173 3	2.053 717 3E+01
deciliter/day	0.295 735 3	2.957 353 0E–01
dekaliter/day	0.002 957 4	2.957 353 0E–03
gallon/day [UK]	0.006 505 3	6.505 267 1E–03
gallon/day [US, liquid]	0.007 812 5	7.812 500 0E–03
lambda/minute	20.537 173 3	2.053 717 3E+01
liter/day	0.029 573 5	2.957 353 0E–02
liter/day [pre-1964]	0.029 572 7	2.957 270 2E–02
milliliter/hour	1.232 230	1.232 230 4E+00
ounce/day [UK, liquid]	1.040 842 7	1.040 842 7E+00

ounce/foot \<linear density\>

	Standard	Scientific
denier	837,092.22	8.370 922 2E+05
drex	930,102.46	9.301 024 6E+05
kilogram/meter	0.093 010 2	9.301 024 6E–02
kilotex	93.010 246	9.301 024 6E+01
ounce/yard	3	3.000 000 0E+00
pli	0.005 208 3	5.208 333 3E–03
pound/yard	0.187 5	1.875 000 0E–01
tex	93,010.246	9.301 024 6E+04

ounce/gallon [-/UK, liquid] \<density\>

	Standard	Scientific
grain/cubic inch	1.577 034 4	1.577 034 4E+00
grain/gallon [-/UK, liquid]	437.5	4.375 000 0E+02
grain/gallon [-/US, liquid]	364.294 96	3.642 949 6E+02
kilogram/cubic meter	6.236 023 3	6.236 023 3E+00
ounce/cubic foot	6.228 835 5	6.228 835 5E+00
pound/cubic foot	0.389 302 2	3.893 022 2E–01
pound/gallon [-/UK, liquid]	0.062 5	6.250 000 0E–02
pound/gallon [-/US, liquid]	0.052 042 1	5.204 213 7E–02
slug/cubic yard	0.326 696 8	3.266 968 4E–01
ton/cubic yard [short]	0.005 255 6	5.255 579 9E–03
tonne/cubic meter	0.006 236	6.236 023 3E–03

ounce/gallon [-/US, liquid] \<density\>

	Standard	Scientific
grain/cubic inch	1.893 939 4	1.893 939 4E+00
gram/cubic decimeter	7.489 151 7	7.489 151 7E+00
gram/liter	7.489 151 7	7.489 151 7E+00
kilogram/cubic meter	7.489 151 7	7.489 151 7E+00
milligram/milliliter	7.489 151 7	7.489 151 7E+00
ounce/cubic foot	7.480 519 5	7.480 519 5E+00
pound/cubic yard	12.623 377	1.262 337 7E+01
pound/gallon [-/UK, liquid]	0.075 059 4	7.505 937 0E–02
pound/gallon [-/US, liquid]	0.062 5	6.250 000 0E–02
slug/cubic foot	0.014 531 4	1.453 135 3E–02
ton/cubic yard [short]	0.006 311 7	6.311 688 3E–03
tonne/cubic meter	0.007 489 2	7.489 151 7E–03

ounce/gallon [troy/UK, liquid] \<density\>

	Standard	Scientific
grain/cubic inch	1.730 232 1	1.730 232 1E+00
grain/gallon [-/UK, liquid]	480	4.800 000 0E+02

grain/gallon [-/US, liquid]	399.683 61	3.996 836 1E+02
gram/liter	6.841 808 4	6.841 808 4E+00
kilogram/cubic meter	6.841 808 4	6.841 808 4E+00
ounce/cubic foot	6.833 922 3	6.833 922 3E+00
ounce/cubic foot [troy]	6.228 835 5	6.228 835 5E+00
ounce/gallon [-/UK, liquid]	1.097 142 9	1.097 142 9E+00
ounce/gallon [troy/US, liquid]	0.832 674 2	8.326 741 8E-01
pound/cubic yard	11.532 244	1.153 224 4E+01
slug/cubic yard	0.358 433 1	3.584 331 0E-01
ton/cubic yard [short]	0.005 766 1	5.766 122 0E-03

ounce/gallon [troy/US, liquid] <density>

grain/cubic inch	2.077 922 1	2.077 922 1E+00
grain/gallon [-/US, liquid]	480	4.800 000 0E+02
gram/liter	8.216 669 3	8.216 669 3E+00
kilogram/cubic meter	8.216 669 3	8.216 669 3E+00
ounce/cubic foot	8.207 198 5	8.207 198 5E+00
ounce/cubic foot [troy]	7.480 519 5	7.480 519 5E+00
ounce/gallon [troy/UK, liquid]	1.200 949 9	1.200 949 9E+00
pound/cubic yard	13.849 647	1.384 964 7E+01
slug/cubic yard	0.430 460 2	4.304 602 0E-01
ton/cubic yard [short]	0.006 924 8	6.924 823 7E-03
tonne/cubic meter	0.008 216 7	8.216 669 3E-03

ounce/hour [UK, liquid] <flow rate, volume basis>

barrel/day [UK]	0.004 166 7	4.166 666 7E-03
barrel/day [US, federal]	0.005 811 0	5.811 048 0E-03
barrel/day [US, liquid]	0.005 718 8	5.718 809 2E-03
barrel/day [US, petroleum]	0.004 289 1	4.289 106 9E-03
centiliter/hour	2.841 306 3	2.841 306 3E+00
cubic centimeter/hour	28.413 062 5	2.841 306 3E+01
cubic foot/day	0.024 081 5	2.408 154 8E-02
cubic inch/hour	1.733 871 5	1.733 871 5E+00
cubic millimeter/second	7.892 517 4	7.892 517 4E+00
deciliter/day	6.819 135	6.819 135 0E+00
gallon/day [UK]	0.15	1.500 000 0E-01
gallon/day [US, liquid]	0.180 142 5	1.801 424 9E-01
hectoliter/day	0.006 819 1	6.819 135 0E-03
lambda/second	7.892 517 4	7.892 517 4E+00
liter/day	0.681 913 5	6.819 135 0E-01
liter/day [pre-1964]	0.681 894 4	6.818 944 1E-01
milliliter/hour	28.413 062 5	2.841 306 3E+01
ounce/day [UK, liquid]	24	2.400 000 0E+01
ounce/day [US, liquid]	23.058 239	2.305 823 9E+01
ounce/hour [US, liquid]	0.960 759 9	9.607 599 4E-01

ounce/hour [US, liquid] <flow rate, volume basis>

barrel/day [UK]	0.004 336 8	4.336 844 7E-03
barrel/day [US, federal]	0.006 048 4	6.048 387 1E-03
barrel/day [US, liquid]	0.005 952 4	5.952 381 0E-03
barrel/day [US, petroleum]	0.004 464 3	4.464 285 7E-03
centiliter/hour	2.957 353	2.957 353 0E+00
cubic centimeter/hour	29.573 529 6	2.957 353 0E+01
cubic decimeter/day	0.709 764 7	7.097 647 1E-01
cubic foot/day	0.025 065 1	2.506 510 4E-02
cubic inch/hour	1.804 687 5	1.804 687 5E+00
cubic meter/second	<<<	8.214 869 3E-09
cubic millimeter/second	8.214 869 3	8.214 869 3E+00
deciliter/day	7.097 647 1	7.097 647 1E+00
gallon/day [UK]	0.156 126 4	1.561 264 1E-01
gallon/day [US, liquid]	0.187 5	1.875 000 0E-01
hectoliter/day	0.007 097 6	7.097 647 1E-03
lambda/second	8.214 869 3	8.214 869 3E+00
liter/day	0.709 764 7	7.097 647 1E-01
liter/day [pre-1964]	0.709 744 8	7.097 448 4E-01
milliliter/hour	29.573 529 6	2.957 353 0E+01

	Standard	Scientific
ounce/day [UK, liquid]	24.980 226	2.498 022 6E+01
ounce/day [US, liquid]	24	2.400 000 0E+01
ounce/hour [UK, liquid]	1.040 842 7	1.040 842 7E+00
ounce/inch		**\<linear density\>**
denier	>>>	1.004 510 7E+07
drex	>>>	1.116 123 0E+07
kilogram/meter	1.116 123	1.116 123 0E+00
ounce/foot	12	1.200 000 0E+01
pli	0.062 5	6.250 000 0E-02
pound/yard	2.25	2.250 000 0E+00
tex	1,116,123	1.116 123 0E+06
ounce/minute [UK, liquid]		**\<flow rate, volume basis\>**
barrel/day [UK]	0.25	2.500 000 0E-01
barrel/day [US, federal]	0.348 662 9	3.486 628 8E-01
barrel/day [US, liquid]	0.343 128 6	3.431 285 5E-01
barrel/day [US, petroleum]	0.257 346 4	2.573 464 1E-01
centiliter/minute	2.841 306 3	2.841 306 3E+00
cubic centimeter/minute	28.413 062 5	2.841 306 3E+01
cubic decimeter/hour	1.704 783 8	1.704 783 8E+00
cubic foot/day	1.444 892 9	1.444 892 9E+00
cubic inch/minute	1.733 871 5	1.733 871 5E+00
cubic millimeter/second	473.551 042	4.735 510 4E+02
cubic yard/day	0.053 514 6	5.351 455 1E-02
deciliter/hour	17.047 837 5	1.704 783 8E+01
dekaliter/day	4.091 481	4.091 481 0E+00
gallon/day [UK]	9	9.000 000 0E+00
gallon/day [US, liquid]	10.808 549 3	1.080 854 9E+01
hectoliter/day	0.409 148 1	4.091 481 0E-01
kiloliter/day	0.040 914 8	4.091 481 0E-02
lambda/second	473.551 042	4.735 510 4E+02
liter/hour	1.704 783 8	1.704 783 8E+00
liter/hour [pre-1964]	1.704 736	1.704 736 0E+00
milliliter/minute	28.413 062 5	2.841 306 3E+01
ounce/hour [UK, liquid]	60	6.000 000 0E+01
ounce/hour [US, liquid]	57.645 596	5.764 559 6E+01
ounce/minute [US, liquid]	0.960 759 9	9.607 599 4E-01
stere/day	0.040 914 8	4.091 481 0E-02
thousand cubic foot/day	0.001 444 9	1.444 892 9E-03
ounce/minute [US, liquid]		**\<flow rate, volume basis\>**
barrel/day [UK]	0.260 210 7	2.602 106 8E-01
barrel/day [US, federal]	0.362 903 2	3.629 032 3E-01
barrel/day [US, liquid]	0.357 142 9	3.571 428 6E-01
barrel/day [US, petroleum]	0.267 857 1	2.678 571 4E-01
centiliter/minute	2.957 353	2.957 353 0E+00
cubic centimeter/minute	29.573 529 6	2.957 353 0E+01
cubic decimeter/hour	1.774 411 8	1.774 411 8E+00
cubic foot/day	1.503 906 3	1.503 906 3E+00
cubic inch/minute	1.804 687 5	1.804 687 5E+00
cubic meter/day	0.042 585 9	4.258 588 3E-02
cubic meter/second	0.000 000 0	4.928 921 6E-07
cubic millimeter/second	492.892 159	4.928 921 6E+02
cubic yard/day	0.055 700 2	5.570 023 2E-02
deciliter/hour	17.744 117 7	1.774 411 8E+01
dekaliter/day	4.258 588 3	4.258 588 3E+00
gallon/day [UK]	9.367 584 6	9.367 584 6E+00
gallon/day [US, liquid]	11.25	1.125 000 0E+01
hectoliter/day	0.425 858 8	4.258 588 3E-01
kiloliter/day	0.042 585 9	4.258 588 3E-02
liter/hour	1.774 411 8	1.774 411 8E+00
liter/hour [pre-1964]	1.774 362 1	1.774 362 1E+00
milliliter/minute	29.573 529 6	2.957 353 0E+01
ounce/hour [UK, liquid]	62.450 564	6.245 056 4E+01
ounce/hour [US, liquid]	60	6.000 000 0E+01

	Standard	Scientific
ounce/minute [UK, liquid]	1.040 842 7	1.040 842 7E+00
stere/day	0.042 585 9	4.258 588 2E-02
thousand cubic foot/day	0.001 503 9	1.503 906 3E-03

ounce/second [UK, liquid] — \<flow rate, volume basis\>

	Standard	Scientific
acre foot/day	0.001 990 2	1.990 210 6E-03
acre foot/day [US, survey]	0.001 990 2	1.990 198 6E-03
acre inch/day	0.023 882 5	2.388 252 7E-02
barrel/day [UK]	15	1.500 000 0E+01
barrel/day [US, federal]	20.919 772 9	2.091 977 3E+01
barrel/day [US, liquid]	20.587 713	2.058 771 3E+01
barrel/day [US, petroleum]	15.440 784 8	1.544 078 5E+01
centiliter/second	2.841 306 3	2.841 306 3E+00
cubic centimeter/second	28.413 062 5	2.841 306 3E+01
cubic decimeter/minute	1.704 783 8	1.704 783 8E+00
cubic foot/hour	3.612 232 2	3.612 232 2E+00
cubic inch/second	1.733 871 5	1.733 871 5E+00
cubic meter/day	2.454 888 6	2.454 888 6E+00
cubic meter/second	0.000 028 4	2.841 306 3E-05
cubic yard/day	3.210 873 1	3.210 873 1E+00
dekaliter/hour	10.228 702 5	1.022 870 3E+01
deciliter/minute	17.047 837 5	1.704 783 8E+00
gallon/hour [UK]	22.5	2.250 000 0E+01
gallon/hour [US, liquid]	27.021 373 3	2.702 137 3E+01
hectoliter/hour	1.022 870 3	1.022 870 3E+00
kiloliter/day	2.454 888 6	2.454 888 6E+00
liter/minute	1.704 783 8	1.704 783 8E+00
liter/minute [pre-1964]	1.704 736	1.704 736 0E+00
milliliter/second	28.413 062 5	2.841 306 3E+01
ounce/minute [UK, liquid]	60	6.000 000 0E+01
ounce/minute [US, liquid]	57.645 596	5.764 559 6E+01
ounce/second [US, liquid]	0.960 759 9	9.607 599 4E-01
petrograd standard/day	0.525 415 6	5.254 155 9E-01
stere/day	2.454 888 6	2.454 888 6E+00

ounce/second [US, liquid] — \<flow rate, volume basis\>

	Standard	Scientific
acre foot/day	0.002 071 5	2.071 496 2E-03
acre foot/day [US, survey]	0.002 071 5	2.071 483 8E-03
acre inch/day	0.024 858	2.485 795 5E-02
barrel/day [UK]	15.612 641	1.561 264 1E+01
barrel/day [US, federal]	21.774 193 5	2.177 419 4E+01
barrel/day [US, liquid]	21.428 571 4	2.142 857 1E+01
barrel/day [US, petroleum]	16.071 428 6	1.607 142 9E+01
centiliter/second	2.957 353	2.957 353 0E+00
cubic centimeter/second	29.573 529 6	2.957 353 0E+01
cubic decimeter/minute	1.774 411 8	1.774 411 8E+00
cubic decimeter/second	0.029 573 5	2.957 353 0E-02
cubic foot/hour	3.759 765 6	3.759 765 6E+00
cubic inch/second	1.804 687 5	1.804 687 5E+00
cubic meter/day	2.555 153	2.555 153 0E+00
cubic mile/second	<<<	6.130 137 9E-10
cubic yard/day	3.342 013 9	3.342 013 9E+00
deciliter/minute	17.744 117 7	1.774 411 8E+00
dekaliter/hour	10.646 470 6	1.064 647 1E+01
gallon/hour [UK]	23.418 961 4	2.341 896 1E+01
gallon/hour [US, liquid]	28.125	2.812 500 0E+01
hectoliter/hour	1.064 647 1	1.064 647 1E+00
kiloliter/day	2.555 153	2.555 153 0E+00
liter/minute	1.774 411 8	1.774 411 8E+00
liter/minute [pre-1964]	1.774 362	1.774 362 0E+00
milliliter/second	29.573 529 6	2.957 353 0E+01
ounce/minute [UK, liquid]	62.450 564	6.245 056 4E+01
ounce/minute [US, liquid]	60	6.000 000 0E+01
ounce/second [UK, liquid]	1.040 842 7	1.040 842 7E+00
petrograd standard/day	0.546 875	5.468 750 0E-01

	Standard	Scientific
stere/day	2.555 153	2.555 153 0E+00
thousand cubic foot/day	0.090 234 4	9.023 437 5E-02
ounce/square foot		**<surface density>**
grain/square inch	3.038 194 4	3.038 194 4E+00
kilogram/are	30.515 173	3.051 517 3E+01
kilogram/square meter	0.305 151 7	3.051 517 3E-01
ounce/square yard	9	9.000 000 0E+00
pound/acre	2,722.5	2.722 500 0E+03
pound/square yard	0.562 5	5.625 000 0E-01
slug/square yard	0.017 483	1.748 303 4E-02
ton/square yard [short]	0.000 281 3	2.812 502 0E-04
tonne/square meter	0.000 305 2	3.051 517 3E-04
ounce/square foot second		**<flow rate/unit area, mass basis>**
gram/square meter second	305.151 73	3.051 517 3E+02
kilogram/are second	30.515 173	3.051 517 3E+01
kilogram/square meter second	0.305 151 7	3.051 517 3E-01
pound/square foot second	0.062 5	6.250 000 0E-02
ounce/square inch		**<surface density>**
grain/square inch	437.5	4.375 000 0E+02
gram/square centimeter	4.394 184 9	4.394 184 9E+00
kilogram/are	4,394.184 9	4.394 184 9E+03
kilogram/square meter	43.941 849	4.394 184 9E+01
ounce/square foot	144	1.440 000 0E+02
pound/square foot	9	9.000 000 0E+00
slug/square yard	2.517 557	2.517 557 0E+00
ton/square foot [short]	0.004 5	4.500 000 0E-03
ton/square yard [short]	0.040 5	4.050 000 0E-02
tonne/square meter	0.043 941 8	4.394 184 9E-02
ounce/square yard		**<surface density>**
grain/square foot	48.611 111	4.861 111 1E+01
gram/square meter	33.905 747	3.390 574 7E+01
kilogram/are	3.390 574 7	3.390 574 7E+00
kilogram/square meter	0.033 905 7	3.390 574 7E-02
ounce/square foot	0.111 111 1	1.111 111 1E-01
pound/acre	302.5	3.025 000 0E+02
pound/square yard	0.062 5	6.250 000 0E-02
slug/square yard	0.001 942 6	1.942 559 4E-03
ton/square yard [short]	0.000 031 3	3.125 000 0E-05
tonne/square meter	0.000 033 9	3.390 574 7E-05
ounce/ton [-/long]		**<concentration, mass basis>**
gram/ton [-/long]	28.349 523 1	2.834 952 3E+01
karat	0.000 669 6	6.696 428 6E-04
kilogram/kilogram	0.000 027 9	2.790 178 6E-05
milligram/ton [-/long]	28,349.523 1	2.834 952 3E+04
ounce/ton [troy/long]	0.911 458 3	9.114 583 3E-01
part/million	27.901 785 7	2.790 178 6E+01
pennyweight/ton [troy/long]	18.229 166 7	1.822 916 7E+01
percent	0.002 790 2	2.790 178 6E-03
pound/ton [-/long]	0.062 5	6.250 000 0E-02
ounce/ton [-/metric]		**<concentration, mass basis>**
karat	0.000 680 4	6.803 885 6E-04
kilogram/kilogram	0.000 028 3	2.834 952 3E-05
ounce/ton [-/long]	1.016 046 9	1.016 046 9E+00
ounce/ton [troy/metric]	0.911 458 3	9.114 583 3E-01
part/million	28.349 523 1	2.834 952 3E+01
pennyweight/ton [troy/long]	18.521 688 4	1.852 168 8E+01
percent	0.002 835	2.834 952 3E-03
pound/ton [-/metric]	0.062 5	6.250 000 0E-02
ounce/ton [-/short]		**<concentration, mass basis>**
karat	0.000 75	7.500 000 0E-04
kilogram/kilogram	0.000 031 3	3.125 000 0E-05

milligram/ton [-/UK, assay or assay, long]	1.020 833 3	1.020 833 3E+00
ounce/ton [-/long]	1.12	1.120 000 0E+00
ounce/ton [-/metric]	1.102 311 3	1.102 311 3E+00
ounce/ton [troy/long]	1.020 833 3	1.020 833 3E+00
ounce/ton [troy/metric]	1.004 710 8	1.004 710 8E+00
part/million	31.25	3.125 000 0E+01
percent	0.003 125	3.125 000 0E-03
pound/ton [-/long]	0.07	7.000 000 0E-02

ounce/ton [-/UK, assay or assay, long] \<concentration, mass basis\>

gram/ton [-/US, assay or assay, short]	25.312 074 2	2.531 207 4E+01
karat	20.828 221 1	2.082 822 1E+01
kilogram/kilogram	0.867 842 5	8.678 425 5E-01
ounce/ton [-/US, assay or assay, short]	0.892 857 1	8.928 571 4E-01
ounce/ton [troy/UK, assay or assay, long]	0.911 458 3	9.114 583 3E-01
part/million	867,842.545	8.678 425 5E+05
pennyweight/ton [troy/US, assay or assay, short]	16.276 041 7	1.627 604 2E+01
percent	86.784 254 5	8.678 425 5E+01
pound/ton [-/UK, assay or assay, long]	0.062 5	6.250 000 0E-02

ounce/ton [-/US, assay or assay, short] \<concentration, mass basis\>

gram/ton [-/US, assay or assay, short]	28.349 523 1	2.834 952 3E+01
karat	23.327 607 6	2.332 760 8E+01
kilogram/kilogram	0.971 983 7	9.719 836 5E-01
ounce/ton [-/UK, assay or assay, long]	1.12	1.120 000 0E+00
ounce/ton [troy/UK, assay or assay, long]	1.020 833 3	1.020 833 3E+00
part/million	971,983.65	9.719 836 5E+05
percent	97.198 365	9.719 836 5E+01
pound/ton [-/UK, assay or assay, long]	0.07	7.000 000 0E-02

ounce/ton [troy/long] \<concentration, mass basis\>

gram/ton [-/UK, assay or assay, long]	0.001	1.000 000 0E-03
karat	0.000 734 7	7.346 938 8E-04
kilogram/kilogram	0.000 030 6	3.061 224 5E-05
milligram/ton [-/UK, assay or assay, long]	1	1.000 000 0E+00
ounce/ton [-/long]	1.097 142 9	1.097 142 9E+00
ounce/ton [-/metric]	1.079 815 2	1.079 815 2E+00
part/million	30.612 244 9	3.061 224 5E+01
pennyweight/ton [troy/long]	20	2.000 000 0E+01
percent	0.003 061 2	3.061 224 5E-03

ounce/ton [troy/metric] \<concentration, mass basis\>

karat	0.000 746 5	7.464 859 4E-04
kilogram/kilogram	0.000 031 1	3.110 347 7E-05
milligram/ton [-/UK, assay or assay, long]	1.016 046 9	1.016 046 9E+00
ounce/ton [-/long]	1.114 748 6	1.114 748 6E+00
ounce/ton [-/metric]	1.097 142 9	1.097 142 9E+00
ounce/ton [troy/long]	1.016 046 9	1.016 046 9E+00
pennyweight/ton [troy/metric]	20	2.000 000 0E+01
pound/ton [-/UK, assay or assay, long]	0.000 002 2	2.240 000 0E-06
pound/ton [-/US, assay or assay, short]	0.000 002	2.000 000 0E-06

ounce/ton [troy/short] \<concentration, mass basis\>

gram/ton [-/US, assay or assay, short]	0.001	1.000 000 0E-03
karat	0.000 822 9	8.228 571 4E-04
kilogram/kilogram	0.000 034 3	3.428 571 4E-05
milligram/ton [-/UK, assay or assay, long]	1.12	1.120 000 0E+00
milligram/ton [-/US, assay or assay, short]	1	1.000 000 0E+00
ounce/ton [-/long]	1.228 8	1.228 800 0E+00
ounce/ton [-/metric]	1.209 393	1.209 393 0E+00
ounce/ton [-/short]	1.097 142 9	1.097 142 9E+00
ounce/ton [troy/long]	1.12	1.120 000 0E+00
part/million	34.285 714 3	3.428 571 4E+01
percent	0.003 428 6	3.428 571 4E-03

ounce/ton [troy/UK, assay or assay, long] \<concentration, mass basis\>

karat	22.851 534	2.285 153 4E+01
kilogram/kilogram	0.952 147 2	9.521 472 5E-01

Convert From		<Type of Unit>
Convert To	Standard	Scientific
ounce/ton [-/UK, assay or assay, long]		
part/million	1.097 142 9	1.097 142 9E+00
pennyweight/ton [troy/UK, assay or assay, long]	952,147.249	9.521 472 5E+05
percent	20	2.000 000 0E+01
	95.214 724 9	9.521 472 5E+01
ounce/ton [troy/US, assay or assay, short]		<concentration, mass basis>
karat	25.593 718 1	2.559 371 8E+01
kilogram/kilogram	1.066 404 9	1.066 404 9E+00
ounce/ton [-/UK, assay or assay, long]	1.228 8	1.228 800 0E+00
ounce/ton [-/US, assay or assay, short]	1.097 142 9	1.097 142 9E+00
ounce/ton [troy/UK, assay or assay, long]	1.12	1.120 000 0E+00
part/million	1,066,404.92	1.066 404 9E+06
pennyweight/ton [troy/UK, assay or assay, long]	22.4	2.240 000 0E+01
pennyweight/ton [troy/US, assay or assay, short]	20	2.000 000 0E+01
percent	106.640 492	1.066 404 9E+02
pound/ton [-/UK, assay or assay, long]	0.076 8	7.680 000 0E-02
ounce/yard		<linear density>
denier	279,030.74	2.790 307 4E+05
drex	310,034.15	3.100 341 5E+05
kilogram/meter	0.031 003 4	3.100 341 5E-02
ounce/foot	0.333 333 3	3.333 333 3E-01
poumar	62,500	6.250 000 0E+04
pound/yard	0.062 5	6.250 000 0E-02
tex	31,003.415	3.100 341 5E+04
ouncedal		<force>
newton	0.008 640 9	8.640 934 6E-03
ounce foot/square second	1	1.000 000 0E+00
pound foot/square second	0.062 5	6.250 000 0E-02
poundal	0.062 5	6.250 000 0E-02
ourob [Iran]		<length, special - see page 29>
centimeter	13	1.300 000 0E+01
ouroub [Iran]		<length, special - see page 29>
centimeter	13	1.300 000 0E+01
out [US, survey]		<length>
chain [Gunter or US, survey]	5	5.000 000 0E+00
chain [Ramden or Engineer]	3.300 006 6	3.300 006 6E+00
fathom [US, survey]	55	5.500 000 0E+01
foot [international]	330.000 66	3.300 006 6E+02
foot [US, survey]	330	3.300 000 0E+02
furlong [US, survey]	0.5	5.000 000 0E-01
link [Gunter or US, survey]	500	5.000 000 0E+02
link [Ramden or Engineer]	330.000 66	3.300 006 6E+02
meter	100.584 2	1.005 842 0E+02
mile [international]	0.062 500 1	6.250 012 5E-02
mile [US, survey]	0.062 5	6.250 000 0E-02
pace [US, survey]	132	1.320 000 0E+02
perch [US, survey]	20	2.000 000 0E+01
range [US, survey]	0.010 416 7	1.041 666 7E-02
vara [US, survey, California]	120	1.200 000 0E+02
vara [US, survey, Texas]	118.8	1.188 000 0E+02
yard [based on US, survey foot]	110	1.100 000 0E+02
yard [international]	110.000 22	1.100 002 2E+02
outava [Brazil, gold and silver]		<mass, special - see page 29>
gram	3.6	3.600 000 0E+00
outava [Italy, gold, silver and jewels]		<mass, special - see page 29>
gram	1.7	1.700 000 0E+00
outava [Portugal, gold and silver]		<mass, special - see page 29>
gram	3.6	3.600 000 0E+00
ovido [Saudi Arabia, ancient]		<length, special - see page 29>
centimeter	45.7	4.570 000 0E+01

Convert From
Convert To		**\<Type of Unit\>**
	Standard	Scientific

oxhoft [Germany]   \<volume, special - see page 29\>
liter --- 206.106 --- 2.061 060 0E+02

oxhoft [Russia]   \<volume, special - see page 29\>
liter --- 221.389 4 --- 2.213 894 0E+02

oxhuvud [Sweden]   \<volume, special - see page 29\>
liter --- 235.54 --- 2.355 400 0E+02

oxybaphon [Greece, ancient]   \<volume, special - see page 29\>
milliliter -- 73 --- 7.300 000 0E+01

pa [India]   \<mass, special - see page 29\>
gram -- 233.28 --- 2.332 800 0E+02

paal [Java]   \<length, special - see page 29\>
kilometer --- 1.507 --- 1.507 000 0E+00

paal [Sumatra]   \<length, special - see page 29\>
kilometer --- 1.852 --- 1.852 000 0E+00

paca [Venezuela]   \<mass, special - see page 29\>
kilogram --- 50 --- 5.000 000 0E+01

pace [geometrical]   \<length\>

	Standard	Scientific
chain [Gunter or US, survey]	0.757 574 2	7.575 742 4E−01
chain [Ramden or Engineer]	0.5	5.000 000 0E−01
cubit	33.333 333	3.333 333 3E+01
dekameter	1.524	1.524 000 0E+00
digit	800	8.000 000 0E+02
foot [international]	50	5.000 000 0E+01
foot [US, survey]	49.999 9	4.999 990 0E+01
inch [based on US, survey foot]	599.998 8	5.999 988 0E+02
inch [international]	600	6.000 000 0E+02
link [Gunter or US, survey]	75.757 424	7.575 742 4E+01
link [Ramden or Engineer]	50	5.000 000 0E+01
meter	15.24	1.524 000 0E+01
mile [international]	0.009 469 7	9.469 697 0E−03
mile [US, survey]	0.009 469 7	9.469 678 0E−03
out [US, survey]	0.151 514 9	1.515 148 5E−01
pace [US, survey]	19.999 96	1.999 996 0E+01
palm	200	2.000 000 0E+02
rope	2.5	2.500 000 0E+00
yard [based on US, survey foot]	16.666 633	1.666 663 3E+01
yard [international]	16.666 667	1.666 666 7E+01

pace [Greece, ancient]   \<length, special - see page 29\>
meter -- 0.77 --- 7.700 000 0E−01

pace [Hebrew, ancient]   \<length, special - see page 29\>
centimeter --- 56.018 658 --- 5.601 865 8E+01

pace [US, survey]   \<length\>

	Standard	Scientific
decimeter	7.620 015 2	7.620 015 2E+00
foot [international]	2.500 005	2.500 005 0E+00
foot [US, survey]	2.5	2.500 000 0E+00
furlong [US, survey]	0.003 787 9	3.787 878 8E−03
inch [based on US, survey foot]	30	3.000 000 0E+01
inch [international]	30.000 06	3.000 006 0E+01
link [Gunter or US, survey]	3.787 878 8	3.787 878 8E+00
link [Ramden or Engineer]	2.500 005	2.500 005 0E+00
meter	0.762 001 5	7.620 015 2E−01
mile [international]	0.000 473 5	4.734 858 0E−04
mile [US, survey]	0.000 473 5	4.734 848 5E−04
out [US, survey]	0.007 575 8	7.575 757 6E−03
pace [geometrical]	0.050 000 1	5.000 010 0E−02
perch [US, survey]	0.151 515 2	1.515 151 5E−01
vara [US, survey, California]	0.909 090 9	9.090 909 1E−01
vara [US, survey, Texas]	0.9	9.000 000 0E−01
yard [based on US, survey foot]	0.833 333 3	8.333 333 3E−01
yard [international]	0.833 335	8.333 350 0E−01

| Convert From | <Type of Unit> | |
Convert To	Standard	Scientific
pachen [Russia]	<mass, special - see page 29>	
kilogram	491.414 9	4.914 149 0E+02
pack [UK]	<mass, special - see page 29>	
kilogram	108.862	1.088 620 0E+02
package [Bangladesh, tea]	<mass, special - see page 29>	
kilogram	47.174	4.717 400 0E+01
packen [Russia]	<mass, special - see page 29>	
kilogram	490.79	4.907 900 0E+02
paegel [Denmark]	<volume, special - see page 29>	
liter	0.242	2.420 000 0E−01
paegl [Denmark]	<volume, special - see page 29>	
liter	0.242	2.420 000 0E−01
paegle [Denmark]	<volume, special - see page 29>	
milliliter	241.53	2.415 300 0E+02
paele [Germany, liquid]	<volume, special - see page 29>	
milliliter	215	2.150 000 0E+02
pagoda [India]	<mass, special - see page 29>	
gram	3.499 1	3.499 100 0E+00
pai [Burma]	<mass, special - see page 29>	
gram	1.021	1.021 000 0E+00
pai [Thailand]	<mass, special - see page 29>	
gram	0.468 75	4.687 500 0E−01
paimoneh [Iran]	<volume, special - see page 29>	
liter	1	1.000 000 0E+00
pair		<units>
brace	1	1.000 000 0E+00
couple	1	1.000 000 0E+00
one	2	2.000 000 0E+00
single	2	2.000 000 0E+00
unit	2	2.000 000 0E+00
pajak [Russia]	<volume, special - see page 29>	
liter	52.48	5.248 000 0E+01
pajmaneh [Iran]	<volume, special - see page 29>	
liter	1	1.000 000 0E+00
pajok [Russia]	<volume, special - see page 29>	
liter	52.48	5.248 000 0E+01
pal [Indonesia]	<length, special - see page 29>	
kilometer	1.507	1.507 000 0E+00
pala [Hindu, ancient, gold]	<mass, special - see page 29>	
gram	39.68	3.968 000 0E+01
pala [India, ancient]	<mass, special - see page 29>	
gram	39.68	3.968 000 0E+01
palag [Yugoslavia]	<length, special - see page 29>	
centimeter	3.634	3.634 000 0E+00
palaiste [Greece, ancient]	<length, special - see page 29>	
centimeter	7.7	7.700 000 0E+00
palame [Greece]	<length, special - see page 29>	
meter	1	1.000 000 0E+00
palaz [Yugoslavia]	<length, special - see page 29>	
millimeter	36.34	3.634 000 0E+01
paleste [Greece, ancient]	<length, special - see page 29>	
centimeter	1.92	1.920 000 0E+00
paletz [Russia]	<length, special - see page 29>	
centimeter	1.27	1.270 000 0E+00
palgat [Burma]	<length, special - see page 29>	
centimeter	2.54	2.540 000 0E+00

Convert From	<Type of Unit>	
Convert To	Standard	Scientific

pali [Oman, cereals]   `<mass, special - see page 29>`
  gram --- 280 --- 2.800 000 0E+02

palie [India]   `<mass, special - see page 29>`
  kilogram --- 1.701 --- 1.701 000 0E+00

pallie [India, Calcutta, grain]   `<mass, special - see page 29>`
  gram --- 4,119 --- 4.119 000 0E+03

pallie [India]   `<mass, special - see page 29>`
  kilogram --- 1.701 --- 1.701 000 0E+00

pally [India]   `<volume, special - see page 29>`
  liter --- 5.44 --- 5.440 000 0E+00

pally [India]   `<mass, special - see page 29>`
  kilogram --- 4.665 522 --- 4.665 522 0E+00

palm   `<length>`
  barleycorn --- 9 --- 9.000 000 0E+00
  caliber -- 300 --- 3.000 000 0E+02
  centimeter --- 7.62 --- 7.620 000 0E+00
  cubit --- 0.166 666 7 --- 1.666 666 7E-01
  digit -- 4 --- 4.000 000 0E+00
  foot [international] -- 0.25 --- 2.500 000 0E-01
  foot [US, survey] ---------------------------------- 0.249 999 5 --- 2.499 995 0E-01
  hand [horses] -- 0.75 --- 7.500 000 0E-01
  inch [based on US, survey foot] ----------------- 2.999 994 --- 2.999 994 0E+00
  inch [international] -- 3 --- 3.000 000 0E+00
  line [print] -- 36 --- 3.600 000 0E+01
  meter --- 0.076 2 --- 7.620 000 0E-02
  mil --- 3,000 --- 3.000 000 0E+03
  nail [cloth] --------------------------------------- 1.333 333 3 --- 1.333 333 3E+00
  pace [geometrical] --------------------------------------- 0.005 --- 5.000 000 0E-03
  span --- 0.333 333 3 --- 3.333 333 3E-01
  yard [based on US, survey foot] ------------- 0.083 333 2 --- 8.333 316 7E-02
  yard [international] --------------------------------- 0.083 333 3 --- 8.333 333 3E-02

palm [Egypt, ancient]   `<length, special - see page 29>`
  centimeter -- 7.5 --- 7.500 000 0E+00

palm [Greece, ancient]   `<length, special - see page 29>`
  centimeter -- 1.92 --- 1.920 000 0E+00

palm [Hebrew, ancient]   `<length, special - see page 29>`
  meter -- 0.08 --- 8.000 000 0E-02

palm [Iraq, ancient]   `<length, special - see page 29>`
  centimeter -- 9.9 --- 9.900 000 0E+00

palm [Netherlands]   `<length, special - see page 29>`
  meter --- 0.1 --- 1.000 000 0E-01

palma [Rome, ancient]   `<length, special - see page 29>`
  centimeter -- 7.39 --- 7.390 000 0E+00

palma [Spain]   `<length, special - see page 29>`
  meter -- 0.208 976 --- 2.089 760 0E-01

palmi [Libya]   `<length, special - see page 29>`
  centimeter --- 25 --- 2.500 000 0E+01

palmi [Malta]   `<length, special - see page 29>`
  centimeter --- 26.19 --- 2.619 000 0E+01

palmi [Spain]   `<length, special - see page 29>`
  centimeter -- 20.9 --- 2.090 000 0E+01

palmipes [Rome, ancient]   `<length, special - see page 29>`
  centimeter --- 37 --- 3.700 000 0E+01

palmo [Brazil]   `<length, special - see page 29>`
  centimeter --- 22 --- 2.200 000 0E+01

palmo [Ecuador]   `<length, special - see page 29>`
  centimeter --- 21 --- 2.100 000 0E+01

Convert From	<Type of Unit>	
Convert To	Standard	Scientific
palmo [Italy]	<length, special - see page 29>	
centimeter	10	1.000 000 0E+01
palmo [Libya]	<length, special - see page 29>	
centimeter	25	2.500 000 0E+01
palmo [Malta]	<length, special - see page 29>	
centimeter	26.19	2.619 000 0E+01
palmo [Portugal]	<length, special - see page 29>	
centimeter	22	2.200 000 0E+01
palmo [Spain]	<length, special - see page 29>	
centimeter	20.9	2.090 000 0E+01
palmo cuadrada [Macao]	<area, special - see page 29>	
square meter	0.048 4	4.840 000 0E-02
palmo cubica [Macao]	<volume, special - see page 29>	
cubic meter	0.010 65	1.065 000 0E-02
palmus [Rome, ancient]	<length, special - see page 29>	
centimeter	7.4	7.400 000 0E+00
palmus maior [Rome, ancient]	<length, special - see page 29>	
centimeter	22.2	2.220 000 0E+01
paloin [India]	<mass, special - see page 29>	
kilogram	1.701	1.701 000 0E+00
panchang [Malaysia]	<volume, special - see page 29>	
cubic meter	3.06	3.060 000 0E+00
panchar [Indonesia]	<area, special - see page 29>	
hectare	2.839	2.839 000 0E+00
pank [India]	<mass, special - see page 29>	
milligram	7.593 623	7.593 623 0E+00
panu [Babylon, ancient]	<volume, special - see page 29>	
liter	36	3.600 000 0E+01
pao [Bangladesh]	<mass, special - see page 29>	
gram	233.276	2.332 760 0E+02
pao [India, Calcutta]	<mass, special - see page 29>	
gram	233.276 1	2.332 761 0E+02
pao [India, Madras]	<mass, special - see page 29>	
gram	69.983	6.998 300 0E+01
pao [Nepal]	<mass, special - see page 29>	
gram	194.4	1.944 000 0E+02
pao [Pakistan]	<mass, special - see page 29>	
gram	233.276 1	2.332 761 0E+02
para [Ceylon]	<volume, special - see page 29>	
liter	25.4	2.540 000 0E+01
para [Malaysia]	<volume, special - see page 29>	
liter	45.46	4.546 000 0E+01
para [Singapore]	<volume, special - see page 29>	
liter	45.46	4.546 000 0E+01
para [Straits Settlements]	<volume, special - see page 29>	
liter	45.46	4.546 000 0E+01
paraffin [Zambia]	<volume, special - see page 29>	
liter	18.184	1.818 400 0E+01
parah [Ceylon]	<volume, special - see page 29>	
liter	25.4	2.540 000 0E+01
parah [Sri Lanka, dry]	<volume, special - see page 29>	
liter	25.5	2.550 000 0E+01
parah [Straits Settlements]	<volume, special - see page 29>	
liter	45.46	4.546 000 0E+01

Convert From Convert To	<Type of Unit> Standard	Scientific

parah [Sumatra, rice, milled]   <mass, special - see page 29>
kilogram -- 47.435 --- 4.743 500 0E+01

parak [Malaysia]   <volume, special - see page 29>
liter -- 45.459 6 --- 4.545 960 0E+01

parak [Singapore]   <volume, special - see page 29>
liter -- 45.459 6 --- 4.545 960 0E+01

parasang [Greece, ancient]   <length, special - see page 29>
kilometer -- 5.544 --- 5.544 000 0E+00

parasang [Hebrew, ancient]   <length, special - see page 29>
centimeter ---------------------------------------448,149.26 --- 4.481 492 6E+05

parasang [Iran]   <length, special - see page 29>
kilometer -- 6.24 --- 6.240 000 0E+00

parasang [Iraq, ancient]   <length, special - see page 29>
kilometer -- 5.69 --- 5.690 000 0E+00

parasange [Iran]   <length, special - see page 29>
kilometer -- 6.24 --- 6.240 000 0E+00

parcela [Puerto Rico]   <area, special - see page 29>
square meter -- 982.6 --- 9.826 000 0E+02

Paris foot [Canada, Quebec]   <length, special - see page 29>
meter -- 0.324 84 --- 3.248 400 0E-01

Paris foot [France]   <length, special - see page 29>
meter -- 0.324 84 --- 3.248 400 0E-01

Paris inch [France]   <length, special - see page 29>
centimeter -- 2.707 --- 2.707 000 0E+00

Paris line [France]   <length, special - see page 29>
millimeter -- 2.256 --- 2.256 000 0E+00

parmack [Turkey]   <length, special - see page 29>
centimeter -- 4.17 --- 4.170 000 0E+00

parmah [Turkey]   <length, special - see page 29>
centimeter -- 4.17 --- 4.170 000 0E+00

parmak [Turkey, land]   <length, special - see page 29>
centimeter -- 3.157 --- 3.157 000 0E+00

parrah [Ceylon]   <volume, special - see page 29>
liter -- 25.4 --- 2.540 000 0E+01

parrah [Straits Settlements]   <volume, special - see page 29>
liter -- 45.46 --- 4.546 000 0E+01

parrak [India]   <volume, special - see page 29>
liter -- 110.1 --- 1.101 000 0E+02

parsec   <length>
astronomical unit -----------------------------------206,264.81 --- 2.062 648 1E+05
bevameter-->>> --- 3.085 677 6E+07
kiloparsec -- 0.001 --- 1.000 000 0E-03
light year [based on mean Julian year] ----------- 3.261 563 8 --- 3.261 563 8E+00
megaparsec --0.000 001 --- 1.000 000 0E-06
meter -->>> --- 3.085 677 6E+16
mile [international]--->>> --- 1.917 351 1E+13
mile [US, survey]-->>> --- 1.917 347 3E+13
petameter -- 30.856 776 --- 3.085 677 6E+01
siriometer--- 0.206 264 8 --- 2.062 648 1E-01
spat -- 30,856.776 --- 3.085 677 6E+04
terameter -- 30,856.776 --- 3.085 677 6E+04

part/million   <concentration, mass basis>
gram/ton [-/metric]-- 1 --- 1.000 000 0E+00
gram/tonne-- 1 --- 1.000 000 0E+00
karat --0.000 024 --- 2.400 000 0E-05
kilogram/kilogram--0.000 001 --- 1.000 000 0E-06
milligram/kilogram-- 1 --- 1.000 000 0E+00
milligram/ton [-/metric]---------------------------------- 1,000 --- 1.000 000 0E+03

Convert From Convert To	Standard	<Type of Unit> Scientific
pennyweight/ton [troy/long]	0.653 333 3	6.533 333 3E−01
percent	0.000 1	1.000 000 0E−04
pound/ton [-/short]	0.002	2.000 000 0E−03
parto [Italy, gold]		<mass, special - see page 29>
gram	0.011	1.100 000 0E−02
pas [Belgium]		<length, special - see page 29>
meter	0.9	9.000 000 0E−01
pascal		<pressure>
atmosphere [metric]	0.000 010 2	1.019 716 2E−05
atmosphere [physical]	0.000 009 9	9.869 232 7E−06
atmosphere [standard]	0.000 009 9	9.869 232 7E−06
atmosphere [technical]	0.000 010 2	1.019 716 2E−05
bar	0.000 01	1.000 000 0E−05
barad	10	1.000 000 0E+01
barye [France]	10	1.000 000 0E+01
centibar	0.001	1.000 000 0E−03
centihg	0.000 750 1	7.500 615 8E−04
centimeter of mercury [0 °C, by convention]	0.000 750 1	7.500 615 8E−04
centimeter of water [4 °C, by convention]	0.010 197 2	1.019 716 2E−02
centitorr	0.750 061 7	7.500 616 8E−01
dyne/square centimeter	10	1.000 000 0E+01
foot of air [dry, CO_2 free, at 101325 Pa and 0 °C]	0.258 552	2.585 519 6E−01
foot of air [dry, CO_2 free, at 101325 Pa and 15 °C]	0.272 836 3	2.728 363 4E−01
foot of mercury [0 °C, by convention]	0.000 024 6	2.460 831 9E−05
foot of water [4 °C, by convention]	0.000 334 6	3.345 525 6E−04
gram-force/square centimeter	0.010 197 2	1.019 716 2E−02
inch of air [dry, CO_2 free, at 101325 Pa and 0 °C]	3.102 623 6	3.102 623 6E+00
inch of air [dry, CO_2 free, at 101325 Pa and 15 °C]	3.274 036 1	3.274 036 1E+00
inch of mercury [0 °C, by convention]	0.000 295 3	2.952 998 3E−04
inch of water [4 °C, by convention]	0.004 014 6	4.014 630 8E−03
kilogram-force/square centimeter	0.000 010 2	1.019 716 2E−05
kilogram-force/square meter	0.101 971 6	1.019 716 2E−01
kilogram-force/square millimeter	0.000 000 1	1.019 716 2E−07
kilogram/meter square second	1	1.000 000 0E+00
kilopond/square centimeter	0.000 010 2	1.019 716 2E−05
kilopond/square meter	0.101 971 6	1.019 716 2E−01
kilopond/square millimeter	0.000 000 1	1.019 716 2E−07
kip/square foot	0.000 020 9	2.088 543 4E−05
kip/square inch	0.000 000 1	1.450 377 4E−07
meter of air [dry, CO_2 free, at 101325 Pa and 0 °C]	0.078 806 6	7.880 663 9E−02
meter of air [dry, CO_2 free, at 101325 Pa and 15 °C]	0.083 160 5	8.316 051 7E−02
micrometer of mercury [0 °C, by convention]	7.500 615 8	7.500 615 8E+00
micrometer of water [4 °C, by convention]	101.971 62	1.019 716 2E+02
micron of mercury [0 °C, by convention]	7.500 615 8	7.500 615 8E+00
millihg	0.007 500 6	7.500 615 8E−03
millimeter of mercury [0 °C, by convention]	0.007 500 6	7.500 615 8E−03
millimeter of water [4 °C, by convention]	0.101 971 6	1.019 716 2E−01
millitorr	7.500 616 8	7.500 616 8E+00
newton/square meter	1	1.000 000 0E+00
newton/square millimeter	0.000 001	1.000 000 0E−06
ounce-force/square inch	0.002 320 6	2.320 603 8E−03
pieze [France]	0.001	1.000 000 0E−03
pound-force/square foot	0.020 885 4	2.088 543 4E−02
pound-force/square inch	0.000 145	1.450 377 4E−04
poundal/square foot	0.671 969	6.719 689 8E−01
sthene/square meter [France]	0.001	1.000 000 0E−03
ton-force/square foot [long]	0.000 009 3	9.323 854 6E−06
ton-force/square foot [short]	0.000 010 4	1.044 271 7E−05
ton-force/square inch [long]	<<<	6.474 899 0E−08
ton-force/square inch [short]	<<<	7.251 886 9E−08
ton-force/square meter [metric]	0.000 102	1.019 716 2E−04
torr	0.007 500 6	7.500 616 8E−03

Convert From
Convert To
<Type of Unit>
Standard   Scientific

pascal second   <dynamic viscosity>

Convert To	Standard	Scientific
centipoise	1,000	1.000 000 0E+03
dyne second/square centimeter	10	1.000 000 0E+01
gram-force second/square centimeter	0.010 197 2	1.019 716 2E−02
gram/centimeter second	10	1.000 000 0E+01
hyl/meter second	0.101 971 6	1.019 716 2E−01
kilogram-force second/square meter	0.101 971 6	1.019 716 2E−01
kilogram/meter hour	3,600	3.600 000 0E+03
kilogram/meter second	1	1.000 000 0E+00
newton second/square meter	1	1.000 000 0E+00
poise	10	1.000 000 0E+01
poiseuille [France]	1	1.000 000 0E+00
pound-force second/square foot	0.020 885 4	2.088 543 4E−02
pound-force second/square inch	0.000 145	1.450 377 4E−04
pound/foot hour	2,419.088 31	2.419 088 3E+03
pound/foot second	0.671 969	6.719 689 8E−01
poundal hour/square foot	2,419.088 31	2.419 088 3E+03
poundal second/square foot	0.671 969	6.719 689 8E−01
reyn	0.671 969	6.719 689 8E−01
slug/foot second	0.020 885 4	2.088 543 4E−02

pascal second/cubic meter   <acoustic impedance>

Convert To	Standard	Scientific
acoustic ohm	0.000 01	1.000 000 0E−05
dyne second/centimeter^5	0.000 01	1.000 000 0E−05
newton second/meter^5	1	1.000 000 0E+00

pascal second/meter   <specific acoustic impedance>

Convert To	Standard	Scientific
kilogram-force second/cubic meter	0.101 971 6	1.019 716 2E−01
newton second/cubic meter	1	1.000 000 0E+00
pound-force second/cubic foot	0.006 365 9	6.365 880 4E−03
poundal second/cubic foot	0.204 816 1	2.048 161 4E−01

pascal square meter   <force>

Convert To	Standard	Scientific
crinal	10	1.000 000 0E+01
dyne	100,000	1.000 000 0E+05
gram-force	101.971 621	1.019 716 2E+02
joule/meter	1	1.000 000 0E+00
kilogram meter/square second	1	1.000 000 0E+00
newton	1	1.000 000 0E+00
ounce-force	3.596 943 1	3.596 943 1E+00
pond	101.971 621	1.019 716 2E+02
pound-force	0.224 808 9	2.248 089 4E−01
poundal	7.233 013 9	7.233 013 9E+00

pascal/kelvin   <pressure coefficient>

Convert To	Standard	Scientific
pound-force/square inch °F	0.000 080 6	8.057 652 1E−05

pascal/meter   <pressure gradient>

Convert To	Standard	Scientific
kilogram/square meter square second	1	1.000 000 0E+00
pound-force/square foot foot	0.006 365 9	6.365 880 4E−03
pound/square foot square second	0.204 816 1	2.048 161 4E−01

paso [Spain]   <length, special - see page 29>

Convert To	Standard	Scientific
meter	1.39	1.390 000 0E+00

passeree [India]   <mass, special - see page 29>

Convert To	Standard	Scientific
kilogram	4.665	4.665 000 0E+00

passo [Brazil]   <length, special - see page 29>

Convert To	Standard	Scientific
meter	1.65	1.650 000 0E+00

passo [Libya]   <length, special - see page 29>

Convert To	Standard	Scientific
meter	1	1.000 000 0E+00

passus [Rome, ancient]   <length, special - see page 29>

Convert To	Standard	Scientific
meter	1.478	1.478 000 0E+00

pathi [Nepal]   <volume, special - see page 29>

Convert To	Standard	Scientific
liter	4.546	4.546 000 0E+00

pau [Brunei]   <volume, special - see page 29>

Convert To	Standard	Scientific
milliliter	284	2.840 000 0E+02

Convert From Convert To	**<Type of Unit>** Standard	Scientific
pau [Malaysia]	**<volume, special - see page 29>**	
milliliter	284	2.840 000 0E+02
pau [North Borneo]	**<volume, special - see page 29>**	
liter	0.284 122 5	2.841 225 0E-01
pau [Singapore]	**<volume, special - see page 29>**	
milliliter	284	2.840 000 0E+02
pau [Straits Settlements]	**<volume, special - see page 29>**	
liter	0.284	2.840 000 0E-01
pauseri [India]	**<mass, special - see page 29>**	
kilogram	4.665 522	4.665 522 0E+00
payim [Hebrew, ancient]	**<mass, special - see page 29>**	
gram	7.624	7.624 000 0E+00
pe [Brazil]	**<length, special - see page 29>**	
centimeter	33	3.300 000 0E+01
pe [Cape Verde]	**<length, special - see page 29>**	
meter	0.304 8	3.048 000 0E-01
pe [Macao]	**<length, special - see page 29>**	
centimeter	33	3.300 000 0E+01
pe [Portugal]	**<length, special - see page 29>**	
centimeter	33	3.300 000 0E+01
pe cuadrada [Macao]	**<area, special - see page 29>**	
square meter	0.108 9	1.089 000 0E-01
pe cubica [Macao]	**<volume, special - see page 29>**	
cubic meter	0.035 94	3.594 000 0E-02
pearl [print]	**<length>**	
agate [print]	0.909 090 9	9.090 909 1E-01
barleycorn	0.207 555	2.075 550 0E-01
caliber	6.918 5	6.918 500 0E+00
didot point [print]	4.667 662 4	4.667 662 4E+00
douzieme [print]	9.962 64	9.962 640 0E+00
em [pica, print]	0.416 666 7	4.166 666 7E-01
inch [based on US, survey foot]	0.069 184 9	6.918 486 2E-02
inch [international]	0.069 185	6.918 500 0E-02
iron [print]	0.016 666 7	1.666 666 7E-02
ligne [print]	0.830 22	8.302 200 0E-01
line [print]	0.830 22	8.302 200 0E-01
meter	0.001 757 3	1.757 299 9E-03
mil	69.185	6.918 500 0E+01
millimeter	1.757 299	1.757 299 0E+00
nonpareil [print]	0.833 333 3	8.333 333 3E-01
pica [print]	0.416 666 7	4.166 666 7E-01
point [print]	5	5.000 000 0E+00
pechus [Greece, ancient]	**<length, special - see page 29>**	
meter	0.456	4.560 000 0E-01
peck [UK]	**<volume>**	
barrel [UK]	0.055 555 6	5.555 555 6E-02
board foot	3.853 047 7	3.853 047 7E+00
bushel [UK]	0.25	2.500 000 0E-01
bushel [US, dry]	0.258 014 2	2.580 141 9E-01
cubic decimeter	9.092 18	9.092 180 0E+00
cubic foot	0.321 087 3	3.210 873 1E-01
cubic inch	554.838 87	5.548 388 7E+02
cubic meter	0.009 092 2	9.092 180 0E-03
cubic yard	0.011 892 1	1.189 212 2E-02
cup [Canada, measuring]	40	4.000 000 0E+01
cup [US, measuring]	38.430 398	3.843 039 8E+01
drachm [UK, liquid]	2,560	2.560 000 0E+03
dram [Canada, liquid]	2,560	2.560 000 0E+03
dram [US, liquid]	2,459.545 4	2.459 545 4E+03

Convert From		<Type of Unit>
Convert To	Standard	Scientific

firkin [UK]	0.222 222 2	2.222 222 2E-01
firkin [US]	0.266 877 8	2.668 777 6E-01
gallon [Canada, liquid]	2	2.000 000 0E+00
gallon [UK, dry or liquid]	2	2.000 000 0E+00
gallon [US, dry]	2.064 113 5	2.064 113 5E+00
gill [UK]	64	6.400 000 0E+01
gill [US]	76.860 795	7.686 079 5E+01
liter	9.092 18	9.092 180 0E+00
minim [UK]	153,600	1.536 000 0E+05
minim [US]	147,572.73	1.475 727 3E+05
ounce [UK, liquid]	320	3.200 000 0E+02
ounce [US, liquid]	307.443 18	3.074 431 8E+02
peck [US]	1.032 056 7	1.032 056 7E+00
pint [UK]	16	1.600 000 0E+01
pint [US, dry]	16.512 908	1.651 290 8E+01
quart [UK]	8	8.000 000 0E+00
quart [US, dry]	8.256 453 9	8.256 453 9E+00
quarter [UK]	0.031 25	3.125 000 0E-02
scruple [UK, liquid]	7,680	7.680 000 0E+03
tablespoon [Canada, measuring]	640.001 08	6.400 010 8E+02
tablespoon [US, measuring]	614.886 36	6.148 863 6E+02
teaspoon [Canada, measuring]	1,920.003 2	1.920 003 2E+03
teaspoon [US, measuring]	1,844.659 1	1.844 659 1E+03
Winchester wine gallon [UK]	2.401 899 9	2.401 899 9E+00

peck [US]		<volume>
barrel [UK]	0.053 829 9	5.382 994 3E-02
barrel [US, dry]	0.076 191 2	7.619 118 5E-02
board foot	3.733 368 1	3.733 368 1E+00
bushel [UK]	0.242 234 7	2.422 347 4E-01
bushel [UK, struck measure]	0.242 234 3	2.422 342 5E-01
bushel [US, dry]	0.25	2.500 000 0E-01
bushel [US, heaped]	0.195 655 3	1.956 553 0E-01
bushel [US, struck measure]	0.25	2.500 000 0E-01
cubic decimeter	8.809 767 5	8.809 767 5E+00
cubic foot	0.311 114	3.111 140 0E-01
cubic inch	537.605	5.376 050 0E+02
cubic meter	0.008 809 8	8.809 767 5E-03
cubic yard	0.011 522 7	1.152 274 1E-02
gallon [UK, dry or liquid]	1.937 877 9	1.937 877 9E+00
gallon [US, dry]	2	2.000 000 0E+00
gill [UK]	62.012 094	6.201 209 4E+01
gill [US]	74.473 42	7.447 342 0E+01
liter	8.809 767 5	8.809 767 5E+00
peck [UK]	0.968 939	9.689 389 7E-01
pint [UK]	15.503 024	1.550 302 4E+01
pint [US, dry]	16	1.600 000 0E+01
quart [UK]	7.751 511 8	7.751 511 8E+00
quart [US, dry]	8	8.000 000 0E+00

pecul [Batavia]		<mass, special - see page 29>
kilogram	49.052	4.905 200 0E+01

pecul [Brunei]		<mass, special - see page 29>
kilogram	60.479	6.047 900 0E+01

pecul [Cambodia]		<mass, special - see page 29>
kilogram	60	6.000 000 0E+01

pecul [China, Canton]		<mass, special - see page 29>
kilogram	60.478	6.047 800 0E+01

pecul [China]		<mass, special - see page 29>
kilogram	50	5.000 000 0E+01

pecul [Hong Kong]		<mass, special - see page 29>
kilogram	60.479	6.047 900 0E+01

Convert From / Convert To	Standard	Scientific
pecul [India, Madras]	<mass, special - see page 29>	
kilogram	59.875	5.987 500 0E+01
pecul [India]	<mass, special - see page 29>	
kilogram	59.052	5.905 200 0E+01
pecul [Indonesia]	<mass, special - see page 29>	
kilogram	61.761	6.176 100 0E+01
pecul [Japan]	<mass, special - see page 29>	
kilogram	60	6.000 000 0E+01
pecul [Laos]	<mass, special - see page 29>	
kilogram	60	6.000 000 0E+01
pecul [Macao]	<mass, special - see page 29>	
kilogram	60.479	6.047 900 0E+01
pecul [Malaysia]	<mass, special - see page 29>	
kilogram	60.479	6.047 900 0E+01
pecul [Philippines]	<mass, special - see page 29>	
kilogram	63.249	6.324 900 0E+01
pecul [Thailand]	<mass, special - see page 29>	
kilogram	60	6.000 000 0E+01
pecul [Vietnam]	<mass, special - see page 29>	
kilogram	60.453	6.045 300 0E+01
pedra [Cape Verde]	<mass, special - see page 29>	
kilogram	1.377	1.377 000 0E+00
pegel [Germany, liquid]	<volume, special - see page 29>	
milliliter	215	2.150 000 0E+02
peiktha [Burma]	<mass, special - see page 29>	
kilogram	1.633	1.633 000 0E+00
pekul [India]	<mass, special - see page 29>	
kilogram	59.052	5.905 200 0E+01
peninkulma [Finland]	<length, special - see page 29>	
kilometer	10	1.000 000 0E+01
penjuru [Malaysia]	<area, special - see page 29>	
hectare	0.133 78	1.337 800 0E-01
penjuru [Singapore]	<area, special - see page 29>	
hectare	0.134	1.340 000 0E-01
pennyweight [troy]		<mass>
carat [international]	7.775 869 2	7.775 869 2E+00
carat [UK]	6	6.000 000 0E+00
carat [US, after 1913]	7.775 869 2	7.775 869 2E+00
drachm [UK, apothecary]	0.4	4.000 000 0E-01
dram [avoirdupois]	0.877 714 3	8.777 142 9E-01
dram [US, apothecary]	0.4	4.000 000 0E-01
grain [avoirdupois]	24	2.400 000 0E+01
grain [troy]	24	2.400 000 0E+01
gram	1.555 173 8	1.555 173 8E+00
kilogram	0.001 555 2	1.555 173 8E-03
ounce [apothecary]	0.05	5.000 000 0E-02
ounce [avoirdupois]	0.054 857 1	5.485 714 3E-02
ounce [troy]	0.05	5.000 000 0E-02
point [jewelers']	777.586 92	7.775 869 2E+02
pound	0.003 428 6	3.428 571 4E-03
pound [avoirdupois]	0.003 428 6	3.428 571 4E-03
pound [troy]	0.004 166 7	4.166 666 7E-03
scruple [UK]	1.2	1.200 000 0E+00
scruple [US, apothecary]	1.2	1.200 000 0E+00
ton [UK, assay or assay, long]	0.047 607 4	4.760 736 2E-02
ton [US, assay or assay, short]	0.053 320 2	5.332 024 6E-02
pennyweight/ton [troy/long]		<concentration, mass basis>
gram/ton [-/short]	1.388 548 1	1.388 548 1E+00

Convert From Convert To	Standard	<Type of Unit> Scientific
gram/ton [-/UK, assay or assay, long]	0.000 05	5.000 000 0E−05
gram/tonne	1.530 612 2	1.530 612 2E+00
kilogram/kilogram	0.000 001 5	1.530 612 2E−06
milligram/kilogram	1.530 612 2	1.530 612 2E+00
milligram/ton [-/UK, assay or assay, long]	0.05	5.000 000 0E−02
ounce/ton [troy/long]	0.05	5.000 000 0E−02
part/million	1.530 612 2	1.530 612 2E+00
percent	0.000 153 1	1.530 612 2E−04
pound/ton [-/long]	0.003 428 6	3.428 571 4E−03
pennyweight/ton [troy/metric]		<concentration, mass basis>
gram/ton [-/short]	1.410 83	1.410 830 0E+00
karat	0.000 037 3	3.732 417 2E−05
kilogram/kilogram	0.000 001 6	1.555 173 8E−06
milligram/kilogram	1.555 173 8	1.555 173 8E+00
ounce/ton [troy/metric]	0.05	5.000 000 0E−02
part/million	1.555 173 8	1.555 173 8E+00
pennyweight/ton [troy/long]	1.016 046 9	1.016 046 9E+00
percent	0.000 155 5	1.555 173 8E−04
pound/ton [-/US, assay or assay, short]	0.000 000 1	1.000 000 0E−07
pennyweight/ton [troy/short]		<concentration, mass basis>
gram/ton [-/US, assay or assay, short]	0.000 05	5.000 000 0E−05
karat	0.000 041 1	4.114 285 7E−05
kilogram/kilogram	0.000 001 7	1.714 285 7E−06
milligram/ton [-/US, assay or assay, short]	0.05	5.000 000 0E−02
ounce/ton [troy/short]	0.05	5.000 000 0E−02
part/million	1.714 285 7	1.714 285 7E+00
pennyweight/ton [troy/long]	1.12	1.120 000 0E+00
percent	0.000 171 4	1.714 285 7E−04
pound/ton [-/long]	0.003 84	3.840 000 0E−03
pennyweight/ton [troy/UK, assay or assay, long]		<concentration, mass basis>
gram/ton [-/US, assay or assay, short]	1.388 548 1	1.388 548 1E+00
karat	1.142 576 7	1.142 576 7E+00
kilogram/kilogram	0.047 607 4	4.760 736 2E−02
ounce/ton [troy/UK, assay or assay, long]	0.05	5.000 000 0E−02
part/million	47,607.362 4	4.760 736 2E+04
percent	4.760 736 2	4.760 736 2E+00
pound/ton [-/long]	106.640 492	1.066 404 9E+02
pennyweight/ton [troy/US, assay or assay, short]		<concentration, mass basis>
gram/ton [-/US, assay or assay, short]	1.555 173 8	1.555 173 8E+00
karat	1.279 685 9	1.279 685 9E+00
kilogram/kilogram	0.053 320 2	5.332 024 6E−02
ounce/ton [troy/US, assay or assay, short]	0.05	5.000 000 0E−02
part/million	53,320.245 9	5.332 024 6E+04
pennyweight/ton [troy/UK, assay or assay, long]	1.12	1.120 000 0E+00
percent	5.332 024 6	5.332 024 6E+00
pound/ton [-/UK, assay or assay, long]	0.003 84	3.840 000 0E−03
percent		<concentration, mass basis>
gram/ton [-/metric]	10,000	1.000 000 0E+04
karat	0.24	2.400 000 0E−01
kilogram/kilogram	0.01	1.000 000 0E−02
milligram/gram	10	1.000 000 0E+00
ounce/ton [-/short]	320	3.200 000 0E+02
part/million	10,000	1.000 000 0E+04
pennyweight/ton [troy/short]	5,833.333 33	5.833 333 3E+03
pound/ton [-/long]	22.4	2.240 000 0E+01
pound/ton [-/short]	20	2.000 000 0E+01
perch [Canada, Quebec]		<area, special - see page 29>
square meter	34.19	3.419 000 0E+01
perch [Ireland]		<length, special - see page 29>
meter	6.400 8	6.400 800 0E+00

perch [US, survey]   **<length>**

Convert To	Standard	Scientific
chain [Gunter or US, survey]	0.25	2.500 000 0E−01
chain [Ramden or Engineer]	0.165 000 3	1.650 003 3E−01
fathom [US, survey]	2.75	2.750 000 0E+00
foot [international]	16.500 033	1.650 003 3E+01
foot [US, survey]	16.5	1.650 000 0E+01
furlong [US, survey]	0.025	2.500 000 0E−02
inch [based on US, survey foot]	198	1.980 000 0E+02
inch [international]	198.000 4	1.980 004 0E+02
link [Gunter or US, survey]	25	2.500 000 0E+01
link [Ramden or Engineer]	16.500 033	1.650 003 3E+01
meter	5.029 210 1	5.029 210 1E+00
out [US, survey]	0.05	5.000 000 0E−02
pace [geometrical]	0.330 000 7	3.300 006 6E−01
pace [US, survey]	6.6	6.600 000 0E+00
perche [France]	0.860 115 9	8.601 158 8E−01
pole [US, survey]	1	1.000 000 0E+00
rod [US, survey]	1	1.000 000 0E+00
vara [US, survey, California]	6	6.000 000 0E+00
vara [US, survey, Texas]	5.94	5.940 000 0E+00
yard [based on US, survey foot]	5.5	5.500 000 0E+00
yard [international]	5.500 011	5.500 011 0E+00

perche [Belgium]   **<length, special - see page 29>**

Convert To	Standard	Scientific
meter	6.497	6.497 000 0E+00

perche [Canada, Quebec]   **<length, special - see page 29>**

Convert To	Standard	Scientific
meter	5.847	5.847 000 0E+00

perche [Canada, Quebec]   **<area, special - see page 29>**

Convert To	Standard	Scientific
square meter	34.19	3.419 000 0E+01

perche [France]   **<length, special - see page 29>**

Convert To	Standard	Scientific
meter	7.146	7.146 000 0E+00

perche [France]   **<area, special - see page 29>**

Convert To	Standard	Scientific
square meter	51.072	5.107 200 0E+01

perche [France]   **<length>**

Convert To	Standard	Scientific
arpent [France]	0.1	1.000 000 0E−01
chain [Gunter or US, survey]	0.290 658 5	2.906 585 1E−01
chain [Ramden or Engineer]	0.191 835	1.918 350 0E−01
foot [France]	18	1.800 000 0E+01
foot [international]	19.183 5	1.918 350 0E+01
foot [US, survey]	19.183 462	1.918 346 2E+01
inch [based on US, survey foot]	230.201 54	2.302 015 4E+02
inch [international]	230.202	2.302 020 0E+02
meter	5.847 130 8	5.847 130 8E+00
perch [US, survey]	1.162 634	1.162 634 0E+00
pied [France]	18	1.800 000 0E+01
yard [based on US, survey foot]	6.394 487 2	6.394 487 2E+00
yard [international]	6.394 5	6.394 500 0E+00

perche [Switzerland]   **<length, special - see page 29>**

Convert To	Standard	Scientific
meter	3	3.000 000 0E+00

perestril [Ukraine]   **<length, special - see page 29>**

Convert To	Standard	Scientific
meter	65	6.500 000 0E+01

perm [20 °C]   **<permeability, water>**

Convert To	Standard	Scientific
darcy [20 °C]	2,275.497 2	2.275 497 2E+03
square centimeter	0.000 022 5	2.245 741 1E−05
square foot	<<<	2.417 295 6E−08
square meter	<<<	2.245 741 1E−09

perma [Russia, hay]   **<mass, special - see page 29>**

Convert To	Standard	Scientific
kilogram	3,926.4	3.926 400 0E+03

persakh [Iran]   **<length, special - see page 29>**

Convert To	Standard	Scientific
kilometer	6.24	6.240 000 0E+00

pertica [Rome, ancient]		<length, special - see page 29>
meter	2.96	2.960 000 0E+00
pes [Rome, ancient]		<length, special - see page 29>
centimeter	29.57	2.957 000 0E+01
pes drusianus [Rome, ancient]		<length, special - see page 29>
centimeter	33.4	3.340 000 0E+01
pes quadratus [Rome, ancient]		<area, special - see page 29>
square meter	0.087 6	8.760 000 0E-02
pes sestertius [Rome, ancient]		<length, special - see page 29>
meter	0.74	7.400 000 0E-01
pesiah [Hebrew, ancient]		<length, special - see page 29>
centimeter	56.018 658	5.601 865 8E+01
pesikta [Hebrew, ancient, dry]		<volume, special - see page 29>
cubic centimeter	197,766.6	1.977 666 0E+05
peso [Italy]		<mass, special - see page 29>
kilogram	9.053	9.053 000 0E+00
peso grosso [Italy, Genoa]		<mass, special - see page 29>
kilogram	26.162	2.616 200 0E+01
peso grosso [Italy, Venice]		<mass, special - see page 29>
gram	477	4.770 000 0E+02
peso sottile [Italy, Genoa]		<mass, special - see page 29>
gram	316.97	3.169 700 0E+02
peso sottile [Italy, Venice]		<mass, special - see page 29>
gram	301.25	3.012 500 0E+02
petabar		<pressure>
atmosphere [standard]	>>>	9.869 232 7E+14
atmosphere [technical]	>>>	1.019 716 2E+15
bar	>>>	1.000 000 0E+15
foot of mercury [0 °C, by convention]	>>>	2.460 831 9E+15
foot of water [4 °C, by convention]	>>>	3.345 525 6E+16
kilogram-force/square millimeter	>>>	1.019 716 2E+13
kilopond/square millimeter	>>>	1.019 716 2E+13
kip/square inch	>>>	1.450 377 4E+13
newton/square millimeter	>>>	1.000 000 0E+14
pascal	>>>	1.000 000 0E+20
pound-force/square inch	>>>	1.450 377 4E+16
ton-force/square inch [short]	>>>	7.251 886 9E+12
torr	>>>	7.500 616 8E+17
zettapascal	0.1	1.000 000 0E-01
petacandela		<luminous intensity>
candela	>>>	1.000 000 0E+15
petacoulomb		<electric charge>
ampere hour	>>>	2.777 777 8E+11
coulomb	>>>	1.000 000 0E+15
faraday [based on carbon-12]	>>>	1.036 427 2E+10
gigacoulomb	1,000,000	1.000 000 0E+06
megacoulomb	>>>	1.000 000 0E+09
teracoulomb	1,000	1.000 000 0E+03
petagram		<mass>
kilogram	>>>	1.000 000 0E+12
kiloton [metric]	1,000,000	1.000 000 0E+06
kilotonne	1,000,000	1.000 000 0E+06
megaton [metric]	1,000	1.000 000 0E+03
megatonne	1,000	1.000 000 0E+03
millier	>>>	1.000 000 0E+09
quarter [long]	>>>	3.936 826 1E+09
quarter [short]	>>>	4.409 245 2E+09
quarter [UK]	>>>	7.873 652 2E+10
quarter [US]	>>>	8.818 490 5E+10

| Convert From | | <Type of Unit> |
| Convert To | Standard | Scientific |

quintal [metric]	>>>	1.000 000 0E+10
quintal [UK]	>>>	1.968 413 1E+10
quintal [US]	>>>	2.204 622 6E+10
slug	>>>	6.852 176 6E+10
ton [long]	>>>	9.842 065 3E+08
ton [metric]	>>>	1.000 000 0E+09
ton [short]	>>>	1.102 311 3E+09

petajoule		**<energy>**
cheval vapeur heure [France]	>>>	3.776 726 7E+08
coal equivalent kilogram [UN, standard]	>>>	3.412 084 2E+07
coal equivalent metric ton [UN, standard]	34,120.842	3.412 084 2E+04
exawatthour	0.000 000 3	2.777 777 8E−07
gigawatthour	277.777 78	2.777 777 8E+02
gram [atomic physics, eq. energy]	11.126 501	1.112 650 1E+01
horsepower hour	>>>	3.725 061 4E+08
horsepower hour [metric]	>>>	3.776 726 7E+08
joule	>>>	1.000 000 0E+15
kilogram [atomic physics, eq. energy]	0.011 126 5	1.112 650 1E−02
kiloton [metric, explosive energy]	239.005 74	2.390 057 4E+02
kilowatthour	>>>	2.777 777 8E+08
megaton [metric, explosive energy]	0.239 005 7	2.390 057 4E−01
megawatthour	277,777.78	2.777 777 8E+05
myriawatthour	>>>	2.777 777 8E+07
petawatthour	0.000 277 8	2.777 777 8E−04
quad	0.000 947 8	9.478 171 2E−04
terajoule	1,000	1.000 000 0E+03
terawatthour	0.277 777 8	2.777 777 8E−01
therm [EEC]	9,478,171.2	9.478 171 2E+06
therm [US]	9,480,434.3	9.480 434 3E+06
thermie [France]	>>>	2.389 029 6E+08
ton [metric, explosive energy]	239,005.74	2.390 057 4E+05
watthour	>>>	2.777 777 8E+11

petaliter		**<volume>**
acre foot	>>>	8.107 131 9E+08
billion cubic foot	35,314.667	3.531 466 7E+04
cubem	239.912 76	2.399 127 6E+02
cubic foot	>>>	3.531 466 7E+13
cubic meter	>>>	1.000 000 0E+12
cubic mile	239.912 76	2.399 127 6E+02
cubic yard	>>>	1.307 950 6E+12
hectare meter	>>>	1.000 000 0E+08
liter	>>>	1.000 000 0E+15
million acre foot	810.713 19	8.107 131 9E+02
million board foot	>>>	4.237 760 0E+08
petrograd standard	>>>	2.140 282 8E+11
stere	>>>	1.000 000 0E+12
trillion cubic foot	35.314 667	3.531 466 7E+01

petameter		**<length>**
astronomical unit	6,684.587 2	6.684 587 2E+03
bevameter	1,000,000	1.000 000 0E+06
foot [international]	>>>	3.280 839 9E+15
foot [US, survey]	>>>	3.280 833 3E+15
kiloparsec	0.000 032 4	3.240 779 3E−05
light year [based on mean Julian year]	0.105 700 1	1.057 000 8E−01
megaparsec	<<<	3.240 779 3E−08
meter	>>>	1.000 000 0E+15
mile [international]	>>>	6.213 711 9E+11
mile [US, survey]	>>>	6.213 699 5E+11
parsec	0.032 407 8	3.240 779 3E−02

| **petamole** | | **<amount of substance>** |
| mole | >>> | 1.000 000 0E+15 |

| Convert From | | <Type of Unit> |
| Convert To | Standard | Scientific |

petanewton <force>
crinal	>>> ---	1.000 000 0E+16
dyne	>>> ---	1.000 000 0E+20
gram-force	>>> ---	1.019 716 2E+17
newton	>>> ---	1.000 000 0E+15
ounce-force	>>> ---	3.596 943 1E+15
pond	>>> ---	1.019 716 2E+17
pound-force	>>> ---	2.248 089 4E+14
poundal	>>> ---	7.233 013 9E+15

petapascal <pressure>
atmosphere [standard]	>>> ---	9.869 232 7E+09
atmosphere [technical]	>>> ---	1.019 716 2E+10
bar	>>> ---	1.000 000 0E+10
foot of mercury [0 °C, by convention]	>>> ---	2.460 831 9E+10
foot of water [4 °C, by convention]	>>> ---	3.345 525 6E+11
kilogram-force/square millimeter	>>> ---	1.019 716 2E+08
kilopond/square millimeter	>>> ---	1.019 716 2E+08
kip/square inch	>>> ---	1.450 377 4E+08
newton/square millimeter	>>> ---	1.000 000 0E+09
pascal	>>> ---	1.000 000 0E+15
pound-force/square inch	>>> ---	1.450 377 4E+11
ton-force/square inch [long]	>>> ---	6.474 899 0E+07
ton-force/square inch [short]	>>> ---	7.251 886 9E+07
torr	>>> ---	7.500 616 8E+12

petawatt <power>
Btu/second [I.T.]	>>> ---	9.478 171 2E+11
Btu/second [thermoc.]	>>> ---	9.484 514 1E+11
calorie/second [I.T.]	>>> ---	2.388 459 0E+14
calorie/second [thermoc.]	>>> ---	2.390 057 4E+14
centigrade heat unit/second [mean]	>>> ---	5.261 590 5E+11
cubic meter atmosphere/second	>>> ---	9.869 232 7E+15
dyne centimeter/second	>>> ---	1.000 000 0E+22
erg/second	>>> ---	1.000 000 0E+22
foot pound-force/second	>>> ---	7.375 621 5E+14
foot poundal/second	>>> ---	2.373 036 0E+16
gram-force centimeter/second	>>> ---	1.019 716 2E+19
horsepower	>>> ---	1.341 022 1E+12
horsepower [metric]	>>> ---	1.359 621 6E+12
joule/second	>>> ---	1.000 000 0E+15
kilocalorie/second [I.T.]	>>> ---	2.388 459 0E+11
kilogram-force meter/second	>>> ---	1.019 716 2E+14
kilopond meter/second	>>> ---	1.019 716 2E+14
newton meter/second	>>> ---	1.000 000 0E+15
volt ampere	>>> ---	1.000 000 0E+15
watt	>>> ---	1.000 000 0E+15

petawatthour <energy>
cheval vapeur heure [France]	>>> ---	1.359 621 6E+12
coal equivalent kilogram [UN, standard]	>>> ---	1.228 350 3E+11
coal equivalent metric ton [UN, standard]	>>> ---	1.228 350 3E+08
gram [atomic physics, eq. energy]	40,055.402 ---	4.005 540 2E+04
joule	>>> ---	3.600 000 0E+18
kilogram [atomic physics, eq. energy]	40.055 402 ---	4.005 540 2E+01
kilogram calorie [15 °C, NBS, 1939]	>>> ---	8.600 506 5E+14
kilogram square meter/square second	>>> ---	3.600 000 0E+18
kilopond meter	>>> ---	3.670 978 4E+17
kiloton [metric, explosive energy]	860,420.65 ---	8.604 206 5E+05
kilowatthour	>>> ---	1.000 000 0E+12
liter atmosphere	>>> ---	3.552 923 8E+16
megaton [metric, explosive energy]	860.420 65 ---	8.604 206 5E+02
meter kilogram-force	>>> ---	3.670 978 4E+17
newton meter	>>> ---	3.600 000 0E+18
quad	3.412 141 6 ---	3.412 141 6E+00

Convert From / Convert To	Standard	Scientific
therm [EEC]	>>>	3.412 141 6E+10
therm [US]	>>>	3.412 956 3E+10
thermie [France]	>>>	8.600 506 5E+11
ton [metric, explosive energy]	>>>	8.604 206 5E+08
watthour	>>>	1.000 000 0E+15

petit arpent codastral [Hungary] — <area, special - see page 29>

	Standard	Scientific
are	43.159 4	4.315 900 0E+01

petrograd standard — <volume>

	Standard	Scientific
barrel [US, dry]	40.408 163	4.040 816 3E+00
board foot	1,980	1.980 000 0E+03
bushel [UK]	128.469 73	1.284 697 3E+02
bushel [US, dry]	132.588 05	1.325 880 5E+02
chaldron [UK, dry]	3.568 603 6	3.568 603 6E+00
chaldron [US, dry]	3.683 001 5	3.683 001 5E+00
cord [firewood]	1.289 062 5	1.289 062 5E+00
cord foot [timber]	10.312 5	1.031 250 0E+01
cubic foot	165	1.650 000 0E+02
cubic inch	285,120	2.851 200 0E+05
cubic meter	4.672 279 7	4.672 279 7E+00
cubic yard	6.111 111 1	6.111 111 1E+00
English water ton [UK]	4.588 204 7	4.588 204 7E+00
freight ton	4.125	4.125 000 0E+00
gallon [US, dry]	1,060.704 4	1.060 704 4E+03
kiloliter	4.672 279 7	4.672 279 7E+00
liter	4,672.279 7	4.672 279 7E+03
measurement ton	4.125	4.125 000 0E+00
million board foot	0.001 98	1.980 000 0E−03
ocean ton	4.125	4.125 000 0E+00
register ton	1.65	1.650 000 0E+00
shipping ton	4.125	4.125 000 0E+00
stere	4.672 279 7	4.672 279 7E+00
thousand board foot	1.98	1.980 000 0E+00
thousand cubic foot	0.165	1.650 000 0E−01
trillion cubic foot	<<<	1.650 000 0E−10

petrograd standard/day — <flow rate, volume basis>

	Standard	Scientific
acre foot/day	0.003 787 9	3.787 878 8E−03
acre foot/day [US, survey]	0.003 787 9	3.787 856 1E−03
acre inch/day	0.045 454 5	4.545 454 6E−02
barrel/hour [UK]	1.189 534 6	1.189 534 6E+00
barrel/hour [US, federal]	1.658 986 2	1.658 986 2E+00
barrel/hour [US, liquid]	1.632 653 1	1.632 653 1E+00
barrel/hour [US, petroleum]	1.224 489 8	1.224 489 8E+00
centiliter/second	5.407 731 1	5.407 731 1E+00
cubic centimeter/second	54.077 311 2	5.407 731 1E+01
cubic decimeter/minute	3.244 638 7	3.244 638 7E+00
cubic foot/hour	6.875	6.875 000 0E+00
cubic inch/second	3.3	3.300 000 0E+00
cubic meter/day	4.672 279 7	4.672 279 7E+00
cubic meter/second	0.000 054 1	5.407 731 1E−05
cubic yard/day	6.111 111 1	6.111 111 1E+00
deciliter/minute	32.446 386 7	3.244 638 7E+01
dekaliter/hour	19.467 832	1.946 783 2E+01
gallon/hour [UK]	42.823 243 8	4.282 324 4E+01
gallon/hour [US, liquid]	51.428 571 4	5.142 857 1E+01
hectoliter/hour	1.946 783 2	1.946 783 2E+00
kiloliter/day	4.672 279 7	4.672 279 7E+00
liter/minute	3.244 638 7	3.244 638 7E+00
liter/minute [pre-1964]	3.244 547 8	3.244 547 8E+00
milliliter/second	54.077 311 2	5.407 731 1E+01
ounce/second [UK, liquid]	1.903 255 3	1.903 255 3E+00
ounce/second [US, liquid]	1.828 571 4	1.828 571 4E+00
petrograd standard/hour	0.041 666 7	4.166 666 7E−02
stere/day	4.672 279 7	4.672 279 7E+00

Convert From		<Type of Unit>
Convert To	Standard	Scientific

thousand cubic foot/day --------------------------------- 0.165 --- 1.650 000 0E−01

petrograd standard/hour <flow rate, volume basis>
acre foot/day-- 0.090 909 1 --- 9.090 909 1E−02
acre foot/day [US, survey] ------------------------------ 0.090 908 5 --- 9.090 854 5E−02
acre inch/day--- 1.090 909 1 --- 1.090 909 1E+00
barrel/hour [UK] --------------------------------------28.548 829 2 --- 2.854 882 9E+01
barrel/hour [US, federal]-------------------------------39.815 668 2 --- 3.981 566 8E+01
barrel/hour [US, liquid]---------------------------------39.183 673 5 --- 3.918 367 4E+01
barrel/hour [US, petroleum]-----------------------------29.387 755 1 --- 2.938 775 5E+01
centiliter/second --------------------------------------- 129.785 547 --- 1.297 855 5E+02
cubic centimeter/second -----------------------------1,297.855 47 --- 1.297 855 5E+03
cubic decimeter/second -------------------------------- 1.297 855 5 --- 1.297 855 5E+00
cubic dekameter/day ----------------------------------- 0.112 134 7 --- 1.121 347 1E−01
cubic foot/minute --- 2.75 --- 2.750 000 0E+00
cubic inch/minute---4,752 --- 4.752 000 0E+03
cubic inch/second--79.2 --- 7.920 000 0E+01
cubic meter/hour --------------------------------------- 4.672 279 7 --- 4.672 279 7E+00
cubic meter/second------------------------------------ 0.001 297 9 --- 1.297 855 5E−03
cubic yard/hour -- 6.111 111 1 --- 6.111 111 1E+00
deciliter/second ---------------------------------------12.978 554 7 --- 1.297 855 5E+01
dekaliter/second --------------------------------------- 7.787 132 8 --- 7.787 132 8E+00
gallon/minute [UK] -------------------------------------17.129 297 5 --- 1.712 929 8E+01
gallon/minute [US, liquid]-------------------------------20.571 428 6 --- 2.057 142 9E+01
hectare meter/day -------------------------------------- 0.011 213 5 --- 1.121 347 1E−02
hectoliter/hour --46.722 796 9 --- 4.672 279 7E+01
kiloliter/hour --- 4.672 279 7 --- 4.672 279 7E+00
liter/second -- 1.297 855 5 --- 1.297 855 5E+00
liter/second [pre-1964] --------------------------------- 1.297 819 1 --- 1.297 819 1E+00
milliliter/second ---------------------------------------1,297.855 47 --- 1.297 855 5E+03
ounce/second [UK, liquid] ------------------------------45.678 127 --- 4.567 812 7E+01
ounce/second [US, liquid] ------------------------------43.885 714 --- 4.388 571 4E+01
petrograd standard/day---------------------------------------24 --- 2.400 000 0E+01
stere/hour --- 4.672 279 7 --- 4.672 279 7E+00
thousand cubic foot/day -------------------------------------- 3.96 --- 3.960 000 0E+00

petrograd standard/minute <flow rate, volume basis>
acre foot/day-- 5.454 545 5 --- 5.454 545 5E+00
acre foot/day [US, survey] ------------------------------ 5.454 512 7 --- 5.454 512 7E+00
acre inch/hour-- 2.727 272 7 --- 2.727 272 7E+00
barrel/minute [UK] -------------------------------------28.548 829 2 --- 2.854 882 9E+01
barrel/minute [US, federal]------------------------------39.815 668 2 --- 3.981 566 8E+01
barrel/minute [US, liquid]--------------------------------39.183 673 5 --- 3.918 367 4E+01
barrel/minute [US, petroleum]----------------------------29.387 755 1 --- 2.938 775 5E+01
cubic dekameter/day ----------------------------------- 6.728 082 8 --- 6.728 082 8E+00
cubic foot/second --- 2.75 --- 2.750 000 0E+00
cubic meter/minute ------------------------------------ 4.672 279 7 --- 4.672 279 7E+00
cubic meter/second------------------------------------ 0.077 871 3 --- 7.787 132 8E−02
cubic yard/minute -------------------------------------- 6.111 111 1 --- 6.111 111 1E+00
dekaliter/second --------------------------------------- 7.787 132 8 --- 7.787 132 8E+00
gallon/second [UK]-------------------------------------17.129 297 5 --- 1.712 929 8E+01
gallon/second [US, liquid] -------------------------------20.571 428 6 --- 2.057 142 9E+01
hectoliter/minute --------------------------------------46.722 796 9 --- 4.672 279 7E+01
kiloliter/minute--- 4.672 279 7 --- 4.672 279 7E+00
liter/second ---77.871 328 1 --- 7.787 132 8E+01
liter/second [pre-1964] --------------------------------77.869 147 8 --- 7.786 914 8E+01
ounce/second [UK, liquid] -----------------------------2,740.687 6 --- 2.740 687 6E+03
ounce/second [US, liquid] -----------------------------2,633.142 9 --- 2.633 142 9E+03
petrograd standard/hour-------------------------------------60 --- 6.000 000 0E+01
stere/minute --- 4.672 279 7 --- 4.672 279 7E+00
thousand cubic foot/hour -------------------------------------9.9 --- 9.900 000 0E+00

petrograd standard/second <flow rate, volume basis>
acre foot/hour--13.636 363 6 --- 1.363 636 4E+01
acre foot/hour [US, survey] -----------------------------13.636 281 8 --- 1.363 628 2E+01
acre inch/minute--- 2.727 272 7 --- 2.727 272 7E+00

Convert From	<Type of Unit>	
Convert To	Standard	Scientific

barrel/second [UK]	28.548 829 2	2.854 882 9E+01
barrel/second [US, federal]	39.815 668 2	3.981 566 8E+01
barrel/second [US, liquid]	39.183 673 5	3.918 367 4E+01
barrel/second [US, petroleum]	29.387 755 1	2.938 775 5E+01
billion cubic foot/day	0.014 256	1.425 600 0E−02
cubic dekameter/hour	16.820 206 9	1.682 020 7E+01
cubic foot/second	165	1.650 000 0E+02
cubic meter/second	4.672 279 7	4.672 279 7E+00
cubic yard/second	6.111 111 1	6.111 111 1E+00
dekaliter/second	467.227 969	4.672 279 7E+02
gallon/second [UK]	1,027.757 85	1.027 757 7E+03
gallon/second [US, liquid]	1,234.285 71	1.234 285 7E+03
hectare meter/hour	1.682 020 7	1.682 020 7E+00
hectoliter/second	46.722 796 9	4.672 279 7E+01
kiloliter/second	4.672 279 7	4.672 279 7E+00
liter/second	4,672.279 69	4.672 279 7E+03
liter/second [pre-1964]	4,672.148 87	4.672 148 9E+03
petrograd standard/minute	60	6.000 000 0E+01
stere/second	4.672 279 7	4.672 279 7E+00
thousand cubic foot/minute	9.9	9.900 000 0E+00

pfennig [Austria] — <mass, special - see page 29>

gram	1.093 8	1.093 800 0E+00

pferdestarke [Germany] — <power>

Btu/minute [I.T.]	41.827 098	4.182 709 8E+01
Btu/minute [thermoc.]	41.855 09	4.185 509 0E+01
calorie/second [I.T.]	175.670 86	1.756 708 6E+02
calorie/second [thermoc.]	175.788 42	1.757 884 2E+02
centigrade heat unit/minute [mean]	23.219 359	2.321 935 9E+01
cheval vapeur [France]	1	1.000 000 0E+00
cubic meter atmosphere/second	7,258.808 3	7.258 808 3E+03
dyne centimeter/second	>>>	7.354 987 5E+09
erg/second	>>>	7.354 987 5E+09
foot pound-force/second	542.476 04	5.424 760 4E+02
foot poundal/second	17,453.65	1.745 365 0E+04
gram-force centimeter/second	7,500.000 0	7.500 000 0E+06
hectowatt	7.354 987 5	7.354 987 5E+00
horsepower	0.986 320 1	9.863 200 7E−01
horsepower [metric]	1	1.000 000 0E+00
joule/second	735.498 75	7.354 987 5E+02
kilocalorie/minute [I.T.]	10.540 252	1.054 025 2E+01
kilogram square meter/cubic second	735.498 75	7.354 987 5E+02
kilogram-force meter/second	75	7.500 000 0E+01
kilopond meter/second	75	7.500 000 0E+01
newton meter/second	735.498 75	7.354 987 5E+02
poncelet [France]	0.75	7.500 000 0E−01
ton of refrigeration	0.209 135 5	2.091 354 9E−01
volt ampere	735.498 75	7.354 987 5E+02
watt	735.498 75	7.354 987 5E+02

pferdestarkenstunde [Germany] — <energy>

Btu [I.T.]	2,509.625 9	2.509 625 9E+03
calorie [I.T.]	632,415.09	6.324 150 9E+05
calorie [kilogram, I.T.]	632.415 09	6.324 150 9E+02
centigrade heat unit [I.T.]	1,394.236 6	1.394 236 6E+03
cheval vapeur heure [France]	1	1.000 000 0E+00
coal equivalent kilogram [UN, standard]	0.090 345	9.034 501 3E−02
coal equivalent metric ton [UN, standard]	0.000 090 3	9.034 501 3E−05
cubic centimeter atmosphere	>>>	2.613 171 0E+07
cubic foot atmosphere	922.832 62	9.228 326 2E+02
foot pound-force	1,952,913.7	1.952 913 7E+06
foot poundal	>>>	6.283 314 1E+07
gram calorie	632,566.18	6.325 661 8E+05
horsepower hour	0.986 320 1	9.863 200 7E−01
horsepower hour [metric]	1	1.000 000 0E+00

Convert From / Convert To	Standard	\<Type of Unit\> Scientific
joule	2,647,795.5	2.647 795 5E+06
kilocalorie [I.T.]	632.415 09	6.324 150 9E+02
kilogram calorie [15 °C, NBS, 1939]	632.566 18	6.325 661 8E+02
kilopond meter	270,000	2.700 000 0E+05
meter kilogram-force	270,000	2.700 000 0E+05
newton meter	2,647,795.5	2.647 795 5E+06
therm [EEC]	0.025 096 3	2.509 625 9E−02
therm [US]	0.025 102 3	2.510 225 1E−02
thermie [France]	0.632 566 2	6.325 661 8E−01
watthour	735.498 75	7.354 987 5E+02
wattsecond	2,647,795.5	2.647 795 5E+06
pfiff [Austria]		\<volume, special - see page 29\>
liter	0.18	1.800 000 0E−01
pfund [Austria]		\<mass, special - see page 29\>
kilogram	0.5	5.000 000 0E−01
pfund [Brazil, gold and silver]		\<mass, special - see page 29\>
gram	454.25	4.542 500 0E+02
pfund [Denmark]		\<mass, special - see page 29\>
kilogram	0.5	5.000 000 0E−01
pfund [Germany]		\<mass, special - see page 29\>
kilogram	0.5	5.000 000 0E−01
pfund [Poland]		\<mass, special - see page 29\>
gram	404.6	4.046 000 0E+02
pfund [Switzerland]		\<mass, special - see page 29\>
kilogram	0.5	5.000 000 0E−01
phai mu [Laos]		\<volume, special - see page 29\>
liter	1.25	1.250 000 0E+00
phai mu louang [Laos]		\<volume, special - see page 29\>
liter	0.25	2.500 000 0E−01
phan [Laos]		\<mass, special - see page 29\>
kilogram	1.2	1.200 000 0E+00
phan [Vietnam]		\<mass, special - see page 29\>
milligram	377.8	3.778 000 0E+02
phan [Vietnam]		\<length, special - see page 29\>
millimeter	4	4.000 000 0E+00
phan [Vietnam]		\<area, special - see page 29\>
square meter	0.24	2.400 000 0E−01
pharoagh [Turkey]		\<length, special - see page 29\>
kilometer	10	1.000 000 0E+01
phlan [Cambodia]		\<volume, special - see page 29\>
cubic meter	0.1	1.000 000 0E−01
phlang [Cambodia]		\<volume, special - see page 29\>
liter	100	1.000 000 0E+02
phon		\<loudness level\>
loudness unit	25	2.500 000 0E+01
noy	0.025	2.500 000 0E−02
sone	0.025	2.500 000 0E−02
phot		\<illuminance\>
footcandle	929.030 4	9.290 304 0E+02
lumen/square centimeter	1	1.000 000 0E+00
lumen/square inch	6.451 6	6.451 600 0E+00
lumen/square meter	10,000	1.000 000 0E+04
lux	10,000	1.000 000 0E+04
milliphot	1,000	1.000 000 0E+03
nox	\>\>\>	1.000 000 0E+07
phot second		\<light exposure\>
lumen second/square centimeter	1	1.000 000 0E+00
lumen second/square inch	6.451 6	6.451 600 0E+00

| Convert From | <Type of Unit> | |
Convert To	Standard	Scientific
lux hour	2.777 777 8	2.777 777 8E+00
lux second	10,000	1.000 000 0E+04
phuong [Vietnam]	<volume, special - see page 29>	
liter	30	3.000 000 0E+01
phyeam [Cambodia]	<length, special - see page 29>	
meter	2	2.000 000 0E+00
pic [Bahrain]	<length, special - see page 29>	
centimeter	48.26	4.826 000 0E+01
pic [Cyprus, textiles]	<length, special - see page 29>	
meter	0.609 6	6.096 000 0E−01
pic [Cyprus]	<length, special - see page 29>	
centimeter	60.96	6.096 000 0E+01
pic [Cyprus]	<area, special - see page 29>	
square meter	22.296 73	2.229 673 0E+01
pic [Greece]	<length, special - see page 29>	
centimeter	75	7.500 000 0E+01
pic [India]	<mass, special - see page 29>	
kilogram	59.052	5.905 200 0E+01
pic [Iraq, Baghdad]	<length, special - see page 29>	
centimeter	74.5	7.450 000 0E+01
pic [Iraq, Mosul]	<length, special - see page 29>	
centimeter	70	7.000 000 0E+01
pic [Jordan, land]	<length, special - see page 29>	
centimeter	75.8	7.580 000 0E+01
pic [Jordan, textiles]	<length, special - see page 29>	
centimeter	68	6.800 000 0E+01
pic [Lebanon, land]	<length, special - see page 29>	
centimeter	75.8	7.580 000 0E+01
pic [Lebanon, textiles]	<length, special - see page 29>	
centimeter	67.9	6.790 000 0E+01
pic [Morocco]	<length, special - see page 29>	
centimeter	55.88	5.588 000 0E+01
pic [Russia]	<length, special - see page 29>	
centimeter	71.12	7.112 000 0E+01
pic [Saudi Arabia]	<length, special - see page 29>	
centimeter	45.7	4.570 000 0E+01
pic [Spanish North Africa]	<length, special - see page 29>	
centimeter	61	6.100 000 0E+01
pic [Syria, textiles]	<length, special - see page 29>	
centimeter	70	7.000 000 0E+01
pic [Turkey, land]	<length, special - see page 29>	
centimeter	75.77	7.577 000 0E+01
pic [Turkey, textiles]	<length, special - see page 29>	
centimeter	68	6.800 000 0E+01
pic arabe [Tunisia]	<length, special - see page 29>	
centimeter	49.3	4.930 000 0E+01
pic carre [Egypt]	<area, special - see page 29>	
square meter	0.562 5	5.625 000 0E−01
pic turc [Tunisia]	<length, special - see page 29>	
centimeter	64.4	6.440 000 0E+01
pica [print]	<length>	
agate [print]	2.181 818 2	2.181 818 2E+00
barleycorn	0.498 132	4.981 320 0E−01
caliber	16.604 4	1.660 440 0E+01
didot point [print]	11.202 39	1.120 239 0E+01
douzieme [print]	23.910 336	2.391 033 6E+01

	Standard	Scientific
em [pica, print]	1	1.000 000 0E+00
inch [based on US, survey foot]	0.166 043 7	1.660 436 7E−01
inch [international]	0.166 044	1.660 440 0E−01
iron [print]	0.04	4.000 000 0E−02
ligne [print]	1.992 528	1.992 528 0E+00
line [print]	1.992 528	1.992 528 0E+00
meter	0.004 217 5	4.217 517 6E−03
mil	166.044	1.660 440 0E+02
millimeter	4.217 517 6	4.217 517 6E+00
nonpareil [print]	2	2.000 000 0E+00
pearl [print]	2.4	2.400 000 0E+00
point [print]	12	1.200 000 0E+01

picheus [Greece]		**<length, special - see page 29>**
meter	1.5	1.500 000 0E+00

picki [Greece]		**<length, special - see page 29>**
centimeter	75	7.500 000 0E+01

pico [Brunei]		**<mass, special - see page 29>**
kilogram	60.479	6.047 900 0E+01

pico [Cambodia]		**<mass, special - see page 29>**
kilogram	60	6.000 000 0E+01

pico [China]		**<mass, special - see page 29>**
kilogram	50	5.000 000 0E+01

pico [Hong Kong]		**<mass, special - see page 29>**
kilogram	60.479	6.047 900 0E+01

pico [Indonesia]		**<mass, special - see page 29>**
kilogram	61.761	6.176 100 0E+01

pico [Japan]		**<mass, special - see page 29>**
kilogram	60	6.000 000 0E+01

pico [Laos]		**<mass, special - see page 29>**
kilogram	60	6.000 000 0E+01

pico [Macao]		**<mass, special - see page 29>**
kilogram	60.479	6.047 900 0E+01

pico [Malaysia]		**<mass, special - see page 29>**
kilogram	60.479	6.047 900 0E+01

pico [Philippines]		**<mass, special - see page 29>**
kilogram	63.249	6.324 900 0E+01

pico [Singapore]		**<mass, special - see page 29>**
kilogram	60.479	6.047 900 0E+01

pico [Thailand]		**<mass, special - see page 29>**
kilogram	60	6.000 000 0E+01

pico [Vietnam]		**<mass, special - see page 29>**
kilogram	60.453	6.045 300 0E+01

picoampere		**<electric current>**
abampere	<<<	1.000 000 0E−13
ampere	<<<	1.000 000 0E−12
electrostatic unit of current [cgs system]	0.002 997 9	2.997 924 6E−03
statampere	0.002 997 9	2.997 924 6E−03

picobar		**<pressure>**
atmosphere [standard]	<<<	9.869 232 7E−13
atmosphere [technical]	<<<	1.019 716 2E−12
bar	<<<	1.000 000 0E−12
barye [France]	0.000 001	1.000 000 0E−06
dyne/square centimeter	0.000 001	1.000 000 0E−06
gram-force/square centimeter	<<<	1.019 716 2E−09
kilogram-force/square meter	<<<	1.019 716 2E−08
kilopond/square meter	<<<	1.019 716 2E−08
micrometer of mercury [0 °C, by convention]	0.000 000 8	7.500 615 8E−07
micrometer of water [4 °C, by convention]	0.000 010 2	1.019 716 2E−05
newton/square meter	0.000 000 1	1.000 000 0E−07

	Standard	Scientific
pascal	0.000 000 1	1.000 000 0E-07
poundal/square foot	<<<	6.719 689 8E-08
ton-force/square foot [short]	<<<	1.044 271 7E-12
torr	<<<	7.500 616 8E-10
picocandela		**\<luminous intensity\>**
candela	<<<	1.000 000 0E-12
picocoulomb		**\<electric charge\>**
coulomb	<<<	1.000 000 0E-12
electrostatic unit of charge [cgs system]	0.002 997 9	2.997 924 6E-03
franklin	0.002 997 9	2.997 924 6E-03
statcoulomb	0.002 997 9	2.997 924 6E-03
picocoulomb/kilogram		**\<exposure, gamma and X rays\>**
coulomb/kilogram	<<<	1.000 000 0E-12
roentgen	<<<	3.875 969 0E-09
röntgen	<<<	3.875 969 0E-09
picocoulomb/kilogram second		**\<exposure rate, gamma and X rays\>**
coulomb/kilogram second	<<<	1.000 000 0E-12
roentgen/second	<<<	3.875 969 0E-09
röntgen/second	<<<	3.875 969 0E-09
picofarad		**\<capacitance\>**
abfarad	<<<	1.000 000 0E-21
coulomb/volt	<<<	1.000 000 0E-12
farad	<<<	1.000 000 0E-12
puff	1	1.000 000 0E+00
statfarad	0.898 755 2	8.987 551 8E-01
picofarad/meter		**\<electric permittivity\>**
abfarad/centimeter	<<<	1.000 000 0E-19
farad/meter	<<<	1.000 000 0E-12
statfarad/centimeter	89.875 517 9	8.987 551 8E+01
picogram		**\<mass\>**
gamma	0.000 001	1.000 000 0E-06
grain	<<<	1.543 235 8E-11
kilogram	<<<	1.000 000 0E-15
point [jewelers']	<<<	5.000 000 0E-10
picohenry		**\<electric inductance\>**
abhenry	0.001	1.000 000 0E-03
electromagnetic unit of inductance [cgs system]	0.001	1.000 000 0E-03
electrostatic unit of inductance [cgs system]	<<<	1.112 650 1E-24
henry	<<<	1.000 000 0E-12
stathenry	<<<	1.112 650 1E-24
picojoule		**\<energy\>**
atomic mass unit [unified, C-12, 1986, eq. energy]	0.006 700 5	6.700 530 8E-03
centimeter gram-force	<<<	1.019 716 2E-08
deuteron rest mass [atomic physics, eq. energy]	0.003 327 7	3.327 714 8E-03
dyne centimeter	0.000 01	1.000 000 0E-05
electron rest mass [atomic physics, eq. energy]	12.214 321	1.221 432 1E+01
electronvolt	6,241,506.4	6.241 506 4E+06
erg	0.000 01	1.000 000 0E-05
gigaelectronvolt	0.006 241 5	6.241 506 4E-03
hartree [atomic physics, eq. energy]	229,371.04	2.293 710 4E+05
joule	<<<	1.000 000 0E-12
kiloelectronvolt	6,241.506 4	6.241 506 4E+03
megaelectronvolt	6.241 506 4	6.241 506 4E+00
muon rest mass [atomic physics, eq. energy]	0.059 072 5	5.907 251 1E-02
neutron rest mass [atomic physics, eq. energy]	0.006 643	6.642 970 1E-03
proton rest mass [atomic physics, eq. energy]	0.006 652 1	6.652 126 8E-03
rydberg [atomic physics, eq. energy , eq. energy]	458,736.64	4.587 366 4E+05
teraelectronvolt	0.000 006 2	6.241 506 4E-06
picol [Brunei]		**\<mass, special - see page 29\>**
kilogram	60.479	6.047 900 0E+01

Convert From Convert To	Standard	**<Type of Unit>** Scientific
picol [Cambodia]		**<mass, special - see page 29>**
kilogram	60	6.000 000 0E+01
picol [China]		**<mass, special - see page 29>**
kilogram	60.478	6.047 800 0E+01
picol [Hong Kong]		**<mass, special - see page 29>**
kilogram	60.479	6.047 900 0E+01
picol [India]		**<mass, special - see page 29>**
kilogram	59.052	5.905 200 0E+01
picol [Indonesia]		**<mass, special - see page 29>**
kilogram	61.761	6.176 100 0E+01
picol [Japan]		**<mass, special - see page 29>**
kilogram	60	6.000 000 0E+01
picol [Laos]		**<mass, special - see page 29>**
kilogram	60	6.000 000 0E+01
picol [Macao]		**<mass, special - see page 29>**
kilogram	60.479	6.047 900 0E+01
picol [Malaysia]		**<mass, special - see page 29>**
kilogram	60.479	6.047 900 0E+01
picol [Philippines]		**<mass, special - see page 29>**
kilogram	63.249	6.324 900 0E+01
picol [Singapore]		**<mass, special - see page 29>**
kilogram	60.479	6.047 900 0E+01
picol [Thailand]		**<mass, special - see page 29>**
kilogram	60	6.000 000 0E+01
picol [Vietnam]		**<mass, special - see page 29>**
kilogram	60.453	6.045 300 0E+01
picoliter		**<volume>**
barrel [UK]	<<<	6.110 256 9E−15
barrel [US, liquid]	<<<	8.386 414 4E−15
barrel [US, petroleum]	<<<	6.289 810 8E−15
cubic foot	<<<	3.531 466 7E−14
cubic inch	<<<	6.102 374 4E−11
cubic meter	<<<	1.000 000 0E−15
drachm [UK, liquid]	<<<	2.815 606 4E−10
dram [Canada, liquid]	<<<	2.815 606 4E−10
dram [US, liquid]	<<<	2.705 121 8E−10
drop [US, liquid]	<<<	1.217 304 8E−08
gallon [Canada, liquid]	<<<	2.199 692 5E−13
gallon [UK, dry or liquid]	<<<	2.199 692 5E−13
gallon [US, liquid]	<<<	2.641 720 5E−13
gill [UK]	<<<	7.039 015 9E−12
gill [US]	<<<	8.453 505 7E−12
lambda	0.000 001	1.000 000 0E−06
liter	<<<	1.000 000 0E−12
ounce [UK, liquid]	<<<	3.519 508 0E−11
ounce [US, liquid]	<<<	3.381 402 3E−11
pint [UK]	<<<	1.759 754 0E−12
pint [US, liquid]	<<<	2.113 376 4E−12
quart [UK]	<<<	8.798 769 9E−13
quart [US, liquid]	<<<	1.056 688 2E−12
scruple [UK, liquid]	<<<	8.446 819 1E−10
tablespoon [Canada, measuring]	<<<	7.039 027 9E−11
tablespoon [US, measuring]	<<<	6.762 804 5E−11
teaspoon [Canada, measuring]	<<<	2.111 708 4E−10
teaspoon [US, measuring]	<<<	2.028 841 4E−10
picometer		**<length>**
angstrom	0.01	1.000 000 0E−02
bicron	1	1.000 000 0E+00
fermi	1,000	1.000 000 0E+03

	Standard	Scientific
inch [based on US, survey foot]	<<<	3.937 000 0E−11
inch [international]	<<<	3.937 007 9E−11
meter	<<<	1.000 000 0E−12
micromicron	1	1.000 000 0E+00
stigma	1	1.000 000 0E+00
tenthmeter	0.01	1.000 000 0E−02
wavelength of orange-red spectral line of krypton-86	0.000 001 7	1.650 763 7E−06
x-unit	9.979 320 9	9.979 320 9E+00

picomole <amount of substance>
	Standard	Scientific
mole	<<<	1.000 000 0E−12

piconewton <force>
	Standard	Scientific
crinal	<<<	1.000 000 0E−11
dyne	0.000 000 1	1.000 000 0E−07
gram-force	<<<	1.019 716 2E−10
newton	<<<	1.000 000 0E−12
ounce-force	<<<	3.596 943 1E−12
pond	<<<	1.019 716 2E−10
pound-force	<<<	2.248 089 4E−13
poundal	<<<	7.233 013 9E−12

picoohm <electric resistance>
	Standard	Scientific
1/ siemens	<<<	1.000 000 0E−12
abohm	0.001	1.000 000 0E−03
ohm	<<<	1.000 000 0E−12
statohm	<<<	1.112 650 1E−24

picopascal <pressure>
	Standard	Scientific
atmosphere [standard]	<<<	9.869 232 7E−18
atmosphere [technical]	<<<	1.019 716 2E−17
bar	<<<	1.000 000 0E−17
barye [France]	<<<	1.000 000 0E−11
dyne/square centimeter	<<<	1.000 000 0E−11
kilogram-force/square meter	<<<	1.019 716 2E−13
kilopond/square meter	<<<	1.019 716 2E−13
micrometer of mercury [0 °C, by convention]	<<<	7.500 615 8E−12
micrometer of water [4 °C, by convention]	<<<	1.019 716 2E−10
newton/square meter	<<<	1.000 000 0E−12
pascal	<<<	1.000 000 0E−12
pound-force/square foot	<<<	2.088 543 4E−14
poundal/square foot	<<<	6.719 689 8E−13
torr	<<<	7.500 616 8E−15

picosecond <sedimentation coefficient>
	Standard	Scientific
svedberg	10	1.000 000 0E+01

picosiemens <electric conductance>
	Standard	Scientific
electrostatic unit of conductance [cgs system]	0.898 755 2	8.987 551 8E−01
gaussian electric conductance	0.898 755 2	8.987 551 8E−01
siemens	<<<	1.000 000 0E−12
statsiemens	0.898 755 2	8.987 551 8E−01

picotesla <magnetic flux density>
	Standard	Scientific
gamma	0.001	1.000 000 0E−03
line/square centimeter [of magnetic force]	<<<	1.000 000 0E−08
maxwell/square meter	<<<	1.000 000 0E−12
nanotesla	0.001	1.000 000 0E−03
tesla	<<<	1.000 000 0E−12

picovolt <electric potential>
	Standard	Scientific
abvolt	0.000 1	1.000 000 0E−04
electromagnetic unit of electric potential [cgs system]	0.000 1	1.000 000 0E−04
electrostatic unit of electric potential [cgs system]	<<<	3.335 641 0E−15
statvolt	<<<	3.335 641 0E−15
volt	<<<	1.000 000 0E−12

picowatt <power>
	Standard	Scientific
Btu/hour [I.T.]	<<<	3.412 141 6E−12
Btu/hour [thermoc.]	<<<	3.414 425 1E−12

Convert From Convert To	Standard	<Type of Unit> Scientific
calorie/hour [I.T.]	<<<	8.598 452 3E–10
calorie/hour [thermoc.]	<<<	8.604 206 5E–10
centigrade heat unit/hour [mean]	<<<	1.894 172 6E–12
cubic meter atmosphere/hour	<<<	3.552 923 8E–08
dyne centimeter/hour	0.036	3.600 000 0E–02
erg/hour	0.036	3.600 000 0E–02
foot pound-force/hour	<<<	2.655 223 7E–09
foot poundal/hour	<<<	8.542 929 7E–08
gram-force centimeter/hour	0.000 036 7	3.670 978 4E–05
horsepower	<<<	1.341 022 1E–15
horsepower [metric]	<<<	1.359 621 6E–15
joule/hour	<<<	3.600 000 0E–09
kilocalorie/hour [I.T.]	<<<	8.598 452 3E–13
kilogram-force meter/hour	<<<	3.670 978 4E–10
kilopond meter/hour	<<<	3.670 978 4E–10
newton meter/hour	<<<	3.600 000 0E–09
volt ampere	<<<	1.000 000 0E–12
watt	<<<	1.000 000 0E–12
picowatt/square meter		**<heat flux density>**
Btu/day square foot [I.T.]	<<<	7.607 959 9E–12
Btu/day square foot [thermoc.]	<<<	7.613 051 3E–12
calorie/day square centimeter [I.T.]	<<<	2.063 628 5E–12
calorie/day square centimeter [thermoc.]	<<<	2.065 009 6E–12
watt/square foot	<<<	9.290 304 0E–14
watt/square meter	<<<	1.000 000 0E–12
picoweber		**<magnetic flux>**
gauss square centimeter	0.000 1	1.000 000 0E–04
maxwell	0.000 1	1.000 000 0E–04
statweber	<<<	3.335 641 0E–15
unit pole	0.000 008	7.957 747 5E–06
weber	<<<	1.000 000 0E–12
picul [Brunei]		**<mass, special - see page 29>**
kilogram	60.479	6.047 900 0E+01
picul [Cambodia]		**<mass, special - see page 29>**
kilogram	60	6.000 000 0E+01
picul [China]		**<mass, special - see page 29>**
kilogram	60.478 98	6.047 898 0E+01
picul [Hong Kong]		**<mass, special - see page 29>**
kilogram	60.479	6.047 900 0E+01
picul [India]		**<mass, special - see page 29>**
kilogram	59.052	5.905 200 0E+01
picul [Indonesia]		**<mass, special - see page 29>**
kilogram	61.761	6.176 100 0E+01
picul [Japan]		**<mass, special - see page 29>**
kilogram	60	6.000 000 0E+01
picul [Laos]		**<mass, special - see page 29>**
kilogram	60	6.000 000 0E+01
picul [Macao]		**<mass, special - see page 29>**
kilogram	60.479	6.047 900 0E+01
picul [Malaysia]		**<mass, special - see page 29>**
kilogram	60.479	6.047 900 0E+01
picul [North Borneo]		**<mass, special - see page 29>**
kilogram	60.478 98	6.047 898 0E+01
picul [Philippines]		**<mass, special - see page 29>**
kilogram	63.249	6.324 900 0E+01
picul [Singapore]		**<mass, special - see page 29>**
kilogram	60.479	6.047 900 0E+01
picul [South Korea]		**<mass, special - see page 29>**
kilogram	60.477 5	6.047 750 0E+01

picul [Thailand] \<mass, special - see page 29\>
kilogram ---60----6.000 000 0E+01

picul [Vietnam] \<mass, special - see page 29\>
kilogram ---------------------------------------60.453----6.045 300 0E+01

pie [Argentina] \<length, special - see page 29\>
centimeter--28.89----2.889 000 0E+01

pie [Bolivia] \<length, special - see page 29\>
meter---0.289----2.890 000 0E-01

pie [Chile] \<length, special - see page 29\>
centimeter--30.48----3.048 000 0E+01

pie [Costa Rica] \<length, special - see page 29\>
meter---0.279----2.790 000 0E-01

pie [Cuba] \<length, special - see page 29\>
meter--0.282 7----2.827 000 0E-01

pie [Ecuador] \<length, special - see page 29\>
meter--0.304 8----3.048 000 0E-01

pie [El Salvador] \<length, special - see page 29\>
centimeter--27.86----2.786 000 0E+01

pie [Guatemala] \<length, special - see page 29\>
meter---0.279----2.790 000 0E-01

pie [Haiti] \<length, special - see page 29\>
meter--0.324 8----3.248 000 0E-01

pie [Honduras] \<length, special - see page 29\>
centimeter---------------------------------------27.833----2.783 300 0E+01

pie [Italy] \<length, special - see page 29\>
meter---0.28----2.800 000 0E-01

pie [Mexico] \<length, special - see page 29\>
meter---0.279----2.790 000 0E-01

pie [Nicaragua] \<length, special - see page 29\>
meter---0.28----2.800 000 0E-01

pie [Paraguay] \<length, special - see page 29\>
meter---0.289----2.890 000 0E-01

pie [Spain] \<length, special - see page 29\>
meter---0.279----2.790 000 0E-01

pie cuadrada [Mexico] \<area, special - see page 29\>
square centimeter----------------------------------780.27----7.802 700 0E+02

pie cuadrada [Spain] \<area, special - see page 29\>
square centimeter--------------------------------776.375----7.763 750 0E+02

pie cuadrado [Honduras] \<area, special - see page 29\>
square centimeter-----------------------------------774.7----7.747 000 0E+02

pie cubica [Mexico] \<volume, special - see page 29\>
cubic centimeter----------------------------------21,796----2.179 600 0E+04

pie de madera [Cuba] \<volume, special - see page 29\>
liter--2.36----2.360 000 0E+00

pied [Belgium] \<length, special - see page 29\>
centimeter--32.49----3.249 000 0E+01

pied [Canada, Quebec] \<length, special - see page 29\>
meter---0.324 84----3.248 400 0E-01

pied [Costa Rica] \<length, special - see page 29\>
meter---0.279----2.790 000 0E-01

pied [Cuba] \<length, special - see page 29\>
meter--0.282 7----2.827 000 0E-01

pied [France] \<length, special - see page 29\>
meter---0.324 84----3.248 400 0E-01

Convert From Convert To	Standard	<Type of Unit> Scientific
pied [France]		**<length>**
arpent [France]	0.005 555 6	5.555 555 6E-03
decimeter	3.248 406	3.248 406 0E+00
foot [France]	1	1.000 000 0E+00
foot [international]	1.065 75	1.065 750 0E+00
foot [US, survey]	1.065 747 9	1.065 747 9E+00
inch [based on US, survey foot]	12.788 974	1.278 897 4E+01
inch [international]	12.789	1.278 900 0E+01
link [Gunter or US, survey]	1.614 769 5	1.614 769 5E+00
link [Ramden or Engineer]	1.065 75	1.065 750 0E+00
meter	0.324 840 6	3.248 406 0E-01
nail [cloth]	5.684	5.684 000 0E+00
palm	4.263	4.263 000 0E+00
perche [France]	0.055 555 6	5.555 555 6E-02
span	1.421	1.421 000 0E+00
yard [based on US, survey foot]	0.355 249 3	3.552 492 9E-01
yard [international]	0.355 25	3.552 500 0E-01
pied [Guatemala]		**<length, special - see page 29>**
meter	0.279	2.790 000 0E-01
pied [Haiti]		**<length, special - see page 29>**
meter	0.324 8	3.248 000 0E-01
pied [Mexico]		**<length, special - see page 29>**
meter	0.279	2.790 000 0E-01
pied [Nicaragua]		**<length, special - see page 29>**
meter	0.28	2.800 000 0E-01
pied [Paraguay]		**<length, special - see page 29>**
meter	0.289	2.890 000 0E-01
pied [Spain]		**<length, special - see page 29>**
meter	0.279	2.790 000 0E-01
pied [Switzerland]		**<length, special - see page 29>**
centimeter	30	3.000 000 0E+01
pied anglais [Haiti]		**<length, special - see page 29>**
centimeter	30.48	3.048 000 0E+01
pied carre [Haiti]		**<area, special - see page 29>**
square centimeter	929.030 4	9.290 304 0E+02
pied de perche [UK, land]		**<length, special - see page 29>**
millimeter	279	2.790 000 0E+02
pied de roi [France]		**<length, special - see page 29>**
centimeter	32.487	3.248 700 0E+01
piede [Paraguay]		**<length, special - see page 29>**
centimeter	28.89	2.889 000 0E+01
pieze [France]		**<pressure>**
atmosphere [standard]	0.009 869 2	9.869 232 7E-03
atmosphere [technical]	0.010 197 2	1.019 716 2E-02
bar	0.01	1.000 000 0E-02
barye [France]	10,000	1.000 000 0E+04
centibar	1	1.000 000 0E+00
dyne/square centimeter	10,000	1.000 000 0E+04
gram-force/square centimeter	10.197 162	1.019 716 2E+01
inch of mercury [0 °C, by convention]	0.295 299 8	2.952 998 3E-01
inch of water [4 °C, by convention]	4.014 630 8	4.014 630 8E+00
kilogram-force/square meter	101.971 62	1.019 716 2E+02
kilopascal	1	1.000 000 0E+00
kilopond/square meter	101.971 62	1.019 716 2E+02
kip/square foot	0.020 885 4	2.088 543 4E-02
millimeter of mercury [0 °C, by convention]	7.500 615 8	7.500 615 8E+00
millimeter of water [4 °C, by convention]	101.971 62	1.019 716 2E+02
newton/square meter	1,000	1.000 000 0E+03
ounce-force/square inch	2.320 603 8	2.320 603 8E+00
pascal	1,000	1.000 000 0E+03

Convert From Convert To	<Type of Unit>	
	Standard	Scientific
pound-force/square foot	20.885 434	2.088 543 4E+01
poundal/square foot	671.968 98	6.719 689 8E+02
sthene/square meter [France]	1	1.000 000 0E+00
ton-force/square foot [short]	0.010 442 7	1.044 271 7E-02
ton-force/square meter [metric]	0.101 971 6	1.019 716 2E-01
torr	7.500 616 8	7.500 616 8E+00
pijp [Netherlands]	<volume, special - see page 29>	
hectoliter	5.4	5.400 000 0E+00
pik [Algeria]	<length, special - see page 29>	
meter	0.495	4.950 000 0E-01
pik [Bahrain]	<length, special - see page 29>	
centimeter	48.26	4.826 000 0E+01
pik [Cyprus]	<length, special - see page 29>	
centimeter	60.96	6.096 000 0E+01
pik [Egypt]	<length, special - see page 29>	
centimeter	58	5.800 000 0E+01
pik [Greece]	<length, special - see page 29>	
centimeter	75	7.500 000 0E+01
pik [Iraq]	<length, special - see page 29>	
centimeter	74.5	7.450 000 0E+01
pik [Jordan, land]	<length, special - see page 29>	
centimeter	75.8	7.580 000 0E+01
pik [Jordan, textiles]	<length, special - see page 29>	
centimeter	68	6.800 000 0E+01
pik [Lebanon, land]	<length, special - see page 29>	
centimeter	75.8	7.580 000 0E+01
pik [Lebanon, textiles]	<length, special - see page 29>	
centimeter	68	6.800 000 0E+01
pik [Libya]	<length, special - see page 29>	
centimeter	68	6.800 000 0E+01
pik [Morocco]	<length, special - see page 29>	
centimeter	55.88	5.588 000 0E+01
pik [Russia]	<length, special - see page 29>	
centimeter	71.12	7.112 000 0E+01
pik [Saudi Arabia]	<length, special - see page 29>	
centimeter	45.7	4.570 000 0E+01
pik [Syria, textiles]	<length, special - see page 29>	
centimeter	70	7.000 000 0E+01
pik [Turkey, land]	<length, special - see page 29>	
centimeter	75.8	7.580 000 0E+01
pik andoulsi [Tunisia, wool]	<length, special - see page 29>	
centimeter	64.9	6.490 000 0E+01
pik arbi [Tunisia, linen]	<length, special - see page 29>	
centimeter	49.3	4.930 000 0E+01
pik baladi [Sudan]	<length, special - see page 29>	
centimeter	57.99	5.799 000 0E+01
pik turki [Tunisia, silk]	<length, special - see page 29>	
centimeter	64.5	6.450 000 0E+01
pike [Greece]	<length, special - see page 29>	
centimeter	75	7.500 000 0E+01
pikul [Brunei]	<mass, special - see page 29>	
kilogram	60.479	6.047 900 0E+01
pikul [Cambodia]	<mass, special - see page 29>	
kilogram	60	6.000 000 0E+01
pikul [China]	<mass, special - see page 29>	
kilogram	60.479	6.047 900 0E+01

| Convert From | | <Type of Unit> | |
Convert To		Standard	Scientific

pikul [Hong Kong]   **<mass, special - see page 29>**
  kilogram --- 60.479 --- 6.047 900 0E+01

pikul [Indonesia]   **<mass, special - see page 29>**
  kilogram --- 61.761 --- 6.176 100 0E+01

pikul [Japan]   **<mass, special - see page 29>**
  kilogram -- 60 --- 6.000 000 0E+01

pikul [Laos]   **<mass, special - see page 29>**
  kilogram -- 60 --- 6.000 000 0E+01

pikul [Macao]   **<mass, special - see page 29>**
  kilogram --- 60.479 --- 6.047 900 0E+01

pikul [Malaysia]   **<mass, special - see page 29>**
  kilogram --- 60.479 --- 6.047 900 0E+01

pikul [North Borneo]   **<mass, special - see page 29>**
  kilogram -- 60.478 98 --- 6.047 898 0E+01

pikul [Philippines]   **<mass, special - see page 29>**
  kilogram --- 63.249 --- 6.324 900 0E+01

pikul [Singapore]   **<mass, special - see page 29>**
  kilogram --- 60.479 --- 6.047 900 0E+01

pikul [Thailand]   **<mass, special - see page 29>**
  kilogram -- 60 --- 6.000 000 0E+01

pikul [Vietnam]   **<mass, special - see page 29>**
  kilogram --- 60.453 --- 6.045 300 0E+01

pim [Hebrew, ancient]   **<mass, special - see page 29>**
  gram -- 7.61 --- 7.610 000 0E+00

pin [UK]   **<volume, special - see page 29>**
  liter -- 20.5 --- 2.050 000 0E+01

pinch [US, an approximate measurement]   **<volume>**
  teaspoon -- less than 1/8 teaspoon

pinar [Iran]   **<mass, special - see page 29>**
  gram --- 93.75 --- 9.375 000 0E+01

pinometer [Czechoslovakia]   **<volume, special - see page 29>**
  cubic meter --- 1 --- 1.000 000 0E+00

pint [Netherlands]   **<volume, special - see page 29>**
  liter -- 0.606 3 --- 6.063 000 0E-01

pint [UK]   **<volume>**
  bushel [UK] --- 0.015 625 --- 1.562 500 0E-02
  bushel [US, dry] --- 0.016 125 9 --- 1.612 588 7E-02
  cubic foot --- 0.020 068 --- 2.006 795 7E-02
  cubic inch --- 34.677 429 --- 3.467 742 9E+01
  cubic meter --- 0.000 568 3 --- 5.682 612 5E-04
  cup [Canada, measuring] --- 2.5 --- 2.500 000 0E+00
  cup [US, measuring] --- 2.401 899 9 --- 2.401 899 9E+00
  deciliter -- 5.682 612 5 --- 5.682 612 5E+00
  drachm [UK, liquid] --- 160 --- 1.600 000 0E+02
  dram [Canada, liquid] --- 160 --- 1.600 000 0E+02
  dram [US, liquid] --- 153.721 59 --- 1.537 215 9E+02
  gallon [Canada, liquid] --- 0.125 --- 1.250 000 0E-01
  gallon [UK, dry or liquid] --- 0.125 --- 1.250 000 0E-01
  gallon [US, liquid] --- 0.150 118 7 --- 1.501 187 4E-01
  gill [UK] --- 4 --- 4.000 000 0E+00
  gill [US] --- 4.803 799 7 --- 4.803 799 7E+00
  lambda --- 568,261.25 --- 5.682 612 5E+05
  liter -- 0.568 261 3 --- 5.682 612 5E-01
  minim [UK] --- 9,600 --- 9.600 000 0E+03
  minim [US] --- 9,223.295 4 --- 9.223 295 4E+03
  ounce [UK, liquid] --- 20 --- 2.000 000 0E+01
  ounce [US, liquid] --- 19.215 199 --- 1.921 519 9E+01
  pint [US, dry] --- 1.032 056 7 --- 1.032 056 7E+00

Convert From Convert To	Standard	**\<Type of Unit\>** Scientific
pint [US, liquid] --	1.200 949 9	1.200 949 9E+00
pipe [UK] --	0.001 157 4	1.157 407 4E−03
pipe [US, liquid] ---	0.001 191 4	1.191 418 6E−03
quart [UK] ---	0.5	5.000 000 0E−01
quart [US, dry] --	0.516 028 4	5.160 283 7E−01
quart [US, liquid] ---	0.600 475	6.004 749 6E−01
scruple [UK, liquid] --	480	4.800 000 0E+02
tablespoon [Canada, measuring] -------------------------	40.000 068	4.000 006 8E+01
tablespoon [US, measuring] -----------------------------	38.430 398	3.843 039 8E+01
teaspoon [Canada, measuring] ---------------------------	120.000 2	1.200 002 0E+02
teaspoon [US, measuring] --------------------------------	115.291 19	1.152 911 9E+02
Winchester wine gallon [UK] -----------------------------	0.150 118 7	1.501 187 4E−01
pint [US, dry]		**\<volume\>**
barrel [UK] --	0.003 364 4	3.364 371 4E−03
barrel [US, dry] ---	0.004 761 9	4.761 949 1E−03
bushel [UK] --	0.015 139 7	1.513 967 1E−02
bushel [US, dry] --	0.015 625	1.562 500 0E−02
cubic decimeter---	0.550 610 5	5.506 104 7E−01
cubic foot --	0.019 444 6	1.944 462 5E−02
cubic inch --	33.600 313	3.360 031 3E+01
cubic meter ---	0.000 550 6	5.506 104 7E−04
cubic yard ---	0.000 720 2	7.201 713 1E−04
cup [Canada, measuring] --------------------------------	2.422 347 4	2.422 347 4E+00
cup [US, measuring] ---------------------------------------	2.327 294 4	2.327 294 4E+00
deciliter ---	5.506 104 7	5.506 104 7E+00
gallon [UK, dry or liquid] --------------------------------	0.121 117 4	1.211 173 7E−01
gallon [US, dry] --	0.125	1.250 000 0E−01
gill [UK] ---	3.875 755 9	3.875 755 9E+00
gill [US] ---	4.654 588 7	4.654 588 7E+00
liter ---	0.550 610 5	5.506 104 7E−01
peck [UK] --	0.060 558 7	6.055 868 6E−02
peck [US] --	0.062 5	6.250 000 0E−02
pint [UK] ---	0.968 939	9.689 389 7E−01
quart [UK] ---	0.484 469 5	4.844 694 9E−01
quart [US, dry] --	0.5	5.000 000 0E−01
tablespoon [Canada, measuring] -------------------------	38.757 624	3.875 762 4E+01
tablespoon [US, measuring] -----------------------------	37.236 71	3.723 671 0E+01
teaspoon [Canada, measuring] ---------------------------	116.272 87	1.162 728 7E+02
teaspoon [US, measuring] --------------------------------	111.710 13	1.117 101 3E+02
pint [US, liquid]		**\<volume\>**
barrel [UK] --	0.002 891 2	2.891 229 8E−03
barrel [US, federal proof spirits] -------------------------	0.003 125	3.125 000 0E−03
barrel [US, liquid] --	0.003 968 3	3.968 254 0E−03
barrel [US, petroleum] ---------------------------------------	0.002 976 2	2.976 190 5E−03
cubic foot --	0.016 710 1	1.671 006 9E−02
cubic inch --	28.875	2.887 500 0E+01
cubic meter ---	0.000 473 2	4.731 764 7E−04
cup [Canada, measuring] --------------------------------	2.081 685 5	2.081 685 5E+00
cup [US, measuring] ---------------------------------------	2	2.000 000 0E+00
deciliter ---	4.731 764 7	4.731 764 7E+00
drachm [UK, liquid] --	133.227 87	1.332 278 7E+02
dram [Canada, liquid] ---	133.227 87	1.332 278 7E+02
dram [US, liquid] --	128	1.280 000 0E+02
drop [US, liquid] --	5,760	5.760 000 0E+03
gallon [Canada, liquid] ---------------------------------------	0.104 084 3	1.040 842 7E−01
gallon [UK, dry or liquid] --------------------------------	0.104 084 3	1.040 842 7E−01
gallon [US, liquid] --	0.125	1.250 000 0E−01
gill [UK] ---	3.330 696 7	3.330 696 7E+00
gill [US] ---	4	4.000 000 0E+00
liter ---	0.473 176 5	4.731 764 7E−01
minim [UK] --	7,993.672 2	7.993 672 2E+03
minim [US] --	7,680	7.680 000 0E+03
ounce [UK, liquid] --	16.653 484	1.665 348 4E+01

	Standard	Scientific
ounce [US, liquid]	16	1.600 000 0E+01
pint [UK]	0.832 674 2	8.326 741 8E-01
quart [UK]	0.416 337 1	4.163 370 9E-01
quart [US, liquid]	0.5	5.000 000 0E-01
scruple [UK, liquid]	399.683 61	3.996 836 1E+02
tablespoon [Canada, measuring]	33.307 024	3.330 702 4E+01
tablespoon [US, measuring]	32	3.200 000 0E+01
teaspoon [Canada, measuring]	99.921 071	9.992 107 1E+01
teaspoon [US, measuring]	96	9.600 000 0E+01
Winchester wine gallon [UK]	0.125	1.250 000 0E-01
pinta [Chile]	\<volume, special - see page 29\>	
liter	0.56	5.600 000 0E-01
pinta [Malta, beer, wine and spirits]	\<volume, special - see page 29\>	
milliliter	142	1.420 000 0E+02
pinte [France]	\<volume, special - see page 29\>	
liter	0.931	9.310 000 0E-01
pintji [Netherlands Antilles]	\<mass, special - see page 29\>	
kilogram	0.375	3.750 000 0E-01
pipa [Argentina]	\<volume, special - see page 29\>	
hectoliter	4.56	4.560 000 0E+00
pipa [Brazil]	\<volume, special - see page 29\>	
liter	479.16	4.791 600 0E+02
pipa [Cuba]	\<volume, special - see page 29\>	
liter	476.93	4.769 300 0E+02
pipa [Dominican Republic]	\<volume, special - see page 29\>	
hectoliter	5.728	5.728 000 0E+00
pipa [Paraguay]	\<volume, special - see page 29\>	
hectoliter	5.816	5.816 000 0E+00
pipa [Portugal]	\<volume, special - see page 29\>	
liter	435.3	4.353 000 0E+02
pipa [Singapore]	\<volume, special - see page 29\>	
hectoliter	5.728	5.728 000 0E+00
pipa [Sweden]	\<volume, special - see page 29\>	
liter	471.081	4.710 810 0E+02
pipe [Argentina]	\<volume, special - see page 29\>	
hectoliter	4.56	4.560 000 0E+00
pipe [Cuba]	\<volume, special - see page 29\>	
hectoliter	4.769	4.769 000 0E+00
pipe [Dominican Republic]	\<volume, special - see page 29\>	
hectoliter	5.728	5.728 000 0E+00
pipe [Netherlands, wine]	\<volume, special - see page 29\>	
hectoliter	4.122 5	4.122 500 0E+00
pipe [Paraguay]	\<volume, special - see page 29\>	
hectoliter	5.816	5.816 000 0E+00
pipe [Portugal, Lisbon]	\<volume, special - see page 29\>	
liter	530	5.300 000 0E+02
pipe [Portugal, wine]	\<volume, special - see page 29\>	
liter	535	5.350 000 0E+02
pipe [Russia, liquid]	\<volume, special - see page 29\>	
hectoliter	4.428	4.428 000 0E+00
pipe [Singapore]	\<volume, special - see page 29\>	
hectoliter	5.728	5.728 000 0E+00
pipe [South Africa]	\<volume, special - see page 29\>	
liter	416.383 6	4.163 836 0E+02
pipe [Spain, wine]	\<volume, special - see page 29\>	
liter	4.355	4.355 000 0E+00

Convert From Convert To	Standard	\<Type of Unit\> Scientific
pipe [UK]		**\<volume\>**
barrel [UK]	3	3.000 000 0E+00
barrel [US, dry]	4.246 215 8	4.246 215 8E+00
barrel [US, liquid]	4.117 542 6	4.117 542 6E+00
barrel [US, petroleum]	3.088 157	3.088 157 0E+00
bushel [UK]	13.5	1.350 000 0E+01
bushel [US, dry]	13.932 766	1.393 276 6E+01
chaldron [UK, dry]	0.375	3.750 000 0E−01
chaldron [UK, liquid]	0.375	3.750 000 0E−01
cord foot [timber]	1.083 669 7	1.083 669 7E+00
cubic foot	17.338 715	1.733 871 5E+01
cubic inch	29,961.299	2.996 129 9E+04
cubic meter	0.490 977 7	4.909 777 2E−01
cubic yard	0.642 174 6	6.421 746 1E−01
cup [Canada, measuring]	2,160	2.160 000 0E+03
cup [US, measuring]	2,075.241 5	2.075 241 5E+03
drachm [UK, liquid]	138,240	1.382 400 0E+05
dram [Canada, liquid]	138,240	1.382 400 0E+05
dram [US, liquid]	132,815.45	1.328 154 5E+05
drum [US, liquid]	2.358 228 9	2.358 228 9E+00
firkin [UK]	12	1.200 000 0E+01
firkin [US]	14.411 399	1.441 139 9E+01
gallon [Canada, liquid]	108	1.080 000 0E+02
gallon [UK, dry or liquid]	108	1.080 000 0E+02
gallon [US, liquid]	129.702 59	1.297 025 9E+02
gill [UK]	3,456	3.456 000 0E+03
gill [US]	4,150.482 9	4.150 482 9E+03
hectoliter	4.909 777 2	4.909 777 2E+00
hogshead [UK]	1.714 285 7	1.714 285 7E+00
hogshead [US]	2.058 771 3	2.058 771 3E+00
liter	490.977 72	4.909 777 2E+02
ounce [UK, liquid]	17,280	1.728 000 0E+04
ounce [US, liquid]	16,601.932	1.660 193 2E+04
pint [UK]	864	8.640 000 0E+02
pint [US, liquid]	1,037.620 7	1.037 620 7E+03
pipe [US, liquid]	1,029 385 7	1.029 385 7E+00
quart [UK]	432	4.320 000 0E+02
quart [US, liquid]	518.810 37	5.188 103 7E+02
quarter [UK]	1.687 5	1.687 500 0E+00
stere	0.490 977 7	4.909 777 2E−01
tun [UK, liquid]	0.5	5.000 000 0E−01
tun [US, liquid]	0.514 692 8	5.146 928 3E−01
Winchester wine gallon [UK]	129.702 59	1.297 025 9E+02
pipe [US, liquid]		**\<volume\>**
barrel [UK]	2.914 359 6	2.914 359 6E+00
barrel [US, federal proof spirits]	3.15	3.150 000 0E+00
barrel [US, liquid]	4	4.000 000 0E+00
barrel [US, petroleum]	3	3.000 000 0E+00
cubic foot	16.843 75	1.684 375 0E+01
cubic inch	29,106	2.910 600 0E+04
cubic meter	0.476 961 9	4.769 618 8E−01
cubic yard	0.623 842 6	6.238 425 9E−01
cup [Canada, measuring]	2,098.338 9	2.098 338 9E+03
cup [US, measuring]	2,016	2.016 000 0E+03
drachm [UK, liquid]	134,293.69	1.342 936 9E+05
dram [Canada, liquid]	134,293.69	1.342 936 9E+05
dram [US, liquid]	129,024	1.290 240 0E+05
drum [US, liquid]	2.290 909 1	2.290 909 1E+00
firkin [UK]	11.657 439	1.165 743 9E+01
firkin [US]	14	1.400 000 0E+01
gallon [Canada, liquid]	104.916 95	1.049 169 5E+02
gallon [UK, dry or liquid]	104.916 95	1.049 169 5E+02
gallon [US, liquid]	126	1.260 000 0E+02

| Convert From | | <Type of Unit> |
Convert To	Standard	Scientific
gill [UK]	3,357.342 3	3.357 342 3E+03
gill [US]	4,032	4.032 000 0E+03
hectoliter	4.769 618 8	4.769 618 8E+00
hogshead [UK]	1.665 348 4	1.665 348 4E+00
hogshead [US]	2	2.000 000 0E+00
liter	476.961 88	4.769 618 8E+02
ounce [UK, liquid]	16,786.712	1.678 671 2E+04
ounce [US, liquid]	16,128	1.612 800 0E+04
pint [UK]	839.335 58	8.393 355 8E+02
pint [US, liquid]	1,008	1.008 000 0E+03
pipe [UK]	0.971 453 2	9.714 532 2E-01
quart [UK]	419.667 79	4.196 677 9E+02
quart [US, liquid]	504	5.040 000 0E+02
quarter [UK]	1.639 327 3	1.639 327 3E+00
stere	0.476 961 9	4.769 618 8E-01
tun [UK, liquid]	0.485 726 6	4.857 266 1E-01
tun [US, liquid]	0.5	5.000 000 0E-01
Winchester wine gallon [UK]	126	1.260 000 0E+02

piq [Lebanon, land]   <length - see page 29>
centimeter	75.8	7.580 000 0E+01

piq [Lebanon, textiles]   <length - see page 29>
centimeter	68	6.800 000 0E+01

pishi [Tanganyika]   <volume, special - see page 29>
liter	4	4.000 000 0E+00

pishi [Tanzania]   <volume, special - see page 29>
liter	4	4.000 000 0E+00

pjak [Russia]   <volume, special - see page 29>
liter	52.477 47	5.247 747 0E+01

planck   <moment of momentum>
joule second	1	1.000 000 0E+00
kilogram square meter/second	1	1.000 000 0E+00
newton meter second	1	1.000 000 0E+00
pound square foot/second	23.730 36	2.373 036 0E+01

planken [Germany, liquid]   <volume, special - see page 29>
milliliter	429	4.290 000 0E+02

plethron [Greece, ancient]   <length - see page 29>
meter	30.8	3.080 000 0E+01

pli   <linear density>
kilogram/meter	17.857 967	1.785 796 7E+01
ounce/foot	192	1.920 000 0E+02
ounce/inch	16	1.600 000 0E+01
pound/foot	12	1.200 000 0E+01
pound/inch	1	1.000 000 0E+00
pound/yard	36	3.600 000 0E+01

pliashka [Russia, liquid]   <volume, special - see page 29>
liter	0.61	6.100 000 0E-01

pocket [Swaziland, rice, milled]   <mass, special - see page 29>
kilogram	45.359	4.535 900 0E+01

pocket [Zambia, rice, milled]   <mass, special - see page 29>
kilogram	45	4.500 000 0E+01

podd [Portuguese India]   <volume, special - see page 29>
liter	0.998 3	9.983 000 0E-01

poids de marc [France]   <mass, special - see page 29>
gram	489.5	4.895 000 0E+02

poids de Paris [France]   <mass, special - see page 29>
kilogram	489.51	4.895 100 0E+02

poids de soie [France]   <mass, special - see page 29>
gram	458.912	4.589 120 0E+02

| Convert From | <Type of Unit> | |
Convert To	Standard	Scientific
poids de ville [France]	<mass, special - see page 29>	
gram	418.76	4.187 600 0E+02
point [Denmark]	<length, special - see page 29>	
millimeter	0.181 63	1.816 300 0E-01
point [France]	<length, special - see page 29>	
millimeter	0.188	1.880 000 0E-01
point [jewelers']		<mass>
carat [gemstones]	0.01	1.000 000 0E-02
carat [metric]	0.01	1.000 000 0E-02
carat [US, after 1913]	0.01	1.000 000 0E-02
dram [avoirdupois]	0.001 128 8	1.128 766 8E-03
gamma	2,000	2.000 000 0E+03
grain	0.030 864 7	3.086 471 7E-02
grain [avoirdupois]	0.030 864 7	3.086 471 7E-02
grain [troy]	0.030 864 7	3.086 471 7E-02
kilogram	0.000 002	2.000 000 0E-06
milligram	2	2.000 000 0E+00
ounce	0.000 070 5	7.054 792 4E-05
ounce [apothecary]	0.000 064 3	6.430 149 3E-05
ounce [avoirdupois]	0.000 070 5	7.054 792 4E-05
ounce [troy]	0.000 064 3	6.430 149 3E-05
pennyweight [troy]	0.001 286	1.286 029 9E-03
scruple [UK]	0.001 543 2	1.543 235 8E-03
scruple [US, apothecary]	0.001 543 2	1.543 235 8E-03
point [print]		<length>
agate [print]	0.181 818 2	1.818 181 8E-01
caliber	1.383 7	1.383 700 0E+00
didot point [print]	0.933 532 5	9.335 324 9E-01
douzieme [print]	1.992 528	1.992 528 0E+00
em [pica, print]	0.083 333 3	8.333 333 0E-02
inch [based on US, survey foot]	0.013 837	1.383 697 2E-02
inch [international]	0.013 837	1.383 700 0E-02
iron [print]	0.003 333 3	3.333 333 0E-03
ligne [print]	0.166 044	1.660 440 0E-01
line [print]	0.166 044	1.660 440 0E-01
meter	0.000 351 5	3.514 598 0E-04
micron	351.459 8	3.514 598 0E+02
mil	13.837	1.383 700 0E+01
millimeter	0.351 459 8	3.514 598 0E-01
nonpareil [print]	0.166 666 7	1.666 666 7E-01
pearl [print]	0.2	2.000 000 0E-01
pica [print]	0.083 333 3	8.333 333 0E-02
poise		<dynamic viscosity>
dyne second/square centimeter	1	1.000 000 0E+00
gram/centimeter second	1	1.000 000 0E+00
kilogram/meter second	0.1	1.000 000 0E-01
newton second/square meter	0.1	1.000 000 0E-01
pascal second	0.1	1.000 000 0E-01
poiseuille [France]	0.1	1.000 000 0E-01
pound/foot hour	241.908 831	2.419 088 3E+02
poundal hour/square foot	241.908 831	2.419 088 3E+02
poise cubic centimeter/gram		<kinematic viscosity>
lentor	1	1.000 000 0E+00
liter/centimeter hour	3.6	3.600 000 0E+00
square centimeter/second	1	1.000 000 0E+00
square foot/hour	3.875 007 8	3.875 007 8E+00
square inch/minute	9.300 018 6	9.300 018 6E+00
square meter/day	8.64	8.640 000 0E+00
square meter/second	0.000 1	1.000 000 0E-04
square millimeter/second	100	1.000 000 0E+02
stokes	1	1.000 000 0E+00

Convert From Convert To	Standard	<Type of Unit> Scientific
poiseuille [France]		<dynamic viscosity>
dyne second/square centimeter	10	1.000 000 0E+01
gram/centimeter second	10	1.000 000 0E+01
kilogram/meter second	1	1.000 000 0E+00
newton second/square meter	1	1.000 000 0E+00
pascal second	1	1.000 000 0E+00
poise	10	1.000 000 0E+01
pound/foot second	0.671 969	6.719 689 8E-01
poundal second/square foot	0.671 969	6.719 689 8E-01
poisson [France]		<volume, special - see page 29>
liter	0.116	1.160 000 0E-01
pole [Ireland]		<length, special - see page 29>
meter	6.400 8	6.400 800 0E+00
pole [US, survey]		<length>
cable length [US, survey]	0.022 916 7	2.291 666 7E-02
chain [Gunter or US, survey]	0.25	2.500 000 0E-01
chain [Ramden or Engineer]	0.165 000 3	1.650 003 3E-01
fathom [US, survey]	2.75	2.750 000 0E+00
foot [international]	16.500 033	1.650 003 3E+01
foot [US, survey]	16.5	1.650 000 0E+01
furlong [US, survey]	0.025	2.500 000 0E-02
inch [based on US, survey foot]	198	1.980 000 0E+02
inch [international]	198.000 4	1.980 004 0E+02
link [Gunter or US, survey]	25	2.500 000 0E+01
link [Ramden or Engineer]	16.500 033	1.650 003 3E+01
meter	5.029 210 1	5.029 210 1E+00
out [US, survey]	0.05	5.000 000 0E-02
pace [geometrical]	0.330 000 7	3.300 006 6E-01
pace [US, survey]	6.6	6.600 000 0E+00
perch [US, survey]	1	1.000 000 0E+00
rod [US, survey]	1	1.000 000 0E+00
vara [US, survey, California]	6	6.000 000 0E+00
vara [US, survey, Texas]	5.94	5.940 000 0E+00
yard [based on US, survey foot]	5.5	5.500 000 0E+00
yard [international]	5.500 011	5.500 011 0E+00
polegada [Brazil]		<length, special - see page 29>
centimeter	2.75	2.750 000 0E+00
polegada [Macao]		<length, special - see page 29>
millimeter	27.5	2.750 000 0E+01
polegada [Portugal]		<length, special - see page 29>
centimeter	2.75	2.750 000 0E+00
pollam [India]		<mass, special - see page 29>
gram	23.327	2.332 700 0E+01
pollegada [Portugal]		<length, special - see page 29>
centimeter	2.738	2.738 000 0E+00
polugarnetz [Russia]		<volume, special - see page 29>
liter	1.64	1.640 000 0E+00
polygarnetz [Russia]		<volume, special - see page 29>
liter	1.64	1.640 000 0E+00
poncelet [France]		<power>
Btu/minute [I.T.]	55.769 465	5.576 946 5E+01
Btu/minute [thermoc.]	55.806 786	5.580 678 6E+01
calorie/second [I.T.]	234.227 81	2.342 278 1E+02
calorie/second [thermoc.]	234.384 56	2.343 845 6E+02
centigrade heat unit/minute [mean]	30.959 146	3.095 914 6E+01
cheval vapeur [France]	1.333 333 3	1.333 333 3E+00
cubic meter atmosphere/second	9,678.411 1	9.678 411 1E+03
dyne centimeter/second	>>>	9.806 650 0E+09
erg/second	>>>	9.806 650 0E+09
foot pound-force/second	723.301 39	7.233 013 9E+02

Convert From	<Type of Unit>	
Convert To	Standard	Scientific

foot poundal/second	23,271.534	2.327 153 4E+04
gram-force centimeter/second	>>>	1.000 000 0E+07
hectowatt	9.806 65	9.806 650 0E+00
horsepower	1.315 093 4	1.315 093 4E+00
horsepower [metric]	1.333 333 3	1.333 333 3E+00
joule/second	980.665	9.806 650 0E+02
kilocalorie/minute [I.T.]	14.053 669	1.405 366 9E+01
kilogram square meter/cubic second	980.665	9.806 650 0E+02
kilogram-force meter/second	100	1.000 000 0E+02
kilopond meter/second	100	1.000 000 0E+02
newton meter/second	980.665	9.806 650 0E+02
pferdestarke [Germany]	1.333 333 3	1.333 333 3E+00
ton of refrigeration	0.278 847 3	2.788 473 2E−01
volt ampere	980.665	9.806 650 0E+02
watt	980.665	9.806 650 0E+02

pond		<force>
crinal	0.098 066 5	9.806 650 0E−02
dyne	980.665	9.806 650 0E+02
gram-force	1	1.000 000 0E+00
millinewton	9.806 65	9.806 650 0E+00
newton	0.009 806 7	9.806 650 0E−03
ounce-force	0.035 274	3.527 396 2E−02
pound-force	0.002 204 6	2.204 622 6E−03
poundal	0.070 931 6	7.093 163 5E−02

pond [Indonesia]		<mass, special - see page 29>
gram	494.1	4.941 000 0E+02

pond [Netherlands]		<mass, special - see page 29>
gram	494.1	4.941 000 0E+02

pond [Surinam]		<mass, special - see page 29>
gram	500	5.000 000 0E+02

pond centimeter square second		<moment of inertia of a mass>
gram-force centimeter square second	1	1.000 000 0E+00
kilogram square meter	0.000 098 1	9.806 650 0E−05
ounce square inch	5.361 761 4	5.361 761 4E+00
pond meter square second	0.01	1.000 000 0E−02
pound square inch	0.335 110 1	3.351 100 9E−01
slug square inch	0.010 415 5	1.041 554 0E−02

pond meter square second		<moment of inertia of a mass>
gram square meter	9.806 65	9.806 650 0E+00
gram-force meter square second	1	1.000 000 0E+00
kilogram square meter	0.009 806 7	9.806 650 0E−03
ounce square foot	3.723 445 4	3.723 445 4E+00
ounce-force inch square second	1.388 738 7	1.388 738 7E+00
pond centimeter square second	100	1.000 000 0E+02
slug square inch	1.041 554	1.041 554 0E+00

pondermaat [Netherlands]		<area, special - see page 29>
are	36.75	3.675 000 0E+01

pondo [Rome, ancient]		<mass, special - see page 29>
gram	327.45	3.274 500 0E+02

pong [Laos, opium]		<mass, special - see page 29>
gram	375	3.750 000 0E+02

pong chay [Cambodia]		<length, special - see page 29>
millimeter	0.018 1	1.810 000 0E−02

ponto [Brazil]		<length, special - see page 29>
millimeter	0.191	1.910 000 0E−01

ponto [Macao]		<length, special - see page 29>
centimeter	3.76	3.760 000 0E+00

pony [US, liquid]		<volume>
cubic inch	1.804 687 5	1.804 687 5E+00
cubic meter	0.000 029 6	2.957 353 0E−05

drop [US, liquid]	360	3.600 000 0E+02
liter	0.029 573 5	2.957 353 0E-02
ounce [US, liquid]	1	1.000 000 0E+00
shot [US, liquid]	1	1.000 000 0E+00
pood [Russia]		<mass, special - see page 29>
kilogram	16.38	1.638 000 0E+01
posson [France, liquid]		<volume, special - see page 29>
milliliter	116.4	1.164 000 0E+02
postav [Ukraine]		<length, special - see page 29>
meter	28	2.800 000 0E+01
pot [Belgium, dry]		<volume, special - see page 29>
liter	1.5	1.500 000 0E+00
pot [Belgium, liquid]		<volume, special - see page 29>
liter	0.5	5.000 000 0E-01
pot [Denmark]		<volume, special - see page 29>
liter	0.97	9.700 000 0E-01
pot [France]		<volume, special - see page 29>
liter	1.86	1.860 000 0E+00
pot [Hebrew, ancient]		<volume, special - see page 29>
liter	0.53	5.300 000 0E-01
pot [Norway]		<volume, special - see page 29>
liter	1	1.000 000 0E+00
pot [Portugal, liquid]		<volume, special - see page 29>
liter	8.27	8.270 000 0E+00
pot [Switzerland]		<volume, special - see page 29>
liter	1.5	1.500 000 0E+00
pot beaujolais [France]		<volume, special - see page 29>
centiliter	45	4.500 000 0E+01
pottar [Iceland]		<volume, special - see page 29>
liter	0.966 06	9.660 600 0E-01
pottle [UK]		<volume, special - see page 29>
liter	2.272 98	2.272 980 0E+00
pottur [Iceland]		<volume, special - see page 29>
liter	0.97	9.700 000 0E-01
pou [China]		<area, special - see page 29>
square meter	1.67	1.670 000 0E+00
pouce [Belgium]		<length, special - see page 29>
centimeter	3	3.000 000 0E+00
pouce [France]		<length, special - see page 29>
centimeter	2.707	2.707 000 0E+00
pouce [Haiti]		<length, special - see page 29>
millimeter	27.07	2.707 000 0E+01
pouce [Paraguay]		<length, special - see page 29>
centimeter	2.407	2.407 000 0E+00
pouce [Switzerland]		<length, special - see page 29>
centimeter	3	3.000 000 0E+00
poud [Russia]		<mass, special - see page 29>
kilogram	16.38	1.638 000 0E+01
poumar		<linear density>
kilogram/meter	0.000 000 5	4.960 546 5E-07
ounce/yard	0.000 016	1.600 000 0E-05
pound/inch	<<<	2.777 777 8E-08
pound/yard	0.000 001	1.000 000 0E-06
pound		<mass>
bag of cement [US, dry]	0.010 638 3	1.063 829 8E-02
carat [international]	2,267.961 9	2.267 961 9E+03
carat [UK]	1,750	1.750 000 0E+03

Convert From	<Type of Unit>	
Convert To	Standard	Scientific

	Standard	Scientific
carat [US, after 1913]	2,267.961 9	2.267 961 9E+03
cental [US]	0.01	1.000 000 0E-02
cubic foot of cement [US, dry, in bag]	0.010 638 3	1.063 829 8E-02
drachm [UK, apothecary]	116.666 67	1.166 666 7E+02
dram [avoirdupois]	256	2.560 000 0E+02
dram [US, apothecary]	116.666 67	1.166 666 7E+02
grain	7,000	7.000 000 0E+03
grain [avoirdupois]	7,000	7.000 000 0E+03
grain [troy]	7,000	7.000 000 0E+03
hectogram	4.535 923 7	4.535 923 7E+00
hundredweight [long]	0.008 928 6	8.928 571 4E-03
hundredweight [short]	0.01	1.000 000 0E-02
kilogram	0.453 592 4	4.535 923 7E-01
newton square second/meter	0.453 592 4	4.535 923 7E-01
ounce	16	1.600 000 0E+01
ounce [troy]	14.583 333	1.458 333 3E+01
pennyweight [troy]	291.666 67	2.916 666 7E+02
pound [avoirdupois]	1	1.000 000 0E+00
pound [international]	1	1.000 000 0E+00
pound [troy]	1.215 277 8	1.215 277 8E+00
poundal square second/foot	1	1.000 000 0E+00
quarter [short]	0.002	2.000 000 0E-03
quarter [US]	0.04	4.000 000 0E-02
quintal [US]	0.01	1.000 000 0E-02
scruple [UK]	350	3.500 000 0E+02
scruple [US, apothecary]	350	3.500 000 0E+02
slug	0.031 081	3.108 095 0E-02
slug [metric]	0.046 253 5	4.625 354 9E-02
stone [UK]	0.071 428 6	7.142 857 1E-02
ton [long]	0.000 446 4	4.464 285 7E-04
ton [metric]	0.000 453 6	4.535 923 7E-04
ton [short]	0.000 5	5.000 000 0E-04

pound [apothecary]   `<mass>`

	Standard	Scientific
drachm [UK, apothecary]	96	9.600 000 0E+01
dram [US, apothecary]	96	9.600 000 0E+01
grain	5,760	5.760 000 0E+03
grain [apothecary]	5,760	5.760 000 0E+03
grain [avoirdupois]	5,760	5.760 000 0E+03
grain [troy]	5,760	5.760 000 0E+03
hectogram	3.732 417 2	3.732 417 2E+00
kilogram	0.373 241 7	3.732 417 2E-01
ounce	13.165 714	1.316 571 4E+01
ounce [apothecary]	12	1.200 000 0E+01
ounce [avoirdupois]	13.165 714	1.316 571 4E+01
ounce [troy]	12	1.200 000 0E+01
pennyweight [troy]	240	2.400 000 0E+02
pound	0.822 857 1	8.228 571 4E-01
pound [avoirdupois]	0.822 857 1	8.228 571 4E-01
pound [troy]	1	1.000 000 0E+00
scruple [US, apothecary]	288	2.880 000 0E+02

pound [Argentina]   `<mass, special - see page 29>`

	Standard	Scientific
kilogram	0.458 75	4.587 500 0E-01

pound [Austria, Vienna, commercial]   `<mass, special - see page 29>`

	Standard	Scientific
gram	560.012	5.600 120 0E+02

pound [Austria, Vienna, medicinal]   `<mass, special - see page 29>`

	Standard	Scientific
gram	420.009	4.200 090 0E+02

pound [avoirdupois]   `<mass>`

	Standard	Scientific
carat [international]	2,267.961 9	2.267 961 9E+03
carat [UK]	1,750	1.750 000 0E+03
carat [US, after 1913]	2,267.961 9	2.267 961 9E+03
cental [US]	0.01	1.000 000 0E-02
dram [avoirdupois]	256	2.560 000 0E+02

	Standard	Scientific
grain	7,000	7.000 000 0E+03
grain [apothecary]	7,000	7.000 000 0E+03
grain [avoirdupois]	7,000	7.000 000 0E+03
grain [troy]	7,000	7.000 000 0E+03
hectogram	4.535 923 7	4.535 923 7E+00
hundredweight [long]	0.008 928 6	8.928 571 4E-03
hundredweight [short]	0.01	1.000 000 0E-02
kilogram	0.453 592 4	4.535 923 7E-01
ounce	16	1.600 000 0E+01
ounce [apothecary]	14.583 333	1.458 333 3E+01
ounce [avoirdupois]	16	1.600 000 0E+01
pound	1	1.000 000 0E+00
pound [apothecary]	1.215 277 8	1.215 277 8E+00
pound [international]	1	1.000 000 0E+00
pound [troy]	1.215 277 8	1.215 277 8E+00
pound [UK]	1.000 000 1	1.000 000 1E+00
pound [unified]	1	1.000 000 0E+00
pound [US, avoirdupois]	0.999 999 9	9.999 998 7E-01
pound [US, troy]	1.215 277 6	1.215 277 6E+00
poundal square second/foot	1	1.000 000 0E+00
quarter [short]	0.002	2.000 000 0E-03
quarter [US]	0.04	4.000 000 0E-02
quintal [US]	0.01	1.000 000 0E-02
scruple [UK]	350	3.500 000 0E+02
scruple [US, apothecary]	350	3.500 000 0E+02
ton [long]	0.000 446 4	4.464 285 7E-04
ton [metric]	0.000 453 6	4.535 923 7E-04
ton [short]	0.000 5	5.000 000 0E-04
pound [Belgium, Antwerp]	\<mass, special - see page 29\>	
gram	468.8	4.688 000 0E+02
pound [Belgium, Brussels]	\<mass, special - see page 29\>	
gram	467.67	4.676 700 0E+02
pound [Czechoslovakia]	\<mass, special - see page 29\>	
gram	514.35	5.143 500 0E+02
pound [Denmark]	\<mass, special - see page 29\>	
kilogram	0.5	5.000 000 0E-01
pound [France]	\<mass, special - see page 29\>	
kilogram	0.5	5.000 000 0E-01
pound [Germany]	\<mass, special - see page 29\>	
gram	560.06	5.600 600 0E+02
pound [Hebrew, ancient]	\<mass, special - see page 29\>	
gram	317	3.170 000 0E+02
pound [international]		\<mass\>
cental [US]	0.01	1.000 000 0E-02
drachm [UK, apothecary]	116.666 67	1.166 666 7E+02
dram [avoirdupois]	256	2.560 000 0E+02
dram [US, apothecary]	116.666 67	1.166 666 7E+02
grain	7,000	7.000 000 0E+03
grain [apothecary]	7,000	7.000 000 0E+03
grain [avoirdupois]	7,000	7.000 000 0E+03
grain [troy]	7,000	7.000 000 0E+03
hectogram	4.535 923 7	4.535 923 7E+00
hundredweight [long]	0.008 928 6	8.928 571 4E-03
hundredweight [short]	0.01	1.000 000 0E-02
kilogram	0.453 592 4	4.535 923 7E-01
ounce	16	1.600 000 0E+01
ounce [avoirdupois]	16	1.600 000 0E+01
pound	1	1.000 000 0E+00
pound [avoirdupois]	1	1.000 000 0E+00
pound [unified]	1	1.000 000 0E+00
quarter [short]	0.002	2.000 000 0E-03

Convert From / Convert To	Standard	Scientific
quarter [US]	0.04	4.000 000 0E−02
quintal [US]	0.01	1.000 000 0E−02
scruple [UK]	350	3.500 000 0E+02
scruple [US, apothecary]	350	3.500 000 0E+02
ton [long]	0.000 446 4	4.464 285 7E−04
ton [metric]	0.000 453 6	4.535 923 7E−04
ton [short]	0.000 5	5.000 000 0E−04
pound [Italy, heavy]	<mass, special - see page 29>	
gram	348.687	3.486 870 0E+02
pound [Italy, light]	<mass, special - see page 29>	
gram	316.97	3.169 700 0E+02
pound [Latvia]	<mass, special - see page 29>	
gram	418.83	4.188 300 0E+02
pound [Lebanon]	<mass, special - see page 29>	
gram	508.63	5.086 300 0E+02
pound [Malta, gold and silver]	<mass, special - see page 29>	
gram	316.61	3.166 100 0E+02
pound [Netherlands, Amsterdam]	<mass, special - see page 29>	
kilogram	0.494	4.940 000 0E−01
pound [Netherlands, medicinal]	<mass, special - see page 29>	
gram	375	3.750 000 0E+02
pound [Netherlands, troy]	<mass, special - see page 29>	
gram	492.168	4.921 680 0E+02
pound [Pakistan]	<mass, special - see page 29>	
gram	453.592 37	4.535 923 7E+02
pound [Portugal]	<mass, special - see page 29>	
gram	459	4.590 000 0E+02
pound [Rome, ancient]	<mass, special - see page 29>	
kilogram	0.326	3.260 000 0E−01
pound [Russia, apothecary]	<mass, special - see page 29>	
gram	358.323	3.583 230 0E+02
pound [Russia, avoirdupois]	<mass, special - see page 29>	
kilogram	0.409 512 4	4.095 124 1E−01
pound [Spain, Valencia, small]	<mass, special - see page 29>	
gram	356.01	3.560 100 0E+02
pound [Spain]	<mass, special - see page 29>	
kilogram	0.46	4.600 000 0E−01
pound [Sweden]	<mass, special - see page 29>	
gram	425.34	4.253 400 0E+02
pound [Switzerland, apothecary]	<mass, special - see page 29>	
gram	500	5.000 000 0E+02
pound [troy]	<mass>	
carat [international]	1,866.208 6	1.866 208 6E+03
carat [UK]	1,440	1.440 000 0E+03
drachm [UK, apothecary]	96	9.600 000 0E+01
dram [US, apothecary]	96	9.600 000 0E+01
grain	5,760	5.760 000 0E+03
grain [apothecary]	5,760	5.760 000 0E+03
grain [avoirdupois]	5,760	5.760 000 0E+03
grain [troy]	5,760	5.760 000 0E+03
hectogram	3.732 417 2	3.732 417 2E+00
kilogram	0.373 241 7	3.732 417 2E−01
ounce	13.165 714	1.316 571 4E+01
ounce [apothecary]	12	1.200 000 0E+01
ounce [avoirdupois]	13.165 714	1.316 571 4E+01
ounce [troy]	12	1.200 000 0E+01
pennyweight [troy]	240	2.400 000 0E+02
point [jewelers']	186,620.86	1.866 208 6E+05

pound	0.822 857 1	8.228 571 4E-01
pound [apothecary]	1	1.000 000 0E+00
pound [US, troy]	0.999 999 9	9.999 998 7E-01
scruple [UK]	288	2.880 000 0E+02
scruple [US, apothecary]	288	2.880 000 0E+02

pound [UK]   `<mass>`

carat [UK]	1,749.999 9	1.749 999 9E+03
centner [UK]	0.008 928 6	8.928 570 8E-03
drachm [UK, apothecary]	116.666 66	1.166 666 6E+02
grain	6,999.999 5	6.999 999 5E+03
hectogram	4.535 923 4	4.535 923 4E+00
hundredweight [UK]	0.008 928 6	8.928 570 8E-03
kilogram	0.453 592 3	4.535 923 4E-01
pound	0.999 999 9	9.999 999 3E-01
quarter [UK]	0.035 714 3	3.571 428 3E-02
quintal [metric]	0.004 535 9	4.535 923 4E-03
quintal [UK]	0.008 928 6	8.928 570 8E-03
scruple [UK]	349.999 98	3.499 999 8E+02
stone [UK]	0.071 428 6	7.142 856 6E-02

pound [unified]   `<mass>`

carat [international]	2,267.961 9	2.267 961 9E+03
carat [UK]	1,750	1.750 000 0E+03
cental [US]	0.01	1.000 000 0E-02
dram [avoirdupois]	256	2.560 000 0E+02
grain	7,000	7.000 000 0E+03
grain [apothecary]	7,000	7.000 000 0E+03
grain [avoirdupois]	7,000	7.000 000 0E+03
grain [troy]	7,000	7.000 000 0E+03
hectogram	4.535 923 7	4.535 923 7E+00
hundredweight [short]	0.01	1.000 000 0E-02
kilogram	0.453 592 4	4.535 923 7E-01
ounce	16	1.600 000 0E+01
ounce [avoirdupois]	16	1.600 000 0E+01
pound	1	1.000 000 0E+00
pound [avoirdupois]	1	1.000 000 0E+00
pound [international]	1	1.000 000 0E+00
pound [UK]	1.000 000 1	1.000 000 1E+00
pound [US, avoirdupois]	0.999 999 9	9.999 998 7E-01
poundal square second/foot	1	1.000 000 0E+00
quarter [short]	0.002	2.000 000 0E-03
quarter [US]	0.04	4.000 000 0E-02
quintal [metric]	0.004 535 9	4.535 923 7E-03
quintal [US]	0.01	1.000 000 0E-02
scruple [UK]	350	3.500 000 0E+02
scruple [US, apothecary]	350	3.500 000 0E+02
slug	0.031 081	3.108 095 0E-02
ton [long]	0.000 446 4	4.464 285 7E-04
ton [metric]	0.000 453 6	4.535 923 7E-04
ton [short]	0.000 5	5.000 000 0E-04

pound [US, avoirdupois]   `<mass>`

dram [avoirdupois]	256.000 03	2.560 000 3E+02
grain	7,000.000 9	7.000 000 9E+03
grain [apothecary]	7,000.000 9	7.000 000 9E+03
grain [avoirdupois]	7,000.000 9	7.000 000 9E+03
grain [troy]	7,000.000 9	7.000 000 9E+03
hectogram	4.535 924 3	4.535 924 3E+00
hundredweight [short]	0.01	1.000 000 1E-02
kilogram	0.453 592 4	4.535 924 3E-01
ounce	16.000 002	1.600 000 2E+01
pound	1.000 000 1	1.000 000 1E+00
pound [UK]	1.000 000 2	1.000 000 2E+00
pound [unified]	1.000 000 1	1.000 000 1E+00

Convert From Convert To	Standard	\<Type of Unit\> Scientific
pound [US, troy]		**\<mass\>**
grain	5,760.000 7	5.760 000 7E+03
grain [troy]	5,760.000 7	5.760 000 7E+03
hectogram	3.732 417 7	3.732 417 7E+00
kilogram	0.373 241 8	3.732 417 7E−01
ounce	13.165 716	1.316 571 6E+01
pennyweight [troy]	240.000 03	2.400 000 3E+02
pound	0.822 857 3	8.228 572 5E−01
pound [troy]	1.000 000 1	1.000 000 1E+00
pound foot/second		**\<momentum\>**
bole	13,825.495	1.382 549 5E+04
gram centimeter/second	13,825.495	1.382 549 5E+04
newton second	0.138 255	1.382 549 5E−01
poundal second	1	1.000 000 0E+00
slug foot/second	0.031 081	3.108 095 0E−02
pound foot/square second		**\<force\>**
crinal	1.382 549 5	1.382 549 5E+00
dyne	13,825.495	1.382 549 5E+04
gram-force	14.098 081 9	1.409 808 2E+01
newton	0.138 255	1.382 549 5E−01
ounce foot/square second	16	1.600 000 0E+01
ounce-force	0.497 295 2	4.972 952 0E−01
ouncedal	16	1.600 000 0E+01
pond	14.098 081 9	1.409 808 2E+01
pound-force	0.031 081	3.108 095 0E−02
poundal	1	1.000 000 0E+00
ton foot/square second [long]	0.000 446 4	4.464 285 7E−04
ton foot/square second [short]	0.000 5	5.000 000 0E−04
tondal	0.000 446 4	4.464 285 7E−04
pound of water [at 4 °C, 101.325 kPa, using IST-90 density equation]		**\<volume\>**
cubic foot	0.016 018 9	1.601 891 2E−02
cubic inch	27.680 68	2.768 068 0E+01
cubic meter	0.000 453 6	4.536 050 8E−04
gallon [US, liquid]	0.119 829 8	1.198 297 8E−01
liter	0.453 605 1	4.536 050 8E−01
pound of water [at 60 °F, 14.696 pound-force/square inch, using IST-90 density equation]		**\<volume\>**
cubic foot	0.016 034 3	1.603 428 2E−02
cubic inch	27.707 239	2.770 723 9E+01
cubic meter	0.000 454	4.540 402 9E−04
gallon [US, liquid]	0.119 944 8	1.199 447 6E−01
liter	0.454 040 3	4.540 402 9E−01
pound of water [evaporated from and at 100 °C]		**\<energy\>**
Btu [I.T.]	970.335 34	9.703 353 4E+02
joule	1,023,758	1.023 758 0E+06
pound of water [heated from 16.7 °C to 100 °C]		**\<energy\>**
Btu [I.T.]	149.893 44	1.498 934 4E+02
joule	158,145.96	1.581 459 6E+05
pound square foot		**\<moment of inertia of a mass\>**
gram-force meter square second	4.297 095 3	4.297 095 3E+00
kilogram square meter	0.042 140 1	4.214 011 0E−02
ounce-force inch square second	5.967 542 4	5.967 542 4E+00
pond meter square second	4.297 095 3	4.297 095 3E+00
slug square inch	4.475 656 8	4.475 656 8E+00
pound square foot/cubic second		**\<power\>**
Btu/hour [I.T.]	0.143 788	1.437 880 2E−01
Btu/hour [thermoc.]	0.143 884 3	1.438 842 5E−01
calorie/hour [I.T.]	36.233 973	3.623 397 3E+01
calorie/hour [thermoc.]	36.258 221	3.625 822 1E+01
centigrade heat unit/hour [mean]	0.079 820 6	7.982 064 1E−02
centiwatt	4.214 011	4.214 011 0E+00

cubic meter atmosphere/minute	24.953 433	2.495 343 3E+01
dyne centimeter/second	421,401.1	4.214 011 0E+05
erg/second	421,401.1	4.214 011 0E+05
foot pound-force/minute	1.864 857	1.864 857 0E+00
foot poundal/second	1	1.000 000 0E+00
gram-force centimeter/second	429.709 53	4.297 095 3E+02
horsepower	0.000 056 5	5.651 081 8E-05
horsepower [metric]	0.000 057 3	5.729 460 5E-05
joule/minute	2.528 406 6	2.528 406 6E+00
kilocalorie/hour [I.T.]	0.036 234	3.623 397 3E-02
kilogram square meter/cubic second	0.042 140 1	4.214 011 0E-02
kilogram-force meter/hour	15.469 543	1.546 954 3E+01
kilopond meter/hour	15.469 543	1.546 954 3E+01
lumen [green light at 100% efficiency]	28.865 975	2.886 597 5E+01
lumen [green light at 5,550 angstrom]	28.655 276	2.865 527 6E+01
newton meter/minute	2.528 406 6	2.528 406 6E+00
volt ampere	0.042 140 1	4.214 011 0E-02
watt	0.042 140 1	4.214 011 0E-02
pound square foot/second		**\<moment of momentum\>**
joule second	0.042 140 1	4.214 011 0E-02
kilogram square meter/second	0.042 140 1	4.214 011 0E-02
newton meter second	0.042 140 1	4.214 011 0E-02
planck	0.042 140 1	4.214 011 0E-02
pound square inch		**\<moment of inertia of a mass\>**
gram-force centimeter square second	2.984 094	2.984 094 0E+00
kilogram square centimeter	2.926 396 5	2.926 396 5E+00
kilogram square meter	0.000 292 6	2.926 396 5E-04
ounce square inch	16	1.600 000 0E+01
pond centimeter square second	2.984 094	2.984 094 0E+00
pound-force		**\<force\>**
crinal	44.482 216 2	4.448 221 6E+01
dyne	444,822.162	4.448 221 6E+05
grain-force	7,000	7.000 000 0E+03
gram-force	453.592 37	4.535 923 7E+02
kip	0.001	1.000 000 0E-03
newton	4.448 221 6	4.448 221 6E+00
ounce-force	16	1.600 000 0E+01
pond	453.592 37	4.535 923 7E+02
poundal	32.174 048 6	3.217 404 9E+01
slug foot/square second	1	1.000 000 0E+00
ton-force [short]	0.000 5	5.000 000 0E-04
pound-force foot square second		**\<moment of inertia of a mass\>**
kilogram square meter	1.355 817 9	1.355 817 9E+00
kilopond centimeter square second	13.825 495	1.382 549 5E+01
ounce-force foot square second	16	1.600 000 0E+01
pound square foot	32.174 049	3.217 404 9E+01
pound-force inch square second	12	1.200 000 0E+01
slug square foot	1	1.000 000 0E+00
pound-force inch square second		**\<moment of inertia of a mass\>**
kilogram square meter	0.112 984 8	1.129 848 3E-01
kilogram-force centimeter square second	1.152 124 6	1.152 124 6E+00
kilopond centimeter square second	1.152 124 6	1.152 124 6E+00
ounce-force foot square second	1.333 333 3	1.333 333 3E+00
pound square foot	2.681 170 7	2.681 170 7E+00
slug square inch	12	1.200 000 0E+01
pound-force second		**\<momentum\>**
bole	444,822.16	4.448 221 6E+05
dyne second	444,822.16	4.448 221 6E+05
newton second	4.448 221 6	4.448 221 6E+00
poundal second	32.174 049	3.217 404 9E+01
slug foot/second	1	1.000 000 0E+00

pound-force second/cubic foot — \<specific acoustic impedance\>
	Standard	Scientific
kilogram-force second/cubic meter	16.018 463 4	1.601 846 3E+01
pascal second/meter	157.087 464	1.570 874 6E+02
poundal second/cubic foot	32.174 048 6	3.217 404 9E+01

pound-force second/foot — \<mechanical impedance\>
	Standard	Scientific
joule second/square meter	14.593 902 9	1.459 390 3E+01
kilogram-force second/meter	1.488 163 9	1.488 163 9E+00
newton second/meter	14.593 902 9	1.459 390 3E+01
poundal second/foot	32.174 048 6	3.217 404 9E+01

pound-force second/square foot — \<dynamic viscosity\>
	Standard	Scientific
hyl/meter second	4.882 427 6	4.882 427 6E+00
kilogram-force second/square meter	4.882 427 6	4.882 427 6E+00
pascal second	47.880 259	4.788 025 9E+01
pound/foot second	32.174 048 6	3.217 404 9E+01
poundal second/square foot	32.174 048 6	3.217 404 9E+01
slug/foot second	1	1.000 000 0E+00

pound-force second/square inch — \<dynamic viscosity\>
	Standard	Scientific
gram-force second/square centimeter	70.306 958	7.030 695 8E+01
hyl/meter second	703.069 58	7.030 695 8E+02
kilogram-force second/square meter	703.069 58	7.030 695 8E+02
pascal second	6,894.757 29	6.894 757 3E+03
poise	68,947.572 9	6.894 757 3E+04
pound-force second/square foot	144	1.440 000 0E+02

pound-force square second/foot — \<mass\>
	Standard	Scientific
geepound	1	1.000 000 0E+00
hyl	14.593 903	1.459 390 3E+01
kilogram	14.593 903	1.459 390 3E+01
kilogram-force square second/meter	1.488 163 9	1.488 163 9E+00
ounce	514.784 78	5.147 847 8E+02
pound	32.174 049	3.217 404 9E+01
quarter [UK]	1.149 073 2	1.149 073 2E+00
quarter [US]	1.286 961 9	1.286 961 9E+00
slug	1	1.000 000 0E+00
slug [metric]	1.488 163 9	1.488 163 9E+00
stone [UK]	2.298 146 3	2.298 146 3E+00

pound-force/foot — \<surface tension\>
	Standard	Scientific
dyne/centimeter	14,593.903	1.459 390 3E+04
gram-force/centimeter	14.881 639	1.488 163 9E+00
kilogram-force/meter	1.488 163 9	1.488 163 9E+00
kilopond/meter	1.488 163 9	1.488 163 9E+00
newton/meter	14.593 903	1.459 390 3E+01
ounce-force/foot	16	1.600 000 0E+01
ounce-force/inch	1.333 333 3	1.333 333 3E+00
pound-force/inch	0.083 333 3	8.333 333 3E−02

pound-force/inch — \<surface tension\>
	Standard	Scientific
gram-force/centimeter	178.579 67	1.785 796 7E+02
kilogram-force/meter	17.857 967	1.785 796 7E+01
kilopond/meter	17.857 967	1.785 796 7E+01
newton/centimeter	1.751 268 4	1.751 268 4E+00
newton/meter	175.126 84	1.751 268 4E+02
ounce-force/foot	192	1.920 000 0E+02
ounce-force/inch	16	1.600 000 0E+01
pound-force/foot	12	1.200 000 0E+01

pound-force/square foot — \<pressure\>
	Standard	Scientific
atmosphere [standard]	0.000 472 5	4.725 414 2E−04
atmosphere [technical]	0.000 488 2	4.882 427 6E−04
bar	0.000 478 8	4.788 025 9E−04
barye [France]	478.802 59	4.788 025 9E+02
centimeter of mercury [0 °C, by convention]	0.035 913 1	3.591 314 3E−02
centimeter of water [4 °C, by convention]	0.488 242 8	4.882 427 6E−01
dyne/square centimeter	478.802 59	4.788 025 9E+02

Convert From / Convert To	Standard	Type of Unit / Scientific
gram-force/square centimeter	0.488 242 8	4.882 427 6E-01
inch of mercury [0 °C, by convention]	0.014 139	1.413 903 2E-02
inch of water [4 °C, by convention]	0.192 221 6	1.922 215 6E-01
kilogram-force/square meter	4.882 427 6	4.882 427 6E+00
kilopond/square meter	4.882 427 6	4.882 427 6E+00
kip/square foot	0.001	1.000 000 0E-03
millimeter of mercury [0 °C, by convention]	0.359 131 4	3.591 314 3E-01
millimeter of water [4 °C, by convention]	4.882 427 6	4.882 427 6E+00
newton/square meter	47.880 259	4.788 025 9E+01
ounce-force/square inch	0.111 111 1	1.111 111 1E-01
pascal	47.880 259	4.788 025 9E+01
poundal/square foot	32.174 049	3.217 404 9E+01
ton-force/square foot [short]	0.000 5	5.000 000 0E-04
ton-force/square meter [metric]	0.004 882 4	4.882 427 6E-03
torr	0.359 131 5	3.591 314 8E-01

pound-force/square foot foot   **\<pressure gradient\>**

Convert To	Standard	Scientific
kilogram/square meter square second	157.087 46	1.570 874 6E+02
pascal/meter	157.087 46	1.570 874 6E+02
pound/square foot square second	32.174 049	3.217 404 9E+01

pound-force/square inch   **\<pressure\>**

Convert To	Standard	Scientific
atmosphere [standard]	0.068 046	6.804 596 4E-02
atmosphere [technical]	0.070 307	7.030 695 8E-02
bar	0.068 947 6	6.894 757 3E-02
barad	68,947.573	6.894 757 3E+04
barye [France]	68,947.573	6.894 757 3E+04
centibar	6.894 757 3	6.894 757 3E+00
centihg	5.171 492 5	5.171 492 5E+00
centimeter of mercury [0 °C, by convention]	5.171 492 5	5.171 492 5E+00
centimeter of water [4 °C, by convention]	70.306 958	7.030 695 8E+01
dyne/square centimeter	68,947.573	6.894 757 3E+04
foot of mercury [0 °C, by convention]	0.169 668 4	1.696 683 9E-01
foot of water [4 °C, by convention]	2.306 658 7	2.306 658 7E+00
gram-force/square centimeter	70.306 958	7.030 695 8E+01
inch of mercury [0 °C, by convention]	2.036 020 7	2.036 020 7E+00
inch of water [4 °C, by convention]	27.670 905	2.767 990 5E+01
kilogram-force/square meter	703.069 58	7.030 695 8E+02
kilopascal	6.894 757 3	6.894 757 3E+00
kilopond/square meter	703.069 58	7.030 695 8E+02
kip/square foot	0.144	1.440 000 0E-01
millimeter of mercury [0 °C, by convention]	51.714 925	5.171 492 5E+01
millimeter of water [4 °C, by convention]	703.069 58	7.030 695 8E+02
newton/square meter	6,894.757 3	6.894 757 3E+03
ounce-force/square inch	16	1.600 000 0E+01
pascal	6,894.757 3	6.894 757 3E+03
pieze [France]	6.894 757 3	6.894 757 3E+00
pound-force/square foot	144	1.440 000 0E+02
poundal/square foot	4,633.063	4.633 063 0E+03
sthene/square meter [France]	6.894 757 3	6.894 757 3E+00
ton-force/square foot [long]	0.064 285 7	6.428 571 4E-02
ton-force/square foot [short]	0.072	7.200 000 0E-02
ton-force/square inch [short]	0.000 5	5.000 000 0E-04
ton-force/square meter [metric]	0.703 069 6	7.030 695 8E-01
torr	51.714 933	5.171 493 3E+01

pound-force/square inch °F   **\<pressure coefficient\>**

Convert To	Standard	Scientific
pascal/kelvin	12,410.563	1.241 056 3E+04

pound/acre   **\<surface density\>**

Convert To	Standard	Scientific
grain/square yard	1.446 281	1.446 281 0E+00
kilogram/hectare	1.120 851 2	1.120 851 2E+00
kilogram/square meter	0.000 112 1	1.120 851 2E-04
ounce/square yard	0.003 305 8	3.305 785 1E-03
pound/square yard	0.000 206 6	2.066 115 7E-04

pound/acre second \<flow rate/unit area, mass basis\>

gram/square meter second	0.112 085 1	1.120 851 2E-01
kilogram/hectare second	1.120 851 2	1.120 851 2E+00
kilogram/square meter second	0.000 112 1	1.120 851 2E-04
ounce/square foot second	0.000 367 3	3.673 094 6E-04

pound/Btu [-/ I.T.] \<specific fuel consumption, mass basis\>

kilogram/joule	0.000 429 9	4.299 226 1E-04
kilogram/kilocalorie [-/ I.T.]	1.8	1.800 000 0E+00
pound/horsepower hour	2,544.433 6	2.544 433 6E+03

pound/circular mil foot \<density\>

kilogram/cubic meter	>>>	2.936 929 1E+09
pound/cubic inch	106,103.3	1.061 033 0E+05
ton/cubic inch [short]	53.051 648	5.305 164 8E+01

pound/cubic foot \<density\>

grain/cubic foot	7,000	7.000 000 0E+03
grain/cubic inch	4.050 925 9	4.050 925 9E+00
gram/liter	16.018 463	1.601 846 3E+01
kilogram/cubic meter	16.018 463	1.601 846 3E+01
ounce/cubic foot	16	1.600 000 0E+01
ounce/cubic yard	432	4.320 000 0E+02
ounce/gallon [-/-US, liquid]	2.138 888 9	2.138 888 9E+00
pound/cubic yard	27	2.700 000 0E+01
slug/cubic yard	0.839 185 7	8.391 856 5E-01
ton/cubic foot [short]	0.000 5	5.000 000 0E-04
ton/cubic yard [short]	0.013 5	1.350 000 0E-02
tonne/cubic meter	0.016 018 5	1.601 846 3E-02

pound/cubic inch \<density\>

grain/cubic inch	7,000	7.000 000 0E+03
kilogram/cubic meter	27,679.905	2.767 990 5E+04
ounce/cubic inch	16	1.600 000 0E+01
ounce/cubic inch [troy]	14.583 333	1.458 333 3E+01
ounce/gallon [-/-US, liquid]	3,696	3.696 000 0E+03
pound/circular mil foot	0.000 009 4	9.424 778 0E-06
pound/cubic foot	1,728	1.728 000 0E+03
pound/gallon [-/-US, liquid]	231	2.310 000 0E+02
slug/cubic foot	53.707 882	5.370 788 2E+01
ton/cubic foot [short]	0.864	8.640 000 0E-01
ton/cubic inch [short]	0.000 5	5.000 000 0E-04
ton/cubic yard [short]	23.328	2.332 800 0E+01
ton/gallon [short/US, liquid]	0.115 5	1.155 000 0E-01

pound/cubic yard \<density\>

gammil	593.276 42	5.932 764 2E+02
grain/cubic yard	7,000	7.000 000 0E+03
grain/gallon [-/-US, liquid]	34.657 922	3.465 792 2E+01
gram/liter	0.593 276 4	5.932 764 2E-01
kilogram/cubic meter	0.593 276 4	5.932 764 2E-01
micril	593.276 42	5.932 764 2E+02
ounce/cubic yard	16	1.600 000 0E+01
ounce/cubic yard [troy]	14.583 333	1.458 333 3E+01
pound/cubic foot	0.037 037	3.703 703 7E-02
slug/cubic yard	0.031 081	3.108 095 0E-02
ton/cubic yard [short]	0.000 5	5.000 000 0E-04
tonne/cubic meter	0.000 593 3	5.932 764 2E-04

pound/foot \<linear density\>

denier	>>>	1.339 347 5E+07
drex	>>>	1.488 163 9E+07
kilogram/meter	1.488 163 9	1.488 163 9E+00
ounce/inch	1.333 333 3	1.333 333 3E+00
pli	0.083 333 3	8.333 333 3E-02
pound/yard	3	3.000 000 0E+00
tex	1,488,163.9	1.488 163 9E+06

Convert From		<Type of Unit>
Convert To	Standard	Scientific

pound/foot hour   **<dynamic viscosity>**

	Standard	Scientific
kilogram/meter hour	1.488 163 9	1.488 163 9E+00
millipoise	4.133 788 7	4.133 788 7E+00
pascal second	0.000 413 4	4.133 788 7E−04
poise	0.004 133 8	4.133 788 7E−03
poundal hour/square foot	1	1.000 000 0E+00

pound/foot second   **<dynamic viscosity>**

	Standard	Scientific
kilogram/meter second	1.488 163 9	1.488 163 9E+00
newton second/square meter	1.488 163 9	1.488 163 9E+00
pascal second	1.488 163 9	1.488 163 9E+00
poise	14.881 639 4	1.488 163 9E+01
poiseuille [France]	1.488 163 9	1.488 163 9E+00
poundal second/square foot	1	1.000 000 0E+00
reyn	1	1.000 000 0E+00
slug/foot second	0.031 081	3.108 095 0E−02

pound/gallon [-/UK, liquid]   **<density>**

	Standard	Scientific
grain/gallon [-/UK, liquid]	7,000	7.000 000 0E+03
grain/gallon [-/US, liquid]	5,828.719 3	5.828 719 3E+03
gram/liter	99.776 373	9.977 637 3E+01
kilogram/cubic meter	99.776 373	9.977 637 3E+01
ounce/gallon [-/UK, liquid]	16	1.600 000 0E+01
ounce/gallon [-/US, liquid]	13.322 787	1.332 278 7E+01
pound/cubic foot	6.228 835 5	6.228 835 5E+00
slug/cubic yard	5.227 149 4	5.227 149 4E+00
ton/cubic yard [short]	0.084 089 3	8.408 927 9E−02
ton/gallon [short/UK, liquid]	0.000 5	5.000 000 0E−04
tonne/cubic meter	0.099 776 4	9.977 637 3E−02

pound/gallon [-/US, liquid]   **<density>**

	Standard	Scientific
grain/cubic inch	30.303 03	3.030 303 0E+01
grain/gallon [-/US, liquid]	7,000	7.000 000 0E+03
gram/cubic centimeter	0.119 826 4	1.198 264 3E−01
kilogram/cubic meter	119.826 43	1.198 264 3E+02
ounce/cubic foot	119.688 31	1.196 883 1E+02
ounce/cubic foot [troy]	109.090 91	1.090 909 1E+02
ounce/gallon [-/US, liquid]	16	1.600 000 0E+01
pound/cubic foot	7.480 519 5	7.480 519 5E+00
pound/gallon [-/UK, liquid]	1.200 949 9	1.200 949 9E+00
slug/cubic yard	6.277 544 6	6.277 544 6E+00
ton/cubic yard [short]	0.100 987	1.009 870 1E−01
tonne/cubic meter	0.119 826 4	1.198 264 3E−01

pound/horsepower hour   **<specific fuel consumption, mass basis>**

	Standard	Scientific
kilogram/joule	0.000 000 2	1.689 659 4E−07
kilogram/kilocalorie [-/ I.T.]	0.000 707 4	7.074 266 0E−04
pound/Btu [-/ I.T.]	0.000 393	3.930 147 8E−04

pound/hour   **<flow rate, mass basis>**

	Standard	Scientific
gram/minute	7.559 872 8	7.559 872 8E+00
kilogram/second	0.000 126	1.259 978 8E−04
pound/minute	0.016 666 7	1.666 666 7E−02

pound/inch   **<linear density>**

	Standard	Scientific
denier	>>>	1.607 217 1E+08
drex	>>>	1.785 796 7E+08
kilogram/meter	17.857 967	1.785 796 7E+01
ounce/inch	16	1.600 000 0E+01
pli	1	1.000 000 0E+00
poumar	>>>	3.600 000 0E+07
pound/foot	12	1.200 000 0E+01
tex	>>>	1.785 796 7E+07

pound/minute   **<flow rate, mass basis>**

	Standard	Scientific
gram/second	7.559 872 8	7.559 872 8E+00
kilogram/second	0.007 559 9	7.559 872 8E−03
pound/hour	60	6.000 000 0E+01

Convert From		<Type of Unit>
Convert To	Standard	Scientific
pound/second		<flow rate, mass basis>
kilogram/second	0.453 592 4	4.535 923 7E-01
pound/minute	60	6.000 000 0E+01
pound/square foot		<surface density>
grain/square inch	48.611 111	4.861 111 1E+01
kilogram/are	488.242 76	4.882 427 6E+02
kilogram/square meter	4.882 427 6	4.882 427 6E+00
ounce/square foot	16	1.600 000 0E+01
ounce/square yard	144	1.440 000 0E+02
pound/square yard	9	9.000 000 0E+00
slug/square yard	0.279 728 6	2.797 285 5E-01
ton/square foot [short]	0.000 5	5.000 000 0E-04
ton/square yard [short]	0.004 5	4.500 000 0E-03
tonne/square meter	0.004 882 4	4.882 427 6E-03
pound/square foot second		<flow rate/unit area, mass basis>
gram/square meter second	4,882.427 6	4.882 427 6E+03
kilogram/are second	488.242 76	4.882 427 6E+02
kilogram/square meter second	4.882 427 6	4.882 427 6E+00
ounce/square foot second	16	1.600 000 0E+01
slug/square foot second	0.031 081	3.108 095 0E-02
pound/square foot square second		<pressure gradient>
kilogram/square meter square second	4.882 427 6	4.882 427 6E+00
pascal/meter	4.882 427 6	4.882 427 6E+00
pound-force/square foot foot	0.031 081	3.108 095 0E-02
pound/square inch		<surface density>
grain/square inch	7,000	7.000 000 0E+03
kilogram/are	70,306.958	7.030 695 8E+04
kilogram/square meter	703.069 58	7.030 695 8E+02
ounce/square inch	16	1.600 000 0E+01
slug/square foot	4.475 656 8	4.475 656 8E+00
ton/square foot [short]	0.072	7.200 000 0E-02
ton/square inch [short]	0.000 5	5.000 000 0E-04
ton/square yard [short]	0.648	6.480 000 0E-01
tonne/square meter	0.703 069 6	7.030 695 8E-01
pound/square yard		<surface density>
grain/square inch	5.401 234 6	5.401 234 6E+00
grain/square yard	7,000	7.000 000 0E+03
kilogram/are	54.249 196	5.424 919 6E+01
kilogram/square meter	0.542 492	5.424 919 6E-01
ounce/square foot	1.777 777 8	1.777 777 8E+00
ounce/square yard	16	1.600 000 0E+01
pound/acre	4,840	4.840 000 0E+03
pound/square foot	0.111 111 1	1.111 111 1E-01
slug/square yard	0.031 081	3.108 095 0E-02
ton/square yard [short]	0.000 5	5.000 000 0E-04
pound/ton [-/long]		<concentration, mass basis>
karat	0.010 714 3	1.071 428 6E-02
kilogram/kilogram	0.000 446 4	4.464 285 7E-04
ounce/ton [-/long]	16	1.600 000 0E+01
part/million	446.428 571	4.464 285 7E+02
pennyweight/ton [troy/long]	291.666 667	2.916 666 7E+02
percent	0.044 642 9	4.464 285 7E-02
pound/ton [-/metric]	0.984 206 5	9.842 065 3E-01
pound/ton [-/metric]		<concentration, mass basis>
karat	0.010 886 2	1.088 621 7E-02
kilogram/kilogram	0.000 453 6	4.535 923 7E-04
ounce/ton [-/metric]	16	1.600 000 0E+01
part/million	453.592 37	4.535 923 7E+02
pennyweight/ton [troy/metric]	291.666 667	2.916 666 7E+02
percent	0.045 359 2	4.535 923 7E-02
pound/ton [-/long]	1.016 046 9	1.016 046 9E+00

pound/ton [-/short]   <concentration, mass basis>

	Standard	Scientific
gram/ton [-/metric]	500	5.000 000 0E+02
gram/tonne	500	5.000 000 0E+02
karat	0.012	1.200 000 0E-02
kilogram/kilogram	0.000 5	5.000 000 0E-04
milligram/kilogram	500	5.000 000 0E+02
milligram/ton [-/metric]	500,000	5.000 000 0E+05
ounce/ton [-/short]	16	1.600 000 0E+01
part/million	500	5.000 000 0E+02
pennyweight/ton [troy/long]	326.666 667	3.266 666 7E+02
percent	0.05	5.000 000 0E-02
pound/ton [-/long]	1.12	1.120 000 0E+00

pound/ton [-/UK, assay or assay, long]   <concentration, mass basis>

	Standard	Scientific
karat	333.251 537	3.332 515 4E+02
kilogram/kilogram	13.885 480 7	1.388 548 1E+01
ounce/ton [-/UK, assay or assay, long]	16	1.600 000 0E+01
ounce/ton [troy/UK, assay or assay, long]	14.583 333 3	1.458 333 3E+01
part/million	>>>	1.388 548 1E+07
percent	1,388.548 07	1.388 548 1E+03

pound/ton [-/US, assay or assay, short]   <concentration, mass basis>

	Standard	Scientific
karat	373.241 722	3.732 417 2E+02
kilogram/kilogram	15.551 738 4	1.555 173 8E+01
ounce/ton [-/US, assay or assay, short]	16	1.600 000 0E+01
ounce/ton [troy/metric]	500,000	5.000 000 0E+05
part/million	>>>	1.555 173 8E+07
pennyweight/ton [troy/metric]	>>>	1.000 000 0E+05
percent	1,555.173 84	1.555 173 8E+03
pound/ton [-/UK, assay or assay, long]	1.12	1.120 000 0E+00

pound/yard   <linear density>

	Standard	Scientific
denier	4,464,491.8	4.464 491 8E+06
drex	4,960,546.5	4.960 546 5E+06
kilogram/meter	0.496 054 7	4.960 546 5E-01
ounce/foot	5.333 333 3	5.333 333 3E+00
pli	0.027 777 8	2.777 777 8E-02
poumar	1,000,000	1.000 000 0E+06
pound/foot	0.333 333 3	3.333 333 3E-01
tex	496,054.65	4.960 546 5E+05

poundal   <force>

	Standard	Scientific
crinal	1.382 549 5	1.382 549 5E+00
dyne	13,825.495 4	1.382 549 5E+04
gram-force	14.098 081 9	1.409 808 2E+01
newton	0.138 255	1.382 549 5E-01
ounce foot/square second	16	1.600 000 0E+01
ounce-force	0.497 295 2	4.972 952 0E-01
ouncedal	16	1.600 000 0E+01
pond	14.098 081 9	1.409 808 2E+01
pound foot/square second	1	1.000 000 0E+00
pound-force	0.031 081	3.108 095 0E-02
ton foot/square second [long]	0.000 446 4	4.464 285 7E-04
ton foot/square second [short]	0.000 5	5.000 000 0E-04
tondal	0.000 446 4	4.464 285 7E-04

poundal hour/square foot   <dynamic viscosity>

	Standard	Scientific
kilogram/meter hour	1.488 163 9	1.488 163 9E+00
millipoise	4.133 788 7	4.133 788 7E+00
pascal second	0.000 413 4	4.133 788 7E-04
poise	0.004 133 8	4.133 788 7E-03
pound/foot hour	1	1.000 000 0E+00

poundal second   <momentum>

	Standard	Scientific
dyne second	13,825.495	1.382 549 5E+04
newton second	0.138 255	1.382 549 5E-01
pound foot/second	1	1.000 000 0E+00
slug foot/second	0.031 081	3.108 095 0E-02

Convert From / Convert To	Standard	Scientific `<Type of Unit>`

poundal second/cubic foot — `<specific acoustic impedance>`

	Standard	Scientific
kilogram-force second/cubic meter	0.497 869 1	4.978 690 6E-01
pascal second/meter	4.882 427 6	4.882 427 6E+00
pound-force second/cubic foot	0.031 081	3.108 095 0E-02

poundal second/foot — `<mechanical impedance>`

	Standard	Scientific
joule second/square meter	0.453 592 4	4.535 923 7E-01
kilogram-force second/meter	0.046 253 5	4.625 354 9E-02
newton second/meter	0.453 592 4	4.535 923 7E-01
pound-force second/foot	0.031 081	3.108 095 0E-02

poundal second/square foot — `<dynamic viscosity>`

	Standard	Scientific
dyne second/square centimeter	14.881 639 4	1.488 163 9E+01
gram/centimeter second	14.881 639 4	1.488 163 9E+01
kilogram/meter second	1.488 163 9	1.488 163 9E+00
newton second/square meter	1.488 163 9	1.488 163 9E+00
pascal second	1.488 163 9	1.488 163 9E+00
poise	14.881 639 4	1.488 163 9E+01
poiseuille [France]	1.488 163 9	1.488 163 9E+00
pound/foot second	1	1.000 000 0E+00
reyn	1	1.000 000 0E+00

poundal square second/foot — `<mass>`

	Standard	Scientific
cental [US]	0.01	1.000 000 0E-02
dram [avoirdupois]	256	2.560 000 0E+02
grain	7,000	7.000 000 0E+03
hectogram	4.535 923 7	4.535 923 7E+00
hundredweight [short]	0.01	1.000 000 0E-02
ounce	16	1.600 000 0E+01
pound	1	1.000 000 0E+00
quarter [short]	0.002	2.000 000 0E-03
quarter [US]	0.04	4.000 000 0E-02
quintal [US]	0.01	1.000 000 0E-02
scruple [UK]	350	3.500 000 0E+02
scruple [US, apothecary]	350	3.500 000 0E+02
ton [long]	0.000 446 4	4.464 285 7E-04
ton [short]	0.000 5	5.000 000 0E-04
ton [UK]	0.000 446 4	4.464 285 7E-04

poundal/square foot — `<pressure>`

	Standard	Scientific
atmosphere [standard]	0.000 014 7	1.468 703 6E-05
atmosphere [technical]	0.000 015 2	1.517 504 9E-05
bar	0.000 014 9	1.488 163 9E-05
barye [France]	14.881 639	1.488 163 9E+01
centitorr	1.116 214 8	1.116 214 8E+00
dyne/square centimeter	14.881 639	1.488 163 9E+01
gram-force/square centimeter	0.015 175	1.517 504 9E-02
inch of mercury [0 °C, by convention]	0.000 439 5	4.394 545 6E-04
inch of water [4 °C, by convention]	0.005 974 4	5.974 428 7E-03
kilogram-force/square meter	0.151 750 5	1.517 504 9E-01
kilopond/square meter	0.151 750 5	1.517 504 9E-01
micrometer of mercury [0 °C, by convention]	11.162 146	1.116 214 6E+01
micrometer of water [4 °C, by convention]	151.750 49	1.517 504 9E+02
millimeter of mercury [0 °C, by convention]	0.011 162 1	1.116 214 6E-02
millimeter of water [4 °C, by convention]	0.151 750 5	1.517 504 9E-01
newton/square meter	1.488 163 9	1.488 163 9E+00
ounce-force/square inch	0.003 453 4	3.453 438 9E-03
pascal	1.488 163 9	1.488 163 9E+00
pound-force/square foot	0.031 081	3.108 095 0E-02
ton-force/square foot [short]	0.000 015 5	1.554 047 5E-05
ton-force/square meter [metric]	0.000 151 8	1.517 504 9E-04
torr	0.011 162 1	1.116 214 8E-02

pous [Greece, ancient] — `<length, special - see page 29>`

	Standard	Scientific
centimeter	31.23	3.123 000 0E+01

pow [Afghanistan] — `<mass, special - see page 29>`

	Standard	Scientific
gram	441.625	4.416 250 0E+02

Convert From		<Type of Unit>
Convert To	Standard	Scientific

powa [Bangladesh] <mass, special - see page 29>
gram --- 233.276 --- 2.332 760 0E+02

powa [India] <mass, special - see page 29>
gram --- 233.276 1 --- 2.332 761 0E+02

powa [Pakistan] <mass, special - see page 29>
gram --- 233.276 --- 2.332 760 0E+02

powa chhatak [Bangladesh] <mass, special - see page 29>
gram -- 14.58 --- 1.458 000 0E+01

preece <electric resistivity>
ohm circular mil/foot ------------------------------->>> --- 6.015 304 9E+21
ohm foot --->>> --- 3.280 839 9E+13
ohm meter -->>> --- 1.000 000 0E+13

pret [Poland] <length, special - see page 29>
meter --- 4.32 --- 4.320 000 0E+00

probmetze [Austria] <volume, special - see page 29>
liter -- 0.060 048 --- 6.004 800 0E-02

proton rest mass [atomic physics, eq. energy] <energy>
atomic mass unit [unified, C-12, 1986, eq. energy] ----- 1.007 276 5 --- 1.007 276 5E+00
centimeter gram-force ------------------------------- 0.000 001 5 --- 1.532 917 6E-06
deuteron rest mass [atomic physics, eq. energy] -------- 0.500 248 2 --- 5.002 482 5E-01
dyne centimeter -------------------------------------- 0.001 503 3 --- 1.503 278 6E-03
electron rest mass [atomic physics, eq. energy] -------- 1,836.152 7 --- 1.836 152 7E+03
electronvolt --->>> --- 9.382 723 1E+08
erg --- 0.001 503 3 --- 1.503 278 6E-03
gigaelectronvolt ------------------------------------- 0.938 272 3 --- 9.382 723 1E-01
joule ---<<< --- 1.503 278 6E-10
kiloelectronvolt ------------------------------------- 938,272.31 --- 9.382 723 1E+05
megaelectronvolt ------------------------------------ 938.272 31 --- 9.382 723 1E+02
muon rest mass [atomic physics, eq. energy] ---------- 8.880 244 3 --- 8.880 244 3E+00
neutron rest mass [atomic physics, eq. energy] -------- 0.998 623 5 --- 9.986 234 9E-01
teraelectronvolt ------------------------------------- 0.000 938 3 --- 9.382 723 1E-04

pu [China] <length, special - see page 29>
meter --- 1.8 --- 1.800 000 0E+00

pu [Macao] <area, special - see page 29>
square meter -- 3.172 5 --- 3.172 500 0E+00

pud [Russia] <mass, special - see page 29>
kilogram -- 16.3 --- 1.630 000 0E+01

puddee [India] <volume, special - see page 29>
liter -- 1.533 --- 1.533 000 0E+00

puff <capacitance>
farad --<<< --- 1.000 000 0E-12
picofarad -- 1 --- 1.000 000 0E+00

puili [Portuguese India] <volume, special - see page 29>
liter -- 3.993 --- 3.993 000 0E+00

pulgada [Argentina] <length, special - see page 29>
centimeter --- 2.407 --- 2.407 000 0E+00

pulgada [Bolivia] <length, special - see page 29>
centimeter --- 2.406 --- 2.406 000 0E+00

pulgada [Colombia] <length, special - see page 29>
centimeter --- 2.5 --- 2.500 000 0E+00

pulgada [Cuba] <length, special - see page 29>
millimeter -- 23.6 --- 2.360 000 0E+01

pulgada [El Salvador] <length, special - see page 29>
centimeter --- 2.322 --- 2.322 000 0E+00

pulgada [Guatemala] <length, special - see page 29>
centimeter --- 2.322 --- 2.322 000 0E+00

pulgada [Honduras] <length, special - see page 29>
millimeter -- 23.2 --- 2.320 000 0E+01

Convert From Convert To	Standard	<Type of Unit> Scientific
pulgada [Mexico] millimeter	<length, special - see page 29> 23.3	2.330 000 0E+01
pulgada [Nicaragua] millimeter	<length, special - see page 29> 23.3	2.330 000 0E+01
pulgada [Panama] centimeter	<length, special - see page 29> 2.32	2.320 000 0E+00
pulgada [Paraguay] millimeter	<length, special - see page 29> 24.1	2.410 000 0E+01
pulgada [Philippines] centimeter	<length, special - see page 29> 2.322	2.322 000 0E+00
pulgada [Spain] centimeter	<length, special - see page 29> 2.32	2.320 000 0E+00
pulgada cuadrada [Mexico] square centimeter	<area, special - see page 29> 5.418 5	5.418 500 0E+00
pulgada cubica [Mexico] cubic centimeter	<volume, special - see page 29> 12.613	1.261 300 0E+01
pulgada inglesa [Chile] centimeter	<length, special - see page 29> 2.54	2.540 000 0E+00
pulgada maderera [Chile] cubic decimeter	<volume, special - see page 29> 23.597	2.359 700 0E+01
pulzier [Malta] millimeter	<length, special - see page 29> 21.83	2.183 000 0E+01
pun [Mongolia] milligram	<mass, special - see page 29> 375	3.750 000 0E+02
pun [Mongolia] millimeter	<length, special - see page 29> 3.2	3.200 000 0E+00
pun [South Korea] millimeter	<length, special - see page 29> 3.03	3.030 000 0E+00
puncheon [UK] cubic meter	<volume, special - see page 29> 0.317 975 1	3.179 751 0E−01
pund [Denmark] kilogram	<mass, special - see page 29> 0.5	5.000 000 0E−01
pund [Germany] kilogram	<mass, special - see page 29> 0.5	5.000 000 0E−01
pund [Iceland] kilogram	<mass, special - see page 29> 0.5	5.000 000 0E−01
pund [Norway] gram	<mass, special - see page 29> 498.1	4.981 000 0E+02
pund [Sweden] gram	<mass, special - see page 29> 500	5.000 000 0E+02
punk [India] milligram	<mass, special - see page 29> 9.11	9.110 000 0E+00
punkho [India] milligram	<mass, special - see page 29> 9.11	9.110 000 0E+00
punko [India] milligram	<mass, special - see page 29> 7.593 623	7.593 623 0E+00
punkt [Austria] centimeter	<length, special - see page 29> 0.183	1.830 000 0E−01
punto [Honduras] millimeter	<length, special - see page 29> 0.161	1.610 000 0E−01
punto [Italy] millimeter	<length, special - see page 29> 3.57	3.570 000 0E+00
punto [Philippines] gram	<mass, special - see page 29> 210.8	2.108 000 0E+02

punto [Venezuela] — <mass, special - see page 29>
kilogram -- 600 --- 6.000 000 0E+02

purana [Hindu, ancient, silver] — <mass, special - see page 29>
gram --- 3.968 --- 3.968 000 0E+00

pushuri [Bangladesh] — <mass, special - see page 29>
kilogram -- 4.666 --- 4.666 000 0E+00

pygme [Greece, ancient] — <length, special - see page 29>
centimeter--- 34.6 --- 3.460 000 0E+01

pygon [Greece, ancient] — <length, special - see page 29>
centimeter--- 38.5 --- 3.850 000 0E+01

pyi [Burma, dry] — <volume, special - see page 29>
liter --- 2.557 --- 2.557 000 0E+00

pyi [Burma, rice, milled] — <mass, special - see page 29>
kilogram -- 2.126 --- 2.126 000 0E+00

pyong [North Korea] — <area, special - see page 29>
square meter -- 3.305 785 1 --- 3.305 785 1E+00

pyong [South Korea, timber] — <volume, special - see page 29>
cubic meter --- 2.003 5 --- 2.003 500 0E+00

pyong [South Korea] — <area, special - see page 29>
square meter -- 3.306 --- 3.306 000 0E+00

pyron — <heat flux density>
Btu/minute square foot [I.T.]---------------------------- 3.686 690 6 --- 3.686 690 6E+00
Btu/minute square foot [thermoc.]---------------------- 3.689 157 8 --- 3.689 157 8E+00
kilocalorie/hour square meter [I.T.] --------------------- 600 --- 6.000 000 0E+02
kilocalorie/hour square meter [thermoc.] ------------- 600.401 53 --- 6.004 015 3E+02
watt/square foot--- 64.827 741 --- 6.482 774 1E+01
watt/square meter--------------------------------------- 697.8 --- 6.978 000 0E+02

pyung [South Korea] — <area, special - see page 29>
square meter -- 3.305 79 --- 3.305 790 0E+00

q-unit — <energy>
Btu [I.T.]-->>> 1.000 000 0E+18
joule -->>> 1.055 055 9E+21

qab [Hebrew, ancient] — <volume, special - see page 29>
liter --- 1.276 --- 1.276 000 0E+00

qabdah [Egypt] — <length, special - see page 29>
centimeter--- 12.5 --- 1.250 000 0E+01

qabh [Hebrew, ancient] — <volume, special - see page 29>
liter --- 1.277 --- 1.277 000 0E+00

qabim [Hebrew, ancient] — <volume, special - see page 29>
liter --- 2.1 --- 2.100 000 0E+00

qabin [Hebrew, ancient, dry] — <volume, special - see page 29>
liter --- 2.1 --- 2.100 000 0E+00

qada [Sudan] — <area, special - see page 29>
are --- 220.54 --- 2.205 400 0E+02

qadaa [Sudan] — <area, special - see page 29>
hectare -- 2.204 --- 2.204 000 0E+00

qadah [Egypt] — <volume, special - see page 29>
liter --- 2.06 --- 2.060 000 0E+00

qadah [Sudan] — <volume, special - see page 29>
liter --- 2.062 5 --- 2.062 500 0E+00

qadah [Yemen] — <mass, special - see page 29>
kilogram -- 90.72 --- 9.072 000 0E+01

qadam [Sudan] — <length, special - see page 29>
meter -- 0.304 8 --- 3.048 000 0E-01

qama [Yemen] — <length, special - see page 29>
meter -- 1.65 --- 1.650 000 0E+00

| Convert From | | <Type of Unit> |
Convert To	Standard	Scientific
qamhah [Egypt]	<mass, special - see page 29>	
gram	0.048 75	4.875 000 0E-02
qantar [Cyprus]	<mass, special - see page 29>	
kilogram	55.883	5.588 300 0E+01
qantar [Egypt]	<mass, special - see page 29>	
kilogram	44.928	4.492 800 0E+01
qantar [Greece]	<mass, special - see page 29>	
kilogram	56.32	5.632 000 0E+01
qantar [Iraq, ancient]	<mass, special - see page 29>	
kilogram	44.928	4.492 800 0E+01
qantar [Islam]	<mass, special - see page 29>	
kilogram	44.688	4.468 800 0E+01
qantar [Lebanon]	<mass, special - see page 29>	
kilogram	256.4	2.564 000 0E+02
qantar [Libya]	<mass, special - see page 29>	
kilogram	51.28	5.128 000 0E+01
qantar [Malta]	<mass, special - see page 29>	
kilogram	79.379	7.937 900 0E+01
qantar [Morocco]	<mass, special - see page 29>	
kilogram	100	1.000 000 0E+02
qantar [Sudan, large]	<mass, special - see page 29>	
kilogram	141.5	1.415 000 0E+02
qantar [Sudan, small]	<mass, special - see page 29>	
kilogram	44.928	4.492 800 0E+01
qantar [Syria]	<mass, special - see page 29>	
kilogram	256.5	2.565 000 0E+02
qantar [Turkey]	<mass, special - see page 29>	
kilogram	56.45	5.645 000 0E+01
qasa [Yemen]	<mass, special - see page 29>	
kilogram	1.134	1.134 000 0E+00
qasab [Egypt, ancient]	<length, special - see page 29>	
meter	3.55	3.550 000 0E+00
qasaba [Egypt]	<length, special - see page 29>	
meter	3.55	3.550 000 0E+00
qasba [Malta]	<length, special - see page 29>	
meter	2.095	2.095 000 0E+00
qasba kwadra [Malta and Gozo]	<area, special - see page 29>	
square meter	4.391 12	4.391 120 0E+00
qasba xubu [Malta and Gozo]	<volume, special - see page 29>	
cubic meter	9.201 59	9.201 590 0E+00
qassabeh [Lebanon]	<area, special - see page 29>	
square meter	23.814	2.381 400 0E+01
qav [Hebrew, ancient]	<volume, special - see page 29>	
liter	2.1	2.100 000 0E+00
qdt [Egypt, ancient]	<mass, special - see page 29>	
gram	9.1	9.100 000 0E+00
qesita [Arabia, ancient]	<mass, special - see page 29>	
gram	1,429	1.429 000 0E+03
qilli [Lebanon, olive oil]	<mass, special - see page 29>	
kilogram	33.345	3.334 500 0E+01
qing [China]	<area, special - see page 29>	
hectare	6.666 666 7	6.666 666 7E+00
qintar [Egypt, ancient]	<mass, special - see page 29>	
kilogram	44.928	4.492 800 0E+01

Convert From	<Type of Unit>	
Convert To	Standard	Scientific

qintar [Iraq, ancient]   <mass, special - see page 29>
kilogram ---- 44.928 --- 4.492 800 0E+01

qirat [Egypt, ancient]   <length, special - see page 29>
millimeter ---- 0.87 --- 8.700 000 0E-01

qirat [Egypt]   <volume, special - see page 29>
liter ---- 0.064 453 --- 6.445 300 0E-02

qirat [Egypt]   <mass, special - see page 29>
gram ---- 0.195 --- 1.950 000 0E-01

qirat [Egypt]   <area, special - see page 29>
square meter ---- 175.03 --- 1.750 300 0E+02

qirat barsoun [Egypt]   <length, special - see page 29>
centimeter ---- 0.087 --- 8.700 000 0E-02

qirath [Islam]   <mass, special - see page 29>
gram ---- 0.195 --- 1.950 000 0E-01

qu [Babylon, ancient]   <volume, special - see page 29>
liter ---- 1 --- 1.000 000 0E+00

quad   <energy>
cheval vapeur heure [France] ---->>> 3.984 657 6E+11
coal equivalent kilogram [UN, standard] ---->>> 3.599 939 4E+10
coal equivalent metric ton [UN, standard] ---->>> 3.599 939 4E+07
exawatthour ---- 0.000 293 1 --- 2.930 710 7E-04
gigawatthour ---- 293,071.07 --- 2.930 710 7E+05
gram [atomic physics, eq. energy] ---- 11,739.08 --- 1.173 908 0E+04
horsepower hour ---->>> 3.930 147 8E+11
horsepower hour [metric] ---->>> 3.984 657 6E+11
joule ---->>> 1.055 055 9E+18
kilogram [atomic physics, eq. energy] ---- 11.739 08 --- 1.173 908 0E+01
kilogram calorie [15 °C, NBS, 1939] ---->>> 2.520 559 6E+14
kilogram square meter/square second ---->>> 1.055 055 9E+18
kilopond meter ---->>> 1.075 857 6E+17
kiloton [metric, explosive energy] ---- 252,164.4 --- 2.521 644 0E+05
kilowatthour ---->>> 2.930 710 7E+11
liter atmosphere ---->>> 1.041 259 2E+16
megaton [metric, explosive energy] ---- 252.164 4 --- 2.521 644 0E+02
therm [EEC] ---->>> 1.000 000 0E+10
therm [US] ---->>> 1.000 238 8E+10
thermie [France] ---->>> 2.520 559 6E+11
ton [metric, explosive energy] ---->>> 2.521 644 0E+08
watthour ---->>> 2.930 710 7E+14

quadra [Brazil]   <area, special - see page 29>
are ---- 1.742 --- 1.742 000 0E+00

quadra de sesmaria [Brazil]   <area, special - see page 29>
hectare ---- 87.1 --- 8.710 000 0E+01

quadran [Rome, ancient]   <mass, special - see page 29>
gram ---- 3.1 --- 3.100 000 0E+00

quadrantal [Rome, ancient, liquid]   <volume, special - see page 29>
liter ---- 25.8 --- 2.580 000 0E+01

quadrat [Germany]   <area, special - see page 29>
square meter ---- 14.18 --- 1.418 000 0E+01

quadrato [Italy]   <area, special - see page 29>
are ---- 50.5 --- 5.050 000 0E+01

quadrennial   <time>
year [normal calendar] ---- 4 --- 4.000 000 0E+00

quadrennium   <time>
year [normal calendar] ---- 4 --- 4.000 000 0E+00

quadrillion [UK]   <units>
septillion [US] ---- 1 --- 1.000 000 0E+00
unit ---->>> 1.000 000 0E+24

Convert From		<Type of Unit>
Convert To	Standard	Scientific

quadrillion [US] — <units>
unit -------- >>> ---- 1.000 000 0E+15

quamha [Islam] — <mass, special - see page 29>
gram -------- 0.05 ---- 5.000 000 0E-02

quan diem xich [Vietnam] — <length, special - see page 29>
centimeter -------- 47 ---- 4.700 000 0E+01

quantar [Cyprus] — <mass, special - see page 29>
kilogram -------- 55.883 ---- 5.588 300 0E+01

quantar [Egypt] — <mass, special - see page 29>
kilogram -------- 44.928 ---- 4.492 800 0E+01

quantar [Greece] — <mass, special - see page 29>
kilogram -------- 56.32 ---- 5.632 000 0E+01

quantar [Lebanon] — <mass, special - see page 29>
kilogram -------- 256.4 ---- 2.564 000 0E+02

quantar [Libya] — <mass, special - see page 29>
kilogram -------- 51.28 ---- 5.128 000 0E+01

quantar [Malta] — <mass, special - see page 29>
kilogram -------- 79.38 ---- 7.938 000 0E+01

quantar [Morocco] — <mass, special - see page 29>
kilogram -------- 100 ---- 1.000 000 0E+02

quantar [Sudan, large] — <mass, special - see page 29>
kilogram -------- 141.5 ---- 1.415 000 0E+02

quantar [Sudan, small] — <mass, special - see page 29>
kilogram -------- 44.928 ---- 4.492 800 0E+01

quantar [Syria] — <mass, special - see page 29>
kilogram -------- 256.5 ---- 2.565 000 0E+02

quantar [Turkey] — <mass, special - see page 29>
kilogram -------- 56.45 ---- 5.645 000 0E+01

quart [Germany] — <volume, special - see page 29>
liter -------- 1.145 04 ---- 1.145 040 0E+00

quart [Hebrew, ancient] — <volume, special - see page 29>
liter -------- 1.08 ---- 1.080 000 0E+00

quart [UK] — <volume>

Convert To	Standard	Scientific
bushel [UK]	0.031 25	3.125 000 0E-02
bushel [US, dry]	0.032 251 8	3.225 177 3E-02
cubic decimeter	1.136 522 5	1.136 522 5E+00
cubic foot	0.040 135 9	4.013 591 3E-02
cubic inch	69.354 858	6.935 485 8E+01
cubic meter	0.001 136 5	1.136 522 5E-03
cup [Canada, measuring]	5	5.000 000 0E+00
cup [US, measuring]	4.803 799 7	4.803 799 7E+00
drachm [UK, liquid]	320	3.200 000 0E+02
dram [Canada, liquid]	320	3.200 000 0E+02
dram [US, liquid]	307.443 18	3.074 431 8E+02
gallon [Canada, liquid]	0.25	2.500 000 0E-01
gallon [UK, dry or liquid]	0.25	2.500 000 0E-01
gallon [US, liquid]	0.300 237 5	3.002 374 8E-01
gill [UK]	8	8.000 000 0E+00
gill [US]	9.607 599 4	9.607 599 4E+00
liter	1.136 522 5	1.136 522 5E+00
minim [UK]	19,200	1.920 000 0E+04
minim [US]	18,446.591	1.844 659 1E+04
ounce [UK, liquid]	40	4.000 000 0E+01
ounce [US, liquid]	38.430 398	3.843 039 8E+01
peck [UK]	0.125	1.250 000 0E-01
peck [US]	0.129 007 1	1.290 070 9E-01
pint [UK]	2	2.000 000 0E+00
pint [US, liquid]	2.401 899 9	2.401 899 9E+00
quart [US, liquid]	1.200 949 9	1.200 949 9E+00

Convert From / Convert To	Standard	Scientific
scruple [UK, liquid]	960	9.600 000 0E+02
tablespoon [Canada, measuring]	80.000 135	8.000 013 5E+01
tablespoon [US, measuring]	76.860 795	7.686 079 5E+01
teaspoon [Canada, measuring]	240.000 41	2.400 004 1E+02
teaspoon [US, measuring]	230.582 39	2.305 823 9E+02
Winchester wine gallon [UK]	0.300 237 5	3.002 374 8E−01
quart [US, dry]		**<volume>**
barrel [US, dry]	0.009 523 9	9.523 898 1E−03
bushel [UK]	0.030 279 3	3.027 934 3E−02
bushel [US]	0.031 25	3.125 000 0E−02
bushel [US, struck measure]	0.031 25	3.125 000 0E−02
cubic decimeter	1.101 220 9	1.101 220 9E+00
cubic foot	0.038 889 3	3.888 925 1E−02
cubic inch	67.200 625	6.720 062 5E+01
cubic meter	0.001 101 2	1.101 220 9E−03
cubic yard	0.001 440 3	1.440 342 6E−03
gallon [US, dry]	0.25	2.500 000 0E−01
liter	1.101 220 9	1.101 220 9E+00
peck [UK]	0.121 117 4	1.211 173 7E−01
peck [US]	0.125	1.250 000 0E−01
pint [UK]	1.937 877 9	1.937 877 9E+00
pint [US, dry]	2	2.000 000 0E+00
quart [UK]	0.968 939	9.689 389 7E−01
stere	0.001 101 2	1.101 220 9E−03
quart [US, liquid]		**<volume>**
barrel [UK]	0.005 782 5	5.782 459 6E−03
barrel [US, federal proof spirits]	0.006 25	6.250 000 0E−03
barrel [US, liquid]	0.007 936 5	7.936 507 9E−03
barrel [US, petroleum]	0.005 952 4	5.952 381 0E−03
cubic foot	0.033 420 1	3.342 013 9E−02
cubic inch	57.75	5.775 000 0E+01
cubic meter	0.000 946 4	9.463 529 5E−04
cubic yard	0.001 237 8	1.237 782 9E−03
cup [Canada, measuring]	4.163 370 9	4.163 370 9E+00
cup [US, measuring]	4	4.000 000 0E+00
deciliter	9.463 529	9.463 529 5E+00
drachm [UK, liquid]	266.455 74	2.664 557 4E+02
dram [Canada, liquid]	266.455 74	2.664 557 4E+02
dram [US, liquid]	256	2.560 000 0E+02
drop [US, liquid]	11,520	1.152 000 0E+04
drum [US, liquid]	0.004 545 5	4.545 454 5E−03
gallon [Canada, liquid]	0.208 168 6	2.081 685 5E−01
gallon [UK, dry or liquid]	0.208 168 6	2.081 685 5E−01
gallon [US, liquid]	0.25	2.500 000 0E−01
gill [UK]	6.661 393 5	6.661 393 5E+00
gill [US]	8	8.000 000 0E+00
hogshead [UK]	0.003 304 3	3.304 262 6E−03
hogshead [US]	0.003 968 3	3.968 254 0E−03
liter	0.946 353	9.463 529 5E−01
minim [UK]	15,987.344	1.598 734 4E+04
minim [US]	15,360	1.536 000 0E+04
ounce [UK, liquid]	33.306 967	3.330 696 7E+01
ounce [US, liquid]	32	3.200 000 0E+01
pint [UK]	1.665 348 4	1.665 348 4E+00
pint [US, liquid]	2	2.000 000 0E+00
quart [UK]	0.832 674 2	8.326 741 8E−01
tablespoon [Canada, measuring]	66.614 048	6.661 404 8E+01
tablespoon [US, measuring]	64	6.400 000 0E+01
teaspoon [Canada, measuring]	199.842 14	1.998 421 4E+02
teaspoon [US, measuring]	192	1.920 000 0E+02
Winchester wine gallon [UK]	0.25	2.500 000 0E−01
quart de bouteille [Mauritius]		**<volume, special - see page 29>**
centiliter	75.77	7.577 000 0E+01

quarta [Cape Verde, dry] — <volume, special - see page 29>
liter ---- 10.398 ---- 1.039 800 0E+01

quarta [Cape Verde] — <area, special - see page 29>
hectare ---- 0.464 64 ---- 4.646 400 0E-01

quartarella [Italy, dry] — <volume, special - see page 29>
liter ---- 36.8 ---- 3.680 000 0E+01

quartarius [Rome, ancient, dry] — <volume, special - see page 29>
liter ---- 0.136 ---- 1.360 000 0E-01

quartarius [Rome, ancient, liquid] — <volume, special - see page 29>
liter ---- 0.137 ---- 1.370 000 0E-01

quartarius [Rome, ancient] — <volume, special - see page 29>
liter ---- 0.136 ---- 1.360 000 0E-01

quartaut [France] — <volume, special - see page 29>
liter ---- 67.06 ---- 6.706 000 0E+01

quartaut [Portugal, wine] — <volume, special - see page 29>
liter ---- 134 ---- 1.340 000 0E+02

quarte [France] — <volume, special - see page 29>
liter ---- 3.25 ---- 3.250 000 0E+00

quarteau [France, dry] — <volume, special - see page 29>
hectoliter ---- 4.683 ---- 4.683 000 0E+00

quartel [Germany, liquid] — <volume, special - see page 29>
milliliter ---- 429 ---- 4.290 000 0E+02

quarter [cloth] — <length>

	Standard	Scientific
barleycorn	27	2.700 000 0E+01
bolt [cloth]	0.006 25	6.250 000 0E-03
caliber	900	9.000 000 0E+02
cubit	0.5	5.000 000 0E-01
decimeter	2.286	2.286 000 0E+00
digit	12	1.200 000 0E+01
ell [cloth]	0.2	2.000 000 0E-01
foot [international]	0.75	7.500 000 0E-01
hand [horses]	2.25	2.250 000 0E+00
inch [international]	9	9.000 000 0E+00
iron [shoe leather]	432	4.320 000 0E+02
meter	0.228 6	2.286 000 0E-01
nail [cloth]	4	4.000 000 0E+00
pace [geometrical]	0.015	1.500 000 0E-02
palm	3	3.000 000 0E+00
skein [cloth]	0.002 083 3	2.083 333 3E-03
span	1	1.000 000 0E+00
yard [international]	0.25	2.500 000 0E-01

quarter [long] — <mass>

	Standard	Scientific
cental [US]	5.6	5.600 000 0E+00
centner [UK]	5	5.000 000 0E+00
decitonne	2.540 117 3	2.540 117 3E+00
doppelzentner [Germany]	2.540 117 3	2.540 117 3E+00
dram [avoirdupois]	143,360	1.433 600 0E+05
grain	3,920,000	3.920 000 0E+06
hundredweight [long]	5	5.000 000 0E+00
hundredweight [short]	5.6	5.600 000 0E+00
kilogram	254.011 73	2.540 117 3E+02
ounce	8,960	8.960 000 0E+03
pound	560	5.600 000 0E+02
quarter [short]	1.12	1.120 000 0E+00
quarter [UK]	20	2.000 000 0E+01
quarter [US]	22.4	2.240 000 0E+01
quintal [UK]	5	5.000 000 0E+00
quintal [US]	5.6	5.600 000 0E+00
stone [UK]	40	4.000 000 0E+01
ton [long]	0.25	2.500 000 0E-01

| Convert From | | |
Convert To	Standard	Scientific
ton [short]	0.28	2.800 000 0E−01
quarter [short]		**\<mass\>**
cental [US]	5	5.000 000 0E+00
dram [avoirdupois]	128,000	1.280 000 0E+05
grain	3,500,000	3.500 000 0E+06
hundredweight [long]	4.464 285 7	4.464 285 7E+00
hundredweight [short]	5	5.000 000 0E+00
kilogram	226.796 19	2.267 961 9E+02
ounce	8,000	8.000 000 0E+03
ounce [avoirdupois]	8,000	8.000 000 0E+03
pound	500	5.000 000 0E+02
pound [avoirdupois]	500	5.000 000 0E+02
pound [international]	500	5.000 000 0E+02
pound [unified]	500	5.000 000 0E+02
poundal square second/foot	500	5.000 000 0E+02
quarter [US]	20	2.000 000 0E+01
quintal [US]	5	5.000 000 0E+00
ton [long]	0.223 214 3	2.232 142 9E−01
ton [short]	0.25	2.500 000 0E−01
quarter [UK]		**\<mass\>**
carat [international]	63,502.932	6.350 293 2E+04
carat [UK]	49,000	4.900 000 0E+04
cental [US]	0.28	2.800 000 0E−01
centner [UK]	0.25	2.500 000 0E−01
dram [avoirdupois]	7,168	7.168 000 0E+03
grain	196,000	1.960 000 0E+05
hundredweight [short]	0.28	2.800 000 0E−01
hundredweight [UK]	0.25	2.500 000 0E−01
kilogram	12.700 586	1.270 058 6E+01
ounce	448	4.480 000 0E+02
pound	28	2.800 000 0E+01
pound [UK]	28.000 002	2.800 000 2E+01
quarter [long]	0.05	5.000 000 0E−02
quarter [short]	0.056	5.600 000 0E−02
quarter [US]	1.12	1.120 000 0E+00
quintal [UK]	0.25	2.500 000 0E−01
scruple [UK]	9,800	9.800 000 0E+03
stone	2	2.000 000 0E+00
ton [long]	0.012 5	1.250 000 0E−02
ton [short]	0.014	1.400 000 0E−02
ton [UK]	0.012 5	1.250 000 0E−02
quarter [UK]		**\<volume\>**
barrel [UK]	1.777 777 8	1.777 777 8E+00
barrel [US, dry]	2.516 276	2.516 276 0E+00
bushel [UK]	8	8.000 000 0E+00
bushel [UK, struck measure]	7.999 983 6	7.999 983 6E+00
bushel [US, dry]	8.256 453 9	8.256 453 9E+00
bushel [US, heaped]	6.461 675 9	6.461 675 9E+00
bushel [US, struck measure]	8.256 453 9	8.256 453 9E+00
chaldron [UK, dry]	0.222 222 2	2.222 222 2E−01
chaldron [UK, liquid]	0.222 222 2	2.222 222 2E−01
chaldron [US, dry]	0.229 345 9	2.293 459 4E−01
cubic foot	10.274 794	1.027 479 4E+01
cubic inch	17,754.844	1.775 484 4E+04
cubic meter	0.290 949 8	2.909 497 6E−01
cup [Canada, measuring]	1,280	1.280 000 0E+03
cup [US, measuring]	1,229.772 7	1.229 772 7E+03
drachm [UK, liquid]	81,920	8.192 000 0E+04
dram [Canada, liquid]	81,920	8.192 000 0E+04
dram [US, liquid]	78,705.454	7.870 545 4E+04
gallon [Canada, liquid]	64	6.400 000 0E+01
gallon [UK, dry or liquid]	64	6.400 000 0E+01
gallon [US, dry]	66.051 632	6.605 163 2E+01

Convert To	Standard	Scientific
gill [UK]	2,048	2.048 000 0E+03
gill [US]	2,459.545 4	2.459 545 4E+03
hectoliter	2.909 497 6	2.909 497 6E+00
liter	290.949 76	2.909 497 6E+02
ounce [UK, liquid]	10,240	1.024 000 0E+04
ounce [US, liquid]	9,838.181 8	9.838 181 8E+03
peck [UK]	32	3.200 000 0E+01
peck [US]	33.025 816	3.302 581 6E+01
pint [UK]	512	5.120 000 0E+02
pint [US, dry]	528.413 05	5.284 130 5E+02
pint [US, liquid]	614.886 36	6.148 863 6E+02
quart [UK]	256	2.560 000 0E+02
quart [US, dry]	264.206 53	2.642 065 3E+02
quart [US, liquid]	307.443 18	3.074 431 8E+02
scruple [UK, liquid]	245,760	2.457 600 0E+05
stere	0.290 949 8	2.909 497 6E−01

quarter [US]   <mass>

Convert To	Standard	Scientific
cental [US]	0.25	2.500 000 0E−01
dram [avoirdupois]	6,400	6.400 000 0E+03
grain	175,000	1.750 000 0E+05
hundredweight [short]	0.25	2.500 000 0E−01
kilogram	11.339 809	1.133 980 9E+01
ounce	400	4.000 000 0E+02
pound	25	2.500 000 0E+01
poundal square second/foot	25	2.500 000 0E+01
quarter [short]	0.05	5.000 000 0E−02
quintal [US]	0.25	2.500 000 0E−01
scruple [US, apothecary]	8,750	8.750 000 0E+03
ton [long]	0.011 160 7	1.116 071 4E−02
ton [short]	0.012 5	1.250 000 0E−02

quartern [UK, dry]   <volume, special - see page 29>

Convert To	Standard	Scientific
liter	2.272 98	2.272 980 0E+00

quartern [UK, liquid]   <volume, special - see page 29>

Convert To	Standard	Scientific
liter	0.142 061 3	1.420 613 0E−01

quarteron [France]   <area, special - see page 29>

Convert To	Standard	Scientific
square meter	1,076	1.076 000 0E+03

quarteron [Switzerland]   <volume, special - see page 29>

Convert To	Standard	Scientific
liter	15	1.500 000 0E+01

quartia [Belize]   <volume, special - see page 29>

Convert To	Standard	Scientific
liter	2.841	2.841 000 0E+00

quartier [Germany]   <volume, special - see page 29>

Convert To	Standard	Scientific
liter	0.859	8.590 000 0E−01

quartilho [Brazil]   <volume, special - see page 29>

Convert To	Standard	Scientific
liter	0.665 5	6.655 000 0E−01

quartilho [Portugal, liquid]   <volume, special - see page 29>

Convert To	Standard	Scientific
liter	0.345	3.450 000 0E−01

quartillo [Portugal]   <volume, special - see page 29>

Convert To	Standard	Scientific
liter	0.349	3.490 000 0E−01

quarto [Brazil]   <volume, special - see page 29>

Convert To	Standard	Scientific
liter	9.07	9.070 000 0E+00

quarto [Italy, dry]   <volume, special - see page 29>

Convert To	Standard	Scientific
hectoliter	0.736	7.360 000 0E−01

quarto [Portugal]   <volume, special - see page 29>

Convert To	Standard	Scientific
liter	3.46	3.460 000 0E+00

quartuccio [Italy, liquid]   <volume, special - see page 29>

Convert To	Standard	Scientific
milliliter	114	1.140 000 0E+02

quarter   <time>

Convert To	Standard	Scientific
year [normal calendar]	0.25	2.500 000 0E−01

quattuordecillion [UK]
unit -->>> --- 1.000 000 0E+84 <units>

quattuordecillion [US]
unit -->>> --- 1.000 000 0E+45 <units>

que [Vietnam, cereal] <volume, special - see page 29>
milliliter --- 0.02 --- 2.000 000 0E-02

quei [China] <volume, special - see page 29>
milliliter --- 0.01 --- 1.000 000 0E-02

quentchen [Austria] <mass, special - see page 29>
gram --- 4.375 1 --- 4.375 100 0E+00

quenten [Norway] <mass, special - see page 29>
gram --- 3.89 --- 3.890 000 0E+00

quiba [Tunisia, cereals] <volume, special - see page 29>
liter --- 36.369 --- 3.636 900 0E+01

quilat [Austria, jewels and pearls] <mass, special - see page 29>
gram --- 0.208 --- 2.080 000 0E-01

quilat [Batavia, jewels and pearls] <mass, special - see page 29>
gram --- 0.198 --- 1.980 000 0E-01

quilat [Germany, gold and silver] <mass, special - see page 29>
gram --- 10.62 --- 1.062 000 0E+01

quilat [Germany, jewels and pearls] <mass, special - see page 29>
gram --- 0.206 --- 2.060 000 0E-01

quilat [India, jewels and pearls] <mass, special - see page 29>
gram --- 0.198 --- 1.980 000 0E-01

quilat [Netherlands, jewels and pearls] <mass, special - see page 29>
gram --- 0.207 --- 2.070 000 0E-01

quilat [Portugal, jewels] <mass, special - see page 29>
gram --- 0.205 8 --- 2.058 000 0E-01

quilat [Switzerland, gold and silver] <mass, special - see page 29>
gram --- 10.2 --- 1.020 000 0E+01

quilat [UK, jewels and pearls] <mass, special - see page 29>
gram --- 0.209 --- 2.090 000 0E-01

quilate [Brazil] <mass, special - see page 29>
milligram --- 199.24 --- 1.992 400 0E+02

quilate [Colombia] <mass, special - see page 29>
milligram --- 20 --- 2.000 000 0E+01

quilate [Philippines] <mass, special - see page 29>
gram --- 0.205 --- 2.050 000 0E-01

quilate [Spain] <mass, special - see page 29>
gram --- 0.199 693 --- 1.996 930 0E-01

quilo [Greece] <volume, special - see page 29>
liter --- 37.7 --- 3.770 000 0E+01

quincentenary <time>
quincentennial --- 1 --- 1.000 000 0E+00
year [normal calendar] ------------------------------------- 500 --- 5.000 000 0E+02

quincentennial <time>
quincentenary --- 1 --- 1.000 000 0E+00
year [normal calendar] ------------------------------------- 500 --- 5.000 000 0E+02

quincunx [Rome, ancient] <mass, special - see page 29>
gram --- 136.44 --- 1.364 400 0E+02

quindecennial <time>
year [normal calendar] ------------------------------------- 15 --- 1.500 000 0E+01

quindecillion [UK] <units>
unit -->>> --- 1.000 000 0E+90

quindecillion [US] <units>
octillion [UK] --- 1 --- 1.000 000 0E+00

unit-- >>>----1.000 000 0E+48

quinon [Philippines]   <area, special - see page 29>
  hectare--2.795----2.795 000 0E+00

quinquagesimal   <time>
  day-- 50----5.000 000 0E+01

quinquennium   <time>
  year [normal calendar]--5----5.000 000 0E+00

quintal [Algiers, copper and wax]   <mass, special - see page 29>
  kilogram--54.05----5.405 000 0E+01

quintal [Algiers, cotton and almonds]   <mass, special - see page 29>
  kilogram-- 59.455----5.945 500 0E+01

quintal [Algiers, flax]   <mass, special - see page 29>
  kilogram-- 108.1----1.081 000 0E+02

quintal [Algiers, iron, lead, and wool]   <mass, special - see page 29>
  kilogram--81.075----8.107 500 0E+01

quintal [Algiers, oil, soap, butter, honey, and dates] <mass, special - see page 29>
  kilogram--89.723----8.972 300 0E+01

quintal [Argentina]   <mass, special - see page 29>
  gram--45.94----4.594 000 0E+01

quintal [Belize]   <mass, special - see page 29>
  gram--45.36----4.536 000 0E+01

quintal [Bolivia]   <mass, special - see page 29>
  kilogram--46----4.600 000 0E+01

quintal [Brazil]   <mass, special - see page 29>
  kilogram--58.758 4----5.875 840 0E+01

quintal [British Honduras]   <mass, special - see page 29>
  kilogram---------------------------------- 45.359 237----4.535 923 7E+01

quintal [Chile]   <mass, special - see page 29>
  kilogram--46.009 3----4.600 930 0E+01

quintal [Colombia]   <mass, special - see page 29>
  kilogram-- 50----5.000 000 0E+01

quintal [Costa Rica]   <mass, special - see page 29>
  kilogram--46----4.600 000 0E+01

quintal [Cuba]   <mass, special - see page 29>
  kilogram-- 46.009----4.600 900 0E+01

quintal [Czechoslovakia]   <mass, special - see page 29>
  kilogram-- 50----5.000 000 0E+01

quintal [Dominican Republic]   <mass, special - see page 29>
  kilogram-- 45.36----4.536 000 0E+01

quintal [Ecuador]   <mass, special - see page 29>
  kilogram--46----4.600 000 0E+01

quintal [Egypt, ancient]   <mass, special - see page 29>
  kilogram-- 44.928----4.492 800 0E+01

quintal [El Salvador]   <mass, special - see page 29>
  kilogram-- 45.378----4.537 800 0E+01

quintal [France, Paris]   <mass, special - see page 29>
  kilogram-- 100----1.000 000 0E+02

quintal [France]   <mass, special - see page 29>
  kilogram-- 48.951----4.895 100 0E+01

quintal [Greece]   <mass, special - see page 29>
  kilogram--56.32----5.632 000 0E+01

quintal [Guatemala]   <mass, special - see page 29>
  kilogram--46----4.600 000 0E+01

quintal [Honduras]   <mass, special - see page 29>
  kilogram -- 46----4.600 000 0E+01

Convert From Convert To	Standard	<Type of Unit> Scientific

quintal [Iraq, ancient]   <mass, special - see page 29>
	Standard	Scientific
kilogram	44.928	4.492 800 0E+01

quintal [Macao]   <mass, special - see page 29>
kilogram	58.752	5.875 200 0E+01

quintal [metric]   <mass>
carat [international]	500,000	5.000 000 0E+05
cental [US]	2.204 622 6	2.204 622 6E+00
decitonne	1	1.000 000 0E+00
doppelzentner [Germany]	1	1.000 000 0E+00
hundredweight [long]	1.968 413 1	1.968 413 1E+00
hundredweight [short]	2.204 622 6	2.204 622 6E+00
kilogram	100	1.000 000 0E+02
megagram	0.1	1.000 000 0E-01
myriagram	10	1.000 000 0E+01
ounce	3,527.396 2	3.527 396 2E+03
point [jewelers']	>>>	5.000 000 0E+07
pound	220.462 26	2.204 622 6E+02
quarter [US]	8.818 490 5	8.818 490 5E+00
quintal [US]	2.204 622 6	2.204 622 6E+00
slug	6.852 176 6	6.852 176 6E+00
ton [long]	0.098 420 7	9.842 065 3E-02
ton [metric]	0.1	1.000 000 0E-01
ton [short]	0.110 231 1	1.102 311 3E-01
tonne	0.1	1.000 000 0E-01

quintal [Mexico]   <mass, special - see page 29>
kilogram	46.02	4.602 000 0E+01

quintal [Morocco]   <mass, special - see page 29>
kilogram	51.26	5.126 000 0E+01

quintal [Nicaragua]   <mass, special - see page 29>
kilogram	46	4.600 000 0E+01

quintal [Paraguay]   <mass, special - see page 29>
kilogram	45.9	4.590 000 0E+01

quintal [Peru]   <mass, special - see page 29>
kilogram	46	4.600 000 0E+01

quintal [Philippines]   <mass, special - see page 29>
kilogram	46	4.600 000 0E+01

quintal [Portugal]   <mass, special - see page 29>
kilogram	60	6.000 000 0E+01

quintal [Romania]   <mass, special - see page 29>
kilogram	56.726	5.672 600 0E+01

quintal [Spain]   <mass, special - see page 29>
kilogram	46.009	4.600 900 0E+01

quintal [Switzerland]   <mass, special - see page 29>
kilogram	100	1.000 000 0E+02

quintal [Turkey]   <mass, special - see page 29>
kilogram	100	1.000 000 0E+02

quintal [UK]   <mass>
cental [US]	1.12	1.120 000 0E+00
centner [UK]	1	1.000 000 0E+00
drachm [UK, apothecary]	13,066.667	1.306 666 7E+04
geepound	3.481 066 4	3.481 066 4E+00
hundredweight [long]	1	1.000 000 0E+00
hundredweight [short]	1.12	1.120 000 0E+00
hundredweight [UK]	1	1.000 000 0E+00
kilogram	50.802 345	5.080 234 5E+01
ounce	1,792	1.792 000 0E+03
pound	112	1.120 000 0E+02
quarter [long]	0.2	2.000 000 0E-01
quarter [short]	0.224	2.240 000 0E-01

	Standard	Scientific
quarter [UK]	4	4.000 000 0E+00
quarter [US]	4.48	4.480 000 0E+00
quintal [US]	1.12	1.120 000 0E+00
scruple [UK]	39,200	3.920 000 0E+04
stone [UK]	8	8.000 000 0E+00
ton [long]	0.05	5.000 000 0E-02
ton [short]	0.056	5.600 000 0E-02
ton [UK]	0.05	5.000 000 0E-02

quintal [Uruguay]   <mass, special - see page 29>
| kilogram | 45.94 | 4.594 000 0E+01 |

quintal [US]   <mass>
	Standard	Scientific
cental [US]	1	1.000 000 0E+00
dram [avoirdupois]	25,600	2.560 000 0E+04
grain	700,000	7.000 000 0E+05
hundredweight [long]	0.892 857 1	8.928 571 4E-01
hundredweight [short]	1	1.000 000 0E+00
kilogram	45.359 237	4.535 923 7E+01
ounce	1,600	1.600 000 0E+03
pound	100	1.000 000 0E+02
poundal square second/foot	100	1.000 000 0E+02
quarter [short]	0.2	2.000 000 0E-01
quarter [US]	4	4.000 000 0E+00
scruple [US, apothecary]	35,000	3.500 000 0E+04
ton [long]	0.044 642 9	4.464 285 7E-02
ton [short]	0.05	5.000 000 0E-02

quintal [Venezuela]   <mass, special - see page 29>
| kilogram | 46.09 | 4.609 000 0E+01 |

quintar [Saudi Arabia]   <mass, special - see page 29>
| kilogram | 50.804 | 5.080 400 0E+01 |

quintaux [France]   <mass, special - see page 29>
| kilogram | 48.95 | 4.895 000 0E+01 |

quintillion [UK]   <units>
| nonillion [US] | 1 | 1.000 000 0E+00 |
| unit | >>> | 1.000 000 0E+30 |

quintillion [US]   <units>
| trillion [UK] | 1 | 1.000 000 0E+00 |
| unit | >>> | 1.000 000 0E+18 |

rabaa [Morocco]   <mass, special - see page 29>
| gram | 250 | 2.500 000 0E+02 |

rabia [Morocco]   <area, special - see page 29>
| square meter | 450 | 4.500 000 0E+02 |

racin [Spain]   <volume, special - see page 29>
| liter | 0.289 07 | 2.890 700 0E-01 |

racione [Spain, dry]   <volume, special - see page 29>
| liter | 0.29 | 2.900 000 0E-01 |

rad   <absorbed dose>
| gray | 0.01 | 1.000 000 0E-02 |
| rep | 1.193 317 4 | 1.193 317 4E+00 |

rad/second   <absorbed dose rate>
| gray/second | 0.01 | 1.000 000 0E-02 |
| rep/second | 1.193 317 4 | 1.193 317 4E+00 |

radian   <plane angle>
centrad	100	1.000 000 0E+02
circle [angular]	0.159 154 9	1.591 549 4E-01
degree [angular]	57.295 78	5.729 578 0E+01
gon [angular]	63.661 977	6.366 197 7E+01
grade [angular]	63.661 977	6.366 197 7E+01
mil [military artillery, angle, NATO]	1,018.591 6	1.018 591 6E+03
mil [military artillery, angle, US, WWII]	636.619 77	6.366 197 7E+02

mil [military artillery, angle, USSR]	1,002.676 1	1.002 676 1E+03
mil [military infantry, angle, UK]	1,000	1.000 000 0E+03
minute [angular]	3,437.746 8	3.437 746 8E+03
revolution [angular]	0.159 154 9	1.591 549 4E−01
right angle	0.636 619 8	6.366 197 7E−01
second [angular]	206,264.81	2.062 648 1E+05
sign	1.909 859 3	1.909 859 3E+00

radian/hour \<frequency\>

1/second	0.000 044 2	4.420 970 6E−05
degree/hour	57.295 78	5.729 578 0E+01
millihertz	0.044 209 7	4.420 970 6E−02
radian/minute	0.016 666 7	1.666 666 7E−02
revolution/hour	0.159 154 9	1.591 549 4E−01

radian/meter \<reciprocal length, phase coefficient\>

1/centimeter	0.01	1.000 000 0E−02
1/inch	0.025 4	2.540 000 0E−02
1/meter	1	1.000 000 0E+00
degree/foot	17.463 754	1.746 375 4E+01
degree/inch	1.455 312 8	1.455 312 8E+00
diopter	1	1.000 000 0E+00

radian/minute \<frequency\>

1/second	0.002 652 6	2.652 582 4E−03
degree/minute	57.295 78	5.729 578 0E+01
millihertz	2.652 582 4	2.652 582 4E+00
radian/hour	60	6.000 000 0E+01
revolution/hour	9.549 296 6	9.549 296 6E+00

radian/second \<frequency\>

1/second	0.159 154 9	1.591 549 4E−01
degree/second	57.295 78	5.729 578 0E+01
millihertz	159.154 94	1.591 549 4E+02
radian/hour	3,600	3.600 000 0E+03
radian/minute	60	6.000 000 0E+01
revolution/minute	9.549 296 6	9.549 296 6E+00

radian/second [atomic physics, eq. energy] \<energy\>

cheval vapeur heure [France]	\>\>\>	3.581 286 4E+27
coal equivalent kilogram [UN, standard]	\>\>\>	3.235 513 6E+26
coal equivalent metric ton [UN, standard]	\>\>\>	3.235 513 6E+23
gram [atomic physics, eq. energy]	\>\>\>	1.055 072 0E+20
joule	\>\>\>	9.482 513 9E+33
kilogram [atomic physics, eq. energy]	\>\>\>	1.055 072 0E+17
kiloton [metric, explosive energy]	\>\>\>	2.266 375 2E+21
megaton [metric, explosive energy]	\>\>\>	2.266 375 2E+18
quad	\>\>\>	8.987 689 0E+15
therm [EEC]	\>\>\>	8.987 689 0E+25
therm [US]	\>\>\>	8.989 835 0E+25
thermie [France]	\>\>\>	2.265 400 6E+27
ton [metric, explosive energy]	\>\>\>	2.266 375 2E+24
watthour	\>\>\>	2.634 031 6E+30

radian/square second \<angular acceleration\>

degree/square second	57.295 78	5.729 578 0E+01

rafa [Bahrain] \<mass, special - see page 29\>

kilogram	254	2.540 000 0E+02

rageil [Sudan] \<length, special - see page 29\>

meter	1.676	1.676 000 0E+00

ragil [Sudan] \<length, special - see page 29\>

meter	1.676	1.676 000 0E+00

ragil bergedawi [Sudan] \<length, special - see page 29\>

meter	2.438	2.438 000 0E+00

rai [Laos] \<area, special - see page 29\>

hectare	0.16	1.600 000 0E−01

Convert From	<Type of Unit>	
Convert To	Standard	Scientific

rai [Thailand] <area, special - see page 29>
hectare-- 0.16 ---- 1.600 000 0E-01

raik [India] <volume, special - see page 29>
liter -- 1.376 ---- 1.376 000 0E+00

raik [India] <mass, special - see page 29>
kilogram -- 1.166 38 ---- 1.166 380 0E+00

rajabah [Oman] <length, special - see page 29>
centimeter -- 3 ---- 3.000 000 0E+00

ralica [Yugoslavia] <area, special - see page 29>
are --- 25 ---- 2.500 000 0E+01

ralo [Yugoslavia] <area, special - see page 29>
are --- 25 ---- 2.500 000 0E+01

range [US, survey] <length>
cable length [US, survey] --------------------------------------- 44 ---- 4.400 000 0E+01
chain [Gunter or US, survey] ----------------------------------- 480 ---- 4.800 000 0E+02
chain [Ramden or Engineer] ------------------------------ 316.800 63 ---- 3.168 006 3E+02
fathom [US, survey] -- 5,280 ---- 5.280 000 0E+03
foot [international] -- 31,680.063 ---- 3.168 006 3E+04
foot [US, survey] --- 31,680 ---- 3.168 000 0E+04
furlong [US, survey] --- 48 ---- 4.800 000 0E+00
kilometer -- 9.656 083 3 ---- 9.656 083 3E+00
league [international, nautical] ------------------------------ 1.737 956 ---- 1.737 956 0E+00
league [US, statute] --- 2 ---- 2.000 000 0E+00
meter --- 9,656.083 3 ---- 9.656 083 3E+03
mile [international] -- 6.000 012 ---- 6.000 012 0E+00
mile [US, statute] --- 6 ---- 6.000 000 0E+00
mile [US, survey] -- 6 ---- 6.000 000 0E+00
myriameter -- 0.965 608 3 ---- 9.656 083 3E-01
out [US, survey] -- 96 ---- 9.600 000 0E+01
perch [US, survey] --- 1,920 ---- 1.920 000 0E+03
township [US, survey] -- 1 ---- 1.000 000 0E+00
yard [based on US, survey foot] ---------------------------- 10,560 ---- 1.056 000 0E+04
yard [international] -- 10,560.021 ---- 1.056 002 1E+04

ratal [Egypt] <mass, special - see page 29>
kilogram --- 0.449 ---- 4.490 000 0E-01

ratal [Iran] <mass, special - see page 29>
kilogram --- 0.469 ---- 4.690 000 0E-01

ratal [Jordan] <mass, special - see page 29>
kilogram --- 2.564 ---- 2.564 000 0E+00

ratal [Lebanon] <mass, special - see page 29>
kilogram --- 2.564 ---- 2.564 000 0E+00

ratal [Libya] <mass, special - see page 29>
kilogram --- 0.513 ---- 5.130 000 0E-01

ratal [Malta] <mass, special - see page 29>
kilogram --- 0.794 ---- 7.940 000 0E-01

ratal [Morocco] <mass, special - see page 29>
gram --- 500 ---- 5.000 000 0E+02

ratal [Saudi Arabia] <mass, special - see page 29>
kilogram --- 0.462 ---- 4.620 000 0E-01

ratal [Somalia] <mass, special - see page 29>
kilogram --- 0.448 ---- 4.480 000 0E-01

ratal [Sudan] <mass, special - see page 29>
kilogram --- 0.449 ---- 4.490 000 0E-01

ratal [Syria] <mass, special - see page 29>
kilogram --- 2.565 ---- 2.565 000 0E+00

ratal [Tanzania] <mass, special - see page 29>
kilogram --- 0.454 ---- 4.540 000 0E-01

Convert From Convert To	Standard	<Type of Unit> Scientific
ratel [Egypt] kilogram	<mass, special - see page 29> 0.449 ---	4.490 000 0E-01
ratel [Iran] kilogram	<mass, special - see page 29> 0.469 ---	4.690 000 0E-01
ratel [Jordan] kilogram	<mass, special - see page 29> 2.564 ---	2.564 000 0E+00
ratel [Lebanon] kilogram	<mass, special - see page 29> 2.564 ---	2.564 000 0E+00
ratel [Libya] kilogram	<mass, special - see page 29> 0.513 ---	5.130 000 0E-01
ratel [Malta] kilogram	<mass, special - see page 29> 0.794 ---	7.940 000 0E-01
ratel [Morocco] gram	<mass, special - see page 29> 500 ---	5.000 000 0E+02
ratel [Saudi Arabia] kilogram	<mass, special - see page 29> 0.462 ---	4.620 000 0E-01
ratel [Somalia] kilogram	<mass, special - see page 29> 0.448 ---	4.480 000 0E-01
ratel [Sudan] kilogram	<mass, special - see page 29> 0.449 ---	4.490 000 0E-01
ratel [Syria] kilogram	<mass, special - see page 29> 2.565 ---	2.565 000 0E+00
ratel [Tanzania] kilogram	<mass, special - see page 29> 0.454 ---	4.540 000 0E-01
rati [Bangladesh, precious metals] milligram	<mass, special - see page 29> 121.5 ---	1.215 000 0E+02
rati [India] milligram	<mass, special - see page 29> 120 ---	1.200 000 0E+02
ratili [Egypt] kilogram	<mass, special - see page 29> 0.449 ---	4.490 000 0E-01
ratili [Iran] kilogram	<mass, special - see page 29> 0.469 ---	4.690 000 0E-01
ratili [Jordan] kilogram	<mass, special - see page 29> 2.564 ---	2.564 000 0E+00
ratili [Lebanon] kilogram	<mass, special - see page 29> 2.564 ---	2.564 000 0E+00
ratili [Libya] kilogram	<mass, special - see page 29> 0.513 ---	5.130 000 0E-01
ratili [Malta] kilogram	<mass, special - see page 29> 0.794 ---	7.940 000 0E-01
ratili [Morocco] gram	<mass, special - see page 29> 500 ---	5.000 000 0E+02
ratili [Saudi Arabia] kilogram	<mass, special - see page 29> 0.462 ---	4.620 000 0E-01
ratili [Somalia] kilogram	<mass, special - see page 29> 0.448 ---	4.480 000 0E-01
ratili [Sudan] kilogram	<mass, special - see page 29> 0.449 ---	4.490 000 0E-01
ratili [Syria] kilogram	<mass, special - see page 29> 2.565 ---	2.565 000 0E+00
ratili [Tanganyika] gram	<mass, special - see page 29> 453.592 37 ---	4.535 923 7E+02
ratili [Tanzania] kilogram	<mass, special - see page 29> 0.454 ---	4.540 000 0E-01

Convert From	<Type of Unit>	
Convert To	Standard	Scientific

ratl [Bahrain] <mass, special - see page 29>
kilogram ---0.454----4.540 000 0E-01

ratl [Egypt] <mass, special - see page 29>
kilogram ---0.449----4.490 000 0E-01

ratl [Iran] <mass, special - see page 29>
kilogram ---0.469----4.690 000 0E-01

ratl [Iraq] <mass, special - see page 29>
gram-- 401.674----4.016 740 0E+02

ratl [Jordan] <mass, special - see page 29>
kilogram ---2.564----2.564 000 0E+00

ratl [Lebanon] <mass, special - see page 29>
kilogram ---2.564----2.564 000 0E+00

ratl [Libya] <mass, special - see page 29>
kilogram ---0.513----5.130 000 0E-01

ratl [Malta] <mass, special - see page 29>
kilogram ---0.794----7.940 000 0E-01

ratl [Morocco] <mass, special - see page 29>
gram-- 500----5.000 000 0E+02

ratl [North Africa] <mass, special - see page 29>
gram-- 490.7----4.907 000 0E+02

ratl [Saudi Arabia] <mass, special - see page 29>
kilogram ---0.462----4.620 000 0E-01

ratl [Somalia] <mass, special - see page 29>
kilogram ---0.448----4.480 000 0E-01

ratl [Spain] <mass, special - see page 29>
gram-- 503.68----5.036 800 0E+02

ratl [Sudan] <mass, special - see page 29>
kilogram ---0.449----4.490 000 0E-01

ratl [Syria, heavy] <mass, special - see page 29>
kilogram ---1.853----1.853 000 0E+00

ratl [Syria] <mass, special - see page 29>
kilogram ---2.565----2.565 000 0E+00

ratl [Tanzania] <mass, special - see page 29>
kilogram ---0.454----4.540 000 0E-01

ratl [Yemen] <mass, special - see page 29>
gram-- 453.6----4.536 000 0E+02

ratl djarwi [Islam] <mass, special - see page 29>
gram-- 964----9.640 000 0E+02

ratl laythi [Islam] <mass, special - see page 29>
gram-- 617.96----6.179 600 0E+02

ratl rumi [Muslim, ancient] <mass, special - see page 29>
gram-- 370.776----3.707 760 0E+02

rattel [Egypt] <mass, special - see page 29>
kilogram ---0.449----4.490 000 0E-01

rattel [Iran] <mass, special - see page 29>
kilogram ---0.469----4.690 000 0E-01

rattel [Jordan] <mass, special - see page 29>
kilogram ---2.564----2.564 000 0E+00

rattel [Lebanon] <mass, special - see page 29>
kilogram ---2.564----2.564 000 0E+00

rattel [Libya] <mass, special - see page 29>
kilogram ---0.513----5.130 000 0E-01

rattel [Malta] <mass, special - see page 29>
kilogram ---0.794----7.940 000 0E-01

Convert From		<Type of Unit>
Convert To	Standard	Scientific
rattel [Morocco]	<mass, special - see page 29>	
gram	500	5.000 000 0E+02
rattel [Saudi Arabia]	<mass, special - see page 29>	
kilogram	0.462	4.620 000 0E-01
rattel [Somalia]	<mass, special - see page 29>	
kilogram	0.448	4.480 000 0E-01
rattel [Sudan]	<mass, special - see page 29>	
kilogram	0.449	4.490 000 0E-01
rattel [Syria]	<mass, special - see page 29>	
kilogram	2.565	2.565 000 0E+00
rattel [Tanzania]	<mass, special - see page 29>	
kilogram	0.454	4.540 000 0E-01
raummeter [Austria, piled wood]	<volume, special - see page 29>	
cubic meter	1	1.000 000 0E+00
rayl	<specific acoustic impedance>	
dyne second/cubic centimeter	1	1.000 000 0E+00
kilogram-force second/cubic meter	1.019 716 2	1.019 716 2E+00
pascal second/meter	10	1.000 000 0E+01
pound-force second/cubic foot	0.063 658 8	6.365 880 4E-02
poundal second/cubic foot	2.048 161 4	2.048 161 4E+00
real [Indonesia, precious metals]	<mass, special - see page 29>	
gram	27.045	2.704 500 0E+01
rebah [Hebrew, ancient]	<mass, special - see page 29>	
gram	3.2	3.200 000 0E+00
rebee [Syria]	<volume, special - see page 29>	
liter	4.75	4.750 000 0E+00
rebia [Algeria]	<length, special - see page 29>	
centimeter	12.4	1.240 000 0E+01
red [Honduras, maize or corn]	<mass, special - see page 29>	
kilogram	45.359	4.535 900 0E+01
reed [Egypt, ancient]	<length, special - see page 29>	
meter	3.15	3.150 000 0E+00
reed [Hebrew, ancient]	<length, special - see page 29>	
meter	3.1	3.100 000 0E+00
reed [Israel]	<length, special - see page 29>	
meter	2.679	2.679 000 0E+00
ref [Sweden]	<length, special - see page 29>	
meter	29.69	2.969 000 0E+01
register ton	<volume>	
barrel [UK]	17.302 321	1.730 232 1E+01
barrel [US, dry]	24.489 796	2.448 979 6E+01
board foot	1,200	1.200 000 0E+03
bushel [UK]	77.860 443	7.786 044 3E+01
bushel [US, dry]	80.356 395	8.035 639 5E+01
cord [firewood]	0.781 25	7.812 500 0E-01
cord foot [timber]	6.25	6.250 000 0E+00
cubic foot	100	1.000 000 0E+02
cubic inch	172,800	1.728 000 0E+05
cubic meter	2.831 684 7	2.831 684 7E+00
cubic yard	3.703 703 7	3.703 703 7E+00
English water ton [UK]	2.780 730 1	2.780 730 1E+00
freight ton	2.5	2.500 000 0E+00
gallon [Canada, liquid]	622.883 55	6.228 835 5E+02
gallon [UK, dry or liquid]	622.883 55	6.228 835 5E+02
gallon [US, dry]	642.851 16	6.428 511 6E+02
kiloliter	2.831 684 7	2.831 684 7E+00
liter	2,831.684 7	2.831 684 7E+03
measurement ton	2.5	2.500 000 0E+00

Convert From / Convert To	Standard	Scientific
[rehoboam continued]		
million board foot	0.001 2	1.200 000 0E-03
ocean ton	2.5	2.500 000 0E+00
petrograd standard	0.606 060 6	6.060 606 1E-01
shipping ton	2.5	2.500 000 0E+00
stere	2.831 684 7	2.831 684 7E+00
thousand board foot	1.2	1.200 000 0E+00
thousand cubic foot	0.1	1.000 000 0E-01
rehoboam [champagne bottle]	**<champagne bottle size>**	
bottle [wine, standard]	6	6.000 000 0E+00
liter	4.5	4.500 000 0E+00
relong [Malaysia]	**<area, special - see page 29>**	
hectare	0.287	2.870 000 0E-01
relong [Singapore]	**<area, special - see page 29>**	
hectare	0.287	2.870 000 0E-01
rem	**<dose equivalent>**	
sievert	0.01	1.000 000 0E-02
remen [Egypt, ancient]	**<length, special - see page 29>**	
centimeter	44.9	4.490 000 0E+01
rep	**<absorbed dose>**	
gray	0.008 38	8.380 000 0E-03
rad	0.838	8.380 000 0E-01
rep/second	**<absorbed dose rate>**	
gray/second	0.008 38	8.380 000 0E-03
rad/second	0.838	8.380 000 0E-01
retal [Algeria]	**<mass, special - see page 29>**	
gram	500	5.000 000 0E+02
retti [India]	**<mass, special - see page 29>**	
milligram	146	1.460 000 0E+02
revaim [Hebrew, ancient]	**<mass, special - see page 29>**	
gram	3.2	3.200 000 0E+00
revolution [angular]	**<plane angle>**	
circle [angular]	1	1.000 000 0E+00
degree [angular]	360	3.600 000 0E+02
grade [angular]	400	4.000 000 0E+02
mil [military artillery, angle, US, WWII]	4,000	4.000 000 0E+03
radian	6.283 185 3	6.283 185 3E+00
right angle	4	4.000 000 0E+00
revolution/hour	**<frequency>**	
1/second	0.000 277 8	2.777 777 8E-04
degree/minute	6	6.000 000 0E+00
millihertz	0.277 777 8	2.777 777 8E-01
radian/hour	6.283 185 3	6.283 185 3E+00
revolution/minute	0.016 666 7	1.666 666 7E-02
revolution/minute	**<frequency>**	
1/second	0.016 666 7	1.666 666 7E-02
degree/second	6	6.000 000 0E+00
millihertz	16.666 667	1.666 666 7E+01
radian/minute	6.283 185 3	6.283 185 3E+00
revolution/hour	60	6.000 000 0E+01
revolution/second	**<frequency>**	
1/second	1	1.000 000 0E+00
cycle/second	1	1.000 000 0E+00
degree/second	360	3.600 000 0E+02
hertz	1	1.000 000 0E+00
millihertz	1,000	1.000 000 0E+03
radian/second	6.283 185 3	6.283 185 3E+00
revolution/minute	60	6.000 000 0E+01
rey [Iran]	**<mass, special - see page 29>**	
kilogram	12	1.200 000 0E+01

Convert From Convert To	Standard	<Type of Unit> Scientific

reyn — <dynamic viscosity>
pascal second	1.488 163 9	1.488 163 9E+00
pound/foot second	1	1.000 000 0E+00
poundal second/square foot	1	1.000 000 0E+00

rhine [Germany] — <volume, special - see page 29>
centiliter	70	7.000 000 0E+01

rhineland acre [Surinam] — <area, special - see page 29>
hectare	0.426 4	4.264 000 0E-01

rhynland acre [Guyana] — <area, special - see page 29>
hectare	0.426	4.260 000 0E-01

ri [Japan] — <length, special - see page 29>
kilometer	3.93	3.930 000 0E+00

ri [North Korea] — <length, special - see page 29>
meter	392.727	3.927 270 0E+02

ri [South Korea] — <length, special - see page 29>
millimeter	0.303	3.030 000 0E-01

rif [Yugoslavia] — <length, special - see page 29>
meter	0.777	7.770 000 0E-01

right angle — <plane angle>
degree [angular]	90	9.000 000 0E+01
grade [angular]	100	1.000 000 0E+02
mil [military artillery, angle, NATO]	1,600	1.600 000 0E+03
mil [military artillery, angle, US, WWII]	1,000	1.000 000 0E+03
minute [angular]	5,400	5.400 000 0E+03
radian	1.570 796 3	1.570 796 3E+00
revolution [angular]	0.25	2.500 000 0E-01

rin [Japan] — <mass, special - see page 29>
milligram	37.5	3.750 000 0E+01

rin [Japan] — <length, special - see page 29>
millimeter	0.303	3.030 000 0E-01

river [Egypt, ancient] — <length, special - see page 29>
kilometer	2	2.000 000 0E+00

rob [Egypt, ancient] — <volume, special - see page 29>
liter	8.25	8.250 000 0E+00

roba [Bahrain] — <mass, special - see page 29>
kilogram	1.814	1.814 000 0E+00

robbah [Egypt] — <volume, special - see page 29>
liter	0.516	5.160 000 0E-01

robo kibaba [Tanganyika] — <volume, special - see page 29>
liter	0.25	2.500 000 0E-01

robo kibaba [Tanzania] — <volume, special - see page 29>
liter	0.25	2.500 000 0E-01

rod [Egypt, ancient] — <length, special - see page 29>
meter	52.3	5.230 000 0E+01

rod [Mesopotamia, ancient] — <length, special - see page 29>
meter	3	3.000 000 0E+00

rod [US, survey] — <length>
chain [Gunter or US, survey]	0.25	2.500 000 0E-01
chain [Ramden or Engineer]	0.165 000 3	1.650 003 3E-01
fathom [US, survey]	2.75	2.750 000 0E+00
foot [international]	16.500 033	1.650 003 3E+01
foot [US, survey]	16.5	1.650 000 0E+01
furlong [US, survey]	0.025	2.500 000 0E-02
inch [based on US, survey foot]	198	1.980 000 0E+02
inch [international]	198.000 4	1.980 004 0E+02
link [Gunter or US, survey]	25	2.500 000 0E+01
link [Ramden or Engineer]	16.500 033	1.650 003 3E+01
meter	5.029 210 1	5.029 210 1E+00

Convert From Convert To	Standard	\<Type of Unit\> Scientific
out [US, survey]	0.05	5.000 000 0E−02
pace [geometrical]	0.330 000 7	3.300 006 6E−01
pace [US, survey]	6.6	6.600 000 0E+00
perch [US, survey]	1	1.000 000 0E+00
pole [US, survey]	1	1.000 000 0E+00
vara [US, survey, California]	6	6.000 000 0E+00
vara [US, survey, Texas]	5.94	5.940 000 0E+00
yard [based on US, survey foot]	5.5	5.500 000 0E+00
yard [international]	5.500 011	5.500 011 0E+00
rode [Denmark]		\<length, special - see page 29\>
meter	3.138	3.138 000 0E+00
roe [Netherlands]		\<length, special - see page 29\>
meter	3.77	3.770 000 0E+00
roede [Belgium]		\<area, special - see page 29\>
are	1	1.000 000 0E+00
roede [Indonesia]		\<length, special - see page 29\>
meter	3.767 4	3.767 400 0E+00
roede [Netherlands]		\<length, special - see page 29\>
meter	3.679 77	3.679 770 0E+00
roeneng [Thailand]		\<length, special - see page 29\>
kilometer	4	4.000 000 0E+00
roentgen		\<exposure, gamma and X rays\>
coulomb/kilogram	0.000 258	2.580 000 0E−04
röntgen	1	1.000 000 0E+00
roentgen/second		\<exposure rate, gamma and X rays\>
coulomb/kilogram second	0.000 258	2.580 000 0E−04
röntgen/second	1	1.000 000 0E+00
rolo [Yugoslavia]		\<area, special - see page 29\>
are	25	2.500 000 0E+01
rom		\<electric conductivity\>
1/ohm meter	1	1.000 000 0E+00
mho/meter	1	1.000 000 0E+00
siemens/meter	1	1.000 000 0E+00
röntgen		\<exposure, gamma and X rays\>
coulomb/kilogram	0.000 258	2.580 000 0E−04
roentgen	1	1.000 000 0E+00
röntgen/second		\<exposure rate, gamma and X rays\>
coulomb/kilogram second	0.000 258	2.580 000 0E−04
roentgen/second	1	1.000 000 0E+00
rood		\<area\>
acre [commerical]	0.302 501 2	3.025 012 1E−01
acre [international]	0.250 001	2.500 010 0E−01
acre [US, survey]	0.25	2.500 000 0E−01
are	10.117 182	1.011 718 2E+01
hectare	0.101 171 8	1.011 718 2E−01
labor [US, survey]	0.001 411 3	1.411 313 1E−03
square arpent [US, survey]	0.295 917 5	2.959 175 0E−01
square chain [Gunter or US, survey]	2.5	2.500 000 0E+00
square chain [Ramden or Engineer]	1.089	1.089 000 0E+00
square foot [international]	10,890.044	1.089 004 4E+04
square foot [US, survey]	10,890	1.089 000 0E+04
square furlong [US, survey]	0.025	2.500 000 0E−02
square meter	1,011.718 2	1.011 718 2E+03
square mile [international]	0.000 390 6	3.906 265 6E−04
square mile [US, statute]	0.000 390 6	3.906 250 0E−04
square mile [US, survey]	0.000 390 6	3.906 250 0E−04
square perch [US, survey]	40	4.000 000 0E+01
rood [Swaziland]		\<length, special - see page 29\>
meter	3.778 3	3.778 300 0E+00

Convert From Convert To	Standard	Scientific

ropani [Nepal]   `<area, special - see page 29>`
 square meter ---- 94.05 --- 9.405 000 0E+01

rope   `<length>`
 barleycorn ---- 720 --- 7.200 000 0E+02
 caliber ---- 24,000 --- 2.400 000 0E+04
 chain [Gunter or US, survey] ---- 0.303 029 7 --- 3.030 297 0E-01
 chain [Ramden or Engineer] ---- 0.2 --- 2.000 000 0E-01
 cubit ---- 13.333 333 --- 1.333 333 3E+01
 digit ---- 320 --- 3.200 000 0E+02
 foot [international] ---- 20 --- 2.000 000 0E+01
 foot [US, survey] ---- 19.999 96 --- 1.999 996 0E+01
 hand [horses] ---- 60 --- 6.000 000 0E+01
 inch [based on US, survey foot] ---- 239.999 52 --- 2.399 995 2E+02
 inch [international] ---- 240 --- 2.400 000 0E+02
 meter ---- 6.096 --- 6.096 000 0E+00
 pace [geometrical] ---- 0.4 --- 4.000 000 0E-01
 pace [US, survey] ---- 7.999 984 --- 7.999 984 0E+00
 palm ---- 80 --- 8.000 000 0E+01
 span ---- 26.666 667 --- 2.666 666 7E+01
 yard [based on US, survey foot] ---- 6.666 653 3 --- 6.666 653 3E+00
 yard [international] ---- 6.666 666 7 --- 6.666 666 7E+00

rope [Mesopotamia, ancient, rope]   `<length, special - see page 29>`
 meter ---- 60 --- 6.000 000 0E+01

rope [UK]   `<length, special - see page 29>`
 meter ---- 6.096 --- 6.096 000 0E+00

roquille [France]   `<volume, special - see page 29>`
 liter ---- 0.029 1 --- 2.910 000 0E-02

rosa [Cuba]   `<area, special - see page 29>`
 hectare ---- 0.746 --- 7.460 000 0E-01

rotal [Egypt]   `<mass, special - see page 29>`
 kilogram ---- 0.449 --- 4.490 000 0E-01

rotal [Morocco]   `<mass, special - see page 29>`
 gram ---- 513 --- 5.130 000 0E+02

rotal [Saudi Arabia]   `<mass, special - see page 29>`
 kilogram ---- 0.462 --- 4.620 000 0E-01

rotal [Somalia]   `<mass, special - see page 29>`
 kilogram ---- 0.448 --- 4.480 000 0E-01

rotal [Spanish North Africa]   `<mass, special - see page 29>`
 gram ---- 507.5 --- 5.075 000 0E+02

rotal [Sudan]   `<mass, special - see page 29>`
 kilogram ---- 0.449 --- 4.490 000 0E-01

rotal [Syria]   `<mass, special - see page 29>`
 kilogram ---- 2.565 --- 2.565 000 0E+00

rotal [Tanzania]   `<mass, special - see page 29>`
 kilogram ---- 0.454 --- 4.540 000 0E-01

rotel fedhy [Algeria, silver]   `<mass, special - see page 29>`
 gram ---- 497.435 --- 4.974 350 0E+02

rotl [Egypt, ancient]   `<mass, special - see page 29>`
 kilogram ---- 0.449 --- 4.490 000 0E-01

rotl [Eritrea]   `<mass, special - see page 29>`
 gram ---- 449 --- 4.490 000 0E+02

rotl [Ethiopia]   `<mass, special - see page 29>`
 gram ---- 311 --- 3.110 000 0E+02

rotl [Iran]   `<mass, special - see page 29>`
 kilogram ---- 0.469 --- 4.690 000 0E-01

rotl [Israel, North]   `<mass, special - see page 29>`
 kilogram ---- 2.4 --- 2.400 000 0E+00

rotl [Israel, South]
kilogram -- `<mass, special - see page 29>`
2.88----2.880 000 0E+00

rotl [Jordan]
kilogram -- `<mass, special - see page 29>`
2.564----2.564 000 0E+00

rotl [Lebanon]
kilogram -- `<mass, special - see page 29>`
2.564----2.564 000 0E+00

rotl [Libya]
kilogram -- `<mass, special - see page 29>`
0.513----5.130 000 0E-01

rotl [Morocco]
gram -- `<mass, special - see page 29>`
500----5.000 000 0E+02

rotl [Saudi Arabia]
gram -- `<mass, special - see page 29>`
453.6----4.536 000 0E+02

rotl [Somalia]
kilogram -- `<mass, special - see page 29>`
0.448----4.480 000 0E-01

rotl [Sudan, liquid]
liter -- `<volume, special - see page 29>`
0.568 245----5.682 450 0E-01

rotl [Sudan]
kilogram -- `<mass, special - see page 29>`
0.449----4.490 000 0E-01

rotl [Syria]
kilogram -- `<mass, special - see page 29>`
2.565----2.565 000 0E+00

rotl [Tanzania]
kilogram -- `<mass, special - see page 29>`
0.454----4.540 000 0E-01

rotle [Yemen]
gram -- `<mass, special - see page 29>`
672----6.720 000 0E+02

rotol [Egypt]
kilogram -- `<mass, special - see page 29>`
0.449----4.490 000 0E-01

rotol [Libya]
kilogram -- `<mass, special - see page 29>`
0.513----5.130 000 0E-01

rotol [Malta]
kilogram -- `<mass, special - see page 29>`
0.794----7.940 000 0E-01

rotol [Morocco]
gram -- `<mass, special - see page 29>`
500----5.000 000 0E+02

rotol [Saudi Arabia]
kilogram -- `<mass, special - see page 29>`
0.462----4.620 000 0E-01

rotol [Somalia]
kilogram -- `<mass, special - see page 29>`
0.448----4.480 000 0E-01

rotol [Sudan]
kilogram -- `<mass, special - see page 29>`
0.449----4.490 000 0E-01

rotol [Syria]
kilogram -- `<mass, special - see page 29>`
2.565----2.565 000 0E+00

rotol [Tanzania]
kilogram -- `<mass, special - see page 29>`
0.454----4.540 000 0E-01

rotoli [Egypt]
gram -- `<mass, special - see page 29>`
449.3----4.493 000 0E+02

rotoli [Turkey]
gram -- `<mass, special - see page 29>`
641.472 5----6.414 725 0E+02

rotolo [Egypt]
kilogram -- `<mass, special - see page 29>`
0.449----4.490 000 0E-01

rotolo [Iran]
kilogram -- `<mass, special - see page 29>`
0.469----4.690 000 0E-01

rotolo [Jordan]
kilogram -- `<mass, special - see page 29>`
2.564----2.564 000 0E+00

rotolo [Lebanon]
kilogram -- `<mass, special - see page 29>`
2.564----2.564 000 0E+00

Convert From		<Type of Unit>
Convert To	Standard	Scientific

rotolo [Libya]
kilogram --- <mass, special - see page 29>
0.513 --- 5.130 000 0E−01

rotolo [Malta]
kilogram --- <mass, special - see page 29>
0.794 --- 7.940 000 0E−01

rotolo [Morocco]
gram -- <mass, special - see page 29>
500 --- 5.000 000 0E+02

rotolo [Saudi Arabia]
kilogram --- <mass, special - see page 29>
0.462 --- 4.620 000 0E−01

rotolo [Somalia]
kilogram --- <mass, special - see page 29>
0.448 --- 4.480 000 0E−01

rotolo [Sudan]
kilogram --- <mass, special - see page 29>
0.449 --- 4.490 000 0E−01

rotolo [Syria]
kilogram --- <mass, special - see page 29>
2.565 --- 2.565 000 0E+00

rotolo [Tanzania]
kilogram --- <mass, special - see page 29>
0.454 --- 4.540 000 0E−01

rottel [Egypt]
kilogram --- <mass, special - see page 29>
0.449 --- 4.490 000 0E−01

rottel [Iran]
kilogram --- <mass, special - see page 29>
0.469 --- 4.690 000 0E−01

rottel [Jordan]
kilogram --- <mass, special - see page 29>
2.564 --- 2.564 000 0E+00

rottel [Lebanon]
kilogram --- <mass, special - see page 29>
2.564 --- 2.564 000 0E+00

rottel [Libya]
kilogram --- <mass, special - see page 29>
0.513 --- 5.130 000 0E−01

rottel [Malta]
kilogram --- <mass, special - see page 29>
0.794 --- 7.940 000 0E−01

rottel [Saudi Arabia]
kilogram --- <mass, special - see page 29>
0.462 --- 4.620 000 0E−01

rottel [Somalia]
kilogram --- <mass, special - see page 29>
0.448 --- 4.480 000 0E−01

rottel [Sudan]
kilogram --- <mass, special - see page 29>
0.449 --- 4.490 000 0E−01

rottel [Syria]
kilogram --- <mass, special - see page 29>
2.565 --- 2.565 000 0E+00

rottel [Tanzania]
kilogram --- <mass, special - see page 29>
0.454 --- 4.540 000 0E−01

rottel [Tunisia]
gram -- <mass, special - see page 29>
503.8 --- 5.038 000 0E+02

rottle [Egypt]
kilogram --- <mass, special - see page 29>
0.449 --- 4.490 000 0E−01

rottle [Iran]
kilogram --- <mass, special - see page 29>
0.469 --- 4.690 000 0E−01

rottle [Jordan]
kilogram --- <mass, special - see page 29>
2.564 --- 2.564 000 0E+00

rottle [Lebanon]
kilogram --- <mass, special - see page 29>
2.564 --- 2.564 000 0E+00

rottle [Libya]
kilogram --- <mass, special - see page 29>
0.513 --- 5.130 000 0E−01

rottle [Malta]
kilogram --- <mass, special - see page 29>
0.794 --- 7.940 000 0E−01

rottle [Morocco]
gram -- <mass, special - see page 29>
500 --- 5.000 000 0E+02

| Convert From | <Type of Unit> | |
Convert To	Standard	Scientific
rottle [Saudi Arabia, ancient]	<mass, special - see page 29>	
gram	462.5	4.625 000 0E+02
rottle [Saudi Arabia]	<mass, special - see page 29>	
gram	453.6	4.536 000 0E+02
rottle [Somalia]	<mass, special - see page 29>	
kilogram	0.448	4.480 000 0E−01
rottle [Sudan]	<mass, special - see page 29>	
kilogram	0.449	4.490 000 0E−01
rottle [Syria]	<mass, special - see page 29>	
kilogram	2.565	2.565 000 0E+00
rottle [Tanzania]	<mass, special - see page 29>	
kilogram	0.454	4.540 000 0E−01
rotto [Syria]	<mass, special - see page 29>	
kilogram	2.217	2.217 000 0E+00
rottol [Egypt]	<mass, special - see page 29>	
kilogram	0.449	4.490 000 0E−01
rottol [Iran]	<mass, special - see page 29>	
kilogram	0.469	4.690 000 0E−01
rottol [Jordan]	<mass, special - see page 29>	
kilogram	2.564	2.564 000 0E+00
rottol [Lebanon]	<mass, special - see page 29>	
kilogram	2.565	2.565 000 0E+00
rottol [Libya]	<mass, special - see page 29>	
kilogram	0.513	5.130 000 0E−01
rottol [Malta]	<mass, special - see page 29>	
kilogram	0.794	7.940 000 0E−01
rottol [Morocco]	<mass, special - see page 29>	
gram	500	5.000 000 0E+02
rottol [Saudi Arabia]	<mass, special - see page 29>	
kilogram	0.462	4.620 000 0E−01
rottol [Somalia]	<mass, special - see page 29>	
kilogram	0.448	4.480 000 0E−01
rottol [Sudan]	<mass, special - see page 29>	
kilogram	0.449	4.490 000 0E−01
rottol [Syria]	<mass, special - see page 29>	
kilogram	2.565	2.565 000 0E+00
rottol [Tanzania]	<mass, special - see page 29>	
kilogram	0.454	4.540 000 0E−01
rottol [Turkey]	<volume, special - see page 29>	
liter	1.6	1.600 000 0E+00
rottol [Turkey]	<mass, special - see page 29>	
kilogram	2.566	2.566 000 0E+00
rottolo [Abyssinia, ancient]	<mass, special - see page 29>	
gram	311	3.110 000 0E+02
rottolo [Cyprus]	<mass, special - see page 29>	
gram	558.825 8	5.588 258 0E+02
rottolo [Egypt]	<mass, special - see page 29>	
kilogram	0.449	4.490 000 0E−01
rottolo [Ethiopia]	<mass, special - see page 29>	
gram	311	3.110 000 0E+02
rottolo [Iran]	<mass, special - see page 29>	
kilogram	0.469	4.690 000 0E−01
rottolo [Jordan]	<mass, special - see page 29>	
kilogram	2.564	2.564 000 0E+00

rottolo [Lebanon]
kilogram -- <mass, special - see page 29>
2.564 --- 2.564 000 0E+00

rottolo [Libya]
kilogram -- <mass, special - see page 29>
0.513 --- 5.130 000 0E-01

rottolo [Malta]
kilogram -- <mass, special - see page 29>
0.794 --- 7.940 000 0E-01

rottolo [Morocco]
gram -- <mass, special - see page 29>
526.3 --- 5.263 000 0E+02

rottolo [Somalia]
kilogram -- <mass, special - see page 29>
0.448 --- 4.480 000 0E-01

rottolo [Somaliland]
gram -- <mass, special - see page 29>
453 --- 4.530 000 0E+02

rottolo [Sudan]
kilogram -- <mass, special - see page 29>
0.449 --- 4.490 000 0E-01

rottolo [Syria]
kilogram -- <mass, special - see page 29>
2.565 --- 2.565 000 0E+00

rottolo [Tanzania]
kilogram -- <mass, special - see page 29>
0.454 --- 4.540 000 0E-01

rottolo [Tunisia]
gram -- <mass, special - see page 29>
503.6 --- 5.036 000 0E+02

rottolo a kebyr [Algeria]
gram -- <mass, special - see page 29>
819.1 --- 8.191 000 0E+02

rottolo a khadhary [Algeria]
gram -- <mass, special - see page 29>
614.3 --- 6.143 000 0E+02

rottolo a thary [Algeria]
gram -- <mass, special - see page 29>
546.1 --- 5.461 000 0E+02

rottolo attari [Tunisia]
gram -- <mass, special - see page 29>
503.924 --- 5.039 240 0E+02

roub [Egypt]
liter -- <volume, special - see page 29>
8.25 --- 8.250 000 0E+00

roubouh [Egypt]
liter -- <volume, special - see page 29>
8.25 --- 8.250 000 0E+00

roupi [Cyprus]
centimeter -- <length, special - see page 29>
7.62 --- 7.620 000 0E+00

roupi [Greece]
centimeter -- <length, special - see page 29>
8.1 --- 8.100 000 0E+00

rova [Hebrew, ancient]
gram -- <mass, special - see page 29>
3.2 --- 3.200 000 0E+00

roza [Cuba]
hectare -- <area, special - see page 29>
0.746 --- 7.460 000 0E-01

rtel [Morocco]
gram -- <mass, special - see page 29>
500 --- 5.000 000 0E+02

ruay [Burma]
milligram -- <mass, special - see page 29>
255 --- 2.550 000 0E+02

rub [Egypt]
liter -- <volume, special - see page 29>
8.25 --- 8.250 000 0E+00

rub [Eritrea]
liter -- <volume, special - see page 29>
1.8 --- 1.800 000 0E+00

ruba [Bahrain]
kilogram -- <mass, special - see page 29>
1.814 --- 1.814 000 0E+00

ruba [Saudi Arabia]
kilogram -- <mass, special - see page 29>
9.321 3 --- 9.321 300 0E+00

ruba [Sudan]
liter -- <volume, special - see page 29>
8.25 --- 8.250 000 0E+00

Convert From / Convert To	Standard	Scientific

Convert From Convert To	<Type of Unit> 	
	Standard	Scientific
rubbiatella [Italy, dry]	<volume, special - see page 29>	
hectoliter	1.472	1.472 000 0E+00
rubbio [Italy]	<mass, special - see page 29>	
kilogram	7.919 5	7.919 500 0E+00
rubia [Eritrea]	<volume, special - see page 29>	
liter	1.8	1.800 000 0E+00
rundlet [UK]	<volume, special - see page 29>	
liter	82	8.200 000 0E+01
ruplagi [Turkey]	<volume, special - see page 29>	
liter	25.2	2.520 000 0E+01
rute [Germany]	<length, special - see page 29>	
meter	3.766	3.766 000 0E+00
rute [Switzerland]	<length, special - see page 29>	
meter	3	3.000 000 0E+00
ruthe [Denmark]	<length, special - see page 29>	
meter	3.138 57	3.138 570 0E+00
ruthe [Germany]	<length, special - see page 29>	
meter	2.918 6	2.918 600 0E+00
ruthe [Switzerland]	<length, special - see page 29>	
meter	1.8	1.800 000 0E+00
rutherford	<radionuclide activity>	
1/second	1,000,000	1.000 000 0E+06
becquerel	1,000,000	1.000 000 0E+06
curie	0.000 027	2.702 702 7E−05
megabecquerel	1	1.000 000 0E+00
rutherford/cubic meter	<radionuclide volume activity>	
becquerel/cubic meter	1,000,000	1.000 000 0E+06
curie/cubic meter	0.000 027	2.702 702 7E−05
megabecquerel/cubic meter	1	1.000 000 0E+00
millicurie/cubic meter	0.027 027	2.702 702 7E−02
rutherford/kilogram	<radionuclide specific activity>	
becquerel/kilogram	1,000,000	1.000 000 0E+06
curie/kilogram	0.000 027	2.702 702 7E−05
ruttee [India]	<mass, special - see page 29>	
milligram	146	1.460 000 0E+02
ruttee [Pakistan]	<mass, special - see page 29>	
milligram	121.5	1.215 000 0E+02
rydberg [atomic physics, eq. energy]	<energy>	
1/centimeter [atomic physics, eq. energy]	109,738.62	1.097 386 2E+05
1/meter [atomic physics, eq. energy]	>>>	1.097 386 2E+07
atomic mass unit [unified, C-12, 1986, eq. energy]	<<<	1.460 648 7E−08
centimeter gram-force	<<<	2.222 879 4E−14
cubic centimeter atmosphere	<<<	2.151 394 0E−17
deuteron rest mass [atomic physics, eq. energy]	<<<	7.254 085 4E−09
dyne centimeter	<<<	2.179 900 0E−11
electron rest mass [atomic physics, eq. energy]	0.000 026 6	2.662 599 8E−05
electronvolt	13.605 86	1.360 586 0E+01
erg	<<<	2.179 900 0E−11
gigaelectronvolt	<<<	1.360 586 0E−08
hartree [atomic physics, eq. energy]	0.500 005 9	5.000 059 4E−01
hertz [atomic physics, eq. energy]	>>>	3.289 881 2E+15
joule	<<<	2.179 900 0E−18
kayser [atomic physics, eq. energy]	109,738.62	1.097 386 2E+05
kelvin [atomic physics, eq. energy]	157,888.49	1.578 884 9E+05
kiloelectronvolt	0.013 605 9	1.360 586 0E−02
megaelectronvolt	0.000 013 6	1.360 586 0E−05
muon rest mass [atomic physics, eq. energy]	0.000 000 1	1.287 721 7E−07
neutron rest mass [atomic physics, eq. energy]	<<<	1.448 101 0E−08
proton rest mass [atomic physics, eq. energy]	<<<	1.450 097 1E−08

| Convert From | | <Type of Unit> | |
Convert To		Standard	Scientific
wattsecond		<<<	2.179 900 0E–18
ryutsubo [Japan]		<volume, special - see page 29>	
cubic meter		6.01	6.010 000 0E+00
sa [Tunisia, cereals]		<volume, special - see page 29>	
liter		3.031	3.031 000 0E+00
saa [Jordan, oil]		<volume, special - see page 29>	
liter		6	6.000 000 0E+00
saa [Libya, dry]		<volume, special - see page 29>	
liter		118.8	1.188 000 0E+02
saa [Libya]		<area, special - see page 29>	
are		96	9.600 000 0E+01
saa [Morocco]		<area, special - see page 29>	
square meter		900	9.000 000 0E+02
saa [Tunisia, dry]		<volume, special - see page 29>	
liter		3.33	3.330 000 0E+00
saa [Tunisia, liquid]		<volume, special - see page 29>	
liter		1.134	1.134 000 0E+00
saagh [Syria]		<volume, special - see page 29>	
liter		9.73	9.730 000 0E+00
saah [Algeria]		<volume, special - see page 29>	
liter		58	5.800 000 0E+01
sabbath day's journey [Hebrew, ancient]		<length, special - see page 29>	
meter		970	9.700 000 0E+02
sabbitha [Iran]		<volume, special - see page 29>	
liter		7.237	7.237 000 0E+00
sabin		<sound absorption>	
square foot		1	1.000 000 0E+00
square meter		0.092 903	9.290 304 0E–02
sac [Colombia]		<mass, special - see page 29>	
kilogram		62.5	6.250 000 0E+01
sac [Haiti, coffee]		<mass, special - see page 29>	
kilogram		60	6.000 000 0E+01
sac [Switzerland, dry]		<volume, special - see page 29>	
hectoliter		1.5	1.500 000 0E+00
sac [Zaire, coffee]		<mass, special - see page 29>	
kilogram		60	6.000 000 0E+01
sacco [Brazil, coffee]		<mass, special - see page 29>	
kilogram		60	6.000 000 0E+01
sacco [Colombia, coffee]		<mass, special - see page 29>	
kilogram		69	6.900 000 0E+01
sacco [Costa Rica, coffee]		<mass, special - see page 29>	
kilogram		69	6.900 000 0E+01
sacco [Cuba, coffee]		<mass, special - see page 29>	
kilogram		90	9.000 000 0E+01
sacco [Eritrea]		<volume, special - see page 29>	
liter		108	1.080 000 0E+02
sacco [Guatemala, coffee]		<mass, special - see page 29>	
kilogram		69	6.900 000 0E+01
sack [Brazil, rice paddy]		<mass, special - see page 29>	
kilogram		50	5.000 000 0E+01
sack [Egypt, ancient]		<volume, special - see page 29>	
hectoliter		0.96	9.600 000 0E–01
sack [Egypt, rice, milled]		<mass, special - see page 29>	
kilogram		100	1.000 000 0E+02
sack [Ghana, rice paddy]		<mass, special - see page 29>	
kilogram		76.204	7.620 400 0E+01

| Convert From | \<Type of Unit\> | |
Convert To	Standard	Scientific
sack [Ghana, rice, milled]	\<mass, special - see page 29\>	
kilogram	108.862	1.088 620 0E+02
sack [Malawi, rice paddy]	\<mass, special - see page 29\>	
kilogram	72.575	7.257 500 0E+01
sack [Malawi, rice, milled]	\<mass, special - see page 29\>	
kilogram	90.718	9.071 800 0E+01
sack [Philippines]	\<volume, special - see page 29\>	
liter	75	7.500 000 0E+01
sack [South Africa, rice paddy]	\<mass, special - see page 29\>	
kilogram	68.039	6.803 900 0E+01
sack [South Africa, rice, milled]	\<mass, special - see page 29\>	
kilogram	72.575	7.257 500 0E+01
sack [Surinam, rice paddy]	\<mass, special - see page 29\>	
kilogram	70	7.000 000 0E+01
sack [Surinam, rice, milled]	\<mass, special - see page 29\>	
kilogram	100	1.000 000 0E+02
sack [Taiwan, rice paddy]	\<mass, special - see page 29\>	
kilogram	118	1.180 000 0E+02
sack [Taiwan, rice, milled]	\<mass, special - see page 29\>	
kilogram	100	1.000 000 0E+02
sack [UK]	\<mass, special - see page 29\>	
kilogram	127.006	1.270 060 0E+02
sack [Zambia, rice paddy]	\<mass, special - see page 29\>	
kilogram	68	6.800 000 0E+01
saco [Colombia, coffee]	\<mass, special - see page 29\>	
kilogram	70	7.000 000 0E+01
saco [Colombia]	\<mass, special - see page 29\>	
kilogram	62.5	6.250 000 0E+01
saco [Cuba, coffee]	\<mass, special - see page 29\>	
kilogram	70	7.000 000 0E+01
saco [Cuba]	\<mass, special - see page 29\>	
kilogram	62.5	6.250 000 0E+01
saco [Dominican Republic, coffee]	\<mass, special - see page 29\>	
kilogram	75	7.500 000 0E+01
saco [Haiti]	\<mass, special - see page 29\>	
kilogram	60	6.000 000 0E+01
saco [Honduras, coffee]	\<mass, special - see page 29\>	
kilogram	69	6.900 000 0E+01
saco [Nicaragua, coffee]	\<mass, special - see page 29\>	
kilogram	69	6.900 000 0E+01
saco [Peru, coffee]	\<mass, special - see page 29\>	
kilogram	69	6.900 000 0E+01
saco de cafe [Colombia, coffee]	\<mass, special - see page 29\>	
kilogram	62.5	6.250 000 0E+01
saco de cafe [Costa Rica, coffee]	\<mass, special - see page 29\>	
kilogram	69	6.900 000 0E+01
saddirham [Iran]	\<mass, special - see page 29\>	
kilogram	1.5	1.500 000 0E+00
sadzhen [Russia]	\<length, special - see page 29\>	
meter	2.133 6	2.133 600 0E+00
saga [Malaysia, precious metals]	\<mass, special - see page 29\>	
milligram	280.8	2.808 000 0E+02
saga [Singapore, precious metals]	\<mass, special - see page 29\>	
milligram	280.8	2.808 000 0E+02

Convert From	<Type of Unit>	
Convert To	Standard	Scientific

sagen [Russia]   <length, special - see page 29>
meter --- 2.134 --- 2.134 000 0E+00

sagene [Russia]   <length, special - see page 29>
meter -- 2.133 6 --- 2.133 600 0E+00

sah [Czechoslovakia]   <length, special - see page 29>
meter -- 1.896 --- 1.896 000 0E+00

saha [Syria]   <volume, special - see page 29>
liter --- 13 --- 1.300 000 0E+01

saha [Tunisia, cereals]   <volume, special - see page 29>
liter -- 3.031 --- 3.031 000 0E+00

sahh [Morocco]   <volume, special - see page 29>
liter -- 56 --- 5.600 000 0E+01

sahh [Spanish North Africa] <volume, special - see page 29>
liter -- 56 --- 5.600 000 0E+01

sahm [Egypt]   <area, special - see page 29>
square meter -------------------------------------- 7.293 1 --- 7.293 100 0E+00

sahme [Egypt]   <area, special - see page 29>
square meter -- 7.29 --- 7.290 000 0E+00

sahtout [Egypt]   <area, special - see page 29>
square meter --------------------------------------- 0.303 88 --- 3.038 800 0E-01

sai [Japan]   <volume, special - see page 29>
cubic decimeter ------------------------------------- 27.826 --- 2.782 600 0E+01

sajon [Russia]   <length, special - see page 29>
meter --- 2.134 --- 2.134 000 0E+00

sale [Burma]   <volume, special - see page 29>
liter -- 0.639 275 6 --- 6.392 756 0E-01

salm [Malta]   <mass, special - see page 29>
kilogram -- 222.3 --- 2.223 000 0E+02

salma tumoli [Malta, cereals] <volume, special - see page 29>
hectoliter --- 2.909 --- 2.909 000 0E+00

salmanazar [champagne bottle] <champagne bottle size>
bottle [wine, standard]------------------------------------- 12 --- 1.200 000 0E+01
liter --- 9 --- 9.000 000 0E+00

salme [Malta and Gozo]   <mass, special - see page 29>
kilogram --- 222.25 --- 2.222 500 0E+02

saltus [Rome, ancient]   <area, special - see page 29>
hectare -- 202 --- 2.020 000 0E+02
square kilometer -------------------------------- 2.013 --- 2.013 000 0E+00

salung [Laos]   <mass, special - see page 29>
gram --- 3.75 --- 3.750 000 0E+00

salung [Thailand]   <mass, special - see page 29>
gram --- 3.75 --- 3.750 000 0E+00

sandong [Burma]   <length, special - see page 29>
centimeter -- 55.88 --- 5.588 000 0E+01

sang [Iran]   <mass, special - see page 29>
kilogram -- 1 --- 1.000 000 0E+00

sang [Laos]   <mass, special - see page 29>
kilogram --- 1.2 --- 1.200 000 0E+00

sao [Thailand]   <length, special - see page 29>
meter --- 7.309 5 --- 7.309 500 0E+00

sao [Vietnam, cereal]   <volume, special - see page 29>
milliliter -- 2 --- 2.000 000 0E+00

sao [Vietnam, soil measure] <volume, special - see page 29>
cubic meter --- 144 --- 1.440 000 0E+02

sao [Vietnam]   <area, special - see page 29>
square meter -- 360 --- 3.600 000 0E+02

Convert From	<Type of Unit>	
Convert To	Standard	Scientific

sar [Iraq, ancient]
square meter — <area, special - see page 29>
————— 15—1.500 000 0E+01

saschen [Russia]
meter — <length, special - see page 29>
————— 2.134—2.134 000 0E+00

sat [Egypt, ancient]
liter — <volume, special - see page 29>
————— 11.7—1.170 000 0E+01

sat [Hebrew, ancient, dry]
liter — <volume, special - see page 29>
————— 12.7—1.270 000 0E+01

sat [Laos]
liter — <volume, special - see page 29>
————— 200—2.000 000 0E+02

sat [Thailand]
liter — <volume, special - see page 29>
————— 20—2.000 000 0E+01

satlijh [Yugoslavia]
kilogram — <mass, special - see page 29>
————— 0.32—3.200 000 0E−01

saton [Hebrew, ancient, dry]
liter — <volume, special - see page 29>
————— 12.7—1.270 000 0E+01

sauk [Laos]
centimeter — <length, special - see page 29>
————— 40—4.000 000 0E+01

sauk [Thailand]
centimeter — <length, special - see page 29>
————— 50—5.000 000 0E+01

saum [Austria]
kilogram — <mass, special - see page 29>
————— 154—1.540 000 0E+02

saum [Switzerland]
liter — <volume, special - see page 29>
————— 150—1.500 000 0E+02

saw [Tunisia, cereals]
liter — <volume, special - see page 29>
————— 3.031—3.031 000 0E+00

sawk [Laos]
centimeter — <length, special - see page 29>
————— 40—4.000 000 0E+01

sawk [Thailand]
centimeter — <length, special - see page 29>
————— 50—5.000 000 0E+01

sayut [Burma]
liter — <volume, special - see page 29>
————— 5.114—5.114 000 0E+00

sazem [Poland]
meter — <length, special - see page 29>
————— 1.73—1.730 000 0E+00

sazhen [Ukraine]
meter — <length, special - see page 29>
————— 1.9—1.900 000 0E+00

sazhene [Russia]
meter — <length, special - see page 29>
————— 2.134—2.134 000 0E+00

scala [Cyprus]
square meter — <area, special - see page 29>
————— 1,337.8—1.337 800 0E+03

scala [Israel]
square meter — <area, special - see page 29>
————— 1,000—1.000 000 0E+03

scala [Jordan]
square meter — <area, special - see page 29>
————— 1,000—1.000 000 0E+03

scala [Lebanon]
square meter — <area, special - see page 29>
————— 919—9.190 000 0E+02

scala [Libya]
square meter — <area, special - see page 29>
————— 919—9.190 000 0E+02

scala [Syria]
square meter — <area, special - see page 29>
————— 919—9.190 000 0E+02

scala [Turkey]
square meter — <area, special - see page 29>
————— 919—9.190 000 0E+02

scala [Yugoslavia]
square meter — <area, special - see page 29>
————— 1,000—1.000 000 0E+03

Convert From / Convert To	Standard	Scientific
scale cubit [Islam]	<length, special - see page 29>	
centimeter	145.6	1.456 000 0E+02
scheffel [Germany, Bavaria]	<volume, special - see page 29>	
liter	222.36	2.223 600 0E+02
scheffel [Germany, Prussia]	<volume, special - see page 29>	
liter	54.961 8	5.496 180 0E+01
scheffel [Germany, Wurttemberg]	<volume, special - see page 29>	
liter	177.22	1.772 200 0E+02
schepel [Netherlands]	<volume, special - see page 29>	
liter	10	1.000 000 0E+01
scheppel [South Africa]	<volume, special - see page 29>	
liter	27.275 76	2.727 576 0E+01
schibr [Egypt, ancient]	<length, special - see page 29>	
centimeter	22.5	2.250 000 0E+01
schoenus [Rome, ancient]	<length, special - see page 29>	
kilometer	5.912	5.912 000 0E+00
schoinos [Greece, ancient]	<length, special - see page 29>	
kilometer	5.6	5.600 000 0E+00
schoppe [Germany]	<volume, special - see page 29>	
liter	0.459 25	4.592 500 0E-01
schoppen [Germany]	<volume, special - see page 29>	
liter	0.5	5.000 000 0E-01
schtaff [Russia]	<volume, special - see page 29>	
liter	1.229 941	1.229 941 0E+00
schuh [Switzerland]	<length, special - see page 29>	
centimeter	30	3.000 000 0E+01
score		<units>
decade	2	2.000 000 0E+00
single	20	2.000 000 0E+01
ten	2	2.000 000 0E+00
unit	20	2.000 000 0E+01
scripula [Iceland]	<mass, special - see page 29>	
gram	0.954	9.540 000 0E-01
scripula [Norway]	<mass, special - see page 29>	
gram	0.954	9.540 000 0E-01
scripula [Sweden]	<mass, special - see page 29>	
gram	0.954	9.540 000 0E-01
scripulum [Rome, ancient]	<mass, special - see page 29>	
gram	1.137	1.137 000 0E+00
scrupel [Austria, apothecary]	<mass, special - see page 29>	
gram	1.458 4	1.458 400 0E+00
scrupel [Netherlands]	<mass, special - see page 29>	
gram	1.286 699	1.286 699 0E+00
scruple [France]	<mass, special - see page 29>	
gram	1.275	1.275 000 0E+00
scruple [Rome, ancient]	<area, special - see page 29>	
square meter	8.74	8.740 000 0E+00
scruple [Switzerland]	<mass, special - see page 29>	
gram	1.302	1.302 000 0E+00
scruple [UK, liquid]		<volume>
cubic centimeter	1.183 877 6	1.183 877 6E+00
cubic foot	0.000 041 8	4.180 824 3E-05
cubic inch	0.072 244 6	7.224 464 4E-02
cubic meter	0.000 001 2	1.183 877 6E-06
drachm [UK, liquid]	0.333 333 3	3.333 333 3E-01
dram [Canada, liquid]	0.333 333 3	3.333 333 3E-01
dram [US, liquid]	0.320 253 3	3.202 533 1E-01

drop [US, liquid]	14.411 399	1.441 139 9E+01
liter	0.001 183 9	1.183 877 6E-03
milliliter	1.183 877 6	1.183 877 6E+00
minim [UK]	20	2.000 000 0E+01
minim [US]	19.215 199	1.921 519 9E+01
ounce [UK, liquid]	0.041 666 7	4.166 666 7E-02
ounce [US, liquid]	0.040 031 7	4.003 166 4E-02
tablespoon [Canada, measuring]	0.083 333 5	8.333 347 4E-02
tablespoon [US, measuring]	0.080 063 3	8.006 332 8E-02
teaspoon [Canada, measuring]	0.250 000 4	2.500 004 2E-01
teaspoon [US, measuring]	0.240 19	2.401 899 9E-01

scruple [UK] \<mass\>

carat [international]	6.479 891	6.479 891 0E+00
carat [UK]	5	5.000 000 0E+00
carat [US, after 1913]	6.479 891	6.479 891 0E+00
drachm [UK, apothecary]	0.333 333 3	3.333 333 3E-01
dram [avoirdupois]	0.731 428 6	7.314 285 7E-01
dram [US, apothecary]	0.333 333 3	3.333 333 3E-01
grain	20	2.000 000 0E+01
grain [apothecary]	20	2.000 000 0E+01
grain [avoirdupois]	20	2.000 000 0E+01
grain [troy]	20	2.000 000 0E+01
gram	1.295 978 2	1.295 978 2E+00
kilogram	0.001 296	1.295 978 2E-03
ounce	0.045 714 3	4.571 428 6E-02
pennyweight [troy]	0.833 333 3	8.333 333 3E-01
point [jewelers']	647.989 1	6.479 891 0E+02
pound	0.002 857 1	2.857 142 9E-03
scruple [US, apothecary]	1	1.000 000 0E+00

scruple [US, apothecary] \<mass\>

carat [international]	6.479 891	6.479 891 0E+00
carat [UK]	5	5.000 000 0E+00
drachm [UK, apothecary]	0.333 333 3	3.333 333 3E-01
dram [avoirdupois]	0.731 428 6	7.314 285 7E-01
dram [US, apothecary]	0.333 333 3	3.333 333 3E-01
grain	20	2.000 000 0E+01
grain [apothecary]	20	2.000 000 0E+01
grain [avoirdupois]	20	2.000 000 0E+01
grain [troy]	20	2.000 000 0E+01
gram	1.295 978 2	1.295 978 2E+00
kilogram	0.001 296	1.295 978 2E-03
ounce [apothecary]	0.041 666 7	4.166 666 7E-02
ounce [avoirdupois]	0.045 714 3	4.571 428 6E-02
pennyweight [troy]	0.833 333 3	8.333 333 3E-01
pound	0.002 857 1	2.857 142 9E-03
pound [US, troy]	0.003 472 2	3.472 221 8E-03
scruple [UK]	1	1.000 000 0E+00
ton [UK, assay or assay, long]	0.039 672 8	3.967 280 2E-02
ton [US, assay or assay, short]	0.044 433 5	4.443 353 8E-02

scruplum [Rome, ancient] \<mass, special - see page 29\>

gram	1.14	1.140 000 0E+00

scruplum [Rome, ancient] \<area, special - see page 29\>

square meter	8.76	8.760 000 0E+00

scruplum [Russia, apothecary] \<mass, special - see page 29\>

gram	1.244	1.244 000 0E+00

sdal [Morocco] \<area, special - see page 29\>

hectare	0.18	1.800 000 0E-01

se [Iraq, ancient] \<mass, special - see page 29\>

milligram	45	4.500 000 0E+01

se [Japan] \<area, special - see page 29\>

square meter	99.174	9.917 400 0E+01

| Convert From | | \<Type of Unit\> |
| Convert To | Standard | Scientific |

sea [Hebrew, ancient] — \<volume, special - see page 29\>
liter -- 7.7 --- 7.700 000 0E+00

seah [Babylon, ancient] — \<volume, special - see page 29\>
liter -- 6.6 --- 6.600 000 0E+00

seah [Hebrew, ancient] — \<volume, special - see page 29\>
liter --- 15 --- 1.500 000 0E+01

seak [Macao] — \<volume, special - see page 29\>
liter -------------------------------------- 103.1 --- 1.031 000 0E+02

seam [UK] — \<volume, special - see page 29\>
liter --------------------------------- 290.941 4 --- 2.909 414 0E+02

second — \<sedimentation coefficient\>
svedberg ------------------------------------ >>> --- 1.000 000 0E+13

second — \<time\>

Convert To	Standard	Scientific
blink	1.157 407 4	1.157 407 4E+00
day	0.000 011 6	1.157 407 4E−05
day [Coordinated Universal Time (UTC)]	0.000 011 6	1.157 407 4E−05
day [mean sidereal]	0.000 011 6	1.160 576 3E−05
day [mean solar]	0.000 011 6	1.157 407 4E−05
hour	0.000 277 8	2.777 777 8E−04
hour [Coordinated Universal Time (UTC)]	0.000 277 8	2.777 777 8E−04
hour [mean sidereal]	0.000 278 5	2.785 383 1E−04
hour [mean solar]	0.000 277 8	2.777 777 8E−04
minute	0.016 666 7	1.666 666 7E−02
minute [Coordinated Universal Time (UTC)]	0.016 666 7	1.666 666 7E−02
minute [mean sidereal]	0.016 712 3	1.671 229 9E−02
minute [mean solar]	0.016 666 7	1.666 666 7E−02
month [anomalistic or perihelion]	0.000 000 4	4.200 422 1E−07
month [draconic]	0.000 000 4	4.253 263 3E−07
month [lunar or phase or synodic]	0.000 000 4	3.919 350 9E−07
month [mean sidereal]	0.000 000 4	4.236 226 2E−07
month [seasonal or tropical]	0.000 000 4	4.236 238 6E−07
second [Coordinated Universal Time (UTC)]	1	1.000 000 0E+00
second [mean sidereal]	1.002 737 9	1.002 737 9E+00
second [mean solar]	1	1.000 000 0E+00
shake	>>>	1.000 000 0E+08
year [anomalistic or perihelion]	<<<	3.168 725 2E−08
year [elipse]	<<<	3.339 124 0E−08
year [leap]	<<<	3.162 315 3E−08
year [mean Gregorian]	<<<	3.168 873 9E−08
year [mean Julian]	<<<	3.168 808 8E−08
year [mean sidereal]	<<<	3.168 753 6E−08
year [normal calendar]	<<<	3.170 979 2E−08
year [seasonal or tropical]	<<<	3.168 876 5E−08

second [angular] — \<plane angle\>

Convert To	Standard	Scientific
degree [angular]	0.000 277 8	2.777 777 8E−04
grade [angular]	0.000 308 6	3.086 419 8E−04
microradian	4.848 136 8	4.848 136 8E+00
radian	0.000 004 8	4.848 136 8E−06

second [Coordinated Universal Time (UTC)] — \<time\>

Convert To	Standard	Scientific
day	0.000 011 6	1.157 407 4E−05
day [Coordinated Universal Time (UTC)]	0.000 011 6	1.157 407 4E−05
hour	0.000 277 8	2.777 777 8E−04
hour [Coordinated Universal Time (UTC)]	0.000 277 8	2.777 777 8E−04
minute	0.016 666 7	1.666 666 7E−02
minute [Coordinated Universal Time (UTC)]	0.016 666 7	1.666 666 7E−02
month [mean sidereal]	0.000 000 4	4.236 226 2E−07
second	1	1.000 000 0E+00
second [mean sidereal]	1.002 737 9	1.002 737 9E+00
second [mean solar]	1	1.000 000 0E+00
year [mean sidereal]	<<<	3.168 753 6E−08
year [normal calendar]	<<<	3.170 979 2E−08

Convert From / Convert To	Standard	Scientific
second [mean sidereal]		**<time>**
day	0.000 011 5	1.154 247 2E-05
day [mean sidereal]	0.000 011 6	1.157 407 4E-05
hour	0.000 277	2.770 193 2E-04
hour [mean sidereal]	0.000 277 8	2.777 777 8E-04
minute	0.016 621 2	1.662 115 9E-02
minute [mean sidereal]	0.016 666 7	1.666 666 7E-02
month [mean sidereal]	0.000 000 4	4.224 659 5E-07
second	0.997 269 6	9.972 695 7E-01
second [mean solar]	0.997 269 6	9.972 695 7E-01
year [mean sidereal]	<<<	3.160 101 5E-08
year [normal calendar]	<<<	3.162 321 1E-08
second [mean solar]		**<time>**
day	0.000 011 6	1.157 407 4E-05
day [mean solar]	0.000 011 6	1.157 407 4E-05
hour	0.000 277 8	2.777 777 8E-04
hour [mean solar]	0.000 277 8	2.777 777 8E-04
minute	0.016 666 7	1.666 666 7E-02
minute [mean solar]	0.016 666 7	1.666 666 7E-02
month [mean sidereal]	0.000 000 4	4.236 226 2E-07
month [seasonal or tropical]	0.000 000 4	4.236 238 6E-07
second	1	1.000 000 0E+00
second [Coordinated Universal Time (UTC)]	1	1.000 000 0E+00
second [mean sidereal]	1.002 737 9	1.002 737 9E+00
year [mean sidereal]	<<<	3.168 753 6E-08
year [normal calendar]	<<<	3.170 979 2E-08
second centimeter °C/calorie [-/ I.T.]		**<thermal resistivity>**
meter kelvin/watt	0.002 388 5	2.388 459 0E-03
second centimeter °C/calorie [-/ thermoc.]		**<thermal resistivity>**
meter kelvin/watt	0.002 390 1	2.390 057 4E-03
second °C/calorie [-/ I.T.]		**<thermal resistance>**
hour °C/kilocalorie [-/ I.T.]	0.277 777 8	2.777 777 8E-01
hour °F/Btu [-/ I.T.]	0.125 997 9	1.259 978 8E-01
kelvin/watt	0.238 845 9	2.388 459 0E-01
second °C/kilogram-force		**<thermal resistivity>**
meter kelvin/watt	0.101 971 6	1.019 716 2E-01
second foot °F/Btu [-/ I.T.]		**<thermal resistivity>**
meter kelvin/watt	0.000 160 5	1.604 970 3E-04
second foot degree Rankine/Btu [-/ I.T.]		**<thermal resistivity>**
meter kelvin/watt	0.000 160 5	1.604 970 3E-04
second kelvin/joule		**<thermal resistance>**
hour °C/kilocalorie [-/ I.T.]	1.163	1.163 000 0E+00
hour °F/Btu [-/ I.T.]	0.527 527 9	5.275 279 3E-01
kelvin/watt	1	1.000 000 0E+00
second °C/calorie [-/ I.T.]	4.186 8	4.186 800 0E+00
second kelvin/newton		**<thermal resistivity>**
meter kelvin/watt	1	1.000 000 0E+00
second meter kelvin/joule		**<thermal resistivity>**
meter kelvin/watt	1	1.000 000 0E+00
meter kelvin/watt	1	1.000 000 0E+00
second square centimeter °C/calorie centimeter [-/ I.T.]		**<thermal resistivity>**
meter kelvin/watt	0.002 388 5	2.388 459 0E-03
second square foot °F/Btu foot [-/ I.T.]		**<thermal resistivity>**
meter kelvin/watt	0.000 160 5	1.604 970 3E-04
second square foot °F/Btu inch [-/ I.T.]		**<thermal resistivity>**
meter kelvin/watt	0.001 926	1.925 964 4E-03
second square foot °F/Btu inch [-/ thermoc.]		**<thermal resistivity>**
meter kelvin/watt	0.001 927 3	1.927 253 8E-03

Convert From		<Type of Unit>
Convert To	Standard	Scientific

second square foot degree Rankine/Btu foot [-/ I.T.]   <thermal resistivity>
meter kelvin/watt --- 0.000 160 5 --- 1.604 970 3E−04

second square foot degree Rankine/Btu inch [-/ I.T.]   <thermal resistivity>
meter kelvin/watt --- 0.001 926 --- 1.925 964 4E−03

second/henry   <electric conductance>
1/ohm --- 1 --- 1.000 000 0E+00
absiemens --- <<< --- 1.000 000 0E−09
ampere/volt --- 1 --- 1.000 000 0E+00
mho --- 1 --- 1.000 000 0E+00
siemens -- 1 --- 1.000 000 0E+00
statsiemens --- >>> --- 8.987 551 8E+11

second/ohm   <capacitance>
abfarad --- <<< --- 1.000 000 0E−09
ampere second/volt --- 1 --- 1.000 000 0E+00
coulomb/volt --- 1 --- 1.000 000 0E+00
farad --- 1 --- 1.000 000 0E+00
statfarad --- >>> --- 8.987 551 8E+11

second/ohm meter   <electric permittivity>
abfarad/centimeter -- 0.000 000 1 --- 1.000 000 0E−07
farad/meter --- 1 --- 1.000 000 0E+00
statfarad/centimeter -- >>> --- 8.987 551 8E+13

section [Canada]   <area, special - see page 29>
square kilometer --- 2.59 --- 2.590 000 0E+00

section [US, survey]   <area>
acre [commerical] --- 774.403 1 --- 7.744 031 0E+02
acre [international] -- 640.002 56 --- 6.400 025 6E+02
acre [US, survey] --- 640 --- 6.400 000 0E+02
hectare --- 258.999 85 --- 2.589 998 5E+02
labor [US, survey] --- 3.612 961 5 --- 3.612 961 5E+00
rood -- 2,560 --- 2.560 000 0E+03
square arpent [US, survey] ----------------------------------- 757.548 8 --- 7.575 488 0E+02
square chain [Gunter or US, survey] ------------------------------ 6,400 --- 6.400 000 0E+03
square chain [Ramden or Engineer] -------------------------- 2,787.84 --- 2.787 840 0E+03
square furlong [US, survey] --- 64 --- 6.400 000 0E+01
square kilometer --- 2.589 998 5 --- 2.589 998 5E+00
square league [US, statute] ------------------------------- 0.111 111 1 --- 1.111 111 1E−01
square meter --- 2,589,998.5 --- 2.589 998 5E+06
square mile [international] ---------------------------------- 1.000 004 --- 1.000 004 0E+00
square mile [US, statute] -- 1 --- 1.000 000 0E+00
square mile [US, survey] --- 1 --- 1.000 000 0E+00
square myriameter -- 0.025 9 --- 2.589 998 5E−02
township [US, survey] -- 0.027 777 8 --- 2.777 777 8E−02

sedri [Eritrea]   <length, special - see page 29>
centimeter --- 23 --- 2.300 000 0E+01

seer [Afghanistan]   <mass, special - see page 29>
kilogram -- 7.066 --- 7.066 000 0E+00

seer [Bangladesh]   <mass, special - see page 29>
kilogram --- 0.933 --- 9.330 000 0E−01

seer [Ceylon]   <mass, special - see page 29>
kilogram --- 0.933 104 3 --- 9.331 043 0E−01

seer [India]   <mass, special - see page 29>
gram -- 0.933 1 --- 9.331 000 0E−01

seer [Iran]   <mass, special - see page 29>
gram --- 75 --- 7.500 000 0E+01

seer [Nepal]   <mass, special - see page 29>
kilogram --- 0.933 1 --- 9.331 000 0E−01

seer [Pakistan]   <mass, special - see page 29>
kilogram --- 0.933 --- 9.330 000 0E−01

Convert From Convert To	<Type of Unit>	
	Standard	Scientific
seer [Sri Lanka, liquid]	<volume, special - see page 29>	
liter	1.06	1.060 000 0E+00
seer [Yemen]	<mass, special - see page 29>	
kilogram	0.933	9.330 000 0E-01
seh [Hong Kong]	<volume, special - see page 29>	
hectoliter	1	1.000 000 0E+00
seidel [Austria, beer]	<volume, special - see page 29>	
liter	0.353 6	3.536 000 0E-01
seidel [Germany, liquid]	<volume, special - see page 29>	
milliliter	429	4.290 000 0E+02
seik [Burma, dry]	<volume, special - see page 29>	
liter	10.229	1.022 900 0E+01
seik [Burma, liquid]	<volume, special - see page 29>	
liter	2.02	2.020 000 0E+00
seim [Hebrew, ancient, dry]	<volume, special - see page 29>	
liter	12.7	1.270 000 0E+01
seit [Burma, dry]	<volume, special - see page 29>	
liter	10.288 41	1.028 841 0E+01
seit [Burma, liquid]	<volume, special - see page 29>	
liter	2.02	2.020 000 0E+00
selemin [Portugal]	<volume, special - see page 29>	
liter	0.436 2	4.362 000 0E-01
semimodius [Rome, ancient, dry]	<volume, special - see page 29>	
liter	4.36	4.360 000 0E+00
semis [Rome, ancient]	<mass, special - see page 29>	
gram	163.73	1.637 300 0E+02
semisextula [Rome, ancient]	<mass, special - see page 29>	
gram	2.28	2.280 000 0E+00
semiuncia [Rome, ancient]	<mass, special - see page 29>	
gram	13.7	1.370 000 0E+01
semodius [Rome, ancient, dry]	<volume, special - see page 29>	
liter	4.3	4.300 000 0E+00
semuncia [Rome, ancient]	<mass, special - see page 29>	
gram	13.644	1.364 400 0E+01
sen [Cambodia]	<length, special - see page 29>	
meter	40	4.000 000 0E+01
sen [Laos]	<length, special - see page 29>	
meter	40	4.000 000 0E+01
sen [Thailand]	<length, special - see page 29>	
meter	40	4.000 000 0E+01
sene [Laos]	<mass, special - see page 29>	
kilogram	120	1.200 000 0E+02
senh [Cambodia]	<length, special - see page 29>	
meter	40	4.000 000 0E+01
senh [Laos]	<length, special - see page 29>	
meter	40	4.000 000 0E+01
senh [Thailand]	<length, special - see page 29>	
meter	40	4.000 000 0E+01
sentner [Scandinavia]	<mass, special - see page 29>	
kilogram	50.802 08	5.080 208 0E+01
senzer [Eritrea]	<length, special - see page 29>	
centimeter	23	2.300 000 0E+01
senzer [Ethiopia]	<length, special - see page 29>	
meter	0.23	2.300 000 0E-01

sep [Egypt, ancient] <mass, special - see page 29>
kilogram -- 0.94 --- 9.400 000 0E−01

septendecillion [UK] <units>
unit --->>> --1.000 000 0E+102

septendecillion [US] <units>
nonillion [UK]-- 1 --- 1.000 000 0E+00
unit --->>> --1.000 000 0E+54

septillion [UK] <units>
tredecillion [US]------------------------------------- 1 --- 1.000 000 0E+00
unit --->>> --1.000 000 0E+42

septillion [US] <units>
quadrillion [UK]-------------------------------------- 1 --- 1.000 000 0E+00
unit --->>> --1.000 000 0E+24

septunx [Rome, ancient] <mass, special - see page 29>
gram --- 191.02 --- 1.910 200 0E+02

seqel [Hebrew, ancient] <mass, special - see page 29>
gram -- 11.42 --- 1.142 000 0E+01

ser [Bangladesh] <mass, special - see page 29>
kilogram -- 0.933 1 --- 9.331 000 0E−01

ser [Muslim India] <mass, special - see page 29>
kilogram -- 0.933 --- 9.330 000 0E−01

sescuncia [Rome, ancient] <mass, special - see page 29>
gram -- 40.93 --- 4.093 000 0E+01

sesma [Spain] <length, special - see page 29>
meter -- 0.139 318 --- 1.393 180 0E−01

sesquicentennial <time>
year [normal calendar]------------------------------ 150 --- 1.500 000 0E+02

seste [Thailand] <volume, special - see page 29>
liter --- 800 --- 8.000 000 0E+02

sesterce [Rome, ancient] <mass, special - see page 29>
gram --- 25.4 --- 2.540 000 0E+01

set [Egypt, ancient] <area, special - see page 29>
hectare --- 0.275 --- 2.750 000 0E−01

setier [France, dry] <volume, special - see page 29>
hectoliter--- 1.561 --- 1.561 000 0E+00

setier [France, liquid] <volume, special - see page 29>
liter -- 0.465 7 --- 4.657 000 0E−01

setier [Switzerland] <volume, special - see page 29>
liter --- 37.5 --- 3.750 000 0E+01

sett [Antigua] <length, special - see page 29>
centimeter-- 22.9 --- 2.290 000 0E+01

seu [Babylon, ancient] <mass, special - see page 29>
gram --- 0.046 --- 4.600 000 0E−02

seu [Thailand] <length, special - see page 29>
meter ------------------------------------ 208.333 33 --- 2.083 333 3E+02

sexdecillion [UK] <units>
unit --->>> --1.000 000 0E+96

sexdecillion [US] <units>
unit --->>> --1.000 000 0E+51

sextan [Rome, ancient] <mass, special - see page 29>
gram -- 54.58 --- 5.458 000 0E+01

sextario [Iran] <volume, special - see page 29>
milliliter --- 329 --- 3.290 000 0E+02

sextarius [Babylon, ancient] <volume, special - see page 29>
liter --- 0.5 --- 5.000 000 0E−01

Convert From Convert To	Standard	<Type of Unit> Scientific
sextarius [Rome, ancient] liter	<volume, special - see page 29> 0.546	5.460 000 0E-01
sextillion [UK] undecillion [US] unit	<units> 1 >>>	1.000 000 0E+00 1.000 000 0E+36
sextillion [US] unit	<units> >>>	1.000 000 0E+21
sexto [Venezuela] liter	<volume, special - see page 29> 0.166	1.660 000 0E-01
sextula [Rome, ancient] gram	<mass, special - see page 29> 4.55	4.550 000 0E+00
shake microsecond second	<time> 0.01 <<<	1.000 000 0E-02 1.000 000 0E-08
shaku [Japan] milliliter	<volume, special - see page 29> 18.039	1.803 900 0E+01
shaku [Japan] meter	<length, special - see page 29> 0.303	3.030 000 0E-01
shaku [Japan] square meter	<area, special - see page 29> 0.033 058	3.305 800 0E-02
shan [India] milligram	<mass, special - see page 29> 30.374 49	3.037 449 0E+01
shao [China] centiliter	<volume, special - see page 29> 1	1.000 000 0E+00
shatamana [Hindu, ancient, silver] gram	<mass, special - see page 29> 39.68	3.968 000 0E+01
she [Iraq, ancient] milligram	<mass, special - see page 29> 45	4.500 000 0E+01
she [Iraq, ancient] square centimeter	<area, special - see page 29> 14	1.400 000 0E+01
shekalim [Hebrew, ancient] gram	<mass, special - see page 29> 12.7	1.270 000 0E+01
shekel [Babylon, ancient] gram	<mass, special - see page 29> 8.22	8.220 000 0E+00
shekel [Egypt, ancient] gram	<mass, special - see page 29> 15.6	1.560 000 0E+01
shekel [Greece, ancient] gram	<mass, special - see page 29> 9.72	9.720 000 0E+00
shekel [Hebrew, ancient] gram	<mass, special - see page 29> 11.42	1.142 000 0E+01
shekel [Iraq, ancient, silver] gram	<mass, special - see page 29> 8.02	8.020 000 0E+00
shekel [Mesopotamia, ancient] gram	<mass, special - see page 29> 8	8.000 000 0E+00
shekel [Palestine, ancient] gram	<mass, special - see page 29> 16.33	1.633 000 0E+01
shekel [Rome, ancient] gram	<mass, special - see page 29> 14.27	1.427 000 0E+01
shekel hamelech [Hebrew, ancient] gram	<mass, special - see page 29> 14.55	1.455 000 0E+01
shen [China] liter	<volume, special - see page 29> 1.035 44	1.035 440 0E+00
sheng [China] liter	<volume, special - see page 29> 1.035	1.035 000 0E+00
sheqel [Hebrew, ancient] gram	<mass, special - see page 29> 176.29	1.762 900 0E+02

Convert From		<Type of Unit>
Convert To	Standard	Scientific

shi [Japan] <length, special - see page 29>
millimeter -- 0.003 030 3 --- 3.030 303 0E−03

shi ke [China] <mass, special - see page 29>
gram -- 10 --- 1.000 000 0E+01

shi mi [China] <length, special - see page 29>
meter --- 10 --- 1.000 000 0E+01

shi sheng [China] <volume, special - see page 29>
liter --- 10 --- 1.000 000 0E+01

shibiri [Tanganyika] <length, special - see page 29>
centimeter -- 23 --- 2.300 000 0E+01

shibr [Oman] <length, special - see page 29>
centimeter -- 24 --- 2.400 000 0E+01

shibr [Saudi Arabia] <length, special - see page 29>
centimeter -- 17.78 --- 1.778 000 0E+01

shiglu [Babylon, ancient] <mass, special - see page 29>
gram --- 8.3 --- 8.300 000 0E+00

shih chang [China] <length, special - see page 29>
meter -- 3.333 333 3 --- 3.333 333 3E+00

shih chien [China] <mass, special - see page 29>
gram --- 3.125 --- 3.125 000 0E+00

shih chih [China] <length, special - see page 29>
centimeter --- 33.333 333 --- 3.333 333 3E+01

shih chin [China] <mass, special - see page 29>
gram -- 500 --- 5.000 000 0E+02

shih ching [China] <area, special - see page 29>
hectare --- 6.666 666 7 --- 6.666 666 7E+00

shih dan [China] <volume, special - see page 29>
hectoliter --- 1 --- 1.000 000 0E+00

shih dao [China] <volume, special - see page 29>
dekaliter -- 1 --- 1.000 000 0E+00

shih fen [China] <mass, special - see page 29>
milligram -- 312.5 --- 3.125 000 0E+02

shih fen [China] <length, special - see page 29>
millimeter --- 3.333 333 3 --- 3.333 333 3E+00

shih fen [China] <area, special - see page 29>
square meter --- 66.666 667 --- 6.666 666 7E+01

shih hao [China] <mass, special - see page 29>
milligram -- 3.125 --- 3.125 000 0E+00

shih hao [China] <length, special - see page 29>
millimeter -- 0.033 333 3 --- 3.333 333 3E−02

shih hao [China] <area, special - see page 29>
square meter --- 0.666 666 7 --- 6.666 666 7E−01

shih ho [China] <volume, special - see page 29>
deciliter --- 1 --- 1.000 000 0E+00

shih li [China] <mass, special - see page 29>
milligram --- 31.25 --- 3.125 000 0E+01

shih li [China] <length, special - see page 29>
millimeter --- 0.333 333 3 --- 3.333 333 3E−01

shih li [China] <area, special - see page 29>
square meter --- 6.666 666 7 --- 6.666 666 7E+00

shih liang [China] <mass, special - see page 29>
gram --- 31.25 --- 3.125 000 0E+01

shih mow [China] <area, special - see page 29>
are -- 6.666 666 7 --- 6.666 666 7E+00

Convert From Convert To	<Type of Unit> Standard	Scientific
shih se [China]	<volume, special - see page 29>	
mililiter	1	1.000 000 0E+00
shih sen [China]	<volume, special - see page 29>	
liter	1	1.000 000 0E+00
shih sho [China]	<volume, special - see page 29>	
centiliter	1	1.000 000 0E+00
shih sze [China]	<mass, special - see page 29>	
milligram	0.312 5	3.125 000 0E−01
shih tan [China]	<mass, special - see page 29>	
kilogram	50	5.000 000 0E+01
shih tsun [China]	<length, special - see page 29>	
centimeter	3.333 333 3	3.333 333 3E+00
shih tze [China]	<length, special - see page 29>	
millimeter	0.003 333 3	3.333 333 3E−03
shih yin [China]	<length, special - see page 29>	
meter	33.333 333	3.333 333 3E+01
shin [Mongolia]	<volume, special - see page 29>	
centiliter	65	6.500 000 0E+01
shinik [Turkey]	<volume, special - see page 29>	
liter	10	1.000 000 0E+01
ship last [France]	<mass, special - see page 29>	
kilogram	2,000	2.000 000 0E+03
ship last [Sweden]	<mass, special - see page 29>	
tonne	2.45	2.450 000 0E+00
ship pound [Russia]	<mass, special - see page 29>	
kilogram	163.597	1.635 970 0E+02
ship pund [Sweden]	<mass, special - see page 29>	
kilogram	170	1.700 000 0E+02
shipping ton	<volume>	
barrel [UK]	6.920 928 3	6.920 928 3E+00
barrel [US, dry]	9.795 918 4	9.795 918 4E+00
billion cubic foot	<<<	4.000 000 0E−08
board foot	480	4.800 000 0E+02
bushel [UK]	31.144 177	3.114 417 7E+01
bushel [US, dry]	32.142 558	3.214 255 8E+01
cord [firewood]	0.312 5	3.125 000 0E−01
cord foot [timber]	2.5	2.500 000 0E+00
cubic foot	40	4.000 000 0E+01
cubic inch	69,120	6.912 000 0E+04
cubic meter	1.132 673 9	1.132 673 9E+00
cubic yard	1.481 481 5	1.481 481 5E+00
English water ton [UK]	1.112 292	1.112 292 0E+00
freight ton	1	1.000 000 0E+00
gallon [US, dry]	257.140 47	2.571 404 7E+02
kiloliter	1.132 673 9	1.132 673 9E+00
liter	1,132.673 9	1.132 673 9E+03
measurement ton	1	1.000 000 0E+00
million board foot	0.000 48	4.800 000 0E−04
ocean ton	1	1.000 000 0E+00
petrograd standard	0.242 424 2	2.424 242 4E−01
register ton	0.4	4.000 000 0E−01
stere	1.132 673 9	1.132 673 9E+00
thousand board foot	0.48	4.800 000 0E−01
thousand cubic foot	0.04	4.000 000 0E−02
shippond [Norway]	<mass, special - see page 29>	
kilogram	159.4	1.594 000 0E+02
sho [China]	<volume, special - see page 29>	
liter	0.010 354 4	1.035 440 0E−02

Convert From Convert To	**\<Type of Unit\>**	
	Standard	Scientific

sho [Japan] — \<volume, special - see page 29\>
liter ------- 1.803 907 --- 1.803 907 0E+00

shot [US, liquid] — \<volume\>
cubic inch ------- 1.804 687 5 --- 1.804 687 5E+00
cubic meter ------- 0.000 029 6 --- 2.957 353 0E-05
drop [US, liquid] ------- 360 --- 3.600 000 0E+02
liter ------- 0.029 573 5 --- 2.957 353 0E-02
ounce [US, liquid] ------- 1 --- 1.000 000 0E+00
pony [US, liquid] ------- 1 --- 1.000 000 0E+00

shushack [Belize] — \<volume, special - see page 29\>
liter ------- 22.73 --- 2.273 000 0E+01

shusi [Iraq, ancient] — \<length, special - see page 29\>
centimeter ------- 1.65 --- 1.650 000 0E+00

si [China] — \<mass, special - see page 29\>
milligram ------- 0.5 --- 5.000 000 0E-01

si mi [China] — \<length, special - see page 29\>
millimeter ------- 0.1 --- 1.000 000 0E-01

sicca [India, gold and silver] — \<mass, special - see page 29\>
gram ------- 15 --- 1.500 000 0E+01

sicilicus [Rome, ancient] — \<mass, special - see page 29\>
gram ------- 6.83 --- 6.830 000 0E+00

side of a besana [Cuba] — \<length, special - see page 29\>
meter ------- 50.88 --- 5.088 000 0E+01

side of a beswa [Afghanistan] — \<length, special - see page 29\>
meter ------- 9.879 --- 9.879 000 0E+00

side of a beswasa [Afghanistan] — \<length, special - see page 29\>
meter ------- 22.09 --- 2.209 000 0E+01

side of a gereeb [Afghanistan] — \<length, special - see page 29\>
meter ------- 44.18 --- 4.418 000 0E+01

side of a jerib [Afghanistan] — \<length, special - see page 29\>
meter ------- 44.18 --- 4.418 000 0E+01

siegbahn — \<length\>
angstrom ------- 0.001 002 1 --- 1.002 072 2E-03
meter ------- <<< --- 1.002 072 2E-13
x-unit ------- 1 --- 1.000 000 0E+00

siegh [Malta] — \<area, special - see page 29\>
square meter ------- 187.354 --- 1.873 540 0E+02

siemens — \<electric conductance\>
1/ohm ------- 1 --- 1.000 000 0E+00
abmho ------- <<< --- 1.000 000 0E-09
absiemens ------- <<< --- 1.000 000 0E-09
ampere/volt ------- 1 --- 1.000 000 0E+00
electromagnetic unit of conductance [cgs system] ------- <<< --- 1.000 000 0E-09
electrostatic unit of conductance [cgs system] ------- >>> --- 8.987 551 8E+11
gaussian electric conductance ------- >>> --- 8.987 551 8E+11
gemmho ------- 1,000,000 --- 1.000 000 0E+06
mho ------- 1 --- 1.000 000 0E+00
second/henry ------- 1 --- 1.000 000 0E+00
statmho ------- >>> --- 8.987 551 8E+11
statsiemens ------- >>> --- 8.987 551 8E+11

siemens meter/square millimeter — \<electric conductivity\>
absiemens/centimeter ------- 0.000 01 --- 1.000 000 0E-05
mho/meter ------- 1,000,000 --- 1.000 000 0E+06
siemens/meter ------- 1,000,000 --- 1.000 000 0E+06
statsiemens/centimeter ------- >>> --- 8.987 551 8E+15

siemens volt — \<electric current\>
abampere ------- 0.1 --- 1.000 000 0E-01
ampere ------- 1 --- 1.000 000 0E+00

| Convert From | | <Type of Unit> |
Convert To	Standard	Scientific
electromagnetic unit of current [cgs system]	0.1	1.000 000 0E−01
statampere	>>>	2.997 924 6E+09
siemens/meter		**<electric conductivity>**
1/ohm meter	1	1.000 000 0E+00
absiemens/centimeter	<<<	1.000 000 0E−11
mho/meter	1	1.000 000 0E+00
rom	1	1.000 000 0E+00
siemens meter/square millimeter	0.000 001	1.000 000 0E−06
statsiemens/centimeter	>>>	8.987 551 8E+09
sievert		**<dose equivalent>**
joule/kilogram	1	1.000 000 0E+00
newton meter/kilogram	1	1.000 000 0E+00
rem	100	1.000 000 0E+02
square meter/square second	1	1.000 000 0E+00
siglos [Greece, ancient]		**<mass, special - see page 29>**
gram	5.6	5.600 000 0E+00
siglos [Hebrew, ancient]		**<mass, special - see page 29>**
gram	86.5	8.650 000 0E+01
sign		**<plane angle>**
degree [angular]	30	3.000 000 0E+01
minute [angular]	1,800	1.800 000 0E+03
radian	0.523 598 8	5.235 987 8E−01
sihr [Afghanistan]		**<mass, special - see page 29>**
kilogram	7.066	7.066 000 0E+00
sihr [Bangladesh]		**<mass, special - see page 29>**
kilogram	0.933	9.330 000 0E−01
sihr [India]		**<mass, special - see page 29>**
kilogram	0.933	9.330 000 0E−01
sihr [Iran]		**<mass, special - see page 29>**
gram	75	7.500 000 0E+01
sihr [Pakistan]		**<mass, special - see page 29>**
kilogram	0.933	9.330 000 0E−01
sihr [Yemen]		**<mass, special - see page 29>**
kilogram	0.933	9.330 000 0E−01
siki [Bangladesh]		**<mass, special - see page 29>**
gram	2.92	2.920 000 0E+00
siki [India]		**<mass, special - see page 29>**
gram	2.915 952	2.915 952 0E+00
sila [Iraq, ancient]		**<volume, special - see page 29>**
liter	0.963	9.630 000 0E−01
sila [Mesopotamia, ancient]		**<volume, special - see page 29>**
liter	0.82	8.200 000 0E−01
sila [Sumeria, ancient]		**<volume, special - see page 29>**
liter	1	1.000 000 0E+00
sildar mal [Iceland]		**<volume, special - see page 29>**
hectoliter	1.5	1.500 000 0E+00
siliqua [Rome, ancient]		**<mass, special - see page 29>**
gram	0.189	1.890 000 0E−01
simri [Germany]		**<volume, special - see page 29>**
liter	22.153	2.215 300 0E+01
sing [Hong Kong]		**<volume, special - see page 29>**
liter	1	1.000 000 0E+00
single		**<units>**
couple	0.5	5.000 000 0E−01
one	1	1.000 000 0E+00
unit	1	1.000 000 0E+00

sinik [Turkey] \<volume, special - see page 29\>
liter ---------- 9.2 --- 9.200 000 0E+00

sinjer [Abyssinia, ancient] \<length, special - see page 29\>
centimeter ---------- 23 --- 2.300 000 0E+01

sinjer [Ethiopia] \<length, special - see page 29\>
meter ---------- 0.23 --- 2.300 000 0E-01

sinzer [Abyssinia, ancient] \<length, special - see page 29\>
centimeter ---------- 23 --- 2.300 000 0E+01

sinzer [Ethiopia] \<length, special - see page 29\>
centimeter ---------- 22.86 --- 2.286 000 0E+01

sir [Iran] \<mass, special - see page 29\>
gram ---------- 74.233 6 --- 7.423 360 0E+01

siriometer \<length\>
astronomical unit ---------- 1,000,000 --- 1.000 000 0E+06
kilometer ---------- >>> --- 1.495 978 7E+14
kiloparsec ---------- 0.004 848 1 --- 4.848 136 8E-03
megaparsec ---------- 0.000 004 8 --- 4.848 136 8E-06
meter ---------- >>> --- 1.495 978 7E+17
mile [international] ---------- >>> --- 9.295 580 7E+13
parsec ---------- 4.848 136 8 --- 4.848 136 8E+00

sitarion [Greece, ancient] \<mass, special - see page 29\>
milligram ---------- 68 --- 6.800 000 0E+01

sitio [Mexico] \<area, special - see page 29\>
hectare ---------- 1,755.61 --- 1.755 610 0E+03

sitio de ganado mayor [Mexico] \<area, special - see page 29\>
square kilometer ---------- 17.556 --- 1.755 600 0E+01

six [UK] \<volume, special - see page 29\>
liter ---------- 27.3 --- 2.730 000 0E+01

sjomil [Finland] \<length, special - see page 29\>
meter ---------- 1,852 --- 1.852 000 0E+03

sjomila [Iceland] \<length, special - see page 29\>
meter ---------- 1,855 --- 1.855 000 0E+03

sjomill [Finland] \<length, special - see page 29\>
meter ---------- 1,852 --- 1.852 000 0E+03

skaalpund [Netherlands] \<mass, special - see page 29\>
kilogram ---------- 0.422 --- 4.220 000 0E-01

skaalpund [Norway] \<mass, special - see page 29\>
kilogram ---------- 0.498 1 --- 4.981 000 0E-01

skaalpund [Sweden] \<mass, special - see page 29\>
gram ---------- 425.15 --- 4.251 500 0E+02

skaepper [Denmark] \<volume, special - see page 29\>
liter ---------- 17.39 --- 1.739 000 0E+01

skaepper [Denmark] \<area, special - see page 29\>
square meter ---------- 689.528 --- 6.895 280 0E+02

skalpund [Sweden] \<mass, special - see page 29\>
gram ---------- 425.15 --- 4.251 500 0E+02

skalpunt [Finland] \<mass, special - see page 29\>
kilogram ---------- 0.425 076 --- 4.250 760 0E-01

skein [cloth] \<length\>
bolt [cloth] ---------- 3 --- 3.000 000 0E+00
cubit ---------- 240 --- 2.400 000 0E+02
ell [cloth] ---------- 96 --- 9.600 000 0E+01
foot [international] ---------- 360 --- 3.600 000 0E+02
foot [US, survey] ---------- 359.999 28 --- 3.599 992 8E+02
hand [horses] ---------- 1,080 --- 1.080 000 0E+03
hectometer ---------- 1.097 28 --- 1.097 280 0E+00
inch [based on US, survey foot] ---------- 4,319.991 4 --- 4.319 991 4E+03

Convert From		
Convert To	Standard	Scientific

	Standard	Scientific
inch [international]	4,320	4.320 000 0E+03
meter	109.728	1.097 280 0E+02
nail [cloth]	1,920	1.920 000 0E+03
pace [geometrical]	7.2	7.200 000 0E+00
palm	1,440	1.440 000 0E+03
quarter [cloth]	480	4.800 000 0E+02
rope	18	1.800 000 0E+01
span	480	4.800 000 0E+02
yard [based on US, survey foot]	119.999 76	1.199 997 6E+02
yard [international]	120	1.200 000 0E+02

skeppe [Denmark]   `<volume, special - see page 29>`
liter	17.39	1.739 000 0E+01

skeppslast [Sweden]   `<mass, special - see page 29>`
kilogram	4,250.76	4.250 760 0E+03

skeppund [Sweden]   `<mass, special - see page 29>`
kilogram	170.03	1.700 300 0E+02

skiblast [Denmark]   `<mass, special - see page 29>`
kilogram	2,600	2.600 000 0E+03

skibpund [Denmark]   `<mass, special - see page 29>`
kilogram	160	1.600 000 0E+02

skieppe [Denmark]   `<volume, special - see page 29>`
liter	17.39	1.739 000 0E+01

skippund [Iceland]   `<mass, special - see page 29>`
kilogram	160	1.600 000 0E+02

skippunt [Finland]   `<mass, special - see page 29>`
kilogram	170.03	1.700 300 0E+02

skjeppe [Norway]   `<volume, special - see page 29>`
liter	17.37	1.737 000 0E+01

skot   `<luminance>`
apostilb [international]	0.001	1.000 000 0E-03
blondel	0.001	1.000 000 0E-03
bril	0.01	1.000 000 0E-02
candela/square meter	0.000 318 3	3.183 098 9E-04
lambert	0.000 000 1	1.000 000 0E-07

skrupel [Sweden]   `<length, special - see page 29>`
centimeter	0.002 969	2.969 010 0E-03

slug   `<mass>`
carat [international]	72,969.515	7.296 951 5E+04
cental [US]	0.321 740 5	3.217 404 9E-01
dyne square second/centimeter	14,593.903	1.459 390 3E+04
geepound	1	1.000 000 0E+00
hundredweight [long]	0.287 268 3	2.872 682 9E-01
hundredweight [short]	0.321 740 5	3.217 404 9E-01
hyl	1.488 163 9	1.488 163 9E+00
kilogram	14.593 903	1.459 390 3E+01
kilogram-force square second/meter	1.488 163 9	1.488 163 9E+00
myriagram	1.459 390 3	1.459 390 3E+00
newton square second/meter	14.593 903	1.459 390 3E+01
ounce	514.784 78	5.147 847 8E+02
pound	32.174 049	3.217 404 9E+01
pound-force square second/foot	1	1.000 000 0E+00
poundal square second/foot	32.174 049	3.217 404 9E+01
quarter [UK]	1.149 073 2	1.149 073 2E+00
quarter [US]	1.286 961 9	1.286 961 9E+00
slug [metric]	1.488 163 9	1.488 163 9E+00
stone [UK]	2.298 146 3	2.298 146 3E+00
ton [long]	0.014 363 4	1.436 341 5E-02
ton [metric]	0.014 593 9	1.459 390 3E-02
ton [short]	0.016 087	1.608 702 4E-02
tonne	0.014 593 9	1.459 390 3E-02

slug [metric] <mass>

doppelzentner [Germany]	0.098 066 5	9.806 650 0E-02
glug	10	1.000 000 0E+01
hundredweight [long]	0.193 035 4	1.930 353 8E-01
hundredweight [short]	0.216 199 6	2.161 996 2E-01
hyl	1	1.000 000 0E+00
kilogram	9.806 65	9.806 650 0E+00
kilogram-force square second/meter	1	1.000 000 0E+00
newton square second/meter	9.806 65	9.806 650 0E+00
ounce	345.919 4	3.459 194 0E+02
pound	21.619 962	2.161 996 2E+01
pound-force square second/foot	0.671 969	6.719 689 8E-01
poundal square second/foot	21.619 962	2.161 996 2E+01
stone [UK]	1.544 283	1.544 283 0E+00
ton [long]	0.009 651 8	9.651 768 9E-03
ton [short]	0.010 81	1.080 998 1E-02

slug foot/second <momentum>

gram centimeter/second	444,822.16	4.448 221 6E+05
newton second	4.448 221 6	4.448 221 6E+00
pound foot/second	32.174 049	3.217 404 9E+01
pound-force second	1	1.000 000 0E+00

slug foot/square second <force>

crinal	44.482 216 2	4.448 221 6E+01
dyne	444,822.162	4.448 221 6E+05
grain-force	7,000	7.000 000 0E+03
gram-force	453.592 37	4.535 923 7E+02
kip	0.001	1.000 000 0E-03
newton	4.448 221 6	4.448 221 6E+00
ounce-force	16	1.600 000 0E+01
pond	453.592 37	4.535 923 7E+02
pound-force	1	1.000 000 0E+00
poundal	32.174 048 6	3.217 404 9E+01
ton-force [short]	0.000 5	5.000 000 0E-04

slug square foot <moment of inertia of a mass>

kilogram square meter	1.355 817 9	1.355 817 9E+00
kilogram-force centimeter square second	13.825 495	1.382 549 5E+01
ounce-force foot square second	16	1.600 000 0E+01
pound square foot	32.174 049	3.217 404 9E+01
pound-force foot square second	1	1.000 000 0E+00
pound-force inch square second	12	1.200 000 0E+01

slug square inch <moment of inertia of a mass>

gram square meter	9.415 402 4	9.415 402 4E+00
kilogram square meter	0.009 415 4	9.415 402 4E-03
ounce square foot	3.574 894 3	3.574 894 3E+00
ounce-force inch square second	1.333 333 3	1.333 333 3E+00
pond centimeter square second	96.010 385	9.601 038 5E+01

slug/cubic foot <density>

grain/cubic inch	130.334 69	1.303 346 9E+02
gram/cubic centimeter	0.515 378 8	5.153 788 2E-01
kilogram/cubic meter	515.378 82	5.153 788 2E+02
ounce/cubic inch	0.297 907 9	2.979 078 6E-01
pound/cubic foot	32.174 049	3.217 404 9E+01
pound/gallon [-/UK, liquid]	5.165 339 3	5.165 339 3E+00
pound/gallon [-/US, liquid]	4.301 044 7	4.301 044 7E+00
slug/cubic yard	27	2.700 000 0E+01
ton/cubic yard [short]	0.434 349 7	4.343 496 6E-01
tonne/cubic meter	0.515 378 8	5.153 788 2E-01

slug/cubic inch <density>

grain/cubic inch	225,218.34	2.252 183 4E+05
gram/cubic centimeter	890.574 6	8.905 746 0E+02
kilogram/cubic meter	890,574.6	8.905 746 0E+05
ounce/cubic inch	514.784 78	5.147 847 8E+02

Convert From Convert To	Standard	<Type of Unit> Scientific
pound/cubic inch	32.174 049	3.217 404 9E+01
slug/cubic foot	1,728	1.728 000 0E+03
slug/gallon [-/US, liquid]	231	2.310 000 0E+02
ton/gallon [long/US, liquid]	3.317 948 8	3.317 948 8E+00
ton/gallon [short/US, liquid]	3.716 102 6	3.716 102 6E+00
tonne/liter	0.890 574 6	8.905 746 0E−01
slug/cubic yard		**<density>**
grain/cubic inch	4.827 210 6	4.827 210 6E+00
gram/cubic decimeter	19.088 104	1.908 810 4E+01
kilogram/cubic meter	19.088 104	1.908 810 4E+01
milligram/milliliter	19.088 104	1.908 810 4E+01
ounce/cubic foot	19.066 103	1.906 610 3E+01
ounce/gallon [-/US, liquid]	2.548 767 2	2.548 767 2E+00
pound/cubic foot	1.191 631 4	1.191 631 4E+00
pound/gallon [-/US, liquid]	0.159 298	1.592 979 5E−01
slug/cubic foot	0.037 037	3.703 703 7E−02
ton/cubic yard [short]	0.016 087	1.608 702 4E−02
tonne/cubic meter	0.019 088 1	1.908 810 4E−02
slug/foot second		**<dynamic viscosity>**
hyl/meter second	4.882 427 6	4.882 427 6E+00
kilogram-force second/square meter	4.882 427 6	4.882 427 6E+00
newton second/square meter	47.880 259	4.788 025 9E+01
pascal second	47.880 259	4.788 025 9E+01
poise	478.802 59	4.788 025 9E+02
pound-force second/square foot	1	1.000 000 0E+00
poundal second/square foot	32.174 048 6	3.217 404 9E+01
slug/gallon [-/UK, liquid]		**<density>**
grain/cubic inch	811.833 32	8.118 333 2E+02
gram/milliliter	3.210 209 9	3.210 209 9E+00
kilogram/cubic meter	3,210.209 9	3.210 209 9E+03
kilogram/liter	3.210 209 9	3.210 209 9E+00
ounce/cubic inch	1.855 619	1.855 619 0E+00
pound/cubic inch	0.115 976	1.159 761 9E−01
slug/cubic foot	6.228 835 5	6.228 835 5E+00
slug/gallon [-/US, liquid]	0.832 674 2	8.326 741 8E−01
ton/cubic yard [short]	2.705 492 5	2.705 492 5E+00
tonne/cubic meter	3.210 209 9	3.210 209 9E+00
slug/gallon [-/US, liquid]		**<density>**
grain/cubic inch	974.971 17	9.749 711 7E+02
gram/milliliter	3.855 301 3	3.855 301 3E+00
kilogram/cubic meter	3,855.301 3	3.855 301 3E+03
kilogram/liter	3.855 301 3	3.855 301 3E+00
ounce/cubic inch	2.228 505 5	2.228 505 5E+00
pound/cubic inch	0.139 281 6	1.392 816 0E−01
pound/gallon [-/US, liquid]	32.174 049	3.217 404 9E+01
slug/cubic foot	7.480 519 5	7.480 519 5E+00
ton/cubic yard [short]	3.249 161 1	3.249 161 1E+00
tonne/cubic meter	3.855 301 3	3.855 301 3E+00
slug/square foot		**<surface density>**
grain/square inch	1,564.016 2	1.564 016 2E+03
kilogram/are	15,708.746	1.570 874 6E+04
kilogram/square meter	157.087 46	1.570 874 6E+02
ounce/square inch	3.574 894 3	3.574 894 3E+00
pound/square foot	32.174 049	3.217 404 9E+01
slug/square yard	9	9.000 000 0E+00
ton/square foot [short]	0.016 087	1.608 702 4E−02
ton/square yard [short]	0.144 783	1.447 832 2E−01
tonne/square meter	0.157 087 46	1.570 874 6E−01
slug/square foot second		**<flow rate/unit area, mass basis>**
kilogram/square meter second	157.087 46	1.570 874 6E+02
ounce/square foot second	514.784 78	5.147 847 8E+02
pound/square foot second	32.174 049	3.217 404 9E+01

	Standard	Scientific
ton/square foot second [short]	0.016 087	1.608 702 4E−02
tonne/square meter second	0.157 087 5	1.570 874 6E−01
slug/square inch		**<surface density>**
grain/square inch	225,218.34	2.252 183 4E+05
kilogram/square centimeter	2.262 059 5	2.262 059 5E+00
kilogram/square meter	22,620.595	2.262 059 5E+04
ounce/square inch	514.784 78	5.147 847 8E+02
pound/square inch	32.174 049	3.217 404 9E+01
slug/square foot	144	1.440 000 0E+02
slug/square yard	1,296	1.296 000 0E+03
ton/square foot [short]	2.316 531 5	2.316 531 5E+00
ton/square inch [short]	0.016 087	1.608 702 4E−02
ton/square yard [short]	20.848 783	2.084 878 3E+01
tonne/square meter	22.620 595	2.262 059 5E+01
slug/square yard		**<surface density>**
grain/square inch	173.779 58	1.737 795 8E+02
gram/square centimeter	1.745 416 3	1.745 416 3E+00
kilogram/are	1,745.416 3	1.745 416 3E+03
kilogram/square meter	17.454 163	1.745 416 3E+01
ounce/square foot	57.198 309	5.719 830 9E+01
pound/square yard	3.574 894 3	3.574 894 3E+00
ton/square foot [short]	0.001 787 4	1.787 447 1E−03
ton/square yard [short]	0.016 087	1.608 702 4E−02
tonne/square meter	0.017 454 2	1.745 416 3E−02
sok [Laos]		**<length, special - see page 29>**
centimeter	40	4.000 000E+01
sok [Thailand]		**<length, special - see page 29>**
centimeter	50	5.000 000E+01
sok louang [Laos]		**<length, special - see page 29>**
centimeter	50	5.000 000E+01
solar [Costa Rica]		**<area, special - see page 29>**
square meter	873.6	8.736 000E+02
solar [Ecuador]		**<area, special - see page 29>**
square meter	1,764	1.764 000E+03
solares [Ecuador]		**<area, special - see page 29>**
are	17.468	1.746 800E+01
solidus [Rome, ancient]		**<mass, special - see page 29>**
gram	4.548	4.548 000E+00
solotnik [Russia]		**<mass, special - see page 29>**
gram	4.25	4.250 000E+00
solung [Thailand]		**<mass, special - see page 29>**
gram	3.75	3.750 000E+00
sompay [Thailand]		**<mass, special - see page 29>**
gram	0.937 5	9.375 000E−01
sone		**<loudness level>**
loudness unit	1,000	1.000 000E+03
noy	1	1.000 000E+00
phon	40	4.000 000E+01
sossus [Iraq, ancient]		**<length, special - see page 29>**
millimeter	1.65	1.650 000E+00
sotka [Russia]		**<length, special - see page 29>**
centimeter	2.134	2.134 000E+00
sound absorption unit		**<sound absorption>**
square foot	1	1.000 000E+00
square meter	0.092 903	9.290 304E−02
span		**<length>**
barleycorn	27	2.700 000E+01
caliber	900	9.000 000E+02
cubit	0.5	5.000 000E−01

| Convert From | | \<Type of Unit\> |
Convert To	Standard	Scientific
decimeter	2.286	2.286 000 0E+00
digit	12	1.200 000 0E+01
foot [international]	0.75	7.500 000 0E−01
foot [US, survey]	0.749 998 5	7.499 985 0E−01
hand [horses]	2.25	2.250 000 0E+00
inch [based on US, survey foot]	8.999 982	8.999 982 0E+00
inch [international]	9	9.000 000 0E+00
iron [shoe leather]	432	4.320 000 0E+02
meter	0.228 6	2.286 000 0E−01
mil	9,000	9.000 000 0E+03
nail [cloth]	4	4.000 000 0E+00
pace [geometrical]	0.015	1.500 000 0E−02
palm	3	3.000 000 0E+00
quarter [cloth]	1	1.000 000 0E+00
yard [based on US, survey foot]	0.249 999 5	2.499 995 0E−01
yard [international]	0.25	2.500 000 0E−01

span [Egypt, ancient]	\<length, special - see page 29\>	
meter	0.225	2.250 000 0E−01

span [Greece, ancient]	\<length, special - see page 29\>	
centimeter	23.1	2.310 000 0E+01

span [Hebrew, ancient]	\<length, special - see page 29\>	
centimeter	22.5	2.250 000 0E+01

spanland [Sweden]	\<area, special - see page 29\>	
hectare	0.247	2.470 000 0E−01

spann [Sweden]	\<volume, special - see page 29\>	
liter	73.28	7.328 000 0E+01

spannland [Sweden]	\<area, special - see page 29\>	
square meter	2,468.21	2.468 210 0E+03

spat	\<length\>	
bevameter	1,000	1.000 000 0E+03
gigameter	1,000	1.000 000 0E+03
light year [based on mean Julian year]	0.000 105 7	1.057 000 8E−04
meter	>>>	1.000 000 0E+12
mile [international]	>>>	6.213 711 9E+08
parsec	0.000 032 4	3.240 779 3E−05
terameter	1	1.000 000 0E+00

spat	\<solid angle\>	
hemisphere	2	2.000 000 0E+00
spheradian	12.566 371	1.256 637 1E+01
sphere	1	1.000 000 0E+00
spherical degree	720	7.200 000 0E+02
spherical right angle	8	8.000 000 0E+00
spherical solid angle	1	1.000 000 0E+00
square degree	41,252.961	4.125 296 1E+04
square grade	50,929.582	5.092 958 2E+04
sterad	12.566 371	1.256 637 1E+01
steradian	12.566 371	1.256 637 1E+01
steregon	1	1.000 000 0E+00

speed of light	\<velocity\>	
dekameter/second	>>>	2.997 924 6E+07
foot/second	>>>	9.835 710 6E+08
hectometer/second	2,997,924.58	2.997 924 6E+06
inch/second	>>>	1.180 285 3E+10
kilometer/second	299,792.458	2.997 924 6E+05
knot [international]	>>>	5.827 499 8E+08
megameter/second	299.792 458	2.997 924 6E+02
meter/second	>>>	2.997 924 6E+08
mile/second	186,282.397	1.862 824 0E+05
nautical mile/second [international]	161,874.977	1.618 749 8E+05
yard/second	>>>	3.278 570 2E+08

Convert From		**\<Type of Unit\>**
Convert To	Standard	Scientific

spheradian \<solid angle\>
hemisphere	0.159 154 9	1.591 549 4E−01
spat	0.079 577 5	7.957 747 2E−02
sphere	0.079 577 5	7.957 747 2E−02
spherical degree	57.295 78	5.729 578 0E+01
spherical right angle	0.636 619 8	6.366 197 7E−01
spherical solid angle	0.079 577 5	7.957 747 2E−02
square degree	3,282.806 4	3.282 806 4E+03
square grade	4,052.847 3	4.052 847 3E+03
sterad	1	1.000 000 0E+00
steradian	1	1.000 000 0E+00
steregon	0.079 577 5	7.957 747 2E−02

sphere \<solid angle\>
hemisphere	2	2.000 000 0E+00
spat	1	1.000 000 0E+00
spheradian	12.566 371	1.256 637 1E+01
spherical degree	720	7.200 000 0E+02
spherical right angle	8	8.000 000 0E+00
spherical solid angle	1	1.000 000 0E+00
square degree	41,252.961	4.125 296 1E+04
square grade	50,929.582	5.092 958 2E+04
sterad	12.566 371	1.256 637 1E+01
steradian	12.566 371	1.256 637 1E+01
steregon	1	1.000 000 0E+00

spherical degree \<solid angle\>
hemisphere	0.002 777 8	2.777 777 8E−03
spat	0.001 388 9	1.388 888 9E−03
spheradian	0.017 453 3	1.745 329 3E−02
sphere	0.001 388 9	1.388 888 9E−03
spherical right angle	0.011 111 1	1.111 111 1E−02
spherical solid angle	0.001 388 9	1.388 888 9E−03
square degree	57.295 78	5.729 578 0E+01
square grade	70.735 53	7.073 553 0E+01
sterad	0.017 453 3	1.745 329 3E−02
steradian	0.017 453 3	1.745 329 3E−02
steregon	0.001 388 9	1.388 888 9E−03

spherical right angle \<solid angle\>
hemisphere	0.25	2.500 000 0E−01
spat	0.125	1.250 000 0E−01
spheradian	1.570 796 3	1.570 796 3E+00
sphere	0.125	1.250 000 0E−01
spherical degree	90	9.000 000 0E+01
spherical solid angle	0.125	1.250 000 0E−01
square degree	5,156.620 2	5.156 620 2E+03
square grade	6,366.197 7	6.366 197 7E+03
sterad	1.570 796 3	1.570 796 3E+00
steradian	1.570 796 3	1.570 796 3E+00
steregon	0.125	1.250 000 0E−01

spherical solid angle \<solid angle\>
hemisphere	2	2.000 000 0E+00
spat	1	1.000 000 0E+00
spheradian	12.566 371	1.256 637 1E+01
sphere	1	1.000 000 0E+00
spherical degree	720	7.200 000 0E+02
spherical right angle	8	8.000 000 0E+00
square degree	41,252.961	4.125 296 1E+04
square grade	50,929.582	5.092 958 2E+04
sterad	12.566 371	1.256 637 1E+01
steradian	12.566 371	1.256 637 1E+01
steregon	1	1.000 000 0E+00

spint [Netherlands] \<volume, special - see page 29\>
liter	5	5.000 000 0E+00

Convert From Convert To	Standard	<Type of Unit> Scientific

spithame [Greece, ancient]   <length, special - see page 29>
	Standard	Scientific
centimeter	23.1	2.310 000 0E+01

square   <area>
	Standard	Scientific
centiare	9.290 304	9.290 304 0E+00
circular foot [international]	127.323 95	1.273 239 5E+02
circular foot [US, survey]	127.323 45	1.273 234 5E+02
hectare	0.000 929	9.290 304 0E−04
square chain [Gunter or US, survey]	0.022 956 7	2.295 674 9E−02
square chain [Ramden or Engineer]	0.01	9.999 960 0E−03
square foot [international]	100	1.000 000 0E+02
square foot [US, survey]	99.999 6	9.999 960 0E+01
square link [Gunter or US, survey]	229.567 49	2.295 674 9E+02
square link [Ramden or Engineer]	99.999 6	9.999 960 0E+01
square meter	9.290 304	9.290 304 0E+00
square perch [US, survey]	0.367 308	3.673 079 9E−01
square vara [US, survey, California]	13.223 088	1.322 308 8E+01
square vara [US, survey, Texas]	12.959 948	1.295 994 8E+01
square yard [based on US, survey foot]	11.111 067	1.111 106 7E+01
square yard [international]	11.111 111	1.111 111 1E+01

square [Sri Lanka]   <area, special - see page 29>
	Standard	Scientific
square meter	83.61	8.361 000 0E+01

square aldan [Mongolia]   <area, special - see page 29>
	Standard	Scientific
square meter	2.56	2.560 000 0E+00

square alen [Denmark]   <area, special - see page 29>
	Standard	Scientific
square meter	0.394 016	3.940 160 0E−01

square ampere/joule   <electric reluctance>
	Standard	Scientific
1/abhenry	<<<	1.000 000 0E−09
1/henry	1	1.000 000 0E+00
1/stathenry	>>>	8.987 551 8E+11

square angstrom   <area>
	Standard	Scientific
barn	>>>	1.000 000 0E+08
circular microinch	0.000 019 7	1.973 525 2E−05
circular micrometer	<<<	1.273 239 5E−08
circular mil	<<<	1.973 525 2E−11
square bicron	10,000	1.000 000 0E+04
square femtometer	>>>	1.000 000 0E+10
square fermi	>>>	1.000 000 0E+10
square meter	<<<	1.000 000 0E−20
square microinch	0.000 015 5	1.550 003 1E−05
square micromicron	10,000	1.000 000 0E+04
square micron	<<<	1.000 000 0E−08
square mil	<<<	1.550 003 1E−11
square millimicron	0.01	1.000 000 0E−02
square stigma	10,000	1.000 000 0E+04
square tenthmeter	1	1.000 000 0E+00
square thou	<<<	1.550 003 1E−11
square x-unit	995,868.45	9.958 684 5E+05

square archine [Russia]   <area, special - see page 29>
	Standard	Scientific
square meter	0.505 805 4	5.058 054 0E−01

square arpent [US, survey]   <area>
	Standard	Scientific
acre [commerical]	1.022 248 5	1.022 248 5E+00
acre [international]	0.844 833 4	8.448 334 4E−01
acre [US, survey]	0.844 830 1	8.448 300 0E−01
are	34.189 196	3.418 919 6E+01
hectare	0.341 892	3.418 919 6E−01
labor [US, survey]	0.004 769 3	4.769 278 9E−03
rood	3.379 320 2	3.379 320 2E+00
section [US, survey]	0.001 32	1.320 047 0E−03
square	368.009 45	3.680 094 5E+02
square chain [Gunter or US, survey]	8.448 300 6	8.448 300 6E+00
square chain [Ramden or Engineer]	3.680 079 8	3.680 079 8E+00

	Standard	Scientific
square foot [international]	36,800.945	3.680 094 5E+04
square foot [US, survey]	36,800.798	3.680 079 8E+04
square furlong [US, survey]	0.084 483	8.448 300 6E−02
square meter	3,418.919 6	3.418 919 6E+03
square mile [international]	0.001 320 1	1.320 052 3E−03
square mile [US, statute]	0.001 32	1.320 047 0E−03
square mile [US, survey]	0.001 32	1.320 047 0E−03
square perch [US, survey]	135.172 81	1.351 728 1E+02
square astronomical unit		**<area>**
square bevameter	22,379.523	2.237 952 3E+04
square gigameter	22,379.523	2.237 952 3E+04
square light year	<<<	2.500 354 1E−10
square megameter	>>>	2.237 952 3E+10
square meter	>>>	2.237 952 3E+22
square parsec	<<<	2.350 442 4E−11
square petameter	<<<	2.237 952 3E−08
square terameter	0.022 379 5	2.237 952 3E−02
square attometer		**<area>**
barn	<<<	1.000 000 0E−08
square bicron	<<<	1.000 000 0E−12
square fermi	0.000 001	1.000 000 0E−06
square meter	<<<	1.000 000 0E−36
square microinch	<<<	1.550 003 1E−21
square micromicron	<<<	1.000 000 0E−12
square mil	<<<	1.550 003 1E−27
square stigma	<<<	1.000 000 0E−12
square x-unit	<<<	9.958 684 5E−11
square yoctometer	>>>	1.000 000 0E+12
square zeptometer	1,000,000	1.000 000 0E+06
square baa [Saudi Arabia]		**<area, special - see page 29>**
square meter	2.810 317	2.810 317 0E+00
square barleycorn		**<area>**
circular inch [based on US, survey foot]	0.141 470 5	1.414 704 9E−01
circular inch [international]	0.141 471 1	1.414 710 6E−01
circular millimeter	91.271 469	9.127 146 9E+01
square caliber	1,111.111 1	1.111 111 1E+03
square foot [international]	0.000 771 6	7.716 049 4E−04
square foot [US, survey]	0.000 771 6	7.716 018 5E−04
square inch [based on US, survey foot]	0.111 110 7	1.111 106 7E−01
square inch [international]	0.111 111 1	1.111 111 1E−01
square link [Gunter or US, survey]	0.001 771 4	1.771 364 1E−03
square link [Ramden or Engineer]	0.000 771 6	7.716 018 5E−04
square meter	0.000 071 7	7.168 444 4E−05
square millimeter	71.684 444	7.168 444 4E+01
square pace	0.000 123 5	1.234 567 9E−04
square palm	0.012 345 7	1.234 567 9E−02
square span	0.001 371 7	1.371 742 1E−03
square bevameter		**<area>**
square astronomical unit	0.000 044 7	4.468 370 5E−05
square gigameter	1	1.000 000 0E+00
square meter	>>>	1.000 000 0E+18
square mile [international]	>>>	3.861 021 6E+11
square mile [US, statute]	>>>	3.861 006 1E+11
square mile [US, survey]	>>>	3.861 006 1E+11
square myriameter	>>>	1.000 000 0E+10
township [US, survey]	>>>	1.072 501 7E+10
square bicron		**<area>**
barn	10,000	1.000 000 0E+04
circular microinch	<<<	1.973 525 2E−09
square angstrom	0.000 1	1.000 000 0E−04
square fermi	1,000,000	1.000 000 0E+06
square microinch	<<<	1.550 003 1E−09

Convert From	<Type of Unit>	
Convert To	Standard	Scientific

square micromicron	1	1.000 000 0E+00
square micron	<<<	1.000 000 0E-12
square millimicron	0.000 001	1.000 000 0E-06
square picometer	1	1.000 000 0E+00
square stigma	1	1.000 000 0E+00
square tenthmeter	0.000 1	1.000 000 0E-04
square x-unit	99.586 845	9.958 684 5E+01

square braca [Cape Verde] — <length, special - see page 29>
meter	2.2	2.200 000 0E+00

square braca [Cape Verde] — <area, special - see page 29>
square meter	4.84	4.840 000 0E+00

square busa [Saudi Arabia] — <area, special - see page 29>
square centimeter	6.451 6	6.451 600 0E+00

square cable length [US, survey] — <area>
acre [commerical]	14.400 058	1.440 005 8E+01
acre [international]	11.900 874	1.190 087 4E+01
acre [US, survey]	11.900 826	1.190 082 6E+01
hectare	4.816 112 9	4.816 112 9E+00
labor [US, survey]	0.067 183 2	6.718 316 8E-02
rood	47.603 306	4.760 330 6E+01
section [US, survey]	0.018 595	1.859 504 1E-02
square arpent [US, survey]	14.086 651	1.408 665 1E+01
square chain [Gunter or US, survey]	119.008 26	1.190 082 6E+02
square chain [Ramden or Engineer]	51.84	5.184 000 0E+01
square foot [international]	518,402.07	5.184 020 7E+05
square foot [US, survey]	518,400	5.184 000 0E+05
square furlong [US, survey]	1.190 082 6	1.190 082 6E+00
square hectometer	4.816 112 9	4.816 112 9E+00
square meter	48,161.129	4.816 112 9E+04
square mile [international]	0.018 595 1	1.859 511 6E-02
square mile [US, statute]	0.018 595	1.859 504 1E-02
square mile [US, survey]	0.018 595	1.859 504 1E-02

square caliber — <area>
circular inch [based on US, survey foot]	0.000 127 3	1.273 234 5E-04
circular inch [international]	0.000 127 3	1.273 234 5E-04
circular micrometer	82,144.322	8.214 432 2E+04
circular mil	127.323 95	1.273 239 5E+02
square centimeter	0.000 645 2	6.451 600 0E-04
square inch [based on US, survey foot]	0.000 1	9.999 960 0E-05
square inch [international]	0.000 1	1.000 000 0E-04
square meter	<<<	6.451 600 0E-08
square micrometer	64,516	6.451 600 0E+04
square micron	64,516	6.451 600 0E+04
square mil	100	1.000 000 0E+02
square thou	100	1.000 000 0E+02

square cape foot [South Africa] — <area, special - see page 29>
square centimeter	991.356	9.913 560 0E+02

square cape foot [Swaziland] — <area, special - see page 29>
square centimeter	991.356	9.913 560 0E+02

square cape rood [South Africa] — <area, special - see page 29>
are	0.142 75	1.427 500 0E-01

square cape rood [Swaziland] — <area, special - see page 29>
square meter	14.275 5	1.427 550 0E+01

square cassaba [Iraq, ancient] — <area, special - see page 29>
square meter	14.4	1.440 000 0E+01

square centimeter — <permeability, water>
darcy [20 °C]	>>>	1.013 250 0E+08
perm [20 °C]	44,528.73	4.452 873 0E+04

square centimeter — <area, special - see page 29>
ferthumiungur [Iceland]	0.146 198	1.461 988 0E-01

Convert To	Standard	Scientific
ly [Vietnam]	0.002 999 9	2.999 850 0E−03
pie cuadrada [Mexico]	0.001 281 6	1.281 607 6E−03
pie cuadrada [Spain]	0.001 288	1.288 037 4E−03
pie cuadrado [Honduras]	0.001 290 8	1.290 822 3E−03
pied carre [Haiti]	0.001 076 4	1.076 391 0E−03
pulgada cuadrada [Mexico]	0.184 552 9	1.845 529 2E−01
she [Iraq, ancient]	0.071 428 6	7.142 857 1E−02
square busa [Saudi Arabia]	0.155 000 3	1.550 003 1E−01
square cape foot [South Africa]	0.001 008 7	1.008 719 4E−03
square cape foot [Swaziland]	0.001 008 7	1.008 719 4E−03
square dira [Saudi Arabia]	0.000 517 9	5.178 932 1E−04
square duim [Russia]	0.155 000 3	1.550 003 1E−01
square fitr [Saudi Arabia]	0.004 305 6	4.305 564 2E−03
square hindaza [Saudi Arabia]	0.000 209 5	2.095 030 6E−04
square shibr [Saudi Arabia]	0.003 163 3	3.163 271 6E−03
square centimeter		**<area>**
circular centimeter	1.273 239 5	1.273 239 5E+00
circular foot [international]	0.001 370 5	1.370 503 6E−03
circular foot [US, survey]	0.001 370 5	1.370 498 2E−03
circular inch [based on US, survey foot]	0.197 351 7	1.973 517 3E−01
circular inch [international]	0.197 352 5	1.973 525 2E−01
square caliber	1,550.003 1	1.550 003 1E+03
square foot [international]	0.001 076 4	1.076 391 0E−03
square foot [US, survey]	0.001 076 4	1.076 386 7E−03
square inch [based on US, survey foot]	0.154 999 7	1.549 996 9E−01
square inch [international]	0.155 000 3	1.550 003 1E−01
square meter	0.000 1	1.000 000 0E−04
square millimeter	100	1.000 000 0E+02
square centimeter °C/watt		**<thermal insulation coefficient>**
square centimeter second °C/calorie [-/ I.T.]	4.186 8	4.186 800 0E+00
square centimeter second °C/calorie [-/ thermoc.]	4.184	4.184 000 0E+00
square foot °C/watt	0.001 076 4	1.076 391 0E−03
square foot hour °F/Btu [-/ I.T.]	0.000 567 8	5.678 263 3E−04
square foot hour °F/Btu [-/ thermoc.]	0.000 567 4	5.674 464 5E−04
square meter hour °C/kilocalorie [-/ I.T.]	0.000 116 3	1.163 000 0E−04
square meter kelvin/watt	0.000 1	1.000 000 0E−04
square centimeter °C/watt centimeter		**<thermal resistivity>**
meter kelvin/watt	0.01	1.000 000 0E−02
square centimeter kelvin/watt		**<thermal insulation coefficient>**
square centimeter second °C/calorie [-/ I.T.]	4.186 8	4.186 800 0E+00
square centimeter second °C/calorie [-/ thermoc.]	4.184	4.184 000 0E+00
square foot °C/watt	0.001 076 4	1.076 391 0E−03
square foot hour °F/Btu [-/ I.T.]	0.000 567 8	5.678 263 3E−04
square foot hour °F/Btu [-/ thermoc.]	0.000 567 4	5.674 464 5E−04
square meter hour °C/kilocalorie [-/ I.T.]	0.000 116 3	1.163 000 0E−04
square meter kelvin/watt	0.000 1	1.000 000 0E−04
square centimeter second °C/calorie [-/ I.T.]		**<thermal insulation coefficient>**
square centimeter second °C/calorie [-/ thermoc.]	0.999 331 2	9.993 312 3E−01
square foot °C/watt	0.000 257 1	2.570 915 8E−04
square foot hour °F/Btu [-/ I.T.]	0.000 135 6	1.356 229 9E−04
square foot hour °F/Btu [-/ thermoc.]	0.000 135 5	1.355 322 6E−04
square meter hour °C/kilocalorie [-/ I.T.]	0.000 027 8	2.777 777 8E−05
square meter kelvin/watt	0.000 023 9	2.388 459 0E−05
square centimeter second °C/calorie [-/ thermoc.]		**<thermal insulation coefficient>**
square centimeter second °C/calorie [-/ I.T.]	1.000 669 2	1.000 669 2E+00
square foot °C/watt	0.000 257 3	2.572 636 3E−04
square foot hour °F/Btu [-/ I.T.]	0.000 135 7	1.357 137 5E−04
square foot hour °F/Btu [-/ thermoc.]	0.000 135 6	1.356 229 6E−04
square meter hour °C/kilocalorie [-/ I.T.]	0.000 027 8	2.779 636 7E−05
square meter kelvin/watt	0.000 023 9	2.390 057 4E−05

Convert From / Convert To	Standard	Scientific
square centimeter/day		**<kinematic viscosity>**
square centimeter/hour	0.041 666 7	4.166 666 7E−02
square inch/day	0.155 000 3	1.550 003 1E−01
square meter/second	<<<	1.157 407 4E−09
square millimeter/hour	4.166 666 7	4.166 666 7E+00
square centimeter/dyne		**<compressibility>**
1/pascal	10	1.000 000 0E+01
square foot/poundal	14.881 639	1.488 163 9E+01
square meter/kilogram-force	98.066 5	9.806 650 0E+01
square meter/newton	10	1.000 000 0E+01
square centimeter/erg		**<spectral cross-section>**
centimeter/dyne	1	1.000 000 0E+00
foot/pound-force	14,593.903	1.459 390 3E+04
meter/newton	1,000	1.000 000 0E+03
square meter/joule	1,000	1.000 000 0E+03
square centimeter/gram		**<specific area>**
square foot/pound	0.488 242 8	4.882 427 6E−01
square meter/kilogram	0.1	1.000 000 0E−01
square centimeter/gram-force		**<compressibility>**
1/pascal	0.010 197 2	1.019 716 2E−02
square foot/pound-force	0.488 242 8	4.882 427 6E−01
square inch/pound-force	70.306 958	7.030 695 8E+01
square meter/kilogram-force	0.1	1.000 000 0E−01
square centimeter/hour		**<kinematic viscosity>**
square centimeter/day	24	2.400 000 0E+01
square foot/day	0.025 833 4	2.583 338 5E−02
square inch/day	3.720 007 4	3.720 007 4E+00
square meter/second	<<<	2.777 777 8E−08
square millimeter/minute	1.666 666 7	1.666 666 7E+00
square centimeter/minute		**<kinematic viscosity>**
centistokes	1.666 666 7	1.666 666 7E+00
liter/centimeter day	1.44	1.440 000 0E+00
square foot/day	1.550 003 1	1.550 003 1E+00
square inch/hour	9.300 018 6	9.300 018 6E+00
square meter/second	0.000 001 7	1.666 666 7E−06
square millimeter/second	1.666 666 7	1.666 666 7E+00
square centimeter/second		**<kinematic viscosity>**
lentor	1	1.000 000 0E+00
liter/centimeter hour	3.6	3.600 000 0E+00
poise cubic centimeter/gram	1	1.000 000 0E+00
square foot/hour	3.875 007 8	3.875 007 8E+00
square inch/minute	9.300 018 6	9.300 018 6E+00
square meter/day	8.64	8.640 000 0E+00
square meter/second	0.000 1	1.000 000 0E−04
stokes	1	1.000 000 0E+00
square chain [Gunter or US, survey]		**<area>**
acre [commerical]	0.121 000 5	1.210 004 8E−01
acre [international]	0.100 000 4	1.000 000 0E−01
acre [US, survey]	0.1	1.000 000 0E−01
hectare	0.040 468 7	4.046 872 6E−02
rood	0.4	4.000 000 0E−01
square arpent [US, survey]	0.118 367	1.183 670 0E−01
square chain [Ramden or Engineer]	0.435 6	4.356 000 0E−01
square dekameter	4.046 872 6	4.046 872 6E+00
square foot [international]	4,356.017 4	4.356 017 4E+03
square foot [US, survey]	4,356	4.356 000 0E+03
square furlong [US, survey]	0.01	1.000 000 0E−02
square link [Gunter or US, survey]	10,000	1.000 000 0E+04
square link [Ramden or Engineer]	4,356	4.356 000 0E+03
square meter	404.687 26	4.046 872 6E+02
square mile [international]	0.000 156 3	1.562 506 3E−04

Convert From / Convert To	Standard	Scientific
square mile [US, statute]	0.000 156 3	1.562 500 0E−04
square mile [US, survey]	0.000 156 3	1.562 500 0E−04
square perch [US, survey]	16	1.600 000 0E+01
square vara [US, survey, California]	576	5.760 000 0E+02
square vara [US, survey, Texas]	564.537 6	5.645 376 0E+02
square yard [based on US, survey foot]	484	4.840 000 0E+02
square yard [international]	484.001 94	4.840 019 4E+02
square chain [Ramden or Engineer]		**<area>**
acre [commerical]	0.277 778 9	2.777 788 9E−01
acre [international]	0.229 569 3	2.295 693 3E−01
acre [US, survey]	0.229 568 4	2.295 684 1E−01
hectare	0.092 903 4	9.290 341 2E−02
labor [US, survey]	0.001 296	1.295 971 6E−03
square	100.000 4	1.000 004 0E+02
square arpent [US, survey]	0.271 733 2	2.717 332 4E−01
square chain [Gunter or US, survey]	2.295 684 1	2.295 684 1E+00
square foot [international]	10,000.04	1.000 004 0E+04
square foot [US, survey]	10,000	1.000 000 0E+04
square furlong [US, survey]	0.022 956 8	2.295 684 1E−02
square link [Gunter or US, survey]	22,956.841	2.295 684 1E+04
square link [Ramden or Engineer]	10,000	1.000 000 0E+04
square meter	929.034 12	9.290 341 2E+02
square mile [international]	0.000 358 7	3.587 020 8E−04
square mile [US, statute]	0.000 358 7	3.587 006 4E−04
square mile [US, survey]	0.000 358 7	3.587 006 4E−04
square perch [US, survey]	36.730 946	3.673 094 6E+01
square vara [US, survey, California]	1,322.314	1.322 314 0E+03
square vara [US, survey, Texas]	1,296	1.296 000 0E+03
square yard [based on US, survey foot]	1,111.111 1	1.111 111 1E+03
square yard [international]	1,111.115 6	1.111 115 6E+03
square chok [South Korea]		**<area, special - see page 29>**
square meter	0.091 827	9.182 700 0E−02
square cordel [Cuba]		**<area, special - see page 29>**
square meter	414.204	4.142 040 0E+02
square cuadra [Chile]		**<area, special - see page 29>**
hectare	1.572	1.572 000 0E+00
square cuadra [Ecuador]		**<area, special - see page 29>**
hectare	0.705 6	7.056 000 0E−01
square cuadra [Uruguay]		**<volume, special - see page 29>**
hectoliter	1.373	1.373 000 0E+00
square cubit		**<area>**
are	0.002 090 3	2.090 318 4E−03
square	0.022 5	2.250 000 0E−02
square digit	576	5.760 000 0E+02
square foot [international]	2.25	2.250 000 0E+00
square foot [US, survey]	2.249 991	2.249 991 0E+00
square inch [based on US, survey foot]	323.998 7	3.239 987 0E+02
square inch [international]	324	3.240 000 0E+02
square meter	0.209 031 8	2.090 318 4E−01
square pace	0.36	3.600 000 0E−01
square palm	36	3.600 000 0E+01
square span	4	4.000 000 0E+00
square yard [based on US, survey foot]	0.249 999	2.499 990 0E−01
square yard [international]	0.25	2.500 000 0E−01
square cubit [Egypt, ancient]		**<area, special - see page 29>**
square meter	0.275	2.750 000 0E−01
square decimeter		**<area>**
centiare	0.01	1.000 000 0E−02
circular centimeter	127.323 95	1.273 239 5E+02
circular foot [international]	0.137 050 4	1.370 503 6E−01
circular foot [US, survey]	0.137 049 8	1.370 498 2E−01

square foot [international]	0.107 639 1	1.076 391 0E-01
square foot [US, survey]	0.107 638 7	1.076 386 7E-01
square inch [based on US, survey foot]	15.499 969	1.549 996 9E+01
square inch [international]	15.500 031	1.550 003 1E+01
square link [Gunter or US, survey]	0.247 104 4	2.471 043 9E-01
square link [Ramden or Engineer]	0.107 638 7	1.076 386 7E-01
square meter	0.01	1.000 000 0E-02
square vara [US, survey, California]	0.014 233 2	1.423 321 3E-02
square vara [US, survey, Texas]	0.013 95	1.394 997 2E-02
square yard [based on US, survey foot]	0.011 959 9	1.195 985 3E-02
square yard [international]	0.011 959	1.195 990 0E-02

square degree | | **<solid angle>** |
hemisphere	0.000 048 5	4.848 136 8E-05
spat	0.000 024 2	2.424 068 4E-05
spheradian	0.000 304 6	3.046 174 2E-04
sphere	0.000 024 2	2.424 068 4E-05
spherical degree	0.017 453 3	1.745 329 3E-02
spherical right angle	0.000 193 9	1.939 254 7E-04
spherical solid angle	0.000 024 2	2.424 068 4E-05
square grade	1.234 567 9	1.234 567 9E+00
sterad	0.000 304 6	3.046 174 2E-04
steradian	0.000 304 6	3.046 174 2E-04
steregon	0.000 024 2	2.424 068 4E-05

square dekameter | | **<area>** |
acre [commercial]	0.029 899 8	2.989 975 1E-02
acre [international]	0.024 710 5	2.471 053 8E-02
acre [US, survey]	0.024 710 4	2.471 043 9E-02
are	1	1.000 000 0E+00
hectare	0.01	1.000 000 0E-02
rood	0.098 841 8	9.884 175 7E-02
square chain [Gunter or US, survey]	0.247 104 4	2.471 043 9E-01
square chain [Ramden or Engineer]	0.107 638 7	1.076 386 7E-01
square foot [international]	1,076.391	1.076 391 0E+03
square foot [US, survey]	1,076.386 7	1.076 386 7E+03
square meter	100	1.000 000 0E+02
square perch [US, survey]	3.953 670 3	3.953 670 3E+00
square yard [based on US, survey foot]	119.598 53	1.195 985 3E+02
square yard [international]	119.599	1.195 990 0E+02

square depa [Malaysia] | | **<area, special - see page 29>** |
| square meter | 3.345 | 3.345 000 0E+00 |

square depa [Singapore] | | **<area, special - see page 29>** |
| square meter | 3.345 | 3.345 000 0E+00 |

square digit | | **<area>** |
circular foot [international]	0.004 973 6	4.973 592 0E-03
circular foot [US, survey]	0.004 973 6	4.973 572 1E-03
circular inch [based on US, survey foot]	0.716 194 4	7.161 943 8E-01
circular inch [international]	0.716 197 2	7.161 972 4E-01
square barleycorn	5.062 5	5.062 500 0E+00
square centimeter	3.629 025	3.629 025 0E+00
square cubit	0.001 736 1	1.736 111 1E-03
square foot [international]	0.003 906 2	3.906 250 0E-03
square foot [US, survey]	0.003 906 2	3.906 234 0E-03
square inch [based on US, survey foot]	0.562 497 5	5.624 977 5E-01
square inch [international]	0.562 5	5.625 000 0E-01
square meter	0.000 362 9	3.629 025 0E-04
square pace	0.000 625	6.250 000 0E-04
square palm	0.062 5	6.250 000 0E-02

square dira [Saudi Arabia] | | **<area, special - see page 29>** |
| square centimeter | 1,930.9 | 1.930 900 0E+03 |

square diraa meman [Egypt, ancient] | | **<area, special - see page 29>** |
| square meter | 0.562 5 | 5.625 000 0E-01 |

square dra maghmari [Syria]   `<area, special - see page 29>`
square meter --- 0.575 --- 5.750 000 0E−01

square duim [Russia]   `<area, special - see page 29>`
square centimeter --- 6.451 6 --- 6.451 600 0E+00

square estado [Spain]   `<area, special - see page 29>`
square meter --- 11.182 --- 1.118 200 0E+01

square exameter   `<area>`
square astronomical unit --->>> --- 4.468 370 5E+13
square bevameter --->>> --- 1.000 000 0E+18
square gigameter --->>> --- 1.000 000 0E+18
square light year --- 11,172.509 --- 1.117 250 9E+04
square meter --->>> --- 1.000 000 0E+36
square parsec --- 1,050.264 8 --- 1.050 264 8E+03
square petameter --- 1,000,000 --- 1.000 000 0E+06

square fathom [US, survey]   `<area>`
acre [international] --- 0.000 826 4 --- 8.264 495 9E−04
acre [US, survey] --- 0.000 826 4 --- 8.264 462 8E−04
hectare --- 0.000 334 5 --- 3.344 522 8E−04
square chain [Gunter or US, survey] --- 0.008 264 5 --- 8.264 462 8E−03
square chain [Ramden or Engineer] --- 0.003 6 --- 3.600 000 0E−03
square foot [international] --- 36.000 144 --- 3.600 014 4E+01
square foot [US, survey] --- 36 --- 3.600 000 0E+01
square meter --- 3.344 522 8 --- 3.344 522 8E+00
square mile [international] --- 0.000 001 3 --- 1.291 327 5E−06
square mile [US, statute] --- 0.000 001 3 --- 1.291 322 3E−06
square mile [US, survey] --- 0.000 001 3 --- 1.291 322 3E−06
square perch [US, survey] --- 0.132 231 4 --- 1.322 314 0E−01
square yard [based on US, survey foot] --- 4 --- 4.000 000 0E+00
square yard [international] --- 4.000 016 --- 4.000 016 0E+00

square femtometer   `<area>`
barn --- 0.01 --- 1.000 000 0E−02
circular microinch --- <<< --- 1.973 525 2E−15
square angstrom --- <<< --- 1.000 000 0E−10
square bicron --- 0.000 001 --- 1.000 000 0E−06
square fermi --- 1 --- 1.000 000 0E+00
square meter --- <<< --- 1.000 000 0E−30
square microinch --- <<< --- 1.550 003 1E−15
square micromicron --- 0.000 001 --- 1.000 000 0E−06
square millimicron --- <<< --- 1.000 000 0E−12
square stigma --- 0.000 001 --- 1.000 000 0E−06
square tenthmeter --- <<< --- 1.000 000 0E−10
square x-unit --- 0.000 099 6 --- 9.958 684 5E−05

square fermi   `<area>`
barn --- 0.01 --- 1.000 000 0E−02
circular microinch --- <<< --- 1.973 525 2E−15
square angstrom --- <<< --- 1.000 000 0E−10
square bicron --- 0.000 001 --- 1.000 000 0E−06
square femtometer --- 1 --- 1.000 000 0E+00
square meter --- <<< --- 1.000 000 0E−30
square microinch --- <<< --- 1.550 003 1E−15
square micromicron --- 0.000 001 --- 1.000 000 0E−06
square millimicron --- <<< --- 1.000 000 0E−12
square stigma --- 0.000 001 --- 1.000 000 0E−06
square tenthmeter --- <<< --- 1.000 000 0E−10
square x-unit --- 0.000 099 6 --- 9.958 684 5E−05

square fitr [Saudi Arabia]   `<area, special - see page 29>`
square centimeter --- 232.257 6 --- 2.322 576 0E+02

square food [Luxembourg, hide processing]   `<area, special - see page 29>`
square meter --- 0.304 8 --- 3.048 000 0E−01

square foot   `<permeability, water>`
darcy [20 ºC] --->>> --- 9.413 400 5E+10

Convert From Convert To	**<Type of Unit>**	
	Standard	Scientific

Convert From / Convert To	Standard	Scientific
millidarcy [20 °C]	>>>	9.413 400 5E+13
perm [20 °C]	>>>	4.136 854 4E+07
square foot		**<sound absorption>**
open window unit	1	1.000 000 0E+00
sabin	1	1.000 000 0E+00
sound absorption unit	1	1.000 000 0E+00
square-foot unit of absorption	1	1.000 000 0E+00
square foot [international]		**<area>**
acre [commerical]	0.000 027 8	2.777 777 8E-05
acre [international]	0.000 023	2.295 684 1E-05
acre [US, survey]	0.000 023	2.295 674 9E-05
are	0.000 929	9.290 304 0E-04
base box [for tin-plated steel sheet]	0.004 591 8	4.591 836 7E-03
circular foot [international]	1.273 239 5	1.273 239 5E+00
circular foot [US, survey]	1.273 234 5	1.273 234 5E+00
hectare	0.000 009 3	9.290 304 0E-06
square	0.01	1.000 000 0E-02
square decimeter	9.290 304	9.290 304 0E+00
square foot [US, survey]	0.999 996	9.999 960 0E-01
square inch [based on US, survey foot]	143.999 42	1.439 994 2E+02
square inch [international]	144	1.440 000 0E+02
square link [Gunter or US, survey]	2.295 674 9	2.295 674 9E+00
square link [Ramden or Engineer]	0.999 996	9.999 960 0E-01
square meter	0.092 903	9.290 304 0E-02
square mile [international]	<<<	3.587 006 4E-08
square mile [US, statute]	<<<	3.586 992 1E-08
square mile [US, survey]	<<<	3.586 992 1E-08
square pace	0.16	1.600 000 0E-01
square palm	16	1.600 000 0E+01
square yard [based on US, survey foot]	0.111 110 7	1.111 106 7E-01
square yard [international]	0.111 111 1	1.111 111 1E-01
square foot [US, survey]		**<area>**
acre [commerical]	0.000 027 8	2.777 788 9E-05
acre [international]	0.000 023	2.295 693 3E-05
acre [US, survey]	0.000 023	2.295 684 1E-05
circular foot [international]	1.273 244 6	1.273 244 6E+00
circular foot [US, survey]	1.273 239 5	1.273 239 5E+00
hectare	0.000 009 3	9.290 341 2E-06
labor [US, survey]	0.000 000 1	1.295 971 6E-07
section [US, survey]	<<<	3.587 006 4E-08
square arpent [US, survey]	0.000 027 2	2.717 332 4E-05
square cable length [US, survey]	0.000 001 9	1.929 012 3E-06
square chain [Gunter or US, survey]	0.000 229 6	2.295 684 1E-04
square chain [Ramden or Engineer]	0.000 1	1.000 000 0E-04
square fathom [US, survey]	0.027 777 8	2.777 777 8E-02
square foot [international]	1.000 004	1.000 004 0E+00
square furlong [US, survey]	0.000 002 3	2.295 684 1E-06
square inch [based on US, survey foot]	144	1.440 000 0E+02
square inch [international]	144.000 58	1.440 005 8E+02
square league [US, statute]	<<<	3.985 562 7E-09
square link [Gunter or US, survey]	2.295 684 1	2.295 684 1E+00
square link [Ramden or Engineer]	1	1.000 000 0E+00
square meter	0.092 903 4	9.290 341 2E-02
square mile [international]	<<<	3.587 020 8E-08
square mile [US, survey]	<<<	3.587 006 4E-08
square perch [US, survey]	0.003 673 1	3.673 094 6E-03
square vara [US, survey, California]	0.132 231 4	1.322 314 0E-01
square vara [US, survey, Texas]	0.129 6	1.296 000 0E-01
square yard [based on US, survey foot]	0.111 111 1	1.111 111 1E-01
square yard [international]	0.111 111 6	1.111 115 6E-01
township [US, survey]	<<<	9.963 906 7E-10

square foot °C/watt <thermal insulation coefficient>
square centimeter second °C/calorie [-/ I.T.]	3,889.664 5	3.889 664 5E+03
square centimeter second °C/calorie [-/ thermoc.]	3,887.063 2	3.887 063 2E+03
square foot hour °F/Btu [-/ I.T.]	0.527 527 9	5.275 279 E-01
square foot hour °F/Btu [-/ thermoc.]	0.527 175	5.271 750 0E-01
square meter hour °C/kilocalorie [-/ I.T.]	0.108 046 2	1.080 462 4E-01
square meter kelvin/watt	0.092 903	9.290 304 0E-02

square foot hour °F/Btu [-/ I.T.] <thermal insulation coefficient>
square centimeter second °C/calorie [-/ I.T.]	7,373.381 2	7.373 381 2E+03
square centimeter second °C/calorie [-/ thermoc.]	7,368.450 1	7.368 450 1E+03
square foot °C/watt	1.895 634 2	1.895 634 2E+00
square foot hour °F/Btu [-/ thermoc.]	0.999 331	9.993 309 8E-01
square meter hour °C/kilocalorie [-/ I.T.]	0.204 816 1	2.048 161 4E-01
square meter kelvin/watt	0.176 110 2	1.761 101 8E-01

square foot hour °F/Btu [-/ thermoc.] <thermal insulation coefficient>
square centimeter second °C/calorie [-/ I.T.]	7,378.317 4	7.378 317 4E+03
square centimeter second °C/calorie [-/ thermoc.]	7,373.383	7.373 383 0E+03
square foot °C/watt	1.896 903 3	1.896 903 3E+00
square foot hour °F/Btu [-/ I.T.]	1.000 669 5	1.000 669 5E+00
square meter hour °C/kilocalorie [-/ I.T.]	0.204 953 3	2.049 532 6E-01
square meter kelvin/watt	0.176 228 1	1.762 280 8E-01

square foot/cubic foot <area/unit volume>
square meter/cubic meter	3.280 839 9	3.280 839 9E+00
square yard/cubic yard	3	3.000 000 0E+00

square foot/day <kinematic viscosity>
centistokes	1.075 266 7	1.075 266 7E+00
square centimeter/hour	38.709 6	3.870 960 0E+01
square inch/hour	6	6.000 000 0E+00
square meter/second	0.000 001 1	1.075 266 7E-06
square millimeter/second	1.075 266 7	1.075 266 7E+00

square foot/hour <kinematic viscosity>
centistokes	25.806 4	2.580 640 0E+01
lentor	0.258 064	2.580 640 0E-01
liter/centimeter day	22.296 729 6	2.229 673 0E+01
square foot/day	24	2.400 000 0E+01
square inch/minute	2.4	2.400 000 0E+00
square meter/day	2.229 673	2.229 673 0E+00
square meter/second	0.000 025 8	2.580 640 0E-05
square millimeter/second	25.806 4	2.580 640 0E+01

square foot/minute <kinematic viscosity>
liter/centimeter hour	55.741 824	5.574 182 4E+01
poise cubic centimeter/gram	15.483 84	1.548 384 0E+01
square centimeter/second	15.483 84	1.548 384 0E+01
square foot/hour	60	6.000 000 0E+01
square inch/second	2.4	2.400 000 0E+00
square meter/hour	5.574 182 4	5.574 182 4E+00
square meter/second	0.001 548 4	1.548 384 0E-03
stokes	15.483 84	1.548 384 0E+01

square foot/pound <specific area>
acre/pound	0.000 023	2.295 684 1E-05
hectare/kilogram	0.000 020 5	2.048 161 4E-05
square centimeter/gram	2.048 161 4	2.048 161 4E+00
square meter/kilogram	0.204 816 1	2.048 161 4E-01

square foot/pound-force <compressibility>
1/pascal	0.020 885 4	2.088 543 4E-02
square centimeter/gram-force	2.048 161 4	2.048 161 4E+00
square foot/poundal	0.031 081	3.108 095 0E-02
square meter/kilogram-force	0.204 816 1	2.048 161 4E-01

square foot/poundal <compressibility>
1/pascal	0.671 969	6.719 689 0E-01
square foot/pound-force	32.174 049	3.217 404 9E+01

square meter/kilogram-force	6.589 764 6	6.589 764 6E+00
square foot/second		**<kinematic viscosity>**
liter/centimeter minute	55.741 824	5.574 182 4E+01
poise cubic centimeter/gram	929.030 4	9.290 304 0E+02
square centimeter/second	929.030 4	9.290 304 0E+02
square foot/minute	60	6.000 000 0E+01
square inch/second	144	1.440 000 0E+02
square meter/second	0.092 903	9.290 304 0E−02
stokes	929.030 4	9.290 304 0E+02
square foot/ton-force [-/long]		**<compressibility>**
1/pascal	0.000 009 3	9.323 854 6E−06
square foot/ton-force [-/short]	0.892 857 1	8.928 571 4E−01
square inch/pound-force	0.064 285 7	6.428 571 4E−02
square foot/ton-force [-/short]		**<compressibility>**
1/pascal	0.000 010 4	1.044 271 7E−05
square foot/ton-force [-/long]	1.12	1.120 000 0E+00
square inch/pound-force	0.072	7.200 000 0E−02
square meter/kilogram-force	0.000 102 4	1.024 080 7E−04
square furlong [US, survey]		**<area>**
acre [commerical]	12.100 048	1.210 004 8E+01
acre [international]	10.000 04	1.000 004 0E+01
acre [US, survey]	10	1.000 000 0E+01
hectare	4.046 872 6	4.046 872 6E+00
labor [US, survey]	0.056 452 5	5.645 252 3E−02
rood	40	4.000 000 0E+01
section [US, survey]	0.015 625	1.562 500 0E−02
square arpent [US, survey]	11.836 7	1.183 670 0E+01
square cable length [US, survey]	0.840 277 8	8.402 777 8E−01
square chain [Gunter or US, survey]	100	1.000 000 0E+02
square chain [Ramden or Engineer]	43.56	4.356 000 0E+01
square foot [international]	435,601.74	4.356 017 4E+05
square foot [US, survey]	435,600	4.356 000 0E+05
square hectometer	4.046 872 6	4.046 872 6E+00
square league [US, statute]	0.001 736 1	1.736 111 1E−03
square meter	40,468.726	4.046 872 6E+04
square mile [international]	0.015 625 1	1.562 506 3E−02
square mile [US, statute]	0.015 625	1.562 500 0E−02
square mile [US, survey]	0.015 625	1.562 500 0E−02
square yard [based on US, survey foot]	48,400	4.840 000 0E+04
square yard [international]	48,400.194	4.840 019 4E+04
square fut [Russia]		**<area, special - see page 29>**
square meter	0.092 903	9.290 304 0E−02
square gaz gereeb [Afghanistan]		**<area, special - see page 29>**
square meter	0.543	5.430 000 0E−01
square gaz memar [Afghanistan]		**<area, special - see page 29>**
square meter	0.702	7.020 000 0E−01
square gaz sha [Afghanistan]		**<area, special - see page 29>**
square meter	1.136	1.136 000 0E+00
square gazi jerib [Afghanistan]		**<area, special - see page 29>**
square meter	0.542 6	5.426 000 0E−01
square gigameter		**<area>**
square astronomical unit	0.000 044 7	4.468 370 5E−05
square bevameter	1	1.000 000 0E+00
square light year	<<<	1.117 250 9E−14
square megameter	1,000,000	1.000 000 0E+06
square meter	>>>	1.000 000 0E+18
square mile [international]	>>>	3.861 021 6E+11
square mile [US, statute]	>>>	3.861 006 1E+11
square mile [US, survey]	>>>	3.861 006 1E+11
square myriameter	>>>	1.000 000 0E+10
township [US, survey]	>>>	1.072 501 7E+10

square grade   <solid angle>

	Standard	Scientific
hemisphere	0.000 039 3	3.926 990 8E-05
spat	0.000 019 6	1.963 495 4E-05
spheradian	0.000 246 7	2.467 401 1E-04
sphere	0.000 019 6	1.963 495 4E-05
spherical degree	0.014 137 2	1.413 716 7E-02
spherical right angle	0.000 157 1	1.570 796 3E-04
spherical solid angle	0.000 019 6	1.963 495 4E-05
square degree	0.81	8.100 000 0E-01
sterad	0.000 246 7	2.467 401 1E-04
steradian	0.000 246 7	2.467 401 1E-04
steregon	0.000 019 6	1.963 495 4E-05

square guz [Iran]   <area, special - see page 29>

	Standard	Scientific
square meter	1.08	1.080 000 0E+00

square hectometer   <area>

	Standard	Scientific
acre [commerical]	2.989 975 1	2.989 975 1E+00
acre [international]	2.471 053 8	2.471 053 8E+00
acre [US, survey]	2.471 043 9	2.471 043 9E+00
hectare	1	1.000 000 0E+00
labor [US, survey]	0.013 949 7	1.394 966 7E-02
rood	9.884 175 7	9.884 175 7E+00
section [US, survey]	0.003 861	3.861 006 1E-03
square arpent [US, survey]	2.924 900 6	2.924 900 6E+00
square chain [Gunter or US, survey]	24.710 439	2.471 043 9E+01
square chain [Ramden or Engineer]	10.763 867	1.076 386 7E+01
square foot [international]	107,639.1	1.076 391 0E+05
square foot [US, survey]	107,638.67	1.076 386 7E+05
square furlong [US, survey]	0.247 104 4	2.471 043 9E-01
square meter	10,000	1.000 000 0E+04
square mile [international]	0.003 861	3.861 021 6E-03
square mile [US, statute]	0.003 861	3.861 006 1E-03
square mile [US, survey]	0.003 861	3.861 006 1E-03
square perch [US, survey]	395.367 03	3.953 670 3E+02

square hindaza [Saudi Arabia]   <area, special - see page 29>

	Standard	Scientific
square centimeter	4,773.2	4.773 200 0E+03

square hvat [Yugoslavia]   <area, special - see page 29>

	Standard	Scientific
square meter	3.597	3.597 000 0E+00

square inch [based on US, survey foot]   <area>

	Standard	Scientific
circular centimeter	8.214 465 1	8.214 465 1E+00
circular foot [international]	0.008 842	8.841 976 7E-03
circular foot [US, survey]	0.008 841 9	8.841 941 3E-03
circular inch [based on US, survey foot]	1.273 239 5	1.273 239 5E+00
circular inch [international]	1.273 244 6	1.273 244 6E+00
circular mil	1,273,244.6	1.273 244 6E+06
square caliber	10,000.04	1.000 004 0E+04
square centimeter	6.451 625 8	6.451 625 8E+00
square foot [international]	0.006 944 5	6.944 472 2E-03
square foot [US, survey]	0.006 944 4	6.944 444 4E-03
square inch [international]	1.000 004	1.000 004 0E+00
square link [Gunter or US, survey]	0.015 942 3	1.594 225 1E-02
square link [Ramden or Engineer]	0.006 944 4	6.944 444 4E-03
square meter	0.000 645 2	6.451 625 8E-04
square vara [US, survey, California]	0.000 918 3	9.182 736 5E-04
square vara [US, survey, Texas]	0.000 9	9.000 000 0E-04
square yard [based on US, survey foot]	0.000 771 6	7.716 049 4E-04
square yard [international]	0.000 771 6	7.716 080 2E-04

square inch [international]   <area>

	Standard	Scientific
base box [for tin-plated steel sheet]	0.000 031 9	3.188 775 5E-05
circular centimeter	8.214 432 2	8.214 432 2E+00
circular inch [based on US, survey foot]	1.273 234 5	1.273 234 5E+00
circular inch [international]	1.273 239 5	1.273 239 5E+00
circular mil	1,273,239.5	1.273 239 5E+06

	Standard	Scientific
circular millimeter	821.443 22	8.214 432 2E+02
square caliber	10,000	1.000 000 0E+04
square centimeter	6.451 6	6.451 600 0E+00
square foot [international]	0.006 944 4	6.944 444 4E−03
square foot [US, survey]	0.006 944 4	6.944 416 7E−03
square inch [based on US, survey foot]	0.999 996	9.999 960 0E−01
square link [Gunter or US, survey]	0.015 942 2	1.594 218 7E−02
square link [Ramden or Engineer]	0.006 944 4	6.944 416 7E−03
square meter	0.000 645 2	6.451 600 0E−04
square mil	1,000,000	1.000 000 0E+06
square millimeter	645.16	6.451 600 0E+02
square inch/day		**<kinematic viscosity>**
centistokes	0.007 467 1	7.467 129 6E−03
liter/centimeter day	0.006 451 6	6.451 600 0E−03
square centimeter/day	6.451 6	6.451 600 0E+00
square foot/day	0.006 944 4	6.944 444 4E−03
square inch/hour	0.041 666 7	4.166 666 7E−02
square meter/second	<<<	7.467 129 6E−09
square millimeter/hour	26.881 666 7	2.688 166 7E+01
square inch/hour		**<kinematic viscosity>**
centistokes	0.179 211 1	1.792 111 1E−01
liter/centimeter day	0.154 838 4	1.548 384 0E−01
square centimeter/hour	6.451 6	6.451 600 0E+00
square foot/day	0.166 666 7	1.666 666 7E−01
square inch/day	24	2.400 000 0E+01
square meter/second	0.000 000 2	1.792 111 1E−07
square millimeter/minute	10.752 666 7	1.075 266 7E+01
square inch/minute		**<kinematic viscosity>**
centistokes	10.752 666 7	1.075 266 7E+01
liter/centimeter day	9.290 304	9.290 304 0E+00
square centimeter/minute	6.451 6	6.451 600 0E+00
square foot/day	10	1.000 000 0E+01
square meter/second	0.000 010 8	1.075 266 7E−05
square millimeter/second	10.752 666 7	1.075 266 7E+01
square inch/pound-force		**<compressibility>**
1/pascal	0.000 145	1.450 377 4E−04
square centimeter/gram-force	0.014 223 3	1.422 334 3E−02
square foot/ton-force [-/long]	15.555 556	1.555 555 6E+01
square foot/ton-force [-/short]	13.888 889	1.388 889 9E+01
square inch/second		**<kinematic viscosity>**
liter/centimeter hour	23.225 76	2.322 576 0E+01
poise cubic centimeter/gram	6.451 6	6.451 600 0E+00
square foot/hour	25	2.500 000 0E+01
square inch/minute	60	6.000 000 0E+01
square meter/hour	2.322 576	2.322 576 0E+00
square meter/second	0.000 645 2	6.451 600 0E−04
stokes	6.451 6	6.451 600 0E+00
square jareeb [Pakistan]		**<area, special - see page 29>**
square meter	404.69	4.046 900 0E+02
square jemba [Malaysia]		**<area, special - see page 29>**
square meter	13.378 04	1.337 804 0E+01
square jemba [Singapore]		**<area, special - see page 29>**
square meter	13.378 04	1.337 804 0E+01
square kafiz [Iran]		**<area, special - see page 29>**
are	1	1.000 000 0E+00
square karam [Pakistan]		**<area, special - see page 29>**
square meter	2.81	2.810 000 0E+00
square kilometer		**<area>**
acre [commerical]	298.997 51	2.989 975 1E+02
acre [international]	247.105 38	2.471 053 8E+02

	Standard	Scientific
acre [US, survey]	247.104 39	2.471 043 9E+02
fan gong li [China]	1	1.000 000 0E+00
fermila [Iceland]	0.017 624 9	1.762 487 2E−02
hectare	100	1.000 000 0E+02
labor [US, survey]	1.394 966 7	1.394 966 7E+00
legua cuadrada [Paraguay]	0.053 276 5	5.327 650 5E−02
legua cuadrada [Uruguay]	0.037 594	3.759 398 5E−02
legua quadrada [Brazil]	0.022 935 8	2.293 578 0E−02
milha quadrada [Brazil]	0.206 611 6	2.066 115 7E−01
rood	988.417 57	9.884 175 7E+02
saltus [Rome, ancient]	0.496 771	4.967 709 1E−01
section [Canada]	0.386 100 4	3.861 003 9E−01
section [US, survey]	0.386 100 6	3.861 006 1E−01
sitio de ganado mayor [Mexico]	0.056 960 6	5.696 058 3E−02
square arpent [US, survey]	292.490 06	2.924 900 6E+02
square cable length [US, survey]	20.763 633	2.076 363 3E+01
square chain [Gunter or US, survey]	2,471.043 9	2.471 043 9E+03
square chain [Ramden or Engineer]	1,076.386 7	1.076 386 7E+03
square furlong [US, survey]	24.710 439	2.471 043 9E+01
square league [US, statute]	0.042 900 1	4.290 006 8E−02
square lieue [Switzerland]	0.043 402 8	4.340 277 8E−02
square meile [Hungary]	0.014 330 1	1.433 013 8E−02
square meter	1,000,000	1.000 000 0E+06
square mile [international]	0.386 102 2	3.861 021 6E−01
square mile [US, statute]	0.386 100 6	3.861 006 1E−01
square mile [US, survey]	0.386 100 6	3.861 006 1E−01
square myriameter	0.01	1.000 000 0E−02
square ri [Japan]	0.064 836 3	6.483 625 3E−02
suerte [Uruguay]	0.050 200 8	5.020 080 3E−02
township [US, survey]	0.010 725	1.072 501 7E−02

square lanca [Cape Verde] <area, special - see page 29>

	Standard	Scientific
square meter	19.36	1.936 000 0E+01

square league [nautical] <area>

	Standard	Scientific
square foot [international]	>>>	3.322 726 1E+08
square foot [US, survey]	>>>	3.322 712 9E+08
square furlong [US, survey]	762.789 91	7.627 899 1E+02
square league [US, statute]	1.324 288	1.324 288 0E+00
square meter	>>>	3.086 913 6E+07
square mile [international]	11.918 64	1.191 864 0E+01
square mile [international nautical]	9	9.000 000 0E+00
square mile [US, nautical]	9	9.000 000 0E+00
square mile [US, survey]	11.918 592	1.191 859 2E+01
square myriameter	0.308 691 4	3.086 913 6E−01

square league [US, statute] <area>

	Standard	Scientific
acre [commerical]	6,969.627 9	6.969 627 9E+03
acre [international]	5,760.023	5.760 023 0E+03
acre [US, survey]	5,760	5.760 000 0E+03
hectare	2,330.998 6	2.330 998 6E+03
labor [US, survey]	32.516 653	3.251 665 3E+01
section [US, survey]	9	9.000 000 0E+00
square chain [Gunter or US, survey]	57,600	5.760 000 0E+04
square chain [Ramden or Engineer]	25,090.56	2.509 056 0E+04
square foot [international]	>>>	2.509 066 0E+08
square foot [US, survey]	>>>	2.509 056 0E+08
square furlong [US, survey]	576	5.760 000 0E+02
square league [nautical]	0.755 122 7	7.551 227 3E−01
square meter	>>>	2.330 998 6E+07
square mile [international]	9.000 036	9.000 036 0E+00
square mile [US, statute]	9	9.000 000 0E+00
square mile [US, survey]	9	9.000 000 0E+00
square perch [US, survey]	921,600	9.216 000 0E+05
square yard [based on US, survey foot]	>>>	2.787 840 0E+07
square yard [international]	>>>	2.787 851 2E+07

Convert From Convert To	Standard	<Type of Unit> Scientific
township [US, survey]---	0.25----	2.500 000 0E-01
square lieue [Switzerland]		**<area, special - see page 29>**
square kilometer--	23.04----	2.304 000 0E+01
square light year		**<area>**
square astronomical unit--	>>>----	3.999 433 5E+09
square bevameter --	>>>----	8.950 541 2E+13
square meter--	>>>----	8.950 541 2E+31
square mile [international]---------------------------------------	>>>----	3.455 823 3E+25
square mile [US, statute]--	>>>----	3.455 809 5E+25
square mile [US, survey]--	>>>----	3.455 809 5E+25
square parsec---	0.094 004 4----	9.400 438 0E-02
square petameter--	89.505 412----	8.950 541 2E+01
square linija [Russia]		**<area, special - see page 29>**
square millimeter---	6.451 6----	6.451 600 0E+00
square link [Gunter or US, survey]		**<area>**
circular foot [international] --------------------------------------	0.554 625 4----	5.546 253 6E-01
circular foot [US, survey]---------------------------------------	0.554 623 2----	5.546 231 5E-01
circular inch [based on US, survey foot] --------------------------	79.865 733----	7.986 573 3E+01
circular inch [international]--------------------------------------	79.866 052----	7.986 605 2E+01
square chain [Gunter or US, survey]------------------------------	0.000 1----	1.000 000 0E-04
square chain [Ramden or Engineer] ------------------------------	0.000 043 5----	4.356 017 4E-05
square foot [international]---------------------------------------	0.435 601 7----	4.356 017 4E-01
square foot [US, survey]--	0.435 6----	4.356 000 0E-01
square inch [based on US, survey foot]----------------------------	62.726 4----	6.272 640 0E+01
square inch [international] --------------------------------------	62.726 651----	6.272 665 1E+01
square link [Ramden or Engineer] -------------------------------	0.435 6----	4.356 000 0E-01
square meter --	0.040 468 7----	4.046 872 6E-02
square mile [international] --------------------------------------	<<<----	1.562 506 3E-08
square mile [US, statute]--	<<<----	1.562 500 0E-08
square mile [US, survey]--	<<<----	1.562 500 0E-08
square perch [US, survey]---------------------------------------	0.001 6----	1.600 000 0E-03
square yard [based on US, survey foot]----------------------------	0.048 4----	4.840 000 0E-02
square yard [international]---------------------------------------	0.048 400 2----	4.840 019 4E-02
square link [Ramden or Engineer]		**<area>**
circular foot [international] --------------------------------------	1.273 244 6----	1.273 244 6E+00
circular foot [US, survey]---------------------------------------	1.273 239 5----	1.273 239 5E+00
circular inch [based on US, survey foot] --------------------------	183.346 49----	1.833 464 9E+02
circular inch [international]--------------------------------------	183.347 23----	1.833 472 3E+02
square chain [Gunter or US, survey]------------------------------	0.000 229 6----	2.295 684 1E-04
square chain [Ramden or Engineer] ------------------------------	0.000 1----	1.000 000 0E-04
square foot [international]---------------------------------------	1.000 004----	1.000 004 0E+00
square foot [US, survey]--	1----	1.000 000 0E+00
square inch [based on US, survey foot]----------------------------	144----	1.440 000 0E+02
square inch [international] --------------------------------------	144.000 58----	1.440 005 8E+02
square link [Gunter or US, survey] ------------------------------	2.295 684 1----	2.295 684 1E+00
square meter --	0.092 903 4----	9.290 341 2E-02
square mile [international] --------------------------------------	<<<----	3.587 020 8E-08
square mile [US, statute]--	<<<----	3.587 006 4E-08
square mile [US, survey]--	<<<----	3.587 006 4E-08
square yard [based on US, survey foot]----------------------------	0.111 111 1----	1.111 111 1E-01
square yard [international]---------------------------------------	0.111 111 6----	1.111 115 6E-01
square megameter		**<area>**
acre [commerical]---	>>>----	2.989 975 1E+08
acre [international]--	>>>----	2.471 053 8E+08
acre [US, survey]---	>>>----	2.471 043 9E+08
hectare--	>>>----	1.000 000 0E+08
labor [US, survey]--	1,394,966.7----	1.394 966 7E+06
rood--	>>>----	9.884 175 7E+08
section [US, survey]---	386,100.61----	3.861 006 1E+05
square bevameter --	0.000 001----	1.000 000 0E-06
square meter --	>>>----	1.000 000 0E+12
square mile [international] --------------------------------------	386,102.16----	3.861 021 6E+05

	Standard	Scientific
square mile [US, statute]	386,100.61	3.861 006 1E+05
square mile [US, survey]	386,100.61	3.861 006 1E+05
township [US, survey]	10,725,017	1.072 501 7E+04
square meile [Hungary]	\<area, special - see page 29\>	
square kilometer	69.783	6.978 300 0E+01
square meter	\<permeability, water\>	
darcy [20 °C]	>>>	1.013 250 0E+12
kilogram meter/pascal square second	1	1.000 000 0E+00
millidarcy [20 °C]	>>>	1.013 250 0E+15
perm [20 °C]	>>>	4.452 873 0E+08
square meter	\<sound absorption\>	
open window unit	10.763 91	1.076 391 0E+01
sabin	10.763 91	1.076 391 0E+01
sound absorption unit	10.763 91	1.076 391 0E+01
square-foot unit of absorption	10.763 91	1.076 391 0E+01
square-foot meter	\<area\>	
acre [commerical]	0.000 299	2.989 975 1E-04
acre [international]	0.000 247 1	2.471 053 8E-04
acre [US, survey]	0.000 247 1	2.471 043 9E-04
actus simplex [Rome, ancient]	0.023 753	2.375 296 9E-02
aftari [Morocco]	0.001 111 1	1.111 111 1E-03
album [Denmark]	0.017 403 1	1.740 310 8E-02
anna [Pakistan]	0.059 304 9	5.930 494 6E-02
are	0.01	1.000 000 0E-02
aroura [Egypt, ancient]	0.000 491 4	4.914 222 3E-04
base box [for tin-plated steel sheet]	0.049 426 1	4.942 611 9E-02
beit sea [Hebrew, ancient]	0.001 351 4	1.351 351 4E-03
besana [Cuba]	0.000 386 3	3.862 838 3E-04
beswa [Afghanistan]	0.010 245 9	1.024 590 2E-02
bin [Taiwan]	0.302 480 3	3.024 803 4E-01
bing fang kung chih [Taiwan]	1	1.000 000 0E+00
braca quadrada [Brazil]	0.206 611 6	2.066 115 7E-01
bu [Japan]	0.302 480 3	3.024 803 4E-01
cadastral denum [Lebanon]	0.001	1.000 000 0E-03
cantero [Ecuador]	0.002 267 6	2.267 573 7E-03
cao [Vietnam]	0.002 777 8	2.777 777 8E-03
carree [France]	0.019 580 2	1.958 020 1E-02
catta [India]	0.014 949 9	1.494 987 6E-02
centiare	1	1.000 000 0E+00
chast [Russia]	0.026 315 8	2.631 578 9E-02
chattak [India]	0.239 198	2.391 980 1E-01
ching [China]	0.088 960 1	8.896 005 7E-02
chuo [China]	0.005 930 5	5.930 494 6E-03
circular foot [international]	13.705 036	1.370 503 6E+01
circular foot [US, survey]	13.704 982	1.370 498 2E+01
circular inch [based on US, survey foot]	1,973.517 3	1.973 517 3E+03
circular inch [international]	1,973.525 2	1.973 525 2E+03
clima [Rome, ancient]	0.003 174 6	3.174 603 2E-03
cong [Vietnam]	0.001	1.000 000 0E-03
cordel cuadrado [Cuba]	0.002 414 3	2.414 292 6E-03
courd [Morocco]	0.002 222 2	2.222 222 2E-03
cuadra [El Salvador]	0.014 233 3	1.423 325 5E-02
cuadra cuadrada [Uruguay]	0.000 135 5	1.355 013 6E-04
cuartilla [Venezuela]	0.01	1.000 000 0E-02
daneq [Egypt]	0.034 279 4	3.427 944 6E-02
dau chung [Hong Kong]	0.001 482 6	1.482 579 7E-03
decempeda quadrata [Rome, ancient]	0.114 155 3	1.141 552 5E-01
denum [Cyprus]	0.000 747 5	7.474 958 7E-04
denum [Syria]	0.001 25	1.250 000 0E-03
deunam [Near East]	0.000 4	4.000 000 0E-04
deunam [Cyprus]	0.000 747 5	7.474 958 7E-04
deunam [Middle East]	0.001 088 1	1.088 139 3E-03

square meter (continued)

<area>

	Standard	Scientific
dhur [Nepal]	0.059 070 2	5.907 023 5E-02
donum [Cyprus]	0.000 747 5	7.474 958 9E-04
donum [Israel]	0.001	1.000 000 0E-03
donum [Jordan]	0.001	1.000 000 0E-03
donum [Lebanon]	0.001 088 1	1.088 139 3E-03
donum [Libya]	0.001 088 1	1.088 139 3E-03
donum [Syria]	0.001 088 1	1.088 139 3E-03
donum [Turkey]	0.001 088 1	1.088 139 3E-03
donum [Yugoslavia]	0.001 428 6	1.428 571 4E-03
dulum [Cyprus]	0.000 747 5	7.474 958 9E-04
dulum [Israel]	0.001	1.000 000 0E-03
dulum [Jordan]	0.001	1.000 000 0E-03
dulum [Lebanon]	0.001 088 1	1.088 139 3E-03
dulum [Libya]	0.001 088 1	1.088 139 3E-03
dulum [Syria]	0.001 088 1	1.088 139 3E-03
dulum [Turkey]	0.001 088 1	1.088 139 3E-03
dulum [Yugoslavia]	0.001	1.000 000 0E-03
dunam [Cyprus]	0.000 747 5	7.474 958 9E-04
dunam [Israel]	0.001	1.000 000 0E-03
dunam [Jordan]	0.001	1.000 000 0E-03
dunam [Lebanon]	0.001 088 1	1.088 139 3E-03
dunam [Libya]	0.001 088 1	1.088 139 3E-03
dunam [Syria]	0.001 088 1	1.088 139 3E-03
dunam [Turkey]	0.001 088 1	1.088 139 3E-03
dunum [Cyprus]	0.000 747 5	7.474 958 9E-04
dunum [Israel]	0.001	1.000 000 0E-03
dunum [Jordan]	0.001	1.000 000 0E-03
dunum [Lebanon]	0.001 088 1	1.088 139 3E-03
dunum [Libya]	0.001 088 1	1.088 139 3E-03
dunum [Syria]	0.001 088 1	1.088 139 3E-03
dunum [Turkey]	0.001 088 1	1.088 139 3E-03
dunum [Yugoslavia]	0.001	1.000 000 0E-03
erlek [Cyprus]	0.002 99	2.989 975 5E-03
estadal [Nicaragua]	0.088 652 5	8.865 248 2E-02
estadal [Spain]	0.089 445 4	8.944 543 8E-02
estodal [Spain]	0.089 447	8.944 703 7E-02
evieh [Turkey]	0.001	1.000 000 0E-03
evlek [Cyprus]	0.002 989 5	2.989 536 6E-03
evlek [Turkey]	6.944 444 4	6.944 444 4E+00
fan mi [China]	1	1.000 000 0E+00
fanega [Peru]	0.000 153	1.529 987 8E-04
fanegada [Spain]	0.000 156 3	1.562 500 0E-04
feralin [Iceland]	2.538 006 6	2.538 006 6E+00
ferfathmur [Iceland]	0.282 007 9	2.820 079 0E-01
ferfet [Iceland]	10.152 284	1.015 228 4E+01
feun [China]	0.025	2.500 000 0E-02
fjerdingkar [Denmark]	0.005 801 1	5.801 069 7E-03
gadula [Libya]	0.081 632 7	8.163 265 3E-02
gang [Vietnam]	25	2.500 000 0E+01
garmida [Hebrew, ancient]	3.333 333 3	3.333 333 3E+00
gereeb [Afghanistan]	0.000 512 3	5.122 950 8E-04
ghe [Vietnam]	6.25	6.250 000 0E+00
gin [Iraq, ancient]	4	4.000 000 0E+00
go [Japan]	3.024 986 4	3.024 986 4E+00
gradula [Libya]	0.081 632 7	8.163 265 3E-02
guntha [Pakistan]	0.009 884 4	9.884 353 1E-03
habba [Egypt]	0.017 139 7	1.713 972 3E-02
hectare	0.000 1	1.000 000 0E-04
hout [Netherlands]	0.000 703 6	7.035 812 3E-04
iugerum [Rome, ancient]	0.000 396 3	3.963 064 2E-04
jabia [Libya]	0.000 816 3	8.163 265 3E-04
jak [South Korea]	30.249 864	3.024 986 4E+01

square meter (continued) \<area\>

	Standard	Scientific
jemba [Malaysia]	0.074 749 6	7.474 958 9E-02
jemba [Singapore]	0.074 749 6	7.474 958 9E-02
jirib [Afghanistan]	0.512 295 1	5.122 950 8E-01
kanal [Pakistan]	0.001 976 8	1.976 831 5E-03
kannland [Sweden]	0.022 686	2.268 602 5E-02
kappland [Sweden]	0.006 482 4	6.482 435 8E-03
kassabe [Syria]	0.041 992 1	4.199 210 5E-02
katha [Bangladesh]	0.014 836 8	1.483 679 5E-02
kattha [Nepal]	0.002 953 6	2.953 599 0E-03
kejla [Malta]	0.053 376	5.337 603 4E-02
khau [Vietnam]	6.25	6.250 000 0E+00
kirat [Egypt]	0.005 713 3	5.713 306 3E-03
kirat [Egypt, ancient]	0.005 713 1	5.713 143 1E-03
koltuk [Turkey]	0.675 675 7	6.756 756 8E-01
kvadratfot [Sweden]	11.344 274	1.134 427 4E+01
kvadratni khvat [Yugoslavia]	0.278 040 4	2.780 403 7E-01
labor [Canada]	0.001 395 1	1.395 089 3E-03
labor [US, survey]	0.000 001 4	1.394 966 7E-06
lekha [Bulgaria]	0.004 351 6	4.351 610 1E-03
lelong [Malaysia]	0.004 484 9	4.484 908 3E-03
lelong [Singapore]	0.004 484 9	4.484 908 3E-03
lino [Paraguay]	0.013 315 6	1.331 557 9E-02
litro [Venezuela]	0.001 6	1.600 000 0E-03
marasseh [Lebanon]	0.02	2.000 000 0E-02
marla [India]	0.006 090 1	6.090 134 0E-03
marla [Pakistan]	0.039 536 6	3.953 663 1E-02
matomana [Nepal]	1.257 861 6	1.257 861 6E+00
matomuri [Nepal]	0.007 862 9	7.862 871 5E-03
matopathi [Nepal]	0.157 257 4	1.572 574 3E-01
maz [Macao]	0.001 313 4	1.313 370 1E-03
mecate [British Honduras]	0.001 915 7	1.915 708 8E-03
medida [Venezuela]	0.001 6	1.600 000 0E-03
merice [Czechoslovakia]	0.521 376 4	5.213 764 3E-01
merrassi [Syria]	0.02	2.000 000 0E-02
mesana [Cuba]	0.000 386 3	3.862 838 3E-04
mieng [Vietnam]	0.027 777 8	2.777 777 8E-02
moreas stremma [Greece, ancient]	0.000 787 4	7.874 015 7E-04
motyka [Yugoslavia]	0.001 25	1.250 000 0E-03
moud [Morocco]	0.002 222 2	2.222 222 2E-03
mow [Hong Kong]	0.001 186 5	1.186 521 1E-03
myo [South Korea]	0.010 083 3	1.008 331 8E-02
ngan [Laos]	0.002 5	2.500 000 0E-03
ngan [Thailand]	0.002 5	2.500 000 0E-03
ngane [Laos]	0.002 5	2.500 000 0E-03
ngane [Thailand]	0.002 5	2.500 000 0E-03
o [Vietnam]	6.25	6.250 000 0E+00
olc [Iraq]	0.01	1.000 000 0E-02
onca [Cape Verde]	0.000 860 9	8.608 815 4E-04
palmo cuadrada [Macao]	20.661 157	2.066 115 7E+01
parcela [Puerto Rico]	0.001 017 7	1.017 708 1E-03
pe cuadrada [Macao]	9.182 736 5	9.182 736 5E+00
perch [Canada, Quebec]	0.029 248 3	2.924 831 8E-02
perche [Canada, Quebec]	0.029 248 3	2.924 831 8E-02
perche [France]	0.019 580 2	1.958 020 1E-02
pes quadratus [Rome, ancient]	11.415 525	1.141 552 5E+01
phan [Vietnam]	4.166 666 7	4.166 666 7E+00
pic [Cyprus]	0.044 849 6	4.484 962 6E-02
pic carre [Egypt]	1.777 777 8	1.777 777 8E+00
pou [China]	0.598 802 4	5.988 024 0E-01
pu [Macao]	0.315 208 8	3.152 088 3E-01
pyong [North Korea]	0.302 5	3.025 000 0E-01
pyong [South Korea]	0.302 480 3	3.024 803 4E-01

square meter (continued) **\<area>**

	Standard	Scientific
pyung [South Korea]	0.302 499 6	3.024 995 5E-01
qasba kwadra [Malta and Gozo]	0.227 732 3	2.277 323 3E-01
qassabeh [Lebanon]	0.041 992 1	4.199 210 5E-02
qirat [Egypt]	0.005 713 3	5.713 306 3E-03
quadrat [Germany]	0.070 521 9	7.052 186 2E-02
quarteron [France]	0.000 929 4	9.293 680 3E-04
rabia [Morocco]	0.002 222 2	2.222 222 2E-03
rood	0.000 988 4	9.884 175 7E-04
ropani [Nepal]	0.010 632 6	1.063 264 2E-02
saa [Morocco]	0.001 111 1	1.111 111 1E-03
sahm [Egypt]	0.137 115 9	1.371 159 0E-01
sahme [Egypt]	0.137 174 2	1.371 742 1E-01
sahtout [Egypt]	3.290 772 7	3.290 772 7E+00
sao [Vietnam]	0.002 777 8	2.777 777 8E-03
sar [Iraq, ancient]	0.066 666 7	6.666 666 7E-02
scala [Cyprus]	0.000 747 5	7.474 958 9E-04
scala [Israel]	0.001	1.000 000 0E-03
scala [Jordan]	0.001	1.000 000 0E-03
scala [Lebanon]	0.001 088 1	1.088 139 3E-03
scala [Libya]	0.001 088 1	1.088 139 3E-03
scala [Syria]	0.001 088 1	1.088 139 3E-03
scala [Turkey]	0.001 088 1	1.088 139 3E-03
scala [Yugoslavia]	0.001	1.000 000 0E-03
scruple [Rome, ancient]	0.114 416 5	1.144 164 8E-01
scrupulum [Rome, ancient]	0.114 155 3	1.141 552 5E-01
se [Japan]	0.010 083 3	1.008 328 8E-02
section [US, survey]	0.000 000 4	3.861 006 1E-07
shaku [Japan]	30.249 864	3.024 986 4E+01
shih fen [China]	0.015	1.500 000 0E-02
shih hao [China]	1.5	1.500 000 0E+00
shih li [China]	0.15	1.500 000 0E-01
siegh [Malta]	0.005 337 5	5.337 489 5E-03
skaepper [Denmark]	0.001 450 3	1.450 267 4E-03
solar [Costa Rica]	0.001 144 7	1.144 688 6E-03
solar [Ecuador]	0.000 566 9	5.668 934 2E-04
spannland [Sweden]	0.000 405 2	4.051 519 1E-04
square	0.107 639 1	1.076 391 0E-01
square [Sri Lanka]	0.011 960 3	1.196 029 2E-02
square aldan [Mongolia]	0.390 625	3.906 250 0E-01
square alen [Denmark]	2.537 968	2.537 968 0E+00
square angstrom	>>>	1.000 000 0E+20
square archine [Russia]	1.977 044 9	1.977 044 9E+00
square arpent [US, survey]	0.000 292 5	2.924 900 6E-04
square astronomical unit	<<<	4.468 370 5E-23
square baa [Saudi Arabia]	0.355 831 7	3.558 317 4E-01
square barleycorn	13,950.028	1.395 002 8E+04
square bevameter	<<<	1.000 000 0E-18
square bicron	>>>	1.000 000 0E+24
square braca [Cape Verde]	0.206 611 6	2.066 115 7E-01
square cable length [US, survey]	0.000 020 8	2.076 363 3E-05
square caliber	>>>	1.550 003 1E+07
square cape rood [Swaziland]	0.070 050 1	7.005 008 6E-02
square cassaba [Iraq, ancient]	0.069 444 4	6.944 444 4E-02
square chain [Gunter or US, survey]	0.002 471	2.471 043 9E-03
square chain [Ramden or Engineer]	0.001 076 4	1.076 386 7E-03
square chok [South Korea]	10.890 043	1.089 004 3E+01
square cordel [Cuba]	0.002 414 3	2.414 269 3E-03
square cubit [Egypt, ancient]	3.636 363 6	3.636 363 6E+00
square cubit	4.783 960 2	4.783 960 2E+00
square depa [Malaysia]	0.298 953 7	2.989 536 6E-01
square depa [Singapore]	0.298 953 7	2.989 536 6E-01
square digit	2,755.561 1	2.755 561 1E+03

square meter (continued) \<area\>

square diraa meman [Egypt, ancient]	1.777 777 8	1.777 777 8E+00
square dra maghmari [Syria]	1.739 130 4	1.739 130 4E+00
square estado [Spain]	0.089 429 4	8.942 944 0E-02
square fathom [US, survey]	0.298 996 3	2.989 963 2E-01
square food [Luxembourg, hide processing]	3.280 839 9	3.280 839 9E+00
square foot [international]	10.763 91	1.076 391 0E+01
square foot [US, survey]	10.763 867	1.076 386 7E+01
square furlong [US, survey]	0.000 024 7	2.471 043 9E-05
square fut [Russia]	10.763 91	1.076 391 0E+01
square gaz gereeb [Afghanistan]	1.841 620 6	1.841 620 6E+00
square gaz memar [Afghanistan]	1.424 501 4	1.424 501 4E+00
square gaz sha [Afghanistan]	0.880 281 7	8.802 816 9E-01
square gazi jerib [Afghanistan]	1.842 978 3	1.842 978 3E+00
square guz [Iran]	0.925 925 9	9.259 259 3E-01
square hvat [Yugoslavia]	0.278 009 5	2.780 094 5E-01
square inch [based on US, survey foot]	1.549.996 9	1.549 996 9E+03
square inch [international]	1.550.003 1	1.550 003 1E+03
square jareeb [Pakistan]	0.002 471	2.471 027 2E-03
square jemba [Malaysia]	0.074 749 4	7.474 936 5E-02
square jemba [Singapore]	0.074 749 4	7.474 936 5E-02
square karam [Pakistan]	0.355 871 9	3.558 718 9E-01
square lanca [Cape Verde]	0.051 652 9	5.165 289 3E-02
square league [nautical]	\<\<\<	3.239 481 7E-08
square league [US, statute]	\<\<\<	4.290 006 8E-08
square light year	\<\<\<	1.117 250 9E-32
square link [Gunter or US, survey]	24.710 439	2.471 043 9E+01
square link [Ramden or Engineer]	10.763 867	1.076 386 7E+01
square mile [international]	0.000 000 4	3.861 021 6E-07
square mile [international nautical]	0.000 000 3	2.915 533 5E-07
square mile [US, nautical]	0.000 000 3	2.915 533 5E-07
square mile [US, statute]	0.000 000 4	3.861 006 1E-07
square mile [US, survey]	0.000 000 4	3.861 006 1E-07
square mimar [Turkey]	1.739 130 4	1.739 130 4E+00
square Paris foot [Canada, Quebec]	9.478 673	9.478 673 0E+00
square parsec	\<\<\<	1.050 264 8E-33
square perch [Ireland]	0.024 408 1	2.440 810 3E-02
square perch [US, survey]	0.039 536 7	3.953 670 3E-02
square perche [France]	0.019 580 2	1.958 020 1E-02
square perche [Mauritius]	0.023 692 2	2.369 219 1E-02
square perche [Switzerland]	0.111 111 1	1.111 111 1E-01
square pes [Rome, ancient]	11.494 253	1.149 425 3E+01
square pic [Greece]	1.777 777 8	1.777 777 8E+00
square rod [Netherlands]	0.01	1.000 000 0E-02
square ruthe [Germany, Bavaria]	0.117 395 7	1.173 956 9E-01
square ruthe [Germany, Prussia]	0.070 497	7.049 700 4E-02
square ruthe [Germany, Wurttemberg]	0.121 836 8	1.218 368 1E-01
square sagene [Russia]	0.219 671 6	2.196 716 4E-01
square sajon [Russia]	0.219 683 7	2.196 836 6E-01
square sazhen [Russia]	0.219 780 2	2.197 802 2E-01
square stigma	\>\>\>	1.000 000 0E+24
square taim [India]	4.784 689	4.784 689 0E+00
square tenthmeter	\>\>\>	1.000 000 0E+20
square terameter	\<\<\<	1.000 000 0E-24
square vara [Canada]	1.394 700 1	1.394 700 1E+00
square vara [Colombia]	1.562 5	1.562 500 0E+00
square vara [Costa Rica]	1.430 615 2	1.430 615 2E+00
square vara [Cuba]	1.390 820 6	1.390 820 6E+00
square vara [El Salvador]	1.423 325 5	1.423 325 5E+00
square vara [Guatemala]	1.428 571 4	1.428 571 4E+00
square vara [Honduras]	1.434 257 2	1.434 257 2E+00
square vara [Nicaragua]	1.417 233 6	1.417 233 6E+00
square vara [Paraguay]	1.331 557 9	1.331 557 9E+00

square meter (continued) \<area\>

	Standard	Scientific
square wa [Thailand]	0.25	2.500 000 0E−01
square yard [based on US, survey foot]	1.195 985 3	1.195 985 3E+00
square yard [international]	1.195 99	1.195 990 0E+00
square zar [Iran]	0.925 925 9	9.259 259 3E−01
stt [Egypt, ancient]	0.000 365 6	3.656 307 1E−04
tac [Vietnam]	0.416 666 7	4.166 666 7E−01
talangva [Laos]	0.25	2.500 000 0E−01
tamna [Morocco]	0.004 444 4	4.444 444 4E−03
tan [South Korea]	0.001 008 3	1.008 328 8E−03
tarabiit [Morocco]	0.002 222 2	2.222 222 2E−03
tarang ngu [Thailand]	0.168 449 4	1.684 494 2E−01
tarang sao [Thailand]	0.018 716 4	1.871 642 7E−02
tarang sen [Thailand]	0.000 625	6.250 000 0E−04
tarang wah [Thailand]	0.25	2.500 000 0E−01
tarea [Cuba]	0.014 486 5	1.448 645 5E−02
tarea [Dominican Republic]	0.001 590 3	1.590 330 8E−03
tarefa [Brazil]	0.001 033 1	1.033 057 9E−03
tartous [Cyprus]	0.000 747 5	7.474 958 9E−04
tartous [Israel]	0.001	1.000 000 0E−03
tartous [Jordan]	0.001	1.000 000 0E−03
tartous [Lebanon]	0.001 088 1	1.088 139 3E−03
tartous [Libya]	0.001 088 1	1.088 139 3E−03
tartous [Syria]	0.001 088 1	1.088 139 3E−03
tartous [Turkey]	0.001 088 1	1.088 139 3E−03
tartous [Yugoslavia]	0.001	1.000 000 0E−03
task [British Honduras]	0.001 915 7	1.915 708 8E−03
tavola [Italy]	0.026 315 8	2.631 578 9E−02
than [Vietnam]	0.25	2.500 000 0E−01
thon [Vietnam]	0.416 666 7	4.166 666 7E−01
thuoc [Vietnam]	0.041 666 7	4.166 666 7E−02
tmen [Morocco]	0.001 111 1	1.111 111 1E−03
town lot [Sierra Leone]	0.002 870 3	2.870 346 5E−03
township [US, survey]	\<\<\<	1.072 501 7E−08
tsubo [Japan]	0.302 498 6	3.024 986 4E−01
ure [Mongolia]	0.001 085 1	1.085 069 4E−03
vara [Cape Verde]	0.826 446 3	8.264 462 8E−01
vara cuadrada [Argentina]	1.331 557 9	1.331 557 9E+00
vara cuadrada [Chile]	1.430 819 9	1.430 819 9E+00
vara cuadrada [Colombia]	1.562 5	1.562 500 0E+00
vara cuadrada [Costa Rica]	1.430 819 9	1.430 819 9E+00
vara cuadrada [Cuba]	1.562 5	1.562 500 0E+00
vara cuadrada [El Salvador]	1.428 979 7	1.428 979 7E+00
vara cuadrada [Honduras]	1.434 308 7	1.434 308 7E+00
vara cuadrada [Macao]	0.826 446 3	8.264 462 8E−01
vara cuadrada [Mexico]	1.424 014 6	1.424 014 6E+00
vara cuadrada [Nicaragua]	1.419 647 9	1.419 647 9E+00
vara cuadrada [Paraguay]	1.331 557 9	1.331 557 9E+00
vara cuadrada [Spain]	1.431 153 6	1.431 153 6E+00
vara cuadrada [Uruguay]	1.355 013 6	1.355 013 6E+00
vierkante duim [Netherlands]	10,000	1.000 000 0E+04
vierkante el [Netherlands]	1	1.000 000 0E+00
vierkante palm [Netherlands]	100	1.000 000 0E+02
vierkante roede [Netherlands]	0.01	1.000 000 0E−02
vierkante roede [Netherlands]	0.01	1.000 000 0E−02
xich [Vietnam]	0.041 666 7	4.166 666 7E−02

square meter °C/kilowatt \<thermal insulation coefficient\>

	Standard	Scientific
square centimeter second °C/calorie [-/ I.T.]	41.868	4.186 800 0E+01
square centimeter second °C/calorie [-/ thermoc.]	41.84	4.184 000 0E+01
square foot °C/watt	0.010 763 9	1.076 391 0E−02
square foot hour °F/Btu [-/ I.T.]	0.005 678 3	5.678 263 3E−03
square foot hour °F/Btu [-/ thermoc.]	0.005 674 5	5.674 464 5E−03

Convert From / Convert To	Standard	Scientific
square meter hour °C/kilocalorie [-/ I.T.]	0.001 163	1.163 000 0E-03
square meter kelvin/watt	0.001	1.000 000 0E-03
square meter °C/watt		**<thermal insulation coefficient>**
clo [for clothing]	6.451 612 9	6.451 612 9E+00
square centimeter second °C/calorie [-/ I.T.]	41,868	4.186 800 0E+04
square centimeter second °C/calorie [-/ thermoc.]	41,840	4.184 000 0E+04
square foot °C/watt	10.763 91	1.076 391 0E+01
square foot hour °F/Btu [-/ I.T.]	5.678 263 3	5.678 263 3E+00
square foot hour °F/Btu [-/ thermoc.]	5.674 464 5	5.674 464 5E+00
square meter °C/kilocalorie [-/ I.T.]	1.163	1.163 000 0E+00
square meter kelvin/watt	1	1.000 000 0E+00
tog [for clothing]	10	1.000 000 0E+01
square meter hour °C/kilocalorie [-/ I.T.]		**<thermal insulation coefficient>**
square centimeter second °C/calorie [-/ I.T.]	36,000	3.600 000 0E+04
square centimeter second °C/calorie [-/ thermoc.]	35,975.924	3.597 592 4E+04
square foot °C/watt	9.255 297	9.255 297 0E+00
square foot hour °F/Btu [-/ I.T.]	4.882 427 6	4.882 427 6E+00
square foot hour °F/Btu [-/ thermoc.]	4.879 161 2	4.879 161 2E+00
square meter kelvin/watt	0.859 845 2	8.598 452 3E-01
square meter hour °C/kilocalorie meter [-/ I.T.]		**<thermal resistivity>**
meter kelvin/watt	0.859 845 2	8.598 452 3E-01
square meter kelvin/kilowatt		**<thermal insulation coefficient>**
square centimeter second °C/calorie [-/ I.T.]	41,868	4.186 800 0E+01
square centimeter second °C/calorie [-/ thermoc.]	41.84	4.184 000 0E+01
square foot °C/watt	0.010 763 9	1.076 391 0E-02
square foot hour °F/Btu [-/ I.T.]	0.005 678 3	5.678 263 3E-03
square foot hour °F/Btu [-/ thermoc.]	0.005 674 5	5.674 464 5E-03
square meter hour °C/kilocalorie [-/ I.T.]	0.001 163	1.163 000 0E-03
square meter kelvin/watt	0.001	1.000 000 0E-03
square meter kelvin/watt		**<thermal insulation coefficient>**
clo [for clothing]	6.451 612 9	6.451 612 9E+00
square centimeter °C/watt	10,000	1.000 000 0E+04
square centimeter kelvin/watt	10,000	1.000 000 0E+04
square centimeter second °C/calorie [-/ I.T.]	41,868	4.186 800 0E+04
square centimeter second °C/calorie [-/ thermoc.]	41,840	4.184 000 0E+04
square foot °C/watt	10.763 91	1.076 391 0E+01
square foot hour °F/Btu [-/ I.T.]	5.678 263 3	5.678 263 3E+00
square foot hour °F/Btu [-/ thermoc.]	5.674 464 5	5.674 464 5E+00
square meter °C/kilowatt	1,000	1.000 000 0E+03
square meter °C/watt	1	1.000 000 0E+00
square meter hour °C/kilocalorie [-/ I.T.]	1.163	1.163 000 0E+00
square meter kelvin/kilowatt	1,000	1.000 000 0E+03
square meter second kelvin/joule	1	1.000 000 0E+00
tog [for clothing]	10	1.000 000 0E+01
square meter second kelvin/joule		**<thermal insulation coefficient>**
square centimeter second °C/calorie [-/ I.T.]	41,868	4.186 800 0E+04
square centimeter second °C/calorie [-/ thermoc.]	41,840	4.184 000 0E+04
square foot °C/watt	10.763 91	1.076 391 0E+01
square foot hour °F/Btu [-/ I.T.]	5.678 263 3	5.678 263 3E+00
square foot hour °F/Btu [-/ thermoc.]	5.674 464 5	5.674 464 5E+00
square meter °C/kilocalorie [-/ I.T.]	1.163	1.163 000 0E+00
square meter kelvin/watt	1	1.000 000 0E+00
square meter/cubic meter		**<area/unit volume>**
square foot/cubic foot	0.304 8	3.048 000 0E-01
square yard/cubic yard	0.914 4	9.144 000 0E-01
square meter/day		**<kinematic viscosity>**
centistokes	11.574 074 1	1.157 407 4E+01
liter/centimeter day	10	1.000 000 0E+01
poise cubic centimeter/gram	0.115 740 7	1.157 407 4E-01
square centimeter/minute	6.944 444 4	6.944 444 4E+00
square foot/day	10.763 910 4	1.076 391 0E+01

Convert From Convert To	Standard	<Type of Unit> Scientific
square inch/minute	1.076 391	1.076 391 0E+00
square meter/second	0.000 011 6	1.157 407 4E−05
square meter/hour		**<kinematic viscosity>**
liter/centimeter hour	10	1.000 000 0E+01
poise cubic centimeter/gram	2.777 777 8	2.777 777 8E+00
square centimeter/second	2.777 777 8	2.777 777 8E+00
square foot/hour	10.763 910 4	1.076 391 0E+01
square inch/minute	25.833 385	2.583 338 5E+01
square meter/second	0.000 277 8	2.777 777 8E−04
stokes	2.777 777 8	2.777 777 8E+00
square meter/joule		**<spectral cross-section>**
barn/electronvolt	>>>	1.602 177 3E+09
centimeter/dyne	0.001	1.000 000 0E−03
foot/pound-force	14.593 903	1.459 390 3E+01
meter/newton	1	1.000 000 0E+00
square second/kilogram	1	1.000 000 0E+00
square meter/kilogram		**<specific area>**
acre/pound	0.000 112 1	1.120 851 2E−04
hectare/kilogram	0.000 1	1.000 000 0E−04
square centimeter/gram	10	1.000 000 0E+01
square foot/pound	4.882 427 6	4.882 427 6E+00
square meter/kilogram-force		**<compressibility>**
1/pascal	0.101 971 6	1.019 716 2E−01
square foot/pound-force	4.882 427 6	4.882 427 6E+00
square foot/poundal	0.151 750 5	1.517 504 9E−01
square meter/kilopond	1	1.000 000 0E+00
square meter/kilopond		**<compressibility>**
1/pascal	0.101 971 6	1.019 716 2E−01
square foot/pound-force	4.882 427 6	4.882 427 6E+00
square foot/poundal	0.151 750 5	1.517 504 9E−01
square meter/kilogram-force	1	1.000 000 0E+00
square meter/minute		**<kinematic viscosity>**
liter/centimeter minute	10	1.000 000 0E+01
poise cubic centimeter/gram	166.666 667	1.666 666 7E+02
square centimeter/second	166.666 667	1.666 666 7E+02
square foot/minute	10.763 910 4	1.076 391 0E+01
square inch/second	25.833 385	2.583 338 5E+01
square meter/second	0.016 666 7	1.666 666 7E−02
stokes	166.666 667	1.666 666 7E+02
square meter/newton		**<compressibility>**
1/pascal	1	1.000 000 0E+00
square centimeter/dyne	0.1	1.000 000 0E−01
square foot/pound-force	47.880 259	4.788 025 9E+01
square foot/poundal	1.488 163 9	1.488 163 9E+00
square meter/kilogram-force	9.806 65	9.806 650 0E+00
square meter/pascal second		**<mobility>**
cubic foot second/pound	16.018 463	1.601 846 3E+01
cubic inch second/pound	27,679.905	2.767 990 5E+04
cubic meter second/kilogram	1	1.000 000 0E+00
square meter/second		**<kinematic viscosity>**
lentor	10,000	1.000 000 0E+04
liter/centimeter second	10	1.000 000 0E+01
poise cubic centimeter/gram	10,000	1.000 000 0E+04
square foot/second	10.763 910 4	1.076 391 0E+01
square inch/second	1,550.003 1	1.550 003 1E+03
square meter/minute	60	6.000 000 0E+01
stokes	10,000	1.000 000 0E+04
square meter/square second		**<dose equivalent>**
joule/kilogram	1	1.000 000 0E+00
newton meter/kilogram	1	1.000 000 0E+00
sievert	1	1.000 000 0E+00

square meter/volt second   \<9

	Standard	Scientific
square meter/weber	1	1.000 000 0E+00
square second ampere/kilogram	1	1.000 000 0E+00

square meter/weber   \<9

	Standard	Scientific
square meter/volt second	1	1.000 000 0E+00
square second ampere/kilogram	1	1.000 000 0E+00

square microinch   \<area\>

	Standard	Scientific
circular inch [based on US, survey foot]	<<<	1.273 234 5E-12
circular inch [international]	<<<	1.273 239 5E-12
circular microinch	1.273 239 5	1.273 239 5E+00
circular micrometer	0.000 821 4	8.214 432 2E-04
circular mil	0.000 001 3	1.273 239 5E-06
square angstrom	64,516	6.451 600 0E+04
square bicron	>>>	6.451 600 0E+08
square caliber	<<<	1.000 000 0E-08
square inch [based on US, survey foot]	<<<	9.999 960 0E-13
square inch [international]	<<<	1.000 000 0E-12
square micromicron	>>>	6.451 600 0E+08
square micron	0.000 645 2	6.451 600 0E-04
square mil	0.000 001	1.000 000 0E-06
square millimicron	645.16	6.451 600 0E+02
square nanometer	645.16	6.451 600 0E+02
square stigma	>>>	6.451 600 0E+08
square tenthmeter	64,516	6.451 600 0E+04
square thou	0.000 001	1.000 000 0E-06
square x-unit	>>>	6.424 944 9E+10

square micrometer   \<area\>

	Standard	Scientific
circular inch [based on US, survey foot]	<<<	1.973 517 3E-09
circular inch [international]	<<<	1.973 525 2E-09
circular microinch	1,973.525 2	1.973 525 2E+03
circular micrometer	1.273 239 5	1.273 239 5E+00
circular mil	0.001 973 5	1.973 525 2E-03
square angstrom	>>>	1.000 000 0E+08
square caliber	0.000 015 5	1.550 003 1E-05
square foot [international]	<<<	1.076 391 0E-11
square foot [US, survey]	<<<	1.076 386 7E-11
square inch [based on US, survey foot]	<<<	1.549 996 9E-09
square inch [international]	<<<	1.550 003 1E-09
square meter	<<<	1.000 000 0E-12
square microinch	1,550.003 1	1.550 003 1E+03
square micron	1	1.000 000 0E+00
square mil	0.001 55	1.550 003 1E-03
square millimicron	1,000,000	1.000 000 0E+06
square tenthmeter	>>>	1.000 000 0E+08
square thou	0.001 55	1.550 003 1E-03

square micromicron   \<area\>

	Standard	Scientific
barn	10,000	1.000 000 0E+04
circular microinch	<<<	1.973 525 2E-09
square angstrom	0.000 1	1.000 000 0E-04
square bicron	1	1.000 000 0E+00
square femtometer	1,000,000	1.000 000 0E+06
square fermi	1,000,000	1.000 000 0E+06
square meter	<<<	1.000 000 0E-24
square microinch	<<<	1.550 003 1E-09
square picometer	1	1.000 000 0E+00
square stigma	1	1.000 000 0E+00
square tenthmeter	0.000 1	1.000 000 0E-04
square x-unit	99.586 845	9.958 684 5E+01

square micron   \<area\>

	Standard	Scientific
circular microinch	1,973.525 2	1.973 525 2E+03
circular micrometer	1.273 239 5	1.273 239 5E+00
circular mil	0.001 973 5	1.973 525 2E-03

	Standard	Scientific
circular millimeter	0.000 001 3	1.273 239 5E–06
square angstrom	>>>	1.000 000 0E+08
square inch [based on US, survey foot]	<<<	1.549 996 9E–09
square inch [international]	<<<	1.550 003 1E–09
square meter	<<<	1.000 000 0E–12
square microinch	1,550.003 1	1.550 003 1E+03
square micrometer	1	1.000 000 0E+00
square mil	0.001 55	1.550 003 1E–03
square millimicron	1,000,000	1.000 000 0E+06
square tenthmeter	>>>	1.000 000 0E+08
square thou	0.001 55	1.550 003 1E–03

square mil \<area\>

	Standard	Scientific
circular centimeter	0.000 008 2	8.214 432 2E–06
circular inch [based on US, survey foot]	0.000 001 3	1.273 234 5E–06
circular inch [international]	0.000 001 3	1.273 239 5E–06
circular microinch	1,273,239.5	1.273 239 5E+06
circular micrometer	821.443 22	8.214 432 2E+02
circular mil	1.273 239 5	1.273 239 5E+00
square caliber	0.01	1.000 000 0E–02
square inch [based on US, survey foot]	0.000 001	9.999 960 0E–07
square inch [international]	0.000 001	1.000 000 0E–06
square meter	<<<	6.451 600 0E–10
square microinch	1,000,000	1.000 000 0E+06
square micrometer	645.16	6.451 600 0E+02
square micron	645.16	6.451 600 0E+02
square thou	1	1.000 000 0E+00

square mile [international nautical] \<area\>

	Standard	Scientific
acre [commerical]	1,025.532 8	1.025 532 8E+03
acre [international]	847.547 74	8.475 477 4E+02
acre [US, survey]	847.544 35	8.475 443 5E+02
hectare	342.990 4	3.429 904 0E+02
section [US, survey]	1.324 288	1.324 288 0E+00
square foot [international]	>>>	3.691 917 9E+07
square foot [US, survey]	>>>	3.691 903 2E+07
square kilometer	3.429 904	3.429 904 0E+00
square league [nautical]	0.111 111 1	1.111 111 1E–01
square league [US, statute]	0.147 143 1	1.471 431 2E–01
square meter	3,429,904	3.429 904 0E+06
square mile [international]	1.324 293 3	1.324 293 3E+00
square mile [US, nautical]	1	1.000 000 0E+00
square mile [US, statute]	1.324 288	1.324 288 0E+00
square mile [US, survey]	1.324 288	1.324 288 0E+00
square perch [US, survey]	135,607.1	1.356 071 0E+05
square yard [based on US, survey foot]	4,102,114.6	4.102 114 6E+06
square yard [international]	4,102,131	4.102 131 0E+06
township [US, survey]	0.036 785 8	3.678 577 9E–02

square mile [international] \<area\>

	Standard	Scientific
acre [commerical]	774.4	7.744 000 0E+02
acre [international]	640	6.400 000 0E+02
acre [US, survey]	639.997 44	6.399 974 4E+02
hectare	258.998 81	2.589 988 1E+02
labor [US, survey]	3.612 947	3.612 947 0E+00
section [US, survey]	0.999 996	9.999 960 0E–01
square arpent [US, survey]	757.545 77	7.575 457 7E+02
square chain [Gunter or US, survey]	6,399.974 4	6.399 974 4E+03
square chain [Ramden or Engineer]	2,787.828 8	2.787 828 8E+03
square foot [international]	>>>	2.787 840 0E+07
square foot [US, survey]	>>>	2.787 828 8E+07
square kilometer	2.589 988 1	2.589 988 1E+00
square league [US, statute]	0.111 110 7	1.111 106 7E–01
square meter	2,589,988.1	2.589 988 1E+06
square mile [US, statute]	0.999 996	9.999 960 0E–01
square mile [US, survey]	0.999 996	9.999 960 0E–01

	Standard	Scientific
square yard [based on US, survey foot]	3,097,587.6	3.097 587 6E+06
square yard [international]	3,097,600	3.097 600 0E+06
township [US, survey]	0.027 777 7	2.777 766 7E-02
square mile [US, nautical]		**\<area\>**
hectare	342.990 4	3.429 904 0E+02
square foot [international]	>>>	3.691 917 9E+07
square foot [US, survey]	>>>	3.691 903 2E+07
square kilometer	3.429 904	3.429 904 0E+00
square league [nautical]	0.111 111 1	1.111 111 1E-01
square league [US, statute]	0.147 143 1	1.471 431 2E-01
square meter	3,429,904	3.429 904 0E+06
square mile [international]	1.324 293 3	1.324 293 3E+00
square mile [international nautical]	1	1.000 000 0E+00
square mile [US, statute]	1.324 288	1.324 288 0E+00
square mile [US, survey]	1.324 288	1.324 288 0E+00
square mile [US, statute]		**\<area\>**
acre [commerical]	774.403 1	7.744 031 0E+02
acre [international]	640.002 56	6.400 025 6E+02
acre [US, survey]	640	6.400 000 0E+02
hectare	258.999 85	2.589 998 5E+02
labor [US, survey]	3.612 961 5	3.612 961 5E+00
section [US, survey]	1	1.000 000 0E+00
square chain [Gunter or US, survey]	6,400	6.400 000 0E+03
square chain [Ramden or Engineer]	2,787.84	2.787 840 0E+03
square furlong [US, survey]	64	6.400 000 0E+01
square kilometer	2.589 998 5	2.589 998 5E+00
square league [US, statute]	0.111 111 1	1.111 111 1E-01
square meter	2,589,998.5	2.589 998 5E+06
square mile [international]	1.000 004	1.000 004 0E+00
square mile [international nautical]	0.755 122 7	7.551 227 3E-01
square mile [US, nautical]	0.755 122 7	7.551 227 3E-01
square mile [US, survey]	1	1.000 000 0E+00
square yard [based on US, survey foot]	3,097,600	3.097 600 0E+06
square yard [international]	3,097,612.4	3.097 612 4E+06
township [US, survey]	0.027 777 8	2.777 777 8E-02
square mile [US, survey]		**\<area\>**
acre [commerical]	774.403 1	7.744 031 0E+02
acre [international]	640.002 56	6.400 025 6E+02
acre [US, survey]	640	6.400 000 0E+02
hectare	258.999 85	2.589 998 5E+02
labor [US, survey]	3.612 961 5	3.612 961 5E+00
rood	2,560	2.560 000 0E+03
section [US, survey]	1	1.000 000 0E+00
square chain [Gunter or US, survey]	6,400	6.400 000 0E+03
square chain [Ramden or Engineer]	2,787.84	2.787 840 0E+03
square foot [international]	>>>	2.787 851 2E+07
square foot [US, survey]	>>>	2.787 840 0E+07
square furlong [US, survey]	64	6.400 000 0E+01
square kilometer	2.589 998 5	2.589 998 5E+00
square meter	2,589,998.5	2.589 998 5E+06
square mile [international]	1.000 004	1.000 004 0E+00
square mile [international nautical]	0.755 122 7	7.551 227 3E-01
square mile [US, nautical]	0.755 122 7	7.551 227 3E-01
square mile [US, statute]	1	1.000 000 0E+00
square yard [based on US, survey foot]	3,097,600	3.097 600 0E+06
square yard [international]	3,097,612.4	3.097 612 4E+06
township [US, survey]	0.027 777 8	2.777 777 8E-02
square millimeter		**\<area\>**
circular inch [based on US, survey foot]	0.001 973 5	1.973 517 3E-03
circular inch [international]	0.001 973 5	1.973 525 2E-03
circular mil	1,973.525 2	1.973 525 2E+03
circular millimeter	1.273 239 5	1.273 239 5E+00

| Convert From | | <Type of Unit> |
Convert To	Standard	Scientific
linea cuadrada [Mexico]	0.265 752 5	2.657 524 8E-01
square caliber	15.500 031	1.550 003 1E+01
square foot [international]	0.000 010 8	1.076 391 0E-05
square foot [US, survey]	0.000 010 8	1.076 386 7E-05
square inch [based on US, survey foot]	0.001 55	1.549 996 9E-03
square inch [international]	0.001 55	1.550 003 1E-03
square linija [Russia]	0.155 000 3	1.550 003 1E-01
square meter	0.000 001	1.000 000 0E-06
square mil	1,550.003 1	1.550 003 1E+03
square thou	1,550.003 1	1.550 003 1E+03
square yard [based on US, survey foot]	0.000 001 2	1.195 985 3E-06
square yard [international]	0.000 001 2	1.195 990 0E-06
vierkante streep [Netherlands]	1	1.000 000 0E+00
square millimeter/day		**<kinematic viscosity>**
centistokes	0.000 011 6	1.157 407 4E-05
liter/centimeter day	0.000 01	1.000 000 0E-05
square centimeter/day	0.01	1.000 000 0E-02
square foot/day	0.000 010 8	1.076 391 0E-05
square inch/day	0.001 55	1.550 003 1E-03
square meter/day	0.000 001	1.000 000 0E-06
square meter/second	<<<	1.157 407 4E-11
stokes	0.000 000 1	1.157 407 4E-07
square millimeter/hour		**<kinematic viscosity>**
centistokes	0.000 277 8	2.777 777 8E-04
liter/centimeter day	0.000 24	2.400 000 0E-04
square centimeter/day	0.24	2.400 000 0E-01
square foot/day	0.000 258 3	2.583 338 5E-04
square inch/day	0.037 200 1	3.720 007 4E-02
square meter/second	<<<	2.777 777 8E-10
square millimeter/day	24	2.400 000 0E+01
square millimeter/minute		**<kinematic viscosity>**
centistokes	0.016 666 7	1.666 666 7E-02
liter/centimeter day	0.014 4	1.440 000 0E-02
square centimeter/day	14.4	1.440 000 0E+01
square foot/day	0.015 5	1.550 003 1E-02
square inch/day	2.232 004 5	2.232 004 5E+00
square meter/second	<<<	1.666 666 7E-08
square millimeter/second		**<kinematic viscosity>**
centistokes	1	1.000 000 0E+00
liter/centimeter day	0.864	8.640 000 0E-02
poise cubic centimeter/gram	0.01	1.000 000 0E-02
square centimeter/hour	36	3.600 000 0E+01
square foot/day	0.930 018 9	9.300 018 6E-01
square inch/hour	5.580 011 2	5.580 011 2E+00
square meter/day	0.000 001	1.000 000 0E-06
square millimeter/minute	60	6.000 000 0E+01
square millimicron		**<area>**
barn	>>>	1.000 000 0E+10
circular microinch	0.001 973 5	1.973 525 2E-03
circular micrometer	0.000 001 3	1.273 239 5E-06
circular mil	<<<	1.973 525 2E-09
square angstrom	100	1.000 000 0E+02
square bicron	1,000,000	1.000 000 0E+06
square caliber	<<<	1.550 003 1E-11
square fermi	>>>	1.000 000 0E+12
square meter	<<<	1.000 000 0E-18
square microinch	0.001 55	1.550 003 1E-03
square micromicron	1,000,000	1.000 000 0E+06
square micron	0.000 001	1.000 000 0E-06
square nanometer	1	1.000 000 0E+00
square stigma	1,000,000	1.000 000 0E+06
square tenthmeter	100	1.000 000 0E+02

	Standard	Scientific
square thou	<<<	1.550 003 1E−09
square x-unit	>>>	9.958 684 5E+07
square mimar [Turkey]	**<area, special - see page 29>**	
square meter	0.575	5.750 000 0E−01
square myriameter		**<area>**
acre [commerical]	29,899.751	2.989 975 1E+04
acre [international]	24,710.538	2.471 053 8E+04
acre [US, survey]	24,710.439	2.471 043 9E+04
hectare	10,000	1.000 000 0E+04
labor [US, survey]	139.496 67	1.394 966 7E+02
rood	98,841.757	9.884 175 7E+04
section [US, survey]	38.610 061	3.861 006 1E+01
square foot [international]	>>>	1.076 391 0E+09
square foot [US, survey]	>>>	1.076 386 7E+09
square kilometer	100	1.000 000 0E+02
square league [US, statute]	4.290 006 8	4.290 006 8E+00
square meter	>>>	1.000 000 0E+08
square mile [international]	38.610 216	3.861 021 6E+01
square mile [US, statute]	38.610 061	3.861 006 1E+01
square mile [US, survey]	38.610 061	3.861 006 1E+01
township [US, survey]	1.072 501 7	1.072 501 7E+00
square nanometer		**<area>**
barn	>>>	1.000 000 0E+10
circular microinch	0.001 973 5	1.973 525 2E−03
circular mil	<<<	1.973 525 2E−09
square angstrom	100	1.000 000 0E+02
square bicron	1,000,000	1.000 000 0E+06
square fermi	>>>	1.000 000 0E+12
square inch [based on US, survey foot]	<<<	1.549 996 9E−15
square inch [international]	<<<	1.550 003 1E−15
square meter	<<<	1.000 000 0E−18
square microinch	0.001 55	1.550 003 1E−03
square micromicron	1,000,000	1.000 000 0E+06
square micron	0.000 001	1.000 000 0E−06
square millimicron	1	1.000 000 0E+00
square stigma	1,000,000	1.000 000 0E+06
square tenthmeter	100	1.000 000 0E+02
square thou	<<<	1.550 003 1E−09
square x-unit	>>>	9.958 684 5E+07
square pace		**<area>**
circular foot [international]	7.957 747 2	7.957 747 2E+00
circular foot [US, survey]	7.957 715 3	7.957 715 3E+00
hectare	0.000 058 1	5.806 440 0E−05
square	0.062 5	6.250 000 0E−02
square cubit	2.777 777 8	2.777 777 8E+00
square foot [international]	6.25	6.250 000 0E+00
square foot [US, survey]	6.249 975	6.249 975 0E+00
square inch [based on US, survey foot]	899.996 4	8.999 964 0E+02
square inch [international]	900	9.000 000 0E+02
square link [Gunter or US, survey]	14.347 968	1.434 796 8E+01
square link [Ramden or Engineer]	6.249 975	6.249 975 0E+00
square meter	0.580 644	5.806 440 0E−01
square palm	100	1.000 000 0E+02
square pole [US, survey]	0.022 956 7	2.295 674 9E−02
square span	11.111 111	1.111 111 1E+01
square yard [based on US, survey foot]	0.694 441 7	6.944 416 7E−01
square yard [international]	0.694 444 4	6.944 444 4E−01
square palm		**<area>**
hectare	0.000 000 6	5.806 440 0E−07
square	0.000 625	6.250 000 0E−04
square barleycorn	81	8.100 000 0E+01
square caliber	90,000	9.000 000 0E+04

	Standard	Scientific
square cubit	0.027 777 8	2.777 777 8E-02
square digit	16	1.600 000 0E+01
square foot [international]	0.062 5	6.250 000 0E-02
square foot [US, survey]	0.062 499 8	6.249 975 0E-02
square inch [based on US, survey foot]	8.999 964	8.999 964 0E+00
square inch [international]	9	9.000 000 0E+00
square meter	0.005 806 4	5.806 440 0E-03
square mil	9,000,000	9.000 000 0E+06
square pace	0.01	1.000 000 0E-02
square span	0.111 111 1	1.111 111 1E-01
square thou	9,000,000	9.000 000 0E+06

square Paris foot [Canada, Quebec]   <area, special - see page 29>

	Standard	Scientific
square meter	0.105 5	1.055 000 0E-01

square parsec   <area>

	Standard	Scientific
square astronomical unit	>>>	4.254 518 2E+10
square bevameter	>>>	9.521 408 7E+14
square exameter	0.000 952 1	9.521 408 7E-04
square light year	10.637 802	1.063 780 2E+01
square meter	>>>	9.521 408 7E+32
square petameter	952.140 87	9.521 408 7E+02

square perch [Ireland]   <area, special - see page 29>

	Standard	Scientific
square meter	40.97	4.097 000 0E+01

square perch [US, survey]   <area>

	Standard	Scientific
acre [commerical]	0.007 562 5	7.562 530 3E-03
acre [international]	0.006 25	6.250 025 0E-03
acre [US, survey]	0.006 25	6.250 000 0E-03
hectare	0.002 529 3	2.529 295 4E-03
rood	0.025	2.500 000 0E-02
square	2.722 510 9	2.722 510 9E+00
square chain [Gunter or US, survey]	0.062 5	6.250 000 0E-02
square chain [Ramden or Engineer]	0.027 225	2.722 500 0E-02
square foot [international]	272.251 09	2.722 510 9E+02
square foot [US, survey]	272.25	2.722 500 0E+02
square furlong [US, survey]	0.000 625	6.250 000 0E-04
square link [Gunter or US, survey]	625	6.250 000 0E+02
square link [Ramden or Engineer]	272.25	2.722 500 0E+02
square meter	25.292 954	2.529 295 4E+01
square pole [US, survey]	1	1.000 000 0E+00
square rod [US, survey]	1	1.000 000 0E+00
square yard [based on US, survey foot]	30.25	3.025 000 0E+01
square yard [international]	30.250 121	3.025 012 1E+01

square perche [France]   <area, special - see page 29>

	Standard	Scientific
square meter	51.072	5.107 200 0E+01

square perche [Mauritius]   <area, special - see page 29>

	Standard	Scientific
square meter	42.208	4.220 800 0E+01

square perche [Switzerland]   <area, special - see page 29>

	Standard	Scientific
square meter	9	9.000 000 0E+00

square pes [Rome, ancient]   <area, special - see page 29>

	Standard	Scientific
square meter	0.087	8.700 000 0E-02

square petameter   <area>

	Standard	Scientific
square astronomical unit	>>>	4.468 370 5E+07
square bevameter	>>>	1.000 000 0E+12
square light year	0.011 172 5	1.117 250 9E-02
square meter	>>>	1.000 000 0E+30
square mile [international]	>>>	3.861 021 6E+23
square mile [US, statute]	>>>	3.861 006 1E+23
square mile [US, survey]	>>>	3.861 006 1E+23
square myriameter	>>>	1.000 000 0E+22
square parsec	0.001 050 3	1.050 264 8E-03

square pic [Greece]   <area, special - see page 29>

	Standard	Scientific
square meter	0.562 5	5.625 000 0E-01

square picometer <area>

barn	10,000	1.000 000 0E+04
circular microinch	<<<	1.973 525 2E-09
square angstrom	0.000 1	1.000 000 0E-04
square bicron	1	1.000 000 0E+00
square fermi	1,000,000	1.000 000 0E+06
square meter	<<<	1.000 000 0E-24
square microinch	<<<	1.550 003 1E-09
square micromicron	1	1.000 000 0E+00
square mil	<<<	1.550 003 1E-15
square millimicron	0.000 001	1.000 000 0E-06
square stigma	1	1.000 000 0E+00
square tenthmeter	0.000 1	1.000 000 0E-04
square thou	<<<	1.550 003 1E-15
square x-unit	99.586 845	9.958 684 5E+01

square pole [US, survey] <area>

acre [commerical]	0.007 562 5	7.562 530 3E-03
acre [international]	0.006 25	6.250 025 0E-03
acre [US, survey]	0.006 25	6.250 000 0E-03
hectare	0.002 529 3	2.529 295 4E-03
rood	0.025	2.500 000 0E-02
square	2.722 510 9	2.722 510 9E+00
square chain [Gunter or US, survey]	0.062 5	6.250 000 0E-02
square chain [Ramden or Engineer]	0.027 225	2.722 500 0E-02
square foot [international]	272.251 09	2.722 510 9E+02
square foot [US, survey]	272.25	2.722 500 0E+02
square link [Gunter or US, survey]	625	6.250 000 0E+02
square link [Ramden or Engineer]	272.25	2.722 500 0E+02
square meter	25.292 954	2.529 295 4E+01
square perch [US, survey]	1	1.000 000 0E+00
square rod [US, survey]	1	1.000 000 0E+00
square vara [US, survey, California]	36	3.600 000 0E+01
square vara [US, survey, Texas]	35.283 6	3.528 360 0E+01
square yard [based on US, survey foot]	30.25	3.025 000 0E+01
square yard [international]	30.250 121	3.025 012 1E+01

square ri [Japan] <area, special - see page 29>

square kilometer	15.423 47	1.542 347 0E+01

square rod [Netherlands] <area, special - see page 29>

square meter	100	1.000 000 0E+02

square rod [US, survey] <area>

acre [commerical]	0.007 562 5	7.562 530 3E-03
acre [international]	0.006 25	6.250 025 0E-03
acre [US, survey]	0.006 25	6.250 000 0E-03
hectare	0.002 529 3	2.529 295 4E-03
rood	0.025	2.500 000 0E-02
square	2.722 510 9	2.722 510 9E+00
square chain [Gunter or US, survey]	0.062 5	6.250 000 0E-02
square chain [Ramden or Engineer]	0.027 225	2.722 500 0E-02
square foot [international]	272.251 09	2.722 510 9E+02
square foot [US, survey]	272.25	2.722 500 0E+02
square link [Gunter or US, survey]	625	6.250 000 0E+02
square link [Ramden or Engineer]	272.25	2.722 500 0E+02
square meter	25.292 954	2.529 295 4E+01
square perch [US, survey]	1	1.000 000 0E+00
square pole [US, survey]	1	1.000 000 0E+00
square vara [US, survey, California]	36	3.600 000 0E+01
square vara [US, survey, Texas]	35.283 6	3.528 360 0E+01
square yard [based on US, survey foot]	30.25	3.025 000 0E+01
square yard [international]	30.250 121	3.025 012 1E+01

square rope <area>

acre [commerical]	0.011 111 1	1.111 111 1E-02
acre [international]	0.009 182 7	9.182 736 5E-03

	Standard	Scientific
acre [US, survey]	0.009 182 7	9.182 699 7E-03
hectare	0.003 716 1	3.716 121 6E-03
rood	0.036 730 8	3.673 079 9E-02
square	4	4.000 000 0E+00
square chain [Gunter or US, survey]	0.091 827	9.182 699 7E-02
square chain [Ramden or Engineer]	0.039 999 8	3.999 984 0E-02
square foot [international]	400	4.000 000 0E+02
square foot [US, survey]	399.998 4	3.999 984 0E+02
square link [Gunter or US, survey]	918.269 97	9.182 699 7E+02
square link [Ramden or Engineer]	399.998 4	3.999 984 0E+02
square meter	37.161 216	3.716 121 6E+01
square pace	64	6.400 000 0E+01
square palm	6,400	6.400 000 0E+03
square perch [US, survey]	1.469 232	1.469 232 0E+00
square yard [based on US, survey foot]	44.444 267	4.444 426 7E+01
square yard [international]	44.444 444	4.444 444 4E+01

square ruthe [Germany, Bavaria] <area, special - see page 29>

	Standard	Scientific
square meter	8.518 2	8.518 200 0E+00

square ruthe [Germany, Prussia] <area, special - see page 29>

	Standard	Scientific
square meter	14.185	1.418 500 0E+01

square ruthe [Germany, Wurttemberg] <area, special - see page 29>

	Standard	Scientific
square meter	8.207 7	8.207 700 0E+00

square sagene [Russia] <area, special - see page 29>

	Standard	Scientific
square meter	4.552 249	4.552 249 0E+00

square sajon [Russia] <area, special - see page 29>

	Standard	Scientific
square meter	4.552	4.552 000 0E+00

square sazhen [Russia] <area, special - see page 29>

	Standard	Scientific
square meter	4.55	4.550 000 0E+00

square second ampere/kilogram <9

	Standard	Scientific
square meter/volt second	1	1.000 000 0E+00
square meter/weber	1	1.000 000 0E+00

square second/kilogram <spectral cross-section>

	Standard	Scientific
barn/erg	>>>	1.000 000 0E+21
foot/pound-force	14.593 903	1.459 390 3E+01
meter/newton	1	1.000 000 0E+00
square meter/joule	1	1.000 000 0E+00

square sen [Thailand] <area, special - see page 29>

	Standard	Scientific
hectare	0.16	1.600 000 0E-01

square shibr [Saudi Arabia] <area, special - see page 29>

	Standard	Scientific
square centimeter	316.128 4	3.161 284 0E+02

square span <area>

	Standard	Scientific
circular foot [international]	0.716 197 2	7.161 972 4E-01
circular foot [US, survey]	0.716 194 4	7.161 943 8E-01
circular inch [based on US, survey foot]	103.131 99	1.031 319 9E+02
circular inch [international]	103.132 4	1.031 324 0E+02
square	0.005 625	5.625 000 0E-03
square cubit	0.25	2.500 000 0E-01
square decimeter	5.225 796	5.225 796 0E+00
square digit	144	1.440 000 0E+02
square foot [international]	0.562 5	5.625 000 0E-01
square foot [US, survey]	0.562 497 8	5.624 977 5E-01
square inch [based on US, survey foot]	80.999 676	8.099 967 6E+01
square inch [international]	81	8.100 000 0E+01
square meter	0.052 258	5.225 796 0E-02
square pace	0.09	9.000 000 0E-02
square palm	9	9.000 000 0E+00
square yard [based on US, survey foot]	0.062 499 8	6.249 975 0E-02
square yard [international]	0.062 5	6.250 000 0E-02

square stigma <area>

	Standard	Scientific
barn	10,000	1.000 000 0E+04

Convert From		\<Type of Unit\>
Convert To	Standard	Scientific

circular microinch	\<\<\<	1.973 525 2E−09
circular mil	\<\<\<	1.973 525 2E−15
square angstrom	0.000 1	1.000 000 0E−04
square bicron	1	1.000 000 0E+00
square fermi	1,000,000	1.000 000 0E+06
square meter	\<\<\<	1.000 000 0E−24
square microinch	\<\<\<	1.550 003 1E−09
square micromicron	1	1.000 000 0E+00
square micron	\<\<\<	1.000 000 0E−12
square millimicron	0.000 001	1.000 000 0E−06
square picometer	1	1.000 000 0E+00
square tenthmeter	0.000 1	1.000 000 0E−04
square x-unit	99.586 845	9.958 684 5E+01

square taim [India] \<area, special - see page 29\>
square meter	0.209	2.090 000 0E−01

square tenthmeter \<area\>
barn	\>\>\>	1.000 000 0E+08
circular microinch	0.000 019 7	1.973 525 2E−05
circular micrometer	\<\<\<	1.273 239 5E−08
circular mil	\<\<\<	1.973 525 2E−11
square angstrom	1	1.000 000 0E+00
square bicron	10,000	1.000 000 0E+04
square fermi	\>\>\>	1.000 000 0E+10
square meter	\<\<\<	1.000 000 0E−20
square microinch	0.000 015 5	1.550 003 1E−05
square micromicron	10,000	1.000 000 0E+04
square mil	\<\<\<	1.550 003 1E−11
square millimicron	0.01	1.000 000 0E−02
square nanometer	0.01	1.000 000 0E−02
square stigma	10,000	1.000 000 0E+04
square thou	\<\<\<	1.550 003 1E−11
square x-unit	995,868.45	9.958 684 5E+05

square terameter \<area\>
hectare	\>\>\>	1.000 000 0E+20
square astronomical unit	44.683 705	4.468 370 5E+01
square bevameter	1,000,000	1.000 000 0E+06
square light year	\<\<\<	1.117 250 9E−08
square meter	\>\>\>	1.000 000 0E+24
square mile [international]	\>\>\>	3.861 021 6E+17
square mile [US, statute]	\>\>\>	3.861 006 1E+17
square mile [US, survey]	\>\>\>	3.861 006 1E+17
square myriameter	\>\>\>	1.000 000 0E+16
square parsec	\>\>\>	1.050 264 8E−09

square thou \<area\>
circular micrometer	821.443 22	8.214 432 2E+02
circular mil	1.273 239 5	1.273 239 5E+00
square angstrom	\>\>\>	6.451 600 0E+10
square caliber	0.01	1.000 000 0E−02
square inch [based on US, survey foot]	0.000 001	9.999 960 0E−07
square inch [international]	0.000 001	1.000 000 0E−06
square meter	\<\<\<	6.451 600 0E−10
square microinch	1,000,000	1.000 000 0E+06
square micrometer	645.16	6.451 600 0E+02
square micron	645.16	6.451 600 0E+02
square mil	1	1.000 000 0E+00

square vara [Canada] \<area, special - see page 29\>
square meter	0.717	7.170 000 0E−01

square vara [Colombia] \<area, special - see page 29\>
square meter	0.64	6.400 000 0E−01

square vara [Costa Rica] \<area, special - see page 29\>
square meter	0.699	6.990 000 0E−01

Convert From Convert To	<Type of Unit> Standard	Scientific

square vara [Cuba] — \<area, special - see page 29\>
| square meter | 0.719 | 7.190 000 0E-01 |

square vara [El Salvador] — \<area, special - see page 29\>
| square meter | 0.702 58 | 7.025 800 0E-01 |

square vara [Guatemala] — \<area, special - see page 29\>
| square meter | 0.7 | 7.000 000 0E-01 |

square vara [Honduras] — \<area, special - see page 29\>
| square meter | 0.697 225 | 6.972 250 0E-01 |

square vara [Nicaragua] — \<area, special - see page 29\>
| square meter | 0.705 6 | 7.056 000 0E-01 |

square vara [Paraguay] — \<area, special - see page 29\>
| square meter | 0.751 | 7.510 000 0E-01 |

square vara [US, survey, California] — \<area\>
Convert To	Standard	Scientific
acre [commerical]	0.000 210 1	2.100 702 8E-04
acre [international]	0.000 173 6	1.736 118 1E-04
acre [US, survey]	0.000 173 6	1.736 111 1E-04
hectare	0.000 070 3	7.025 820 5E-05
square arpent [US, survey]	0.000 205 5	2.054 982 6E-04
square chain [Gunter or US, survey]	0.001 736 1	1.736 111 1E-03
square chain [Ramden or Engineer]	0.000 756 3	7.562 500 0E-04
square foot [international]	7.562 530 3	7.562 530 3E+00
square foot [US, survey]	7.562 5	7.562 500 0E+00
square inch [based on US, survey foot]	1,089.	1.089 000 0E+03
square inch [international]	1,089.004 4	1.089 004 4E+03
square link [Gunter or US, survey]	17.361 111	1.736 111 1E+01
square link [Ramden or Engineer]	7.562 5	7.562 500 0E+00
square meter	0.702 582 1	7.025 820 5E-01
square perch [US, survey]	0.027 777 8	2.777 777 8E-02
square vara [US, survey, Texas]	0.980 1	9.801 000 0E-01
square yard [based on US, survey foot]	0.840 277 8	8.402 777 8E-01
square yard [international]	0.840 281 1	8.402 811 4E-01

square vara [US, survey, Texas] — \<area\>
Convert To	Standard	Scientific
acre [commerical]	0.000 214 3	2.143 355 6E-04
acre [international]	0.000 177 1	1.771 368 3E-04
acre [US, survey]	0.000 177 1	1.771 361 0E-04
hectare	0.000 071 7	7.168 473 1E-05
square arpent [US, survey]	0.000 209 7	2.096 707 1E-04
square chain [Gunter or US, survey]	0.001 771 4	1.771 361 2E-03
square chain [Ramden or Engineer]	0.000 771 6	7.716 049 4E-04
square foot [international]	7.716 080 2	7.716 080 2E+00
square foot [US, survey]	7.716 049 4	7.716 049 4E+00
square link [Gunter or US, survey]	17.713 612	1.771 361 2E+01
square link [Ramden or Engineer]	7.716 049 4	7.716 049 4E+00
square meter	0.716 847 3	7.168 473 1E-01
square perch [US, survey]	0.028 341 8	2.834 177 9E-02
square vara [US, survey, California]	1.020 304 1	1.020 304 1E+00
square yard [based on US, survey foot]	0.857 338 8	8.573 388 2E-01
square yard [international]	0.857 342 3	8.573 422 5E-01

square wa [Thailand] — \<area, special - see page 29\>
| square meter | 4 | 4.000 000 0E+00 |

square x-unit — \<area\>
Convert To	Standard	Scientific
barn	100.414 87	1.004 148 7E+02
circular microinch	<<<	1.981 712 8E-11
circular micrometer	<<<	1.278 521 8E-14
square angstrom	0.000 001	1.004 148 7E-06
square bicron	0.010 041 5	1.004 148 7E-02
square fermi	10,041.487	1.004 148 7E+04
square meter	<<<	1.004 148 7E-26
square microinch	<<<	1.556 433 6E-11
square micromicron	0.010 041 5	1.004 148 7E-02
square micron	<<<	1.004 148 7E-14

Convert From / Convert To	Standard	<Type of Unit> Scientific

Convert To	Standard	Scientific
square millimicron	<<<	1.004 148 7E−08
square picometer	0.010 041 5	1.004 148 7E−02
square stigma	0.010 041 5	1.004 148 7E−02
square tenthmeter	0.000 001	1.004 148 7E−06
square thou	<<<	1.556 433 6E−17

square yard [based on US, survey foot] <area>

Convert To	Standard	Scientific
acre [commerical]	0.000 25	2.500 000 0E−04
acre [international]	0.000 206 6	2.066 124 0E−04
acre [US, survey]	0.000 206 6	2.066 115 7E−04
circular foot [international]	11.459 202	1.145 920 2E+01
circular foot [US, survey]	11.459 156	1.145 915 6E+01
hectare	0.000 083 6	8.361 307 0E−05
square fathom [US, survey]	0.25	2.500 000 0E−01
square foot [international]	9.000 036	9.000 036 0E+00
square foot [US, survey]	9	9.000 000 0E+00
square inch [based on US, survey foot]	1,296	1.296 000 0E+03
square inch [international]	1,296.005 2	1.296 005 2E+03
square link [Gunter or US, survey]	20.661 157	2.066 115 7E+01
square link [Ramden or Engineer]	9	9.000 000 0E+00
square meter	0.836 130 7	8.361 307 0E−01
square perch [US, survey]	0.033 057 9	3.305 785 1E−02
square vara [US, survey, California]	1.190 082 6	1.190 082 6E+00
square vara [US, survey, Texas]	1.166 4	1.166 400 0E+00
square yard [international]	1.000 004	1.000 004 0E+00

square yard [international] <area>

Convert To	Standard	Scientific
acre [commerical]	0.000 25	2.500 000 0E−04
acre [international]	0.000 206 6	2.066 115 7E−04
acre [US, survey]	0.000 206 6	2.066 107 4E−04
hectare	0.000 083 6	8.361 273 6E−05
square	0.09	9.000 000 0E−02
square foot [international]	9	9.000 000 0E+00
square foot [US, survey]	8.999 964	8.999 964 0E+00
square inch [based on US, survey foot]	1,295.994 8	1.295 994 8E+03
square inch [international]	1,296	1.296 000 0E+03
square link [Gunter or US, survey]	20.661 074	2.066 107 4E+01
square link [Ramden or Engineer]	8.999 964	8.999 964 0E+00
square meter	0.836 127 4	8.361 273 6E−01
square pace	1.44	1.440 000 0E+00
square perch [US, survey]	0.033 057 7	3.305 771 9E−02
square span	16	1.600 000 0E+01
square yard [based on US, survey foot]	0.999 996	9.999 960 0E−01

square yard/cubic yard <area/unit volume>

Convert To	Standard	Scientific
square foot/cubic foot	0.333 333 3	3.333 333 3E−01
square meter/cubic meter	1.093 613 3	1.093 613 3E+00

square yoctometer <area>

Convert To	Standard	Scientific
barn	<<<	1.000 000 0E−20
square angstrom	<<<	1.000 000 0E−28
square bicron	<<<	1.000 000 0E−24
square fermi	<<<	1.000 000 0E−18
square meter	<<<	1.000 000 0E−48
square micromicron	<<<	1.000 000 0E−24
square millimicron	<<<	1.000 000 0E−30
square stigma	<<<	1.000 000 0E−24
square tenthmeter	<<<	1.000 000 0E−28
square x-unit	<<<	9.958 684 5E−23

square yottameter <area>

Convert To	Standard	Scientific
square astronomical unit	>>>	4.468 370 5E+25
square bevameter	>>>	1.000 000 0E+30
square light year	>>>	1.117 250 9E+16
square meter	>>>	1.000 000 0E+48
square myriameter	>>>	1.000 000 0E+40
square parsec	>>>	1.050 264 8E+15

square zar [Iran] · \<area, special - see page 29\>
  square meter-- 1.08----1.080 000 0E+00

square zeptometer · \<area\>
  barn-- \<\<\<----1.000 000 0E-14
  circular microinch -- \<\<\<----1.973 525 2E-27
  circular micrometer -- \<\<\<----1.273 239 5E-30
  square angstrom -- \<\<\<----1.000 000 0E-22
  square bicron --- \<\<\<----1.000 000 0E-18
  square fermi--- \<\<\<----1.000 000 0E-12
  square meter-- \<\<\<----1.000 000 0E-42
  square microinch-- \<\<\<----1.550 003 1E-27
  square micromicron -- \<\<\<----1.000 000 0E-18
  square micron--- \<\<\<----1.000 000 0E-30
  square millimicron -- \<\<\<----1.000 000 0E-24
  square stigma--- \<\<\<----1.000 000 0E-18
  square tenthmeter -- \<\<\<----1.000 000 0E-22
  square x-unit-- \<\<\<----9.958 684 5E-17

square zettameter · \<area\>
  square astronomical unit----------------------------------- \>\>\>----4.468 370 5E+19
  square bevameter -- \>\>\>----1.000 000 0E+24
  square light year -- \>\>\>----1.117 250 9E+10
  square meter-- \>\>\>----1.000 000 0E+42
  square parsec--- \>\>\>----1.050 264 8E+09

square-foot unit of absorption · \<sound absorption\>
  square foot--1----1.000 000 0E+00
  square meter-- 0.092 903----9.290 304 0E-02

ssu [China] · \<mass, special - see page 29\>
  milligram--- 0.377 993 7----3.779 937 0E-01

staab [Switzerland] · \<length, special - see page 29\>
  meter--- 1.2----1.200 000 0E+00

stab [Germany] · \<length, special - see page 29\>
  meter---1----1.000 000 0E+00

stade [Greece, ancient] · \<length, special - see page 29\>
  meter--- 185----1.850 000 0E+02

stadia [Greece, ancient] · \<length, special - see page 29\>
  meter--- 184.7----1.847 000 0E+02

stadion [Greece, ancient, olympic] · \<length, special - see page 29\>
  meter--- 192----1.920 000 0E+02

stadion [Hebrew, ancient] · \<length, special - see page 29\>
  meter--- 161.856----1.618 560 0E+02

stadion [Iraq, ancient] · \<length, special - see page 29\>
  meter--- 711----7.110 000 0E+02

stadion [Mesopotamia, ancient] · \<length, special - see page 29\>
  meter--- 180----1.800 000 0E+02

stadion [Rome, ancient] · \<length, special - see page 29\>
  meter-- 184.83----1.848 300 0E+02

stadium [Hebrew, ancient] · \<length, special - see page 29\>
  centimeter--- 14,938.309----1.493 830 9E+04

stadium [Rome, ancient] · \<length, special - see page 29\>
  meter-- 185.42----1.854 200 0E+02

stajo [Italy, dry] · \<volume, special - see page 29\>
  liter-- 24.53----2.453 000 0E+01

stang [Sweden] · \<length, special - see page 29\>
  meter-- 2.97----2.970 000 0E+00

stangiew [Poland] · \<volume, special - see page 29\>
  liter--- 273.08----2.730 800 0E+02

stanjen [Romania] · \<length, special - see page 29\>
  meter-- 2.23----2.230 000 0E+00

star pagoda [India, gold and silver]   \<mass, special - see page 29\>
gram -- 3.405 --- 3.405 000 0E+00

starello [Italy, dry]   \<volume, special - see page 29\>
liter --- 18.4 --- 1.840 000 0E+01

statampere   \<electric current\>
ampere --- <<< --- 3.335 641 0E-10
electrostatic unit of current [cgs system] ----------------- 1 --- 1.000 000 0E+00
franklin/second -- 1 --- 1.000 000 0E+00
gaussian electric current ------------------------------------ 1 --- 1.000 000 0E+00

statampere square centimeter   \<electromagnetic moment\>
ampere square inch -- <<< --- 5.170 253 8E-11
ampere square meter -- <<< --- 3.335 641 0E-14

statampere/centimeter   \<magnetic field strength\>
abampere/centimeter -- <<< --- 3.335 641 0E-11
ampere/inch -- <<< --- 8.472 528 0E-10
ampere/meter -- <<< --- 3.335 641 0E-08
oersted --- <<< --- 4.191 690 0E-10

statampere/square centimeter   \<electric current density\>
ampere/square inch -- <<< --- 2.152 022 1E-09
ampere/square meter ----------------------------- 0.000 003 3 --- 3.335 641 0E-06
kiloampere/square meter ------------------------------------ <<< --- 3.335 641 0E-09

statcoulomb   \<electric charge\>
coulomb -- <<< --- 3.335 641 0E-10
electrostatic unit of charge [cgs system] ------------------ 1 --- 1.000 000 0E+00
franklin --- 1 --- 1.000 000 0E+00
gaussian electric charge ------------------------------------ 1 --- 1.000 000 0E+00
picocoulomb -- 333.564 095 --- 3.335 641 0E+02

statcoulomb centimeter   \<electric dipole moment\>
abcoulomb centimeter --------------------------------------- <<< --- 3.335 641 0E-11
ampere second meter --------------------------------------- <<< --- 3.335 641 0E-12
coulomb meter --- <<< --- 3.335 641 0E-12
franklin centimeter --- 1 --- 1.000 000 0E+00

statcoulomb/centimeter   \<electric dipole moment/unit area\>
coulomb/meter --- <<< --- 3.335 641 0E-08
franklin/centimeter --- 1 --- 1.000 000 0E+00

statcoulomb/cubic centimeter   \<electric charge density\>
coulomb/cubic meter ---------------------------------- 0.000 333 6 --- 3.335 641 0E-04
franklin/cubic centimeter ----------------------------------- 1 --- 1.000 000 0E+00
microcoulomb/cubic meter ------------------------- 333.564 095 --- 3.335 641 0E+02

statcoulomb/square centimeter   \<electric flux density\>
abcoulomb/square centimeter ------------------------------ <<< --- 3.335 641 0E-11
ampere hour/square meter --------------------------------- <<< --- 9.265 669 3E-10
coulomb/square inch --- <<< --- 2.152 022 1E-09
coulomb/square meter --------------------------- 0.000 003 3 --- 3.335 641 0E-06
franklin/square centimeter ---------------------------------- 1 --- 1.000 000 0E+00
microcoulomb/square meter ----------------------- 3.335 641 --- 3.335 641 0E+00

stater [Greece, ancient]   \<mass, special - see page 29\>
gram --- 9.72 --- 9.720 000 0E+00

stater [Greece]   \<mass, special - see page 29\>
kilogram -- 56.32 --- 5.632 000 0E+01

statfarad   \<capacitance\>
abfarad -- <<< --- 1.112 650 1E-21
coulomb/volt -- <<< --- 1.112 650 1E-12
electrostatic unit of capacitance [cgs system]----------- 1 --- 1.000 000 0E+00
farad --- <<< --- 1.112 650 1E-12
gaussian electric capacitance----------------------------- 1 --- 1.000 000 0E+00
jar --- 0.001 --- 1.000 000 0E-03

statfarad/centimeter   \<electric permittivity\>
abfarad/centimeter -- <<< --- 1.112 650 1E-21

	Standard	Scientific
ampere second/volt meter	\<\<\<	1.112 650 1E-14
farad/meter	\<\<\<	1.112 650 1E-14
picofarad/meter	0.011 126 5	1.112 650 1E-02

stathenry — \<electric inductance\>

	Standard	Scientific
abhenry	\>\>\>	8.987 551 8E+20
electrostatic unit of inductance [cgs system]	1	1.000 000 0E+00
gaussian electric inductance	1	1.000 000 0E+00
henry	\>\>\>	8.987 551 8E+11
ohm second	\>\>\>	8.987 551 8E+11

statmho — \<electric conductance\>

	Standard	Scientific
absiemens	\<\<\<	1.112 650 1E-21
electrostatic unit of conductance [cgs system]	1	1.000 000 0E+00
gaussian electric conductance	1	1.000 000 0E+00
picosiemens	1.112 650 1	1.112 650 1E+00
siemens	\<\<\<	1.112 650 1E-12
statsiemens	1	1.000 000 0E+00

statmho/centimeter — \<electric conductivity\>

	Standard	Scientific
abmho/centimeter	\<\<\<	1.112 650 1E-21
mho/meter	\<\<\<	1.112 650 1E-10
siemens/meter	\<\<\<	1.112 650 1E-10

statohm — \<electric resistance\>

	Standard	Scientific
1/ siemens	\>\>\>	8.987 551 8E+11
abohm	\>\>\>	8.987 551 8E+20
electrostatic unit of resistance [cgs system]	1	1.000 000 0E+00
gaussian electric resistance	1	1.000 000 0E+00
ohm	\>\>\>	8.987 551 8E+11

statohm centimeter — \<electric resistivity\>

	Standard	Scientific
abohm centimeter	\>\>\>	8.987 551 8E+20
gigaohm meter	8.987 551 8	8.987 551 8E+00
microhm inch	\>\>\>	3.538 406 2E+17
ohm circular mil/foot	\>\>\>	5.406 286 5E+18
ohm meter	\>\>\>	8.987 551 8E+09
ohm square millimeter/meter	\>\>\>	8.987 551 8E+15

statsiemens — \<electric conductance\>

	Standard	Scientific
electrostatic unit of conductance [cgs system]	1	1.000 000 0E+00
gaussian electric conductance	1	1.000 000 0E+00
picosiemens	1.112 650 1	1.112 650 1E+00
siemens	\<\<\<	1.112 650 1E-12
statmho	1	1.000 000 0E+00

statsiemens/centimeter — \<electric conductivity\>

	Standard	Scientific
absiemens/centimeter	\<\<\<	1.112 650 1E-21
mho/meter	\<\<\<	1.112 650 1E-10
siemens/meter	\<\<\<	1.112 650 1E-10

stattesla — \<magnetic flux density\>

	Standard	Scientific
electrostatic unit of magnetic flux density [cgs system]	1	1.000 000 0E+00
gaussian magnetic flux density	1	1.000 000 0E+00
tesla	2,997,924.6	2.997 924 6E+06

statvolt — \<electric potential\>

	Standard	Scientific
abvolt	\>\>\>	2.997 924 6E+10
electrostatic unit of electric potential [cgs system]	1	1.000 000 0E+00
erg/franklin	1	1.000 000 0E+00
gaussian electric potential	1	1.000 000 0E+00
hectovolt	2.997 924 6	2.997 924 6E+00
volt	299.792 458	2.997 924 6E+02

statvolt/centimeter — \<electric field strength\>

	Standard	Scientific
kilovolt/meter	29.979 245 8	2.997 924 6E+01
volt/inch	761.472 843	7.614 728 4E+02
volt/meter	29,979.245 8	2.997 924 6E+04

statweber — \<magnetic flux\>

	Standard	Scientific
electrostatic unit of magnetic flux [cgs system]	1	1.000 000 0E+00

gauss square centimeter	>>>	2.997 924 6E+10
gaussian magnetic flux	1	1.000 000 0E+00
hectoweber	2.997 924 6	2.997 924 6E+00
maxwell	>>>	2.997 924 6E+10
unit pole	>>>	2.385 672 7E+09
weber	299.792 458	2.997 924 6E+02

statweber centimeter <magnetic dipole moment>

abweber centimeter	>>>	2.997 924 6E+10
weber meter	37.673 031 3	3.767 303 1E+01

statweber/centimeter <magnetic vector potential>

abweber/centimeter	>>>	2.997 924 6E+10
weber/meter	29,979.245 8	2.997 924 6E+04

steekkan [Netherlands] <volume, special - see page 29>

liter	19.4	1.940 000 0E+01

stein [Austria] <mass, special - see page 29>

kilogram	11.2	1.120 000 0E+01

stein [Germany] <volume, special - see page 29>

centiliter	75	7.500 000 0E+01

stemma [Greece, ancient] <area, special - see page 29>

are	12.702	1.270 200 0E+01

step [Greece, ancient] <length, special - see page 29>

meter	0.77	7.700 000 0E-01

sterad <solid angle>

hemisphere	0.159 154 9	1.591 549 4E-01
spat	0.079 577 5	7.957 747 2E-02
spheradian	1	1.000 000 0E+00
sphere	0.079 577 5	7.957 747 2E-02
spherical degree	57.295 78	5.729 578 0E+01
spherical right angle	0.636 619 8	6.366 197 7E-01
spherical solid angle	0.079 577 5	7.957 747 2E-02
square degree	3,282.806 4	3.282 806 4E+03
square grade	4,052.847 3	4.052 847 3E+03
steradian	1	1.000 000 0E+00
steregon	0.079 577 5	7.957 747 2E-02

steradian <solid angle>

hemisphere	0.159 154 9	1.591 549 4E-01
spat	0.079 577 5	7.957 747 2E-02
spheradian	1	1.000 000 0E+00
sphere	0.079 577 5	7.957 747 2E-02
spherical degree	57.295 78	5.729 578 0E+01
spherical right angle	0.636 619 8	6.366 197 7E-01
spherical solid angle	0.079 577 5	7.957 747 2E-02
square degree	3,282.806 4	3.282 806 4E+03
square grade	4,052.847 3	4.052 847 3E+03
sterad	1	1.000 000 0E+00
steregon	0.079 577 5	7.957 747 2E-02

stere <volume>

barrel [UK]	6.110 256 9	6.110 256 9E+00
barrel [US, dry]	8.648 489 8	8.648 489 8E+00
board foot	423.776	4.237 760 0E+02
bushel [UK]	27.496 156	2.749 615 6E+01
bushel [US, dry]	28.377 593	2.837 759 3E+01
cord [firewood]	0.275 895 8	2.758 958 3E-01
cord foot [timber]	2.207 166 7	2.207 166 7E+00
cubic foot	35.314 667	3.531 466 7E+01
cubic inch	61,023.744	6.102 374 4E+04
cubic meter	1	1.000 000 0E+00
cubic yard	1.307 950 6	1.307 950 6E+00
English water ton [UK]	0.982 005 6	9.820 055 7E-01
freight ton	0.882 866 7	8.828 666 7E-01
gallon [US, dry]	227.020 75	2.270 207 5E+02

kiloliter	1	1.000 000 0E+00
liter	1,000	1.000 000 0E+03
measurement ton	0.882 866 7	8.828 666 7E-01
million board foot	0.000 423 8	4.237 760 7E-04
ocean ton	0.882 866 7	8.828 666 7E-01
peck [UK]	109.984 62	1.099 846 2E+02
peck [US]	113.510 37	1.135 103 7E+02
petrograd standard	0.214 028 3	2.140 282 8E-01
quarter [UK]	3.437 019 5	3.437 019 5E+00
register ton	0.353 146 7	3.531 466 7E-01
shipping ton	0.882 866 7	8.828 666 7E-01
thousand board foot	0.423 776	4.237 760 0E-01
thousand cubic foot	0.035 314 7	3.531 466 7E-02

stere/day   \<flow rate, volume basis\>

acre inch/day	0.009 728 6	9.728 558 3E-03
barrel/day [UK]	6.110 256 9	6.110 256 9E+00
barrel/day [US, federal]	8.521 679 1	8.521 679 1E+00
barrel/day [US, liquid]	8.386 414 4	8.386 414 4E+00
barrel/day [US, petroleum]	6.289 810 8	6.289 810 8E+00
centiliter/second	1.157 407 4	1.157 407 4E+00
cubic centimeter/second	11.574 074 1	1.157 407 4E+01
cubic decimeter/hour	41.666 666 7	4.166 666 7E+01
cubic dekameter/day	0.001	1.000 000 0E-03
cubic foot/hour	1.471 444 5	1.471 444 5E+00
cubic inch/minute	42.377 600 1	4.237 760 0E+01
cubic meter/day	1	1.000 000 0E+00
cubic meter/second	0.000 011 6	1.157 407 4E-05
cubic yard/day	1.307 950 6	1.307 950 6E+00
deciliter/minute	6.944 444 4	6.944 444 4E+00
dekaliter/hour	4.166 666 7	4.166 666 7E+00
gallon/hour [UK]	9.165 385 3	9.165 385 3E+00
gallon/hour [US, liquid]	11.007 168 0	1.100 716 9E+01
hectoliter/day	10	1.000 000 0E+01
kiloliter/day	1	1.000 000 0E+00
liter/hour	41.666 666 7	4.166 666 7E+01
liter/hour [pre-1964]	41.665 5	4.166 550 0E+01
milliliter/second	11.574 074 1	1.157 407 4E+01
ounce/minute [UK, liquid]	24.441 028	2.444 102 8E+01
ounce/minute [US, liquid]	23.481 96	2.348 196 0E+01
petrograd standard/day	0.214 028 3	2.140 282 8E-01
thousand cubic foot/day	0.035 314 7	3.531 466 7E-02

stere/hour   \<flow rate, volume basis\>

acre foot/day	0.019 457 1	1.945 711 7E-02
acre foot/day [US, survey]	0.019 457	1.945 700 0E-02
acre inch/day	0.233 485 4	2.334 854 0E-01
barrel/hour [UK]	6.110 256 9	6.110 256 9E+00
barrel/hour [US, federal]	8.521 679 1	8.521 679 1E+00
barrel/hour [US, liquid]	8.386 414 4	8.386 414 4E+00
barrel/hour [US, petroleum]	6.289 810 8	6.289 810 8E+00
centiliter/second	27.777 777 8	2.777 777 8E+01
cubic centimeter/second	277.777 778	2.777 777 8E+02
cubic decimeter/minute	16.666 666 7	1.666 666 7E+01
cubic dekameter/day	0.024	2.400 000 0E-02
cubic foot/hour	35.314 666 7	3.531 466 7E+01
cubic inch/second	16.951 04	1.695 104 0E+01
cubic meter/hour	1	1.000 000 0E+00
cubic yard/hour	1.307 950 6	1.307 950 6E+00
deciliter/second	2.777 777 8	2.777 777 8E+00
dekaliter/minute	1.666 666 7	1.666 666 7E+00
gallon/minute [UK]	3.666 154 1	3.666 154 1E+00
gallon/minute [US, liquid]	4.402 867 5	4.402 867 5E+00
hectare meter/day	0.002 4	2.400 000 0E-03
hectoliter/hour	10	1.000 000 0E+01

	Standard	Scientific
kiloliter/hour	1	1.000 000 0E+00
liter/minute	16.666 666 7	1.666 666 7E+01
liter/minute [pre-1964]	16.666 2	1.666 620 0E+01
milliliter/second	277.777 778	2.777 777 8E+02
ounce/second [UK, liquid]	9.776 411	9.776 411 0E+00
ounce/second [US, liquid]	9.392 784 1	9.392 784 1E+00
petrograd standard/day	5.136 678 8	5.136 678 8E+00
stere/day	24	2.400 000 0E+01
thousand cubic foot/day	0.847 552	8.475 520 0E-01

stere/minute — <flow rate, volume basis>

	Standard	Scientific
acre foot/day	1.167 427	1.167 427 0E+00
acre foot/day [US, survey]	1.167 42	1.167 420 0E+00
acre inch/day	14.009 124	1.400 912 4E+01
barrel/minute [UK]	6.110 256 9	6.110 256 9E+00
barrel/minute [US, federal]	8.521 679 1	8.521 679 1E+00
barrel/minute [US, liquid]	8.386 414 4	8.386 414 4E+00
barrel/minute [US, petroleum]	6.289 810 8	6.289 810 8E+00
cubic decimeter/second	16.666 666 7	1.666 666 7E+01
cubic dekameter/day	1.44	1.440 000 0E+00
cubic foot/minute	35.314 666 7	3.531 466 7E+01
cubic inch/second	1,017.062 4	1.017 062 4E+03
cubic meter/minute	1	1.000 000 0E+00
cubic yard/minute	1.307 950 6	1.307 950 6E+00
deciliter/second	166.666 667	1.666 666 7E+02
dekaliter/second	1.666 666 7	1.666 666 7E+00
gallon/second [UK]	3.666 154 1	3.666 154 1E+00
gallon/second [US, liquid]	4.402 867 5	4.402 867 5E+00
hectare meter/day	0.144	1.440 000 0E-01
hectoliter/minute	10	1.000 000 0E+01
kiloliter/minute	1	1.000 000 0E+00
liter/second	16.666 666 7	1.666 666 7E+01
liter/second [pre-1964]	16.666 2	1.666 620 0E+01
ounce/second [UK, liquid]	586.584 66	5.865 846 6E+02
ounce/second [US, liquid]	563.567 05	5.635 670 5E+02
petrograd standard/hour	12.841 697	1.284 169 7E+01
stere/hour	60	6.000 000 0E+01
thousand cubic foot/hour	2.118 88	2.118 880 0E+00

stere/second — <flow rate, volume basis>

	Standard	Scientific
acre foot/hour	2.918 567 5	2.918 567 5E+00
acre foot/hour [US, survey]	2.918 55	2.918 550 0E+00
acre inch/hour	35.022 81	3.502 281 0E+01
barrel/second [UK]	6.110 256 9	6.110 256 9E+00
barrel/second [US, federal]	8.521 679 1	8.521 679 1E+00
barrel/second [US, liquid]	8.386 414 4	8.386 414 4E+00
barrel/second [US, petroleum]	6.289 810 8	6.289 810 8E+00
billion cubic foot/day	0.003 051 2	3.051 187 2E-03
cubic dekameter/hour	3.6	3.600 000 0E+00
cubic foot/second	35.314 666 7	3.531 466 7E+01
cubic meter/second	1	1.000 000 0E+00
cubic yard/second	1.307 950 6	1.307 950 6E+00
dekaliter/second	100	1.000 000 0E+02
gallon/second [UK]	219.969 248	2.199 692 5E+02
gallon/second [US, liquid]	264.172 052	2.641 720 5E+02
hectare meter/day	8.64	8.640 000 0E+00
hectoliter/second	10	1.000 000 0E+01
kiloliter/second	1	1.000 000 0E+00
liter/second	1,000	1.000 000 0E+03
liter/second [pre-1964]	999.972 001	9.999 720 0E+02
petrograd standard/minute	12.841 697	1.284 169 7E+01
stere/minute	60	6.000 000 0E+01
thousand cubic foot/minute	2.118 88	2.118 880 0E+00

steregon — <solid angle>

	Standard	Scientific
hemisphere	2	2.000 000 0E+00

spat	1	1.000 000 0E+00
spheradian	12.566 371	1.256 637 1E+01
sphere	1	1.000 000 0E+00
spherical degree	720	7.200 000 0E+02
spherical right angle	8	8.000 000 0E+00
spherical solid angle	1	1.000 000 0E+00
square degree	41,252.961	4.125 296 1E+04
square grade	50,929.582	5.092 958 2E+04
sterad	12.566 371	1.256 637 1E+01
steradian	12.566 371	1.256 637 1E+01

stero [Italy]   **<volume, special - see page 29>**

cubic meter	1	1.000 000 0E+00

sthene   **<force>**

crinal	10,000	1.000 000 0E+04
dyne	>>>	1.000 000 0E+08
funal	1	1.000 000 0E+00
gram-force	101,971.621	1.019 716 2E+05
kilonewton	1	1.000 000 0E+00
newton	1,000	1.000 000 0E+03
ounce-force	3,596.943 09	3.596 943 1E+03
pond	101,971.621	1.019 716 2E+05
pound-force	224.808 943	2.248 089 4E+02
poundal	7,233.013 85	7.233 013 9E+03
ton meter/square second [metric]	1	1.000 000 0E+00

sthene/square meter [France]   **<pressure>**

atmosphere [standard]	0.009 869 2	9.869 232 7E−03
atmosphere [technical]	0.010 197 2	1.019 716 2E−02
bar	0.01	1.000 000 0E−02
barye [France]	10,000	1.000 000 0E+04
centibar	1	1.000 000 0E+00
centimeter of mercury [0 °C, by convention]	0.750 061 2	7.500 615 8E−01
centimeter of water [4 °C, by convention]	10.197 162	1.019 716 2E+01
dyne/square centimeter	10,000	1.000 000 0E+04
gram-force/square centimeter	10.197 162	1.019 716 2E+01
inch of mercury [0 °C, by convention]	0.295 299 8	2.952 998 3E−01
inch of water [4 °C, by convention]	4.014 630 8	4.014 630 8E+00
kilogram-force/square meter	101.971 62	1.019 716 2E+02
kilopascal	1	1.000 000 0E+00
kilopond/square meter	101.971 62	1.019 716 2E+02
kip/square foot	0.020 885 4	2.088 543 4E−02
millimeter of mercury [0 °C, by convention]	7.500 615 8	7.500 615 8E+00
millimeter of water [4 °C, by convention]	101.971 62	1.019 716 2E+02
newton/square meter	1,000	1.000 000 0E+03
ounce-force/square inch	2.320 603 8	2.320 603 8E+00
pascal	1,000	1.000 000 0E+03
pieze [France]	1	1.000 000 0E+00
pound-force/square foot	20.885 434	2.088 543 4E+01
poundal/square foot	671.968 98	6.719 689 8E+02
ton-force/square foot [short]	0.010 442 7	1.044 271 7E−02
ton-force/square meter [metric]	0.101 971 6	1.019 716 2E−01
torr	7.500 616 8	7.500 616 8E+00

stich [Germany]   **<length, special - see page 29>**

millimeter	1	1.000 000 0E+00

stigma   **<length>**

angstrom	0.01	1.000 000 0E−02
bicron	1	1.000 000 0E+00
fermi	1,000	1.000 000 0E+03
inch [based on US, survey foot]	<<<	3.937 007 9E−11
inch [international]	<<<	3.937 007 9E−11
meter	<<<	1.000 000 0E−12
micromicron	1	1.000 000 0E+00
millimicron	0.001	1.000 000 0E−03

Convert From Convert To		Standard	<Type of Unit> Scientific

		Standard	Scientific
picometer			
tenthmeter		1	1.000 000 0E+00
		0.01	1.000 000 0E-02
wavelength of orange-red spectral line of krypton-86		0.000 001 7	1.650 763 7E-06
x-unit		9.979 320 9	9.979 320 9E+00
stilb			**<luminance>**
apostilb [international]		31,415.927	3.141 592 7E+04
blondel		31,415.927	3.141 592 7E+04
candela/square inch		6.451 6	6.451 600 0E+00
candela/square meter		10,000	1.000 000 0E+04
footlambert		2,918.635 1	2.918 635 1E+03
lambert		3.141 592 7	3.141 592 7E+00
nit		10,000	1.000 000 0E+04
stina [Ukraine]			**<length, special - see page 29>**
meter		7	7.000 000 0E+00
stinka [Ukraine]			**<length, special - see page 29>**
meter		7	7.000 000 0E+00
stof [Russia]			**<volume, special - see page 29>**
liter		0.153 742 6	1.537 426 0E-01
stokes			**<kinematic viscosity>**
centistokes		100	1.000 000 0E+02
lentor		1	1.000 000 0E+00
liter/centimeter hour		3.6	3.600 000 0E+00
poise cubic centimeter/gram		1	1.000 000 0E+00
square centimeter/second		1	1.000 000 0E+00
square foot/hour		3.875 007 8	3.875 007 8E+00
square inch/minute		9.300 018 6	9.300 018 6E+00
square meter/day		8.64	8.640 000 0E+00
square meter/second		0.000 1	1.000 000 0E-04
stone [Cyprus]			**<mass, special - see page 29>**
kilogram		6.350 293	6.350 293 0E+00
stone [Scotland]			**<mass, special - see page 29>**
kilogram		10.886	1.088 600 0E+01
stone [UK]			**<mass>**
carat [international]		31,751.466	3.175 146 6E+04
carat [UK]		24,500	2.450 000 0E+04
cental [US]		0.14	1.400 000 0E-01
centner [UK]		0.125	1.250 000 0E-01
drachm [UK, apothecary]		1,633.333 3	1.633 333 3E+03
dram [avoirdupois]		3,584	3.584 000 0E+03
dram [US, apothecary]		1,633.333 3	1.633 333 3E+03
grain		98,000	9.800 000 0E+04
grain [apothecary]		98,000	9.800 000 0E+04
grain [avoirdupois]		98,000	9.800 000 0E+04
grain [troy]		98,000	9.800 000 0E+04
hundredweight [long]		0.125	1.250 000 0E-01
hundredweight [short]		0.14	1.400 000 0E-01
hundredweight [UK]		0.125	1.250 000 0E-01
kilogram		6.350 293 2	6.350 293 2E+00
ounce		224	2.240 000 0E+02
ounce [avoirdupois]		224	2.240 000 0E+02
pound		14	1.400 000 0E+01
poundal square second/foot		14	1.400 000 0E+01
quarter [UK]		0.5	5.000 000 0E-01
quarter [US]		0.56	5.600 000 0E-01
quintal [UK]		0.125	1.250 000 0E-01
quintal [US]		0.14	1.400 000 0E-01
scruple [UK]		4,900	4.900 000 0E+03
scruple [US, apothecary]		4,900	4.900 000 0E+03
stong [Sweden]			**<length, special - see page 29>**
meter		2.969 2	2.969 200 0E+00

Convert From / Convert To	Standard	Scientific
stoop [Netherlands]	<volume, special - see page 29>	
liter	2.425	2.425 000 0E+00
stop [Sweden]	<volume, special - see page 29>	
liter	1.308 56	1.308 560 0E+00
stopa [Czechoslovakia, Bohemia]	<length, special - see page 29>	
meter	0.296 3	2.963 000 0E-01
stopa [Czechoslovakia, Moravia]	<length, special - see page 29>	
meter	0.284	2.840 000 0E-01
stopa [Poland]	<length, special - see page 29>	
centimeter	28.8	2.880 000 0E+01
stopa [Russia]	<length, special - see page 29>	
centimeter	30.48	3.048 000 0E+01
stopa [Yugoslavia]	<length, special - see page 29>	
centimeter	31.6	3.160 000 0E+01
stoppa [Poland]	<length, special - see page 29>	
meter	0.288	2.880 000 0E-01
stopy [Ukraine]	<length, special - see page 29>	
centimeter	31.6	3.160 000 0E+01
streep [Netherlands]	<length, special - see page 29>	
millimeter	1	1.000 000 0E+00
stremma [Greece, ancient]	<area, special - see page 29>	
are	12.702	1.270 200 0E+01
stremma [Switzerland]	<area, special - see page 29>	
are	10	1.000 000 0E+01
strich [Germany]	<length, special - see page 29>	
millimeter	1	1.000 000 0E+00
strich [Switzerland]	<length, special - see page 29>	
millimeter	2.083 333	2.083 333 0E+00
strike [UK]	<volume, special - see page 29>	
liter	72.735 36	7.273 536 0E+01
stringene [Romania]	<length, special - see page 29>	
meter	1.96	1.960 000 0E+00
stritch [Switzerland]	<length, special - see page 29>	
millimeter	0.3	3.000 000 0E-01
strych [Czechoslovakia]	<volume, special - see page 29>	
liter	93.592	9.359 200 0E+01
strych [Czechoslovakia]	<area, special - see page 29>	
are	28.78	2.878 000 0E+01
stt [Egypt, ancient]	<area, special - see page 29>	
square meter	2,735	2.735 000 0E+03
stubchen [Denmark]	<volume, special - see page 29>	
liter	3.864	3.864 000 0E+00
stunde [Switzerland]	<length, special - see page 29>	
kilometer	4.8	4.800 000 0E+00
su bad [Sumeria, ancient]	<length, special - see page 29>	
centimeter	25	2.500 000 0E+01
suerte [Nicaragua]	<area, special - see page 29>	
hectare	1.41	1.410 000 0E+00
suerte [Uruguay]	<area, special - see page 29>	
square kilometer	19.92	1.992 000 0E+01
suk [South Korea, barley]	<mass, special - see page 29>	
kilogram	99	9.900 000 0E+01
suk [South Korea, rice paddy]	<mass, special - see page 29>	
kilogram	100	1.000 000 0E+02

Convert From	<Type of Unit>	
Convert To	Standard	Scientific

suk [South Korea, rice, milled]   `<mass, special - see page 29>`
  kilogram --------------------------------- 144 --- 1.440 000 0E+02

suk [South Korea, wheat]   `<mass, special - see page 29>`
  kilogram --------------------------------- 138 --- 1.380 000 0E+02

suk [South Korea]   `<volume, special - see page 29>`
  liter ------------------------------ 180.391 --- 1.803 910 0E+02

suku [Indonesia]   `<mass, special - see page 29>`
  gram ----------------------------- 6.761 --- 6.761 000 0E+00

sulga [Mongolia]   `<volume, special - see page 29>`
  liter ---------------------------------- 6.5 --- 6.500 000 0E+00

sultchek [Turkey]   `<volume, special - see page 29>`
  liter ------------------------------------ 1 --- 1.000 000 0E+00

sun [Japan, textiles]   `<length, special - see page 29>`
  centimeter ------------------------- 3.788 --- 3.788 000 0E+00

sun [Japan]   `<volume, special - see page 29>`
  milliliter -------------------- 0.018 039 1 --- 1.803 907 0E-02

sun [Japan]   `<length, special - see page 29>`
  centimeter --------------------------- 3.03 --- 3.030 000 0E+00

sus [Somalia]   `<mass, special - see page 29>`
  kilogram ------------------------- 1.475 --- 1.475 000 0E+00

susi [Sumeria, ancient]   `<length, special - see page 29>`
  centimeter -------------------------- 1.67 --- 1.670 000 0E+00

sutu [Assyrian, ancient]   `<volume, special - see page 29>`
  liter ---------------------------------- 13.4 --- 1.340 000 0E+01

sutu [Babylon, ancient]   `<volume, special - see page 29>`
  liter -------------------------------------- 6 --- 6.000 000 0E+00

suvarna [Hindu, ancient, gold]   `<mass, special - see page 29>`
  gram ------------------------------- 9.92 --- 9.920 000 0E+00

suvarna [India, ancient]   `<mass, special - see page 29>`
  gram ------------------------------- 9.92 --- 9.920 000 0E+00

suvarnamasha [India, ancient]   `<mass, special - see page 29>`
  milligram ---------------------------- 620 --- 6.200 000 0E+02

svedberg   `<sedimentation coefficient>`
  picosecond----------------------------- 0.1 --- 1.000 000 0E-01
  second ------------------------------- <<< --- 1.000 000 0E-13

swin [China, silver]   `<mass, special - see page 29>`
  gram ----------------------------- 0.378 --- 3.780 000 0E-01

syli [Finland]   `<volume, special - see page 29>`
  cubic meter -------------------------------- 4 --- 4.000 000 0E+00

ta [Brunei]   `<mass, special - see page 29>`
  kilogram ---------------------------- 60.479 --- 6.047 900 0E+01

ta [Cambodia]   `<mass, special - see page 29>`
  kilogram --------------------------------- 60 --- 6.000 000 0E+01

ta [China]   `<mass, special - see page 29>`
  kilogram ---------------------------- 60.479 --- 6.047 900 0E+01

ta [Hong Kong]   `<mass, special - see page 29>`
  kilogram ---------------------------- 60.479 --- 6.047 900 0E+01

ta [Indonesia]   `<mass, special - see page 29>`
  kilogram ---------------------------- 61.761 --- 6.176 100 0E+01

ta [Japan]   `<mass, special - see page 29>`
  kilogram --------------------------------- 60 --- 6.000 000 0E+01

ta [Laos]   `<mass, special - see page 29>`
  kilogram --------------------------------- 60 --- 6.000 000 0E+01

ta [Macao]   `<mass, special - see page 29>`
  kilogram ---------------------------- 60.479 --- 6.047 900 0E+01

Convert From	<Type of Unit>	
Convert To	Standard	Scientific

ta [Malaysia]   **<mass, special - see page 29>**
kilogram --- 60.479----6.047 900 0E+01

ta [Philippines]   **<mass, special - see page 29>**
kilogram --- 63.249----6.324 900 0E+01

ta [Singapore]   **<mass, special - see page 29>**
kilogram --- 60.479----6.047 900 0E+01

ta [Thailand]   **<mass, special - see page 29>**
kilogram --- 60----6.000 000 0E+01

ta [Vietnam, rice paddy]   **<mass, special - see page 29>**
kilogram --- 68----6.800 000 0E+01

ta [Vietnam, rice, milled]   **<mass, special - see page 29>**
kilogram --- 100----1.000 000 0E+02

ta [Vietnam]   **<mass, special - see page 29>**
kilogram --- 60.45----6.045 000 0E+01

taam [Brunei]   **<mass, special - see page 29>**
kilogram --- 60.479----6.047 900 0E+01

taam [Cambodia]   **<mass, special - see page 29>**
kilogram --- 60----6.000 000 0E+01

taam [China]   **<mass, special - see page 29>**
kilogram --- 60.479----6.047 900 0E+01

taam [Hong Kong]   **<mass, special - see page 29>**
kilogram --- 60.479----6.047 900 0E+01

taam [Indonesia]   **<mass, special - see page 29>**
kilogram --- 61.761----6.176 100 0E+01

taam [Japan]   **<mass, special - see page 29>**
kilogram --- 60----6.000 000 0E+01

taam [Laos]   **<mass, special - see page 29>**
kilogram --- 60----6.000 000 0E+01

taam [Macao]   **<mass, special - see page 29>**
kilogram --- 60.479----6.047 900 0E+01

taam [Malaysia]   **<mass, special - see page 29>**
kilogram --- 60.479----6.047 900 0E+01

taam [Philippines]   **<mass, special - see page 29>**
kilogram --- 63.249----6.324 900 0E+01

taam [Singapore]   **<mass, special - see page 29>**
kilogram --- 60.479----6.047 900 0E+01

taam [Thailand]   **<mass, special - see page 29>**
kilogram --- 60----6.000 000 0E+01

taam [Vietnam]   **<mass, special - see page 29>**
kilogram --- 60.453----6.045 300 0E+01

tabla [Somalia]   **<volume, special - see page 29>**
liter --- 20.385----2.038 500 0E+01

tabla [Somaliland]   **<volume, special - see page 29>**
liter --- 20.4----2.040 000 0E+01

table [Lebanon, cereals]   **<mass, special - see page 29>**
kilogram --- 15----1.500 000 0E+01

tablespoon [Canada, measuring]   **<volume>**
bushel [UK] --	0.000 390 6	3.906 243 4E–04
bushel [US, dry] --------------------------------------	0.000 403 1	4.031 464 8E–04
centiliter --	1.420 650 7	1.420 650 7E+00
cubic foot --	0.000 501 7	5.016 980 7E–04
cubic inch --	0.866 934 3	8.669 342 6E–01
cubic meter ---	0.000 014 2	1.420 650 7E–05
cup [Canada, measuring] -------------------------------	0.062 499 9	6.249 989 4E–02
cup [US, measuring] -----------------------------------	0.060 047 4	6.004 739 5E–02
drachm [UK, liquid] -----------------------------------	3.999 993 2	3.999 993 2E+00
dram [Canada, liquid] ---------------------------------	3.999 993 2	3.999 993 2E+00

Convert From		<Type of Unit>
Convert To	Standard	Scientific

dram [US, liquid]	3.843 033 3	3.843 033 3E+00
drop [US, liquid]	172.936 5	1.729 365 0E+02
gallon [Canada, liquid]	0.003 125	3.124 994 7E-03
gallon [UK, dry or liquid]	0.003 125	3.124 994 7E-03
gallon [US, liquid]	0.003 753	3.752 962 2E-03
liter	0.014 206 5	1.420 650 7E-02
ounce [UK, liquid]	0.499 999 2	4.999 991 5E-01
ounce [US, liquid]	0.480 379 2	4.803 791 6E-01
tablespoon [US, measuring]	0.960 758 3	9.607 583 1E-01
teaspoon [Canada, measuring]	3	3.000 000 0E+00
teaspoon [US, measuring]	2.882 274 9	2.882 274 9E+00

tablespoon [US, measuring]		<volume>
centiliter	1.478 676 5	1.478 676 5E+00
cubic foot	0.000 522 2	5.221 896 7E-04
cubic inch	0.902 343 8	9.023 437 5E-01
cubic meter	0.000 014 8	1.478 676 5E-05
cup [Canada, measuring]	0.065 052 7	6.505 267 1E-02
cup [US, measuring]	0.062 5	6.250 000 0E-02
drachm [UK, liquid]	4.163 370 9	4.163 370 9E+00
dram [Canada, liquid]	4.163 370 9	4.163 370 9E+00
dram [US, liquid]	4	4.000 000 0E+00
drop [US, liquid]	180	1.800 000 0E+02
gill [UK]	0.104 084 3	1.040 842 7E-01
gill [US]	0.125	1.250 000 0E-01
liter	0.014 786 8	1.478 676 5E-02
minim [UK]	249.802 26	2.498 022 6E+02
minim [US]	240	2.400 000 0E+02
ounce [UK, liquid]	0.520 421 4	5.204 213 7E-01
ounce [US, liquid]	0.5	5.000 000 0E-01
pint [UK]	0.026 021 1	2.602 106 8E-02
pint [US, liquid]	0.031 25	3.125 000 0E-02
tablespoon [Canada, measuring]	1.040 844 5	1.040 844 5E+00
teaspoon [Canada, measuring]	3.122 533 5	3.122 533 5E+00
teaspoon [US, measuring]	3	3.000 000 0E+00

tac [Vietnam]		<length, special - see page 29>
centimeter	4	4.000 000 0E+00

tac [Vietnam]		<area, special - see page 29>
square meter	2.4	2.400 000 0E+00

tael [Brunei]		<mass, special - see page 29>
gram	37.8	3.780 000 0E+01

tael [Cambodia]		<mass, special - see page 29>
gram	37.5	3.750 000 0E+01

tael [China]		<mass, special - see page 29>
gram	37.78	3.778 000 0E+01

tael [Hong Kong]		<mass, special - see page 29>
gram	37.799	3.779 900 0E+01

tael [Japan]		<mass, special - see page 29>
gram	37.5	3.750 000 0E+01

tael [Macao]		<mass, special - see page 29>
gram	37.799	3.779 900 0E+01

tael [Philippines]		<mass, special - see page 29>
gram	39.531	3.953 100 0E+01

tael [Singapore, precious metals and medicine]		<mass, special - see page 29>
gram	34.447 4	3.444 740 0E+01

tael [Thailand]		<mass, special - see page 29>
gram	60	6.000 000 0E+01

tael [Vietnam]		<mass, special - see page 29>
gram	37.783	3.778 300 0E+01

Convert From / Convert To	Standard	Scientific
tagwerk [Germany, Bavaria]	<area, special - see page 29>	
are	34.073	3.407 300 0E+01
tagwerk [Germany, Wurttemberg]	<area, special - see page 29>	
are	1.168 2	1.168 200 0E+00
tahil [Brunei]	<mass, special - see page 29>	
gram	37.8	3.780 000 0E+01
tahil [Cambodia]	<mass, special - see page 29>	
gram	37.5	3.750 000 0E+01
tahil [China]	<mass, special - see page 29>	
gram	50	5.000 000 0E+01
tahil [Hong Kong]	<mass, special - see page 29>	
gram	37.8	3.780 000 0E+01
tahil [Macao]	<mass, special - see page 29>	
gram	37.8	3.780 000 0E+01
tahil [Malaysia]	<mass, special - see page 29>	
gram	37.798	3.779 800 0E+01
tahil [North Borneo]	<mass, special - see page 29>	
gram	37.799 36	3.779 936 0E+01
tahil [Sarawak]	<mass, special - see page 29>	
gram	37.799 36	3.779 936 0E+01
tahil [Singapore]	<mass, special - see page 29>	
gram	37.799	3.779 900 0E+01
tai [Taiwan]	<mass, special - see page 29>	
gram	600	6.000 000 0E+02
taim [Burma]	<length, special - see page 29>	
meter	0.457 2	4.572 000 0E-01
taim [Cambodia]	<length, special - see page 29>	
meter	0.5	5.000 000 0E-01
taim [India]	<length, special - see page 29>	
centimeter	45.72	4.572 000 0E+01
taim [Malaysia]	<length, special - see page 29>	
meter	0.457 2	4.572 000 0E-01
taim [Pakistan]	<length, special - see page 29>	
meter	0.457 2	4.572 000 0E-01
taim [Singapore]	<length, special - see page 29>	
meter	0.457	4.570 000 0E-01
taim [Somalia]	<length, special - see page 29>	
meter	0.558 8	5.588 000 0E-01
taing [Burma]	<length, special - see page 29>	
kilometer	3.91	3.910 000 0E+00
talangva [Laos]	<area, special - see page 29>	
square meter	4	4.000 000 0E+00
talanton [Greece, ancient]	<mass, special - see page 29>	
kilogram	29.2	2.920 000 0E+01
talbot	<quantity of light>	
candela second steradian	1	1.000 000 0E+00
joule	0.001 464 1	1.464 128 8E-03
lumen second	1	1.000 000 0E+00
lux second square meter	1	1.000 000 0E+00
wattsecond [light at 540 THz]	0.001 464 1	1.464 128 8E-03
tale [China]	<mass, special - see page 29>	
gram	37.78	3.778 000 0E+01
tale [Sumatra, gold and silver]	<mass, special - see page 29>	
gram	61.52	6.152 000 0E+01
talent [Babylon, ancient]	<mass, special - see page 29>	
gram	49.11	4.911 000 0E+01

talent [Egypt, ancient]
kilogram -- \<mass, special - see page 29\>
------ 46.7 --- 4.670 000 0E+01

talent [Greece, ancient]
kilogram -- \<mass, special - see page 29\>
------ 26.196 --- 2.619 600 0E+01

talent [Hebrew, ancient]
kilogram -- \<mass, special - see page 29\>
------ 34.3 --- 3.430 000 0E+01

talent [Mesopotamia, ancient]
kilogram -- \<mass, special - see page 29\>
------ 28.8 --- 2.880 000 0E+01

talenton [Greece, ancient]
kilogram -- \<mass, special - see page 29\>
------ 150 --- 1.500 000 0E+02

talentum [Rome, ancient]
kilogram -- \<mass, special - see page 29\>
------ 25.8 --- 2.580 000 0E+01

taler [Germany, silver]
gram -- \<mass, special - see page 29\>
------ 16.67 --- 1.667 000 0E+01

tali [Indonesia]
gram -- \<mass, special - see page 29\>
------ 3.381 --- 3.381 000 0E+00

tam [Brunei]
kilogram -- \<mass, special - see page 29\>
------ 60.479 --- 6.047 900 0E+01

tam [Cambodia]
kilogram -- \<mass, special - see page 29\>
------ 60 --- 6.000 000 0E+01

tam [China]
kilogram -- \<mass, special - see page 29\>
------ 60.479 --- 6.047 900 0E+01

tam [Hong Kong]
kilogram -- \<mass, special - see page 29\>
------ 60.479 --- 6.047 900 0E+01

tam [Indonesia]
kilogram -- \<mass, special - see page 29\>
------ 61.761 --- 6.176 100 0E+01

tam [Japan]
kilogram -- \<mass, special - see page 29\>
------ 60 --- 6.000 000 0E+01

tam [Laos]
kilogram -- \<mass, special - see page 29\>
------ 60 --- 6.000 000 0E+01

tam [Macao]
kilogram -- \<mass, special - see page 29\>
------ 60.479 --- 6.047 900 0E+01

tam [Malaysia]
kilogram -- \<mass, special - see page 29\>
------ 60.479 --- 6.047 900 0E+01

tam [Philippines]
kilogram -- \<mass, special - see page 29\>
------ 63.249 --- 6.324 900 0E+01

tam [Singapore]
kilogram -- \<mass, special - see page 29\>
------ 60.479 --- 6.047 900 0E+01

tam [Thailand]
kilogram -- \<mass, special - see page 29\>
------ 60 --- 6.000 000 0E+01

tam [Vietnam]
kilogram -- \<mass, special - see page 29\>
------ 60.453 --- 6.045 300 0E+01

tamlaum [Thailand]
liter --- \<volume, special - see page 29\>
------ 400 --- 4.000 000 0E+02

tamlung [Thailand]
gram -- \<mass, special - see page 29\>
------ 60 --- 6.000 000 0E+01

tamna [Morocco]
square meter -- \<area, special - see page 29\>
------ 225 --- 2.250 000 0E+02

tamuga [Costa Rica, solidified sugar cane juice]
kilogram -- \<mass, special - see page 29\>
------ 2.07 --- 2.070 000 0E+00

tan [Brunei]
kilogram -- \<mass, special - see page 29\>
------ 60.479 --- 6.047 900 0E+01

tan [Cambodia]
kilogram -- \<mass, special - see page 29\>
------ 60 --- 6.000 000 0E+01

Convert From Convert To	Standard	**\<Type of Unit\>** Scientific
tan [China]	\<volume, special - see page 29\>	
hectoliter	1.035 5	1.035 500 0E+00
tan [China]	\<mass, special - see page 29\>	
kilogram	50	5.000 000 0E+01
tan [Hong Kong]	\<mass, special - see page 29\>	
kilogram	60.479	6.047 900 0E+01
tan [Japan]	\<mass, special - see page 29\>	
kilogram	60	6.000 000 0E+01
tan [Japan]	\<area, special - see page 29\>	
are	9.92	9.920 000 0E+00
tan [Laos]	\<mass, special - see page 29\>	
kilogram	60	6.000 000 0E+01
tan [Macao]	\<mass, special - see page 29\>	
kilogram	60.479	6.047 900 0E+01
tan [Malaysia]	\<mass, special - see page 29\>	
kilogram	60.479	6.047 900 0E+01
tan [Philippines]	\<mass, special - see page 29\>	
kilogram	63.249	6.324 900 0E+01
tan [Singapore]	\<mass, special - see page 29\>	
kilogram	60.479	6.047 900 0E+01
tan [South Korea]	\<area, special - see page 29\>	
square meter	991.74	9.917 400 0E+02
tan [Thailand]	\<mass, special - see page 29\>	
kilogram	60	6.000 000 0E+01
tan [Vietnam]	\<mass, special - see page 29\>	
kilogram	60.453	6.045 300 0E+01
tanan [Thailand]	\<volume, special - see page 29\>	
liter	1	1.000 000 0E+00
tang [India, pearls]	\<mass, special - see page 29\>	
gram	12.96	1.296 000 0E+01
tanica [Eritrea]	\<volume, special - see page 29\>	
liter	18	1.800 000 0E+01
tanica [Iraq]	\<volume, special - see page 29\>	
liter	18.184	1.818 400 0E+01
tanica [Somalia]	\<volume, special - see page 29\>	
liter	18	1.800 000 0E+01
tanica [Somaliland]	\<volume, special - see page 29\>	
liter	18	1.800 000 0E+01
tank [India, pearls]	\<mass, special - see page 29\>	
gram	12.96	1.296 000 0E+01
tao [Cambodia, rice paddy]	\<mass, special - see page 29\>	
kilogram	12	1.200 000 0E+01
tao [Cambodia, rice, milled]	\<mass, special - see page 29\>	
kilogram	15	1.500 000 0E+01
tao [Cambodia]	\<volume, special - see page 29\>	
liter	15	1.500 000 0E+01
tar [Burma]	\<length, special - see page 29\>	
meter	3.2	3.200 000 0E+00
tarabiit [Morocco]	\<area, special - see page 29\>	
square meter	450	4.500 000 0E+02
tarang ngu [Thailand]	\<area, special - see page 29\>	
square meter	5.936 5	5.936 500 0E+00
tarang sao [Thailand]	\<area, special - see page 29\>	
square meter	53.429	5.342 900 0E+01

Convert From	Convert To	<Type of Unit>	Standard	Scientific
tarang sen [Thailand]	square meter	**<area, special - see page 29>**	1,600	1.600 000 0E+03
tarang wah [Thailand]	square meter	**<area, special - see page 29>**	4	4.000 000 0E+00
tarea [Cuba]	square meter	**<area, special - see page 29>**	69.03	6.903 000 0E+01
tarea [Dominican Republic]	square meter	**<area, special - see page 29>**	628.8	6.288 000 0E+02
tarefa [Brazil]	square meter	**<area, special - see page 29>**	968	9.680 000 0E+02
tarialte [Morocco]	hectare	**<area, special - see page 29>**	0.36	3.600 000 0E–01
tarri [Algeria]	liter	**<volume, special - see page 29>**	19.842	1.984 200 0E+01
tartimar [Hebrew, ancient]	gram	**<mass, special - see page 29>**	179.25	1.792 500 0E+02
tartous [Cyprus]	square meter	**<area, special - see page 29>**	1,337.8	1.337 800 0E+03
tartous [Israel]	square meter	**<area, special - see page 29>**	1,000	1.000 000 0E+03
tartous [Jordan]	square meter	**<area, special - see page 29>**	1,000	1.000 000 0E+03
tartous [Lebanon]	square meter	**<area, special - see page 29>**	919	9.190 000 0E+02
tartous [Libya]	square meter	**<area, special - see page 29>**	919	9.190 000 0E+02
tartous [Syria]	square meter	**<area, special - see page 29>**	919	9.190 000 0E+02
tartous [Turkey]	square meter	**<area, special - see page 29>**	919	9.190 000 0E+02
tartous [Yugoslavia]	square meter	**<area, special - see page 29>**	1,000	1.000 000 0E+03
task [Belize]	are	**<area, special - see page 29>**	5.22	5.220 000 0E+00
task [British Honduras]	square meter	**<area, special - see page 29>**	522	5.220 000 0E+02
task [Costa Rica]	meter	**<length, special - see page 29>**	20.064	2.006 400 0E+01
task [Guatemala]	meter	**<length, special - see page 29>**	20.064	2.006 400 0E+01
task [Nicaragua]	meter	**<length, special - see page 29>**	20.16	2.016 000 0E+01
tat [Abyssinia, ancient]	centimeter	**<length, special - see page 29>**	2.5	2.500 000 0E+00
tat [Ethiopia]	cubic meter	**<volume, special - see page 29>**	0.025	2.500 000 0E–02
tat [Ethiopia]	centimeter	**<length, special - see page 29>**	2	2.000 000 0E+00
tau [China]	liter	**<volume, special - see page 29>**	10.354 7	1.035 470 0E+01
tauk [India, pearls]	gram	**<mass, special - see page 29>**	4.67	4.670 000 0E+00
taung [Burma]	meter	**<length, special - see page 29>**	0.457 2	4.572 000 0E–01

taung [Cambodia]
  meter-- <length, special - see page 29>
  --- 0.5----5.000 000 0E-01

taung [India]
  meter-- <length, special - see page 29>
  -- 0.457 2----4.572 000 0E-01

taung [Malaysia]
  meter-- <length, special - see page 29>
  -- 0.457 2----4.572 000 0E-01

taung [Pakistan]
  meter-- <length, special - see page 29>
  -- 0.457 2----4.572 000 0E-01

taung [Singapore]
  meter-- <length, special - see page 29>
  --- 0.457----4.570 000 0E-01

taung [Somalia]
  meter-- <length, special - see page 29>
  -- 0.558 8----5.588 000 0E-01

tavola [Italy]
  square meter----------------------------------- <area, special - see page 29>
  --- 38----3.800 000 0E+01

taza [Cuba]
  milliliter--- <volume, special - see page 29>
  --- 236----2.360 000 0E+02

tcharak [Iran]
  gram-- <mass, special - see page 29>
  -- 0.75----7.500 000 0E-01

tcharak [Iran]
  centimeter------------------------------------- <length, special - see page 29>
  --- 26----2.600 000 0E+01

tcharka [Russia]
  liter--- <volume, special - see page 29>
  -- 0.122 994 1----1.229 941 0E-01

tchast [Russia]
  liter--- <volume, special - see page 29>
  -- 0.109 328 1----1.093 281 0E-01

tcheirek [Iran]
  kilogram --------------------------------------- <mass, special - see page 29>
  -- 0.742 336----7.423 360 0E-01

tcheirek [Iran]
  centimeter------------------------------------- <length, special - see page 29>
  --- 26----2.600 000 0E+01

tcheki [Turkey]
  kilogram --------------------------------------- <mass, special - see page 29>
  --- 225.8----2.258 000 0E+02

tchetverik [Russia]
  liter--- <volume, special - see page 29>
  -- 26.238 74----2.623 874 0E+01

tchetvert [Russia, dry]
  liter--- <volume, special - see page 29>
  -- 209.909 9----2.099 099 0E+02

tchetvert [Russia]
  hectare--- <area, special - see page 29>
  -- 0.546 269----5.462 699 0E-01

teacup [Scandinavia]
  milliliter-- <volume, special - see page 29>
  --- 125----1.250 000 0E+02

teacup [UK]
  centiliter--------------------------------------- <volume, special - see page 29>
  --- 25----2.500 000 0E+01

teaspoon [Canada, measuring]
                                                                    <volume>
  cubic centimeter------------------------------------ 4.735 502 4----4.735 502 4E+00
  cubic foot--- 0.000 167 2----1.672 326 9E-04
  cubic inch-- 0.288 978 1----2.889 780 9E-01
  cubic meter-- 0.000 004 7----4.735 502 4E-06
  cup [Canada, measuring] ------------------------- 0.020 833 3----2.083 329 8E-02
  cup [US, measuring] ---------------------------------- 0.020 015 8----2.001 579 8E-02
  drachm [UK, liquid] ----------------------------------- 1.333 331 1----1.333 331 1E+00
  dram [Canada, liquid] -------------------------------- 1.333 331 1----1.333 331 1E+00
  dram [US, liquid] -------------------------------------- 1.281 011 1----1.281 011 0E+00
  liter-- 0.004 735 5----4.735 502 4E-03
  milliliter--- 4.735 502 4----4.735 502 4E+00
  ounce [UK, liquid] ------------------------------------- 0.166 666 4----1.666 663 8E-01
  ounce [US, liquid] ------------------------------------- 0.160 126 4----1.601 263 9E-01
  pint [UK] --- 0.008 333 3----8.333 319 2E-03
  pint [US, dry] -- 0.008 600 5----8.600 458 7E-03
  pint [US, liquid] --------------------------------------- 0.010 007 9----1.000 789 9E-02
  quart [UK] -- 0.004 166 7----4.166 659 6E-03

Convert From Convert To	Standard	<Type of Unit> Scientific
quart [US, dry]	0.004 300 2	4.300 229 2E-03
quart [US, liquid]	0.005 003 9	5.003 949 6E-03
scruple [UK, liquid]	3.999 993 2	3.999 993 2E+00
tablespoon [Canada, measuring]	0.333 333 3	3.333 333 3E-01
tablespoon [US, measuring]	0.320 252 8	3.202 527 7E-01
teaspoon [US, measuring]	0.960 758 3	9.607 583 1E-01

teaspoon [US, measuring]		**<volume>**
cubic centimeter	4.928 921 6	4.928 921 6E+00
cubic foot	0.000 174 1	1.740 632 2E-04
cubic inch	0.300 781 3	3.007 812 5E-01
cubic meter	0.000 004 9	4.928 921 6E-06
cup [Canada, measuring]	0.021 684 2	2.168 422 4E-02
cup [US, measuring]	0.020 833 3	2.083 333 3E-02
drachm [UK, liquid]	1.387 790 3	1.387 790 3E+00
dram [Canada, liquid]	1.387 790 3	1.387 790 3E+00
dram [US, liquid]	1.333 333 3	1.333 333 3E+00
drop [US, liquid]	60	6.000 000 0E+01
liter	0.004 928 9	4.928 921 6E-03
milliliter	4.928 921 6	4.928 921 6E+00
minim [UK]	83.267 418	8.326 741 8E+01
minim [US]	80	8.000 000 0E+01
ounce [UK, liquid]	0.173 473 8	1.734 737 9E-01
ounce [US, liquid]	0.166 666 7	1.666 666 7E-01
scruple [UK, liquid]	4.163 370 9	4.163 370 9E+00
tablespoon [Canada, measuring]	0.346 948 2	3.469 481 6E-01
tablespoon [US, measuring]	0.333 333 3	3.333 333 3E-01
teaspoon [Canada, measuring]	1.040 844 5	1.040 844 5E+00

tefah [Hebrew, ancient]		**<length, special - see page 29>**
centimeter	7.8	7.800 000 0E+00

teman [Arabia]		**<volume, special - see page 29>**
liter	85	8.500 000 0E+01

teman [Libya]		**<volume, special - see page 29>**
liter	26.82	2.682 000 0E+01

teminye [Syria]		**<volume, special - see page 29>**
liter	2.41	2.410 000 0E+00

ten		**<units>**
decade	1	1.000 000 0E+00
single	10	1.000 000 0E+01
unit	10	1.000 000 0E+01

ten drachma [Greece, ancient]		**<mass, special - see page 29>**
gram	63.04	6.304 000 0E+01

teneka [Iraq]		**<volume, special - see page 29>**
liter	18.184	1.818 400 0E+01

teneka [Somalia]		**<volume, special - see page 29>**
liter	18	1.800 000 0E+01

teng [Burma, dry]		**<volume, special - see page 29>**
liter	40.915	4.091 500 0E+01

teningsfet [Iceland]		**<volume, special - see page 29>**
cubic meter	0.030 9	3.090 000 0E-02

tenthmeter		**<length>**
angstrom	1	1.000 000 0E+00
bicron	100	1.000 000 0E+02
fermi	100,000	1.000 000 0E+05
meter	<<<	1.000 000 0E-10
microinch	0.003 937	3.937 007 9E-03
micromicron	100	1.000 000 0E+02
micron	0.000 1	1.000 000 0E-04
millimicron	0.1	1.000 000 0E-01
nanometer	0.1	1.000 000 0E-01
stigma	100	1.000 000 0E+02

wavelength of orange-red spectral line of krypton-86	0.000 165 1	1.650 763 7E−04
x-unit	997.932 09	9.979 320 9E+02

tepah [Hebrew, ancient]   <length, special - see page 29>
meter	0.074	7.400 000 0E−02

tephah [Hebrew, ancient]   <length, special - see page 29>
centimeter	9.3	9.300 000 0E+00

terabar   <pressure>
atmosphere [standard]	>>>	9.869 232 7E+11
atmosphere [technical]	>>>	1.019 716 2E+12
bar	>>>	1.000 000 0E+12
centimeter of mercury [0 °C, by convention]	>>>	7.500 615 8E+13
centimeter of water [4 °C, by convention]	>>>	1.019 716 2E+15
foot of mercury [0 °C, by convention]	>>>	2.460 831 9E+12
foot of water [4 °C, by convention]	>>>	3.345 525 6E+13
kilogram-force/square millimeter	>>>	1.019 716 2E+10
kilopond/square millimeter	>>>	1.019 716 2E+10
kip/square inch	>>>	1.450 377 4E+10
newton/square millimeter	>>>	1.000 000 0E+11
pascal	>>>	1.000 000 0E+17
pound-force/square inch	>>>	1.450 377 4E+13
ton-force/square inch [long]	>>>	6.474 899 0E+09
ton-force/square inch [short]	>>>	7.251 886 9E+09
torr	>>>	7.500 616 8E+14
zettapascal	0.000 1	1.000 000 0E−04

terabecquerel   <radionuclide activity>
1/second	>>>	1.000 000 0E+12
becquerel	>>>	1.000 000 0E+12
curie	27.027 027	2.702 702 7E+01
rutherford	1,000,000	1.000 000 0E+06

teracandela   <luminous intensity>
candela	>>>	1.000 000 0E+12

teracoulomb   <electric charge>
abcoulomb	>>>	1.000 000 0E+11
coulomb	>>>	1.000 000 0E+12
faraday [based on carbon-12]	>>>	1.036 427 2E+07
statcoulomb	>>>	2.997 924 6E+21

teraelectronvolt   <energy>
atomic mass unit [unified, C-12, 1986, eq. energy]	1,073.543 9	1.073 543 9E+03
Btu [I.T.]	<<<	1.518 571 1E−10
calorie [I.T.]	<<<	3.826 734 8E−08
calorie [kilogram, I.T.]	<<<	3.826 734 8E−11
centigrade heat unit [I.T.]	<<<	8.436 506 1E−11
centimeter gram-force	0.001 633 8	1.633 766 2E−03
cubic centimeter atmosphere	0.000 001 6	1.581 226 1E−06
cubic foot atmosphere	<<<	5.584 047 2E−11
deuteron rest mass [atomic physics, eq. energy]	533.158 92	5.331 589 2E+02
dyne centimeter	1.602 177 3	1.602 177 3E+00
electron rest mass [atomic physics, eq. energy]	1,956,950.8	1.956 950 8E+06
erg	1.602 177 3	1.602 177 3E+00
foot pound-force	0.000 000 1	1.181 705 4E−07
foot poundal	0.000 003 8	3.802 024 5E−06
gigaelectronvolt	1,000	1.000 000 0E+03
gram calorie	<<<	3.827 649 0E−08
inch ounce-force	0.000 022 7	2.268 874 3E−05
inch pound-force	0.000 001 4	1.418 046 4E−06
joule	0.000 000 2	1.602 177 3E−07
kilogram square meter/square second	0.000 000 2	1.602 177 3E−07
kilopond meter	<<<	1.633 766 2E−08
liter atmosphere	<<<	1.581 226 1E−09
meter kilogram-force	<<<	1.633 766 2E−08
muon rest mass [atomic physics, eq. energy]	9,464.463 8	9.464 463 8E+03

	Standard	Scientific
neutron rest mass [atomic physics, eq. energy]	1,064.321 6	1.064 321 6E+03
newton meter	0.000 000 2	1.602 177 3E-07
proton rest mass [atomic physics, eq. energy]	1,065.788 7	1.065 788 7E+03
wattsecond	0.000 000 2	1.602 177 3E-07
terafarad		**\<capacitance\>**
abfarad	1,000	1.000 000 0E+03
coulomb/volt	>>>	1.000 000 0E+12
electromagnetic unit of capacitance [cgs system]	1,000	1.000 000 0E+03
farad	>>>	1.000 000 0E+12
teragram		**\<mass\>**
kilogram	>>>	1.000 000 0E+09
megaton [metric]	1	1.000 000 0E+00
megatonne	1	1.000 000 0E+00
ounce	>>>	3.527 396 2E+10
pound	>>>	2.204 622 6E+09
quintal [metric]	>>>	1.000 000 0E+07
ton [long]	984,206.53	9.842 065 3E+05
ton [metric]	1,000,000	1.000 000 0E+06
ton [short]	1,102,311.3	1.102 311 3E+06
tonne	1,000,000	1.000 000 0E+06
terahenry		**\<electric inductance\>**
abhenry	>>>	1.000 000 0E+21
electrostatic unit of inductance [cgs system]	1.112 650 1	1.112 650 1E+00
gaussian electric inductance	1.112 650 1	1.112 650 1E+00
henry	>>>	1.000 000 0E+12
stathenry	1.112 650 1	1.112 650 1E+00
terahertz		**\<frequency\>**
1/second	>>>	1.000 000 0E+12
degree/second	>>>	3.600 000 0E+14
fresnel	1	1.000 000 0E+00
gigahertz	1,000	1.000 000 0E+03
radian/second	>>>	6.283 185 3E+12
revolution/second	>>>	1.000 000 0E+12
terajoule		**\<energy\>**
cheval vapeur heure [France]	377,672.67	3.776 726 7E+05
coal equivalent kilogram [UN, standard]	34,120.842	3.412 084 2E+04
coal equivalent metric ton [UN, standard]	34.120 842	3.412 084 2E+01
gigawatthour	0.277 777 8	2.777 777 8E-01
gram [atomic physics, eq. energy]	0.011 126 5	1.112 650 1E-02
hectowatthour	2,777,777.8	2.777 777 8E+06
horsepower hour	372,506.14	3.725 061 4E+05
horsepower hour [metric]	377,672.67	3.776 726 7E+05
joule	>>>	1.000 000 0E+12
kilogram [atomic physics, eq. energy]	0.000 011 1	1.112 650 1E-05
kilogram calorie [15 °C, NBS, 1939]	>>>	2.389 029 6E+08
kiloton [metric, explosive energy]	0.239 005 7	2.390 057 4E-01
kilowatthour	277,777.78	2.777 777 8E+05
megaton [metric, explosive energy]	0.000 239	2.390 057 4E-04
pferdestarkenstunde [Germany]	377,672.67	3.776 726 7E+05
quad	0.000 000 9	9.478 171 2E-07
therm [EEC]	9,478.171 2	9.478 171 2E+03
therm [US]	9,480.434 3	9.480 434 3E+03
thermie [France]	238,902.96	2.389 029 6E+05
ton [metric, explosive energy]	239.005 74	2.390 057 4E+02
watthour	>>>	2.777 777 8E+08
teraliter		**\<volume\>**
acre foot	810,713.19	8.107 131 9E+05
acre inch	9,728,558.3	9.728 558 3E+06
barrel [UK]	>>>	6.110 256 9E+09
barrel [US, federal]	>>>	8.521 679 1E+09
barrel [US, federal proof spirits]	>>>	6.604 301 3E+09
barrel [US, liquid]	>>>	8.386 414 4E+09

Convert From Convert To	Standard	<Type of Unit> Scientific
barrel [US, petroleum]	>>>	6.289 810 8E+09
cubem	0.239 912 8	2.399 127 6E−01
cubic kilometer	1	1.000 000 0E+00
cubic meter	>>>	1.000 000 0E+09
cubic mile	0.239 912 8	2.399 127 6E−01
cubic yard	>>>	1.307 950 6E+09
drum [US, liquid]	>>>	4.803 128 2E+09
gallon [Canada, liquid]	>>>	2.199 692 5E+11
gallon [UK, dry or liquid]	>>>	2.199 692 5E+11
gallon [US, liquid]	>>>	2.641 720 5E+11
hectare meter	100,000	1.000 000 0E+05
liter	>>>	1.000 000 0E+12
pipe [UK]	>>>	2.036 752 3E+09
pipe [US, liquid]	>>>	2.096 603 6E+09
stere	>>>	1.000 000 0E+09
trillion cubic foot	0.035 314 7	3.531 466 7E−02
terameter		**<length>**
astronomical unit	6.684 587 2	6.684 587 2E+00
bevameter	1,000	1.000 000 0E+03
kiloparsec	<<<	3.240 779 3E−08
light year [based on mean Julian year]	0.000 105 7	1.057 000 8E−04
meter	>>>	1.000 000 0E+12
mile [international]	>>>	6.213 711 9E+08
mile [US, survey]	>>>	6.213 699 5E+08
myriameter	>>>	1.000 000 0E+08
parsec	0.000 032 4	3.240 779 3E−05
spat	1	1.000 000 0E+00
teramole		**<amount of substance>**
mole	>>>	1.000 000 0E+12
teranewton		**<force>**
crinal	>>>	1.000 000 0E+13
dyne	>>>	1.000 000 0E+17
gram-force	>>>	1.019 716 2E+14
newton	>>>	1.000 000 0E+12
ounce-force	>>>	3.596 943 1E+12
pond	>>>	1.019 716 2E+14
pound-force	>>>	2.248 089 4E+11
poundal	>>>	7.233 013 9E+12
teraohm		**<electric resistance>**
1/ siemens	>>>	1.000 000 0E+12
abohm	>>>	1.000 000 0E+21
ohm	>>>	1.000 000 0E+12
statohm	1.112 650 1	1.112 650 1E+00
terapascal		**<pressure>**
atmosphere [standard]	9,869,232.7	9.869 232 7E+06
atmosphere [technical]	>>>	1.019 716 2E+07
bar	>>>	1.000 000 0E+07
centimeter of mercury [0 °C, by convention]	>>>	7.500 615 8E+08
centimeter of water [4 °C, by convention]	>>>	1.019 716 2E+10
foot of mercury [0 °C, by convention]	>>>	2.460 831 9E+07
foot of water [4 °C, by convention]	>>>	3.345 525 6E+08
kilogram-force/square millimeter	101,971.62	1.019 716 2E+05
kilopond/square millimeter	101,971.62	1.019 716 2E+05
kip/square inch	145,037.74	1.450 377 4E+05
newton/square millimeter	1,000,000	1.000 000 0E+06
pascal	>>>	1.000 000 0E+12
terabar	0.000 01	1.000 000 0E−05
ton-force/square inch [short]	72,518.869	7.251 886 9E+04
torr	>>>	7.500 616 8E+09
terasiemens		**<electric conductance>**
abmho	1,000	1.000 000 0E+03
absiemens	1,000	1.000 000 0E+03

| Convert From | | <Type of Unit> |
| Convert To | Standard | Scientific |

electromagnetic unit of conductance [cgs system]	1,000	1.000 000 0E+03
siemens	>>>	1.000 000 0E+12
statsiemens	>>>	8.987 551 8E+23

teratesla   <magnetic flux density>

electrostatic unit of magnetic flux density [cgs system]	333,564.095	3.335 641 0E+05
gaussian magnetic flux density	333,564.095	3.335 641 0E+05
line/square centimeter [of magnetic force]	>>>	1.000 000 0E+16
maxwell/square meter	>>>	1.000 000 0E+12
tesla	>>>	1.000 000 0E+12

teravolt   <electric potential>

abvolt	>>>	1.000 000 0E+20
erg/franklin	>>>	3.335 641 0E+09
statvolt	>>>	3.335 641 0E+09
volt	>>>	1.000 000 0E+12

terawatt   <power>

Btu/second [I.T.]	>>>	9.478 171 2E+08
Btu/second [thermoc.]	>>>	9.484 514 1E+08
calorie/second [I.T.]	>>>	2.388 459 2E+11
calorie/second [thermoc.]	>>>	2.390 057 4E+11
centigrade heat unit/second [mean]	>>>	5.261 590 5E+08
cubic meter atmosphere/second	>>>	9.869 232 7E+12
dyne centimeter/second	>>>	1.000 000 0E+19
erg/second	>>>	1.000 000 0E+19
foot pound-force/second	>>>	7.375 621 5E+11
foot poundal/second	>>>	2.373 036 0E+13
gram-force centimeter/second	>>>	1.019 716 2E+16
horsepower	>>>	1.341 022 1E+09
horsepower [metric]	>>>	1.359 621 6E+09
joule/second	>>>	1.000 000 0E+12
kilocalorie/second [I.T.]	>>>	2.388 459 0E+08
kilogram-force meter/second	>>>	1.019 716 2E+11
kilopond meter/second	>>>	1.019 716 2E+11
million Btu/hour [I.T.]	3,412,141.6	3.412 141 6E+06
newton meter/second	>>>	1.000 000 0E+12
volt ampere	>>>	1.000 000 0E+12
watt	>>>	1.000 000 0E+12

terawatthour   <energy>

cheval vapeur heure [France]	>>>	1.359 621 6E+09
coal equivalent kilogram [UN, standard]	>>>	1.228 350 3E+08
coal equivalent metric ton [UN, standard]	122,835.03	1.228 350 3E+05
gram [atomic physics, eq. energy]	40.055 402	4.005 540 2E+01
gram calorie	>>>	8.600 506 5E+14
horsepower hour	>>>	1.341 022 1E+09
horsepower hour [metric]	>>>	1.359 621 6E+09
joule	>>>	3.600 000 0E+15
kilocalorie [I.T.]	>>>	8.598 452 3E+11
kilogram [atomic physics, eq. energy]	0.040 055 4	4.005 540 2E-02
kiloton [metric, explosive energy]	860.420 65	8.604 206 5E+02
megaton [metric, explosive energy]	0.860 420 7	8.604 206 5E-01
quad	0.003 412 1	3.412 141 6E-03
therm [EEC]	>>>	3.412 141 6E+07
therm [US]	>>>	3.412 956 3E+07
thermie [France]	>>>	8.600 506 5E+08
ton [metric, explosive energy]	860,420.65	8.604 206 5E+05

teraweber   <magnetic flux>

gauss square centimeter	>>>	1.000 000 0E+20
maxwell	>>>	1.000 000 0E+20
statweber	>>>	3.335 641 0E+09
unit pole	>>>	7.957 747 5E+18
weber	>>>	1.000 000 0E+12

tercia [Colombia]   <length, special - see page 29>

centimeter	27.87	2.787 000 0E+01

tercia [Costa Rica] — \<length, special - see page 29\>
meter ---- 0.279 ---- 2.790 000 0E−01

tercia [Cuba] — \<length, special - see page 29\>
meter ---- 0.282 7 ---- 2.827 000 0E−01

tercia [Guatemala] — \<length, special - see page 29\>
meter ---- 0.279 ---- 2.790 000 0E−01

tercia [Haiti] — \<length, special - see page 29\>
meter ---- 0.324 8 ---- 3.248 000 0E−01

tercia [Mexico] — \<length, special - see page 29\>
meter ---- 0.279 ---- 2.790 000 0E−01

tercia [Nicaragua] — \<length, special - see page 29\>
meter ---- 0.28 ---- 2.800 000 0E−01

tercia [Paraguay] — \<length, special - see page 29\>
meter ---- 0.289 ---- 2.890 000 0E−01

tercia [Spain] — \<length, special - see page 29\>
meter ---- 0.279 ---- 2.790 000 0E−01

tercio [Cuba, tobacco] — \<mass, special - see page 29\>
kilogram ---- 50.55 ---- 5.055 000 0E+01

tercio [Ecuador] — \<mass, special - see page 29\>
kilogram ---- 36.8 ---- 3.680 000 0E+01

tercio [Mexico] — \<mass, special - see page 29\>
kilogram ---- 73.64 ---- 7.364 000 0E+01

tercio [Venezuela] — \<mass, special - see page 29\>
kilogram ---- 40 ---- 4.000 000 0E+01

tereia [Spain] — \<length, special - see page 29\>
meter ---- 0.278 635 ---- 2.786 350 0E−01

termini [Tunisia] — \<mass, special - see page 29\>
gram ---- 3.936 ---- 3.936 000 0E+00

terto [Egypt, ancient] — \<length, special - see page 29\>
centimeter ---- 22.5 ---- 2.250 000 0E+01

teruncius [Rome, ancient] — \<mass, special - see page 29\>
gram ---- 81.86 ---- 8.186 000 0E+01

terz [Malta, beer, wine and spirits] — \<volume, special - see page 29\>
milliliter ---- 284.1 ---- 2.841 000 0E+02

terz [Malta, oil and milk] — \<volume, special - see page 29\>
milliliter ---- 319.6 ---- 3.196 000 0E+02

tesla — \<magnetic flux density\>
abtesla ---- 10,000 ---- 1.000 000 0E+04
ampere henry/square meter ---- 1 ---- 1.000 000 0E+00
electromagnetic unit of magnetic flux density [cgs system] -- 10,000 ---- 1.000 000 0E+04
electrostatic unit of magnetic flux density [cgs system] 0.000 000 3 ---- 3.335 641 0E−07
gamma ---- >>> ---- 1.000 000 0E+09
gauss ---- 10,000 ---- 1.000 000 0E+04
gaussian magnetic flux density ---- 0.000 000 3 ---- 3.335 641 0E−07
joule/ampere square meter ---- 1 ---- 1.000 000 0E+00
line/square centimeter [of magnetic force] ---- 10,000 ---- 1.000 000 0E+04
maxwell/square meter ---- 1 ---- 1.000 000 0E+00
newton/ampere meter ---- 1 ---- 1.000 000 0E+00
stattesla ---- 0.000 000 3 ---- 3.335 641 0E−07
volt second/square meter ---- 1 ---- 1.000 000 0E+00
weber/square meter ---- 1 ---- 1.000 000 0E+00

tesla square meter — \<magnetic flux\>
ampere henry ---- 1 ---- 1.000 000 0E+00
gauss square centimeter ---- >>> ---- 1.000 000 0E+08
joule/ampere ---- 1 ---- 1.000 000 0E+00
maxwell ---- >>> ---- 1.000 000 0E+08
statweber ---- 0.003 335 6 ---- 3.335 641 0E−03
unit pole ---- 7,957,747.54 ---- 7.957 747 5E+06

Convert From Convert To	<Type of Unit>	
	Standard	Scientific
volt second	1	1.000 000 0E+00
weber	1	1.000 000 0E+00
tetradrachm [Egypt, ancient]	<mass, special - see page 29>	
gram	15.6	1.560 000 0E+01
tetradrachm [Greece, ancient]	<mass, special - see page 29>	
gram	19.4	1.940 000 0E+01
tetradrachma [Greece, ancient]	<mass, special - see page 29>	
gram	17.4	1.740 000 0E+01
tetradrachma [Hebrew, ancient]	<mass, special - see page 29>	
gram	14	1.400 000 0E+01
tex	<linear density>	
denier	9	9.000 000 0E+00
drex	10	1.000 000 0E+01
gram/kilometer	1	1.000 000 0E+00
kilogram/meter	0.000 001	1.000 000 0E−06
milligram/meter	1	1.000 000 0E+00
ounce/foot	0.000 010 8	1.075 150 4E−05
pound/yard	0.000 002	2.015 906 9E−06
thail [Indonesia, diamonds]	<mass, special - see page 29>	
gram	54.09	5.409 000 0E+01
thail [Indonesia, opium]	<mass, special - see page 29>	
gram	38.601	3.860 100 0E+01
thail [Indonesia, precious metals]	<mass, special - see page 29>	
gram	54.09	5.409 000 0E+01
thaler [Oman, Maria Theresa]	<mass, special - see page 29>	
gram	28.05	2.805 000 0E+01
thamardi tin [Burma, dry]	<volume, special - see page 29>	
liter	40.915	4.091 500 0E+01
thamardi tinn [Burma]	<volume, special - see page 29>	
liter	122.740 9	1.227 409 0E+02
thamin [Yemen]	<mass, special - see page 29>	
kilogram	2.381	2.381 000 0E+00
than [Vietnam, soil measure]	<volume, special - see page 29>	
cubic meter	1.6	1.600 000 0E+00
than [Vietnam]	<area, special - see page 29>	
square meter	4	4.000 000 0E+00
thanan [Thailand]	<volume, special - see page 29>	
liter	1	1.000 000 0E+00
thang [Cambodia, rice paddy]	<mass, special - see page 29>	
kilogram	24	2.400 000 0E+01
thang [Cambodia, rice, milled]	<mass, special - see page 29>	
kilogram	30	3.000 000 0E+01
thang [Cambodia]	<volume, special - see page 29>	
liter	30	3.000 000 0E+01
thang [Laos]	<volume, special - see page 29>	
liter	200	2.000 000 0E+02
thang [Thailand]	<volume, special - see page 29>	
liter	20	2.000 000 0E+01
thang [Vietnam]	<volume, special - see page 29>	
liter	2	2.000 000 0E+00
thang louang [Laos]	<volume, special - see page 29>	
liter	40	4.000 000 0E+01
theb [Egypt, ancient]	<length, special - see page 29>	
centimeter	1.87	1.870 000 0E+00
then [Tunisia]	<mass, special - see page 29>	
gram	3.936 91	3.936 910 0E+00

therm [EEC] <energy>

Convert To	Standard	Scientific
Btu [I.T.]	100,000	1.000 000 0E+05
calorie [I.T.]	>>>	2.519 957 6E+07
calorie [kilogram, I.T.]	25,199.576	2.519 957 6E+04
centigrade heat unit [I.T.]	55,555.556	5.555 555 6E+04
cheval vapeur heure [France]	39.846 576	3.984 657 6E+01
coal equivalent kilogram [UN, standard]	3.599 939 4	3.599 939 4E+00
coal equivalent metric ton [UN, standard]	0.003 599 9	3.599 939 4E−03
cubic centimeter atmosphere	>>>	1.041 259 2E+09
cubic foot atmosphere	36,771.721	3.677 172 1E+04
foot pound-force	>>>	7.781 692 6E+07
foot poundal	>>>	2.503 685 6E+09
frigorie [France]	25,205.596	2.520 559 6E+04
gram [atomic physics, eq. energy]	0.000 001 2	1.173 908 0E−06
hectowatthour	293.071 07	2.930 710 7E+02
horsepower hour	39.301 478	3.930 147 8E+01
horsepower hour [metric]	39.846 576	3.984 657 6E+01
joule	>>>	1.055 055 9E+08
kilocalorie [I.T.]	25,199.576	2.519 957 6E+04
kilogram calorie [15 °C, NBS, 1939]	25,205.596	2.520 559 6E+04
kilogram square meter/square second	>>>	1.055 055 9E+08
kilopond meter	>>>	1.075 857 6E+07
kilowatthour	29.307 107	2.930 710 7E+01
liter atmosphere	1,041,259.2	1.041 259 2E+06
meter kilogram-force	>>>	1.075 857 6E+07
myriawatthour	2.930 710 7	2.930 710 7E+00
newton meter	>>>	1.055 055 9E+08
pferdestarkenstunde [Germany]	39.846 576	3.984 657 6E+01
therm [US]	1.000 238 8	1.000 238 8E+00
thermie [France]	25.205 596	2.520 559 6E+01
ton [metric, explosive energy]	0.025 216 4	2.521 644 0E−02
watthour	29,307.107	2.930 710 7E+04
wattsecond	>>>	1.055 055 9E+08

therm [US] <energy>

Convert To	Standard	Scientific
Btu [15 °C]	100,000	1.000 000 0E+05
Btu [I.T.]	99,976.129	9.997 612 9E+04
Btu [I.T. , pre-1956]	99,977.631	9.997 763 1E+04
calorie [I.T.]	>>>	2.519 356 1E+07
calorie [kilogram, I.T.]	25,193.561	2.519 356 1E+04
centigrade heat unit [I.T.]	55,542.294	5.554 229 4E+04
cheval vapeur heure [France]	39.837 064	3.983 706 4E+01
coal equivalent kilogram [UN, standard]	3.599 080 1	3.599 080 1E+00
coal equivalent metric ton [UN, standard]	0.003 599 1	3.599 080 1E−03
frigorie [France]	25,199.58	2.519 958 0E+04
gram [atomic physics, eq. energy]	0.000 001 2	1.173 627 7E−06
horsepower hour	39.292 096	3.929 209 6E+01
horsepower hour [metric]	39.837 064	3.983 706 4E+01
joule	>>>	1.054 804 0E+08
kilocalorie [I.T.]	25,193.561	2.519 356 1E+04
kilowatthour	29.300 111	2.930 011 1E+01
megaton [metric, explosive energy]	<<<	2.521 042 1E−08
newton meter	>>>	1.054 804 0E+08
pferdestarkenstunde [Germany]	39.837 064	3.983 706 4E+01
therm [EEC]	0.999 761 3	9.997 612 9E−01
thermie [France]	25.199 58	2.519 958 0E+01
ton [metric, explosive energy]	0.025 210 4	2.521 042 1E−02
watthour	29,300.111	2.930 011 1E+04

thermie [France] <energy>

Convert To	Standard	Scientific
Btu [I.T.]	3,967.372 9	3.967 372 9E+03
calorie [15 °C, NBS, 1939]	1,000,000	1.000 000 0E+06
calorie [I.T.]	999,761.15	9.997 611 5E+05
calorie [kilogram, I.T.]	999.761 15	9.997 611 5E+02
centigrade heat unit [15 °C]	2,204.622 3	2.204 622 3E+03

Convert From Convert To	Standard	\<Type of Unit\> Scientific
centigrade heat unit [I.T.]	2,204.096 1	2.204 096 1E+03
cheval vapeur heure [France]	1.580 862 3	1.580 862 3E+00
coal equivalent kilogram [UN, standard]	0.142 823	1.428 230 2E−01
cubic centimeter atmosphere	>>>	4.131 063 4E+07
cubic foot atmosphere	1,458.871 3	1.458 871 3E+03
frigorie [France]	1,000	1.000 000 0E+03
horsepower hour	1.559 236 2	1.559 236 2E+00
horsepower hour [metric]	1.580 862 3	1.580 862 3E+00
joule	4,185,800	4.185 800 0E+06
kilocalorie [I.T.]	999.761 15	9.997 611 5E+02
kilogram calorie [15 °C, NBS, 1939]	1,000	1.000 000 0E+03
kilowatthour	1.162 722 2	1.162 722 2E+00
liter atmosphere	41,310.634	4.131 063 4E+04
megajoule	4.185 8	4.185 800 0E+00
newton meter	4,185,800	4.185 800 0E+06
pferdestarkenstunde [Germany]	1.580 862 3	1.580 862 3E+00
therm [EEC]	0.039 673 7	3.967 372 9E−02
therm [US]	0.039 683 2	3.968 320 2E−02
ton [metric, explosive energy]	0.001 000 4	1.000 430 2E−03
watthour	1,162.722 2	1.162 722 2E+03

thneap [Cambodia]		\<length, special - see page 29\>
centimeter	2.083	2.083 000 0E+00

thon [Vietnam]		\<area, special - see page 29\>
square meter	2.4	2.400 000 0E+00

thou		\<length\>
angstrom	254,000	2.540 000 0E+05
barleycorn	0.003	3.000 000 0E−03
caliber	0.1	1.000 000 0E−01
inch [based on US, survey foot]	0.001	9.999 980 0E−04
inch [international]	0.001	1.000 000 0E−03
meter	0.000 025 4	2.540 000 0E−05
microinch	1,000	1.000 000 0E+03
micrometer	25.4	2.540 000 0E+01
micron	25.4	2.540 000 0E+01
mil	1	1.000 000 0E+00
millimicron	25,400	2.540 000 0E+04
wavelength of orange-red spectral line of krypton-86	41.929 399	4.192 939 9E+01

thoum [Yemen]		\<volume, special - see page 29\>
liter	50	5.000 000 0E+01

thousand		\<units\>
unit	1,000	1.000 000 0E+03

thousand board foot		\<volume\>
barrel [UK]	14.418 601	1.441 860 1E+01
barrel [US, dry]	20.408 163	2.040 816 3E+01
board foot	1,000	1.000 000 0E+03
bushel [UK]	64.883 703	6.488 370 3E+01
bushel [US, dry]	66.963 663	6.696 366 3E+01
chaldron [UK, dry]	1.802 325 1	1.802 325 1E+00
chaldron [US, dry]	1.860 101 7	1.860 101 7E+00
cord [firewood]	0.651 041 7	6.510 416 7E−01
cord foot [timber]	5.208 333 3	5.208 333 3E+00
cubic foot	83.333 333	8.333 333 3E+01
cubic inch	144,000	1.440 000 0E+05
cubic meter	2.359 737 2	2.359 737 2E+00
cubic yard	3.086 419 8	3.086 419 8E+00
English water ton [UK]	2.317 275 1	2.317 275 1E+00
freight ton	2.083 333 3	2.083 333 3E+00
gallon [UK, dry or liquid]	519.069 62	5.190 696 2E+02
gallon [US, dry]	535.709 3	5.357 093 0E+02
hectare meter	0.000 236	2.359 737 2E−04
kiloliter	2.359 737 2	2.359 737 2E+00
liter	2,359.737 2	2.359 737 2E+03

	Standard	Scientific
measurement ton	2.083 333 3	2.083 333 3E+00
million board foot	0.001	1.000 000 0E−03
ocean ton	2.083 333 3	2.083 333 3E+00
peck [UK]	259.534 81	2.595 348 1E+02
peck [US]	267.854 65	2.678 546 5E+02
petrograd standard	0.505 050 5	5.050 505 1E−01
pint [UK]	4,152.557	4.152 557 0E+03
pint [US, dry]	4,285.674 4	4.285 674 4E+03
quart [UK]	2,076.278 5	2.076 278 5E+03
quart [US, dry]	2,142.837 2	2.142 837 2E+03
register ton	0.833 333 3	8.333 333 3E−01
shipping ton	2.083 333 3	2.083 333 3E+00
stere	2.359 737 2	2.359 737 2E+00
thousand cubic foot	0.083 333 3	8.333 333 3E−02

thousand cubic foot \<volume\>

	Standard	Scientific
acre foot	0.022 956 8	2.295 684 1E−02
acre inch	0.275 482 1	2.754 820 9E−01
barrel [UK]	173.023 21	1.730 232 1E+02
barrel [US, dry]	244.897 96	2.448 979 6E+02
billion cubic foot	0.000 001	1.000 000 0E−06
board foot	12,000	1.200 000 0E+04
bushel [UK]	778.604 43	7.786 044 3E+02
bushel [US, dry]	803.563 95	8.035 639 5E+02
chaldron [UK, dry]	21.627 901	2.162 790 1E+01
chaldron [US, dry]	22.321 221	2.232 122 1E+01
cord [firewood]	7.812 5	7.812 500 0E+00
cord foot [timber]	62.5	6.250 000 0E+01
cubic foot	1,000	1.000 000 0E+03
cubic inch	1,728,000	1.728 000 0E+06
cubic meter	28.316 847	2.831 684 7E+01
cubic yard	37.037 037	3.703 703 7E+01
English water ton [UK]	27.807 301	2.780 730 1E+01
firkin [UK]	692.092 83	6.920 928 3E+02
firkin [US]	831.168 83	8.311 688 3E+02
freight ton	25	2.500 000 0E+01
gallon [Canada, liquid]	6,228.835 5	6.228 835 5E+03
gallon [UK, dry or liquid]	6,228.835 5	6.228 835 5E+03
gallon [US, dry]	6,428.511 6	6.428 511 6E+03
gallon [US, liquid]	7,480.519 5	7.480 519 5E+03
hectare meter	0.002 831 7	2.831 684 7E−03
hogshead [UK]	98.870 404	9.887 040 4E+01
hogshead [US]	118.738 4	1.187 384 0E+02
liter	28,316.847	2.831 684 7E+04
measurement ton	25	2.500 000 0E+01
million board foot	0.012	1.200 000 0E−02
ocean ton	25	2.500 000 0E+01
peck [UK]	3,114.417 7	3.114 417 7E+03
peck [US]	3,214.255 8	3.214 255 8E+03
petrograd standard	6.060 606 1	6.060 606 1E+00
quarter [UK]	97.325 554	9.732 555 4E+01
register ton	10	1.000 000 0E+01
shipping ton	25	2.500 000 0E+01
stere	28.316 847	2.831 684 7E+01
thousand board foot	12	1.200 000 0E+01

thousand cubic foot/day \<flow rate, volume basis\>

	Standard	Scientific
acre foot/day	0.022 956 8	2.295 684 1E−02
acre foot/day [US, survey]	0.022 956 7	2.295 670 3E−02
acre inch/day	0.275 482 1	2.754 820 9E−01
barrel/hour [UK]	7.209 303	7.209 300 3E+00
barrel/hour [US, federal]	10.054 461 7	1.005 446 2E+01
barrel/hour [US, liquid]	9.894 867	9.894 867 0E+00
barrel/hour [US, petroleum]	7.421 150 3	7.421 150 3E+00
centiliter/second	32.774 128	3.277 412 8E+01

Convert To	Standard	Scientific
cubic centimeter/second	327.741 28	3.277 412 8E+02
cubic decimeter/minute	19.664 476 8	1.966 447 7E+01
cubic foot/day	1,000	1.000 000 0E+03
cubic foot/hour	41.666 666 7	4.166 666 7E+01
cubic inch/second	20	2.000 000 0E+01
cubic meter/hour	1.179 868 6	1.179 868 6E+00
cubic meter/second	0.000 327 7	3.277 412 8E−04
cubic yard/hour	1.543 209 9	1.543 209 9E+00
deciliter/second	3.277 412 8	3.277 412 8E+00
dekaliter/minute	1.966 447 7	1.966 447 7E+00
gallon/minute [UK]	4.325 580 2	4.325 580 2E+00
gallon/minute [US, liquid]	5.194 805 2	5.194 805 2E+00
hectare meter/day	0.002 831 7	2.831 684 5E−03
hectoliter/hour	11.798 686 1	1.179 868 6E+00
kiloliter/hour	1.179 868 6	1.179 868 6E+00
liter/minute	19.664 476 8	1.966 447 7E+01
liter/minute [pre-1964]	19.663 926 2	1.966 392 6E+01
milliliter/second	327.741 28	3.277 412 8E+02
ounce/second [UK, liquid]	11.534 88	1.153 488 0E+01
ounce/second [US, liquid]	11.082 251	1.108 225 1E+01
petrograd standard/day	6.060 606 1	6.060 606 1E+00
stere/hour	1.179 868 6	1.179 868 6E+00
thousand cubic foot/hour	0.041 666 7	4.166 666 7E−02

thousand cubic foot/hour	**<flow rate, volume basis>**	
acre foot/day	0.550 964 2	5.509 641 9E−01
acre foot/day [US, survey]	0.550 960 9	5.509 608 8E−01
acre inch/day	6.611 570 3	6.611 570 3E+00
barrel/minute [UK]	2.883 720 1	2.883 720 1E+00
barrel/minute [US, federal]	4.021 784 7	4.021 784 7E+00
barrel/minute [US, liquid]	3.957 946 8	3.957 946 8E+00
barrel/minute [US, petroleum]	2.968 460 1	2.968 460 1E+00
centiliter/second	786.579 072	7.865 790 7E+02
cubic decimeter/second	7.865 790 7	7.865 790 7E+00
cubic dekameter/day	0.679 604 3	6.796 043 2E−01
cubic foot/minute	16.666 666 7	1.666 666 7E+01
cubic inch/second	480	4.800 000 0E+02
cubic meter/second	0.007 865 8	7.865 790 7E−03
cubic yard/hour	37.037 037	3.703 703 7E+01
deciliter/second	78.657 907 2	7.865 790 7E+01
dekaliter/minute	47.194 744 4	4.719 474 4E+01
gallon/second [UK]	1.730 232 1	1.730 232 1E+00
gallon/second [US, liquid]	2.077 922 1	2.077 922 1E+00
hectoliter/minute	4.719 474 4	4.719 474 4E+00
liter/second	7.865 790 7	7.865 790 7E+00
liter/second [pre-1964]	7.865 570 5	7.865 570 5E+00
ounce/second [UK, liquid]	276.837 13	2.768 371 3E+02
ounce/second [US, liquid]	265.974 03	2.659 740 3E+02
petrograd standard/hour	6.060 606 1	6.060 606 1E+00
stere/hour	28.316 847	2.831 684 7E+01
thousand cubic foot/day	24	2.400 000 0E+01

thousand cubic foot/minute	**<flow rate, volume basis>**	
acre foot/hour	1.377 410 5	1.377 410 5E+00
acre foot/hour [US, survey]	1.377 402 2	1.377 402 2E+00
acre inch/hour	16.528 925 6	1.652 892 6E+01
barrel/second [UK]	2.883 720 1	2.883 720 1E+00
barrel/second [US, federal]	4.021 784 7	4.021 784 7E+00
barrel/second [US, liquid]	3.957 946 8	3.957 946 8E+00
barrel/second [US, petroleum]	2.968 460 1	2.968 460 1E+00
billion cubic foot/day	0.001 44	1.440 000 0E−03
cubic dekameter/hour	1.699 010 8	1.699 010 8E+00
cubic foot/second	16.666 666 7	1.666 666 7E+01
cubic meter/second	0.471 947 4	4.719 474 4E−01
cubic yard/minute	37.037 037	3.703 703 7E+01

Convert From	<Type of Unit>	
Convert To	Standard	Scientific

dekaliter/second	47.194 744 3	4.719 474 4E+01
gallon/second [UK]	103.813 924	1.038 139 2E+02
gallon/second [US, liquid]	124.675 325	1.246 753 3E+02
hectare meter/day	4.077 625 9	4.077 625 9E+00
hectoliter/second	4.719 474 4	4.719 474 4E+00
kiloliter/minute	28.316 846 6	2.831 684 7E+01
liter/second	471.947 443	4.719 474 4E+02
liter/second [pre-1964]	471.934 229	4.719 342 3E+02
ounce/second [UK, liquid]	16,610.228	1.661 022 8E+04
ounce/second [US, liquid]	15,958.442	1.595 844 2E+04
petrograd standard/minute	6.060 606 1	6.060 606 1E+00
stere/minute	28.316 847	2.831 684 7E+01
thousand cubic foot/hour	60	6.000 000 0E+01

thousand cubic foot/second	<flow rate, volume basis>	
acre foot/minute	1.377 410 5	1.377 410 5E+00
acre foot/minute [US, survey]	1.377 402 2	1.377 402 2E+00
acre inch/minute	16.528 925 6	1.652 892 6E+01
barrel/second [UK]	173.023 207	1.730 232 1E+02
barrel/second [US, federal]	241.307 08	2.413 070 8E+02
barrel/second [US, liquid]	237.476 809	2.374 768 1E+02
barrel/second [US, petroleum]	178.107 607	1.781 076 1E+02
billion cubic foot/day	0.086 4	8.640 000 0E-02
cubic dekameter/minute	1.699 010 8	1.699 010 8E+00
cubic foot/second	1,000	1.000 000 0E+03
cubic meter/second	28.316 846 6	2.831 684 7E+01
cubic yard/second	37.037 037	3.703 703 7E+01
dekaliter/second	2,831.684 66	2.831 684 7E+03
gallon/second [UK]	6,228.835 46	6.228 835 5E+03
gallon/second [US, liquid]	7,480.519 48	7.480 519 5E+03
hectare meter/hour	10.194 064 5	1.019 406 5E+01
hectoliter/second	283.168 466	2.831 684 7E+02
kiloliter/second	28.316 846 6	2.831 684 7E+01
liter/second	28,316.846 6	2.831 684 7E+04
liter/second [pre-1964]	28,316.053 7	2.831 605 4E+04
million acre foot/day	0.001 983 5	1.983 471 1E-03
ounce/second [UK, liquid]	996,613.67	9.966 136 7E+05
ounce/second [US, liquid]	957,506.49	9.575 064 9E+05
petrograd standard/second	6.060 606 1	6.060 606 1E+00
stere/second	28.316 847	2.831 684 7E+01
thousand cubic foot/minute	60	6.000 000 0E+01

thumlumgur [Iceland]	<length, special - see page 29>	
centimeter	2.6	2.600 000 0E+00

thumn [Muslim Spain, olive oil]	<mass, special - see page 29>	
kilogram	1.12	1.120 000 0E+00

thung [Vietnam]	<volume, special - see page 29>	
liter	20	2.000 000 0E+01

thuoc [Thailand]	<length, special - see page 29>	
meter	0.487 3	4.873 000 0E-01

thuoc [Vietnam, cereal]	<volume, special - see page 29>	
centiliter	2	2.000 000 0E+00

thuoc [Vietnam]	<area, special - see page 29>	
square meter	24	2.400 000 0E+01

thuoc may [Vietnam]	<length, special - see page 29>	
centimeter	62.5	6.250 000 0E+01

thuoc moc [Vietnam]	<length, special - see page 29>	
centimeter	40	4.000 000 0E+01

ti [Vietnam]	<mass, special - see page 29>	
milligram	0.377 8	3.778 000 0E-01

ti [Vietnam]	<length, special - see page 29>	
micrometer	4	4.000 000 0E+00

	<Type of Unit>	
	Standard	Scientific

tia [Yemen]
gram --- <mass, special - see page 29>
1.166 --- 1.166 000 0E+00

tical [Burma]
gram --- <mass, special - see page 29>
16.33 --- 1.633 000 0E+01

tical [Laos]
gram --- <mass, special - see page 29>
15 --- 1.500 000 0E+01

tical [Thailand]
gram --- <mass, special - see page 29>
15 --- 1.500 000 0E+01

tien [Vietnam]
gram --- <mass, special - see page 29>
3.778 --- 3.778 000 0E+00

tierce [UK]
liter --- <volume, special - see page 29>
191 --- 1.910 000 0E+02

tiercon [Mauritius]
hectoliter --- <volume, special - see page 29>
1.71 --- 1.710 000 0E+00

tikal [Burma]
gram --- <mass, special - see page 29>
16.33 --- 1.633 000 0E+01

tillis [Islam, flour]
kilogram --- <mass, special - see page 29>
66.735 --- 6.673 500 0E+01

timbang [Indonesia, opium]
milligram -- <mass, special - see page 29>
386.01 --- 3.860 100 0E+02

tin [Burma]
liter --- <volume, special - see page 29>
40.913 64 --- 4.091 364 0E+01

tin han [Burma]
liter --- <volume, special - see page 29>
40.913 64 --- 4.091 364 0E+01

tinaja [Philippines]
liter --- <volume, special - see page 29>
48 --- 4.800 000 0E+01

tinja [Philippines]
liter --- <volume, special - see page 29>
48 --- 4.800 000 0E+01

tipree [Ceylon]
liter --- <volume, special - see page 29>
0.861 --- 8.610 000 0E−01

tipree [India]
liter --- <volume, special - see page 29>
0.860 2 --- 8.602 000 0E−01

tiya [Nigeria]
kilogram --- <mass, special - see page 29>
2.27 --- 2.270 000 0E+00

tjaere tonde [Denmark]
hectoliter --- <volume, special - see page 29>
1.159 34 --- 1.159 340 0E+00

tjengkal [Indonesia]
meter --- <length, special - see page 29>
3.767 4 --- 3.767 400 0E+00

tji [Indonesia, opium]
gram --- <mass, special - see page 29>
3.86 --- 3.860 000 0E+00

tmen [Morocco]
square meter --- <area, special - see page 29>
900 --- 9.000 000 0E+02

to [Japan]
liter --- <volume, special - see page 29>
18.039 --- 1.803 900 0E+01

toat [Vietnam]
milliliter -- <volume, special - see page 29>
0.2 --- 2.000 000 0E−01

tod [UK, avoirdupois]
kilogram --- <mass, special - see page 29>
12.701 --- 1.270 100 0E+01

toesa [Macao]
meter --- <length, special - see page 29>
1.98 --- 1.980 000 0E+00

tog [for clothing]
clo [for clothing] ------------------------------------- <thermal insulation coefficient>
0.645 161 3 --- 6.451 612 9E−01
square meter °C/watt -------------------------------- 0.1 --- 1.000 000 0E−01
square meter kelvin/watt --------------------------- 0.1 --- 1.000 000 0E−01

toise [Belgium]
meter --- <length, special - see page 29>
2.015 --- 2.015 000 0E+00

Convert From / Convert To	Standard	Scientific
toise [France]	<length, special - see page 29>	
meter	1.949	1.949 000 0E+00
toise [Mauritius]	<length, special - see page 29>	
meter	1.949	1.949 000 0E+00
toise [Switzerland]	<length, special - see page 29>	
meter	1.8	1.800 000 0E+00
tokhoi [Mongolia]	<length, special - see page 29>	
centimeter	32	3.200 000 0E+01
tola [Bahrain]	<mass, special - see page 29>	
gram	11.66	1.166 000 0E+01
tola [Bangladesh]	<mass, special - see page 29>	
gram	11.664	1.166 400 0E+01
tola [Ceylon]	<mass, special - see page 29>	
gram	11.663 8	1.166 380 0E+01
tola [India]	<mass, special - see page 29>	
gram	11.664	1.166 400 0E+01
tola [Pakistan]	<mass, special - see page 29>	
gram	11.664	1.166 400 0E+01
tola [Yemen]	<mass, special - see page 29>	
gram	11.664	1.166 400 0E+01
tola [Zanzibar and Pemba]	<mass, special - see page 29>	
gram	11.398	1.139 800 0E+01
tolah [India, gold and silver]	<mass, special - see page 29>	
gram	14.55	1.455 000 0E+01
tomande [Saudi Arabia, ancient]	<mass, special - see page 29>	
kilogram	84.9	8.490 000 0E+01
tomin [Spain]	<mass, special - see page 29>	
gram	0.599 079	5.990 790 0E-01
tomini [Morocco]	<volume, special - see page 29>	
liter	5.83	5.830 000 0E+00
tomini [Morocco]	<length, special - see page 29>	
centimeter	7.14	7.140 000 0E+00
tomma [Iceland]	<length, special - see page 29>	
centimeter	2.54	2.540 000 0E+00
tomme [Denmark]	<length, special - see page 29>	
centimeter	2.615 48	2.615 480 0E+00
tomna [Malta]	<volume, special - see page 29>	
liter	18.184	1.818 400 0E+01
tomna [Malta]	<area, special - see page 29>	
hectare	0.112	1.120 000 0E-01
ton [Canada]	<mass, special - see page 29>	
tonne	0.907 18	9.071 800 0E-01
ton [dead weight]		<mass>
cental [US]	22.4	2.240 000 0E+01
centner [UK]	20	2.000 000 0E+01
hundredweight [long]	20	2.000 000 0E+01
hundredweight [short]	22.4	2.240 000 0E+01
hundredweight [UK]	20	2.000 000 0E+01
kilogram	1 016.046 9	1.016 046 9E+03
megagram	1.016 046 9	1.016 046 9E+00
millier	1.016 046 9	1.016 046 9E+00
pound	2,240	2.240 000 0E+03
quarter [long]	4	4.000 000 0E+00
quarter [short]	4.48	4.480 000 0E+00
quarter [UK]	80	8.000 000 0E+01
quarter [US]	89.6	8.960 000 0E+01
quintal [UK]	20	2.000 000 0E+01

Convert From Convert To	<Type of Unit> Standard	Scientific
quintal [US]	22.4	2.240 000 0E+01
ton [long]	1	1.000 000 9E+00
ton [metric]	1.016 046 9	1.016 046 9E+00
ton [short]	1.12	1.120 000 0E+00
ton [UK]	1	1.000 000 0E+00
ton [US, displacement]	1	1.000 000 0E+00
ton [US, gross]	1	1.000 000 0E+00
ton [US, shipping]	1	1.000 000 0E+00

ton [long]		**<mass>**
cental [US]	22.4	2.240 000 0E+01
centner [UK]	20	2.000 000 0E+01
hundredweight [long]	20	2.000 000 0E+01
hundredweight [short]	22.4	2.240 000 0E+01
hundredweight [UK]	20	2.000 000 0E+01
kilogram	1,016.046 9	1.016 046 9E+03
pound	2,240	2.240 000 0E+03
quarter [long]	4	4.000 000 0E+00
quarter [short]	4.48	4.480 000 0E+00
quintal [UK]	20	2.000 000 0E+01
quintal [US]	22.4	2.240 000 0E+01
stone [UK]	160	1.600 000 0E+02
ton [dead weight]	1	1.000 000 0E+00
ton [metric]	1	1.000 000 0E+00
ton [short]	1.12	1.120 000 0E+00
ton [UK]	1	1.000 000 0E+00
ton [US, displacement]	1	1.000 000 0E+00
ton [US, gross]	1	1.000 000 0E+00
ton [US, net]	1.12	1.120 000 0E+00
ton [US, shipping]	1	1.000 000 0E+00

ton [metric, explosive energy]		**<energy>**
Btu [I.T.]	3,965,666.8	3.965 666 8E+06
calorie [I.T.]	>>>	9.993 312 3E+08
calorie [kilogram, I.T.]	999,331.23	9.993 312 3E+05
cheval vapeur heure [France]	1,580.182 5	1.580 182 5E+03
coal equivalent kilogram [UN, standard]	142.761 6	1.427 616 0E+02
coal equivalent metric ton [UN, standard]	0.142 761 6	1.427 616 0E-01
cubic foot atmosphere	1,458,243.9	1.458 243 9E+06
frigorie [France]	999,569.97	9.995 699 7E+05
hectowatthour	11,622.222	1.162 222 2E+04
horsepower hour	1,558.565 7	1.558 565 7E+03
horsepower hour [metric]	1,580.182 5	1.580 182 5E+03
joule	>>>	4.184 000 0E+09
kilocalorie [I.T.]	999,331.23	9.993 312 3E+05
kilogram calorie [15 °C, NBS, 1939]	999,569.97	9.995 699 7E+05
kiloton [metric, explosive energy]	0.001	1.000 000 0E-03
kilowatthour	1,162.222 2	1.162 222 2E+03
liter atmosphere	>>>	4.129 286 9E+07
megaton [metric, explosive energy]	0.000 001	1.000 000 0E-06
meter kilogram-force	>>>	4.266 492 6E+08
pferdestarkenstunde [Germany]	1,580.182 5	1.580 182 5E+03
quad	<<<	3.965 666 8E-09
therm [EEC]	39.656 668	3.965 666 8E+01
therm [US]	39.666 137	3.966 613 7E+01
thermie [France]	999.569 97	9.995 699 7E+02
watthour	1,162,222.2	1.162 222 2E+06

ton [metric]		**<mass>**
carat [metric]	5,000,000	5.000 000 0E+06
cental [US]	22.046 226	2.204 622 6E+01
centner [UK]	19.684 131	1.968 413 1E+01
decitonne	10	1.000 000 0E+01
doppelzentner [Germany]	10	1.000 000 0E+01
grain	>>>	1.543 235 8E+07
kilogram	1,000	1.000 000 0E+03
kiloton [metric]	0.001	1.000 000 0E-03

Convert From Convert To	Standard	Scientific
\<Type of Unit\>		

Convert From / Convert To	Standard	Scientific
kilotonne	0.001	1.000 000 0E−03
megagram	1	1.000 000 0E+00
millier	1	1.000 000 0E+00
newton square second/meter	1,000	1.000 000 0E+03
pound	2,204.622 6	2.204 622 6E+03
quarter [long]	3.936 826 1	3.936 826 1E+00
quarter [short]	4.409 245 2	4.409 245 2E+00
quintal [metric]	10	1.000 000 0E+01
quintal [US]	22.046 226	2.204 622 6E+01
ton [long]	0.984 206 5	9.842 065 3E−01
ton [short]	1.102 311 3	1.102 311 3E+00
tonne	1	1.000 000 0E+00
ton [Pakistan]	**\<mass, special - see page 29\>**	
kilogram	1,016.047	1.016 047 0E+03
ton [short]	**\<mass\>**	
cental [US]	20	2.000 000 0E+01
centner [UK]	17.857 143	1.785 714 3E+01
decitonne	9.071 847 4	9.071 847 4E+00
doppelzentner [Germany]	9.071 847 4	9.071 847 4E+00
hundredweight [long]	17.857 143	1.785 714 3E+01
hundredweight [short]	20	2.000 000 0E+01
kilogram	907.184 74	9.071 847 4E+02
ounce	32,000	3.200 000 0E+04
pound	2,000	2.000 000 0E+03
poundal square second/foot	2,000	2.000 000 0E+03
quarter [short]	4	4.000 000 0E+00
quarter [US]	80	8.000 000 0E+01
quintal [US]	20	2.000 000 0E+01
ton [long]	0.892 857 1	8.928 571 4E−01
ton [metric]	0.907 184 7	9.071 847 4E−01
ton [US, net]	1	1.000 000 0E+00
ton [Spanish, long]	**\<mass, special - see page 29\>**	
tonne	1.030 6	1.030 600 0E+00
ton [Spanish, short]	**\<mass, special - see page 29\>**	
tonne	0.920 2	9.202 000 0E−01
ton [UK, assay or assay, long]	**\<mass\>**	
carat [international]	163.333 33	1.633 333 3E+02
carat [UK]	126.030 93	1.260 309 3E+02
dekagram	3.266 666 7	3.266 666 7E+00
drachm [UK, apothecary]	8.402 061 8	8.402 061 8E+00
dram [US, apothecary]	8.402 061 8	8.402 061 8E+00
kilogram	0.032 666 7	3.266 666 7E−02
ounce	1.152 282 8	1.152 282 8E+00
ounce [apothecary]	1.050 257 7	1.050 257 7E+00
ounce [avoirdupois]	1.152 282 8	1.152 282 8E+00
ounce [troy]	1.050 257 7	1.050 257 7E+00
pound	0.072 017 7	7.201 767 2E−02
ton [US, assay or assay, short]	1.12	1.120 000 0E+00
ton [UK]	**\<mass\>**	
carat [international]	5,080,234.5	5.080 234 5E+06
carat [UK]	3,920,000	3.920 000 0E+06
cental [US]	22.4	2.240 000 0E+01
centner [UK]	20	2.000 000 0E+01
hundredweight [long]	20	2.000 000 0E+01
hundredweight [short]	22.4	2.240 000 0E+01
hundredweight [UK]	20	2.000 000 0E+01
kilogram	1,016.046 9	1.016 046 9E+03
megagram	1.016 046 9	1.016 046 9E+00
millier	1.016 046 9	1.016 046 9E+00
ounce	35,840	3.584 000 0E+04
pound	2,240	2.240 000 0E+03
poundal square second/foot	2,240	2.240 000 0E+03

quarter [long]	4	4.000 000 0E+00
quarter [short]	4.48	4.480 000 0E+00
quarter [UK]	80	8.000 000 0E+01
quarter [US]	89.6	8.960 000 0E+01
quintal [UK]	20	2.000 000 0E+01
quintal [US]	22.4	2.240 000 0E+01
stone [UK]	160	1.600 000 0E+02
ton [dead weight]	1	1.000 000 0E+00
ton [long]	1	1.000 000 0E+00
ton [metric]	1.016 046 9	1.016 046 9E+00
ton [short]	1.12	1.120 000 0E+00
ton [US, displacement]	1	1.000 000 0E+00
ton [US, gross]	1	1.000 000 0E+00
ton [US, shipping]	1	1.000 000 0E+00
tonne	1.016 046 9	1.016 046 9E+00

ton [US, assay or assay, short] — <mass>

carat [international]	145.833 33	1.458 333 3E+02
dekagram	2.916 666 7	2.916 666 7E+00
drachm [UK, apothecary]	7.501 840 9	7.501 840 9E+00
dram [US, apothecary]	7.501 840 9	7.501 840 9E+00
grain	450.110 45	4.501 104 5E+02
kilogram	0.029 166 7	2.916 666 7E-02
ounce	1.028 823 9	1.028 823 9E+00
ounce [troy]	0.937 730 1	9.377 301 1E-01
pennyweight [troy]	18.754 602	1.875 460 2E+01
pound	0.064 301 5	6.430 149 3E-02
pound [troy]	0.078 144 2	7.814 417 6E-02
scruple [US, apothecary]	22.505 523	2.250 552 3E+01

ton [US, displacement] — <mass>

cental [US]	22.4	2.240 000 0E+01
centner [UK]	20	2.000 000 0E+01
hundredweight [long]	20	2.000 000 0E+01
hundredweight [short]	22.4	2.240 000 0E+01
kilogram	1,016.046 9	1.016 046 9E+03
pound	2,240	2.240 000 0E+03
quarter [long]	4	4.000 000 0E+00
quarter [short]	4.48	4.480 000 0E+00
quarter [US]	89.6	8.960 000 0E+01
quintal [US]	22.4	2.240 000 0E+01
stone [UK]	160	1.600 000 0E+02
ton [dead weight]	1	1.000 000 0E+00
ton [long]	1	1.000 000 0E+00
ton [short]	1.12	1.120 000 0E+00
ton [UK]	1	1.000 000 0E+00
ton [US, gross]	1	1.000 000 0E+00
ton [US, net]	1.12	1.120 000 0E+00
ton [US, shipping]	1	1.000 000 0E+00

ton [US, gross] — <mass>

cental [US]	22.4	2.240 000 0E+01
centner [UK]	20	2.000 000 0E+01
hundredweight [long]	20	2.000 000 0E+01
hundredweight [short]	22.4	2.240 000 0E+01
hundredweight [US, gross]	20	2.000 000 0E+01
kilogram	1,016.046 9	1.016 046 9E+03
pound	2,240	2.240 000 0E+03
quarter [long]	4	4.000 000 0E+00
quarter [short]	4.48	4.480 000 0E+00
quintal [UK]	20	2.000 000 0E+01
quintal [US]	22.4	2.240 000 0E+01
stone [UK]	160	1.600 000 0E+02
ton [dead weight]	1	1.000 000 0E+00
ton [long]	1	1.000 000 0E+00
ton [short]	1.12	1.120 000 0E+00

Convert From		<Type of Unit>
Convert To	Standard	Scientific

ton [UK]	1	1.000 000 0E+00
ton [US, displacement]	1	1.000 000 0E+00
ton [US, net]	1.12	1.120 000 0E+00
ton [US, shipping]	1	1.000 000 0E+00

ton [US, net]   **<mass>**

cental [US]	20	2.000 000 0E+01
centner [UK]	17.857 143	1.785 714 3E+01
hundredweight [long]	17.857 143	1.785 714 3E+01
hundredweight [short]	20	2.000 000 0E+01
hundredweight [US, net]	20	2.000 000 0E+01
kilogram	907.184 74	9.071 847 4E+02
ounce	32,000	3.200 000 0E+04
pound	2,000	2.000 000 0E+03
poundal square second/foot	2,000	2.000 000 0E+03
quarter [short]	4	4.000 000 0E+00
quarter [US]	80	8.000 000 0E+01
quintal [US]	20	2.000 000 0E+01
scruple [US, apothecary]	700,000	7.000 000 0E+05
ton [long]	0.892 857 1	8.928 571 4E-01
ton [short]	1	1.000 000 0E+00

ton [US, shipping]   **<mass>**

cental [US]	22.4	2.240 000 0E+01
centner [UK]	20	2.000 000 0E+01
hundredweight [long]	20	2.000 000 0E+01
hundredweight [short]	22.4	2.240 000 0E+01
hundredweight [UK]	20	2.000 000 0E+01
kilogram	1,016.046 9	1.016 046 9E+03
pound	2,240	2.240 000 0E+03
quarter [long]	4	4.000 000 0E+00
quarter [short]	4.48	4.480 000 0E+00
quintal [UK]	20	2.000 000 0E+01
quintal [US]	22.4	2.240 000 0E+01
stone [UK]	160	1.600 000 0E+02
ton [dead weight]	1	1.000 000 0E+00
ton [long]	1	1.000 000 0E+00
ton [short]	1.12	1.120 000 0E+00
ton [UK]	1	1.000 000 0E+00
ton [US, displacement]	1	1.000 000 0E+00
ton [US, gross]	1	1.000 000 0E+00

ton foot/square second [long]   **<force>**

newton	309.691 1	3.096 911 0E+02
pound foot/square second	2,240	2.240 000 0E+03
poundal	2,240	2.240 000 0E+03
ton foot/square second [short]	1.12	1.120 000 0E+00
tondal	1	1.000 000 0E+00

ton foot/square second [short]   **<force>**

newton	276.509 91	2.765 099 1E+02
pound foot/square second	2,000	2.000 000 0E+03
poundal	2,000	2.000 000 0E+03
ton foot/square second [long]	0.892 857 1	8.928 571 4E-01
tondal	0.892 857 1	8.928 571 4E-01

ton meter/square second [metric]   **<force>**

funal	1	1.000 000 0E+00
kilonewton	1	1.000 000 0E+00
newton	1,000	1.000 000 0E+03
sthene	1	1.000 000 0E+00

ton of anthracite coal [short]   **<energy>**

joule	>>>	2.678 400 0E+10
kilowatthour	7,440	7.440 000 0E+00

ton of bituminous coal [short]   **<energy>**

joule	>>>	2.606 400 0E+10

Convert From Convert To	Standard	\<Type of Unit> Scientific
kilowatthour	7,240	7.240 000 0E+03
ton of refrigeration		**\<power>**
Btu/second [I.T.]	3.333 333 3	3.333 333 3E+00
Btu/second [thermoc.]	3.335 564 1	3.335 564 1E+00
calorie/second [I.T.]	839.985 87	8.399 858 7E+02
calorie/second [thermoc.]	840.548	8.405 480 0E+02
centigrade heat unit/second [mean]	1.850 423 9	1.850 423 9E+00
cheval vapeur [France]	4.781 589 1	4.781 589 1E+00
cubic meter atmosphere/second	34,708.639	3.470 863 9E+04
dyne centimeter/second	>>>	3.516 852 8E+10
erg/second	>>>	3.516 852 8E+10
foot pound-force/second	2,593.897 5	2.593 897 5E+03
foot poundal/second	83,456.185	8.345 618 5E+04
gram-force centimeter/second	>>>	3.586 191 9E+07
horsepower	4.716 177 3	4.716 177 3E+00
horsepower [metric]	4.781 589 1	4.781 589 1E+00
joule/second	3,516.852 8	3.516 852 8E+03
kilocalorie/minute [I.T.]	50.399 152	5.039 915 2E+01
kilogram-force meter/second	358.619 19	3.586 191 9E+02
kilopond meter/second	358.619 19	3.586 191 9E+02
kilowatt	3.516 852 8	3.516 852 8E+00
million Btu/hour [I.T.]	0.012	1.200 000 0E−02
newton meter/second	3,516.852 8	3.516 852 8E+03
pferdestarke [Germany]	4.781 589 1	4.781 589 1E+00
poncelet [France]	3.586 191 9	3.586 191 9E+00
volt ampere	3,516.852 8	3.516 852 8E+03
watt	3,516.852 8	3.516 852 8E+03
ton-force [long]		**\<force>**
crinal	99,640.164 2	9.964 016 4E+04
newton	9,964.016 42	9.964 016 4E+03
ounce-force	35,840	3.584 000 0E+04
pond	1,016,046.91	1.016 046 9E+06
pound-force	2,240	2.240 000 0E+03
poundal	72,069.868 8	7.206 986 9E+04
ton-force [metric]	1.016 046 9	1.016 046 9E+00
ton-force [short]	1.12	1.120 000 0E+00
ton-force [metric]		**\<force>**
crinal	98,066.5	9.806 650 0E+04
kilogram-force	1,000	1.000 000 0E+03
kilonewton	9.806 65	9.806 650 0E+00
newton	9,806.65	9.806 650 0E+03
ounce-force	35,273.961 9	3.527 396 2E+04
pond	1,000,000	1.000 000 0E+06
pound-force	2,204.622 62	2.204 622 6E+03
poundal	70,931.635 3	7.093 163 5E+04
ton-force [long]	0.984 206 5	9.842 065 3E−01
ton-force [short]	1.102 311 3	1.102 311 3E+00
ton-force [short]		**\<force>**
crinal	88,964.432 3	8.896 443 2E+04
kip	2	2.000 000 0E+00
newton	8,896.443 23	8.896 443 2E+03
ounce-force	32,000	3.200 000 0E+04
pound-force	2,000	2.000 000 0E+03
poundal	64,348.097 1	6.434 809 7E+04
slug foot/square second	2,000	2.000 000 0E+03
ton-force [long]	0.892 857 1	8.928 571 4E−01
ton-force [metric]	0.907 184 7	9.071 847 4E−01
ton-force/square foot [long]		**\<pressure>**
atmosphere [standard]	1.058 492 8	1.058 492 8E+00
atmosphere [technical]	1.093 663 8	1.093 663 8E+00
bar	1.072 517 8	1.072 517 8E+00
centimeter of mercury [0 °C, by convention]	80.445 439	8.044 543 9E+01

| Convert From | | <Type of Unit> |
Convert To	Standard	Scientific
centimeter of water [4 °C, by convention]	1,093.663 8	1.093 663 8E+03
foot of mercury [0 °C, by convention]	2.639 286 1	2.639 286 1E+00
foot of water [4 °C, by convention]	35.881 358	3.588 135 8E+01
gram-force/square centimeter	1,093.663 8	1.093 663 8E+03
kilogram-force/square centimeter	1.093 663 8	1.093 663 8E+00
kilopond/square centimeter	1.093 663 8	1.093 663 8E+00
kip/square foot	2.24	2.240 000 0E+00
newton/square millimeter	0.107 251 8	1.072 517 8E-01
ounce-force/square inch	248.888 89	2.488 888 9E+02
pascal	107,251.78	1.072 517 8E+05
pound-force/square foot	2,240	2.240 000 0E+03
pound-force/square inch	15.555 556	1.555 555 6E+01
ton-force/square foot [short]	1.12	1.120 000 0E+00
ton-force/square meter [metric]	10.936 638	1.093 663 8E+01
torr	804.454 51	8.044 545 1E+02

ton-force/square foot [short] <pressure>

Convert To	Standard	Scientific
atmosphere [standard]	0.945 082 8	9.450 828 3E-01
atmosphere [technical]	0.976 485 5	9.764 855 3E-01
bar	0.957 605 2	9.576 051 8E-01
barye [France]	957,605.18	9.576 051 8E+05
centimeter of mercury [0 °C, by convention]	71.826 285	7.182 628 5E+01
centimeter of water [4 °C, by convention]	976.485 53	9.764 855 3E+02
decibar	9.576 051 8	9.576 051 8E+00
dyne/square centimeter	957,605.18	9.576 051 8E+05
foot of mercury [0 °C, by convention]	2.356 505 4	2.356 505 4E+00
foot of water [4 °C, by convention]	32.036 927	3.203 692 7E+01
gram-force/square centimeter	976.485 53	9.764 855 3E+02
inch of mercury [0 °C, by convention]	28.278 065	2.827 806 5E+01
inch of water [4 °C, by convention]	384.443 12	3.844 431 2E+02
kilogram-force/square centimeter	0.976 485 5	9.764 855 3E-01
kilopond/square centimeter	0.976 485 5	9.764 855 3E-01
kip/square foot	2	2.000 000 0E+00
newton/square millimeter	0.095 760 5	9.576 051 8E-02
ounce-force/square inch	222.222 22	2.222 222 2E+02
pascal	95,760.518	9.576 051 8E+04
pound-force/square foot	2,000	2.000 000 0E+03
pound-force/square inch	13.888 889	1.388 888 9E+01
poundal/square foot	64,348.097	6.434 809 7E+04
ton-force/square foot [long]	0.892 857 1	8.928 571 4E-01
ton-force/square meter [metric]	9.764 855 3	9.764 855 3E+00
torr	718.262 95	7.182 629 5E+02

ton-force/square inch [long] <pressure>

Convert To	Standard	Scientific
atmosphere [standard]	152.422 96	1.524 229 6E+02
atmosphere [technical]	157.487 59	1.574 875 9E+02
bar	154.442 56	1.544 425 6E+02
centimeter of mercury [0 °C, by convention]	11,584.143	1.158 414 3E+04
centimeter of water [4 °C, by convention]	157,487.59	1.574 875 9E+05
foot of mercury [0 °C, by convention]	380.057 19	3.800 571 9E+02
foot of water [4 °C, by convention]	5,166.915 5	5.166 915 5E+03
gram-force/square centimeter	157,487.59	1.574 875 9E+05
hectobar	1.544 425 6	1.544 425 6E+00
kilogram-force/square millimeter	1.574 875 9	1.574 875 9E+00
kilopond/square millimeter	1.574 875 9	1.574 875 9E+00
kip/square inch	2.24	2.240 000 0E+00
newton/square millimeter	15.444 256	1.544 425 6E+01
pascal	>>>	1.544 425 6E+07
pound-force/square inch	2,240	2.240 000 0E+03
ton-force/square foot [long]	144	1.440 000 0E+02
ton-force/square foot [short]	161.28	1.612 800 0E+02
ton-force/square inch [short]	1.12	1.120 000 0E+00
torr	115,841.45	1.158 414 5E+05

ton-force/square inch [short] <pressure>

Convert To	Standard	Scientific
atmosphere [standard]	136.091 93	1.360 919 3E+02

Convert From Convert To	Standard	**\<Type of Unit\>** Scientific
atmosphere [technical]	140.613 92	1.406 139 2E+02
bar	137.895 15	1.378 951 5E+02
centimeter of mercury [0 °C, by convention]	10,342.985	1.034 298 5E+04
centimeter of water [4 °C, by convention]	140,613.92	1.406 139 2E+05
dyne/square centimeter	\>\>\>	1.378 951 5E+08
foot of mercury [0 °C, by convention]	339.336 78	3.393 367 8E+02
foot of water [4 °C, by convention]	4,613.317 5	4.613 317 5E+03
gram-force/square centimeter	140,613.92	1.406 139 2E+05
hectobar	1.378 951 5	1.378 951 5E+00
inch of mercury [0 °C, by convention]	4,072.041 4	4.072 041 4E+03
inch of water [4 °C, by convention]	55,359.809	5.535 980 9E+04
kilogram-force/square millimeter	1.406 139 2	1.406 139 2E+00
kilopond/square millimeter	1.406 139 2	1.406 139 2E+00
kip/square inch	2	2.000 000 0E+00
newton/square millimeter	13.789 515	1.378 951 5E+01
ounce-force/square inch	32,000.	3.200 000 0E+04
pascal	\>\>\>	1.378 951 5E+07
pound-force/square foot	288,000.	2.880 000 0E+05
pound-force/square inch	2,000.	2.000 000 0E+03
ton-force/square foot [short]	144.	1.440 000 0E+02
ton-force/square inch [long]	0.892 857 1	8.928 571 4E-01
ton-force/square meter [metric]	1,406.139 2	1.406 139 2E+03
torr	103,429.87	1.034 298 7E+05

ton-force/square meter [metric]		**\<pressure\>**
atmosphere [standard]	0.096 784 1	9.678 411 1E-02
atmosphere [technical]	0.1	1.000 000 0E-01
bar	0.098 066 5	9.806 650 0E-02
barye [France]	98,066.5	9.806 650 0E+04
centibar	9.806 65	9.806 650 0E+00
centihg	7.355 591 4	7.355 591 4E+00
centimeter of mercury [0 °C, by convention]	7.355 591 4	7.355 591 4E+00
centimeter of water [4 °C, by convention]	100	1.000 000 0E+02
dyne/square centimeter	98,066.5	9.806 650 0E+04
foot of mercury [0 °C, by convention]	0.241 325 2	2.413 251 8E-01
foot of water [4 °C, by convention]	3.280 839 9	3.280 839 9E+00
gram-force/square centimeter	100	1.000 000 0E+02
inch of mercury [0 °C, by convention]	2.895 902 1	2.895 902 1E+00
inch of water [4 °C, by convention]	39.370 079	3.937 007 9E+01
kilogram-force/square centimeter	0.1	1.000 000 0E-01
kilopascal	9.806 65	9.806 650 0E+00
kilopond/square centimeter	0.1	1.000 000 0E-01
kip/square foot	0.204 816 1	2.048 161 4E-01
millimeter of mercury [0 °C, by convention]	73.555 914	7.355 591 4E+01
millimeter of water [4 °C, by convention]	1,000	1.000 000 0E+03
newton/square meter	9,806.65	9.806 650 0E+03
ounce-force/square inch	22.757 349	2.275 734 9E+01
pascal	9,806.65	9.806 650 0E+03
pieze [France]	9.806 65	9.806 650 0E+00
pound-force/square foot	204.816 14	2.048 161 4E+02
pound-force/square inch	1.422 334 3	1.422 334 3E+00
poundal/square foot	6,589.764 6	6.589 764 6E+03
sthene/square meter [France]	9.806 65	9.806 650 0E+00
ton-force/square foot [short]	0.102 408 1	1.024 080 7E-01
torr	73.555 924	7.355 592 4E+01

ton/cubic foot [long]		**\<density\>**
grain/cubic inch	9,074.074 1	9.074 074 1E+03
gram/cubic centimeter	35.881 358	3.588 135 8E+01
gram/milliliter	35.881 358	3.588 135 8E+01
kilogram/cubic meter	35,881.358	3.588 135 8E+04
ounce/cubic inch	20.740 741	2.074 074 1E+01
pound/cubic inch	1.296 296 3	1.296 296 3E+00
slug/cubic foot	69.621 328	6.962 132 8E+01
slug/gallon [-/US, liquid]	9.307 017 9	9.307 017 9E+00

	Standard	Scientific
ton/cubic foot [short]	1.12	1.120 000 0E+00
ton/cubic yard [long]	27	2.700 000 0E+01
ton/cubic yard [short]	30.24	3.024 000 0E+01
tonne/cubic meter	35.881 358	3.588 135 8E+01

ton/cubic foot [short] <density>

	Standard	Scientific
grain/cubic inch	8,101.851 9	8.101 851 9E+03
gram/cubic centimeter	32.036 927	3.203 692 7E+01
kilogram/cubic meter	32,036.927	3.203 692 7E+04
ounce/cubic inch	18.518 519	1.851 851 9E+01
pound/cubic foot	2,000	2.000 000 0E+03
pound/cubic inch	1.157 407 4	1.157 407 4E+00
pound/cubic yard	54,000	5.400 000 0E+04
slug/cubic foot	62.161 9	6.216 190 0E+01
slug/gallon [-/US, liquid]	8.309 837 4	8.309 837 4E+00
ton/cubic yard [short]	27	2.700 000 0E+01
tonne/cubic meter	32.036 927	3.203 692 7E+01

ton/cubic inch [long] <density>

	Standard	Scientific
grain/cubic inch	>>>	1.568 000 0E+07
gram/cubic centimeter	62,002.987	6.200 298 7E+04
kilogram/cubic meter	>>>	6.200 298 7E+07
ounce/cubic inch	35,840	3.584 000 0E+04
pound/cubic inch	2,240	2.240 000 0E+03
slug/cubic foot	69.621 328	6.962 132 8E+01
ton/cubic inch [short]	1.12	1.120 000 0E+00
tonne/liter	62.002 987	6.200 298 7E+01

ton/cubic inch [short] <density>

	Standard	Scientific
grain/cubic inch	>>>	1.400 000 0E+07
gram/cubic centimeter	55,359.809	5.535 980 9E+04
kilogram/cubic meter	>>>	5.535 980 9E+07
megagram/liter	55.359 809	5.535 980 9E+01
ounce/cubic inch	32,000	3.200 000 0E+04
pound/circular mil foot	0.018 849 6	1.884 955 6E-02
pound/cubic inch	2,000	2.000 000 0E+03
pound/gallon [-/US, liquid]	462,000	4.620 000 0E+05
slug/cubic foot	62.161 9	6.216 190 0E+01
ton/cubic foot [short]	1,728	1.728 000 0E+03
ton/cubic inch [long]	0.892 857 1	8.928 571 4E-01
ton/gallon [short/US, liquid]	231	2.310 000 0E+02
tonne/liter	55.359 809	5.535 980 9E+01

ton/cubic yard [long] <density>

	Standard	Scientific
grain/cubic inch	336.076 82	3.360 768 2E+02
gram/cubic centimeter	1.328 939 2	1.328 939 2E+00
kilogram/cubic meter	1,328.939 2	1.328 939 2E+03
ounce/cubic inch	0.768 175 6	7.681 755 8E-01
pound/cubic yard	2,240	2.240 000 0E+03
slug/cubic foot	2.578 567 7	2.578 567 7E+00
ton/cubic yard [short]	1.12	1.120 000 0E+00
tonne/cubic meter	1.328 939 2	1.328 939 2E+00

ton/cubic yard [short] <density>

	Standard	Scientific
grain/cubic yard	>>>	1.400 000 0E+07
gram/cubic centimeter	1.186 552 8	1.186 552 8E+00
kilogram/cubic meter	1,186.552 8	1.186 552 8E+03
ounce/cubic yard	32,000	3.200 000 0E+04
pound/cubic yard	2,000	2.000 000 0E+03
slug/cubic foot	2.302 292 6	2.302 292 6E+00
ton/cubic foot [short]	0.037 037	3.703 703 7E-02
tonne/cubic meter	1.186 552 8	1.186 552 8E+00

ton/gallon [long/UK, liquid] <density>

	Standard	Scientific
gram/milliliter	223.499 07	2.234 990 7E+02
kilogram/cubic meter	223,499.07	2.234 990 7E+05
ounce/cubic inch	129.190 66	1.291 906 6E+02
pound/cubic inch	8.074 416 3	8.074 416 3E+00

Convert From Convert To	\<Type of Unit\> Standard	Scientific
pound/gallon [-/UK, liquid]	2,240	2.240 000 0E+03
pound/gallon [-/US, liquid]	1,865.190 2	1.865 190 2E+03
slug/cubic inch	0.250 960 5	2.509 605 3E−01
ton/cubic foot [short]	6.976 295 7	6.976 295 7E+00
ton/gallon [long/US, liquid]	0.832 674 2	8.326 741 8E−01
ton/gallon [short/UK, liquid]	1.12	1.120 000 0E+00
ton/gallon [short/US, liquid]	0.932 595 1	9.325 950 9E−01
tonne/liter	0.223 499 1	2.234 990 7E−01

ton/gallon [long/US, liquid] — \<density\>

gram/milliliter	268.411 2	2.684 112 0E+02
kilogram/cubic meter	268,411.2	2.684 112 0E+05
ounce/cubic inch	155.151 52	1.551 515 2E+02
ounce/gallon [-/US, liquid]	35,840	3.584 000 0E+04
pound/cubic inch	9.696 969 7	9.696 969 7E+00
pound/gallon [-/US, liquid]	2,240	2.240 000 0E+03
slug/cubic inch	0.301 391	3.013 910 3E−01
ton/cubic foot [long]	7.480 519 5	7.480 519 5E+00
ton/gallon [short/US, liquid]	1.12	1.120 000 0E+00
tonne/liter	0.268 411 2	2.684 112 0E−01

ton/gallon [short/UK, liquid] — \<density\>

grain/gallon [-/UK, liquid]	>>>	1.400 000 0E+07
grain/gallon [-/US, liquid]	>>>	1.165 743 9E+07
kilogram/cubic meter	199,552.75	1.995 527 5E+05
ounce/cubic inch	115.394	1.153 940 6E+02
ounce/gallon [-/UK, liquid]	32,000	3.200 000 0E+04
ounce/gallon [-/US, liquid]	26,645.574	2.664 557 4E+04
pound/cubic inch	7.209 300 3	7.209 300 3E+00
pound/gallon [-/UK, liquid]	2,000	2.000 000 0E+03
pound/gallon [-/US, liquid]	1,665.348 4	1.665 348 4E+03
slug/cubic inch	0.224 071 9	2.240 719 0E−01
ton/cubic foot [long]	5.561 460 2	5.561 460 2E+00
ton/cubic foot [short]	6.228 835 5	6.228 835 5E+00
ton/gallon [short/US, liquid]	0.832 674 2	8.326 741 8E−01
tonne/liter	0.199 552 8	1.995 527 5E−01

ton/gallon [short/US, liquid] — \<density\>

grain/gallon [-/UK, liquid]	>>>	1.681 329 9E+07
grain/gallon [-/US, liquid]	>>>	1.400 000 0E+07
gram/milliliter	239.652 85	2.396 528 5E+02
kilogram/cubic meter	239,652.85	2.396 528 5E+05
ounce/cubic inch	138.528 14	1.385 281 4E+02
ounce/gallon [-/US, liquid]	32,000	3.200 000 0E+04
pound/cubic inch	8.658 008 7	8.658 008 7E+00
pound/gallon [-/US, liquid]	2,000	2.000 000 0E+03
slug/cubic inch	0.269 099 1	2.690 991 4E−01
ton/cubic foot [short]	7.480 519 5	7.480 519 5E+00
ton/gallon [short/UK, liquid]	1.200 949 9	1.200 949 9E+00
tonne/liter	0.239 652 9	2.396 528 5E−01

ton/hour [long] — \<flow rate, mass basis\>

kilogram/second	0.282 235 3	2.822 352 5E−01

ton/hour [metric] — \<flow rate, mass basis\>

kilogram/second	0.277 777 8	2.777 777 8E−01

ton/hour [short] — \<flow rate, mass basis\>

kilogram/second	0.251 995 8	2.519 957 6E−01

ton/minute [long] — \<flow rate, mass basis\>

kilogram/second	16.934 115 1	1.693 411 5E+01

ton/minute [metric] — \<flow rate, mass basis\>

kilogram/second	16.666 666 7	1.666 666 7E+01

ton/minute [short] — \<flow rate, mass basis\>

kilogram/second	15.119 745 7	1.511 974 6E+01

ton/second [long] — \<flow rate, mass basis\>

kilogram/second	1,016.046 908 8	1.016 046 9E+03

ton/second [metric] <flow rate, mass basis>
| kilogram/second | 1,000 | 1.000 000 0E+03 |

ton/second [short] <flow rate, mass basis>
| kilogram/second | 907.184 74 | 9.071 847 4E+02 |

ton/square foot [long] <surface density>
grain/square inch	108,888.89	1.088 888 9E+05
kilogram/are	1,093,663.8	1.093 663 8E+06
kilogram/square centimeter	1.093 663 8	1.093 663 8E+00
kilogram/square meter	10,936.638	1.093 663 8E+04
ounce/square inch	248.888 89	2.488 888 9E+02
pound/square inch	15.555 556	1.555 555 6E+01
pound/square yard	20,160	2.016 000 0E+04
slug/square foot	69.621 328	6.962 132 8E+01
ton/square foot [short]	1.12	1.120 000 0E+00
ton/square yard [long]	9	9.000 000 0E+00
ton/square yard [short]	10.08	1.008 000 0E+01
tonne/square meter	10.936 638	1.093 663 8E+01

ton/square foot [short] <surface density>
grain/square inch	97,222.222	9.722 222 2E+04
kilogram/are	976,485.53	9.764 855 3E+05
kilogram/square meter	9,764.855 3	9.764 855 3E+03
ounce/square inch	222.222 22	2.222 222 2E+02
pound/square foot	2,000	2.000 000 0E+03
pound/square inch	13.888 889	1.388 888 9E+01
pound/square yard	18,000	1.800 000 0E+04
slug/square foot	62.161 9	6.216 190 0E+01
ton/square foot [long]	0.892 857 1	8.928 571 4E-01
ton/square yard [long]	8.035 714 3	8.035 714 3E+00
ton/square yard [short]	9	9.000 000 0E+00
tonne/square meter	9.764 855 3	9.764 855 3E+00

ton/square foot second [long] <flow rate/unit area, mass basis>
kilogram/square meter second	10,936.638	1.093 663 8E+04
pound/square foot second	2,240	2.240 000 0E+03
slug/square foot second	69.621 328	6.962 132 8E+01
ton/square foot second [short]	1.12	1.120 000 0E+00
tonne/square meter second	10.936 638	1.093 663 8E+01

ton/square foot second [short] <flow rate/unit area, mass basis>
kilogram/square meter second	9,764.855 3	9.764 855 3E+03
pound/square foot second	2,000	2.000 000 0E+03
slug/square foot second	62.161 9	6.216 190 0E+01
ton/square foot second [long]	0.892 857 1	8.928 571 4E-01
tonne/square meter second	9.764 855 3	9.764 855 3E+00

ton/square inch [long] <surface density>
gram/square centimeter	157,487.59	1.574 875 9E+05
kilogram/square meter	1,574,875.9	1.574 875 9E+06
ounce/square inch	35,840	3.584 000 0E+04
pound/square inch	2,240	2.240 000 0E+03
slug/square inch	69.621 328	6.962 132 8E+01
ton/square foot [long]	144	1.440 000 0E+02
ton/square inch [short]	1.12	1.120 000 0E+00
ton/square yard [long]	1,296	1.296 000 0E+03
tonne/square centimeter	0.157 487 6	1.574 875 9E-01

ton/square inch [short] <surface density>
kilogram/square meter	1,406,139.2	1.406 139 2E+06
ounce/square inch	32,000	3.200 000 0E+04
pound/square foot	288,000	2.880 000 0E+05
pound/square inch	2,000	2.000 000 0E+03
pound/square yard	2,592,000	2.592 000 0E+06
slug/square inch	62.161 9	6.216 190 0E+01
ton/square foot [short]	144	1.440 000 0E+02
ton/square inch [long]	0.892 857 1	8.928 571 4E-01

Convert From Convert To	\<Type of Unit\> Standard	Scientific
ton/square yard [short]	1,296	1.296 000 0E+03
tonne/square centimeter	0.140 613 9	1.406 139 2E−01
ton/square yard [long]	**\<surface density\>**	
grain/square inch	12,098.765	1.209 876 5E+04
kilogram/are	121,518.2	1.215 182 0E+05
kilogram/square meter	1,215.182	1.215 182 0E+03
ounce/square inch	27.654 321	2.765 432 1E+01
ounce/square yard	35,840	3.584 000 0E+04
pound/square inch	1.728 395 1	1.728 395 1E+00
pound/square yard	2,240	2.240 000 0E+03
slug/square foot	7.735 703 2	7.735 703 2E+00
ton/square foot [long]	0.111 111 1	1.111 111 1E−01
ton/square foot [short]	0.124 444 4	1.244 444 4E−01
ton/square yard [short]	1.12	1.120 000 0E+00
tonne/square meter	1.215 182	1.215 182 0E+00
ton/square yard [short]	**\<surface density\>**	
grain/square inch	10,802.469	1.080 246 9E+04
grain/square yard	>>>	1.400 000 0E+07
kilogram/are	108,498.39	1.084 983 9E+05
kilogram/square meter	1,084.983 9	1.084 983 9E+03
ounce/square inch	24.691 358	2.469 135 8E+01
ounce/square yard	32,000	3.200 000 0E+04
pound/acre	9,680,000	9.680 000 0E+06
pound/square inch	1.543 209 9	1.543 209 9E+00
pound/square yard	2,000	2.000 000 0E+03
slug/square foot	6.906 877 8	6.906 877 8E+00
ton/square foot [short]	0.111 111 1	1.111 111 1E−01
ton/square yard [long]	0.892 857 1	8.928 571 4E−01
tonne/square meter	1.084 983 9	1.084 983 9E+00
tondal	**\<force\>**	
newton	309.691 1	3.096 911 0E+02
pound foot/square second	2,240	2.240 000 0E+03
poundal	2,240	2.240 000 0E+03
ton foot/square second [long]	1	1.000 000 0E+00
ton foot/square second [short]	1.12	1.120 000 0E+00
tonde [Denmark, dry]	**\<volume, special - see page 29\>**	
liter	139.1	1.391 000 0E+02
tonde [Denmark, liquid]	**\<volume, special - see page 29\>**	
liter	131.4	1.314 000 0E+02
tonde [Denmark]	**\<area, special - see page 29\>**	
hectare	2.836 9	2.836 900 0E+00
tonde hartkorn [Denmark]	**\<area, special - see page 29\>**	
are	283.69	2.836 900 0E+02
tonde korn [Denmark]	**\<volume, special - see page 29\>**	
hectoliter	1.391 21	1.391 210 0E+00
tonde land [Denmark]	**\<area, special - see page 29\>**	
hectare	0.552	5.520 000 0E−01
tonde ol [Denmark]	**\<volume, special - see page 29\>**	
hectoliter	1.313 92	1.313 920 0E+00
tonde sild [Denmark]	**\<volume, special - see page 29\>**	
hectoliter	1.082 05	1.082 050 0E+00
tonel [Argentina]	**\<volume, special - see page 29\>**	
cubic meter	1.029	1.029 000 0E+00
tonel [Argentina]	**\<mass, special - see page 29\>**	
tonne	0.919	9.190 000 0E−01
tonel [Bolivia]	**\<mass, special - see page 29\>**	
tonne	0.92	9.200 000 0E−01
tonel [Brazil]	**\<volume, special - see page 29\>**	
hectoliter	9.583 2	9.583 200 0E+00

Convert From Convert To	Standard	<Type of Unit> Scientific
tonel [Colombia] tonne	<mass, special - see page 29> 1	1.000 000 0E+00
tonel [Costa Rica] tonne	<mass, special - see page 29> 0.92	9.200 000 0E-01
tonel [Cuba, long] tonne	<mass, special - see page 29> 1.030 6	1.030 600 0E+00
tonel [Cuba, short] tonne	<mass, special - see page 29> 0.920 2	9.202 000 0E-01
tonel [El Salvador] tonne	<mass, special - see page 29> 0.92	9.200 000 0E-01
tonel [Guatemala] tonne	<mass, special - see page 29> 0.92	9.200 000 0E-01
tonel [Nicaragua] tonne	<mass, special - see page 29> 0.92	9.200 000 0E-01
tonel [Paraguay] tonne	<mass, special - see page 29> 0.918	9.180 000 0E-01
tonel [Peru] tonne	<mass, special - see page 29> 0.92	9.200 000 0E-01
tonel [Portugal] liter	<volume, special - see page 29> 860	8.600 000 0E+02
tonel [Portugal] tonne	<mass, special - see page 29> 0.793	7.930 000 0E-01
tonel [Spain, long] tonne	<mass, special - see page 29> 1.030 6	1.030 600 0E+00
tonel [Spain, short] tonne	<mass, special - see page 29> 0.920 2	9.202 000 0E-01
tonelada [Argentina] liter	<volume, special - see page 29> 1,028.98	1.028 980 0E+03
tonelada [Bolivia] tonne	<mass, special - see page 29> 0.92	9.200 000 0E-01
tonelada [Brazil] kilogram	<mass, special - see page 29> 793.238	7.932 380 0E+02
tonelada [Colombia] tonne	<mass, special - see page 29> 1	1.000 000 0E+00
tonelada [Costa Rica] tonne	<mass, special - see page 29> 0.92	9.200 000 0E-01
tonelada [Cuba, long] tonne	<mass, special - see page 29> 1.030 6	1.030 600 0E+00
tonelada [Cuba, short] tonne	<mass, special - see page 29> 0.920 2	9.202 000 0E-01
tonelada [El Salvador] tonne	<mass, special - see page 29> 0.92	9.200 000 0E-01
tonelada [Guatemala] tonne	<mass, special - see page 29> 0.92	9.200 000 0E-01
tonelada [Honduras] kilogram	<mass, special - see page 29> 907.184 74	9.071 847 4E+02
tonelada [Nicaragua] tonne	<mass, special - see page 29> 0.92	9.200 000 0E-01
tonelada [Paraguay] tonne	<mass, special - see page 29> 0.918	9.180 000 0E-01
tonelada [Peru] tonne	<mass, special - see page 29> 0.92	9.200 000 0E-01
tonelada [Portugal] liter	<volume, special - see page 29> 870.5	8.705 000 0E+02

Convert From	<Type of Unit>	
Convert To	Standard	Scientific

tonelada [Portugal] — <mass, special - see page 29>
  tonne — 0.793 — 7.930 000 0E-01

tonelada [Spain] — <mass, special - see page 29>
  kilogram — 920.186 — 9.201 860 0E+02

tonelada [Spanish] — <mass, special - see page 29>
  kilogram — 919.886 — 9.198 860 0E+02

tonelada corta [El Salvador] — <mass, special - see page 29>
  tonne — 0.92 — 9.200 000 0E-01

tonna [Hungary] — <mass, special - see page 29>
  tonne — 1 — 1.000 000 0E+00

tonne — <mass>

Convert To	Standard	Scientific
carat [metric]	5,000,000	5.000 000 0E+06
cental [US]	22.046 226	2.204 622 6E+01
centner [UK]	19.684 131	1.968 413 1E+01
decitonne	10	1.000 000 0E+01
doppelzentner [Germany]	10	1.000 000 0E+01
geepound	68.521 766	6.852 176 6E+01
hundredweight [long]	19.684 131	1.968 413 1E+01
hundredweight [short]	22.046 226	2.204 622 6E+01
kandy [Burma]	0.122 474	1.224 739 7E-01
kilogram	1,000	1.000 000 0E+03
kung tun [Taiwan]	1	1.000 000 0E+00
last [US]	0.551 146 4	5.511 463 8E-01
megagram	1	1.000 000 0E+00
millier	1	1.000 000 0E+00
newton square second/meter	1,000	1.000 000 0E+03
pound	2,204.622 6	2.204 622 6E+03
quarter [long]	3.936 826 1	3.936 826 1E+00
quarter [short]	4.409 245 2	4.409 245 2E+00
quintal [metric]	10	1.000 000 0E+01
ship last [Sweden]	0.408 163 3	4.081 632 7E-01
ton [Canada]	1.102 311 7	1.102 311 7E+00
ton [long]	0.984 206 5	9.842 065 3E-01
ton [metric]	1	1.000 000 0E+00
ton [short]	1.102 311 3	1.102 311 3E+00
ton [Spanish, long]	0.970 308 6	9.703 085 6E-01
ton [Spanish, short]	1.086 720 3	1.086 720 3E+00
tonel [Argentina]	1.088 139 3	1.088 139 3E+00
tonel [Bolivia]	1.086 956 5	1.086 956 5E+00
tonel [Colombia]	1	1.000 000 0E+00
tonel [Costa Rica]	1.086 956 5	1.086 956 5E+00
tonel [Cuba, long]	0.970 308 6	9.703 085 6E-01
tonel [Cuba, short]	1.086 720 3	1.086 720 3E+00
tonel [El Salvador]	1.086 956 5	1.086 956 5E+00
tonel [Guatemala]	1.086 956 5	1.086 956 5E+00
tonel [Nicaragua]	1.086 956 5	1.086 956 5E+00
tonel [Paraguay]	1.089 324 6	1.089 324 6E+00
tonel [Peru]	1.086 956 5	1.086 956 5E+00
tonel [Portugal]	1.261 034	1.261 034 0E+00
tonel [Spain, long]	0.970 308 6	9.703 085 6E-01
tonel [Spain, short]	1.086 720 3	1.086 720 3E+00
tonelada [Bolivia]	1.086 956 5	1.086 956 5E+00
tonelada [Colombia]	1	1.000 000 0E+00
tonelada [Costa Rica]	1.086 956 5	1.086 956 5E+00
tonelada [Cuba, long]	0.970 308 6	9.703 085 6E-01
tonelada [Cuba, short]	1.086 720 3	1.086 720 3E+00
tonelada [El Salvador]	1.086 956 5	1.086 956 5E+00
tonelada [Guatemala]	1.086 956 5	1.086 956 5E+00
tonelada [Nicaragua]	1.086 956 5	1.086 956 5E+00
tonelada [Paraguay]	1.089 324 6	1.089 324 6E+00
tonelada [Peru]	1.086 956 5	1.086 956 5E+00
tonelada [Portugal]	1.261 034	1.261 034 0E+00

Convert From / Convert To	Standard	Scientific

Convert From   **\<Type of Unit\>**
Convert To   Standard   Scientific

tonne (continued)   \<mass\>

Convert To	Standard	Scientific
tonelada corta [El Salvador]	1.086 956 5	1.086 956 5E+00
tonna [Hungary]	1	1.000 000 0E+00
tonneau [Argentina]	1.088 139 3	1.088 139 3E+00
tonneau [Bolivia]	1.086 956 5	1.086 956 5E+00
tonneau [Colombia]	1	1.000 000 0E+00
tonneau [Costa Rica]	1.086 956 5	1.086 956 5E+00
tonneau [Cuba, long]	0.970 308 6	9.703 085 6E−01
tonneau [Cuba, short]	1.086 720 3	1.086 720 3E+00
tonneau [El Salvador]	1.086 956 5	1.086 956 5E+00
tonneau [Guatemala]	1.086 956 5	1.086 956 5E+00
tonneau [Nicaragua]	1.086 956 5	1.086 956 5E+00
tonneau [Paraguay]	1.089 324 6	1.089 324 6E+00
tonneau [Peru]	1.086 956 5	1.086 956 5E+00
tonneau [Portugal]	1.261 034	1.261 034 0E+00
tonneau [Spain, long]	0.970 308 6	9.703 085 6E−01
tonneau [Spain, short]	1.086 720 3	1.086 720 3E+00
tonnelada [Argentina]	1.088 139 3	1.088 139 3E+00
tonnelada [Bolivia]	1.086 956 5	1.086 956 5E+00
tonnelada [Colombia]	1	1.000 000 0E+00
tonnelada [Costa Rica]	1.086 956 5	1.086 956 5E+00
tonnelada [Cuba, long]	0.970 308 6	9.703 085 6E−01
tonnelada [Cuba, short]	1.086 720 3	1.086 720 3E+00
tonnelada [El Salvador]	1.086 956 5	1.086 956 5E+00
tonnelada [Guatemala]	1.086 956 5	1.086 956 5E+00
tonnelada [Nicaragua]	1.086 956 5	1.086 956 5E+00
tonnelada [Paraguay]	1.089 324 6	1.089 324 6E+00
tonnelada [Peru]	1.086 956 5	1.086 956 5E+00
tonnelada [Portugal]	1.261 034	1.261 034 0E+00
tonnelada [Spain, long]	0.970 308 6	9.703 085 6E−01
tonnelada [Spain, short]	1.086 720 3	1.086 720 3E+00
tonos [Greece]	0.666 666 7	6.666 666 7E−01
vagon [Hungary]	0.1	1.000 000 0E−01
vagon [Yugoslavia]	0.1	1.000 000 0E−01
wagon [Yugoslavia]	0.1	1.000 000 0E−01

tonne/cubic centimeter   \<density\>

Convert To	Standard	Scientific
grain/cubic inch	>>>	2.528 910 4E+08
gram/cubic centimeter	1,000,000	1.000 000 0E+06
kilogram/cubic meter	>>>	1.000 000 0E+09
ounce/cubic inch	578,036.67	5.780 366 7E+05
pound/cubic inch	36,127.292	3.612 729 2E+04
slug/cubic inch	1,122.870 6	1.122 870 6E+03
ton/cubic inch [short]	18.063 646	1.806 364 6E+01
tonne/milliliter	1	1.000 000 0E+00

tonne/cubic decimeter   \<density\>

Convert To	Standard	Scientific
kilogram/cubic centimeter	1	1.000 000 0E+00
kilogram/cubic meter	1,000,000	1.000 000 0E+06
kilogram/milliliter	1	1.000 000 0E+00
megagram/cubic decimeter	1	1.000 000 0E+00
megagram/liter	1	1.000 000 0E+00
ounce/cubic inch	578.036 67	5.780 366 7E+02
pound/cubic inch	36.127 292	3.612 729 2E+01
slug/cubic inch	1.122 870 6	1.122 870 6E+00
ton/cubic foot [short]	31.213 98	3.121 398 0E+01
ton/gallon [long/US, liquid]	3.725 627	3.725 627 0E+00
ton/gallon [short/US, liquid]	4.172 702 2	4.172 702 2E+00
tonne/liter	1	1.000 000 0E+00

tonne/cubic meter   \<density\>

Convert To	Standard	Scientific
grain/cubic inch	252.891 04	2.528 910 4E+02
gram/cubic centimeter	1	1.000 000 0E+00
gram/milliliter	1	1.000 000 0E+00
kilogram/cubic decimeter	1	1.000 000 0E+00

Convert From		**\<Type of Unit\>**
Convert To	Standard	Scientific

	Standard	Scientific
kilogram/cubic meter	1,000	1.000 000 0E+03
kilogram/liter	1	1.000 000 0E+00
megagram/cubic meter	1	1.000 000 0E+00
ounce/cubic inch	0.578 036 7	5.780 366 7E−01
pound/cubic foot	62.427 961	6.242 796 1E+01
pound/gallon [-/US, liquid]	8.345 404 5	8.345 404 5E+00
slug/cubic foot	1.940 320 3	1.940 320 3E+00
ton/cubic yard [short]	0.842 777 5	8.427 774 7E−01
tonne/cubic decimeter	0.001	1.000 000 0E−03

tonne/kilometer   **\<linear density\>**

	Standard	Scientific
denier	9,000,000	9.000 000 0E+06
drex	>>>	1.000 000 0E+07
kilogram/meter	1	1.000 000 0E+00
ounce/foot	10.751 504	1.075 150 4E+01
pound/yard	2.015 906 9	2.015 906 9E+00
tex	1,000,000	1.000 000 0E+06

tonne/liter   **\<density\>**

	Standard	Scientific
grain/cubic inch	252,891.04	2.528 910 4E+05
gram/milliliter	1,000	1.000 000 0E+03
kilogram/cubic meter	1,000,000	1.000 000 0E+06
kilogram/milliliter	1	1.000 000 0E+00
megagram/liter	1	1.000 000 0E+00
ounce/cubic inch	578.036 67	5.780 366 7E+02
pound/cubic inch	36.127 292	3.612 729 2E+01
slug/cubic foot	1,122.870 6	1.122 870 6E+03
ton/cubic foot [long]	27.869 625	2.786 962 5E+01
ton/cubic foot [short]	31.213 98	3.121 398 0E+01
ton/gallon [long/US, liquid]	3.725 627	3.725 627 0E+00
ton/gallon [short/US, liquid]	4.172 702 2	4.172 702 2E+00
tonne/cubic decimeter	1	1.000 000 0E+00

tonne/milliliter   **\<density\>**

	Standard	Scientific
grain/cubic inch	>>>	2.528 910 4E+08
gram/cubic centimeter	1,000,000	1.000 000 0E+06
kilogram/cubic meter	>>>	1.000 000 0E+09
megagram/milliliter	1	1.000 000 0E+00
ounce/cubic inch	578,036.67	5.780 366 7E+05
pound/cubic inch	36,127.292	3.612 729 2E+04
slug/cubic inch	1,122.870 6	1.122 870 6E+03
ton/cubic inch [short]	18.063 646	1.806 364 6E+01
tonne/cubic centimeter	1	1.000 000 0E+00

tonne/square centimeter   **\<surface density\>**

	Standard	Scientific
gram/square centimeter	1,000,000	1.000 000 0E+06
kilogram/square centimeter	1,000	1.000 000 0E+03
kilogram/square meter	>>>	1.000 000 0E+07
ounce/square inch	227,573.49	2.275 734 9E+05
pound/square inch	14,223.343	1.422 334 3E+04
slug/square inch	442.075 02	4.420 750 2E+02
ton/square foot [short]	1,024.080 7	1.024 080 7E+03
ton/square inch [short]	7.111 671 7	7.111 671 7E+00
ton/square yard [short]	9,216.726 5	9.216 726 5E+03

tonne/square meter   **\<surface density\>**

	Standard	Scientific
grain/square inch	9,956.340 3	9.956 340 3E+03
kilogram/are	100,000	1.000 000 0E+05
kilogram/square meter	1,000	1.000 000 0E+03
ounce/square inch	22.757 349	2.275 734 9E+01
pound/square inch	1.422 334 3	1.422 334 3E+00
slug/square foot	6.365 880 4	6.365 880 4E+00
ton/square foot [short]	0.102 408 1	1.024 080 7E−01
ton/square yard [short]	0.921 672 7	9.216 726 5E−01
tonne/square centimeter	0.000 1	1.000 000 0E−04

tonne/square meter second   **\<flow rate/unit area, mass basis\>**

	Standard	Scientific
kilogram/square meter second	1,000	1.000 000 0E+03

Convert From / Convert To	Standard	Scientific
ounce/square foot second	3,277.058 3	3.277 058 3E+03
pound/square foot second	204.816 14	2.048 161 4E+02
slug/square foot second	6.365 880 4	6.365 880 4E+00
ton/square foot second [long]	0.091 435 8	9.143 577 8E−02
ton/square foot second [short]	0.102 408 1	1.024 080 7E−01
tonneau [Argentina]	\<volume, special - see page 29\>	
cubic meter	1.029	1.029 000 0E+00
tonneau [Argentina]	\<mass, special - see page 29\>	
tonne	0.919	9.190 000 0E−01
tonneau [Belgium, wine]	\<volume, special - see page 29\>	
liter	100	1.000 000 0E+02
tonneau [Bolivia]	\<mass, special - see page 29\>	
tonne	0.92	9.200 000 0E−01
tonneau [Colombia]	\<mass, special - see page 29\>	
tonne	1	1.000 000 0E+00
tonneau [Costa Rica]	\<mass, special - see page 29\>	
tonne	0.92	9.200 000 0E−01
tonneau [Cuba, long]	\<mass, special - see page 29\>	
tonne	1.030 6	1.030 600 0E+00
tonneau [Cuba, short]	\<mass, special - see page 29\>	
tonne	0.920 2	9.202 000 0E−01
tonneau [El Salvador]	\<mass, special - see page 29\>	
tonne	0.92	9.200 000 0E−01
tonneau [France, wine]	\<volume, special - see page 29\>	
hectoliter	9.048	9.048 000 0E+00
tonneau [Greece]	\<mass, special - see page 29\>	
kilogram	65.28	6.528 000 0E+01
tonneau [Guatemala]	\<mass, special - see page 29\>	
tonne	0.92	9.200 000 0E−01
tonneau [Nicaragua]	\<mass, special - see page 29\>	
tonne	0.92	9.200 000 0E−01
tonneau [Paraguay]	\<mass, special - see page 29\>	
tonne	0.918	9.180 000 0E−01
tonneau [Peru]	\<mass, special - see page 29\>	
tonne	0.92	9.200 000 0E−01
tonneau [Portugal]	\<volume, special - see page 29\>	
liter	860	8.600 000 0E+02
tonneau [Portugal]	\<mass, special - see page 29\>	
tonne	0.793	7.930 000 0E−01
tonneau [Spain, long]	\<mass, special - see page 29\>	
tonne	1.030 6	1.030 600 0E+00
tonneau [Spain, short]	\<mass, special - see page 29\>	
tonne	0.920 2	9.202 000 0E−01
tonneau de jauge international [France]	\<volume, special - see page 29\>	
cubic meter	2.831 684 7	2.831 684 7E+00
tonneau de mer [France]	\<volume, special - see page 29\>	
cubic meter	1.44	1.440 000 0E+00
tonnelada [Argentina]	\<volume, special - see page 29\>	
cubic meter	1.029	1.029 000 0E+00
tonnelada [Argentina]	\<mass, special - see page 29\>	
tonne	0.919	9.190 000 0E−01
tonnelada [Bolivia]	\<mass, special - see page 29\>	
tonne	0.92	9.200 000 0E−01
tonnelada [Colombia]	\<mass, special - see page 29\>	
tonne	1	1.000 000 0E+00

Convert From / Convert To	Type of Unit Standard	Scientific
tonnelada [Costa Rica]	<mass, special - see page 29>	
tonne	0.92	9.200 000 0E−01
tonnelada [Cuba, long]	<mass, special - see page 29>	
tonne	1.030 6	1.030 600 0E+00
tonnelada [Cuba, short]	<mass, special - see page 29>	
tonne	0.920 2	9.202 000 0E−01
tonnelada [El Salvador]	<mass, special - see page 29>	
tonne	0.92	9.200 000 0E−01
tonnelada [Guatemala]	<mass, special - see page 29>	
tonne	0.92	9.200 000 0E−01
tonnelada [Nicaragua]	<mass, special - see page 29>	
tonne	0.92	9.200 000 0E−01
tonnelada [Paraguay]	<mass, special - see page 29>	
tonne	0.918	9.180 000 0E−01
tonnelada [Peru]	<mass, special - see page 29>	
tonne	0.92	9.200 000 0E−01
tonnelada [Portugal]	<volume, special - see page 29>	
liter	871	8.710 000 0E+02
tonnelada [Portugal]	<mass, special - see page 29>	
tonne	0.793	7.930 000 0E−01
tonnelada [Spain, long]	<mass, special - see page 29>	
tonne	1.030 6	1.030 600 0E+00
tonnelada [Spain, short]	<mass, special - see page 29>	
tonne	0.920 2	9.202 000 0E−01
tonni [Spanish North Africa]	<length, special - see page 29>	
centimeter	7.625	7.625 000 0E+00
tonos [Greece]	<mass, special - see page 29>	
tonne	1.5	1.500 000 0E+00
top [Somalia]	<length, special - see page 29>	
meter	3.91	3.910 000 0E+00
top [Somaliland]	<length, special - see page 29>	
meter	3.91	3.910 000 0E+00
tophah [Hebrew, ancient]	<length, special - see page 29>	
centimeter	7.8	7.800 000 0E+00
topo [Peru]	<area, special - see page 29>	
are	27.06	2.706 000 0E+01
toque [Seychelles]	<volume, special - see page 29>	
liter	22	2.200 000 0E+01
torr	<pressure>	
atmosphere [standard]	0.001 315 8	1.315 789 5E−03
atmosphere [technical]	0.001 359 5	1.359 509 8E−03
bar	0.001 333 2	1.333 223 7E−03
barye [France]	1,333.223 7	1.333 223 7E+03
centimeter of mercury [0 °C, by convention]	0.1	9.999 998 6E−02
centimeter of water [4 °C, by convention]	1.359 509 8	1.359 509 8E+00
dyne/square centimeter	1,333.223 7	1.333 223 7E+03
foot of mercury [0 °C, by convention]	0.003 280 8	3.280 839 4E−03
foot of water [4 °C, by convention]	0.044 603 3	4.460 334 0E−02
gram-force/square centimeter	1.359 509 8	1.359 509 8E+00
hectopascal	1.333 223 7	1.333 223 7E+00
inch of mercury [0 °C, by convention]	0.039 370 1	3.937 007 3E−02
inch of water [4 °C, by convention]	0.535 240 1	5.352 400 8E−01
kilogram-force/square meter	13.595 098	1.359 509 8E+01
kilopond/square meter	13.595 098	1.359 509 8E+01
kip/square foot	0.002 784 5	2.784 495 6E−03
millibar	1.333 223 7	1.333 223 7E+00
millimeter of mercury [0 °C, by convention]	0.999 999 9	9.999 998 6E−01
millimeter of water [4 °C, by convention]	13.595 098	1.359 509 8E+01

	Standard	Scientific
newton/square meter	133.322 37	1.333 223 7E+02
ounce-force/square inch	0.309 388 4	3.093 884 0E-01
pascal	133.322 37	1.333 223 7E+02
pound-force/square foot	2.784 495 6	2.784 495 6E+00
poundal/square foot	89.588 495	8.958 849 5E+01
ton-force/square foot [long]	0.001 243 1	1.243 078 4E-03
ton-force/square foot [short]	0.001 392 2	1.392 247 8E-03
ton-force/square meter [metric]	0.013 595 1	1.359 509 8E-02

tot [UK] <volume, special - see page 29>
milliliter	23.677	2.367 700 0E+01

totchka [Russia] <length, special - see page 29>
millimeter	0.254	2.540 000 0E-01

totschka [Russia] <length, special - see page 29>
millimeter	0.254	2.540 000 0E-01

totska [Russia] <length, special - see page 29>
millimeter	0.254	2.540 000 0E-01

tou [China] <volume, special - see page 29>
liter	10	1.000 000 0E+01

toumnah [Egypt] <volume, special - see page 29>
liter	0.257 8	2.578 000 0E-01

touque [Cambodia] <volume, special - see page 29>
liter	18	1.800 000 0E+01

touque [Seychelles] <volume, special - see page 29>
liter	22.739 8	2.273 980 0E+01

tovar [Bulgaria] <mass, special - see page 29>
kilogram	128.8	1.288 000 0E+02

tovar [Yugoslavia] <mass, special - see page 29>
kilogram	128	1.280 000 0E+02

town lot [Sierra Leone] <area, special - see page 29>
square meter	348.39	3.483 900 0E+02

township [US, survey] <length>
	Standard	Scientific
cable length [US, survey]	44	4.400 000 0E+01
chain [Gunter or US, survey]	480	4.800 000 0E+02
chain [Ramden or Engineer]	316.800 63	3.168 006 3E+02
fathom [US, survey]	5,280	5.280 000 0E+03
foot [international]	31,680.063	3.168 006 3E+04
foot [US, survey]	31,680	3.168 000 0E+04
furlong [US, survey]	48	4.800 000 0E+01
kilometer	9.656 083 3	9.656 083 3E+00
league [international, nautical]	1.737 956	1.737 956 0E+00
league [US, statute]	2	2.000 000 0E+00
meter	9,656.083 3	9.656 083 3E+03
mile [international]	6.000 012	6.000 012 0E+00
mile [US, statute]	6	6.000 000 0E+00
mile [US, survey]	6	6.000 000 0E+00
out [US, survey]	96	9.600 000 0E+01
pace [US, survey]	12,672	1.267 200 0E+04
perch [US, survey]	1,920	1.920 000 0E+03
range [US, survey]	1	1.000 000 0E+00
yard [based on US, survey foot]	10,560	1.056 000 0E+04
yard [international]	10,560.021	1.056 002 1E+04

township [US, survey] <area>
	Standard	Scientific
acre [commerical]	27,878.512	2.787 851 2E+04
acre [international]	23,040.092	2.304 009 2E+04
acre [US, survey]	23,040	2.304 000 0E+04
hectare	9,323.994 5	9.323 994 5E+03
labor [US, survey]	130.066 61	1.300 666 1E+02
rood	92,160	9.216 000 0E+04
section [US, survey]	36	3.600 000 0E+01
square arpent [US, survey]	27,271.757	2.727 175 7E+04

Convert From Convert To	<Type of Unit> Standard	Scientific
square chain [Gunter or US, survey]	230,400	2.304 000 0E+05
square chain [Ramden or Engineer]	100,362.24	1.003 622 4E+05
square furlong [US, survey]	2,304	2.304 000 0E+03
square league [US, statute]	4	4.000 000 0E+00
square meter	>>>	9.323 994 5E+07
square mile [international]	36.000 144	3.600 014 4E+01
square mile [US, statute]	36	3.600 000 0E+01
square mile [US, survey]	36	3.600 000 0E+01
square myriameter	0.932 399 5	9.323 994 5E−01
square yard [based on US, survey foot]	>>>	1.115 136 8E+08
square yard [international]	>>>	1.115 140 5E+08
trait [Switzerland]	**<length, special - see page 29>**	
millimeter	0.3	3.000 000 0E−01
tredecillion [UK]	**<units>**	
unit	>>>	1.000 000 0E+78
tredecillion [US]	**<units>**	
septillion [UK]	1	1.000 000 0E+00
unit	>>>	1.000 000 0E+42
tricentennial	**<time>**	
year [normal calendar]	300	3.000 000 0E+02
triennium	**<time>**	
year [normal calendar]	3	3.000 000 0E+00
triens [Rome, ancient]	**<mass, special - see page 29>**	
gram	109.15	1.091 500 0E+02
trillion [UK]	**<units>**	
quintillion [US]	1	1.000 000 0E+00
unit	>>>	1.000 000 0E+18
trillion [US]	**<units>**	
billion [UK]	1	1.000 000 0E+00
unit	>>>	1.000 000 0E+12
trillion cubic foot	**<volume>**	
billion cubic foot	1,000	1.000 000 0E+03
cubem	6.793 572 8	6.793 572 8E+00
cubic foot	>>>	1.000 000 0E+12
cubic kilometer	28.316 847	2.831 684 7E+01
cubic meter	>>>	2.831 684 7E+10
cubic mile	6.793 572 8	6.793 572 8E+00
cubic yard	>>>	3.703 703 7E+10
freight ton	>>>	2.500 000 0E+10
liter	>>>	2.831 684 7E+13
million acre foot	22.956 841	2.295 684 1E+01
million board foot	>>>	1.200 000 0E+07
ocean ton	>>>	2.500 000 0E+10
petrograd standard	>>>	6.060 606 1E+09
register ton	>>>	1.000 000 0E+10
shipping ton	>>>	2.500 000 0E+10
thousand board foot	>>>	1.200 000 0E+10
thousand cubic foot	>>>	1.000 000 0E+09
trillion cubic foot/day	**<flow rate, volume basis>**	
acre foot/second	265.704 18	2.657 041 8E+02
acre foot/second [US, survey]	265.702 586	2.657 025 9E+02
acre inch/second	3,188.450 16	3.188 450 2E+03
billion cubic foot/day	1,000	1.000 000 0E+03
billion cubic foot/hour	41.666 666 7	4.166 666 7E+01
cubem/day	6.793 572 8	6.793 572 8E+00
cubic dekameter/second	327.741 28	3.277 412 8E+02
cubic kilometer/hour	1.179 868 6	1.179 868 6E+00
cubic meter/second	327,741.28	3.277 412 8E+05
cubic mile/day	6.793 572 8	6.793 572 8E+00
hectare meter/second	32.774 128	3.277 412 8E+01
petrograd standard/second	70,145.903	7.014 590 3E+04

| Convert From | <Type of Unit> | |
Convert To	Standard	Scientific
thousand cubic foot/second	11,574.074	1.157 407 4E+04
trillion cubic foot/hour	0.041 666 7	4.166 666 7E−02
trillion cubic foot/hour	<flow rate, volume basis>	
acre foot/second	6,376.900 32	6.376 900 3E+03
acre foot/second [US, survey]	6,376.862 05	6.376 862 1E+03
billion cubic foot/minute	16.666 666 7	1.666 666 7E+01
cubem/hour	6.793 572 8	6.793 572 8E+00
cubic dekameter/second	7,865.790 72	7.865 790 7E+03
cubic kilometer/hour	28.316 846 6	2.831 684 7E+01
cubic meter/second	7,865,790.72	7.865 790 7E+06
cubic mile/hour	6.793 572 8	6.793 572 8E+00
hectare meter/second	786.579 072	7.865 790 7E+02
million acre foot/hour	22.956 841 1	2.295 684 1E+01
trillion cubic foot/day	24	2.400 000 0E+01
trillion cubic foot/minute	<flow rate, volume basis>	
acre foot/second	382,614.019	3.826 140 2E+05
acre foot/second [US, survey]	382,611.723	3.826 117 2E+05
billion cubic foot/second	16.666 666 7	1.666 666 7E+01
cubem/minute	6.793 572 8	6.793 572 8E+00
cubic kilometer/minute	28.316 846 6	2.831 684 7E+01
cubic meter/second	>>>	4.719 474 4E+08
cubic mile/minute	6.793 572 8	6.793 572 8E+00
hectare meter/second	47,194.744 3	4.719 474 4E+04
million acre foot/minute	22.956 841 1	2.295 684 1E+01
trillion cubic foot/second	60	6.000 000 0E+01
trillion cubic foot/second	<flow rate, volume basis>	
billion cubic foot/second	1,000	1.000 000 0E+03
cubem/second	6.793 572 8	6.793 572 8E+00
cubic kilometer/second	28.316 846 6	2.831 684 7E+01
cubic meter/second	>>>	2.831 684 7E+10
cubic mile/second	6.793 572 8	6.793 572 8E+00
million acre foot/second	22.956 841 1	2.295 684 1E+01
trillion cubic foot/minute	60	6.000 000 0E+01
trug [US, mortar]	<volume, special - see page 29>	
liter	23.491 8	2.349 180 0E+01
truong [Vietnam]	<length, special - see page 29>	
meter	4	4.000 000 0E+00
tsal [Ukraine]	<length, special - see page 29>	
millimeter	24.8	2.480 000 0E+01
tschak [Iran]	<mass, special - see page 29>	
kilogram	0.742 336	7.423 360 0E−01
tschak [Iran]	<length, special - see page 29>	
centimeter	26	2.600 000 0E+01
tscheki [Turkey]	<mass, special - see page 29>	
gram	318.667	3.186 670 0E+02
tsein [China]	<mass, special - see page 29>	
gram	3.779 9	3.779 900 0E+00
tser [Egypt, ancient]	<length, special - see page 29>	
centimeter	36	3.600 000 0E+01
tsin [Cambodia]	<mass, special - see page 29>	
gram	3.75	3.750 000 0E+00
tsin [Hong Kong]	<mass, special - see page 29>	
gram	3.78	3.780 000 0E+00
tsin [Mongolia]	<mass, special - see page 29>	
gram	3.75	3.750 000 0E+00
tsubo [Japan]	<area, special - see page 29>	
square meter	3.305 8	3.305 800 0E+00
tsun [China]	<length, special - see page 29>	
centimeter	3.581 4	3.581 400 0E+00

tsun [Hong Kong]	\<length, special - see page 29\>	
centimeter	3.714 75	3.714 750 0E+00
tu [China]	\<length, special - see page 29\>	
kilometer	161.16	1.611 600 0E+02
tuc [Vietnam, cereal]	\<volume, special - see page 29\>	
milliliter	0.003 3	3.300 000 0E-03
tughar [Iraq]	\<mass, special - see page 29\>	
kilogram	2,032.094	2.032 094 0E+03
tuht [Turkey]	\<mass, special - see page 29\>	
gram	160.4	1.604 000 0E+02
tum [Finland]	\<length, special - see page 29\>	
centimeter	2.47	2.470 000 0E+00
tum [Sweden]	\<length, special - see page 29\>	
centimeter	2.97	2.970 000 0E+00
tuman [Hebrew, ancient]	\<volume, special - see page 29\>	
cubic centimeter	274.695 67	2.746 956 7E+02
tumma [Finland]	\<length, special - see page 29\>	
centimeter	2.47	2.470 000 0E+00
tumna [Sudan]	\<mass, special - see page 29\>	
kilogram	5.616	5.616 000 0E+00
tumoli [Malta, cereals]	\<volume, special - see page 29\>	
hectoliter	72.737	7.273 700 0E+01
tun [Malaysia]	\<volume, special - see page 29\>	
hectoliter	11.456	1.145 600 0E+01
tun [Singapore]	\<volume, special - see page 29\>	
hectoliter	11.456	1.145 600 0E+01
tun [Straits Settlements]	\<volume, special - see page 29\>	
liter	1,145.6	1.145 600 0E+03
tun [UK, liquid]	\<volume\>	
acre foot	0.000 796 1	7.960 842 3E-04
acre inch	0.009 553	9.553 010 8E-03
barrel [UK]	6	6.000 000 0E+00
barrel [US, federal]	8.367 909 2	8.367 909 2E+00
barrel [US, federal proof spirits]	6.485 129 6	6.485 129 6E+00
barrel [US, liquid]	8.235 085 2	8.235 085 2E+00
barrel [US, petroleum]	6.176 313 9	6.176 313 9E+00
bushel [UK]	27	2.700 000 0E+01
chaldron [UK, liquid]	0.75	7.500 000 0E-01
cubic foot	34.677 429	3.467 742 9E+01
cubic inch	59,922.597	5.992 259 7E+04
cubic meter	0.981 955 4	9.819 554 4E-01
cubic yard	1.284 349 2	1.284 349 2E+00
cup [Canada, measuring]	4,320	4.320 000 0E+03
cup [US, measuring]	4,150.482 9	4.150 482 9E+03
drum [US, liquid]	4.716 457 9	4.716 457 9E+00
firkin [UK]	24	2.400 000 0E+01
firkin [US]	28.822 798	2.882 279 8E+01
gallon [Canada, liquid]	216	2.160 000 0E+02
gallon [UK, dry or liquid]	216	2.160 000 0E+02
gallon [US, liquid]	259.405 18	2.594 051 8E+02
gill [UK]	6,912	6.912 000 0E+03
gill [US]	8,300.965 9	8.300 965 9E+03
hectoliter	9.819 554 4	9.819 554 4E+00
hogshead [UK]	3.428 571 4	3.428 571 4E+00
hogshead [US]	4.117 542 6	4.117 542 6E+00
liter	981.955 44	9.819 554 4E+02
ounce [UK, liquid]	34,560	3.456 000 0E+04
ounce [US, liquid]	33,203.864	3.320 386 4E+04
peck [UK]	108	1.080 000 0E+02

	Standard	Scientific
peck [US]	111.462 13	1.114 621 3E+02
pint [UK]	1,728	1.728 000 0E+03
pint [US, liquid]	2,075.241 5	2.075 241 5E+03
pipe [UK]	2	2.000 000 0E+00
pipe [US, liquid]	2.058 771 3	2.058 771 3E+00
quart [UK]	864	8.640 000 0E+02
quart [US, liquid]	1,037.620 7	1.037 620 7E+03
quarter [UK]	3.375	3.375 000 0E+00
scruple [UK, liquid]	829,440	8.294 400 0E+05
tun [US, liquid]	1.029 385 7	1.029 385 7E+00
Winchester wine gallon [UK]	259.405 18	2.594 051 8E+02

tun [US, liquid]   \<volume\>

	Standard	Scientific
acre foot	0.000 773 4	7.733 585 9E−04
acre inch	0.009 280 3	9.280 303 0E−03
barrel [UK]	5.828 719 3	5.828 719 3E+00
barrel [US, federal proof spirits]	6.3	6.300 000 0E+00
barrel [US, liquid]	8	8.000 000 0E+00
barrel [US, petroleum]	6	6.000 000 0E+00
chaldron [UK, liquid]	0.728 589 9	7.285 899 1E−01
cubic foot	33.687 5	3.368 750 0E+01
cubic inch	58,212	5.821 200 0E+04
cubic meter	0.953 923 8	9.539 237 7E−01
cubic yard	1.247 685 2	1.247 685 2E+00
cup [Canada, measuring]	4,196.677 9	4.196 677 9E+03
cup [US, measuring]	4,032	4.032 000 0E+03
drum [US, liquid]	4.581 818 2	4.581 818 2E+00
firkin [UK]	23.314 877	2.331 487 7E+01
firkin [US]	28	2.800 000 0E+01
gallon [Canada, liquid]	209.833 89	2.098 338 9E+02
gallon [UK, dry or liquid]	209.833 89	2.098 338 9E+02
gallon [US, liquid]	252	2.520 000 0E+02
gill [UK]	6,714.684 6	6.714 684 6E+03
gill [US]	8,064	8.064 000 0E+03
hectare meter	0.000 095 4	9.539 237 7E−05
hectoliter	9.539 237 7	9.539 237 7E+00
hogshead [UK]	3.330 696 7	3.330 696 7E+00
hogshead [US]	4	4.000 000 0E+00
liter	953.923 77	9.539 237 7E+02
ounce [UK, liquid]	33,573.423	3.357 342 3E+04
ounce [US, liquid]	32,256	3.225 600 0E+04
pint [UK]	1,678.671 2	1.678 671 2E+03
pint [US, liquid]	2,016	2.016 000 0E+03
pipe [UK]	1.942 906 4	1.942 906 4E+00
pipe [US, liquid]	2	2.000 000 0E+00
quart [UK]	839.335 58	8.393 355 8E+02
quart [US, liquid]	1,008	1.008 000 0E+03
quarter [UK]	3.278 654 6	3.278 654 6E+00
stere	0.953 923 8	9.539 237 7E−01
tun [UK, liquid]	0.971 453 2	9.714 532 2E−01
Winchester wine gallon [UK]	252	2.520 000 0E+02

tundagslatta [Iceland]   \<area, special - see page 29\>

	Standard	Scientific
are	31.915	3.191 500 0E+01

tunland [Finland]   \<area, special - see page 29\>

	Standard	Scientific
are	49.36	4.936 000 0E+01

tunland [Sweden]   \<area, special - see page 29\>

	Standard	Scientific
are	49.36	4.936 000 0E+01

tunna [Finland]   \<volume, special - see page 29\>

	Standard	Scientific
liter	125.63	1.256 300 0E+02

tunna [Sweden]   \<volume, special - see page 29\>

	Standard	Scientific
liter	146.6	1.466 000 0E+02

Convert From	<Type of Unit>	
Convert To	Standard	Scientific

tunna smjors [Iceland] <mass, special - see page 29>
kilogram --- 112 --- 1.120 000 0E+02

tunnia [Finland, grain] <volume, special - see page 29>
liter -- 164.88 --- 1.648 800 0E+02

tunnia [Finland, liquid] <volume, special - see page 29>
liter -- 125.63 --- 1.256 300 0E+02

tunnland [Finland] <area, special - see page 29>
are -- 49.36 --- 4.936 000 0E+01

tunnland [Sweden] <area, special - see page 29>
are -- 49.36 --- 4.936 000 0E+01

tzemed [Mesopotamia, ancient] <area, special - see page 29>
hectare -- 0.2 --- 2.000 000 0E-01

ubanu [Akkadian, ancient] <length, special - see page 29>
centimeter --- 1.67 --- 1.670 000 0E+00

uckir [Tunisia] <mass, special - see page 29>
gram --- 31.495 3 --- 3.149 530 0E+01

ud [Sudan] <length, special - see page 29>
meter -- 2.32 --- 2.320 000 0E+00

ueba [Libya] <volume, special - see page 29>
hectoliter -- 2.905 --- 2.905 000 0E+00

ugga [Sudan] <mass, special - see page 29>
kilogram --- 1.248 --- 1.248 000 0E+00

ughia [Somaliland] <mass, special - see page 29>
gram --- 28.313 --- 2.831 300 0E+01

ugija [Malta and Gozo] <mass, special - see page 29>
gram --- 26.459 56 --- 2.645 956 0E+01

ukia [Ethiopia] <mass, special - see page 29>
gram -- 25.9 --- 2.590 000 0E+01

ukia [Iraq] <mass, special - see page 29>
kilogram --- 1.042 --- 1.042 000 0E+00

ukia [Jordan, Nabulsi] <mass, special - see page 29>
gram --- 240.4 --- 2.404 000 0E+02

ukia [Lebanon] <mass, special - see page 29>
gram --- 213.7 --- 2.137 000 0E+02

ukia [Libya] <mass, special - see page 29>
gram --- 32.05 --- 3.205 000 0E+01

ukia [Somalia] <mass, special - see page 29>
gram --- 28 --- 2.800 000 0E+01

ukia [Sudan] <mass, special - see page 29>
gram --- 37.44 --- 3.744 000 0E+01

ukia [Syria, Damascus] <mass, special - see page 29>
gram --- 213.7 --- 2.137 000 0E+02

ukie [Libya, ostrich feathers and spinning wools] <mass, special - see page 29>
gram --- 32.05 --- 3.205 000 0E+01

ukkia [Algeria] <mass, special - see page 29>
gram --- 34.13 --- 3.413 000 0E+01

ukla [Hebrew, ancient] <volume, special - see page 29>
cubic centimeter --- 109.874 3 --- 1.098 743 0E+02

ulna [Rome, ancient] <length, special - see page 29>
centimeter --- 44.34 --- 4.434 000 0E+01

una [Iran] <mass, special - see page 29>
milligram -- 12.21 --- 1.221 000 0E+01

uncia [Rome, ancient] <mass, special - see page 29>
gram -- 27.288 --- 2.728 800 0E+01

uncia [Rome, ancient] — \<length, special - see page 29>
centimeter ---------- 2.464 ---- 2.464 000 0E+00

uncya [Poland] — \<mass, special - see page 29>
gram ---------- 25.344 ---- 2.534 400 0E+01

undecillion [UK] — \<units>
unit ---------- >>> ---- 1.000 000 0E+66

undecillion [US] — \<units>
sextillion [UK] ---------- 1 ---- 1.000 000 0E+00
unit ---------- >>> ---- 1.000 000 0E+36

unglee [India] — \<length, special - see page 29>
centimeter ---------- 1.89 ---- 1.890 000 0E+00

unglie [Pakistan] — \<length, special - see page 29>
centimeter ---------- 1.905 ---- 1.905 000 0E+00

ungul [India] — \<length, special - see page 29>
centimeter ---------- 1.905 ---- 1.905 000 0E+00

ungul [Pakistan] — \<length, special - see page 29>
centimeter ---------- 1.905 ---- 1.905 000 0E+00

unguli [India] — \<length, special - see page 29>
centimeter ---------- 1.905 ---- 1.905 000 0E+00

unit — \<units>
centillion [UK] ---------- <<< ---- 0.000 000 0E−600
one ---------- 1 ---- 1.000 000 0E+00
single ---------- 1 ---- 1.000 000 0E+00

unit pole — \<magnetic flux>
gauss square centimeter ---------- 12.566 37 ---- 1.256 637 0E+01
maxwell ---------- 12.566 37 ---- 1.256 637 0E+01
statweber ---------- <<< ---- 4.191 690 8E−10
weber ---------- 0.000 000 1 ---- 1.256 637 0E−07

uns [Sweden] — \<mass, special - see page 29>
gram ---------- 26.567 3 ---- 2.656 730 0E+01

unser [Denmark] — \<mass, special - see page 29>
gram ---------- 29.412 ---- 2.941 200 0E+01

unze [Algeria] — \<mass, special - see page 29>
gram ---------- 34.13 ---- 3.413 000 0E+01

unze [Austria] — \<mass, special - see page 29>
gram ---------- 35.001 ---- 3.500 100 0E+01

unze [France, 1800 definition] — \<mass, special - see page 29>
gram ---------- 100 ---- 1.000 000 0E+02

unze [Germany] — \<mass, special - see page 29>
gram ---------- 31.25 ---- 3.125 000 0E+01

unze [Switzerland] — \<mass, special - see page 29>
gram ---------- 31.25 ---- 3.125 000 0E+01

unzen [Germany] — \<mass, special - see page 29>
gram ---------- 29.23 ---- 2.923 000 0E+01

uqija [Malta] — \<mass, special - see page 29>
gram ---------- 26.5 ---- 2.650 000 0E+01

uqije [Islam] — \<mass, special - see page 29>
gram ---------- 39 ---- 3.900 000 0E+01

ure [Mongolia] — \<area, special - see page 29>
square meter ---------- 921.6 ---- 9.216 000 0E+02

urna [Rome, ancient, liquid] — \<volume, special - see page 29>
liter ---------- 13 ---- 1.300 000 0E+01

usbaa [Egypt] — \<length, special - see page 29>
centimeter ---------- 3.3 ---- 3.300 000 0E+00

ush [Iraq, ancient] — \<length, special - see page 29>
meter ---------- 711 ---- 7.110 000 0E+02

Convert From		
Convert To	**Standard**	**Scientific**

uye [Lebanon]	<mass, special - see page 29>	
gram	200	2.000 000 0E+02
uyen [Vietnam, rice, milled]	<volume, special - see page 29>	
liter	1	1.000 000 0E+00
uzan [Tunisia]	<mass, special - see page 29>	
gram	31.487	3.148 700 0E+01
va [Laos]	<length, special - see page 29>	
meter	2	2.000 000 0E+00
va [Thailand]	<length, special - see page 29>	
meter	2	2.000 000 0E+00
va louang [Laos]	<length, special - see page 29>	
meter	2	2.000 000 0E+00
va yiet [Laos]	<length, special - see page 29>	
meter	2	2.000 000 0E+00
vadem [Netherlands]	<length, special - see page 29>	
meter	1.83	1.830 000 0E+00
vadra [Romania]	<volume, special - see page 29>	
liter	15.2	1.520 000 0E+01
vagon [Hungary]	<mass, special - see page 29>	
tonne	10	1.000 000 0E+01
vagon [Yugoslavia]	<mass, special - see page 29>	
tonne	10	1.000 000 0E+01
vall [India, gold and silver]	<mass, special - see page 29>	
gram	3.768	3.768 000 0E+00
vamfort [Hungary]	<mass, special - see page 29>	
kilogram	0.5	5.000 000 0E−01
vammazsa [Hungary]	<mass, special - see page 29>	
kilogram	50	5.000 000 0E+01
var		<power>
Btu/hour [I.T.]	3.412 141 6	3.412 141 6E+00
watt	1	1.000 000 0E+00
vara [Argentina]	<length, special - see page 29>	
centimeter	86.6	8.660 000 0E+01
vara [Bolivia]	<length, special - see page 29>	
meter	0.866	8.660 000 0E−01
vara [Brazil]	<length, special - see page 29>	
meter	1.1	1.100 000 0E+00
vara [Canada]	<length, special - see page 29>	
meter	0.847	8.470 000 0E−01
vara [Cape Verde]	<area, special - see page 29>	
square meter	1.21	1.210 000 0E+00
vara [Chile]	<length, special - see page 29>	
centimeter	83.59	8.359 000 0E+01
vara [Colombia]	<length, special - see page 29>	
centimeter	80	8.000 000 0E+01
vara [Costa Rica]	<length, special - see page 29>	
centimeter	83.6	8.360 000 0E+01
vara [Cuba]	<length, special - see page 29>	
centimeter	84.8	8.480 000 0E+01
vara [Dominican Republic]	<length, special - see page 29>	
centimeter	83.6	8.360 000 0E+01
vara [Ecuador]	<length, special - see page 29>	
centimeter	84	8.400 000 0E+01
vara [El Salvador]	<length, special - see page 29>	
centimeter	83.6	8.360 000 0E+01

vara [Guatemala] — <length, special - see page 29>
centimeter -- 83.6 ---- 8.360 000 0E+01

vara [Honduras] — <length, special - see page 29>
centimeter -- 83.5 ---- 8.350 000 0E+01

vara [Macao] — <length, special - see page 29>
meter --- 1.1 ---- 1.100 000 0E+00

vara [Mexico] — <length, special - see page 29>
centimeter -- 83.8 ---- 8.380 000 0E+01

vara [Nicaragua] — <length, special - see page 29>
centimeter --- 84 ---- 8.400 000 0E+01

vara [Panama] — <length, special - see page 29>
centimeter --- 80 ---- 8.000 000 0E+01

vara [Paraguay] — <length, special - see page 29>
centimeter -- 86.7 ---- 8.670 000 0E+01

vara [Peru] — <length, special - see page 29>
centimeter -- 83.8 ---- 8.380 000 0E+01

vara [Philippines] — <length, special - see page 29>
meter --------------------------------------- 0.835 92 ---- 8.359 200 0E−01

vara [Portugal] — <length, special - see page 29>
meter --- 1.1 ---- 1.100 000 0E+00

vara [Spain] — <length, special - see page 29>
centimeter -------------------------------------- 83.59 ---- 8.359 000 0E+01

vara [Uruguay] — <length, special - see page 29>
centimeter -- 85.9 ---- 8.590 000 0E+01

vara [US, survey, California] — <length>
chain [Gunter or US, survey]	0.041 666 7	4.166 666 7E−02
chain [Ramden or Engineer]	0.027 500 1	2.750 005 5E−02
decimeter	8.382 016 8	8.382 016 8E+00
fathom [US, survey]	0.458 333 3	4.583 333 3E−01
foot [international]	2.750 005 5	2.750 005 5E+00
foot [US, survey]	2.75	2.750 000 0E+00
furlong [US, survey]	0.004 166 7	4.166 666 7E−03
inch [based on US, survey foot]	33	3.300 000 0E+01
inch [international]	33.000 066	3.300 006 6E+01
link [Gunter or US, survey]	4.166 666 7	4.166 666 7E+00
link [Ramden or Engineer]	2.750 005 5	2.750 005 5E+00
meter	0.838 201 7	8.382 016 8E−01
out [US, survey]	0.008 333 3	8.333 333 3E−03
pace [geometrical]	0.055 000 1	5.500 011 0E−02
pace [US, survey]	1.1	1.100 000 0E+00
perch [US, survey]	0.166 666 7	1.666 666 7E−01
vara [US, survey, Texas]	0.99	9.900 000 0E−01
yard [based on US, survey foot]	0.916 666 7	9.166 666 7E−01
yard [international]	0.916 668 5	9.166 685 0E−01

vara [US, survey, Texas] — <length>
cable length [US, survey]	0.003 858	3.858 024 7E−03
chain [Gunter or US, survey]	0.042 087 5	4.208 754 2E−02
chain [Ramden or Engineer]	0.027 777 8	2.777 783 3E−02
decimeter	8.466 683 6	8.466 683 6E+00
fathom [US, survey]	0.462 963	4.629 629 6E−01
foot [international]	2.777 783	2.777 783 3E+00
foot [US, survey]	2.777 777 8	2.777 777 8E+00
furlong [US, survey]	0.004 208 8	4.208 754 2E−03
inch [based on US, survey foot]	33.333 333	3.333 333 3E+01
inch [international]	33.333 34	3.333 340 0E+01
link [Gunter or US, survey]	4.208 754 2	4.208 754 2E+00
link [Ramden or Engineer]	2.777 783	2.777 783 3E+00
meter	0.846 668 4	8.466 683 6E−01
out [US, survey]	0.008 417 5	8.417 508 4E−03
pace [US, survey]	1.111 111 1	1.111 111 1E+00

Convert From / Convert To	Standard	Scientific
perch [US, survey]	0.168 350 2	1.683 501 7E−01
vara [US, survey, California]	1.010 101	1.010 101 0E+00
yard [based on US, survey foot]	0.925 925 9	9.259 259 3E−01
yard [international]	0.925 927 8	9.259 277 8E−01
vara [Venezuela]	\<length, special - see page 29\>	
meter	0.8	8.000 000 0E−01
vara cuadrada [Argentina]	\<area, special - see page 29\>	
square meter	0.751	7.510 000 0E−01
vara cuadrada [Chile]	\<area, special - see page 29\>	
square meter	0.698 9	6.989 000 0E−01
vara cuadrada [Colombia]	\<area, special - see page 29\>	
square meter	0.64	6.400 000 0E−01
vara cuadrada [Costa Rica]	\<area, special - see page 29\>	
square meter	0.698 9	6.989 000 0E−01
vara cuadrada [Cuba]	\<area, special - see page 29\>	
square meter	0.64	6.400 000 0E−01
vara cuadrada [El Salvador]	\<area, special - see page 29\>	
square meter	0.699 8	6.998 000 0E−01
vara cuadrada [Guatemala]	\<area, special - see page 29\>	
are	0.006 987	6.987 000 0E−03
vara cuadrada [Honduras]	\<area, special - see page 29\>	
square meter	0.697 2	6.972 000 0E−01
vara cuadrada [Macao]	\<area, special - see page 29\>	
square meter	1.21	1.210 000 0E+00
vara cuadrada [Mexico]	\<area, special - see page 29\>	
square meter	0.702 24	7.022 400 0E−01
vara cuadrada [Nicaragua]	\<area, special - see page 29\>	
square meter	0.704 4	7.044 000 0E−01
vara cuadrada [Paraguay]	\<area, special - see page 29\>	
square meter	0.751	7.510 000 0E−01
vara cuadrada [Spain]	\<area, special - see page 29\>	
square meter	0.698 737	6.987 370 0E−01
vara cuadrada [Uruguay]	\<area, special - see page 29\>	
square meter	0.738	7.380 000 0E−01
vara cubica [Macao]	\<volume, special - see page 29\>	
cubic meter	1.331	1.331 000 0E+00
vara cubica [Mexico]	\<volume, special - see page 29\>	
cubic meter	0.588 48	5.884 800 0E−01
vara cubica [Spain]	\<volume, special - see page 29\>	
cubic meter	0.584 078	5.840 780 0E−01
vara granadina [Colombia]	\<length, special - see page 29\>	
centimeter	80	8.000 000 0E+01
vat [Belgium]	\<volume, special - see page 29\>	
hectoliter	1	1.000 000 0E+00
vat [Netherlands]	\<volume, special - see page 29\>	
liter	931.2	9.312 000 0E+02
vedro [Bulgaria]	\<volume, special - see page 29\>	
liter	10	1.000 000 0E+01
vedro [Russia]	\<volume, special - see page 29\>	
liter	12.3	1.230 000 0E+01
velte [France, liquid]	\<volume, special - see page 29\>	
liter	7.451	7.451 000 0E+00
velte [Mauritius]	\<volume, special - see page 29\>	
liter	7.450 5	7.450 500 0E+00
ver [India]	\<length, special - see page 29\>	
meter	0.685 8	6.858 000 0E−01

ver [Iran]
meter -- `<length, special - see page 29>`
1.04 ---- 1.040 000 0E+00

ver [Pakistan]
meter -- `<length, special - see page 29>`
0.914 4 ---- 9.144 000 0E-01

verchok [Russia]
centimeter -- `<length, special - see page 29>`
4.445 ---- 4.445 000 0E+00

verge [France]
meter -- `<length, special - see page 29>`
7.146 ---- 7.146 000 0E+00

verklinje [Sweden]
centimeter -- `<length, special - see page 29>`
0.206 181 ---- 2.061 810 0E-01

verktum [Sweden]
centimeter -- `<length, special - see page 29>`
2.474 17 ---- 2.474 170 0E+00

versock [Russia]
centimeter -- `<length, special - see page 29>`
4.445 ---- 4.445 000 0E+00

verst [Russia]
kilometer --- `<length, special - see page 29>`
1.067 ---- 1.067 000 0E+00

versta [Russia]
kilometer --- `<length, special - see page 29>`
1.067 ---- 1.067 000 0E+00

verste [Finland]
meter -- `<length, special - see page 29>`
1,069 ---- 1.069 000 0E+03

verste [Russia]
kilometer --- `<length, special - see page 29>`
1.066 8 ---- 1.066 800 0E+00

vi [Vietnam]
milligram --- `<mass, special - see page 29>`
0.003 778 ---- 3.778 000 0E-03

vi [Vietnam]
nanometer -- `<length, special - see page 29>`
40 ---- 4.000 000 0E+01

viacka [Romania]
liter --- `<volume, special - see page 29>`
14.15 ---- 1.415 000 0E+01

vicenary
vicennial -- `<time>`
1 ---- 1.000 000 0E+00
year [normal calendar] ------------------------- 20 ---- 2.000 000 0E+01

vicennial
vicenary -- `<time>`
1 ---- 1.000 000 0E+00
year [normal calendar] ------------------------- 20 ---- 2.000 000 0E+01

vidro [Russia]
liter --- `<volume, special - see page 29>`
12.3 ---- 1.230 000 0E+01

vierd [Netherlands]
liter --- `<volume, special - see page 29>`
6.815 ---- 6.815 000 0E+00

vierding [Austria]
gram --- `<mass, special - see page 29>`
140 ---- 1.400 000 0E+02

vierkante duim [Netherlands]
square meter ------------------------------------ `<area, special - see page 29>`
0.000 1 ---- 1.000 000 0E-04

vierkante el [Netherlands]
square meter ------------------------------------ `<area, special - see page 29>`
1 ---- 1.000 000 0E+00

vierkante mijl [Netherlands]
hectare --- `<area, special - see page 29>`
100 ---- 1.000 000 0E+02

vierkante palm [Netherlands]
square meter ------------------------------------ `<area, special - see page 29>`
0.01 ---- 1.000 000 0E-02

vierkante roede [Netherlands]
square meter ------------------------------------ `<area, special - see page 29>`
100 ---- 1.000 000 0E+02

vierkante roedo [Netherlands]
square meter ------------------------------------ `<area, special - see page 29>`
100 ---- 1.000 000 0E+02

vierkante streep [Netherlands]
square millimeter ------------------------------- `<area, special - see page 29>`
1 ---- 1.000 000 0E+00

vierling [Germany]
liter --- `<volume, special - see page 29>`
5.538 2 ---- 5.538 200 0E+00

viertel [Austria] — \<volume, special - see page 29\>
liter -- 15.4 --- 1.540 000 0E+01

viertel [Denmark] — \<volume, special - see page 29\>
liter -- 7.73 --- 7.730 000 0E+00

viertel [Germany, dry] — \<volume, special - see page 29\>
liter -- 13.74 --- 1.374 000 0E+01

viertel [Germany, liquid] — \<volume, special - see page 29\>
milliliter -- 429 --- 4.290 000 0E+02

viertel [Switzerland] — \<volume, special - see page 29\>
liter -- 15 --- 1.500 000 0E+01

viertelein [Germany] — \<volume, special - see page 29\>
liter -- 0.173 07 --- 1.730 700 0E-01

viertellot [Switzerland] — \<mass, special - see page 29\>
gram -- 3.906 --- 3.906 000 0E+00

viertelsaum [Switzerland, liquid] — \<volume, special - see page 29\>
liter -- 37.5 --- 3.750 000 0E+01

vigintillion [UK] — \<units\>
unit -- >>> --1.000 000 0E+120

vigintillion [US] — \<units\>
unit -- >>> --1.000 000 0E+63

vilasti [Ceylon] — \<length, special - see page 29\>
meter --- 0.328 --- 3.280 000 0E-01

vilasti [India] — \<length, special - see page 29\>
centimeter --------------------------------------- 32.08 --- 3.208 000 0E+01

vingerhoed [Netherlands] — \<volume, special - see page 29\>
centiliter -- 1 --- 1.000 000 0E+00

violle — \<luminous intensity\>
candela -- 20.17 --- 2.017 000 0E+01
lumen/steradian ---------------------------------- 20.17 --- 2.017 000 0E+01

vis [Burma] — \<mass, special - see page 29\>
kilogram --- 1.633 --- 1.633 000 0E+00

vis [India] — \<mass, special - see page 29\>
kilogram --- 4.665 --- 4.665 000 0E+00

vis [Romania] — \<mass, special - see page 29\>
kilogram --- 1.633 --- 1.633 000 0E+00

visham [India] — \<mass, special - see page 29\>
kilogram --- 4.665 --- 4.665 000 0E+00

viss [Burma] — \<mass, special - see page 29\>
kilogram --- 1.633 --- 1.633 000 0E+00

viss [India] — \<mass, special - see page 29\>
kilogram --- 4.665 --- 4.665 000 0E+00

vloka [Poland] — \<area, special - see page 29\>
hectare --- 16.796 --- 1.679 600 0E+01

voet [Netherlands] — \<length, special - see page 29\>
centimeter --------------------------------------- 28.3 --- 2.830 000 0E+01

volt — \<electric potential\>
abvolt --------------------------------------- >>> --- 1.000 000 0E+08
ampere ohm ------------------------------------- 1 --- 1.000 000 0E+00
coulomb/farad ----------------------------------- 1 --- 1.000 000 0E+00
crocodile ---------------------------------- 0.000 001 --- 1.000 000 0E-06
electromagnetic unit of electric potential [cgs system] --- >>> --- 1.000 000 0E+08
electrostatic unit of electric potential [cgs system] ------ 0.003 335 6 --- 3.335 641 0E-03
erg/franklin -------------------------------- 0.003 335 6 --- 3.335 641 0E-03
gaussian electric potential ----------------- 0.003 335 6 --- 3.335 641 0E-03
joule/coulomb ---------------------------------- 1 --- 1.000 000 0E+00
statvolt ------------------------------------ 0.003 335 6 --- 3.335 641 0E-03
volt [international] ------------------------- 0.999 662 1 --- 9.996 621 1E-01

Convert From Convert To	<Type of Unit>
	Standard	Scientific

Convert From / Convert To	Standard	Scientific
watt/ampere	1	1.000 000 0E+00
weber/second	1	1.000 000 0E+00

volt [international] <electric potential>

	Standard	Scientific
ampere ohm	1.000 338	1.000 338 0E+00
coulomb/farad	1.000 338	1.000 338 0E+00
erg/franklin	0.003 336 8	3.336 768 4E-03
statvolt	0.003 336 8	3.336 768 4E-03
volt	1.000 338	1.000 338 0E+00

volt ampere <power>

	Standard	Scientific
Btu/hour [I.T.]	3.412 141 6	3.412 141 6E+00
Btu/hour [thermoc.]	3.414 425 1	3.414 425 1E+00
calorie/minute [I.T.]	14.330 754	1.433 075 4E+01
calorie/minute [thermoc.]	14.340 344	1.434 034 4E+01
centigrade heat unit/hour [mean]	1.894 172 6	1.894 172 6E+00
cubic meter atmosphere/second	9.869 232 7	9.869 232 7E+00
dyne centimeter/second	>>>	1.000 000 0E+07
erg/second	>>>	1.000 000 0E+07
foot pound-force/minute	44.253 729	4.425 372 9E+01
foot poundal/second	23.730 36	2.373 036 0E+01
gram-force centimeter/second	10,197.162	1.019 716 2E+04
horsepower	0.001 341	1.341 022 1E-03
horsepower [metric]	0.001 359 6	1.359 621 6E-03
joule/second	1	1.000 000 0E+00
kilocalorie/hour [I.T.]	0.859 845 2	8.598 452 3E-01
kilogram square meter/cubic second	1	1.000 000 0E+00
kilogram-force meter/minute	6.118 297 3	6.118 297 3E+00
kilopond meter/minute	6.118 297 3	6.118 297 3E+00
lumen [green light at 100% efficiency]	685	6.850 000 0E+02
lumen [green light at 5,550 angstrom]	680.000 02	6.800 000 2E+02
newton meter/second	1	1.000 000 0E+00
pound square foot/cubic second	23.730 36	2.373 036 0E+01
watt	1	1.000 000 0E+00

volt ampere second/meter <force>

	Standard	Scientific
crinal	10	1.000 000 0E+01
gram-force	101.971 621	1.019 716 2E+02
joule/meter	1	1.000 000 0E+00
kilogram meter/square second	1	1.000 000 0E+00
newton	1	1.000 000 0E+00
ounce-force	3.596 943 1	3.596 943 1E+00
pascal square meter	1	1.000 000 0E+00
pound-force	0.224 808 9	2.248 089 4E-01
poundal	7.233 013 9	7.233 013 9E+00
watt second/meter	1	1.000 000 0E+00

volt second <magnetic flux>

	Standard	Scientific
ampere henry	1	1.000 000 0E+00
gauss square centimeter	>>>	1.000 000 0E+08
joule/ampere	1	1.000 000 0E+00
maxwell	>>>	1.000 000 0E+08
statweber	0.003 335 6	3.335 641 0E-03
tesla square meter	1	1.000 000 0E+00
unit pole	7,957,747.54	7.957 747 5E+06
weber	1	1.000 000 0E+00

volt second meter <magnetic dipole moment>

	Standard	Scientific
abweber centimeter	>>>	7.957 747 2E+08
newton square meter/ampere	1	1.000 000 0E+00
statweber centimeter	0.026 544 2	2.654 418 7E-02
weber meter	1	1.000 000 0E+00

volt second/ampere <electric inductance>

	Standard	Scientific
abhenry	>>>	1.000 000 0E+09
henry	1	1.000 000 0E+00
joule/square ampere	1	1.000 000 0E+00
ohm second	1	1.000 000 0E+00

Convert From		<Type of Unit>
Convert To	Standard	Scientific

stathenry	<<<	1.112 650 1E−12
weber/ampere	1	1.000 000 0E+00

volt second/meter <magnetic vector potential>

abweber/centimeter	1,000,000	1.000 000 0E+06
newton/ampere	1	1.000 000 0E+00
statweber/centimeter	0.000 033 4	3.335 641 0E−05
weber/meter	1	1.000 000 0E+00

volt second/square meter <magnetic flux density>

ampere henry/square meter	1	1.000 000 0E+00
electromagnetic unit of magnetic flux density [cgs system]	10,000	1.000 000 0E+04
gauss	10,000	1.000 000 0E+04
joule/ampere square meter	1	1.000 000 0E+00
line/square centimeter [of magnetic force]	10,000	1.000 000 0E+04
maxwell/square meter	1	1.000 000 0E+00
newton/ampere meter	1	1.000 000 0E+00
tesla	1	1.000 000 0E+00
weber/square meter	1	1.000 000 0E+00

volt/ampere <electric resistance>

1/ siemens	1	1.000 000 0E+00
1/mho	1	1.000 000 0E+00
abohm	>>>	1.000 000 0E+09
henry/second	1	1.000 000 0E+00
ohm	1	1.000 000 0E+00
statohm	<<<	1.112 650 1E−12

volt/centimeter <electric field strength>

statvolt/centimeter	0.003 335 6	3.335 641 0E−03
volt/inch	2.54	2.540 000 0E+00
volt/meter	100	1.000 000 0E+02
volt/millimeter	0.1	1.000 000 0E−01

volt/°C <seebeck coefficient>

volt/°F	0.555 555 6	5.555 555 6E−01
volt/kelvin	1	1.000 000 0E+00

volt/°F <seebeck coefficient>

volt/°C	1.8	1.800 000 0E+00
volt/kelvin	1.8	1.800 000 0E+00

volt/inch <electric field strength>

joule/coulomb meter	39.370 078 7	3.937 007 9E+01
statvolt/centimeter	0.001 313 2	1.313 244 5E−03
volt/meter	39.370 078 7	3.937 007 9E+01
volt/mil	0.001	1.000 000 0E−03

volt/kelvin <seebeck coefficient>

volt/°C	1	1.000 000 0E+00
volt/°F	0.555 555 6	5.555 555 6E−01

volt/meter <electric field strength>

ampere ohm/meter	1	1.000 000 0E+00
coulomb/farad meter	1	1.000 000 0E+00
joule/coulomb meter	1	1.000 000 0E+00
newton/coulomb	1	1.000 000 0E+00
statvolt/centimeter	0.000 033 4	3.335 641 0E−05
volt/inch	0.025 4	2.540 000 0E−02
watt/ampere meter	1	1.000 000 0E+00
weber/second meter	1	1.000 000 0E+00

volt/mil <electric field strength>

abvolt/centimeter	>>>	3.937 007 9E+10
statvolt/centimeter	1.313 244 5	1.313 244 5E+00
volt/inch	1,000	1.000 000 0E+03
volt/meter	39,370.078 7	3.937 007 9E+04

volt/millimeter <electric field strength>

kilovolt/meter	1	1.000 000 0E+00
volt/inch	25.4	2.540 000 0E+01

| Convert From | | <Type of Unit> |
Convert To	Standard	Scientific
volt/meter	1,000	1.000 000 0E+03
volt/ohm		<electric current>
ampere	1	1.000 000 0E+00
coulomb/second	1	1.000 000 0E+00
gilbert	1.256 637 1	1.256 637 1E+00
siemens volt	1	1.000 000 0E+00
watt/volt	1	1.000 000 0E+00
weber/henry	1	1.000 000 0E+00
wa [Laos]		<length, special - see page 29>
meter	2	2.000 000 0E+00
wa [Thailand]		<length, special - see page 29>
meter	2	2.000 000 0E+00
wag [Netherlands, wool]		<mass, special - see page 29>
kilogram	77.353	7.735 300 0E+01
wagia [Ethiopia]		<mass, special - see page 29>
gram	25.9	2.590 000 0E+01
wagia [Iraq]		<mass, special - see page 29>
gram	128.3	1.283 000 0E+02
wagia [Jordan]		<mass, special - see page 29>
gram	240.4	2.404 000 0E+02
wagia [Lebanon]		<mass, special - see page 29>
gram	213.7	2.137 000 0E+02
wagia [Libya]		<mass, special - see page 29>
gram	32.05	3.205 000 0E+01
wagia [Somalia]		<mass, special - see page 29>
gram	28	2.800 000 0E+01
wagia [Sudan]		<mass, special - see page 29>
gram	37.44	3.744 000 0E+01
wagia [Syria]		<mass, special - see page 29>
gram	213.7	2.137 000 0E+02
wagia dahabia [Sudan, gold]		<mass, special - see page 29>
gram	32	3.200 000 0E+01
wagla [Iraq]		<mass, special - see page 29>
kilogram	1.042	1.042 000 0E+00
wagon [Yugoslavia]		<mass, special - see page 29>
tonne	10	1.000 000 0E+01
wah [Laos]		<length, special - see page 29>
meter	2	2.000 000 0E+00
wah [Thailand]		<length, special - see page 29>
meter	2	2.000 000 0E+00
wakea [Ethiopia]		<mass, special - see page 29>
gram	25.9	2.590 000 0E+01
wakea [Iraq]		<mass, special - see page 29>
kilogram	1.042	1.042 000 0E+00
wakea [Jordan]		<mass, special - see page 29>
gram	240.4	2.404 000 0E+02
wakea [Lebanon]		<mass, special - see page 29>
gram	213.7	2.137 000 0E+02
wakea [Libya]		<mass, special - see page 29>
gram	32.05	3.205 000 0E+01
wakea [Somalia]		<mass, special - see page 29>
gram	28	2.800 000 0E+01
wakea [Sudan]		<mass, special - see page 29>
gram	37.44	3.744 000 0E+01
wakea [Syria]		<mass, special - see page 29>
gram	213.7	2.137 000 0E+02

wakega [Yemen]   \<mass, special - see page 29\>
  gram -- 31.6 --- 3.160 000 0E+01

wakia [Tanganyika]   \<mass, special - see page 29\>
  gram ------------------------------------- 28.349 52 --- 2.834 952 0E+01

wakiah [Zanzibar and Pemba]   \<mass, special - see page 29\>
  gram -- 28 --- 2.800 000 0E+01

walk of a Babylonian hour [Mesopotamia, ancient] \<length, special - see page 29\>
  kilometer --- 11.82 --- 1.182 000 0E+01

wanche [Ethiopia]   \<volume, special - see page 29\>
  liter --- 0.3 --- 3.000 000 0E-01

wang [Indonesia]   \<mass, special - see page 29\>
  gram --- 1.127 --- 1.127 000 0E+00

war [Yemen]   \<length, special - see page 29\>
  meter -- 0.914 4 --- 9.144 000 0E-01

wari [Tanganyika]   \<length, special - see page 29\>
  centimeter -- 91 --- 9.100 000 0E+01

wari [Tanzania]   \<length, special - see page 29\>
  meter -- 0.914 4 --- 9.144 000 0E-01

watt   \<power\>

Convert To	Standard	Scientific
Btu/hour [15 °C]	3.412 956 3	3.412 956 3E+00
Btu/hour [15.6 °C]	3.413 357 6	3.413 357 6E+00
Btu/hour [15.8 °C, Canada]	3.413 568	3.413 568 0E+00
Btu/hour [15.8 °C, ISO]	3.413 940 3	3.413 940 3E+00
Btu/hour [3.9 °C]	3.397 284 1	3.397 284 1E+00
Btu/hour [I.T.]	3.412 141 6	3.412 141 6E+00
Btu/hour [I.T., pre-1956]	3.412 192 9	3.412 192 9E+00
Btu/hour [mean]	3.409 510 6	3.409 510 6E+00
Btu/hour [thermoc.]	3.414 425 1	3.414 425 1E+00
Btu/minute [15 °C]	0.056 882 6	5.688 260 6E-02
Btu/minute [15.6 °C]	0.056 889 3	5.688 929 3E-02
Btu/minute [15.8 °C, Canada]	0.056 892 8	5.689 280 0E-02
Btu/minute [15.8 °C, ISO]	0.056 899	5.689 900 4E-02
Btu/minute [3.9 °C]	0.056 621 4	5.662 140 1E-02
Btu/minute [I.T.]	0.056 869	5.686 902 7E-02
Btu/minute [I.T., pre-1956]	0.056 869 9	5.686 988 2E-02
Btu/minute [mean]	0.056 825 2	5.682 517 7E-02
Btu/minute [thermoc.]	0.056 907 1	5.690 708 5E-02
Btu/second [15 °C]	0.000 948	9.480 434 3E-04
Btu/second [15.6 °C]	0.000 948 2	9.481 548 9E-04
Btu/second [15.8 °C, Canada]	0.000 948 2	9.482 133 3E-04
Btu/second [15.8 °C, ISO]	0.000 948 3	9.483 167 4E-04
Btu/second [3.9 °C]	0.000 943 7	9.436 900 2E-04
Btu/second [I.T.]	0.000 947 8	9.478 171 2E-04
Btu/second [I.T., pre-1956]	0.000 947 8	9.478 313 6E-04
Btu/second [mean]	0.000 947 1	9.470 862 9E-04
Btu/second [thermoc.]	0.000 948 5	9.484 514 1E-04
calorie/hour [15 °C, CIPM, 1950]	860.112 29	8.601 122 9E+02
calorie/hour [15 °C, NBS, 1939]	860.050 65	8.600 506 5E+02
calorie/hour [20 °C]	860.852 72	8.608 527 2E+02
calorie/hour [I.T.]	859.845 23	8.598 452 3E+02
calorie/hour [mean]	859.184 44	8.591 844 4E+02
calorie/hour [thermoc.]	860.420 65	8.604 206 5E+02
calorie/minute [15 °C, CIPM, 1950]	14.335 205	1.433 520 5E+01
calorie/minute [15 °C, NBS, 1939]	14.334 177	1.433 417 7E+01
calorie/minute [20 °C]	14.347 545	1.434 754 5E+01
calorie/minute [I.T.]	14.330 754	1.433 075 4E+01
calorie/minute [mean]	14.319 741	1.431 974 1E+01
calorie/minute [thermoc.]	14.340 344	1.434 034 4E+01
calorie/second [15 °C, CIPM, 1950]	0.238 920 1	2.389 200 8E-01
calorie/second [15 °C, NBS, 1939]	0.238 903	2.389 029 6E-01
calorie/second [20 °C]	0.239 125 8	2.391 257 6E-01

watt (continued)   <power>

calorie/second [I.T.]	0.238 845 9	2.388 459 0E-01
calorie/second [mean]	0.238 662 4	2.386 623 5E-01
calorie/second [thermoc.]	0.239 005 7	2.390 057 4E-01
centigrade heat unit/hour [mean]	1.894 172 6	1.894 172 6E+00
centigrade heat unit/minute [mean]	0.031 569 5	3.156 954 3E-02
centigrade heat unit/second [mean]	0.000 526 2	5.261 590 5E-04
cheval vapeur [France]	0.001 359 6	1.359 621 6E-03
clusec	750,061.67	7.500 616 7E+05
cubic meter atmosphere/hour	35,529.238	3.552 923 8E+04
cubic meter atmosphere/minute	592.153 96	5.921 539 6E+02
cubic meter atmosphere/second	9.869 232 7	9.869 232 7E+00
dyne centimeter/hour	>>>	3.600 000 0E+10
dyne centimeter/minute	>>>	6.000 000 0E+08
dyne centimeter/second	>>>	1.000 000 0E+07
erg/hour	>>>	3.600 000 0E+10
erg/minute	>>>	6.000 000 0E+08
erg/second	>>>	1.000 000 0E+07
foot pound-force/hour	2,655.223 7	2.655 223 7E+03
foot pound-force/minute	44.253 729	4.425 372 9E+01
foot pound-force/second	0.737 562 2	7.375 621 5E-01
foot poundal/hour	85,429.297	8.542 929 7E+04
foot poundal/minute	1,423.821 6	1.423 821 6E+03
foot poundal/second	23.730 36	2.373 036 0E+01
gram-force centimeter/hour	>>>	3.670 978 4E+07
gram-force centimeter/minute	611,829.73	6.118 297 3E+05
gram-force centimeter/second	10,197.162	1.019 716 2E+04
horsepower	0.001 341	1.341 022 1E-03
horsepower [550 foot pound-force/second]	0.001 341	1.341 022 1E-03
horsepower [boiler]	0.000 101 9	1.019 420 0E-04
horsepower [electric]	0.001 340 5	1.340 482 6E-03
horsepower [mechanical]	0.001 341	1.341 022 1E-03
horsepower [metric]	0.001 359 6	1.359 621 6E-03
horsepower [UK]	0.001 341	1.341 022 1E-03
horsepower [US]	0.001 341	1.341 022 1E-03
horsepower [water]	0.001 340 4	1.340 405 3E-03
inch ounce-force revolution/minute	1,532.294 3	1.532 294 3E+03
joule/hour	3,600	3.600 000 0E+03
joule/minute	60	6.000 000 0E+01
joule/second	1	1.000 000 0E+00
kilocalorie/hour [I.T.]	0.859 845 2	8.598 452 3E-01
kilocalorie/hour [mean]	0.859 184 4	8.591 844 4E-01
kilocalorie/hour [thermoc.]	0.860 420 7	8.604 206 5E-01
kilocalorie/minute [I.T.]	0.014 330 8	1.433 075 4E-02
kilocalorie/minute [mean]	0.014 319 7	1.431 974 1E-02
kilocalorie/minute [thermoc.]	0.014 340 3	1.434 034 4E-02
kilocalorie/second [I.T.]	0.000 238 8	2.388 459 0E-04
kilocalorie/second [mean]	0.000 238 7	2.386 623 5E-04
kilocalorie/second [thermoc.]	0.000 239	2.390 057 4E-04
kilogram square meter/cubic second	1	1.000 000 0E+00
kilogram-force meter/hour	367.097 84	3.670 978 4E+02
kilogram-force meter/minute	6.118 297 3	6.118 297 3E+00
kilogram-force meter/second	0.101 971 6	1.019 716 2E-01
kilopond meter/hour	367.097 84	3.670 978 4E+02
kilopond meter/minute	6.118 297 3	6.118 297 3E+00
kilopond meter/second	0.101 971 6	1.019 716 2E-01
lumen [green light at 100% efficiency]	685	6.850 000 0E+02
lumen [green light at 5,550 angstrom]	680.000 02	6.800 000 2E+02
lumen [monochromatic radiation of 540 THz]	683	6.830 000 0E+02
million Btu/hour [I.T.]	0.000 003 4	3.412 141 6E-06
newton meter/hour	3,600	3.600 000 0E+03
newton meter/minute	60	6.000 000 0E+01
newton meter/second	1	1.000 000 0E+00

watt (continued)   `<power>`

	Standard	Scientific
pferdestarke [Germany]	0.001 359 6	1.359 621 6E-03
poncelet [France]	0.001 019 7	1.019 716 2E-03
pound square foot/cubic second	23.730 36	2.373 036 0E+01
ton of refrigeration	0.000 284 3	2.843 451 4E-04
var	1	1.000 000 0E+00
volt ampere	1	1.000 000 0E+00
watt [international, 1948]	0.999 835	9.998 350 3E-01
watt [international, US, 1948]	0.999 818	9.998 180 3E-01
watt [legal, US, 1948]	0.999 983	9.999 830 0E-01

watt [at 540 THz]   `<luminous flux>`

	Standard	Scientific
lumen	683	6.830 000 0E+02
watt [at 5550 angstrom]	1.004 411 8	1.004 411 8E+00
watt [green light at 100% efficiency]	0.997 080 3	9.970 802 9E-01

watt [at 5550 angstrom]   `<luminous flux>`

	Standard	Scientific
lumen	680	6.800 000 0E+02
watt [at 540 THz]	0.995 607 6	9.956 076 1E-01
watt [green light at 100% efficiency]	0.992 700 7	9.927 007 3E-01

watt [green light at 100% efficiency]   `<luminous flux>`

	Standard	Scientific
lumen	685	6.850 000 0E+02
watt [at 540 THz]	1.002 928 3	1.002 928 3E+00
watt [at 5550 angstrom]	1.007 352 9	1.007 352 9E+00

watt [international, 1948]   `<power>`

	Standard	Scientific
Btu/hour [I.T.]	3.412 704 6	3.412 704 6E+00
Btu/hour [thermoc.]	3.414 988 5	3.414 988 5E+00
calorie/minute [I.T.]	14.333 118	1.433 311 8E+01
calorie/minute [thermoc.]	14.342 71	1.434 271 0E+01
centigrade heat unit/hour [mean]	1.894 485 1	1.894 485 1E+00
cubic meter atmosphere/second	9.870 861 1	9.870 861 1E+00
dyne centimeter/second	>>>	1.000 165 0E+07
erg/second	>>>	1.000 165 0E+07
foot pound-force/minute	44.261 031	4.426 103 1E+01
foot poundal/second	23.734 276	2.373 427 6E+01
gram-force centimeter/second	10,198.845	1.019 884 5E+04
horsepower	0.001 341 2	1.341 243 4E-03
horsepower [metric]	0.001 359 8	1.359 846 0E-03
joule/second	1.000 165	1.000 165 0E+00
kilocalorie/hour [I.T.]	0.859 987 1	8.599 871 0E-01
kilogram square meter/cubic second	1.000 165	1.000 165 0E+00
kilogram-force meter/minute	6.119 306 8	6.119 306 8E+00
kilopond meter/minute	6.119 306 8	6.119 306 8E+00
lumen [green light at 100% efficiency]	685.113 03	6.851 130 3E+02
lumen [green light at 5,550 angstrom]	680.112 22	6.801 122 2E+02
newton meter/second	1.000 165	1.000 165 0E+00
pound square foot/cubic second	23.734 276	2.373 427 6E+01
volt ampere	1.000 165	1.000 165 0E+00
watt	1.000 165	1.000 165 0E+00

watt [international, US, 1948]   `<power>`

	Standard	Scientific
Btu/hour [I.T.]	3.412 762 6	3.412 762 6E+00
Btu/hour [thermoc.]	3.415 046 5	3.415 046 5E+00
calorie/minute [I.T.]	14.333 362	1.433 336 2E+01
calorie/minute [thermoc.]	14.342 954	1.434 295 4E+01
centigrade heat unit/hour [mean]	1.894 517 3	1.894 517 3E+00
cubic meter atmosphere/second	9.871 028 9	9.871 028 9E+00
dyne centimeter/second	>>>	1.000 182 0E+07
erg/second	>>>	1.000 182 0E+07
foot pound-force/minute	44.261 783	4.426 178 3E+01
foot poundal/second	23.734 679	2.373 467 9E+01
gram-force centimeter/second	10,199.018	1.019 901 8E+04
horsepower	0.001 341 3	1.341 266 2E-03
horsepower [metric]	0.001 359 9	1.359 869 1E-03

Convert From Convert To	Standard	\<Type of Unit\> Scientific
joule/second	1.000 182	1.000 182 0E+00
kilocalorie/hour [I.T.]	0.860 001 7	8.600 017 2E−01
kilogram square meter/cubic second	1.000 182	1.000 182 0E+00
kilogram-force meter/minute	6.119 410 8	6.119 410 8E+00
kilopond meter/minute	6.119 410 8	6.119 410 8E+00
lumen [green light at 100% efficiency]	685.124 67	6.851 246 7E+02
lumen [green light at 5,550 angstrom]	680.123 78	6.801 237 8E+02
newton meter/second	1.000 182	1.000 182 0E+00
pound square foot/cubic second	23.734 679	2.373 467 9E+01
volt ampere	1.000 182	1.000 182 0E+00
watt	1.000 182	1.000 182 0E+00
watt [legal, US, 1948]		**\<power\>**
Btu/hour [I.T.]	3.412 199 6	3.412 199 6E+00
Btu/hour [thermoc.]	3.414 483 1	3.414 483 1E+00
calorie/minute [I.T.]	14.330 997	1.433 099 7E+01
calorie/minute [thermoc.]	14.340 584	1.434 058 8E+01
centigrade heat unit/hour [mean]	1.894 204 8	1.894 204 8E+00
cubic meter atmosphere/second	9.869 400 4	9.869 400 4E+00
dyne centimeter/second	>>>	1.000 017 0E+07
erg/second	>>>	1.000 017 0E+07
foot pound-force/minute	44.254 481	4.425 448 1E+01
foot poundal/second	23.730 764	2.373 076 4E+01
gram-force centimeter/second	10,197.335	1.019 733 5E+04
horsepower	0.001 341	1.341 044 9E−03
horsepower [metric]	0.001 359 6	1.359 644 7E−03
joule/second	1.000 017	1.000 017 0E+00
kilocalorie/hour [I.T.]	0.859 859 9	8.598 598 5E−01
kilogram square meter/cubic second	1.000 017	1.000 017 0E+00
kilogram-force meter/minute	6.118 401 3	6.118 401 3E+00
kilopond meter/minute	6.118 401 3	6.118 401 3E+00
lumen [green light at 100% efficiency]	685.011 65	6.850 116 5E+02
lumen [green light at 5,550 angstrom]	680.011 58	6.800 115 8E+02
newton meter/second	1.000 017	1.000 017 0E+00
pound square foot/cubic second	23.730 764	2.373 076 4E+01
volt ampere	1.000 017	1.000 017 0E+00
watt	1.000 017	1.000 017 0E+00
watt centimeter/square centimeter °C		**\<thermal conductivity\>**
Btu foot/hour square foot °F [I.T.]	57.778 932	5.777 893 2E+01
Btu foot/hour square foot °F [thermoc.]	57.817 613	5.781 761 3E+01
Btu inch/second square foot °F [I.T.]	0.192 596 4	1.925 964 4E−01
Btu inch/second square foot °F [thermoc.]	0.192 725 4	1.927 253 8E−01
Btu/hour foot °F [I.T.]	57.778 932	5.777 893 2E+01
Btu/hour foot °F [thermoc.]	57.817 613	5.781 761 3E+01
calorie centimeter/second square centimeter °C [I.T.]	0.238 845 9	2.388 459 0E−01
calorie/second centimeter °C [I.T.]	0.238 845 9	2.388 459 0E−01
calorie/second centimeter °C [thermoc.]	0.239 005 7	2.390 057 4E−01
kilocalorie/hour meter °C [I.T.]	85.984 523	8.598 452 3E+01
watt/centimeter kelvin	1	1.000 000 0E+00
watt/foot °C	30.48	3.048 000 0E+01
watt/meter kelvin	100	1.000 000 0E+02
watt second/kilogram		**\<specific thermodynamic energy\>**
joule/kilogram	1	1.000 000 0E+00
watt/ampere		**\<electric potential\>**
ampere ohm	1	1.000 000 0E+00
coulomb/farad	1	1.000 000 0E+00
joule/coulomb	1	1.000 000 0E+00
statvolt	0.003 335 6	3.335 641 0E−03
volt	1	1.000 000 0E+00
watt/ampere meter		**\<electric field strength\>**
joule/coulomb meter	1	1.000 000 0E+00
statvolt/centimeter	0.000 033 4	3.335 641 0E−05
volt/inch	0.025 4	2.540 000 0E−02

	Standard	Scientific
volt/meter	1	1.000 000 0E+00
watt/centimeter kelvin		**\<thermal conductivity\>**
Btu foot/hour square foot °F [I.T.]	57.778 932	5.777 893 2E+01
Btu foot/hour square foot °F [thermoc.]	57.817 613	5.781 761 3E+01
Btu inch/second square foot °F [I.T.]	0.192 596 4	1.925 964 1E-01
Btu inch/second square foot °F [thermoc.]	0.192 725 4	1.927 253 8E-01
Btu/hour foot °F [I.T.]	57.778 932	5.777 893 2E+01
Btu/hour foot °F [thermoc.]	57.817 613	5.781 761 3E+01
calorie centimeter/second square centimeter °C [I.T.]	0.238 845 9	2.388 459 0E-01
calorie/second centimeter °C [I.T.]	0.238 845 9	2.388 459 0E-01
calorie/second centimeter °C [thermoc.]	0.239 005 7	2.390 057 4E-01
kilocalorie/hour meter °C [I.T.]	85.984 523	8.598 452 3E+01
watt centimeter/square centimeter °C	1	1.000 000 0E+00
watt/foot °C	30.48	3.048 000 0E+01
watt/meter kelvin	100	1.000 000 0E+02
watt/cubic foot		**\<heat release rate\>**
watt/cubic meter	35.314 666 7	3.531 466 7E+01
watt/cubic meter		**\<heat release rate\>**
Btu/cubic foot hour [I.T.]	0.096 621 1	9.662 109 1E-02
joule/cubic meter second	1	1.000 000 0E+00
kilocalorie/cubic meter hour [I.T.]	0.859 845 2	8.598 452 3E-01
watt/cubic foot	0.028 316 8	2.831 684 7E-02
watt/cubic meter kelvin		**\<heat transfer coefficient\>**
Btu/cubic foot hour °F [I.T.]	0.053 678 4	5.367 838 4E-02
calorie/second cubic centimeter °C [I.T.]	0.000 000 2	2.388 459 0E-07
joule/second cubic meter kelvin	1	1.000 000 0E+00
kilocalorie/hour cubic meter °C [I.T.]	0.859 845 2	8.598 452 3E-01
kilowatt/cubic meter kelvin	0.001	1.000 000 0E-03
watt/foot °C		**\<thermal conductivity\>**
Btu foot/hour square foot °F [I.T.]	1.895 634 2	1.895 634 2E+00
Btu foot/hour square foot °F [thermoc.]	1.896 903 3	1.896 903 3E+00
Btu inch/hour square foot °F [I.T.]	22.747 611	2.274 761 1E+01
Btu inch/hour square foot °F [thermoc.]	22.762 84	2.276 284 0E+01
Btu/hour foot °F [I.T.]	1.895 634 2	1.895 634 2E+00
Btu/hour foot °F [thermoc.]	1.896 903 3	1.896 903 3E+00
calorie centimeter/hour square centimeter °C [I.T.]	28.210 145	2.821 014 5E+01
kilocalorie/hour meter °C [I.T.]	2.821 014 5	2.821 014 5E+00
watt/meter kelvin	3.280 839 9	3.280 839 9E+00
watt/kelvin		**\<thermal conductance\>**
Btu/second °F [I.T.]	0.000 526 6	5.265 650 7E-04
calorie/second °C [I.T.]	0.238 845 9	2.388 459 0E-01
joule/second kelvin	1	1.000 000 0E+00
kilocalorie/second °C [I.T.]	0.000 238 8	2.388 459 0E-04
watt/kilogram		**\<absorbed dose rate\>**
gray/second	1	1.000 000 0E+00
rad/second	100	1.000 000 0E+02
rep/second	119.331 74	1.193 317 4E+02
watt/meter °C		**\<thermal conductivity\>**
Btu foot/hour square foot °F [I.T.]	0.577 789 3	5.777 893 2E-01
Btu foot/hour square foot °F [thermoc.]	0.578 176 1	5.781 761 3E-01
Btu inch/hour square foot °F [I.T.]	6.933 471 8	6.933 471 8E+00
Btu inch/hour square foot °F [thermoc.]	6.938 113 5	6.938 113 5E+00
Btu/hour foot °F [I.T.]	0.577 789 3	5.777 893 2E-01
Btu/hour foot °F [thermoc.]	0.578 176 1	5.781 761 3E-01
calorie centimeter/hour square centimeter °C [I.T.]	8.598 452 3	8.598 452 3E+00
joule/second meter kelvin	1	1.000 000 0E+00
kilocalorie/hour meter °C [I.T.]	0.859 845 2	8.598 452 3E-01
watt/foot °C	0.304 8	3.048 000 0E-01
watt/meter kelvin	1	1.000 000 0E+00
watt/meter kelvin		**\<thermal conductivity\>**
Btu foot/hour square foot °F [I.T.]	0.577 789 3	5.777 893 2E-01

| Convert From | <Type of Unit> | |
Convert To	Standard	Scientific
Btu foot/hour square foot °F [thermoc.]	0.578 176 1	5.781 761 3E-01
Btu foot/hour square foot degree Rankine [I.T.]	0.577 789 3	5.777 893 2E-01
Btu foot/second square foot °F [I.T.]	0.000 160 5	1.604 970 3E-04
Btu foot/second square foot degree Rankine [I.T.]	0.000 160 5	1.604 970 3E-04
Btu inch/day square foot °F [I.T.]	166.403 32	1.664 033 2E+02
Btu inch/day square foot degree Rankine [I.T.]	166.403 32	1.664 033 2E+02
Btu inch/hour square foot °F [I.T.]	6.933 471 8	6.933 471 8E+00
Btu inch/hour square foot °F [thermoc.]	6.938 113 5	6.938 113 5E+00
Btu inch/hour square foot degree Rankine [I.T.]	6.933 471 8	6.933 471 8E+00
Btu inch/second square foot °F [I.T.]	0.001 926	1.925 964 4E-03
Btu inch/second square foot °F [thermoc.]	0.001 927 3	1.927 253 8E-03
Btu inch/second square foot degree Rankine [I.T.]	0.001 926	1.925 964 4E-03
Btu/hour foot °F [I.T.]	0.577 789 3	5.777 893 2E-01
Btu/hour foot °F [thermoc.]	0.578 176 1	5.781 761 3E-01
Btu/hour foot degree Rankine [I.T.]	0.577 789 3	5.777 893 2E-01
Btu/second foot °F [I.T.]	0.000 160 5	1.604 970 3E-04
Btu/second foot degree Rankine [I.T.]	0.000 160 5	1.604 970 3E-04
calorie centimeter/hour square centimeter °C [I.T.]	8.598 452 3	8.598 452 3E+00
calorie centimeter/second square centimeter °C [I.T.]	0.002 388 5	2.388 459 0E-03
calorie/second centimeter °C [I.T.]	0.002 388 5	2.388 459 0E-03
calorie/second centimeter °C [thermoc.]	0.002 390 1	2.390 057 4E-03
erg/centimeter second °C	100,000	1.000 000 0E+05
joule/second meter kelvin	1	1.000 000 0E+00
kilocalorie meter/square meter hour °C	0.859 845 2	8.598 452 3E-01
kilocalorie/hour meter °C [I.T.]	0.859 845 2	8.598 452 3E-01
kilogram-force/second °C	0.101 971 6	1.019 716 2E-01
kilowatt/meter °C	0.001	1.000 000 0E-03
kilowatt/meter kelvin	0.001	1.000 000 0E-03
newton/second kelvin	1	1.000 000 0E+00
watt centimeter/square centimeter °C	0.01	1.000 000 0E-02
watt/centimeter kelvin	0.01	1.000 000 0E-02
watt/foot °C	0.304 8	3.048 000 0E-01
watt/meter °C	1	1.000 000 0E+00
watt/square centimeter	**<heat flux density>**	
Btu/minute square foot [I.T.]	52.833 055	5.283 305 5E+01
Btu/minute square foot [thermoc.]	52.868 412	5.286 841 2E+01
calorie/second square centimeter [I.T.]	0.238 845 9	2.388 459 0E-01
calorie/second square centimeter [thermoc.]	0.239 005 7	2.390 057 4E-01
finsen unit	0.1	1.000 000 0E-01
watt/square inch	6.451 6	6.451 600 0E+00
watt/square meter	10,000	1.000 000 0E+04
watt/square centimeter °C	**<heat transfer coefficient>**	
Btu/second square foot °F [I.T.]	0.489 195	4.891 949 5E-01
Btu/second square foot °F [thermoc.]	0.489 522 5	4.895 224 5E-01
calorie/second square centimeter °C [I.T.]	0.238 845 9	2.388 459 0E-01
calorie/second square centimeter °C [thermoc.]	0.239 005 7	2.390 057 4E-01
watt/square foot °C	929.030 4	9.290 304 0E+02
watt/square meter kelvin	10,000	1.000 000 0E+04
watt/square centimeter kelvin	**<heat transfer coefficient>**	
Btu/second square foot °F [I.T.]	0.489 195	4.891 949 5E-01
Btu/second square foot °F [thermoc.]	0.489 522 5	4.895 224 5E-01
calorie/second square centimeter °C [I.T.]	0.238 845 9	2.388 459 0E-01
calorie/second square centimeter °C [thermoc.]	0.239 005 7	2.390 057 4E-01
watt/square foot °C	929.030 4	9.290 304 0E+02
watt/square meter kelvin	10,000	1.000 000 0E+04
watt/square foot	**<heat flux density>**	
Btu/hour square foot [I.T.]	3.412 141 6	3.412 141 6E+00
Btu/hour square foot [thermoc.]	3.414 425 1	3.414 425 1E+00
kilocalorie/hour square meter [I.T.]	9.255 297	9.255 297 0E+00
kilocalorie/hour square meter [thermoc.]	9.261 490 8	9.261 490 8E+00
pyron	0.015 425 5	1.542 549 5E-02
watt/square meter	10.763 91	1.076 391 0E+01

| Convert From | | <Type of Unit> |
| Convert To | Standard | Scientific |

watt/square foot °C   **\<heat transfer coefficient\>**

Btu/hour square foot °F [I.T.]	1.895 634 2	1.895 634 2E+00
Btu/hour square foot °F [thermoc.]	1.896 903 3	1.896 903 3E+00
calorie/hour square centimeter °C [I.T.]	0.925 529 7	9.255 297 0E-01
watt/square meter kelvin	10.763 391	1.076 391 0E+01

watt/square foot °F   **\<heat transfer coefficient\>**

Btu/hour square foot °F [I.T.]	3.412 141 6	3.412 141 6E+00
watt/square meter kelvin	19.375 039	1.937 503 9E+01

watt/square inch   **\<heat flux density\>**

Btu/minute square foot [I.T.]	8.189 139 9	8.189 139 9E+00
Btu/minute square foot [thermoc.]	8.194 620 2	8.194 620 2E+00
kilocalorie/hour square meter [I.T.]	1,332.762 8	1.332 762 8E+03
kilocalorie/hour square meter [thermoc.]	1,333.654 7	1.333 654 7E+03
pyron	2.221 271 3	2.221 271 3E+00
watt/square meter	1,550.003 1	1.550 003 1E+03

watt/square meter   **\<heat flux density\>**

Btu/day square foot [I.T.]	7.607 959 9	7.607 959 9E+00
Btu/day square foot [thermoc.]	7.613 051 3	7.613 051 3E+00
calorie/day square centimeter [I.T.]	2.063 628 5	2.063 628 5E+00
calorie/day square centimeter [thermoc.]	2.065 009 6	2.065 009 6E+00
calorie/minute square centimeter [I.T.]	0.001 433 1	1.433 075 4E-03
calorie/minute square centimeter [thermoc.]	0.001 434	1.434 034 4E-03
erg/second square centimeter	1,000.	1.000 000 0E+03
finsen unit	0.000 01	1.000 000 0E-05
joule/second square meter	1	1.000 000 0E+00
pyron	0.001 433 1	1.433 075 4E-03
watt/square foot	0.092 903	9.290 304 0E-02
watt/square inch	0.000 645 2	6.451 600 0E-04

watt/square meter °C   **\<heat transfer coefficient\>**

Btu/hour square foot °F [I.T.]	4.226 644 4	4.226 644 4E+00
calorie/hour square centimeter °C [I.T.]	0.085 984 5	8.598 452 3E-02
joule/second square meter kelvin	1	1.000 000 0E+00
watt/square meter kelvin	1	1.000 000 0E+00

watt/square meter hertz   **\<energy flux density\>**

flux unit	>>>	1.000 000 0E+26

watt/square meter kelvin   **\<heat transfer coefficient\>**

Btu/day square foot °F [I.T.]	4.226 644 4	4.226 644 4E+00
Btu/hour square foot °F [I.T.]	0.176 110 2	1.761 101 8E-01
Btu/hour square foot °F [thermoc.]	0.176 228 1	1.762 280 8E-01
Btu/second square foot °F [I.T.]	0.000 048 9	4.891 949 5E-05
Btu/second square foot °F [thermoc.]	0.000 049	4.895 224 5E-05
calorie/hour square centimeter °C [I.T.]	0.085 984 5	8.598 452 3E-02
calorie/second square centimeter °C [I.T.]	0.000 023 9	2.388 459 0E-05
calorie/second square centimeter °C [thermoc.]	0.000 023 9	2.390 057 4E-05
erg/square centimeter second °C	1,000.	1.000 000 0E+03
joule/second square meter kelvin	1	1.000 000 0E+00
kilocalorie/hour square meter °C [I.T.]	0.859 845 2	8.598 452 3E-01
kilogram-force/meter second °C	0.101 971 6	1.019 716 2E-01
kilogram/cubic second kelvin	1	1.000 000 0E+00
kilowatt/square meter °C	0.001	1.000 000 0E-03
kilowatt/square meter kelvin	0.001	1.000 000 0E-03
watt/square centimeter °C	0.000 1	1.000 000 0E-04
watt/square centimeter kelvin	0.000 1	1.000 000 0E-04
watt/square foot °C	0.092 903	9.290 304 0E-02
watt/square foot °F	0.051 612 8	5.161 280 0E-02
watt/square meter °C	1	1.000 000 0E+00

watt/square millimeter   **\<heat flux density\>**

Btu/second square foot [I.T.]	88.055 092	8.805 509 2E+01
Btu/second square foot [thermoc.]	88.114 02	8.811 402 0E+01
calorie/second square centimeter [I.T.]	23.884 59	2.388 459 0E+01
calorie/second square centimeter [thermoc.]	23.900 574	2.390 057 4E+01

Convert From	\<Type of Unit\>	
Convert To	Standard	Scientific
pyron	1,433.075 4	1.433 075 4E+03
watt/square inch	645.16	6.451 600 0E+02
watt/square meter	1,000,000	1.000 000 0E+06

watt/steradian   **\<radiant intensity\>**

erg/second steradian	>>>	1.000 000 0E+07
joule/second steradian	1	1.000 000 0E+00

watt/steradian [at 540 THz]   **\<luminous intensity\>**

candela	683	6.830 000 0E+02
watt/steradian [at 5550 angstrom]	1.004 411 8	1.004 411 8E+00
watt/steradian [green light at 100% efficiency]	0.997 080 3	9.970 802 9E−01

watt/steradian [at 5550 angstrom]   **\<luminous intensity\>**

candela	680	6.800 000 0E+02
watt/steradian [at 540 THz]	0.995 607 6	9.956 076 1E−01
watt/steradian [green light at 100% efficiency]	0.992 700 7	9.927 007 3E−01

watt/steradian [green light at 100% efficiency]   **\<luminous intensity\>**

candela	685	6.850 000 0E+02
watt/steradian [at 540 THz]	1.002 928 3	1.002 928 3E+00
watt/steradian [at 5550 angstrom]	1.007 352 9	1.007 352 9E+00

watt/steradian square meter   **\<radiance\>**

erg/second steradian square centimeter	1,000	1.000 000 0E+03
joule/second steradian square meter	1	1.000 000 0E+00

watt/volt   **\<electric current\>**

ampere	1	1.000 000 0E+00
coulomb/second	1	1.000 000 0E+00
gilbert	1.256 637 1	1.256 637 1E+00
siemens volt	1	1.000 000 0E+00
volt/ohm	1	1.000 000 0E+00
weber/henry	1	1.000 000 0E+00

watthour   **\<energy\>**

Btu [I.T.]	3.412 141 6	3.412 141 6E+00
calorie [I.T.]	859.845 23	8.598 452 3E+02
calorie [kilogram, I.T.]	0.859 845 2	8.598 452 3E−01
centigrade heat unit [I.T.]	1.895 634 2	1.895 634 2E+00
centimeter gram-force	>>>	3.670 978 4E+07
cheval vapeur heure [France]	0.001 359 6	1.359 621 6E−03
coal equivalent kilogram [UN, standard]	0.000 122 8	1.228 350 3E−04
coal equivalent metric ton [UN, standard]	0.000 000 1	1.228 350 3E−07
cubic centimeter atmosphere	35,529.238	3.552 923 8E+04
cubic foot atmosphere	1.254 703 2	1.254 703 2E+00
foot pound-force	2,655.223 7	2.655 223 7E+03
foot poundal	85,429.297	8.542 929 7E+04
frigorie [France]	0.860 050 7	8.600 506 5E−01
gram calorie	860.050 65	8.600 506 5E+02
horsepower hour	0.001 341	1.341 022 1E−03
horsepower hour [metric]	0.001 359 6	1.359 621 6E−03
inch ounce-force	509,802.96	5.098 029 6E+05
inch pound-force	31,862.685	3.186 268 5E+04
joule	3,600	3.600 000 0E+03
kilocalorie [I.T.]	0.859 845 2	8.598 452 3E−01
kilogram calorie [15 °C, NBS, 1939]	0.860 050 7	8.600 506 5E−01
kilogram square meter/square second	3,600	3.600 000 0E+03
kilopond meter	367.097 84	3.670 978 4E+02
liter atmosphere	35.529 238	3.552 923 8E+01
meter kilogram-force	367.097 84	3.670 978 4E+02
newton meter	3,600	3.600 000 0E+03
pferdestarkenstunde [Germany]	0.001 359 6	1.359 621 6E−03
therm [EEC]	0.000 034 1	3.412 141 6E−05
therm [US]	0.000 034 1	3.412 956 3E−05
thermie [France]	0.000 860 1	8.600 506 5E−04
ton [metric, explosive energy]	0.000 000 9	8.604 206 5E−07
wattsecond	3,600	3.600 000 0E+03

wattsecond		**\<energy\>**
Btu [I.T.]	0.000 947 8	9.478 171 2E−04
calorie [I.T.]	0.238 845 9	2.388 459 0E−01
calorie [kilogram, I.T.]	0.000 238 8	2.388 459 0E−04
centigrade heat unit [I.T.]	0.000 526 6	5.265 650 7E−04
centimeter gram-force	10,197.162	1.019 716 2E+04
cheval vapeur heure [France]	0.000 000 4	3.776 726 7E−07
cubic centimeter atmosphere	9.869 232 7	9.869 232 7E+00
cubic foot atmosphere	0.000 348 5	3.485 286 6E−04
dyne centimeter	>>>	1.000 000 0E+07
erg	>>>	1.000 000 0E+07
foot pound-force	0.737 562 2	7.375 621 5E−01
foot poundal	23.730 36	2.373 036 0E+01
frigorie [France]	0.000 238 9	2.389 029 6E−04
gram calorie	0.238 903	2.389 029 6E−01
horsepower hour	0.000 000 4	3.725 061 4E−07
horsepower hour [metric]	0.000 000 4	3.776 726 7E−07
inch ounce-force	141.611 93	1.416 119 3E+02
inch pound-force	8.850 745 8	8.850 745 8E+00
joule	1	1.000 000 0E+00
kilocalorie [I.T.]	0.000 238 8	2.388 459 0E−04
kilogram square meter/square second	1	1.000 000 0E+00
kilopond meter	0.101 971 6	1.019 716 2E−01
liter atmosphere	0.009 869 2	9.869 232 7E−03
megaerg	10	1.000 000 0E+01
megalerg	10	1.000 000 0E+01
meter kilogram-force	0.101 971 6	1.019 716 2E−01
newton meter	1	1.000 000 0E+00
pferdestarkenstunde [Germany]	0.000 000 4	3.776 726 7E−07
thermie [France]	0.000 000 2	2.389 029 6E−07
watthour	0.000 277 8	2.777 777 8E−04
wattsecond [green light at 100% efficiency]		**\<quantity of light\>**
joule	1.002 928 3	1.002 928 3E+00
lumen second	685	6.850 000 0E+02
wattsecond [light at 540 THz]	1.002 928 3	1.002 928 3E+00
wattsecond [light at 5550 angstrom]	1.007 352 9	1.007 352 9E+00
wattsecond [light at 540 THz]		**\<quantity of light\>**
joule	1	1.000 000 0E+00
lumen second	683	6.830 000 0E+02
talbot	683	6.830 000 0E+02
wattsecond [green light at 100% efficiency]	0.997 080 3	9.970 802 9E−01
wattsecond [light at 5550 angstrom]	1.004 411 8	1.004 411 8E+00
wattsecond [light at 5550 angstrom]		**\<quantity of light\>**
joule	0.995 607 6	9.956 076 1E−01
lumen second	680	6.800 000 0E+02
wattsecond [green light at 100% efficiency]	0.992 700 7	9.927 007 3E−01
wattsecond [light at 540 THz]	0.995 607 6	9.956 076 1E−01
wattsecond/meter		**\<force\>**
crinal	10	1.000 000 0E+01
gram-force	101.971 621	1.019 716 2E+02
joule/meter	1	1.000 000 0E+00
kilogram meter/square second	1	1.000 000 0E+00
newton	1	1.000 000 0E+00
ounce-force	3.596 943 1	3.596 943 1E+00
pascal square meter	1	1.000 000 0E+00
pound foot/square second	7.233 013 9	7.233 013 9E+00
pound-force	0.224 808 9	2.248 089 4E−01
poundal	7.233 013 9	7.233 013 9E+00
volt ampere second/meter	1	1.000 000 0E+00
wavelength of orange-red spectral line of krypton-86		**\<length\>**
angstrom	6,057.802 1	6.057 802 1E+03
bicron	605,780.21	6.057 802 1E+05

Convert From / Convert To	Standard	<Type of Unit> Scientific
fermi	>>>	6.057 802 1E+08
inch [international]	0.000 023 8	2.384 961 5E−05
meter	0.000 000 6	6.057 802 1E−07
microinch	23.849 615	2.384 961 5E+01
micrometer	0.605 780 2	6.057 802 1E−01
micromicron	605,780.21	6.057 802 1E+05
micron	0.605 780 2	6.057 802 1E−01
mil	0.023 849 6	2.384 961 5E−02
stigma	605,780.21	6.057 802 1E+05
tenthmeter	6,057.802 1	6.057 802 1E+03
thou	0.023 849 6	2.384 961 5E−02
x-unit	6,045,275.1	6.045 275 1E+06
wazma [Iraq]	<mass, special - see page 29>	
kilogram	101.604 7	1.016 047 0E+02
wazna [Saudi Arabia]	<mass, special - see page 29>	
kilogram	1.587 6	1.587 600 0E+00
weba [Tunisia, cereals]	<volume, special - see page 29>	
liter	36.369	3.636 900 0E+01
weber	<magnetic flux>	
abweber	>>>	1.000 000 0E+08
ampere henry	1	1.000 000 0E+00
electromagnetic unit of magnetic flux [cgs system]	>>>	1.000 000 0E+08
electrostatic unit of magnetic flux [cgs system]	0.003 335 6	3.335 641 0E−03
gauss square centimeter	>>>	1.000 000 0E+08
gaussian magnetic flux	0.003 335 6	3.335 641 0E−03
joule/ampere	1	1.000 000 0E+00
line [of magnetic force]	>>>	1.000 000 0E+08
maxwell	>>>	1.000 000 0E+08
statweber	0.003 335 6	3.335 641 0E−03
tesla square meter	1	1.000 000 0E+00
unit pole	7,957,747.54	7.957 747 5E+06
volt second	1	1.000 000 0E+00
weber centimeter	<magnetic dipole moment>	
abweber centimeter	7,957,747.15	7.957 747 2E+06
statweber centimeter	0.000 265 4	2.654 418 7E−04
weber meter	0.01	1.000 000 0E−02
weber meter	<magnetic dipole moment>	
abweber centimeter	>>>	7.957 747 2E+08
newton square meter/ampere	1	1.000 000 0E+00
statweber centimeter	0.026 544 2	2.654 418 7E−02
volt second meter	1	1.000 000 0E+00
weber millimeter	<magnetic dipole moment>	
abweber centimeter	795,774.715	7.957 747 2E+05
statweber centimeter	0.000 026 5	2.654 418 7E−05
weber meter	0.001	1.000 000 0E−03
weber/ampere	<electric inductance>	
abhenry	>>>	1.000 000 0E+09
henry	1	1.000 000 0E+00
joule/square ampere	1	1.000 000 0E+00
ohm second	1	1.000 000 0E+00
stathenry	<<<	1.112 650 1E−12
volt second/ampere	1	1.000 000 0E+00
weber/centimeter	<magnetic vector potential>	
abweber/centimeter	>>>	1.000 000 0E+08
statweber/centimeter	0.003 335 6	3.335 641 0E−03
weber/meter	100	1.000 000 0E+02
weber/henry	<electric current>	
ampere	1	1.000 000 0E+00
coulomb/second	1	1.000 000 0E+00
gilbert	1.256 637 1	1.256 637 1E+00
siemens volt	1	1.000 000 0E+00

volt/ohm	1	1.000 000 0E+00
watt/volt	1	1.000 000 0E+00
weber/meter		**\<magnetic vector potential\>**
abweber/centimeter	1,000,000	1.000 000 0E+06
newton/ampere	1	1.000 000 0E+00
statweber/centimeter	0.000 033 4	3.335 641 0E−05
volt second/meter	1	1.000 000 0E+00
weber/millimeter		**\<magnetic vector potential\>**
abweber/centimeter	>>>	1.000 000 0E+09
statweber/centimeter	0.033 356 4	3.335 641 0E−02
weber/meter	1,000	1.000 000 0E+03
weber/second		**\<electric potential\>**
ampere ohm	1	1.000 000 0E+00
coulomb/farad	1	1.000 000 0E+00
joule/coulomb	1	1.000 000 0E+00
statvolt	0.003 335 6	3.335 641 0E−03
volt	1	1.000 000 0E+00
watt/ampere	1	1.000 000 0E+00
weber/second meter		**\<electric field strength\>**
joule/coulomb meter	1	1.000 000 0E+00
statvolt/centimeter	0.000 033 4	3.335 641 0E−05
volt/inch	0.025 4	2.540 000 0E−02
volt/meter	1	1.000 000 0E+00
watt/ampere meter	1	1.000 000 0E+00
weber/square meter		**\<magnetic flux density\>**
ampere henry/square meter	1	1.000 000 0E+00
electromagnetic unit of magnetic flux density [cgs system]	10,000	1.000 000 0E+04
gauss	10,000	1.000 000 0E+04
joule/ampere square meter	1	1.000 000 0E+00
line/square centimeter [of magnetic force]	10,000	1.000 000 0E+04
maxwell/square meter	1	1.000 000 0E+00
newton/ampere meter	1	1.000 000 0E+00
tesla	1	1.000 000 0E+00
volt second/square meter	1	1.000 000 0E+00
wedro [Russia]		**\<volume, special - see page 29\>**
liter	12.3	1.230 000 0E+01
week		**\<time\>**
day	7	7.000 000 0E+00
fortnight	0.5	5.000 000 0E−01
wei mi [China]		**\<length, special - see page 29\>**
micrometer	1	1.000 000 0E+00
weiba [Egypt]		**\<volume, special - see page 29\>**
liter	33	3.300 000 0E+01
werchok [Russia]		**\<length, special - see page 29\>**
centimeter	4.445	4.445 000 0E+00
werst [Russia]		**\<length, special - see page 29\>**
kilometer	1.067	1.067 000 0E+00
wey [UK]		**\<volume, special - see page 29\>**
liter	1,454.707	1.454 707 0E+03
whiba [Tunisia]		**\<volume, special - see page 29\>**
liter	40	4.000 000 0E+01
wiba [Tunisia, cereals]		**\<volume, special - see page 29\>**
liter	36.369	3.636 900 0E+01
wichtje [Netherlands]		**\<mass, special - see page 29\>**
gram	1	1.000 000 0E+00
Winchester wine gallon [UK]		**\<volume\>**
barrel [UK]	0.023 129 8	2.312 983 8E−02
barrel [UK, wine]	0.026 434 1	2.643 410 1E−02
barrel [US, federal proof spirits]	0.025	2.500 000 0E−02

	Standard	Scientific
barrel [US, liquid]	0.031 746	3.174 603 2E−02
cubic decimeter	3.785 411 8	3.785 411 8E+00
cubic foot	0.133 680 6	1.336 805 6E−01
cubic inch	231	2.310 000 0E+02
cubic meter	0.003 785 4	3.785 411 8E−03
cubic yard	0.004 951 1	4.951 131 7E−03
cup [Canada, measuring]	16.653 484	1.665 348 4E+01
cup [US, measuring]	16	1.600 000 0E+01
drachm [UK, liquid]	1,065.823	1.065 823 0E+03
dram [Canada, liquid]	1,065.823	1.065 823 0E+03
dram [US, liquid]	1,024	1.024 000 0E+03
drop [US, liquid]	46,080	4.608 000 0E+04
drum [US, liquid]	0.018 181 8	1.818 181 8E−02
gallon [Canada, liquid]	0.832 674 2	8.326 741 8E−01
gallon [UK, dry or liquid]	0.832 674 2	8.326 741 8E−01
gallon [US, liquid]	1	1.000 000 0E+00
gill [UK]	26.645 574	2.664 557 4E+01
gill [US]	32	3.200 000 0E+01
liter	3.785 411 8	3.785 411 8E+00
minim [UK]	63,949.377	6.394 937 7E+04
minim [US]	61,440	6.144 000 0E+04
ounce [UK, liquid]	133.227 87	1.332 278 7E+02
ounce [US, liquid]	128	1.280 000 0E+02
pint [UK]	6.661 393 5	6.661 393 5E+00
pint [US, liquid]	8	8.000 000 0E+00
quart [UK]	3.330 696 7	3.330 696 7E+00
quart [US, liquid]	4	4.000 000 0E+00
scruple [UK, liquid]	3,197.468 9	3.197 468 9E+03
stere	0.003 785 4	3.785 411 8E−03
tablespoon [Canada, measuring]	266.456 19	2.664 561 9E+02
tablespoon [US, measuring]	256	2.560 000 0E+02
teaspoon [Canada, measuring]	799.368 57	7.993 685 7E+02
teaspoon [US, measuring]	768	7.680 000 0E+02
tun [UK, liquid]	0.003 855	3.854 973 1E−03
tun [US, liquid]	0.003 968 3	3.968 254 0E−03

windle [UK, wheat] \<mass, special - see page 29\>
| kilogram | 99.79 | 9.979 000 0E+01 |

winspel [Germany, dry] \<volume, special - see page 29\>
| hectoliter | 13.19 | 1.319 000 0E+01 |

wise [Netherlands] \<volume, special - see page 29\>
| liter | 1,000 | 1.000 000 0E+03 |

wisse [Netherlands] \<volume, special - see page 29\>
| cubic meter | 1 | 1.000 000 0E+00 |

wizna [Malta] \<mass, special - see page 29\>
| kilogram | 3.969 | 3.969 000 0E+00 |

wog [Netherlands, wool] \<mass, special - see page 29\>
| kilogram | 77.353 | 7.735 300 0E+01 |

woket [Eritrea] \<mass, special - see page 29\>
| gram | 28.1 | 2.810 000 0E+01 |

woket [Ethiopia] \<mass, special - see page 29\>
| gram | 25.9 | 2.590 000 0E+01 |

woket [Iraq] \<mass, special - see page 29\>
| kilogram | 1.042 | 1.042 000 0E+00 |

woket [Jordan] \<mass, special - see page 29\>
| gram | 240.4 | 2.404 000 0E+02 |

woket [Lebanon] \<mass, special - see page 29\>
| gram | 213.7 | 2.137 000 0E+02 |

woket [Libya] \<mass, special - see page 29\>
| gram | 32.05 | 3.205 000 0E+01 |

Convert From		<Type of Unit>
Convert To	Standard	Scientific

woket [Somalia] <mass, special - see page 29>
  gram -- 28 --- 2.800 000 0E+01

woket [Sudan] <mass, special - see page 29>
  gram --- 37.44 --- 3.744 000 0E+01

woket [Syria] <mass, special - see page 29>
  gram -- 213.7 --- 2.137 000 0E+02

woog [Denmark] <mass, special - see page 29>
  kilogram -- 18 --- 1.800 000 0E+01

wukiyeh [Iraq, ancient] <mass, special - see page 29>
  gram --- 37.4 --- 3.740 000 0E+01

x-unit <length>
  angstrom -- 0.001 002 1 --- 1.002 072 2E−03
  bicron --- 0.100 207 2 --- 1.002 072 2E−01
  femtometer --- 100.207 22 --- 1.002 072 2E+02
  fermi --- 100.207 22 --- 1.002 072 2E+02
  inch [international] ----------------------------------- <<< --- 3.945 166 1E−12
  meter --- <<< --- 1.002 072 2E−13
  microinch -- 0.000 003 9 --- 3.945 166 1E−06
  micrometer -- 0.000 000 1 --- 1.002 072 2E−07
  micromicron --------------------------------------- 0.100 207 2 --- 1.002 072 2E−01
  micron --- 0.000 000 1 --- 1.002 072 2E−07
  mil -- <<< --- 3.945 166 1E−09
  millimicron --------------------------------------- 0.000 100 2 --- 1.002 072 2E−04
  picometer --- 0.100 207 2 --- 1.002 072 2E−01
  siegbahn -- 1 --- 1.000 000 0E+00
  stigma --- 0.100 207 2 --- 1.002 072 2E−01
  tenthmeter -- 0.001 002 1 --- 1.002 072 2E−03
  wavelength of orange-red spectral line of krypton-86 --- 0.000 000 2 --- 1.654 184 4E−07

xang [Laos] <mass, special - see page 29>
  kilogram -- 1.2 --- 1.200 000 0E+00

xeste [Greece, ancient] <volume, special - see page 29>
  liter --- 0.53 --- 5.300 000 0E−01

xeste [Hebrew, ancient] <volume, special - see page 29>
  cubic centimeter ------------------------------ 549.391 34 --- 5.493 913 4E+02

xiber [Libya] <length, special - see page 29>
  centimeter --- 25 --- 2.500 000 0E+01

xiber [Macao] <length, special - see page 29>
  centimeter --- 22 --- 2.200 000 0E+01

xiber [Malta] <length, special - see page 29>
  centimeter --- 26.19 --- 2.619 000 0E+01

xiber [Spain] <length, special - see page 29>
  centimeter -- 20.9 --- 2.090 000 0E+01

xiber xubu [Malta and Gozo] <volume, special - see page 29>
  cubic meter ------------------------------------- 0.017 971 9 --- 1.797 190 0E−02

xich [Vietnam] <length, special - see page 29>
  meter --- 0.4 --- 4.000 000 0E−01

xich [Vietnam] <area, special - see page 29>
  square meter --- 24 --- 2.400 000 0E+01

yan [China] <mass, special - see page 29>
  kilogram --- 120.958 --- 1.209 580 0E+02

yang [South Korea] <mass, special - see page 29>
  gram --- 37.5 --- 3.750 000 0E+01

yard [based on US, survey foot] <length>
  cable length [US, survey] ------------------------ 0.004 166 7 --- 4.166 666 7E−03
  chain [Gunter or US, survey] ------------------- 0.045 454 5 --- 4.545 454 5E−02
  chain [Ramden or Engineer] ----------------- 0.030 000 1 --- 3.000 006 0E−02
  decimeter -- 9.144 018 3 --- 9.144 018 3E+00
  fathom [US, survey] --------------------------------- 0.5 --- 5.000 000 0E−01

Convert From		<Type of Unit>
Convert To	Standard	Scientific

foot [international]	3.000 006	3.000 006 0E+00
foot [US, survey]	3	3.000 000 0E+00
furlong [US, survey]	0.004 545 5	4.545 454 5E−03
inch [based on US, survey foot]	36	3.600 000 0E+01
inch [international]	36.000 072	3.600 007 2E+01
league [US, statute]	0.000 189 4	1.893 939 4E−04
link [Gunter or US, survey]	4.545 454 5	4.545 454 5E+00
link [Ramden or Engineer]	3.000 006	3.000 006 0E+00
meter	0.914 401 8	9.144 018 3E−01
mile [international]	0.000 568 2	5.681 829 5E−04
mile [US, statute]	0.000 568 2	5.681 818 2E−04
mile [US, survey]	0.000 568 2	5.681 818 2E−04
out [US, survey]	0.009 090 9	9.090 909 1E−03
pace [geometrical]	0.060 000 1	6.000 012 0E−02
pace [US, survey]	1.2	1.200 000 0E+00
perch [US, survey]	0.181 818 2	1.818 181 8E−01
pole [US, survey]	0.181 818 2	1.818 181 8E−01
range [US, survey]	0.000 094 7	9.469 697 0E−05
rod [US, survey]	0.181 818 2	1.818 181 8E−01
township [US, survey]	0.000 094 7	9.469 697 0E−05
vara [US, survey, California]	1.090 909 1	1.090 909 1E+00
vara [US, survey, Texas]	1.08	1.080 000 0E+00
yard [international]	1.000 002	1.000 002 0E+00
yard [UK]	1.000 003 7	1.000 003 7E+00

yard [international]		<length>
astronomical unit	<<<	6.112 386 5E−12
barleycorn	108	1.080 000 0E+02
bolt [cloth]	0.025	2.500 000 0E−02
cable length [US, survey]	0.004 166 7	4.166 658 3E−03
chain [Gunter or US, survey]	0.045 454 5	4.545 445 5E−02
chain [Ramden or Engineer]	0.03	3.000 000 0E−02
cubit	2	2.000 000 0E+00
decimeter	9.144	9.144 000 0E+00
digit	48	4.800 000 0E+01
foot [international]	3	3.000 000 0E+00
foot [US, survey]	2.999 994	2.999 994 0E+00
hand [horses]	9	9.000 000 0E+00
inch [based on US, survey foot]	35.999 928	3.599 992 8E+01
inch [international]	36	3.600 000 0E+01
kilometer	0.000 914 4	9.144 000 0E−04
lea [US, cotton yarn]	0.008 333 3	8.333 333 3E−03
lea [US, linen yarn]	0.003 333 3	3.333 333 3E−03
lea [US, silk yarn]	0.008 333 3	8.333 333 3E−03
lea [US, wool yarn]	0.012 5	1.250 000 0E−02
light year [based on mean Julian year]	<<<	9.665 215 6E−17
link [Gunter or US, survey]	4.545 445 5	4.545 445 5E+00
link [Ramden or Engineer]	3	3.000 000 0E+00
meter	0.914 4	9.144 000 0E−01
mile [international]	0.000 568 2	5.681 818 2E−04
mile [US, statute]	0.000 568 2	5.681 806 8E−04
mile [US, survey]	0.000 568 2	5.681 806 8E−04
pace [geometrical]	0.06	6.000 000 0E−02
palm	12	1.200 000 0E+01
quarter [cloth]	4	4.000 000 0E+00
rope	0.15	1.500 000 0E−01
span	4	4.000 000 0E+00
yard [based on US, survey foot]	0.999 998	9.999 980 0E−01
yard [UK]	1.000 001 7	1.000 001 7E+00

yard [Pakistan]		<length, special - see page 29>
meter	0.914 4	9.144 000 0E−01

yard [UK]		<length>
decimeter	9.143 984 1	9.143 984 1E+00
foot [international]	2.999 994 8	2.999 994 8E+00

Convert From	<Type of Unit>	
Convert To	Standard	Scientific

	Standard	Scientific
inch [based on US, survey foot]	35.999 865	3.599 986 5E+01
inch [international]	35.999 937	3.599 993 7E+01
meter	0.914 398 4	9.143 984 1E-01
mile [international]	0.000 568 2	5.681 808 3E-04
mile [UK, nautical]	0.000 493 4	4.934 201 9E-04
mile [US, survey]	0.000 568 2	5.681 796 9E-04
yard [based on US, survey foot]	0.999 996 3	9.999 962 6E-01
yard [international]	0.999 998 3	9.999 982 6E-01

yard/day <velocity>

	Standard	Scientific
centimeter/hour	3.81	3.810 000 0E+00
foot/day	3	3.000 000 0E+00
inch/hour	1.5	1.500 000 0E+00
knot [international]	0.000 020 6	2.057 235 4E-05
meter/day	0.914 4	9.144 000 0E-01
mile/day	0.000 568 2	5.681 818 2E-04
millimeter/hour	38.1	3.810 000 0E+01
nautical mile/day [international]	0.000 493 7	4.937 365 0E-04
yard/hour	0.041 666 7	4.166 666 7E-02

yard/hour <velocity>

	Standard	Scientific
centimeter/minute	1.524	1.524 000 0E+00
dekameter/day	2.194 56	2.194 560 0E+00
foot/hour	3	3.000 000 0E+00
hectometer/day	0.219 456	2.194 560 0E-01
inch/hour	36	3.600 000 0E+01
kilometer/day	0.021 945 6	2.194 560 0E-02
knot [international]	0.000 493 7	4.937 365 0E-04
meter/day	21.945 6	2.194 560 0E+01
meter/second	0.000 254	2.540 000 0E-04
mile/day	0.013 636 4	1.363 636 4E-02
millimeter/minute	15.24	1.524 000 0E+01
nautical mile/day [international]	0.011 849 7	1.184 967 6E-02
yard/day	24	2.400 000 0E+01

yard/minute <velocity>

	Standard	Scientific
centimeter/second	1.524	1.524 000 0E+00
dekameter/hour	5.486 4	5.486 400 0E+00
foot/minute	3	3.000 000 0E+00
hectometer/day	13.167 36	1.316 736 0E+01
inch/minute	36	3.600 000 0E+01
kilometer/day	1.316 736	1.316 736 0E+00
knot [international]	0.029 624 2	2.962 419 0E-02
meter/hour	54.864	5.486 400 0E+01
meter/second	0.015 24	1.524 000 0E-02
mile/day	0.818 181 8	8.181 818 2E-01
millimeter/second	15.24	1.524 000 0E+01
nautical mile/day [international]	0.710 980 6	7.109 805 6E-01
yard/hour	60	6.000 000 0E+01

yard/second <velocity>

	Standard	Scientific
centimeter/second	91.44	9.144 000 0E+01
dekameter/minute	5.486 4	5.486 400 0E+00
foot/second	3	3.000 000 0E+00
hectometer/hour	32.918 4	3.291 840 0E+01
inch/second	36	3.600 000 0E+01
kilometer/hour	3.291 84	3.291 840 0E+00
knot [international]	1.777 451 4	1.777 451 4E+00
megameter/day	0.079 004 2	7.900 416 0E-02
meter/minute	54.864	5.486 400 0E+01
mile/hour	2.045 454 6	2.045 454 6E+00
millimeter/second	914.4	9.144 000 0E+02
nautical mile/hour [international]	1.777 451 4	1.777 451 4E+00
yard/minute	60	6.000 000 0E+01

yarda [Colombia] <length, special - see page 29>

	Standard	Scientific
meter	0.9	9.000 000 0E-01

Convert From	<Type of Unit>	
Convert To	Standard	Scientific

yarda [Yemen] <length, special - see page 29>
  meter ---- 0.914 4 ---- 9.144 000 0E-01

year [anomalistic or perihelion] <time>
  day ---- 365.259 635 ---- 3.652 596 4E+02
  hour ---- 8,766.231 24 ---- 8.766 231 2E+03
  minute ---- 525,973.874 ---- 5.259 738 7E+05
  month [mean sidereal] ---- 13.368 865 9 ---- 1.336 886 6E+01
  second ---- >>> ---- 3.155 843 3E+07
  year [elipse] ---- 1.053 775 2 ---- 1.053 775 2E+00
  year [mean sidereal] ---- 1.000 009 ---- 1.000 009 0E+00
  year [normal calendar] ---- 1.000 711 3 ---- 1.000 711 3E+00

year [elipse] <time>
  day ---- 346.620 074 ---- 3.466 200 7E+02
  hour ---- 8,318.881 78 ---- 8.318 881 8E+03
  minute ---- 499,132.907 ---- 4.991 329 1E+05
  month [mean sidereal] ---- 12.686 639 4 ---- 1.268 663 9E+01
  second ---- >>> ---- 2.994 797 4E+07
  year [mean sidereal] ---- 0.948 977 5 ---- 9.489 775 1E-01
  year [normal calendar] ---- 0.949 644 ---- 9.496 440 4E-01

year [leap] <time>
  day ---- 366 ---- 3.660 000 0E+02
  hour ---- 8,784 ---- 8.784 000 0E+03
  minute ---- 527,040 ---- 5.270 400 0E+05
  month [mean sidereal] ---- 13.395 964 ---- 1.339 596 4E+01
  month [seasonal or tropical] ---- 13.396 003 2 ---- 1.339 600 3E+01
  second ---- >>> ---- 3.162 240 0E+07
  year [mean sidereal] ---- 1.002 035 9 ---- 1.002 035 9E+00
  year [normal calendar] ---- 1.002 739 7 ---- 1.002 739 7E+00

year [mean Gregorian] <time>
  day ---- 365.242 5 ---- 3.652 425 0E+02
  hour ---- 8,765.82 ---- 8.765 820 0E+03
  minute ---- 525,949.2 ---- 5.259 492 0E+05
  month [mean sidereal] ---- 13.368 238 7 ---- 1.336 823 9E+01
  second ---- >>> ---- 3.155 695 2E+07
  year [normal calendar] ---- 1.000 664 4 ---- 1.000 664 4E+00
  year [seasonal or tropical] ---- 1.000 000 9 ---- 1.000 000 9E+00

year [mean Julian] <time>
  day ---- 365.25 ---- 3.652 500 0E+02
  hour ---- 8,766 ---- 8.766 000 0E+03
  minute ---- 525,960 ---- 5.259 600 0E+05
  month [mean sidereal] ---- 13.368 513 2 ---- 1.336 851 3E+01
  month [seasonal or tropical] ---- 13.368 552 4 ---- 1.336 855 2E+01
  second ---- >>> ---- 3.155 760 0E+07
  year [normal calendar] ---- 1.000 684 9 ---- 1.000 684 9E+00
  year [seasonal or tropical] ---- 1.000 021 4 ---- 1.000 021 4E+00

year [mean sidereal] <time>
  day ---- 365.256 363 ---- 3.652 563 6E+02
  day [mean sidereal] ---- 366.256 402 ---- 3.662 564 0E+02
  hour ---- 8,766.152 71 ---- 8.766 152 7E+03
  hour [mean sidereal] ---- 8,790.153 64 ---- 8.790 153 6E+03
  minute ---- 525,969.163 ---- 5.259 691 6E+05
  minute [mean sidereal] ---- 527,409.218 ---- 5.274 092 2E+05
  month [mean sidereal] ---- 13.368 746 1 ---- 1.336 874 6E+01
  second ---- >>> ---- 3.155 815 0E+07
  second [mean sidereal] ---- >>> ---- 3.164 455 3E+07
  year [normal calendar] ---- 1.000 702 4 ---- 1.000 702 4E+00

year [normal calendar] <time>
  day ---- 365 ---- 3.650 000 0E+02
  hour ---- 8,760 ---- 8.760 000 0E+03
  minute ---- 525,600 ---- 5.256 000 0E+05
  month [mean sidereal] ---- 13.359 363 ---- 1.335 936 3E+01

Convert From Convert To	Standard	\<Type of Unit\> Scientific
second --->>> ---		3.153 600 0E+07
year [mean sidereal]---	0.999 298 1 ---	9.992 981 3E-01
year [seasonal or tropical]		**\<time\>**
day ---	365.242 19 ---	3.652 421 9E+02
hour --	8,765.812 56 ---	8.765 812 6E+03
minute ---	525,948.754 ---	5.259 487 5E+05
month [seasonal or tropical]-----------------------------	13.368 266 5 ---	1.336 826 7E+01
second --->>> ---		3.155 692 7E+07
year [mean sidereal]---------------------------------------	0.999 961 2 ---	9.999 612 0E-01
year [normal calendar] ---------------------------------	1.000 663 5 ---	1.000 663 5E+00
yen [Vietnam]		**\<mass, special - see page 29\>**
kilogram ---	6 ---	6.000 000 0E+00
yin [China]		**\<length, special - see page 29\>**
meter ---	35.814 ---	3.581 400 0E+01
ying [China]		**\<length, special - see page 29\>**
meter ---	35.814 ---	3.581 400 0E+01
yoch [Cambodia]		**\<length, special - see page 29\>**
kilometer ---	16 ---	1.600 000 0E+01
yoch [Thailand]		**\<length, special - see page 29\>**
kilometer ---	16 ---	1.600 000 0E+01
yoctobar		**\<pressure\>**
atmosphere [standard]---<<< ---		9.869 232 7E-25
atmosphere [technical]---<<< ---		1.019 716 2E-24
bar --<<< ---		1.000 000 0E-24
micrometer of mercury [0 °C, by convention] ------------------------<<< ---		7.500 615 8E-19
micrometer of water [4 °C, by convention]--------------------<<< ---		1.019 716 2E-17
pascal ---<<< ---		1.000 000 0E-19
pound-force/square foot---------------------------------------<<< ---		2.088 543 4E-21
poundal/square foot---<<< ---		6.719 689 8E-20
ton-force/square foot [short]------------------------------<<< ---		1.044 271 7E-24
torr --<<< ---		7.500 616 8E-22
zeptopascal---	100 ---	1.000 000 0E+02
yoctocandela		**\<luminous intensity\>**
candela --<<< ---		1.000 000 0E-24
yoctogram		**\<mass\>**
atomic mass unit [unified, C-12,1986] -------------	0.602 213 7 ---	6.022 136 7E-01
avogram --	0.602 213 7 ---	6.022 136 7E-01
dalton ---	0.602 213 7 ---	6.022 136 7E-01
kilogram ---<<< ---		1.000 000 0E-27
yoctojoule		**\<energy\>**
1/centimeter [atomic physics, eq. energy] -------	0.050 341 1 ---	5.034 112 5E-02
1/meter [atomic physics, eq. energy]----------------	5.034 112 5 ---	5.034 112 5E+00
atomic mass unit [unified, C-12, 1986, eq. energy]------------<<< ---		6.700 530 8E-15
attojoule---	0.000 001 ---	1.000 000 0E-06
deuteron rest mass [atomic physics, eq. energy] ---------------<<< ---		3.327 714 8E-15
electron rest mass [atomic physics, eq. energy] ---------------<<< ---		1.221 432 1E-11
electronvolt --	0.000 006 2 ---	6.241 506 4E-06
gigaelectronvolt--<<< ---		6.241 506 4E-15
hartree [atomic physics, eq. energy] ---------------	0.000 000 2 ---	2.293 710 4E-07
hertz [atomic physics, eq. energy] -------------------------------->>> ---		1.509 189 0E+09
joule ---<<< ---		1.000 000 0E-24
kayser [atomic physics, eq. energy] ---------------	0.050 341 1 ---	5.034 112 5E-02
kelvin [atomic physics, eq. energy] ---------------	0.072 429 2 ---	7.242 923 3E-02
kiloelectronvolt--<<< ---		6.241 506 4E-09
megaelectronvolt--<<< ---		6.241 506 4E-12
muon rest mass [atomic physics, eq. energy] ----------------<<< ---		5.907 251 1E-14
neutron rest mass [atomic physics, eq. energy] --------------<<< ---		6.642 970 1E-15
proton rest mass [atomic physics, eq. energy]----------------<<< ---		6.652 126 8E-15
rydberg [atomic physics, eq. energy , eq. energy] -------	0.000 000 5 ---	4.587 366 4E-07

yoctoliter   \<volume\>

	Standard	Scientific
cubic inch	<<<	6.102 374 4E-23
cubic meter	<<<	1.000 000 0E-27
cubic nanometer	1	1.000 000 0E+00
drachm [UK, liquid]	<<<	2.815 606 4E-22
dram [Canada, liquid]	<<<	2.815 606 4E-22
dram [US, liquid]	<<<	2.705 121 8E-22
drop [US, liquid]	<<<	1.217 304 8E-20
liter	<<<	1.000 000 0E-24
ounce [UK, liquid]	<<<	3.519 508 0E-23
ounce [US, liquid]	<<<	3.381 402 3E-23

yoctometer   \<length\>

	Standard	Scientific
angstrom	<<<	1.000 000 0E-14
bicron	<<<	1.000 000 0E-12
fermi	<<<	1.000 000 0E-09
meter	<<<	1.000 000 0E-24
micromicron	<<<	1.000 000 0E-12
mil	<<<	3.937 007 9E-20
millimicron	<<<	1.000 000 0E-15
stigma	<<<	1.000 000 0E-12
tenthmeter	<<<	1.000 000 0E-14
wavelength of orange-red spectral line of krypton-86	<<<	1.650 763 7E-18
x-unit	<<<	9.979 320 9E-12

yoctomole   \<amount of substance\>

	Standard	Scientific
mole	<<<	1.000 000 0E-24

yoctonewton   \<force\>

	Standard	Scientific
crinal	<<<	1.000 000 0E-23
dyne	<<<	1.000 000 0E-19
gram-force	<<<	1.019 716 2E-22
newton	<<<	1.000 000 0E-24
pound-force	<<<	2.248 089 4E-25
poundal	<<<	7.233 013 9E-24

yoctopascal   \<pressure\>

	Standard	Scientific
atmosphere [standard]	<<<	9.869 232 7E-30
atmosphere [technical]	<<<	1.019 716 2E-29
bar	<<<	1.000 000 0E-29
foot of mercury [0 °C, by convention]	<<<	2.460 831 9E-29
foot of water [4 °C, by convention]	<<<	3.345 525 6E-28
kilogram-force/square meter	<<<	1.019 716 2E-25
kilopond/square meter	<<<	1.019 716 2E-25
newton/square meter	<<<	1.000 000 0E-24
pascal	<<<	1.000 000 0E-24
ton-force/square foot [short]	<<<	1.044 271 7E-29
ton-force/square meter [metric]	<<<	1.019 716 2E-28
yoctobar	0.000 01	1.000 000 0E-05

yoctowatt   \<power\>

	Standard	Scientific
Btu/hour [I.T.]	<<<	3.412 141 6E-24
Btu/hour [thermoc.]	<<<	3.414 425 1E-24
calorie/hour [I.T.]	<<<	8.598 452 3E-22
calorie/hour [thermoc.]	<<<	8.604 206 5E-22
cubic meter atmosphere/hour	<<<	3.552 923 8E-20
dyne centimeter/hour	<<<	3.600 000 0E-14
erg/hour	<<<	3.600 000 0E-14
foot pound-force/hour	<<<	2.655 223 7E-21
foot poundal/hour	<<<	8.542 929 7E-20
gram-force centimeter/hour	<<<	3.670 978 4E-17
horsepower	<<<	1.341 022 1E-27
horsepower [metric]	<<<	1.359 621 6E-27
joule/hour	<<<	3.600 000 0E-21
kilocalorie/hour [I.T.]	<<<	8.598 452 3E-25
kilogram-force meter/hour	<<<	3.670 978 4E-22
kilopond meter/hour	<<<	3.670 978 4E-22

Convert From Convert To	Standard	Scientific
		\<Type of Unit\>

Convert From / Convert To	Standard	Scientific
newton meter/hour	<<< ---	3.600 000 0E-21
volt ampere	<<< ---	1.000 000 0E-24
watt	<<< ---	1.000 000 0E-24

yoke [Austria] — \<area, special - see page 29\>
are	57.55 ---	5.755 000 0E+01

yoke [Hungary] — \<area, special - see page 29\>
are	43.16 ---	4.316 000 0E+01

yot [Thailand] — \<length, special - see page 29\>
kilometer	4 ---	4.000 000 0E+00

yote [Cambodia] — \<length, special - see page 29\>
kilometer	16 ---	1.600 000 0E+01

yote [Thailand] — \<length, special - see page 29\>
kilometer	16 ---	1.600 000 0E+01

yottabar — \<pressure\>
atmosphere [standard]	>>> ---	9.869 232 7E+23
atmosphere [technical]	>>> ---	1.019 716 2E+24
bar	>>> ---	1.000 000 0E+24
foot of mercury [0 °C, by convention]	>>> ---	2.460 831 9E+24
foot of water [4 °C, by convention]	>>> ---	3.345 525 6E+25
kilogram-force/square millimeter	>>> ---	1.019 716 2E+22
kilopond/square millimeter	>>> ---	1.019 716 2E+22
kip/square inch	>>> ---	1.450 377 4E+22
newton/square millimeter	>>> ---	1.000 000 0E+23
pascal	>>> ---	1.000 000 0E+29
pound-force/square inch	>>> ---	1.450 377 4E+25
ton-force/square inch [short]	>>> ---	7.251 886 9E+21
torr	>>> ---	7.500 616 8E+26
yottapascal	100,000 ---	1.000 000 0E+05

yottacandela — \<luminous intensity\>
candela	>>> ---	1.000 000 0E+24

yottagram — \<mass\>
kilogram	>>> ---	1.000 000 0E+21
pound	>>> ---	2.204 622 6E+21
quintal [metric]	>>> ---	1.000 000 0E+19
ton [long]	>>> ---	9.842 065 3E+17
ton [metric]	>>> ---	1.000 000 0E+18
ton [short]	>>> ---	1.102 311 3E+18

yottajoule — \<energy\>
cheval vapeur heure [France]	>>> ---	3.776 726 7E+17
coal equivalent kilogram [UN, standard]	>>> ---	3.412 084 2E+16
coal equivalent metric ton [UN, standard]	>>> ---	3.412 084 2E+13
gram [atomic physics, eq. energy]	>>> ---	1.112 650 1E+10
horsepower hour	>>> ---	3.725 061 4E+17
horsepower hour [metric]	>>> ---	3.776 726 7E+17
joule	>>> ---	1.000 000 0E+24
kilogram [atomic physics, eq. energy]	>>> ---	1.112 650 1E+07
kiloton [metric, explosive energy]	>>> ---	2.390 057 4E+11
kilowatthour	>>> ---	2.777 777 8E+17
megaton [metric, explosive energy]	>>> ---	2.390 057 4E+08
megawatthour	>>> ---	2.777 777 8E+14
petawatthour	277,777.78 ---	2.777 777 8E+05
quad	947,817.12 ---	9.478 171 2E+05
radian/second [atomic physics, eq. energy]	<<< ---	1.054 572 7E-10
therm [EEC]	>>> ---	9.478 171 2E+15
therm [US]	>>> ---	9.480 434 3E+15
thermie [France]	>>> ---	2.389 029 6E+17
ton [metric, explosive energy]	>>> ---	2.390 057 4E+14

yottaliter — \<volume\>
acre foot	>>> ---	8.107 131 9E+17
barrel [UK]	>>> ---	6.110 256 9E+21
barrel [US, liquid]	>>> ---	8.386 414 4E+21

Convert From Convert To	Standard	\<Type of Unit\> Scientific
barrel [US, petroleum] -- >>>		6.289 810 8E+21
billion cubic foot -- >>>		3.531 466 7E+13
chaldron [UK, dry] -- >>>		7.637 821 1E+20
chaldron [UK, liquid] --- >>>		7.637 821 1E+20
chaldron [US, dry] -- >>>		7.882 664 8E+20
cubem -- >>>		2.399 127 6E+11
cubic foot --- >>>		3.531 466 7E+22
cubic megameter --- 1,000		1.000 000 0E+03
cubic meter --- >>>		1.000 000 0E+21
cubic mile --- >>>		2.399 127 6E+11
cubic yard --- >>>		1.307 950 6E+21
gallon [Canada, liquid] --- >>>		2.199 692 5E+23
gallon [UK, dry or liquid] --- >>>		2.199 692 5E+23
gallon [US, dry] --- >>>		2.270 207 5E+23
gallon [US, liquid] -- >>>		2.641 720 5E+23
hectare meter --- >>>		1.000 000 0E+17
liter -- >>>		1.000 000 0E+24
million acre foot -- >>>		8.107 131 9E+11
million board foot --- >>>		4.237 760 0E+17
trillion cubic foot --- >>>		3.531 466 7E+10

yottameter \<length\>

Convert To	Standard	Scientific
astronomical unit -- >>>		6.684 587 2E+12
bevameter --- >>>		1.000 000 0E+15
kiloparsec -- 32,407.793		3.240 779 3E+04
light year [based on mean Julian year] ----------------------- >>>		1.057 000 8E+08
megaparsec --- 32.407 793		3.240 779 3E+01
meter -- >>>		1.000 000 0E+24
mile [international] --- >>>		6.213 711 9E+20
mile [US, statute] -- >>>		6.213 699 5E+20
mile [US, survey] --- >>>		6.213 699 5E+20
myriameter --- >>>		1.000 000 0E+20
parsec --- >>>		3.240 779 3E+07

yottamole \<amount of substance\>

Convert To	Standard	Scientific
mole --- >>>		1.000 000 0E+24

yottanewton \<force\>

Convert To	Standard	Scientific
crinal --- >>>		1.000 000 0E+25
dyne -- >>>		1.000 000 0E+29
gram-force -- >>>		1.019 716 2E+26
newton --- >>>		1.000 000 0E+24
ounce-force --- >>>		3.596 943 1E+24
pond -- >>>		1.019 716 2E+26
pound-force --- >>>		2.248 089 4E+23
poundal -- >>>		7.233 013 9E+24

yottapascal \<pressure\>

Convert To	Standard	Scientific
atmosphere [standard] -- >>>		9.869 232 7E+18
atmosphere [technical] -- >>>		1.019 716 2E+19
bar --- >>>		1.000 000 0E+19
centimeter of mercury [0 °C, by convention] ----------------- >>>		7.500 615 8E+20
centimeter of water [4 °C, by convention] -------------------- >>>		1.019 716 2E+22
exabar -- 10		1.000 000 0E+01
foot of mercury [0 °C, by convention] -------------------------- >>>		2.460 831 9E+19
foot of water [4 °C, by convention] ------------------------------ >>>		3.345 525 6E+20
kilogram-force/square millimeter ----------------------------- >>>		1.019 716 2E+17
kilopond/square millimeter ------------------------------------- >>>		1.019 716 2E+17
pascal --- >>>		1.000 000 0E+24
pound-force/square inch --------------------------------------- >>>		1.450 377 4E+20
ton-force/square inch [short] --------------------------------- >>>		7.251 886 9E+16
torr --- >>>		7.500 616 8E+21
zettabar -- 0.01		1.000 000 0E-02

yottawatt \<power\>

Convert To	Standard	Scientific
Btu/second [I.T.] --- >>>		9.478 171 2E+20
Btu/second [thermoc.] --- >>>		9.484 514 1E+20

| Convert From | | \<Type of Unit\> |
Convert To	Standard	Scientific
calorie/second [I.T.]	>>>	2.388 459 0E+23
calorie/second [thermoc.]	>>>	2.390 057 4E+23
centigrade heat unit/second [mean]	>>>	5.261 590 5E+20
cubic meter atmosphere/second	>>>	9.869 232 7E+24
dyne centimeter/second	>>>	1.000 000 0E+31
erg/second	>>>	1.000 000 0E+31
foot pound-force/second	>>>	7.375 621 5E+23
foot poundal/second	>>>	2.373 036 0E+25
gram-force centimeter/second	>>>	1.019 716 2E+28
horsepower	>>>	1.341 022 1E+21
horsepower [metric]	>>>	1.359 621 6E+21
joule/second	>>>	1.000 000 0E+24
kilocalorie/second [I.T.]	>>>	2.388 459 0E+20
kilogram-force meter/second	>>>	1.019 716 2E+23
kilopond meter/second	>>>	1.019 716 2E+23
newton meter/second	>>>	1.000 000 0E+24
volt ampere	>>>	1.000 000 0E+24
watt	>>>	1.000 000 0E+24
yottawatthour		**\<energy\>**
cheval vapeur heure [France]	>>>	1.359 621 6E+21
coal equivalent kilogram [UN, standard]	>>>	1.228 350 3E+20
coal equivalent metric ton [UN, standard]	>>>	1.228 350 3E+17
gram [atomic physics, eq. energy]	>>>	4.005 540 2E+13
joule	>>>	3.600 000 0E+27
kilogram [atomic physics, eq. energy]	>>>	4.005 540 2E+10
kiloton [metric, explosive energy]	>>>	8.604 206 5E+14
megaton [metric, explosive energy]	>>>	8.604 206 5E+11
quad	>>>	3.412 141 6E+09
radian/second [atomic physics, eq. energy]	0.000 000 4	3.796 461 6E−07
ton [metric, explosive energy]	>>>	8.604 206 5E+17
yoyana [India]		**\<length, special - see page 29\>**
kilometer	7.92	7.920 000 0E+00
yugada [Peru]		**\<area, special - see page 29\>**
hectare	32.3	3.230 000 0E+01
yugada [Spain]		**\<area, special - see page 29\>**
hectare	32.198	3.219 800 0E+01
yusdroman [Iraq, ancient]		**\<mass, special - see page 29\>**
gram	374	3.740 000 0E+02
yuzanar [Burma]		**\<length, special - see page 29\>**
kilometer	75.834	7.583 400 0E+01
ywegale [Burma]		**\<mass, special - see page 29\>**
milligram	255	2.550 000 0E+02
ywegi [Burma]		**\<mass, special - see page 29\>**
gram	0.510 291 4	5.102 914 0E−01
ywegyi [Burma]		**\<mass, special - see page 29\>**
gram	0.51	5.100 000 0E−01
zah [Tunisia, cereals]		**\<volume, special - see page 29\>**
liter	3.031	3.031 000 0E+00
zak [Netherlands]		**\<volume, special - see page 29\>**
liter	81.78	8.178 000 0E+01
zalay [Burma]		**\<volume, special - see page 29\>**
liter	0.126 3	1.263 000 0E−01
zar [India]		**\<length, special - see page 29\>**
meter	0.685 8	6.858 000 0E−01
zar [Iran]		**\<length, special - see page 29\>**
meter	1.04	1.040 000 0E+00
zar [Pakistan]		**\<length, special - see page 29\>**
meter	0.914 4	9.144 000 0E−01

Convert From / Convert To — <Type of Unit> Standard / Scientific

Convert From / Convert To	Standard	Scientific

zarf [Turkey] <volume, special - see page 29>
liter -- 2.3 ---- 2.300 000 0E+00

zayoot [Burma] <volume, special - see page 29>
liter -- 1.01 ---- 1.010 000 0E+00

zaz [Iran] <length, special - see page 29>
meter -- 1.04 ---- 1.040 000 0E+00

zebo [Egypt, ancient] <length, special - see page 29>
millimeter -- 18.72 ---- 1.872 000 0E+01

zentner [Austria] <mass, special - see page 29>
kilogram -- 56.001 ---- 5.600 100 0E+01

zentner [Denmark] <mass, special - see page 29>
kilogram -- 50 ---- 5.000 000 0E+01

zentner [Germany] <mass, special - see page 29>
kilogram -- 50 ---- 5.000 000 0E+01

zentner [Switzerland] <mass, special - see page 29>
kilogram -- 50 ---- 5.000 000 0E+01

zentner [UK] <mass, special - see page 29>
kilogram -- 45.36 ---- 4.536 000 0E+01

zeptobar <pressure>
atmosphere [standard] --- <<< ---- 9.869 232 7E−22
atmosphere [technical] --- <<< ---- 1.019 716 2E−21
attopascal -- 100 ---- 1.000 000 0E+02
bar --- <<< ---- 1.000 000 0E−21
centimeter of mercury [0 °C, by convention] -------------------- <<< ---- 7.500 615 8E−20
centimeter of water [4 °C, by convention] ----------------------- <<< ---- 1.019 716 2E−18
foot of mercury [0 °C, by convention] ---------------------------- <<< ---- 2.460 831 9E−21
foot of water [4 °C, by convention] -------------------------------- <<< ---- 3.345 526 5E−20
kilogram-force/square meter -------------------------------------- <<< ---- 1.019 716 2E−17
kilopond/square meter -- <<< ---- 1.019 716 2E−17
ton-force/square foot [short] -------------------------------------- <<< ---- 1.044 271 7E−21
torr --- <<< ---- 7.500 616 8E−19
zeptopascal -- 100,000 ---- 1.000 000 0E+05

zeptocandela <luminous intensity>
candela -- <<< ---- 1.000 000 0E−21

zeptogram <mass>
atomic mass unit [unified, C-12,1986] ---------------- 602.213 67 ---- 6.022 136 7E+02
avogram -- 602.213 67 ---- 6.022 136 7E+02
dalton -- 602.213 67 ---- 6.022 136 7E+02
gamma -- <<< ---- 1.000 000 0E−15
kilogram -- <<< ---- 1.000 000 0E−24

zeptojoule <energy>
1/centimeter [atomic physics, eq. energy] ------------------- 50.341 125 ---- 5.034 112 5E+01
1/meter [atomic physics, eq. energy] ------------------- 5,034.112 5 ---- 5.034 112 5E+03
atomic mass unit [unified, C-12, 1986, eq. energy] ----------- <<< ---- 6.700 530 8E−12
deuteron rest mass [atomic physics, eq. energy] ------------- <<< ---- 3.327 714 8E−12
electron rest mass [atomic physics, eq. energy] -------------- <<< ---- 1.221 432 1E−08
electronvolt --- 0.006 241 5 ---- 6.241 506 4E−03
gigaelectronvolt --- <<< ---- 6.241 506 4E−12
hartree [atomic physics, eq. energy] --------------------- 0.000 229 4 ---- 2.293 710 4E−04
hertz [atomic physics, eq. energy] ------------------------------ >>> ---- 1.509 189 0E+12
joule --- <<< ---- 1.000 000 0E−21
kayser [atomic physics, eq. energy] ------------------------- 50.341 125 ---- 5.034 112 5E+01
kelvin [atomic physics, eq. energy] ----------------------- 72.429 233 ---- 7.242 923 3E+01
kiloelectronvolt --- 0.000 006 2 ---- 6.241 506 4E−06
megaelectronvolt --- <<< ---- 6.241 506 4E−09
muon rest mass [atomic physics, eq. energy] ----------------- <<< ---- 5.907 251 1E−11
neutron rest mass [atomic physics, eq. energy] -------------- <<< ---- 6.642 970 1E−12
proton rest mass [atomic physics, eq. energy] --------------- <<< ---- 6.652 126 8E−12
rydberg [atomic physics, eq. energy , eq. energy] ------- 0.000 458 7 ---- 4.587 366 4E−04

Convert From		\<Type of Unit\>
Convert To	Standard	Scientific

zeptoliter <volume>
cubic inch		6.102 374 4E-20
cubic meter		1.000 000 0E-24
cubic nanometer	1,000	1.000 000 0E+03
drop [US, liquid]		1.217 304 8E-17
liter		1.000 000 0E-21
ounce [UK, liquid]		3.519 508 0E-20
ounce [US, liquid]		3.381 402 3E-20

zeptometer <length>
angstrom		1.000 000 0E-11
bicron		1.000 000 0E-09
fermi	0.000 001	1.000 000 0E-06
microinch		3.937 007 9E-14
micromicron		1.000 000 0E-09
micron		1.000 000 0E-15
millimicron		1.000 000 0E-12
stigma		1.000 000 0E-09
tenthmeter		1.000 000 0E-11
wavelength of orange-red spectral line of krypton-86		1.650 763 7E-15
x-unit		9.979 320 9E-09

zeptomole <amount of substance>
mole		1.000 000 0E-21

zeptonewton <force>
crinal		1.000 000 0E-20
dyne		1.000 000 0E-16
gram-force		1.019 716 2E-19
newton		1.000 000 0E-21
ounce-force		3.596 943 1E-21
pound-force		2.248 089 4E-22
poundal		7.233 013 9E-21

zeptopascal <pressure>
atmosphere [standard]		9.869 232 7E-27
atmosphere [technical]		1.019 716 2E-26
attobar		1.000 000 0E-08
centimeter of mercury [0 °C, by convention]		7.500 615 8E-25
centimeter of water [4 °C, by convention]		1.019 716 2E-23
foot of mercury [0 °C, by convention]		2.460 831 9E-26
foot of water [4 °C, by convention]		3.345 526 6E-25
kilogram-force/square meter		1.019 716 2E-22
kilopond/square meter		1.019 716 2E-22
pascal		1.000 000 0E-21
pound-force/square foot		2.088 543 4E-23
poundal/square foot		6.719 689 8E-22
ton-force/square foot [short]		1.044 271 7E-26
torr		7.500 616 8E-24
yoctobar	0.01	1.000 000 0E-02

zeptowatt <power>
Btu/hour [I.T.]		3.412 141 6E-21
Btu/hour [thermoc.]		3.414 425 1E-21
calorie/hour [I.T.]		8.598 452 3E-19
calorie/hour [thermoc.]		8.604 206 5E-19
dyne centimeter/hour		3.600 000 0E-11
erg/hour		3.600 000 0E-11
foot pound-force/minute		4.425 372 9E-20
foot poundal/second		2.373 036 0E-20
gram-force centimeter/hour		3.670 978 4E-14
horsepower [metric]		1.359 621 6E-24
joule/hour		3.600 000 0E-18
kilocalorie/hour [I.T.]		8.598 452 3E-22
kilogram-force meter/hour		3.670 978 4E-19
kilopond meter/hour		3.670 978 4E-19
newton meter/hour		3.600 000 0E-18

Convert From Convert To	Standard	\<Type of Unit> Scientific
volt ampere	<<<	1.000 000 0E–21
watt	<<<	1.000 000 0E–21
zer [Iran]		**\<length, special - see page 29>**
meter	1.04	1.040 000 0E+00
zer [Sumeria, ancient]		**\<length, special - see page 29>**
meter	60	6.000 000 0E+01
zeret [Hebrew, ancient]		**\<length, special - see page 29>**
meter	0.221	2.210 000 0E–01
zereth [Hebrew, ancient]		**\<length, special - see page 29>**
centimeter	23	2.300 000 0E+01
zettabar		**\<pressure>**
atmosphere [standard]	>>>	9.869 232 7E+20
atmosphere [technical]	>>>	1.019 716 2E+21
bar	>>>	1.000 000 0E+21
centimeter of mercury [0 °C, by convention]	>>>	7.500 615 8E+22
centimeter of water [4 °C, by convention]	>>>	1.019 716 2E+24
foot of mercury [0 °C, by convention]	>>>	2.460 831 9E+21
foot of water [4 °C, by convention]	>>>	3.345 525 6E+22
newton/square millimeter	>>>	1.000 000 0E+20
pascal	>>>	1.000 000 0E+26
pound-force/square inch	>>>	1.450 377 4E+22
ton-force/square inch [short]	>>>	7.251 886 9E+18
torr	>>>	7.500 616 8E+23
yottapascal	100	1.000 000 0E+02
zettacandela		**\<luminous intensity>**
candela	>>>	1.000 000 0E+21
zettagram		**\<mass>**
kilogram	>>>	1.000 000 0E+18
millier	>>>	1.000 000 0E+15
newton square second/meter	>>>	1.000 000 0E+18
pound	>>>	2.204 622 6E+18
quintal [metric]	>>>	1.000 000 0E+16
ton [long]	>>>	9.842 065 3E+14
ton [metric]	>>>	1.000 000 0E+15
ton [short]	>>>	1.102 311 3E+15
zettajoule		**\<energy>**
cheval vapeur heure [France]	>>>	3.776 726 7E+14
coal equivalent kilogram [UN, standard]	>>>	3.412 084 2E+13
coal equivalent metric ton [UN, standard]	>>>	3.412 084 2E+10
cubic foot atmosphere	>>>	3.485 286 6E+19
gram [atomic physics, eq. energy]	>>>	1.112 650 1E+07
horsepower hour	>>>	3.725 061 4E+14
horsepower hour [metric]	>>>	3.776 726 7E+14
joule	>>>	1.000 000 0E+21
kilogram [atomic physics, eq. energy]	11,126.501	1.112 650 1E+04
kiloton [metric, explosive energy]	>>>	2.390 057 4E+08
liter atmosphere	>>>	9.869 232 7E+18
megaton [metric, explosive energy]	239,005.74	2.390 057 4E+05
pferdestarkenstunde [Germany]	>>>	3.776 726 7E+14
quad	947.817 12	9.478 171 2E+02
radian/second [atomic physics, eq. energy]	<<<	1.054 572 7E–13
therm [EEC]	>>>	9.478 171 2E+12
therm [US]	>>>	9.480 434 3E+12
thermie [France]	>>>	2.389 029 6E+14
ton [metric, explosive energy]	>>>	2.390 057 4E+11
zettaliter		**\<volume>**
acre foot	>>>	8.107 131 9E+14
cubem	>>>	2.399 127 6E+08
cubic foot	>>>	3.531 466 7E+19
cubic megameter	1	1.000 000 0E+00
cubic meter	>>>	1.000 000 0E+18

| Convert From | | <Type of Unit> |
Convert To	Standard	Scientific
cubic mile	>>>	2.399 127 6E+08
cubic yard	>>>	1.307 950 6E+18
gallon [Canada, liquid]	>>>	2.199 692 5E+20
gallon [UK, dry or liquid]	>>>	2.199 692 5E+20
gallon [US, dry]	>>>	2.270 207 5E+20
gallon [US, liquid]	>>>	2.641 720 5E+20
hectare meter	>>>	1.000 000 0E+14
liter	>>>	1.000 000 0E+21
million acre foot	>>>	8.107 131 9E+08
million board foot	>>>	4.237 760 0E+14
stere	>>>	1.000 000 0E+18
thousand board foot	>>>	4.237 760 0E+17
thousand cubic foot	>>>	3.531 466 7E+16
trillion cubic foot	>>>	3.531 466 7E+07

zettameter <length>

Convert To	Standard	Scientific
astronomical unit	>>>	6.684 587 2E+09
bevameter	>>>	1.000 000 0E+12
kiloparsec	32.407 793	3.240 779 3E+01
light year [based on mean Julian year]	105,700.08	1.057 000 8E+05
megaparsec	0.032 407 8	3.240 779 3E−02
meter	>>>	1.000 000 0E+21
mile [international]	>>>	6.213 711 9E+17
mile [US, statute]	>>>	6.213 699 5E+17
mile [US, survey]	>>>	6.213 699 5E+17
myriameter	>>>	1.000 000 0E+17
parsec	32,407.793	3.240 779 3E+04
terameter	>>>	1.000 000 0E+09

zettamole <amount of substance>

Convert To	Standard	Scientific
mole	>>>	1.000 000 0E+21

zettanewton <force>

Convert To	Standard	Scientific
crinal	>>>	1.000 000 0E+22
dyne	>>>	1.000 000 0E+26
gram-force	>>>	1.019 716 2E+23
newton	>>>	1.000 000 0E+21
ounce-force	>>>	3.596 943 1E+21
pound-force	>>>	2.248 089 4E+20
poundal	>>>	7.233 013 9E+21

zettapascal <pressure>

Convert To	Standard	Scientific
atmosphere [standard]	>>>	9.869 232 7E+15
atmosphere [technical]	>>>	1.019 716 2E+16
bar	>>>	1.000 000 0E+16
centimeter of mercury [0 °C, by convention]	>>>	7.500 615 8E+17
centimeter of water [4 °C, by convention]	>>>	1.019 716 2E+19
exabar	0.01	1.000 000 0E−02
foot of mercury [0 °C, by convention]	>>>	2.460 831 9E+16
foot of water [4 °C, by convention]	>>>	3.345 525 6E+17
kilogram-force/square millimeter	>>>	1.019 716 2E+14
kilopond/square millimeter	>>>	1.019 716 2E+14
pascal	>>>	1.000 000 0E+21
petabar	10	1.000 000 0E+01
ton-force/square inch [short]	>>>	7.251 886 9E+13
torr	>>>	7.500 616 8E+18

zettawatt <power>

Convert To	Standard	Scientific
Btu/second [I.T.]	>>>	9.478 171 2E+17
Btu/second [thermoc.]	>>>	9.484 514 1E+17
calorie/second [I.T.]	>>>	2.388 459 0E+20
calorie/second [thermoc.]	>>>	2.390 057 4E+20
centigrade heat unit/second [mean]	>>>	5.261 590 5E+17
cubic meter atmosphere/second	>>>	9.869 232 7E+21
foot pound-force/second	>>>	7.375 621 5E+20
foot poundal/second	>>>	2.373 036 0E+22
horsepower	>>>	1.341 022 1E+18

Convert From / Convert To	Standard	\<Type of Unit\> Scientific
horsepower [metric] --- >>>---		1.359 621 6E+18
joule/second --- >>>---		1.000 000 0E+21
kilocalorie/second [I.T.] -- >>>---		2.388 459 0E+17
kilogram-force meter/second--- >>>---		1.019 716 2E+20
kilopond meter/second-- >>>---		1.019 716 2E+20
million Btu/hour [I.T.] -- >>>---		3.412 141 6E+15
volt ampere -- >>>---		1.000 000 0E+21
watt -- >>>---		1.000 000 0E+21
zettawatthour		\<energy\>
cheval vapeur heure [France]--- >>>---		1.359 621 6E+18
coal equivalent kilogram [UN, standard] ------------------------------- >>>---		1.228 350 3E+17
coal equivalent metric ton [UN, standard] ----------------------------- >>>---		1.228 350 3E+14
cubic foot atmosphere -- >>>---		1.254 703 2E+21
gram [atomic physics, eq. energy] ------------------------------------- >>>---		4.005 540 2E+10
joule --- >>>---		3.600 000 0E+24
kilogram [atomic physics, eq. energy] --------------------------------- >>>---		4.005 540 2E+07
kiloton [metric, explosive energy] ------------------------------------- >>>---		8.604 206 5E+11
megaton [metric, explosive energy] ----------------------------------- >>>---		8.604 206 5E+08
quad -- 3,412,141.6-		3.412 141 6E+06
radian/second [atomic physics, eq. energy]------------------------- <<<---		3.796 461 6E-10
ton [metric, explosive energy]--- >>>---		8.604 206 5E+14
zevre [Turkey]	\<mass, special - see page 29\>	
milligram--- 2.09-		2.090 000 0E+00
zhang [China]	\<length, special - see page 29\>	
meter --- 3.581-		3.581 000 0E+00
zhang [Thailand]	\<mass, special - see page 29\>	
kilogram--- 1.2-		1.200 000 0E+00
zira [Turkey]	\<length, special - see page 29\>	
meter--- 1-		1.000 000 0E+00
ziraa [Iraq]	\<length, special - see page 29\>	
centimeter--- 74.5-		7.450 000 0E+01
zirah [Lebanon, land]	\<length, special - see page 29\>	
centimeter--- 75.8-		7.580 000 0E+01
zirah [Lebanon, textiles]	\<length, special - see page 29\>	
centimeter--- 67.9-		6.790 000 0E+01
zirai [Turkey]	\<length, special - see page 29\>	
meter--- 1-		1.000 000 0E+00
zogol [Hungary]	\<length, special - see page 29\>	
meter-- 1.896-		1.896 000 0E+00
zoll [Austria]	\<length, special - see page 29\>	
centimeter--- 2.634-		2.634 000 0E+00
zoll [Germany, Bavaria]	\<length, special - see page 29\>	
centimeter--- 2.432 2-		2.432 200 0E+00
zoll [Germany, Prussia]	\<length, special - see page 29\>	
centimeter-- 2.615 48-		2.615 480 0E+00
zoll [Germany, Wurttemberg]	\<length, special - see page 29\>	
centimeter--- 2.864 9-		2.864 900 0E+00
zoll [Germany]	\<length, special - see page 29\>	
centimeter-- 2.62-		2.620 000 0E+00
zoll [Sweden]	\<length, special - see page 29\>	
centimeter--- 2.969-		2.969 000 0E+00
zoll [Switzerland]	\<length, special - see page 29\>	
centimeter--- 3-		3.000 000 0E+00
zollcentner [Germany]	\<mass, special - see page 29\>	
kilogram--- 50-		5.000 000 0E+01
zollpfund [Austria]	\<length, special - see page 29\>	
centimeter--- 2.634-		2.634 000 0E+00

zollpfund [Germany]	<mass, special - see page 29>	
gram	500	5.000 000 0E+02
zollverein pound [Germany]	<mass, special - see page 29>	
gram	500	5.000 000 0E+02
zolotnik [Russia]	<mass, special - see page 29>	
gram	4.266	4.266 000 0E+00
zudda [Arabia]	<volume, special - see page 29>	
liter	6.32	6.320 000 0E+00
zugtierlast [Switzerland]	<mass, special - see page 29>	
kilogram	750	7.500 000 0E+02
zuz [Hebrew, ancient]	<mass, special - see page 29>	
gram	3.585	3.585 000 0E+00

A ppendix

Units Grouped by Type

Absorbed Dose
erg/gram
gray
joule/kilogram
milligray
millijoule/kilogram
rad
rep

Absorbed Dose Rate
erg/gram second
gray/second
joule/second kilogram
milligray/second
millijoule/kilogram second
rad/second
rep/second

Acceleration
celo
centigal
centimeter/square second
decigal
decimeter/square second
dekameter/square second
foot/square second
g-unit
gal
galileo
gn
grav
hectometer/square second
inch/square second
kilometer/hour second
kilometer/square second
leo
meter/square second
mile/hour minute
mile/hour second
mile/square second
milligal
millimeter/square second

Acceleration Gradient
Eötvös unit
gal/centimeter
gal/foot

gal/inch
gal/meter

Acoustic Impedance
acoustic ohm
dyne second/centimeter^5
newton second/meter^5
pascal second/cubic meter

Amount of Substance
attomole
centimole
decimole
dekamole
examole
femtomole
gigamole
hectomole
kilomole
megamole
micromole
millimole
mole
nanomole
number of atoms in 0.012 kg of carbon-12
one atom of carbon-12
petamole
picomole
teramole
yoctomole
yottamole
zeptomole
zettamole

Angular Acceleration
degree/square second
radian/square second

Area
abraa
acre
actus quadratus
actus simplex
aftari
albrun
album
alqueire carree

anna
aranjada
ardeb
are
aroura
arpent
arpent codatral
bahu
balita
barn
base box
bau
beit sea
beit zemed
besana
beswa
bigha
bin
bing fang kung chih
bouw
braca quadrada
braza
braza carree
bu
bunder
caballeria
cadastral denum
cadastral yoke
cadne
cantero
cao
cape morgen
carga
caro
carreau
carreau de terre
carree
catta
cawney
cawnie
celemin
centiare
centuria
chast
chattak
chia
ching
chungbo

Area (cont.)

chuo
circular centimeter
circular foot
circular inch
circular microinch
circular micrometer
circular mil
circular millimeter
clima
cong
cordel cuadrado
courd
cuadra
cuadra cuadrada
cuadro
cuarta
cuartilla
cuerda
cunningham acre
dan chung
dan oranja
daneq
darat
dareb
dau chung
decempeda quadrata
deciatine
denum
desatine
desiatyny
dessetine
dessiatina
deunam
deunum
dhumd
dhur
diciatine
djarib
djerib
djevil
djung
donum
dulum
dunam
dunum
engjateigur
erlek
estadal
estodal
evieh
evlek
faddan
fan gong li
fan mi
fanega
fanegada
fanga
fanga carree
feddan
feddan masri
feralin
ferfathmur

ferfet
fermila
ferrado
ferthumiungur
feun
fjerdingkar
gadula
gan
gang
garmida
gasha
geira
gereeb
ghamaon
ghe
ghumaon
gin
giornata
girib
go
gong mu
gong qing
gouffa
gradula
gubiar
guntha
habba
hectare
heredium
hold
hout
iugerum
izenbi
jabia
jak
jareeb
jemba
jerib
jirib
jitro
joch
juchart
juger
jugerum
jungbo
kadastral hold
kalad
kanal
kanee
kannland
kappland
kassabe
katastarsko jutro
katasztralis hold
katha
kattha
keila
kejla
kerad kamel
khau
khedem
kila
kin
king

kirat
kish
ko
koltuk
kordofan
kordofan mukhamas
korec
kulba
kung ching
kung mou
kung mu
kvadratfot
kvadratni khvat
labor
lan
lanac
lanaz
legua cuadrada
legua quadrada
lekha
lelong
line
linea cuadrada
lino
litro
loan
ly
maal
makhammus
mal
man
manzana
marabba
marasseh
marco real
marla
matomana
matomuri
matopathi
mau
maw
maz
mecate
medida
medio
merice
merrassi
mesana
meshara
metze
mieng
mil covas
milha quadrada
mira
mishara
modd
moraba
moreas stremma
morg
morga
morgan
morgen
motyka
mou

Area (cont.)
square stigma
square taim
square tenthmeter
square terameter
square thou
square vara
square wa
square x-unit
square yard
square yoctometer
square yottameter
square zar
square zeptometer
square zettameter
stemma
stremma
strych
stt
suerte
tac
tagwerk
talangva
tamna
tan
tarabiit
tarang ngu
tarang sao
tarang sen
tarang wah
tarea
tarefa
tarialte
tartous
task
tavola
tchetvert
than
thon
thuoc
tmen
tomna
tonde
tonde hartkorn
tonde land
topo
town lot
township
tsubo
tundagslatta
tunland
tunnland
tzemed
ure
vara
vara cuadrada
vierkante duim
vierkante el
vierkante mijl
vierkante palm
vierkante roede
vierkante roedo
vierkante streep

vloka
xich
yoke
yugada

Area Per Unit Volume
square foot/cubic foot
square meter/cubic meter
square yard/cubic yard

Atomic Activity
1/second
becquerel
curie
disintegration/second
gigabecquerel
kilobecquerel
megabecquerel
millicurie
rutherford
terabecquerel

Champagne Bottle Size
balthazar
bottle
jeroboam
magnum
methuselah
nebuchadnezzar
rehoboam
salmanazar

Coefficient of Heat Transfer or Thermal Conductance
Btu/day square foot degree Fahrenheit
Btu/hour square foot degree Fahrenheit
Btu/second square foot degree Fahrenheit
calorie/hour square centimeter degree Celsius
calorie/second square centimeter degree Celsius
erg/square centimeter second degree Celsius
joule/second square meter kelvin
kilocalorie/hour square meter degree Celsius
kilogram-force/meter second degree Celsius
kilogram/cubic second kelvin
kilowatt/square meter degree Celsius
kilowatt/square meter kelvin
watt/square centimeter degree Celsius

watt/square centimeter kelvin
watt/square foot degree Celsius
watt/square foot degree Fahrenheit
watt/square meter degree Celsius
watt/square meter kelvin

Coefficient of Thermal Insulation or Thermal Insulance
clo
square centimeter degree Celsius/watt
square centimeter kelvin/watt
square centimeter second degree Celsius/calorie
square foot degree Celsius/watt
square foot hour degree Fahrenheit/Btu
square meter degree Celsius/kilowatt
square meter degree Celsius/watt
square meter hour degree Celsius/kilocalorie
square meter kelvin/kilowatt
square meter kelvin/watt
square meter second kelvin/joule
tog

Compressibility
1/pascal
brewster
square centimeter/dyne
square centimeter/gram-force
square foot/pound-force
square foot/poundal
square foot/ton-force
square inch/pound-force
square meter/kilogram-force
square meter/kilopond
square meter/newton
square meter/tonne

Concentration (Mole Basis)
Amagat density unit
kilomole/cubic meter
micromole/cubic centimeter
micromole/liter
millimole/cubic centimeter
millimole/cubic meter
millimole/liter

Concentration (Mole Basis) (cont.)

millimole/milliliter
mole/cubic decimeter
mole/cubic meter
mole/liter

Concentration (Volume Basis)

cubic foot/cubic foot
cubic foot/gallon
cubic meter/cubic meter
cubic meter/liter
gallon/cubic foot
liter/cubic meter

Density

gammil
grain/cubic foot
grain/cubic inch
grain/cubic yard
grain/gallon
gram/cubic centimeter
gram/cubic decimeter
gram/cubic meter
gram/liter
gram/milliliter
kilogram/cubic centimeter
kilogram/cubic decimeter
kilogram/cubic meter
kilogram/liter
kilogram/milliliter
megagram/cubic centimeter
megagram/cubic decimeter
megagram/cubic meter
megagram/liter
megagram/milliliter
micril
milligram/cubic centimeter
milligram/cubic decimeter
milligram/cubic meter
milligram/liter
milligram/milliliter
ounce/cubic foot
ounce/cubic inch
ounce/cubic yard
ounce/gallon
pound/circular mil foot
pound/cubic foot
pound/cubic inch
pound/cubic yard
pound/gallon
slug/cubic foot
slug/cubic inch
slug/cubic yard
slug/gallon
ton/cubic foot
ton/cubic inch
ton/cubic yard
ton/gallon
tonne/cubic centimeter
tonne/cubic decimeter

tonne/cubic meter
tonne/liter
tonne/milliliter

Density of States

1/Btu cubic foot
1/calorie cubic centimeter
1/electronvolt cubic meter
1/erg cubic centimeter
1/joule cubic meter
1/watt hour cubic meter

Dose Equivalent

joule/kilogram
millisievert
newton meter/kilogram
rem
sievert
square meter/square second

Electric Capacitance

abfarad
ampere second/volt
centifarad
coulomb/volt
decifarad
dekafarad
electromagnetic unit of capacitance
electrostatic unit of capacitance
farad
gaussian electric capacitance
gigafarad
hectofarad
jar
kilofarad
megafarad
microfarad
millifarad
nanofarad
picofarad
puff
second/ohm
statfarad
terafarad

Electric Charge

abcoulomb
ampere hour
ampere minute
ampere second
centicoulomb
coulomb
decicoulomb
dekacoulomb
electromagnetic unit of charge
electron charge
electrostatic unit of charge
elementary charge

farad volt
faraday
franklin
gaussian electric charge
gigacoulomb
hectocoulomb
kilocoulomb
megacoulomb
microcoulomb
millicoulomb
nanocoulomb
petacoulomb
picocoulomb
statcoulomb
teracoulomb

Electric Charge Density

abcoulomb/cubic centimeter
ampere hour/cubic meter
ampere second/cubic meter
coulomb/cubic centimeter
coulomb/cubic meter
coulomb/cubic millimeter
franklin/cubic centimeter
gigacoulomb/cubic meter
kilocoulomb/cubic meter
megacoulomb/cubic meter
microcoulomb/cubic meter
millicoulomb/cubic meter
statcoulomb/cubic centimeter

Electric Conductance

1/ohm
abmho
absiemens
ampere/volt
centisiemens
decisiemens
dekasiemens
electromagnetic unit of conductance
electrostatic unit of conductance
gaussian electric conductance
gemmho
gigasiemens
hectosiemens
kilosiemens
megamho
megasiemens
mho
micromho
microsiemens
millimho
millisiemens
nanosiemens
picosiemens
second/henry
siemens
statmho

Electric Conductance (continued)
statsiemens
terasiemens

Electric Conductivity
1/ohm meter
abmho/centimeter
absiemens/centimeter
kilosiemens/meter
megasiemens/meter
mho/meter
rom
siemens meter/square millimeter
siemens/meter
statmho/centimeter
statsiemens/centimeter

Electric Current
abampere
ampere
biot
centiampere
coulomb/second
deciampere
dekaampere
electromagnetic unit of current
electrostatic unit of current
franklin/second
gaussian electric current
gilbert
hectoampere
kiloampere
megaampere
microampere
milliampere
nanoampere
picoampere
siemens volt
statampere
volt/ohm
watt/volt
weber/henry

Electric Current Density
abampere/square centimeter
ampere/square centimeter
ampere/square inch
ampere/square meter
ampere/square millimeter
kiloampere/square meter
megaampere/square meter
statampere/square centimeter

Electric Dipole Moment
abcoulomb centimeter
ampere hour meter
ampere second meter
coulomb centimeter
coulomb meter
coulomb millimeter
debye unit
farad volt meter
franklin centimeter
kilocoulomb meter
millicoulomb meter
statcoulomb centimeter

Electric Dipole Moment Per Unit Area
abcoulomb/centimeter
ampere hour/meter
ampere second/meter
coulomb/centimeter
coulomb/meter
coulomb/millimeter
debye unit/square angstrom
farad volt/meter
franklin/centimeter
helmholtz
kilocoulomb/meter
millicoulomb/meter
statcoulomb/centimeter

Electric Elastance
1/farad
daraf

Electric Field Strength
abvolt/centimeter
ampere ohm/meter
coulomb/farad meter
joule/coulomb meter
kilovolt/meter
megavolt/meter
microvolt/meter
millivolt/meter
newton/coulomb
statvolt/centimeter
volt/centimeter
volt/inch
volt/meter
volt/mil
volt/millimeter
watt/ampere meter
weber/second meter

Electric Inductance
abhenry
centihenry
decihenry
dekahenry
electromagnetic unit of inductance

electrostatic unit of inductance
gaussian electric inductance
gigahenry
hectohenry
henry
joule/square ampere
kilohenry
megahenry
microhenry
millihenry
nanohenry
ohm second
picohenry
stathenry
terahenry
volt second/ampere
weber/ampere

Electric Mobility
square meter/volt second
square meter/weber
square second ampere/kilogram

Electric Permeability
henry/centimeter
henry/meter
henry/millimeter
magn
microhenry/meter
nanohenry/meter

Electric Permittivity
abfarad/centimeter
ampere second/volt meter
coulomb/volt meter
farad/meter
kilofarad/meter
microfarad/meter
millifarad/meter
nanofarad/meter
picofarad/meter
second/ohm meter
statfarad/centimeter

Electric Polarizability
coulomb square centimeter/volt
coulomb square meter/volt
farad square meter

Electric Potential
abvolt
ampere ohm
centivolt
coulomb/farad
crocodile
decivolt
dekavolt
electromagnetic unit of electric potential

Electric Potential (continued)

electrostatic unit of electric potential
erg/franklin
gaussian electric potential
gigavolt
hectovolt
joule/coulomb
kilovolt
megavolt
microvolt
millivolt
nanovolt
picovolt
statvolt
teravolt
volt
watt/ampere
weber/second

Electric Reluctance

1/abhenry
1/henry
1/ohm second
1/stathenry
ampere/volt second
ampere/weber
square ampere/joule

Electric Resistance

1/mho
1/siemens
abohm
centiohm
deciohm
dekaohm
electromagnetic unit of resistance
electrostatic unit of resistance
gaussian electric resistance
gigaohm
hectohm
henry/second
kilohm
megohm
microhm
milliohm
nanoohm
ohm
picoohm
statohm
teraohm
volt/ampere

Electric Resistivity

abohm centimeter
gigaohm meter
kilohm meter
megohm meter
microhm centimeter

microhm inch
microhm meter
milliohm meter
nanoohm meter
ohm centimeter
ohm circular mil/foot
ohm foot
ohm inch
ohm meter
ohm square millimeter/meter
preece
statohm centimeter

Electromagnetic Energy Density

Btu/cubic foot
calorie/cubic centimeter
dyne/square centimeter
erg/cubic centimeter
joule/cubic meter
kilocalorie/cubic meter
newton/square meter

Electromagnetic Moment

abampere square centimeter
ampere circular mil
ampere square centimeter
ampere square inch
ampere square meter
ampere square millimeter
kiloampere square meter
milliampere square meter
statampere square centimeter

Energy

1/centimeter
1/meter
atomic mass unit
attojoule
Board of Trade Unit
Btu
calorie
centigrade heat unit
centijoule
centimeter gram-force
cheval vapeur heure
coal equivalent kilogram
coal equivalent metric ton
cubic centimeter atmosphere
cubic foot atmosphere
cubic foot of liquified petroleum gas
cubic foot of natural gas
cubic meter atmosphere
decijoule
dekajoule
dekawatthour

deuteron rest mass
dyne centimeter
electron rest mass
electronvolt
erg
exajoule
exawatthour
femtojoule
foot pound-force
foot poundal
frigorie
gallon of automotive gasoline
gallon of aviation gasoline
gallon of diesel oil
gallon of distillate #2 fuel oil
gallon of jet fuel, kerosene type
gallon of jet fuel, naphtha type
gallon of kerosene
gallon of residual fuel oil
gigaelectronvolt
gigajoule
gigawatthour
gram
gram calorie
hartree
hectojoule
hectowatthour
hertz
horsepower hour
inch pound-force
joule
kayser
kelvin
kilocalorie
kiloelectronvolt
kilogram
kilogram calorie
kilogram of water
kilogram square meter/square second
kilojoule
kilopond meter
kiloton
kilowatthour
liter atmosphere
megaelectronvolt
megaerg
megajoule
megalerg
megaton
megawatthour
meter kilogram-force
microjoule
millijoule
muon rest mass
myriawatthour
nanojoule
neutron rest mass
newton meter
petajoule
petawatthour

Energy (continued)
pferdestarkenstunde
picojoule
pound of water
proton rest mass
q-unit
quad
radian/second
rydberg
teraelectronvolt
terajoule
terawatthour
therm
thermie
ton
ton of anthracite coal
ton of bituminous coal
watthour
wattsecond
yoctojoule
yottajoule
yottawatthour
zeptojoule
zettajoule
zettawatthour

Energy Fluence or Radiant Exposure
Btu/square foot
calorie/square centimeter
dyne/centimeter
electronvolt/square meter
erg/square centimeter
joule/square meter
kilocalorie/square meter
langley
newton/meter

Energy Flux Density
flux unit
watt/square meter hertz

Exposure
ampere second/kilogram
ampere square meter/joule second
coulomb/kilogram
microcoulomb/kilogram
millicoulomb/kilogram
nanocoulomb/kilogram
picocoulomb/kilogram
röntgen
roentgen

Exposure Rate
ampere/kilogram
coulomb/kilogram second
microcoulomb/kilogram second
millicoulomb/kilogram second

nanocoulomb/kilogram second
picocoulomb/kilogram second
röntgen/second
roentgen/second

Flow Rate (Mass Basis)
gram/hour
gram/minute
gram/second
kilogram/hour
kilogram/minute
kilogram/second
milligram/hour
milligram/minute
milligram/second
pound/hour
pound/minute
pound/second
ton/hour
ton/minute
ton/second

Flow Rate (Mole Basis)
millimole/hour
millimole/minute
millimole/second
mole/hour
mole/minute
mole/second

Flow Rate (Volume Basis)
acre foot/day
acre foot/hour
acre foot/minute
acre foot/second
acre inch/day
acre inch/hour
acre inch/minute
acre inch/second
barrel/day
barrel/hour
barrel/minute
barrel/second
billion cubic foot/day
billion cubic foot/hour
billion cubic foot/minute
billion cubic foot/second
centiliter/day
centiliter/hour
centiliter/minute
centiliter/second
cubem/day
cubem/hour
cubem/minute
cubem/second
cubic centimeter/day
cubic centimeter/hour

cubic centimeter/minute
cubic centimeter/second
cubic decimeter/day
cubic decimeter/hour
cubic decimeter/minute
cubic decimeter/second
cubic dekameter/day
cubic dekameter/hour
cubic dekameter/minute
cubic dekameter/second
cubic foot/day
cubic foot/hour
cubic foot/minute
cubic foot/second
cubic inch/day
cubic inch/hour
cubic inch/minute
cubic inch/second
cubic kilometer/day
cubic kilometer/hour
cubic kilometer/minute
cubic kilometer/second
cubic meter/day
cubic meter/hour
cubic meter/minute
cubic meter/second
cubic mile/day
cubic mile/hour
cubic mile/minute
cubic mile/second
cubic millimeter/day
cubic millimeter/hour
cubic millimeter/minute
cubic millimeter/second
cubic yard/day
cubic yard/hour
cubic yard/minute
cubic yard/second
cusec
deciliter/day
deciliter/hour
deciliter/minute
deciliter/second
dekaliter/day
dekaliter/hour
dekaliter/minute
dekaliter/second
gallon/day
gallon/hour
gallon/minute
gallon/second
hectare meter/day
hectare meter/hour
hectare meter/minute
hectare meter/second
hectoliter/day
hectoliter/hour
hectoliter/minute
hectoliter/second
kiloliter/day
kiloliter/hour
kiloliter/minute
kiloliter/second
lambda/day

Flow Rate (Volume Basis) (continued)

lambda/hour
lambda/minute
lambda/second
liter/day
liter/hour
liter/minute
liter/second
milliliter/day
milliliter/hour
milliliter/minute
milliliter/second
million acre foot/day
million acre foot/hour
million acre foot/minute
million acre foot/second
miner's inch
ounce/day
ounce/hour
ounce/minute
ounce/second
petrograd standard/day
petrograd standard/hour
petrograd standard/minute
petrograd standard/second
stere/day
stere/hour
stere/minute
stere/second
thousand cubic foot/day
thousand cubic foot/hour
thousand cubic foot/minute
thousand cubic foot/second
trillion cubic foot/day
trillion cubic foot/hour
trillion cubic foot/minute
trillion cubic foot/second

Flow Rate Per Unit Area (Mass Basis)

gram/square meter second
kilogram/are second
kilogram/hectare second
kilogram/square meter second
milligram/square meter second
ounce/square foot second
pound/acre second
pound/square foot second
slug/square foot second
ton/square foot second
tonne/square meter second

Force

attonewton
centinewton
crinal
decigram-force
decinewton
dekagram-force
dekanewton
dyne
erg/centimeter
exanewton
femtonewton
funal
giganewton
grain-force
gram centimeter/square second
gram-force
hectonewton
hyl meter/square second
joule/meter
kilogram meter/square second
kilogram-force
kilonewton
kilopond
kip
meganewton
micronewton
millinewton
nanonewton
newton
ounce foot/square second
ounce-force
ouncedal
pascal square meter
petanewton
piconewton
pond
pound foot/square second
pound-force
poundal
slug foot/square second
sthene
teranewton
ton foot/square second
ton meter/square second
ton-force
tondal
volt ampere second/meter
watt second/meter
yoctonewton
yottanewton
zeptonewton
zettanewton

Frequency or Circular Frequency or Angluar Velocity

1/second
cycle/second
degree/hour
degree/minute
degree/second
fresnel
gigahertz
hertz
kilohertz
megahertz
millihertz
radian/hour
radian/minute
radian/second
revolution/hour
revolution/minute
revolution/second
terahertz

Fuel Consumption (SI)

cubic meter/meter
gallon/mile
liter/meter
liter/100 kilometer
liter/kilometer

Fuel Consumption (US)

kilometer/cubic meter
kilometer/liter
meter/cubic meter
meter/liter
mile/gallon

Geothermal Gradient

degree Celsius/meter
degree Fahrenheit/foot
kelvin/meter

Geothermal Step

foot/degree Fahrenheit
meter/degree Celsius
meter/kelvin

Heat Capacity or Entropy

Btu/degree Fahrenheit
calorie/degree Celsius
clausius
erg/kelvin
joule/kelvin
kilocalorie/degree Celsius

Heat Flow Rate or Radiant Exitance or Sound Intensity

Btu/day square foot
Btu/hour square foot
Btu/minute square foot
Btu/second square foot
Btu/second square inch
calorie/day square centimeter
calorie/minute square centimeter
calorie/second square centimeter
erg/second square centimeter
finsen unit
joule/second square meter

Heat Flow Rate or Radiant Exitance or Sound Intensity (continued)

kilocalorie/hour square meter
kilowatt/square meter
megawatt/square meter
microwatt/square meter
milliwatt/square meter
nanowatt/square meter
picowatt/square meter
pyron
watt/square centimeter
watt/square foot
watt/square inch
watt/square meter
watt/square millimeter

Heat Release Rate

Btu/cubic foot hour
calorie/cubic centimeter second
erg/cubic centimeter second
joule/cubic meter second
kilocalorie/cubic meter hour
watt/cubic foot
watt/cubic meter

Heat Transfer Coefficient

Btu/hour cubic foot degree Fahrenheit
calorie/second cubic centimeter degree Celsius
joule/second cubic meter kelvin
kilocalorie/hour cubic meter degree Celsius
kilowatt/cubic meter kelvin
watt/cubic meter kelvin

Length

abdah
actus
ady
agate
aldan
alen
alin
aln
amma
ammah
angstrom
angula
anguli
annuk
anukabiet
archin
arine

arish
arkana
arpent
arsheen
arshin
arshyn
asba
astronomical unit
attometer
aune
azba
baa
bahar
bamboo
bandle
barleycorn
behar
bei mi
bema
beru
bevameter
bicron
bitta
bolt
boo
bow
braca
braccio d'ara
brache
brasse
braza
brazada
busa
cabda
cable length
cabulla
cal
caliber
calow
canna
cape foot
cape inch
cape rood
carsi
cassaba
cay
centimeter
cha
chabba
chain
cham am
chang
charac
chauseemeile
che
check
cheh
chek
cheung
chhek
chi
chih
chinese foot
chinese inch

chinese mile
chinese yard
cho
chok
choryos
chuhm
chum
chung
chungbo
codo
cordel
coss
coudee
covada
covado
covido
crosh
cuada
cuadra
cuarta
cuarto
cubi
cubit
cubito
cubitus
cuerda
cuerda
cun
dain
daktylos
decempeda
decimeter
dedo
deido
dekameter
depa
deraga
deraga akhdam
deraga cabda
derah
dha
dhanu
dhara
dhira
dhiraa
dhra
dhra d'alep
didot point
digit
digitus
dira
dira baladi
dira minari
diraa
diraa baladi
diraa memari
dong
doron
double stadion
douzieme
dra
dra arbi
dra maghmari
draa arbi

Length (continued)

draa milki
drah
drahi
duim
duime
dynia
el
ell
elle
em
emmet
encablure
endaze
endazeh
endere
esba
estadel
estadio
estado
etzba
etzbah
exameter
ezba
famn
fan
faon
farsakh
farsakh song
fatar
fathmur
fathom
faust
favn
femtometer
fen
fen mi
fermi
fershi kadim
fet
finger
fingerbreadth
fitr
fod
foot
fot
fun
furlong
fuss
fusz
fut
gana
ganu
gar
gareh
garwoke
gasab
gat
gatsar
gaulette
gaz
gaz gareeb
gaz memar

gaz sha
gazi jerib
gazi memar
gazi sha
geerah
gereh gaz sha
gereh gazi sha
gi
gigameter
girah
gireh
gis
gon
gong li
gradus
gramme
gran
great ovido
greater pic
gudge
guereh
guz
haat
habba shair
habl
halibin
hand
handaza
hao mi
hasit
hasta
hat
hath
hatt
haut
hectometer
hema
hemipodion
hesta
hindaza
hippicon
hiro
hollegada
hong euk louang
hot
hu mi
huvelik
hvat
imagu
inch
iron
jacob
jalka
jaob
jarda
jareeb
jarib
java paal
jenghal
jengkal
jo
jow
jumba

jungbo
kabda
kabellangd
kabellengte
kabiet
kabiet louang
kairi
kala
kam
kam louang
kama
kaneh
karam
kasaba
kasaba hakimiyya
kasbu
kassaba
kassabah
kathouah
kawtha
ken
kend
kerat
kette
keup
khalad
khat
khet
khluon chay
khos aldan
khub
khub louang
khubi
khup
khvat
kilometer
kiloparsec
kind
kirat
klafter
konak
kondylos
kor
kosh
koss
kovid
krap sran
kujira shaku
kung
kung chang
kung chih
kung fen
kung fun
kung li
kung tsun
kung yin
kup
kus
kvarter
lackilo
lan
lanca
landmil
lasta

Length (continued)

lath
latro
lea
league
legoa
legua
lei
lesser pic
li
li mi
lichar
lieue
lieue de poste
light year
ligne
liin
likot
lina
line
linea
linha
linhada
linia
linie
liniya
linja
linje
link
loket
lokiec
ly
ma
marfold
marhala
marok
mecate
megameter
megaparsec
meile
mekyas cubit
merfold
mertfold
meter
mi
microinch
micrometer
micromicron
micron
miglio
mijl
mil
mila
mila a landi
mile
mile passum
milha
miliarum
milion
mill
milla
mille
mille passus

mille passuum
milliare
millimeter
millimicron
million
mimar
mimari
min
mira
mkono
mo
moolum
moot
moreas plethron
mou
mylia
myriameter
nail
nanometer
ngu
niew
ninda
niou
niou louang
niranja
niu
nocktat
node
noeud de loch
nonpareil
nus
nymil
oke thapa
oke thapal
ona
orguia
orgyia
ourob
ouroub
out
ovido
paal
pace
pal
palag
palaiste
palame
palaz
paleste
paletz
palgat
palm
palma
palmi
palmipes
palmo
palmus
palmus maior
parasang
parasange
Paris foot
Paris inch
Paris line
parmah

parmak
parsec
pas
paso
passo
passus
pe
pearl
pechus
peninkulma
perch
perche
perestril
persakh
pertica
pes
pes drusianus
pes sestertius
pesiah
petameter
phan
pharoagh
phyeam
pic
pic arabe
pic turc
pica
picheus
picki
picometer
pie
pied
pied anglais
pied de perche
pied de roi
piede
pik
pik andoulsi
pik arbi
pik baladi
pik turki
pike
piq
plethron
point
pole
polegada
pollegada
pong chay
ponto
postav
pouce
pous
pret
pu
pulgada
pulgada inglesa
pulzier
pun
punkt
punto
pygme
pygon

Length (continued)

verst
versta
verste
vi
vilasti
voet
wa
wah
walk of a Babylonian hour
war
wari
wavelength of orange-red
  spectral line of krypton-86
wei mi
werchok
werst
x-unit
xiber
xich
yard
yarda
yin
ying
yoch
yoctometer
yot
yote
yottameter
yoyana
yuzanar
zar
zaz
zebo
zeptometer
zer
zeret
zereth
zettameter
zhang
zira
ziraa
zirah
zirai
zogol
zoll
zollpfund

Light Exposure

footcandle second
kilolux second
lumen second/square
  centimeter
lumen second/square foot
lumen second/square inch
lumen second/square meter
lux hour
lux second
metercandle second
milliphot second
nox second
phot second

Linear Density

denier
drex
gram/kilometer
gram/meter
kilogram/kilometer
kilogram/meter
kilotex
milligram/kilometer
milligram/meter
ounce/foot
ounce/inch
ounce/yard
pli
poumar
pound/foot
pound/inch
pound/yard
tex
tonne/kilometer

Linear Electric Current Density

abampere/centimeter
ampere/centimeter
ampere/inch
ampere/meter
ampere/millimeter
gilbert/centimeter
kiloampere/meter
newton/weber
oersted
statampere/centimeter

Linear Energy Transfer

Btu/foot
dyne
electronvolt/meter
erg/centimeter
joule/meter
kilocalorie/meter
newton

Luminance

apostilb
blondel
bril
candela/square centimeter
candela/square foot
candela/square inch
candela/square meter
footlambert
kilocandela/square meter
lambert
lumen/steradian square
  meter
lux steradian
millilambert
nit
skot
stilb

Luminous Efficacy

candela steradian/watt
lumen/watt
lux square meter/watt

Luminous Flux

candela steradian
lumen
lux square meter
watt

Luminous Flux Density

candela steradian/square
  meter
footcandle
kilolux
lumen/square centimeter
lumen/square foot
lumen/square inch
lumen/square meter
lux
metercandle
milliphot
nox
phot

Luminous Intensity

attocandela
bougie decimale
bougie nouvelle
candela
candle
carcel
centicandela
decicandela
dekacandela
exacandela
femtocandela
gigacandela
hectocandela
Hefner candle
hefnerkerze
kilocandela
lumen/steradian
lux square meter/steradian
megacandela
microcandela
millicandela
nanocandela
petacandela
picocandela
teracandela
violle
watt/steradian
yoctocandela
yottacandela
zeptocandela
zettacandela

Magnetic Dipole Moment
abweber centimeter
kiloweber meter
milliweber meter
newton square
  meter/ampere
statweber centimeter
volt second meter
weber centimeter
weber meter
weber millimeter

Magnetic Flux
abweber
ampere henry
centiweber
deciweber
dekaweber
electromagnetic unit of
  magnetic flux
electrostatic unit of
  magnetic flux
gauss square centimeter
gaussian magnetic flux
gigaweber
hectoweber
joule/ampere
kiloweber
line
maxwell
megaweber
microweber
milliweber
nanoweber
picoweber
statweber
teraweber
tesla square meter
unit pole
volt second
weber

Magnetic Flux Density
abtesla
ampere henry/square meter
centitesla
decitesla
dekatesla
electromagnetic unit of
  magnetic flux density
electrostatic unit of
  magnetic flux density
gamma
gauss
gaussian magnetic flux
  density
gigatesla
hectotesla
joule/ampere square meter
kilotesla
line/square centimeter
maxwell/square meter

megatesla
microtesla
millitesla
nanotesla
newton/ampere meter
picotesla
stattesla
teratesla
tesla
volt second/square meter
weber/square meter

Magnetic Vector Potential
abweber/centimeter
kiloweber/meter
milliweber/meter
newton/ampere
statweber/centimeter
volt second/meter
weber/centimeter
weber/meter
weber/millimeter

Mass Moment of Inertia
gram square centimeter
gram square meter
gram-force centimeter
  square second
gram-force meter square
  second
kilogram square centimeter
kilogram square meter
kilogram-force centimeter
  square second
kilogram-force meter
  square second
kilopond centimeter square
  second
kilopond meter square
  second
ounce square foot
ounce square inch
ounce-force foot square
  second
ounce-force inch square
  second
pond centimeter square
  second
pond meter square second
pound square foot
pound square inch
pound-force foot square
  second
pound-force inch square
  second
slug square foot
slug square inch

Mass
abada

abas
abbas
abbassi
abucco
acheintaya
acino
adarme
adowlie
adowly
agito
akey
almane
almud
almude
amat
anna
ansyr
aratel
argienco
argienso
arratel
arroa
arroba
artal
as
ass
atado
atomic mass unit
attogram
aureus
avogram
baar
baer
bag of cement
bahar
baht
bai
bak
bale
ballen
baquila
bar
bara
bat
bath
batman
batmar
batt
bazer
behar
bei ke
beka
bekah
bekaim
benda
beqa
bercherect
berkovec
berkovet
berkovetz
berkowetz
berkowitz
bes
bhar

Mass (continued)

bhara
bhari
bia
biltu
binae sextulae
bis
bismar pound
bismerpund
bissmar pound
bohar
bojote
boll
bongkal
botija
botijuela
botsa
briquette
bugday
bulto
buncal
bundle
bunkal
buttima
cabulla
cafa
cafla
caja
calc
can
cana
candareen
candarin
candil
candy
cantar
cantara
cantarelli
cantaro
cantaro barbaresco
cantaro grosso
cantaro sottile
caractero
carak
carat
carate
carga
carga de papa
cargo
case
cash
castellano
cate
catti
cattie
catty
cavan
ceira
ceki
cekirdek
cental
centenaar
centigram

centnar
centner
central
chabba
chalkos
chalque
chang
chapah
charak
charge
chariot
charruba
chattack
chattak
chattauck
chawal
chee
cheky
cheli
chequi
chhatak
chi
chien
chin
chinanda
chinbul
chittack
chittak
chombol
chong
chuchok
clove
coccio
cojang
cola
commerzlast
coyan
crith
crown
cuartilla
cubic foot of cement
custom centner
custom quintal
dalton
dam
damleng
dan
danar
danich
darchini
dareikos
daric
darm
dartung
dawala
dawulla
dbn
deben
decigram
decina
decitonne
decunx
dekagram
demikilo

denaro
denat
denheiro
denier
denk
derham
derhem
derime
deunx
deusquin
dextan
dhan
dharana
dharni
dhura
dhurree
didrachm
didrachma
dilepton
dimidia sextula
dinar
dipondium
dirham
dirhem
dodran
doli
dolia
dolja
doly
don
donchung
dong
doon
doppelzentner
drachm
drachma
drachme
dram
drame
dramm
dramma
dramme
ducat
ducat ass
duella
duelle
dun
dung
dyne square
   second/centimeter
dzhin
el cotejo
engel
engelot
engelsen
escropulo
escrupulo
esschen
estelin
exagram
fan
fanega
fanoe
farasala

Mass (continued)

farasalah
fardo
fardo de tabaco
farsalah
fatil
felin
femtogram
fen
fen ke
ferasla
ferlino
fern
ferrah
fierding
firlot
fisk
fitil
flask of mercury
foring
fount
founte
fout
frail
frasala
frasilla
frasla
frasoulla
frazila
frazula
fuen
funda
funt
funta
gamma
gandom
gandum
garsa
gauza
gedang
geepound
gera
gerah
gerbe
gerot
ghirara
gian
giarra
gigagram
gin
girla
giro
gisla
gizla
glied
glug
gon
gorraf
grain
gram
gramma

gran
grande litra
grani
granottino
granow
granum
grao
great mina
grein
grivna
gros
gros poid
gun
gunja
gyrath
hab
habba
habbe
hal
half chest
half mina
haml
hang
hao
hao ke
hap
harbour ton
hardal
harruba
harsela
hebbeh
hectogram
heller
hembl
heml
hemla
hiyaka me
hogga
hoi
hong
hoon
hot
houn
huitieme
hukka
hundredweight
hyaku me
hyl
imeru
jin
ka
kahun
kaila
kalvar
kambeh
kamha
kamian
kamlah
kamme
kan
kancha
kanchha
kandi
kandy

kantar
kantar attari
kantar d'leppo
kantje
kara
karaat
karat
karch
karsha
karshapana
karvar
kasm
kat
kati
katti
kdt
ke
kedet
kela
keml
kemple
kental
keun
khandi
kharvar
kharwar
khashkha
khaskha
khord
khou
kiccar
kikar
kikkar
kikkor
kila
kile
kilogram
kilogram-force square
    second/meter
kilolitra
kiloton
kilotonne
kin
kinn
kintar
kirat
kite
kitmir
kiya
kiyak kin
kiyaka me
klam
klender
kleud
klom
kolle
kon
kona
koret
korn
korn tonde
korrel
kouna
koyan

Mass (continued)

koyang
kramergewicht
krat
krinne
krishnala
kula
kulack
kung chien
kung chin
kung chu
kung fen
kung hao
kung heng
kung ko
kung liang
kung shi
kung sun
kung szu
kung tan
kung ton
kung tun
kunke
kunna
kupang
kurr
kvint
kvintin
kwamme
kwan
kyaku me
kyat
lachsa
ladan
lagel
lan
lana
lane
lang
last
lata
le
lea
leang
leung
li
li ke
liang
libbra
libbra metrica
libra
libra de farmacia
libre subtile
liespfund
liespund
lin
lira
lispond
lispound
lispund
litra
litre
litro

littre
livre
livre commune
livre de Charlemagne
livre de pharmacie
livre esterlin
livre francaise
livre poids de marc
livre poids de table
livre usuelle
load
lod
logarike litra
lolti
lood
loode
loot
lot
loth
ludra
luong
lut
lutow
ly
lyang
mace
mahn
mahnd
mahs
mahud
maille
makkuk
man
man chah
man i bandar abbassi
man i hashemi
man i kahneh
man i noh abbassi
man i rey
man i shah
man i tabriz
man tabriz
mancuerna
mandel gewichtsgran
mane
maneh
mangal
mangalis
mangelin
manhe
manim
mann
manne
mano
manojo
manu
mao
maon
maqar
marc
marca
marck
marco
marco real

marfold
mario
mark
markgewicht
mas
masha
massa
mat
mata
matar
maund
mayam
mazsa
me
media
megagram
megaton
megatonne
meile
mesghal
meteka
meterzentner
methgal
methkal
metical
metir
metkal
metric-technical unit of
    mass
metrischer
metska
metskal
mian
microgram
migr
migrab
mil
milli-mass-unit
millier
milligram
mina
minah
miscal
miskal
mismal
misqal
misri
mite
mithkal
mitiga
mitkal
mitqal
mitqual
mitsal
mna
mo
mocha
modd
moio
mokka pound
momme
mon
monme
moo

Mass (continued)

moosa
mounce
mound
mozetta
mudd
mudu
mula
mule load
mun
mune
mutagalla
myriagram
nagel
nail
nakhod
nakir
nanogram
naqir
nass
natr
nawa
neal
nelli
nesef
neseph
neter
netir
netseph
newton square
  second/meter
ngamu
nijo
nim man
nishka
nohod
nokhod
nouaia
nsp
nuge
obol
obolos
obolus
occa
ochava
ock
ocque
octava
ogga
oitava
oka
oke
oket
okia
okiya
okka
onca
once
once arabi
oncia
onckie
ons
onza

opuia
oqa
oqiya
oquia
ore
ort
osira
ottava
oukeia
ounce
outava
pa
paca
pachen
pack
package
packen
pagoda
pai
pala
pali
palie
pallie
pally
paloin
pank
pao
parah
parto
passeree
pauseri
payim
pecul
pedra
peiktha
pekul
pennyweight
perma
peso
peso grosso
peso sottile
petagram
pfennig
pfund
phan
pic
pico
picogram
picol
picul
pikul
pim
pinar
pintji
pocket
poids de marc
poids de Paris
poids de soie
poids de ville
point
pollam
pond
pondo
pong

pood
poud
pound
pound-force square
  second/foot
poundal square second/foot
pow
powa
powa chhatak
pud
pun
pund
punk
punkho
punko
punto
purana
pushuri
pyi
qadah
qamhah
qantar
qasa
qdt
qesita
qilli
qintar
qirat
qirath
quadran
quamha
quantar
quarter
quentchen
quenten
quilat
quilate
quincunx
quintal
quintar
quintaux
rabaa
rafa
raik
ratal
ratel
rati
ratili
ratl
ratl djarwi
ratl laythi
ratl rumi
rattel
real
rebah
red
retal
retti
revaim
rey
rin
roba
rotal
rotel fedhy

Mass (continued)

rotl	shiglu	tang
rotle	shih chien	tank
rotol	shih chin	tao
rotoli	shih fen	tartimar
rotolo	shih hao	tauk
rottel	shih li	tcharak
rottle	shih liang	tcheirek
rotto	shih sze	tcheki
rottol	shih tan	ten drachma
rottolo	ship last	teragram
rottolo a kebyr	ship pound	tercio
rottolo a khadhary	ship pund	termini
rottolo a thary	shippond	teruncius
rottolo attari	si	tetradrachm
rova	sicca	tetradrachma
rtel	sicilicus	thail
ruay	siglos	thaler
ruba	sihr	thamin
rubbio	siki	thang
ruttee	siliqua	then
sac	sir	thumn
sacco	sitarion	ti
sack	skaalpund	tia
saco	skalpund	tical
saco de cafe	skalpunt	tien
saddirham	skeppslast	tikal
saga	skeppund	tillis
salm	skiblast	timbang
salme	skibpund	tiya
salung	skippund	tji
sang	skippunt	tod
satlijh	slug	tola
saum	solidus	tolah
scripula	solotnik	tomande
scripulum	solung	tomin
scrupel	sompay	ton
scruple	ssu	tonel
scrupulum	star pagoda	tonelada
se	stater	tonelada corta
seer	stein	tonna
semis	stone	tonne
semisextula	suk	tonneau
semiuncia	suku	tonnelada
sene	sus	tonos
sentner	suvarna	tovar
sep	suvarnamasha	triens
septunx	swin	tschak
seqel	ta	tscheki
ser	taam	tsein
sescuncia	table	tsin
sesterce	tael	tughar
seu	tahil	tuht
sextan	tai	tumna
sextula	talanton	tunna smjors
shan	tale	uckir
shatamana	talent	ugga
she	talenton	ughia
shekalim	talentum	ugija
shekel	taler	ukia
shekel hamelech	tali	ukie
sheqel	tam	ukkia
shi ke	tamlung	una
	tamuga	uncia
	tan	uncya

Mass (continued)
uns
unser
unze
unzen
uqija
uqijje
uye
uzan
vagon
vall
vamfort
vammazsa
vi
vierding
viertellot
vis
visham
viss
wag
wagia
wagia dahabia
wagla
wagon
wakea
wakega
wakia
wakiah
wang
wazma
wazna
wichtje
windle
wizna
wog
woket
woog
wukiyeh
xang
yan
yang
yen
yoctogram
yottagram
yusdroman
ywegale
ywegi
ywegyi
zentner
zeptogram
zettagram
zevre
zhang
zollcentner
zollpfund
zollverein pound
zolotnik
zugtierlast
zuz

Mechanical Impedance
dyne second/centimeter

joule second/square meter
kilogram-force
    second/meter
newton second/meter
pound-force second/foot
poundal second/foot

Mobility
cubic centimeter
    second/gram
cubic foot second/pound
cubic inch second/pound
cubic meter
    second/kilogram
square meter/pascal
    second
kilomole/kilogram
micromole/gram
millimole/gram
millimole/kilogram
mole/gram
mole/kilogram

Molar Heat Capacity
joule/mole kelvin
kilojoule/mole kelvin
millijoule/mole kelvin

Molar Mass
gram/mole
kilogram/kilomole
kilogram/mole

Molar Thermodynamic Energy
joule/mole
kilojoule/mole
millijoule/mole

Molar Volume
cubic centimeter/mole
cubic decimeter/mole
cubic meter/mole
liter/mole

Moment of Momentum or Angular Momentum or Angular Impulse
dyne centimeter second
erg second
gram square
    centimeter/second
joule second
kilogram square
    meter/second
newton meter second
planck
pound square foot/second

Momentum or Impulse
bole
dyne second
gram centimeter/second
kilogram meter/second
newton second
pound foot/second
pound-force second
poundal second
slug foot/second

Neutron Source Density
1/cubic centimeter day
1/cubic foot minute
1/cubic meter second
1/cubic yard second

Noise or Loudness Level
loudness unit
noy
phon
sone

Ore Grading or Concentration (Mass Basis)
gram/ton
gram/tonne
karat
kilogram/kilogram
milligram/gram
milligram/kilogram
milligram/ton
ounce/ton
part/million
pennyweight/ton
percent
pound/ton

Permeability - Water
darcy
kilogram meter/pascal
    square second
millidarcy
perm
square centimeter
square foot
square meter
square yard

Phase Coefficient or Angular Repetency or Reciprocal Length
1/centimeter
1/foot
1/inch
1/meter
degree/foot

Phase Coefficient or Angular Repetency or Reciprocal Length (continued)

degree/inch
diopter
radian/meter

Plane Angle

centrad
circle
degree
gon
grade
microradian
mil
milliradian
minute
radian
revolution
right angle
second
sign

Power

attowatt
Btu/hour
Btu/minute
Btu/second
calorie/hour
calorie/minute
calorie/second
centigrade heat unit/hour
centigrade heat unit/minute
centigrade heat unit/second
centiwatt
cheval vapeur
clusec
cubic meter atmosphere/hour
cubic meter atmosphere/minute
cubic meter atmosphere/second
deciwatt
dekawatt
dyne centimeter/hour
dyne centimeter/minute
dyne centimeter/second
erg/hour
erg/minute
erg/second
exawatt
femtowatt
foot pound-force/hour
foot pound-force/minute
foot pound-force/second
foot poundal/hour
foot poundal/minute
foot poundal/second
gigawatt
gram-force centimeter/hour

gram-force centimeter/minute
gram-force centimeter/second
hectowatt
horsepower
inch ounce-force revolution/minute
joule/hour
joule/minute
joule/second
kilocalorie/hour
kilocalorie/minute
kilocalorie/second
kilogram square meter/cubic second
kilogram-force meter/hour
kilogram-force meter/minute
kilogram-force meter/second
kilopond meter/hour
kilopond meter/minute
kilopond meter/second
kilowatt
lumen
megawatt
microwatt
million Btu/hour
milliwatt
nanowatt
newton meter/hour
newton meter/minute
newton meter/second
petawatt
pferdestarke
picowatt
poncelet
pound square foot/cubic second
terawatt
ton of refrigeration
var
volt ampere
watt
yoctowatt
yottawatt
zeptowatt
zettawatt

Pressure

atmosphere
attobar
attopascal
bar
barad
barye
centibar
centihg
centimeter of mercury
centimeter of water
centipascal
centitorr
decibar

decipascal
decitorr
dekabar
dekapascal
dyne/square centimeter
exabar
exapascal
femtobar
femtopascal
foot of air
foot of mercury
foot of water
gigabar
gigapascal
gram-force/square centimeter
hectobar
hectopascal
inch of air
inch of mercury
inch of water
kilobar
kilogram-force/square centimeter
kilogram-force/square meter
kilogram-force/square millimeter
kilogram/meter square second
kilopascal
kilopond/square centimeter
kilopond/square meter
kilopond/square millimeter
kip/square foot
kip/square inch
megabar
megapascal
meter of air
microbar
micrometer of mercury
micrometer of water
micron of mercury
micropascal
millibar
millihg
millimeter of mercury
millimeter of water
millipascal
millitorr
nanobar
nanopascal
newton/square meter
newton/square millimeter
ounce-force/square inch
pascal
petabar
petapascal
picobar
picopascal
pieze
pound-force/square foot
pound-force/square inch
poundal/square foot

Pressure (continued)
sthene/square meter
terabar
terapascal
ton-force/square foot
ton-force/square inch
ton-force/square meter
torr
yoctobar
yoctopascal
yottabar
yottapascal
zeptobar
zeptopascal
zettabar
zettapascal

Pressure Coefficient
pascal/kelvin
pound-force/square inch
  degree Fahrenheit

Pressure Gradient
kilogram/square meter
  square second
pascal/meter
pound-force/square foot
  foot
pound/square foot square
  second

Pure Numbers or Count or Units
baker's dozen
billion
brace
centillion
couple
decade
decillion
dozen
duodecal
duodecillion
googol
googolplex
great gross
gross
heptad
hexad
hundred
milliard
million
nonillion
novemdecillion
octad
octillion
octodecillion
one
pair
quadrillion
quattuordecillion
quindecillion

quintillion
score
septendecillion
septillion
sexdecillion
sextillion
single
ten
thousand
tredecillion
trillion
undecillion
unit
vigintillion

Quantity of Light
candela second steradian
joule
lumen hour
lumen second
lux second square meter
talbot
watt second

Radiance
erg/second steradian
  square centimeter
joule/second steradian
  square meter
watt/steradian square meter

Radiant Intensity
erg/second steradian
joule/second steradian
watt/steradian

Second Moment or Moment of Inertia of an Area
$centimeter^4$
$foot^4$
$inch^4$
$meter^4$
$millimeter^4$

Sedimentation Coefficient
femtosecond
picosecond
second
svedberg

Seebeck Coefficient
volt/degree Celsius
volt/degree Fahrenheit
volt/kelvin

Solid Angle
hemisphere
microsteradian
spat

spheradian
sphere
spherical degree
spherical right angle
spherical solid angle
square degree
square grade
sterad
steradian
steregon

Sound Absorbtion
open window unit
sabin
sound absorption unit
square foot
square meter
square-foot unit of
  absorption

Sound Pressure Level or Power Ratio
bel
brig
decibel
decineper
dex
neper

Specific Acoustic Impedance
dyne second/cubic
  centimeter
kilogram-force
  second/cubic meter
newton second/cubic meter
pascal second/meter
pound-force second/cubic
  foot
poundal second/cubic foot
rayl

Specific Activity
becquerel/kilogram
curie/kilogram
kilobecquerel/kilogram
megabecquerel/kilogram
millicurie/kilogram
rutherford/kilogram

Specific Area
acre/pound
hectare/kilogram
square centimeter/gram
square foot/pound
square meter/kilogram

Specific Fuel Consumption (Mass Basis)

gram/calorie
kilogram/joule
kilogram/kilocalorie
pound/Btu
pound/horsepower hour

Specific Fuel Consumption (Volume Basis)

cubic centimeter/calorie
cubic foot/Btu
cubic meter/joule
cubic meter/kilocalorie
gallon/horsepower hour
liter/joule
liter/kilowatthour

Specific Heat Capacity or Specific Entropy

Btu/pound degree Fahrenheit
calorie/gram degree Celsius
erg/gram degree Celsius
foot pound-force/pound degree Fahrenheit
joule/kilogram kelvin
kilocalorie/kilogram degree Celsius
kilogram-force meter/kilogram degree Celsius
kilopond meter/kilogram degree Celsius
mayer

Specific Thermodynamic Energy or Specific Energy

Btu/pound
calorie/gram
electronvolt/gram
erg/gram
foot pound-force/pound
joule/kilogram
kilocalorie/kilogram
kilogram-force meter/kilogram
kilojoule/kilogram
megajoule/kilogram
newton meter/kilogram
watt second/kilogram

Specific Volume

cubic centimeter/gram

cubic foot/pound
cubic inch/pound
cubic meter/kilogram

Spectral Cross-section

barn/electronvolt
barn/erg
centimeter/dyne
foot/pound-force
meter/newton
square centimeter/erg
square meter/joule
square second/kilogram

Surface Charge Density

abcoulomb/square centimeter
ampere hour/square meter
ampere second/square meter
coulomb/square centimeter
coulomb/square inch
coulomb/square meter
coulomb/square millimeter
franklin/square centimeter
kilocoulomb/square meter
megacoulomb/square meter
microcoulomb/square meter
millicoulomb/square meter
statcoulomb/square centimeter

Surface Concentration

gibbs
mole/square meter

Surface Density

grain/square foot
grain/square inch
grain/square yard
gram/square centimeter
gram/square meter
kilogram/are
kilogram/hectare
kilogram/square centimeter
kilogram/square meter
milligram/square centimeter
milligram/square meter
ounce/square foot
ounce/square inch
ounce/square yard
pound/acre
pound/square foot
pound/square inch
pound/square yard
slug/square foot
slug/square inch
slug/square yard
ton/square foot

ton/square inch
ton/square yard
tonne/square centimeter
tonne/square meter

Surface Tension

dyne/centimeter
dyne/meter
gram-force/centimeter
gram-force/meter
kilogram-force/centimeter
kilogram-force/meter
kilopond/centimeter
kilopond/meter
millinewton/centimeter
millinewton/meter
newton/centimeter
newton/meter
ounce-force/foot
ounce-force/inch
pound-force/foot
pound-force/inch

Temperature

degree Celsius
degree Fahrenheit
degree Rankine
degree Reaumur
kelvin

Thermal Conductance

Btu/second degree Fahrenheit
calorie/second degree Celsius
joule/second kelvin
kilocalorie/second degree Celsius
watt/kelvin

Thermal Conductivity

Btu foot/hour square foot degree Fahrenheit
Btu foot/hour square foot degree Rankine
Btu foot/second square foot degree Fahrenheit
Btu foot/second square foot degree Rankine
Btu inch/day square foot degree Fahrenheit
Btu inch/day square foot degree Rankine
Btu inch/hour square foot degree Fahrenheit
Btu inch/hour square foot degree Rankine
Btu inch/second square foot degree Fahrenheit
Btu inch/second square foot degree Rankine
Btu/hour foot degree Fahrenheit

Thermal Conductivity (continued)

Btu/hour foot degree Rankine
Btu/second foot degree Fahrenheit
Btu/second foot degree Rankine
calorie centimeter/hour square centimeter degree Celsius
calorie centimeter/second square centimeter degree Celsius
calorie/second centimeter degree Celsius
erg/centimeter second degree Celsius
joule/second meter kelvin
kilocalorie meter/square meter hour degree Celsius
kilocalorie/hour meter degree Celsius
kilogram-force/second degree Celsius
kilowatt/meter degree Celsius
kilowatt/meter kelvin
newton/second kelvin
watt centimeter/square centimeter degree Celsius
watt/centimeter kelvin
watt/foot degree Celsius
watt/meter degree Celsius
watt/meter kelvin

Thermal Resistance

degree Celsius/kilowatt
degree Celsius/watt
hour degree Celsius/kilocalorie
hour degree Fahrenheit/Btu
kelvin/kilowatt
kelvin/watt
second degree Celsius/calorie
second kelvin/joule

Thermal Resistivity

centimeter kelvin/watt
centimeter second degree Celsius/erg
day square foot degree Fahrenheit/Btu inch
day square foot degree Rankine/Btu inch
foot degree Celsius/watt
hour foot degree Fahrenheit/Btu
hour foot degree Rankine/Btu

hour meter degree Celsius/kilocalorie
hour square centimeter degree Celsius/calorie centimeter
hour square foot degree Fahrenheit/Btu foot
hour square foot degree Fahrenheit/Btu inch
hour square foot degree Rankine/Btu foot
hour square foot degree Rankine/Btu inch
meter degree Celsius/kilowatt
meter degree Celsius/watt
meter kelvin/kilowatt
meter kelvin/watt
second centimeter degree Celsius/calorie
second degree Celsius/kilogram-force
second foot degree Fahrenheit/Btu
second foot degree Rankine/Btu
second kelvin/newton
second meter kelvin/joule
second square centimeter degree Celsius/calorie centimeter
second square foot degree Fahrenheit/Btu foot
second square foot degree Fahrenheit/Btu inch
second square foot degree Rankine/Btu foot
second square foot degree Rankine/Btu inch
square centimeter degree Celsius/watt centimeter
square meter hour degree Celsius/kilocalorie meter

Time

annual
bicentennial
biennial
biennium
blink
centenary
centennial
centisecond
century
chiliad
day
decade
decennary
decennial
decennium
fortnight
hectosecond
hour

kilosecond
megasecond
microsecond
millenarian
millenary
millennium
millisecond
minute
month
quadrennial
quadrennium
quarter
quincentenary
quincentennial
quindecennial
quinquagesimal
quinquennium
second
sesquicentennial
tricentennial
triennium
vicenary
vicennial
week
year

Torque or Moment of Force or Bending Moment

centimeter gram-force
dyne centimeter
foot ounce-force
foot pound-force
foot poundal
inch ounce-force
inch pound-force
kilonewton meter
kilopond meter
meganewton meter
meter kilogram-force
micronewton meter
millinewton meter
newton meter

Torque Per Unit Length

foot pound-force/inch
inch pound-force/inch
newton meter/meter

Total Mass Stopping Power

Btu square foot/pound
calorie square centimeter/gram
erg square centimeter/gram
joule square meter/kilogram
kilocalorie square meter/kilogram

Velocity or Speed

benz
centimeter/day
centimeter/hour
centimeter/minute
centimeter/second
dekameter/day
dekameter/hour
dekameter/minute
dekameter/second
foot/day
foot/hour
foot/minute
foot/second
hectometer/day
hectometer/hour
hectometer/minute
hectometer/second
inch/day
inch/hour
inch/minute
inch/second
kilometer/day
kilometer/hour
kilometer/minute
kilometer/second
knot
megameter/day
megameter/hour
megameter/minute
megameter/second
meter/day
meter/hour
meter/minute
meter/second
mile/day
mile/hour
mile/minute
mile/second
millimeter/day
millimeter/hour
millimeter/minute
millimeter/second
nautical mile/day
nautical mile/hour
nautical mile/minute
nautical mile/second
speed of light
yard/day
yard/hour
yard/minute
yard/second

Viscosity (Dynamic)

centipoise
decipoise
dyne second/square
    centimeter
gram-force second/square
    centimeter
gram/centimeter second
hyl/meter second

kilogram-force
    second/square meter
kilogram/meter hour
kilogram/meter second
millipascal second
millipoise
newton second/square
    meter
pascal second
poise
poiseuille
pound-force second/square
    foot
pound-force second/square
    Inch
pound/foot hour
pound/foot second
poundal hour/square foot
poundal second/square foot
reyn
slug/foot second

Viscosity (Kinematic)

centistokes
lentor
liter/centimeter day
liter/centimeter hour
liter/centimeter minute
liter/centimeter second
poise cubic centime-
    ter/gram
square centimeter/day
square centimeter/hour
square centimeter/minute
square centimeter/second
square foot/day
square foot/hour
square foot/minute
square foot/second
square Inch/day
square Inch/hour
square Inch/minute
square Inch/second
square meter/day
square meter/hour
square meter/minute
square meter/second
square millimeter/day
square millimeter/hour
square millimeter/minute
square millimeter/second
stokes

Volume Activity

becquerel/cubic meter
curie/cubic meter
kilobecquerel/cubic meter
megabecquerel/cubic meter
millicurie/cubic meter
rutherford/cubic meter

Volume or Capacity

aam

abe
acetabulum
achtel
acre foot
acre inch
adoulie
ahm
aime
aimer
ako
akov
alma
almenn turma
almud
almude
alqueire
alquier
am
Amagat volume unit
ambar
ammonam
amomam
amphora
amunam
ancre
ankare
anker
ankre
anoman
antal
antel
apatan
ardab
ardeb
arroba
artaba
artabe
atting
attoliter
aum
azumbre
bag
balde
balli
ban
bandu
baril
barile
barmil
barrel
barril
barrique
barzina
basket
bat
bath
batos
battim
becher
beczka
bei sheng
benequen
bezah
billion cubic foot

Volume or Capacity (continued)

board foot
boccale
bochka
bocka
bocoy
bois equarris
bois ronds
bois scies
boisseau
bok
bok louang
boot
bota
botchka
botella
botellon
botte
bottle
boutylka
bozze
brente
bucket
bulto
bushel
byce
byee
cab
caba
cabaho
caban
cadaa
caffiso
cafiso
cafisso
cafiz
cahaho
cahia
cahiz
cajon
cajuela
camionada
can
canada
candel
candil
caneca
cantara
cantaro
cap
capicha
carga
cargo
carretada
cass
cast
cavan
cazuela
centiliter
ceston
chai meu

chaldron
chang awn
charka
chela
chemica
chetverik
chetvert
chetvertinka
chevron
chkalik
choinix
chomor
chopin
chopine
chou
chous
chu
chupa
cob
cochliarion
codo
collothum
conge
congius
coomb
copa
cor
cord
cord foot
cotyla
cuarta
cuarter
cuarteron
cuartilla
cuartillo
cuartillo habanero
cubem
cubic archine
cubic attometer
cubic centimeter
cubic cubit
cubic decimeter
cubic dekameter
cubic duim
cubic exameter
cubic femtometer
cubic fod
cubic foot
cubic fot
cubic fut
cubic gareh
cubic gigameter
cubic hectometer
cubic inch
cubic kilometer
cubic klafter
cubic megameter
cubic meter
cubic micrometer
cubic mile
cubic millimeter
cubic nanometer
cubic petameter
cubic picometer

cubic sagene
cubic terameter
cubic verchok
cubic yard
cubic yoctometer
cubic yottameter
cubic zeptometer
cubic zettameter
cubic zoll
cuddy
culleus
cup
curo
cwierc
cyathus
cyathys
dai
dan
dariba
daribah
dau
daula
debbie
deciliter
dekaliter
dimerlie
doi
dou
double fanega
drachm
dram
dreiling
dreissiger
drop
drum
du
efa
efot
egg
eimer
emine
encaa
English water ton
entelam
epha
ephah
erklein
ertragsfestmeter
exaliter
fad ol
famn
fan sheng
fanega
fanga
fass
fat
favn
favn braende
favne
femtoliter
feuillette
fifth
fillette angevine
firkin

Volume or Capacity (continued)

fjarding
fjerding
fjerdingkar
flagon
foder
foglietta
folha
forten
fortin
frasco
frasila
freight ton
fudder
fuder
futtermassel
gab
galao
gallon
galon
ganta
gantang
garava
garce
garnetz
garniec
garra
garrafa
garrafon
geriwa
ghebeta
gia
gia chiec
gia nan
gian sheng
giarra
gigaliter
gill
gin
gisla
gizla
go
goduk
gomari
gomor
goundo
great hin
gur
gur
gurraf
hak
halbe
halbstuck
half anker
half barrel
half hogshead
half homer
halvstop
hao sheng
he
hectare meter
hectoliter

hekat
hekt
hemikotylion
hemina
hen
henu
hin
hinim
hkt
hoc
hog
hogshead
holzklafter
homer
hop
hu
huacal
imi
immi
ippyong
issaron
itce
itcze
jae
jak
jarra
jigger
jizla
jumfru
jungfru
kab
kada
kadah
kaledje
kalong
kam meu
kan
kanahn
kande
kanna
kanne
kannu
kantaing
kapiza
kappa
kappe
kard
kartocc
kartos
katang
kav
kavan
keddah
keila
keleh
kettle
kfiz
khakoon
khanan
khanan louang
khar
kharouba
kharrouba
kharruba

khoinix
khoubhie
khous
khwe
khwet
kibaba
kila
kilah
kilderkin
kile
kileh
kilesi
kilo
kiloliter
kirat
kist
ko
kob
kob louang
koddi
koibon
koilon
koku
kolla
kollast
koltunna
konge
kop
kor
korce
korec
korn skeppa
korn tonde
korn topmaal
korn tunna
koros
kortab
koryec
korzec
kotyle
kouza
koyan
krina
krouchka
kruska
kuba
kubieke duim
kubieke el
kubieke palm
kubikfot
kul tonde
kula
kulimet
kulla
kulmet
kuna
kuncha
kung ho
kung ping
kung sheng
kung shih
kung so
kung tan
kung tou

Volume or Capacity (continued)

kung tso	mass	muthmassel
kunna	masse	mutsje
kurru	massel	mystram
kutu	masskanne	nafer
kuza	mattaro	nalih
kvarter	mau	nanoliter
kwai	measure	nigida
kwak	measurement ton	niou
kwarta	measurette	nisf kadah
kwarteka	medida	nisf keddah
kwarterka	medimno	noessel
kwarti	medimnos	nofs
kwe	medimnus	noggin
kwien	medio	nozibu
kyathos	medio almud	nusfiah
kyathys	megaliter	o
laang	megarikon	ocean ton
lai	meias canada	ock
lamang	meio	octava
lamany	mengel	octavillo
lambda	menor	ohm
lame	mercal	oitava
lang	merica	oka
last	merice	oke
lastre	messe	okka
le	metarta	okshoofd
leaguer	meter	olcek
legana	metreta	ollock
legger	metretes	oltonde
letakhim	metro	oltunna
letek	mettar	omarium
letekh	metter	omer
lethech	metze	oms
lethek	microliter	oner
lethekh	mid	onza
li sheng	midd	orna
ligula	mieng	ort
linea cubica	millerole	osmin
liter	milliliter	osmina
litre	million acre foot	ottinger
litron	million board foot	ottingkar
load	minae	ottinkar
lof	mine	ouiba
log	mingel	ounce
logh	minim	oxhoft
lugim	minot	oxhuvud
maass	mirze	oxybaphon
maatje	misura	paegel
maess	modd	paegl
makuk	modion	paegle
mal	modios	paele
malouah	modius	paimoneh
maltaro	moio	pajak
malter	moselle	pajmaneh
malwa	moule	pajok
mana	moyo	pally
mandu	mud	palmo cubica
marcal	mudd	panchang
marco real	mudde	panu
maris	muid	para
marta	mula	paraffin
	musa kibaba	parah
	musu kibaba	parak
	muth	parrah

Volume or Capacity (continued)

parrak
pathi
pau
pe cubica
peck
pegel
pesikta
petaliter
petrograd standard
pfiff
phai mu
phai mu louang
phlan
phlang
phuong
picoliter
pie cubica
pie de madera
pijp
pin
pinometer
pint
pinta
pinte
pipa
pipe
pishi
pjak
planken
pliashka
podd
poisson
polugarnetz
polygarnetz
pony
posson
pot
pot beaujolais
pottar
pottle
pottur
pound of water
probmetze
puddee
puili
pulgada cubica
pulgada maderera
puncheon
pyi
pyong
qab
qabh
qabim
qabin
qadah
qasba xubu
qav
qirat
qu
quadrantal
quart

quart de bouteille
quarta
quartarella
quartarius
quartaut
quarte
quarteau
quartel
quarter
quartern
quarteron
quartia
quartier
quartilho
quartillo
quarto
quartuccio
que
quei
quiba
quilo
racin
racione
raik
raummeter
rebee
register ton
rhine
rob
robbah
robo kibaba
roquille
rotl
rottol
roub
roubouh
rub
ruba
rubbiatella
rubia
rundlet
ruplagi
ryutsubo
sa
saa
saagh
saah
sabbitha
sac
sacco
sack
saha
sahh
sai
sale
salma tumoli
sao
sat
saton
saum
saw
sayut
scheffel
schepel

scheppel
schoppe
schoppen
schtaff
scruple
sea
seah
seak
seam
seer
seh
seidel
seik
seim
seit
selemin
semimodius
semodius
seste
setier
sextario
sextarius
sexto
shaku
shao
shen
sheng
shi sheng
shih dan
shih dao
shih ho
shih se
shih sen
shih sho
shin
shinik
shipping ton
sho
shot
shushack
sila
sildar mal
simri
sing
sinik
six
skaepper
skeppe
skieppe
spann
spint
square cuadra
stajo
stangiew
starello
steekkan
stein
stere
stero
stof
stoop
stop
strike
strych

**Volume or Capacity
(continued)**

stubchen
suk
sulga
sultchek
sun
sutu
syli
tabla
tablespoon
tamlaum
tan
tanan
tanica
tao
tarri
tat
tau
taza
tcharka
tchast
tchetverik
tchetvert
teacup
teaspoon
teman
teminye
teneka
teng
teningsfet
teraliter
terz
thamardi tin
thamardi tinn
than
thanan
thang
thang louang
thoum
thousand board foot
thousand cubic foot
thung
thuoc
tierce
tiercon
tin
tin han
tinaja
tinja
tipree
tjaere tonde
to
toat
tomini
tomna
tonde
tonde korn
tonde ol
tonde sild
tonel
tonelada
tonneau

tonneau de jauge
   international
tonneau de mer
tonnelada
toque
tot
tou
toumnah
touque
trillion cubic foot
trug
tuc
tuman
tumoli
tun
tunna
tunnia
ueba
ukla
urna
uyen
vadra
vara cubica
vat
vedro
velte
viacka
vidro
vierd
vierling
viertel
viertelein
viertelsaum
vingerhoed
wanche
weba
wedro
weiba
wey
whiba
wiba
Winchester wine gallon
winspel
wise
wisse
xeste
xiber xubu
yoctoliter
yottaliter
zah
zak
zalay
zarf
zayoot
zeptoliter
zettaliter
zudda

Units Not Currently in
Measure For Measure

bodge (volume)
butt (volume)
centimeter candle (illumination)
decilit (sound intensity level)
decilog (sound intensity level)
decilu (sound intensity level)
duty (energy)
E-unit (absorbed dose rate)
eman (dose equivalent)
ergon (angular momentum)
fors (acceleration)
fourier (thermal resistance)
galvat (electric current)
grave (mass)
herschel (radiance)
kapp line (magnetic flux)
kine (velocity)
logit (sound level)
lumberg (quantity of light)
mache (volume activity)
mic (electric inductance)
mug (mass)
octave (volume)
par (mass)
perm inch (permeability)
photon (angular momentum)
piece (volume)
queue (volume)
rum (pressure)
runlet (volume)
speck (volume, approximate)
stab (length)
stack (volume)
stathm (mass)
tor (pressure)

treice (volume)
vac (pressure)